Conflict of the Ages

(The Complete Series)

by Ellen G. White

The Story of Patriarchs and Prophets
The Story of Prophets and Kings
The Desire of Ages
The Acts of the Apostles
The Great Controversy Between Christ and Satan

Cover Image © Can Stock Photo Inc. / Hasenonkel

©2015 Wilder Publications, Inc.

Wilder Publications, Inc.
PO Box 632
Floyd Va 24091

ISBN: 978-1-5154-2274-7

First Edition

10 9 8 7 6 5 4 3 2 1

The Story of Patriarchs and Prophets

CONTENTS

Why was Sin Permitted?

"God is love." 1 John 4:16. His nature, His law, is love. It ever has been; it ever will be. "The high and lofty One that inhabiteth eternity," whose "ways are everlasting," changeth not. With Him "is no variableness, neither shadow of turning." Isaiah 57:15; Habakkuk 3:6; James 1:17.

Every manifestation of creative power is an expression of infinite love. The sovereignty of God involves fullness of blessing to all created beings. The psalmist says:

"Strong is Thy hand, and high is Thy right hand.
Righteousness and judgment are the foundation of Thy throne:
Mercy and truth go before Thy face.
Blessed is the people that know the joyful sound:
They walk, O Lord, in the light of Thy countenance.
In Thy name do they rejoice all the day:
And in Thy righteousness are they exalted.
For Thou art the glory of their strength: . . .
or our shield belongeth unto Jehovah,
And our king to the Holy One."
Psalm 89:13-18, R.V.

The history of the great conflict between good and evil, from the time it first began in heaven to the final overthrow of rebellion and the total eradication of sin, is also a demonstration of God's unchanging love.

The Sovereign of the universe was not alone in His work of beneficence. He had an associate—a co-worker who could appreciate His purposes, and could share His joy in giving happiness to created beings. "In the beginning was the Word, and the Word was with God, and the Word was God. The same was in the beginning with God." John 1:1, 2. Christ, the Word, the only begotten of God, was one with the eternal Father—one in nature, in character, in purpose—the only being that could enter into all the counsels and purposes of God. "His name shall be called Wonderful, Counselor, The mighty God, The everlasting Father, The Prince of Peace." Isaiah 9:6. His "goings forth have been from of old, from everlasting." Micah 5:2. And the Son of God declares concerning Himself: "The Lord possessed Me in the beginning of His way, before His works of old. I was set up from everlasting. . . . When He appointed the foundations of the earth: then I was by Him, as one brought up with Him: and I was daily His delight, rejoicing always before Him." Proverbs 8:22-30.

The Father wrought by His Son in the creation of all heavenly beings. "By Him were all things created, . . . whether they be thrones, or dominions, or principalities, or powers: all things were created by Him, and for Him." Colossians 1:16. Angels are God's ministers, radiant with the light ever flowing from His presence and speeding on rapid wing to execute His will. But the Son, the anointed of God, the "express image of His person," "the brightness of His glory," "upholding all things by the word of His power," holds supremacy over them all. Hebrews 1:3. "A glorious high throne from the beginning," was the place of His sanctuary (Jeremiah 17:12); "a scepter of righteousness," the scepter of His kingdom. Hebrews 1:8. "Honor and majesty are before Him: strength and beauty are in His sanctuary." Psalm 96:6. Mercy and truth go before His face. Psalm 89:14.

The law of love being the foundation of the government of God, the happiness of all intelligent beings depends upon their perfect accord with its great principles of righteousness. God desires from all His creatures the service of love—service that springs from an appreciation of His character. He takes no pleasure in a forced obedience; and to all He grants freedom of will, that they may render Him voluntary service.

So long as all created beings acknowledged the allegiance of love, there was perfect harmony throughout the universe of God. It was the joy of the heavenly host to fulfill the purpose of their Creator. They delighted in reflecting His glory and showing forth His praise. And while love to God was supreme, love for one another was confiding and unselfish. There was no note of discord to mar the celestial harmonies. But a change came over this happy state. There was one who perverted the freedom that God had granted to His creatures. Sin originated with him who, next to Christ, had been most honored of God and was highest in power and glory among the inhabitants of heaven. Lucifer, "son of the morning," was first of the covering cherubs, holy and undefiled. He stood in the presence of the great Creator, and the ceaseless beams of glory enshrouding the eternal God rested upon him. "Thus saith the Lord God; Thou sealest up the sum, full of wisdom, and perfect in beauty. Thou hast been in Eden the garden of God; every precious stone was thy covering. . . . Thou art the anointed cherub that covereth; and I have set thee so: thou wast upon the holy mountain of God; thou hast walked up and down in the midst of the stones of fire. Thou wast perfect in thy ways from the day that thou wast created, till iniquity was found in thee." Ezekiel 28:12-15.

Little by little Lucifer came to indulge the desire for self-exaltation. The Scripture says, "Thine heart was lifted up because of thy beauty, thou hast corrupted thy wisdom by reason of thy brightness." Ezekiel 28:17. "Thou hast said in thine heart, . . . I will exalt my throne above the stars of God. . . . I will be like the Most High." Isaiah 14:13, 14. Though all his glory was from God, this mighty angel came to regard it as pertaining to himself. Not content with his position, though honored above the heavenly host, he ventured to covet homage due alone to the Creator. Instead of seeking to make God supreme in the affections and allegiance of all created beings, it was his endeavor to secure their service and loyalty to himself. And coveting the glory with which the infinite Father had invested His Son, this prince of angels aspired to power that was the prerogative of Christ alone.

Now the perfect harmony of heaven was broken. Lucifer's disposition to serve himself instead of his Creator aroused a feeling of apprehension when observed by those who considered that the glory of God should be supreme. In heavenly council the angels pleaded with Lucifer. The Son of God presented before him the greatness, the goodness, and the justice of the Creator, and the sacred, unchanging nature of His law. God Himself had established the order of heaven;

and in departing from it, Lucifer would dishonor his Maker and bring ruin upon himself. But the warning, given in infinite love and mercy, only aroused a spirit of resistance. Lucifer allowed his jealousy of Christ to prevail, and became the more determined.

To dispute the supremacy of the Son of God, thus impeaching the wisdom and love of the Creator, had become the purpose of this prince of angels. To this object he was about to bend the energies of that master mind, which, next to Christ's, was first among the hosts of God. But He who would have the will of all His creatures free, left none unguarded to the bewildering sophistry by which rebellion would seek to justify itself. Before the great contest should open, all were to have a clear presentation of His will, whose wisdom and goodness were the spring of all their joy.

The King of the universe summoned the heavenly hosts before Him, that in their presence He might set forth the true position of His Son and show the relation He sustained to all created beings. The Son of God shared the Father's throne, and the glory of the eternal, self-existent One encircled both. About the throne gathered the holy angels, a vast, unnumbered throng—"ten thousand times ten thousand, and thousands of thousands" (Revelation 5:11.), the most exalted angels, as ministers and subjects, rejoicing in the light that fell upon them from the presence of the Deity. Before the assembled inhabitants of heaven the King declared that none but Christ, the Only Begotten of God, could fully enter into His purposes, and to Him it was committed to execute the mighty counsels of His will. The Son of God had wrought the Father's will in the creation of all the hosts of heaven; and to Him, as well as to God, their homage and allegiance were due. Christ was still to exercise divine power, in the creation of the earth and its inhabitants. But in all this He would not seek power or exaltation for Himself contrary to God's plan, but would exalt the Father's glory and execute His purposes of beneficence and love.

The angels joyfully acknowledged the supremacy of Christ, and prostrating themselves before Him, poured out their love and adoration. Lucifer bowed with them, but in his heart there was a strange, fierce conflict. Truth, justice, and loyalty were struggling against envy and jealousy. The influence of the holy angels seemed for a time to carry him with them. As songs of praise ascended in melodious strains, swelled by thousands of glad voices, the spirit of evil seemed vanquished; unutterable love thrilled his entire being; his soul went out, in harmony with the sinless worshippers, in love to the Father and the Son. But again he was filled with pride in his own glory. His desire for supremacy returned, and envy of Christ was once more indulged. The high honors conferred upon Lucifer were not appreciated as God's special gift, and therefore, called forth no gratitude to his Creator. He glorified in his brightness and exaltation and aspired to be equal with God. He was beloved and reverenced by the heavenly host, angels delighted to execute his commands, and he was clothed with wisdom and glory above them all. Yet the Son of God was exalted above him, as one in power and authority with the Father. He shared the Father's counsels, while Lucifer did not thus enter into the purposes of God. "Why," questioned this mighty angel, "should Christ have the supremacy? Why is He honored above Lucifer?"

Leaving his place in the immediate presence of the Father, Lucifer went forth to diffuse the spirit of discontent among the angels. He worked with mysterious secrecy, and for a time concealed his real purpose under an appearance of reverence for God. He began to insinuate doubts concerning the laws that governed heavenly beings, intimating that though laws might be necessary for the inhabitants of the worlds, angels, being more exalted, needed no such restraint, for their own wisdom was a sufficient guide. They were not beings that could bring dishonor to God; all their thoughts were holy; it was no more possible for them than for God Himself to err. The exaltation of the Son of God as equal with the Father was represented as an injustice to Lucifer, who, it was claimed, was also entitled to reverence and honor. If this prince of angels could but attain to his true, exalted position, great good would accrue to the entire host of heaven; for it was his object to secure freedom for all. But now even the liberty which they had hitherto enjoyed was at an end; for an absolute Ruler had been appointed them, and to His authority all must pay homage. Such were the subtle deceptions that through the wiles of Lucifer were fast obtaining in the heavenly courts.

There had been no change in the position or authority of Christ. Lucifer's envy and misrepresentation and his claims to equality with Christ had made necessary a statement of the true position of the Son of God; but this had been the same from the beginning. Many of the angels were, however, blinded by Lucifer's deceptions.

Taking advantage of the loving, loyal trust reposed in him by the holy beings under his command, he had so artfully instilled into their minds his own distrust and discontent that his agency was not discerned. Lucifer had presented the purposes of God in a false light—misconstruing and distorting them to excite dissent and dissatisfaction. He cunningly drew his hearers on to give utterance to their feelings; then these expressions were repeated by him when it would serve his purpose, as evidence that the angels were not fully in harmony with the government of God. While claiming for himself perfect loyalty to God, he urged that changes in the order and laws of heaven were necessary for the stability of the divine government. Thus while working to excite opposition to the law of God and to instill his own discontent into the minds of the angels under him, he was ostensibly seeking to remove dissatisfaction and to reconcile disaffected angels to the order of heaven. While secretly fomenting discord and rebellion, he with consummate craft caused it to appear as his sole purpose to promote loyalty and to preserve harmony and peace.

The spirit of dissatisfaction thus kindled was doing its baleful work. While there was no open outbreak, division of feeling imperceptibly grew up among the angels. There were some who looked with favor upon Lucifer's insinuations against the government of God. Although they had heretofore been in perfect harmony with the order which God had established, they were now discontented and unhappy because they could not penetrate His unsearchable counsels; they were dissatisfied with His purpose in exalting Christ. These stood ready to second Lucifer's demand for equal authority with the Son of God. But angels who were loyal and true maintained the wisdom and justice of the divine decree and endeavored to reconcile this disaffected being to the will of God. Christ was the Son of God; He had been one with Him before the angels were called into existence. He had ever stood at the right hand of the Father; His supremacy, so full of blessing to all who came under its benignant control, had not heretofore been questioned. The harmony of heaven had never been interrupted; wherefore should there now be discord? The loyal angels could see only terrible consequences from this dissension, and with earnest entreaty they counseled the disaffected ones to renounce their purpose and prove themselves loyal to God by fidelity to His government.

In great mercy, according to His divine character, God bore long with Lucifer. The spirit of discontent and disaffection had never before been known in heaven. It was a new element, strange, mysterious, unaccountable. Lucifer himself had not at first been acquainted with the real nature of his feelings; for a time he had feared to express the workings and imaginings of his mind; yet he did not dismiss them. He did not see whither he was drifting. But such efforts as infinite love and wisdom only could devise, were made to convince him of his error. His disaffection was proved to be without cause, and he was made to see what would be the result of persisting in revolt. Lucifer was convinced that he was in the wrong. He saw that "the Lord is righteous in all His ways, and holy in all His works" (Psalm 145:17); that the divine statutes are just, and that he ought to acknowledge them as such before all heaven. Had he done this, he might have saved himself and many angels. He had not at that time fully cast off his allegiance to God. Though he had left his position as covering cherub, yet if he had been willing to return to God, acknowledging the Creator's wisdom, and satisfied to fill the place appointed him in God's great plan, he would have been reinstated in his office. The time had come for a final decision; he must fully yield to the divine sovereignty or place himself in open rebellion. He nearly reached the decision to return, but pride forbade him. It was too great a sacrifice for one who had been so highly honored to confess that he had been in error, that his imaginings were false, and to yield to the authority which he had been working to prove unjust.

A compassionate Creator, in yearning pity for Lucifer and his followers, was seeking to draw them back from the abyss of ruin into which they were about to plunge. But His mercy was misinterpreted. Lucifer pointed to the long-suffering of God as an evidence of his own superiority, an indication that the King of the universe would yet accede to his terms. If the angels would stand firmly with him, he declared, they could yet gain all that they desired. He persistently defended his own course, and fully committed himself to the great controversy against his Maker. Thus it was that Lucifer, "the light bearer," the sharer of God's glory, the attendant of His throne, by transgression became Satan, "the adversary" of God and holy beings and the destroyer of those whom Heaven had committed to his guidance and guardianship.

Rejecting with disdain the arguments and entreaties of the loyal angels, he denounced them as deluded slaves. The preference shown to Christ he declared an act of injustice both to himself and to all the heavenly host, and announced that he would no longer submit to this invasion of his rights and theirs. He would never again acknowledge the supremacy of Christ. He had determined to claim the honor which should have been given him, and take command of all who would become his followers; and he promised those would enter his ranks a new and better government, under which all would enjoy freedom. Great numbers of the angels signified their purpose to accept him as their leader. Flattered by the favor with which his advances were received, he hoped to win all the angels to his side, to become equal with God Himself, and to be obeyed by the entire host of heaven.

Still the loyal angels urged him and his sympathizers to submit to God; and they set before them the inevitable result should they refuse: He who had created them could overthrow their power and signally punish their rebellious daring. No angel could successfully oppose the law of God, which was as sacred as Himself. They warned all to close their ears against Lucifer's deceptive reasoning, and urged him and his followers to seek the presence of God without delay and confess the error of questioning His wisdom and authority.

Many were disposed to heed this counsel, to repent of their disaffection, and seek to be again received into favor with the Father and His Son. But Lucifer had another deception ready. The mighty revolter now declared that the angels who had united with him had gone too far to return; that he was acquainted with the divine law, and knew that God would not forgive. He declared that all who should submit to the authority of Heaven would be stripped of their honor, degraded from their position. For himself, he was determined never again to acknowledge the authority of Christ. The only course remaining for him and his followers, he said, was to assert their liberty, and gain by force the rights which had not been willingly accorded them.

So far as Satan himself was concerned, it was true that he had now gone too far to return. But not so with those who had been blinded by his deceptions. To them the counsel and entreaties of the loyal angels opened a door of hope; and had they heeded the warning, they might have broken away from the snare of Satan. But pride, love for their leader, and the desire for unrestricted freedom were permitted to bear sway, and the pleadings of divine love and mercy were finally rejected.

God permitted Satan to carry forward his work until the spirit of disaffection ripened into active revolt. It was necessary for his plans to be fully developed, that their true nature and tendency might be seen by all. Lucifer, as the anointed cherub, had been highly exalted; he was greatly loved by the heavenly beings, and his influence over them was strong. God's government included not only the inhabitants of heaven, but of all the worlds that He had created; and Lucifer had concluded that if he could carry the angels of heaven with him in rebellion, he could carry also all the worlds. He had artfully presented his side of the question, employing sophistry and fraud to secure his objects. His power to deceive was very great. By disguising himself in a cloak of falsehood, he had gained an advantage. All his acts were so clothed with mystery that it was difficult to disclose to the angels the true nature of his work. Until fully developed, it could not be made to appear the evil thing it was; his disaffection would not be seen to be rebellion. Even the loyal angels could not fully discern his character or see to what his work was leading.

Lucifer had at first so conducted his temptations that he himself stood uncommitted. The angels whom he could not bring fully to his side, he accused of indifference to the interests of heavenly beings. The very work which he himself was doing, he charged upon the loyal angels. It was his policy to perplex with subtle arguments concerning the purposes of God. Everything that was simple he shrouded in mystery, and by artful perversion cast doubt upon the plainest statements of Jehovah. And his high position, so closely connected with the divine government, gave greater force to his representations. God could employ only such means as were consistent with truth and righteousness. Satan could use what God could not— flattery and deceit. He had sought to falsify the word of God and had misrepresented His plan of government, claiming that God was not just in imposing laws upon the angels; that in requiring submission and obedience from His creatures, He was seeking merely the exaltation of Himself. It was therefore necessary to demonstrate before the inhabitants of heaven, and of all the worlds, that God's government is just, His law perfect. Satan had made it appear that he himself was seeking to promote the good of the universe. The true character of the usurper and his real object must be understood by all. He must have time to manifest himself by his wicked works.

The discord which his own course had caused in heaven, Satan charged upon the government of God. All evil he declared to be the result of the divine administration. He claimed that it was his own object to improve upon the statutes of Jehovah. Therefore God permitted him to demonstrate the nature of his claims, to show the working out of his proposed changes in the divine law. His own work must condemn him. Satan had claimed from the first that he was not in rebellion. The whole universe must see the deceiver unmasked.

Even when he was cast out of heaven. Infinite Wisdom did not destroy Satan. Since only the service of love can be acceptable to God, the allegiance of His creatures must rest upon a conviction of His justice and benevolence. The inhabitants of heaven and of the worlds, being unprepared to comprehend the nature or consequences of sin, could not then have seen the justice of God in the destruction of Satan. Had he been immediately blotted out of existence, some would have served God from fear rather than from love. The influence of the deceiver would not have been fully destroyed, nor would be the spirit of rebellion have been utterly eradicated. For the good of the entire universe through ceaseless ages, he must more fully developed his principles, that his charges against the divine government might be seen in their true light by all created beings, and that the justice and mercy of God and the immutability of His law might be forever placed beyond all question.

Satan's rebellion was to be a lesson to the universe through all coming ages—a perpetual testimony to the nature of sin and its terrible results. The working out of Satan's rule, its effects upon both men and angels, would show what must be the fruit of setting aside the divine authority. It would testify that with the existence of God's government is bound up the well-being of all the creatures He has made. Thus the history of this terrible experiment of rebellion was to be a perpetual safeguard to all holy beings, to prevent them from being deceived as to the nature of transgression, to save them from committing sin, and suffering its penalty.

He that ruleth in the heavens is the one who sees the end from the beginning—the one before whom the mysteries of the past and the future are alike outspread, and who, beyond the woe and darkness and ruin that sin has wrought, beholds the accomplishment of His own purposes of love and blessing. Though "clouds and darkness are round about Him: righteousness and judgment are the foundation of His throne." Psalm 97:2, R.V. And this the inhabitants of the universe, both loyal and disloyal, will one day understand. "His work is perfect: for all His ways are judgment: a God of truth and without iniquity, just and right is He." Deuteronomy 32:4.

The Creation

"By the word of the Lord were the heavens made; and all the host of them by the breath of His mouth." "For He spake, and it was;" "He commanded, and it stood fast." Psalm 33:6,9. He "laid the foundations of the earth, that it should not be removed forever." Psalm 104:5.

As the earth came forth from the hand of its Maker, it was exceedingly beautiful. Its surface was diversified with mountains, hills, and plains, interspersed with noble rivers and lovely lakes; but the hills and mountains were not abrupt and rugged, abounding in terrific steeps and frightful chasms, as they now do; the sharp, ragged edges of earth's rocky framework were buried beneath the fruitful soil, which everywhere produced a luxuriant growth of verdure. There were no loathsome swamps or barren deserts. Graceful shrubs and delicate flowers greeted the eye at every turn. The heights were crowned with trees more majestic than any that now exist. The air, untainted by foul miasma, was clear and healthful. The entire landscape outvied in beauty the decorated grounds of the proudest palace. The angelic host viewed the scene with delight, and rejoiced at the wonderful works of God.

After the earth with its teeming animal and vegetable life had been called into existence, man, the crowning work of the Creator, and the one for whom the beautiful earth had been fitted up, was brought upon the stage of action. To him was given dominion over all that his eye could behold; for "God said, Let Us make man in Our image, after Our likeness: and let them have dominion over . . . all the earth. . . . So God created man in His own image; . . . male and female created He them." Here is clearly set forth the origin of the human race; and the divine record is so plainly stated that there is no occasion for erroneous conclusions. God created man in His own image. Here is no mystery. There is no ground for the supposition that man was evolved by slow degrees of development from the lower forms of animal or vegetable life. Such teaching lowers the great work of the Creator to the level of man's narrow, earthly conceptions. Men are so intent upon excluding God from the sovereignty of the universe that they degrade man and defraud him of the dignity of his origin. He who set the starry worlds on high and tinted with delicate skill the flowers of the field, who filled the earth and the heavens with the wonders of His power, when He came to crown His glorious work, to place one in the midst to stand as ruler of the fair earth, did not fail to create a being worthy of the hand that gave him life. The genealogy of our race, as given by inspiration, traces back its origin, not to a line of developing germs, mollusks, and quadrupeds, but to the great Creator. Though formed from the dust, Adam was "the son of God."

He was placed, as God's representative, over the lower orders of being. They cannot understand or acknowledge the sovereignty of God, yet they were made capable of loving and serving man. The psalmist says, "Thou madest him to have dominion over the works of Thy hands; Thou hast put all things under his feet: . . . the beasts of the field; the fowl of the air, . . . and whatsoever passeth through the paths of the seas." Psalm 8:6-8.

Man was to bear God's image, both in outward resemblance and in character. Christ alone is "the express image" (Hebrews 1:3) of the Father; but man was formed in the likeness of God. His nature was in harmony with the will of God. His mind was capable of comprehending divine things. His affections were pure; his appetites and passions were under the control of reason. He was holy and happy in bearing the image of God and in perfect obedience to His will.

As man came forth from the hand of his Creator, he was of lofty stature and perfect symmetry. His countenance bore the ruddy tint of health and glowed with the light of life and joy. Adam's height was much greater than that of men who now inhabit the earth. Eve was somewhat less in stature; yet her form was noble, and full of beauty. The sinless pair wore no artificial garments; they were clothed with a covering of light and glory, such as the angels wear. So long as they lived in obedience to God, this robe of light continued to enshroud them.

After the creation of Adam every living creature was brought before him to receive its name; he saw that to each had been given a companion, but among them "there was not found an help meet for him." Among all the creatures that God had made on the earth, there was not one equal to man. And God said, "It is not good that the man should be alone; I will make him an help meet for him." Man was not made to dwell in solitude; he was to be a social being. Without companionship the beautiful scenes and delightful employments of Eden would have failed to yield perfect happiness. Even communion with angels could not have satisfied his desire for sympathy and companionship. There was none of the same nature to love and to be loved.

God Himself gave Adam a companion. He provided "an help meet for him"—a helper corresponding to him-one who was fitted to be his companion, and who could be one with him in love and sympathy. Eve was created from a rib taken from the side of Adam, signifying that she was not to control him as the head, nor to be trampled under his feet as an inferior, but to stand by his side as an equal, to be loved and protected by him. A part of man, bone of his bone, and flesh of his flesh, she was his second self, showing the close union and the affectionate attachment that should exist in this relation. "For no man ever yet hated his own flesh; but nourisheth and cherisheth it." Ephesians 5:29. "Therefore shall a man leave his father and his mother, and shall cleave unto his wife; and they shall be one."

God celebrated the first marriage. Thus the institution has for its originator the Creator of the universe. "Marriage is honorable" (Hebrews 13:4); it was one of the first gifts of God to man, and it is one of the two institutions that, after the Fall, Adam brought with him beyond the gates of Paradise. When the divine principles are recognized and obeyed in this relation, marriage is a blessing; it guards the purity and happiness of the race, it provides for man's social needs, it elevates the physical, the intellectual, and the moral nature.

"And the Lord God planted a garden eastward in Eden; and there He put the man whom He had formed." Everything that God had made was the perfection of beauty, and nothing seemed wanting that could contribute to the happiness of the holy pair; yet the Creator gave them still another token of His love, by preparing a garden especially for their home. In this garden were trees of every variety, many of them laden with fragrant and delicious fruit. There were lovely vines, growing upright, yet presenting a most graceful appearance, with their branches drooping under their load of tempting fruit of the richest and most varied hues. It was the work of Adam and Eve to train the branches of the vine to form bowers, thus making for themselves a dwelling from living trees covered with foliage and fruit. There were fragrant flowers of every hue in rich profusion. In the midst of the garden stood the tree of life, surpassing in glory all other trees. Its fruit appeared like apples of gold and silver, and had the power to perpetuate life.

The creation was now complete. "The heavens and the earth were finished, and all the host of them." "And God saw everything that He had made, and, behold, it was very good." Eden bloomed on earth. Adam and Eve had free access to the tree of life. No taint of sin or shadow of death marred the fair creation. "The morning stars sang together, and all the sons of God shouted for joy." Job 38:7.

The great Jehovah had laid the foundations of the earth; He had dressed the whole world in the garb of beauty and had filled it with things useful to man; He had created all the wonders of the land and of the sea. In six days the great work of creation had been accomplished. And God "rested on the seventh day from all His work which He had made. And God blessed the seventh day, and sanctified it: because that in it He had rested from all His work which God created and made." God looked with satisfaction upon the work of His hands. All was perfect, worthy of its divine Author, and He rested, not as one weary, but as well pleased with the fruits of His wisdom and goodness and the manifestations of His glory.

After resting upon the seventh day, God sanctified it, or set it apart, as a day of rest for man. Following the example of the Creator, man was to rest upon this sacred day, that as he should look upon the heavens and the earth, he might reflect upon God's great work of creation; and that as he should behold the evidences of God's wisdom and goodness, his heart might be filled with love and reverence for his Maker.

In Eden, God set up the memorial of His work of creation, in placing His blessing upon the seventh day. The Sabbath was committed to Adam, the father and representative of the whole human family. Its observance was to be an act of grateful acknowledgment, on the part of all who should dwell upon the earth, that God was their Creator and their rightful Sovereign; that they were the work of His hands and the subjects of His authority. Thus the institution was wholly commemorative, and given to all mankind. There was nothing in it shadowy or of restricted application to any people.

God saw that a Sabbath was essential for man, even in Paradise. He needed to lay aside his own interests and pursuits for one day of the seven, that he might more fully contemplate the works of God and meditate upon His power and goodness. He needed a Sabbath to remind him more vividly of God and to awaken gratitude because all that he enjoyed and possessed came from the beneficent hand of the Creator.

God designs that the Sabbath shall direct the minds of men to the contemplation of His created works. Nature speaks to their senses, declaring that there is a living God, the Creator, the Supreme Ruler of all. "The heavens declare the glory of God; and the firmament showeth His handiwork. Day unto day uttereth speech, and night unto night showeth knowledge." Psalm 19:1, 2. The beauty that clothes the earth is token of God's love. We may behold it in the everlasting hills, in the lofty trees, in the opening buds and the delicate flowers. All speak to us of God. The Sabbath, ever pointing to Him who made them all, bids men open the great book of nature and trace therein the wisdom, the power, and the love of the Creator.

Our first parents, though created innocent and holy, were not placed beyond the possibility of wrongdoing. God made them free moral agents, capable of appreciating the wisdom and benevolence of His character and the justice of His requirements, and with full liberty to yield or to withhold obedience. They were to enjoy communion with God and with holy angels; but before they could be rendered eternally secure, their loyalty must be tested. At the very beginning of man's existence a check was placed upon the desire for self-indulgence, the fatal passion that lay at the foundation of Satan's fall. The tree of knowledge, which stood near the tree of life in the midst of the garden, was to be a test of the obedience, faith, and love of our parents. While permitted to eat freely of every other tree, they were forbidden to taste of this, on pain of death. They were also to be exposed to the temptations of Satan; but if they endured the trial, they would finally be placed beyond his power, to enjoy perpetual favor with God.

God placed man under law, as an indispensable condition of his very existence. He was a subject of the divine government, and there can be no government without law. God might have created man without the power to transgress His law; He might have withheld the hand of Adam from touching the forbidden fruit; but in that case man would have been, not a free moral agent, but a mere automaton. Without freedom of choice, his obedience would not have been voluntary, but forced. There could have been no development of character. Such a course would have been contrary to God's plan in dealing with the inhabitants of other worlds. It would have been unworthy of man as an intelligent being, and would have sustained Satan's charge of God's arbitrary rule.

God made upright; He gave him noble traits of character, with no bias toward evil. He endowed him with high intellectual powers, and presented before him the strongest possible inducements to be true to his allegiance. Obedience, perfect and perpetual, was the condition of eternal happiness. On this condition he was to have access to the tree of life.

The home of our first parents was to be a pattern for other homes as their children should go forth to occupy the earth. That home, beautified by the hand of God Himself, was not a gorgeous palace. Men, in their pride, delight in magnificent and costly edifices and glory in the works of their own hands; but God placed Adam in a garden. This was his dwelling. The blue heavens were its dome; the earth, with its delicate flowers and carpet of living green, was its floor; and the leafy branches of the goodly trees were its canopy. Its walls were hung with the most magnificent adornings—the handiwork of the great Master Artist. In the surroundings of the holy pair was a lesson for all time—that true happiness is found, not in the indulgence of pride and luxury, but in communion with God through His created works. If men would give less attention to the artificial, and would cultivate greater simplicity, they would come far nearer to answering the purpose of God in their creation. Pride and ambition are never satisfied, but those who are truly wise will find substantial and elevating pleasure in the sources of enjoyment that God has placed within the reach of all.

To the dwellers in Eden was committed the care of the garden, "to dress it and to keep it." Their occupation was not wearisome, but pleasant and invigorating. God appointed labor as a blessing to man, to occupy his mind, to strengthen his body, and to develop his faculties. In mental and physical activity Adam found one of the highest pleasures of his holy existence. And when, as a result of his disobedience, he was driven from his beautiful home, and forced to struggle with a stubborn soil to gain his daily bread, that very labor, although widely different from his pleasant occupation in the garden, was a safeguard against temptation and a source of happiness. Those who regard work as a curse, attended though it be with weariness and pain, are cherishing an error. The rich often look down with contempt upon the working classes, but this is wholly at variance with God's purpose in creating man. What are the possessions of even the most wealthy in comparison with the heritage given to the lordly Adam? Yet Adam was not to be idle. Our Creator, who understands what is for man's happiness, appointed Adam his work. The true joy of life is found only by the working men and women. The angels are diligent workers; they are the ministers of God to the children of men. The Creator has prepared no place for the stagnating practice of indolence.

While they remained true to God, Adam and his companion were to bear rule over the earth. Unlimited control was given them over every living thing. The lion and the lamb sported peacefully around them or lay down together at their feet. The happy birds flitted about them without fear; and as their glad songs ascended to the praise of their Creator, Adam and Eve united with them in thanksgiving to the Father and the Son.

The holy pair were not only children under the fatherly care of God but students receiving instruction from the all-wise Creator. They were visited by angels, and were granted communion with their Maker, with no obscuring veil between. They were full of the vigor imparted by the tree of life, and their intellectual power was but little less than that of the angels. The mysteries of the visible universe—"the wondrous works of Him which is perfect in knowledge" (Job 37:16)—afforded them an exhaustless source of instruction and delight. The laws and operations of nature, which have engaged men's study for six thousand years, were opened to their minds by the infinite Framer and Upholder of all. They held converse with leaf and flower and tree, gathering from each the secrets of its life. With every living creature, from the mighty leviathan that playeth among the waters to the insect mote that floats in the sunbeam, Adam was familiar. He had given to each its name, and he was acquainted with the nature and habits of all. God's glory in the heavens, the

innumerable worlds in their orderly revolutions, "the balancings of the clouds," the mysteries of light and sound, of day and night—all were open to the study of our first parents. On every leaf of the forest or stone of the mountains, in every shining star, in earth and air and sky, God's name was written. The order and harmony of creation spoke to them of infinite wisdom and power. They were ever discovering some attraction that filled their hearts with deeper love and called forth fresh expressions of gratitude.

So long as they remained loyal to the divine law, their capacity to know, to enjoy, and to love would continually increase. They would be constantly gaining new treasures of knowledge, discovering fresh springs of happiness, and obtaining clearer and yet clearer conceptions of the immeasurable, unfailing love of God.

The Temptation and Fall

No longer free to stir up rebellion in heaven, Satan's enmity against God found a new field in plotting the ruin of the human race. In the happiness and peace of the holy pair in Eden he beheld a vision of the bliss that to him was forever lost. Moved by envy, he determined to incite them to disobedience, and bring upon them the guilt and penalty of sin. He would change their love to distrust and their songs of praise to reproaches against their Maker. Thus he would not only plunge these innocent beings into the same misery which he was himself enduring, but would cast dishonor upon God, and cause grief in heaven.

Our first parents were not left without a warning of the danger that threatened them. Heavenly messengers opened to them the history of Satan's fall and his plots for their destruction, unfolding more fully the nature of the divine government, which the prince of evil was trying to overthrow. It was by disobedience to the just commands of God that Satan and his host had fallen. How important, then, that Adam and Eve should honor that law by which alone it was possible for order and equity to be maintained.

The law of God is as sacred as God Himself. It is a revelation of His will, a transcript of His character, the expression of divine love and wisdom. The harmony of creation depends upon the perfect conformity of all beings, of everything, animate and inanimate, to the law of the Creator. God has ordained laws for the government, not only of living beings, but of all the operations of nature. Everything is under fixed laws, which cannot be disregarded. But while everything in nature is governed by natural laws, man alone, of all that inhabits the earth, is amenable to moral law. To man, the crowning work of creation, God has given power to understand His requirements, to comprehend the justice and beneficence of His law, and its sacred claims upon him; and of man unswerving obedience is required.

Like the angels, the dwellers in Eden had been placed upon probation; their happy estate could be retained only on condition of fidelity to the Creator's law. They could obey and live, or disobey and perish. God had made them the recipients of rich blessings; but should they disregard His will, He who spared not the angels that sinned, could not spare them; transgression would forfeit His gifts and bring upon them misery and ruin.

The angels warned them to be on their guard against the devices of Satan, for his efforts to ensnare them would be unwearied. While they were obedient to God the evil one could not harm them; for, if need be, every angel in heaven would be sent to their help. If they steadfastly repelled his first insinuations, they would be as secure as the heavenly messengers. But should they once yield to temptation, their nature would become so depraved that in themselves they would have no power and no disposition to resist Satan.

The tree of knowledge had been made a test of their obedience and their love to God. The Lord had seen fit to lay upon them but one prohibition as to the use of all that was in the garden; but if they should disregard His will in this particular, they would incur the guilt of transgression. Satan was not to follow them with continual temptations; he could have access to them only at the forbidden tree. Should they attempt to investigate its nature, they would be exposed to his wiles. They were admonished to give careful heed to the warning which God had sent them and to be content with the instruction which He had seen fit to impart.

In order to accomplish his work unperceived, Satan chose to employ as his medium the serpent—a disguise well adapted for his purpose of deception. The serpent was then one of the wisest and most beautiful creatures on the earth. It had wings, and while flying through the air presented an appearance of dazzling brightness, having the color and brilliancy of burnished gold. Resting in the rich-laden branches of the forbidden tree and regaling itself with the delicious fruit, it was an object to arrest the attention and delight the eye of the beholder. Thus in the garden of peace lurked the destroyer, watching for his prey.

The angels had cautioned Eve to beware of separating herself from her husband while occupied in their daily labor in the garden; with him she would be in less danger from temptation than if she were alone. But absorbed in her pleasing task, she unconsciously wandered from his side. On perceiving that she was alone, she felt an apprehension of danger, but dismissed her fears, deciding that she had sufficient wisdom and strength to discern evil and to withstand it. Unmindful of the angels' caution, she soon found herself gazing with mingled curiosity and admiration upon the forbidden tree. The fruit was very beautiful, and she questioned with herself why God had withheld it from them. Now was the tempter's opportunity. As if he were able to discern the workings of her mind, he addressed her: "Yea, hath God said, Ye shall not eat of every tree of the garden?" Eve was surprised and startled as she thus seemed to hear the echo of her thoughts. But the serpent continued, in a musical voice, with subtle praise of her surpassing loveliness; and his words were not displeasing. Instead of fleeing from the spot she lingered wonderingly to hear a serpent speak. Had she been addressed by a being like the angels, her fears would have been excited; but she had no thought that the fascinating serpent could become the medium of the fallen foe.

To the tempter's ensnaring question she replied: "We may eat of the fruit of the trees of the garden: but of the fruit of the tree which is in the midst of the garden, God hath said, Ye shall not eat of it, neither shall ye touch it, lest ye die. And the serpent said unto the woman, Ye shall not surely die: for God doth know that in the day ye eat thereof, then your eyes shall be opened, and ye shall be as gods, knowing good and evil."

By partaking of this tree, he declared, they would attain to a more exalted sphere of existence and enter a broader field of knowledge. He himself had eaten of the forbidden fruit, and as a result had acquired the power of speech. And he insinuated that the Lord jealously desired to withhold it from them, lest they should be exalted to equality with Himself. It was because of its wonderful properties, imparting wisdom and power, that He had prohibited them from tasting or even touching it. The tempter intimated that the divine warning was not to be actually fulfilled; it was designed merely to intimidate them. How could it be possible for them to die? Had they not eaten of the tree of life? God had been seeking to prevent them from reaching a nobler development and finding greater happiness.

Such has been Satan's work from the days of Adam to the present, and he has pursued it with great success. He tempts men to distrust God's love and to doubt His wisdom. He is constantly seeking to excite a spirit of irreverent curiosity, a restless, inquisitive desire to penetrate the secrets of divine wisdom and power. In their efforts to search out what God has been pleased to withhold, multitudes overlook the truths which He has revealed, and which are essential to salvation. Satan tempts men to disobedience by leading them to believe they are entering a wonderful field of knowledge. But this is all a deception. Elated with their ideas of progression, they are, by trampling on God's requirements, setting their feet in the path that leads to degradation and death.

Satan represented to the holy pair that they would be gainers by breaking the law of God. Do we not today hear similar reasoning? Many talk of the narrowness of those who obey God's commandments, while they themselves claim to have broader ideas and to enjoy greater liberty. What is this but an echo of the voice from Eden, "In the day ye eat thereof"—transgress the divine requirement—"ye shall be as gods"? Satan claimed to have received great good by eating of the forbidden fruit, but he did not let it appear that by transgression he had become an outcast from heaven. Though he had found sin to result in infinite loss, he concealed his own misery in order to draw others into the same position. So now the transgressor seeks to disguise his true character; he may claim to be holy; but his exalted profession only makes him the more dangerous as a deceiver. He is on the side of Satan, trampling upon the law of God, and leading others to do the same, to their eternal ruin.

Eve really believed the words of Satan, but her belief did not save her from the penalty of sin. She disbelieved the words of God, and this was what led to her fall. In the judgment men will not be condemned because they conscientiously believed a lie, but because they did not believe the truth, because they neglected the opportunity of learning what is truth. Notwithstanding the sophistry of Satan to the contrary, it is always disastrous to disobey God. We must set our hearts to know what is truth. All the lessons which God has caused to be placed on record in His word are for our warning and instruction. They are given to save us from deception. Their neglect will result in ruin to ourselves. Whatever contradicts God's word, we may be sure proceeds from Satan.

The serpent plucked the fruit of the forbidden tree and placed it in the hands of the half-reluctant Eve. Then he reminded her of her own words, that God had forbidden them to touch it, lest they die. She would receive no more harm from eating the fruit, he declared, than from touching it. Perceiving no evil results from what she had done, Eve grew bolder. When she "saw that the tree was good for food, and that it was pleasant to the eyes, and a tree to be desired to make one wise, she took of the fruit thereof, and did eat." It was grateful to the taste, and as she ate, she seemed to feel a vivifying power, and imagined herself entering upon a higher state of existence. Without a fear she plucked and ate. And now, having herself transgressed, she became the agent of Satan in working the ruin of her husband. In a state of strange, unnatural excitement, with her hands filled with the forbidden fruit, she sought his presence, and related all that had occurred.

An expression of sadness came over the face of Adam. He appeared astonished and alarmed. To the words of Eve he replied that this must be the foe against whom they had been warned; and by the divine sentence she must die. In answer she urged him to eat, repeating the words of the serpent, that they should not surely die. She reasoned that this must be true, for she felt no evidence of God's displeasure, but on the contrary realized a delicious, exhilarating influence, thrilling every faculty with new life, such, she imagined, as inspired the heavenly messengers.

Adam understood that his companion had transgressed the command of God, disregarded the only prohibition laid upon them as a test of their fidelity and love. There was a terrible struggle in his mind. He mourned that he had permitted Eve to wander from his side. But now the deed was done; he must be separated from her whose society had been his joy. How could he have it thus? Adam had enjoyed the companionship of God and of holy angels. He had looked upon the glory of the Creator. He understood the high destiny opened to the human race should they remain faithful to God. Yet all these blessings were lost sight of in the fear of losing that one gift which in his eyes outvalued every other. Love, gratitude, loyalty to the Creator—all were overborne by love to Eve. She was a part of himself, and he could not endure the thought of

separation. He did not realize that the same Infinite Power who had from the dust of the earth created him, a living, beautiful form, and had in love given him a companion, could supply her place. He resolved to share her fate; if she must die, he would die with her. After all, he reasoned, might not the words of the wise serpent be true? Eve was before him, as beautiful and apparently as innocent as before this act of disobedience. She expressed greater love for him than before. No sign of death appeared in her, and he decided to brave the consequences. He seized the fruit and quickly ate.

After his transgression Adam at first imagined himself entering upon a higher state of existence. But soon the thought of his sin filled him with terror. The air, which had hitherto been of a mild and uniform temperature, seemed to chill the guilty pair. The love and peace which had been theirs was gone, and in its place they felt a sense of sin, a dread of the future, a nakedness of soul. The robe of light which had enshrouded them, now disappeared, and to supply its place they endeavored to fashion for themselves a covering; for they could not, while unclothed, meet the eye of God and holy angels.

They now began to see the true character of their sin. Adam reproached his companion for her folly in leaving his side and permitting herself to be deceived by the serpent; but they both flattered themselves that He who had given them so many evidences of His love, would pardon this one transgression, or that they would not be subjected to so dire a punishment as they had feared.

Satan exulted in his success. He had tempted the woman to distrust God's love, to doubt His wisdom, and to transgress His law, and through her he had caused the overthrow of Adam.

But the great Lawgiver was about to make known to Adam and Eve the consequences of their transgression. The divine presence was manifested in the garden. In their innocence and holiness they had joyfully welcomed the approach of their Creator; but now they fled in terror, and sought to hide in the deepest recesses of the garden. But "the Lord God called unto Adam, and said unto him, Where art thou? And he said, I heard Thy voice in the garden, and I was afraid, because I was naked; and I hid myself. And He said, Who told thee that thou wast naked? Hast thou eaten of the tree, whereof I commanded thee that thou shouldest not eat?"

Adam could neither deny nor excuse his sin; but instead of manifesting penitence, he endeavored to cast the blame upon his wife, and thus upon God Himself: "The woman whom Thou gavest to be with me, she gave me of the tree, and I did eat." He who, from love to Eve, had deliberately chosen to forfeit the approval of God, his home in Paradise, and an eternal life of joy, could now, after his fall, endeavor to make his companion, and even the Creator Himself, responsible for the transgression. So terrible is the power of sin.

When the woman was asked, "What is this that thou hast done?" she answered, "The serpent beguiled me, and I did eat." "Why didst Thou create the serpent? Why didst Thou suffer him to enter Eden?"—these were the questions implied in her excuse for her sin. Thus, like Adam, she charged God with the responsibility of their fall. The spirit of self-justification originated in the father of lies; it was indulged by our first parents as soon as they yielded to the influence of Satan, and has been exhibited by all the sons and daughters of Adam. Instead of humbly confessing their sins, they try to shield themselves by casting the blame upon others, upon circumstances, or upon God—making even His blessings an occasion of murmuring against Him.

The Lord then passed sentence upon the serpent: "Because thou hast done this, thou art cursed above all cattle, and above every beast of the field; upon thy belly shalt thou go, and dust shalt thou eat all the days of thy life." Since it had been employed as Satan's medium, the serpent was to share the visitation of divine judgment. From the most beautiful and admired of the creatures of the field, it was to become the most groveling and detested of them all, feared and hated by both man and beast. The words next addressed to the serpent applied directly to Satan himself, pointing forward to his ultimate defeat and destruction: "I will put enmity between thee and the woman, and between thy seed and her seed; it shall bruise thy head, and thou shalt bruise his heel."

Eve was told of the sorrow and pain that must henceforth be her portion. And the Lord said, "Thy desire shall be to thy husband, and he shall rule over thee." In the creation God had made her the equal of Adam. Had they remained obedient to God—in harmony with His great law of love—they would ever have been in harmony with each other; but sin had brought discord, and now their union could be maintained and harmony preserved only by submission on the part of the one or the other. Eve had been the first in transgression; and she had fallen into temptation by separating from her companion, contrary to the divine direction. It was by her solicitation that Adam sinned, and she was now placed in subjection to her husband. Had the principles joined in the law of God been cherished by the fallen race, this sentence, though growing out of the results of sin, would have proved a blessing to them; but man's abuse of the supremacy thus given him has too often rendered the lot of woman very bitter and made her life a burden.

Eve had been perfectly happy by her husband's side in her Eden home; but, like restless modern Eves, she was flattered with the hope of entering a higher sphere than that which God had assigned her. In attempting to rise above her original position, she fell far below it. A similar result will be reached by all who are unwilling to take up cheerfully their life duties in accordance with God's plan. In their efforts to reach positions for which He has not fitted them, many are leaving vacant the place where they might be a blessing. In their desire for a higher sphere, many have sacrificed true womanly dignity and nobility of character, and have left undone the very work that Heaven appointed them.

To Adam the Lord declared: "Because thou hast hearkened unto the voice of thy wife, and hast eaten of the tree, of which I commanded thee, saying, Thou shalt not eat of it: cursed is the ground for thy sake; in sorrow shalt thou eat of it all the days of thy life; thorns also and thistles shall it bring forth to thee; and thou shalt eat the herb of the field; in the sweat of thy face shalt thou eat bread, till thou return unto the ground; for out of it was thou taken: for dust thou art, and unto dust shalt thou return."

It was not the will of God that the sinless pair should know aught of evil. He had freely given them the good, and had withheld the evil. But, contrary to His command, they had eaten of the forbidden tree, and now they would continue to eat of it—they would have the knowledge of evil—all the days of their life. From that time the race would be afflicted by Satan's temptations. Instead of the happy labor heretofore appointed them, anxiety and toil were to be their lot. They would be subject to disappointment, grief, and pain, and finally to death.

Under the curse of sin all nature was to witness to man of the character and results of rebellion against God. When God made man He made him rule over the earth and all living creatures. So long as Adam remained loyal to Heaven, all nature was in subjection to him. But when he rebelled against the divine law, the inferior creatures were in rebellion against his rule. Thus the Lord, in His great mercy, would show men the sacredness of His law, and lead them, by their own experience, to see the danger of setting it aside, even in the slightest degree.

And the life of toil and care which was henceforth to be man's lot was appointed in love. It was a discipline rendered needful by his sin, to place a check upon the indulgence of appetite and passion, to develop habits of self-control. It was a part of God's great plan of man's recovery from the ruin and degradation of sin.

The warning given to our first parents—"In the day that thou eatest thereof thou shalt surely die" (Genesis 2:17)—did not imply that they were to die on the very day when they partook of the forbidden fruit. But on the day the irrevocable sentence would be pronounced. Immortality was promised them on condition of obedience; by transgression they would forfeit eternal life. That very day would be doomed to death.

In order to possess an endless existence, man must continue to partake of the tree of life. Deprived of this, his vitality would gradually diminish until life should become extinct. It was Satan's plan that Adam and Eve should by disobedience incur God's displeasure; and then, if they failed to obtain forgiveness, he hoped that they would eat of the tree of life, and thus perpetuate an existence of sin and misery. But after man's fall, holy angels were immediately commissioned to guard the tree of life. Around these angels flashed beams of light having the appearance of a glittering sword. None of the family of Adam were permitted to pass the barrier to partake of the life-giving fruit; hence there is not an immortal sinner.

The tide of woe that flowed from the transgression of our first parents is regarded by many as too awful a consequence for so small a sin, and they impeach the wisdom and justice of

God in His dealings with man. But if they would look more deeply into this question, they might discern their error. God created man after His own likeness, free from sin. The earth was to be peopled with beings only a little lower than the angels; but their obedience must be tested; for God would not permit the world to be filled with those who would disregard His law. Yet, in His great mercy, He appointed Adam no severe test. And the very lightness of the prohibition made the sin exceedingly great. If Adam could not bear the smallest of tests, he could not have endured a greater trial had he been entrusted with higher responsibilities.

Had some great test been appointed Adam, then those whose hearts incline to evil would have excused themselves by saying, "This is a trivial matter, and God is not so particular about little things." And there would be continual transgression in things looked upon as small, and which pass unrebuked among men. But the Lord has made it evident that sin in any degree is offensive to Him.

To Eve it seemed a small thing to disobey God by tasting the fruit of the forbidden tree, and to tempt her husband also to transgress; but their sin opened the floodgates of woe upon the world. Who can know, in the moment of temptation, the terrible consequences that will result from one wrong step?

Many who teach that the law of God is not binding upon man, urge that it is impossible for him to obey its precepts. But if this were true, why did Adam suffer the penalty of transgression? The sin of our first parents brought guilt and sorrow upon the world, and had it not been for the goodness and mercy of God, would have plunged the race into hopeless despair. Let none deceive themselves. "The wages of sin is death." Romans 6:23. The law of God can no more be transgressed with impunity now than when sentence was pronounced upon the father of mankind.

After their sin Adam and Eve were no longer to dwell in Eden. They earnestly entreated that they might remain in the home of their innocence and joy. They confessed that they had forfeited all right to that happy abode, but pledged themselves for the future to yield strict obedience to God. But they were told that their nature had become depraved by sin; they had lessened their strength to resist evil and had opened the way for Satan to gain more ready access to them. In their innocence they had yielded to temptation; and now, in a state of conscious guilt, they would have less power to maintain their integrity.

In humility and unutterable sadness they bade farewell to their beautiful home and went forth to dwell upon the earth, where rested the curse of sin. The atmosphere, once so mild and uniform in temperature, was now subject to marked changes, and the Lord mercifully provided them with a garment of skins as a protection from the extremes of heat and cold.

As they witnessed in drooping flower and falling leaf the first signs of decay, Adam and his companion mourned more deeply than men now mourn over their dead. The death of the frail, delicate flowers was indeed a cause of sorrow; but when the goodly trees cast off their leaves, the scene brought vividly to mind the stern fact that death is the portion of every living thing.

The Garden of Eden remained upon the earth long after man had become an outcast from its pleasant paths. The fallen race were long permitted to gaze upon the home of innocence, their entrance barred only by the watching angels. At the cherubim-guarded gate of Paradise the divine glory was revealed. Hither came Adam and his sons to worship God. Here they renewed their vows of obedience to that law the transgression of which had banished them from Eden. When the tide of iniquity overspread the world, and the wickedness of men determined their destruction by a flood of waters, the hand that had planted Eden withdrew it from the earth. But in the final restitution, when there shall be "a new heaven and a new earth" (Revelation 21:1), it is to be restored more gloriously adorned than at the beginning.

Then they that have kept God's commandments shall breathe in immortal vigor beneath the tree of life; and through unending ages the inhabitants of sinless worlds shall behold, in that garden of delight, a sample of the perfect work of God's creation, untouched by the curse of sin—a sample of what the whole earth would have become, had man but fulfilled the Creator's glorious plan.

The Plan of Redemption

The fall of man filled all heaven with sorrow. The world that God had made was blighted with the curse of sin and inhabited by beings doomed to misery and death. There appeared no escape for those who had transgressed the law. Angels ceased their songs of praise. Throughout the heavenly courts there was mourning for the ruin that sin had wrought.

The Son of God, heaven's glorious Commander, was touched with pity for the fallen race. His heart was moved with infinite compassion as the woes of the lost world rose up before Him. But divine love had conceived a plan whereby man might be redeemed. The broken law of God demanded the life of the sinner. In all the universe there was but one who could, in behalf of man, satisfy its claims. Since the divine law is as sacred as God Himself, only one equal with God could make atonement for its transgression. None but Christ could redeem fallen man from the curse of the law and bring him again into harmony with Heaven. Christ would take upon Himself the guilt and shame of sin—sin so offensive to a holy God that it must separate the Father and His Son. Christ would reach to the depths of misery to rescue the ruined race.

Before the Father He pleaded in the sinner's behalf, while the host of heaven awaited the result with an intensity of interest that words cannot express. Long continued was that mysterious communing—"the counsel of peace" (Zechariah 6:13) for the fallen sons of men. The plan of salvation had been laid before the creation of the earth; for Christ is "the Lamb slain from the foundation of the world" (Revelation

13:8); yet it was a struggle, even with the King of the universe, to yield up His Son to die for the guilty race. But "God so loved the world, that He gave His only-begotten Son, that whosoever believeth in Him should not perish, but have everlasting life." John 3:16. Oh, the mystery of redemption! the love of God for a world that did not love Him! Who can know the depths of that love which "passeth knowledge"? Through endless ages immortal minds, seeking to comprehend the mystery of that incomprehensible love, will wonder and adore.

God was to be manifest in Christ, "reconciling the world unto Himself." 2 Corinthians 5:19. Man had become so degraded by sin that it was impossible for him, in himself, to come into harmony with Him whose nature is purity and goodness. But Christ, after having redeemed man from the condemnation of the law, could impart divine power to unite with human effort. Thus by repentance toward God and faith in Christ the fallen children of Adam might once more become "sons of God." 1 John 3:2.

The plan by which alone man's salvation could be secured, involved all heaven in its infinite sacrifice. The angels could not rejoice as Christ opened before them the plan of redemption, for they saw that man's salvation must cost their loved Commander unutterable woe. In grief and wonder they listened to His words as He told them how He must descend from heaven's purity and peace, its joy and glory and immortal life, and come in contact with the degradation of earth, to endure its sorrow, shame, and death. He was to stand between the sinner and the penalty of sin; yet few would receive Him as the Son of God. He would leave His high position as the Majesty of heaven, appear upon earth and humble Himself as a man, and by His own experience become acquainted with the sorrows and temptations which man would have to endure. All this would be necessary in order that He might be able to succor them that should be tempted. Hebrews 2:18. When His mission as a teacher should be ended, He must be delivered into the hands of wicked men and be subjected to every insult and torture that Satan could inspire them to inflict. He must die the cruelest of deaths, lifted up between the heavens and the earth as a guilty sinner. He must pass long hours of agony so terrible that angels could not look upon it, but would veil their faces from the sight. He must endure anguish of soul, the hiding of His Father's face, while the guilt of transgression —the weight of the sins of the whole world—should be upon Him.

The angels prostrated themselves at the feet of their Commander and offered to become a sacrifice for man. But an angel's life could not pay the debt; only He who created man had power to redeem him. Yet the angels were to have a part to act in the plan of redemption. Christ was to be made "a little lower than the angels for the suffering of death." Hebrews 2:9. As He should take human nature upon Him, His strength would not be equal to theirs, and they were to minister to Him, to strengthen and soothe Him under His sufferings. They were also to be ministering spirits, sent forth to minister for them who should be heirs of salvation. Hebrews 1:14. They would guard the subjects of grace from the power of evil angels and from the darkness constantly thrown around them by Satan.

When the angels should witness the agony and humiliation of their Lord, they would be filled with grief and indignation and would wish to deliver Him from His murderers; but they were not to interpose in order to prevent anything which they should behold. It was a part of the plan of redemption that Christ should suffer the scorn and abuse of wicked men, and He consented to all this when He became the Redeemer of man.

Christ assured the angels that by His death He would ransom many, and would destroy him who had the power of death. He would recover the kingdom which man had lost by transgression, and the redeemed were to inherit it with Him, and dwell therein forever. Sin and sinners would be blotted out, nevermore to disturb the peace of heaven or earth. He bade the angelic host to be in accord with the plan that His Father had accepted, and rejoice that, through His death, fallen man could be reconciled to God.

Then joy, inexpressible joy, filled heaven. The glory and blessedness of a world redeemed, outmeasured even the anguish and sacrifice of the Prince of life. Through the celestial courts echoed the first strains of that song which was to ring out above the hills of Bethlehem—"Glory to God in the highest, and on earth peace, good will toward men." Luke 2:14. With a deeper gladness now than in the rapture of the new creation, "the morning stars sang together, and all the sons of God shouted for joy." Job 38:7.

To man the first intimation of redemption was communicated in the sentence pronounced upon Satan in the garden. The Lord declared, "I will put enmity between thee and the woman, and between thy seed and her seed; it shall bruise thy head, and thou shalt bruise his heel." Genesis 3:15. This sentence, uttered in the hearing of our first parents, was to them a promise. While it foretold war between man and Satan, it declared that the power of the great adversary would finally be broken. Adam and Eve stood as criminals before the righteous Judge, awaiting the sentence which transgression had incurred; but before they heard of the life of toil and sorrow which must be their portion, or of the decree that they must return to dust, they listened to words that could not fail to give them hope. Though they must suffer from the power of their mighty foe, they could look forward to final victory.

When Satan heard that enmity should exist between himself and the woman, and between his seed and her seed, he knew that his work of depraving human nature would be interrupted; that by some means man would be enabled to resist his power. Yet as the plan of salvation was more fully unfolded, Satan rejoiced with his angels that, having caused man's fall, he could bring down the Son of God from His exalted position. He declared that his plans had thus far been successful upon the earth, and that when Christ should take upon Himself human nature, He also might be overcome, and thus the redemption of the fallen race might be prevented.

Heavenly angels more fully opened to our first parents the plan that had been devised for their salvation. Adam and his companion were assured that notwithstanding their great sin, they were not to be abandoned to the control of Satan. The Son of God had offered to atone, with His own life, for their transgression. A period of probation would be granted them, and through repentance and faith in Christ they might again become the children of God.

The sacrifice demanded by their transgression revealed to Adam and Eve the sacred character of the law of God; and they saw, as they had never seen before, the guilt of sin and its dire results. In their remorse and anguish they pleaded that the penalty might not fall upon Him whose love had been the source of all their joy; rather let it descend upon them and their prosperity.

They were told that since the law of Jehovah is the foundation of His government in heaven as well as upon the earth, even the life of an angel could not be accepted as a sacrifice for its transgression. Not one of its precepts could be abrogated or changed to meet man in his fallen condition; but the Son of God, who had created man, could make an atonement for him. As Adam's transgression had brought wretchedness and death, so the sacrifice of Christ would bring life and immortality.

Not only man but the earth had by sin come under the power of the wicked one, and was to be restored by the plan of redemption. At his creation Adam was placed in dominion over the earth. But by yielding to temptation, he was brought under the power of Satan. "Of whom a man is overcome, of the same is he brought in bondage." 2 Peter 2:19. When man became Satan's captive, the dominion which he held, passed to his conqueror. Thus Satan became "the god of this world." 2 Corinthians 4:4. He had usurped that dominion over the earth which had been originally given to Adam. But Christ, by His sacrifice paying the penalty of sin, would not only redeem man, but recover the dominion which he had forfeited. All that was lost by the first Adam will be restored by the second. Says the prophet, "O tower of the flock, the stronghold of the daughter of Zion, unto thee shall it come, even the first dominion." Micah 4:8. And the apostle Paul points forward to the "redemption of the purchased possession." Ephesians 1:14. God created the earth to be the abode of holy, happy beings. The Lord "formed the earth and made it; He hath established it, He created it not in vain, He formed it to be inhabited." Isaiah 45:18. That purpose will be fulfilled, when, renewed by the power of God, and freed from sin and sorrow, it shall become the eternal abode of the redeemed. "The righteous shall inherit the land, and dwell therein forever." "And there shall be no more curse: but the throne of God and of the Lamb shall be in it; and His servants shall serve Him." Psalm 37:29; Revelation 22:3.

Adam, in his innocence, had enjoyed open communion with his Maker; but sin brought separation between God and man, and the atonement of Christ alone could span the abyss and make possible the communication of blessing or salvation from heaven to earth. Man was still cut off from direct approach to his Creator, but God would communicate with him through Christ and angels.

Thus were revealed to Adam important events in the history of mankind, from the time when the divine sentence was pronounced in Eden, to the Flood, and onward to the first advent of the Son of God. He was shown that while the sacrifice of Christ would be of sufficient value to save the whole world, many would choose a life of sin rather than of repentance and obedience. Crime would increase through successive generations, and the curse of sin would rest more and more heavily upon the human race, upon the beasts, and upon the earth. The days of man would be shortened by his own course of sin; he would deteriorate in physical stature and endurance and in moral and intellectual power, until the world would be filled with misery of every type. Through the indulgence of appetite and passion men would become incapable of appreciating the great truths of the plan of redemption. Yet Christ, true to the purpose for which He left heaven, would continue His interest in men, and still invite them to hide their weakness and deficiencies in Him. He would supply the needs of all who would come unto Him in faith. And there would ever be a few who would preserve the knowledge of God and would remain unsullied amid the prevailing iniquity.

The sacrificial offerings were ordained by God to be to man a perpetual reminder and a penitential acknowledgment of his sin and a confession of his faith in the promised Redeemer. They were intended to impress upon the fallen race the solemn truth that it was sin that caused death. To Adam, the offering of the first sacrifice was a most painful ceremony. His hand must be raised to take life, which only God could give. It was the first time he had ever witnessed death, and he knew that had he been obedient to God, there would have been no death of man or beast. As he slew the innocent victim, he trembled at the thought that his sin must shed the blood of the spotless Lamb of God. This scene gave him a deeper and more vivid sense of the greatness of his transgression, which nothing but the death of God's dear Son could expiate. And he marveled at the infinite goodness that would give such a ransom to save the guilty. A star of hope illumined the dark and terrible future and relieved it of its utter desolation.

But the plan of redemption had a yet broader and deeper purpose than the salvation of man. It was not for this alone that Christ came to the earth; it was not merely that the inhabitants of this little world might regard the law of God as it should be regarded; but it was to vindicate the character of God before the universe. To this result of His great sacrifice—its influence upon the intelligences of other worlds, as well as upon man—the Saviour looked forward when just before His crucifixion He said: "Now is the judgment of this world: now shall the prince of this world be cast out. And I, if I be lifted up from the earth, will draw all unto Me." John 12:31, 32. The act of Christ in dying for the salvation of man would not only make heaven accessible to men, but before all the universe it would justify God and His Son in their dealing with the rebellion of Satan. It would establish the perpetuity of the law of God and would reveal the nature and the results of sin.

From the first the great controversy had been upon the law of God. Satan had sought to prove that God was unjust, that His law was faulty, and that the good of the universe required it to be changed. In attacking the law he aimed to overthrow the authority of its Author. In the controversy it was to be shown whether the divine statutes were defective and subject to change, or perfect and immutable.

When Satan was thrust out of heaven, he determined to make the earth his kingdom. When he tempted and overcame Adam and Eve, he thought that he had gained possession of this world; "because," said he, "they have chosen me as their ruler." He claimed that it was impossible that forgiveness should be granted to the sinner, and therefore the fallen race were his rightful subjects, and the world was his. But God gave His own dear Son— one equal with Himself—to bear the penalty of transgression, and thus He provided a way by which they might be restored to His favor, and brought back to their Eden home. Christ undertook to redeem man and to rescue the world from the grasp of Satan. The great controversy begun in heaven was to be decided in the very world, on the very same field, that Satan claimed as his.

It was the marvel of all the universe that Christ should humble Himself to save fallen man. That He who had passed from star to star, from world to world, superintending all, by His providence supplying the needs of every order of being in His vast creation—that He should consent to leave His glory and take upon Himself human nature, was a mystery which the sinless intelligences of other worlds desired to understand. When Christ came to our world in the form of humanity, all were intensely interested in following Him as He traversed, step by step, the bloodstained path from the manger to Calvary. Heaven marked the insult and mockery that He received, and knew that it was at Satan's instigation. They marked the work of counteragencies going forward; Satan constantly pressing darkness, sorrow, and suffering upon the race, and Christ counteracting it. They watched the battle between light and darkness as it waxed stronger. And as Christ in His expiring agony upon the cross cried out, "It is finished" (John 19:30), a shout of triumph rang through every world and through heaven itself. The great contest that had been so long in progress in this world was now decided, and Christ was conqueror. His death had answered the question whether the Father and the Son had sufficient love for man to exercise self-denial and a spirit of sacrifice. Satan had revealed his true character as a liar and a murderer. It was seen that the very same spirit with which he had ruled the children of men who were under his power, he would have manifested if permitted to control the intelligences of heaven. With one voice the loyal universe united in extolling the divine administration.

If the law could be changed, man might have been saved without the sacrifice of Christ; but the fact that it was necessary for Christ to give His life for the fallen race, proves that the law of God will not release the sinner from its claims upon him. It is demonstrated that the wages of sin is death. When Christ died, the destruction of Satan was made certain. But if the law was abolished at the cross, as many claim, then the agony and death of God's dear Son were endured only to give to Satan just what he asked; then the prince of evil triumphed, his charges against the divine government were sustained. The very fact that Christ bore the penalty of man's transgression is a mighty argument to all created intelligences that the law is changeless; that God is righteous, merciful, and self-denying; and that infinite justice and mercy unite in the administration of His government.

Cain and Abel Tested

Cain and Abel, the sons of Adam, differed widely in character. Abel had a spirit of loyalty to God; he saw justice and mercy in the Creator's dealings with the fallen race, and gratefully accepted the hope of redemption. But Cain cherished feelings of rebellion, and murmured against God because of the curse pronounced upon the earth and upon the human race for Adam's sin. He permitted his mind to run in the same channel that led to Satan's fall—indulging the desire for self-exaltation and questioning the divine justice and authority.

These brothers were tested, as Adam had been tested before them, to prove whether they would believe and obey the word of God. They were acquainted with the provision made for the salvation of man, and understood the system of offerings which God had ordained. They knew that in these offerings they were to express faith in the Saviour whom the offerings typified, and at the same time to acknowledge their total dependence on Him for pardon; and they knew that by thus conforming to the divine plan for their redemption, they were giving proof of their obedience to the will of God. Without the shedding of blood there could be no remission of sin; and they were to show their faith in the blood of Christ as the promised atonement by offering the firstlings of the flock in sacrifice. Besides this, the first fruits of the earth were to be presented before the Lord as a thank offering.

The two brothers erected their altars alike, and each brought an offering. Abel presented a sacrifice from the flock, in accordance with the Lord's directions. "And the Lord had respect unto Abel and to his offering." Fire flashed from heaven and consumed the sacrifice. But Cain, disregarding the Lord's direct and explicit command, presented only an offering of fruit. There was no token from heaven to show that it was accepted. Abel pleaded with his brother to approach God in the divinely prescribed way, but his entreaties only made Cain the more determined to follow his own will. As the eldest, he felt above being admonished by his brother, and despised his counsel.

Cain came before God with murmuring and infidelity in his heart in regard to the promised sacrifice and the necessity of the sacrificial offerings. His gift expressed no penitence for sin. He felt, as many now feel, that it would be an acknowledgment of weakness to follow the exact plan marked out by God, of trusting his salvation wholly to the atonement of the promised Saviour. He chose the course of self-dependence. He would come in his own merits. He would not bring the lamb, and mingle its blood with his offering, but would present his fruits, the products of his labor. He presented his offering as a favor done to God, through which he expected to secure the divine approval. Cain obeyed in building an altar, obeyed in bringing a sacrifice; but he rendered only a partial obedience. The essential part, the recognition of the need of a Redeemer, was left out.

So far as birth and religious instruction were concerned, these brothers were equal. Both were sinners, and both acknowledged the claims of God to reverence and worship. To outward appearance their religion was the same up to a certain point, but beyond this the difference between the two was great.

"By faith Abel offered unto God a more excellent sacrifice than Cain." Hebrews 11:4. Abel grasped the great principles of redemption. He saw himself a sinner, and he saw sin and its penalty, death, standing between his soul and communion with God. He brought the slain victim, the sacrificed life, thus acknowledging the claims of the law that had been transgressed. Through the shed blood he looked to the future sacrifice, Christ dying on the cross of Calvary; and trusting in the atonement that was there to be made, he had the witness that he was righteous, and his offering accepted.

Cain had the same opportunity of learning and accepting these truths as had Abel. He was not the victim of an arbitrary purpose. One brother was not elected to be accepted of God, and the other to be rejected. Abel chose faith and obedience; Cain, unbelief and rebellion. Here the whole matter rested.

Cain and Abel represent two classes that will exist in the world till the close of time. One class avail themselves of the appointed sacrifice for sin; the other venture to depend upon their own merits; theirs is a sacrifice without the virtue of divine mediation, and thus it is not able to bring man into favor with God. It is only through the merits of Jesus that our transgressions can be pardoned. Those who feel no need of the blood of Christ, who feel that without divine grace they can by their own works secure the approval of God, are making the same mistake as did Cain. If they do not accept the cleansing blood, they are under condemnation. There is no other provision made whereby they can be released from the thralldom of sin.

The class of worshipers who follow the example of Cain includes by far the greater portion of the world; for nearly every false religion has been based on the same principle—that man can depend upon his own efforts for salvation. It is claimed by some that the human race is in need, not of

redemption, but of development—that it can refine, elevate, and regenerate itself. As Cain thought to secure the divine favor by an offering that lacked the blood of a sacrifice, so do these expect to exalt humanity to the divine standard, independent of the atonement. The history of Cain shows what must be the results. It shows what man will become apart from Christ. Humanity has no power to regenerate itself. It does not tend upward, toward the divine, but downward, toward the satanic. Christ is our only hope. "There is none other name under heaven given among men, whereby we must be saved." "Neither is there salvation in any other." Acts 4:12.

True faith, which relies wholly upon Christ, will be manifested by obedience to all the requirements of God. From Adam's day to the present time the great controversy has been concerning obedience to God's law. In all ages there have been those who claimed a right to the favor of God even while they were disregarding some of His commands. But the Scriptures declare that by works is "faith made perfect;" and that, without the works of obedience, faith "is dead." James 2:22, 17. He that professes to know God, "and keepeth not His commandments, is a liar, and the truth is not in him." 1 John 2:4.

When Cain saw that his offering was rejected, he was angry with the Lord and with Abel; he was angry that God did not accept man's substitute in place of the sacrifice divinely ordained, and angry with his brother for choosing to obey God instead of joining in rebellion against Him. Notwithstanding Cain's disregard of the divine command, God did not leave him to himself; but He condescended to reason with the man who had shown himself so unreasonable. And the Lord said unto Cain, "Why art thou wroth? and why is thy countenance fallen?" Through an angel messenger the divine warning was conveyed: "If thou doest well, shalt thou not be accepted? And if thou doest not well, sin lieth at the door." The choice lay with Cain himself. If he would trust to the merits of the promised Saviour, and would obey God's requirements, he would enjoy His favor. But should he persist in unbelief and transgression, he would have no ground for complaint because he was rejected by the Lord.

But instead of acknowledging his sin, Cain continued to complain of the injustice of God and to cherish jealousy and hatred of Abel. He angrily reproached his brother, and attempted to draw him into controversy concerning God's dealings with them. In meekness, yet fearlessly and firmly, Abel defended the justice and goodness of God. He pointed out Cain's error, and tried to convince him that the wrong was in himself. He pointed to the compassion of God in sparing the life of their parents when He might have punished them with instant death, and urged that God loved them, or He would not have given His Son, innocent and holy, to suffer the penalty which they had incurred. All this caused Cain's anger to burn the hotter. Reason and conscience told him that Abel was in the right; but he was enraged that one who had been wont to heed his counsel should now presume to disagree with him, and that he could gain no sympathy in his rebellion. In the fury of his passion he slew his brother.

Cain hated and killed his brother, not for any wrong that Abel had done, but "because his own works were evil, and his brother's righteous." 1 John 3:12. So in all ages the wicked have hated those who were better than themselves. Abel's life of obedience and unswerving faith was to Cain a perpetual reproof. "Everyone that doeth evil hateth the light, neither cometh to the light, lest his deeds should be reproved." John 3:20. The brighter the heavenly light that is reflected from the character of God's faithful servants, the more clearly the sins of the ungodly are revealed, and the more determined will be their efforts to destroy those who disturb their peace.

The murder of Abel was the first example of the enmity that God had declared would exist between the serpent and the seed of the woman—between Satan and his subjects and Christ and His followers. Through man's sin, Satan had gained control of the human race, but Christ would enable them to cast off his yoke. Whenever, through faith in the Lamb of God, a soul renounces the service of sin, Satan's wrath is kindled. The holy life of Abel testified against Satan's claim that it is impossible for man to keep God's law. When Cain, moved by the spirit of the wicked one, saw that he could not control Abel, he was so enraged that he destroyed his life. And wherever there are any who will stand in vindication of the righteousness of the law of God, the same spirit will be manifested against them. It is the spirit that through all the ages has set up the stake and kindled the burning pile for the disciples of Christ. But the cruelties heaped upon the follower of Jesus are instigated by Satan and his hosts because they cannot force him to submit to their control. It is the rage of a vanquished foe. Every martyr of Jesus has died a conqueror. Says the prophet, "They overcame him by the blood of the Lamb, and by the word of their testimony; and they loved not their lives unto the death." Revelation 12:11, 9.

Cain the murderer was soon called to answer for his crime. "The Lord said unto Cain, Where is Abel thy brother? And he said, I know not: Am I my brother's keeper?" Cain had gone so far in sin that he had lost a sense of the continual presence of God and of His greatness and omniscience. So he resorted to falsehood to conceal his guilt.

Again the Lord said to Cain, "What hast thou done? The voice of thy brother's blood crieth unto Me from the ground." God had given Cain an opportunity to confess his sin. He had had time to reflect. He knew the enormity of the deed he had done, and of the falsehood he had uttered to conceal it; but he was rebellious still, and sentence was no longer deferred. The divine voice that had been heard in entreaty and admonition pronounced the terrible words: "And now art thou cursed from the earth, which hath opened her mouth to receive thy brother's blood from thy hand. When thou tillest the ground, it shall not henceforth yield unto thee her strength; a fugitive and a vagabond shalt thou be in the earth."

Notwithstanding that Cain had by his crimes merited the sentence of death, a merciful Creator still spared his life, and granted him opportunity for repentance. But Cain lived only to harden his heart, to encourage rebellion against the divine authority, and to become the head of a line of bold, abandoned sinners. This one apostate, led on by Satan, became a tempter to others; and his example and influence exerted their demoralizing power, until the earth became so corrupt and filled with violence as to call for its destruction.

In sparing the life of the first murderer, God presented before the whole universe a lesson bearing upon the great controversy. The dark history of Cain and his descendants was an illustration of what would have been the result of permitting the sinner to live on forever, to carry out his rebellion against God. The forbearance of God only rendered the wicked more bold and defiant in their iniquity. Fifteen centuries after the sentence pronounced upon Cain, the universe witnessed the fruition of his influence and example, in the crime and pollution that flooded the earth. It was made manifest that the sentence of death pronounced upon the fallen race for the transgression of God's law was both just and merciful. The longer men lived in sin, the more abandoned they became. The divine sentence cutting short a career of unbridled iniquity, and freeing the world from the influence of those who had become hardened in rebellion, was a blessing rather than a curse.

Satan is constantly at work, with intense energy and under a thousand disguises, to misrepresent the character and government of God. With extensive, well-organized plans and marvelous power, he is working to hold the inhabitants of the world under his deceptions. God, the One infinite and all-wise, sees the end from the beginning, and in dealing with evil His plans were far-reaching and comprehensive. It was His purpose, not merely to put down the rebellion, but to demonstrate to all the universe the nature of the rebellion. God's plan was unfolding, showing both His justice and His mercy, and fully vindicating His wisdom and righteousness in His dealings with evil.

The holy inhabitants of other worlds were watching with the deepest interest the events taking place on the earth. In the condition of the world that existed before the Flood they saw illustrated the results of the administration which Lucifer had endeavored to establish in heaven, in rejecting the authority of Christ and casting aside the law of God. In those high-handed sinners of the antediluvian world they saw the subjects over whom Satan held sway. The thoughts of men's hearts were only evil continually. Genesis 6:5. Every emotion, every impulse and imagination, was at war with the divine principles of purity and peace and love. It was an example of the awful depravity resulting from Satan's policy to remove from God's creatures the restraint of His holy law.

By the facts unfolded in the progress of the great controversy, God will demonstrate the principles of His rules of government, which have been falsified by Satan and by all whom he has deceived. His justice will finally be acknowledged by the whole world, though the acknowledgment will be made too late to save the rebellious. God carries with Him the sympathy and approval of the whole universe as step by step His great plan advances to its complete fulfillment. He will carry it with Him in the final eradication of rebellion. It will be seen that all who have forsaken the divine precepts have placed themselves on the side of Satan, in warfare against Christ. When the prince of this world shall be judged, and all who have united with him shall share his fate, the whole universe as witnesses to the sentence will declare, "Just and true are Thy ways, Thou King of saints." Revelation 15:3.

Seth and Enoch

To Adam was given another son, to be the inheritor of the divine promise, the heir of the spiritual birthright. The name Seth, given to this son, signified "appointed," or "compensation;" "for," said the mother, "God hath appointed me another seed instead of Abel, whom Cain slew." Seth was of more noble stature than Cain or Abel, and resembled Adam more closely than did his other sons. He was a worthy character, following in the steps of Abel. Yet he inherited no more natural goodness than did Cain. Concerning the creation of Adam it is said, "In the likeness of God made He him;" but man, after the Fall, "begat a son in his own likeness, after his image." While Adam was created sinless, in the likeness of God, Seth, like Cain, inherited the fallen nature of his parents. But he received also the knowledge of the Redeemer and instruction in righteousness. By divine grace he served and honored God; and he labored, as Abel would have done, had he lived, to turn the minds of sinful men to revere and obey their Creator.

"To Seth, to him also there was born a son; and he called his name Enos: then began men to call upon the name of Jehovah." The faithful had worshiped God before; but as men increased, the distinction between the two classes became more marked. There was an open profession of loyalty to God on the part of one, as there was of contempt and disobedience on the part of the other.

Before the Fall our first parents had kept the Sabbath, which was instituted in Eden; and after their expulsion from Paradise they continued its observance. They had tasted the bitter fruits of disobedience, and had learned what every one that tramples upon God's commandments will sooner or later learn—that the divine precepts are sacred and immutable, and that the penalty of transgression will surely be inflicted. The Sabbath was honored by all the children of Adam that remained loyal to God. But Cain and his descendants did not respect the day upon which God had rested. They chose their own time for labor and for rest, regardless of Jehovah's express command.

Upon receiving the curse of God, Cain had withdrawn from his father's household. He had first chosen his occupation as a tiller of the soil, and he now founded a city, calling it after the name of his eldest son. He had gone out from the presence of the Lord, cast away the promise of the restored Eden, to seek his possessions and enjoyment in the earth under the curse of sin, thus standing at the head of that great class of men who worship the god of this world. In that which pertains to mere earthly and material progress, his descendants became distinguished. But they were regardless of God, and in opposition to His purposes for man. To the crime of murder, in which Cain had led the way, Lamech, the fifth in descent, added polygamy, and, boastfully defiant, he acknowledged God, only to draw from the avenging of Cain an assurance of his own safety. Abel had led a pastoral life, dwelling in tents or booths, and the descendants of Seth followed the same course, counting themselves "strangers and pilgrims on the earth," seeking "a better country, that is, an heavenly." Hebrews 11:13, 16.

For some time the two classes remained separate. The race of Cain, spreading from the place of their first settlement, dispersed over the plains and valleys where the children of Seth had dwelt; and the latter, in order to escape from their contaminating influence, withdrew to the mountains, and there made their home. So long as this separation continued, they maintained the worship of God in its purity. But in the lapse of time they ventured, little by little, to mingle with the inhabitants of the valleys. This association was productive of the worst results. "The sons of God saw the daughters of men that they were fair." The children of Seth, attracted by the beauty of the daughters of Cain's descendants, displeased the Lord by intermarrying with them. Many of the worshipers of God were beguiled into sin by the allurements that were now constantly before them, and they lost their peculiar, holy character. Mingling with the depraved, they became like them in spirit and in deeds; the restrictions of the seventh commandment were disregarded, "and they took them wives of all which they chose." The children of Seth went "in the way of Cain" (Jude 11); they fixed their minds upon worldly prosperity and enjoyment and neglected the commandments of the Lord. Men "did not like to retain God in their knowledge;" they "became vain in their imaginations, and their foolish heart was darkened." Romans 1:21. Therefore "God gave them over to a mind void of judgment." Verse 28, margin. Sin spread abroad in the earth like a deadly leprosy.

For nearly a thousand years Adam lived among men, a witness to the results of sin. Faithfully he sought to stem the tide of evil. He had been commanded to instruct his posterity in the way of the Lord; and he carefully treasured what God had revealed to him, and repeated it to succeeding generations. To his children and children's children, to the ninth generation, he described man's holy and happy estate in Paradise, and repeated the history of his fall, telling them of the sufferings by which God had taught him the necessity of strict adherence to His law, and explaining to them the merciful provisions for their salvation. Yet there were but few who gave heed to his words. Often he was met with bitter reproaches for the sin that had brought such woe upon his posterity.

Adam's life was one of sorrow, humility, and contrition. When he left Eden, the thought that he must die thrilled him with horror. He was first made acquainted with the reality of death in the human family when Cain, his first-born son, became the murderer of his brother. Filled with the keenest remorse for his own sin, and doubly bereaved in the death of Abel and the rejection of Cain, Adam was bowed down with anguish. He witnessed the wide-spreading corruption that was finally to cause the destruction of the world by a flood; and though the sentence of death pronounced upon him by His Maker had at first appeared terrible, yet after beholding for nearly a thousand years the results of sin, he felt that it was merciful in God to bring to an end a life of suffering and sorrow.

Notwithstanding the wickedness of the antediluvian world, that age was not, as has often been supposed, an era of ignorance and barbarism. The people were granted the opportunity of reaching a high standard of moral and intellectual attainment. They possessed great physical and mental strength, and their advantages for acquiring both religious and scientific knowledge were unrivaled. It is a mistake to suppose that because they lived to a great age their minds matured late; their mental powers were early developed, and those who cherished the fear of God and lived in harmony with His will continued to increase in knowledge and wisdom throughout their life. Could illustrious scholars of our time be placed in contrast with men of the same age who lived before the Flood, they would appear as greatly inferior in mental as in physical strength. As the years of man have decreased, and his physical strength has diminished, so his mental capacities have lessened. There are men who now apply themselves to study during a period of from twenty to fifty years, and the world is filled with admiration of their attainments. But how limited are these acquirements in comparison with those of men whose mental and physical powers were developing for centuries!

It is true that the people of modern times have the benefit of the attainments of their predecessors. The men of masterly minds, who planned and studied and wrote, have left their work for those who follow. But even in this respect, and so far as merely human knowledge is concerned, how much greater the advantages of the men of that olden time! They had among them for hundreds of years him who was formed in God's image, whom the Creator Himself pronounced "good"—the man whom God had instructed in all the wisdom pertaining to the material world. Adam had learned from the Creator the history of creation; he himself witnessed the events of nine centuries; and he imparted his knowledge to his descendants. The antediluvians were without books, they had no written records; but with their great physical and mental vigor, they had strong memories, able to grasp and to retain that which was communicated to them, and in turn to transmit it unimpaired to their posterity. And for hundreds of years there were seven generations living upon the earth contemporaneously, having the opportunity of consulting together and profiting each by the knowledge and experience of all.

The advantages enjoyed by men of that age to gain a knowledge of God through His works have never been equaled since. And so far from being an era of religious darkness, that was an age of great light. All the world had opportunity to receive instruction from Adam, and those who feared the Lord had also Christ and angels for their teachers. And they had a silent witness to the truth, in the garden of God, which for so many centuries remained among men. At the cherubim-guarded gate of Paradise the glory of God was revealed, and hither came the first worshipers. Here their altars were reared, and their offerings presented. It was here that Cain and Abel had brought their sacrifices, and God had condescended to communicate with them.

Skepticism could not deny the existence of Eden while it stood just in sight, its entrance barred by watching angels. The order of creation, the object of the garden, the history of its two trees so closely connected with man's destiny, were undisputed facts. And the existence and supreme authority of God, the obligation of His law, were truths which men were slow to question while Adam was among them.

Notwithstanding the prevailing iniquity, there was a line of holy men who, elevated and ennobled by communion with God, lived as in the companionship of heaven. They were men of massive intellect, of wonderful attainments. They had a great and holy mission—to develop a character of righteousness, to teach a lesson of godliness, not only to the men of their time, but for future generations. Only a few of the most prominent are mentioned in the Scriptures; but all through the ages God had faithfully witnesses, truehearted worshipers.

Of Enoch it is written that he lived sixty-five years, and begat a son. After that he walked with God three hundred years. During these earlier years Enoch had loved and feared God and had kept His commandments. He was one of the holy line, the preservers of the true faith, the progenitors of the promised seed. From the lips of Adam he had learned the dark story of the Fall, and the cheering one of God's grace as seen in the promise; and he relied upon the Redeemer to come. But after the birth of his first son, Enoch reached a higher experience; he was drawn into a closer relationship with God. He realized more fully his own obligations and responsibility as a son of God. And as he saw the child's love for its father, its simple trust in his protection; as he felt the deep, yearning tenderness of his own heart for that first-born son, he learned a precious lesson of the wonderful love of God to men in the gift of His Son, and the confidence which the children of God may repose in their heavenly Father. The infinite, unfathomable love of God through Christ became the subject of his meditations day and night; and with all the fervor of his soul he sought to reveal that love to the people among whom he dwelt.

Enoch's walk with God was not in a trance or vision, but in all the duties of his daily life. He did not become a hermit, shutting himself entirely from the world; for he had a work to do for God in the world. In the family and in his intercourse with men, as a husband and father, a friend, a citizen, he was the steadfast, unwavering servant of the Lord.

His heart was in harmony with God's will; for "can two walk together, except they be agreed?" Amos 3:3. And this holy walk was continued for three hundred years. There are few Christians who would not be far more earnest and devoted if they knew that they had but a short time to live, or that the coming of Christ was about to take place. But Enoch's faith waxed the stronger, his love became more ardent, with the lapse of centuries.

Enoch was a man of strong and highly cultivated mind and extensive knowledge; he was honored with special revelations from God; yet being in constant communion with Heaven, with a sense of the divine greatness and perfection ever before him, he was one of the humblest of men. The closer the connection with God, the deeper was the sense of his own weakness and imperfection.

Distressed by the increasing wickedness of the ungodly, and fearing that their infidelity might lessen his reverence for God, Enoch avoided constant association with them, and spent much time in solitude, giving himself to meditation and prayer. Thus he waited before the Lord, seeking a clearer knowledge of His will, that he might perform it. To him prayer was as the breath of the soul; he lived in the very atmosphere of heaven.

Through holy angels God revealed to Enoch His purpose to destroy the world by a flood, and He also opened more fully to him the plan of redemption. By the spirit of prophecy He carried him down through the generations that should live after the Flood, and showed him the great events connected with the second coming of Christ and the end of the world.

Enoch had been troubled in regard to the dead. It had seemed to him that the righteous and the wicked would go to the dust together, and that this would be their end. He could not see the life of the just beyond the grave. In prophetic vision he was instructed concerning the death of Christ, and was shown His coming in glory, attended by all the holy angels, to ransom His people from the grave. He also saw the corrupt state of the world when Christ should appear the second time—that there would be a boastful, presumptuous, self-willed generation, denying the only God and the Lord Jesus Christ, trampling upon the law, and despising the atonement. He saw the righteous crowned with glory and honor, and the wicked banished from the presence of the Lord, and destroyed by fire.

Enoch became a preacher of righteousness, making known to the people what God had revealed to him. Those who feared the Lord sought out this holy man, to share his instruction and his prayers. He labored publicly also, bearing God's messages to all who would hear the words or warning. His labors were not restricted to the Sethites. In the land where Cain had sought to flee from the divine Presence, the prophet of God made known the wonderful scenes that had passed before his vision. "Behold," he declared, "the Lord cometh with ten thousands of His saints, to execute judgment upon all, and to convince all that are ungodly among them of all their ungodly deeds." Jude 14, 15.

He was a fearless reprover of sin. While he preached the love of God in Christ to the people of his time, and pleaded with them to forsake their evil ways, he rebuked the prevailing iniquity and warned the men of his generation that judgment would surely be visited upon the transgressor. It was the Spirit of Christ that spoke through Enoch; that Spirit is manifested, not alone in utterances of love, compassion, and entreaty; it is not smooth things only that are spoken by holy men. God puts into the heart and lips of His messengers truths to utter that are keen and cutting as a two-edged sword.

The power of God that wrought with His servant was felt by those who heard. Some gave heed to the warning, and renounced their sins; but the multitudes mocked at the solemn message, and went on more boldly in their evil ways. The servants of God are to bear a similar message to the world in the last days, and it will also be received with unbelief and mockery. The antediluvian world rejected the warning words of him who walked with God. So will the last generation make light of the warnings of the Lord's messengers.

In the midst of a life of active labor, Enoch steadfastly maintained his communion with God. The greater and more pressing his labors, the more constant and earnest were his prayers. He continued to exclude himself, at certain periods, from all society. After remaining for a time among the people, laboring to benefit them by instruction and example, he would withdraw, to spend a season in solitude, hungering and thirsting for that divine knowledge which God alone can impart. Communing thus with God, Enoch came more and more to reflect the divine image. His face was radiant with a holy light, even the light that shineth in the face of Jesus. As he came forth from these divine communings, even the ungodly beheld with awe the impress of heaven upon his countenance.

The wickedness of men had reached such a height that destruction was pronounced against them. As year after year passed on, deeper and deeper grew the tide of human guilt, darker and darker gathered the clouds of divine judgment. Yet Enoch, the witness of faith, held on his way, warning, pleading, entreating, striving to turn back the tide of guilt and to stay the bolts of vengeance. Though his warnings were disregarded by a sinful, pleasure-loving people, he had the testimony that God approved, and he continued to battle faithfully against the prevailing evil, until God removed him from a world of sin to the pure joys of heaven.

The men of that generation had mocked the folly of him who sought not to gather gold or silver or to build up possessions here. But Enoch's heart was upon eternal treasures. He had looked upon the celestial city. He had seen the King in His glory in the midst of Zion. His mind, his heart, his conversation, were in heaven. The greater the existing iniquity, the more earnest was his longing for the home of

God. While still on earth, he dwelt, by faith, in the realms of light.

"Blessed are the pure in heart: for they shall see God." Matthew 5:8. For three hundred years Enoch had been seeking purity of soul, that he might be in harmony with Heaven. For three centuries he had walked with God. Day by day he had longed for a closer union; nearer and nearer had grown the communion, until God took him to Himself. He had stood at the threshold of the eternal world, only a step between him and the land of the blest; and now the portals opened, the walk with God, so long pursued on earth, continued, and he passed through the gates of the Holy City—the first from among men to enter there.

His loss was felt on earth. The voice that had been heard day after day in warning and instruction was missed. There were some, both of the righteous and the wicked, who had witnessed his departure; and hoping that he might have been conveyed to some one of his places of retirement, those who loved him made diligent search, as afterward the sons of the prophets searched for Elijah; but without avail. They reported that he was not, for God had taken him.

By the translation of Enoch the Lord designed to teach an important lesson. There was danger that men would yield to discouragement, because of the fearful results of Adam's sin. Many were ready to exclaim, "What profit is it that we have feared the Lord and have kept His ordinances, since a heavy curse is resting upon the race, and death is the portion of us all?" But the instructions which God gave to Adam, and which were repeated by Seth, and exemplified by Enoch, swept away the gloom and darkness, and gave hope to man, that as through Adam came death, so through the promised Redeemer would come life and immortality. Satan was urging upon men the belief that there was no reward for the righteous or punishment for the wicked, and that it was impossible for men to obey the divine statutes. But in the case of Enoch, God declares "that He is, and that He is a rewarder of them that diligently seek Him." Hebrews 11:6. He shows what He will do for those who keep His commandments. Men were taught that it is possible to obey the law of God; that even while living in the midst of the sinful and corrupt, they were able, by the grace of God, to resist temptation, and become pure and holy. They saw in his example the blessedness of such a life; and his translation was an evidence of the truth of his prophecy concerning the hereafter, with its award of joy and glory and immortal life to the obedient, and of condemnation, woe, and death to the transgressor.

By faith Enoch "was translated that he should not see death; . . . for before his translation he had this testimony, that he pleased God." Hebrews 11:5. In the midst of a world by its iniquity doomed to destruction, Enoch lived a life of such close communion with God that he was not permitted to fall under the power of death. The godly character of this prophet represents the state of holiness which must be attained by those who shall be "redeemed from the earth" (Revelation 14:3) at the time of Christ's second advent. Then, as in the world before the Flood, iniquity will prevail. Following the promptings of their corrupt hearts and the teachings of a deceptive philosophy, men will rebel against the authority of Heaven. But like Enoch, God's people will seek for purity of heart and conformity to His will, until they shall reflect the likeness of Christ. Like Enoch, they will warn the world of the Lord's second coming and of the judgments to be visited upon transgression, and by their holy conversation and example they will condemn the sins of the ungodly. As Enoch was translated to heaven before the destruction of the world by water, so the living righteous will be translated from the earth before its destruction by fire. Says the apostle: "We shall not all sleep, but we shall all be changed, in a moment, in the twinkling of an eye, at the last trump." "For the Lord Himself shall descend from heaven with a shout, with the voice of the Archangel, and with the trump of God;" "the trumpet shall sound, and the dead shall be raised incorruptible, and we shall be changed." "The dead in Christ shall rise first: then we which are alive and remain shall be caught up together with them in the clouds, to meet the Lord in the air: and so shall we ever be with the Lord. Wherefore comfort one another with these words." 1 Corinthians 15:51, 52; 1 Thessalonians 4:16-18.

The Flood

In the days of Noah a double curse was resting upon the earth in consequence of Adam's transgression and of the murder committed by Cain. Yet this had not greatly changed the face of nature. There were evident tokens of decay, but the earth was still rich and beautiful in the gifts of God's providence. The hills were crowned with majestic trees supporting the fruit-laden branches of the vine. The vast, gardenlike plains were clothed with verdure, and sweet with the fragrance of a thousand flowers. The fruits of the earth were in great variety, and almost without limit. The trees far surpassed in size, beauty, and perfect proportion any now to be found; their wood was of fine grain and hard substance, closely resembling stone, and hardly less enduring. Gold, silver, and precious stones existed in abundance.

The human race yet retained much of its early vigor. But a few generations had passed since Adam had access to the tree which was to prolong life; and man's existence was still measured by centuries. Had that long-lived people, with their rare powers to plan and execute, devoted themselves to the service of God, they would have made their Creator's name a praise in the earth, and would have answered the purpose for which He gave them life. But they failed to do this. There were many giants, men of great stature and strength, renowned for wisdom, skillful in devising the most cunning and wonderful works; but their guilt in giving loose rein to iniquity was in proportion to their skill and mental ability.

God bestowed upon these antediluvians many and rich gifts; but they used His bounties to glorify themselves, and turned them into a curse by fixing their affections upon the gifts instead of the Giver. They employed the gold and silver, the precious stones and the choice wood, in the construction of habitations for themselves, and endeavored to excel one another in beautifying their dwellings with the most skillful workmanship. They sought only to gratify the desires of their own proud hearts, and reveled in scenes of pleasure and wickedness. Not desiring to retain God in their knowledge, they soon came to deny His existence. They adored nature in place of the God of nature. They glorified human genius, worshiped the works of their own hands, and taught their children to bow down to graven images.

In the green fields and under the shadow of the goodly trees they set up the altars of their idols. Extensive groves, that retained their foliage throughout the year, were dedicated to the worship of false gods. With these groves were connected beautiful gardens, their long, winding avenues overhung with fruit-bearing trees of all descriptions, adorned with statuary, and furnished with all that could delight the senses or minister to the voluptuous desires of the people, and thus allure them to participate in the idolatrous worship.

Men put God out of their knowledge and worshiped the creatures of their own imagination; and as the result, they became more and more debased. The psalmist describes the effect produced upon the worshiper by the adoration of idols. He says, "They that make them are like unto them; so is every one that trusteth in them." Psalm 115:8. It is a law of the human mind that by beholding we become changed. Man will rise no higher than his conceptions of truth, purity, and holiness. If the mind is never exalted above the level of humanity, if it is not uplifted by faith to contemplate infinite wisdom and love, the man will be constantly sinking lower and lower. The worshipers of false gods clothed their deities with human attributes and passions, and thus their standard of character was degraded to the likeness of sinful humanity. They were defiled in consequence. "God saw that the wickedness of man was great in the earth, and that every imagination of the thoughts of his heart was only evil continually. . . . The earth also was corrupt before God; and the earth was filled with violence." God had given men His commandments as a rule of life, but His law was transgressed, and every conceivable sin was the result. The wickedness of men was open and daring, justice was trampled in the dust, and the cries of the oppressed reached unto heaven.

Polygamy had been early introduced, contrary to the divine arrangement at the beginning. The Lord gave to Adam one wife, showing His order in that respect. But after the Fall, men chose to follow their own sinful desires; and as the result, crime and wretchedness rapidly increased. Neither the marriage relation nor the rights of property were respected. Whoever coveted the wives or the possessions of his neighbor, took them by force, and men exulted in their deeds of violence. They delighted in destroying the life of animals; and the use of flesh for food rendered them still more cruel and bloodthirsty, until they came to regard human life with astonishing indifference.

The world was in its infancy; yet iniquity had become so deep and widespread that God could no longer bear with it; and He said, "I will destroy man whom I have created from the face of the earth." He declared that His Spirit should not always strive with the guilty race. If they did not cease to pollute with their sins the world and its rich treasures, He would blot them from His creation, and would destroy the things with which He had delighted to bless them; He would sweep away the beasts of the field, and the vegetation which furnished such an abundant supply of food, and would transform the fair earth into one vast scene of desolation and ruin.

Amid the prevailing corruption, Methuselah, Noah, and many others labored to keep alive the knowledge of the true God and to stay the tide of moral evil. A hundred and twenty years before the Flood, the Lord by a holy angel declared to Noah His purpose, and directed him to build an ark. While building the ark he was to preach that God would bring a flood of water upon the earth to destroy the wicked. Those who would believe the message, and would prepare for that event by repentance and reformation, should find pardon and be saved. Enoch had repeated to his children what God had shown him in regard to the Flood, and Methuselah and his sons, who lived to hear the preaching of Noah, assisted in building the ark.

God gave Noah the exact dimensions of the ark and explicit directions in regard to its construction in every particular. Human wisdom could not have devised a structure of so great strength and durability. God was the designer, and Noah the master builder. It was constructed like the hull of a ship, that it might float upon the water, but in some respects it more nearly resembled a house. It was three stories high, with but one door, which was in the side. The light was admitted at the top, and the different apartments were so arranged that all were lighted. The material employed in the construction of the ark was the cypress, or gopher wood, which would be untouched by decay for hundreds of years. The building of this immense structure was a slow and laborious process. On account of the great size of the trees and the nature of the wood, much more labor was required then than now to prepare timber, even with the greater strength which men then possessed. All that man could do was done to render the work perfect, yet the ark could not of itself have withstood the storm which was to come upon the earth. God alone could preserve His servants upon the tempestuous waters.

"By faith Noah, being warned of God of things not seen as yet, moved with fear, prepared an ark to the saving of his house; by the which he condemned the world, and became heir of the righteousness which is by faith." Hebrews 11:7. While Noah was giving his warning message to the world, his works testified of his sincerity. It was thus that his faith was perfected and made evident. He gave the world an example of believing just what God says. All that he possessed, he invested in the ark. As he began to construct that immense boat on dry ground, multitudes came from every direction to see the strange sight and to hear the earnest, fervent words of the singular preacher. Every blow struck upon the ark was a witness to the people.

Many at first appeared to receive the warning; yet they did not turn to God with true repentance. They were unwilling to renounce their sins. During the time that elapsed before the coming of the Flood, their faith was tested, and they failed to endure the trial. Overcome by the prevailing unbelief, they finally joined their former associates in rejecting the solemn message. Some were deeply convicted, and would have heeded the words of warning; but there were so many to jest and ridicule, that they partook of the same spirit, resisted the invitations of mercy, and were soon among the boldest and most defiant scoffers; for none are so reckless and go to such lengths in sin as do those who have once had light, but have resisted the convicting Spirit of God.

The men of that generation were not all, in the fullest acceptation of the term, idolaters. Many professed to be worshipers of God. They claimed that their idols were representations of the Deity, and that through them the people could obtain a clearer conception of the divine Being. This class were foremost in rejecting the preaching of Noah. As they endeavored to represent God by material objects, their minds were blinded to His majesty and power; they ceased to realize the holiness of His character, or the sacred, unchanging nature of His requirements. As sin became general, it appeared less and less sinful, and they finally declared that the divine law was no longer in force; that it was contrary to the character of God to punish transgression; and they denied that His judgments were to be visited upon the earth. Had the men of that generation obeyed the divine law, they would have recognized the voice of God in the warning of His servant; but their minds had become so blinded by rejection of light that they really believed Noah's message to be a delusion.

It was not multitudes or majorities that were on the side of right. The world was arrayed against God's justice and His laws, and Noah was regarded as a fanatic. Satan, when tempting Eve to disobey God, said to her, "Ye shall not surely die." Genesis 3:4. Great men, worldly, honored, and wise men, repeated the same. "The threatenings of God," they said, "are for the purpose of intimidating, and will never be verified. You need not be alarmed. Such an event as the destruction of the world by the God who made it, and the punishment of the beings He has created, will never take place. Be at peace; fear not. Noah is a wild fanatic." The world made merry at the folly of the deluded old man. Instead of humbling the heart before God, they continued their disobedience and wickedness, the same as though God had not spoken to them through His servant.

But Noah stood like a rock amid the tempest. Surrounded by popular contempt and ridicule, he distinguished himself by his holy integrity and unwavering faithfulness. A power attended his words, for it was the voice of God to man through His servant. Connection with God made him strong in the strength of infinite power, while for one hundred and twenty years his solemn voice fell upon the ears of that generation in regard to events, which, so far as human wisdom could judge, were impossible.

The world before the Flood reasoned that for centuries the laws of nature had been fixed. The recurring seasons had come in their order. Heretofore rain had never fallen; the earth had been watered by a mist or dew. The rivers had never yet passed their boundaries, but had borne their waters safely to the sea. Fixed decrees had kept the waters from overflowing their banks. But these reasoners did not recognize the hand of Him who had stayed the waters, saying, "Hitherto shalt thou come, but no further." Job 38:11.

As time passed on, with no apparent change in nature, men whose hearts had at times trembled with fear, began to be reassured. They reasoned, as many reason now, that nature is above the God of nature, and that her laws are so firmly established that God Himself could not change them. Reasoning that if the message of Noah were correct, nature would be turned out of her course, they made that message, in the minds of the world, a delusion—a grand deception. They manifested their contempt for the warning of God by doing just as they had done before the warning was given. They continued their festivities and their gluttonous feasts; they ate and drank, planted and builded, laying their plans in reference to advantages they hoped to gain in the future; and they went to greater lengths in wickedness, and in defiant disregard of God's requirements, to testify that they had no fear of the Infinite One. They asserted that if there were any truth in what Noah had said, the men of renown—the wise, the prudent, the great men—would understand the matter.

Had the antediluvians believed the warning, and repented of their evil deeds, the Lord would have turned aside His wrath, as He afterward did from Nineveh. But by their obstinate resistance to the reproofs of conscience and the warnings of God's prophet, that generation filled up the measure of their iniquity, and became ripe for destruction.

The period of their probation was about to expire. Noah had faithfully followed the instructions which he had received from God. The ark was finished in every part as the Lord had directed, and was stored with food for man and beast. And now the servant of God made his last solemn appeal to the people. With an agony of desire that words cannot express, he entreated them to seek a refuge while it might be found. Again they rejected his words, and raised their voices in jest and scoffing. Suddenly a silence fell upon the mocking throng. Beasts of every description, the fiercest as well as the most gentle, were seen coming from mountain and forest and quietly making their way toward the ark. A noise as of a rushing wind was heard, and lo, birds were flocking from all directions, their numbers darkening the heavens, and in perfect order they passed to the ark. Animals obeyed the command of God, while men were disobedient. Guided by holy angels, they "went in two and two unto Noah into the ark," and the clean beasts by sevens. The world looked on in wonder, some in fear. Philosophers were called upon to account for the singular occurrence, but in vain. It was a mystery which they could not fathom. But men had become so hardened by their persistent rejection of light that even this scene produced but a momentary impression. As the doomed race beheld the sun shining in its glory, and the earth clad in almost Eden beauty, they banished their rising fears by boisterous merriment, and by their deeds of violence they seemed to invite upon themselves the visitation of the already awakened wrath of God.

God commanded Noah, "Come thou and all thy house into the ark; for thee have I seen righteous before Me in this generation." Noah's warnings had been rejected by the world, but his influence and example resulted in blessings to his family. As a reward for his faithfulness and integrity, God saved all the members of his family with him. What encouragement to parental fidelity!

Mercy had ceased its pleadings for the guilty race. The beasts of the field and the birds of the air had entered the place of refuge. Noah and his household were within the ark, "and the Lord shut him in." A flash of dazzling light was seen, and a cloud of glory more vivid than the lightning descended from heaven and hovered before the entrance of the ark. The massive door, which it was impossible for those within to close, was slowly swung to its place by unseen hands. Noah was shut in, and the rejecters of God's mercy were shut out. The seal of Heaven was on that door; God had shut it, and God alone could open it. So when Christ shall cease His intercession for guilty men, before His coming in the clouds of heaven, the door of mercy will be shut. Then divine grace will no longer restrain the wicked, and Satan will have full control of those who have rejected mercy. They will endeavor to destroy God's people; but as Noah was shut into the ark, so the righteous will be shielded by divine power.

For seven days after Noah and his family entered the ark, there appeared no sign of the coming storm. During this period their faith was tested. It was a time of triumph to the world without. The apparent delay confirmed them in the belief that Noah's message was a delusion, and that the Flood would never come. Notwithstanding the solemn scenes which they had witnessed—the beasts and birds entering the ark, and the angel of God closing the door—they still continued their sport and revelry, even making a jest of these signal manifestations of God's power. They gathered in crowds about the ark, deriding its inmates with a daring violence which they had never ventured upon before.

But upon the eighth day dark clouds overspread the heavens. There followed the muttering of thunder and the flash of lightning. Soon large drops of rain began to fall. The world had never witnessed anything like this, and the hearts of men were struck with fear. All were secretly inquiring, "Can it be that Noah was in the right, and that the world is doomed to destruction?" Darker and darker grew the heavens, and faster came the falling rain. The beasts were roaming about in the wildest terror, and their discordant cries seemed to moan out their own destiny and the fate of man. Then "the fountains of the great deep" were "broken up, and the windows of heaven were opened." Water appeared to come from the clouds in mighty cataracts. Rivers broke away from their boundaries, and overflowed the valleys. Jets of water burst from the earth with indescribable force, throwing massive rocks hundreds of feet into the air, and these, in falling, buried themselves deep in the ground.

The people first beheld the destruction of the works of their own hands. Their splendid buildings, and the beautiful gardens and groves where they had placed their idols, were destroyed by lightning from heaven, and the ruins were scattered far and wide. The altars on which human sacrifices had been offered were torn down, and the worshipers were made to tremble at the power of the living God, and to know that it was their corruption and idolatry which had called down their destruction.

As the violence of the storm increased, trees, buildings, rocks, and earth were hurled in every direction. The terror of man and beast was beyond description. Above the roar of the tempest was heard the wailing of a people that had despised the authority of God. Satan himself, who was compelled to remain in the midst of the warring elements, feared for his own existence. He had delighted to control so powerful a race, and desired them to live to practice their abominations and continue their rebellion against the Ruler of heaven. He now uttered imprecations against God, charging Him with injustice and cruelty. Many of the people, like Satan, blasphemed God, and had they been able, they would have torn Him from the throne of power. Others were frantic with fear, stretching their hands toward the ark and pleading for admittance. But their entreaties were in vain. Conscience was at last aroused to know that there is a God who ruleth in the heavens. They called upon Him earnestly, but His ear was not open to their cry. In that terrible hour they saw that the transgression of God's law had caused their ruin. Yet while, through fear of punishment, they acknowledged their sin, they felt no true contrition, no abhorrence of evil. They would have returned to their defiance of Heaven, had the judgment been removed. So when God's judgments shall fall upon the earth before its deluge by fire, the impenitent will know just where and what their sin is—the despising of His holy law. Yet they will have no more true repentance than did the old-world sinners.

Some in their desperation endeavored to break into the ark, but the firm-made structure withstood their efforts. Some clung to the ark until they were borne away by the surging waters, or their hold was broken by collision with rocks and trees. The massive ark trembled in every fiber as it was beaten by the merciless winds and flung from billow to billow. The cries of the beasts within expressed their fear and pain. But amid the warring elements it continued to ride safely. Angels that excel in strength were commissioned to preserve it.

The beasts, exposed to the tempest, rushed toward man, as though expecting help from him. Some of the people bound their children and themselves upon powerful animals, knowing that these were tenacious of life, and would climb to the highest points to escape the rising waters. Some fastened themselves to lofty trees on the summit of hills or mountains; but the trees were uprooted, and with their burden of living beings were hurled into the seething billows. One spot after another that promised safety was abandoned. As the waters rose higher and higher, the people fled for refuge to the loftiest mountains. Often man and beast would struggle together for a foothold, until both were swept away.

From the highest peaks men looked abroad upon a shoreless ocean. The solemn warnings of God's servant no longer seemed a subject for ridicule and scorning. How those doomed sinners longed for the opportunities which they had slighted! How they pleaded for one hour's probation, one more privilege of mercy, one call from the lips of Noah! But the sweet voice of mercy was no more to be heard by them. Love, no less than justice, demanded that God's judgments should put a check on sin. The avenging waters swept over the last retreat, and the despisers of God perished in the black depths.

"By the word of God . . . the world that then was, being overflowed with water, perished: but the heavens and the earth, which are now, by the same word are kept in store, reserved unto fire against the day of judgment and perdition of ungodly men." 2 Peter 3:5-7. Another storm is coming. The earth will again be swept by the desolating wrath of God, and sin and sinners will be destroyed.

The sins that called for vengeance upon the antediluvian world exist today. The fear of God is banished from the hearts of men, and His law is treated with indifference and contempt. The intense worldliness of that generation is equaled by that of the generation now living. Said Christ, "As in the days that were before the Flood they were eating and drinking, marrying and giving in marriage, until the day that Noah entered into the ark, and knew not until the Flood came, and took them all away; so shall also the coming of the Son of man be." Matthew 24:38, 39. God did not condemn the antediluvians for eating and drinking; He had given them the fruits of the earth in great abundance to supply their physical wants. Their sin consisted in taking these gifts without gratitude to the Giver, and debasing themselves by indulging appetite without restraint. It was lawful for them to marry. Marriage was in God's order; it was one of the first institutions which He established. He gave special directions concerning this ordinance, clothing it with sanctity and beauty; but these directions were forgotten, and marriage was perverted and made to minister to passion.

A similar condition of things exists now. That which is lawful in itself is carried to excess. Appetite is indulged without restraint. Professed followers of Christ are today eating and drinking with the drunken, while their names stand in honored church records. Intemperance benumbs the moral and spiritual powers and prepares the way for indulgence of the lower passions. Multitudes feel under no moral obligation to curb their sensual desires, and they become the slaves of lust. Men are living for the pleasures of

sense; for this world and this life alone. Extravagance pervades all circles of society. Integrity is sacrificed for luxury and display. They that make haste to be rich pervert justice and oppress the poor, and "slaves and souls of men" are still bought and sold. Fraud and bribery and theft stalk unrebuked in high places and in low. The issues of the press teem with records of murder—crimes so cold-blooded and causeless that it seems as though every instinct of humanity were blotted out. And these atrocities have become of so common occurrence that they hardly elicit a comment or awaken surprise. The spirit of anarchy is permeating all nations, and the outbreaks that from time to time excite the horror of the world are but indications of the pent-up fires of passion and lawlessness that, having once escaped control, will fill the earth with woe and desolation. The picture which Inspiration has given of the antediluvian world represents too truly the condition to which modern society is fast hastening. Even now, in the present century, and in professedly Christian lands, there are crimes daily perpetrated as black and terrible as those for which the old-world sinners were destroyed.

Before the Flood God sent Noah to warn the world, that the people might be led to repentance, and thus escape the threatened destruction. As the time of Christ's second appearing draws near, the Lord sends His servants with a warning to the world to prepare for that great event. Multitudes have been living in transgression of God's law, and now He in mercy calls them to obey its sacred precepts. All who will put away their sins by repentance toward God and faith in Christ are offered pardon. But many feel that it requires too great a sacrifice to put away sin. Because their life does not harmonize with the pure principles of God's moral government, they reject His warnings and deny the authority of His law.

Of the vast population of the earth before the Flood, only eight souls believed and obeyed God's word through Noah. For a hundred and twenty years the preacher of righteousness warned the world of the coming destruction, but his message was rejected and despised. So it will be now. Before the Lawgiver shall come to punish the disobedient, transgressors are warned to repent, and return to their allegiance; but with the majority these warnings will be in vain. Says the apostle Peter, "There shall come in the last days scoffers, walking after their own lusts, and saying, Where is the promise of His coming? for since the fathers fell asleep, all things continue as they were from the beginning." 2 Peter 3:3, 4. Do we not hear these very words repeated, not merely by the openly ungodly, but by many who occupy the pulpits of our land? "There is no cause for alarm," they cry. "Before Christ shall come, all the world is to be converted, and righteousness is to reign for a thousand years. Peace, peace! all things continue as they were from the beginning. Let none be disturbed by the exciting message of these alarmists." But this doctrine of the millennium does not harmonize with the teachings of Christ and His apostles. Jesus asked the significant question, "When the Son of man cometh, shall He find faith on the earth?"

Luke 18:8. And, as we have seen, He declares that the state of the world will be as in the days of Noah. Paul warns us that we may look for wickedness to increase as the end draws near: "The Spirit speaketh expressly, that in the latter times some shall depart from the faith, giving heed to seducing spirits, and doctrines of devils." 1 Timothy 4:1. The apostle says that "in the last days perilous times shall come." 2 Timothy 3:1. And he gives a startling list of sins that will be found among those who have a form of godliness.

As the time of their probation was closing, the antediluvians gave themselves up to exciting amusements and festivities. Those who possessed influence and power were bent on keeping the minds of the people engrossed with mirth and pleasure, lest any should be impressed by the last solemn warning. Do we not see the same repeated in our day? While God's servants are giving the message that the end of all things is at hand, the world is absorbed in amusements and pleasure seeking. There is a constant round of excitement that causes indifference to God and prevents the people from being impressed by the truths which alone can save them from the coming destruction.

In Noah's day philosophers declared that it was impossible for the world to be destroyed by water; so now there are men of science who endeavor to show that the world cannot be destroyed by fire—that this would be inconsistent with the laws of nature. But the God of nature, the Maker and Controller of her laws, can use the works of His hands to serve His own purpose.

When great and wise men had proved to their satisfaction that it was impossible for the world to be destroyed by water, when the fears of the people were quieted, when all regarded Noah's prophecy as a delusion, and looked upon him as a fanatic—then it was that God's time had come. "The fountains of the great deep" were "broken up, and the windows of heaven were opened," and the scoffers were overwhelmed in the waters of the Flood. With all their boasted philosophy, men found too late that their wisdom was foolishness, that the Lawgiver is greater than the laws of nature, and that Omnipotence is at no loss for means to accomplish His purposes. "As it was in the days of Noah," "even thus shall it be in the days when the Son of man is revealed." Luke 17:26, 30. "The day of the Lord will come as a thief in the night; in the which the heavens shall pass away with a great noise, and the elements shall melt with fervent heat, the earth also and the works that are therein shall be burned up." 2 Peter 3:10. When the reasoning of philosophy has banished the fear of God's judgments; when religious teachers are pointing forward to long ages of peace and prosperity, and the world are absorbed in their rounds of business and pleasure, planting and building, feasting and merrymaking, rejecting God's warnings and mocking His messengers—then it is that sudden destruction cometh upon them, and they shall not escape. 1 Thessalonians 5:3.

After the Flood

The waters rose fifteen cubits above the highest mountains. It often seemed to the family within the ark that they must perish, as for five long months their boat was tossed about, apparently at the mercy of wind and wave. It was a trying ordeal; but Noah's faith did not waver, for he had the assurance that the divine hand was upon the helm.

As the waters began to subside, the Lord caused the ark to drift into a spot protected by a group of mountains that had been preserved by His power. These mountains were but a little distance apart, and the ark moved about in this quiet haven, and was no longer driven upon the boundless ocean. This gave great relief to the weary, tempest-tossed voyagers.

Noah and his family anxiously waited for the decrease of the waters, for they longed to go forth again upon the earth. Forty days after the tops of the mountains became visible, they sent out a raven, a bird of quick scent, to discover whether the earth had become dry. This bird, finding nothing but water, continued to fly to and from the ark. Seven days later a dove was sent forth, which, finding no footing, returned to the ark. Noah waited seven days longer, and again sent forth the dove. When she returned at evening with an olive leaf in her mouth, there was great rejoicing. Later "Noah removed the covering of the ark, and looked, and, behold, the face of the ground was dry." Still he waited patiently within the ark. As he had entered at God's command, he waited for special directions to depart.

At last an angel descended from heaven, opened the massive door, and bade the patriarch and his household go forth upon the earth and take with them every living thing. In the joy of their release Noah did not forget Him by whose gracious care they had been preserved. His first act after leaving the ark was to build an altar and offer from every kind of clean beast and fowl a sacrifice, thus manifesting his gratitude to God for deliverance and his faith in Christ, the great sacrifice. This offering was pleasing to the Lord; and a blessing resulted, not only to the patriarch and his family, but to all who should live upon the earth. "The Lord smelled a sweet savor; and the Lord said in His heart, I will not again curse the ground any more for man's sake. . . . While the earth remaineth, seedtime and harvest, and cold and heat, and summer and winter, and day and night shall not cease." Here was a lesson for all succeeding generations. Noah had come forth upon a desolate earth, but before preparing a house for himself he built an altar to God. His stock of cattle was small, and had been preserved at great expense; yet he cheerfully gave a part to the Lord as an acknowledgment that all was His. In like manner it should be our first care to render our freewill offerings to God. Every manifestation of His mercy and love toward us should be gratefully acknowledged, both by acts of devotion and by gifts to His cause.

Lest the gathering clouds and falling rain should fill men with constant terror, from fear of another flood, the Lord encouraged the family of Noah by a promise: "I will establish

My covenant with you; . . . neither shall there any more be a flood to destroy the earth. . . . I do set My bow in the cloud, and it shall be for a token of a covenant between Me and the earth. And it shall come to pass, when I bring a cloud over the earth, that the bow shall be seen in the cloud. . . . And I will look upon it, that I may remember the everlasting covenant between God and every living creature."

How great the condescension of God and His compassion for His erring creatures in thus placing the beautiful rainbow in the clouds as a token of His covenant with men! The Lord declares that when He looks upon the bow, He will remember His covenant. This does not imply that He would ever forget; but He speaks to us in our own language, that we may better understand Him. It was God's purpose that as the children of after generations should ask the meaning of the glorious arch which spans the heavens, their parents should repeat the story of the Flood, and tell them that the Most High had bended the bow and placed it in the clouds as an assurance that the waters should never again overflow the earth. Thus from generation to generation it would testify of divine love to man and would strengthen his confidence in God.

In heaven the semblance of a rainbow encircles the throne and overarches the head of Christ. The prophet says, "As the appearance of the bow that is in the cloud in the day of rain, so was the appearance of the brightness round about. This was the appearance of the likeness of the glory of Jehovah." Ezekiel 1:28. The revelator declares, "Behold, a throne was set in heaven, and one sat on the throne. . . . There was a rainbow round about the throne, in sight like unto an emerald." Revelation 4:2, 3. When man by his great wickedness invites the divine judgments, the Saviour, interceding with the Father in his behalf, points to the bow in the clouds, to the rainbow around the throne and above His own head, as a token of the mercy of God toward the repentant sinner.

With the assurance given to Noah concerning the Flood, God Himself has linked one of the most precious promises of His grace: "As I have sworn that the waters of Noah should no more go over the earth; so have I sworn that I would not be wroth with thee, nor rebuke thee. For the mountains shall depart, and the hills be removed; but My kindness shall not depart from thee, neither shall the covenant of My peace be removed, saith Jehovah that hath mercy on thee." Isaiah 54:9, 10.

As Noah looked upon the powerful beasts of prey that came forth with him from the ark, he feared that his family, numbering only eight persons, would be destroyed by them. But the Lord sent an angel to His servant with the assuring message: "The fear of you and the dread of you shall be upon every beast of the earth, and upon every fowl of the air, upon all that moveth upon the earth, and upon all the fishes of the sea; into your hand are they delivered. Every moving thing that liveth shall be meat for you; even as the green herb have I given you all things." Before this time God had given man no permission to eat animal food; He intended that the race should subsist wholly upon the productions of the earth; but now that every green thing had been destroyed. He allowed them to eat the flesh of the clean beasts that had been preserved in the ark.

The entire surface of the earth was changed at the Flood. A third dreadful curse rested upon it in consequence of sin. As the water began to subside, the hills and mountains were surrounded by a vast, turbid sea, Everywhere were strewn the dead bodies of men and beasts. The Lord would not permit these to remain to decompose and pollute the air, therefore He made of the earth a vast burial ground. A violent wind which was caused to blow for the purpose of drying up the waters, moved them with great force, in some instances even carrying away the tops of the mountains and heaping up trees, rocks, and earth above the bodies of the dead. By the same means the silver and gold, the choice wood and precious stones, which had enriched and adorned the world before the Flood, and which the inhabitants had idolized, were concealed from the sight and search of men, the violent action of the waters piling earth and rocks upon these treasures, and in some cases even forming mountains above them. God saw that the more He enriched and prospered sinful men, the more they would corrupt their ways before Him. The treasures that should have led them to glorify the bountiful Giver had been worshiped, while God had been dishonored and despised.

The earth presented an appearance of confusion and desolation impossible to describe. The mountains, once so beautiful in their perfect symmetry, had become broken and irregular. Stones, ledges, and ragged rocks were now scattered upon the surface of the earth. In many places hills and mountains had disappeared, leaving no trace where they once stood; and plains had given place to mountain ranges. These changes were more marked in some places than in others. Where once had been earth's richest treasures of gold, silver, and precious stones, were seen the heaviest marks of the curse. And upon countries that were not inhabited, and those where there had been the least crime, the curse rested more lightly.

At this time immense forests were buried. These have since been changed to coal, forming the extensive coal beds that now exist, and also yielding large quantities of oil. The coal and oil frequently ignite and burn beneath the surface of the earth. Thus rocks are heated, limestone is burned, and iron ore melted. The action of the water upon the lime adds fury to the intense heat, and causes earthquakes, volcanoes, and fiery issues. As the fire and water come in contact with ledges of rock and ore, there are heavy explosions underground, which sound like muffled thunder. The air is hot and suffocating. Volcanic eruptions follow; and these often failing to give sufficient vent to the heated elements, the earth itself is convulsed, the ground heaves and swells like the waves of the sea, great fissures appear, and sometimes cities, villages, and burning mountains are swallowed up. These wonderful manifestations will be more and more frequent and terrible just before the second coming of Christ and the end of the world, as signs of its speedy destruction.

The depths of the earth are the Lord's arsenal, whence were drawn weapons to be employed in the destruction of the old world. Waters gushing from the earth united with the waters from heaven to accomplish the work of desolation. Since the Flood, fire as well as water has been God's agent to destroy very wicked cities. These judgments are sent that those who lightly regard God's law and trample upon His authority may be led to tremble before His power and to confess His just sovereignty. As men have beheld burning mountains pouring forth fire and flames and torrents of melted ore, drying up rivers, overwhelming populous cities, and everywhere spreading ruin and desolation, the stoutest heart has been filled with terror and infidels and blasphemers have been constrained to acknowledge the infinite power of God.

Said the prophets of old, referring to scenes like these: "Oh that Thou wouldest rend the heavens, that Thou wouldest come down, that the mountains might flow down at Thy presence, as when the melting fire burneth, the fire causeth the waters to boil, to make Thy name known to Thine adversaries, that the nations may tremble at Thy presence! When Thou didst terrible things which we looked not for, Thou camest down, the mountains flowed down at Thy presence." Isaiah 64:1-3. "The Lord hath His way in the whirlwind and in the storm, and the clouds are the dust of His feet. He rebuketh the sea, and maketh it dry, and drieth up all the rivers." Nahum 1:3, 4.

More terrible manifestations than the world has ever yet beheld, will be witnessed at the second advent of Christ. "The mountains quake at Him, and the hills melt, and the earth is burned at His presence, yea, the world, and all that dwell therein. Who can stand before His indignation? and who can abide in the fierceness of His anger?" Nahum 1:5, 6. "Bow Thy heavens, O Lord, and come down: touch the mountains, and they shall smoke. Cast forth lightning, and scatter them: shoot out Thine arrows, and destroy them." Psalm 144:5, 6.

"I will show wonders in heaven above, and signs in the earth beneath; blood, and fire, and vapor of smoke." Acts 2:19. "And there were voices, and thunders, and lightnings; and there was a great earthquake, such as was not since men were upon the earth, so mighty an earthquake, and so great." "And every island fled away, and the mountains were not found. And there fell upon men a great hail out of heaven, every stone about the weight of a talent." Revelation 16:18, 20, 21.

As lightnings from heaven unite with the fire in the earth, the mountains will burn like a furnace, and will pour forth terrific streams of lava, overwhelming gardens and fields, villages and cities. Seething molten masses thrown into the rivers will cause the waters to boil, sending forth massive rocks with indescribable violence and scattering their broken fragments upon the land. Rivers will be dried up. The earth will be convulsed; everywhere there will be dreadful earthquakes and eruptions.

Thus God will destroy the wicked from off the earth. But the righteous will be preserved in the midst of these commotions, as Noah was preserved in the ark. God will be their refuge, and under His wings shall they trust. Says the psalmist: "Because thou hast made the Lord, which is my refuge, even the Most High, thy habitation; there shall no evil befall thee." Psalm 91:9, 10. "In the time of trouble He shall hide me in His pavilion: in the secret of His tabernacle shall He hide me." Psalm 27:5. God's promise is, "Because he hath set his love upon Me, therefore will I deliver him: I will set him on high, because he hath known My name." Psalm 91:14.

The Literal Week

Like the Sabbath, the week originated at creation, and it has been preserved and brought down to us through Bible history. God Himself measured off the first week as a sample for successive weeks to the close of time. Like every other, it consisted of seven literal days. Six days were employed in the work of creation; upon the seventh, God rested, and He then blessed this day and set it apart as a day of rest for man.

In the law given from Sinai, God recognized the week, and the facts upon which it is based. After giving the command, "Remember the Sabbath day, to keep it holy," and specifying what shall be done on the six days, and what shall not be done on the seventh, He states the reason for thus observing the week, by pointing back to His own example: "For in six days the Lord made heaven and earth, the sea, and all that in them is, and rested the seventh day: wherefore the Lord blessed the Sabbath day, and hallowed it." Exodus 20:8-11. This reason appears beautiful and forcible when we understand the days of creation to be literal. The first six days of each week are given to man for labor, because God employed the same period of the first week in the work of creation. On the seventh day man is to refrain from labor, in commemoration of the Creator's rest.

But the assumption that the events of the first week required thousands upon thousands of years, strikes directly at the foundation of the fourth commandment. It represents the Creator as commanding men to observe the week of literal days in commemoration of vast, indefinite periods. This is unlike His method of dealing with His creatures. It makes indefinite and obscure that which He has made very plain. It is infidelity in its most insidious and hence most dangerous form; its real character is so disguised that it is held and taught by many who profess to believe the Bible.

"By the word of the Lord were the heavens made; and all the host of them by the breath of His mouth." "For He spake, and it was done; He commanded, and it stood fast." Psalm 33:6, 9. The Bible recognizes no long ages in which the earth was slowly evolved from chaos. Of each successive day of creation, the sacred record declares that it consisted of the evening and the morning, like all other days that have followed. At the close of each day is given the result of the

Creator's work. The statement is made at the close of the first week's record, "These are the generations of the heavens and of the earth when they were created." Genesis 2:4. But this does not convey the idea that the days of creation were other than literal days. Each day was called a generation, because that in it God generated, or produced, some new portion of His work.

Geologists claim to find evidence from the earth itself that it is very much older than the Mosaic record teaches. Bones of men and animals, as well as instruments of warfare, petrified trees, etcetera, much larger than any that now exist, or that have existed for thousands of years, have been discovered, and from this it is inferred that the earth was populated long before the time brought to view in the record of creation, and by a race of beings vastly superior in size to any men now living. Such reasoning has led many professed Bible believers to adopt the position that the days of creation were vast, indefinite periods.

But apart from Bible history, geology can prove nothing. Those who reason so confidently upon its discoveries have no adequate conception of the size of men, animals, and trees before the Flood, or of the great changes which then took place. Relics found in the earth do give evidence of conditions differing in many respects from the present, but the time when these conditions existed can be learned only from the Inspired Record. In the history of the Flood, inspiration has explained that which geology alone could never fathom. In the days of Noah, men, animals, and trees, many times larger than now exist, were buried, and thus preserved as an evidence to later generations that the antediluvians perished by a flood. God designed that the discovery of these things should establish faith in inspired history; but men, with their vain reasoning, fall into the same error as did the people before the Flood—the things which God gave them as a benefit, they turn into a curse by making a wrong use of them.

It is one of Satan's devices to lead the people to accept the fables of infidelity; for he can thus obscure the law of God, in itself very plain, and embolden men to rebel against the divine government. His efforts are especially directed against the fourth commandment, because it so clearly points to the living God, the Maker of the heavens and the earth.

There is a constant effort made to explain the work of creation as the result of natural causes; and human reasoning is accepted even by professed Christians, in opposition to plain Scripture facts. There are many who oppose the investigation of the prophecies, especially those of Daniel and the Revelation, declaring them to be so obscure that we cannot understand them; yet these very persons eagerly receive the suppositions of geologists, in contradiction of the Mosaic record. But if that which God has revealed is so difficult to understand, how inconsistent it is to accept mere suppositions in regard to that which He has not revealed!

"The secret things belong unto the Lord our God: but those things which are revealed belong unto us and to our children forever." Deuteronomy 29:29. Just how God accomplished the work of creation He has never revealed to men; human science cannot search out the secrets of the Most High. His creative power is as incomprehensible as His existence.

God has permitted a flood of light to be poured upon the world in both science and art; but when professedly scientific men treat upon these subjects from a merely human point of view, they will assuredly come to wrong conclusions. It may be innocent to speculate beyond what God's word has revealed, if our theories do not contradict facts found in the Scriptures; but those who leave the word of God, and seek to account for His created works upon scientific principles, are drifting without chart or compass upon an unknown ocean. The greatest minds, if not guided by the word of God in their research, become bewildered in their attempts to trace the relations of science and revelation. Because the Creator and His works are so far beyond their comprehension that they are unable to explain them by natural laws, they regard Bible history as unreliable. Those who doubt the reliability of the records of the Old and New Testaments, will be led to go a step further, and doubt the existence of God; and then, having lost their anchor, they are left to beat about upon the rocks of infidelity.

These persons have lost the simplicity of faith. There should be a settled belief in the divine authority of God's Holy Word. The Bible is not to be tested by men's ideas of science. Human knowledge is an unreliable guide. Skeptics who read the Bible for the sake of caviling, may, through an imperfect comprehension of either science or revelation, claim to find contradictions between them; but rightly understood, they are in perfect harmony. Moses wrote under the guidance of the Spirit of God, and a correct theory of geology will never claim discoveries that cannot be reconciled with his statements. All truth, whether in nature or in revelation, is consistent with itself in all its manifestations.

In the word of God many queries are raised that the most profound scholars can never answer. Attention is called to these subjects to show us how much there is, even among the common things of everyday life, that finite minds, with all their boasted wisdom, can never fully understand.

Yet men of science think that they can comprehend the wisdom of God, that which He has done or can do. The idea largely prevails that He is restricted by His own laws. Men either deny or ignore His existence, or think to explain everything, even the operation of His Spirit upon the human heart; and they no longer reverence His name or fear His power. They do not believe in the supernatural, not understanding God's laws or His infinite power to work His will through them. As commonly used, the term "laws of nature" comprises what men have been able to discover with regard to the laws that govern the physical world; but how limited is their knowledge, and how vast the field in which the Creator can work in harmony with His own laws and yet wholly beyond the comprehension of finite beings!

Many teach that matter possesses vital power—that certain properties are imparted to matter, and it is then left to act through its own inherent energy; and that the operations of nature are conducted in harmony with fixed laws, with which God Himself cannot interfere. This is false science, and is not sustained by the word of God. Nature is the servant of her Creator. God does not annul His laws or work contrary to them, but He is continually using them as His instruments. Nature testifies of an intelligence, a presence, an active energy, that works in and through her laws. There is in nature the continual working of the Father and the Son. Christ says, "My Father worketh hitherto, and I work." John 5:17.

The Levites, in their hymn recorded by Nehemiah, sang, "Thou, even Thou, art Lord alone; Thou hast made heaven, the heaven of heavens, with all their host, the earth, and all things therein, . . . and Thou preservest them all." Nehemiah 9:6. As regards this world, God's work of creation is completed. For "the works were finished from the foundation of the world." Hebrews 4:3. But His energy is still exerted in upholding the objects of His creation. It is not because the mechanism that has once been set in motion continues to act by its own inherent energy that the pulse beats and breath follows breath; but every breath, every pulsation of the heart, is an evidence of the all-pervading care of Him in whom "we live, and move, and have our being." Acts 17:28. It is not because of inherent power that year by year the earth produces her bounties and continues her motion around the sun. The hand of God guides the planets and keeps them in position in their orderly march through the heavens. He "bringeth out their host by number: He calleth them all by names by the greatness of His might, for that He is strong in power; not one faileth." Isaiah 40:26. It is through His power that vegetation flourishes, that the leaves appear and the flowers bloom. He "maketh grass to grow upon the mountains" (Psalm 147:8), and by Him the valleys are made fruitful. "All the beasts of the forest . . . seek their meat from God," and every living creature, from the smallest insect up to man, is daily dependent upon His providential care. In the beautiful words of the psalmist, "These wait all upon Thee. . . . That Thou givest them they gather: Thou openest Thine hand, they are filled with good." Psalm 104:20, 21, 27, 28. His word controls the elements; He covers the heavens with clouds and prepares rain for the earth. "He giveth snow like wool: He scattereth the hoarfrost like ashes." Psalm 147:16. "When He uttereth His voice, there is a multitude of waters in the heavens, and He causeth the vapors to ascend from the ends of the earth; He maketh lightnings with rain, and bringeth forth the wind out of His treasuries." Jeremiah 10:13.

God is the foundation of everything. All true science is in harmony with His works; all true education leads to obedience to His government. Science opens new wonders to our view; she soars high, and explores new depths; but she brings nothing from her research that conflicts with divine revelation. Ignorance may seek to support false views of God by appeals to science, but the book of nature and the written word shed light upon each other. We are thus led to adore the Creator and to have an intelligent trust in His word.

No finite mind can fully comprehend the existence, the power, the wisdom, or the works of the Infinite One. Says the sacred writer: "Canst thou by searching find out God? canst thou find out the Almighty unto perfection? It is as high as heaven; what canst thou do? deeper than hell; what canst thou know? The measure thereof is longer than the earth, and broader than the sea." Job 11:7-9. The mightiest intellects of earth cannot comprehend God. Men may be ever searching, ever learning, and still there is an infinity beyond.

Yet the works of creation testify of God's power and greatness. "The heavens declare the glory of God; and the firmament showeth His handiwork." Psalm 19:1. Those who take the written word as their counselor will find in science an aid to understand God. "The invisible things of Him from the creation of the world are clearly seen, being understood by the things that are made, even His eternal power and Godhead." Romans 1:20.

The Tower of Babel

To repeople the desolate earth, which the Flood had so lately swept from its moral corruption, God had preserved but one family, the household of Noah, to whom He had declared, "Thee have I seen righteous before Me in this generation." Genesis 7:1. Yet in the three sons of Noah was speedily developed the same great distinction seen in the world before the Flood. In Shem, Ham, and Japheth, who were to be the founders of the human race, was foreshadowed the character of their posterity.

Noah, speaking by divine inspiration, foretold the history of the three great races to spring from these fathers of mankind. Tracing the descendants of Ham, through the son rather than the father, he declared, "Cursed be Canaan; a servant of servants shall he be unto his brethren." The unnatural crime of Ham declared that filial reverence had long before been cast from his soul, and it revealed the impiety and vileness of his character. These evil characteristics were perpetuated in Canaan and his posterity, whose continued guilt called upon them the judgments of God.

On the other hand, the reverence manifested by Shem and Japheth for their father, and thus for the divine statutes, promised a brighter future for their descendants. Concerning these sons it was declared: "Blessed be Jehovah, God of Shem; and Canaan shall be his servant. God shall enlarge Japheth, and he shall dwell in the tents of Shem; and Canaan shall be his servant." The line of Shem was to be that of the chosen people, of God's covenant, of the promised Redeemer. Jehovah was the God of Shem. From him would descend Abraham, and the people of Israel, through whom Christ was to come. "Happy is that people, whose God is the Lord." Psalm 144:15. And Japheth "shall dwell in the tents of Shem." In the blessings of the gospel the descendants of Japheth were especially to share.

The posterity of Canaan descended to the most degrading forms of heathenism. Though the prophetic curse had doomed them to slavery, the doom was withheld for centuries. God bore with their impiety and corruption until they passed the limits of divine forbearance. Then they were dispossessed, and became bondmen to the descendants of Shem and Japheth.

The prophecy of Noah was no arbitrary denunciation of wrath or declaration of favor. It did not fix the character and destiny of his sons. But it showed what would be the result of the course of life they had severally chosen and the character they had developed. It was an expression of God's purpose toward them and their posterity in view of their own character and conduct. As a rule, children inherit the dispositions and tendencies of their parents, and imitate their example; so that the sins of the parents are practiced by the children from generation to generation. Thus the vileness and irreverence of Ham were reproduced in his posterity, bringing a curse upon them for many generations. "One sinner destroyeth much good." Ecclesiastes 9:18.

On the other hand, how richly rewarded was Shem's respect for his father; and what an illustrious line of holy men appears in his posterity! "The Lord knoweth the days of the upright," "and his seed is blessed." Psalm 37:18, 26. "Know therefore that the Lord thy God He is God, the faithful God, which keepeth covenant and mercy with them that love Him and keep His commandments to a thousand generations." Deuteronomy 7:9.

For a time the descendants of Noah continued to dwell among the mountains where the ark had rested. As their numbers increased, apostasy soon led to division. Those who desired to forget their Creator and to cast off the restraint of His law felt a constant annoyance from the teaching and example of their God-fearing associates, and after a time they decided to separate from the worshipers of God. Accordingly they journeyed to the plain of Shinar, on the banks of the river Euphrates. They were attracted by the beauty of the situation and the fertility of the soil, and upon this plain they determined to make their home.

Here they decided to build a city, and in it a tower of such stupendous height as should render it the wonder of the world. These enterprises were designed to prevent the people from scattering abroad in colonies. God had directed men to disperse throughout the earth, to replenish and subdue it; but these Babel builders determined to keep their community united in one body, and to found a monarchy that should eventually embrace the whole earth. Thus their city would become the metropolis of a universal empire; its glory would command the admiration and homage of the world and render the founders illustrious. The magnificent tower, reaching to the heavens, was intended to stand as a monument of the power and wisdom of its builders, perpetuating their fame to the latest generations.

The dwellers on the plain of Shinar disbelieved God's covenant that He would not again bring a flood upon the earth. Many of them denied the existence of God and attributed the Flood to the operation of natural causes. Others believed in a Supreme Being, and that it was He who had destroyed the antediluvian world; and their hearts, like that of Cain, rose up in rebellion against Him. One object before them in the erection of the tower was to secure their own safety in case of another deluge. By carrying the structure to a much greater height than was reached by the waters of the Flood, they thought to place themselves beyond all possibility of danger. And as they would be able to ascend to the region of the clouds, they hoped to ascertain the cause of the Flood. The whole undertaking was designed to exalt still further the pride of its projectors and to turn the minds of future generations away from God and lead them into idolatry.

When the tower had been partially completed, a portion of it was occupied as a dwelling place for the builders; other apartments, splendidly furnished and adorned, were devoted to their idols. The people rejoiced in their success, and praised the gods of silver and gold, and set themselves against the Ruler of heaven and earth. Suddenly the work that had been advancing so prosperously was checked. Angels were sent to bring to naught the purpose of the builders. The tower had reached a lofty height, and it was impossible for the workmen at the top to communicate directly with those at the base; therefore men were stationed at different points, each to receive and report to the one next below him the orders for needed material or other directions concerning the work. As messages were thus passing from one to another the language was confounded, so that material was called for which was not needed, and the directions delivered were often the reverse of those that had been given. Confusion and dismay followed. All work came to a standstill. There could be no further harmony or co-operation. The builders were wholly unable to account for the strange misunderstandings among them, and in their rage and disappointment they reproached one another. Their confederacy ended in strife and bloodshed. Lightnings from heaven, as an evidence of God's displeasure, broke off the upper portion of the tower and cast it to the ground. Men were made to feel that there is a God who ruleth in the heavens.

Up to this time all men had spoken the same language; now those that could understand one another's speech united in companies; some went one way, and some another. "The Lord scattered them abroad from thence upon the face of all the earth." This dispersion was the means of peopling the earth, and thus the Lord's purpose was accomplished through the very means that men had employed to prevent its fulfillment.

But at what a loss to those who had set themselves against God! It was His purpose that as men should go forth to found nations in different parts of the earth they should carry with them a knowledge of His will, that the light of truth might shine undimmed to succeeding generations. Noah, the faithful preacher of righteousness, lived for three hundred and fifty years after the Flood, Shem for five hundred years, and thus their descendants had an opportunity to become acquainted with the requirements of God and the history of His dealings with their fathers. But they were unwilling to listen to these unpalatable truths; they had no desire to retain God in their knowledge; and by the confusion of tongues they were, in a great measure, shut out from intercourse with those who might have given them light.

The Babel builders had indulged the spirit of murmuring against God. Instead of gratefully remembering His mercy to Adam and His gracious covenant with Noah, they had complained of His severity in expelling the first pair from Eden and destroying the world by a flood. But while they murmured against God as arbitrary and severe, they were accepting the rule of the cruelest of tyrants. Satan was seeking to bring contempt upon the sacrificial offerings that prefigured the death of Christ; and as the minds of the people were darkened by idolatry, he led them to counterfeit these offerings and sacrifice their own children upon the altars of their gods. As men turned away from God, the divine attributes—justice, purity, and love—were supplanted by oppression, violence, and brutality.

The men of Babel had determined to establish a government that should be independent of God. There were some among them, however, who feared the Lord, but who had been deceived by the pretensions of the ungodly and drawn into their schemes. For the sake of these faithful ones the Lord delayed His judgments and gave the people time to reveal their true character. As this was developed, the sons of God labored to turn them from their purpose; but the people were fully united in their Heaven-daring undertaking. Had they gone on unchecked, they would have demoralized the world in its infancy. Their confederacy was founded in rebellion; a kingdom established for self-exaltation, but in which God was to have no rule or honor. Had this confederacy been permitted, a mighty power would have borne sway to banish righteousness—and with it peace, happiness, and security—from the earth. For the divine statutes, which are "holy and just and good" (Romans 7:12), men were endeavoring to substitute laws to suit the purpose of their own selfish and cruel hearts.

Those that feared the Lord cried unto Him to interpose. "And the Lord came down to see the city and the tower, which the children of men builded." In mercy to the world He defeated the purpose of the tower builders and overthrew the memorial of their daring. In mercy He confounded their speech, thus putting a check on their purposes of rebellion. God bears long with the perversity of men, giving them ample opportunity for repentance; but He marks all their devices to resist the authority of His just and holy law. From time to time the unseen hand that holds the scepter of government is stretched out to restrain iniquity. Unmistakable evidence is given that the Creator of the universe, the One infinite in wisdom and love and truth, is the Supreme Ruler of heaven and earth, and that none can with impunity defy His power.

The schemes of the Babel builders ended in shame and defeat. The monument to their pride became the memorial of their folly. Yet men are continually pursuing the same course—depending upon self, and rejecting God's law. It is the principle that Satan tried to carry out in heaven; the same

that governed Cain in presenting his offering.

There are tower builders in our time. Infidels construct their theories from the supposed deductions of sciences, and reject the revealed word of God. They presume to pass sentence upon God's moral government; they despise His law and boast of the sufficiency of human reason. They, "because sentence against an evil work is not executed speedily, therefore the heart of the sons of men is fully set in them to do evil." Ecclesiastes 8:11.

In the professedly Christian world many turn away from the plain teachings of the Bible and build up a creed from human speculations and pleasing fables, and they point to their tower as a way to climb up to heaven. Men hang with admiration upon the lips of eloquence while it teaches that the transgressor shall not die, that salvation may be secured without obedience to the law of God. If the professed followers of Christ would accept God's standard, it would bring them into unity; but so long as human wisdom is exalted above His Holy Word, there will be divisions and dissension. The existing confusion of conflicting creeds and sects is fitly represented by the term "Babylon," which prophecy (Revelation 14:8; 18:2) applies to the world-loving churches of the last days.

Many seek to make a heaven for themselves by obtaining riches and power. They "speak wickedly concerning oppression: they speak loftily" (Psalm 73:8), trampling upon human rights and disregarding divine authority. The proud may be for a time in great power, and may see success in all that they undertake; but in the end they will find only disappointment and wretchedness.

The time of God's investigation is at hand. The Most High will come down to see that which the children of men have builded. His sovereign power will be revealed; the works of human pride will be laid low. "The Lord looketh from heaven; He beholdeth all the sons of men. From the place of His habitation He looketh upon all the inhabitants of the earth." "The Lord bringeth the counsel of the heathen to nought: He maketh the devices of the people of none effect. The counsel of the Lord standeth forever, the thoughts of His heart to all generations." Psalm 33:13, 14, 10, 11.

The Call of Abraham

After the dispersion from Babel idolatry again became well-nigh universal, and the Lord finally left the hardened transgressors to follow their evil ways, while He chose Abraham, of the line of Shem, and made him the keeper of His law for future generations. Abraham had grown up in the midst of superstition and heathenism. Even his father's household, by whom the knowledge of God had been preserved, were yielding to the seductive influences surrounding them, and they "served other gods" than Jehovah. But the true faith was not to become extinct. God has ever preserved a remnant to serve Him. Adam, Seth, Enoch, Methuselah, Noah, Shem, in unbroken line, had preserved from age to age the precious revealings of His will. The son of Terah became the inheritor of this holy trust. Idolatry invited him on every side, but in vain. Faithful among the faithless, uncorrupted by the prevailing apostasy, he steadfastly adhered to the worship of the one true God. "The Lord is nigh unto all them that call upon Him, to all that call upon Him in truth." Psalm 145:18. He communicated His will to Abraham, and gave him a distinct knowledge of the requirements of His law and of the salvation that would be accomplished through Christ.

There was given to Abraham the promise, especially dear to the people of that age, of a numerous posterity and of national greatness: "I will make of thee a great nation, and I will bless thee, and make thy name great; and thou shalt be a blessing." And to this was added the assurance, precious above every other to the inheritor of faith, that of his line the Redeemer of the world should come: "In thee shall all families of the earth be blessed." Yet, as the first condition of fulfillment, there was to be a test of faith; a sacrifice was demanded.

The message of God came to Abraham, "Get thee out of thy country, and from thy kindred, and from thy father's house, unto a land that I will show thee." In order that God might qualify him for his great work as the keeper of the sacred oracles, Abraham must be separated from the associations of his early life. The influence of kindred and friends would interfere with the training which the Lord purposed to give His servant. Now that Abraham was, in a special sense, connected with heaven, he must dwell among strangers. His character must be peculiar, differing from all the world. He could not even explain his course of action so as to be understood by his friends. Spiritual things are spiritually discerned, and his motives and actions were not comprehended by his idolatrous kindred.

"By faith Abraham, when he was called to go out into a place which he should after receive for an inheritance, obeyed; and he went out, not knowing whither he went." Hebrews 11:8. Abraham's unquestioning obedience is one of the most striking evidences of faith to be found in all the Bible. To him, faith was "the substance of things hoped for, the evidence of things not seen." Verse 1. Relying upon the divine promise, without the least outward assurance of its fulfillment, he abandoned home and kindred and native land, and went forth, he knew not whither, to follow where God should lead. "By faith he became a sojourner in the land of promise, as in a land not his own, dwelling in tents, with Isaac and Jacob, the heirs with him of the same promise." Hebrews 11:9, R.V.

It was no light test that was thus brought upon Abraham, no small sacrifice that was required of him. There were strong ties to bind him to his country, his kindred, and his home. But he did not hesitate to obey the call. He had no question to ask concerning the land of promise—whether the soil was fertile and the climate healthful; whether the country afforded agreeable surroundings and would afford opportunities for amassing wealth. God has spoken, and His servant must obey;

the happiest place on earth for him was the place where God would have him to be.

Many are still tested as was Abraham. They do not hear the voice of God speaking directly from the heavens, but He calls them by the teachings of His word and the events of His providence. They may be required to abandon a career that promises wealth and honor, to leave congenial and profitable associations and separate from kindred, to enter upon what appears to be only a path of self-denial, hardship, and sacrifice. God has a work for them to do; but a life of ease and the influence of friends and kindred would hinder the development of the very traits essential for its accomplishment. He calls them away from human influences and aid, and leads them to feel the need of His help, and to depend upon Him alone, that He may reveal Himself to them. Who is ready at the call of Providence to renounce cherished plans and familiar associations? Who will accept new duties and enter untried fields, doing God's work with firm and willing heart, for Christ's sake counting his losses gain? He who will do this has the faith of Abraham, and will share with him that "far more exceeding and eternal weight of glory," with which "the sufferings of this present time are not worthy to be compared." 2 Corinthians 4:17; Romans 8:18.

The call from heaven first came to Abraham while he dwelt in "Ur of the Chaldees" and in obedience to it he removed to Haran. Thus far his father's family accompanied him, for with their idolatry they united the worship of the true God. Here Abraham remained till the death of Terah. But from his father's grave the divine Voice bade him go forward. His brother Nahor with his household clung to their home and their idols. Besides Sarah, the wife of Abraham, only Lot, the son of Haran long since dead, chose to share the patriarch's, pilgrim life. Yet it was a large company that set out from Mesopotamia. Abraham already possessed extensive flocks and herds, the riches of the East, and he was surrounded by a numerous body of servants and retainers. He was departing from the land of his fathers, never to return, and he took with him all that he had, "their substance that they had gathered, and the souls that they had gotten in Haran." Among these were many led by higher considerations than those of service and self-interest. During their stay in Haran, both Abraham and Sarah had led others to the worship and service of the true God. These attached themselves to the patriarch's household, and accompanied him to the land of promise. "And they went forth to go into the land of Canaan; and into the land of Canaan they came."

The place where they first tarried was Shechem. Under the shade of the oaks of Moreh, in a wide, grassy valley, with its olive groves and gushing springs, between Mount Ebal on the one side and Mount Gerizim on the other, Abraham made his encampment. It was a fair and goodly country that the patriarch had entered—"a land of brooks of water, of fountains and depths that spring out of valleys and hills; a land of wheat, and barley, and vines, and fig trees, and pomegranates; a land of oil olive, and honey." Deuteronomy 8:7, 8. But to the worshiper of Jehovah, a heavy shadow rested upon wooded hill and fruitful plain. "The Canaanite was then in the land." Abraham had reached the goal of his hopes to find a country occupied by an alien race and overspread with idolatry. In the groves were set up the altars of false gods, and human sacrifices were offered upon the neighboring heights. While he clung to the divine promise, it was not without distressful forebodings that he pitched his tent. Then "the Lord appeared unto Abram, and said, Unto thy seed will I give this land." His faith was strengthened by this assurance that the divine presence was with him, that he was not left to the mercy of the wicked. "And there builded he an altar unto the Lord, who appeared unto him." Still a wayfarer, he soon removed to a spot near Bethel, and again erected an altar, and called upon the name of the Lord.

Abraham, "the friend of God," set us a worthy example. His was a life of prayer. Wherever he pitched his tent, close beside it was set up his altar, calling all within his encampment to the morning and evening sacrifice. When his tent was removed, the altar remained. In following years, there were those among the roving Canaanites who received instruction from Abraham; and whenever one of these came to that altar, he knew who had been there before him; and when he had pitched his tent, he repaired the altar, and there worshiped the living God.

Abraham continued to journey southward, and again his faith was tested. The heavens withheld their rain, the brooks ceased to flow in the valleys, and the grass withered on the plains. The flocks and herds found no pasture, and starvation threatened the whole encampment. Did not the patriarch now question the leadings of Providence? Did he not look back with longing to the plenty of the Chaldean plains? All were eagerly watching to see what Abraham would do, as trouble after trouble came upon him. So long as his confidence appeared unshaken, they felt that there was hope; they were assured that God was his Friend, and that He was still guiding him.

Abraham could not explain the leadings of Providence; he had not realized his expectations; but he held fast the promise, "I will bless thee, and make thy name great; and thou shalt be a blessing." With earnest prayer he considered how to preserve the life of his people and his flocks, but he would not allow circumstances to shake his faith in God's word. To escape the famine he went down into Egypt. He did not forsake Canaan, or in his extremity turn back to the Chaldean land from which he came, where there was no scarcity of bread; but he sought a temporary refuge as near as possible to the Land of Promise, intending shortly to return where God had placed him.

The Lord in His providence had brought this trial upon Abraham to teach him lessons of submission, patience, and faith— lessons that where to be placed on record for the benefit of all who should afterward be called to endure affliction. God leads His children by a way that they know not, but He does not forget or cast off those who put their trust in Him. He permitted affliction to come upon Job, but He did not forsake him. He allowed the beloved John to be exiled to lonely Patmos, but the Son of God met him there, and his vision was filled with scenes of immortal glory. God permits trials to assail His people, that by their constancy and obedience they themselves may be spiritually enriched, and that their example may be a source of strength to others. "I know the thoughts that I think toward you, saith the Lord, thoughts of peace, and not of evil." Jeremiah 29:11. The very trials that task our faith most severely and make it seem that God has forsaken us, are to lead us closer to Christ, that we may lay all our burdens at His feet and experience the peace which He will give us in exchange.

God has always tried His people in the furnace of affliction. It is in the heat of the furnace that the dross is separated from the true gold of the Christian character. Jesus watches the test; He knows what is needed to purify the precious metal, that it may reflect the radiance of His love. It is by close, testing trials that God disciplines His servants. He sees that some have powers which may be used in the advancement of His work, and He puts these persons upon trial; in His providence He brings them into positions that test their character and reveal defects and weaknesses that have been hidden from their own knowledge. He gives them opportunity to correct these defects and to fit themselves for His service. He shows them their own weakness, and teaches them to lean upon Him; for He is their only help and safeguard. Thus His object is attained. They are educated, trained, and disciplined, prepared to fulfill the grand purpose for which their powers were given them. When God calls them to action, they are ready, and heavenly angels can unite with them in the work to be accomplished on the earth.

During his stay in Egypt, Abraham gave evidence that he was not free from human weakness and imperfection. In concealing the fact that Sarah was his wife, he betrayed a distrust of the divine care, a lack of that lofty faith and courage so often and nobly exemplified in his life. Sarah was fair to look upon, and he doubted not that the dusky Egyptians would covet the beautiful stranger, and that in order to secure her, they would not scruple to slay her husband. He reasoned that he was not guilty of falsehood in representing Sarah as his sister, for she was the daughter of his father, though not of his mother. But this concealment of the real relation between them was deception. No deviation from strict integrity can meet God's approval. Through Abraham's lack of faith, Sarah was placed in great peril. The king of Egypt, being informed of her beauty, caused her to be taken to his palace, intending to make her his wife. But the Lord, in His great mercy, protected Sarah by sending judgments upon the royal household. By this means the monarch learned the truth in the matter, and, indignant at the deception practiced upon him, he reproved Abraham and restored to him his wife, saying, "What is this that thou hast done unto me? . . . Why saidst thou, She is my sister? So I might have taken her to me to wife. Now therefore behold thy wife, take her, and go thy way."

Abraham had been greatly favored by the king; even now Pharaoh would permit no harm to be done him or his company, but ordered a guard to conduct them in safety out of his dominions. At this time laws were made prohibiting the Egyptians from intercourse with foreign shepherds in any such familiarity as eating or drinking with them. Pharaoh's dismissal of Abraham was kind and generous; but he bade him leave Egypt, for he dared not permit him to remain. He had ignorantly been about to do him a serious injury, but God had interposed, and saved the monarch from committing so great a sin. Pharaoh saw in this stranger a man whom the God of heaven honored, and he feared to have in his kingdom one who was so evidently under divine favor. Should Abraham remain in Egypt, his increasing wealth and honor would be likely to excite the envy or covetousness of the Egyptians, and some injury might be done him, for which the monarch would be held responsible, and which might again bring judgments upon the royal house.

The warning that had been given to Pharaoh proved a protection to Abraham in his after-intercourse with heathen peoples; for the matter could not be kept secret, and it was seen that the God whom Abraham worshiped would protect His servant, and that any injury done him would be avenged. It is a dangerous thing to wrong one of the children of the King of heaven. The psalmist refers to this chapter in Abraham's experience when he says, in speaking of the chosen people, that God "reproved kings for their sakes; saying, Touch not Mine anointed, and do My prophets no harm." Psalm 105:14, 15.

There is an interesting similarity between Abraham's experience in Egypt and that of his posterity, centuries later. Both went down into Egypt on account of a famine, and both sojourned there. Through the manifestation of divine judgments in their behalf, the fear of them fell upon the Egyptians; and, enriched by the gifts of the heathen, they went out with great substance.

Abraham in Canaan

Abraham returned to Canaan "very rich in cattle, in silver, and in gold." Lot was still with him, and again they came to Bethel, and pitched their tents by the altar which they had before erected. They soon found that increased possessions brought increased trouble. In the midst of hardships and trials they had dwelt together in harmony, but in their prosperity there was danger of strife between them. The pasturage was not sufficient for the flocks and herds of both, and the frequent disputes among the herdsmen were brought for settlement to their masters. It was evident that they must separate. Abraham was Lot's senior in years, and his superior in relation, in wealth, and in position; yet he was the first to propose plans for preserving peace. Although the whole land had been given him by God Himself, he courteously waived this right.

"Let there be no strife," he said, "between me and thee, and between my herdmen and thy herdmen; for we be brethren. Is not the whole land before thee? separate thyself, I pray thee, from me: if thou wilt take the left hand, then I will go to the right; or if thou depart to the right hand, then I will go to the left."

Here the noble, unselfish spirit of Abraham was displayed. How many under similar circumstances would, at all hazards, cling to their individual rights and preferences! How many households have thus been rent asunder! How many churches have been divided, making the cause of truth a byword and a reproach among the wicked! "Let there be no strife between me and thee," said Abraham, "for we be brethren;" not only by natural relationship, but as worshipers of the true God. The children of God the world over are one family, and the same spirit of love and conciliation should govern them. "Be kindly affectioned one to another with brotherly love; in honor preferring one another" (Romans 12:10), is the teaching of our Saviour. The cultivation of a uniform courtesy, a willingness to do to others as we would wish them to do to us, would annihilate half the ills of life. The spirit of self-aggrandizement is the spirit of Satan; but the heart in which the love of Christ is cherished, will possess that charity which seeketh not her own. Such will heed the divine injunction, "Look not every man on his own things, but every man also on the things of others." Philippians 2:4.

Although Lot owed his prosperity to his connection with Abraham, he manifested no gratitude to his benefactor. Courtesy would have dictated that he yield the choice to Abraham, but instead of this he selfishly endeavored to grasp all its advantages. He "lifted up his eyes, and beheld all the plain of Jordan, that it was well watered everywhere, . . . even as the garden of the Lord, like the land of Egypt, as thou comest unto Zoar." The most fertile region in all Palestine was the Jordan Valley, reminding the beholders of the lost Paradise and equaling the beauty and productiveness of the Nile-enriched plains they had so lately left. There were cities also, wealthy and beautiful, inviting to profitable traffic in their crowded marts. Dazzled with visions of worldly gain, Lot overlooked the moral and spiritual evils that would be encountered there. The inhabitants of the plain were "sinners before the Lord exceedingly;" but of this he was ignorant, or, knowing, gave it but little weight. He "chose him all the plain of Jordan," and "pitched his tent toward Sodom." How little did he foresee the terrible results of that selfish choice!

After the separation from Lot, Abraham again received from the Lord a promise of the whole country. Soon after this he removed to Hebron, pitching his tent under the oaks of Mamre and erecting beside it an altar to the Lord. In the free air of those upland plains, with their olive groves and vineyards, their fields of waving grain, and the wide pasture grounds of the encircling hills, he dwelt, well content with his simple, patriarchal life, and leaving to Lot the perilous luxury of the vale of Sodom.

Abraham was honored by the surrounding nations as a

mighty prince and a wise and able chief. He did not shut away his influence from his neighbors. His life and character, in their marked contrast with those of the worshipers of idols, exerted a telling influence in favor of the true faith. His allegiance to God was unswerving, while his affability and benevolence inspired confidence and friendship and his unaffected greatness commanded respect and honor.

His religion was not held as a precious treasure to be jealously guarded and enjoyed solely by the possessor. True religion cannot be thus held, for such a spirit is contrary to the principles of the gospel. While Christ is dwelling in the heart it is impossible to conceal the light of His presence, or for that light to grow dim. On the contrary, it will grow brighter and brighter as day by day the mists of selfishness and sin that envelop the soul are dispelled by the bright beams of the Sun of Righteousness.

The people of God are His representatives upon the earth, and He intends that they shall be lights in the moral darkness of this world. Scattered all over the country, in the towns, cities, and villages, they are God's witnesses, the channels through which He will communicate to an unbelieving world the knowledge of His will and the wonders of His grace. It is His plan that all who are partakers of the great salvation shall be missionaries for Him. The piety of the Christian constitutes the standard by which worldlings judge the gospel. Trials patiently borne, blessings gratefully received, meekness, kindness, mercy, and love, habitually exhibited, are the lights that shine forth in the character before the world, revealing the contrast with the darkness that comes of the selfishness of the natural heart.

Rich in faith, noble in generosity, unfaltering in obedience, and humble in the simplicity of his pilgrim life, Abraham was also wise in diplomacy and brave and skillful in war. Notwithstanding he was known as the teacher of a new religion, three royal brothers, rulers of the Amorite plains in which he dwelt, manifested their friendship by inviting him to enter into an alliance with them for greater security; for the country was filled with violence and oppression. An occasion soon arose for him to avail himself of this alliance.

Chedorlaomer, king of Elam, had invaded Canaan fourteen years before, and made it tributary to him. Several of the princes now revolted, and the Elamite king, with four allies, again marched into the country to reduce them to submission. Five kings of Canaan joined their forces and met the invaders in the vale of Siddim, but only to be completely overthrown. A large part of the army was cut to pieces, and those who escaped fled for safety to the mountains. The victors plundered the cities of the plain and departed with rich spoil and many captives, among whom were Lot and his family.

Abraham, dwelling in peace in the oak groves at Mamre, learned from one of the fugitives the story of the battle and the calamity that had befallen his nephew. He had cherished no unkind memory of Lot's ingratitude. All his affection for him was awakened, and he determined that he should be rescued. Seeking, first of all, divine counsel, Abraham

prepared for war. From his own encampment he summoned three hundred and eighteen trained servants, men trained in the fear of God, in the service of their master, and in the practice of arms. His confederates, Mamre, Eschol, and Aner, joined him with their bands, and together they started in pursuit of the invaders. The Elamites and their allies had encamped at Dan, on the northern border of Canaan. Flushed with victory, and having no fear of an assault from their vanquished foes, they had given themselves up to reveling. The patriarch divided his force so as to approach from different directions, and came upon the encampment by night. His attack, so vigorous and unexpected, resulted in speedy victory. The king of Elam was slain and his panic-stricken forces were utterly routed. Lot and his family, with all the prisoners and their goods, were recovered, and a rich booty fell into the hands of the victors. To Abraham, under God, the triumph was due. The worshiper of Jehovah had not only rendered a great service to the country, but had proved himself a man of valor. It was seen that righteousness is not cowardice, and that Abraham's religion made him courageous in maintaining the right and defending the oppressed. His heroic act gave him a widespread influence among the surrounding tribes. On his return, the king of Sodom came out with his retinue to honor the conqueror. He bade him take the goods, begging only that the prisoners should be restored. By the usage of war, the spoils belonged to the conquerors; but Abraham had undertaken this expedition with no purpose of gain, and he refused to take advantage of the unfortunate, only stipulating that his confederates should receive the portion to which they entitled.

Few, if subjected to such a test, would have shown themselves as noble as did Abraham. Few would have resisted the temptation to secure so rich a booty. His example is a rebuke to self-seeking, mercenary spirits. Abraham regarded the claims of justice and humanity. His conduct illustrates the inspired maxim, "Thou shalt love thy neighbor as thyself." Leviticus 19:18. "I have lifted up my hand," he said, "unto the Lord, the most high God, the possessor of heaven and earth, that I will not take from a thread even to a shoe latchet, and that I will not take anything that is thine, lest thou shouldest say, I have made Abram rich." He would give them no occasion to think that he had engaged in warfare for the sake of gain, or to attribute his prosperity to their gifts or favor. God had promised to bless Abraham, and to Him the glory should be ascribed.

Another who came out to welcome the victorious patriarch was Melchizedek, king of Salem, who brought forth bread and wine for the refreshment of his army. As "priest of the most high God," he pronounced a blessing upon Abraham, and gave thanks to the Lord, who had wrought so great a deliverance by his servant. And Abraham "gave him tithes of all."

Abraham gladly returned to his tents and his flocks, but his mind was disturbed by harassing thoughts. He had been a man of peace, so far as possible shunning enmity and strife; and with horror he recalled the scene of carnage he had witnessed. But the nations whose forces he had defeated would doubtless renew the invasion of Canaan, and make him the special object of their vengeance. Becoming thus involved in national quarrels, the peaceful quiet of his life would be broken. Furthermore, he had not entered upon the possession of Canaan, nor could he now hope for an heir, to whom the promise might be fulfilled.

In a vision of the night the divine Voice was again heard. "Fear not, Abram," were the words of the Prince of princes; "I am thy shield, and thy exceeding great reward." But his mind was so oppressed by forebodings that he could not now grasp the promise with unquestioning confidence as heretofore. He prayed for some tangible evidence that it would be fulfilled. And how was the covenant promise to be realized, while the gift of a son was withheld? "What wilt thou give me," he said, "seeing I go childless?" "And, lo, one born in my house is mine heir." He proposed to make his trusty servant Eliezer his son by adoption, and the inheritor of his possessions. But he was assured that a child of his own was to be his heir. Then he was led outside his tent, and told to look up to the unnumbered stars glittering in the heavens; and as he did so, the words were spoken, "So shall thy seed be." "Abraham believed God, and it was counted unto him for righteousness." Romans 4:3.

Still the patriarch begged for some visible token as a confirmation of his faith and as an evidence to after-generations that God's gracious purposes toward them would be accomplished. The Lord condescended to enter into a covenant with His servant, employing such forms as were customary among men for the ratification of a solemn engagement. By divine direction, Abraham sacrificed a heifer, a she-goat, and a ram, each three years old, dividing the bodies and laying the pieces a little distance apart. To these he added a turtledove and a young pigeon, which, however, were not divided. This being done, he reverently passed between the parts of the sacrifice, making a solemn vow to God of perpetual obedience. Watchful and steadfast, he remained beside the carcasses till the going down of the sun, to guard them from being defiled or devoured by birds of prey. About sunset he sank into a deep sleep; and, "lo, a horror of great darkness fell upon him." And the voice of God was heard, bidding him not to expect immediate possession of the Promised Land, and pointing forward to the sufferings of his posterity before their establishment in Canaan. The plan of redemption was here opened to him, in the death of Christ, the great sacrifice, and His coming in glory. Abraham saw also the earth restored to its Eden beauty, to be given him for an everlasting possession, as the final and complete fulfillment of the promise.

As a pledge of this covenant of God with men, a smoking furnace and a burning lamp, symbols of the divine presence, passed between the severed victims, totally consuming them. And again a voice was heard by Abraham, confirming the gift of the land of Canaan to his descendants, "from the river of Egypt unto the great river, the river Euphrates."

When Abraham had been nearly twenty-five years in Canaan, the Lord appeared unto him, and said, "I am the Almighty God; walk before Me, and be thou perfect." In awe, the patriarch fell upon his face, and the message continued: "Behold, My covenant is with thee, and thou shalt be a father of many nations." In token of the fulfillment of this covenant, his name, heretofore called Abram, was changed to Abraham, which signifies, "father of a great multitude." Sarai's name became Sarah—"princess;" for, said the divine Voice, "she shall be a mother of nations; kings of people shall be of her."

At this time the rite of circumcision was given to Abraham as "a seal of the righteousness of the faith which he had yet being uncircumcised." Romans 4:11. It was to be observed by the patriarch and his descendants as a token that they were devoted to the service of God and thus separated from idolaters, and that God accepted them as His peculiar treasure. By this rite they were pledged to fulfill, on their part, the conditions of the covenant made with Abraham. They were not to contact marriages with the heathen; for by so doing they would lose their reverence for God and His holy law; they would be tempted to engage in the sinful practices of other nations, and would be seduced into idolatry.

God conferred great honor upon Abraham. Angels of heaven walked and talked with him as friend with friend. When judgments were about to be visited upon Sodom, the fact was not hidden from him, and he became an intercessor with God for sinners. His interview with the angels presents also a beautiful example of hospitality.

In the hot summer noontide the patriarch was sitting in his tent door, looking out over the quiet landscape, when he saw in the distance three travelers approaching. Before reaching his tent, the strangers halted, as if consulting as to their course. Without waiting for them to solicit favors, Abraham rose quickly, and as they were apparently turning in another direction, he hastened after them, and with the utmost courtesy urged them to honor him by tarrying for refreshment. With his own hands he brought water that they might wash the dust of travel from their feet. He himself selected their food, and while they were at rest under the cooling shade, an entertainment was made ready, and he stood respectfully beside them while they partook of his hospitality. This act of courtesy God regarded of sufficient importance to record in His word; and a thousand years later it was referred to by an inspired apostle: "Be not forgetful to entertain strangers: for thereby some have entertained angels unawares." Hebrews 13:2.

Abraham had seen in his guests only three tired wayfarers, little thinking that among them was One whom he might worship without sin. But the true character of the heavenly messengers was now revealed. Though they were on their way as ministers of wrath, yet to Abraham, the man of faith, they spoke first of blessings. Though God is strict to mark iniquity and to punish transgression, He takes no delight in vengeance. The work of destruction is a "strange work" to Him who is infinite in love.

"The secret of the Lord is with them that fear Him." Psalm 25:14. Abraham had honored God, and the Lord honored him, taking him into His counsels, and revealing to him His purposes. "Shall I hide from Abraham that thing which I do?" said the Lord. "The cry of Sodom and Gomorrah is great, and because their sin is very grievous, I will go down now, and see whether they have done altogether according to the cry of it, which is come unto me; and if not, I will know." God knew well the measure of Sodom's guilt; but He expressed Himself after the manner of men, that the justice of His dealings might be understood. Before bringing judgment upon the transgressors He would go Himself, to institute an examination of their course; if they had not passed the limits of divine mercy, He would still grant them space for repentance.

Two of the heavenly messengers departed, leaving Abraham alone with Him whom he now knew to be the Son of God. And the man of faith pleaded for the inhabitants of Sodom. Once he had saved them by his sword, now he endeavored to save them by prayer. Lot and his household were still dwellers there; and the unselfish love that prompted Abraham to their rescue from the Elamites, now sought to save them, if it were God's will, from the storm of divine judgment.

With deep reverence and humility he urged his plea: "I have taken upon me to speak unto the Lord, which am but dust and ashes." There was no self-confidence, no boasting of his own righteousness. He did not claim favor on the ground of his obedience, or of the sacrifices he had made in doing God's will. Himself a sinner, he pleaded in the sinner's behalf. Such a spirit all who approach God should possess. Yet Abraham manifested the confidence of a child pleading with a loved father. He came close to the heavenly Messenger, and fervently urged his petition. Though Lot had become a dweller in Sodom, he did not partake in the iniquity of its inhabitants. Abraham thought that in that populous city there must be other worshipers of the true God. And in view of this he pleaded, "That be far from Thee, to do after this manner, to slay the righteous with the wicked: . . . that be far from Thee: Shall not the Judge of all the earth do right?" Abraham asked not once merely, but many times. Waxing bolder as his requests were granted, he continued until he gained the assurance that if even ten righteous persons could be found in it, the city would be spared.

Love for perishing souls inspired Abraham's prayer. While he loathed the sins of that corrupt city, he desired that the sinners might be saved. His deep interest for Sodom shows the anxiety that we should feel for the impenitent. We should cherish hatred of sin, but pity and love for the sinner. All around us are souls going down to ruin as hopeless, as terrible, as that which befell Sodom. Every day the probation of some is closing. Every hour some are passing beyond the reach of mercy. And where are the voices of warning and entreaty to bid the sinner flee from this fearful doom? Where are the hands stretched out to draw him back from death? Where are

those who with humility and persevering faith are pleading with God for him?

The spirit of Abraham was the spirit of Christ. The Son of God is Himself the great Intercessor in the sinner's behalf. He who has paid the price for its redemption knows the worth of the human soul. With an antagonism to evil such as can exist only in a nature spotlessly pure, Christ manifested toward the sinner a love which infinite goodness alone could conceive. In the agonies of the crucifixion, Himself burdened with the awful weight of the sins of the whole world, He prayed for His revilers and murderers, "Father, forgive them; for they know not what they do." Luke 23:34.

Of Abraham it is written that "he was called the friend of God," "the father of all them that believe." James 2:23; Romans 4:11. The testimony of God concerning this faithful patriarch is, "Abraham obeyed My voice, and kept My charge, My commandments, My statutes, and My laws." And again, "I know him, that he will command his children and his household after him, and they shall keep the way of the Lord, to do justice and judgment; that the Lord may bring upon Abraham that which he hath spoken of him." It was a high honor to which Abraham was called, that of being the father of the people who for centuries were the guardians and preservers of the truth of God for the world—of that people through whom all the nations of the earth should be blessed in the advent of the promised Messiah. But He who called the patriarch judged him worthy. It is God that speaks. He who understands the thoughts afar off, and places the right estimate upon men, says, "I know him." There would be on the part of Abraham no betraying of the truth for selfish purposes. He would keep the law and deal justly and righteously. And he would not only fear the Lord himself, but would cultivate religion in his home. He would instruct his family in righteousness. The law of God would be the rule in his household.

Abraham's household comprised more than a thousand souls. Those who were led by his teachings to worship the one God, found a home in his encampment; and here, as in a school, they received such instruction as would prepare them to be representatives of the true faith. Thus a great responsibility rested upon him. He was training heads of families, and his methods of government would be carried out in the households over which they should preside.

In early times the father was the ruler and priest of his own family, and he exercised authority over his children, even after they had families of their own. His descendants were taught to look up to him as their head, in both religious and secular matters. This patriarchal system of government Abraham endeavored to perpetuate, as it tended to preserve the knowledge of God. It was necessary to bind the members of the household together, in order to build up a barrier against the idolatry that had become so widespread and so deep-seated. Abraham sought by every means in his power to guard the inmates of his encampment against mingling with the heathen and witnessing their idolatrous practices, for he knew that familiarity with evil would insensibly corrupt the principles. The greatest care was exercised to shut out every form of false religion and to impress the mind with the majesty and glory of the living God as the true object of worship.

It was a wise arrangement, which God Himself had made, to cut off His people, so far as possible, from connection with the heathen, making them a people dwelling alone, and not reckoned among the nations. He had separated Abraham from his idolatrous kindred, that the patriarch might train and educate his family apart from the seductive influences which would have surrounded them in Mesopotamia, and that the true faith might be preserved in its purity by his descendants from generation to generation.

Abraham's affection for his children and his household led him to guard their religious faith, to impart to them a knowledge of the divine statutes, as the most precious legacy he could transmit to them, and through them to the world. All were taught that they were under the rule of the God of heaven. There was to be no oppression on the part of parents and no disobedience on the part of children. God's law had appointed to each his duties, and only in obedience to it could any secure happiness or prosperity.

His own example, the silent influence of his daily life, was a constant lesson. The unswerving integrity, the benevolence and unselfish courtesy, which had won the admiration of kings, were displayed in the home. There was a fragrance about the life, a nobility and loveliness of character, which revealed to all that he was connected with Heaven. He did not neglect the soul of the humblest servant. In his household there was not one law for the master and another for the servant; a royal way for the rich and another for the poor. All were treated with justice and compassion, as inheritors with him of the grace of life.

"He will command his . . . household." There would be no sinful neglect to restrain the evil propensities of his children, no weak, unwise, indulgent favoritism; no yielding of his conviction of duty to the claims of mistaken affection. Abraham would not only give right instruction, but he would maintain the authority of just and righteous laws.

How few there are in our day who follow this example! On the part of too many parents there is a blind and selfish sentimentalism, miscalled love, which is manifested in leaving children, with their unformed judgment and undisciplined passions, to the control of their own will. This is the veriest cruelty to the youth and a great wrong to the world. Parental indulgence causes disorder in families and in society. It confirms in the young the desire to follow inclination, instead of submitting to the divine requirements. Thus they grow up with a heart averse to doing God's will, and they transmit their irreligious, insubordinate spirit to their children and children's children. Like Abraham, parents should command their households after them. Let obedience to parental authority be taught and enforced as the first step in obedience to the authority of God.

The light esteem in which the law of God is held, even by religious leaders, has been productive of great evil. The teaching which has become so widespread, that the divine statutes are no longer binding upon men, is the same as idolatry in its effect upon the morals of the people. Those who seek to lessen the claims of God's holy law are striking directly at the foundation of the government of families and nations. Religious parents, failing to walk in His statutes, do not command their household to keep the way of the Lord. The law of God is not made the rule of life. The children, as they make homes of their own, feel under no obligation to teach their children what they themselves have never been taught. And this is why there are so many godless families; this is why depravity is so deep and widespread.

Not until parents themselves walk in the law of the Lord with perfect hearts will they be prepared to command their children after them. A reformation in this respect is needed—a reformation which shall be deep and broad. Parents need to reform; ministers need to reform; they need God in their households. If they would see a different state of things, they must bring His word into their families and must make it their counselor. They must teach their children that it is the voice of God addressed to them, and is to be implicitly obeyed. They should patiently instruct their children, kindly and untiringly teach them how to live in order to please God. The children of such a household are prepared to meet the sophistries of infidelity. They have accepted the Bible as the basis of their faith, and they have a foundation that cannot be swept away by the incoming tide of skepticism.

In too many households prayer is neglected. Parents feel that they have no time for morning and evening worship. They cannot spare a few moments to be spent in thanksgiving to God for His abundant mercies—for the blessed sunshine and the showers of rain, which cause vegetation to flourish, and for the guardianship of holy angels. They have no time to offer prayer for divine help and guidance and for the abiding presence of Jesus in the household. They go forth to labor as the ox or the horse goes, without one thought of God or heaven. They have souls so precious that rather than permit them to be hopelessly lost, the Son of God gave His life to ransom them; but they have little more appreciation of His great goodness than have the beasts that perish.

Like the patriarchs of old, those who profess to love God should erect an altar to the Lord wherever they pitch their tent. If ever there was a time when every house should be a house of prayer, it is now. Fathers and mothers should often lift up their hearts to God in humble supplication for themselves and their children. Let the father, as priest of the household, lay upon the altar of God the morning and evening sacrifice, while the wife and children unite in prayer and praise. In such a household Jesus will love to tarry.

From every Christian home a holy light should shine forth. Love should be revealed in action. It should flow out in all home intercourse, showing itself in thoughtful kindness, in gentle, unselfish courtesy. There are homes where this principle is carried out—homes where God is worshiped and truest love reigns. From these homes morning and evening prayer ascends to God as sweet incense, and His mercies and blessings descend upon the suppliants like the morning dew.

A well-ordered Christian household is a powerful argument in favor of the reality of the Christian religion—an argument that the infidel cannot gainsay. All can see that there is an influence at work in the family that affects the children, and that the God of Abraham is with them. If the homes of professed Christians had a right religious mold, they would exert a mighty influence for good. They would indeed be the "light of the world." The God of heaven speaks to every faithful parent in the words addressed to Abraham: "I know him, that he will command his children and his household after him, and they shall keep the way of the Lord, to do justice and judgment; that the Lord may bring upon Abraham that which He hath spoken of him."

The Test of Faith

Abraham had accepted without question the promise of a son, but he did not wait for God to fulfill His word in His own time and way. A delay was permitted, to test his faith in the power of God; but he failed to endure the trial. Thinking it impossible that a child should be given her in her old age, Sarah suggested, as a plan by which the divine purpose might be fulfilled, that one of her handmaidens should be taken by Abraham as a secondary wife. Polygamy had become so widespread that it had ceased to be regarded as a sin, but it was no less a violation of the law of God, and was fatal to the sacredness and peace of the family relation. Abraham's marriage with Hagar resulted in evil, not only to his own household, but to future generations.

Flattered with the honor of her new position as Abraham's wife, and hoping to be the mother of the great nation to descend from him, Hagar became proud and boastful, and treated her mistress with contempt. Mutual jealousies disturbed the peace of the once happy home. Forced to listen to the complaints of both, Abraham vainly endeavored to restore harmony. Though it was at Sarah's earnest entreaty that he had married Hagar, she now reproached him as the one at fault. She desired to banish her rival; but Abraham refused to permit this; for Hagar was to be the mother of this child, as he fondly hoped, the son of promise. She was Sarah's servant, however, and he still left her to the control of her mistress. Hagar's haughty spirit would not brook the harshness which her insolence had provoked. "When Sarai dealt hardly with her, she fled from her face."

She made her way to the desert, and as she rested beside a fountain, lonely and friendless, an angel of the Lord, in human form, appeared to her. Addressing her as "Hagar, Sarai's maid," to remind her of her position and her duty, he bade her, "Return to thy mistress, and submit thyself under her hands." Yet with the reproof there were mingled words of comfort. "The Lord hath heard thy affliction." "I will multiply

thy seed exceedingly, that it shall not be numbered for multitude." And as a perpetual reminder of His mercy, she was bidden to call her child Ishmael, "God shall hear."

When Abraham was nearly one hundred years old, the promise of a son was repeated to him, with the assurance that the future heir should be the child of Sarah. But Abraham did not yet understand the promise. His mind at once turned to Ishmael, clinging to the belief that through him God's gracious purposes were to be accomplished. In his affection for his son he exclaimed, "O that Ishmael might live before Thee!" Again the promise was given, in words that could not be mistaken: "Sarah thy wife shall bear thee a son indeed; and thou shalt call his name Isaac: and I will establish My covenant with him." Yet God was not unmindful of the father's prayer. "As for Ishmael," He said, "I have heard thee: Behold, I have blessed him, . . . and I will make him a great nation."

The birth of Isaac, bringing, after a lifelong waiting, the fulfillment of their dearest hopes, filled the tents of Abraham and Sarah with gladness. But to Hagar this event was the overthrow of her fondly cherished ambitions. Ishmael, now a youth, had been regarded by all in the encampment as the heir of Abraham's wealth and the interior of the blessings promised to his descendants. Now he was suddenly set aside; and in their disappointment, mother and son hated the child of Sarah. The general rejoicing increased their jealousy, until Ishmael dared openly to mock the heir of God's promise. Sarah saw in Ishmael's turbulent disposition a perpetual source of discord, and she appealed to Abraham, urging that Hagar and Ishmael be sent away from the encampment. The patriarch was thrown into great distress. How could he banish Ishmael his son, still dearly beloved? In his perplexity he pleaded for divine guidance. The Lord, through a holy angel, directed him to grant Sarah's desire; his love for Ishmael or Hagar ought not to stand in the way, for only thus could he restore harmony and happiness to his family. And the angel gave him the consoling promise that though separated from his father's home, Ishmael should not be forsaken by God; his life should be preserved, and he should become the father of a great nation. Abraham obeyed the angel's word, but it was not without keen suffering. The father's heart was heavy with unspoken grief as he sent away Hagar and his son.

The instruction given to Abraham touching the sacredness of the marriage relation was to be a lesson for all ages. It declares that the rights and happiness of this relation are to be carefully guarded, even at a great sacrifice. Sarah was the only true wife of Abraham. Her rights as a wife and mother no other person was entitled to share. She reverenced her husband, and in this she is presented in the New Testament as a worthy example. But she was unwilling that Abraham's affections should be given to another, and the Lord did not reprove her for requiring the banishment of her rival. Both Abraham and Sarah distrusted the power of God, and it was this error that led to the marriage with Hagar.

God had called Abraham to be the father of the faithful,

and his life was to stand as an example of faith to succeeding generations. But his faith had not been perfect. He had shown distrust of God in concealing the fact that Sarah was his wife, and again in his marriage with Hagar. That he might reach the highest standard, God subjected him to another test, the closest which man was ever called to endure. In a vision of the night he was directed to repair to the land of Moriah, and there offer up his son as a burnt offering upon a mountain that should be shown him.

At the time of receiving this command, Abraham had reached the age of a hundred and twenty years. He was regarded as an old man, even in his generation. In his earlier years he had been strong to endure hardship and to brave danger, but now the ardor of his youth had passed away. One in the vigor of manhood may with courage meet difficulties and afflictions that would cause his heart to fail later in life, when his feet are faltering toward the grave. But God had reserved His last, most trying test for Abraham until the burden of years was heavy upon him, and he longed for rest from anxiety and toil.

The patriarch was dwelling at Beersheba, surrounded by prosperity and honor. He was very rich, and was honored as a mighty prince by the rulers of the land. Thousands of sheep and cattle covered the plains that spread out beyond his encampment. On every side were the tents of his retainers, the home of hundreds of faithful servants. The son of promise had grown up to manhood by his side. Heaven seemed to have crowned with its blessing a life of sacrifice in patient endurance of hope deferred.

In the obedience of faith, Abraham had forsaken his native country—had turned away from the graves of his fathers and the home of his kindred. He had wandered as a stranger in the land of his inheritance. He had waited long for the birth of the promised heir. At the command of God he had sent away his son Ishmael. And now, when the child so long desired was entering upon manhood, and the patriarch seemed able to discern the fruition of his hopes, a trial greater than all others was before him.

The command was expressed in words that must have wrung with anguish that father's heart: "Take now thy son, thine only son Isaac, whom thou lovest, . . . and offer him there for a burnt offering." Isaac was the light of his home, the solace of his old age, above all else the inheritor of the promised blessing. The loss of such a son by accident or disease would have been heart rending to the fond father; it would have bowed down his whitened head with grief; but he was commanded to shed the blood of that son with his own hand. It seemed to him a fearful impossibility.

Satan was at hand to suggest that he must be deceived, for the divine law commands, "Thou shalt not kill," and God would not require what He had once forbidden. Going outside his tent, Abraham looked up to the calm brightness of the unclouded heavens, and recalled the promise made nearly fifty years before, that his seed should be innumerable as the stars. If this promise was to be fulfilled through Isaac, how could he be put to death? Abraham was tempted to believe that he might be under a delusion. In his doubt and anguish he bowed upon the earth, and prayed, as he had never prayed before, for some confirmation of the command if he must perform this terrible duty. He remembered the angels sent to reveal to him God's purpose to destroy Sodom, and who bore to him the promise of this same son Isaac, and he went to the place where he had several times met the heavenly messengers, hoping to meet them again, and receive some further direction; but none came to his relief. Darkness seemed to shut him in; but the command of God was sounding in his ears, "Take now thy son, thine only son Isaac, whom thou lovest." That command must be obeyed, and he dared not delay. Day was approaching, and he must be on his journey.

Returning to his tent, he went to the place where Isaac lay sleeping the deep, untroubled sleep of youth and innocence. For a moment the father looked upon the dear face of his son, then turned tremblingly away. He went to the side of Sarah, who was also sleeping. Should he awaken her, that she might once more embrace her child? Should he tell her of God's requirement? He longed to unburden his heart to her, and share with her this terrible responsibility; but he was restrained by the fear that she might hinder him. Isaac was her joy and pride; her life was bound up in him, and the mother's love might refuse the sacrifice.

Abraham at last summoned his son, telling him of the command to offer sacrifice upon a distant mountain. Isaac had often gone with his father to worship at some one of the various altars that marked his wanderings, and this summons excited no surprise. The preparations for the journey were quickly completed. The wood was made ready and put upon the ass, and with two menservants they set forth.

Side by side the father and the son journeyed in silence. The patriarch, pondering his heavy secret, had no heart for words. His thoughts were of the proud, fond mother, and the day when he should return to her alone. Well he knew that the knife would pierce her heart when it took the life of her son.

That day—the longest that Abraham had ever experienced—dragged slowly to its close. While his son and the young men were sleeping, he spent the night in prayer, still hoping that some heavenly messenger might come to say that the trial was enough, that the youth might return unharmed to his mother. But no relief came to his tortured soul. Another long day, another night of humiliation and prayer, while ever the command that was to leave him childless was ringing in his ears. Satan was near to whisper doubts and unbelief, but Abraham resisted his suggestions. As they were about to begin the journey of the third day, the patriarch, looking northward, saw the promised sign, a cloud of glory hovering over Mount Moriah, and he knew that the voice which had spoken to him was from heaven.

Even now he did not murmur against God, but strengthened his soul by dwelling upon the evidences of the Lord's goodness and faithfulness. This son had been unexpectedly given; and had not He who bestowed the precious gift a right to recall His own? Then faith repeated the promise, "In Isaac shall they seed be called"—a seed numberless as the grains of sand upon the shore. Isaac was the child of a miracle, and could not the power that gave him life restore it? Looking beyond that which was seen, Abraham grasped the divine word, "accounting that God was able to raise him up, even from the dead." Hebrews 11:19.

Yet none but God could understand how great was the father's sacrifice in yielding up his son to death; Abraham desired that none but God should witness the parting scene. He bade his servants remain behind, saying, "I and the lad will go yonder and worship, and come again to you." The wood was laid upon Isaac, the one to be offered, the father took the knife and the fire, and together they ascended toward the mountain summit, the young man silently wondering whence, so far from folds and flocks, the offering was to come. At last he spoke, "My father," "behold the fire and the wood: but where is the lamb for a burnt offering?" Oh, what a test was this! How the endearing words, "my father," pierced Abraham's heart! Not yet—he could not tell him now . "My son," he said, "God will provide Himself a lamb for a burnt offering."

At the appointed place they built the altar and laid the wood upon it. Then, with trembling voice, Abraham unfolded to his son the divine message. It was with terror and amazement that Isaac learned his fate, but he offered no resistance. He could have escaped his doom, had he chosen to do so; the grief-stricken old man, exhausted with the struggle of those three terrible days, could not have opposed the will of the vigorous youth. But Isaac had been trained from childhood to ready, trusting obedience, and as the purpose of God was opened before him, he yielded a willing submission. He was a sharer in Abraham's faith, and he felt that he was honored in being called to give his life as an offering to God. He tenderly seeks to lighten the father's grief, and encourages his nerveless hands to bind the cords that confine him to the altar.

And now the last words of love are spoken, the last tears are shed, the last embrace is given. The father lifts the knife to slay his son, when suddenly his arm is stayed. An angel of God calls to the patriarch out of heaven, "Abraham, Abraham!" He quickly answers, "Here am I," And again the voice is heard, "Lay not thine hand upon the lad, neither do thou any thing unto him: for now I know that thou fearest God, seeing thou hast not withheld thy son, thine only son, from Me."

Then Abraham saw "a ram caught in a thicket," and quickly bringing the new victim, he offered it "in the stead of his son." In his joy and gratitude Abraham gave a new name to the sacred spot—"Jehovah-jireh," "the Lord will provide."

On Mount Moriah, God again renewed His covenant, confirming with a solemn oath the blessing to Abraham and to his seed through all coming generations: "By myself have I sworn, saith Jehovah, for because thou hast done this thing, and hast not withheld thy son, thine only son, that in blessing I will bless thee, and in multiplying I will multiply thy seed as the stars of the heaven, and as the sand which is upon the seashore; and thy seed shall possess the gate of his enemies; and in thy seed shall all the nations of the earth be blessed; because thou hast obeyed My voice."

Abraham's great act of faith stands like a pillar of light, illuminating the pathway of God's servants in all succeeding ages. Abraham did not seek to excuse himself from doing the will of God. During that three days' journey he had sufficient time to reason, and to doubt God, if he was disposed to doubt. He might have reasoned that the slaying of his son would cause him to be looked upon as a murderer, a second Cain; that it would cause his teaching to be rejected and despised; and thus destroy his power to do good to his fellow men. He might have pleaded that age should excuse him from obedience. But the patriarch did not take refuge in any of these excuses. Abraham was human; his passions and attachments were like ours; but he did not stop to question how the promise could be fulfilled if Isaac should be slain. He did not stay to reason with his aching heart. He knew that God is just and righteous in all His requirements, and he obeyed the command to the very letter.

"Abraham believed God, and it was imputed unto him for righteousness: an he was called the friend of God." James 2:23. And Paul says, "They which are of faith, the same are the children of Abraham." Galatians 3:7. But Abraham's faith was made manifest by his works. "Was not Abraham our father justified by works, when he had offered Isaac his son upon the altar? Seest thou how faith wrought with his works, and by works was faith made perfect?" James 2:21, 22. There are many who fail to understand the relation of faith and works. They say, "Only believe in Christ, and you are safe. You have nothing to do with keeping the law." But genuine faith will be manifest in obedience. Said Christ to the unbelieving Jews, "If ye were Abraham's children, ye would do the works of Abraham." John 8:39. And concerning the father of the faithful the Lord declares, "Abraham obeyed My voice, and kept My charge, My commandments, My statutes, and My laws." Genesis 26:5. Says the apostle James, "Faith, if it hath not works, is dead, being alone." James 2:17. And John, who dwells so fully upon love, tells us, "This is the love of God, that we keep His commandments." 1 John 5:3.

Through type and promise God "preached before the gospel unto Abraham." Galatians 3:8. And the patriarch's faith was fixed upon the Redeemer to come. Said Christ to the Jews. "Your father Abraham rejoiced that he should see My day; and he saw it, and was glad." John 8:56, R.V., margin. The ram offered in the place of Isaac represented the Son of God, who was to be sacrificed in our stead. When man was doomed to death by transgression of the law of God, the Father, looking upon His Son, said to the sinner, "Live: I have found a ransom."

It was to impress Abraham's mind with the reality of the gospel, as well as to test his faith, that God commanded him to slay his son. The agony which he endured during the dark days of that fearful trial was permitted that he might understand from his own experience something of the greatness of the sacrifice made by the infinite God for man's redemption. No other test could have caused Abraham such torture of soul as did the offering of his son. God gave His Son to a death of agony and shame. The angels who witnessed the humiliation and soul anguish of the Son of God were not permitted to interpose, as in the case of Isaac. There was no voice to cry, "It is enough." To save the fallen race, the King of glory yielded up His life. What stronger proof can be given of the infinite compassion and love of God? "He that spared not His own Son, but delivered Him up for us all, how shall He not with Him also freely give us all things?" Romans 8:32.

The sacrifice required of Abraham was not alone for his own good, nor solely for the benefit of succeeding generations; but it was also for the instruction of the sinless intelligences of heaven and of other worlds. The field of the controversy between Christ and Satan—the field on which the plan of redemption is wrought out—is the lesson book of the universe. Because Abraham had shown a lack of faith in God's promises, Satan had accused him before the angels and before God of having failed to comply with the conditions of the covenant, and as unworthy of its blessings. God desired to prove the loyalty of His servant before all heaven, to demonstrate that nothing less than perfect obedience can be accepted, and to open more fully before them the plan of salvation.

Heavenly beings were witnesses of the scene as the faith of Abraham and the submission of Isaac were tested. The trial was far more severe than that which had been brought upon Adam. Compliance with the prohibition laid upon our first parents involved no suffering, but the command to Abraham demanded the most agonizing sacrifice. All heaven beheld with wonder and admiration Abraham's unfaltering obedience. All heaven applauded his fidelity. Satan's accusations were shown to be false. God declared to His servant, "Now I know that thou fearest God, seeing thou hast not withheld thy son, thine only son from Me." God's covenant, confirmed to Abraham by an oath before the intelligences of other worlds, testified that obedience will be rewarded.

It had been difficult even for the angels to grasp the mystery of redemption—to comprehend that the Commander of heaven, the Son of God, must die for guilty man. When the command was given to Abraham to offer up his son, the interest of all heavenly beings was enlisted. With intense earnestness they watched each step in the fulfillment of this command. When to Isaac's question, "Where is the lamb for a burnt offering?" Abraham made answer, "God will provide Himself a lamb;" and when the father's hand was stayed as he was about to slay his son, and the ram which God had provided was offered in the place of Isaac—then light was shed upon the mystery of redemption, and even the angels understood more clearly the wonderful provision that God had made for man's salvation. 1 Peter 1:12.

Destruction of Sodom

Fairest among the cities of the Jordan Valley was Sodom, set in a plain which was "as the garden of the Lord" in its fertility and beauty. Here the luxuriant vegetation of the tropics flourished. Here was the home of the palm tree, the olive, and the vine; and flowers shed their fragrance throughout the year. Rich harvests clothed the fields, and flocks and herds covered the encircling hills. Art and commerce contributed to enrich the proud city of the plain. The treasures of the East adorned her palaces, and the caravans of the desert brought their stores of precious things to supply her marts of trade. With little thought or labor, every want of life could be supplied, and the whole year seemed one round of festivity.

The profusion reigning everywhere gave birth to luxury and pride. Idleness and riches make the heart hard that has never been oppressed by want or burdened by sorrow. The love of pleasure was fostered by wealth and leisure, and the people gave themselves up to sensual indulgence. "Behold," says the prophet, "this was the iniquity of thy sister Sodom, pride, fullness of bread, and abundance of idleness was in her and in her daughters, neither did she strengthen the hand of the poor and needy. And they were haughty, and committed abomination before Me: therefore I took them away as I saw good." Ezekiel 16:49, 50. There is nothing more desired among men than riches and leisure, and yet these gave birth to the sins that brought destruction upon the cities of the plain. Their useless, idle life made them a prey to Satan's temptations, and they defaced the image of God, and became satanic rather than divine. Idleness is the greatest curse that can fall upon man, for vice and crime follow in its train. It enfeebles the mind, perverts the understanding, and debases the soul. Satan lies in ambush, ready to destroy those who are unguarded, whose leisure gives him opportunity to insinuate himself under some attractive disguise. He is never more successful than when he comes to men in their idle hours.

In Sodom there was mirth and revelry, feasting and drunkenness. The vilest and most brutal passions were unrestrained. The people openly defied God and His law and delighted in deeds of violence. Though they had before them the example of the antediluvian world, and knew how the wrath of God had been manifested in their destruction, yet they followed the same course of wickedness.

At the time of Lot's removal to Sodom, corruption had not become universal, and God in His mercy permitted rays of light to shine amid the moral darkness. When Abraham rescued the captives from the Elamites, the attention of the people was called to the true faith. Abraham was not a stranger to the people of Sodom, and his worship of the unseen God had been a matter of ridicule among them; but his victory over greatly superior forces, and his magnanimous disposition of the prisoners and spoil, excited wonder and admiration. While his skill and valor were extolled, none could avoid the conviction that a divine power had made him conqueror. And his noble and unselfish spirit, so foreign to the self-seeking inhabitants of Sodom, was another evidence of the superiority of the religion which he had honored by his courage and fidelity.

Melchizedek, in bestowing the benediction upon Abraham, had acknowledged Jehovah as the source of his strength and the author of the victory: "Blessed be Abram of the most high God, possessor of heaven and earth: and blessed be the most high God, which hath delivered thine enemies into thy hand." Genesis 14:19, 20. God was speaking to that people by His providence, but the last ray of light was rejected as all before had been.

And now the last night of Sodom was approaching. Already the clouds of vengeance cast their shadows over the devoted city. But men perceived it not. While angels drew near on their mission of destruction, men were dreaming of prosperity and pleasure. The last days was like every other that had come and gone. Evening fell upon a scene of loveliness and security. A landscape of unrivaled beauty was bathed in the rays of the declining sun. The coolness of eventide had called forth the inhabitants of the city, and the pleasure-seeking throngs were passing to and fro, intent upon the enjoyment of the hour.

In the twilight two strangers drew near to the city gate. They were apparently travelers coming in to tarry for the night. None could discern in those humble wayfarers the mighty heralds of divine judgment, and little dreamed the gay, careless multitude that in their treatment of these heavenly messengers that very night they would reach the climax of the guilt which doomed their proud city. But there was one man who manifested kindly attention toward the strangers and invited them to his home. Lot did not know their true character, but politeness and hospitality were habitual with him; they were a part of his religion—lessons that he had learned from the example of Abraham. Had he not cultivated a spirit of courtesy, he might have been left to perish with the rest of Sodom. Many a household, in closing its doors against a stranger, has shut out God's messenger, who would have brought blessing and hope and peace.

Every act of life, however small, has its bearing for good or for evil. Faithfulness or neglect in what are apparently the smallest duties may open the door for life's richest blessings or its greatest calamities. It is little things that test the character. It is the unpretending acts of daily self-denial, performed with a cheerful, willing heart, that God smiles upon. We are not to live for self, but for others. And it is only by self-forgetfulness, by cherishing a loving, helpful spirit, that we can make our life a blessing. The little attentions, the small, simple courtesies, go far to make up the sum of life's happiness, and the neglect of these constitutes no small share of human wretchedness.

Seeing the abuse to which strangers were exposed in Sodom, Lot made it one of his duties to guard them at their entrance, by offering them entertainment at his own house. He was sitting at the gate as the travelers approached, and upon observing them, he rose from his place to meet them, and bowing courteously, said, "Behold now, my lords, turn in, I pray you, into your servant's house, and tarry all night." They seemed to decline his hospitality, saying, "Nay; but we will abide in the street." Their object in this answer was twofold—to test the sincerity of Lot and also to appear ignorant of the character of the men of Sodom, as if they supposed it safe to remain in the street at night. Their answer made Lot the more determined not to leave them to the mercy of the rabble. He pressed his invitation until they yielded, and accompanied him to his house.

He had hoped to conceal his intention from the idlers at the gate by bringing the strangers to his home by a circuitous route; but their hesitation and delay, and his persistent urging, caused them to be observed, and before they had retired for the night, a lawless crowd gathered about the house. It was an immense company, youth and aged men alike inflamed by the vilest passions. The strangers had been making inquiry in regard to the character of the city, and Lot had warned them not to venture out of his door that night, when the hooting and jeers of the mob were heard, demanding that the men be brought out to them.

Knowing that if provoked to violence they could easily break into his house, Lot went out to try the effect of persuasion upon them. "I pray you, brethren," he said, "do not so wickedly," using the term "brethren" in the sense of neighbors, and hoping to conciliate them and make them ashamed of their vile purposes. But his words were like oil upon the flames. Their rage became like the roaring of a tempest. They mocked Lot as making himself a judge over them, and threatened to deal worse with him than they had purposed toward his guests. They rushed upon him, and would have torn him in pieces had he not been rescued by the angels of God. The heavenly messengers "put forth their hand, and pulled Lot into the house to them, and shut to the door." The events that followed, revealed the character of the guests he had entertained. "They smote the men that were at the door of the house with blindness, both small and great: so that they wearied themselves to find the door." Had they not been visited with double blindness, being given up to hardness of heart, the stroke of God upon them would have caused them to fear, and to desist from their evil work. That last night was marked by no greater sins than many others before it; but mercy, so long slighted, had at last ceased its pleading. The inhabitants of Sodom had passed the limits of divine forbearance—"the hidden boundary between God's patience and His wrath." The fires of His vengeance were about to be kindled in the vale of Siddim.

The angels revealed to Lot the object of their mission: "We will destroy this place, because the cry of them is waxen great before the face of the Lord; and the Lord hath sent us to destroy it." The strangers whom Lot had endeavored to protect, now promised to protect him, and to save also all the members of his family who would flee with him from the wicked city. The mob had wearied themselves out and departed, and Lot went out to warn his children. He repeated the words of the angels, "Up, get you out of this place; for the Lord will destroy this city." But he seemed to them as one that mocked. They laughed at what they called his superstitious fears. His daughters were influenced by their husbands. They were well enough off where they were. They could see no evidence of danger. Everything was just as it had been. They had great possessions, and they could not believe it possible that beautiful Sodom would be destroyed.

Lot returned sorrowfully to his home and told the story of his failure. Then the angels bade him arise and take his wife and the two daughters who were yet in his house and leave the city. But Lot delayed. Though daily distressed at beholding deeds of violence, he had no true conception of the debasing and abominable iniquity practiced in that vile city. He did not realize the terrible necessity for God's judgments to put a check on sin. Some of his children clung to Sodom, and his wife refused to depart without them. The thought of leaving those whom he held dearest on earth seemed more than he could bear. It was hard to forsake his luxurious home and all the wealth acquired by the labors of his whole life, to go forth a destitute wanderer. Stupefied with sorrow, he lingered, loath to depart. But for the angels of God, they would all have perished in the ruin of Sodom. The heavenly messengers took him and his wife and daughters by the hand and led them out of the city.

Here the angels left them, and turned back to Sodom to accomplish their work of destruction. Another—He with whom Abraham had pleaded—drew near to Lot. In all the cities of the plain, even ten righteous persons had not been found; but in answer to the patriarch's prayer, the one man who feared God was snatched from destruction. The command was given with startling vehemence: "Escape for thy life; look not behind thee, neither stay thou in all the plain; escape to the mountain, lest thou be consumed." Hesitancy or delay now would be fatal. To cast one lingering look upon the devoted city, to tarry for one moment from regret to leave so beautiful a home, would have cost their life. The storm of divine judgment was only waiting that these poor fugitives might make their escape.

But Lot, confused and terrified, pleaded that he could not do as he was required lest some evil should overtake him and he should die. Living in that wicked city, in the midst of unbelief, his faith had grown dim. The Prince of heaven was by his side, yet he pleaded for his own life as though God, who had manifested such care and love for him, would not still preserve him. He should have trusted himself wholly to the divine Messenger, giving his will and his life into the Lord's hands without a doubt or a question. But like so many others, he endeavored to plan for himself: "Behold now, this city is near to flee unto, and it is a little one: O, let me escape thither, (is it not a little one?) and my soul shall live." The city here mentioned was Bela, afterward called Zoar. It was but a few miles from Sodom, and, like it, was corrupt and doomed to destruction. But Lot asked that it might be spared, urging that this was but a small request; and his desire was granted. The Lord assured him, "I have accepted thee concerning this thing also, that I will not overthrow this city, for the which thou hast spoken." Oh, how great the mercy of God toward His erring creatures!

Again the solemn command was given to hasten, for the fiery storm would be delayed but little longer. But one of the fugitives ventured to cast a look backward to the doomed city, and she became a monument of God's judgment. If Lot himself had manifested no hesitancy to obey the angels' warning, but had earnestly fled toward the mountains, without one word of pleading or remonstrance, his wife also would have made her escape. The influence of his example would have saved her from the sin that sealed her doom. But his hesitancy and delay caused her to lightly regard the divine warning. While her body was upon the plain, her heart clung to Sodom, and she perished with it. She rebelled against God because His judgments involved her possessions and her children in the ruin. Although so greatly favored in being called out from the wicked city, she felt that she was severely dealt with, because the wealth that it had taken years to accumulate must be left to destruction. Instead of thankfully accepting deliverance, she presumptuously looked back to desire the life of those who had rejected the divine warning. Her sin showed her to be unworthy of life, for the preservation of which she felt so little gratitude.

We should beware of treating lightly God's gracious provisions for our salvation. There are Christians who say, "I do not care to be saved unless my companion and children are saved with me." They feel that heaven would not be heaven to them without the presence of those who are so dear. But have those who cherish this feeling a right conception of their own relation to God, in view of His great goodness and mercy toward them? Have they forgotten that they are bound by the strongest ties of love and honor and loyalty to the service of their Creator and Redeemer? The invitations of mercy are addressed to all; and because our friends reject the Saviour's pleading love, shall we also turn away? The redemption of the soul is precious. Christ has paid an infinite price for our salvation, and no one who appreciates the value of this great sacrifice or the worth of the soul will despise God's offered mercy because others choose to do so. The very fact that others are ignoring His just claims should arouse us to greater diligence, that we may honor God ourselves, and lead all whom we can influence, to accept His love.

"The sun was risen upon the earth when Lot entered into Zoar." The bright rays of the morning seemed to speak only prosperity and peace to the cities of the plain. The stir of active life began in the streets; men were going their various ways, intent on the business or the pleasures of the day. The sons-in law of Lot were making merry at the fears and warnings of the weak-minded old man. Suddenly and unexpectedly as would be a thunder peal from an unclouded sky, the tempest broke. The Lord rained brimstone and fire out of heaven upon the cities and the fruitful plain; its palaces and temples, costly dwellings, gardens and vineyards, and the gay, pleasure-seeking throngs that only the night before had insulted the messengers of heaven—all were consumed. The smoke of the conflagration went up like the smoke of a great furnace. And the fair vale of Siddim became a desolation, a place never to be built up or inhabited—a witness to all generations of the certainty of God's judgments upon transgression.

The flames that consumed the cities of the plain shed their warning light down even to our time. We are taught the fearful and solemn lesson that while God's mercy bears long with the transgressor, there is a limit beyond which men may not go on in sin. When that limit is reached, then the offers of mercy are withdrawn, and the ministration of judgment begins.

The Redeemer of the world declares that there are greater sins than that for which Sodom and Gomorrah were destroyed. Those who hear the gospel invitation calling sinners to repentance, and heed it not, are more guilty before God than were the dwellers in the vale of Siddim. And still greater sin is theirs who profess to know God and to keep His commandments, yet who deny Christ in their character and their daily life. In the light of the Saviour's warning, the fate of Sodom is a solemn admonition, not merely to those who are guilty of outbreaking sin, but to all who are trifling with Heaven-sent light and privileges.

Said the True Witness to the church at Ephesus: "I have somewhat against thee, because thou hast left thy first love. Remember therefore from whence thou art fallen, and repent, and do the first works; or else I will come unto thee quickly, and will remove thy candlestick out of his place, except thou repent." Revelation 2:4, 5. The Saviour watches for a response to His offers of love and forgiveness, with a more tender compassion than that which moves the heart of an earthly parent to forgive a wayward, suffering son. He cries after the wanderer, "Return unto Me, and I will return unto you." Malachi 3:7. But if the erring one persistently refuses to heed the voice that calls him with pitying, tender love, he will at last be left in darkness. The heart that has long slighted God's mercy, becomes hardened in sin, and is no longer susceptible to the influence of the grace of God. Fearful will be the doom of that soul of whom the pleading Saviour shall finally declare, he "is joined to idols: let him alone." Hosea 4:17. It will be more tolerable in the day of judgment for the cities of the plain than for those who have known the love of Christ, and yet have turned away to choose the pleasures of a world of sin.

You who are slighting the offers of mercy, think of the long array of figures accumulating against you in the books of heaven; for there is a record kept of the impieties of nations, of families, of individuals. God may bear long while the account goes on, and calls to repentance and offers of pardon may be given; yet a time will come when the account will be full; when the soul's decision has been made; when by his own choice man's destiny has been fixed. Then the signal will be given for judgment to be executed.

There is cause for alarm in the condition of the religious world today. God's mercy has been trifled with. The multitudes make void the law of Jehovah, "teaching for doctrines the commandments of men." Matthew 15:9. Infidelity prevails in many of the churches in our land; not infidelity in its broadest sense—an open denial of the Bible—but an infidelity that is robed in the garb of Christianity, while it is undermining faith in the Bible as a revelation from God. Fervent devotion and vital piety have given place to hollow formalism. As the result, apostasy and sensualism prevail. Christ declared, "As it was in the days of Lot, . . . even thus shall it be in the day when the Son of man is revealed." Luke 17:28, 30. The daily record of passing events testifies to the fulfillment of His words. The world is fast becoming ripe for destruction. Soon the judgments of God are to be poured out, and sin and sinners are to be consumed.

Said our Saviour: "Take heed to yourselves, lest at any time your hearts be overcharged with surfeiting, and drunkenness, and cares of this life, and so that day come upon you unawares. For as a snare shall it come on all them that dwell on the face of the whole earth"—upon all whose interests are centered in this world. "Watch ye therefore, and pray always, that ye may be accounted worthy to escape all these things that shall come to pass, and to stand before the Son of man." Luke 21:34-36.

Before the destruction of Sodom, God sent a message to Lot, "Escape for thy life; look not behind thee, neither stay thou in all the plain; escape to the mountain, lest thou be consumed." The same voice of warning was heard by the disciples of Christ before the destruction of Jerusalem: "When ye shall see Jerusalem compassed with armies, then know that the desolation thereof is nigh. Then let them which are in Judea flee to the mountains." Luke 21:20, 21. They must not tarry to secure anything from their possessions, but must make the most of the opportunity to escape.

There was a coming out, a decided separation from the wicked, an escape for life. So it was in the days of Noah; so with Lot; so with the disciples prior to the destruction of Jerusalem; and so it will be in the last days. Again the voice of God is heard in a message of warning, bidding His people separate themselves from the prevailing iniquity.

The state of corruption and apostasy that in the last days would exist in the religious world, was presented to the prophet John in the vision of Babylon, "that great city, which reigneth over the kings of the earth." Revelation 17:18. Before its destruction the call is to be given from heaven, "Come out of her, My people, that ye be not partakers of her sins, and that ye receive not of her plagues." Revelation 18:4. As in the days of Noah and Lot, there must be a marked separation from sin and sinners. There can be no compromise between God and the world, no turning back to secure earthly treasures. "Ye cannot serve God and mammon." Matthew 6:24.

Like the dwellers in the vale of Siddim, the people are

dreaming of prosperity and peace. "Escape for thy life," is the warning from the angels of God; but other voices are heard saying, "Be not excited; there is no cause for alarm." The multitudes cry, "Peace and safety," while Heaven declares that swift destruction is about to come upon the transgressor. On the night prior to their destruction, the cities of the plain rioted in pleasure and derided the fears and warnings of the messenger of God; but those scoffers perished in the flames; that very night the door of mercy was forever closed to the wicked, careless inhabitants of Sodom. God will not always be mocked; He will not long be trifled with. "Behold, the day of the Lord cometh, cruel both with wrath and fierce anger, to lay the land desolate: and He shall destroy the sinners thereof out of it." Isaiah 13:9. The great mass of the world will reject God's mercy, and will be overwhelmed in swift and irretrievable ruin. But those who heed the warning shall dwell "in the secret place of the Most High," and "abide under the shadow of the Almighty." His truth shall be their shield and buckler. For them is the promise, "With long life will I satisfy him, and show him My salvation." Psalm 91:1, 4, 16.

Lot dwelt but a short time in Zoar. Iniquity prevailed there as in Sodom, and he feared to remain, lest the city should be destroyed. Not long after, Zoar was consumed, as God had purposed. Lot made his way to the mountains, and abode in a cave, stripped of all for which he had dared to subject his family to the influences of a wicked city. But the curse of Sodom followed him even here. The sinful conduct of his daughters was the result of the evil associations of that vile place. Its moral corruption had become so interwoven with their character that they could not distinguish between good and evil. Lot's only posterity, the Moabites and Ammonites, were vile, idolatrous tribes, rebels against God and bitter enemies of His people.

In how wide contrast to the life of Abraham was that of Lot! Once they had been companions, worshiping at one altar, dwelling side by side in their pilgrim tents; but how widely separated now! Lot had chosen Sodom for its pleasure and profit. Leaving Abraham's altar and its daily sacrifice to the living God, he had permitted his children to mingle with a corrupt and idolatrous people; yet he had retained in his heart the fear of God, for he is declared in the Scriptures to have been a "just" man; his righteous soul was vexed with the vile conversation that greeted his ears daily and the violence and crime he was powerless to prevent. He was saved at last as "a brand plucked out of the fire" (Zechariah 3:2), yet stripped of his possessions, bereaved of his wife and children, dwelling in caves, like the wild beasts, covered with infamy in his old age; and he gave to the world, not a race of righteous men, but two idolatrous nations, at enmity with God and warring upon His people, until, their cup of iniquity being full, they were appointed to destruction. How terrible were the results that followed one unwise step!

Says the wise man, "Labor not to be rich: cease from thine own wisdom." "He that is greedy of gain troubleth his own house; but he that hateth gifts shall live." Proverbs 23:4; 15:27. And the apostle Paul declares, "They that will be rich fall into temptation and a snare, and into many foolish and hurtful lusts, which drown men in destruction and perdition." 1 Timothy 6:9.

When Lot entered Sodom he fully intended to keep himself free from iniquity and to command his household after him. But he signally failed. The corrupting influences about him had an effect upon his own faith, and his children's connection with the inhabitants of Sodom bound up his interest in a measure with theirs. The result is before us.

Many are still making a similar mistake. In selecting a home they look more to the temporal advantages they may gain than to the moral and social influences that will surround themselves and their families. They choose a beautiful and fertile country, or remove to some flourishing city, in the hope of securing greater prosperity; but their children are surrounded by temptation, and too often they form associations that are unfavorable to the development of piety and the formation of a right character. The atmosphere of lax morality, of unbelief, of indifference to religious things, has a tendency to counteract the influence of the parents. Examples of rebellion against parental and divine authority are ever before the youth; many form attachments for infidels and unbelievers, and cast in their lot with the enemies of God.

In choosing a home, God would have us consider, first of all, the moral and religious influences that will surround us and our families. We may be placed in trying positions, for many cannot have their surroundings what they would; and whenever duty calls us, God will enable us to stand uncorrupted, if we watch and pray, trusting in the grace of Christ. But we should not needlessly expose ourselves to influences that are unfavorable to the formation of Christian character. When we voluntarily place ourselves in an atmosphere of worldliness and unbelief, we displease God and drive holy angels from our homes.

Those who secure for their children worldly wealth and honor at the expense of their eternal interests, will find in the end that these advantages are a terrible loss. Like Lot, many see their children ruined, and barely save their own souls. Their lifework is lost; their life is a sad failure. Had they exercised true wisdom, their children might have had less of worldly prosperity, but they would have made sure of a title to the immortal inheritance.

The heritage that God has promised to His people is not in this world. Abraham had no possession in the earth, "no, not so much as to set his foot on." Acts 7:5. He possessed great substance, and he used it to the glory of God and the good of his fellow men; but he did not look upon this world as his home. The Lord had called him to leave his idolatrous countrymen, with the promise of the land of Canaan as an everlasting possession; yet neither he nor his son nor his son's son received it. When Abraham desired a burial place for his dead, he had to buy it of the Canaanites. His sole possession in the Land of Promise was that rock-hewn tomb in the cave of Machpelah.

But the word of God had not failed; neither did it meet its final accomplishment in the occupation of Canaan by the Jewish people. "To Abraham and his seed were the promises made." Galatians 3:16. Abraham himself was to share the inheritance. The fulfillment of God's promise may seem to be long delayed—for "one day is with the Lord as a thousand years, and a thousand years as one day" (2 Peter 3:8); it may appear to tarry; but at the appointed time "it will surely come, it will not tarry." Habakkuk 2:3. The gift to Abraham and his seed included not merely the land of Canaan, but the whole earth. So says the apostle, "The promise, that he should be the heir of the world, was not to Abraham, or to his seed, through the law, but through the righteousness of faith." Romans 4:13. And the Bible plainly teaches that the promises made to Abraham are to be fulfilled through Christ. All that are Christ's are "Abraham's seed, and heirs according to the promise"—heirs to "an inheritance incorruptible, and undefiled, and that fadeth not away"—the earth freed from the curse of sin. Galatians 3:29; 1 Peter 1:4. For "the kingdom and dominion, and the greatness of the kingdom under the whole heaven, shall be given to the people of the saints of the Most High;" and "the meek shall inherit the earth; and shall delight themselves in the abundance of peace." Daniel 7:27; Psalm 37:11.

God gave to Abraham a view of this immortal inheritance, and with this hope he was content. "By faith he sojourned in the Land of Promise, as in a strange country, dwelling in tabernacles with Isaac and Jacob, the heirs with him of the same promise: for he looked for a city which hath foundations, whose builder and maker is God." Hebrews 11:9, 10.

Of the posterity of Abraham it is written, "These all died in faith, not having received the promises, but having seen them afar off, and were persuaded of them, and embraced them, and confessed that they were strangers and pilgrims on the earth." Verse 13. We must dwell as pilgrims and strangers here if we would gain "a better country, that is, an heavenly." Verse 16. Those who are children of Abraham will be seeking the city which he looked for, "whose builder and maker is God."

The Marriage of Isaac

Abraham had become an old man, and expected soon to die; yet one act remained for him to do in securing the fulfillment of the promise to his posterity. Isaac was the one divinely appointed to succeed him as the keeper of the law of God and the father of the chosen people, but he was yet unmarried. The inhabitants of Canaan were given to idolatry, and God had forbidden intermarriage between His people and them, knowing that such marriages would lead to apostasy. The patriarch feared the effect of the corrupting influences surrounding his son. Abraham's habitual faith in God and submission to His will were reflected in the character of Isaac; but the young man's affections were strong, and he was gentle and yielding in disposition. If united with one who did not fear God, he would be in danger of sacrificing principle for the sake of harmony. In the mind of Abraham the choice of a wife for his son was a matter of grave importance; he was anxious to have him marry one who would not lead him from God.

In ancient times marriage engagements were generally made by the parents, and this was the custom among those who worshiped God. None were required to marry those whom they could not love; but in the bestowal of their affections the youth were guided by the judgment of their experienced, God-fearing parents. It was regarded as a dishonor to parents, and even a crime, to pursue a course contrary to this.

Isaac, trusting to his father's wisdom and affection, was satisfied to commit the matter to him, believing also that God Himself would direct in the choice made. The patriarch's thoughts turned to his father's kindred in the land of Mesopotamia. Though not free from idolatry, they cherished the knowledge and the worship of the true God. Isaac must not leave Canaan to go to them, but it might be that among them could be found one who would leave her home and unite with him in maintaining the pure worship of the living God. Abraham committed the important matter to "his eldest servant," a man of piety, experience, and sound judgment, who had rendered him long and faithful service. He required this servant to make a solemn oath before the Lord, that he would not take a wife for Isaac of the Canaanites, but would choose a maiden from the family of Nahor in Mesopotamia. He charged him not to take Isaac thither. If a damsel could not be found who would leave her kindred, then the messenger would be released from his oath. The patriarch encouraged him in his difficult and delicate undertaking with the assurance that God would crown his mission with success. "The Lord God of heaven," he said, "which took me from my father's house, and from the land of my kindred, . . . He shall send His angel before thee."

The messenger set out without delay. Taking with him ten camels for the use of his own company and the bridal party that might return with him, provided also with gifts for the intended wife and her friends, he made the long journey beyond Damascus, and onward to the rich plains that border on the great river of the East. Arrived at Haran, "the city of Nahor," he halted outside the walls, near the well to which the women of the place came at evening for water. It was a time of anxious thought with him. Important results, not only to his master's household, but to future generations, might follow from the choice he made; and how was he to choose wisely among entire strangers? Remembering the words of Abraham, that God would send His angel with him, he prayed earnestly for positive guidance. In the family of his master he was accustomed to the constant exercise of kindness and hospitality, and he now asked that an act of courtesy might indicate the maiden whom God had chosen.

Hardly was the prayer uttered before the answer was given. Among the women who were gathered at the well, the courteous manners of one attracted his attention. As she came from the well, the stranger went to meet her, asking for some water from the pitcher upon her shoulder. The request received a kindly answer, with an offer to draw water for the camels also, a service which it was customary even for the daughters of princes to perform for their fathers' flocks and herds. Thus the desired sign was given. The maiden "was very fair to look upon," and her ready courtesy gave evidence of a kind heart and an active, energetic nature. Thus far the divine hand had been with him. After acknowledging her kindness by rich gifts, the messengers asked her parentage, and on learning that she was the daughter of Bethuel, Abraham's nephew, he "bowed down his head, and worshiped the Lord."

The man had asked for entertainment at her father's house, and in his expressions of thanksgiving had revealed the fact of his connection with Abraham. Returning home, the maiden told what had happened, and Laban, her brother, at once hastened to bring the stranger and his attendants to share their hospitality.

Eliezer would not partake of food until he had told his errand, his prayer at the well, with all the circumstances attending it. Then he said, "And now, if ye will deal kindly and truly with my master, tell me: and if not, tell me; that I may turn to the right hand, or to the left." The answer was, "The thing proceedeth from the Lord: we cannot speak unto thee bad or good. Behold, Rebekah is before thee; take her, and go, and let her be thy master's son's wife, as the Lord hath spoken."

After the consent of the family had been obtained, Rebekah herself was consulted as to whether she would go to so great a distance from her father's house, to marry the son of Abraham. She believed, from what had taken place, that God had selected her to be Isaac's wife, and she said, "I will go."

The servant, anticipating his master's joy at the success of his mission, was impatient to be gone; and with the morning they set out on the homeward journey. Abraham dwelt at Beersheba, and Isaac, who had been attending to the flocks in the adjoining country, had returned to his father's tent to await the arrival of the messenger from Haran. "And Isaac went out to meditate in the field at the eventide: and he lifted up his eyes, and saw, and, behold, the camels were coming. And Rebekah lifted up her eyes, and when she saw Isaac, she lighted off the camel. For she had said unto the servant, What man is that that walketh in the field to meet us? And the servant had said, It is my master: therefore she took a veil, and covered herself. And the servant told Isaac all things that he had done. And Isaac brought her into his mother Sarah's tent, and took Rebekah, and she became his wife; and he loved her: and Isaac was comforted after his mother's death."

Abraham had marked the result of the intermarriage of those who feared God and those who feared Him not, from the days of Cain to his own time. The consequences of his own marriage with Hagar, and of the marriage connections of Ishmael and Lot, were before him. The lack of faith on the part of Abraham and Sarah had resulted in the birth of Ishmael, the mingling of the righteous seed with the ungodly. The father's influence upon his son was counteracted by that of the mother's idolatrous kindred and by Ishmael's connection with heathen wives. The jealousy of Hagar, and of the wives whom she chose for Ishmael, surrounded his family with a barrier that Abraham endeavored in vain to overcome.

Abraham's early teachings had not been without effect upon Ishmael, but the influence of his wives resulted in establishing idolatry in his family. Separated from his father, and embittered by the strife and contention of a home destitute of the love and fear of God, Ishmael was driven to choose the wild, marauding life of the desert chief, "his hand" "against every man, and every man's hand against him." Genesis 16:12. In his latter days he repented of his evil ways and returned to his father's God, but the stamp of character given to his posterity remained. The powerful nation descended from him were a turbulent, heathen people, who were ever an annoyance and affliction to the descendants of Isaac.

The wife of Lot was a selfish, irreligious woman, and her influence was exerted to separate her husband from Abraham. But for her, Lot would not have remained in Sodom, deprived of the counsel of the wise, God-fearing patriarch. The influence of his wife and the associations of that wicked city would have led him to apostatize from God had it not been for the faithful instruction he had early received from Abraham. The marriage of Lot and his choice of Sodom for a home were the first links in a chain of events fraught with evil to the world for many generations.

No one who fears God can without danger connect himself with one who fears Him not. "Can two walk together, except they be agreed?" Amos 3:3. The happiness and prosperity of the marriage relation depends upon the unity of the parties; but between the believer and the unbeliever there is a radical difference of tastes, inclinations, and purposes. They are serving two masters, between whom there can be no concord. However pure and correct one's principles may be, the influence of an unbelieving companion will have a tendency to lead away from God.

He who has entered the marriage relation while unconverted, is by his conversion placed under stronger obligation to be faithful to his companion, however widely they may differ in regard to religious faith; yet the claims of God should be placed above every earthly relationship, even though trials and persecution may be the result. With the spirit of love and meekness, this fidelity may have an influence to win the unbelieving one. But the marriage of Christians with the ungodly is forbidden in the Bible. The Lord's direction is, "Be ye not unequally yoked together with unbelievers." 2 Corinthians 6:14, 17, 18.

Isaac was highly honored by God in being made inheritor of the promises through which the world was to be blessed; yet when he was forty years of age he submitted to his father's judgment in appointing his experience, God-fearing servant to choose a wife for him. And the result of that marriage, as presented in the Scriptures, is a tender and beautiful picture of domestic happiness: "Isaac brought her into his mother Sarah's tent, and took Rebekah, and she became his wife; and he loved her: and Isaac was comforted after his mother's death."

What a contrast between the course of Isaac and that pursued by the youth of our time, even among professed Christians! Young people too often feel that the bestowal of their affections is a matter in which self alone should be consulted—a matter that neither God nor their parents should in any wise control. Long before they have reached manhood or womanhood they think themselves competent to make their own choice, without the aid of their parents. A few years of married life are usually sufficient to show them their error, but often too late to prevent its baleful results. For the same lack of wisdom and self-control that dictated the hasty choice is permitted to aggravate the evil, until the marriage relation a galling yoke. Many have thus wrecked their happiness in this life and their hope of the life to come.

If there is any subject which should be carefully considered and in which the counsel of older and more experienced persons should be sought, it is the subject of marriage; if ever the Bible was needed as a counselor, if ever divine guidance should be sought in prayer, it is before taking a step that binds persons together for life.

Parents should never lose sight of their own responsibility for the future happiness of their children. Isaac's deference to his father's judgment was the result of the training that had taught him to love a life of obedience. While Abraham required his children to respect parental authority, his daily life testified that that authority was not a selfish or arbitrary control, but was founded in love, and had their welfare and happiness in view.

Fathers and mothers should feel that a duty devolves upon them to guide the affections of the youth, that they may be placed upon those who will be suitable companions. They should feel it a duty, by their own teaching and example, with the assisting grace of God, to so mold the character of the children from their earliest years that they will be pure and noble and will be attracted to the good and true. Like attracts like; like appreciates like. Let the love for truth and purity and goodness be early implanted in the soul, and the youth will seek the society of those who possess these characteristics.

Let parents seek, in their own character and in their home life, to exemplify the love and beneficence of the heavenly Father. Let the home be full of sunshine. This will be worth far more to your children than lands or money. Let the home love be kept alive in their hearts, that they may look back upon the home of their childhood as a place of peace and happiness next to heaven. The members of the family do not all have the same stamp of character, and there will be frequent occasion for the exercise of patience and forbearance; but through love and self-discipline all may be bound together in the closest union.

True love is a high and holy principle, altogether different in character from that love which is awakened by impulse and which suddenly dies when severely tested. It is by faithfulness to duty in the parental home that the youth are to prepare themselves for homes of their own. Let them here practice self-denial and manifest kindness, courtesy, and Christian sympathy. Thus love will be kept warm in the heart, and he who goes out from such a household to stand at the head of a family of his own will know how to promote the happiness of her whom he has chosen as a companion for life. Marriage, instead of being the end of love, will be only its beginning.

Jacob and Esau

Jacob and Esau, the twin sons of Isaac, present a striking contrast, both in character and in life. This unlikeness was foretold by the angel of God before their birth. When in answer to Rebekah's troubled prayer he declared that two sons would be given her, he opened to her their future history, that each would become the head of a mighty nation, but that one would be greater than the other, and that the younger would have the pre-eminence.

Esau grew up loving self-gratification and centering all his interest in the present. Impatient of restraint, he delighted in the wild freedom of the chase, and early chose the life of a hunter. Yet he was the father's favorite. The quiet, peace-loving shepherd was attracted by the daring and vigor of this elder son, who fearlessly ranged over mountain and desert, returning home with game for his father and with exciting accounts of his adventurous life. Jacob, thoughtful, diligent, and care-taking, ever thinking more of the future than the present, was content to dwell at home, occupied in the care of the flocks and the tillage of the soil. His patient perseverance, thrift, and foresight were valued by the mother. His affections were deep and strong, and his gentle, unremitting attentions added far more to her happiness than did the boisterous and occasional kindnesses of Esau. To Rebekah, Jacob was the dearer son.

The promises made to Abraham and confirmed to his son were held by Isaac and Rebekah as the great object of their desires and hopes. With these promises Esau and Jacob were familiar. They were taught to regard the birthright as a matter of great importance, for it included not only an inheritance of worldly wealth but spiritual pre-eminence. He who received it was to be the priest of his family, and in the line of his posterity the Redeemer of the world would come. On the other hand, there were obligations resting upon the possessor of the birthright. He who should inherit its blessings must devote his life to the service of God. Like Abraham, he must be obedient to the divine requirements. In marriage, in his family relations, in public life, he must consult the will of God.

Isaac made known to his sons these privileges and conditions, and plainly stated that Esau, as the eldest, was the one entitled to the birthright. But Esau had no love for devotion, no inclination to a religious life. The requirements that accompanied the spiritual birthright were an unwelcome and even hateful restraint to him. The law of God, which was the condition of the divine covenant with Abraham, was regarded by Esau as a yoke of bondage. Bent on self-indulgence, he desired nothing so much as liberty to do as he pleased. To him power and riches, feasting and reveling, were happiness. He gloried in the unrestrained freedom of his wild, roving life. Rebekah remembered the words of the angel, and she read with clearer insight than did her husband the character of their sons. She was convinced that the heritage of divine promise was intended for Jacob. She repeated to Isaac the angel's words; but the father's affections were centered upon the elder son, and he was unshaken in his purpose.

Jacob had learned from his mother of the divine intimation that the birthright should fall to him, and he was filled with an unspeakable desire for the privileges which it would confer. It was not the possession of his father's wealth that he craved; the spiritual birthright was the object of his longing. To commune with God as did righteous Abraham, to offer the sacrifice of atonement for his family, to be the progenitor of the chosen people and of the promised Messiah, and to inherit the immortal possessions embraced in the blessings of the covenant—here were the privileges and honors that kindled his most ardent desires. His mind was ever reaching forward to the future, and seeking to grasp its unseen blessings.

With secret longing he listened to all that his father told concerning the spiritual birthright; he carefully treasured what he had learned from his mother. Day and night the subject occupied his thoughts, until it became the absorbing interest of his life. But while he thus esteemed eternal above temporal blessings, Jacob had not an experimental knowledge of the God whom he revered. His heart had not been renewed by divine grace. He believed that the promise concerning himself could not be fulfilled so long as Esau retained the rights of the first-born, and he constantly studied to devise some way whereby he might secure the blessing which his brother held so lightly, but which was so precious to himself.

When Esau, coming home one day faint and weary from the chase, asked for the food that Jacob was preparing, the latter, with whom one thought was ever uppermost, seized upon his advantage, and offered to satisfy his brother's hunger at the price of the birthright. "Behold, I am at the point to die," cried the reckless, self-indulgent hunter, "and what profit shall this birthright do to me?" And for a dish of red pottage he parted with his birthright, and confirmed the transaction by an oath. A short time at most would have secured him food in his father's tents, but to satisfy the desire of the moment he carelessly bartered the glorious heritage that God Himself had promised to his fathers. His whole interest was in the present. He was ready to sacrifice the heavenly to the earthly, to exchange a future good for a momentary indulgence.

"Thus Esau despised his birthright." In disposing of it he felt a sense of relief. Now his way was unobstructed; he could do as he liked. For this wild pleasure, miscalled freedom, how many are still selling their birthright to an inheritance pure and undefiled, eternal in the heavens!

Ever subject to mere outward and earthly attractions, Esau took two wives of the daughters of Heth. They were worshipers of false gods, and their idolatry was a bitter grief to Isaac and Rebekah. Esau had violated one of the conditions of the covenant, which forbade intermarriage between the chosen people and the heathen; yet Isaac was still unshaken in his determination to bestow upon him the birthright. The reasoning of Rebekah, Jacob's strong desire for the blessing, and Esau's indifference to its obligations had no effect to change the father's purpose.

Years passed on, until Isaac, old and blind, and expecting soon to die, determined no longer to delay the bestowal of the blessing upon his elder son. But knowing the opposition of Rebekah and Jacob, he decided to perform the solemn ceremony in secret. In accordance with the custom of making a feast upon such occasions, the patriarch bade Esau, "Go out to the field, and take me some venison; and make me savory meat, . . . that my soul may bless thee before I die."

Rebekah divined his purpose. She was confident that it was contrary to what God had revealed as His will. Isaac was in danger of incurring the divine displeasure and of debarring his younger son from the position to which God had called him. She had in vain tried the effect of reasoning with Isaac, and she determined to resort to stratagem.

No sooner had Esau departed on his errand than Rebekah set about the accomplishment of her purpose. She told Jacob what had taken place, urging the necessity of immediate action to prevent the bestowal of the blessing, finally and irrevocably, upon Esau. And she assured her son that if he would follow her directions, he might obtain it as God had promised. Jacob did not readily consent to the plan that she proposed. The thought of deceiving his father caused him great distress. He felt that such a sin would bring a curse rather than a blessing. But his scruples were overborne, and he proceeded to carry out his mother's suggestions. It was not his intention to utter a direct falsehood, but once in the presence of his father he seemed to have gone too far to retreat, and he obtained by fraud the coveted blessing.

Jacob and Rebekah succeeded in their purpose, but they gained only trouble and sorrow by their deception. God had declared that Jacob should receive the birthright, and His word would have been fulfilled in His own time had they waited in faith for Him to work for them. But like many who now profess to be children of God, they were unwilling to leave the matter in His hands. Rebekah bitterly repented the wrong counsel she had given her son; it was the means of separating him from her, and she never saw his face again. From the hour when he received the birthright, Jacob was weighed down with self-condemnation. He had sinned against his father, his brother, his own soul, and against God. In one short hour he had made work for a lifelong repentance. This scene was vivid before him in afteryears, when the wicked course of his sons oppressed his soul.

No sooner had Jacob left his father's tent than Esau entered. Though he had sold his birthright, and confirmed the transfer by a solemn oath, he was now determined to secure its blessings, regardless of his brother's claim. With the spiritual was connected the temporal birthright, which would give him the headship of the family and possession of a double portion of his father's wealth. These were blessings that he could value. "Let my father arise," he said, "and eat of his son's venison, that thy soul may bless me."

Trembling with astonishment and distress, the blind old father learned the deception that had been practiced upon him. His long and fondly cherished hopes had been thwarted, and he keenly felt the disappointment that must come upon his elder son. Yet the conviction flashed upon him that it was God's providence which had defeated his purpose and brought about the very thing he had determined to prevent. He remembered the words of the angel to Rebekah, and notwithstanding the sin of which Jacob was now guilty, he saw in him the one best fitted to accomplish the purposes of God. While the words of blessing were upon his lips, he had felt the Spirit of inspiration upon him; and now, knowing all the circumstances, he ratified the benediction unwittingly pronounced upon Jacob: "I have blessed him; yea, and he shall be blessed."

Esau had lightly valued the blessing while it seemed within his reach, but he desired to possess it now that it was gone from him forever. All the strength of his impulsive, passionate nature was aroused, and his grief and rage were terrible. He cried with an exceeding bitter cry, "Bless me, even me also, O my father!" "Hast thou not reserved a blessing for me?" But the promise given was not to be recalled. The birthright which he had so carelessly bartered he could not now regain. "For one morsel of meat," for a momentary gratification of appetite that had never been restrained, Esau sold his inheritance; but when he saw his folly, it was too late to recover the blessing. "He found no place of repentance, though he sought it carefully with tears." Hebrews 12:16, 17. Esau was not shut out from the privilege of seeking God's favor by repentance, but he could find no means of recovering the birthright. His grief did not spring from conviction of sin; he did not desire to be reconciled to God. He sorrowed because of the results of his sin, but not for the sin itself.

Because of his indifference to the divine blessings and requirements, Esau is called in Scripture "a profane person." Verse 16. He represents those who lightly value the redemption purchased for them by Christ, and are ready to sacrifice their heirship to heaven for the perishable things of earth. Multitudes live for the present, with no thought or care for the future. Like Esau they cry, "Let us eat and drink; for tomorrow we die." 1 Corinthians 15:32. They are controlled by inclination; and rather than practice self-denial, they will forgo the most valuable considerations. If one must be relinquished, the gratification of a depraved appetite or the heavenly blessings promised only to the self-denying and God-fearing, the claims of appetite prevail, and God and heaven are virtually despised. How many, even of professed Christians, cling to indulgences that are injurious to health and that benumb the sensibilities of the soul. When the duty is presented of cleansing themselves from all filthiness of the flesh and spirit, perfecting holiness in the fear of God, they are offended. They see that they cannot retain these hurtful gratifications and yet secure heaven, and they conclude that since the way to eternal life is so strait, they will no longer walk therein.

Multitudes are selling their birthright for sensual indulgence. Health is sacrificed, the mental faculties are enfeebled, and heaven is forfeited; and all for a mere temporary pleasure—an indulgence at once both weakening and debasing in its character. As Esau awoke to see the folly of his rash exchange when it was too late to recover his loss, so it will be in the day of God with those who have bartered their heirship to heaven for selfish gratifications.

Jacob's Flight and Exile

Threatened with death by the wrath of Esau, Jacob went out from his father's home a fugitive; but he carried with him the father's blessing; Isaac had renewed to him the covenant promise, and had bidden him, as its inheritor, to seek a wife of his mother's family in Mesopotamia. Yet it was with a deeply troubled heart that Jacob set out on his lonely journey. With only his staff in his hand he must travel hundreds of miles through a country inhabited by wild, roving tribes. In his remorse and timidity he sought to avoid men, lest he should be traced by his angry brother. He feared that he had lost forever the blessing that God had purposed to give him; and Satan was at hand to press temptations upon him.

The evening of the second day found him far away from his father's tents. He felt that he was an outcast, and he knew that all this trouble had been brought upon him by his own wrong course. The darkness of despair pressed upon his soul, and he hardly dared to pray. But he was so utterly lonely that he felt the need of protection from God as he had never felt it before. With weeping and deep humiliation he confessed his sin, and entreated for some evidence that he was not utterly forsaken. Still his burdened heart found no relief. He had lost all confidence in himself, and he feared that the God of his fathers had cast him off.

But God did not forsake Jacob. His mercy was still extended to His erring, distrustful servant. The Lord compassionately revealed just what Jacob needed—a Saviour. He had sinned, but his heart was filled with gratitude as he saw revealed a way by which he could be restored to the favor of God.

Wearied with his journey, the wanderer lay down upon the ground, with a stone for his pillow. As he slept he beheld a ladder, bright and shining, whose base rested upon the earth, while the top reached to heaven. Upon this ladder angels were ascending and descending; above it was the Lord of glory, and from the heavens His voice was heard: "I am the Lord God of Abraham thy father, and the God of Isaac." The land whereon he lay as an exile and fugitive was promised to him and to his posterity, with the assurance, "In thee and in thy seed shall all the families of the earth be blessed." This promise had been given to Abraham and to Isaac, and now it was renewed to Jacob. Then in special regard to his present loneliness and distress, the words of comfort and encouragement were spoken: "Behold, I am with thee, and will keep thee in all places whither thou goest, and will bring thee again into this land; for I will not leave thee, until I have done that which I have spoken to thee of."

The Lord knew the evil influences that would surround Jacob, and the perils to which he would be exposed. In mercy He opened up the future before the repentant fugitive, that he might understand the divine purpose with reference to himself, and be prepared to resist the temptations that would surely come to him when alone amid idolaters and scheming men. There would be ever before him the high standard at which he must aim; and the knowledge that through him the purpose of God was reaching its accomplishment, would constantly prompt him to faithfulness.

In the vision the plan of redemption was presented to Jacob, not fully, but in such parts as were essential to him at that time. The mystic ladder revealed to him in his dream was the same to which Christ referred in His conversation with Nathanael. Said He, "Ye shall see heaven open, and the angels of God ascending and descending upon the Son of man." John 1:51. Up to the time of man's rebellion against the government of God, there had been free communion between God and man. But the sin of Adam and Eve separated earth from heaven, so that man could not have communion with his Maker. Yet the world was not left in solitary hopelessness. The ladder represents Jesus, the appointed medium of communication. Had He not with His own merits bridged the gulf that sin had made, the ministering angels could have held no communion with fallen man. Christ connects man in his weakness and helplessness with the source of infinite power.

All this was revealed to Jacob in his dream. Although his mind at once grasped a part of the revelation, its great and mysterious truths were the study of his lifetime, and unfolded to his understanding more and more.

Jacob awoke from his sleep in the deep stillness of night. The shining forms of his vision had disappeared. Only the dim outline of the lonely hills, and above them the heavens bright with stars, now met his gaze. But he had a solemn sense that God was with him. An unseen presence filled the solitude. "Surely the Lord is in this place," he said, "and I knew it not. . . . This is none other but the house of God, and this is the gate of heaven."

"And Jacob rose up early in the morning, and took the stone that he had put for his pillows, and set it up for a pillar, and poured oil upon the top of it." In accordance with the custom of commemorating important events, Jacob set up a memorial of God's mercy, that whenever he should pass that way he might tarry at this sacred spot to worship the Lord. And he called the place Bethel, or the "house of God." With deep gratitude he repeated the promise that God's presence would be with him; and then he made the solemn vow, "If

God will be with me, and will keep me in this way that I go, and will give me bread to eat, and raiment to put on, so that I come again to my father's house in peace; then shall the Lord be my God: and this stone, which I have set for a pillar, shall be God's house: and of all that Thou shalt give me I will surely give the tenth unto Thee."

Jacob was not here seeking to make terms with God. The Lord had already promised him prosperity, and this vow was the outflow of a heart filled with gratitude for the assurance of God's love and mercy. Jacob felt that God had claims upon him which he must acknowledge, and that the special tokens of divine favor granted him demanded a return. So does every blessing bestowed upon us call for a response to the Author of all our mercies. The Christian should often review his past life and recall with gratitude the precious deliverances that God has wrought for him, supporting him in trial, opening ways before him when all seemed dark and forbidding, refreshing him when ready to faint. He should recognize all of them as evidences of the watchcare of heavenly angels. In view of these innumerable blessings he should often ask, with subdued and grateful heart, "What shall I render unto the Lord for all His benefits toward me?" Psalm 116:12.

Our time, our talents, our property, should be sacredly devoted to Him who has given us these blessings in trust. Whenever a special deliverance is wrought in our behalf, or new and unexpected favors are granted us, we should acknowledge God's goodness, not only by expressing our gratitude in words, but, like Jacob, by gifts and offerings to His cause. As we are continually receiving the blessings of God, so we are to be continually giving.

"Of all that Thou shalt give me," said Jacob, "I will surely give the tenth unto Thee." Shall we who enjoy the full light and privileges of the gospel be content to give less to God than was given by those who lived in the former, less favored dispensation? Nay, as the blessings we enjoy are greater, are not our obligations correspondingly increased? But how small the estimate; how vain the endeavor to measure with mathematical rules, time, money, and love, against a love so immeasurable and a gift of such inconceivable worth. Tithes for Christ! Oh, meager pittance, shameful recompense for that which cost so much! From the cross of Calvary, Christ calls for an unreserved consecration. All that we have, all that we are, should be devoted to God.

With a new and abiding faith in the divine promises, and assured of the presence and guardianship of heavenly angels, Jacob pursued his journey to "the land of the children of the East." Genesis 29:1, margin. But how different his arrival from that of Abraham's messenger nearly a hundred years before! The servant had come with a train of attendants riding upon camels, and with rich gifts of gold and silver; the son was a lonely, footsore traveler, with no possession save his staff. Like Abraham's servant, Jacob tarried beside a well, and it was here that he met Rachel, Laban's younger daughter. It was Jacob now who rendered service, rolling the stone from the well and watering the flocks. On making known his kinship, he was welcomed to the home of Laban. Though he came portionless and unattended, a few weeks showed the worth of his diligence and skill, and he was urged to tarry. It was arranged that he should render Laban seven years' service for the hand of Rachel.

In early times custom required the bridegroom, before the ratification of a marriage engagement, to pay a sum of money or its equivalent in other property, according to his circumstances, to the father of his wife. This was regarded as a safeguard to the marriage relation. Fathers did not think it safe to trust the happiness of their daughters to men who had not made provision for the support of a family. If they had not sufficient thrift and energy to manage business and acquire cattle or lands, it was feared that their life would prove worthless. But provision was made to test those who had nothing to pay for a wife. They were permitted to labor for the father whose daughter they loved, the length of time being regulated by the value of the dowry required. When the suitor was faithful in his services, and proved in other respects worthy, he obtained the daughter as his wife; and generally the dowry which the father had received was given her at her marriage. In the case of both Rachel and Leah, however, Laban selfishly retained the dowry that should have been given them; they referred to this when they said, just before the removal from Mesopotamia, "He hath sold us, and hath quite devoured also our money."

The ancient custom, though sometimes abused, as by Laban, was productive of good results. When the suitor was required to render service to secure his bride, a hasty marriage was prevented, and there was opportunity to rest the depth of his affections, as well as his ability to provide for a family. In our time many evils result from pursuing an opposite course. It is often the case that persons before marriage have little opportunity to become acquainted with each other's habits and disposition, and, so far as everyday life is concerned, they are virtually strangers when they unite their interests at the altar. Many find, too late, that they are not adapted to each other, and lifelong wretchedness is the result of their union. Often the wife and children suffer from the indolence and inefficiency or the vicious habits of the husband and father. If the character of the suitor had been tested before marriage, according to the ancient custom, great unhappiness might have been prevented.

Seven years of faithful service Jacob gave for Rachel, and the years that he served "seemed unto him but a few days, for the love he had to her." But the selfish and grasping Laban, desiring to retain so valuable a helper, practiced a cruel deception in substituting Leah for Rachel. The fact that Leah herself was a party to the cheat, caused Jacob to feel that he could not love her. His indignant rebuke to Laban was met with the offer of Rachel for another seven years' service. But the father insisted that Leah should not be discarded, since this would bring disgrace upon the family. Jacob was thus placed in a most painful and trying position; he finally decided to retain Leah and marry Rachel. Rachel was ever the one best loved; but his preference for her excited envy and jealousy, and his life was embittered by the rivalry between the sister-wives.

For twenty years Jacob remained in Mesopotamia, laboring in the service of Laban, who, disregarding the ties of kinship, was bent upon securing to himself all the benefits of their connection. Fourteen years of toil he demanded for his two daughters; and during the remaining period, Jacob's wages were ten times changed. Yet Jacob's service was diligent and faithful. His words to Laban in their last interview vividly describe the untiring vigilance which he had given to the interests of his exacting master: "This twenty years have I been with thee; thy ewes and thy she-goats have not cast their young, and the rams of thy flock have I not eaten. That which was torn of beasts I brought not unto thee; I bare the loss of it; of my hand didst thou require it, whether stolen by day, or stolen by night. Thus I was; in the day the drought consumed me, and the frost by night; and my sleep departed from mine eyes."

It was necessary for the shepherd to watch his flocks day and night. They were in danger from robbers, and also from wild beasts, which were numerous and bold, often committing great havoc in flocks that were not faithfully guarded. Jacob had many assistants in caring for the extensive flocks of Laban, but he himself was held responsible for them all. During some portions of the year it was necessary for him to be constantly with the flocks in person, to guard them in the dry season against perishing from thirst, and during the coldest months from becoming chilled with the heavy night frosts. Jacob was the chief shepherd; the servants in his employ were the undershepherds. If any of the sheep were missing, the chief shepherd suffered the loss; and he called the servants to whom he entrusted the care of the flock to a strict account if it was not found in a flourishing condition.

The shepherd's life of diligence and care-taking, and his tender compassion for the helpless creatures entrusted to his charge, have been employed by the inspired writers to illustrate some of the most precious truths of the gospel. Christ, in His relation to His people, is compared to a shepherd. After the Fall He saw His sheep doomed to perish in the dark ways of sin. To save these wandering ones He left the honors and glories of His Father's house. He says, "I will seek that which was lost, and bring again that which was driven away, and will bind up that which was broken, and will strengthen that which was sick." I will "save My flock, and they shall no more be a prey." "Neither shall the beast of the land devour them." Ezekiel 34:16, 22, 28. His voice is heard calling them to His fold, "a shadow in the daytime from the heat, and for a place of refuge, and for a covert from storm and from rain." Isaiah 4:6. His care for the flock is unwearied. He strengthens the weak, relieves the suffering, gathers the lambs in His arms, and carries them in His bosom. His sheep love Him. "And a stranger will they not follow, but will flee from him; for they know not the voice of strangers." John 10:5.

Christ says, "The good shepherd giveth his life for the

sheep. But he that is an hireling, and not the shepherd, whose own the sheep are not, seeth the wolf coming, and leaveth the sheep, and fleeth; and the wolf catcheth them, and scattereth the sheep. The hireling fleeth, because he is an hireling, and careth not for the sheep. I am the Good Shepherd, and know My sheep, and am known of Mine." Verses 11-14.

Christ, the Chief Shepherd, has entrusted the care of His flock to His ministers as undershepherds; and He bids them have the same interest that He has manifested, and feel the sacred responsibility of the charge He has entrusted to them. He has solemnly commanded them to be faithful, to feed the flock, to strengthen the weak, to revive the fainting, and to shield them from devouring wolves.

To save His sheep, Christ laid down His own life; and He points His shepherds to the love thus manifested, as their example. But "he that is an hireling, . . . whose own the sheep are not," has no real interest in the flock. He is laboring merely for gain, and he cares only for himself. He studies his own profit instead of the interest of his charge; and in time of peril or danger he will flee, and leave the flock.

The apostle Peter admonishes the undershepherds: "Feed the flock of God which is among you, taking the oversight thereof, not by constraint, but willingly; not for filthy lucre, but of a ready mind; neither as being lords over God's heritage, but being ensamples to the flock." 1 Peter 5:2, 3. Paul says, "Take heed therefore unto yourselves, and to all the flock, over the which the Holy Ghost hath made you overseers, to feed the church of God, which He hath purchased with His own blood. For I know this, that after my departing shall grievous wolves enter in among you, not sparing the flock." Acts 20:28, 29.

All who regard as an unwelcome task the care and burdens that fall to the lot of the faithful shepherd, are reproved by the apostle: "Not by constraint, but willingly; not for filthy lucre, but of a ready mind." 1 Peter 5:2. All such unfaithful servants the Chief Shepherd would willingly release. The church of Christ has been purchased with His blood, and every shepherd should realize that the sheep under his care cost an infinite sacrifice. He should regard them each as of priceless worth, and should be unwearied in his efforts to keep them in a healthy, flourishing condition. The shepherd who is imbued with the spirit of Christ will imitate His self-denying example, constantly laboring for the welfare of his charge; and the flock will prosper under his care.

All will be called to render a strict account of their ministry. The Master will demand of every shepherd, "Where is the flock that was given thee, thy beautiful flock?" Jeremiah 13:20. He that is found faithful, will receive a rich reward. "When the Chief Shepherd shall appear," says the apostle, "ye shall receive a crown of glory that fadeth not away." 1 Peter 5:4.

When Jacob, growing weary of Laban's service, proposed to return to Canaan, he said to his father-in-law, "Send me away, that I may go unto mine own place, and to my country. Give me my wives and my children, for whom I have served thee,

and let me go: for thou knowest my service which I have done thee." But Laban urged him to remain, declaring, "I have learned by experience that the Lord hath blessed me for thy sake." He saw that his property was increasing under the care of his son-in-law.

Said Jacob, "It was little which thou hadst before I came, and it is now increased unto a multitude." But as time passed on, Laban became envious of the greater prosperity of Jacob, who "increased exceedingly, and had much cattle, and maidservants, and menservants, and camels, and asses." Laban's sons shared their father's jealousy, and their malicious speeches came to Jacob's ears: He "hath taken away all that was our father's, and of that which was our father's hath he gotten all this glory. And Jacob beheld the countenance of Laban, and, behold, it was not toward him as before."

Jacob would have left his crafty kinsman long before but for the fear of encountering Esau. Now he felt that he was in danger from the sons of Laban, who, looking upon his wealth as their own, might endeavor to secure it by violence. He was in great perplexity and distress, not knowing which way to turn. But mindful of the gracious Bethel promise, he carried his case to God, and sought direction from Him. In a dream his prayer was answered: "Return unto the land of thy fathers, and to thy kindred; and I will be with thee."

Laban's absence afforded opportunity for departure. The flocks and herds were speedily gathered and sent forward, and with his wives, children, and servants, Jacob crossed the Euphrates, urging his way toward Gilead, on the borders of Canaan. After three days Laban learned of their flight, and set forth in pursuit, overtaking the company on the seventh day of their journey. He was hot with anger, and bent on forcing them to return, which he doubted not he could do, since his band was much the stronger. The fugitives were indeed in great peril.

That he did not carry out his hostile purpose was due to the fact that God Himself had interposed for the protection of His servant. "It is in the power of my hand to do you hurt," said Laban, "but the God of your father spake unto me yesternight, saying, Take thou heed that thou speak not to Jacob either good or bad;" that is, he should not force him to return, or urge him by flattering inducements.

Laban had withheld the marriage dowry of his daughters and had ever treated Jacob with craft and harshness; but with characteristic dissimulation he now reproached him for his secret departure, which had given the father no opportunity to make a parting feast or even to bid farewell to his daughters and their children.

In reply Jacob plainly set forth Laban's selfish and grasping policy, and appealed to him as a witness to his own faithfulness and honesty. "Except the God of my father, the God of Abraham, and the fear of Isaac, had been with me," said Jacob, "surely thou hadst sent me away now empty. God hath seen mine affliction, and the labor of my hands, and rebuked thee yesternight."

Laban could not deny the facts brought forward, and he now

proposed to enter into a covenant of peace. Jacob consented to the proposal, and a pile of stones was erected as a token of the compact. To this pillar Laban gave the name Mizpah, "watchtower," saying, "The Lord watch between me and thee, when we are absent one from another."

"And Laban said to Jacob, Behold this heap, and behold this pillar, which I have cast betwixt me and thee; this heap be witness, and this pillar be witness, that I will not pass over this heap to thee, and that thou shalt not pass over this heap and this pillar unto me, for harm. The God of Abraham, and the God of Nahor, the God of their father, judge betwixt us. And Jacob sware by the fear of his father Isaac." To confirm the treaty, the parties held a feast. The night was spent in friendly communing; and at the dawn of day, Laban and his company departed. With this separation ceased all trace of connection between the children of Abraham and the dwellers in Mesopotamia.

The Night of Wrestling

Though Jacob had left Padan-aram in obedience to the divine direction, it was not without many misgivings that he retraced the road which he had trodden as a fugitive twenty years before. His sin in the deception of his father was ever before him. He knew that his long exile was the direct result of that sin, and he pondered over these things day and night, the reproaches of an accusing conscience making his journey very sad. As the hills of his native land appeared before him in the distance, the heart of the patriarch was deeply moved. All the past rose vividly before him. With the memory of his sin came also the thought of God's favor toward him, and the promises of divine help and guidance.

As he drew nearer his journey's end, the thought of Esau brought many a troubled foreboding. After the flight of Jacob, Esau had regarded himself as the sole heir of their father's possessions. The news of Jacob's return would excite the fear that he was coming to claim the inheritance. Esau was now able to do his brother great injury, if so disposed, and he might be moved to violence against him, not only by the desire for revenge, but in order to secure undisturbed possession of the wealth which he had so long looked upon as his own.

Again the Lord granted Jacob a token of the divine care. As he traveled southward from Mount Gilead, two hosts of heavenly angels seemed to encompass him behind and before, advancing with his company, as if for their protection. Jacob remembered the vision at Bethel so long before, and his burdened heart grew lighter at this evidence that the divine messengers who had brought him hope and courage at his flight from Canaan were to be the guardians of his return. And he said, "This is God's host: and he called the name of that place Mahanaim"—"two hosts, or, camps."

Yet Jacob felt that he had something to do to secure his own safety. He therefore dispatched messengers with a conciliatory greeting to his brother. He instructed them as to the exact words in which they were to address Esau. It had been foretold before the birth of the two brothers that the elder should serve the younger, and, lest the memory of this should be a cause of bitterness, Jacob told the servants they were sent to "my lord Esau;" when brought before him, they were to refer to their master as "thy servant Jacob;" and to remove the fear that he was returning, a destitute wanderer, to claim the paternal inheritance, Jacob was careful to state in his message, "I have oxen, an asses, flocks, and menservants, and womenservants: and I have sent to tell my lord, that I may find grace in thy sight."

But the servants returned with the tidings that Esau was approaching with four hundred men, and no response was sent to the friendly message. It appeared certain that he was coming to seek revenge. Terror pervaded the camp. "Jacob was greatly afraid and distressed." He could not go back, and he feared to advance. His company, unarmed and defenseless, were wholly unprepared for a hostile encounter. He accordingly divided them into two bands, so that if one should be attacked, the other might have an opportunity to escape. He sent from his vast flocks generous presents to Esau, with a friendly message. He did all in his power to atone for the wrong to his brother and to avert the threatened danger, and then in humiliation and repentance he pleaded for divine protection: Thou "saidst unto me, Return unto thy country, and to thy kindred, and I will deal well with thee: I am not worthy of the least of all the mercies, and of all the truth, which Thou hast showed unto Thy servant; for with my staff I passed over this Jordan; and now I am become two bands. Deliver me, I pray Thee, from the hand of my brother, from the hand of Esau: for I fear him, lest he will come and smite me, and the mother with the children."

They had now reached the river Jabbok, and as night came on, Jacob sent his family across the ford of the river, while he alone remained behind. He had decided to spend the night in prayer, and he desired to be alone with God. God could soften the heart of Esau. In Him was the patriarch's only hope.

It was in a lonely, mountainous region, the haunt of wild beasts and the lurking place of robbers and murderers. Solitary and unprotected, Jacob bowed in deep distress upon the earth. It was midnight. All that made life dear to him were at a distance, exposed to danger and death. Bitterest of all was the thought that it was his own sin which had brought this peril upon the innocent. With earnest cries and tears he made his prayer before God. Suddenly a strong hand was laid upon him. He thought that an enemy was seeking his life, and he endeavored to wrest himself from the grasp of his assailant. In the darkness the two struggled for the mastery. Not a word was spoken, but Jacob put forth all his strength, and did not relax his efforts for a moment. While he was thus battling for his life, the sense of his guilt pressed upon his soul; his sins rose up before him, to shut him out from God. But in his terrible extremity he remembered God's promises, and his whole heart went out in entreaty for His mercy. The struggle continued until near the break of day, when the stranger placed his finger upon Jacob's thigh, and he was crippled instantly. The patriarch now discerned the character of his antagonist. He knew that he had been in conflict with a heavenly messenger, and this was why his almost superhuman effort had not gained the victory. It was Christ, "the Angel of the covenant," who had revealed Himself to Jacob. The patriarch was now disabled and suffering the keenest pain, but he would not loosen his hold. All penitent and broken, he clung to the Angel; "he wept, and made supplication" (Hosea 12:4), pleading for a blessing. He must have the assurance that his sin was pardoned. Physical pain was not sufficient to divert his mind from this object. His determination grew stronger, his faith more earnest and persevering, until the very last. The Angel tried to release Himself; He urged, "Let Me go, for the day breaketh;" but Jacob answered, "I will not let Thee go, except Thou bless me." Had this been a boastful, presumptuous confidence, Jacob would have been instantly destroyed; but his was the assurance of one who confesses his own unworthiness, yet trusts the faithfulness of a covenant-keeping God.

Jacob "had power over the Angel, and prevailed." Hosea 12:4. Through humiliation, repentance, and self-surrender, this sinful, erring mortal prevailed with the Majesty of heaven. He had fastened his trembling grasp upon the promises of God, and the heart of Infinite Love could not turn away the sinner's plea.

The error that had led to Jacob's sin in obtaining the birthright by fraud was now clearly set before him. He had not trusted God's promises, but had sought by his own efforts to bring about that which God would have accomplished in His own time and way. As an evidence that he had been forgiven, his name was changed from one that was a reminder of his sin, to one that commemorated his victory. "Thy name," said the Angel, "shall be called no more Jacob, but Israel: for as a prince hast thou power with God and with men, and hast prevailed."

Jacob had received the blessing for which his soul had longed. His sin as a supplanter and deceiver had been pardoned. The crisis in his life was past. Doubt, perplexity, and remorse had embittered his existence, but now all was changed; and sweet was the peace of reconciliation with God. Jacob no longer feared to meet his brother. God, who had forgiven his sin, could move the heart of Esau also to accept his humiliation and repentance.

While Jacob was wrestling with the Angel, another heavenly messenger was sent to Esau. In a dream, Esau beheld his brother for twenty years an exile from his father's house; he witnessed his grief at finding his mother dead; he saw him encompassed by the hosts of God. This dream was related by Esau to his soldiers, with the charge not to harm Jacob, for the God of his father was with him.

The two companies at last approached each other, the desert chief leading his men of war, and Jacob with his wives and children, attended by shepherds and handmaidens, and followed by long lines of flocks and herds. Leaning upon his staff, the patriarch went forward to meet the band of soldiers.

He was pale and disabled from his recent conflict, and he walked slowly and painfully, halting at every step; but his countenance was lighted up with joy and peace.

At sight of that crippled sufferer, "Esau ran to meet him, and embraced him, and fell on his neck, and kissed him: and they wept." As they looked upon the scene, even the hearts of Esau's rude soldiers were touched. Notwithstanding he had told them of his dream, they could not account for the change that had come over their captain. Though they beheld the patriarch's infirmity, they little thought that this his weakness had been made his strength.

In his night of anguish beside the Jabbok, when destruction seemed just before him, Jacob had been taught how vain is the help of man, how groundless is all trust in human power. He saw that his only help must come from Him against whom he had so grievously sinned. Helpless and unworthy, he pleaded God's promise of mercy to the repentant sinner. That promise was his assurance that God would pardon and accept him. Sooner might heaven and earth pass than that word could fail; and it was this that sustained him through that fearful conflict.

Jacob's experience during that night of wrestling and anguish represents the trial through which the people of God must pass just before Christ's second coming. The prophet Jeremiah, in holy vision looking down to this time, said, "We have heard a voice of trembling, of fear, and not of peace. . . . All faces are turned into paleness. Alas! for that day is great, so that none is like it: it is even the time of Jacob's trouble; but he shall be saved out of it." Jeremiah 30:5-7.

When Christ shall cease His work as mediator in man's behalf, then this time of trouble will begin. Then the case of every soul will have been decided, and there will be no atoning blood to cleanse from sin. When Jesus leaves His position as man's intercessor before God, the solemn announcement is made, "He that is unjust, let him be unjust still: and he which is filthy, let him be filthy still: and he that is righteous, let him be righteous still: and he that is holy, let him be holy still." Revelation 22:11. Then the restraining Spirit of God is withdrawn from the earth. As Jacob was threatened with death by his angry brother, so the people of God will be in peril from the wicked who are seeking to destroy them. And as the patriarch wrestled all night for deliverance from the hand of Esau, so the righteous will cry to God day and night for deliverance from the enemies that surround them.

Satan had accused Jacob before the angels of God, claiming the right to destroy him because of his sin; he had moved upon Esau to march against him; and during the patriarch's long night of wrestling, Satan endeavored to force upon him a sense of his guilt, in order to discourage him, and break his hold upon God. When in his distress Jacob laid hold of the Angel, and made supplication with tears, the heavenly Messenger, in order to try his faith, also reminded him of his sin, and endeavored to escape from him. But Jacob would not be turned away. He had learned that God is merciful, and he cast himself upon His mercy. He pointed back to his repentance for his sin, and pleaded for deliverance. As he reviewed his life, he was driven almost to despair; but he held fast the Angel, and with earnest, agonizing cries urged his petition until he prevailed.

Such will be the experience of God's people in their final struggle with the powers of evil. God will test their faith, their perseverance, their confidence in His power to deliver them. Satan will endeavor to terrify them with the thought that their cases are hopeless; that their sins have been too great to receive pardon. They will have a deep sense of their shortcomings, and as they review their lives their hopes will sink. But remembering the greatness of God's mercy, and their own sincere repentance, they will plead His promises made through Christ to helpless, repenting sinners. Their faith will not fail because their prayers are not immediately answered. They will lay hold of the strength of God, as Jacob laid hold of the Angel, and the language of their souls will be, "I will not let Thee go, except Thou bless me."

Had not Jacob previously repented of his sin in obtaining the birthright by fraud, God could not have heard his prayer and mercifully preserved his life. So in the time of trouble, if the people of God had unconfessed sins to appear before them while tortured with fear and anguish, they would be overwhelmed; despair would cut off their faith, and they could not have confidence to plead with God for deliverance. But while they have a deep sense of their unworthiness, they will have no concealed wrongs to reveal. Their sins will have been blotted out by the atoning blood of Christ, and they cannot bring them to remembrance.

Satan leads many to believe that God will overlook their unfaithfulness in the minor affairs of life; but the Lord shows in His dealing with Jacob that He can in no wise sanction or tolerate evil. All who endeavor to excuse or conceal their sins, and permit them to remain upon the books of heaven, unconfessed and unforgiven, will be overcome by Satan. The more exalted their profession, and the more honorable the position which they hold, the more grievous is their course in the sight of God, and the more certain the triumph of the great adversary.

Yet Jacob's history is an assurance that God will not cast off those who have been betrayed into sin, but who have returned unto Him with true repentance. It was by self-surrender and confiding faith that Jacob gained what he had failed to gain by conflict in his own strength. God thus taught His servant that divine power and grace alone could give him the blessing he craved. Thus it will be with those who live in the last days. As dangers surround them, and despair seizes upon the soul, they must depend solely upon the merits of the atonement. We can do nothing of ourselves. In all our helpless unworthiness we must trust in the merits of the crucified and risen Saviour. None will ever perish while they do this. The long, black catalogue of our delinquencies is before the eye of the Infinite. The register is complete; none of our offenses are forgotten. But He who listened to the cries of His servants of old, will hear the prayer of faith and pardon our transgressions. He has promised, and He will fulfill His word.

Jacob prevailed because he was persevering and determined. His experience testifies to the power of importunate prayer. It is now that we are to learn this lesson of prevailing prayer, of unyielding faith. The greatest victories to the church of Christ or to the individual Christian are not those that are gained by talent or education, by wealth or the favor of men. They are those victories that are gained in the audience chamber with God, when earnest, agonizing faith lays hold upon the mighty arm of power.

Those who are unwilling to forsake every sin and to seek earnestly for God's blessing, will not obtain it. But all who will lay hold of God's promises as did Jacob, and be as earnest and persevering as he was, will succeed as he succeeded. "Shall not God avenge His own elect, which cry day and night unto Him, though He bear long with them? I tell you that He will avenge them speedily." Luke 18:7, 8.

The Return to Canaan

Crossing the Jordan, "Jacob came in peace to the city of Shechem, which is in the land of Canaan." Genesis 33:18, R.V. Thus the patriarch's prayer at Bethel, that God would bring him again in peace to his own land, had been granted. For a time he dwelt in the vale of Shechem. It was here that Abraham, more than a hundred years before, had made his first encampment and erected his first altar in the Land of Promise. Here Jacob "bought the parcel of ground where he had spread his tent, at the hand of the children of Hamor, Shechem's father, for a hundred pieces of money. And he erected there an altar, and called it El-elohe-Israel" (verses 19, 20)—God, the God of Israel." Like Abraham, Jacob set up beside his tent an altar unto the Lord, calling the members of his household to the morning and the evening sacrifice. It was here also that he dug the well to which, seventeen centuries later, came Jacob's Son and Saviour, and beside which, resting during the noontide heat, He told His wondering hearers of that "well of water springing up into everlasting life." John 4:14.

The tarry of Jacob and his sons at Shechem ended in violence and bloodshed. The one daughter of the household had been brought to shame and sorrow, two brothers were involved in the guilt of murder, a whole city had been given to ruin and slaughter, in retaliation for the lawless deed of one rash youth. The beginning that led to results so terrible was the act of Jacob's daughter, who "went out to see the daughters of the land," thus venturing into association with the ungodly. He who seeks pleasure among those that fear not God is placing himself on Satan's ground and inviting his temptations.

The treacherous cruelty of Simeon and Levi was not unprovoked; yet in their course toward the Shechemites they committed a grievous sin. They had carefully concealed from Jacob their intentions, and the tidings of their revenge filled him with horror. Heartsick at the deceit and violence of his sons, he only said, "Ye have troubled me to make me to stink among the inhabitants of the land: . . . and I being few in number, they shall gather themselves together against me, and slay me; and I shall be destroyed, I and my house." But the grief and abhorrence with which he regarded their bloody deed is shown by the words in which, nearly fifty years later, he referred to it, as he lay upon his deathbed in Egypt: "Simeon and Levi are brethren; instruments of cruelty are in their habitations. O my soul, come not thou into their secret; unto their assembly, mine honor, be not thou united. . . . Cursed be their anger, for it was fierce; and their wrath, for it was cruel." Genesis 49:5-7.

Jacob felt that there was cause for deep humiliation. Cruelty and falsehood were manifest in the character of his sons. There were false gods in the camp, and idolatry had to some extent gained a foothold even in his household. Should the Lord deal with them according to their deserts, would He not leave them to the vengeance of the surrounding nations?

While Jacob was thus bowed down with trouble, the Lord directed him to journey southward to Bethel. The thought of this place reminded the patriarch not only of his vision of the angels and of God's promises of mercy, but also of the vow which he had made there, that the Lord should be his God. He determined that before going to this sacred spot his household should be freed from the defilement of idolatry. He therefore gave direction to all in the encampment, "Put away the strange gods that are among you, and be clean, and change your garments: and let us arise, and go up to Bethel; and I will make there an altar unto God, who answered me in the day of my distress, and was with me in the way which I went."

With deep emotion Jacob repeated the story of his first visit to Bethel, when he left his father's tent a lonely wanderer, fleeing for his life, and how the Lord had appeared to him in the night vision. As he reviewed the wonderful dealings of God with him, his own heart was softened, his children also were touched by a subduing power; he had taken the most effectual way to prepare them to join in the worship of God when they should arrive at Bethel. "And they gave unto Jacob all the strange gods which were in their hand, and all their earrings which were in their ears; and Jacob hid them under the oak which was by Shechem."

God caused a fear to rest upon the inhabitants of the land, so that they made no attempt to avenge the slaughter at Shechem. The travelers reached Bethel unmolested. Here the Lord again appeared to Jacob and renewed to him the covenant promise. "And Jacob set up a pillar in the place where He talked with him, even a pillar of stone."

At Bethel, Jacob was called to mourn the loss of one who had long been an honored member of his father's family—Rebekah's nurse, Deborah, who had accompanied her mistress from Mesopotamia to the land of Canaan. The presence of this aged woman had been to Jacob a precious tie that bound him to his early life, and especially to the mother

whose love for him had been so strong and tender. Deborah was buried with expressions of so great sorrow that the oak under which her grave was made, was called "the oak of weeping." It should not be passed unnoticed that the memory of her life of faithful service and of the mourning over this household friend has been accounted worthy to be preserved in the word of God.

From Bethel it was only a two days' journey to Hebron, but it brought to Jacob a heavy grief in the death of Rachel. Twice seven years' service he had rendered for her sake, and his love had made the toil but light. How deep and abiding that love had been, was shown when long afterward, as Jacob in Egypt lay near his death, Joseph came to visit his father, and the aged patriarch, glancing back upon his own life, said, "As for me, when I came from Padan, Rachel died by me in the land of Canaan in the way, when yet there was but a little way to come unto Ephrath: and I buried her there in the way of Ephrath." Genesis 48:7. In the family history of his long and troubled life the loss of Rachel was alone recalled.

Before her death Rachel gave birth to a second son. With her parting breath she named the child Benoni, "son of my sorrow." But his father called him Benjamin, "son of my right hand," or "my strength." Rachel was buried where she died, and a pillar was raised upon the spot to perpetuate her memory.

On the way to Ephrath another dark crime stained the family of Jacob, causing Reuben, the first-born son, to be denied the privileges and honors of the birthright.

At last Jacob came to his journey's end, "unto Isaac his father unto Mamre, . . . which is Hebron, where Abraham and Isaac sojourned." Here he remained during the closing years of his father's life. To Isaac, infirm and blind, the kind attentions of this long-absent son were a comfort during years of loneliness and bereavement.

Jacob and Esau met at the deathbed of their father. Once the elder brother had looked forward to this event as an opportunity for revenge, but his feelings had since greatly changed. And Jacob, well content with the spiritual blessings of the birthright, resigned to the elder brother the inheritance of their father's wealth—the only inheritance that Esau sought or valued. They were no longer estranged by jealousy or hatred, yet they parted, Esau removing to Mount Seir. God, who is rich in blessing, had granted to Jacob worldly wealth, in addition to the higher good that he had sought. The possessions of the two brothers "were more than that they might dwell together; and the land wherein they were strangers could not bear them because of their cattle." This separation was in accordance with the divine purpose concerning Jacob. Since the brothers differed so greatly in regard to religious faith, it was better for them to dwell apart.

Esau and Jacob had alike been instructed in the knowledge of God, and both were free to walk in His commandments and to receive His favor; but they had not both chosen to do this. The two brothers had walked in different ways, and their paths would continue to diverge more and more widely.

There was no arbitrary choice on the part of God by which Esau was shut out from the blessings of salvation. The gifts of His grace through Christ are free to all. There is no election but one's own by which any may perish. God has set forth in His word the conditions upon which every soul will be elected to eternal life—obedience to His commandments, through faith in Christ. God has elected a character in harmony with His law, and anyone who shall reach the standard of His requirement will have an entrance into the kingdom of glory. Christ Himself said, "He that believeth on the Son hath everlasting life: and he that believeth not the Son shall not see life." John 3:36. "Not everyone that saith unto Me, Lord, Lord, shall enter into the kingdom of heaven; but he that doeth the will of My Father which is in heaven." Matthew 7:21. And in the Revelation He declares, "Blessed are they that do His commandments, that they may have right to the tree of life, and may enter in through the gates into the city." Revelation 22:14. As regards man's final salvation, this is the only election brought to view in the word of God.

Every soul is elected who will work out his own salvation with fear and trembling. He is elected who will put on the armor and fight the good fight of faith. He is elected who will watch unto prayer, who will search the Scriptures, and flee from temptation. He is elected who will have faith continually, and who will be obedient to every word that proceedeth out of the mouth of God. The provisions of redemption are free to all; the results of redemption will be enjoyed by those who have complied with the conditions.

Esau had despised the blessings of the covenant. He had valued temporal above spiritual good, and he had received that which he desired. It was by his own deliberate choice that he was separated from the people of God. Jacob had chosen the inheritance of faith. He had endeavored to obtain it by craft, treachery, and falsehood; but God had permitted his sin to work out its correction. Yet through all the bitter experience of his later years, Jacob had never swerved from his purpose or renounced his choice. He had learned that in resorting to human skill and craft to secure the blessing, he had been warring against God. From that night of wrestling beside the Jabbok, Jacob had come forth a different man. Self-confidence had been uprooted. Henceforth the early cunning was no longer seen. In place of craft and deception, his life was marked by simplicity and truth. He had learned the lesson of simple reliance upon the Almighty Arm, and amid trial and affliction he bowed in humble submission to the will of God. The baser elements of character were consumed in the furnace fire, the true gold was refined, until the faith of Abraham and Isaac appeared undimmed in Jacob.

The sin of Jacob, and the train of events to which it led, had not failed to exert an influence for evil—an influence that revealed its bitter fruit in the character and life of his sons. As these sons arrived at manhood they developed serious faults. The results of polygamy were manifest in the household. This terrible evil tends to dry up the very springs of love, and its influence weakens the most sacred ties. The jealousy of the several mothers had embittered the family relation, the children had grown up contentious and impatient of control, and the father's life was darkened with anxiety and grief.

There was one, however, of a widely different character—the elder son of Rachel, Joseph, whose rare personal beauty seemed but to reflect an inward beauty of mind and heart. Pure, active, and joyous, the lad gave evidence also of moral earnestness and firmness. He listened to his father's instructions, and loved to obey God. The qualities that afterward distinguished him in Egypt—gentleness, fidelity, and truthfulness—were already manifest in his daily life. His mother being dead, his affections clung the more closely to the father, and Jacob's heart was bound up in this child of his old age. He "loved Joseph more than all his children."

But even this affection was to become a cause of trouble and sorrow. Jacob unwisely manifested his preference for Joseph, and this excited the jealousy of his other sons. As Joseph witnessed the evil conduct of his brothers, he was greatly troubled; he ventured gently to remonstrate with them, but only aroused still further their hatred and resentment. He could not endure to see them sinning against God, and he laid the matter before his father, hoping that his authority might lead them to reform.

Jacob carefully avoided exciting their anger by harshness or severity. With deep emotion he expressed his solicitude for his children, and implored them to have respect for his gray hairs, and not to bring reproach upon his name, and above all not to dishonor God by such disregard of His precepts. Ashamed that their wickedness was known, the young men seemed to be repentant, but they only concealed their real feelings, which were rendered more bitter by this exposure.

The father's injudicious gift to Joseph of a costly coat, or tunic, such as was usually worn by persons of distinction, seemed to them another evidence of his partiality, and excited a suspicion that he intended to pass by his elder children, to bestow the birthright upon the son of Rachel. Their malice was still further increased as the boy one day told them of a dream that he had had. "Behold," he said, "we were binding sheaves in the field, and, lo, my sheaf arose, and also stood upright; and, behold, your sheaves stood round about, and made obeisance to my sheaf."

"Shalt thou indeed reign over us? or shalt thou indeed have dominion over us?" exclaimed his brothers in envious anger.

Soon he had another dream, of similar import, which he also related: "Behold, the sun and the moon and the eleven stars made obeisance to me." This dream was interpreted as readily as the first. The father, who was present, spoke reprovingly—"What is this dream that thou hast dreamed? Shall I and thy mother and thy brethren indeed come to bow down ourselves to thee to the earth?" Notwithstanding the apparent severity of his words, Jacob believed that the Lord was revealing the future to Joseph.

As the lad stood before his brothers, his beautiful countenance lighted up with the Spirit of inspiration, they could not withhold their admiration; but they did not choose to renounce their evil ways, and they hated the purity that reproved their sins. The same spirit that actuated Cain was kindling in their hearts.

The brothers were obliged to move from place to place to secure pasturage for their flocks, and frequently they were absent from home for months together. After the circumstances just related, they went to the place which their father had bought at Shechem. Some time passed, bringing no tidings from them, and the father began to fear for their safety, on account of their former cruelty toward the Shechemites. He therefore sent Joseph to find them, and bring him words as to their welfare. Had Jacob known the real feeling of his sons toward Joseph, he would not have trusted him alone with them; but this they had carefully concealed.

With a joyful heart, Joseph parted from his father, neither the aged man nor the youth dreaming of what would happen before they should meet again. When, after his long and solitary journey, Joseph arrived at Shechem, his brothers and their flocks were not to be found. Upon inquiring for them, he was directed to Dothan. He had already traveled more than fifty miles, and now an additional distance of fifteen lay before him, but he hastened on, forgetting his weariness in the thought of relieving the anxiety of his father, and meeting the brothers, whom, despite their unkindness, he still loved.

His brothers saw him approaching; but no thought of the long journey he had made to meet them, of his weariness and hunger, of his claims upon their hospitality and brotherly love, softened the bitterness of their hatred. The sight of the coat, the token of their father's love, filled them with frenzy. "Behold, this dreamer cometh," they cried in mockery. Envy and revenge, long secretly cherished, now controlled them. "Let us slay him," they said, "and cast him into some pit, and we will say, Some evil beast hath devoured him; and we shall see what will become of his dreams."

They would have executed their purpose but for Reuben. He shrank from participating in the murder of his brother, and proposed that Joseph be cast alive into a pit, and left there to perish; secretly intending, however, to rescue him and return him to his father. Having persuaded all to consent to this plan, Reuben left the company, fearing that he might fail to control his feelings, and that his real intentions would be discovered.

Joseph came on, unsuspicious of danger, and glad that the object of his long search was accomplished; but instead of the expected greeting, he was terrified by the angry and revengeful glances which he met. He was seized and his coat stripped from him. Taunts and threats revealed a deadly purpose. His entreaties were unheeded. He was wholly in the power of those maddened men. Rudely dragging him to a deep pit, they thrust him in, and having made sure that there was no possibility of his escape, they left him there to perish from hunger, while they "sat down to eat bread."

But some of them were ill at ease; they did not feel the satisfaction they had anticipated from their revenge. Soon a company of travelers was seen approaching. It was a caravan of Ishmaelites from beyond Jordan, on their way to Egypt with spices and other merchandise. Judah now proposed to sell their brother to these heathen traders instead of leaving him to die. While he would be effectually put out of their way, they would remain clear of his blood; "for," he urged, "he is our brother and our flesh." To this proposition all agreed, and Joseph was quickly drawn out of the pit.

As he saw the merchants the dreadful truth flashed upon him. To become a slave was a fate more to be feared than death. In an agony of terror he appealed to one and another of his brothers, but in vain. Some were moved with pity, but fear of derision kept them silent; all felt that they had now gone too far to retreat. If Joseph were spared, he would doubtless report them to the father, who would not overlook their cruelty toward his favorite son. Steeling their hearts against his entreaties, they delivered him into the hands of the heathen traders. The caravan moved on, and was soon lost to view.

Reuben returned to the pit, but Joseph was not there. In alarm and self-reproach he rent his garments, and sought his brothers, exclaiming, "The child is not; and I, whither shall I go?" Upon learning the fate of Joseph, and that it would now be impossible to recover him, Reuben was induced to unite with the rest in the attempt to conceal their guilt. Having killed a kid, they dipped Joseph's coat in its blood, and took it to their father, telling him that they had found it in the fields, and that they feared it was their brother's. "Know now," they said, "whether it be thy son's coat or no." They had looked forward to this scene with dread, but they were not prepared for the heart-rending anguish, the utter abandonment of grief, which they were compelled to witness. "It is my son's coat," said Jacob; "an evil beast hath devoured him. Joseph is without doubt rent in pieces." Vainly his sons and daughters attempted to comfort him. He "rent his clothes, and put sackcloth upon his loins, and mourned for his son many days." Time seemed to bring no alleviation of his grief. "I will go down into the grave unto my son mourning," was his despairing cry. The young men, terrified at what they had done, yet dreading their father's reproaches, still hid in their own hearts the knowledge of their guilt, which even to themselves seemed very great.

Joseph in Egypt

Meanwhile, Joseph with his captors was on the way to Egypt. As the caravan journeyed southward toward the borders of Canaan, the boy could discern in the distance the hills among which lay his father's tents. Bitterly he wept at thought of that loving father in his loneliness and affliction. Again the scene at Dothan came up before him. He saw his angry brothers and felt their fierce glances bent upon him. The stinging, insulting words that had met his agonized entreaties were ringing in his ears. With a trembling heart he looked forward to the future. What a change in situation—from the tenderly cherished son to the despised and helpless slave! Alone and friendless, what would be his lot in the strange land to which he was going? For a time Joseph gave himself up to uncontrolled grief and terror.

But, in the providence of God, even this experience was to be a blessing to him. He had learned in a few hours that which years might not otherwise have taught him. His father, strong and tender as his love had been, had done him wrong by his partiality and indulgence. This unwise preference had angered his brothers and provoked them to the cruel deed that had separated him from his home. Its effects were manifest also in his own character. Faults had been encouraged that were now to be corrected. He was becoming self-sufficient and exacting. Accustomed to the tenderness of his father's care, he felt that he was unprepared to cope with the difficulties before him, in the bitter, uncared-for life of a stranger and a slave.

Then his thoughts turned to his father's God. In his childhood he had been taught to love and fear Him. Often in his father's tent he had listened to the story of the vision that Jacob saw as he fled from his home an exile and a fugitive. He had been told of the Lord's promises to Jacob, and how they had been fulfilled—how, in the hour of need, the angels of God had come to instruct, comfort, and protect him. And he had learned of the love of God in providing for men a Redeemer. Now all these precious lessons came vividly before him. Joseph believed that the God of his fathers would be his God. He then and there gave himself fully to the Lord, and he prayed that the Keeper of Israel would be with him in the land of his exile.

His soul thrilled with the high resolve to prove himself true to God—under all circumstances to act as became a subject of the King of heaven. He would serve the Lord with undivided heart; he would meet the trials of his lot with fortitude and perform every duty with fidelity. One day's experience had been the turning point in Joseph's life. Its terrible calamity had transformed him from a petted child to a man, thoughtful, courageous, and self-possessed.

Arriving in Egypt, Joseph was sold to Potiphar, captain of the king's guard, in whose service he remained for ten years. He was here exposed to temptations of no ordinary character. He was in the midst of idolatry. The worship of false gods was surrounded by all the pomp of royalty, supported by the wealth and culture of the most highly civilized nation then in existence. Yet Joseph preserved his simplicity and his fidelity to God. The sights and sounds of vice were all about him, but he was as one who saw and heard not. His thoughts were not permitted to linger upon forbidden subjects. The desire to gain the favor of the Egyptians could not cause him to conceal his principles. Had he attempted to do this, he would have been overcome by temptation; but he was not ashamed of the religion of his fathers, and he made no effort to hide the fact that he was a worshiper of Jehovah.

"And the Lord was with Joseph, and he was a prosperous man. . . . And his master saw that the Lord was with him, and that the Lord made all that he did to prosper in his hand."

Potiphar's confidence in Joseph increased daily, and he finally promoted him to be his steward, with full control over all his possessions. "And he left all that he had in Joseph's hand; and he knew not aught he had, save the bread which he did eat."

The marked prosperity which attended everything placed under Joseph's care was not the result of a direct miracle; but his industry, care, and energy were crowned with the divine blessing. Joseph attributed his success to the favor of God, and even his idolatrous master accepted this as the secret of his unparalleled prosperity. Without steadfast, well-directed effort, however, success could never have been attained. God was glorified by the faithfulness of His servant. It was His purpose that in purity and uprightness the believer in God should appear in marked contrast to the worshipers of idols—that thus the light of heavenly grace might shine forth amid the darkness of heathenism.

Joseph's gentleness and fidelity won the heart of the chief captain, who came to regard him as a son rather than a slave. The youth was brought in contact with men of rank and learning, and he acquired a knowledge of science, of languages, and of affairs—an education needful to the future prime minister of Egypt.

But Joseph's faith and integrity were to be tested by fiery trials. His master's wife endeavored to entice the young man to transgress the law of God. Heretofore he had remained untainted by the corruption teeming in that heathen land; but this temptation, so sudden, so strong, so seductive—how should it be met? Joseph knew well what would be the consequence of resistance. On the one hand were concealment, favor, and rewards; on the other, disgrace, imprisonment, perhaps death. His whole future life depended upon the decision of the moment. Would principle triumph? Would Joseph still be true to God? With inexpressible anxiety, angels looked upon the scene.

Joseph's answer reveals the power of religious principle. He would not betray the confidence of his master on earth, and, whatever the consequences, he would be true to his Master in heaven. Under the inspecting eye of God and holy angels many take liberties of which they would not be guilty in the presence of their fellow men, but Joseph's first thought was of God. "How can I do this great wickedness, and sin against God?" he said.

If we were to cherish an habitual impression that God sees and hears all that we do and say and keeps a faithful record of our words and actions, and that we must meet it all, we would fear to sin. Let the young ever remember that wherever they are, and whatever they do, they are in the presence of God. No part of our conduct escapes observation. We cannot hide our ways from the Most High. Human laws, though sometimes severe, are often transgressed without detection, and hence with impunity. But not so with the law of God. The deepest midnight is no cover for the guilty one. He may think himself alone, but to every deed there is an unseen witness. The very motives of his heart are open to divine inspection. Every act, every word, every thought, is as distinctly marked as though there were only one person in the whole world, and the attention of heaven were centered upon him.

Joseph suffered for his integrity, for his tempter revenged herself by accusing him of a foul crime, and causing him to be thrust into prison. Had Potiphar believed his wife's charge against Joseph, the young Hebrew would have lost his life; but the modesty and uprightness that had uniformly characterized his conduct were proof of his innocence; and yet, to save the reputation of his master's house, he was abandoned to disgrace and bondage.

At the first Joseph was treated with great severity by his jailers. The psalmist says, "His feet they hurt with fetters; he was laid in chains of iron: until the time that his word came to pass; the word of the Lord tried him." Psalm 105:18, 19, R.V. But Joseph's real character shines out, even in the darkness of the dungeon. He held fast his faith and patience; his years of faithful service had been most cruelly repaid, yet this did not render him morose or distrustful. He had the peace that comes from conscious innocence, and he trusted his case with God. He did not brood upon his own wrongs, but forgot his sorrow in trying to lighten the sorrows of others. He found a work to do, even in the prison. God was preparing him in the school of affliction for greater usefulness, and he did not refuse the needful discipline. In the prison, witnessing the results of oppression and tyranny and the effects of crime, he learned lessons of justice, sympathy, and mercy, that prepared him to exercise power with wisdom and compassion.

Joseph gradually gained the confidence of the keeper of the prison, and was finally entrusted with the charge of all the prisoners. It was the part he acted in the prison—the integrity of his daily life and his sympathy for those who were in trouble and distress—that opened the way for his future prosperity and honor. Every ray of light that we shed upon others is reflected upon ourselves. Every kind and sympathizing word spoken to the sorrowful, every act to relieve the oppressed, and every gift to the needy, if prompted by a right motive, will result in blessings to the giver.

The chief baker and chief butler of the king had been cast into prison for some offense, and they came under Joseph's charge. One morning, observing that they appeared very sad, he kindly inquired the cause and was told that each had had a remarkable dream, of which they were anxious to learn the significance. "Do not interpretations belong to God?" said Joseph, "tell me them, I pray you." As each related his dream, Joseph made known its import: In three days the butler was to be reinstated in his position, and give the cup into Pharaoh's hand as before, but the chief baker would be put to death by the king's command. In both cases the event occurred as foretold.

The king's cupbearer had professed the deepest gratitude to Joseph, both for the cheering interpretation of his dream and for many acts of kind attention; and in return the latter, referring in a most touching manner to his own unjust captivity, entreated that his case be brought before the king.

"Think on me," he said, "when it shall be well with thee, and show kindness, I pray thee, unto me, and make mention of me unto Pharaoh, and bring me out of this house: for indeed I was stolen away out of the land of the Hebrews: and here also have I done nothing that they should put me into the dungeon." The chief butler saw the dream fulfilled in every particular; but when restored to royal favor, he thought no more of his benefactor. For two years longer Joseph remained a prisoner. The hope that had been kindled in his heart gradually died out, and to all other trials was added the bitter sting of ingratitude.

But a divine hand was about to open the prison gates. The king of Egypt had in one night two dreams, apparently pointing to the same event and seeming to foreshadow some great calamity. He could not determine their significance, yet they continued to trouble his mind. The magicians and wise men of his realm could give no interpretation. The king's perplexity and distress increased, and terror spread throughout his palace. The general agitation recalled to the chief butler's mind the circumstances of his own dream; with it came the memory of Joseph, and a pang of remorse for his forgetfulness and ingratitude. He at once informed the king how his own dream and that of the chief baker had been interpreted by a Hebrew captive, and how the predictions had been fulfilled.

It was humiliating to Pharaoh to turn away from the magicians and wise men of his kingdom to consult an alien and a slave, but he was ready to accept the lowliest service if his troubled mind might find relief. Joseph was immediately sent for; he put off his prison attire, and shaved himself, for his hair had grown long during the period of his disgrace and confinement. He was then conducted to the presence of the king.

"And Pharaoh said unto Joseph, I have dreamed a dream, and there is none that can interpret it: and I have heard say of thee, that thou canst understand a dream to interpret it. And Joseph answered Pharaoh, saying, It is not in me: God shall give Pharaoh an answer of peace." Joseph's reply to the king reveals his humility and his faith in God. He modestly disclaims the honor of possessing in himself superior wisdom. "It is not in me." God alone can explain these mysteries.

Pharaoh then proceeded to relate his dreams: "Behold, I stood upon the bank of the river: and, behold, there came up out of the river seven kine, fat-fleshed and well-favored; and they fed in a meadow: and, behold, seven other kine came up after them, poor and very ill-favored and lean-fleshed, such as I never saw in all the land of Egypt for badness: and the lean and the ill-favored kine did eat up the first seven fat kine: and when they had eaten them up, it could not be known that they had eaten them; but they were still ill-favored, as at the beginning. So I awoke. And I saw in my dream, and, behold, seven ears came up in one stalk, full and good: and, behold, seven ears, withered, thin, and blasted with the east wind, sprung up after them: and the thin ears devoured the seven good ears: and I told this unto the magicians; but there was none that could declare it to me."

"The dream of Pharaoh is one," said Joseph. "God hath showed Pharaoh what He is about to do." There were to be seven years of great plenty. Field and garden would yield more abundantly than ever before. And this period was to be followed by seven years of famine. "And the plenty shall not be known in the land by reason of that famine following; for it shall be very grievous." The repetition of the dream was evidence both of the certainty and nearness of the fulfillment. "Now therefore," he continued, "let Pharaoh look out a man discreet and wise, and set him over the land of Egypt. Let Pharaoh do this, and let him appoint officers over the land, and take up the fifth part of the land of Egypt in the seven plenteous years. And let them gather all the food of those good years that come, and lay up corn under the hand of Pharaoh, and let them keep food in the cities. And that food shall be for store to the land against the seven years of famine."

The interpretation was so reasonable and consistent, and the policy which it recommended was so sound and shrewd, that its correctness could not be doubted. But who was to be entrusted with the execution of the plan? Upon the wisdom of this choice depended the nation's preservation. The king was troubled. For some time the matter of the appointment was under consideration. Through the chief butler the monarch had learned of the wisdom and prudence displayed by Joseph in the management of the prison; it was evident that he possessed administrative ability in a pre-eminent degree. The cupbearer, now filled with self-reproach, endeavored to atone for his former ingratitude, by the warmest praise of his benefactor; and further inquiry by the king proved the correctness of his report. In all the realm Joseph was the only man gifted with wisdom to point out the danger that threatened the kingdom and the preparation necessary to meet it; and the king was convinced that he was the one best qualified to execute the plans which he had proposed. It was evident that a divine power was with him, and that there were none among the king's officers of state so well qualified to conduct the affairs of the nation at this crisis. The fact that he was a Hebrew and a slave was of little moment when weighed against his evident wisdom and sound judgment. "Can we find such a one as this is, a man in whom the Spirit of God is?" said the king to his counselors.

The appointment was decided upon, and to Joseph the astonishing announcement was made, "Forasmuch as God hath showed thee all this, there is none so discreet and wise as thou art: thou shalt be over my house, and according unto thy word shall all my people be ruled: only in the throne will I be greater than thou." The king proceeded to invest Joseph with the insignia of his high office. "And Pharaoh took off his ring from his hand, and put it upon Joseph's hand, and arrayed him in vestures of fine linen, and put a gold chain about his neck; and he made him to ride in the second chariot which he had; and they cried before him, Bow the knee."

"He made him lord of his house, and ruler of all his substance: to bind his princes at his pleasure; and teach his senators wisdom." Psalm 105:21, 22. From the dungeon Joseph was exalted to be ruler over all the land of Egypt. It was a position of high honor, yet it was beset with difficulty and peril. One cannot stand upon a lofty height without danger. As the tempest leaves unharmed the lowly flower of the valley, while it uproots the stately tree upon the mountaintop, so those who have maintained their integrity in humble life may be dragged down to the pit by the temptations that assail worldly success and honor. But Joseph's character bore the test alike of adversity and prosperity. The same fidelity to God was manifest when he stood in the palace of the Pharaohs as when in a prisoner's cell. He was still a stranger in a heathen land, separated from his kindred, the worshipers of God; but he fully believed that the divine hand had directed his steps, and in constant reliance upon God he faithfully discharged the duties of his position. Through Joseph the attention of the king and great men of Egypt was directed to the true God; and though they adhered to their idolatry, they learned to respect the principles revealed in the life and character of the worshiper of Jehovah.

How was Joseph enabled to make such a record of firmness of character, uprightness, and wisdom?—In his early years he had consulted duty rather than inclination; and the integrity, the simple trust, the noble nature, of the youth bore fruit in the deeds of the man. A pure and simple life had favored the vigorous development of both physical and intellectual powers. Communion with God through His works and the contemplation of the grand truths entrusted to the inheritors of faith had elevated and ennobled his spiritual nature, broadening and strengthening the mind as no other study could do. Faithful attention to duty in every station, from the lowliest to the most exalted, had been training every power for its highest service. He who lives in accordance with the Creator's will is securing to himself the truest and noblest development of character. "The fear of the Lord, that is wisdom; and to depart from evil is understanding." Job 28:28.

There are few who realize the influence of the little things of life upon the development of character. Nothing with which we have to do is really small. The varied circumstances that we meet day by day are designed to test our faithfulness and to qualify us for greater trusts. By adherence to principle in the transactions of ordinary life, the mind becomes accustomed to hold the claims of duty above those of pleasure and inclination. Minds thus disciplined are not wavering between right and wrong, like the reed trembling in the wind; they are loyal to duty because they have trained themselves to habits of fidelity and truth. By faithfulness in that which is least they acquire strength to be faithful in greater matters.

An upright character is of greater worth than the gold of Ophir. Without it none can rise to an honorable eminence. But character is not inherited. It cannot be bought. Moral excellence and fine mental qualities are not the result of accident. The most precious gifts are of no value unless they are improved. The formation of a noble character is the work of a lifetime and must be the result of diligent and persevering effort. God gives opportunities; success depends upon the use made of them.

Joseph and His Brothers

At the very opening of the fruitful years began the preparation for the approaching famine. Under the direction of Joseph, immense storehouses were erected in all the principal places throughout the land of Egypt, and ample arrangements were made for preserving the surplus of the expected harvest. The same policy was continued during the seven years of plenty, until the amount of grain laid in store was beyond computation.

And now the seven years of dearth began to come, according to Joseph's prediction. "And the dearth was in all lands; but in all the land of Egypt there was bread. And when all the land of Egypt was famished, the people cried to Pharaoh for bread: and Pharaoh said unto all the Egyptians, Go unto Joseph; what he saith to you, do. And the famine was over all the face of the earth: and Joseph opened all the storehouses, and sold unto the Egyptians."

The famine extended to the land of Canaan and was severely felt in that part of the country where Jacob dwelt. Hearing of the abundant provision made by the king of Egypt, ten of Jacob's sons journeyed thither to purchase grain. On their arrival they were directed to the king's deputy, and with other applicants they came to present themselves before the ruler of the land. And they "bowed down themselves before him with their faces to the earth." "Joseph knew his brethren, but they knew not him." His Hebrew name had been exchanged for the one bestowed upon him by the king, and there was little resemblance between the prime minister of Egypt and the stripling whom they had sold to the Ishmaelites. As Joseph saw his brothers stooping and making obeisance, his dreams came to his mind, and the scenes of the past rose vividly before him. His keen eye, surveying the group, discovered that Benjamin was not among them. Had he also fallen a victim to the treacherous cruelty of those savage men? He determined to learn the truth. "Ye are spies," he said sternly; "to see the nakedness of the land ye are come."

They answered, "Nay, my lord, but to buy food are thy servants come. We are all one man's sons; we are true men; thy servants are no spies." He wished to learn if they possessed the same haughty spirit as when he was with them, and also to draw from them some information in regard to their home; yet he well knew how deceptive their statements might be. He repeated the charge, and they replied, "Thy servants are twelve brethren, the sons of one man in the land of Canaan; and, behold, the youngest is this day with our father, and one is not."

Professing to doubt the truthfulness of their story, and to still look upon them as spies, the governor declared that he would prove them, by requiring them to remain in Egypt till one of their number should go and bring their youngest brother down. If they would not consent to this, they were to be treated as spies. But to such an arrangement the sons of Jacob could not agree, since the time required for carrying it out would cause their families to suffer for food; and who among them would undertake the journey alone, leaving his brothers in prison? How could he meet his father under such circumstances? It appeared probable that they were to be put to death or to be made slaves; and if Benjamin were brought, it might be only to share their fate. They decided to remain and suffer together, rather than bring additional sorrow upon their father by the loss of his only remaining son. They were accordingly cast into prison, where they remained three days.

During the years since Joseph had been separated from his brothers, these sons of Jacob had changed in character. Envious, turbulent, deceptive, cruel, and revengeful they had been; but now, when tested by adversity, they were shown to be unselfish, true to one another, devoted to their father, and, themselves middle-aged men, subject to his authority.

The three days in the Egyptian prison were days of bitter sorrow as the brothers reflected upon their past sins. Unless Benjamin could be produced their conviction as spies appeared certain, and they had little hope of gaining their father's consent to Benjamin's absence. On the third day Joseph caused the brothers to be brought before him. He dared not detain them longer. Already his father and the families with him might be suffering for food. "This do, and live," he said; "for I fear God; if ye be true men, let one of your brethren be bound in the house of your prison: go ye, carry corn for the famine of your houses: but bring your youngest brother unto me; so shall your words be verified, and ye shall not die." This proposition they agreed to accept, though expressing little hope that their father would let Benjamin return with them. Joseph had communicated with them through an interpreter, and having no thought that the governor understood them, they conversed freely with one another in his presence. They accused themselves in regard to their treatment of Joseph: "We are verily guilty concerning our brother, in that we saw the anguish of his soul, when he besought us, and we would not hear; therefore is this distress come upon us." Reuben, who had formed the plan for delivering him at Dothan, added, "Spake I not unto you, saying, Do not sin against the child; and ye would not hear? therefore, behold, also his blood is required." Joseph, listening, could not control his emotions, and he went out and wept. On his return he commanded that Simeon be bound before them and again committed to prison. In the cruel treatment of their brother, Simeon had been the instigator and chief actor, and it was for this reason that the choice fell upon him.

Before permitting his brothers to depart, Joseph gave directions that they should be supplied with grain, and also that each man's money should be secretly placed in the mouth of his sack. Provender for the beasts on the homeward journey was also supplied. On the way one of the company, opening his sack, was surprised to find his bag of silver. On his making known the fact to the others, they were alarmed and perplexed, and said one to another, "What is this that God hath done unto us?"—should they regard it as a token of good from the Lord, or had He suffered it to occur to punish them for their sins and plunge them still deeper in affliction? They acknowledged that God had seen their sins, and that He was now punishing them.

Jacob was anxiously awaiting the return of his sons, and on their arrival the whole encampment gathered eagerly around them as they related to their father all that had occurred. Alarm and apprehension filled every heart. The conduct of the Egyptian governor seemed to imply some evil design, and their fears were confirmed, when, as they opened their sacks, the owner's money was found in each. In his distress the aged father exclaimed, "Me have ye bereaved of my children: Joseph is not, and Simeon is not, and ye will take Benjamin away: all these things are against me." Reuben answered, "Slay my two sons, if I bring him not to thee: deliver him into my hand, and I will bring him to thee again." This rash speech did not relieve the mind of Jacob. His answer was, "My son shall not go down with you; for his brother is dead, and he is left alone: if mischief befall him by the way in the which ye go, then shall ye bring down my gray hairs with sorrow to the grave."

But the drought continued, and in process of time the supply of grain that had been brought from Egypt was nearly exhausted. The sons of Jacob well knew that it would be in vain to return to Egypt without Benjamin. They had little hope of changing their father's resolution, and they awaited the issue in silence. Deeper and deeper grew the shadow of approaching famine; in the anxious faces of all in the encampment the old man read their need; at last he said, "Go again, buy us a little food."

Judah answered, "The man did solemnly protest unto us, saying, Ye shall not see my face, except your brother be with you. If thou wilt send our brother with us, we will go down and buy thee food: but if thou wilt not send him, we will not go down: for the man said unto us, Ye shall not see my face, except your brother be with you." Seeing that his father's resolution began to waver, he added, "Send the lad with me, and we will arise and go; that we may live, and not die, both we, and thou, and also our little ones;" and he offered to be surety for his brother and to bear the blame forever if he failed to restore Benjamin to his father.

Jacob could no longer withhold his consent, and he directed his sons to prepare for the journey. He bade them also take to the ruler a present of such things as the famine-wasted country afforded—"a little balm, and a little honey, spices and myrrh, nuts and almonds," also a double quantity of money. "Take also your brother," he said, "and arise, go again unto the man." As his sons were about to depart on their doubtful journey the aged father arose, and raising his hands to heaven, uttered the prayer, "God Almighty give you mercy before the man, that he may send away your other brother, and Benjamin. If I be bereaved of my children, I am bereaved."

Again they journeyed to Egypt and presented themselves before Joseph. As his eye fell upon Benjamin, his own mother's son, he was deeply moved. He concealed his emotion, however, but ordered that they be taken to his house, and that preparation be made for them to dine with him. Upon being conducted to the governor's palace, the brothers were greatly alarmed, fearing that they were to be called to account for the money found in their sacks. They thought that it might have been intentionally placed there, to furnish occasion for making them slaves. In their distress they consulted with the steward of the house, relating to him the circumstances of their visit to Egypt; and in proof of their innocence informed him that they had brought back the money found in their sacks, also other money to buy food; and they added, "We cannot tell who put our money in our sacks." The man replied, "Peace be to you, fear not: your God, and the God of your father, hath given you treasure in your sacks: I had your money." Their anxiety was relieved, and when Simeon, who had been released from prison, joined them, they felt that God was indeed gracious unto them.

When the governor again met them they presented their gifts and humbly "bowed themselves to him to the earth." Again his dreams came to his mind, and after saluting his guests he hastened to ask, "Is your father well, the old man of whom ye spake? Is he yet alive?" "Thy servant our father is in good health, he is yet alive," was the answer, as they again made obeisance. Then his eye rested upon Benjamin, and he said, "Is this your younger brother, of whom ye spake unto me?" "God be gracious unto thee, my son;" but, overpowered by feelings of tenderness, he could say no more. "He entered into his chamber, and wept there."

Having recovered his self-possession, he returned, and all proceeded to the feast. By the laws of caste the Egyptians were forbidden to eat with people of any other nation. The sons of Jacob had therefore a table by themselves, while the governor, on account of his high rank, ate by himself, and the Egyptians also had separate tables. When all were seated the brothers were surprised to see that they were arranged in exact order, according to their ages. Joseph "sent messes unto them from before him;" but Benjamin's was five times as much as any of theirs. By this token of favor to Benjamin he hoped to ascertain if the youngest brother was regarded with the envy and hatred that had been manifested toward himself. Still supposing that Joseph did not understand their language, the brothers freely conversed with one another; thus he had a good opportunity to learn their real feelings. Still he desired to test them further, and before their departure he ordered that his own drinking cup of silver should be concealed in the sack of the youngest.

Joyfully they set out on their return. Simeon and Benjamin were with them, their animals were laden with grain, and all felt that they had safely escaped the perils that had seemed to surround them. But they had only reached the outskirts of the city when they were overtaken by the governor's steward, who uttered the scathing inquiry, "Wherefore have ye rewarded evil for good? Is not this it in which my lord drinketh, and whereby indeed he divineth? ye have done evil in so doing." This cup was supposed to possess the power of detecting any poisonous substance placed therein. At that day cups of this kind were highly valued as a safeguard against murder by poisoning.

To the steward's accusation the travelers answered, "Wherefore saith my lord these words? God forbid that thy servants should do according to this thing: behold, the money, which we found in our sack's mouths, we brought again unto thee out of the land of Canaan: how then should we steal out of thy lord's house silver or gold? With whomsoever of thy servants it be found, both let him die, and we also will be my lord's bondmen."

"Now also let it be according unto your words," said the steward; "he with whom it is found shall be my servant; and ye shall be blameless."

The search began immediately. "They speedily took down every man his sack to the ground," and the steward examined each, beginning with Reuben's, and taking them in order down to that of the youngest. In Benjamin's sack the cup was found.

The brothers rent their garments in token of utter wretchedness, and slowly returned to the city. By their own promise Benjamin was doomed to a life of slavery. They followed the steward to the palace, and finding the governor yet there, they prostrated themselves before him. "What deed is this that ye have done?" he said. "Wot ye not that such a man as I can certainly divine?" Joseph designed to draw from them an acknowledgment of their sin. He had never claimed the power of divination, but was willing to have them believe that he could read the secrets of their lives.

Judah answered, "What shall we say unto my Lord? what shall we speak? or how shall we clear ourselves? God hath found out the iniquity of thy servants: behold, we are my lord's servants, both we, and he also with whom the cup is found."

"God forbid that I should do so," was the reply; "but the man in whose hand the cup is found, he shall be my servant; and as for you, get you up in peace unto your father."

In his deep distress Judah now drew near to the ruler and exclaimed, "O my lord, let thy servant, I pray thee, speak a word in my lord's ears, and let not thine anger burn against thy servant: for thou art even as Pharaoh." In words of touching eloquence he described his father's grief at the loss of Joseph and his reluctance to let Benjamin come with them to Egypt, as he was the only son left of his mother, Rachel, whom Jacob so dearly loved. "Now therefore," he said, "when I come to thy servant my father, and the lad be not with us; seeing that his life is bound up in the lad's life; it shall come to pass, when he seeth that the lad is not with us, that he will die: and thy servants shall bring down the gray hairs of thy servant our father with sorrow to the grave. For thy servant became surety for the lad unto my father, saying, If I bring him not unto thee, then I shall bear the blame to my father forever. Now therefore, I pray thee, let thy servant abide instead of the lad a bondman to my lord; and let the lad go up with his brethren. For how shall I go up to my father, and the lad be not with me? lest peradventure I see the evil that shall come on my father."

Joseph was satisfied. He had seen in his brothers the fruits of true repentance. Upon hearing Judah's noble offer he gave orders that all but these men should withdraw; then, weeping aloud, he cried, "I am Joseph; doth my father yet live?"

His brothers stood motionless, dumb with fear and amazement. The ruler of Egypt their brother Joseph, whom they had envied and would have murdered, and finally sold as a slave! All their ill treatment of him passed before them. They remembered how they had despised his dreams and had labored to prevent their fulfillment. Yet they had acted their part in fulfilling these dreams; and now that they were completely in his power he would, no doubt, avenge the wrong that he had suffered.

Seeing their confusion, he said kindly, "Come near to me, I pray you;" and as they came near, he continued, "I am Joseph your brother, whom ye sold into Egypt. Now therefore be not grieved, nor angry with yourselves, that ye sold me hither: for God did send me before you to preserve life." Feeling that they had already suffered enough for their cruelty toward him, he nobly sought to banish their fears and lessen the bitterness of their self-reproach.

"For these two years," he continued, "hath the famine been in the land: and yet there are five years, in the which there shall neither be earing not harvest. And God sent me before you to preserve you a posterity in the earth, and to save your lives by a great deliverance. So now it was not you that sent me hither, but God: and He hath made me a father to Pharaoh, and lord of all his house, and a ruler throughout all the land of Egypt. Haste ye, and go up to my father, and say unto him, Thus saith thy son Joseph, God hath made me lord of all Egypt: come down unto me tarry not: and thou shalt dwell in the land of Goshen, and thou shalt be near unto me, thou, and thy children, and thy children's children, and thy flocks, and thy herds, and all that thou hast: and there will I nourish thee; for yet there are five years of famine; lest thou, and thy household, and all that thou hast, come to poverty. And, behold, your eyes see, and the eyes of my brother Benjamin, that it is my mouth that speaketh unto you." "And he fell upon his brother Benjamin's neck, and wept; and Benjamin wept upon his neck. Moreover he kissed all his brethren, and wept upon them: and after that his brethren talked with him." They humbly confessed their sin and entreated his forgiveness. They had long suffered anxiety and remorse, and now they rejoiced that he was still alive.

The news of what had taken place was quickly carried to the king, who, eager to manifest his gratitude to Joseph, confirmed the governor's invitation to his family, saying, "The good of all the land of Egypt is yours." The brothers were sent away abundantly supplied with provision and carriages and everything necessary for the removal of all their families and attendants to Egypt. On Benjamin, Joseph bestowed more valuable gifts than upon the others. Then, fearing that disputes would arise among them on the homeward journey, he gave them, as they were about to leave him, the charge, "See that ye fall not out by the way."

The sons of Jacob returned to their father with the joyful tidings, "Joseph is yet alive, and he is governor over all the land of Egypt." At first the aged man was overwhelmed; he could not believe what he heard; but when he saw the long train of wagons and loaded animals, and when Benjamin was with him once more, he was convinced, and in the fullness of his joy exclaimed, "It is enough; Joseph my son is yet alive: I will go and see him before I die."

Another act of humiliation remained for the ten brothers. They now confessed to their father the deceit and cruelty that for so many years had embittered his life and theirs. Jacob had not suspected them of so base a sin, but he saw that all had been overruled for good, and he forgave and blessed his erring children.

The father and his sons, with their families, their flocks and herds, and numerous attendants, were soon on the way to Egypt. With gladness of heart they pursued their journey, and when they came to Beersheba the patriarch offered grateful sacrifices and entreated the Lord to grant them an assurance that He would go with them. In a vision of the night the divine word came to him: "Fear not to go down into Egypt; for I will there make of thee a great nation. I will go down with thee into Egypt; and I will also surely bring thee up again."

The assurance, "Fear not to go down into Egypt; for I will there make of thee a great nation," was significant. The promise had been given to Abraham of a posterity numberless as the stars, but as yet the chosen people had increased but slowly. And the land of Canaan now offered no field for the development of such a nation as had been foretold. It was in the possession of powerful heathen tribes, that were not to be dispossessed until "the fourth generation." If the descendants of Israel were here to become a numerous people, they must either drive out the inhabitants of the land or disperse themselves among them. The former, according to the divine arrangement, they could not do; and should they mingle with the Canaanites, they would be in danger of being seduced into idolatry. Egypt, however, offered the conditions necessary to the fulfillment of the divine purpose. A section of country well-watered and fertile was open to them there, affording every advantage for their speedy increase. And the antipathy they must encounter in Egypt on account of their occupation—for every shepherd was "an abomination unto the Egyptians"—would enable them to remain a distinct and separate people and would thus serve to shut them out from participation in the idolatry of Egypt.

Upon reaching Egypt the company proceeded directly to the land of Goshen. Thither came Joseph in his chariot of state, attended by a princely retinue. The splendor of his surroundings and the dignity of his position were alike forgotten; one thought alone filled his mind, one longing thrilled his heart. As he beheld the travelers approaching, the love whose yearnings had for so many long years been repressed, would no longer be controlled. He sprang from his chariot and hastened forward to bid his father welcome. "And he fell on his neck, and wept on his neck a good while. And Israel said unto Joseph, Now let me die, since I have seen thy face, because thou art ye alive."

Joseph took five of his brothers to present to Pharaoh and receive from him the grant of land for their future home. Gratitude to his prime minister would have led the monarch to honor them with appointments to offices of state; but Joseph, true to the worship of Jehovah, sought to save his brothers from the temptations to which they would be exposed at a heathen court; therefore he counseled them, when questioned by the king, to tell him frankly their occupation. The sons of Jacob followed this counsel, being careful also to state that they had come to sojourn in the land, not to become permanent dwellers there, thus reserving the right to depart if they chose. The king assigned them a home, as offered, in "the best of the land," the country of Goshen.

Not long after their arrival Joseph brought his father also to be presented to the king. The patriarch was a stranger in royal courts; but amid the sublime scenes of nature he had communed with a mightier Monarch; and now, in conscious superiority, he raised his hands and blessed Pharaoh.

In his first greeting to Joseph, Jacob had spoken as if, with this joyful ending to his long anxiety and sorrow, he was ready to die. But seventeen years were yet to be granted him in the peaceful retirement of Goshen. These years were in happy contrast to those that had preceded them. He saw in his sons evidence of true repentance; he saw his family surrounded by all the conditions needful for the development of a great nation; and his faith grasped the sure promise of their future establishment in Canaan. He himself was surrounded with every token of love and favor that the prime minister of Egypt could bestow; and happy in the society of his long-lost son, he passed down gently and peacefully to the grave.

As he felt death approaching, he sent for Joseph. Still holding fast the promise of God respecting the possession of Canaan, he said, "Bury me not, I pray thee, in Egypt: but I will lie with my fathers, and thou shalt carry me out of Egypt, and bury me in their burying place." Joseph promised to do so, but Jacob was not satisfied; he exacted a solemn oath to lay him beside his fathers in the cave of Machpelah.

Another important matter demanded attention; the sons of Joseph were to be formally instated among the children of Israel. Joseph, coming for a last interview with his father, brought with him Ephraim and Manasseh. These youths were connected, through their mother, with the highest order of the Egyptian priesthood; and the position of their father opened to them the avenues to wealth and distinction, should they choose to connect themselves with the Egyptians. It was Joseph's desire, however, that they should unite with their own people. He manifested his faith in the covenant promise, in behalf of his sons renouncing all the honors that the court of Egypt offered, for a place among the despised shepherd tribes, to whom had been entrusted the oracles of God.

Said Jacob, "Thy two sons, Ephraim, and Manasseh, which were born unto thee in the land of Egypt, before I came unto thee into Egypt, are mine; as Reuben and Simeon, they shall be mine." They were to be adopted as his own, and to become the heads of separate tribes. Thus one of the birthright privileges, which Reuben had forfeited, was to fall to Joseph—a double portion in Israel.

Jacob's eyes were dim with age, and he had not been aware of the presence of the young men; but now, catching the outline of their forms, he said, "Who are these?" On being told, he added, "Bring them, I pray thee, unto me, and I will bless them." As they came nearer, the patriarch embraced and kissed them, solemnly laying his hands upon their heads in benediction. Then he uttered the prayer, "God, before whom my fathers Abraham and Isaac did walk, the God which fed me all my life long unto this day, the Angel which redeemed me from all evil, bless the lads." There was no spirit of self-dependence, no reliance upon human power or cunning now. God had been his preserver and support. There was no complaint of the evil days in the past. Its trials and sorrows were no longer regarded as things that were "against" him. Memory recalled only His mercy and loving-kindness who had been with him throughout his pilgrimage.

The blessing ended, Jacob gave his son the assurance—leaving for the generations to come, through long years of bondage and sorrow, this testimony to his faith—"Behold, I die; but God shall be with you, and bring you again unto the land of your fathers."

At the last all the sons of Jacob were gathered about his dying bed. And Jacob called unto his sons, and said, "Gather yourselves together, and hear, ye sons of Jacob; and hearken unto Israel your father," "that I may tell you that which shall befall you in the last days." Often and anxiously he had thought of their future, and had endeavored to picture to himself the history of the different tribes. Now as his children waited to receive his last blessing the Spirit of Inspiration rested upon him, and before him in prophetic vision the future of his descendants was unfolded. One after another the names of his sons were mentioned, the character of each was described, and the future history of the tribes was briefly foretold.

"Reuben, thou art my first-born,
My might, and the beginning of my strength,
The excellency of dignity, and the excellency of power."

Thus the father pictured what should have been the position of Reuben as the first-born son; but his grievous sin at Edar had made him unworthy of the birthright blessing. Jacob continued—

"Unstable as water,
Thou shalt not excel."

The priesthood was apportioned to Levi, the kingdom and the Messianic promise to Judah, and the double portion of the inheritance to Joseph. The tribe of Reuben never rose to any eminence in Israel; it was not so numerous as Judah, Joseph, or Dan, and was among the first that were carried into captivity.

Next in age to Reuben were Simeon and Levi. They had been united in their cruelty toward the Shechemites, and they had also been the most guilty in the selling of Joseph. Concerning them it was declared—

"I will divide them in Jacob,
And scatter them in Israel."

At the numbering of Israel, just before their entrance to Canaan, Simeon was the smallest tribe. Moses, in his last blessing, made no reference to Simeon. In the settlement of Canaan this tribe had only a small portion of Judah's lot, and such families as afterward became powerful formed different colonies and settled in territory outside the borders of the Holy Land. Levi also received no inheritance except forty-eight cities scattered in different parts of the land. In the case of this tribe, however, their fidelity of Jehovah when the other tribes apostatized, secured their appointment to the sacred service of the sanctuary, and thus the curse was changed into a blessing.

The crowning blessings of the birthright were transferred to Judah. The significance of the name—which denotes praise,—is unfolded in the prophetic history of this tribe:

"Judah, thou art he whom thy brethren shall praise:
Thy hand shall be in the neck of thine enemies;
Thy father's children shall bow down before thee.
Judah is a lion's whelp:
From the prey, my son, thou art gone up:
He stooped down, he couched as a lion,
And as an old lion: who shall rouse him up?
The scepter shall not depart from Judah,
Nor a lawgiver from between his feet,
Until Shiloh come;
And unto Him shall the gathering of the people be."

The lion, king of the forest, is a fitting symbol of this tribe, from which came David, and the Son of David, Shiloh, the true "Lion of the tribe of Judah," to whom all powers shall finally bow and all nations render homage.

For most of his children Jacob foretold a prosperous future. At last the name of Joseph was reached, and the father's heart overflowed as he invoked blessings upon "the head of him that was separate from his brethren":

"Joseph is a fruitful bough,
Even a fruitful bough by a well;
Whose branches run over the wall:
The archers have sorely grieved him,
And shot at him, and hated him:

But his bow abode in strength,
And the arms of his hands were made strong
By the hands of the mighty God of Jacob;
(From thence is the shepherd, the stone of Israel;)

Even by the God of thy father, who shall help thee;
And by the Almighty, who shall bless thee
With blessings of heaven above,
Blessings of the deep that lieth under,
Blessings of the breasts, and of the womb:
The blessings of thy father have prevailed
Above the blessings of my progenitors
Unto the utmost bound of the everlasting hills:
They shall be on the head of Joseph,
And on the crown of the head of him that was separate from
his brethren."

Jacob had even been a man of deep and ardent affection; his love for his sons was strong and tender, and his dying testimony to them was not the utterance of partiality or resentment. He had forgiven them all, and he loved them to the last. His paternal tenderness would have found expression only in words of encouragement and hope; but the power of God rested upon him, and under the influence of Inspiration he was constrained to declare the truth, however painful.

The last blessings pronounced, Jacob repeated the charge concerning his burial place: "I am to be gathered unto my people: bury me with my fathers . . . in the cave that is in the field of Machpelah." "There they buried Abraham and Sarah his wife; there they buried Isaac and Rebekah his wife; and there I buried Leah." Thus the last act of his life was to manifest his faith in God's promise.

Jacob's last years brought an evening of tranquillity and repose after a troubled and weary day. Clouds had gathered dark above his path, yet his sun set clear, and the radiance of heaven illumined his parting hours. Says the Scripture, "At evening time it shall be light." Zechariah 14:7. "Mark the perfect man, and behold the upright: for the end of that man is peace." Psalm 37:37.

Jacob had sinned, and had deeply suffered. Many years of toil, care, and sorrow had been his since the day when his great sin caused him to flee from his father's tents. A homeless fugitive, separated from his mother, whom he never saw again; laboring seven years for her whom he loved, only to be basely cheated; toiling twenty years in the service of a covetous and grasping kinsman; seeing his wealth increasing, and sons rising around him, but finding little joy in the contentious and divided household; distressed by his daughter's shame, by her brothers' revenge, by the death of Rachel, by the unnatural crime of Reuben, by Judah's sin, by the cruel deception and malice practiced toward Joseph—how long and dark is the catalogue of evils spread out to view! Again and again he had reaped the fruit of that first wrong deed. Over and over he saw repeated among his sons the sins of which he himself had

been guilty. But bitter as had been the discipline, it had accomplished its work. The chastening, though grievous, had yielded "the peaceable fruit of righteousness." Hebrews 12:11.

Inspiration faithfully records the faults of good men, those who were distinguished by the favor of God; indeed, their faults are more fully presented than their virtues. This has been a subject of wonder to many, and has given the infidel occasion to scoff at the Bible. But it is one of the strongest evidences of the truth of Scripture, that facts are not glossed over, nor the sins of its chief characters suppressed. The minds of men are so subject to prejudice that it is not possible for human histories to be absolutely impartial. Had the Bible been written by uninspired persons, it would no doubt have presented the character of its honored men in a more flattering light. But as it is, we have a correct record of their experiences.

Men whom God favored, and to whom He entrusted great responsibilities, were sometimes overcome by temptation and committed sin, even as we at the present day strive, waver, and frequently fall into error. Their lives, with all their faults and follies, are open before us, both for our encouragement and warning. If they had been represented as without fault, we, with our sinful nature, might despair at our own mistakes and failures. But seeing where others struggled through discouragements like our own, where they fell under temptations as we have done, and yet took heart again and conquered through the grace of God, we are encouraged in our striving after righteousness. As they, though sometimes beaten back, recovered their ground, and were blessed of God, so we too may be overcomers in the strength of Jesus. On the other hand, the record of their lives may serve as a warning to us. It shows that God will by no means clear the guilty. He sees sin in His most favored ones, and He deals with it in them even more strictly than in those who have less light and responsibility.

After the burial of Jacob fear again filled the hearts of Joseph's brothers. Notwithstanding his kindness toward them, conscious guilt made them distrustful and suspicious. It might be that he had but delayed his revenge, out of regard to their father, and that he would now visit upon them the long-deferred punishment for their crime. They dared not appear before him in person, but sent a message: "Thy father did command before he died, saying, So shall ye say unto Joseph, Forgive, I pray thee now, the trespass of thy brethren, and their sin; for they did unto thee evil: and now, we pray thee, forgive the trespass of the servants of the God of thy father." This message affected Joseph to tears, and, encouraged by this, his brothers came and fell down before him, with the words, "Behold, we be thy servants." Joseph's love for his brothers was deep and unselfish, and he was pained at the thought that they could regard him as cherishing a spirit of revenge toward them. "Fear not," he said; "for am I in the place of God? But as for you, ye thought evil against me; but God meant it unto good, to bring to pass, as it is this day, to save much people alive. Now therefore fear ye not: I will nourish you, and your little ones."

The life of Joseph illustrates the life of Christ. It was envy that moved the brothers of Joseph to sell him as a slave; they hoped to prevent him from becoming greater than themselves. And when he was carried to Egypt, they flattered themselves that they were to be no more troubled with his dreams, that they had removed all possibility of their fulfillment. But their own course was overruled by God to bring about the very event that they designed to hinder. So the Jewish priests and elders were jealous of Christ, fearing that He would attract the attention of the people from them. They put Him to death, to prevent Him from becoming king, but they were thus bringing about this very result.

Joseph, through his bondage in Egypt, became a savior to his father's family; yet this fact did not lessen the guilt of his brothers. So the crucifixion of Christ by His enemies made Him the Redeemer of mankind, the Saviour of the fallen race, and Ruler over the whole world; but the crime of His murderers was just as heinous as though God's providential hand had not controlled events for His own glory and the good of man.

As Joseph was sold to the heathen by his own brothers, so Christ was sold to His bitterest enemies by one of His disciples. Joseph was falsely accused and thrust into prison because of his virtue; so Christ was despised and rejected because His righteous, self-denying life was a rebuke to sin; and though guilty of no wrong, He was condemned upon the testimony of false witnesses. And Joseph's patience and meekness under injustice and oppression, his ready forgiveness and noble benevolence toward his unnatural brothers, represent the Saviour's uncomplaining endurance of the malice and abuse of wicked men, and His forgiveness, not only of His murderers, but of all who have come to Him confessing their sins and seeking pardon.

Joseph outlived his father fifty-four years. He lived to see "Ephraim's children of the third generation: the children also of Machir the son of Manasseh were brought up upon Joseph's knees." He witnessed the increase and prosperity of his people, and through all the years his faith in God's restoration of Israel to the Land of Promise was unshaken.

When he saw that his end was near, he summoned his kinsmen about him. Honored as he had been in the land of the Pharaohs, Egypt was to him but the place of his exile; his last act was to signify that his lot was cast with Israel. His last words were, "God will surely visit you, and bring you out of this land unto the land which He sware to Abraham, to Isaac, and to Jacob." And he took a solemn oath of the children of Israel that they would carry up his bones with them to the land of Canaan. "So Joseph died, being an hundred and ten years old: and they embalmed him, and he was put in a coffin in Egypt." And through the centuries of toil which followed, the coffin, a reminder of the dying words of Joseph, testified to Israel that they were only sojourners in Egypt, and bade them keep their hopes fixed upon the Land of Promise, for the time of deliverance would surely come.

Moses

The people of Egypt, in order to supply themselves with food during the famine, had sold to the crown their cattle and lands, and had finally bound themselves to perpetual serfdom. Joseph wisely provided for their release; he permitted them to become royal tenants, holding their lands of the king, and paying an annual tribute of one fifth of the products of their labor.

But the children of Jacob were not under the necessity of making such conditions. On account of the service that Joseph had rendered the Egyptian nation, they were not only granted a part of the country as a home, but were exempted from taxation, and liberally supplied with food during the continuance of the famine. The king publicly acknowledged that it was through the merciful interposition of the God of Joseph that Egypt enjoyed plenty while other nations were perishing from famine. He saw, too, that Joseph's management had greatly enriched the kingdom, and his gratitude surrounded the family of Jacob with royal favor.

But as time rolled on, the great man to whom Egypt owed so much, and the generation blessed by his labors, passed to the grave. And "there arose up a new king over Egypt, which knew not Joseph." Not that he was ignorant of Joseph's services to the nation, but he wished to make no recognition of them, and, so far as possible, to bury them in oblivion. "And he said unto his people, Behold, the people of the children of Israel are more and mightier than we: come on, let us deal wisely with them; lest they multiply, and it come to pass, that, when there falleth out any war, they join also unto our enemies, and fight against us, and so get them up out of the land."

The Israelites had already become very numerous; they "were fruitful, and increased abundantly, and multiplied, and waxed exceeding mighty; and the land was filled with them." Under Joseph's fostering care, and the favor of the king who was then ruling, they had spread rapidly over the land. But they had kept themselves a distinct race, having nothing in common with the Egyptians in customs or religion; and their increasing numbers now excited the fears of the king and his people, lest in case of war they should join themselves with the enemies of Egypt. Yet policy forbade their banishment from the country. Many of them were able and understanding workmen, and they added greatly to the wealth of the nation; the king needed such laborers for the erection of his magnificent palaces and temples. Accordingly he ranked them with the Egyptians who had sold themselves with their possessions to the kingdom. Soon taskmasters were set over them, and their slavery became complete. "And the Egyptians made the children of Israel to serve with rigor: and they made their lives bitter with hard bondage, in mortar, and in brick, and in all manner of service in the field: all their service, wherein they made them serve, was with rigor." "But the more they afflicted them, the more they multiplied and grew."

The king and his counselors had hoped to subdue the

Israelites with hard labor, and thus decrease their numbers and crush out their independent spirit. Failing to accomplish their purpose, they proceeded to more cruel measures. Orders were issued to the women whose employment gave them opportunity for executing the command, to destroy the Hebrew male children at their birth. Satan was the mover in this matter. He knew that a deliverer was to be raised up among the Israelites; and by leading the king to destroy their children he hoped to defeat the divine purpose. But the women feared God, and dared not execute the cruel mandate. The Lord approved their course, and prospered them. The king, angry at the failure of his design, made the command more urgent and extensive. The whole nation was called upon to hunt out and slaughter his helpless victims. "And Pharaoh charged all his people, saying, Every son that is born ye shall cast into the river, and every daughter ye shall save alive."

While this decree was in full force a son was born to Amram and Jochebed, devout Israelites of the tribe of Levi. The babe was "a goodly child;" and the parents, believing that the time of Israel's release was drawing near, and that God would raise up a deliverer for His people, determined that their little one should not be sacrificed. Faith in God strengthened their hearts, "and they were not afraid of the king's commandment." Hebrews 11:23.

The mother succeeded in concealing the child for three months. Then, finding that she could no longer keep him safely, she prepared a little ark of rushes, making it watertight by means of slime and pitch; and laying the babe therein, she placed it among the flags at the river's brink. She dared not remain to guard it, lest the child's life and her own should be forfeited; but his sister, Miriam, lingered near, apparently indifferent, but anxiously watching to see what would become of her little brother. And there were other watchers. The mother's earnest prayers had committed her child to the care of God; and angels, unseen, hovered above his lowly resting place. Angels directed Pharaoh's daughter thither. Her curiosity was excited by the little basket, and as she looked upon the beautiful child within, she read the story at a glance. The tears of the babe awakened her compassion, and her sympathies went out to the unknown mother who had resorted to this means to preserve the life of her precious little one. She determined that he should be saved; she would adopt him as her own.

Miriam had been secretly noting every movement; perceiving that the child was tenderly regarded, she ventured nearer, and at last said, "Shall I go and call thee a nurse of the Hebrew women, that she may nurse the child for thee?" And permission was given.

The sister hastened to her mother with the happy news, and without delay returned with her to the presence of Pharaoh's daughter. "Take this chid away, and nurse it for me, and I will give thee thy wages," said the princess.

God had heard the mother's prayers; her faith had been rewarded. It was with deep gratitude that she entered upon her now safe and happy task. She faithfully improved her opportunity to educate her child for God. She felt confident that he had been preserved for some great work, and she knew that he must soon be given up to his royal mother, to be surrounded with influences that would tend to lead him away from God. All this rendered her more diligent and careful in his instruction than in that of her other children. She endeavored to imbue his mind with the fear of God and the love of truth and justice, and earnestly prayed that he might be preserved from every corrupting influence. She showed him the folly and sin of idolatry, and early taught him to bow down and pray to the living God, who alone could hear him and help him in every emergency.

She kept the boy as long as she could, but was obliged to give him up when he was about twelve years old. From his humble cabin home he was taken to the royal palace, to the daughter of Pharaoh, "and he became her son." Yet even here he did not lose the impressions received in childhood. The lessons learned at his mother's side could not be forgotten. They were a shield from the pride, the infidelity, and the vice that flourished amid the splendor of the court.

How far-reaching in its results was the influence of that one Hebrew woman, and she an exile and a slave! The whole future life of Moses, the great mission which he fulfilled as the leader of Israel, testifies to the importance of the work of the Christian mother. There is no other work that can equal this. To a very great extent the mother holds in her own hands the destiny of her children. She is dealing with developing minds and characters, working not alone for time, but for eternity. She is sowing seed that will spring up and bear fruit, either for good or for evil. She has not to paint a form of beauty upon canvas or to chisel it from marble, but to impress upon a human soul the image of the divine. Especially during their early years the responsibility rests upon her of forming the character of her children. The impressions now made upon their developing minds will remain with them all through life. Parents should direct the instruction and training of their children while very young, to the end that they may be Christians. They are placed in our care to be trained, not as heirs to the throne of an earthly empire, but as kings unto God, to reign through unending ages.

Let every mother feel that her moments are priceless; her work will be tested in the solemn day of accounts. Then it will be found that many of the failures and crimes of men and women have resulted from the ignorance and neglect of those whose duty it was to guide their childish feet in the right way. Then it will be found that many who have blessed the world with the light of genius and truth and holiness, owe the principles that were the mainspring of their influence and success to a praying, Christian mother.

At the court of Pharaoh, Moses received the highest civil and military training. The monarch had determined to make his adopted grandson his successor on the throne, and the youth was educated for his high station. "And Moses was learned in all the wisdom of the Egyptians, and was mighty in words and in deeds." Acts 7:22. His ability as a military leader made him a favorite with the armies of Egypt, and he was generally regarded as a remarkable character. Satan had been defeated in his purpose. The very decree condemning the Hebrew children to death had been overruled by God for the training and education of the future leader of His people.

The elders of Israel were taught by angels that the time for their deliverance was near, and that Moses was the man whom God would employ to accomplish this work. Angels instructed Moses also that Jehovah had chosen him to break the bondage of His people. He, supposing that they were to obtain their freedom by force of arms, expected to lead the Hebrew host against the armies of Egypt, and having this in view, he guarded his affections, lest in his attachment to his foster mother or to Pharaoh he would not be free to do the will of God.

By the laws of Egypt all who occupied the throne of the Pharaohs must become members of the priestly caste; and Moses, as the heir apparent, was to be initiated into the mysteries of the national religion. This duty was committed to the priests. But while he was an ardent and untiring student, he could not be induced to participate in the worship of the gods. He was threatened with the loss of the crown, and warned that he would be disowned by the princess should he persist in his adherence to the Hebrew faith. But he was unshaken in his determination to render homage to none save the one God, the Maker of heaven and earth. He reasoned with priests and worshipers, showing the folly of their superstitious veneration of senseless objects. None could refute his arguments or change his purpose, yet for the time his firmness was tolerated on account of his high position and the favor with which he was regarded by both the king and the people.

"By faith Moses, when he was come to years, refused to be called the son of Pharaoh's daughter; choosing rather to suffer affliction with the people of God, than to enjoy the pleasures of sin for a season; esteeming the reproach of Christ greater riches than the treasures in Egypt: for he had respect unto the recompense of the reward." Hebrews 11:24-26. Moses was fitted to take pre-eminence among the great of the earth, to shine in the courts of its most glorious kingdom, and to sway the scepter of its power. His intellectual greatness distinguishes him above the great men of all ages. As historian, poet, philosopher, general of armies, and legislator, he stands without a peer. Yet with the world before him, he had the moral strength to refuse the flattering prospects of wealth and greatness and fame, "choosing rather to suffer affliction with the people of God, than to enjoy the pleasures of sin for a season."

Moses had been instructed in regard to the final reward to be given to the humble and obedient servants of God, and worldly gain sank to its proper insignificance in comparison. The magnificent palace of Pharaoh and the monarch's throne were held out as an inducement to Moses; but he knew that the sinful pleasures that make men forget God were in its lordly courts. He looked beyond the gorgeous palace, beyond a monarch's crown, to the high honors that will be bestowed on the saints of the Most High in a kingdom untainted by sin. He saw by faith an imperishable crown that the King of heaven would place on the brow of the overcomer. This faith led him to turn away from the lordly ones of earth and join the humble, poor, despised nation that had chosen to obey God rather than to serve sin.

Moses remained at court until he was forty years of age. His thoughts often turned upon the abject condition of his people, and he visited his brethren in their servitude, and encouraged them with the assurance that God would work for their deliverance. Often, stung to resentment by the sight of injustice and oppression, he burned to avenge their wrongs. One day, while thus abroad, seeing an Egyptian smiting an Israelite, he sprang forward and slew the Egyptian. Except the Israelite, there had been no witness to the deed, and Moses immediately buried the body in the sand. He had now shown himself ready to maintain the cause of his people, and he hoped to see them rise to recover their liberty. "He supposed his brethren would have understood how that God by his hand would deliver them; but they understood not." Acts 7:25. They were not yet prepared for freedom. On the following day Moses saw two Hebrews striving together, one of them evidently at fault. Moses reproved the offender, who at once retaliated upon the reprover, denying his right to interfere, and basely accusing him of crime: "Who made thee a prince and a judge over us?" he said. "Intendest thou to kill me, as thou killedst the Egyptian?"

The whole matter was quickly made known to the Egyptians, and, greatly exaggerated, soon reached the ears of Pharaoh. It was represented to the king that this act meant much; that Moses designed to lead his people against the Egyptians, to overthrow the government, and to seat himself upon the throne; and that there could be no security for the kingdom while he lived. It was at once determined by the monarch that he should die; but, becoming aware of his danger, he made his escape and fled toward Arabia.

The Lord directed his course, and he found a home with Jethro, the priest and prince of Midian, who was also a worshiper of God. After a time Moses married one of the daughters of Jethro; and here, in the service of his father-in-law, as keeper of his flocks, he remained forty years.

In slaying the Egyptian, Moses had fallen into the same error so often committed by his fathers, of taking into their own hands the work that God had promised to do. It was not God's will to deliver His people by warfare, as Moses thought, but by His own mighty power, that the glory might be ascribed to Him alone. Yet even this rash act was overruled by God to accomplish His purposes. Moses was not prepared for his great work. He had yet to learn the same lesson of faith that Abraham and Jacob had been taught—not to rely upon human strength or wisdom, but upon the power of God for the fulfillment of His promises. And there were other lessons that, amid the solitude of the mountains, Moses was to receive. In the school of self-denial and hardship he was to learn patience, to temper his passions. Before he could govern wisely, he must be trained to obey. His own heart must be fully in harmony with God before he could teach the knowledge of His will to Israel. By his own experience he must be prepared to exercise a fatherly care over all who needed his help.

Man would have dispensed with that long period of toil and obscurity, deeming it a great loss of time. But Infinite Wisdom called him who was to become the leader of his people to spend forty years in the humble work of a shepherd. The habits of caretaking, of self-forgetfulness and tender solicitude for his flock, thus developed, would prepare him to become the compassionate, longsuffering shepherd of Israel. No advantage that human training or culture could bestow, could be a substitute for this experience.

Moses had been learning much that he must unlearn. The influences that had surrounded him in Egypt—the love of his foster mother, his own high position as the king's grandson, the dissipation on every hand, the refinement, the subtlety, and the mysticism of a false religion, the splendor of idolatrous worship, the solemn grandeur of architecture and sculpture—all had left deep impressions upon his developing mind and had molded, to some extent, his habits and character. Time, change of surroundings, and communion with God could remove these impressions. It would require on the part of Moses himself a struggle as for life to renounce error and accept truth, but God would be his helper when the conflict should be too severe for human strength.

In all who have been chosen to accomplish a work for God the human element is seen. Yet they have not been men of stereotyped habits and character, who were satisfied to remain in that condition. They earnestly desired to obtain wisdom from God and to learn to work for Him. Says the apostle, "If any of you lack wisdom, let him ask of God, that giveth to all men liberally, and upbraideth not; and it shall be given him." James 1:5. But God will not impart to men divine light while they are content to remain in darkness. In order to receive God's help, man must realize his weakness and deficiency; he must apply his own mind to the great change to be wrought in himself; he must be aroused to earnest and persevering prayer and effort. Wrong habits and customs must be shaken off; and it is only by determined endeavor to correct these errors and to conform to right principles that the victory can be gained. Many never attain to the position that they might occupy, because they wait for God to do for them that which He has given them power to do for themselves. All who are fitted for usefulness must be trained by the severest mental and moral discipline, and God will assist them by uniting divine power with human effort.

Shut in by the bulwarks of the mountains, Moses was alone with God. The magnificent temples of Egypt no longer impressed his mind with their superstition and falsehood. In the solemn grandeur of the everlasting hills he beheld the majesty of the Most High, and in contrast realized how powerless and insignificant were the gods of Egypt.

Everywhere the Creator's name was written. Moses seemed to stand in His presence and to be over-shadowed by His power. Here his pride and self-sufficiency were swept away. In the stern simplicity of his wilderness life, the results of the ease and luxury of Egypt disappeared. Moses became patient, reverent, and humble, "very meek, above all the men which were upon the face of the earth" (Numbers 12:3), yet strong in faith in the mighty God of Jacob.

As the years rolled on, and he wandered with his flocks in solitary places, pondering upon the oppressed condition of his people, he recounted the dealings of God with his fathers and the promises that were the heritage of the chosen nation, and his prayers for Israel ascended by day and by night. Heavenly angels shed their light around him. Here, under the inspiration of the Holy Spirit, he wrote the book of Genesis. The long years spent amid the desert solitudes were rich in blessing, not alone to Moses and his people, but to the world in all succeeding ages.

"And it came to pass in process of time, that the king of Egypt died: and the children of Israel sighed by reason of the bondage, and they cried, and their cry came up unto God by reason of the bondage. And God heard their groaning, and God remembered His covenant with Abraham, with Isaac, and with Jacob. And God looked upon the children of Israel, and God had respect unto them." The time for Israel's deliverance had come. But God's purpose was to be accomplished in a manner to pour contempt on human pride. The deliverer was to go forth as a humble shepherd, with only a rod in his hand; but God would make that rod the symbol of His power. Leading his flocks one day near Horeb, "the mountain of God," Moses saw a bush in flames, branches, foliage, and trunk, all burning, yet seeming not to be consumed. He drew near to view the wonderful sight, when a voice from out of the flame called him by name. With trembling lips he answered, "Here am I." He was warned not to approach irreverently: "Put off thy shoes from off thy feet; for the place whereon thou standest is holy ground. . . . I am the God of thy father, the God of Abraham, the God of Isaac, and the God of Jacob." It was He who, as the Angel of the covenant, had revealed Himself to the fathers in ages past. "And Moses hid his face; for he was afraid to look upon God."

Humility and reverence should characterize the deportment of all who come into the presence of God. In the name of Jesus we may come before Him with confidence, but we must not approach Him with the boldness of presumption, as though He were on a level with ourselves. There are those who address the great and all-powerful and holy God, who dwelleth in light unapproachable, as they would address an equal, or even an inferior. There are those who conduct themselves in His house as they would not presume to do in the audience chamber of an earthly ruler. These should remember that they are in His sight whom seraphim adore, before whom angels veil their faces. God is greatly to be reverenced; all who truly realize His presence will bow in humility before Him, and, like Jacob beholding the vision of

God, they will cry out, "How dreadful is this place! This is none other but the house of God, and this is the gate of heaven."

As Moses waited in reverent awe before God the words continued: "I have surely seen the affliction of My people which are in Egypt, and have heard their cry by reason of their taskmasters; for I know their sorrows; and I am come down to deliver them out of the hand of the Egyptians, and to bring them up out of that land unto a good land and a large, unto a land flowing with milk and honey. . . . Come now therefore, and I will send thee unto Pharaoh, that thou mayest bring forth My people the children of Israel out of Egypt."

Amazed and terrified at the command, Moses drew back, saying, "Who am I, that I should go unto Pharaoh, and that I should bring forth the children of Israel out of Egypt?" The reply was, "Certainly I will be with thee; and this shall be a token unto thee, that I have sent thee: When thou hast brought forth the people out of Egypt, ye shall serve God upon this mountain."

Moses thought of the difficulties to be encountered, of the blindness, ignorance, and unbelief of his people, many of whom were almost destitute of a knowledge of God. "Behold," he said, "when I come unto the children of Israel, and shall say unto them, The God of your fathers hath sent me unto you; and they shall say to me, What is His name? what shall I say unto them?" The answer was—

"I Am That I Am." "Thus shalt thou say unto the children of Israel, I Am hath sent me unto you."

Moses was commanded first to assemble the elders of Israel, the most noble and righteous among them, who had long grieved because of their bondage, and to declare to them a message from God, with a promise of deliverance. Then he was to go with the elders before the king, and say to him—

"The Lord God of the Hebrews hath met with us: and now let us go, we beseech thee, three days' journey into the wilderness, that we may sacrifice to the Lord our God."

Moses was forewarned that Pharaoh would resist the appeal to let Israel go. Yet the courage of God's servant must not fail; for the Lord would make this the occasion to manifest His power before the Egyptians and before His people. "And I will stretch out My hand, and smite Egypt with all My wonders which I will do in the midst thereof: and after that he will let you go."

Direction was also given concerning the provision they were to make for the journey. The Lord declared, "It shall come to pass, that, when ye go, ye shall not go empty: but every woman shall borrow of her neighbor, and of her that sojourneth in her house, jewels of silver, and jewels of gold, and raiment." The Egyptians had been enriched by the labor unjustly exacted from the Israelites, and as the latter were to start on the journey to their new home, it was right for them to claim the reward of their years of toil. They were to ask for articles of value, such as could be easily transported, and God would give them favor in the sight of the Egyptians. The mighty miracles wrought for their deliverance would strike terror to the oppressors, so that the requests of the bondmen would be granted.

Moses saw before him difficulties that seemed insurmountable. What proof could he give his people that God had indeed sent him? "Behold," he said, "they will not believe me, nor hearken unto my voice: for they will say, The Lord hath not appeared unto thee." Evidence that appealed to his own senses was now given. He was told to cast his rod upon the ground. As he did so, "it became a serpent; and Moses fled from before it." He was commanded to seize it, and in his hand it became a rod. He was bidden to put his hand into his bosom. He obeyed, and "when he took it out, behold, his hand was leprous as snow." Being told to put it again into his bosom, he found on withdrawing it that it had become like the other. By these signs the Lord assured Moses that His own people, as well as Pharaoh, should be convinced that One mightier than the king of Egypt was manifest among them.

But the servant of God was still overwhelmed by the thought of the strange and wonderful work before him. In his distress and fear he now pleaded as an excuse a lack of ready speech: "O my Lord, I am not eloquent, neither heretofore, nor since Thou hast spoken unto Thy servant; but I am slow of speech, and of a slow tongue." He had been so long away from the Egyptians that he had not so clear knowledge and ready use of their language as when he was among them.

The Lord said unto him, "Who hath made man's mouth? or who maketh the dumb, or deaf, or the seeing, or the blind? have not I the Lord?" To this was added another assurance of divine aid: "Now therefore go, and I will be with thy mouth, and teach thee what thou shalt say." But Moses still entreated that a more competent person be selected. These excuses at first proceeded from humility and diffidence; but after the Lord had promised to remove all difficulties, and to give him final success, then any further shrinking back and complaining of his unfitness showed distrust of God. It implied a fear that God was unable to qualify him for the great work to which He had called him, or that He had made a mistake in the selection of the man.

Moses was now directed to Aaron, his elder brother, who, having been in daily use of the language of the Egyptians, was able to speak it perfectly. He was told that Aaron was coming to meet him. The next words from the Lord were an unqualified command:

"Thou shalt speak unto him, and put words in his mouth: and I will be with thy mouth, and with his mouth, and will teach you what ye shall do. And he shall be thy spokesman unto the people: and he shall be, even he shall be to thee instead of a mouth, and thou shalt be to him instead of God. And thou shalt take this rod in thine hand, wherewith thou shalt do signs." He could make no further resistance, for all ground for excuse was removed.

The divine command given to Moses found him self-distrustful, slow of speech, and timid. He was overwhelmed with a sense of his incapacity to be a mouthpiece for God to Israel. But having once accepted the work, he entered upon it with his whole heart, putting all his trust in the Lord. The greatness of his mission called into exercise the best powers of his mind. God blessed his ready obedience, and he became eloquent, hopeful, self-possessed, and well fitted for the greatest work ever given to man. This is an example of what God does to strengthen the character of those who trust Him fully and give themselves unreservedly to His commands.

A man will gain power and efficiency as he accepts the responsibilities that God places upon him, and with his whole soul seeks to qualify himself to bear them aright. However humble his position or limited his ability, that man will attain true greatness who, trusting to divine strength, seeks to perform his work with fidelity. Had Moses relied upon his own strength and wisdom, and eagerly accepted the great charge, he would have evinced his entire unfitness for such a work. The fact that a man feels his weakness is at least some evidence that he realizes the magnitude of the work appointed him, and that he will make God his counselor and his strength.

Moses returned to his father-in-law and expressed his desire to visit his brethren in Egypt. Jethro's consent was given, with his blessing, "Go in peace." With his wife and children, Moses set forth on the journey. He had not dared to make known the object of his mission, lest they should not be allowed to accompany him. Before reaching Egypt, however, he himself thought it best for their own safety to send them back to the home in Midian.

A secret dread of Pharaoh and the Egyptians, whose anger had been kindled against him forty years before, had rendered Moses still more reluctant to return to Egypt; but after he had set out to obey the divine command, the Lord revealed to him that his enemies were dead.

On the way from Midian, Moses received a startling and terrible warning of the Lord's displeasure. An angel appeared to him in a threatening manner, as if he would immediately destroy him. No explanation was given; but Moses remembered that he had disregarded one of God's requirements; yielding to the persuasion of his wife, he had neglected to perform the rite of circumcision upon their youngest son. He had failed to comply with the condition by which his child could be entitled to the blessings of God's covenant with Israel; and such a neglect on the part of their chosen leader could not but lessen the force of the divine precepts upon the people. Zipporah, fearing that her husband would be slain, performed the rite herself, and the angel then permitted Moses to pursue his journey. In his mission to Pharaoh, Moses was to be placed in a position of great peril; his life could be preserved only through the protection of holy angels. But while living in neglect of a known duty, he would not be secure; for he could not be shielded by the angels of God.

In the time of trouble just before the coming of Christ, the righteous will be preserved through the ministration of heavenly angels; but there will be no security for the transgressor of God's law. Angels cannot then protect those who are disregarding one of the divine precepts.

The Plagues of Egypt

Aaron, being instructed by angels, went forth to meet his brother, from whom he had been so long separated; and they met amid the desert solitudes, near Horeb. Here they communed together, and Moses told Aaron "all the words of the Lord who had sent him, and all the signs which He had commanded him." Exodus 4:28. Together they journeyed to Egypt; and having reached the land of Goshen, they proceeded to assemble the elders of Israel. Aaron repeated to them all the dealings of God with Moses, and then the signs which God had given Moses were shown before the people. "The people believed: and when they heard that the Lord had visited the children of Israel, and that He had looked upon their affliction, then they bowed their heads and worshiped." Verse 31.

Moses had been charged also with a message for the king. The two brothers entered the palace of the Pharaohs as ambassadors from the King of kings, and they spoke in His name: "Thus saith Jehovah, God of Israel, Let My people go, that they may hold a feast unto Me in the wilderness."

"Who is Jehovah, that I should obey His voice to let Israel go?" demanded the monarch; "I know not Jehovah, neither will I let Israel go."

Their answer was, "The God of the Hebrews hath met with us: let us go, we pray thee, three days' journey into the desert, and sacrifice unto the Lord our God; lest He fall upon us with pestilence, or with the sword."

Tidings of them and of the interest they were exciting among the people had already reached the king. His anger was kindled. "Wherefore do ye, Moses and Aaron, let the people from their works?" he said. "Get you unto your burdens." Already the kingdom had suffered loss by the interference of these strangers. At thought of this he added, "Behold, the people of the land now are many, and ye make them rest from their burdens."

In their bondage the Israelites had to some extent lost the knowledge of God's law, and they had departed from its precepts. The Sabbath had been generally disregarded, and the exactions of their taskmasters made its observance apparently impossible. But Moses had shown his people that obedience to God was the first condition of deliverance; and the efforts made to restore the observance of the Sabbath had come to the notice of their oppressors.

The king, thoroughly roused, suspected the Israelites of a design to revolt from his service. Disaffection was the result of idleness; he would see that no time was left them for dangerous scheming. And he at once adopted measures to tighten their bonds and crush out their independent spirit. The same day orders were issued that rendered their labor still more cruel and oppressive. The most common building material of that country was sun-dried brick; the walls of the finest edifices were made of this, and then faced with stone; and the manufacture of brick employed great numbers of the bondmen. Cut straw being intermixed with the clay, to hold it together, large quantities of straw were required for the work; the king now directed that no more straw be furnished; the laborers must find it for themselves, while the same amount of brick should be exacted.

This order produced great distress among the Israelites throughout the land. The Egyptian taskmasters had appointed Hebrew officers to oversee the work of the people, and these officers were responsible for the labor performed by those under their charge. When the requirement of the king was put in force, the people scattered themselves throughout the land, to gather stubble instead of straw; but they found it impossible to accomplish the usual amount of labor. For this failure the Hebrew officers were cruelly beaten.

These officers supposed that their oppression came from their taskmasters, and not from the king himself; and they went to him with their grievances. Their remonstrance was met by Pharaoh with a taunt: "Ye are idle, ye are idle: therefore ye say, Let us go and do sacrifice to the Lord." They were ordered back to their work, with the declaration that their burdens were in no case to be lightened. Returning, they met Moses and Aaron, and cried out to them, "The Lord look upon you, and judge; because ye have made our savor to be abhorred in the eyes of Pharaoh, and in the eyes of his servants, to put a sword in their hand to slay us."

As Moses listened to these reproaches he was greatly distressed. The sufferings of the people had been much increased. All over the land a cry of despair went up from old and young, and all united in charging upon him the disastrous change in their condition. In bitterness of soul he went before God, with the cry, "Lord, wherefore hast Thou so evil entreated this people? why is it that Thou hast sent me? For since I came to Pharaoh to speak in Thy name, he hath done evil to this people; neither hast Thou delivered Thy people at all." The answer was, "Now shalt thou see what I will do to Pharaoh: for with a strong hand shall he let them go, and with a strong hand shall he drive them out of his land." Again he was pointed back to the covenant which God had made with the fathers, and was assured that it would be fulfilled.

During all the years of servitude in Egypt there had been among the Israelites some who adhered to the worship of Jehovah. These were solely troubled as they saw their children daily witnessing the abominations of the heathen, and even bowing down to their false gods. In their distress they cried unto the Lord for deliverance from the Egyptian yoke, that they might be freed from the corrupting influence of idolatry. They did not conceal their faith, but declared to the Egyptians that the object of their worship was the Maker of heaven and earth, the only true and living God. They rehearsed the evidences of His existence and power, from creation down to the days of Jacob. The Egyptians thus had an opportunity to become acquainted with the religion of the Hebrews; but disdaining to be instructed by their slaves, they tried to seduce the worshipers of God by promises of reward, and, this failing, by threats and cruelty.

The elders of Israel endeavored to sustain the sinking faith of their brethren by repeating the promises made to their fathers, and the prophetic words of Joseph before his death, foretelling their deliverance from Egypt. Some would listen and believe. Others, looking at the circumstances that surrounded them, refused to hope. The Egyptians, being informed of what was reported among their bondmen, derided their expectations and scornfully denied the power of their God. They pointed to their situation as a nation of slaves, and tauntingly said, "If your God is just and merciful, and possesses power above that of the Egyptian gods, why does He not make you a free people?" They called attention to their own condition. They worshiped deities termed by the Israelites false gods, yet they were a rich and powerful nation. They declared that their gods had blessed them with prosperity, and had given them the Israelites as servants, and they gloried in their power to oppress and destroy the worshipers of Jehovah. Pharaoh himself boasted that the God of the Hebrews could not deliver them from his hand.

Words like these destroyed the hopes of many of the Israelites. The case appeared to them very much as the Egyptians had represented. It was true that they were slaves, and must endure whatever their cruel taskmasters might choose to inflict. Their children had been hunted and slain, and their own lives were a burden. Yet they were worshiping the God of heaven. If Jehovah were indeed above all gods, surely He would not thus leave them in bondage to idolaters. But those who were true to God understood that it was because of Israel's departure from Him—because of their disposition to marry with heathen nations, thus being led into idolatry—that the Lord had permitted them to become bondmen; and they confidently assured their brethren that He would soon break the yoke of the oppressor.

The Hebrews had expected to obtain their freedom without any special trial of their faith or any real suffering or hardship. But they were not yet prepared for deliverance. They had little faith in God, and were unwilling patiently to endure their afflictions until He should see fit to work for them. Many were content to remain in bondage rather than meet the difficulties attending removal to a strange land; and the habits of some had become so much like those of the Egyptians that they preferred to dwell in Egypt. Therefore the Lord did not deliver them by the first manifestation of His power before Pharaoh. He overruled events more fully to develop the tyrannical spirit of the Egyptian king and also to reveal Himself to His people. Beholding His justice, His power, and His love, they would choose to leave Egypt and give themselves to His service. The task of Moses would have been much less difficult had not many of the Israelites become so corrupted that they were unwilling to leave Egypt.

The Lord directed Moses to go again to the people and repeat the promise of deliverance, with a fresh assurance of divine favor. He went as he was commanded; but they would not listen. Says the Scripture, "They hearkened not . . . for anguish of spirit, and for cruel bondage." Again the divine message came to Moses, "Go in, speak unto Pharaoh king of Egypt, that he let the children of Israel go out of his land." In discouragement he replied, "Behold, the children of Israel have not hearkened unto me; how then shall Pharaoh hear me?" He was told to take Aaron with him and go before Pharaoh, and again demand "that he send the children of Israel out of his land."

He was informed that the monarch would not yield until God should visit judgments upon Egypt and bring out Israel by the signal manifestation of His power. Before the infliction of each plague, Moses was to describe its nature and effects, that the king might save himself from it if he chose. Every punishment rejected would be followed by one more severe, until his proud heart would be humbled, and he would acknowledge the Maker of heaven and earth as the true and living God. The Lord would give the Egyptians an opportunity to see how vain was the wisdom of their mighty men, how feeble the power of their gods, when opposed to the commands of Jehovah. He would punish the people of Egypt for their idolatry and silence their boasting of the blessings received from their senseless deities. God would glorify His own name, that other nations might hear of His power and tremble at His mighty acts, and that His people might be led to turn from their idolatry and render Him pure worship.

Again Moses and Aaron entered the lordly halls of the king of Egypt. There, surrounded by lofty columns and glittering adornments, by the rich paintings and sculptured images of heathen gods, before the monarch of the most powerful kingdom then in existence, stood the two representatives of the enslaved race, to repeat the command from God for Israel's release. The king demanded a miracle, in evidence of their divine commission. Moses and Aaron had been directed how to act in case such a demand should be made, and Aaron now took the rod and cast it down before Pharaoh. It became a serpent. The monarch sent for his "wise men and the sorcerers," who "cast down every man his rod and they became serpents: but Aaron's rod swallowed up their rods." Then the king, more determined than before, declared his magicians equal in power with Moses and Aaron; he denounced the servants of the Lord as impostors, and felt himself secure in resisting their demands. Yet while he despised their message, he was restrained by divine power from doing them harm.

It was the hand of God, and no human influence or power possessed by Moses and Aaron, that wrought the miracles which they showed before Pharaoh. Those signs and wonders were designed to convince Pharaoh that the great "I AM" had sent Moses, and that it was the duty of the king to let Israel go, that they might serve the living God. The magicians also showed signs and wonders; for they wrought not by their own skill alone, but by the power of their god, Satan, who assisted them in counterfeiting the work of Jehovah.

The magicians did not really cause their rods to become serpents; but by magic, aided by the great deceiver, they were able to produce this appearance. It was beyond the power of Satan to change the rods to living serpents. The prince of evil, though possessing all the wisdom and might of an angel fallen, has not power to create, or to give life; this is the prerogative of God alone. But all that was in Satan's power to do, he did; he produced a counterfeit. To human sight the rods were changed to serpents. Such they were believed to be by Pharaoh and his court. There was nothing in their appearance to distinguish them from the serpent produced by Moses. Though the Lord caused the real serpent to swallow up the spurious ones, yet even this was regarded by Pharaoh, not as a work of God's power, but as the result of a kind of magic superior to that of his servants.

Pharaoh desired to justify his stubbornness in resisting the divine command, and hence he was seeking some pretext for disregarding the miracles that God had wrought through Moses. Satan gave him just what he wanted. By the work that he wrought through the magicians he made it appear to the Egyptians that Moses and Aaron were only magicians and sorcerers, and that the message they brought could not claim respect as coming from a superior being. Thus Satan's counterfeit accomplished its purpose of emboldening the Egyptians in their rebellion and causing Pharaoh to harden his heart against conviction. Satan hoped also to shake the faith of Moses and Aaron in the divine origin of their mission, that his instruments might prevail. He was unwilling that the children of Israel should be released from bondage to serve the living God.

But the prince of evil had a still deeper object in manifesting his wonders through the magicians. He well knew that Moses, in breaking the yoke of bondage from off the children of Israel, pre-figured Christ, who was to break the reign of sin over the human family. He knew that when Christ should appear, mighty miracles would be wrought as an evidence to the world that God had sent Him. Satan trembled for his power. By counterfeiting the work of God through Moses, he hoped not only to prevent the deliverance of Israel, but to exert an influence through future ages to destroy faith in the miracles of Christ. Satan is constantly seeking to counterfeit the work of Christ and to establish his own power and claims. He leads men to account for the miracles of Christ by making them appear to be the result of human skill and power. In many minds he thus destroys faith in Christ as the Son of God, and leads them to reject the gracious offers of mercy through the plan of redemption.

Moses and Aaron were directed to visit the riverside next morning, where the king was accustomed to repair. The overflowing of the Nile being the source of food and wealth for all Egypt, the river was worshiped as a god, and the monarch came thither daily to pay his devotions. Here the two brothers again repeated the message to him, and then they stretched out the rod and smote upon the water. The sacred stream ran blood, the fish died, and the river became offensive to the smell. The water in the houses, the supply preserved in cisterns, was likewise changed to blood. But "the magicians of Egypt did so with their enchantments," and "Pharaoh turned and went into his house, neither did he set his heart to this also." For seven days the plague continued, but without effect.

Again the rod was stretched out over the waters, and frogs came up from the river and spread over the land. They overran the houses, took possession of the bed chambers, and even the ovens and kneading troughs. The frog was regarded as sacred by the Egyptians, and they would not destroy it; but the slimy pests had now become intolerable. They swarmed even in the palace of the Pharaohs, and the king was impatient to have them removed. The magicians had appeared to produce frogs, but they could not remove them. Upon seeing this, Pharaoh was somewhat humbled. He sent for Moses and Aaron, and said, "Entreat the Lord, that He may take away the frogs from me, and from my people; and I will let the people go, that they may do sacrifice unto the Lord." After reminding the king of his former boasting, they requested him to appoint a time when they should pray for the removal of the plague. He set the next day, secretly hoping that in the interval the frogs might disappear of themselves, and thus save him from the bitter humiliation of submitting to the God of Israel. The plague, however, continued till the time specified, when throughout all Egypt the frogs died, but their putrid bodies, which remained, polluted the atmosphere.

The Lord could have caused them to return to dust in a moment; but He did not do this lest after their removal the king and his people should pronounce it the result of sorcery or enchantment, like the work of the magicians. The frogs died, and were then gathered together in heaps. Here the king and all Egypt had evidence which their vain philosophy could not gainsay, that this work was not accomplished by magic, but was a judgment from the God of heaven.

"When Pharaoh saw that there was respite, he hardened his heart." At the command of God, Aaron stretched out his hand, and the dust of the earth became lice throughout all the land of Egypt. Pharaoh called upon the magicians to do the same, but they could not. The work of God was thus shown to be superior to that of Satan. The magicians themselves acknowledged, "This is the finger of God." But the king was still unmoved.

Appeal and warning were ineffectual, and another judgment was inflicted. The time of its occurrence was foretold, that it might not be said to have come by chance. Flies filled the houses and swarmed upon the ground, so that "the land was corrupted by reason of the swarms of flies." These flies were large and venomous, and their bite was extremely painful to man and beast. As had been foretold, this visitation did not extend to the land of Goshen.

Pharaoh now offered the Israelites permission to sacrifice in Egypt, but they refused to accept such conditions. "It is not meet," said Moses; "lo, shall we sacrifice the abomination of the Egyptians before their eyes, and will they not stone us?" The animals which the Hebrews would be required to sacrifice were among those regarded as sacred by the Egyptians; and such was the reverence in which these creatures were held, that to slay one, even accidentally, was a crime punishable with death. It would be impossible for the Hebrews to worship in Egypt without giving offense to their masters. Moses again proposed to go three days' journey into the wilderness. The monarch consented, and begged the servants of God to entreat that the plague might be removed. They promised to do this, but warned him against dealing deceitfully with them. The plague was stayed, but the king's heart had become hardened by persistent rebellion, and he still refused to yield.

A more terrible stroke followed—murrain upon all the Egyptian cattle that were in the field. Both the sacred animals and the beasts of burden—kine and oxen and sheep, horses and camels and asses—were destroyed. It had been distinctly stated that the Hebrews were to be exempt; and Pharaoh, on sending messengers to the home of the Israelites, proved the truth of this declaration of Moses. "Of the cattle of the children of Israel died not one." Still the king was obstinate.

Moses was next directed to take ashes of the furnace, and "sprinkle it toward heaven in the sight of Pharaoh." This act was deeply significant. Four hundred years before, God had shown to Abraham the future oppression of His people, under the figure of a smoking furnace and a burning lamp. He had declared that He would visit judgments upon their oppressors, and would bring forth the captives with great substance. In Egypt, Israel had long languished in the furnace of affliction. This act of Moses was an assurance to them that God was mindful of His covenant, and that the time for their deliverance had come.

As the ashes were sprinkled toward heaven, the fine particles spread over all the land of Egypt, and wherever they settled, produced boils "breaking forth with blains upon man, and upon beast." The priests and magicians had hitherto encouraged Pharaoh in his stubbornness, but now a judgment had come that reached even them. Smitten with a loathsome and painful disease, their vaunted power only making them contemptible, they were no longer able to contend against the God of Israel. The whole nation was made to see the folly of trusting in the magicians, when they were not able to protect even their own persons.

Still the heart of Pharaoh grew harder. And now the Lord sent a message to him, declaring, "I will at this time send all My plagues upon thy heart, and upon thy servants, and upon thy people; that thou mayest know that there is none like Me in all the earth. . . . And in very deed for this cause have I raised thee up, for to show in thee My power." Not that God had given him an existence for this purpose, but His providence had overruled events to place him upon the throne at the very time appointed for Israel's deliverance. Though this haughty tyrant had by his crimes forfeited the mercy of God, yet his life had been preserved that through his stubbornness the Lord might manifest His wonders in the land of Egypt. The disposing of events is of God's providence. He could have placed upon the throne a more merciful king, who would not have dared to withstand the mighty manifestations of divine power. But in that case the Lord's purposes would not have been accomplished. His people were permitted to experience the grinding cruelty of the Egyptians, that they might not be deceived concerning the debasing influence of idolatry. In His dealing with Pharaoh, the Lord manifested His hatred of idolatry and His determination to punish cruelty and oppression.

God had declared concerning Pharaoh, "I will harden his heart, that he shall not let the people go." Exodus 4:21. There was no exercise of supernatural power to harden the heart of the king. God gave to Pharaoh the most striking evidence of divine power, but the monarch stubbornly refused to heed the light. Every display of infinite power rejected by him, rendered him the more determined in his rebellion. The seeds of rebellion that he sowed when he rejected the first miracle, produced their harvest. As he continued to venture on in his own course, going from one degree of stubbornness to another, his heart became more and more hardened, until he was called to look upon the cold, dead faces of the first-born.

God speaks to men through His servants, giving cautions and warnings, and rebuking sin. He gives to each an opportunity to correct his errors before they become fixed in the character; but if one refuses to be corrected, divine power does not interpose to counteract the tendency of his own action. He finds it more easy to repeat the same course. He is hardening the heart against the influence of the Holy Spirit. A further rejection of light places him where a far stronger influence will be ineffectual to make an abiding impression.

He who has once yielded to temptation will yield more readily the second time. Every repetition of the sin lessens his power of resistance, blinds his eyes, and stifles conviction. Every seed of indulgence sown will bear fruit. God works no miracle to prevent the harvest. "Whatsoever a man soweth, that shall he also reap." Galatians 6:7. He who manifests an infidel hardihood, a stolid indifference to divine truth, is but reaping the harvest of that which he has himself sown. It is thus that multitudes come to listen with stoical indifference to the truths that once stirred their very souls. They sowed neglect and resistance to the truth, and such is the harvest which they reap.

Those who are quieting a guilty conscience with the thought that they can change a course of evil when they choose, that they can trifle with the invitations of mercy, and yet be again and again impressed, take this course at their peril. They think that after casting all their influence on the side of the great rebel, in a moment of utmost extremity, when danger compasses them about, they will change leaders. But this is not so easily done. The experience, the education, the discipline of a life of sinful indulgence, has so thoroughly molded the character that they cannot then receive the image of Jesus. Had no light shone upon their pathway, the case would have been different. Mercy might interpose, and give them an opportunity to accept her overtures; but after light has been long rejected and despised, it will be finally withdrawn.

A plague of hail was next threatened upon Pharaoh, with the warning, "Send therefore now, and gather thy cattle, and all that thou hast in the field; for upon every man and beast which shall be found in the field, and shall not be brought home, the hail shall come down upon them, and they shall die." Rain or hail was unusual in Egypt, and such a storm as was foretold had never been witnessed. The report spread rapidly, and all who believed the word of the Lord gathered in their cattle, while those who despised the warning left them in the field. Thus in the midst of judgment the mercy of God was displayed, the people were tested, and it was shown how many had been led to fear God by the manifestation of His power.

The storm came as predicted—thunder and hail, and fire mingled with it, "very grievous, such as there was none like it in all the land of Egypt since it became a nation. And the hail smote throughout all the land of Egypt all that was in the field, both man and beast; and the hail smote every herb of the field, and brake every tree of the field." Ruin and desolation marked the path of the destroying angel. The land of Goshen alone was spared. It was demonstrated to the Egyptians that the earth is under the control of the living God, that the elements obey His voice, and that the only safety is in obedience to Him.

All Egypt trembled before the awful outpouring of divine judgment. Pharaoh hastily sent for the two brothers, and cried out, "I have sinned this time: the Lord is righteous, and I and my people are wicked. Entreat the Lord (for it is enough) that there be no more mighty thunderings and hail; and I will let you go, and ye shall stay no longer." The answer was, "As soon as I am gone out of the city, I will spread abroad my hands unto the Lord; and the thunder shall cease, neither shall there be any more hail; that thou mayest know how that the earth is the Lord's. But as for thee and thy servants, I know that ye will not yet fear the Lord God."

Moses knew that the contest was not ended. Pharaoh's confessions and promises were not the effect of any radical change in his mind or heart, but were wrung from him by terror and anguish. Moses promised, however, to grant his request; for he would give him no occasion for further stubbornness. The prophet went forth, unheeding the fury of the tempest, and Pharaoh and all his host were witnesses to the power of Jehovah to preserve His messenger. Having passed without the city, Moses "spread abroad his hands unto the Lord: and the thunders and hail ceased, and the rain was not poured upon the earth." But no sooner had the king recovered from his fears than his heart returned to its perversity.

Then the Lord said unto Moses, "Go in unto Pharaoh: for I have hardened his heart, and the heart of his servants, that I might show these My signs before him; and that thou mayest tell in the ears of thy son, and of thy son's son, what things I have wrought in Egypt, and My signs which I have done among them; that ye may know how that I am Jehovah." The

Lord was manifesting His power, to confirm the faith of Israel in Him as the only true and living God. He would give unmistakable evidence of the difference He placed between them and the Egyptians, and would cause all nations to know that the Hebrews, whom they had despised and oppressed, were under the protection of the God of heaven.

Moses warned the monarch that if he still remained obstinate, a plague of locusts would be sent, which would cover the face of the earth and eat up every green thing that remained; they would fill the houses, even the palace itself; such a scourge, he said, as "neither thy fathers, nor thy fathers' fathers have seen, since the day that they were upon the earth unto this day."

The counselors of Pharaoh stood aghast. The nation had sustained great loss in the death of their cattle. Many of the people had been killed by the hail. The forests were broken down and the crops destroyed. They were fast losing all that had been gained by the labor of the Hebrews. The whole land was threatened with starvation. Princes and courtiers pressed about the king and angrily demanded, "How long shall this man be a snare unto us? let the men go, that they may serve the Lord their God: knowest thou not yet that Egypt is destroyed?"

Moses and Aaron were again summoned, and the monarch said to them, "Go, serve the Lord your God: but who are they that shall go?"

The answer was, "We will go with our young and with our old, with our sons and with our daughters, with our flocks and with our herds will we go; for we must hold a feast unto the Lord."

The king was filled with rage. "Let the Lord be so with you," he cried, "as I will let you go, and your little ones: look to it; for evil is before you. Not so: go now ye that are men, and serve the Lord; for that ye did desire. And they were driven out from Pharaoh's presence." Pharaoh had endeavored to destroy the Israelites by hard labor, but he now pretended to have a deep interest in their welfare and a tender care for their little ones. His real object was to keep the women and children as surety for the return of the men.

Moses now stretched forth his rod over the land, and an east wind blew, and brought locusts. "Very grievous were they; before them there were no such locusts as they, neither after them shall be such." They filled the sky till the land was darkened, and devoured every green thing remaining. Pharaoh sent for the prophets in haste, and said, "I have sinned against the Lord your God, and against you. Now therefore, forgive, I pray thee, my sin only this once, and entreat the Lord your God, that He may take away from me this death only." They did so, and a strong west wind carried away the locusts toward the Red Sea. Still the king persisted in his stubborn resolution.

The people of Egypt were ready to despair. The scourges that had already fallen upon them seemed almost beyond endurance, and they were filled with fear for the future. The nation had worshiped Pharaoh as a representative of their god, but many were now convinced that he was opposing himself to One who made all the powers of nature the ministers of His will. The Hebrew slaves, so miraculously favored, were becoming confident of deliverance. Their taskmasters dared not oppress them as heretofore. Throughout Egypt there was a secret fear that the enslaved race would rise and avenge their wrongs. Everywhere men were asking with bated breath, What will come next?

Suddenly a darkness settled upon the land, so thick and black that it seemed a "darkness which may be felt." Not only were the people deprived of light, but the atmosphere was very oppressive, so that breathing was difficult. "They saw not one another, neither rose any from his place for three days: but all the children of Israel had light in their dwellings." The sun and moon were objects of worship to the Egyptians; in this mysterious darkness the people and their gods alike were smitten by the power that had undertaken the cause of the bondmen. Yet fearful as it was, this judgment is an evidence of God's compassion and His unwillingness to destroy. He would give the people time for reflection and repentance before bringing upon them the last and most terrible of the plagues.

Fear at last wrung from Pharaoh a further concession. At the end of the third day of darkness he summoned Moses, and consented to the departure of the people, provided the flocks and herds were permitted to remain. "There shall not an hoof be left behind," replied the resolute Hebrew. "We know not with what we must serve the Lord, until we come thither." The king's anger burst forth beyond control. "Get thee from me," he cried, "take heed to thyself, see my face no more; for in that day thou seest my face thou shalt die."

The answer was, "Thou hast spoken well, I will see thy face again no more."

"The man Moses was very great in the land of Egypt, in the sight of Pharaoh's servants, and in the sight of the people." Moses was regarded with awe by the Egyptians. The king dared not harm him, for the people looked upon him as alone possessing power to remove the plagues. They desired that the Israelites might be permitted to leave Egypt. It was the king and the priests that opposed to the last the demands of Moses.

The Passover

When the demand for Israel's release had been first presented to the king of Egypt, the warning of the most terrible of the plagues had been given. Moses was directed to say to Pharaoh, "Thus saith the Lord, Israel is My son, even My first-born: and I say unto thee, Let My son go, that he may serve Me: and if thou refuse to let him go, behold, I will slay thy son, even thy first-born." Exodus 4:22, 23. Though despised by the Egyptians, the Israelites had been honored by God, in that they were singled out to be the depositaries of His law. In the special blessings and privileges accorded them, they had pre-eminence among the nations, as the first-born son had among brothers.

The judgment of which Egypt had first been warned, was to be the last visited. God is long-suffering and plenteous in mercy. He has a tender care for the beings formed in His image. If the loss of their harvests and their flocks and herds had brought Egypt to repentance, the children would not have been smitten; but the nation had stubbornly resisted the divine command, and now the final blow was about to fall.

Moses had been forbidden, on pain of death, to appear again in Pharaoh's presence; but a last message from God was to be delivered to the rebellious monarch, and again Moses came before him, with the terrible announcement: "Thus saith the Lord, About midnight will I go out into the midst of Egypt: and all the first-born in the land of Egypt shall die, from the first-born of Pharaoh that sitteth upon his throne, even unto the first-born of the maidservant that is behind the mill; and all the first-born of beasts. And there shall be a great cry throughout all the land of Egypt, such as there was none like it, nor shall be like it any more. But against any of the children of Israel shall not a dog move his tongue, against man or beast: that ye may know how that the Lord doth put a difference between the Egyptians and Israel. And all these thy servants shall come down unto me, and bow down themselves unto me, saying, Get thee out, and all the people that follow thee: and after that I will go out."

Before the execution of this sentence the Lord through Moses gave direction to the children of Israel concerning their departure from Egypt, and especially for their preservation from the coming judgment. Each family, alone or in connection with others, was to slay a lamb or a kid "without blemish," and with a bunch of hyssop sprinkle its blood on "the two side posts and on the upper doorpost" of the house, that the destroying angel, coming at midnight, might not enter that dwelling. They were to eat the flesh roasted, with unleavened bread and bitter herbs, at night, as Moses said, "with your loins girded, your shoes on your feet, and your staff in your hand; and ye shall eat it in haste: it is the Lord's Passover."

The Lord declared: "I will pass through the land of Egypt this night, and will smite all the first-born in the land of Egypt, both man and beast; and against all the gods of Egypt I will execute judgment. . . . And the blood shall be to you for a token upon the houses where ye are: and when I see the blood, I will pass over you, and the plague shall not be upon you to destroy you, when I smite the land of Egypt."

In commemoration of this great deliverance a feast was to be observed yearly by the people of Israel in all future generations. "This day shall be unto you for a memorial; and ye shall keep it a feast to the Lord throughout your generations: ye shall keep it a feast by an ordinance forever." As they should keep the feast in future years, they were to repeat to their children the story of this great deliverance, as Moses bade them: "Ye shall say, It is the sacrifice of the Lord's Passover, who passed over the houses of the children of Israel in Egypt, when He smote the Egyptians, and delivered our houses."

Furthermore, the first-born of both man and beast were to be the Lord's, to be bought back only by a ransom, in acknowledgment that when the first-born in Egypt perished, that of Israel, though graciously preserved, had been justly exposed to the same doom but for the atoning sacrifice. "All the first-born are Mine," the Lord declared; "for on the day that I smote all the first-born in the land of Egypt, I hallowed unto Me all the first-born in Israel, both man and beast: Mine they shall be," Numbers 3:13. After the institution of the tabernacle service the Lord chose unto Himself the tribe of Levi for the work of the sanctuary, instead of the first-born of the people. "They are wholly given unto Me from among the children of Israel," He said. "Instead of the first-born of all the children of Israel, have I taken them unto Me." Numbers 8:16. All the people were, however, still required, in acknowledgment of God's mercy, to pay a redemption price for the first-born son. Numbers 18:15, 16.

The Passover was to be both commemorative and typical, not only pointing back to the deliverance from Egypt, but forward to the greater deliverance which Christ was to accomplish in freeing His people from the bondage of sin. The sacrificial lamb represents "the Lamb of God," in whom is our only hope of salvation. Says the apostle, "Christ our Passover is sacrificed for us." 1 Corinthians 5:7. It was not enough that the paschal lamb be slain; its blood must be sprinkled upon the doorposts; so the merits of Christ's blood must be applied to the soul. We must believe, not only that He died for the world, but that He died for us individually. We must appropriate to ourselves the virtue of the atoning sacrifice.

The hyssop used in sprinkling the blood was the symbol of purification, being thus employed in the cleansing of the leper and of those defiled by contact with the dead. In the psalmist's prayer also its significance is seen: "Purge me with hyssop, and I shall be clean: wash me, and I shall be whiter than snow." Psalm 51:7.

The lamb was to be prepared whole, not a bone of it being broken: so not a bone was to be broken of the Lamb of God, who was to die for us. John 19:36. Thus was also represented the completeness of Christ's sacrifice.

The flesh was to be eaten. It is not enough even that we believe on Christ for the forgiveness of sin; we must by faith be constantly receiving spiritual strength and nourishment from Him through His word. Said Christ, "Except ye eat the flesh of the Son of man, and drink His blood, ye have no life in you. Whoso eateth My flesh, and drinketh My blood, hath eternal life." John 6:53, 54. And to explain His meaning He said, "The words that I speak unto you, they are spirit, and they are life." Verse 63. Jesus accepted His Father's law, wrought out its principles in His life, manifested its spirit, and showed its beneficent power in the heart. Says John, "The Word was made flesh and dwelt among us, (and we beheld His glory, the glory as of the only begotten of the Father,) full of grace and truth." John 1:14. The followers of Christ must be partakers of His experience. They must receive and assimilate the word of God so that it shall become the motive power of life and action. By the power of Christ they must be changed into His likeness, and reflect the divine attributes. They must eat the flesh and drink the blood of the Son of God, or there is no life in them. The spirit and work of Christ must become the spirit and work of His disciples.

The lamb was to be eaten with bitter herbs, as pointing back to the bitterness of the bondage in Egypt. So when we feed upon Christ, it should be with contrition of heart, because of our sins. The use of unleavened bread also was significant. It was expressly enjoined in the law of the Passover, and as strictly observed by the Jews in their practice, that no leaven should be found in their houses during the feast. In like manner the leaven of sin must be put away from all who would receive life and nourishment from Christ. So Paul writes to the Corinthian church, "Purge out therefore the old leaven, that ye may be a new lump. . . . For even Christ our Passover is sacrificed for us: therefore let us keep the feast, not with old leaven, neither with the leaven of malice and wickedness; but with the unleavened bread of sincerity and truth." 1 Corinthians 5:7, 8.

Before obtaining freedom, the bondmen must show their faith in the great deliverance about to be accomplished. The token of blood must be placed upon their houses, and they must separate themselves and their families from the Egyptians, and gather within their own dwellings. Had the Israelites disregarded in any particular the directions given them, had they neglected to separate their children from the Egyptians, had they slain the lamb, but failed to strike the doorpost with blood, or had any gone out of their houses, they would not have been secure. They might have honestly believed that they had done all that was necessary, but their sincerity would not have saved them. All who failed to heed the Lord's directions would lose their first-born by the hand of the destroyer.

By obedience the people were to give evidence of their faith. So all who hope to be saved by the merits of the blood of Christ should realize that they themselves have something to do in securing their salvation. While it is Christ only that can redeem us from the penalty of transgression, we are to turn from sin to obedience. Man is to be saved by faith, not by works; yet his faith must be shown by his works. God has given His Son to die as a propitiation for sin, He has manifested the light of truth, the way of life, He has given facilities, ordinances, and privileges; and now man must co-operate with these saving agencies; he must appreciate and use the helps that God has provided—believe and obey all the divine requirements.

As Moses rehearsed to Israel the provisions of God for their deliverance, "the people bowed the head and worshiped." The glad hope of freedom, the awful knowledge of the impending judgment upon their oppressors, the cares and labors incident to their speedy departure—all were for the time swallowed up in gratitude to their gracious Deliverer. Many of the Egyptians had been led to acknowledge the God of the Hebrews as the only true God, and these now begged to be permitted to find shelter in the homes of Israel when the destroying angel should pass through the land. They were gladly welcomed, and they pledged themselves henceforth to serve the God of Jacob and to go forth from Egypt with His people.

The Israelites obeyed the directions that God had given. Swiftly and secretly they made their preparations for departure. Their families were gathered, the paschal lamb slain, the flesh roasted with fire, the unleavened bread and bitter herbs prepared. The father and priest of the household sprinkled the blood upon the doorpost, and joined his family within the dwelling. In haste and silence the paschal lamb was eaten. In awe the people prayed and watched, the heart of the eldest born, from the strong man down to the little child, throbbing with indefinable dread. Fathers and mothers clasped in their arms their loved first-born as they thought of the fearful stroke that was to fall that night. But no dwelling of Israel was visited by the death-dealing angel. The sign of blood—the sign of a Saviour's protection—was on their doors, and the destroyer entered not.

At midnight "there was a great cry in Egypt: for there was not a house where there was not one dead." All the first-born in the land, "from the firstborn of Pharaoh that sat on his throne unto the firstborn of the captive that was in the dungeon; and all the firstborn of cattle" had been smitten by the destroyer. Throughout the vast realm of Egypt the pride of every household had been laid low. The shrieks and wails of the mourners filled the air. King and courtiers, with blanched faces and trembling limbs, stood aghast at the overmastering horror. Pharaoh remembered how he had once exclaimed, "Who is Jehovah, that I should obey His voice to let Israel go? I know not Jehovah, neither will I let Israel go." Now, his heaven-daring pride humbled in the dust, he "called for Moses and Aaron by night, and said, Rise up, and get you forth from among my people, both ye and the children of Israel; and go, serve the Lord, as ye have said. Also take your flocks and your herds, as ye have said. . . . And be gone; and bless me also." The royal counselors also and the people entreated the Israelites to depart "out of the land in haste; for they said, We be all dead men."

The Exodus

With their loins girt, with sandaled feet, and staff in hand, the people of Israel had stood, hushed, awed, yet expectant, awaiting the royal mandate that should bid them go forth. Before the morning broke, they were on their way. During the plagues, as the manifestation of God's power had kindled faith in the hearts of the bondmen and had struck terror to their oppressors, the Israelites had gradually assembled themselves in Goshen; and notwithstanding the suddenness of their flight, some provision had already been made for the necessary organization and control of the moving multitudes, they being divided into companies, under appointed leaders.

And they went out, "about six hundred thousand on foot that were men, beside children. And a mixed multitude went up also with them." In this multitude were not only those who were actuated by faith in the God of Israel, but also a far greater number who desired only to escape from the plagues, or who followed in the wake of the moving multitudes merely from excitement and curiosity. This class were ever a hindrance and a snare to Israel.

The people took also with them "flocks, and herds, even very much cattle." These were the property of the Israelites, who had never sold their possessions to the king, as had the Egyptians. Jacob and his sons had brought their flocks and herds with them to Egypt, where they had greatly increased. Before leaving Egypt, the people, by the direction of Moses, claimed a recompense for their unpaid labor; and the Egyptians were too eager to be freed from their presence to refuse them. The bondmen went forth laden with the spoil of their oppressors.

That day completed the history revealed to Abraham in prophetic vision centuries before: "Thy seed shall be a stranger in a land that is not theirs, and shall serve them; and they shall afflict them four hundred years; and also that nation, whom they shall serve, will I judge: and afterward shall they come out with great substance." Genesis 15:13, 14. The four hundred years had been fulfilled. "And it came to pass the selfsame day, that the Lord did bring the children of Israel out of the land of Egypt by their armies." In their departure from Egypt the Israelites bore with them a precious legacy, in the bones of Joseph, which had so long awaited the fulfillment of God's promise, and which, during the dark years of bondage, had been a reminder of Israel's deliverance.

Instead of pursuing the direct route to Canaan, which lay through the country of the Philistines, the Lord directed their course southward, toward the shores of the Red Sea. "For God said, Lest peradventure the people repent when they see war, and they return to Egypt." Had they attempted to pass through Philistia, their progress would have been opposed; for the Philistines, regarding them as slaves escaping from their masters, would not have hesitated to make war upon them. The Israelites were poorly prepared for an encounter with that powerful and warlike people. They had little knowledge of God and little faith in Him, and they would have become terrified and disheartened. They were unarmed and unaccustomed to war, their spirits were depressed by long bondage, and they were encumbered with women and children, flocks and herds. In leading them by the way of the Red Sea, the Lord revealed Himself as a God of compassion as well as of judgment.

"And they took their journey from Succoth, and encamped in Etham, in the edge of the wilderness. And the Lord went before them by day in a pillar of cloud, to lead them the way; and by night in a pillar of fire, to give them light; to go by day and night. He took not away the pillar of the cloud by day, nor the pillar of fire by night, from before the people." Says the psalmist, "He spread a cloud for a covering; and fire to give light in the night." Psalm 105:39. See also I Corinthians 10:1, 2. The standard of their invisible Leader was ever with them. By day the cloud directed their journeyings or spread as a canopy above the host. It served as a protection from the burning heat, and by its coolness and moisture afforded grateful refreshment in the parched, thirsty desert. By night it became a pillar of fire, illuminating their encampment and constantly assuring them of the divine presence.

In one of the most beautiful and comforting passages of Isaiah's prophecy, reference is made to the pillar of cloud and of fire to represent God's care for His people in the great final struggle with the powers of evil: "The Lord will create upon every dwelling place of Mount Zion, and upon her assemblies, a cloud and smoke by day, and the shining of a flaming fire by night: for above all the glory shall be a covering. And there shall be a tabernacle for a shadow in the daytime from the heat, and for a place of refuge, and for a covert from storm and from rain." Isaiah 4:5, 6, margin.

Across a dreary, desertlike expanse they journeyed. Already they began to wonder whither their course would lead; they were becoming weary with the toilsome way, and in some hearts began to arise a fear of pursuit by the Egyptians. But the cloud went forward, and they followed. And now the Lord directed Moses to turn aside into a rocky defile, and encamp beside the sea. It was revealed to him that Pharaoh would pursue them, but that God would be honored in their deliverance.

In Egypt the report was spread that the children of Israel, instead of tarrying to worship in the desert, were pressing on toward the Red Sea. Pharaoh's counselors declared to the king that their bondmen had fled, never to return. The people deplored their folly in attributing the death of the first-born to the power of God. Their great men, recovering from their fears, accounted for the plagues as the result of natural causes. "Why have we done this, that we have let Israel go from serving us?" was the bitter cry.

Pharaoh collected his forces, "six hundred chosen chariots, and all the chariots of Egypt," horsemen, captains, and foot soldiers. The king himself, attended by the great men of his realm, headed the attacking army. To secure the favor of the gods, and thus ensure the success of their undertaking, the priests also accompanied them. The king was resolved to intimidate the Israelites by a grand display of his power. The Egyptians feared lest their forced submission to the God of Israel should subject them to the derision of other nations; but if they should now go forth with a great show of power and bring back the fugitives, they would redeem their glory, as well as recover the services of their bondmen.

The Hebrews were encamped beside the sea, whose waters presented a seemingly impassable barrier before them, while on the south a rugged mountain obstructed their further progress. Suddenly they beheld in the distance the flashing armor and moving chariots betokening the advance guard of a great army. As the force drew nearer, the hosts of Egypt were seen in full pursuit. Terror filled the hearts of Israel. Some cried unto the Lord, but far the greater part hastened to Moses with their complaints: "Because there were no graves in

full of joy in the consciousness of freedom, and every thought of discontent was hushed.

But for three days, as they journeyed, they could find no water. The supply which they had taken with them was exhausted. There was nothing to quench their burning thirst as they dragged wearily over the sun-burnt plains. Moses, who was familiar with this region, knew what the others did not, that at Marah, the nearest station where springs were to be found, the water was unfit for use. With intense anxiety he watched the guiding cloud. With a sinking heart he heard the glad shout. "Water! water!" echoed along the line. Men, women, and children in joyous haste crowded to the fountain, when, lo, a cry of anguish burst forth from the host—the water was bitter.

In their horror and despair they reproached Moses for having led them in such a way, not remembering that the divine presence in that mysterious cloud had been leading him as well as them. In his grief at their distress Moses did what they had forgotten to do; he cried earnestly to God for help. "And the Lord showed him a tree, which when he had cast into the waters, the waters were made sweet." Here the promise was given to Israel through Moses, "If thou wilt diligently hearken to the voice of the Lord thy God, and wilt do that which is right in His sight, and wilt give ear to His commandments, and keep all His statutes, I will put none of these diseases upon thee, which I have brought upon the Egyptians: for I am the Lord that healeth thee."

From Marah the people journeyed to Elim, where they found "twelve wells of water, and threescore and ten palm trees." Here they remained several days before entering the wilderness of Sin. When they had been a month absent from Egypt, they made their first encampment in the wilderness. Their store of provisions had now begun to fail. There was scanty herbage in the wilderness, and their flocks were diminishing. How was food to be supplied for these vast multitudes? Doubts filled their hearts, and again they murmured. Even the rulers and elders of the people joined in complaining against the leaders of God's appointment: "Would to God we had died by the hand of the Lord in the land of Egypt, when we sat by the fleshpots, and when we did eat bread to the full; for ye have brought us forth into this wilderness, to kill this whole assembly with hunger."

They had not as yet suffered from hunger; their present wants were supplied, but they feared for the future. They could not understand how these vast multitudes were to subsist in their travels through the wilderness, and in imagination they saw their children famishing. The Lord permitted difficulties to surround them, and their supply of food to be cut short, that their hearts might turn to Him who had hitherto been their Deliverer. If in their want they would call upon Him, He would still grant them manifest tokens of His love and care. He had promised that if they would obey His commandments, no disease should come upon them, and it was sinful unbelief on their part to anticipate that they or their children might die for hunger.

God had promised to be their God, to take them to Himself as a people, and to lead them to a large and good land; but they were ready to faint at every obstacle encountered in the way to that land. In a marvelous manner He had brought them out from their bondage in Egypt, that He might elevate and ennoble them and make them a praise in the earth. But it was necessary for them to encounter difficulties and to endure privations. God was bringing them from a state of degradation and fitting them to occupy an honorable place among the nations and to receive important and sacred trusts. Had they possessed faith in Him, in view of all that He had wrought for them, they would cheerfully have borne inconvenience, privation, and even real suffering; but they were unwilling to trust the Lord any further than they could witness the continual evidences of His power. They forgot their bitter service in Egypt. They forgot the goodness and power of God displayed in their behalf in their deliverance from bondage. They forgot how their children had been spared when the destroying angel slew all the first-born of Egypt. They forgot the grand exhibition of divine power at the Red Sea. They forgot that while they had crossed safely in the path that had been opened for them, the armies of their enemies, attempting to follow them, had been overwhelmed by the waters of the sea. They saw and felt only their present inconveniences and trials; and instead of saying, "God has done great things for us; whereas we were slaves, He is making of us a great nation," they talked of the hardness of the way, and wondered when their weary pilgrimage would end.

The history of the wilderness life of Israel was chronicled for the benefit of the Israel of God to the close of time. The record of God's dealings with the wanderers of the desert in all their marchings to and fro, in their exposure to hunger, thirst, and weariness, and in the striking manifestations of His power for their relief, is fraught with warning and instruction for His people in all ages. The varied experience of the Hebrews was a school of preparation for their promised home in Canaan. God would have His people in these days review with a humble heart and teachable spirit the trials through which ancient Israel passed, that they may be instructed in their preparation for the heavenly Canaan.

Many look back to the Israelites, and marvel at their unbelief and murmuring, feeling that they themselves would not have been so ungrateful; but when their faith is tested, even by little trials, they manifest no more faith or patience than did ancient Israel. When brought into strait places, they murmur at the process by which God has chosen to purify them. Though their present needs are supplied, many are unwilling to trust God for the future, and they are in constant anxiety lest poverty shall come upon them, and their children shall be left to suffer. Some are always anticipating evil or magnifying the difficulties that really exist, so that their eyes are blinded to the many blessings which demand their gratitude. The obstacles they encounter, instead of leading them to seek help from God, the only Source of strength, separate them from Him, because they awaken unrest and repining.

Do we well to be thus unbelieving? Why should we be ungrateful and distrustful? Jesus is our friend; all heaven is interested in our welfare; and our anxiety and fear grieve the Holy Spirit of God. We should not indulge in a solicitude that only frets and wears us, but does not help us to bear trials. No place should be given to that distrust of God which leads us to make a preparation against future want the chief pursuit of life, as though our happiness consisted in these earthly things. It is not the will of God that His people should be weighed down with care. But our Lord does not tell us that there are no dangers in our path. He does not propose to take His people out of the world of sin and evil, but He points us to a never-failing refuge. He invites the weary and care-laden, "Come unto Me, all ye that labor and are heavy-laden, and I will give you rest." Lay off the yoke of anxiety and worldly care that you have placed on your own neck, and "take My yoke upon you, and learn of Me; for I am meek and lowly in heart: and ye shall find rest unto your souls." Matthew 11:28, 29. We may find rest and peace in God, casting all our care upon Him; for He careth for us. See 1 Peter 5:7.

Says the apostle Paul, "Take heed, brethren, lest there be in any of you an evil heart of unbelief, in departing from the living God." Hebrews 3:12. In view of all that God has wrought for us, our faith should be strong, active, and enduring. Instead of murmuring and complaining, the language of our hearts should be, "Bless the Lord, O my soul: and all that is within me, bless His holy name. Bless the Lord, O my soul, and forget not all His benefits." Psalm 103:1, 2.

God was not unmindful of the wants of Israel. He said to their leader, "I will rain bread from heaven for you." And directions were given that the people gather a daily supply, with a double amount on the sixth day, that the sacred observance of the Sabbath might be maintained.

Moses assured the congregation that their wants were to be supplied: "The Lord shall give you in the evening flesh to eat, and in the morning bread to the full." And he added, "What are we? your murmurings are not against us, but against the Lord." He further bade Aaron say to them, "Come near before the Lord: for He hath heard your murmurings." While Aaron was speaking, "they looked toward the wilderness, and, behold, the glory of the Lord appeared in the cloud." A splendor such as they had never witnessed symbolized the divine Presence. Through manifestations addressed to their senses, they were to obtain a knowledge of God. They must be taught that the Most High, and not merely the man Moses, was their leader, that they might fear His name and obey His voice.

At nightfall the camp was surrounded by vast flocks of quails, enough to supply the entire company. In the morning there lay upon the surface of the ground "a small round thing, as small as the hoarfrost." "It was like coriander seed, white." The people called it "manna." Moses said, "This is the bread which the Lord hath given you to eat." The people gathered the manna, and found that there was an abundant supply for all. They "ground it in mills, or beat it in a mortar, and baked it in pans, and made cakes of it." Numbers 11:8. "And the taste of it was like wafers made with honey." They were directed to gather daily an omer for every person; and they were not to leave of it until the morning. Some attempted to keep a supply until the next day, but it was then found to be unfit for food. The provision for the day must be gathered in the morning; for all that remained upon the ground was melted by the sun.

In the gathering of the manna it was found that some obtained more and some less than the stipulated amount; but "when they did mete it with an omer, he that gathered much had nothing over, and he that gathered little had no lack." An explanation of this scripture, as well as a practical lesson from it, is given by the apostle Paul in his second epistle to the Corinthians. He says, "I mean not that other men be eased, and ye burdened: but by an equality, that now at this time your abundance may be a supply for their want, that their abundance also may be a supply for your want: that there may be equality: as it is written, He that had gathered much had nothing over; and he that had gathered little had no lack." 2 Corinthians 8:13-15.

On the sixth day the people gathered two omers for every person. The rulers hastened to acquaint Moses with what had been done. His answer was, "This is that which the Lord hath said, Tomorrow is the rest of the holy Sabbath unto the Lord: bake that which ye will bake today, and seethe that ye will seethe; and that which remaineth over lay up for you to be kept until the morning." They did so, and found that it remained unchanged. "And Moses said, Eat that today; for today is a Sabbath unto the Lord: today ye shall not find it in the field. Six days ye shall gather it; but on the seventh day, which is the Sabbath, in it there shall be none."

God requires that His holy day be as sacredly observed now as in the time of Israel. The command given to the Hebrews should be regarded by all Christians as an injunction from Jehovah to them. The day before the Sabbath should be made a day of preparation, that everything may be in readiness for its sacred hours. In no case should our own business be allowed to encroach upon holy time. God has directed that the sick and suffering be cared for; the labor required to make them comfortable is a work of mercy, and no violation of the Sabbath; but all unnecessary work should be avoided. Many carelessly put off till the beginning of the Sabbath little things that might have been done on the day of preparation. This should not be. Work that is neglected until the beginning of the Sabbath should remain undone until it is past. This course might help the memory of these thoughtless ones, and make them careful to do their own work on the six working days.

Every week during their long sojourn in the wilderness the Israelites witnessed a threefold miracle, designed to impress their minds with the sacredness of the Sabbath: a double quantity of manna fell on the sixth day, none on the seventh, and the portion needed for the Sabbath was preserved sweet and pure, when if any were kept over at any other time it became unfit for use.

In the circumstances connected with the giving of the manna, we have conclusive evidence that the Sabbath was not instituted, as many claim, when the law was given at Sinai. Before the Israelites came to Sinai they understood the Sabbath to be obligatory upon them. In being obliged to gather every Friday a double portion of manna in preparation for the Sabbath, when none would fall, the sacred nature of the day of rest was continually impressed upon them. And when some of the people went out on the Sabbath to gather manna, the Lord asked, "How long refuse ye to keep My commandments and My laws?"

"The children of Israel did eat manna forty years, until they came to a land inhabited: they did eat manna, until they came unto the borders of the land of Canaan." For forty years they were daily reminded by this miraculous provision, of God's unfailing care and tender love. In the words of the psalmist, God gave them "of the corn of heaven. Man did eat angels' food" (Psalm 78:24, 25)—that is, food provided for them by the angels. Sustained by "the corn of heaven," they were daily taught that, having God's promise, they were as secure from want as if surrounded by fields of waving grain on the fertile plains of Canaan.

The manna, falling from heaven for the sustenance of Israel, was a type of Him who came from God to give life to the world. Said Jesus, "I am that Bread of life. Your fathers did eat manna in the wilderness, and are dead. This is the bread which cometh down from heaven. . . . If any man eat of this bread, he shall live forever: and the bread that I will give is My flesh, which I will give for the life of the world." John 6:48-51. And among the promises of blessing to God's people in the future life it is written, "To him that overcometh will I give to eat of the hidden manna." Revelation 2:17.

After leaving the wilderness of Sin, the Israelites encamped in Rephidim. Here there was no water, and again they distrusted the providence of God. In their blindness and presumption the people came to Moses with the demand, "Give us water that we may drink." But his patience failed not. "Why chide ye with me?" he said; "wherefore do ye tempt the Lord?" They cried in anger, "Wherefore is this, that thou hast brought us up out of Egypt, to kill us and our children and our cattle with thirst?" When they had been so abundantly supplied with food, they remembered with shame their unbelief and murmurings, and promised to trust the Lord in the future; but they soon forgot their promise, and failed at the first trial of their faith. The pillar of cloud that was leading them seemed to veil a fearful mystery. And Moses—who was he? they questioned, and what could be his object in bringing them from Egypt? Suspicion and distrust filled their hearts, and they boldly accused him of designing to kill them and their children by privations and hardships that he might enrich himself with their possessions. In the tumult of rage and indignation they were about to stone him.

In distress Moses cried to the Lord, "What shall I do unto this people?" He was directed to take the elders of Israel and the rod wherewith he had wrought wonders in Egypt, and to go on before the people. And the Lord said unto him, "Behold, I will stand before thee there upon the rock in Horeb; and thou shalt smite the rock, and there shall come water out of it, that the people may drink." He obeyed, and the waters burst forth in a living stream that abundantly supplied the encampment. Instead of commanding Moses to lift up his rod and call down some terrible plague, like those on Egypt, upon the leaders in this wicked murmuring, the Lord in His great mercy made the rod His instrument to work their deliverance.

"He clave the rocks in the wilderness, and gave them drink as out of the great depths. He brought streams also out of the rock, and caused waters to run down like rivers." Psalm 78:15, 16. Moses smote the rock, but it was the Son of God who, veiled in the cloudy pillar, stood beside Moses, and caused the life-giving water to flow. Not only Moses and the elders, but all the congregation who stood at a distance, beheld the glory of the Lord; but had the cloud been removed, they would have been slain by the terrible brightness of Him who abode therein.

In their thirst the people had tempted God, saying, "Is the Lord among us, or not?"—"If God has brought us here, why does He not give us water as well as bread?" The unbelief thus manifested was criminal, and Moses feared that the judgments of God would rest upon them. And he called the name of the place Massah, "temptation," and Meribah, "chiding," as a memorial of their sin.

A new danger now threatened them. Because of their murmuring against Him, the Lord suffered them to be attacked by their enemies. The Amalekites, a fierce, warlike tribe inhabiting that region, came out against them and smote those who, faint and weary, had fallen into the rear. Moses, knowing that the masses of the people were unprepared for battle, directed Joshua to choose from the different tribes a body of soldiers, and lead them on the morrow against the enemy, while he himself would stand on an eminence near by with the rod of God in his hand. Accordingly the next day Joshua and his company attacked the foe, while Moses and Aaron and Hur were stationed on a hill overlooking the battlefield. With arms outstretched toward heaven, and holding the rod of God in his right hand, Moses prayed for the success of the armies of Israel. As the battle progressed, it was observed that so long as his hands were reaching upward, Israel prevailed, but when they were lowered, the enemy was victorious. As Moses became weary, Aaron and Hur stayed up his hands until the going down of the sun, when the enemy was put to flight.

As Aaron and Hur supported the hands of Moses, they showed the people their duty to sustain him in his arduous work while he should receive the word from God to speak to them. And the act of Moses also was significant, showing that God held their destiny in His hands; while they made Him their trust, He would fight for them and subdue their enemies; but when they should let go their hold upon Him, and trust in their own power, they would be even weaker than those who had not the knowledge of God, and their foes would prevail against them.

As the Hebrews triumphed when Moses was reaching his hands toward heaven and interceding in their behalf, so the Israel of God prevail when they by faith take hold upon the strength of their mighty Helper. Yet divine strength is to be combined with human effort. Moses did not believe that God would overcome their foes while Israel remained inactive. While the great leader was pleading with the Lord, Joshua and his brave followers were putting forth their utmost efforts to repulse the enemies of Israel and of God.

After the defeat of the Amalekites, God directed Moses, "Write this for a memorial in a book, and rehearse it in the ears of Joshua: for I will utterly put out the remembrance of Amalek from under heaven." Just before his death the great leader delivered to his people the solemn charge: "Remember what Amalek did unto thee by the way, when ye were come forth out of Egypt; how he met thee by the way, and smote the hindmost of thee, even all that were feeble behind thee, when thou wast faint and weary; and he feared not God. . . . Thou shalt blot out the remembrance of Amalek from under heaven; thou shalt not forget it." Deuteronomy 25:17-19. Concerning this wicked people the Lord declared, "The hand of Amalek is against the throne of Jehovah." Exodus 17:16, margin.

The Amalekites were not ignorant of God's character or of His sovereignty, but instead of fearing before Him, they had set themselves to defy His power. The wonders wrought by Moses before the Egyptians were made a subject of mockery by the people of Amalek, and the fears of surrounding nations were ridiculed. They had taken oath by their gods that they would destroy the Hebrews, so that not one should escape, and they boasted that Israel's God would be powerless to resist them. They had not been injured or threatened by the Israelites. Their assault was wholly unprovoked. It was to manifest their hatred and defiance of God that they sought to destroy His people. The Amalekites had long been high-handed sinners, and their crimes had cried to God for vengeance, yet His mercy had still called them to repentance; but when the men of Amalek fell upon the wearied and defenseless ranks of Israel, they sealed their nation's doom. The care of God is over the weakest of His children. No act of cruelty or oppression toward them is unmarked by Heaven. Over all who love and fear Him, His hand extends as a shield; let men beware that they smite not that hand; for it wields the sword of justice.

Not far distant from where the Israelites were now encamped was the home of Jethro, the father-in-law of Moses. Jethro had heard of the deliverance of the Hebrews, and he now set out to visit them, and restore to Moses his wife and two sons. The great leader was informed by messengers of their approach, and he went out with joy to meet them, and, the first greetings over, conducted them to his tent. He had sent back his family when on his way to the perils of leading Israel from Egypt, but now he could again enjoy the relief and comfort of their society. To Jethro he recounted the wonderful dealings of God with Israel, and the patriarch rejoiced and blessed the Lord, and with Moses and the elders he united in offering sacrifice and holding a solemn feast in commemoration of God's mercy.

As Jethro remained in the camp, he soon saw how heavy were the burdens that rested upon Moses. To maintain order and discipline among that vast, ignorant, and untrained multitude was indeed a stupendous task. Moses was their recognized leader and magistrate, and not only the general interests and duties of the people, but the controversies that arose among them, were referred to him. He had permitted this, for it gave him an opportunity to instruct them; as he said, "I do make them know the statutes of God, and His laws." But Jethro remonstrated against this, saying, "This thing is too heavy for thee; thou art not able to perform it thyself alone." "Thou wilt surely wear away," and he counseled Moses to appoint proper persons as rulers of thousands, and others as rulers of hundreds, and others of tens. They should be "able men, such as fear God, men of truth, hating covetousness." These were to judge in all matters of minor consequence, while the most difficult and important cases should still be brought before Moses, who was to be to the people, said Jethro, "to God-ward, that thou mayest bring the causes unto God: and thou shalt teach them ordinances and laws, and shalt show them the way wherein they must walk, and the work that they must do." This counsel was accepted, and it not only brought relief to Moses, but resulted in establishing more perfect order among the people.

The Lord had greatly honored Moses, and had wrought wonders by his hand; but the fact that he had been chosen to instruct others did not lead him to conclude that he himself needed no instruction. The chosen leader of Israel listened gladly to the suggestions of the godly priest of Midian, and adopted his plan as a wise arrangement.

From Rephidim the people continued their journey, following the movement of the cloudy pillar. Their route had led across barren plains, over steep ascents, and through rocky defiles. Often as they had traversed the sandy wastes, they had seen before them rugged mountains, like huge bulwarks, piled up directly across their course, and seeming to forbid all further progress. But as they approached, openings here and there appeared in the mountain wall, and beyond, another plain opened to view. Through one of the deep, gravelly passes they were now led. It was a grand and impressive scene. Between the rocky cliffs rising hundreds of feet on either side, flowed in a living tide, far as the eye could reach, the hosts of Israel with their flocks and herds. And now before them in solemn majesty Mount Sinai lifted its massive front. The cloudy pillar rested upon its summit, and the people spread their tents upon the plain beneath. Here was to be their home for nearly a year. At night the pillar of fire assured them of the divine protection, and while they were locked in slumber, the bread of heaven fell gently upon the encampment.

The dawn gilded the dark ridges of the mountains, and the sun's golden rays pierced the deep gorges, seeming to these weary travelers like beams of mercy from the throne of God. On every hand vast, rugged heights seemed in their solitary grandeur to speak of eternal endurance and majesty. Here the mind was impressed with solemnity and awe. Man was made to feel his ignorance and weakness in the presence of Him who "weighed the mountains in scales, and the hills in a balance." Isaiah 40:12. Here Israel was to receive the most wonderful revelation ever made by God to men. Here the Lord had gathered His people that He might impress upon them the sacredness of His requirements by declaring with His own voice His holy law. Great and radical changes were to be wrought in them; for the degrading influences of servitude and a long-continued association with idolatry had left their mark upon habits and character. God was working to lift them to a higher moral level by giving them a knowledge of Himself.

The Law Given to Israel

Soon after the encampment at Sinai, Moses was called up into the mountain to meet with God. Alone he climbed the steep and rugged path, and drew near to the cloud that marked the place of Jehovah's presence. Israel was now to be taken into a close and peculiar relation to the Most High—to be incorporated as a church and a nation under the government of God. The message to Moses for the people was:

"Ye have seen what I did unto the Egyptians, and how I bare you on eagles' wings, and brought you unto Myself. Now therefore, if ye will obey My voice indeed, and keep My covenant, then ye shall be a peculiar treasure unto Me above all people: for all the earth is Mine: and ye shall be unto Me a kingdom of priests, and an holy nation."

Moses returned to the camp, and having summoned the elders of Israel, he repeated to them the divine message. Their answer was, "All that the Lord hath spoken we will do." Thus they entered into a solemn covenant with God, pledging themselves to accept Him as their ruler, by which they became, in a special sense, the subjects of His authority.

Again their leader ascended the mountain, and the Lord said unto him, "Lo, I come unto thee in a thick cloud, that the people may hear when I speak with thee, and believe thee forever." When they met with difficulties in the way, they were disposed to murmur against Moses and Aaron, and accuse them of leading the hosts of Israel from Egypt to destroy them. The Lord would honor Moses before them, that they might be led to confide in his instructions.

God purposed to make the occasion of speaking His law a scene of awful grandeur, in keeping with its exalted character. The people were to be impressed that everything connected with the service of God must be regarded with the greatest reverence. The Lord said to Moses, "Go unto the people, and sanctify them today and tomorrow, and let them wash their clothes, and be ready against the third day: for the third day

the Lord will come down in the sight of all the people upon Mount Sinai." During these intervening days all were to occupy the time in solemn preparation to appear before God. Their person and their clothing must be freed from impurity. And as Moses should point out their sins, they were to devote themselves to humiliation, fasting, and prayer, that their hearts might be cleansed from iniquity.

The preparations were made, according to the command; and in obedience to a further injunction, Moses directed that a barrier be placed about the mount, that neither man nor beast might intrude upon the sacred precinct. If any ventured so much as to touch it, the penalty was instant death.

On the morning of the third day, as the eyes of all the people were turned toward the mount, its summit was covered with a thick cloud, which grew more black and dense, sweeping downward until the entire mountain was wrapped in darkness and awful mystery. Then a sound as of a trumpet was heard, summoning the people to meet with God; and Moses led them forth to the base of the mountain. From the thick darkness flashed vivid lightnings, while peals of thunder echoed and re-echoed among the surrounding heights. "And Mount Sinai was altogether on a smoke, because the Lord descended upon it in fire: and the smoke thereof ascended as the smoke of a furnace, and the whole mount quaked greatly." "The glory of the Lord was like devouring fire on the top of the mount" in the sight of the assembled multitude. And "the voice of the trumpet sounded long, and waxed louder and louder." So terrible were the tokens of Jehovah's presence that the hosts of Israel shook with fear, and fell upon their faces before the Lord. Even Moses exclaimed, "I exceedingly fear and quake." Hebrews 12:21.

And now the thunders ceased; the trumpet was no longer heard; the earth was still. There was a period of solemn silence, and then the voice of God was heard. Speaking out of the thick darkness that enshrouded Him, as He stood upon the mount, surrounded by a retinue of angels, the Lord made known His law. Moses, describing the scene, says: "The Lord came from Sinai, and rose up from Seir unto them; He shined forth from Mount Paran, and He came with ten thousands of saints: from His right hand went a fiery law for them. Yea, He loved the people; all His saints are in Thy hand: and they sat down at Thy feet; every one shall receive of Thy words." Deuteronomy 33:2, 3.

Jehovah revealed Himself, not alone in the awful majesty of the judge and lawgiver, but as the compassionate guardian of His people: "I am the Lord thy God, which have brought thee out of the land of Egypt, out of the house of bondage." He whom they had already known as their Guide and Deliverer, who had brought them forth from Egypt, making a way for them through the sea, and overthrowing Pharaoh and his hosts, who had thus shown Himself to be above all the gods of Egypt—He it was who now spoke His law.

The law was not spoken at this time exclusively for the benefit of the Hebrews. God honored them by making them the guardians and keepers of His law, but it was to be held as a sacred trust for the whole world. The precepts of the Decalogue are adapted to all mankind, and they were given for the instruction and government of all. Ten precepts, brief, comprehensive, and authoritative, cover the duty of man to God and to his fellow man; and all based upon the great fundamental principle of love. "Thou shalt love the Lord thy God with all thy heart, and with all thy soul, and with all thy strength, and with all thy mind; and thy neighbor as thyself." Luke 10:27. See also Deuteronomy 6:4, 5; Leviticus 19:18. In the Ten Commandments these principles are carried out in detail, and made applicable to the condition and circumstances of man.

"Thou shalt have no other gods before Me."

Jehovah, the eternal, self-existent, uncreated One, Himself the Source and Sustainer of all, is alone entitled to supreme reverence and worship. Man is forbidden to give to any other object the first place in his affections or his service. Whatever we cherish that tends to lessen our love for God or to interfere with the service due Him, of that do we make a god.

"Thou shalt not make unto thee any graven image, or any likeness of anything that is in heaven above, or that is in the earth beneath, or that is in the water under the earth: thou shalt not bow down thyself to them, nor serve them."

The second commandment forbids the worship of the true God by images or similitudes. Many heathen nations claimed that their images were mere figures or symbols by which the Deity was worshiped, but God has declared such worship to be sin. The attempt to represent the Eternal One by material objects would lower man's conception of God. The mind, turned away from the infinite perfection of Jehovah, would be attracted to the creature rather than to the Creator. And as his conceptions of God were lowered, so would man become degraded.

"I the Lord thy God am a jealous God." The close and sacred relation of God to His people is represented under the figure of marriage. Idolatry being spiritual adultery, the displeasure of God against it is fitly called jealousy.

"Visiting the iniquity of the fathers upon the children unto the third and fourth generation of them that hate Me." It is inevitable that children should suffer from the consequences of parental wrongdoing, but they are not punished for the parents' guilt, except as they participate in their sins. It is usually the case, however, that children walk in the steps of their parents. By inheritance and example the sons become partakers of the father's sin. Wrong tendencies, perverted appetites, and debased morals, as well as physical disease and degeneracy, are transmitted as a legacy from father to son, to the third and fourth generation. This fearful truth should have a solemn power to restrain men from following a course of sin.

"Showing mercy unto thousands of them that love Me, and keep My commandments." In prohibiting the worship of false gods, the second commandment by implication enjoins the worship of the true God. And to those who are faithful in His service, mercy is promised, not merely to the third and fourth generation as is the wrath threatened against those who hate Him, but to thousands of generations.

"Thou shalt not take the name of the Lord thy God in vain: for the Lord will not hold him guiltless that taketh His name in vain."

This commandment not only prohibits false oaths and common swearing, but it forbids us to use the name of God in a light or careless manner, without regard to its awful significance. By the thoughtless mention of God in common conversation, by appeals to Him in trivial matters, and by the frequent and thoughtless repetition of His name, we dishonor Him. "Holy and reverend is His name." Psalm 111:9. All should meditate upon His majesty, His purity and holiness, that the heart may be impressed with a sense of His exalted character; and His holy name should be uttered with reverence and solemnity.

"Remember the Sabbath day, to keep it holy. Six days shalt thou labor, and do all thy work: but the seventh day is the Sabbath of the Lord thy God: in it thou shalt not do any work, thou, nor thy son, nor thy daughter, thy manservant, nor thy maidservant, nor thy cattle, nor thy stranger that is within thy gates: for in six days the Lord made heaven and earth, the sea, and all that in them is, and rested the seventh day: wherefore the Lord blessed the Sabbath day, and hallowed it."

The Sabbath is not introduced as a new institution but as having been founded at creation. It is to be remembered and observed as the memorial of the Creator's work. Pointing to God as the Maker of the heavens and the earth, it distinguishes the true God from all false gods. All who keep the seventh day signify by this act that they are worshipers of Jehovah. Thus the Sabbath is the sign of man's allegiance to God as long as there are any upon the earth to serve Him. The fourth commandment is the only one of all the ten in which are found both the name and the title of the Lawgiver. It is the only one that shows by whose authority the law is given. Thus it contains the seal of God, affixed to His law as evidence of its authenticity and binding force.

God has given me six days wherein to labor, and He requires that their own work be done in the six working days. Acts of necessity and mercy are permitted on the Sabbath, the sick and suffering are at all times to be cared for; but unnecessary labor is to be strictly avoided. "Turn away thy foot from the Sabbath, from doing thy pleasure on My holy day; and call the Sabbath a delight, the holy of the Lord, honorable; and . . . honor Him, not doing thine own ways, nor finding thine own pleasure." Isaiah 58:13. Nor does the prohibition end here. "Nor speaking thine own words," says the prophet. Those who discuss business matters or lay plans on the Sabbath are regarded by God as though engaged in the actual transaction of business. To keep the Sabbath holy, we should not even allow our minds to dwell upon things of a worldly character. And the commandment includes all within our gates. The inmates of the house are to lay aside their worldly business during the sacred hours. All should unite to honor God by willing service upon His holy day.

"Honor thy father and thy mother: that thy days may be long upon the land which the Lord thy God giveth thee."

Parents are entitled to a degree of love and respect which is due to no other person. God Himself, who has placed upon them a responsibility for the souls committed to their charge, has ordained that during the earlier years of life, parents shall stand in the place of God to their children. And he who rejects the rightful authority of his parents is rejecting the authority of God. The fifth commandment requires children not only to yield respect, submission, and obedience to their parents, but also to give them love and tenderness, to lighten their cares, to guard their reputation, and to succor and comfort them in old age. It also enjoins respect for ministers and rulers and for all others to whom God has delegated authority.

This, says the apostle, "is the first commandment with promise." Ephesians 6:2. To Israel, expecting soon to enter Canaan, it was a pledge to the obedient, of long life in that good, land; but it has a wider meaning, including all the Israel of God, and promising eternal life upon the earth when it shall be freed from the curse of sin.

"Thou shalt not kill."

All acts of injustice that tend to shorten life; the spirit of hatred and revenge, or the indulgence of any passion that leads to injurious acts toward others, or causes us even to wish them harm (for "whosoever hateth his brother is a murderer"); a selfish neglect of caring for the needy or suffering; all self-indulgence or unnecessary deprivation or excessive labor that tends to injure health—all these are, to a greater or less degree, violations of the sixth commandment.

"Thou shalt not commit adultery."

This commandment forbids not only acts of impurity, but sensual thoughts and desires, or any practice that tends to excite them. Purity is demanded not only in the outward life but in the secret intents and emotions of the heart. Christ, who taught the far-reaching obligation of the law of God, declared the evil thought or look to be as truly sin as is the unlawful deed.

"Thou shalt not steal."

Both public and private sins are included in this prohibition. The eighth commandment condemns manstealing and slave dealing, and forbids wars of conquest. It condemns theft and robbery. It demands strict integrity in the minutest details of the affairs of life. It forbids overreaching in trade, and requires the payment of just debts or wages. It declares that every attempt to advantage oneself by the ignorance, weakness, or misfortune of another is registered as fraud in the books of heaven.

"Thou shalt not bear false witness against thy neighbor."

False speaking in any matter, every attempt or purpose to deceive our neighbor, is here included. An intention to deceive is what constitutes falsehood. By a glance of the eye, a motion of the hand, an expression of the countenance, a falsehood may be told as effectually as by words. All intentional overstatement, every hint or insinuation calculated to convey an erroneous or exaggerated impression, even the statement of facts in such a manner as to mislead, is falsehood. This precept forbids every effort to injure our neighbor's reputation by misrepresentation or evil surmising, by slander or tale bearing. Even the intentional suppression of truth, by which injury may result to others, is a violation of the ninth commandment.

"Thou shalt not covet thy neighbor's house, thou shalt not covet thy neighbor's wife, nor his manservant, nor his maidservant, nor his ox, nor his ass, nor anything that is thy neighbor's."

The tenth commandment strikes at the very root of all sins, prohibiting the selfish desire, from which springs the sinful act. He who in obedience to God's law refrains from indulging even a sinful desire for that which belongs to another will not be guilty of an act of wrong toward his fellow creatures.

Such were the sacred precepts of the Decalogue, spoken amid thunder and flame, and with a wonderful display of the power and majesty of the great Lawgiver. God accompanied the proclamation of His law with exhibitions of His power and glory, that His people might never forget the scene, and that they might be impressed with profound veneration for the Author of the law, the Creator of heaven and earth. He would also show to all men the sacredness, the importance, and the permanence of His law.

The people of Israel were overwhelmed with terror. The awful power of God's utterances seemed more than their trembling hearts could bear. For as God's great rule of right was presented before them, they realized as never before the offensive character of sin, and their own guilt in the sight of a holy God. They shrank away from the mountain in fear and awe. The multitude cried out to Moses, "Speak thou with us, and we will hear: but let not God speak with us, lest we die." The leader answered, "Fear not: for God is come to prove you, and that His fear may be before your faces, that ye sin not." The people, however, remained at a distance, gazing in terror upon the scene, while Moses "drew near unto the thick darkness where God was."

The minds of the people, blinded and debased by slavery and heathenism, were not prepared to appreciate fully the far-reaching principles of God's ten precepts. That the obligations of the Decalogue might be more fully understood and enforced, additional precepts were given, illustrating and applying the principles of the Ten Commandments. These laws were called judgments, both because they were framed in infinite wisdom and equity and because the magistrates were to give judgment according to them. Unlike the Ten Commandments, they were delivered privately to Moses, who was to communicate them to the people.

The first of these laws related to servants. In ancient times criminals were sometimes sold into slavery by the judges; in some cases, debtors were sold by their creditors; and poverty even led persons to sell themselves or their children. But a Hebrew could not be sold as a slave for life. His term of service was limited to six years; on the seventh he was to be set at liberty. Manstealing, deliberate murder, and rebellion against parental authority were to be punished with death. The holding of slaves not of Israelitish birth was permitted, but their life and person were strictly guarded. The murderer of a slave was to be punished; an injury inflicted upon one by his master, though no more than the loss of a tooth, entitled him to his freedom.

The Israelites had lately been servants themselves, and now that they were to have servants under them, they were to beware of indulging the spirit of cruelty and exaction from which they had suffered under their Egyptian taskmasters. The memory of their own bitter servitude should enable them to put themselves in the servant's place, leading them to be kind and compassionate, to deal with others as they would wish to be dealt with.

The rights of widows and orphans were especially guarded, and a tender regard for their helpless condition was enjoined. "If thou afflict them in any wise," the Lord declared, "and they cry at all unto Me, I will surely hear their cry; and My wrath shall wax hot, and I will kill you with the sword; and your wives shall be widows, and your children fatherless." Aliens who united themselves with Israel were to be protected from wrong or oppression. "Thou shalt not oppress a stranger: for ye know the heart of a stranger, seeing ye were strangers in the land of Egypt."

The taking of usury from the poor was forbidden. A poor man's raiment or blanket taken as a pledge, must be restored to him at nightfall. He who was guilty of theft was required to restore double. Respect for magistrates and rulers was enjoined, and judges were warned against perverting judgment, aiding a false cause, or receiving bribes. Calumny and slander were prohibited, and acts of kindness enjoined, even toward personal enemies.

Again the people were reminded of the sacred obligation of the Sabbath. Yearly feasts were appointed, at which all the men of the nation were to assemble before the Lord, bringing to Him their offerings of gratitude and the first fruits of His bounties. The object of all these regulations was stated: they proceeded from no exercise of mere arbitrary sovereignty; all were given for the good of Israel. The Lord said, "Ye shall be holy men unto Me"—worthy to be acknowledged by a holy God.

These laws were to be recorded by Moses, and carefully treasured as the foundation of the national law, and, with the ten precepts which they were given to illustrate, the condition of the fulfillment of God's promises to Israel.

The message was now given them from Jehovah: "Behold, I send an Angel before thee, to keep thee in the way, and to bring thee into the place which I have prepared. Beware of Him, and obey His voice, provoke Him not; for He will not pardon your transgressions: for My name is in Him. But if thou shalt indeed obey His voice, and do all that I speak; then I will be an enemy unto thine enemies, and an adversary unto thine adversaries." During all the wanderings of Israel, Christ, in the pillar of cloud and of fire, was their Leader. While there

were types pointing to a Saviour to come, there was also a present Saviour, who gave commands to Moses for the people, and who was set forth before them as the only channel of blessing.

Upon descending from the mountain, "Moses came and told the people all the words of the Lord, and all the judgments: and all the people answered with one voice, and said, All the words which the Lord hath said will we do." This pledge, together with the words of the Lord which it bound them to obey, was written by Moses in a book.

Then followed the ratification of the covenant. An altar was built at the foot of the mountain, and beside it twelve pillars were set up, "according to the twelve tribes of Israel," as a testimony to their acceptance of the covenant. Sacrifices were then presented by young men chosen for the service.

Having sprinkled the altar with the blood of the offerings, Moses "took the book of the covenant, and read in the audience of the people." Thus the conditions of the covenant were solemnly repeated, and all were at liberty to choose whether or not they would comply with them. They had at the first promised to obey the voice of God; but they had since heard His law proclaimed; and its principles had been particularized, that they might know how much this covenant involved. Again the people answered with one accord, "All that the Lord hath said will we do, and be obedient." "When Moses had spoken every precept to all the people according to the law, he took the blood, . . . and sprinkled both the book and all the people, saying, This is the blood of the testament which God hath enjoined unto you." Hebrews 9:19, 20.

Arrangements were now to be made for the full establishment of the chosen nation under Jehovah as their king. Moses had received the command, "Come up unto the Lord, thou, and Aaron, Nadab, and Abihu, and seventy of the elders of Israel; and worship ye afar off. And Moses alone shall come near the Lord." While the people worshiped at its foot, these chosen men were called up into the mount. The seventy elders were to assist Moses in the government of Israel, and God put upon them His Spirit, and honored them with a view of His power and greatness. "And they saw the God of Israel: and there was under His feet as it were a paved work of a sapphire stone, and as it were the body of heaven in his clearness." They did not behold the Deity, but they saw the glory of His presence. Before this they could not have endured such a scene; but the exhibition of God's power had awed them to repentance; they had been contemplating His glory, purity, and mercy, until they could approach nearer to Him who was the subject of their meditations.

Moses and "his minister Joshua" were now summoned to meet with God. And as they were to be some time absent, the leader appointed Aaron and Hur, assisted by the elders, to act in his stead. "And Moses went up into the mount, and a cloud covered the mount. And the glory of the Lord abode upon Mount Sinai." For six days the cloud covered the mountain as a token of God's special presence; yet there was no revelation of Himself or communication of His will.

During this time Moses remained in waiting for a summons to the presence chamber of the Most High. He had been directed, "Come up to Me into the mount, and be there," and though his patience and obedience were tested, he did not grow weary of watching, or forsake his post. This period of waiting was to him a time of preparation, of close self-examination. Even this favored servant of God could not at once approach into His presence and endure the exhibitions of His glory. Six days must be employed in devoting himself to God by searching of heart, meditation, and prayer before he could be prepared for direct communication with his Maker.

Upon the seventh day, which was the Sabbath, Moses was called up into the cloud. The thick cloud opened in the sight of all Israel, and the glory of the Lord broke forth like devouring fire. "And Moses went into the midst of the cloud, and gat him up into the mount; and Moses was in the mount forty days and forty nights." The forty days' tarry in the mount did not include the six days of preparation. During the six days Joshua was with Moses, and together they ate of the manna and drank of "the brook that descended out of the mount." But Joshua did not enter with Moses into the cloud. He remained without, and continued to eat and drink daily while awaiting the return of Moses, but Moses fasted during the entire forty days.

During his stay in the mount, Moses received directions for the building of a sanctuary in which the divine presence would be specially manifested. "Let them make Me a sanctuary; that I may dwell among them" (Exodus 25:8), was the command of God. For the third time the observance of the Sabbath was enjoined. "It is a sign between Me and the children of Israel forever," the Lord declared, "that ye may know that I am Jehovah that doth sanctify you. Ye shall keep the Sabbath therefore; for it is holy unto you. . . . Whosoever doeth any work therein, that soul shall be cut off from among his people." Exodus 31:17, 13, 14. Directions had just been given for the immediate erection of the tabernacle for the service of God; and now the people might conclude, because the object had in view was the glory of God, and also because of their great need of a place of worship, that they would be justified in working at the building upon the Sabbath. To guard them from this error, the warning was given. Even the sacredness and urgency of that special work for God must not lead them to infringe upon His holy rest day.

Henceforth the people were to be honored with the abiding presence of their King. "I will dwell among the children of Israel, and will be their God," "and the tabernacle shall be sanctified by My glory" (Exodus 29:45, 43), was the assurance given to Moses. As the symbol of God's authority and the embodiment of His will, there was delivered to Moses a copy of the Decalogue engraved by the finger of God Himself upon two tables of stone (Deuteronomy 9:10; Exodus 32:15, 16), to be sacredly enshrined in the sanctuary, which, when made, was to be the visible center of the nation's worship.

From a race of slaves the Israelites had been exalted above all peoples to be the peculiar treasure of the King of kings. God had separated them from the world, that He might commit to them a sacred trust. He had made them the depositaries of His law, and He purposed, through them, to preserve among men the knowledge of Himself. Thus the light of heaven was to shine out to a world enshrouded in darkness, and a voice was to be heard appealing to all peoples to turn from their idolatry to serve the living God. If the Israelites would be true to their trust, they would become a power in the world. God would be their defense, and He would exalt them above all other nations. His light and truth would be revealed through them, and they would stand forth under His wise and holy rule as an example of the superiority of His worship over every form of idolatry.

Idolatry at Sinai

While Moses was absent it was a time of waiting and suspense to Israel. The people knew that he had ascended the mount with Joshua, and had entered the cloud of thick darkness which could be seen from the plain below, resting on the mountain peak, illuminated from time to time with the lightnings of the divine Presence. They waited eagerly for his return. Accustomed as they had been in Egypt to material representations of deity, it had been hard for them to trust in an invisible being, and they had come to rely upon Moses to sustain their faith. Now he was taken from them. Day after day, week after week passed, and still he did not return. Notwithstanding the cloud was still in view, it seemed to many in the camp that their leader had deserted them, or that he had been consumed by the devouring fire.

During this period of waiting, there was time for them to meditate upon the law of God which they had heard, and to prepare their hearts to receive the further revelations that He might make to them. They had none too much time for this work; and had they been thus seeking a clearer understanding of God's requirements, and humbling their hearts before Him, they would have been shielded from temptation. But they did not do this, and they soon became careless, inattentive, and lawless. Especially was this the case with the mixed multitude. They were impatient to be on their way to the Land of Promise—the land flowing with milk and honey. It was only on condition of obedience that the goodly land was promised them, but they had lost sight of this. There were some who suggested a return to Egypt, but whether forward to Canaan or backward to Egypt, the masses of the people were determined to wait no longer for Moses.

Feeling their helplessness in the absence of their leader, they returned to their old superstitions. The "mixed multitude" had been the first to indulge murmuring and impatience, and they were the leaders in the apostasy that followed. Among the objects regarded by the Egyptians as symbols of deity was the ox or calf; and it was at the suggestion of those who had practiced this form of idolatry in Egypt that a calf was now made and worshiped. The people desired some image to represent God, and to go before them in the place of Moses. God had given no manner of similitude of Himself, and He had prohibited any material representation for such a purpose. The mighty miracles in Egypt and at the Red Sea were designed to establish faith in Him as the invisible, all-powerful Helper of Israel, the only true God. And the desire for some visible manifestation of His presence had been granted in the pillar of cloud and of fire that guided their hosts, and in the revealing of His glory upon Mount Sinai. But with the cloud of the Presence still before them, they turned back in their hearts to the idolatry of Egypt, and represented the glory of the invisible God by the similitude of an ox!

In the absence of Moses, the judicial authority had been delegated to Aaron, and a vast crowd gathered about his tent, with the demand, "Make us gods, which shall go before us; for as for this Moses, the man that brought us up out of the land of Egypt, we wot not what is become of him. The cloud, they said, that had heretofore led them, now rested permanently upon the mount; it would no longer direct their travels. They must have an image in its place; and if, as had been suggested, they should decide to return to Egypt, they would find favor with the Egyptians by bearing this image before them and acknowledging it as their god.

Such a crisis demanded a man of firmness, decision, and unflinching courage; one who held the honor of God above popular favor, personal safety, or life itself. But the present leader of Israel was not of this character. Aaron feebly remonstrated with the people, but his wavering and timidity at the critical moment only rendered them the more determined. The tumult increased. A blind, unreasoning frenzy seemed to take possession of the multitude. There were some who remained true to their covenant with God, but the greater part of the people joined in the apostasy. A few who ventured to denounce the proposed image making as idolatry, were set upon and roughly treated, and in the confusion and excitement they finally lost their lives.

Aaron feared for his own safety; and instead of nobly standing up for the honor of God, he yielded to the demands of the multitude. His first act was to direct that the golden earrings be collected from all the people and brought to him, hoping that pride would lead them to refuse such a sacrifice. But they willingly yielded up their ornaments; and from these he made a molten calf, in imitation of the gods of Egypt. The people proclaimed, "These be thy gods, O Israel, which brought thee up out of the land of Egypt." And Aaron basely permitted this insult to Jehovah. He did more. Seeing with what satisfaction the golden god was received, he built an altar before it, and made proclamation, "Tomorrow is a feast to the Lord." The announcement was heralded by trumpeters from company to company throughout the camp. "And they rose up early on the morrow, and offered burnt offerings, and brought peace offerings; and the people sat down to eat and to drink and rose up to play." Under the pretense of holding "a feast to the Lord," they gave themselves up to gluttony and licentious reveling.

How often, in our own day, is the love of pleasure disguised by a "form of godliness"! A religion that permits men, while observing the rites of worship, to devote themselves to selfish or sensual gratification, is as pleasing to the multitudes now as in the days of Israel. And there are still pliant Aarons, who, while holding positions of authority in the church, will yield to the desires of the unconsecrated, and thus encourage them in sin.

Only a few days had passed since the Hebrews had made a solemn covenant with God to obey His voice. They had stood trembling with terror before the mount, listening to the words of the Lord, "Thou shalt have no other gods before Me." The glory of God still hovered above Sinai in the sight of the congregation; but they turned away, and asked for other gods. "They made a calf in Horeb, and worshiped the molten image. Thus they changed their glory into the similitude of an ox." Psalm 106:19, 20. How could greater ingratitude have been shown, or more daring insult offered, to Him who had revealed Himself to them as a tender father and an all-powerful king!

Moses in the mount was warned of the apostasy in the camp and was directed to return without delay. "Go, get thee down," were the words of God; "thy people, which thou broughtest out of the land of Egypt, have corrupted themselves: they have turned aside quickly out of the way which I commanded them. They have made them a molten calf, and have worshiped it." God might have checked the movement at the outset; but He suffered it to come to this height that He might teach all a lesson in His punishment of treason and apostasy.

God's covenant with His people had been disannulled, and He declared to Moses, "Let Me alone, that My wrath may wax hot against them, and that I may consume them: and I will make of thee a great nation." The people of Israel, especially the mixed multitude, would be constantly disposed to rebel against God. They would also murmur against their leader, and would grieve him by their unbelief and stubbornness, and it would be a laborious and soul-trying work to lead them through to the Promised Land. Their sins had already forfeited the favor of God, and justice called for their destruction. The Lord therefore proposed to destroy them, and make of Moses a mighty nation.

"Let Me alone, . . . that I may consume them," were the words of God. If God had purposed to destroy Israel, who could plead for them? How few but would have left the sinners to their fate! How few but would have gladly exchanged a lot of toil and burden and sacrifice, repaid with ingratitude and murmuring, for a position of ease and honor, when it was God Himself that offered the release.

But Moses discerned ground for hope where there appeared only discouragement and wrath. The words of God, "Let Me alone," he understood not to forbid but to encourage intercession, implying that nothing but the prayers of Moses could save Israel, but that if thus entreated, God would spare His people. He "besought the Lord his God, and said, Lord, why doth Thy wrath wax hot against Thy people, which Thou hast brought forth out of the land of Egypt with great power, and with a mighty hand?"

God had signified that He disowned His people. He had spoken of them to Moses as "thy people, which thou broughtest out of Egypt." But Moses humbly disclaimed the leadership of Israel. They were not his, but God's— "Thy people, which Thou has brought forth . . . with great power, and with a mighty hand. Wherefore," he urged, "should the Egyptians speak, and say, For mischief did He bring them out, to slay them in the mountains, and to consume them from the face of the earth?"

During the few months since Israel left Egypt, the report of their wonderful deliverance had spread to all the surrounding nations. Fear and terrible foreboding rested upon the heathen. All were watching to see what the God of Israel would do for His people. Should they now be destroyed, their enemies would triumph, and God would be dishonored. The Egyptians would claim that their accusations were true—instead of leading His people into the wilderness to sacrifice, He had caused them to be sacrificed. They would not consider the sins of Israel; the destruction of the people whom He had so signally honored, would bring reproach upon His name. How great the responsibility resting upon those whom God has highly honored, to make His name a praise in the earth! With what care should they guard against committing sin, to call down His judgments and cause His name to be reproached by the ungodly!

As Moses interceded for Israel, his timidity was lost in his deep interest and love for those for whom he had, in the hands of God, been the means of doing so much. The Lord listened to his pleadings, and granted his unselfish prayer. God had proved His servant; He had tested his faithfulness and his love for that erring, ungrateful people, and nobly had Moses endured the trial. His interest in Israel sprang from no selfish motive. The prosperity of God's chosen people was dearer to him than personal honor, dearer than the privilege of becoming the father of a mighty nation. God was pleased with his faithfulness, his simplicity of heart, and his integrity, and He committed to him, as a faithful shepherd, the great charge of leading Israel to the Promised Land.

As Moses and Joshua came down from the mount, the former bearing the "tables of the testimony," they heard the shouts and outcries of the excited multitude, evidently in a state of wild uproar. To Joshua the soldier, the first thought was of an attack from their enemies. "There is a noise of war in the camp," he said. But Moses judged more truly the nature of the commotion. The sound was not that of combat, but of revelry. "It is not the voice of them that shout for mastery, neither is it the voice of them that cry for being overcome; but the noise of them that sing do I hear."

As they drew near the encampment, they beheld the people shouting and dancing around their idol. It was a scene of heathen riot, an imitation of the idolatrous feasts of Egypt; but how unlike the solemn and reverent worship of God! Moses was overwhelmed. He had just come from the presence of God's glory, and though he had been warned of what was taking place, he was unprepared for that dreadful exhibition of the degradation of Israel. His anger was hot. To show his abhorrence of their crime, he threw down the tables of stone, and they were broken in the sight of all the people, thus signifying that as they had broken their covenant with God, so God had broken His covenant with them.

Entering the camp, Moses passed through the crowds of revelers, and seizing upon the idol, cast it into the fire. He afterward ground it to powder, and having strewed it upon the stream that descended from the mount, he made the people drink of it. Thus was shown the utter worthlessness of the god which they had been worshiping.

The great leader summoned his guilty brother and sternly demanded, "What did this people unto thee, that thou hast brought so great a sin upon them?" Aaron endeavored to shield himself by relating the clamors of the people; that if he had not complied with their wishes, he would have been put to death. "Let not the anger of my lord wax hot," he said; "thou knowest the people, that they are set on mischief. For they said unto me, Make us gods, which shall go before us: for as for this Moses, the man that brought us up out of the land of Egypt, we wot not what is become of him. And I said unto them, Whosoever hath any gold, let them break it off. So they gave it me: then I cast it into the fire, and there came out this calf." He would lead Moses to believe that a miracle had been wrought—that the gold had been cast into the fire, and by supernatural power changed to a calf. But his excuses and prevarications were of no avail. He was justly dealt with as the chief offender.

The fact that Aaron had been blessed and honored so far above the people was what made his sin so heinous. It was Aaron "the saint of the Lord" (Psalm 106:16), that had made the idol and announced the feast. It was he who had been appointed as spokesman for Moses, and concerning whom God Himself had testified, "I know that he can speak well" (Exodus 4:14), that had failed to check the idolaters in their heaven-daring purpose. He by whom God had wrought in bringing judgments both upon the Egyptians and upon their gods, had heard unmoved the proclamation before the molten image, "These be thy gods, O Israel, which brought thee up out of the land of Egypt." It was he who had been with Moses on the mount, and had there beheld the glory of the Lord, who had seen that in the manifestation of that glory there was nothing of which an image could be made—it was he who had changed that glory into the similitude of an ox. He to whom God had committed the government of the people in the absence of Moses, was found sanctioning their rebellion. "The Lord was very angry with Aaron to have destroyed him." Deuteronomy 9:20. But in answer to the earnest intercession of Moses, his life was spared; and in penitence and humiliation for his great sin, he was restored to the favor of God.

If Aaron had had courage to stand for the right, irrespective of consequences, he could have prevented that apostasy. If he had unswervingly maintained his own allegiance to God, if he had cited the people to the perils of Sinai, and had reminded them of their solemn covenant with God to obey His law, the evil would have been checked. But his compliance with the desires of the people and the calm assurance with which he proceeded to carry out their plans, emboldened them to go to greater lengths in sin than had before entered their minds.

When Moses, on returning to the camp, confronted the rebels, his severe rebukes and the indignation he displayed in breaking the sacred tables of the law were contrasted by the people with his brother's pleasant speech and dignified demeanor, and their sympathies were with Aaron. To justify himself, Aaron endeavored to make the people responsible for his weakness in yielding to their demand; but notwithstanding this, they were filled with admiration of his gentleness and patience. But God seeth not as man sees. Aaron's yielding spirit and his desire to please had blinded his eyes to the enormity of the crime he was sanctioning. His course in giving his influence to sin in Israel cost the life of thousands. In what contrast with this was the course of Moses, who, while faithfully executing God's judgments, showed that the welfare of Israel was dearer to him than prosperity or honor or life.

Of all the sins that God will punish, none are more grievous in His sight than those that encourage others to do evil. God would have His servants prove their loyalty by faithfully rebuking transgression, however painful the act may be. Those who are honored with a divine commission are not to be weak, pliant time-servers. They are not to aim at self-exaltation, or to shun disagreeable duties, but to perform God's work with unswerving fidelity.

Though God had granted the prayer of Moses in sparing Israel from destruction, their apostasy was to be signally punished. The lawlessness and insubordination into which Aaron had permitted them to fall, if not speedily crushed, would run riot in wickedness, and would involve the nation in irretrievable ruin. By terrible severity the evil must be put away. Standing in the gate of the camp, Moses called to the people, "Who is on the Lord's side? let him come unto me." Those who had not joined in the apostasy were to take their position at the right of Moses; those who were guilty but repentant, at the left. The command was obeyed. It was found that the tribe of Levi had taken no part in the idolatrous worship. From among other tribes there were great numbers who, although they had sinned, now signified their repentance. But a large company, mostly of the mixed multitude that instigated the making of the calf, stubbornly persisted in their rebellion. In the name of "the Lord God of Israel," Moses now commanded those upon his right hand, who had kept themselves clear of idolatry, to gird on their swords and slay all who persisted in rebellion. "And there fell of the people that day about three thousand men." Without regard to position, kindred, or friendship, the ringleaders in wickedness were cut off; but all who repented and humbled themselves were spared.

Those who performed this terrible work of judgment were acting by divine authority, executing the sentence of the King of heaven. Men are to beware how they, in their human blindness, judge and condemn their fellow men; but when God commands them to execute His sentence upon iniquity, He is to be obeyed. Those who performed this painful act, thus manifested their abhorrence of rebellion and idolatry, and consecrated themselves more fully to the service of the true God. The Lord honored their faithfulness by bestowing special distinction upon the tribe of Levi.

The Israelites had been guilty of treason, and that against a King who had loaded them with benefits and whose authority they had voluntarily pledged themselves to obey. That the divine government might be maintained justice must be visited upon the traitors. Yet even here God's mercy was displayed. While He maintained His law, He granted freedom of choice and opportunity for repentance to all. Only those were cut off who persisted in rebellion.

It was necessary that this sin should be punished, as a testimony to surrounding nations of God's displeasure against idolatry. By executing justice upon the guilty, Moses, as God's instrument, must leave on record a solemn and public protest against their crime. As the Israelites should hereafter condemn the idolatry of the neighboring tribes, their enemies would throw back upon them the charge that the people who claimed Jehovah as their God had made a calf and worshiped it in Horeb. Then though compelled to acknowledge the disgraceful truth, Israel could point to the terrible fate of the transgressors, as evidence that their sin had not been sanctioned or excused.

Love no less than justice demanded that for this sin judgment should be inflicted. God is the guardian as well as the sovereign of His people. He cuts off those who are determined upon rebellion, that they may not lead others to ruin. In sparing the life of Cain, God had demonstrated to the universe what would be the result of permitting sin to go unpunished. The influence exerted upon his descendants by his life and teaching led to the state of corruption that demanded the destruction of the whole world by a flood. The history of the antediluvians testifies that long life is not a blessing to the sinner; God's great forbearance did not repress their wickedness. The longer men lived, the more corrupt they became.

So with the apostasy at Sinai. Unless punishment had been speedily visited upon transgression, the same results would again have been seen. The earth would have become as corrupt as in the days of Noah. Had these transgressors been spared, evils would have followed, greater than resulted from sparing the life of Cain. It was the mercy of God that thousands should suffer, to prevent the necessity of visiting judgments upon millions. In order to save the many, He must punish the few. Furthermore, as the people had cast off their allegiance to God, they had forfeited the divine protection, and, deprived of their defense, the whole nation was exposed to the power of their enemies. Had not the evil been promptly put away, they would soon have fallen a prey to their numerous and powerful foes. It was necessary for the good of Israel, and also as a lesson to all succeeding generations, that crime should be promptly punished. And it was no less a mercy to the sinners themselves that they should be cut short in their evil course. Had their life been spared, the same spirit that led them to rebel against God would have been manifested in hatred and strife among themselves, and they would eventually have destroyed one another. It was in love to the world, in love to Israel, and even to the transgressors, that crime was punished with swift and terrible severity.

As the people were roused to see the enormity of their guilt, terror pervaded the entire encampment. It was feared that every offender was to be cut off. Pitying their distress, Moses promised to plead once more with God for them.

"Ye have sinned a great sin," he said, "and now I will go up unto the Lord; peradventure I shall make an atonement for your sin." He went, and in his confession before God he said, "Oh, this people have sinned a great sin, and have made them gods of gold. Yet now if Thou wilt forgive their sin—; and if not, blot me, I pray Thee, out of Thy book which Thou hast written." The answer was, "Whosoever hath sinned against Me, him will I blot out of My book. Therefore now go, lead the people into the place of which I have spoken unto thee: behold, Mine Angel shall go before thee: nevertheless, in the day when I visit, I will visit their sin upon them."

In the prayer of Moses our minds are directed to the heavenly records in which the names of all men are inscribed, and their deeds, whether good or evil, are faithfully registered. The book of life contains the names of all who have ever entered the service of God. If any of these depart from Him, and by stubborn persistence in sin become finally hardened against the influences of His Holy Spirit, their names will in the judgment be blotted from the book of life, and they themselves will be devoted to destruction. Moses realized how dreadful would be the fate of the sinner; yet if the people of Israel were to be rejected by the Lord, he desired his name to be blotted out with theirs; he could not endure to see the judgments of God fall upon those who had been so graciously delivered. The intercession of Moses in behalf of Israel illustrates the mediation of Christ for sinful men. But the Lord did not permit Moses to bear, as did Christ, the guilt of the transgressor. "Whosoever hath sinned against Me," He said, "him will I blot out of My book."

In deep sadness the people had buried their dead. Three thousand had fallen by the sword; a plague had soon after broken out in the encampment; and now the message came to them that the divine Presence would no longer accompany them in their journeyings. Jehovah had declared, "I will not go up in the midst of thee; for thou art a stiffnecked people: lest I consume thee in the way." And the command was given, "Put off thy ornaments from thee, that I may know what to do unto thee." Now there was mourning throughout the encampment. In penitence and humiliation "the children of Israel stripped themselves of their ornaments by the mount Horeb."

By the divine direction the tent that had served as a temporary place of worship was removed "afar off from the camp." This was still further evidence that God had withdrawn His presence from them. He would reveal Himself to Moses, but not to such a people. The rebuke was keenly felt, and to the conscience-smitten multitudes it seemed a foreboding of greater calamity. Had not the Lord separated Moses from the camp that He might utterly destroy them? But they were not left without hope. The tent was pitched without the encampment, but Moses called it "the tabernacle of the congregation." All who were truly penitent, and desired to return to the Lord, were directed to repair thither to confess their sins and seek His mercy. When they returned to their tents Moses entered the tabernacle. With agonizing interest the people watched for some token that his intercessions in their behalf were accepted. If God should condescend to meet with him, they might hope that they were not to be utterly consumed. When the cloudy pillar descended, and stood at the entrance of the tabernacle, the people wept for joy, and they "rose up and worshiped, every man in his tent door."

Moses knew well the perversity and blindness of those who were placed under his care; he knew the difficulties with which he must contend. But he had learned that in order to prevail with the people, he must have help from God. He pleaded for a clearer revelation of God's will and for an assurance of His presence: "See, Thou sayest unto me, Bring up this people: and Thou hast not let me know whom Thou wilt send with me. Yet Thou hast said, I know thee by name, and thou hast also found grace in My sight. Now therefore, I pray Thee, if I have found grace in Thy sight, show me now Thy way, that I may know Thee, that I may find grace in Thy sight: and consider that this nation is Thy people."

The answer was, "My presence shall go with thee, and I will give thee rest." But Moses was not yet satisfied. There pressed upon his soul a sense of the terrible results should God leave Israel to hardness and impenitence. He could not endure that his interests should be separated from those of his brethren, and he prayed that the favor of God might be restored to His people, and that the token of His presence might continue to direct their journeyings: "If Thy presence go not with me, carry us not up hence. For wherein shall it be known here that I and Thy people have found grace in Thy sight? is it not in that Thou goest with us? So shall we be separated, I and Thy people, from all the people that are upon the face of the earth."

And the Lord said, "I will do this thing also that thou hast spoken: for thou hast found grace in My sight, and I know thee by name." Still the prophet did not cease pleading. Every prayer had been answered, but he thirsted for greater tokens of God's favor. He now made a request that no human being had ever made before: "I beseech Thee, show me Thy glory."

God did not rebuke his request as presumptuous; but the gracious words were spoken, "I will make all My goodness pass before thee." The unveiled glory of God, no man in this mortal state can look upon and live; but Moses was assured that he should behold as much of the divine glory as he could endure. Again he was summoned to the mountain summit; then the hand that made the world, that hand that "removeth the mountains, and they know not" (Job 9:5), took this creature of the dust, this mighty man of faith, and placed him in a cleft of the rock, while the glory of God and all His goodness passed before him.

This experience—above all else the promise that the divine Presence would attend him—was to Moses an assurance of success in the work before him; and he counted it of infinitely greater worth than all the learning of Egypt or all his attainments as a statesman or a military leader. No earthly power or skill or learning can supply the place of God's abiding presence.

To the transgressor it is a fearful thing to fall into the hands of the living God; but Moses stood alone in the presence of the Eternal One, and he was not afraid; for his soul was in harmony with the will of his Maker. Says the psalmist, "If I regard iniquity in my heart, the Lord will not hear me." Psalm 66:18. But "the secret of the Lord is with them that fear Him; and He will show them His covenant." Psalm 25:14.

The Deity proclaimed Himself, "The Lord, The Lord God, merciful and gracious, long-suffering, and abundant in goodness and truth, keeping mercy for thousands, forgiving iniquity and transgression and sin, and that will by no means clear the guilty."

"Moses made haste, and bowed his head toward the earth, and worshiped." Again he entreated that God would pardon the iniquity of His people, and take them for His inheritance. His prayer was granted. The Lord graciously promised to renew His favor to Israel, and in their behalf to do marvels such as had not been done "in all the earth, nor in any nation."

Forty days and nights Moses remained in the mount; and during all this time, as at the first, he was miraculously sustained. No man had been permitted to go up with him, nor during the time of his absence were any to approach the mount. At God's command he had prepared two tables of stone, and had taken them with him to the summit; and again the Lord "wrote upon the tables the words of the covenant, the Ten Commandments."

During that long time spent in communion with God, the face of Moses had reflected the glory of the divine Presence; unknown to himself his face shown with a dazzling light when he descended from the mountain. Such a light illumined the countenance of Stephen when brought before his judges; "and all that sat in the council, looking steadfastly on him, saw his face as it had been the face of an angel." Acts 6:15. Aaron as well as the people shrank away from Moses, and "they were afraid to come nigh him." Seeing their confusion and terror, but ignorant of the cause, he urged them to come near. He held out to them the pledge of God's reconciliation, and assured them of His restored favor. They perceived in his voice nothing but love and entreaty, and at last one ventured to approach him. Too awed to speak, he silently pointed to the countenance of Moses, and then toward heaven. The great leader understood his meaning. In their conscious guilt, feeling themselves still under the divine displeasure, they could not endure the heavenly light, which, had they been obedient to God, would have filled them with joy. There is fear in guilt. The soul that is free from sin will not wish to hide from the light of heaven.

Moses had much to communicate to them; and compassionating their fear, he put a veil upon his face, and continued to do so thereafter whenever he returned to the camp from communion with God.

By this brightness God designed to impress upon Israel the sacred, exalted character of His law, and the glory of the gospel revealed through Christ. While Moses was in the mount, God presented to him, not only the tables of the law, but also the plan of salvation. He saw that the sacrifice of Christ was pre-figured by all the types and symbols of the Jewish age; and it was the heavenly light streaming from Calvary, no less than the glory of the law of God, that shed such a radiance upon the face of Moses. That divine illumination symbolized the glory of the dispensation of which Moses was the visible mediator, a representative of the one true Intercessor.

The glory reflected in the countenance of Moses illustrates the blessings to be received by God's commandment-keeping people through the mediation of Christ. It testifies that the closer our communion with God, and the clearer our knowledge of His requirements, the more fully shall we be conformed to the divine image, and the more readily do we become partakers of the divine nature.

Moses was a type of Christ. As Israel's intercessor veiled his countenance, because the people could not endure to look upon its glory, so Christ, the divine Mediator, veiled His divinity with humanity when He came to earth. Had He come clothed with the brightness of heaven, he could not have found access to men in their sinful state. They could not have endured the glory of His presence. Therefore He humbled Himself, and was made "in the likeness of sinful flesh (Romans 8:3), that He might reach the fallen race, and lift them up.

Satan's Enmity Against the Law

The very first effort of Satan to overthrow God's law—undertaken among the sinless inhabitants of heaven—seemed for a time to be crowned with success. A vast number of the angels were seduced; but Satan's apparent triumph resulted in defeat and loss, separation from God, and banishment from heaven.

When the conflict was renewed upon the earth, Satan again won a seeming advantage. By transgression, man became his captive, and man's kingdom also was betrayed into the hands of the archrebel. Now the way seemed open for Satan to establish an independent kingdom, and to defy the authority of God and His Son. But the plan of salvation made it possible for man again to be brought into harmony with God, and to render obedience to His law, and for both man and the earth to be finally redeemed from the power of the wicked one.

Again Satan was defeated, and again he resorted to deception, in the hope of converting his defeat into a victory. To stir up rebellion in the fallen race, he now represented God as unjust in having permitted man to transgress His law. "Why," said the artful tempter, "when God knew what would be the result, did He permit man to be placed on trial, to sin, and bring in misery and death?" And the children of Adam, forgetful of the long-suffering mercy that had granted man another trial, regardless of the amazing, the awful sacrifice which his rebellion had cost the King of heaven, gave ear to the tempter, and murmured against the only Being who could save them from the destructive power of Satan.

There are thousands today echoing the same rebellious complaint against God. They do not see that to deprive man of the freedom of choice would be to rob him of his prerogative as an intelligent being, and make him a mere automaton. It is not God's purpose to coerce the will. Man was created a free moral agent. Like the inhabitants of all other worlds, he must be subjected to the test of obedience; but he is never brought into such a position that yielding to evil becomes a matter of necessity. No temptation or trial is permitted to come to him which he is unable to resist. God made such ample provision that man need never have been defeated in the conflict with Satan.

As men increased upon the earth, almost the whole world joined the ranks of rebellion. Once more Satan seemed to have gained the victory. But omnipotent power again cut short the working of iniquity, and the earth was cleansed by the Flood from its moral pollution.

Says the prophet, "When Thy judgments are in the earth, the inhabitants of the world will learn righteousness. Let favor be showed to the wicked, yet will he not learn righteousness, . . . and will not behold the majesty of Jehovah." Isaiah 26:9, 10. Thus it was after the Flood. Released from His judgments, the inhabitants of the earth again rebelled against the Lord. Twice God's covenant and His statutes had been rejected by the world. Both the people before the Flood and the descendants of Noah cast off the divine authority. Then God entered into covenant with Abraham, and took to Himself a people to become the depositaries of His law. To seduce and destroy this people, Satan began at once to lay his snares. The children of Jacob were tempted to contract marriages with the heathen and to worship their idols. But Joseph was faithful to God, and his fidelity was a constant testimony to the true faith. It was to quench this light that Satan worked through the envy of Joseph's brothers to cause him to be sold as a slave in a heathen land. God overruled events, however, so that the knowledge of Himself should be given to the people of Egypt. Both in the house of Potiphar and in the prison Joseph received an education and training that, with the fear of God,

prepared him for his high position as prime minister of the nation. From the palace of the Pharaohs his influence was felt throughout the land, and the knowledge of God spread far and wide. The Israelites in Egypt also became prosperous and wealthy, and such as were true to God exerted a widespread influence. The idolatrous priests were filled with alarm as they saw the new religion finding favor. Inspired by Satan with his own enmity toward the God of heaven, they set themselves to quench the light. To the priests was committed the education of the heir to the throne, and it was this spirit of determined opposition to God and zeal for idolatry that molded the character of the future monarch, and led to cruelty and oppression toward the Hebrews.

During the forty years after the flight of Moses from Egypt, idolatry seemed to have conquered. Year by year the hopes of the Israelites grew fainter. Both king and people exulted in their power, and mocked the God of Israel. This grew until it culminated in the Pharaoh who was confronted by Moses. When the Hebrew leader came before the king with a message from "Jehovah, God of Israel," it was not ignorance of the true God, but defiance of His power, that prompted the answer, "Who is Jehovah, that I should obey His voice? . . . I know not Jehovah." From first to last, Pharaoh's opposition to the divine command was not the result of ignorance, but of hatred and defiance.

Though the Egyptians had so long rejected the knowledge of God, the Lord still gave them opportunity for repentance. In the days of Joseph, Egypt had been an asylum for Israel; God had been honored in the kindness shown His people; and now the long-suffering One, slow to anger, and full of compassion, gave each judgment time to do its work; the Egyptians, cursed through the very objects they had worshiped, had evidence of the power of Jehovah, and all who would, might submit to God and escape His judgments. The bigotry and stubbornness of the king resulted in spreading the knowledge of God, and bringing many of the Egyptians to give themselves to His service.

It was because the Israelites were so disposed to connect themselves with the heathen and imitate their idolatry that God had permitted them to go down into Egypt, where the influence of Joseph was widely felt, and where circumstances were favorable for them to remain a distinct people. Here also the gross idolatry of the Egyptians and their cruelty and oppression during the latter part of the Hebrew sojourn should have inspired in them an abhorrence of idolatry, and should have led them to flee for refuge to the God of their fathers. This very providence Satan made a means to serve his purpose, darkening the minds of the Israelites and leading them to imitate the practices of their heathen masters. On account of the superstitious veneration in which animals were held by the Egyptians, the Hebrews were not permitted, during their bondage, to present the sacrificial offerings. Thus their minds were not directed by this service to the great Sacrifice, and their faith was weakened. When the time came for Israel's deliverance, Satan set himself to resist the purposes of God. It was his determination that that great people, numbering more than two million souls, should be held in ignorance and superstition. The people whom God had promised to bless and multiply, to make a power in the earth, and through whom he was to reveal the knowledge of His will—the people whom He was to make the keepers of His law—this very people Satan was seeking to keep in obscurity and bondage, that he might obliterate from their minds the remembrance of God.

When the miracles were wrought before the king, Satan was on the ground to counteract their influence and prevent Pharaoh from acknowledging the supremacy of God and obeying His mandate. Satan wrought to the utmost of his power to counterfeit the work of God and resist His will. The only result was to prepare the way for greater exhibitions of the divine power and glory, and to make more apparent, both to the Israelites and to all Egypt, the existence and sovereignty of the true and living God.

God delivered Israel with the mighty manifestations of His power, and with judgments upon all the gods of Egypt. "He brought forth his people with joy, and His chosen with gladness: . . . that they might observe His statutes, and keep His laws." Psalm 105:43-45. He rescued them from their servile state, that He might bring them to a good land—a land which in His providence had been prepared for them as a refuge from their enemies, where they might dwell under the shadow of His wings. He would bring them to Himself, and encircle them in His everlasting arms; and in return for all His goodness and mercy to them they were required to have no other gods before Him, the living God, and to exalt His name and make it glorious in the earth.

During the bondage in Egypt many of the Israelites had, to a great extent, lost the knowledge of God's law, and had mingled its precepts with heathen customs and traditions. God brought them to Sinai, and there with His own voice declared His law.

Satan and evil angels were on the ground. Even while God was proclaiming His law to His people, Satan was plotting to tempt them to sin. This people whom God had chosen, he would wrench away, in the very face of Heaven. By leading them into idolatry, he would destroy the efficacy of all worship; for how can man be elevated by adoring what is no higher than himself and may be symbolized by his own handiwork? If men could become so blinded to the power, the majesty, and the glory of the infinite God as to represent Him by a graven image, or even by a beast or reptile; if they could so forget their own divine relationship, formed in the image of their Maker as to bow down to these revolting and senseless objects—then the way was open for foul license; the evil passions of the heart would be unrestrained, and Satan would have full sway.

At the very foot of Sinai, Satan began to execute his plans for overthrowing the law of God, thus carrying forward the same work he had begun in heaven. During the forty days while Moses was in the mount with God, Satan was busy exciting doubt, apostasy, and rebellion. While God was writing down His law, to be committed to His covenant people, the Israelites, denying their loyalty to Jehovah, were demanding gods of gold! When Moses came from the awful presence of the divine glory, with the precepts of the law which they had pledged themselves to obey, he found them, in open defiance of its commands, bowing in adoration before a golden image.

By leading Israel to this daring insult and blasphemy to Jehovah, Satan had planned to cause their ruin. Since they had proved themselves to be so utterly degraded, so lost to all sense of the privileges and blessings that God had offered them, and to their own solemn and repeated pledges of loyalty, the Lord would, he believed, divorce them from Himself and devote them to destruction. Thus would be secured the extinction of the seed of Abraham, that seed of promise that was to preserve the knowledge of the living God, and through whom He was to come—the true Seed, that was to conquer Satan. The great rebel had planned to destroy Israel, and thus thwart the purposes of God. But again he was defeated. Sinful as they were, the people of Israel were not destroyed. While those who stubbornly ranged themselves on the side of Satan were cut off, the people, humbled and repentant, were mercifully pardoned. The history of this sin was to stand as a perpetual testimony to the guilt and punishment of idolatry, and the justice and long-suffering mercy of God.

The whole universe had been witness to the scenes at Sinai. In the working out of the two administrations was seen the contrast between the government of God and that of Satan. Again the sinless inhabitants of other worlds beheld the results of Satan's apostasy, and the kind of government he would have established in heaven had he been permitted to bear sway.

By causing men to violate the second commandment, Satan aimed to degrade their conceptions of the Divine Being. By setting aside the fourth, he would cause them to forget God altogether. God's claim to reverence and worship, above the gods of the heathen, is based upon the fact that He is the Creator, and that to Him all other beings owe their existence. Thus it is presented in the Bible. Says the prophet Jeremiah: "The Lord is the true God, He is the living God, and an everlasting King. . . . The gods that have not made the heavens and the earth, even they shall perish from the earth, and from under these heavens. He hath made the earth by His power, He hath established the world by His wisdom, and hath stretched out the heavens by His discretion." "Every man is brutish in his knowledge: every founder is confounded by the graven image: for his molten image is falsehood, and there is no breath in them. They are vanity, and the work of errors: in the time of their visitation they shall perish. The portion of Jacob is not like them: for He is the former of all things." Jeremiah 10:10-12, 14-16. The Sabbath, as a memorial of God's creative power, points to Him as the maker of the heavens and the earth. Hence it is a constant witness to His existence and a reminder of His greatness, His wisdom, and His love. Had the Sabbath always been sacredly observed, there could never have been an atheist or an idolater.

The Sabbath institution, which originated in Eden, is as old as the world itself. It was observed by all the patriarchs, from creation down. During the bondage in Egypt, the Israelites were forced by their taskmasters to violate the Sabbath, and to a great extent they lost the knowledge of its sacredness. When the law was proclaimed at Sinai the very first words of the fourth commandment were, "Remember the Sabbath day, to keep it holy"—showing that the Sabbath was not then instituted; we are pointed back for its origin to creation. In order to obliterate God from the minds of men, Satan aimed to tear down this great memorial. If men could be led to forget their Creator, they would make no effort to resist the power of evil, and Satan would be sure of his prey.

Satan's enmity against God's law had impelled him to war against every precept of the Decalogue. To the great principle of love and loyalty to God, the Father of all, the principle of filial love and obedience is closely related. Contempt for parental authority will soon lead to contempt for the authority of God. Hence Satan's efforts to lessen the obligation of the fifth commandment. Among heathen peoples the principle enjoined in this precept was little heeded. In many nations parents were abandoned or put to death as soon as age had rendered them incapable of providing for themselves. In the family the mother was treated with little respect, and upon the death of her husband she was required to submit to the authority of her eldest son. Filial obedience was enjoined by Moses; but as the Israelites departed from the Lord, the fifth commandment, with others, came to be disregarded.

Satan was "a murderer from the beginning" (John 8:44); and as soon as he had obtained power over the human race, he not only prompted them to hate and slay one another, but, the more boldly to defy the authority of God, he made the violation of the sixth commandment a part of their religion.

By perverted conceptions of divine attributes, heathen nations were led to believe human sacrifices necessary to secure the favor of their deities; and the most horrible cruelties have been perpetrated under the various forms of idolatry. Among these was the practice of causing their children to pass through the fire before their idols. When one of them came through this ordeal unharmed, the people believed that their offerings were accepted; the one thus delivered was regarded as specially favored by the gods, was loaded with benefits, and ever afterward held in high esteem; and however aggravated his crimes, he was never punished. But should one be burned in passing through the fire, his fate was sealed; it was believed that the anger of the gods could be appeased only by taking the life of the victim, and he was accordingly offered as a sacrifice. In times of great apostasy these abominations prevailed, to some extent, among the Israelites.

The violation of the seventh commandment also was early practiced in the name of religion. The most licentious and abominable rites were made a part of the heathen worship. The gods themselves were represented as impure, and their worshipers gave the rein to the baser passions. Unnatural vices prevailed and the religious festivals were characterized by universal and open impurity.

Polygamy was practiced at an early date. It was one of the sins that brought the wrath of God upon the antediluvian world. Yet after the Flood it again became widespread. It was Satan's studied effort to pervert the marriage institution, to weaken its obligations and lessen its sacredness; for in no surer way could he deface the image of God in man and open the door to misery and vice.

From the opening of the great controversy it has been Satan's purpose to misrepresent God's character and to excite rebellion against His law, and this work appears to be crowned with success. The multitudes give ear to Satan's deceptions and set themselves against God. But amid the working of evil, God's purposes move steadily forward to their accomplishment; to all created intelligences He is making manifest His justice and benevolence. Through Satan's temptations the whole human race have become transgressors of God's law, but by the sacrifice of His Son a way is opened whereby they may return to God. Through the grace of Christ they may be enabled to render obedience to the Father's law. Thus in every age, from the midst of apostasy and rebellion, God gathers out a people that are true to Him—a people "in whose heart is His law." Isaiah 51:7.

It was by deception that Satan seduced angels; thus he has in all ages carried forward his work among men, and he will continue this policy to the last. Should he openly profess to be warring against God and His law, men would beware; but he disguises himself, and mixes truth with error. The most dangerous falsehoods are those that are mingled with truth. It is thus that errors are received that captivate and ruin the soul. By this means Satan carries the world with him. But a day is coming when his triumph will be forever ended.

God's dealings with rebellion will result in fully unmasking the work that has so long been carried on under cover. The results of Satan's rule, the fruits of setting aside the divine statutes, will be laid open to the view of all created intelligences. The law of God will stand fully vindicated. It will be seen that all the dealings of God have been conducted with reference to the eternal good of His people, and the good of all the worlds that He has created. Satan himself, in the presence of the witnessing universe, will confess the justice of God's government and the righteousness of His law.

The time is not far distant when God will arise to vindicate His insulted authority. "The Lord cometh out of His place to punish the inhabitants of the earth for their iniquity." Isaiah 26:21. "But who may abide the day of His coming? and who shall stand when He appeareth?" Malachi 3:2. The people of Israel, because of their sinfulness, were forbidden to approach the mount when God was about to descend upon it to proclaim His law, lest they should be consumed by the burning glory of His presence. If such manifestations of His power marked the place chosen for the proclamation of God's law, how terrible must be His tribunal when He comes for the execution of these sacred statutes. How will those who have trampled upon His authority endure His glory in the great day of final retribution? The terrors of Sinai were to represent to the people the scenes of the judgment. The sound of a trumpet summoned Israel to meet with God. The voice of the Archangel and the trump of God shall summon, from the whole earth, both the living and the dead to the presence of their Judge. The Father and the Son, attended by a multitude of angels, were present upon the mount. At the great judgment day Christ will come "in the glory of His Father with His angels." Matthew 16:27. He shall then sit upon the throne of His glory, and before Him shall be gathered all nations.

When the divine Presence was manifested upon Sinai, the glory of the Lord was like devouring fire in the sight of all Israel. But when Christ shall come in glory with His holy angels the whole earth shall be ablaze with the terrible light of His presence. "Our God shall come, and shall not keep silence: a fire shall devour before Him, and it shall be very tempestuous round about Him. He shall call to the heavens from above, and to the earth, that He may judge His people." Psalm 50:3, 4. A fiery stream shall issue and come forth from before Him, which shall cause the elements to melt with fervent heat, the earth also, and the works that are therein shall be burned up. "The Lord Jesus shall be revealed from heaven with His mighty angels, in

flaming fire taking vengeance on them that know not God, and that obey not the gospel." 2 Thessalonians 1:7, 8.

Never since man was created had there been witnessed such a manifestation of divine power as when the law was proclaimed from Sinai. "The earth shook, the heavens also dropped at the presence of God: even Sinai itself was moved at the presence of God, the God of Israel." Psalm 68:8. Amid the most terrific convulsions of nature the voice of God, like a trumpet, was heard from the cloud. The mountain was shaken from base to summit, and the hosts of Israel, pale and trembling with terror, lay upon their faces upon the earth. He whose voice then shook the earth has declared, "Yet once more I shake not the earth only, but also heaven." Hebrews 12:26. Says the Scripture, "The Lord shall roar from on high, and utter His voice from His holy habitation;" "and the heavens and the earth shall shake." Jeremiah 25:30; Joel 3:16. In that great coming day, the heaven itself shall depart "as a scroll when it is rolled together." Revelation 6:14. And every mountain and island shall be moved out of its place. "The earth shall reel to and fro like a drunkard, and shall be removed like a cottage; and the transgression thereof shall be heavy upon it; and it shall fall, and not rise again." Isaiah 24:20.

"Therefore shall all hands be faint," all faces shall be "turned into paleness," "and every man's heart shall melt. And they shall be afraid: pangs and sorrows shall take hold of

them." "And I will punish the world for their evil," saith the Lord, "and I will cause the arrogancy of the proud to cease, and will lay low the haughtiness of the terrible." Isaiah 13:7, 8, 11; Jeremiah 30:6.

When Moses came from the divine Presence in the mount, where he had received the tables of the testimony, guilty Israel could not endure the light that glorified his countenance. How much less can transgressors look upon the Son of God when He shall appear in the glory of His Father, surrounded by all the heavenly host, to execute judgment upon the transgressors of His law and the rejecters of His atonement. Those who have disregarded the law of God and trodden under foot the blood of Christ, "the kings of the earth, and the great men, and the rich men, and the chief captains, and the mighty men," shall hide themselves "in the dens and in the rocks of the mountains," and they shall say to the mountains and rocks, "Fall on us, and hide us from the face of Him that sitteth on the throne, and from the wrath of the Lamb: for the great day of His wrath is come; and who shall be able to stand?" Revelation 6:15-17. "In that day a man shall cast his idols of silver, and his idols of gold, . . . to the moles and to the bats; to go into the clefts of the rocks, and into the tops of the ragged rocks, for fear of the Lord, and for the glory of His majesty, when He ariseth to shake terribly the earth." Isaiah 2:20, 21.

Then it will be seen that Satan's rebellion against God has resulted in ruin to himself and to all that chose to become his subjects. He has represented that great good would result from transgression; but it will be seen that "the wages of sin is death." "For, behold, the day cometh, that shall burn as an oven; and all the proud, yea, and all that do wickedly, shall be stubble: and the day that cometh shall burn them up, saith the Lord of hosts, that it shall leave them neither root nor branch." Malachi 4:1. Satan, the root of every sin, and all evil workers, who are his branches, shall be utterly cut off. An end will be made of sin, with all the woe and ruin that have resulted from it. Says the psalmist, "Thou hast destroyed the wicked, thou hast put out their name forever and ever. O thou enemy, destructions are come to a perpetual end." Psalm 9:5, 6.

But amid the tempest of divine judgment the children of God will have no cause for fear. "The Lord will be the hope of His people, and the strength of the children of Israel." Joel 3:16. The day that brings terror and destruction to the transgressors of God's law will bring to the obedient "joy unspeakable and full of glory" "Gather My saints together unto Me," saith the Lord, "those that have made a covenant with Me by sacrifice. And the heavens shall declare His righteousness: for God is Judge Himself."

"Then shall ye return, and discern between the righteous and the wicked, between him that serveth God and him that serveth Him not." Malachi 3:18. "Hearken unto Me, ye that know righteousness, the people in whose heart is My law." "Behold, I have taken out of thine hand the cup of trembling, . . . thou shalt no more drink it again." I, even I, am He that comforteth you." Isaiah 51:7, 22, 12. "For the mountains shall depart, and the hills be removed; but My kindness shall not depart from thee, neither shall the covenant of My peace be removed, saith the Lord that hath mercy on thee." Isaiah 54:10.

The great plan of redemption results in fully bringing back the world into God's favor. All that was lost by sin is restored. Not only man but the earth is redeemed, to be the eternal abode of the obedient. For six thousand years Satan has struggled to maintain possession of the earth. Now God's original purpose in its creation is accomplished. "The saints of the Most High shall take the kingdom, and possess the kingdom forever, even forever and ever." Daniel 7:18.

"From the rising of the sun unto the going down of the same the Lord's name is to be praised." Psalm 113:3. "In that day shall there be one Lord, and His name one." "And Jehovah shall be king over all the earth." Zechariah 14:9. Says the Scripture, "Forever, O Lord, Thy word is settled in heaven." "All His commandments are sure. They stand fast forever and ever." Psalms 119:89; 111:7, 8. The sacred statutes which Satan has hated and sought to destroy, will be honored throughout a sinless universe. And "as the earth bringeth forth her bud, and as the garden causeth the things that are sown in it to spring forth; so the Lord God will cause righteousness and praise to spring forth before all nations." Isaiah 61:11.

The Tabernacle and Its Services

The command was communicated to Moses while in the mount with God, "Let them make Me a sanctuary; that I may dwell among them;" and full directions were given for the construction of the tabernacle. By their apostasy the Israelites forfeited the blessing of the divine Presence, and for the time rendered impossible the erection of a sanctuary for God among them. But after they were again taken into favor with Heaven, the great leader proceeded to execute the divine command.

Chosen men were especially endowed by God with skill and wisdom for the construction of the sacred building. God Himself gave to Moses the plan of that structure, with particular directions as to its size and form, the materials to be employed, and every article of furniture which it was to contain. The holy places made with hands were to be "figures of the true," "patterns of things in the heavens" (Hebrews 9:24, 23)—a miniature representation of the heavenly temple where Christ, our great High Priest, after offering His life as a sacrifice, was to minister in the sinner's behalf. God presented before Moses in the mount a view of the heavenly sanctuary, and commanded him to make all things according to the pattern shown him. All these directions were carefully recorded by Moses, who communicated them to the leaders of the people.

For the building of the sanctuary great and expensive preparations were necessary; a large amount of the most precious and costly material was required; yet the Lord accepted only freewill offerings. "Of every man that giveth it willingly with his heart ye shall take My offering" was the divine command repeated by Moses to the congregation. Devotion to God and a spirit of sacrifice were the first requisites in preparing a dwelling place for the Most High.

All the people responded with one accord. "They came, every one whose heart stirred him up, and every one whom his spirit made willing, and they brought the Lord's offering to the work of the tabernacle of the congregation, and for all His service, and for the holy garments. And they came, both men and women, as many as were willinghearted, and brought bracelets, and earrings, and rings, and tablets, all jewels of gold: and every man that offered, offered an offering of gold unto the Lord."

"And every man with whom was found blue, and purple, and scarlet, and fine linen, and goats' hair, and rams' skins dyed red, and sealskins, brought them. Everyone that did offer an offering of silver and brass brought the Lord's offering: and every man, with whom was found acacia wood for any work of the service, brought it.

"And all the women that were wisehearted did spin with their hands, and brought that which they had spun, the blue, and the purple, the scarlet, and the fine linen. And all the women whose heart stirred them up in wisdom spun the goats' hair.

"And the rulers brought the onyx stones, and the stones to be set, for the ephod, and for the breastplate; and the spice, and the oil; for the light, and for the anointing oil, and for the sweet incense." Exodus 35:23-28, R.V.

While the building of the sanctuary was in progress the people, old and young—men, women, and children—continued to bring their offerings, until those in charge of the work found that they had enough, and even more than could be used. And Moses caused to be proclaimed throughout the camp, "Let neither man nor woman make any more work for the offering of the sanctuary. So the people were restrained from bringing." The murmurings of the Israelites and the visitations of God's judgments because of their sins are recorded as a warning to after-generations. And their devotion, their zeal and liberality, are an example worthy of imitation. All who love the worship of God and prize the blessing of His sacred presence will manifest the same spirit of sacrifice in preparing a house where He may meet with them. They will desire to bring to the Lord an offering of the very best that they possess. A house built for God should not be left in debt, for He is thereby dishonored. An amount sufficient to accomplish the work should be freely given, that the workmen may be able to say, as did the builders of the tabernacle, "Bring no more offerings."

The tabernacle was so constructed that it could be taken apart and borne with the Israelites in all their journeyings. It was therefore small, being not more than fifty-five feet in length, and eighteen in breadth and height. Yet it was a magnificent structure. The wood employed for the building and its furniture was that of the acacia tree, which was less subject to decay than any other to be obtained at Sinai. The walls consisted of upright boards, set in silver sockets, and held firm by pillars and connecting bars; and all were overlaid with gold, giving to the building the appearance of solid gold. The roof was formed of four sets of curtains, the innermost of "fine twined linen, and blue, and purple, and scarlet: with cherubim of cunning work;" the other three respectively were of goats' hair, rams' skins dyed red, and sealskins, so arranged as to afford complete protection.

The building was divided into two apartments by a rich and beautiful curtain, or veil, suspended from gold-plated pillars; and a similar veil closed the entrance of the first apartment. These, like the inner covering, which formed the ceiling, were of the most gorgeous colors, blue, purple, and scarlet, beautifully arranged, while inwrought with threads of gold and silver were cherubim to represent the angelic host who are connected with the work of the heavenly sanctuary and who are ministering spirits to the people of God on earth.

The sacred tent was enclosed in an open space called the court, which was surrounded by hangings, or screens, of fine linen, suspended from pillars of brass. The entrance to this enclosure was at the eastern end. It was closed by curtains of costly material and beautiful workmanship, though inferior to those of the sanctuary. The hangings of the court being only about half as high as the walls of the tabernacle, the building could be plainly seen by the people without. In the court, and nearest the entrance, stood the brazen altar of burnt offering. Upon this altar were consumed all the sacrifices made by fire unto the Lord, and its horns were sprinkled with the atoning blood. Between the altar and the door of the tabernacle was the laver, which was also of brass, made from the mirrors that had been the freewill offering of the women of Israel. At the laver the priests were to wash their hands and their feet whenever they went into the sacred apartments, or approached the altar to offer a burnt offering unto the Lord.

In the first apartment, or holy place, were the table of showbread, the candlestick, or lampstand, and the altar of incense. The table of showbread stood on the north. With its ornamental crown, it was overlaid with pure gold. On this table the priests were each Sabbath to place twelve cakes, arranged in two piles, and sprinkled with frankincense. The loaves that were removed, being accounted holy, were to be eaten by the priests. On the south was the seven-branched candlestick, with its seven lamps. Its branches were ornamented with exquisitely wrought flowers, resembling lilies, and the whole was made from one solid piece of gold. There being no windows in the tabernacle, the lamps were never all extinguished at one time, but shed their light by day and by night. Just before the veil separating the holy place from the most holy and the immediate presence of God, stood the golden altar of incense. Upon this altar the priest was to burn incense every morning and evening; its horns were touched with the blood of the sin offering, and it was sprinkled with blood upon the great Day of Atonement. The fire upon this altar was kindled by God Himself and was sacredly cherished. Day and night the holy incense diffused its fragrance throughout the sacred apartments, and without, far around the tabernacle.

Beyond the inner veil was the holy of holies, where centered the symbolic service of atonement and intercession, and which formed the connecting link between heaven and earth. In this apartment was the ark, a chest of acacia wood, overlaid within and without with gold, and having a crown of gold about the top. It was made as a depository for the tables of stone, upon which God Himself had inscribed the Ten Commandments. Hence it was called the ark of God's testament, or the ark of the covenant, since the Ten Commandments were the basis of the covenant made between God and Israel.

The cover of the sacred chest was called the mercy seat. This was wrought of one solid piece of gold, and was surmounted by golden cherubim, one standing on each end. One wing of each angel was stretched forth on high, while the other was folded over the body (see Ezekiel 1:11) in token of reverence and humility. The position of the cherubim, with their faces turned toward each other, and looking reverently downward toward the ark, represented the reverence with which the heavenly host regard the law of God and their interest in the plan of redemption.

Above the mercy seat was the Shekinah, the manifestation of the divine Presence; and from between the cherubim, God made known His will. Divine messages were sometimes communicated to the high priest by a voice from the cloud. Sometimes a light fell upon the angel at the right, to signify approval or acceptance, or a shadow or cloud rested upon the one at the left to reveal disapproval or rejection.

The law of God, enshrined within the ark, was the great rule of righteousness and judgment. That law pronounced death upon the transgressor; but above the law was the mercy seat, upon which the presence of God was revealed, and from which, by virtue of the atonement, pardon was granted to the repentant sinner. Thus in the work of Christ for our redemption, symbolized by the sanctuary service, "mercy and truth are met together; righteousness and peace have kissed each other." Psalm 85:10.

No language can describe the glory of the scene presented within the sanctuary—the gold-plated walls reflecting the light from the golden candlestick, the brilliant hues of the richly embroidered curtains with their shining angels, the table, and the altar of incense, glittering with gold; beyond the second veil the sacred ark, with its mystic cherubim, and above it the holy Shekinah, the visible manifestation of Jehovah's presence; all but a dim reflection of the glories of the temple of God in heaven, the great center of the work for man's redemption.

A period of about half a year was occupied in the building of the tabernacle. When it was completed, Moses examined all the work of the builders, comparing it with the pattern shown him in the mount and the directions he had received from God. "As the Lord had commanded, even so had they done it: and Moses blessed them." With eager interest the multitudes of Israel crowded around to look upon the sacred structure. While they were contemplating the scene with reverent satisfaction, the pillar of cloud floated over the sanctuary and, descending, enveloped it. "And the glory of the Lord filled the tabernacle." There was a revealing of the divine majesty, and for a time even Moses could not enter. With deep emotion the people beheld the token that the work of their hands was accepted. There were no loud demonstrations of rejoicing. A solemn awe rested upon all. But the gladness of their hearts welled up in tears of joy, and they murmured low, earnest words of gratitude that God had condescended to abide with them.

By divine direction the tribe of Levi was set apart for the service of the sanctuary. In the earliest times every man was the priest of his own household. In the days of Abraham the priesthood was regarded as the birthright of the eldest son. Now, instead of the first-born of all Israel, the Lord accepted the tribe of Levi for the work of the sanctuary. By this signal honor He manifested His approval of their fidelity, both in adhering to His service and in executing His judgments when Israel apostatized in the worship of the golden calf. The priesthood, however, was restricted to the family of Aaron. Aaron and his sons alone were permitted to minister before the Lord; the rest of the tribe were entrusted with the charge of the tabernacle and its furniture, and they were to attend upon the priests in their ministration, but they were not to sacrifice, to burn incense, or to see the holy things till they were covered.

In accordance with their office, a special dress was appointed for the priests. "Thou shalt make holy garments for Aaron thy brother, for glory and for beauty," was the divine direction to Moses. The robe of the common priest was of white linen, and woven in one piece. It extended nearly to the feet and was confined about the waist by a white linen girdle embroidered in blue, purple, and red. A linen turban, or miter, completed his outer costume. Moses at the burning bush was directed to put off his sandals, for the ground whereon he stood was holy. So the priests were not to enter the sanctuary with shoes upon their feet. Particles of dust cleaving to them would desecrate the holy place. They were to leave their shoes in the court before entering the sanctuary, and also to wash both their hands and their feet before ministering in the tabernacle or at the altar of burnt offering. Thus was constantly taught the lesson that all defilement must be put away from those who would approach into the presence of God.

The garments of the high priest were of costly material and beautiful workmanship, befitting his exalted station. In addition to the linen dress of the common priest, he wore a robe of blue, also woven in one piece. Around the skirt it was ornamented with golden bells, and pomegranates of blue, purple, and scarlet. Outside of this was the ephod, a shorter garment of gold, blue, purple, scarlet, and white. It was confined by a girdle of the same colors, beautifully wrought. The ephod was sleeveless, and on its gold-embroidered shoulder pieces were set two onyx stones, bearing the names of the twelve tribes of Israel.

Over the ephod was the breastplate, the most sacred of the priestly vestments. This was of the same material as the ephod. It was in the form of a square, measuring a span, and was suspended from the shoulders by a cord of blue from golden rings. The border was formed of a variety of precious stones, the same that form the twelve foundations of the City of God. Within the border were twelve stones set in gold, arranged in rows of four, and, like those in the shoulder pieces, engraved with the names of the tribes. The Lord's direction was, "Aaron shall bear the names of the children of Israel in the breastplate of judgment upon his heart, when he goeth in unto the holy place, for a memorial before the Lord continually." Exodus 28:29. So Christ, the great High Priest, pleading His blood before the Father in the sinner's behalf, bears upon His heart the name of every repentant, believing soul. Says the psalmist, "I am poor and needy; yet the Lord thinketh upon me." Psalm 40:17.

At the right and left of the breastplate were two large stones of great brilliancy. These were known as the Urim and Thummim. By them the will of God was made known through the high priest. When questions were brought for decision before the Lord, a halo of light encircling the precious stone at the right was a token of the divine consent or approval, while a cloud shadowing the stone at the left was an evidence of denial or disapprobation.

The miter of the high priest consisted of the white linen turban, having attached to it by a lace of blue, a gold plate bearing the inscription, "Holiness to Jehovah." Everything connected with the apparel and deportment of the priests was to be such as to impress the beholder with a sense of the holiness of God, the sacredness of His worship, and the purity required of those who came into His presence.

Not only the sanctuary itself, but the ministration of the priests, was to "serve unto the example and shadow of heavenly things." Hebrews 8:5. Thus it was of great importance; and the Lord, through Moses, gave the most definite and explicit instruction concerning every point of this typical service. The ministration of the sanctuary consisted of two divisions, a daily and a yearly service. The daily service was performed at the altar of burnt offering in the court of the tabernacle and in the holy place; while the yearly service was in the most holy.

No mortal eye but that of the high priest was to look upon the inner apartment of the sanctuary. Only once a year could the priest enter there, and that after the most careful and solemn preparation. With trembling he went in before God, and the people in reverent silence awaited his return, their hearts uplifted in earnest prayer for the divine blessing. Before the mercy seat the high priest made the atonement for Israel; and in the cloud of glory, God met with him. His stay here beyond the accustomed time filled them with fear, lest because of their sins or his own he had been slain by the glory of the Lord.

The daily service consisted of the morning and evening burnt offering, the offering of sweet incense on the golden altar, and the special offerings for individual sins. And there were also offerings for sabbaths, new moons, and special feasts.

Every morning and evening a lamb of a year old was burned upon the altar, with its appropriate meat offering, thus symbolizing the daily consecration of the nation to Jehovah, and their constant dependence upon the atoning blood of Christ. God expressly directed that every offering presented for the service of the sanctuary should be "without blemish." Exodus 12:5. The priests were to examine all animals brought as a sacrifice, and were to reject every one in which a defect was discovered. Only an offering "without blemish" could be a symbol of His perfect purity who was to offer Himself as "a lamb without blemish and without spot." 1 Peter 1:19. The apostle Paul points to these sacrifices as an illustration of what the followers of Christ are to become. He says, "I beseech you therefore, brethren, by the mercies of God, that ye present your bodies a living sacrifice, holy, acceptable unto God, which is your reasonable service." Romans 12:1. We are to give ourselves to the service of God, and we should seek to make the offering as nearly perfect as possible. God will not be pleased with anything less than the best we can offer. Those who love Him with all the heart, will desire to give Him the best service of the life, and they will be constantly seeking to bring every power of their being into harmony with the laws that will promote their ability to do His will.

In the offering of incense the priest was brought more directly into the presence of God than in any other act of the daily ministration. As the inner veil of the sanctuary did no extend to the top of the building, the glory of God, which was manifested above the mercy seat, was partially visible from the first apartment. When the priest offered incense before the Lord, he looked toward the ark; and as the cloud of incense arose, the divine glory descended upon the mercy seat and filled the most holy place, and often so filled both apartments that the priest was obliged to retire to the door of the tabernacle. As in that typical service the priest looked by faith to the mercy seat which he could not see, so the people of God are now to direct their prayers to Christ, their great High Priest, who, unseen by human vision, is pleading in their behalf in the sanctuary above.

The incense, ascending with the prayers of Israel, represents the merits and intercession of Christ, His perfect righteousness, which through faith is imputed to His people, and which can alone make the worship of sinful beings acceptable to God. Before the veil of the most holy place was an altar of perpetual intercession, before the holy, an altar of continual atonement. By blood and by incense God was to be approached—symbols pointing to the great Mediator, through whom sinners may approach Jehovah, and through whom alone mercy and salvation can be granted to the repentant, believing soul.

As the priests morning and evening entered the holy place at the time of incense, the daily sacrifice was ready to be offered upon the altar in the court without. This was a time of intense interest to the worshipers who assembled at the tabernacle. Before entering into the presence of God through the ministration of the priest, they were to engage in earnest searching of heart and confession of sin. They united in silent prayer, with their faces toward the holy place. Thus their petitions ascended with the cloud of incense, while faith laid hold upon the merits of the promised Saviour prefigured by the atoning sacrifice. The hours appointed for the morning and the evening sacrifice were regarded as sacred, and they came to be observed as the set time for worship throughout the Jewish nation. And when in later times the Jews were scattered as captives in distant lands, they still at the appointed hour turned their faces toward Jerusalem and offered up their petitions to the God of Israel. In this custom Christians have an example for morning and evening prayer. While God condemns a mere round of ceremonies, without the spirit of worship, He looks with great pleasure upon those who love Him, bowing morning and evening to seek pardon for sins committed and to present their requests for needed blessings.

The showbread was kept ever before the Lord as a perpetual offering. Thus it was a part of the daily sacrifice. It was called showbread, or "bread of the presence," because it was ever before the face of the Lord. It was an acknowledgment of man's dependence upon God for both temporal and spiritual food, and that it is received only through the mediation of Christ. God had fed Israel in the wilderness with bread from heaven, and they were still dependent upon His bounty, both for temporal food and spiritual blessings. Both the manna and the showbread pointed to Christ, the living Bread, who is ever in the presence of God for us. He Himself said, "I am the living Bread which came down from heaven." John 6:48-51. Frankincense was placed upon the loaves. When the bread was removed every Sabbath, to be replaced by fresh loaves, the frankincense was burned upon the altar as a memorial before God.

The most important part of the daily ministration was the service performed in behalf of individuals. The repentant sinner brought his offering to the door of the tabernacle, and, placing his hand upon the victim's head, confessed his sins, thus in figure transferring them from himself to the innocent sacrifice. By his own hand the animal was then slain, and the blood was carried by the priest into the holy place and sprinkled before the veil, behind which was the ark containing the law that the sinner had transgressed. By this ceremony the sin was, through the blood, transferred in figure to the sanctuary. In some cases the blood was not taken into the holy place; but the flesh was then to be eaten by the priest, as Moses directed the sons of Aaron, saying, "God hath given it you to bear the iniquity of the congregation." Leviticus 10:17. Both ceremonies alike symbolized the transfer of the sin from the penitent to the sanctuary.

Such was the work that went on day by day throughout the year. The sins of Israel being thus transferred to the sanctuary, the holy places were defiled, and a special work became necessary for the removal of the sins. God commanded that an atonement be made for each of the sacred apartments, as for the altar, to "cleanse it, and hallow it from the uncleanness of the children of Israel." Leviticus 16:19.

Once a year, on the great Day of Atonement, the priest entered the most holy place for the cleansing of the sanctuary. The work there performed completed the yearly round of ministration.

On the Day of Atonement two kids of the goats were brought to the door of the tabernacle, and lots were cast upon them, "one lot for the Lord, and the other lot for the scapegoat." The goat upon which the first lot fell was to be slain as a sin offering for the people. And the priest was to bring his blood within the veil, and sprinkle it upon the mercy seat. "And he shall make an atonement for the holy place, because of the uncleanness of the children of Israel, and because of their transgression in all their sins; and so shall he do for the tabernacle of the congregation, that remaineth among them in the midst of their uncleanness."

"And Aaron shall lay both his hands upon the head of the live goat, and confess over him all the iniquities of the children of Israel, and all their transgressions in all their sins, putting them upon the head of the goat, and shall send him away by the hand of a fit man into the wilderness: and the goat shall bear upon him all their iniquities into a land not inhabited." Not until the goat had been thus sent away did the people regard themselves as freed from the burden of their sins. Every man was to afflict his soul while the work of atonement was going forward. All business was laid aside, and the whole congregation of Israel spent the day in solemn humiliation before God, with prayer, fasting, and deep searching of heart.

Important truths concerning the atonement were taught the people by this yearly service. In the sin offerings presented during the year, a substituted had been accepted in the sinner's stead; but the blood of the victim had not made full atonement for the sin. It had only provided a means by which the sin was transferred to the sanctuary. By the offering of blood, the sinner acknowledged the authority of the law, confessed the guilt of his transgression, and expressed his faith in Him who was to take away the sin of the world; but he was not entirely released from the condemnation of the law. On the Day of Atonement the high priest, having taken an offering for the congregation, went into the most holy place with the blood and sprinkled it upon the mercy seat, above the tables of the law. Thus the claims of the law, which demanded the life of the sinner, were satisfied. Then in his character of mediator the priest took the sins upon himself, and, leaving the sanctuary, he bore with him the burden of Israel's guilt. At the door of the tabernacle he laid his hands upon the head of the scapegoat and confessed over him "all the iniquities of the children of Israel, and all their

transgressions in all their sins, putting them upon the head of the goat." And as the goat bearing these sins was sent away, they were, with him, regarded as forever separated from the people. Such was the service performed "unto the example and shadow of heavenly things." Hebrews 8:5.

As has been stated, the earthly sanctuary was built by Moses according to the pattern shown him in the mount. It was "a figure for the time then present, in which were offered both gifts and sacrifices;" its two holy places were "patterns of things in the heavens;" Christ, our great High Priest, is "a minister of the sanctuary, and of the true tabernacle, which the Lord pitched, and not man." Hebrews 9:9, 23; 8:2. As in vision the apostle John was granted a view of the temple of God in heaven, he beheld there "seven lamps of fire burning before the throne." He saw an angel "having a golden censer; and there was given unto him much incense, that he should offer it with the prayers of all saints upon the golden altar which was before the throne." Revelation 4:5; 8:3. Here the prophet was permitted to behold the first apartment of the sanctuary in heaven; and he saw there the "seven lamps of fire" and the "golden altar" represented by the golden candlestick and the altar of incense in the sanctuary on earth. Again, "the temple of God was opened" (Revelation 11:19), and he looked within the inner veil, upon the holy of holies. Here he beheld "the ark of His testament" (Revelation 11:19), represented by the sacred chest constructed by Moses to contain the law of God.

Moses made the earthly sanctuary, "according to the fashion that he had seen." Paul declares that "the tabernacle, and all the vessels of the ministry," when completed, were "the patterns of things in the heavens." Acts 7:44; Hebrews 9:21, 23. And John says that he saw the sanctuary in heaven. That sanctuary, in which Jesus ministers in our behalf, is the great original, of which the sanctuary built by Moses was a copy.

The heavenly temple, the abiding place of the King of kings, where "thousand thousands ministered unto Him, and ten thousand times ten thousand stood before Him" (Daniel 7:10), that temple filled with the glory of the eternal throne, where seraphim, its shining guardians, veil their faces in adoration—no earthly structure could represent its vastness and its glory. Yet important truths concerning the heavenly sanctuary and the great work there carried forward for man's redemption were to be taught by the earthly sanctuary and its services.

After His ascension, our Saviour was to begin His work as our High Priest. Says Paul, "Christ is not entered into the holy places made with hands, which are the figures of the true; but into heaven itself, now to appear in the presence of God for us." Hebrews 9:24. As Christ's ministration was to consist of two great divisions, each occupying a period of time and having a distinctive place in the heavenly sanctuary, so the typical ministration consisted of two divisions, the daily and the yearly service, and to each a department of the tabernacle was devoted.

As Christ at His ascension appeared in the presence of God

to plead His blood in behalf of penitent believers, so the priest in the daily ministration sprinkled the blood of the sacrifice in the holy place in the sinner's behalf.

The blood of Christ, while it was to release the repentant sinner from the condemnation of the law, was not to cancel the sin; it would stand on record in the sanctuary until the final atonement; so in the type the blood of the sin offering removed the sin from the penitent, but it rested in the sanctuary until the Day of Atonement.

In the great day of final award, the dead are to be "judged out of those things which were written in the books, according to their works." Revelation 20:12. Then by virtue of the atoning blood of Christ, the sins of all the truly penitent will be blotted from the books of heaven. Thus the sanctuary will be freed, or cleansed, from the record of sin. In the type, this great work of atonement, or blotting out of sins, was represented by the services of the Day of Atonement—the cleansing of the earthly sanctuary, which was accomplished by the removal, by virtue of the blood of the sin offering, of the sins by which it had been polluted.

As in the final atonement the sins of the truly penitent are to be blotted from the records of heaven, no more to be remembered or come into mind, so in the type they were borne away into the wilderness, forever separated from the congregation.

Since Satan is the originator of sin, the direct instigator of all the sins that caused the death of the Son of God, justice demands that Satan shall suffer the final punishment. Christ's work for the redemption of men and the purification of the universe from sin will be closed by the removal of sin from the heavenly sanctuary and the placing of these sins upon Satan, who will bear the final penalty. So in the typical service, the yearly round of ministration closed with the purification of the sanctuary, and the confessing of the sins on the head of the scapegoat.

Thus in the ministration of the tabernacle, and of the temple that afterward took its place, the people were taught each day the great truths relative to Christ's death and ministration, and once each year their minds were carried forward to the closing events of the great controversy between Christ and Satan, the final purification of the universe from sin and sinners.

The Sin of Nadab and Abihu

After the dedication of the tabernacle, the priests were consecrated to their sacred office. These services occupied seven days, each marked by special ceremonies. On the eight day they entered upon their ministration. Assisted by his sons, Aaron offered the sacrifices that God required, and he lifted up his hands and blessed the people. All had been done as God commanded, and He accepted the sacrifice, and revealed His glory in a remarkable manner; fire came from the Lord and consumed the offering upon the altar. The people looked upon this wonderful manifestation of divine power with awe and intense interest. They saw in it a token of God's glory and favor, and they raised a universal shout of praise and adoration and fell on their faces as if in the immediate presence of Jehovah.

But soon afterward a sudden and terrible calamity fell upon the family of the high priest. At the hour of worship, as the prayers and praise of the people were ascending to God, two of the sons of Aaron took each his censer and burned fragrant incense thereon, to rise as a sweet odor before the Lord. But they transgressed His command by the use of "strange fire." For burning the incense they took common instead of the sacred fire which God Himself had kindled, and which He had commanded to be used for this purpose. For this sin a fire went out from the Lord and devoured them in the sight of the people.

Next to Moses and Aaron, Nadab and Abihu had stood highest in Israel. They had been especially honored by the Lord, having been permitted with the seventy elders to behold His glory in the mount. But their transgression was not therefore to be excused or lightly regarded. All this rendered their sin more grievous. Because men have received great light, because they have, like the princes of Israel, ascended to the mount, and been privileged to have communion with God, and to dwell in the light of His glory, let them not flatter themselves that they can afterward sin with impunity, that because they have been thus honored, God will not be strict to punish their iniquity. This is a fatal deception. The great light and privileges bestowed require returns of virtue and holiness corresponding to the light given. Anything short of this, God cannot accept. Great blessings or privileges should never lull to security or carelessness. They should never give license to sin or cause the recipients to feel that God will not be exact with them. All the advantages which God has given are His means to throw ardor into the spirit, zeal into effort, and vigor into the carrying out of His holy will.

Nadab and Abihu had not in their youth been trained to habits of self-control. The father's yielding disposition, his lack of firmness for right, had led him to neglect the discipline of his children. His sons had been permitted to follow inclination. Habits of self-indulgence, long cherished, obtained a hold upon them which even the responsibility of the most sacred office had not power to break. They had not been taught to respect the authority of their father, and they did not realize the necessity of exact obedience to the requirements of God. Aaron's mistaken indulgence of his sons prepared them to become the subjects of the divine judgments.

God designed to teach the people that they must approach Him with reverence and awe, and in His own appointed manner. He cannot accept partial obedience. It was not enough that in this solemn season of worship nearly everything was done as He had directed. God has pronounced a curse upon those who depart from His commandments, and put no difference between common and holy things. He declares by the prophet: "Woe unto them that call evil good, and good evil; that put darkness for light, and light for darkness! . . . Woe unto them that are wise in their own eyes, and prudent in their own sight! . . . which justify the wicked for reward, and take away the righteousness of the righteous from him! . . . They have cast away the law of the Lord of hosts, and despised the word of the Holy One of Israel." Isaiah 5:20-24. Let no one deceive himself with the belief that a part of God's commandments are nonessential, or that He will accept a substitute for that which He has required. Said the prophet Jeremiah, "Who is he that saith, and it cometh to pass, when the Lord commandeth it not?" Lamentations 3:37. God has placed in His word no command which men may obey or disobey at will and not suffer the consequences. If men choose any other path than that of strict obedience, they will find that "the end thereof are the ways of death." Proverbs 14:12.

"Moses said unto Aaron, and unto Eleazar and unto Ithamar, his sons, Uncover not your heads, neither rend your clothes; lest ye die, . . . for the anointing oil of the Lord is upon you." The great leader reminded his brother of the words of God, "I will be sanctified in them that come nigh Me, and before all the people I will be glorified." Aaron was silent. The death of his sons, cut down without warning, in so terrible a sin—a sin which he now saw to be the result of his own neglect of duty—wrung the father's heart with anguish, but he gave his feelings no expression. By no manifestation of grief must he seem to sympathize with sin. The congregation must not be led to murmur against God.

The Lord would teach His people to acknowledge the justice of His corrections, that others may fear. There were those in Israel whom the warning of this terrible judgment might save from presuming upon God's forbearance until they, too, should seal their own destiny. The divine rebuke is upon that false sympathy for the sinner which endeavors to excuse his sin. It is the effect of sin to deaden the moral perceptions, so that the wrongdoer does not realize the enormity of transgression, and without the convicting power of the Holy Spirit he remains in partial blindness to his sin. It is the duty of Christ's servants to show these erring ones their peril. Those who destroy the effect of the warning by blinding the eyes of sinners to the real character and results of sin often flatter themselves that they thus give evidence of their charity; but they are working directly to oppose and hinder the work of God's Holy Spirit; they are lulling the sinner to rest on the brink of destruction; they are making themselves partakers in his guilt and incurring a fearful responsibility for his impenitence. Many, many, have gone down to ruin as the result of this false and deceptive sympathy.

Nadab and Abihu would never have committed that fatal sin had they not first become partially intoxicated by the free use of wine. They understood that the most careful and solemn preparation was necessary before presenting themselves in the sanctuary, where the divine Presence was manifested; but by intemperance they were disqualified for their holy office. Their minds became confused and their moral perceptions dulled so that they could not discern the difference between the sacred and the common. To Aaron and his surviving sons was given the warning: "Do not drink wine nor strong drink, thou, nor thy sons with thee, when ye go into the tabernacle of the congregation, lest ye die: it shall be a statute forever throughout your generations: and that ye may put difference between holy and unholy, and between unclean and clean; and that ye may teach the children of Israel all the statutes which the Lord hath spoken." The use of spirituous liquors has the effect to weaken the body, confuse the mind, and debase the morals. It prevents men from realizing the sacredness of holy things or the binding force of God's requirements. All who occupied positions of sacred responsibility were to be men of strict temperance, that their minds might be clear to discriminate between right and wrong, that they might possess firmness of principle, and wisdom to administer justice and to show mercy.

The same obligation rests upon every follower of Christ. The apostle Peter declares, "Ye are a chosen generation, a royal priesthood, an holy nation, a peculiar people. 1 Peter 2:9. We are required by God to preserve every power in the best possible condition, that we may render acceptable service to our Creator. When intoxicants are used, the same effects will follow as in the case of those priests of Israel. The conscience will lose its sensibility to sin, and a process of hardening to iniquity will most certainly take place, till the common and the sacred will lose all difference of significance. How can we then meet the standard of the divine requirements?" "Know ye not that your body is the temple of the Holy Ghost which is in you, which ye have of God, and ye are not your own? For ye are bought with a price: therefore glorify God in your body, and in your spirit, which are Gods." 1 Corinthians 6:19, 20. "Whether therefore ye eat, or drink, or whatsoever ye do, do all to the glory of God." 1 Corinthians 10:31. To the church of Christ in all ages is addressed the solemn and fearful warning, "If any man defile the temple of God, him shall God destroy; for the temple of God is holy, which temple ye are." 1 Corinthians 3:17.

The Law and the Covenants

Adam and Eve, at their creation, had a knowledge of the law of God; they were acquainted with its claims upon them; its precepts were written upon their hearts. When man fell by transgression the law was not changed, but a remedial system was established to bring him back to obedience. The promise of a Saviour was given, and sacrificial offerings pointing forward to the death of Christ as the great sin offering were established. But had the law of God never been transgressed, there would have been no death, and no need of a Saviour; consequently there would have been no need of sacrifices.

Adam taught his descendants the law of God, and it was handed down from father to son through successive generations. But notwithstanding the gracious provision for man's redemption, there were few who accepted it and rendered obedience. By transgression the world became so vile that it was necessary to cleanse it by the Flood from its corruption. The law was preserved by Noah and his family, and Noah taught his descendants the Ten Commandments. As men again departed from God, the Lord chose Abraham, of whom He declared, "Abraham obeyed My voice, and kept My charge, My commandments, My statutes, and My laws." Genesis 26:5. To him was given the rite of circumcision, which was a sign that those who received it were devoted to the service of God—a pledge that they would remain separate from idolatry, and would obey the law of God. The failure of Abraham's descendants to keep this pledge, as shown in their disposition to form alliances with the heathen and adopt their practices, was the cause of their sojourn and bondage in Egypt. But in their intercourse with idolaters, and their forced submission to the Egyptians, the divine precepts became still further corrupted with the vile and cruel teachings of heathenism. Therefore when the Lord brought them forth from Egypt, He came down upon Sinai, enshrouded in glory and surrounded by His angels, and in awful majesty spoke His law in the hearing of all the people.

He did not even then trust His precepts to the memory of a people who were prone to forget His requirements, but wrote them upon tables of stone. He would remove from Israel all possibility of mingling heathen traditions with His holy precepts, or of confounding His requirements with human ordinances or customs. But He did not stop with giving them the precepts of the Decalogue. The people had shown themselves so easily led astray that He would leave no door of temptation unguarded. Moses was commanded to write, as God should bid him, judgments and laws giving minute instruction as to what was required. These directions relating to the duty of the people to God, to one another, and to the stranger were only the principles of the Ten Commandments amplified and given in a specific manner, that none need err. They were designed to guard the sacredness of the ten precepts engraved on the tables of stone.

If man had kept the law of God, as given to Adam after his fall, preserved by Noah, and observed by Abraham, there would have been no necessity for the ordinance of circumcision. And if the descendants of Abraham had kept the covenant, of which circumcision was a sign, they would never have been seduced into idolatry, nor would it have been necessary for them to suffer a life of bondage in Egypt; they would have kept God's law in mind, and there would have been no necessity for it to be proclaimed from Sinai or engraved upon the tables of stone. And had the people practiced the principles of the Ten Commandments, there would have been no need of the additional directions given to Moses.

The sacrificial system, committed to Adam, was also perverted by his descendants. Superstition, idolatry, cruelty, and licentiousness corrupted the simple and significant service that God had appointed. Through long intercourse with idolaters the people of Israel had mingled many heathen customs with their worship; therefore the Lord gave them at Sinai definite instruction concerning the sacrificial service. After the completion of the tabernacle He communicated with Moses from the cloud of glory above the mercy seat, and gave him full directions concerning the system of offerings and the forms of worship to be maintained in the sanctuary. The ceremonial law was thus given to Moses, and by him written in a book. But the law of Ten Commandments spoken from Sinai had been written by God Himself on the tables of stone, and was sacredly preserved in the ark.

There are many who try to blend these two systems, using the texts that speak of the ceremonial law to prove that the moral law has been abolished; but this is a perversion of the Scriptures. The distinction between the two systems is broad and clear. The ceremonial system was made up of symbols pointing to Christ, to His sacrifice and His priesthood. This ritual law, with its sacrifices and ordinances, was to be performed by the Hebrews until type met antitype in the death of Christ, the Lamb of God that taketh away the sin of the world. Then all the sacrificial offerings were to cease. It is this law that Christ "took . . . out of the way, nailing it to His cross." Colossians 2:14. But concerning the law of Ten Commandments the psalmist declares, "Forever, O Lord, Thy word is settled in heaven." Psalm 119:89. And Christ Himself says, "Think not that I am come to destroy the law. . . . Verily I say unto you"—making the assertion as emphatic as possible—"Till heaven and earth pass, one jot or one tittle shall in no wise pass from the law, till all be fulfilled." Matthew 5:17, 18. Here He teaches, not merely what the claims of God's law had been, and were then, but that these claims should hold as long as the heavens and the earth remain. The law of God is as immutable as His throne. It will maintain its claims upon mankind in all ages.

Concerning the law proclaimed from Sinai, Nehemiah says, "Thou camest down also upon Mount Sinai, and spakest with them from heaven, and gavest them right judgments, and true laws, good statutes and commandments." Nehemiah 9:13. And Paul, "the apostle to the Gentiles," declares, "The law is holy, and the commandment holy, and just, and good." Romans 7:12. This can be no other than the Decalogue; for it is the law that says, "Thou shalt not covet." Verse 7.

While the Saviour's death brought to an end the law of types and shadows, it did not in the least detract from the obligation of the moral law. On the contrary, the very fact that it was necessary for Christ to die in order to atone for the transgression of that law, proves it to be immutable.

Those who claim that Christ came to abrogate the law of God and to do away with the Old Testament, speak of the Jewish age as one of darkness, and represent the religion of the Hebrews as consisting of mere forms and ceremonies. But this is an error. All through the pages of scared history, where the dealings of God with His chosen people are recorded, there are burning traces of the great I Am. Never has He given to the sons of men more open manifestations of His power and glory than when He alone was acknowledged as Israel's ruler, and gave the law to His people. Here was a scepter swayed by no human hand; and the stately goings forth of Israel's invisible King were unspeakably grand and awful.

In all these revelations of the divine presence the glory of God was manifested through Christ. Not alone at the Saviour's advent, but through all the ages after the Fall and the promise of redemption, "God was in Christ, reconciling the world unto Himself." 2 Corinthians 5:19. Christ was the foundation and center of the sacrificial system in both the patriarchal and the Jewish age. Since the sin of our first parents there has been no direct communication between God and man. The Father has given the world into the hands of Christ, that through His mediatorial work He may redeem man and vindicate the authority and holiness of the law of God. All the communion between heaven and the fallen race has been through Christ. It was the Son of God that gave to our first parents the promise of redemption. It was He who revealed Himself to the patriarchs. Adam, Noah, Abraham, Isaac, Jacob, and Moses understood the gospel. They looked for salvation through man's Substitute and Surety. These holy men of old held communion with the Saviour who was to come to our world in human flesh; and some of them talked with Christ and heavenly angels face to face.

Christ was not only the leader of the Hebrews in the wilderness—the Angel in whom was the name of Jehovah, and who, veiled in the cloudy pillar, went before the host—but it was He who gave the law to Israel. Amid the awful glory of Sinai, Christ declared in the hearing of all the people the ten precepts of His Father's law. It was He who gave to Moses the law engraved upon the tables of stone.

It was Christ that spoke to His people through the prophets. The apostle Peter, writing to the Christian church, says that the prophets "prophesied of the grace that should come unto you: searching what, or what manner of time the Spirit of Christ which was in them did signify, when it testified beforehand the sufferings of Christ and the glory that should follow." 1 Peter 1:10, 11. It is the voice of Christ that speaks to us through the Old Testament. "The testimony of Jesus is the spirit of prophecy." Revelation 19:10.

In His teachings while personally among men Jesus directed the minds of the people to the Old Testament. He said to the Jews, "Ye search the Scriptures, because ye think that in them ye have eternal life; and these are they which bear witness of Me." John 5:39, R.V. At this time the books of the Old Testament were the only part of the Bible in existence. Again the Son of God declared, "They have Moses and the prophets; let them hear them." And He added, "If they hear not Moses and the prophets, neither will they be persuaded, though one rose from the dead." Luke 16:29, 31.

The ceremonial law was given by Christ. Even after it was no longer to be observed, Paul presented it before the Jews in its true position and value, showing its place in the plan of redemption and its relation to the work of Christ; and the great apostle pronounces this law glorious, worthy of its divine Originator. The solemn service of the sanctuary typified the grand truths that were to be revealed through successive generations. The cloud of incense ascending with the prayers of Israel represents His righteousness that alone can make the sinner's prayer acceptable to God; the bleeding victim on the altar of sacrifice testified of a Redeemer to come; and from the holy of holies the visible token of the divine Presence shone forth. Thus through age after age of darkness and apostasy faith was kept alive in the hearts of men until the time came for the advent of the promised Messiah.

Jesus was the light of His people—the Light of the world—before He came to earth in the form of humanity. The first gleam of light that pierced the gloom in which sin had wrapped the world, came from Christ. And from Him has come every ray of heaven's brightness that has fallen upon the inhabitants of the earth. In the plan of redemption Christ is the Alpha and the Omega—the First and the Last.

Since the Saviour shed His blood for the remission of sins, and ascended to heaven "to appear in the presence of God for us" (Hebrews 9:24), light has been streaming from the cross of Calvary and from the holy places of the sanctuary above. But the clearer light granted us should not cause us to despise that which in earlier times was received through the types pointing to the coming Saviour. The gospel of Christ sheds light upon the Jewish economy and gives significance to the ceremonial law. As new truths are revealed, and that which has been known from the beginning is brought into clearer light, the character and purposes of God are made manifest in His dealings with His chosen people. Every additional ray of light that we receive gives us a clearer understanding of the plan of redemption, which is the working out of the divine will in the salvation of man. We see new beauty and force in the inspired word, and we study its pages with a deeper and more absorbing interest.

The opinion is held by many that God placed a separating wall between the Hebrews and the outside world; that His care and love, withdrawn to a great extent from the rest of mankind, were centered upon Israel. But God did not design that His people should build up a wall of partition between themselves and their fellow men. The heart of Infinite Love was reaching out toward all the inhabitants of the earth. Though they had rejected Him, He was constantly seeking to reveal Himself to them and make them partakers of His love and grace. His blessing was granted to the chosen people, that they might bless others.

God called Abraham, and prospered and honored him; and the patriarch's fidelity was a light to the people in all the countries of his sojourn. Abraham did not shut himself away from the people around him. He maintained friendly relations with the kings of the surrounding nations, by some of whom he was treated with great respect; and his integrity and unselfishness, his valor and benevolence, were representing the character of God. In Mesopotamia, in Canaan, in Egypt, and even to the inhabitants of Sodom, the God of heaven was revealed through His representative.

So to the people of Egypt and of all the nations connected

with that powerful kingdom, God manifested Himself through Joseph. Why did the Lord choose to exalt Joseph so highly among the Egyptians? He might have provided some other way for the accomplishment of His purposes toward the children of Jacob; but He desired to make Joseph a light, and He placed him in the palace of the king, that the heavenly illumination might extend far and near. By his wisdom and justice, by the purity and benevolence of his daily life, by his devotion to the interests of the people—and that people a nation of idolaters—Joseph was a representative of Christ. In their benefactor, to whom all Egypt turned with gratitude and praise, that heathen people were to behold the love of their Creator and Redeemer. So in Moses also God placed a light beside the throne of the earth's greatest kingdom, that all who would, might learn of the true and living God. And all this light was given to the Egyptians before the hand of God was stretched out over them in judgments.

In the deliverance of Israel from Egypt a knowledge of the power of God spread far and wide. The warlike people of the stronghold of Jericho trembled. "As soon as we had heard these things," said Rahab, "our hearts did melt, neither did there remain any more courage in any man, because of you: for Jehovah your God, He is God in heaven above, and in earth beneath." Joshua 2:11. Centuries after the exodus the priests of the Philistines reminded their people of the plagues of Egypt, and warned them against resisting the God of Israel.

God called Israel, and blessed and exalted them, not that by obedience to His law they alone might receive His favor and become the exclusive recipients of His blessings, but in order to reveal Himself through them to all the inhabitants of the earth. It was for the accomplishment of this very purpose that He commanded them to keep themselves distinct from the idolatrous nations around them.

Idolatry and all the sins that followed in its train were abhorrent to God, and He commanded His people not to mingle with other nations, to "do after their works," and forget God. He forbade their marriage with idolaters, lest their hearts should be led away from Him. It was just as necessary then as it is now that God's people should be pure, "unspotted from the world." They must keep themselves free from its spirit, because it is opposed to truth and righteousness. But God did not intend that His people, in self-righteous exclusiveness, should shut themselves away from the world, so that they could have no influence upon it.

Like their Master, the followers of Christ in every age were to be the light of the world. The Saviour said, "A city that is set on an hill cannot be hid. Neither do men light a candle, and put it under a bushel, but on a candlestick; and it giveth light unto all that are in the house"—that is, in the world. And He adds, "Let your light so shine before men, that they may see your good works, and glorify your Father which is in heaven." Matthew 5:14-16. This is just what Enoch, and Noah, Abraham, Joseph, and Moses did. It is just what God designed that His people Israel should do.

It was their own evil heart of unbelief, controlled by Satan, that led them to hide their light, instead of shedding it upon surrounding peoples; it was that same bigoted spirit that caused them either to follow the iniquitous practices of the heathen or to shut themselves away in proud exclusiveness, as if God's love and care were over them alone.

As the Bible presents two laws, one changeless and eternal, the other provisional and temporary, so there are two covenants. The covenant of grace was first made with man in Eden, when after the Fall there was given a divine promise that the seed of the woman should bruise the serpent's head. To all men this covenant offered pardon and the assisting grace of God for future obedience through faith in Christ. It also promised them eternal life on condition of fidelity to God's law. Thus the patriarchs received the hope of salvation.

This same covenant was renewed to Abraham in the promise, "In thy seed shall all the nations of the earth be blessed." Genesis 22:18. This promise pointed to Christ. So Abraham understood it (see Galatians 3:8, 16), and he trusted in Christ for the forgiveness of sins. It was this faith that was accounted unto him for righteousness. The covenant with Abraham also maintained the authority of God's law. The Lord appeared unto Abraham, and said, "I am the Almighty God; walk before Me, and be thou perfect." Genesis 17:1. The testimony of God concerning His faithful servant was, "Abraham obeyed My voice, and kept My charge, My commandments, My statutes, and My laws." Genesis 26:5. And the Lord declared to him, "I will establish My covenant between Me and thee and thy seed after thee in their generations, for an everlasting covenant, to be a God unto thee and to thy seed after thee." Genesis 17:7.

Though this covenant was made with Adam and renewed to Abraham, it could not be ratified until the death of Christ. It had existed by the promise of God since the first intimation of redemption had been given; it had been accepted by faith; yet when ratified by Christ, it is called a new covenant. The law of God was the basis of this covenant, which was simply an arrangement for bringing men again into harmony with the divine will, placing them where they could obey God's law.

Another compact—called in Scripture the "old" covenant—was formed between God and Israel at Sinai, and was then ratified by the blood of a sacrifice. The Abrahamic covenant was ratified by the blood of Christ, and it is called the "second," or "new," covenant, because the blood by which it was sealed was shed after the blood of the first covenant. That the new covenant was valid in the days of Abraham is evident from the fact that it was then confirmed both by the promise and by the oath of God—the "two immutable things, in which it was impossible for God to lie." Hebrews 6:18.

But if the Abrahamic covenant contained the promise of redemption, why was another covenant formed at Sinai? In their bondage the people had to a great extent lost the knowledge of God and of the principles of the Abrahamic covenant. In delivering them from Egypt, God sought to reveal to them His power and His mercy, that they might be led to love and trust Him. He brought them down to the Red Sea—where, pursued by the Egyptians, escape seemed impossible—that they might realize their utter helplessness, their need of divine aid; and then He wrought deliverance for them. Thus they were filled with love and gratitude to God and with confidence in His power to help them. He had bound them to Himself as their deliverer from temporal bondage.

But there was a still greater truth to be impressed upon their minds. Living in the midst of idolatry and corruption, they had no true conception of the holiness of God, of the exceeding sinfulness of their own hearts, their utter inability, in themselves, to render obedience to God's law, and their need of a Saviour. All this they must be taught.

God brought them to Sinai; He manifested His glory; He gave them His law, with the promise of great blessings on condition of obedience: "If ye will obey My voice indeed, and keep My covenant, then . . . ye shall be unto Me a kingdom of priests, and an holy nation." Exodus 19:5, 6. The people did not realize the sinfulness of their own hearts, and that without Christ it was impossible for them to keep God's law; and they readily entered into covenant with God. Feeling that they were able to establish their own righteousness, they declared, "All that the Lord hath said will we do, and be obedient." Exodus 24:7. They had witnessed the proclamation of the law in awful majesty, and had trembled with terror before the mount; and yet only a few weeks passed before they broke their covenant with God, and bowed down to worship a graven image. They could not hope for the favor of God through a covenant which they had broken; and now, seeing their sinfulness and their need of pardon, they were brought to feel their need of the Saviour revealed in the Abrahamic covenant and shadowed forth in the sacrificial offerings. Now by faith and love they were bound to God as their deliverer from the bondage of sin. Now they were prepared to appreciate the blessings of the new covenant.

The terms of the "old covenant" were, Obey and live: "If a man do, he shall even live in them" (Ezekiel 20:11; Leviticus 18:5); but "cursed be he that confirmeth not all the words of this law to do them." Deuteronomy 27:26. The "new covenant" was established upon "better promises"—the promise of forgiveness of sins and of the grace of God to renew the heart and bring it into harmony with the principles of God's law. "This shall be the covenant that I will make with the house of Israel; After those days, saith the Lord, I will put my law in their inward parts, and write it in their hearts . . . . I will forgive their iniquity, and will remember their sin no more." Jeremiah 31:33, 34.

The same law that was engraved upon the tables of stone is written by the Holy Spirit upon the tables of the heart. Instead of going about to establish our own righteousness we accept the righteousness of Christ. His blood atones for our sins. His obedience is accepted for us. Then the heart renewed by the Holy Spirit will bring forth "the fruits of the Spirit." Through the grace of Christ we shall live in obedience to the law of God written upon our hearts. Having the Spirit of Christ, we shall walk even as He walked. Through the prophet He declared of Himself, "I delight to do Thy will, O My God: yea, Thy law is within My heart." Psalm 40:8. And when among men He said, "The Father hath not left Me alone; for I do always those things that please Him." John 8:29.

The apostle Paul clearly presents the relation between faith and the law under the new covenant. He says: "Being justified by faith, we have peace with God through our Lord Jesus Christ." "Do we then make void the law through faith? God forbid: yea, we establish the law." "For what the law could not do, in that it was weak through the flesh"—it could not justify man, because in his sinful nature he could not keep the law—"God sending His own Son in the likeness of sinful flesh, and for sin, condemned sin in the flesh: that the righteousness of the law might be fulfilled in us, who walk not after the flesh, but after the Spirit." Romans 5:1, 3:31, 8:3, 4.

God's work is the same in all time, although there are different degrees of development and different manifestations of His power, to meet the wants of men in the different ages. Beginning with the first gospel promise, and coming down through the patriarchal and Jewish ages, and even to the present time, there has been a gradual unfolding of the purposes of God in the plan of redemption. The Saviour typified in the rites and ceremonies of the Jewish law is the very same that is revealed in the gospel. The clouds that enveloped His divine form have rolled back; the mists and shades have disappeared; and Jesus, the world's Redeemer, stands revealed. He who proclaimed the law from Sinai, and delivered to Moses the precepts of the ritual law, is the same that spoke the Sermon on the Mount. The great principles of love to God, which He set forth as the foundation of the law and the prophets, are only a reiteration of what He had spoken through Moses to the Hebrew people: "Hear, O Israel: The Lord our God is one Lord: and thou shalt love the Lord thy God with all thine heart, and with all thy soul, and with all thy might." Deuteronomy 6:4, 5. "Thou shalt love thy neighbor as thyself." Leviticus 19:18. The teacher is the same in both dispensations. God's claims are the same. The principles of His government are the same. For all proceed from Him "with whom is no variableness, neither shadow of turning." James 1:17.

From Sinai to Kadesh

The building of the tabernacle was not begun for some time after Israel arrived at Sinai; and the sacred structure was first set up at the opening of the second year from the Exodus. This was followed by the consecration of the priests, the celebration of the Passover, the numbering of the people, and the completion of various arrangements essential to their civil or religious system, so that nearly a year was spent in the encampment at Sinai. Here their worship had taken a more definite form, the laws had been given for the government of the nation, and a more efficient organization had been effected preparatory to their entrance into the land of Canaan.

The government of Israel was characterized by the most thorough organization, wonderful alike for its completeness and its simplicity. The order so strikingly displayed in the perfection and arrangement of all God's created works was manifest in the Hebrew economy. God was the center of authority and government, the sovereign of Israel. Moses stood as their visible leader, by God's appointment, to administer the laws in His name. From the elders of the tribes a council of seventy was afterward chosen to assist Moses in the general affairs of the nation. Next came the priests, who consulted the Lord in the sanctuary. Chiefs, or princes, ruled over the tribes. Under these were "captains over thousands, and captains over hundreds, and captains over fifties, and captains over tens," and, lastly, officers who might be employed for special duties. Deuteronomy 1:15.

The Hebrew camp was arranged in exact order. It was separated into three great divisions, each having its appointed position in the encampment. In the center was the tabernacle, the abiding place of the invisible King. Around it were stationed the priests and Levites. Beyond these were encamped all the other tribes.

To the Levites was committed the charge of the tabernacle and all that pertained thereto, both in the camp and on the journey. When the camp set forward they were to strike the sacred tent; when a halting place was reached they were to set it up. No person of another tribe was allowed to come near, on pain of death. The Levites were separated into three divisions, the descendants of the three sons of Levi, and each was assigned its special position and work. In front of the tabernacle, and nearest to it, were the tents of Moses and Aaron. On the south were the Kohathites, whose duty it was to care for the ark and the other furniture; on the north Merarites, who were placed in charge of the pillars, sockets, boards, etc.; in the rear the Gershonites, to whom the care of the curtains and hangings was committed.

The position of each tribe also was specified. Each was to march and to encamp beside its own standard, as the Lord had commanded: "Every man of the children of Israel shall pitch by his own standard, with the ensign of their father's house: far off about the tabernacle of the congregation shall they pitch." "As they encamp, so shall they set forward, every man in his place by their standards." Numbers 2:2, 17. The mixed multitude that had accompanied Israel from Egypt were not permitted to occupy the same quarters with the tribes, but were to abide upon the outskirts of the camp; and their offspring were to be excluded from the community until the third generation. Deuteronomy 23:7, 8.

Scrupulous cleanliness as well as strict order throughout the encampment and its environs was enjoined. Through sanitary regulations were enforced. Every person who was unclean from any cause was forbidden to enter the camp. These measures were indispensable to the preservation of health among so vast a multitude; and it was necessary also that perfect order and purity be maintained, that Israel might enjoy the presence of a holy God. Thus He declared: "The Lord thy God walketh in the midst of thy camp, to deliver thee, and to give up thine enemies before thee; therefore shall thy camp he holy."

In all the journeyings of Israel, "the ark of the covenant of the Lord went before them, . . . to search out a resting place for them." Numbers 10:33. Borne by the sons of Kohath, the sacred chest containing God's holy law was to lead the van. Before it went Moses and Aaron; and the priests, bearing silver trumpets, were stationed near. These priests received directions from Moses, which they communicated to the people by the trumpets. It was the duty of the leaders of each company to give definite directions concerning all the movements to be made, as indicated by the trumpets. Whoever neglected to comply with the directions given was punished with death.

God is a God of order. Everything connected with heaven is in perfect order; subjection and thorough discipline mark the movements of the angelic host. Success can only attend order and harmonious action. God requires order and system in His work now no less than in the days of Israel. All who are working for Him are to labor intelligently, not in a careless, haphazard manner. He would have His work done with faith and exactness, that He may place the seal of His approval upon it.

God Himself directed the Israelites in all their travels. The place of their encampment was indicated by the descent of the pillar of cloud; and so long as they were to remain in camp, the cloud rested over the tabernacle. When they were to continue their journey it was lifted high above the sacred tent. A solemn invocation marked both the halt and the departure. "It came to pass, when the ark set forward, that Moses said, Rise up, Lord, and let Thine enemies be scattered; and let them that hate Thee flee before Thee. And when it rested, he said, Return, O Lord, unto the many thousands of Israel." Numbers 10:35, 36.

A distance of only eleven days' journey lay between Sinai and Kadesh, on the borders of Canaan; and it was with the prospect of speedily entering the goodly land that the hosts of Israel resumed their march when the cloud at last gave the signal for an onward movement. Jehovah had wrought wonders in bringing them from Egypt, and what blessings might they not expect now that they had formally covenanted to accept Him as their Sovereign, and had been acknowledged as the chosen people of the Most High?

Yet it was almost with reluctance that many left the place where they had so long encamped. They had come almost to regard it as their home. Within the shelter of those granite walls God had gathered His people, apart from all other nations, to repeat to them His holy law. They loved to look upon the sacred mount, on whose hoary peaks and barren ridges the divine glory had so often been displayed. The scene was so closely associated with the presence of God and holy angels that it seemed too sacred to be left thoughtlessly, or even gladly.

At the signal from the trumpeters, however, the entire camp set forward, the tabernacle borne in the midst, and each tribe in its appointed position, under its own standard. All eyes were turned anxiously to see in what direction the cloud would lead. As it moved toward the east, where were only mountain masses huddled together, black and desolate, a feeling of sadness and doubt arose in many hearts.

As they advanced, the way became more difficult. Their route lay through stony ravine and barren waste. All around them was the great wilderness—"a land of deserts and of pits," "a land of drought, and of the shadow of death," "a land that no man passed through, and where no man dwelt." Jeremiah 2:6. The rocky gorges, far and near, were thronged with men, women, and children, with beasts and wagons, and long lines of flocks and herds. Their progress was necessarily slow and toilsome; and the multitudes, after their long encampment, were not prepared to endure the perils and discomforts of the way.

After three days' journey open complaints were heard. These originated with the mixed multitude, many of whom were not fully united with Israel, and were continually watching for some cause of censure. The complainers were not pleased with the direction of the march, and they were continually finding fault with the way in which Moses was leading them, though they well knew that he, as well as they, was following the guiding cloud. Dissatisfaction is contagious, and it soon spread in the encampment.

Again they began to clamor for flesh to eat. Though abundantly supplied with manna, they were not satisfied. The Israelites, during their bondage in Egypt, had been compelled to subsist on the plainest and simplest food; but then keen appetite induced by privation and hard labor had made it palatable. Many of the Egyptians, however, who were now among them, had been accustomed to a luxurious diet; and these were the first to complain. At the giving of the manna, just before Israel reached Sinai, the Lord had granted them flesh in answer to their clamors; but it was furnished them for only one day.

God might as easily have provided them with flesh as with manna, but a restriction was placed upon them for their good. It was His purpose to supply them with food better suited to their wants than the feverish diet to which many had become accustomed in Egypt. The perverted appetite was to be brought into a more healthy state, that they might enjoy the food originally provided for man—the fruits of the earth, which God gave to Adam and Eve in Eden. It was for this reason that the Israelites had been deprived, in a great measure, of animal food.

Satan tempted them to regard this restriction as unjust and cruel. He caused them to lust after forbidden things, because he saw that the unrestrained indulgence of appetite would tend to produce sensuality, and by this means the people could be more easily brought under his control. The author of disease and misery will assail men where he can have the greatest success. Through temptations addressed to the appetite he has, to a large extent, led men into sin from the time when he induced Eve to eat of the forbidden fruit. It was by this same means that he led Israel to murmur against God. Intemperance in eating and drinking, leading as it does to the indulgence of the lower passions, prepares the way for men to disregard all moral obligations. When assailed by temptation, they have little power of resistance.

God brought the Israelites from Egypt, that He might establish them in the land of Canaan, a pure, holy, and happy people. In the accomplishment of this object He subjected them to a course of discipline, both for their own good and for the good of their posterity. Had they been willing to deny appetite, in obedience to His wise restrictions, feebleness and disease would have been unknown among them. Their descendants would have possessed both physical and mental strength. They would have had clear perceptions of truth and duty, keen discrimination, and sound judgment. But their unwillingness to submit to the restrictions and requirements of God, prevented them, to a great extent, from reaching the high standard which He desired them to attain, and from receiving the blessings which He was ready to bestow upon them.

Says the psalmist: "They tempted God in their heart by asking meat for their lust. Yea, they spake against God; they said, Can God furnish a table in the wilderness? Behold, He smote the rock, that the waters gushed out, and the streams overflowed; can He give bread also? can He provide flesh for His people? Therefore the Lord heard this, and was wroth." Psalm 78:18-21. Murmuring and tumults had been frequent during the journey from the Red Sea to Sinai, but in pity for their ignorance and blindness God had not then visited the sin with judgments. But since that time He had revealed Himself to them at Horeb. They had received great light, as they had been witnesses to the majesty, the power, and the mercy of God; and their unbelief and discontent incurred the greater guilt. Furthermore, they had covenanted to accept Jehovah as their king and to obey His authority. Their murmuring was now rebellion, and as such it must receive prompt and signal punishment, if Israel was to be preserved from anarchy and ruin. "The fire of Jehovah burnt among them, and consumed them that were in the uttermost parts of the camp." The most guilty of the complainers were slain by lightning from the cloud.

The people in terror besought Moses to entreat the Lord for them. He did so, and the fire was quenched. In memory of this judgment he called the name of the place Taberah, "a burning."

But the evil was soon worse than before. Instead of leading the survivors to humiliation and repentance, this fearful judgment seemed only to increase their murmurings. In all directions the people were gathered at the door of their tents, weeping and lamenting. "The mixed multitude that was among them fell a lusting: and the children of Israel also wept again, and said, Who shall give us flesh to eat? We remember the fish, which we did eat in Egypt freely; the cucumbers, and the melons, and the leeks, and the onions, and the garlic: but now our soul is dried away: there is nothing at all, beside this manna, before our eyes." Thus they manifested their discontent with the food provided for them by their Creator. Yet they had constant evidence that it was adapted to their wants; for notwithstanding the hardships they endured, there was not a feeble one in all their tribes.

The heart of Moses sank. He had pleaded that Israel should not be destroyed, even though his own posterity might then become a great nation. In his love for them he had prayed that his name might be blotted from the book of life rather than that they should be left to perish. He had imperiled all for them, and this was their response. All their hardships, even their imaginary sufferings, they charged upon him; and their wicked murmurings made doubly heavy the burden of care and responsibility under which he staggered. In his distress he was tempted even to distrust God. His prayer was almost a complaint. "Wherefore hast Thou afflicted Thy servant? and wherefore have I not found favor in Thy sight, that Thou layest the burden of all this people upon me? . . . Whence should I have flesh to give unto all this people? for they weep unto me, saying, Give us flesh, that we may eat. I am not able to bear all this people alone, because it is too heavy for me."

The Lord hearkened to his prayer, and directed him to summon seventy men of the elders of Israel—men not only advanced in years, but possessing dignity, sound judgment, and experience. "And bring them unto the tabernacle of the congregation," He said, "that they may stand there with thee. And I will come down and talk with thee there: and I will take of the spirit which is upon thee, and will put it upon them; and they shall bear the burden of the people with thee, that thou bear it not thyself alone."

The Lord permitted Moses to choose for himself the most faithful and efficient men to share the responsibility with him. Their influence would assist in holding in check the violence of the people, and quelling insurrection; yet serious evils would eventually result from their promotion. They would never have been chosen had Moses manifested faith corresponding to the evidences he had witnessed of God's power and goodness. But he had magnified his own burdens and services, almost losing sight of the fact that he was only the instrument by which God had wrought. He was not excusable in indulging, in the slightest degree, the spirit of murmuring that was the curse of Israel. Had he relied fully upon God, the Lord would have guided him continually and would have given him strength for every emergency.

Moses was directed to prepare the people for what God was about to do for them. "Sanctify yourselves against tomorrow, and ye shall eat flesh: for ye have wept in the ears of the Lord, saying, Who shall give us flesh to eat? for it was well with us in Egypt: therefore the Lord will give you flesh, and ye shall eat. Ye shall not eat one day, nor two days, nor five days, neither ten days, nor twenty days; but even a whole month, until it come out at your nostrils, and it be loathsome unto

you: because that ye have despised the Lord which is among you, and have wept before Him, saying, Why came we forth out of Egypt?"

"The people, among whom I am," exclaimed Moses, "are six hundred thousand footmen; and Thou has said, I will give them flesh, that they may eat a whole month. Shall the flocks and the herds be slain for them, to suffice them? or shall all the fish of the sea be gathered together for them?"

He was reproved for his distrust: "Is the Lord's hand waxed short? thou shalt see now whether My word shall come to pass unto thee or not."

Moses repeated to the congregation the words of the Lord, and announced the appointment of the seventy elders. The great leader's charge to these chosen men might well serve as a model of judicial integrity for the judges and legislators of modern times: "Hear the causes between your brethren, and judge righteously between every man and his brother, and the stranger that is with him. Ye shall not respect persons in judgment; but ye shall hear the small as well as the great; ye shall not be afraid of the face of man; for the judgment is God's." Deuteronomy 1:16, 17.

Moses now summoned the seventy to the tabernacle. "And the Lord came down in a cloud, and spake unto him, and took of the spirit that was upon him, and gave it unto the seventy elders: and it came to pass, that, when the spirit rested upon them, they prophesied, and did not cease." Like the disciples on the Day of Pentecost, they were endued with "power from on high." It pleased the Lord thus to prepare them for their work, and to honor them in the presence of the congregation, that confidence might be established in them as men divinely chosen to unite with Moses in the government of Israel.

Again evidence was given of the lofty, unselfish spirit of the great leader. Two of the seventy, humbly counting themselves unworthy of so responsible a position, had not joined their brethren at the tabernacle; but the Spirit of God came upon them where they were, and they, too, exercised the prophetic gift. On being informed of this, Joshua desired to check such irregularity, fearing that it might tend to division. Jealous for the honor of his master, "My lord Moses," he said, "forbid them." The answer was, "Enviest thou for my sake? would God that all the Lord's people were prophets, and that the Lord would put His Spirit upon them."

A strong wind blowing from the sea now brought flocks of quails, "about a day's journey on this side, and a day's journey on the other side, round about the camp, and about two cubits above the face of the earth." Numbers 11:31, R.V. All that day and night, and the following day, the people labored in gathering the food miraculously provided. Immense quantities were secured. "He that gathered least gathered ten homers." All that was not needed for present use was preserved by drying, so that the supply, as promised, was sufficient for a whole month.

God gave the people that which was not for their highest good, because they persisted in desiring it; they would not be satisfied with those things that would prove a benefit to them.

Their rebellious desires were gratified, but they were left to suffer the result. They feasted without restraint, and their excesses were speedily punished. "The Lord smote the people with a very great plague." Large numbers were cut down by burning fevers, while the most guilty among them were smitten as soon as they tasted the food for which they had lusted.

At Hazeroth, the next encampment after leaving Taberah, a still more bitter trial awaited Moses. Aaron and Miriam had occupied a position of high honor and leadership in Israel. Both were endowed with the prophetic gift, and both had been divinely associated with Moses in the deliverance of the Hebrews. "I sent before thee Moses, Aaron, and Miriam" (Micah 6:4), are the words of the Lord by the prophet Micah. Miriam's force of character had been early displayed when as a child she watched beside the Nile the little basket in which was hidden the infant Moses. Her self-control and tact God had made instrumental in preserving the deliverer of His people. Richly endowed with the gifts of poetry and music, Miriam had led the women of Israel in song and dance on the shore of the Red Sea. In the affections of the people and the honor of Heaven she stood second only to Moses and Aaron. But the same evil that first brought discord in heaven sprang up in the heart of this woman of Israel, and she did not fail to find a sympathizer in her dissatisfaction.

In the appointment of the seventy elders Miriam and Aaron had not been consulted, and their jealousy was excited against Moses. At the time of Jethro's visit, while the Israelites were on the way to Sinai, the ready acceptance by Moses of the counsel of his father-in-law had aroused in Aaron and Miriam a fear that his influence with the great leader exceeded theirs. In the organization of the council of elders they felt that their position and authority had been ignored. Miriam and Aaron had never known the weight of care and responsibility which had rested upon Moses; yet because they had been chosen to aid him they regarded themselves as sharing equally with him the burden of leadership, and they regarded the appointment of further assistants as uncalled for.

Moses felt the importance of the great work committed to him as no other man had ever felt it. He realized his own weakness, and he made God his counselor. Aaron esteemed himself more highly, and trusted less in God. He had failed when entrusted with responsibility, giving evidence of the weakness of his character by his base compliance in the matter of the idolatrous worship at Sinai. But Miriam and Aaron, blinded by jealousy and ambition, lost sight of this. Aaron had been highly honored by God in the appointment of his family to the sacred office of the priesthood; yet even this now added to the desire for self-exaltation. "And they said, Hath the Lord indeed spoken only by Moses? hath He not spoken also by us?" Regarding themselves as equally favored by God, they felt that they were entitled to the same position and authority.

Yielding to the spirit of dissatisfaction, Miriam found cause of complaint in events that God had especially overruled. The marriage of Moses had been displeasing to her. That he should choose a woman of another nation, instead of taking a wife from among the Hebrews, was an offense to her family and national pride. Zipporah was treated with ill-disguised contempt.

Though called a "Cushite woman" (Numbers 12:1, R.V.), the wife of Moses was a Midianite, and thus a descendant of Abraham. In personal appearance she differed from the Hebrews in being of a somewhat darker complexion. Though not an Israelite, Zipporah was a worshiper of the true God. She was of a timid, retiring disposition, gentle and affectionate, and greatly distressed at the sight of suffering; and it was for this reason that Moses, when on the way to Egypt, had consented to her return to Midian.

He desired to spare her the pain of witnessing the judgments that were to fall on the Egyptians.

When Zipporah rejoined her husband in the wilderness, she saw that his burdens were wearing away his strength, and she made known her fears to Jethro, who suggested measures for his relief. Here was the chief reason for Miriam's antipathy to Zipporah. Smarting under the supposed neglect shown to herself and Aaron, she regarded the wife to Moses as the cause, concluding that her influence had prevented him from taking them into his counsels as formerly. Had Aaron stood up firmly for the right, he might have checked the evil; but instead of showing Miriam the sinfulness of her conduct, he sympathized with her, listened to her words of complaint, and thus came to share her jealousy.

Their accusations were borne by Moses in uncomplaining silence. It was the experience gained during the years of toil and waiting in Midian—the spirit of humility and long-suffering there developed—that prepared Moses to meet with patience the unbelief and murmuring of the people and the pride and envy of those who should have been his unswerving helpers. Moses "was very meek, above all he men which were upon the face of the earth," and this is why he was granted divine wisdom and guidance above all others. Says the Scripture, "The meek will He guide in judgment: and the meek will He teach His way." Psalm 25:9. The meek are guided by the Lord, because they are teachable, willing to be instructed. They have a sincere desire to know and to do the will of God. The Saviour's promise is, "If any man will do His will, he shall know of the doctrine." John 7:17. And He declares by the apostle James, "If any of you lack wisdom, let him ask of God, that giveth to all men liberally, and upbraideth not; and it shall be given him." James 1:5. But His promise is only to those who are willing to follow the Lord wholly. God does not force the will of any; hence He cannot lead those who are too proud to be taught, who are bent upon having their own way. Of the double-minded man—he who seeks to follow his own will, while professing to do the will of God—it is written, "Let not that man think that he shall receive anything of the Lord." James 1:7.

God had chosen Moses, and had put His Spirit upon him; and Miriam and Aaron, by their murmurings, were guilty of disloyalty, not only to their appointed leader, but to God

Himself. The seditious whisperers were summoned to the tabernacle, and brought face to face with Moses. "And Jehovah came down in the pillar of the cloud, and stood in the door of the tabernacle, and called Aaron and Miriam." Their claim to the prophetic gift was not denied; God might have spoken to them in visions and dreams. But to Moses, whom the Lord Himself declared "faithful in all Mine house," a nearer communion had been granted. With him God spake mouth to mouth. "Wherefore then were ye not afraid to speak against My servant Moses? And the anger of the Lord was kindled against them; and He departed." The cloud disappeared from the tabernacle in token of God's displeasure, and Miriam was smitten. She "became leprous, white as snow." Aaron was spared, but he was severely rebuked in Miriam's punishment. Now, their pride humbled in the dust, Aaron confessed their sin, and entreated that his sister might not be left to perish by that loathsome and deadly scourge. In answer to the prayers of Moses the leprosy was cleansed. Miriam was, however, shut out of the camp for seven days. Not until she was banished from the encampment did the symbol of God's favor again rest upon the tabernacle. In respect for her high position, and in grief at the blow that had fallen upon her, the whole company abode in Hazeroth, awaiting her return.

This manifestation of the Lord's displeasure was designed to be a warning to all Israel, to check the growing spirit of discontent and insubordination. If Miriam's envy and dissatisfaction had not been signally rebuked, it would have resulted in great evil. Envy is one of the most satanic traits that can exist in the human heart, and it is one of the most baleful in its effects. Says the wise man, "Wrath is cruel, and anger is outrageous; but who is able to stand before envy?" Proverbs 27:4. It was envy that first caused discord in heaven, and its indulgence has wrought untold evil among men. "Where envying and strife is, there is confusion and every evil work." James 3:16.

It should not be regarded as a light thing to speak evil of others or to make ourselves judges of their motives or actions. "He that speaketh evil of his brother, and judgeth his brother, speaketh evil of the law, and judgeth the law: but if thou judge the law, thou art not a doer of the law, but a judge." James 4:11. There is but one judge—He "who both will bring to light the hidden things of darkness, and will make manifest the counsels of the hearts." 1 Corinthians 4:5. And whoever takes it upon himself to judge and condemn his fellow men is usurping the prerogative of the Creator.

The Bible specially teaches us to beware of lightly bringing accusation against those whom God has called to act as His ambassadors. The apostle Peter, describing a class who are abandoned sinners, says, "Presumptuous are they, self-willed, they are not afraid to speak evil of dignities. Whereas angels, which are greater in power and might, bring not railing accusation against them before the Lord." 2 Peter 2:10, 11. And Paul, in his instruction for those who are placed over the church, says, "Against an elder receive not an accusation, but before two or three witnesses." 1 Timothy 5:19. He who has placed upon men the heavy responsibility of leaders and teachers of His people will hold the people accountable for the manner in which they treat His servants. We are to honor those whom God has honored. The judgment visited upon Miriam should be a rebuke to all who yield to jealousy, and murmur against those upon whom God lays the burden of His work.

The Twelve Spies

Eleven days after leaving Mount Horeb the Hebrew host encamped at Kadesh, in the wilderness of Paran, which was not far from the borders of the Promised Land. Here it was proposed by the people that spies be sent up to survey the country. The matter was presented before the Lord by Moses, and permission was granted, with the direction that one of the rulers of each tribe should be selected for this purpose. The men were chosen as had been directed, and Moses bade them go and see the country, what it was, its situation and natural advantages; and the people that dwelt therein, whether they were strong or weak, few or many; also to observe the nature of the soil and its productiveness and to bring of the fruit of the land.

They went, and surveyed the whole land, entering at the southern border and proceeding to the northern extremity. They returned after an absence of forty days. The people of Israel were cherishing high hopes and were waiting in eager expectancy. The news of the spies' return was carried from tribe to tribe and was hailed with rejoicing. The people rushed out to meet the messengers, who had safely escaped the dangers of their perilous undertaking. The spies brought specimens of the fruit, showing the fertility of the soil. It was in the time of ripe grapes, and they brought a cluster of grapes so large that it was carried between two men. They also brought of the figs and pomegranates which grew there in abundance.

The people rejoiced that they were to come into possession of so goodly a land, and they listened intently as the report was brought to Moses, that not a word should escape them. "We came unto the land whither thou sentest us," the spies began, "and surely it floweth with milk and honey; and this is the fruit of it." The people were enthusiastic; they would eagerly obey the voice of the Lord, and go up at once to possess the land. But after describing the beauty and fertility of the land, all but two of the spies enlarged upon the difficulties and dangers that lay before the Israelites should they undertake the conquest of Canaan. They enumerated the powerful nations located in various parts of the country, and said that the cities were walled and very great, and the people who dwelt therein were strong, and it would be impossible to conquer them. They also stated that they had seen giants, the sons of Anak, there, and it was useless to think of possessing the land.

Now the scene changed. Hope and courage gave place to

cowardly despair, as the spies uttered the sentiments of their unbelieving hearts, which were filled with discouragement prompted by Satan. Their unbelief cast a gloomy shadow over the congregation, and the mighty power of God, so often manifested in behalf of the chosen nation, was forgotten. The people did not wait to reflect; they did not reason that He who had brought them thus far would certainly give them the land; they did not call to mind how wonderfully God had delivered them from their oppressors, cutting a path through the sea and destroying the pursuing hosts of Pharaoh. They left God out of the question, and acted as though they must depend solely on the power of arms.

In their unbelief they limited the power of God and distrusted the hand that had hitherto safely guided them. And they repeated their former error of murmuring against Moses and Aaron. "This, then, is the end of our high hopes," they said. "This is the land we have traveled all the way from Egypt to possess." They accused their leaders of deceiving the people and bringing trouble upon Israel.

The people were desperate in their disappointment and despair. A wail of agony arose and mingled with the confused murmur of voices. Caleb comprehended the situation, and, bold to stand in defense of the word of God, he did all in his power to counteract the evil influence of his unfaithful associates. For an instant the people were stilled to listen to his words of hope and courage respecting the goodly land. He did not contradict what had already been said; the walls were high and the Canaanites strong. But God had promised the land to Israel. "Let us go up at once and possess it," urged Caleb; "for we are well able to overcome it."

But the ten, interrupting him, pictured the obstacles in darker colors than at first. "We be not able to go up against the people," they declared; "for they are stronger than we. . . . All the people that we saw in it are men of a great stature. And there we saw the giants, the sons of Anak, which come of the giants: and we were in our own sight as grasshoppers, and so we were in their sight."

These men, having entered upon a wrong course, stubbornly set themselves against Caleb and Joshua, against Moses, and against God. Every advance step rendered them the more determined. They were resolved to discourage all effort to gain possession of Canaan. They distorted the truth in order to sustain their baleful influence. It "is a land that eateth up the inhabitants thereof," they said. This was not only an evil report, but it was also a lying one. It was inconsistent with itself. The spies had declared the country to be fruitful and prosperous, and the people of giant stature, all of which would be impossible if the climate were so unhealthful that the land could be said to "eat up the inhabitants." But when men yield their hearts to unbelief they place themselves under the control of Satan, and none can tell to what lengths he will lead them.

"And all the congregation lifted up their voice, and cried; and the people wept that night." Revolt and open mutiny quickly followed; for Satan had full sway, and the people seemed bereft of reason. They cursed Moses and Aaron, forgetting that God hearkened to their wicked speeches, and that, enshrouded in the cloudy pillar, the Angel of His presence was witnessing their terrible outburst of wrath. In bitterness they cried out, "Would God that we had died in the land of Egypt! or would God we had died in this wilderness!" Then their feelings rose against God: "Wherefore hath the Lord brought us unto this land, to fall by the sword, that our wives and our children should be a prey? were it not better for us to return into Egypt? And they said one to another, Let us make a captain, and let us return into Egypt." Thus they accused not only Moses, but God Himself, of deception, in promising them a land which they were not able to possess. And they went so far as to appoint a captain to lead them back to the land of their suffering and bondage, from which they had been delivered by the strong arm of Omnipotence.

In humiliation and distress "Moses and Aaron fell on their faces before all the assembly of the congregation of the children of Israel," not knowing what to do to turn them from their rash and passionate purpose. Caleb and Joshua attempted to quiet the tumult. With their garments rent in token of grief and indignation, they rushed in among the people, and their ringing voices were heard above the tempest of lamentation and rebellious grief: "The land, which we passed through to search it, is an exceeding good land. If the Lord delight in us, then He will bring us into this land, and give it us; a land which floweth with milk and honey. Only rebel not ye against the Lord, neither fear ye the people of the land; for they are bread for us: their defense is departed from them, and the Lord is with us: fear them not."

The Canaanites had filled up the measure of their iniquity, and the Lord would no longer bear with them. His protection being removed, they would be an easy prey. By the covenant of God the land was ensured to Israel. But the false report of the unfaithful spies was accepted, and through it the whole congregation were deluded. The traitors had done their work. If only the two men had brought the evil report, and all the ten had encouraged them to possess the land in the name of the Lord, they would still have taken the advice of the two in preference to the ten, because of their wicked unbelief. But there were only two advocating the right, while ten were on the side of rebellion.

The unfaithful spies were loud in denunciation of Caleb and Joshua, and the cry was raised to stone them. The insane mob seized missiles with which to slay those faithful men. They rushed forward with yells of madness, when suddenly the stones dropped from their hands, a hush fell upon them, and they shook with fear. God had interposed to check their murderous design. The glory of His presence, like a flaming light, illuminated the tabernacle. All the people beheld the signal of the Lord. A mightier one than they had revealed Himself, and none dared continue their resistance. The spies who brought the evil report crouched terror-stricken, and with bated breath sought their tents.

Moses now arose and entered the tabernacle. The Lord

declared to him, "I will smite them with the pestilence, and disinherit them, and will make of thee a greater nation." But again Moses pleaded for his people. He could not consent to have them destroyed, and he himself made a mightier nation. Appealing to the mercy of God, he said: "I beseech Thee, let the power of my Lord be great according as Thou hast spoken, saying, The Lord is long-suffering, and of great mercy. . . . Pardon, I beseech Thee, the iniquity of this people according to the greatness of Thy mercy, and as Thou hast forgiven this people, from Egypt even until now."

The Lord promised to spare Israel from immediate destruction; but because of their unbelief and cowardice He could not manifest His power to subdue their enemies. Therefore in His mercy He bade them, as the only safe course, to turn back toward the Red Sea.

In their rebellion the people had exclaimed, "Would God we had died in this wilderness!" Now this prayer was to be granted. The Lord declared: "As ye have spoken in Mine ears, so will I do to you: your carcasses shall fall in this wilderness, and all that were numbered of you, according to your whole number, from twenty years old and upward. . . . But your little ones, which ye said should be a prey, them will I bring in, and they shall know the land which ye have despised." And of Caleb He said, "My servant Caleb, because he had another spirit with him, and hath followed Me fully, him will I bring into the land whereinto he went; and his seed shall possess it." As the spies had spent forty days in their journey, so the hosts of Israel were to wander in the wilderness forty years.

When Moses made known to the people the divine decision, their rage was changed to mourning. They knew that their punishment was just. The ten unfaithful spies, divinely smitten by the plague, perished before the eyes of all Israel; and in their fate the people read their own doom.

Now they seemed sincerely to repent of their sinful conduct; but they sorrowed because of the result of their evil course rather than from a sense of their ingratitude and disobedience. When they found that the Lord did not relent in His decree, their self-will again arose, and they declared that they would not return into the wilderness. In commanding them to retire from the land of their enemies, God tested their apparent submission and proved that it was not real. They knew that they had deeply sinned in allowing their rash feelings to control them and in seeking to slay the spies who had urged them to obey God; but they were only terrified to find that they had made a fearful mistake, the consequences of which would prove disastrous to themselves. Their hearts were unchanged, and they only needed an excuse to occasion a similar outbreak. This presented itself when Moses, by the authority of God, commanded them to go back into the wilderness.

The decree that Israel was not to enter Canaan for forty years was a bitter disappointment to Moses and Aaron, Caleb and Joshua; yet without a murmur they accepted the divine decision. But those who had been complaining of God's dealings with them, and declaring that they would return to Egypt, wept and mourned greatly when the blessings which they had despised were taken from them. They had complained at nothing, and now God gave them cause to weep. Had they mourned for their sin when it was faithfully laid before them, this sentence would not have been pronounced; but they mourned for the judgment; their sorrow was not repentance, and could not secure a reversing of their sentence.

The night was spent in lamentation, but with the morning came a hope. They resolved to redeem their cowardice. When God had bidden them go up and take the land, they had refused; and now when He directed them to retreat they were equally rebellious. They determined to seize upon the land and possess it; it might be that God would accept their work and change His purpose toward them.

God had made it their privilege and their duty to enter the land at the time of His appointment, but through their willful neglect that permission had been withdrawn. Satan had gained his object in preventing them from entering Canaan; and now he urged them on to do the very thing, in the face of the divine prohibition, which they had refused to do when God required it. Thus the great deceiver gained the victory by leading them to rebellion the second time. They had distrusted the power of God to work with their efforts in gaining possession of Canaan; yet now they presumed upon their own strength to accomplish the work independent of divine aid. "We have sinned against the Lord," they cried; "we will go up and fight, according to all that the Lord our God commanded us." Deuteronomy 1:41. So terribly blinded had they become by transgression. The Lord had never commanded them to "go up and fight." It was not His purpose that they should gain the land by warfare, but by strict obedience to His commands.

Though their hearts were unchanged, the people had been brought to confess the sinfulness and folly of their rebellion at the report of the spies. They now saw the value of the blessing which they had so rashly cast away. They confessed that it was their own unbelief which had shut them out from Canaan. "We have sinned," they said, acknowledging that the fault was in themselves, and not in God, whom they had so wickedly charged with failing to fulfill His promises to them. Though their confession did not spring from true repentance, it served to vindicate the justice of God in His dealings with them.

The Lord still works in a similar manner to glorify His name by bringing men to acknowledge His justice. When those who profess to love Him complain of His providence, despise His promises, and, yielding to temptation, unite with evil angels to defeat the purposes of God, the Lord often so overrules circumstances as to bring these persons where, though they may have no real repentance, they will be convinced of their sin and will be constrained to acknowledge the wickedness of their course and the justice and goodness of God in His dealings with them. It is thus that God sets counteragencies at work to make manifest the works of darkness. And though the spirit which prompted to the evil course is not radically changed, confessions are made that vindicate the honor of God and justify His faithful reprovers, who have been opposed and misrepresented. Thus it will be when the wrath of God shall be finally poured out. When "the Lord cometh with ten thousand of His saints, to execute judgment upon all," He will also "convince all that are ungodly among them of all their ungodly deeds." Jude 14, 15. Every sinner will be brought to see and acknowledge the justice of his condemnation.

Regardless of the divine sentence, the Israelites prepared to undertake the conquest of Canaan. Equipped with armor and weapons of war, they were, in their own estimation, fully prepared for conflict; but they were sadly deficient in the sight of God and His sorrowful servants. When, nearly forty years later, the Lord directed Israel to go up and take Jericho, He promised to go with them. The ark containing His law was borne before their armies. His appointed leaders were to direct their movements, under the divine supervision. With such guidance, no harm could come to them. But now, contrary to the command of God and the solemn prohibition of their leaders, without the ark, and without Moses, they went out to meet the armies of the enemy.

The trumpet sounded an alarm, and Moses hastened after them with the warning, "Wherefore now do ye transgress the commandment of the Lord? but it shall not prosper. Go not up, for the Lord is not among you; that ye be not smitten before your enemies. For the Amalekites and the Canaanites are there before you, and ye shall fall by the sword."

The Canaanites had heard of the mysterious power that seemed to be guarding this people and of the wonders wrought in their behalf, and they now summoned a strong force to repel the invaders. The attacking army had no leader. No prayer was offered that God would give them the victory. They set forth with the desperate purpose to reverse their fate or to die in battle. Though untrained in war, they were a vast multitude of armed men, and they hoped by a sudden and fierce assault to bear down all opposition. They presumptuously challenged the foe that had not dared to attack them.

The Canaanites had stationed themselves upon a rocky tableland reached only by difficult passes and a steep and dangerous ascent. The immense numbers of the Hebrews could only render their defeat more terrible. They slowly threaded the mountain paths, exposed to the deadly missiles of their enemies above. Massive rocks came thundering down, marking their path with the blood of the slain. Those who reached the summit, exhausted with their ascent, were fiercely repulsed, and driven back with great loss. The field of carnage was strewn with the bodies of the dead. The army of Israel was utterly defeated. Destruction and death was the result of that rebellious experiment.

Forced to submission at last, the survivors "returned, and wept before the Lord;" but "the Lord would not hearken" to their voice. Deuteronomy 1:45. By their signal victory the enemies of Israel, who had before awaited with trembling the approach of that mighty host, were inspired with confidence to resist them. All the reports they had heard concerning the marvelous things that God had wrought for His people, they now regarded as false, and they felt that there was no cause for fear. That first defeat of Israel, by inspiring the Canaanites with courage and resolution, had greatly increased the difficulties of the conquest. Nothing remained for Israel but to fall back from the face of their victorious foes, into the wilderness, knowing that here must be the grave of a whole generation.

The Rebellion of Korah

The judgments visited upon the Israelites served for a time to restrain their murmuring and insubordination, but the spirit of rebellion was still in the heart and eventually brought forth the bitterest fruits. The former rebellions had been mere popular tumults, arising from the sudden impulse of the excited multitude; but now a deep-laid conspiracy was formed, the result of a determined purpose to overthrow the authority of the leaders appointed by God Himself.

Korah, the leading spirit in this movement, was a Levite, of the family of Kohath, and a cousin of Moses; he was a man of ability and influence. Though appointed to the service of the tabernacle, he had become dissatisfied with his position and aspired to the dignity of the priesthood. The bestowal upon Aaron and his house of the priestly office, which had formerly devolved upon the first-born son of every family, had given rise to jealousy and dissatisfaction, and for some time Korah had been secretly opposing the authority of Moses and Aaron, though he had not ventured upon any open act of rebellion. He finally conceived the bold design of overthrowing both the civil and the religious authority. He did not fail to find sympathizers. Close to the tents of Korah and the Kohathites, on the south side of the tabernacle, was the encampment of the tribe of Reuben, the tents of Dathan and Abiram, two princes of this tribe, being near that of Korah. These princes readily joined in his ambitious schemes. Being descendants from the eldest son of Jacob, they claimed that the civil authority belonged to them, and they determined to divide with Korah the honors of the priesthood.

The state of feeling among the people favored the designs of Korah. In the bitterness of their disappointment, their former doubts, jealousy, and hatred had returned, and again their complaints were directed against their patient leader. The Israelites were continually losing sight of the fact that they were under divine guidance. They forgot that the Angel of the covenant was their invisible leader, that, veiled by the cloudy pillar, the presence of Christ went before them, and that from Him Moses received all his directions.

They were unwilling to submit to the terrible sentence that they must all die in the wilderness, and hence they were ready to seize upon every pretext for believing that it was not God but Moses who was leading them and who had pronounced their doom. The best efforts of the meekest man upon the earth could not quell the insubordination of this people; and although the marks of God's displeasure at their former perverseness were still before them in their broken ranks and missing numbers, they did not take the lesson to heart. Again they were overcome by temptation.

The humble shepherd's life of Moses had been far more peaceful and happy than his present position as leader of that vast assembly of turbulent spirits. Yet Moses dared not choose. In place of a shepherd's crook a rod of power had been given him, which he could not lay down until God should release him.

He who reads the secrets of all hearts had marked the purposes of Korah and his companions and had given His people such warning and instruction as might have enabled them to escape the deception of these designing men. They had seen the judgment of God fall upon Miriam because of her jealousy and complaints against Moses. The Lord had declared that Moses was greater than a prophet. "With him will I speak mouth to mouth." "Wherefore, then," He added, "were ye not afraid to speak against My servant Moses?" Numbers 12:8. These instructions were not intended for Aaron and Miriam alone, but for all Israel.

Korah and his fellow conspirators were men who had been favored with special manifestations of God's power and greatness. They were of the number who went up with Moses into the mount and beheld the divine glory. But since that time a change had come. A temptation, slight at first, had been harbored, and had strengthened as it was encouraged, until their minds were controlled by Satan, and they ventured upon their work of disaffection. Professing great interest in the prosperity of the people, they first whispered their discontent to one another and then to leading men of Israel. Their insinuations were so readily received that they ventured still further, and at last they really believed themselves to be actuated by zeal for God.

They were successful in alienating two hundred and fifty princes, men of renown in the congregation. With these strong and influential supporters they felt confident of making a radical change in the government and greatly improving upon the administration of Moses and Aaron.

Jealousy had given rise to envy, and envy to rebellion. They had discussed the question of the right of Moses to so great authority and honor, until they had come to regard him as occupying a very enviable position, which any of them could fill as well as he. And they deceived themselves and one another into thinking that Moses and Aaron had themselves assumed the positions they held. The discontented ones said that these leaders had exalted themselves above the congregation of the Lord, in taking upon them the priesthood and government, but their house was not entitled to distinction above others in Israel; they were no more holy than the people, and it should be enough for them to be on a level with their brethren, who were equally favored with God's special presence and protection.

The next work of the conspirators was with the people. To those who are in the wrong, and deserving of reproof, there is nothing more pleasing than to receive sympathy and praise. And thus Korah and his associates gained the attention and enlisted the support of the congregation. The charge that the murmurings of the people had brought upon them the wrath of God was declared to be a mistake. They said that the congregation were not at fault, since they desired nothing more than their rights; but that Moses was an overbearing ruler; that he had reproved the people as sinners, when they were a holy people, and the Lord was among them.

Korah reviewed the history of their travels through the wilderness, where they had been brought into strait places, and many had perished because of their murmuring and disobedience. His hearers thought they saw clearly that their troubles might have been prevented if Moses had pursued a different course. They decided that all their disasters were chargeable to him, and that their exclusion from Canaan was in consequence of the mismanagement of Moses and Aaron; that if Korah would be their leader, and would encourage them by dwelling upon their good deeds, instead of reproving their sins, they would have a very peaceful, prosperous journey; instead of wandering to and fro in the wilderness, they would proceed directly to the Promised Land.

In this work of disaffection there was greater union and harmony among the discordant elements of the congregation than had ever before existed. Korah's success with the people increased his confidence and confirmed him in his belief that the usurpation of authority by Moses, if unchecked, would be fatal to the liberties of Israel; he also claimed that God had opened the matter to him, and had authorized him to make a change in the government before it should be too late. But many were not ready to accept Korah's accusations against Moses. The memory of his patient, self-sacrificing labors came up before them, and conscience was disturbed. It was therefore necessary to assign some selfish motive for his deep interest for Israel; and the old charge was reiterated, that he had led them out to perish in the wilderness, that he might seize upon their possessions.

For a time this work was carried on secretly. As soon, however, as the movement had gained sufficient strength to warrant an open rupture, Korah appeared at the head of the faction, and publicly accused Moses and Aaron of usurping authority which Korah and his associates were equally entitled to share. It was charged, further, that the people had been deprived of their liberty and independence. "Ye take too much upon you," said the conspirators, "seeing all the congregation are holy, every one of them, and the Lord is among them: wherefore then lift ye up yourselves above the congregation of the Lord?"

Moses had not suspected this deep-laid plot, and when its terrible significance burst upon him, he fell upon his face in silent appeal to God. He arose sorrowful indeed, but calm and strong. Divine guidance had been granted him. "Even tomorrow," he said, "the Lord will show who are His, and who is holy; and will cause him to come near unto Him: even him whom He hath chosen will He cause to come near unto Him." The test was to be deferred until the morrow, that all might have time for reflection. Then those who aspired to the priesthood were to come each with a censer, and offer incense at the tabernacle in the presence of the congregation. The law was very explicit that only those who had been ordained to the sacred office should minister in the sanctuary. And even the priests, Nadab and Abihu, had been destroyed for venturing to offer "strange fire," in disregard of a divine command. Yet Moses challenged his accusers, if they dared enter upon so perilous an appeal, to refer the matter to God.

Singling out Korah and his fellow Levites, Moses said, "Seemeth it but a small thing unto you, that the God of Israel hath separated you from the congregation of Israel, to bring you near to Himself to do the service of the tabernacle of the Lord, and to stand before the congregation to minister unto them? And He hath brought thee near to Him, and all thy brethren the sons of Levi with thee: and seek ye the priesthood also? for which cause both thou and all thy company are gathered together against the Lord. And what is Aaron, that ye murmur against him?"

Dathan and Abiram had not taken so bold a stand as had Korah; and Moses, hoping that they might have been drawn into the conspiracy without having become wholly corrupted, summoned them to appear before him, that he might hear their charges against him. But they would not come, and they insolently refused to acknowledge his authority. Their reply, uttered in the hearing of the congregation, was, "Is it a small thing that thou hast brought us up out of a land that floweth with milk and honey, to kill us in the wilderness, except thou make thyself altogether a prince over us? Moreover thou hast not brought us into a land that floweth with milk and honey, or given us inheritance of fields and vineyards: wilt thou put out the eyes of these men? We will not come up."

Thus they applied to the scene of their bondage the very language in which the Lord had described the promised inheritance. They accused Moses of pretending to act under divine guidance, as a means of establishing his authority; and they declared that they would no longer submit to be led about like blind men, now toward Canaan, and now toward the wilderness, as best suited his ambitious designs. Thus he who had been as a tender father, a patient shepherd, was represented in the blackest character of a tyrant and usurper. The exclusion from Canaan, in punishment of their own sins, was charged upon him.

It was evident that the sympathies of the people were with the disaffected party; but Moses made no effort at self-vindication. He solemnly appealed to God, in the presence of the congregation, as a witness to the purity of his motives and the uprightness of his conduct, and implored Him to be his judge.

On the morrow, the two hundred and fifty princes, with Korah at their head, presented themselves, with their censers. They were brought into the court of the tabernacle, while the people gathered without, to await the result. It was not Moses who assembled the congregation to behold the defeat of Korah and his company, but the rebels, in their blind presumption, had called them together to witness their victory. A large part of the congregation openly sided with Korah, whose hopes were high of carrying his point against Aaron.

As they were thus assembled before God, "the glory of the Lord appeared unto all the congregation." The divine warning was communicated to Moses and Aaron, "Separate yourselves from among this congregation, that I may consume them in a moment." But they fell upon their faces, with the prayer, "O God, the God of the spirits of all flesh, shall one man sin, and wilt Thou be wroth with all the congregation?"

Korah had withdrawn from the assembly to join Dathan and Abiram when Moses, accompanied by the seventy elders, went down with a last warning to the men who had refused to come to him. The multitudes followed, and before delivering his message, Moses, by divine direction, bade the people, "Depart, I pray you, from the tents of these wicked men, and touch nothing of theirs, lest ye be consumed in all their sins." The warning was obeyed, for an apprehension of impending judgment rested upon all. The chief rebels saw themselves abandoned by those whom they had deceived, but their hardihood was unshaken. They stood with their families in the door of their tents, as if in defiance of the divine warning.

In the name of the God of Israel, Moses now declared, in the hearing of the congregation: "Hereby ye shall know that the Lord hath sent me to do all these works; for I have not done them of mine own mind. If these men die the common death of all men, or if they be visited after the visitation of all men, then the Lord hath not sent me. But if the Lord make a new thing, and the earth open her mouth, and swallow them up, with all that appertain unto them, and they go down quick into the pit, then ye shall understand that these men have provoked the Lord."

The eyes of all Israel were fixed upon Moses as they stood, in terror and expectation, awaiting the event. As he ceased speaking, the solid earth parted, and the rebels went down alive into the pit, with all that pertained to them, and "they perished from among the congregation." The people fled, self-condemned as partakers in the sin.

But the judgments were not ended. Fire flashing from the cloud consumed the two hundred and fifty princes who had offered incense. These men, not being the first in rebellion, were not destroyed with the chief conspirators. They were permitted to see their end, and to have an opportunity for repentance; but their sympathies were with the rebels, and they shared their fate.

When Moses was entreating Israel to flee from the coming destruction, the divine judgment might even then have been stayed, if Korah and his company had repented and sought forgiveness. But their stubborn persistence sealed their doom. The entire congregation were sharers in their guilt, for all had, to a greater or less degree, sympathized with them. Yet God in His great mercy made a distinction between the leaders in rebellion and those whom they had led. The people who had permitted themselves to be deceived were still granted space for repentance. Overwhelming evidence had been given that they were wrong, and that Moses was right. The signal manifestation of God's power had removed all uncertainty.

Jesus, the Angel who went before the Hebrews, sought to save them from destruction. Forgiveness was lingering for them. The judgment of God had come very near, and appealed to them to repent. A special, irresistible interference from heaven had arrested their rebellion. Now, if they would respond to the interposition of God's providence, they might be saved. But while they fled from the judgments, through fear of destruction, their rebellion was not cured. They returned to their tents that night terrified, but not repentant.

They had been flattered by Korah and his company until they really believed themselves to be very good people, and that they had been wronged and abused by Moses. Should they admit that Korah and his company were wrong, and Moses right, then they would be compelled to receive as the word of God the sentence that they must die in the wilderness. They were not willing to submit to this, and they tried to believe that Moses had deceived them. They had fondly cherished the hope that a new order of things was about to be established, in which praise would be substituted for reproof, and ease for anxiety and conflict.

The men who had perished had spoken flattering words and had professed great interest and love for them, and the people concluded that Korah and his companions must have been good men, and that Moses had by some means been the cause of their destruction.

It is hardly possible for men to offer greater insult to God than to despise and reject the instrumentalities He would use for their salvation. The Israelites had not only done this, but had purposed to put both Moses and Aaron to death. Yet they did not realize the necessity of seeking pardon of God for their grievous sin. That night of probation was not passed in repentance and confession, but in devising some way to resist the evidences which showed them to be the greatest of sinners. They still cherished hatred of the men of God's appointment, and braced themselves to resist their authority. Satan was at hand to pervert their judgment and lead them blindfold to destruction.

All Israel had fled in alarm at the cry of the doomed sinners who went down into the pit, for they said, "Lest the earth swallow us up also." "But on the morrow all the congregation of the children of Israel murmured against Moses and against Aaron, saying, ye have killed the people of the Lord." And they were about to proceed to violence against their faithful, self-sacrificing leaders.

A manifestation of the divine glory was seen in the cloud above the tabernacle, and a voice from the cloud spoke to Moses and Aaron, "Get you up from among this congregation, that I may consume them as in a moment."

The guilt of sin did not rest upon Moses, and hence he did not fear and did not hasten away and leave the congregation to perish. Moses lingered, in this fearful crisis manifesting the true shepherd's interest for the flock of his care. He pleaded that the wrath of God might not utterly destroy the people of His choice. By his intercession he stayed the arm of vengeance, that a full end might not be made of disobedient, rebellious Israel.

But the minister of wrath had gone forth; the plague was doing its work of death. By his brother's direction, Aaron took a censer and hastened into the midst of the congregation to "make an atonement for them." "And he stood between the dead and the living." As the smoke of the incense ascended, the prayers of Moses in the tabernacle went up to God; and the plague was stayed; but not until fourteen thousand of Israel lay dead, an evidence of the guilt of murmuring and rebellion.

But further evidence was given that the priesthood had been established in the family of Aaron. By divine direction each tribe prepared a rod and wrote upon it the name of the tribe. The name of Aaron was upon that of Levi. The rods were laid up in the tabernacle, "before the testimony." The blossoming of any rod was to be a token that the Lord had chosen that tribe for the priesthood. On the morrow, "behold, the rod of Aaron for the house of Levi was budded, and brought forth buds, and bloomed blossoms, and yielded almonds." It was shown to the people, and afterward laid up in the tabernacle as a witness to succeeding generations. This miracle effectually settled the question of the priesthood.

It was now fully established that Moses and Aaron had spoken by divine authority, and the people were compelled to believe the unwelcome truth that they were to die in the wilderness. "Behold," they exclaimed, "we die, we perish, we all perish." They confessed that they had sinned in rebelling against their leaders, and that Korah and his company had suffered from the just judgment of God.

In the rebellion of Korah is seen the working out, upon a narrower stage, of the same spirit that led to the rebellion of Satan in heaven. It was pride and ambition that prompted Lucifer to complain of the government of God, and to seek the overthrow of the order which had been established in heaven. Since his fall it has been his object to infuse the same spirit of envy and discontent, the same ambition for position and honor, into the minds of men. He thus worked upon the minds of Korah, Dathan, and Abiram, to arouse the desire for self-exaltation and excite envy, distrust, and rebellion. Satan caused them to reject God as their leader, by rejecting the men of God's appointment. Yet while in their murmuring against Moses and Aaron they blasphemed God, they were so deluded as to think themselves righteous, and to regard those who had faithfully reproved their sins as actuated by Satan.

Do not the same evils still exist that lay at the foundation of Korah's ruin? Pride and ambition are widespread; and when these are cherished, they open the door to envy, and a striving for supremacy; the soul is alienated from God, and unconsciously drawn into the ranks of Satan. Like Korah and his companions, many, even of the professed followers of

Christ, are thinking, planning, and working so eagerly for self-exaltation that in order to gain the sympathy and support of the people they are ready to pervert the truth, falsifying and misrepresenting the Lord's servants, and even charging them with the base and selfish motives that inspire their own hearts. By persistently reiterating falsehood, and that against all evidence, they at last come to believe it to be truth. While endeavoring to destroy the confidence of the people in the men of God's appointment, they really believe that they are engaged in a good work, verily doing God service.

The Hebrews were not willing to submit to the directions and restrictions of the Lord. They were restless under restraint, and unwilling to receive reproof. This was the secret of their murmuring against Moses. Had they been left free to do as they pleased, there would have been fewer complaints against their leader. All through the history of the church God's servants have had the same spirit to meet.

It is by sinful indulgence that men give Satan access to their minds, and they go from one stage of wickedness to another. The rejection of light darkens the mind and hardens the heart, so that it is easier for them to take the next step in sin and to reject still clearer light, until at last their habits of wrongdoing become fixed. Sin ceases to appear sinful to them. He who faithfully preaches God's word, thereby condemning their sins, too often incurs their hatred. Unwilling to endure the pain and sacrifice necessary to reform, they turn upon the Lord's servant and denounce his reproofs as uncalled for and severe. Like Korah, they declare that the people are not at fault; it is the reprover that causes all the trouble. And soothing their consciences with this deception, the jealous and disaffected combine to sow discord in the church and weaken the hands of those who would build it up.

Every advance made by those whom God has called to lead in His work has excited suspicion; every act has been misrepresented by the jealous and faultfinding. Thus it was in the time of Luther, of the Wesleys and other reformers. Thus it is today.

Korah would not have taken the course he did had he known that all the directions and reproofs communicated to Israel were from God. But he might have known this. God had given overwhelming evidence that He was leading Israel. But Korah and his companions rejected light until they became so blinded that the most striking manifestations of His power were not sufficient to convince them; they attributed them all to human or satanic agency. The same thing was done by the people, who the day after the destruction of Korah and his company came to Moses and Aaron, saying, "Ye have killed the people of the Lord." Notwithstanding they had had the most convincing evidence of God's displeasure at their course, in the destruction of the men who had deceived them, they dared to attribute His judgments to Satan, declaring that through the power of the evil one, Moses and Aaron had caused the death of good and holy men. It was this act that sealed their doom. They had committed the sin against the Holy Spirit, a sin by which man's heart is

effectually hardened against the influence of divine grace. "Whosoever speaketh a word against the Son of man," said Christ, "it shall be forgiven him: but whosoever speaketh against the Holy Ghost, it shall not be forgiven him." Matthew 12:32. These words were spoken by our Saviour when the gracious works which He had performed through the power of God were attributed by the Jews to Beelzebub. It is through the agency of the Holy Spirit that God communicates with man; and those who deliberately reject this agency as satanic, have cut off the channel of communication between the soul and Heaven.

God works by the manifestation of His Spirit to reprove and convict the sinner; and if the Spirit's work is finally rejected, there is no more that God can do for the soul. The last resource of divine mercy has been employed. The transgressor has cut himself off from God, and sin has no remedy to cure itself. There is no reserved power by which God can work to convict and convert the sinner. "Let him alone" (Hosea 4:17) is the divine command. Then "there remaineth no more sacrifice for sins, but a certain fearful looking for of judgment and fiery indignation, which shall devour the adversaries." Hebrews 10:26, 27.

In the Wilderness

For nearly forty years the children of Israel are lost to view in the obscurity of the desert. "The space," says Moses, "in which we came from Kadesh-barnea, until we were come over the brook Zered, was thirty and eight years; until all the generation of the men of war were wasted out from among the host, as the Lord sware unto them. For indeed the hand of the Lord was against them, to destroy them from among the host, until they were consumed." Deuteronomy 2:14, 15.

During these years the people were constantly reminded that they were under the divine rebuke. In the rebellion at Kadesh they had rejected God, and God had for the time rejected them. Since they had proved unfaithful to His covenant, they were not to receive the sign of the covenant, the rite of circumcision. Their desire to return to the land of slavery had shown them to be unworthy of freedom, and the ordinance of the Passover, instituted to commemorate the deliverance from bondage, was not to be observed.

Yet the continuance of the tabernacle service testified that God had not utterly forsaken His people. And His providence still supplied their wants. "The Lord thy God hath blessed thee in all the works of thy hand," said Moses, in rehearsing the history of their wanderings. "He knoweth thy walking through this great wilderness; these forty years the Lord thy God hath been with thee; thou hast lacked nothing." And the Levites' hymn, recorded by Nehemiah, vividly pictures God's care for Israel, even during these years of rejection and banishment: "Thou in Thy manifold mercies forsookest them not in the wilderness: the pillar of the cloud departed not from them by day, to lead them in the way; neither the pillar of fire by night, to show them light, and the way wherein they should go. Thou gavest also Thy good Spirit to instruct them, and withheldest not Thy manna from their mouth, and gavest them water for their thirst. Yea, forty years didst Thou sustain them in the wilderness; . . . their clothes waxed not old, and their feet swelled not." Nehemiah 9:19-21.

The wilderness wandering was not only ordained as a judgment upon the rebels and murmurers, but it was to serve as a discipline for the rising generation, preparatory to their entrance into the Promised Land. Moses declared to them, "As a man chasteneth his son, so the Lord thy God chasteneth thee," "to humble thee, and to prove thee, to know what was in thine heart, whether thou wouldest keep His commandments, or no. And He . . . suffered thee to hunger, and fed thee with manna, which thou knewest not, neither did thy fathers know; that He might make thee know that man doth not live by bread only, but by every word that proceedeth out of the mouth of the Lord doth man live." Deuteronomy 8:5, 2, 3.

"He found him in a desert land, and in the waste howling wilderness; He led him about, He instructed him, He kept him as the apple of His eyes." "In all their affliction He was afflicted, and the Angel of His presence saved them; in His love and in His pity He redeemed them; and He bare them, and carried them all the days of old." Deuteronomy 32:10; Isaiah 63:9.

Yet the only records of their wilderness life are instances of rebellion against the Lord. The revolt of Korah had resulted in the destruction of fourteen thousand of Israel. And there were isolated cases that showed the same spirit of contempt for the divine authority.

On one occasion the son of an Israelitish woman and of an Egyptian, one of the mixed multitude that had come up with Israel from Egypt, left his own part of the camp, and entering that of the Israelites, claimed the right to pitch his tent there. This the divine law forbade him to do, the descendants of an Egyptian being excluded from the congregation until the third generation. A dispute arose between him and an Israelite, and the matter being referred to the judges was decided against the offender.

Enraged at this decision, he cursed the judge, and in the heat of passion blasphemed the name of God. He was immediately brought before Moses. The command had been given, "He that curseth his father, or his mother, shall surely be put to death" (Exodus 21:17); but no provision had been made to meet this case. So terrible was the crime that there was felt to be a necessity for special direction from God. The man was placed in ward until the will of the Lord could be ascertained. God Himself pronounced the sentence; by the divine direction the blasphemer was conducted outside the camp and stoned to death. Those who had been witness to the sin placed their hands upon his head, thus solemnly testifying to the truth of the charge against him. Then they threw the first stones, and the people who stood by afterward joined in executing the sentence.

This was followed by the announcement of a law to meet similar offenses: "Thou shalt speak unto the children of Israel, saying, Whosoever curseth his God shall bear his sin. And he that blasphemeth the name of the Lord, he shall surely be put to death, and all the congregation shall certainly stone him: as well the stranger, as he that is born in the land, when he blasphemeth the name of the Lord, shall be put to death." Leviticus 24:15, 16.

There are those who will question God's love and His justice in visiting so severe punishment for words spoken in the heat of passion. But both love and justice require it to be shown that utterances prompted by malice against God are a great sin. The retribution visited upon the first offender would be a warning to others, that God's name is to be held in reverence. But had this man's sin been permitted to pass unpunished, others would have been demoralized; and as the result many lives must eventually have been sacrificed.

The mixed multitude that came up with the Israelites from Egypt were a source of continual temptation and trouble. They professed to have renounced idolatry and to worship the true God; but their early education and training had molded their habits and character, and they were more or less corrupted with idolatry and with irreverence for God. They were oftenest the ones to stir up strife and were the first to complain, and they leavened the camp with their idolatrous practices and their murmurings against God.

Soon after the return into the wilderness, an instance of Sabbath violation occurred, under circumstances that rendered it a case of peculiar guilt. The Lord's announcement that He would disinherit Israel had roused a spirit of rebellion. One of the people, angry at being excluded from Canaan, and determined to show his defiance of God's law, ventured upon the open transgression of the fourth commandment by going out to gather sticks upon the Sabbath. During the sojourn in the wilderness the kindling of fires upon the seventh day had been strictly prohibited. The prohibition was not to extend to the land of Canaan, where the severity of the climate would often render fires a necessity; but in the wilderness, fire was not needed for warmth. The act of this man was a willful and deliberate violation of the fourth commandment—a sin, not of thoughtlessness or ignorance, but of presumption.

He was taken in the act and brought before Moses. It had already been declared that Sabbathbreaking should be punished with death, but it had not yet been revealed how the penalty was to be inflicted. The case was brought by Moses before the Lord, and the direction was given, "The man shall be surely put to death: all the congregation shall stone him with stones without the camp." Numbers 15:35. The sins of blasphemy and willful Sabbathbreaking received the same punishment, being equally an expression of contempt for the authority of God.

In our day there are many who reject the creation Sabbath as a Jewish institution and urge that if it is to be kept, the penalty of death must be inflicted for its violation; but we see that blasphemy received the same punishment as did Sabbathbreaking. Shall we therefore conclude that the third commandment also is to be set aside as applicable only to the Jews? Yet the argument drawn from the death penalty applies to the third, the fifth, and indeed to nearly all the ten precepts, equally with the fourth. Though God may not now punish the transgression of His law with temporal penalties, yet His word declares that the wages of sin is death; and in the final execution of the judgment it will be found that death is the portion of those who violate His sacred precepts.

During the entire forty years in the wilderness, the people were every week reminded of the sacred obligation of the Sabbath, by the miracle of the manna. Yet even this did not lead them to obedience. Though they did not venture upon so open and bold transgression as had received such signal punishment, yet there was great laxness in the observance of the fourth commandment. God declares through His prophet, "My Sabbaths they greatly polluted." Ezekiel 20:13-24. And this is enumerated among the reasons for the exclusion of the first generation from the Promised Land. Yet their children did not learn the lesson. Such was their neglect of the Sabbath during the forty years' wandering, that though God did not prevent them from entering Canaan, He declared that they should be scattered among the heathen after the settlement in the Land of Promise.

From Kadesh the children of Israel had turned back into the wilderness; and the period of their desert sojourn being ended, they came, "even the whole congregation, into the desert of Zin in the first month: and the people abode in Kadesh." Numbers 20:1.

Here Miriam died and was buried. From that scene of rejoicing on the shores of the Red Sea, when Israel went forth with song and dance to celebrate Jehovah's triumph, to the wilderness grave which ended a lifelong wandering—such had been the fate of millions who with high hopes had come forth from Egypt. Sin had dashed from their lips the cup of blessing. Would the next generation learn the lesson?

"For all this they sinned still, and believed not for His wondrous works. . . . When He slew them, then they sought Him: and they returned and inquired early after God. And they remembered that God was their Rock, and the high God their Redeemer." Psalm 78:32-35. Yet they did not turn to God with a sincere purpose. Though when afflicted by their enemies they sought help from Him who alone could deliver, yet "their heart was not right with Him, neither were they steadfast in His covenant. But He, being full of compassion, forgave their iniquity, and destroyed them not: yea, many a time turned He His anger away. . . . For He remembered that they were but flesh; a wind that passeth away, and cometh not again." Verses 37-39.

The Smitten Rock

From the smitten rock in Horeb first flowed the living stream that refreshed Israel in the desert. During all their wanderings, wherever the need existed, they were supplied with water by a miracle of God's mercy. The water did not, however, continue to flow from Horeb. Wherever in their journeyings they wanted water, there from the clefts of the rock it gushed out beside their encampment.

It was Christ, by the power of His word, that caused the refreshing stream to flow for Israel. "They drank of that spiritual Rock that followed them: and that Rock was Christ." 1 Corinthians 10:4. He was the source of all temporal as well as spiritual blessings. Christ, the true Rock, was with them in all their wanderings. "They thirsted not when He led them through the deserts: He caused the waters to flow out of the rock for them; He clave the rock also, and the waters gushed out." "They ran in the dry places like a river." Isaiah 48:21; Psalm 105:41.

The smitten rock was a figure of Christ, and through this symbol the most precious spiritual truths are taught. As the life-giving waters flowed from the smitten rock, so from Christ, "smitten of God," "wounded for our transgressions," "bruised for our iniquities" (Isaiah 53:4, 5), the stream of salvation flows for a lost race. As the rock had been once smitten, so Christ was to be "once offered to bear the sins of many." Hebrews 9:28. Our Saviour was not to be sacrificed a second time; and it is only necessary for those who seek the blessings of His grace to ask in the name of Jesus, pouring forth the heart's desire in penitential prayer. Such prayer will bring before the Lord of hosts the wounds of Jesus, and then will flow forth afresh the life-giving blood, symbolized by the flowing of the living water for Israel.

The flowing of the water from the rock in the desert was celebrated by the Israelites, after their establishment in Canaan, with demonstrations of great rejoicing. In the time of Christ this celebration had become a most impressive ceremony. It took place on the occasion of the Feast of Tabernacles, when the people from all the land were assembled at Jerusalem. On each of the seven days of the feast the priests went out with music and the choir of Levites to draw water in a golden vessel from the spring of Siloam. They were followed by multitudes of the worshipers, as many as could get near the stream drinking of it, while the jubilant strains arose, "With joy shall ye draw water out of the wells of salvation." Isaiah 12:3. Then the water drawn by the priests was borne to the temple amid the sounding of trumpets and the solemn chant, "Our feet shall stand within thy gates, O Jerusalem." Psalm 122:2. The water was poured out upon the altar of burnt offering, while songs of praise rang out, the multitudes joining in triumphant chorus with musical instruments and deep-toned trumpets.

The Saviour made use of this symbolic service to direct the minds of the people to the blessings that He had come to bring them. "In the last day, that great day of the feast," His voice was heard in tones that rang through the temple courts, "If any man thirst, let him come unto Me, and drink. He that believeth on Me, as the Scripture hath said, out of his belly shall flow rivers of living water." "This," said John, "spake He of the Spirit, which they that believe on Him should receive." John 7:37-39. The refreshing water, welling up in a parched and barren land, causing the desert place to blossom, and flowing out to give life to the perishing, is an emblem of the divine grace which Christ alone can bestow, and which is as the living water, purifying, refreshing, and invigorating the soul. He in whom Christ is abiding has within him a never-failing fountain of grace and strength. Jesus cheers the life and brightens the path of all who truly seek Him. His love, received into the heart, will spring up in good works unto eternal life. And not only does it bless the soul in which it springs, but the living stream will flow out in words and deeds of righteousness, to refresh the thirsting around him.

The same figure Christ had employed in His conversation with the woman of Samaria at Jacob's well: "Whosoever drinketh of the water that I shall give him shall never thirst; but the water that I shall give him shall be in him a well of water springing up into everlasting life." John 4:14. Christ combines the two types. He is the rock, He is the living water.

The same beautiful and expressive figures are carried throughout the Bible. Centuries before the advent of Christ, Moses pointed to Him as the rock of Israel's salvation (Deuteronomy 32:15); the psalmist sang of Him as "my Redeemer," "the rock of my strength," "the rock that is higher than I," "a rock of habitation," "rock of my heart," "rock of my refuge." In David's song His grace is pictured also as the cool, "still waters," amid green pastures, beside which the heavenly Shepherd leads His flock. Again, "Thou shalt make them," he says, "drink of the river of Thy pleasures. For with Thee is the fountain of life." Psalms 19:14; 62:7; 61:2; 71:3. (margin); 73:26 (margin); 94:22; 23:2; 36:8, 9. And the wise man declares, "The wellspring of wisdom as a flowing brook." Proverbs 18:4. To Jeremiah, Christ is "the fountain of living waters;" to Zechariah, "a fountain opened . . . for sin and for uncleanness." Jeremiah 2:13; Zechariah 13:1.

Isaiah describes Him as the "rock of ages," and "the shadow of a great rock in a weary land." Isaiah 26:4. (margin); 32:2. And he records the precious promise, bringing vividly to mind the living stream that flowed for Israel: "When the poor and needy seek water, and there is none, and their tongue faileth for thirst, I the Lord will hear them, I the God of Israel will not forsake them." "I will pour water upon him that is thirsty, and floods upon the dry ground;" "in the wilderness shall waters break out, and streams in the desert." The invitation is given, "Ho, every one that thirsteth, come ye to the waters." Isaiah 41:17; 44:3; 35:6; 55:1. And in the closing pages of the Sacred Word this invitation is echoed. The river of the water of life, "clear as crystal," proceeds from the throne of God and the Lamb; and the gracious call is ringing down through the ages, "Whosoever will, let him take the water of life freely." Revelation 22:17.

Just before the Hebrew host reached Kadesh, the living stream ceased that for so many years had gushed out beside their encampment. It was the Lord's purpose again to test His people. He would prove whether they would trust His providence or imitate the unbelief of their fathers.

They were now in sight of the hills of Canaan. A few days' march would bring them to the borders of the Promised Land. They were but a little distance from Edom, which belonged to the descendants of Esau, and through which lay the appointed route to Canaan. The direction had been given to Moses, "Turn you northward. And command thou the people, saying, Ye are to pass through the coast of your brethren the children of Esau, which dwell in Seir; and they shall be afraid of you. . . . Ye shall buy meat of them for money, that ye may eat; and ye shall also buy water of them for money, that ye may drink." Deuteronomy 2:3-6. These directions should have been sufficient to explain why their supply of water had been cut off; they were about to pass through a well-watered, fertile country, in a direct course to the land of Canaan. God had promised them an unmolested passage through Edom, and an opportunity to purchase food, and also water sufficient to supply the host. The cessation of the miraculous flow of water should therefore have been a cause of rejoicing, a token that the wilderness wandering was ended. Had they not been blinded by their unbelief, they would have understood this. But that which should have been an evidence of the fulfillment of God's promise was made the occasion of doubt and murmuring. The people seemed to have given up all hope that God would bring them into possession of Canaan, and they clamored for the blessings of the wilderness.

Before God permitted them to enter Canaan, they must show that they believed His promise. The water ceased before they had reached Edom. Here was an opportunity for them, for a little time, to walk by faith instead of sight. But the first trial developed the same turbulent, unthankful spirit that had been manifested by their fathers. No sooner was the cry for water heard in the encampment than they forgot the hand that had for so many years supplied their wants, and instead of turning to God for help, they murmured against Him, in their desperation exclaiming, "Would God that we had died when our brethren died before the Lord!" (Numbers 20:1-13); that is, they wished they had been of the number who were destroyed in the rebellion of Korah.

Their cries were directed against Moses and Aaron: "Why have ye brought up the congregation of the Lord into this wilderness, that we and our cattle should die there? And wherefore have ye made us to come up out of Egypt, to bring us in unto this evil place? it is no place of seed, or of figs, or of vines, or of pomegranates; neither is there any water to drink."

The leaders went to the door of the tabernacle and fell upon their faces. Again "the glory of the Lord appeared," and Moses was directed, "Take the rod, and gather thou the assembly together, thou and Aaron thy brother, and speak ye unto the rock before their eyes; and it shall give forth his water, and thou shalt bring forth to them water out of the rock."

The two brothers went on before the multitude, Moses with the rod of God in his hand. They were now aged men. Long had they borne with the rebellion and obstinacy of Israel; but now, at last, even the patience of Moses gave way. "Hear now, ye rebels," he cried; "must we fetch you water out of this rock?" and instead of speaking to the rock, as God had commanded him, he smote it twice with the rod.

The water gushed forth in abundance to satisfy the host. But a great wrong had been done. Moses had spoken from irritated feeling; his words were an expression of human passion rather than of holy indignation because God had been dishonored. "Hear now, ye rebels," he said. This accusation was true, but even truth is not to be spoken in passion or impatience. When God had bidden Moses to charge upon Israel their rebellion, the words had been painful to him, and hard for them to bear, yet God had sustained him in delivering the message. But when he took it upon himself to accuse them, he grieved the Spirit of God and wrought only harm to the people. His lack of patience and self-control was evident. Thus the people were given occasion to question whether his past course had been under the direction of God, and to excuse their own sins. Moses, as well as they, had offended God. His course, they said, had from the first been open to criticism and censure. They had now found the pretext which they desired for rejecting all the reproofs that God had sent them through His servant.

Moses manifested distrust of God. "Shall we bring water?" he questioned, as if the Lord would not do what He promised. "Ye believed Me not," the Lord declared to the two brothers, "to sanctify Me in the eyes of the children of Israel." At the time when the water failed, their own faith in the fulfillment of God's promise had been shaken by the murmuring and rebellion of the people. The first generation had been condemned to perish in the wilderness because of their unbelief, yet the same spirit appeared in their children. Would these also fail of receiving the promise? Wearied and disheartened, Moses and Aaron had made no effort to stem the current of popular feeling. Had they themselves manifested unwavering faith in God, they might have set the matter before the people in such a light as would have enabled them to bear this test. By prompt, decisive exercise of the authority vested in them as magistrates, they might have quelled the murmuring. It was their duty to put forth every effort in their power to bring about a better state of things before asking God to do the work for them. Had the murmuring at Kadesh been promptly checked, what a train of evil might have been prevented!

By his rash act Moses took away the force of the lesson that God purposed to teach. The rock, being a symbol of Christ, had been once smitten, as Christ was to be once offered. The second time it was needful only to speak to the rock, as we have only to ask for blessings in the name of Jesus. By the second smiting of the rock the significance of this beautiful figure of Christ was destroyed.

More than this, Moses and Aaron had assumed power that belongs only to God. The necessity for divine interposition made the occasion one of great solemnity, and the leaders of Israel should have improved it to impress the people with reverence for God and to strengthen their faith in His power and goodness. When they angrily cried, "Must we fetch you water out of this rock?" they put themselves in God's place, as though the power lay with themselves, men possessing human frailties and passions. Wearied with the continual murmuring and rebellion of the people, Moses had lost sight of his Almighty Helper, and without the divine strength he had been left to mar his record by an exhibition of human weakness. The man who might have stood pure, firm, and unselfish to the close of his work had been overcome at last. God had been dishonored before the congregation of Israel, when He should have been magnified and exalted.

God did not on this occasion pronounce judgments upon those whose wicked course had so provoked Moses and Aaron. All the reproof fell upon the leaders. Those who stood as God's representatives had not honored Him. Moses and Aaron had felt themselves aggrieved, losing sight of the fact that the murmuring of the people was not against them but against God. It was by looking to themselves, appealing to their own sympathies, that they unconsciously fell into sin, and failed to set before the people their great guilt before God.

Bitter and deeply humiliating was the judgment immediately pronounced. "The Lord spake unto Moses and Aaron, Because ye believed Me not, to sanctify Me in the eyes of the children of Israel, therefore ye shall not bring this congregation into the land which I have given them." With rebellious Israel they must die before the crossing of the Jordan. Had Moses and Aaron been cherishing self-esteem or indulging a passionate spirit in the face of divine warning and reproof, their guilt would have been far greater. But they were not chargeable with willful or deliberate sin; they had been overcome by a sudden temptation, and their contrition was immediate and heartfelt. The Lord accepted their repentance, though because of the harm their sin might do among the people, He could not remit its punishment.

Moses did not conceal his sentence, but told the people that since he had failed to ascribe glory to God, he could not lead them into the Promised Land. He bade them mark the severe punishment visited upon him, and then consider how God must regard their murmurings in charging upon a mere man the judgments which they had by their sins brought upon themselves. He told them how he had pleaded with God for a remission of the sentence, and had been refused. "The Lord was wroth with me for your sakes," he said, "and would not hear me." Deuteronomy 3:26.

On every occasion of difficulty or trial the Israelites had been ready to charge Moses with having led them from Egypt, as though God had had no agency in the matter. Throughout their journeyings, as they had complained of the difficulties in the way, and murmured against their leaders, Moses had told them, "Your murmurings are against God. It is not I, but God, who has wrought in your deliverance." But his hasty words before the rock, "shall we bring water?" were a virtual admission of their charge, and would thus confirm them in their unbelief and justify their murmurings. The Lord would remove this impression forever from their minds, by forbidding Moses to enter the Promised Land. Here was unmistakable evidence that their leader was not Moses, but the mighty Angel of whom the Lord had said, "Behold, I send an Angel before thee, to keep thee in the way, and to bring thee into the place which I have prepared. Beware of Him, and obey His voice: . . . for My name is in Him." Exodus 23:20, 21.

"The Lord was wroth with me for your sakes," said Moses. The eyes of all Israel were upon Moses, and his sin cast a reflection upon God, who had chosen him as the leader of His people. The transgression was known to the whole congregation; and had it been passed by lightly, the impression would have been given that unbelief and impatience under great provocation might be excused in those in responsible positions. But when it was declared that because of that one sin Moses and Aaron were not to enter Canaan, the people knew that God is no respecter of persons, and that He will surely punish the transgressor.

The history of Israel was to be placed on record for the instruction and warning of coming generations. Men of all future time must see the God of heaven as an impartial ruler, in no case justifying sin. But few realize the exceeding sinfulness of sin. Men flatter themselves that God is too good to punish the transgressor. But in the light of Bible history it is evident that God's goodness and His love engage Him to deal with sin as an evil fatal to the peace and happiness of the universe.

Not even the integrity and faithfulness of Moses could avert the retribution of his fault. God had forgiven the people greater transgressions, but He could not deal with sin in the leaders as in those who were led. He had honored Moses above every other man upon the earth. He had revealed to him His glory, and through him He had communicated His statutes to Israel. The fact that Moses had enjoyed so great light and knowledge made his sin more grievous. Past faithfulness will not atone for one wrong act. The greater the light and privileges granted to man, the greater is his responsibility, the more aggravated his failure, and the heavier his punishment.

Moses was not guilty of a great crime, as men would view the matter; his sin was one of common occurrence. The psalmist says that "he spake unadvisedly with his lips." Psalm 106:33. To human judgment this may seem a light thing; but if God dealt so severely with this sin in His most faithful and honored servant, He will not excuse it in others. The spirit of self-exaltation, the disposition to censure our brethren, is displeasing to God. Those who indulge in these evils cast doubt upon the work of God, and give the skeptical an excuse for their unbelief. The more important one's position, and the greater his influence, the greater is the necessity that he should cultivate patience and humility.

If the children of God, especially those who stand in positions of responsibility, can be led to take to themselves the glory that is due to God, Satan exults. He has gained a victory. It was thus that he fell. Thus he is most successful in tempting others to ruin. It is to place us on our guard against his devices that God has given in His word so many lessons teaching the danger of self-exaltation. There is not an impulse of our nature, not a faculty of the mind or an inclination of the heart, but needs to be, moment by moment, under the control of the Spirit of God. There is not a blessing which God bestows upon man, nor a trial which He permits to befall him, but Satan both can and will seize upon it to tempt, to harass and destroy the soul, if we give him the least advantage. Therefore however great one's spiritual light, however much he may enjoy of the divine favor and blessing, he should ever walk humbly before the Lord, pleading in faith that God will direct every thought and control every impulse.

All who profess godliness are under the most sacred obligation to guard the spirit, and to exercise self-control under the greatest provocation. The burdens placed upon Moses were very great; few men will ever be so severely tried as he was; yet this was not allowed to excuse his sin. God has made ample provision for His people; and if they rely upon His strength, they will never become the sport of circumstances. The strongest temptation cannot excuse sin. However great the pressure brought to bear upon the soul, transgression is our own act. It is not in the power of earth or hell to compel anyone to do evil. Satan attacks us at our weak points, but we need not be overcome. However severe or unexpected the assault, God has provided help for us, and in His strength we may conquer.

The Journey Around Edom

The encampment of Israel at Kadesh was but a short distance from the borders of Edom, and both Moses and the people greatly desired to follow the route through this country to the Promised Land; accordingly they sent a message, as God had directed them, to the Edomite king—

"Thus saith thy brother Israel, Thou knowest all the travail that hath befallen us: how our fathers went down into Egypt, and we have dwelt in Egypt a long time; and the Egyptians vexed us, and our fathers: and when we cried unto the Lord, He heard our voice, and sent an Angel, and hath brought us forth out of Egypt: and, behold, we are in Kadesh, a city in the uttermost of thy border. Let us pass, I pray thee, through thy country: we will not pass through the fields, or through the vineyards, neither will we drink of the water of the wells: we will go by the king's highway, we will not turn to the right hand nor to the left, until we have passed thy borders."

To this courteous request a threatening refusal was returned: "Thou shalt not pass by me, lest I come out against thee with the sword."

Surprised at this repulse, the leaders of Israel sent a second appeal to the king, with the promise, "We will go by the highway: and if I and my cattle drink of thy water, then I will pay for it: I will only, without doing anything else, go through on my feet."

"Thou shalt not go through," was the answer. Armed bands of Edomites were already posted at the difficult passes, so that any peaceful advance in that direction was impossible, and the

Hebrews were forbidden to resort to force. They must make the long journey around the land of Edom.

Had the people, when brought into trial, trusted in God, the Captain of the Lord's host would have led them through Edom, and the fear of them would have rested upon the inhabitants of the land, so that, instead of manifesting hostility, they would have shown them favor. But the Israelites did not act promptly upon God's word, and while they were complaining and murmuring, the golden opportunity passed. When they were at last ready to present their request to the king, it was refused. Ever since they left Egypt, Satan had been steadily at work to throw hindrances and temptations in their way, that they might not inherit Canaan. And by their own unbelief they had repeatedly opened the door for him to resist the purpose of God.

It is important to believe God's word and act upon it promptly, while His angels are waiting to work for us. Evil angels are ready to contest every step of advance. And when God's providence bids His children go forward, when He is ready to do great things for them. Satan tempts them to displease the Lord by hesitation and delay; he seeks to kindle a spirit of strife or to arouse murmuring or unbelief, and thus deprive them of the blessings that God desired to bestow. God's servants should be minutemen, ever ready to move as fast as His providence opens the way. And delay on their part gives time for Satan to work to defeat them.

In the directions first given to Moses concerning their passage through Edom, after declaring that the Edomites should be afraid of Israel, the Lord had forbidden His people to make use of this advantage against them. Because the power of God was engaged for Israel, and the fears of the Edomites would make them an easy prey, the Hebrews were not therefore to prey upon them. The command given them was, "Take ye good heed unto yourselves therefore: meddle not with them; for I will not give you of their land, no, not so much as a foot breadth; because I have given Mount Seir unto Esau for a possession." Deuteronomy 2:4, 5. The Edomites were descendants of Abraham and Isaac, and for the sake of these His servants, God had shown favor to the children of Esau. He had given them Mount Seir for a possession, and they were not to be disturbed unless by their sins they should place themselves beyond the reach of His mercy. The Hebrews were to dispossess and utterly destroy the inhabitants of Canaan, who had filled up the measure of their iniquity but the Edomites were still probationers, and as such were to be mercifully dealt with. God delights in mercy, and He manifests His compassion before He inflicts His judgments. He teaches Israel to spare the people of Edom, before requiring them to destroy the inhabitants of Canaan.

The ancestors of Edom and Israel were brothers, and brotherly kindness and courtesy should exist between them. The Israelites were forbidden, either then or at any future time, to revenge the affront given them in the refusal of passage through the land. They must not expect to possess any part of the land of Edom. While the Israelites were the chosen and favored people of God, they must heed the restrictions which He placed upon them. God had promised them a goodly inheritance; but they were not to feel that they alone had any rights in the earth, and seek to crowd out all others. They were directed, in all their intercourse with the Edomites, to beware of doing them injustice. They were to trade with them, buying such supplies as were needed, and promptly paying for all they received. As an encouragement to Israel to trust in God and obey His word they were reminded, "The Lord thy God hath blessed thee; . . . thou hast lacked nothing." Deuteronomy 2:7. They were not dependent upon the Edomites, for they had a God rich in resources. They must not by force or fraud seek to obtain anything pertaining to them; but in all their intercourse they should exemplify the principle of the divine law, "Thou shalt love thy neighbor as thyself."

Had they in this manner passed through Edom, as God had purposed, the passage would have proved a blessing, not only to themselves, but to the inhabitants of the land; for it would have given them an opportunity to become acquainted with God's people and His worship and to witness how the God of Jacob prospered those who loved and feared Him. But all this the unbelief of Israel had prevented. God had given the people water in answer to their clamors, but He permitted their unbelief to work out its punishment. Again they must traverse the desert and quench their thirst from the miraculous spring, which, had they but trusted in Him, they would no longer have needed.

Accordingly the hosts of Israel again turned toward the south, and made their way over sterile wastes, that seemed even more dreary after a glimpse of the green spots among the hills and valleys of Edom. From the mountain range overlooking this gloomy desert, rises Mount Hor, whose summit was to be the place of Aaron's death and burial. When the Israelites came to this mountain, the divine command was addressed to Moses—

"Take Aaron and Eleazar his son, and bring them up unto Mount Hor: and strip Aaron of his garments, and put them upon Eleazar his son: and Aaron shall be gathered unto his people, and shall die there."

Together these two aged men and the younger one toiled up the mountain height. The heads of Moses and Aaron were white with the snows of sixscore winters. Their long and eventful lives had been marked with the deepest trials and the greatest honors that had ever fallen to the lot of man. They were men of great natural ability, and all their powers had been developed, exalted, and dignified by communion with the Infinite One. Their life had been spent in unselfish labor for God and their fellow men; their countenances gave evidence of great intellectual power, firmness and nobility of purpose, and strong affections.

Many years Moses and Aaron had stood side by side in their cares and labors. Together they had breasted unnumbered dangers, and had shared together the signal blessing of God; but the time was at hand when they must be separated. They moved on very slowly, for every moment in each other's society was precious. The ascent was steep and toilsome; and as they often paused to rest, they communed together of the past and the future. Before them, as far as the eye could reach, was spread out the scene of their desert wanderings. In the plain below were encamped the vast hosts of Israel, for whom these chosen men had spent the best portion of their lives; for whose welfare they had felt so deep an interest, and made so great sacrifices. Somewhere beyond the mountains of Edom was the path leading to the Promised Land—that land whose blessings Moses and Aaron were not to enjoy. No rebellious feelings found a place in their hearts, no expression of murmuring escaped their lips; yet a solemn sadness rested upon their countenances as they remembered what had debarred them from the inheritance of their fathers.

Aaron's work for Israel was done. Forty years before, at the age of eighty-three, God had called him to unite with Moses in his great and important mission. He had co-operated with his brother in leading the children of Israel from Egypt. He had held up the great leader's hands when the Hebrew hosts gave battle to Amalek. He had been permitted to ascend Mount Sinai, to approach into the presence of God, and to behold the divine glory. The Lord had conferred upon the family of Aaron the office of the priesthood, and had honored him with the sacred consecration of high priest. He had sustained him in the holy office by the terrible manifestations of divine judgment in the destruction of Korah and his company. It was through Aaron's intercession that the plague was stayed. When his two sons were slain for disregarding God's express command, he did not rebel or even murmur. Yet the record of his noble life had been marred. Aaron committed a grievous sin when he yielded to the clamors of the people and made the golden calf at Sinai; and again, when he united with Miriam in envy and murmuring against Moses. And he, with Moses, offended the Lord at Kadesh by disobeying the command to speak to the rock that it might give forth its water.

God intended that these great leaders of His people should be representatives of Christ. Aaron bore the names of Israel upon his breast. He communicated to the people the will of God. He entered the most holy place on the Day of Atonement, "not without blood," as a mediator for all Israel. He came forth from that work to bless the congregation, as Christ will come forth to bless His waiting people when His work of atonement in their behalf shall be ended. It was the exalted character of that sacred office as representative of our great High Priest that made Aaron's sin at Kadesh of so great magnitude.

With deep sorrow Moses removed from Aaron the holy vestments, and placed them upon Eleazar, who thus became his successor by divine appointment. For his sin at Kadesh, Aaron was denied the privilege of officiating as God's high priest in Canaan—of offering the first sacrifice in the goodly land, and thus consecrating the inheritance of Israel. Moses was to continue to bear his burden in leading the people to the very borders of Canaan. He was to come within sight of the Promised Land, but was not to enter it. Had these servants of God, when they stood before the rock at Kadesh, borne unmurmuringly the test there brought upon them, how different would have been their future! A wrong act can never be undone. It may be that the work of a lifetime will not recover what has been lost in a single moment of temptation or even thoughtlessness.

The absence from the camp of the two great leaders, and the fact that they had been accompanied by Eleazar, who, it was well known, was to be Aaron's successor in holy office, awakened a feeling of apprehension, and their return was anxiously awaited. As the people looked about them, upon their vast congregation, they saw that nearly all the adults who left Egypt had perished in the wilderness. All felt a foreboding of evil as they remembered the sentence pronounced against Moses and Aaron. Some were aware of the object of that mysterious journey to the summit of Mount Hor, and their solicitude for their leaders was heightened by bitter memories and self-accusings.

The forms of Moses and Eleazar were at last discerned, slowly descending the mountainside, but Aaron was not with them. Upon Eleazar were the sacerdotal garments, showing that he had succeeded his father in the sacred office. As the people with heavy hearts gathered about their leader, Moses told them that Aaron had died in his arms upon Mount Hor, and that they there buried him. The congregation broke forth in mourning and lamentation, for they all loved Aaron, though they had so often caused him sorrow. "They mourned for Aaron thirty days, even all the house of Israel."

Concerning the burial of Israel's high priest, the Scriptures give only the simple record, "There Aaron died, and there he was buried." Deuteronomy 10:6. In what striking contrast to the customs of the present day was this burial, conducted according to the express command of God. In modern times the funeral services of a man of high position are often made the occasion of ostentatious and extravagant display. When Aaron died, one of the most illustrious men that ever lived, there were only two of his nearest friends to witness his death and to attend his burial. And that lonely grave upon Mount Hor was forever hidden from the sight of Israel. God is not honored in the great display so often made over the dead, and the extravagant expense incurred in returning their bodies to the dust.

The whole congregation sorrowed for Aaron, yet they could not feel the loss so keenly as did Moses. The death of Aaron forcibly reminded Moses that his own end was near; but short as the time of his stay on earth must be, he deeply felt the loss of his constant companion—the one who had shared his joys and sorrows, his hopes and fears, for so many long years. Moses must now continue the work alone; but he knew that God was his friend, and upon Him he leaned more heavily.

Soon after leaving Mount Hor the Israelites suffered defeat in an engagement with Arad, one of the Canaanite kings. But as they earnestly sought help from God, divine aid was granted them, and their enemies were routed. This victory, instead of inspiring gratitude and leading the people to feel their dependence upon God, made them boastful and self-confident. Soon they fell into the old habit of murmuring. They were now dissatisfied because the armies of Israel had not been permitted to advance upon Canaan immediately after their rebellion at the report of the spies nearly forty years before. They pronounced their long sojourn in the wilderness an unnecessary delay, reasoning that they might have conquered their enemies as easily heretofore as now.

As they continued their journey toward the south, their route lay through a hot, sandy valley, destitute of shade or vegetation. The way seemed long and difficult, and they suffered from weariness and thirst. Again they failed to endure the test of their faith and patience. By continually dwelling on the dark side of their experiences, they separated themselves farther and farther from God. They lost sight of the fact that but for their murmuring when the water ceased at Kadesh, they would have been spared the journey around Edom. God had purposed better things for them. Their hearts should have been filled with gratitude to Him that He had punished their sin so lightly. But instead of this, they flattered themselves that if God and Moses had not interfered, they might now have been in possession of the Promised Land. After bringing trouble upon themselves, making their lot altogether harder than God designed, they charged all their misfortunes upon Him. Thus they cherished bitter thoughts concerning His dealings with them, and finally they became discontented with everything. Egypt looked brighter and more desirable than liberty and the land to which God was leading them.

As the Israelites indulged the spirit of discontent, they were disposed to find fault even with their blessings. "And the people spake against God, and against Moses, Wherefore have ye brought us up out of Egypt to die in the wilderness? for there is no bread, neither is there any water; and our soul loatheth this light bread."

Moses faithfully set before the people their great sin. It was God's power alone that had preserved them in "that great and terrible wilderness, wherein were fiery serpents, and scorpions, and drought, where there was no water." Deuteronomy 8:15. Every day of their travels they had been kept by a miracle of divine mercy. In all the way of God's leading they had found water to refresh the thirsty, bread from heaven to satisfy their hunger, and peace and safety under the shadowy cloud by day and the pillar of fire by night. Angels had ministered to them as they climbed the rocky heights or threaded the rugged paths of the wilderness. Notwithstanding the hardships they had endured, there was not a feeble one in all their ranks. Their feet had not swollen in their long journeys, neither had their clothes grown old. God had subdued before them the fierce beasts of prey and the venomous reptiles of the forest and the desert. If with all these tokens of His love the people still continued to complain, the Lord would withdraw His protection until they should be led to appreciate His merciful care, and return to Him with repentance and humiliation.

Because they had been shielded by divine power they had not realized the countless dangers by which they were continually surrounded. In their ingratitude and unbelief they had anticipated death, and now the Lord permitted death to come upon them. The poisonous serpents that infested the wilderness were called fiery serpents, on account of the terrible effects produced by their sting, it causing violent inflammation and speedy death. As the protecting hand of God was removed from Israel, great numbers of the people were attacked by these venomous creatures.

Now there was terror and confusion throughout the encampment. In almost every tent were the dying or the dead. None were secure. Often the silence of night was broken by piercing cries that told of fresh victims. All were busy in ministering to the sufferers, or with agonizing care endeavoring to protect those who were not yet stricken. No murmuring now escaped their lips. When compared with the present suffering, their former difficulties and trials seemed unworthy of a thought.

The people now humbled themselves before God. They came to Moses with their confessions and entreaties. "We have sinned," they said, "for we have spoken against the Lord, and against thee." Only a little before, they had accused him of being their worst enemy, the cause of all their distress and afflictions. But even when the words were upon their lips, they knew that the charge was false; and as soon as real trouble came they fled to him as the only one who could intercede with God for them. "Pray unto the Lord," was their cry, "that He take away the serpents from us."

Moses was divinely commanded to make a serpent of brass resembling the living ones, and to elevate it among the people. To this, all who had been bitten were to look, and they would find relief. He did so, and the joyful news was sounded throughout the encampment that all who had been bitten might look upon the brazen serpent and live. Many had already died, and when Moses raised the serpent upon the pole, some would not believe that merely gazing upon that metallic image would heal them; these perished in their unbelief. Yet there were many who had faith in the provision which God had made. Fathers, mothers, brothers, and sisters were anxiously engaged in helping their suffering, dying friends to fix their languid eyes upon the serpent. If these, though faint and dying, could only once look, they were perfectly restored.

The people well knew that there was no power in the serpent of brass to cause such a change in those who looked upon it. The healing virtue was from God alone. In His wisdom He chose this way of displaying His power. By this simple means the people were made to realize that this affliction had been brought upon them by their sins. They were also assured that while obeying God they had no reason to fear, for He would preserve them.

The lifting up of the brazen serpent was to teach Israel an important lesson. They could not save themselves from the fatal effect of the poison in their wounds. God alone was able to heal them. Yet they were required to show their faith in the provision which He had made. They must look in order to live. It was their faith that was acceptable with God, and by looking upon the serpent their faith was shown. They knew that there was no virtue in the serpent itself, but it was a symbol of Christ; and the necessity of faith in His merits was thus presented to their minds. Heretofore many had brought their offerings to God, and had felt that in so doing they made ample atonement for their sins. They did not rely upon the Redeemer to come, of whom these offerings were only a type. The Lord would now teach them that their sacrifices, in themselves, had no more power or virtue than the serpent of brass, but were, like that, to lead their minds to Christ, the great sin offering.

"As Moses lifted up the serpent in the wilderness," even so was the Son of man "lifted up: that whosoever believeth in Him should not perish, but have eternal life." John 3:14, 15. All who have ever lived upon the earth have felt the deadly sting of "that old serpent, called the devil, and Satan." Revelation 12:9. The fatal effects of sin can be removed only by the provision that God has made. The Israelites saved their lives by looking upon the uplifted serpent. That look implied faith. They lived because they believed God's word, and trusted in the means provided for their recovery. So the sinner may look to Christ, and live. He receives pardon through faith in the atoning sacrifice. Unlike the inert and lifeless symbol, Christ has power and virtue in Himself to heal the repenting sinner.

While the sinner cannot save himself, he still has something to do to secure salvation. "Him that cometh to Me," says Christ, "I will in no wise cast out." John 6:37. But we must come to Him; and when we repent of our sins, we must believe that He accepts and pardons us. Faith is the gift of God, but the power to exercise it is ours. Faith is the hand by which the soul takes hold upon the divine offers of grace and mercy.

Nothing but the righteousness of Christ can entitle us to one of the blessings of the covenant of grace. There are many who have long desired and tried to obtain these blessings, but have not received them, because they have cherished the idea that they could do something to make themselves worthy of them. They have not looked away from self, believing that Jesus is an all-sufficient Saviour. We must not think that our own merits will save us; Christ is our only hope of salvation. "For there is none other name under heaven given among men, whereby we must be saved." Acts 4:12.

When we trust God fully, when we rely upon the merits of Jesus as a sin-pardoning Saviour, we shall receive all the help that we can desire. Let none look to self, as though they had power to save themselves. Jesus died for us because we were helpless to do this. In Him is our hope, our justification, our righteousness. When we see our sinfulness we should not despond and fear that we have no Saviour, or that He has no thoughts of mercy toward us. At this very time He is inviting us to come to Him in our helplessness and be saved.

Many of the Israelites saw no help in the remedy which Heaven had appointed. The dead and dying were all around them, and they knew that, without divine aid, their own fate was certain; but they continued to lament their wounds, their pains, their sure death, until their strength was gone, and their eyes were glazed, when they might have had instant healing. If we are conscious of our needs, we should not devote all our powers to mourning over them. While we realize our helpless condition without Christ, we are not to yield to discouragement, but rely upon the merits of a crucified and risen Saviour. Look and live. Jesus has pledged His word; He will save all who come unto Him. Though millions who need to be healed will reject His offered mercy, not one who trusts in His merits will be left to perish.

Many are unwilling to accept of Christ until the whole mystery of the plan of salvation shall be made plain to them. They refuse the look of faith, although they see that thousands have looked, and have felt the efficacy of looking, to the cross of Christ. Many wander in the mazes of philosophy, in search of reasons and evidence which they will never find, while they reject the evidence which God has been pleased to give. They refuse to walk in the light of the Sun of Righteousness, until the reason of its shining shall be explained. All who persist in this course will fail to come to a knowledge of the truth. God will never remove every occasion for doubt. He gives sufficient evidence on which to base faith, and if this is not accepted, the mind is left in darkness. If those who were bitten by the serpents had stopped to doubt and question before they would consent to look, they would have perished. It is our duty, first, to look; and the look of faith will give us life.

The Conquest of Bashan

After passing to the south of Edom, the Israelites turned northward, and again set their faces toward the Promised Land. Their route now lay over a vast, elevated plain, swept by cool, fresh breezes from the hills. It was a welcome change from the parched valley through which they had been traveling, and they pressed forward, buoyant and hopeful. Having crossed the brook Zered, they passed to the east of the land of Moab; for the command had been given, "Distress not the Moabites, neither contend with them in battle: for I will not give thee of their land for a possession; because I have given Ar unto the children of Lot." And the same direction was repeated concerning the Ammonites, who were also descendants of Lot.

Still pushing northward, the hosts of Israel soon reached the country of the Amorites. This strong and warlike people originally occupied the southern part of the land of Canaan; but, increasing in numbers, they crossed the Jordan, made war upon the Moabites, and gained possession of a portion of their territory. Here they had settled, holding undisputed sway over all the land from the Arnon as far north as the Jabbok. The route to the Jordan which the Israelites desired to pursue lay directly through this territory, and Moses sent a friendly message to Sihon, the Amorite king, at his capital: "Let me pass through thy land: I will go along by the highway, I will neither turn unto the right hand nor to the left. Thou shalt sell me meat for money, that I may eat; and give me water for money, that I may drink: only I will pass through on my feet." The answer was a decided refusal, and all the hosts of the Amorites were summoned to oppose the progress of the invaders. This formidable army struck terror to the Israelites, who were poorly prepared for an encounter with well-armed and well-disciplined forces. So far as skill in warfare was concerned, their enemies had the advantage. To all human appearance, a speedy end would be made of Israel.

But Moses kept his gaze fixed upon the cloudy pillar, and encouraged the people with the thought that the token of God's presence was still with them. At the same time he directed them to do all that human power could do in preparing for war. Their enemies were eager for battle, and confident that they would blot out the unprepared Israelites from the land. But from the Possessor of all lands the mandate had gone forth to the leader of Israel: "Rise ye up, take your journey, and pass over the river Arnon: behold, I have given into thine hand Sihon the Amorite, king of Heshbon, and his land: begin to possess it, and contend with him in battle. This day will I begin to put the dread of thee and the fear of thee upon the nations that are under the whole heaven, who shall hear report of thee, and shall tremble, and be in anguish because of thee."

These nations on the borders of Canaan would have been spared, had they not stood, in defiance of God's word, to oppose the progress of Israel. The Lord had shown Himself to be long-suffering, of great kindness and tender pity, even to these heathen peoples. When Abraham was shown in vision that his seed, the children of Israel, should be strangers in a strange land four hundred years, the Lord gave him the promise, "In the fourth generation they shall come hither again: for the iniquity of the Amorites is not yet full." Genesis 15:16. Although the Amorites were idolaters, whose life was justly forfeited by their great wickedness, God spared them four hundred years to give them unmistakable evidence that He was the only true God, the Maker of heaven and earth. All His wonders in bringing Israel from Egypt were known to them. Sufficient evidence was given; they might have known the truth, had they been willing to turn from their idolatry and licentiousness. But they rejected the light and clung to their idols.

When the Lord brought His people a second time to the borders of Canaan, additional evidence of His power was granted to those heathen nations. They saw that God was with Israel in the victory gained over King Arad and the Canaanites, and in the miracle wrought to save those who were perishing from the sting of the serpents. Although the Israelites had been refused a passage through the land of Edom, thus being compelled to take the long and difficult route by the Red Sea, yet in all their journeyings and encampments, past the land of Edom, of Moab and Ammon,

they had shown no hostility, and had done no injury to the people or their possessions. On reaching the border of the Amorites, Israel had asked permission only to travel directly through the country, promising to observe the same rules that had governed their intercourse with other nations. When the Amorite king refused this courteous solicitation, and defiantly gathered his hosts for battle, their cup of iniquity was full, and God would now exercise His power for their overthrow.

The Israelites crossed the river Arnon and advanced upon the foe. An engagement took place, in which the armies of Israel were victorious; and, following up the advantage gained, they were soon in possession of the country of the Amorites. It was the Captain of the Lord's host who vanquished the enemies of His people; and He would have done the same thirty-eight years before had Israel trusted in Him.

Filled with hope and courage, the army of Israel eagerly pressed forward, and, still journeying northward, they soon reached a country that might well test their courage and their faith in God. Before them lay the powerful and populous kingdom of Bashan, crowded with great stone cities that to this day excite the wonder of the world—"threescore cities . . . with high walls, gates, and bars; besides unwalled towns a great many." Deuteronomy 3:1-11. The houses were constructed of huge black stones, of such stupendous size as to make the buildings absolutely impregnable to any force that in those times could have been brought against them. It was a country filled with wild caverns, lofty precipices, yawning gulfs, and rocky strongholds. The inhabitants of this land, descendants from a giant race, were themselves of marvelous size and strength, and so distinguished for violence and cruelty as to be the terror of all surrounding nations; while Og, the king of the country, was remarkable for size and prowess, even in a nation of giants.

But the cloudy pillar moved forward, and following its guidance the Hebrew hosts advanced to Edrei, where the giant king, with his forces, awaited their approach. Og had skillfully chosen the place of battle. The city of Edrei was situated upon the border of a tableland rising abruptly from the plain, and covered with jagged, volcanic rocks. It could be approached only by narrow pathways, steep and difficult of ascent. In case of defeat, his forces could find refuge in that wilderness of rocks, where it would be impossible for strangers to follow them.

Confident of success, the king came forth with an immense army upon the open plain, while shouts of defiance were heard from the tableland above, where might be seen the spears of thousands, eager for the fray. When the Hebrews looked upon the lofty form of that giant of giants towering above the soldiers of his army; when they saw the hosts that surrounded him, and beheld the seemingly impregnable fortress, behind which unseen thousands were entrenched, the hearts of many in Israel quaked with fear. But Moses was calm and firm; the Lord had said concerning the king of Bashan, "Fear him not: for I will deliver him, and all his people, and his land, into thy hand; and thou shalt do unto him as thou didst unto Sihon king of the Amorites, which dwelt at Heshbon."

The calm faith of their leader inspired the people with confidence in God. They trusted all to His omnipotent arm, and He did not fail them. Not mighty giants nor walled cities, armed hosts nor rocky fortresses, could stand before the Captain of the Lord's host. The Lord led the army; the Lord discomfited the enemy; the Lord conquered in behalf of Israel. The giant king and his army were destroyed, and the Israelites soon took possession of the whole country. Thus was blotted from the earth that strange people who had given themselves up to iniquity and abominable idolatry.

In the conquest of Gilead and Bashan there were many who recalled the events which nearly forty years before had, in Kadesh, doomed Israel to the long desert wandering. They saw that the report of the spies concerning the Promised Land was in many respects correct. The cities were walled and very great, and were inhabited by giants, in comparison with whom the Hebrews were mere pygmies. But they could now see that the fatal mistake of their fathers had been in distrusting the power of God. This alone had prevented them from at once entering the goodly land.

When they were at the first preparing to enter Canaan, the undertaking was attended with far less difficulty than now. God had promised His people that if they would obey His voice He would go before them and fight for them; and He would also send hornets to drive out the inhabitants of the land. The fears of the nations had not been generally aroused, and little preparation had been made to oppose their progress. But when the Lord now bade Israel go forward, they must advance against alert and powerful foes, and must contend with large and well-trained armies that had been preparing to resist their approach.

In their contest with Og and Sihon the people were brought to the same test beneath which their fathers had so signally failed. But the trial was now far more severe than when God had commanded Israel to go forward. The difficulties in their way had greatly increased since they refused to advance when bidden to do so in the name of the Lord. It is thus that God still tests His people. And if they fail to endure the trial, He brings them again to the same point, and the second time the trial will come closer, and be more severe than the preceding. This is continued until they bear the test, or, if they are still rebellious, God withdraws His light from them and leaves them in darkness.

The Hebrews now remembered how once before, when their forces had gone to battle, they had been routed, and thousands slain. But they had then gone in direct opposition to the command of God. They had gone out without Moses, God's appointed leader, without the cloudy pillar, the symbol of the divine presence, and without the ark. But now Moses was with them, strengthening their hearts with words of hope and faith; the Son of God, enshrined in the cloudy pillar, led the way; and the sacred ark accompanied the host. This experience has a lesson for us. The mighty God of Israel is our God. In Him we may trust, and if we obey His requirements He will work for us in as signal a manner as He did for His ancient people. Everyone who seeks to follow the path of duty will at times be assailed by doubt and unbelief. The way will sometimes be so barred by obstacles, apparently insurmountable, as to dishearten those who will yield to discouragement; but God is saying to such, Go forward. Do your duty at any cost. The difficulties that seem so formidable, that fill your soul with dread, will vanish as you move forward in the path of obedience, humbly trusting in God.

Balaam

Returning to the Jordan from the conquest of Bashan, the Israelites, in preparation for the immediate invasion of Canaan, encamped beside the river, above its entrance into the Dead Sea, and just opposite the plain of Jericho. They were upon the very borders of Moab, and the Moabites were filled with terror at the close proximity of the invaders.

The people of Moab had not been molested by Israel, yet they had watched with troubled forebodings all that had taken place in the surrounding countries. The Amorites, before whom they had been forced to retreat, had been conquered by the Hebrews, and the territory which the Amorites had wrested from Moab was now in the possession of Israel. The hosts of Bashan had yielded before the mysterious power enshrouded in the cloudy pillar, and the giant strongholds were occupied by the Hebrews. The Moabites dared not risk an attack upon them; an appeal to arms was hopeless in face of the supernatural agencies that wrought in their behalf. But they determined, as Pharaoh had done, to enlist the power of sorcery to counteract the work of God. They would bring a curse upon Israel.

The people of Moab were closely connected with the Midianites, both by the ties of nationality and religion. And Balak, the king of Moab, aroused the fears of the kindred people, and secured their co-operation in his designs against Israel by the message, "Now shall this company lick up all that are round about us, as the ox licketh up the grass of the field." Balaam, an inhabitant of Mesopotamia, was reported to possess supernatural powers, and his fame had reached to the land of Moab. It was determined to call him to their aid. Accordingly, messengers of "the elders of Moab and the elders of Midian," were sent to secure his divinations and enchantments against Israel.

The ambassadors at once set out on their long journey over the mountains and across the deserts to Mesopotamia; and upon finding Balaam, they delivered to him the message of their king: "Behold, there is a people come out from Egypt: behold, they cover the face of the earth, and they abide over against me: come now therefore, I pray thee, curse me this people; for they are too mighty for me: peradventure I shall prevail, that we may smite them, and that I may drive them out of the land: for I wot that he whom thou blessest is blessed, and he whom thou cursest is cursed."

Balaam was once a good man and a prophet of God; but he had apostatized, and had given up to covetousness; yet he still professed to be a servant of the Most High. He was not ignorant of God's work in behalf of Israel; and when the messengers announced their errand, he well knew that it was his duty to refuse the rewards of Balak and to dismiss the ambassadors. But he ventured to dally with temptation, and urged the messengers to tarry with him that night, declaring that he could give no decided answer till he had asked counsel of the Lord. Balaam knew that his curse could not harm Israel. God was on their side, and so long as they were true to Him no adverse power of earth or hell could prevail against them. But his pride was flattered by the words of the ambassadors, "He whom thou blessest is blessed, and he whom thou cursest is cursed." The bribe of costly gifts and prospective exaltation excited his covetousness. He greedily accepted the offered treasures, and then, while professing strict obedience to the will of God, he tried to comply with the desires of Balak.

In the night season the angel of God came to Balaam with the message, "Thou shalt not go with them; thou shalt not curse the people: for they are blessed."

In the morning Balaam reluctantly dismissed the messengers, but he did not tell them what the Lord had said. Angry that his visions of gain and honor had been suddenly dispelled, he petulantly exclaimed, "Get you into your land: for the Lord refuseth to give me leave to go with you."

Balaam "loved the wages of unrighteousness." 2 Peter 2:15. The sin of covetousness, which God declares to be idolatry, had made him a timeserver, and through this one fault Satan gained

entire control of him. It was this that caused his ruin. The tempter is ever presenting worldly gain and honor to entice men from the service of God. He tells them it is their overconscientiousness that keeps them from prosperity. Thus many are induced to venture out of the path of strict integrity. One wrong step makes the next easier, and they become more and more presumptuous. They will do and dare most terrible things when once they have given themselves to the control of avarice and a desire for power. Many flatter themselves that they can depart from strict integrity for a time, for the sake of some worldly advantage, and that having gained their object, they can change their course when they please. Such are entangling themselves in the snare of Satan, and it is seldom that they escape.

When the messengers reported to Balak the prophet's refusal to accompany them, they did not intimate that God had forbidden him. Supposing that Balaam's delay was merely to secure a richer reward, the king sent princes more in number and more honorable than the first, with promises of higher honors, and with authority to concede to any terms that Balaam might demand. Balak's urgent message to the prophet was, "Let nothing, I pray thee, hinder thee from coming unto me: for I will promote thee unto very great honor, and I will do whatsoever thou sayest unto me: come

therefore, I pray thee, curse me this people."

A second time Balaam was tested. In response to the solicitations of the ambassadors he professed great conscientiousness and integrity, assuring them that no amount of gold and silver could induce him to go contrary to the will of God. But he longed to comply with the king's request; and although the will of God had already been definitely made known to him, he urged the messengers to tarry, that he might further inquire of God; as though the Infinite One were a man, to be persuaded.

In the night season the Lord appeared to Balaam and said, "If the men come to call thee, rise up, and go with them; but yet the word which I shall say unto thee, that shalt thou do." Thus far the Lord would permit Balaam to follow his own will, because he was determined upon it. He did not seek to do the will of God, but chose his own course, and then endeavored to secure the sanction of the Lord.

There are thousands at the present day who are pursuing a similar course. They would have no difficulty in understanding their duty if it were in harmony with their inclinations. It is plainly set before them in the Bible or is clearly indicated by circumstances and reason. But because these evidences are contrary to their desires and inclinations they frequently set them aside and presume to go to God to learn their duty. With great apparent conscientiousness they pray long and earnestly for light. But God will not be trifled with. He often permits such persons to follow their own desires and to suffer the result. "My people would not hearken to My voice. . . . So I gave them up unto their own hearts' lust: and they walked in their own counsels." Psalm 81:11, 12. When one clearly sees a duty, let him not presume to go to God with the prayer that he may be excused from performing it. He should rather, with a humble, submissive spirit, ask for divine strength and wisdom to meet its claims.

The Moabites were a degraded, idolatrous people; yet according to the light which they had received their guilt was not so great in the sight of Heaven as was that of Balaam. As he professed to be God's prophet, however, all he should say would be supposed to be uttered by divine authority. Hence he was not to be permitted to speak as he chose, but must deliver the message which God should give him. "The word which I shall say unto thee, that shalt thou do," was the divine command.

Balaam had received permission to go with the messengers from Moab if they came in the morning to call him. But, annoyed at his delay, and expecting another refusal, they set out on their homeward journey without further consultation with him. Every excuse for complying with the request of Balak had now been removed. But Balaam was determined to secure the reward; and, taking the beast upon which he was accustomed to ride, he set out on the journey. He feared that even now the divine permission might be withdrawn, and he pressed eagerly forward, impatient lest he should by some means fail to gain the coveted reward.

But "the angel of the Lord stood in the way for an adversary against him." The animal saw the divine messenger, who was unperceived by the man, and turned aside from the highway into a field. With cruel blows Balaam brought the beast back into the path; but again, in a narrow place shut in by walls, the angel appeared, and the animal, trying to avoid the menacing figure, crushed her master's foot against the wall. Balaam was blinded to the heavenly interposition, and knew not that God was obstructing his path. The man became exasperated, and beating the ass unmercifully, forced it to proceed.

Again, "in a narrow place, where was no way to turn either to the right hand or to the left," the angel appeared, as before, in a threatening attitude; and the poor beast, trembling with terror, made a full stop, and fell to the earth under its rider. Balaam's rage was unbounded, and with his staff he smote the animal more cruelly than before. God now opened its mouth, and by "the dumb ass speaking with man's voice," he "forbade the madness of the prophet." 2 Peter 2:16. "What have I done unto thee," it said, "that thou hast smitten me these three times?"

Furious at being thus hindered in his journey, Balaam answered the beast as he would have addressed an intelligent being—"Because thou hast mocked me: I would there were a sword in mine hand, for now would I kill thee." Here was a professed magician, on his way to pronounce a curse upon a whole people with the intent to paralyze their strength, while he had not power even to slay the animal upon which he rode!

The eyes of Balaam were now opened, and he beheld the angel of God standing with drawn sword ready to slay him. In terror "he bowed down his head, and fell flat on his face." The angel said to him, "Wherefore hast thou smitten thine ass these three times? Behold, I went out to withstand thee, because thy way is perverse before me: and the ass saw me, and turned from me these three times: unless she had turned from me surely now also I had slain thee, and saved her alive."

Balaam owed the preservation of his life to the poor animal that he had treated so cruelly. The man who claimed to be a prophet of the Lord, who declared that his eyes were open, and he saw the "vision of the Almighty," was so blinded by covetousness and ambition that he could not discern the angel of God visible to his beast. "The god of this world hath blinded the minds of them which believe not." 2 Corinthians 4:4. How many are thus blinded! They rush on in forbidden paths, transgressing the divine law, and cannot discern that God and His angels are against them. Like Balaam they are angry at those who would prevent their ruin.

Balaam had given evidence of the spirit that controlled him, by his treatment of his beast. "A righteous man regardeth the life of his beast: but the tender mercies of the wicked are cruel."

Proverbs 12:10. Few realize as they should the sinfulness of abusing animals or leaving them to suffer from neglect. He who created man made the lower animals also, and "His tender mercies are over all His works." Psalm 145:9. The animals were created to serve man, but he has no right to cause them pain by harsh treatment or cruel exaction.

It is because of man's sin that "the whole creation groaneth and travaileth in pain together." Romans 8:22. Suffering and death were thus entailed, not only upon the human race, but upon the animals. Surely, then, it becomes man to seek to lighten, instead of increasing, the weight of suffering which his transgression has brought upon God's creatures. He who will abuse animals because he has them in his power is both a coward and a tyrant. A disposition to cause pain, whether to our fellow men or to the brute creation, is satanic. Many do not realize that their cruelty will ever be known, because the poor dumb animals cannot reveal it. But could the eyes of these men be opened, as were those of Balaam, they would see an angel of God standing as a witness, to testify against them in the courts above. A record goes up to heaven, and a day is coming when judgment will be pronounced against those who abuse God's creatures.

When he beheld the messenger of God, Balaam exclaimed in terror, "I have sinned; for I knew not that thou stoodest in the way against me: now therefore, if it displease thee, I will get me back again." The Lord suffered him to proceed on his journey, but gave him to understand that his words should be controlled by divine power. God would give evidence to Moab that the Hebrews were under the guardianship of Heaven, and this He did effectually when He showed them how powerless Balaam was even to utter a curse against them without divine permission.

The king of Moab, being informed of the approach of Balaam, went out with a large retinue to the borders of his kingdom, to receive him. When he expressed his astonishment at Balaam's delay, in view of the rich rewards awaiting him, the prophet's answer was, "Lo, I am come unto thee: have I now any power at all to say anything? the word that God putteth in my mouth, that shall I speak." Balaam greatly regretted this restriction; he feared that his purpose could not be carried out, because the Lord's controlling power was upon him.

With great pomp the king, with the chief dignitaries of his kingdom, escorted Balaam to "the high places of Baal," from which he could survey the Hebrew host. Behold the prophet as he stands upon the lofty height, looking down over the encampment of God's chosen people. How little do the Israelites know of what is taking place so near them! How little do they know of the care of God, extended over them by day and by night! How dull are the perceptions of God's people! How slow are they, in every age, to comprehend His great love and mercy! If they could discern the wonderful power of God constantly exerted in their behalf, would not their hearts be filled with gratitude for His love, and with awe at the thought of His majesty and power?

Balaam had some knowledge of the sacrificial offerings of the Hebrews, and he hoped that by surpassing them in costly gifts he might secure the blessing of God and ensure the accomplishment of his sinful projects. Thus the sentiments of the idolatrous Moabites were gaining control of his mind. His wisdom had become foolishness; his spiritual vision was beclouded; he had brought blindness upon himself by yielding to the power of Satan.

By Balaam's direction seven altars were erected, and he offered a sacrifice upon each. He then withdrew to a "high place," to meet with God, promising to make known to Balak whatever the Lord should reveal.

With the nobles and princes of Moab the king stood beside the sacrifice, while around them gathered the eager multitude, watching for the return of the prophet. He came at last, and the people waited for the words that should paralyze forever that strange power exerted in behalf of the hated Israelites. Balaam said:

> "The king of Moab hath brought me from Aram,
> Out of the mountains of the east,
> Saying, Come, curse me Jacob,
> And come, defy Israel.
> How shall I curse, whom God hath not cursed?
> Or how shall I defy, whom the Lord hath not defied?
> For from the top of the rocks I see him,
> And from the hills I behold him:
> Lo, the people shall dwell alone,
> And shall not be reckoned among the nations.
> Who can count the dust of Jacob,
> And the number of the fourth part of Israel?
> Let me die the death of the righteous,
> And let my last end be like his!"

Balaam confessed that he came with the purpose of cursing Israel, but the words he uttered were directly contrary to the sentiments of his heart. He was constrained to pronounce blessings, while his soul was filled with curses.

As Balaam looked upon the encampment of Israel he beheld with astonishment the evidence of their prosperity. They had been represented to him as a rude, disorganized multitude, infesting the country in roving bands that were a pest and terror to the surrounding nations; but their appearance was the reverse of all this. He saw the vast extent and perfect arrangement of their camp, everything bearing the marks of thorough discipline and order. He was shown the favor with which God regarded Israel, and their distinctive character as His chosen people. They were not to stand upon a level with other nations, but to be exalted above them all. "The people shall dwell alone, and shall not be reckoned among the nations." At the time when these words were spoken the Israelites had no permanent settlement, and their peculiar character, their manners and customs, were not familiar to Balaam. But how strikingly was this prophecy fulfilled in the afterhistory of Israel! Through all the years of their captivity, through all the ages since they were dispersed among the nations, they have remained a distinct people. So the people of God—the true Israel—though scattered throughout all nations, are on earth but sojourners, whose citizenship is in heaven.

Not only was Balaam shown the history of the Hebrew people as a nation, but he beheld the increase and prosperity of the true Israel of God to the close of time. He saw the special favor of the Most High attending those who love and fear Him. He saw them supported by His arm as they enter the dark valley of the shadow of death. And he beheld them coming forth from their graves, crowned with glory, honor, and immortality. He saw the redeemed rejoicing in the unfading glories of the earth made new. Gazing upon the scene, he exclaimed, "Who can count the dust of Jacob, and the number of the fourth part of Israel?" And as he saw the crown of glory on every brow, the joy beaming from every countenance, and looked forward to that endless life of unalloyed happiness, he uttered the solemn prayer, "Let me die the death of the righteous, and let my last end be like his!"

If Balaam had had a disposition to accept the light that God had given, he would now have made true his words; he would at once have severed all connection with Moab. He would no longer have presumed upon the mercy of God, but would have returned to Him with deep repentance. But Balaam loved the wages of unrighteousness, and these he was determined to secure.

Balak had confidently expected a curse that would fall like a withering blight upon Israel; and at the words of the prophet he passionately exclaimed, "What hast thou done unto me? I took thee to curse mine enemies, and, behold, thou hast blessed them altogether." Balaam, seeking to make a virtue of necessity, professed to have spoken from a conscientious regard for the will of God the words that had been forced from his lips by divine power. His answer was, "Must I not take heed to speak that which the Lord hath put in my mouth?"

Balak could not even now relinquish his purpose. He decided that the imposing spectacle presented by the vast encampment of the Hebrews had so intimidated Balaam that he dared not practice his divinations against them. The king determined to take the prophet to some point where only a small part of the host might be seen. If Balaam could be induced to curse them in detached parties, the whole camp would soon be devoted to destruction. On the top of an elevation called Pisgah another trial was made. Again seven altars were erected, whereon were placed the same offerings as at the first. The king and his princes remained by the sacrifices, while Balaam retired to meet with God. Again the prophet was entrusted with a divine message, which he was powerless to alter or withhold.

When he appeared to the anxious, expectant company the question was put to him, "What hath the Lord spoken?" The answer, as before, struck terror to the heart of king and princes:

> "God is not a man, that He should lie;
> Neither the son of man, that He should repent:
> Hath He said, and shall He not do it?
> Or hath He spoken, and shall He not make it good?

Behold, I have received commandment to bless:
And He hath blessed; and I cannot reverse it.
He hath not beheld iniquity in Jacob,
Neither hath He seen perverseness in Israel:
The Lord his God is with him,
And the shout of a king is among them."

Awed by these revelations, Balaam exclaimed, "Surely there is no enchantment against Jacob, neither is there any divination against Israel." The great magician had tried his power of enchantment, in accordance with the desire of the Moabites; but concerning this very occasion it should be said of Israel, "What hath God wrought!" While they were under the divine protection, no people or nation, though aided by all the power of Satan, should be able to prevail against them. All the world should wonder at the marvelous work of God in behalf of His people— that a man determined to pursue a sinful course should be so controlled by divine power as to utter, instead of imprecations, the richest and most precious promises, in the language of sublime and impassioned poetry. And the favor of God at this time manifested toward Israel was to be an assurance of His protecting care for His obedient, faithful children in all ages. When Satan should inspire evil men to misrepresent, harass, and destroy God's people, this very occurrence would be brought to their remembrance, and would strengthen their courage and their faith in God.

The king of Moab, disheartened and distressed, exclaimed, "Neither curse them at all, nor bless them at all." Yet a faint hope still lingered in his heart, and he determined to make another trial. He now conducted Balaam to Mount Peor, where was a temple devoted to the licentious worship of Baal, their god. Here the same number of altars were erected as before, and the same number of sacrifices were offered; but Balaam went not alone, as at other times, to learn God's will. He made no pretense of sorcery, but standing beside the altars, he looked abroad upon the tents of Israel. Again the Spirit of God rested upon him, and the divine message came from his lips:

"How goodly are thy tents, O Jacob,
And thy tabernacles, O Israel!
As the valleys are they spread forth, as gardens by the river's side,
As the trees of lignaloes which the Lord hath planted, and as cedar trees beside the waters.
He shall pour the water out of his buckets, and his seed shall be in many waters,
And his King shall be higher than Agag, and his kingdom shall be exalted. . . .
He couched, he lay down as a lion, and as a great lion: who shall stir him up?
Blessed is he that blesseth thee, and cursed is he that curseth thee."

The prosperity of God's people is here represented by some of the most beautiful figures to be found in nature. The prophet likens Israel to fertile valleys covered with abundant harvests; to flourishing gardens watered by never-failing springs; to the fragrant sandal tree and the stately cedar. The figure last mentioned is one of the most strikingly beautiful and appropriate to be found in the inspired word. The cedar of Lebanon was honored by all the people of the East. The class of trees to which it belongs is found wherever man has gone throughout the earth. From the arctic regions to the tropic zone they flourish, rejoicing in the heat, yet braving the cold; springing in rich luxuriance by the riverside, yet towering aloft upon the parched and thirsty waste. They plant their roots deep among the rocks of the mountains and boldly stand in defiance of the tempest. Their leaves are fresh and green when all else has perished at the breath of winter. Above all other trees the cedar of Lebanon is distinguished for its strength, its firmness, its undecaying vigor; and this is used as a symbol of those whose life is "hid with Christ in God." Colossians 3:3. Says the Scripture, "The righteous . . . shall grow like a cedar." Psalm 92:12. The divine hand has exalted the cedar as king over the forest. "The fir trees were not like his boughs, and the chestnut trees were not like his branches" (Ezekiel 31:8); nor any tree in the garden of God. The cedar is repeatedly employed as an emblem of royalty, and its use in Scripture to represent the righteous shows how Heaven regards those who do the will of God.

Balaam prophesied that Israel's King would be greater and more powerful than Agag. This was the name given to the kings of the Amalekites, who were at this time a very powerful nation; but Israel, if true to God, would subdue all her enemies. The King of Israel was the Son of God; and His throne was one day to be established in the earth, and His power to be exalted above all earthly kingdoms.

As he listened to the prophet's words Balak was overwhelmed with disappointed hope, with fear and rage. He was indignant that Balaam could have given him the least encouragement of a favorable response, when everything was determined against him. He regarded with scorn the prophet's compromising, deceptive course. The king exclaimed fiercely, "Therefore now flee thou to thy place: I thought to promote thee unto great honor; but, lo, the Lord hath kept thee back from honor." The answer was that the king had been forewarned that Balaam could speak only the message given him from God.

Before returning to his people, Balaam uttered a most beautiful and sublime prophecy of the world's Redeemer and the final destruction of the enemies of God:

"I shall see Him, but not now: I shall behold Him, but not nigh:
There shall come a Star out of Jacob, and a Scepter shall rise out of Israel,
And shall smite the corners of Moab, and destroy all the children of Sheth."

And he closed by predicting the complete destruction of Moab and Edom, of Amalek and the Kenites, thus leaving to the Moabitish king no ray of hope.

Disappointed in his hopes of wealth and promotion, in disfavor with the king, and conscious that he had incurred the displeasure of God, Balaam returned from his self-chosen mission. After he had reached his home the controlling power of the Spirit of God left him, and his covetousness, which had been merely held in check, prevailed. He was ready to resort to any means to gain the reward promised by Balak. Balaam knew that the prosperity of Israel depended upon their obedience to God, and that there was no way to cause their overthrow but by seducing them into sin. He now decided to secure Balak's favor by advising the Moabites of the course to be pursued to bring a curse upon Israel.

He immediately returned to the land of Moab and laid his plans before the king. The Moabites themselves were convinced that so long as Israel remained true to God, He would be their shield. The plan proposed by Balaam was to separate them from God by enticing them into idolatry. If they could be led to engage in the licentious worship of Baal and Ashtaroth, their omnipotent Protector would become their enemy, and they would soon fall a prey to the fierce, warlike nations around them. This plan was readily accepted by the king, and Balaam himself remained to assist in carrying it into effect.

Balaam witnessed the success of his diabolical scheme. He saw the curse of God visited upon His people, and thousands falling under His judgments; but the divine justice that punished sin in Israel did not permit the tempters to escape. In the war of Israel against the Midianites, Balaam was slain. He had felt a presentiment that his own end was near when he exclaimed, "Let me die the death of the righteous, and let my last end be like his!" But he had not chosen to live the life of the righteous, and his destiny was fixed with the enemies of God.

The fate of Balaam was similar to that of Judas, and their characters bear a marked resemblance to each other. Both these men tried to unite the service of God and mammon, and met with signal failure. Balaam acknowledged the true God, and professed to serve Him; Judas believed in Jesus as the Messiah, and united with His followers. But Balaam hoped to make the service of Jehovah the steppingstone to the acquirement of riches and worldly honor; and failing in this he stumbled and fell and was broken. Judas expected by his connection with Christ to secure wealth and promotion in that worldly kingdom which, as he believed, the Messiah was about to set up. The failure of his hopes drove him to apostasy and ruin. Both Balaam and Judas had received great light and enjoyed special privileges, but a single cherished sin poisoned the entire character and caused their destruction.

It is a perilous thing to allow an unchristian trait to live in the heart. One cherished sin will, little by little, debase the character, bringing all its nobler powers into subjection to the evil desire. The removal of one safeguard from the conscience, the indulgence of one evil habit, one neglect of the high claims of duty, breaks down the defenses of the soul and opens the way for Satan to come in and lead us astray. The only safe course is to let our prayers go forth daily from a sincere heart, as did David, "Hold up my goings in Thy paths, that my footsteps slip not." Psalm 17:5.

Apostasy at the Jordan

With joyful hearts and renewed faith in God, the victorious armies of Israel had returned from Bashan. They had already gained possession of a valuable territory, and they were confident of the immediate conquest of Canaan. Only the river Jordan lay between them and the Promised Land. Just across the river was a rich plain, covered with verdure, watered with streams from copious fountains, and shaded by luxuriant palm trees. On the western border of the plain rose the towers and palaces of Jericho, so embosomed in its palm-tree groves that it was called "the city of palm trees."

On the eastern side of Jordan, between the river and the high tableland which they had been traversing, was also a plain, several miles in width and extending some distance along the river. This sheltered valley had the climate of the tropics; here flourished the shittim, or acacia, tree, giving to the plain the name, "Vale of Shittim." It was here that the Israelites encamped, and in the acacia groves by the riverside they found an agreeable retreat.

But amid these attractive surroundings they were to encounter an evil more deadly than mighty hosts of armed men or the wild beasts of the wilderness. That country, so rich in natural advantages, had been defiled by the inhabitants. In the public worship of Baal, the leading deity, the most degrading and iniquitous scenes were constantly enacted. On every side were places noted for idolatry and licentiousness, the very names being suggestive of the vileness and corruption of the people.

These surroundings exerted a polluting influence upon the Israelites. Their minds became familiar with the vile thoughts constantly suggested; their life of ease and inaction produced its demoralizing effect; and almost unconsciously to themselves they were departing from God and coming into a condition where they would fall an easy prey to temptation.

During the time of their encampment beside Jordan, Moses was preparing for the occupation of Canaan. In this work the great leader was fully employed; but to the people this time of suspense and expectation was most trying, and before many weeks had elapsed their history was marred by the most frightful departures from virtue and integrity.

At first there was little intercourse between the Israelites and their heathen neighbors, but after a time Midianitish women began to steal into the camp. Their appearance excited no alarm, and so quietly were their plans conducted that the attention of Moses was not called to the matter. It was the object of these women, in their association with the Hebrews, to seduce them into transgression of the law of God, to draw their attention to heathen rites and customs, and lead them into idolatry. These motives were studiously concealed under the garb of friendship, so that they were not suspected, even by the guardians of the people.

At Balaam's suggestion, a grand festival in honor of their gods was appointed by the king of Moab, and it was secretly arranged that Balaam should induce the Israelites to attend. He was regarded by them as a prophet of God, and hence had little difficulty in accomplishing his purpose. Great numbers of the people joined him in witnessing the festivities. They ventured upon the forbidden ground, and were entangled in the snare of Satan. Beguiled with music and dancing, and allured by the beauty of heathen vestals, they cast off their fealty to Jehovah. As they united in mirth and feasting, indulgence in wine beclouded their senses and broke down the barriers of self-control. Passion had full sway; and having defiled their consciences by lewdness, they were persuaded to bow down to idols. They offered sacrifice upon heathen altars and participated in the most degrading rites.

It was not long before the poison had spread, like a deadly infection, through the camp of Israel. Those who would have conquered their enemies in battle were overcome by the wiles of heathen women. The people seemed to be infatuated. The rulers and the leading men were among the first to transgress, and so many of the people were guilty that the apostasy became national. "Israel joined himself unto Baalpeor." When Moses was aroused to perceive the evil, the plots of their enemies had been so successful that not only were the Israelites participating in the licentious worship at Mount Peor, but the heathen rites were coming to be observed in the camp of Israel. The aged leader was filled with indignation, and the wrath of God was kindled.

Their iniquitous practices did that for Israel which all the enchantments of Balaam could not do—they separated them from God. By swift-coming judgments the people were awakened to the enormity of their sin. A terrible pestilence broke out in the camp, to which tens of thousands speedily fell a prey. God commanded that the leaders in this apostasy be put to death by the magistrates. This order was promptly obeyed. The offenders were slain, then their bodies were hung up in sight of all Israel that the congregation, seeing the leaders so severely dealt with, might have a deep sense of God's abhorrence of their sin and the terror of His wrath against them.

All felt that the punishment was just, and the people hastened to the tabernacle, and with tears and deep humiliation confessed their sin. While they were thus weeping before God, at the door of the tabernacle, while the plague was still doing its work of death, and the magistrates were executing their terrible commission, Zimri, one of the nobles of Israel, came boldly into the camp, accompanied by a Midianitish harlot, a princess "of a chief house in Midian," whom he escorted to his tent. Never was vice bolder or more stubborn. Inflamed with wine, Zimri declared his "sin as Sodom," and gloried in his shame. The priests and leaders had prostrated themselves in grief and humiliation, weeping "between the porch and the altar," and entreating the Lord to spare His people, and give not His heritage to reproach, when this prince in Israel flaunted his sin in the sight of the congregation, as if to defy the vengeance of God and mock the judges of the nation. Phinehas, the son of Eleazar the high priest, rose up from among the congregation, and seizing a javelin, "he went after the man of Israel into the tent," and slew them both. Thus the plague was stayed, while the priest who had executed the divine judgment was honored before all Israel, and the priesthood was confirmed to him and to his house forever.

Phinehas "hath turned My wrath away from the children of Israel," was the divine message; "wherefore say, Behold, I give unto him My covenant of peace: and he shall have it, and his seed after him, even the covenant of an everlasting priesthood; because he was zealous for His God, and made an atonement for the children of Israel."

The judgments visited upon Israel for their sin at Shittim, destroyed the survivors of that vast company, who, nearly forty years before, had incurred the sentence, "They shall surely die in the wilderness." The numbering of the people by divine direction, during their encampment on the plains of Jordan, showed that "of them whom Moses and Aaron the priest numbered, when they numbered the children of Israel in the wilderness of Sinai, . . . there was not left a man of them, save Caleb the son of Jephunneh, and Joshua the son of Nun." Numbers 26:64, 65.

God had sent judgments upon Israel for yielding to the enticements of the Midianites; but the tempters were not to escape the wrath of divine justice. The Amalekites, who had attacked Israel at Rephidim, falling upon those who were faint and weary behind the host, were not punished till long after; but the Midianites who seduced them into sin were speedily made to feel God's judgments, as being the more dangerous enemies. "Avenge the children of Israel of the Midianites" (Numbers 31:2), was the command of God to Moses; "afterward shalt thou be gathered unto thy people." This mandate was immediately obeyed. One thousand men were chosen from each of the tribes and sent out under the leadership of Phinehas. "And they warred against the Midianites, as the Lord commanded Moses. . . . And they slew the kings of Midian, beside the rest of them that were slain; . . . five kings of Midian: Balaam also the son of Beor they slew with the sword." Verses 7, 8. The women also, who had been made captives by the attacking army, were put to death at the command of Moses, as the most guilty and most dangerous of the foes of Israel.

Such was the end of them that devised mischief against God's people. Says the psalmist: "The heathen are sunk down in the pit that they made: in the net which they hid is their own foot taken." Psalm 9:15. "For the Lord will not cast off His people, neither will He forsake His inheritance. But judgment shall return unto righteousness." When men "gather themselves together against the soul of the righteous," the

Lord "shall bring upon them their own iniquity, and shall cut them off in their own wickedness." Psalm 94:14, 15, 21, 23.

When Balaam was called to curse the Hebrews he could not, by all his enchantments, bring evil upon them; for the Lord had not "beheld iniquity in Jacob," neither had He "seen perverseness in Israel." Numbers 23:21, 23. But when through yielding to temptation they transgressed God's law, their defense departed from them. When the people of God are faithful to His commandments, "there is no enchantment against Jacob, neither is there any divination against Israel." Hence all the power and wily arts of Satan are exerted to seduce them into sin. If those who profess to be the depositaries of God's law become transgressors of its precepts, they separate themselves from God, and they will be unable to stand before their enemies.

The Israelites, who could not be overcome by the arms or by the enchantments of Midian, fell a prey to her harlots. Such is the power that woman, enlisted in the service of Satan, has exerted to entrap and destroy souls. "She hath cast down many wounded: yea, many strong men have been slain by her." Proverbs 7:26. It was thus that the children of Seth were seduced from their integrity, and the holy seed became corrupt. It was thus that Joseph was tempted. Thus Samson betrayed his strength, the defense of Israel, into the hands of the Philistines. Here David stumbled. And Solomon, the wisest of kings, who had thrice been called the beloved of his God, became a slave of passion, and sacrificed his integrity to the same bewitching power.

"Now all these things happened unto them for ensamples: and they are written for our admonition, upon whom the ends of the world are come. Wherefore let him that thinketh he standeth take heed lest he fall." 1 Corinthians 10:11, 12. Satan well knows the material with which he has to deal in the human heart. He knows—for he has studied with fiendish intensity for thousands of years—the points most easily assailed in every character; and through successive generations he has wrought to overthrow the strongest men, princes in Israel, by the same temptations that were so successful at Baalpeor. All along through the ages there are strewn wrecks of character that have been stranded upon the rocks of sensual indulgence. As we approach the close of time, as the people of God stand upon the borders of the heavenly Canaan, Satan will, as of old, redouble his efforts to prevent them from entering the goodly land. He lays his snares for every soul. It is not the ignorant and uncultured merely that need to be guarded; he will prepare his temptations for those in the highest positions, in the most holy office; if he can lead them to pollute their souls, he can through them destroy many. And he employs the same agents now as he employed three thousand years ago. By worldly friendships, by the charms of beauty, by pleasure seeking, mirth, feasting, or the wine cup, he tempts to the violation of the seventh commandment.

Satan seduced Israel into licentiousness before leading them to idolatry. Those who will dishonor God's image and defile His temple in their own persons will not scruple at any dishonor to God that will gratify the desire of their depraved hearts. Sensual indulgence weakens the mind and debases the soul. The moral and intellectual powers are benumbed and paralyzed by the gratification of the animal propensities; and it is impossible for the slave of passion to realize the sacred obligation of the law of God, to appreciate the atonement, or to place a right value upon the soul. Goodness, purity, and truth, reverence for God, and love for sacred things—all those holy affections and noble desires that link men with the heavenly world—are consumed in the fires of lust. The soul becomes a blackened and desolate waste, the habitation of the evil spirits, and the "cage of every unclean and hateful bird." Beings formed in the image of God are dragged down to a level with the brutes.

It was by associating with idolaters and joining in their festivities that the Hebrews were led to transgress God's law and bring His judgments upon the nation. So now it is by leading the followers of Christ to associate with the ungodly and unite in their amusements that Satan is most successful in alluring them into sin. "Come out from among them, and be ye separate, saith the Lord, and touch not the unclean." 2 Corinthians 6:17. God requires of His people now as great a distinction from the world, in customs, habits, and principles, as He required of Israel anciently. If they faithfully follow the teachings of His word, this distinction will exist; it cannot be otherwise. The warnings given to the Hebrews against assimilating with the heathen were not more direct or explicit than are those forbidding Christians to conform to the spirit and customs of the ungodly. Christ speaks to us, "Love not the world, neither the things that are in the world. If any man love the world, the love of the Father is not in him." 1 John 2:15. "The friendship of the world is enmity with God; whosoever therefore will be a friend of the world is the enemy of God." James 4:4. The followers of Christ are to separate themselves from sinners, choosing their society only when there is opportunity to do them good. We cannot be too decided in shunning the company of those who exert an influence to draw us away from God. While we pray, "Lead us not into temptation," we are to shun temptation, so far as possible.

It was when the Israelites were in a condition of outward ease and security that they were led into sin. They failed to keep God ever before them, they neglected prayer and cherished a spirit of self-confidence. Ease and self-indulgence left the citadel of the soul unguarded, and debasing thoughts found entrance. It was the traitors within the walls that overthrew the strongholds of principle and betrayed Israel into the power of Satan. It is thus that Satan still seeks to compass the ruin of the soul. A long preparatory process, unknown to the world, goes on in the heart before the Christian commits open sin. The mind does not come down at once from purity and holiness to depravity, corruption, and crime. It takes time to degrade those formed in the image of God to the brutal or the satanic. By beholding we become changed. By the indulgence of impure thoughts man can so educate his mind that sin which he once loathed will become pleasant to him.

Satan is using every means to make crime and debasing vice popular. We cannot walk the streets of our cities without encountering flaring notices of crime presented in some novel, or to be acted at some theater. The mind is educated to familiarity with sin. The course pursued by the base and vile is kept before the people in the periodicals of the day, and everything that can excite passion is brought before them in exciting stories. They hear and read so much of debasing crime that the once tender conscience, which would have recoiled with horror from such scenes, becomes hardened, and they dwell upon these things with greedy interest.

Many of the amusements popular in the world today, even with those who claim to be Christians, tend to the same end as did those of the heathen. There are indeed few among them that Satan does not turn to account in destroying souls. Through the drama he has worked for ages to excite passion and glorify vice. The opera, with its fascinating display and bewildering music, the masquerade, the dance, the card table, Satan employs to break down the barriers of principle and open the door to sensual indulgence. In every gathering for pleasure where pride is fostered or appetite indulged, where one is led to forget God and lose sight of eternal interests, there Satan is binding his chains about the soul.

"Keep thy heart with all diligence," is the counsel of the wise man; "for out of it are the issues of life." Proverbs 4:23. As man "thinketh in his heart, so is he." Proverbs 23:7. The heart must be renewed by divine grace, or it will be in vain to seek for purity of life. He who attempts to build up a noble, virtuous character independent of the grace of Christ is building his house upon the shifting sand. In the fierce storms of temptation it will surely be overthrown. David's prayer should be the petition of every soul: "Create in me a clean heart, O God; and renew a right spirit within me." Psalm 51:10. And having become partakers of the heavenly gift, we are to go on unto perfection, being "kept by the power of God through faith." 1 Peter 1:5.

Yet we have a work to do to resist temptation. Those who would not fall a prey to Satan's devices must guard well the avenues of the soul; they must avoid reading, seeing, or hearing that which will suggest impure thoughts. The mind should not be left to wander at random upon every subject that the adversary of souls may suggest. "Girding up the loins of your mind," says the apostle Peter, "Be sober, . . . not fashioning yourselves according to your former lusts in . . . your ignorance: but like as He which called you is holy, be ye yourselves also holy in all manner of living." 1 Peter 1:13-15, R.V. Says Paul, "Whatsoever things are true, whatsoever things are honest, whatsoever things are just, whatsoever things are pure, whatsoever things are lovely, whatsoever things are of good report; if there be any virtue, and if there be any praise, think on these things." Philippians 4:8. This will require earnest prayer and unceasing watchfulness. We must be aided by the abiding influence of the Holy Spirit, which will attract the mind upward, and habituate it to dwell on pure and holy things. And we must give diligent study to the word of God. "Wherewithal shall a young man cleanse his way? by taking heed thereto according to Thy word." "Thy word," says the psalmist, "have I hid in mine heart, that I might not sin against Thee." Psalm 119:9, 11.

Israel's sin at Beth-peor brought the judgments of God upon the nation, and though the same sins may not now be punished as speedily, they will as surely meet retribution. "If any man defile the temple of God, him shall God destroy." 1 Corinthians 3:17. Nature has affixed terrible penalties to these crimes—penalties which, sooner or later, will be inflicted upon every transgressor. It is these sins more than any other that have caused the fearful degeneracy of our race, and the weight of disease and misery with which the world is cursed. Men may succeed in concealing their transgression from their fellow men, but they will no less surely reap the result, in suffering, disease, imbecility, or death. And beyond this life stands the tribunal of the judgment, with its award of eternal penalties. "They which do such things shall not inherit the kingdom of God," but with Satan and evil angels shall have their part in that "lake of fire" which "is the second death." Galatians 5:21; Revelation 20:14.

"The lips of a strange woman drop as an honeycomb, and her mouth is smoother than oil: but her end is bitter as wormwood, sharp as a two-edged sword." Proverbs 5:3, 4. "Remove thy way far from her, and come not nigh the door of her house: lest thou give thine honor unto others, and thy years unto the cruel: lest strangers be filled with thy wealth; and thy labors be in the house of a stranger; and thou mourn at the last, when thy flesh and thy body are consumed." Verses 8-11. "Her house inclineth unto death." "None that go unto her return again." Proverbs 2:18, 19. "Her guests are in the depths of hell." Proverbs 9:18.

The Law Repeated

The Lord announced to Moses that the appointed time for the possession of Canaan was at hand; and as the aged prophet stood upon the heights overlooking the river Jordan and the Promised Land, he gazed with deep interest upon the inheritance of his people. Would it be possible that the sentence pronounced against him for his sin at Kadesh might be revoked? With deep earnestness he pleaded, "O Lord God, Thou hast begun to show Thy servant Thy greatness, and Thy mighty hand; for what god is there in heaven or in earth, that can do according to Thy works, and according to Thy might? I pray Thee, let me go over, and see the good land that is beyond Jordan, that goodly mountain, and Lebanon." Deuteronomy 3:24-27.

The answer was, "Let it suffice thee; speak no more unto Me of this matter. Get thee up into the top of Pisgah, and lift up thine eyes westward, and northward, and southward, and eastward, and behold it with thine eyes; for thou shalt not go over this Jordan."

Without a murmur Moses submitted to the decree of God.

And now his great anxiety was for Israel. Who would feel the interest for their welfare that he had felt? From a full heart he poured forth the prayer, "Let the Lord, the God of the spirits of all flesh, set a man over the congregation, which may go out before them, and which may go in before them, and which may lead them out, and which may bring them in; that the congregation of the Lord be not as sheep which have no shepherd." Numbers 27:16, 17.

The Lord hearkened to the prayer of His servant; and the answer came, "Take thee Joshua, the son of Nun, a man in whom is the Spirit, and lay thine hand upon him; and set him before Eleazar the priest, and before all the congregation; and give him a charge in their sight. And thou shalt put some of thine honor upon him, that all the congregation of the people of Israel may be obedient." Verses 18-20. Joshua had long attended Moses; and being a man of wisdom, ability, and faith, he was chosen to succeed him.

Through the laying on of hands by Moses, accompanied by a most impressive charge, Joshua was solemnly set apart as the leader of Israel. He was also admitted to a present share in the government. The words of the Lord concerning Joshua came through Moses to the congregation, "He shall stand before Eleazar the priest, who shall ask counsel for him, after the judgment of Urim before the Lord. At his word shall they go out, and at his word they shall come in, both he, and all the children of Israel with him, even all the congregation." Verses 21-23.

Before relinquishing his position as the visible leader of Israel, Moses was directed to rehearse to them the history of their deliverance from Egypt and their journeyings in the wilderness, and also to recapitulate the law spoken from Sinai. When the law was given, but few of the present congregation were old enough to comprehend the awful solemnity of the occasion. As they were soon to pass over Jordan and take possession of the Promised Land, God would present before them the claims of His law and enjoin upon them obedience as the condition of prosperity.

Moses stood before the people to repeat his last warnings and admonitions. His face was illumined with a holy light. His hair was white with age; but his form was erect, his countenance expressed the unabated vigor of health, and his eye was clear and undimmed. It was an important occasion, and with deep feeling he portrayed the love and mercy of their Almighty Protector:

"Ask now of the days that are past, which were before thee, since the day that God created man upon the earth, and ask from the one side of heaven unto the other, whether there hath been any such thing as this great thing is, or hath been heard like it? Did ever people hear the voice of God speaking out of the midst of the fire, as thou hast heard, and live? or hath God assayed to go and take Him a nation from the midst of another nation, by temptations, by signs, and by wonders, and by war, and by a mighty hand, and by a stretched-out arm, and by great terrors, according to all that the Lord your God did for you in Egypt before your eyes? Unto thee it was showed, that thou mightest know that the Lord He is God; there is none else beside Him."

"The Lord did not set His love upon you, nor choose you, because ye were more in number than any people; for ye were the fewest of all people: but because the Lord loved you, and because He would keep the oath which He had sworn unto your fathers, hath the Lord brought you out with a mighty hand, and redeemed you out of the house of bondmen, from the hand of Pharaoh king of Egypt. Know therefore that Jehovah thy God, He is God, the faithful God, which keepeth covenant and mercy with them that love Him and keep His commandments to a thousand generations." Deuteronomy 7:7-9.

The people of Israel had been ready to ascribe their troubles to Moses; but now their suspicions that he was controlled by pride, ambition, or selfishness, were removed, and they listened with confidence to his words. Moses faithfully set before them their errors and the transgressions of their fathers. They had often felt impatient and rebellious because of their long wandering in the wilderness; but the Lord had not been chargeable with this delay in possessing Canaan; He was more grieved than they because He could not bring them into immediate possession of the Promised Land, and thus display before all nations His mighty power in the deliverance of His people. With their distrust of God, with their pride and unbelief, they had not been prepared to enter Canaan. They would in no way represent that people whose God is the Lord; for they did not bear His character of purity, goodness, and benevolence. Had their fathers yielded in faith to the direction of God, being governed by His judgments and walking in His ordinances, they would long before have been settled in Canaan, a prosperous, holy, happy people. Their delay to enter the goodly land dishonored God and detracted from His glory in the sight of surrounding nations.

Moses, who understood the character and value of the law of God, assured the people that no other nation had such wise, righteous, and merciful rules as had been given to the Hebrews. "Behold," he said, "I have taught you statutes and judgments, even as the Lord my God commanded me, that ye should do so in the land whither ye go to possess it. Keep therefore and do them; for this is your wisdom and your understanding in the sight of the nations, which shall hear all these statutes, and say, Surely this great nation is a wise and understanding people."

Moses called their attention to the "day that thou stoodest before the Lord thy God in Horeb." And he challenged the Hebrew host: "What nation is there so great, who hath God so nigh unto them, as the Lord our God is in all things that we call upon Him for? And what nation is there so great, that hath statutes and judgments so righteous as all this law, which I set before you this day?" Today the challenge to Israel might be repeated. The laws which God gave His ancient people were wiser, better, and more humane than those of the most civilized nations of the earth. The laws of the nations bear marks of the infirmities and passions of the unrenewed heart;

but God's law bears the stamp of the divine.

"The Lord hath taken you, and brought you forth out of the iron furnace," declared Moses, "to be unto Him a people of inheritance." The land which they were soon to enter, and which was to be theirs on condition of obedience to the law of God, was thus described to them—and how must these words have moved the hearts of Israel, as they remembered that he who so glowingly pictured the blessings of the goodly land had been, through their sin, shut out from sharing the inheritance of his people:

"The Lord thy God bringeth thee into a good land," "not as the land of Egypt, from whence ye came out, where thou sowedst thy seed, and wateredst it with thy foot, as a garden of herbs: but the land, whither ye go to possess it, is a land of hills and valleys, and drinketh water of the rain of heaven;" "a land of brooks of water, of fountains and depths that spring out of valleys and hills; a land of wheat, and barley, and vines, and fig trees, and pomegranates; a land of oil olive, and honey; a land wherein thou shalt eat bread without scarceness, thou shalt not lack anything in it; a land whose stones are iron, and out of whose hills thou mayest dig brass;" "a land which the Lord thy God careth for: the eyes of the Lord thy God are always upon it, from the beginning of the year even unto the end of the year." Deuteronomy 8:7-9; 11:10-12.

"And it shall be, when the Lord thy God shall have brought thee into the land which He sware unto thy fathers, to Abraham, to Isaac, and to Jacob, to give thee great and goodly cities, which thou buildedst not, and houses full of all good things, which thou filledst not, and wells digged, which thou diggedst not, vineyards and olive trees, which thou plantedst not; when thou shalt have eaten and be full; then beware lest thou forget the Lord." "Take heed unto yourselves, lest ye forget the covenant of the Lord your God. . . . For the Lord thy God is a consuming fire, even a jealous God." If they should do evil in the sight of the Lord, then, said Moses, "Ye shall soon utterly perish from off the land whereunto ye go over Jordan to possess it."

After the public rehearsal of the law, Moses completed the work of writing all the laws, the statutes, and the judgments which God had given him, and all the regulations concerning the sacrificial system. The book containing these was placed in charge of the proper officers, and was for safe keeping deposited in the side of the ark. Still the great leader was filled with fear that the people would depart from God. In a most sublime and thrilling address he set before them the blessings that would be theirs on condition of obedience, and the curses that would follow upon transgression:

"If thou shalt hearken diligently unto the voice of the Lord thy God, to observe and to do all His commandments which I command thee this day," "blessed shalt thou be in the city, and blessed shalt thou be in the field," in "the fruit of thy body, and the fruit of thy ground, and the fruit of thy cattle. . . . Blessed shall be thy basket and thy store. Blessed shalt thou be when thou comest in, and blessed shalt thou be when thou goest out. The Lord shall cause thine enemies that rise up against thee to be smitten before thy face. . . . The Lord shall command the blessing upon thee in thy storehouses, and in all that thou settest thine hand unto."

"But it shall come to pass, if thou wilt not hearken unto the voice of the Lord thy God, to observe to do all His commandments and His statutes which I command thee this day; that all these curses shall come upon thee," "and thou shalt become an astonishment, a proverb, and a byword, among all nations whither the Lord shall lead thee." "And the Lord shall scatter thee among all people, from the one end of the earth even unto the other; and there thou shalt serve other gods, which neither thou nor thy fathers have known, even wood and stone. And among these nations shalt thou find no ease, neither shall the sole of thy foot have rest: but the Lord shall give thee there a trembling heart, and failing of eyes, and sorrow of mind: and thy life shall hang in doubt before thee; and thou shalt fear day and night, and shalt have none assurance of thy life: in the morning thou shalt say, Would God it were even! and at even thou shalt say, Would God it were morning! for the fear of thine heart wherewith thou shalt fear, and for the sight of thine eyes which thou shalt see."

By the Spirit of Inspiration, looking far down the ages, Moses pictured the terrible scenes of Israel's final overthrow as a nation, and the destruction of Jerusalem by the armies of Rome: "The Lord shall bring a nation against thee from far, from the end of the earth, as swift as the eagle flieth; a nation whose tongue thou shalt not understand; a nation of fierce countenance, which shall not regard the person of the old, nor show favor to the young."

The utter wasting of the land and the horrible suffering of the people during the siege of Jerusalem under Titus centuries later, were vividly portrayed: "He shall eat the fruit of thy cattle, and the fruit of thy land, until thou be destroyed. . . . And he shall besiege thee in all thy gates, until thy high and fenced walls come down, wherein thou trustedst, throughout all thy land. . . . Thou shalt eat the fruit of thine own body, the flesh of thy sons and of thy daughters, which the Lord thy God hath given thee, in the siege, and in the straitness, wherewith thine enemies shall distress thee." "The tender and delicate woman among you, which would not adventure to set the sole of her foot upon the ground for delicateness and tenderness, her eye shall be evil toward the husband of her bosom, . . . and toward her children which she shall bear: for she shall eat them for want of all things secretly in the siege and straitness, wherewith thine enemy shall distress thee in thy gates."

Moses closed with these impressive words: "I call heaven and earth to record this day against you, that I have set before you life and death, blessing and cursing: therefore choose life, that both thou and thy seed may live: that thou mayest love the Lord thy God, and that thou mayest obey His voice, and that thou mayest cleave unto Him: for He is thy life, and the length of thy days: that thou mayest dwell in the land which the Lord sware unto thy fathers, to Abraham, to Isaac, and to

Jacob, to give them." Deuteronomy 30:19, 20.

The more deeply to impress these truths upon all minds, the great leader embodied them in sacred verse. This song was not only historical, but prophetic. While it recounted the wonderful dealings of God with His people in the past, it also foreshadowed the great events of the future, the final victory of the faithful when Christ shall come the second time in power and glory. The people were directed to commit to memory this poetic history, and to teach it to their children and children's children. It was to be chanted by the congregation when they assembled for worship, and to be repeated by the people as they went about their daily labors. It was the duty of parents to so impress these words upon the susceptible minds of their children that they might never be forgotten.

Since the Israelites were to be, in a special sense, the guardians and keepers of God's law, the significance of its precepts and the importance of obedience were especially to be impressed upon them, and through them, upon their children and children's children. The Lord commanded concerning His statutes: "Thou shalt teach them diligently unto thy children, and shalt talk of them when thou sittest in thine house, and when thou walkest by the way, and when thou liest down, and when thou risest up. . . . And thou shalt write them upon the posts of thy house, and on thy gates."

When their children should ask in time to come, "What mean the testimonies, and the statutes, and the judgments, which the Lord our God hath commanded you? then the parents were to repeat the history of God's gracious dealings with them—how the Lord had wrought for their deliverance that they might obey His Law—and to declare to them, "The Lord commanded us to do all these statutes, to fear the Lord our God, for our good always, that He might preserve us alive, as it is at this day. And it shall be our righteousness, if we observe to do all these commandments before the Lord our God as He hath commanded us."

The Death of Moses

In all the dealings of God with His people there is, mingled with His love and mercy, the most striking evidence of His strict and impartial justice. This is exemplified in the history of the Hebrew people. God had bestowed great blessings upon Israel. His loving-kindness toward them is touchingly portrayed: "As an eagle stirreth up her nest, fluttereth over her young, spreadeth abroad her wings, taketh them, beareth them on her wings: so the Lord alone did lead him." And yet what swift and severe retribution was visited upon them for their transgressions!

The infinite love of God has been manifested in the gift of His only-begotten Son to redeem a lost race. Christ came to the earth to reveal to men the character of His Father, and His life was filled with deeds of divine tenderness and compassion. And yet Christ Himself declares, "Till heaven and earth pass, one jot or one title shall in no wise pass from the law." Matthew 5:18. The same voice that with patient, loving entreaty invites the sinner to come to Him and find pardon and peace, will in the judgment bid the rejecters of His mercy, "Depart from Me, ye cursed." Matthew 25:41. In all the Bible, God is represented not only as a tender father but as a righteous judge. Though He delights in showing mercy, and "forgiving iniquity and transgression and sin," yet He "will by no means clear the guilty." Exodus 34:7.

The great Ruler of nations had declared that Moses was not to lead the congregation of Israel into the goodly land, and the earnest pleading of God's servant could not secure a reversing of His sentence. He knew that he must die. Yet he had not for a moment faltered in his care for Israel. He had faithfully sought to prepare the congregation to enter upon the promised inheritance. At the divine command Moses and Joshua repaired to the tabernacle, while the pillar of cloud came and stood over the door. Here the people were solemnly committed to the charge of Joshua. The work of Moses as leader of Israel was ended. Still he forgot himself in his interest for his people. In the presence of the assembled multitude Moses, in the name of God, addressed to his successor these words of holy cheer: "Be strong and of a good courage: for thou shalt bring the children of Israel into the land which I sware unto them: and I will be with thee." He then turned to the elders and officers of the people, giving them a solemn charge to obey faithfully the instructions he had communicated to them from God.

As the people gazed upon the aged man, so soon to be taken from them, they recalled, with a new and deeper appreciation, his parental tenderness, his wise counsels, and his untiring labors. How often, when their sins had invited the just judgments of God, the prayers of Moses had prevailed with Him to spare them! Their grief was heightened by remorse. They bitterly remembered that their own perversity had provoked Moses to the sin for which he must die.

The removal of their beloved leader would be a far stronger rebuke to Israel than any which they could have received had his life and mission been continued. God would lead them to feel that they were not to make the life of their future leader as trying as they had made that of Moses. God speaks to His people in blessings bestowed; and when these are not appreciated, He speaks to them in blessings removed, that they may be led to see their sins, and return to Him with all the heart.

That very day there came to Moses the command, "Get thee up . . . unto Mount Nebo, . . . and behold the land of Canaan, which I give unto the children of Israel for a possession: and die in the mount whither thou goest up, and be gathered unto thy people." Moses had often left the camp, in obedience to the divine summons, to commune with God; but he was now to depart on a new and mysterious errand. He must go forth to resign his life into the hands of his Creator. Moses knew that he was to die alone; no earthly friend would be permitted to minister to him in his last hours. There was a mystery and awfulness about the scene before him, from which his heart shrank. The severest trial was his separation from the people of his care and love—the people with whom his interest and his life had so long been united. But he had learned to trust in God, and with unquestioning faith he committed himself and his people to His love and mercy.

For the last time Moses stood in the assembly of his people. Again the Spirit of God rested upon him, and in the most sublime and touching language he pronounced a blessing upon each of the tribes, closing with a benediction upon them all:

"There is none like unto God, O Jeshurun,
Who rideth upon the heaven for thy help,
And in His excellency on the skies.
The eternal God is thy dwelling place,
And underneath are the everlasting arms:
And He thrust out the enemy from before thee,
And said, Destroy.
And Israel dwelleth in safety,
The fountain of Jacob alone,
In a land of corn and wine;
Yea, His heavens drop down dew.
Happy art thou, O Israel:
Who is like unto thee, a people saved by Jehovah,
The shield of thy help."
Deuteronomy 33:26-29, R.V.

Moses turned from the congregation, and in silence and alone made his way up the mountainside. He went to "the mountain of Nebo, to the top of Pisgah." Upon that lonely height he stood, and gazed with undimmed eye upon the scene spread out before him. Far away to the west lay the blue waters of the Great Sea; in the north, Mount Hermon stood out against the sky; to the east was the tableland of Moab, and beyond lay Bashan, the scene of Israel's triumph; and away to the south stretched the desert of their long wanderings.

In solitude Moses reviewed his life of vicissitudes and hardships since he turned from courtly honors and from a prospective kingdom in Egypt, to cast in his lot with God's chosen people. He called to mind those long years in the desert with the flocks of Jethro, the appearance of the Angel in the burning bush, and his own call to deliver Israel. Again he beheld the mighty miracles of God's power displayed in behalf of the chosen people, and His long-suffering mercy during the years of their wandering and rebellion. Notwithstanding all that God had wrought for them, notwithstanding his own prayers and labors, only two of all the adults in the vast army that left Egypt had been found so faithful that they could enter the Promised Land. As Moses reviewed the result of his labors, his life of trial and sacrifice seemed to have been almost in vain.

Yet he did not regret the burdens he had borne. He knew that his mission and work were of God's own appointing. When first called to become the leader of Israel from bondage, he shrank from the responsibility; but since he had taken up the work he had not cast aside the burden. Even when the Lord had proposed to release him, and destroy rebellious Israel, Moses could not consent. Though his trials had been great, he had enjoyed special tokens of God's favor; he had obtained a rich experience during the sojourn in the wilderness, in witnessing the manifestations of God's power and glory, and in the communion of His love; he felt that he had made a wise decision in choosing to suffer affliction with the people of God, rather than to enjoy the pleasures of sin for a season.

As he looked back upon his experience as a leader of God's people, one wrong act marred the record. If that transgression could be blotted out, he felt that he would not shrink from death. He was assured that repentance, and faith in the promised Sacrifice, were all that God required, and again Moses confessed his sin and implored pardon in the name of Jesus.

And now a panoramic view of the Land of Promise was presented to him. Every part of the country was spread out before him, not faint and uncertain in the dim distance, but standing out clear, distinct, and beautiful to his delighted vision. In this scene it was presented, not as it then appeared, but as it would become, with God's blessing upon it, in the possession of Israel. He seemed to be looking upon a second Eden. There were mountains clothed with cedars of Lebanon, hills gray with olives and fragrant with the odor of the vine, wide green plains bright with flowers and rich in fruitfulness, here the palm trees of the tropics, there waving fields of wheat and barley, sunny valleys musical with the ripple of brooks and the song of birds, goodly cities and fair gardens, lakes rich in "the abundance of the seas," grazing flocks upon the hillsides, and even amid the rocks the wild bee's hoarded treasures. It was indeed such a land as Moses, inspired by the Spirit of God, had described to Israel: "Blessed of the Lord . . . for the precious things of heaven, for the dew, and for the deep that coucheth beneath, and for the precious fruits brought forth by the sun, . . . and for the chief things of the ancient mountains, . . . and for the precious things of the earth and fullness thereof."

Moses saw the chosen people established in Canaan, each of the tribes in its own possession. He had a view of their history after the settlement of the Promised Land; the long, sad story of their apostasy and its punishment was spread out before him. He saw them, because of their sins, dispersed among the heathen, the glory departed from Israel, her beautiful city in ruins, and her people captives in strange lands. He saw them restored to the land of their fathers, and at last brought under the dominion of Rome.

He was permitted to look down the stream of time and behold the first advent of our Saviour. He saw Jesus as a babe in Bethlehem. He heard the voices of the angelic host break forth in the glad song of praise to God and peace on earth. He beheld in the heavens the star guiding the Wise Men of the East to Jesus, and a great light flooded his mind as he called those prophetic words, "There shall come a Star out of Jacob, and a Scepter shall rise out of Israel." Numbers 24:17. He beheld Christ's humble life in Nazareth, His ministry of love and sympathy and healing, His rejection by a proud, unbelieving nation. Amazed he listened to their boastful exaltation of the law of God, while they despised and rejected Him by whom the law was given. He saw Jesus upon Olivet as with weeping He bade farewell to the city of His love. As Moses beheld the final rejection of that people so highly blessed of Heaven—that people for whom he had toiled and prayed and sacrificed, for whom he had been willing that his own name should be blotted from the book of life; as he listened to those fearful words, "Behold your house is left unto you desolate" (Matthew 23:38), his heart was wrung with anguish, and bitter tears fell from his eyes, in sympathy with the sorrow of the Son of God.

He followed the Saviour to Gethsemane, and beheld the agony in the garden, the betrayal, the mockery and scourging—the crucifixion. Moses saw that as he had lifted up the serpent in the wilderness, so the Son of God must be lifted up, that whosoever would believe on Him "should not perish, but have eternal life." John 3:15. Grief, indignation, and horror filled the heart of Moses as he viewed the hypocrisy and satanic hatred manifested by the Jewish nation against their Redeemer, the mighty Angel who had gone before their fathers. He heard Christ's agonizing cry, "My God, My God, why hast Thou forsaken Me?" Mark 15:34. He saw Him lying in Joseph's new tomb. The darkness of hopeless despair seemed to enshroud the world. But he looked again, and beheld Him coming forth a conqueror, and ascending to heaven escorted by adoring angels and leading a multitude of captives. He saw the shining gates open to receive Him, and the host of heaven with songs of triumph welcoming their Commander. And it was there revealed to him that he himself would be one who should attend the Saviour, and open to Him the everlasting gates. As he looked upon the scene, his countenance shone with a holy radiance. How small appeared the trials and sacrifices of his life when compared with those of the Son of God! how light in contrast with the "far more exceeding and eternal weight of glory"! 2 Corinthians 4:17. He rejoiced that he had been permitted, even in a small measure, to be a partaker in the sufferings of Christ.

Moses beheld the disciples of Jesus as they went forth to carry His gospel to the world. He saw that though the people of Israel "according to the flesh" had failed of the high destiny to which God had called them, in their unbelief had failed to become the light of the world, though they had despised God's mercy and forfeited their blessings as His chosen people—yet God had not cast off the seed of Abraham; the glorious purposes which He had undertaken to accomplish through Israel were to be fulfilled. All who through Christ should become the children of faith were to be counted as Abraham's seed; they were inheritors of the covenant promises; like Abraham, they were called to guard and to make known to the world the law of God and the gospel of His Son. Moses saw the light of the gospel shining out through the disciples of Jesus to them "which sat in darkness" (Matthew 4:16), and thousands from the lands of the Gentiles flocking to the brightness of its rising. And beholding, he rejoiced in the increase and prosperity of Israel.

And now another scene passed before him. He had been shown the work of Satan in leading the Jews to reject Christ, while they professed to honor His Father's law. He now saw the Christian world under a similar deception in professing to accept Christ while they rejected God's law. He had heard from the priests and elders the frenzied cry, "Away with Him!" "Crucify Him, crucify Him!" and now he heard from professedly Christian teachers the cry, "Away with the law!" He saw the Sabbath trodden under foot, and a spurious institution established in its place. Again Moses was filled with astonishment and horror. How could those who believed in Christ reject the law spoken by His own voice upon the sacred mount? How could any that feared God set aside the law which is the foundation of His government in heaven and earth? With joy Moses saw the law of God still honored and exalted by a faithful few. He saw the last great struggle of earthly powers to destroy those who keep God's law. He looked forward to the time when God shall arise to punish the inhabitants of the earth for their iniquity, and those who have feared His name shall be covered and hid in the day of His anger. He heard God's covenant of peace with those who have kept His law, as He utters His voice from His holy habitation and the heavens and the earth do shake. He saw the second coming of Christ in glory, the righteous dead raised to immortal life, and the living saints translated without seeing death, and together ascending with songs of gladness to the City of God.

Still another scene opens to his view—the earth freed from the curse, lovelier than the fair Land of Promise so lately spread out before him. There is no sin, and death cannot enter. There the nations of the saved find their eternal home. With joy unutterable Moses looks upon the scene—the fulfillment of a more glorious deliverance than his brightest hopes have ever pictured. Their earthly wanderings forever past, the Israel of God have at last entered the goodly land.

Again the vision faded, and his eyes rested upon the land of Canaan as it spread out in the distance. Then, like a tired warrior, he lay down to rest. "So Moses the servant of the Lord died there in the land of Moab, according to the word of the Lord. And He buried him in a valley in the land of Moab, over against Beth-peor: but no man knoweth of his sepulcher." Many who had been unwilling to heed the counsels of Moses while he was with them would have been in danger of committing idolatry over his dead body had they known the place of his burial. For this reason it was concealed from men. But angels of God buried the body of His faithful servant and watched over the lonely grave.

"There arose not a prophet since in Israel like unto Moses, whom Jehovah knew face to face, in all the signs and the wonders which Jehovah sent him to do . . . and in all that mighty hand, and in all the great terror which Moses showed in the sight of all Israel."

Had not the life of Moses been marred with that one sin, in failing to give God the glory of bringing water from the rock at Kadesh, he would have entered the Promised Land, and would have been translated to heaven without seeing death. But he was not long to remain in the tomb. Christ Himself, with the angels who had buried Moses, came down from heaven to call forth the sleeping saint. Satan had exulted at his success in causing Moses to sin against God, and thus come under the dominion of death. The great adversary declared that the divine sentence—"Dust thou art, and unto dust shalt thou return" (Genesis 3:19)—gave him possession of the dead. The power of the grave had never been broken, and all who were in the tomb he claimed as his captives, never to be released from his dark prison house.

For the first time Christ was about to give life to the dead. As the Prince of life and the shining ones approached the grave, Satan was alarmed for his supremacy. With his evil angels he stood to dispute an invasion of the territory that he claimed as his own. He boasted that the servant of God had become his prisoner. He declared that even Moses was not able to keep the law of God; that he had taken to himself the glory due to Jehovah—the very sin which had caused Satan's banishment from heaven—and by transgression had come under the dominion of Satan. The archtraitor reiterated the original charges that he had made against the divine government, and repeated his complaints of God's injustice toward him.

Christ did not stoop to enter into controversy with Satan. He might have brought against him the cruel work which his deceptions had wrought in heaven, causing the ruin of a vast number of its inhabitants. He might have pointed to the falsehoods told in Eden, that had led to Adam's sin and brought death upon the human race. He might have reminded Satan that it was his own work in tempting Israel to murmuring and rebellion, which had wearied the long-suffering patience of their leader, and in an unguarded moment had surprised him into the sin for which he had fallen under the power of death. But Christ referred all to His Father, saying, "The Lord rebuke thee." Jude 9. The Saviour entered into no dispute with His adversary, but He then and there began His work of breaking the power of the fallen foe, and bringing the dead to life. Here was an evidence that Satan could not controvert, of the supremacy of the Son of God. The resurrection was forever made certain. Satan was despoiled of his prey; the righteous dead would live again.

In consequence of sin Moses had come under the power of Satan. In his own merits he was death's lawful captive; but he was raised to immortal life, holding his title in the name of the Redeemer. Moses came forth from the tomb glorified, and ascended with his Deliverer to the City of God.

Never, till exemplified in the sacrifice of Christ, were the justice and the love of God more strikingly displayed than in His dealings with Moses. God shut Moses out of Canaan, to teach a lesson which should never be forgotten—that He requires exact obedience, and that men are to beware of taking to themselves the glory which is due to their Maker. He could not grant the prayer of Moses that he might share the inheritance of Israel, but He did not forget or forsake His servant. The God of heaven understood the suffering that Moses had endured; He had noted every act of faithful service through those long years of conflict and trial. On the top of Pisgah, God called Moses to an inheritance infinitely more glorious than the earthly Canaan.

Upon the mount of transfiguration Moses was present with Elijah, who had been translated. They were sent as bearers of light and glory from the Father to His Son. And thus the prayer of Moses, uttered so many centuries before, was at last fulfilled. He stood upon the "goodly mountain," within the heritage of his people, bearing witness to Him in whom all the promises to Israel centered. Such is the last scene revealed to mortal vision in the history of that man so highly honored of Heaven.

Moses was a type of Christ. He himself had declared to Israel, "The Lord thy God will raise up unto thee a Prophet from the midst of thee, of thy brethren, like unto me; unto Him ye shall hearken." Deuteronomy 18:15. God saw fit to discipline Moses in the school of affliction and poverty before he could be prepared to lead the hosts of Israel to the earthly Canaan. The Israel of God, journeying to the heavenly Canaan, have a Captain who needed no human teaching to prepare Him for His mission as a divine leader; yet He was made perfect through sufferings; and "in that He Himself hath suffered being tempted, He is able to succor them that are tempted." Hebrews 2:10, 18. Our Redeemer manifested no human weakness or imperfection; yet He died to obtain for us an entrance into the Promised Land.

"And Moses verily was faithful in all his house as a servant, for a testimony of those things which were to be spoken after; but Christ as a son over His own house; whose house are we, if we hold fast the confidence and the rejoicing of the hope firm unto the end." Hebrews 3:5, 6.

Crossing the Jordan

The Israelites deeply mourned for their departed leader, and thirty days were devoted to special services in honor of his memory. Never till he was taken from them had they so fully realized the value of his wise counsels, his parental tenderness, and his unswerving faith. With a new and deeper appreciation they recalled the precious lessons he had given while still with them.

Moses was dead, but his influence did not die with him. It was to live on, reproducing itself in the hearts of his people. The memory of that holy, unselfish life would long be cherished, with silent, persuasive power molding the lives even of those who had neglected his living words. As the glow of the descending sun lights up the mountain peaks long after the sun itself has sunk behind the hills, so the works of the pure, the holy, and the good shed light upon the world long after the actors themselves have passed away. Their works, their words, their example, will forever live. "The righteous shall be in everlasting remembrance." Psalm 112:6.

While they were filled with grief at their great loss, the people knew that they were not left alone. The pillar of cloud rested over the tabernacle by day, and the pillar of fire by night, an assurance that God would still be their guide and helper if they would walk in the way of His commandments.

Joshua was now the acknowledged leader of Israel. He had been known chiefly as a warrior, and his gifts and virtues were especially valuable at this stage in the history of his people. Courageous, resolute, and persevering, prompt, incorruptible, unmindful of selfish interests in his care for those committed to his charge, and, above all, inspired by a living faith in God—such was the character of the man divinely chosen to conduct the armies of Israel in their entrance upon the Promised Land. During the sojourn in the wilderness he had acted as prime minister to Moses, and by his quiet, unpretending fidelity, his steadfastness when others wavered, his firmness to maintain the truth in the midst of danger, he had given evidence of his fitness to succeed Moses, even before he was called to the position by the voice of God.

It was with great anxiety and self-distrust that Joshua had looked forward to the work before him; but his fears were removed by the assurance of God, "As I was with Moses, so I will be with thee: I will not fail thee, nor forsake thee. . . . Unto this people shalt thou divide for an inheritance the land, which I sware unto their fathers to give them." "Every place that the sole of your foot shall tread upon, that have I given unto you, as I said unto Moses." To the heights of Lebanon in the far distance, to the shores of the Great Sea, and away to the banks of the Euphrates in the east—all was to be theirs.

To this promise was added the injunction, "Only be thou strong and very courageous, that thou mayest observe to do according to all the law, which Moses My servant commanded." The Lord's direction was, "This book of the law shall not depart out of thy mouth; but thou shalt meditate therein day and night;" "turn not from it to the right hand or to the left;" "for then thou shalt make thy way prosperous, and then thou shalt have good success."

The Israelites were still encamped on the east side of Jordan, which presented the first barrier to the occupation of Canaan. "Arise," had been the first message of God to Joshua, "go over this Jordan, thou, and all this people, unto the land which I do give to them." No instruction was given as to the way in which they were to make the passage. Joshua knew, however, that whatever God should command, He would make a way for His people to perform, and in this faith the intrepid leader at once began his arrangements for an advance.

A few miles beyond the river, just opposite the place where the Israelites were encamped, was the large and strongly fortified city of Jericho. This city was virtually the key to the whole country, and it would present a formidable obstacle to the success of Israel. Joshua therefore sent two young men as spies to visit this city and ascertain something as to its population, its resources, and the strength of its fortifications. The inhabitants of the city, terrified and suspicious, were constantly on the alert, and the messengers were in great danger. They were, however, preserved by Rahab, a woman of Jericho, at the peril of her own life. In return for her kindness they gave her a promise of protection when the city should be taken.

The spies returned in safety with the tidings, "Truly the Lord hath delivered into our hands all the land; for even all the inhabitants of the country do faint because of us." It had been declared to them in Jericho, "We have heard how the Lord dried up the water of the Red Sea for you, when ye came out of Egypt; and what ye did unto the two kings of the Amorites, that were on the other side Jordan, Sihon and Og, whom ye utterly destroyed. And as soon as we had heard these things, our hearts did melt, neither did there remain any more courage in any man, because of you: for the Lord your God, He is God in heaven above, and in earth beneath."

Orders were now issued to make ready for an advance. The people were to prepare a three days' supply of food, and the army was to be put in readiness for battle. All heartily acquiesced in the plans of their leader and assured him of their confidence and support: "All that thou commandest us we will do, and whithersoever thou sendest us, we will go. According as we hearkened unto Moses in all things, so will we hearken unto thee: only the Lord thy God be with thee, as He was with Moses."

Leaving their encampment in the acacia groves of Shittim, the host descended to the border of the Jordan. All knew, however, that without divine aid they could not hope to make the passage. At this time of the year—in the spring season—the melting snows of the mountains had so raised the Jordan that the river overflowed its banks, making it impossible to cross at the usual fording places. God willed that the passage of Israel over Jordan should be miraculous. Joshua, by divine direction, commanded the people to sanctify themselves; they must put away their sins and free themselves from all outward impurity; "for tomorrow," he said, "the Lord will do wonders among you." The "ark of the covenant" was to lead the way before the host. When they should see the token of Jehovah's presence, borne by the priests, remove from its place in the center of the camp, and advance toward the river, then they were to remove from their place, "and go after it.' The circumstances of the passage were minutely foretold; and said Joshua, "Hereby ye shall know that the living God is among you, and that He will without fail drive out from before you the Canaanites. . . . Behold, the ark of the covenant of the Lord of all the earth passeth over before you into Jordan."

At the appointed time began the onward movement, the ark, borne upon the shoulders of the priests, leading the van. The people had been directed to fall back, so that there was a vacant space of more than half a mile about the ark. All watched with deep interest as the priests advanced down the bank of the Jordan. They saw them with the sacred ark move steadily forward toward the angry, surging stream, till the feet of the bearers were dipped into the waters. Then suddenly the tide above was swept back, while the current below flowed on, and the bed of the river was laid bare.

At the divine command the priests advanced to the middle of the channel and stood there while the entire host descended and crossed to the farther side. Thus was impressed upon the minds of all Israel the fact that the power that stayed the waters of Jordan was the same that had opened the Red Sea to their fathers forty years before. When the people had all passed over, the ark itself was borne to the western shore. No sooner had it reached a place of security, and "the soles of the priests' feet were lifted up unto the dry land," than the imprisoned waters, being set free, rushed down, a resistless flood, in the natural channel of the stream.

Coming generations were not to be without a witness to this great miracle. While the priests bearing the ark were still in the midst of Jordan, twelve men previously chosen, one from each tribe, took up each a stone from the river bed where the priests were standing, and carried it over to the western side. These stones were to be set up as a monument in the first camping place beyond the river. The people were bidden to repeat to their children and children's children the story of the deliverance that God had wrought for them, as Joshua said, "That all the people of the earth might know the hand of the Lord, that it is mighty: that ye might fear the Lord your God forever."

The influence of this miracle, both upon the Hebrews and upon their enemies, was of great importance. It was an assurance to Israel of God's continued presence and protection—an evidence that He would work for them through Joshua as He had wrought through Moses. Such an assurance was needed to strengthen their hearts as they entered upon the conquest of the land—the stupendous task that had staggered the faith of their fathers forty years before. The Lord had declared to Joshua before the crossing, "This day will I begin to magnify thee in the sight of all Israel, that they may know that, as I was with Moses, so I will be with thee." And the result fulfilled the promise. "On that day the Lord magnified Joshua in the sight of all Israel; and they feared him, as they feared Moses, all the days of his life."

This exercise of divine power in behalf of Israel was designed also to increase the fear with which they were regarded by the surrounding nations, and thus prepare the way for their easier and complete triumph. When the tidings that God had stayed the waters of Jordan before the children of Israel, reached the kings of the Amorites and of the Canaanites, their hearts melted with fear. The Hebrews had already slain the five kings of Midian, the powerful Sihon, king of the Amorites, and Og of Bashan, and now the passage over the swollen and impetuous Jordan filled all the surrounding nations with terror. To the Canaanites, to all Israel, and to Joshua himself, unmistakable evidence had been given that the living God, the King of heaven and earth, was among His people, and that He would not fail them nor forsake them.

A short distance from Jordan the Hebrews made their first encampment in Canaan. Here Joshua "circumcised the children of Israel;" "and the children of Israel encamped in Gilgal, and kept the Passover." The suspension of the rite of circumcision since the rebellion at Kadesh had been a constant witness to Israel that their covenant with God, of which it was the appointed symbol, had been broken. And the discontinuance of the Passover, the memorial of their deliverance from Egypt, had been an evidence of the Lord's displeasure at their desire to return to the land of bondage. Now, however, the years of rejection were ended. Once more God acknowledged Israel as His people, and the sign of the covenant was restored. The rite of circumcision was performed upon all the people who had been born in the wilderness. And the Lord declared to Joshua, "This day have I rolled away the reproach of Egypt from off you," and in allusion to this the place of their encampment was called Gilgal, "a rolling away," or "rolling off."

Heathen nations had reproached the Lord and His people because the Hebrews had failed to take possession of Canaan, as they expected, soon after leaving Egypt. Their enemies had triumphed because Israel had wandered so long in the wilderness, and they had mockingly declared that the God of the Hebrews was not able to bring them into the Promised Land. The Lord had now signally manifested His power and favor in opening the Jordan before His people, and their enemies could no longer reproach them.

"On the fourteenth day of the month at even," the Passover was celebrated on the plains of Jericho. "And they did eat of the old corn of the land on the morrow after the Passover, unleavened cakes, and parched corn in the selfsame day. And the manna ceased on the morrow after they had eaten of the old corn of the land; neither had the children of Israel manna any more; but they did eat of the fruit of the land of Canaan." The long years of their desert wanderings were ended. The feet of Israel were at last treading the Promised Land.

The Fall of Jericho

The Hebrews had entered Canaan, but they had not subdued it; and to human appearance the struggle to gain possession of the land must be long and difficult. It was inhabited by a powerful race, who stood ready to oppose the invasion of their territory. The various tribes were bound together by the fear of a common danger. Their horses and iron battle chariots, their knowledge of the country, and their training in war, would give them great advantage. Furthermore, the country was guarded by fortresses—"cities great and fenced up to heaven." Deuteronomy 9:1. Only in the assurance of a strength not their own could the Israelites hope for success in the impending conflict.

One of the strongest fortresses in the land—the large and wealthy city of Jericho—lay just before them, but a little distance from their camp at Gilgal. On the border of a fertile plain abounding with the rich and varied productions of the tropics, its palaces and temples the abode of luxury and vice, this proud city, behind its massive battlements, offered defiance to the God of Israel. Jericho was one of the principal seats of idol worship, being especially devoted to Ashtaroth, the goddess of the moon. Here centered all that was vilest and most degrading in the religion of the Canaanites. The people of Israel, in whose minds were fresh the fearful results of their sin at Beth-peor, could look upon this heathen city only with disgust and horror.

To reduce Jericho was seen by Joshua to be the first step in the conquest of Canaan. But first of all he sought an assurance of divine guidance, and it was granted him. Withdrawing from the encampment to meditate and to pray that the God of Israel would go before His people, he beheld an armed warrior, of lofty stature and commanding presence, "with his sword drawn in his hand." To Joshua's challenge, "Art thou for us, or for our adversaries?" the answer was given, "As Captain of the host of the Lord am I now come." The same command given to Moses in Horeb, "Loose thy shoe from off thy foot; for the place whereon thou standest is holy," revealed the true character of the mysterious stranger. It was Christ, the Exalted One, who stood before the leader of Israel. Awe-stricken, Joshua fell upon his face and worshiped, and heard the assurance, "I have given into thine hand Jericho, and the king thereof, and the mighty men of valor," and he received instruction for the capture of the city.

In obedience to the divine command Joshua marshaled the armies of Israel. No assault was to be made. They were simply to make the circuit of the city, bearing the ark of God and blowing upon trumpets. First came the warriors, a body of chosen men, not now to conquer by their own skill and prowess, but by obedience to the directions given them from God. Seven priests with trumpets followed. Then the ark of God, surrounded by a halo of divine glory, was borne by priests clad in the dress denoting their sacred office. The army of Israel followed, each tribe under its standard. Such was the procession that compassed the doomed city. No sound was heard but the tread of that mighty host and the solemn peal of the trumpets, echoing among the hills and resounding through the streets of Jericho. The circuit completed, the army returned in silence to their tents, and the ark was restored to its place in the tabernacle.

With wonder and alarm the watchmen of the city marked every move, and reported to those in authority. They knew not the meaning of all this display; but when they beheld that mighty host marching around their city once each day, with the sacred ark and the attendant priests, the mystery of the scene struck terror to the hearts of priest and people. Again they would inspect their strong defenses, feeling certain they could successfully resist the most powerful attack. Many ridiculed the thought that any harm could come to them through these singular demonstrations. Others were awed as they beheld the procession that each day wound about the city. They remembered that the Red Sea had once parted before this people, and that a passage had just been opened for them through the river Jordan. They knew not what further wonders God might work for them.

For six days the host of Israel made the circuit of the city. The seventh day came, and with the first dawn of light, Joshua marshaled the armies of the Lord. Now they were directed to march seven times around Jericho, and at a mighty peal from the trumpets to shout with a loud voice, for God had given them the city.

The vast army marched solemnly around the devoted walls. All was silent, save the measured tread of many feet, and the occasional sound of the trumpet, breaking the stillness of the early morning. The massive walls of solid stone seemed to defy the siege of men. The watchers on the walls looked on with rising fear, as, the first circuit ended, there followed a second, then a third, a fourth, a fifth, a sixth. What could be the object of these mysterious movements? What mighty event was impending? They had not long to wait. As the seventh circuit was completed, the long procession paused. The trumpets, which for an interval had been silent, now broke forth in a blast that shook the very earth. The walls of solid stone, with their massive towers and battlements, tottered and heaved from their foundations, and with a crash fell in ruin to the earth. The inhabitants of Jericho were paralyzed with terror, and the hosts of Israel marched in and took possession of the city.

The Israelites had not gained the victory by their own power; the conquest had been wholly the Lord's; and as the first fruits of the land, the city, with all that it contained, was to be devoted as a sacrifice to God. It was to be impressed upon Israel that in the conquest of Canaan they were not to fight for themselves, but simply as instruments to execute the will of God; not to seek for riches or self-exaltation, but the glory of Jehovah their King. Before the capture the command had been given, "The city shall be accursed, even it, and all that are therein." "Keep yourselves from the accursed thing, lest ye make yourselves accursed . . . and make the camp of Israel a curse, and trouble it."

All the inhabitants of the city, with every living thing that it contained, "both man and woman, young and old, and ox, and sheep, and ass," were put to the sword. Only faithful Rahab, with her household, was spared, in fulfillment of the promise of the spies. The city itself was burned; its palaces and temples, its magnificent dwellings with all their luxurious appointments, the rich draperies and the costly garments, were given to the flames. That which could not be destroyed by fire, "the silver, and the gold, and the vessels of brass and of iron," was to be devoted to the service of the tabernacle. The very site of the city was accursed; Jericho was never to be rebuilt as a stronghold; judgments were threatened upon anyone who should presume to restore the walls that divine power had cast down. The solemn declaration was made in the presence of all Israel, "Cursed be the man before the Lord, that riseth up and buildeth this city Jericho: he shall lay the foundation thereof in his first-born, and in his youngest son shall he set up the gates of it."

The utter destruction of the people of Jericho was but a fulfillment of the commands previously given through Moses concerning the inhabitants of Canaan: "Thou shalt smite them, and utterly destroy them." Deuteronomy 7:2. "Of the cities of these people, . . . thou shalt save alive nothing that breatheth." Deuteronomy 20:16. To many these commands seem to be contrary to the spirit of love and mercy enjoined in other portions of the Bible, but they were in truth the dictates of infinite wisdom and goodness. God was about to establish Israel in Canaan, to develop among them a nation and government that should be a manifestation of His kingdom upon the earth. They were not only to be inheritors of the true religion, but to disseminate its principles throughout the world. The Canaanites had abandoned themselves to the foulest and most debasing heathenism, and it was necessary that the land should be cleared of what would so surely prevent the fulfillment of God's gracious purposes.

The inhabitants of Canaan had been granted ample opportunity for repentance. Forty years before, the opening of the Red Sea and the judgments upon Egypt had testified to the supreme power of the God of Israel. And now the overthrow of the kings of Midian, of Gilead and Bashan, had further shown that Jehovah was above all gods. The holiness of His character and His abhorrence of impurity had been evinced in the judgments visited upon Israel for their participation in the abominable rites of Baalpeor. All these events were known to the inhabitants of Jericho, and there were many who shared Rahab's conviction, though they refused to obey it, that Jehovah, the God of Israel, "is God in heaven above, and upon the earth beneath." Like the men before the Flood, the Canaanites lived only to blaspheme Heaven and defile the earth. And both love and justice demanded the prompt execution of these rebels against God and foes to man.

How easily the armies of heaven brought down the walls of Jericho, that proud city whose bulwarks, forty years before, had struck terror to the unbelieving spies! Thy Mighty One of Israel had said, "I have given into thine hand Jericho." Against that word human strength was powerless.

"By faith the walls of Jericho fell down." Hebrews 11:30. The Captain of the Lord's host communicated only with Joshua; He did not reveal Himself to all the congregation, and it rested with them to believe or doubt the words of Joshua, to obey the commands given by him in the name of the Lord, or to deny his authority. They could not see the host of angels who attended them under the leadership of the Son of God. They might have reasoned: "What unmeaning movements are these, and how ridiculous the performance of marching daily around the walls of the city, blowing trumpets of rams' horns. This can have no effect upon those towering fortifications." But the very plan of continuing this ceremony through so long a time prior to the final overthrow of the walls afforded opportunity for the development of faith among the Israelites. It was to be impressed upon their minds that their strength was not in the wisdom of man, nor in his might, but only in the God of their salvation. They were thus to become accustomed to relying wholly upon their divine Leader.

God will do great things for those who trust in Him. The reason why His professed people have no greater strength is that they trust so much to their own wisdom, and do not give the Lord an opportunity to reveal His power in their behalf. He will help His believing children in every emergency if they will place their entire confidence in Him and faithfully obey him.

Soon after the fall of Jericho, Joshua determined to attack Ai, a small town among the ravines a few miles to the west of the Jordan Valley. Spies sent to this place brought back the report that the inhabitants were but few, and that only a small force would be needed to overthrow it.

The great victory that God had gained for them had made the Israelites self-confident. Because He had promised them the land of Canaan they felt secure, and failed to realize that divine help alone could give them success. Even Joshua laid his plans for the conquest of Ai without seeking counsel from God.

The Israelites had begun to exalt their own strength and to look with contempt upon their foes. An easy victory was expected, and three thousand men were thought sufficient to take the place. These rushed to the attack without the assurance that God would be with them. They advanced nearly to the gate of the city, only to encounter the most determined resistance. Panic-stricken at the numbers and thorough preparation of their enemies, they fled in confusion down the steep descent. The Canaanites were in hot pursuit; "they chased them from before the gate, . . . and smote them in the going down." Though the loss was small as to numbers—but thirty-six men being slain—the defeat was disheartening to the whole congregation. "The hearts of the people melted, and became as water." This was the first time they had met the Canaanites in actual battle, and if put to flight before the defenders of this little town, what would be the result in the greater conflicts before them? Joshua looked upon their ill success as an expression of God's displeasure, and in distress and apprehension he "rent his clothes, and fell to the earth upon his face before the ark of the Lord until the eventide, he and the elders of Israel, and put dust upon their heads."

"Alas, O Lord God," he cried, "wherefore hast Thou at all brought this people over Jordan, to deliver us into the hand of the Amorites, to destroy us? . . . O Lord, what shall I say, when Israel turneth their backs before their enemies! For the Canaanites and all the inhabitants of the land shall hear of it, and shall environ us round, and cut off our name from the earth: and what wilt Thou do unto Thy great name?"

The answer from Jehovah was, "Get thee up; wherefore liest thou thus upon thy face? Israel hath . . . transgressed My covenant which I commanded them." It was a time for prompt and decided action, and not for despair and lamentation. There was secret sin in the camp, and it must be searched out and put away before the presence and blessing of the Lord could be with His people. "Neither will I be with you any more, except ye destroy the accursed from among you."

God's command had been disregarded by one of those appointed to execute His judgments. And the nation was held accountable for the guilt of the transgressor: " They have even taken of the accursed thing, and have also stolen, and dissembled also." Instruction was given to Joshua for the discovery and punishment of the criminal. The lot was to be employed for the detection of the guilty. The sinner was not directly pointed out, the matter being left in doubt for a time, that the people might feel their responsibility for the sins existing among them, and thus be led to searching of heart and humiliation before God.

Early in the morning, Joshua gathered the people together by their tribes, and the solemn and impressive ceremony began. Step by step the investigation went on. Closer and still closer came the fearful test. First the tribe, then the family, then the household, then the man was taken, and Achan the son of Carmi, of the tribe of Judah, was pointed out by the finger of God as the troubler of Israel.

To establish his guilt beyond all question, leaving no ground for the charge that he had been unjustly condemned, Joshua solemnly adjured Achan to acknowledge the truth. The wretched man made full confession of his crime: "Indeed I have sinned against the Lord God of Israel. . . . When I saw among the spoils a goodly Babylonish garment, and two hundred shekels of silver, and a wedge of gold of fifty shekel's weight, then I coveted them, and took them; and, behold, they are hid in the earth in the midst of my tent." Messengers were immediately dispatched to the tent, where they removed the earth at the place specified, and "behold, it was hid in his tent, and the silver under it. And they took them out of the midst of the tent, and brought them unto Joshua, . . . and laid them out before the Lord."

Sentence was pronounced and immediately executed. "Why hast thou troubled us?" said Joshua, "the Lord shall trouble thee this day." As the people had been held responsible for Achan's sin, and had suffered from its consequences, they were, through their representatives, to take part in its punishment. "All Israel stoned him with stones."

Then there was raised over him a great pile of stones—a witness to the sin and its punishment. "Wherefore the name of that place was called, The valley of Achor," that is, "trouble." In the book of Chronicles his memorial is written—"Achar, the troubler of Israel." 1 Chronicles 2:7.

Achan's sin was committed in defiance of the most direct and solemn warnings and the most mighty manifestations of God's power. "Keep yourselves from the accursed thing, lest ye make yourselves accursed," had been the proclamation to all Israel. The command was given immediately after the miraculous passage of the Jordan, and the recognition of God's covenant by the circumcision of the people—after the observance of the Passover, and the appearance of the Angel of the covenant, the Captain of the Lord's host. It had been

followed by the overthrow of Jericho, giving evidence of the destruction which will surely overtake all transgressors of God's law. The fact that divine power alone had given the victory to Israel, that they had not come into possession of Jericho by their own strength, gave solemn weight to the command prohibiting them from partaking of the spoils. God, by the might of His own word, had overthrown this stronghold; the conquest was His, and to Him alone the city with all that it contained was to be devoted.

Of the millions of Israel there was but one man who, in that solemn hour of triumph and of judgment, had dared to transgress the command of God. Achan's covetousness was excited by the sight of that costly robe of Shinar; even when it had brought him face to face with death he called it "a goodly Babylonish garment." One sin had led to another, and he appropriated the gold and silver devoted to the treasury of the Lord—he robbed God of the first fruits of the land of Canaan.

The deadly sin that led to Achan's ruin had its root in covetousness, of all sins one of the most common and the most lightly regarded. While other offenses meet with detection and punishment, how rarely does the violation of the tenth commandment so much as call forth censure. The enormity of this sin, and its terrible results, are the lessons of Achan's history.

Covetousness is an evil of gradual development. Achan had cherished greed of gain until it became a habit, binding him in fetters well-nigh impossible to break. While fostering this evil, he would have been filled with horror at the thought of bringing disaster upon Israel; but his perceptions were deadened by sin, and when temptation came, he fell an easy prey.

Are not similar sins still committed, in the face of warnings as solemn and explicit? We are as directly forbidden to indulge covetousness as was Achan to appropriate the spoils of Jericho. God has declared it to be idolatry. We are warned, "Ye cannot serve God and mammon." Matthew 6:24. "Take heed, and beware of covetousness." Luke 12:15. "Let it not be once named among you." Ephesians 5:3. We have before us the fearful doom of Achan, of Judas, of Ananias and Sapphira. Back of all these we have that of Lucifer, the "son of the morning," who, coveting a higher state, forfeited forever the brightness and bliss of heaven. And yet, notwithstanding all these warnings, covetousness abounds.

Everywhere its slimy track is seen. It creates discontent and dissension in families; it excites envy and hatred in the poor against the rich; it prompts the grinding oppression of the rich toward the poor. And this evil exists not in the world alone, but in the church. How common even here to find selfishness, avarice, overreaching, neglect of charities, and robbery of God "in tithes and offerings." Among church members "in good and regular standing" there are, alas! many Achans. Many a man comes stately to church, and sits at the table of the Lord, while among his possessions are hidden unlawful gains, the things that God has cursed. For a goodly

Babylonish garment, multitudes sacrifice the approval of conscience and their hope of heaven. Multitudes barter their integrity, and their capabilities for usefulness, for a bag of silver shekels. The cries of the suffering poor are unheeded; the gospel light is hindered in its course; the scorn of worldlings is kindled by practices that give the lie to the Christian profession; and yet the covetous professor continues to heap up treasures. "Will a man rob God? Yet ye have robbed Me" (Malachi 3:8), saith the Lord.

Achan's sin brought disaster upon the whole nation. For one man's sin the displeasure of God will rest upon His church till the transgression is searched out and put away. The influence most to be feared by the church is not that of open opposers, infidels, and blasphemers, but of inconsistent professors of Christ. These are the ones that keep back the blessing of the God of Israel and bring weakness upon His people.

When the church is in difficulty, when coldness and spiritual declension exist, giving occasion for the enemies of God to triumph, then, instead of folding their hands and lamenting their unhappy state, let its members inquire if there is not an Achan in the camp. With humiliation and searching of heart, let each seek to discover the hidden sins that shut out God's presence.

Achan acknowledged his guilt, but when it was too late for the confession to benefit himself. He had seen the armies of Israel return from Ai defeated and disheartened; yet he did not come forward and confess his sin. He had seen Joshua and the elders of Israel bowed to the earth in grief too great for words. Had he then made confession, he would have given some proof of true penitence; but he still kept silence. He had listened to the proclamation that a great crime had been committed, and had even heard its character definitely stated. But his lips were sealed. Then came the solemn investigation. How his soul thrilled with terror as he saw his tribe pointed out, then his family and his household! But still he uttered no confession, until the finger of God was placed upon him. Then, when his sin could no longer be concealed, he admitted the truth. How often are similar confessions made. There is a vast difference between admitting facts after they have been proved and confessing sins known only to ourselves and to God. Achan would not have confessed had he not hoped by so doing to avert the consequences of his crime. But his confession only served to show that his punishment was just. There was no genuine repentance for sin, no contrition, no change of purpose, no abhorrence of evil.

So confessions will be made by the guilty when they stand before the bar of God, after every case has been decided for life or death. The consequences to result to himself will draw from each an acknowledgment of his sin. It will be forced from the soul by an awful sense of condemnation and a fearful looking for of judgment. But such confessions cannot save the sinner.

So long as they can conceal their transgressions from their fellow men, many, like Achan, feel secure, and flatter themselves that God will not be strict to mark iniquity. All too late their sins will find them out in that day when they shall not be purged with sacrifice or offering forever. When the records of heaven shall be opened, the Judge will not in words declare to man his guilt, but will cast one penetrating, convicting glance, and every deed, every transaction of life, will be vividly impressed upon the memory of the wrongdoer. The person will not, as in Joshua's day, need to be hunted out from tribe to family, but his own lips will confess his shame. The sins hidden from the knowledge of men will then be proclaimed to the whole world.

The Blessings and the Curses

After the execution of the sentence upon Achan, Joshua was commanded to marshal all the men of war and again advance against Ai. The power of God was with His people, and they were soon in possession of the city.

Military operations were now suspended, that all Israel might engage in a solemn religious service. The people were eager to obtain a settlement in Canaan; as yet they had not homes or lands for their families, and in order to gain these they must drive out the Canaanites; but this important work must be deferred, for a higher duty demanded their first attention.

Before taking possession of their inheritance, they must renew their covenant of loyalty to God. In the last instructions of Moses, direction had been twice given for a convocation of the tribes upon Mounts Ebal and Gerizim, at Shechem, for the solemn recognition of the law of God. In obedience to these injunctions the whole people, not only men, but "the women, and the little ones, and the strangers that were conversant among them" left their camp at Gilgal, and marched through the country of their enemies, to the vale of Shechem, near the center of the land. Though surrounded by unconquered foes, they were safe under the protection of God as long as they were faithful to Him. Now, as in the days of Jacob, "the terror of God was upon the cities that were round about them" (Genesis 35:5), and the Hebrews were unmolested.

The place appointed for this solemn service was one already sacred from its association with the history of their fathers. It was here that Abraham raised his first altar to Jehovah in the land of Canaan. Here both Abraham and Jacob had pitched their tents. Here the latter bought the field in which the tribes were to bury the body of Joseph. Here also was the well that Jacob had dug, and the oak under which he had buried the idolatrous images of his household.

The spot chosen was one of the most beautiful in all Palestine, and worthy to be the theater where this grand and impressive scene was to be enacted. The lovely valley, its green fields dotted with olive groves, watered with brooks from living fountains, and gemmed with wild flowers, spread out invitingly between the barren hills. Ebal and Gerizim, upon opposite sides of the valley, nearly approach each other, their lower spurs seeming to form a natural pulpit, every word spoken on one being distinctly audible on the other, while the mountainsides, receding, afford space for a vast assemblage.

According to the directions given by Moses, a monument of great stones was erected upon Mount Ebal. Upon these stones, previously prepared by a covering of plaster, the law was inscribed—not only the ten precepts spoken from Sinai and engraved on the tables of stone, but the laws communicated to Moses, and by him written in a book. Beside this monument was built an altar of unhewn stone, upon which sacrifices were offered unto the Lord. The fact that the altar was set up on Mount Ebal, the mountain upon which the curse was put, was significant, denoting that because of their transgressions of God's law, Israel had justly incurred His wrath, and that it would be at once visited, but for the atonement of Christ, represented by the altar of sacrifice.

Six of the tribes—all descended from Leah and Rachel—were stationed upon Mount Gerizim; while those that descended from the handmaids, together with Reuben and Zebulun, took their position on Ebal, the priests with the ark occupying the valley between them. Silence was proclaimed by the sound of the signal trumpet; and then in the deep stillness, and in the presence of this vast assembly, Joshua, standing beside the sacred ark, read the blessings that were to follow obedience to God's law. All the tribes on Gerizim responded by an Amen. He then read the curses, and the tribes on Ebal in like manner gave their assent, thousands upon thousands of voices uniting as the voice of one man in the solemn response. Following this came the reading of the law of God, together with the statutes and judgments that had been delivered to them by Moses.

Israel had received the law directly from the mouth of God at Sinai; and its sacred precepts, written by His own hand, were still preserved in the ark. Now it had been again written where all could read it. All had the privilege of seeing for themselves the conditions of the covenant under which they were to hold possession of Canaan. All were to signify their acceptance of the terms of the covenant and give their assent to the blessings or curses for its observance or neglect. The law was not only written upon the memorial stones, but was read by Joshua himself in the hearing of all Israel. It had not been many weeks since Moses gave the whole book of Deuteronomy in discourses to the people, yet now Joshua read the law again.

Not alone the men of Israel, but "all the women and the little ones" listened to the reading of the law; for it was important that they also should know and do their duty. God had commanded Israel concerning His statutes: "Therefore shall ye lay up these My words in your heart and in your soul, and bind them for a sign upon your hand, that they may be as frontlets between your eyes. And ye shall teach them your children, . . . that your days may be multiplied, and the days of your children, in the land which the Lord sware unto your fathers to give them, as the days of heaven upon the earth."

Deuteronomy 11:18-21.

Every seventh year the whole law was to be read in the assembly of all Israel, as Moses commanded: "At the end of every seven years, in the solemnity of the year of release, in the feast of tabernacles, when all Israel is come to appear before the Lord thy God in the place which He shall choose, thou shalt read this law before all Israel in their hearing. Gather the people together, men, and women, and children, and thy stranger that is within thy gates, that they may hear, and that they may learn, and fear the Lord your God, and observe to do all the words of this law: and that their children, which have not known anything, may hear, and learn to fear the Lord your God, as long as ye live in the land whither ye go over Jordan to possess it." Deuteronomy 31:10-13.

Satan is ever at work endeavoring to pervert what God has spoken, to blind the mind and darken the understanding, and thus lead men into sin. This is why the Lord is so explicit, making His requirements so very plain that none need err. God is constantly seeking to draw men close under His protection, that Satan may not practice his cruel, deceptive power upon them. He has condescended to speak to them with His own voice, to write with His own hand the living oracles. And these blessed words, all instinct with life and luminous with truth, are committed to men as a perfect guide. Because Satan is so ready to catch away the mind and divert the affections from the Lord's promises and requirements, the greater diligence is needed to fix them in the mind and impress them upon the heart.

Greater attention should be given by religious teachers to instructing the people in the facts and lessons of Bible history and the warnings and requirements of the Lord. These should be presented in simple language, adapted to the comprehension of children. It should be a part of the work both of ministers and parents to see that the young are instructed in the Scriptures.

Parents can and should interest their children in the varied knowledge found in the sacred pages. But if they would interest their sons and daughters in the word of God, they must be interested in it themselves. They must be familiar with its teachings, and, as God commanded Israel, speak of it, "when thou sittest in thine house, and when thou walkest by the way, when thou liest down, and when thou risest up." Deuteronomy 11:19. Those who desire their children to love and reverence God must talk of His goodness, His majesty, and His power, as revealed in His word and in the works of creation.

Every chapter and every verse of the Bible is a communication from God to men. We should bind its precepts as signs upon our hands and as frontlets between our eyes. If studied and obeyed, it would lead God's people, as the Israelites were led, by the pillar of cloud by day and the pillar of fire by night.

League With the Gibeonites

From Shechem the Israelites returned to their encampment at Gilgal. Here they were soon after visited by a strange deputation, who desired to enter into treaty with them. The ambassadors represented that they had come from a distant country, and this seemed to be confirmed by their appearance. Their clothing was old and worn, their sandals were patched, their provisions moldy, and the skins that served them for wine bottles were rent and bound up, as if hastily repaired on the journey.

In their far-off home—professedly beyond the limits of Palestine—their fellow countrymen, they said, had heard of the wonders which God had wrought for His people, and had sent them to make a league with Israel. The Hebrews had been specially warned against entering into any league with the idolaters of Canaan, and a doubt as to the truth of the strangers' words arose in the minds of the leaders. "Peradventure ye dwell among us," they said. To this the ambassadors only replied, "We are thy servants." But when Joshua directly demanded of them, "Who are ye? and from whence come ye?" they reiterated their former statement, and added, in proof of their sincerity, "This our bread we took hot for our provision out of our houses on the day we came forth to go unto you; but now, behold, it is dry, and it is moldy: and these bottles of wine, which we filled, were new; and, behold, they be rent: and these our garments and our shoes are become old by reason of the very long journey."

These representations prevailed. The Hebrews "asked not counsel at the mouth of the Lord. And Joshua made peace with them, and made a league with them, to let them live: and the princes of the congregation sware unto them." Thus the treaty was entered into. Three days afterward the truth was discovered. "They heard that they were their neighbors, and that they dwelt among them." Knowing that it was impossible to resist the Hebrews, the Gibeonites had resorted to stratagem to preserve their lives.

Great was the indignation of the Israelites as they learned the deception that had been practiced upon them. And this was heightened when, after three days' journey, they reached the cities of the Gibeonites, near the center of the land. "All the congregation murmured against the princes;" but the latter refused to break the treaty, though secured by fraud, because they had "sworn unto them by the Lord God of Israel." "And the children of Israel smote them not." The Gibeonites had pledged themselves to renounce idolatry, and accept the worship of Jehovah; and the preservation of their lives was not a violation of God's command to destroy the idolatrous Canaanites. Hence the Hebrews had not by their oath pledged themselves to commit sin. And though the oath had been secured by deception, it was not to be disregarded. The obligation to which one's word is pledged—if it do not bind him to perform a wrong act—should be held sacred. No consideration of gain, of revenge, or of self-interest can in any way affect the inviolability of an oath or pledge. "Lying lips are abomination to the Lord." Proverbs 12:22. He that "shall ascend into the hill of the Lord," and "stand in His holy place," is "he that sweareth to his own hurt, and changeth not." Psalms 24:3; 15:4.

The Gibeonites were permitted to live, but were attached as bondmen to the sanctuary, to perform all menial services. "Joshua made them that day hewers of wood and drawers of water for the congregation, and for the altar of the Lord." These conditions they gratefully accepted, conscious that they had been at fault, and glad to purchase life on any terms. "Behold, we are in thine hand," they said to Joshua; "as it seemeth good and right unto thee to do unto us, do." For centuries their descendants were connected with the service of the sanctuary.

The territory of the Gibeonites comprised four cities. The people were not under the rule of a king, but were governed by elders, or senators. Gibeon, the most important of their towns, "was a great city, as one of the royal cities," "and all the men thereof were mighty." It is a striking evidence of the terror with which the Israelites had inspired the inhabitants of Canaan, that the people of such a city should have resorted to so humiliating an expedient to save their lives.

But it would have fared better with the Gibeonites had they dealt honestly with Israel. While their submission to Jehovah secured the preservation of their lives, their deception brought them only disgrace and servitude. God had made provision that all who would renounce heathenism, and connect themselves with Israel, should share the blessings of the covenant. They were included under the term, "the stranger that sojourneth among you," and with few exceptions this class were to enjoy equal favors and privileges with Israel. The Lord's direction was—

"If a stranger sojourn with thee in your land, ye shall not vex him. But the stranger that dwelleth with you shall be unto you as one born among you, and thou shalt love him as thyself." Leviticus 19:33, 34. Concerning the Passover and the offering of sacrifices it was commanded, "One ordinance shall be both for you of the congregation, and also for the stranger that sojourneth with you: . . . as ye are, so shall the stranger be before the Lord." Numbers 15:15.

Such was the footing on which the Gibeonites might have been received, but for the deception to which they had resorted. It was no light humiliation to those citizens of a "royal city," "all the men whereof were mighty," to be made hewers of wood and drawers of water throughout their generations. But they had adopted the garb of poverty for the purpose of deception, and it was fastened upon them as a badge of perpetual servitude. Thus through all their generations their servile condition would testify to God's hatred of falsehood.

The submission of Gibeon to the Israelites filled the kings of Canaan with dismay. Steps were at once taken for revenge upon those who had made peace with the invaders. Under the leadership of Adonizedek, king of Jerusalem, five of the Canaanite kings entered into a confederacy against Gibeon.

Their movements were rapid. The Gibeonites were unprepared for defense, and they sent a message to Joshua at Gilgal: "Slack not thy hand from thy servants; come up to us quickly, and save us, and help us: for all the kings of the Amorites that dwell in the mountains are gathered together against us." The danger threatened not the people of Gibeon alone, but also Israel. This city commanded the passes to central and southern Palestine, and it must be held if the country was to be conquered.

Joshua prepared to go at once to the relief of Gibeon. The inhabitants of the besieged city had feared that he would reject their appeal, because of the fraud which they had practiced; but since they had submitted to the control of Israel, and had accepted the worship of God, he felt himself under obligation to protect them. He did not this time move without divine counsel, and the Lord encouraged him in the undertaking. "Fear them not," was the divine message; "for I have delivered them into thine hand; there shall not a man of them stand before thee." "So Joshua ascended from Gilgal, he, and all the people of war with him, and all the mighty men of valor."

By marching all night he brought his forces before Gibeon in the morning. Scarcely had the confederate princes mustered their armies about the city when Joshua was upon them. The attack resulted in the utter discomfiture of the assailants. The immense host fled before Joshua up the mountain pass to Beth-horon; and having gained the height, they rushed down the precipitous descent upon the other side. Here a fierce hailstorm burst upon them. "The Lord cast down great stones from heaven: . . . they were more which died with hailstones than they whom the children of Israel slew with the sword."

While the Amorites were continuing their headlong flight, intent on finding refuge in the mountain strongholds, Joshua, looking down from the ridge above, saw that the day would be too short for the accomplishment of his work. If not fully routed, their enemies would again rally, and renew the struggle. "Then spake Joshua to the Lord, . . . and he said in the sight of Israel, Sun, stand thou still upon Gibeon; and thou, Moon, in the valley of Ajalon. And the sun stood still, and the moon stayed, until the people had avenged themselves upon their enemies. . . . The sun stood still in the midst of heaven, and hasted not to go down about a whole day."

Before the evening fell, God's promise to Joshua had been fulfilled. The entire host of the enemy had been given into his hand. Long were the events of that day to remain in the memory of Israel. "There was no day like that before it or after it, that Jehovah hearkened unto the voice of a man: for the Lord fought for Israel." "The sun and moon stood still in their habitation: at the light of Thine arrows they went, and at the shining of Thy glittering spear. Thou didst march through the land in indignation, Thou didst thresh the heathen in anger. Thou wentest forth for the salvation of Thy people." Habakkuk 3:11-13.

The Spirit of God inspired Joshua's prayer, that evidence might again be given of the power of Israel's God. Hence the request did not show presumption on the part of the great leader. Joshua had received the promise that God would surely overthrow these enemies of Israel, yet he put forth as earnest effort as though success depended upon the armies of Israel alone. He did all that human energy could do, and then he cried in faith for divine aid. The secret of success is the union of divine power with human effort. Those who achieve the greatest results are those who rely most implicitly upon the Almighty Arm. The man who commanded, "Sun, stand thou still upon Gibeon; and thou, Moon, in the valley of Ajalon," is the man who for hours lay prostrate upon the earth in prayer in the camp of Gilgal. The men of prayer are the men of power.

This mighty miracle testifies that the creation is under the control of the Creator. Satan seeks to conceal from men the divine agency in the physical world—to keep out of sight the unwearied working of the first great cause. In this miracle all who exalt nature above the God of nature stand rebuked.

At His own will God summons the forces of nature to overthrow the might of His enemies—"fire, and hail; snow, and vapor; stormy wind fulfilling His word." Psalm 148:8. When the heathen Amorites had set themselves to resist His purposes, God interposed, casting down "great stones from heaven" upon the enemies of Israel. We are told of a greater battle to take place in the closing scenes of earth's history, when "Jehovah hath opened His armory, and hath brought forth the weapons of His indignation." Jeremiah 50:25. "Hast thou," he inquires, "entered into the treasures of the snow? or hast thou seen the treasures of the hail, which I have reserved against the time of trouble, against the day of battle and war?" Job 38:22, 23.

The revelator describes the destruction that is to take place when the "great voice out of the temple of heaven" announces, "It is done." He says, "There fell upon men a great hail out of heaven, every stone about the weight of a talent." Revelation 16:17, 21.

The Division of Canaan

The victory at Beth-horon was speedily followed by the conquest of southern Canaan. "Joshua smote all the country of the hills, and of the south, and of the vale. . . . And all these kings and their land did Joshua take at one time, because the Lord God of Israel fought for Israel. And Joshua returned, and all Israel with him, unto the camp at Gilgal."

The tribes of northern Palestine, terrified at the success which had attended the armies of Israel, now entered into a league against them. At the head of this confederacy was Jabin, king of Hazor, a territory to the west of Lake Merom. "And they went out, they and all their hosts with them." This army was much larger than any that the Israelites had before encountered in Canaan—"much people, even as the sand that is upon the seashore in multitude, with horses and chariots very many. And when all these kings were met together, they came and pitched together at the waters of Merom, to fight against Israel." Again a message of encouragement was given to Joshua: "Be not afraid because of them: for tomorrow about this time will I deliver them up all slain before Israel."

Near Lake Merom he fell upon the camp of the allies and utterly routed their forces. "The Lord delivered them into the hand of Israel, who smote them, and chased them . . . until they left them none remaining." The chariots and horses that had been the pride and boast of the Canaanites were not to be appropriated by Israel. At the command of God the chariots were burned, and the horses lamed, and thus rendered unfit for use in battle. The Israelites were not to put their trust in chariots or horses, but "in the name of the Lord their God."

One by one the cities were taken, and Hazor, the stronghold of the confederacy, was burned. The war was continued for several years, but its close found Joshua master of Canaan. "And the land had rest from war."

But though the power of the Canaanites had been broken, they had not been fully dispossessed. On the west the Philistines still held a fertile plain along the seacoast, while north of them was the territory of the Sidonians. Lebanon also was in the possession of the latter people; and to the south, toward Egypt, the land was still occupied by the enemies of Israel.

Joshua was not, however, to continue the war. There was another work for the great leader to perform before he should relinquish the command of Israel. The whole land, both the parts already conquered and that which was yet unsubdued, was to be apportioned among the tribes. And it was the duty of each tribe to fully subdue its own inheritance. If the people should prove faithful to God, He would drive out their enemies from before them; and He promised to give them still greater possessions if they would but be true to His covenant.

To Joshua, with Eleazar the high priest, and the heads of the tribes, the distribution of the land was committed, the location of each tribe being determined by lot. Moses himself had fixed the bounds of the country as it was to be divided among the tribes when they should come in possession of Canaan, and had appointed a prince from each tribe to attend to the distribution. The tribe of Levi, being devoted to the sanctuary service, was not counted in this allotment; but forty-eight cities in different parts of the country were assigned the Levites as their inheritance.

Before the distribution of the land had been entered upon, Caleb, accompanied by the heads of his tribe, came forward with a special claim. Except Joshua, Caleb was now the oldest man in Israel. Caleb and Joshua were the only ones among the spies who had brought a good report of the Land of Promise, encouraging the people to go up and possess it in the name of the Lord. Caleb now reminded Joshua of the promise then made, as the reward of his faithfulness: "The land whereon thy feet have trodden shall be thine inheritance, and thy children's forever, because thou hast wholly followed the Lord." He therefore presented a request that Hebron be given

him for a possession. Here had been for many years the home of Abraham, Isaac, and Jacob; and here, in the cave of Machpelah, they were buried. Hebron was the seat of the dreaded Anakim, whose formidable appearance had so terrified the spies, and through them destroyed the courage of all Israel. This, above all others, was the place which Caleb, trusting in the strength of God, chose for his inheritance.

"Behold, the Lord hath kept me alive," he said, "these forty and five years, even since the Lord spake this word unto Moses: . . . and now, lo, I am this day fourscore and five years old. As yet I am as strong this day as I was in the day that Moses sent me: as my strength was then, even so is my strength now, for war, both to go out, and to come in. Now therefore give me this mountain, whereof the Lord spake in that day: for thou heardest in that day how the Anakim were there, and that the cities were great and fenced: if so be the Lord will be with me, then I shall be able to drive them out, as the Lord said." This request was supported by the chief men of Judah. Caleb himself being the one appointed from this tribe to apportion the land, he had chosen to unite these men with him in presenting his claim, that there might be no appearance of having employed his authority for selfish advantage.

His claim was immediately granted. To none could the conquest of this giant stronghold be more safely entrusted. "Joshua blessed him, and gave unto Caleb the son of Jephunneh Hebron for an inheritance," "because that he wholly followed the Lord God of Israel." Caleb's faith now was just what it was when his testimony had contradicted the evil report of the spies. He had believed God's promise that He would put His people in possession of Canaan, and in this he had followed the Lord fully. He had endured with his people the long wandering in the wilderness, thus sharing the disappointments and burdens of the guilty; yet he made no complaint of this, but exalted the mercy of God that had preserved him in the wilderness when his brethren were cut off. Amid all the hardships, perils, and plagues of the desert wanderings, and during the years of warfare since entering Canaan, the Lord had preserved him; and now at upwards of fourscore his vigor was unabated. He did not ask for himself a land already conquered, but the place which above all others the spies had thought it impossible to subdue. By the help of God he would wrest his stronghold from the very giants whose power had staggered the faith of Israel. It was no desire for honor or aggrandizement that prompted Caleb's request. The brave old warrior was desirous of giving to the people an example that would honor God, and encourage the tribes fully to subdue the land which their fathers had deemed unconquerable.

Caleb obtained the inheritance upon which his heart had been set for forty years, and, trusting in God to be with him, he "drove thence the three sons of Anak." Having thus secured a possession for himself and his house, his zeal did not abate; he did not settle down to enjoy his inheritance, but pushed on to further conquests for the benefit of the nation and the glory of God.

The cowards and rebels had perished in the wilderness, but the righteous spies ate of the grapes of Eschol. To each was given according to his faith. The unbelieving had seen their fears fulfilled. Notwithstanding God's promise, they had declared that it was impossible to inherit Canaan, and they did not possess it. But those who trusted in God, looking not so much to the difficulties to be encountered as to the strength of their Almighty Helper, entered the goodly land. It was through faith that the ancient worthies "subdued kingdoms, . . . escaped the edge of the sword, out of weakness were made strong, waxed valiant in fight, turned to flight the armies of the aliens." Hebrews 11:33, 34. "This is the victory that overcometh the world, even our faith." 1 John 5:4.

Another claim concerning the division of the land revealed a spirit widely different from that of Caleb. It was presented by the children of Joseph, the tribe of Ephraim with the half tribe of Manasseh. In consideration of their superior numbers, these tribes demanded a double portion of territory. The lot designated for them was the richest in the land, including the fertile plain of Sharon; but many of the principal towns in the valley were still in possession of the Canaanites, and the tribes shrank from the toil and danger of conquering their possessions, and desired an additional portion in territory already subdued. The tribe of Ephraim was one of the largest in Israel, as well as the one to which Joshua himself belonged, and its members naturally regarded themselves as entitled to special consideration. "Why hast thou given me but one lot and one portion to inherit," they said, "seeing I am a great people?" But no departure from strict justice could be won from the inflexible leader.

His answer was, "If thou be a great people, then get thee up to the wood country, and cut down for thyself there in the land of the Perizzites and of the giants, if Mount Ephraim be too narrow for thee."

Their reply showed the real cause of complaint. They lacked faith and courage to drive out the Canaanites. "The hill is not enough for us," they said; "and all the Canaanites that dwell in the land of the valley have chariots of iron."

The power of the God of Israel had been pledged to His people, and had the Ephraimites possessed the courage and faith of Caleb, no enemy could have stood before them. Their evident desire to shun hardship and danger was firmly met by Joshua. "Thou art a great people, and hast great power," he said; "thou shalt drive out the Canaanites, though they have iron chariots, and though they be strong." Thus their own arguments were turned against them. Being a great people, as they claimed, they were fully able to make their own way, as did their brethren. With the help of God they need not fear the chariots of iron.

Heretofore Gilgal had been the headquarters of the nation and the seat of the tabernacle. But now the tabernacle was to be removed to the place chosen for its permanent location. This was Shiloh, a little town in the lot of Ephraim. It was near the center of the land, and was easy of access to all the tribes. Here a portion of country had been thoroughly subdued, so that the worshipers would not be molested. "And the whole congregation of the children of Israel assembled together at Shiloh, and set up the tabernacle of the congregation there." The tribes that were still encamped when the tabernacle was removed from Gilgal followed it, and pitched near Shiloh. Here these tribes remained until they dispersed to their possessions.

The ark remained at Shiloh for three hundred years, until, because of the sins of Eli's house, it fell into the hands of the Philistines, and Shiloh was ruined. The ark was never returned to the tabernacle here, the sanctuary service was finally transferred to the temple at Jerusalem, and Shiloh fell into insignificance. There are only ruins to mark the spot where it once stood. Long afterward its fate was made use of as a warning to Jerusalem. "Go ye now unto My place which was in Shiloh," the Lord declared by the prophet Jeremiah, "where I set My name at the first, and see what I did to it for the wickedness of My people Israel. . . . Therefore will I do unto this house, which is called by My name, wherein ye trust, and unto the place which I gave to you and to your fathers, as I have done to Shiloh." Jeremiah 7:12-14.

"When they had made an end of dividing the land," and all the tribes had been allotted their inheritance. Joshua presented his claim. To him, as to Caleb, a special promise of inheritance had been given; yet he asked for no extensive province, but only a single city. "They gave him the city which he asked, . . . and he built the city, and dwelt therein." The name given to the city was Timnath-serah, "the portion that remains"—a standing testimony to the noble character and unselfish spirit of the conqueror, who, instead of being the first to appropriate the spoils of conquest, deferred his claim until the humblest of his people had been served.

Six of the cities assigned to the Levites—three on each side the Jordan—were appointed as cities of refuge, to which the manslayer might flee for safety. The appointment of these cities had been commanded by Moses, "that the slayer may flee thither, which killeth any person at unawares. And they shall be unto you cities for refuge," he said, "that the manslayer die not, until he stand before the congregation in judgment." Numbers 35:11, 12. This merciful provision was rendered necessary by the ancient custom of private vengeance, by which the punishment of the murderer devolved on the nearest relative or the next heir of the deceased. In cases where guilt was clearly evident it was not necessary to wait for a trial by the magistrates. The avenger might pursue the criminal anywhere and put him to death wherever he should be found. The Lord did not see fit to abolish this custom at that time, but He made provision to ensure the safety of those who should take life unintentionally.

The cities of refuge were so distributed as to be within a half day's journey of every part of the land. The roads leading to them were always to be kept in good repair; all along the way signposts were to be erected bearing the word "Refuge" in plain, bold characters, that the fleeing one might not be delayed for a moment. Any person—Hebrew, stranger, or sojourner—might avail himself of this provision. But while the guiltless were not to be rashly slain, neither were the guilty to escape punishment. The case of the fugitive was to be fairly tried by the proper authorities, and only when found innocent of intentional murder was he to be protected in the city of refuge. The guilty were given up to the avenger. And those who were entitled to protection could receive it only on condition of remaining within the appointed refuge. Should one wander away beyond the prescribed limits, and be found by the avenger of blood, his life would pay the penalty of his disregard of the Lord's provision. At the death of the high priest, however, all who had sought shelter in the cities of refuge were at liberty to return to their possessions.

In a trial for murder the accused was not to be condemned on the testimony of one witness, even though circumstantial evidence might be strong against him. The Lord's direction was, "Whoso killeth any person, the murderer shall be put to death by the mouth of witnesses: but one witness shall not testify against any person to cause him to die." Numbers 35:30. It was Christ who gave to Moses these directions for Israel; and when personally with His disciples on earth, as He taught them how to treat the erring, the Great Teacher repeated the lesson that one man's testimony is not to acquit or condemn. One man's views and opinions are not to settle disputed questions. In all these matters two or more are to be associated, and together they are to bear the responsibility, "that in the mouth of two or three witnesses every word may be established." Matthew 18:16.

If the one tried for murder were proved guilty, no atonement or ransom could rescue him. "Whoso sheddeth man's blood, by man shall his blood be shed." Genesis 9:6. "Ye shall take no satisfaction for the life of a murderer, which is guilty of death: but he shall be surely put to death." "Thou shalt take him from Mine altar, that he may die," was the command of God; "the land cannot be cleansed of the blood that is shed therein, but by the blood of him that shed it." Numbers 35:31, 33; Exodus 21:14. The safety and purity of the nation demanded that the sin of murder be severely punished. Human life, which God alone could give, must be sacredly guarded.

The cities of refuge appointed for God's ancient people were a symbol of the refuge provided in Christ. The same merciful Saviour who appointed those temporal cities of refuge has by the shedding of His own blood provided for the transgressors of God's law a sure retreat, into which they may flee for safety from the second death. No power can take out of His hands the souls that go to Him for pardon. "There is therefore now no condemnation to them which are in Christ Jesus." "Who is he that condemneth? It is Christ that died, yea rather, that is risen again, who is even at the right hand of God, who also maketh intercession for us;" that "we might have a strong consolation, who have fled for refuge to lay hold upon the hope set before us." Romans 8:1, 34; Hebrews 6:18.

He who fled to the city of refuge could make no delay. Family and employment were left behind. There was no time to say farewell to loved ones. His life was at stake, and every other interest must be sacrificed to the one purpose—to reach the place of safety. Weariness was forgotten, difficulties were unheeded. The fugitive dared not for one moment slacken his pace until he was within the wall of the city.

The sinner is exposed to eternal death, until he finds a hiding place in Christ; and as loitering and carelessness might rob the fugitive of his only chance for life, so delays and indifference may prove the ruin of the soul. Satan, the great adversary, is on the track of every transgressor of God's holy law, and he who is not sensible of his danger, and does not earnestly seek shelter in the eternal refuge, will fall a prey to the destroyer.

The prisoner who at any time went outside the city of refuge was abandoned to the avenger of blood. Thus the people were taught to adhere to the methods which infinite wisdom appointed for their security. Even so, it is not enough that the sinner believe in Christ for the pardon of sin; he must, by faith and obedience, abide in Him. "For if we sin willfully after that we have received the knowledge of the truth, there remaineth no more sacrifice for sins, but a certain fearful looking for of judgment and fiery indignation, which shall devour the adversaries." Hebrews 10:26, 27.

Two of the tribes of Israel, Gad and Reuben, with half the tribe of Manasseh, had received their inheritance before crossing the Jordan. To a pastoral people, the wide upland plains and rich forests of Gilead and Bashan, offering extensive grazing land for their flocks and herds, had attractions which were not to be found in Canaan itself, and the two and a half tribes, desiring to settle here, had pledged themselves to furnish their proportion of armed men to accompany their brethren across the Jordan and to share their battles till they also should enter upon their inheritance. The obligation had been faithfully discharged. When the ten tribes entered Canaan forty thousand of "the children of Reuben, and the children of Gad, and half the tribe of Manasseh . . . prepared for war passed over before the Lord unto battle, to the plains of Jericho." Joshua 4:12, 13. For years they had fought bravely by the side of their brethren. Now the time had come for them to get unto the land of their possession. As they had united with their brethren in the conflicts, so they had shared the spoils; and they returned "with much riches . . . and with very much cattle, with silver, and with gold, and with brass, and with iron, and with very much raiment," all of which they were to share with those who had remained with the families and flocks.

They were now to dwell at a distance from the sanctuary of the Lord, and it was with an anxious heart that Joshua witnessed their departure, knowing how strong would be the temptations, in their isolated and wandering life, to fall into the customs of the heathen tribes that dwelt upon their borders.

While the minds of Joshua and other leaders were still

oppressed with anxious forebodings, strange tidings reached them. Beside the Jordan, near the place of Israel's miraculous passage of the river, the two and a half tribes had erected a great altar, similar to the altar of burnt offering at Shiloh. The law of God prohibited, on pain of death, the establishment of another worship than that at the sanctuary. If such was the object of this altar, it would, if permitted to remain, lead the people away from the true faith.

The representatives of the people assembled at Shiloh, and in the heat of their excitement and indignation proposed to make war at once upon the offenders. Through the influence of the more cautious, however, it was decided to send first a delegation to obtain from the two and a half tribes an explanation of their conduct. Ten princes, one from each tribe, were chosen. At their head was Phinehas, who had distinguished himself by his zeal in the matter of Peor.

The two and a half tribes had been at fault in entering, without explanation, upon an act open to such grave suspicions. The ambassadors, taking it for granted that their brethren were guilty, met them with sharp rebuke. They accused them of rebelling against the Lord, and bade them remember how judgments had been visited upon Israel for joining themselves to Baalpeor. In behalf of all Israel, Phinehas stated to the children of Gad and Reuben that if they were unwilling to abide in that land without an altar for sacrifice, they would be welcome to a share in the possessions and privileges of their brethren on the other side.

In reply the accused explained that their altar was not intended for sacrifice, but simply as a witness that, although separated by the river, they were of the same faith as their brethren in Canaan. They had feared that in future years their children might be excluded from the tabernacle, as having no part in Israel. Then this altar, erected after the pattern of the altar of the Lord at Shiloh, would be a witness that its builders were also worshipers of the living God.

With great joy the ambassadors accepted this explanation, and immediately carried back the tidings to those who sent them. All thoughts of war were dismissed, and the people united in rejoicing, and praise to God.

The children of Gad and Reuben now placed upon their altar an inscription pointing out the purpose for which it was erected; and they said, "It shall be a witness between us that Jehovah is God." Thus they endeavored to prevent future misapprehension and to remove what might be a cause of temptation.

How often serious difficulties arise from a simple misunderstanding, even among those who are actuated by the worthiest motives; and without the exercise of courtesy and forbearance, what serious and even fatal results may follow. The ten tribes remembered how, in Achan's case, God had rebuked the lack of vigilance to discover the sins existing among them. Now they resolved to act promptly and earnestly; but in seeking to shun their first error, they had gone to the opposite extreme. Instead of making courteous inquiry to learn the facts in the case, they had met their brethren with censure and condemnation. Had the men of Gad and Reuben retorted in the same spirit, war would have been the result. While it is important on the one hand that laxness in dealing with sin be avoided, it is equally important on the other to shun harsh judgment and groundless suspicion.

While very sensitive to the least blame in regard to their own course, many are too severe in dealing with those whom they suppose to be in error. No one was ever reclaimed from a wrong position by censure and reproach; but many are thus driven further from the right path and led to harden their hearts against conviction. A spirit of kindness, a courteous, forbearing deportment may save the erring and hide a multitude of sins.

The wisdom displayed by the Reubenites and their companions is worthy of imitation. While honestly seeking to promote the cause of true religion, they were misjudged and severely censured; yet they manifested no resentment. They listened with courtesy and patience to the charges of their brethren before attempting to make their defense, and then fully explained their motives and showed their innocence. Thus the difficulty which had threatened such serious consequences was amicably settled.

Even under false accusation those who are in the right can afford to be calm and considerate. God is acquainted with all that is misunderstood and misinterpreted by men, and we can safely leave our case in His hands. He will as surely vindicate the cause of those who put their trust in Him as He searched out the guilt of Achan. Those who are actuated by the spirit of Christ will possess that charity which suffers long and is kind.

It is the will of God that union and brotherly love should exist among His people. The prayer of Christ just before His crucifixion was that His disciples might be one as He is one with the Father, that the world might believe that God had sent Him. This most touching and wonderful prayer reaches down the ages, even to our day; for His words were, "Neither pray I for these alone, but for them also which shall believe on Me through their word." John 17:20. While we are not to sacrifice one principle of truth, it should be our constant aim to reach this state of unity. This is the evidence of our discipleship. Said Jesus, "By this shall all men know that ye are My disciples, if ye have love one to another." John 13:35. The apostle Peter exhorts the church, "Be ye all of one mind, having compassion one of another; love as brethren, be pitiful, be courteous: not rendering evil for evil, or railing for railing: but contrariwise blessing; knowing that ye are thereunto called, that ye should inherit a blessing." 1 Peter 3:8, 9.

The Last Words of Joshua

The wars and conquest ended, Joshua had withdrawn to the peaceful retirement of his home at Timnath-serah. "And it came to pass, a long time after that the Lord had given rest unto Israel from all their enemies round about, that Joshua .

. . called for all Israel, and for their elders, and for their heads, and for their judges, and for their officers."

Some years had passed since the people had settled in their possessions, and already could be seen cropping out the same evils that had heretofore brought judgments upon Israel. As Joshua felt the infirmities of age stealing upon him, and realized that his work must soon close, he was filled with anxiety for the future of his people. It was with more than a father's interest that he addressed them, as they gathered once more about their aged chief. "Ye have seen," he said, "all that the Lord your God hath done unto all these nations because of you; for the Lord your God is He that hath fought for you." Although the Canaanites had been subdued, they still possessed a considerable portion of the land promised to Israel, and Joshua exhorted his people not to settle down at ease and forget the Lord's command to utterly dispossess these idolatrous nations.

The people in general were slow to complete the work of driving out the heathen. The tribes had dispersed to their possessions, the army had disbanded, and it was looked upon as a difficult and doubtful undertaking to renew the war. But Joshua declared: "The Lord your God, He shall expel them from before you, and drive them from out of your sight; and ye shall possess their land, as the Lord your God hath promised unto you. Be ye therefore very courageous to keep and to do all that is written in the book of the law of Moses, that ye turn not aside therefrom to the right hand or to the left."

Joshua appealed to the people themselves as witnesses that, so far as they had complied with the conditions, God had faithfully fulfilled His promises to them. "Ye know in all your hearts and in all your souls," he said, "that not one thing hath failed of all the good things which the Lord your God spake concerning you; all are come to pass unto you, and not one thing hath failed thereof." He declared to them that as the Lord had fulfilled His promises, so He would fulfill His threatenings. "It shall come to pass, that as all good things are come upon you, which the Lord your God promised you; so shall the Lord bring upon you all evil things. . . . When ye have transgressed the covenant of the Lord, . . . then shall the anger of the Lord be kindled against you, and ye shall perish quickly from off the good land which He hath given unto you."

Satan deceives many with the plausible theory that God's love for His people is so great that He will excuse sin in them; he represents that while the threatenings of God's word are to serve a certain purpose in His moral government, they are never to be literally fulfilled. But in all His dealings with his creatures God has maintained the principles of righteousness by revealing sin in its true character—by demonstrating that its sure result is misery and death. The unconditional pardon of sin never has been, and never will be. Such pardon would show the abandonment of the principles of righteousness, which are the very foundation of the government of God. It would fill the unfallen universe with consternation. God has faithfully pointed out the results of sin, and if these warnings were not true, how could we be sure that His promises would be fulfilled? That so-called benevolence which would set aside justice is not benevolence but weakness.

God is the life-giver. From the beginning all His laws were ordained to life. But sin broke in upon the order that God had established, and discord followed. So long as sin exists, suffering and death are inevitable. It is only because the Redeemer has borne the curse of sin in our behalf that man can hope to escape, in his own person, its dire results.

Before the death of Joshua the heads and representatives of the tribes, obedient to his summons, again assembled at Shechem. No spot in all the land possessed so many sacred associations, carrying their minds back to God's covenant with Abraham and Jacob, and recalling also their own solemn vows upon their entrance into Canaan. Here were the mountains Ebal and Gerizim, the silent witnesses of those vows which now, in the presence of their dying leader, they had assembled to renew. On every side were evidences of what God had wrought for them; how He had given them a land for which they did not labor, and cities which they built not, vineyards and oliveyards which they planted not. Joshua reviewed once more the history of Israel, recounting the wonderful works of God, that all might have a sense of His love and mercy and might serve Him "in sincerity and in truth."

By Joshua's direction the ark had been brought from Shiloh. The occasion was one of great solemnity, and this symbol of God's presence would deepen the impression he wished to make upon the people. After presenting the goodness of God toward Israel, he called upon them, in the name of Jehovah, to choose whom they would serve. The worship of idols was still to some extent secretly practiced, and Joshua endeavored now to bring them to a decision that should banish this sin from Israel. "If it seem evil unto you to serve Jehovah," he said, "choose you this day whom ye will serve." Joshua desired to lead them to serve God, not by compulsion, but willingly. Love to God is the very foundation of religion. To engage in His service merely from hope of reward or fear of punishment would avail nothing. Open apostasy would not be more offensive to God than hypocrisy and mere formal worship.

The aged leader urged the people to consider, in all its bearings, what he had set before them, and to decide if they really desired to live as did the degraded idolatrous nations around them. If it seemed evil to them to serve Jehovah, the source of power, the fountain of blessing, let them that day choose whom they would serve—"the gods which your fathers served," from whom Abraham was called out, "or the gods of the Amorites, in whose land ye dwell." These last words were a keen rebuke to Israel. The gods of the Amorites had not been able to protect their worshipers. Because of their abominable and debasing sins, that wicked nation had been destroyed, and the good land which they once possessed had been given to God's people. What folly for Israel to choose the deities for whose worship the Amorites had been destroyed! "As for me and my house," said Joshua, "we will serve Jehovah." The same holy zeal that inspired the leader's heart was communicated to the people. His appeals called forth the unhesitating response, "God forbid that we should forsake Jehovah, to serve other gods."

"Ye cannot serve the Lord," said Joshua: "for He is a holy God; . . . He will not forgive your transgressions nor your sins." Before there could be any permanent reformation the people must be led to feel their utter inability in themselves to render obedience to God. They had broken His law, it condemned them as transgressors, and it provided no way of escape. While they trusted in their own strength and righteousness, it was impossible for them to secure the pardon of their sins; they could not meet the claims of God's perfect law, and it was in vain that they pledged themselves to serve God. It was only by faith in Christ that they could secure pardon of sin and receive strength to obey God's law. They must cease to rely upon their own efforts for salvation, they must trust wholly in the merits of the promised Saviour, if they would be accepted of God.

Joshua endeavored to lead his hearers to weigh well their words, and refrain from vows which they would be unprepared to fulfill. With deep earnestness they repeated the declaration: "Nay; but we will serve the Lord." Solemnly consenting to the witness against themselves that they had chosen Jehovah, they once more reiterated their pledge of loyalty: "The Lord our God will we serve, and His voice will we obey.

"So Joshua made a covenant with the people that day, and set them a statute and an ordinance in Shechem." Having written an account of this solemn transaction, he placed it, with the book of the law, in the side of the ark. And he set up a pillar as a memorial, saying, "Behold, this stone shall be a witness unto us; for it hath heard all the words of the Lord which He spake unto us; it shall be therefore a witness unto you, lest ye deny your God. So Joshua let the people depart, every man unto his inheritance."

Joshua's work for Israel was done. He had "wholly followed the Lord;" and in the book of God he is written, "The servant of Jehovah." The noblest testimony to his character as a public leader is the history of the generation that had enjoyed his labors: "Israel served the Lord all the days of Joshua, and all the days of the elders that overlived Joshua."

Tithes and Offerings

In the Hebrew economy one tenth of the income of the people was set apart to support the public worship of God. Thus Moses declared to Israel: "All the tithe of the land, whether of the seed of the land, or of the fruit of the tree, is the Lord's: it is holy unto the Lord." "And concerning the tithe of the herd, or of the flock, . . . the tenth shall be holy unto the Lord." Leviticus 27:30, 32.

But the tithing system did not originate with the Hebrews. From the earliest times the Lord claimed a tithe as His, and this claim was recognized and honored. Abraham paid tithes to Melchizedek, the priest of the most high God. Genesis 14:20. Jacob, when at Bethel, an exile and a wanderer, promised the Lord, "Of all that Thou shalt give me I will surely give the tenth unto Thee." Genesis 28:22. As the Israelites were about to be established as a nation, the law of tithing was reaffirmed as one of the divinely ordained statutes upon obedience to which their prosperity depended.

The system of tithes and offerings was intended to impress the minds of men with a great truth—that God is the source of every blessing to His creatures, and that to Him man's gratitude is due for the good gifts of His providence.

"He giveth to all life, and breath, and all things." Acts 17:25. The Lord declares, "Every beast of the forest is Mine, and the cattle upon a thousand hills." Psalm 50:10. "The silver is Mine, and the gold is Mine." Haggai 2:8. And it is God who gives men power to get wealth. Deuteronomy 8:18. As an acknowledgment that all things came from Him, the Lord directed that a portion of His bounty should be returned to Him in gifts and offerings to sustain His worship.

"The tithe . . . is the Lord's." Here the same form of expression is employed as in the law of the Sabbath. "The seventh day is the Sabbath of the Lord thy God." Exodus 20:10. God reserved to Himself a specified portion of man's time and of his means, and no man could, without guilt, appropriate either for his own interests.

The tithe was to be exclusively devoted to the use of the Levites, the tribe that had been set apart for the service of the sanctuary. But this was by no means the limit of the contributions for religious purposes. The tabernacle, as afterward the temple, was erected wholly by freewill offerings; and to provide for necessary repairs and other expenses, Moses directed that as often as the people were numbered, each should contribute a half shekel for "the service of the tabernacle." In the time of Nehemiah a contribution was made yearly for this purpose. See Exodus 30:12-16; 2 Kings 12:4, 5; 2 Chronicles 24:4-13; Nehemiah 10:32, 33. From time to time sin offerings and thank offerings were brought to God. These were presented in great numbers at the annual feasts. And the most liberal provision was made for the poor.

Even before the tithe could be reserved there had been an acknowledgment of the claims of God. The first that ripened of every product of the land was consecrated to Him. The first of the wool when the sheep were shorn, of the grain when the wheat was threshed, the first of the oil and the wine, was set apart for God. So also were the first-born of all animals; and a redemption price was paid for the first-born son. The first fruits were to be presented before the Lord at the sanctuary, and were then devoted to the use of the priests.

Thus the people were constantly reminded that God was the true proprietor of their fields, their flocks, and their herds; that He sent them sunshine and rain for their seedtime and harvest, and that everything they possessed was of His creation, and He had made them stewards of His goods.

As the men of Israel, laden with the first fruits of field and orchard and vineyard, gathered at the tabernacle, there was made a public acknowledgment of God's goodness. When the priest accepted the gift, the offerer, speaking as in the presence of Jehovah, said, "A Syrian ready to perish was my father;" and he described the sojourn in Egypt and the affliction from which God had delivered Israel "with an outstretched arm, and with great terribleness, and with signs, and with wonders." And he said, "He hath brought us into this place, and hath given us this land, even a land that floweth with milk and honey. And now, behold, I have brought the first fruits of the land, which Thou, Jehovah, hast given me." Deuteronomy 26:5, 8-11.

The contributions required of the Hebrews for religious and charitable purposes amounted to fully one fourth of their income. So heavy a tax upon the resources of the people might be expected to reduce them to poverty; but, on the contrary, the faithful observance of these regulations was one of the conditions of their prosperity. On condition of their obedience God made them this promise: "I will rebuke the devourer for your sakes, and he shall not destroy the fruits of your ground; neither shall your vine cast her fruit before the time in the field. . . . And all nations shall call you blessed: for ye shall be a delightsome land, saith the Lord of hosts." Malachi 3:11.

A striking illustration of the results of selfishly withholding even freewill offerings from the cause of God was given in the days of the prophet Haggai. After their return from the captivity in Babylon, the Jews undertook to rebuild the temple of the Lord; but meeting determined opposition from their enemies, they discontinued the work; and a severe drought, by which they were reduced to actual want, convinced them that it was impossible to complete the building of the temple. "The time is not come," they said, "the time that the Lord's house should be built." But a message was sent them by the Lord's prophet: "Is it time for you, O ye, to dwell in your ceiled houses, and this house lie waste? Now therefore thus saith the Lord of hosts; Consider your ways. Ye have sown much, and bring in little; ye eat, but ye have not enough; ye drink, but ye are not filled with drink; ye clothe you, but there is none warm; and he that earneth wages, earneth wages to put it into a bag with holes." Haggai 1:2-6. And then the reason is given: "Ye looked for much, and, lo, it came to little; and when ye brought it home, I did blow upon it. Why? saith the Lord of hosts. Because of Mine house that is waste, and ye run every man unto his own house. Therefore the heaven over you is stayed from dew, and the earth is stayed from her fruit. And I called for a drought upon the land, and upon the mountains, and upon the corn, and upon the new wine, and upon the oil, and upon that which the ground bringeth forth, and upon men, and upon cattle, and upon all the labor of the hands." Verses 9-12. "When one came to a heap of twenty measures, there were but ten: when one came to the pressfat for to draw out fifty vessels out of the press, there were but twenty. I smote you with blasting and with mildew and with hail in all the labors of your hands." Haggai 2:16, 19.

Roused by these warnings, the people set themselves to build the house of God. Then the word of the Lord came to them: "Consider now from this day and upward, from the four and twentieth day of the ninth month, even from the day that the foundation of the Lord's temple was laid, . . . from this day will I bless you." Verses 18, 19.

Says the wise man, "There is that scattereth, and yet increaseth; and there is that withholdeth more than is meet, but it tendeth to poverty." Proverbs 11:24. And the same lesson is taught in the New Testament by the apostle Paul: "He which soweth sparingly shall reap also sparingly; and he which soweth bountifully shall reap also bountifully." "God is able to make all grace abound toward you; that ye, always having all sufficiency in all things, may abound to every good work." 2 Corinthians 9:6, 8.

God intended that His people Israel should be light bearers to all the inhabitants of the earth. In maintaining His public worship they were bearing a testimony to the existence and sovereignty of the living God. And this worship it was their privilege to sustain, as an expression of their loyalty and their love to Him. The Lord has ordained that the diffusion of light and truth in the earth shall be dependent upon the efforts and offerings of those who are partakers of the heavenly gift. He might have made angels the ambassadors of His truth; He might have made known His will, as He proclaimed the law from Sinai, with His own voice; but in His infinite love and wisdom He called men to become colaborers with Himself, by choosing them to do this work.

In the days of Israel the tithe and freewill offerings were needed to maintain the ordinances of divine service. Should the people of God give less in this age? The principle laid down by Christ is that our offerings to God should be in proportion to the light and privileges enjoyed. "Unto whomsoever much is given, of him shall be much required." Luke 12:48. Said the Saviour to His disciples as He sent them forth, "Freely ye have received, freely give." Matthew 10:8. As our blessings and privileges are increased—above all, as we have before us the unparalleled sacrifice of the glorious Son of God—should not our gratitude find expression in more abundant gifts to extend to others the message of salvation? The work of the gospel, as it widens, requires greater provision to sustain it than was called for anciently; and this makes the law of tithes and offerings of even more urgent necessity now than under the Hebrew economy. If His people were liberally to sustain His cause by their voluntary gifts, instead of resorting to unchristian and unhallowed methods to fill the treasury, God would be honored, and many more souls would be won to Christ.

The plan of Moses to raise means for the building of the tabernacle was highly successful. No urging was necessary. Nor did he employ any of the devices to which churches in our day so often resort. He made no grand feast. He did not invite the people to scenes of gaiety, dancing, and general amusement; neither did he institute lotteries, nor anything of this profane order, to obtain means to erect the tabernacle for God. The Lord directed Moses to invite the children of Israel to bring their offerings. He was to accept gifts from everyone that gave willingly, from his heart. And the offerings came in so great abundance that Moses bade the people cease bringing, for they had supplied more than could be used.

God has made men His stewards. The property which He has placed in their hands is the means that He has provided for the spread of the gospel. To those who prove themselves faithful stewards He will commit greater trusts, Saith the Lord, "Them that honor Me I will honor." 1 Samuel 2:30. "God loveth a cheerful giver," and when His people, with grateful hearts, bring their gifts and offerings to Him, "not grudgingly, or of necessity," His blessing will attend them, as He has promised. "Bring ye all the tithes into the storehouse, that there may be meat in Mine house, and prove Me now herewith, saith the Lord of hosts, if I will not open you the windows of heaven, and pour you out a blessing, that there shall not be room enough to receive it." Malachi 3:10.

God's Care for the Poor

To promote the assembling of the people for religious service, as well as to provide for the poor, a second tithe of all the increase was required. Concerning the first tithe, the Lord had declared, "I have given the children of Levi all the tenth in Israel." Numbers 18:21. But in regard to the second He commanded, "Thou shalt eat before the Lord thy God, in the place which He shall choose to place His name there, the tithe of thy corn, of thy wine, and of thine oil, and the firstlings of thy herds and of thy flocks; that thou mayest learn to fear the Lord thy God always." Deuteronomy 14:23, 29; 16:11-14. This tithe, or its equivalent in money, they were for two years to bring to the place where the sanctuary was established. After presenting a thank offering to God, and a specified portion to the priest, the offerers were to use the remainder for a religious feast, in which the Levite, the stranger, the fatherless, and the widow should participate. Thus provision was made for the thank offerings and feasts at the yearly festivals, and the people were drawn to the society of the priests and Levites, that they might receive instruction and encouragement in the service of God.

Every third year, however, this second tithe was to be used at home, in entertaining the Levite and the poor, as Moses said, "That they may eat within thy gates, and be filled." Deuteronomy 26:12. This tithe would provide a fund for the uses of charity and hospitality.

And further provision was made for the poor. There is nothing, after their recognition of the claims of God, that more distinguishes the laws given by Moses than the liberal, tender, and hospitable spirit enjoined toward the poor. Although God had promised greatly to bless His people, it was not His design that poverty should be wholly unknown among them. He declared that the poor should never cease out of the land. There would ever be those among His people who would call into exercise their sympathy, tenderness, and benevolence. Then, as now, persons were subject to misfortune, sickness, and loss of property; yet so long as they

followed the instruction given by God, there were no beggars among them, neither any who suffered for food.

The law of God gave the poor a right to a certain portion of the produce of the soil. When hungry, a man was at liberty to go to his neighbor's field or orchard or vineyard, and eat of the grain or fruit to satisfy his hunger. It was in accordance with this permission that the disciples of Jesus plucked and ate of the standing grain as they passed through a field upon the Sabbath day.

All the gleanings of harvest field, orchard, and vineyard, belonged to the poor. "When thou cuttest down thine harvest in thy field," said Moses, "and hast forgot a sheaf in the field, thou shalt not go again to fetch it. . . . When thou beatest thine olive tree, thou shalt not go over the boughs again. . . . When thou gatherest the grapes of thy vineyard, thou shalt not glean it afterward: it shall be for the stranger, for the fatherless, and for the widow. And thou shalt remember that thou wast a bondman in the land of Egypt." Deuteronomy 24:19-22; Leviticus 19:9, 10.

Every seventh year special provision was made for the poor. The sabbatical year, as it was called, began at the end of the harvest. At the seedtime, which followed the ingathering, the people were not to sow; they should not dress the vineyard in the spring; and they must expect neither harvest nor vintage. Of that which the land produced spontaneously they might eat while fresh, but they were not to lay up any portion of it in their storehouses. The yield of this year was to be free for the stranger, the fatherless, and the widow, and even for the creatures of the field. Exodus 23:10, 11; Leviticus 25:5.

But if the land ordinarily produced only enough to supply the wants of the people, how were they to subsist during the year when no crops were gathered? For this the promise of God made ample provision. "I will command My blessing upon you in the sixth year," He said, "and it shall bring forth fruit for three years. And ye shall sow the eighth year, and eat yet of old fruit until the ninth year; until her fruits come in ye shall eat of the old store." Leviticus 25:21,22.

The observance of the sabbatical year was to be a benefit to both the land and the people. The soil, lying untilled for one season, would afterward produce more plentifully. The people were released from the pressing labors of the field; and while there were various branches of work that could be followed during this time, all enjoyed greater leisure, which afforded opportunity for the restoration of their physical powers for the exertions of the following years. They had more time for meditation and prayer, for acquainting themselves with the teachings and requirements of the Lord, and for the instruction of their households.

In the sabbatical year the Hebrew slaves were to be set at liberty, and they were not to be sent away portionless. The Lord's direction was: "When thou sendest him out free from thee, thou shalt not let him go away empty. Thou shalt furnish him liberally out of thy flock, and out of thy floor, and out of thy winepress: of that wherewith the Lord thy God hath blessed thee thou shalt give unto him." Deuteronomy

15:13, 14.

The hire of a laborer was to be promptly paid: "Thou shalt not oppress a hired servant that is poor and needy, whether he be of thy brethren, or of thy strangers that are in thy land: . . . at his day thou shalt give him his hire, neither shall the sun go down upon it; for he is poor, and setteth his heart upon it." Deuteronomy 24:14, 15.

Special directions were also given concerning the treatment of fugitives from service: "Thou shalt not deliver unto his master the servant which is escaped from his master unto thee. He shall dwell with thee, even among you, in that place which he shall choose in one of thy gates, where it liketh him best: thou shalt not oppress him." Deuteronomy 23:15, 16.

To the poor, the seventh year was a year of release from debt. The Hebrews were enjoined at all times to assist their needy brethren by lending them money without interest. To take usury from a poor man was expressly forbidden: "If thy brother be waxen poor, and fallen in decay with thee; then thou shalt relieve him: yea, though he be a stranger, or a sojourner; that he may live with thee. Take thou no usury of him, or increase: but fear thy God; that thy brother may live with thee. Thou shalt not give him thy money upon usury, nor lend him thy victuals for increase." Leviticus 25:35-37. If the debt remained unpaid until the year of release, the principal itself could not be recovered. The people were expressly warned against withholding from their brethren needed assistance on account of this: "If there be among you a poor man of one of thy brethren, . . . thou shalt not harden thine heart, nor shut thine hand from thy poor brother. . . . Beware that there be not a thought in thy wicked heart, saying, The seventh year, the year of release, is at hand; and thine eye be evil against thy poor brother, and thou givest him nought; and he cry unto the Lord against thee, and it be sin unto thee." "The poor shall never cease out of the land; therefore I command thee, saying, Thou shalt open thine hand wide unto thy brother, to thy poor, and to thy needy, in thy land," "and shalt surely lend him sufficient for his need, in that which he wanteth." Deuteronomy 15:7-9, 11, 8.

None need fear that their liberality would bring them to want. Obedience to God's commandments would surely result in prosperity. "Thou shalt lend unto many nations," He said, "but thou shalt not borrow; and thou shalt reign over many nations, but they shall not reign over thee." Deuteronomy 15:6.

After "seven sabbaths of years," "seven times seven years," came that great year of release—the jubilee. "Then shalt thou cause the trumpet of the jubilee to sound . . . throughout all your land. And ye shall hallow the fiftieth year, and proclaim liberty throughout all the land unto all the inhabitants thereof: it shall be a jubilee unto you; and ye shall return every man unto his possession, and ye shall return every man unto his family." Leviticus 25:9, 10.

"On the tenth day of the seventh month, in the Day of Atonement," the trumpet of the jubilee was sounded. Throughout the land, wherever the Jewish people dwelt, the sound was heard, calling upon all the children of Jacob to welcome the year of release. On the great Day of Atonement satisfaction was made for the sins of Israel, and with gladness of heart the people would welcome the jubilee.

As in the sabbatical year, the land was not to be sown or reaped, and all that it produced was to be regarded as the rightful property of the poor. Certain classes of Hebrew slaves—all who did not receive their liberty in the sabbatical year—were now set free. But that which especially distinguished the year of jubilee was the reversion of all landed property to the family of the original possessor. By the special direction of God the land had been divided by lot. After the division was made no one was at liberty to trade his estate. Neither was he to sell his land unless poverty compelled him to do so, and then, whenever he or any of his kindred might desire to redeem it, the purchaser must not refuse to sell it; and if unredeemed, it would revert to its first possessor or his heirs in the year of jubilee.

The Lord declared to Israel: "The land shall not be sold forever: for the land is Mine; for ye are strangers and sojourners with Me." Leviticus 25:23. The people were to be impressed with the fact that it was God's land which they were permitted to possess for a time; that He was the rightful owner, the original proprietor, and that He would have special consideration made for the poor and unfortunate. It was to be impressed upon the minds of all that the poor have as much right to a place in God's world as have the more wealthy.

Such were the provisions made by our merciful Creator, to lessen suffering, to bring some ray of hope, to flash some gleam of sunshine, into the life of the destitute and distressed.

The Lord would place a check upon the inordinate love of property and power. Great evils would result from the continued accumulation of wealth by one class, and the poverty and degradation of another. Without some restraint the power of the wealthy would become a monopoly, and the poor, though in every respect fully as worthy in God's sight, would be regarded and treated as inferior to their more prosperous brethren. The sense of this oppression would arouse the passions of the poorer class. There would be a feeling of despair and desperation which would tend to demoralize society and open the door to crimes of every description. The regulations that God established were designed to promote social equality. The provisions of the sabbatical year and the jubilee would, in a great measure, set right that which during the interval had gone wrong in the social and political economy of the nation.

These regulations were designed to bless the rich no less than the poor. They would restrain avarice and a disposition for self-exaltation, and would cultivate a noble spirit of benevolence; and by fostering good will and confidence between all classes, they would promote social order, the stability of government. We are all woven together in the great web of humanity, and whatever we can do to benefit and uplift others will reflect in blessing upon ourselves. The law of mutual dependence runs through all classes of society. The poor are not more dependent upon the rich than are the rich upon the poor. While the one class ask a share in the blessings which God has bestowed upon their wealthier neighbors, the other need the faithful service, the strength of brain and bone and muscle, that are the capital of the poor.

Great blessings were promised to Israel on condition of obedience to the Lord's directions. "I will give you rain in due season," He declared, "and the land shall yield her increase, and the trees of the field shall yield their fruit. And your threshing shall reach unto the vintage, and the vintage shall reach unto the sowing time: and ye shall eat your bread to the full, and dwell in your land safely. And I will give peace in the land, and ye shall lie down, and none shall make you afraid: and I will rid evil beasts out of the land, neither shall the sword go through your land. . . . I will walk among you, and will be your God, and ye shall be My people. . . . But if ye will not hearken unto Me, and will not do all these commandments; and . . . ye break My covenant: . . . ye shall sow your seed in vain, for your enemies shall eat it. And I will set My face against you, and ye shall be slain before your enemies: they that hate you shall reign over you; and ye shall flee when none pursueth you." Leviticus 26: 4-17.

There are many who urge with great enthusiasm that all men should have an equal share in the temporal blessings of God. But this was not the purpose of the Creator. A diversity of condition is one of the means by which God designs to prove and develop character. Yet He intends that those who have worldly possessions shall regard themselves merely as stewards of His goods, as entrusted with means to be employed for the benefit of the suffering and the needy.

Christ has said that we shall have the poor always with us, and He unites His interest with that of His suffering people. The heart of our Redeemer sympathizes with the poorest and lowliest of His earthly children. He tells us that they are His representatives on earth. He has placed them among us to awaken in our hearts the love that He feels toward the suffering and oppressed. Pity and benevolence shown to them are accepted by Christ as if shown to Himself. An act of cruelty or neglect toward them is regarded as though done to Him.

If the law given by God for the benefit of the poor had continued to be carried out, how different would be the present condition of the world, morally, spiritually, and temporally! Selfishness and self-importance would not be manifested as now, but each would cherish a kind regard for the happiness and welfare of others; and such widespread destitution as is now seen in many lands would not exist.

The principles which God has enjoined, would prevent the terrible evils that in all ages have resulted from the oppression of the rich toward the poor and the suspicion and hatred of the poor toward the rich. While they might hinder the amassing of great wealth and the indulgence of unbounded luxury, they would prevent the consequent ignorance and degradation of tens of thousands whose ill-paid servitude is required to build up these colossal fortunes. They would bring a peaceful solution of those problems that now threaten to fill the world with anarchy and bloodshed.

The Annual Feasts

There were three annual assemblies of all Israel for worship at the sanctuary. Exodus 23:14-16. Shiloh was for a time the place of these gatherings; but Jerusalem afterward became the center of the nation's worship, and here the tribes convened for the solemn feasts.

The people were surrounded by fierce, warlike tribes, that were eager to seize upon their lands; yet three times every year all the able-bodied men and all the people who could make the journey were directed to leave their homes and repair to the place of assembly, near the center of the land. What was to hinder their enemies from sweeping down upon those unprotected households, to lay them waste with fire and sword? What was to prevent an invasion of the land, that would bring Israel into captivity to some foreign foe? God had promised to be the protector of His people. "The angel of Jehovah encampeth round about them that fear Him, and delivereth them." Psalm 34:7. While the Israelites went up to worship, divine power would place a restraint upon their enemies. God's promise was, "I will cast out the nations before thee, and enlarge thy borders: neither shall any man desire thy land, when thou shalt go up to appear before the Lord thy God thrice in the year." Exodus 34:24.

The first of these festivals, the Passover, the feast of unleavened bread, occurred in Abib, the first month of the Jewish year, corresponding to the last of March and the beginning of April. The cold of winter was past, the latter rain had ended, and all nature rejoiced in the freshness and beauty of the springtime. The grass was green on the hills and valleys, and wild flowers everywhere brightened the fields. The moon, now approaching the full, made the evenings delightful. It was the season so beautifully pictured by the sacred singer:

"The winter is past,
The rain is over and gone;
The flowers appear on the earth;
The time of the singing of birds is come,
And the voice of the turtle is heard in our land;
The fig tree ripeneth her green figs,
And the vines are in blossom,
They give forth their fragrance." Song of Solomon 2:11-13, R.V.

Throughout the land bands of pilgrims were making their way toward Jerusalem. The shepherds from their flocks, the herdsmen from the mountains, fishers from the Sea of Galilee, the husbandmen from their fields, and sons of the prophets from the sacred schools—all turned their steps toward the place where God's presence was revealed. They journeyed by short stages, for many went on foot. The caravans were constantly receiving accessions, and often became very large before reaching the Holy City.

Nature's gladness awakened joy in the hearts of Israel and gratitude to the Giver of all good. The grand Hebrew psalms were chanted, exalting the glory and majesty of Jehovah. At the sound of the signal trumpet, with the music of cymbals, the chorus of thanksgiving arose, swelled by hundreds of voices:

"I was glad when they said unto me,
Let us go unto the house of the Lord.
Our feet are standing
Within thy gates, O Jerusalem. . . .
Whither the tribes go up, even the tribes of the Lord, . . .
To give thanks unto the name of Jehovah. . . .
Pray for the peace of Jerusalem:
They shall prosper that love thee." Psalm 122:1-6, R.V.

As they saw around them the hills where the heathen had been wont to kindle their altar fires, the children of Israel sang:

"Shall I lift up mine eyes to the hills?
Whence should my help come?
My help cometh from Jehovah,
Which made heaven and earth." Psalm 121:1, 2 (margin).

"They that trust in the Lord
Are as Mount Zion, which cannot be moved, but abideth forever.
As the mountains are round about Jerusalem,
So the Lord is round about His people,
From this time forth and forevermore." Psalm 125:1, 2, R.V.

Surmounting the hills in view of the Holy City, they looked with reverent awe upon the throngs of worshipers wending their way to the temple. They saw the smoke of the incense ascending, and as they heard the trumpets of the Levites heralding the sacred service, they caught the inspiration of the hour, and sang:

"Great is the Lord, and greatly to be praised
In the city of our God, in the mountain of His holiness.
Beautiful for situation, the joy of the whole earth,
Is Mount Zion, on the sides of the north,
The city of the great King."
Psalm 48:1, 2.

"Peace be within thy walls,
And prosperity within thy palaces."
"Open to me the gates of righteousness:
I will go into them, and I will praise the Lord."
"I will pay my vows unto the Lord
Now in the presence of all His people,
In the courts of the Lord's house,

In the midst of thee, O Jerusalem,
Praise ye the Lord."
Psalm 122:7; 118:19; 116:18, 19.

All the houses in Jerusalem were thrown open to the pilgrims, and rooms were furnished free; but this was not sufficient for the vast assembly, and tents were pitched in every available space in the city and upon the surrounding hills.

On the fourteenth day of the month, at even, the Passover was celebrated, its solemn, impressive ceremonies commemorating the deliverance from bondage in Egypt, and pointing forward to the sacrifice that should deliver from the bondage of sin. When the Saviour yielded up His life on Calvary, the significance of the Passover ceased, and the ordinance of the Lord's Supper was instituted as a memorial of the same event of which the Passover had been a type.

The Passover was followed by the seven day's feast of unleavened bread. The first and the seventh day were days of holy convocation, when no servile work was to be performed. On the second day of the feast, the first fruits of the year's harvest were presented before God. Barley was the earliest grain in Palestine, and at the opening of the feast it was beginning to ripen. A sheaf of this grain was waved by the priest before the altar of God, as an acknowledgment that all was His. Not until this ceremony had been performed was the harvest to be gathered.

Fifty days from the offering of first fruits, came the Pentecost, called also the feast of harvest and the feast of weeks. As an expression of gratitude for the grain prepared as food, two loaves baked with leaven were presented before God. The Pentecost occupied but one day, which was devoted to religious service.

In the seventh month came the Feast of Tabernacles, or of ingathering. This feast acknowledged God's bounty in the products of the orchard, the olive grove, and the vineyard. It was the crowning festal gathering of the year. The land had yielded its increase, the harvests had been gathered into the granaries, the fruits, the oil, and the wine had been stored, the first fruits had been reserved, and now the people came with their tributes of thanksgiving to God, who had thus richly blessed them.

This feast was to be pre-eminently an occasion of rejoicing. It occurred just after the great Day of Atonement, when the assurance had been given that their iniquity should be remembered no more. At peace with God, they now came before Him to acknowledge His goodness and to praise Him for His mercy. The labors of the harvest being ended, and the toils of the new year not yet begun, the people were free from care, and could give themselves up to the sacred, joyous influences of the hour. Though only the fathers and sons were commanded to appear at the feasts, yet, so far as possible, all the household were to attend them, and to their hospitality the servants, the Levites, the stranger, and the poor were made welcome.

Like the Passover, the Feast of Tabernacles was commemorative. In memory of their pilgrim life in the wilderness the people were now to leave their houses and dwell in booths, or arbors, formed from the green branches "of goodly trees, branches of palm trees, and the boughs of thick trees, and willows of the brook." Leviticus 23:40, 42, 43.

The first day was a holy convocation, and to the seven days of the feast an eighth day was added, which was observed in like manner.

At these yearly assemblies the hearts of old and young would be encouraged in the service of God, while the association of the people from the different quarters of the land would strengthen the ties that bound them to God and to one another. Well would it be for the people of God at the present time to have a Feast of

Tabernacles—a joyous commemoration of the blessings of God to them. As the children of Israel celebrated the deliverance that God had wrought for their fathers, and His miraculous preservation of them during their journeyings from Egypt, so should we gratefully call to mind the various ways He has devised for bringing us out from the world, and from the darkness of error, into the precious light of His grace and truth.

With those who lived at a distance from the tabernacle, more than a month of every year must have been occupied in attendance upon the annual feasts. This example of devotion to God should emphasize the importance of religious worship and the necessity of subordinating our selfish, worldly interests to those that are spiritual and eternal. We sustain a loss when we neglect the privilege of associating together to strengthen and encourage one another in the service of God. The truths of His word lose their vividness and importance in our minds. Our hearts cease to be enlightened and aroused by the sanctifying influence, and we decline in spirituality. In our intercourse as Christians we lose much by lack of sympathy with one another. He who shuts himself up to himself is not filling the position that God designed he should. We are all children of one Father, dependent upon one another for happiness. The claims of God and of humanity are upon us. It is the proper cultivation of the social elements of our nature that brings us into sympathy with our brethren and affords us happiness in our efforts to bless others.

The Feast of Tabernacles was not only commemorative but typical. It not only pointed back to the wilderness sojourn, but, as the feast of harvest, it celebrated the ingathering of the fruits of the earth, and pointed forward to the great day of final ingathering, when the Lord of the harvest shall send forth His reapers to gather the tares together in bundles for the fire, and to gather the wheat into His garner. At that time the wicked will all be destroyed. They will become "as though they had not been." Obadiah 16. And every voice in the whole universe will unite in joyful praise to God. Says the revelator, "Every creature which is in heaven, and on the earth, and under the earth, and such as are in the sea, and all that are in them, heard I saying, Blessing, and honor, and glory, and power, be unto Him that sitteth upon the throne, and unto the Lamb forever and ever." Revelation 5:13.

The people of Israel praised God at the Feast of Tabernacles, as they called to mind His mercy in their deliverance from the bondage of Egypt and His tender care for them during their pilgrim life in the wilderness. They rejoiced also in the consciousness of pardon and acceptance, through the service of the Day of Atonement, just ended. But when the ransomed of the Lord shall have been safely gathered into the heavenly Canaan, forever delivered from the bondage of the curse, under which "the whole creation groaneth and travaileth in pain together until now" (Romans 8:22), they will rejoice with joy unspeakable and full of glory. Christ's great work of atonement for men will then have been completed, and their sins will have been forever blotted out.

"The wilderness and the solitary place shall be glad for them;
And the desert shall rejoice, and blossom as the rose.
It shall blossom abundantly, and rejoice even with joy and singing:
The glory of Lebanon shall be given unto it,
The excellency of Carmel and Sharon;
They shall see the glory of the Lord, and the excellency of our
God.

"Then the eyes of the blind shall be opened,
And the ears of the deaf shall be unstopped.
Then shall the lame man leap as an hart,
And the tongue of the dumb sing:
"For in the wilderness shall waters break out,
And streams in the desert.
And the parched ground shall become a pool,
And the thirsty land springs of water: . . .
"And an highway shall be there, and a way,
And it shall be called The way of holiness;
The unclean shall not pass over it;
But it shall be for those:
The wayfaring men, though fools, shall not err therein.

"No lion shall be there,
Nor any ravenous beast shall go up thereon,
It shall not be found there;
But the redeemed shall walk there:
"And the ransomed of the Lord shall return,
And come to Zion with songs
And everlasting joy upon their heads:
They shall obtain joy and gladness,
And sorrow and sighing shall flee away."
Isaiah 35:1, 2, 5-10.

The Earlier Judges

After the settlement in Canaan the tribes made no vigorous

effort to complete the conquest of the land. Satisfied with the territory already gained, their zeal soon flagged, and the war was discontinued. "When Israel was strong, . . . they put the Canaanites to tribute, and did not utterly drive them out." Judges 1:28.

The Lord had faithfully fulfilled, on His part, the promises made to Israel; Joshua had broken the power of the Canaanites, and had distributed the land to the tribes. It only remained for them, trusting in the assurance of divine aid, to complete the work of dispossessing the inhabitants of the land. But this they failed to do. By entering into league with the Canaanites they directly transgressed the command of God, and thus failed to fulfill the condition on which He had promised to place them in possession of Canaan.

From the very first communication of God with them at Sinai, they had been warned against idolatry. Immediately after the proclamation of the law the message was sent them by Moses concerning the nations of Canaan: "Thou shalt not bow down to their gods, nor serve them, nor do after their works: but thou shalt utterly overthrow them, and quite break down their images. And ye shall serve the Lord your God, and He shall bless thy bread, and thy water; and I will take sickness away from the midst of thee." Exodus 23:24, 25. The assurance was given that so long as they remained obedient, God would subdue their enemies before them: "I will send My fear before thee, and will destroy all the people to whom thou shalt come; and I will make all thine enemies turn their backs unto thee. And I will send hornets before thee, which shall drive out the Hivite, the Canaanite, and the Hittite, from before thee. I will not drive them out from before thee in one year; lest the land become desolate, and the beast of the field multiply against thee. By little and little I will drive them out from before thee, until thou be increased, and inherit the land. . . . I will deliver the inhabitants of the land into your hand; and thou shalt drive them out before thee. Thou shalt make no covenant with them, nor with their gods. They shall not dwell in thy land, lest they make the sin against Me: for if thou serve their gods, it will surely be a snare unto thee." Exodus 23:27-33. These directions were reiterated in the most solemn manner by Moses before his death, and they were repeated by Joshua.

God had placed His people in Canaan as a mighty breastwork to stay the tide of moral evil, that it might not flood the world. If faithful to Him, God intended that Israel should go on conquering and to conquer. He would give into their hands nations greater and more powerful than the Canaanites. The promise was: "If ye shall diligently keep all these commandments which I command you, . . . then will the Lord drive out all these nations from before you, and ye shall possess greater nations and mightier than yourselves. Every place whereon the soles of your feet shall tread shall be yours: from the wilderness and Lebanon, from the river, the river Euphrates, even unto the uttermost sea shall your coast be. There shall no man be able to stand before you: for the Lord your God shall lay the fear of you and the dread of you

upon all the land that ye shall tread upon, as He hath said unto you." Deuteronomy 11:22-25.

But regardless of their high destiny, they chose the course of ease and self-indulgence; they let slip their opportunities for completing the conquest of the land; and for many generations they were afflicted by the remnant of these idolatrous peoples, that were, as the prophet had foretold, as "pricks" in their eyes, and as "thorns" in their sides. Numbers 33:55.

The Israelites were "mingled among the heathen, and learned their works." Psalm 106:35. They intermarried with the Canaanites, and idolatry spread like a plague throughout the land. "They served their idols: which were a snare unto them. Yea, they sacrificed their sons and their daughters unto devils: . . . and the land was polluted with blood. . . . Therefore was the wrath of the Lord kindled against His people, insomuch that He abhorred His own inheritance." Psalm 106:36-40.

Until the generation that had received instruction from Joshua became extinct, idolatry made little headway; but the parents had prepared the way for the apostasy of their children. The disregard of the Lord's restrictions on the part of those who came in possession of Canaan sowed seed of evil that continued to bring forth bitter fruit for many generations. The simple habits of the Hebrews had secured them physical health; but association with the heathen led to the indulgence of appetite and passion, which gradually lessened physical strength and enfeebled the mental and moral powers. By their sins the Israelites were separated from God; His strength was removed from them, and they could no longer prevail against their enemies. Thus they were brought into subjection to the very nations that through God they might have subdued.

"They forsook the Lord God of their fathers, which brought them out of the land of Egypt," "and guided them in the wilderness like a flock." "They provoked Him to anger with their high places, and moved Him to jealousy with their graven images." Therefore the Lord "forsook the tabernacle of Shiloh, the tent which He placed among them; and delivered His strength into captivity, and His glory into the enemy's hand." Judges 2:12; Psalm 78:52, 58, 60, 61. Yet He did not utterly forsake His people. There was ever a remnant who were true to Jehovah; and from time to time the Lord raised up faithful and valiant men to put down idolatry and to deliver the Israelites from their enemies. But when the deliverer was dead, and the people were released from his authority, they would gradually return to their idols. And thus the story of backsliding and chastisement, of confession and deliverance, was repeated again and again.

The king of Mesopotamia, the king of Moab, and after them the Philistines, and the Canaanites of Hazor, led by Sisera, in turn became the oppressors of Israel. Othniel, Shamgar, and Ehud, Deborah and Barak, were raised up as deliverers of their people. But again "the children of Israel did evil in the sight of the Lord; and the Lord delivered them into the hand of Midian." Heretofore the hand of the oppressor had fallen but lightly on the tribes dwelling east of the Jordan, but in the present calamities they were the first sufferers.

The Amalekites on the south of Canaan, as well as the Midianites on its eastern border, and in the deserts beyond, were still the unrelenting enemies of Israel. The latter nation had been nearly destroyed by the Israelites in the days of Moses, but they had since increased greatly, and had become numerous and powerful. They had thirsted for revenge; and now that the protecting hand of God was withdrawn from Israel, the opportunity had come. Not alone the tribes east of Jordan, but the whole land suffered from their ravages. The wild, fierce inhabitants of the desert, "as locusts for multitude" (Judges 6:5, R.V.), came swarming into the land, with their flocks and herds. Like a devouring plague they spread over the country, from the river Jordan to the Philistine plain. They came as soon as the harvests began to ripen, and remained until the last fruits of the earth had been gathered. They stripped the fields of their increase and robbed and maltreated the inhabitants and then returned to the deserts. Thus the Israelites dwelling in the open country were forced to abandon their homes, and to congregate in walled towns, to seek refuge in fortresses, or even to find shelter in caves and rocky fastnesses among the mountains. For seven years this oppression continued, and then, as the people in their distress gave heed to the Lord's reproof, and confessed their sins, God again raised up a helper for them.

Gideon was the son of Joash, of the tribe of Manasseh. The division to which this family belonged held no leading position, but the household of Joash was distinguished for courage and integrity. Of his brave sons it is said, "Each one resembled the children of a king." All but one had fallen in the struggles against the Midianites, and he had caused his name to be feared by the invaders. To Gideon came the divine call to deliver his people. He was engaged at the time in threshing wheat. A small quantity of grain had been concealed, and not daring to beat it out on the ordinary threshing floor, he had resorted to a spot near the winepress; for the season of ripe grapes being still far off, little notice was now taken of the vineyards. As Gideon labored in secrecy and silence, he sadly pondered upon the condition of Israel and considered how the oppressor's yoke might be broken from off his people.

Suddenly the "Angel of the Lord" appeared and addressed him with the words, "Jehovah is with thee, thou mighty man of valor."

"O my Lord," was his answer, "if the Lord be with us, why then is all this befallen us? and where be all His miracles which our fathers told us of, saying, Did not the Lord bring us up from Egypt? but now the Lord hath forsaken us, and delivered us into the hands of the Midianites."

The Messenger of heaven replied, "Go in this thy might, and thou shalt save Israel from the hand of the Midianites: have not I sent thee?"

Gideon desired some token that the one now addressing him was the Covenant Angel, who in time past had wrought for Israel. Angels of God, who communed with Abraham, had once tarried to share his hospitality; and Gideon now entreated the divine Messenger to remain as his guest. Hastening to his tent, he prepared from his scanty store a kid and unleavened cakes, which he brought forth and set before Him. But the Angel bade him, "Take the flesh and the unleavened cakes, and lay them upon this rock, and pour out the broth." Gideon did so, and then the sign which he had desired was given: with the staff in His hand, the Angel touched the flesh and the unleavened cakes, and a flame bursting from the rock consumed the sacrifice. Then the Angel vanished from his sight.

Gideon's father, Joash, who shared in the apostasy of his countrymen, had erected at Ophrah, where he dwelt, a large altar to Baal, at which the people of the town worshiped. Gideon was commanded to destroy this altar and to erect an altar to Jehovah over the rock on which the offering had been consumed, and there to present a sacrifice to the Lord. The offering of sacrifice to God had been committed to the priests, and had been restricted to the altar at Shiloh; but He who had established the ritual service, and to whom all its offerings pointed, had power to change its requirements. The deliverance of Israel was to be preceded by a solemn protest against the worship of Baal. Gideon must declare war upon idolatry before going out to battle with the enemies of his people.

The divine direction was faithfully carried out. Knowing that he would be opposed if it were attempted openly, Gideon performed the work in secret; with the aid of his servants, accomplishing the whole in one night. Great was the rage of the men of Ophrah when they came next morning to pay their devotions to Baal. They would have taken Gideon's life had not Joash—who had been told of the Angel's visit—stood in defense of his son. "Will ye plead for Baal?" said Joash. "Will ye save him? he that will plead for him, let him be put to death whilst it is yet morning: if he be a god, let him plead for himself, because one hath cast down his altar." If Baal could not defend his own altar, how could he be trusted to protect his worshipers?

All thoughts of violence toward Gideon were dismissed; and when he sounded the trumpet of war, the men of Ophrah were among the first to gather to his standard. Heralds were dispatched to his own tribe of Manasseh, and also to Asher, Zebulum, and Naphthali, and all answered to the call.

Gideon dared not place himself at the head of the army without still further evidence that God had called him to his work, and that He would be with him. He prayed, "If Thou wilt save Israel by mine hand, as Thou hast said, behold, I will put a fleece of wool in the floor; and if the dew be on the fleece only, and it be dry upon all the earth besides, then shall I know that Thou wilt save Israel by mine hand, as Thou hast said." In the morning the fleece was wet, while the ground was dry. But now a doubt arose, since wool naturally absorbs moisture when there is any in the air; the test might not be decisive. Hence he asked that the sign be reversed, pleading that his extreme caution might not displease the Lord. His request was granted.

Thus encouraged, Gideon led out his forces to give battle to the invaders. "All the Midianites and the Amalekites and the children of the east were gathered together, and went over, and pitched in the valley of Jezreel." The entire force under Gideon's command numbered only thirty-two thousand men; but with the vast host of the enemy spread out before him, the word of the Lord came to him: "The people that are with thee are too many for Me to give the Midianites into their hands, lest Israel vaunt themselves against Me, saying, Mine own hand hath saved me. Now therefore go to, proclaim in the ears of the people, saying, Whosoever is fearful and afraid, let him return and depart early from Mount Gilead." Those who were unwilling to face danger and hardships, or whose worldly interests would draw their hearts from the work of God, would add no strength to the armies of Israel. Their presence would prove only a cause of weakness.

It had been made a law in Israel that before they went to battle the following proclamation should be made throughout the army: "What man is there that hath built a new house, and hath not dedicated it? let him go and return to his house, lest he die in the battle, and another man dedicate it. And what man is he that hath planted a vineyard, and hath not yet eaten of it? let him also go and return unto his house, lest he die in the battle, and another man eat of it. And what man is there that hath betrothed a wife, and hath not taken her? let him go and return unto his house, lest he die in the battle, and another man take her." And the officers were to speak further to the people, saying, "What man is there that is fearful and fainthearted? let him go and return unto his house, lest his brethren's heart faint as well as his heart." Deuteronomy 20:5-8.

Because his numbers were so few compared with those of the enemy, Gideon had refrained from making the usual proclamation. He was filled with astonishment at the declaration that his army was too large. But the Lord saw the pride and unbelief existing in the hearts of His people. Aroused by the stirring appeals of Gideon, they had readily enlisted; but many were filled with fear when they saw the multitudes of the Midianites. Yet, had Israel triumphed, those very ones would have taken the glory to themselves instead of ascribing the victory to God.

Gideon obeyed the Lord's direction, and with a heavy heart he saw twenty-two thousand, or more than two thirds of his entire force, depart for their homes. Again the word of the Lord came to him: "The people are yet too many; bring them down unto the water, and I will try them for thee there: and it shall be, that of whom I say unto thee, This shall go with thee, the same shall go with thee; and of whomsoever I say unto thee, This shall not go with thee, the same shall not go." The people were led down to the waterside, expecting to make an immediate advance upon the enemy. A few hastily took a little water in the hand and sucked it up as they went on; but nearly all bowed upon their knees, and leisurely drank from the surface of the stream. Those who took of the water in their hands were but three hundred out of ten thousand; yet these were selected; all the rest were permitted to return to their homes.

By the simplest means character is often tested. Those who in time of peril were intent upon supplying their own wants were not the men to be trusted in an emergency. The Lord has no place in His work for the indolent and self-indulgent. The men of His choice were the few who would not permit their own wants to delay them in the discharge of duty. The three hundred chosen men not only possessed courage and self-control, but they were men of faith. They had not defiled themselves with idolatry. God could direct them, and through them He could work deliverance for Israel. Success does not depend upon numbers. God can deliver by few as well as by many. He is honored not so much by the great numbers as by the character of those who serve Him.

The Israelites were stationed on the brow of a hill overlooking the valley where the hosts of the invaders lay encamped. "And the Midianites and the Amalekites and all the children of the east lay along in the valley like locusts for multitude; and their camels were without number, as the sand which is upon the seashore for multitude." Judges 7:12, R.V. Gideon trembled as he thought of the conflict of the morrow. But the Lord spoke to him in the night season and bade him, with Phurah his attendant, go down to the camp of the Midianites, intimating that he would there hear something for his encouragement. He went, and, waiting in the darkness and silence, he heard a soldier relating a dream to his companion: "Lo, a cake of barley bread tumbled into the host of Midian, and came unto a tent, and smote it that it fell, and overturned it, that the tent lay along." The other answered in words that stirred the heart of that unseen listener, "This is nothing else save the sword of Gideon the son of Joash, a man of Israel: for into his hand hath God delivered Midian, and all the host." Gideon recognized the voice of God speaking to him through those Midianitish strangers. Returning to the few men under his command, he said, "Arise; for the Lord hath delivered into your hand the host of Midian."

By divine direction a plan of attack was suggested to him, which he immediately set out to execute. The three hundred men were divided into three companies. To every man were given a trumpet, and a torch concealed in an earthen pitcher. The men were stationed in such a manner as to approach the Midianite camp from different directions. In the dead of night, at a signal from Gideon's war horn, the three companies sounded their trumpets; then, breaking their pitchers and displaying the blazing torches, they rushed upon the enemy with the terrible war cry, "The sword of the Lord, and of Gideon!"

The sleeping army was suddenly aroused. Upon every side was seen the light of the flaming torches. In every direction was heard the sound of trumpets, with the cry of the assailants. Believing themselves at the mercy of an overwhelming force, the Midianites were panic-stricken. With wild cries of alarm they fled for life, and, mistaking their own companions for enemies, they slew one another. As news of the victory spread, thousands of the men of Israel who had been dismissed to their homes returned and joined in pursuit of their fleeing enemies. The Midianites were making their way toward the Jordan, hoping to reach their own territory, beyond the river. Gideon sent messengers to the tribe of Ephraim, rousing them to intercept the fugitives at the southern fords. Meanwhile, with his three hundred, "faint, yet pursuing," Gideon crossed the stream hard after those who had already gained the farther side. The two princes, Zebah and Zalmunna, who had been over the entire host, and who had escaped with an army of fifteen thousand men, were overtaken by Gideon, their force completely scattered, and the leaders captured and slain.

In this signal defeat not less than one hundred and twenty thousand of the invaders perished. The power of the Midianites was broken, so that they were never again able to make war upon Israel. The tidings spread swiftly far and wide, that Israel's God had again fought for His people. No words can describe the terror of the surrounding nations when they learned what simple means had prevailed against the power of a bold, warlike people.

The leader whom God chose to overthrow the Midianites occupied no prominent position in Israel. He was not a ruler, a priest, or a Levite. He thought himself the least in his father's house. But God saw in him a man of courage and integrity. He was distrustful of himself and willing to follow the guidance of the Lord. God does not always choose for His work men of the greatest talents, but He selects those whom He can best use. "Before honor is humility." Proverbs 15:33. The Lord can work most effectually through those who are most sensible of their own insufficiency, and who will rely upon Him as their leader and source of strength. He will make them strong by uniting their weakness to His might, and wise by connecting their ignorance with His wisdom.

If they would cherish true humility, the Lord could do much more for His people; but there are few who can be trusted with any large measure of responsibility or success without becoming self-confident and forgetful of their dependence upon God. This is why, in choosing the instruments for His work, the Lord passes by those whom the world honors as great, talented, and brilliant. They are too often proud and self-sufficient. They feel competent to act without counsel from God.

The simple act of blowing a blast upon the trumpet by the army of Joshua around Jericho, and by Gideon's little band about the hosts of Midian, was made effectual, through the power of God, to overthrow the might of His enemies. The most complete system that men have ever devised, apart from the power and wisdom of God, will prove a failure, while the most unpromising methods will succeed when divinely appointed and entered upon with humility and faith. Trust in God and obedience to His will are as essential to the Christian in the spiritual warfare as to Gideon and Joshua in their

battles with the Canaanites. By the repeated manifestations of His power in behalf of Israel, God would lead them to have faith in Him—with confidence to seek His help in every emergency. He is just as willing to work with the efforts of His people now and to accomplish great things through weak instrumentalities. All heaven awaits our demand upon its wisdom and strength. God is "able to do exceeding abundantly above all that we ask or think." Ephesians 3:20.

Gideon returned from pursuing the enemies of the nation, to meet censure and accusation from his own countrymen. When at his call the men of Israel had rallied against the Midianites, the tribe of Ephraim had remained behind. They looked upon the effort as a perilous undertaking; and as Gideon sent them no special summons, they availed themselves of this excuse not to join their brethren. But when the news of Israel's triumph reached them, the Ephraimites were envious because they had not shared it. After the rout of the Midianites, the men of Ephraim had, by Gideon's direction, seized the fords of the Jordan, thus preventing the escape of the fugitives. By this means a large number of the enemy were slain, among whom were two princes, Oreb and Zeeb. Thus the men of Ephraim followed up the battle, and helped complete the victory. Nevertheless, they were jealous and angry, as though Gideon had been led by his own will and judgment. They did not discern God's hand in the triumph of Israel, they did not appreciate His power and mercy in their deliverance; and this very fact showed them unworthy to be chosen as His special instruments.

Returning with the trophies of victory, they angrily reproached Gideon: "Why hast thou served us thus, that thou calledst us not, when thou wentest to fight with the Midianites?"

"What have I done now, in comparison of you?" said Gideon. "Is not the gleaning of the grapes of Ephraim better than the vintage of Abiezer? God hath delivered into your hands the princes of Midian, Oreb and Zeeb: and what was I able to do in comparison of you?"

The spirit of jealousy might easily have been fanned into a quarrel that would have caused strife and bloodshed; but Gideon's modest answer soothed the anger of the men of Ephraim, and they returned in peace to their homes. Firm and uncompromising where principle was concerned, and in war a "mighty man of valor," Gideon displayed also a spirit of courtesy that is rarely witnessed.

The people of Israel, in their gratitude at deliverance from the Midianites, proposed to Gideon that he should become their king, and that the throne should be confirmed to his descendants. This proposition was in direct violation of the principles of the theocracy. God was the king of Israel, and for them to place a man upon the throne would be a rejection of their Divine Sovereign. Gideon recognized this fact; his answer shows how true and noble were his motives. "I will not rule over you," he declared; "neither shall my son rule over you: the Lord shall rule over you."

But Gideon was betrayed into another error, which brought

disaster upon his house and upon all Israel. The season of inactivity that succeeds a great struggle is often fraught with greater danger than is the period of conflict. To this danger Gideon was now exposed. A spirit of unrest was upon him. Hitherto he had been content to fulfill the directions given him from God; but now, instead of waiting for divine guidance, he began to plan for himself. When the armies of the Lord have gained a signal victory, Satan will redouble his efforts to overthrow the work of God. Thus thoughts and plans were suggested to the mind of Gideon, by which the people of Israel were led astray.

Because he had been commanded to offer sacrifice upon the rock where the Angel appeared to him, Gideon concluded that he had been appointed to officiate as a priest. Without waiting for the divine sanction, he determined to provide a suitable place, and to institute a system of worship similar to that carried on at the tabernacle. With the strong popular feeling in his favor he found no difficulty in carrying out his plan. At his request all the earrings of gold taken from the Midianites were given him as his share of the spoil. The people also collected many other costly materials, together with the richly adorned garments of the princes of Midian. From the material thus furnished, Gideon constructed an ephod and a breastplate, in imitation of those worn by the high priest. His course proved a snare to himself and his family, as well as to Israel. The unauthorized worship led many of the people finally to forsake the Lord altogether, to serve idols. After Gideon's death great numbers, among whom were his own family, joined in this apostasy. The people were led away from God by the very man who had once overthrown their idolatry.

There are few who realize how far-reaching is the influence of their words and acts. How often the errors of parents produce the most disastrous effects upon their children and children's children, long after the actors themselves have been laid in the grave. Everyone is exerting an influence upon others, and will be held accountable for the result of that influence. Words and actions have a telling power, and the long hereafter will show the effect of our life here. The impression made by our words and deeds will surely react upon ourselves in blessing or in cursing. This thought gives an awful solemnity to life, and should draw us to God in humble prayer that He will guide us by His wisdom.

Those who stand in the highest positions may lead astray. The wisest err; the strongest may falter and stumble. There is need that light from above should be constantly shed upon our pathway. Our only safety lies in trusting our way implicitly to Him who has said, "Follow Me."

After the death of Gideon "the children of Israel remembered not the Lord their God, who had delivered them out of the hands of all their enemies on every side: neither showed they kindness to the house of Jerubbaal, namely, Gideon, according to all the goodness which he had showed unto Israel." Forgetful of all that they owed to Gideon, their judge and deliverer, the people of Israel accepted his baseborn son Abimelech as their king, who, to sustain his power, murdered all but one of Gideon's lawful children. When men cast off the fear of God they are not long in departing from honor and integrity. An appreciation of the Lord's mercy will lead to an appreciation of those who, like Gideon, have been employed as instruments to bless His people. The cruel course of Israel toward the house of Gideon was what might be expected from a people who manifested so great ingratitude to God.

After the death of Abimelech the rule of judges who feared the Lord served for a time to put a check upon idolatry, but erelong the people returned to the practices of the heathen communities around them. Among the northern tribes the gods of Syria and Sidon had many worshipers. On the southwest the idols of the Philistines, and on the east those of Moab and Ammon, had turned the hearts of Israel from the God of their fathers. But apostasy speedily brought its punishment. The Ammonites subdued the eastern tribes and, crossing the Jordan, invaded the territory of Judah and Ephraim. On the west the Philistines came up from their plain beside the sea, burning and pillaging far and near. Again Israel seemed to be abandoned to the power of relentless foes.

Again the people sought help from Him whom they had so forsaken and insulted. "The children of Israel cried unto the Lord, saying, We have sinned against Thee, both because we have forsaken our God, and also served Baalim." But sorrow had not worked true repentance. The people mourned because their sins had brought suffering upon themselves, but not because they had dishonored God by transgression of His holy law. True repentance is more than sorrow for sin. It is a resolute turning away from evil.

The Lord answered them through one of His prophets: "Did I not deliver you from the Egyptians, and from the Amorites, from the children of Ammon, and from the Philistines? The Zidonians also, and the Amalekites, and the Maonites, did oppress you; and ye cried to Me, and I delivered you out of their hand. Yet ye have forsaken Me, and served other gods: wherefore I will deliver you no more. Go and cry unto the gods which ye have chosen; let them deliver you in the time of your tribulation."

These solemn and fearful words carry the mind forward to another scene—the great day of final judgment—when the rejecters of God's mercy and the despisers of His grace shall be brought face to face with His justice. At that tribunal must they render an account who have devoted their God-given talents of time, of means, or of intellect, to serving the gods of this world. They have forsaken their true and loving Friend, to follow the path of convenience and worldly pleasure. They intended at some time to return to God; but the world with its follies and deceptions absorbed the attention. Frivolous amusements, pride of dress, indulgence of appetite, hardened the heart and benumbed the conscience, so that the voice of truth was not heard. Duty was despised. Things of infinite value were lightly esteemed, until the heart lost all desire to sacrifice for Him who has given so much for man. But in the reaping time they will gather that which they have sown.

Saith the Lord: "I have called, and ye refused; I have stretched out My hand, and no man regarded; but ye have set at nought all My counsel, and would none of My reproof: . . . when your fear cometh as desolation, and your destruction cometh as a whirlwind; when distress and anguish cometh upon you. Then shall they call upon Me, but I will not answer; they shall seek Me early, but they shall not find Me: for that they hated knowledge, and did not choose the fear of the Lord: they would none of My counsel: they despised all My reproof. Therefore shall they eat of the fruit of their own way, and be filled with their own devices." "But whoso hearkeneth unto Me shall dwell safely, and shall be quiet from fear of evil." Proverbs 1:24-31, 33.

The Israelites now humbled themselves before the Lord. "And they put away the strange gods from among them, and served Jehovah." And the Lord's heart of love was grieved—"was grieved for the misery of Israel." Oh, the long-suffering mercy of our God! When His people put away the sins that had shut out His presence, He heard their prayers and at once began to work for them.

A deliverer was raised up in the person of Jephthah, a Gileadite, who made war upon the Ammonites and effectually destroyed their power. For eighteen years at this time Israel had suffered under the oppression of her foes, yet again the lesson taught by suffering was forgotten.

As His people returned to their evil ways, the Lord permitted them to be still oppressed by their powerful enemies, the Philistines. For many years they were constantly harassed, and at times completely subjugated, by this cruel and warlike nation. They had mingled with these idolaters, uniting with them in pleasure and in worship, until they seemed to be one with them in spirit and interest. Then these professed friends of Israel became their bitterest enemies and sought by every means to accomplish their destruction.

Like Israel, Christians too often yield to the influence of the world and conform to its principles and customs, in order to secure the friendship of the ungodly; but in the end it will be found that these professed friends are the most dangerous of foes. The Bible plainly teaches that there can be no harmony between the people of God and the world. "Marvel not, my brethren, if the world hate you." 1 John 3:13. Our Saviour says, "Ye know that it hated Me before it hated you." John 15:18. Satan works through the ungodly, under cover of a pretended friendship, to allure God's people into sin, that he may separate them from Him; and when their defense is removed, then he will lead his agents to turn against them and seek to accomplish their destruction.

Samson

Amid the widespread apostasy the faithful worshipers of God continued to plead with Him for the deliverance of Israel. Though there was apparently no response, though year after year the power of the oppressor continued to rest more heavily upon the land, God's providence was preparing help for them. Even in the early years of the Philistine oppression a child was born through whom God designed to humble the power of these mighty foes.

On the border of the hill country overlooking the Philistine plain was the little town of Zorah. Here dwelt the family of Manoah, of the tribe of Dan, one of the few households that amid the general defection had remained true to Jehovah. To the childless wife of Manoah "the Angel of Jehovah" appeared with the message that she should have a son, through whom God would begin to deliver Israel. In view of this the Angel gave her instruction concerning her own habits, and also for the treatment of her child: "Now therefore beware, I pray thee, and drink not wine nor strong drink, and eat not any unclean thing." And the same prohibition was to be imposed, from the first, upon the child, with the addition that his hair should not be cut; for he was to be consecrated to God as a Nazarite from his birth.

The woman sought her husband, and, after describing the Angel, she repeated His message. Then, fearful that they should make some mistake in the important work committed to them, the husband prayed, "Let the Man of God which Thou didst send come again unto us, and teach us what we shall do unto the child that shall be born."

When the Angel again appeared, Manoah's anxious inquiry was, "How shall we order the child, and how shall we do unto him?" The previous instruction was repeated—"Of all that I said unto the woman let her beware. She may not eat of anything that cometh of the vine, neither let her drink wine or strong drink, nor eat any unclean thing: all that I commanded her let her observe."

God had an important work for the promised child of Manoah to do, and it was to secure for him the qualifications necessary for this work that the habits of both the mother and the child were to be carefully regulated. "Neither let her drink wine or strong drink," was the Angel's instruction for the wife of Manoah, "nor eat any unclean thing. All that I commanded her let her observe." The child will be affected for good or for evil by the habits of the mother. She must herself be controlled by principle and must practice temperance and self-denial, if she would seek the welfare of her child. Unwise advisers will urge upon the mother the necessity of gratifying every wish and impulse, but such teaching is false and mischievous. The mother is by the command of God Himself placed under the most solemn obligation to exercise self-control.

And fathers as well as mothers are involved in this responsibility. Both parents transmit their own characteristics, mental and physical, their dispositions and appetites, to their children. As the result of parental intemperance children often lack physical strength and mental and moral power. Liquor drinkers and tobacco users may, and do, transmit their insatiable craving, their inflamed blood and irritable nerves, to their children. The licentious often bequeath their unholy desires, and even loathsome diseases, as a legacy to their offspring. And as the children have less power to resist temptation than had the parents, the tendency is for each generation to fall lower and lower. To a great degree parents are responsible not only for the violent passions and perverted appetites of their children but for the infirmities of the thousands born deaf, blind, diseased, or idiotic.

The inquiry of every father and mother should be, "What shall we do unto the child that shall be born unto us?" The effect of prenatal influences has been by many lightly regarded; but the instruction sent from heaven to those Hebrew parents, and twice repeated in the most explicit and solemn manner, shows how this matter is looked upon by our Creator.

And it was not enough that the promised child should receive a good legacy from the parents. This must be followed by careful training and the formation of right habits. God directed that the future judge and deliverer of Israel should be trained to strict temperance from infancy. He was to be a Nazarite from his birth, thus being placed under a perpetual prohibition against the use of wine or strong drink. The lessons of temperance, self-denial, and self-control are to be taught to children even from babyhood.

The angel's prohibition included "every unclean thing." The distinction between articles of food as clean and unclean was not a merely ceremonial and arbitrary regulation, but was based upon sanitary principles. To the observance of this distinction may be traced, in a great degree, the marvelous vitality which for thousands of years has distinguished the Jewish people. The principles of temperance must be carried further than the mere use of spirituous liquors. The use of stimulating and indigestible food is often equally injurious to health, and in many cases sows the seeds of drunkenness. True temperance teaches us to dispense entirely with everything hurtful and to use judiciously that which is healthful. There are few who realize as they should how much their habits of diet have to do with their health, their character, their usefulness in this world, and their eternal destiny. The appetite should ever be in subjection to the moral and intellectual powers. The body should be servant to the mind, and not the mind to the body.

The divine promise to Manoah was in due time fulfilled in the birth of a son, to whom the name of Samson was given. As the boy grew up it became evident that he possessed extraordinary physical strength. This was not, however, as Samson and his parents well knew, dependent upon his well-knit sinews, but upon his condition as a Nazarite, of which his unshorn hair was a symbol. Had Samson obeyed the divine commands as faithfully as his parents had done, his would have been a nobler and happier destiny. But association with idolaters corrupted him. The town of Zorah being near the country of the Philistines, Samson came to mingle with them on friendly terms. Thus in his youth intimacies sprang up, the influence of which darkened his whole life. A young woman dwelling in the Philistine town of Timnath engaged

Samson's affections, and he determined to make her his wife. To his God-fearing parents, who endeavored to dissuade him from his purpose, his only answer was, "She pleaseth me well." The parents at last yielded to his wishes, and the marriage took place.

Just as he was entering upon manhood, the time when he must execute his divine mission—the time above all others when he should have been true to God—Samson connected himself with the enemies of Israel. He did not ask whether he could better glorify God when united with the object of his choice, or whether he was placing himself in a position where he could not fulfill the purpose to be accomplished by his life. To all who seek first to honor Him, God has promised wisdom; but there is no promise to those who are bent upon self-pleasing.

How many are pursuing the same course as did Samson! How often marriages are formed between the godly and the ungodly, because inclination governs in the selection of husband or wife! The parties do not ask counsel of God, nor have His glory in view. Christianity ought to have a controlling influence upon the marriage relation, but it is too often the case that the motives which lead to this union are not in keeping with Christian principles. Satan is constantly seeking to strengthen his power over the people of God by inducing them to enter into alliance with his subjects; and in order to accomplish this he endeavors to arouse unsanctified passions in the heart. But the Lord has in His word plainly instructed His people not to unite themselves with those who have not His love abiding in them. "What concord hath Christ with Belial? or what part hath he that believeth with an infidel? and what agreement hath the temple of God with idols?" 2 Corinthians 6:15, 16.

At his marriage feast Samson was brought into familiar association with those who hated the God of Israel. Whoever voluntarily enters into such relations will feel it necessary to conform, to some degree, to the habits and customs of his companions. The time thus spent is worse than wasted. Thoughts are entertained and words are spoken that tend to break down the strongholds of principle and to weaken the citadel of the soul.

The wife, to obtain whom Samson had transgressed the command of God, proved treacherous to her husband before the close of the marriage feast. Incensed at her perfidy, Samson forsook her for the time, and went alone to his home at Zorah. When, afterward relenting, he returned for his bride, he found her the wife of another. His revenge, in the wasting of all the fields and vineyards of the Philistines, provoked them to murder her, although their threats had driven her to the deceit with which the trouble began. Samson had already given evidence of his marvelous strength by slaying, singlehanded, a young lion, and by killing thirty of the men of Askelon. Now, moved to anger by the barbarous murder of his wife, he attacked the Philistines and smote them "with a great slaughter." Then, wishing a safe retreat from his enemies, he withdrew to "the rock Etam," in the tribe of Judah.

To this place he was pursued by a strong force, and the inhabitants of Judah, in great alarm, basely agreed to deliver him to his enemies. Accordingly three thousand men of Judah went up to him. But even at such odds they would not have dared approach him had they not felt assured that he would not harm his own countrymen. Samson consented to be bound and delivered to the Philistines, but first exacted from the men of Judah a promise not to attack him themselves, and thus compel him to destroy them. He permitted them to bind him with two new ropes, and he was led into the camp of his enemies amid demonstrations of great joy. But while their shouts were waking the echoes of the hills, "the Spirit of Jehovah came mightily upon him." He burst asunder the strong new cords as if they had been flax burned in the fire. Then seizing the first weapon at hand, which, though only the jawbone of an ass, was rendered more effective than sword or spear, he smote the Philistines until they fled in terror, leaving a thousand men dead upon the field.

Had the Israelites been ready to unite with Samson and follow up the victory, they might at this time have freed themselves from the power of their oppressors. But they had become dispirited and cowardly. They had neglected the work which God commanded them to perform, in dispossessing the heathen, and had united with them in their degrading practices, tolerating their cruelty, and, so long as it was not directed against themselves, even countenancing their injustice. When themselves brought under the power of the oppressor, they tamely submitted to the degradation which they might have escaped, had they only obeyed God. Even when the Lord raised up a deliverer for them, they would, not infrequently, desert him and unite with their enemies.

After his victory the Israelites made Samson judge, and he ruled Israel for twenty years. But one wrong step prepares the way for another. Samson had transgressed the command of God by taking a wife from the Philistines, and again he ventured among them—now his deadly enemies—in the indulgence of unlawful passion. Trusting to his great strength, which had inspired the Philistines with such terror, he went boldly to Gaza, to visit a harlot of that place. The inhabitants of the city learned of his presence, and they were eager for revenge. Their enemy was shut safely within the walls of the most strongly fortified of all their cities; they felt sure of their prey, and only waited till the morning to complete their triumph. At midnight Samson was aroused. The accusing voice of conscience filled him with remorse, as he remembered that he had broken his vow as a Nazarite. But notwithstanding his sin, God's mercy had not forsaken him. His prodigious strength again served to deliver him. Going to the city gate, he wrenched it from its place and carried it, with its posts and bars, to the top of a hill on the way to Hebron.

But even this narrow escape did not stay his evil course. He did not again venture among the Philistines, but he continued to seek those sensuous pleasures that were luring him to ruin. "He loved a woman in the valley of Sorek," not far from his own birthplace. Her name was Delilah, "the consumer." The vale of Sorek was celebrated for its vineyards; these also had a temptation for the wavering Nazarite, who had already indulged in the use of wine, thus breaking another tie that bound him to purity and to God. The Philistines kept a vigilant watch over the movements of their enemy, and when he degraded himself by this new attachment, they determined, through Delilah, to accomplish his ruin.

A deputation consisting of one leading man from each of the Philistine provinces was sent to the vale of Sorek. They dared not attempt to seize him while in possession of his great strength, but it was their purpose to learn, if possible, the secret of his power. They therefore bribed Delilah to discover and reveal it.

As the betrayer plied Samson with her questions, he deceived her by declaring that the weakness of other men would come upon him if certain processes were tried. When she put the matter to the test, the cheat was discovered. Then she accused him of falsehood, saying, "How canst thou say, I love thee, when thine heart is not with me? Thou hast mocked me these three times, and hast not told me wherein thy great strength lieth." Three times Samson had the clearest evidence that the Philistines had leagued with his charmer to destroy him; but when her purpose failed, she treated the matter as a jest, and he blindly banished fear.

Day by day Delilah urged him, until "his soul was vexed unto death;" yet a subtle power kept him by her side. Overcome at last, Samson made known the secret: "There hath not come a razor upon mine head; for I have been a Nazarite unto God from my mother's womb: if I be shaven, then my strength will go from me, and I shall become weak, and be like any other man." A messenger was immediately dispatched to the lords of the Philistines, urging them to come to her without delay. While the warrior slept, the heavy masses of his hair were severed from his head. Then, as she had done three times before, she called, "The Philistines be upon thee, Samson!" Suddenly awaking, he thought to exert his strength as before and destroy them; but his powerless arms refused to do his bidding, and he knew that "Jehovah was departed from him." When he had been shaven, Delilah began to annoy him and cause him pain, thus making a trial of his strength; for the Philistines dared not approach him till fully convinced that his power was gone. Then they seized him and, having put out both his eyes, they took him to Gaza. Here he was bound with fetters in their prison house and confined to hard labor.

What a change to him who had been the judge and champion of Israel!—now weak, blind, imprisoned, degraded to the most menial service! Little by little he had violated the conditions of his sacred calling. God had borne long with him; but when he had so yielded himself to the power of sin as to betray his secret, the Lord departed from him. There was no virtue in his long hair merely, but it was a token of his loyalty to God; and when the symbol was sacrificed in the indulgence of passion, the blessings of which it was a token were also forfeited.

In suffering and humiliation, a sport for the Philistines, Samson learned more of his own weakness than he had ever known before; and his afflictions led him to repentance. As his hair grew, his power gradually returned; but his enemies, regarding him as a fettered and helpless prisoner, felt no apprehensions.

The Philistines ascribed their victory to their gods; and, exulting, they defied the God of Israel. A feast was appointed in honor of Dagon, the fish god, "the protector of the sea." From town and country throughout the Philistine plain the people and their lords assembled. Throngs of worshipers filled the vast temple and crowded the galleries about the roof. It was a scene of festivity and rejoicing. There was the pomp of the sacrificial service, followed by music and feasting. Then, as the crowning trophy of Dagon's power, Samson was brought in. Shouts of exultation greeted his appearance. People and rulers mocked his misery and adored the god who had overthrown "the destroyer of their country." After a time, as if weary, Samson asked permission to rest against the two central pillars which supported the temple roof. Then he silently uttered the prayer, "O Lord God, remember me, I pray Thee, and strengthen me, I pray Thee, only this once, O God, that I may be at once avenged of the Philistines." With these words he encircled the pillars with his mighty arms; and crying, "Let me die with the Philistines!" he bowed himself, and the roof fell, destroying at one crash all that vast multitude. "So the dead which he slew at his death were more than they which he slew in his life."

The idol and its worshipers, priest and peasant, warrior and noble, were buried together beneath the ruins of Dagon's temple. And among them was the giant form of him whom God had chosen to be the deliverer of His people. Tidings of the terrible overthrow were carried to the land of Israel, and Samson's kinsmen came down from their hills, and, unopposed, rescued the body of the fallen hero. And they "brought him up, and buried him between Zorah and Eshtaol, in the burying place of Manoah his father."

God's promise that through Samson He would "begin to deliver Israel out of the hand of the Philistines" was fulfilled; but how dark and terrible the record of that life which might have been a praise to God and a glory to the nation! Had Samson been true to his divine calling, the purpose of God could have been accomplished in his honor and exaltation. But he yielded to temptation and proved untrue to his trust, and his mission was fulfilled in defeat, bondage, and death.

Physically, Samson was the strongest man upon the earth; but in self-control, integrity, and firmness, he was one of the weakest of men. Many mistake strong passions for a strong character, but the truth is that he who is mastered by his passions is a weak man. The real greatness of the man is measured by the power of the feelings that he controls, not by those that control him.

God's providential care had been over Samson, that he might be prepared to accomplish the work which he was called to do. At the very outset of life he was surrounded with favorable conditions for physical strength, intellectual vigor, and moral purity. But under the influence of wicked associates he let go that hold upon God which is man's only safeguard, and he was swept away by the tide of evil. Those who in the way of duty are brought into trial may be sure that God will preserve them; but if men willfully place themselves under the power of temptation, they will fall, sooner or later.

The very ones whom God purposes to use as His instruments for a special work, Satan employs his utmost power to lead astray. He attacks us at our weak points, working through defects in the character to gain control of the whole man; and he knows that if these defects are cherished, he will succeed. But none need be overcome. Man is not left alone to conquer the power of evil by his own feeble efforts. Help is at hand and will be given to every soul who really desires it. Angels of God, that ascend and descend the ladder which Jacob saw in vision, will help every soul who will, to climb even to the highest heaven.

The Child Samuel

Elkanah, a Levite of Mount Ephraim, was a man of wealth and influence, and one who loved and feared the Lord. His wife, Hannah, was a woman of fervent piety. Gentle and unassuming, her character was marked with deep earnestness and a lofty faith.

The blessing so earnestly sought by every Hebrew was denied this godly pair; their home was not gladdened by the voice of childhood; and the desire to perpetuate his name led the husband—as it had led many others—to contract a second marriage. But this step, prompted by a lack of faith in God, did not bring happiness. Sons and daughters were added to the household; but the joy and beauty of God's sacred institution had been marred and the peace of the family was broken. Peninnah, the new wife, was jealous and narrow-minded, and she bore herself with pride and insolence. To Hannah, hope seemed crushed and life a weary burden; yet she met the trial with uncomplaining meekness.

Elkanah faithfully observed the ordinances of God. The worship at Shiloh was still maintained, but on account of irregularities in the ministration his services were not required at the sanctuary, to which, being a Levite, he was to give attendance. Yet he went up with his family to worship and sacrifice at the appointed gatherings.

Even amid the sacred festivities connected with the service of God the evil spirit that had cursed his home intruded. After presenting the thank offerings, all the family, according to the established custom, united in a solemn yet joyous feast. Upon these occasions Elkanah gave the mother of his children a portion for herself and for each of her sons and daughters; and in token of regard for Hannah, he gave her a double portion, signifying that his affection for her was the same as if she had had a son. Then the second wife, fired with jealousy, claimed the precedence as one highly favored of God, and taunted Hannah with her childless state as evidence of the Lord's displeasure. This was repeated from year to year, until Hannah could endure it no longer. Unable to hide her grief, she wept without restraint, and withdrew from the feast. Her husband vainly sought to comfort her. "Why weepest thou? and why eatest thou not? and why is thy heart grieved?" he said; "am I not better to thee than ten sons?"

Hannah uttered no reproach. The burden which she could share with no earthly friend she cast upon God. Earnestly she pleaded that He would take away her reproach and grant her the precious gift of a son to nurture and train for Him. And she made a solemn vow that if her request were granted, she would dedicate her child to God, even from its birth. Hannah had drawn near to the entrance of the tabernacle, and in the anguish of her spirit she "prayed, . . . and wept sore." Yet she communed with God in silence, uttering no sound. In those evil times such scenes of worship were rarely witnessed. Irreverent feasting and even drunkenness were not uncommon, even at the religious festivals; and Eli the high priest, observing Hannah, supposed that she was overcome with wine. Thinking to administer a deserved rebuke, he said sternly, "How long wilt thou be drunken? put away thy wine from thee."

Pained and startled, Hannah answered gently, "No, my lord, I am a woman of a sorrowful spirit: I have drunk neither wine nor strong drink, but have poured out my soul before the Lord. Count not thine handmaid for a daughter of Belial: for out of the abundance of my complaint and grief have I spoken hitherto."

The high priest was deeply moved, for he was a man of God; and in place of rebuke he uttered a blessing: "Go in peace: and the God of Israel grant thee thy petition that thou hast asked of Him."

Hannah's prayer was granted; she received the gift for which she had so earnestly entreated. As she looked upon the child, she called him Samuel—"asked of God." As soon as the little one was old enough to be separated from his mother, she fulfilled her vow. She loved her child with all the devotion of a mother's heart; day by day, as she watched his expanding powers and listened to his childish prattle, her affections entwined about him more closely. He was her only son, the special gift of Heaven; but she had received him as a treasure consecrated to God, and she would not withhold from the Giver His own.

Once more Hannah journeyed with her husband to Shiloh and presented to the priest, in the name of God, her precious gift, saying, "For this child I prayed; and the Lord hath given me my petition which I asked of Him: therefore also I have lent him to the Lord; as long as he liveth he shall be lent to the Lord." Eli was deeply impressed by the faith and devotion of this woman of Israel. Himself as overindulgent father, he was awed and humbled as he beheld this mother's great sacrifice in parting with her only child, that she might devote him to the service of God. He felt reproved for his own selfish love, and in humiliation and reverence he bowed before the Lord and worshiped.

The mother's heart was filled with joy and praise, and she longed to pour forth her gratitude to God. The Spirit of Inspiration came upon her; "and Hannah prayed, and said:

"My heart rejoiceth in the Lord;
Mine horn is exalted in the Lord;
My mouth is enlarged over mine enemies;
Because I rejoice in Thy salvation.
There is none holy as the Lord:
For there is none beside Thee:
Neither is there any rock like our God.
Talk no more so exceeding proudly;
Let not arrogancy come out of your mouth;
For Jehovah is a God of knowledge,
And by Him actions are weighed. . . .
The Lord killeth, and maketh alive:
He bringeth down to the grave, and bringeth up.
The Lord maketh poor, and maketh rich:
He bringeth low, and lifteth up.
He raiseth up the poor out of the dust,
And lifteth up the beggar from the dunghill,
To set them among princes,
And to make them inherit the throne of glory:
For the pillars of the earth are the Lord's,
And He hath set the world upon them.
He will keep the feet of His saints,
And the wicked shall be silent in darkness;
For by strength shall no man prevail.
The adversaries of the Lord shall be broken to pieces;

Out of heaven shall He thunder upon them:
The Lord shall judge the ends of the earth;
And He shall give strength unto His king,
And exalt the horn of His anointed."

Hannah's words were prophetic, both of David, who should reign as king of Israel, and of the Messiah, the Lord's Anointed. Referring first to the boasting of an insolent and contentious woman, the song points to the destruction of the enemies of God and the final triumph of His redeemed people.

From Shiloh, Hannah quietly returned to her home at Ramah, leaving the child Samuel to be trained for service in the house of God, under the instruction of the high priest. From the earliest dawn of intellect she had taught her son to love and reverence God and to regard himself as the Lord's. By every familiar object surrounding him she had sought to lead his thoughts up to the Creator. When separated from her child, the faithful mother's solicitude did not cease. Every day he was the subject of her prayers. Every year she made, with her own hands, a robe of service for him; and as she went up with her husband to worship at Shiloh, she gave the child this reminder of her love. Every fiber of the little garment had been woven with a prayer that he might be pure, noble, and true. She did not ask for her son worldly greatness, but she earnestly pleaded that he might attain that greatness which Heaven values—that he might honor God and bless his fellow men.

What a reward was Hannah's! and what an encouragement to faithfulness is her example! There are opportunities of inestimable worth, interests infinitely precious, committed to every mother. The humble round of duties which women have come to regard as a wearisome task should be looked upon as a grand and noble work. It is the mother's privilege to bless the world by her influence, and in doing this she will bring joy to her own heart. She may make straight paths for the feet of her children, through sunshine and shadow, to the glorious heights above. But it is only when she seeks, in her own life, to follow the teachings of Christ that the mother can hope to form the character of her children after the divine pattern. The world teems with corrupting influences. Fashion and custom exert a strong power over the young. If the mother fails in her duty to instruct, guide, and restrain, her children will naturally accept the evil, and turn from the good. Let every mother go often to her Saviour with the prayer, "Teach us, how shall we order the child, and what shall we do unto him?" Let her heed the instruction which God has given in His word, and wisdom will be given her as she shall have need.

"The child Samuel grew on, and was in favor both with the Lord, and also with men." Though Samuel's youth was passed at the tabernacle devoted to the worship of God, he was not free from evil influences or sinful example. The sons of Eli feared not God, nor honored their father; but Samuel did not seek their company nor follow their evil ways. It was his constant endeavor to become what God would have him. This is the privilege of every youth. God is pleased when even little children give themselves to His service.

Samuel had been placed under the care of Eli, and the loveliness of his character drew forth the warm affection of the aged priest. He was kind, generous, obedient, and respectful. Eli, pained by the waywardness of his own sons, found rest and comfort and blessing in the presence of his charge. Samuel was helpful and affectionate, and no father ever loved his child more tenderly than did Eli this youth. It was a singular thing that between the chief magistrate of the nation and the simple child so warm an affection should exist. As the infirmities of age came upon Eli, and he was filled with anxiety and remorse by the profligate course of his own sons, he turned to Samuel for comfort.

It was not customary for the Levites to enter upon their peculiar services until they were twenty-five years of age, but Samuel had been an exception to this rule. Every year saw more important trusts committed to him; and while he was yet a child, a linen ephod was placed upon him as a token of his consecration to the work of the sanctuary. Young as he was when brought to minister in the tabernacle, Samuel had even then duties to perform in the service of God, according to his capacity. These were at first very humble, and not always pleasant; but they were performed to the best of his ability, and with a willing heart. His religion was carried into every duty of life. He regarded himself as God's servant, and his work as God's work. His efforts were accepted, because they were prompted by love to God and a sincere desire to do His will. It was thus that Samuel became a co-worker with the Lord of heaven and earth. And God fitted him to accomplish a great work for Israel.

If children were taught to regard the humble round of everyday duties as the course marked out for them by the Lord, as a school in which they were to be trained to render faithful and efficient service, how much more pleasant and honorable would their work appear. To perform every duty as unto the Lord, throws a charm around the humblest employment and links the workers on earth with the holy beings who do God's will in heaven.

Success in this life, success in gaining the future life, depends upon a faithful, conscientious attention to the little things. Perfection is seen in the least, no less than in the greatest, of the works of God. The hand that hung the worlds in space is the hand that wrought with delicate skill the lilies of the field. And as God is perfect in His sphere, so we are to be perfect in ours. The symmetrical structure of a strong, beautiful character is built up by individual acts of duty. And faithfulness should characterize our life in the least as well as in the greatest of its details. Integrity in little things, the performance of little acts of fidelity and little deeds of kindness, will gladden the path of life; and when our work on earth is ended, it will be found that every one of the little duties faithfully performed has exerted an influence for good—an influence that can never perish.

The youth of our time may become as precious in the sight of God as was Samuel. By faithfully maintaining their Christian integrity, they may exert a strong influence in the work of reform. Such men are needed at this time. God has a work for every one of them. Never did men achieve greater results for God and humanity than may be achieved in this our day by those who will be faithful to their God-given trust.

Eli and His Sons

Eli was priest and judge in Israel. He held the highest and most responsible positions among the people of God. As a man divinely chosen for the sacred duties of the priesthood, and set over the land as the highest judicial authority, he was looked up to as an example, and he wielded a great influence over the tribes of Israel. But although he had been appointed to govern the people, he did not rule his own household. Eli was an indulgent father. Loving peace and ease, he did not exercise his authority to correct the evil habits and passions of his children. Rather than contend with them or punish them, he would submit to their will and give them their own way. Instead of regarding the education of his sons as one of the most important of his responsibilities, he treated the matter as of little consequence. The priest and judge of Israel had not been left in darkness as to the duty of restraining and governing the children that God had given to his care. But Eli shrank from this duty, because it involved crossing the will of his sons, and would make it necessary to punish and deny them. Without weighing the terrible consequences that would follow his course, he indulged his children in whatever they desired and neglected the work of fitting them for the service of God and the duties of life.

God had said of Abraham, "I know him, that he will command his children and his household after him, and they shall keep the way of the Lord, to do justice and judgment." Genesis 18:19. But Eli allowed his children to control him. The father became subject to the children. The curse of transgression was apparent in the corruption and evil that marked the course of his sons. They had no proper appreciation of the character of God or of the sacredness of His law. His service was to them a common thing. From childhood they had been accustomed to the sanctuary and its service; but instead of becoming more reverent, they had lost all sense of its holiness and significance. The father had not corrected their want of reverence for his authority, had not checked their disrespect for the solemn services of the sanctuary; and when they reached manhood, they were full of the deadly fruits of skepticism and rebellion.

Though wholly unfit for the office, they were placed as priests in the sanctuary to minister before God. The Lord had given the most specific directions in regard to offering sacrifices; but these wicked men carried their disregard of authority into the service of God, and did not give attention to the law of the offerings, which were to be made in the most solemn manner. The sacrifices, pointing forward to the death of Christ, were designed to preserve in the hearts of the people faith in the Redeemer to come; hence it was of the greatest importance that the Lord's directions concerning them should be strictly heeded. The peace offerings were especially an expression of thanksgiving to God. In these offerings the fat alone was to be burned upon the altar; a certain specified portion was reserved for the priests, but the greater part was returned to the offerer, to be eaten by him and his friends in a sacrificial feast. Thus all hearts were to be directed, in gratitude and faith, to the great Sacrifice that was to take away the sin of the world.

The sons of Eli, instead of realizing the solemnity of this symbolic service, only thought how they could make it a means of self-indulgence. Not content with the part of the peace offerings allotted them, they demanded an additional portion; and the great number of these sacrifices presented at the annual feasts gave the priests an opportunity to enrich themselves at the expense of the people. They not only demanded more than their right, but refused to wait even until the fat had been burned as an offering to God. They persisted in claiming whatever portion pleased them, and, if denied, threatened to take it by violence.

This irreverence on the part of the priests soon robbed the service of its holy and solemn significance, and the people "abhorred the offering of the Lord." The great antitypical sacrifice to which they were to look forward was no longer recognized. "Wherefore the sin of the young men was very great before the Lord."

These unfaithful priests also transgressed God's law and dishonored their sacred office by their vile and degrading practices; yet they continued to pollute by their presence the tabernacle of God. Many of the people, filled with indignation at the corrupt course of Hophni and Phinehas, ceased to come up to the appointed place of worship. Thus the service which God had ordained was despised and neglected because associated with the sins of wicked men, while those whose hearts were inclined to evil were emboldened in sin. Ungodliness, profligacy, and even idolatry prevailed to a fearful extent.

Eli had greatly erred in permitting his sons to minister in holy office. By excusing their course, on one pretext and another, he became blinded to their sins; but at last they reached a pass where he could no longer hide his eyes from the crimes of his sons. The people complained of their violent deeds, and the high priest was grieved and distressed. He dared remain silent no longer. But his sons had been brought up to think of no one but themselves, and now they cared for no one else. They saw the grief of their father, but their hard hearts were not touched. They heard his mild admonitions, but they were not impressed, nor would they change their evil course though warned of the consequences of their sins. Had Eli dealt justly with his wicked sons, they would have been rejected from the priestly office and punished with death. Dreading thus to bring public disgrace and condemnation upon them, he sustained them in the most sacred positions of trust. He still permitted them to mingle their corruption with the holy service of God and to inflict upon the cause of truth an injury which years could not efface. But when the judge of Israel neglected his work, God took the matter in hand.

"There came a man of God unto Eli, and said unto him, Thus saith the Lord, Did I plainly appear unto the house of thy father, when they were in Egypt in Pharaoh's house? And did I choose him out of all the tribes of Israel to be My priest, to offer upon Mine altar, to burn incense, to wear an ephod before Me? and did I give unto the house of thy father all the offerings made by fire of the children of Israel? Wherefore kick ye at My sacrifice and at Mine offering, which I have commanded in My habitation; and honorest thy sons above Me, to make yourselves fat with the chiefest of all the offerings of Israel My people? Wherefore the Lord God of Israel saith, I said indeed that thy house, and the house of thy father, should walk before Me forever: but now the Lord saith, Be it far from Me; for them that honor Me I will honor, and they that despise Me shall be lightly esteemed. . . . And I will raise Me up a faithful priest, that shall do according to that which is in Mine heart and in My mind: and I will build him a sure house; and he shall walk before Mine anointed forever."

God charged Eli with honoring his sons above the Lord. Eli had permitted the offering appointed by God as a blessing to Israel to be made a thing of abhorrence, rather than bring his sons to shame for their impious and abominable practices. Those who follow their own inclination, in blind affection for their children, indulging them in the gratification of their selfish desires, and do not bring to bear the authority of God to rebuke sin and correct evil, make it manifest that they are honoring their wicked children more than they honor God. They are more anxious to shield their reputation than to glorify God; more desirous to please their children than to please the Lord and to keep His service from every appearance of evil.

God held Eli, as a priest and judge of Israel, accountable for the moral and religious standing of his people, and in a special sense for the character of his sons. He should first have attempted to restrain evil by mild measures; but if these did not avail, he should have subdued the wrong by the severest means. He incurred the Lord's displeasure by not reproving sin and executing justice upon the sinner. He could not be depended upon to keep Israel pure. Those who have too little courage to reprove wrong, or who through indolence or lack of interest make no earnest effort to purify the family or the church of God, are held accountable for the evil that may result from their neglect of duty. We are just as responsible for evils that we might have checked in others by exercise of parental or pastoral authority as if the acts had been our own.

Eli did not manage his household according to God's rules for family government. He followed his own judgment. The fond father overlooked the faults and sins of his sons in their childhood, flattering himself that after a time they would outgrow their evil tendencies. Many are now making a similar mistake. They think they know a better way of training their children than that which God has given in His word. They foster wrong tendencies in them, urging as an excuse, "They are too young to be punished. Wait till they become older, and can be reasoned with." Thus wrong habits are left to strengthen until they become second nature. The children grow up without restraint, with traits of character that are a lifelong curse to them and are liable to be reproduced in others.

There is no greater curse upon households than to allow the youth to have their own way. When parents regard every wish of their children and indulge them in what they know is not for their good, the children soon lose all respect for their parents, all regard for the authority of God or man, and are led captive at the will of Satan. The influence of an ill-regulated family is widespread and disastrous to all society. It accumulates in a tide of evil that affects families, communities, and governments.

Because of Eli's position, his influence was more extended than if he had been an ordinary man. His family life was imitated throughout Israel. The baleful results of his negligent, ease-loving ways were seen in thousands of homes that were molded by his example. If children are indulged in evil practices, while the parents make a profession of religion, the truth of God is brought into reproach. The best test of the Christianity of a home is the type of character begotten by its influence. Actions speak louder than the most positive profession of godliness. If professors of religion, instead of putting forth earnest, persistent, and painstaking effort to bring up a well-ordered household as a witness to the benefits of faith in God, are lax in their government and indulgent to the evil desires of their children, they are doing as did Eli, and are bringing disgrace on the cause of Christ and ruin upon themselves and their households. But great as are the evils of parental unfaithfulness under any circumstances, they are tenfold greater when they exist in the families of those appointed as teachers of the people. When these fail to control their own households, they are, by their wrong example, misleading many. Their guilt is as much greater than that of others as their position is more responsible.

The promise had been made that the house of Aaron should walk before God forever; but this promise had been made on condition that they should devote themselves to the work of the sanctuary with singleness of heart and honor God in all their ways, not serving self nor following their own perverse inclinations. Eli and his sons had been tested, and the Lord had found them wholly unworthy of the exalted position of priests in His service. And God declared, "Be it far from Me." He could not accomplish the good that He had meant to do them, because they failed to do their part.

The example of those who minister in holy things should be such as to impress the people with reverence for God and with fear to offend Him. When men, standing "in Christ's stead" (2 Corinthians 5:20) to speak to the people God's message of mercy and reconciliation, use their sacred calling as a cloak for selfish or sensual gratification, they make themselves the most effective agents of Satan. Like Hophni and Phinehas, they cause men to "abhor the offering of the Lord." They may pursue their evil course in secret for a time; but when at last their true character is exposed, the faith of the people receives a shock that often results in destroying their confidence in religion. There is left upon the mind a distrust of all who profess to teach the word of God. The message of the true servant of Christ is doubtfully received. The question constantly arises, "Will not this man prove to be like the one we thought so holy, and found so corrupt?" Thus the word of God loses its power upon the souls of men.

In Eli's reproof to his sons are words of solemn and fearful import—words that all who minister in sacred things would do well to ponder: "If one man sin against another, the judge shall judge him: but if a man sin against the Lord, who shall entreat for him.?" Had their crimes injured only their fellow men, the judge might have made reconciliation by appointing a penalty and requiring restitution; and thus the offenders might have been pardoned. Or had they not been guilty of a presumptuous sin, a sin offering might have been presented for them. But their sins were so interwoven with their ministration as priests of the Most High, in offering sacrifice for sin, the work of God was so profaned and dishonored before the people, that no expiation could be accepted for them. Their own father, though himself high priest, dared not make intercession in their behalf; he could not shield them from the wrath of a holy God. Of all sinners, those are most guilty who cast contempt upon the means that Heaven has provided for man's redemption—who "crucify to themselves the Son of God afresh, and put Him to an open shame." Hebrews 6:6.

The Ark Taken by the Philistines

Another warning was to be given to Eli's house. God could not communicate with the high priest and his sons; their sins, like a thick cloud, had shut out the presence of His Holy Spirit. But in the midst of evil the child Samuel remained true to Heaven, and the message of condemnation to the house of Eli was Samuel's commission as a prophet of the Most High.

"The word of the Lord was precious in those days; there was no open vision. And it came to pass at that time, when Eli was laid down in his place, and his eyes began to wax dim, that he could not see; and ere the lamp of God went out in the temple of the Lord, where the ark of God was, and Samuel was laid down to sleep; that the Lord called Samuel." Supposing the voice to be that of Eli, the child hastened to the bedside of the priest, saying, "Here am I; for thou calledst me." The answer was, "I called not, my son; lie down again." Three times Samuel was called, and thrice he responded in like manner. And then Eli was convinced that the mysterious call was the voice of God. The Lord had passed by His chosen servant, the man of hoary hairs, to commune with a child. This in itself was a bitter yet deserved rebuke to Eli and his house.

No feeling of envy or jealousy was awakened in Eli's heart. He directed Samuel to answer, if again called, "Speak, Lord; for Thy servant heareth." Once more the voice was heard, and the child answered, "Speak; for Thy servant heareth." So awed was he at the thought that the great God should speak to him that he could not remember the exact words which Eli bade him say.

"And the Lord said to Samuel, Behold, I will do a thing in Israel, at which both the ears of everyone that heareth it shall tingle. In that day I will perform against Eli all things which I have spoken concerning his house: when I begin, I will also make an end. For I have told him that I will judge his house forever for the iniquity which he knoweth; because his sons made themselves vile, and he restrained them not. And therefore I have sworn unto the house of Eli, that the iniquity of Eli's house shall not be purged with sacrifice nor offering forever."

Before receiving this message from God, "Samuel did not yet know the Lord, neither was the word of the Lord yet revealed unto him;" that is, he was not acquainted with such direct manifestations of God's presence as were granted to the prophets. It was the Lord's purpose to reveal Himself in an unexpected manner, that Eli might hear of it through the surprise and inquiry of the youth.

Samuel was filled with fear and amazement at the thought of having so terrible a message committed to him. In the morning he went about his duties as usual, but with a heavy burden upon his young heart. The Lord had not commanded him to reveal the fearful denunciation, hence he remained silent, avoiding, as far as possible, the presence of Eli. He trembled, lest some question should compel him to declare the divine judgments against one whom he loved and reverenced. Eli was confident that the message foretold some great calamity to him and his house. He called Samuel, and charged him to relate faithfully what the Lord had revealed. The youth obeyed, and the aged man bowed in humble submission to the appalling sentence. "It is the Lord," he said: "let Him do what seemeth Him good."

Yet Eli did not manifest the fruits of true repentance. He confessed his guilt, but failed to renounce the sin. Year after year the Lord delayed His threatened judgments. Much might have been done in those years to redeem the failures of the past, but the aged priest took no effective measures to correct the evils that were polluting the sanctuary of the Lord and leading thousands in Israel to ruin. The forbearance of God caused Hophni and Phinehas to harden their hearts and to become still bolder in transgression. The messages of warning and reproof to his house were made known by Eli to the whole nation. By this means he hoped to counteract, in some measure, the evil influence of his past neglect. But the warnings were disregarded by the people, as they had been by the priests. The people of surrounding nations also, who were not ignorant of the iniquities openly practiced in Israel, became still bolder in their idolatry and crime. They felt no sense of guilt for their sins, as they would have felt had the Israelites preserved their integrity. But a day of retribution was approaching. God's authority had been set aside, and His worship neglected and despised, and it became necessary for Him to interpose, that the honor of His name might be maintained.

"Now Israel went out against the Philistines to battle, and pitched beside Ebenezer: and the Philistines pitched in Aphek." This expedition was undertaken by the Israelites without counsel from God, without the concurrence of high priest or prophet. "And the Philistines put themselves in array against Israel: and when they joined battle, Israel was smitten before the Philistines: and they slew of the army in the field about four thousand men." As the shattered and disheartened force returned to their encampment, "the elders of Israel said, Wherefore hath the Lord smitten us today before the Philistines?" The nation was ripe for the judgments of God, yet they did not see that their own sins had been the cause of this terrible disaster. And they said, "Let us fetch the ark of the covenant of the Lord out of Shiloh unto us, that, when it cometh among us, it may save us out of the hand of our enemies." The Lord had given no command or permission that the ark should come into the army; yet the Israelites felt confident that victory would be theirs, and uttered a great shout when it was borne into the camp by the sons of Eli.

The Philistines looked upon the ark as the god of Israel. All the mighty works that Jehovah had wrought for His people were attributed to its power. As they heard the shouts of joy at its approach, they said, "What meaneth the noise of this great shout in the camp of the Hebrews? And they understood that the ark of the Lord was come into the camp. And the

Philistines were afraid; for they said, God has come into the camp. And they said, Woe unto us! for there hath not been such a thing heretofore. Woe unto us! who shall deliver us out of the hand of these mighty Gods? These are the Gods that smote the Egyptians with all the plagues in the wilderness. Be strong, and quit yourselves like men, O ye Philistines, that ye be not servants unto the Hebrews, as they have been to you: quit yourselves like men, and fight."

The Philistines made a fierce assault, which resulted in the defeat of Israel, with great slaughter. Thirty thousand men lay dead upon the field, and the ark of God was taken, the two sons of Eli having fallen while fighting to defend it. Thus again was left upon the page of history a testimony for all future ages—that the iniquity of God's professed people will not go unpunished. The greater the knowledge of God's will, the greater the sin of those who disregard it.

The most terrifying calamity that could occur had befallen Israel. The ark of God had been captured, and was in the possession of the enemy. The glory had indeed departed from Israel when the symbol of the abiding presence and power of Jehovah was removed from the midst of them. With this sacred chest were associated the most wonderful revelations of God's truth and power. In former days miraculous victories had been achieved whenever it appeared. It was shadowed by the wings of the golden cherubim, and the unspeakable glory of the Shekinah, the visible symbol of the most high God, had rested over it in the holy of holies. But now it had brought no victory. It had not proved a defense on this occasion, and there was mourning throughout Israel.

They had not realized that their faith was only a nominal faith, and had lost its power to prevail with God. The law of God, contained in the ark, was also a symbol of His presence; but they had cast contempt upon the commandments, had despised their requirements, and had grieved the Spirit of the Lord from among them. When the people obeyed the holy precepts, the Lord was with them to work for them by His infinite power; but when they looked upon the ark, and did not associate it with God, nor honor His revealed will by obedience to His law, it could avail them little more than a common box. They looked to the ark as the idolatrous nations looked to their gods, as if it possessed in itself the elements of power and salvation. They transgressed the law it contained; for their very worship of the ark led to formalism, hypocrisy, and idolatry. Their sin had separated them from God, and He could not give them the victory until they had repented of and forsaken their iniquity.

It was not enough that the ark and the sanctuary were in the midst of Israel. It was not enough that the priests offered sacrifices, and that the people were called the children of God. The Lord does not regard the request of those who cherish iniquity in the heart; it is written that "he that turneth away his ear from hearing the law, even his prayer shall be abomination." Proverbs 28:9.

When the army went out to battle, Eli, blind and old, had tarried at Shiloh. It was with troubled forebodings that he awaited the result of the conflict; "for his heart trembled for the ark of God." Taking his position outside the gate of the tabernacle, he sat by the highway side day after day, anxiously expecting the arrival of a messenger from the battlefield.

At length a Benjamite from the army, "with his clothes rent, and with earth upon his head," came hurrying up the ascent leading to the city. Passing heedlessly the aged man beside the way, he rushed on to the town, and repeated to eager throngs the tidings of defeat and loss.

The sound of wailing and lamentation reached the watcher beside the tabernacle. The messenger was brought to him. And the man said unto Eli, "Israel is fled before the Philistines, and there hath been also a great slaughter among the people, and thy two sons also, Hophni and Phinehas, are dead." Eli could endure all this, terrible as it was, for he had expected it. But when the messenger added, "And the ark of God is taken," a look of unutterable anguish passed over his countenance. The thought that his sin had thus dishonored God and caused Him to withdraw His presence from Israel was more than he could bear; his strength was gone, he fell, "and his neck brake, and he died."

The wife of Phinehas, notwithstanding the impiety of her husband, was a woman who feared the Lord. The death of her father-in-law and her husband, and above all, the terrible tidings that the ark of God was taken, caused her death. She felt that the last hope of Israel was gone; and she named the child born in this hour of adversity, Ichabod, or "inglorious;" with her dying breath mournfully repeating the words, "The glory is departed from Israel: for the ark of God is taken."

But the Lord had not wholly cast aside His people, nor would He long suffer the exultation of the heathen. He had used the Philistines as the instrument to punish Israel, and He employed the ark to punish the Philistines. In time past the divine Presence had attended it, to be the strength and glory of His obedient people. That invisible Presence would still attend it, to bring terror and destruction to the transgressors of His holy law. The Lord often employs His bitterest enemies to punish the unfaithfulness of His professed people. The wicked may triumph for a time as they see Israel suffering chastisement, but the time will come when they, too, must meet the sentence of a holy, sin-hating God. Whenever iniquity is cherished, there, swift and unerring, the divine judgments will follow.

The Philistines removed the ark in triumph to Ashdod, one of their five principal cities, and placed it in the house of their god Dagon. They imagined that the power which had hitherto attended the ark would be theirs, and that this, united with the power of Dagon, would render them invincible. But upon entering the temple on the following day, they beheld a sight which filled them with consternation. Dagon had fallen upon his face to the earth before the ark of Jehovah. The priests reverently lifted the idol and restored it to its place. But the next morning they found it, strangely mutilated, again lying upon the earth before the ark. The upper part of this idol was like that of a man, and the lower part was in the likeness of a fish. Now every part that resembled the human form had been cut off, and only the body of the fish remained. Priests and people were horror-struck; they looked upon this mysterious event as an evil omen, foreboding destruction to themselves and their idols before the God of the Hebrews. They now removed the ark from their temple and placed it in a building by itself.

The inhabitants of Ashdod were smitten with a distressing and fatal disease. Remembering the plagues that were inflicted upon Egypt by the God of Israel, the people attributed their afflictions to the presence of the ark among them. It was decided to convey it to Gath. But the plague followed close upon its removal, and the men of that city sent it to Ekron. Here the people received it with terror, crying, "They have brought about the ark of the God of Israel to us, to slay us and our people." They turned to their gods for protection, as the people of Gath and Ashdod had done; but the work of the destroyer went on, until, in their distress, "the cry of the city went up to heaven." Fearing longer to retain the ark among the homes of men, the people next placed it in the open field. There followed a plague of mice, which infested the land, destroying the products of the soil, both in the storehouse and in the field. Utter destruction, by disease or famine, now threatened the nation.

For seven months the ark remained in Philistia, and during all this time the Israelites made no effort for its recovery. But the Philistines were now as anxious to free themselves from its presence as they had been to obtain it. Instead of being a source of strength to them, it was a great burden and a heavy curse. Yet they knew not what course to pursue; for wherever it went the judgments of God followed. The people called for the princes of the nation, with the priests and diviners, and eagerly inquired, "What shall we do to the ark of Jehovah? tell us wherewith we shall send it to his place?" They were advised to return it with a costly trespass offering. "Then," said the priests, "ye shall be healed, and it shall be known to you why His hand is not removed from you."

To ward off or to remove a plague, it was anciently the custom among the heathen to make an image in gold, silver, or other material, of that which caused the destruction, or of the object or part of the body specially affected. This was set up on a pillar or in some conspicuous place, and was supposed to be an effectual protection against the evils thus represented. A similar practice still exists among some heathen peoples. When a person suffering from disease goes for cure to the temple of his idol, he carries with him a figure of the part affected, which he presents as an offering to his god.

It was in accordance with the prevailing superstition that the Philistine lords directed the people to make representations of the plagues by which they had been afflicted—"five golden emerods, and five golden mice, according to the number of the lords of the Philistines: for," said they, "one plague was on you all, and on your lords."

These wise men acknowledged a mysterious power accompanying the ark—a power which they had no wisdom to meet. Yet they did not counsel the people to turn from their idolatry to serve the Lord. They still hated the God of Israel, though compelled by overwhelming judgments to submit to His authority. Thus sinners may be convinced by the judgments of God that it is in vain to contend against Him. They may be compelled to submit to His power, while at heart they rebel against His control. Such submission cannot save the sinner. The heart must be yielded to God—must be subdued by divine grace—before man's repentance can be accepted.

How great is the long-suffering of God toward the wicked! The idolatrous Philistines and backsliding Israel had alike enjoyed the gifts of His providence. Ten thousand unnoticed mercies were silently falling in the pathway of ungrateful, rebellious men. Every blessing spoke to them of the Giver, but they were indifferent to His love. The forbearance of God was very great toward the children of men; but when they stubbornly persisted in their impenitence, He removed from them His protecting hand. They refused to listen to the voice of God in His created works, and in the warnings, counsels, and reproofs of His word, and thus He was forced to speak to them through judgments.

There were some among the Philistines who stood ready to oppose the return of the ark to its own land. Such an acknowledgment of the power of Israel's God would be humiliating to the pride of Philistia. But "the priests and the diviners" admonished the people not to imitate the stubbornness of Pharaoh and the Egyptians, and thus bring upon themselves still greater afflictions. A plan which won the consent of all was now proposed, and immediately put in execution. The ark, with the golden trespass offering, was placed upon a new cart, thus precluding all danger of defilement; to this cart, or car, were attached two kine upon whose necks a yoke had never been placed. Their calves were shut up at home, and the cows were left free to go where they pleased. If the ark should thus be returned to the Israelites by the way of Beth-shemesh, the nearest city of the Levites, the Philistines would accept this as evidence that the God of Israel had done unto them this great evil; "but if not," they said, "then we shall know that it is not His hand that smote us; it was a chance that happened to us."

On being set free, the kine turned from their young and, lowing as they went, took the direct road to Beth-shemesh. Guided by no human hand, the patient animals kept on their way. The divine Presence accompanied the ark, and it passed on safely to the very place designated.

It was now the time of wheat harvest, and the men of Beth-shemesh were reaping in the valley. "And they lifted up their eyes, and saw the ark, and rejoiced to see it. And the cart came into the field of Joshua, a Beth-shemite, and stood there, where there was a great stone: and they clave the wood of the cart, and offered the kine of burnt-offering unto the Lord." The lords of the Philistines, who had followed the ark "unto the border of Beth-shemesh," and had witnessed its reception, now returned to Ekron. The plague had ceased, and they were convinced that their calamities had been a judgment from the God of Israel.

The men of Beth-shemesh quickly spread the tidings that the ark was in their possession, and the people from the surrounding country flocked to welcome its return. The ark had been placed upon the stone that first served for an altar, and before it additional sacrifices were offered unto the Lord. Had the worshipers repented of their sins, God's blessing would have attended them. But they were not faithfully obeying His law; and while they rejoiced at the return of the ark as a harbinger of good, they had no true sense of its sacredness. Instead of preparing a suitable place for its reception, they permitted it to remain in the harvest field. As they continued to gaze upon the sacred chest and to talk of the wonderful manner in which it had been restored, they began to conjecture wherein lay its peculiar power. At last, overcome by curiosity, they removed the coverings and ventured to open it.

All Israel had been taught to regard the ark with awe and reverence. When required to remove it from place to place the Levites were not so much as to look upon it. Only once a year was the high priest permitted to behold the ark of God. Even the heathen Philistines had not dared to remove its coverings. Angels of heaven, unseen, ever attended it in all its journeyings. The irreverent daring of the people at Beth-shemesh was speedily punished. Many were smitten with sudden death.

The survivors were not led by this judgment to repent of their sin, but only to regard the ark with superstitious fear. Eager to be free from its presence, yet not daring to remove it, the Beth-shemites sent a message to the inhabitants of Kirjath-jearim, inviting them to take it away. With great joy the men of this place welcomed the sacred chest. They knew that it was the pledge of divine favor to the obedient and faithful. With solemn gladness they brought it to their city and placed it in the house of Abinadab, a Levite. This man appointed his son Eleazar to take charge of it, and it remained there for many years.

During the years since the Lord first manifested Himself to the son of Hannah, Samuel's call to the prophetic office had come to be acknowledged by the whole nation. By faithfully delivering the divine warning to the house of Eli, painful and trying as the duty had been, Samuel had given proof of his fidelity as Jehovah's messenger; "and the Lord was with him, and did let none of his words fall to the ground. And all Israel from Dan even to Beersheba knew that Samuel was established to be a prophet of the Lord."

The Israelites as a nation still continued in a state of irreligion and idolatry, and as a punishment they remained in subjection to the Philistines. During this time Samuel visited the cities and villages throughout the land, seeking to turn the hearts of the people to the God of their fathers; and his efforts were not without good results. After suffering the oppression of their enemies for twenty years, the Israelites "mourned after the Lord." Samuel counseled them, "If ye do return unto the Lord with all your hearts, then put away the strange gods and Ashtaroth from among you, and prepare your hearts unto the Lord, and serve Him only." Here we see that practical piety, heart religion, was taught in the days of Samuel as taught by Christ when He was upon the earth. Without the grace of Christ the outward forms of religion were valueless to ancient Israel. They are the same to modern Israel.

There is need today of such a revival of true heart religion as was experienced by ancient Israel. Repentance is the first step that must be taken by all who would return to God. No one can do this work for another. We must individually humble our souls before God and put away our idols. When we have done all that we can do, the Lord will manifest to us His salvation.

With the co-operation of the heads of the tribes, a large assembly was gathered at Mizpeh. Here a solemn fast was held. With deep humiliation the people confessed their sins; and as an evidence of their determination to obey the instructions they had heard, they invested Samuel with the authority of judge.

The Philistines interpreted this gathering to be a council of war, and with a strong force set out to disperse the Israelites before their plans could be matured. The tidings of their approach caused great terror in Israel. The people entreated Samuel, "Cease not to cry unto the Lord our God for us, that He will save us out of the hand of the Philistines."

While Samuel was in the act of presenting a lamb as a burnt offering, the Philistines drew near for battle. Then the Mighty One who had descended upon Sinai amid fire and smoke and thunder, who had parted the Red Sea and made a way through Jordan for the children of Israel, again manifested His power. A terrible storm burst upon the advancing host, and the earth was strewn with the dead bodies of mighty warriors.

The Israelites had stood in silent awe, trembling with hope and fear. When they beheld the slaughter of their enemies, they knew that God had accepted their repentance. Through unprepared for battle, they seized the weapons of the slaughtered Philistines and pursued the fleeing host to Beth-car. This signal victory was gained upon the very field where, twenty years before, Israel had been smitten before the Philistines, the priests slain, and the ark of God taken. For nations as well as for individuals, the path of obedience to God is the path of safety and happiness, while that of transgression leads only to disaster and defeat. The Philistines were now so completely subdued that they surrendered the strongholds which had been taken from Israel and refrained from acts of hostility for many years. Other nations followed this example, and the Israelites enjoyed peace until the close of Samuel's sole administration.

That the occasion might never be forgotten, Samuel set up, between Mizpeh and Shen, a great stone as a memorial. He called the name of it Ebenezer, "the stone of help," saying to the people, "hitherto hath Jehovah helped us."

The Lord Himself directed the education of Israel. His care was not restricted to their religious interests; whatever affected their mental or physical well-being was also the subject of divine providence, and came within the sphere of divine law.

God had commanded the Hebrews to teach their children His requirements and to make them acquainted with all His dealings with their fathers. This was one of the special duties of every parent—one that was not to be delegated to another. In the place of stranger lips the loving hearts of the father and mother were to give instruction to their children. Thoughts of God were to be associated with all the events of daily life. The mighty works of God in the deliverance of His people and the promises of the Redeemer to come were to be often recounted in the homes of Israel; and the use of figures and symbols caused the lessons given to be more firmly fixed in the memory. The great truths of God's providence and of the future life were impressed on the young mind. It was trained to see God alike in the scenes of nature and the words of revelation. The stars of heaven, the trees and flowers of the field, the lofty mountains, the rippling brooks—all spoke of the Creator. The solemn service of sacrifice and worship at the sanctuary and the utterances of the prophets were a revelation of God.

Such was the training of Moses in the lowly cabin home in Goshen; of Samuel, by the faithful Hannah; of David, in the hill dwelling at Bethlehem; of Daniel, before the scenes of the captivity separated him from the home of his fathers. Such, too, was the early life of Christ at Nazareth; such the training by which the child Timothy learned from the lips of his grandmother Lois, and his mother Eunice (2 Timothy 1:5; 3:15), the truths of Holy Writ.

Further provision was made for the instruction of the young, by the establishment of the schools of the prophets. If a youth desired to search deeper into the truths of the word of God and to seek wisdom from above, that he might become a teacher in Israel, these schools were open to him. The schools of the prophets were founded by Samuel to serve as a barrier against the widespread corruption, to provide for the moral and spiritual welfare of the youth, and to promote the future prosperity of the nation by furnishing it with men qualified to act in the fear of God as leaders and counselors. In the accomplishment of this object Samuel gathered companies of young men who were pious, intelligent, and studious. These were called the sons of the prophets. As they communed with God and studied His word and His works, wisdom from above was added to their natural endowments. The instructors were men not only well versed in divine truth, but those who had themselves enjoyed communion with God and had received the special endowment of His Spirit. They enjoyed the respect and confidence of the people, both for learning and piety.

In Samuel's day there were two of these schools—one at Ramah, the home of the prophet, and the other at Kirjath-jearim, where the ark then was. Others were established in later times.

The pupils of these schools sustained themselves by their own labor in tilling the soil or in some mechanical employment. In Israel this was not thought strange or degrading; indeed, it was regarded a crime to allow children to grow up in ignorance of useful labor. By the command of God every child was taught some trade, even though he was to be educated for holy office. Many of the religious teachers supported themselves by manual labor. Even so late as the time of the apostles, Paul and Aquila were no less honored because they earned a livelihood by their trade of tentmaking.

The chief subjects of study in these schools were the law of God, with the instructions given to Moses, sacred history, sacred music, and poetry. The manner of instruction was far different from that in the theological schools of the present day, from which many students graduate with less real knowledge of God and religious truth than when they entered. In those schools of the olden time it was the grand object of all study to learn the will of God and man's duty toward Him. In the records of sacred history were traced the footsteps of Jehovah. The great truths set forth by the types were brought to view, and faith grasped the central object of all that system—the Lamb of God that was to take away the sin of the world.

A spirit of devotion was cherished. Not only were students taught the duty of prayer, but they were taught how to pray, how to approach their Creator, how to exercise faith in Him, and how to understand and obey the teachings of His Spirit. Sanctified intellects brought forth from the treasure house of God things new and old, and the Spirit of God was manifested in prophecy and sacred song.

Music was made to serve a holy purpose, to lift the thoughts to that which is pure, noble, and elevating, and to awaken in the soul devotion and gratitude to God. What a contrast between the ancient custom and the uses to which music is now too often devoted! How many employ this gift to exalt self, instead of using it to Glorify God! A love for music leads the unwary to unite with world lovers in pleasure gatherings where God has forbidden His children to go. Thus that which is a great blessing when rightly used, becomes one of the most successful agencies by which Satan allures the mind from duty and from the contemplation of eternal things.

Music forms a part of God's worship in the courts above, and we should endeavor, in our songs of praise, to approach as nearly as possible to the harmony of the heavenly choirs. The proper training of the voice is an important feature in education and should not be neglected. Singing, as a part of religious service, is as much an act of worship as is prayer. The heart must feel the spirit of the song to give it right expression.

How wide the difference between those schools taught by the prophets of God and our modern institutions of learning! How few schools are to be found that are not governed by the maxims and customs of the world! There is a deplorable lack of proper restraint and judicious discipline. The existing ignorance of God's word among a people professedly Christian is alarming. Superficial talk, mere sentimentalism, passes for instruction in morals and religion. The justice and mercy of God, the beauty of holiness and the sure reward of rightdoing, the heinous character of sin and the certainty of its terrible results, are not impressed upon the minds of the young. Evil associates are instructing the youth in the ways of crime, dissipation, and licentiousness.

Are there not some lessons which the educators of our day might learn with profit from the ancient schools of the Hebrews? He who created man has provided for his development in body and mind and soul. Hence, real success in education depends upon the fidelity with which men carry out the Creator's plan.

The true object of education is to restore the image of God in the soul. In the beginning God created man in His own likeness. He endowed him with noble qualities. His mind was well balanced, and all the powers of his being were harmonious. But the Fall and its effects have perverted these gifts. Sin has marred and well-nigh obliterated the image of God in man. It was to restore this that the plan of salvation was devised, and a life of probation was granted to man. To bring him back to the perfection in which he was first created is the great object of life—the object that underlies every other. It is the work of parents and teachers, in the education of the youth, to co-operate with the divine purpose; and is so doing they are "laborers together with God." 1 Corinthians 3:9.

All the varied capabilities that men possess—of mind and soul and body—are given them by God, to be so employed as to reach the highest possible degree of excellence. But this cannot be a selfish and exclusive culture; for the character of God, whose likeness we are to receive, is benevolence and love. Every faculty, every attribute, with which the Creator has endowed us is to be employed for His glory and for the uplifting of our fellow men. And in this employment is found its purest, noblest, and happiest exercise.

Were this principle given the attention which its importance demands, there would be a radical change in some of the current methods of education. Instead of appealing to pride and selfish ambition, kindling a spirit of emulation, teachers would endeavor to awaken the love for goodness and truth and beauty—to arouse the desire for excellence. The student would seek the development of God's gifts in himself, not to excel others, but to fulfill the purpose of the Creator and to receive His likeness. Instead of being directed to mere earthly standards, or being actuated by the desire for self-exaltation, which in itself dwarfs and belittles, the mind would be directed to the Creator, to know Him and to become like Him.

"The fear of the Lord is the beginning of wisdom: and the knowledge of the Holy is understanding." Proverbs 9:10. The great work of life is character building, and a knowledge of God is the foundation of all true education. To impart this knowledge and to mold the character in harmony with it should be the object of the teacher's work. The law of God is a reflection of His character. Hence the psalmist says, "All Thy commandments are righteousness;" and "through Thy precepts I get understanding." Psalm 119:172, 104. God has revealed Himself to us in His word and in the works of creation. Through the volume of inspiration and the book of nature we are to obtain a knowledge of God.

It is a law of the mind that it gradually adapts itself to the subjects upon which it is trained to dwell. If occupied with commonplace matters only, it will become dwarfed and enfeebled. If never required to grapple with difficult problems, it will after a time almost lose the power of growth. As an educating power the Bible is without a rival. In the word of God the mind finds subject for the deepest thought, the loftiest aspiration. The Bible is the most instructive history that men possess. It came fresh from the fountain of eternal truth, and a divine hand has preserved its purity through all the ages. It lights up the far-distant past, where human research seeks vainly to penetrate. In God's word we behold the power that laid the foundation of the earth and that stretched out the heavens. Here only can we find a history of our race unsullied by human prejudice or human pride. Here are recorded the struggles, the defeats, and the victories of the greatest men this world has ever known. Here the great problems of duty and destiny are unfolded. The curtain that separates the visible from the invisible world is lifted, and we behold the conflict of the opposing forces of good and evil, from the first entrance of sin to the final triumph of righteousness and truth; and all is but a revelation of the character of God. In the reverent contemplation of the truths presented in His word the mind of the student is brought into communion with the infinite mind. Such a study will not only refine and ennoble the character, but it cannot fail to expand and invigorate the mental powers.

The teaching of the Bible has a vital bearing upon man's prosperity in all the relations of this life. It unfolds the principles that are the cornerstone of a nation's prosperity—principles with which is bound up the well-being of society, and which are the safeguard of the family—principles without which no man can attain usefulness, happiness, and honor in this life, or can hope to secure the future, immortal life. There is no position in life, no phase of human experience, for which the teaching of the Bible is not an essential preparation. Studied and obeyed, the word of God would give to the world men of stronger and more active intellect than will the closest application to all the subjects that human philosophy embraces. It would give men of strength and solidity of character, of keen perception and sound judgment—men who would be an honor to God and a blessing to the world.

In the study of the sciences also we are to obtain a knowledge of the Creator. All true science is but an interpretation of the handwriting of God in the material world. Science brings from her research only fresh evidences of the wisdom and power of God. Rightly understood, both the book of nature and the written word make us acquainted with God by teaching us something of the wise and beneficent laws through which He works.

The student should be led to see God in all the works of creation. Teachers should copy the example of the Great Teacher, who from the familiar scenes of nature drew illustrations that simplified His teachings and impressed them more deeply upon the minds of His hearers. The birds caroling in the leafy branches, the flowers of the valley, the lofty trees, the fruitful lands, the springing grain, the barren soil, the setting sun gilding the heavens with its golden beams—all served as means of instruction. He connected the visible works of the Creator with the words of life which He spoke, that whenever these objects should be presented to the eyes of His hearers, their thoughts might revert to the lessons of truth He had linked with them.

The impress of Deity, manifest in the pages of revelation, is seen upon the lofty mountains, the fruitful valleys, the broad, deep ocean. The things of nature speak to man of his Creator's love. He has linked us to Himself by unnumbered tokens in heaven and in earth. This world is not all sorrow and misery. "God is love," is written upon every opening bud, upon the petals of every flower, and upon every spire of grass. Though the curse of sin has caused the earth to bring forth thorns and thistles, there are flowers upon the thistles and the thorns are hidden by roses. All things in nature testify to the tender, fatherly care of our God and to His desire to make His children happy. His prohibitions and injunctions are not intended merely to display His authority, but in all that He does He has the well-being of His children in view. He does not require them to give up anything that it would be for their best interest to retain.

The opinion which prevails in some classes of society, that religion is not conductive to health or to happiness in this life, is one of the most mischievous of errors. The Scripture says: "The fear of the Lord tendeth to life: and he that hath it shall abide satisfied." Proverbs 19:23. "What man is he that desireth life, and loveth many days, that he may see good? Keep thy tongue from evil, and thy lips from speaking guile. Depart from evil, and do good; seek peace, and pursue it." Psalm 34:12-14. The words of wisdom "are life unto those that find them, and health to all their flesh." Proverbs 4:22.

True religion brings man into harmony with the laws of God, physical, mental, and moral. It teaches self-control, serenity, temperance. Religion ennobles the mind, refines the taste, and sanctifies the judgment. It makes the soul a partaker of the purity of heaven. Faith in God's love and overruling providence lightens the burdens of anxiety and care. It fills the heart with joy and contentment in the highest or the lowliest lot. Religion tends directly to promote health, to lengthen life, and to heighten our enjoyment of all its blessings. It opens to the soul a never-failing fountain of happiness. Would that all who have not chosen Christ might realize that He has something vastly better to offer them that they are seeking for themselves. Man is doing the greatest injury and injustice to his own soul when he thinks and acts contrary to the will of God. No real joy can be found in the path forbidden by Him who knows what is best, and who plans for the good of His creatures. The path of transgression leads to misery and destruction; but wisdom's "ways are ways of pleasantness, and all her paths are peace." Proverbs 3:17.

The physical as well as the religious training practiced in the schools of the Hebrews may be profitably studied. The worth of such training is not appreciated. There is an intimate relation between the mind and the body, and in order to reach a high standard of moral and intellectual attainment the laws that control our physical being must be heeded. To secure a strong, well-balanced character, both the mental and the physical powers must be exercised and developed. What study can be more important for the young than that which treats of this wonderful organism that God has committed to us, and of the laws by which it may be preserved in health?

And now, as in the days of Israel, every youth should be instructed in the duties of practical life. Each should acquire a knowledge of some branch of manual labor by which, if need be, he may obtain a livelihood. This is essential, not only as a safeguard against the vicissitudes of life, but from its bearing upon physical, mental, and moral development. Even if it were certain that one would never need to resort to manual labor for his support, still he should be taught to work. Without physical exercise, no one can have a sound constitution and vigorous health; and the discipline of well-regulated labor is no less essential to the securing of a strong and active mind and a noble character.

Every student should devote a portion of each day to active labor. Thus habits of industry would be formed and a spirit of self-reliance encouraged, while the youth would be shielded from many evil and degrading practices that are so often the result of idleness. And this is all in keeping with the primary object of education, for in encouraging activity, diligence, and purity we are coming into harmony with the Creator.

Let the youth be led to understand the object of their creation, to honor God and bless their fellow men; let them see the tender love which the Father in heaven has manifested toward them, and the high destiny for which the discipline of this life is to prepare them, the dignity and honor to which they are called, even to become the sons of God, and thousands would turn with contempt and loathing from the low and selfish aims and the frivolous pleasures that have hitherto engrossed them. They would learn to hate sin and to shun it, not merely from hope of reward or fear of punishment, but from a sense of its inherent baseness, because it would be a degrading of their God-given powers, a stain upon their Godlike manhood.

God does not bid the youth to be less aspiring. The elements of character that make a man successful and honored among men—the irrepressible desire for some greater good, the indomitable will, the strenuous exertion, the untiring perseverance—are not to be crushed out. By the grace of God they are to be directed to objects as much higher than mere selfish and temporal interests as the heavens are higher than the earth. And the education begun in this life will be continued in the life to come. Day by day the wonderful works of God, the evidences of His wisdom and power in creating and sustaining the universe, the infinite mystery of love and wisdom in the plan of redemption, will open to the mind in new beauty. "Eye hath not seen, nor ear heard, neither have entered into the heart of man, the things which God hath prepared for them that love Him." 1 Corinthians 2:9. Even in this life we may catch glimpses of His presence and may taste the joy of communion with Heaven, but the fullness of its joy and blessing will be reached in the hereafter. Eternity alone can reveal the glorious destiny to which man, restored to God's image, may attain.

The First King of Israel

The government of Israel was administered in the name and by the authority of God. The work of Moses, of the seventy elders, of the rulers and judges, was simply to enforce the laws that God had given; they had no authority to legislate for the nation. This was, and continued to be, the condition of Israel's existence as a nation. From age to age men inspired by God were sent to instruct the people and to direct in the enforcement of the laws.

The Lord foresaw that Israel would desire a king, but He did not consent to a change in the principles upon which the state was founded. The king was to be the vicegerent of the Most High. God was to be recognized as the Head of the nation, and His law was to be enforced as the supreme law of the land.

When the Israelites first settled in Canaan they acknowledged the principles of the theocracy, and the nation prospered under the rule of Joshua. But increase of population and intercourse with other nations brought a change. The people adopted many of the customs of their heathen neighbors and thus sacrificed to a great degree their own peculiar, holy character. Gradually they lost their reverence for God and ceased to prize the honor of being His chosen people. Attracted by the pomp and display of heathen monarchs, they tired of their own simplicity. Jealousy and envy sprang up between the tribes. Internal dissensions made them weak; they were continually exposed to the invasion of their heathen foes, and the people were coming to believe that in order to maintain their standing among the nations, the tribes must be united under a strong central government. As they departed from obedience to God's law, they desired to be freed from the rule of their divine Sovereign; and thus the demand for a monarchy became widespread throughout Israel.

Since the days of Joshua the government had never been conducted with so great wisdom and success as under Samuel's administration. Divinely invested with the threefold office of judge, prophet, and priest, he had labored with untiring and disinterested zeal for the welfare of his people, and the nation had prospered under his wise control. Order had been restored, and godliness promoted, and the spirit of discontent was checked for the time. But with advancing years the prophet was forced to share with others the cares of government, and he appointed his two sons to act as his assistants. While Samuel continued the duties of his office at Ramah, the young men were stationed at Beersheba, to administer justice among the people near the southern border of the land.

It was with the full assent of the nation that Samuel had appointed his sons to office, but they did not prove themselves worthy of their father's choice. The Lord had, through Moses, given special directions to His people that the rulers of Israel should judge righteously, deal justly with the widow and the fatherless, and receive no bribes. But the sons of Samuel "turned aside after lucre, and took bribes, and perverted judgment." The sons of the prophet had not heeded the precepts which he had sought to impress upon their minds. They had not copied the pure, unselfish life of their father. The warning given to Eli had not exerted the influence upon the mind of Samuel that it should have done. He had been to some extent too indulgent with his sons, and the result was apparent in their character and life.

The injustice of these judges caused much dissatisfaction, and a pretext was thus furnished for urging the change that had long been secretly desired. "All the elders of Israel gathered themselves together, and came to Samuel unto Ramah, and said unto him, Behold, thou art old, and thy sons walk not in thy ways: now make us a king to judge us like all the nations." The cases of abuse among the people had not been referred to Samuel. Had the evil course of his sons been known to him, he would have removed them without delay; but this was not what the petitioners desired. Samuel saw that their real motive was discontent and pride, and that their demand was the result of a deliberate and determined purpose. No complaint had been made against Samuel. All acknowledged the integrity and wisdom of his administration; but the aged prophet looked upon the request as a censure upon himself, and a direct effort to set him aside. He did not, however, reveal his feelings; he uttered no reproach, but carried the matter to the Lord in prayer and sought counsel from Him alone.

And the Lord said unto Samuel: "Hearken unto the voice of the people in all that they say unto thee: for they have not rejected thee, but they have rejected Me, that I should not reign over them. According to all the works which they have done since the day that I brought them up out of Egypt even unto this day, wherewith they have forsaken Me, and served other gods, so do they also unto thee." The prophet was reproved for grieving at the conduct of the people toward himself as an individual. They had not manifested disrespect for him, but for the authority of God, who had appointed the rulers of His people. Those who despise and reject the faithful servant of God show contempt, not merely for the man, but for the Master who sent him. It is God's words, His reproofs and counsel, that are set at nought; it is His authority that is rejected.

The days of Israel's greatest prosperity had been those in which they acknowledged Jehovah as their King—when the laws and the government which He had established were regarded as superior to those of all other nations. Moses had declared to Israel concerning the commandments of the Lord: "This is your wisdom and your understanding in the sight of the nations, which shall hear all these statutes, and say, Surely this great nation is a wise and understanding people." Deuteronomy 4:6. But by departing from God's law the Hebrews had failed to become the people that God desired to make them, and then all the evils which were the result of their own sin and folly they charged upon the government of God. So completely had they become blinded by sin.

The Lord had, through His prophets, foretold that Israel would be governed by a king; but it does not follow that this form of government was best for them or according to His will. He permitted the people to follow their own choice, because they refused to be guided by His counsel. Hosea declares that God gave them a king in His anger. Hosea 13:11. When men choose to have their own way, without seeking counsel from God, or in opposition to His revealed will, He often grants their desires, in order that, through the bitter experience that follows, they may be led to realize their folly and to repent of their sin. Human pride and wisdom will prove a dangerous guide. That which the heart desires contrary to the will of God will in the end be found a curse rather than a blessing.

God desired His people to look to Him alone as their Law-giver and their Source of strength. Feeling their dependence upon God, they would be constantly drawn nearer to Him. They would become elevated and ennobled, fitted for the high destiny to which He had called them as His chosen people. But when a man was placed upon the throne, it would tend to turn the minds of the people from God. They would trust more to human strength, and less to divine power, and the errors of their king would lead them into sin and separate the nation from God.

Samuel was instructed to grant the request of the people, but to warn them of the Lord's disapproval, and also make known what would be the result of their course. "And Samuel told all the words of the Lord unto the people that asked of him a king." He faithfully set before them the burdens that would be laid upon them, and showed the contrast between such a state of oppression and their present comparatively free and prosperous condition. Their king would imitate the pomp and luxury of other monarchs, to support which, grievous exactions upon their persons and property would be necessary. The goodliest of their young men he would require for his service. They would be made charioteers and horsemen and runners before him. They must fill the ranks of his army, and they would be required to till his fields, to reap his harvests, and to manufacture implements of war for his service. The daughters of Israel would be for confectioners and bakers for the royal household. To support his kingly state he would seize upon the best of their lands, bestowed upon the people by Jehovah Himself. The most valuable of their servants also, and of their cattle, he would take, and "put them to his work." Besides all this, the king would require a tenth of all their income, the profits of their labor, or the products of the soil. "Ye shall be his servants," concluded the prophet. "And ye shall cry out in that day because of your king which ye shall have chosen you; and the Lord will not hear you in that day." However burdensome its exactions should be found, when once a monarchy was established, they could not set it aside at pleasure.

But the people returned the answer, "Nay; but we will have a king over us; that we also may be like all the nations; and that our king may judge us, and go out before us, and fight our battles."

"Like all the nations." The Israelites did not realize that to be in this respect unlike other nations was a special privilege and blessing. God had separated the Israelites from every other people, to make them His own peculiar treasure. But they, disregarding this high honor, eagerly desired to imitate the example of the heathen! And still the longing to conform to worldly practices and customs exists among the professed people of God. As they depart from the Lord they become ambitious for the gains and honors of the world. Christians are constantly seeking to imitate the practices of those who worship the god of this world. Many urge that by uniting with worldlings and conforming to their customs they might exert a stronger influence over the ungodly. But all who pursue this course thereby separate from the Source of their strength. Becoming the friends of the world, they are the enemies of God. For the sake of earthly distinction they sacrifice the unspeakable honor to which God has called them, of showing forth the praises of Him who hath called us out of darkness into His marvelous light. 1 Peter 2:9.

With deep sadness Samuel listened to the words of the people; but the Lord said unto him, "Hearken unto their voice, and make them a king." The prophet had done his duty. He had faithfully presented the warning, and it had been rejected. With a heavy heart he dismissed the people, and himself departed to prepare for the great change in the government.

Samuel's life of purity and unselfish devotion was a perpetual rebuke both to self-serving priests and elders and to the proud, sensual congregation of Israel. Although he assumed no pomp and made no display, his labors bore the signet of Heaven. He was honored by the world's Redeemer, under whose guidance he ruled the Hebrew nation. But the people had become weary of his piety and devotion; they despised his humble authority and rejected him for a man who should rule them as a king.

In the character of Samuel we see reflected the likeness of Christ. It was the purity of our Saviour's life that provoked the wrath of Satan. That life was the light of the world, and revealed the hidden depravity in the hearts of men. It was the holiness of Christ that stirred up against Him the fiercest passions of falsehearted professors of godliness. Christ came not with the wealth and honors of earth, yet the works which He wrought showed Him to possess power greater than that of any human prince. The Jews looked for the Messiah to break the oppressor's yoke, yet they cherished the sins that had bound it upon their necks. Had Christ cloaked their sins and applauded their piety, they would have accepted Him as their king; but they would not bear His fearless rebuke of their vices. The loveliness of a character in which benevolence, purity, and holiness reigned supreme, which entertained no hatred except for sin, they despised. Thus it has been in every age of the world. The light from heaven brings condemnation on all who refuse to walk in it. When rebuked by the example of those who hate sin, hypocrites will become agents of Satan to harass and persecute the faithful. "All that will live godly in Christ Jesus shall suffer persecution." 2 Timothy 3:12.

Though a monarchical form of government for Israel had been foretold in prophecy, God had reserved to Himself the right to choose their king. The Hebrews so far respected the authority of God as to leave the selection entirely to Him. The choice fell upon Saul, a son of Kish, of the tribe of Benjamin.

The personal qualities of the future monarch were such as to gratify that pride of heart which prompted the desire for a king. "There was not among the children of Israel a goodlier person than he." 1 Samuel 9:2. Of noble and dignified bearing, in the prime of life, comely and tall, he appeared like one born to command. Yet with these external attractions, Saul was destitute of those higher qualities that constitute true wisdom. He had not in youth learned to control his rash, impetuous passions; he had never felt the renewing power of divine grace.

Saul was the son of a powerful and wealthy chief, yet in accordance with the simplicity of the times he was engaged with his father in the humble duties of a husbandman. Some of his father's animals having strayed upon the mountains, Saul went with a servant to seek for them. For three days they searched in vain, when, as they were not far from Ramah, the home of Samuel, the servant proposed that they should inquire of the prophet concerning the missing property. "I have here at hand the fourth part of a shekel of silver," he said: "that will I give to the man of God, to tell us our way." This was in accordance with the custom of the times. A person approaching a superior in rank or office made him a small present, as an expression of respect.

As they drew near to the city they met some young maidens who had come out to draw water, and inquired of them for the seer. In reply they were told that a religious service was about to take place, that the prophet had already arrived, there was to be an offering upon "the high place," and after that a sacrificial feast. A great change had taken place under Samuel's administration. When the call of God first came to him the services of the sanctuary were held in contempt. "Men abhorred the offering of the Lord." 1 Samuel 2:17. But the worship of God was now maintained throughout the land,

and the people manifested an interest in religious services. There being no ministration in the tabernacle, sacrifices were for the time offered elsewhere; and the cities of the priests and Levites, where the people resorted for instruction, were chosen for this purpose. The highest points in these cities were usually selected as the place of sacrifice, and hence were called "the high places."

At the gate of the city Saul was met by the prophet himself. God had revealed to Samuel that at that time the chosen king of Israel would present himself before him. As they now stood face to face, the Lord said to Samuel, "Behold the man whom I spake to thee of! this same shall reign over My people."

To the request of Saul, "Tell me, I pray thee, where the seer's house is," Samuel replied, "I am the seer." Assuring him also that the lost animals had been found, he urged him to tarry and attend the feast, at the same time giving some intimation of the great destiny before him: "On whom is all the desire of Israel? Is it not on thee, and on all thy father's house?" The listener's heart thrilled at the prophet's words. He could not but perceive something of their significance, for the demand for a king had become a matter of absorbing interest to the whole nation. Yet with modest self-depreciation Saul replied, "Am not I a Benjamite, of the smallest of the tribes of Israel? and my family the least of all the families of the tribe of Benjamin? wherefore then speakest thou so to me?"

Samuel conducted the stranger to the place of assembly, where the principal men of the town were gathered. Among them, at the prophet's direction, the place of honor was given to Saul, and at the feast the choicest portion was set before him. The services over, Samuel took his guest to his own home, and there upon the housetop he communed with him, setting forth the great principles on which the government of Israel had been established, and thus seeking to prepare him, in some measure, for his high station.

When Saul departed, early next morning, the prophet went forth with him. Having passed through the town, he directed the servant to go forward. Then he bade Saul stand still to receive a message sent him from God. "Then Samuel took a vial of oil, and poured it upon his head, and kissed him, and said, Is it not because Jehovah hath anointed thee to be captain over His inheritance?" As evidence that this was done by divine authority, he foretold the incidents that would occur on the homeward journey and assured Saul that he would be qualified by the Spirit of God for the station awaiting him. "The Spirit of Jehovah will come upon thee," said the prophet, and thou "shalt be turned into another man. And let it be, when these signs are come unto thee, that thou do as occasion serve thee; for God is with thee."

As Saul went on his way, all came to pass as the prophet had said. Near the border of Benjamin he was informed that the lost animals had been found. In the plain of Tabor he met three men who were going to worship God at Bethel. One of them carried three kids for sacrifice, another three loaves of bread, and the third a bottle of wine, for the sacrificial feast.

They gave Saul the usual salutation and also presented him with two of the three loaves of bread. At Gibeah, his own city, a band of prophets returning from "the high place" were singing the praise of God to the music of the pipe and the harp, the psaltery and the tabret. As Saul approached them the Spirit of the Lord came upon him also, and he joined in their song of praise, and prophesied with them. He spoke with so great fluency and wisdom, and joined so earnestly in the service, that those who had known him exclaimed in astonishment, "What is this that is come unto the son of Kish? Is Saul also among the prophets?"

As Saul united with the prophets in their worship, a great change was wrought in him by the Holy Spirit. The light of divine purity and holiness shone in upon the darkness of the natural heart. He saw himself as he was before God. He saw the beauty of holiness. He was now called to begin the warfare against sin and Satan, and he was made to feel that in this conflict his strength must come wholly from God. The plan of salvation, which had before seemed dim and uncertain, was opened to his understanding. The Lord endowed him with courage and wisdom for his high station. He revealed to him the Source of strength and grace, and enlightened his understanding as to the divine claims and his own duty.

The anointing of Saul as king had not been made known to the nation. The choice of God was to be publicly manifested by lot. For this purpose Samuel convoked the people at Mizpeh. Prayer was offered for divine guidance; then followed the solemn ceremony of casting the lot. In silence the assembled multitude awaited the issue. The tribe, the family, and the household were successively designated, and then Saul, the son of Kish, was pointed out as the individual chosen. But Saul was not in the assembly. Burdened with a sense of the great responsibility about to fall upon him, he had secretly withdrawn. He was brought back to the congregation, who observed with pride and satisfaction that he was of kingly bearing and noble form, being "higher than any of the people from his shoulders and upward." Even Samuel, when presenting him to the assembly, exclaimed, "See ye him whom the Lord hath chosen, that there is none like him among all the people?" And in response arose from the vast throng one long, loud shout of joy, "God save the king!"

Samuel then set before the people "the manner of the kingdom," stating the principles upon which the monarchial government was based, and by which it should be controlled. The king was not to be an absolute monarch, but was to hold his power in subjection to the will of the Most High. This address was recorded in a book, wherein were set forth the prerogatives of the prince and the rights and privileges of the people. Though the nation had despised Samuel's warning, the faithful prophet, while forced to yield to their desires, still endeavored, as far as possible, to guard their liberties.

While the people in general were ready to acknowledge Saul as their king, there was a large party in opposition. For a monarch to be chosen from Benjamin, the smallest of the tribes of Israel—and that to the neglect of both Judah and Ephraim, the largest and most powerful—was a slight which they could not brook. They refused to profess allegiance to Saul or to bring him the customary presents. Those who had been most urgent in their demand for a king were the very ones that refused to accept with gratitude the man of God's appointment. The members of each faction had their favorite, whom they wished to see placed on the throne, and several among the leaders had desired the honor for themselves. Envy and jealousy burned in the hearts of many. The efforts of pride and ambition had resulted in disappointment and discontent.

In this condition of affairs Saul did not see fit to assume the royal dignity. Leaving Samuel to administer the government as formerly, he returned to Gibeah. He was honorably escorted thither by a company, who, seeing the divine choice in his selection, were determined to sustain him. But he made no attempt to maintain by force his right to the throne. In his home among the uplands of Benjamin he quietly occupied himself in the duties of a husbandman, leaving the establishment of his authority entirely to God.

Soon after Saul's appointment the Ammonites, under their king, Nahash, invaded the territory of the tribes east of Jordan and threatened the city of Jabesh-gilead. The inhabitants tried to secure terms of peace by offering to become tributary to the Ammonites. To this the cruel king would not consent but on condition that he might put out the right eye of every one of them, thus making them abiding witnesses to his power.

The people of the besieged city begged a respite of seven days. To this the Ammonites consented, thinking thus to heighten the honor of their expected triumph. Messengers were at once dispatched from Jabesh, to seek help from the tribes west of Jordan. They carried the tidings to Gibeah, creating widespread terror. Saul, returning at night from following the oxen in the field, heard the loud wail that told of some great calamity. He said, "What aileth the people that they weep?" When the shameful story was repeated, all his dormant powers were roused. "The Spirit of God came upon Saul. . . . And he took a yoke of oxen, and hewed them in pieces, and sent them throughout all the coasts of Israel by the hands of messengers, saying, Whosoever cometh nor forth after Saul and after Samuel, so shall it be done unto his oxen."

Three hundred and thirty thousand men gathered on the plain of Bezek, under the command of Saul. Messengers were immediately sent to the besieged city with the assurance that they might expect help on the morrow, the very day on which they were to submit to the Ammonites. By a rapid night march Saul and his army crossed the Jordan and arrived before Jabesh in "the morning watch." Like Gideon, dividing his force into three companies, he fell upon the Ammonite camp at that early hour, when, not suspecting danger, they were least secure. In the panic that followed they were routed with great slaughter. And "they which remained were scattered, so that two of them were not left together."

The promptness and bravery of Saul, as well as the generalship shown in the successful conduct of so large a force, were qualities which the people of Israel had desired in a monarch, that they might be able to cope with other nations. They now greeted him as their king, attributing the honor of the victory to human agencies and forgetting that without God's special blessing all their efforts would have been in vain. In their enthusiasm some proposed to put to death those who had at first refused to acknowledge the authority of Saul. But the king interfered, saying, "There shall not a man be put to death this day: for today the Lord hath wrought salvation in Israel." Here Saul gave evidence of the change that had taken place in his character. Instead of taking honor to himself, he gave the glory to God. Instead of showing a desire for revenge, he manifested a spirit of compassion and forgiveness. This is unmistakable evidence that the grace of God dwells in the heart.

Samuel now proposed that a national assembly should be convoked at Gilgal, that the kingdom might there be publicly confirmed to Saul. It was done; "and there they sacrificed sacrifices of peace offerings before the Lord; and there Saul and all the men of Israel rejoiced greatly."

Gilgal had been the place of Israel's first encampment in the Promised Land. It was here that Joshua, by divine direction, set up the pillar of twelve stones to commemorate the miraculous passage of the Jordan. Here circumcision had been renewed. Here they had kept the first Passover after the sin at Kadesh and the desert sojourn. Here the manna ceased. Here the Captain of the Lord's host had revealed Himself as chief in command of the armies of Israel. From this place they marched to the overthrow of Jericho and the conquest of Ai. Here Achan met the penalty of his sin, and here was made that treaty with the Gibeonites which punished Israel's neglect to ask counsel of God. Upon this plain, linked with so many thrilling associations, stood Samuel and Saul; and when the shouts of welcome to the king had died away, the aged prophet gave his parting words as ruler of the nation.

"Behold," he said, "I have hearkened unto your voice in all that ye said unto me, and have made a king over you. And now, behold, the king walketh before you: and I am old and gray-headed; . . . and I have walked before you from my childhood unto this day. Behold, here I am: witness against me before the Lord, and before His anointed: whose ox have I taken? or whose ass have I taken? or whom have I defrauded? whom have I oppressed? or of whose hand have I received any bribe to blind mine eyes therewith? and I will restore it you."

With one voice the people answered, "Thou hast not defrauded us, nor oppressed us, neither hast thou taken ought of any man's hand."

Samuel was not seeking merely to justify his own course. He had previously set forth the principles that should govern both the king and the people, and he desired to add to his words the weight of his own example. From childhood he had been connected with the work of God, and during his long life one object had been ever before him—the glory of God and the highest good of Israel.

Before there could be any hope of prosperity for Israel they must be led to repentance before God. In consequence of sin they had lost their faith in God and their discernment of His power and wisdom to rule the nation—lost their confidence in His ability to vindicate His cause. Before they could find true peace they must be led to see and confess the very sin of which they had been guilty. They had declared the object of the demand for a king to be, "That our king may judge us, and go out before us, and fight our battles." Samuel recounted the history of Israel, from the day when God brought them from Egypt. Jehovah, the King of kings, had gone out before them and had fought their battles. Often their sins had sold them into the power of their enemies, but no sooner did they turn from their evil ways than God's mercy raised up a deliverer. The Lord sent Gideon and Barak, and "Jephthah, and Samuel, and delivered you out of the hand of your enemies on every side, and ye dwelt safe." Yet when threatened with danger they had declared, "A king shall reign over us," when, said the prophet, "Jehovah your God was your King."

"Now therefore," continued Samuel, "stand and see this great thing, which the Lord will do before your eyes. Is it not wheat harvest today? I will call unto the Lord, and He shall send thunder and rain; that ye may perceive and see that your wickedness is great, which ye have done in the sight of the Lord, in asking you a king. So Samuel called unto the Lord; and the Lord sent thunder and rain that day." At the time of wheat harvest, in May and June, no rain fell in the East. The sky was cloudless, and the air serene and mild. So violent a storm at this season filled all hearts with fear. In humiliation the people now confessed their sin—the very sin of which they had been guilty: "Pray for thy servants unto the Lord thy God, that we die not: for we have added unto all our sins this evil, to ask us a king."

Samuel did not leave the people in a state of discouragement, for this would have prevented all effort for a better life. Satan would lead them to look upon God as severe and unforgiving, and they would thus be exposed to manifold temptations. God is merciful and forgiving, ever desiring to show favor to His people when they will obey His voice. "Fear not," was the message of God by His servant: "ye have done all this wickedness: yet turn not aside from following the Lord, but serve the Lord with all your heart; and turn ye not aside: for then should ye go after vain things, which cannot profit nor deliver; for they are vain. For the Lord will not forsake His people."

Samuel said nothing of the slight which had been put upon himself; he uttered no reproach for the ingratitude with which Israel had repaid his lifelong devotion; but he assured them of his unceasing interest for them: "God forbid that I should sin against the Lord in ceasing to pray for you: but I will teach you the good and the right way: only fear the Lord, and serve Him in truth with all your heart: for consider how great things He hath done for you. But if ye shall still do wickedly, ye shall be consumed, both ye and your king."

The Presumption of Saul

After the assembly at Gilgal, Saul disbanded the army that had at his call arisen to overthrow the Ammonites, reserving only two thousand men to be stationed under his command at Michmash and one thousand to attend his son Jonathan at Gibeah. Here was a serious error. His army was filled with hope and courage by the recent victory; and had he proceeded at once against other enemies of Israel, a telling blow might have been struck for the liberties of the nation.

Meanwhile their warlike neighbors, the Philistines, were active. After the defeat at Ebenezer they had still retained possession of some hill fortresses in the land of Israel, and now they established themselves in the very heart of the country. In facilities, arms, and equipments the Philistines had great advantage over Israel. During the long period of their oppressive rule they had endeavored to strengthen their power by forbidding the Israelites to practice the trade of smiths, lest they should make weapons of war. After the conclusion of peace the Hebrews had still resorted to the Philistine garrisons for such work as needed to be done. Controlled by love of ease and the abject spirit induced by long oppression, the men of Israel had, to a great extent, neglected to provide themselves with weapons of war. Bows and slings were used in warfare, and these the Israelites could obtain; but there were none among them, except Saul and his son Jonathan, who possessed a spear or a sword.

It was not until the second year of Saul's reign that an attempt was made to subdue the Philistines. The first blow was struck by Jonathan, the king's son, who attacked and overcame their garrison at Geba. The Philistines, exasperated by this defeat, made ready for a speedy attack upon Israel. Saul now caused war to be proclaimed by the sound of the trumpet throughout the land, calling upon all the men of war, including the tribes across the Jordan, to assemble at Gilgal. This summons was obeyed.

The Philistines had gathered an immense force at Michmash—"thirty thousand chariots, and six thousand horsemen, and people as the sand which is on the seashore in multitude." When the tidings reached Saul and his army at Gilgal, the people were appalled at thought of the mighty forces they would have to encounter in battle. They were not prepared to meet the enemy, and many were so terrified that they dared not come to the test of an encounter. Some crossed the Jordan, while others hid themselves in caves and pits and amid the rocks that abounded in that region. As the time for the encounter drew near, the number of desertions rapidly increased, and those who did not withdraw from the ranks were filled with foreboding and terror.

When Saul was first anointed king of Israel, he had received from Samuel explicit directions concerning the course to be pursued at this time. "Thou shalt go down before me to Gilgal," said the prophet; "and, behold, I will come down unto thee, to offer burnt offerings, and to sacrifice sacrifices of peace offerings: seven days shalt thou tarry, till I come to thee, and show thee what thou shalt do." I Samuel 10:8.

Day after day Saul tarried, but without making decided efforts toward encouraging the people and inspiring confidence in God. Before the time appointed by the prophet had fully expired, he became impatient at the delay and allowed himself to be discouraged by the trying circumstances that surrounded him. Instead of faithfully seeking to prepare the people for the service that Samuel was coming to perform, he indulged in unbelief and foreboding. The work of seeking God by sacrifice was a most solemn and important work; and God required that His people should search their hearts and repent of their sins, that the offering might be made with acceptance before Him, and that His blessing might attend their efforts to conquer the enemy. But Saul had grown restless; and the people, instead of trusting in God for help, were looking to the king whom they had chosen, to lead and direct them.

Yet the Lord still cared for them and did not give them up to the disasters that would have come upon them if the frail arm of flesh had become their only support. He brought them into close places, that they might be convicted of the folly of depending on man, and that they might turn to Him as their only help. The time for the proving of Saul had come. He was now to show whether or not he would depend on God and patiently wait according to His command, thus revealing himself as one whom God could trust in trying places as the ruler of His people, or whether he would be vacillating and unworthy of the sacred responsibility that had devolved upon him. Would the king whom Israel had chosen, listen to the Ruler of all kings? Would he turn the attention of his fainthearted soldiers to the One in whom is everlasting strength and deliverance?

With growing impatience he awaited the arrival of Samuel and attributed the confusion and distress and desertion of his army to the absence of the prophet. The appointed time came, but the man of God did not immediately appear. God's providence had detained His servant. But Saul's restless, impulsive spirit would no longer be restrained. Feeling that something must be done to calm the fears of the people, he determined to summon an assembly for religious service, and by sacrifice entreat the divine aid. God had directed that only those consecrated to the office should present sacrifices before Him. But Saul commanded, "Bring hither a burnt offering;" and, equipped as he was with armor and weapons of war, he approached the altar and offered sacrifice before God.

"And it came to pass, that as soon as he had made an end of offering the burnt offering, behold, Samuel came; and Saul went out to meet him, that he might salute him." Samuel saw at once that Saul had gone contrary to the express directions that had been given him. The Lord had spoken by His prophet that at this time He would reveal what Israel must do in this crisis. If Saul had fulfilled the conditions upon which divine help was promised, the Lord would have wrought a marvelous deliverance for Israel, with the few who were loyal to the king. But Saul was so well satisfied with himself and his work that he went out to meet the prophet as one who should be commended rather than disapproved.

Samuel's countenance was full of anxiety and trouble; but to his inquiry, "What hast thou done?" Saul offered excuses for his presumptuous act. He said: "I saw that the people were scattered from me, and that thou camest not within the days appointed, and that the Philistines gathered themselves together at Michmash; therefore said I, The Philistines will come down now upon me to Gilgal, and I have not made supplication unto the Lord: I forced myself therefore, and offered a burnt offering.

"And Samuel said to Saul, Thou hast done foolishly: thou hast not kept the commandment of the Lord thy God, which He commanded thee: for now would the Lord have established thy kingdom upon Israel forever. But now thy kingdom shall not continue: the Lord hath sought Him a man after His own heart, and the Lord hath commanded him to be captain over His people. . . . And Samuel arose, and gat him up from Gilgal unto Gibeah of Benjamin."

Either Israel must cease to be the people of God, or the principle upon which the monarchy was founded must be maintained, and the nation must be governed by a divine power. If Israel would be wholly the Lord's, if the will of the human and earthly were held in subjection to the will of God, He would continue to be the Ruler of Israel. So long as the king and the people would conduct themselves as subordinate to God, so long He could be their defense. But in Israel no monarchy could prosper that did not in all things acknowledge the supreme authority of God.

If Saul had shown a regard for the requirements of God in this time of trial, God could have worked His will through him. His failure now proved him unfit to be the vicegerent of God to His people. He would mislead Israel. His will, rather than the will of God, would be the controlling power. If Saul had been faithful, his kingdom would have been established forever; but since he had failed, the purpose of God must be accomplished by another. The government of Israel must be committed to one who would rule the people according to the will of Heaven.

We do not know what great interests may be at stake in the proving of God. There is no safety except in strict obedience to the word of God. All His promises are made upon condition of faith and obedience, and a failure to comply with His commands cuts off the fulfillment to us of the rich provisions of the Scriptures. We should not follow impulse, nor rely on the judgment of men; we should look to the revealed will of God and walk according to His definite commandment, no matter what circumstances may surround us. God will take care of the results; by faithfulness to His word we may in time of trial prove before men and angels that the Lord can trust us in difficult places to carry out His will, honor His name, and bless His people.

Saul was in disfavor with God, and yet unwilling to humble his heart in penitence. What he lacked in real piety he would try to make up by his zeal in the forms of religion. Saul was not ignorant of Israel's defeat when the ark of God was brought into the camp by Hophni and Phinehas; and yet, knowing all this, he determined to send for the sacred chest and its attendant priest. Could he by this means inspire confidence in the people, he hoped to reassemble his scattered army and give battle to the Philistines. He would now dispense with Samuel's presence and support, and thus free himself from the prophet's unwelcome criticisms and reproofs.

The Holy Spirit had been granted to Saul to enlighten his understanding and soften his heart. He had received faithful instruction and reproof from the prophet of God. And yet how great was his perversity! The history of Israel's first king presents a sad example of the power of early wrong habits. In his youth Saul did not love and fear God; and that impetuous spirit, not early trained to submission, was ever ready to rebel against divine authority. Those who in their youth cherish a sacred regard for the will of God, and who faithfully perform the duties of their position, will be prepared for higher service in afterlife. But men cannot for years pervert the powers that God has given them, and then, when they choose to change, find these powers fresh and free for an entirely opposite course.

Saul's efforts to arouse the people proved unavailing. Finding his force reduced to six hundred men, he left Gilgal and retired to the fortress at Geba, lately taken from the Philistines. This stronghold was on the south side of a deep, rugged valley, or gorge, a few miles north of the site of Jerusalem. On the north side of the same valley, at Michmash, the Philistine force lay encamped while detachments of troops went out in different directions to ravage the country.

God had permitted matters to be thus brought to a crisis that He might rebuke the perversity of Saul and teach His people a lesson of humility and faith. Because of Saul's sin in his presumptuous offering, the Lord would not give him the honor of vanquishing the Philistines. Jonathan, the king's son, a man who feared the Lord, was chosen as the instrument to deliver Israel. Moved by a divine impulse, he proposed to his armor-bearer that they should make a secret attack upon the enemy's camp. "It may be," he urged, "that the Lord will work for us: for there is no restraint to the Lord to save by many or by few."

The armor-bearer, who also was a man of faith and prayer, encouraged the design, and together they withdrew from the camp, secretly, lest their purpose should be opposed. With earnest prayer to the Guide of their fathers, they agreed upon a sign by which they might determine how to proceed. Then passing down into the gorge separating the two armies, they silently threaded their way, under the shadow of the cliff, and partially concealed by the mounds and ridges of the valley. Approaching the Philistine fortress, they were revealed to the view of their enemies, who said, tauntingly, "Behold, the Hebrews come forth out of the holes where they had hid themselves," then challenged them, "Come up to us, and we will show you a thing," meaning that they would punish the two Israelites for their daring. This challenge was the token that Jonathan and his companion had agreed to accept as evidence that the Lord would prosper their undertaking.

Passing now from the sight of the Philistines, and choosing a secret and difficult path, the warriors made their way to the summit of a cliff that had been deemed inaccessible, and was not very strongly guarded. Thus they penetrated the enemy's camp and slew the sentinels, who, overcome with surprise and fear, offered no resistance.

Angels of heaven shielded Jonathan and his attendant, angels fought by their side, and the Philistines fell before them. The earth trembled as though a great multitude with horsemen and chariots were approaching. Jonathan recognized the tokens of divine aid, and even the Philistines knew that God was working for the deliverance of Israel. Great fear seized upon the host, both in the field and in the garrison. In the confusion, mistaking their own soldiers for enemies, the Philistines began to slay one another.

Soon the noise of the battle was heard in the camp of Israel. The king's sentinels reported that there was great confusion among the Philistines, and that their numbers were decreasing. Yet it was not known that any part of the Hebrew army had left the camp. Upon inquiry it was found that none were absent except Jonathan and his armor-bearer. But seeing that the Philistines were meeting with a repulse, Saul led his army to join the assault. The Hebrews who had deserted to the enemy now turned against them; great numbers also came out of their hiding places, and as the Philistines fled, discomfited, Saul's army committed terrible havoc upon the fugitives.

Determined to make the most of his advantage, the king rashly forbade his soldiers to partake of food for the entire day, enforcing his command by the solemn imprecation, "Cursed be the man that eateth any food until evening, that I may be avenged on mine enemies." The victory had already been gained, without Saul's knowledge or co-operation, but he hoped to distinguish himself by the utter destruction of the vanquished army. The command to refrain from food was prompted by selfish ambition, and it showed the king to be indifferent to the needs of his people when these conflicted with his desire for self-exaltation. To confirm his prohibition by a solemn oath showed Saul to be both rash and profane. The very words of the curse give evidence that Saul's zeal was for himself, and not for the honor of God. He declared his object to be, not "that the Lord may be avenged on His enemies," but "that I may be avenged on mine enemies."

The prohibition resulted in leading the people to transgress the command of God. They had been engaged in warfare all day, and were faint for want of food; and as soon as the hours of restriction were over, they fell upon the spoil and devoured the flesh with the blood, thus violating the law that forbade the eating of blood.

During the day's battle Jonathan, who had not heard of the king's command, unwittingly offended by eating a little honey as he passed through a wood. Saul learned of this at evening. He had declared that the violation of his edict should be punished with death; and though Jonathan had not been guilty of a willful sin, though God had miraculously preserved his life and had wrought deliverance through him, the king declared that the sentence must be executed. To spare the life of his son would have been an acknowledgment on the part of Saul that he had sinned in making so rash a vow. This would have been humiliating to his pride. "God do so, and more also," was his terrible sentence: "thou shalt surely die, Jonathan."

Saul could not claim the honor of the victory, but he hoped to be honored for his zeal in maintaining the sacredness of his oath. Even at the sacrifice of his son, he would impress upon his subjects the fact that the royal authority must be maintained. At Gilgal, but a short time before, Saul had presumed to officiate as priest, contrary to the command of God. When reproved by Samuel, he had stubbornly justified himself. Now, when his own command was disobeyed—though the command was unreasonable and had been violated through ignorance—the king and father sentenced his son to death.

The people refused to allow the sentence to be executed. Braving the anger of the king, they declared, "Shall Jonathan die, who hath wrought this great salvation in Israel? God forbid: as the Lord liveth, there shall not one hair of his head fall to the ground; for he hath wrought with God this day." The proud monarch dared not disregard this unanimous verdict, and the life of Jonathan was preserved.

Saul could not but feel that his son was preferred before him, both by the people and by the Lord. Jonathan's deliverance was a severe reproof to the king's rashness. He felt a presentiment that his curses would return upon his own head. He did not longer continue the war with the Philistines, but returned to his home, moody and dissatisfied.

Those who are most ready to excuse or justify themselves in sin are often most severe in judging and condemning others. Many, like Saul, bring upon themselves the displeasure of God, but they reject counsel and despise reproof. Even when convinced that the Lord is not with them, they refuse to see in themselves the cause of their trouble. They cherish a proud, boastful spirit, while they indulge in cruel judgment or severe rebuke of others who are better than they. Well would it be for such self-constituted judges to ponder those words of Christ: "With what judgment ye judge, ye shall be judged: and with what measure ye mete, it shall be measured to you again." Matthew 7:2.

Often those who are seeking to exalt themselves are brought into positions where their true character is revealed. So it was in the case of Saul. His own course convinced the people that kingly honor and authority were dearer to him than justice, mercy, or benevolence. Thus the people were led to see their error in rejecting the government that God had given them. They had exchanged the pious prophet, whose prayers had brought down blessings, for a king who in his blind zeal had prayed for a curse upon them.

Had not the men of Israel interposed to save the life of Jonathan, their deliverer would have perished by the king's decree. With what misgivings must that people afterward have followed Saul's guidance! How bitter the thought that he had been placed upon the throne by their own act! The Lord bears long with the waywardness of men, and to all He grants opportunity to see and forsake their sins; but while He may seem to prosper those who disregard His will and despise His warnings, He will, in His own time, surely make manifest their folly.

Saul Rejected

Saul had failed to bear the test of faith in the trying situation at Gilgal, and had brought dishonor upon the service of God; but his errors were not yet irretrievable, and the Lord would grant him another opportunity to learn the lesson of unquestioning faith in His word and obedience to His commands.

When reproved by the prophet at Gilgal, Saul saw no great sin in the course he had pursued. He felt that he had been treated unjustly, and endeavored to vindicate his actions and offered excuses for his error. From that time he had little intercourse with the prophet. Samuel loved Saul as his own son, while Saul, bold and ardent in temper, had held the prophet in high regard; but he resented Samuel's rebuke, and thenceforth avoided him so far as possible.

But the Lord sent His servant with another message to Saul. By obedience he might still prove his fidelity to God and his worthiness to walk before Israel. Samuel came to the king and delivered the word of the Lord. That the monarch might realize the importance of heeding the command, Samuel expressly declared that he spoke by divine direction, by the same authority that had called Saul to the throne. The prophet said, "Thus saith the Lord of hosts, I remember that which Amalek did to Israel, how he laid wait for him in the way, when he came up from Egypt. Now go and smite Amalek, and utterly destroy all that they have, and spare them not; but slay both man and woman, infant and suckling, ox and sheep, camel and ass." The Amalekites had been the first to make war upon Israel in the wilderness; and for this sin, together with their defiance of God and their debasing idolatry, the Lord, through Moses, had pronounced sentence upon them. By divine direction the history of their cruelty toward Israel had been recorded, with the command, "Thou shalt blot out the remembrance of Amalek from under heaven; thou shalt not forget it." Deuteronomy 25:19. For four hundred years the execution of this sentence had been deferred; but the Amalekites had not turned from their sins. The Lord knew that this wicked people would, if it were possible, blot out His people and His worship from the earth. Now the time had come for the sentence, so long delayed, to be executed.

The forbearance that God has exercised toward the wicked, emboldens men in transgression; but their punishment will be none the less certain and terrible for being long delayed. "The Lord shall rise up as in Mount Perazim, He shall be wroth as in the valley of Gibeon, that He may do His work, His strange work; and bring to pass His act, His strange act." Isaiah 28:21. To our merciful God the act of punishment is a strange act. "As I live, saith the Lord God, I have no pleasure in the death of the wicked; but that the wicked turn from his way and live." Ezekiel 33:11. The Lord is "merciful and gracious, long-suffering, and abundant in goodness and truth, . . . forgiving iniquity and transgression and sin." Yet He will "by no means clear the guilty." Exodus 34:6, 7. While He does not delight in vengeance, He will execute judgment upon the transgressors of His law. He is forced to do this, to preserve the inhabitants of the earth from utter depravity and ruin. In order to save some He must cut off those who have become hardened in sin. "The Lord is slow to anger, and great in power, and will not at all acquit the wicked." Nahum 1:3. By terrible things in righteousness He will vindicate the authority of His downtrodden law. And the very fact of His reluctance to execute justice testifies to the enormity of the sins that call forth His judgments and to the severity of the retribution awaiting the transgressor.

But while inflicting judgment, God remembered mercy. The Amalekites were to be destroyed, but the Kenites, who dwelt among them, were spared. This people, though not wholly free from idolatry, were worshipers of God and were friendly to Israel. Of this tribe was the brother-in-law of Moses, Hobab, who had accompanied the Israelites in their travels through the wilderness, and by his knowledge of the country had rendered them valuable assistance.

Since the defeat of the Philistines at Michmash, Saul had made war against Moab, Ammon, and Edom, and against the Amalekites and the Philistines; and wherever he turned his arms, he gained fresh victories. On receiving the commission against the Amalekites, he at once proclaimed war. To his own authority was added that of the prophet, and at the call to battle the men of Israel flocked to his standard. The expedition was not to be entered upon for the purpose of self-aggrandizement; the Israelites were not to receive either the honor of the conquest or the spoils of their enemies. They were to engage in the war solely as an act of obedience to God, for the purpose of executing His judgment upon the Amalekites. God intended that all nations should behold the doom of that people that had defied His sovereignty, and should mark that they were destroyed by the very people whom they had despised.

"Saul smote the Amalekites from Havilah until thou comest to Shur, that is over against Egypt. And he took Agag the king of the Amalekites alive, and utterly destroyed all the people with the edge of the sword. But Saul and the people spared Agag, and the best of the sheep, and of the oxen, and of the fatlings, and the lambs, and all that was good, and would not utterly destroy them: but everything that was vile and refuse, that they destroyed utterly."

This victory over the Amalekites was the most brilliant victory that Saul had ever gained, and it served to rekindle the pride of heart that was his greatest peril. The divine edict devoting the enemies of God to utter destruction was but partially fulfilled. Ambitious to heighten the honor of his triumphal return by the presence of a royal captive, Saul ventured to imitate the customs of the nations around him and spared Agag, the fierce and warlike king of the Amalekites. The people reserved for themselves the finest of the flocks, herds, and beasts of burden, excusing their sin on the ground that the cattle were reserved to be offered as sacrifices to the Lord. It was their purpose, however, to use these merely as a substitute, to save their own cattle.

Saul had now been subjected to the final test. His presumptuous disregard of the will of God, showing his determination to rule as an independent monarch, proved that he could not be trusted with royal power as the vicegerent of the Lord. While Saul and his army were marching home in the flush of victory, there was deep anguish in the home of Samuel the prophet. He had received a message from the Lord denouncing the course of the king: "It repenteth Me that I have set up Saul to be king: for he is turned back from following Me, and hath not performed My commandments." The prophet was deeply grieved over the course of the rebellious king, and he wept and prayed all night for a reversing of the terrible sentence.

God's repentance is not like man's repentance. "The Strength of Israel will not lie nor repent: for He is not a man, that He should repent." Man's repentance implies a change of mind. God's repentance implies a change of circumstances and relations. Man may change his relation to God by complying with the conditions upon which he may be brought into the divine favor, or he may, by his own action, place himself outside the favoring condition; but the Lord is the same "yesterday, and today, and forever." Hebrews 13:8. Saul's disobedience changed his relation to God; but the conditions of acceptance with God were unaltered—God's requirements were still the same, for with Him there "is no variableness, neither shadow of turning." James 1:17.

With an aching heart the prophet set forth the next morning to meet the erring king. Samuel cherished a hope that, upon reflection, Saul might become conscious of his sin, and by repentance and humiliation be again restored to the divine favor. But when the first step is taken in the path of transgression the way becomes easy. Saul, debased by his disobedience, came to meet Samuel with a lie upon his lips. He exclaimed, "Blessed be thou of the Lord: I have performed the commandment of the Lord."

The sounds that fell on the prophet's ears disproved the statement of the disobedient king. To the pointed question, "What meaneth then this bleating of the sheep in mine ears, and the lowing of the oxen which I hear?" Saul made answer, "They have brought them from the Amalekites: for the people spared the best of the sheep and of the oxen, to sacrifice unto the Lord thy God; and the rest we have utterly destroyed." The people had obeyed Saul's directions; but in order to shield himself, he was willing to charge upon them the sin of his disobedience.

The message of Saul's rejection brought unspeakable grief to the heart of Samuel. It had to be delivered before the whole army of Israel, when they were filled with pride and triumphal rejoicing over a victory that was accredited to the valor and generalship of their king, for Saul had not associated God with the success of Israel in this conflict; but when the prophet saw the evidence of Saul's rebellion, he was stirred with indignation that he, who had been so highly favored of God, should transgress the commandment of Heaven and lead Israel into sin. Samuel was not deceived by the subterfuge of the king. With mingled grief and indignation he declared, "Stay, and I will tell thee what the Lord hath said to me this night. . . . When thou wast little in thine own sight, wast thou not made the head of the tribes of Israel, and the Lord anointed thee king over Israel?" He repeated the command of the Lord concerning Amalek, and demanded the reason of the king's disobedience.

Saul persisted in self-justification: "Yea, I have obeyed the voice of the Lord, and have gone the way which the Lord sent me, and have brought Agag the king of Amalek, and have utterly destroyed the Amalekites. But the people took of the spoil, sheep and oxen, the chief of the things which should have been utterly destroyed, to sacrifice unto the Lord thy God in Gilgal."

In stern and solemn words the prophet swept away the refuge of lies and pronounced the irrevocable sentence: "Hath the Lord as great delight in burnt offerings and sacrifices, as in obeying the voice of the Lord? Behold, to obey is better than sacrifice, and to hearken than the fat of rams. For rebellion is as the sin of witchcraft, and stubbornness is as iniquity and idolatry. Because thou hast rejected the word of the Lord, He hath also rejected thee from being king."

As the king heard this fearful sentence he cried out, "I have sinned: for I have transgressed the commandment of the Lord, and thy words: because I feared the people, and obeyed their voice." Terrified by the denunciation of the prophet, Saul acknowledged his guilt, which he had before stubbornly denied; but he still persisted in casting blame upon the people, declaring that he had sinned through fear of them.

It was not sorrow for sin, but fear of its penalty, that actuated the king of Israel as he entreated Samuel, "I pray thee, pardon my sin, and turn again with me, that I may worship the Lord." If Saul had had true repentance, he would have made public confession of his sin; but it was his chief anxiety to maintain his authority and retain the allegiance of the people. He desired the honor of Samuel's presence in order to strengthen his own influence with the nation.

"I will not return with thee," was the answer of the prophet: "for thou hast rejected the word of the Lord, and the Lord hath rejected thee from being king over Israel." As Samuel turned to depart, the king, in an agony of fear, laid hold of his mantle to hold him back, but it rent in his hands. Upon this, the prophet declared, "The Lord hath rent the kingdom of Israel from thee this day, and hath given it to a neighbor of thine, that is better than thou."

Saul was more disturbed by the alienation of Samuel than

by the displeasure of God. He knew that the people had greater confidence in the prophet than in himself. Should another by divine command be now anointed king, Saul felt that it would be impossible to maintain his own authority. He feared an immediate revolt should Samuel utterly forsake him. Saul entreated the prophet to honor him before the elders and the people by publicly uniting with him in a religious service. By divine direction Samuel yielded to the king's request, that no occasion might be given for a revolt. But he remained only as a silent witness of the service.

An act of justice, stern and terrible, was yet to be performed. Samuel must publicly vindicate the honor of God and rebuke the course of Saul. He commanded that the king of the Amalekites be brought before him. Above all who had fallen by the sword of Israel, Agag was the most guilty and merciless; one who had hated and sought to destroy the people of God, and whose influence had been strongest to promote idolatry. He came at the prophet's command, flattering himself that the danger of death was past. Samuel declared: "As thy sword hath made women childless, so shall thy mother be childless among women. And Samuel hewed Agag in pieces before the Lord." This done, Samuel returned to his home at Ramah, Saul to his at Gibeah. Only once thereafter did the prophet and the king ever meet each other.

When called to the throne, Saul had a humble opinion of his own capabilities, and was willing to be instructed. He was deficient in knowledge and experience and had serious defects of character. But the Lord granted him the Holy Spirit as a guide and helper, and placed him in a position where he could develop the qualities requisite for a ruler of Israel. Had he remained humble, seeking constantly to be guided by divine wisdom, he would have been enabled to discharge the duties of his high position with success and honor. Under the influence of divine grace every good quality would have been gaining strength, while evil tendencies would have lost their power. This is the work which the Lord proposes to do for all who consecrate themselves to Him. There are many whom He has called to positions in His work because they have a humble and teachable spirit. In His providence He places them where they may learn of Him. He will reveal to them their defects of character, and to all who seek His aid He will give strength to correct their errors.

But Saul presumed upon his exaltation, and dishonored God by unbelief and disobedience. Though when first called to the throne he was humble and self-distrustful, success made him self-confident. The very first victory of his reign had kindled that pride of heart which was his greatest danger. The valor and military skill displayed in the deliverance of Jabesh-gilead had roused the enthusiasm of the whole nation. The people honored their king, forgetting that he was but the agent by whom God had wrought; and though at first Saul ascribed the glory to God, he afterward took honor to himself. He lost sight of his dependence upon God, and in heart departed from the Lord. Thus the way was prepared for his sin of presumption and sacrilege at Gilgal. The same blind self-confidence led him to reject Samuel's reproof. Saul acknowledged Samuel to be a prophet sent from God; hence he should have accepted the reproof, though he could not himself see that he had sinned. Had he been willing to see and confess his error, this bitter experience would have proved a safeguard for the future.

If the Lord had then separated Himself entirely from Saul, He would not have again spoken to him through His prophet, entrusting him with a definite work to perform, that he might correct the errors of the past. When one who professes to be a child of God becomes careless in doing His will, thereby influencing others to be irreverent and unmindful of the Lord's injunctions, it is still possible for his failures to be turned into victories if he will but accept reproof with true contrition of soul and return to God in humility and faith. The humiliation of defeat often proves a blessing by showing us our inability to do the will of God without His aid.

When Saul turned away from the reproof sent him by God's Holy Spirit, and persisted in his stubborn self-justification, he rejected the only means by which God could work to save him from himself. He had willfully separated himself from God. He could not receive divine help or guidance until he should return to God by confession of his sin.

At Gilgal, Saul had made an appearance of great conscientiousness, as he stood before the army of Israel offering up a sacrifice to God. But his piety was not genuine. A religious service performed in direct opposition to the command of God only served to weaken Saul's hands, placing him beyond the help that God was so willing to grant him.

In his expedition against Amalek, Saul thought he had done all that was essential of that which the Lord had commanded him; but the Lord was not pleased with partial obedience, nor willing to pass over what had been neglected through so plausible a motive. God has given men no liberty to depart from His requirements. The Lord had declared to Israel, "Ye shall not do . . . every man whatsoever is right in his own eyes;" but ye shall "observe and hear all these words which I command thee." Deuteronomy 12:8, 28. In deciding upon any course of action we are not to ask whether we can see that harm will result from it, but whether it is in keeping with the will of God. "There is a way which seemeth right unto a man; but the end thereof are the ways of death." Proverbs 14:12.

"To obey is better than sacrifice." The sacrificial offerings were in themselves of no value in the sight of God. They were designed to express on the part of the offerer penitence for sin and faith in Christ and to pledge future obedience to the law of God. But without penitence, faith, and an obedient heart, the offerings were worthless. When, in direct violation of God's command, Saul proposed to present a sacrifice of that which God had devoted to destruction, open contempt was shown for the divine authority. The service would have been an insult to Heaven. Yet with the sin of Saul and its result before us, how many are pursuing a similar course. While they refuse to believe and obey some requirement of the Lord, they persevere in offering up to God their formal services of religion. There is no response of the Spirit of God to such service. No matter how zealous men may be in their observance of religious ceremonies, the Lord cannot accept them if they persist in willful violation of one of His commands.

"Rebellion is as the sin of witchcraft, and stubbornness is as iniquity and idolatry." Rebellion originated with Satan, and all rebellion against God is directly due to satanic influence. Those who set themselves against the government of God have entered into an alliance with the archapostate, and he will exercise his power and cunning to captivate the senses and mislead the understanding. He will cause everything to appear in a false light. Like our first parents, those who are under his bewitching spell see only the great benefits to be received by transgression.

No stronger evidence can be given of Satan's delusive power than that many who are thus led by him deceive themselves with the belief that they are in the service of God. When Korah, Dathan, and Abiram rebelled against the authority of Moses, they thought they were opposing only a human leader, a man like themselves; and they came to believe that they were verily doing God service. But in rejecting God's chosen instrument they rejected Christ; they insulted the Spirit of God. So, in the days of Christ, the Jewish scribes and elders, who professed great zeal for the honor of God, crucified His Son. The same spirit still exists in the hearts of those who set themselves to follow their own will in opposition to the will of God.

Saul had had the most ample proof that Samuel was divinely inspired. His venturing to disregard the command of God through the prophet was against the dictates of reason and sound judgment. His fatal presumption must be attributed to satanic sorcery. Saul had manifested great zeal in suppressing idolatry and witchcraft; yet in his disobedience to the divine command he had been actuated by the same spirit of opposition to God and had been as really inspired by Satan as are those who practice sorcery; and when reproved, he had added stubbornness to rebellion. He could have offered no greater insult to the Spirit of God had he openly united with idolaters.

It is a perilous step to slight the reproofs and warnings of God's word or of His Spirit. Many, like Saul, yield to temptation until they become blind to the true character of sin. They flatter themselves that they have had some good object in view, and have done no wrong in departing from the Lord's requirements. Thus they do despite to the Spirit of grace, until its voice is no longer heard, and they are left to the delusions which they have chosen.

In Saul, God had given to Israel a king after their own heart, as Samuel said when the kingdom was confirmed to Saul at Gilgal, "Behold the king whom ye have chosen, and whom ye have desired." 1 Samuel 12:13. Comely in person, of noble stature and princely bearing, his appearance accorded with their conceptions of royal dignity; and his personal valor and his ability in the conduct of armies were the qualities which they regarded as best calculated to secure respect and honor from other nations. They felt little solicitude that their king should possess those higher qualities which alone could fit him to rule which justice and equity. They did not ask for one who had true nobility of character, who possessed the love and fear of God. They had not sought counsel from God as to the qualities a ruler should possess, in order to preserve their distinctive, holy character as His chosen people. They were not seeking God's way, but their own way. Therefore God gave them such a king as they desired—one whose character was a reflection of their own. Their hearts were not in submission to God, and their king also was unsubdued by divine grace. Under the rule of this king they would obtain the experience necessary in order that they might see their error, and return to their allegiance to God.

Yet the Lord, having placed on Saul the responsibility of the kingdom, did not leave him to himself. He caused the Holy Spirit to rest upon Saul to reveal to him his own weakness and his need of divine grace; and had Saul relied upon God, God would have been with him. So long as his will was controlled by the will of God, so long as he yielded to the discipline of His Spirit, God could crown his efforts with success. But when Saul chose to act independently of God, the Lord could no longer be his guide, and was forced to set him aside. Then He called to the throne "a man after His own heart" (1 Samuel 13:14)—not one who was faultless in character, but who, instead of trusting to himself, would rely upon God, and be guided by His Spirit; who, when he sinned, would submit to reproof and correction.

The Anointing of David

A few miles south of Jerusalem, "the city of the great King," is Bethlehem, where David, the son of Jesse, was born more than a thousand years before the infant Jesus was cradled in the manger and worshiped by the Wise Men from the East. Centuries before the advent of the Saviour, David, in the freshness of boyhood, kept watch of his flocks as they grazed on the hills surrounding Bethlehem. The simple shepherd boy sang the songs of his own composing, and the music of his harp made a sweet accompaniment to the melody of his fresh young voice. The Lord had chosen David, and was preparing him, in his solitary life with his flocks, for the work He designed to commit to his trust in after years.

While David was thus living in the retirement of his humble shepherd's life, the Lord God was speaking about him to the prophet Samuel. "And the Lord said unto Samuel, How long wilt thou mourn for Saul, seeing I have rejected him from reigning over Israel? fill thine horn with oil, and go, I will send thee to Jesse the Bethlehemite: for I have provided Me a king among his sons. . . . Take an heifer with thee, and say, I am come to sacrifice to the Lord. And call Jesse to the sacrifice, and I will show thee what thou shalt do: and thou shalt anoint unto Me him whom I name unto thee. And Samuel did that which the Lord spake, and came to

Bethlehem. And the elders of the town trembled at his coming, and said, Comest thou peaceably? And he said, Peaceably." The elders accepted an invitation to the sacrifice, and Samuel called also Jesse and his sons. The altar was built and the sacrifice was ready. All the household of Jesse were present, with the exception of David, the youngest son, who had been left to guard the sheep, for it was not safe to leave the flocks unprotected.

When the sacrifice was ended, and before partaking of the offering feast, Samuel began his prophetic inspection of the noble-appearing sons of Jesse. Eliab was the eldest, and more nearly resembled Saul for stature and beauty than the others. His comely features and finely developed form attracted the attention of the prophet. As Samuel looked upon his princely bearing, he thought, "This is indeed the man whom God has chosen as successor to Saul," and he waited for the divine sanction that he might anoint him. But Jehovah did not look upon the outward appearance. Eliab did not fear the Lord. Had he been called to the throne, he would have been a proud, exacting ruler. The Lord's word to Samuel was, "Look not on his countenance, or on the height of his stature; because I have refused him: for the Lord seeth not as man seeth; for man looketh on the outward appearance, but the Lord looketh on the heart." No outward beauty can recommend the soul to God. The wisdom and excellence revealed in the character and deportment, express the true beauty of the man; and it is the inner worth, the excellency of the heart, that determines our acceptance with the Lord of hosts. How deeply should we feel this truth in the judgment of ourselves and others. We may learn from the mistake of Samuel how vain is the estimation that rests on beauty of face or nobility of stature. We may see how incapable is man's wisdom of understanding the secrets of the heart or of comprehending the counsels of God without special enlightenment from heaven. The thoughts and ways of God in relation to His creatures are above our finite minds; but we may be assured that His children will be brought to fill the very place for which they are qualified, and will be enabled to accomplish the very work committed to their hands, if they will but submit their will to God, that His beneficent plans may not be frustrated by the perversity of man.

Eliab passed from the inspection of Samuel, and the six brothers who were in attendance at the service followed in succession to be observed by the prophet; but the Lord did not signify His choice of any one of them. With painful suspense Samuel had looked upon the last of the young men; the prophet was perplexed and bewildered. He inquired of Jesse, "Are here all thy children?" The father answered, "There remaineth yet the youngest, and behold, he keepeth the sheep." Samuel directed that he should be summoned, saying, "We will not sit down till he come hither."

The lonely shepherd was startled by the unexpected call of the messenger, who announced that the prophet had come to Bethlehem and had sent for him. With surprise he questioned why the prophet and judge of Israel should desire to see him; but without delay he obeyed the call. "Now he was ruddy, and withal of a beautiful countenance, and goodly to look to." As Samuel beheld with pleasure the handsome, manly, modest shepherd boy, the voice of the Lord spoke to the prophet, saying, "Arise, anoint him: for this is he." David had proved himself brave and faithful in the humble office of a shepherd, and now God had chosen him to be captain of His people. "Then Samuel took the horn of oil, and anointed him in the midst of his brethren: and the Spirit of the Lord came upon David from that day forward." The prophet had accomplished his appointed work, and with a relieved heart he returned to Ramah.

Samuel had not made known his errand, even to the family of Jesse, and the ceremony of anointing David had been performed in secret. It was an intimation to the youth of the high destiny awaiting him, that amid all the varied experiences and perils of his coming years, this knowledge might inspire him to be true to the purpose of God to be accomplished by his life.

The great honor conferred upon David did not serve to elate him. Notwithstanding the high position which he was to occupy, he quietly continued his employment, content to await the development of the Lord's plans in His own time and way. As humble and modest as before his anointing, the shepherd boy returned to the hills and watched and guarded his flocks as tenderly as ever. But with new inspiration he composed his melodies and played upon his harp. Before him spread a landscape of rich and varied beauty. The vines, with their clustering fruit, brightened in the sunshine. The forest trees, with their green foliage, swayed in the breeze. He beheld the sun flooding the heavens with light, coming forth as a bridegroom out of his chamber and rejoicing as a strong man to run a race. There were the bold summits of the hills reaching toward the sky; in the faraway distance rose the barren cliffs of the mountain wall of Moab; above all spread the tender blue of the overarching heavens. And beyond was God. He could not see Him, but His works were full of His praise. The light of day, gilding forest and mountain, meadow and stream, carried the mind up to behold the Father of lights, the Author of every good and perfect gift. Daily revelations of the character and majesty of his Creator filled the young poet's heart with adoration and rejoicing. In contemplation of God and His works the faculties of David's mind and heart were developing and strengthening for the work of his afterlife. He was daily coming into a more intimate communion with God. His mind was constantly penetrating into new depths for fresh themes to inspire his song and to wake the music of his harp. The rich melody of his voice poured out upon the air, echoed from the hills as if responsive to the rejoicing of the angels' songs in heaven.

Who can measure the results of those years of toil and wandering among the lonely hills? The communion with nature and with God, the care of his flocks, the perils and deliverances, the griefs and joys, of his lowly lot, were not only to mold the character of David and to influence his future life, but through the psalms of Israel's sweet singer they were in all coming ages to kindle love and faith in the hearts of God's people, bringing them nearer to the ever-loving heart of Him in whom all His creatures live.

David, in the beauty and vigor of his young manhood, was preparing to take a high position with the noblest of the earth. His talents, as precious gifts from God, were employed to extol the glory of the divine Giver. His opportunities of contemplation and meditation served to enrich him with that wisdom and piety that made him beloved of God and angels. As he contemplated the perfections of his Creator, clearer conceptions of God, opened before his soul. Obscure themes were illuminated, difficulties were made plain, perplexities were harmonized, and each ray of new light called forth fresh bursts of rapture, and sweeter anthems of devotion, to the glory of God and the Redeemer. The love that moved him, the sorrows that beset him, the triumphs that attended him, were all themes for his active thought; and as he beheld the love of God in all the providences of his life, his heart throbbed with more fervent adoration and gratitude, his voice rang out in a richer melody, his harp was swept with more exultant joy; and the shepherd boy proceeded from strength to strength, from knowledge to knowledge; for the Spirit of the Lord was upon him.

David and Goliath

When King Saul realized that he had been rejected by God, and when he felt the force of the words of denunciation that had been addressed to him by the prophet, he was filled with bitter rebellion and despair. It was not true repentance that had bowed the proud head of the king. He had no clear perception of the offensive character of his sin, and did not arouse to the work of reforming his life, but brooded over what he thought was the injustice of God in depriving him of the throne of Israel and in taking the succession away from his posterity. He was ever occupied in the anticipating the ruin that had been brought upon his house. He felt that the valor which he had displayed in encountering his enemies should offset his sin of disobedience. He did not accept with meekness the chastisement of God; but his haughty spirit became desperate, until he was on the verge of losing his reason. His counselors advised him to seek for the services of a skillful musician, in the hope that the soothing notes of a sweet instrument might calm his troubled spirit. In the providence of God, David, as a skillful performer upon the harp, was brought before the king. His lofty and heaven-inspired strains had the desired effect. The brooding melancholy that had settled like a dark cloud over the mind of Saul was charmed away.

When his services were not required at the court of Saul, David returned to his flocks among the hills and continued to maintain his simplicity of spirit and demeanor. Whenever it was necessary, he was recalled to minister before the king, to soothe the mind of the troubled monarch till the evil spirit

should depart from him. But although Saul expressed delight in David and his music, the young shepherd went from the king's house to the fields and hills of his pasture with a sense of relief and gladness.

David was growing in favor with God and a man. He had been instructed in the way of the Lord, and he now set his heart more fully to do the will of God than ever before. He had new themes for thought. He had been in the court of the king and had seen the responsibilities of royalty. He had discovered some of the temptations that beset the soul of Saul and had penetrated some of the mysteries in the character and dealings of Israel's first king. He had seen the glory of royalty shadowed with a dark cloud of sorrow, and he knew that the household of Saul, in their private life, were far from happy. All these things served to bring troubled thoughts to him who had been anointed to be king over Israel. But while he was absorbed in deep meditation, and harassed by thoughts of anxiety, he turned to his harp, and called forth strains that elevated his mind to the Author of every good, and the dark clouds that seemed to shadow the horizon of the future were dispelled.

God was teaching David lessons of trust. As Moses was trained for his work, so the Lord was fitting the son of Jesse to become the guide of His chosen people. In his watchcare for his flocks, he was gaining an appreciation of the care that the Great Shepherd has for the sheep of His pasture.

The lonely hills and the wild ravines where David wandered with his flocks were the lurking place of beasts of prey. Not infrequently the lion from the thickets by the Jordan, or the bear from his lair among the hills, came, fierce with hunger, to attack the flocks. According to the custom of his time, David was armed only with his sling and shepherd's staff; yet he early gave proof of his strength and courage in protecting his charge. Afterward describing these encounters, he said: "When there came a lion, or a bear, and took a lamb out of the flock, I went out after him, and smote him, and delivered it out of his mouth: and when he arose against me, I caught him by his beard, and smote him, and slew him." 1 Samuel 17:34, 35, R.V. His experience in these matters proved the heart of David and developed in him courage and fortitude and faith.

Even before he was summoned to the court of Saul, David had distinguished himself by deeds of valor. The officer who brought him to the notice of the king declared him to be "a mighty valiant man, and a man of war, and prudent in matters," and he said, "The Lord is with him."

When war was declared by Israel against the Philistines, three of the sons of Jesse joined the army under Saul; but David remained at home. After a time, however, he went to visit the camp of Saul. By his father's direction he was to carry a message and a gift to his elder brothers and to learn if they were still in safety and health. But, unknown to Jesse, the youthful shepherd had been entrusted with a higher mission. The armies of Israel were in peril, and David had been directed by an angel to save his people.

As David drew near to the army, he heard the sound of commotion, as if an engagement was about to begin. And "the host was going forth to the fight, and shouted for the battle." Israel and the Philistines were drawn up in array, army against army. David ran to the army, and came and saluted his brothers. While he was talking with them, Goliath, the champion of the Philistines, came forth, and with insulting language defied Israel and challenged them to provide a man from their ranks who would meet him in single combat. He repeated his challenge, and when David saw that all Israel were filled with fear, and learned that the Philistine's defiance was hurled at them day after day, without arousing a champion to silence the boaster, his spirit was stirred within him. He was fired with zeal to preserve the honor of the living God and the credit of His people.

The armies of Israel were depressed. Their courage failed. They said one to another, "Have ye seen this man that is come up? surely to defy Israel is he come up." In shame and indignation, David exclaimed, "Who is this uncircumcised Philistine, that he should defy the armies of the living God?"

Eliab, David's eldest brother, when he heard these words, knew well the feelings that were stirring the young man's soul. Even as a shepherd, David had manifested daring, courage, and strength but rarely witnessed; and the mysterious visit of Samuel to their father's house, and his silent departure, had awakened in the minds of the brothers suspicions of the real object of his visit. Their jealousy had been aroused as they saw David honored above them, and they did not regard him with the respect and love due to his integrity and brotherly tenderness. They looked upon him as merely a stripling shepherd, and now the question which he asked was regarded by Eliab as a censure upon his own cowardice in making no attempt to silence the giant of the Philistines. The elder brother exclaimed angrily, "Why camest thou down hither? and with whom hast thou left those few sheep in the wilderness? I know thy pride, and the naughtiness of thine heart; for thou art come down that thou mightest see the battle." David's answer was respectful but decided: "What have I now done? Is there not a cause?"

The words of David were repeated to the king, who summoned the youth before him. Saul listened with astonishment to the words of the shepherd, as he said, "Let no man's heart fail because of him; thy servant will go and fight with this Philistine." Saul strove to turn David from his purpose, but the young man was not to be moved. He replied in a simple, unassuming way, relating his experiences while guarding his father's flocks. And he said, "The Lord that delivered me out of the paw of the lion, and out of the paw of the bear, He will deliver me out of the hand of this Philistine. And Saul said unto David, Go, and the Lord be with thee."

For forty days the host of Israel had trembled before the haughty challenge of the Philistine giant. Their hearts failed within them as they looked upon his massive form, in height measuring six cubits and a span. Upon his head was a helmet of brass, he was clothed with a coat of mail that weighed five thousand shekels, and he had greaves of brass upon his legs. The coat was made of plates of brass that overlaid one another, like the scales of a fish, and they were so closely joined that no dart or arrow could possibly penetrate the armor. At his back the giant bore a huge javelin, or lance, also of brass. "The staff of his spear was like a weaver's beam; and his spear's head weighed six hundred shekels of iron; and one bearing a shield went before him."

Morning and evening Goliath had approached the camp of Israel, saying with a loud voice, "Why are ye come out to set your battle in array? am not I a Philistine, and ye servants to Saul? choose you a man for you, and let him come down to me. If he be able to fight with me, and to kill me, then will we be your servants: but if I prevail against him, and kill him, then shall ye be our servants, and serve us. And the Philistine said, I defy the armies of Israel this day; give me a man, that we may fight together."

Though Saul had given David permission to accept Goliath's challenge, the king had small hope that David would be successful in his courageous undertaking. Command was given to clothe the youth in the king's own armor. The heavy helmet of brass was put upon his head, and the coat of mail was placed upon his body; the monarch's sword was at his side. Thus equipped, he started upon his errand, but erelong began to retrace his steps. The first thought in the minds of the anxious spectators was that David had decided not to risk his life in meeting an antagonist in so unequal an encounter. But this was far from the thought of the brave young man. When he returned to Saul he begged permission to lay aside the heavy armor, saying, "I cannot go with these; for I have not proved them." He laid off the king's armor, and in its stead took only his staff in his hand, with his shepherd's scrip and a simple sling. Choosing five smooth stones out of the brook, he put them in his bag, and, with his sling in his hand, drew near to the Philistine. The giant strode boldly forward, expecting to meet the mightiest of the warriors of Israel. His armor-bearer walked before him, and he looked as if nothing could withstand him. As he came nearer to David he saw but a stripling, called a boy because of his youth. David's countenance was ruddy with health, and his well-knit form, unprotected by armor, was displayed to advantage; yet between its youthful outline and the massive proportions of the Philistine, there was a marked contrast.

Goliath was filled with amazement and anger. "Am I a dog," he exclaimed, "that thou comest to me with staves?" Then he poured upon David the most terrible curses by all the gods of his knowledge. He cried in derision, "Come to me, and I will give thy flesh unto the fowls of the air, and to the beasts of the field."

David did not weaken before the champion of the Philistines. Stepping forward, he said to his antagonist: "Thou comest to me with a sword, and with a spear, and with a shield: but I come to thee in the name of the Lord of hosts, the God of the armies of Israel, whom thou hast defied. This day will the Lord deliver thee into mine hand; and I will smite thee, and take thine head from thee; and I will give the carcasses of the host of the Philistines this day unto the fowls of the air, and to the wild beasts of the earth; that all the earth may know that there is a God in Israel. And all this assembly shall know that the Lord saveth not with sword and spear: for the battle is the Lord's, and He will give you into our hands."

There was a ring of fearlessness in his tone, a look of triumph and rejoicing upon his fair countenance. This speech, given in a clear, musical voice, rang out on the air, and was distinctly heard by the listening thousands marshaled for war. The anger of Goliath was roused to the very highest heat. In his rage he pushed up the helmet that protected his forehead and rushed forward to wreak vengeance upon his opponent. The son of Jesse was preparing for his foe. "And it came to pass, when the Philistine arose, and came and drew nigh to meet David, that David hasted, and ran toward the army to meet the Philistine. And David put his hand in his bag, and took thence a stone, and slang it, and smote the Philistine in the forehead, that the stone sunk into his forehead; and he fell upon his face to the earth."

Amazement spread along the lines of the two armies. They had been confident that David would be slain; but when the stone went whizzing through the air, straight to the mark, they saw the mighty warrior tremble, and reach forth his hands, as if he were struck with sudden blindness. The giant reeled, and staggered, and like a smitten oak, fell to the ground. David did not wait an instant. He sprang upon the prostrate form of the Philistine, and with both hands laid hold of Goliath's heavy sword. A moment before, the giant had boasted that with it he would sever the youth's head from his shoulders and give his body to the fowls of the air. Now it was lifted in the air, and then the head of the boaster rolled from his trunk, and a shout of exultation went up from the camp of Israel.

The Philistines were smitten with terror, and the conclusion which ensued resulted in a precipitate retreat. The shouts of the triumphant Hebrews echoed along the summits of the mountains, as they rushed after their fleeing enemies; and they "pursued the Philistines, until thou come to the valley, and to the gates of Ekron. And the wounded of the Philistines fell down by the way to Shaaraim, even unto Gath, and unto Ekron. And the children of Israel returned from chasing after the Philistines, and they spoiled their tents. And David took the head of the Philistine, and brought it to Jerusalem; but he put his armor in his tent."

David a Fugitive

After the slaying of Goliath, Saul kept David with him, and would not permit him to return to his father's house. And it came to pass that "the soul of Jonathan was knit with the soul of David, and Jonathan loved him as his own soul." Jonathan and David made a covenant to be united as brethren, and the king's son "stripped himself of the robe that was upon him, and gave it to David, and his garments, even to his sword, and

to his bow, and to his girdle." David was entrusted with important responsibilities, yet he preserved his modesty, and won the affection of the people as well as the royal household.

"David went out whithersoever Saul sent him, and behaved himself wisely: and Saul set him over the men of war." David was prudent and faithful, and it was evident that the blessing of God was with him. Saul at times realized his own unfitness for the government of Israel, and he felt that the kingdom would be more secure if there could be connected with him one who received instruction from the Lord. Saul hoped also that his connection with David would be a safeguard to himself. Since David was favored and shielded by the Lord, his presence might be a protection to Saul when he went out with him to war.

It was the providence of God that had connected David with Saul. David's position at court would give him a knowledge of affairs, in preparation for his future greatness. It would enable him to gain the confidence of the nation. The vicissitudes and hardships which befell him, through the enmity of Saul, would lead him to feel his dependence upon God, and to put his whole trust in Him. And the friendship of Jonathan for David was also of God's providence, to preserve the life of the future ruler of Israel. In all these things God was working out His gracious purposes, both for David and for the people of Israel.

Saul, however, did not long remain friendly to David. When Saul and David were returning from battle with the Philistines, "the women came out of all cities of Israel, singing and dancing, to meet King Saul, with tabrets, with joy, and with instruments of music." One company sang, "Saul hath slain his thousands," while another company took up the strain, and responded, "And David his ten thousands." The demon of jealousy entered the heart of the king. He was angry because David was exalted above himself in the song of the women of Israel. In place of subduing these envious feelings, he displayed the weakness of his character, and exclaimed. "They have ascribed unto David ten thousands, and to me they have ascribed but thousands: and what can he have more but the kingdom?"

One great defect in the character of Saul was his love of approbation. This trait had had a controlling influence over his actions and thoughts; everything was marked by his desire for praise and self-exaltation. His standard of right and wrong was the low standard of popular applause. No man is safe who lives that he may please men, and does not seek first for the approbation of God. It was the ambition of Saul to be first in the estimation of men; and when this song of praise was sung, a settled conviction entered the mind of the king that David would obtain the hearts of the people and reign in his stead.

Saul opened his heart to the spirit of jealousy by which his soul was poisoned. Notwithstanding the lessons which he had received from the prophet Samuel, instructing him that God would accomplish whatsoever He chose, and that no one could hinder it, the king made it evident that he had no true knowledge of the plans or power of God. The monarch of Israel was opposing his will to the will of the Infinite One. Saul had not learned, while ruling the kingdom of Israel, that he should rule his own spirit. He allowed his impulses to control his judgment, until he was plunged into a fury of passion. He had paroxysms of rage, when he was ready to take the life of any who dared oppose his will. From this frenzy he would pass into a state of despondency and self-contempt, and remorse would take possession of his soul.

He loved to hear David play upon his harp, and the evil spirit seemed to be charmed away for the time; but one day when the youth was ministering before him, and bringing sweet music from his instrument, accompanying his voice as he sang the praises of God, Saul suddenly threw his spear at the musician, for the purpose of putting an end to his life. David was preserved by the interposition of God, and without injury fled from the rage of the maddened king.

As Saul's hatred of David increased, he became more and more watchful to find an opportunity to take his life; but none of his plans against the anointed of the Lord were successful. Saul gave himself up to the control of the wicked spirit that ruled over him; while David trusted in Him who is mighty in counsel, and strong to deliver. "The fear of the Lord is the beginning of wisdom" (Proverbs 9:10), and David's prayer was continually directed to God, that he might walk before Him in a perfect way.

Desiring to be freed from the presence of his rival, the king "removed him from him, and made him his captain over a thousand. . . . But all Israel and Judah loved David." The people were not slow to see that David was a competent person, and that the affairs entrusted to his hands were managed with wisdom and skill. The counsels of the young man were of a wise and discreet character, and proved to be safe to follow; while the judgment of Saul was at times unreliable, and his decisions were not wise.

Though Saul was ever on the alert for an opportunity to destroy David, he stood in fear of him, since it was evident that the Lord was with him. David's blameless character aroused the wrath of the king; he deemed that the very life and presence of David cast a reproach upon him, since by contrast it presented his own character to disadvantage. It was envy that made Saul miserable and put the humble subject of his throne in jeopardy. What untold mischief has this evil trait of character worked in our world! The same enmity existed in the heart of Saul that stirred the heart of Cain against his brother Abel, because Abel's works were righteous, and God honored him, and his own works were evil, and the Lord could not bless him. Envy is the offspring of pride, and if it is entertained in the heart, it will lead to hatred, and eventually to revenge and murder. Satan displayed his own character in exciting the fury of Saul against him who had never done him harm.

The king kept a strict watch upon David, hoping to find some occasion of indiscretion or rashness that might serve as an excuse to bring him into disgrace. He felt that he could not be satisfied until he could take the young man's life and still be justified before the nation for his evil act. He laid a snare for the feet of David, urging him to conduct the war against the Philistines with still greater vigor, and promising, as a reward of his valor, an alliance with the eldest daughter of the royal house. To this proposal David's modest answer was, "Who am I? and what is my life, or my father's family in Israel, that I should be son-in-law to the king?" The monarch manifested his insincerity by wedding the princess to another.

An attachment for David on the part of Michal, Saul's youngest daughter, afforded the king another opportunity to plot against his rival. Michal's hand was offered the young man on condition that evidence should be given of the defeat and slaughter of a specified number of their national foes. "Saul thought to make David fall by the hand of the Philistines," but God shielded His servant. David returned a victor from the battle, to become the king's son-in-law. "Michal Saul's daughter loved him," and the monarch, enraged, saw that his plots had resulted in the elevation of him whom he sought to destroy. He was still more assured that this was the man whom the Lord had said was better than he, and who should reign on the throne of Israel in his place. Throwing off all disguise, he issued a command to Jonathan and to the officers of the court to take the life of the one he hated.

Jonathan revealed the king's intention to David and bade him conceal himself while he would plead with his father to spare the life of the deliverer of Israel. He presented before the king what David had done to preserve the honor and even the life of the nation, and what terrible guilt would rest upon the murderer of the one whom God had used to scatter their enemies. The conscience of the king was touched, and his heart was softened. "And Saul sware, As the Lord liveth, he shall not be slain." David was brought to Saul, and he ministered in his presence, as he had done in the past.

Again war was declared between the Israelites and the Philistines, and David led the army against their enemies. A great victory was gained by the Hebrews, and the people of the realm praised his wisdom and heroism. This served to stir up the former bitterness of Saul against him. While the young man was playing before the king, filling the palace with sweet harmony, Saul's passion overcame him, and he hurled a javelin at David, thinking to pin the musician to the wall; but the angel of the Lord turned aside the deadly weapon. David escaped and fled to his own house. Saul sent spies that they might take him as he should come out in the morning, and put an end to his life.

Michal informed David of the purpose of her father. She urged him to flee for his life, and let him down from the window, thus enabling him to make his escape. He fled to Samuel at Ramah, and the prophet, fearless of the king's displeasure, welcomed the fugitive. The home of Samuel was a peaceful place in contrast with the royal palace. It was here, amid the hills, that the honored servant of the Lord continued his work. A company of seers was with him, and they studied closely the will of God and listened reverently to the words of instruction that fell from the lips of Samuel. Precious were the lessons that David learned from the teacher of Israel. David believed that the troops of Saul would not be ordered to invade this sacred place, but no place seemed to be sacred to the darkened mind of the desperate king. David's connection with Samuel aroused the jealousy of the king, lest he who was revered as a prophet of God throughout all Israel should lend his influence to the advancement of Saul's rival. When the king learned where David was, he sent officers to bring him to Gibeah, where he intended to carry out his murderous design.

The messengers went on their way, intent upon taking David's life; but One greater than Saul controlled them. They were met by unseen angels, as was Balaam when he was on his way to curse Israel. They began to utter prophetic sayings of what would occur in the future, and proclaimed the glory and majesty of Jehovah. Thus God overruled the wrath of man and manifested His power to restrain evil, while He walled in His servant by a guard of angels.

The tidings reached Saul as he eagerly waited to have David in his power; but instead of feeling the rebuke of God, he was still more exasperated, and sent other messengers. These also were overpowered by the Spirit of God, and united with the first in prophesying. The third embassage was sent by the king; but when they came into the company of the prophets, the divine influence fell upon them also, and they prophesied. Saul then decided that he himself would go, for his fierce enmity had become uncontrollable. He was determined to wait for no further chance to kill David; as soon as he should come within reach of him, he intended with his own hand to slay him, whatever might be the consequences.

But an angel of God met him on the way and controlled him. The Spirit of God held him in Its power, and he went forward uttering prayers to God, interspersed with predictions and sacred melodies. He prophesied of the coming Messiah as the world's Redeemer. When he came to the prophet's home in Ramah, he laid aside the outer garments that betokened his rank, and all day and all night he lay before Samuel and his pupils, under the influence of the divine Spirit. The people were drawn together to witness this strange scene, and the experience of the king was reported far and wide. Thus again, near the close of his reign, it became a proverb in Israel that Saul also was among the prophets.

Again the persecutor was defeated in his purpose. He assured David that he was at peace with him, but David had little confidence in the king's repentance. He took this opportunity to escape, lest the mood of the king should change, as formerly. His heart was wounded within him, and he longed to see his friend Jonathan once more. Conscious of his innocence, he sought the king's son and made a most touching appeal. "What have I done?" he asked, "what is mine iniquity? and what is my sin before thy father, that he seeketh my life?" Jonathan believed that his father had changed his purpose and no longer intended to take the life of David. And Jonathan said unto him, "God forbid; thou shalt not die: behold, my father will do nothing either great or small, but that he will show it me: and why should my father hide this thing from me? It is not so." After the remarkable exhibition of the power of God, Jonathan could not believe that his father would still harm David, since this would be manifest rebellion against God. But David was not convinced. With intense earnestness he declared to Jonathan, "As the Lord liveth, and as thy soul liveth, there is but a step between me and death."

At the time of the new moon a sacred festival was celebrated in Israel. This festival recurred upon the day following the interview between David and Jonathan. At this feast it was expected that both the young men would appear at the king's table; but David feared to be present, and it was arranged that he should visit his brothers in Bethlehem. On his return he was to hide himself in a field not far from the banqueting hall, for three days absenting himself from the presence of the king; and Jonathan would note the effect upon Saul. If inquiry should be made as to the whereabouts of the son of Jesse, Jonathan was to say that he had gone home to attend the sacrifice offered by his father's household. If no angry demonstrations were made by the king, but he should answer, "It is well," then it would be safe for David to return to the court. But if he should become enraged at his absence, it would decide the matter of David's flight.

On the first day of the feast the king made no inquiry concerning the absence of David; but when his place was vacant the second day, he questioned, "Wherefore cometh not the son of Jesse to meat, neither yesterday nor today? And Jonathan answered Saul, David earnestly asked leave of me to go to Bethlehem: and he said, Let me go, I pray thee; for our family hath a sacrifice in the city; and my brother, he hath commanded me to be there: and now, if I have found favor in thine eyes, let me get away, I pray thee, and see my brethren. Therefore he cometh not unto the king's table." When Saul heard these words, his anger was ungovernable. He declared that as long as David lived, Jonathan could not come to the throne of Israel, and he demanded that David should be sent for immediately, that he might be put to death. Jonathan again made intercession for his friend, pleading, "Wherefore shall he be slain? what hath he done?" This appeal to the king only made him more satanic in his fury, and the spear which he had intended for David he now hurled at his own son.

The prince was grieved and indignant, and leaving the royal presence, he was no more a guest at the feast. His soul was bowed down with sorrow as he repaired at the appointed time to the spot where David was to learn the king's intentions toward him. Each fell upon the other's neck, and they wept bitterly. The dark passion of the king cast its shadow upon the life of the young men, and their grief was too intense for expression. Jonathan's last words fell upon the ear of David as they separated to pursue their different paths, "Go in peace, forasmuch as we have sworn both of us in the name of the Lord, saying, The Lord be between me and thee, and between my seed and thy seed forever."

The king's son returned to Gibeah, and David hastened to reach Nob, a city but a few miles distant, and also belonging to the tribe of Benjamin. The tabernacle had been taken to this place from Shiloh, and here Ahimelech the high priest ministered. David knew not whither to flee for refuge, except to the servant of God. The priest looked upon him with astonishment, as he came in haste and apparently alone, with a countenance marked by anxiety and sorrow. He inquired what had brought him there. The young man was in constant fear of discovery, and in his extremity he resorted to deception. David told the priest that he had been sent by the king on a secret errand, one which required the utmost expedition. Here he manifested a want of faith in God, and his sin resulted in causing the death of the high priest. Had the facts been plainly stated, Ahimelech would have known what course to pursue to preserve his life. God requires that truthfulness shall mark His people, even in the greatest peril. David asked the priest for five loaves of bread. There was nothing but hallowed bread in the possession of the man of God, but David succeeded in removing his scruples, and obtained the bread to satisfy his hunger.

A new danger now presented itself. Doeg, the chief of Saul's herdsmen, who had professed the faith of the Hebrews, was now paying his vows in the place of worship. At sight of this man David determined to make haste to secure another place of refuge, and to obtain some weapon with which to defend himself if defense should become necessary. He asked Ahimelech for a sword, and was told that he had none except the sword of Goliath, which had been kept as a relic in the tabernacle. David replied, "There is none like that; give it me." His courage revived as he grasped the sword that he had once used in destroying the champion of the Philistines.

David fled to Achish, the king of Gath; for he felt that there was more safety in the midst of the enemies of his people than in the dominions of Saul. But it was reported to Achish that David was the man who had slain the Philistine champion years before; and now he who had sought refuge with the foes of Israel found himself in great peril. But, feigning madness, he deceived his enemies and thus made his escape.

The first error of David was his distrust of God at Nob, and his second mistake was his deception before Achish. David had displayed noble traits of character, and his moral worth had won him favor with the people; but as trial came upon him, his faith was shaken, and human weakness appeared. He saw in every man a spy and a betrayer. In a great emergency David had looked up to God with a steady eye of faith, and had vanquished the Philistine giant. He believed in God, he went in His name. But as he had been hunted and persecuted, perplexity and distress had nearly hidden his heavenly Father from his sight.

Yet this experience was serving to teach David wisdom; for it led him to realize his weakness and the necessity of constant dependence upon God. Oh, how precious is the sweet influence of the Spirit of God as it comes to depressed or despairing souls, encouraging the fainthearted, strengthening the feeble, and imparting courage and help to the tried servants of the Lord! Oh, what a God is ours, who deals gently with the erring and manifests His patience and tenderness in adversity, and when we are overwhelmed with some great sorrow!

Every failure on the part of the children of God is due to their lack of faith. When shadows encompass the soul, when we want light and guidance, we must look up; there is light beyond the darkness. David ought not to have distrusted God for one moment. He had cause for trusting in Him: he was the Lord's anointed, and in the midst of danger he had been protected by the angels of God; he had been armed with courage to do wonderful things; and if he had but removed his mind from the distressing situation in which he was placed, and had thought of God's power and majesty, he would have been at peace even in the midst of the shadows of death; he could with confidence have repeated the promise of the Lord, "The mountains shall depart, and the hills be removed; but My kindness shall not depart from thee, neither shall the covenant of My peace be removed." Isaiah 54:10.

Among the mountains of Judah, David sought refuge from the pursuit of Saul. He made good his escape to the cave of Adullam, a place that, with a small force, could be held against a large army. "And when his brethren and all his father's house heard it, they went down thither to him." The family of David could not feel secure, knowing that at any time the unreasonable suspicions of Saul might be directed against them on account of their relation to David. They had now learned—what was coming to be generally known in Israel—that God had chosen David as the future ruler of His people; and they believed that they would be safer with him, even though he was a fugitive in a lonely cave, than they could be while exposed to the insane madness of a jealous king.

In the cave of Adullam the family were united in sympathy and affection. The son of Jesse could make melody with voice and harp as he sang, "Behold, how good and how pleasant it is for brethren to dwell together in unity!" Psalm 133:1. He had tasted the bitterness of distrust on the part of his own brothers; and the harmony that had taken the place of discord brought joy to the exile's heart. It was here that David composed the fifty-seventh psalm.

It was not long before David's company was joined by others who desired to escape the exactions of the king. There were many who had lost confidence in the ruler of Israel, for they could see that he was no longer guided by the Spirit of the Lord. "And everyone that was in distress, and everyone that was in debt, and everyone that was discontented," resorted to David, "and he became a captain over them: and there were with him about four hundred men." Here David had a little kingdom of his own, and in it order and discipline prevailed. But even in his retreat in the mountains he was far from feeling secure, for he received continual evidence that the king had not relinquished his murderous purpose.

He found a refuge for his parents with the king of Moab, and then, at a warning of danger from a prophet of the Lord, he fled from his hiding place to the forest of Hareth. The experience through which David was passing was not unnecessary or fruitless. God was giving him a course of discipline to fit him to become a wise general as well as a just and merciful king. With his band of fugitives he was gaining a preparation to take up the work that Saul, because of his murderous passion and blind indiscretion, was becoming wholly unfitted to do. Men cannot depart from the counsel of God and still retain that calmness and wisdom which will enable them to act with justice and discretion. There is no insanity so dreadful, so hopeless, as that of following human wisdom, unguided by the wisdom of God.

Saul had been preparing to ensnare and capture David in the cave of Adullam, and when it was discovered that David had left this place of refuge, the king was greatly enraged. The flight of David was a mystery to Saul. He could account for it only by the belief that there had been traitors in his camp, who had informed the son of Jesse of his proximity and design.

He affirmed to his counselors that a conspiracy had been formed against him, and with the offer of rich gifts and positions of honor he bribed them to reveal who among his people had befriended David. Doeg the Edomite turned informer. Moved by ambition and avarice, and by hatred of the priest, who had reproved his sins, Doeg reported David's visit to Ahimelech, representing the matter in such a light as to kindle Saul's anger against the man of God. The words of that mischievous tongue, set on fire of hell, stirred up the worst passions in Saul's heart. Maddened with rage, he declared that the whole family of the priest should perish. And the terrible decree was executed. Not only Ahimelech, but the members of his father's house—"four-score and five persons that did wear a linen ephod"—were slain at the king's command, by the murderous hand of Doeg.

"And Nob, the city of the priests, smote he with the edge of the sword, both men and women, children and sucklings, and oxen, and asses, and sheep." This is what Saul could do under the control of Satan. When God had said that the iniquity of the Amalekites was full, and had commanded him to destroy them utterly, he thought himself too compassionate to execute the divine sentence, and he spared that which was devoted to destruction; but now, without a command from God, under the guidance of Satan, he could slay the priests of the Lord and bring ruin upon the inhabitants of Nob. Such is the perversity of the human heart that has refused the guidance of God.

This deed filled all Israel with horror. It was the king whom they had chosen that had committed this outrage, and he had only done after the manner of the kings of other nations that feared not God. The ark was with them, but the priests of whom they had inquired were slain with the sword. What would come next?

The Magnanimity of David

After Saul's atrocious slaughter of the priests of the Lord, "one of the sons of Ahimelech the son of Ahitub, named Abiathar, escaped, and fled after David. And Abiathar showed David that Saul had slain the Lord's priests. And David said unto Abiathar, I knew it that day, when Doeg the Edomite was there, that he would surely tell Saul: I have occasioned the death of all the persons of thy father's house. Abide thou with me, fear not: for he that seeketh my life seeketh thy life: but with me thou shalt be in safeguard."

Still hunted by the king, David found no place of rest or security. At Keilah his brave band saved the town from capture by the Philistines, but they were not safe, even among the people whom they had delivered. From Keilah they repaired to the wilderness of Ziph.

At this time, when there were so few bright spots in the path of David, he was rejoiced to receive an unexpected visit from Jonathan, who had learned the place of his refuge. Precious were the moments which these two friends passed in each other's society. They related their varied experiences, and Jonathan strengthened the heart of David, saying, "Fear not: for the hand of Saul my father shall not find thee; and thou shalt be king over Israel, and I shall be next unto thee; and that also Saul my father knoweth." As they talked of the wonderful dealings of God with David, the hunted fugitive was greatly encouraged. "And they two made a covenant before the Lord: and David abode in the wood, and Jonathan went to his house."

After the visit of Jonathan, David encouraged his soul with songs of praise, accompanying his voice with his harp as he sang:

"In the Lord put I my trust:
How say ye to my soul,
Flee as a bird to your mountain?
For, lo, the wicked bend their bow,
They make ready their arrow upon the string,
That they may privily shoot at the upright in heart.
If the foundations be destroyed,
What can the righteous do?
The Lord is in His holy temple,
The Lord's throne is in heaven:
His eyes behold, His eyelids try, the children of men.
The Lord trieth the righteous:
But the wicked and him that loveth violence His soul hateth." Psalm 11:1-5.

The Ziphites, into whose wild regions David went from Keilah, sent word to Saul in Gibeah that they knew where David was hiding, and that they would guide the king to his retreat. But David, warned of their intentions, changed his position, seeking refuge in the mountains between Maon and the Dead Sea.

Again word was sent to Saul, "Behold, David is in the wilderness of Engedi. Then Saul took three thousand chosen men out of all Israel, and went to seek David and his men upon the rocks of the wild goats." David had only six hundred men in his company, while Saul advanced against him with an army of three thousand. In a secluded cave the son of Jesse and his men waited for the guidance of God as to what should be done. As Saul was pressing his way up the mountains, he turned aside, and entered, alone, the very cavern in which David and his band were hidden. When David's men saw this they urged their leader to kill Saul. The fact that the king was now in their power was interpreted by them as certain evidence that God Himself had delivered the enemy into their hand, that they might destroy him. David was tempted to take this view of the matter; but the voice of conscience spoke to him, saying, "Touch not the anointed of the Lord."

David's men were still unwilling to leave Saul in peace, and they reminded their commander of the words of God, "Behold, I will deliver thine enemy into thine hand, that thou mayest do to him as it shall seem good unto thee. Then David arose, and cut off the skirt of Saul's robe privily." But his conscience smote him afterward, because he had even marred the garment of the king.

Saul rose up and went out of the cave to continue his search, when a voice fell upon his startled ears, saying, "My lord the king." He turned to see who was addressing him, and lo! it was the son of Jesse, the man whom he had so long desired to have in his power that he might kill him. David bowed himself to the king, acknowledging him as his master. Then he addressed Saul in these words: "Wherefore hearest thou men's words, saying, Behold, David seeketh thy hurt? Behold, this day thine eyes have seen how that the Lord hath delivered thee today into mine hand in the cave: and some bade me kill thee; but mine eye spared thee; and I said, I will not put forth mine hand against my lord; for he is the Lord's anointed. Moreover, my father, see, yea, see the skirt of thy robe in my hand: for in that I cut off the skirt of thy robe, and killed thee not, know thou and see that there is neither evil nor transgression in mine hand, and I have not sinned against thee; yet thou huntest my soul to take it."

When Saul heard the words of David he was humbled, and could not but admit their truthfulness. His feelings were deeply moved as he realized how completely he had been in the power of the man whose life he sought. David stood before him in conscious innocence. With a softened spirit, Saul exclaimed, "Is this thy voice, my son David? And Saul lifted up his voice, and wept." Then he declared to David: "Thou art more righteous than I: for thou hast rewarded me good, whereas I have rewarded thee evil. . . .For if a man find his enemy, will he let him go well away? wherefore the Lord reward thee good for that thou hast done unto me this day. And now, behold, I know well that thou shalt surely be king, and that the kingdom of Israel shall be established in thine hand." And David made a covenant with Saul that when this should take place he would favorably regard the house of Saul, and not cut off his name.

Knowing what he did of Saul's past course, David could put no confidence in the assurances of the king, nor hope that his penitent condition would long continue. So when Saul returned to his home David remained in the strongholds of the mountains.

The enmity that is cherished toward the servants of God by those who have yielded to the power of Satan changes at times to a feeling of reconciliation and favor, but the change does not always prove to be lasting. After evil-minded men have engaged in doing and saying wicked things against the Lord's servants, the conviction that they have been in the wrong sometimes takes deep hold upon their minds. The Spirit of the Lord strives with them, and they humble their hearts before God, and before those whose influence they have sought to destroy, and they may change their course toward them. But as they again open the door to the suggestions of the evil one, the old doubts are revived, the old enmity is awakened, and they return to engage in the same work which they repented of, and for a time abandoned. Again they speak evil, accusing and condemning in the bitterest manner the very ones to whom they made most humble confession. Satan can use such souls with far greater power after such a course has been pursued than he could before, because they have sinned against greater light.

"And Samuel died; and all the Israelites were gathered together, and lamented him, and buried him in his house at Ramah." The death of Samuel was regarded as an irreparable loss by the nation of Israel. A great and good prophet and an eminent judge had fallen in death, and the grief of the people was deep and heartfelt. From his youth up Samuel had walked before Israel in the integrity of his heart; although Saul had been the acknowledged king, Samuel had wielded a more powerful influence than he, because his record was one of faithfulness, obedience, and devotion. We read that he judged Israel all the days of his life.

As the people contrasted the course of Saul with that of Samuel, they saw what a mistake they had made in desiring a king that they might not be different from the nations around them. Many looked with alarm at the condition of society, fast becoming leavened with irreligion and godlessness. The example of their ruler was exerting a widespread influence, and well might Israel mourn that Samuel, the prophet of the Lord, was dead.

The nation had lost the founder and president of its sacred schools, but that was not all. It had lost him to whom the people had been accustomed to go with their great troubles—lost one who had constantly interceded with God in behalf of the best interests of its people. The intercession of Samuel had given a feeling of security; for "the effectual fervent prayer of a righteous man availeth much." James 5:16. The people felt now that God was forsaking them. The king seemed little less than a madman. Justice was perverted, and order was turned to confusion.

It was when the nation was racked with internal strife, when the calm, God-fearing counsel of Samuel seemed to be most needed, that God gave His aged servant rest. Bitter were the reflections of the people as they looked upon his quiet resting place, and remembered their folly in rejecting him as their ruler; for he had had so close a connection with Heaven that he seemed to bind all Israel to the throne of Jehovah. It was Samuel who had taught them to love and obey God; but now that he was dead, the people felt that they were left to the mercies of a king who was joined to Satan, and who would divorce the people from God and heaven.

David could not be present at the burial of Samuel, but he mourned for him as deeply and tenderly as a faithful son could mourn for a devoted father. He knew that Samuel's death had broken another bond of restraint from the actions of Saul, and he felt less secure than when the prophet lived. While the attention of Saul was engaged in mourning for the death of Samuel, David took the opportunity to seek a place of greater security; so he fled to the wilderness of Paran. It was here that he composed the one hundred and twentieth and twenty-first psalms. In these desolate wilds, realizing that the prophet was dead, and the king was his enemy, he sang:

"My help cometh from the Lord,
Which made heaven and earth.
He will not suffer thy foot to be moved:
He that keepeth thee will not slumber.
Behold, He that keepeth Israel
Shall neither slumber nor sleep. . . .
The Lord shall preserve thee from all evil:
He shall preserve thy soul.
The Lord shall preserve thy going out and thy coming in
From this time forth, and even forevermore."
Psalm 121:2-8.

While David and his men were in the wilderness of Paran, they protected from the depredations of marauders the flocks and herds of a wealthy man named Nabal, who had vast possessions in that region. Nabal was a descendant of Caleb, but his character was churlish and niggardly.

It was the time of sheepshearing, a season of hospitality. David and his men were in sore need of provisions; and in accordance with the custom of the times, the son of Jesse sent ten young men to Nabal, bidding them greet him in their master's name; and he added: "Thus shall ye say to him that liveth in prosperity, Peace be both to thee, and peace be to thine house, and peace be unto all that thou hast. And now I have heard that thou hast shearers: now thy shepherds which were with us, we hurt them not, neither was there aught missing unto them, all the while they were in Carmel. Ask thy young men, and they will show thee. Wherefore let the young men find favor in thine eyes; for we come in a good day: give, I pray thee, whatsoever cometh to thine hand unto thy servants, and to thy son David."

David and his men had been like a wall of protection to the shepherds and flocks of Nabal; and now this rich man was asked to furnish from his abundance some relief to the necessities of those who had done him such valuable service.

David and his men might have helped themselves from the flocks and herds, but they did not. They behaved themselves in an honest way. Their kindness, however, was lost upon Nabal. The answer he returned to David was indicative of his character: "Who is David? and who is the son of Jesse? There be many servants nowadays that break away every man from his master. Shall I then take my bread, and my water, and my flesh that I have killed for my shearers, and give it unto men, whom I know not whence they be?"

When the young men returned empty-handed and related the affair to David, he was filled with indignation. He commanded his men to equip themselves for an encounter; for he had determined to punish the man who had denied him what was his right, and had added insult to injury. This impulsive movement was more in harmony with the character of Saul than with that of David, but the son of Jesse had yet to learn of patience in the school of affliction.

One of Nabal's servants hastened to Abigail, the wife of Nabal, after he had dismissed David's young men, and told her what had happened. "Behold," he said, "David sent messengers out of the wilderness to salute our master; and he railed on them. But the men were very good unto us, and we were not hurt, neither missed we anything, as long as we were conversant with them, when we were in the fields. They were a wall unto us both by night and day, all the while we were with them keeping the sheep. Now therefore know and consider what thou wilt do; for evil is determined against our master, and against all his household."

Without consulting her husband or telling him of her intention, Abigail made up an ample supply of provisions, which, laded upon asses, she sent forward in the charge of servants, and herself started out to meet the band of David. She met them in a covert of a hill. "And when Abigail saw David, she hasted, and lighted off the ass, and fell before David on her face, and bowed herself to the ground, and fell at his feet, and said, Upon me, my lord, upon me let this iniquity be: and let thine handmaid, I pray thee, speak in thine audience." Abigail addressed David with as much reverence as though speaking to a crowned monarch. Nabal had scornfully exclaimed, "Who is David?" but Abigail called him, "my lord." With kind words she sought to sooth his irritated feelings, and she pleaded with him in behalf of her husband. With nothing of ostentation or pride, but full of the wisdom and love of God, Abigail revealed the strength of her devotion to her household; and she made it plain to David that the unkind course of her husband was in no wise premeditated against him as a personal affront, but was simply the outburst of an unhappy and selfish nature.

"Now therefore, my lord, as the Lord liveth, and as thy soul liveth, seeing the Lord hath withholden thee from coming to shed blood, and from avenging thyself with thine own hand, now let thine enemies, and they that seek evil to my lord, be as Nabal." Abigail did not take to herself the credit of this reasoning to turn David from his hasty purpose, but gave to God the honor and the praise. She then offered her rich provision as a peace offering to the men of David, and still pleaded as if she herself were the one who had so excited the resentment of the chief.

"I pray thee," she said, "forgive the trespass of thine handmaid: for the Lord will certainly make my lord a sure house; because my lord fighteth the battles of the Lord, and evil hath not been found in thee all thy days." Abigail presented by implication the course that David ought to pursue. He should fight the battles of the Lord. He was not to seek revenge for personal wrongs, even though persecuted as a traitor. She continued: "Though man be risen up to pursue thee, and to seek thy soul, yet the soul of my lord shall be bound in the bundle of life with the Lord thy God. . . . And it shall come to pass, when the Lord shall have done to my lord according to all the good that He hath spoken concerning thee, and shall have appointed thee prince over Israel; that this shall be no grief unto thee, nor offense of heart unto my lord, either that thou hast shed blood causeless, or that my lord hath avenged himself: and when the Lord shall have dealt well with my lord, then remember thine handmaid." 1 Samuel 25:29-31, R. V.

These words could have come only from the lips of one who had partaken of the wisdom from above. The piety of Abigail, like the fragrance of a flower, breathed out all unconsciously in face and word and action. The Spirit of the Son of God was abiding in her soul. Her speech, seasoned with grace, and full of kindness and peace, shed a heavenly influence. Better impulses came to David, and he trembled as he thought what might have been the consequences of his rash purpose. "Blessed are the peacemakers: for they shall be called the children of God." Matthew 5:9. Would that there were many more like this woman of Israel, who would soothe the irritated feelings, prevent rash impulses, and quell great evils by words of calm and well-directed wisdom.

A consecrated Christian life is ever shedding light and comfort and peace. It is characterized by purity, tact, simplicity, and usefulness. It is controlled by that unselfish love that sanctifies the influence. It is full of Christ, and leaves a track of light wherever its possessor may go. Abigail was a wise reprover and counselor. David's passion died away under the power of her influence and reasoning. He was convinced that he had taken an unwise course and had lost control of his own spirit.

With a humble heart he received the rebuke, in harmony with his own words, "Let the righteous smite me; it shall be a kindness: and let him reprove me; it shall be an excellent oil." Psalm 141:5. He gave thanks and blessings because she advised him righteously. There are many who, when they are reproved, think it praiseworthy if they receive the rebuke without becoming impatient; but how few take reproof with gratitude of heart and bless those who seek to save them from pursuing an evil course.

When Abigail returned home she found Nabal and his guests in the enjoyment of a great feast, which they had converted into a scene of drunken revelry. Not until the next morning did she relate to her husband what had occurred in her interview with David. Nabal was a coward at heart; and when he realized how near his folly had brought him to a sudden death, he seemed smitten with paralysis. Fearful that David would still pursue his purpose of revenge, he was filled with horror, and sank down in a condition of helpless insensibility. After ten days he died. The life that God had given him had been only a curse to the world. In the midst of his rejoicing and making merry, God had said to him, as He said to the rich man of the parable, "This night thy soul shall be required of thee." Luke 12:20.

David afterward married Abigail. He was already the husband of one wife, but the custom of the nations of his time had perverted his judgment and influenced his actions. Even great and good men have erred in following the practices of the world. The bitter result of marrying many wives was sorely felt throughout all the life of David.

After the death of Samuel, David was left in peace for a few months. Again he repaired to the solitude of the Ziphites; but these enemies, hoping to secure the favor of the king, informed him of David's hiding place. This intelligence aroused the demon of passion that had been slumbering in Saul's breast. Once more he summoned his men of arms and led them out in pursuit of David. But friendly spies brought tidings to the son of Jesse that Saul was again pursuing him; and with a few of his men, David started out to learn the location of his enemy. It was night when, cautiously advancing, they came upon the encampment, and saw before them the tents of the king and his attendants. They were unobserved, for the camp was quiet in slumber. David called upon his friends to go with him into the very midst of the foe. In answer to his question, "Who will go down with me to Saul to the camp?" Abishai promptly responded, "I will go down with thee."

Hidden by the deep shadows of the hills, David and his attendant entered the encampment of the enemy. As they sought to ascertain the exact number of their foes, they came upon Saul sleeping, his spear stuck in the ground, and a cruse of water at his head. Beside him lay Abner, his chief commander, and all around them were the soldiers, locked in slumber. Abishai raised his spear, and said to David, "God hath delivered thine enemy into thine hand this day: now therefore let me smite him, I pray thee, with the spear even to the earth at once, and I will not smite him the second time." He waited for the word of permission; but there fell upon his ear the whispered words: "Destroy him not: for who can stretch forth his hand against the Lord's anointed, and be guiltless? . . . As the Lord liveth, the Lord shall smite him; or his day shall come to die; or he shall descend into battle, and perish. The Lord forbid that I should stretch forth mine hand against the Lord's anointed: but, I pray thee, take thou now the spear that is at his bolster, and the cruse of water, and let us go. So David took the spear and the cruse of water from Saul's bolster; and they gat them away, and no man saw it, nor knew it, neither awaked: for they were all asleep; because a deep sleep from the Lord was fallen upon them." How easily the Lord can weaken the strongest, remove prudence from the wisest, and baffle the skill of the most watchful!

When David was at a safe distance from the camp he stood on the top of a hill and cried with a loud voice to the people and to Abner, saying, "Art not thou a valiant man? and who is like to thee in Israel? wherefore then hast thou not kept thy lord the king? for there came one of the people in to destroy the king thy lord. This thing is not good that thou hast done. As the Lord liveth, ye are worthy to die, because ye have not kept your master the Lord's anointed. And now see where the king's spear is, and the cruse of water that was at his bolster. And Saul knew David's voice, and said, Is this thy voice, my son David? And David said, It is my voice, my lord, O king. And he said, Wherefore doth my lord thus pursue after his servant? for what have I done? or what evil is in mine hand? Now therefore, I pray thee, let my lord the king hear the words of his servant." Again the acknowledgment fell from the lips of the king, "I have sinned: return, my son David; for I will no more do thee harm, because my soul was precious in thine eyes this day: behold, I have played the fool, and have erred exceedingly. And David answered and said, Behold the king's spear! and let one of the young men come over and fetch it." Although Saul had made the promise, "I will no more do thee harm," David did not place himself in his power.

The second instance of David's respect for his sovereign's life made a still deeper impression upon the mind of Saul and brought from him a more humble acknowledgment of his fault. He was astonished and subdued at the manifestation of such kindness. In parting from David, Saul exclaimed, "Blessed be thou, my son David: thou shalt both do great things, and also shalt still prevail." But the son of Jesse had no hope that the king would long continue in this frame of mind.

David despaired of a reconciliation with Saul. It seemed inevitable that he should at last fall a victim to the malice of the king, and he determined again to seek refuge in the land of the Philistines. With the six hundred men under his command, he passed over to Achish, the king of Gath.

David's conclusion that Saul would certainly accomplish his murderous purpose was formed without the counsel of God. Even while Saul was plotting and seeking to accomplish his destruction, the Lord was working to secure David the kingdom. God works out His plans, though to human eyes they are veiled in mystery. Men cannot understand the ways of God; and, looking at appearances, they interpret the trials and tests and provings that God permits to come upon them as things that are against them, and that will only work their ruin. Thus David looked on appearances, and not at the promises of God. He doubted that he would ever come to the throne. Long trials had wearied his faith and exhausted his patience.

The Lord did not send David for protection to the Philistines, the most bitter foes of Israel. This very nation would be among his worst enemies to the last, and yet he had fled to them for help in his time of need. Having lost all confidence in Saul and in those who served him, he threw himself upon the mercies of the enemies of his people. David was a brave general, and had proved himself a wise and successful warrior; but he was working directly against his own interests when he went to the Philistines. God had appointed him to set up his standard in the land of Judah, and it was want of faith that led him to forsake his post of duty without a command from the Lord.

God was dishonored by David's unbelief. The Philistines had feared David more than they had feared Saul and his armies; and by placing himself under the protection of the Philistines, David discovered to them the weakness of his own people. Thus he encouraged these relentless foes to oppress Israel. David had been anointed to stand in defense of the people of God; and the Lord would not have His servants give encouragement to the wicked by disclosing the weakness of His people or by an appearance of indifference to their welfare. Furthermore, the impression was received by his brethren that he had gone to the heathen to serve their gods. By this act he gave occasion for misconstruing his motives, and many were led to hold prejudice against him. The very thing that Satan desired to have him do he was led to do; for, in seeking refuge among the Philistines, David caused great exultation to the enemies of God and His people. David did not renounce his worship of God nor cease his devotion to His cause; but he sacrificed his trust in Him to his personal safety, and thus tarnished the upright and faithful character that God requires His servants to possess.

David was cordially received by the king of the Philistines. The warmth of this reception was partly due to the fact that the king admired him and partly to the fact that it was flattering to his vanity to have a Hebrew seek his protection. David felt secure from betrayal in the dominions of Achish. He brought his family, his household, and his possessions, as did also his men; and to all appearance he had come to settle permanently in the land of Philistia. All this was gratifying to Achish, who promised to protect the fugitive Israelites.

At David's request for a residence in the country, removed from the royal city, the king graciously granted Ziklag as a possession. David realized that it would be dangerous for himself and his men to be under the influence of idolaters. In a town wholly separated for their use they might worship God with more freedom than they could if they remained in Gath, where the heathen rites could not but prove a source of evil and annoyance.

While dwelling in this isolated town David made war upon the Geshurites, the Gezrites, and the Amalekites, and he left none alive to bring tidings to Gath. When he returned from battle he gave Achish to understand that he had been warring against those of his own nation, the men of Judah. By this dissembling he was the means of strengthening the hand of the Philistines; for the king said, "He hath made his people Israel utterly to abhor him; therefore he shall be my servant forever." David knew that it was the will of God that those heathen tribes should be destroyed, and he knew that he was appointed to do this work; but he was not walking in the counsel of God when he practiced deception.

"And it came to pass in those days, that the Philistines gathered their armies together for warfare, to fight with Israel. And Achish said unto David, Know thou assuredly, that thou shalt go out with me to battle, thou and thy men." David had no intention of lifting his hand against his people; but he was not certain as to what course he would pursue, until circumstances should indicate his duty. He answered the king evasively, and said, "Surely thou shalt know what thy servant can do." Achish understood these words as a promise of assistance in the approaching war, and pledged his word to bestow upon David great honor, and give him a high position at the Philistine court.

But although David's faith had staggered somewhat at the promises of God, he still remembered that Samuel had anointed him king of Israel. He recalled the victories that God had given him over his enemies in the past. He reviewed the great mercy of God in preserving him from the hand of Saul, and determined not to betray a sacred trust. Even though the king of Israel had sought his life, he would not join his forces with the enemies of his people.

The Death of Saul

Again war was declared between Israel and the Philistines. "The Philistines gathered themselves together, and came and pitched in Shunem," on the northern edge of the plain of Jezreel; while Saul and his forces encamped but a few miles distant, at the foot of Mount Gilboa, on the southern border of the plain. It was on this plain that Gideon, with three hundred men, had put to flight the hosts of Midian. But the spirit that inspired Israel's deliverer was widely different from that which now stirred the heart of the king. Gideon went forth strong in faith in the mighty God of Jacob; but Saul felt himself to be alone and defenseless, because God had forsaken him. As he looked abroad upon the Philistine host, "he was afraid, and his heart greatly trembled."

Saul had learned that David and his force were with the Philistines, and he expected that the son of Jesse would take this opportunity to revenge the wrongs he had suffered. The king was in sore distress. It was his own unreasoning passion, spurring him on to destroy the chosen of God, that had involved the nation in so great peril. While he had been engrossed in pursuing David he had neglected the defense of his kingdom. The Philistines, taking advantage of its unguarded condition, had penetrated into the very heart of the country. Thus while Satan had been urging Saul to employ every energy in hunting David, that he might destroy him, the same malignant spirit had inspired the Philistines to seize their opportunity to work Saul's ruin and overthrow the people of God. How often is the same policy still employed by the archenemy! He moves upon some unconsecrated heart to kindle envy and strife in the church, and then, taking advantage of the divided condition of God's people, he stirs up his agents to work their ruin.

On the morrow Saul must engage the Philistines in battle. The shadows of impending doom gathered dark about him; he longed for help and guidance. But it was in vain that he sought counsel from God. "The Lord answered him not, neither by dreams, nor by Urim, nor by prophets." The Lord never turned away a soul that came to Him in sincerity and humility. Why did he turn Saul away unanswered? The king had by his own act forfeited the benefits of all the methods of inquiring of God. He had rejected the counsel of Samuel the prophet; he had exiled David, the chosen of God; he had slain the priests of the Lord. Could he expect to be answered by God when he had cut off the channels of communication that Heaven had ordained? He had sinned away the Spirit of grace, and could he be answered by dreams and revelations from the Lord? Saul did not turn to God with humility and repentance. It was not pardon for sin and reconciliation with God, that he sought, but deliverance from his foes. By his own stubbornness and rebellion he had cut himself off from God. There could be no return but by the way of penitence and contrition; but the proud monarch, in his anguish and despair, determined to seek help from another source.

"Then said Saul unto his servants, Seek me a woman that hath a familiar spirit, that I may go to her, and inquire of her." Saul had a full knowledge of the character of necromancy. If had been expressly forbidden by the Lord, and the sentence of death was pronounced against all who practiced its unholy arts. During the life of Samuel, Saul had commanded that all wizards and those that had familiar spirits should be put to death; but now, in the rashness of desperation, he had recourse to that oracle which he had condemned as an abomination.

It was told the king that a woman who had a familiar spirit was living in concealment at Endor. This woman had entered into covenant with Satan to yield herself to his control, to fulfill his purposes; and in return, the prince of evil wrought wonders for her and revealed secret things to her.

Disguising himself, Saul went forth by night with but two attendants, to seek the retreat of the sorceress. Oh, pitiable sight! the king of Israel led captive by Satan at his will! What path so dark for human feet to tread as that chosen by one who has persisted in having his own way, resisting the holy influences of the Spirit of God! What bondage so terrible as that of him who is given over to the control of the worst of tyrants—himself! Trust in God and obedience to His will were the only conditions upon which Saul could be king of Israel. Had he complied with these conditions throughout his reign, his kingdom would have been secure; God would have been his guide, the Omnipotent his shield. God had borne long with Saul; and although his rebellion and obstinacy had well-nigh silenced the divine voice in the soul, there was still opportunity for repentance. But when in his peril he turned from God to obtain light from a confederate of Satan, he had cut the last tie that bound him to his Maker; he had placed himself fully under the control of that demoniac power which for years had been exercised upon him, and which had brought him to the verge of destruction.

Under the cover of darkness Saul and his attendants made their way across the plain, and, safely passing the Philistine host, they crossed the mountain ridge, to the lonely home of the sorceress of Endor. Here the woman with a familiar spirit had hidden herself away that she might secretly continue her profane incantations. Disguised as he was, Saul's lofty stature and kingly port declared that he was no common soldier. The woman suspected that her visitor was Saul, and his rich gifts strengthened her suspicions. To his request, "I pray thee, divine unto me by the familiar spirit, and bring me him up, whom I shall name unto thee," the woman answered, "Behold, thou knowest what Saul hath done, how he hath cut off those that have familiar spirits, and the wizards, out of the land: wherefore then layest thou a snare for my life, to cause me to die?" Then "Saul sware to her by the Lord, saying, As the Lord liveth, there shall no punishment happen to thee for this thing." And when she said, "Whom shall I bring up unto thee?" he answered, "Samuel."

After practicing her incantations, she said, "I saw gods ascending out of the earth. . . . An old man cometh up; and he is covered with a mantle. And Saul perceived that it was Samuel, and he stooped with his face to the ground, and bowed himself."

It was not God's holy prophet that came forth at the spell of a sorcerer's incantation. Samuel was not present in that haunt of evil spirits. That supernatural appearance was produced solely by the power of Satan. He could as easily assume the form of Samuel as he could assume that of an angel of light, when he tempted Christ in the wilderness.

The woman's first words under the spell of her incantation had been addressed to the king, "Why hast thou deceived me? for thou art Saul." Thus the first act of the evil spirit which personated the prophet was to communicate secretly with this wicked woman, to warn her of the deception that had been practiced upon her. The message to Saul from the pretended prophet was, "Why hast thou disquieted me, to bring me up? And Saul answered, I am sore distressed; for the Philistines make war against me, and God is departed from me, and answereth me no more, neither by prophets, nor by dreams: therefore I have called thee, that thou mayest make known unto me what I shall do."

When Samuel was living, Saul had despised his counsel and had resented his reproofs. But now, in the hour of his distress and calamity, he felt that the prophet's guidance was his only hope, and in order to communicate with Heaven's ambassador he vainly had recourse to the messenger of hell! Saul had placed himself fully in the power of Satan; and now he whose only delight is in causing misery and destruction, made the most of his advantage, to work the ruin of the unhappy king. In answer to Saul's agonized entreaty came the terrible message, professedly from the lips of Samuel:

"Wherefore then dost thou ask of me, seeing the Lord is departed from thee, and is become thine enemy? And the Lord hath done to him, as he spake by me: for the Lord hath rent the kingdom out of thine hand, and given it to thy neighbor, even to David: because thou obeyedst not the voice of the Lord, nor executedst His fierce wrath upon Amalek, therefore hath the Lord done this thing unto thee this day. Moreover the Lord will also deliver Israel with thee into the hand of the Philistines."

All through his course of rebellion Saul had been flattered and deceived by Satan. It is the tempter's work to belittle sin, to make the path of transgression easy and inviting, to blind the mind to the warnings and threatenings of the Lord. Satan, by his bewitching power, had led Saul to justify himself in defiance of Samuel's reproofs and warning. But now, in his extremity, he turned upon him, presenting the enormity of his sin and the hopelessness of pardon, that he might goad him to desperation. Nothing could have been better chosen to destroy his courage and confuse his judgment, or to drive him to despair and self-destruction.

Saul was faint with weariness and fasting; he was terrified and conscience-stricken. As the fearful prediction fell upon his ear, his form swayed like an oak before the tempest, and he fell prostrate to the earth.

The sorceress was filled with alarm. The king of Israel lay before her like one dead. Should he perish in her retreat, what would be the consequences to herself? She besought him to arise and partake of food, urging that since she had imperiled her life in granting his desire, he should yield to her request for the preservation of his own. His servants joining their entreaties, Saul yielded at last, and the woman set before him the fatted calf and unleavened bread hastily prepared. What a scene!—In the wild cave of the sorceress, which but a little before had echoed with the words of doom—in the presence of Satan's messenger—he who had been anointed of God as king over Israel sat down to eat, in preparation for the day's deadly strife.

Before the break of day he returned with his attendants to the camp of Israel to make ready for the conflict. By consulting that spirit of darkness Saul had destroyed himself. Oppressed by the horror of despair, it would be impossible for him to inspire his army with courage. Separated from the Source of strength, he could not lead the minds of Israel to look to God as their helper. Thus the prediction of evil would work its own accomplishment.

On the plain of Shunem and the slopes of Mount Gilboa the armies of Israel and the hosts of the Philistines closed in mortal combat. Though the fearful scene in the cave of Endor had driven all hope from his heart, Saul fought with desperate valor for his throne and his kingdom. But it was in vain. "The men of Israel fled from before the Philistines, and fell down slain in Mount Gilboa." Three brave sons of the king died at his side. The archers pressed upon Saul. He had seen his soldiers falling around him and his princely sons cut down by the sword. Himself wounded, he could neither fight not fly. Escape was impossible, and determined not to be taken alive by the Philistines, he bade his armor-bearer, "Draw thy sword, and thrust me through therewith." When the man refused to lift his hand against the Lord's anointed, Saul took his own life by falling upon his sword.

Thus the first king of Israel perished, with the guilt of self-murder upon his soul. His life had been a failure, and he went down in dishonor and despair, because he had set up his own perverse will against the will of God.

The tidings of defeat spread far and wide, carrying terror to all Israel. The people fled from the cities, and the Philistines took undisturbed possession. Saul's reign, independent of God, had well-nigh proved the ruin of his people.

On the day following the engagement, the Philistines, searching the battlefield to rob the slain, discovered the bodies of Saul and his three sons. To complete their triumph, they cut off the head of Saul and stripped him of his armor; then the head and the armor, reeking with blood, were sent to the country of the Philistines as a trophy of victory, "to publish it in the house of their idols, and among the people." The armor was finally put in "the house of Ashtaroth," while the head was fastened in the temple of Dagon. Thus the glory of the victory was ascribed to the power of these false gods, and the name of Jehovah was dishonored.

The dead bodies of Saul and his sons were dragged to Beth-shan, a city not far from Gilboa, and near the river Jordan. Here they were hung up in chains, to be devoured by birds of prey. But the brave men of Jabesh-gilead, remembering Saul's deliverance of their city in his earlier and happier years, now manifested their gratitude by rescuing the bodies of the king and princes, and giving them honorable burial. Crossing the Jordan by night, they "took the body of Saul and the bodies of his sons from the wall of Beth-shan, and came to Jabesh, and burnt them there, And they took their bones, and buried them under a tree at Jabesh, and fasted seven days." Thus the noble deed performed forty years before, secured for Saul and his sons burial by tender and pitying hands in that dark hour of defeat and dishonor.

Ancient and Modern Sorcery

The Scripture account of Saul's visit to the woman of Endor has been a source of perplexity to many students of the Bible. There are some who take the position that Samuel was actually present at the interview with Saul, but the Bible itself furnishes sufficient ground for a contrary conclusion. If, as claimed by some, Samuel was in heaven, he must have been summoned thence, either by the power of God or by that of Satan. None can believe for a moment that Satan had power to call the holy prophet of God from heaven to honor the incantations of an abandoned woman. Nor can we conclude that God summoned him to the witch's cave; for the Lord had already refused to communicate with Saul, by dreams, by Urim, or by prophets. 1 Samuel 28:6. These were God's own appointed mediums of communication, and He did not pass them by to deliver the message through the agent of Satan.

The message itself is sufficient evidence of its origin. Its object was not to lead Saul to repentance, but to urge him on to ruin; and this is not the work of God, but of Satan. Furthermore, the act of Saul in consulting a sorceress is cited in Scripture as one reason why he was rejected by God and abandoned to destruction: "Saul died for his transgression which he committed against the Lord, even against the word of the Lord, which he kept not, and also for asking counsel of one that had a familiar spirit, to inquire of it; and inquired not of the Lord: therefore He slew him, and turned the kingdom unto David the son of Jesse." 1 Chronicles 10:13, 14. Here it is distinctly stated that Saul inquired of the familiar spirit, not of the Lord. He did not communicate with Samuel, the prophet of God; but through the sorceress he held intercourse with Satan. Satan could not present the real Samuel, but he did present a counterfeit, that served his purpose of deception.

Nearly all forms of ancient sorcery and witchcraft were founded upon a belief in communion with the dead. Those who practiced the arts of necromancy claimed to have intercourse with departed spirits, and to obtain through them a knowledge of future events. This custom of consulting the dead is referred to in the prophecy of Isaiah: "When they shall say unto you, Seek unto them that have familiar spirits, and unto wizards that peep and that mutter: should not a people seek unto their God? for the living to the dead?" Isaiah 8:19.

This same belief in communion with the dead formed the cornerstone of heathen idolatry. The gods of the heathen were believed to be the deified spirits of departed heroes. Thus the religion of the heathen was a worship of the dead. This is evident from the Scriptures. In the account of the sin of Israel at Bethpeor, it is stated: "Israel abode in Shittim, and the people began to commit whoredom with the daughters of Moab. And they called the people unto the sacrifices of their gods: and the people did eat, and bowed down to their gods. And Israel joined himself unto Baalpeor." Numbers 25:1-3. The psalmist tells us to what kind of gods these sacrifices were offered. Speaking of the same apostasy of the Israelites, he says, "They joined themselves also unto Baalpeor, and ate the sacrifices of the dead" (Psalm 106:28); that is, sacrifices that had been offered to the dead.

The deification of the dead has held a prominent place in nearly every system of heathenism, as has also the supposed communion with the dead. The gods were believed to communicate their will to men, and also, when consulted, to give them counsel. Of this character were the famous oracles of Greece and Rome.

The belief in communion with the dead is still held, even in professedly Christian lands. Under the name of spiritualism the practice of communicating with beings claiming to be the spirits of the departed has become widespread. It is calculated to take hold of the sympathies of those who have laid their loved ones in the grave. Spiritual beings sometimes appear to persons in the form of their deceased friends, and relate incidents connected with their lives and perform acts which they performed while living. In this way they lead men to believe that their dead friends are angels, hovering over them and communicating with them. Those who thus assume to be the spirits of the departed are regarded with a certain idolatry, and with many their word has greater weight than the word of God.

There are many, however, who regard spiritualism as a mere imposture. The manifestations by which it supports its claims to a supernatural character are attributed to fraud on the part of the medium. But while it is true that the results of trickery have often been palmed off as genuine manifestations, there have also been marked evidences of supernatural power. And many who reject spiritualism as the result of human skill or cunning will, when confronted with manifestations which they cannot account for upon this ground, be led to acknowledge its claims.

Modern spiritualism and the forms of ancient witchcraft and idol worship—all having communion with the dead as their vital principle—are founded upon that first lie by which Satan beguiled Eve in Eden: "Ye shall not surely die: for God doth know that in the day ye eat thereof, . . . ye shall be as gods." Genesis 3:4, 5. Alike based upon falsehood and perpetuating the same, they are alike from the father of lies.

The Hebrews were expressly forbidden to engage in any manner in pretended communion with the dead. God closed this door effectually when He said: "The dead know not anything. . . . Neither have they any more a portion forever in anything that is done under the sun." Ecclesiastes 9:5, 6. "His breath goeth forth, he returneth to his earth; in that very day his thoughts perish." Psalm 146:4. And the Lord declared to Israel: "The soul that turneth after such as have familiar spirits, and after wizards, to go a whoring after them, I will even set My face against that soul, and will cut him off from among his people." Leviticus 20:6.

The "familiar spirits" were not the spirits of the dead, but evil angels, the messengers of Satan. Ancient idolatry, which, as we have seen, comprises both worship of the dead and pretended communion with them, is declared by the Bible to have been demon worship. The apostle Paul, in warning his brethren against participating, in any manner, in the idolatry of their heathen neighbors, says, "The things which the Gentiles sacrifice, they sacrifice to devils, and not to God, and I would not that ye should have fellowship with devils." 1 Corinthians 10:20. The psalmist, speaking of Israel, says that "they sacrificed their sons and their daughters unto devils," and in the next verse he explains that they sacrificed them "unto the idols of Canaan." Psalm 106:37, 38. In their supposed worship of dead men they were in reality worshiping demons.

Modern spiritualism, resting upon the same foundation, is but a revival in a new form of the witchcraft and demon worship that God condemned and prohibited of old. It is foretold in the Scriptures, which declare that "in the latter times some shall depart from the faith, giving heed to seducing spirits, and doctrines of devils." 1 Timothy 4:1. Paul, in his second letter to the Thessalonians, points to the special working of Satan in spiritualism as an event to take place immediately before the second advent of Christ. Speaking of Christ's second coming, he declares that it is "after the working of Satan with all power and signs and lying wonders." 2 Thessalonians 2:9. And Peter, describing the dangers to which the church was to be exposed in the last days, says that as there were false prophets who led Israel into sin, so there will be false teachers, "who privily shall bring in damnable heresies, even denying the Lord that bought them. . . . And many shall follow their pernicious ways." 2 Peter 2:1, 2. Here the apostle has pointed out one of the marked characteristics of spiritualist teachers. They refuse to acknowledge Christ as the Son of God. Concerning such teachers the beloved John declares: "Who is a liar but he that denieth that Jesus is the Christ? He is antichrist, that denieth the Father and the Son. Whosoever denieth the Son, the same hath not the Father." 1 John 2:22, 23. Spiritualism, by denying Christ, denies both the Father and the Son, and the Bible pronounces it the manifestation of antichrist.

By the prediction of Saul's doom, given through the woman of Endor, Satan planned to ensnare the people of Israel. He hoped that they would be inspired with confidence in the sorceress, and would be led to consult her. Thus they would turn from God as their counselor and would place themselves under the guidance of Satan. The lure by which spiritualism attracts the multitudes is its pretended power to draw aside the veil from the future and reveal to men what God has hidden. God has in His word opened before us the great events of the future—all that it is essential for us to know—and He has given us a safe guide for our feet amid all its perils; but it is Satan's purpose to destroy men's confidence in God, to make them dissatisfied with their condition in life, and to lead them to seek a knowledge of what God has wisely veiled from them, and to despise what He has revealed in His Holy Word.

There are many who become restless when they cannot know the definite outcome of affairs. They cannot endure uncertainty, and in their impatience they refuse to wait to see the salvation of God. Apprehended evils drive them nearly distracted. They give way to their rebellious feelings, and run hither and thither in passionate grief, seeking intelligence concerning that which has not been revealed. If they would but trust in God, and watch unto prayer, they would find divine consolation. Their spirit would be calmed by communion with God. The weary and the heavy-laden would find rest unto their souls if they would only go to Jesus; but when they neglect the means that God has ordained for their comfort, and resort to other sources, hoping to learn what God has withheld, they commit the error of Saul, and thereby gain only a knowledge of evil.

God is not pleased with this course, and has expressed it in the most explicit terms. This impatient haste to tear away the veil from the future reveals a lack of faith in God and leaves the soul open to the suggestions of the master deceiver. Satan leads men to consult those that have familiar spirits; and by revealing hidden things of the past, he inspires confidence in his power to foretell things to come. By experience gained through the long ages he can reason from cause to effect and often forecast, with a degree of accuracy, some of the future events of man's life. Thus he in enabled to deceive poor, misguided souls and bring them under his power and lead them captive at his will.

God has given us the warning by His prophet: "When they shall say unto you, Seek unto them that have familiar spirits, and unto wizards that peep and that mutter: should not a people seek unto their God? for the living to the dead? To the law and to the testimony: if they speak not according to this word, it is because there is no light in them." Isaiah 8:19, 20.

Shall those who have a holy God, infinite in wisdom and power, go unto wizards, whose knowledge comes from intimacy with the enemy of our Lord? God Himself is the light of His people; He bids them fix their eyes by faith upon the glories that are veiled from human sight. The Sun of Righteousness sends its bright beams into their hearts; they have light from the throne of heaven, and they have no desire to turn away from the source of light to the messengers of Satan.

The demon's message to Saul, although it was a denunciation of sin and a prophecy of retribution, was not meant to reform him, but to goad him to despair and ruin. Oftener, however, it serves the tempter's purpose best to lure men to destruction by flattery. The teaching of the demon gods in ancient times fostered the vilest license. The divine precepts condemning sin and enforcing righteousness were set aside; truth was light regarded, and impurity was not only permitted but enjoined. Spiritualism declares that there is no death, no sin, no judgment, no retribution; that "men are unfallen demigods;" that desire is the highest law; and that man is accountable only to himself. The barriers that God has erected to guard truth, purity, and reverence are broken down, and many are thus emboldened in sin. Does not such teaching suggest an origin similar to that of demon worship?

The Lord presented before Israel the results of holding communion with evil spirits, in the abominations of the Canaanites: they were without natural affection, idolaters, adulterers, murderers, and abominable by every corrupt thought and revolting practice. Men do not know their own hearts; for "the heart is deceitful above all things, and desperately wicked." Jeremiah 17:9. But God understands the tendencies of the depraved nature of man. Then, as now, Satan was watching to bring about conditions favorable to rebellion, that the people of Israel might make themselves as abhorrent to God as were the Canaanites. The adversary of souls is ever on the alert to open channels for the unrestrained flow of evil in us; for he desires that we may be ruined, and be condemned before God.

Satan was determined to keep his hold on the land of Canaan, and when it was made the habitation of the children of Israel, and the law of God was made the law of the land, he hated Israel with a cruel and malignant hatred and plotted their destruction. Through the agency of evil spirits strange gods were introduced; and because of transgression, the chosen people were finally scattered from the Land of Promise. This history Satan is striving to repeat in our day. God is leading His people out from the abominations of the world, that they may keep His law; and because of this, the rage of "the accuser of our brethren" knows no bounds. "The devil is come down unto you, having great wrath, because he knoweth that he hath but a short time." Revelation 12:10, 12. The antitypical land of promise is just before us, and Satan is determined to destroy the people of God and cut them off from their inheritance. The admonition, "Watch ye and pray, lest ye enter into temptation" (Mark 14:38), was never more needed than now.

The word of the Lord to ancient Israel is addressed also to His people in this age: "Regard not them that have familiar spirits, neither seek after wizards, to be defiled by them;" "for all that do these things are an abomination unto the Lord." Leviticus 19:31; Deuteronomy 18:12.

David at Ziklag

David and his men had not taken part in the battle between Saul and the Philistines, though they had marched with the Philistines to the field of conflict. As the two armies prepared to join battle the son of Jesse found himself in a situation of great perplexity. It was expected that he would fight for the Philistines. Should he in the engagement quit the post assigned him and retire from the field, he would not only brand himself with cowardice, but with ingratitude and treachery to Achish, who had protected him and confided in him. Such an act would cover his name with infamy, and would expose him to the wrath of enemies more to be feared than Saul. Yet he could not for a moment consent to fight against Israel. Should he do this, he would become a traitor to his country—the enemy of God and of His people. It would forever bar his way to the throne of Israel; and should Saul be slain in the engagement, his death would be charged upon David.

David was caused to feel that he had missed his path. Far better would it have been for him to find refuge in God's strong fortresses of the mountains than with the avowed enemies of Jehovah and His people. But the Lord in His great mercy did not punish this error of His servant by leaving him to himself in his distress and perplexity; for though David, losing his grasp on divine power, had faltered and turned aside from the path of strict integrity, it was still the purpose of his heart to be true to God. While Satan and his host were busy helping the adversaries of God and of Israel to plan against a king who had forsaken God, and the angels of the Lord were working to deliver David from the peril into which he had fallen. Heavenly messengers moved upon the Philistine princes to protest against the presence of David and his force with the army in the approaching conflict.

"What do these Hebrews here?" cried the Philistine lords, pressing about Achish. The latter, unwilling to part with so important an ally, answered, "Is not this David, the servant of Saul the king of Israel, which hath been with me these days, or these years, and I have found no fault in him since he fell unto me unto this day?"

But the princes angrily persisted in their demand: "Make this fellow return, that he may go again to his place which thou hast appointed him, and let him not go down with us to battle, lest in the battle he be an adversary to us: for wherewith should he reconcile himself unto his master? should it not be with the heads of these men? Is not this David, of whom they sang one to another in dances, saying, Saul slew his thousands, and David his ten thousands?" The slaughter of their famed champion and the triumph of Israel upon that occasion were still fresh in the memory of the Philistine lords. They did not believe that David would fight against his own people; and should he, in the heat of battle, take sides with them, he could inflict greater harm on the Philistines than would the whole of Saul's army.

Thus Achish was forced to yield, and calling David, said unto him, "Surely as Jehovah liveth, thou hast been upright, and thy going out and thy coming in with me in the host is good in my sight: for I have not found evil in thee since the day of thy coming unto me unto this day. Nevertheless the lords favor thee not. Wherefore now return, and go in peace, that thou displease not the lords of the Philistines."

David, fearing to betray his real feelings, answered, "But what have I done? and what hast thou found in thy servant so long as I have been with thee unto this day, that I may not go fight against the enemies of my lord the king?"

The reply of Achish must have sent a thrill of shame and remorse through David's heart, as he thought how unworthy of a servant of Jehovah were the deceptions to which he had stooped. "I know that thou art good in my sight, as an angel of God," said the king: "notwithstanding, the princes of the Philistines have said, He shall not go up with us to the battle. Wherefore now rise up early in the morning with thy master's servants that are come with thee: and as soon as ye be up early in the morning, and have light, depart." Thus the snare in which David had become entangled was broken, and he was set free.

After three days' travel David and his band of six hundred men reached Ziklag, their Philistine home. But a scene of desolation met their view. The Amalekites, taking advantage of David's absence, with his force, had avenged themselves for his incursions into their territory. They had surprised the city while it was left unguarded, and having sacked and burned it, had departed, taking all the women and children as captives, with much spoil.

Dumb with horror and amazement, David and his men for a little time gazed in silence upon the blackened and smoldering ruins. Then as a sense of their terrible desolation burst upon them, those battle-scarred warriors "lifted up their voice and wept, until they had no more power to weep."

Here again David was chastened for the lack of faith that had led him to place himself among the Philistines. He had

opportunity to see how much safety could be found among the foes of God and His people. David's followers turned upon him as the cause of their calamities. He had provoked the vengeance of the Amalekites by his attack upon them; yet, too confident of security in the midst of his enemies, he had left the city unguarded. Maddened with grief and rage, his soldiers were now ready for any desperate measures, and they threatened even to stone their leader.

David seemed to be cut off from every human support. All that he held dear on earth had been swept from him. Saul had driven him from his country; the Philistines had driven him from the camp; the Amalekites had plundered his city; his wives and children had been made prisoners; and his own familiar friends had banded against him, and threatened him even with death. In this hour of utmost extremity David, instead of permitting his mind to dwell upon these painful circumstances, looked earnestly to God for help. He "encouraged himself in the Lord." He reviewed his past eventful life. Wherein had the Lord ever forsaken him? His soul was refreshed in recalling the many evidences of God's favor. The followers of David, by their discontent and impatience, made their affliction doubly grievous; but the man of God, having even greater cause for grief, bore himself with fortitude. "What time I am afraid, I will trust in Thee" (Psalm 56:3), was the language of his heart. Though he himself could not discern a way out of the difficulty, God could see it, and would teach him what to do.

Sending for Abiathar the priest, the son of Ahimelech, "David inquired of the Lord, saying, If I pursue after this troop, shall I overtake them?" The answer was, "Pursue: for thou shalt surely overtake them, and shalt without fail recover all." 1 Samuel 30:8, R.V.

At these words the tumult of grief and passion ceased. David and his soldiers at once set out in pursuit of their fleeing foe. So rapid was their march, that upon reaching the brook Besor, which empties near Gaza into the Mediterranean Sea, two hundred of the band were compelled by exhaustion to remain behind. But David with the remaining four hundred pressed forward, nothing daunted.

Advancing, they came upon an Egyptian slave apparently about to perish from weariness and hunger. Upon receiving food and drink, however, he revived, and they learned that he had been left to die by his cruel master, an Amalekite belonging to the invading force. He told the story of the raid and pillage; and then, having exacted a promise that he should not be slain or delivered to his master, he consented to lead David's company to the camp of their enemies.

As they came in sight of the encampment a scene of revelry met their gaze. The victorious host were holding high festival. "They were spread abroad upon all the earth, eating and drinking, and dancing, because of all the great spoil that they had taken out of the land of the Philistines, and out of the land of Judah." An immediate attack was ordered, and the pursuers rushed fiercely upon their prey. The Amalekites were surprised and thrown into confusion. The battle was continued all that night and the following day, until nearly the entire host was slain. Only a band of four hundred men, mounted upon camels, succeeded in making their escape. The word of the Lord was fulfilled. "David recovered all that the Amalekites had carried away: and David rescued his two wives. And there was nothing lacking to them, neither small nor great, neither sons nor daughters, neither spoil, nor anything that they had taken to them: David recovered all."

When David had invaded the territory of the Amalekites, he had put to the sword all the inhabitants that fell into his hands. But for the restraining power of God the Amalekites would have retaliated by destroying the people of Ziklag. They decided to spare the captives, desiring to heighten the honor of the triumph by leading home a large number of prisoners, and intending afterward to sell them as slaves. Thus, unwittingly, they fulfilled God's purpose, keeping the prisoners unharmed, to be restored to their husbands and fathers.

All earthly powers are under the control of the Infinite One. To the mightiest ruler, to the most cruel oppressor, He says, "Hitherto shalt thou come, but no further." Job 38:11. God's power is constantly exercised to counteract the agencies of evil; He is ever at work among men, not for their destruction, but for their correction and preservation.

With great rejoicing the victors took up their homeward march. Upon reaching their companions who had remained behind, the more selfish and unruly of the four hundred urged that those who had had no part in the battle should not share the spoils; that it was enough for them to recover each his wife and children. But David would permit no such arrangement. "Ye shall not do so, my brethren," he said, "with that which the Lord hath given us. . . . As his part is that goeth down to the battle, so shall his part be that tarrieth by the stuff; they shall part alike." Thus the matter was settled, and it afterward became a statute in Israel that all who were honorably connected with a military campaign should share the spoils equally with those who engaged in actual combat.

Besides recovering all the spoil that had been taken from Ziklag, David and his band had captured extensive flocks and herds belonging to the Amalekites. These were called "David's spoil;" and upon returning to Ziklag, he sent from this spoil presents to the elders of his own tribe of Judah. In this distribution all those were remembered who had befriended him and his followers in the mountain fastnesses, when he had been forced to flee from place to place for his life. Their kindness and sympathy, so precious to the hunted fugitive, were thus gratefully acknowledged.

It was the third day since David and his warriors returned to Ziklag. As they labored to restore their ruined homes, they watched with anxious hearts for tidings of the battle which they knew must have been fought between Israel and the Philistines. Suddenly a messenger entered the town, "with his clothes rent, and earth upon his head." He was at once brought to David, before whom he bowed with reverence, expressing recognition of him as a powerful prince, whose favor he desired. David eagerly inquired how the battle had gone. The fugitive reported Saul's defeat and death, and the death of Jonathan. But he went beyond a simple statement of facts. Evidently supposing that David must cherish enmity toward his relentless persecutor, the stranger hoped to secure honor to himself as the slayer of the king. With an air of boasting the man went on to relate that during the battle he found the monarch of Israel wounded, and sore pressed by his foes, and that at his own request the messenger had slain him. The crown from his head and the golden bracelets from his arm he had brought to David. He confidently expected that these tidings would be hailed with joy, and that a rich reward would be his for the part that he had acted.

But "David took hold on his clothes, and rent them; and likewise all the men that were with him: and they mourned, and wept, and fasted until even, for Saul, and for Jonathan his son, and for the people of the Lord, and for the house of Israel; because they were fallen by the sword."

The first shock of the fearful tidings past, David's thoughts returned to the stranger herald, and the crime of which, according to his own statement, he was guilty. The chief demanded of the young man, "Whence art thou?" And he answered, "I am the son of a stranger, an Amalekite. And David said unto him, How wast thou not afraid to stretch forth thine hand to destroy the Lord's anointed?" Twice David had had Saul in his power; but when urged to slay him, he had refused to lift his hand against him who had been consecrated by the command of God to rule over Israel. Yet the Amalekite feared not to boast that he had slain the king of Israel. He had accused himself of a crime worthy of death, and the penalty was inflicted at once. David said, "Thy blood be upon thy head; for thy mouth hath testified against thee, saying, I have slain the Lord's anointed."

David's grief at the death of Saul was sincere and deep, evincing the generosity of a noble nature. He did not exult in the fall of his enemy. The obstacle that had barred his access to the throne of Israel was removed, but at this he did not rejoice. Death had obliterated the remembrance of Saul's distrust and cruelty, and now nothing in his history was thought of but that which was noble and kingly. The name of Saul was linked with that of Jonathan, whose friendship had been so true and so unselfish.

The song in which David gave utterance to the feelings of his heart became a treasure to his nation, and to the people of God in all subsequent ages:

"Thy glory, O Israel, is slain upon thy high places!
How are the mighty fallen!
Tell it not in Gath,
Publish it not in the streets of Ashkelon;
Lest the daughters of the Philistines rejoice,
Lest the daughters of the uncircumcised triumph.
Ye mountains of Gilboa,
Let there be no dew nor rain upon you, neither fields of offerings:

For there the shield of the mighty was vilely cast away,
The shield of Saul as of one not anointed with oil. . . .
Saul and Jonathan were lovely and pleasant in their lives,
And in their death they were not divided;
They were swifter than eagles,
They were stronger than lions.
Ye daughters of Israel, weep over Saul,
Who clothed you in scarlet delicately,
Who put ornaments of gold upon your apparel.
How are the mighty fallen in the midst of the battle!
Jonathan is slain upon thy high places.
I am distressed for thee, my brother Jonathan:
Very pleasant hast thou been unto me:
Thy love to me was wonderful,
Passing the love of women.
How are the mighty fallen,
And the weapons of war perished!"
Samuel 1:19-27, R.V.

David Called to the Throne

The death of Saul removed the dangers that had made David an exile. The way was now open for him to return to his own land. When the days of mourning for Saul and Jonathan were ended, "David inquired of the Lord, saying, Shall I go up into any of the cities of Judah? And the Lord said unto him, Go up. And David said, Whither shall I go up? And He said, Unto Hebron."

Hebron was twenty miles north from Beersheba, and about midway between that city and the future site of Jerusalem. It was originally called Kirjath-arba, the city of Arba, the father of Anak. Later it was called Mamre, and here was the burial place of the patriarchs, "the cave of Machpelah." Hebron had been the possession of Caleb and was now the chief city of Judah. It lies in a valley surrounded by fertile hill country and fruitful lands. The most beautiful vineyards of Palestine were on its borders, together with numerous plantations of olive and other fruit trees.

David and his followers immediately prepared to obey the instruction which they had received from God. The six hundred armed men, with their wives and children, their flocks and herds, were soon on the way to Hebron. As the caravan entered the city the men of Judah were waiting to welcome David as the future king of Israel. Arrangements were at once made for his coronation. "And there they anointed David king over the house of Judah." But no effort was made to establish his authority by force over the other tribes.

One of the first acts of the new-crowned monarch was to express his tender regard for the memory of Saul and Jonathan. Upon learning of the brave deed of the men of Jabesh-gilead in rescuing the bodies of the fallen leaders and giving them honorable burial, David sent an embassy to Jabesh with the message, "Blessed be ye of the Lord, that ye have showed this kindness unto your lord, even unto Saul,

and have buried him. And now the Lord show kindness and truth unto you: and I also will requite you this kindness." And he announced his own accession to the throne of Judah and invited the allegiance of those who had proved themselves so truehearted.

The Philistines did not oppose the action of Judah in making David king. They had befriended him in his exile, in order to harass and weaken the kingdom of Saul, and now they hoped that because of their former kindness to David the extension of his power would, in the end, work to their advantage. But David's reign was not to be free from trouble. With his coronation began the dark record of conspiracy and rebellion. David did not sit upon a traitor's throne; God had chosen him to be king of Israel, and there had been no occasion for distrust or opposition. Yet hardly had his authority been acknowledged by the men of Judah, when through the influence of Abner, Ishbosheth, the son of Saul, was proclaimed king, and set upon a rival throne in Israel.

Ishbosheth was but a weak and incompetent representative of the house of Saul, while David was pre-eminently qualified to bear the responsibilities of the kingdom. Abner, the chief agent in raising Ishbosheth to kingly power, had been commander-in-chief of Saul's army, and was the most distinguished man in Israel. Abner knew that David had been appointed by the Lord to the throne of Israel, but having so long hunted and pursued him, he was not now willing that the son of Jesse should succeed to the kingdom over which Saul had reigned.

The circumstances under which Abner was placed served to develop his real character and showed him to be ambitious and unprincipled. He had been intimately associated with Saul and had been influenced by the spirit of the king to despise the man whom God had chosen to reign over Israel. His hatred had been increased by the cutting rebuke that David had given him at the time when the cruse of water and the spear of the king had been taken from the side of Saul as he slept in the camp. He remembered how David had cried in the hearing of the king and the people of Israel, "Art not thou a valiant man? and who is like to thee in Israel? wherefore then hast thou not kept thy lord the king? . . . This thing is not good that thou hast done. As the Lord liveth, ye are worthy to die, because ye have not kept your master, the Lord's anointed." This reproof had rankled in his breast, and he determined to carry out his revengeful purpose and create division in Israel, whereby he himself might be exalted. He employed the representative of departed royalty to advance his own selfish ambitions and purposes. He knew that the people loved Jonathan. His memory was cherished, and Saul's first successful campaigns had not been forgotten by the army. With determination worthy a better cause, this rebellious leader went forward to carry out his plans.

Mahanaim, on the farther side of Jordan, was chosen as the royal residence, since it offered the greatest security against attack, either from David or from the Philistines. Here the coronation of Ishbosheth took place. His reign was first accepted by the tribes east of Jordan, and was finally extended over all Israel except Judah. For two years the son of Saul enjoyed his honors in his secluded capital. But Abner, intent upon extending his power over all Israel, prepared for aggressive warfare. And "there was long war between the house of Saul and the house of David: but David waxed stronger and stronger, and the house of Saul waxed weaker and weaker."

At last treachery overthrew the throne that malice and ambition had established. Abner, becoming incensed against the weak and incompetent Ishbosheth, deserted to David, with the offer to bring over to him all the tribes of Israel. His proposals were accepted by the king, and he was dismissed with honor to accomplish his purpose. But the favorable reception of so valiant and famed a warrior excited the jealousy of Joab, the commander-in-chief of David's army. There was a blood feud between Abner and Joab, the former having slain Asahel, Joab's brother, during the war between Israel and Judah. Now Joab, seeing an opportunity to avenge his brother's death and rid himself of a prospective rival, basely took occasion to waylay and murder Abner.

David, upon hearing of this treacherous assault, exclaimed, "I and my kingdom are guiltless before the Lord forever from the blood of Abner the son of Ner. Let it rest on the head of Joab; and on all his father's house." In view of the unsettled state of the kingdom, and the power and position of the murderers—for Joab's brother Abishai had been united with him—David could not visit the crime with just retribution, yet he publicly manifested his abhorrence of the bloody deed. The burial of Abner was attended with public honors. The army, with Joab at their head, were required to take part in the services of mourning, with rent garments and clothed in sackcloth. The king manifested his grief by keeping a fast upon the day of burial; he followed the bier as chief mourner; and at the grave he pronounced an elegy which was a cutting rebuke of the murderers. "The king lamented over Abner, and said:

"Died Abner as a fool dieth?
Thy hands were not bound,
Nor thy feet put into fetters:
As a man falleth before wicked men,
So fellest thou."

David's magnanimous recognition of one who had been his bitter enemy won the confidence and admiration of all Israel. "All the people took notice of it, and it pleased them: as whatsoever the king did pleased all the people. For all the people and all Israel understood that day that it was not of the king to slay Abner the son of Ner." In the private circle of his trusted counselors and attendants the king spoke of the crime, and recognizing his own inability to punish the murderers as he desired, he left them to the justice of God: "Know ye not that there is a prince and a great man fallen this day in Israel? And I am this day weak, though anointed king; and these

men the sons of Zeruiah be too hard for me: the Lord shall reward the doer of evil according to his wickedness."

Abner had been sincere in his offers and representations to David, yet his motives were base and selfish. He had persistently opposed the king of God's appointment, in the expectation of securing honor to himself. It was resentment, wounded pride, and passion that led him to forsake the cause he had so long served; and in deserting to David he hoped to receive the highest position of honor in his service. Had he succeeded in his purpose, his talents and ambition, his great influence and want of godliness, would have endangered the throne of David and the peace and prosperity of the nation.

"When Saul's son heard that Abner was dead in Hebron, his hands were feeble, and all the Israelites were troubled." It was evident that the kingdom could not long be maintained. Soon another act of treachery completed the downfall of the waning power. Ishbosheth was foully murdered by two of his captains, who, cutting off his head, hastened with it to the king of Judah, hoping thus to ingratiate themselves in his favor.

They appeared before David with the gory witness to their crime, saying, "Behold the head of Ishbosheth the son of Saul thine enemy, which sought thy life; and the Lord hath avenged my lord the king this day of Saul, and of his seed." But David, whose throne God Himself had established, and whom God had delivered from his adversaries, did not desire the aid of treachery to establish his power. He told these murderers of the doom visited upon him who boasted of slaying Saul. "How much more," he added, "when wicked men have slain a righteous person in his own house upon his bed? shall I not therefore now require his blood of your hand, and take you away from the earth? And David commanded his young men, and they slew them. . . . But they took the head of Ishbosheth and buried it in the sepulchre of Abner in Hebron."

After the death of Ishbosheth there was a general desire among the leading men of Israel that David should become king of all the tribes. "Then came all the tribes of Israel to David unto Hebron, and spake, saying, Behold, we are thy bone and thy flesh." They declared, "Thou wast he that leddest out and broughtest in Israel: and the Lord said to thee, Thou shalt feed My people Israel, and thou shalt be a captain over Israel. So all the elders of Israel came to the king to Hebron; and King David made a league with them in Hebron before the Lord." Thus through the providence of God the way had been opened for him to come to the throne. He had no personal ambition to gratify, for he had not sought the honor to which he had been brought.

More than eight thousand of the descendants of Aaron and of the Levites waited upon David. The change in the sentiments of the people was marked and decisive. The revolution was quiet and dignified, befitting the great work they were doing. Nearly half a million souls, the former subjects of Saul, thronged Hebron and its environs. The very hills and valleys were alive with the multitudes. The hour for the coronation was appointed; the man who had been expelled from the court of Saul, who had fled to the mountains and hills and to the caves of the earth to preserve his life, was about to receive the highest honor that can be conferred upon man by his fellow man. Priests and elders, clothed in the garments of their sacred office, officers and soldiers with glittering spear and helmet, and strangers from long distances, stood to witness the coronation of the chosen king. David was arrayed in the royal robe. The sacred oil was put upon his brow by the high priest, for the anointing by Samuel had been prophetic of what would take place at the inauguration of the king. The time had come, and David, by solemn rite, was consecrated to his office as God's vicegerent. The scepter was placed in his hands. The covenant of his righteous sovereignty was written, and the people gave their pledges of loyalty. The diadem was placed upon his brow, and the coronation ceremony was over. Israel had a king by divine appointment. He who had waited patiently for the Lord, beheld the promise of God fulfilled. "And David went on, and grew great, and the Lord God of hosts was with him." 2 Samuel 5:10.

The Reign of David

As soon as David was established on the throne of Israel he began to seek a more appropriate location for the capital of his realm. Twenty miles from Hebron a place was selected as the future metropolis of the kingdom. Before Joshua had led the armies of Israel over Jordan it had been called Salem. Near this place Abraham had proved his loyalty to God. Eight hundred years before the coronation of David it had been the home of Melchizedek, the priest of the most high God. It held a central and elevated position in the country and was protected by an environment of hills. Being on the border between Benjamin and Judah, it was in close proximity to Ephraim and was easy of access to the other tribes.

In order to secure this location the Hebrews must dispossess a remnant of the Canaanites, who held a fortified position on the mountains of Zion and Moriah. This stronghold was called Jebus, and its inhabitants were known as Jebusites. For centuries Jebus had been looked upon as impregnable; but it was besieged and taken by the Hebrews under the command of Joab, who, as the reward of his valor, was made commander-in-chief of the armies of Israel. Jebus now became the national capital, and its heathen name was changed to Jerusalem.

Hiram, king of the wealthy city of Tyre, on the Mediterranean Sea, now sought an alliance with the king of Israel, and lent his aid to David in the work of erecting a palace at Jerusalem. Ambassadors were sent from Tyre, accompanied by architects and workmen and long trains laden with costly wood, cedar trees, and other valuable material.

The increasing strength of Israel in its union under David, the acquisition of the stronghold of Jebus, and the alliance with Hiram, king of Tyre, excited the hostility of the Philistines, and they again invaded the country with a strong force, taking up their position in the valley of Rephaim, but a short distance from Jerusalem. David with his men of war retired to the stronghold of Zion, to await divine direction. "And David inquired of the Lord, saying, Shall I go up to the Philistines? wilt thou deliver them into mine hand? And the Lord said unto David, Go up: for I will doubtless deliver the Philistines into thine hand."

David advanced upon the enemy at once, defeated and destroyed them, and took from them the gods which they had brought with them to ensure their victory. Exasperated by the humiliation of their defeat, the Philistines gathered a still larger force, and returned to the conflict. And again they "spread themselves in the valley of Rephaim." Again David sought the Lord and the great I Am took the direction of the armies of Israel.

God instructed David, saying, "Thou shalt not go up; but fetch a compass behind them, and come upon them over against the mulberry trees. And let it be, when thou hearest the sound of a going in the tops of the mulberry trees, that then thou shalt bestir thyself: for then shall the Lord go out before thee, to smite the host of the Philistines." If David, like Saul, had chosen his own way, success would not have attended him. But he did as the Lord had commanded, and he "smote the host of the Philistines from Gibeon even to Gazer. And the fame of David went out into all lands; and the Lord brought the fear of him upon all nations." 1 Chronicles 14:16, 17.

Now that David was firmly established upon the throne and free from the invasions of foreign foes, he turned to the accomplishment of a cherished purpose—to bring up the ark of God to Jerusalem. For many years the ark had remained at Kirjath-jearim, nine miles distant; but it was fitting that the capital of the nation should be honored with the token of the divine Presence.

David summoned thirty thousand of the leading men of Israel, for it was his purpose to make the occasion a scene of great rejoicing and imposing display. The people responded gladly to the call. The high priest, with his brethren in sacred office and the princes and leading men of the tribes, assembled at Kirjath-jearim. David was aglow with holy zeal. The ark was brought out from the house of Abinadab and placed upon a new cart drawn by oxen, while two of the sons of Abinadab attended it.

The men of Israel followed with exultant shouts and songs of rejoicing, a multitude of voices joining in melody with the sound of musical instruments; "David and all the house of Israel played before the Lord . . . on harps, and on psalteries, and on timbrels, and on cornets, and on cymbals." It had been long since Israel had witnessed such a scene of triumph. With solemn gladness the vast procession wound its way along the hills and valleys toward the Holy City.

But "when they came to Nachon's threshing floor, Uzzah put forth his hand to the ark of God, and took hold of it; for the oxen shook it. And the anger of the Lord was kindled against Uzzah, and God smote him there for his rashness; and there he died by the ark of God." A sudden terror fell upon the rejoicing throng. David was astonished and greatly alarmed, and in his heart he questioned the justice of God. He had been seeking to honor the ark as the symbol of the divine presence. Why, then, had that fearful judgment been sent to turn the season of gladness into an occasion of grief and mourning? Feeling that it would be unsafe to have the ark near him, David determined to let it remain where it was. A place was found for it nearby, at the house of Obed-edom the Gittite.

The fate of Uzzah was a divine judgment upon the violation of a most explicit command. Through Moses the Lord had given special instruction concerning the transportation of the ark. None but the priests, the descendants of Aaron, were to touch it, or even to look upon it uncovered. The divine direction was, "The sons of Kohath shall come to bear it: but they shall not touch any holy thing, lest they die." Numbers 4:15. The priests were to cover the ark, and then the Kohathites must lift it by the staves, which were placed in rings upon each side of the ark and were never removed. To the Gershonites and Merarites, who had in charge the curtains and boards and pillars of the tabernacle, Moses gave carts and oxen for the transportation of that which was committed to them. "But unto the sons of Kohath he gave none: because the service of the sanctuary belonging unto them was that they should bear upon their shoulders." Numbers 7:9. Thus in the bringing of the ark from Kirjath-jearim there had been a direct and inexcusable disregard of the Lord's directions.

David and his people had assembled to perform a sacred work, and they had engaged in it with glad and willing hearts; but the Lord could not accept the service, because it was not performed in accordance with His directions. The Philistines, who had not a knowledge of God's law, had placed the ark upon a cart when they returned it to Israel, and the Lord accepted the effort which they made. But the Israelites had in their hands a plain statement of the will of God in all these matters, and their neglect of these instructions was dishonoring to God. Upon Uzzah rested the greater guilt of presumption. Transgression of God's law had lessened his sense of its sacredness, and with unconfessed sins upon him he had, in face of the divine prohibition, presumed to touch the symbol of God's presence. God can accept no partial obedience, no lax way of treating His commandments. By the judgment upon Uzzah He designed to impress upon all Israel the importance of giving strict heed to His requirements. Thus the death of that one man, by leading the people to repentance, might prevent the necessity of inflicting judgments upon thousands.

Feeling that his own heart was not wholly right with God, David, seeing the stroke upon Uzzah, had feared the ark, lest some sin on his part should bring judgments upon him. But Obed-edom, though he rejoiced with trembling, welcomed the sacred symbol as the pledge of God's favor to the obedient.

The attention of all Israel was now directed to the Gittite and his household; all watched to see how it would fare with them. "And the Lord blessed Obed-edom, and all his household."

Upon David the divine rebuke accomplished its work. He was led to realize as he had never realized before the sacredness of the law of God and the necessity of strict obedience. The favor shown to the house of Obed-edom led David again to hope that the ark might bring a blessing to him and to his people.

At the end of three months he resolved to make another attempt to remove the ark, and he now gave earnest heed to carry out in every particular the directions of the Lord. Again the chief men of the nation were summoned, and a vast assemblage gathered about the dwelling place of the Gittite. With reverent care the ark was now placed upon the shoulders of men of divine appointment, the multitude fell into line, and with trembling hearts the vast procession again set forth. After advancing six paces the trumpet sounded a halt. By David's direction sacrifices of "oxen and fatlings" were to be offered. Rejoicing now took the place of trembling and terror. The king had laid aside his royal robes and had attired himself in a plain linen ephod, such as was worn by the priests. He did not by this act signify that he assumed priestly functions, for the ephod was sometimes worn by others besides the priests. But in this holy service he would take his place as, before God, on an equality with his subjects. Upon that day Jehovah was to be adored. He was to be the sole object of reverence.

Again the long train was in motion, and the music of harp and cornet, trumpet and cymbal, floated heavenward, blended with the melody of many voices. "And David danced before the Lord," in his gladness keeping time to the measure of the song.

David's dancing in reverent joy before God has been cited by pleasure lovers in justification of the fashionable modern dance, but there is no ground for such an argument. In our day dancing is associated with folly and midnight reveling. Health and morals are sacrificed to pleasure. By the frequenters of the ballroom God is not an object of thought and reverence; prayer or the song of praise would be felt to be out of place in their assemblies. This test should be decisive. Amusements that have a tendency to weaken the love for sacred things and lessen our joy in the service of God are not to be sought by Christians. The music and dancing in joyful praise to God at the removal of the ark had not the faintest resemblance to the dissipation of modern dancing. The one tended to the remembrance of God and exalted His holy name. The other is a device of Satan to cause men to forget God and to dishonor Him.

The triumphal procession approached the capital, following the sacred symbol of their invisible King. Then a burst of song demanded of the watchers upon the walls that the gates of the Holy City should be thrown open:

"Lift up your heads, O ye gates;
And be ye lift up, ye everlasting doors;

And the King of glory shall come in."

A band of singers and players answered:

"Who is this King of glory?"

From another company came the response:

"The Lord strong and mighty,
The Lord mighty in battle."

Then hundreds of voices, uniting, swelled the triumphal chorus:

"Lift up your heads, O ye gates;
Even lift them up, ye everlasting doors;
And the King of glory shall come in."

Again the joyful interrogation was heard, "Who is this King of glory?" And the voice of the great multitude, like "the sound of many waters," was heard in the rapturous reply:

"The Lord of hosts,
He is the King of glory." Psalm 24:7-10.

Then the gates were opened wide, the procession entered, and with reverent awe the ark was deposited in the tent that had been prepared for its reception. Before the sacred enclosure altars for sacrifice were erected; the smoke of peace offerings and burnt offerings, and the clouds of incense, with the praises and supplications of Israel, ascended to heaven. The service ended, the king himself pronounced a benediction upon his people. Then with regal bounty he caused gifts of food and wine to be distributed for their refreshment.

All the tribes had been represented in this service, the celebration of the most sacred event that had yet marked the reign of David. The Spirit of divine inspiration had rested upon the king, and now as the last beams of the setting sun bathed the tabernacle in a hallowed light, his heart was uplifted in gratitude to God that the blessed symbol of His presence was now so near the throne of Israel.

Thus musing, David turned toward his palace, "to bless his household." But there was one who had witnessed the scene of rejoicing with a spirit widely different from that which moved the heart of David. "As the ark of the Lord came into the city of David, Michal Saul's daughter looked through a window, and saw King David leaping and dancing before the Lord; and she despised him in her heart." In the bitterness of her passion she could not await David's return to the palace, but went out to meet him, and to his kindly greeting poured forth a torrent of bitter words. Keen and cutting was the irony of her speech:

"How glorious was the king of Israel today, who uncovered himself today in the eyes of the handmaids of his servants, as one of the vain fellows shamelessly uncovereth himself!"

David felt that it was the service of God which Michal had despised and dishonored, and he sternly answered: "It was before the Lord, which chose me before thy father, and before all his house, to appoint me ruler over the people of the Lord, over Israel: therefore will I play before the Lord. And I will yet be more vile than thus, and will be base in mine own sight: and of the maidservants which thou hast spoken of, of them shall I be had in honor." To David's rebuke was added that of the Lord: because of her pride and arrogance, Michal "had no child unto the day of her death."

The solemn ceremonies attending the removal of the ark had made a lasting impression upon the people of Israel, arousing a deeper interest in the sanctuary service and kindling anew their zeal for Jehovah. David endeavored by every means in his power to deepen these impressions. The service of song was made a regular part of religious worship, and David composed psalms, not only for the use of the priests in the sanctuary service, but also to be sung by the people in their journeys to the national altar at the annual feasts. The influence thus exerted was far-reaching, and it resulted in freeing the nation from idolatry. Many of the surrounding peoples, beholding the prosperity of Israel, were led to think favorably of Israel's God, who had done such great things for His people.

The tabernacle built by Moses, with all that appertained to the sanctuary service, except the ark, was still at Gibeah. It was David's purpose to make Jerusalem the religious center of the nation. He had erected a palace for himself, and he felt that it was not fitting for the ark of God to rest within a tent. He determined to build for it a temple of such magnificence as should express Israel's appreciation of the honor granted the nation in the abiding presence of Jehovah their King. Communicating his purpose to the prophet Nathan, he received the encouraging response, "Do all that is in thine heart; for the Lord is with thee."

But that same night the word of the Lord came to Nathan, giving him a message for the king. David was to be deprived of the privilege of building a house for God, but he was granted an assurance of the divine favor to him, to his posterity, and to the kingdom of Israel: "Thus saith Jehovah of hosts; I took thee from the sheepcote, from following the sheep, to be ruler over My people, over Israel; and I was with thee whithersoever thou wentest, and have cut off all thine enemies out of thy sight, and have made thee a great name, like unto the name of the great men that are in the earth. Moreover I will appoint a place for My people Israel, and will plant them, that they may dwell in a place of their own, and move no more; neither shall the children of wickedness afflict them any more, as beforetime."

As David had desired to build a house for God, the promise was given. "The Lord telleth thee that He will make thee a house. . . . I will set up thy seed after thee. . . . He shall build a house for My name, and I will stablish the throne of his kingdom forever."

The reason why David was not to build the temple was

declared: "Thou hast shed blood abundantly, and hast made great wars: thou shalt not build a house unto My name. . . . Behold, a son shall be born to thee, who shall be a man of rest; and I will give him rest from all his enemies: . . . his name shall be Solomon, and I will give peace and quietness unto Israel in his days. He shall build a house for My name." 1 Chronicles 22:8-10.

Though the cherished purpose of his heart had been denied, David received the message with gratitude. "Who am I, O Lord God?" he exclaimed, "and what is my house, that Thou hast brought me hitherto? And this was yet a small thing in Thy sight, O Lord God; but Thou hast spoken also of Thy servant's house for a great while to come;" and he then renewed his covenant with God.

David knew that it would be an honor to his name and would bring glory to his government to perform the work that he had purposed in his heart to do, but he was ready to submit his will to the will of God. The grateful resignation thus manifested is rarely seen, even among Christians. How often do those who have passed the strength of manhood cling to the hope of accomplishing some great work upon which their hearts are set, but which they are unfitted to perform! God's providence may speak to them, as did His prophet to David, declaring that the work which they so much desire is not committed to them. It is theirs to prepare the way for another to accomplish it. But instead of gratefully submitting to the divine direction, many fall back as if slighted and rejected, feeling that if they cannot do the one thing which they desire to do, they will do nothing. Many cling with desperate energy to responsibilities which they are incapable of bearing, and vainly endeavor to accomplish a work for which they are insufficient, while that which they might do, lies neglected. And because of this lack of co-operation on their part the greater work is hindered or frustrated.

David, in his covenant with Jonathan, had promised that when he should have rest from his enemies he would show kindness to the house of Saul. In his prosperity, mindful of this covenant, the king made inquiry, "Is there yet any that is left of the house of Saul, that I may show him kindness for Jonathan's sake?" He was told of a son of Jonathan, Mephibosheth, who had been lame from childhood. At the time of Saul's defeat by the Philistines at Jezreel, the nurse of this child, attempting to flee with him, had let him fall, thus making him a lifelong cripple. David now summoned the young man to court and received him with great kindness. The private possessions of Saul were restored to him for the support of his household; but the son of Jonathan was himself to be the constant guest of the king, sitting daily at the royal table. Through reports from the enemies of David, Mephibosheth had been led to cherish a strong prejudice against him as a usurper; but the monarch's generous and courteous reception of him and his continued kindness won the heart of the young man; he became strongly attached to David, and, like his father Jonathan, he felt that his interest was one with that of the king whom God had chosen.

After David's establishment upon the throne of Israel the nation enjoyed a long interval of peace. The surrounding peoples, seeing the strength and unity of the kingdom, soon thought it prudent to desist from open hostilities; and David, occupied with the organization and upbuilding of his kingdom, refrained from aggressive war. At last, however, he made war upon Israel's old enemies, the Philistines, and upon the Moabites, and succeeded in overcoming both and making them tributary.

Then there was formed against the kingdom of David a vast coalition of the surrounding nations, out of which grew the greatest wars and victories of his reign and the most extensive accessions to his power. This hostile alliance, which really sprang from jealousy of David's increasing power, had been wholly unprovoked by him. The circumstances that led to its rise were these:

Tidings were received at Jerusalem announcing the death of Nahash, king of the Ammonites—a monarch who had shown kindness to David when he was a fugitive from the rage of Saul. Now, desiring to express his grateful appreciation of the favor shown him in his distress, David sent ambassadors with a message of sympathy to Hanun, the son and successor of the Ammonite king. "Said David, I will show kindness unto Hanun the son of Nahash, as his father showed kindness unto me."

But his courteous act was misinterpreted. The Ammonites hated the true God and were the bitter enemies of Israel. The apparent kindness of Nahash to David had been prompted wholly by hostility to Saul as king of Israel. The message of David was misconstrued by Hanun's counselors. They "said unto Hanun their lord, Thinkest thou that David doth honor thy father, that he hath sent comforters unto thee? hath not David rather sent his servants unto thee, to search the city, and to spy it out, and to overthrow it?" It was by the advice of his counselors that Nahash, half a century before, had been led to make the cruel condition required of the people of Jabesh-gilead, when, besieged by the Ammonites, they sued for a covenant of peace. Nahash had demanded the privilege of thrusting out all their right eyes. The Ammonites still vividly remembered how the king of Israel had foiled their cruel design, and had rescued the people whom they would have humbled and mutilated. The same hatred of Israel still prompted them. They could have no conception of the generous spirit that had inspired David's message. When Satan controls the minds of men he will excite envy and suspicion which will misconstrue the very best intentions. Listening to his counselors, Hanun regarded David's messengers as spies, and loaded them with scorn and insult.

The Ammonites had been permitted to carry out the evil purposes of their hearts without restraint, that their real character might be revealed to David. It was not God's will that Israel should enter into a league with this treacherous heathen people.

In ancient times, as now, the office of ambassador was held sacred. By the universal law of nations it ensured protection from personal violence or insult. The ambassador standing as a representative of his sovereign, any indignity offered to him demanded prompt retaliation. The Ammonites, knowing that the insult offered to Israel would surely be avenged, made preparation for war. "When the children of Ammon saw that they had made themselves odious to David, Hanun and the children of Ammon sent a thousand talents of silver to hire them chariots and horsemen out of Mesopotamia, and out of Syria-maachah, and out of Zobah. So they hired thirty and two thousand chariots. . . . And the children of Ammon gathered themselves together from their cities, and came to battle." 1 Chronicles 19:6, 7.

It was indeed a formidable alliance. The inhabitants of the region lying between the river Euphrates and the Mediterranean Sea had leagued with the Ammonites. The north and east of Canaan was encircled with armed foes, banded together to crush the kingdom of Israel.

The Hebrews did not wait for the invasion of their country. Their forces, under Joab, crossed the Jordan and advanced toward the Ammonite capital. As the Hebrew captain led his army to the field he sought to inspire them for the conflict, saying, "Be of good courage, and let us behave ourselves valiantly for our people, and for the cities of our God: and let the Lord do that which is good in His sight." 1 Chronicles 19:13. The united forces of the allies were overcome in the first engagement. But they were not yet willing to give over the contest, and the next year renewed the war. The king of Syria gathered his forces, threatening Israel with an immense army. David, realizing how much dependent upon the result of this contest, took the field in person, and by the blessing of God inflicted upon the allies a defeat so disastrous that the Syrians, from Lebanon to the Euphrates, not only gave up the war, but became tributary to Israel. Against the Ammonites David pushed the war with vigor, until their strongholds fell and the whole region came under the dominion of Israel.

The dangers which had threatened the nation with utter destruction proved, through the providence of God, to be the very means by which it rose to unprecedented greatness. In commemorating his remarkable deliverances, David sings:

"The Lord liveth; and blessed be my rock; and exalted be the
God of my salvation:
Even the God that executeth vengeance for me, and subdueth peoples under me.

He rescueth me from mine enemies:
Yea, Thou liftest me up above them that rise up against me:
Thou deliverest me from the violent man.
Therefore I will give thanks unto Thee, O Lord, among the nations,
And will sing praises unto Thy name.
Great deliverance giveth He to His king;
And sheweth loving-kindness to His anointed,
To David and to his seed, forevermore."

Psalm 18:46-50, R.V.

And throughout the songs of David the thought was impressed on his people that Jehovah was their strength and deliverer:

"There is no king saved by the multitude of a host:
A mighty man is not delivered by much strength.
A horse is a vain thing for safety:
Neither shall he deliver any by his great strength."
Psalm 33:16, 17.

"Thou art my King, O God:
Command deliverances for Jacob.
Through Thee will we push down our enemies:
Through Thy name will we tread them under that rise up against us.
For I will not trust in my bow,
Neither shall my sword save me.
But Thou hast saved us from our enemies,
And hast put them to shame that hated us." Psalm 44:4-7.

"Some trust in chariots, and some in horses:
But we will remember the name of Jehovah our God."
Psalm 20:7.

The kingdom of Israel had now reached in extent the fulfillment of the promise given to Abraham, and afterward repeated to Moses: "Unto thy seed have I given this land, from the river of Egypt unto the great river, the river Euphrates." Genesis 15:18. Israel had become a mighty nation, respected and feared by surrounding peoples. In his own realm David's power had become very great. He commanded, as few sovereigns in any age have been able to command, the affections and allegiance of his people. He had honored God, and God was now honoring him.

But in the midst of prosperity lurked danger. In the time of his greatest outward triumph David was in the greatest peril, and met his most humiliating defeat.

David's Sin and Repentance

The Bible has little to say in praise of men. Little space is given to recounting the virtues of even the best men who have ever lived. This silence is not without purpose; it is not without a lesson. All the good qualities that men possess are the gift of God; their good deeds are performed by the grace of God through Christ. Since they owe all to God the glory of whatever they are or do belongs to Him alone; they are but instruments in His hands. More than this—as all the lessons of Bible history teach—it is a perilous thing to praise or exalt men; for if one comes to lose sight of his entire dependence on God, and to trust to his own strength, he is sure to fall. Man is contending with foes who are stronger than he. "We wrestle not against flesh and blood, but against principalities, against powers, against the rulers of the darkness of this world, against wicked spirits in high places." Ephesians 6:12, margin. It is impossible for us in our own strength to maintain the conflict; and whatever diverts the mind from God, whatever leads to self-exaltation or to self-dependence, is surely preparing the way for our overthrow. The tenor of the Bible is to inculcate distrust of human power and to encourage trust in divine power.

It was the spirit of self-confidence and self-exaltation that prepared the way for David's fall. Flattery and the subtle allurements of power and luxury were not without effect upon him. Intercourse with surrounding nations also exerted an influence for evil. According to the customs prevailing among Eastern rulers, crimes not to be tolerated in subjects were uncondemned in the king; the monarch was not under obligation to exercise the same self-restraint as the subject. All this tended to lessen David's sense of the exceeding sinfulness of sin. And instead of relying in humility upon the power of Jehovah, he began to trust to his own wisdom and might. As soon as Satan can separate the soul from God, the only Source of strength, he will seek to arouse the unholy desires of man's carnal nature. The work of the enemy is not abrupt; it is not, at the outset, sudden and startling; it is a secret undermining of the strongholds of principle. It begins in apparently small things—the neglect to be true to God and to rely upon Him wholly, the disposition to follow the customs and practices of the world.

Before the conclusion of the war with the Ammonites, David, leaving the conduct of the army to Joab, returned to Jerusalem. The Syrians had already submitted to Israel, and the complete overthrow of the Ammonites appeared certain. David was surrounded by the fruits of victory and the honors of his wise and able rule. It was now, while he was at ease and unguarded, that the tempter seized the opportunity to occupy his mind. The fact that God had taken David into so close connection with Himself and had manifested so great favor toward him, should have been to him the strongest of incentives to preserve his character unblemished. But when in ease and self-security he let go his hold upon God, David yielded to Satan and brought upon his soul the stain of guilt. He, the Heaven-appointed leader of the nation, chosen by God to execute His law, himself trampled upon its precepts. He who should have been a terror to evildoers, by his own act strengthened their hands.

Amid the perils of his earlier life David in conscious integrity could trust his case with God. The Lord's hand had guided him safely past the unnumbered snares that had been laid for his feet. But now, guilty and unrepentant, he did not ask help and guidance from Heaven, but sought to extricate himself from the dangers in which sin had involved him. Bathsheba, whose fatal beauty had proved a snare to the king, was the wife of Uriah the Hittite, one of David's bravest and most faithful officers. None could foresee what would be the result should the crime become known. The law of God pronounced the adulterer guilty of death, and the proud-spirited soldier, so shamefully wronged, might avenge himself by taking the life of the king or by exciting the nation to revolt.

Every effort which David made to conceal his guilt proved unavailing. He had betrayed himself into the power of Satan; danger surrounded him, dishonor more bitter than death was before him. There appeared but one way of escape, and in his desperation he was hurried on to add murder to adultery. He who had compassed the destruction of Saul was seeking to lead David also to ruin. Though the temptations were different, they were alike in leading to transgression of God's law. David reasoned that if Uriah were slain by the hand of enemies in battle, the guilt of his death could not be traced home to the king, Bathsheba would be free to become David's wife, suspicion could be averted, and the royal honor would be maintained.

Uriah was made the bearer of his own death warrant. A letter sent by his hand to Joab from the king commanded, "Set ye Uriah in the forefront of the hottest battle, and retire ye from him, that he may be smitten, and die." Joab, already stained with the guilt of one wanton murder, did not hesitate to obey the king's instructions, and Uriah fell by the sword of the children of Ammon.

Heretofore David's record as a ruler had been such as few monarchs have ever equaled. It is written of him that he "executed judgment and justice unto all his people." 2 Samuel 8:15. His integrity had won the confidence and fealty of the nation. But as he departed from God and yielded himself to the wicked one, he became for the time the agent of Satan; yet he still held the position and authority that God had given him, and because of this, claimed obedience that would imperil the soul of him who should yield it. And Joab, whose allegiance had been given to the king rather than to God, transgressed God's law because the king commanded it.

David's power had been given him by God, but to be exercised only in harmony with the divine law. When he commanded that which was contrary to God's law, it became sin to obey. "The powers that be are ordained of God" (Romans 13:1), but we are not to obey them contrary to God's law. The apostle Paul, writing to the Corinthians, sets forth the principle by which we should be governed. He says, "Be ye followers of me, even as I also am of Christ." 1 Corinthians 11:1.

An account of the execution of his order was sent to David, but so carefully worded as not to implicate either Joab or the king. Joab "charged the messenger saying, When thou hast made an end of telling the matters of the war unto the king, and if so be that the king's wrath arise, . . .then say thou, Thy servant Uriah the Hittite is dead also. So the messenger went, and came and showed David all that Joab had sent him for."

The king's answer was, "Thus shalt thou say unto Joab, Let not this thing displease thee, for the sword devoureth one as well as another: make thy battle more strong against the city, and overthrow it: and encourage thou him."

Bathsheba observed the customary days of mourning for her

husband; and at their close "David sent and fetched her to his house, and she became his wife." He whose tender conscience and high sense of honor would not permit him, even when in peril of his life, to put forth his hand against the Lord's anointed, had so fallen that he could wrong and murder one of his most faithful and most valiant soldiers, and hope to enjoy undisturbed the reward of his sin. Alas! how had the fine gold become dim! how had the most fine gold changed!

From the beginning Satan has portrayed to men the gains to be won by transgression. Thus he seduced angels. Thus he tempted Adam and Eve to sin. And thus he is still leading multitudes away from obedience to God. The path of transgression is made to appear desirable; "but the end thereof are the ways of death." Proverbs 14:12. Happy they who, having ventured in this way, learn how bitter are the fruits of sin, and turn from it betimes. God in His mercy did not leave David to be lured to utter ruin by the deceitful rewards of sin.

For the sake of Israel also there was a necessity for God to interpose. As time passed on, David's sin toward Bathsheba became known, and suspicion was excited that he had planned the death of Uriah. The Lord was dishonored. He had favored and exalted David, and David's sin misrepresented the character of God and cast reproach upon His name. It tended to lower the standard of godliness in Israel, to lessen in many minds the abhorrence of sin; while those who did not love and fear God were by it emboldened in transgression.

Nathan the prophet was bidden to bear a message of reproof to David. It was a message terrible in its severity. To few sovereigns could such a reproof be given but at the price of certain death to the reprover. Nathan delivered the divine sentence unflinchingly, yet with such heaven-born wisdom as to engage the sympathies of the king, to arouse his conscience, and to call from his lips the sentence of death upon himself. Appealing to David as the divinely appointed guardian of his people's rights, the prophet repeated a story of wrong and oppression that demanded redress.

"There were two men in one city," he said, "the one rich, and the other poor. The rich man had exceeding many flocks and herds: but the poor man had nothing, save one little ewe lamb, which he had bought and nourished up: and it grew up together with him, and with his children; it did eat of his own meat, and drank of his own cup, and lay in his bosom, and was unto him as a daughter. And there came a traveler unto the rich man, and he spared to take of his own flock and of his own herd, to dress for the wayfaring man that was come unto him; but took the poor man's lamb, and dressed it for the man that was come to him."

The anger of the king was roused, and he exclaimed, "As the Lord liveth, the man that hath done this thing is worthy to die. And he shall restore the lamb fourfold, because he did this thing, and because he had no pity." 2 Samuel 12:5, 6, margin.

Nathan fixed his eyes upon the king; then, lifting his right hand to heaven, he solemnly declared, "Thou art the man."

"Wherefore," he continued, "hast thou despised the commandment of the Lord, to do evil in His sight?" The guilty may attempt, as David had done, to conceal their crime from men; they may seek to bury the evil deed forever from human sight or knowledge; but "all things are naked and opened unto the eyes of Him with whom we have to do." Hebrews 4:13. "There is nothing covered, that shall not be revealed; and hid, that shall not be known." Matthew 10:26.

Nathan declared: "Thus saith the Lord God of Israel, I anointed thee king over Israel, and I delivered thee out of the hand of Saul. . . . Wherefore hast thou despised the commandment of the Lord, to do evil in His sight? thou hast killed Uriah the Hittite with the sword, and hast taken his wife to be thy wife, and hast slain him with the sword of the children of Ammon. Now therefore the sword shall never depart from thine house. . . . Behold, I will raise up evil against thee out of thine own house, and I will take thy wives before thine eyes, and give them unto thy neighbor. . . . For thou didst it secretly; but I will do this thing before all Israel, and before the sun."

The prophet's rebuke touched the heart of David; conscience was aroused; his guilt appeared in all its enormity. His soul was bowed in penitence before God. With trembling lips he said, "I have sinned against the Lord." All wrong done to others reaches back from the injured one to God. David had committed a grievous sin, toward both Uriah and Bathsheba, and he keenly felt this. But infinitely greater was his sin against God.

Though there would be found none in Israel to execute the sentence of death upon the anointed of the Lord, David trembled, lest, guilty and unforgiven, he should be cut down by the swift judgment of God. But the message was sent him by the prophet, "The Lord also hath put away thy sin; thou shalt not die." Yet justice must be maintained. The sentence of death was transferred from David to the child of his sin. Thus the king was given opportunity for repentance; while to him the suffering and death of the child, as a part of his punishment, was far more bitter than his own death could have been. The prophet said, "Because by this deed thou hast given great occasion to the enemies of the Lord to blaspheme, the child also that is born unto thee shall surely die."

When his child was stricken, David, with fasting and deep humiliation, pleaded for its life. He put off his royal robes, he laid aside his crown, and night after night he lay upon the earth, in heartbroken grief interceding for the innocent one suffering for his guilt. "The elders of his house arose, and went to him, to raise him up from the earth: but he would not." Often when judgments had been pronounced upon persons or cities, humiliation and repentance had turned aside the blow, and the Ever-Merciful, swift to pardon, had sent messengers of peace. Encouraged by this thought, David persevered in his supplication so long as the child was spared. Upon learning that it was dead, he quietly submitted to the decree of God. The first stroke had fallen of that retribution which he himself had declared just; but David, trusting in God's mercy, was not without comfort.

Very many, reading the history of David's fall, have inquired, "Why has this record been made public? Why did God see fit to throw open to the world this dark passage in the life of one so highly honored of Heaven?" The prophet, in his reproof to David, had declared concerning his sin, "By this deed thou hast given great occasion to the enemies of the Lord to blaspheme." Through successive generations infidels have pointed to the character of David, bearing this dark stain, and have exclaimed in triumph and derision, "This is the man after God's own heart!" Thus a reproach has been brought upon religion, God and His word have been blasphemed, souls have been hardened in unbelief, and many, under a cloak of piety, have become bold in sin.

But the history of David furnishes no countenance to sin. It was when he was walking in the counsel of God that he was called a man after God's own heart. When he sinned, this ceased to be true of him until by repentance he had returned to the Lord. The word of God plainly declares, "The thing that David had done was evil in the eyes of the Lord." 2 Samuel 11:27, margin. And the Lord said to David by the prophet, "Wherefore hast thou despised the commandment of the Lord, to do evil in His sight? . . . Now therefore the sword shall never depart from thine house; because thou hast despised Me." Though David repented of his sin and was forgiven and accepted by the Lord, he reaped the baleful harvest of the seed he himself had sown. The judgments upon him and upon his house testify to God's abhorrence of the sin.

Heretofore God's providence had preserved David against all the plottings of his enemies, and had been directly exercised to restrain Saul. But David's transgression had changed his relation to God. The Lord could not in any wise sanction iniquity. He could not exercise His power to protect David from the results of his sin as he had protected him from the enmity of Saul.

There was a great change in David himself. He was broken in spirit by the consciousness of his sin and its far-reaching results. He felt humbled in the eyes of his subjects. His influence was weakened. Hitherto his prosperity had been attributed to his conscientious obedience to the commandments of the Lord. But now his subjects, having a knowledge of his sin, would be led to sin more freely. His authority in his own household, his claim to respect and obedience from his sons, was weakened. A sense of his guilt kept him silent when he should have condemned sin; it made his arm feeble to execute justice in his house. His evil example exerted its influence upon his sons, and God would not interpose to prevent the result. He would permit things to take their natural course, and thus David was severely chastised.

For a whole year after his fall David lived in apparent security; there was no outward evidence of God's displeasure. But the divine sentence was hanging over him. Swiftly and surely a day of judgment and retribution was approaching, which no repentance could avert, agony and shame that would darken his whole earthly life. Those who, by pointing to the example of David, try to lessen the guilt of their own sins, should learn from the Bible record that the way of transgression is hard. Though like David they should turn from their evil course, the results of sin, even in this life, will be found bitter and hard to bear.

God intended the history of David's fall to serve as a warning that even those whom He has greatly blessed and favored are not to feel secure and neglect watchfulness and prayer. And thus it has proved to those who in humility have sought to learn the lesson that God designed to teach. From generation to generation thousands have thus been led to realize their own danger from the tempter's power. The fall of David, one so greatly honored by the Lord, has awakened in them distrust of self. They have felt that God alone could keep them by His power through faith. Knowing that in Him was their strength and safety, they have feared to take the first step on Satan's ground.

Even before the divine sentence was pronounced against David he had begun to reap the fruit of transgression. His conscience was not at rest. The agony of spirit which he then endured is brought to view in the thirty-second psalm. He says:

"Blessed is he whose transgression is forgiven, whose sin is covered.

Blessed is the man unto whom the Lord imputeth not iniquity,

And in whose spirit there is no guile.

When I kept silence, my bones waxed old

Through my roaring all the day long.

For day and night Thy hand was heavy upon me:

My moisture was changed as with the drought of summer." Psalm 32:1-4, R.V.

And the fifty-first psalm is an expression of David's repentance, when the message of reproof came to him from God:

"Have mercy upon me, O God, according to Thy loving-kindness:

According unto the multitude of Thy tender mercies blot out

my transgressions.

Wash me thoroughly from mine iniquity, and cleanse me from

my sin.

For I acknowledge my transgressions: and my sin is ever before

me. . . .

Purge me with hyssop, and I shall be clean: wash me, and I shall be whiter than snow.

Make me to hear joy and gladness;

That the bones which Thou hast broken may rejoice.

Hide Thy face from my sins,

And blot out all mine iniquities.

Create in me a clean heart, O God;
And renew a right spirit within me.
Cast me not away from Thy presence;
And take not Thy Holy Spirit from me.
Restore unto me the joy of Thy salvation;
And uphold me with Thy free Spirit.
Then will I teach transgressors Thy ways;
And sinners shall be converted unto Thee.
Deliver me from bloodguiltiness, O God, Thou God of my
salvation:
And my tongue shall sing aloud of Thy righteousness."
Psalm 51:1-14.

Thus in a sacred song to be sung in the public assemblies of his people, in the presence of the court—priests and judges, princes and men of war—and which would preserve to the latest generation the knowledge of his fall, the king of Israel recounted his sin, his repentance, and his hope of pardon through the mercy of God. Instead of endeavoring to conceal his guilt he desired that others might be instructed by the sad history of his fall.

David's repentance was sincere and deep. There was no effort to palliate his crime. No desire to escape the judgments threatened, inspired his prayer. But he saw the enormity of his transgression against God; he saw the defilement of his soul; he loathed his sin. It was not for pardon only that he prayed, but for purity of heart. David did not in despair give over the struggle. In the promises of God to repentant sinners he saw the evidence of his pardon and acceptance.

"For Thou desirest not sacrifice; else would I give it:
Thou delightest not in burnt offering.
The sacrifices of God are a broken spirit:
A broken and a contrite heart, O God, Thou wilt not despise."
Psalm 51:16, 17.

Though David had fallen, the Lord lifted him up. He was now more fully in harmony with God and in sympathy with his fellow men than before he fell. In the joy of his release he sang:

"I acknowledged my sin unto Thee, and mine iniquity have I
not hid.
I said, I will confess my transgressions unto the Lord;
And Thou forgavest the iniquity of my sin. . . .
Thou art my hiding place; Thou shalt preserve me from
trouble;
Thou shalt compass me about with songs of deliverance."
Psalm 32:5-7.

Many have murmured at what they called God's injustice in sparing David, whose guilt was so great, after having rejected Saul for what appear to them to be far less flagrant sins. But David humbled himself and confessed his sin, while Saul despised reproof and hardened his heart in impenitence.

This passage in David's history is full of significance to the repenting sinner. It is one of the most forcible illustrations given us of the struggles and temptations of humanity, and of genuine repentance toward God and faith in our Lord Jesus Christ. Through all the ages it has proved a source of encouragement to souls that, having fallen into sin, were struggling under the burden of their guilt. Thousands of the children of God, who have been betrayed into sin, when ready to give up to despair have remembered how David's sincere repentance and confession were accepted by God, notwithstanding he suffered for his transgression; and they also have taken courage to repent and try again to walk in the way of God's commandments.

Whoever under the reproof of God will humble the soul with confession and repentance, as did David, may be sure that there is hope for him. Whoever will in faith accept God's promises, will find pardon. The Lord will never cast away one truly repentant soul. He has given this promise: "Let him take hold of My strength, that he may make peace with Me; and he shall make peace with Me." Isaiah 27:5. "Let the wicked forsake his way, and the unrighteous man his thoughts: and let him return unto the Lord, and He will have mercy upon him; and to our God, for He will abundantly pardon." Isaiah 55:7.

The Rebellion of Absalom

"He shall restore fourfold," had been David's unwitting sentence upon himself, on listening to the prophet Nathan's parable; and according to his own sentence he was to be judged. Four of his sons must fall, and the loss of each would be a result of the father's sin.

The shameful crime of Amnon, the first-born, was permitted by David to pass unpunished and unrebuked. The law pronounced death upon the adulterer, and the unnatural crime of Amnon made him doubly guilty. But David, self-condemned for his own sin, failed to bring the offender to justice. For two full years Absalom, the natural protector of the sister so foully wronged, concealed his purpose of revenge, but only to strike more surely at the last. At a feast of the king's sons the drunken, incestuous Amnon was slain by his brother's command.

Twofold judgment had been meted out to David. The terrible message was carried to him, "Absalom hath slain all the king's sons, and there is not one of them left. Then the king arose, and tare his garments, and lay on the earth; and all his servants stood by with their clothes rent." The king's sons, returning in alarm to Jerusalem, revealed to their father the truth; Amnon alone had been slain; and they "lifted up their voice and wept: and the king also and all his servants wept very sore." But Absalom fled to Talmai, the king of Geshur, his mother's father.

Like other sons of David, Amnon had been left to selfish indulgence. He had sought to gratify every thought of his heart, regardless of the requirements of God. Notwithstanding his great sin, God had borne long with him. For two years he had been granted opportunity for repentance; but he continued in sin, and with his guilt upon him, he was cut down by death, to await the awful tribunal of the judgment.

David had neglected the duty of punishing the crime of Amnon, and because of the unfaithfulness of the king and father and the impenitence of the son, the Lord permitted events to take their natural course, and did not restrain Absalom. When parents or rulers neglect the duty of punishing iniquity, God Himself will take the case in hand. His restraining power will be in a measure removed from the agencies of evil, so that a train of circumstances will arise which will punish sin with sin.

The evil results of David's unjust indulgence toward Amnon were not ended, for it was here that Absalom's alienation from his father began. After he fled to Geshur, David, feeling that the crime of his son demanded some punishment, refused him permission to return. And this had a tendency to increase rather than to lessen the inextricable evils in which the king had come to be involved. Absalom, energetic, ambitious, and unprincipled, shut out by his exile from participation in the affairs of the kingdom, soon gave himself up to dangerous scheming.

At the close of two years Joab determined to effect a reconciliation between the father and his son. And with this object in view he secured the services of a woman of Tekoah, reputed for wisdom. Instructed by Joab, the woman represented herself to David as a widow whose two sons had been her only comfort and support. In a quarrel one of these had slain the other, and now all the relatives of the family demanded that the survivor should be given up to the avenger of blood. "And so," said the mother, "they shall quench my coal which is left, and shall not leave to my husband neither name nor remainder upon the earth." The king's feelings were touched by this appeal, and he assured the woman of the royal protection for her son.

After drawing from him repeated promises for the young man's safety, she entreated the king's forbearance, declaring that he had spoken as one at fault, in that he did not fetch home again his banished. "For," she said, "we must needs die, and are as water spilt on the ground, which cannot be gathered up again; neither doth God respect any person; ye doth He devise means, that His banished be not expelled from Him." This tender and touching portrayal of the love of God toward the sinner—coming as it did from Joab, the rude soldier—is a striking evidence of the familiarity of the Israelites with the great truths of redemption. The king, feeling his own need of God's mercy, could not resist this appeal. To Joab the command was given, "Go therefore, bring the young man Absalom again."

Absalom was permitted to return to Jerusalem, but not to appear at court or to meet his father. David had begun to see the evil effects of his indulgence toward his children; and tenderly as he loved this beautiful and gifted son, he felt it necessary, as a lesson both to Absalom and to the people, that abhorrence for such a crime should be manifested. Absalom lived two years in his own house, but banished from the court. His sister dwelt with him, and her presence kept alive the memory of the irreparable wrong she had suffered. In the popular estimation the prince was a hero rather than an offender. And having this advantage, he set himself to gain the hearts of the people. His personal appearance was such as to win the admiration of all beholders. "In all Israel there was none to be so much praised as Absalom for his beauty: from the sole of his foot even to the crown of his head there was no blemish in him." It was not wise for the king to leave a man of Absalom's character—ambitious, impulsive, and passionate—to brood for two years over supposed grievances. And David's action in permitting him to return to Jerusalem, and yet refusing to admit him to his presence, enlisted in his behalf the sympathies of the people.

With the memory ever before him of his own transgression of the law of God, David seemed morally paralyzed; he was weak and irresolute, when before his sin he had been courageous and decided. His influence with the people had been weakened. And all this favored the designs of his unnatural son.

Through the influence of Joab, Absalom was again admitted to his father's presence; but though there was an outward reconciliation, he continued his ambitious scheming. He now assumed an almost royal state, having chariots and horses, and fifty men to run before him. And while the king was more and more inclined to desire retirement and solitude, Absalom sedulously courted the popular favor.

The influence of David's listlessness and irresolution extended to his subordinates; negligence and delay characterized the administration of justice. Absalom artfully turned every cause of dissatisfaction to his own advantage. Day by day this man of noble mien might be seen at the gate of the city, where a crowd of suppliants waited to present their wrongs for redness. Absalom mingled with them and listened to their grievances, expressing sympathy with their sufferings and regret at the inefficiency of the government. Having thus listened to the story of a man of Israel, the prince would reply, "Thy matters are good and right; but there is no man deputed of the king to hear thee;" adding, "O that I were made judge in the land, that every man which hath any suit or cause might come unto me, and I would do him justice! And it was so, that when any man came nigh to him to do him obeisance, he put forth his hand, and took him, and kissed him."

Fomented by the artful insinuations of the prince, discontent with the government was fast spreading. The praise of Absalom was on the lips of all. He was generally regarded as heir to the kingdom; the people looked upon him with pride as worthy of this high station, and a desire was kindled that he might occupy the throne. "So Absalom stole the hearts of the men of Israel." Yet the king, blinded by affection for his son, suspected nothing. The princely state which

Absalom had assumed, was regarded by David as intended to do honor to his court—as an expression of joy at the reconciliation.

The minds of the people being prepared for what was to follow, Absalom secretly sent picked men throughout the tribes, to concert measures for a revolt. And now the cloak of religious devotion was assumed to conceal his traitorous designs. A vow made long before while he was in exile must be paid in Hebron. Absalom said to the king, "I pray thee, let me go and pay my vow, which I have vowed unto the Lord, in Hebron. For thy servant vowed a vow while I abode at Geshur in Syria, saying, If the Lord shall bring me again indeed to Jerusalem, then I will serve the Lord." The fond father, comforted with this evidence of piety in his son, dismissed him with his blessing. The conspiracy was now fully matured. Absalom's crowning act of hypocrisy was designed not only to blind the king but to establish the confidence of the people, and thus to lead them on to rebellion against the king whom God had chosen.

Absalom set forth for Hebron, and there went with him "two hundred men out of Jerusalem, that were called; and they went in their simplicity, and they knew not anything." These men went with Absalom, little thinking that their love for the son was leading them into rebellion against the father. Upon arriving at Hebron, Absalom immediately summoned Ahithophel, one of the chief counselors of David, a man in high repute for wisdom, whose opinion was thought to be as safe and wise as that of an oracle. Ahithophel joined the conspirators, and his support made the cause of Absalom appear certain of success, attracting to his standard many influential men from all parts of the land. As the trumpet of revolt was sounded, the prince's spies throughout the country spread the tidings that Absalom was king, and many of the people gathered to him.

Meanwhile the alarm was carried to Jerusalem, to the king. David was suddenly aroused, to see rebellion breaking out close beside his throne. His own son—the son whom he had loved and trusted—had been planning to seize his crown and doubtless to take his life. In his great peril David shook off the depression that had so long rested upon him, and with the spirit of his earlier years he prepared to meet this terrible emergency. Absalom was mustering his forces at Hebron, only twenty miles away. The rebels would soon be at the gates of Jerusalem.

From his palace David looked out upon his capital—"beautiful for situation, the joy of the whole earth, . . . the city of the great King." Psalm 48:2. He shuddered at the thought of exposing it to carnage and devastation. Should he call to his help the subjects still loyal to his throne, and make a stand to hold his capital? Should he permit Jerusalem to be deluged with blood? His decision was taken. The horrors of war should not fall upon the chosen city. He would leave Jerusalem, and then test the fidelity of his people, giving them an opportunity to rally to his support. In this great crisis it was his duty to God and to his people to maintain the authority with which Heaven had invested him. The issue of the conflict he would trust with God.

In humility and sorrow David passed out of the gate of Jerusalem—driven from his throne, from his palace, from the ark of God, by the insurrection of his cherished son. The people followed in long, sad procession, like a funeral train. David's bodyguard of Cherethites, Pelethites, and six hundred Gittites from Gath, under the command of Ittai, accompanied the king. But David, with characteristic unselfishness, could not consent that these strangers who had sought his protection should be involved in his calamity. He expressed surprise that they should be ready to make this sacrifice for him. Then said the king to Ittai the Gittite, "Wherefore goest thou also with us? return to thy place, and abide with the king: for thou art a stranger, and also an exile. Whereas thou camest but yesterday, should I this day make thee go up and down with us? seeing I go whither I may, return thou, and take back thy brethren: mercy and truth be with thee."

Ittai answered, "As the Lord liveth, and as my lord the king liveth, surely in what place my lord the king shall be, whether in death or life, even there also will thy servant be." These men had been converted from paganism to the worship of Jehovah, and nobly they now proved their fidelity to their God and their king. David, with grateful heart, accepted their devotion to his apparently sinking cause, and all passed over the brook Kidron on the way toward the wilderness.

Again the procession halted. A company clad in holy vestments was approaching. "And lo Zadok also, and all the Levites were with him, bearing the ark of the covenant of God." The followers of David looked upon this as a happy omen. The presence of that sacred symbol was to them a pledge of their deliverance and ultimate victory. It would inspire the people with courage to rally to the king. Its absence from Jerusalem would bring terror to the adherents of Absalom.

At sight of the ark joy and hope for a brief moment thrilled the heart of David. But soon other thoughts came to him. As the appointed ruler of God's heritage he was under solemn responsibility. Not personal interests, but the glory of God and the good of his people, were to be uppermost in the mind of Israel's king. God, who dwelt between the cherubim, had said of Jerusalem, "This is My rest" (Psalm 132:14); and without divine authority neither priest nor king had a right to remove therefrom the symbol of His presence. And David knew that his heart and life must be in harmony with the divine precepts, else the ark would be the means of disaster rather than of success. His great sin was ever before him. He recognized in this conspiracy the just judgment of God. The sword that was not to depart from his house had been unsheathed. He knew not what the result of the struggle might be. It was not for him to remove from the capital of the nation the sacred statutes which embodied the will of their divine Sovereign, which were the constitution of the realm and the foundation of its prosperity.

He commanded Zadok, "Carry back the ark of God into the

city: if I shall find favor in the eyes of the Lord, He will bring me again, and show me both it and His habitation: but if He thus say, I have no delight in thee; behold, here am I, let Him do to me as seemeth good unto Him."

David added, "Art not thou a seer?"—a man appointed of God to instruct the people. "Return into the city in peace, and your two sons with you, Ahimaaz thy son, and Jonathan the son of Abiathar. See, I will tarry in the plain of the wilderness, until there come word from you to certify me." In the city the priests might do him good service by learning the movements and purposes of the rebels, and secretly communicating them to the king by their sons, Ahimaaz and Jonathan.

As the priests turned back toward Jerusalem a deeper shadow fell upon the departing throng. Their king a fugitive, themselves outcasts, forsaken even by the ark of God—the future was dark with terror and foreboding. "And David went up by the ascent of Mount Olivet, and wept as he went up, and had his head covered, and he went barefoot: and all the people that was with him covered every man his head, and they went up, weeping as they went up. And one told David, saying, Ahithophel is among the conspirators with Absalom." Again David was forced to recognize in his calamities the results of his own sin. The defection of Ahithophel, the ablest and most wily of political leaders, was prompted by revenge for the family disgrace involved in the wrong to Bathsheba, who was his granddaughter.

"And David said, O Lord, I pray Thee, turn the counsel of Ahithophel into foolishness." Upon reaching the top of the mount, the king bowed in prayer, casting upon God the burden of his soul and humbly supplicating divine mercy. His prayer seemed to be at once answered. Hushai the Archite, a wise and able counselor, who had proved himself a faithful friend to David, now came to him with his robes rent and with earth upon his head, to cast in his fortunes with the dethroned and fugitive king. David saw, as by a divine enlightenment, that this man, faithful and truehearted, was the one needed to serve the interests of the king in the councils at the capital. At David's request Hushai returned to Jerusalem to offer his services to Absalom and defeat the crafty counsel of Ahithophel.

With this gleam of light in the darkness, the king and his followers pursued their way down the eastern slope of Olivet, through a rocky and desolate waste, through wild ravines, and along stony and precipitous paths, toward the Jordan. "And when King David came to Bahurim, behold, thence came out a man of the family of the house of Saul, whose name was Shimei, the son of Gera: he came forth, and cursed still as he came. And he cast stones at David, and at all the servants of King David: and all the people and all the mighty men were on his right hand and on his left. And thus said Shimei when he cursed, Come out, come out, thou bloody man, and thou man of Belial. The Lord hath returned upon thee all the blood of the house of Saul, in whose stead thou hast reigned; and the Lord hath delivered the kingdom into the hand of Absalom thy son: and, behold, thou art taken in thy mischief, because thou art a bloody man."

In David's prosperity Shimei had not shown by word or act that he was not a loyal subject. But in the affliction of the king this Benjamite revealed his true character. He had honored David upon his throne, but he cursed him in his humiliation. Base and selfish, he looked upon others as of the same character as himself, and, inspired by Satan, he wreaked his hatred upon him whom God had chastened. The spirit that leads man to triumph over, to revile or distress, one who is in affliction is the spirit of Satan.

Shimei's accusations against David were utterly false—a baseless and malignant slander. David had not been guilty of wrong toward Saul or his house. When Saul was wholly in his power, and he could have slain him, he merely cut the skirt of his robe, and he reproached himself for showing even this disrespect for the Lord's anointed.

Of David's sacred regard for human life, striking evidence had been given, even while he himself was hunted like a beast of prey. One day while he was hidden in the cave of Adullam, his thoughts turning back to the untroubled freedom of his boyhood life, the fugitive exclaimed, "Oh that one would give me drink of the water of the well of Bethlehem, which is by the gate!" 2 Samuel 23:13-17. Bethlehem was at that time in the hands of the Philistines; but three mighty men of David's band broke through the guard, and brought of the water of Bethlehem to their master. David could not drink it. "Be it far from me," he cried; "is not this the blood of the men that went in jeopardy of their lives?" And he reverently poured out the water as an offering to God. David had been a man of war, much of his life had been spent amid scenes of violence; but of all who have passed through such an ordeal, few indeed have been so little affected by its hardening, demoralizing influence as was David.

David's nephew, Abishai, one of the bravest of his captains, could not listen patiently to Shimei's insulting words. "Why," he exclaimed, "should this dead dog curse my lord the king? let me go over, I pray thee, and take off his head." But the king forbade him. "Behold," he said, "my son . . . seeketh my life: how much more now may this Benjamite do it? let him alone, and let him curse; for the Lord hath bidden him. It may be that the Lord will look on mine affliction, and that the Lord will requite me good for his cursing this day."

Conscience was uttering bitter and humiliating truths to David. While his faithful subjects wondered at his sudden reverse of fortune, it was no mystery to the king. He had often had forebodings of an hour like this. He had wondered that God had so long borne with his sins, and had delayed the merited retribution. And now in his hurried and sorrowful flight, his feet bare, his royal robes changed for sackcloth, the lamentations of his followers awaking the echoes of the hills, he thought of his loved capital—of the place which had been the scene of his sin— and as he remembered the goodness and long-suffering of God, he was not altogether without hope. He felt that the Lord would still deal with him in mercy.

Many a wrongdoer has excused his own sin by pointing to David's fall, but how few there are who manifest David's penitence and humility. How few would bear reproof and retribution with the patience and fortitude that he manifested. He had confessed his sin, and for years had sought to do his duty as a faithful servant of God; he had labored for the upbuilding of his kingdom, and under his rule it had attained to strength and prosperity never reached before. He had gathered rich stores of material for the building of the house of God, and now was all the labor of his life to be swept away? Must the results of years of consecrated toil, the work of genius and devotion and statesmanship, pass into the hands of his reckless and traitorous son, who regarded not the honor of God nor the prosperity of Israel? How natural it would have seemed for David to murmur against God in this great affliction!

But he saw in his own sin the cause of his trouble. The words of the prophet Micah breathe the spirit that inspired David's heart. "When I sit in darkness, the Lord shall be a light unto me. I will bear the indignation of the Lord, because I have sinned against Him, until He plead my cause, and execute judgment for me." Micah 7:8, 9. And the Lord did not forsake David. This chapter in his experience, when, under cruelest wrong and insult, he shows himself to be humble, unselfish, generous, and submissive, is one of the noblest in his whole experience. Never was the ruler of Israel more truly great in the sight of heaven than at this hour of his deepest outward humiliation.

Had God permitted David to go on unrebuked in sin, and while transgressing the divine precepts, to remain in peace and prosperity upon his throne, the skeptic and infidel might have had some excuse for citing the history of David as a reproach to the religion of the Bible. But in the experience through which He caused David to pass, the Lord shows that He cannot tolerate or excuse sin. And David's history enables us to see also the great ends which God has in view in His dealings with sin; it enables us to trace, even through darkest judgments, the working out of His purposes of mercy and beneficence. He caused David to pass under the rod, but He did not destroy him; the furnace is to purify, but not to consume. The Lord says, "If they break My statutes, and keep not My commandments; then will I visit their transgression with the rod, and their iniquity with stripes. Nevertheless My loving-kindness will I not utterly take from him, nor suffer My faithfulness to fail." Psalm 89:31-33.

Soon after David left Jerusalem, Absalom and his army entered, and without a struggle took possession of the stronghold of Israel. Hushai was among the first to greet the new-crowned monarch, and the prince was surprised and gratified at the accession of his father's old friend and counselor. Absalom was confident of success. Thus far his schemes had prospered, and eager to strengthen his throne and secure the confidence of the nation, he welcomed Hushai to his court.

Absalom was now surrounded by a large force, but it was mostly composed of men untrained for war. As yet they had not been brought into conflict. Ahithophel well knew that David's situation was far from hopeless. A large part of the nation were still true to him; he was surrounded by tried warriors, who were faithful to their king, and his army was commanded by able and experienced generals. Ahithophel knew that after the first burst of enthusiasm in favor of the new king, a reaction would come. Should the rebellion fail, Absalom might be able to secure a reconciliation with his father; then Ahithophel, as his chief counselor, would be held most guilty for the rebellion; upon him the heaviest punishment would fall. To prevent Absalom from retracing his steps, Ahithophel counseled him to an act that in the eyes of the whole nation would make reconciliation impossible. With hellish cunning this wily and unprincipled statesman urged Absalom to add the crime of incest to that of rebellion. In the sight of all Israel he was to take to himself his father's concubines, according to the custom of oriental nations, thus declaring that he succeeded to his father's throne. And Absalom carried out the vile suggestion. Thus was fulfilled the word of God to David by the prophet, "Behold, I will raise up evil against thee out of thine own house, and I will take thy wives before thine eyes, and give them unto thy neighbor. . . . For thou didst it secretly: but I will do this thing before all Israel, and before the sun." 2 Samuel 12:11, 12. Not that God prompted these acts of wickedness, but because of David's sin He did not exercise His power to prevent them.

Ahithophel had been held in high esteem for his wisdom, but he was destitute of the enlightenment which comes from God. "The fear of the Lord is the beginning of wisdom" (Proverbs 9:10); and this, Ahithophel did not possess, or he could hardly have based the success of treason upon the crime of incest. Men of corrupt hearts plot wickedness, as if there were no overruling Providence to cross their designs; but "He that sitteth in the heavens shall laugh: the Lord shall have them in derision." Psalm 2:4. The Lord declares: "They would none of My counsel: they despised all My reproof. Therefore shall they eat of the fruit of their own way, and be filled with their own devices. For the turning away of the simple shall slay them, and the prosperity of fools shall destroy them." Proverbs 1:30-32.

Having succeeded in the plot for securing his own safety, Ahithophel urged upon Absalom the necessity of immediate action against David. "Let me now choose out twelve thousand men," he said, "and I will arise and pursue after David this night: and I will come upon him while he is weary and weak-handed, and will make him afraid: and all the people that are with him shall flee; and I will smite the king only: and I will bring back all the people unto thee." This plan was approved by the king's counselors. Had it been followed, David would surely have been slain, unless the Lord had directly interposed to save him. But a wisdom higher than that of the renowned Ahithophel was directing events. "The Lord had appointed to defeat the good counsel of Ahithophel, to the intent that the Lord might bring evil upon Absalom."

Hushai had not been called to the council, and he would not intrude himself unasked, lest suspicion should be drawn upon him as a spy; but after the assembly had dispersed, Absalom, who had a high regard for the judgment of his father's counselor, submitted to him the plan of Ahithophel. Hushai saw that if the proposed plan were followed, David would be lost. And he said, "The counsel that Ahithophel hath given is not good at this time. For, said Hushai, thou knowest thy father and his men, that they be mighty men, and they be chafed in their minds, as a bear robbed of her whelps in the field: and thy father is a man of war, and will not lodge with the people. Behold, he is hid now in some pit, or in some other place;" he argued that, if Absalom's forces should pursue David, they would not capture the king; and should they suffer a reverse, it would tend to dishearten them and work great harm to Absalom's cause. "For," he said, "all Israel knoweth that thy father is a mighty man, and they which be with him are valiant men." And he suggested a plan attractive to a vain and selfish nature, fond of the show of power: "I counsel that all Israel be generally gathered unto thee, from Dan even to Beer-sheba, as the sand that is by the sea for multitude; and that thou go to battle in thine own person. So shall we come upon him in some place where he shall be found, and we will light upon him as the dew falleth on the ground: and of him and of all the men that are with him there shall not be left so much as one. Moreover, if he be gotten into a city, then shall all Israel bring ropes to that city, and we will draw it into the river, until there be not one small stone found there.

"And Absalom and all the men of Israel said, The counsel of Hushai the Archite is better than the counsel of Ahithophel." But there was one who was not deceived—one who clearly foresaw the result of this fatal mistake of Absalom's. Ahithophel knew that the cause of the rebels was lost. And he knew that whatever might be the fate of the prince, there was no hope for the counselor who had instigated his greatest crimes. Ahithophel had encouraged Absalom in rebellion; he had counseled him to the most abominable wickedness, to the dishonor of his father; he had advised the slaying of David and had planned its accomplishment; he had cut off the last possibility of his own reconciliation with the king; and now another was preferred before him, even by Absalom. Jealous, angry, and desperate, Ahithophel "gat him home to his house, to his city, and put his household in order, and hanged himself, and died." Such was the result of the wisdom of one, who, with all his high endowments, did not make God his counselor. Satan allures men with flattering promises, but in the end it will be found by every soul, that the "wages of sin is death." Romans 6:23.

Hushai, not certain that his counsel would be followed by the fickle king, lost no time in warning David to escape beyond Jordan without delay. To the priests, who were to forward it by their sons, Hushai sent the message: "Thus and thus did Ahithophel counsel Absalom and the elders of Israel; and thus and thus have I counseled. Now therefore . . . lodge not this night in the plains of the wilderness, but speedily pass over; lest the king be swallowed up, and all the people that are with him."

The young men were suspected and pursued, yet they succeeded in performing their perilous mission. David, spent with toil and grief after that first day of flight, received the message that he must cross the Jordan that night, for his son was seeking his life.

What were the feelings of the father and king, so cruelly wronged, in this terrible peril? "A mighty valiant man," a man of war, a king, whose word was law, betrayed by his son whom he had loved and indulged and unwisely trusted, wronged and deserted by subjects bound to him by the strongest ties of honor and fealty—in what words did David pour out the feelings of his soul? In the hour of his darkest trial David's heart was stayed upon God, and he sang:

"Lord, how are they increased that trouble me!
Many are they that rise up against me.
Many there be which say of my soul,
There is no help for him in God.
But Thou, O Lord, art a shield for me;
My glory, and the lifter up of mine head.
I cried unto the Lord with my voice,
And He heard me out of His holy hill.
I laid me down and slept;
I awaked; for the Lord sustained me.
I will not be afraid of ten thousands of people,
That have set themselves against me round about. . . .
Salvation belongeth unto the Lord:
Thy blessing is upon Thy people." Psalm 3:1-8.

David and all his company—warriors and statesmen, old men and youth, the women and the little children—in the darkness of night crossed the deep and swift-flowing river. "By the morning light there lacked not one of them that was not gone over Jordan."

David and his forces fell back to Mahanaim, which had been the royal seat of Ishbosheth. This was a strongly fortified city, surrounded by a mountainous district favorable for retreat in case of war. The country was well-provisioned, and the people were friendly to the cause of David. Here many adherents joined him, while wealthy tribesmen brought abundant gifts of provision, and other needed supplies.

Hushai's counsel had achieved its object, gaining for David opportunity for escape; but the rash and impetuous prince could not be long restrained, and he soon set out in pursuit of his father. "And Absalom passed over Jordan, he and all the men of Israel with him." Absalom made Amasa, the son of David's sister Abigail, commander-in-chief of his forces. His army was large, but it was undisciplined and poorly prepared to cope with the tried soldiers of his father.

David divided his forces into three battalions under the command of Joab, Abishai, and Ittai the Gittite. It had been his purpose himself to lead his army in the field; but against this the officers of the army, the counselors, and the people vehemently protested. "Thou shalt not go forth," they said: "for if we flee away, they will not care for us; neither if half of us die, will they care for us: but thou art worth ten thousand of us: therefore now it is better that thou be ready to succour us out of the city. And the king said unto them, What seemeth you best I will do." 2 Samuel 18:3, 4, R.V.

From the walls of the city the long lines of the rebel army were in full view. The usurper was accompanied by a vast host, in comparison with which David's force seemed but a handful. But as the king looked upon the opposing forces, the thought uppermost in his mind was not of the crown and the kingdom, nor of his own life, that depended upon the wage of battle. The father's heart was filled with love and pity for his rebellious son. As the army filed out from the city gates David encouraged his faithful soldiers, bidding them go forth trusting that the God of Israel would give them the victory. But even here he could not repress his love for Absalom. As Joab, leading the first column, passed his king, the conqueror of a hundred battlefields stooped his proud head to hear the monarch's last message, as with trembling voice he said, "Deal gently for my sake with the young man, even with Absalom." And Abishai and Ittai received the same charge—"Deal gently for my sake with the young man, even with Absalom." But the king's solicitude, seeming to declare that Absalom was dearer to him than his kingdom, dearer even than the subjects faithful to his throne, only increased the indignation of the soldiers against the unnatural son.

The place of battle was a wood near the Jordan, in which the great numbers of Absalom's army were only a disadvantage to him. Among the thickets and marshes of the forest these undisciplined troops became confused and unmanageable. And "the people of Israel were slain before the servants of David, and there was there a great slaughter that day of twenty thousand men." Absalom, seeing that the day was lost, had turned to flee, when his head was caught between the branches of a widespreading tree, and his mule going out from under him, he was left helplessly suspended, a prey to his enemies. In this condition he was found by a soldier, who, for fear of displeasing the king, spared Absalom, but reported to Joab what he had seen. Joab was restrained by no scruples. He had befriended Absalom, having twice secured his reconciliation with David, and the trust had been shamelessly betrayed. But for the advantages gained by Absalom through Joab's intercession, this rebellion, with all its horrors, could never have occurred. Now it was in Joab's power at one blow to destroy the instigator of all this evil. "And he took three darts in his hand, and thrust them through the heart of Absalom. . . . And they took Absalom, and cast him into a great pit in the wood, and laid a very great heap of stones upon him."

Thus perished the instigators of rebellion in Israel. Ahithophel had died by his own hand. The princely Absalom, whose glorious beauty had been the pride of Israel, had been cut down in the vigor of his youth, his dead body thrust into a pit, and covered with a heap of stones, in token of everlasting reproach. During his lifetime Absalom had reared for himself a costly monument in the king's dale, but the only memorial which marked his grave was that heap of stones in the wilderness.

The leader of the rebellion being slain, Joab by the sound of the trumpet recalled his army from the pursuit of the fleeing host, and messengers were at once dispatched to bear the tidings to the king.

The watchman upon the city wall, looking out toward the battlefield, discovered a man running alone. Soon a second came in sight. As the first drew nearer, the watchman said to the king, who was waiting beside the gate, "Methinketh the running of the foremost is like the running of Ahimaaz the son of Zadok. And the king said, He is a good man, and cometh with good tidings. And Ahimaaz called, and said unto the king, All is well. And he fell down to the earth upon his face before the king, and said, Blessed be the Lord thy God, which hath delivered up the men that lifted up their hand against my lord the king." To the king's eager inquiry, "Is the young man Absalom safe?" Ahimaaz returned an evasive answer.

The second messenger came, crying, "Tidings, my lord the king: for the Lord hath avenged thee this day of all them that rose up against thee." Again from the father's lips came the absorbing question, "Is the young man Absalom safe?" Unable to conceal the heavy tidings, the herald answered, "The enemies of my lord the king, and all that rise against thee to do thee hurt, be as that young man is." It was enough. David questioned no further, but with bowed head he "went up to the chamber over the gate, and wept: and as he went, thus he said, O my son Absalom! my son, my son Absalom! would God I had died for thee, O Absalom, my son, my son!"

The victorious army, returning from the field, approached the city, their shouts of triumph awaking the echoes of the hills. But as they entered the city gate the shout died away, their banners drooped in their hands, and with downcast gaze they advanced more like those who had suffered defeat than like conquerors. For the king was not waiting to bid them welcome, but from the chamber above the gate his wailing cry was heard, "O my son Absalom! my son, my son Absalom! would God I had died for thee, O Absalom, my son, my son!"

"The victory that day was turned into mourning unto all the people; for the people heard say that day how the king was grieved for his son. And the people gat them by stealth that day into the city, as people being ashamed steal away when they flee in battle."

Joab was filled with indignation. God had given them reason for triumph and gladness; the greatest rebellion that had ever been known in Israel had been crushed; and yet this great victory was turned to mourning for him whose crime had cost the blood of thousands of brave men. The rude, blunt captain pushed his way into the presence of the king, and boldly said, "Thou hast shamed this day the faces of all thy servants, which this day have saved thy life, and the lives of thy sons and of thy daughters; . . . in that thou lovest thine enemies, and hatest thy friends. For thou hast declared this day, that thou regardest neither princes nor servants: for this day I perceive, that if Absalom had lived, and all we had died this day, then it had pleased thee well. Now therefore arise, go forth, and speak comfortably unto thy servants: for I swear by the Lord, if thou go not forth, there will not tarry one with thee this night: and that will be worse unto thee than all the evil that befell thee from thy youth until now."

Harsh and even cruel as was the reproof to the heart-stricken king, David did not resent it. Seeing that his general was right, he went down to the gate, and with words of courage and commendation greeted his brave soldiers as they marched past him.

The Last Years of David

The overthrow of Absalom did not at once bring peace to the kingdom. So large a part of the nation had joined in revolt that David would not return to his capital and resume his authority without an invitation from the tribes. In the confusion that followed Absalom's defeat there was no prompt and decided action to recall the king, and when at last Judah undertook to bring back David, the jealousy of the other tribes was roused, and a counterrevolution followed. This, however, was speedily quelled, and peace returned to Israel.

The history of David affords one of the most impressive testimonies ever given to the dangers that threaten the soul from power and riches and worldly honor—those things that are most eagerly desired among men. Few have ever passed through an experience better adapted to prepare them for enduring such a test. David's early life as a shepherd, with its lessons of humility, of patient toil, and of tender care for his flocks; the communion with nature in the solitude of the hills, developing his genius for music and poetry, and directing his thoughts to the Creator; the long discipline of his wilderness life, calling into exercise courage, fortitude, patience, and faith in God, had been appointed by the Lord as a preparation for the throne of Israel. David had enjoyed precious experiences of the love of God, and had been richly endowed with His Spirit; in the history of Saul he had seen the utter worthlessness of mere human wisdom. And yet worldly success and honor so weakened the character of David that he was repeatedly overcome by the temper.

Intercourse with heathen peoples led to a desire to follow their national customs and kindled ambition for worldly greatness. As the people of Jehovah, Israel was to be honored; but as pride and self-confidence increased, the Israelites were not content with this pre-eminence. They cared rather for their standing among other nations. This spirit could not fail to invite temptation. With a view to extending his conquests among foreign nations, David determined to increase his army by requiring military service from all who were of proper age. To effect this, it became necessary to take a census of the population. It was pride and ambition that prompted this action of the king. The numbering of the people would show the contrast between the weakness of the kingdom when David ascended the throne and its strength and prosperity under his rule. This would tend still further to foster the already too great self-confidence of both king and people. The Scripture says, "Satan stood up against Israel, and provoked David to number Israel." The prosperity of Israel under David had been due to the blessing of God rather than to the ability of her king or the strength of her armies. But the increasing of the military resources of the kingdom would give the impression to surrounding nations that Israel's trust was in her armies, and not in the power of Jehovah.

Though the people of Israel were proud of their national greatness, they did not look with favor upon David's plan for so greatly extending the military service. The proposed enrollment caused much dissatisfaction; consequently it was thought necessary to employ the military officers in place of the priests and magistrates, who had formerly taken the census. The object of the undertaking was directly contrary to the principles of a theocracy. Even Joab remonstrated, unscrupulous as he had heretofore shown himself. He said, "The Lord make His people a hundred times so many more as they be: but, my lord the king, are they not all my lord's servants? why then doth my lord require this thing? why will he be a cause of trespass to Israel? Nevertheless the king's word prevailed against Joab. Wherefore Joab departed, and went throughout all Israel, and came to Jerusalem." The numbering was not finished when David was convicted of his sin. Self-condemned, he "said unto God, I have sinned greatly, because I have done this thing: but now, I beseech Thee, do away the iniquity of Thy servant; for I have done very foolishly." The next morning a message was brought to David by the prophet Gad: "Thus saith the Lord, Choose thee either three years' famine; or three months to be destroyed before thy foes, while that the sword of thine enemies overtaketh thee; or else three days the sword of the Lord, even the pestilence, in the land, and the angel of the Lord destroying throughout all the coasts of Israel. Now therefore," said the prophet, "advise thyself what word I shall bring again to Him that sent me."

The king's answer was, "I am in a great strait: let us fall now into the hand of the Lord; for His mercies are great: and let me not fall into the hand of man."

The land was smitten with pestilence, which destroyed seventy thousand in Israel. The scourge had not yet entered the capital, when "David lifted up his eyes, and saw the angel of the Lord stand between the earth and the heaven, having a drawn sword in his hand stretched out over Jerusalem. Then David and the elders of Israel, who were clothed in sackcloth, fell upon their faces." The king pleaded with God in behalf of Israel: "Is it not I that commanded the people to be numbered? even I it is that have sinned and done evil indeed; but as for these sheep, what have they done? let Thine hand, I pray Thee, O Lord my God, be on me, and on my father's house; but not on Thy people, that they should be plagued."

The taking of the census had caused disaffection among the people; yet they had themselves cherished the same sins that prompted David's action. As the Lord through Absalom's sin visited judgment upon David, so through David's error He punished the sins of Israel.

The destroying angel had stayed his course outside Jerusalem. He stood upon Mount Moriah, "in the threshing floor of Ornan the Jebusite." Directed by the prophet, David went to the mountain, and there built an altar to the Lord, "and offered burnt offerings and peace offerings, and called upon the Lord; and He answered him from heaven by fire upon the altar of burnt offering." "So the Lord was entreated for the land, and the plague was stayed from Israel."

The spot upon which the altar was erected, henceforth ever to be regarded as holy ground, was tendered to the king by Ornan as a gift. But the king declined thus to receive it. "I will verily buy it for the full price," he said; "for I will not take that which is thine for the Lord, not offer burnt offerings without cost. So David gave to Ornan for the place six hundred shekels of gold by weight." This spot, memorable as the place where Abraham had built the altar to offer up his son, and now hallowed by this great deliverance, was afterward chosen as the site of the temple erected by Solomon.

Still another shadow was to gather over the last years of David. He had reached the age of threescore and ten. The hardships and exposures of his early wanderings, his many wars, the cares and afflictions of his later years, had sapped the fountain of life. Though his mind retained its clearness and strength, feebleness and age, with their desire for seclusion, prevented a quick apprehension of what was passing in the kingdom, and again rebellion sprang up in the very shadow of the throne. Again the fruit of David's parental indulgence was manifest. The one who now aspired to the throne was Adonijah, "a very goodly man" in person and bearing, but unprincipled and reckless. In his youth he had been subjected to but little restraint; for "his father had not displeased him at any time in saying, Why hast thou done so?" He now rebelled against the authority of God, who had appointed Solomon to the throne. Both by natural endowments and religious character Solomon was better qualified than his elder brother to become ruler of Israel; yet although the choice of God had been clearly indicated, Adonijah did not fail to find sympathizers. Joab, though guilty of many crimes, had heretofore been loyal to the throne; but he now joined the conspiracy against Solomon, as did also Abiathar the priest.

The rebellion was ripe; the conspirators had assembled at a great feast just without the city to proclaim Adonijah king, when their plans were thwarted by the prompt action of a few faithful persons, chief among whom were Zadok the priest, Nathan the prophet, and Bathsheba the mother of Solomon. They represented the state of affairs to the king, reminding him of the divine direction that Solomon should succeed to the throne. David at once abdicated in favor of Solomon, who was immediately anointed and proclaimed king. The conspiracy was crushed. Its chief actors had incurred the penalty of death. Abiathar's life was spared, out of respect to his office and his former fidelity to David; but he was degraded from the office of high priest, which passed to the line of Zadok. Joab and Adonijah were spared for the time, but after the death of David they suffered the penalty of their crime. The execution of the sentence upon the son of David completed the fourfold judgment that testified to God's abhorrence of the father's sin.

From the very opening of David's reign one of his most cherished plans had been that of erecting a temple to the Lord. Though he had not been permitted to execute this design, he had manifested no less zeal and earnestness in its behalf. He had provided an abundance of the most costly material—gold, silver, onyx stones, and stones of divers colors; marble, and the most precious woods. And now these valuable treasures that he had collected must be committed to others; for other hands must build the house for the ark, the symbol of God's presence.

Seeing that his end was near, the king summoned the princes of Israel, with representative men from all parts of the kingdom, to receive this legacy in trust. He desired to commit to them his dying charge and secure their concurrence and support in the great work to be accomplished. Because of his physical weakness, it had not been expected that he would attend to this transfer in person; but the inspiration of God came upon him, and with more than his wonted fervor and power, he was able, for the last time, to address his people. He told them of his own desire to build the temple, and of the Lord's command that the work should be committed to Solomon his son. The divine assurance was, "Solomon thy son, he shall build My house and My courts; for I have chosen him to be My son, and I will be his Father. Moreover I will establish his kingdom forever, if he be constant to do My commandments and My judgments, as at this day." "Now therefore," David said, "in the sight of all Israel the congregation of the Lord, and in the audience of our God, keep and seek for all the commandments of the Lord your God: that ye may possess this good land, and leave it for an inheritance for your children after you forever."

David had learned by his own experience how hard is the path of him who departs from God. He had felt the condemnation of the broken law, and had reaped the fruits of transgression; and his whole soul was moved with solicitude that the leaders of Israel should be true to God, and that Solomon should obey God's law, shunning the sins that had weakened his father's authority, embittered his life, and dishonored God. David knew that it would require humility of heart, a constant trust in God, and unceasing watchfulness to withstand the temptations that would surely beset Solomon in his exalted station; for such prominent characters are a special mark for the shafts of Satan. Turning to his son, already acknowledged as his successor on the throne, David said: "And thou, Solomon my son, know thou the God of thy father, and serve Him with a perfect heart and with a willing mind: for the Lord searcheth all hearts, and understandeth all the imaginations of the thoughts: if thou seek Him, He will be found of thee; but if thou forsake Him, He will cast thee off forever. Take heed now; for the Lord hath chosen thee to build a house for the sanctuary: be strong, and do it."

David gave Solomon minute directions for building the temple, with patterns of every part, and of all its instruments of service, as had been revealed to him by divine inspiration. Solomon was still young, and shrank from the weighty responsibilities that would devolve upon him in the erection of the temple and in the government of God's people. David said to his son, "Be strong and of good courage, and do it: fear not, nor be dismayed, for the Lord God, even my God, will be with thee; He will not fail thee, nor forsake thee."

Again David appealed to the congregation: "Solomon my son, whom alone God hath chosen, is yet young and tender, and the work is great: for the palace is not for man, but for the Lord God." He said, "I have prepared with all my might for the house of my God," and he went on to enumerate the materials he had gathered. More than this, he said, "I have set my affection to the house of my God, I have of mine own proper good, of gold and silver, which I have given to the house of my God, over and above all that I have prepared for the holy house, even three thousand talents of gold, of the gold of Ophir, and seven thousand talents of refined silver, to overlay the walls of the houses withal." "Who then," he asked of the assembled multitude that had brought their liberal gifts—"who then is willing to consecrate his service this day unto the Lord?"

There was a ready response from the assembly. "The chief of the fathers and princes of the tribes of Israel, and the captains of thousands and of hundreds, with the rulers of the king's work, offered willingly, and gave, for the service of the house of God, of gold five thousand talents and ten thousand drams, and of silver ten thousand talents, and of brass eighteen thousand talents, and one hundred thousand talents of iron. And they with whom precious stones were found gave them to the treasure of the house of the Lord. . . . Then the people rejoiced, for that they offered willingly, because with perfect heart they offered willingly to the Lord: and David the king also rejoiced with great joy.

"Wherefore David blessed the Lord before all the congregation: and David said, Blessed be Thou, Lord God of Israel our father, forever and ever. Thine, O Lord, is the greatness, and the power, and the glory, and the victory, and the majesty: for all that is in the heaven and in the earth is Thine; Thine is the kingdom, O Lord, and Thou art exalted as head above all. Both riches and honor come of Thee, and Thou reignest over all; and in Thine hand is power and might; and in Thine hand it is to make great, and to give strength unto all. Now therefore, our God, we thank Thee, and praise Thy glorious name. But who am I, and what is my people, that we should be able to offer so willingly after this sort? for all things come of Thee, and of Thine own have we given Thee. For we are strangers before Thee, and sojourners,

as were all our fathers: our days on the earth are as a shadow, and there is none abiding. O Lord our God, all this store that we have prepared to build Thee an house for Thine holy name cometh of Thine hand, and is all Thine own. I know also, my God, that Thou triest the heart, and hast pleasure in uprightness.

"As for me, in the uprightness of mine heart I have willingly offered all these things: and now have I seen with joy Thy people, which are present here, to offer willingly unto Thee. O Lord God of Abraham, Isaac and of Israel, our fathers, keep this forever in the imagination of the thoughts of the heart of Thy people, and prepare their heart unto Thee: and give unto Solomon my son a perfect heart, to keep Thy commandments, Thy testimonies, and Thy statutes, and to do all these things, and to build the palace, for the which I have made provision. And David said to all the congregation, Now bless the Lord your God. And all the congregation blessed the Lord God of their fathers, and bowed down their heads, and worshiped the Lord."

With deepest interest the king had gathered the rich material for building and beautifying the temple. He had composed the glorious anthems that in afteryears should echo through its courts. Now his heart was made glad in God, as the chief of the fathers and the princes of Israel so nobly responded to his appeal, and offered themselves to the important work before them. And as they gave their service, they were disposed to do more. They swelled the offerings, giving of their own possessions into the treasury. David had felt deeply his own unworthiness in gathering the material for the house of God, and the expression of loyalty in the ready response of the nobles of his kingdom, as with willing hearts they dedicated their treasures to Jehovah and devoted themselves to His service, filled him with joy. But it was God alone who had imparted this disposition to His people. He, not man, must be glorified. It was He who had provided the people with the riches of earth, and His Spirit had made them willing to bring their precious things for the temple. It was all of the Lord; if His love had not moved upon the hearts of the people, the king's efforts would have been vain, and the temple would never have been erected.

All that man receives of God's bounty still belongs to God. Whatever God has bestowed in the valuable and beautiful things of earth is placed in the hands of men to test them—to sound the depths of their love for Him and their appreciation of His favors. Whether it be the treasures of wealth or of intellect, they are to be laid, a willing offering, at the feet of Jesus; the giver saying, meanwhile, with David, "All things come of Thee, and of Thine own have we given Thee."

When he felt that death was approaching, the burden of David's heart was still for Solomon and for the kingdom of Israel, whose prosperity must so largely depend upon the fidelity of her king. "And he charged Solomon his son, saying, I go the way of all the earth: be thou strong therefore, and show thyself a man; and keep the charge of the Lord thy God, to walk in His ways, to keep His statutes, and His commandments, and His judgments, and His testimonies, . . . that thou mayest prosper in all that thou doest, and whithersoever thou turnest thyself: that the Lord may continue His word which He spake concerning me, saying, If thy children take heed to their way, to walk before Me in truth with all their heart and with all their soul, there shall not fail thee (said He) a man on the throne of Israel." 1 Kings 2:1-4.

David's "last words," as recorded, are a song—a song of trust, of loftiest principle, and undying faith:

"David the son of Jesse saith,
And the man who was raised on high saith,
The anointed of the God of Jacob,
And the sweet psalmist of Israel:
The Spirit of Jehovah spake by me: . . .
One that ruleth over men righteously,
That ruleth in the fear of God,
He shall be as the light of the morning, when the sun riseth,
A morning without clouds;
When the tender grass springeth out of the earth,
Through clear shining after rain.
Verily my house is not so with God;
Yet He hath made me an everlasting covenant,
Ordered in all things, and sure:
For it is all my salvation, and all my desire."
2 Samuel 23:1-5, R.V.

Great had been David's fall, but deep was his repentance, ardent was his love, and strong his faith. He had been forgiven much, and therefore he loved much. Luke 7:48.

The psalms of David pass through the whole range of experience, from the depths of conscious guilt and self-condemnation to the loftiest faith and the most exalted communing with God. His life record declares that sin can bring only shame and woe, but that God's love and mercy can reach to the deepest depths, that faith will lift up the repenting soul to share the adoption of the sons of God. Of all the assurances which His word contains, it is one of the strongest testimonies to the faithfulness, the justice, and the covenant mercy of God.

Man "fleeth also as a shadow, and continueth not," "but the word of our God shall stand forever." "The mercy of Jehovah is from everlasting to everlasting upon them that fear Him, and His righteousness unto children's children; to such as keep His covenant, and to those that remember His commandments to do them." Job 14:2; Isaiah 40:8; Psalm 103:17, 18.

"Whatsoever God doeth, it shall be forever." Ecclesiastes 3:14.

Glorious are the promises made to David and his house, promises that look forward to the eternal ages, and find their complete fulfillment in Christ. The Lord declared:

"I have sworn unto David My servant . . . with whom My hand shall be established: Mine arm also shall strengthen him. . . . My faithfulness and My mercy shall be with him: and in My name shall his horn be exalted. I will set his hand also in the sea, and his right hand in the rivers. He shall cry unto Me, Thou art my Father, my God, and the Rock of my salvation. Also I will make him My first-born, higher than the kings of the earth. My mercy will I keep for him forevermore, and My covenant shall stand fast with him." Psalm 89:3-28.

"His seed also will I make to endure forever,
And his throne as the days of heaven." Psalm 89:29.

"He shall judge the poor of the people,
He shall save the children of the needy,
And shall break in pieces the oppressor.
They shall fear thee while the sun endureth,
And so long as the moon, throughout all generations. . . .
In his days shall the righteous flourish;
And abundance of peace, till the moon be no more.
He shall have dominion also from sea to sea,
And from the river unto the ends of the earth."
"His name shall endure forever:
His name shall be continued as long as the sun:
And men shall be blessed in him:
All nations shall call him blessed."
Psalm 72:4-8, R.V., 17.

"For unto us a Child is born, unto us a Son is given: and the government shall be upon His shoulder: and His name shall be called Wonderful, Counselor, The mighty God, The everlasting Father, The Prince of Peace." "He shall be great, and shall be called the Son of the Highest; and the Lord God shall give unto Him the throne of His father David: and He shall reign over the house of Jacob forever; and of His kingdom there shall be no end." Isaiah 9:6; Luke 1:32, 33.

The Story of Prophets and Kings

CONTENTS

The Vineyard of the Lord

It was for the purpose of bringing the best gifts of Heaven to all the peoples of earth that God called Abraham out from his idolatrous kindred and bade him dwell in the land of Canaan. "I will make of thee a great nation," He said, "and I will bless thee, and make thy name great; and thou shalt be a blessing." Genesis 12:2. It was a high honor to which Abraham was called—that of being the father of the people who for centuries were to be the guardians and preservers of the truth of God to the world, the people through whom all the nations of the earth should be blessed in the advent of the promised Messiah.

Men had well-nigh lost the knowledge of the true God. Their minds were darkened by idolatry. For the divine statutes, which are "holy, and just, and good" (Romans 7:12), men were endeavoring to substitute laws in harmony with the purposes of their own cruel, selfish hearts. Yet God in His mercy did not blot them out of existence. He purposed to give them opportunity for becoming acquainted with Him through His church. He designed that the principles revealed through His people should be the means of restoring the moral image of God in man.

God's law must be exalted, His authority maintained; and to the house of Israel was given this great and noble work. God separated them from the world, that He might commit to them a sacred trust. He made them the depositaries of His law, and He purposed through them to preserve among men the knowledge of Himself. Thus the light of heaven was to shine out to a world enshrouded in darkness, and a voice was to be heard appealing to all peoples to turn from idolatry to serve the living God.

"With great power, and with a mighty hand," God brought His chosen people out of the land of Egypt. Exodus 32:11. "He sent Moses His servant; and Aaron whom He had chosen. They showed His signs among them, and wonders in the land of Ham." "He rebuked the Red Sea also, and it was dried up: so He led them through the depths." Psalms 105:26, 27; 106:9. He rescued them from their servile state, that He might bring them to a good land, a land which in His providence He had prepared for them as a refuge from their enemies. He would bring them to Himself and encircle them in His everlasting arms; and in return for His goodness and mercy they were to exalt His name and make it glorious in the earth.

"The Lord's portion is His people; Jacob is the lot of His inheritance. He found him in a desert land, and in the waste howling wilderness; He led him about, He instructed him, He kept him as the apple of His eye. As an eagle stirreth up her nest, fluttereth over her young, spreadeth abroad her wings, taketh them, beareth them on her wings: so the Lord alone did lead him, and there was no strange god with him." Deuteronomy 32:9-12. Thus He brought the Israelites unto Himself, that they might dwell as under the shadow of the Most High. Miraculously preserved from the perils of the wilderness wandering, they were finally established in the Land of Promise as a favored nation.

By means of a parable, Isaiah has told with touching pathos the story of Israel's call and training to stand in the world as Jehovah's representatives, fruitful in every good work:

"Now will I sing to my well-beloved a song of my beloved touching His vineyard. My well-beloved hath a vineyard in a very fruitful hill: and He fenced it, and gathered out the stones thereof, and planted it with the choicest vine, and built a tower in the midst of it, and also made a wine press therein: and He looked that it should bring forth grapes." Isaiah 5:1, 2.

Through the chosen nation, God had purposed to bring blessing to all mankind. "The vineyard of the Lord of hosts," the prophet declared, "is the house of Israel, and the men of Judah His pleasant plant." Isaiah 5:7.

To this people were committed the oracles of God. They were hedged about by the precepts of His law, the everlasting principles of truth, justice, and purity. Obedience to these principles was to be their protection, for it would save them from destroying themselves by sinful practices. And as the tower in the vineyard, God placed in the midst of the land His holy temple.

Christ was their instructor. As He had been with them in the wilderness, so He was still to be their teacher and guide. In the tabernacle and the temple His glory dwelt in the holy Shekinah above the mercy seat. In their behalf He constantly manifested the riches of His love and patience.

Through Moses the purpose of God was set before them and the terms of their prosperity made plain. "Thou art an holy people unto the Lord thy God," he said; "the Lord thy God hath chosen thee to be a special people unto Himself, above all people that are upon the face of the earth."

"Thou hast avouched the Lord this day to be thy God, and to walk in His ways, and to keep His statutes, and His commandments, and His judgments, and to hearken unto His voice: and the Lord hath avouched thee this day to be His peculiar people, as He hath promised thee, and that thou shouldest keep all His commandments; and to make thee high above all nations which He hath made, in praise, and in name, and in honor; and that thou mayest be an holy people unto the Lord thy God, as He hath spoken." Deuteronomy 7:6; 26:17-19.

The children of Israel were to occupy all the territory which God appointed them. Those nations that rejected the worship and service of the true God were to be dispossessed. But it was God's purpose that by the revelation of His character through Israel men should be drawn unto Him. To all the world the gospel invitation was to be given. Through the teaching of the sacrificial service, Christ was to be uplifted before the nations, and all who would look unto Him should live. All who, like Rahab the Canaanite and Ruth the Moabitess, turned from idolatry to the worship of the true God were to unite themselves with His chosen people. As the numbers of Israel increased, they were to enlarge their borders until their kingdom should embrace the world.

But ancient Israel did not fulfill God's purpose. The Lord declared, "I had planted thee a noble vine, wholly a right seed: how then art thou turned into the degenerate plant of a strange vine unto Me?" "Israel is an empty vine, he bringeth forth fruit unto himself." "And now, O inhabitants of Jerusalem, and men of Judah, judge, I pray you, betwixt Me and My vineyard. What could have been done more to My vineyard, that I have not done in it? Wherefore, when I looked that it should bring forth grapes, brought it forth wild grapes? And now go to; I will tell you what I will do to My vineyard: I will take away the hedge thereof, and it shall be eaten up; and break down the wall thereof, and it shall be trodden down: and I will lay it waste: it shall not be pruned, nor digged; but there shall come up briers and thorns: I will also command the clouds that they rain no rain upon it. For . . . He looked for judgment, but behold oppression; for righteousness, but behold a cry." Jeremiah 2:21; Hosea 10:1; Isaiah 5:3-7.

The Lord had through Moses set before His people the result of unfaithfulness. By refusing to keep His covenant, they would cut themselves off from the life of God, and His blessing could not come upon them. At times these warnings were heeded, and rich blessings were bestowed upon the Jewish nation and through them upon surrounding peoples. But more often in their history they forgot God and lost sight of their high privilege as His representatives. They robbed Him of the service He required of them, and they robbed their fellow men of religious guidance and a holy example. They desired to appropriate to themselves the fruits of the vineyard over which they had been made stewards. Their covetousness and greed caused them to be despised even by the heathen. Thus the Gentile world was given occasion to misinterpret the character of God and the laws of His kingdom.

With a father's heart, God bore with His people. He pleaded with them by mercies given and mercies withdrawn. Patiently He set their sins before them and in forbearance waited for their acknowledgment. Prophets and messengers were sent to urge His claim upon the husbandmen; but, instead of being welcomed, these men of discernment and spiritual power were treated as enemies. The husbandmen persecuted and killed them. God sent still other messengers, but they received the same treatment as the first, only that the husbandmen showed still more determined hatred.

The withdrawal of divine favor during the period of the Exile led many to repentance, yet after their return to the Land of Promise the Jewish people repeated the mistakes of former generations and brought themselves into political conflict with surrounding nations. The prophets whom God sent to correct the prevailing evils were received with the same suspicion and scorn that had been accorded the messengers of earlier times; and thus, from century to century, the keepers of the vineyard added to their guilt.

The goodly vine planted by the divine Husbandman upon the hills of Palestine was despised by the men of Israel and was finally cast over the vineyard wall; they bruised it and trampled it under their feet and hoped that they had destroyed it forever. The Husbandman removed the vine and concealed it from their sight. Again He planted it, but on the other side of the wall and in such a manner that the stock was no longer visible. The branches hung over the wall, and grafts might be joined to it; but the stem itself was placed beyond the power of men to reach or harm.

Of special value to God's church on earth today—the keepers of His vineyard—are the messages of counsel and admonition given through the prophets who have made plain His eternal purpose in behalf of mankind. In the teachings of the prophets, His love for the lost race and His plan for their salvation are clearly revealed. The story of Israel's call, of their successes and failures, of their restoration to divine favor, of their rejection of the Master of the vineyard, and of the carrying out of the plan of the ages by a goodly remnant to whom are to be fulfilled all the covenant promises—this has been the theme of God's messengers to His church throughout the centuries that have passed. And today God's message to His church—to those who are occupying His vineyard as faithful husbandmen—is none other than that spoken through the prophet of old:

"Sing ye unto her, A vineyard of red wine. I the Lord do keep it; I will water it every moment: lest any hurt it, I will keep it night and day." Isaiah 27:2, 3.

Let Israel hope in God. The Master of the vineyard is even now gathering from among men of all nations and peoples the precious fruits for which He has long been waiting. Soon He will come unto His own; and in that glad day His eternal purpose for the house of Israel will finally be fulfilled. "He shall cause them that come of Jacob to take root: Israel shall blossom and bud, and fill the face of the world with fruit." Verse 6.

"Thus saith the Lord, Let not the wise man glory in his wisdom, neither let the mighty man glory in his might, let not the rich man glory in his riches: but let him that glorieth glory in this, that he understandeth and knoweth Me, that I am the Lord which exercise loving-kindness, judgment, and righteousness, in the earth: for in these things I delight, saith the Lord." Jeremiah 9:23, 24.

Solomon

In the reign of David and Solomon, Israel became strong among the nations and had many opportunities to wield a mighty influence in behalf of truth and the right. The name of Jehovah was exalted and held in honor, and the purpose for which the Israelites had been established in the Land of Promise bade fair of meeting with fulfillment. Barriers were broken down, and seekers after truth from the lands of the heathen were not turned away unsatisfied. Conversions took place, and the church of God on earth was enlarged and prospered.

Solomon was anointed and proclaimed king in the closing years of his father David, who abdicated in his favor. His early life was bright with promise, and it was God's purpose that he should go on from strength to strength, from glory to glory, ever approaching nearer the similitude of the character of

God, and thus inspiring His people to fulfill their sacred trust as the depositaries of divine truth.

David knew that God's high purpose for Israel could be met only as rulers and people should seek with unceasing vigilance to attain to the standard placed before them. He knew that in order for his son Solomon to fulfill the trust with which God was pleased to honor him, the youthful ruler must be not merely a warrior, a statesman, and a sovereign, but a strong, good man, a teacher of righteousness, an example of fidelity.

With tender earnestness David entreated Solomon to be manly and noble, to show mercy and loving-kindness to his subjects, and in all his dealings with the nations of earth to honor and glorify the name of God and to make manifest the beauty of holiness. The many trying and remarkable experiences through which David had passed during his lifetime had taught him the value of the nobler virtues and led him to declare in his dying charge to Solomon: "He that ruleth over men must be just, ruling in the fear of God. And he shall be as the light of the morning, when the sun riseth, even a morning without clouds; as the tender grass springing out of the earth by clear shining after rain." 2 Samuel 23:3, 4.

Oh, what an opportunity was Solomon's! Should he follow the divinely inspired instruction of his father, his reign would be a reign of righteousness, like that described in the seventy-second psalm:

"Give the king Thy judgments, O God,
And Thy righteousness unto the king's son.
He shall judge Thy people with righteousness,
And Thy poor with judgment. . . .
He shall come down like rain upon the mown grass:
As showers that water the earth.
In his days shall the righteous flourish;
And abundance of peace so long as the moon endureth.
He shall have dominion also from sea to sea,
And from the river unto the ends of the earth. . . .
The kings of Tarshish and of the isles shall bring presents:
The kings of Sheba and Seba shall offer gifts.
Yea, all kings shall fall down before him:
All nations shall serve him.
For he shall deliver the needy when he crieth;
The poor also, and him that hath no helper. . . .
Prayer also shall be made for him continually;
And daily shall he be praised. . . .
His name shall endure forever:
His name shall be continued as long as the sun: And men shall be blessed in him:
All nations shall call him blessed.
"Blessed be the Lord God, the God of Israel,
Who only doeth wondrous things.
And blessed be His glorious name forever:
And let the whole earth be filled with His glory;
Amen, and Amen."

In his youth Solomon made David's choice his own, and for many years he walked uprightly, his life marked with strict obedience to God's commands. Early in his reign he went with his counselors of state to Gibeon, where the tabernacle that had been built in the wilderness still was, and there he united with his chosen advisers, "the captains of thousands and of hundreds," "the judges," and "every governor in all Israel, the chief of the fathers," in offering sacrifices to God and in consecrating themselves fully to the Lord's service. 2 Chronicles 1:2. Comprehending something of the magnitude of the duties connected with the kingly office, Solomon knew that those bearing heavy burdens must seek the Source of Wisdom for guidance, if they would fulfill their responsibilities acceptably. This led him to encourage his counselors to unite with him heartily in making sure of their acceptance with God.

Above every earthly good, the king desired wisdom and understanding for the accomplishment of the work God had given him to do. He longed for quickness of mind, for largeness of heart, for tenderness of spirit. That night the Lord appeared to Solomon in a dream and said, "Ask what I shall give thee." In his answer the young and inexperienced ruler gave utterance to his feeling of helplessness and his desire for aid. "Thou hast showed unto Thy servant David my father great mercy," he said, "according as he walked before Thee in truth, and in righteousness, and in uprightness of heart with Thee; and Thou hast kept for him this great kindness, that Thou hast given him a son to sit on his throne, as it is this day.

"And now, O Lord my God, Thou hast made Thy servant king instead of David my father: and I am but a little child: I know not how to go out or come in. And Thy servant is in the midst of Thy people which Thou hast chosen, a great people, that cannot be numbered nor counted for multitude. Give therefore Thy servant an understanding heart to judge Thy people, that I may discern between good and bad: for who is able to judge this Thy so great a people?

"And the speech pleased the Lord, that Solomon had asked this thing." "Because this was in thine heart," God said to Solomon, "and thou hast not asked riches, wealth, or honor, nor the life of thine enemies, neither yet hast asked long life; but hast asked wisdom and knowledge for thyself, that thou mayest judge My people," "behold, I have done according to thy words: lo, I have given thee a wise and an understanding heart; so that there was none like thee before thee, neither after thee shall any arise like unto thee. And I have also given thee that which thou hast not asked, both riches, and honor," "such as none of the kings have had that have been before thee, neither shall there any after thee have the like."

"And if thou wilt walk in My ways, to keep My statutes and My commandments, as thy father David did walk, then I will lengthen thy days." 1 Kings 3:5-14; 2 Chronicles 1:7-12.

God promised that as He had been with David, so He would be with Solomon. If the king would walk before the Lord in uprightness, if he would do what God had commanded him, his throne would be established and his reign would be the means of exalting Israel as "a wise and understanding people," the light of the surrounding nations. Deuteronomy 4:6.

The language used by Solomon while praying to God before the ancient altar at Gibeon reveals his humility and his strong desire to honor God. He realized that without divine aid he was as helpless as a little child to fulfill the responsibilities resting on him. He knew that he lacked discernment, and it was a sense of his great need that led him to seek God for wisdom. In his heart there was no selfish aspirations for a knowledge that would exalt him above others. He desired to discharge faithfully the duties devolving upon him, and he chose the gift that would be the means of causing his reign to bring glory to God. Solomon was never so rich or so wise or so truly great as when he confessed, "I am but a little child: I know not how to go out or come in."

Those who today occupy positions of trust should seek to learn the lesson taught by Solomon's prayer. The higher the position a man occupies, the greater the responsibility that he has to bear, the wider will be the influence that he exerts and the greater his need of dependence on God. Ever should he remember that with the call to work comes the call to walk circumspectly before his fellow men. He is to stand before God in the attitude of a learner. Position does not give holiness of character. It is by honoring God and obeying His commands that a man is made truly great.

The God whom we serve is no respecter of persons. He who gave to Solomon the spirit of wise discernment is willing to impart the same blessing to His children today. "If any of you lack wisdom," His word declares, "let him ask of God, the giveth to all men liberally, and upbraideth not; and it shall be given him." James 1:5. When a burden bearer desires wisdom more than he desires wealth, power, or fame, he will not be disappointed. Such a one will learn from the Great Teacher not only what to do, but how to do it in a way that will meet with the divine approval.

So long as he remains consecrated, the man whom God has endowed with discernment and ability will not manifest an eagerness for high position, neither will he seek to rule or control. Of necessity men must bear responsibilities; but instead of striving for the supremacy, he who is a true leader will pray for an understanding heart, to discern between good and evil.

The path of men who are placed as leaders is not an easy one. But they are to see in every difficulty a call to prayer. Never are they to fail of consulting the great Source of all wisdom. Strengthened and enlightened by the Master Worker, they will be enabled to stand firm against unholy influences and to discern right from wrong, good from evil. They will approve that which God approves, and will strive earnestly against the introduction of wrong principles into His cause.

The wisdom that Solomon desired above riches, honor, or long life, God gave him. His petition for a quick mind, a large heart, and a tender spirit was granted. "God gave Solomon wisdom and understanding exceeding much, and largeness of heart, even as the sand that is on the seashore. And Solomon's wisdom excelled the wisdom of all the children of the east country, and all the wisdom of Egypt. For he was wiser than all men; . . . and his fame was in all nations round about." 1 Kings 4:29-31.

"And all Israel . . . feared the king: for they saw that the wisdom of God was in him, to do judgment." I Kings 3:28. The hearts of the people were turned toward Solomon, as they had been toward David, and they obeyed him in all things. "Solomon . . . was strengthened in his kingdom, and the Lord his God was with him, and magnified him exceedingly." 2 Chronicles 1:1.

For many years Solomon's life was marked with devotion to God, with uprightness and firm principle, and with strict obedience to God's commands. He directed in every important enterprise and managed wisely the business matters connected with the kingdom. His wealth and wisdom, the magnificent buildings and public works that he constructed during the early years of his reign, the energy, piety, justice, and magnanimity that he revealed in word and deed, won the loyalty of his subjects and the admiration and homage of the rulers of many lands.

The name of Jehovah was greatly honored during the first part of Solomon's reign. The wisdom and righteousness revealed by the king bore witness to all nations of the excellency of the attributes of the God whom he served. For a time Israel was as the light of the world, showing forth the greatness of Jehovah. Not in the surpassing wisdom, the fabulous riches, the far-reaching power and fame that were his, lay the real glory of Solomon's early reign; but in the honor that he brought to the name of the God of Israel through a wise use of the gifts of Heaven.

As the years went by and Solomon's fame increased, he sought to honor God by adding to his mental and spiritual strength, and by continuing to impart to others the blessings he received. None understood better than he that it was through the favor of Jehovah that he had come into possession of power and wisdom and understanding, and that these gifts were bestowed that he might give to the world a knowledge of the King of kings.

Solomon took an especial interest in natural history, but his researchers were not confined to any one branch of learning. Through a diligent study of all created things, both animate and inanimate, he gained a clear conception of the Creator. In the forces of nature, in the mineral and the animal world, and in every tree and shrub and flower, he saw a revelation of God's wisdom; and as he sought to learn more and more, his knowledge of God and his love for Him constantly increased.

Solomon's divinely inspired wisdom found expression in songs of praise and in many proverbs. "He spake three thousand proverbs: and his songs were a thousand and five. And he spake of trees, from the cedar tree that is in Lebanon even unto the hyssop that springeth out of the wall: he spake also of beasts, and of fowl, and of creeping things, and of fishes." 1 Kings 4:32, 33.

In the proverbs of Solomon are outlined principles of holy living and high endeavor, principles that are heaven-born and that lead to godliness, principles that should govern every act of life. It was the wide dissemination of these principles, and the recognition of God as the One to whom all praise and honor belong, that made Solomon's early reign a time of moral uplift as well as of material prosperity.

"Happy is the man that findeth wisdom," he wrote, "and the man that getteth understanding. For the merchandise of it is better than the merchandise of silver, and the gain thereof than fine gold. She is more precious than rubies: and all things thou canst desire are not to be compared unto her. Length of days is in her right hand; and in her left hand riches and honor. Her ways are ways of pleasantness, and all her paths are peace. She is a tree of life to them that lay hold upon her: and happy is every one that retaineth her." Proverbs 3:13-18.

"Wisdom is the principal thing; therefore get wisdom: and with all thy getting get understanding." Proverbs 4:7 . "The fear of the Lord is the beginning of wisdom." Psalm 111:10. "The fear of the Lord is to hate evil: pride, and arrogancy, and the evil way, and the froward mouth, do I hate." Proverbs 8:13.

O that in later years Solomon had heeded these wonderful words of wisdom! O that he who had declared, "The lips of the wise disperse knowledge" (Proverbs 15:17), and who had himself taught the kings of the earth to render to the King of kings the praise they desired to give to an earthly ruler, had never with a "froward mouth," in "pride and arrogancy," taken to himself the glory due to God alone!

The Temple and Its Dedication

The long-cherished plan of David to erect a temple to the Lord, Solomon wisely carried out. For seven years Jerusalem was filled with busy workers engaged in leveling the chosen site, in building vast retaining walls, in laying broad foundations,—"great stones, costly stones, and hewed stones,"—in shaping the heavy timbers brought from the Lebanon forests, and in erecting the magnificent sanctuary. 1 Kings 5:17.

Simultaneously with the preparation of wood and stone, to which task many thousands were bending their energies, the manufacture of the furnishings for the temple was steadily progressing under the leadership of Hiram of Tyre, "a cunning man, endued with understanding, . . . skillful to work in gold, and in silver, in brass, in iron, in stone, and in timber, in purple, in blue, and in fine linen, and in crimson." 2 Chronicles 2:13, 14.

Thus as the building on Mount Moriah was noiselessly upreared with "stone made ready before it was brought thither: so that there was neither hammer nor ax nor any tool of iron heard in the house, while it was in building," the beautiful fittings were perfected according to the patterns committed by David to his son, "all the vessels that were for the house of God." 1 Kings 6:7; 2 Chronicles 4:19. These included the altar of incense, the table of shewbread, the candlestick and lamps, with the vessels and instruments connected with the ministrations of the priests in the holy place, all "of gold, and that perfect gold." 2 Chronicles 4:21. The brazen furniture,—the altar of burnt offering, the great laver supported by twelve oxen, the lavers of smaller size, with many other vessels,—"in the plain of Jordan did the king cast them, in the clay ground between Succoth and Zeredathah." 2 Chronicles 4:17. These furnishings were provided in abundance, that there should be no lack.

Of surpassing beauty and unrivaled splendor was the palatial building which Solomon and his associates erected for God and His worship. Garnished with precious stones, surrounded by spacious courts with magnificent approaches, and lined with carved cedar and burnished gold, the temple structure, with its broidered hangings and rich furnishings, was a fit emblem of the living church of God on earth, which through the ages has been building in accordance with the divine pattern, with materials that have been likened to "gold, silver, precious stones," "polished after the similitude of a palace." 1 Corinthians 3:12; Psalm 144:12 . Of this spiritual temple Christ is "the chief Cornerstone; in whom all the building fitly framed together groweth unto an holy temple in the Lord." Ephesians 2:20, 21.

At last the temple planned by King David, and built by Solomon his son, was completed. "All that came into Solomon's heart to make in the house of the Lord," he had "prosperously effected." 2 Chronicles 7:11. And now, in order that the palace crowning the heights of Mount Moriah might indeed be, as David had so much desired, a dwelling place "not for man, but for the Lord God" (1 Chronicles 29:1), there remained the solemn ceremony of formally dedicating it to Jehovah and His worship.

The spot on which the temple was built had long been regarded as a consecrated place. It was here that Abraham, the father of the faithful, had revealed his willingness to sacrifice his only son in obedience to the command of Jehovah. Here God had renewed with Abraham the covenant of blessing, which included the glorious Messianic promise to the human race of deliverance through the sacrifice of the Son of the Most High. See Genesis 22:9, 16:18. Here it was that when David offered burnt offerings and peace offerings to stay the avenging sword of the destroying angel, God had answered him by fire from heaven. See 1 Chronicles 21. And now once more the worshipers of Jehovah were here to meet their God and renew their vows of allegiance to Him.

The time chosen for the dedication was a most favorable one—the seventh month, when the people from every part of the kingdom were accustomed to assemble at Jerusalem to celebrate the Feast of Tabernacles. This feast was preeminently an occasion of rejoicing. The labors of the harvest being ended and the toils of the new year not yet begun, the people were free from care and could give themselves up to the sacred, joyous influences of the hour.

At the appointed time the hosts of Israel, with richly clad representatives from many foreign nations, assembled in the temple courts. The scene was one of unusual splendor. Solomon, with the elders of Israel and the most influential men among the people, had returned from another part of the city, whence they had brought the ark of the testament. From the sanctuary on the heights of Gibeon had been transferred the ancient "tabernacle of the congregation, and all the holy vessels that were in the tabernacle" (2 Chronicles 5:5); and these cherished reminders of the earlier experiences of the children of Israel during their wanderings in the wilderness and their conquest of Canaan, now found a permanent home in the splendid building that had been erected to take the place of the portable structure.

In bringing to the temple the sacred ark containing the two tables of stone on which were written by the finger of God the precepts of the Decalogue, Solomon had followed the example of his father David. Every six paces he sacrificed. With singing and with music and with great ceremony, "the priests brought in the ark of the covenant of the Lord unto his place, to the oracle of the house, into the most holy place." Verse 7. As they came out of the inner sanctuary, they took the positions assigned them. The singers —Levites arrayed in white linen, having cymbals and psalteries and harps—stood at the east end of the altar, and with them a hundred and twenty priests sounding with trumpets. See verse 12.

"It came even to pass, as the trumpeters and singers were as one, to make one sound to be heard in praising and thanking the Lord; and when they lifted up their voice with the trumpets and cymbals and instruments of music, and praised the Lord, saying, For He is good; for His mercy endureth forever: that then the house was filled with a cloud, even the house of the Lord; so that the priests could not stand to minister by reason of the cloud: for the glory of the Lord had filled the house of God." Verses 13, 14.

Realizing the significance of this cloud, Solomon declared: "The Lord hath said that He would dwell in the thick darkness. But I have built an house of habitation for Thee, and a place for Thy dwelling forever." 2 Chronicles 6:1, 2.

"The Lord reigneth;
Let the people tremble:
He sitteth between the cherubims;
Let the earth be moved.
"The Lord is great in Zion;
And He is high above all the people.
Let them praise Thy great and terrible name;
For it is holy. . . .
"Exalt ye the Lord our God,
And worship at His footstool;
For He is holy." Psalm 99:1-5.

"In the midst of the court" of the temple had been erected "a brazen scaffold," or platform, "five cubits long, and five cubits broad, and three cubits high." Upon this Solomon stood and with uplifted hands blessed the vast multitude before him. "And all the congregation of Israel stood." 2 Chronicles 6:13, 3.

"Blessed be the Lord God of Israel," Solomon exclaimed, "who hath with His hands fulfilled that which He spake with His mouth to my father David, saying, . . . I have chosen Jerusalem, that My name might be there." Verses 4-6.

Solomon then knelt upon the platform, and in the hearing of all the people offered the dedicatory prayer. Lifting his hands toward heaven, while the congregation were bowed with their faces to the ground, the king pleaded: "Lord God of Israel, there is no God like Thee in the heaven, nor in the earth; which keepest covenant, and showest mercy unto Thy servants, that walk before Thee with all their heart."

"Will God in very deed dwell with men on the earth? Behold, heaven and the heaven of heavens cannot contain Thee; how much less this house which I have built? Have respect therefore to the prayer of Thy servant, and to his supplication, O Lord my God, to hearken unto the cry and the prayer which Thy servant prayeth before Thee: that Thine eyes may be open upon this house day and night, upon the place whereof Thou hast said that Thou wouldest put Thy name there; to hearken unto the prayer which Thy servant prayeth toward this place. Hearken therefore unto the supplications of Thy servant, and of Thy people Israel, which they shall make toward this place: hear Thou from Thy dwelling place, even from heaven; and when Thou hearest, forgive. . . .

"If Thy people Israel be put to the worse before the enemy, because they have sinned against Thee; and shall return and confess Thy name, and pray and make supplication before Thee in this house; then hear Thou from the heavens, and forgive the sin of Thy people Israel, and bring them again unto the land which Thou gavest to them and to their fathers.

"When the heaven is shut up, and there is no rain, because they have sinned against Thee; yet if they pray toward this place, and confess Thy name, and turn from their sin, when Thou dost afflict them; then hear Thou from heaven, and forgive the sin of Thy servants, and of Thy people Israel, when Thou hast taught them the good way, wherein they should walk; and send rain upon Thy land, which Thou hast given unto Thy people for an inheritance.

"If there be dearth in the land, if there be pestilence, if there be blasting, or mildew, locusts, or caterpillars; if their enemies besiege them in the cities of their land; whatsoever sore or whatsoever sickness there be: then what prayer or what supplication soever shall be made of any man, or of all Thy people Israel, when everyone shall know his own sore and his own grief, and shall spread forth his hands in his house: then hear Thou from heaven Thy dwelling place, and forgive, and render unto every man according unto all his ways, whose heart Thou knowest; . . . that they may fear Thee, to walk in Thy ways, so long as they live in the land which Thou gavest unto our fathers.

"Moreover concerning the stranger, which is not of Thy people Israel, but is come from a far country for Thy great name's sake, and Thy mighty hand, and Thy stretched-out arm; if they come and pray in this house; then hear Thou from the heavens, even from Thy dwelling place, and do according to all that the stranger calleth to Thee for; that all people of the earth may know Thy name, and fear Thee, as doth Thy people Israel, and may know that this house which I have built is called by Thy name.

"If Thy people go out to war against their enemies by the way that Thou shalt send them, and they pray unto Thee toward this city which Thou hast chosen, and the house which I have built for Thy name; then hear Thou from the heavens their prayer and their supplication, and maintain their cause.

"If they sin against Thee, (for there is no man which sinneth not,) and Thou be angry with them, and deliver them over before their enemies, and they carry them away captives unto a land far off or near; yet if they bethink themselves in the land whither they are carried captive, and turn and pray unto Thee in the land of their captivity, saying, We have sinned, we have done amiss, and have dealt wickedly; if they return to Thee with all their heart and with all their soul in the land of their captivity, whither they have carried them captives, and pray toward their land, which Thou gavest unto their fathers, and toward the city which Thou hast chosen, and toward the house which I have built for Thy name: then hear Thou from the heavens, even from Thy dwelling place, their prayer and their supplications, and maintain their cause, and forgive Thy people which have sinned against Thee.

"Now, my God, let, I beseech Thee, Thine eyes be open, and let Thine ears be attent unto the prayer that is made in this place. Now therefore arise, O Lord God, into Thy resting place, Thou, and the ark of Thy strength: let Thy priests, O Lord God, be clothed with salvation, and let Thy saints rejoice in goodness. O Lord God, turn not away the face of Thine anointed: remember the mercies of David Thy servant." Verses 14:42.

As Solomon ended his prayer, "fire came down from heaven, and consumed the burnt offering and the sacrifices." The priests could not enter the temple because "the glory of the Lord had filled the Lord's house." "When all the children of Israel saw . . . the glory of the Lord upon the house, they bowed themselves with their faces to the ground upon the pavement, and worshiped, and praised the Lord, saying, For He is good; for His mercy endureth forever."

Then king and people offered sacrifices before the Lord. "So the king and all the people dedicated the house of God." 2 Chronicles 7:1-5. For seven days the multitudes from every part of the kingdom, from the borders "of Hamath unto the river of Egypt," "a very great congregation," kept a joyous feast. The week following was spent by the happy throng in observing the Feast of Tabernacles. At the close of the season of reconsecration and rejoicing the people returned to their homes, "glad and merry in heart for the goodness that the Lord had showed unto David, and to Solomon, and to Israel His people." Verses 8, 10.

The king had done everything within his power to encourage the people to give themselves wholly to God and His service, and to magnify His holy name. And now once more, as at Gibeon early in his reign, Israel's ruler was given evidence of divine acceptance and blessing. In a night vision the Lord appeared to him with the message: "I have heard thy prayer, and have chosen this place to Myself for an house of sacrifice. If I shut up heaven that there be no rain, or if I command the locusts to devour the land, or if I send pestilence among My people; if My people, which are called by My name, shall humble themselves, and pray, and seek My face, and turn from their wicked ways; then will I hear from heaven, and will forgive their sin, and will heal their land. Now Mine eyes shall be open, and Mine ears attent unto the prayer that is made in this place. For now have I chosen and sanctified this house, that My name may be there forever: and Mine eyes and Mine heart shall be there perpetually." Verses 12-16.

Had Israel remained true to God, this glorious building would have stood forever, a perpetual sign of God's especial favor to His chosen people. "The sons of the stranger," God declared, "that join themselves to the Lord, to serve Him, and to love the name of the Lord, to be His servants, everyone that keepeth the Sabbath from polluting it, and taketh hold of My covenant; even them will I bring to My holy mountain, and make them joyful in My house of prayer: their burnt offerings and their sacrifices shall be accepted upon Mine altar; for Mine house shall be called an house of prayer for all people." Isaiah 56:6, 7.

In connection with these assurances of acceptance, the Lord made very plain the path of duty before the king. "As for thee," He declared, "if thou wilt walk before Me, as David thy father walked, and do according to all that I have commanded thee, and shalt observe My statutes and My judgments; then will I establish the throne of thy kingdom, according as I have covenanted with David thy father, saying, There shall not fail thee a man to be ruler in Israel." 2 Chronicles 7:17, 18. Had Solomon continued to serve the Lord in humility, his entire reign would have exerted a powerful influence for good over the surrounding nations, nations that had been so favorably impressed by the reign of David his father and by the wise words and the magnificent works of the earlier years of his own reign. Foreseeing the terrible temptations that attend prosperity and worldly honor, God warned Solomon against the evil of apostasy and foretold the awful results of sin. Even the beautiful temple that had just been dedicated, He declared, would become "a proverb and a byword among all nations" should the Israelites forsake "the Lord God of their fathers" and persist in idolatry. Verses 20, 22.

Strengthened in heart and greatly cheered by the message from heaven that his prayer in behalf of Israel had been heard, Solomon now entered upon the most glorious period of his reign, when "all the kings of the earth" began to seek his presence, "to hear his wisdom, that God had put in his heart." 2 Chronicles 9:23. Many came to see the manner of his government and to receive instruction regarding the conduct of difficult affairs.

As these people visited Solomon, he taught them of God as the Creator of all things, and they returned to their homes with clearer conceptions of the God of Israel and of His love for the human race. In the works of nature they now beheld an expression of His love and a revelation of His character; and many were led to worship Him as their God.

The humility of Solomon at the time he began to bear the burdens of state, when he acknowledged before God, "I am but a little child" (1 Kings 3:7), his marked love of God, his profound reverence for things divine, his distrust of self, and his exaltation of the infinite Creator of all—all these traits of character, so worthy of emulation, were revealed during the services connected with the completion of the temple, when during his dedicatory prayer he knelt in the humble position of a petitioner. Christ's followers today should guard against the tendency to lose the spirit of reverence and godly fear. The Scriptures teach men how they should approach their Maker—with humility and awe, through faith in a divine Mediator. The psalmist has declared:

"The Lord is a great God,

And a great King above all gods. . . .

O come, let us worship and bow down:

Let us kneel before the Lord our Maker."

Psalm 95:3-6. Both in public and in private worship it is our privilege to bow on our knees before God when we offer our petitions to Him. Jesus, our example, "kneeled down, and prayed." Luke 22:41. Of his disciples it is recorded that they, too, "kneeled down, and prayed." Acts 9:40. Paul declared, "I bow my knees unto the Father of our Lord Jesus Christ." Ephesians 3:14. In confessing before God the sins of Israel, Ezra knelt. See Ezra 9:5. Daniel "kneeled upon his knees three times a day, and prayed, and gave thanks before his God." Daniel 6:10.

True reverence for God is inspired by a sense of His infinite greatness and a realization of His presence. With this sense of the Unseen, every heart should be deeply impressed. The hour and place of prayer are sacred, because God is there. And as reverence is manifested in attitude and demeanor, the feeling that inspires it will be deepened. "Holy and reverend is His name," the psalmist declares. Psalm 111:9. Angels, when they speak that name, veil their faces. With what reverence, then, should we, who are fallen and sinful, take it upon our lips!

Well would it be for old and young to ponder those words of Scripture that show how the place marked by God's special presence should be regarded. "Put off thy shoes from off thy feet," He commanded Moses at the burning bush, "for the place whereon thou standest is holy ground." Exodus 3:5. Jacob, after beholding the vision of the angel, exclaimed, "The Lord is in this place; and I knew it not. . . . This is none other but the house of God, and this is the gate of heaven." Genesis 28:16, 17.

In that which was said during the dedicatory services, Solomon had sought to remove from the minds of those present the superstitions in regard to the Creator, that had beclouded the minds of the heathen. The God of heaven is not, like the gods of the heathen, confined to temples made with hands; yet He would meet with His people by His Spirit when they should assemble at the house dedicated to His worship.

Centuries later Paul taught the same truth in the words: "God that made the world and all things therein, seeing that He is Lord of heaven and earth, dwelleth not in temples made with hands; neither is worshiped with men's hands, as though He needed anything, seeing He giveth to all life, and breath, and all things; . . . that they should seek the Lord, if haply they might feel after Him, and find Him, though He be not far from every one of us: for in Him we live, and move, and have our being." Acts 17:24-28.

"Blessed is the nation whose God is the Lord;

And the people whom He hath chosen for His own inheritance.

The Lord looketh from heaven; He beholdeth all the sons of men.

From the place of His habitation He looketh upon all the inhabitants of the earth."

"The Lord hath prepared His throne in the heavens;

And His kingdom ruleth over all."

"Thy way, O God, is in the sanctuary:

Who is so great a God as our God?

Thou art the God that doest wonders:

Thou hast declared Thy strength among the people."

Psalms 33:12-14; 103:19; 77:13, 14.

Although God dwells not in temples made with hands, yet He honors with His presence the assemblies of His people. He has promised that when they come together to seek Him, to acknowledge their sins, and to pray for one another, He will meet with them by His Spirit. But those who assemble to worship Him should put away every evil thing. Unless they worship Him in spirit and truth and in the beauty of holiness, their coming together will be of no avail. Of such the Lord declares, "This people draweth nigh unto Me with their mouth, and honoreth Me with their lips; but their heart is far from Me." Matthew 15:8, 9. Those who worship God must worship Him "in spirit and in truth: for the Father seeketh such to worship Him." John 4:23.

"The Lord is in His holy temple: let all the earth keep silence before Him." Habakkuk 2:20.

Pride of Prosperity

While Solomon exalted the law of heaven, God was with him, and wisdom was given him to rule over Israel with impartiality and mercy. At first, as wealth and worldly honor came to him, he remained humble, and great was the extent of his influence. "Solomon reigned over all kingdoms from the river unto the land of the Philistines, and unto the border of Egypt." "He . . . had peace on all sides round about him. And Judah and Israel dwelt safely, every man under his vine and under his fig tree, . . . all the days of Solomon." 1 Kings 4:21,

24, 25.

But after a morning of great promise his life was darkened by apostasy. History records the melancholy fact that he who had been called Jedidiah,—"Beloved of the Lord" (2 Samuel 12:25, margin),—he who had been honored by God with tokens of divine favor so remarkable that his wisdom and uprightness gained for him world-wide fame, he who had led others to ascribe honor to the God of Israel, turned from the worship of Jehovah to bow before the idols of the heathen.

Hundreds of years before Solomon came to the throne, the Lord, foreseeing the perils that would beset those who might be chosen as rulers of Israel, gave Moses instruction for their guidance. Directions were given that he who should sit on the throne of Israel should "write him a copy" of the statutes of Jehovah "in a book out of that which is before the priests the Levites." "It shall be with him," the Lord said, "and he shall read therein all the days of his life: that he may learn to fear the Lord his God, to keep all the words of this law and these statutes, to do them: that his heart be not lifted up above his brethren, and that he turn not aside from the commandment, to the right hand, or to the left: to the end that he may prolong his days in his kingdom, he, and his children, in the midst of Israel." Deuteronomy 17:18-20.

In connection with this instruction the Lord particularly cautioned the one who might be anointed king not to "multiply wives to himself, that his heart turn not away: neither shall he greatly multiply to himself silver and gold." Verse 17.

With these warnings Solomon was familiar, and for a time he heeded them. His greatest desire was to live and rule in accordance with the statutes given at Sinai. His manner of conducting the affairs of the kingdom was in striking contrast with the customs of the nations of his time—nations who feared not God and whose rulers trampled underfoot His holy law.

In seeking to strengthen his relations with the powerful kingdom lying to the southward of Israel, Solomon ventured upon forbidden ground. Satan knew the results that would attend obedience; and during the earlier years of Solomon's reign—years glorious because of the wisdom, the beneficence, and the uprightness of the king—he sought to bring in influences that would insidiously undermine Solomon's loyalty to principle and cause him to separate from God. That the enemy was successful in this effort, we know from the record: "Solomon made affinity with Pharaoh king of Egypt, and took Pharaoh's daughter, and brought her into the City of David." 1 Kings 3:1.

From a human point of view, this marriage, though contrary to the teachings of God's law, seemed to prove a blessing; for Solomon's heathen wife was converted and united with him in the worship of the true God. Furthermore, Pharaoh rendered signal service to Israel by taking Gezer, slaying "the Canaanites that dwelt in the city," and giving it "for a present unto his daughter, Solomon's wife." 1 Kings 9:16. This city Solomon rebuilt and thus apparently greatly strengthened his kingdom along the Mediterranean seacoast. But in forming an alliance with a heathen nation, and sealing the compact by marriage with an idolatrous princess, Solomon rashly disregarded the wise provision that God had made for maintaining the purity of His people. The hope that his Egyptian wife might be converted was but a feeble excuse for the sin.

For a time God in His compassionate mercy overruled this terrible mistake; and the king, by a wise course, could have checked at least in a large measure the evil forces that his imprudence had set in operation. But Solomon had begun to lose sight of the Source of his power and glory. As inclination gained the ascendancy over reason, self-confidence increased, and he sought to carry out the Lord's purpose in his own way. He reasoned that political and commercial alliances with the surrounding nations would bring these nations to a knowledge of the true God; and he entered into unholy alliance with nation after nation. Often these alliances were sealed by marriages with heathen princesses. The commands of Jehovah were set aside for the customs of surrounding peoples.

Solomon flattered himself that his wisdom and the power of his example would lead his wives from idolatry to the worship of the true God, and also that the alliances thus formed would draw the nations round about into close touch with Israel. Vain hope! Solomon's mistake in regarding himself as strong enough to resist the influence of heathen associates was fatal. And fatal, too, the deception that led him to hope that notwithstanding a disregard of God's law on his part, others might be led to revere and obey its sacred precepts.

The king's alliances and commercial relations with heathen nations brought him renown, honor, and the riches of this world. He was enabled to bring gold from Ophir and silver from Tarshish in great abundance. "The king made silver and gold at Jerusalem as plenteous as stones, and cedar trees made he as the sycamore trees that are in the vale for abundance." 2 Chronicles 1:15. Wealth, with all its attendant temptations, came in Solomon's day to an increasingly large number of people; but the fine gold of character was dimmed and marred.

So gradual was Solomon's apostasy that before he was aware of it; he had wandered far from God. Almost imperceptibly he began to trust less and less in divine guidance and blessing, and to put confidence in his own strength. Little by little he withheld from God that unswerving obedience which was to make Israel a peculiar people, and he conformed more and more closely to the customs of the surrounding nations. Yielding to the temptations incident to his success and his honored position, he forgot the Source of his prosperity. An ambition to excel all other nations in power and grandeur led him to pervert for selfish purposes the heavenly gifts hitherto employed for the glory of God. The money which should have been held in sacred trust for the benefit of the worthy poor and for the extension of principles of holy living throughout the world, was selfishly absorbed in ambitious projects.

Engrossed in an overmastering desire to surpass other

nations in outward display, the king overlooked the need of acquiring beauty and perfection of character. In seeking to glorify himself before the world, he sold his honor and integrity. The enormous revenues acquired through commerce with many lands were supplemented by heavy taxes. Thus pride, ambition, prodigality, and indulgence bore fruit in cruelty and exaction. The conscientious, considerate spirit that had marked his dealings with the people during the early part of his reign, was now changed. From the wisest and most merciful of rulers, he degenerated into a tyrant. Once the compassionate, God-fearing guardian of the people, he became oppressive and despotic. Tax after tax was levied upon the people, that means might be forthcoming to support the luxurious court.

The people began to complain. The respect and admiration they had once cherished for their king was changed into disaffection and abhorrence.

As a safeguard against dependence on the arm of flesh, the Lord had warned those who should rule over Israel not to multiply horses to themselves. But in utter disregard of this command, "Solomon had horses brought out of Egypt." "And they brought unto Solomon horses out of Egypt, and out of all lands." "Solomon gathered together chariots and horsemen: and he had a thousand and four hundred chariots, and twelve thousand horsemen, whom he bestowed in the cities for chariots, and with the king at Jerusalem." 2 Chronicles 1:16; 9:28; 1 Kings 10:26.

More and more the king came to regard luxury, self-indulgence, and the favor of the world as indications of greatness. Beautiful and attractive women were brought from Egypt, Phoenicia, Edom, and Moab, and from many other places. These women were numbered by hundreds. Their religion was idol worship, and they had been taught to practice cruel and degrading rites. Infatuated with their beauty, the king neglected his duties to God and to his kingdom.

His wives exerted a strong influence over him and gradually prevailed on him to unite with them in their worship. Solomon had disregarded the instruction that God had given to serve as a barrier against apostasy, and now he gave himself up to the worship of the false gods. "It came to pass, when Solomon was old, that his wives turned away his heart after other gods: and his heart was not perfect with the Lord his God, as was the heart of David his father. For Solomon went after Ashtoreth the goddess of the Zidonians, and after Milcom the abomination of the Ammonites." 1 Kings 2:4, 5.

On the southern eminence of the Mount of Olives, opposite Mount Moriah, where stood the beautiful temple of Jehovah, Solomon erected an imposing pile of buildings to be used as idolatrous shrines. To please his wives, he placed huge idols, unshapely images of wood and stone, amidst the groves of myrtle and olive. There, before the altars of heathen deities, "Chemosh, the abomination of Moab," and "Molech, the abomination of the children of Ammon," were practiced the most degrading rites of heathenism. Verse 7.

Solomon's course brought its sure penalty. His separation from God through communication with idolaters was his ruin. As he cast off his allegiance to God, he lost the mastery of himself. His moral efficiency was gone. His fine sensibilities became blunted, his conscience seared. He who in his early reign had displayed so much wisdom and sympathy in restoring a helpless babe to its unfortunate mother (see 1 Kings 3:16-28), fell so low as to consent to the erection of an idol to whom living children were offered as sacrifices. He who in his youth was endowed with discretion and understanding, and who in his strong manhood had been inspired to write, "There is a way which seemeth right unto a man, but the end thereof are the ways of death" (Proverbs 14:12), in later years departed so far from purity as to countenance licentious, revolting rites connected with the worship of Chemosh and Ashtoreth. He who at the dedication of the temple had said to his people, "Let your heart therefore be perfect with the Lord our God" (1 Kings 8:61), became himself an offender, in heart and life denying his own words. He mistook license for liberty. He tried—but at what cost!—to unite light with darkness, good with evil, purity with impurity, Christ with Belial.

From being one of the greatest kings that ever wielded a scepter, Solomon became a profligate, the tool and slave of others. His character, once noble and manly, became enervated and effeminate. His faith in the living God was supplanted by atheistic doubts. Unbelief marred his happiness, weakened his principles, and degraded his life. The justice and magnanimity of his early reign were changed to despotism and tyranny. Poor, frail human nature! God can do little for men who lose their sense of dependence upon Him.

During these years of apostasy, the spiritual decline of Israel progressed steadily. How could it be otherwise when their king had united his interests with satanic agencies? Through these agencies the enemy worked to confuse the minds of the Israelites in regard to true and false worship, and they became an easy prey. Commerce with other nations brought them into intimate contact with those who had no love for God, and their own love for Him was greatly lessened. Their keen sense of the high, holy character of God was deadened. Refusing to follow in the path of obedience, they transferred their allegiance to the enemy of righteousness. It came to be a common practice to intermarry with idolaters, and the Israelites rapidly lost their abhorrence of idol worship. Polygamy was countenanced. Idolatrous mothers brought their children up to observe heathen rites. In the lives of some, the pure religious service instituted by God was replaced by idolatry of the darkest hue.

Christians are to keep themselves distinct and separate from the world, its spirit, and its influences. God is fully able to keep us in the world, but we are not to be of the world. His love is not uncertain and fluctuating. Ever He watches over His children with a care that is measureless. But He requires undivided allegiance. "No man can serve two masters: for either he will hate the one, and love the other; or else he will hold to the one, and despise the other. Ye cannot serve God and mammon." Matthew 6:24.

Solomon was endued with wonderful wisdom, but the world drew him away from God. Men today are no stronger than he; they are as prone to yield to the influences that caused his downfall. As God warned Solomon of his danger, so today He warns His children not to imperil their souls by affinity with the world. "Come out from among them," He pleads, "and be ye separate, . . . and touch not the unclean thing, and I will receive you, and will be a Father unto you, and ye shall be My sons and daughters, saith the Lord Almighty." 2 Corinthians 6:17, 18.

In the midst of prosperity lurks danger. Throughout the ages, riches and honor have ever been attended with peril to humility and spirituality. It is not the empty cup that we have difficulty in carrying; it is the cup full to the brim that must be carefully balanced. Affliction and adversity may cause sorrow, but it is prosperity that is most dangerous to spiritual life. Unless the human subject is in constant submission to the will of God, unless he is sanctified by the truth, prosperity will surely arouse the natural inclination to presumption.

In the valley of humiliation, where men depend on God to teach them and to guide their every step, there is comparative safety. But the men who stand, as it were, on a lofty pinnacle, and who, because of their position, are supposed to possess great wisdom—these are in gravest peril. Unless such men make God their dependence, they will surely fall.

Whenever pride and ambition are indulged, the life is marred, for pride, feeling no need, closes the heart against the infinite blessings of Heaven. He who makes self-glorification his aim will find himself destitute of the grace of God, through whose efficiency the truest riches and the most satisfying joys are won. But he who gives all and does all for Christ will know the fulfillment of the promise, "The blessing of the Lord, it maketh rich, and He addeth no sorrow with it." Proverbs 10:22. With the gentle touch of grace the Saviour banishes from the soul unrest and unholy ambition, changing enmity to love and unbelief to confidence. When He speaks to the soul, saying, "Follow Me," the spell of the world's enchantment is broken. At the sound of His voice the spirit of greed and ambition flees from the heart, and men arise, emancipated, to follow Him.

Results of Transgression

Prominent among the primary causes that led Solomon into extravagance and oppression was his failure to maintain and foster the spirit of self-sacrifice.

When, at the foot of Sinai, Moses told the people of the divine command, "Let them make Me a sanctuary; that I may dwell among them," the response of the Israelites was accompanied by the appropriate gifts. "They came, everyone whose heart stirred him up, and everyone whom his spirit made willing," and brought offerings. Exodus 25:8; 35:21. For the building of the sanctuary, great and extensive preparations were necessary; a large amount of the most precious and costly material was required, but the Lord accepted only freewill offerings. "Of every man that giveth it willingly with his heart ye shall take My offering," was the command repeated by Moses to the congregation. Exodus 25:2. Devotion to God and a spirit of sacrifice were the first requisites in preparing a dwelling place for the Most High.

A similar call to self-sacrifice was made when David turned over to Solomon the responsibility of building the temple. Of the assembled multitude David asked, "Who then is willing to consecrate his service this day unto the Lord?" 1 Chronicles 29:5. This call to consecration and willing service should ever have been kept in mind by those who had to do with the erection of the temple.

For the construction of the wilderness tabernacle, chosen men were endowed by God with special skill and wisdom. "Moses said unto the children of Israel, See, the Lord hath called by name Bezaleel, . . . of the tribe of Judah; and He hath filled him with the Spirit of God, in wisdom, in understanding, and in knowledge, and in all manner of workmanship. . . . And He hath put in his heart that he may teach, both he, and Aholiab, . . . of the tribe of Dan. Them hath He filled with wisdom of heart, to work all manner of work, of the engraver, and of the cunning workman, and of the embroiderer, . . . and of the weaver, even of them that do any work. . . . Then wrought Bezaleel and Aholiab, and every wisehearted man, in whom the Lord put wisdom and understanding." Exodus 35:30-35; 36:1. Heavenly intelligences co-operated with the workmen whom God Himself had chosen.

The descendants of these workmen inherited to a large degree the talents conferred on their forefathers. For a time these men of Judah and Dan remained humble and unselfish; but gradually, almost imperceptibly, they lost their hold upon God and their desire to serve Him unselfishly. They asked higher wages for their services, because of their superior skill as workmen in the finer arts. In some instances their request was granted, but more often they found employment in the surrounding nations. In place of the noble spirit of self-sacrifice that had filled the hearts of their illustrious ancestors, they indulged a spirit of covetousness, of grasping for more and more. That their selfish desires might be gratified, they used their God-given skill in the service of heathen kings, and lent their talent to the perfecting of works which were a dishonor to their Maker.

It was among these men that Solomon looked for a master workman to superintend the construction of the temple on Mount Moriah. Minute specifications, in writing, regarding every portion of the sacred structure, had been entrusted to the king; and he could have looked to God in faith for consecrated helpers, to whom would have been granted special skill for doing with exactness the work required. But Solomon lost sight of this opportunity to exercise faith in God. He sent to the king of Tyre for a man, "cunning to work in gold, and in silver, and in brass, and in iron, and in purple, and crimson, and blue, and that can skill to grave with the cunning men . . . in Judah and in Jerusalem." 2 Chronicles 2:7.

The Phoenician king responded by sending Huram, "the son of a woman of the daughters of Dan, and his father was a man of Tyre." Verse 14. Huram was a descendant, on his mother's side, of Aholiab, to whom, hundreds of years before, God had given special wisdom for the construction of the tabernacle.

Thus at the head of Solomon's company of workmen there was placed a man whose efforts were not prompted by an unselfish desire to render service to God. He served the god of this world, mammon. The very fibers of his being were inwrought with the principles of selfishness.

Because of his unusual skill, Huram demanded large wages. Gradually the wrong principles that he cherished came to be accepted by his associates. As they labored with him day after day, they yielded to the inclination to compare his wages with their own, and they began to lose sight of the holy character of their work. The spirit of self-denial left them, and in its place came the spirit of covetousness. The result was a demand for higher wages, which was granted.

The baleful influences thus set in operation permeated all branches of the Lord's service, and extended throughout the kingdom. The high wages demanded and received gave to many an opportunity to indulge in luxury and extravagance. The poor were oppressed by the rich; the spirit of self-sacrifice was well-nigh lost. In the far-reaching effects of these influences may be traced one of the principal causes of the terrible apostasy of him who once was numbered among the wisest of mortals.

The sharp contrast between the spirit and motives of the people building the wilderness tabernacle, and of those engaged in erecting Solomon's temple, has a lesson of deep significance. The self-seeking that characterized the workers on the temple finds its counterpart today in the selfishness that rules in the world. The spirit of covetousness, of seeking for the highest position and the highest wage, is rife. The willing service and joyous self-denial of the tabernacle workers is seldom met with. But this is the only spirit that should actuate the followers of Jesus. Our divine Master has given an example of how His disciples are to work. To those whom He bade, "Follow Me, and I will make you fishers of men" (Matthew 4:19), He offered no stated sum as a reward for their services. They were to share with Him in self-denial and sacrifice.

Not for the wages we receive are we to labor. The motive that prompts us to work for God should have in it nothing akin to self-serving. Unselfish devotion and a spirit of sacrifice have always been and always will be the first requisite of acceptable service. Our Lord and Master designs that not one thread of selfishness shall be woven into His work. Into our efforts we are to bring the tact and skill, the exactitude and wisdom, that the God of perfection required of the builders of the earthly tabernacle; yet in all our labors we are to remember that the greatest talents or the most splendid services are acceptable only when self is laid upon the altar, a living, consuming sacrifice.

Another of the deviations from right principles that finally led to the downfall of Israel's king was his yielding to the temptation to take to himself the glory that belongs to God alone.

From the day that Solomon was entrusted with the work of building the temple, to the time of its completion, his avowed purpose was "to build an house for the name of the Lord God of Israel." 2 Chronicles 6:7. This purpose was fully recognized before the assembled hosts of Israel at the time of the dedication of the temple. In his prayer the king acknowledged that Jehovah had said, "My name shall be there." 1 Kings 8:29.

One of the most touching portions of Solomon's dedicatory prayer was his plea to God for the strangers that should come from countries afar to learn more of Him whose fame had been spread abroad among the nations. "They shall hear," the king pleaded, "of Thy great name, and of Thy strong hand, and of Thy stretched-out arm." In behalf of every one of these stranger worshipers Solomon had petitioned: "Hear Thou, . . . and do according to all that the stranger calleth to Thee for: that all people of the earth may know Thy name, to fear Thee, as do Thy people Israel; and that they may know that this house, which I have builded, is called by Thy name." Verses 42, 43.

At the close of the service, Solomon had exhorted Israel to be faithful and true to God, in order that "all the people of the earth may know," he said, "that the Lord is God, and that there is none else." Verse 60.

A Greater than Solomon was the designer of the temple; the wisdom and glory of God stood there revealed. Those who were unacquainted with this fact naturally admired and praised Solomon as the architect and builder; but the king disclaimed any honor for its conception or erection.

Thus it was when the Queen of Sheba came to visit Solomon. Hearing of his wisdom and of the magnificent temple he had built, she determined "to prove him with hard questions" and to see for herself his famous works. Attended by a retinue of servants, and with camels bearing "spices, and gold in abundance, and precious stones," she made the long journey to Jerusalem. "And when she was come to Solomon, she communed with him of all that was in her heart." She talked with him of the mysteries of nature; and Solomon taught her of the God of nature, the great Creator, who dwells in the highest heaven and rules over all. "Solomon told her all her questions: there was not anything hid from the king, which he told her not." 1 Kings 10:1-3; 2 Chronicles 9:1, 2.

"When the Queen of Sheba had seen all Solomon's wisdom, and the house that he had built, . . . there was no more spirit in her." "It was a true report," she acknowledged, "which I heard in mine own land of thine acts, and of thy wisdom: howbeit I believed not their words, until I came, and mine eyes had seen it:" "and, behold, the half was not told me: thy wisdom and prosperity exceedeth the fame which I heard. Happy are thy men, happy are these thy servants, which stand continually before thee, and that hear thy wisdom." 1 Kings 10:4-8; 2 Chronicles 9:3-6.

By the time of the close of her visit the queen had been so fully taught by Solomon as to the source of his wisdom and prosperity that she was constrained, not to extol the human agent, but to exclaim, "Blessed be the Lord thy God, which delighted in thee, to set thee on the throne of Israel: because the Lord loved Israel forever, therefore made He thee king, to do judgment and justice." 1 Kings 10:9. This is the impression that God designed should be made upon all peoples. And when "all the kings of the earth sought the presence of Solomon, to hear his wisdom, that God had put in his heart" (2 Chronicles 9:23), Solomon for a time honored God by reverently pointing them to the Creator of the heavens and the earth, the Ruler of the universe, the All-wise.

Had Solomon continued in humility of mind to turn the attention of men from himself to the One who had given him wisdom and riches and honor, what a history might have been his! But while the pen of inspiration records his virtues, it also bears faithful witness to his downfall. Raised to pinnacle of greatness and surrounded with the gifts of fortune, Solomon became dizzy, lost his balance, and fell. Constantly extolled by men of the world, he was at length unable to withstand the flattery offered him. The wisdom entrusted to him that he might glorify the Giver, filled him with pride. He finally permitted men to speak of him as the one most worthy of praise for the matchless splendor of the building planned and erected for the honor of "the name of the Lord God of Israel."

Thus it was that the temple of Jehovah came to be known throughout the nations as "Solomon's temple." The human agent had taken to himself the glory that belonged to the One "higher than the highest." Ecclesiastes 5:8. Even to this day the temple of which Solomon declared, "This house which I have built is called by Thy name" (2 Chronicles 6:33), is oftenest spoken of, not as the temple of Jehovah, but as "Solomon's temple."

Man cannot show greater weakness than by allowing men to ascribe to him the honor for gifts that are Heaven-bestowed. The true Christian will make God first and last and best in everything. No ambitious motives will chill his love for God; steadily, perseveringly, will he cause honor to redound to his heavenly Father. It is when we are faithful in exalting the name of God that our impulses are under divine supervision, and we are enabled to develop spiritual and intellectual power.

Jesus, the divine Master, ever exalted the name of His heavenly Father. He taught His disciples to pray, "Our Father who art in heaven, hallowed be Thy name." Matthew 6:9, A.R.V. And they were not to forget to acknowledge, "Thine is . . . the glory." Verse 13. So careful was the great Healer to direct attention from Himself to the Source of His power, that the wondering multitude, "when they saw the dumb to speak, the maimed to be whole, the lame to walk, and the blind to see," did not glorify Him, but "glorified the God of Israel."

Matthew 15:31. In the wonderful prayer that Christ offered just before His crucifixion, He declared, "I have glorified Thee on the earth." "Glorify Thy Son," He pleaded, "that Thy Son also may glorify Thee." "O righteous Father, the world hath not known Thee: but I have known Thee, and these have known that Thou hast sent Me. And I have declared unto them Thy name, and will declare it: that the love wherewith Thou hast loved Me may be in them, and I in them." John 17:1, 4, 25, 26.

"Thus saith the Lord, Let not the wise man glory in his wisdom, neither let the mighty man glory in his might, let not the rich man glory in his riches: but let him that glorieth glory in this, that he understandeth and knoweth Me, that I am the Lord which exercise loving-kindness, judgment, and righteousness, in the earth: for in these things I delight, saith the Lord." Jeremiah 9:23, 24.

"I will praise the name of God, . . .
And will magnify Him with thanksgiving."
"Thou art worthy, O Lord, to receive glory and honor and power."
"I will praise Thee, O Lord my God, with all my heart:
And I will glorify Thy name forevermore."
"O magnify the Lord with me,
And let us exalt His name together."
Psalm 69:30; Revelation 4:11; Psalms 86:12; 34:3.

The introduction of principles leading away from a spirit of sacrifice and tending toward self-glorification, was accompanied by yet another gross perversion of the divine plan for Israel. God had designed that His people should be the light of the world. From them was to shine forth the glory of His law as revealed in the life practice. For the carrying out of this design, He had caused the chosen nation to occupy a strategic position among the nations of earth.

In the days of Solomon the kingdom of Israel extended from Hamath on the north to Egypt on the south, and from the Mediterranean Sea to the river Euphrates. Through this territory ran many natural highways of the world's commerce, and caravans from distant lands were constantly passing to and fro. Thus there was given to Solomon and his people opportunity to reveal to men of all nations the character of the King of kings, and to teach them to reverence and obey Him. To all the world this knowledge was to be given. Through the teaching of the sacrificial offerings, Christ was to be uplifted before the nations, that all who would might live.

Placed at the head of a nation that had been set as a beacon light to the surrounding nations, Solomon should have used his God-given wisdom and power of influence in organizing and directing a great movement for the enlightenment of those who were ignorant of God and His truth. Thus multitudes would have been won to allegiance to the divine precepts, Israel would have been shielded from the evils practiced by the heathen, and the Lord of glory would have been greatly honored. But Solomon lost sight of this high purpose. He failed of improving his splendid opportunities for enlightening those who were continually passing through his territory or tarrying at the principal cities.

The missionary spirit that God had implanted in the heart of Solomon and in the hearts of all true Israelites was supplanted by a spirit of commercialism. The opportunities afforded by contact with many nations were used for personal aggrandizement. Solomon sought to strengthen his position politically by building fortified cities at the gateways of commerce. He rebuilt Gezer, near Joppa, lying along the road between Egypt and Syria; Beth-horon, to the westward of Jerusalem, commanding the passes of the highway leading from the heart of Judea to Gezer and the seacoast; Megiddo, situated on the caravan road from Damascus to Egypt, and from Jerusalem to the northward; and "Tadmor in the wilderness" (2 Chronicles 8:4), along the route of caravans from the east. All these cities were strongly fortified. The commercial advantages of an outlet at the head of the Red Sea were developed by the construction of "a navy of ships in Ezion-geber, . . . on the shore of the Red Sea, in the land of Edom." Trained sailors from Tyre, "with the servants of Solomon," manned these vessels on voyages "to Ophir, and fetched from thence gold," and "great plenty of almug trees, and precious stones." Verse 18; 1 Kings 9:26, 28; 10:11.

The revenue of the king and of many of his subjects was greatly increased, but at what a cost! Through the cupidity and shortsightedness of those to whom had been entrusted the oracles of God, the countless multitudes who thronged the highways of travel were allowed to remain in ignorance of Jehovah.

In striking contrast to the course pursued by Solomon was the course followed by Christ when He was on this earth. The Saviour, though possessing "all power," never used this power for self-aggrandizement. No dream of earthly conquest, of worldly greatness, marred the perfection of His service for mankind. "Foxes have holes, and the birds of the air have nests," He said, "but the Son of man hath not where to lay His head." Matthew 8:20. Those who, in response to the call of the hour, have entered the service of the Master Worker, may well study His methods. He took advantage of the opportunities to be found along the great thoroughfares of travel.

In the intervals of His journeys to and fro, Jesus dwelt at Capernaum, which came to be known as "His own city." Matthew 9:1. Situated on the highway from Damascus to Jerusalem and Egypt and to the Mediterranean Sea, it was well adapted to be the center of the Saviour's work. People from many lands passed through the city or tarried for rest. There Jesus met with those of all nations and all ranks, and thus His lessons were carried to other countries and into many households. By this means interest was aroused in the prophecies pointing forward to the Messiah, attention was directed to the Saviour, and His mission was brought before the world.

In this our day the opportunities for coming into contact with men and women of all classes and many nationalities are much greater than in the days of Israel. The thoroughfares of travel have multiplied a thousandfold.

Like Christ, the messengers of the Most High today should take their position in these great thoroughfares, where they can meet the passing multitudes from all parts of the world. Like Him, hiding self in God, they are to sow the gospel seed, presenting before others the precious truths of Holy Scripture that will take deep root in mind and heart, and spring up unto life eternal.

Solemn are the lessons of Israel's failure during the years when ruler and people turned from the high purpose they had been called to fulfill. Wherein they were weak, even to the point of failure, the Israel of God today, the representatives of heaven that make up the true church of Christ, must be strong; for upon them devolves the task of finishing the work that has been committed to man, and of ushering in the day of final awards. Yet the same influences that prevailed against Israel in the time when Solomon reigned are to be met with still. The forces of the enemy of all righteousness are strongly entrenched; only by the power of God can the victory be gained. The conflict before us calls for the exercise of a spirit of self-denial, for distrust of self and for dependence on God alone, for the wise use of every opportunity for the saving of souls. The Lord's blessing will attend His church as they advance unitedly, revealing to a world lying in the darkness of error the beauty of holiness as manifested in a Christlike spirit of self-sacrifice, in an exaltation of the divine rather than the human, and in loving and untiring service for those so much in need of the blessings of the gospel.

Solomon's Repentance

Twice during Solomon's reign the Lord had appeared to him with words of approval and counsel—in the night vision at Gibeon, when the promise of wisdom, riches, and honor was accompanied by an admonition to remain humble and obedient; and after the dedication of the temple, when once more the Lord exhorted him to faithfulness. Plain were the admonitions, wonderful the promises, given to Solomon; yet of him who in circumstances, in character, and in life seemed abundantly fitted to heed the charge and meet the expectation of Heaven, it is recorded: "He kept not that which the Lord commanded." "His heart was turned from the Lord God of Israel, which had appeared unto him twice, and had commanded him concerning this thing, that he should not go after other gods." 1 Kings 11:9, 10. And so complete was his apostasy, so hardened his heart in transgression, that his case seemed well-nigh hopeless.

From the joy of divine communion, Solomon turned to find satisfaction in the pleasures of sense. Of this experience he says: "I made me great works; I builded me houses; I planted me vineyards: I made me gardens and orchards: . . . I got me servants and maidens: . . . I gathered me also silver and gold, and the peculiar treasure of kings and of the provinces: I gat me men singers and women singers, and the delights of the sons of men, as musical instruments, and that of all sorts. So

I was great, and increased more than all that were before me in Jerusalem. . . .

"And whatsoever mine eyes desired I kept not from them, I withheld not my heart from any joy; for my heart rejoiced in all my labor. . . . Then I looked on all the works that my hands had wrought, and on the labor that I had labored to do: and, behold, all was vanity and vexation of spirit, and there was no profit under the sun.

"And I turned myself to behold wisdom, and madness, and folly: for what can the man do that cometh after the king? even that which hath been already done. . . . I hated life. . . . Yea, I hated all my labor which I had taken under the sun." Ecclesiastes 2:4-18.

By his own bitter experience, Solomon learned the emptiness of a life that seeks in earthly things its highest good. He erected altars to heathen gods, only to learn how vain is their promise of rest to the spirit. Gloomy and soul-harassing thoughts troubled him night and day. For him there was no longer any joy of life or peace of mind, and the future was dark with despair.

Yet the Lord forsook him not. By messages of reproof and by severe judgments, He sought to arouse the king to a realization of the sinfulness of his course. He removed His protecting care and permitted adversaries to harass and weaken the kingdom. "The Lord stirred up an adversary unto Solomon, Hadad the Edomite. . . . And God stirred him up another adversary, Rezon, . . . captain over a band," who "abhorred Israel, and reigned over Syria. And Jeroboam, . . . Solomon's servant," "a mighty man of valor," "even he lifted up his hand against the king." 1 Kings 11:14-28.

At last the Lord, through a prophet, delivered to Solomon the startling message: "Forasmuch as this is done of thee, and thou hast not kept My covenant and My statutes, which I have commanded thee, I will surely rend the kingdom from thee, and will give it to thy servant. Notwithstanding in thy days I will not do it for David thy father's sake: but I will rend it out of the hand of thy son." Verses 11, 12.

Awakened as from a dream by this sentence of judgment pronounced against him and his house, Solomon with quickened conscience began to see his folly in its true light. Chastened in spirit, with mind and body enfeebled, he turned wearied and thirsting from earth's broken cisterns, to drink once more at the fountain of life. For him at last the discipline of suffering had accomplished its work. Long had he been harassed by the fear of utter ruin because of inability to turn from folly; but now he discerned in the message given him a ray of hope. God had not utterly cut him off, but stood ready to deliver him from a bondage more cruel than the grave, and from which he had had no power to free himself.

In gratitude Solomon acknowledged the power and the loving-kindness of the One who is "higher than the highest" (Ecclesiastes 5:8); in penitence he began to retrace his steps toward the exalted plane of purity and holiness from whence he had fallen so far. He could never hope to escape the blasting results of sin, he could never free his mind from all remembrance of the self-indulgent course he had been pursuing, but he would endeavor earnestly to dissuade others from following after folly. He would humbly confess the error of his ways and lift his voice in warning lest others be lost irretrievably because of the influences for evil he had been setting in operation.

The true penitent does not put his past sins from his remembrance. He does not, as soon as he has obtained peace, grow unconcerned in regard to the mistakes he has made. He thinks of those who have been led into evil by his course, and tries in every possible way to lead them back into the true path. The clearer the light that he has entered into, the stronger is his desire to set the feet of others in the right way. He does not gloss over his wayward course, making his wrong a light thing, but lifts the danger signal, that others may take warning.

Solomon acknowledged that "the heart of the sons of men is full of evil, and madness is in their heart." Ecclesiastes 9:3. And again he declared, "Because sentence against an evil work is not executed speedily, therefore the heart of the sons of men is fully set in them to do evil. Though a sinner do evil an hundred times, and his days be prolonged, yet surely I know that it shall be well with them that fear God, which fear before Him: but it shall not be well with the wicked, neither shall he prolong his days, which are as a shadow; because he feareth not before God." Ecclesiastes 8:11-13.

By the spirit of inspiration the king recorded for after generations the history of his wasted years with their lessons of warning. And thus, although the seed of his sowing was reaped by his people in harvests of evil, his life-work was not wholly lost. With meekness and lowliness Solomon in his later years "taught the people knowledge; yea, he gave good heed, and sought out, and set in order many proverbs." He "sought to find out acceptable words: and that which was written was upright, even words of truth." "The words of the wise are as goads, and as nails fastened by the masters of assemblies, which are given from one shepherd. And further, by these, my son, be admonished." Ecclesiastes 12:9-12.

"Let us hear the conclusion of the whole matter," he wrote: "Fear God, and keep His commandments: for this is the whole duty of man. For God shall bring every work into judgment, with every secret thing, whether it be good, or whether it be evil." Verses 13, 14.

Solomon's later writings reveal that as he realized more and still more the wickedness of his course, he gave special attention to warning the youth against falling into the errors that had led him to squander for nought Heaven's choicest gifts. With sorrow and shame he confessed that in the prime of manhood, when he should have found God his comfort, his support, his life, he turned from the light of Heaven and the wisdom of God, and put idolatry in the place of the worship of Jehovah. And now, having learned through sad experience the folly of such a life, his yearning desire was to save others from entering into the bitter experience through which he had passed.

With touching pathos he wrote concerning the privileges and responsibilities before the youth in God's service:

"Truly the light is sweet, and a pleasant thing it is for the eyes to behold the sun: but if a man live many years, and rejoice in them all; yet let him remember the days of darkness; for they shall be many. All that cometh is vanity. Rejoice, O young man, in thy youth; and let thy heart cheer thee in the days of thy youth, and walk in the ways of thine heart, and in the sight of thine eyes: but know thou, that for all these things God will bring thee into judgment. Therefore remove sorrow from thy heart, and put away evil from thy flesh: for childhood and youth are vanity." Ecclesiastes 11:7-10.

"Remember now thy Creator in the days of thy youth,
While the evil days come not,
Nor the years draw nigh,
When thou shalt say, I have no pleasure in them;
"While the sun,
Or the light,
Or the moon,
Or the stars,
Be not darkened,
Nor the clouds return after the rain:
"In the day when the keepers of the house shall tremble,
And the strong men shall bow themselves,
And the grinders cease because they are few,
And those that look out of the windows be darkened,
And the doors shall be shut in the streets,
"When the sound of the grinding is low,
And he shall rise up at the voice of the bird,
And all the daughters of music shall be brought low;
"Also when they shall be afraid of that which is high,
And fears shall be in the way,
"And the almond tree shall flourish,
And the grasshopper shall be a burden,
And desire shall fail:
"Because man goeth to his long home,
And the mourners go about the streets:
"Or ever the silver cord be loosed,
Or the golden bowl be broken,
Or the pitcher be broken at the fountain,
Or the wheel broken at the cistern.
"Then shall the dust return to the earth As it was:
And the spirit shall return unto God Who gave it."
Ecclesiastes 12:1-7.

Not only to the youth, but to those of mature years, and to those who are descending the hill of life and facing the western sun, the life of Solomon is full of warning. We see and hear of unsteadiness in youth, the young wavering between right and wrong, and the current of evil passions proving too strong for them. In those of maturer years, we do not look for this unsteadiness and unfaithfulness; we expect the character to be established, the principles firmly rooted. But this is not always so. When Solomon should have been in character as a sturdy oak, he fell from his steadfastness under the power of temptation. When his strength should have been the firmest, he was found to be the weakest.

From such examples we should learn that in watchfulness and prayer is the only safety for both young and old. Security does not lie in exalted position and great privileges. One may for many years have enjoyed a genuine Christian experience, but he is still exposed to Satan's attacks. In the battle with inward sin and outward temptation, even the wise and powerful Solomon was vanquished. His failure teaches us that, whatever a man's intellectual qualities may be, and however faithfully he may have served God in the past, he can never with safety trust in his own wisdom and integrity.

In every generation and in every land the true foundation and pattern for character building have been the same. The divine law, "Thou shalt love the Lord thy God with all thy heart, . . . and thy neighbor as thyself," the great principle made manifest in the character and life of our Saviour, is the only secure foundation, the only sure guide. Luke 10:27. "Wisdom and knowledge shall be the stability of thy times, and strength of salvation," the wisdom and knowledge which God's word alone can impart. Isaiah 33:6.

It is as true now as when the words were spoken to Israel of obedience to His commandments: "This is your wisdom and your understanding in the sight of the nations." Deuteronomy 4:6. Here is the only safeguard for individual integrity, for the purity of the home, the well-being of society, or the stability of the nation. Amidst all life's perplexities and dangers and conflicting claims, the one safe and sure rule is to do what God says. "The statutes of the Lord are right," and "he that doeth these things shall never be moved." Psalms 19:8; 15:5.

Those who heed the warning of Solomon's apostasy will shun the first approach of those sins that overcame him. Only obedience to the requirements of Heaven will keep man from apostasy. God has bestowed upon man great light and many blessings; but unless this light and these blessings are accepted, they are no security against disobedience and apostasy. When those whom God has exalted to positions of high trust turn from Him to human wisdom, their light becomes darkness. Their entrusted capabilities become a snare.

Till the conflict is ended, there will be those who will depart from God. Satan will so shape circumstances that unless we are kept by divine power, they will almost imperceptibly weaken the fortifications of the soul. We need to inquire at every step, "Is this the way of the Lord?" So long as life shall last, there will be need of guarding the affections and the passions with a firm purpose. Not one moment can we be secure except as we rely upon God, the life hidden with Christ. Watchfulness and prayer are the safeguards of purity.

All who enter the City of God will enter through the strait gate—by agonizing effort; for "there shall in no wise enter into it anything that defileth." Revelation 21:27. But none who have fallen need give up to despair. Aged men, once honored of God, may have defiled their souls, sacrificing virtue on the altar of lust; but if they repent, forsake sin, and turn to God, there is still hope for them. He who declares, "Be thou faithful unto death, and I will give thee a crown of life," also gives the invitation, "Let the wicked forsake his way, and the unrighteous man his thoughts: and let him return unto the Lord, and He will have mercy upon him; and to our God, for He will abundantly pardon." Revelation 2:10; Isaiah 55:7. God hates sin, but He loves the sinner. "I will heal their backsliding," He declares; "I will love them freely." Hosea 14:4.

Solomon's repentance was sincere; but the harm that his example of evil-doing had wrought could not be undone. During his apostasy there were in the kingdom men who remained true to their trust, maintaining their purity and loyalty. But many were led astray; and the forces of evil set in operation by the introduction of idolatry and worldly practices could not easily be stayed by the penitent king. His influence for good was greatly weakened. Many hesitated to place full confidence in his leadership. Though the king confessed his sin and wrote out for the benefit of after generations a record of his folly and repentance, he could never hope entirely to destroy the baleful influence of his wrong deeds. Emboldened by his apostasy, many continued to do evil, and evil only. And in the downward course of many of the rulers who followed him may be traced the sad influence of the prostitution of his God-given powers.

In the anguish of bitter reflection on the evil of his course, Solomon was constrained to declare, "Wisdom is better than weapons of war: but one sinner destroyeth much good." "There is an evil which I have seen under the sun, as an error which proceedeth from the ruler: folly is set in great dignity." "Dead flies cause the ointment of the apothecary to send forth a stinking savor: so doth a little folly him that is in reputation for wisdom and honor." Ecclesiastes 9:18, 10:5, 6, 1.

Among the many lessons taught by Solomon's life, none is more strongly emphasized than the power of influence for good or for ill. However contracted may be our sphere, we still exert an influence for weal or woe. Beyond our knowledge or control, it tells upon others in blessing or cursing. It may be heavy with the gloom of discontent and selfishness, or poisonous with the deadly taint of some cherished sin; or it may be charged with the life-giving power of faith, courage, and hope, and sweet with the fragrance of love. But potent for good or for ill it will surely be.

That our influence should be a savor of death unto death is a fearful thought, yet it is possible. One soul misled, forfeiting eternal bliss—who can estimate the loss! And yet one rash act, one thoughtless word, on our part may exert so deep an influence on the life of another that it will prove the ruin of his soul. One blemish on the character may turn many away from Christ.

As the seed sown produces a harvest, and this in turn is sown, the harvest is multiplied. In our relation to others, this law holds true. Every act, every word, is a seed that will bear fruit. Every deed of thoughtful kindness, of obedience, of self-denial, will reproduce itself in others, and through them in still others. So every act of envy, malice, or dissension is a seed that will spring up in a "root of bitterness" whereby many shall be defiled. Hebrews 12:15. And how much larger number will the "many" poison! Thus the sowing of good and evil goes on for time and for eternity.

The Rending of the Kingdom

"Solomon slept with his fathers, and was buried in the City of David his father: and Rehoboam his son reigned in his stead." 1 Kings 11:43.

Soon after his accession to the throne, Rehoboam went to Shechem, where he expected to receive formal recognition from all the tribes. "To Shechem were all Israel come to make him king." 2 Chronicles 10:1.

Among those present was Jeroboam the son of Nebat —the same Jeroboam who during Solomon's reign had been known as "a mighty man of valor," and to whom the prophet Ahijah the Shilonite had delivered the startling message, "Behold, I will rend the kingdom out of the hand of Solomon, and will give ten tribes to thee." 1 Kings 11:28, 31.

The Lord through His messenger had spoken plainly to Jeroboam regarding the necessity of dividing the kingdom. This division must take place, He had declared, "because that they have forsaken Me, and have worshiped Ashtoreth the goddess of the Zidonians, Chemosh the god of the Moabites, and Milcom the god of the children of Ammon, and have not walked in My ways, to do that which is right in Mine eyes, and to keep My statutes and My judgments, as did David." Verse 33.

Jeroboam had been further instructed that the kingdom was not to be divided before the close of Solomon's reign. "I will not take the whole kingdom out of his hand," the Lord had declared; "but I will make him prince all the days of his life for David My servant's sake, whom I chose, because he kept My commandments and My statutes: but I will take the kingdom out of his son's hand, and will give it unto thee, even ten tribes." Verses 34, 35.

Although Solomon had longed to prepare the mind of Rehoboam, his chosen successor, to meet with wisdom the crisis foretold by the prophet of God, he had never been able to exert a strong molding influence for good over the mind of his son, whose early training had been so grossly neglected. Rehoboam had received from his mother, an Ammonitess, the stamp of a vacillating character. At times he endeavored to serve God and was granted a measure of prosperity; but he was not steadfast, and at last he yielded to the influences for evil that had surrounded him from infancy. In the mistakes of Rehoboam's life and in his final apostasy is revealed the fearful result of Solomon's union with idolatrous women.

The tribes had long suffered grievous wrongs under the oppressive measures of their former ruler. The extravagance of Solomon's reign during his apostasy had led him to tax the people heavily and to require of them much menial service.

Before going forward with the coronation of a new ruler, the leading men from among the tribes determined to ascertain whether or not it was the purpose of Solomon's son to lessen these burdens. "So Jeroboam and all Israel came and spake to Rehoboam, saying, Thy father made our yoke grievous: now therefore ease thou somewhat the grievous servitude of thy father, and his heavy yoke that he put upon us, and we will serve thee."

Desirous of taking counsel with his advisers before outlining his policy, Rehoboam answered, "Come again unto me after three days. And the people departed.

"And King Rehoboam took counsel with the old men that had stood before Solomon his father while he yet lived, saying, What counsel give ye me to return answer to this people? And they spake unto him, saying, If thou be kind to this people, and please them, and speak good words to them, they will be thy servants forever." 2 Chronicles 10:3-7.

Dissatisfied, Rehoboam turned to the younger men with whom he had associated during his youth and early manhood, and inquired of them, "What counsel give ye that we may answer this people, who have spoken to me, saying, Make the yoke which thy father did put upon us lighter?" 1 Kings 12:9. The young men suggested that he deal sternly with the subjects of his kingdom and make plain to them that from the very beginning he would brook no interference with his personal wishes.

Flattered by the prospect of exercising supreme authority, Rehoboam determined to disregard the counsel of the older men of his realm, and to make the younger men his advisers. Thus it came to pass that on the day appointed, when "Jeroboam and all the people came to Rehoboam" for a statement concerning the policy he intended to pursue, Rehoboam "answered the people roughly, . . . saying, May father made your yoke heavy, and I will add to your yoke: my father also chastised you with whips, but I will chastise you with scorpions." Verses 12-14.

Had Rehoboam and his inexperienced counselors understood the divine will concerning Israel, they would have listened to the request of the people for decided reforms in the administration of the government. But in the hour of opportunity that came to them during the meeting in Shechem, they failed to reason from cause to effect, and thus forever weakened their influence over a large number of the people. Their expressed determination to perpetuate and add to the oppression introduced during Solomon's reign was in direct conflict with God's plan for Israel, and gave the people ample occasion to doubt the sincerity of their motives. In this unwise and unfeeling attempt to exercise power, the king and his chosen counselors revealed the pride of position and authority.

The Lord did not allow Rehoboam to carry out the policy he had outlined. Among the tribes were many thousands who had become thoroughly aroused over the oppressive measures of Solomon's reign, and these now felt that they could not do otherwise than rebel against the house of David. "When all Israel saw that the king hearkened not unto them, the people answered the king, saying, What portion have we in David? neither have we inheritance in the son of Jesse: to your tents, O Israel: now see to thine own house, David. So Israel departed unto their tents." Verse 16.

The breach created by the rash speech of Rehoboam proved irreparable. Thenceforth the twelve tribes of Israel were divided, the tribes of Judah and Benjamin composing the lower or southern kingdom of Judah, under the rulership of Rehoboam; while the ten northern tribes formed and maintained a separate government, known as the kingdom of Israel, with Jeroboam as their ruler. Thus was fulfilled the prediction of the prophet concerning the rending of the kingdom. "The cause was from the Lord." Verse 15.

When Rehoboam saw the ten tribes withdrawing their allegiance from him, he was aroused to action. Through one of the influential men of his kingdom, "Adoram, who was over the tribute," he made an effort to conciliate them. But the ambassador of peace received treatment which bore witness to the feeling against Rehoboam. "All Israel stoned him with stones, that he died." Startled by this evidence of the strength of revolt, "King Rehoboam made speed to get him up to his chariot, to flee to Jerusalem." Verse 18.

At Jerusalem "he assembled all the house of Judah, with the tribe of Benjamin, an hundred and fourscore thousand chosen men, which were warriors, to fight against the house of Israel, to bring the kingdom again to Rehoboam the son of Solomon. But the word of God came unto Shemaiah the man of God, saying, Speak unto Rehoboam, the son of Solomon, king of Judah, and unto all the house of Judah and Benjamin, and to the remnant of the people, saying, Thus saith the Lord, Ye shall not go up, nor fight against your brethren the children of Israel: return every man to his house; for this thing is from Me. They hearkened therefore to the word of the Lord, and returned to depart, according to the word of the Lord." Verses 21-24.

For three years Rehoboam tried to profit by his sad experience at the beginning of his reign; and in this effort he was prospered. He "built cities for defense in Judah," and "fortified the strongholds, and put captains in them, and store of victual, and of oil and wine." He was careful to make these fortified cities "exceeding strong." 2 Chronicles 11:5, 11, 12. But the secret of Judah's prosperity during the first years of Rehoboam's reign lay not in these measures. It was their recognition of God as the Supreme Ruler that placed the tribes of Judah and Benjamin on vantage ground. To their number were added many God-fearing men from the northern tribes. "Out of all the tribes of Israel," the record reads, "such as set their hearts to seek the Lord God of Israel came to Jerusalem, to sacrifice unto the Lord God of their fathers. So they strengthened the kingdom of Judah, and made Rehoboam the son of Solomon strong, three years: for three years they walked in the way of David and Solomon." Verses 16, 17.

In continuing this course lay Rehoboam's opportunity to

redeem in large measure the mistakes of the past and to restore confidence in his ability to rule with discretion. But the pen of inspiration has traced the sad record of Solomon's successor as one who failed to exert a strong influence for loyalty to Jehovah. Naturally headstrong, confident, self-willed, and inclined to idolatry, nevertheless, had he placed his trust wholly in God, he would have developed strength of character, steadfast faith, and submission to the divine requirements. But as time passed, the king put his trust in the power of position and in the strongholds he had fortified. Little by little he gave way to inherited weakness, until he threw his influence wholly on the side of idolatry. "It came to pass, when Rehoboam had established the kingdom, and had strengthened himself, he forsook the law of the Lord, and all Israel with him." 2 Chronicles 12:1.

How sad, how filled with significance, the words, "And all Israel with him"! The people whom God had chosen to stand as a light to the surrounding nations were turning from their Source of strength and seeking to become like the nations about them. As with Solomon, so with Rehoboam—the influence of wrong example led many astray. And as with them, so to a greater or less degree is it today with everyone who gives himself up to work evil—the influence of wrongdoing is not confined to the doer. No man liveth unto himself. None perish alone in their iniquity. Every life is a light that brightens and cheers the pathway of others, or a dark and desolating influence that tends toward despair and ruin. We lead others either upward to happiness and immortal life, or downward to sorrow and eternal death. And if by our deeds we strengthen or force into activity the evil powers of those around us, we share their sin.

God did not allow the apostasy of Judah's ruler to remain unpunished. "In the fifth year of King Rehoboam Shishak king of Egypt came up against Jerusalem, because they had transgressed against the Lord, with twelve hundred chariots, and three score thousand horsemen: and the people were without number that came with him out of Egypt. . . . And he took the fenced cities which pertained to Judah, and came to Jerusalem.

"Then came Shemaiah the prophet to Rehoboam, and to the princes of Judah, that were gathered together to Jerusalem because of Shishak, and said unto them, Thus saith the Lord, Ye have forsaken Me, and therefore have I also left you in the hand of Shishak." Verses 2-5.

The people had not yet gone to such lengths in apostasy that they despised the judgments of God. In the losses sustained by the invasion of Shishak, they recognized the hand of God and for a time humbled themselves. "The Lord is righteous," they acknowledged.

"And when the Lord saw that they humbled themselves, the word of the Lord came to Shemaiah, saying, They have humbled themselves; therefore I will not destroy them, but I will grant them some deliverance; and My wrath shall not be poured out upon Jerusalem by the hand of Shishak. Nevertheless they shall be his servants; that they may know My service, and the service of the kingdoms of the countries.

"So Shishak king of Egypt came up against Jerusalem, and took away the treasures of the house of the Lord, and the treasures of the king's house; he took all: he carried away also the shields of gold which Solomon had made. Instead of which King Rehoboam made shields of brass, and committed them to the hands of the chief of the guard, that kept the entrance of the king's house.... And when he humbled himself, the wrath of the Lord turned from him, that He would not destroy him altogether: and also in Judah things went well." Verses 6-12.

But as the hand of affliction was removed, and the nation prospered once more, many forgot their fears and turned again to idolatry. Among these was King Rehoboam himself. Though humbled by the calamity that had befallen him, he failed to make this experience a decisive turning point in his life. Forgetting the lesson that God had endeavored to teach him, he relapsed into the sins that had brought judgments on the nation. After a few inglorious years, during which the king "did evil, because he prepared not his heart to seek the Lord," "Rehoboam slept with his fathers, and was buried in the City of David: and Abijah his son reigned in his stead." Verses 14, 16. With the rending of the kingdom early in Rehoboam's reign the glory of Israel began to depart, never again to be regained in its fullness. At times during the centuries that followed, the throne of David was occupied by men of moral worth and far-seeing judgment, and under the rulership of these sovereigns the blessings resting upon the men of Judah were extended to the surrounding nations. At times the name of Jehovah was exalted above every false god, and His law was held in reverence. From time to time mighty prophets arose to strengthen the hands of the rulers and to encourage the people to continued faithfulness. But the seeds of evil already springing up when Rehoboam ascended the throne were never to be wholly uprooted; and at times the once-favored people of God were to fall so low as to become a byword among the heathen.

Yet notwithstanding the perversity of those who leaned toward idolatrous practices, God in mercy would do everything in His power to save the divided kingdom from utter ruin. And as the years rolled on and His purpose concerning Israel seemed to be utterly thwarted by the devices of men inspired by satanic agencies, He still manifested His beneficent designs through the captivity and restoration of the chosen nation.

The rending of the kingdom was but the beginning of a wonderful history, wherein are revealed the long-sufferance and tender mercy of God. From the crucible of affliction through which they were to pass because of hereditary and cultivated tendencies to evil, those whom God was seeking to purify unto Himself a peculiar people, zealous of good works, were finally to acknowledge:

"There is none like unto Thee, O Lord; Thou art great, and Thy name is great in might. Who would not fear Thee, O King of nations? . . . Among all the wise men of the nations, and in all their kingdoms, there is none like unto Thee." "The Lord is the true God, He is the living God, and an everlasting King." Jeremiah 10:6, 7, 10.

And the worshipers of idols were at last to learn the lesson that false gods are powerless to uplift and save. "The gods that have not made the heavens and the earth, even they shall perish from the earth, and from under these heavens." Verse 11. Only in allegiance to the living God, the Creator of all and the Ruler over all, can man find rest and peace.

With one accord the chastened and penitent of Israel and Judah were at last to renew their covenant relationship with Jehovah of hosts, the God of their fathers; and of Him they were to declare:

"He hath made the earth by His power,
He hath established the world by His wisdom,
And hath stretched out the heavens by His discretion.
"When He uttereth His voice, there is a multitude of waters in the heavens.
And He causeth the vapors to ascend from the ends of the earth;
He maketh lightnings with rain, and bringeth forth the wind out of His treasures.
"Every man is brutish in his knowledge:
Every founder is confounded by the graven image:
For his molten image is falsehood, and there is no breath in them.
"They are vanity, and the work of errors:
In the time of their visitation they shall perish.
The portion of Jacob is not like them:
"For He is the former of all things;
And Israel is the rod of His inheritance:
The Lord of hosts is His name."
Verses 12-16.

Jeroboam

Placed on the throne by the ten tribes of Israel who had rebelled against the house of David, Jeroboam, the former servant of Solomon, was in a position to bring about wise reforms in both civil and religious affairs. Under the rulership of Solomon he had shown aptitude and sound judgment; and the knowledge he had gained during years of faithful service fitted him to rule with discretion. But Jeroboam failed to make God his trust.

Jeroboam's greatest fear was that at some future time the hearts of his subjects might be won over by the ruler occupying the throne of David. He reasoned that if the ten tribes should be permitted to visit often the ancient seat of the Jewish monarchy, where the services of the temple were still conducted as in the years of Solomon's reign, many might feel inclined to renew their allegiance to the government centering at Jerusalem. Taking counsel with His advisers, Jeroboam determined by one bold stroke to lessen, so far as possible, the probability of a revolt from his rule. He would bring this about by creating within the borders of his newly formed kingdom two centers of worship, one at Bethel and the other at Dan. In these places the ten tribes should be invited to assemble, instead of at Jerusalem, to worship God.

In arranging this transfer, Jeroboam thought to appeal to the imagination of the Israelites by setting before them some visible representation to symbolize the presence of the invisible God. Accordingly he caused to be made two calves of gold, and these were placed within shrines at the appointed centers of worship. In this effort to represent the Deity, Jeroboam violated the plain command of Jehovah: "Thou shalt not make unto thee any graven image. . . . Thou shalt not bow down thyself to them, nor serve them." Exodus 20:4, 5.

So strong was Jeroboam's desire to keep the ten tribes away from Jerusalem that he lost sight of the fundamental weakness of his plan. He failed to take into consideration the great peril to which he was exposing the Israelites by setting before them the idolatrous symbol of the deity with which their ancestors had been so familiar during the centuries of Egyptian bondage. Jeroboam's recent residence in Egypt should have taught him the folly of placing before the people such heathen representations. But his set purpose of inducing the northern tribes to discontinue their annual visits to the Holy City led him to adopt the most imprudent of measures. "It is too much for you to go up to Jerusalem," he urged; "behold thy gods, O Israel, which brought thee up out of the land of Egypt." 1 Kings 12:28. Thus they were invited to bow down before the golden images and adopt strange forms of worship.

The king tried to persuade the Levites, some of whom were living within his realm, to serve as priests in the newly erected shrines at Bethel and Dan; but in this effort he met with failure. He was therefore compelled to elevate to the priesthood men from "the lowest of the people." Verse 31. Alarmed over the prospect, many of the faithful, including a great number of the Levites, fled to Jerusalem, where they might worship in harmony with the divine requirements.

"Jeroboam ordained a feast in the eighth month, on the fifteenth day of the month, like unto the feast that is in Judah, and he offered upon the altar. So did he in Bethel, sacrificing unto the calves that he had made: and he placed in Bethel the priests of the high places which he had made." Verse 32.

The king's bold defiance of God in thus setting aside divinely appointed institutions was not allowed to pass unrebuked. Even while he was officiating and burning incense during the dedication of the strange altar he had set up at Bethel, there appeared before him a man of God from the kingdom of Judah, sent to denounce him for presuming to introduce new forms of worship. The prophet "cried against the altar, . . . and said, O altar, altar, thus saith the Lord; Behold, a child shall be born unto the house of David, Josiah by name; and upon thee shall he offer the priests of the high places that burn incense upon thee, and men's bones shall be burnt upon thee.

"And he gave a sign the same day, saying, This is the sign

which the Lord hath spoken; Behold, the altar shall be rent, and the ashes that are upon it shall be poured out." Immediately the altar "was rent, and the ashes poured out from the altar, according to the sign which the man of God had given by the word of the Lord." 1 Kings 13:2, 3, 5.

On seeing this, Jeroboam was filled with a spirit of defiance against God and attempted to restrain the one who had delivered the message. In wrath "he put forth his hand from the altar" and cried out, "Lay hold on him." His impetuous act met with swift rebuke. The hand outstretched against the messenger of Jehovah suddenly became powerless and withered, and could not be withdrawn.

Terror-stricken, the king appealed to the prophet to intercede with God in his behalf. "Entreat now the face of the Lord thy God," he pleaded, "and pray for me, that my hand may be restored me again, And the man of God besought the Lord, and the king's hand was restored him again, and become as it was before." Verses 4, 6.

Vain had been Jeroboam's effort to invest with solemnity the dedication of a strange altar, respect for which would have led to disrespect for the worship of Jehovah in the temple at Jerusalem. By the message of the prophet, the king of Israel should have been led to repent and to renounce his wicked purposes, which were turning the people away from the true worship of God. But he hardened his heart and determined to follow a way of his own choosing.

At the time of the feast at Bethel the hearts of the Israelites were not fully hardened. Many were susceptible to the influence of the Holy Spirit. The Lord designed that those who were taking rapid steps in apostasy should be checked in their course before it should be too late. He sent His messenger to interrupt the idolatrous proceedings and to reveal to king and people what the outworking of this apostasy would be. The rending of the altar was a sign of God's displeasure at the abomination that was being wrought in Israel.

The Lord seeks to save, not to destroy. He delights in the rescue of sinners. "As I live, saith the Lord God, I have no pleasure in the death of the wicked." Ezekiel 33:11. By warnings and entreaties He calls the wayward to cease from their evil-doing and to turn to Him and live. He gives His chosen messengers a holy boldness, that those who hear may fear and be brought to repentance. How firmly the man of God rebuked the king! And this firmness was essential; in no other way could the existing evils have been rebuked. The Lord gave His servant boldness, that an abiding impression might be made on those who heard. The messengers of the Lord are never to fear the face of man, but are to stand unflinchingly for the right. So long as they put their trust in God, they need not fear; for He who gives them their commission gives them also the assurance of His protecting care.

Having delivered his message, the prophet was about to return, when Jeroboam said to him, "Come home with me, and refresh thyself, and I will give thee a reward." "If thou wilt give me half thine house," the prophet replied, "I will not go in with thee, neither will I eat bread nor drink water in this place: for so was it charged me by the word of the Lord, saying, Eat no bread, nor drink water, nor turn again by the same way that thou camest." 1 Kings 13:7-9.

Well would it have been for the prophet had he adhered to his purpose to return to Judea without delay. While traveling homeward by another route, he was overtaken by an aged man who claimed to be a prophet and who made false representations to the man of God, declaring, "I am a prophet also as thou art; and an angel spake unto me by the word of the Lord, saying, Bring him back with thee into thine house, that he may eat bread and drink water." Again and again the lie was repeated and the invitation urged until the man of God was persuaded to return.

Because the true prophet allowed himself to take a course contrary to the line of duty, God permitted him to suffer the penalty of transgression. While he and the one who had invited him to return to Bethel were sitting together at the table, the inspiration of the Almighty came upon the false prophet, "and he cried unto the man of God that came from Judah, saying, Thus saith the Lord, Forasmuch as thou hast disobeyed the mouth of the Lord, and hast not kept the commandment which the Lord thy God commanded thee, . . . thy carcass shall not come unto the sepulcher of thy fathers." Verses 18-22.

This prophecy of doom was soon literally fulfilled. "It came to pass, after he had eaten bread, and after he had drunk, that he saddled for him the ass. . . . And when he was gone, a lion met him by the way, and slew him: and his carcass was cast in the way, and the ass stood by it, the lion also stood by the carcass. And, behold, men passed by, and saw the carcass cast in the way, . . . and they came and told it in the city where the old prophet dwelt. And when the prophet that brought him back from the way heard thereof, he said, It is the man of God, who was disobedient unto the word of the Lord." Verses 23-26.

The penalty that overtook the unfaithful messenger was a still further evidence of the truth of the prophecy uttered over the altar. If, after disobeying the word of the Lord, the prophet had been permitted to go on in safety, the king would have used this fact in an attempt to vindicate his own disobedience. In the rent altar, in the palsied arm, and in the terrible fate of the one who dared disobey an express command of Jehovah, Jeroboam should have discerned the swift displeasure of an offended God, and these judgments should have warned him not to persist in wrongdoing. But, far from repenting, Jeroboam "made again of the lowest of the people priests of the high places: whosoever would, he consecrated him, and he became one of the priests of the high places." Thus he not only sinned greatly himself, but "made Israel to sin;" and "this thing became sin unto the house of Jeroboam, even to cut it off, and to destroy it from off the face of the earth." Verses 33, 34; 14:16.

Toward the close of a troubled reign of twenty-two years,

Jeroboam met with a disastrous defeat in a war with Abijah, the successor of Rehoboam. "Neither did Jeroboam recover strength again in the days of Abijah: and the Lord struck him, and he died." 2 Chronicles 13:20.

The apostasy introduced during Jeroboam's reign became more and more marked, until finally it resulted in the utter ruin of the kingdom of Israel. Even before the death of Jeroboam, Ahijah, the aged prophet at Shiloh who many years before had predicted the elevation of Jeroboam to the throne, declared: "The Lord shall smite Israel, as a reed is shaken in the water, and He shall root up Israel out of this good land, which He gave to their fathers, and shall scatter them beyond the river, because they have made their groves, provoking the Lord to anger. And He shall give Israel up because of the sins of Jeroboam, who did sin, and who made Israel to sin." 1 Kings 14:15, 16.

Yet the Lord did not give Israel up without first doing all that could be done to lead them back to their allegiance to Him. Through long, dark years when ruler after ruler stood up in bold defiance of Heaven and led Israel deeper and still deeper into idolatry, God sent message after message to His backslidden people. Through His prophets He gave them every opportunity to stay the tide of apostasy and to return to Him. During the years that were to follow the rending of the kingdom, Elijah and Elisha were to live and labor, and the tender appeals of Hosea and Amos and Obadiah were to be heard in the land. Never was the kingdom of Israel to be left without noble witnesses to the mighty power of God to save from sin. Even in the darkest hours some would remain true to their divine Ruler and in the midst of idolatry would live blameless in the sight of a holy God. These faithful ones were numbered among the goodly remnant through whom the eternal purpose of Jehovah was finally to be fulfilled.

National Apostasy

From the time of Jeroboam's death to Elijah's appearance before Ahab the people of Israel suffered a steady spiritual decline. Ruled by men who did not fear Jehovah and who encouraged strange forms of worship, the larger number of the people rapidly lost sight of their duty to serve the living God and adopted many of the practices of idolatry.

Nadab, the son of Jeroboam, occupied the throne of Israel for only a few months. His career of evil was suddenly stopped by a conspiracy headed by Baasha, one of his generals, to gain control of the government. Nadab was slain, with all his kindred in the line of succession, "according unto the saying of the Lord, which He spake by His servant Ahijah the Shilonite: because of the sins of Jeroboam which he sinned, and which he made Israel sin." 1 Kings 15:29, 30.

Thus perished the house of Jeroboam. The idolatrous worship introduced by him had brought upon the guilty offenders the retributive judgments of Heaven; and yet the rulers who followed—Baasha, Elah, Zimri, and Omri—during a period of nearly forty years, continued in the same fatal course of evil-doing.

During the greater part of this time of apostasy in Israel, Asa was ruling in the kingdom of Judah. For many years "Asa did that which was good and right in the eyes of the Lord his God: for he took away the altars of the strange gods, and the high places, and brake down the images, and cut down the groves: and commanded Judah to seek the Lord God of their fathers, and to do the law and the commandment. Also he took away out of all the cities of Judah the high places and the sun images: and the kingdom was quiet before him." 2 Chronicles 14:2-5.

The faith of Asa was put to a severe test when "Zerah the Ethiopian with an host of a thousand thousand, and three hundred chariots," invaded his kingdom. Verse 9. In this crisis Asa did not put his trust in the "fenced cities in Judah" that he had built, with "walls, and towers, gates, and bars," nor in the "mighty men of valor" in his carefully trained army. Verses 6-8. The king's trust was in Jehovah of hosts, in whose name marvelous deliverances had been wrought in behalf of Israel of old. Setting his forces in battle array, he sought the help of God.

The opposing armies now stood face to face. It was a time of test and trial to those who served the Lord. Had every sin been confessed? Had the men of Judah full confidence in God's power to deliver? Such thoughts as these were in the minds of the leaders. From every human viewpoint the vast host from Egypt would sweep everything before it. But in time of peace Asa had not been giving himself to amusement and pleasure; he had been preparing for any emergency. He had an army trained for conflict; he had endeavored to lead his people to make their peace with God. And now, although his forces were fewer in number than the enemy, his faith in the One whom he had made his trust did not weaken. Having sought the Lord in the days of prosperity, the king could now rely upon Him in the day of adversity. His petitions showed that he was not a stranger to God's wonderful power. "It is nothing with Thee to help," he pleaded, "whether with many, or with them that have no power: help us, O Lord our God; for we rest on Thee, and in Thy name we go against this multitude. O Lord, Thou art our God; let not man prevail against Thee." Verse 11.

The prayer of Asa is one that every Christian believer may fittingly offer. We fight in a warfare, not against flesh and blood, but against principalities and powers, and against spiritual wickedness in high places. See Ephesians 6:12. In life's conflict we must meet evil agencies that have arrayed themselves against the right. Our hope is not in man, but in the living God. With full assurance of faith we may expect that He will unite His omnipotence with the efforts of human instrumentalities, for the glory of His name. Clad with the armor of His righteousness, we may gain the victory over every foe.

King Asa's faith was signally rewarded. "The Lord smote the Ethiopians before Asa, and before Judah; and the Ethiopians fled. And Asa and the people that were with him pursued them unto Gerar: and the Ethiopians were overthrown, that they could not recover themselves; for the were destroyed before the Lord, and before His host." 2 Chronicles 14:12, 13.

As the victorious armies of Judah and Benjamin were returning to Jerusalem, "the Spirit of God came upon Azariah the son of Oded: and he went out to meet Asa, and said unto him, Hear ye me, Asa, and all Judah and Benjamin; The Lord is with you, while ye be with Him; and if ye seek Him, He will be found of you; but if ye forsake Him, He will forsake you." "Be ye strong therefore, and let not your hands be weak: for your work shall be rewarded." 2 Chronicles 15:1, 2, 7.

Greatly encouraged by these words, Asa soon led out in a second reformation in Judah. He "put away the abominable idols out of all the land of Judah and Benjamin, and out of the cities which he had taken from Mount Ephraim, and renewed the altar of the Lord, that was before the porch of the Lord.

"And he gathered all Judah and Benjamin, and the strangers with them out of Ephraim and Manasseh, and out of Simeon: for they fell to him out of Israel in abundance, when they saw that the Lord his God was with him. So they gathered themselves together at Jerusalem in the third month, in the fifteenth year of the reign of Asa. And they offered unto the Lord the same time, of the spoil which they had brought, seven hundred oxen and seven thousand sheep. And they entered into a covenant to seek the Lord God of their fathers with all their heart and with all their soul." "And He was found of them: and the Lord gave them rest round about." Verses 8-12, 15. Asa's long record of faithful service was marred by some mistakes, made at times when he failed to put his trust fully in God. When, on one occasion, the king of Israel entered the kingdom of Judah and seized Ramah, a fortified city only five miles from Jerusalem, Asa sought deliverance by forming an alliance with Benhadad, king of Syria. This failure to trust God alone in time of need was sternly rebuked by Hanani the prophet, who appeared before Asa with the message:

"Because thou hast relied on the king of Syria, and not relied on the Lord thy God, therefore is the host of the king of Syria escaped out of thine hand. Were not the Ethiopians and the Lubims a huge host, with very many chariots and horsemen? yet, because thou didst rely on the Lord, He delivered them into thine hand. For the eyes of the Lord run to and fro throughout the whole earth, to show Himself strong in the behalf of them whose heart is perfect toward Him. Herein thou hast done foolishly: therefore from henceforth thou shalt have wars." 2 Chronicles 16:7-9.

Instead of humbling himself before God because of his mistake, "Asa was wroth with the seer, and put him in a prison house; for he was in a rage with him because of this thing. And Asa oppressed some of the people the same time." Verse 10.

"In the thirty and ninth year of his reign," Asa was "diseased in his feet, until his disease was exceeding great: yet in his disease he sought not to the Lord, but to the physicians." Verse 12. The king died in the forty-first year of his reign and was succeeded by Jehoshaphat, his son.

Two years before the death of Asa, Ahab began to rule in the kingdom of Israel. From the beginning his reign was marked by a strange and terrible apostasy. His father, Omri, the founder of Samaria, had "wrought evil in the eyes of the Lord, and did worse than all that were before him" (1 Kings 16:25); but the sins of Ahab were even greater. He "did more to provoke the Lord God of Israel to anger than all the kings of Israel that were before him," acting "as if it had been a light thing for him to walk in the sins of Jeroboam the son of Nebat." Verses 33, 31. Not content with encouraging the forms of religious service followed at Bethel and Dan, he boldly led the people into the grossest heathenism, by setting aside the worship of Jehovah for Baal worship.

Taking to wife Jezebel, "the daughter of Ethbaal king of the Zidonians" and high priest of Baal, Ahab "served Baal, and worshiped him. And he reared up an altar for Baal in the house of Baal, which he had built in Samaria." Verses 31, 32.

Not only did Ahab introduce Baal worship at the capital city, but under the leadership of Jezebel he erected heathen altars in many "high places," where in the shelter of surrounding groves the priests and others connected with this seductive form of idolatry exerted their baleful influence, until well-nigh all Israel were following after Baal. "There was none like unto Ahab," who "did sell himself to work wickedness in the sight of the Lord, whom Jezebel his wife stirred up. And he did very abominably in following idols, according to all things as did the Amorites, whom the Lord cast out before the children of Israel." 1 Kings 21:25, 26.

Ahab was weak in moral power. His union by marriage with an idolatrous woman of decided character and positive temperament resulted disastrously both to himself and to the nation. Unprincipled, and with no high standard of rightdoing, his character was easily molded by the determined spirit of Jezebel. His selfish nature was incapable of appreciating the mercies of God to Israel and his own obligations as the guardian and leader of the chosen people.

Under the blighting influence of Ahab's rule, Israel wandered far from the living God and corrupted their ways before Him. For many years they had been losing their sense of reverence and godly fear; and now it seemed as if there were none who dared expose their lives by openly standing forth in opposition to the prevailing blasphemy. The dark shadow of apostasy covered the whole land. Images of Baalim and Ashtoreth were everywhere to be seen. Idolatrous temples and consecrated groves, wherein were worshiped the works of men's hands, were multiplied. The air was polluted with the smoke of the sacrifices offered to false gods. Hill and vale resounded with the drunken cries of a heathen priesthood who sacrificed to the sun, moon, and stars.

Through the influence of Jezebel and her impious priests, the people were taught that the idol gods that had been set up were deities, ruling by their mystic power the elements of earth, fire, and water. All the bounties of heaven—the running brooks, the streams of living water, the gentle dew, the showers of rain which refreshed the earth and caused the fields to bring forth abundantly—were ascribed to the favor of Baal and Ashtoreth, instead of to the Giver of every good and perfect gift. The people forgot that the hills and valleys, the streams and fountains, were in the hand of the living God, that He controlled the sun, the clouds of heaven, and all the powers of nature.

Through faithful messengers the Lord sent repeated warnings to the apostate king and the people, but in vain were these words of reproof. In vain aid the inspired messengers assert Jehovah's right to be the only God in Israel; in vain did they exalt the laws that He had entrusted to them. Captivated by the gorgeous display and the fascinating rites of idol worship, the people followed the example of the king and his court, and gave themselves up to the intoxicating, degrading pleasures of a sensual worship. In their blind folly they chose to reject God and His worship. The light so graciously given them had become darkness. The fine gold had become dim. Alas, how had the glory of Israel departed! Never before had the chosen people of God fallen so low in apostasy. Of "the prophets of Baal" there were "four hundred and fifty," besides four hundred "prophets of the groves." 1 Kings 18:19. Nothing short of the miracle-working power of God could preserve the nation from utter destruction. Israel had voluntarily separated herself from Jehovah, yet the Lord in compassion still yearned after those who had been led into sin, and He was about to send to them one of the mightiest of His prophets, through whom many were to be led back to allegiance to the God of their fathers.

"Who is wise, and he shall understand these things? Prudent, and he shall know them? For the ways of the Lord are right, And the just shall walk in them: But the transgressors shall fall therein." Hosea 14:9.

Elijah the Tishbite

Among the mountains of Gilead, east of the Jordan, there dwelt in the days of Ahab a man of faith and prayer whose fearless ministry was destined to check the rapid spread of apostasy in Israel. Far removed from any city of renown, and occupying no high station in life, Elijah the Tishbite nevertheless entered upon his mission confident in God's purpose to prepare the way before him and to give him abundant success. The word of faith and power was upon his lips, and his whole life was devoted to the work of reform. His was the voice of one crying in the wilderness to rebuke sin and press back the tide of evil. And while he came to the people as a reprover of sin, his message offered the balm of Gilead to the sin-sick souls of all who desired to be healed.

As Elijah saw Israel going deeper and deeper into idolatry, his soul was distressed and his indignation aroused. God had done great things for His people. He had delivered them from bondage and given them "the lands of the heathen, . . . that they might observe His statutes, and keep His laws." Psalm 105:44, 45. But the beneficent designs of Jehovah were now well-nigh forgotten. Unbelief was fast separating the chosen nation from the Source of their strength. Viewing this apostasy from his mountain retreat, Elijah was overwhelmed with sorrow. In anguish of soul he besought God to arrest the once-favored people in their wicked course, to visit them with judgments, if need be, that they might be led to see in its true light their departure from Heaven. He longed to see them brought to repentance before they should go to such lengths in evil-doing as to provoke the Lord to destroy them utterly.

Elijah's prayer was answered. Oft-repeated appeals, remonstrances, and warnings had failed to bring Israel to repentance. The time had come when God must speak to them by means of judgments. Inasmuch as the worshipers of Baal claimed that the treasures of heaven, the dew and the rain, came not from Jehovah, but from the ruling forces of nature, and that it was through the creative energy of the sun that the earth was enriched and made to bring forth abundantly, the curse of God was to rest heavily upon the polluted land. The apostate tribes of Israel were to be shown the folly of trusting to the power of Baal for temporal blessings. Until they should turn to God with repentance, and acknowledge Him as the source of all blessing, there should fall upon the land neither dew nor rain.

To Elijah was entrusted the mission of delivering to Ahab Heaven's message of judgment. He did not seek to be the Lord's messenger; the word of the Lord came to him. And jealous for the honor of God's cause, he did not hesitate to obey the divine summons, though to obey seemed to invite swift destruction at the hand of the wicked king. The prophet set out at once and traveled night and day until he reached Samaria. At the palace he solicited no admission, nor waited to be formally announced. Clad in the coarse garments usually worn by the prophets of that time, he passed the guards, apparently unnoticed, and stood for a moment before the astonished king.

Elijah made no apology for his abrupt appearance. A Greater than the ruler of Israel had commissioned him to speak; and, lifting his hand toward heaven, he solemnly affirmed by the living God that the judgments of the Most High were about to fall upon Israel. "As the Lord God of Israel liveth, before whom I stand," he declared, "there shall not be dew nor rain these years, but according to my word."

It was only by the exercise of strong faith in the unfailing power of God's word that Elijah delivered his message. Had he not possessed implicit confidence in the One whom he served, he would never have appeared before Ahab. On his way to Samaria, Elijah had passed by ever-flowing streams, hills covered with verdure, and stately forests that seemed beyond the reach of drought. Everything on which the eye rested was clothed with beauty. The prophet might have wondered how the streams that had never ceased their flow could become dry, or how those hills and valleys could be burned with drought. But he gave no place to unbelief. He fully believed that God would humble apostate Israel, and that through judgments they would be brought to repentance. The fiat of

Heaven had gone forth; God's word could not fail; and at the peril of his life Elijah fearlessly fulfilled his commission. Like a thunderbolt from a clear sky, the message of impending judgment fell upon the ears of the wicked king; but before Ahab could recover from his astonishment, or frame a reply, Elijah disappeared as abruptly as he had come, without waiting to witness the effect of his message. And the Lord went before him, making plain the way. "Turn thee eastward," the prophet was bidden, "and hide thyself by the brook Cherith, that is before Jordan. And it shall be, that thou shalt drink of the brook; and I have commanded the ravens to feed thee."

The king made diligent inquiry, but the prophet was not to be found. Queen Jezebel, angered over the message that had locked up the treasures of heaven, lost no time in conferring with the priests of Baal, who united with her in cursing the prophet and in defying the wrath of Jehovah. But notwithstanding their desire to find him who had uttered the word of woe, they were destined to meet with disappointment. Nor could they conceal from others a knowledge of the judgment pronounced in consequence of the prevailing apostasy. Tidings of Elijah's denunciation of the sins of Israel, and of his prophecy of swift-coming punishment, quickly spread throughout the land. The fears of some were aroused, but in general the heavenly message was received with scorn and ridicule.

The prophet's words went into immediate effect. Those who were at first inclined to scoff at the thought of calamity, soon had occasion for serious reflection; for after a few months the earth, unrefreshed by dew or rain, became dry, and vegetation withered. As time passed, streams that had never been known to fail began to decrease, and brooks began to dry up. Yet the people were urged by their leaders to have confidence in the power of Baal and to set aside as idle words the prophecy of Elijah. The priests still insisted that it was through the power of Baal that the showers of rain fell. Fear not the God of Elijah, nor tremble at His word, they urged, it is Baal that brings forth the harvest in its season and provides for man and beast.

God's message to Ahab gave Jezebel and her priests and all the followers of Baal and Ashtoreth opportunity to test the power of their gods, and, if possible, to prove the word of Elijah false. Against the assurances of hundreds of idolatrous priests, the prophecy of Elijah stood alone. If, notwithstanding the prophet's declaration, Baal could still give dew and rain, causing the streams to continue to flow and vegetation to flourish, then let the king of Israel worship him and the people say that he is God.

Determined to keep the people in deception, the priests of Baal continue to offer sacrifices to their gods and to call upon them night and day to refresh the earth. With costly offerings the priests attempt to appease the anger of their gods; with a zeal and a perseverance worthy of a better cause they linger round their pagan altars and pray earnestly for rain. Night after night, throughout the doomed land, their cries and entreaties arise. But no clouds appear in the heavens by day to hide the burning rays of the sun. No dew or rain refreshes the thirsty earth. The word of Jehovah stands unchanged by anything the priests of Baal can do.

A year passes, and yet there is no rain. The earth is parched as if with fire. The scorching heat of the sun destroys what little vegetation has survived. Streams dry up, and lowing herds and bleating flocks wander hither and thither in distress. Once-flourishing fields have become like burning desert sands, a desolate waste. The groves dedicated to idol worship are leafless; the forest trees, gaunt skeletons of nature, afford no shade. The air is dry and suffocating; dust storms blind the eyes and nearly stop the breath. Once-prosperous cities and villages have become places of mourning. Hunger and thirst are telling upon man and beast with fearful mortality. Famine, with all its horror, comes closer and still closer.

Yet notwithstanding these evidences of God's power, Israel repented not, nor learned the lesson that God would have them learn. They did not see that He who created nature controls her laws, and can make of them instruments of blessing or of destruction. Proudhearted, enamored of their false worship, they were unwilling to humble themselves under the mighty hand of God, and they began to cast about for some other cause to which to attribute their sufferings.

Jezebel utterly refused to recognize the drought as a judgment from Jehovah. Unyielding in her determination to defy the God of heaven, she, with nearly the whole of Israel, united in denouncing Elijah as the cause of all their misery. Had he not borne testimony against their forms of worship? If only he could be put out of the way, she argued, the anger of their gods would be appeased, and their troubles would end.

Urged on by the queen, Ahab instituted a most diligent search for the hiding place of the prophet. To the surrounding nations, far and near, he sent messengers to seek for the man whom he hated, yet feared; and in his anxiety to make the search as thorough as possible, he required of these kingdoms and nations an oath that they knew nothing of the whereabouts of the prophet. But the search was in vain. The prophet was safe from the malice of the king whose sins had brought upon the land the denunciation of an offended God.

Failing in her efforts against Elijah, Jezebel determined to avenge herself by slaying all the prophets of Jehovah in Israel. Not one should be left alive. The infuriated woman carried out her purpose in the massacre of many of God's servants. Not all, however, perished. Obadiah, the governor of Ahab's house, yet faithful to God, "took an hundred prophets," and at the risk of his own life, "hid them by fifty in a cave, and fed them with bread and water." 1 Kings 18:4.

The second year of famine passed, and still the pitiless heavens gave no sign of rain. Drought and famine continued their devastation throughout the kingdom. Fathers and mothers, powerless to relieve the sufferings of their children, were forced to see them die. Yet still apostate Israel refused to humble their hearts before God and continued to murmur against the man by whose word these terrible judgments had been brought upon them. They seemed unable to discern in their suffering and distress a call to repentance, a divine interposition to save them from taking the fatal step beyond the boundary of Heaven's forgiveness.

The apostasy of Israel was an evil more dreadful than all the multiplied horrors of famine. God was seeking to free the people from their delusion and lead them to understand their accountability to the One to whom they owed their life and all things. He was trying to help them to recover their lost faith, and He must needs bring upon them great affliction.

"Have I any pleasure at all that the wicked should die? saith the Lord God: and not that he should return from his ways, and live?" "Cast away from you all your transgressions, whereby ye have transgressed; and make you a new heart and a new spirit: for why will ye die, O house of Israel? For I have no pleasure in the death of him that dieth, saith the Lord God: wherefore turn yourselves, and live ye." "Turn ye, turn ye from your evil ways; for why will ye die, O house of Israel?" Ezekiel 18:23, 31, 32; 33:11.

God had sent messengers to Israel, with appeals to return to their allegiance. Had they heeded these appeals, had they turned from Baal to the living God, Elijah's message of judgment would never have been given. But the warnings that might have been a savor of life unto life had proved to them a savor of death unto death. Their pride had been wounded, their anger had been aroused against the messengers, and now they regarded with intense hatred the prophet Elijah. If only he should fall into their hands, gladly they would deliver him to Jezebel—as if by silencing his voice they could stay the fulfillment of his words! In the face of calamity they continued to stand firm in their idolatry. Thus they were adding to the guilt that had brought the judgments of Heaven upon the land.

For stricken Israel there was but one remedy—a turning away from the sins that had brought upon them the chastening hand of the Almighty, and a turning to the Lord with full purpose of heart. To them had been given the assurance, "If I shut up heaven that there be no rain, or if I command the locusts to devour the land, or if I send pestilence among My people; if My people, which are called by My name, shall humble themselves, and pray, and seek My face, and turn from their wicked ways; then will I hear from heaven, and will forgive their sin, and will heal their land." 2 Chronicles 7:13, 14. It was to bring to pass this blessed result that God continued to withhold from them the dew and the rain until a decided reformation should take place.

The Voice of Stern Rebuke

For a time Elijah remained hidden in the mountains by the brook Cherith. There for many months he was miraculously provided with food. Later on, when, because of the continued drought, the brook became dry, God bade His servant find refuge in a heathen land. "Arise," He bade him, "get thee to Zarephath, which belongeth to Zidon, and dwell there: behold, I have commanded a widow woman there to sustain thee."

This woman was not an Israelite. She had never had the privileges and blessings that the chosen people of God had enjoyed; but she was a believer in the true God and had walked in all the light that was shining on her pathway. And now, when there was no safety for Elijah in the land of Israel, God sent him to this woman to find a asylum in her home.

"So he arose and went to Zarephath. And when he came to the gate of the city, behold, the widow woman was there gathering of sticks: and he called to her, and said, Fetch me, I pray thee, a little water in a vessel, that I may drink. And as she was going to fetch it, he called to her, and said, Bring me, I pray thee, a morsel of bread in thine hand."

In this poverty-stricken home the famine pressed sore, and the pitifully meager fare seemed about to fail. The coming of Elijah on the very day when the widow feared that she must give up the struggle to sustain life tested to the utmost her faith in the power of the living God to provide for her necessities. But even in her dire extremity she bore witness to her faith by a compliance with the request of the stranger who was asking her to share her last morsel with him.

In response to Elijah's request for food and drink, the widow said, "As the Lord thy God liveth, I have not a cake, but an handful of meal in a barrel, and a little oil in a cruse: and, behold, I am gathering two sticks, that I may go in and dress it for me and my son, that we may eat it, and die." Elijah said to her, "Fear not; go and do as thou hast said: but make me thereof a little cake first, and bring it unto me, and after make for thee and for thy son. For thus saith the Lord of Israel, The barrel of meal shall not waste, neither shall the cruse of oil fail, until the day that the Lord sendeth rain upon the earth."

No greater test of faith than this could have been required. The widow had hitherto treated all strangers with kindness and liberality. Now, regardless of the suffering that might result to herself and child, and trusting in the God of Israel to supply her every need, she met this supreme test of hospitality by doing "according to the saying of Elijah."

Wonderful was the hospitality shown to God's prophet by this Phoenician woman, and wonderfully were her faith and generosity rewarded. "She, and he, and her house, did eat many days. And the barrel of meal wasted not, neither did the cruse of oil fail, according to the word of the Lord, which He spake by Elijah.

"And it came to pass after these things, that the son of the woman, the mistress of the house, fell sick; and his sickness was so sore, that there was no breath left in him. And she said unto Elijah, What have I to do with thee, O thou man of God? art thou come unto me to call my sin to remembrance, and to slay my son?

"And he said unto her, Give me thy son. And he took him out of her bosom, and carried him up into a loft, where he abode, and laid him upon his own bed. . . . And he stretched himself upon the child three times, and cried unto the Lord. . . . And the Lord heard the voice of Elijah; and the soul of the child came into him again, and he revived.

"And Elijah took the child, and brought him down out of the chamber into the house, and delivered him unto his mother: and Elijah said, See, thy son liveth. And the woman said to Elijah, Now by this I know that thou art a man of God, and that the word of the Lord in thy mouth is truth."

The widow of Zarephath shared her morsel with Elijah, and in return her life and that of her son were preserved. And to all who, in time of trial and want, give sympathy and assistance to others more needy, God has promise great blessing. He has not changed. His power is no less now than in the days of Elijah. No less sure now than when spoken by our Saviour is the promise, "He that receiveth a prophet in the name of a prophet shall receive a prophet's reward." Matthew 10:41.

"Be not forgetful to entertain strangers: for thereby some have entertained angels unawares." Hebrews 13:2. These words have lost none of their force through the lapse of time. Our heavenly Father still continues to place in the pathway of His children opportunities that are blessings in disguise; and those who improve these opportunities find great joy. "If thou draw out thy soul to the hungry, and satisfy the afflicted soul; then shall thy light rise in obscurity, and thy darkness be as the noonday: and the Lord shall guide thee continually, and satisfy thy soul in drought, and make fat thy bones: and thou shalt be like a watered garden, and like a spring of water, whose waters fail not." Isaiah 58:10, 11. To His faithful servants today Christ says, "He that receiveth you receiveth Me, and he that receiveth Me receiveth Him that sent Me." No act of kindness shown in His name will fail to be recognized and rewarded. And in the same tender recognition Christ includes even the feeblest and lowliest of the family of God. "Whosoever shall give to drink," He says, "unto one of these little ones"—those who are as children in their faith and their knowledge of Christ—"a cup of cold water only in the name of a disciple, verily I say unto you, he shall in no wise lose his reward." Matthew 10:40, 42.

Through the long years of drought and famine, Elijah prayed earnestly that the hearts of Israel might be turned from idolatry to allegiance to God. Patiently the prophet waited, while the hand of the Lord rested heavily on the stricken land. As he saw evidences of suffering and want multiplying on every side, his heart was wrung with sorrow, and he longed for power to bring about a reformation quickly. But God Himself was working out His plan, and all that His servant could do was to pray on in faith and await the time for decided action.

The apostasy prevailing in Ahab's day was the result of many years of evil-doing. Step by step, year after year, Israel had been departing from the right way. For generation after generation they had refused to make straight paths for their feet, and at last the great majority of the people had yielded themselves to the leadership of the powers of darkness.

About a century had passed since, under the rulership of King David, Israel had joyfully united in chanting hymns of praise to the Most High, in recognition of their entire dependence on Him for daily mercies. Listen to their words of adoration as then they sang:

"O God of our salvation, . . .
Thou makest the outgoings of the morning and evening to rejoice.
Thou visitest the earth, and waterest it:
Thou greatly enrichest it with the river of God, which is full of water:
Thou preparest them corn, when Thou hast so provided for it.
Thou waterest the ridges thereof abundantly: Thou causest rain to descend into the furrows thereof:
Thou makest it soft with showers: Thou blessest the springing thereof.
Thou crownest the year with Thy goodness; And Thy paths drop fatness.
They drop upon the pastures of the wilderness:
And the little hills rejoice on every side.
The pastures are clothed with flocks;
The valleys also are covered over with corn;
They shout for joy, they also sing."
Psalm 65:5, 8-13, margin.

Israel had then recognized God as the One who "laid the foundations of the earth." In expression of their faith they had sung:

"Thou coveredst it with the deep as with a garment:
The waters stood above the mountains.
At Thy rebuke they fled;
At the voice of Thy thunder they hasted away.
They go up by the mountains; they go down by the valleys
Unto the place which Thou hast founded for them.
Thou hast set a bound that they may not pass over;
That they turn not again to cover the earth."
Psalm 104:5-9.

It is by the mighty power of the Infinite One that the elements of nature in earth and sea and sky are kept within bounds. And these elements He uses for the happiness of His creatures. "His good treasure" is freely expended "to give the rain . . . in his season, and to bless all the work" of man's hands. Deuteronomy 28:12.

"He sendeth the springs into the valleys,
Which run among the hills.
They give drink to every beast of the field:
The wild asses quench their thirst.
By them shall the fowls of the heaven have their habitation,
Which sing among the branches. . . .
He causeth the grass to grow for the cattle,
And herb for the service of man:
That He may bring forth food out of the earth;
And wine that maketh glad the heart of man,
And oil to make his face to shine,
And bread which strengtheneth man's heart. . . .

"O Lord, how manifold are Thy works!
In wisdom hast Thou made them all: The earth is full of Thy riches.
So is this great and wide sea,
Wherein are things creeping innumerable,
Both small and great beasts. . . .
These wait all upon Thee;
That Thou mayest give them their meat in due season.
That Thou givest them they gather:
"Thou openest Thine hand,
They are filled with good."
Psalm 104:10-15,24-28.

Israel had had abundant occasion for rejoicing. The land to which the Lord had brought them was a land flowing with milk and honey. During the wilderness wandering, God had assured them that He was guiding them to a country where they need never suffer for lack of rain. "The land, whither thou goest in to possess it," He had told them, "is not as the land of Egypt, from whence ye came out, where thou sowedst thy seed, and wateredst it with thy foot, as a garden of herbs: but the land, whither ye go to possess it, is a land of hills and valleys, and drinketh water of the rain of heaven: a land which the Lord thy God careth for: the eyes of the Lord thy God are always upon it, from the beginning of the year even unto the end of the year." The promise of abundance of rain had been given on condition of obedience. "It shall come to pass," the Lord had declared, "if ye shall hearken diligently unto My commandments which I command you this day, to love the Lord your God, and to serve Him with all your heart and with all your soul, that I will give you the rain of your land in his due season, the first rain and the latter rain, that thou mayest gather in thy corn, and thy wine, and thine oil. And I will send grass in thy fields for thy cattle, that thou mayest eat and be full.

"Take heed to yourselves," the Lord had admonished His people, "that your heart be not deceived, and ye turn aside, and serve other gods, and worship them; and then the Lord's wrath be kindled against you, and He shut up the heaven, that there be no rain, and that the land yield not her fruit; and lest ye perish quickly from off the good land which the Lord giveth you." Deuteronomy 11:10-17.

"If thou wilt not hearken unto the voice of the Lord thy God, to observe to do all His commandments and His statutes," the Israelites had been warned, "thy heaven that is over thy head shall be brass, and the earth that is under thee shall be iron. The Lord shall make the rain of thy land powder and dust: from heaven shall it come down upon thee, until thou be destroyed." Deuteronomy 28:15, 23, 24.

These were among the wise counsels of Jehovah to ancient Israel. "Lay up these My words in your heart and in your soul," He had commanded His chosen people, "and bind them for a sign upon your hand, that they may be as frontlets between your eyes. And ye shall teach them your children, speaking of them when thou sittest in thine house, and when thou walkest by the way, when thou liest down, and when thou risest up." Deuteronomy 11:18, 19. Plain were these commands, yet as the centuries passed, and generation after generation lost sight of the provision made for their spiritual welfare, the ruinous influences of apostasy threatened to sweep aside every barrier of divine grace.

Thus it had come to pass that God was now visiting His people with the severest of His judgments. The prediction of Elijah was meeting with terrible fulfillment. For three years the messenger of woe was sought for in city after city and nation after nation. At the mandate of Ahab, many rulers had given their oath of honor that the strange prophet could not be found in their dominions. Yet the search was continued, for Jezebel and the prophets of Baal hated Elijah with a deadly hatred, and they spared no effort to bring him within reach of their power. And still there was no rain.

At last, "after many days," the word of the Lord came to Elijah, "Go, show thyself unto Ahab; and I will send rain upon the earth."

In obedience to the command, "Elijah went to show himself unto Ahab." About the time that the prophet set forth on his journey to Samaria, Ahab had proposed to Obadiah, the governor of his household, that they make thorough search for springs and brooks of water, in the hope of finding pasture for their starving flocks and herds. Even in the royal court the effect of the long-continued drought was keenly felt. The king, deeply concerned over the outlook for his household, decided to unite personally with his servant in a search for some favored spots where pasture might be had. "So they divided the land between them to pass throughout it: Ahab went one way by himself, and Obadiah went another way by himself."

"As Obadiah was in the way, behold, Elijah met him: and he knew him, and fell on his face, and said, Art thou that my lord Elijah?"

During the apostasy of Israel, Obadiah had remained faithful. His master, the king, had been unable to turn him from his allegiance to the living God. Now he was honored with a commission from Elijah, who said, "Go, tell thy lord, Behold, Elijah is here."

Greatly terrified, Obadiah exclaimed, "What have I sinned, that thou wouldest deliver thy servant into the hand of Ahab, to slay me?" To take such a message as this to Ahab was to court certain death. "As the Lord thy God liveth," he explained to the prophet, "there is no nation or kingdom, whither my lord hath not sent to seek thee: and when they said, He is not there; he took an oath of the kingdom and nation, that they found thee not. And now thou sayest, Go, tell thy lord, Behold, Elijah is here. And it shall come to pass, as soon as I am gone from thee, that the Spirit of the Lord shall carry thee whither I know not; and so when I come and tell Ahab, and he cannot find thee, he shall slay me."

Earnestly Obadiah pleaded with the prophet not to urge him. "I thy servant," he urged, "fear the Lord from my youth. Was it not told my lord what I did when Jezebel slew the prophets of the Lord, how I hid an hundred men of the Lord's prophets by fifty in a cave, and fed them with bread and water? And now thou sayest, Go, tell thy lord, Behold, Elijah is here: and he shall slay me."

With a solemn oath Elijah promised Obadiah that the errand should not be in vain. "As the Lord of hosts liveth, before whom I stand," he declared, "I will surely show myself unto him today." Thus assured, "Obadiah went to meet Ahab, and told him."

In astonishment mingled with terror the king listened to the message from the man whom he feared and hated, and for whom he had sought so untiringly. Well he knew that Elijah would not endanger his life merely for the sake of meeting him. Could it be possible that the prophet was about to utter another woe against Israel? The king's heart was seized with dread. He remembered the withered arm of Jeroboam. Ahab could not avoid obeying the summons, neither dared he lift up his hand against the messenger of God. And so, accompanied by a bodyguard of soldiers, the trembling monarch went to meet the prophet.

The king and the prophet stand face to face. Though Ahab is filled with passionate hatred, yet in the presence of Elijah he seems unmanned, powerless. In his first faltering words, "Art thou he that troubleth Israel?" he unconsciously reveals the inmost feelings of his heart. Ahab knew that it was by the word of God that the heavens had become as brass, yet he sought to cast upon the prophet the blame for the heavy judgments resting on the land.

It is natural for the wrongdoer to hold the messengers of God responsible for the calamities that come as the sure result of a departure from the way of righteousness. Those who place themselves in Satan's power are unable to see things as God sees them. When the mirror of truth is held up before them, they become indignant at the thought of receiving reproof. Blinded by sin, they refuse to repent; they feel that God's servants have turned against them and are worthy of severest censure.

Standing in conscious innocence before Ahab, Elijah makes no attempt to excuse himself or to flatter the king. Nor does he seek to evade the king's wrath by the good news that the drought is almost over. He has no apology to offer. Indignant, and jealous for the honor of God, he casts back the imputation of Ahab, fearlessly declaring to the king that it is his sins, and the sins of his fathers, that have brought upon Israel this terrible calamity. "I have not troubled Israel," Elijah boldly asserts, "but thou, and thy father's house, in that ye have forsaken the commandments of the Lord, and thou hast followed Baalim."

Today there is need of the voice of stern rebuke; for grievous sins have separated the people from God. Infidelity is fast becoming fashionable. "We will not have this man to reign over us," is the language of thousands. Luke 19:14. The smooth sermons so often preached make no lasting impression; the trumpet does not give a certain sound. Men are not cut to the heart by the plain, sharp truths of God's word.

There are many professed Christians who, if they should express their real feelings, would say, What need is there of speaking so plainly? They might as well ask, Why need John the Baptist have said to the Pharisees, "O generation of vipers, who hath warned you to flee from the wrath to come?" Luke 3:7. Why need he have provoked the anger of Herodias by telling Herod that it was unlawful for him to live with his brother's wife? The forerunner of Christ lost his life by his plain speaking. Why could he not have moved along without incurring the displeasure of those who were living in sin?

So men who should be standing as faithful guardians of God's law have argued, till policy has taken the place of faithfulness, and sin is allowed to go unreproved. When will the voice of faithful rebuke be heard once more in the church?

"Thou art the man." 2 Samuel 12:7. Words as unmistakably plain as these spoken by Nathan to David are seldom heard in the pulpits of today, seldom seen in the public press. If they were not so rare, we should see more of the power of God revealed among men. The Lord's messengers should not complain that their efforts are without fruit until they repent of their own love of approbation and their desire to please men, which leads them to suppress truth.

Those ministers who are men pleasers, who cry, Peace, peace, when God has not spoken peace, might well humble their hearts before God, asking pardon for their insincerity and their lack of moral courage. It is not from love for their neighbor that they smooth down the message entrusted to them, but because they are self-indulgent and ease-loving. True love seeks first the honor of God and the salvation of souls. Those who have this love will not evade the truth to save themselves from the unpleasant results of plain speaking. When souls are in peril, God's ministers will not consider self, but will speak the word given them to speak, refusing to excuse or palliate evil.

Would that every minister might realize the sacredness of his office and the holiness of his work, and show the courage that Elijah showed! As divinely appointed messengers, ministers are in a position of awful responsibility. They are to "reprove, rebuke, exhort will all long-suffering." 2 Timothy 4:2. In Christ's stead they are to labor as stewards of the mysteries of heaven, encouraging the obedient and warning the disobedient. With them worldly policy is to have no weight. Never are they to swerve from the path in which Jesus has bidden them walk. They are to go forward in faith, remembering that they are surrounded by a cloud of witnesses. They are not to speak their own words, but words which One greater than the potentates of earth has bidden them speak. Their message is to be, "Thus saith the Lord." God calls for men like Elijah, Nathan, and John the Baptist—men who will bear His message with faithfulness, regardless of the consequences; men who will speak the truth bravely, though it call for the sacrifice of all they have.

God cannot use men who, in time of peril, when the strength, courage, and influence of all are needed, are afraid to take a firm stand for the right. He calls for men who will do faithful battle against wrong, warring against principalities and powers, against the rulers of the darkness of this world, against spiritual wickedness in high places. It is to such as these that He will speak the words: "Well done, good and faithful servant; . . . enter thou into the joy of thy Lord." Matthew 25:23.

Carmel

Standing before Ahab, Elijah demanded that all Israel be assembled to meet him and the prophets of Baal and Ashtoreth on Mount Carmel. "Send," he commanded, "and gather to me all Israel unto Mount Carmel, and the prophets of Baal four hundred and fifty, and the prophets of the groves four hundred, which eat at Jezebel's table."

The command was issued by one who seemed to stand in the very presence of Jehovah; and Ahab obeyed at once, as if the prophet were monarch, and the king a subject. Swift messengers were sent throughout the kingdom with the summons to meet Elijah and the prophets of Baal and Ashtoreth. In every town and village the people prepared to assemble at the appointed time. As they journeyed toward the place, the hearts of many were filled with strange forebodings. Something unusual was about to happen; else why this summons to gather at Carmel? What new calamity was about to fall upon the people and the land?

Before the drought, Mount Carmel had been a place of beauty, its streams fed from never-failing springs, and its fertile slopes covered with fair flowers and flourishing groves. But now its beauty languished under a withering curse. The altars erected to the worship of Baal and Ashtoreth stood now in leafless groves. On the summit of one of the highest ridges, in sharp contrast with these was the broken-down altar of Jehovah.

Carmel overlooked a wide expanse of country; its heights were visible from many parts of the kingdom of Israel. At the foot of the mount there were vantage points from which could be seen much of what took place above. God had been signally dishonored by the idolatrous worship carried on under cover of its wooded slopes; and Elijah chose this elevation as the most conspicuous place for the display of God's power and for the vindication of the honor of His name.

Early on the morning of the day appointed, the hosts of apostate Israel, in eager expectancy, gather near the top of the mountain. Jezebel's prophets march up in imposing array. In regal pomp the king appears and takes his position at the head of the priests, and the idolaters shout his welcome. But there is apprehension in the hearts of the priests as they remember that at the word of the prophet the land of Israel for three years and a half has been destitute of dew and rain. Some fearful crisis is at hand, they feel sure. The gods in whom they have trusted have been unable to prove Elijah a false prophet. To their frantic cries, their prayers, their tears, their humiliation, their revolting ceremonies, their costly and ceaseless sacrifices, the objects of their worship have been

strangely indifferent. Facing King Ahab and the false prophets, and surrounded by the assembled hosts of Israel, Elijah stands, the only one who has appeared to vindicate the honor of Jehovah. He whom the whole kingdom has charged with its weight of woe is now before them, apparently defenseless in the presence of the monarch of Israel, the prophets of Baal, the men of war, and the surrounding thousands. But Elijah is not alone. Above and around him are the protecting hosts of heaven, angels that excel in strength.

Unashamed, unterrified, the prophet stands before the multitude, fully aware of his commission to execute the divine command. His countenance is lighted with an awful solemnity. In anxious expectancy the people wait for him to speak. Looking first upon the broken-down altar of Jehovah, and then upon the multitude, Elijah cries out in clear, trumpetlike tones, "How long halt ye between two opinions? if the Lord be God, follow Him: but if Baal, then follow him."

The people answer him not a word. Not one in that vast assembly dare reveal loyalty to Jehovah. Like a dark cloud, deception and blindness had overspread Israel. Not all at once had this fatal apostasy closed about them, but gradually, as from time to time they had failed to heed the words of warning and reproof that the Lord sent them. Each departure from rightdoing, each refusal to repent, had deepened their guilt and driven them farther from Heaven. And now, in this crisis, they persisted in refusing to take their stand for God.

The Lord abhors indifference and disloyalty in a time of crisis in His work. The whole universe is watching with inexpressible interest the closing scenes of the great controversy between good and evil. The people of God are nearing the borders of the eternal world; what can be of more importance to them than that they be loyal to the God of heaven? All through the ages, God has had moral heroes, and He has them now—those who, like Joseph and Elijah and Daniel, are not ashamed to acknowledge themselves His peculiar people. His special blessing accompanies the labors of men of action, men who will not be swerved from the straight line of duty, but who with divine energy will inquire, "Who is on the Lord's side?" (Exodus 32:26), men who will not stop merely with the inquiry, but who will demand that those who choose to identify themselves with the people of God shall step forward and reveal unmistakably their allegiance to the King of kings and Lord of lords. Such men make their wills and plans subordinate to the law of God. For love of Him they count not their lives dear unto themselves. Their work is to catch the light from the Word and let it shine forth to the world in clear, steady rays. Fidelity to God is their motto.

While Israel on Carmel doubt and hesitate, the voice of Elijah again breaks the silence: "I, even I only, remain a prophet of the Lord; but Baal's prophets are four hundred and fifty men. Let them therefore give us two bullocks; and let them choose one bullock for themselves, and cut it in pieces, and lay it on wood, and put no fire under: and I will dress the other bullock, and lay it on wood, and put no fire under: and call ye on the name of your gods, and I will call on the name of the Lord: and the God that answereth by fire, let him be God."

The proposal of Elijah is so reasonable that the people cannot well evade it, so they find courage to answer, "It is well spoken." The prophets of Baal dare not lift their voices in dissent; and, addressing them, Elijah directs, "Choose you one bullock for yourselves, and dress it first; for ye are many; and call on the name of your gods, but put no fire under."

Outwardly bold and defiant, but with terror in their guilty hearts, the false priests prepare their altar, laying on the wood and the victim; and then they begin their incantations. Their shrill cries echo and re-echo through the forests and the surrounding heights, as they call on the name of their god, saying, "O Baal, hear us." The priests gather about their altar, and with leaping and writhing and screaming, with tearing of hair and cutting of flesh, they beseech their god to help them.

The morning passes, noon comes, and yet there is no evidence that Baal hears the cries of his deluded followers. There is no voice, no reply to their frantic prayers. The sacrifice remains unconsumed.

As they continue their frenzied devotions, the crafty priests are continually trying to devise some means by which they may kindle a fire upon the altar and lead the people to believe that the fire has come direct from Baal. But Elijah watches every movement; and the priests, hoping against hope for some opportunity to deceive, continue to carry on their senseless ceremonies.

"It came to pass at noon, that Elijah mocked them, and said, Cry aloud: for he is a god; either he is talking, or he is pursuing, or he is in a journey, or peradventure he sleepeth, and must be awaked. And they cried aloud, and cut themselves after their manner with knives and lancets, till the blood gushed out upon them. And it came to pass, when midday was past, and they prophesied until the time of the offering of the evening sacrifice, that there was neither voice, nor any to answer, nor any that regarded."

Gladly would Satan have come to the help of those whom he had deceived, and who were devoted to his service. Gladly would he have sent the lightning to kindle their sacrifice. But Jehovah has set Satan's bounds, restrained his power, and not all the enemy's devices can convey one spark to Baal's altar.

At last, their voices hoarse with shouting, their garments stained with blood from self-inflicted wounds, the priests become desperate. With unabated frenzy they now mingle with their pleading terrible cursings of their sun-god, and Elijah continues to watch intently; for he knows that if by any device the priests should succeed in kindling their altar fire, he would instantly be torn in pieces.

Evening draws on. The prophets of Baal are weary, faint, confused. One suggests one thing, and another something else, until finally they cease their efforts. Their shrieks and curses no longer resound over Carmel. In despair they retire from the contest.

All day long the people have witnessed the demonstrations of the baffled priests. They have beheld their wild leaping round the altar, as if they would grasp the burning rays of the sun to serve their purpose. They have looked with horror on the frightful, self-inflicted mutilations of the priests, and have had opportunity to reflect on the follies of idol worship. Many in the throng are weary of the exhibitions of demonism, and they now await with deepest interest the movements of Elijah.

It is the hour of the evening sacrifice, and Elijah bids the people, "Come near unto me." As they tremblingly draw near, he turns to the broken-down altar where once men worshiped the God of heaven, and repairs it. To him this heap of ruins is more precious than all the magnificent altars of heathendom.

In the reconstruction of this ancient altar, Elijah revealed his respect for the covenant that the Lord made with Israel when they crossed the Jordan into the Promised Land. Choosing "twelve stones, according to the number of the tribes of the sons of Jacob, . . . he built an altar in the name of the Lord."

The disappointed priests of Baal, exhausted by their vain efforts, wait to see what Elijah will do. They hate the prophet for proposing a test that has exposed the weakness and inefficiency of their gods; yet they fear his power. The people, fearful also, and almost breathless with expectancy, watch while Elijah continues his preparations. The calm demeanor of the prophet stands out in sharp contrast with the fanatical, senseless frenzy of the followers of Baal.

The altar completed, the prophet makes a trench about it, and, having put the wood in order and prepared the bullock, he lays the victim on the altar and commands the people to flood the sacrifice and the altar with water. "Fill four barrels," he directed, "and pour it on the burnt sacrifice, and on the wood. And he said, Do it the second time. And they did it the second time. And he said, Do it the third time. And they did it the third time. And the water ran round about the altar; and he filled the trench also with water."

Reminding the people of the long-continued apostasy that has awakened the wrath of Jehovah, Elijah calls upon them to humble their hearts and turn to the God of their fathers, that the curse upon the land of Israel may be removed. Then, bowing reverently before the unseen God, he raises his hands toward heaven and offers a simple prayer. Baal's priests have screamed and foamed and leaped, from early morning until late in the afternoon; but as Elijah prays, no senseless shrieks resound over Carmel's height. He prays as if he knows Jehovah is there, a witness to the scene, a listener to his appeal. The prophets of Baal have prayed wildly, incoherently. Elijah prays simply and fervently, asking God to show His superiority over Baal, that Israel may be led to turn to Him.

"Lord God of Abraham, Isaac, and of Israel," the prophet pleads, "let it be known this day that Thou art God in Israel, and that I am Thy servant, and that I have done all these things at Thy word. Hear me, O Lord, hear me, that this people may know that Thou art the Lord God, and that Thou hast turned their heart back again."

A silence, oppressive in its solemnity, rests upon all. The

priests of Baal tremble with terror. Conscious of their guilt, they look for swift retribution.

No sooner is the prayer of Elijah ended than flames of fire, like brilliant flashes of lightning, descend from heaven upon the upreared altar, consuming the sacrifice, licking up the water in the trench, and consuming even the stones of the altar. The brilliancy of the blaze illumines the mountain and dazzles the eyes of the multitude. In the valleys below, where many are watching in anxious suspense the movements of those above, the descent of fire is clearly seen, and all are amazed at the sight. It resembles the pillar of fire which at the Red Sea separated the children of Israel from the Egyptian host.

The people on the mount prostrate themselves in awe before the unseen God. They dare not continue to look upon the Heaven-sent fire. They fear that they themselves will be consumed; and, convicted of their duty to acknowledge the God of Elijah as the God of their fathers, to whom they owe allegiance, they cry out together as with one voice, "The Lord, He is the God; the Lord, He is the God." With startling distinctness the cry resounds over the mountain and echoes in the plain below. At last Israel is aroused, undeceived, penitent. At last the people see how greatly they have dishonored God. The character of Baal worship, in contrast with the reasonable service required by the true God, stands fully revealed. The people recognize God's justice and mercy in withholding the dew and the rain until they have been brought to confess His name. They are ready now to admit that the God of Elijah is above every idol.

The priests of Baal witness with consternation the wonderful revelation of Jehovah's power. Yet even in their discomfiture and in the presence of divine glory, they refuse to repent of their evil-doing. They would still remain the prophets of Baal. Thus they showed themselves ripe for destruction. That repentant Israel may be protected from the allurements of those who have taught them to worship Baal, Elijah is directed by the Lord to destroy these false teachers. The anger of the people has already been aroused against the leaders in transgression; and when Elijah gives the command, "Take the prophets of Baal; let not one of them escape," they are ready to obey. They seize the priests, and take them to the brook Kishon, and there, before the close of the day that marked the beginning of decided reform, the ministers of Baal are slain. Not one is permitted to live.

From Jezreel to Horeb

With the slaying of the prophets of Baal, the way was opened for carrying forward a mighty spiritual reformation among the ten tribes of the northern kingdom. Elijah had set before the people their apostasy; he had called upon them to humble their hearts and turn to the Lord. The judgments of Heaven had been executed; the people had confessed their sins, and had acknowledged the God of their fathers as the living God; and now the curse of Heaven was to be withdrawn, and the temporal blessings of life renewed. The land was to be refreshed with rain. "Get thee up, eat and drink," Elijah said to Ahab; "for there is a sound of abundance of rain." Then the prophet went to the top of the mount to pray.

It was not because of any outward evidence that the showers were about to fall, that Elijah could so confidently bid Ahab prepare for rain. The prophet saw no clouds in the heavens; he heard no thunder. He simply spoke the word that the Spirit of the Lord had moved him to speak in response to his own strong faith. Throughout the day he had unflinchingly performed the will of God and had revealed his implicit confidence in the prophecies of God's word; and now, having done all that was in his power to do, he knew that Heaven would freely bestow the blessings foretold. The same God who had sent the drought had promised an abundance of rain as the reward of rightdoing; and now Elijah waited for the promised outpouring. In an attitude of humility, "his face between his knees," he interceded with God in behalf of penitent Israel.

Again and again Elijah sent his servant to a point overlooking the Mediterranean, to learn whether there were any visible token that God had heard his prayer. Each time the servant returned with the word, "There is nothing." The prophet did not become impatient or lose faith, but continued his earnest pleading. Six times the servant returned with the word that there was no sign of rain in the brassy heavens. Undaunted, Elijah sent him forth once more; and this time the servant returned with the word, "Behold, there ariseth a little cloud out of the sea like a man's hand."

This was enough. Elijah did not wait for the heavens to gather blackness. In that small cloud he beheld by faith an abundance of rain; and he acted in harmony with his faith, sending his servant quickly to Ahab with the message, "Prepare thy chariot, and get thee down, that the rain stop thee not."

It was because Elijah was a man of large faith that God could use him in this grave crisis in the history of Israel. As he prayed, his faith reached out and grasped the promises of Heaven, and he persevered in prayer until his petitions were answered. He did not wait for the full evidence that God had heard him, but was willing to venture all on the slightest token of divine favor. And yet what he was enabled to do under God, all may do in their sphere of activity in God's service; for of the prophet from the mountains of Gilead it is written: "Elias was a man subject to like passions as we are, and he prayed earnestly that it might not rain: and it rained not on the earth by the space of three years and six months." James 5:17.

Faith such as this is needed in the world today—faith that will lay hold on the promises of God's word and refuse to let go until Heaven hears. Faith such as this connects us closely with Heaven, and brings us strength for coping with the powers of darkness. Through faith God's children have "subdued kingdoms, wrought righteousness, obtained promises, stopped the mouths of lions, quenched the violence of fire, escaped the edge of the sword, out of weakness were made strong, waxed valiant in fight, turned to flight the armies of the aliens." Hebrews 11:33, 34. And through faith we today are to reach the heights of God's purpose for us. "If thou canst believe, all things are possible to him that believeth." Mark 9:23.

Faith is an essential element of prevailing prayer. "He that cometh to God must believe that He is, and that He is a rewarder of them that diligently seek Him." "If we ask anything according to His will, He heareth us: and if we know that He hear us, whatsoever we ask, we know that we have the petitions that we desired of Him." Hebrews 11:6, 1 John 5:14, 15. With the persevering faith of Jacob, with the unyielding persistence of Elijah, we may present our petitions to the Father, claiming all that He has promised. The honor of His throne is staked for the fulfillment of His word.

The shades of night were gathering about Mount Carmel as Ahab prepared for the descent. "It came to pass in the meanwhile, that the heaven was black with clouds and wind, and there was a great rain. And Ahab rode, and went to Jezreel." As he journeyed toward the royal city through the darkness and the blinding rain, Ahab was unable to see his way before him. Elijah, who, as the prophet of God, had that day humiliated Ahab before his subjects and slain his idolatrous priests, still acknowledged him as Israel's king; and now, as an act of homage, and strengthened by the power of God, he ran before the royal chariot, guiding the king to the entrance of the city.

In this gracious act of God's messenger shown to a wicked king is a lesson for all who claim to be servants of God, but who are exalted in their own estimation. There are those who feel above performing duties that to them appear menial. They hesitate to perform even needful service, fearing that they will be found doing the work of a servant. These have much to learn from the example of Elijah. By his word the treasures of heaven had been for three years withheld from the earth; he had been signally honored of God as, in answer to his prayer on Carmel, fire had flashed from heaven and consumed the sacrifice; his hand had executed the judgment of God in slaying the idolatrous prophets; his petition for rain had been granted. And yet, after the signal triumphs with which God had been pleased to honor his public ministry, he was willing to perform the service of a menial.

At the gate of Jezreel, Elijah and Ahab separated. The prophet, choosing to remain outside the walls, wrapped himself in his mantle, and lay down upon the bare earth to sleep. The king, passing within, soon reached the shelter of his palace and there related to his wife the wonderful events of the day and the marvelous revelation of divine power that had proved to Israel that Jehovah is the true God and Elijah His chosen messenger. As Ahab told the queen of the slaying of the idolatrous prophets, Jezebel, hardened and impenitent, became infuriated. She refused to recognize in the events on Carmel the overruling providence of God, and, still defiant, she boldly declared that Elijah should die.

That night a messenger aroused the weary prophet and delivered to him the word of Jezebel: "So let the gods do to me, and more also, if I make not thy life as the life of one of them by tomorrow about this time."

It would seem that after showing courage so undaunted, after triumphing so completely over king and priests and people, Elijah could never afterward have given way to despondency nor been awed into timidity. But he who had been blessed with so many evidences of God's loving care was not above the frailties of mankind, and in this dark hour his faith and courage forsook him. Bewildered, he started from his slumber. The rain was pouring from the heavens, and darkness was on every side. Forgetting that three years before, God had directed his course to a place of refuge from the hatred of Jezebel and the search of Ahab, the prophet now fled for his life. Reaching Beersheba, he "left his servant there. But he himself went a day's journey into the wilderness." Elijah should not have fled from his post of duty. He should have met the threat of Jezebel with an appeal for protection to the One who had commissioned him to vindicate the honor of Jehovah. He should have told the messenger that the God in whom he trusted would protect him against the hatred of the queen. Only a few hours had passed since he had witnessed a wonderful manifestation of divine power, and this should have given him assurance that he would not now be forsaken. Had he remained where he was, had he made God his refuge and strength, standing steadfast for the truth, he would have been shielded from harm. The Lord would have given him another signal victory by sending His judgments on Jezebel; and the impression made on the king and the people would have wrought a great reformation.

Elijah had expected much from the miracle wrought on Carmel. He had hoped that after this display of God's power, Jezebel would no longer have influence over the mind of Ahab, and that there would be a speedy reform throughout Israel. All day on Carmel's height he had toiled without food. Yet when he guided the chariot of Ahab to the gate of Jezreel, his courage was strong, despite the physical strain under which he had labored.

But a reaction such as frequently follows high faith and glorious success was pressing upon Elijah. He feared that the reformation begun on Carmel might not be lasting; and depression seized him. He had been exalted to Pisgah's top; now he was in the valley. While under the inspiration of the Almighty, he had stood the severest trial of faith; but in this time of discouragement, with Jezebel's threat sounding in his ears, and Satan still apparently prevailing through the plotting of this wicked woman, he lost his hold on God. He had been exalted above measure, and the reaction was tremendous. Forgetting God, Elijah fled on and on, until he found himself in a dreary waste, alone. Utterly wearied, he sat down to rest under a juniper tree. And sitting there, he requested for himself that he might die. "It is enough; now, O Lord," he said, "take away my life; for I am not better than my fathers."

A fugitive, far from the dwelling places of men, his spirits crushed by bitter disappointment, he desired never again to look upon the face of man. At last, utterly exhausted, he fell asleep.

Into the experience of all there come times of keen disappointment and utter discouragement—days when sorrow is the portion, and it is hard to believe that God is still the kind benefactor of His earthborn children; days when troubles harass the soul, till death seems preferable to life. It is then that many lose their hold on God and are brought into the slavery of doubt, the bondage of unbelief. Could we at such times discern with spiritual insight the meaning of God's providences we should see angels seeking to save us from ourselves, striving to plant our feet upon a foundation more firm than the everlasting hills, and new faith, new life, would spring into being.

The faithful Job, in the day of his affliction and darkness, declared:

"Let the day perish wherein I was born."
"O that my grief were throughly weighed,
And my calamity laid in the balances together!"
"O that I might have my request;
And that God would grant me the thing that I long for!
Even that it would please God to destroy me;
That He would let loose His hand, and cut me off!
Then should I yet have comfort."
"I will not refrain my mouth;
I will speak in the anguish of my spirit;
I will complain in the bitterness of my soul."
"My soul chooseth . . . death rather than my life.
I loathe it;
I would not live alway:
Let me alone;
For my days are vanity."
Job 3:3; 6:2, 8-10; 7:11, 15, 16.

But though weary of life, Job was not allowed to die. To him were pointed out the possibilities of the future, and there was given him the message of hope:

"Thou shalt be steadfast, and shalt not fear:
Because thou shalt forget thy misery,
And remember it as waters that pass away:
And thine age shall be clearer than the noonday;
Thou shalt shine forth, thou shalt be as the morning. And thou shalt be secure,
Because there is hope. . . .
Thou shalt lie down,
And none shall make thee afraid;
Yea, many shall make suit unto thee.
But the eyes of the wicked shall fail,
And they shall not escape,
And their hope shall be as the giving up of the ghost."
Job 11:15-20.

From the depths of discouragement and despondency Job rose to the heights of implicit trust in the mercy and the saving power of God. Triumphantly he declared:

"Though He slay me, yet will I trust in Him: . . .
He also shall be my salvation."
"I know that my Redeemer liveth,
And that He shall stand at the latter day upon the earth:
And though after my skin worms destroy this body,
Yet in my flesh shall I see God:
Whom I shall see for myself,
And mine eyes shall behold, and not another."
Job 13:15, 16; 19:25-27.

"The Lord answered Job out of the whirlwind" (Job 38:1), and revealed to His servant the might of His power. When Job caught a glimpse of his Creator, he abhorred himself and repented in dust and ashes. Then the Lord was able to bless him abundantly and to make his last years the best of his life.

Hope and courage are essential to perfect service for God. These are the fruit of faith. Despondency is sinful and unreasonable. God is able and willing "more abundantly" (Hebrews 6:17) to bestow upon His servants the strength they need for test and trial. The plans of the enemies of His work may seem to be well laid and firmly established, but God can overthrow the strongest of these. And this He does in His own time and way, when He sees that the faith of His servants has been sufficiently tested.

For the disheartened there is a sure remedy—faith, prayer, work. Faith and activity will impart assurance and satisfaction that will increase day by day. Are you tempted to give way to feelings of anxious foreboding or utter despondency? In the darkest days, when appearances seem most forbidding, fear not. Have faith in God. He knows your need. He has all power. His infinite love and compassion never weary. Fear not that He will fail of fulfilling His promise. He is eternal truth. Never will He change the covenant He has made with those who love Him. And He will bestow upon His faithful servants the measure of efficiency that their need demands. The apostle Paul has testified: "He said unto me, My grace is sufficient for thee: for My strength is made perfect in weakness. . . . Therefore I take pleasure in infirmities, in reproaches, in necessities, in persecutions, in distresses for Christ's sake: for when I am weak, then am I strong." 2 Corinthians 12:9, 10.

Did God forsake Elijah in his hour of trial? Oh, no! He loved His servant no less when Elijah felt himself forsaken of God and man than when, in answer to his prayer, fire flashed from heaven and illuminated the mountaintop. And now, as Elijah slept, a soft touch and a pleasant voice awoke him. He started up in terror, as if to flee, fearing that the enemy had discovered him. But the pitying face bending over him was not the face of an enemy, but of a friend. God had sent an angel from heaven with food for His servant. "Arise and eat," the angel said. "And he looked, and, behold, there was a cake baken on the coals, and a cruse of water at his head."

After Elijah had partaken of the refreshment prepared for him, he slept again. A second time the angel came. Touching the exhausted man, he said with pitying tenderness, "Arise and eat; because the journey is too great for thee." "And he arose, and did eat and drink;" and in the strength of that food he was able to journey "forty days and forty nights unto Horeb the mount of God," where he found refuge in a cave.

"What Doest Thou Here?"

Elijah's retreat on Mount Horeb, though hidden from man, was known to God; and the weary and discouraged prophet was not left to struggle alone with the powers of darkness that were pressing upon him. At the entrance to the cave wherein Elijah had taken refuge, God met with him, through a mighty angel sent to inquire into his needs and to make plain the divine purpose for Israel.

Not until Elijah had learned to trust wholly in God could he complete his work for those who had been seduced into Baal worship. The signal triumph on the heights of Carmel had opened the way for still greater victories; yet from the wonderful opportunities opening before him, Elijah had been turned away by the threat of Jezebel. The man of God must be made to understand the weakness of his present position as compared with the vantage ground the Lord would have him occupy.

God met His tried servant with the inquiry, "What doest thou here, Elijah? I sent you to the brook Cherith and afterward to the widow of Sarepta. I commissioned you to return to Israel and to stand before the idolatrous priests on Carmel, and I girded you with strength to guide the chariot of the king to the gate of Jezreel. But who sent you on this hasty flight into the wilderness? What errand have you here?

In bitterness of soul Elijah mourned out his complaint: "I have been very jealous for the Lord God of hosts: for the children of Israel have forsaken Thy covenant, thrown down Thine altars, and slain Thy prophets with the sword; and I, even I only, am left; and they seek my life, to take it away."

Calling upon the prophet to leave the cave, the angel bade him stand before the Lord on the mount, and listen to His word. "And, behold, the Lord passed by, and a great and strong wind rent the mountains, and brake in pieces the rocks before the Lord; but the Lord was not in the wind: and after the wind an earthquake; but the Lord was not in the earthquake: and after the earthquake a fire; but the Lord was not in the fire: and after the fire a still small voice. And it was so, when Elijah heard it, that he wrapped his face in his mantle, and went out, and stood in the entering in of the cave."

Not in mighty manifestations of divine power, but by "a still small voice," did God choose to reveal Himself to His servant. He desired to teach Elijah that it is not always the work that makes the greatest demonstration that is most successful in accomplishing His purpose. While Elijah waited for the revelation of the Lord, a tempest rolled, the lightnings flashed, and a devouring fire swept by; but God was not in all this. Then there came a still, small voice, and the prophet covered his head before the presence of the Lord. His petulance was silenced, his spirit softened and subdued. He now knew that a quiet trust, a firm reliance on God, would ever find for him a present help in time of need.

It is not always the most learned presentation of God's truth that convicts and converts the soul. Not by eloquence or logic are men's hearts reached, but by the sweet influences of the Holy Spirit, which operate quietly yet surely in transforming and developing character. It is the still, small voice of the Spirit of God that has power to change the heart.

"What doest thou here, Elijah?" the voice inquired; and again the prophet answered, "I have been very jealous for the Lord God of hosts: because the children of Israel have forsaken Thy covenant, thrown down Thine altars, and slain Thy prophets with the sword; and I, even I only, am left; and they seek my life, to take it away."

The Lord answered Elijah that the wrongdoers in Israel should not go unpunished. Men were to be especially chosen to fulfill the divine purpose in the punishment of the idolatrous kingdom. There was stern work to be done, that all might be given opportunity to take their position on the side of the true God. Elijah himself was to return to Israel, and share with others the burden of bringing about a reformation.

"Go," the Lord commanded Elijah, "return on thy way to the wilderness of Damascus: and when thou comest, anoint Hazael to be king over Syria: and Jehu the son of Nimshi shalt thou anoint to be king over Israel: and Elisha the son of Shaphat of Abel-meholah shalt thou anoint to be prophet in thy room. And it shall come to pass, that him that escapeth the sword of Hazael shall Jehu slay: and him that escapeth from the sword of Jehu shall Elisha slay."

Elijah had thought that he alone in Israel was a worshiper of the true God. But He who reads the hearts of all revealed to the prophet that there were many others who, through the long years of apostasy, had remained true to Him. "I have left Me," God said, "seven thousand in Israel, all the knees which have not bowed unto Baal, and every mouth which hath not kissed him."

From Elijah's experience during those days of discouragement and apparent defeat there are many lessons to be drawn, lessons invaluable to the servants of God in this age, marked as it is by general departure from right. The apostasy prevailing today is similar to that which in the prophet's day overspread Israel. In the exaltation of the human above the divine, in the praise of popular leaders, in the worship of mammon, and in the placing of the teachings of science above the truths of revelation, multitudes today are following after Baal. Doubt and unbelief are exercising their baleful influence over mind and heart, and many are substituting for the oracles of God the theories of men. It is publicly taught that we have reached a time when human reason should be exalted above the teachings of the Word. The law of God, the divine standard of righteousness, is declared to be of no effect. The enemy of all truth is working with deceptive power to cause men and women to place human institutions where God should be, and to forget that which was ordained for the happiness and salvation of mankind.

Yet this apostasy, widespread as it has come to be, is not universal. Not all in the world are lawless and sinful; not all have taken sides with the enemy. God has many thousands who have not bowed the knee to Baal, many who long to understand more fully in regard to Christ and the law, many who are hoping against hope that Jesus will come soon to end the reign of sin and death. And there are many who have been worshiping Baal ignorantly, but with whom the Spirit of God is still striving.

These need the personal help of those who have learned to know God and the power of His word. In such a time as this, every child of God should be actively engaged in helping others. As those who have an understanding of Bible truth try to seek out the men and women who are longing for light, angels of God will attend them. And where angels go, none need fear to move forward. As a result of the faithful efforts of consecrated workers, many will be turned from idolatry to the worship of the living God. Many will cease to pay homage to man-made institutions and will take their stand fearlessly on the side of God and His law.

Much depends on the unceasing activity of those who are true and loyal, and for this reason Satan puts forth every possible effort to thwart the divine purpose to be wrought out through the obedient. He causes some to lose sight of their high and holy mission, and to become satisfied with the pleasures of this life. He leads them to settle down at ease, or, for the sake of greater worldly advantages, to remove from places where they might be a power for good. Others he causes to flee in discouragement from duty, because of opposition or persecution. But all such are regarded by Heaven with tenderest pity. To every child of God whose voice the enemy of souls had succeeded in silencing, the question is addressed, "What doest thou here?" I commissioned you to go into all the world and preach the gospel, to prepare a people for the day of God. Why are you here? Who sent you?

The joy set before Christ, the joy that sustained Him through sacrifice and suffering, was the joy of seeing sinners saved. This should be the joy of every follower of His, the spur to his ambition. Those who realize, even in a limited degree, what redemption means to them and to their fellow men, will comprehend in some measure the vast needs of humanity. Their hearts will be moved to compassion as they see the moral and spiritual destitution of thousands who are under the shadow of a terrible doom, in comparison with which physical suffering fades into nothingness.

Of families, as of individuals, the question is asked, "What doest thou here?" In many churches there are families well instructed in the truths of God's word, who might widen the sphere of their influence by moving to places in need of the ministry they are capable of giving. God calls for Christian families to go into the dark places of the earth and work wisely and perseveringly for those who are enshrouded in spiritual gloom. To answer this call requires self-sacrifice. While many are waiting to have every obstacle removed, souls are dying, without hope and without God. For the sake of worldly advantage, for the sake of acquiring scientific knowledge, men are willing to venture into pestilential regions and to endure hardship and privation. Where are those who are willing to do as much for the sake of telling others of the Saviour?

If, under trying circumstances, men of spiritual power, pressed beyond measure, become discouraged and desponding, if at times they see nothing desirable in life, that they should choose it, this is nothing strange or new. Let all such remember that one of the mightiest of the prophets fled for his life before the rage of an infuriated woman. A fugitive, weary and travel-worn, bitter disappointment crushing his spirits, he asked that he might die. But it was when hope was gone and his lifework seemed threatened with defeat, that he learned one of the most precious lessons of his life. In the hour of his greatest weakness he learned the need and the possibility of trusting God under circumstances the most forbidding.

Those who, while spending their life energies in self-sacrificing labor, are tempted to give way to despondency and distrust, may gather courage from the experience of Elijah. God's watchful care, His love, His power, are especially manifest in behalf of His servants whose zeal is misunderstood or unappreciated, whose counsels and reproofs are slighted, and whose efforts toward reform are repaid with hatred and opposition.

It is at the time of greatest weakness that Satan assails the soul with the fiercest temptations. It was thus that he hoped to prevail over the Son of God; for by this policy he had gained many victories over man. When the will power weakened and faith failed, then those who had stood long and valiantly for the right yielded to temptation. Moses, wearied with forty years of wandering and unbelief, lost for a moment his hold on Infinite Power. He failed just on the borders of the Promised Land. So with Elijah. He who had maintained his trust in Jehovah during the years of drought and famine, he who had stood undaunted before Ahab, he who throughout that trying day on Carmel had stood before the whole nation of Israel the sole witness to the true God, in a moment of weariness allowed the fear of death to overcome his faith in God.

And so it is today. When we are encompassed with doubt, perplexed by circumstances, or afflicted by poverty or distress, Satan seeks to shake our confidence in Jehovah. It is then that he arrays before us our mistakes and tempts us to distrust God, to question His love. He hopes to discourage the soul and break our hold on God. Those who, standing in the forefront of the conflict, are impelled by the Holy Spirit to do a special work, will frequently feel a reaction when the pressure is removed. Despondency may shake the most heroic faith and weaken the most steadfast will. But God understands, and He still pities and loves. He reads the motives and the purposes of the heart. To wait patiently, to trust when everything looks dark, is the lesson that the leaders in God's work need to learn. Heaven will not fail them in their day of adversity. Nothing is apparently more helpless, yet really more invincible, than the soul that feels its nothingness and relies wholly on God.

Not alone for men in positions of large responsibility is the lesson of Elijah's experience in learning anew how to trust God in the hour of trial. He who was Elijah's strength is strong to uphold every struggling child of His, no matter how weak. Of everyone He expects loyalty, and to everyone He grants power according to the need. In his own strength man is strengthless; but in the might of God he may be strong to overcome evil and to help others to overcome. Satan can never gain advantage of him who makes God his defense. "Surely, shall one say, in the Lord have I righteousness and strength." Isaiah 45:24.

Fellow Christian, Satan knows your weakness; therefore cling to Jesus. Abiding in God's love, you may stand every test. The righteousness of Christ alone can give you power to stem the tide of evil that is sweeping over the world. Bring faith into your experience. Faith lightens every burden, relieves every weariness. Providences that are now mysterious you may solve by continued trust in God. Walk by faith in the path He marks out. Trials will come, but go forward. This will strengthen your faith and fit you for service. The records of sacred history are written, not merely that we may read and wonder, but that the same faith which wrought in God's servants of old may work in us. In no less marked manner will the Lord work now, wherever there are hearts of faith to be channels of His power.

To us, as to Peter, the word is spoken, "Satan hath desired to have you, that he may sift you as wheat: but I have prayed for thee, that thy faith fail not." Luke 22:31, 32. Christ will never abandon those for whom He has died. We may leave Him and be overwhelmed with temptation, but Christ can never turn from one for whom He has paid the ransom of His own life. Could our spiritual vision be quickened, we should see souls bowed under oppression and burdened with grief, pressed as a cart beneath sheaves, and ready to die in discouragement. We should see angels flying quickly to the aid of these tempted ones, forcing back the hosts of evil that encompass them, and placing their feet on the sure foundation. The battles waging between the two armies are as real as those fought by the armies of this world, and on the issue of the spiritual conflict eternal destinies depend.

In the vision of the prophet Ezekiel there was the appearance of a hand beneath the wings of the cherubim. This is to teach God's servants that it is divine power that gives success. Those whom God employs as His messengers are not to feel that His work is dependent on them. Finite beings are not left to carry this burden of responsibility. He who slumbers not, who is continually at work for the accomplishment of His designs, will carry forward His work. He will thwart the purposes of wicked men and will bring to confusion the counsels of those who plot mischief against His people. He who is the King, the Lord of hosts, sitteth between the cherubim, and amidst the strife and tumult of nations. He guards His children still. When the strongholds of kings shall be overthrown, when the arrows of wrath shall strike through the hearts of His enemies, His people will be safe in His hands.

"In the Spirit and Power of Elias"

Through the long centuries that have passed since Elijah's time, the record of his lifework has brought inspiration and courage to those who have been called to stand for the right in the midst of apostasy. And for us, "upon whom the ends of the world are come" (1 Corinthians 10:11), it has special significance. History is being repeated. The world today has its Ahabs and its Jezebels. The present age is one of idolatry, as verily as was that in which Elijah lived. No outward shrine may be visible; there may be no image for the eye to rest upon; yet thousands are following after the gods of this world—after riches, fame, pleasure, and the pleasing fables that permit man to follow the inclinations of the unregenerate heart. Multitude have a wrong conception of God and His attributes, and are as truly serving a false god as were the worshipers of Baal. Many even of those who claim to be Christians have allied themselves with influences that are unalterably opposed to God and His truth. Thus they are led to turn away from the divine and to exalt the human.

The prevailing spirit of our time is one of infidelity and apostasy—a spirit of avowed illumination because of a knowledge of truth, but in reality of the blindest presumption. Human theories are exalted and placed where God and His law should be. Satan tempts men and women to disobey, with the promise that in disobedience they will find liberty and freedom that will make them as gods. There is seen a spirit of opposition to the plain word of God, of idolatrous exaltation of human wisdom above divine revelation. Men have allowed their minds to become so darkened and confused by conformity to worldly customs and influences that they seem to have lost all power to discriminate between light and darkness, truth and error. So far have they departed from the right way that they hold the opinions of a few philosophers, so-called, to be more trustworthy than the truths of the Bible. The entreaties and promises of God's word, its threatenings against disobedience and idolatry—these seem powerless to melt their hearts. A faith such as actuated Paul, Peter, and John they regard as old-fashioned, mystical, and unworthy of the intelligence of modern thinkers.

In the beginning, God gave His law to mankind as a means of attaining happiness and eternal life. Satan's only hope of thwarting the purpose of God is to lead men and women to disobey this law, and his constant effort has been to misrepresent its teachings and belittle its importance. His master stroke has been an attempt to change the law itself, so as to lead men to violate its precepts while professing to obey it.

One writer has likened the attempt to change the law of God to an ancient mischievous practice of turning in a wrong direction a signpost erected at an important junction where two roads met. The perplexity and hardship which this practice often caused was great.

A signpost was erected by God for those journeying through this world. One arm of this signpost pointed out willing obedience to the Creator as the road to felicity and life, while the other arm indicated disobedience as the path to misery and death. The way to happiness was as clearly defined as was the way to the city of refuge under the Jewish dispensation. But in an evil hour for our race, the great enemy of all good turned the signpost around, and multitudes have mistaken the way.

Through Moses the Lord instructed the Israelites: "Verily My Sabbaths ye shall keep: for it is a sign between Me and you throughout your generations; that ye may know that I am the Lord that doth sanctify you. Ye shall keep the Sabbath therefore; for it is holy unto you: everyone that defileth it shall surely be put to death: for whosoever doeth any work. . . in the Sabbath day, he shall surely be put to death. Wherefore the children of Israel shall keep the Sabbath, to observe the Sabbath throughout their generations, for a perpetual covenant. It is a sign between Me and the children of Israel forever: for in six days the Lord made heaven and earth, and on the seventh day He rested, and was refreshed." Exodus 31:13-17.

In these words the Lord clearly defined obedience as the way to the City of God; but the man of sin has changed the signpost, making it point in the wrong direction. He has set up a false sabbath and has caused men and women to think that by resting on it they were obeying the command of the Creator.

God has declared that the seventh day is the Sabbath of the Lord. When "the heavens and the earth were finished," He exalted this day as a memorial of His creative work. Resting on the seventh day "from all His work which He had made," "God blessed the seventh day, and sanctified it." Genesis 2:1-3. At the time of the Exodus from Egypt, the Sabbath institution was brought prominently before the people of God. While they were still in bondage, their taskmasters had attempted to force them to labor on the Sabbath by increasing the amount of work required each week. Again and again the conditions of labor had been made harder and more exacting. But the Israelites were delivered from bondage and brought to a place where they might observe unmolested all the precepts of Jehovah. At Sinai the law was spoken; and a copy of it, on two tables of stone, "written with the finger of God" was delivered to Moses. Exodus 31:18. And through nearly forty years of wandering the Israelites were constantly reminded of God's appointed rest day, by the withholding of the manna every seventh day and the miraculous preservation of the double portion that fell on the preparation day.

Before entering the Promised Land, the Israelites were admonished by Moses to "keep the Sabbath day to sanctify it." Deuteronomy 5:12. The Lord designed that by a faithful observance of the Sabbath command, Israel should continually be reminded of their accountability to Him as their Creator and their Redeemer. While they should keep the Sabbath in the proper spirit, idolatry could not exist; but should the claims of this precept of the Decalogue be set aside as no longer binding, the Creator would be forgotten and men would worship other gods. "I gave them My Sabbaths," God declared, "to be a sign between Me and them, that they might know that I am the Lord that sanctify them." Yet "they despised My judgments, and walked not in My statutes, but polluted My Sabbaths: for their heart went after their idols." And in His appeal to them to return to Him, He called their attention anew to the importance of keeping the Sabbath holy. "I am the Lord your God," He said; "walk in My statutes, and keep My judgments, and do them; and hallow My Sabbaths; and they shall be a sign between Me and you, that ye may know that I am the Lord your God." Ezekiel 20:12, 16, 19, 20.

In calling the attention of Judah to the sins that finally brought upon them the Babylonian Captivity, the Lord declared: "Thou hast. . . profaned My Sabbaths." "Therefore have I poured out Mine indignation upon them; I have consumed them with the fire of My wrath: their own way have I recompensed upon their heads." Ezekiel 22:8, 31.

At the restoration of Jerusalem, in the days of Nehemiah, Sabbathbreaking was met with the stern inquiry, "Did not your fathers thus, and did not our God bring all this evil upon us, and upon this city? yet ye bring more wrath upon Israel by profaning the Sabbath." Nehemiah 13:18.

Christ, during His earthly ministry, emphasized the binding claims of the Sabbath; in all His teaching He showed reverence for the institution He Himself had given. In His days the Sabbath had become so perverted that its observance reflected the character of selfish and arbitrary men rather than the character of God. Christ set aside the false teaching by which those who claimed to know God had misrepresented Him. Although followed with merciless hostility by the rabbis, He did not even appear to conform to their requirements, but went straight forward keeping the Sabbath according to the law of God.

In unmistakable language He testified to His regard for the law of Jehovah. "Think not that I am come to destroy the law, or the prophets," He said; "I am not come to destroy, but to fulfill. For verily I say unto you, Till heaven and earth pass, one jot or one tittle shall in no wise pass from the law, till all be fulfilled. Whosoever therefore shall break one of these least commandments, and shall teach men so, he shall be called the least in the kingdom of heaven: but whosoever shall do and teach them, the same shall be called great in the kingdom of heaven." Matthew 5:17-19.

During the Christian dispensation, the great enemy of man's happiness has made the Sabbath of the fourth commandment an object of special attack. Satan says, "I will work at cross purposes with God. I will empower my followers to set aside God's memorial, the seventh-day Sabbath. Thus I will show the world that the day sanctified and blessed by God has been changed. That day shall not live in the minds of the people. I will obliterate the memory of it. I will place in its stead a day that does not bear the credentials of God, a day that cannot be a sign between God and His people. I will lead those who accept this day to place upon it the sanctity that God placed upon the seventh day.

"Through my vicegerent, I will exalt myself. The first day will be extolled, and the Protestant world will receive this spurious sabbath as genuine. Through the nonobservance of the Sabbath that God instituted, I will bring His law into contempt. The words, 'A sign between Me and you throughout your generations,' I will make to serve on the side of my sabbath.

"Thus the world will become mine. I will be the ruler of the earth, the prince of the world. I will so control the minds under my power that God's Sabbath shall be a special object of contempt. A sign? I will make the observance of the seventh day a sign of disloyalty to the authorities of earth. Human laws will be made so stringent that men and women will not dare to observe the seventh-day Sabbath. For fear of wanting food and clothing, they will join with the world in transgressing God's law. The earth will be wholly under my dominion."

Through the setting up of a false sabbath, the enemy thought to change times and laws. But has he really succeeded in changing God's law? The words of the thirty-first Chapter of Exodus are the answer. He who is the same yesterday, today, and forever, has declared of the seventh-day Sabbath: "It is a sign between Me and you throughout your generations." "It is a sign . . . forever." Exodus 31:13, 17. The changed signpost is pointing the wrong way, but God has not changed. He is still the mighty God of Israel. "Behold, the nations are as a drop of a bucket, and are counted as the small dust of the balance: behold, He taketh up the isles as a very little thing. And Lebanon is not sufficient to burn, nor the beasts thereof sufficient for a burnt offering. All nations before His are as nothing; and they are counted to Him less than nothing, and vanity." Isaiah 40:15-17. And He is just as jealous for His law now as He was in the days of Ahab and Elijah.

But how is that law disregarded! Behold the world today in open rebellion against God. This is in truth a froward generation, filled with ingratitude, formalism, insincerity, pride, and apostasy. Men neglect the Bible and hate truth. Jesus sees His law rejected, His love despised, His ambassadors treated with indifference. He has spoken by His mercies, but these have been unacknowledged; He has spoken by warnings, but these have been unheeded. The temple courts of the human soul have been turned into places of unholy traffic. Selfishness, envy, pride, malice— all are cherished.

Many do not hesitate to sneer at the word of God. Those who believe that word just as it reads are held up to ridicule.

There is a growing contempt for law and order, directly traceable to a violation of the plain commands of Jehovah. Violence and crime are the result of turning aside from the path of obedience. Behold the wretchedness and misery of multitudes who worship at the shrine of idols and who seek in vain for happiness and peace.

Behold the well-nigh universal disregard of the Sabbath commandment. Behold also the daring impiety of those who, while enacting laws to safeguard the supposed sanctity of the first day of the week, at the same time are making laws legalizing the liquor traffic. Wise above that which is written, they attempt to coerce the consciences of men, while lending their sanction to an evil that brutalizes and destroys the beings created in the image of God. It is Satan himself who inspires such legislation. He well knows that the curse of God will rest on those who exalt human enactments above the divine, and he does all in his power to lead men into the broad road that ends in destruction.

So long have men worshiped human opinions and human institutions that almost the whole world is following after idols. And he who has endeavored to change God's law is using every deceptive artifice to induce men and women to array themselves against God and against the sign by which the righteous are known. But the Lord will not always suffer His law to be broken and despised with impunity. There is a time coming when "the lofty looks of man shall be humbled, and the haughtiness of men shall be bowed down, and the Lord alone shall be exalted in that day." Isaiah 2:11. Skepticism may treat the claims of God's law with jest, scoffing, and denial. The spirit of worldliness may contaminate the many and control the few, the cause of God may hold its ground only by great exertion and continual sacrifice, yet in the end the truth will triumph gloriously.

In the closing work of God in the earth, the standard of His law will be again exalted. False religion may prevail, iniquity may abound, the love of many may wax cold, the cross of Calvary may be lost sight of, and darkness, like the pall of death, may spread over the world; the whole force of the popular current may be turned against the truth; plot after plot may be formed to overthrow the people of God; but in the hour of greatest peril the God of Elijah will raise up human instrumentalities to bear a message that will not be silenced. In the populous cities of the land, and in the places where men have gone to the greatest lengths in speaking against the Most High, the voice of stern rebuke will be heard. Boldly will men of God's appointment denounce the union of the church with the world. Earnestly will they call upon men and women to turn from the observance of a man-made institution to the observance of the true Sabbath. "Fear God, and give glory to Him," they will proclaim to every nation; "for the hour of His judgment is come: and worship Him that made heaven, and earth, and the sea, and the fountains of waters. . . . If any man worship the beast and his image, and receive his mark in his forehead, or in his hand, the same shall drink of the wine of the wrath of God, which is poured out without mixture into the cup of His indignation." Revelation 14:7-10.

God will not break His covenant, nor alter the thing that has gone out of His lips. His word will stand fast forever as unalterable as His throne. At the judgment this covenant will be brought forth, plainly written with the finger of God, and the world will be arraigned before the bar of Infinite Justice to receive sentence.

Today, as in the days of Elijah, the line of demarcation between God's commandment-keeping people and the worshipers of false gods in clearly drawn. "How long halt ye between two opinions?" Elijah cried; "if the Lord be God, follow Him: but if Baal, then follow him." 1 Kings 18:21. And the message for today is: "Babylon the great is fallen, is fallen. . . . Come out of her, My people, that ye be not partakers of her sins, and that ye receive not of her plagues. For her sins have reached unto heaven, and God hath remembered her iniquities." Revelation 18:2, 4, 5.

The time is not far distant when the test will come to every soul. The observance of the false sabbath will be urged upon us. The contest will be between the commandments of God and the commandments of men. Those who have yielded step by step to worldly demands and conformed to worldly customs will then yield to the powers that be, rather than subject themselves to derision, insult, threatened imprisonment, and death. At that time the gold will be separated from the dross. True godliness will be clearly distinguished from the appearance and tinsel of it. Many a star that we have admired for its brilliance will then go out in darkness. Those who have assumed the ornaments of the sanctuary, but are not clothed with Christ's righteousness, will then appear in the shame of their own nakedness.

Among earth's inhabitants, scattered in every land, there are those who have not bowed the knee to Baal. Like the stars of heaven, which appear only at night, these faithful ones will shine forth when darkness covers the earth and gross darkness the people. In heathen Africa, in the Catholic lands of Europe and of South America, in China, in India, in the islands of the sea, and in all the dark corners of the earth, God has in reserve a firmament of chosen ones that will yet shine forth amidst the darkness, revealing clearly to an apostate world the transforming power of obedience to His law. Even now they are appearing in every nation, among every tongue and people; and in the hour of deepest apostasy, when Satan's supreme effort is made to cause "all, both small and great, rich and poor, free and bond," to receive, under penalty of death, the sign of allegiance to a false rest day, these faithful ones, "blameless and harmless, the sons of God, without rebuke," will "shine as lights in the world." Revelation 13:16; Philippians 2:15. The darker the night, the more brilliantly will they shine.

What strange work Elijah would have done in numbering Israel at the time when God's judgments were falling upon the backsliding people! He could count only one on the Lord's side. But when he said, "I, even I only, am left; and they seek my life," the word of the Lord surprised him, "Yet I have left Me seven thousand in Israel, all the knees which have not bowed unto Baal." 1 Kings 19:14, 18.

Then let no man attempt to number Israel today, but let everyone have a heart of flesh, a heart of tender sympathy, a heart that, like the heart of Christ, reaches out for the salvation of a lost world.

Jehoshaphat

Until called to the throne at the age of thirty-five, Jehoshaphat had before him the example of good King Asa, who in nearly every crisis had done "that which was right in the eyes of the Lord." 1 Kings 15:11. During a prosperous reign of twenty-five years, Jehoshaphat sought to walk "in all the ways of Asa his father; he turned not aside."

In his efforts to rule wisely, Jehoshaphat endeavored to persuade his subjects to take a firm stand against idolatrous practices. Many of the people in his realm "offered and burnt incense yet in the high places." 1 Kings 22:43. The king did not at once destroy these shrines; but from the beginning he tried to safeguard Judah from the sins characterizing the northern kingdom under the rule of Ahab, of whom he was a contemporary for many years. Jehoshaphat himself was loyal to God. He "sought not unto Baalim; but sought to the Lord God of his father, and walked in His commandments, and not after the doings of Israel." Because of his integrity, the Lord was with him, and "stablished the kingdom in his hand." 2 Chronicles 17:3-5.

"All Judah brought to Jehoshaphat presents; and he had riches and honor in abundance. And his heart was lifted up in the ways of the Lord." As time passed and reformations were wrought, the king "took away the high places and groves out of Judah." Verses 5, 6. "And the remnant of the Sodomites, which remained in the days of his father Asa, he took out of the land." 1 Kings 22:46. Thus gradually the inhabitants of Judah were freed from many of the perils that had been threatening to retard seriously their spiritual development.

Throughout the kingdom the people were in need of instruction in the law of God. In an understanding of this law lay their safety; by conforming their lives to its requirements they would become loyal both to God and to man. Knowing this, Jehoshaphat took steps to ensure to his people thorough instruction in the Holy Scriptures. The princes in charge of the different portions of his realm were directed to arrange for the faithful ministry of teaching priests. By royal appointment these instructors, working under the direct supervision of the princes, "went about throughout all the cities of Judah, and taught the people." 2 Chronicles 17:7-9. And as many endeavored to understand God's requirements and to put away sin, a revival was effected.

To this wise provision for the spiritual needs of his subjects, Jehoshaphat owed much of his prosperity as a ruler. In obedience to God's law there is great gain. In conformity to the divine requirements there is a transforming power that brings peace and good will among men. If the teachings of

God's word were made the controlling influence in the life of every man and woman, if mind and heart were brought under its restraining power, the evils that now exist in national and in social life would find no place. From every home would go forth an influence that would make men and women strong in spiritual insight and in moral power, and thus nations and individuals would be placed on vantage ground.

For many years Jehoshaphat lived in peace, unmolested by surrounding nations. "The fear of the Lord fell upon all the kingdoms of the lands that were round about Judah." Verse 10. From Philistia he received tribute money and presents; from Arabia, large flocks of sheep and goats. "Jehoshaphat waxed great exceedingly; and he built in Judah castles, and cities of stores. . . . Men of war, mighty men of valor, . . . waited on the king, beside those whom the king put in the fenced cities throughout all Judah." Verses 12-19. Blessed abundantly with "riches and honor," he was enabled to wield a mighty influence for truth and righteousness. 2 Chronicles 18:1. Some years after coming to the throne, Jehoshaphat, now in the height of his prosperity, consented to the marriage of his son, Jehoram, to Athaliah, daughter of Ahab and Jezebel. By this union there was formed between the kingdoms of Judah and Israel an alliance which was not in the order of God and which in a time of crisis brought disaster to the king and to many of his subjects.

On one occasion Jehoshaphat visited the king of Israel at Samaria. Special honor was shown the royal guest from Jerusalem, and before the close of his visit he was persuaded to unite with the king of Israel in war against the Syrians. Ahab hoped that by joining his forces with those of Judah he might regain Ramoth, one of the old cities of refuge, which, he contended, rightfully belonged to the Israelites.

Although Jehoshaphat in a moment of weakness had rashly promised to join the king of Israel in his war against the Syrians, yet his better judgment led him to seek to learn the will of God concerning the undertaking. "Inquire, I pray thee, at the word of the Lord today," he suggested to Ahab. In response, Ahab called together four hundred of the false prophets of Samaria, and asked of them, "Shall we go to Ramothgilead to battle, or shall I forbear?" And they answered, "Go up; for God will deliver it into the kings's hand." Verses 4, 5.

Unsatisfied, Jehoshaphat sought to learn for a certainty the will of God. "Is there not here a prophet of the Lord," he asked, "that we might inquire of him?" Verse 6. "There is yet one man, Micaiah to son of Imlah, by whom we may inquire of the Lord," Ahab answered; "but I hate him" for he doth not prophesy good concerning me, but evil." 1 Kings 22:8. Jehoshaphat was firm in his request that the man of God be called; and upon appearing before them and being adjured by Ahab to tell "nothing but that which is true in the name of the Lord," Micaiah said: "I saw all Israel scattered upon the hills, as sheep that have not a shepherd: and the Lord said, These have no master: let them return every man to his house in peace." Verses 16, 17.

The words of the prophet should have been enough to show the kings that their project was not favored by Heaven, but neither ruler felt inclined to heed the warning. Ahab had marked out his course, and he was determined to follow it. Jehoshaphat had given his word of honor, "We will be with thee in the war;" and after making such a promise, he was reluctant to withdraw his forces. 2 Chronicles 18:3. "So the king of Israel and Jehoshaphat the king of Judah went up to Ramothgilead." 1 Kings 22:29.

During the battle that followed, Ahab was shot by an arrow, and at eventide he died. "About the going down of the sun," "there went a proclamation throughout the host," "Every man to his city, and every man to his own country." Verse 36. Thus was fulfilled the word of the prophet. From this disastrous battle Jehoshaphat returned to Jerusalem. As he approached the city, the prophet Jehu met him with the reproof: "Shouldest thou help the ungodly, and love them that hate the Lord? therefore is wrath upon thee from before the Lord. Nevertheless there are good things found in thee, in that thou hast taken away the groves out of the land, and hast prepared thine heart to seek God." 2 Chronicles 19:2, 3.

The later years of Jehoshaphat's reign were largely spent in strengthening the national and spiritual defenses of Judah. He "went out again through the people from Beersheba to Mount Ephraim, and brought them back unto the Lord God of their fathers." Verse 4.

One of the important steps taken by the king was the establishment and maintenance of efficient courts of justice. He "set judges in the land throughout all the fenced cities of Judah, city by city;" and in the charge given them he urged: "Take heed what ye do: for ye judge not for man, but for the Lord, who is with you in the judgment. Wherefore now let the fear of the Lord be upon you; take heed and do it: for there is no iniquity with the Lord our God, nor respect of persons, nor taking of gifts." Verses 5-7.

The judicial system was perfected by the founding of a court of appeal at Jerusalem, where Jehoshaphat "set of the Levites, and of the priests, and of the chief of the fathers of Israel, for the judgement of the Lord, and for controversies." Verse 8.

The king exhorted these judges to be faithful. "Thus shall ye do in the fear of the Lord, faithfully, and with a perfect heart," he charged them. "And what cause soever shall come to you of your brethren that dwell in their cities, between blood and blood, between law and commandment, statutes and judgments, ye shall even warn them that they trespass not against the Lord, and so wrath come upon you, and upon your brethren: this do, and ye shall not trespass.

"And, behold, Amariah the chief priest is over you in all matters of the Lord; and Zebadiah the son of Ishmael, the ruler of the house of Judah, for all the king's matters: also the Levites shall be officers before you.

"Deal courageously, and the Lord shall be with the good." Verses 9-11.

In his careful safeguarding of the rights and liberties of his subjects, Jehoshaphat emphasized the consideration that every

Jezebel soon learned the particulars, and, indignant that anyone should refuse the request of the king, she assured Ahab that he need no longer be sad. "Dost thou now govern the kingdom of Israel?" she said. "Arise, and eat bread, and let thine heart be merry: I will give thee the vineyard of Naboth the Jezreelite."

Ahab cared not by what means his wife might accomplish the desired object, and Jezebel immediately proceeded to carry out her wicked purpose. She wrote letters in the name of the king, sealed them with his signet, and sent them to the elders and nobles of the city where Naboth dwelt, saying: "Proclaim a fast, and set Naboth on high among the people: and set two men, sons of Belial, before him, to bear witness against him, saying, Thou didst blaspheme God and the king. And then carry him out, and stone him, that he may die."

The command was obeyed. "The men of his city, even the elders and the nobles, . . . did as Jezebel had . . . written in the letters which she had sent unto them." Then Jezebel went to the king and bade him arise and take the vineyard. And Ahab, heedless of the consequences, blindly followed her counsel and went down to take possession of the coveted property.

The king was not allowed to enjoy unrebuked that which he had gained by fraud and bloodshed. "The word of the Lord came to Elijah the Tishbite, saying, Arise, go down to meet Ahab king of Israel, which is in Samaria: behold, he is in the vineyard of Naboth, whither he is gone down to possess it. And thou shalt speak unto him, saying, Thus saith the Lord, Hast thou killed, and also taken possession?" And the Lord further instructed Elijah to pronounce upon Ahab a terrible judgment.

The prophet hastened to carry out the divine command. The guilty ruler, meeting the stern messenger of Jehovah face to face in the vineyard, gave voice to his startled fear in the words, "Hast thou found me, O mine enemy?"

Without hesitation the messenger of the Lord replied, "I have found thee: because thou hast sold thyself to work evil in the sight of the Lord. Behold, I will bring evil upon thee, and will take away thy posterity." No mercy was to be shown. The house of Ahab was to be utterly destroyed, "like the house of Jeroboam the son of Nebat, and like the house of Baasha the son of Ahijah," the Lord declared through His servant, "for the provocation wherewith thou hast provoked Me to anger, and made Israel to sin."

And of Jezebel the Lord declared, "The dogs shall eat Jezebel by the wall of Jezreel. Him that dieth of Ahab in the city the dogs shall eat; and him that dieth in the field shall the fowls of the air eat."

When the king heard this fearful message, "he rent his clothes, and put sackcloth upon his flesh, and fasted, and lay in sackcloth, and went softly.

"And the word of the Lord came to Elijah the Tishbite, saying, Seest thou how Ahab humbleth himself before Me? because he humbleth himself before Me, I will not bring the evil in his days: but in his son's days will I bring the evil upon his house."

It was less than three years later that King Ahab met his death at the hands of the Syrians. Ahaziah, his successor, "did evil in the sight of the Lord, and walked in the way of his father, and in the way of his mother, and in the way of Jeroboam." "He served Baal, and worshiped him, and provoked to anger the Lord God of Israel," as his father Ahab had done. 1 Kings 22:52, 53. But judgments followed close upon the sins of the rebellious king. A disastrous war with Moab, and then an accident by which his own life was threatened, attested to God's wrath against him.

Having fallen "through a lattice in his upper chamber," Ahaziah, seriously injured, and fearful of the possible outcome, sent some of his servants to make inquiry of Baalzebub, the god of Ekron, whether he should recover or not. The god of Ekron was supposed to give information, through the medium of its priests, concerning future events. Large numbers of people went to inquire of it; but the predictions there uttered, and the information given, proceeded from the prince of darkness.

Ahaziah's servants were met by a man of God, who directed them to return to the king with the message: "Is it because there is no God in Israel, that ye go to inquire of Baal-zebub, the god of Ekron? Now therefore thus saith Jehovah, Thou shalt not come down from the bed whither thou art gone up, but shalt surely die." Having delivered his message, the prophet departed.

The astonished servants hastened back to the king, and repeated to him the words of the man of God. The king inquired, "What manner of man was he?" They answered, "He was an hairy man, and girt with a girdle of leather about his loins." "It is Elijah the Tishbite," Ahaziah exclaimed. He knew that if the stranger whom his messengers had met was indeed Elijah, the words of doom pronounced would surely come to pass. Anxious to avert, if possible, the threatened judgment, he determined to send for the prophet.

Twice Ahaziah sent a company of soldiers to intimidate the prophet, and twice the wrath of God fell upon them in judgment. The third company of soldiers humbled themselves before God; and their captain, as he approached the Lord's messenger, "fell on his knees before Elijah, and besought him, and said unto him, O man of God, I pray thee, let my life, and the life of these fifty thy servants, be precious in thy sight."

"The angel of Jehovah said unto Elijah, Go down with him: be not afraid of him. And he arose, and went down with him unto the king. And he said unto him, Thus saith Jehovah, Forasmuch as thou hast sent messengers to inquire of Baal-zebub, the god of Ekron, is it because there is no God in Israel to inquire of His word? therefore thou shalt not come down from the bed whither thou art gone up, but shalt surely die."

During the father's reign, Ahaziah had witnessed the wondrous works of the Most High. He had seen the terrible evidences that God had given apostate Israel of the way in which He regards those who set aside the binding claims of

His law. Ahaziah had acted as if these awful realities were but idle tales. Instead of humbling his heart before the Lord, he had followed after Baal, and at last he had ventured upon this, his most daring act of impiety. Rebellious, and unwilling to repent, Ahaziah died, "according to the word of the Lord which Elijah had spoken."

The history of King Ahaziah's sin and its punishment has in it a warning which none can disregard with impunity. Men today may not pay homage to heathen gods, yet thousands are worshiping at Satan's shrine as verily as did the king of Israel. The spirit of idolatry is rife in the world today, although, under the influence of science and education, it has assumed forms more refined and attractive than in the days when Ahaziah sought to the god of Ekron. Every day adds its sorrowful evidence that faith in the sure word of prophecy is decreasing, and that in its stead superstition and satanic witchery are captivating the minds of many.

Today the mysteries of heathen worship are replaced by the secret association and seances, the obscurities and wonders, of spiritistic mediums. The disclosures of these mediums are eagerly received by thousands who refuse to accept light from God's word or through His Spirit. Believers in spiritism may speak with scorn of the magicians of old, but the great deceiver laughs in triumph as they yield to his arts under a different form.

There are many who shrink with horror from the thought of consulting spirit mediums, but who are attracted by more pleasing forms of spiritism. Others are led astray by the teachings of Christian Science, and by the mysticism of Theosophy and other Oriental religions.

The apostles of nearly all forms of spiritism claim to have power to heal. They attribute this power to electricity, magnetism, the so-called "sympathetic remedies," or to latent forces within the mind of man. And there are not a few, even in this Christian age, who go to these healers, instead of trusting in the power of the living God and the skill of well-qualified physicians. The mother, watching by the sickbed of her child, exclaims, "I can do no more. Is there no physician who has power to restore my child?" She is told of the wonderful cures performed by some clairvoyant or magnetic healer, and she trusts her dear one to his charge, placing it as verily in the hand of Satan as if he were standing by her side. In many instances the future life of the child is controlled by a satanic power which it seems impossible to break.

God had cause for displeasure at Ahaziah's impiety. What had He not done to win the hearts of the people of Israel and to inspire them with confidence in Himself? For ages He had been giving His people manifestations of unexampled kindness and love. From the beginning He had shown that His "delights were with the sons of men." Proverbs 8:31. He had been a very present help to all who sought Him in sincerity. Yet now the king of Israel, turning from God to ask help of the worst enemy of his people, proclaimed to the heathen that he had more confidence in their idols than in the God of heaven. In the same manner do men and women dishonor Him when they turn from the Source of strength and wisdom to ask help or counsel from the powers of darkness. If God's wrath was kindled by Ahaziah's act, how does He regard those who, having still greater light, choose to follow a similar course?

Those who give themselves up to the sorcery of Satan, may boast of great benefit received; but does this prove their course to be wise or safe? What if life should be prolonged? What if temporal gain should be secured? Will it pay in the end to have disregarded the will of God? All such apparent gain will prove at last an irrecoverable loss. We cannot with impunity break down a single barrier which God has erected to guard His people from Satan's power.

As Ahaziah had no son, he was succeeded by Jehoram, his brother, who reigned over the ten tribes for twelve years. Throughout these years his mother, Jezebel, was still living, and she continued to exercise her evil influence over the affairs of the nation. Idolatrous customs were still practiced by many of the people. Jehoram himself "wrought evil in the sight of the Lord; but not like his father, and like his mother: for he put away the image of Baal that his father had made. Nevertheless he cleaved unto the sins of Jereboam the son of Nebat, which made Israel to sin; he departed not therefrom." 2 Kings 3:2, 3.

It was during Jehoram's reign over Israel that Jehoshaphat died, and Jehoshaphat's son, also named Jehoram, ascended the throne of the kingdom of Judah. By his marriage with the daughter of Ahab and Jezebel, Jehoram of Judah was closely connected with the king of Israel; and in his reign he followed after Baal, "like as did the house of Ahab." "Moreover he made high places in the mountains of Judah, and caused the inhabitants of Jerusalem to commit fornication, and compelled Judah thereto." 2 Chronicles 21:6, 11.

The king of Judah was not permitted to continue his terrible apostasy unreproved. The prophet Elijah had not yet been translated, and he could not remain silent while the kingdom of Judah was pursuing the same course that had brought the northern kingdom to the verge of ruin. The prophet sent to Jehoram of Judah a written communication, in which the wicked king read the awful words:

"Thus saith the Lord God of David thy father, Because thou hast not walked in the ways of Jehoshaphat thy father, nor in the ways of Asa king of Judah, but hast walked in the way of the kings of Israel, and hast made Judah and the inhabitants of Jerusalem to go a whoring, like to the whoredoms of the house of Ahab, and also hast slain thy brethren of thy father's house, which were better than thyself: behold, with a great plague will the Lord smite thy people, and thy children, and thy wives, and all thy goods: and thou shalt have great sickness."

In fulfillment of this prophecy "the Lord stirred up against Jehoram the spirit of the Philistines, and of the Arabians, that were near the Ethiopians: and they came up into Judah, and brake into it, and carried away all the substance that was found in the king's house, and his sons also, and his wives; so that there was never a son left him, save Jehoahaz, the youngest of his sons.

"And after all this the Lord smote him in his bowels with an incurable disease. And it came to pass, that in process of time, after the end of two years, . . . he died of sore diseases." "And Ahaziah his son reigned in his stead." Verses 12:19; 2 Kings 8:24.

Jehoram the son of Ahab was still reigning in the kingdom of Israel when his nephew, Ahaziah, came to the throne of Judah. Ahaziah ruled only one year, and during this time, influenced by his mother, Athaliah, "his counselor to do wickedly," "he walked in the way of the house of Ahab, and did evil in the sight of the Lord." 2 Chronicles 22:3, 4; 2 Kings 8:27. Jezebel, his grandmother, was still living, and he allied himself boldly with Jehoram of Israel, his uncle.

Ahaziah of Judah soon met a tragic end. The surviving members of the house of Ahab were indeed "his counselors after the death of his father to his destruction." 2 Chronicles 22:3, 4. While Ahaziah was visiting his uncle at Jezreel, the prophet Elisha was divinely directed to send one of the sons of the prophets to Ramothgilead to anoint Jehu king of Israel. The combined forces of Judah and Israel were at that time engaged in a military campaign against the Syrians of Ramothgilead. Jehoram had been wounded in battle, and had returned to Jezreel, leaving Jehu in charge of the royal armies.

In anointing Jehu, the messenger of Elisha declared, "I have anointed thee king over the people of the Lord, even over Israel." And then he solemnly charged Jehu with a special commission from heaven. "Thou shalt smite the house of Ahab thy master," the Lord declared through His messenger, "that I may avenge the blood of My servants the prophets, and the blood of all the servants of the Lord, at the hand of Jezebel. For the whole house of Ahab shall perish." 2 Kings 9:6-8.

After he had been proclaimed king by the army, Jehu hastened to Jezreel, where he began his work of execution on those who had deliberately chosen to continue in sin and to lead others into sin. Jehoram of Israel, Ahaziah of Judah, and Jezebel the queen mother, with "all that remained of the house of Ahab in Jezreel, and all his great men, and his kinsfolks, and his priests," were slain. "All the prophets of Baal, all his servants, and all his priests" dwelling at the center of Baal worship near Samaria, were put to the sword. The idolatrous images were broken down and burned, and the temple of Baal was laid in ruins. "Thus Jehu destroyed Baal out of Israel." 2 Kings 10:11, 19, 28.

Tidings of this general execution reached Athaliah, Jezebel's daughter, who still occupied a commanding position in the kingdom of Judah. When she saw that her son, the king of Judah, was dead, "she arose and destroyed all the seed royal of the house of Judah." In this massacre all the descendants of David who were eligible to the throne were destroyed, save one, a babe named Joash, whom the wife of Jehoiada the high priest hid within the precincts of the temple. For six years the

child remained hidden, while "Athaliah reigned over the land." 2 Chronicles 22:10, 12.

At the end of this time, "the Levites and all Judah" (2 Chronicles 23:8) united with Jehoiada the high priest in crowning and anointing the child Joash and acclaiming him their king. "And they clapped their hands, and said, God save the king." 2 Kings 11:12.

"Now when Athaliah heard the noise of the people running and praising the king, she came to the people into the house of the Lord." 2 Chronicles 23:12. "And when she looked, behold, the king stood by a pillar, as the manner was, and the princes and the trumpeters by the king, and all the people of the land rejoiced, and blew with trumpets."

"Athaliah rent her clothes, and cried, Treason, Treason." 2 Kings 11:14. But Jehoiada commanded the officers to lay hold of Athaliah and all her followers and lead them out of the temple to a place of execution, where they were to be slain.

Thus perished the last member of the house of Ahab. The terrible evil that had been wrought through his alliance with Jezebel, continued till the last of his descendants was destroyed. Even in the land of Judah, where the worship of the true God had never been formally set aside, Athaliah had succeeded in seducing many. Immediately after the execution of the impenitent queen "all the people of the land went into the house of Baal, and brake it down; his altars and his images brake they in pieces thoroughly, and slew Mattan the priest of Baal before the altars." Verse 18.

A reformation followed. Those who took part in acclaiming Joash king, had solemnly covenanted "that they should be the Lord's people." And now that the evil influence of the daughter of Jezebel had been removed from the kingdom of Judah, and the priests of Baal had been slain and their temple destroyed, "all the people of the land rejoiced: and the city was quiet." 2 Chronicles 23:16, 21.

The Call of Elisha

God had bidden Elijah anoint another to be prophet in his stead. "Elisha the son of Shaphat . . . shalt thou anoint to be prophet in thy room" (1 Kings 19:16), He had said; and in obedience to the command, Elijah went to find Elisha. As he journeyed northward, how changed was the scene from what it had been only a short while before! Then the ground was parched, the farming districts unworked, for neither dew nor rain had fallen for three and a half years. Now on every hand vegetation was springing up as if to redeem the time of drought and famine.

Elisha's father was a wealthy farmer, a man whose household were among the number that in a time of almost universal apostasy had not bowed the knee to Baal. Theirs was a home where God was honored and where allegiance to the faith of ancient Israel was the rule of daily life. In such surroundings the early years of Elisha were passed. In the quietude of country life, under the teaching of God and nature and the discipline of useful work, he received the training in habits of simplicity and of obedience to his parents and to God that helped to fit him for the high position he was afterward to occupy.

The prophetic call came to Elisha while, with his father's servants, he was plowing in the field. He had taken up the work that lay nearest. He possessed both the capabilities of a leader among men and the meekness of one who is ready to serve. Of a quiet and gentle spirit, he was nevertheless energetic and steadfast. Integrity, fidelity, and the love and fear of God were his, and in the humble round of daily toil he gained strength of purpose and nobleness of character, constantly increasing in grace and knowledge. While co-operating with his father in the home-life duties, he was learning to co-operate with God.

By faithfulness in little things, Elisha was preparing for weightier trusts. Day by day, through practical experience, he gained a fitness for a broader, higher work. He learned to serve; and in learning this, he learned also how to instruct and lead. The lesson is for all. None can know what may be God's purpose in His discipline; but all may be certain that faithfulness in little things is the evidence of fitness for greater responsibilities. Every act of life is a revelation of character, and he only who in small duties proves himself "a workman that needeth not to be ashamed" can be honored by God with higher service. 2 Timothy 2:15.

He who feels that it is of no consequence how he performs the smaller tasks proves himself unfit for a more honored position. He may think himself fully competent to take up the larger duties; but God looks deeper than the surface. After test and trial, there is written against him the sentence, "Thou art weighed in the balances, and art found wanting." His unfaithfulness reacts upon himself. He fails of gaining the grace, the power, the force of character, which is received through unreserved surrender.

Because they are not connected with some directly religious work, many feel that their lives are useless, that they are doing nothing for the advancement of God's kingdom. If they could do some great thing how gladly they would undertake it! But because they can serve only in little things, they think themselves justified in doing nothing. In this they err. A man may be in the active service of God while engaged in the ordinary, everyday duties—while felling trees, clearing the ground, or following the plow. The mother who trains her children for Christ is as truly working for God as is the minister in the pulpit.

Many long for special talent with which to do a wonderful work, while the duties lying close at hand, the performance of which would make the life fragrant, are lost sight of. Let such ones take up the duties lying directly in their pathway. Success depends not so much on talent as on energy and willingness. It is not the possession of splendid talents that enables us to render acceptable service, but the conscientious performance of daily duties, the contented spirit, the unaffected, sincere interest in the welfare of others. In the humblest lot true excellence may be found. The commonest tasks, wrought with loving faithfulness, are beautiful in God's sight.

As Elijah, divinely directed in seeking a successor, passed the field in which Elisha was plowing, he cast upon the young man's shoulders the mantle of consecration. During the famine the family of Shaphat had become familiar with the work and mission of Elijah, and now the Spirit of God impressed Elisha's heart as to the meaning of the prophet's act. To him it was the signal that God had called him to be the successor of Elijah.

"And he left the oxen, and ran after Elijah, and said, Let me, I pray thee, kiss my father and my mother, and then I will follow thee." "Go back again," was Elijah's answer, "for what have I done to thee?" This was not a repulse, but a test of faith. Elisha must count the cost—decide for himself to accept or reject the call. If his desires clung to his home and its advantages, he was at liberty to remain there. But Elisha understood the meaning of the call. He knew it was from God, and he did not hesitate to obey, Not for any worldly advantage would he forgo the opportunity of becoming God's messenger or sacrifice the privilege of association with His servant. He "took a yoke of oxen, and slew them, and boiled their flesh with the instruments of the oxen, and gave unto the people, and they did eat. Then he arose, and went after Elijah, and ministered unto him." 1 Kings 19:20, 21. Without hesitation he left a home where he was beloved, to attend the prophet in his uncertain life.

Had Elisha asked Elijah what was expected of him,—what would be his work,—he would have been answered: God knows; He will make it known to you. If you wait upon the Lord, He will answer your every question. You may come with me if you have evidence that God has called you. Know for yourself that God stands back of me, and that it is His voice you hear. If you can count everything but dross that you may win the favor of God, come.

Similar to the call that came to Elisha was the answer given by Christ to the young ruler who asked Him the question, "What good thing shall I do, that I may have eternal life?" "If thou wilt be perfect," Christ replied, "go and sell that thou hast, and give to the poor, and thou shalt have treasure in heaven: and come and follow Me." Matthew 19:16, 21.

Elisha accepted the call to service, casting no backward glance at the pleasures and comforts he was leaving. The young ruler, when he heard the Saviour's words, "went away sorrowful: for he had great possessions." Verse 22. He was not willing to make the sacrifice. His love for his possessions was greater than his love for God. By his refusal to renounce all for Christ, he proved himself unworthy of a place in the Master's service.

The call to place all on the altar of service comes to each one. We are not all asked to serve as Elisha served, nor are we all bidden to sell everything we have; but God asks us to give His service the first place in our lives, to allow no day to pass without doing something to advance His work in the earth. He does not expect from all the same kind of service. One may be called to ministry in a foreign land; another may be asked to give of his means for the support of gospel work. God accepts the offering of each. It is the consecration of the life and all its interests, that is necessary. Those who make this consecration will hear and obey the call of Heaven.

To everyone who becomes a partaker of His grace, the Lord appoints a work for others. Individually we are to stand in our lot, saying, "Here am I; send me." Whether a man be a minister of the Word or a physician, whether he be merchant or farmer, professional man or mechanic, the responsibility rests upon him. It is his work to reveal to others the gospel of their salvation. Every enterprise is which he engages should be a means to this end.

It was no great work that was at first required of Elisha; commonplace duties still constituted his discipline. He is spoken of as pouring water on the hands of Elijah, his master. He was willing to do anything that the Lord directed, and at every step he learned lessons of humility and service. As the prophet's personal attendant, he continued to prove faithful in little things, while with daily strengthening purpose he devoted himself to the mission appointed him by God.

Elisha's life after uniting with Elijah was not without temptations. Trials he had in abundance; but in every emergency he relied on God. He was tempted to think of the home that he had left, but to this temptation he gave no heed. Having put his hand to the plow, he was resolved not to turn back, and through test and trial he proved true to his trust.

Ministry comprehends far more than preaching the word. It means training young men as Elijah trained Elisha, taking them from their ordinary duties, and giving them responsibilities to bear in God's work—small responsibilities at first, and larger ones as they gain strength and experience. There are in the ministry men of faith and prayer, men who can say, "That which was from the beginning, which we have heard, which we have seen with our eyes, which we have looked upon, and our hands have handled, of the Word of life; . . . that which we have seen and heard declare we unto you." 1 John 1:1-3. Young, inexperienced workers should be trained by actual labor in connection with these experienced servants of God. Thus they will learn how to bear burdens.

Those who undertake this training of young workers are doing noble service. The Lord Himself co-operates with their efforts. And the young men to whom the word of consecration has been spoken, whose privilege it is to be brought into close association with earnest, godly workers, should make the most of their opportunity. God has honored them by choosing them for His service and by placing them where they can gain greater fitness for it, and they should be humble, faithful, obedient, and willing to sacrifice. If they submit to God's discipline, carrying out His directions and choosing His servants as their counselors, they will develop into righteous, high-principled, steadfast men, whom God can entrust with responsibilities.

As the gospel is proclaimed in its purity, men will be called from the plow and from the common commercial business vocations that largely occupy the mind and will be educated in connection with men of experience. As they learn to labor effectively, they will proclaim the truth with power. Through most wonderful workings of divine providence, mountains of difficulty will be removed and cast into the sea. The message that means so much to the dwellers upon the earth will be heard and understood. Men will know what is truth. Onward and still onward the work will advance until the whole earth shall have been warned, and then shall the end come.

For several years after the call of Elisha, Elijah and Elisha labored together, the younger man daily gaining greater preparedness for his work. Elijah had been God's instrument for the overthrow of gigantic evils. The idolatry which, supported by Ahab and the heathen Jezebel, had seduced the nation, had been given a decided check. Baal's prophets had been slain. The whole people of Israel had been deeply stirred, and many were returning to the worship of God. As Elijah's successor, Elisha, by careful, patient instruction, must endeavor to guide Israel in safe paths. His association with Elijah, the greatest prophet since the days of Moses, prepared him for the work that he was soon to take up alone.

During these years of united ministry, Elijah from time to time was called upon to meet flagrant evils with stern rebuke. When wicked Ahab seized Naboth's vineyard, it was the voice of Elijah that prophesied his doom and the doom of all his house. And when Ahaziah, after the death of his father Ahab, turned from the living God to Baal-zebub, the god of Ekron, it was Elijah's voice that was heard once more in earnest protest.

The schools of the prophets, established by Samuel, had fallen into decay during the years of Israel's apostasy. Elijah re-established these schools, making provision for young men to gain an education that would lead them to magnify the law and make it honorable. Three of these schools, one at Gilgal, one at Bethel, and one at Jericho, are mentioned in the record. Just before Elijah was taken to heaven, he and Elisha visited these centers of training. The lessons that the prophet of God had given them on former visits, he now repeated. Especially did he instruct them concerning their high privilege of loyally maintaining their allegiance to the God of heaven. He also impressed upon their minds the importance of letting simplicity mark every feature of their education. Only in this way could they receive the mold of heaven and go forth to work in the ways of the Lord.

The heart of Elijah was cheered as he saw what was being accomplished by means of these schools. The work of reformation was not complete, but he could see throughout the kingdom a verification of the word of the Lord, "Yet I have left Me seven thousand in Israel, all the knees which have not bowed unto Baal." 1 Kings 19:18.

As Elisha accompanied the prophet on his round of service from school to school, his faith and resolution were once more tested. At Gilgal, and again at Bethel and Jericho, he was invited by the prophet to turn back. "Tarry here, I pray thee,"

Elijah said; "for the Lord hath sent me to Bethel." But in his early labor of guiding the plow, Elisha had learned not to fail or to become discouraged, and now that he had set his hand to the plow in another line of duty he would not be diverted from his purpose. He would not be parted from his master, so long as opportunity remained for gaining a further fitting up for service. Unknown to Elijah, the revelation that he was to be translated had been made known to his disciples in the schools of the prophets, and in particular to Elisha. And now the tried servant of the man of God kept close beside him. As often as the invitation to turn back was given, his answer was, "As the Lord liveth, and as thy soul liveth, I will not leave thee."

"And they two went on. . . . And they two stood by Jordan. And Elijah took his mantle, and wrapped it together, and smote the waters, and they were divided hither and thither, so that they two went over on dry ground. And it came to pass, when they were gone over, that Elijah said unto Elisha, Ask what I shall do for thee, before I be taken away from thee."

Elisha asked not for worldly honor, or for a high place among the great men of earth. That which he craved was a large measure of the Spirit that God had bestowed so freely upon the one about to be honored with translation. He knew that nothing but the Spirit which had rested upon Elijah could fit him to fill the place in Israel to which God had called him, and so he asked, "I pray thee, let a double portion of thy Spirit be upon me."

In response to this request, Elijah said, "Thou hast asked a hard thing: nevertheless, if thou see me when I am taken from thee, it shall be so unto thee; but if not, it shall not be so. And it came to pass, as they still went on, and talked, that, behold, there appeared a chariot of fire, and horses of fire, and parted them both asunder; and Elijah went up by a whirlwind into heaven." See 2 Kings 2:1-11.

Elijah was a type of the saints who will be living on the earth at the time of the second advent of Christ and who will be "changed, in a moment, in the twinkling of an eye, at the last trump," without tasting of death. 1 Corinthians 15:51, 52. It was as a representative of those who shall be thus translated that Elijah, near the close of Christ's earthly ministry, was permitted to stand with Moses by the side of the Saviour on the mount of transfiguration. In these glorified ones, the disciples saw in miniature a representation of the kingdom of the redeemed. They beheld Jesus clothed with the light of heaven; they heard the "voice out of the cloud" (Luke 9:35), acknowledging Him as the Son of God; they saw Moses, representing those who will be raised from the dead at the time of the second advent; and there also stood Elijah, representing those who at the close of earth's history will be changed from mortal to immortal and be translated to heaven without seeing death.

In the desert, in loneliness and discouragement, Elijah had said that he had had enough of life and had prayed that he might die. But the Lord in His mercy had not taken him at his word. There was yet a great work for Elijah to do; and when his work was done, he was not to perish in discouragement and solitude. Not for him the descent into the tomb, but the ascent with God's angels to the presence of His glory.

"And Elisha saw it, and he cried, My father, my father, the chariot of Israel, and the horsemen thereof. And he saw him no more: and he took hold of his own clothes, and rent them in two pieces. He took up also the mantle of Elijah that fell from him, and went back, and stood by the bank of Jordan; and he took the mantle of Elijah that fell from him, and smote the waters, and said, Where is the Lord God of Elijah? and when he also had smitten the waters, they parted hither and thither: and Elisha went over. And when the sons of the prophets which were to view at Jericho saw him, they said, The Spirit of Elijah doth rest on Elisha. And they came to meet him, and bowed themselves to the ground before him." 2 Kings 2:12-15.

When the Lord in His providence sees fit to remove from His work those to whom He has given wisdom, He helps and strengthens their successors, if they will look to Him for aid and will walk in His ways. They may be even wiser than their predecessors; for they may profit by their experience and learn wisdom from their mistakes.

Henceforth Elisha stood in Elijah's place. He who had been faithful in that which was least was to prove himself faithful also in much.

The Healing of the Waters

In Patriarchal times the Jordan Valley was "well watered everywhere, . . . even as the garden of the Lord." It was in this fair valley that Lot chose to make his home when he "pitched his tent toward Sodom." Genesis 13:10, 12. At the time that the cities of the plain were destroyed, the region round about became a desolate waste, and it has since formed a part of the wilderness of Judea.

A portion of the beautiful valley remained, with its life-giving springs and streams, to gladden the heart of man. In this valley, rich with fields of grain and forests of date palms and other fruit-bearing trees, the hosts of Israel had encamped after crossing the Jordan and had first partaken of the fruits of the Promised Land. Before them had stood the walls of Jericho, a heathen stronghold, the center of the worship of Ashtoreth, vilest and most degrading of all Canaanitish forms of idolatry. Soon its walls were thrown down and its inhabitants slain, and at the time of its fall the solemn declaration was made, in the presence of all Israel: "Cursed be the man before the Lord, that riseth up and buildeth this city Jericho: he shall lay the foundation thereof in his first-born, and in his youngest son shall he set up the gates of it." Joshua 6:26.

Five centuries passed. The spot lay desolate, accursed of God. Even the springs that had made residence in this portion of the valley so desirable suffered the blighting effects of the curse. But in the days of Ahab's apostasy, when through Jezebel's influence the worship of Ashtoreth was revived,

Jericho, the ancient seat of this worship, was rebuilt, though at a fearful cost to the builder. Hiel the Bethelite "laid the foundation thereof in Abiram his first-born, and set up the gates thereof in his youngest son Segub, according to the world of the Lord." 1 Kings 16:34.

Not far from Jericho, in the midst of fruitful groves, was one of the schools of the prophets, and thither, after the ascension of Elijah, Elisha went. During his sojourn among them the men of the city came to the prophet and said, "Behold, I pray thee, the situation of this city is pleasant, as my lord seeth: but the water is nought, and the ground barren." The spring that in former years had been pure and life-giving, and had contributed largely to the water supply of the city and the surrounding district, was now unfit for use.

In response to the plea of the men of Jericho, Elisha said, "Bring me a new cruse, and put salt therein." Having received this, "he went forth unto the spring of the waters, and cast the salt in there, and said, Thus saith the Lord, I have healed these waters; there shall not be from thence any more death or barren land." 2 Kings 2:19-21.

The healing of the waters of Jericho was accomplished, not by any wisdom of man, but by the miraculous interposition of God. Those who had rebuilt the city were undeserving of the favor of Heaven; yet He who "maketh His sun to rise on the evil and on the good, and sendeth rain on the just and on the unjust," saw fit in this instance to reveal, through this token of compassion, His willingness to heal Israel of their spiritual maladies. Matthew 5:45. The restoration was permanent; "the waters were healed unto this day, according to the saying of Elisha which he spake." 2 Kings 2:22. From age to age the waters have flowed on, making that portion of the valley an oasis of beauty.

Many are the spiritual lessons to be gathered from the story of the healing of the waters. The new cruse, the salt, the spring—all are highly symbolic.

In casting salt into the bitter spring, Elisha taught the same spiritual lesson imparted centuries later by the Saviour to His disciples when He declared, "Ye are the salt of the earth." Matthew 5:13. The salt mingling with the polluted spring purified its waters and brought life and blessing where before had been blighting and death. When God compares His children to salt, He would teach them that His purpose in making them the subjects of His grace is that they may become agents in saving others. The object of God in choosing a people before all the world was not only that He might adopt them as His sons and daughters, but that through them the world might receive the grace that bringeth salvation. When the Lord chose Abraham, it was not simply to be the special friend of God, but to be a medium of the peculiar privileges the Lord desired to bestow upon the nations.

The world needs evidences of sincere Christianity. The poison of sin is at work at the heart of society. Cities and towns are steeped in sin and moral corruption. The world is full of sickness, suffering, and iniquity. Nigh and afar off are souls in poverty and distress, weighed down with a sense of guilt and perishing for want of a saving influence. The gospel of truth is kept ever before them, yet they perish because the example of those who should be a savor of life to them is a savor of death. Their souls drink in bitterness because the springs are poisoned, when they should be like a well of water springing up unto everlasting life.

Salt must be mingled with the substance to which it is added; it must penetrate, infuse it, that it may be preserved. So it is through personal contact and association that men are reached by the saving power of the gospel. They are not saved as masses, but as individuals. Personal influence is a power. It is to work with the influence of Christ, to lift where Christ lifts, to impart correct principles, and to stay the progress of the world's corruption. It is to diffuse that grace which Christ alone can impart. It is to uplift, to sweeten the lives and characters of others by the power of a pure example united with earnest faith and love.

Of the hitherto polluted spring at Jericho, the Lord declared, "I have healed these waters; there shall not be from thence any more death or barren land." The polluted stream represents the soul that is separate from God. Sin not only shuts away from God, but destroys in the human soul both the desire and the capacity for knowing Him. Through sin, the whole human organism is deranged, the mind is perverted, the imagination corrupted; the faculties of the soul are degraded. There is an absence of pure religion, of heart holiness. The converting power of God has not wrought in transforming the character. The soul is weak, and for want of moral force to overcome, is polluted and debased.

To the heart that has become purified, all is changed. Transformation of character is the testimony to the world of an indwelling Christ. The Spirit of God produces a new life in the soul, bringing the thoughts and desires into obedience to the will of Christ; and the inward man is renewed in the image of God. Weak and erring men and women show to the world that the redeeming power of grace can cause the faulty character to develop into symmetry and abundant fruitfulness.

The heart that receives the word of God is not as a pool that evaporates, not like a broken cistern that loses its treasure. It is like the mountain stream, fed by unfailing springs, whose cool, sparkling waters leap from rock to rock, refreshing the weary, the thirsty, the heavy-laden. It is like a river constantly flowing and, as it advances, becoming deeper and wider, until its life-giving waters are spread over all the earth. The stream that goes singing on its way leaves behind its gift of verdure and fruitfulness. The grass on its banks is a fresher green, the trees have a richer verdure, the flowers are more abundant. When the earth lies bare and brown under the summer's scorching heat, a line of verdure marks the river's course.

So it is with the true child of God. The religion of Christ reveals itself as a vitalizing, pervading principle, a living, working, spiritual energy. When the heart is opened to the heavenly influence of truth and love, these principles will flow forth again like streams in the desert, causing fruitfulness to appear where now are barrenness and dearth.

As those who have been cleansed and sanctified through a knowledge of Bible truth engage heartily in the work of soulsaving, they will become indeed a savor of life unto life. And as daily they drink of the inexhaustible fountain of grace and knowledge, they will find that their own hearts are filled to overflowing with the Spirit of their Master, and that through their unselfish ministry many are benefited physically, mentally, and spiritually. The weary are refreshed, the sick restored to health, and the sin-burdened relieved. In far-off countries thanksgiving is heard from the lips of those whose hearts are turned from the service of sin unto righteousness.

"Give, and it shall be given unto you;" for the word of God is "a fountain of gardens, a well of living waters, and streams from Lebanon." Luke 6:38; Song of Solomon 4:15.

A Prophet of Peace

The work of Elisha as a prophet was in some respects very different from that of Elijah. To Elijah had been committed messages of condemnation and judgment; his was the voice of fearless reproof, calling king and people to turn from their evil ways. Elisha's was a more peaceful mission; his it was to build up and strengthen the work that Elijah had begun; to teach the people the way of the Lord. Inspiration pictures him as coming into personal touch with the people, surrounded by the sons of the prophets, bringing by his miracles and his ministry healing and rejoicing.

Elisha was a man of mild and kindly spirit; but that he could also be stern is shown by his course when, on the way to Bethel, he was mocked by ungodly youth who had come out of the city. These youth had heard of Elijah's ascension, and they made this solemn event the subject of their jeers, saying to Elisha, "Go up, thou bald head; go up, thou bald head." At the sound of their mocking words the prophet turned back, and under the inspiration of the Almighty he pronounced a curse upon them. The awful judgment that followed was of God. "There came forth two she-bears out of the wood, and tare forty and two" of them. 2 Kings 2:23, 24.

Had Elisha allowed the mockery to pass unnoticed, he would have continued to be ridiculed and reviled by the rabble, and his mission to instruct and save in a time of grave national peril might have been defeated. This one instance of terrible severity was sufficient to command respect throughout his life. For fifty years he went in and out of the gate of Bethel, and to and fro in the land, from city to city, passing through crowds of idle, rude, dissolute youth; but none mocked him or made light of his qualifications as the prophet of the Most High.

Even kindness should have its limits. Authority must be maintained by a firm severity, or it will be received by many with mockery and contempt. The so-called tenderness, the coaxing and indulgence, used toward youth by parents and guardians, is one of the worst evils which can come upon them. In every family, firmness, decision, positive requirements, are essential.

Reverence, in which the youth who mocked Elisha were so lacking, is a grace that should be carefully cherished. Every child should be taught to show true reverence for God. Never should His name be spoken lightly or thoughtlessly. Angels, as they speak it, veil their faces. With what reverence should we, who are fallen and sinful, take it upon our lips!

Reverence should be shown for God's representatives— for ministers, teachers, and parents, who are called to speak and act in His stead. In the respect shown them, God is honored.

Courtesy, also, is one of the graces of the Spirit and should be cultivated by all. It has power to soften natures which without it would grow hard and rough. Those who profess to be followers of Christ, and are at the same time rough, unkind, and uncourteous, have not learned of Jesus. Their sincerity may not be doubted, their uprightness may not be questioned; but sincerity and uprightness will not atone for a lack of kindness and courtesy.

The kindly spirit that enabled Elisha to exert a powerful influence over the lives of many in Israel, is revealed in the story of his friendly relations with a family dwelling at Shunem. In his journeyings to and fro throughout the kingdom "it fell on a day, that Elisha passed to Shunem, where was a great woman; and she constrained him to eat bread. And so it was, that as oft as he passed by, he turned in thither to eat bread." The mistress of the house perceived that Elisha was "an holy man of God," and she said to her husband: "Let us make a little chamber, I pray thee, on the wall; and let us set for him there a bed, and a table, and a stool, and a candlestick: and it shall be, when he cometh to us, that he shall turn in thither." To this retreat Elisha often came, thankful for its quiet peace. Nor was God unmindful of the woman's kindness. Her home had been childless; and now the Lord rewarded her hospitality by the gift of a son.

Years passed. The child was old enough to be out in the field with the reapers. One day he was stricken down by the heat, "and he said unto his father, My head, my head." The father bade a lad carry the child to his mother; "and when he had taken him, and brought him to his mother, he sat on her knees till noon, and then died. And she went up, and laid him on the bed of the man of God, and shut the door upon him, and went out."

In her distress, the Shunammite determined to go to Elisha for help. The prophet was then at Mount Carmel, and the woman, accompanied by her servant, set forth immediately. "And it came to pass, when the man of God saw her afar off, that he said to Gehazi his servant, Behold, yonder is that Shunammite: run now, I pray thee, to meet her, and say unto her, Is it well with thee? is it well with thy husband? is it well with the child?" The servant did as he was bidden, but not till she had reached Elisha did the stricken mother reveal the cause of her sorrow. Upon hearing of her loss, Elisha bade Gehazi: "Gird up thy loins, and take my staff in thine hand,

and go thy way: if thou meet any man, salute him not; and if any salute thee, answer him not again: and lay my staff upon the face of the child."

But the mother would not be satisfied till Elisha himself came with her. "As the Lord liveth, and as thy soul liveth, I will not leave thee," she declared. "And he arose, and followed her. And Gehazi passed on before them, and laid the staff upon the face of the child; but there was neither voice, nor hearing. Wherefore he went again to meet him, and told him, saying, The child is not awaked."

When they reached the house, Elisha went into the room where the dead child lay, "and shut the door upon them twain, and prayed unto the Lord. And he went up, and lay upon the child, and put his mouth upon his mouth, and his eyes upon his eyes, and his hands upon his hands: and he stretched himself upon the child; and the flesh of the child waxed warm. Then he returned, and walked in the house to and fro; and went up, and stretched himself upon him: and the child sneezed seven times, and the child opened his eyes."

Calling Gehazi, Elisha bade him send the mother to him. "And when she was come in unto him, he said, Take up thy son. Then he went in, and fell at his feet, and bowed herself to the ground, and took up her son, and went out."

So was the faith of this woman rewarded. Christ, the great Life-giver, restored her son to her. In like manner will His faithful ones be rewarded, when, at His coming, death loses its sting and the grave is robbed of the victory it has claimed. Then will He restore to His servants the children that have been taken from them by death. "Thus saith the Lord; A voice was heard in Ramah, lamentation, and bitter weeping; Rachel weeping for her children refused to be comforted for her children, because they were not. Thus saith the Lord; Refrain thy voice from weeping, and thine eyes from tears: for thy work shall be rewarded, . . . and they shall come again from the land of the enemy. And there is hope in thine end, saith the Lord, that thy children shall come again to their own border." Jeremiah 31:15-17.

Jesus comforts our sorrow for the dead with a message of infinite hope: "I will ransom them from the power of the grave; I will redeem them from death: O death, I will be thy plagues; O grave, I will be thy destruction." Hosea 13:14. "I am He that liveth, and was dead; and, behold, I am alive for evermore, . . . and have the keys of hell and of death." Revelation 1:18. "The Lord Himself shall descend from heaven with a shout, with the voice of the Archangel, and with the trump of God: and the dead in Christ shall rise first: then we which are alive and remain shall be caught up together with them in the clouds, to meet the Lord in the air: and so shall we ever be with the Lord." 1 Thessalonians 4:16, 17.

Like the Saviour of mankind, of whom he was a type, Elisha in his ministry among men combined the work of healing with that of teaching. Faithfully, untiringly, throughout his long and effective labors, Elisha endeavored to foster and advance the important educational work carried on by the schools of the prophets. In the providence of God his words of instruction to the earnest groups of young men assembled were confirmed by the deep movings of the Holy Spirit, and at times by other unmistakable evidences of his authority as a servant of Jehovah.

It was on the occasion of one of his visits to the school established at Gilgal that he healed the poisoned pottage. "There was a dearth in the land; and the sons of the prophets were sitting before him: and he said unto his servant, Set on the great pot, and seethe pottage for the sons of the prophets. And one went out into the field to gather herbs, and found a wild vine, and gathered thereof wild gourds his lap full, and came and shred them into the pot of pottage: for they knew them not. So they poured out for the men to eat. And it came to pass, as they were eating of the pottage, that they cried out, and said, O thou man of God, there is death in the pot. And they could not eat thereof. But he said, Then bring meal. And he cast it into the pot; and he said, Pour out for the people, that they may eat. And there was no harm in the pot."

At Gilgal, also, while the dearth was still in the land, Elisha fed one hundred men with the present brought to him by "a man from Baalshalisha," "bread of the first fruits, twenty loaves of barley, and full ears of corn in the husk thereof." There were those with him who were sorely in need of food. When the offering came, he said to his servant, "Give unto the people, that they may eat. And his servitor said, What, should I set this before an hundred men? He said again, Give the people, that they may eat: for thus saith the Lord, They shall eat, and shall leave thereof. So he set it before them, and they did eat, and left thereof, according to the word of the Lord."

What condescension it was on the part of Christ, through His messenger, to work this miracle to satisfy hunger! Again and again since that time, though not always in so marked and perceptible a manner, has the Lord Jesus worked to supply human need. If we had clearer spiritual discernment we would recognize more readily than we do God's compassionate dealing with the children of men.

It is the grace of God on the small portion that makes it all-sufficient. God's hand can multiply it a hundredfold. From His resources He can spread a table in the wilderness. By the touch of His hand He can increase the scanty provision and make it sufficient for all. It was His power that increased the loaves and corn in the hands of the sons of the prophets.

In the days of Christ's earthly ministry, when He performed a similar miracle in feeding the multitudes, the same unbelief was manifested as was shown by those associated with the prophet of old. "What!" said Elisha's servant; "should I set this before an hundred men?" And when Jesus bade His disciples give the multitude to eat, they answered, "We have no more but five loaves and two fishes; except we should go and buy meat for all this people." Luke 9:13. What is that among so many?

The lesson is for God's children in every age. When the Lord gives a work to be done, let not men stop to inquire into the reasonableness of the command or the probable result of their efforts to obey. The supply in their hands may seem to fall short of the need to be filled; but in the hands of the Lord it will prove more than sufficient. The servitor "set it before them, and they did eat, and left thereof, according to the word of the Lord."

A fuller sense of God's relationship to those whom He has purchased with the gift of His Son, a greater faith in the onward progress of His cause in the earth—this is the great need of the church today. Let none waste time in deploring the scantiness of their visible resources. The outward appearance may be unpromising, but energy and trust in God will develop resources. The gift brought to Him with thanksgiving and with prayer for His blessing, He will multiply as He multiplied the food given to the sons of the prophets and to the weary multitude.

Naaman

"Now Naaman, captain of the host of the king of Syria, was a great man with his master, and honorable, because by him the Lord had given deliverance unto Syria: he was also a mighty man in valor, but he was a leper."

Ben-hadad, king of Syria, had defeated the armies of Israel in the battle which resulted in the death of Ahab. Since that time the Syrians had maintained against Israel a constant border warfare, and in one of their raids they had carried away a little maid who, in the land of her captivity, "waited on Naaman's wife." A slave, far from her home, this little maid was nevertheless one of God's witnesses, unconsciously fulfilling the purpose for which God had chosen Israel as His people. As she ministered in that heathen home, her sympathies were aroused in behalf of her master; and, remembering the wonderful miracles of healing wrought through Elisha, she said to her mistress, "Would God my lord were with the prophet that is in Samaria! for he would recover him of his leprosy." She knew that the power of Heaven was with Elisha, and she believed that by this power Naaman could be healed.

The conduct of the captive maid, the way that she bore herself in that heathen home, is a strong witness to the power of early home training. There is no higher trust than that committed to fathers and mothers in the care and training of their children. Parents have to do with the very foundations of habit and character. By their example and teaching the future of their children is largely decided.

Happy are the parents whose lives are a true reflection of the divine, so that the promises and commands of God awaken in the child gratitude and reverence; the parents whose tenderness and justice and long-suffering interpret to the child the love and justice and long-suffering of God, and who by teaching the child to love and trust and obey them, are teaching him to love and trust and obey his Father in heaven. Parents who impart to the child such a gift have endowed him with a treasure more precious than the wealth of all the ages, a treasure as enduring as eternity.

We know not in what line our children may be called to serve. They may spend their lives within the circle of the home; they may engage in life's common vocations, or go as teachers of the gospel to heathen lands; but all are alike called to be missionaries for God, ministers of mercy to the world. They are to obtain an education that will help them to stand by the side of Christ in unselfish service.

The parents of that Hebrew maid, as they taught her of God, did not know the destiny that would be hers. But they were faithful to their trust; and in the home of the captain of the Syrian host, their child bore witness to the God whom she had learned to honor.

Naaman heard of the words that the maid had spoken to her mistress; and, obtaining permission from the king, he went forth to seek healing, taking with him "ten talents of silver, and six thousand pieces of gold, and ten changes of raiment." He also carried a letter from the king of Syria to the king of Israel, in which was written the message, "Behold, I have . . . sent Naaman my servant to thee, that thou mayest recover him of his leprosy." When the king of Israel read the letter, "he rent his clothes, and said, Am I God, to kill and to make alive, that this man doth send unto me to recover a man of his leprosy? wherefore consider, I pray you, and see how he seeketh a quarrel against me."

Tidings of the matter reached Elisha, and he sent word to the king, saying, "Wherefore hast thou rent thy clothes? let him come now to me, and he shall know that there is a prophet in Israel."

"So Naaman came with his horses and with his chariot, and stood at the door of the house of Elisha." Through a messenger the prophet bade him, "Go and wash in Jordan seven times, and thy flesh shall come again to thee, and thou shalt be clean."

Naaman had expected to see some wonderful manifestation of power from heaven. "I thought," he said, "he will surely come out to me, and stand, and call on the name of the Lord his God, and strike his hand over the place, and recover the leper." When told to wash in the Jordan, his pride was touched, and in mortification and disappointment he exclaimed, "Are not Abana and Pharpar, rivers of Damascus, better than all the waters of Israel? may I not wash in them, and be clean?" "So he turned and went away in a rage."

The proud spirit of Naaman rebelled against following the course outlined by Elisha. The rivers mentioned by the Syrian captain were beautified by surrounding groves, and many flocked to the banks of these pleasant streams to worship their idol gods. It would have cost Naaman no great humiliation of soul to descend into one of those streams. But it was only through following the specific directions of the prophet that he could find healing. Willing obedience alone would bring the desired result.

Naaman's servants entreated him to carry out Elisha's directions: "If the prophet had bid thee do some great thing," they urged, "wouldest thou not have done it? how much rather then, when he saith to thee, Wash, and be clean?" The faith of Naaman was being tested, while pride struggled for the mastery. But faith conquered, and the haughty Syrian yielded his pride of heart and bowed in submission to the revealed will of Jehovah. Seven times he dipped himself in Jordan, "according to the saying of the man of God." And his faith was honored; "his flesh came again like unto the flesh of a little child, and he was clean."

Gratefully "he returned to the man of God, he and all his company," with the acknowledgment, "Behold, now I know that there is no God in all the earth, but in Israel."

In accordance with the custom of the times, Naaman now asked Elisha to accept a costly present. But the prophet refused. It was not for him to take payment for a blessing that God had in mercy bestowed. "As the Lord liveth," he said, "I will receive none." The Syrian "urged him to take it; but he refused."

"And Naaman said, Shall there not then, I pray thee, be given to thy servant two mules' burden of earth? for thy servant will henceforth offer neither burnt offering nor sacrifice unto other gods, but unto the Lord. In this thing the Lord pardon thy servant, that when my master goeth into the house of Rimmon to worship there, and he leaneth on my hand, and I bow myself in the house of Rimmon: when I bow down myself in the house of Rimmon, the Lord pardon thy servant in this thing.

"And he said unto him, Go in peace. So he departed from him a little way."

Gehazi, Elisha's servant, had had opportunity during the years to develop the spirit of self-denial characterizing his master's lifework. It had been his privilege to become a noble standard-bearer in the army of the Lord. The best gifts of Heaven had long been within his reach; yet, turning from these, he had coveted instead the base alloy of worldly wealth. And now the hidden longings of his avaricious spirit led him to yield to an overmastering temptation. "Behold," he reasoned within himself, "my master hath spared Naaman this Syrian, in not receiving at his hands that which he brought: but . . . I will run after him, and take somewhat of him." And thus it came about that in secrecy "Gehazi followed after Naaman."

When Naaman saw him running after him, he lighted down from the chariot to meet him, and said, Is all well? And he said, All is well." Then Gehazi uttered a deliberate lie. "My master," he said, "hath sent me, saying, Behold, even now there be come to me from Mount Ephraim two young men of the sons of the prophets: give them, I pray thee, a talent of silver, and two changes of garments." To the request Naaman gladly acceded, pressing upon Gehazi two talents of silver instead of one, "with two changes of garments," and commissioning servants to bear the treasure back.

As Gehazi neared Elisha's home, he dismissed the servants and placed the silver and the garments in hiding. This accomplished, "he went in, and stood before his master;" and, to shield himself from censure, he uttered a second lie. In response to the inquiry of the prophet, "Whence comest thou?" Gehazi answered, "Thy servant went no whither."

Then came the stern denunciation, showing that Elisha knew all. "Went not mine heart with thee," he asked, "when the man turned again from his chariot to meet thee? Is it a time to receive money, and to receive garments, and olive yards, and vineyards, and sheep, and oxen, and menservants, and maidservants? The leprosy therefore of Naaman shall cleave unto thee, and unto thy seed forever." Swift was the retribution that overtook the guilty man. He went out from Elisha's presence "a leper as white as snow."

Solemn are the lessons taught by this experience of one to whom had been given high and holy privileges. The course of Gehazi was such as to place a stumbling block in the pathway of Naaman, upon whose mind had broken a wonderful light, and who was favorably disposed toward the service of the living God. For the deception practiced by Gehazi there could be pleaded no excuse. To the day of his death he remained a leper, cursed of God and shunned by his fellow men.

"A false witness shall not be unpunished, and he that speaketh lies shall not escape." Proverbs 19:5. Men may think to hide their evil deeds from human eyes, but they cannot deceive God. "All things are naked and opened unto the eyes of Him with whom we have to do." Heb. 4:13. Gehazi thought to deceive Elisha, but God revealed to His prophet the words that Gehazi had spoken to Naaman, and every detail of the scene between the two men.

Truth is of God; deception in all its myriad forms is of Satan, and whoever in any way departs from the straight line of truth is betraying himself into the power of the wicked one. Those who have learned of Christ will "have no fellowship with the unfruitful works of darkness." Ephesians 5:11. In speech, as in life, they will be simple, straightforward, and true, for they are preparing for the fellowship of those holy ones in whose mouth is found no guile. See Revelation 14:5.

Centuries after Naaman returned to his Syrian home, healed in body and converted in spirit, his wonderful faith was referred to and commended by the Saviour as an object lesson for all who claim to serve God. "Many lepers were in Israel in the time of Eliseus the prophet," the Saviour declared; "and none of them was cleansed, saving Naaman the Syrian." Luke 4:27. God passed over the many lepers in Israel because their unbelief closed the door of good to them. A heathen nobleman who had been true to his convictions of right, and who felt his need of help, was in the sight of God more worthy of His blessing than were the afflicted in Israel, who had slighted and despised their God-given privileges. God works for those who appreciate His favors and respond to the light given them from heaven.

Today in every land there are those who are honest in heart, and upon these the light of heaven is shining. If they continue faithful in following that which they understand to be duty, they will be given increased light, until, like Naaman of old, they will be constrained to acknowledge that "there is no God in all the earth," save the living God, the Creator.

To every sincere soul "that walketh in darkness, and hath no light," is given the invitation, "Let him trust in the name of the Lord, and stay upon his God." "For since the beginning of the world men have not heard, nor perceived by the ear, neither hath the eye seen, O God, beside Thee, what He hath prepared for him that waiteth for Him. Thou meetest him that rejoiceth and worketh righteousness, those that remember Thee in Thy ways." Isaiah 50:10; 64:4, 5.

Elisha's Closing Ministry

Called to the prophetic office while Ahab was still reigning, Elisha had lived to see many changes take place in the kingdom of Israel. Judgment upon judgment had befallen the Israelites during the reign of Hazael the Syrian, who had been anointed to be the scourge of the apostate nation. The stern measures of reform instituted by Jehu had resulted in the slaying of all the house of Ahab. In continued wars with the Syrians, Jehoahaz, Jehu's successor, had lost some of the cities lying east of the Jordan. For a time it had seemed as if the Syrians might gain control of the entire kingdom. But the reformation begun by Elijah and carried forward by Elisha had led many to inquire after God. The altars of Baal were being forsaken, and slowly yet surely God's purpose was being fulfilled in the lives of those who chose to serve Him with all the heart.

It was because of His love for erring Israel that God permitted the Syrians to scourge them. It was because of His compassion for those whose moral power was weak that He raised up Jehu to slay wicked Jezebel and all the house of Ahab. Once more, through a merciful providence, the priests of Baal and of Ashtoreth were set aside and their heathen altars thrown down. God in His wisdom foresaw that if temptation were removed, some would forsake heathenism and turn their faces heavenward, and this is why He permitted calamity after calamity to befall them. His judgments were tempered with mercy; and when His purpose was accomplished, He turned the tide in favor of those who had learned to inquire after Him.

While influences for good and for evil were striving for the ascendancy, and Satan was doing all in his power to complete the ruin he had wrought during the reign of Ahab and Jezebel, Elisha continued to bear his testimony. He met with opposition, yet none could gainsay his words. Throughout the kingdom he was honored and venerated. Many came to him for counsel. While Jezebel was still living, Joram, the king of Israel, sought his advice; and once, when in Damascus, he was visited by messengers from Benhadad, king of Syria, who desired to learn whether a sickness then upon him would result in death. To all the prophet bore faithful witness in a time when, on every hand, truth was being perverted and the great majority of the people were in open rebellion against Heaven.

And God never forsook His chosen messenger. On one occasion, during a Syrian invasion, the king of Syria sought to destroy Elisha because of his activity in apprising the king of Israel of the plans of the enemy. The Syrian king had taken counsel with his servants, saying, "In such and such a place shall be my camp." This plan was revealed by the Lord to Elisha, who "sent unto the king of Israel, saying, Beware that thou pass not such a place; for thither the Syrians are come down. And the king of Israel sent to the place which the man of God told him and warned him of, and saved himself there, not once nor twice.

"Therefore the heart of the king of Syria was sore troubled for this thing; and he called his servants, and said unto them, Will ye not show me which of us is for the king of Israel? And one of his servants said, None, my lord, O king: but Elisha, the prophet that is in Israel, telleth the king of Israel the words that thou speakest in thy bedchamber."

Determined to make away with the prophet, the Syrian king commanded, "Go and spy where he is, that I may send and fetch him." The prophet was in Dothan; and, learning this, the king sent thither "horses, and chariots, and a great host: and they came by night, and compassed the city about. And when the servant of the man of God was risen early, and gone forth, behold, an host compassed the city both with horses and chariots."

In terror Elisha's servant sought him with the tidings. "Alas, my master!" he said, "how shall we do?"

"Fear not," was the answer of the prophet; "for they that be with us are more than they that be with them." And then, that the servant might know this for himself, "Elisha prayed, and said, Lord, I pray Thee, open his eyes, that he may see." "The Lord opened the eyes of the young man; and he saw: and, behold, the mountain was full of horses and chariots of fire round about Elisha." Between the servant of God and the hosts of armed foemen was an encircling band of heavenly angels. They had come down in mighty power, not to destroy, not to exact homage, but to encamp round about and minister to the Lord's weak and helpless ones.

When the people of God are brought into strait places, and apparently there is no escape for them, the Lord alone must be their dependence.

As the company of Syrian soldiers boldly advanced, ignorant of the unseen hosts of heaven, "Elisha prayed unto the Lord, and said, Smite this people, I pray Thee, with blindness. And He smote them with blindness according to the word of Elisha. And Elisha said unto them, This is not the way, neither is this the city: follow me, and I will bring you to the man whom ye seek. But he led them to Samaria.

"And it came to pass, when they were come into Samaria, that Elisha said, Lord, open the eyes of these men, that they may see. And the Lord opened their eyes, and they saw; and, behold, they were in the midst of Samaria. And the king of Israel said unto Elisha, when he saw them, My father, shall I smite them? shall I smite them? And he answered, Thou shalt not smite them: wouldest thou smite those whom thou hast taken captive with thy sword and with thy bow? set bread and water before them, that they may eat and drink, and go to their master. And he prepared great provision for them: and when they had eaten and drunk, he sent them away, and they went to their master." See 2 Kings 6.

For a time after this, Israel was free from the attacks of the Syrians. But later, under the energetic direction of a determined king, Hazael, the Syrian hosts surrounded Samaria and besieged it. Never had Israel been brought into so great a strait as during this siege. The sins of the fathers were indeed being visited upon the children and the children's children. The horrors of prolonged famine were driving the king of Israel to desperate measures, when Elisha predicted deliverance the following day.

As the next morning was about to dawn, the Lord "made the host of the Syrians to hear a noise of chariots, and a noise of horses, even the noise of a great host;" and they, seized with fear, "arose and fled in the twilight," leaving "their tents, and their horses, and their asses, even the camp as it was," with rich stores of food. They "fled for their life," not tarrying until after the Jordan had been crossed.

During the night of the flight, four leprous men at the gate of the city, made desperate by hunger, had proposed to visit the Syrian camp and throw themselves upon the mercy of the besiegers, hoping thereby to arouse sympathy and obtain food. What was their astonishment when, entering the camp, they found "no man there." With none to molest or forbid, "they went into one tent, and did eat and drink, and carried thence silver, and gold, and raiment, and went and hid it; and came again, and entered into another tent, and carried thence also, and went and hid it. Then they said one to another, We do not well: this day is a day of good tidings, and we hold our peace." Quickly they returned to the city with the glad news.

Great was the spoil; so abundant were the supplies that on that day "a measure of fine flour was sold for a shekel, and two measures of barley for a shekel," as had been foretold by Elisha the day before. Once more the name of God was exalted before the heathen "according to the word of the Lord" through His prophet in Israel. See 2 Kings 7:5-16.

Thus the man of God continued to labor from year to year, drawing close to the people in faithful ministry, and in times of crisis standing by the side of kings as a wise counselor. The long years of idolatrous backsliding on the part of rulers and people had wrought their baleful work; the dark shadow of apostasy was still everywhere apparent, yet here and there were those who had steadfastly refused to bow the knee to Baal. As Elisha continued his work of reform, many were reclaimed from heathenism, and these learned to rejoice in the service of the true God. The prophet was cheered by these miracles of divine grace, and he was inspired with a great longing to reach all who were honest in heart. Wherever he was he endeavored to be a teacher of righteousness.

From a human point of view the outlook for the spiritual regeneration of the nation was as hopeless as is the outlook today before God's servants who are laboring in the dark places of the earth. But the church of Christ is God's agency for the proclamation of truth; she is empowered by Him to do a special work; and if she is loyal to God, obedient to His commandments, there will dwell within her the excellency of divine power. If she will be true to her allegiance, there is no power that can stand against her. The forces of the enemy will be no more able to overwhelm her than is the chaff to resist the whirlwind.

There is before the church the dawn of a bright, glorious day, if she will put on the robe of Christ's righteousness, withdrawing from all allegiance to the world.

God calls upon His faithful ones, who believe in Him, to talk courage to those who are unbelieving and hopeless. Turn to the Lord, ye prisoners of hope. Seek strength from God, the living God. Show an unwavering, humble faith in His power and His willingness to save. When in faith we take hold of His strength, He will change, wonderfully change, the most hopeless, discouraging outlook. He will do this for the glory of His name.

So long as Elisha was able to journey from place to place throughout the kingdom of Israel, he continued to take an active interest in the upbuilding of the schools of the prophets. Wherever he was, God was with him, giving him words to speak and power to work miracles. On one occasion "the sons of the prophets said unto Elisha, Behold now, the place where we dwell with thee is too strait for us. Let us go, we pray thee, unto Jordan, and take thence every man a beam, and let us make us a place there, where we may dwell." 2 Kings 6:1, 2. Elisha went with them to Jordan, encouraging them by his presence, giving them instruction, and even performing a miracle to aid them in their work. "As one was felling a beam, the axhead fell into the water: and he cried, and said, Alas, master! for it was borrowed. And the man of God said, Where fell it? And he showed him the place. And he cut down a stick, and cast it in thither; and the iron did swim. Therefore said he, Take it up to thee. And he put out his hand, and took it." Verses 5-7.

So effectual had been his ministry and so widespread his influence that, as he lay upon his deathbed, even the youthful King Joash, an idolater with but little respect for God, recognized in the prophet a father in Israel, and acknowledged that his presence among them was of more value in time of trouble than the possession of an army of horses and chariots. The record reads: "Now Elisha was fallen sick of his sickness whereof he died. And Joash the king of Israel came down unto him, and wept over his face, and said, O my father, my father, the chariot of Israel, and the horsemen thereof." 2 Kings 13:14.

To many a troubled soul in need of help the prophet had acted the part of a wise, sympathetic father. And in this instance he turned not from the godless youth before him, so unworthy of the position of trust he was occupying, and yet so greatly in need of counsel. God in His providence was bringing to the king an opportunity to redeem the failures of the past and to place his kingdom on vantage ground. The Syrian foe, now occupying the territory east of the Jordan, was to be repulsed. Once more the power of God was to be manifested in behalf of erring Israel.

The dying prophet bade the king, "Take bow and arrows." Joash obeyed. Then the prophet said, "Put thine hand upon the bow." Joash "put his hand upon it: and Elisha put his hands upon the king's hands. And he said, Open the window eastward"—toward the cities beyond the Jordan in possession of the Syrians. The king having opened the latticed window, Elisha bade him shoot. As the arrow sped on its way, the prophet was inspired to say, "The arrow of the Lord's deliverance, and the arrow of deliverance from Syria: for thou shalt smite the Syrians in Aphek, till thou have consumed them."

And now the prophet tested the faith of the king. Bidding Joash take up the arrows, he said, "Smite upon the ground." Thrice the king smote the ground, and then he stayed his hand. "Thou shouldest have smitten five or six times," Elisha exclaimed in dismay; "then hadst thou smitten Syria till thou hadst consumed it: whereas now thou shalt smite Syria but thrice." 2 Kings 13:15-19.

The lesson is for all in positions of trust. When God opens the way for the accomplishment of a certain work and gives assurance of success, the chosen instrumentality must do all in his power to bring about the promised result. In proportion to the enthusiasm and perseverance with which the work is carried forward will be the success given. God can work miracles for His people only as they act their part with untiring energy. He calls for men of devotion to His work, men of moral courage, with ardent love for souls, and with a zeal that never flags. Such workers will find no task too arduous, no prospect too hopeless; they will labor on, undaunted, until apparent defeat is turned into glorious victory. Not even prison walls nor the martyr's stake beyond, will cause them to swerve from their purpose of laboring together with God for the upbuilding of His kingdom.

With the counsel and encouragement given Joash, the work of Elisha closed. He upon whom had fallen in full measure the spirit resting upon Elijah, had proved faithful to the end. Never had he wavered. Never had he lost his trust in the power of Omnipotence. Always, when the way before him seemed utterly closed, he had still advanced by faith, and God had honored his confidence and opened the way before him.

It was not given Elisha to follow his master in a fiery chariot. Upon him the Lord permitted to come a lingering illness. During the long hours of human weakness and suffering his faith laid fast hold on the promises of God, and he beheld ever about him heavenly messengers of comfort and peace. As on the heights of Dothan he had seen the encircling hosts of heaven, the fiery chariots of Israel and the horsemen thereof, so now he was conscious of the presence of sympathizing angels, and he was sustained. Throughout his life he had exercised strong faith, and as he had advanced in a knowledge of God's providences and of His merciful kindness, faith had ripened into an abiding trust in his God, and when death called him he was ready to rest from his labors.

"Precious in the sight of the Lord is the death of His saints." Psalm 116:15. "The righteous hath hope in his death." Proverbs 14:32. With the psalmist, Elisha could say in all confidence, "God will redeem my soul from the power of the grave: for He shall receive me." Psalm 49:15. And with rejoicing he could testify, "I know that my Redeemer liveth, and that He shall stand at the latter day upon the earth." Job 19:25. "As for me, I will behold Thy face in righteousness: I shall be satisfied, when I awake, with Thy likeness." Psalm 17:15.

"Nineveh, That Great City"

Among the cities of the ancient world in the days of divided Israel one of the greatest was Nineveh, the capital of the Assyrian realm. Founded on the fertile bank of the Tigris, soon after the dispersion from the tower of Babel, it had flourished through the centuries until it had become "an exceeding great city of three days' journey." Jonah 3:3.

In the time of its temporal prosperity Nineveh was a center of crime and wickedness. Inspiration has characterized it as "the bloody city, . . . full of lies and robbery." In figurative language the prophet Nahum compared the Ninevites to a cruel, ravenous lion. "Upon whom," he inquired, "hath not thy wickedness passed continually?" Nahum 3:1, 19.

Yet Nineveh, wicked though it had become, was not wholly given over to evil. He who "beholdeth all the sons of men" (Psalm 33:13) and "seeth every precious thing" (Job 28:10) perceived in that city many who were reaching out after something better and higher, and who, if granted opportunity to learn of the living God, would put away their evil deeds and worship Him. And so in His wisdom God revealed Himself to them in an unmistakable manner, to lead them, if possible, to repentance.

The instrument chosen for this work was the prophet Jonah, the son of Amittai. To him came the word of the Lord, "Arise, go to Nineveh, that great city, and cry against it; for their wickedness is come up before Me." Jonah 1:1, 2.

As the prophet thought of the difficulties and seeming impossibilities of this commission, he was tempted to question the wisdom of the call. From a human viewpoint it seemed as if nothing could be gained by proclaiming such a message in that proud city. He forgot for the moment that the God whom he served was all-wise and all-powerful. While he hesitated, still doubting, Satan overwhelmed him with discouragement. The prophet was seized with a great dread, and he "rose up to flee unto Tarshish." Going to Joppa, and finding there a ship ready to sail, "he paid the fare thereof and went down into it, to go with them." Verse 3.

In the charge given him, Jonah had been entrusted with a heavy responsibility; yet He who had bidden him go was able to sustain His servant and grant him success. Had the prophet obeyed unquestioningly, he would have been spared many bitter experiences, and would have been blessed abundantly. Yet in the hour of Jonah's despair the Lord did not desert him. Through a series of trials and strange providences, the

upon the inhabitants of the cities, because of the steady increase of determined wickedness. The corruption that prevails is beyond the power of the human pen to describe. Every day brings fresh revelations of strife, bribery, and fraud; every day brings its heart-sickening record of violence and lawlessness, of indifference to human suffering, of brutal, fiendish destruction of human life. Every day testifies to the increase of insanity, murder, and suicide.

From age to age Satan has sought to keep men in ignorance of the beneficent designs of Jehovah. He has endeavored to remove from their sight the great things of God's law— the principles of justice, mercy, and love therein set forth. Men boast of the wonderful progress and enlightenment of the age in which we are now living; but God sees the earth filled with iniquity and violence. Men declare that the law of God has been abrogated, that the Bible is not authentic; and as a result, a tide of evil, such as has not been seen since the days of Noah and of apostate Israel, is sweeping over the world. Nobility of soul, gentleness, piety, are battered away to gratify the lust for forbidden things. The black record of crime committed for the sake of gain is enough to chill the blood and fill the soul with horror.

Our God is a God of mercy. With long-sufferance and tender compassion He deals with the transgressors of His law. And yet, in this our day, when men and women have so many opportunities for becoming familiar with the divine law as revealed in Holy Writ, the great Ruler of the universe cannot behold with any satisfaction the wicked cities, where reign violence and crime. The end of God's forbearance with those who persist in disobedience is approaching rapidly.

Ought men to be surprised over a sudden and unexpected change in the dealings of the Supreme Ruler with the inhabitants of a fallen world? Ought they to be surprised when punishment follows transgression and increasing crime? Ought they to be surprised that God should bring destruction and death upon those whose ill-gotten gains have been obtained through deception and fraud? Notwithstanding the fact that increasing light regarding God's requirements has been shining on their pathway, many have refused to recognize Jehovah's rulership, and have chosen to remain under the black banner of the originator of all rebellion against the government of heaven.

The forbearance of God has been very great—so great that when we consider the continuous insult to His holy commandments, we marvel. The Omnipotent One has been exerting a restraining power over His own attributes. But He will certainly arise to punish the wicked, who so boldly defy the just claims of the Decalogue. God allows men a period of probation; but there is a point beyond which divine patience is exhausted, and the judgments of God are sure to follow. The Lord bears long with men, and with cities, mercifully giving warnings to save them from divine wrath; but a time will come when pleadings for mercy will no longer be heard, and the rebellious element that continues to reject the light of truth will be blotted out, in mercy to themselves and to those who would otherwise be influenced by their example.

The time is at hand when there will be sorrow in the world that no human balm can heal. The Spirit of God is being withdrawn. Disasters by sea and by land follow one another in quick succession. How frequently we hear of earthquakes and tornadoes, of destruction by fire and flood, with great loss of life and property! Apparently these calamities are capricious outbreaks of disorganized, unregulated forces of nature, wholly beyond the control of man; but in them all, God's purpose may be read. They are among the agencies by which He seeks to arouse men and women to a sense of their danger.

God's messengers in the great cities are not to become discouraged over the wickedness, the injustice, the depravity, which they are called upon to face while endeavoring to proclaim the glad tidings of salvation. The Lord would cheer every such worker with the same message that He gave to the apostle Paul in wicked Corinth: "Be not afraid, but speak, and hold not thy peace: for I am with thee, and no man shall set on thee to hurt thee: for I have much people in this city." Acts 18:9, 10. Let those engaged in soul-saving ministry remember that while there are many who will not heed the counsel of God in His word, the whole world will not turn from light and truth, from the invitations of a patient, forbearing Saviour. In every city, filled though it may be with violence and crime, there are many who with proper teaching may learn to become followers of Jesus. Thousands may thus be reached with saving truth and be led to receive Christ as a personal Saviour.

God's message for the inhabitants of earth today is, "Be ye also ready: for in such an hour as ye think not the Son of man cometh." Matthew 24:44. The conditions prevailing in society, and especially in the great cities of the nations, proclaim in thunder tones that the hour of God's judgment is come and that the end of all things earthly is at hand. We are standing on the threshold of the crisis of the ages. In quick succession the judgments of God will follow one another—fire, and flood, and earthquake, with war and bloodshed. We are not to be surprised at this time by events both great and decisive; for the angel of mercy cannot remain much longer to shelter the impenitent.

"Behold, the Lord cometh out of His place to punish the inhabitants of the earth for their iniquity: the earth also shall disclose her blood, and shall no more cover her slain." Isaiah 26:21. The storm of God's wrath is gathering; and those only will stand who respond to the invitations of mercy, as did the inhabitants of Nineveh under the preaching of Jonah, and become sanctified through obedience to the laws of the divine Ruler. The righteous alone shall be hid with Christ in God till the desolation be overpast. Let the language of the soul be:

"Other refuge have I none,
Hangs my helpless soul on Thee;
Leave, O, leave me not alone!
Still support and comfort me.
"Hide me, O my Saviour, hide!

Till the storm of life is past;
Safe into the haven guide,
O receive my soul at last!"

The Assyrian Captivity

The closing years of the ill-fated kingdom of Israel were marked with violence and bloodshed such as had never been witnessed even in the worst periods of strife and unrest under the house of Ahab. For two centuries and more the rulers of the ten tribes had been sowing the wind; now they were reaping the whirlwind. King after king was assassinated to make way for others ambitious to rule. "They have set up kings," the Lord declared of these godless usurpers, "but not by Me: they have made princes, and I knew it not." Hosea 8:4. Every principle of justice was set aside; those who should have stood before the nations of earth as the depositaries of divine grace, "dealt treacherously against the Lord" and with one another. Hosea 5:7.

With the severest reproofs, God sought to arouse the impenitent nation to a realization of its imminent danger of utter destruction. Through Hosea and Amos He sent the ten tribes message after message, urging full and complete repentance, and threatening disaster as the result of continued transgression. "Ye have plowed wickedness," declared Hosea, "ye have reaped iniquity; ye have eaten the fruit of lies: because thou didst trust in thy way, in the multitude of thy mighty men. Therefore shall a tumult arise among thy people, and all thy fortresses shall be spoiled. . . . In a morning shall the king of Israel utterly be cut off." Hosea 10:13-15.

Of Ephraim the prophet testified, "Strangers have devoured his strength, and he knoweth it not: yea, gray hairs are here and there upon him, yet he knoweth not." "Israel hath cast off the thing that is good." "Broken in judgment," unable to discern the disastrous outcome of their evil course, the ten tribes were soon to be "wanderers among the nations." Hosea 7:9; 8:3; 5:11; 9:17.

Some of the leaders in Israel felt keenly their loss of prestige and wished that this might be regained. But instead of turning away from those practices which had brought weakness to the kingdom, they continued in iniquity, flattering themselves that when occasion arose, they would attain to the political power they desired by allying themselves with the heathen. "When Ephraim saw his sickness, and Judah saw his wound, then went Ephraim to the Assyrian." "Ephraim also is like a silly dove without heart: they call to Egypt, they go to Assyria." "They do make a covenant with the Assyrians." Hosea 5:13, 7:11; 12:1.

Through the man of God that had appeared before the altar at Bethel, through Elijah and Elisha, through Amos and Hosea, the Lord had repeatedly set before the ten tribes the evils of disobedience. But notwithstanding reproof and entreaty, Israel had sunk lower and still lower in apostasy. "Israel slideth back as a backsliding heifer," the Lord declared; "My people are bent to backsliding from Me." Hosea 4:16; 11:7.

There were times when the judgments of Heaven fell very heavily on the rebellious people. "I hewed them by the prophets," God declared; "I have slain them by the words of My mouth: and thy judgments are as the light that goeth forth. For I desired mercy, and not sacrifice; and the knowledge of God more than burnt offerings. But they like men have transgressed the covenant: there have they dealt treacherously against Me." Hosea 6:5-7.

"Hear the word of the Lord, ye children of Israel," was the message that finally came to them: "Seeing thou hast forgotten the law of thy God, I will also forget thy children. As they were increased, so they sinned against Me: therefore will I change their glory into shame. . . . I will punish them for their ways, and reward them their doings." Hosea 4:1, 6-9.

The iniquity in Israel during the last half century before the Assyrian captivity was like that of the days of Noah, and of every other age when men have rejected God and have given themselves wholly to evil-doing. The exaltation of nature above the God of nature, the worship of the creature instead of the Creator, has always resulted in the grossest of evils. Thus when the people of Israel, in their worship of Baal and Ashtoreth, paid supreme homage to the forces of nature, they severed their connection with all that is uplifting and ennobling, and fell an easy prey to temptation. With the defenses of the soul broken down, the misguided worshipers had no barrier against sin and yielded themselves to the evil passions of the human heart.

Against the marked oppression, the flagrant injustice, the unwonted luxury and extravagance, the shameless feasting and drunkenness, the gross licentiousness and debauchery, of their age, the prophets lifted their voices; but in vain were their protests, in vain their denunciation of sin. "Him that rebuketh in the gate," declared Amos, "they hate, . . . and they abhor him that speaketh uprightly." "They afflict the just, they take a bribe, and they turn aside the poor in the gate from their right." Amos 5:10, 12.

Such were some of the results that had followed the setting up of two calves of gold by Jeroboam. The first departure from established forms of worship had led to the introduction of grosser forms of idolatry, until finally nearly all the inhabitants of the land had given themselves over to the alluring practices of nature worship. Forgetting their Maker, Israel "deeply corrupted themselves." Hosea 9:9.

The prophets continued to protest against these evils and to plead for rightdoing. "Sow to yourselves in righteousness, reap in mercy," Hosea urged; "break up your fallow ground: for it is time to seek the Lord, till He come and rain righteousness upon you." "Turn thou to thy God: keep mercy and judgment, and wait on thy God continually." "O Israel, return unto the Lord thy God; for thou hast fallen by thine iniquity: . . . say unto Him, Take away all iniquity, and receive us graciously." Hosea 10:12; 12:6; 14:1, 2.

The transgressors were given many opportunities to repent. In their hour of deepest apostasy and greatest need, God's message to them was one of forgiveness and hope. "O Israel," He declared, "thou hast destroyed thyself; but in Me is thine help. I will be thy King: where is any other that may save thee?" Hosea 13:9, 10.

"Come, and let us return unto the Lord," the prophet entreated; "for He hath torn, and He will heal us; He hath smitten, and He will bind us up. After two days will He revive us: in the third day He will raise us up, and we shall live in His sight. Then shall we know, if we follow on to know the Lord: His going forth is prepared as the morning; and He shall come unto us as the rain, as the latter and former rain unto the earth." Hosea 6:1-3.

To those who had lost sight of the plan of the ages for the deliverance of sinners ensnared by the power of Satan, the Lord offered restoration and peace. "I will heal their backsliding, I will love them freely," He declared: "for Mine anger is turned away from him. I will be as the dew unto Israel: he shall grow as the lily, and cast forth his roots as Lebanon. His branches shall spread, and his beauty shall be as the olive tree, and his smell as Lebanon. They that dwell under His shadow shall return; they shall revive as the corn, and grow as the vine: the scent thereof shall be as the wine of Lebanon. Ephraim shall say, What have I to do any more with idols? I have heard him, and observed him: I am like a green fir tree. From Me is thy fruit found.

"Who is wise, and he shall understand these things?
Prudent, and he shall know them?
For the ways of the Lord are right,
And the just shall walk in them:
But the transgressors shall fall therein."
Hosea 14:4-9.

The benefits of seeking God were strongly urged. "Seek ye Me," the Lord invited, "and ye shall live: but seek not Bethel, nor enter into Gilgal, and pass not to Beersheba: for Gilgal shall surely go into captivity, and Bethel shall come to nought."

"Seek good, and not evil, that ye may live: and so the Lord, the God of hosts, shall be with you, as ye have spoken. Hate the evil, and love the good, and establish judgment in the gate: it may be that the Lord God of hosts will be gracious unto the remnant of Joseph." Amos 5:4, 5, 14, 15.

By far the greater number of those who heard these invitations refused to profit by them. So contrary to the evil desires of the impenitent were the words of God's messengers, that the idolatrous priest at Bethel sent to the ruler in Israel, saying, "Amos hath conspired against thee in the midst of the house of Israel: the land is not able to bear all his words." Amos 7:10.

Through Hosea the Lord declared, "When I would have healed Israel, then the iniquity of Ephraim was discovered, and the wickedness of Samaria." "The pride of Israel testifieth to his face: and they do not return to the Lord their God, nor seek Him for all this." Hosea 7:1, 10.

From generation to generation the Lord had borne with His wayward children, and even now, in the face of defiant rebellion, He still longed to reveal Himself to them as willing to save. "O Ephraim," He cried, "what shall I do unto thee? O Judah, what shall I do unto thee? for your goodness is as a morning cloud, and as the early dew it goeth away." Hosea 6:4.

The evils that had overspread the land had become incurable; and upon Israel was pronounced the dread sentence: "Ephraim is joined to idols: let him alone." "The days of visitation are come, the days of recompense are come; Israel shall know it." Hosea 4:17; 9:7.

The ten tribes of Israel were not to reap the fruitage of the apostasy that had taken form with the setting up of the strange altars at Bethel and at Dan. God's message to them was: "Thy calf, O Samaria, hath cast thee off; Mine anger is kindled against them: how long will it be ere they attain to innocency? For from Israel was it also: the workman made it; therefore it is not God: but the calf of Samaria shall be broken in pieces." "The inhabitants of Samaria shall fear because of the calves of Beth-aven: for the people thereof shall mourn over it, and the priests thereof that rejoiced on it. . . . It shall be also carried unto Assyria for a present to King Jareb" (Sennacherib). Hosea 8:5, 6; 10:5, 6.

"Behold, the eyes of the Lord God are upon the sinful kingdom, and I will destroy it from off the face of the earth; saying that I will not utterly destroy the house of Jacob, saith the Lord. For, lo, I will command, and I will sift the house of Israel among all nations, like as corn is sifted in a sieve, yet shall not the least grain fall upon the earth. All the sinners of My people shall die by the sword, which say, The evil shall not overtake nor prevent us."

"The houses of ivory shall perish, and the great houses shall have an end, saith the Lord." "The Lord God of hosts is He that toucheth the land, and it shall melt, and all that dwell therein shall mourn." "Thy sons and thy daughters shall fall by the sword, and thy land shall be divided by line; and thou shalt die in a polluted land: and Israel shall surely go into captivity forth of his land." "Because I will do this unto thee, prepare to meet thy God, O Israel." Amos 9:8-10; 3:15; 9:5; 7:17; 4:12.

For a season these predicted judgments were stayed, and during the long reign of Jeroboam II the armies of Israel gained signal victories; but this time of apparent prosperity wrought no change in the hearts of the impenitent, and it was finally decreed, "Jeroboam shall die by the sword, and Israel shall surely be led away captive out of their own land." Amos 7:11.

The boldness of this utterance was lost on king and people, so far had they gone in impenitence. Amaziah, a leader among the idolatrous priests at Bethel, stirred by the plain words spoken by the prophet against the nation and their king, said to Amos, "O thou seer, go, flee thee away into the land of Judah, and there eat bread, and prophesy there: but prophesy not again any more at Bethel: for it is the king's chapel, and it is the king's court." Verses 12, 13.

To this the prophet firmly responded: "Thus saith the Lord, . . . Israel shall surely go into captivity." Verse 17.

The words spoken against the apostate tribes were literally fulfilled; yet the destruction of the kingdom came gradually. In judgment the Lord remembered mercy, and at first, when "Pul the king of Assyria came against the land," Menahem, then king of Israel, was not taken captive, but was permitted to remain on the throne as a vassal of the Assyrian realm. "Menahem gave Pul a thousand talents of silver, that his hand might be with him to confirm the kingdom in his hand. And Menahem exacted the money of Israel, even of all the mighty men of wealth, of each man fifty shekels of silver, to give to the king of Assyria." 2 Kings 15:19, 20. The Assyrians, having humbled the ten tribes, returned for a season to their own land.

Menahem, far from repenting of the evil that had wrought ruin in his kingdom, continued in "the sins of Jeroboam the son of Nebat, who made Israel to sin." Pekahiah and Pekah, his successors, also "did that which was evil in the sight of the Lord." Verses 18, 24, 28. "In the days of Pekah," who reigned twenty years, Tiglath-pileser, king of Assyria, invaded Israel and carried away with him a multitude of captives from among the tribes living in Galilee and east of the Jordan. "The Reubenites, and the Gadites, and the half tribe of Manasseh," with others of the inhabitants of "Gilead, and Galilee, all the land of Naphtali" (1 Chronicles 5:26; 2 Kings 15:29), were scattered among the heathen in lands far removed from Palestine.

From this terrible blow the northern kingdom never recovered. The feeble remnant continued the forms of government, though no longer possessed of power. Only one more ruler, Hoshea, was to follow Pekah. Soon the kingdom was to be swept away forever. But in that time of sorrow and distress God still remembered mercy, and gave the people another opportunity to turn from idolatry. In the third year of Hoshea's reign, good King Hezekiah began to rule in Judah and as speedily as possible instituted important reforms in the temple service at Jerusalem. A Passover celebration was arranged for, and to this feast were invited not only the tribes of Judah and Benjamin, over which Hezekiah had been anointed king, but all the northern tribes as well. A proclamation was sounded "throughout all Israel, from Beersheba even to Dan, that they should come to keep the Passover unto the Lord God of Israel at Jerusalem: for they had not done it of a long time in such sort as it was written.

"So the posts went with the letters from the king and his princes throughout all Israel and Judah," with the pressing invitation, "Ye children of Israel, turn again unto the Lord of God of Abraham, Isaac, and Israel, and He will return to the remnant of you, that are escaped out of the hand of the kings of Assyria. . . . Be ye not stiff-necked, as your fathers were, but yield yourselves unto the Lord, and enter into His sanctuary, which He hath sanctified forever: and serve the Lord your God, that the fierceness of His wrath may turn away from you.

For if ye turn again unto the Lord, your brethren and your children shall find compassion before them that lead them captive, so that they shall come again into this land: for the Lord your God is gracious and merciful, and will not turn away His face from you; if ye return unto Him." 2 Chronicles 30:5-9.

"From city to city through the country of Ephraim and Manasseh even unto Zebulun," the couriers sent out by Hezekiah carried the message. Israel should have recognized in this invitation an appeal to repent and turn to God. But the remnant of the ten tribes still dwelling within the territory of the once-flourishing northern kingdom treated the royal messengers from Judah with indifference and even with contempt. "They laughed them to scorn, and mocked them." There were a few, however, who gladly responded. "Divers of Asher and Manasseh and of Zebulun humbled themselves, and came to Jerusalem, . . . to keep the feast of unleavened bread." Verses 10-13.

About two years later, Samaria was invested by the hosts of Assyria under Shalmaneser; and in the siege that followed, multitudes perished miserably of hunger and disease as well as by the sword. The city and nation fell, and the broken remnant of the ten tribes were carried away captive and scattered in the provinces of the Assyrian realm.

The destruction that befell the northern kingdom was a direct judgment from Heaven. The Assyrians were merely the instruments that God used to carry out His purpose. Through Isaiah, who began to prophesy shortly before the fall of Samaria, the Lord referred to the Assyrian hosts as "the rod of Mine anger." "The staff in their hand," He said, "is Mine indignation." Isaiah 10:5.

Grievously had the children of Israel "sinned against the Lord their God, . . . and wrought wicked things." "They would not hear, but . . . rejected His statutes, and His covenant that He made with their fathers, and His testimonies which He testified against them." It was because they had "left all the commandments of the Lord their God, and made them molten images, even two calves, and made a grove, and worshiped all the host of heaven, and served Baal," and refused steadfastly to repent, that the Lord "afflicted them, and delivered them into the hand of spoilers, until He had cast them out of His sight," in harmony with the plain warnings He had sent them "by all His servants the prophets."

"So was Israel carried away out of their own land to Assyria," "because they obeyed not the voice of the Lord their God, but transgressed His covenant, and all that Moses the servant of the Lord commanded." 2 Kings 17:7, 11,14-16, 20, 23; 18:12.

In the terrible judgments brought upon the ten tribes the Lord had a wise and merciful purpose. That which He could no longer do through them in the land of their fathers He would seek to accomplish by scattering them among the heathen. His plan for the salvation of all who should choose to avail themselves of pardon through the Saviour of the human race must yet be fulfilled; and in the afflictions brought upon Israel, He was preparing the way for His glory to be revealed to the nations of earth. Not all who were carried captive were impenitent. Among them were some who had remained true to God, and others who had humbled themselves before Him. Through these, "the sons of the living God" (Hosea 1:10), He would bring multitudes in the Assyrian realm to a knowledge of the attributes of His character and the beneficence of His law.

"Destroyed for Lack of Knowledge"

God's favor toward Israel had always been conditional on their obedience. At the foot of Sinai they had entered into covenant relationship with Him as His "peculiar treasure. . . above all people." Solemnly they had promised to follow in the path of obedience. "All that the Lord hath spoken we will do," they had said. Exodus 19:5, 8. And when, a few days afterward, God's law was spoken from Sinai, and additional instruction in the form of statutes and judgments was communicated through Moses, the Israelites with one voice had again promised, "All the words which the Lord hath said will we do." At the ratification of the covenant, the people had once more united in declaring, "All that the Lord hath said will we do, and be obedient," Exodus 24:3, 7. God had chosen Israel as His people, and they had chosen Him as their King.

Near the close of the wilderness wandering the conditions of the covenant had been repeated. At Baalpeor, on the very borders of the Promised Land, where many fell a prey to subtle temptation, those who remained faithful renewed their vows of allegiance. Through Moses they were warned against the temptations that would assail them in the future; and they were earnestly exhorted to remain separate from the surrounding nations and to worship God alone.

"Now therefore hearken," Moses had instructed Israel, "unto the statutes and unto the judgments, which I teach you, for to do them, that ye may live, and go in and possess the land which the Lord God of your fathers giveth you. Ye shall not add unto the word which I command you, neither shall ye diminish aught from it, that ye may keep the commandments of the Lord your God which I command you. . . . Keep therefore and do them; for this is your wisdom and your understanding in the sight of the nations, which shall hear all these statutes, and say, Surely this great nation is a wise and understanding people." Deuteronomy 4:1-6.

The Israelites had been specially charged not to lose sight of the commandments of God, in obedience to which they would find strength and blessing. "Take heed to thyself, and keep thy soul diligently," had been the word of the Lord to them through Moses, "lest thou forget the things which thine eyes have seen, and lest they depart from thy heart all the days of thy life: but teach them thy sons, and thy sons' sons." Verse 9. The awe-inspiring scenes connected with the giving of the law at Sinai were never to be forgotten. Plain and decided were the warnings that had been given Israel against the idolatrous customs prevailing among the neighboring nations. "Take ye . . . good heed unto yourselves," was the counsel given; "lest ye corrupt yourselves, and make you a graven image, the similitude of any figure," "and lest thou lift up thine eyes unto heaven, and when thou seest the sun, and the moon, and the stars, even all the host of heaven, shouldest be driven to worship them, and serve them, which the Lord thy God hath divided unto all nations under the whole heaven." "Take heed unto yourselves, lest ye forget the covenant of the Lord your God, which He made with you, and make you a graven image, or the likeness of anything, which the Lord thy God hath forbidden thee." Verses 15, 16, 19, 23.

Moses traced the evils that would result from a departure from the statutes of Jehovah. Calling heaven and earth to witness, he declared that if, after having dwelt long in the Land of Promise, the people should introduce corrupt forms of worship and bow down to graven images and should refuse to return to the worship of the true God, the anger of the Lord would be aroused, and they would be carried away captive and scattered among the heathen. "Ye shall soon utterly perish from off the land whereunto ye go over Jordan to possess it," he warned them; "ye shall not prolong your days upon it, but shall utterly be destroyed. And the Lord shall scatter you among the nations, and ye shall be left few in number among the heathen, whither the Lord shall lead you. And there ye shall serve gods, the work of men's hands, wood and stone, which neither see, nor hear, nor eat, nor smell." Verses 26-28.

This prophecy, fulfilled in part in the time of the judges, met a more complete and literal fulfillment in the captivity of Israel in Assyria and of Judah in Babylon.

The apostasy of Israel had developed gradually. From generation to generation, Satan had made repeated attempts to cause the chosen nation to forget "the commandments, the statutes, and the judgments" that they had promised to keep forever. Deuteronomy 6:1. He knew that if he could only lead Israel to forget God, and to "walk after other gods, and serve them, and worship them," they would "surely perish." Deuteronomy 8:19.

The enemy of God's church upon the earth had not, however, taken fully into account the compassionate nature of Him who "will by no means clear the guilty," yet whose glory it is to be "merciful and gracious, long-suffering, and abundant in goodness and truth, keeping mercy for thousands, forgiving iniquity and transgression and sin." Exodus 34:6, 7. Despite the efforts of Satan to thwart God's purpose for Israel, nevertheless even in some of the darkest hours of their history, when it seemed as if the forces of evil were about to gain the victory, the Lord graciously revealed Himself. He spread before Israel the things that were for the welfare of the nation. "I have written to him the great things of My law," He declared through Hosea, "but they were counted as a strange thing." "I taught Ephraim also to go, taking them by their arms; but they knew not that I healed them." Hosea 8:12; 11:3. Tenderly had the Lord dealt with them, instructing them by His prophets line upon line, precept upon precept.

Had Israel heeded the messages of the prophets, they would have been spared the humiliation that followed. It was because they had persisted in turning aside from His law that God was compelled to let them go into captivity. "My people are destroyed for lack of knowledge," was His message to them through Hosea. "Because thou hast rejected knowledge, I will also reject thee: . . . seeing thou hast forgotten the law of thy God." Hosea 4:6.

In every age, transgression of God's law has been followed by the same result. In the days of Noah, when every principle of rightdoing was violated, and iniquity became so deep and widespread that God could no longer bear with it, the decree went forth, "I will destroy man whom I have created from the face of the earth." Genesis 6:7. In Abraham's day the people of Sodom openly defied God and His law; and there followed the same wickedness, the same corruption, the same unbridled indulgence, that had marked the antediluvian world. The inhabitants of Sodom passed the limits of divine forbearance, and there was kindled against them the fire of God's vengeance.

The time preceding the captivity of the ten tribes of Israel was one of similar disobedience and of similar wickedness. God's law was counted as a thing of nought, and this opened the floodgates of iniquity upon Israel. "The Lord hath a controversy with the inhabitants of the land," Hosea declared, "because there is no truth, nor mercy, nor knowledge of God in the land. By swearing, and lying, and killing, and stealing, and committing adultery, they break out, and blood toucheth blood." Hosea 4:1, 2.

The prophecies of judgment delivered by Amos and Hosea were accompanied by predictions of future glory. To the ten tribes, long rebellious and impenitent, was given no promise of complete restoration to their former power in Palestine. Until the end of time, they were to be "wanderers among the nations." But through Hosea was given a prophecy that set before them the privilege of having a part in the final restoration that is to be made to the people of God at the close of earth's history, when Christ shall appear as King of kings and Lord of lords. "Many days," the prophet declared, the ten tribes were to abide "without a king, and without a prince, and without a sacrifice, and without an image, and without an ephod, and without teraphim." "Afterward," the prophet continued, "shall the children of Israel return, and seek the Lord their God, and David their king; and shall fear the Lord and His goodness in the latter days." Hosea 3:4, 5.

In symbolic language Hosea set before the ten tribes God's plan of restoring to every penitent soul who would unite with His church on earth, the blessings granted Israel in the days of their loyalty to Him in the Promised Land. Referring to Israel as one to whom He longed to show mercy, the Lord declared, "I will allure her, and bring her into the wilderness, and speak comfortably unto her. And I will give her her vineyards from thence, and the valley of Achor for a door of hope: and she shall sing there, as in the days of her youth, and as in the day when she came up out of the land of Egypt. And it shall be at that day, saith the Lord, that thou shalt call Me Ishi; and shalt call Me no more Baali. For I will take away the names of Baalim out of her mouth, and they shall no more be remembered by their name." Hosea 2:14-17.

In the last days of this earth's history, God's covenant with His commandment-keeping people is to be renewed. "In that day will I make a covenant for them with the beasts of the field, and with the fowls of heaven, and with the creeping things of the ground: and I will break the bow and the sword and the battle out of the earth, and will make them to lie down safely. And I will betroth thee unto Me forever; yea, I will betroth thee unto Me in righteousness, and in judgment, and in loving-kindness, and in mercies. I will even betroth thee unto Me in faithfulness: and thou shalt know the Lord.

"And it shall come to pass in that day, I will hear, saith the Lord, I will hear the heavens, and they shall hear the earth; and the earth shall hear the corn, and the wine, and the oil; and they shall hear Jezreel. And I will sow her unto Me in the earth; and I will have mercy upon her that had not obtained mercy; and I will say to them which were not My people, Thou art My people; and they shall say, Thou art my God." Verses 18-23.

"In that day" "the remnant of Israel, and such as are escaped of the house of Jacob, . . . shall stay upon the Lord, the Holy One of Israel, in truth." Isaiah 10:20. From "every nation, and kindred, and tongue, and people" there will be some who will gladly respond to the message, "Fear God, and give glory to Him; for the hour of His judgment is come." They will turn from every idol that binds them to earth, and will "worship Him that made heaven, and earth, and the sea, and the fountains of waters." They will free themselves from every entanglement and will stand before the world as monuments of God's mercy. Obedient to the divine requirements, they will be recognized by angels and by men as those that have kept "the commandments of God, and the faith of Jesus." Revelation 14:6, 7, 12.

"Behold, the days come, saith the Lord, that the plowman shall overtake the reaper, and the treader of grapes him that soweth seed; and the mountains shall drop sweet wine, and all the hills shall melt. And I will bring again the captivity of My people of Israel, and they shall build the waste cities, and inhabit them; and they shall plant vineyards, and drink the wine thereof; they shall also make gardens, and eat the fruit of them. And I will plant them upon their land, and they shall no more be pulled up out of their land which I have given them, saith the Lord thy God." Amos 9:13-15.

"Shall the prey be taken from the mighty, or the lawful captive delivered?" "Thus saith the Lord, Even the captives of the mighty shall be taken away, and the prey of the terrible shall be delivered." "They shall be greatly ashamed, that trust in graven images, that say to the molten images, Ye are our gods." Isaiah 49:24, 25; 42:17.

The Call of Isaiah

The long reign of Uzziah in the land of Judah and Benjamin was characterized by a prosperity greater than that of any other ruler since the death of Solomon, nearly two centuries before. For many years the king ruled with discretion. Under the blessing of Heaven his armies regained some of the territory that had been lost in former years. Cities were rebuilt and fortified, and the position of the nation among the surrounding peoples was greatly strengthened. Commerce revived, and the riches of the nations flowed into Jerusalem. Uzziah's name "spread far abroad; for he was marvellously helped, till he was strong." 2 Chronicles 26:15.

This outward prosperity, however, was not accompanied by a corresponding revival of spiritual power. The temple services were continued as in former years, and multitudes assembled to worship the living God; but pride and formality gradually took the place of humility and sincerity. Of Uzziah himself it is written: "When he was strong, his heart was lifted up to his destruction: for he transgressed against the Lord his God." Verse 16.

The sin that resulted so disastrously to Uzziah was one of presumption. In violation of a plain command of Jehovah, that none but the descendants of Aaron should officiate as priests, the king entered the sanctuary "to burn incense upon the altar." Azariah the high priest and his associates remonstrated, and pleaded with him to turn from his purpose. "Thou hast trespassed," they urged; "neither shall it be for thine honor." Verses 16, 18.

Uzziah was filled with wrath that he, the king, should be thus rebuked. But he was not permitted to profane the sanctuary against the united protest of those in authority. While standing there, in wrathful rebellion, he was suddenly smitten with a divine judgment. Leprosy appeared on his forehead. In dismay he fled, never again to enter the temple courts. Unto the day of his death, some years later, Uzziah remained a leper—a living example of the folly of departing from a plain "Thus saith the Lord." Neither his exalted position nor his long life of service could be pleaded as an excuse for the presumptuous sin by which he marred the closing years of his reign, and brought upon himself the judgment of Heaven.

God is no respecter of persons. "The soul that doeth aught presumptuously, whether he be born in the land, or a stranger, the same reproacheth the Lord; and that soul shall be cut off from among his people." Numbers 15:30.

The judgment that befell Uzziah seemed to have a restraining influence on his son. Jotham bore heavy responsibilities during the later years of his father's reign and succeeded to the throne after Uzziah's death. Of Jotham it is written: "He did that which was right in the sight of the Lord: he did according to all that his father Uzziah had done. Howbeit the high places were not removed: the people sacrificed and burned incense still in the high places." 2 Kings 15:34, 35.

The reign of Uzziah was drawing to a close, and Jotham was already bearing many of the burdens of state, when Isaiah, of the royal line, was called, while yet a young man, to the prophetic mission. The times in which Isaiah was to labor were fraught with peculiar peril to the people of God. The prophet was to witness the invasion of Judah by the combined armies of northern Israel and of Syria; he was to behold the Assyrian hosts encamped before the chief cities of the kingdom. During his lifetime, Samaria was to fall, and the ten tribes of Israel were to be scattered among the nations. Judah was again and again to be invaded by the Assyrian armies, and Jerusalem was to suffer a siege that would have resulted in her downfall had not God miraculously interposed. Already grave perils were threatening the peace of the southern kingdom. The divine protection was being removed, and the Assyrian forces were about to overspread the land of Judah.

But the dangers from without, overwhelming though they seemed, were not so serious as the dangers from within. It was the perversity of his people that brought to the Lord's servant the greatest perplexity and the deepest depression. By their apostasy and rebellion those who should have been standing as light bearers among the nations were inviting the judgments of God. Many of the evils which were hastening the swift destruction of the northern kingdom, and which had recently been denounced in unmistakable terms by Hosea and Amos, were fast corrupting the kingdom of Judah.

The outlook was particularly discouraging as regards the social conditions of the people. In their desire for gain, men were adding house to house and field to field. See Isaiah 5:8. Justice was perverted, and no pity was shown the poor. Of these evils God declared, "The spoil of the poor is in your houses." Ye beat My people to pieces, and grind the faces of the poor." Isaiah 3:14, 15. Even the magistrates, whose duty it was to protect the helpless, turned a deaf ear to the cries of the poor and needy, the widows and the fatherless. See Isaiah 10:1, 2.

With oppression and wealth came pride and love of display, gross drunkenness, and a spirit of revelry. See Isaiah 2:11, 12; 3:16, 18-23; 5:22, 11, 12. And in Isaiah's day idolatry itself no longer provoked surprise. See Isaiah 2:8, 9. Iniquitous practices had become so prevalent among all classes that the few who remained true to God were often tempted to lose heart and to give way to discouragement and despair. It seemed as if God's purpose for Israel were about to fail and that the rebellious nation was to suffer a fate similar to that of Sodom and Gomorrah.

In the face of such conditions it is not surprising that when, during the last year of Uzziah's reign, Isaiah was called to bear to Judah God's messages of warning and reproof, he shrank from the responsibility. He well knew that he would encounter obstinate resistance. As he realized his own inability to meet the situation and thought of the stubbornness and unbelief of the people for whom he was to labor, his task seemed hopeless. Should he in despair relinquish his mission and leave Judah undisturbed to their idolatry? Were the gods of Nineveh to rule the earth in defiance of the God of heaven?

Such thoughts as these were crowding through Isaiah's mind as he stood under the portico of the temple. Suddenly the gate and the inner veil of the temple seemed to be uplifted or withdrawn, and he was permitted to gaze within, upon the holy of holies, where even the prophet's feet might not enter. There rose up before him a vision of Jehovah sitting upon a throne high and lifted up, while the train of His glory filled the temple. On each side of the throne hovered the seraphim, their faces veiled in adoration, as they ministered before their Maker and united in the solemn invocation, "Holy, holy holy, is the Lord of hosts: the whole earth is full of His glory," until post and pillar and cedar gate seemed shaken with the sound, and the house was filled with their tribute of praise. Isaiah 6:3.

As Isaiah beheld this revelation of the glory and majesty of his Lord, he was overwhelmed with a sense of the purity and holiness of God. How sharp the contrast between the matchless perfection of his Creator, and the sinful course of those who, with himself, had long been numbered among the chosen people of Israel and Judah! "Woe is me!" he cried; "for I am undone; because I am a man of unclean lips, and I dwell in the midst of a people of unclean lips: for mine eyes have seen the King, the Lord of hosts." Verse 5. Standing, as it were, in the full light of the divine presence within the inner sanctuary, he realized that if left to his own imperfection and inefficiency, he would be utterly unable to accomplish the mission to which he had been called. But a seraph was sent to relieve him of his distress and to fit him for his great mission. A living coal from the altar was laid upon his lips, with the words, "Lo, this hath touched thy lips; and thine iniquity is taken away, and thy sin purged." Then the voice of God was heard saying, "Whom shall I send, and who will go for Us?" and Isaiah responded, "Here am I; send me." Verses 7, 8.

The heavenly visitant bade the waiting messenger,
"Go, and tell this people,
"Here ye indeed, but understand not;
And see ye indeed, but perceive not.
Make the heart of this people fat,
And make their ears heavy, and shut their eyes;
Lest they see with their eyes, and hear with their ears,
And understand with their heart,
And convert, and be healed."
Verses 9, 10.

The prophet's duty was plain; he was to lift his voice in protest against the prevailing evils. But he dreaded to undertake the work without some assurance of hope. "Lord, how long?" he inquired. Verse 11. Are none of Thy chosen people ever to understand and repent and be healed?

His burden of soul in behalf of erring Judah was not to be borne in vain. His mission was not to be wholly fruitless. Yet the evils that had been multiplying for many generations could not be removed in his day. Throughout his lifetime he must be a patient, courageous teacher—a prophet of hope as

well as of doom. The divine purpose finally accomplished, the full fruitage of his efforts, and of the labors of all God's faithful messengers, would appear. A remnant should be saved. That this might be brought about, the messages of warning and entreaty were to be delivered to the rebellious nation, the Lord declared:

"Until the cities be wasted without inhabitant,
And the houses without man,
And the land be utterly desolate,
And the Lord have removed men far away,
And there be a great forsaking in the midst of the land."
Verses 11, 12.

The heavy judgments that were to befall the impenitent, —war, exile, oppression, the loss of power and prestige among the nations,—all these were to come in order that those who would recognize in them the hand of an offended God might be led to repent. The ten tribes of the northern kingdom were soon to be scattered among the nations and their cities left desolate; the destroying armies of hostile nations were to sweep over their land again and again; even Jerusalem was finally to fall, and Judah was to be carried away captive; yet the Promised Land was not to remain wholly forsaken forever. The assurance of the heavenly visitant to Isaiah was:

"In it shall be a tenth,
And it shall return, and shall be eaten:
As a teil tree, and as an oak,
Whose substance is in them, when they cast their leaves:
So the holy seed shall be the substance thereof."
Verse 13.

This assurance of the final fulfillment of God's purpose brought courage to the heart of Isaiah. What though earthly powers array themselves against Judah? What though the Lord's messenger meet with opposition and resistance? Isaiah had seen the King, the Lord of hosts; he had heard the song of the seraphim, "The whole earth is full of His glory;" he had the promise that the messages of Jehovah to backsliding Judah would be accompanied by the convicting power of the Holy Spirit; and the prophet was nerved for the work before him. Verse 3. Throughout his long and arduous mission he carried with him the memory of this vision. For sixty years or more he stood before the children of Judah as a prophet of hope, waxing bolder and still bolder in his predictions of the future triumph of the church.

"Behold Your God!"

In Isaiah's day the spiritual understanding of mankind was dark through misapprehension of God. Long had Satan sought to lead men to look upon their Creator as the author of sin and suffering and death. Those whom he had thus deceived, imagined that God was hard and exacting. They regarded

Him as watching to denounce and condemn, unwilling to receive the sinner so long as there was a legal excuse for not helping him. The law of love by which heaven is ruled had been misrepresented by the archdeceiver as a restriction upon men's happiness, a burdensome yoke from which they should be glad to escape. He declared that its precepts could not be obeyed and that the penalties of transgression were bestowed arbitrarily.

In losing sight of the true character of Jehovah, the Israelites were without excuse. Often had God revealed Himself to them as one "full of compassion, and gracious, long-suffering, and plenteous in mercy and truth." Psalm 86:15. "When Israel was a child," He testified, "then I loved him, and called My son out of Egypt." Hosea 11:1.

Tenderly had the Lord dealt with Israel in their deliverance from Egyptian bondage and in their journey to the Promised Land. "In all their affliction He was afflicted, and the angel of His presence saved them: in His love and in His pity He redeemed them; and He bare them, and carried them all the days of old. Isaiah 63:9.

"My presence shall go with thee," was the promise given during the journey through the wilderness. Exodus 33:14. This assurance was accompanied by a marvelous revelation of Jehovah's character, which enabled Moses to proclaim to all Israel the goodness of God, and to instruct them fully concerning the attributes of their invisible King. "The Lord passed by before him, and proclaimed, The Lord, The Lord God, merciful and gracious, long-suffering, and abundant in goodness and truth, keeping mercy for thousands, forgiving iniquity and transgression and sin, and that will by no means clear the guilty." Exodus 34:6, 7.

It was upon his knowledge of the long-sufferance of Jehovah and of His infinite love and mercy, that Moses based his wonderful plea for the life of Israel when, on the borders of the Promised Land, they refused to advance in obedience to the command of God. At the height of their rebellion the Lord had declared, "I will smite them with the pestilence, and disinherit them;" and He had proposed to make of the descendants of Moses "a greater nation and mightier than they." Numbers 14:12. But the prophet pleaded the marvelous providences and promises of God in behalf of the chosen nation. And then, as the strongest of all pleas, he urged the love of God for fallen man. See verses 17-19.

Graciously the Lord responded, "I have pardoned according to thy word." And then He imparted to Moses, in the form of a prophecy, a knowledge of His purpose concerning the final triumph of Israel. "As truly as I live," He declared, "all the earth shall be filled with the glory of the Lord." Verses 20, 21. God's glory, His character, His merciful kindness and tender love—that which Moses had pleaded in behalf of Israel—were to be revealed to all mankind. And this promise of Jehovah was made doubly sure; it was confirmed by an oath. As surely as God lives and reigns, His glory should be declared "among the heathen, His wonders among all people." Psalm 96:3.

It was concerning the future fulfillment of this prophecy that Isaiah had heard the shining seraphim singing before the throne, "The whole earth is full of His glory." Isaiah 6:3. The prophet, confident of the certainty of these words, himself afterward boldly declared of those who were bowing down to the images of wood and stone, "They shall see the glory of the Lord, and the excellency of our God." Isaiah 35:2.

Today this prophecy is meeting rapid fulfillment. The missionary activities of the church of God on earth are bearing rich fruitage, and soon the gospel message will have been proclaimed to all nations. "To the praise of the glory of His grace," men and women from every kindred, tongue, and people are being made "accepted in the Beloved," "that in the ages to come He might show the exceeding riches of His grace in His kindness toward us through Christ Jesus." Ephesians 1:6; 2:7. "Blessed be the Lord God, the God of Israel, who only doeth wondrous things. And blessed be His glorious name forever: and let the whole earth be filled with His glory." Psalm 72:18, 19.

In the vision that came to Isaiah in the temple court, he was given a clear view of the character of the God of Israel. "The high and lofty One that inhabiteth eternity, whose name is Holy," had appeared before him in great majesty; yet the prophet was made to understand the compassionate nature of his Lord. He who dwells "in the high and holy place" dwells "with him also that is of a contrite and humble spirit, to revive the spirit of the humble, and to revive the heart of the contrite ones." Isaiah 57:15. The angel commissioned to touch Isaiah's lips had brought to him the message, "Thine iniquity is taken away, and thy sin purged." Isaiah 6:7.

In beholding his God, the prophet, like Saul of Tarsus at the gate of Damascus, had not only been given a view of his own unworthiness; there had come to his humbled heart the assurance of forgiveness, full and free; and he had arisen a changed man. He had seen his Lord. He had caught a glimpse of the loveliness of the divine character. He could testify of the transformation wrought through beholding Infinite Love. Henceforth he was inspired with longing desire to see erring Israel set free from the burden and penalty of sin. "Why should ye be stricken any more?" the prophet inquired. "Come now, and let us reason together, saith the Lord: though your sins be as scarlet, they shall be as white as snow; though they be red like crimson, they shall be as wool." "Wash you, make you clean; put away the evil of your doings from before Mine eyes; cease to do evil; learn to do well." Isaiah 1:5, 18, 16, 17.

The God whom they had been claiming to serve, but whose character they had misunderstood, was set before them as the great Healer of spiritual disease. What though the whole head was sick and the whole heart faint? what though from the sole of the foot even unto the crown of the head there was no soundness, but wounds, and bruises, and putrefying sores? See Isaiah 1:6. He who had been walking frowardly in the way of his heart might find healing by turning to the Lord. "I have seen his ways," the Lord declared, "and will heal him: I will lead him also, and restore comforts unto him. . . . Peace,

peace to him that is far off, and to him that is near, saith the Lord; and I will heal him." Isaiah 57:18, 19.

The prophet exalted God as Creator of all. His message to the cities of Judah was, "Behold your God!" Isaiah 40:9. "Thus saith God the Lord, He that created the heavens, and stretched them out; He that spread forth the earth, and that which cometh out of it;" "I am the Lord that maketh all things;" "I form the light, and create darkness;" "I have made the earth, and created man upon it: I, even My hands, have stretched out the heavens, and all their host have I commanded." Isaiah 42:5; 44:24; 45:7, 12. "To whom then will ye liken Me, or shall I be equal? saith the Holy One. Lift up your eyes on high, and behold who hath created these things, that bringeth out their host by number: He calleth them all by names by the greatness of His might, for that He is strong in power; not one faileth." Isaiah 40:25, 26.

To those who feared they would not be received if they should return to God, the prophet declared:

"Why sayest thou, O Jacob, and speakest, O Israel, My way is hid from the Lord, and my judgment is passed over from my God? Hast thou not known? hast thou not heard, that the everlasting God, the Lord, the Creator of the ends of the earth, fainteth not, neither is weary? there is no searching of His understanding. He giveth power to the faint; and to them that have no might He increaseth strength. Even the youths shall faint and be weary, and the young men shall utterly fall: but they that wait upon the Lord shall renew their strength; they shall mount up with wings as eagles; they shall run, and not be weary; and they shall walk, and not faint." Verses 27-31.

The heart of Infinite Love yearns after those who feel powerless to free themselves from the snares of Satan; and He graciously offers to strengthen them to live for Him. "Fear thou not," He bids them; "for I am with thee: be not dismayed; for I am thy God: I will strengthen thee; yea, I will help thee; yea, I will uphold thee with the right hand of My righteousness." "I the Lord thy God will hold thy right hand, saying unto thee, Fear not; I will help thee. Fear not, thou worm Jacob, and ye man of Israel; I will help thee, saith the Lord, and thy Redeemer, the Holy One of Israel." Isaiah 41:10, 13, 14.

The inhabitants of Judah were all undeserving, yet God would not give them up. By them His name was to be exalted among the heathen. Many who were wholly unacquainted with His attributes were yet to behold the glory of the divine character. It was for the purpose of making plain His merciful designs that He kept sending His servants the prophets with the message, "Turn ye again now everyone from his evil way." Jeremiah 25:5. "For My name's sake," He declared through Isaiah, "will I defer Mine anger, and for My praise will I refrain for thee, that I cut thee not off." "For Mine own sake, even for Mine own sake, will I do it: for how should My name be polluted? and I will not give My glory unto another." Isaiah 48:9, 11.

The call to repentance was sounded with unmistakable clearness, and all were invited to return. "Seek ye the Lord while He may be found," the prophet pleaded; "call ye upon Him while He is near: let the wicked forsake his way, and the unrighteous man his thoughts: and let him return unto the Lord, and He will have mercy upon him; and to our God, for He will abundantly pardon." Isaiah 55:6, 7.

Have you, reader, chosen your own way? Have you wandered far from God? Have you sought to feast upon the fruits of transgression, only to find them turn to ashes upon your lips? And now, your life plans thwarted and your hopes dead, do you sit alone and desolate? That voice which has long been speaking to your heart, but to which you would not listen, comes to you distinct and clear, "Arise ye, and depart; for this is not your rest: because it is polluted, it shall destroy you, even with a sore destruction." Micah 2:10. Return to your Father's house. He invites you, saying, "Return unto Me; for I have redeemed thee." "Come unto Me: hear, and your soul shall live; and I will make an everlasting covenant with you, even the sure mercies of David." Isaiah 44:22; 55:3.

Do not listen to the enemy's suggestion to stay away from Christ until you have made yourself better, until you are good enough to come to God. If you wait until then you will never come. When Satan points to your filthy garments, repeat the promise of the Saviour, "Him that cometh to Me I will in no wise cast out." John 6:37. Tell the enemy that the blood of Jesus Christ cleanses from all sin. Make the prayer of David your own: "Purge me with hyssop, and I shall be clean: wash me, and I shall be whiter than snow." Psalm 51:7.

The exhortations of the prophet to Judah to behold the living God, and to accept His gracious offers, were not in vain. There were some who gave earnest heed, and who turned from their idols to the worship of Jehovah. They learned to see in their Maker love and mercy and tender compassion. And in the dark days that were to come in the history of Judah, when only a remnant were to be left in the land, the prophet's words were to continue bearing fruit in decided reformation. "At that day," declared Isaiah, "shall a man look to his Maker, and his eyes shall have respect to the Holy One of Israel. And he shall not look to the altars, the work of his hands, neither shall respect that which his fingers have made, either the groves, or the images." Isaiah 17:7, 8.

Many were to behold the One altogether lovely, the chiefest among ten thousand. "Thine eyes shall see the King in His beauty," was the gracious promise made them. Isaiah 33:17. Their sins were to be forgiven, and they were to make their boast in God alone. In that glad day of redemption from idolatry they would exclaim, "The glorious Lord will be unto us a place of broad rivers and streams. . . . The Lord is our judge, the Lord is our lawgiver, the Lord is our king; He will save us." Verses 21, 22.

The messages borne by Isaiah to those who chose to turn from their evil ways were full of comfort and encouragement. Hear the word of the Lord through His prophet:

"Remember these, O Jacob and Israel;

For thou art My servant:
I have formed thee; thou art My servant:
O Israel, thou shalt not be forgotten of Me.
I have blotted out, as a thick cloud, thy transgressions,
And, as a cloud, thy sins:
Return unto Me; for I have redeemed thee."
Isaiah 44:21, 22.

"In that day thou shalt say,
O Lord, I will praise Thee:
Though Thou wast angry with me,
Thine anger is turned away, and Thou comfortedst me.
"Behold, God is my salvation;
I will trust, and not be afraid:
For the Lord Jehovah is my strength and my song;
He also is become my salvation. . . .
"Sing unto the Lord; for He hath done excellent things:
This is known in all the earth.
Cry out and shout, thou inhabitant of Zion:
For great is the Holy One of Israel in the midst of thee."
Isaiah 12.

Ahaz

The accession of Ahaz to the throne brought Isaiah and his associates face to face with conditions more appalling than any that had hitherto existed in the realm of Judah. Many who had formerly withstood the seductive influence of idolatrous practices were now being persuaded to take part in the worship of heathen deities. Princes in Israel were proving untrue to their trust; false prophets were arising with messages to lead astray; even some of the priests were teaching for hire. Yet the leaders in apostasy still kept up the forms of divine worship and claimed to be numbered among the people of God.

The prophet Micah, who bore his testimony during those troublous times, declared that sinners in Zion, while claiming to "lean upon the Lord," and blasphemously boasting, "Is not the Lord among us? none evil can come upon us," continued to "build up Zion with blood, and Jerusalem with iniquity." Micah 3:11, 10. Against these evils the prophet Isaiah lifted his voice in stern rebuke: "Hear the word of the Lord, ye rulers of Sodom; give ear unto the law of our God, ye people of Gomorrah. To what purpose is the multitude of your sacrifices unto Me? saith the Lord. . . . When ye come to appear before Me, who hath required this at your hand, to tread My courts?" Isaiah 1:10-12.

Inspiration declares, "The sacrifice of the wicked is abomination: how much more, when he bringeth it with a wicked mind?" Proverbs 21:27. The God of heaven is "of purer eyes than to behold evil," and cannot "look on iniquity." Habakkuk 1:13. It is not because He is unwilling to forgive that He turns from the transgressor; it is because the sinner refuses to make use of the abundant provisions of grace, that God is unable to deliver from sin. "The Lord's hand is not shortened, that it cannot save; neither His ear heavy, that it cannot hear: but your iniquities have separated between you and your God, and your sins have hid His face from you, that He will not hear." Isaiah 59:1, 2.

Solomon had written, "Woe to thee, O land, when thy king is a child!" Ecclesiastes 10:16. Thus it was with the land of Judah. Through continued transgression her rulers had become as children. Isaiah called the attention of the people to the weakness of their position among the nations of earth, and he showed that this was the result of wickedness in high places. "Behold," he said, "the Lord, the Lord of hosts, doth take away from Jerusalem and from Judah the stay and the staff, the whole stay of bread, and the whole stay of water, the mighty man, and the man of war, the judge, and the prophet, and the prudent, and the ancient, the captain of fifty, and the honorable man, and the counselor, and the cunning artificer, and the eloquent orator. And I will give children to be their princes, and babes shall rule over them." "For Jerusalem is ruined, and Judah is fallen: because their tongue and their doings are against the Lord." Isaiah 3:1-4, 8.

"They which lead thee," the prophet continued, "cause thee to err, and destroy the way of thy paths." Verse 12. During the reign of Ahaz this was literally true; for of him it is written: "He walked in the ways of the kings of Israel, and made also molten images for Baalim. Moreover he burnt incense in the valley of the son of Hinnom;" "yea, and made his son to pass through the fire, according to the abominations of the heathen, whom the Lord cast out from before the children of Israel." 2 Chronicles 28:2, 3; 2 Kings 16:3.

This was indeed a time of great peril for the chosen nation. Only a few short years, and the ten tribes of the kingdom of Israel were to be scattered among the nations of heathendom. And in the kingdom of Judah also the outlook was dark. The forces for good were rapidly diminishing, the forces for evil multiplying. The prophet Micah, viewing the situation, was constrained to exclaim: "The good man is perished out of the earth: and there is none upright among men." "The best of them is as a brier: the most upright is sharper than a thorn hedge." Micah 7:2, 4. "Except the Lord of hosts had left unto us a very small remnant," declared Isaiah, "we should have been as Sodom, and . . . Gomorrah." Isaiah 1:9.

In every age, for the sake of those who have remained true, as well as because of His infinite love for the erring, God has borne long with the rebellious, and has urged them to forsake their course of evil and return to Him. "Precept upon precept; line upon line, . . . here a little, and there a little," through men of His appointment, He has taught transgressors' the way of righteousness. Isaiah 28:10.

And thus it was during the reign of Ahaz. Invitation upon invitation was sent to erring Israel to return to their allegiance to Jehovah. Tender were the pleadings of the prophets; and as they stood before the people, earnestly exhorting to repentance and reformation, their words bore fruit to the glory of God.

Through Micah came the wonderful appeal, "Hear ye now

what the Lord saith; Arise, contend thou before the mountains, and let the hills hear thy voice. Hear ye, O mountains, the Lord's controversy, and ye strong foundations of the earth: for the Lord hath a controversy with His people, and He will plead with Israel.

"O My people, what have I done unto thee? and wherein have I wearied thee? testify against Me. For I brought thee up out of the land of Egypt, and redeemed thee out of the house of servants; and I sent before thee Moses, Aaron, and Miriam.

"O My people, remember now what Balak king of Moab consulted, and what Balaam the son of Beor answered him from Shittim unto Gilgal; that ye may know the righteousness of the Lord." Micah 6:1-5.

The God whom we serve is long-suffering; "His compassions fail not." Lamentations 3:22. Throughout the period of probationary time His Spirit is entreating men to accept the gift of life. "As I live, saith the Lord God, I have no pleasure in the death of the wicked; but that the wicked turn from his way and live: turn ye, turn ye from your evil ways; for why will ye die?" Ezekiel 33:11. It is Satan's special device to lead man into sin and then leave him there, helpless and hopeless, fearing to seek for pardon. But God invites, "Let him take hold of My strength, that he may make peace with Me; and he shall make peace with Me." Isaiah 27:5. In Christ every provision has been made, every encouragement offered.

In the days of apostasy in Judah and Israel, many were inquiring: "Wherewith shall I come before the Lord, and bow myself before the high God? shall I come before Him with burnt offerings, with calves of a year old? will the Lord be pleased with thousands of rams, or with ten thousands of rivers of oil?" The answer is plain and positive: "He hath showed thee, O man, what is good; and what doth the Lord require of thee, but to do justly, and to love mercy, and to walk humbly with thy God?" Micah 6:6-8.

In urging the value of practical godliness, the prophet was only repeating the counsel given Israel centuries before. Through Moses, as they were about to enter the Promised Land, the word of the Lord had been: "And now, Israel, what doth the Lord thy God require of thee, but to fear the Lord thy God, to walk in all His ways, and to love Him, and to serve the Lord thy God with all thy heart and with all thy soul, to keep the commandments of the Lord, and His statutes, which I command thee this day for thy good?" Deuteronomy 10:12, 13. From age to age these counsels were repeated by the servants of Jehovah to those who were in danger of falling into habits of formalism and of forgetting to show mercy. When Christ Himself, during His earthly ministry, was approached by a lawyer with the question, "Master, which is the great commandment in the law?" Jesus said to him, "Thou shalt love the Lord thy God with all thy heart, and with all thy soul, and with all thy mind. This is the first and great commandment. And the second is like unto it, Thou shalt love thy neighbor as thyself. On these two commandments hang all the law and the prophets." Matthew 22:36-40.

These plain utterances of the prophets and of the Master Himself, should be received by us as the voice of God to every soul. We should lose no opportunity of performing deeds of mercy, of tender forethought and Christian courtesy, for the burdened and the oppressed. If we can do no more, we may speak words of courage and hope to those who are unacquainted with God, and who can be approached most easily by the avenue of sympathy and love.

Rich and abundant are the promises made to those who are watchful of opportunities to bring joy and blessing into the lives of others. "If thou draw out thy soul to the hungry, and satisfy the afflicted soul; then shall thy light rise in obscurity, and thy darkness be as the noonday: and the Lord shall guide thee continually, and satisfy thy soul in drought, and make fat thy bones: and thou shalt be like a watered garden, and like a spring of water, whose waters fail not." Isaiah 58:10, 11.

The idolatrous course of Ahaz, in the face of the earnest appeals of the prophets, could have but one result. "The wrath of the Lord was upon Judah and Jerusalem, and He . . . delivered them to trouble, to astonishment, and to hissing." 2 Chronicles 29:8. The kingdom suffered a rapid decline, and its very existence was soon imperiled by invading armies. "Rezin king of Syria and Pekah son of Remaliah king of Israel came up to Jerusalem to war: and they besieged Ahaz." 2 Kings 16:5.

Had Ahaz and the chief men of his realm been true servants of the Most High, they would have had no fear of so unnatural an alliance as had been formed against them. But repeated transgression had shorn them of strength. Stricken with a nameless dread of the retributive judgments of an offended God, the heart of the king "was moved, and the heart of his people, as the trees of the wood are moved with the wind." Isaiah 7:2. In this crisis the word of the Lord came to Isaiah, bidding him meet the trembling king and say:

"Take heed, and be quiet; fear not, neither be fainthearted . . . . Because Syria, Ephraim, and the son of Remaliah, have taken evil counsel against thee, saying, Let us go up against Judah, and vex it, and let us make a breach therein for us, and set a king in the midst of it: . . . thus saith the Lord God, It shall not stand, neither shall it come to pass." The prophet declared that the kingdom of Israel, and Syria as well, would soon come to an end. "If ye will not believe," he concluded, "surely ye shall not be established." Verses 4-7, 9.

Well would it have been for the kingdom of Judah had Ahaz received this message as from heaven. But choosing to lean on the arm of flesh, he sought help from the heathen. In desperation he sent word to Tiglath-pileser, king of Assyria: "I am thy servant and thy son: come up, and save me out of the hand of the king of Syria, and out of the hand of the king of Israel, which rise up against me." 2 Kings 16:7. The request was accompanied by a rich present from the king's treasure and from the temple storehouse.

The help asked for was sent, and King Ahaz was given temporary relief, but at what a cost to Judah! The tribute offered aroused the cupidity of Assyria, and that treacherous nation soon threatened to overflow and spoil Judah. Ahaz and his unhappy subjects were now harassed by the fear of falling completely into the hands of the cruel Assyrians.

"The Lord brought Judah low" because of continued transgression. In this time of chastisement Ahaz, instead of repenting, trespassed "yet more against the Lord: . . . for he sacrificed unto the gods of Damascus." "Because the gods of the kings of Syria help them," he said, "therefore will I sacrifice to them, that they may help me." 2 Chronicles 28:19, 22, 23.

As the apostate king neared the end of his reign, he caused the doors of the temple to be closed. The sacred services were interrupted. No longer were the candlesticks kept burning before the altar. No longer were offerings made for the sins of the people. No longer did sweet incense ascend on high at the time of the morning and the evening sacrifice. Deserting the courts of the house of God and locking fast its doors, the inhabitants of the godless city boldly set up altars for the worship of heathen deities on the street corners throughout Jerusalem. Heathenism had seemingly triumphed; the powers of darkness had well-nigh prevailed.

But in Judah there dwelt some who maintained their allegiance to Jehovah, steadfastly refusing to be led into idolatry. It was to these that Isaiah and Micah and their associates looked in hope as they surveyed the ruin wrought during the last years of Ahaz. Their sanctuary was closed, but the faithful ones were assured: "God is with us." Sanctify the Lord of hosts Himself; and let Him be your fear, and let Him be your dread. And He shall be for a sanctuary." Isaiah 8:10, 13, 14.

Hezekiah

In sharp contrast with the reckless rule of Ahaz was the reformation wrought during the prosperous reign of his son. Hezekiah came to the throne determined to do all in his power to save Judah from the fate that was overtaking the northern kingdom. The messages of the prophets offered no encouragement to halfway measures. Only by most decided reformation could be threatened judgments be averted.

In the crisis, Hezekiah proved to be a man of opportunity. No sooner had he ascended the throne than he began to plan and to execute. He first turned his attention to the restoration of the temple services, so long neglected; and in this work he earnestly solicited the co-operation of a band of priests and Levites who had remained true to their sacred calling. Confident of their loyal support, he spoke with them freely concerning his desire to institute immediate and far-reaching reforms. "Our fathers have trespassed," he confessed, "and done that which was evil in the eyes of the Lord our God, and have forsaken Him, and have turned away their faces from the habitation of the Lord." "Now it is in mine heart to make a covenant with the Lord God of Israel, that His fierce wrath may turn away from us." 2 Chronicles 29:6, 10.

In a few well-chosen words the king reviewed the situation they were facing—the closed temple and the cessation of all services within its precincts; the flagrant idolatry practiced in the streets of the city and throughout the kingdom; the apostasy of multitudes who might have remained true to God had the leaders in Judah set before them a right example; and the decline of the kingdom and loss of prestige in the estimation of surrounding nations. The northern kingdom was rapidly crumbling to pieces; many were perishing by the sword; a multitude had already been carried away captive; soon Israel would fall completely into the hands of the Assyrians, and be utterly ruined; and this fate would surely befall Judah as well, unless God should work mightily through chosen representatives.

Hezekiah appealed directly to the priests to unite with him in bringing about the necessary reforms. "Be not now negligent," he exhorted them; "for the Lord hath chosen you to stand before Him, to serve Him, and that ye should minister unto Him, and burn incense." "Sanctify now yourselves, and sanctify the house of the Lord God of your fathers." Verses 11, 5.

It was a time for quick action. The priests began at once. Enlisting the co-operation of others of their number who had not been present during this conference, they engaged heartily in the work of cleansing and sanctifying the temple. Because of the years of desecration and neglect, this was attended with many difficulties; but the priests and the Levites labored untiringly, and within a remarkably short time they were able to report their task completed. The temple doors had been repaired and thrown open; the sacred vessels had been assembled and put into place; and all was in readiness for the re-establishment of the sanctuary services.

In the first service held, the rulers of the city united with King Hezekiah and with the priests and Levites in seeking forgiveness for the sins of the nation. Upon the altar were placed sin offerings "to make an atonement for all Israel." "And when they had made an end of offering, the king and all that were present with him bowed themselves, and worshiped." Once more the temple courts resounded with words of praise and adoration. The songs of David and of Asaph were sung with joy, as the worshipers realized that they were being delivered from the bondage of sin and apostasy. "Hezekiah rejoiced, and all the people, that God had prepared the people: for the thing was done suddenly." Verses 24, 29, 36.

God had indeed prepared the hearts of the chief men of Judah to lead out in a decided reformatory movement, that the tide of apostasy might be stayed. Through His prophets He had sent to His chosen people message after message of earnest entreaty—messages that had been despised and rejected by the ten tribes of the kingdom of Israel, now given over to the enemy. But in Judah there remained a goodly remnant, and to these the prophets continued to appeal. Hear Isaiah urging, "Turn ye unto Him from whom the children of Israel have deeply revolted." Isaiah 31:6. Hear Micah declaring with confidence: "I will look unto the Lord; I will wait for the God of my salvation: my God will hear me. Rejoice not against me, O mine enemy; when I fall, I shall arise; when I sit in darkness, the Lord shall be a light unto me. I will bear the indignation of the Lord, because I have sinned against Him, until He plead my cause, and execute judgment for me: He will bring me forth to the light, and I shall behold His righteousness." Micah 7:7-9.

These and other like messages revealing the willingness of God to forgive and accept those who turned to Him with full purpose of heart, had brought hope to many a fainting soul in the dark years when the temple doors remained closed; and now, as the leaders began to institute a reform, a multitude of the people, weary of the thralldom of sin, were ready to respond.

Those who entered the temple courts to seek forgiveness and to renew their vows of allegiance to Jehovah, had wonderful encouragement offered them in the prophetic portions of Scripture. The solemn warnings against idolatry, spoken through Moses in the hearing of all Israel, had been accompanied by prophecies of God's willingness to hear and forgive those who in times of apostasy should seek Him with all the heart. "If thou turn to the Lord thy God," Moses had said, "and shalt be obedient unto His voice; (for the Lord thy God is a merciful God;) He will not forsake thee, neither destroy thee, nor forget the covenant of thy fathers which He sware unto them." Deuteronomy 4:30, 31.

And in the prophetic prayer offered at the dedication of the temple whose services Hezekiah and his associates were now restoring, Solomon had prayed, "When Thy people Israel be smitten down before the enemy, because they have sinned against Thee, and shall turn again to Thee, and confess Thy name, and pray, and make supplication unto Thee in this house: then hear Thou in heaven, and forgive the sin of Thy people Israel." 1 Kings 8:33, 34. The seal of divine approval had been placed upon this prayer; for at its close fire had come down from heaven to consume the burnt offering and the sacrifices, and the glory of the Lord had filled the temple. See 2 Chronicles 7:1. And by night the Lord had appeared to Solomon to tell him that his prayer had been heard, and that mercy would be shown those who should worship there. The gracious assurance was given: "If My people, which are called by My name, shall humble themselves, and pray, and seek My face, and turn from their wicked ways; then will I hear from heaven, and will forgive their sin, and will heal their land." Verse 14.

These promises met abundant fulfillment during the reformation under Hezekiah.

The good beginning made at the time of the purification of the temple was followed by a broader movement, in which Israel as well as Judah participated. In his zeal to make the temple services a real blessing to the people, Hezekiah determined to revive the ancient custom of gathering the Israelites together for the celebration of the Passover feast.

For many years the Passover had not been observed as a national festival. The division of the kingdom after the close of Solomon's reign had made this seem impracticable. But the terrible judgments befalling the ten tribes were awakening in the hearts of some a desire for better things; and the stirring messages of the prophets were having their effect. By royal couriers the invitation to the Passover at Jerusalem was heralded far and wide, "from city to city through the country of Ephraim and Manasseh even unto Zebulun." The bearers of the gracious invitation were usually repulsed. The impenitent turned lightly aside; nevertheless some, eager to seek God for a clearer knowledge of His will, "humbled themselves, and came to Jerusalem." 2 Chronicles 30:10, 11.

In the land of Judah the response was very general; for upon them was "the hand of God," "to give them one heart to do the commandment of the king and of the princes" —a command in accord with the will of God as revealed through His prophets. Verses 22, 21.

The occasion was one of the greatest profit to the multitudes assembled. The desecrated streets of the city were cleared of the idolatrous shrines placed there during the reign of Ahaz. On the appointed day the Passover was observed, and the week was spent by the people in offering peace offerings and in learning what God would have them do. Daily the Levites "taught the good knowledge of the Lord;" and those who had prepared their hearts to seek God, found pardon. A great gladness took possession of the worshiping multitude; "the Levites and the priests praised the Lord day by day, singing with loud instruments;" all were united in their desire to praise Him who had proved so gracious and merciful. Verse 12.

The seven days usually allotted to the Passover feast passed all too quickly, and the worshipers determined to spend another seven days in learning more fully the way of the Lord. The teaching priests continued their work of instruction from the book of the law; daily the people assembled at the temple to offer their tribute of praise and thanksgiving; and as the great meeting drew to a close, it was evident that God had wrought marvelously in the conversion of backsliding Judah and in stemming the tide of idolatry which threatened to sweep all before it. The solemn warnings of the prophets had not been uttered in vain. "There was great joy in Jerusalem: for since the time of Solomon the son of David king of Israel there was not the like in Jerusalem." Verse 26.

The time had come for the return of the worshipers to their homes. "The priests the Levites arose and blessed the people: and their voice was heard, and their prayer came up to His holy dwelling place, even unto heaven." Verse 27. God had accepted those who with broken hearts had confessed their sins and with resolute purpose had turned to Him for forgiveness and help.

There now remained an important work in which those who were returning to their homes must take an active part, and the accomplishment of this work bore evidence to the genuineness of the reformation wrought. The record reads: "All Israel that were present went out to the cities of Judah, and brake the images in pieces, and cut down the groves, and threw down the high places and the altars out of all Judah and Benjamin, in Ephraim also and Manasseh, until they had utterly destroyed them all. Then all the children of Israel returned, every man to his possession, into their own cities." 2 Chronicles 31:1.

Hezekiah and his associates instituted various reforms for the upbuilding of the spiritual and temporal interests of the kingdom. "Throughout all Judah" the king "wrought that which was good and right and truth before the Lord his God. And in every work that he began, . . . he did it with all his heart, and prospered." "He trusted in the Lord God of Israel, . . . and departed not from following Him, but kept His commandments, which the Lord commanded Moses. And the Lord was with him; and he prospered." Verses 20, 21; 2 Kings 18:5-7.

The reign of Hezekiah was characterized by a series of remarkable providences which revealed to the surrounding nations that the God of Israel was with His people. The success of the Assyrians in capturing Samaria and in scattering the shattered remnant of the ten tribes among the nations, during the earlier portion of his reign, was leading many to question the power of the God of the Hebrews. Emboldened by their successes, the Ninevites had long since set aside the message of Jonah and had become defiant in their opposition to the purposes of Heaven. A few years after the fall of Samaria the victorious armies reappeared in Palestine, this time directing their forces against the fenced cities of Judah, with some measure of success; but they withdrew for a season because of difficulties arising in other portions of their realm. Not until some years later, toward the close of Hezekiah's reign, was it to be demonstrated before the nations of the world whether the gods of the heathen were finally to prevail.

The Ambassadors From Babylon

In the midst of his prosperous reign King Hezekiah was suddenly stricken with a fatal malady. "Sick unto death," his case was beyond the power of man to help. And the last vestige of hope seemed removed when the prophet Isaiah appeared before him with the message, "Thus saith the Lord, Set thine house in order: for thou shalt die, and not live." Isaiah 38:1.

The outlook seemed utterly dark; yet the king could still pray to the One who had hitherto been his "refuge and strength, a very present help in trouble." Psalm 46:1. And so "he turned his face to the wall, and prayed unto the Lord, saying, I beseech Thee, O Lord, remember now how I have walked before Thee in truth and with a perfect heart, and have done that which is good in Thy sight. And Hezekiah wept sore." 2 Kings 20:2, 3.

Since the days of David there had reigned no king who had wrought so mightily for the upbuilding of the kingdom of God in a time of apostasy and discouragement as had Hezekiah. The dying ruler had served his God faithfully, and had strengthened the confidence of the people in Jehovah as their Supreme Ruler. And, like David, he could now plead:

"Let my prayer come before Thee:
Incline Thine ear unto my cry;
For my soul is full of troubles:
And my life draweth nigh unto the grave."
Psalm 88:2, 3.
"Thou art my hope, O Lord God:
Thou art my trust from my youth.
By Thee have I been holden up."
"Forsake me not when my strength faileth."
"O God, be not far from me:
O my God, make haste for my help."
"O God, forsake me not;
Until I have showed Thy strength unto this generation,
And Thy power to everyone that is to come."
Psalm 71:5, 6, 9, 12, 18.

He whose "compassions fail not," heard the prayer of His servant. Lamentations 3:22. "It came to pass, afore Isaiah was gone out into the middle court, that the word of the Lord came to him, saying, Turn again, and tell Hezekiah the captain of My people, Thus saith the Lord, the God of David thy father, I have heard thy prayer, I have seen thy tears: behold, I will heal thee: on the third day thou shalt go up unto the house of the Lord. And I will add unto thy days fifteen years; and I will deliver thee and this city out of the hand of the king of Assyria; and I will defend this city for Mine own sake, and for My servant David's sake." 2 Kings 20:4-6.

Gladly the prophet returned with the words of assurance and hope. Directing that a lump of figs be laid upon the diseased part, Isaiah delivered to the king the message of God's mercy and protecting care.

Like Moses in the land of Midian, like Gideon in the presence of the heavenly messenger, like Elisha just before the ascension of his master, Hezekiah pleaded for some sign that the message was from heaven. "What shall be the sign," he inquired of the prophet, "that the Lord will heal me, and that I shall go up into the house of the Lord the third day?"

"This sign shalt thou have of the Lord," the prophet answered, "that the Lord will do the thing that He hath spoken: shall the shadow go forward ten degrees, or go back ten degrees?" "It is a light thing," Hezekiah replied, "for the shadow to go down ten degrees: nay, but let the shadow return backward ten degrees."

Only by the direct interposition of God could the shadow on the sundial be made to turn back ten degrees; and this was to be the sign to Hezekiah that the Lord had heard his prayer. Accordingly, "the prophet cried unto the Lord: and He brought the shadow ten degrees backward, by which it had gone down in the dial of Ahaz." Verses 8-11.

Restored to his wonted strength, the king of Judah acknowledged in words of song the mercies of Jehovah, and vowed to spend his remaining days in willing service to the

King of kings. His grateful recognition of God's compassionate dealing with him is an inspiration to all who desire to spend their years to the glory of their Maker.

> "I said
> In the cutting off of my days,
> I shall go to the gates of the grave:
> I am deprived of the residue of my years.
> "I said,
> I shall not see the Lord, even the Lord, in the land of the living;
> I shall behold man no more with the inhabitants of the world.
> "Mine age is departed,
> And is removed from me as a shepherd's tent:
> "I have cut off like a weaver my life:
> He will cut me off with pining sickness:
> "From day even to night wilt Thou make an end of me.
> I reckoned till morning, that,
> As a lion, so will He break all my bones:
> "From day even to night wilt Thou make an end of me.
> Like a crane or a swallow, so did I chatter:
> I did mourn as a dove:
> Mine eyes fail with looking upward:
> O Lord, I am oppressed; undertake for me.
> "What shall I say?
> He hath both spoken unto me,
> And Himself hath done it:
> I shall go softly all my years in the bitterness of my soul.
> "O Lord, by these things men live,
> And in all these things is the life of my spirit:
> So wilt Thou recover me, and make me to live.
> "Behold, for peace I had great bitterness:
> But Thou hast in love to my soul delivered it from the pit of corruption:
> For Thou hast cast all my sins behind Thy back.
> "For the grave cannot praise Thee,
> Death cannot celebrate Thee:
> They that go down into the pit cannot hope for Thy truth.
> "The living, the living, he shall praise Thee,
> As I do this day:
> The father to the children shall make known Thy truth.
> "The Lord was ready to save me:
> Therefore we will sing my songs to the stringed instruments
> All the days of our life in the house of the Lord."
> Isaiah 38:10-20.

In the fertile valleys of the Tigris and the Euphrates there dwelt an ancient race which, though at that time subject to Assyria, was destined to rule the world. Among its people were wise men who gave much attention to the study of astronomy; and when they noticed that the shadow on the sundial had been turned back ten degrees, they marveled greatly. Their king, Merodachbaladan, upon learning that this miracle had been wrought as a sign to the king of Judah that the God of heaven had granted him a new lease of life, sent ambassadors to Hezekiah to congratulate him on his recovery and to learn, if possible, more of the God who was able to perform so great a wonder.

The visit of these messengers from the ruler of a far-away land gave Hezekiah an opportunity to extol the living God. How easy it would have been for him to tell them of God, the upholder of all created things, through whose favor his own life had been spared when all other hope had fled! What momentous transformations might have taken place had these seekers after truth from the plains of Chaldea been led to acknowledge the supreme sovereignty of the living God!

But pride and vanity took possession of Hezekiah's heart, and in self-exaltation he laid open to covetous eyes the treasures with which God had enriched His people. The king "showed them the house of his precious things, the silver, and the gold, and the spices, and the precious ointment, and all the house of his armor, and all that was found in his treasures: there was nothing in his house, nor in all his dominion, that Hezekiah showed them not." Isaiah 39:2. Not to glorify God did he do this, but to exalt himself in the eyes of the foreign princes. He did not stop to consider that these men were representatives of a powerful nation that had not the fear nor the love of God in their hearts, and that it was imprudent to make them his confidants concerning the temporal riches of the nation.

The visit of the ambassadors to Hezekiah was a test of his gratitude and devotion. The record says, "Howbeit in the business of the ambassadors of the princes of Babylon, who sent unto him to inquire of the wonder that was done in the land, God left him, to try him, that He might know all that was in his heart." 2 Chronicles 32:31. Had Hezekiah improved the opportunity given him to bear witness to the power, the goodness, the compassion, of the God of Israel, the report of the ambassadors would have been as light piercing darkness. But he magnified himself above the Lord of hosts. He "rendered not again according to the benefit done unto him; for his heart was lifted up." Verse 25.

How disastrous the results which were to follow! To Isaiah it was revealed that the returning ambassadors were carrying with them a report of the riches they had seen, and that the king of Babylon and his counselors would plan to enrich their own country with the treasures of Jerusalem. Hezekiah had grievously sinned; "therefore there was wrath upon him, and upon Judah and Jerusalem." Verse 25.

"Then came Isaiah the prophet unto King Hezekiah, and said unto him, What said these men? and from whence came they unto thee? And Hezekiah said, They are come from a far country unto me, even from Babylon. Then said he, What have they seen in thine house? And Hezekiah answered, All that is in mine house have they seen: there is nothing among my treasures that I have not showed them.

"Then said Isaiah to Hezekiah, Hear the word of the Lord of hosts: Behold, the days come, that all that is in thine house, and that which thy fathers have laid up in store until this day, shall be carried to Babylon: nothing shall be left, saith the Lord. And of thy sons that shall issue from thee, which thou shalt beget, shall they take away; and they shall be eunuchs in the palace of the king of Babylon.

"Then said Hezekiah to Isaiah, Good is the word of the Lord which thou hast spoken." Isaiah 39:3-8.

Filled with remorse, "Hezekiah humbled himself for the pride of his heart, both he and the inhabitants of Jerusalem, so that the wrath of the Lord came not upon them in the days of Hezekiah." 2 Chronicles 32:26. But the evil seed had been sown and in time was to spring up and yield a harvest of desolation and woe. During his remaining years the king of Judah was to have much prosperity because of his steadfast purpose to redeem the past and to bring honor to the name of the God whom he served; yet his faith was to be severely tried, and he was to learn that only by putting his trust fully in Jehovah could he hope to triumph over the powers of darkness that were plotting his ruin and the utter destruction of his people.

The story of Hezekiah's failure to prove true to his trust at the time of the visit of the ambassadors is fraught with an important lesson for all. Far more than we do, we need to speak of the precious Chapters in our experience, of the mercy and loving-kindness of God, of the matchless depths of the Saviour's love. When mind and heart are filled with the love of God, it will not be difficult to impart that which enters into the spiritual life. Great thoughts, noble aspirations, clear perceptions of truth, unselfish purposes, yearnings for piety and holiness, will find expression in words that reveal the character of the heart treasure.

Those with whom we associate day by day need our help, our guidance. They may be in such a condition of mind that a word spoken in season will be as a nail in a sure place. Tomorrow some of these souls may be where we can never reach them again. What is our influence over these fellow travelers?

Every day of life is freighted with responsibilities which we must bear. Every day, our words and acts are making impressions upon those with whom we associate. How great the need that we set a watch upon our lips and guard carefully our steps! One reckless movement, one imprudent step, and the surging waves of some strong temptation may sweep a soul into the downward path. We cannot gather up the thoughts we have planted in human minds. If they have been evil, we may have set in motion a train of circumstances, a tide of evil, which we are powerless to stay.

On the other hand, if by our example we aid others in the development of good principles, we give them power to do good. In their turn they exert the same beneficial influence over others. Thus hundreds and thousands are helped by our unconscious influence. The true follower of Christ strengthens the good purposes of all with whom he comes in contact. Before an unbelieving, sin-loving world he reveals the power of God's grace and the perfection of His character.

Deliverance From Assyria

In a time of grave national peril, when the hosts of Assyria were invading the land of Judah and it seemed as if nothing could save Jerusalem from utter destruction, Hezekiah rallied the forces of his realm to resist with unfailing courage their heathen oppressors and to trust in the power of Jehovah to deliver. "Be strong and courageous, be not afraid nor dismayed for the king of Assyria, nor for all the multitude that is with him," Hezekiah exhorted the men of Judah; "for there be more with us than with him: with him is an arm of flesh; but with us is the Lord our God to help us, and to fight our battles." 2 Chronicles 32:7, 8.

It was not without reason that Hezekiah could speak with certainty of the outcome. The boastful Assyrian, while used by God for a season as the rod of His anger for the punishment of the nations, was not always to prevail. See Isaiah 10:5. "Be not afraid of the Assyrian," had been the message of the Lord through Isaiah some years before to those that dwelt in Zion; "for yet a very little while, . . . and the Lord of hosts shall stir up a scourge for him according to the slaughter of Midian at the rock of Oreb: and as His rod was upon the sea, so shall He lift it up after the manner of Egypt. And it shall come to pass in that day, that his burden shall be taken away from off thy shoulder, and his yoke from off thy neck, and the yoke shall be destroyed because of the anointing." Verses 24-27.

In another prophetic message, given "in the year that King Ahaz died," the prophet had declared: "The Lord of hosts hath sworn, saying, Surely as I have thought, so shall it come to pass; and as I have purposed, so shall it stand: that I will break the Assyrian in My land, and upon My mountains tread him underfoot: then shall his yoke depart from off them, and his burden depart from off their shoulders. This is the purpose that is purposed upon the whole earth: and this is the hand that is stretched out upon all the nations. For the Lord of hosts hath purposed, and who shall disannul it? and His hand is stretched out, and who shall turn it back?" Isaiah 14:28, 24-27.

The power of the oppressor was to be broken. Yet Hezekiah, in the earlier years of his reign, had continued to pay tribute to Assyria, in harmony with the agreement entered into by Ahaz. Meanwhile the king had taken "counsel with his princes and his mighty men," and had done everything possible for the defense of his kingdom. He had made sure of a bountiful supply of water within the walls of Jerusalem, while without the city there should be a scarcity. "Also he strengthened himself, and built up all the wall that was broken, and raised it up to the towers, and another wall without, and repaired Millo in the city of David, and made darts and shields in abundance. And he set captains of war over the people." 2 Chronicles 32:3, 5, 6. Nothing had been left undone that could be done in preparation for a siege.

At the time of Hezekiah's accession to the throne of Judah, the Assyrians had already carried captive a large number of the children of Israel from the northern kingdom; and a few years after he had begun to reign, and while he was still strengthening the defenses of Jerusalem, the Assyrians besieged and captured Samaria and scattered the ten tribes among the many provinces of the Assyrian realm. The borders of Judah were only a few miles distant, with Jerusalem less than fifty miles away; and the rich spoils to be found within the temple would tempt the enemy to return.

But the king of Judah had determined to do his part in preparing to resist the enemy; and, having accomplished all that human ingenuity and energy could do, he had assembled his forces and had exhorted them to be of good courage. "Great is the Holy One of Israel in the midst of thee" had been the message of the prophet Isaiah to Judah; and the king with unwavering faith now declared, "With us is the Lord our God to help us, and to fight our battles." Isaiah 12:6; 2 Chronicles 32:8.

Nothing more quickly inspires faith than the exercise of faith. The king of Judah had prepared for the coming storm; and now, confident that the prophecy against the Assyrians would be fulfilled, he stayed his soul upon God. "And the people rested themselves upon the words of Hezekiah." 2 Chronicles 32:8. What though the armies of Assyria, fresh from the conquest of the greatest nations of earth, and triumphant over Samaria in Israel, should now turn their forces against Judah? What though they should boast, "As my hand hath found the kingdoms of the idols, and whose graven images did excel them of Jerusalem and of Samaria; shall I not, as I have done unto Samaria and her idols, so do to Jerusalem and her idols?" Isaiah 10:10, 11. Judah had nothing to fear; for their trust was in Jehovah.

The long-expected crisis finally came. The forces of Assyria, advancing from triumph to triumph, appeared in Judea. Confident of victory, the leaders divided their forces into two armies, one of which was to meet the Egyptian army to the southward, while the other was to besiege Jerusalem.

Judah's only hope was now in God. All possible help from Egypt had been cut off, and no other nations were near to lend a friendly hand.

The Assyrian officers, sure of the strength of their disciplined forces, arranged for a conference with the chief men of Judah, during which they insolently demanded the surrender of the city. This demand was accompanied by blasphemous revilings against the God of the Hebrews. Because of the weakness and apostasy of Israel and Judah, the name of God was no longer feared among the nations, but had become a subject for continual reproach. See Isaiah 52:5.

"Speak ye now to Hezekiah," said Rabshakeh, one of Sennacherib's chief officers, "Thus saith the great king, the king of Assyria, What confidence is this wherein thou trustest? Thou sayest, (but they are but vain words,) I have counsel and strength for the war. Now on whom dost thou trust, that thou rebellest against me?" 2 Kings 18:19, 20.

The officers were conferring outside the gates of the city, but within the hearing of the sentries on the wall; and as the representatives of the Assyrian king loudly urged their proposals upon the chief men of Judah, they were requested to speak in the Syrian rather than the Jewish language, in order that those upon the wall might not have knowledge of the proceedings of the conference. Rabshakeh, scorning this suggestion, lifted his voice still higher, and, continuing to speak in the Jewish language, said:

"Hear ye the words of the great king, the king of Assyria. Thus saith the king, Let not Hezekiah deceive you: for he shall not be able to deliver you. Neither let Hezekiah make you trust in the Lord, saying, The Lord will surely deliver us: this city shall not be delivered into the hand of the king of Assyria.

"Hearken not to Hezekiah: for thus saith the king of Assyria, Make an agreement with me by a present, and come out to me: and eat ye everyone of his vine, and everyone of his fig tree, and drink ye everyone the waters of his own cistern; until I come and take you away to a land like your own land, a land of corn and wine, a land of bread and vineyards.

"Beware lest Hezekiah persuade you, saying, The Lord will deliver us. Hath any of the gods of the nations delivered his land out of the hand of the king of Assyria? Where are the gods of Hamath and Arphad? where are the gods of Sepharvaim? and have they delivered Samaria out of my hand? Who are they among all the gods of these lands, that have delivered their land out of my hand, that the Lord should deliver Jerusalem out of my hand?" Isaiah 36:13-20.

To these taunts the children of Judah "answered him not a word." The conference was at an end. The Jewish representatives returned to Hezekiah "with their clothes rent, and told him the words of Rabshakeh." Verses 21, 22. The king, upon learning of the blasphemous challenge, "rent his clothes, and covered himself with sackcloth, and went into the house of the Lord." 2 Kings 19:1.

A messenger was dispatched to Isaiah to inform him of the outcome of the conference. "This day is a day of trouble, and of rebuke, and blasphemy," was the word the king sent. "It may be the Lord thy God will hear all the words of Rabshakeh, whom the king of Assyria his master hath sent to reproach the living God; and will reprove the words which the Lord thy God hath heard: wherefore lift up thy prayer for the remnant that are left." Verses 3, 4.

"For this cause Hezekiah the king, and the prophet Isaiah the son of Amoz, prayed and cried to Heaven." 2 Chronicles 32:20.

God answered the prayers of His servants. To Isaiah was given the message for Hezekiah: "Thus saith the Lord, Be not afraid of the words which thou hast heard, with which the servants of the king of Assyria have blasphemed Me. Behold, I will send a blast upon him, and he shall hear a rumor, and shall return to his own land; and I will cause him to fall by the sword in his own land." 2 Kings 19:6, 7.

The Assyrian representatives, after taking leave of the chief men of Judah, communicated direct with their king, who was with the division of his army guarding the approach from

Egypt. Upon hearing the report, Sennacherib wrote "letters to rail on the Lord God of Israel, and to speak against Him, saying, As the gods of the nations of other lands have not delivered their people out of mine hand, so shall not the God of Hezekiah deliver His people out of mine hand." 2 Chronicles 32:17.

The boastful threat was accompanied by the message: "Let not thy God in whom thou trustest deceive thee, saying, Jerusalem shall not be delivered into the hand of the king of Assyria. Behold, thou hast heard what the kings of Assyria have done to all lands, by destroying them utterly: and shalt thou be delivered? Have the gods of the nations delivered them which my fathers have destroyed; as Gozan, and Haran, and Rezeph, and the children of Eden which were in Thelasar? Where is the king of Hamath, and the king of Arpad, and the king of the city of Sepharvaim, of Hena, and Ivah?" 2 Kings 19:10-13.

When the king of Judah received the taunting letter, he took it into the temple and "spread it before the Lord" and prayed with strong faith for help from heaven, that the nations of earth might know that the God of the Hebrews still lived and reigned. Verse 14. The honor of Jehovah was at stake; He alone could bring deliverance.

"O Lord God of Israel, which dwellest between the cherubims," Hezekiah pleaded, "Thou art the God, even Thou alone, of all the kingdoms of the earth; Thou hast made heaven and earth. Lord, bow down Thine ear, and hear: open, Lord, Thine eyes, and see: and hear the words of Sennacherib, which hath sent him to reproach the living God. Of a truth, Lord, the kings of Assyria have destroyed the nations and their lands, and have cast their gods into the fire: for they were no gods, but the work of men's hands, wood and stone: therefore they have destroyed them. Now therefore, O Lord our God, I beseech Thee, save Thou us out of his hand, that all the kingdoms of the earth may know that Thou art the Lord God, even Thou only." 2 Kings 19:15-19.

"Give ear, O Shepherd of Israel,
Thou that leadest Joseph like a flock;
Thou that dwellest between the cherubims, shine forth.
Before Ephraim and Benjamin and Manasseh stir up Thy strength,
And come and save us.
Turn us again, O God,
And cause Thy face to shine; and we shall be saved.
"O Lord God of hosts,
How long wilt Thou be angry against the prayer of Thy people?
Thou feedest them with the bread of tears;
And givest them tears to drink in great measure.
Thou makest us a strife unto our neighbors:
And our enemies laugh among themselves.
Turn us again, O God of hosts,
And cause Thy face to shine; and we shall be saved.
"Thou hast brought a vine out of Egypt:

Thou hast cast out the heathen, and planted it. Thou preparedst room before it,
And didst cause it to take deep root, and it filled the land.
The hills were covered with the shadow of it,
And the boughs thereof were like the goodly cedars.
She sent out her boughs unto the sea,
And her branches unto the river.
"Why hast Thou then broken down her hedges,
So that all they which pass by the way do pluck her?
The boar out of the wood doth waste it,
And the wild beast of the field doth devour it.
Return, we beseech Thee, O God of hosts:
Look down from heaven, and behold, and visit this vine;
And the vineyard which Thy right hand hath planted,
And the branch that Thou madest strong for Thyself. . . .
"Quicken us, and we will call upon Thy name.
Turn us again, O Lord God of hosts,
Cause Thy face to shine; and we shall be saved." Psalm 80.

Hezekiah's pleadings in behalf of Judah and of the honor of their Supreme Ruler were in harmony with the mind of God. Solomon, in his benediction at the dedication of the temple, had prayed the Lord to maintain "the cause of His people Israel at all times, as the matter shall require: that all the people of the earth may know that the Lord is God, and that there is none else." 1 Kings 8:59, 60. Especially was the Lord to show favor when, in times of war or of oppression by an army, the chief men of Israel should enter the house of prayer and plead for deliverance. Verses 33, 34.

Hezekiah was not left without hope. Isaiah sent to him, saying, "Thus saith the Lord God of Israel, That which thou hast prayed to Me against Sennacherib king of Assyria I have heard. This is the word that the Lord hath spoken concerning him:

"The virgin the daughter of Zion hath despised thee, and laughed thee to scorn; the daughter of Jerusalem hath shaken her head at thee.

"Whom hast thou reproached and blasphemed? and against whom hast thou exalted thy voice, and lifted up thine eyes on high? even against the Holy One of Israel. By thy messengers thou hast reproached the Lord, and hast said, With the multitude of my chariots I am come up to the height of the mountains, to the sides of Lebanon, and will cut down the tall cedar trees thereof, and the choice fir trees thereof: and I will enter into the lodgings of his borders, and into the forest of his Carmel. I have digged and drunk strange waters, and with the sole of my feet have I dried up all the rivers of besieged places.

"Hast thou not heard long ago how I have done it, and of ancient times that I have formed it? now have I brought it to pass, that thou shouldest be to lay waste fenced cities into ruinous heaps. Therefore their inhabitants were of small power, they were dismayed and confounded; they were as the grass of the field, and as the green herb, as the grass on the housetops, and as corn blasted before it be grown up.

"But I know thy abode, and thy going out, and thy coming

in, and thy rage against Me. Because thy rage against Me and thy tumult is come up into Mine ears, therefore I will put My hook in thy nose, and My bridle in thy lips, and I will turn thee back by the way by which thou camest." 2 Kings 19:20-28.

The land of Judah had been laid waste by the army of occupation, but God had promised to provide miraculously for the needs of the people. To Hezekiah came the message: "This shall be a sign unto thee, Ye shall eat this year such things as grow of themselves, and in the second year that which springeth of the same; and in the third year sow ye, and reap, and plant vineyards, and eat the fruits thereof. And the remnant that is escaped of the house of Judah shall yet again take root downward, and bear fruit upward. For out of Jerusalem shall go forth a remnant, and they that escape out of Mount Zion: the zeal of the Lord of hosts shall do this.

"Therefore thus saith the Lord concerning the king of Assyria, He shall not come into this city, nor shoot an arrow there, nor come before it with shield, nor cast a bank against it. By the way that he came, by the same shall he return, and shall not come into this city, saith the Lord. For I will defend this city, to save it, for Mine own sake, and for My servant David's sake." Verses 29-34.

That very night deliverance came. "The angel of the Lord went out, and smote in the camp of the Assyrians an hundred fourscore and five thousand." Verse 35. "All the mighty men of valor, and the leaders and captains in the camp of the king of Assyria," were slain. 2 Chronicles 32:21.

Tidings of this terrible judgment upon the army that had been sent to take Jerusalem, soon reached Sennacherib, who was still guarding the approach to Judea from Egypt. Stricken with fear, the Assyrian king hasted to depart and "returned with shame of face to his own land." Verse 21. But he had not long to reign. In harmony with the prophecy that had been uttered concerning his sudden end, he was assassinated by those of his own home, "and Esarhaddon his son reigned in his stead." Isaiah 37:38.

The God of the Hebrews had prevailed over the proud Assyrian. The honor of Jehovah was vindicated in the eyes of the surrounding nations. In Jerusalem the hearts of the people were filled with holy joy. Their earnest entreaties for deliverance had been mingled with confession of sin and with many tears. In their great need they had trusted wholly in the power of God to save, and He had not failed them. Now the temple courts resounded with songs of solemn praise.

"In Judah is God known:
His name is great in Israel.
In Salem also is His tabernacle,
And His dwelling place in Zion.
There brake He the arrows of the bow,
The shield, and the sword, and the battle.
"Thou art more glorious and excellent Than the mountains of prey.
The stouthearted are spoiled, they have slept their sleep:

And none of the men of might have found their hands.
At Thy rebuke, O God of Jacob,
Both the chariot and horse are cast into a dead sleep.
"Thou, even Thou, art to be feared:
And who may stand in Thy sight when once Thou art angry?
Thou didst cause judgment to be heard from heaven;
The earth feared, and was still,
When God arose to judgment,
To save all the meek of the earth.
"Surely the wrath of man shall praise Thee:
The remainder of wrath shalt Thou restrain.
Vow, and pay unto the Lord your God:
Let all that be round about Him bring presents unto Him that ought to be feared.
He shall cut off the spirit of princes:
He is terrible to the kings of the earth."
Psalm 76.

The rise and fall of the Assyrian Empire is rich in lessons for the nations of earth today. Inspiration has likened the glory of Assyria at the height of her prosperity to a noble tree in the garden of God, towering above the surrounding trees.

"The Assyrian was a cedar in Lebanon with fair branches, and with a shadowing shroud, and of an high stature; and his top was among the thick boughs. . . . Under his shadow dwelt all great nations. Thus was he fair in his greatness, in the length of his branches: for his root was by great waters. The cedars in the garden of God could not hide him: the fir trees were not like his boughs, and the chestnut trees were not like his branches; nor any tree in the garden of God was like unto him in his beauty. . . . All the trees of Eden, that were in the garden of God, envied him." Ezekiel 31:3-9.

But the rulers of Assyria, instead of using their unusual blessings for the benefit of mankind, became the scourge of many lands. Merciless, with no thought of God or their fellow men, they pursued the fixed policy of causing all nations to acknowledge the supremacy of the gods of Nineveh, whom they exalted above the Most High. God had sent Jonah to them with a message of warning, and for a season they humbled themselves before the Lord of hosts and sought forgiveness. But soon they turned again to idol worship and to the conquest of the world.

The prophet Nahum, in his arraignment of the evildoers in Nineveh, exclaimed:

"Woe to the bloody city!
It is all full of lies and robbery; The prey departeth not;
"The noise of a whip, and the noise of the rattling of the wheels,
And of the prancing horses, and of the jumping chariots.
The horseman lifteth up both the bright sword and the glittering spear:
And there is a multitude of slain. . . .
"Behold, I am against thee,

they were also to impart to others a knowledge of the living God. Many from among the sons of the strangers were to learn to love Him as their Creator and their Redeemer; they were to begin the observance of His holy Sabbath day as a memorial of His creative power; and when He should make "bare His holy arm in the eyes of all the nations," to deliver His people from captivity, "all the ends of the earth" should see of the salvation of God. Verse 10. Many of these converts from heathenism would wish to unite themselves fully with the Israelites and accompany them on the return journey to Judea. None of these were to say, "The Lord hath utterly separated me from His people" (Isaiah 56:3), for the word of God through His prophet to those who should yield themselves to Him and observe His law was that they should thenceforth be numbered among spiritual Israel—His church on earth.

"The sons of the stranger, that join themselves to the Lord, to serve Him, and to love the name of the Lord, to be His servants, everyone that keepeth the Sabbath from polluting it, and taketh hold of My covenant; even them will I bring to My holy mountain, and make them joyful in My house of prayer: their burnt offerings and their sacrifices shall be accepted upon Mine altar; for Mine house shall be called an house of prayer for all people. The Lord God which gathereth the outcasts of Israel saith, Yet will I gather others to Him, beside those that are gathered unto Him." Verses 6-8.

The prophet was permitted to look down the centuries to the time of the advent of the promised Messiah. At first he beheld only "trouble and darkness, dimness of anguish." Isaiah 8:22. Many who were longing for the light of truth were being led astray by false teachers into the bewildering mazes of philosophy and spiritism; others were placing their trust in a form of godliness, but were not bringing true holiness into the life practice. The outlook seemed hopeless; but soon the scene changed, and before the eyes of the prophet was spread a wondrous vision. He saw the Sun of Righteousness arise with healing in His wings; and, lost in admiration, he exclaimed: "The dimness shall not be such as was in her vexation, when at the first He lightly afflicted the land of Zebulun and the land of Naphtali, and afterward did more grievously afflict her by the way of the sea, beyond Jordan, in Galilee of the nations. The people that walked in darkness have seen a great light: they that dwell in the land of the shadow of death, upon them hath the light shined." Isaiah 9:1, 2.

This glorious Light of the world was to bring salvation to every nation, kindred, tongue, and people. Of the work before Him, the prophet heard the eternal Father declare: "It is a light thing that Thou shouldest be My servant to raise up the tribes of Jacob, and to restore the preserved of Israel: I will also give Thee for a light to the Gentiles, that Thou mayest be My salvation unto the end of the earth." "In an acceptable time have I heard Thee, and in a day of salvation have I helped Thee: and I will preserve Thee, and give Thee for a covenant of the people, to establish the earth, to cause to inherit the desolate heritages; that Thou mayest say to the prisoners, Go forth; to them that are in darkness, Show yourselves." "Behold, these shall come from far: and, lo, these from the north and from the west; and these from the land of Sinim." Isaiah 49:6, 8, 9, 12.

Looking on still farther through the ages, the prophet beheld the literal fulfillment of these glorious promises. He saw the bearers of the glad tidings of salvation going to the ends of the earth, to every kindred and people. He heard the Lord saying of the gospel church, "Behold, I will extend peace to her like a river, and the glory of the Gentiles like a flowing stream;" and he heard the commission, "Enlarge the place of thy tent, and let them stretch forth the curtains of thine habitations: spare not, lengthen thy cords, and strengthen thy stakes; for thou shalt break forth on the right hand and on the left; and thy seed shall inherit the Gentiles." Isaiah 66:12; 54:2, 3.

Jehovah declared to the prophet that He would send His witnesses "unto the nations, to Tarshish, Pul, and Lud, . . . to Tubal, and Javan, to the isles afar off." Isaiah 66:19.

"How beautiful upon the mountains
Are the feet of him that bringeth good tidings,
That publisheth peace;
That bringeth good tidings of good,
That publisheth salvation;
That saith unto Zion, Thy God reigneth!"
Isaiah 52:7.

The prophet heard the voice of God calling His church to her appointed work, that the way might be prepared for the ushering in of His everlasting kingdom. The message was unmistakably plain:

"Arise, shine; for thy light is come,
And the glory of the Lord is risen upon thee.
"For, behold, the darkness shall cover the earth,
And gross darkness the people:
But the Lord shall arise upon thee,
And His glory shall be seen upon thee.
And the Gentiles shall come to thy light,
And kings to the brightness of thy rising.
"Lift up thine eyes round about, and see:
All they gather themselves together, they come to thee:
Thy sons shall come from far,
And thy daughters shall be nursed at thy side."
"And the sons of strangers shall build up thy walls,
And their kings shall minister unto thee:
For in My wrath I smote thee, But in My favor have I had mercy on thee.
Therefore thy gates shall be open continually;
They shall not be shut day nor night;
That men may bring unto thee the forces of the Gentiles,
And that their kings may be brought."
"Look unto Me, and be ye saved, all the ends of the earth:
For I am God, and there is none else."

Isaiah 60:1-4, 10, 11; 45:22.

These prophecies of a great spiritual awakening in a time of gross darkness are today meeting fulfillment in the advancing lines of mission stations that are reaching out into the benighted regions of earth. The groups of missionaries in heathen lands have been likened by the prophet to ensigns set up for the guidance of those who are looking for the light of truth.

"In that day," says Isaiah, "there shall be a root of Jesse, which shall stand for an ensign of the people; to it shall the Gentiles seek: and his rest shall be glorious. And it shall come to pass in that day, that the Lord shall set His hand again the second time to recover the remnant of His people. . . . And He shall set up an ensign for the nations, and shall assemble the outcasts of Israel, and gather together the dispersed of Judah from the four corners of the earth." Isaiah 11:10-12.

The day of deliverance is at hand. "The eyes of the Lord run to and fro throughout the whole earth, to show Himself strong in the behalf of them whose heart is perfect toward Him." 2 Chronicles 16:9. Among all nations, kindreds, and tongues, He sees men and women who are praying for light and knowledge. Their souls are unsatisfied; long have they fed on ashes. See Isaiah 44:20. The enemy of all righteousness has turned them aside, and they grope as blind men. But they are honest in heart and desire to learn a better way. Although in the depths of heathenism, with no knowledge of the written law of God nor of His Son Jesus, they have revealed in manifold ways the working of a divine power on mind and character.

At times those who have no knowledge of God aside from that which they have received under the operations of divine grace have been kind to His servants, protecting them at the risk of their own lives. The Holy Spirit is implanting the grace of Christ in the heart of many a noble seeker after truth, quickening his sympathies contrary to his nature, contrary to his former education. The "Light, which lighteth every man that cometh into the world" (John 1:9), is shining in his soul; and this Light, if heeded, will guide his feet to the kingdom of God. The prophet Micah said: "When I sit in darkness, the Lord shall be a light unto me. . . . He will bring me forth to the light, and I shall behold His righteousness." Micah 7:8, 9.

Heaven's plan of salvation is broad enough to embrace the whole world. God longs to breathe into prostrate humanity the breath of life. And He will not permit any soul to be disappointed who is sincere in his longing for something higher and nobler than anything the world can offer. Constantly He is sending His angels to those who, while surrounded by circumstances the most discouraging, pray in faith for some power higher than themselves to take possession of them and bring deliverance and peace. In various ways God will reveal Himself to them and will place them in touch with providences that will establish their confidence in the One who has given Himself a ransom for all, "that they might set their hope in God, and not forget the works of God, but keep His commandments." Psalm 78:7.

"Shall the prey be taken from the mighty, or the lawful captive delivered?" "Thus saith the Lord, Even the captives of the mighty shall be taken away, and the prey of the terrible shall be delivered." Isaiah 49:24, 25. "They shall be greatly ashamed, that trust in graven images, that say to the molten images, Ye are our gods." Isaiah 42:17.

"Happy is he that hath the God of Jacob for his help, whose hope is in the Lord his God!" Psalm 146:5. "Turn you to the stronghold, ye prisoners of hope!" Zechariah 9:12. Unto all the honest in heart in heathen lands—"the upright" in the sight of Heaven—"there ariseth light in the darkness." Psalm 112:4. God hath spoken: "I will bring the blind by a way that they knew not; I will lead them in paths that they have not known: I will make darkness light before them, and crooked things straight. These things will I do unto them, and not forsake them." Isaiah 42:16.

"I will correct thee in measure, and will not leave thee altogether unpunished." Jeremiah 30:11

Manasseh and Josiah

The kingdom of Judah, prosperous throughout the times of Hezekiah, was once more brought low during the long years of Manasseh's wicked reign, when paganism was revived, and many of the people were led into idolatry. "Manasseh made Judah and the inhabitants of Jerusalem to err, and to do worse than the heathen." 2 Chronicles 33:9. The glorious light of former generations was followed by the darkness of superstition and error. Gross evils sprang up and flourished—tyranny, oppression, hatred of all that is good. Justice was perverted; violence prevailed.

Yet those evil times were not without witnesses for God and the right. The trying experiences through which Judah had safely passed during Hezekiah's reign had developed, in the hearts of many, a sturdiness of character that now served as a bulwark against the prevailing iniquity. Their testimony in behalf of truth and righteousness aroused the anger of Manasseh and his associates in authority, who endeavored to establish themselves in evil-doing by silencing every voice of disapproval. "Manasseh shed innocent blood very much, till he had filled Jerusalem from one end to another." 2 Kings 21:16.

One of the first to fall was Isaiah, who for over half a century had stood Judah as the appointed messenger of Jehovah. "Others had trial of cruel mockings and scourgings, yea, moreover of bonds and imprisonment: they were stoned, they were sawn asunder, were tempted, were slain with the sword: they wandered about in sheepskins and goatskins; being destitute, afflicted, tormented; (of whom the world was not worthy:) they wandered in deserts, and in mountains, and in dens and caves of the earth." Hebrews 11:36-38.

Some of those who suffered persecution during Manasseh's reign were commissioned to bear special messages of reproof and of judgment. The king of Judah, the prophets declared, "hath done wickedly above all . . . which were before him." Because of this wickedness, his kingdom was nearing a crisis; soon the inhabitants of the land were to be carried captive to Babylon, there to become "a prey and a spoil to all their enemies." 2 Kings 21:11, 14. But the Lord would not utterly forsake those who in a strange land should acknowledge Him as their Ruler; they might suffer great tribulation, yet He would bring deliverance to them in His appointed time and way. Those who should put their trust wholly in Him would find a sure refuge.

Faithfully the prophets continued their warnings and their exhortations; fearlessly they spoke to Manasseh and to his people; but the messages were scorned; backsliding Judah would not heed. As an earnest of what would befall the people should they continue impenitent, the Lord permitted their king to be captured by a band of Assyrian soldiers, who "bound him with fetters, and carried him to Babylon," their temporary capital. This affliction brought the king to his senses; "he besought the Lord his God, and humbled himself greatly before the God of his fathers, and prayed unto Him: and He was entreated of him, and heard his supplication, and brought him again to Jerusalem into his kingdom. Then Manasseh knew that the Lord He was God." 2 Chronicles 33:11-13. But this repentance, remarkable though it was, came too late to save the kingdom from the corrupting influence of years of idolatrous practices. Many had stumbled and fallen, never again to rise.

Among those whose life experience had been shaped beyond recall by the fatal apostasy of Manasseh, was his own son, who came to the throne at the age of twenty-two. Of King Amon it is written: "He walked in all the way that his father walked in, and served the idols that his father served, and worshiped them: and he forsook the Lord God of his fathers" (2 Kings 21:21, 22); he "humbled not himself before the Lord, as Manasseh his father had humbled himself; but Amon trespassed more and more." The wicked king was not permitted to reign long. In the midst of his daring impiety, only two years from the time he ascended the throne, he was slain in the palace by his own servants; and "the people of the land made Josiah his son king in his stead." 2 Chronicles 33:23, 25.

With the accession of Josiah to the throne, where he was to rule for thirty-one years, those who had maintained the purity of their faith began to hope that the downward course of the kingdom was checked; for the new king, though only eight years old, feared God, and from the very beginning "he did that which was right in the sight of the Lord, and walked in all the way of David his father, and turned not aside to the right hand or to the left." 2 Kings 22:2. Born of a wicked king, beset with temptations to follow in his father's steps, and with few counselors to encourage him in the right way, Josiah nevertheless was true to the God of Israel. Warned by the errors of past generations, he chose to do right, instead of descending to the low level of sin and degradation to which his father and his grandfather had fallen. He "turned not aside

to the right hand or to the left." As one who was to occupy a position of trust, he resolved to obey the instruction that had been given for the guidance of Israel's rulers, and his obedience made it possible for God to use him as a vessel unto honor.

At the time Josiah began to rule, and for many years before, the truehearted in Judah were questioning whether God's promises to ancient Israel could ever be fulfilled. From a human point of view the divine purpose for the chosen nation seemed almost impossible of accomplishment. The apostasy of former centuries had gathered strength with the passing years; ten of the tribes had been scattered among the heathen; only the tribes of Judah and Benjamin remained, and even these now seemed on the verge of moral and national ruin. The prophets had begun to foretell the utter destruction of their fair city, where stood the temple built by Solomon, and where all their earthly hopes of national greatness had centered. Could it be that God was about to turn aside from His avowed purpose of bringing deliverance to those who should put their trust in Him? In the face of the long-continued persecution of the righteous, and of the apparent prosperity of the wicked, could those who had remained true to God hope for better days?

These anxious questionings were voiced by the prophet Habakkuk. Viewing the situation of the faithful in his day, he expressed the burden of his heart in the inquiry: "O Lord, how long shall I cry, and Thou wilt not hear! even cry out unto Thee of violence, and Thou wilt not save! Why dost Thou show me iniquity, and cause me to behold grievance? for spoiling and violence are before me: and there are that raise up strife and contention. Therefore the law is slacked, and judgment doth never go forth: for the wicked doth compass about the righteous; therefore wrong judgment proceedeth." Habakkuk 1:2-4.

God answered the cry of His loyal children. Through His chosen mouthpiece He revealed His determination to bring chastisement upon the nation that had turned from Him to serve the gods of the heathen. Within the lifetime of some who were even then making inquiry regarding the future, He would miraculously shape the affairs of the ruling nations of earth and bring the Babylonians into the ascendancy. These Chaldeans, "terrible and dreadful," were to fall suddenly upon the land of Judah as a divinely appointed scourge. Verse 7. The princes of Judah and the fairest of the people were to be carried captive to Babylon; the Judean cities and villages and the cultivated fields were to be laid waste; nothing was to be spared.

Confident that even in this terrible judgment the purpose of God for His people would in some way be fulfilled, Habakkuk bowed in submission to the revealed will of Jehovah. "Art Thou not from everlasting, O Lord my God, mine Holy One?" he exclaimed. And then, his faith reaching out beyond the forbidding prospect of the immediate future, and laying fast hold on the precious promises that reveal God's love for His trusting children, the prophet added, "We shall not die."

Verse 12. With this declaration of faith he rested his case, and that of every believing Israelite, in the hands of a compassionate God.

This was not Habakkuk's only experience in the exercise of strong faith. On one occasion, when meditating concerning the future, he said, "I will stand upon my watch, and set me upon the tower, and will watch to see what He will say unto me." Graciously the Lord answered him: "Write the vision, and make it plain upon tables, that he may run that readeth it. For the vision is yet for an appointed time, but at the end it shall speak, and not lie: though it tarry, wait for it; because it will surely come, it will not tarry. Behold, his soul which is lifted up is not upright in him: but the just shall live by his faith." Habakkuk 2:1-4.

The faith that strengthened Habakkuk and all the holy and the just in those days of deep trial was the same faith that sustains God's people today. In the darkest hours, under circumstances the most forbidding, the Christian believer may keep his soul stayed upon the source of all light and power. Day by day, through faith in God, his hope and courage may be renewed. "The just shall live by his faith." In the service of God there need be no despondency, no wavering, no fear. The Lord will more than fulfill the highest expectations of those who put their trust in Him. He will give them the wisdom their varied necessities demand.

Of the abundant provision made for every tempted soul, the apostle Paul bears eloquent testimony. To him was given the divine assurance, "My grace is sufficient for thee: for My strength is made perfect in weakness." In gratitude and confidence the tried servant of God responded: "Most gladly therefore will I rather glory in my infirmities, that the power of Christ may rest upon me. Therefore I take pleasure in infirmities, in reproaches, in necessities, in persecutions, in distresses for Christ's sake: for when I am weak, them am I strong." 2 Corinthians 12:9, 10.

We must cherish and cultivate the faith of which prophets and apostles have testified—the faith that lays hold on the promises of God and waits for deliverance in His appointed time and way. The sure word of prophecy will meet its final fulfillment in the glorious advent of our Lord and Saviour Jesus Christ, as King of kings and Lord of lords. The time of waiting may seem long, the soul may be oppressed by discouraging circumstances, many in whom confidence has been placed may fall by the way; but with the prophet who endeavored to encourage Judah in a time of unparalleled apostasy, let us confidently declare, "The Lord is in His holy temple: let all the earth keep silence before Him." Habakkuk 2:20. Let us ever hold in remembrance the cheering message, "The vision is yet for an appointed time, but at the end it shall speak, and not lie: though it tarry, wait for it; because it will surely come, it will not tarry. . . . The just shall live by his faith." Verses 3, 4.

"O Lord, revive Thy work in the midst of the years,
In the midst of the years make known;

In wrath remember mercy.
"God came from Teman,
And the Holy One from Mount Paran.
His glory covered the heavens,
And the earth was full of His praise.
And His brightness was as the light;
He had bright beams out of His side:
And there was the hiding of His power.
Before Him went the pestilence,
And burning coals went forth at His feet.
He stood, and measured the earth:
He beheld, and drove asunder the nations;
And the everlasting mountains were scattered,
The perpetual hills did bow:
His ways are everlasting."
"Thou wentest forth for the salvation of Thy people,
Even for salvation with Thine anointed."
"Although the fig tree shall not blossom,
Neither shall fruit be in the vines;
The labor of the olive shall fail,
And the fields shall yield no meat;
The flock shall be cut off from the fold,
And there shall be no herd in the stalls:
Yet I will rejoice in the Lord,
I will joy in the God of my salvation.
The Lord God is my strength."
Habakkuk 3:2-6, 13, 17-19.

Habakkuk was not the only one through whom was given a message of bright hope and of future triumph as well as of present judgment. During the reign of Josiah the word of the Lord came to Zephaniah, specifying plainly the results of continued apostasy, and calling the attention of the true church to the glorious prospect beyond. His prophecies of impending judgment upon Judah apply with equal force to the judgments that are to fall upon an impenitent world at the time of the second advent of Christ:

"The great day of the Lord is near,
It is near, and hasteth greatly,
Even the voice of the day of the Lord:
The mighty man shall cry there bitterly.
"That day is a day of wrath,
A day of trouble and distress,
A day of wasteness and desolation,
A day of darkness and gloominess,
"A day of clouds and thick darkness,
A day of the trumpet and alarm
Against the fenced cities,
And against the high towers."
Zephaniah 1:14-16.

"I will bring distress upon men, that they shall walk like blind men, because they have sinned against the Lord: and their blood shall be poured out as dust. . . . Neither their silver nor their gold shall be able to deliver them in the day of the Lord's wrath: but the whole land shall be devoured by the fire of His jealousy: for He shall make even a speedy riddance of all them that dwell in the land." Verses 17, 18.

"Gather yourselves together, yea, gather together,
O nation not desired;
Before the decree bring forth,
Before the day pass as the chaff,
Before the fierce anger of the Lord come upon you,
Before the day of the Lord's anger come upon you.
"Seek ye the Lord, all ye meek of the earth,
Which have wrought His judgment;
Seek righteousness,
Seek meekness:
It may be ye shall be hid In the day of the Lord's anger."
Zephaniah 2:1-3.

"Behold, at that time I will deal with all them that afflict thee: and I will save her that halteth, and gather her that was driven away; and I will make them a praise and a name, whose shame hath been in all the earth. At that time will I bring you in, and at that time will I gather you: for I will make you a name and a praise among all the peoples of the earth, when I bring again your captivity before your eyes, saith the Lord." Zephaniah 3:19, 20, R.V.

"Sing, O daughter of Zion; shout, O Israel;
Be glad and rejoice with all the heart,
O daughter of Jerusalem.
The Lord hath taken away thy judgments,
He hath cast out thine enemy:
The King of Israel, even the Lord,
Is in the midst of thee:
Thou shalt not see evil any more.
"In that day it shall be said to Jerusalem, Fear thou not:
And to Zion, Let not thine hands be slack.
The Lord thy God in the midst of thee Is mighty; He will save,
He will rejoice over thee with joy;
He will rest in His love,
He will joy over thee with singing."
Verses 14-17.

The Book of the Law

The silent yet powerful influences set in operation by the messages of the prophets regarding the Babylonian Captivity did much to prepare the way for a reformation that took place in the eighteenth year of Josiah's reign. This reform movement, by which threatened judgments were averted for a season, was brought about in a wholly unexpected manner through the discovery and study of a portion of Holy Scripture that for many years had been strangely misplaced and lost.

Nearly a century before, during the first Passover celebrated by Hezekiah, provision had been made for the daily public reading of the book of the law to the people by teaching priests. It was the observance of the statutes recorded by Moses, especially those given in the book of the covenant, which forms a part of Deuteronomy, that had made the reign of Hezekiah so prosperous. But Manasseh had dared set aside these statutes; and during his reign the temple copy of the book of the law, through careless neglect, had become lost. Thus for many years the people generally were deprived of its instruction.

The long-lost manuscript was found in the temple by Hilkiah, the high priest, while the building was undergoing extensive repairs in harmony with King Josiah's plan for the preservation of the sacred structure. The high priest handed the precious volume to Shaphan, a learned scribe, who read it and then took it to the king with the story of its discovery.

Josiah was deeply stirred as he heard read for the first time the exhortations and warnings recorded in this ancient manuscript. Never before had he realized so fully the plainness with which God had set before Israel "life and death, blessing and cursing" (Deuteronomy 30:19): and how repeatedly they had been urged to choose the way of life, that they might become a praise in the earth, a blessing to all nations. "Be strong and of a good courage, fear not, nor be afraid," Israel had been exhorted through Moses; "for the Lord thy God. He it is that doth go with thee; He will not fail thee, not forsake thee." Deuteronomy 31:6.

The book abounded in assurances of God's willingness to save to the uttermost those who should place their trust fully in Him. As He had wrought in their deliverance from Egyptian bondage, so would He work mightily in establishing them in the Land of Promise and in placing them at the head of the nations of earth.

The encouragements offered as the reward of obedience were accompanied by prophecies of judgments against the disobedient; and as the king heard the inspired words, he recognized, in the picture set before him, conditions that were similar to those actually existing in his kingdom. In connection with these prophetic portrayals of departure from God, he was startled to find plain statements to the effect that the day of calamity would follow swiftly and that there would be no remedy. The language was plain; there could be no mistaking the meaning of the words. And at the close of the volume, in a summary of God's dealings with Israel and a rehearsal of the events of the future, these matters were made doubly plain. In the hearing of all Israel, Moses had declared:

"Give ear, O ye heavens, and I will speak;
And hear, O earth, the words of my mouth.
My doctrine shall drop as the rain,
My speech shall distill as the dew,
As the small rain upon the tender herb,
And as the showers upon the grass:
Because I will publish the name of the Lord:

Ascribe ye greatness unto our God.
He is the Rock, His work is perfect:
For all His ways are judgment:
A God of truth and without iniquity,
Just and right is He."
Deuteronomy 32:1-4.
"Remember the days of old,
Consider the years of many generations:
Ask thy father, and he will show thee;
Thy elders, and they will tell thee.
When the Most High divided to the nations their inheritance,
When He separated the sons of Adam,
He set the bounds of the people
According to the number of the children of Israel.
For the Lord's portion is His people;
Jacob is the lot of His inheritance.
He found him in a desert land,
And in the waste howling wilderness;
He led him about, He instructed him,
He kept him as the apple of His eye."
Verses 7-10.
But Israel "forsook God which made him,
And lightly esteemed the Rock of his salvation.
They provoked Him to jealousy with strange gods,
With abominations provoked they Him to anger.
They sacrificed unto devils, not to God;
To gods whom they knew not,
To new gods that came newly up,
Whom your fathers feared not.
Of the Rock that begat thee thou art unmindful,
And hast forgotten God that formed thee.
"And when the Lord saw it, He abhorred them,
Because of the provoking of His sons, and of His daughters.
And He said, I will hide My face from them,
I will see what their end shall be:
For they are a very froward generation,
Children in whom is no faith.
They have moved Me to jealousy with that which is not God; They have provoked Me to anger with their vanities:
And I will move them to jealousy with those which are not a people;
I will provoke them to anger with a foolish nation."
"I will heap mischiefs upon them;
I will spend Mine arrows upon them.
They shall be burnt with hunger, and devoured with burning heat,
And with bitter destruction."
"For they are a nation void of counsel,
Neither is there any understanding in them.
O that they were wise, that they understood this,
That they would consider their latter end!
How should one chase a thousand,
And two put ten thousand to flight,
Except their rock had sold them,

And the Lord had shut them up?
For their rock is not as our Rock,
Even our enemies themselves being judges."
"Is not this laid up in store with Me,
And sealed up among My treasures?
To Me belongeth vengeance, and recompense;
Their foot shall slide in due time:
For the day of their calamity is at hand,
And the things that shall come upon them make haste."
Verses 15:21, 23, 24, 28-31, 34, 35 .

These and similar passages revealed to Josiah God's love for His people and His abhorrence of sin. As the king read the prophecies of swift judgment upon those who should persist in rebellion, he trembled for the future. The perversity of Judah had been great; what was to be the outcome of their continued apostasy?

In former years the king had not been indifferent to the prevailing idolatry. "In the eighth year of his reign, while he was yet young," he had consecrated himself fully to the service of God. Four years later, at the age of twenty, he had made an earnest effort to remove temptation from his subjects by purging "Judah and Jerusalem from the high places, and the groves, and the carved images, and the molten images." "They brake down the altars of Baalim in his presence; and the images, that were on high above them, he cut down; and the groves, and the carved images, and the molten images, he brake in pieces, and made dust of them, and strowed it upon the graves of them that had sacrificed unto them. And he burnt the bones of the priests upon their altars, and cleansed Judah and Jerusalem." 2 Chronicles 34:3-5.

Not content with doing thorough work in the land of Judah, the youthful ruler had extended his efforts to the portions of Palestine formerly occupied by the ten tribes of Israel, only a feeble remnant of which now remained. "So did he," the record reads, "in the cities of Manasseh, and Ephraim, and Simeon, even unto Naphtali." Not until he had traversed the length and breadth of this region of ruined homes, and "had broken down the altars and the groves, and had beaten the graven images into powder, and cut down all the idols throughout all the land of Israel," did he return to Jerusalem. Verses 6,7.

Thus Josiah, from his earliest manhood, had endeavored to take advantage of his position as king to exalt to principles of God's holy law. And now, while Shaphan the scribe was reading to him out of the book of the law, the king discerned in this volume a treasure of knowledge, a powerful ally, in the work of reform he so much desired to see wrought in the land. He resolved to walk in the light of its counsels, and also to do all in his power to acquaint his people with its teachings and to lead them, if possible, to cultivate reverence and love for the law of heaven.

But was it possible to bring about the needed reform? Israel had almost reached the limit of divine forbearance; soon God would arise to punish those who had brought dishonor upon

His name. Already the anger of the Lord was kindled against the people. Overwhelmed with sorrow and dismay, Josiah rent his garments and bowed before God in agony of spirit, seeking pardon for the sins of an impenitent nation.

At that time the prophetess Huldah was living in Jerusalem, near the temple. The mind of the king, filled with anxious foreboding, reverted to her, and he determined to inquire of the Lord through this chosen messenger to learn, if possible, whether by any means within his power he might save erring Judah, now on the verge of ruin.

The gravity of the situation and the respect in which he held the prophetess led him to choose as his messengers to her the first men of the kingdom. "Go ye," he bade them, "inquire of the Lord for me, and for the people, and for all Judah, concerning the words of this book that is found: for great is the wrath of the Lord that is kindled against us, because our fathers have not hearkened unto the words of this book, to do according unto all that which is written concerning us." 2 Kings 22:13.

Through Huldah the Lord sent Josiah word that Jerusalem's ruin could not be averted. Even should the people now humble themselves before God, they could not escape their punishment. So long had their senses been deadened by wrongdoing that, if judgment should not come upon them, they would soon return to the same sinful course. "Tell the man that sent you to me," the prophetess declared, "Thus saith the Lord, Behold, I will bring evil upon this place, and upon the inhabitants thereof, even all the words of the book which the king of Judah hath read: because they have forsaken Me, and have burned incense unto other gods, that they might provoke Me to anger with all the works of their hands; therefore My wrath shall be kindled against this place, and shall not be quenched." Verses 15-17.

But because the king had humbled his heart before God, the Lord would acknowledge his promptness in seeking forgiveness and mercy. To him was sent the message: "Because thine heart was tender, and thou hast humbled thyself before the Lord, when thou heardest what I spake against this place, and against the inhabitants thereof, that they should become a desolation and a curse, and hast rent thy clothes, and wept before Me; I also have heard thee, saith the Lord. Behold therefore, I will gather thee unto thy fathers, and thou shalt be gathered into thy grave in peace; and thine eyes shall not see all the evil which I will bring upon this place." Verses 19, 20.

The king must leave with God the events of the future; he could not alter the eternal decrees of Jehovah. But in announcing the retributive judgments of Heaven, the Lord had not withdrawn opportunity for repentance and reformation; and Josiah, discerning in this a willingness on the part of God to temper His judgments with mercy, determined to do all in his power to bring about decided reforms. He arranged at once for a great convocation, to which were invited the elders and magistrates in Jerusalem and Judah, together with the common people. These, with the priests and Levites, met the king in the court of the temple.

To this vast assembly the king himself read "all the words of the book of the covenant which was found in the house of the Lord." 2 Kings 23:2. The royal reader was deeply affected, and he delivered his message with the pathos of a broken heart. His hearers were profoundly moved. The intensity of feeling revealed in the countenance of the king, the solemnity of the message itself, the warning of judgments impending—all these had their effect, and many determined to join with the king in seeking forgiveness.

Josiah now proposed that those highest in authority unite with the people in solemnly covenanting before God to co-operate with one another in an effort to institute decided changes. "The king stood by a pillar, and made a covenant before the Lord, to walk after the Lord, and to keep His commandments and His testimonies and His statutes with all their heart and all their soul, to perform the words of this covenant that were written in this book." The response was more hearty than the king had dared hope for: "All the people stood to the covenant." Verse 3.

In the reformation that followed, the king turned his attention to the destruction of every vestige of idolatry that remained. So long had the inhabitants of the land followed the customs of the surrounding nations in bowing down to images of wood and stone, that it seemed almost beyond the power of man to remove every trace of these evils. But Josiah persevered in his effort to cleanse the land. Sternly he met idolatry by slaying "all the priests of the high places;" "moreover the workers with familiar spirits, and the wizards, and the images, and the idols, and all the abominations that were spied in the land of Judah and in Jerusalem, did Josiah put away, that he might perform the words of the law which were written in the book that Hilkiah the priest found in the house of the Lord." Verses 20, 24.

In the days of the rending of the kingdom, centuries before, when Jeroboam the son of Nebat, in bold defiance of the God whom Israel had served, was endeavoring to turn the hearts of the people away from the services of the temple in Jerusalem to new forms of worship, he had set up an unconsecrated altar at Bethel. During the dedication of this altar, where many in years to come were to be seduced into idolatrous practices, there had suddenly appeared a man of God from Judea, with words of condemnation for the sacrilegious proceedings. He had "cried against the altar," declaring:

"O altar, altar, thus saith the Lord; Behold, a child shall be born unto the house of David, Josiah by name; and upon thee shall he offer the priests of the high places that burn incense upon thee, and men's bones shall be burnt upon thee." 1 Kings 13:2. This announcement had been accompanied by a sign that the word spoken was of the Lord.

Three centuries had passed. During the reformation wrought by Josiah, the king found himself in Bethel, where stood this ancient altar. The prophecy uttered so many years before in the presence of Jeroboam, was now to be literally fulfilled. "The altar that was at Bethel, and the high place which

Jeroboam the son of Nebat, who made Israel to sin, had made, both that altar and the high place he brake down, and burned the high place, and stamped it small to powder, and burned the grove.

"And as Josiah turned himself, he spied the sepulchers that were there in the mount, and sent, and took the bones out of the sepulchers, and burned them upon the altar, and polluted it, according to the word of the Lord which the man of God proclaimed, who proclaimed these words.

"Then he said, What title is that that I see? And the men of the city told him, It is the sepulcher of the man of God, which came from Judah, and proclaimed these things that thou hast done against the altar of Bethel. And he said, Let him alone; let no man move his bones. So they let his bones alone, with the bones of the prophet that came out of Samaria." 2 Kings 23:15-18.

On the southern slopes of Olivet, opposite the beautiful temple of Jehovah on Mount Moriah, were the shrines and images that had been placed there by Solomon to please his idolatrous wives. See 1 Kings 11:6-8. For upwards of three centuries the great, misshapen images had stood on the "Mount of Offense," mute witnesses to the apostasy of Israel's wisest king. These, too, were removed and destroyed by Josiah.

The king sought further to establish the faith of Judah in the God of their fathers by holding a great Passover feast, in harmony with the provisions made in the book of the law. Preparation was made by those having the sacred services in charge, and on the great day of the feast, offerings were freely made. "There was not holden such a Passover from the days of the judges that judged Israel, nor in all the days of the kings of Israel, nor of the kings of Judah." 2 Kings 23:22. But the zeal of Josiah, acceptable though it was to God, could not atone for the sins of past generations; nor could the piety displayed by the king's followers effect a change of heart in many who stubbornly refused to turn from idolatry to the worship of the true God.

For more than a decade following the celebration of the Passover, Josiah continued to reign. At the age of thirty-nine he met death in battle with the forces of Egypt, "and was buried in one of the sepulchers of his fathers." "All Judah and Jerusalem mourned for Josiah. And Jeremiah lamented for Josiah: and all the singing men and the singing women spake of Josiah in their lamentations to this day, and made them an ordinance in Israel: and, behold, they are written in the lamentations." 2 Chronicles 35:24, 25. Like unto Josiah "was there no king before him, that turned to the Lord with all his heart, and with all his soul, and with all his might, according to all the law of Moses; neither after him arose there any like him. Notwithstanding the Lord turned not from the fierceness of His great wrath, . . . because of all the provocations that Manasseh had provoked Him withal." 2 Kings 23:25, 26. The time was rapidly approaching when Jerusalem was to be utterly destroyed and the inhabitants of the land carried captive to Babylon, there to learn the lessons they had refused to learn under circumstances more favorable.

Jeremiah

Among those who had hoped for a permanent spiritual revival as the result of the reformation under Josiah was Jeremiah, called of God to the prophetic office while still a youth, in the thirteenth year of Josiah's reign. A member of the Levitical priesthood, Jeremiah had been trained from childhood for holy service. In those happy years of preparation he little realized that he had been ordained from birth to be "a prophet unto the nations;" and when the divine call came, he was overwhelmed with a sense of his unworthiness. "Ah, Lord God!" he exclaimed, "behold, I cannot speak: for I am a child." Jeremiah 1:5, 6.

In the youthful Jeremiah, God saw one who would be true to his trust and who would stand for the right against great opposition. In childhood he had proved faithful; and now he was to endure hardness, as a good soldier of the cross. "Say not, I am a child," the Lord bade His chosen messenger; "for thou shalt go to all that I shall send thee, and whatsoever I command thee thou shalt speak. Be not afraid of their faces: for I am with thee to deliver thee." "Gird up thy loins, and arise, and speak unto them all that I command thee: be not dismayed at their faces, lest I confound thee before them. For, behold, I have made thee this day a defensed city, and an iron pillar, and brazen walls against the whole land, against the kings of Judah, against the princes thereof, against the priests thereof, and against the people of the land. And they shall fight against thee; but they shall not prevail against thee; for I am with thee, saith the Lord, to deliver thee." Verses 7, 8, 17-19.

For forty years Jeremiah was to stand before the nation as a witness for truth and righteousness. In a time of unparalleled apostasy he was to exemplify in life and character the worship of the only true God. During the terrible sieges of Jerusalem he was to be the mouthpiece of Jehovah. He was to predict the downfall of the house of David and the destruction of the beautiful temple built by Solomon. And when imprisoned because of his fearless utterances, he was still to speak plainly against sin in high places. Despised, hated, rejected of men, he was finally to witness the literal fulfillment of his own prophecies of impending doom, and share in the sorrow and woe that should follow the destruction of the fated city.

Yet amid the general ruin into which the nation was rapidly passing, Jeremiah was often permitted to look beyond the distressing scenes of the present to the glorious prospects of the future, when God's people should be ransomed from the land of the enemy and planted again in Zion. He foresaw the time when the Lord would renew His covenant relationship with them. "Their soul shall be as a watered garden; and they shall not sorrow any more at all." Jeremiah 31:12.

Of his call to the prophetic mission, Jeremiah himself wrote: "The Lord put forth His hand, and touched my mouth. And the Lord said unto me, Behold, I have put My words in thy mouth. See, I have this day set thee over the nations and over the kingdoms, to root out, and to pull down, and to destroy, and to throw down, to build, and to plant." Jeremiah 1:9, 10.

Thank God for the words, "to build, and to plant." By these words Jeremiah was assured of the Lord's purpose to restore and to heal. Stern were the messages to be borne in the years that were to follow. Prophecies of swift-coming judgments were to be fearlessly delivered. From the plains of Shinar "an evil" was to "break forth upon all the inhabitants of the land." "I will utter My judgments against them," the Lord declared, "touching all their wickedness, who have forsaken Me." Verses 14, 16. Yet the prophet was to accompany these messages with assurances of forgiveness to all who should turn from their evil-doing.

As a wise master builder, Jeremiah at the very beginning of his lifework sought to encourage the men of Judah to lay the foundations of their spiritual life broad and deep, by making thorough work of repentance. Long had they been building with material likened by the apostle Paul to wood, hay, and stubble, and by Jeremiah himself to dross. "Refuse silver shall men call them," he declared of the impenitent nation, "because the Lord hath rejected them." Jeremiah 6:30, margin. Now they were urged to begin building wisely and for eternity, casting aside the rubbish of apostasy and unbelief, and using as foundation material the pure gold, the refined silver, the precious stones—faith and obedience and good works—which alone are acceptable in the sight of a holy God.

Through Jeremiah the word of the Lord to His people was: "Return, thou backsliding Israel, . . . and I will not cause Mine anger to fall upon you: for I am merciful, saith the Lord, and I will not keep anger forever. Only acknowledge thine iniquity, that thou hast transgressed against the Lord thy God. . . . Turn, O backsliding children, saith the Lord; for I am married unto you." "Thou shalt call Me, My Father; and shalt not turn away from Me." "Return, ye backsliding children, and I will heal your backslidings." Jeremiah 3:12-14, 19, 22.

And in addition to these wonderful pleadings, the Lord gave His erring people the very words with which they might turn to Him. They were to say: "Behold, we come unto Thee; for Thou art the Lord our God. Truly in vain is salvation hoped for from the hills, and from the multitude of mountains: truly in the Lord our God is the salvation of Israel. . . . We lie down in our shame, and our confusion covereth us: for we have sinned against the Lord our God, we and our fathers, from our youth even unto this day, and have not obeyed the voice of the Lord our God." Verses 22-25.

The reformation under Josiah had cleansed the land of the idolatrous shrines, but the hearts of the multitude had not been transformed. The seeds of truth that had sprung up and given promise of an abundant harvest had been choked by thorns. Another such backsliding would be fatal; and the Lord sought to arouse the nation to a realization of their danger. Only as they should prove loyal to Jehovah could they hope for the divine favor and for prosperity.

Jeremiah called their attention repeatedly to the counsels given in Deuteronomy. More than any other of the prophets, he emphasized the teachings of the Mosaic law and showed how these might bring the highest spiritual blessing to the nation and to every individual heart. "Ask for the old paths, where is the good way, and walk therein," he pleaded, "and ye shall find rest for your souls." Jeremiah 6:16.

On one occasion, by command of the Lord, the prophet took his position at one of the principal entrances to the city and there urged the importance of keeping holy the Sabbath day. The inhabitants of Jerusalem were in danger of losing sight of the sanctity of the Sabbath, and they were solemnly warned against following their secular pursuits on that day. A blessing was promised on condition of obedience. "If ye diligently hearken unto Me," the Lord declared, and "hallow the Sabbath day, to do no work therein; then shall there enter into the gates of this city kings and princes sitting upon the throne of David, riding in chariots and on horses, they, and their princes, the men of Judah, and the inhabitants of Jerusalem: and this city shall remain forever." Jeremiah 17:24, 25.

This promise of prosperity as the reward of allegiance was accompanied by a prophecy of the terrible judgments that would befall the city should its inhabitants prove disloyal to God and His law. If the admonitions to obey the Lord God of their fathers and to hallow His Sabbath day were not heeded, the city and its palaces would be utterly destroyed by fire.

Thus the prophet stood firmly for the sound principles of right living so clearly outlined in the book of the law. But the conditions prevailing in the land of Judah were such that only by the most decided measures could a change for the better be brought about; therefore he labored most earnestly in behalf of the impenitent. "Break up your fallow ground," he pleaded, "and sow not among thorns." "O Jerusalem, wash thine heart from wickedness, that thou mayest be saved." Jeremiah 4:3, 14. But by the great mass of the people the call to repentance and reformation was unheeded. Since the death of good King Josiah, those who ruled the nation had been proving untrue to their trust and had been leading many astray. Jehoahaz, deposed by the interference of the king of Egypt, had been followed by Jehoiakim, an older son of Josiah. From the beginning of Jehoiakim's reign, Jeremiah had little hope of saving his beloved land from destruction and the people from captivity. Yet he was not permitted to remain silent while utter ruin threatened the kingdom. Those who had remained loyal to God must be encouraged to persevere in rightdoing, and sinners must, if possible, be induced to turn from iniquity.

The crisis demanded a public and far-reaching effort. Jeremiah was commanded by the Lord to stand in the court of the temple and speak to all the people of Judah who might pass in and out. From the messages given him he must diminish not a word, that sinners in Zion might have the fullest possible opportunity to hearken and to turn from their evil ways.

The prophet obeyed; he stood in the gate of the Lord's house and there lifted his voice in warning and entreaty.

Under the inspiration of the Almighty he declared:

"Hear the word of the Lord, all ye of Judah, that enter in at these gates to worship the Lord. Thus saith the Lord of hosts, the God of Israel, Amend your ways and your doings, and I will cause you to dwell in this place. Trust ye not in lying words, saying, The temple of the Lord, The temple of the Lord, The temple of the Lord, are these. For if ye thoroughly amend your ways and your doings; if ye thoroughly execute judgment between a man and his neighbor; if ye oppress not the stranger, the fatherless, and the widow, and shed not innocent blood in this place, neither walk after other gods to your hurt: then will I cause you to dwell in this place, in the land that I gave to your fathers, forever and ever." Jeremiah 7:2-7.

The unwillingness of the Lord to chastise is here vividly shown. He stays His judgments that He may plead with the impenitent. He who exercises "loving-kindness, judgment, and righteousness, in the earth" yearns over His erring children; in every way possible He seeks to teach them the way of life everlasting. Jeremiah 9:24. He had brought the Israelites out of bondage that they might serve Him, the only true and living God. Though they had wandered long in idolatry and had slighted His warnings, yet He now declares His willingness to defer chastisement and grant yet another opportunity for repentance. He makes plain the fact that only by the most thorough heart reformation could the impending doom be averted. In vain would be the trust they might place in the temple and its services. Rites and ceremonies could not atone for sin. Notwithstanding their claim to be the chosen people of God, reformation of heart and of the life practice alone could save them from the inevitable result of continued transgression.

Thus it was that "in the cities of Judah, and in the streets of Jerusalem" the message of Jeremiah to Judah was, "Hear ye the words of this covenant,"—the plain precepts of Jehovah as recorded in the Sacred Scriptures,—"and do them." Jeremiah 11:6. And this is the message he proclaimed as he stood in the temple courts in the beginning of the reign of Jehoiakim.

Israel's experience from the days of the Exodus was briefly reviewed. God's covenant with them had been, "Obey My voice, and I will be your God, and ye shall be My people: and walk ye in all the ways that I have commanded you, that it may be well unto you." Shamelessly and repeatedly had this covenant been broken. The chosen nation had "walked in the counsels and in the imagination of their evil heart, and went backward, and not forward." Jeremiah 7:23, 24.

"Why," the Lord inquired, "is this people of Jerusalem slidden back by a perpetual backsliding?" Jeremiah 8:5. In the language of the prophet it was because they had obeyed not the voice of the Lord their God and had refused to be corrected. See Jeremiah 5:3. "Truth is perished," he mourned, "and is cut off from their mouth." "The stork in the heaven knoweth her appointed times; and the turtle and the crane and the swallow observe the time of their coming; but My people know not the judgment of the Lord." "Shall I not visit them for these things? saith the Lord: shall not My soul be avenged on such a nation as this?" Jeremiah 7:28; 8:7; 9:9.

The time had come for deep heart searching. While Josiah had been their ruler, the people had had some ground for hope. But no longer could he intercede in their behalf, for he had fallen in battle. The sins of the nation were such that the time for intercession had all but passed by. "Though Moses and Samuel stood before Me," the Lord declared, "yet My mind could not be toward this people: cast them out of My sight, and let them go forth. And it shall come to pass, if they say unto thee, Whither shall we go forth? then thou shalt tell them. Thus saith the Lord; Such as are for death, to death; and such as are for the sword, to the sword; and such as are for the famine, to the famine; and such as are for the captivity, to the captivity." Jeremiah 15:1, 2.

A refusal to heed the invitation of mercy that God was now offering would bring upon the impenitent nation the judgments that had befallen the northern kingdom of Israel over a century before. The message to them now was: "If ye will not hearken to Me, to walk in My law, which I have set before you, to hearken to the words of My servants the prophets, whom I sent unto you, both rising up early, and sending them, but ye have not hearkened; then will I make this house like Shiloh, and will make this city a curse to all the nations of the earth." Jeremiah 26:4-6. Those who stood in the temple court listening to Jeremiah's discourse understood clearly this reference to Shiloh, and to the time in the days of Eli when the Philistines had overcome Israel and carried away the ark of the testament.

The sin of Eli had consisted in passing lightly over the iniquity of his sons in sacred office, and over the evils prevailing throughout the land. His neglect to correct these evils had brought upon Israel a fearful calamity. His sons had fallen in battle, Eli himself had lost his life, the ark of God had been taken from the land of Israel, thirty thousand of the people had been slain—and all because sin had been allowed to flourish unrebuked and unchecked. Israel had vainly thought that, notwithstanding their sinful practices, the presence of the ark would ensure them victory over the Philistines. In like manner, during the days of Jeremiah, the inhabitants of Judah were prone to believe that a strict observance of the divinely appointed services of the temple would preserve them from a just punishment for their wicked course.

What a lesson is this to men holding positions of responsibility today in the church of God! What a solemn warning to deal faithfully with wrongs that bring dishonor to the cause of truth! Let none who claim to be the depositaries of God's law flatter themselves that the regard they may outwardly show toward the commandments will preserve them from the exercise of divine justice. Let none refuse to be reproved for evil, nor charge the servants of God with being too zealous in endeavoring to cleanse the camp from evil-doing. A sin-hating God calls upon those who claim to keep His law to depart from all iniquity. A neglect to repent and to render willing obedience will bring upon men and women today as serious consequences as came upon ancient Israel. There is a limit beyond which the judgments of Jehovah can no longer be delayed. The desolation of Jerusalem in the days of Jeremiah is a solemn warning to modern Israel, that the counsels and admonitions given them through chosen instrumentalities cannot be disregarded with impunity.

Jeremiah's message to priests and people aroused the antagonism of many. With boisterous denunciation they cried out, "Why hast thou prophesied in the name of the Lord, saying, This house shall be like Shiloh, and this city shall be desolate without an inhabitant? And all the people were gathered against Jeremiah in the house of the Lord." Jeremiah 26:9. Priests, false prophets, and people turned in wrath upon him who would not speak to them smooth things or prophesy deceit. Thus was the message of God despised, and His servant threatened with death.

Tidings of the words of Jeremiah were carried to the princes of Judah, and they hastened from the palace of the king to the temple, to learn for themselves the truth of the matter. "Then spake the priests and the prophets unto the princes and to all the people, saying, This man is worthy to die; for he hath prophesied against this city, as ye have heard with your ears." Verse 11. But Jeremiah stood boldly before the princes and the people, declaring: "The Lord sent me to prophesy against this house and against this city all the words that ye have heard. Therefore now amend your ways and your doings, and obey the voice of the Lord your God; and the Lord will repent Him of the evil that He hath pronounced against you. As for me, behold, I am in your hand: do with me as seemeth good and meet unto you. But know ye for certain, that if ye put me to death, ye shall surely bring innocent blood upon yourselves, and upon this city, and upon the inhabitants thereof: for of a truth the Lord hath sent me unto you to speak all these words in your ears." Verses 12-15.

Had the prophet been intimidated by the threatening attitude of those high in authority, his message would have been without effect, and he would have lost his life; but the courage with which he delivered the solemn warning commanded the respect of the people and turned the princes of Israel in his favor. They reasoned with the priests and false prophets, showing them how unwise would be the extreme measures they advocated, and their words produced a reaction in the minds of the people. Thus God raised up defenders for His servant.

The elders also united in protesting against the decision of the priests regarding the fate of Jeremiah. They cited the case of Micah, who had prophesied judgments upon Jerusalem, saying, "Zion shall be plowed like a field, and Jerusalem shall become heaps, and the mountain of the house as the high places of a forest." And they asked: "Did Hezekiah king of Judah and all Judah put him at all to death? did he not fear the Lord, and besought the Lord, and the Lord repented Him of the evil which He had pronounced against them? Thus

might we procure great evil against our souls." Verses 18, 19.

Through the pleading of these men of influence the prophet's life was spared, although many of the priests and false prophets, unable to endure the condemning truths he uttered, would gladly have seen him put to death on the plea of sedition.

From the day of his call to the close of his ministry, Jeremiah stood before Judah as "a tower and a fortress" against which the wrath of man could not prevail. "They shall fight against thee," the Lord had forewarned His servant, "but they shall not prevail against thee: for I am with thee to save thee and to deliver thee, saith the Lord. And I will deliver thee out of the hand of the wicked, and I will redeem thee out of the hand of the terrible." Jeremiah 6:27; 15:20, 21.

Naturally of a timid and shrinking disposition, Jeremiah longed for the peace and quiet of a life of retirement, where he need not witness the continued impenitence of his beloved nation. His heart was wrung with anguish over the ruin wrought by sin. "O that my head were waters, and mine eyes a fountain of tears," he mourned, "that I might weep day and night for the slain of the daughter of my people! O that I had in the wilderness a lodging place of wayfaring men; that I might leave my people, and go from them." Jeremiah 9:1, 2.

Cruel were the mockings he was called upon to endure. His sensitive soul was pierced through and through by the arrows of derision hurled at him by those who despised his messages and made light of his burden for their conversion. "I was a derision to all my people," he declared, "and their song all the day." "I am in derision daily, everyone mocketh me." "All my familiars watched for my halting, saying, Peradventure he will be enticed, and we shall prevail against him, and we shall take our revenge on him." Lamentations 3:14; Jeremiah 20:7, 10.

But the faithful prophet was daily strengthened to endure. "The Lord is with me as a mighty terrible One," he declared in faith; "therefore my persecutors shall stumble, and they shall not prevail: they shall be really ashamed; for they shall not prosper: their everlasting confusion shall never be forgotten." "Sing unto the Lord, praise ye the Lord: for He hath delivered the soul of the poor from the hand of evildoers." Jeremiah 20:11, 13.

The experiences through which Jeremiah passed in the days of his youth and also in the later years of his ministry, taught him the lesson that "the way of man is not in self: it is not in man that walketh to direct his steps." He learned to pray, "O Lord, correct me, but with judgment; not in Thine anger, lest Thou bring me nothing." Jeremiah 10:23, 24.

When called to drink of the cup of tribulation and sorrow, and when tempted in his misery to say, "My strength and my hope is perished from the Lord," he recalled the providences of God in his behalf and triumphantly exclaimed, "It is of the Lord's mercies that we are not consumed, because His compassions fail not. They are new every morning: great is Thy faithfulness. The Lord is my portion, saith my soul; therefore will I hope in Him. The Lord is good unto them that wait for Him, to the soul that seeketh Him. It is good that a man should both hope and quietly wait for the salvation of the Lord." Lamentations 3:18, 22-26.

Approaching Doom

The first years of Jehoiakim's reign were filled with warnings of approaching doom. The word of the Lord spoken by the prophets was about to be fulfilled. The Assyrian power to the northward, long supreme, was no longer to rule the nations. Egypt on the south, in whose power the king of Judah was vainly placing his trust, was soon to receive a decided check. All unexpectedly a new world power, the Babylonian Empire, was rising to the eastward and swiftly overshadowing all other nations.

Within a few short years the king of Babylon was to be used as the instrument of God's wrath upon impenitent Judah. Again and again Jerusalem was to be invested and entered by the besieging armies of Nebuchadnezzar. Company after company—at first a few only, but later on thousands and tens of thousands—were to be taken captive to the land of Shinar, there to dwell in enforced exile. Jehoiakim, Jehoiachin, Zedekiah—all these Jewish kings were in turn to become vassals of the Babylonian ruler, and all in turn were to rebel. Severer and yet more severe chastisements were to be inflicted upon the rebellious nation, until at last the entire land was to become a desolation, Jerusalem was to be laid waste and burned with fire, the temple that Solomon had built was to be destroyed, and the kingdom of Judah was to fall, never again to occupy its former position among the nations of earth.

Those times of change, so fraught with peril to the Israelitish nation, were marked with many messages from Heaven through Jeremiah. Thus the Lord gave the children of Judah ample opportunity of freeing themselves from entangling alliances with Egypt, and of avoiding controversy with the rulers of Babylon. As the threatened danger came closer, he taught the people by means of a series of acted parables, hoping thus to arouse them to a sense of their obligation to God, and also to encourage them to maintain friendly relations with the Babylonian government.

To illustrate the importance of yielding implicit obedience to the requirements of God, Jeremiah gathered some Rechabites into one of the chambers of the temple and set wine before them, inviting them to drink. As was to have been expected, he met with remonstrance and absolute refusal. "We will drink no wine," the Rechabites firmly declared, "for Jonadab the son of Rechab our father commanded us, saying, Ye shall drink no wine, neither ye, nor your sons forever."

"Then came the word of the Lord unto Jeremiah, saying, Thus saith the Lord of hosts, the God of Israel; Go and tell the men of Judah and the inhabitants of Jerusalem, Will ye not receive instruction to hearken to My words? saith the Lord. The words of Jonadab the son of Rechab, that he commanded his sons not to drink wine, are performed; for unto this day they drink none, but obey their father's commandment." Jeremiah 35:6, 12-14.

God sought thus to bring into sharp contrast the obedience of the Rechabites with the disobedience and rebellion of His people. The Rechabites had obeyed the command of their father and now refused to be enticed into transgression. But the men of Judah had hearkened not to the words of the Lord, and were in consequence about to suffer His severest judgments.

"I have spoken unto you, rising early and speaking," the Lord declared, "but ye hearkened not unto Me. I have sent also unto you all My servants the prophets, rising up early and sending them, saying, Return ye now every man from his evil way, and amend your doings, and go not after other gods to serve them, and ye shall dwell in the land which I have given to you and to your fathers: but ye have not inclined your ear, nor hearkened unto Me. Because the sons of Jonadab the son of Rechab have performed the commandment of their father, which he commanded them; but this people hath not hearkened unto Me: therefore thus saith the Lord God of hosts, the God of Israel; Behold, I will bring upon Judah and upon all the inhabitants of Jerusalem all the evil that I have pronounced against them: because I have spoken unto them, but they have not heard; and I have called unto them, but they have not answered." Verses 14-17.

When men's hearts are softened and subdued by the constraining influence of the Holy Spirit, they will give heed to counsel; but when they turn from admonition until their hearts become hardened, the Lord permits them to be led by other influences. Refusing the truth, they accept falsehood, which becomes a snare to their own destruction.

God had pleaded with Judah not to provoke Him to anger, but they had hearkened not. Finally sentence was pronounced against them. They were to be led away captive to Babylon. The Chaldeans were to be used as the instrument by which God would chastise His disobedient people. The sufferings of the men of Judah were to be in proportion to the light they had had and to the warnings they had despised and rejected. Long had God delayed His judgments, but now He would visit His displeasure upon them as a last effort to check them in their evil course.

Upon the house of the Rechabites was pronounced a continued blessing. The prophet declared, "Because ye have obeyed the commandment of Jonadab your father, and kept all his precepts, and done according unto all that he hath commanded you: therefore thus saith the Lord of hosts, the God of Israel; Jonadab the son of Rechab shall not want a man to stand before Me forever." Verses 18, 19. Thus God taught His people that faithfulness and obedience would be reflected back upon Judah in blessing, even as the Rechabites were blessed for obedience to their father's command.

The lesson is for us. If the requirements of a good and wise father, who took the best and most effectual means to secure his posterity against the evils of intemperance, were worthy of strict obedience, surely God's authority should be held in as much greater reverence as He is holier than man. Our Creator and our Commander, infinite in power, terrible in judgment, seeks by every means to bring men to see and repent of their sins. By the mouth of His servants He predicts the dangers of disobedience; He sounds the note of warning and faithfully reproves sin. His people are kept in prosperity only by His mercy, through the vigilant watchcare of chosen instrumentalities. He cannot uphold and guard a people who reject His counsel and despise His reproofs. For a time He may withhold His retributive judgments; yet He cannot always stay His hand.

The children of Judah were numbered among those of whom God had declared, "Ye shall be unto Me a kingdom of priests, and an holy nation." Exodus 19:6. Never did Jeremiah in his ministry lose sight of the vital importance of heart holiness in the varied relationships of life, and especially in the service of the most high God. Plainly he foresaw the downfall of the kingdom and a scattering of the inhabitants of Judah among the nations; but with the eye of faith he looked beyond all this to the times of restoration. Ringing in his ears was the divine promise: "I will gather the remnant of My flock out of all countries whither I have driven them, and will bring them again to their folds. . . . Behold, the days come, saith the Lord, that I will raise unto David a righteous Branch, and a King shall reign and prosper, and shall execute judgment and justice in the earth. In His days Judah shall be saved, and Israel shall dwell safely: and this is His name whereby He shall be called, THE LORD OUR RIGHTEOUSNESS." Jeremiah 23:3-6.

Thus prophecies of oncoming judgment were mingled with promises of final and glorious deliverance. Those who should choose to make their peace with God and live holy lives amid the prevailing apostasy, would receive strength for every trial and be enabled to witness for Him with mighty power. And in the ages to come the deliverance wrought in their behalf would exceed in fame that wrought for the children of Israel at the time of the Exodus. The days were coming, the Lord declared through His prophet, when "they shall no more say, The Lord liveth, which brought up the children of Israel out of the land of Egypt; but, The Lord liveth, which brought up and which led the seed of the house of Israel out of the north country, and from all countries whither I had driven them; and they shall dwell in their own land." Verses 7, 8. Such were the wonderful prophecies uttered by Jeremiah during the closing years of the history of the kingdom of Judah, when the Babylonians were coming unto universal rule, and were even then bringing their besieging armies against the walls of Zion.

Like sweetest music these promises of deliverance fell upon the ears of those who were steadfast in their worship of Jehovah. In the homes of the high and the lowly, where the counsels of a covenant-keeping God were still held in reverence, the words of the prophet were repeated again and again. Even the children were mightily stirred, and upon their young and receptive minds lasting impressions were made.

It was their conscientious observance of the commands of Holy Scripture, that in the days of Jeremiah's ministry brought to Daniel and his fellows opportunities to exalt the true God before the nations of earth. The instruction these Hebrew children had received in the homes of their parents, made them strong in faith and constant in their service of the living God, the Creator of the heavens and the earth. When, early in the reign of Jehoiakim, Nebuchadnezzar for the first time besieged and captured Jerusalem, and carried away Daniel and his companions, with others specially chosen for service in the court of Babylon, the faith of the Hebrew captives was tried to the utmost. But those who had learned to place their trust in the promises of God found these all-sufficient in every experience through which they were called to pass during their sojourn in a strange land. The Scriptures proved to them a guide and a stay.

As an interpreter of the meaning of the judgments beginning to fall upon Judah, Jeremiah stood nobly in defense of the justice of God and of His merciful designs even in the severest chastisements. Untiringly the prophet labored. Desirous of reaching all classes, he extended the sphere of his influence beyond Jerusalem to the surrounding districts by frequent visits to various parts of the kingdom.

In his testimonies to the church, Jeremiah constantly referred to the teachings of the book of the law that had been so greatly honored and exalted during Josiah's reign. He emphasized anew the importance of maintaining a covenant relationship with the all-merciful and compassionate Being who upon the heights of Sinai had spoken the precepts of the Decalogue. Jeremiah's words of warning and entreaty reached every part of the kingdom, and all had opportunity to know the will of God concerning the nation.

The prophet made plain the fact that our heavenly Father allows His judgments to fall, "that the nations may know themselves to be but men." Psalm 9:20. "If ye walk contrary unto Me, and will not hearken unto Me," the Lord had forewarned His people, "I, even I, . . . will scatter you among the heathen, and will draw out a sword after you: and your land shall be desolate, and your cities waste." Leviticus 26:21, 28, 33.

At the very time messages of impending doom were urged upon princes and people, their ruler, Jehoiakim, who should have been a wise spiritual leader, foremost in confession of sin and in reformation and good works, was spending his time in selfish pleasure. "I will build me a wide house and large chambers," he proposed; and this house, "ceiled with cedar, and painted with vermilion" (Jeremiah 22:14), was built with money and labor secured through fraud and oppression.

The wrath of the prophet was aroused, and he was inspired to pronounce judgment upon the faithless ruler. "Woe unto him that buildeth his house by unrighteousness, and his chambers by wrong," he declared; "that useth his neighbor's service without wages, and giveth him not for his work. . . . Shalt thou reign, because thou closest thyself in cedar? Did not thy father eat and drink, and do judgment and justice, and then it was well with him? He judged the cause of the poor and needy; then it was well with him: was not this to know Me? saith the Lord. But thine eyes and thine heart are not but for thy covetousness, and for to shed innocent blood, and for oppression, and for violence, to do it.

"Therefore thus saith the Lord concerning Jehoiakim the son of Josiah king of Judah; They shall not lament for him, saying, Ah my brother! or, Ah sister! they shall not lament for him, saying, Ah lord! or, Ah his glory! He shall be buried with the burial of an ass, drawn and cast forth beyond the gates of Jerusalem." Verses 13-19.

Within a few years this terrible judgment was to be visited upon Jehoiakim; but first the Lord in mercy informed the impenitent nation of His set purpose. In the fourth year of Jehoiakim's reign "Jeremiah the prophet spake unto all the people of Judah, and to all the inhabitants of Jerusalem," pointing out that for over a score of years, "from the thirteenth year of Josiah, . . . even unto this day," he had borne witness of God's desire to save, but that his messages had been despised. Jeremiah 25:2, 3. And now the word of the Lord to them was:

"Thus saith the Lord of hosts; Because ye have not heard My words, behold, I will send and take all the families of the north, saith the Lord, and Nebuchadnezzar the king of Babylon, My servant, and will bring them against this land, and against the inhabitants thereof, and against all these nations round about, and will utterly destroy them, and make them an astonishment, and an hissing, and perpetual desolations. Moreover I will take from them the voice of mirth, and the voice of gladness, the voice of the bridegroom, and the voice of the bride, the sound of the millstones, and the light of the candle. And this whole land shall be a desolation, and an astonishment; and these nations shall serve the king of Babylon seventy years." Verses 8-11.

Although the sentence of doom had been clearly pronounced, its awful import could scarcely be understood by the multitudes who heard. That deeper impressions might be made, the Lord sought to illustrate the meaning of the words spoken. He bade Jeremiah liken the fate of the nation to the draining of a cup filled with the wine of divine wrath. Among the first to drink of this cup of woe was to be "Jerusalem, and the cities of Judah, and the kings thereof." Others were to partake of the same cup—"Pharaoh king of Egypt, and his servants, and his princes, and all his people," and many other nations of earth—until God's purpose should have been fulfilled. See Jeremiah 25.

To illustrate further the nature of the swift-coming judgments, the prophet was bidden to "take of the ancients of the people, and of the ancients of the priests; and go forth unto the valley of the son of Hinnom," and there, after reviewing the apostasy of Judah, he was to dash to pieces "a potter's earthen bottle," and declare in behalf of Jehovah, whose servant he was, "Even so will I break this people and this city, as one breaketh a potter's vessel, that cannot be made whole again."

The prophet did as he was commanded. Then, returning to the city, he stood in the court of the temple and declared in the hearing of all the people. "Thus saith the Lord of hosts, the God of Israel; Behold, I will bring upon this city and upon all her towns all the evil that I have pronounced against it, because they have hardened their necks, that they might not hear My words." See Jeremiah 19.

The prophet's words, instead of leading to confession and repentance, aroused the anger of those high in authority, and as a consequence Jeremiah was deprived of his liberty. Imprisoned, and placed in the stocks, the prophet nevertheless continued to speak the messages of Heaven to those who stood by. His voice could not be silenced by persecution. The word of truth, he declared, "was in mine heart as a burning fire shut up in my bones, and I was weary with forbearing, and I could not stay." Jeremiah 20:9.

It was about this time that the Lord commanded Jeremiah to commit to writing the messages he desired to bear to those for whose salvation his heart of pity was continually yearning. "Take thee a roll of a book," the Lord bade His servant, "and write therein all the words that I have spoken unto thee against Israel, and against Judah, and against all the nations, from the day I spake unto thee, from the days of Josiah, even unto this day. It may be that the house of Judah will hear all the evil which I purpose to do unto them; that they may return every man from his evil way; that I may forgive their iniquity and their sin." Jeremiah 36:2,3.

In obedience to this command, Jeremiah called to his aid a faithful friend, Baruch the scribe, and dictated "all the words of the Lord, which He had spoken unto him." Verse 4. These were carefully written out on a roll of parchment and constituted a solemn reproof for sin, a warning of the sure result of continual apostasy, and an earnest appeal for the renunciation of all evil.

When the writing was completed, Jeremiah, who was still a prisoner, sent Baruch to read the roll to the multitudes who were assembling at the temple on the occasion of a national fast day, "in the fifth year of Jehoiakim the son of Josiah king of Judah, in the ninth month." "It may be," the prophet said, "they will present their supplication before the Lord, and will return everyone from his evil way: for great is the anger and the fury that the Lord hath pronounced against this people." Verses 9, 7. Baruch obeyed, and the roll was read before all the people of Judah. Afterward the scribe was summoned before the princes to read the words to them. They listened with great interest and promised to inform the king concerning all they had heard, but counseled the scribe to hide himself, for they feared the king would reject the testimony and seek to slay those who had prepared and delivered the message.

When King Jehoiakim was told by the princes what Baruch had read, he immediately ordered the roll brought before him and read in his hearing. One of the royal attendants, Jehudi by name, fetched the roll and began reading the words of reproof and warning. It was the time of winter, and the king and his companions of state, the princes of Judah, were gathered about an open fire. Only a small portion had been read, when the king, far from trembling at the danger hanging over himself and his people, seized the roll and in a frenzy of rage "cut it with the penknife and cast it into the fire that was on the hearth, until all the roll was consumed." Verse 23.

Neither the king nor his princes were afraid "nor rent their garments." Certain of the princes, however, "had made intercession to the king that he would not burn the roll: but he would not hear them." The writing having been destroyed, the wrath of the wicked king rose against Jeremiah and Baruch, and he forthwith sent for them to be taken; "but the Lord hid them." Verses 24-26.

In bringing to the attention of the temple worshipers, and of the princes and king, the written admonitions contained in the inspired roll, God was graciously seeking to warn the men of Judah for their good. "It may be," He said, "the house of Judah will hear all the evil which I purpose to do unto them; that they may return every man from his evil way; that I may forgive their iniquity and their sin." Verse 3. God pities men struggling in the blindness of perversity; He seeks to enlighten the darkened understanding by sending reproofs and threatenings designed to cause the most exalted to feel their ignorance and to deplore their errors. He endeavors to help the self-complacent to become dissatisfied with their vain attainments and to seek for spiritual blessing through a close connection with heaven.

God's plan is not to send messengers who will please and flatter sinners; He delivers no messages of peace to lull the unsanctified into carnal security. Instead, He lays heavy burdens upon the conscience of the wrongdoer and pierces his soul with sharp arrows of conviction. Ministering angels present to him the fearful judgments of God, to deepen the sense of need and to prompt the agonizing cry, "What must I do to be saved?" Acts 16:30. But the Hand that humbles to the dust, rebukes sin, and puts pride and ambition to shame, is the Hand that lifts up the penitent, stricken one. With deepest sympathy He who permits the chastisement to fall, inquires, "What wilt thou that I shall do unto thee?" When man has sinned against a holy and merciful God, he can pursue no course so noble as to repent sincerely and confess his errors in tears and bitterness of soul. This God requires of him; He accepts nothing less than a broken heart and a contrite spirit. But King Jehoiakim and his lords, in their arrogance and pride, refused the invitation of God. They would not heed the warning, and repent. The gracious opportunity proffered them at the time of the burning of the sacred roll, was their last. God had declared that if at that time they refused to hear His voice, He would inflict upon them fearful retribution. They did refuse to hear, and He pronounced His final judgments upon Judah, and He would visit with special wrath the man who had proudly lifted himself up against the Almighty.

"Thus saith the Lord of Jehoiakim king of Judah; He shall have none to sit upon the throne of David: and his dead body shall be cast out in the day to the heat, and in the night to the frost. And I will punish him and his seed and his servants

for their iniquity; and I will bring upon them, and upon the inhabitants of Jerusalem, and upon the men of Judah, all the evil that I have pronounced against them." Jeremiah 36:30, 31.

The burning of the roll was not the end of the matter. The written words were more easily disposed of than the reproof and warning they contained and the swift-coming punishment God had pronounced against rebellious Israel. But even the written roll was reproduced. "Take thee again another roll," the Lord commanded His servant, "and write in it all the former words that were in the first roll, which Jehoiakim the king of Judah hath burned." The record of the prophecies concerning Judah and Jerusalem had been reduced to ashes; but the words were still living in the heart of Jeremiah, "as a burning fire," and the prophet was permitted to reproduce that which the wrath of man would fain have destroyed.

Taking another roll, Jeremiah gave it to Baruch, "who wrote therein from the mouth of Jeremiah all the words of the book which Jehoiakim king of Judah had burned in the fire: and there were added besides unto them many like words." Verses 28, 32. The wrath of man had sought to prevent the labors of the prophet of God; but the very means by which Jehoiakim had endeavored to limit the influence of the servant of Jehovah, gave further opportunity for making plain the divine requirements.

The spirit of opposition to reproof, that led to the persecution and imprisonment of Jeremiah, exists today. Many refuse to heed repeated warnings, preferring rather to listen to false teachers who flatter their vanity and overlook their evil-doing. In the day of trouble such will have no sure refuge, no help from heaven. God's chosen servants should meet with courage and patience the trials and sufferings that befall them through reproach, neglect, and misrepresentation. They should continue to discharge faithfully the work God has given them to do, ever remembering that the prophets of old and the Saviour of mankind and His apostles also endured abuse and persecution for the Word's sake.

It was God's purpose that Jehoiakim should heed the counsels of Jeremiah and thus win favor in the eyes of Nebuchadnezzar and save himself much sorrow. The youthful king had sworn allegiance to the Babylonian ruler, and had he remained true to his promise he would have commanded the respect of the heathen, and this would have led to precious opportunities for the conversion of souls.

Scorning the unusual privileges granted him, Judah's king willfully followed a way of his own choosing. He violated his word of honor to the Babylonian ruler, and rebelled. This brought him and his kingdom into a very strait place. Against him were sent "bands of the Chaldees, and bands of the Syrians, and bands of the Moabites, and bands of the children of Ammon," and he was powerless to prevent the land from being overrun by these marauders. 2 Kings 24:2. Within a few years he closed his disastrous reign in ignominy, rejected of Heaven, unloved by his people, and despised by the rulers of Babylon whose confidence he had betrayed—and all as the result of his fatal mistake in turning from the purpose of God as revealed through His appointed messenger.

Jehoiachin, the son of Jehoiakim, occupied the throne only three months and ten days, when he surrendered to the Chaldean armies which, because of the rebellion of Judah's ruler, were once more besieging the fated city. On this occasion Nebuchadnezzar "carried away Jehoiachin to Babylon, and the king's mother, and the king's wives, and his officers, and the mighty of the land," several thousand in number, together with "craftsmen and smiths a thousand." With these the king of Babylon took "all the treasures of the house of the Lord, and the treasures of the king's house." 2 Kings 24:15, 16, 13.

The kingdom of Judah, broken in power and robbed of its strength both in men and in treasure, was nevertheless still permitted to exist as a separate government. At its head Nebuchadnezzar placed Mattaniah, a younger son of Josiah, changing his name to Zedekiah.

The Last King of Judah

Zedekiah at the beginning of his reign was trusted fully by the king of Babylon and had as a tried counselor the prophet Jeremiah. By pursuing an honorable course toward the Babylonians and by paying heed to the messages from the Lord through Jeremiah, he could have kept the respect of many in high authority and have had opportunity to communicate to them a knowledge of the true God. Thus the captive exiles already in Babylon would have been placed on vantage ground and granted many liberties; the name of God would have been honored far and wide; and those that remained in the land of Judah would have been spared the terrible calamities that finally came upon them.

Through Jeremiah, Zedekiah and all Judah, including those taken to Babylon, were counseled to submit quietly to the temporary rule of their conquerors. It was especially important that those in captivity should seek the peace of the land into which they had been carried. This, however, was contrary to the inclinations of the human heart; and Satan, taking advantage of the circumstances, caused false prophets to arise among the people, both in Jerusalem and in Babylon, who declared that the yoke of bondage would soon be broken and the former prestige of the nation restored.

The heeding of such flattering prophecies would have led to fatal moves on the part of the king and the exiles, and would have frustrated the merciful designs of God in their behalf. Lest an insurrection be incited and great suffering ensue, the Lord commanded Jeremiah to meet the crisis without delay, by warning the king of Judah of the sure consequence of rebellion. The captives also were admonished, by written communications, not to be deluded into believing their deliverance near. "Let not your prophets and your diviners, that be in the midst of you, deceive you," he urged. Jeremiah 29:8. In this connection mention was made of the Lord's purpose to restore Israel at the close of the seventy years of captivity foretold by His messengers.

With what tender compassion did God inform His captive people of His plans for Israel! He knew that should they be persuaded by false prophets to look for a speedy deliverance, their position in Babylon would be made very difficult. Any demonstration or insurrection on their part would awaken the vigilance and severity of the Chaldean authorities and would lead to a further restriction of their liberties. Suffering and disaster would result. He desired them to submit quietly to their fate and make their servitude as pleasant as possible; and his counsel to them was: "Build ye houses, and dwell in them; and plant gardens, and eat the fruit of them; . . . and seek the peace of the city whither I have caused you to be carried away captives, and pray unto the Lord for it: for in the peace thereof shall ye have peace." Verses 5-7.

Among the false teachers in Babylon were two men who claimed to be holy, but whose lives were corrupt. Jeremiah had condemned the evil course of these men and had warned them of their danger. Angered by reproof, they sought to oppose the work of the true prophet by stirring up the people to discredit his words and to act contrary to the counsel of God in the matter of subjecting themselves to the king of Babylon. The Lord testified through Jeremiah that these false prophets should be delivered into the hands of Nebuchadnezzar and slain before his eyes. Not long afterward, this prediction was literally fulfilled.

To the end of time, men will arise to create confusion and rebellion among those who claim to be representatives of the true God. Those who prophesy lies will encourage men to look upon sin as a light thing. When the terrible results of their evil deeds are made manifest, they will seek, if possible, to make the one who has faithfully warned them, responsible for their difficulties, even as the Jews charged Jeremiah with their evil fortunes. But as surely as the words of Jehovah through His prophet were vindicated anciently, so surely will the certainty of His messages be established today.

From the first, Jeremiah had followed a consistent course in counseling submission to the Babylonians. This counsel was given not only to Judah, but to many of the surrounding nations. In the earlier portion of Zedekiah's reign, ambassadors from the rulers of Edom, Moab, Tyre, and other nations visited the king of Judah to learn whether in his judgment the time was opportune for a united revolt and whether he would join them in battling against the king of Babylon. While these ambassadors were awaiting a response, the word of the Lord came to Jeremiah, saying, "Make thee bonds and yokes, and put them upon thy neck, and send them to the king of Edom, and to the king of Moab, and to the king of the Ammonites, and to the king of Tyrus, and to the king of Zidon, by the hand of the messengers which come to Jerusalem unto Zedekiah king of Judah." Jeremiah 27:2, 3.

Jeremiah was commanded to instruct the ambassadors to inform their rulers that God had given them all into the hand of Nebuchadnezzar, the king of Babylon, and that they were to "serve him, and his son, and his son's son, until the very time of his land come." Verse 7.

The ambassadors were further instructed to declare to their rulers that if they refused to serve the Babylonian king they should be punished "with the sword, and with the famine, and with the pestilence" till they were consumed. Especially were they to turn from the teaching of false prophets who might counsel otherwise. "Hearken not ye to your prophets," the Lord declared, "nor to your diviners, nor to your dreamers, nor to your enchanters, nor to your sorcerers, which speak unto you, saying, Ye shall not serve the king of Babylon: for they prophesy a lie unto you, to remove you far from your land; and that I should drive you out, and ye should perish. But the nations that bring their neck under the yoke of the king of Babylon, and serve him, those will I let remain still in their own land, saith the Lord; and they shall till it, and dwell therein." Verses 8-11. The lightest punishment that a merciful God could inflict upon so rebellious a people was submission to the rule of Babylon, but if they warred against this decree of servitude they were to feel the full vigor of His chastisement. The amazement of the assembled council of nations knew no bounds when Jeremiah, carrying the yoke of subjection about his neck, made known to them the will of God.

Against determined opposition Jeremiah stood firmly for the policy of submission. Prominent among those who presumed to gainsay the counsel of the Lord was Hananiah, one of the false prophets against whom the people had been warned. Thinking to gain the favor of the king and of the royal court, he lifted his voice in protest, declaring that God had given him words of encouragement for the Jews. Said he: "Thus speaketh the Lord of hosts, the God of Israel, saying, I have broken the yoke of the king of Babylon. Within two full years will I bring again into this place all the vessels of the Lord's house, that Nebuchadnezzar king of Babylon took away from this place, and carried them to Babylon: and I will bring again to this place Jeconiah the son of Jehoiakim king of Judah, with all the captives of Judah, that went into Babylon, saith the Lord: for I will break the yoke of the king of Babylon." Jeremiah 28:2-4.

Jeremiah, in the presence of the priests and people, earnestly entreated them to submit to the king of Babylon for the time the Lord had specified. He cited the men of Judah to the prophecies of Hosea, Habakkuk, Zephaniah, and others whose messages of reproof and warning had been similar to his own. He referred them to events which had taken place in fulfillment of prophecies of retribution for unrepented sin. In the past the judgments of God had been visited upon the impenitent in exact fulfillment of His purpose as revealed through His messengers.

"The prophet which prophesieth of peace," Jeremiah proposed in conclusion, "when the word of the prophet shall come to pass, then shall the prophet be known, that the Lord hath truly sent him." Verse 9. If Israel chose to run the risk, future developments would effectually decide which was the true prophet.

The words of Jeremiah counseling submission aroused Hananiah to a daring challenge of the reliability of the message delivered. Taking the symbolic yoke from Jeremiah's neck, Hananiah broke it, saying, "Thus saith the Lord; Even so will I break the yoke of Nebuchadnezzar king of Babylon from the neck of all nations within the space of two full years.

"And the prophet Jeremiah went his way." Verse II. Apparently he could do nothing more than to retire from the scene of conflict. But Jeremiah was given another message. "Go and tell Hananiah," he was bidden, "Thus saith the Lord; Thou hast broken the yokes of wood; but thou shalt make for them yokes of iron. For thus saith the Lord of hosts, the God of Israel; I have put a yoke of iron upon the neck of all these nations, that they may serve Nebuchadnezzar king of Babylon; and they shall serve him. . . . "Then said the prophet Jeremiah unto Hananiah the prophet, Hear now, Hananiah; The Lord hath not sent thee; but thou makest this people to trust in a lie. Therefore thus saith the Lord; Behold, I will cast thee from off the face of the earth: this year thou shalt die, because thou hast taught rebellion against the Lord. So Hananiah the prophet died the same year in the seventh month." Verses 13-17.

The false prophet had strengthened the unbelief of the people in Jeremiah and his message. He had wickedly declared himself the Lord's messenger, and he suffered death in consequence. In the fifth month Jeremiah prophesied the death of Hananiah, and in the seventh month his words were proved true by their fulfillment.

The unrest caused by the representations of the false prophets brought Zedekiah under suspicion of treason, and only by quick and decisive action on his part was he permitted to continue reigning as a vassal. Opportunity for such action was taken advantage of shortly after the return of the ambassadors from Jerusalem to the surrounding nations, when the king of Judah accompanied Seraiah, "a quiet prince," on an important mission to Babylon. Jeremiah 51:59. During this visit to the Chaldean court, Zedekiah renewed his oath of allegiance to Nebuchadnezzar.

Through Daniel and others of the Hebrew captives, the Babylonian monarch had been made acquainted with the power and supreme authority of the true God; and when Zedekiah once more solemnly promised to remain loyal, Nebuchadnezzar required him to swear to this promise in the name of the Lord God of Israel. Had Zedekiah respected this renewal of his covenant oath, his loyalty would have had a profound influence on the minds of many who were watching the conduct of those who claimed to reverence the name and to cherish the honor of the God of the Hebrews.

But Judah's king lost sight of his high privilege of bringing honor to the name of the living God. Of Zedekiah it is recorded: "He did that which was evil in the sight of the Lord his God, and humbled not himself before Jeremiah the prophet speaking from the mouth of the Lord. And he also rebelled against King Nebuchadnezzar, who had made him swear by God: but he stiffened his neck, and hardened his heart from turning unto the Lord God of Israel." 2 Chronicles 36:12, 13.

While Jeremiah continued to bear his testimony in the land of Judah, the prophet Ezekiel was raised up from among the captives in Babylon, to warn and to comfort the exiles, and also to confirm the word of the Lord that was being spoken through Jeremiah. During the years that remained of Zedekiah's reign, Ezekiel made very plain the folly of trusting to the false predictions of those who were causing the captives to hope for an early return to Jerusalem. He was also instructed to foretell, by means of a variety of symbols and solemn messages, the siege and utter destruction of Jerusalem.

In the sixth year of the reign of Zedekiah, the Lord revealed to Ezekiel in vision some of the abominations that were being practiced in Jerusalem, and within the gate of the Lord's house, and even in the inner court. The chambers of images, and the pictured idols, "every form of creeping things, and abominable beasts, and all the idols of the house of Israel"—all these in rapid succession passed before the astonished gaze of the prophet. Ezekiel 8:10.

Those who should have been spiritual leaders among the people, "the ancients of the house of Israel," to the number of seventy, were seen offering incense before the idolatrous representations that had been introduced into hidden chambers within the sacred precincts of the temple court. "The Lord seeth us not," the men of Judah flattered themselves as they engaged in their heathenish practices; "the Lord hath forsaken the earth," they blasphemously declared. Verses 11, 12.

There were still "greater abominations" for the prophet to behold. At a gate leading from the outer to the inner court he was shown "women weeping for Tammuz," and within "the inner court of the Lord's house, . . . at the door of the temple of the Lord, between the porch and the altar, were about five and twenty men, with their backs toward the temple of the Lord, and their faces toward the east; and they worshiped the sun toward the east." Verses 13-16.

And now the glorious Being who accompanied Ezekiel throughout this astonishing vision of wickedness in high places in the land of Judah, inquired of the prophet: "Hast thou seen this, O son of man? Is it a light thing to the house of Judah that they commit the abominations which they commit here? for they have filled the land with violence, and have returned to provoke Me to anger: and, lo, they put the branch to their nose. Therefore will I also deal in fury: Mine eye shall not spare, neither will I have pity: and though they cry in Mine ears with a loud voice, yet will I not hear them." Verses 17, 18.

Through Jeremiah the Lord had declared of the wicked men who presumptuously dared to stand before the people in His name: "Both prophet and priest are profane; yea, in My house have I found their wickedness." Jeremiah 23:11. In the terrible arraignment of Judah as recorded in the closing narrative of the chronicler of Zedekiah's reign, this charge of violating the sanctity of the temple was repeated.

"Moreover," the sacred writer declared, "all the chief of the priests, and the people, transgressed very much after all the abominations of the heathen; and polluted the house of the Lord which He had hallowed in Jerusalem." 2 Chronicles 36:14.

The day of doom for the kingdom of Judah was fast approaching. No longer could the Lord set before them the hope of averting the severest of His judgments. "Should ye be utterly unpunished?" He inquired. "Ye shall not be unpunished." Jeremiah 25:29.

Even these words were received with mocking derision. "The days are prolonged, and every vision faileth," declared the impenitent. But through Ezekiel this denial of the sure word of prophecy was sternly rebuked. "Tell them," the Lord declared, "I will make this proverb to cease, and they shall no more use it as a proverb in Israel; but say unto them, The days are at hand, and the effect of every vision. For there shall be no more any vain vision nor flattering divination within the house of Israel. For I am the Lord: I will speak, and the word that I shall speak shall come to pass; it shall be no more prolonged: for in your days, O rebellious house, will I say the word, and will perform it, saith the Lord God.

"Again," testifies Ezekiel, "the word of the Lord came to me, saying, Son of man, behold, they of the house of Israel say, The vision that he seeth is for many days to come, and he prophesieth of the times that are far off. Therefore say unto them, Thus saith the Lord God; There shall none of My words be prolonged any more, but the word which I have spoken shall be done, saith the Lord God." Ezekiel 12:22-28.

Foremost among those who were rapidly leading the nation to ruin was Zedekiah their king. Forsaking utterly the counsels of the Lord as given through the prophets, forgetting the debt of gratitude he owed Nebuchadnezzar, violating his solemn oath of allegiance taken in the name of the Lord God of Israel, Judah's king rebelled against the prophets, against his benefactor, and against his God. In the vanity of his own wisdom he turned for help to the ancient enemy of Israel's prosperity, "sending his ambassadors into Egypt, that they might give him horses and much people."

"Shall he prosper?" the Lord inquired concerning the one who had thus basely betrayed every sacred trust; "shall he escape that doeth such things? or shall he break the covenant, and be delivered? As I live, saith the Lord God, surely in the place where the king dwelleth that made him king, whose oath he despised, and whose covenant he brake, even with him in the midst of Babylon he shall die. Neither shall Pharaoh with his mighty army and great company make for him in the war: . . . seeing he despised the oath by breaking the covenant, when, lo, he had given his hand, and hath done all these things, he shall not escape." Ezekiel 17:15-18.

To the "profane wicked prince" had come the day of final reckoning. "Remove the diadem," the Lord decreed, "and take off the crown." Not until Christ Himself should set up His kingdom was Judah again to be permitted to have a king. "I will overturn, overturn, overturn, it," was the divine edict concerning the throne of the house of David; "and it shall be no more, until He come whose right it is; and I will give it Him." Ezekiel 21:25-27.

Carried Captive Into Babylon

In the ninth year of Zedekiah's reign "Nebuchadnezzar king of Babylon came, he, and all his host, against Jerusalem," to besiege the city. 2 Kings 25:1. The outlook for Judah was hopeless. "Behold, I am against thee," the Lord Himself declared through Ezekiel. "I the Lord have drawn forth My sword out of his sheath" it shall not return any more. . . . Every heart shall melt, and all hands shall be feeble, and every spirit shall faint, and all knees shall be weak as water." "I will pour out Mine indignation upon thee, I will blow against thee in the fire of My wrath, and deliver thee into the hand of brutish men, and skillful to destroy." Ezekiel 21:3, 5-7, 31.

The Egyptians endeavored to come to the rescue of the beleaguered city; and the Chaldeans, in order to keep them back, abandoned for a time their siege of the Judean capital. Hope sprang up in the heart of Zedekiah, and he sent a messenger to Jeremiah, asking him to pray to God in behalf of the Hebrew nation.

The prophet's fearful answer was that the Chaldeans would return and destroy the city. The fiat had gone forth; no longer could the impenitent nation avert the divine judgments. "Deceive not yourselves," the Lord warned His people. "The Chaldeans . . . shall not depart. For though ye had smitten the whole army of the Chaldeans that fight against you, and there remained but wounded men among them, yet should they rise up every man in his tent, and burn this city with fire." Jeremiah 37:9, 10. The remnant of Judah were to go into captivity, to learn through adversity the lessons they had refused to learn under circumstances more favorable. From this decree of the holy Watcher there could be no appeal.

Among the righteous still in Jerusalem, to whom had been made plain the divine purpose, were some who determined to place beyond the reach of ruthless hands the sacred ark containing the tables of stone on which had been traced the precepts of the Decalogue. This they did. With mourning and sadness they secreted the ark in a cave, where it was to be hidden from the people of Israel and Judah because of their sins, and was to be no more restored to them. That sacred ark is yet hidden. It has never been disturbed since it was secreted.

For many years Jeremiah had stood before the people as a faithful witness for God; and now, as the fated city was about to pass into the hands of the heathen, he considered his work done and attempted to leave, but was prevented by a son of one of the false prophets, who reported that Jeremiah was about to join the Babylonians, to whom he had repeatedly urged the men of Judah to submit. The prophet denied the lying charge, but nevertheless "the princes were wroth with Jeremiah, and smote him, and put him in prison." Verse 15.

The hopes that had sprung up in the hearts of princes and people when the armies of Nebuchadnezzar turned south to meet the Egyptians, were soon dashed to the ground. The word of the Lord had been, "Behold, I am against thee, Pharaoh king of Egypt." The might of Egypt was but a broken reed. "All the inhabitants of Egypt," Inspiration had declared, "shall know that I am the Lord, because they have been a staff of reed to the house of Israel." "I will strengthen the arms of the king of Babylon, and the arms of Pharaoh shall fall down; and they shall know that I am the Lord, when I shall put My sword into the hand of the king of Babylon, and he shall stretch it out upon the land of Egypt." Ezekiel 29:3, 6; 30:25, 26.

While the princes of Judah were still vainly looking toward Egypt for help, King Zedekiah with anxious foreboding was thinking of the prophet of God that had been thrust into prison. After many days the king sent for him and asked him secretly, "Is there any word from the Lord?" Jeremiah answered, "There is: for, said He, thou shalt be delivered into the hand of the king of Babylon.

"Moreover Jeremiah said unto King Zedekiah, What have I offended against thee, or against thy servants, or against this people, that ye have put me in prison? Where are now your prophets which prophesied unto you, saying, The king of Babylon shall not come against you, nor against this land? Therefore hear now, I pray thee, O my lord the king: let my supplication, I pray thee, be accepted before thee; that thou cause me not to return to the house of Jonathan the scribe, lest I die there." Jeremiah 37:17-20.

At this Zedekiah commanded that they "commit Jeremiah into the court of the prison, and that they should give him daily a piece of bread out of the bakers' street, until all the bread in the city were spent. Thus Jeremiah remained in the court of the prison." Verse 21.

The king dared not openly manifest any faith in Jeremiah. Though his fear drove him to seek information of him privately, yet he was too weak to brave the disapprobation of his princes and of the people by submitting to the will of God as declared by the prophet.

From the court of the prison Jeremiah continued to advise submission to the Babylonian rule. To offer resistance would be to invite sure death. The message of the Lord to Judah was: "He that remaineth in this city shall die by the sword, by the famine, and by the pestilence: but he that goeth forth to the Chaldeans shall live; for he shall have his life for a prey, and shall live." Plain and positive were the words spoken. In the name of the Lord the prophet boldly declared, "This city shall surely be given into the hand of the king of Babylon's army, which shall take it." Jeremiah 38:2, 3.

At last the princes, enraged over the repeated counsels of Jeremiah, which were contrary to their set policy of resistance, made a vigorous protest before the king, urging that the prophet was an enemy to the nation, and that his words had weakened the hands of the people and brought misfortune upon them; therefore he should be put to death.

The cowardly king knew that the charges were false; but in order to propitiate those who occupied high and influential positions in the nation, he feigned to believe their falsehoods and gave Jeremiah into their hands to do with him as they pleased. The prophet was cast "into the dungeon of Malchiah the son of Hammelech, that was in the court of the prison: and they let down Jeremiah with cords. And in the dungeon there was no water, but mire: so Jeremiah sunk in the mire." Verse 6. But God raised up friends for him, who besought the king in his behalf, and had him again removed to the court of the prison.

Once more the king sent privately for Jeremiah, and bade him faithfully relate the purpose of God toward Jerusalem. In response, Jeremiah inquired, "If I declare it unto thee, wilt thou not surely put me to death? and if I give thee counsel, wilt thou not hearken unto me?" The king entered into a secret compact with the prophet. "As the Lord liveth, that made us this soul," Zedekiah promised, "I will not put thee to death, neither will I give thee into the hand of these men that seek thy life." Verses 15, 16.

There was still opportunity for the king to reveal a willingness to heed the warnings of Jehovah, and thus to temper with mercy the judgments even now falling on city and nation. "If thou wilt assuredly go forth unto the king of Babylon's princes," was the message given the king, "then thy soul shall live, and this city shall not be burned with fire; and thou shalt live, and thine house: but if thou wilt not go forth to the king of Babylon's princes, then shall this city be given into the hand of the Chaldeans, and they shall burn it with fire, and thou shalt not escape out of their hand."

"I am afraid of the Jews that are fallen to the Chaldeans," the king replied, "lest they deliver me into their hand, and they mock me." But the prophet promised, "They shall not deliver thee." And he added the earnest entreaty, "Obey, I beseech thee, the voice of the Lord, which I speak unto thee: so it shall be well unto thee, and thy soul shall live." Verses 17-20.

Thus even to the last hour, God made plain His willingness to show mercy to those who would choose to submit to His just requirements. Had the king chosen to obey, the lives of the people might have been spared, and the city saved from conflagration; but he thought he had gone too far to retrace his steps. He was afraid of the Jews, afraid of ridicule, afraid for his life. After years of rebellion against God, Zedekiah thought it too humiliating to say to his people, I accept the word of the Lord, as spoken through the prophet Jeremiah; I dare not venture to war against the enemy in the face of all these warnings.

With tears Jeremiah entreated Zedekiah to save himself and his people. With anguish of spirit he assured him that unless he should heed the counsel of God, he could not escape with his life, and all his possessions would fall to the Babylonians. But the king had started on the wrong course, and he would not retrace his steps. He decided to follow the counsel of the false prophets, and of the men whom he really despised, and who ridiculed his weakness in yielding so readily to their wishes. He sacrificed the noble freedom of his manhood and

became a cringing slave to public opinion. With no fixed purpose to do evil, he was also without resolution to stand boldly for the right. Convicted though he was of the value of the counsel given by Jeremiah, he had not the moral stamina to obey; and as a consequence he advanced steadily in the wrong direction.

The king was even too weak to be willing that his courtiers and people should know that he had held a conference with Jeremiah, so fully had the fear of man taken possession of his soul. If Zedekiah had stood up bravely and declared that he believed the words of the prophet, already half fulfilled, what desolation might have been averted! He should have said, I will obey the Lord, and save the city from utter ruin. I dare not disregard the commands of God because of the fear or favor of man. I love the truth, I hate sin, and I will follow the counsel of the Mighty One of Israel.

Then the people would have respected his courageous spirit, and those who were wavering between faith and unbelief would have taken a firm stand for the right. The very fearlessness and justice of this course would have inspired his subjects with admiration and loyalty. He would have had ample support, and Judah would have been spared the untold woe of carnage and famine and fire.

The weakness of Zedekiah was a sin for which he paid a fearful penalty. The enemy swept down like a resistless avalanche and devastated the city. The Hebrew armies were beaten back in confusion. The nation was conquered. Zedekiah was taken prisoner, and his sons were slain before his eyes. The king was led away from Jerusalem a captive, his eyes were put out, and after arriving in Babylon he perished miserably. The beautiful temple that for more than four centuries had crowned the summit of Mount Zion was not spared by the Chaldeans. "They burnt the house of God, and brake down the wall of Jerusalem, and burnt all the palaces thereof with fire, and destroyed all the goodly vessels thereof." 2 Chronicles 36:19.

At the time of the final overthrow of Jerusalem by Nebuchadnezzar, many had escaped the horrors of the long siege, only to perish by the sword. Of those who still remained, some, notably the chief of the priests and officers, and the princes of the realm, were taken to Babylon and there executed as traitors. Others were carried captive, to live in servitude to Nebuchadnezzar and to his sons "until the reign of the kingdom of Persia: to fulfill the word of the Lord by the mouth of Jeremiah." Verses 20, 21.

Of Jeremiah himself it is recorded: "Nebuchadnezzar king of Babylon gave charge concerning Jeremiah to Nebuchadnezzar-adan the captain of the guard, saying, Take him, and look well to him, and do him no harm; but do unto him even as he shall say unto thee." Jeremiah 39:11, 12.

Released from prison by the Babylonian officers, the prophet chose to cast in his lot with the feeble remnant, "certain poor of the land" left by the Chaldeans to be "vinedressers and husbandmen." Over these the Babylonians set Gedaliah as governor. Only a few months passed before the newly appointed governor was treacherously slain. The poor people, after passing through many trials, were finally persuaded by their leaders to take refuge in the land of Egypt. Against this move, Jeremiah lifted his voice in protest. "Go ye not into Egypt," he pleaded. But the inspired counsel was not heeded, and "all the remnant of Judah, . . . even men, and women, and children," took flight into Egypt. "They obeyed not the voice of the Lord: thus came they even to Tahpanhes." Jeremiah 43:5-7.

The prophecies of doom pronounced by Jeremiah upon the remnant that had rebelled against Nebuchadnezzar by fleeing to Egypt were mingled with promises of pardon to those who should repent of their folly and stand ready to return. While the Lord would not spare those who turned from His counsel to the seductive influences of Egyptian idolatry, yet He would show mercy to those who should prove loyal and true. "A small number that escape the sword shall return out of the land of Egypt into the land of Judah," He declared; "and all the remnant of Judah, that are gone into the land of Egypt to sojourn there, shall know whose words shall stand, Mine, or theirs." Jeremiah 44:28.

The sorrow of the prophet over the utter perversity of those who would have been the spiritual light of the world, his sorrow over the fate of Zion and of the people carried captive to Babylon, is revealed in the lamentations he has left on record as a memorial of the folly of turning from the counsels of Jehovah to human wisdom. Amid the ruin wrought, Jeremiah could still declare, "It is of the Lord's mercies that we are not consumed;" and his constant prayer was, "Let us search and try our ways, and turn again to the Lord." Lamentations 3:22, 40. While Judah was still a kingdom among the nations, he had inquired of his God, "Hast Thou utterly rejected Judah? hath Thy soul loathed Zion?" and he had made bold to plead, "Do not abhor us, for Thy name's sake." Jeremiah 14:19, 21. The prophet's absolute faith in God's eternal purpose to bring order out of confusion, and to demonstrate to the nations of earth and to the entire universe His attributes of justice and love, now led him to plead confidently in behalf of those who might turn from evil to righteousness.

But now Zion was utterly destroyed; the people of God were in their captivity. Overwhelmed with grief, the prophet exclaimed: "How doth the city sit solitary, that was full of people! how is she become as a widow! she that was great among the nations, and princess among the provinces, how is she become tributary! She weepeth sore in the night, and her tears are on her cheeks: among all her lovers she hath none to comfort her: all her friends have dealt treacherously with her, they are become her enemies.

"Judah is gone into captivity because of affliction, and because of great servitude: she dwelleth among the heathen, she findeth no rest: all her persecutors overtook her between the straits. The ways of Zion do mourn, because none come to the solemn feasts: all her gates are desolate: her priests sigh, her virgins are afflicted, and she is in bitterness. Her adversaries are the chief, her enemies prosper; for the Lord hath afflicted her for the multitude of her transgressions: her children are gone into captivity before the enemy."

"How hath the Lord covered the daughter of Zion with a cloud in His anger, and cast down from heaven unto the earth the beauty of Israel, and remembered not His footstool in the day of His anger! The Lord hath swallowed up all the habitations of Jacob, and hath not pitied: He hath thrown down in His wrath the strongholds of the daughter of Judah; He hath brought them down to the ground: He hath polluted the kingdom and the princes thereof. He hath cut off in His fierce anger all the horn of Israel: He hath drawn back His right hand from before the enemy, and He burned against Jacob like a flaming fire, which devoureth round about. He hath bent His bow like an enemy: He stood with His right hand as an adversary, and slew all that were pleasant to the eye in the tabernacle of the daughter of Zion: He poured out His fury like fire."

"What thing shall I take to witness for thee? what thing shall I liken to thee, O daughter of Jerusalem? what shall I equal to thee, that I may comfort thee, O virgin daughter of Zion? for thy breach is great like the sea: who can heal thee?"

"Remember, O Lord, what is come upon us: consider, and behold our reproach. Our inheritance is turned to strangers, our houses to aliens. We are orphans and fatherless, our mothers are as widows. . . . Our fathers have sinned, and are not; and we have borne their iniquities. Servants have ruled over us: there is none that doth deliver us out of their hand. . . . For this our heart is faint; for these things our eyes are dim." "Thou, O Lord, remainest forever; Thy throne from generation to generation. Wherefore dost Thou forget us forever, and forsake us so long time? Turn Thou us unto Thee, O Lord, and we shall be turned; renew our days as of old." Lamentations 1:1-5; 2:1-4, 13; 5:1-3, 7, 8, 17, 19-21.

Light Through Darkness

The dark years of destruction and death marking the end of the kingdom of Judah would have brought despair to the stoutest heart had it not been for the encouragements in the prophetic utterances of God's messengers. Through Jeremiah in Jerusalem, through Daniel in the court of Babylon, through Ezekiel on the banks of the Chebar, the Lord in mercy made clear His eternal purpose and gave assurance of His willingness to fulfill to His chosen people the promises recorded in the writings of Moses. That which He had said He would do for those who should prove true to Him, He would surely bring to pass. "The word of God . . . liveth and abideth forever." 1 Peter 1:23.

In the days of the wilderness wandering the Lord had made abundant provision for His children to keep in remembrance the words of His law. After the settlement in Canaan the divine precepts were to be repeated daily in every home; they were to be written plainly upon the doorposts and gates, and spread upon memorial tablets. They were to be set to music and chanted by young and old. Priests were to teach these holy precepts in public assemblies, and the rulers of the land were to make them their daily study. "Meditate therein day and night," the Lord commanded Joshua concerning the book of the law, "that thou mayest observe to do according to all that is written therein: for then thou shalt make thy way prosperous, and then thou shalt have good success." Joshua 1:8.

The writings of Moses were taught by Joshua to all Israel. "There was not a word of all that Moses commanded, which Joshua read not before all the congregation of Israel, with the women, and the little ones, and the strangers that were conversant among them." Joshua 8:35. This was in harmony with the express command of Jehovah providing for a public rehearsal of the words of the book of the law every seven years, during the Feast of Tabernacles. "Gather the people together, men, and women, and children, and thy stranger that is within thy gates," the spiritual leaders of Israel had been instructed. "that they may hear, and that they may learn, and fear the Lord your God, and observe to do all the words of this law: and that their children, which have not known anything, may hear, and learn to fear the Lord your God, as long as ye live in the land whither ye go over Jordan to possess it." Deuteronomy 31:12, 13.

Had this counsel been heeded through the centuries that followed, how different would have been Israel's history! Only as a reverence for God's Holy Word was cherished in the hearts of the people, could they hope to fulfill the divine purpose. It was regard for the law of God that gave Israel strength during the reign of David and the earlier years of Solomon's rule; it was through faith in the living word that reformation was wrought in the days of Elijah and of Josiah. And it was to these same Scriptures of truth, Israel's richest heritage, that Jeremiah appealed in his efforts toward reform. Wherever he ministered he met the people with the earnest plea, "Hear ye the words of this covenant," words which would bring them a full understanding of God's purpose to extend to all nations a knowledge of saving truth. Jeremiah 11:12.

In the closing years of Judah's apostasy the exhortations of the prophets were seemingly of but little avail; and as the armies of the Chaldeans came for the third and last time to besiege Jerusalem, hope fled from every heart. Jeremiah predicted utter ruin; and it was because of his insistence on surrender that he had finally been thrown into prison. But God left not to hopeless despair the faithful remnant who were still in the city. Even while Jeremiah was kept under close surveillance by those who scorned his messages, there came to him fresh revelations concerning Heaven's willingness to forgive and to save, which have been an unfailing source of comfort to the church of God from that day to this.

Laying fast hold on the promises of God, Jeremiah, by means of an acted parable, illustrated before the inhabitants of the fated city his strong faith in the ultimate fulfillment of God's purpose for His people. In the presence of witnesses, and with careful observance of all necessary legal forms, he purchased for seventeen shekels of silver an ancestral field situated in the neighboring village of Anathoth.

From every human point of view this purchase of land in territory already under the control of the Babylonians, appeared to be an act of folly. The prophet himself had been foretelling the destruction of Jerusalem, the desolation of Judea, and the utter ruin of the kingdom. He had been prophesying a long period of captivity in faraway Babylon. Already advanced in years, he could never hope to receive personal benefit from the purchase he had made. However, his study of the prophecies that were recorded in the Scriptures had created within his heart a firm conviction that the Lord purposed to restore to the children of the captivity their ancient possession of the Land of Promise. With the eye of faith Jeremiah saw the exiles returning at the end of the years of affliction and reoccupying the land of their fathers. Through the purchase of the Anathoth estate he would do what he could to inspire others with the hope that brought so much comfort to his own heart.

Having signed the deeds of transfer and secured the countersignatures of witnesses, Jeremiah charged Baruch his secretary: "Take these evidences, this evidence of the purchase, both which is sealed, and this evidence which is open; and put them in an earthen vessel, that they may continue many days. For thus saith the Lord of hosts, the God of Israel; Houses and fields and vineyards shall be possessed again in this land." Jeremiah 32:14, 15.

So discouraging was the outlook for Judah at the time of this extraordinary transaction that immediately after perfecting the details of the purchase and arranging for the preservation of the written records, the faith of Jeremiah, unshaken though it had been, was now sorely tried. Had he, in his endeavor to encourage Judah, acted presumptuously? In his desire to establish confidence in the promises of God's word, had he given ground for false hope? Those who had entered into covenant relationship with God had long since scorned the provisions made in their behalf. Could the promises to the chosen nation ever meet with complete fulfillment?

Perplexed in spirit, bowed down with sorrow over the sufferings of those who had refused to repent of their sins, the prophet appealed to God for further enlightenment concerning the divine purpose for mankind.

"Ah Lord God!" he prayed, "behold, Thou hast made the heaven and the earth by Thy great power and stretched-out arm, and there is nothing too hard for Thee: Thou showest loving-kindness unto thousands, and recompensest the iniquity of the fathers into the bosom of their children after them: the great, the mighty God, the Lord of hosts, is His name, great in counsel, and mighty in work: for Thine eyes are open upon all the ways of the sons of men: to give everyone according to his ways, and according to the fruit of his doings: which hast set signs and wonders in the land of Egypt, even unto this day, and in Israel, and among other men; and hast made Thee a name, as at this day; and hast brought forth Thy people Israel out of the land of Egypt with signs, and with wonders, and with a strong hand, and with a stretched-out arm, and with great terror; and hast given them this land, which Thou didst swear to their fathers to give them, a land flowing with milk and honey; and they came in, and possessed it; but they obeyed not Thy voice, neither walked in Thy law; they have done nothing of all that Thou commandedst them to do: therefore Thou hast caused all this evil to come upon them." Verses 17-23.

Nebuchadnezzar's armies were about to take the walls of Zion by storm. Thousands were perishing in a last desperate defense of the city. Many thousands more were dying of hunger and disease. The fate of Jerusalem was already sealed. The besieging towers of the enemy's forces were already overlooking the walls. "Behold the mounts," the prophet continued in his prayer to God; "they are come unto the city to take it; and the city is given into the hand of the Chaldeans, that fight against it, because of the sword, and of the famine, and of the pestilence: and what Thou hast spoken is come to pass; and, behold, Thou seest it. And Thou hast said unto me, O Lord God, Buy thee the field for money, and take witnesses; for the city is given into the hand of the Chaldeans." Verses 24, 25.

The prayer of the prophet was graciously answered. "The word of the Lord unto Jeremiah" in that hour of distress, when the faith of the messenger of truth was being tried as by fire, was: "Behold, I am the Lord, the God of all flesh: is there anything too hard for Me?" Verses 26, 27. The city was soon to fall into the hand of the Chaldeans; its gates and palaces were to be set on fire and burned; but, notwithstanding the fact that destruction was imminent and the inhabitants of Jerusalem were to be carried away captive, nevertheless the eternal purpose of Jehovah for Israel was yet to be fulfilled. In further answer to the prayer of His servant, the Lord declared concerning those upon whom His chastisements were falling:

"Behold, I will gather them out of all countries, whither I have driven them in Mine anger, and in My fury, and in great wrath; and I will bring them again unto this place, and I will cause them to dwell safely: and they shall be My people, and I will be their God: and I will give them one heart, and one way, that they may fear Me forever, for the good of them, and of their children after them: and I will make an everlasting covenant with them, that I will not turn away from them, to do them good; but I will put My fear in their hearts, that they shall not depart from Me. Yea, I will rejoice over them to do them good, and I will plant them in this land assuredly with My whole heart and with My whole soul.

"For thus saith the Lord; Like as I have brought all this great evil upon this people, so will I bring upon them all the good that I have promised them. And fields shall be bought in this land, whereof ye say, It is desolate without man or beast; it is given into the hand of the Chaldeans. Men shall buy fields for money, and subscribe evidences, and seal them, and take witnesses in the land of Benjamin, and in the places about Jerusalem, and in the cities of Judah, and in the cities of the mountains, and in the cities of the valley, and in the cities of the south: for I will cause their captivity to return, saith the Lord." Verses 37-44.

In confirmation of these assurances of deliverance and restoration, "the word of the Lord came unto Jeremiah the second time, while he was yet shut up in the court of the prison, saying, "Thus saith the Lord the Maker thereof, the Lord that formed it, to establish it; the Lord is His name; Call unto Me, and I will answer thee, and show thee great and mighty things, which thou knowest not. For thus saith the Lord, the God of Israel, concerning the houses of this city, and concerning the houses of the kings of Judah, which are thrown down by the mounts, and by the sword; . . . Behold, I will bring it health and cure, and I will cure them, and will reveal unto them the abundance of peace and truth. And I will cause the captivity of Judah and the captivity of Israel to return, and will build them, as at the first. And I will cleanse them from all their iniquity, whereby they have sinned against Me; and I will pardon all their iniquities. . . . And it shall be to Me a name of joy, a praise and an honor before all the nations of the earth, which shall hear all the good that I do unto them: and they shall fear and tremble for all the goodness and for all the prosperity that I procure unto it.

"Thus saith the Lord; Again there shall be heard in this place, which ye say shall be desolate without man and without beast, even in the cities of Judah, and in the streets of Jerusalem, . . . the voice of joy, and the voice of gladness, the voice of the bridegroom, and the voice of the bride, the voice of them that shall say, Praise the Lord of hosts: for the Lord is good; for His mercy endureth forever: and of them that shall bring the sacrifice of praise into the house of the Lord. For I will cause to return the captivity of the land, as at the first, saith the Lord.

"Thus saith the Lord of hosts; Again in this place, which is desolate without man and without beast, and in all the cities thereof, shall be an habitation of shepherds causing their flocks to lie down. In the cities of the mountains, and in the cities of the vale, and in the cities of the south, and in the land of Benjamin, and in the places about Jerusalem, and in the cities of Judah, shall the flocks pass again under the hands of him that telleth them, saith the Lord.

"Behold, the days come, saith the Lord, that I will perform that good thing which I have promised unto the house of Israel and to the house of Judah." Jeremiah 33:1-14.

Thus was the church of God comforted in one of the darkest hours of her long conflict with the forces of evil. Satan had seemingly triumphed in his efforts to destroy Israel; but the Lord was overruling the events of the present, and during the years that were to follow, His people were to have opportunity to redeem the past. His message to the church was:

"Fear thou not, O My servant Jacob; . . . neither be dismayed, O Israel: for, lo, I will save thee from afar, and thy seed from the land of their captivity; and Jacob shall return, and shall be in rest, and be quiet, and none shall make him afraid. For I am with thee, saith the Lord, to save thee." "I will restore health unto thee, and I will heal thee of thy wounds." Jeremiah 30:10, 11, 17.

In the glad day of restoration the tribes of divided Israel were to be reunited as one people. The Lord was to be acknowledged as ruler over "all the families of Israel." "They shall be My people." He declared. "Sing with gladness for Jacob, and shout among the chief of the nations: publish ye, praise ye, and say, O Lord, save Thy people, the remnant of Israel. Behold, I will bring them from the north country, and gather them from the coasts of the earth, and with them the blind and the lame; . . . they shall come with weeping, and with supplications will I lead them: I will cause them to walk by the rivers of waters in a straight way, wherein they shall not stumble: for I am a Father to Israel, and Ephraim is My first-born." Jeremiah 31:1, 7-9

Humbled in the sight of the nations, those who once had been recognized as favored of Heaven above all other peoples of the earth were to learn in exile the lesson of obedience so necessary for their future happiness. Until they had learned this lesson, God could not do for them all that He desired to do. "I will correct thee in measure, and will not leave thee altogether unpunished," He declared in explanation of His purpose to chastise them for their spiritual good. Jeremiah 30:11. Yet those who had been the object of His tender love were not forever set aside; before all the nations of earth He would demonstrate His plan to bring victory out of apparent defeat, to save rather than to destroy. To the prophet was given the message:

"He that scattered Israel will gather him, and keep him, as a shepherd doth his flock. For the Lord hath redeemed Jacob, and ransomed him from the hand of him that was stronger than he. Therefore they shall come and sing in the height of Zion, and shall flow together to the goodness of the Lord, for wheat, and for wine, and for oil, and for the young of the flock and of the herd: and their soul shall be as a watered garden; and they shall not sorrow any more at all. . . . I will turn their mourning into joy, and will comfort them, and make them rejoice from their sorrow. And I will satiate the soul of the priests with fatness, and My people shall be satisfied with My goodness, saith the Lord."

"Thus saith the Lord of hosts, the God of Israel; As yet they shall use this speech in the land of Judah and in the cities thereof, when I shall bring again their captivity; The Lord bless thee, O habitation of justice, and mountain of holiness. And there shall dwell in Judah itself, and in all the cities thereof together, husbandmen, and they that go forth with flocks. For I have satiated the weary soul, and I have replenished every sorrowful soul."

"Behold, the days come, saith the Lord, that I will make a new covenant with the house of Israel, and with the house of Judah: not according to the covenant that I made with their fathers in the day that I took them by the hand to bring them out of the land of Egypt; which My covenant they brake, although I was an husband unto them, saith the Lord: but this shall be the covenant that I will make with the house of Israel; After those days, saith the Lord, I will put My law in their inward parts, and write it in their hearts; and will be their God, and they shall be My people. And they shall teach no more every man his neighbor, and every man his brother, saying, Know the Lord: for they shall all know Me, from the least of them unto the greatest of them, saith the Lord: for I will forgive their iniquity, and I will remember their sin no more." Jeremiah 31:10-14, 23-25, 31-34.

Ye are My witnesses, saith the Lord, and My servant whom I have chosen." Isaiah 43:10.

In the Court of Babylon

Among the children of Israel who were carried captive to Babylon at the beginning of the seventy years' captivity were Christian patriots, men who were as true as steel to principle, who would not be corrupted by selfishness, but who would honor God at the loss of all things. In the land of their captivity these men were to carry out God's purpose by giving to heathen nations the blessings that come through a knowledge of Jehovah. They were to be His representatives. Never were they to compromise with idolaters; their faith and their name as worshipers of the living God they were to bear as a high honor. And this they did. In prosperity and adversity they honored God, and God honored them.

The fact that these men, worshipers of Jehovah, were captives in Babylon, and that the vessels of God's house had been placed in the Temple of the Babylonish gods, was boastfully cited by the victors as evidence that their religion and customs were superior to the religion and customs of the Hebrews. Yet through the very humiliations that Israel's departure from Him had invited, God gave Babylon evidence of His supremacy, of the holiness of His requirements, and of the sure results of obedience. And this testimony He gave, as alone it could be given, through those who were loyal to Him.

Among those who maintained their allegiance to God were Daniel and his three companions—illustrious examples of what men may become who unite with the God of wisdom and power. From the comparative simplicity of their Jewish home, these youth of royal line were taken to the most magnificent of cities and into the court of the world's greatest monarch. Nebuchadnezzar "spake unto Ashpenaz the master of his eunuchs, that he should bring certain of the children of Israel, and of the king's seed, and of the princes; children in whom was no blemish, but well favored, and skillful in all wisdom, and cunning in knowledge, and understanding science, and such as had ability in them to stand in the king's palace. . . .

"Now among these were of the children of Judah, Daniel, Hananiah, Mishael, and Azariah. "Seeing in these youth the promise of remarkable ability, Nebuchadnezzar determined that they should be trained to fill important positions in his kingdom. That they might be fully qualified for their lifework, he arranged for them to learn the language of the Chaldeans and for three years to be granted the unusual educational advantages afforded princess of the realm.

The names of Daniel and his companions were changed to names representing Chaldean deities. Great significance was attached to the names given by Hebrew parents to their children. Often these stood for traits of character that the parent desired to see developed in the child. The prince in whose charge the captive youth were placed, "gave unto Daniel the name of Belteshazzar; and to Hananiah, of Shadrach; and to Mishael, of Meshach; and to Azariah, of Abednego."

The king did not compel the Hebrew youth to renounce their faith in favor of idolatry, but he hoped to bring this about gradually. By giving them names significant of idolatry, by bringing them daily into close association with idolatrous customs, and under the influence of the seductive rites of heathen worship, he hoped to induce them to renounce the religion of their nation and to unite with the worship of the Babylonians.

At the very outset of their career there came to them a decisive test of character. It was provided that they should eat of the food and drink of the wine that came from the king's table. In this the king thought to give them an expression of his favor and of his solicitude for their welfare. But a portion having been offered to idols, the food from the king's table was consecrated to idolatry; and one partaking of it would be regarded as offering homage to the gods of Babylon. In such homage, loyalty to Jehovah forbade Daniel and his companions to join. Even a mere pretense of eating the food or drinking the wine would be a denial of their faith. To do this would be to array themselves with heathenism and to dishonor the principles of the law of God.

Nor dared they risk the enervating effect of luxury and dissipation on physical, mental, and spiritual development. They were acquainted with the history of Nadab and Abihu, the record of whose intemperance and its results had been preserved in the parchments of the Pentateuch; and they knew that their own physical and mental power would be injuriously affected by the use of wine.

Daniel and his associates had been trained by their parents to habits of strict temperance. They had been taught that God would hold them accountable for their capabilities, and that they must never dwarf or enfeeble their powers. This education was to Daniel and his companions the means of their preservation amidst the demoralizing influences of the court of Babylon. Strong were the temptations surrounding them in that corrupt and luxurious court, but they remained uncontaminated. No power, no influence, could sway them from the principles they had learned in early life by a study of the word and works of God.

Had Daniel so desired, he might have found in his surroundings a plausible excuse for departing from strictly temperate habits. He might have argued that, dependent as he was on the king's favor and subject to his power, there was no other course for him to pursue than to eat of the king's food and drink of his wine; for should he adhere to the divine teaching, he would offend the king and probably lose his position and his life. Should he disregard the commandment of the Lord he would retain the favor of the king and secure for himself intellectual advantages and flattering worldly prospects.

But Daniel did not hesitate. The approval of God was dearer to him than the favor of the most powerful earthly potentate—dearer than life itself. He determined to stand firm in his integrity, let the result be what it might. He "purposed in his heart that he would not defile himself with the portion of the king's meat, nor with the wine which he drank." And in this resolve he was supported by his three companions.

In reaching this decision, the Hebrew youth did not act presumptuously but in firm reliance upon God. They did not choose to be singular, but they would be so rather than dishonor God. Should they compromise with wrong in this instance by yielding to the pressure of circumstances, their departure from principle would weaken their sense of right and their abhorrence of wrong. The first wrong step would lead to others, until, their connection with Heaven severed, they would be swept away by temptation.

"God had brought Daniel into favor and tender love with the prince of the eunuchs," and the request that he might not defile himself was received with respect. Yet the prince hesitated to grant it. "I fear my lord the king, who hath appointed your meat and your drink," he explained to Daniel; "for why should he see your faces worse liking than the children which are of your sort? then shall ye make me endanger my head to the king."

Daniel then appealed to Melzar, the officer in special charge of the Hebrew youth, requesting that they might be excused from eating the king's meat and drinking his wine. He asked that the matter be tested by a ten days' trial, the Hebrew youth during this time being supplied with simple food, while their companions ate of the king's dainties.

Melzar, though fearful that by complying with this request he would incur the displeasure of the king, nevertheless consented; and Daniel knew that his case was won. At the end of the ten days' trial the result was found to be the opposite of the prince's fears. "Their countenances appeared fairer and fatter in flesh than all the children which did eat the portion of the king's meat." In personal appearance the Hebrew youth showed a marked superiority over their companions. As a result, Daniel and his associates were permitted to continue their simple diet during their entire course of training.

For three years the Hebrew youth studied to acquire "the learning and the tongue of the Chaldeans." During this time they held fast their allegiance to God and depended constantly upon His power. With their habits of self-denial they united earnestness of purpose, diligence, and steadfastness. It was not pride or ambition that had brought them into the king's court, into companionship with those who neither knew nor feared God; they were captives in a strange land, placed there by Infinite Wisdom. Separated from home influences and sacred associations, they sought to acquit themselves creditably, for the honor of their down-trodden people, and for the glory of Him whose servants they were.

The Lord regarded with approval the firmness and self-denial of the Hebrew youth, and their purity of motive; and His blessing attended them. He "gave them knowledge and skill in all learning and wisdom: and Daniel had understanding in all visions and dreams." The promise was fulfilled, "Them that honor Me I will honor." 1 Samuel 2:30. As Daniel clung to God with unwavering trust, the spirit of prophetic power came upon him. While receiving instruction from man in the duties of court life, he was being taught by God to read the mysteries of the future and to record for coming generations, through figures and symbols, events covering the history of this world till the close of time.

When the time came for the youth in training to be tested, the Hebrews were examined, with other candidates, for the service of the kingdom. But "among them all was found none like Daniel, Hananiah, Mishael, and Azariah." Their keen comprehension, their wide knowledge, their choice and exact language, testified to the unimpaired strength and vigor of their mental powers. "In all matters of wisdom and understanding, that the king inquired of them, he found them ten times better than all the magicians and astrologers that were in all his realm;" "therefore stood they before the king."

At the court of Babylon were gathered representatives from all lands, men of the highest talent, men the most richly endowed with natural gifts, and possessed of the broadest culture that the world could bestow; yet among them all, the Hebrew youth were without a peer. In physical strength and beauty, in mental vigor and literary attainment, they stood unrivaled. The erect form, the firm, elastic step, the fair countenance, the undimmed senses, the untainted breath—all were so many certificates of good habits, insignia of the nobility with which nature honors those who are obedient to her laws.

In acquiring the wisdom of the Babylonians, Daniel and his companions were far more successful than their fellow students; but their learning did not come by chance. They obtained their knowledge by the faithful use of their powers, under the guidance of the Holy Spirit. They placed themselves in connection with the Source of all wisdom, making the knowledge of God the foundation of their education. In faith they prayed for wisdom, and they lived their prayers. They placed themselves where God could bless them. They avoided that which would weaken their powers, and improved every opportunity to become intelligent in all lines of learning. They followed the rules of life that could not fail to give them strength of intellect. They sought to acquire knowledge for one purpose—that they might honor God. They realized that in order to stand as representatives of true religion amid the false religions of heathenism they must have clearness of intellect and must perfect a Christian character. And God Himself was their teacher. Constantly praying,

conscientiously studying, keeping in touch with the Unseen, they walked with God as did Enoch.

True success in any line of work is not the result of chance or accident or destiny. It is the outworking of God's providences, the reward of faith and discretion, of virtue and perseverance. Fine mental qualities and a high moral tone are not the result of accident. God gives opportunities; success depends upon the use made of them.

While God was working in Daniel and his companions "to will and to do of His good pleasure," they were working out their own salvation. Philippians 2:13. Herein is revealed the outworking of the divine principle of co-operation, without which no true success can be attained. Human effort avails nothing without divine power; and without human endeavor, divine effort is with many of no avail. To make God's grace our own, we must act our part. His grace is given to work in us to will and to do, but never as a substitute for our effort.

As the Lord co-operated with Daniel and his fellows, so He will co-operate with all who strive to do His will. And by the impartation of His Spirit He will strengthen every true purpose, every noble resolution. Those who walk in the path of obedience will encounter many hindrances. Strong, subtle influences may bind them to the world; but the Lord is able to render futile every agency that works for the defeat of His chosen ones; in His strength they may overcome every temptation, conquer every difficulty.

God brought Daniel and his associates into connection with the great men of Babylon, that in the midst of a nation of idolaters they might represent His character. How did they become fitted for a position of so great trust and honor? It was faithfulness in little things that gave complexion to their whole life. They honored God in the smallest duties, as well as in the larger responsibilities.

As God called Daniel to witness for Him in Babylon, so He calls us to be His witnesses in the world today. In the smallest as well as the largest affairs of life, He desires us to reveal to men the principles of His kingdom. Many are waiting for some great work to be brought to them, while daily they lose opportunities for revealing faithfulness to God. Daily they fail of discharging with wholeheartedness the little duties of life. While they wait for some large work in which they may exercise supposedly great talents, and thus satisfy their ambitious longings, their days pass away.

In the life of the true Christian there are no nonessentials; in the sight of Omnipotence every duty is important. The Lord measures with exactness every possibility for service. The unused capabilities are just as much brought into account as those that are used. We shall be judged by what we ought to have done, but did not accomplish because we did not use our powers to glorify God.

A noble character is not the result of accident; it is not due to special favors or endowments of Providence. It is the result of self-discipline, of subjection of the lower to the higher nature, of the surrender of self to the service of God and man.

Through the fidelity to the principles of temperance shown

by the Hebrew youth God is speaking to the youth of today. There is need of men who like Daniel will do and dare for the cause of right. Pure hearts, strong hands, fearless courage, are needed; for the warfare between vice and virtue calls for ceaseless vigilance. To every soul Satan comes with temptation in many alluring forms on the point of indulgence of appetite.

The body is a most important medium through which the mind and the soul are developed for the upbuilding of character. Hence it is that the adversary of souls directs his temptations to the enfeebling and degrading of the physical powers. His success here often means the surrender of the whole being to evil. The tendencies of the physical nature, unless under the dominion of a higher power, will surely work ruin and death. The body is to be brought into subjection to the higher powers of the being. The passions are to be controlled by the will, which is itself to be under the control of God. The kingly power of reason, sanctified by divine grace, is to bear sway in the life. Intellectual power, physical stamina, and the length of life depend upon immutable laws. Through obedience to these laws, man may stand conqueror of himself, conqueror of his own inclinations, conqueror of principalities and powers, of "the rulers of the darkness of this world," and of "spiritual wickedness in high places." Ephesians 6:12.

In that ancient ritual which is the gospel in symbol, no blemished offering could be brought to God's altar. The sacrifice that was to represent Christ must be spotless. The word of God points to this as an illustration of what His children are to be—"a living sacrifice," "holy and without blemish." Romans 12:1; Ephesians 5:27.

The Hebrew worthies were men of like passions with ourselves; yet, notwithstanding the seductive influences of the court of Babylon, they stood firm, because they depended upon a strength that is infinite. In them a heathen nation beheld an illustration of the goodness and beneficence of God, and of the love of Christ. And in their experience we have an instance of the triumph of principle over temptation, of purity over depravity, of devotion and loyalty over atheism and idolatry.

The spirit that possessed Daniel, the youth of today may have; they may draw from the same source of strength, possess the same power of self-control, and reveal the same grace in their lives, even under circumstances as unfavorable. Though surrounded by temptations to self-indulgence, especially in our large cities, where every form of sensual gratification is made easy and inviting, yet by divine grace their purpose to honor God may remain firm. Through strong resolution and vigilant watchfulness they may withstand every temptation that assails the soul. But only by him who determines to do right because it is right will the victory be gained.

What a lifework was that of these noble Hebrews! As they bade farewell to their childhood home, little did they dream what a high destiny was to be theirs. Faithful and steadfast, they yielded to the divine guiding, so that through them God could fulfill His purpose.

The same mighty truths that were revealed through these men, God desires to reveal through the youth and children today. The life of Daniel and his fellows is a demonstration of what He will do for those who yield themselves to Him and with the whole heart seek to accomplish His purpose.

Nebuchadnezzar's Dream

Soon after Daniel and his companions entered the service of the king of Babylon, events occurred that revealed to an idolatrous nation the power and faithfulness of the God of Israel. Nebuchadnezzar had a remarkable dream, by which "his spirit was troubled, and his sleep brake from him." But although the king's mind was deeply impressed, he found it impossible, when he awoke, to recall the particulars. In his perplexity, Nebuchadnezzar assembled his wise men—"the magicians, and the astrologers, and the sorcerers"—and besought their help. "I have dreamed a dream," he said, "and my spirit was troubled to know the dream." With this statement of his perplexity he requested them to reveal to him that which would bring relief to his mind.

To this the wise men responded, "O king, live forever: tell thy servants the dream, and we will show the interpretation."

Dissatisfied with their evasive answer, and suspicious because, despite their pretentious claims to reveal the secrets of men, they nevertheless seemed unwilling to grant him help, the king commanded his wise men, with promises of wealth and honor on the one hand, and threats of death on the other, to tell him not only the interpretation of the dream, but the dream itself. "The thing is gone from me," he said; "if ye will not make known unto me the dream, with the interpretation thereof, ye shall be cut in pieces, and your houses shall be made a dunghill. But if ye show the dream, and the interpretation thereof, ye shall receive of me gifts and rewards and great honor."

Still the wise men returned the answer, "Let the king tell his servants the dream, and we will show the interpretation of it."

Nebuchadnezzar, now thoroughly aroused and angered by the apparent perfidy of those in whom he had trusted, declared: "I know of certainty that ye would gain the time, because ye see the thing is gone from me. But if ye will not make known unto me the dream, there is but one decree for you: for ye have prepared lying and corrupt words to speak before me, till the time be changed: therefore tell me the dream, and I shall know that ye can show me the interpretation thereof."

Filled with fear for the consequences of their failure, the magicians endeavored to show the king that his request was unreasonable and his test beyond that which had ever been required of any man. "There is not a man upon the earth," they remonstrated, "that can show the king's matter: therefore there is no king, lord, nor ruler, that asked such things at any magician, or astrologer, or Chaldean. And it is a rare thing that the king requireth, and there is none other that can show it before the king, except the gods, whose dwelling is not with flesh."

Then "the king was angry and very furious, and commanded to destroy all the wise men of Babylon."

Among those sought for by the officers who were preparing to fulfill the provisions of the royal decree, were Daniel and his friends. When told that according to the decree they also must die, "with counsel and wisdom" Daniel inquired of Arioch, the captain of the king's guard, "Why is the decree so hasty from the king?" Arioch told him the story of the king's perplexity over his remarkable dream, and of his failure to secure help from those in whom he had hitherto placed fullest confidence. Upon hearing this, Daniel, taking his life in his hands, ventured into the king's presence and begged that time be granted, that he might petition his God to reveal to him the dream and its interpretation.

To this request the monarch acceded. "Then Daniel went to his house, and made the thing known to Hananiah, Mishael, and Azariah, his companions." Together they sought for wisdom from the Source of light and knowledge. Their faith was strong in the consciousness that God had placed them where they were, that they were doing His work and meeting the demands of duty. In times of perplexity and danger they had always turned to Him for guidance and protection, and He had proved an ever-present help. Now with contrition of heart they submitted themselves anew to the Judge of the earth, pleading that He would grant them deliverance in this their time of special need. And they did not plead in vain. The God whom they had honored, now honored them. The Spirit of the Lord rested upon them, and to Daniel, "in a night vision," was revealed the king's dream and its meaning.

Daniel's first act was to thank God for the revelation given him. "Blessed be the name of God forever and ever," he exclaimed; "for wisdom and might are His: and He changeth the times and the reasons: He removeth kings, and setteth up kings: He giveth wisdom unto the wise, and knowledge to them that know understanding: He revealeth the deep and secret things: He knoweth what is in the darkness, and the light dwelleth with Him. I thank Thee, and praise Thee, O Thou God of my fathers, who hast given me wisdom and might, and hast made known unto me now what we desired of Thee: for Thou hast now made known unto us the king's matter."

Going immediately to Arioch, whom the king had commanded to destroy the wise men, Daniel said, "Destroy not the wise men of Babylon: bring me in before the king, and I will show unto the king the interpretation." Quickly the officer ushered Daniel in before the king, with the words, "I have found a man of the captives of Judah, that will make known unto the king the interpretation."

Behold the Jewish captive, calm and self-possessed, in the presence of the monarch of the world's most powerful empire. In his first words he disclaimed honor for himself and exalted God as the source of all wisdom. To the anxious inquiry of the king, "Art thou able to make known unto me the dream which I have seen, and the interpretation thereof?" he replied: "The secret which the king hath demanded cannot the wise men, the astrologers, the magicians, the soothsayers, show unto the king; but there is a God in heaven that revealeth secrets, and maketh known to the king Nebuchadnezzar what shall be in the latter days. "Thy dream," Daniel declared, "and the visions of thy head upon thy bed, are these; As for thee, O king, thy thoughts came into thy mind upon thy bed, what should come to pass hereafter: and He that revealeth secrets maketh known to thee what shall come to pass. But as for me, this secret is not revealed to me for any wisdom that I have more than any living, but for their sakes that shall make known the interpretation to the king, and that thou mightest know the thoughts of thy heart.

"Thou, O king, sawest, and behold a great image. This great image, whose brightness was excellent, stood before thee; and the form thereof was terrible. This image's head was of fine gold, his breast and his arms of silver, his belly and his thighs of brass, his legs of iron, his feet part of iron and part of clay.

"Thou sawest till that a stone was cut out without hands, which smote the image upon his feet that were of iron and clay, and brake them to pieces. Then was the iron, the clay, the brass, the silver, and the gold, broken to pieces together, and became like the chaff of the summer threshing floors; and the wind carried them away, that no place was found for them: and the stone that smote the image became a great mountain, and filled the whole earth.

"This is the dream," confidently declared Daniel; and the king, listening with closest attention to every particular, knew it was the very dream over which he had been so troubled. Thus his mind was prepared to receive with favor the interpretation. The King of kings was about to communicate great truth to the Babylonian monarch. God would reveal that He has power over the kingdoms of the world, power to enthrone and to dethrone kings. Nebuchadnezzar's mind was to be awakened, if possible, to a sense of his responsibility to Heaven. The events of the future, reaching down to the end of time, were to be opened before him.

"Thou, O king, art a king of kings," Daniel continued, "for the God of heaven hath given thee a kingdom, power, and strength, and glory. And wheresoever the children of men dwell, the beasts of the field and fowls of the heaven hath He given into thine hand, and hath made thee ruler over them all. Thou art this head of gold.

"And after thee shall arise another kingdom inferior to thee, and another third kingdom of brass, which shall bear rule over all the earth.

"And the fourth kingdom shall be strong as iron: forasmuch as iron breaketh in pieces and subdueth all things: and as iron that breaketh all these, shall it break in pieces and bruise.

"And whereas thou sawest the feet and toes, part of potters' clay, and part of iron, the kingdom shall be divided; but there shall be in it of the strength of the iron, forasmuch as thou sawest the iron mixed with miry clay. And as the toes of the feet were part of iron, and part of clay, so the kingdom shall be partly strong, and partly broken. And whereas thou sawest iron mixed with miry clay, they shall mingle themselves with the seed of men: but they shall not cleave one to another, even as iron is not mixed with clay."

"In the days of these kings shall the God of heaven set up a kingdom, which shall never be destroyed: and the kingdom shall not be left to other people, but it shall break in pieces and consume all these kingdoms, and it shall stand forever. Forasmuch as thou sawest that the stone was cut out of the mountain without hands, and that it brake in pieces the iron, the brass, the clay, the silver, and the gold; the great God hath made known to the king what shall come to pass hereafter: and the dream is certain, and the interpretation thereof sure."

The king was convinced of the truth of the interpretation, and in humility and awe he "fell upon his face, and worshiped," saying, "Of a truth it is, that your God is a God of gods, and a Lord of kings, and a revealer of secrets, seeing thou couldest reveal this secret."

Nebuchadnezzar revoked the decree for the destruction of the wise men. Their lives were spared because of Daniel's connection with the Revealer of secrets. And "the king made Daniel a great man, and gave him many great gifts, and made him ruler over the whole province of Babylon, and chief of the governors over all the wise men of Babylon. Then Daniel requested of the king, and he set Shadrach, Meshach, and Abednego, over the affairs of the province of Babylon: but Daniel sat in the gate of the king."

In the annals of human history, the growth of nations, the rise and fall of empires, appear as if dependent on the will and prowess of man; the shaping of events seems, to a great degree, to be determined by his power, ambition, or caprice. But in the word of God the curtain is drawn aside, and we behold, above, behind, and through all the play and counterplay of human interest and power and passions, the agencies of the All-merciful One, silently, patiently working out the counsels of His own will.

In words of matchless beauty and tenderness, the apostle Paul set before the sages of Athens the divine purpose in the creation and distribution of races and nations. "God that made the world and all things therein," declared the apostle, "hath made of one blood all nations of men for to dwell on all the face of the earth, and hath determined the times before appointed, and the bounds of their habitation; that they should seek the Lord, if haply they might feel after Him, and find Him." Acts 17:24-27. God has made plain that whosoever will, may come "into the bond of the covenant." Ezekiel 20:37. In the creation it was His purpose that the earth should be inhabited by beings whose existence would be a blessing to themselves and to one another, and an honor to their Creator. All who will may identify themselves with this purpose. Of them it is spoken, "This people have I formed for Myself; they shall show forth My praise." Isaiah 43:21.

In His law God has made known the principles that underlie all true prosperity, both of nations and of individuals. To the Israelites Moses declared of this law: "This is your wisdom and your understanding." "It is not a vain thing for you; because it is your life." Deuteronomy 4:6; 32:47. The blessings thus assured to Israel are, on the same conditions and in the same degree, assured to every nation and to every individual under the broad heavens.

Hundreds of years before certain nations came upon the stage of action, the Omniscient One looked down the ages and predicted the rise and fall of the universal kingdoms. God declared to Nebuchadnezzar that the kingdom of Babylon should fall, and a second kingdom would arise, which also would have its period of trial. Failing to exalt the true God, its glory would fade, and a third kingdom would occupy its place. This also would pass away; and a fourth, strong as iron, would subdue the nations of the world.

Had the rulers of Babylon—that richest of all earthly kingdoms—kept always before them the fear of Jehovah, they would have been given wisdom and power which would have bound them to Him and kept them strong. But they made God their refuge only when harassed and perplexed. At such times, failing to find help in their great men, they sought it from men like Daniel—men who they knew honored the living God and were honored by Him. To these men they appealed to unravel the mysteries of Providence; for though the rulers of proud Babylon were men of the highest intellect, they had separated themselves so far from God by transgression that they could not understand the revelations and the warnings given them concerning the future.

In the history of nations the student of God's word may behold the literal fulfillment of divine prophecy. Babylon, shattered and broken at last, passed away because in prosperity its rulers had regarded themselves as independent of God, and had ascribed the glory of their kingdom to human achievement. The Medo-Persian realm was visited by the wrath of Heaven because in it God's law had been trampled underfoot. The fear of the Lord had found no place in the hearts of the vast majority of the people. Wickedness, blasphemy, and corruption prevailed. The kingdoms that followed were even more base and corrupt; and these sank lower and still lower in the scale of moral worth.

The power exercised by every ruler on the earth is Heaven-imparted; and upon his use of the power thus bestowed, his success depends. To each the word of the divine Watcher is, "I girded thee, though thou hast not known Me." Isaiah 45:5. And to each the words spoken to Nebuchadnezzar of old are the lesson of life: "Break off thy sins by righteousness, and thine iniquities by showing mercy to the poor: if it may be a lengthening of thy tranquillity." Daniel 4:27.

To understand these things,—to understand that "righteousness exalteth a nation;" that "the throne is established by righteousness," and "upholden by mercy;" to recognize the outworking of these principles in the manifestation of His power who "removeth kings, and setteth up kings,"— this is to understand the philosophy of history. Proverbs 14:34; 16:12; 20:28; Daniel 2:21.

In the word of God only is this clearly set forth. Here it is shown that the strength of nations, as of individuals, is not found in the opportunities or facilities that appear to make them invincible; it is not found in their boasted greatness. It is measured by the fidelity with which they fulfill God's purpose.

The Fiery Furnace

The dream of the great image, opening before Nebuchadnezzar events reaching to the close of time, had been given that he might understand the part he was to act in the world's history, and the relation that his kingdom should sustain to the kingdom of heaven. In the interpretation of the dream, he had been plainly instructed regarding the establishment of God's everlasting kingdom. "In the days of these kings," Daniel had declared, "shall the God of heaven set up a kingdom, which shall never be destroyed: and the kingdom shall not be left to other people, but it shall break in pieces and consume all these kingdoms, and it shall stand forever. . . . The dream is certain, and the interpretation thereof sure." Daniel 2:44, 45.

The king had acknowledged the power of God, saying to Daniel, "Of a truth it is, that your God is a God of gods, . . . and a revealer of secrets." Verse 47. For a time afterward, Nebuchadnezzar was influenced by the fear of God;

but his heart was not yet cleansed from worldly ambition and a desire for self-exaltation. The prosperity attending his reign filled him with pride. In time he ceased to honor God, and resumed his idol worship with increased zeal and bigotry.

The words, "Thou art this head of gold," had made a deep impression upon the ruler's mind. Verse 38. The wise men of his realm, taking advantage of this and of his return to idolatry, proposed that he make an image similar to the one seen in his dream, and set it up where all might behold the head of gold, which had been interpreted as representing his kingdom.

Pleased with the flattering suggestion, he determined to carry it out, and to go even farther. Instead of reproducing the image as he had seen it, he would excel the original. His image should not deteriorate in value from the head to the feet, but should be entirely of gold—symbolic throughout of Babylon as an eternal, indestructible, all-powerful kingdom, which should break in pieces all other kingdoms and stand forever.

The thought of establishing the empire and a dynasty that should endure forever, appealed very strongly to the mighty ruler before whose arms the nations of earth had been unable to stand. With an enthusiasm born of boundless ambition and selfish pride, he entered into counsel with his wise men as to how to bring this about. Forgetting the remarkable providences connected with the dream of the great image;

forgetting also that the God of Israel through His servant Daniel had made plain the significance of the image, and that in connection with this interpretation the great men of the realm had been saved an ignominious death; forgetting all except their desire to establish their own power and supremacy, the king and his counselors of state determined that by every means possible they would endeavor to exalt Babylon as supreme, and worthy of universal allegiance.

The symbolic representation by which God had revealed to king and people His purpose for the nations of earth, was now to be made to serve for the glorification of human power. Daniel's interpretation was to be rejected and forgotten; truth was to be misinterpreted and misapplied. The symbol designed of Heaven to unfold to the minds of men important events of the future, was to be used to hinder the spread of the knowledge that God desired the world to receive. Thus through the devisings of ambitious men, Satan was seeking to thwart the divine purpose for the human race. The enemy of mankind knew that truth unmixed with error is a power mighty to save; but that when used to exalt self and to further the projects of men, it becomes a power for evil.

From his rich store of treasure, Nebuchadnezzar caused to be made a great golden image, similar in its general features to that which had been seen in vision, save in the one particular of the material of which it was composed. Accustomed as they were to magnificent representations of their heathen deities, the Chaldeans had never before produced anything so imposing and majestic as this resplendent statue, threescore cubits in height and six cubits in breadth. And it is not surprising that in a land where idol worship was of universal prevalence, the beautiful and priceless image in the plain of Dura, representing the glory of Babylon and its magnificence and power, should be consecrated as an object of worship. This was accordingly provided for, and a decree went forth that on the day of the dedication all should show their supreme loyalty to the Babylonian power by bowing before the image.

The appointed day came, and a vast concourse from all "people, nations, and languages," assembled on the plain of Dura. In harmony with the king's command, when the sound of music was heard, the whole company "fell down and worshipped the golden image." On that eventful day the powers of darkness seemed to be gaining a signal triumph; the worship of the golden image bade fair to become connected permanently with the established forms of idolatry recognized as the state religion of the land. Satan hoped thereby to defeat God's purpose of making the presence of captive Israel in Babylon a means of blessing to all the nations of heathendom.

But God decreed otherwise. Not all had bowed the knee to the idolatrous symbol of human power. In the midst of the worshipping multitude there were three men who were firmly resolved not thus to dishonor the God of heaven. Their God was King of kings and Lord of lords; they would bow to none other.

To Nebuchadnezzar, flushed with triumph, was brought the

word that among his subjects there were some who dared disobey his mandate. Certain of the wise men, jealous of the honors that had been bestowed upon the faithful companions of Daniel, now reported to the king their flagrant violation of his wishes. "O king, live forever," they exclaimed. "There are certain Jews whom thou hast set over the affairs of the province of Babylon, Shadrach, Meshach, and Abednego; these men, O king, have not regarded thee: they serve not thy gods, nor worship the golden image which thou hast set up."

The king commanded that the men be brought before him. "Is it true," he inquired, "do not ye serve my gods, nor worship the golden image which I have set up?" He endeavored by threats to induce them to unite with the multitude. Pointing to the fiery furnace, he reminded them of the punishment awaiting them if they should persist in their refusal to obey his will. But firmly the Hebrews testified to their allegiance to the God of heaven, and their faith in His power to deliver. The act of bowing to the image was understood by all to be an act of worship. Such homage they could render to God alone.

As the three Hebrews stood before the king, he was convinced that they possessed something the other wise men of his kingdom did not have. They had been faithful in the performance of every duty. He would give them another trial. If only they would signify their willingness to unite with the multitude in worshiping the image, all would be well with them; "but if ye worship not," he added, "ye shall be cast the same hour into the midst of a burning fiery furnace." Then with his hand stretched upward in defiance, he demanded, "Who is that God that shall deliver you out of my hands?"

In vain were the king's threats. He could not turn the men from their allegiance to the Ruler of the universe. From the history of their fathers they had learned that disobedience to God results in dishonor, disaster, and death; and that the fear of the Lord is the beginning of wisdom, the foundation of all true prosperity. Calmly facing the furnace, they said, "O Nebuchadnezzar, we are not careful to answer thee in this matter. If it be so, our God whom we serve is able to deliver us from the burning fiery furnace, and He will deliver us out of thine hand, O king." Their faith strengthened as they declared that God would be glorified by delivering them, and with triumphant assurance born of implicit trust in God, they added, "But if not, be it known unto thee, O king, that we will not serve thy gods, nor worship the golden image which thou hast set up."

The king's wrath knew no bounds. "Full of fury," "the form of his visage was changed against Shadrach, Meshach, and Abednego," representatives of a despised and captive race. Directing that the furnace be heated seven times hotter than its wont, he commanded the mighty men of his army to bind the worshipers of Israel's God, preparatory to summary execution.

"Then these men were bound in their coats, their hosen, and their hats, and their other garments, and were cast into the midst of the burning fiery furnace. Therefore because the king's commandment was urgent, and the furnace exceeding hot, the flame of the fire slew those men that took up Shadrach, Meshach, and Abednego."

But the Lord did not forget His own. As His witnesses were cast into the furnace, the Saviour revealed Himself to them in person, and together they walked in the midst of the fire. In the presence of the Lord of heat and cold, the flames lost their power to consume.

From his royal seat the king looked on, expecting to see the men who had defied him utterly destroyed. But his feelings of triumph suddenly changed. The nobles standing near saw his face grow pale as he started from the throne and looked intently into the glowing flames. In alarm the king, turning to his lords, asked, "Did not we cast three men bound into the midst of the fire? . . . Lo, I see four men loose, walking in the midst of the fire, and they have no hurt; and the form of the fourth is like the Son of God."

How did that heathen king know what the Son of God was like? The Hebrew captives filling positions of trust in Babylon had in life and character represented before him the truth. When asked for a reason of their faith, they had given it without hesitation. Plainly and simply they had presented the principles of righteousness, thus teaching those around them of the God whom they worshiped. They had told of Christ, the Redeemer to come; and in the form of the fourth in the midst of the fire the king recognized the Son of God.

And now, his own greatness and dignity forgotten, Nebuchadnezzar descended from his throne and, going to the mouth of the furnace, cried out, "Ye servants of the most high God, come forth, and come hither."

Then Shadrach, Meshach, and Abednego came forth before the vast multitude, showing themselves unhurt. The presence of their Saviour had guarded them from harm, and only their fetters had been burned. "And the princes, governors, and captains, and the king's counselors, being gathered together, saw these men, upon whose bodies the fire had no power, nor was an hair of their head singed, neither were their coats changed, nor the smell of fire had passed on them."

Forgotten was the great golden image, set up with such pomp. In the presence of the living God, men feared and trembled. "Blessed be the God of Shadrach, Meshach, and Abednego," the humbled king was constrained to acknowledge, "who hath sent His angel, and delivered His servants that trusted in Him, and have changed the king's word, and yielded their bodies, that they might not serve nor worship any god, except their own God."

The experiences of that day led Nebuchadnezzar to issue a decree, "that every people, nation, and language, which speak anything amiss against the God of Shadrach, Meshach, and Abednego, shall be cut in pieces, and their houses shall be made a dunghill." "There is no other god," he urged as the reason for the decree, "that can deliver after this sort."

In these and like words the king of Babylon endeavored to spread abroad before all the peoples of earth his conviction that the power and authority of the God of the Hebrews was worthy of supreme adoration. And God was pleased with the effort of the king to show Him reverence, and to make the royal confession of allegiance as widespread as was the Babylonian realm.

It was right for the king to make public confession, and to seek to exalt the God of heaven above all other gods; but in endeavoring to force his subjects to make a similar confession of faith and to show similar reverence, Nebuchadnezzar was exceeding his right as a temporal sovereign. He had no more right, either civil or moral, to threaten men with death for not worshiping God, than he had to make the decree consigning to the flames all who refused to worship the golden image. God never compels the obedience of man. He leaves all free to choose whom they will serve.

By the deliverance of His faithful servants, the Lord declared that He takes His stand with the oppressed, and rebukes all earthly powers that rebel against the authority of Heaven. The three Hebrews declared to the whole nation of Babylon their faith in Him whom they worshiped. They relied on God. In the hour of their trial they remembered the promise, "When thou passest through the waters, I will be with thee; and through the rivers, they shall not overflow thee: when thou walkest through the fire, thou shalt not be burned; neither shall the flame kindle upon thee." Isaiah 43:2. And in a marvelous manner their faith in the living Word had been honored in the sight of all. The tidings of their wonderful deliverance were carried to many countries by the representatives of the different nations that had been invited by Nebuchadnezzar to the dedication. Through the faithfulness of His children, God was glorified in all the earth.

Important are the lessons to be learned from the experience of the Hebrew youth on the plain of Dura. In this our day, many of God's servants, though innocent of wrongdoing, will be given over to suffer humiliation and abuse at the hands of those who, inspired by Satan, are filled with envy and religious bigotry. Especially will the wrath of man be aroused against those who hallow the Sabbath of the fourth commandment; and at last a universal decree will denounce these as deserving of death.

The season of distress before God's people will call for a faith that will not falter. His children must make it manifest that He is the only object of their worship, and that no consideration, not even that of life itself, can induce them to make the least concession to false worship. To the loyal heart the commands of sinful, finite men will sink into insignificance beside the word of the eternal God. Truth will be obeyed though the result be imprisonment or exile or death.

As in the days of Shadrach, Meshach, and Abednego, so in the closing period of earth's history the Lord will work mightily in behalf of those who stand steadfastly for the right. He who walked with the Hebrew worthies in the fiery furnace will be with His followers wherever they are. His abiding presence will comfort and sustain. In the midst of the time of trouble—trouble such as has not been since there was a nation—His chosen ones will stand unmoved. Satan with all the hosts of evil cannot destroy the weakest of God's saints. Angels that excel in strength will protect them, and in their behalf Jehovah will reveal Himself as a "God of gods," able to save to the uttermost those who have put their trust in Him.

True Greatness

Exalted to the pinnacle of worldly honor, and acknowledged even by Inspiration as "a king of kings" (Ezekiel 26:7). Nebuchadnezzar nevertheless at times had ascribed to the favor of Jehovah the glory of his kingdom and the splendor of his reign. Such had been the case after his dream of the great image. His mind had been profoundly influenced by this vision and by the thought that the Babylonian Empire, universal though it was, was finally to fall, and other kingdoms were to bear sway, until at last all earthly powers were to be superseded by a kingdom set up by the God of heaven, which kingdom was never to be destroyed.

Nebuchadnezzar's noble conception of God's purpose concerning the nations was lost sight of later in his experience; yet when his proud spirit was humbled before the multitude on the plain of Dura, he once more had acknowledged that God's kingdom is "an everlasting kingdom, and His dominion is from generation to generation." An idolater by birth and training, and at the head of an idolatrous people, he had nevertheless an innate sense of justice and right, and God was able to use him as an instrument for the punishment of the rebellious and for the fulfillment of the divine purpose. "The terrible of the nations" (Ezekiel 28:7), it was given Nebuchadnezzar, after years of patient and wearing labor, to conquer Tyre; Egypt also fell a prey to his victorious armies; and as he added nation after nation to the Babylonian realm, he added more and more to his fame as the greatest ruler of the age.

It is not surprising that the successful monarch, so ambitious and so proud-spirited, should be tempted to turn aside from the path of humility, which alone leads to true greatness. In the intervals between his wars of conquest he gave much thought to the strengthening and beautifying of his capital, until at length the city of Babylon became the chief glory of his kingdom, "the golden city," "the praise of the whole earth." His passion as a builder, and his signal success in making Babylon one of the wonders of the world, ministered to his pride, until he was in grave danger of spoiling his record as a wise ruler whom God could continue to use as an instrument for the carrying out of the divine purpose.

In mercy God gave the king another dream, to warn him of his peril and of the snare that had been laid for his ruin. In a vision of the night, Nebuchadnezzar saw a great tree growing in the midst of the earth, its top towering to the heavens and its branches stretching to the ends of the earth. Flocks and herds from the mountains and hills enjoyed shelter beneath its shadow, and the birds of the air built their nests in its boughs. "The leaves thereof were fair, and the fruit thereof much, and in it was meat for all: . . . and all flesh was fed of it."

As the king gazed upon the lofty tree, he beheld "a Watcher," even "an Holy One," who approached the tree and in a loud voice cried: "Hew down the tree, and cut off his branches, shake off his leaves, and scatter his fruit: let the beasts get away from under it, and the fowls from his branches: nevertheless leave the stump of his roots in the earth, even with a band of iron and brass, in the tender grass of the field; and let it be wet with the dew of heaven, and let his portion be with the beasts in the grass of the earth: let his heart be changed from man's, and let a beast's heart be given unto him; and let seven times pass over him. This matter is by the decree of the watchers, and the demand by the word of the holy ones: to the intent that the living may know that the Most High ruleth in the kingdom of men, and giveth it to whomsoever He will, and setteth up over it the basest of men."

Greatly troubled by the dream, which was evidently a prediction of adversity, the king repeated it to "the magicians, the astrologers, the Chaldeans, and the soothsayers;" but although the dream was very explicit, none of the wise men could interpret it.

Once more in this idolatrous nation, testimony was to be borne to the fact that only those who love and fear God can understand the mysteries of the kingdom of heaven. The king in his perplexity sent for his servant Daniel, a man esteemed for his integrity and constancy and for his unrivaled wisdom.

When Daniel, in response to the royal summons, stood in the king's presence, Nebuchadnezzar said, "O Belteshazzar, master of the magicians, because I know that the spirit of the holy gods is in thee, and no secret troubleth thee, tell me the visions of my dream that I have seen, and the interpretation thereof." After relating the dream, Nebuchadnezzar said: "O Belteshazzar, declare the interpretation thereof, forasmuch as all the wise men of my kingdom are not able to make known unto me the interpretation: but thou art able; for the spirit of the holy gods is in thee."

To Daniel the meaning of the dream was plain, and its significance startled him. He "was astonied for one hour, and his thoughts troubled him." Seeing Daniel's hesitation and distress, the king expressed sympathy for his servant. "Belteshazzar," he said, "let not the dream, or the interpretation thereof, trouble thee."

"My lord," Daniel answered, "the dream be to them that hate thee, and the interpretation thereof to thine enemies." The prophet realized that upon him God had laid the solemn duty of revealing to Nebuchadnezzar the judgment that was about to fall upon him because of his pride and arrogance. Daniel must interpret the dream in language the king could understand; and although its dreadful import had made him hesitate in dumb amazement, yet he must state the truth, whatever the consequences to himself.

Then Daniel made known the mandate of the Almighty. "The tree that thou sawest," he said, "which grew, and was strong, whose height reached unto the heaven, and the sight

thereof to all the earth; whose leaves were fair, and the fruit thereof much, and in it was meat for all; under which the beast of the field dwelt, and upon whose branches the fowls of the heaven had their habitation: it is thou, O king, that art grown and become strong: for thy greatness is grown, and reacheth unto heaven, and thy dominion to the end of the earth.

"And whereas the king saw a Watcher and an Holy One coming down from heaven, and saying, Hew the tree down, and destroy it; yet leave the stump of the roots thereof in the earth, even with a band of iron and brass, in the tender grass of the field; and let it be wet with the dew of heaven, and let his portion be with the beasts of the field, till seven times pass over him; this is the interpretation, O king, and this is the decree of the Most High, which is come upon my lord the king: that they shall drive thee from men, and thy dwelling shall be with the beasts of the field, and they shall make thee to eat grass as oxen, and they shall wet thee with the dew of heaven, and seven times shall pass over thee, till thou know that the Most High ruleth in the kingdom of men, and giveth it to whomsoever He will. And whereas they commanded to leave the stump of the tree roots; thy kingdom shall be sure unto thee, after that thou shalt have known that the Heavens do rule."

Having faithfully interpreted the dream, Daniel urged the proud monarch to repent and turn to God, that by rightdoing he might avert the threatened calamity. "O king," the prophet pleaded, "let my counsel be acceptable unto thee, and break off thy sins by righteousness, and thine iniquities by showing mercy to the poor; if it may be a lengthening of thy tranquillity."

For a time the impression of the warning and the counsel of the prophet was strong upon Nebuchadnezzar; but the heart that is not transformed by the grace of God soon loses the impressions of the Holy Spirit. Self-indulgence and ambition had not yet been eradicated from the king's heart, and later on these traits reappeared. Notwithstanding the instruction so graciously given him, and the warnings of past experience, Nebuchadnezzar again allowed himself to be controlled by a spirit of jealousy against the kingdoms that were to follow. His rule, which heretofore had been to a great degree just and merciful, became oppressive. Hardening his heart, he used his God-given talents for self-glorification, exalting himself above the God who had given him life and power.

For months the judgment of God lingered. But instead of being led to repentance by this forbearance, the king indulged his pride until he lost confidence in the interpretation of the dream, and jested at his former fears.

A year from the time he had received the warning, Nebuchadnezzar, walking in his palace and thinking with pride of his power as a ruler and of his success as a builder, exclaimed, "Is not this great Babylon, that I have built for the house of the kingdom by the might of my power, and for the honor of my majesty?"

While the proud boast was yet on the king's lips, a voice

from heaven announced that God's appointed time of judgment had come. Upon his ears fell the mandate of Jehovah: "O King Nebuchadnezzar, to thee it is spoken; The kingdom is departed from thee. And they shall drive thee from men, and thy dwelling shall be with the beasts of the field: they shall make thee to eat grass as oxen, and seven times shall pass over thee, until thou know that the Most High ruleth in the kingdom of men, and giveth it to whomsoever He will."

In a moment the reason that God had given him was taken away; the judgment that the king thought perfect, the wisdom on which he prided himself, was removed, and the once mighty ruler was a maniac. His hand could no longer sway the scepter. The messages of warning had been unheeded; now, stripped of the power his Creator had given him, and driven from men, Nebuchadnezzar "did eat grass as oxen, and his body was wet with the dew of heaven, till his hairs were grown like eagles' feathers, and his nails like birds' claws."

For seven years Nebuchadnezzar was an astonishment to all his subjects; for seven years he was humbled before all the world. Then his reason was restored and, looking up in humility to the God of heaven, he recognized the divine hand in his chastisement. In a public proclamation he acknowledged his guilt and the great mercy of God in his restoration. "At the end of the days," he said, "I Nebuchadnezzar lifted up mine eyes unto heaven, and mine understanding returned unto me, and I blessed the Most High, and I praised and honored Him that liveth forever, whose dominion is an everlasting dominion, and His kingdom is from generation to generation: and all the inhabitants of the earth are reputed as nothing: and He doeth according to His will in the army of heaven, and among the inhabitants of the earth: and none can stay His hand, or say unto Him, What doest Thou?

"At the same time my reason returned unto me; and for the glory of my kingdom, mine honor and brightness returned unto me; and my counselors and my lords sought unto me; and I was established in my kingdom, and excellent majesty was added unto me."

The once proud monarch had become a humble child of God; the tyrannical, overbearing ruler, a wise and compassionate king. He who had defied and blasphemed the God of heaven, now acknowledged the power of the Most High and earnestly sought to promote the fear of Jehovah and the happiness of his subjects. Under the rebuke of Him who is King of kings and Lord of lords, Nebuchadnezzar had learned at last the lesson which all rulers need to learn—that true greatness consists in true goodness. He acknowledged Jehovah as the living God, saying, "I Nebuchadnezzar praise and extol and honor the King of heaven, all whose works are truth, and His ways judgment: and those that walk in pride He is able to abase."

God's purpose that the greatest kingdom in the world should show forth His praise was now fulfilled. This public proclamation, in which Nebuchadnezzar acknowledged the mercy and goodness and authority of God, was the last act of his life recorded in sacred history.

The Unseen Watcher

Toward the close of Daniel's life great changes were taking place in the land to which, over threescore years before, he and his Hebrew companions had been carried captive. Nebuchadnezzar, "the terrible of the nations" (Ezekiel 28:7), had died, and Babylon, "the praise of the whole earth" (Jeremiah 51:41), had passed under the unwise rule of his successors, and gradual but sure dissolution was resulting.

Through the folly and weakness of Belshazzar, the grandson of Nebuchadnezzar, proud Babylon was soon to fall. Admitted in his youth to a share in kingly authority, Belshazzar gloried in his power and lifted up his heart against the God of heaven. Many had been his opportunities to know the divine will and to understand his responsibility of rendering obedience thereto. He had known of his grandfather's banishment, by the decree of God, from the society of men; and he was familiar with Nebuchadnezzar's conversion and miraculous restoration. But Belshazzar allowed the love of pleasure and self-glorification to efface the lessons that he should never have forgotten. He wasted the opportunities graciously granted him, and neglected to use the means within his reach for becoming more fully acquainted with truth. That which Nebuchadnezzar had finally gained at the cost of untold suffering and humiliation, Belshazzar passed by with indifference.

It was not long before reverses came. Babylon was besieged by Cyrus, nephew of Darius the Mede, and commanding general of the combined armies of the Medes and Persians. But within the seemingly impregnable fortress, with its massive walls and its gates of brass, protected by the river Euphrates, and stocked with provision in abundance, the voluptuous monarch felt safe and passed his time in mirth and revelry.

In his pride and arrogancy, with a reckless feeling of security Belshazzar "made a great feast to a thousand of his lords, and drank wine before the thousand." All the attractions that wealth and power could command, added splendor to the scene. Beautiful women with their enchantments were among the guests in attendance at the royal banquet. Men of genius and education were there. Princes and statesmen drank wine like water and reveled under its maddening influence.

With reason dethroned through shameless intoxication, and with lower impulses and passions now in the ascendancy, the king himself took the lead in the riotous orgy. As the feast progressed, he "commanded to bring the golden and silver vessels which . . . Nebuchadnezzar had taken out of the temple which was in Jerusalem; that the king, and his princes, his wives, and his concubines, might drink therein." The king would prove that nothing was too sacred for his hands to handle. "They brought the golden vessels; . . . and the king, and his princes, his wives, and his concubines, drank in them."

They drank wine, and praised the gods of gold, and of silver, of brass, of iron, of wood, and of stone."

Little did Belshazzar think that there was a heavenly Witness to his idolatrous revelry; that a divine Watcher, unrecognized, looked upon the scene of profanation, heard the sacrilegious mirth, beheld the idolatry. But soon the uninvited Guest made His presence felt. When the revelry was at its height of bloodless hand came forth and traced upon the walls of the palace characters that gleamed like fire—words which, though unknown to the vast throng, were a portent of doom to the now conscience-stricken king and his guests.

Hushed was the boisterous mirth, while men and women, seized with nameless terror, watched the hand slowly tracing the mysterious characters. Before them passed, as in panoramic view, the deeds of their evil lives; they seemed to be arraigned before the judgment bar of the eternal God, whose power they had just defied. Where but a few moments before had been hilarity and blasphemous witticism, were pallid faces and cries of fear. When God makes men fear, they cannot hide the intensity of their terror.

Belshazzar was the most terrified of them all. He it was who above all others had been responsible for the rebellion against God which that night had reached its height in the Babylonian realm. In the presence of the unseen Watcher, the representative of Him whose power had been challenged and whose name had been blasphemed, the king was paralyzed with fear. Conscience was awakened. "The joints of his loins were loosed, and his knees smote one against another." Belshazzar had impiously lifted himself up against the God of heaven and had trusted in his own might, not supposing that any would dare say, "Why doest thou thus?" but now he realized that he must render an account of the stewardship entrusted him, and that for his wasted opportunities and his defiant attitude he could offer no excuse.

In vain the king tried to read the burning letters. But here was a secret he could not fathom, a power he could neither understand nor gainsay. In despair he turned to the wise men of his realm for help. His wild cry rang out in the assembly, calling upon the astrologers, the Chaldeans, and the soothsayers to read the writing. "Whosoever shall read this writing," he promised, "and show me the interpretation thereof, shall be clothed with scarlet, and have a chain of gold about his neck, and shall be the third ruler in the kingdom." But of no avail was his appeal to his trusted advisers, with offers of rich awards. Heavenly wisdom cannot be bought or sold. "All the king's wise men . . . could not read the writing, nor make known to the king the interpretation thereof." They were no more able to read the mysterious characters than had been the wise men of a former generation to interpret the dreams of Nebuchadnezzar.

Then the queen mother remembered Daniel, who, over half a century before, had made known to King Nebuchadnezzar the dream of the great image and its interpretation. "O king, live forever," she said. "Let not thy thoughts trouble thee, nor let thy countenance be changed: there is a man in thy kingdom, in whom is the spirit of the holy gods; and in the days of thy father light and understanding and wisdom, like the wisdom of the gods, was found in him; whom the king Nebuchadnezzar . . . made master of the magicians, astrologers, Chaldeans, and soothsayers; forasmuch as an excellent spirit, and knowledge, and understanding, interpreting of dreams, and showing of hard sentences, and dissolving of doubts, were found in the same Daniel, whom the king named Belteshazzar: now let Daniel be called, and he will show the interpretation.

"Then was Daniel brought in before the king." Making an effort to regain his composure, Belshazzar said to the prophet: "Art thou that Daniel, which art of the children of the captivity of Judah, whom the king my father brought out of Jewry? I have even heard of thee, that the spirit of the gods is in thee, and that light and understanding and excellent wisdom is found in thee. And now the wise men, the astrologers, have been brought in before me, that they should read this writing, and make known unto me the interpretation thereof: but they could not show the interpretation of the thing: and I have heard of thee, that thou canst make interpretations, and dissolve doubts: now if thou canst read the writing, and make known to me the interpretation thereof, thou shalt be clothed with scarlet, and have a chain of gold about thy neck, and shalt be the third ruler in the kingdom." Before that terror-stricken throng, Daniel, unmoved by the promises of the king, stood in the quiet dignity of a servant of the Most High, not to speak words of flattery, but to interpret a message of doom. "Let thy gifts be to thyself," he said, "and give thy rewards to another; yet I will read the writing unto the king, and make known to him the interpretation."

The prophet first reminded Belshazzar of matters with which he was familiar, but which had not taught him the lesson of humility that might have saved him. He spoke of Nebuchadnezzar's sin and fall, and of the Lord's dealings with him—the dominion and glory bestowed upon him, the divine judgment for his pride, and his subsequent acknowledgment of the power and mercy of the God of Israel; and then in bold and emphatic words he rebuked Belshazzar for his great wickedness. He held the king's sin up before him, showing him the lessons he might have learned but did not. Belshazzar had not read aright the experience of his grandfather, nor heeded the warning of events so significant to himself. The opportunity of knowing and obeying the true God had been given him, but had not been taken to heart, and he was about to reap the consequence of his rebellion.

"Thou, . . . O Belshazzar," the prophet declared, "hast not humbled thine heart, though thou knewest all this; but hast lifted up thyself against the Lord of heaven; and they have brought the vessels of His house before thee, and thou, and thy lords, thy wives, and thy concubines, have drunk wine in them; and thou hast praised the gods of silver, and gold, of brass, iron, wood, and stone, which see not, nor hear, nor know: and the God in whose hand thy breath is, and whose are all thy ways, hast thou not glorified: then was the part of the hand set from Him; and this writing was written."

Turning to the Heaven-sent message on the wall, the prophet read, "Mene, Mene, Tekel, Upharsin." The hand that had traced the characters was no longer visible, but these four words were still gleaming forth with terrible distinctness; and now with bated breath the people listened while the aged prophet declared:

"This is the interpretation of the thing: Mene; God hath numbered thy kingdom, and finished it. Tekel; Thou art weighed in the balances, and art found wanting. Peres; Thy kingdom is divided, and given to the Medes and Persians."

In that last night of mad folly, Belshazzar and his lords had filled up the measure of their guilt and the guilt of the Chaldean kingdom. No longer could God's restraining hand ward off the impending evil. Through manifold providences, God had sought to teach them reverence for His law. "We would have healed Babylon," He declared of those whose judgment was now reaching unto heaven, "but she is not healed." Jeremiah 51:9. Because of the strange perversity of the human heart, God had at last found it necessary to pass the irrevocable sentence. Belshazzar was to fall, and his kingdom was to pass into other hands.

As the prophet ceased speaking, the king commanded that he be awarded the promised honors; and in harmony with this, "they clothed Daniel with scarlet, and put a chain of gold about his neck, and made a proclamation concerning him, that he should be the third ruler in the kingdom." More than a century before, Inspiration had foretold that "the night of . . . pleasure" during which king and counselors would vie with one another in blasphemy against God, would suddenly be changed into a season of fear and destruction. And now, in rapid succession, momentous events followed one another exactly as had been portrayed in the prophetic scriptures years before the principals in the drama had been born.

While still in the festal hall, surrounded by those whose doom has been sealed, the king is informed by a messenger that "his city is taken" by the enemy against whose devices he had felt so secure; "that the passages are stopped, . . . and the men of war are affrighted." Verses 31, 32. Even while he and his nobles were drinking from the sacred vessels of Jehovah, and praising their gods of silver and of gold, the Medes and the Persians, having turned the Euphrates out of its channel, were marching into the heart of the unguarded city. The army of Cyrus now stood under the walls of the palace; the city was filled with the soldiers of the enemy, "as with caterpillars" (verse 14); and their triumphant shouts could be heard above the despairing cries of the astonished revelers.

"In that night was Belshazzar the king of the Chaldeans slain," and an alien monarch sat upon the throne.

Clearly had the Hebrew prophets spoken concerning the manner in which Babylon should fall. As in vision God had revealed to them the events of the future, they had exclaimed: "How is Sheshach taken! and how is the praise of the whole earth surprised! how is Babylon become an astonishment among the nations!" "How is the hammer of the whole earth cut asunder and broken! how is Babylon become a desolation among the nations!" "At the noise of the taking of Babylon the earth is moved, and the cry is heard among the nations."

"Babylon is suddenly fallen and destroyed." "The spoiler is come upon her, even upon Babylon, and her mighty men are taken, every one of their bows is broken: for the Lord God of recompenses shall surely requite. And I will make drunk her princes, and her wise men, her captains, and her rulers, and her mighty men: and they shall sleep a perpetual sleep, and not wake, saith the King, whose name is the Lord of hosts."

"I have laid a snare for thee, and thou art also taken, O Babylon, and thou wast not aware: thou art found, and also caught, because thou hast striven against the Lord. The Lord hath opened His armory, and hath brought forth the weapons of His indignation: for this is the work of the Lord God of hosts in the land of the Chaldeans."

"Thus saith the Lord of hosts; The children of Israel and the children of Judah were oppressed together: and all that took them captives held them fast; they refused to let them go. Their Redeemer is strong; the Lord of hosts is His name: He shall throughly plead their cause, that He may give rest to the land, and disquiet the inhabitants of Babylon." Jeremiah 51:41; 50:23, 46; 51:8, 56, 57; 50:24, 25, 33, 34.

Thus "the broad walls of Babylon" became "utterly broken, and her high gates. . . burned with fire." Thus did Jehovah of hosts "cause the arrogancy of the proud to cease," and lay low "the haughtiness of the terrible." Thus did "Babylon, the glory of kingdoms, the beauty of the Chaldees' excellency," become as Sodom and Gomorrah— a place forever accursed. "It shall never be inhabited," Inspiration has declared, "neither shall it be dwelt in from generation to generation: neither shall the Arabian pitch tent there; neither shall the shepherds make their fold there. But wild beasts of the desert shall lie there; and their houses shall be full of doleful creatures; and owls shall dwell there, and satyrs shall dance there. And the wild beasts of the islands shall cry in their desolate houses, and dragons in their pleasant palaces." "I will also make it a possession for the bittern, and pools of water: and I will sweep it with the besom of destruction, saith the Lord of hosts." Jeremiah 51:58; Isaiah 13:11, 19-22; 14:23.

To the last ruler of Babylon, as in type to its first, had come the sentence of the divine Watcher: "O king, . . . to thee it is spoken; The kingdom is departed from thee." Daniel 4:31.

"Come down, and sit in the dust, O virgin daughter of Babylon,
Sit on the ground: there is no throne. . . .
Sit thou silent,
And get thee into darkness, O daughter of the Chaldeans:
For thou shalt no more be called, The lady of kingdoms.
"I was wroth with My people,
I have polluted Mine inheritance, and given them into thine hand:
Thou didst show them no mercy; . . .

"And thou saidst, I shall be a lady forever:
So that thou didst not lay these things to thy heart,
Neither didst remember the latter end of it.
"Therefore hear now this,
Thou that art given to pleasures
That dwellest carelessly,
That sayest in thine heart,
I am, and none else beside me;
I shall not sit as a widow,
Neither shall I know the loss of children: . . .
"These two things shall come to thee in a moment in one day,
The loss of children, and widowhood:
They shall come upon thee in their perfection for the multitude of thy sorceries, and for the great abundance of thine enchantments.
For thou hast trusted in thy wickedness:
Thou hast said, None seeth me.
"Thy wisdom and thy knowledge, it hath perverted thee;
And thou hast said in thine heart,
I am, and none else beside me.
Therefore shall evil come upon thee;
Thou shalt not know from whence it riseth:
And mischief shall fall upon thee;
Thou shalt not be able to put it off:
And desolation shall come upon thee suddenly, which thou shalt not know.
"Stand now with thine enchantments, and with the multitude of thy sorceries, wherein thou hast labored from thy youth;
If so be thou shalt be able to profit,
If so be thou mayest prevail.
"Thou art wearied in the multitude of thy counsels.
Let now the astrologers, the stargazers, the monthly prognosticators,
Stand up, and save thee from these things that shall come upon thee.
Behold, they shall be as stubble; . . .
They shall not deliver themselves from the power of the flame: . . .
None shall save thee." Isaiah 47:1-15.

Every nation that has come upon the stage of action has been permitted to occupy its place on the earth, that the fact might be determined whether it would fulfill the purposes of the Watcher and the Holy One. Prophecy has traced the rise and progress of the world's great empires—Babylon, Medo-Persia, Greece, and Rome. With each of these, as with the nations of less power, history has repeated itself. Each has had its period of test; each has failed, its glory faded, its power departed.

While nations have rejected God's principles, and in this rejection have wrought their own ruin, yet a divine, overruling purpose has manifestly been at work throughout the ages. It was this that the prophet Ezekiel saw in the wonderful representation given him during his exile in the land of the Chaldeans, when before his astonished gaze were portrayed the symbols that revealed an overruling Power that has to do with the affairs of earthly rulers.

Upon the banks of the river Chebar, Ezekiel beheld a whirlwind seeming to come from the north, "a great cloud, and a fire infolding itself, and a brightness was about it, and out of the midst thereof as the color of amber." A number of wheels intersecting one another were moved by four living beings. High above all these "was the likeness of a throne, as the appearance of a sapphire stone: and upon the likeness of the throne was the likeness as the appearance of a man above upon it." "And there appeared in the cherubims the form of a man's hand under their wings." Ezekiel 1:4, 26; 10:8. The wheels were so complicated in arrangement that at first sight they appeared to be in confusion; yet they moved in perfect harmony. Heavenly beings, sustained and guided by the hand beneath the wings of the cherubim, were impelling those wheels; above them, upon the sapphire throne, was the Eternal One; and round about the throne was a rainbow, the emblem of divine mercy.

As the wheellike complications were under the guidance of the hand beneath the wings of the cherubim, so the complicated play of human events is under divine control. Amidst the strife and tumult of nations He that sitteth above the cherubim still guides the affairs of this earth.

The history of nations speaks to us today. To every nation and to every individual God has assigned a place in His great plan. Today men and nations are being tested by the plummet in the hand of Him who makes no mistake. All are by their own choice deciding their destiny, and God is overruling all for the accomplishment of His purposes.

The prophecies which the great I am has given in His word, uniting link after link in the chain of events, from eternity in the past to eternity in the future, tell us where we are today in the procession of the ages and what may be expected in the time to come. All that prophecy has foretold as coming to pass, until the present time, has been traced on the pages of history, and we may be assured that all which is yet to come will be fulfilled in its order.

Today the signs of the times declare that we are standing on the threshold of great and solemn events. Everything in our world is in agitation. Before our eyes is fulfilling the Saviour's prophecy of the events to precede His coming: "Ye shall hear of wars and rumors of wars. . . . Nation shall rise against nation, and kingdom against kingdom: and there shall be famines, and pestilences, and earthquakes, in divers places." Matthew 24:6, 7.

The present is a time of overwhelming interest to all living. Rulers and statesmen, men who occupy positions of trust and authority, thinking men and women of all classes, have their attention fixed upon the events taking place about us. They are watching the relations that exist among the nations. They observe the intensity that is taking possession of every earthly element, and they recognize that something great and decisive is about to take place—that the world is on the verge of a stupendous crisis.

The Bible, and the Bible only, gives a correct view of these things. Here are revealed the great final scenes in the history of our world, events that already are casting their shadows before, the sound of their approach causing the earth to tremble and men's hearts to fail them for fear.

"Behold, the Lord maketh the earth empty, and maketh it waste, and turneth it upside down, and scattereth abroad the inhabitants thereof; . . . because they have transgressed the laws, changed the ordinance, broken the everlasting covenant. Therefore hath the curse devoured the earth, and they that dwell therein are desolate." Isaiah 24:1-6.

"Alas for the day! for the day of the Lord is at hand, and as a destruction from the Almighty shall it come. . . . The seed is rotten under their clods, the garners are laid desolate, the barns are broken down; for the corn is withered. How do the beasts groan! the herds of cattle are perplexed, because they have no pasture; yea, the flocks of sheep are made desolate." The vine is dried up, and the fig tree languisheth; the pomegranate tree, the palm tree also, and the apple tree, even all the trees of the field, are withered: because joy is withered away from the sons of men." Joel 1:15-18, 12.

"I am pained at my very heart; . . . I cannot hold my peace, because thou hast heard, O my soul, the sound of the trumpet, the alarm of war. Destruction upon destruction is cried; for the whole land is spoiled." Jeremiah 4:19, 20.

"Alas! for that day is great, so that none is like it: it is even the time of Jacob's trouble; but he shall be saved out of it." Jeremiah 30:7.

"Because thou hast made the Lord, which is my refuge,
Even the Most High, thy habitation;
There shall no evil befall thee,
Neither shall any plague come nigh thy dwelling."
Psalm 91:9, 10.

"O daughter of Zion, . . . the Lord shall redeem thee from the hand of thine enemies. Now also many nations are gathered against thee, that say, Let her be defiled, and let our eye look upon Zion. But they know not the thoughts of the Lord, neither understand they His counsel." Micah 4:10-12. God will not fail His church in the hour of her greatest peril. He has promised deliverance. "I will bring again the captivity of Jacob's tents," He has declared, "and have mercy on his dwelling places." Jeremiah 30:18.

Then will the purpose of God be fulfilled; the principles of His kingdom will be honored by all beneath the sun.

In the Lions' Den

When Darius the Median took the throne formerly occupied by the Babylonian rulers, he at once proceeded to reorganize the government. He "set over the kingdom an hundred and twenty princes; . . . and over these three presidents; of whom Daniel was first: that the princes might give accounts unto them, and the king should have no damage. Then this Daniel

was preferred above the presidents and princes, because an excellent spirit was in him; and the king thought to set him over the whole realm." The honors bestowed upon Daniel excited the jealousy of the leading men of the kingdom, and they sought for occasion of complaint against him. But they could find none, "forasmuch as he was faithful, neither was there any error or fault found in him.

Daniel's blameless conduct excited still further the jealousy of his enemies. "We shall not find any occasion against this Daniel," they were constrained to acknowledge, "except we find it against him concerning the law of his God.

Thereupon the presidents and princes, counseling together, devised a scheme whereby they hoped to accomplish the prophet's destruction. They determined to ask the king to sign a decree which they should prepare, forbidding any person in the realm to ask anything of God or man, except of Darius the king, for the space of thirty days. A violation of this decree should be punished by casting the offender into a den of lions.

Accordingly, the princes prepared such a decree, and presented it to Darius for his signature. Appealing to his vanity, they persuaded him that the carrying out of this edict would add greatly to his honor and authority. Ignorant of the subtle purpose of the princes, the king did not discern their animosity as revealed in the decree, and, yielding to their flattery, he signed it.

The enemies of Daniel left the presence of Darius, rejoicing over the snare now securely laid for the servant of Jehovah. In the conspiracy thus formed, Satan had played an important part. The prophet was high in command in the kingdom, and evil angels feared that his influence would weaken their control over its rulers. It was these satanic agencies who had stirred the princes to envy and jealousy; it was they who had inspired the plan for Daniel's destruction; and the princes, yielding themselves as instruments of evil, carried it into effect.

The prophet's enemies counted on Daniel's firm adherence to principle for the success of their plan. And they were not mistaken in their estimate of his character. He quickly read their malignant purpose in framing the decree, but he did not change his course in a single particular. Why should he cease to pray now, when he most needed to pray? Rather would he relinquish life itself, than his hope of help in God. With calmness he performed his duties as chief of the princes; and at the hour of prayer he went to his chamber, and with his windows open toward Jerusalem, in accordance with his usual custom, he offered his petition to the God of >heaven. He did not try to conceal his act. Although he knew full well the consequences of his fidelity to God, his spirit faltered not. Before those who were plotting his ruin, he would not allow it even to appear that his connection with Heaven was severed. In all cases where the king had a right to command, Daniel would obey; but neither the king nor his decree could make him swerve from allegiance to the King of kings.

Thus the prophet boldly yet quietly and humbly declared that no earthly power has a right to interpose between the soul and God. Surrounded by idolaters, he was a faithful witness to this truth. His dauntless adherence to right was a bright light in the moral darkness of that heathen court. Daniel stands before the world today a worthy example of Christian fearlessness and fidelity.

For an entire day the princes watched Daniel. Three times they saw him go to his chamber, and three times they heard his voice lifted in earnest intercession to God. The next morning they laid their complaint before the king. Daniel, his most honored and faithful statesman, had set the royal decree at defiance. "Hast thou not signed a decree," they reminded him, "that every man that shall ask a petition of any god or man within thirty days, save of thee, O king, shall be cast into the den of lions?"

"The thing is true," the king answered, "according to the law of the Medes and Persians, which altereth not."

Exultantly they now informed Darius of the conduct of his most trusted adviser. "That Daniel, which is of the children of the captivity of Judah," they exclaimed, "regardeth not thee, O king, nor the decree that thou hast signed, but maketh his petition three times a day."

When the monarch heard these words, he saw at once the snare that had been set for his faithful servant. He saw that it was not zeal for kingly glory and honor, but jealousy against Daniel, that had led to the proposal for a royal decree. "Sore displeased with himself" for his part in the evil that had been wrought, he "labored till the going down of the sun" to deliver his friend. The princes, anticipating this effort on the part of the king, came to him with the words, "Know, O king, that the law of the Medes and Persians is, that no decree nor statute which the king establisheth may be changed." The decree, though rashly made, was unalterable and must be carried into effect.

"Then the king commanded, and they brought Daniel, and cast him into the den of lions. Now the king spake and said unto Daniel, Thy God whom thou servest continually, He will deliver thee." A stone was laid on the mouth of the den, and the king himself "sealed it with his own signet, and with the signet of his lords; that the purpose might not be changed concerning Daniel. Then the king went to his palace, and passed the night fasting: neither were instruments of music brought before him: and his sleep went from him."

God did not prevent Daniel's enemies from casting him into the lions' den; He permitted evil angels and wicked men thus far to accomplish their purpose; but it was that He might make the deliverance of His servant more marked, and the defeat of the enemies of truth and righteousness more complete. "Surely the wrath of man shall praise Thee" (Psalm 76:10), the psalmist has testified. Through the courage of this one man who chose to follow right rather than policy, Satan was to be defeated, and the name of God was to be exalted and honored.

Early the next morning King Darius hastened to the den and "cried with a lamentable voice," "O Daniel, servant of the living God, is thy God, whom thou servest continually,

able to deliver thee from the lions?"

The voice of the prophet replied: "O king, live forever. My God hath sent His angel, and hath shut the lions' mouths, that they have not hurt me: forasmuch as before Him innocency was found in me; and also before thee, O king, have I done no hurt.

"Then was the king exceeding glad for him, and commanded that they should take Daniel up out of the den. So Daniel was taken up out of the den, and no manner of hurt was found upon him, because he believed in his God.

"And the king commanded, and they brought those men which had accused Daniel, and they cast them into the den of lions, them, their children, and their wives; and the lions had the mastery of them, and brake all their bones in pieces or ever they came at the bottom of the den."

Once more a proclamation was issued by a heathen ruler, exalting the God of Daniel as the true God. "King Darius wrote unto all people, nations, and languages, that dwell in all the earth; Peace be multiplied unto you. I make a decree, that in every dominion of my kingdom men tremble and fear before the God of Daniel: for He is the living God, and steadfast forever, and His kingdom that which shall not be destroyed, and His dominion shall be even unto the end. He delivereth and rescueth, and He worketh signs and wonders in heaven and in earth, who hath delivered Daniel from the power of the lions."

The wicked opposition to God's servant was now completely broken. "Daniel prospered in the reign of Darius, and in the reign of Cyrus the Persian." And through association with him, these heathen monarchs were constrained to acknowledge his God as "the living God, and steadfast forever, and His kingdom that which shall not be destroyed."

From the story of Daniel's deliverance we may learn that in seasons of trial and gloom God's children should be just what they were when their prospects were bright with hope and their surroundings all that they could desire. Daniel in the lions' den was the same Daniel who stood before the king as chief among the ministers of state and as a prophet of the Most High. A man whose heart is stayed upon God will be the same in the hour of his greatest trial as he is in prosperity, when the light and favor of God and of man beam upon him. Faith reaches to the unseen, and grasps eternal realities.

Heaven is very near those who suffer for righteousness' sake. Christ identifies His interests with the interests of His faithful people; He suffers in the person of His saints, and whoever touches His chosen ones touches Him. The power that is near to deliver from physical harm or distress is also near to save from the greater evil, making it possible for the servant of God to maintain his integrity under all circumstances, and to triumph through divine grace.

The experience of Daniel as a statesman in the kingdoms of Babylon and Medo-Persia reveals the truth that a businessman is not necessarily a designing, policy man, but that he may be a man instructed by God at every step. Daniel, the prime minister of the greatest of earthly kingdoms, was at the same time a prophet of God, receiving the light of heavenly inspiration. A man of like passions as ourselves, the pen of inspiration describes him as without fault. His business transactions, when subjected to the closest scrutiny of his enemies, were found to be without one flaw. He was an example of what every businessman may become when his heart is converted and consecrated, and when his motives are right in the sight of God.

Strict compliance with the requirements of Heaven brings temporal as well as spiritual blessings. Unwavering in his allegiance to God, unyielding in his mastery of self, Daniel, by his noble dignity and unswerving integrity, while yet a young man, won the "favor and tender love" of the heathen officer in whose charge he had been placed. Daniel 1:9. The same characteristics marked his afterlife. He rose speedily to the position of prime minister of the kingdom of Babylon. Through the reign of successive monarchs, the downfall of the nation, and the establishment of another world empire, such were his wisdom and statesmanship, so perfect his tact, his courtesy, his genuine goodness of heart, his fidelity to principle, that even his enemies were forced to the confession that "they could find none occasion nor fault; forasmuch as he was faithful."

Honored by men with the responsibilities of state and with the secrets of kingdoms bearing universal sway, Daniel was honored by God as His ambassador, and was given many revelations of the mysteries of ages to come. His wonderful prophecies, as recorded by him in Chapters 7 to 12 of the book bearing his name, were not fully understood even by the prophet himself; but before his life labors closed, he was given the blessed assurance that "at the end of the days"—in the closing period of this world's history—he would again be permitted to stand in his lot and place. It was not given him to understand all that God had revealed of the divine purpose. "Shut up the words, and seal the book," he was directed concerning his prophetic writings; these were to be sealed "even to the time of the end." "Go thy way, Daniel," the angel once more directed the faithful messenger of Jehovah; "for the words are closed up and sealed till the time of the end. . . . Go thou thy way till the end be: for thou shalt rest, and stand in thy lot at the end of the days." Daniel 12:4, 9, 13.

As we near the close of this world's history, the prophecies recorded by Daniel demand our special attention, as they relate to the very time in which we are living. With them should be linked the teachings of the last book of the New Testament Scriptures. Satan has led many to believe that the prophetic portions of the writings of Daniel and of John the revelator cannot be understood. But the promise is plain that special blessing will accompany the study of these prophecies. "The wise shall understand" (verse 10), was spoken of the visions of Daniel that were to be unsealed in the latter days; and of the revelation that Christ gave to His servant John for the guidance of God's people all through the centuries, the promise is, "Blessed is he that readeth, and they that hear the words of this prophecy, and keep those things which are written therein." Revelation 1:3.

From the rise and fall of nations as made plain in the books of Daniel and the Revelation, we need to learn how worthless is mere outward and worldly glory. Babylon, with all its power and magnificence, the like of which our world has never since beheld,—power and magnificence which to the people of that day seemed so stable and enduring, —how completely has it passed away! As "the flower of the grass," it has perished. James 1:10. So perished the Medo-Persian kingdom, and the kingdoms of Grecia and Rome. And so perishes all that has not God for its foundation. Only that which is bound up with His purpose, and expresses His character, can endure. His principles are the only steadfast things our world knows.

A careful study of the working out of God's purpose in the history of nations and in the revelation of things to come, will help us to estimate at their true value things seen and things unseen, and to learn what is the true aim of life. Thus, viewing the things of time in the light of eternity, we may, like Daniel and his fellows, live for that which is true and noble and enduring. And learning in this life the principles of the kingdom of our Lord and Saviour, that blessed kingdom which is to endure for ever and ever, we may be prepared at His coming to enter with Him into its possession.

"The Lord rebuke thee, O Satan; even the Lord that hath chosen Jerusalem rebuke thee: is not this a brand plucked out of the fire?" Zechariah 3:2.

The Return of the Exiles

The advent of the army of Cyrus before the walls of Babylon was to the Jews a sign that their deliverance from captivity was drawing nigh. More than a century before the birth of Cyrus, Inspiration had mentioned him by name, and had caused a record to be made of the actual work he should do in taking the city of Babylon unawares, and in preparing the way for the release of the children of the captivity. Through Isaiah the word had been spoken:

"Thus saith the Lord to His anointed, to Cyrus, whose right hand I have holden, to subdue nations before him; . . . to open before him the two-leaved gates; and the gates shall not be shut; I will go before thee, and make the crooked places straight: I will break in pieces the gates of brass, and cut in sunder the bars of iron: and I will give thee the treasures of darkness, and hidden riches of secret places, that thou mayest know that I, the Lord, which call thee by thy name, am the God of Israel." Isaiah 45:1-3.

In the unexpected entry of the army of the Persian conqueror into the heart of the Babylonian capital by way of the channel of the river whose waters had been turned aside, and through the inner gates that in careless security had been left open and unprotected, the Jews had abundant evidence of the literal fulfillment of Isaiah's prophecy concerning the sudden overthrow of their oppressors. And this should have been to them an unmistakable sign that God was shaping the affairs of nations in their behalf; for inseparably linked with the prophecy outlining the manner of Babylon's capture and fall were the words:

"Cyrus, he is My shepherd, and shall perform all My pleasure: even saying to Jerusalem, Thou shalt be built; and to the temple, Thy foundation shall be laid." "I have raised him up in righteousness, and I will direct all his ways: he shall build My city, and he shall let go My captives, not for price nor reward, saith the Lord of hosts." Isaiah 44:28; 45:13.

Nor were these the only prophecies upon which the exiles had opportunity to base their hope of speedy deliverance. The writings of Jeremiah were within their reach, and in these was plainly set forth the length of time that should elapse before the restoration of Israel from Babylon. "When seventy years are accomplished," the Lord had foretold through His messenger, "I will punish the king of Babylon, and that nation, saith the Lord, for their iniquity, and the land of the Chaldeans, and will make it perpetual desolations." Jeremiah 25:12. Favor would be shown the remnant of Judah, in answer to fervent prayer. "I will be found of you, saith the Lord: and I will turn away your captivity, and I will gather you from all the nations, and from all the places whither I have driven you, saith the Lord; and I will bring you again into the place whence I caused you to be carried away captive." Jeremiah 29:14.

Often had Daniel and his companions gone over these and similar prophecies outlining God's purpose for His people. And now, as the rapid course of events betokened the mighty hand of God at work among the nations, Daniel gave special thought to the promises made to Israel. His faith in the prophetic word led him to enter into experiences foretold by the sacred writers. "After seventy years be accomplished at Babylon," the Lord had declared, "I will visit you, and perform My good word toward you, in causing you to return. . . . I know the thoughts that I think toward you, saith the Lord, thoughts of peace, and not of evil, to give you an expected end. Then shall ye call upon Me, and ye shall go and pray unto Me, and I will hearken unto you. And ye shall seek Me, and find Me, when ye shall search for Me with all your heart." Verses 10-13.

Shortly before the fall of Babylon, when Daniel was meditating on these prophecies and seeking God for an understanding of the times, a series of visions was given him concerning the rise and fall of kingdoms. With the first vision, as recorded in the seventh Chapter of the book of Daniel, an interpretation was given; yet not all was made clear to the prophet. "My cogitations much troubled me," he wrote of his experience at the time, "and my countenance changed in me: but I kept the matter in my heart." Daniel 7:28.

Through another vision further light was thrown upon the events of the future; and it was at the close of this vision that Daniel heard "one saint speaking, and another saint said unto that certain saint which spake, How long shall be the vision?" Daniel 8:13. The answer that was given, "Unto two thousand and three hundred days; then shall the sanctuary be cleansed"

(verse 14), filled him with perplexity. Earnestly he sought for the meaning of the vision. He could not understand the relation sustained by the seventy years' captivity, as foretold through Jeremiah, to the twenty-three hundred years that in vision he heard the heavenly visitant declare should elapse before the cleansing of God's sanctuary. The angel Gabriel gave him a partial interpretation; yet when the prophet heard the words, "The vision . . . shall be for many days," he fainted away. "I Daniel fainted," he records of his experience, "and was sick certain days; afterward I rose up, and did the king's business; and I was astonished at the vision, but none understood it." Verses 26, 27.

Still burdened in behalf of Israel, Daniel studied anew the prophecies of Jeremiah. They were very plain—so plain that he understood by these testimonies recorded in books "the number of the years, whereof the word of the Lord came to Jeremiah the prophet, that He would accomplish seventy years in the desolations of Jerusalem." Daniel 9:2.

With faith founded on the sure word of prophecy, Daniel pleaded with the Lord for the speedy fulfillment of these promises. He pleaded for the honor of God to be preserved. In his petition he identified himself fully with those who had fallen short of the divine purpose, confessing their sins as his own.

"I set my face unto the Lord God," the prophet declared, "to seek by prayer and supplications, with fasting, and sackcloth, and ashes: and I prayed unto the Lord my God, and made my confession." Verses 3, 4. Though Daniel had long been in the service of God, and had been spoken of by heaven as "greatly beloved," yet he now appeared before God as a sinner, urging the great need of the people he loved. His prayer was eloquent in its simplicity, and intensely earnest. Hear him pleading:

"O Lord, the great and dreadful God, keeping the covenant and mercy to them that love Him, and to them that keep His commandments; we have sinned, and have committed iniquity, and have done wickedly, and have rebelled, even by departing from Thy precepts and from Thy judgments; neither have we hearkened unto Thy servants the prophets, which spake in Thy name to our kings, our princes, and our fathers, and to all the people of the land.

"O Lord, righteousness belongeth unto Thee, but unto us confusion of faces, as at this day; to the men of Judah, and to the inhabitants of Jerusalem, and unto all Israel, that are near, and that are far off, through all the countries whither Thou hast driven them, because of their trespass that they have trespassed against Thee. . . .

"To the Lord our God belong mercies and forgiveness, though we have rebelled against Him." "O Lord, according to all Thy righteousness, I beseech Thee, let Thine anger and Thy fury be turned away from Thy city Jerusalem, Thy holy mountain: because for our sins, and for the iniquities of our fathers, Jerusalem and Thy people are become a reproach to all that are about us.

"Now therefore, O our God, hear the prayer of Thy servant,

and his supplications, and cause Thy face to shine upon Thy sanctuary that is desolate, for the Lord's sake. O my God, incline Thine ear, and hear; open Thine eyes, and behold our desolations, and the city which is called by Thy name: for we do not present our supplications before Thee for our righteousness, but for Thy great mercies.

"O Lord, hear; O Lord, forgive; O Lord, hearken and do; defer not, for Thine own sake, O my God: for Thy city and Thy people are called by Thy name." Verses 4-9, 16-19.

Heaven was bending low to hear the earnest supplication of the prophet. Even before he had finished his plea for pardon and restoration, the mighty Gabriel again appeared to him, and called his attention to the vision he had seen prior to the fall of Babylon and the death of Belshazzar. And then the angel outlined before him in detail the period of the seventy weeks, which was to begin at the time of "the going forth of the commandment to restore and to build Jerusalem." Verse 25.

Daniel's prayer had been offered "in the first year of Darius" (verse 1), the Median monarch whose general, Cyrus, had wrested from Babylonia the scepter of universal rule. The reign of Darius was honored of God. To him was sent the angel Gabriel, "to confirm and to strengthen him." Daniel 11:1. Upon his death, within about two years of the fall of Babylon, Cyrus succeeded to the throne, and the beginning of his reign marked the completion of the seventy years since the first company of Hebrews had been taken by Nebuchadnezzar from their Judean home to Babylon.

The deliverance of Daniel from the den of lions had been used of God to create a favorable impression upon the mind of Cyrus the Great. The sterling qualities of the man of God as a statesman of farseeing ability led the Persian ruler to show him marked respect and to honor his judgment. And now, just at the time God had said He would cause His temple at Jerusalem to be rebuilt, He moved upon Cyrus as His agent to discern the prophecies concerning himself, with which Daniel was so familiar, and to grant the Jewish people their liberty.

As the king saw the words foretelling, more than a hundred years before his birth, the manner in which Babylon should be taken; as he read the message addressed to him by the Ruler of the universe, "I girded thee, though thou hast not known Me: that they may know from the rising of the sun, and from the west, that there is none beside Me;" as he saw before his eyes the declaration of the eternal God, "For Jacob My servant's sake, and Israel Mine elect, I have even called thee by thy name: I have surnamed thee, though thou hast not known Me;" as he traced the inspired record, "I have raised him up in righteousness, and I will direct all his ways: he shall build My city, and he shall let go My captives, not for price nor reward," his heart was profoundly moved, and he determined to fulfill his divinely appointed mission. Isaiah 45:5, 6, 4, 13. He would let the Judean captives go free; he would help them restore the temple of Jehovah.

In a written proclamation published "throughout all his kingdom," Cyrus made known his desire to provide for the return of the Hebrews and for the rebuilding of their temple. "The Lord God of heaven hath given me all the kingdoms of the earth," the king gratefully acknowledged in this public proclamation; "and He hath charged me to build Him an house at Jerusalem, which is in Judah. Who is there among you of all His people? his God be with him, and let him go up to Jerusalem, . . . and build the house of the Lord God of Israel, (He is the God,) which is in Jerusalem. And whosoever remaineth in any place where he sojourneth, let the men of his place help him with silver, and with gold, and with goods, and with beasts, beside the freewill offering." Ezra 1:1-4. "Let the house be builded," he further directed regarding the temple structure, "the place where they offered sacrifices, and let the foundations thereof be strongly laid; the height thereof threescore cubits, and the breadth thereof threescore cubits; with three rows of great stones, and a row of new timber: and let the expenses be given out of the king's house: and also let the golden and silver vessels of the house of God, which Nebuchadnezzar took forth out of the temple which is at Jerusalem, and brought unto Babylon, be restored, and brought again unto the temple which is at Jerusalem." Ezra 6:3-5.

Tidings of this decree reached the farthermost provinces of the king's realm, and everywhere among the children of the dispersion there was great rejoicing. Many, like Daniel, had been studying the prophecies, and had been seeking God for His promised intervention in behalf of Zion. And now their prayers were being answered; and with heartfelt joy they could unite in singing:

"When the Lord turned again the captivity of Zion,
We were like them that dream.
Then was our mouth filled with laughter,
And our tongue with singing:
Then said they among the heathen,
The Lord hath done great things for them.
The Lord hath done great things for us;
Whereof we are glad."
Psalm 126:1-3.

"The chief of the fathers of Judah and Benjamin, and the priests, and the Levites, with all them whose spirit God had raised"—these were the goodly remnant, about fifty thousand strong, from among the Jews in the lands of exile, who determined to take advantage of the wonderful opportunity offered them "to go up to build the house of the Lord which is in Jerusalem." Their friends did not permit them to go empty-handed. "All they that were about them strengthened their hands with vessels of silver, with gold, with goods, and with beasts, and with precious things." And to these and many other voluntary offerings were added "the vessels of the house of the Lord, which Nebuchadnezzar had brought forth out of Jerusalem; . . . even those did Cyrus king of Persia bring forth by the hand of Mithredath the treasurer, . . . five thousand and four hundred" in number, for use in the temple that was to be rebuilt. Ezra 1:5-11. Upon Zerubbabel (known also as Sheshbazzar), a descendant of King David, Cyrus placed the responsibility of acting as governor of the company returning to Judea; and with him was associated Joshua the high priest. The long journey across the desert wastes was accomplished in safety, and the happy company, grateful to God for His many mercies, at once undertook the work of re-establishing that which had been broken down and destroyed. "The chief of the fathers" led out in offering of their substance to help defray the expense of rebuilding the temple; and the people, following their example, gave freely of their meager store. See Ezra 2:64-70.

As speedily as possible, an altar was erected on the site of the ancient altar in the temple court. To the exercises connected with the dedication of this altar, the people had "gathered themselves together as one man;" and there they united in re-establishing the sacred services that had been interrupted at the time of the destruction of Jerusalem by Nebuchadnezzar. Before separating to dwell in the homes they were endeavoring to restore, "they kept also the Feast of Tabernacles." Ezra 3:1-6.

The setting up of the altar of daily burnt offerings greatly cheered the faithful remnant. Heartily they entered into the preparations necessary for the rebuilding of the temple, gathering courage as these preparations advanced from month to month. They had for many years been deprived of the visible tokens of God's presence. And now, surrounded as they were by many sad reminders of the apostasy of their fathers, they longed for some abiding token of divine forgiveness and favor. Above the regaining of personal property and ancient privileges, they valued the approval of God. Wonderfully had He wrought in their behalf, and they felt the assurance of His presence with them; yet they desired greater blessings still. With joyous anticipation they looked forward to the time when, with temple rebuilt, they might behold the shining forth of His glory from within.

The workmen engaged in the preparation of the building material, found among the ruins some of the immense stones brought to the temple site in the days of Solomon. These were made ready for use, and much new material was provided; and soon the work was advanced to the point where the foundation stone must be laid. This was done in the presence of many thousands who had assembled to witness the progress of the work and to give expression to their joy in having a part in it. While the cornerstone was being set in position, the people, accompanied by the trumpets of the priests and the cymbals of the sons of Asaph, "sang together by course in praising and giving thanks unto the Lord; because He is good, for His mercy endureth forever toward Israel." Verse 11.

The house that was about to be rebuilt had been the subject of many prophecies concerning the favor that God desired to show Zion, and all who were present at the laying of the cornerstone should have entered heartily into the spirit of the occasion. Yet mingled with the music and the shouts of praise that were heard on that glad day, was a discordant note.

"Many of the priests and Levites and chief of the fathers, who were ancient men, that had seen the first house, when the foundation of this house was laid before their eyes, wept with a loud voice." Verse 12.

It was natural that sadness should fill the hearts of these aged men, as they thought of the results of long-continued impenitence. Had they and their generation obeyed God, and carried out His purpose for Israel, the temple built by Solomon would not have been destroyed and the captivity would not have been necessary. But because of ingratitude and disloyalty they had been scattered among the heathen.

Conditions were now changed. In tender mercy the Lord had again visited His people and allowed them to return to their own land. Sadness because of the mistakes of the past should have given way to feelings of great joy. God had moved upon the heart of Cyrus to aid them in rebuilding the temple, and this should have called forth expressions of profound gratitude. But some failed of discerning God's opening providences. Instead of rejoicing, they cherished thoughts of discontent and discouragement. They had seen the glory of Solomon's temple, and they lamented because of the inferiority of the building now to be erected.

The murmuring and complaining, and the unfavorable comparisons made, had a depressing influence on the minds of many and weakened the hands of the builders. The workmen were led to question whether they should proceed with the erection of a building that at the beginning was so freely criticized and was the cause of so much lamentation.

There were many in the congregation, however, whose larger faith and broader vision did not lead them to view this lesser glory with such dissatisfaction. "Many shouted aloud for joy: so that the people could not discern the noise of the shout of joy from the noise of the weeping of the people: for the people shouted with a loud shout, and the noise was heard afar off." Verses 12, 13.

Could those who failed to rejoice at the laying of the foundation stone of the temple have foreseen the results of their lack of faith on that day, they would have been appalled. Little did they realize the weight of their words of disapproval and disappointment; little did they know how much their expressed dissatisfaction would delay the completion of the Lord's house.

The magnificence of the first temple, and the imposing rites of its religious services, had been a source of pride to Israel before their captivity; but their worship had ofttimes been lacking in those qualities which God regards as most essential. The glory of the first temple, the splendor of its service, could not recommend them to God; for that which is alone of value in His sight, they did not offer. They did not bring Him the sacrifice of a humble and contrite spirit.

It is when the vital principles of the kingdom of God are lost sight of, that ceremonies become multitudinous and extravagant. It is when the character building is neglected, when the adornment of the soul is lacking, when the simplicity of godliness is despised, that pride and love of display demand magnificent church edifices, splendid adornings, and imposing ceremonials. But in all this God is not honored. He values His church, not for its external advantages, but for the sincere piety which distinguishes it from the world. He estimates it according to the growth of its members in the knowledge of Christ, according to their progress in spiritual experience. He looks for the principles of love and goodness. Not all the beauty of art can bear comparison with the beauty of temper and character to be revealed in those who are Christ's representatives.

A congregation may be the poorest in the land. It may be without the attractions of any outward show; but if the members possess the principles of the character of Christ, angels will unite with them in their worship. The praise and thanksgiving from grateful hearts will ascend to God as a sweet oblation.

"Give thanks unto the Lord, for He is good:
For His mercy endureth forever.
Let the redeemed of the Lord say so,
Whom He hath redeemed from the hand of the enemy."
"Sing unto Him, sing psalms unto Him:
Talk ye of all His wondrous works.
Glory ye in His holy name:
Let the heart of them rejoice that seek the Lord."
"For He satisfieth the longing soul,
And filleth the hungry soul with goodness."
Psalms 107:1, 2; 105:2, 3; 107:9.

"The Prophets of God Helping Them"

Close by the Israelites who had set themselves to the task of rebuilding the temple, dwelt the Samaritans, a mixed race that had sprung up through the intermarriage of heathen colonists from the provinces of Assyria with the remnant of the ten tribes which had been left in Samaria and Galilee. In later years the Samaritans claimed to worship the true God, but in heart and practice they were idolaters. It is true, they held that their idols were but to remind them of the living God, the Ruler of the universe; nevertheless the people were prone to reverence graven images.

During the period of the restoration, these Samaritans came to be known as "the adversaries of Judah and Benjamin." Hearing that "the children of the captivity builded the temple unto the Lord God of Israel," "they came to Zerubbabel, and to the chief of the fathers," and expressed a desire to unite with them in its erection. "Let us build with you," they proposed; "for we seek your God, as ye do; and we do sacrifice unto Him since the days of Esarhaddon king of Assur, which brought us up hither." But the privilege they asked was refused them. "Ye have nothing to do with us to build an house unto our God," the leaders of the Israelites declared; "but we ourselves together will build unto the Lord God of Israel, as King Cyrus the king of Persia hath commanded us." Ezra 4:1-3.

Only a remnant had chosen to return from Babylon; and now, as they undertake a work seemingly beyond their strength, their nearest neighbors come with an offer of help. The Samaritans refer to their worship of the true God, and express a desire to share the privileges and blessings connected with the temple service. "We seek your God, as ye do," they declare. "Let us build with you." But had the Jewish leaders accepted this offer of assistance, they would have opened a door for the entrance of idolatry. They discerned the insincerity of the Samaritans. They realized that help gained through an alliance with these men would be as nothing in comparison with the blessing they might expect to receive by following the plain commands of Jehovah.

Regarding the relation that Israel should sustain to surrounding peoples, the Lord had declared through Moses: "Thou shalt make no covenant with them, nor show mercy unto them: neither shalt thou make marriages with them; . . . for they will turn away thy son from following Me, that they may serve other gods: so will the anger of the Lord be kindled against you, and destroy thee suddenly." "Thou art an holy people unto the Lord thy God, and the Lord hath chosen thee to be a peculiar people unto Himself, above all the nations that are upon the earth." Deuteronomy 7:2-4; 14:2.

The result that would follow an entrance into covenant relation with surrounding nations was plainly foretold. "The Lord shall scatter thee among all people, from the one end of the earth even unto the other," Moses had declared; "and there thou shalt serve other gods, which neither thou nor thy fathers have known, even wood and stone. And among these nations shalt thou find no ease, neither shall the sole of thy foot have rest: but the Lord shall give thee there a trembling heart, and failing of eyes, and sorrow of mind: and thy life shall hang in doubt before thee; and thou shalt fear day and night, and shalt have none assurance of thy life: in the morning thou shalt say, Would God it were even! and at even thou shalt say, Would God it were morning! for the fear of thine heart wherewith thou shalt fear, and for the sight of thine eyes which thou shalt see." Deuteronomy 28:64-67. "But if from thence thou shalt seek the Lord thy God," the promise had been, "thou shalt find Him, if thou seek Him with all thy heart and with all thy soul." Deuteronomy 4:29.

Zerubbabel and his associates were familiar with these and many like scriptures; and in the recent captivity they had evidence after evidence of their fulfillment. And now, having repented of the evils that had brought upon them and their fathers the judgments foretold so plainly through Moses; having turned with all the heart to God, and renewed their covenant relationship with Him, they had been permitted to return to Judea, that they might restore that which had been destroyed. Should they, at the very beginning of their undertaking, enter into a covenant with idolaters?

"Thou shalt make no covenant with them," God had said; and those who had recently rededicated themselves to the Lord at the altar set up before the ruins of His temple, realized that the line of demarcation between His people and the world is ever to be kept unmistakably distinct. They refused to enter into alliance with those who, though familiar with the requirements of God's law, would not yield to its claims.

The principles set forth in Deuteronomy for the instruction of Israel are to be followed by God's people to the end of time. True prosperity is dependent on the continuance of our covenant relationship with God. Never can we afford to compromise principle by entering into alliance with those who do not fear Him.

There is constant danger that professing Christians will come to think that in order to have influence with worldlings, they must to a certain extent conform to the world. But though such a course may appear to afford great advantages, it always ends in spiritual loss. Against every subtle influence that seeks entrance by means of flattering inducements from the enemies of truth, God's people must strictly guard. They are pilgrims and strangers in this world, traveling a path beset with danger. To the ingenious subterfuges and alluring inducements held out to tempt from allegiance, they must give no heed.

It is not the open and avowed enemies of the cause of God that are most to be feared. Those who, like the adversaries of Judah and Benjamin, come with smooth words and fair speeches, apparently seeking for friendly alliance with God's children, have greater power to deceive. Against such every soul should be on the alert, lest some carefully concealed and masterly snare take him unaware. And especially today, while earth's history is closing, the Lord requires of His children a vigilance that knows no relaxation. But though the conflict is a ceaseless one, none are left to struggle alone. Angels help and protect those who walk humbly before God. Never will our Lord betray one who trusts in Him. As His children draw near to Him for protection from evil, in pity and love He lifts up for them a standard against the enemy. Touch them not, He says; for they are Mine. I have graven them upon the palms of My hands.

Untiring in their opposition, the Samaritans "weakened the hands of the people of Judah, and troubled them in building, and hired counselors against them, to frustrate their purpose, all the days of Cyrus king of Persia, even until the reign of Darius." Ezra 4:4, 5. By false reports they aroused suspicion in minds easily led to suspect. But for many years the powers of evil were held in check, and the people in Judea had liberty to continue their work.

While Satan was striving to influence the highest powers in the kingdom of Medo-Persia to show disfavor to God's people, angels worked in behalf of the exiles. The controversy was one in which all heaven was interested. Through the prophet Daniel we are given a glimpse of this mighty struggle between the forces of good and the forces of evil. For three weeks Gabriel wrestled with the powers of darkness, seeking to counteract the influences at work on the mind of Cyrus; and before the contest closed, Christ Himself came to Gabriel's aid. "The prince of the kingdom of Persia withstood me one and twenty days," Gabriel declares; "but, lo, Michael, one of the chief princes, came to help me; and I remained there with the kings of Persia." Daniel 10:13. All that heaven could do in behalf of the people of God was done. The victory was finally gained; the forces of the enemy were held in check all the days of Cyrus, and all the days of his son Cambyses, who reigned about seven and a half years.

This was a time of wonderful opportunity for the Jews. The highest agencies of heaven were working on the hearts of kings, and it was for the people of God to labor with the utmost activity to carry out the decree of Cyrus. They should have spared no effort to restore the temple and its services, and to re-establish themselves in their Judean homes. But in the day of God's power many proved unwilling. The opposition of their enemies was strong and determined, and gradually the builders lost heart. Some could not forget the scene at the laying of the cornerstone, when many had given expression to their lack of confidence in the enterprise. And as the Samaritans grew more bold, many of the Jews questioned whether, after all, the time had come to rebuild. The feeling soon became widespread. Many of the workmen, discouraged and disheartened, returned to their homes to take up the ordinary pursuits of life.

During the reign of Cambyses the work on the temple progressed slowly. And during the reign of the false Smerdis (called Artaxerxes in Ezra 4:7) the Samaritans induced the unscrupulous impostor to issue a decree forbidding the Jews to rebuild their temple and city.

For over a year the temple was neglected and well-nigh forsaken. The people dwelt in their homes and strove to attain temporal prosperity, but their situation was deplorable. Work as they might they did not prosper. The very elements of nature seemed to conspire against them. Because they had let the temple lie waste, the Lord sent upon their substance a wasting drought. God had bestowed upon them the fruits of field and garden, the corn and the wine and the oil, as a token of His favor; but because they had used these bountiful gifts so selfishly, the blessings were removed.

Such were the conditions existing during the early part of the reign of Darius Hystaspes. Spiritually as well as temporally, the Israelites were in a pitiable state. So long had they murmured and doubted; so long had they chosen to make personal interests first, while viewing with apathy the Lord's temple in ruins, that many had lost sight of God's purpose in restoring them to Judea; and these were saying, "The time is not come, the time that the Lord's house should be built." Haggai 1:2.

But even this dark hour was not without hope for those whose trust was in God. The prophets Haggai and Zechariah were raised up to meet the crisis. In stirring testimonies these appointed messengers revealed to the people the cause of their troubles. The lack of temporal prosperity was the result of a neglect to put God's interests first, the prophets declared. Had the Israelites honored God, had they shown Him due respect and courtesy, by making the building of His house their first work, they would have invited His presence and blessing.

To those who had become discouraged, Haggai addressed the searching inquiry, "Is it time for you, O ye, to dwell in your ceiled houses, and this house lie waste? Now therefore thus saith the Lord of hosts; Consider your ways." Why have you done so little? Why do you feel concern for your own buildings and unconcern for the Lord's building? Where is the zeal you once felt for the restoration of the Lord's house? What have you gained by serving self? The desire to escape poverty has led you to neglect the temple, but this neglect has brought upon you that which you feared. "Ye have sown much, and bring in little; ye eat, but ye have not enough; ye drink, but ye are not filled with drink; ye clothe you, but there is none warm; and he that earneth wages earneth wages to put it into a bag with holes." Verses 4-6.

And then, in words that they could not fail to understand, the Lord revealed the cause that had brought them to want: "Ye looked for much, and, lo, it came to little; and when ye brought it home, I did blow upon it. Why? saith the Lord of hosts. Because of Mine house that is waste, and ye run every man unto his own house. Therefore the heaven over you is stayed from dew, and the earth is stayed from her fruit. And I called for a drought upon the land, and upon the mountains, and upon the corn, and upon the new wine, and upon the oil, and upon that which the ground bringeth forth, and upon men, and upon cattle, and upon all the labor of the hands." Verses 9-11.

"Consider your ways," the Lord urged. "Go up to the mountain, and bring wood, and build the house; and I will take pleasure in it, and I will be glorified." Verses 7, 8.

The message of counsel and reproof given through Haggai was taken to heart by the leaders and people of Israel. They felt that God was in earnest with them. They dared not disregard the repeated instruction sent them—that their prosperity, both temporal and spiritual, was dependent on faithful obedience to God's commands. Aroused by the warnings of the prophet, Zerubbabel and Joshua, "with all the remnant of the people, obeyed the voice of the Lord their God, and the words of Haggai the prophet." Verse 12.

As soon as Israel decided to obey, the words of reproof were followed by a message of encouragement. "Then spake Haggai . . . unto the people, saying, I am with you, saith the Lord. And the Lord stirred up the spirit of Zerubbabel" and of Joshua, and "of all the remnant of the people; and they came and did work in the house of the Lord of hosts, their God." Verses 13, 14.

In less than a month after the work on the temple was resumed, the builders received another comforting message. "Be strong, O Zerubbabel," the Lord Himself urged through His prophet; "be strong, O Joshua; . . . and be strong, all ye people of the land, saith the Lord, and work: for I am with you, saith the Lord of hosts." Haggai 2:4.

To Israel encamped before Mount Sinai the Lord had declared: "I will dwell among the children of Israel, and will be their God. And they shall know that I am the Lord their God, that brought them forth out of the land of Egypt, that I may dwell among them: I am the Lord their God." Exodus 29:45, 46. And now, notwithstanding the fact that they had repeatedly "rebelled, and vexed His Holy Spirit" (Isaiah 63:10), God once more, through the messages of His prophet, was stretching out His hand to save. As a recognition of their co-operation with His purpose, He was renewing His covenant that His Spirit should remain among them; and He bade them, "Fear not."

To His children today the Lord declares, "Be strong, . . . and work: for I am with you." The Christian always has a strong helper in the Lord. The way of the Lord's helping we may not know; but this we do know: He will never fail those who put their trust in Him. Could Christians realize how many times the Lord has ordered their way, that the purposes of the enemy concerning them might not be accomplished, they would not stumble along complainingly. Their faith would be stayed on God, and no trial would have power to move them. They would acknowledge Him as their wisdom and efficiency, and He would bring to pass that which He desires to work out through them.

The earnest pleadings and the encouragements given through Haggai were emphasized and added to by Zechariah, whom God raised up to stand by his side in urging Israel to carry out the command to arise and build. Zechariah's first message was an assurance that God's word never fails and a promise of blessing to those who would hearken to the sure word of prophecy.

With fields lying waste, with their scant store of provisions rapidly failing, and surrounded as they were by unfriendly peoples, the Israelites nevertheless moved forward by faith in response to the call of God's messengers, and labored diligently to restore the ruined temple. It was a work requiring firm reliance upon God. As the people endeavored to do their part, and sought for a renewal of God's grace in heart and life, message after message was given them through Haggai and Zechariah, with assurances that their faith would be richly rewarded and that the word of God concerning the future glory of the temple whose walls they were rearing would not fail. In this very building would appear, in the fullness of time, the Desire of all nations as the Teacher and Saviour of mankind.

Thus the builders were not left to struggle alone; "with them were the prophets of God helping them;" and the Lord of hosts Himself had declared, "Be strong, . . . and work: for I am with you." Ezra 5:2; Haggai 2:4.

With heartfelt repentance and a willingness to advance by faith, came the promise of temporal prosperity. "From this day," the Lord declared, "will I bless you." Verse 19.

To Zerubbabel their leader—he who, through all the years since their return from Babylon, had been so sorely tried—was given a most precious message. The day was coming, the Lord declared, when all the enemies of His chosen people would be cast down. "In that day, saith the Lord of hosts, will I take thee, O Zerubbabel, My servant, . . . and will make thee as a signet: for I have chosen thee." Verse 23. Now the governor of Israel could see the meaning of the providence that had led him through discouragement and perplexity; he could discern God's purpose in it all.

This personal word to Zerubbabel has been left on record for the encouragement of God's children in every age. God has a purpose in sending trial to His children. He never leads them otherwise than they would choose to be led if they could see the end from the beginning, and discern the glory of the purpose that they are fulfilling. All that He brings upon them in test and trial comes that they may be strong to do and to suffer for Him.

The messages delivered by Haggai and Zechariah roused the people to put forth every possible effort for the rebuilding of the temple; but, as they worked, they were sadly harassed by the Samaritans and others who devised many hindrances. On one occasion the provincial officers of the Medo-Persian realm visited Jerusalem and requested the name of the one who had authorized the restoration of the building. If at that time the Jews had not been trusting in the Lord for guidance, this inquiry might have resulted disastrously to them. "But the eye of their God was upon the elders of the Jews, that they could not cause them to cease, till the matter came to Darius." Ezra 5:5. The officers were answered so wisely that they decided to write a letter to Darius Hystaspes, then the ruler of Medo-Persia, directing his attention to the original decree made by Cyrus, which commanded that the house of God at Jerusalem be rebuilt, and that the expenses for the same be paid from the king's treasury.

Darius searched for this decree, and found it; whereupon he directed those who had made the inquiry to allow the rebuilding of the temple to proceed. "Let the work of this house of God alone," he commanded; "let the governor of the Jews and the elders of the Jews build this house of God in his place.

"Moreover," Darius continued, "I make a decree what ye shall do to the elders of these Jews for the building of this house of God: that of the king's goods, even of the tribute beyond the river, forthwith expenses be given unto these men, that they be not hindered. And that which they have need of, both young bullocks, and rams, and lambs, for the burnt offerings of the God of heaven, wheat, salt, wine, and oil, according to the appointment of the priests which are at Jerusalem, let it be given them day by day without fail: that they may offer sacrifices of sweet savors unto the God of heaven, and pray for the life of the king, and of his sons." Ezra 6:7-10.

The king further decreed that severe penalties be meted out to those who should in any wise alter the decree; and he closed with the remarkable statement: "The God that hath caused His name to dwell there destroy all kings and people, that shall put to their hand to alter and to destroy this house of God which is at Jerusalem. I Darius have made a decree; let it be done with the speed." Verse 12. Thus the Lord prepared the way for the completion of the temple.

For months before this decree was made, the Israelites had kept on working by faith, the prophets of God still helping them by means of timely messages, through which the divine purpose for Israel was kept before the workers. Two months after Haggai's last recorded message was delivered, Zechariah had a series of visions regarding the work of God in the earth. These messages, given in the form of parables and symbols, came at a time of great uncertainty and anxiety, and were of peculiar significance to the men who were advancing in the name of the God of Israel. It seemed to the leaders as if the permission granted the Jews to rebuild was about to be withdrawn; the future appeared very dark. God saw that His people were in need of being sustained and cheered by a revelation of His infinite compassion and love.

In vision Zechariah heard the angel of the Lord inquiring, "O Lord of hosts, how long wilt Thou not have mercy on Jerusalem and on the cities of Judah, against which Thou hast had indignation these threescore and ten years? And the Lord answered the angel that talked with me," Zechariah declared, "with good words and comfortable words.

"So the angel that communed with me said unto me, Cry thou, saying, Thus saith the Lord of hosts; I am jealous for Jerusalem and for Zion with a great jealousy. And I am very sore displeased with the heathen that are at ease: for I was but a little displeased, and they helped forward the affliction. Therefore thus saith the Lord; I am returned to Jerusalem with mercies: My house shall be built in it, . . . and a line shall be stretched forth upon Jerusalem." Zechariah 1:12-16.

The prophet was now directed to predict, "Thus saith the Lord of hosts; My cities through prosperity shall yet be spread abroad; and the Lord shall yet comfort Zion, and shall yet choose Jerusalem." Verse 17.

Zechariah then saw the powers that had "scattered Judah, Israel, and Jerusalem," symbolized by four horns. Immediately afterward he saw four carpenters, representing the agencies used by the Lord in restoring His people and the house of His worship. See verses 18-21.

"I lifted up mine eyes again," Zechariah said, "and looked, and behold a man with a measuring line in his hand. Then said I, Whither goest thou? And he said unto me, To measure Jerusalem, to see what is the breadth thereof, and what is the length thereof. And, behold, the angel that talked with me went forth, and another angel went out to meet him, and said unto him, Run, speak to this young man, saying, Jerusalem shall be inhabited as towns without walls for the multitude of men and cattle therein: for I, saith the Lord, will be unto her a wall of fire round about, and will be the glory in the midst of her." Zechariah 2:1-5.

God had commanded that Jerusalem be rebuilt; the vision of the measuring of the city was an assurance that He would give comfort and strength to His afflicted ones, and fulfill to them the promises of His everlasting covenant. His protecting care, He declared, would be like "a wall of fire round about;" and through them His glory would be revealed to all the sons of men. That which He was accomplishing for His people was to be known in all the earth. "Cry out and shout, thou inhabitant of Zion: for great is the Holy One of Israel in the midst of thee." Isaiah 12:6.

Joshua and the Angel

The steady advancement made by the builders of the temple greatly discomfited and alarmed the hosts of evil. Satan determined to put forth still further effort to weaken and discourage God's people by holding before them their imperfections of character. If those who had long suffered because of transgression could again be induced to disregard God's commandments, they would be brought once more under the bondage of sin.

Because Israel had been chosen to preserve the knowledge of God in the earth, they had ever been the special objects of Satan's enmity; he was determined to cause their destruction. While they were obedient, he could do them no harm; therefore he had bent all his power and cunning to entice them into sin. Ensnared by his temptations, they had transgressed the law of God and had been left to become the prey of their enemies.

Yet though they were carried as captives to Babylon, God did not forsake them. He sent His prophets to them with reproofs and warnings, and aroused them to see their guilt. When they humbled themselves before God and returned to Him with true repentance, He sent them messages of encouragement, declaring that He would deliver them from captivity, restore them to His favor, and once more establish them in their own land. And now that this work of restoration had begun, and a remnant of Israel had already returned to Judea, Satan was determined to frustrate the carrying out of the divine purpose, and to this end he was seeking to move upon the heathen nations to destroy them utterly.

But in this crisis the Lord strengthened His people "with good words and comfortable words." Zechariah 1:13. Through an impressive illustration of the work of Satan and the work of Christ, He showed the power of their Mediator to vanquish the accuser of His people.

In vision the prophet beholds "Joshua the high priest," "clothed with filthy garments" (Zechariah 3:1, 3), standing before the Angel of the Lord, entreating God's mercy in behalf of his afflicted people. As he pleads for the fulfillment of God's promises, Satan stands up boldly to resist him. He points to the transgressions of Israel as a reason why they should not be restored to the favor of God. He claims them as his prey, and demands that they be given into his hands.

The high priest cannot defend himself or his people from Satan's accusations. He does not claim that Israel is free from fault. In filthy garments, symbolizing the sins of the people, which he bears as their representative, he stands before the Angel, confessing their guilt, yet pointing to their repentance and humiliation, and relying upon the mercy of a sin-pardoning Redeemer. In faith he claims the promises of God.

Then the Angel, who is Christ Himself, the Saviour of sinners, puts to silence the accuser of His people, declaring, "The Lord rebuke thee, O Satan; even the Lord that hath chosen Jerusalem rebuke thee: is not this a brand plucked out of the fire?" Verse 2. Long had Israel remained in the furnace of affliction. Because of their sins they had been well-nigh consumed in the flame kindled by Satan and his agents for their destruction, but God had now set His hand to bring them forth.

As the intercession of Joshua is accepted, the command is given, "Take away the filthy garments from him;" and to Joshua the Angel says, "Behold, I have caused thine iniquity to pass from thee, and I will clothe thee with change of raiment." "So they set a fair miter upon his head, and clothed him with garments." Verses 4, 5. His own sins and those of his people were pardoned. Israel was clothed with "change of raiment"—the righteousness of Christ imputed to them. The miter be placed upon Joshua's head was such as was worn by the priests, and bore the inscription, "Holiness to the Lord" (Exodus 28:36), signifying that notwithstanding his former transgressions, he was now qualified to minister before God in His sanctuary.

The Angel now declared to Joshua: "Thus saith the Lord of hosts; If thou wilt walk in My ways, and if thou wilt keep My charge, then thou shalt also judge My house, and shalt also keep My courts, and I will give thee places to walk among these that stand by." Zechariah 3:7. If obedient, he should be honored as the judge, or ruler, over the temple and all its services; he should walk among attending angels, even in this life; and at last he should join the glorified throng around the throne of God.

"Hear now, O Joshua the high priest, thou, and thy fellows that sit before thee: for they are men wondered at: for, behold, I will bring forth My Servant the Branch." Verse 8. In the Branch, the Deliverer to come, lay the hope of Israel. It was by faith in the coming Saviour that Joshua and his people had received pardon. Through faith in Christ they had been restored to God's favor. By virtue of His merits, if they walked in His ways and kept His statutes, they would be "men wondered at," honored as the chosen of Heaven among the nations of the earth. As Satan accused Joshua and his people, so in all ages he accuses those who seek the mercy and favor of God. He is "the accuser of our brethren, . . . which accused them before our God day and night." Revelation 12:10. Over every soul that is rescued from the power of evil, and whose name is registered in the Lamb's book of life, the controversy is repeated. Never is one received into the family of God without exciting the determined resistance of the enemy. But He who was the hope of Israel then, their defense, their justification and redemption, is the hope of the church today.

Satan's accusations against those who seek the Lord are not prompted by displeasure at their sins. He exults in their defective characters; for he knows that only through their transgression of God's law can he obtain power over them. His accusations arise solely from his enmity to Christ.

Through the plan of salvation, Jesus is breaking Satan's hold upon the human family and rescuing souls from his power. All the hatred and malignity of the archrebel is stirred as he beholds the evidences of Christ's supremacy; and with fiendish power and cunning he works to wrest from Him the children of men who have accepted salvation. He leads men into skepticism, causing them to lose confidence in God and to separate from His love; he tempts them to break the law and then claims them as his captives, contesting Christ's right to take them from him.

Satan knows that those who ask God for pardon and grace will obtain it; therefore he presents their sins before them to discourage them. Against those who are trying to obey God, he is constantly seeking occasion for complaint. Even their best and most acceptable service he seeks to make appear corrupt. By countless devices, the most subtle and the most cruel, he endeavors to secure their condemnation.

In his own strength, man cannot meet the charges of the enemy. In sin-stained garments, confessing his guilt, he stands before God. But Jesus, our Advocate, presents an effectual plea in behalf of all who by repentance and faith have committed the keeping of their souls to Him. He pleads their cause, and by the mighty arguments of Calvary, vanquishes their accuser. His perfect obedience to God's law has given Him all power in heaven and in earth, and He claims from His Father mercy and reconciliation for guilty man. To the accuser of His people He declares:

"The Lord rebuke thee, O Satan. These are the purchase of My blood, brands plucked from the burning." And to those who rely on Him in faith, He gives the assurance, "Behold, I have caused thine iniquity to pass from thee, and I will clothe thee with change of raiment." Zechariah 3:4.

All who have put on the robe of Christ's righteousness will stand before Him as chosen and faithful and true. Satan has no power to pluck them out of the hand of the Saviour. Not one soul who in penitence and faith has claimed His protection will Christ permit to pass under the enemy's power. His word is pledged: "Let him take hold of My strength, that he may make peace with Me; and he shall make peace with Me." Isaiah 27:5. The promise given to Joshua is given to all: "If thou wilt keep My charge,. . . . I will give thee places to walk among these that stand by." Zechariah 3:7. Angels of God will walk on either side of them, even in this world, and they will stand at last among the angels that surround the throne of God.

Zechariah's vision of Joshua and the Angel applies with peculiar force to the experience of God's people in the closing scenes of the great day of atonement. The remnant church will then be brought into great trial and distress. Those who keep the commandments of God and the faith of Jesus will feel the ire of the dragon and his hosts. Satan numbers the world as his subjects; he has gained control even of many professing Christians. But here is a little company who are resisting his supremacy. If he could blot them from the earth, his triumph would be complete. As he influenced the heathen nations to destroy Israel, so in the near future he will stir up the wicked powers of earth to destroy the people of God. Men will be required to render obedience to human edicts in violation of the divine law.

Those who are true to God will be menaced, denounced, proscribed. They will be "betrayed both by parents, and brethren, and kinsfolks, and friends," even unto death. Luke 21:16. Their only hope is in the mercy of God; their only defense will be prayer. As Joshua pleaded before the Angel, so the remnant church, with brokenness of heart and unfaltering faith, will plead for pardon and deliverance through Jesus, their Advocate. They are fully conscious of the sinfulness of their lives, they see their weakness and unworthiness; and they are ready to despair.

The tempter stands by to accuse them, as he stood by to resist Joshua. He points to their filthy garments, their defective characters. He presents their weakness and folly, their sins of ingratitude, their unlikeness to Christ, which has dishonored their Redeemer. He endeavors to affright them with the thought that their case is hopeless, that the stain of their defilement will never be washed away. He hopes so to destroy their faith that they will yield to his temptations, and turn from their allegiance to God.

Satan has an accurate knowledge of the sins that he has tempted God's people to commit, and he urges his accusations against them, declaring, that by their sins they have forfeited divine protection, and claiming that he has the right to destroy them. He pronounces them just as deserving as himself of exclusion from the favor of God. "Are these," he says, "the people who are to take my place in heaven, and the place of the angels who united with me? They profess to obey the law of God; but have they kept its precepts? Have they not been lovers of self more than lovers of God? Have they not placed their own interests above His service? Have they not loved the things of the world? Look at the sins that have marked their lives. Behold their selfishness, their malice, their hatred of one another. Will God banish me and my angels from His presence, and yet reward those who have been guilty of the same sins? Thou canst not do this, O Lord, in justice. Justice demands that sentence be pronounced against them."

But while the followers of Christ have sinned, they have not given themselves up to be controlled by the satanic agencies. They have repented of their sins and have sought the Lord in humility and contrition, and the divine Advocate pleads in their behalf. He who has been most abused by their ingratitude, who knows their sin and also their penitence, declares: "The Lord rebuke thee, O Satan. I gave My life for these souls. They are graven upon the palms of My hands. They may have imperfections of character; they may have failed in their endeavors; but they have repented, and I have forgiven and accepted them."

The assaults of Satan are strong, his delusions are subtle; but the Lord's eye is upon His people. Their affliction is great, the flames of the furnace seem about to consume them; but Jesus will bring them forth as gold tried in the fire. Their earthliness will be removed, that through them the image of Christ may be perfectly revealed.

At times the Lord may seem to have forgotten the perils of His church and the injury done her by her enemies. But God has not forgotten. Nothing in this world is so dear to the heart of God as His church. It is not His will that worldly policy shall corrupt her record. He does not leave His people to be overcome by Satan's temptations. He will punish those who misrepresent Him, but He will be gracious to all who sincerely repent. To those who call upon Him for strength for the development of Christian character, He will give all needed help.

In the time of the end the people of God will sigh and cry for the abominations done in the land. With tears they will warn the wicked of their danger in trampling upon the divine law, and with unutterable sorrow they will humble themselves before the Lord in penitence. The wicked will mock their sorrow and ridicule their solemn appeals. But the anguish and humiliation of God's people is unmistakable evidence that they are regaining the strength and nobility of character lost in consequence of sin. It is because they are drawing nearer to Christ, because their eyes are fixed on His perfect purity, that they discern so clearly the exceeding sinfulness of sin. Meekness and lowliness are the conditions of success and victory. A crown of glory awaits those who bow at the foot of the cross.

God's faithful, praying ones are, as it were, shut in with Him. They themselves know not how securely they are shielded. Urged on by Satan, the rulers of this world are seeking to destroy them; but could the eyes of God's children be opened as were the eyes of Elisha's servant at Dothan, they would see angels of God encamped about them, holding in check the hosts of darkness.

As the people of God afflict their souls before Him, pleading for purity of heart, the command is given, "Take away the filthy garments," and the encouraging words are spoken, "Behold, I have caused thine iniquity to pass from thee, and I will clothe thee with change of raiment." Zechariah 3:4. The spotless robe of Christ's righteousness is placed upon the tried, tempted, faithful children of God. The despised remnant are clothed in glorious apparel, nevermore to be defiled by the corruptions of the world. Their names are retained in the Lamb's book of life, enrolled among the faithful of all ages. They have resisted the wiles of the deceiver; they have not been turned from their loyalty by the dragon's roar. Now they are eternally secure from the tempter's devices. Their sins are transferred to the originator of sin. A "fair miter" is set upon their heads.

While Satan has been urging his accusations, holy angels, unseen, have been passing to and fro, placing upon the faithful ones the seal of the living God. These are they that stand upon Mount Zion with the Lamb, having the Father's name written in their foreheads. They sing the new song before the throne, that song which no man can learn save the hundred and forty and four thousand which were redeemed from the earth. "These are they which follow the Lamb whithersoever He goeth. These were redeemed from among men, being the first fruits unto God and to the Lamb. And in their mouth was found no guile: for they are without fault before the throne of God." Revelation 14:4, 5.

Now is reached the complete fulfillment of the words of the Angel: "Hear now, O Joshua the high priest, thou, and thy fellows that sit before thee: for they are men wondered at: for, behold, I will bring forth My Servant the Branch." Zechariah 3:8. Christ is revealed as the Redeemer and Deliverer of His people. Now indeed are the remnant "men wondered at," as the tears and humiliation of their pilgrimage give place to joy and honor in the presence of God and the Lamb. "In that day shall the branch of the Lord be beautiful and glorious, and the fruit of the earth shall be excellent and comely for them that are escaped of Israel. And it shall come to pass, that he that is left in Zion, and he that remaineth in Jerusalem, shall be called holy, even everyone that is written among the living in Jerusalem." Isaiah 4:2, 3.

"Not by Might, nor by Power"

Immediately after Zechariah's vision of Joshua and the Angel, the prophet received a message regarding the work of Zerubbabel. "The Angel that talked with me," Zechariah declares, "came again, and waked me, as a man that is wakened out of his sleep, and said unto me, What seest thou? And I said, I have looked, and behold a candlestick all of gold, with a bowl upon the top of it, and his seven lamps thereon, and seven pipes to the seven lamps, which are upon the top thereof: and two olive trees by it, one upon the right side of the bowl, and the other upon the left side thereof.

"So I answered and spake to the Angel that talked with me, saying, What are these, my Lord? . . . Then He answered and spake unto me, saying, This is the word of the Lord unto Zerubbabel, saying, Not by might, nor by power, but by My Spirit, saith the Lord of hosts."

"Then answered I, and said unto Him, What are these two olive trees upon the right side of the candlestick and upon the left side thereof? And I answered again, and said unto Him, What be these two olive branches which through the two golden pipes empty the golden oil out of themselves? . . . Then said He, These are the two anointed ones, that stand by the Lord of the whole earth." Zechariah 4:1-6, 11-14.

In this vision the two olive trees which stand before God are represented as emptying the golden oil out of themselves through golden tubes into the bowl of the candlestick. From this the lamps of the sanctuary are fed, that they may give a bright, continuous light. So from the anointed ones that stand in God's presence the fullness of divine light and love and power is imparted to His people, that they may impart to others light and joy and refreshing. Those who are thus enriched are to enrich others with the treasure of God's love.

In rebuilding the house of the Lord, Zerubbabel had labored in the face of manifold difficulties. From the beginning, adversaries had "weakened the hands of the people of Judah, and troubled them in building," "and made them to cease by force and power." Ezra 4:4, 23. But the Lord had interposed in behalf of the builders, and now He spoke through His prophet to Zerubbabel, saying, "Who art thou, O great mountain? before Zerubbabel thou shalt become a plain: and he shall bring forth the headstone thereof with shoutings, crying, Grace, grace unto it." Zechariah 4:7.

Throughout the history of God's people great mountains of difficulty, apparently insurmountable, have loomed up before those who were trying to carry out the purposes of Heaven. Such obstacles are permitted by the Lord as a test of faith. When we are hedged about on every side, this is the time above all others to trust in God and in the power of His Spirit. The exercise of a living faith means an increase of spiritual strength and the development of an unfaltering trust. It is thus that the soul becomes a conquering power. Before the demand of faith, the obstacles placed by Satan across the pathway of the Christian will disappear; for the powers of heaven will come to his aid. "Nothing shall be impossible unto you." Matthew 17:20.

The way of the world is to begin with pomp and boasting. God's way is to make the day of small things the beginning of the glorious triumph of truth and righteousness. Sometimes He trains His workers by bringing to them disappointment and apparent failure. It is His purpose that they shall learn to master difficulties.

Often men are tempted to falter before the perplexities and obstacles that confront them. But if they will hold the beginning of their confidence steadfast unto the end, God will make the way clear. Success will come to them as they struggle against difficulties. Before the intrepid spirit and unwavering faith of a Zerubbabel, great mountains of difficulty will become a plain; and he whose hands have laid the foundation, even "his hands shall also finish it." "He shall bring forth the headstone thereof with shoutings, crying, Grace, grace unto it." Zechariah 4:9, 7.

Human power and human might did not establish the church of God, and neither can they destroy it. Not on the rock of human strength, but on Christ Jesus, the Rock of Ages, was the church founded, "and the gates of hell shall not prevail against it." Matthew 16:18. The presence of God gives stability to His cause. "Put not your trust in princes, nor in the son of man," is the word that comes to us. Psalm 146:3. "In quietness and in confidence shall be your strength." Isaiah 30:15. God's glorious work, founded on the eternal principles of right, will never come to nought. It will go on from strength to strength, "not by might, nor by power, but by My Spirit, saith the Lord of hosts." Zechariah 4:6.

The promise, "The hands of Zerubbabel have laid the foundation of this house; his hands shall also finish it," was literally fulfilled. Verse 9. "The elders of the Jews builded, and they prospered through the prophesying of Haggai the prophet and Zechariah the son of Iddo. And they builded, and finished it, according to the commandment of the God of Israel, and

according to the commandment of Cyrus, and Darius, and Artaxerxes king of Persia. And this house was finished on the third day of the month Adar, which was in the sixth year of the reign of Darius the king." Ezra 6:14, 15.

Shortly afterward the restored temple was dedicated. "The children of Israel, the priests, and the Levites, and the rest of the children of the captivity, kept the dedication of this house of God with joy;" and "upon the fourteenth day of the first month" they "kept the Passover." Verses 16, 17, 19.

The second temple did not equal the first in magnificence, nor was it hallowed by those visible tokens of the divine presence which pertained to the first temple. There was no manifestation of supernatural power to mark its dedication. No cloud of glory was seen to fill the newly erected sanctuary. No fire from heaven descended to consume the sacrifice upon its altar. The Shekinah no longer abode between the cherubim in the most holy place; the ark, the mercy seat, and the tables of testimony were not found there. No sign from heaven made known to the inquiring priest the will of Jehovah.

And yet this was the building concerning which the Lord had declared by the prophet Haggai: "The glory of this latter house shall be greater than of the former." "I will shake all nations, and the Desire of all nations shall come: and I will fill this house with glory, saith the Lord of hosts." Haggai 2:9, 7. For centuries learned men have endeavored to show wherein the promise of God, given to Haggai, has been fulfilled; yet in the advent of Jesus of Nazareth, the Desire of all nations, who by His personal presence hallowed the precincts of the temple, many have steadfastly refused to see any special significance. Pride and unbelief have blinded their minds to the true meaning of the prophet's words.

The second temple was honored, not with the cloud of Jehovah's glory, but with the presence of the One in whom dwelt "all the fullness of the Godhead bodily"—God Himself "manifest in the flesh." Colossians 2:9; 1 Timothy 3:16. In being honored with the personal presence of Christ during His earthly ministry, and in this alone, did the second temple exceed the first in glory. The "Desire of all nations" had indeed come to His temple, when the Man of Nazareth taught and healed in the sacred courts.

In the Days of Queen Esther

Under the favor shown them by Cyrus, nearly fifty thousand of the children of the captivity had taken advantage of the decree permitting their return. These, however, in comparison with the hundreds of thousands scattered throughout the provinces of Medo-Persia, were but a mere remnant. The great majority of the Israelites had chosen to remain in the land of their exile rather than undergo the hardships of the return journey and the re-establishment of their desolated cities and homes.

A score or more of years passed by, when a second decree, quite as favorable as the first, was issued by Darius Hystaspes, the monarch then ruling. Thus did God in mercy provide another opportunity for the Jews in the Medo-Persian realm to return to the land of their fathers. The Lord foresaw the troublous times that were to follow during the reign of Xerxes,—the Ahasuerus of the book of Esther,—and He not only wrought a change of feeling in the hearts of men in authority, but also inspired Zechariah to plead with the exiles to return.

"Ho, ho, come forth, and flee from the land of the north," was the message given the scattered tribes of Israel who had become settled in many lands far from their former home. "I have spread you abroad as the four winds of the heaven, saith the Lord. Deliver thyself, O Zion, that dwellest with the daughter of Babylon. For thus saith the Lord of hosts; After the glory hath He sent me unto the nations which spoiled you: for he that toucheth you toucheth the apple of His eye. For, behold, I will shake mine hand upon them, and they shall be a spoil to their servants: and ye shall know that the Lord of hosts hath sent me." Zechariah 2:6-9.

It was still the Lord's purpose, as it have been from the beginning, that His people should be a praise in the earth, to the glory of His name. During the long years of their exile He had given them many opportunities to return to their allegiance to Him. Some had chosen to listen and to learn; some had found salvation in the midst of affliction. Many of these were to be numbered among the remnant that should return. They were likened by Inspiration to "the highest branch of the high cedar," which was to be planted "upon an high mountain and eminent: in the mountain of the height of Israel." Ezekiel 17:22, 23.

It was those "whose spirit God had raised" (Ezra 1:5) who had returned under the decree of Cyrus. But God ceased not to plead with those who voluntarily remained in the land of their exile, and through manifold agencies He made it possible for them also to return. The large number, however, of those who failed to respond to the decree of Cyrus, remained unimpressible to later influences; and even when Zechariah warned them to flee from Babylon without further delay, they did not heed the invitation.

Meanwhile conditions in the Medo-Persian realm were rapidly changing. Darius Hystaspes, under whose reign the Jews had been shown marked favor, was succeeded by Xerxes the Great. It was during his reign that those of the Jews who had failed of heeding the message to flee were called upon to face a terrible crisis. Having refused to take advantage of the way of escape God had provided, now they were brought face to face with death.

Through Haman the Agagite, an unscrupulous man high in authority in Medo-Persia, Satan worked at this time to counterwork the purposes of God. Haman cherished bitter malice against Mordecai, a Jew. Mordecai had done Haman no harm, but had simply refused to show him worshipful reverence. Scorning to "lay hands on Mordecai alone," Haman plotted "to destroy all the Jews that were throughout the whole kingdom of Ahasuerus, even the people of Mordecai." Esther 3:6.

Misled by the false statements of Haman, Xerxes was induced to issue a decree providing for the massacre of all the Jews "scattered abroad and dispersed among the people in all the provinces" of the Medo-Persian kingdom. Verse 8. A certain day was appointed on which the Jews were to be destroyed and their property confiscated. Little did the king realize the far-reaching results that would have accompanied the complete carrying out of this decree. Satan himself, the hidden instigator of the scheme, was trying to rid the earth of those who preserved the knowledge of the true God.

"In every province, whithersoever the king's commandment and his decree came, there was great mourning among the Jews, and fasting, and weeping, and wailing; and many lay in sackcloth and ashes." Esther 4:3. The decree of the Medes and Persians could not be revoked; apparently there was no hope; all the Israelites were doomed to destruction.

But the plots of the enemy were defeated by a Power that reigns among the children of men. In the providence of God, Esther, a Jewess who feared the Most High, had been made queen of the Medo-Persian kingdom. Mordecai was a near relative of hers. In their extremity they decided to appeal to Xerxes in behalf of their people. Esther was to venture into his presence as an intercessor. "Who knoweth," said Mordecai, "whether thou art come to the kingdom for such a time as this?" Verse 14.

The crisis that Esther faced demanded quick, earnest action; but both she and Mordecai realized that unless God should work mightily in their behalf, their own efforts would be unavailing. So Esther took time for communion with God, the source of her strength. "Go," she directed Mordecai, "gather together all the Jews that are present in Shushan, and fast ye for me, and neither eat nor drink three days, night or day: I also and my maidens will fast likewise; and so will I go in unto the king, which is not according to the law: and if I perish, I perish." Verse 16.

The events that followed in rapid succession,—the appearance of Esther before the king, the marked favor shown her, the banquets of the king and queen with Haman as the only guest, the troubled sleep of the king, the public honor shown Mordecai, and the humiliation and fall of Haman upon the discovery of his wicked plot,—all these are parts of a familiar story. God wrought marvelously for His penitent people; and a counter decree issued by the king, allowing them to fight for their lives, was rapidly communicated to every part of the realm by mounted couriers, who were "hastened and pressed on by the king's commandment." "And in every province, and in every city, whithersoever the king's commandment and his decree came, the Jews had joy and gladness, a feast and a good day. And many of the people of the land became Jews; for the fear of the Jews fell upon them." Esther 8:14, 17.

On the day appointed for their destruction, "the Jews gathered themselves together in their cities throughout all the provinces of the king Ahasuerus, to lay hand on such as sought their hurt: and no man could withstand them; for the fear of them fell upon all people." Angels that excel in strength had been commissioned by God to protect His people while they "stood for their lives." Esther 9:2, 16.

Mordecai was given the position of honor formerly occupied by Haman. He "was next unto King Ahasuerus, and great among the Jews, and accepted of the multitude of his brethren" (Esther 10:3); and he sought to promote the welfare of Israel. Thus did God bring His chosen people once more into favor at the Medo-Persian court, making possible the carrying out of His purpose to restore them to their own land. But it was not until several years later, in the seventh year of Artaxerxes I, the successor of Xerxes the Great, that any considerable number returned to Jerusalem, under Ezra.

The trying experiences that came to God's people in the days of Esther were not peculiar to that age alone. The revelator, looking down the ages to the close of time, has declared, "The dragon was wroth with the woman, and went to make war with the remnant of her seed, which keep the commandments of God, and have the testimony of Jesus Christ." Revelation 12:17. Some who today are living on the earth will see these words fulfilled. The same spirit that in ages past led men to persecute the true church, will in the future lead to the pursuance of a similar course toward those who maintain their loyalty to God. Even now preparations are being made for this last great conflict.

The decree that will finally go forth against the remnant people of God will be very similar to that issued by Ahasuerus against the Jews. Today the enemies of the true church see in the little company keeping the Sabbath commandment, a Mordecai at the gate. The reverence of God's people for His law is a constant rebuke to those who have cast off the fear of the Lord and are trampling on His Sabbath.

Satan will arouse indignation against the minority who refuse to accept popular customs and traditions. Men of position and reputation will join with the lawless and the vile to take counsel against the people of God. Wealth, genius, education, will combine to cover them with contempt. Persecuting rulers, ministers, and church members will conspire against them. With voice and pen, by boasts, threats, and ridicule, they will seek to overthrow their faith. By false representations and angry appeals, men will stir up the passions of the people. Not having a "Thus saith the Scriptures" to bring against the advocates of the Bible Sabbath, they will resort to oppressive enactments to supply the lack. To secure popularity and patronage, legislators will yield to the demand for Sunday laws. But those who fear God, cannot accept an institution that violates a precept of the Decalogue. On this battlefield will be fought the last great conflict in the controversy between truth and error. And we are not left in doubt as to the issue. Today, as in the days of Esther and Mordecai, the Lord will vindicate His truth and His people.

Ezra, the Priest and Scribe

About seventy years after the return of the first company of exiles under Zerubbabel and Joshua, Artaxerxes Longimanus came to the throne of Medo-Persia. The name of this king is connected with sacred history by a series of remarkable providences. It was during his reign that Ezra and Nehemiah lived and labored. He is the one who in 457 B.C. issued the third and final decree for the restoration of Jerusalem. His reign saw the return of a company of Jews under Ezra, the completion of the walls of Jerusalem by Nehemiah and his associates, the reorganization of the temple services, and the great religious reformations instituted by Ezra and Nehemiah. During his long rule he often showed favor to God's people, and in his trusted and well-beloved Jewish friends, Ezra and Nehemiah, he recognized men of God's appointment, raised up for a special work.

The experience of Ezra while living among the Jews who remained in Babylon was so unusual that it attracted the favorable notice of King Artaxerxes, with whom he talked freely regarding the power of the God of heaven, and the divine purpose in restoring the Jews to Jerusalem.

Born of the sons of Aaron, Ezra had been given a priestly training; and in addition to this he had acquired a familiarity with the writings of the magicians, the astrologers, and the wise men of the Medo-Persian realm. But he was not satisfied with his spiritual condition. He longed to be in full harmony with God; he longed for wisdom to carry out the divine will. And so he "prepared his heart to seek the law of the Lord, and to do it." Ezra 7:10. This led him to apply himself diligently to a study of the history of God's people, as recorded in the writings of prophets and kings. He searched the historical and poetical books of the Bible to learn why the Lord had permitted Jerusalem to be destroyed and His people carried captive into a heathen land.

To the experiences of Israel from the time the promise was made to Abraham, Ezra gave special thought. He studied the instruction given at Mount Sinai and through the long period of wilderness wandering. As he learned more and still more concerning God's dealings with His children, and comprehended the sacredness of the law given at Sinai, Ezra's heart was stirred. He experienced a new and thorough conversion and determined to master the records of sacred history, that he might use this knowledge to bring blessing and light to his people.

Ezra endeavored to gain a heart preparation for the work he believed was before him. He sought God earnestly, that he might be a wise teacher in Israel. As he learned to yield mind and will to divine control, there were brought into his life the principles of true sanctification, which, in later years, had a molding influence, not only upon the youth who sought his instruction, but upon all others associated with him.

God chose Ezra to be an instrument of good to Israel, that He might put honor upon the priesthood, the glory of which had been greatly eclipsed during the captivity. Ezra developed into a man of extraordinary learning and became "a ready scribe in the law of Moses." Verse 6. These qualifications made him an eminent man in the Medo-Persian kingdom.

Ezra became a mouthpiece for God, educating those about him in the principles that govern heaven. During the remaining years of his life, whether near the court of the king of Medo-Persia or at Jerusalem, his principal work was that of a teacher. As he communicated to others the truths he learned, his capacity for labor increased. He became a man of piety and zeal. He was the Lord's witness to the world of power of Bible truth to ennoble the daily life.

The efforts of Ezra to revive an interest in the study of the Scriptures were given permanency by his painstaking, lifelong work of preserving and multiplying the Sacred Writings. He gathered all the copies of the law that he could find and had these transcribed and distributed. The pure word, thus multiplied and placed in the hands of many people, gave knowledge that was of inestimable value.

Ezra's faith that God would do a mighty work for His people, led him to tell Artaxerxes of his desire to return to Jerusalem to revive an interest in the study of God's word and to assist his brethren in restoring the Holy City. As Ezra declared his perfect trust in the God of Israel as one abundantly able to protect and care for His people, the king was deeply impressed. He well understood that the Israelites were returning to Jerusalem that they might serve Jehovah; yet so great was the king's confidence in the integrity of Ezra that he showed him marked favor, granting his request and bestowing on him rich gifts for the temple service. He made him a special representative of the Medo-Persian kingdom and conferred on him extensive powers for the carrying out of the purposes that were in his heart.

The decree of Artaxerxes Longimanus for the restoring and building of Jerusalem, the third issued since the close of the seventy years' captivity, is remarkable for its expressions regarding the God of heaven, for its recognition of the attainments of Ezra, and for the liberality of the grants made to the remnant people of God. Artaxerxes refers to Ezra as "the priest, the scribe, even a scribe of the words of the commandments of the Lord, and of His statutes to Israel;" "a scribe of the law of the God of heaven." The king united with his counselors in offering freely "unto the God of Israel, whose habitation is in Jerusalem;" and in addition he made provision for meeting many heavy expenses by ordering that they be paid "out of the king's treasure house." Verses 11, 12, 15, 20.

"Thou art sent of the king, and of his seven counselors," Artaxerxes declared to Ezra, "to inquire concerning Judah and Jerusalem, according to the law of thy God which is in thine hand." And he further decreed: "Whatsoever is commanded by the God of heaven, let it be diligently done for the house of the God of heaven: for why should there be wrath against the realm of the king and his sons?" Verses 14, 23.

In giving permission to the Israelites to return, Artaxerxes arranged for the restoration of the members of the priesthood to their ancient rites and privileges. "We certify you," he declared, "that touching any of the priests and Levites, singers, porters, Nethinims, or ministers of this house of God, it shall not be lawful to impose toll, tribute, or custom, upon them." He also arranged for the appointment of civil officers to govern the people justly in accordance with the Jewish code of laws. "Thou, Ezra, after the wisdom of thy God, that is in thine hand," he directed, "set magistrates and judges, which may judge all the people that are beyond the river, all such as know the laws of thy God; and teach ye them that know them not. And whosoever will not do the law of thy God, and the law of the king, let judgment be executed speedily upon him, whether it be unto death, or to banishment, or to confiscation of goods, or to imprisonment." Verses 24-26.

Thus, "according to the good hand of his God upon him," Ezra had persuaded the king to make abundant provision for the return of all the people of Israel and of the priests and Levites in the Medo-Persian realm, who were minded "of their own free will to go up to Jerusalem." Verses 9, 13. Thus again the children of the dispersion were given opportunity to return to the land with the possession of which were linked the promises to the house of Israel. This decree brought great rejoicing to those who had been uniting with Ezra in a study of God's purposes concerning His people. "Blessed be the Lord God of our fathers," Ezra exclaimed, "which hath put such a thing as this in the king's heart, to beautify the house of the Lord which is in Jerusalem: and hath extended mercy unto me before the king, and his counselors, and before all the king's mighty princes." Verses 27, 28.

In the issuing of this decree by Artaxerxes, God's providence was manifest. Some discerned this and gladly took advantage of the privilege of returning under circumstances so favorable. A general place of meeting was named, and at the appointed time those who were desirous of going to Jerusalem assembled for the long journey. "I gathered them together to the river that runneth to Ahava," Ezra says, "and there abode we in tents three days." Ezra 8:15.

Ezra had expected that a large number would return to Jerusalem, but the number who responded to the call was disappointingly small. Many who had acquired houses and lands had no desire to sacrifice these possessions. They loved ease and comfort and were well satisfied to remain. Their example proved a hindrance to others who otherwise might have chosen to cast in their lot with those who were advancing by faith.

As Ezra looked over the company assembled, he was surprised to find none of the sons of Levi. Where were the members of the tribe that had been set apart for the sacred service of the temple? To the call, Who is on the Lord's side? the Levites should have been the first to respond. During the captivity, and afterward, they had been granted many privileges. They had enjoyed the fullest liberty to minister to the spiritual needs of their brethren in exile. Synagogues had been built, in which the priests conducted the worship of God and instructed the people. The observance of the Sabbath, and the performance of the sacred rites peculiar to the Jewish faith, had been freely allowed.

But with the passing of the years after the close of the captivity, conditions changed, and many new responsibilities rested upon the leaders in Israel. The temple at Jerusalem had been rebuilt and dedicated, and more priests were needed to carry on its services. There was pressing need of men of God to act as teachers of the people. And besides, the Jews remaining in Babylon were in danger of having their religious liberty restricted. Through the prophet Zechariah, as well as by their recent experience during the troublous times of Esther and Mordecai, the Jews in Medo-Persia had been plainly warned to return to their own land. The time had come when it was perilous for them to dwell longer in the midst of heathen influences. In view of these changed conditions, the priests in Babylon should have been quick to discern in the issuance of the decree a special call to them to return to Jerusalem.

The king and his princes had done more than their part in opening the way for the return. They had provided abundant means, but where were the men? The sons of Levi failed at a time when the influence of a decision to accompany their brethren would have led others to follow their example. Their strange indifference is a sad revelation of the attitude of the Israelites in Babylon toward God's purpose for His people.

Once more Ezra appealed to the Levites, sending them an urgent invitation to unite with his company. To emphasize the importance of quick action, he sent with his written plea several of his "chief men" and "men of understanding." Ezra 7:28, 8:16.

While the travelers tarried with Ezra, these trusted messengers hastened back with the plea, "Bring unto us ministers for the house of our God." Ezra 8:17. The appeal was heeded; some who had been halting, made final decision to return. In all, about forty priests and two hundred and twenty Nethinim—men upon whom Ezra could rely as wise ministers and good teachers and helpers—were brought to the camp.

All were now ready to set forth. Before them was a journey that would occupy several months. The men were taking with them their wives and children, and their substance, besides large treasure for the temple and its service. Ezra was aware that enemies lay in wait by the way, ready to plunder and destroy him and his company; yet he had asked from the king no armed force for protection. "I was ashamed," he has explained, "to require of the king a band of soldiers and horsemen to help us against the enemy in the way: because we had spoken unto the king, saying, The hand of our God is upon all them for good that seek Him; but His power and His wrath is against all them that forsake Him." Verse 22.

In this matter, Ezra and his companions saw an opportunity to magnify the name of God before the heathen. Faith in the power of the living God would be strengthened if the Israelites themselves should now reveal implicit faith in their divine Leader. They therefore determined to put their trust wholly in Him. They would ask for no guard of soldiers. They would give the heathen no occasion to ascribe to the strength of man the glory that belongs to God alone. They could not afford to arouse in the minds of their heathen friends one doubt as to the sincerity of their dependence on God as His people. Strength would be gained, not through wealth, not through the power and influence of idolatrous men, but through the favor of God. Only by keeping the law of the Lord before them, and striving to obey it, would they be protected.

This knowledge of the conditions under which they would continue to enjoy the prospering hand of God, lent more than ordinary solemnity to the consecration service that was held by Ezra and his company of faithful souls just before their departure. "I proclaimed a fast there, at the river of Ahava," Ezra has declared of this experience, "that we might afflict ourselves before our God, to seek of Him a right way for us, and for our little ones, and for all our substance." "So we fasted and besought our God for this: and He was entreated of us." Verses 21, 23.

The blessing of God, however, did not make unnecessary the exercise of prudence and forethought. As a special precaution in safeguarding the treasure, Ezra "separated twelve of the chief of the priests"—men whose faithfulness and fidelity had been proved—"and weighed unto them the silver, and the gold, and the vessels, even the offering of the house of our God, which the king, and his counselors, and his lords, and all Israel there present, had offered." These men were solemnly charged to act as vigilant stewards over the treasure entrusted to their care. "Ye are holy unto the Lord," Ezra declared; "the vessels are holy also; and the silver and the gold are a freewill offering unto the Lord God of your fathers. Watch ye, and keep them, until ye weigh them before the chief of the priests and the Levites, and chief of the fathers of Israel, at Jerusalem, in the chambers of the house of the Lord." Verses 24, 25, 28, 29.

The care exercised by Ezra in providing for the transportation and safety of the Lord's treasure, teaches a lesson worthy of thoughtful study. Only those whose trustworthiness had been proved were chosen, and they were instructed plainly regarding the responsibility resting on them. In the appointment of faithful officers to act as treasures of the Lord's goods, Ezra recognized the necessity and value of order and organization in connection with the work of God.

During the few days that the Israelites tarried at the river, every provision was completed for the long journey. "We departed," Ezra writes, "on the twelfth day of the first month, to go unto Jerusalem: and the hand of our God was upon us, and He delivered us from the hand of the enemy, and of such as lay in wait by the way." Verse 31. About four months were occupied on the journey, the multitude that accompanied Ezra, several thousand in all, including women and children, necessitating slow progress. But all were preserved in safety. Their enemies were restrained from harming them. Their journey was a prosperous one, and on the first day of the fifth month, in the seventh year of Artaxerxes, they reached Jerusalem.

A Spiritual Revival

Ezra's arrival in Jerusalem was opportune. There was great need of the influence of his presence. His coming brought courage and hope to the hearts of many who had long labored under difficulties. Since the return of the first company of exiles under the leadership of Zerubbabel and Joshua, over seventy years before, much had been accomplished. The temple had been finished, and the walls of the city had been partially repaired. Yet much remained undone.

Among those who had returned to Jerusalem in former years, there were many who had remained true to God as long as they lived; but a considerable number of the children and the children's children lost sight of the sacredness of God's law. Even some of the men entrusted with responsibilities were living in open sin. Their course was largely neutralizing the efforts made by others to advance the cause of God; for so long as flagrant violations of the law were allowed to go unrebuked, the blessing of Heaven could not rest upon the people.

It was in the providence of God that those who returned with Ezra had had special seasons of seeking the Lord. The experiences through which they had just passed, on their journey from Babylon, unprotected as they had been by any human power, had taught them rich spiritual lessons. Many had grown strong in faith; and as these mingled with the discouraged and the indifferent in Jerusalem, their influence was a powerful factor in the reform soon afterward instituted.

On the fourth day after the arrival, the treasures of silver and gold, with the vessels for the service of the sanctuary, were delivered by the treasures into the hands of the temple officers, in the presence of witnesses, and with the utmost exactitude. Every article was examined "by number and by weight." Ezra 8:34.

The children of the captivity who had returned with Ezra "offered burnt offerings unto the God of Israel" for a sin offering and as a token of their gratitude and thanksgiving for the protection of holy angels during the journey. "And they delivered the king's commissions unto the king's lieutenants, and to the governors on this side the river: and they furthered the people, and the house of God." Verses 35, 36.

Very soon thereafter a few of the chief men of Israel approached Ezra with a serious complaint. Some of "the people of Israel, and the priests, and the Levites" had so far disregarded the holy commands of Jehovah as to intermarry with the surrounding peoples. "They have taken of their daughters for themselves, and for their sons," Ezra was told, "so that the holy seed have mingled themselves with the people" of heathen lands; "yea, the hand of the princes and rulers hath been chief in this trespass." Ezra 9:1, 2.

In his study of the causes leading to the Babylonish captivity, Ezra had learned that Israel's apostasy was largely traceable to their mingling with heathen nations. He had seen that if they had obeyed God's command to keep separate from the nations surrounding them, they would have been spared many sad and humiliating experiences. Now when he learned that notwithstanding the lessons of the past, men of prominence had dared transgress the laws given as a safeguard against apostasy, his heart was stirred within him. He thought of God's goodness in again giving His people a foothold in their native land, and he was overwhelmed with righteous indignation and with grief at their ingratitude. "When I heard this thing," he says, "I rent my garment and my mantle, and plucked off the hair of my head and of my beard, and sat down astonied.

"Then were assembled unto me everyone that trembled at the words of God of Israel, because of the transgression of those that had been carried away; and I sat astonied until the evening sacrifice." Verses 3, 4.

At the time of the evening sacrifice Ezra rose, and, once more rending his garment and his mantle, he fell upon his knees and unburdened his soul in supplication to Heaven. Spreading out his hands unto the Lord, he exclaimed, "O my God, I am ashamed and blush to lift up my face to Thee, my God: for our iniquities are increased over our head, and our trespass is grown up unto the heavens.

"Since the days of our fathers," the suppliant continued, "have we been in a great trespass unto this day; and for our iniquities have we, our kings, and our priests, been delivered into the hand of the kings of the lands, to the sword, to captivity, and to a spoil, and to confusion of face, as it is this day. And now for a little space grace hath been showed from the Lord our God, to leave us a remnant to escape, and to give us a nail in His holy place, that our God may lighten our eyes, and give us a little reviving in our bondage. For we were bondmen; yet our God hath not forsaken us in our bondage, but hath extended mercy unto us in the sight of the kings of Persia, to give us a reviving, to set up the house of our God, and to repair the desolations thereof, and to give us a wall in Judah and in Jerusalem.

"And now, O our God, what shall we say after this? for we have forsaken Thy commandments, which Thou hast commanded by Thy servants the prophets. . . . And after all that is come upon us for our evil deeds, and for our great trespass, seeing that Thou our God hast punished us less than our iniquities deserve, and hast given us such deliverance as this; should we again break Thy commandments, and join in affinity with the people of these abominations? wouldest not Thou be angry with us till Thou hadst consumed us, so that there should be no remnant nor escaping? O Lord God of Israel, Thou art righteous: for we remain yet escaped, as it is this day: behold, we are before Thee in our trespasses: for we cannot stand before Thee because of this." Verses 6-15.

The sorrow of Ezra and his associates over the evils that had insidiously crept into the very heart of the Lord's work, wrought repentance. Many of those who had sinned were deeply affected. "The people wept very sore." Ezra 10:1. In a limited degree they began to realize the heinousness of sin and the horror with which God regards it. They saw the sacredness of the law spoken at Sinai, and many trembled at the thought of their transgressions.

One of those present, Shechaniah by name, acknowledged as true all the words spoken by Ezra. "We have trespassed against our God," he confessed, "and have taken strange wives of the people of the land: yet now there is hope in Israel concerning this thing." Shechaniah proposed that all who had transgressed should make a covenant with God to forsake their sin and to be adjudged "according to the law." "Arise," he bade Ezra; "for this matter belongeth unto thee: we also will be with thee: be of good courage." "Then arose Ezra, and made the chief priests, the Levites, and all Israel, to swear that they should do according to this word." Verses 2-5. This was the beginning of a wonderful reformation. With infinite patience and tact, and with a careful consideration for the rights and welfare of every individual concerned, Ezra and his associates strove to lead the penitent of Israel into the right way. Above all else, Ezra was a teacher of the law; and as he gave personal attention to the examination of every case, he sought to impress the people with the holiness of this law and the blessings to be gained through obedience.

Wherever Ezra labored, there sprang up a revival in the study of the Holy Scriptures. Teachers were appointed to instruct the people; the law of the Lord was exalted and made honorable. The books of the prophets were searched, and the passages foretelling the coming of the Messiah brought hope and comfort to many a sad and weary heart.

More than two thousand years have passed since Ezra "prepared his heart to seek the law of the Lord, and to do it" (Ezra 7:10), yet the lapse of time has not lessened the influence of his pious example. Through the centuries the record of his life of consecration has inspired many with the determination "to seek the law of the Lord, and to do it."

Ezra's motives were high and holy; in all that he did he was actuated by a deep love for souls. The compassion and tenderness that he revealed toward those who had sinned, either willfully or through ignorance, should be an object lesson to all who seek to bring about reforms. The servants of God are to be as firm as a rock where right principles are involved; and yet, withal, they are to manifest sympathy and forbearance. Like Ezra, they are to teach transgressors the way of life by calculating principles that are the foundation of all rightdoing.

In this age of the world, when Satan is seeking, through manifold agencies, to blind the eyes of men and women to the binding claims of the law of God, there is need of men who can cause many to "tremble at the commandment of our God." Ezra 10:3. There is need of true reformers, who will point transgressors to the great Lawgiver and teach them that "the law of the Lord is perfect, converting the soul." Psalm 19:7. There is need of men mighty in the Scriptures, men whose every word and act exalts the statutes of Jehovah, men who seek to strengthen faith. Teachers are needed, oh, so much, who will inspire hearts with reverence and love for the Scriptures.

The widespread iniquity prevalent today may in a great degree be attributed to a failure to study and obey the Scriptures, for when the word of God is set aside, its power to restrain the evil passions of the natural heart is rejected. Men sow to the flesh and of the flesh reap corruption.

With the setting aside of the Bible has come a turning away from God's law. The doctrine that men are released from obedience to the divine precepts, has weakened the force of moral obligation and opened the floodgates of iniquity upon the world. Lawlessness, dissipation, and corruption are sweeping in like an overwhelming flood. Everywhere are seen envy, evil surmising, hypocrisy, estrangement, emulation, strife, betrayal of sacred trusts, indulgence of lust. The whole system of religious principles and doctrines, which should form the foundation and framework of social life, seems to be a tottering mass, ready to fall in ruins.

In the last days of this earth's history the voice that spoke from Sinai is still declaring, "Thou shalt have no other gods before Me." Exodus 20:3. Man has set his will against the will of God, but he cannot silence the word of command. The human mind cannot evade its obligation to a higher power. Theories and speculations may abound; men may try to set science in opposition to revelation, and thus do away with God's law; but stronger and still stronger comes the command, "Thou shalt worship the Lord thy God, and Him only shalt thou serve." Matthew 4:10.

There is no such thing as weakening or strengthening the law of Jehovah. As it has been, so it is. It always has been, and always will be, holy, just, and good, complete in itself. It cannot be repealed or changed. To "honor" or "dishonor" it is but the speech of men.

Between the laws of men and the precepts of Jehovah will come the last great conflict of the controversy between truth and error. Upon this battle we are now entering—a battle not between rival churches contending for the supremacy, but between the religion of the Bible and the religions of fable and tradition. The agencies which have united against truth are now actively at work. God's Holy Word, which has been handed down to us at so great a cost of suffering and bloodshed, is little valued. There are few who really accept it as the rule of life. Infidelity prevails to an alarming extent, not in the world only, but in the church. Many have come to deny doctrines which are the very pillars of the Christian faith. The great facts of creation as presented by the inspired writers, the fall of man, the atonement, the perpetuity of the law—these all are practically rejected by a large share of the professedly Christian world. Thousands who pride themselves on their knowledge regard it as an evidence of weakness to place implicit confidence in the Bible, and a proof of learning to cavil at the Scriptures and to spiritualize and explain away their most important truths.

Christians should be preparing for what is soon to break upon the world as an overwhelming surprise, and this preparation they should make by diligently studying the word of God and striving to conform their lives to its precepts. The tremendous issues of eternity demand of us something besides an imaginary religion, a religion of words and forms, where truth is kept in the outer court. God calls for a revival and a reformation. The words of the Bible and the Bible alone, should be heard from the pulpit. But the Bible has been robbed of its power, and the result is seen in a lowering of the tone of spiritual life. In many sermons of today there is not that divine manifestation which awakens the conscience and brings life to the soul. The hearers cannot say, "Did not our heart burn within us, while He talked with us by the way, and while He opened to us the Scriptures?" Luke 24:32. There are many who are crying out for the living God, longing for the divine presence. Let the word of God speak to the heart. Let those who have heard only tradition and human theories and maxims, hear the voice of Him who can renew the soul unto eternal life.

Great light shone forth from patriarchs and prophets. Glorious things were spoken of Zion, the City of God. Thus the Lord designs that the light shall shine forth through His followers today. If the saints of the Old Testament bore so bright a testimony of loyalty, should not those upon whom is shining the accumulated light of centuries, bear a still more signal witness to the power of truth? The glory of the prophecies sheds their light upon our pathway. Type has met antitype in the death of God's Son. Christ has risen from the dead, proclaiming over the rent sepulcher, "I am the resurrection, and the life." John 11:25. He has sent His Spirit into the world to bring all things to our remembrance. By a miracle of power He has preserved His written word through the ages.

The Reformers whose protest has given us the name of Protestant, felt that God had called them to give the light of the gospel to the world; and in the effort to do this they were ready to sacrifice their possessions, their liberty, even life itself. In the face of persecution and death the gospel was proclaimed far and near. The word of God was carried to the people; and all classes, high and low, rich and poor, learned and ignorant, eagerly studied it for themselves. Are we, in this last conflict of the great controversy, as faithful to our trust as the early Reformers were to theirs?

"Blow the trumpet in Zion, sanctify a fast, call a solemn assembly: gather the people, sanctify the congregation, assemble the elders, gather the children: . . . let the priests, the ministers of the Lord, weep between the porch and the altar, and let them say, Spare Thy people, O Lord, and give not Thine heritage to reproach." "Turn ye even to Me with all your hearts, and with fasting, and with weeping, and with mourning: and rend your heart, and not your garments, and turn unto the Lord your God: for He is gracious and merciful, slow to anger, and of great kindness, and repenteth Him of the evil. Who knoweth if He will return and repent, and leave a blessing behind Him?" Joel 2:15-17, 12-14.

A Man of Opportunity

Nehemiah, one of the Hebrew exiles, occupied a position of influence and honor in the Persian court. As cupbearer to the king he was admitted freely to the royal presence. By virtue of his position, and because of his abilities and fidelity, he had become the monarch's friend and counselor. The recipient of royal favor, however, though surrounded by pomp and splendor, did not forget his God nor his people. With deepest interest his heart turned toward Jerusalem; his hopes and joys were bound up with her prosperity. Through this man, prepared by his residence in the Persian court for the work to which he was to be called, God purposed to bring blessing to His people in the land of their fathers.

By messengers from Judea the Hebrew patriot learned that days of trial had come to Jerusalem, the chosen city. The returned exiles were suffering affliction and reproach. The temple and portions of the city had been rebuilt; but the work of restoration was hindered, the temple services were disturbed, and the people kept in constant alarm by the fact that the walls of the city were still largely in ruins.

Overwhelmed with sorrow, Nehemiah could neither eat nor drink; he "wept, and mourned certain days, and fasted." In his grief he turned to the divine Helper. "I . . . prayed," he said, "before the God of heaven." Faithfully he made confession of his sins and the sins of his people. He pleaded that God would maintain the cause of Israel, restore their courage and strength, and help them to build up the waste places of Judah.

As Nehemiah prayed, his faith and courage grew strong. His mouth was filled with holy arguments. He pointed to the dishonor that would be cast upon God, if His people, now that they had returned to Him, should be left in weakness and oppression; and he urged the Lord to bring to pass His promise: "If ye turn unto Me, and keep My Commandments, and do them; though there were of you cast out unto the uttermost part of the heaven, yet will I gather them from thence, and will bring them unto the place that I have chosen to set My name there." See Deuteronomy 4:29-31. This promise had been given to Israel through Moses before they had entered Canaan, and during the centuries it had stood unchanged. God's people had now returned to Him in penitence and faith, and His promise would not fail.

Nehemiah had often poured out his soul in behalf of his people. But now as he prayed a holy purpose formed in his mind. He resolved that if he could obtain the consent of the king, and the necessary aid in procuring implements and material, he would himself undertake the task of rebuilding the walls of Jerusalem and restoring Israel's national strength. And he asked the Lord to grant him favor in the sight of the king, that this plan might be carried out. "Prosper, I pray Thee, Thy servant this day," he entreated, "and grant him mercy in the sight of this man."

Four months Nehemiah waited for a favorable opportunity to present his request to the king. During this time, though his heart was heavy with grief, he endeavored to bear himself with cheerfulness in the royal presence. In those halls of luxury and splendor all must appear light-hearted and happy. Distress must not cast its shadow over the countenance of any attendant of royalty. But in Nehemiah's seasons of retirement, concealed from human sight, many were the prayers, the confessions, the tears, heard and witnessed by God and angels.

At length the sorrow that burdened the patriot's heart could no longer be concealed. Sleepless nights and care-filled days left their trace upon his countenance. The king, jealous for his own safety, was accustomed to read countenances and to penetrate disguises, and he saw that some secret trouble was preying upon his cupbearer. "Why is thy countenance sad," he inquired, "seeing thou art not sick? this is nothing else but sorrow of heart."

The question filled Nehemiah with apprehension. Would not the king be angry to hear that while outwardly engaged in his service, the courtier's thoughts had been far away with his afflicted people? Would not the offender's life be forfeited? His cherished plan for restoring the strength of Jerusalem—was it about to be overthrown? "Then," he writes, "I was very sore afraid." With trembling lips and tearful eyes he revealed the cause of his sorrow. "Let the king live forever," he answered. "Why should not my countenance be sad, when the city, the place of my fathers' sepulchers, lieth waste, and the gates thereof are consumed with fire?"

The recital of the condition of Jerusalem awakened the sympathy of the monarch without arousing his prejudices. Another question gave the opportunity for which Nehemiah had long waited: "For what dost thou make request?" But the man of God did not venture to reply till he had sought direction from One higher than Artaxerxes. He had a sacred trust to fulfill, in which he required help from the king; and he realized that much depended upon his presenting the matter in such a way as to win his approval and enlist his aid. "I prayed," he said, "to the God of heaven." In that brief prayer Nehemiah pressed into the presence of the King of kings and won to his side a power that can turn hearts as the rivers of waters are turned.

To pray as Nehemiah prayed in his hour of need is a resource at the command of the Christian under circumstances when other forms of prayer may be impossible. Toilers in the busy walks of life, crowded and almost overwhelmed with perplexity, can send up a petition to God for divine guidance. Travelers by sea and land, when threatened with some great danger, can thus commit themselves to Heaven's protection. In times of sudden difficulty or peril the heart may send up its cry for help to One who has pledged Himself to come to the aid of His faithful, believing ones whenever they call upon Him. In every circumstance, under every condition, the soul weighed down with grief and care, or fiercely assailed by temptation, may find assurance, support, and succor in the unfailing love and power of a covenant-keeping God.

Nehemiah, in that brief moment of prayer to the King of kings, gathered courage to tell Artaxerxes of his desire to be released for a time from his duties at the court, and he asked for authority to build up the waste places of Jerusalem and to make it once more a strong and defensed city. Momentous results to the Jewish nation hung upon this request. "And," Nehemiah declares, "the king granted me, according to the good hand of my God upon me."

Having secured the help he sought, Nehemiah with prudence and forethought proceeded to make the arrangements necessary to ensure the success of the enterprise. He neglected no precaution that would tend to its accomplishment. Not even to his own countrymen did he reveal his purpose. While he knew that many would rejoice in his success, he feared that some, by acts of indiscretion, might arouse the jealousy of their enemies and perhaps bring about the defeat of the undertaking.

His request to the king had been so favorably received that Nehemiah was encouraged to ask for still further assistance. To give dignity and authority to his mission, as well as to provide protection on the journey, he asked for and secured a military escort. He obtained royal letters to the governors of the provinces beyond the Euphrates, the territory through which he must pass on his way to Judea; and he obtained, also, a letter to the keeper of the king's forest in the mountains of Lebanon, directing him to furnish such timber as would be needed. That there might be no occasion for complaint that he had exceeded his commission, Nehemiah was careful to have the authority and privileges accorded him, clearly defined.

This example of wise forethought and resolute action should be a lesson to all Christians. God's children are not only to pray in faith, but to work with diligent and provident care. They encounter many difficulties and often hinder the working of Providence in their behalf, because they regard prudence and painstaking effort as having little to do with religion. Nehemiah did not regard his duty done when he had wept and prayed before the Lord. He united his petitions with holy endeavor, putting forth earnest, prayerful efforts for the success of the enterprise in which he was engaged. Careful consideration and well-matured plans are as essential to the carrying forward of sacred enterprises today as in the time of the rebuilding of Jerusalem's walls. Nehemiah did not depend upon uncertainty. The means that he lacked he solicited from those who were able to bestow. And the Lord is still willing to move upon the hearts of those in possession of His goods, in behalf of the cause of truth. Those who labor for Him are to avail themselves of the help that He prompts men to give. These gifts may open ways by which the light of truth shall go to many benighted lands. The donors may have no faith in Christ, no acquaintance with His word; but their gifts are not on this account to be refused.

The Builders on the Wall

Nehemiah's journey to Jerusalem was accomplished in safety. The royal letters to the governors of the provinces along his route secured him honorable reception and prompt assistance. No enemy dared molest the official who was guarded by the power of the Persian king and treated with marked consideration by the provincial rulers. His arrival in Jerusalem, however, with a military escort, showing that he had come on some important mission, excited the jealousy of the heathen tribes living near the city, who had so often indulged their enmity against the Jews by heaping upon them injury and insult. Foremost in this evil work were certain chiefs of these tribes, Sanballat the Horonite, Tobiah the Ammonite, and Geshem the Arabian. From the first these leaders watched with critical eyes the movements of Nehemiah and endeavored by every means in their power to thwart his plans and hinder his work.

Nehemiah continued to exercise the same caution and prudence that had hitherto marked his course. Knowing that bitter and determined enemies stood ready to oppose him, he concealed the nature of his mission from them until a study of the situation should enable him to form his plans. Thus he hoped to secure the co-operation of the people and set them at work before the opposition of his enemies should be aroused.

Choosing a few men whom he knew to be worthy of confidence, Nehemiah told them of the circumstances that had led him to come to Jerusalem, the object that he wished to accomplish, and the plans he proposed to follow. Their interest in his undertaking was at once enlisted and their assistance secured.

On the third night after his arrival Nehemiah rose at midnight and with a few trusted companions went out to view for himself the desolation of Jerusalem. Mounted on his mule, he passed from one part of the city to another, surveying the broken-down walls and gates of the city of his fathers. Painful reflections filled the mind of the Jewish patriot as with sorrow-stricken heart he gazed upon the ruined defenses of his beloved Jerusalem. Memories of Israel's past greatness stood out in sharp contrast with the evidences of her humiliation.

In secrecy and silence Nehemiah completed his circuit of the walls. "The rulers knew not whither I went," he declares, "or what I did; neither had I as yet told it to the Jews, nor to the priests, nor to the nobles, nor to the rulers, nor to the rest that did the work." The remainder of the night he spent in prayer; for he knew that the morning would call for earnest effort to arouse and unite his dispirited and divided countrymen.

Nehemiah bore a royal commission requiring the inhabitants to co-operate with him in rebuilding the walls of the city, but he did not depend upon the exercise of authority. He sought rather to gain the confidence and sympathy of the people, knowing that a union of hearts as well as of hands was essential in the great work before him. When on the morrow he called the people together he presented such arguments as were calculated to arouse their dormant energies and unite their scattered numbers.

Nehemiah's hearers did not know, neither did he tell them, of his midnight circuit of the night before. But the fact that he had made this circuit contributed greatly to his success; for he was able to speak of the condition of the city with an accuracy and a minuteness that astonished his hearers. The impression made upon him as he had looked upon the weakness and degradation of Jerusalem, gave earnestness and power to his words.

Nehemiah presented before the people their reproach among the heathen—their religion dishonored, their God blasphemed. He told them that in a distant land he had heard of their affliction, that he had entreated the favor of Heaven in their behalf, and that, as he was praying, he had determined to ask permission from the king to come to their assistance. He had asked God that the king might not only grant this permission, but might also invest him with the authority and give him the help needed for the work; and his prayer had been answered in such a way as to show that the plan was of the Lord.

All this he related, and then, having shown that he was sustained by the combined authority of the God of Israel and the Persian king, Nehemiah asked the people directly whether they would take advantage of this opportunity and arise and build the wall.

The appeal went straight to their hearts. The thought of how Heaven's favor had been manifested toward them put their fears to shame, and with new courage they said with one voice, "Let us rise up and build." "So they strengthened their hands for this good work."

Nehemiah's whole soul was in the enterprise he had undertaken. His hope, his energy, his enthusiasm, his determination, were contagious, inspiring others with the same high courage and lofty purpose. Each man became a Nehemiah in his turn and helped to make stronger the heart and hand of his neighbor.

When the enemies of Israel heard what the Jews were hoping to accomplish, they laughed them to scorn, saying, "What is this thing that ye do? will ye rebel against the king?" But Nehemiah answered, "The God of heaven, He will prosper us; therefore we His servants will arise and build: but ye have no portion, nor right, nor memorial, in Jerusalem."

Among the first to catch Nehemiah's spirit of zeal and earnestness were the priests. Because of their influential position, these men could do much to advance or hinder the work; and their ready co-operation, at the very outset, contributed not a little to its success. The majority of the princes and rulers of Israel came up nobly to their duty, and these faithful men have honorable mention in the book of God. There were a few, the Tekoite nobles, who "put not their necks to the work of their Lord." The memory of these slothful servants is branded with shame and has been handed down as a warning to all future generations.

In every religious movement there are some who, while they cannot deny that the cause is God's, still hold themselves aloof, refusing to make any effort to help. It were well for such ones to remember the record kept on high—that book in which there are no omissions, no mistakes, and out of which they will be judged. There every neglected opportunity to do service for God is recorded; and there, too, every deed of faith and love is held in everlasting remembrance.

Against the inspiring influence of Nehemiah's presence the example of the Tekoite nobles had little weight. The people in general were animated by patriotism and zeal. Men of ability and influence organized the various classes of citizens into companies, each leader making himself responsible for the erection of a certain part of the wall. And of some it is written that they builded "everyone over against his house."

Nor did Nehemiah's energy abate, now that the work was actually begun. With tireless vigilance he superintended the building, directing the workmen, noting the hindrances, and providing for emergencies. Along the whole extent of that three miles of wall his influence was constantly felt. With timely words he encouraged the fearful, aroused the laggard, and approved the diligent. And ever he watched the movements of their enemies, who from time to time collected at a distance and engaged in conversation, as if plotting mischief, and then, drawing nearer the workmen, attempted to divert their attention.

In his many activities Nehemiah did not forget the source of his strength. His heart was constantly uplifted to God, the great Overseer of all. "The God of heaven," he exclaimed, "He will prosper us;" and the words, echoed and re-echoed, thrilled the hearts of all the workers on the wall.

But the restoration of the defenses of Jerusalem did not go forward unhindered. Satan was working to stir up opposition and bring discouragement. Sanballat, Tobiah, and Geshem, his principal agents in this movement, now set themselves to hinder the work of rebuilding. They endeavored to cause division among the workmen. They ridiculed the efforts of the builders, declaring the enterprise an impossibility and predicting failure.

"What do these feeble Jews?" exclaimed Sanballat mockingly; "will they fortify themselves? . . . will they revive the stones out of the heaps of the rubbish which are burned?" Tobiah, still more contemptuous, added, "Even that which they build, if a fox go up, he shall even break down their stone wall."

The builders were soon beset by more active opposition. They were compelled to guard continually against the plots of their adversaries, who, professing friendliness, sought in various ways to cause confusion and perplexity, and to arouse distrust. They endeavored to destroy the courage of the Jews; they formed conspiracies to draw Nehemiah into their toils; and falsehearted Jews were found ready to aid the treacherous undertaking. The report was spread that Nehemiah was plotting against the Persian monarch, intending to exalt himself as a king over Israel, and that all who aided him were traitors.

But Nehemiah continued to look to God for guidance and support, and "the people had a mind to work." The enterprise went forward until the gaps were filled and the entire wall built up to half its intended height.

As the enemies of Israel saw how unavailing were their efforts, they were filled with rage. Hitherto they had not dared employ violent measures, for they knew that Nehemiah and his companions were acting under the king's commission, and they feared that active opposition against him might bring upon them the monarch's displeasure. But now in their anger they themselves became guilty of the crime of which they had accused Nehemiah. Assembling for counsel, they "conspired all of them together to come and to fight against Jerusalem."

At the same time that the Samaritans were plotting against Nehemiah and his work, some of the leading men among the Jews, becoming disaffected, sought to discourage him by exaggerating the difficulties attending the enterprise. "The strength of the bearers of burdens is decayed," they said, "and there is much rubbish; so that we are not able to build the wall." Discouragement came from still another source. "The Jews which dwelt by," those who were taking no part in the work, gathered up the statements and reports of their enemies and used these to weaken courage and create disaffection.

But taunts and ridicule, opposition and threats, seemed only to inspire Nehemiah with firmer determination and to arouse him to greater watchfulness. He recognized the dangers that must be met in this warfare with their enemies, but his courage was undaunted. "We made our prayer unto our God," he declares, "and set a watch against them day and night." "Therefore set I in the lower places behind the wall, and on the higher places, I even set the people after their families with their swords, their spears, and their bows. And I looked, and rose up, and said unto the nobles, and to the rulers, and to the rest of the people, Be not ye afraid of them: remember the Lord, which is great and terrible, and fight for your brethren, your sons, and your daughters, your wives, and your houses.

"And it came to pass, when our enemies heard that it was known unto us, and God had brought their counsel to nought, that we returned all of us to the wall, everyone unto his work. And it came to pass from that time forth, that the half of my servants wrought in the work, and the other half of them held both the spears, the shields, and the bows, and the habergeons. . . . They which builded on the wall, and they that bare burdens, with those that laded, everyone with one of his hands wrought in the work, and with the other hand held a weapon. For the builders, everyone had his sword girded by his side, and so builded."

Beside Nehemiah stood a trumpeter, and on different parts of the wall were stationed priests bearing the sacred trumpets. The people were scattered in their labors, but on the approach of danger at any point a signal was given for them to repair thither without delay. "So we labored in the work," Nehemiah says, "and half of them held the spears from the rising of the morning till the stars appeared."

Those who had been living in towns and villages outside Jerusalem were now required to lodge within the walls, both to guard the work and to be ready for duty in the morning. This would prevent unnecessary delay, and would cut off the opportunity which the enemy would otherwise improve, of attacking the workmen as they went to and from their homes.

Nehemiah and his companions did not shrink from hardship or trying service. Neither by day nor night, not even during the short time given to sleep, did they put off their clothing or lay aside their armor.

The opposition and discouragement that the builders in Nehemiah's day met from open enemies and pretended friends is typical of the experience that those today will have who work for God. Christians are tried, not only by the anger, contempt, and cruelty of enemies, but by the indolence, inconsistency, lukewarmness, and treachery of avowed friends and helpers. Derision and reproach are hurled at them. And the same enemy that leads to contempt, at a favorable opportunity uses more cruel and violent measures.

Satan takes advantage of every unconsecrated element for the accomplishment of his purposes. Among those who profess to be the supporters of God's cause there are those who unite with His enemies and thus lay His cause open to the attacks of His bitterest foes. Even some who desire the work of God to prosper will yet weaken the hands of His servants by hearing, reporting, and half believing the slanders, boasts, and menaces of His adversaries. Satan works with marvelous success through his agents, and all who yield to their influence are subject to a bewitching power that destroys the wisdom of the wise and the understanding of the prudent. But, like Nehemiah, God's people are neither to fear nor to despise their enemies. Putting their trust in God, they are to go steadily forward, doing His work with unselfishness, and committing to His providence the cause for which they stand.

Amidst great discouragement, Nehemiah made God his trust, his sure defense. And He who was the support of His servant then has been the dependence of His people in every age. In every crisis His people may confidently declare, "If God be for us, who can be against us?" Romans 8:31. However craftily the plots of Satan and his agents may be laid, God can detect them, and bring to nought all their counsels. The response of faith today will be the response made by Nehemiah, "Our God shall fight for us;" for God is in the work, and no man can prevent its ultimate success.

A Rebuke Against Extortion

The wall of Jerusalem had not yet been completed when Nehemiah's attention was called to the unhappy condition of the poorer classes of the people. In the unsettled state of the country, tillage had been to some extent neglected. Furthermore, because of the selfish course pursued by some who had returned to Judea, the Lord's blessing was not resting upon their land, and there was a scarcity of grain.

In order to obtain food for their families, the poor were obliged to buy on credit and at exorbitant prices. They were also compelled to raise money by borrowing on interest to pay the heavy taxes imposed upon them by the kings of Persia. To add to the distress of the poor, the more wealthy among the Jews had taken advantage of their necessities, thus enriching themselves.

The Lord had commanded Israel, through Moses, that every third year a tithe be raised for the benefit of the poor; and a further provision had been made in the suspension of agricultural labor every seventh year, the land lying fallow, its spontaneous products being left to those in need. Faithfulness in devoting these offerings to the relief of the poor and to other benevolent uses would have tended to keep fresh before the people the truth of God's ownership of all, and their opportunity to be channels of blessing. It was Jehovah's purpose that the Israelites should have a training that would eradicate selfishness, and develop breadth and nobility of character.

God had also instructed through Moses: "If thou lend money to any of My people that is poor by thee, thou shalt not be to him as an usurer." "Thou shalt no lend upon usury to thy brother; usury of money, usury of victuals, usury of anything that is lent upon usury." Exodus 22:25; Deuteronomy 23:19. Again He had said, "If there be among you a poor man of one of thy brethren within any of thy gates in thy land which the Lord thy God giveth thee, thou shalt not harden thine heart, nor shut thine hand from thy poor brother: but thou shalt open thine hand wide unto him, and shalt surely lend him sufficient for his need, in that which he wanteth." "For the poor shall never cease out of the land: therefore I command thee, saying, Thou shalt open thine hand wide unto thy brother, to thy poor, and to thy needy, in thy land." Deuteronomy 15:7, 8, 11.

At times following the return of the exiles from Babylon, the wealthy Jews had gone directly contrary to these commands. When the poor were obliged to borrow to pay tribute to the king, the wealthy had lent them money, but had exacted a high rate of interest. By taking mortgages on the lands of the poor, they had gradually reduced the unfortunate debtors to the deepest poverty. Many had been forced to sell their sons and daughters into servitude; and there seemed no hope of improving their condition, no way to redeem either their children or their lands, no prospect before them but ever-increasing distress, with perpetual want and bondage. Yet they were of the same nation, children of the same covenant, as their more favored brethren.

At length the people presented their condition before Nehemiah. "Lo," they said, "we bring into bondage our sons and our daughters to be servants, and some of our daughters are brought into bondage already: neither is it in our power to redeem them; for other men have our lands and vineyards."

As Nehemiah heard of this cruel oppression, his soul was filled with indignation. "I was very angry," he says, "when I heard their cry and these words." He saw that if he succeeded in breaking up the oppressive custom of exaction he must take a decided stand for justice. With characteristic energy and determination he went to work to bring relief to his brethren. The fact that the oppressors were men of wealth, whose support was greatly needed in the work of restoring the city, did not for a moment influence Nehemiah. He sharply rebuked the nobles and rulers, and when he had gathered a great assembly of the people he set before them the requirements of God touching the case.

He called their attention to events that had occurred in the reign of King Ahaz. He repeated the message which God had at the time sent to Israel to rebuke their cruelty and oppression. The children of Judah, because of their idolatry, had been delivered into the hands of their still more idolatrous brethren, the people of Israel. The latter had indulged their enmity by slaying in battle many thousands of the men of Judah and had seized all the women and children, intending to keep them as slaves or to sell them into bondage to the heathen.

Because of the sins of Judah, the Lord had not interposed to prevent the battle; but by the prophet Oded He rebuked the cruel design of the victorious army: "Ye purpose to keep under the children of Judah and Jerusalem for bondmen and bondwomen unto you: but are there not with you, even with you, sins against the Lord your God?" 2 Chronicles 28:10. Oded warned the people of Israel that the anger of the Lord was kindled against them, and that their course of injustice and oppression would call down His judgments. Upon hearing these words, the armed men left the captives and the spoil before the princes and all the congregation. Then certain leading men of the tribe of Ephraim "took the captives, and with the spoil clothed all that were naked among them, and arrayed them, and shod them, and gave them to eat and to drink, and anointed them, and carried all the feeble of them upon asses, and brought them to Jericho, the city of palm trees, to their brethren." Verse 15.

Nehemiah and others had ransomed certain of the Jews who had been sold to the heathen, and he now placed this course in contrast with the conduct of those who for the sake of worldly gain were enslaving their brethren. "It is not good that ye do," he said; "ought ye not to walk in the fear of our God because of the reproach of the heathen our enemies?"

Nehemiah showed them that he himself, being invested with authority from the Persian king, might have demanded large contributions for his personal benefit. But instead of this he had not taken even that which justly belonged to him, but had given liberally to relieve the poor in their need. He urged those among the Jewish rulers who had been guilty of extortion, to cease this iniquitous work; to restore the lands of the poor, and also the increase of money which they had exacted from them; and to lend to them without security or usury.

These words were spoken in the presence of the whole congregation. Had the rulers chosen to justify themselves, they had opportunity to do so. But they offered no excuse. "We will restore them," they declared, "and will require nothing of them; so will we do as thou sayest." At this, Nehemiah in the presence of the priests "took an oath of them, that they should do according to this promise." "And all the congregation said, Amen, and praised the Lord. And the people did according to this promise."

This record teaches an important lesson. "The love of money is the root of all evil." 1 Timothy 6:10. In this generation the desire for gain is the absorbing passion. Wealth is often obtained by fraud. There are multitudes struggling with poverty, compelled to labor hard for small wages, unable to secure even the barest necessities of life. Toil and deprivation, with no hope of better things, make their burden heavy. Careworn and oppressed, they know not where to turn for relief. And all this that the rich may support their extravagance or indulge their desire to hoard!

Love of money and love of display have made this world as a den of thieves and robbers. The Scriptures picture the greed and oppression that will prevail just before Christ's second coming. "Go to now, ye rich men," James writes; "ye have heaped treasure together for the last days. Behold, the hire of the laborers who have reaped down your fields, which is of you kept back by fraud, crieth: and the cries of them which have reaped are entered into the ears of the Lord of Sabaoth. Ye have lived in pleasure on the earth, and been wanton; ye have nourished your hearts, as in a day of slaughter. Ye have condemned and killed the just; and he doth not resist you." James 5:1, 3-6.

Even among those who profess to be walking in the fear of the Lord, there are some who are acting over again the course pursued by the nobles of Israel. Because it is in their power to do so, they exact more than is just, and thus become oppressors. And because avarice and treachery are seen in the lives of those who have named the name of Christ, because the church retains on her books the names of those who have gained their possessions by injustice, the religion of Christ is held in contempt. Extravagance, overreaching, extortion, are corrupting the faith of many and destroying their spirituality. The church is in a great degree responsible for the sins of her members. She gives countenance to evil if she fails to lift her voice against it.

The customs of the world are no criterion for the Christian. He is not to imitate its sharp practices, its overreaching, its extortion. Every unjust act toward a fellow being is a violation of the golden rule. Every wrong done to the children of God is done to Christ Himself in the person of His saints. Every attempt to take advantage of the ignorance, weakness, or misfortune of another is registered as fraud in the ledger of heaven. He who truly fears God, would rather toil day and night, and eat the bread of poverty, than to indulge the passion for gain that oppresses the widow and fatherless or turns the stranger from his right.

The slightest departure from rectitude breaks down the barriers and prepares the heart to do greater injustice. Just to that extent that a man would gain advantage for himself at the disadvantage of another, will his soul become insensible to the influence of the Spirit of God. Gain obtained at such a cost is a fearful loss.

We were all debtors to divine justice, but we had nothing with which to pay the debt. Then the Son of God, who pitied us, paid the price of our redemption. He became poor that through His poverty we might be rich. By deeds of liberality toward His poor we may prove the sincerity of our gratitude for the mercy extended to us. "Let us do good unto all men," the apostle Paul enjoins, "especially unto them who are of the household of faith." Galatians 6:10. And his words accord with those of the Saviour: "Ye have the poor with you always, and whensoever ye will ye may do them good." "Whatsoever ye would that men should do to you, do ye even so to them: for this is the law and the prophets." Mark 14:7; Matthew 7:12.

Heathen Plots

Sanballat and his confederates dared not make open war upon the Jews; but with increasing malice they continued their secret efforts to discourage, perplex, and injure them. The wall about Jerusalem was rapidly approaching completion. When it should be finished and its gates set up, these enemies of Israel could not hope to force an entrance into the city. They were the more eager, therefore, to stop the work without further delay. At last they devised a plan by which they hoped to draw Nehemiah from his station, and while they had him in their power, to kill or imprison him.

Pretending to desire a compromise of the opposing parties, they sought a conference with Nehemiah, and invited him to meet them in a village on the plain on Ono. But enlightened by the Holy Spirit as to their real purpose, he refused. "I sent messengers unto them," he writes, "saying, I am doing a great work, so that I cannot come down: why should the work cease, whilst I leave it, and come down to you?" But the tempters were persistent. Four times they sent a message of similar import, and each time they received the same answer.

Finding this scheme unsuccessful, they resorted to a more daring stratagem. Sanballat sent Nehemiah a messenger bearing an open letter which said: "It is reported among the heathen, and Gashmu saith it, that thou and the Jews think to rebel: for which cause thou buildest the wall, that thou mayest be their king. . . . And thou hast also appointed prophets to preach of thee at Jerusalem, saying, There is a king in Judah: and now shall it be reported to the king according to these words. Come now therefore, and let us take counsel together."

Had the reports mentioned been actually circulated, there would have been cause for apprehension; for they would soon have been carried to the king, whom a slight suspicion might provoke to the severest measures. But Nehemiah was convinced that the letter was wholly false, written to arouse his fears and draw him into a snare. This conclusion was strengthened by the fact that the letter was sent open, evidently that the people might read the contents, and become alarmed and intimidated.

He promptly returned the answer. "There are no such things done as thou sayest, but thou feignest them out of thine own heart." Nehemiah was not ignorant of Satan's devices. He knew that these attempts were made in order to weaken the hands of the builders and thus frustrate their efforts.

Again and again had Satan been defeated; and now, with deeper malice and cunning, he laid a still more subtle and dangerous snare for the servant of God. Sanballat and his companions hired men who professed to be the friends of Nehemiah, to give him evil counsel as the word of the Lord. The chief one engaged in this iniquitous work was Shemaiah, a man previously held in good repute by Nehemiah. This man shut himself up in a chamber near the sanctuary as if fearing that his life was in danger. The temple was at this time protected by walls and gates, but the gates of the city were not yet set up. Professing great concern for Nehemiah's safety, Shemaiah advised him to seek shelter in the temple. "Let us meet together in the house of God, within the temple," he proposed, "and let us shut the doors of the temple: for they will come to slay thee; yea, in the night will they come to slay thee."

Had Nehemiah followed this treacherous counsel, he would have sacrificed his faith in God, and in the eyes of the people he would have appeared cowardly and contemptible. In view of the important work that he had undertaken, and the confidence that he professed to have in the power of God, it would have been altogether inconsistent for him to hide as if in fear. The alarm would have spread among the people, each would have sought his own safety, and the city would have been left unprotected, to fall a prey to its enemies. That one unwise move on the part of Nehemiah would have been a virtual surrender of all that had been gained.

Nehemiah was not long in penetrating the true character and object of his counselor. "I perceived that God had not sent him," he says, "but that he pronounced this prophecy against me: for Tobiah and Sanballat had hired him. Therefore was he hired, that I should be afraid, and do so, and sin, and that they might have matter for an evil report, that they might reproach me."

The infamous counsel given by Shemaiah was seconded by more than one man of high reputation, who, while professing to be Nehemiah's friends, were secretly in league with his enemies. But it was to no avail that they laid their snare. Nehemiah's fearless answer was: "Should such a man as I flee? and who is there, that, being as I am, would go into the temple to save his life? I will not go in."

Notwithstanding the plots of enemies, open and secret, the work of building went steadily forward, and in less than two months from the time of Nehemiah's arrival in Jerusalem the city was girded with its defenses and the builders could walk upon the walls and look down upon their defeated and astonished foes. "When all our enemies heard thereof, and all the heathen that were about us saw these things," Nehemiah writes, "they were much cast down in their own eyes: for they perceived that this work was wrought of our God."

Yet even this evidence of the Lord's controlling hand was not sufficient to restrain discontent, rebellion, and treachery among the Israelites. "The nobles of Judah sent many letters unto Tobiah, and the letters of Tobiah came unto them. For there were many in Judah sworn unto him, because he was the son-in-law of Shechaniah." Here are seen the evil results of intermarriage with idolaters. A family of Judah had become connected with the enemies of God, and the relation had proved a snare. Many others had done the same. These, like the mixed multitude that came up with Israel from Egypt, were a source of constant trouble. They were not wholehearted in His service; and when God's work demanded a sacrifice, they were ready to violate their solemn oath of co-operation and support.

Some who had been foremost in plotting mischief against the Jews, now professed a desire to be on friendly terms with them. The nobles of Judah who had become entangled in idolatrous marriages, and who had held traitorous correspondence with Tobiah and taken oath to serve him, now represented him as a man of ability and foresight, an alliance with whom would be greatly to the advantage of the Jews. At the same time they betrayed to him Nehemiah's plans and movements. Thus the work of God's people was laid open to the attacks of their enemies, and opportunity was given to misconstrue Nehemiah's words and acts, and to hinder his work.

When the poor and oppressed had appealed to Nehemiah for redress of their wrongs, he had stood boldly in their defense and had caused the wrongdoers to remove the reproach that rested on them. But the authority that he had exercised in behalf of his downtrodden countrymen he did not now exercise in his own behalf. His efforts had been met by some with ingratitude and treachery, but he did not use his power to bring the traitors to punishment. Calmly and unselfishly he went forward in his service for the people, never slackening his efforts or allowing his interest to grow less.

Satan's assaults have ever been directed against those who have sought to advance the work and cause of God Though often baffled, he as often renews his attacks with fresh vigor, using means hitherto untried. But it is his secret working through those who avow themselves the friends of God's work, that is most to be feared. Open opposition may be fierce and cruel, but it is fraught with far less peril to God's cause than is the secret enmity of those who, while professing to serve God, are at hear the servants of Satan. These have it in their power to place every advantage in the hands of those who will use their knowledge to hinder the work of God and injure His servants.

Every device that the prince of darkness can suggest will be employed to induce God's servants to form a confederacy with the agents of Satan. Repeated solicitations will come to call them from duty; but, like Nehemiah, they should steadfastly reply, "I am doing a great work, so that I cannot come down." God's workers may safely keep on with their work, letting their efforts refute the falsehoods that malice may coin for their injury. Like the builders on the walls of Jerusalem they must refuse to be diverted from their work by threats or mockery or falsehood. Not for one moment are they to relax their watchfulness or vigilance, for enemies are continually on their track. Ever they must make their prayer to God "and set a watch against them day and night." Nehemiah 4:9.

As the time of the end draws near, Satan's temptations will be brought to bear with greater power upon God's workers. He will employ human agents to mock and revile those who "build the wall." But should the builders come down to meet the attacks of their foes, this would but retard the work. They should endeavor to defeat the purposes of their adversaries, but they should not allow anything to call them from their work. Truth is stronger than error, and right will prevail over wrong.

Neither should they allow their enemies to gain their friendship and sympathy, and thus lure them from their post of duty. He who by any unguarded act exposes the cause of God to reproach, or weakens the hands of his fellow workers, brings upon his own character a stain not easily removed, and places a serious obstacle in the way of his future usefulness.

"They that forsake the law praise the wicked." Proverbs 28:4. When those who are uniting with the world, yet claiming great purity, plead for union with those who have ever been the opposers of the cause of truth, we should fear and shun them as decidedly as did Nehemiah. Such counsel is prompted by the enemy of all good. It is the speech of timeservers, and should be resisted as resolutely today as then. Whatever influence would tend to unsettle the faith of God's people in His guiding power, should be steadfastly withstood.

In Nehemiah's firm devotion to the work of God, and his equally firm reliance on God, lay the reason of the failure of his enemies to draw him into their power. The soul that in indolent falls an easy prey to temptation; but in the life that has a noble aim, an absorbing purpose, evil finds little foothold. The faith of him who is constantly advancing does not weaken; for above, beneath, beyond, he recognizes Infinite Love, working out all things to accomplish His good purpose. God's true servants work with a determination that will not fail because the throne of grace is their constant dependence.

God has provided divine assistance for all the emergencies to which our human resources are unequal. He gives the Holy Spirit to help in every strait, to strengthen our hope and assurance, to illuminate our minds and purify our hearts. He provides opportunities and opens channels of working. If His people are watching the indications of His providence, and are ready to co-operate with Him, they will see mighty results.

Instructed in the Law of God

It was the time of the Feast of Trumpets. Many were gathered at Jerusalem. The scene was one of mournful interest. The wall of Jerusalem had been rebuilt and the gates set up, but a large part of the city was still in ruins.

On a platform of wood, erected in one of the broadest streets, and surrounded on every hand by the sad reminders of Judah's departed glory, stood Ezra, now an aged man. At his right and left were gathered his brother Levites. Looking down from the platform, their eyes swept over a sea of heads. From all the surrounding country the children of the covenant had assembled. "And Ezra blessed the Lord, the great God. And all the people answered, Amen: . . . and they bowed their heads, and worshiped the Lord with their faces to the ground."

Yet even here was evidence of the sin of Israel. Through the intermarriage of the people with other nations, the Hebrew language had become corrupted, and great care was necessary on the part of the speakers to explain the law in the language of the people, that it might be understood by all. Certain of the priests and Levites united with Ezra in explaining the principles of the law. "They read in the book in the law of God distinctly, and gave the sense, and caused them to understand the reading."

"And the ears of all the people were attentive unto the book of the law." They listened, intent and reverent, to the words of the Most High. As the law was explained, they were convinced of their guilt, and they mourned because of their transgressions. But this day was a festival, a day of rejoicing, a holy convocation, a day which the Lord had commanded the people to keep with joy and gladness; and in view of this they were bidden to restrain their grief and to rejoice because of God's great mercy toward them. "This day is holy unto the Lord your God," Nehemiah said. "Mourn not, nor weep. . . . Go your way, eat the fat, and drink the sweet, and send portions unto them for whom nothing is prepared: for this day is holy unto our Lord: neither be ye sorry; for the joy of the Lord is your strength."

The earlier part of the day was devoted to religious exercises, and the people spent the remainder of the time in gratefully recounting the blessings of God and in enjoying the bounties that He had provided. Portions were also sent to the poor, who had nothing to prepare. There was great rejoicing because the words of the law had been read and understood.

On the following day the reading and explaining of the law were continued. And at the time appointed—on the tenth day of the seventh month—the solemn services of the Day of Atonement were performed according to the command of God.

From the fifteenth to the twenty-second of the same month the people and their rulers kept once more the Feast of Tabernacles. It was proclaimed "in all their cities, and in Jerusalem, saying, Go forth unto the mount, and fetch olive branches, and pine branches, and myrtle branches, and palm branches, and branches of thick trees, to make booths, as it is written. So the people went forth, and brought them, and made themselves booths, everyone upon the roof of his house, and in their courts, and in the courts of the house of God. . . . And there was very great gladness. Also day by day, from the first day unto the last day, he read in the book of the law of God."

As they had listened from day to day to the words of the law, the people had been convicted of their transgressions, and of the sins of their nation in past generations. They saw that it was because of a departure from God that His protecting care had been withdrawn and that the children of Abraham had been scattered in foreign lands, and they determined to seek His mercy and to pledge themselves to walk in His commandments. Before entering upon this solemn service, held on the second day after the close of the Feast of Tabernacles, they separated themselves from the heathen among them.

As the people prostrated themselves before the Lord, confessing their sins and pleading for pardon, their leaders encouraged them to believe that God, according to His promise, heard their prayers. They must not only mourn and weep, and repent, but they must believe that God pardoned them. They must show their faith by recounting His mercies and praising Him for His goodness. "Stand up," said these teachers, "and bless the Lord your God for ever and ever."

Then from the assembled throng, as they stood with outstretched hands toward heaven, there arose the song:

"Blessed be Thy glorious name,
Which is exalted above all blessing and praise.
Thou, even Thou, art Lord alone;
Thou hast made heaven, the heaven of heavens, with all their host,
The earth, and all things that are therein,
The seas, and all that is therein,
And Thou preservest them all;
And the host of heaven worshippeth Thee."

The song of praise ended, the leaders of the congregation related the history of Israel, showing how great had been God's goodness toward them, and how great their ingratitude. Then the whole congregation entered into a covenant to keep all the commandments of God. They had suffered punishment for their sins; now they acknowledged the justice of God's dealings with them and pledged themselves to obey His law. And that this might be "a sure covenant," and be preserved in permanent form, as a memorial of the obligation they had taken upon themselves, it was written out, and the priests, Levites, and princes signed it. It was to serve as a reminder of duty and a barrier against temptation. The people took a solemn oath "to walk in God's law, which was given by Moses the servant of God, and to observe and do all the commandments of the Lord our Lord, and His judgments and His statutes." The oath taken at this time included a promise not to intermarry with the people of the land.

Before the day of fasting ended, the people still further manifested their determination to return to the Lord, by pledging themselves to cease from desecrating the Sabbath. Nehemiah did not at this time, as at a later date, exercise his authority to prevent heathen traders from coming into Jerusalem; but in an effort to save the people from yielding to temptation, he bound them, by a solemn covenant, not to transgress the Sabbath law by purchasing from these venders, hoping that this would discourage the traders and put an end to the traffic.

Provision was also made to support the public worship of

God. In addition to the tithe the congregation pledged themselves to contribute yearly a stated sum for the service of the sanctuary. "We cast the lots," Nehemiah writes, "to bring the first fruits of our ground, and the first fruits of all fruit of all trees, year by year, unto the house of the Lord: also the first-born of our sons, and of our cattle, as it is written in the law, and the firstlings of our herds and of our flocks."

Israel had returned to God with deep sorrow for backsliding. They had made confession with mourning and lamentation. They had acknowledged the righteousness of God's dealings with them, and had covenanted to obey His law. Now they must manifest faith in His promises. God had accepted their repentance; they were now to rejoice in the assurance of sins forgiven and their restoration to divine favor.

Nehemiah's efforts to restore the worship of the true God had been crowned with success. As long as the people were true to the oath they had taken, as long as they were obedient to God's word, so long would the Lord fulfill His promise by pouring rich blessings upon them.

For those who are convicted of sin and weighed down with a sense of their unworthiness, there are lessons of faith and encouragement in this record. The Bible faithfully presents the result of Israel's apostasy; but it portrays also the deep humiliation and repentance, the earnest devotion and generous sacrifice, that marked their seasons of return to the Lord.

Every true turning to the Lord brings abiding joy into the life. When a sinner yields to the influence of the Holy Spirit, he sees his own guilt and defilement in contrast with the holiness of the great Searcher of hearts. He sees himself condemned as a transgressor. But he is not, because of this, to give way to despair; for his pardon has already been secured. He may rejoice in the sense of sins forgiven, in the love of a pardoning heavenly Father. It is God's glory to encircle sinful, repentant human beings in the arms of His love, to bind up their wounds, to cleanse them from sin, and to clothe them with the garments of salvation.

Reformation

Solemnly and publicly the people of Judah had pledged themselves to obey the law of God. But when the influence of Ezra and Nehemiah was for a time withdrawn, there were many who departed from the Lord. Nehemiah had returned to Persia. During his absence from Jerusalem, evils crept in that threatened to pervert the nation. Idolaters not only gained a foothold in the city, but contaminated by their presence the very precincts of the temple. Through intermarriage, a friendship had been brought about between Eliashib the high priest and Tobiah the Ammonite, Israel's bitter enemy. As a result of this unhallowed alliance, Eliashib had permitted Tobiah to occupy an apartment connected with the temple, which heretofore had been used as a storeroom for tithes and offerings of the people.

Because of the cruelty and treachery of the Ammonites and Moabites toward Israel, God had declared through Moses that they should be forever shut out from the congregation of His people. See Deuteronomy 23:3-6. In defiance of this word, the high priest had cast out the offerings stored in the chamber of God's house, to make a place for this representative of a proscribed race. Greater contempt for God could not have been shown than to confer such a favor on this enemy of God and His truth.

On returning from Persia, Nehemiah learned of the bold profanation and took prompt measures to expel the intruder. "It grieved me sore," he declares; "therefore I cast forth all the household stuff of Tobiah out of the chamber. Then I commanded, and they cleansed the chambers: and thither brought I again the vessels of the house of God, with the meat offering and the frankincense."

Not only had the temple been profaned, but the offerings had been misapplied. This had tended to discourage the liberalities of the people. They had lost their zeal and fervor, and were reluctant to pay their tithes. The treasuries of the Lord's house were poorly supplied; many of the singers and others employed in the temple service, not receiving sufficient support, had left the work of God to labor elsewhere.

Nehemiah set to work to correct these abuses. He gathered together those who had left the service of the Lord's house, "and set them in their place." This inspired the people with confidence, and all Judah brought "the tithe of the corn and the new wine and the oil." Men who "were counted faithful" were made "treasurers over the treasuries," "and their office was to distribute unto their brethren."

Another result of intercourse with idolaters was a disregard of the Sabbath, the sign distinguishing the Israelites from all other nations as worshipers of the true God. Nehemiah found that heathen merchants and traders from the surrounding country, coming to Jerusalem, had induced many among the Israelites to engage in traffic on the Sabbath. There were some who could not be persuaded to sacrifice principle, but others transgressed and joined with the heathen in their efforts to overcome the scruples of the more conscientious. Many dared openly to violate the Sabbath. "In those days," Nehemiah writes, "saw I in Judah some treading wine presses on the Sabbath, and bringing in sheaves, and lading asses; as also wine, grapes, and figs, and all manner of burdens, which they brought into Jerusalem on the Sabbath day. . . . There dwelt men of Tyre also therein, which brought fish, and all manner of ware, and sold on the Sabbath unto the children of Judah."

This state of things might have been prevented had the rulers exercised their authority; but a desire to advance their own interests had led them to favor the ungodly. Nehemiah fearlessly rebuked them for their neglect of duty. "What evil thing is this that ye do, and profane the Sabbath day?" he sternly demanded. "Did not your fathers thus, and did not our God bring all this evil upon us, and upon this city? yet ye bring more wrath upon Israel by profaning the Sabbath." He then gave command that "when the gates of Jerusalem began to be dark before the Sabbath," they should be shut, and not opened again till the Sabbath was past; and having more confidence in his own servants than in those that the magistrates of Jerusalem might appoint, he stationed them at the gates to see that his orders were enforced.

Not inclined to abandon their purpose, "the merchants and sellers of all kind of ware lodged without Jerusalem once or twice," hoping to find opportunity for traffic, with either the citizens or the country people. Nehemiah warned them that they would be punished if they continued this practice. "Why lodge ye about the wall?" he demanded; "if ye do so again, I will lay hands on you." "From that time forth came they no more on the Sabbath." He also directed the Levites to guard the gates, knowing that they would command greater respect than the common people, while from their close connection with the service of God it was reasonable to expect that they would be more zealous in enforcing obedience to His law.

And now Nehemiah turned his attention to the danger that again threatened Israel from intermarriage and association with idolaters. "In those days," he writes, "saw I Jews that had married wives of Ashdod, of Ammon, and of Moab: and their children spake half in the speech of Ashdod, and could not speak in the Jews' language, but according to the language of each people."

These unlawful alliances were causing great confusion in Israel; for some who entered into them were men in high position, rulers to whom the people had a right to look for counsel and a safe example. Foreseeing the ruin before the nation if this evil were allowed to continue, Nehemiah reasoned earnestly with the wrongdoers. Pointing to the case of Solomon, he reminded them that among all the nations there had risen no king like this man, to whom God had given great wisdom; yet idolatrous women had turned his heart from God, and his example had corrupted Israel. "Shall we then hearken unto you," Nehemiah sternly demanded, "to do all this great evil?" "Ye shall not give your daughters unto their sons, nor take their daughters unto your sons, or for yourselves."

As he set before them God's commands and threatenings, and the fearful judgments visited on Israel in the past for this very sin, their consciences were aroused, and a work of reformation was begun that turned away God's threatened anger and brought His approval and blessings.

There were some in sacred office who pleaded for their heathen wives, declaring that they could not bring themselves to separate from them. But no distinction was made; no respect was shown for rank or position. Whoever among the priests or rulers refused to sever his connection with idolaters was immediately separated from the service of the Lord. A grandson of the high priest, having married a daughter of the notorious Sanballat, was not only removed from office, but promptly banished from Israel. "Remember them, O my God," Nehemiah prayed, "because they have defiled the priesthood, and the covenant of the priesthood, and of the Levites."

How much anguish of soul this needed severity cost the faithful worker for God the judgment alone will reveal. There was a constant struggle with opposing elements, and only by fasting, humiliation, and prayer was advancement made.

Many who had married idolaters chose to go with them into exile, and these, with those who had been expelled from the congregation, joined the Samaritans. Hither some who had occupied high positions in the work of God found their way and after a time cast in their lot fully with them. Desiring to strengthen this alliance, the Samaritans promised to adopt more fully the Jewish faith and customs, and the apostates, determined to outdo their former brethren, erected a temple on Mount Gerizim in opposition to the house of God at Jerusalem. Their religion continued to be a mixture of Judaism and heathenism, and their claim to be the people of God was the source of schism, emulation, and enmity between the two nations, from generation to generation.

In the work of reform to be carried forward today, there is need of men who, like Ezra and Nehemiah, will not palliate or excuse sin, nor shrink from vindicating the honor of God. Those upon whom rests the burden of this work will not hold their peace when wrong is done, neither will they cover evil with a cloak of false charity. They will remember that God is no respecter of persons, and that severity to a few may prove mercy to many. They will remember also that in the one who rebukes evil the spirit of Christ should ever be revealed.

In their work, Ezra and Nehemiah humbled themselves before God, confessing their sins and the sins of their people, and entreating pardon as if they themselves were the offenders. Patiently they toiled and prayed and suffered. That which made their work most difficult was not the open hostility of the heathen, but the secret opposition of pretended friends, who, by lending their influence to the service of evil, increased tenfold the burden God's servants. These traitors furnished the Lord's enemies with material to use in their warfare upon His people. Their evil passions and rebellious wills were ever at war with the plain requirements of God.

The success attending Nehemiah's efforts shows what prayer, faith, and wise, energetic action will accomplish. Nehemiah was not a priest; he was not a prophet; he made no pretension to high title. He was a reformer raised up for an important time. It was his aim to set his people right with God. Inspired with a great purpose, he bent every energy of his being to its accomplishment. High, unbending integrity marked his efforts. As he came into contact with evil and opposition to right he took so determined a stand that the people were roused to labor with fresh zeal and courage. They could not but recognize his loyalty, his patriotism, and his deep love for God; and, seeing this, they were willing to follow where he led.

Industry in a God-appointed duty is an important part of true religion. Men should seize circumstances as God's instruments with which to work His will. Prompt and decisive action at the right time will gain glorious triumphs, while delay and neglect result in failure and dishonor to God. If the leaders in the cause of truth show no zeal, if they are indifferent and purposeless, the church will be careless, indolent, and pleasure-loving; but if they are filled with a holy purpose to serve God and Him alone, the people will be united, hopeful, eager.

The word of God abounds in sharp and striking contrasts. Sin and holiness are placed side by side, that, beholding, we may shun the one and accept the other. The pages that describe the hatred, falsehood, and treachery of Sanballat and Tobiah, describe also the nobility, devotion, and self-sacrifice of Ezra and Nehemiah. We are left free to copy either, as we choose. The fearful results of transgressing God's commands are placed over against the blessings resulting from obedience. We ourselves must decide whether we will suffer the one or enjoy the other.

The work of restoration and reform carried on by the returned exiles, under the leadership of Zerubbabel, Ezra, and Nehemiah, presents a picture of a work of spiritual restoration that is to be wrought in the closing days of this earth's history. The remnant of Israel were a feeble people, exposed to the ravages of their enemies; but through them God purposed to preserve in the earth a knowledge of Himself and of His law. They were the guardians of the true worship, the keepers of the holy oracles. Varied were the experiences that came to them as they rebuilt the temple and the wall of Jerusalem; strong was the opposition that they had to meet. Heavy were the burdens borne by the leaders in this work; but these men moved forward in unwavering confidence, in humility of spirit, and in firm reliance upon God, believing that He would cause His truth to triumph. Like King Hezekiah, Nehemiah "clave to the Lord, and departed not from following Him, but kept His commandments. . . . And the Lord was with him." 2 Kings 18:6, 7.

The spiritual restoration of which the work carried forward in Nehemiah's day was a symbol, is outlined in the words of Isaiah: "They shall build the old wastes, they shall raise up the former desolations, and they shall repair the waste cities." "They that shall be of thee shall build the old waste places: thou shalt raise up the foundations of many generations; and thou shalt be called, The repairer of the breach, The restorer of paths to dwell in." Isaiah 61:4; 58:12.

The prophet here describes a people who, in a time of general departure from truth and righteousness, are seeking to restore the principles that are the foundation of the kingdom of God. They are repairers of a breach that has been made in God's law—the wall that He has placed around His chosen ones for their protection, and obedience to whose precepts of justice, truth, and purity is to be their perpetual safeguard.

In words of unmistakable meaning the prophet points out the specific work of this remnant people who build the wall. "If thou turn away thy foot from the Sabbath, from doing thy pleasure on My holy day; and call the Sabbath a delight, the holy of the Lord, honorable; and shalt honor Him, not doing thine own ways, nor finding thine own pleasure, nor speaking thine own words: then shalt thou delight thyself in the Lord; and I will cause thee to ride upon the high places of the earth, and feed thee with the heritage of Jacob thy father: for the mouth of the Lord hath spoken it." Isaiah 58:13, 14.

In the time of the end every divine institution is to be restored. The breach made in the law at the time the Sabbath was changed by man, is to be repaired. God's remnant people, standing before the world as reformers, are to show that the law of God is the foundation of all enduring reform and that the Sabbath of the fourth commandment is to stand as a memorial of creation, a constant reminder of the power of God. In clear, distinct lines they are to present the necessity of obedience to all the precepts of the Decalogue. Constrained by the love of Christ, they are to co-operate with Him in building up the waste places. They are to be repairers of the breach, restorers of paths to dwell in. See verse 12.

"The kingdom and dominion, and the greatness of the kingdom under the whole heaven, shall be given to the people of the saints of the Most High, whose kingdom is an everlasting kingdom." Daniel 7:27.

The Coming of a Deliverer

Through the long centuries of "trouble and darkness" and "dimness of anguish" (Isaiah 8:22) marking the history of mankind from the day our first parents lost their Eden home, to the time the Son of God appeared as the Saviour of sinners, the hope of the fallen race was centered in the coming of a Deliverer to free men and women from the bondage of sin and the grave.

The first intimation of such a hope was given to Adam and Eve in the sentence pronounced upon the serpent in Eden when the Lord declared to Satan in their hearing, "I will put enmity between thee and the woman, and between thy seed and her seed; it shall bruise thy head, and thou shalt bruise his heel." Genesis 3:15.

As the guilty pair listened to these words, they were inspired with hope; for in the prophecy concerning the breaking of Satan's power they discerned a promise of deliverance from the ruin wrought through transgression. Though they must suffer from the power of their adversary because they had fallen under his seductive influence and had chosen to disobey the plain command of Jehovah, yet they need not yield to utter despair. The Son of God was offering to atone with His own lifeblood for their transgression. To them was to be granted a period of probation, during which, through faith in the power of Christ to save, they might become once more the children of God.

Satan, by means of his success in turning man aside from the path of obedience, became "the god of this world." 2 Corinthians 4:4. The dominion that once was Adam's passed to the usurper. But the Son of God proposed to come to this earth to pay the penalty of sin, and thus not only redeem man, but recover the dominion forfeited. It is of this restoration that Micah prophesied when he said, "O Tower of the flock, the stronghold of the daughter of Zion, unto Thee shall it come, even the first dominion." Micah 4:8. The apostle Paul has referred to it as "the redemption of the purchased possession." Ephesians 1:14. And the psalmist had in mind the same final restoration of man's original inheritance when he declared, "The righteous shall inherit the land, and dwell therein forever." Psalm 37:29.

This hope of redemption through the advent of the Son of God as Saviour and King, has never become extinct in the hearts of men. From the beginning there have been some whose faith has reached out beyond the shadows of the present to the realities of the future. Adam, Seth, Enoch, Methuselah, Noah, Shem, Abraham, Isaac, and Jacob— through these and other worthies the Lord has preserved the precious revealings of His will. And it was thus that to the children of Israel, the chosen people through whom was to be given to the world the promised Messiah, God imparted a knowledge of the requirements of His law, and of the salvation to be accomplished through the atoning sacrifice of His beloved Son.

The hope of Israel was embodied in the promise made at the time of the call of Abraham, and afterward repeated again and again to his posterity, "In thee shall all families of the earth be blessed." Genesis 12:3. As the purpose of God for the redemption of the race was unfolded to Abraham, the Sun of Righteousness shone upon his heart, and his darkness was scattered. And when, at last, the Saviour Himself walked and talked among the sons of men, He bore witness to the Jews of the patriarch's bright hope of deliverance through the coming of a Redeemer. "Your father Abraham rejoiced to see My day," Christ declared; "and he saw it, and was glad." John 8:56.

This same blessed hope was foreshadowed in the benediction pronounced by the dying patriarch Jacob upon his son Judah:

"Judah, thou art he whom thy brethren shall praise:
Thy hand shall be in the neck of thine enemies;
Thy father's children shall bow down before thee. . . .
The scepter shall not depart from Judah,
Nor a lawgiver from between his feet,
Until Shiloh come;
And unto Him shall the gathering of the people be."
Genesis 49:8-10.

Again, on the borders of the Promised Land, the coming of the world's Redeemer was foretold in the prophecy uttered by Balaam:

"I shall see Him, but not now: I shall behold Him, but not nigh:
There shall come a Star out of Jacob, and a Scepter shall rise out of Israel,
And shall smite the corners of Moab, and destroy all the children of Sheth."
Numbers 24:17.

Through Moses, God's purpose to send His Son as the Redeemer of the fallen race, was kept before Israel. On one occasion, shortly before his death, Moses declared, "The Lord thy God will raise up unto thee a Prophet from the midst of thee, of thy brethren, like unto me; unto Him ye shall hearken." Plainly had Moses been instructed for Israel concerning the work of the Messiah to come. "I will raise them up a Prophet from among their brethren, like unto thee," was the word of Jehovah to His servant; "and will put My words in His mouth; and He shall speak unto them all that I shall command Him." Deuteronomy 18:15, 18.

In patriarchal times the sacrificial offerings connected with divine worship constituted a perpetual reminder of the coming of a Saviour, and thus it was with the entire ritual of the sanctuary services throughout Israel's history. In the ministration of the tabernacle, and of the temple that afterward took its place, the people were taught each day, by means of types and shadows, the great truths relative to the advent of Christ as Redeemer, Priest, and King; and once each year their minds were carried forward to the closing events of the great controversy between Christ and Satan, the final purification of the universe from sin and sinners. The sacrifices and offerings of the Mosaic ritual were ever pointing toward a better service, even a heavenly. The earthly sanctuary was "a figure for the time then present," in which were offered both gifts and sacrifices; its two holy places were "patterns of things in the heavens;" for Christ, our great High Priest, is today "a minister of the sanctuary, and of the true tabernacle, which the Lord pitched, and not man." Hebrews 9:9, 23; 8:2.

From the day the Lord declared to the serpent in Eden, "I will put enmity between thee and the woman, and between thy seed and her seed" (Genesis 3:15), Satan has known that he can never hold absolute sway over the inhabitants of this world. When Adam and his sons began to offer the ceremonial sacrifices ordained by God as a type of the coming Redeemer, Satan discerned in these a symbol of communion between earth and heaven. During the long centuries that have followed, it has been his constant effort to intercept this communion. Untiringly has he sought to misrepresent God and to misinterpret the rites pointing to the Saviour, and with a great majority of the members of the human family he has been successful.

While God has desired to teach men that from His own love comes the Gift which reconciles them to Himself, the archenemy of mankind has endeavored to represent God as one who delights in their destruction. Thus the sacrifices and the ordinances designed of Heaven to reveal divine love have been perverted to serve as means whereby sinners have vainly hoped to propitiate, with gifts and good works, the wrath of an offended God. At the same time, Satan has sought to arouse and strengthen the evil passions of men in order that through repeated transgression multitudes might be led on and on, far from God, and hopelessly bound with the fetters of sin.

When God's written word was given through the Hebrew prophets, Satan studied with diligence the messages concerning the Messiah. Carefully he traced the words that outlined with unmistakable clearness Christ's work among men as a suffering sacrifice and as a conquering king. In the parchment rolls of the Old Testament Scriptures he read that the One who was to appear was to be "brought as a lamb to the slaughter," "His visage . . . so marred more than any man, and His form more than the sons of men." Isaiah 53:7; 52:14. The promised Saviour of humanity was to be "despised and rejected of men; a man of sorrows, and acquainted with grief; . . . smitten of God, and afflicted;" yet He was also to exercise His mighty power in order to "judge the poor of the people." He was to "save the children of the needy," and "break in pieces the oppressor." Isaiah 53:3, 4; Psalm 72:4. These prophecies caused Satan to fear and tremble; yet he relinquished not his purpose to thwart, if possible, the merciful provisions of Jehovah for the redemption of the lost race. He determined to blind the eyes of the people, so far as might be possible, to the real significance of the Messianic prophecies, in order to prepare the way for the rejection of Christ at His coming.

During the centuries immediately preceding the Flood, success had attended Satan's efforts to bring about a worldwide prevalence of rebellion against God. And even the lessons of the Deluge were not long held in remembrance. With artful insinuations Satan again led the children of men step by step into bold rebellion. Again he seemed about to triumph, but God's purpose for fallen man was not thus to be set aside. Through the posterity of faithful Abraham, of the line of Shem, a knowledge of Jehovah's beneficent designs was to be preserved for the benefit of future generations. From time to time divinely appointed messengers of truth were to be raised up to call attention to the meaning of the sacrificial ceremonies, and especially to the promise of Jehovah concerning the advent of the One toward whom all the ordinances of the sacrificial system pointed. Thus the world was to be kept from universal apostasy.

Not without the most determined opposition was the divine purpose carried out. In every way possible the enemy of truth and righteousness worked to cause the descendants of Abraham to forget their high and holy calling, and to turn aside to the worship of false gods. And often his efforts were all but successful. For centuries preceding Christ's first advent, darkness covered the earth, and gross darkness the people. Satan was throwing his hellish shadow athwart the pathway of men, that he might prevent them from gaining a knowledge of God and of the future world. Multitudes were sitting in the shadow of death. Their only hope was for this gloom to be lifted, that God might be revealed. With prophetic vision David, the anointed of God, had foreseen that the coming of Christ should be "as the light of the morning, when the sun riseth, even a morning without clouds." 2 Samuel 23:4. And Hosea testified, "His going forth is prepared as the morning." Hosea 6:3. Quietly and gently the daylight breaks upon the earth, dispelling the shadow of darkness and waking the earth to life. So was the Sun of Righteousness to arise, "with healing in His wings." Malachi 4:2. The multitudes dwelling "in the land of the shadow of death" were to see "a great light." Isaiah 9:2.

The prophet Isaiah, looking with rapture upon this glorious deliverance, exclaimed:

"Unto us a Child is born,
Unto us a Son is given:
And the government shall be upon His shoulder:
And His name shall be called Wonderful, Counselor, The mighty God,
The everlasting Father, The Prince of Peace.
Of the increase of His government and peace there shall be no end,
Upon the throne of David,
And upon His kingdom,
To order it, and to establish it With judgment and with justice From henceforth even forever.
The zeal of the Lord of hosts will perform this."
Verses 6, 7.

In the later centuries of Israel's history prior to the first advent it was generally understood that the coming of the Messiah was referred to in the prophecy, "It is a light thing that Thou shouldest be My servant to raise up the tribes of Jacob, and to restore the preserved of Israel: I will also give Thee for a light to the Gentiles, that Thou mayest be My salvation unto the end of the earth." "The glory of the Lord shall be revealed," the prophet had foretold, "and all flesh shall see it together." Isaiah 49:6; 40:5. It was of this light of men that John the Baptist afterward testified so boldly, when he proclaimed, "I am the voice of one crying in the wilderness, Make straight the way of the Lord, as said the prophet Esaias." John 1:23.

It was to Christ that the prophetic promise was given: "Thus saith the Lord, the Redeemer of Israel, and His Holy One, to Him whom man despiseth, to Him whom the nation abhorreth, . . . thus saith the Lord, . . . I will preserve Thee, and give Thee for a covenant of the people, to establish the earth, to cause to inherit the desolate heritages; that Thou mayest say to the prisoners, Go forth; to them that are in darkness, Show yourselves. . . . They shall not hunger nor thirst; neither shall the heat nor sun smite them: for He that hath mercy on them shall lead them, even by the springs of water shall He guided them." Isaiah 49:7-10.

The steadfast among the Jewish nation, descendants of that holy line through whom a knowledge of God had been preserved, strengthened their faith by dwelling on these and similar passages. With exceeding joy they read how the Lord would anoint One "to preach good tidings unto the meek," "to bind up the brokenhearted, to proclaim liberty to the captives," and to declare "the acceptable year of the Lord." Isaiah 61:1, 2. Yet their hearts were filled with sadness as they thought of the sufferings He must endure in order to fulfill the divine purpose. With deep humiliation of soul they traced the words in the prophetic roll:

"Who hath believed our report?
And to whom is the arm of the Lord revealed?
"For He shall grow up before Him as a tender plant,
And as a root out of a dry ground:
He hath no form nor comeliness;
And when we shall see Him,
There is no beauty that we should desire Him.
"He is despised and rejected of men;
A Man of Sorrows, and acquainted with grief:
And we hid as it were our faces from Him;
He was despised, and we esteemed Him not.
"Surely He hath borne our griefs,
And carried our sorrows:
Yet we did esteem Him stricken,
Smitten of God, and afflicted.
"But He was wounded for our transgressions,
He was bruised for our iniquities:
The chastisement of our peace was upon Him;
And with His stripes we are healed.
"All we like sheep have gone astray;
We have turned everyone to his own way;
And the Lord hath laid on Him
The iniquity of us all.
"He was oppressed, and He was afflicted,
Yet He opened not His mouth:
He is brought as a lamb to the slaughter,
And as a sheep before her shearers is dumb,
So He openeth not His mouth.
"He was taken from prison and from judgment:
And who shall declare His generation?
For He was cut off out of the land of the living:
For the transgression of My people was He stricken.
"And He made His grave with the wicked,
And with the rich in His death;
Because He had done no violence,
Neither was any deceit in His mouth."
Isaiah 53:1-9.

Of the suffering Saviour Jehovah Himself declared through Zechariah, "Awake, O sword, against My Shepherd, and against the Man that is My Fellow." Zechariah 13:7. As the substitute and surety for sinful man, Christ was to suffer under divine justice. He was to understand what justice meant. He was to know what it means for sinners to stand before God without an intercessor.

Through the psalmist the Redeemer had prophesied of Himself:

"Reproach hath broken My heart;
And I am full of heaviness:
And I looked for some to take pity,
But there was none;
And for comforters,
But I found none.
They gave Me also gall for My meat;
And in My thirst they gave Me vinegar to drink."
Psalm 69:20, 21.

Of the treatment He was to receive, He prophesied, "Dogs have compassed Me: the assembly of the wicked have enclosed Me: they pierced My hands and My feet. I may tell all My bones: they look and stare upon Me. They part My garments among them, and cast lots upon My vesture." Psalm 22:16-18.

These portrayals of the bitter suffering and cruel death of the Promised One, sad though they were, were rich in promise; for of Him whom "it pleased the Lord to bruise" and to put to grief, in order that He might become "an offering for sin," Jehovah declared:

"He shall see His seed, He shall prolong His days,
And the pleasure of the Lord shall prosper in His hand.
He shall see of the travail of His soul, and shall be satisfied:

"By His knowledge shall My righteous Servant justify many;
For He shall bear their iniquities.
Therefore will I divide Him a portion with the great,
And He shall divide the spoil with the strong;
Because He hath poured out His soul unto death:
And He was numbered with the transgressors;
And He bare the sin of many,
And made intercession for the transgressors."
Isaiah 53:10-12.

It was love for sinners that led Christ to pay the price of redemption. "He saw that there was no man, and wondered that there was no intercessor," none other could ransom men and women from the power of the enemy; "therefore His arm brought salvation unto him; and His righteousness, it sustained him." Isaiah 59:16.

"Behold My Servant, whom I uphold;
Mine Elect, in whom My soul delighteth;
I have put My Spirit upon Him:
He shall bring forth judgment to the Gentiles."
Isaiah 42:1.

In His life no self-assertion was to be mingled. The homage which the world gives to position, to wealth, and to talent, was to be foreign to the Son of God. None of the means that men employ to win allegiance or to command homage, was the Messiah to use. His utter renunciation of self was foreshadowed in the words:

"He shall not cry,
Nor lift up,
Nor cause His voice to be heard in the street.
A bruised reed shall He not break,
And the smoking flax shall He not quench."

Verses 2, 3.

In marked contrast to the teachers of His day was the Saviour to conduct Himself among men. In His life no noisy disputation, no ostentatious worship, no act to gain applause, was ever to be witnessed. The Messiah was to be hid in God, and God was to be revealed in the character of His Son. Without a knowledge of God, humanity would be eternally lost. Without divine help, men and women would sink lower and lower. Life and power must be imparted by Him who made the world. Man's necessities could be met in no other way.

It was further prophesied of the Messiah: "He shall not fail nor be discouraged, till He have set judgment in the earth: and the isles shall wait for His law." The Son of God was to "magnify the law, and make it honorable." Verses 4, 21. He was not to lessen its importance and binding claims; He was rather to exalt it. At the same time He was to free the divine precepts from those burdensome exactions placed upon them by man, whereby many were brought to discouragement in their efforts to serve God acceptably.

Of the mission of the Saviour the word of Jehovah was: "I the Lord have called Thee in righteousness, and will hold Thine hand, and will keep Thee, and give Thee for a covenant of the people, for a light of the Gentiles; to open the blind eyes, to bring out the prisoners from the prison, and them that sit in darkness out of the prison house. I am the Lord: that is My name: and My glory will I not give to another, neither My praise to graven images. Behold, the former things are come to pass, and new things do I declare: before they spring forth I tell you of them." Verses 6-9.

Through the promised Seed, the God of Israel was to bring deliverance to Zion. "There shall come forth a Rod out of the stem of Jesse, and a Branch shall grow out of his roots." "Behold, a virgin shall conceive, and bear a Son, and shall call His name Immanuel. Butter and honey shall He eat, that He may know to refuse the evil, and choose the good." Isaiah 11:1; 7:14, 15.

"And the Spirit of the Lord shall rest upon Him, the Spirit of wisdom and understanding, the Spirit of counsel and might, the Spirit of knowledge and of the fear of the Lord; and shall make Him of quick understanding in the fear of the Lord: and He shall not judge after the sight of His eyes, neither reprove after the hearing of His ears: but with righteousness shall He judge the poor, and reprove with equity for the meek of the earth: and He shall smite the earth with the rod of His mouth, and with the breath of His lips shall He slay the wicked. And righteousness shall be the girdle of His loins, and faithfulness the girdle of His reins." "And in that day there shall be a Root of Jesse, which shall stand for an ensign of the people; to it shall the Gentiles seek: and His rest shall be glorious." Isaiah 11:2-5, 10.

"Behold the Man whose name is the Branch; . . . He shall build the temple of the Lord; and He shall bear the glory, and shall sit and rule upon His throne; and He shall be a priest upon His throne." Zechariah 6:12, 13.

A fountain was to be opened "for sin and for uncleanness" (Zechariah 13:1); the sons of men were to hear the blessed invitation:

"Ho, everyone that thirsteth, come ye to the waters,
And he that hath no money; come ye, buy, and eat;
Yea, come, buy wine and milk
Without money and without price.
"Wherefore do ye spend money for that which is not bread?
And your labor for that which satisfieth not?
Hearken diligently unto Me, and eat ye that which is good,
And let your soul delight itself in fatness.
"Incline your ear, and come unto Me:
Hear, and your soul shall live;
And I will make an everlasting covenant with you,
Even the sure mercies of David."
Isaiah 55:1-3.

To Israel the promise was made: "Behold, I have given Him for a witness to the people, a leader and commander to the people. Behold, thou shalt call a nation that thou knowest not, and nations that knew not thee shall run unto thee because of the Lord thy God, and for the Holy One of Israel; for He hath glorified thee." Verses 4, 5.

"I bring near My righteousness; it shall not be far off, and My salvation shall not tarry: and I will place salvation in Zion for Israel My glory." Isaiah 46:13.

In word and in deed the Messiah, during His earthly ministry, was to reveal to mankind the glory of God the Father. Every act of His life, every word spoken, every miracle wrought, was to make known to fallen humanity the infinite love of God.

"O Zion, that bringest good tidings,
Get thee up into the high mountain;
O Jerusalem, that bringest good tidings,
Lift up thy voice with strength;
Lift it up, be not afraid;
Say unto the cities of Judah, Behold your God!
"Behold, the Lord God will come with strong hand,
And His arm shall rule for Him:
Behold, His reward is with Him,
And His work before Him.
He shall feed His flock like a shepherd:
He shall gather the lambs with His arm,
And carry them in His bosom,
And shall gently lead those that are with young."
Isaiah 40:9-11.
"And in that day shall the deaf hear the words of the Book,
And the eyes of the blind shall see out of obscurity, and out of darkness.
The meek also shall increase their joy in the Lord,
And the poor among men shall rejoice in the Holy One of Israel."

"They also that erred in spirit shall come to understanding,
And they that murmured shall learn doctrine."
Isaiah 29:18, 19, 24.

Thus, through patriarchs and prophets, as well as through types and symbols, God spoke to the world concerning the coming of a Deliverer from sin. A long line of inspired prophecy pointed to the advent of "the Desire of all nations." Haggai 2:7. Even the very place of His birth and the time of His appearance were minutely specified.

The Son of David must be born in David's city. Out of Bethlehem, said the prophet, "shall He come forth . . . that is to be ruler in Israel; whose goings forth have been from of old, from the days of eternity." Micah 5:2, margin. "And thou Bethlehem, land of Judah,

Art in no wise least among the princes of Judah:
For out of thee shall come forth a Governor,
Which shall be Shepherd of My people Israel."
Matthew 2:6, R.V.

The time of the first advent and of some of the chief events clustering about the Saviour's lifework was made known by the angel Gabriel to Daniel. "Seventy weeks," said the angel, "are determined upon thy people and upon thy holy city, to finish the transgression, and to make an end of sins, and to make reconciliation for iniquity, and to bring in everlasting righteousness, and to seal up the vision and prophecy, and to anoint the most holy." Daniel 9:24. A day in prophecy stands for a year. See Numbers 14:34; Ezekiel 4:6. The seventy weeks, or four hundred and ninety days, represent four hundred and ninety years. A starting point for this period is given: "Know therefore and understand, that from the going forth of the commandment to restore and to build Jerusalem unto the Messiah the Prince shall be seven weeks, and threescore and two weeks" (Daniel 9:25), sixty-nine weeks, or four hundred and eighty-three years. The commandment to restore and build Jerusalem, as completed by the decree of Artaxerxes Longimanus, went into effect in the autumn of 457 B.C. See Ezra 6:14; 7:1, 9. From this time four hundred and eighty-three years extend to the autumn of A.D. 27. According to the prophecy, this period was to reach to the Messiah, the Anointed One. In A.D. 27, Jesus at His baptism received the anointing of the Holy Spirit and soon afterward began His ministry. Then the message was proclaimed, "The time is fulfilled." Mark 1:15.

Then, said the angel, "He shall confirm the covenant with many for one week." For seven years after the Saviour entered on His ministry, the gospel was to be preached especially to the Jews; for three and a half years by Christ Himself, and afterward by the apostles. "In the midst of the week He shall cause the sacrifice and the oblation to cease." Daniel 9:27. In the spring of A.D. 31, Christ, the true Sacrifice, was offered on Calvary. Then the veil of the temple was rent in twain, showing that the sacredness and significance of the sacrificial service had departed. The time had come for the earthly sacrifice and oblation to cease.

The one week—seven years—ended in A.D. 34. Then by the stoning of Stephen the Jews finally sealed their rejection of the gospel; the disciples who were scattered abroad by persecution "went everywhere preaching the word" (Acts 8:4); and shortly after, Saul the persecutor was converted and became Paul the apostle to the Gentiles.

The many prophecies concerning the Saviour's advent led the Hebrews to live in an attitude of constant expectancy. Many died in the faith, not having received the promises. But having seen them afar off, they believed and confessed that they were strangers and pilgrims on the earth. From the days of Enoch the promises repeated through patriarchs and prophets had kept alive the hope of His appearing.

Not at first had God revealed the exact time of the first advent; and even when the prophecy of Daniel made this known, not all rightly interpreted the message.

Century after century passed away; finally the voices of the prophets ceased. The hand of the oppressor was heavy upon Israel. As the Jews departed from God, faith grew dim, and hope well-nigh ceased to illuminate the future. The words of the prophets were uncomprehended by many; and those whose faith should have continued strong were ready to exclaim, "The days are prolonged, and every vision faileth." Ezekiel 12:22. But in heaven's council the hour for the coming of Christ had been determined; and "when the fullness of the time was come, God sent forth His Son, . . . to redeem them that were under the law, that we might receive the adoption of sons." Galatians 4:4, 5.

Lessons must be given to humanity in the language of humanity. The Messenger of the covenant must speak. His voice must be heard in His own temple. He, the author of truth, must separate truth from the chaff of man's utterance, which had made it of no effect. The principles of God's government and the plan of redemption must be clearly defined. The lessons of the Old Testament must be fully set before men.

When the Saviour finally appeared "in the likeness of men" (Philippians 2:7), and began His ministry of grace, Satan could but bruise the heel, while by every act of humiliation or suffering Christ was bruising the head of His adversary. The anguish that sin has brought was poured into the bosom of the Sinless; yet while Christ endured the contradiction of sinners against Himself, He was paying the debt for sinful man and breaking the bondage in which humanity had been held. Every pang of anguish, every insult, was working out the deliverance of the race.

Could Satan have induced Christ to yield to a single temptation, could he have led Him by one act or even thought to stain His perfect purity, the prince of darkness would have triumphed over man's Surety and would have gained the whole human family to himself. But while Satan could distress, he could not contaminate. He could cause agony, but not defilement. He made the life of Christ one long scene of conflict and trial, yet with every attack he was losing his hold upon humanity.

In the wilderness of temptation, in the Garden of Gethsemane, and on the cross, our Saviour measured weapons with the prince of darkness. His wounds became the trophies of His victory in behalf of the race. When Christ hung in agony upon the cross, while evil spirits rejoiced and evil men reviled, then indeed His heel was bruised by Satan. But that very act was crushing the serpent's head. Through death He destroyed "him that had the power of death, that is, the devil." Hebrews 2:14. This act decided the destiny of the rebel chief, and made forever sure the plan of salvation. In death He gained the victory over its power; in rising again, He opened the gates of the grave to all His followers. In that last great contest we see fulfilled the prophecy, "It shall bruise thy head, and thou shall bruise his heel." Genesis 3:15.

"Beloved, now are we the sons of God, and it doth not yet appear what we shall be: but we know that, when He shall appear, we shall be like Him; for we shall see Him as He is." 1 John 3:2. Our Redeemer has opened the way, so that the most sinful, the most needy, the most oppressed and despised, may find access to the Father.

"O Lord, Thou art my God;
I will exalt Thee,
I will praise Thy name;
For Thou hast done wonderful things;
Thy counsels of old are faithfulness and truth."
Isaiah 25:1.

"The House of Israel"

In proclaiming the truths of the everlasting gospel to every nation, kindred, tongue, and people, God's church on earth today is fulfilling the ancient prophecy, "Israel shall blossom and bud, and fill the face of the world with fruit." Isaiah 27:6. The followers of Jesus, in co-operation with heavenly intelligences, are rapidly occupying the waste places of the earth; and, as the result of their labors, an abundant fruitage of precious souls is developing. Today, as never before, the dissemination of Bible truth by means of a consecrated church is bringing to the sons of men the benefits foreshadowed centuries ago in the promise to Abraham and to all Israel,—to God's church on earth in every age,—"I will bless thee, . . . and thou shalt be a blessing." Genesis 12:2.

This promise of blessing should have met fulfillment in large measure during the centuries following the return of the Israelites from the lands of their captivity. It was God's design that the whole earth be prepared for the first advent of Christ, even as today the way is preparing for His second coming. At the end of the years of humiliating exile, God graciously gave to His people Israel, through Zechariah, the assurance: "I am returned unto Zion, and will dwell in the midst of Jerusalem: and Jerusalem shall be called a city of truth; and the mountain of the Lord of hosts the holy mountain." And of His people He said, "Behold, . . . I will be their God, in truth and in righteousness." Zechariah 8:3, 7, 8.

These promises were conditional on obedience. The sins that had characterized the Israelites prior to the captivity, were not to be repeated. "Execute true judgment," the Lord exhorted those who were engaged in rebuilding; "and show mercy and compassions every man to his brother: and oppress not the widow, nor the fatherless, the stranger, nor the poor; and let none of you imagine evil against his brother." "Speak ye every man the truth to his neighbor; execute the judgment of truth and peace in your gates." Zechariah 7:9, 10; 8:16.

Rich were the rewards, both temporal and spiritual, promised those who should put into practice these principles of righteousness. "The seed shall be prosperous," the Lord declared; "the vine shall give her fruit, and the ground shall give her increase, and the heavens shall give their dew; and I will cause the remnant of this people to possess all these things. And it shall come to pass, that as ye were a curse among the heathen, O house of Judah, and house of Israel; so I will save you, and ye shall be a blessing." Zechariah 8:12, 13.

By the Babylonish captivity the Israelites were effectually cured of the worship of graven images. After their return, they gave much attention to religious instruction and to the study of that which had been written in the book of the law and in the prophets concerning the worship of the true God. The restoration of the temple enabled them to carry out fully the ritual services of the sanctuary. Under the leadership of Zerubbabel, of Ezra, and of Nehemiah they repeatedly covenanted to keep all the commandments and ordinances of Jehovah. The seasons of prosperity that followed gave ample evidence of God's willingness to accept and forgive, and yet with fatal shortsightedness they turned again and again from their glorious destiny and selfishly appropriated to themselves that which would have brought healing and spiritual life to countless multitudes.

This failure to fulfill the divine purpose was very apparent in Malachi's day. Sternly the Lord's messenger dealt with the evils that were robbing Israel of temporal prosperity and spiritual power. In his rebuke against transgressors the prophet spared neither priests nor people. "The burden of the word of the Lord to Israel" through Malachi was that the lessons of the past be not forgotten and that the covenant made by Jehovah with the house of Israel be kept with fidelity. Only by heartfelt repentance could the blessing of God be realized. "I pray you," the prophet pleaded, "beseech God that He will be gracious unto us." Malachi 1:1, 9.

Not by any temporary failure of Israel, however, was the plan of the ages for the redemption of mankind to be frustrated. Those to whom the prophet was speaking might not heed the message given, but the purposes of Jehovah were nevertheless to move steadily forward to their complete fulfillment. "From the rising of the sun even unto the going down of the same," the Lord declared through His messenger, "My name shall be great among the Gentiles; and in every place incense shall be offered unto My name, and a pure offering: for My name shall be great among the heathen." Malachi 1:11.

The covenant of "life and peace" God had made with the

sons of Levi—the covenant which, if kept, would have brought untold blessing—the Lord now offered to renew with those who once had been spiritual leaders, but who through transgression had become "contemptible and base before all the people." Malachi 2:5, 9.

Solemnly evildoers were warned of the day of judgment to come and of Jehovah's purpose to visit with swift destruction every transgressor. Yet none were left without hope; Malachi's prophecies of judgment were accompanied by invitations to the impenitent to make their peace with God. "Return unto Me," the Lord urged; "and I will return unto you." Malachi 3:7.

It seems as if every heart must respond to such an invitation. The God of heaven is pleading with His erring children to return to Him, that they may again co-operate with Him in carrying forward His work in the earth. The Lord holds out His hand to take the hand of Israel and to help them to the narrow path of self-denial and self-sacrifice, to share with Him the heirship as sons of God. Will they be entreated? Will they discern their only hope?

How sad the record, that in Malachi's day the Israelites hesitated to yield their proud hearts in prompt and loving obedience and hearty co-operation! Self-vindication is apparent in their response, "Wherein shall we return?"

The Lord reveals to His people one of their special sins. "Will a man rob God?" He asks. "Yet ye have robbed Me." Still unconvicted of sin, the disobedient inquire, "Wherein have we robbed Thee?"

Definite indeed is the Lord's answer: "In tithes and offerings. Ye are cursed with a curse: for ye have robbed Me, even this whole nation. Bring ye all the tithes into the store-house, that there may be meat in Mine house, and prove Me now herewith, saith the Lord of hosts, if I will not open you the windows of heaven, and pour you out a blessing, that there shall not be room enough to receive it. And I will rebuke the devourer for your sakes, and he shall not destroy the fruits of your ground; neither shall your vine cast her fruit before the time in the field, saith the Lord of hosts. And all nations shall call you blessed: for ye shall be a delightsome land, saith the Lord of hosts." Verses 7-12.

God blesses the work of men's hands, that they may return to Him His portion. He gives them the sunshine and the rain; He causes vegetation to flourish; He gives health and ability to acquire means. Every blessing comes from His bountiful hand, and He desires men and women to show their gratitude by returning Him a portion in tithes and offerings—in thank offerings, in freewill offerings, in trespass offerings. They are to devote their means to His service, that His vineyard may not remain a barren waste. They are to study what the Lord would do were He in their place. They are to take all difficult matters to Him in prayer. They are to reveal an unselfish interest in the building up of His work in all parts of the world.

Through messages such as those borne by Malachi, the last of the Old Testament prophets, as well as through oppression from heathen foes, the Israelites finally learned the lesson that true prosperity depends upon obedience to the law of God. But with many of the people, obedience was not the outflow of faith and love. Their motives were selfish. Outward service was rendered as a means of attaining to national greatness. The chosen people did not become the light of the world, but shut themselves away from the world as a safeguard against being seduced into idolatry. The restrictions which God had given, forbidding intermarriage between His people and the heathen, and prohibiting Israel from joining in the idolatrous practices of surrounding nations, were so perverted as to build up a wall of partition between the Israelites and all other peoples, thus shutting from others the very blessings which God had commissioned Israel to give to the world.

At the same time the Jews were, by their sins, separating themselves from God. They were unable to discern the deep spiritual significance of their symbolic service. In their self-righteousness they trusted to their own works, to the sacrifices and ordinances themselves, instead of relying upon the merits of Him to whom all these things pointed. Thus "going about to establish their own righteousness" (Romans 10:3), they built themselves up in a self-sufficient formalism. Wanting the Spirit and grace of God, they tried to make up for the lack by a rigorous observance of religious ceremonies and rites. Not content with the ordinances which God Himself had appointed, they encumbered the divine commands with countless exactions of their own devising. The greater their distance from God, the more rigorous they were in the observance of these forms.

With all these minute and burdensome exactions it was a practical impossibility for the people to keep the law. The great principles of righteousness set forth in the Decalogue, and the glorious truths shadowed in the symbolic service, were alike obscured, buried under a mass of human tradition and enactment. Those who were really desirous of serving God, and who tried to observe the whole law as enjoined by the priests and rulers, groaned under a heavy burden.

As a nation, the people of Israel, while desiring the advent of the Messiah, were so far separated from God in heart and life that they could have no true conception of the character or mission of the promised Redeemer. Instead of desiring redemption from sin, and the glory and peace of holiness, their hearts were fixed upon deliverance from their national foes, and restoration to worldly power. They looked for Messiah to come as a conqueror, to break every yoke, and exalt Israel to dominion over all nations. Thus Satan had succeeded in preparing the hearts of the people to reject the Saviour when He should appear. Their own pride of heart, and their false conceptions of His character and mission, would prevent them from honestly weighing the evidences of His Messiahship.

For more than a thousand years the Jewish people had waited the coming of the promised Saviour. Their brightest hopes had rested upon this event. For a thousand years, in song and prophecy, in temple rite and household prayer, His name had been enshrined; and yet when He came, they did not recognize Him as the Messiah for whom they had so long waited. "He came unto His own, and His own received Him not." John 1:11. To their world-loving hearts the Beloved of heaven was "as a root out of a dry ground." In their eyes He had "no form nor comeliness;" they discerned in Him no beauty that they should desire Him. Isaiah 53:2.

The whole life of Jesus of Nazareth among the Jewish people was a reproof to their selfishness, as revealed in their unwillingness to recognize the just claims of the Owner of the vineyard over which they had been placed as husbandmen. They hated His example of truthfulness and piety; and when the final test came, the test which meant obedience unto eternal life or disobedience unto eternal death, they rejected the Holy One of Israel and became responsible for His crucifixion on Calvary's cross.

In the parable of the vineyard, Christ near the close of His earthly ministry called the attention of the Jewish teachers to the rich blessings bestowed upon Israel, and in these showed God's claim to their obedience. Plainly He set before them the glory of God's purpose, which through obedience they might have fulfilled. Withdrawing the veil from the future, He showed how, by failure to fulfill His purpose, the whole nation was forfeiting His blessing and bringing ruin upon itself.

"There was a certain householder," Christ said, "which planted a vineyard, and hedged it round about, and digged a wine press in it, and built a tower, and let it out to husbandmen, and went into a far country." Matthew 21:33.

Thus the Saviour referred to "the vineyard of the Lord of hosts," which the prophet Isaiah centuries before had declared to be "the house of Israel." Isaiah 5:7.

"And when the time of the fruit drew near," Christ continued, the owner of the vineyard "sent his servants to the husbandmen, that they might receive the fruits of it. And the husbandmen took his servants, and beat one, and killed another, and stoned another. Again, he sent other servants more than the first: and they did unto them likewise. But last of all he sent unto them his son, saying, They will reverence my son. But when the husbandmen saw the son, they said among themselves, This is the heir; come, let us kill him, and let us seize on his inheritance. And they caught him, and cast him out of the vineyard, and slew him."

Having portrayed before the priests their crowning act of wickedness, Christ now put to them the question, "When the lord therefore of the vineyard cometh, what will he do unto those husbandmen?" The priests had been following the narrative with deep interest; and without considering the relation of the subject to themselves, they joined with the people in answering, "He will miserably destroy those wicked men, and will let out his vineyard unto other husbandmen, which shall render him the fruits in their seasons."

Unwittingly they had pronounced their own doom. Jesus looked upon them, and under His searching gaze they knew that He read the secrets of their hearts. His divinity flashed out before them with unmistakable power. They saw in the husbandmen a picture of themselves, and they involuntarily exclaimed, "God forbid!"

Solemnly and regretfully Christ asked: "Did ye never read in the Scriptures, The stone which the builders rejected, the same is become the head of the corner: this is the Lord's doing, and it is marvelous in our eyes? Therefore say I unto you, The kingdom of God shall be taken from you, and given to a nation bringing forth the fruits thereof. And whosoever shall fall on this stone shall be broken: but on whomsoever it shall fall, it will grind him to powder." Matthew 21:34-44.

Christ would have averted the doom of the Jewish nation if the people had received Him. But envy and jealousy made them implacable. They determined that they would not receive Jesus of Nazareth as the Messiah. They rejected the Light of the world, and henceforth their lives were surrounded with darkness as the darkness of midnight. The doom foretold came upon the Jewish nation. Their own fierce passions, uncontrolled, wrought their ruin. In their blind rage they destroyed one another. Their rebellious, stubborn pride brought upon them the wrath of their Roman conquerors. Jerusalem was destroyed, the temple laid in ruins, and its site plowed like a field. The children of Judah perished by the most horrible forms of death. Millions were sold to serve as bondmen in heathen lands.

That which God purposed to do for the world through Israel, the chosen nation, He will finally accomplish through His church on earth today. He has "let out His vineyard unto other husbandmen," even to His covenant-keeping people, who faithfully "render Him the fruits in their seasons." Never has the Lord been without true representatives on this earth who have made His interests their own. These witnesses for God are numbered among the spiritual Israel, and to them will be fulfilled all the covenant promises made by Jehovah to His ancient people.

Today the church of God is free to carry forward to completion the divine plan for the salvation of a lost race. For many centuries God's people suffered a restriction of their liberties. The preaching of the gospel in its purity was prohibited, and the severest of penalties were visited upon those who dared disobey the mandates of men. As a consequence, the Lord's great moral vineyard was almost wholly unoccupied. The people were deprived of the light of God's word. The darkness of error and superstition threatened to blot out a knowledge of true religion. God's church on earth was a verily in captivity during this long period of relentless persecution as were the children of Israel held captive in Babylon during the period of the exile.

But, thank God, His church is no longer in bondage. To spiritual Israel have been restored the privileges accorded the people of God at the time of their deliverance from Babylon. In every part of the earth, men and women are responding to the Heaven-sent message which John the revelator prophesied would be proclaimed prior to the second coming of Christ: "Fear God, and give glory to Him; for the hour of His judgment is come." Revelation 14:7.

No longer have the hosts of evil power to keep the church captive; for "Babylon is fallen, is fallen, that great city," which hath "made all nations drink of the wine of the wrath of her fornication;" and to spiritual Israel is given the message, "Come out of her, My people, that ye be not partakers of her sins, and that ye receive not of her plagues." Verse 8; 18:4. As the captive exiles heeded the message, "Flee out of the midst of Babylon" (Jeremiah 51:6), and were restored to the Land of Promise, so those who fear God today are heeding the message to withdraw from spiritual Babylon, and soon they are to stand as trophies of divine grace in the earth made new, the heavenly Canaan.

In Malachi's day the mocking inquiry of the impenitent, "Where is the God of judgment?" met with the solemn response: "The Lord . . . shall suddenly come to His temple, even the Messenger of the covenant. . . . But who may abide the day of His coming? and who shall stand when He appeareth? for He is like a refiner's fire, and like fullers' soap: and He shall sit as a refiner and purifier of silver: and He shall purify the sons of Levi, and purge them as gold and silver, that they may offer unto the Lord an offering in righteousness. Then shall the offering of Judah and Jerusalem be pleasant unto the Lord, as in the days of old, and as in former years." Malachi 2:17; 3:1-4.

When the promised Messiah was about to appear, the message of the forerunner of Christ was: Repent, publicans and sinners; repent, Pharisees and Sadducees; "for the kingdom of heaven is at hand." Matthew 3:2.

Today, in the spirit and power of Elias and of John the Baptist, messengers of God's appointment are calling the attention of a judgment-bound world to the solemn events soon to take place in connection with the closing hours of probation and the appearance of Christ Jesus as King of kings and Lord of lords. Soon every man is to be judged for the deeds done in the body. The hour of God's judgment has come, and upon the members of His church on earth rests the solemn responsibility of giving warning to those who are standing as it were on the very brink of eternal ruin. To every human being in the wide world who will give heed must be made plain the principles at stake in the great controversy being waged, principles upon which hang the destinies of all mankind.

In these final hours of probation for the sons of men, when the fate of every soul is so soon to be decided forever, the Lord of heaven and earth expects His church to arouse to action as never before. Those who have been made free in Christ through a knowledge of precious truth, are regarded by the Lord Jesus as His chosen ones, favored above all other people on the face of the earth; and He is counting on them to show forth the praises of Him who hath called them out of darkness into marvelous light. The blessings which are so liberally bestowed are to be communicated to others. The good news of salvation is to go to every nation, kindred, tongue, and people.

In the visions of the prophets of old the Lord of glory was represented as bestowing special light upon His church in the days of darkness and unbelief preceding His second coming. As the Sun of Righteousness, He was to arise upon His church, "with healing in His wings." Malachi 4:2. And from every true disciple was to be diffused an influence for life, courage, helpfulness, and true healing.

The coming of Christ will take place in the darkest period of this earth's history. The days of Noah and of Lot picture the condition of the world just before the coming of the Son of man. The Scriptures, pointing forward to this time, declare that Satan will work with all power and "with all deceivableness of unrighteousness." 2 Thessalonians 2:9, 10. His working is plainly revealed by the rapidly increasing darkness, the multitudinous errors, heresies, and delusions of these last days. Not only is Satan leading the world captive, but his deceptions are leavening the professed churches of our Lord Jesus Christ. The great apostasy will develop into darkness deep as midnight. To God's people it will be a night of trial, a night of weeping, a night of persecution for the truth's sake. But out of that night of darkness God's light will shine.

He causes "the light to shine out of darkness." 2 Corinthians 4:6. When "the earth was without form, and void; and darkness was upon the face of the deep," "the Spirit of God moved upon the face of the waters. And God said, Let there be light: and there was light." Genesis 1:2, 3. So in the night of spiritual darkness, God's word goes forth, "Let there be light." To His people He says, "Arise, shine; for thy light is come, and the glory of the Lord is risen upon thee." Isaiah 60:1.

"Behold," says the Scripture, "the darkness shall cover the earth, and gross darkness the people: but the Lord shall arise upon thee, and His glory shall be seen upon thee." Verse 2. Christ, the outshining of the Father's glory, came to the world as its light. He came to represent God to men, and of Him it is written that He was anointed "with the Holy Ghost and with power," and "went about doing good." Acts 10:38. In the synagogue at Nazareth He said, "The Spirit of the Lord is upon Me, because He hath anointed Me to preach the gospel to the poor; He hath sent Me to heal the brokenhearted, to preach deliverance to the captives, and recovering of sight to the blind, to set at liberty them that are bruised, to preach the acceptable year of the Lord." Luke 4:18, 19. This was the work He commissioned His disciples to do. "Ye are the light of the world," He said. "Let your light so shine before men, that they may see your good works, and glorify your Father which is in heaven." Matthew 5:14, 16.

This is the work which the prophet Isaiah describes when he says: "Is it not to deal thy bread to the hungry, and that thou bring the poor that are cast out to thy house? when thou seest the naked, that thou cover him; and that thou hide not thyself from thine own flesh? Then shall thy light break forth as the morning, and thine health shall spring forth speedily: and thy righteousness shall go before thee; the glory of the Lord shall be thy rearward." Isaiah 58:7, 8.

Thus in the night of spiritual darkness God's glory is to shine forth through His church in lifting up the bowed down and comforting those that mourn.

All around us are heard the wails of a world's sorrow. On every hand are the needy and distressed. It is ours to aid in relieving and softening life's hardships and misery. The wants of the soul only the love of Christ can satisfy. If Christ is abiding in us, our hearts will be full of divine sympathy. The sealed fountains of earnest, Christlike love will be unsealed.

There are many from whom hope has departed. Bring back the sunshine to them. Many have lost their courage. Speak to them words of cheer. Pray for them. There are those who need the bread of life. Read to them from the word of God. Upon many is a soul sickness which no earthly balm can reach nor physician heal. Pray for these souls. Bring them to Jesus. Tell them that there is a balm in Gilead and a Physician there.

Light is a blessing, a universal blessing, pouring forth its treasures on a world unthankful, unholy, demoralized. So it is with the light of the Sun of Righteousness. The whole earth, wrapped as it is in the darkness of sin and sorrow and pain, is to be lighted with the knowledge of God's love. From no sect, rank, or class of people is the light shining from heaven's throne to be excluded.

The message of hope and mercy is to be carried to the ends of the earth. Whosoever will, may reach forth and take hold of God's strength and make peace with Him, and he shall make peace. No longer are the heathen to be wrapped in midnight darkness. The gloom is to disappear before the bright beams of the Sun of Righteousness.

Christ has made every provision that His church shall be a transformed body, illumined with the Light of the world, possessing the glory of Immanuel. It is His purpose that every Christian shall be surrounded with a spiritual atmosphere of light and peace. He desires that we shall reveal His own joy in our lives.

"Arise, shine; for thy light is come, and the glory of the Lord is risen upon thee." Isaiah 60:1. Christ is coming with power and great glory. He is coming with His own glory and with the glory of the Father. And the holy angels will attend Him on His way. While all the world is plunged in darkness, there will be light in every dwelling of the saints. They will catch the first light of His second appearing. The unsullied light will shine from His splendor, and Christ the Redeemer will be admired by all who have served Him. While the wicked flee, Christ's followers will rejoice in His presence.

Then it is that the redeemed from among men will receive their promised inheritance. Thus God's purpose for Israel will meet with literal fulfillment. That which God purposes, man is powerless to disannul. Even amid the working of evil, God's purposes have been moving steadily forward to their accomplishment. It was thus with the house of Israel throughout the history of the divided monarchy; it is thus with spiritual Israel today.

The seer of Patmos, looking down through the ages to the time of this restoration of Israel in the earth made new, testified:

"I beheld, and lo, a great multitude, which no man could number, of all nations, and kindreds, and people, and tongues, stood before the throne, and before the Lamb, clothed with white robes, and palms in their hands; and cried with a loud voice, saying, Salvation to our God which sitteth upon the throne, and unto the Lamb.

"And all the angels stood round about the throne, and about the elders and the four beasts, and fell before the throne on their faces, and worshiped God, saying, Amen: Blessing, and glory, and wisdom, and thanksgiving, and honor, and power, and might, be unto our God forever and ever."

"And I heard as it were the voice of a great multitude, and as the voice of many waters, and as the voice of mighty thunderings, saying, Alleluia: for the Lord God omnipotent reigneth. Let us be glad and rejoice, and give honor to Him." "He is Lord of lords, and King of kings: and they that are with Him are called, and chosen, and faithful." Revelation 7:9-12; 19:6, 7; 17:14.

Visions of Future Glory

In the darkest days of her long conflict with evil, the church of God has been given revelations of the eternal purpose of Jehovah. His people have been permitted to look beyond the trials of the present to the triumphs of the future, when, the warfare having been accomplished, the redeemed will enter into possession of the promised land. These visions of future glory, scenes pictured by the hand of God, should be dear to His church today, when the controversy of the ages is rapidly closing and the promised blessings are soon to be realized in all their fullness.

Many were the messages of comfort given the church by the prophets of old. "Comfort ye, comfort ye My people" (Isaiah 40:1), was Isaiah's commission from God; and with the commission were given wonderful visions that have been the believers' hope and joy through all the centuries that have followed. Despised of men, persecuted, forsaken, God's children in every age have nevertheless been sustained by His sure promises. By faith they have looked forward to the time when He will fulfill to His church the assurance, "I will make thee an eternal excellency, a joy of many generations." Isaiah 60:15.

Often the church militant is called upon to suffer trial and affliction; for not without severe conflict is the church to triumph. "The bread of adversity," "the water of affliction" (Isaiah 30:20), these are the common lot of all; but none who put their trust in the One mighty to deliver will be utterly overwhelmed. "Thus saith the Lord that created thee, O Jacob, and He that formed thee, O Israel, Fear not: for I have redeemed thee, I have called thee by thy name, thou art Mine. When thou passest through the waters, I will be with thee; and through the rivers, they shall not overflow thee: when thou walkest through the fire, thou shalt not be burned; neither shall the flame kindle upon thee. For I am the Lord thy God, the Holy One of Israel, thy Saviour: I gave Egypt for thy ransom, Ethiopia and Seba for thee. Since thou wast precious in My sight, thou hast been honorable, and I have loved thee: therefore will I give men for thee, and people for thy life." Isaiah 43:1-4.

There is forgiveness with God; there is acceptance full and free through the merits of Jesus, our crucified and risen Lord. Isaiah heard the Lord declaring to His chosen ones: "I, even I, am He that blotteth out thy transgressions for Mine own sake, and will not remember thy sins. Put Me in remembrance: let us plead together: declare thou, that thou mayest be justified." "Thou shalt know that I the Lord am thy Saviour and thy Redeemer, the Mighty One of Jacob." Verses 25, 26; 60:16.

"The rebuke of His people shall He take away," the prophet declared. "They shall call them, The holy people, The redeemed of the Lord." He hath appointed "to give unto them beauty for ashes, the oil of joy for mourning, the garment of praise for the spirit of heaviness; that they might be called trees of righteousness, the planting of the Lord, that He might be glorified."

"Awake, awake; put on thy strength, O Zion;
Put on thy beautiful garments, O Jerusalem, the Holy City:
For henceforth there shall no more come unto thee the uncircumcised and the unclean.
"Shake thyself from the dust;
Arise, and sit down, O Jerusalem:
Loose thyself from the bands of thy neck, O captive daughter of Zion."
"O thou afflicted, tossed with tempest, and not comforted,
Behold, I will lay thy stones with fair colors,
And lay thy foundations with sapphires.
"And I will make thy windows of agates. And thy gates of carbuncles,
And all thy borders of pleasant stones.
"And all thy children shall be taught of the Lord;
And great shall be the peace of thy children.
In righteousness shalt thou be established:
"Thou shalt be far from oppression; for thou shalt not fear:
And from terror; for it shall not come near thee.
Behold, they shall surely gather together, but not by Me:
Whosoever shall gather together against thee shall fall for thy sake. . . .
"No weapon that is formed against thee shall prosper;
And every tongue that shall rise against thee in judgment thou shalt condemn.
This is the heritage of the servants of the Lord,
And their righteousness is of Me, saith the Lord."
Isaiah 25:8; 62:12; 61:3; 52:1, 2; 54:11-17.

Clad in the armor of Christ's righteousness, the church is to enter upon her final conflict. "Fair as the moon, clear as the sun, and terrible as an army with banners" (Song of Solomon 6:10), she is to go forth into all the world, conquering and to conquer.

The darkest hour of the church's struggle with the powers of evil is that which immediately precedes the day of her final deliverance. But none who trust in God need fear; for "when the blast of the terrible ones is as a storm against the wall," God will be to His church "a refuge from the storm." Isaiah 25:4.

In that day only the righteous are promised deliverance. "The sinners in Zion are afraid; fearfulness hath surprised the hypocrites. Who among us shall dwell with the devouring fire? who among us shall dwell with everlasting burnings? He that walketh righteously, and speaketh uprightly; he that despiseth the gain of oppressions, that shaketh his hands from holding of bribes, that stoppeth his ears from hearing of blood, and shutteth his eyes from seeing evil; he shall dwell on high: his place of defense shall be the munitions of rocks: bread shall be given him; his waters shall be sure." Isaiah 33:14-16.

The word of the Lord to His faithful ones is: "Come, My people, enter thou into thy chambers, and shut thy doors about thee: hide thyself as it were for a little moment, until the indignation be overpast. For, behold, the Lord cometh out of His place to punish the inhabitants of the earth for their iniquity." Isaiah 26:20, 21.

In visions of the great judgment day the inspired messengers of Jehovah were given glimpses of the consternation of those unprepared to meet their Lord in peace.

"Behold, the Lord maketh the earth empty, and maketh it waste, and turneth it upside down, and scattereth abroad the inhabitants thereof; . . . because they have transgressed the laws, changed the ordinance, broken the everlasting covenant. Therefore hath the curse devoured the earth, and they that dwell therein are desolate. . . . The mirth of tabrets ceaseth, the noise of them that rejoice endeth, the joy of the harp ceaseth." Isaiah 24:1-8.

"Alas for the day! for the day of the Lord is at hand, and as a destruction from the Almighty shall it come. . . . The seed is rotten under their clods, the garners are laid desolate, the barns are broken down; for the corn is withered. How do the beasts groan! the herds of cattle are perplexed, because they have no pasture; yea, the flocks of sheep are made desolate." "The vine is dried up, and the fig tree languisheth; the pomegranate tree, the palm tree also, and the apple tree, even all the trees of the field, are withered: because joy is withered away from the sons of men." Joel 1:15-18, 12.

"I am pained at my very heart," Jeremiah exclaims as he beholds the desolations wrought during the closing scenes of earth's history. "I cannot hold my peace, because thou hast heard, O my soul, the sound of the trumpet, the alarm of war. Destruction upon destruction is cried; for the whole land is spoiled." Jeremiah 4:19, 20.

"The loftiness of man shall be bowed down," declares Isaiah of the day of God's vengeance, "and the haughtiness of men shall be made low: and the Lord alone shall be exalted in that day. And the idols He shall utterly abolish. . . . In that day a man shall cast his idols of silver, and his idols of gold, which they made each one for himself to worship, to the moles and to the bats; to go into the clefts of the rocks, and into the tops of the ragged rocks, for fear of the Lord, and for the glory of His majesty, when He ariseth to shake terribly the earth." Isaiah 2:17-21.

Of those times of transition, when the pride of man shall be laid low, Jeremiah testifies: "I beheld the earth, and, lo, it was without form, and void; and the heavens, and they had no light. I beheld the mountains, and, lo, they trembled, and all the hills moved lightly. I beheld, and, lo, there was no man, and all the birds of the heavens were fled. I beheld, and, lo, the fruitful place was a wilderness, and all the cities thereof were broken down." "Alas! for that day is great, so that none is like it: it is even the time of Jacob's trouble; but he shall be saved out of it." Jeremiah 4:23-26; 30:7.

The day of wrath to the enemies of God is the day of final deliverance to His church. The prophet declares:

"Strengthen ye the weak hands,
And confirm the feeble knees.
Say to them that are of a fearful heart, Bestrong, fear not:
Behold, your God will come with vengeance,
Even God with a recompense;
He will come and save you."

"He will swallow up death in victory; and the Lord God will wipe away tears from off all faces; and the rebuke of His people shall He take away from off all the earth: for the Lord hath spoken it." Isaiah 35:3, 4; 25:8. And as the prophet beholds the Lord of glory descending from heaven with all the holy angels, to gather the remnant church from among the nations of earth, he hears the waiting ones unite in the exultant cry:

"Lo, this is our God;
We have waited for Him,
And He will save us:
This is the Lord;
We have waited for Him,
We will be glad and rejoice in His salvation."
Isaiah 25:9.

The voice of the Son of God is heard calling forth the sleeping saints, and as the prophet beholds them coming from the prison house of death, he exclaims, "Thy dead men shall live, together with my dead body shall they arise. Awake and sing, ye that dwell in dust: for thy dew is as the dew of herbs, and the earth shall cast out the dead." "Then the eyes of the blind shall be opened,
And the ears of the deaf shall be unstopped.
Then shall the lame man leap as an hart,
And the tongue of the dumb sing."
Isaiah 26:19; 35:5, 6.
In the visions of the prophet, those who have triumphed over sin and the grave are now seen happy in the presence of

their Maker, talking freely with Him as man talked with God in the beginning. "Be ye glad," the Lord bids them, "and rejoice forever in that which I create: for, behold, I create Jerusalem a rejoicing, and her people a joy. And I will rejoice in Jerusalem, and joy in My people: and the voice of weeping shall be no more heard in her, nor the voice of crying." "The inhabitant shall not say, I am sick: the people that dwell therein shall be forgiven their iniquity."

"In the wilderness shall waters break out,
And streams in the desert.
And the parched ground shall become a pool,
And the thirsty land springs of water."
"Instead of the thorn shall come up the fir tree,
And instead of the brier shall come up the myrtle tree."
"And an highway shall be there, and a way,
And it shall be called The way of holiness;
The unclean shall not pass over it;
But it shall be for those:
The wayfaring men, though fools, shall not err therein."
"Speak ye comfortably to Jerusalem, and cry unto her, that her warfare is accomplished, that her iniquity is pardoned: for she hath received of the Lord's hand double for all her sins." Isaiah 65:18, 19; 33:24; 35:6, 7; 55:13; 35:8; 40:2.

As the prophet beholds the redeemed dwelling in the City of God, free from sin and from all marks of the curse, in rapture he exclaims, "Rejoice ye with Jerusalem, and be glad with her, all ye that love her: rejoice for joy with her."

"Violence shall no more be heard in thy land,
Wasting nor destruction within thy borders;
But thou shalt call thy walls Salvation,
And thy gates Praise.
"The sun shall be no more thy light by day;
Neither for brightness shall the moon give light unto thee:
But the Lord shall be unto thee an everlasting light,
And thy God thy glory.
"Thy sun shall no more go down;
Neither shall thy moon withdraw itself:
For the Lord shall be thine everlasting light,
And the days of thy mourning shall be ended.
"Thy people also shall be all righteous:
They shall inherit the land forever,
The branch of My planting,
The work of My hands,
That I may be glorified."
Isaiah 66:10; 60:18-21.

The prophet caught the sound of music there, and song, such music and song as, save in the visions of God, no mortal ear has heard or mind conceived. "The ransomed of the Lord shall return, and come to Zion with songs and everlasting joy upon their heads: they shall obtain joy and gladness, and sorrow and sighing shall flee away." "Joy and gladness shall be found therein, thanksgiving, and the voice of melody." "As well the singers as the players on instruments shall be there." "They shall lift up their voice, they shall sing for the majesty of the Lord." Isaiah 35:10; 51:3; Psalm 87:7; Isaiah 24:14.

In the earth made new, the redeemed will engage in the occupations and pleasures that brought happiness to Adam and Eve in the beginning. The Eden life will be lived, the life in garden and field. "They shall build houses, and inhabit them; and they shall plant vineyards, and eat the fruit of them. They shall not build, and another inhabit; they shall not plant, and another eat: for as the days of a tree are the days of My people, and Mine elect shall long enjoy the work of their hands." Isaiah 65:21, 22.

There every power will be developed, every capability increased. The grandest enterprises will be carried forward, the loftiest aspirations will be reached, the highest ambitions realized. And still there will appear new heights to surmount, new wonders to admire, new truths to comprehend, fresh objects of study to call forth the powers of body and mind and soul.

The prophets to whom these great scenes were revealed longed to understand their full import. They "inquired and searched diligently:. . . searching what, or what manner of time the Spirit of Christ which was in them did signify. . . . Unto whom it was revealed, that not unto themselves, but unto us they did minister the things, which are now reported unto you." 1 Peter 1:10-12.

To us who are standing on the very verge of their fulfillment, of what deep moment, what living interest, are these delineations of the things to come—events for which, since our first parents turned their steps from Eden, God's children have watched and waited, longed and prayed!

Fellow pilgrim, we are still amid the shadows and turmoil of earthly activities; but soon our Saviour is to appear to bring deliverance and rest. Let us by faith behold the blessed hereafter as pictured by the hand of God. He who died for the sins of the world is opening wide the gates of Paradise to all who believe on Him. Soon the battle will have been fought, the victory won. Soon we shall see Him in whom our hopes of eternal life are centered. And in His presence the trials and sufferings of this life will seem as nothingness. The former things "shall not be remembered, nor come into mind." "Cast not away therefore your confidence, which hath great recompense of reward. For ye have need of patience, that, after ye have done the will of God, ye might receive the promise. For yet a little while, and He that shall come will come, and will not tarry." "Israel shall be saved. . . with an everlasting salvation: ye shall not be ashamed nor confounded world without end." Isaiah 65:17; Hebrews 10:35-37; Isaiah 45:17.

Look up, look up, and let your faith continually increase. Let this faith guide you along the narrow path that leads through the gates of the city into the great beyond, the wide, unbounded future of glory that is for the redeemed. "Be patient therefore, brethren, unto the coming of the Lord. Behold, the husbandman waiteth for the precious fruit of the earth, and hath long patience for it, until he receive the early and latter rain. Be ye also patient; stablish your hearts: for the coming of the Lord draweth nigh." James 5:7, 8.

The nations of the saved will know no other law than the law of heaven. All will be a happy, united family, clothed with the garments of praise and thanksgiving. Over the scene the morning stars will sing together, and the sons of God will shout for joy, while God and Christ will unite in proclaiming. "There shall be no more sin, neither shall there be any more death."

"And it shall come to pass, that from one new moon to another, and from one Sabbath to another, shall all flesh come to worship before Me, saith the Lord." "The glory of the Lord shall be revealed, and all flesh shall see it together." "The Lord God will cause righteousness and praise to spring forth before all the nations." "In that day shall the Lord of hosts be for a crown of glory, and for a diadem of beauty, unto the residue of His people."

"The Lord shall comfort Zion: He will comfort all her waste places; and He will make her wilderness like Eden, and her desert like the garden of the Lord." "The glory of Lebanon shall be given unto it, the excellency of Carmel and Sharon." "Thou shalt no more be termed Forsaken; neither shall thy land any more be termed Desolate: but thou shalt be called My Delight, and thy land Beulah. . . . As the bridegroom rejoiceth over the bride, so shall thy God rejoice over thee." Isaiah 66:23; 40:5; 61:11; 28:5; 51:3; 35:2; 62:4, 5, margin.

The Desire of Ages

CONTENTS

"God With Us"

"His name shall be called Immanuel, . . . God with us." "The light of the knowledge of the glory of God" is seen "in the face of Jesus Christ." From the days of eternity the Lord Jesus Christ was one with the Father; He was "the image of God," the image of His greatness and majesty, "the outshining of His glory." It was to manifest this glory that He came to our world. To this sin-darkened earth He came to reveal the light of God's love,—to be "God with us." Therefore it was prophesied of Him, "His name shall be called Immanuel."

By coming to dwell with us, Jesus was to reveal God both to men and to angels. He was the Word of God,—God's thought made audible. In His prayer for His disciples He says, "I have declared unto them Thy name,"—"merciful and gracious, long-suffering, and abundant in goodness and truth,"—"that the love wherewith Thou hast loved Me may be in them, and I in them." But not alone for His earthborn children was this revelation given. Our little world is the lesson book of the universe. God's wonderful purpose of grace, the mystery of redeeming love, is the theme into which "angels desire to look," and it will be their study throughout endless ages. Both the redeemed and the unfallen beings will find in the cross of Christ their science and their song. It will be seen that the glory shining in the face of Jesus is the glory of self-sacrificing love. In the light from Calvary it will be seen that the law of self-renouncing love is the law of life for earth and heaven; that the love which "seeketh not her own" has its source in the heart of God; and that in the meek and lowly One is manifested the character of Him who dwelleth in the light which no man can approach unto.

In the beginning, God was revealed in all the works of creation. It was Christ that spread the heavens, and laid the foundations of the earth. It was His hand that hung the worlds in space, and fashioned the flowers of the field. "His strength setteth fast the mountains." "The sea is His, and He made it." Ps. 65:6; 95:5. It was He that filled the earth with beauty, and the air with song. And upon all things in earth, and air, and sky, He wrote the message of the Father's love.

Now sin has marred God's perfect work, yet that handwriting remains. Even now all created things declare the glory of His excellence. There is nothing, save the selfish heart of man, that lives unto itself. No bird that cleaves the air, no animal that moves upon the ground, but ministers to some other life. There is no leaf of the forest, or lowly blade of grass, but has its ministry. Every tree and shrub and leaf pours forth that element of life without which neither man nor animal could live; and man and animal, in turn, minister to the life of tree and shrub and leaf. The flowers breathe fragrance and unfold their beauty in blessing to the world. The sun sheds its light to gladden a thousand worlds. The ocean, itself the source of all our springs and fountains, receives the streams from every land, but takes to give. The mists ascending from its bosom fall in showers to water the earth, that it may bring forth and bud.

The angels of glory find their joy in giving,—giving love and tireless watchcare to souls that are fallen and unholy. Heavenly beings woo the hearts of men; they bring to this dark world light from the courts above; by gentle and patient ministry they move upon the human spirit, to bring the lost into a fellowship with Christ which is even closer than they themselves can know.

But turning from all lesser representations, we behold God in Jesus. Looking unto Jesus we see that it is the glory of our God to give. "I do nothing of Myself," said Christ; "the living Father hath sent Me, and I live by the Father." "I seek not Mine own glory," but the glory of Him that sent Me. John 8:28; 6:57; 8:50; 7:18. In these words is set forth the great principle which is the law of life for the universe. All things Christ received from God, but He took to give. So in the heavenly courts, in His ministry for all created beings: through the beloved Son, the Father's life flows out to all; through the Son it returns, in praise and joyous service, a tide of love, to the great Source of all. And thus through Christ the circuit of beneficence is complete, representing the character of the great Giver, the law of life.

In heaven itself this law was broken. Sin originated in self-seeking. Lucifer, the covering cherub, desired to be first in heaven. He sought to gain control of heavenly beings, to draw them away from their Creator, and to win their homage to himself. Therefore he misrepresented God, attributing to Him the desire for self-exaltation. With his own evil characteristics he sought to invest the loving Creator. Thus he deceived angels. Thus he deceived men. He led them to doubt the word of God, and to distrust His goodness. Because God is a God of justice and terrible majesty, Satan caused them to look upon Him as severe and unforgiving. Thus he drew men to join him in rebellion against God, and the night of woe settled down upon the world.

The earth was dark through misapprehension of God. That the gloomy shadows might be lightened, that the world might be brought back to God, Satan's deceptive power was to be broken. This could not be done by force. The exercise of force is contrary to the principles of God's government; He desires only the service of love; and love cannot be commanded; it cannot be won by force or authority. Only by love is love awakened. To know God is to love Him; His character must be manifested in contrast to the character of Satan. This work only one Being in all the universe could do. Only He who knew the height and depth of the love of God could make it known. Upon the world's dark night the Sun of Righteousness must rise, "with healing in His wings." Mal. 4:2.

The plan for our redemption was not an afterthought, a plan formulated after the fall of Adam. It was a revelation of "the mystery which hath been kept in silence through times eternal." Rom. 16:25, R. V. It was an unfolding of the principles that from eternal ages have been the foundation of God's throne. From the beginning, God and Christ knew of the apostasy of Satan, and of the fall of man through the deceptive power of the apostate. God did not ordain that sin should exist, but He foresaw its existence, and made provision to meet the terrible emergency. So great was His love for the world, that He covenanted to give His only-begotten Son, "that whosoever believeth in Him should not perish, but have everlasting life." John 3:16.

Lucifer had said, "I will exalt my throne above the stars of God; . . . I will be like the Most High." Isa. 14:13, 14. But Christ, "being in the form of God, counted it not a thing to be grasped to be on an equality with God, but emptied Himself, taking the form of a servant, being made in the likeness of men." Phil. 2:6, 7, R. V., margin.

This was a voluntary sacrifice. Jesus might have remained at the Father's side. He might have retained the glory of heaven, and the homage of the angels. But He chose to give back the scepter into the Father's hands, and to step down from the throne of the universe, that He might bring light to the benighted, and life to the perishing.

Nearly two thousand years ago, a voice of mysterious import was heard in heaven, from the throne of God, "Lo, I come." "Sacrifice and offering Thou wouldest not, but a body hast Thou prepared Me. . . . Lo, I come (in the volume of the Book it is written of Me,) to do Thy will, O God." Heb. 10:5-7. In these words is announced the fulfillment of the purpose that had been hidden from eternal ages. Christ was about to visit our world, and to become incarnate. He says, "A body hast Thou prepared Me." Had He appeared with the glory that was His with the Father before the world was, we could not have endured the light of His presence. That we might behold it and not be destroyed, the manifestation of His glory was shrouded. His divinity was veiled with humanity,—the invisible glory in the visible human form.

This great purpose had been shadowed forth in types and symbols. The burning bush, in which Christ appeared to Moses, revealed God. The symbol chosen for the representation of the Deity was a lowly shrub, that seemingly had no attractions. This enshrined the Infinite. The all-merciful God shrouded His glory in a most humble type, that Moses could look upon it and live. So in the pillar of cloud by day and the pillar of fire by night, God communicated with Israel, revealing to men His will, and imparting to them His grace. God's glory was subdued, and His majesty veiled, that the weak vision of finite men might behold it. So Christ was to come in "the body of our humiliation" (Phil. 3:21, R. V.), "in the likeness of men." In the eyes of the world He possessed no beauty that they should desire Him; yet He was the incarnate God, the light of heaven and earth. His glory was veiled, His greatness and majesty were hidden, that He might draw near to sorrowful, tempted men.

God commanded Moses for Israel, "Let them make Me a sanctuary; that I may dwell among them" (Ex. 25:8), and He abode in the sanctuary, in the midst of His people. Through all their weary wandering in the desert, the symbol of His presence was with them. So Christ set up His tabernacle in the midst of our human encampment. He pitched His tent by the side of the tents of men, that He might dwell among us, and make us familiar with His divine character and life. "The Word became flesh, and tabernacled among us (and we beheld His glory, glory as of the Only Begotten from the Father), full of grace and truth." John 1:14, R. V., margin.

Since Jesus came to dwell with us, we know that God is acquainted with our trials, and sympathizes with our griefs. Every son and daughter of Adam may understand that our Creator is the friend of sinners. For in every doctrine of grace, every promise of joy, every deed of love, every divine attraction presented in the Saviour's life on earth, we see "God with us."

Satan represents God's law of love as a law of selfishness. He declares that it is impossible for us to obey its precepts. The fall of our first parents, with all the woe that has resulted, he charges upon the Creator, leading men to look upon God as the author of sin, and suffering, and death. Jesus was to unveil this deception. As one of us He was to give an example of obedience. For this He took upon Himself our nature, and passed through our experiences. "In all things it behooved Him to be made like unto His brethren." Heb. 2:17. If we had to bear anything which Jesus did not endure, then upon this point Satan would represent the power of God as insufficient for us. Therefore Jesus was "in all points tempted like as we are." Heb. 4:15. He endured every trial to which we are subject. And He exercised in His own behalf no power that is not freely offered to us. As man, He met temptation, and overcame in the strength given Him from God. He says, "I delight to do Thy will, O My God: yea, Thy law is within My heart." Ps. 40:8. As He went about doing good, and healing all who were afflicted by Satan, He made plain to men the character of God's law and the nature of His service. His life testifies that it is possible for us also to obey the law of God.

By His humanity, Christ touched humanity; by His divinity, He lays hold upon the throne of God. As the Son of man, He gave us an example of obedience; as the Son of God, He gives us power to obey. It was Christ who from the bush on Mount Horeb spoke to Moses saying, "I Am That I Am. . . . Thus shalt thou say unto the children of Israel, I Am hath sent me unto you." Ex. 3:14. This was the pledge of Israel's deliverance. So when He came "in the likeness of men," He declared Himself the I Am. The Child of Bethlehem, the meek and lowly Saviour, is God "manifest in the flesh." 1 Tim. 3:16. And to us He says: "I Am the Good Shepherd." "I Am the living Bread." "I Am the Way, the Truth, and the Life." "All power is given unto Me in heaven and in earth." John 10:11; 6:51; 14:6; Matt. 28:18. I Am the assurance of every promise. I Am; be not afraid. "God with us" is the surety of our deliverance from sin, the assurance of our power to obey the law of heaven.

In stooping to take upon Himself humanity, Christ revealed a character the opposite of the character of Satan. But He stepped still lower in the path of humiliation. "Being found in fashion as a man, He humbled Himself, and became obedient unto death, even the death of the cross." Phil. 2:8. As the high priest laid aside his gorgeous pontifical robes, and officiated in the white linen dress of the common priest, so Christ took the form of a servant, and offered sacrifice, Himself the priest, Himself the victim. "He was wounded for our transgressions, He was bruised for our iniquities: the chastisement of our peace was upon Him." Isa. 53:5.

Christ was treated as we deserve, that we might be treated as He deserves. He was condemned for our sins, in which He had no share, that we might be justified by His righteousness, in which we had no share. He suffered the death which was ours, that we might receive the life which was His. "With His stripes we are healed."

By His life and His death, Christ has achieved even more than recovery from the ruin wrought through sin. It was Satan's purpose to bring about an eternal separation between God and man; but in Christ we become more closely united to God than if we had never fallen. In taking our nature, the Saviour has bound Himself to humanity by a tie that is never to be broken. Through the eternal ages He is linked with us. "God so loved the world, that He gave His only-begotten Son." John 3:16. He gave Him not only to bear our sins, and to die as our sacrifice; He gave Him to the fallen race. To assure us of His immutable counsel of peace, God gave His only-begotten Son to become one of the human family, forever to retain His human nature. This is the pledge that God will fulfill His word. "Unto us a child is born, unto us a son is given: and the government shall be upon His shoulder." God has adopted human nature in the person of His Son, and has carried the same into the highest heaven. It is the "Son of man" who shares the throne of the universe. It is the "Son of man" whose name shall be called, "Wonderful, Counselor, The mighty God, The everlasting Father, The Prince of Peace." Isa. 9:6. The I Am is the Daysman between God and humanity, laying His hand upon both. He who is "holy, harmless, undefiled, separate from sinners," is not ashamed to call us brethren. Heb. 7:26; 2:11. In Christ the family of earth and the family of heaven are bound together. Christ glorified is our brother. Heaven is enshrined in humanity, and humanity is enfolded in the bosom of Infinite Love.

Of His people God says, "They shall be as the stones of a crown, lifted up as an ensign upon His land. For how great is His goodness, and how great is His beauty!" Zech. 9:16, 17. The exaltation of the redeemed will be an eternal testimony to God's mercy. "In the ages to come," He will "show the exceeding riches of His grace in His kindness toward us through Christ Jesus." "To the intent that . . . unto the principalities and the powers in the heavenly places might be made known . . . the manifold wisdom of God, according to the eternal purpose which He purposed in Christ Jesus our Lord." Eph. 2:7; 3:10, 11, R. V.

Through Christ's redeeming work the government of God stands justified. The Omnipotent One is made known as the God of love. Satan's charges are refuted, and his character unveiled. Rebellion can never again arise. Sin can never again enter the universe. Through eternal ages all are secure from apostasy. By love's self-sacrifice, the inhabitants of earth and heaven are bound to their Creator in bonds of indissoluble union.

The work of redemption will be complete. In the place where sin abounded, God's grace much more abounds. The earth itself, the very field that Satan claims as his, is to be not only ransomed but exalted. Our little world, under the curse of sin the one dark blot in His glorious creation, will be honored above all other worlds in the universe of God. Here, where the Son of God tabernacled in humanity; where the King of glory lived and suffered and died,—here, when He shall make all things new, the tabernacle of God shall be with men, "and He will dwell with them, and they shall be His people, and God Himself shall be with them, and be their God." And through endless ages as the redeemed walk in the light of the Lord, they will praise Him for His unspeakable Gift,—

Immanuel, "God with us."

The Chosen People

For more than a thousand years the Jewish people had awaited the Saviour's coming. Upon this event they had rested their brightest hopes. In song and prophecy, in temple rite and household prayer, they had enshrined His name. And yet at His coming they knew Him not. The Beloved of heaven was to them "as a root out of a dry ground;" He had "no form nor comeliness;" and they saw in Him no beauty that they should desire Him. "He came unto His own, and His own received Him not." Isa. 53:2; John 1:11.

Yet God had chosen Israel. He had called them to preserve among men the knowledge of His law, and of the symbols and prophecies that pointed to the Saviour. He desired them to be as wells of salvation to the world. What Abraham was in the land of his sojourn, what Joseph was in Egypt, and Daniel in the courts of Babylon, the Hebrew people were to be among the nations. They were to reveal God to men.

In the call of Abraham the Lord had said, "I will bless thee; . . . and thou shalt be a blessing: . . . and in thee shall all families of the earth be blessed." Gen. 12:2, 3. The same teaching was repeated through the prophets. Even after Israel had been wasted by war and captivity, the promise was theirs, "The remnant of Jacob shall be in the midst of many people as a dew from the Lord, as the showers upon the grass, that tarrieth not for man, nor waiteth for the sons of men." Micah 5:7. Concerning the temple at Jerusalem, the Lord declared through Isaiah, "Mine house shall be called an house of prayer for all peoples." Isa. 56:7, R. V.

But the Israelites fixed their hopes upon worldly greatness. From the time of their entrance to the land of Canaan, they departed from the commandments of God, and followed the ways of the heathen. It was in vain that God sent them warning by His prophets. In vain they suffered the chastisement of heathen oppression. Every reformation was followed by deeper apostasy.

Had Israel been true to God, He could have accomplished His purpose through their honor and exaltation. If they had walked in the ways of obedience, He would have made them "high above all nations which He hath made, in praise, and in name, and in honor." "All people of the earth," said

Moses, "shall see that thou art called by the name of the Lord; and they shall be afraid of thee." "The nations which shall hear all these statutes" shall say, "Surely this great nation is a wise and understanding people." Deut. 26:19; 28:10; 4:6. But because of their unfaithfulness, God's purpose could be wrought out only through continued adversity and humiliation.

They were brought into subjection to Babylon, and scattered through the lands of the heathen. In affliction many renewed their faithfulness to His covenant. While they hung their harps upon the willows, and mourned for the holy temple that was laid waste, the light of truth shone out through them, and a knowledge of God was spread among the nations. The heathen systems of sacrifice were a perversion of the system that God had appointed; and many a sincere observer of heathen rites learned from the Hebrews the meaning of the service divinely ordained, and in faith grasped the promise of a Redeemer.

Many of the exiles suffered persecution. Not a few lost their lives because of their refusal to disregard the Sabbath and to observe the heathen festivals. As idolaters were roused to crush out the truth, the Lord brought His servants face to face with kings and rulers, that they and their people might receive the light. Time after time the greatest monarchs were led to proclaim the supremacy of the God whom their Hebrew captives worshiped.

By the Babylonish captivity the Israelites were effectually cured of the worship of graven images. During the centuries that followed, they suffered from the oppression of heathen foes, until the conviction became fixed that their prosperity depended upon their obedience to the law of God. But with too many of the people obedience was not prompted by love. The motive was selfish. They rendered outward service to God as the means of attaining to national greatness. They did not become the light of the world, but shut themselves away from the world in order to escape temptation to idolatry. In the instruction given through Moses, God had placed restrictions upon their association with idolaters; but this teaching had been misinterpreted. It was intended to prevent them from conforming to the practices of the heathen. But it was used to build up a wall of separation between Israel and all other nations. The Jews looked upon Jerusalem as their heaven, and they were actually jealous lest the Lord should show mercy to the Gentiles.

After the return from Babylon, much attention was given to religious instruction. All over the country, synagogues were erected, where the law was expounded by the priests and scribes. And schools were established, which, together with the arts and sciences, professed to teach the principles of righteousness. But these agencies became corrupted. During the captivity, many of the people had received heathen ideas and customs, and these were brought into their religious service. In many things they conformed to the practices of idolaters.

As they departed from God, the Jews in a great degree lost sight of the teaching of the ritual service. That service had been instituted by Christ Himself. In every part it was a symbol of Him; and it had been full of vitality and spiritual beauty. But the Jews lost the spiritual life from their ceremonies, and clung to the dead forms. They trusted to the sacrifices and ordinances themselves, instead of resting upon Him to whom they pointed. In order to supply the place of that which they had lost, the priests and rabbis multiplied requirements of their own; and the more rigid they grew, the less of the love of God was manifested. They measured their holiness by the multitude of their ceremonies, while their hearts were filled with pride and hypocrisy.

With all their minute and burdensome injunctions, it was an impossibility to keep the law. Those who desired to serve God, and who tried to observe the rabbinical precepts, toiled under a heavy burden. They could find no rest from the accusings of a troubled conscience. Thus Satan worked to discourage the people, to lower their conception of the character of God, and to bring the faith of Israel into contempt. He hoped to establish the claim put forth when he rebelled in heaven,—that the requirements of God were unjust, and could not be obeyed. Even Israel, he declared, did not keep the law.

While the Jews desired the advent of the Messiah, they had no true conception of His mission. They did not seek redemption from sin, but deliverance from the Romans. They looked for the Messiah to come as a conqueror, to break the oppressor's power, and exalt Israel to universal dominion. Thus the way was prepared for them to reject the Saviour.

At the time of the birth of Christ the nation was chafing under the rule of her foreign masters, and racked with internal strife. The Jews had been permitted to maintain the form of a separate government; but nothing could disguise the fact that they were under the Roman yoke, or reconcile them to the restriction of their power. The Romans claimed the right of appointing and removing the high priest, and the office was often secured by fraud, bribery, and even murder. Thus the priesthood became more and more corrupt. Yet the priests still possessed great power, and they employed it for selfish and mercenary ends. The people were subjected to their merciless demands, and were also heavily taxed by the Romans. This state of affairs caused widespread discontent. Popular outbreaks were frequent. Greed and violence, distrust and spiritual apathy, were eating out the very heart of the nation.

Hatred of the Romans, and national and spiritual pride, led the Jews still to adhere rigorously to their forms of worship. The priests tried to maintain a reputation for sanctity by scrupulous attention to the ceremonies of religion. The people, in their darkness and oppression, and the rulers, thirsting for power, longed for the coming of One who would vanquish their enemies and restore the kingdom to Israel. They had studied the prophecies, but without spiritual insight. Thus they overlooked those scriptures that point to the humiliation of Christ's first advent, and misapplied those that speak of the glory of His second coming. Pride obscured their vision. They interpreted prophecy in accordance with their selfish desires.

"The Fullness of the Time"

"When the fullness of the time was come, God sent forth His Son, . . . to redeem them that were under the law, that we might receive the adoption of sons." Gal. 4:4, 5.

The Saviour's coming was foretold in Eden. When Adam and Eve first heard the promise, they looked for its speedy fulfillment. They joyfully welcomed their first-born son, hoping that he might be the Deliverer. But the fulfillment of the promise tarried. Those who first received it died without the sight. From the days of Enoch the promise was repeated through patriarchs and prophets, keeping alive the hope of His appearing, and yet He came not. The prophecy of Daniel revealed the time of His advent, but not all rightly interpreted the message. Century after century passed away; the voices of the prophets ceased. The hand of the oppressor was heavy upon Israel, and many were ready to exclaim, "The days are prolonged, and every vision faileth." Ezek. 12:22.

But like the stars in the vast circuit of their appointed path, God's purposes know no haste and no delay. Through the symbols of the great darkness and the smoking furnace, God had revealed to Abraham the bondage of Israel in Egypt, and had declared that the time of their sojourning should be four hundred years. "Afterward," He said, "shall they come out with great substance." Gen. 15:14. Against that word, all the power of Pharaoh's proud empire battled in vain. On "the self-same day" appointed in the divine promise, "it came to pass, that all the hosts of the Lord went out from the land of Egypt." Ex. 12:41. So in heaven's council the hour for the coming of Christ had been determined. When the great clock of time pointed to that hour, Jesus was born in Bethlehem.

"When the fullness of the time was come, God sent forth His Son." Providence had directed the movements of nations, and the tide of human impulse and influence, until the world was ripe for the coming of the Deliverer. The nations were united under one government. One language was widely spoken, and was everywhere recognized as the language of literature. From all lands the Jews of the dispersion gathered to Jerusalem to the annual feasts. As these returned to the places of their sojourn, they could spread throughout the world the tidings of the Messiah's coming.

At this time the systems of heathenism were losing their hold upon the people. Men were weary of pageant and fable. They longed for a religion that could satisfy the heart. While the light of truth seemed to have departed from among men, there were souls who were looking for light, and who were filled with perplexity and sorrow. They were thirsting for a knowledge of the living God, for some assurance of a life beyond the grave.

As the Jews had departed from God, faith had grown dim, and hope had well-nigh ceased to illuminate the future. The words of the prophets were uncomprehended. To the masses of the people, death was a dread mystery; beyond was uncertainty and gloom. It was not alone the wailing of the mothers of Bethlehem, but the cry from the great heart of humanity, that was borne to the prophet across the centuries,—the voice heard in Ramah, "lamentation, and weeping, and great mourning, Rachel weeping for her children, and would not be comforted, because they are not." Matt. 2:18. In "the region and shadow of death," men sat unsolaced. With longing eyes they looked for the coming of the Deliverer, when the darkness should be dispelled, and the mystery of the future should be made plain.

Outside of the Jewish nation there were men who foretold the appearance of a divine instructor. These men were seeking for truth, and to them the Spirit of Inspiration was imparted. One after another, like stars in the darkened heavens, such teachers had arisen. Their words of prophecy had kindled hope in the hearts of thousands of the Gentile world.

For hundreds of years the Scriptures had been translated into the Greek language, then widely spoken throughout the Roman Empire. The Jews were scattered everywhere, and their expectation of the Messiah's coming was to some extent shared by the Gentiles. Among those whom the Jews styled heathen were men who had a better understanding of the Scripture prophecies concerning the Messiah than had the teachers in Israel. There were some who hoped for His coming as a deliverer from sin. Philosophers endeavored to study into the mystery of the Hebrew economy. But the bigotry of the Jews hindered the spread of the light. Intent on maintaining the separation between themselves and other nations, they were unwilling to impart the knowledge they still possessed concerning the symbolic service. The true Interpreter must come. The One whom all these types prefigured must explain their significance.

Through nature, through types and symbols, through patriarchs and prophets, God had spoken to the world. Lessons must be given to humanity in the language of humanity. The Messenger of the covenant must speak. His voice must be heard in His own temple. Christ must come to utter words which should be clearly and definitely understood. He, the author of truth, must separate truth from the chaff of man's utterance, which had made it of no effect. The principles of God's government and the plan of redemption must be clearly defined. The lessons of the Old Testament must be fully set before men.

Among the Jews there were yet steadfast souls, descendants of that holy line through whom a knowledge of God had been preserved. These still looked for the hope of the promise made unto the fathers. They strengthened their faith by dwelling upon the assurance given through Moses, "A Prophet shall the Lord your God raise up unto you of your brethren, like unto me; Him shall ye hear in all things whatsoever He shall say unto you." Acts 3:22. Again, they read how the Lord would anoint One "to preach good tidings unto the meek," "to bind up the brokenhearted, to proclaim liberty to the captives," and to declare the "acceptable year of the Lord."

Isa. 61:1, 2. They read how He would "set judgment in the earth," how the isles should "wait for His law," how the Gentiles should come to His light, and kings to the brightness of His rising. Isa. 42:4; 60:3.

The dying words of Jacob filled them with hope: "The scepter shall not depart from Judah, nor a lawgiver from between his feet, until Shiloh come." Gen. 49:10. The waning power of Israel testified that the Messiah's coming was at hand. The prophecy of Daniel pictured the glory of His reign over an empire which should succeed all earthly kingdoms; and, said the prophet, "It shall stand forever." Dan. 2:44. While few understood the nature of Christ's mission, there was a widespread expectation of a mighty prince who should establish his kingdom in Israel, and who should come as a deliverer to the nations.

The fullness of the time had come. Humanity, becoming more degraded through ages of transgression, called for the coming of the Redeemer. Satan had been working to make the gulf deep and impassable between earth and heaven. By his falsehoods he had emboldened men in sin. It was his purpose to wear out the forbearance of God, and to extinguish His love for man, so that He would abandon the world to satanic jurisdiction.

Satan was seeking to shut out from men a knowledge of God, to turn their attention from the temple of God, and to establish his own kingdom. His strife for supremacy had seemed to be almost wholly successful. It is true that in every generation God had His agencies. Even among the heathen there were men through whom Christ was working to uplift the people from their sin and degradation. But these men were despised and hated. Many of them suffered a violent death. The dark shadow that Satan had cast over the world grew deeper and deeper.

Through heathenism, Satan had for ages turned men away from God; but he won his great triumph in perverting the faith of Israel. By contemplating and worshiping their own conceptions, the heathen had lost a knowledge of God, and had become more and more corrupt. So it was with Israel. The principle that man can save himself by his own works lay at the foundation of every heathen religion; it had now become the principle of the Jewish religion. Satan had implanted this principle. Wherever it is held, men have no barrier against sin.

The message of salvation is communicated to men through human agencies. But the Jews had sought to make a monopoly of the truth which is eternal life. They had hoarded the living manna, and it had turned to corruption. The religion which they tried to shut up to themselves became an offense. They robbed God of His glory, and defrauded the world by a counterfeit of the gospel. They had refused to surrender themselves to God for the salvation of the world, and they became agents of Satan for its destruction.

The people whom God had called to be the pillar and ground of the truth had become representatives of Satan. They were doing the work that he desired them to do, taking a course to misrepresent the character of God, and cause the world to look upon Him as a tyrant. The very priests who ministered in the temple had lost sight of the significance of the service they performed. They had ceased to look beyond the symbol to the thing signified. In presenting the sacrificial offerings they were as actors in a play. The ordinances which God Himself had appointed were made the means of blinding the mind and hardening the heart. God could do no more for man through these channels. The whole system must be swept away.

The deception of sin had reached its height. All the agencies for depraving the souls of men had been put in operation. The Son of God, looking upon the world, beheld suffering and misery. With pity He saw how men had become victims of satanic cruelty. He looked with compassion upon those who were being corrupted, murdered, and lost. They had chosen a ruler who chained them to his car as captives. Bewildered and deceived, they were moving on in gloomy procession toward eternal ruin,—to death in which is no hope of life, toward night to which comes no morning. Satanic agencies were incorporated with men. The bodies of human beings, made for the dwelling place of God, had become the habitation of demons. The senses, the nerves, the passions, the organs of men, were worked by supernatural agencies in the indulgence of the vilest lust. The very stamp of demons was impressed upon the countenances of men. Human faces reflected the expression of the legions of evil with which they were possessed. Such was the prospect upon which the world's Redeemer looked. What a spectacle for Infinite Purity to behold!

Sin had become a science, and vice was consecrated as a part of religion. Rebellion had struck its roots deep into the heart, and the hostility of man was most violent against heaven. It was demonstrated before the universe that, apart from God, humanity could not be uplifted. A new element of life and power must be imparted by Him who made the world.

With intense interest the unfallen worlds had watched to see Jehovah arise, and sweep away the inhabitants of the earth. And if God should do this, Satan was ready to carry out his plan for securing to himself the allegiance of heavenly beings. He had declared that the principles of God's government make forgiveness impossible. Had the world been destroyed, he would have claimed that his accusations were proved true. He was ready to cast blame upon God, and to spread his rebellion to the worlds above. But instead of destroying the world, God sent His Son to save it. Though corruption and defiance might be seen in every part of the alien province, a way for its recovery was provided. At the very crisis, when Satan seemed about to triumph, the Son of God came with the embassage of divine grace. Through every age, through every hour, the love of God had been exercised toward the fallen race. Notwithstanding the perversity of men, the signals of mercy had been continually exhibited. And when the fullness of the time had come, the Deity was glorified by pouring upon the world a flood of healing grace that was never to be obstructed or withdrawn till the plan of salvation should be fulfilled.

Satan was exulting that he had succeeded in debasing the image of God in humanity. Then Jesus came to restore in man the image of his Maker. None but Christ can fashion anew the character that has been ruined by sin. He came to expel the demons that had controlled the will. He came to lift us up from the dust, to reshape the marred character after the pattern of His divine character, and to make it beautiful with His own glory.

Unto You a Saviour

The King of glory stooped low to take humanity. Rude and forbidding were His earthly surroundings. His glory was veiled, that the majesty of His outward form might not become an object of attraction. He shunned all outward display. Riches, worldly honor, and human greatness can never save a soul from death; Jesus purposed that no attraction of an earthly nature should call men to His side. Only the beauty of heavenly truth must draw those who would follow Him. The character of the Messiah had long been foretold in prophecy, and He desired men to accept Him upon the testimony of the word of God.

The angels had wondered at the glorious plan of redemption. They watched to see how the people of God would receive His Son, clothed in the garb of humanity. Angels came to the land of the chosen people. Other nations were dealing in fables and worshiping false gods. To the land where the glory of God had been revealed, and the light of prophecy had shone, the angels came. They came unseen to Jerusalem, to the appointed expositors of the Sacred Oracles, and the ministers of God's house. Already to Zacharias the priest, as he ministered before the altar, the nearness of Christ's coming had been announced. Already the forerunner was born, his mission attested by miracle and prophecy. The tidings of his birth and the wonderful significance of his mission had been spread abroad. Yet Jerusalem was not preparing to welcome her Redeemer.

With amazement the heavenly messengers beheld the indifference of that people whom God had called to communicate to the world the light of sacred truth. The Jewish nation had been preserved as a witness that Christ was to be born of the seed of Abraham and of David's line; yet they knew not that His coming was now at hand. In the temple the morning and the evening sacrifice daily pointed to the Lamb of God; yet even here was no preparation to receive Him. The priests and teachers of the nation knew not that the greatest event of the ages was about to take place. They rehearsed their meaningless prayers, and performed the rites of worship to be seen by men, but in their strife for riches and worldly honor they were not prepared for the revelation of the Messiah. The same indifference pervaded the land of Israel. Hearts selfish and world-engrossed were untouched by the joy that thrilled all heaven. Only a few were longing to behold the Unseen. To these heaven's embassy was sent.

Angels attend Joseph and Mary as they journey from their home in Nazareth to the city of David. The decree of imperial Rome for the enrollment of the peoples of her vast dominion has extended to the dwellers among the hills of Galilee. As in old time Cyrus was called to the throne of the world's empire that he might set free the captives of the Lord, so Caesar Augustus is made the agent for the fulfillment of God's purpose in bringing the mother of Jesus to Bethlehem. She is of the lineage of David, and the Son of David must be born in David's city. Out of Bethlehem, said the prophet, "shall He come forth . . . that is to be ruler in Israel; whose goings forth have been from of old, from the days of eternity." Micah 5:2, margin. But in the city of their royal line, Joseph and Mary are unrecognized and unhonored. Weary and homeless, they traverse the entire length of the narrow street, from the gate of the city to the eastern extremity of the town, vainly seeking a resting place for the night. There is no room for them at the crowded inn. In a rude building where the beasts are sheltered, they at last find refuge, and here the Redeemer of the world is born.

Men know it not, but the tidings fill heaven with rejoicing. With a deeper and more tender interest the holy beings from the world of light are drawn to the earth. The whole world is brighter for His presence. Above the hills of Bethlehem are gathered an innumerable throng of angels. They wait the signal to declare the glad news to the world. Had the leaders in Israel been true to their trust, they might have shared the joy of heralding the birth of Jesus. But now they are passed by.

God declares, "I will pour water upon him that is thirsty, and floods upon the dry ground." "Unto the upright there ariseth light in the darkness." Isa. 44:3; Ps. 112:4. To those who are seeking for light, and who accept it with gladness, the bright rays from the throne of God will shine.

In the fields where the boy David had led his flock, shepherds were still keeping watch by night. Through the silent hours they talked together of the promised Saviour, and prayed for the coming of the King to David's throne. "And, lo, the angel of the Lord came upon them, and the glory of the Lord shone round about them: and they were sore afraid. And the angel said unto them, Fear not: for, behold, I bring you good tidings of great joy, which shall be to all people. For unto you is born this day in the city of David a Saviour, which is Christ the Lord."

At these words, visions of glory fill the minds of the listening shepherds. The Deliverer has come to Israel! Power, exaltation, triumph, are associated with His coming. But the angel must prepare them to recognize their Saviour in poverty and humiliation. "This shall be a sign unto you," he says; "Ye shall find the babe wrapped in swaddling clothes, lying in a manger."

The heavenly messenger had quieted their fears. He had told them how to find Jesus. With tender regard for their human weakness, he had given them time to become accustomed to the divine radiance. Then the joy and glory could no longer be hidden. The whole plain was lighted up with the bright shining of the hosts of God. Earth was hushed, and heaven stooped to listen to the song,—

"Glory to God in the highest,
And on earth peace, good will toward men."

Oh that today the human family could recognize that song! The declaration then made, the note then struck, will swell to the close of time, and resound to the ends of the earth. When the Sun of Righteousness shall arise, with healing in His wings, that song will be re-echoed by the voice of a great multitude, as the voice of many waters, saying, "Alleluia: for the Lord God omnipotent reigneth." Rev. 19:6.

As the angels disappeared, the light faded away, and the shadows of night once more fell on the hills of Bethlehem. But the brightest picture ever beheld by human eyes remained in the memory of the shepherds. "And it came to pass, as the angels were gone away from them into heaven, the shepherds said one to another, Let us now go even unto Bethlehem, and see this thing which is come to pass, which the Lord hath made known unto us. And they came with haste, and found Mary, and Joseph, and the babe lying in a manger."

Departing with great joy, they made known the things they had seen and heard. "And all they that heard it wondered at those things which were told them by the shepherds. But Mary kept all these things, and pondered them in her heart. And the shepherds returned, glorifying and praising God."

Heaven and earth are no wider apart today than when shepherds listened to the angels' song. Humanity is still as much the object of heaven's solicitude as when common men of common occupations met angels at noonday, and talked with the heavenly messengers in the vineyards and the fields. To us in the common walks of life, heaven may be very near. Angels from the courts above will attend the steps of those who come and go at God's command.

The story of Bethlehem is an exhaustless theme. In it is hidden "the depth of the riches both of the wisdom and knowledge of God." Rom. 11:33. We marvel at the Saviour's sacrifice in exchanging the throne of heaven for the manger, and the companionship of adoring angels for the beasts of the stall. Human pride and self-sufficiency stand rebuked in His presence. Yet this was but the beginning of His wonderful condescension. It would have been an almost infinite humiliation for the Son of God to take man's nature, even when Adam stood in his innocence in Eden. But Jesus accepted humanity when the race had been weakened by four thousand years of sin. Like every child of Adam He accepted the results of the working of the great law of heredity. What these results were is shown in the history of His earthly ancestors. He came with such a heredity to share our sorrows and temptations, and to give us the example of a sinless life.

Satan in heaven had hated Christ for His position in the courts of God. He hated Him the more when he himself was dethroned. He hated Him who pledged Himself to redeem a race of sinners. Yet into the world where Satan claimed dominion God permitted His Son to come, a helpless babe, subject to the weakness of humanity. He permitted Him to meet life's peril in common with every human soul, to fight the battle as every child of humanity must fight it, at the risk of failure and eternal loss.

The heart of the human father yearns over his son. He looks into the face of his little child, and trembles at the thought of life's peril. He longs to shield his dear one from Satan's power, to hold him back from temptation and conflict. To meet a bitterer conflict and a more fearful risk, God gave His only-begotten Son, that the path of life might be made sure for our little ones. "Herein is love." Wonder, O heavens! and be astonished, O earth!

The Dedication

About forty days after the birth of Christ, Joseph and Mary took Him to Jerusalem, to present Him to the Lord, and to offer sacrifice. This was according to the Jewish law, and as man's substitute Christ must conform to the law in every particular. He had already been subjected to the rite of circumcision, as a pledge of His obedience to the law.

As an offering for the mother, the law required a lamb of the first year for a burnt offering, and a young pigeon or a turtledove for a sin offering. But the law provided that if the parents were too poor to bring a lamb, a pair of turtledoves or two young pigeons, one for a burnt offering, the other for a sin offering, might be accepted.

The offerings presented to the Lord were to be without blemish. These offerings represented Christ, and from this it is evident that Jesus Himself was free from physical deformity. He was the "lamb without blemish and without spot." 1 Peter 1:19. His physical structure was not marred by any defect; His body was strong and healthy. And throughout His lifetime He lived in conformity to nature's laws. Physically as well as spiritually, He was an example of what God designed all humanity to be through obedience to His laws.

The dedication of the first-born had its origin in the earliest times. God had promised to give the First-born of heaven to save the sinner. This gift was to be acknowledged in every household by the consecration of the first-born son. He was to be devoted to the priesthood, as a representative of Christ among men.

In the deliverance of Israel from Egypt, the dedication of the first-born was again commanded. While the children of Israel were in bondage to the Egyptians, the Lord directed Moses to go to Pharaoh, king of Egypt, and say, "Thus saith the Lord, Israel is My son, even My first-born: and I say unto thee, Let My son go, that he may serve Me: and if thou refuse to let him go, behold, I will slay thy son, even thy first-born." Ex. 4:22, 23.

Moses delivered his message; but the proud king's answer was, "Who is the Lord, that I should obey His voice to let Israel go? I know not the Lord, neither will I let Israel go." Ex.

5:2. The Lord worked for His people by signs and wonders, sending terrible judgments upon Pharaoh. At length the destroying angel was bidden to slay the first-born of man and beast among the Egyptians. That the Israelites might be spared, they were directed to place upon their doorposts the blood of a slain lamb. Every house was to be marked, that when the angel came on his mission of death, he might pass over the homes of the Israelites.

After sending this judgment upon Egypt, the Lord said to Moses, "Sanctify unto Me all the first-born, . . . both of man and of beast: it is Mine;" "for on the day that I smote all the first-born in the land of Egypt I hallowed unto Me all the first-born in Israel, both man and beast: Mine shall they be: I am the Lord." Ex. 13:2; Num. 3:13. After the tabernacle service was established, the Lord chose the tribe of Levi in the place of the first-born of all Israel to minister in the sanctuary. But the first-born were still to be regarded as the Lord's, and were to be bought back by a ransom.

Thus the law for the presentation of the first-born was made particularly significant. While it was a memorial of the Lord's wonderful deliverance of the children of Israel, it prefigured a greater deliverance, to be wrought out by the only-begotten Son of God. As the blood sprinkled on the doorposts had saved the first-born of Israel, so the blood of Christ has power to save the world.

What meaning then was attached to Christ's presentation! But the priest did not see through the veil; he did not read the mystery beyond. The presentation of infants was a common scene. Day after day the priest received the redemption money as the babes were presented to the Lord. Day after day he went through the routine of his work, giving little heed to the parents or children, unless he saw some indication of the wealth or high rank of the parents. Joseph and Mary were poor; and when they came with their child, the priests saw only a man and woman dressed as Galileans, and in the humblest garments. There was nothing in their appearance to attract attention, and they presented only the offering made by the poorer classes.

The priest went through the ceremony of his official work. He took the child in his arms, and held it up before the altar. After handing it back to its mother, he inscribed the name "Jesus" on the roll of the first-born. Little did he think, as the babe lay in his arms, that it was the Majesty of heaven, the King of glory. The priest did not think that this babe was the One of whom Moses had written, "A Prophet shall the Lord your God raise up unto you of your brethren, like unto me; Him shall ye hear in all things whatsoever He shall say unto you." Acts 3:22. He did not think that this babe was He whose glory Moses had asked to see. But One greater than Moses lay in the priest's arms; and when he enrolled the child's name, he was enrolling the name of One who was the foundation of the whole Jewish economy. That name was to be its death warrant; for the system of sacrifices and offerings was waxing old; the type had almost reached its antitype, the shadow its substance.

The Shekinah had departed from the sanctuary, but in the Child of Bethlehem was veiled the glory before which angels bow. This unconscious babe was the promised seed, to whom the first altar at the gate of Eden pointed. This was Shiloh, the peace giver. It was He who declared Himself to Moses as the I am. It was He who in the pillar of cloud and of fire had been the guide of Israel. This was He whom seers had long foretold. He was the Desire of all nations, the Root and the Offspring of David, and the Bright and Morning Star. The name of that helpless little babe, inscribed in the roll of Israel, declaring Him our brother, was the hope of fallen humanity. The child for whom the redemption money had been paid was He who was to pay the ransom for the sins of the whole world. He was the true "high priest over the house of God," the head of "an unchangeable priesthood," the intercessor at "the right hand of the Majesty on high." Heb. 10:21; 7:24; 1:3.

Spiritual things are spiritually discerned. In the temple the Son of God was dedicated to the work He had come to do. The priest looked upon Him as he would upon any other child. But though he neither saw nor felt anything unusual, God's act in giving His Son to the world was acknowledged. This occasion did not pass without some recognition of Christ. "There was a man in Jerusalem, whose name was Simeon; and the same man was just and devout, waiting for the Consolation of Israel: and the Holy Ghost was upon him. And it was revealed unto him by the Holy Ghost, that he should not see death, before he had seen the Lord's Christ."

As Simeon enters the temple, he sees a family presenting their first-born son before the priest. Their appearance bespeaks poverty; but Simeon understands the warnings of the Spirit, and he is deeply impressed that the infant being presented to the Lord is the Consolation of Israel, the One he has longed to see. To the astonished priest, Simeon appears like a man enraptured. The child has been returned to Mary, and he takes it in his arms and presents it to God, while a joy that he has never before felt enters his soul. As he lifts the infant Saviour toward heaven, he says, "Lord, now lettest Thou Thy servant depart in peace, according to Thy word: for mine eyes have seen Thy salvation, which Thou hast prepared before the face of all people; a light to lighten the Gentiles, and the glory of Thy people Israel."

The spirit of prophecy was upon this man of God, and while Joseph and Mary stood by, wondering at his words, he blessed them, and said unto Mary, "Behold, this child is set for the fall and rising again of many in Israel; and for a sign which shall be spoken against; (yea, a sword shall pierce through thy own soul also,) that the thoughts of many hearts may be revealed."

Anna also, a prophetess, came in and confirmed Simeon's testimony concerning Christ. As Simeon spoke, her face lighted up with the glory of God, and she poured out her heartfelt thanks that she had been permitted to behold Christ the Lord.

These humble worshipers had not studied the prophecies in vain. But those who held positions as rulers and priests in

Israel, though they too had before them the precious utterances of prophecy, were not walking in the way of the Lord, and their eyes were not open to behold the Light of life.

So it is still. Events upon which the attention of all heaven is centered are undiscerned, their very occurrence is unnoticed, by religious leaders, and worshipers in the house of God. Men acknowledge Christ in history, while they turn away from the living Christ. Christ in His word calling to self-sacrifice, in the poor and suffering who plead for relief, in the righteous cause that involves poverty and toil and reproach, is no more readily received today than He was eighteen hundred years ago.

Mary pondered the broad and far-reaching prophecy of Simeon. As she looked upon the child in her arms, and recalled the words spoken by the shepherds of Bethlehem, she was full of grateful joy and bright hope. Simeon's words called to her mind the prophetic utterances of Isaiah: "There shall come forth a rod out of the stem of Jesse, and a Branch shall grow out of his roots: and the Spirit of the Lord shall rest upon Him, the spirit of wisdom and understanding, the spirit of counsel and might, the spirit of knowledge and of the fear of the Lord. . . . And righteousness shall be the girdle of His loins, and faithfulness the girdle of His reins." "The people that walked in darkness have seen a great light: they that dwell in the land of the shadow of death, upon them hath the light shined. . . . For unto us a child is born, unto us a son is given: and the government shall be upon His shoulder: and His name shall be called Wonderful, Counselor, The mighty God, The everlasting Father, The Prince of Peace." Isa. 11:1-5; 9:2-6.

Yet Mary did not understand Christ's mission. Simeon had prophesied of Him as a light to lighten the Gentiles, as well as a glory to Israel. Thus the angels had announced the Saviour's birth as tidings of joy to all peoples. God was seeking to correct the narrow, Jewish conception of the Messiah's work. He desired men to behold Him, not merely as the deliverer of Israel, but as the Redeemer of the world. But many years must pass before even the mother of Jesus would understand His mission.

Mary looked forward to the Messiah's reign on David's throne, but she saw not the baptism of suffering by which it must be won. Through Simeon it is revealed that the Messiah is to have no unobstructed passage through the world. In the words to Mary, "A sword shall pierce through thy own soul also," God in His tender mercy gives to the mother of Jesus an intimation of the anguish that already for His sake she had begun to bear.

"Behold," Simeon had said, "this child is set for the fall and rising again of many in Israel; and for a sign which shall be spoken against." They must fall who would rise again. We must fall upon the Rock and be broken before we can be uplifted in Christ. Self must be dethroned, pride must be humbled, if we would know the glory of the spiritual kingdom. The Jews would not accept the honor that is reached through humiliation. Therefore they would not receive their Redeemer. He was a sign that was spoken against.

"That the thoughts of many hearts may be revealed." In the light of the Saviour's life, the hearts of all, even from the Creator to the prince of darkness, are revealed. Satan has represented God as selfish and oppressive, as claiming all, and giving nothing, as requiring the service of His creatures for His own glory, and making no sacrifice for their good. But the gift of Christ reveals the Father's heart. It testifies that the thoughts of God toward us are "thoughts of peace, and not of evil." Jer. 29:11. It declares that while God's hatred of sin is as strong as death, His love for the sinner is stronger than death. Having undertaken our redemption, He will spare nothing, however dear, which is necessary to the completion of His work. No truth essential to our salvation is withheld, no miracle of mercy is neglected, no divine agency is left unemployed. Favor is heaped upon favor, gift upon gift. The whole treasury of heaven is open to those He seeks to save. Having collected the riches of the universe, and laid open the resources of infinite power, He gives them all into the hands of Christ, and says, All these are for man. Use these gifts to convince him that there is no love greater than Mine in earth or heaven. His greatest happiness will be found in loving Me.

At the cross of Calvary, love and selfishness stood face to face. Here was their crowning manifestation. Christ had lived only to comfort and bless, and in putting Him to death, Satan manifested the malignity of his hatred against God. He made it evident that the real purpose of his rebellion was to dethrone God, and to destroy Him through whom the love of God was shown.

By the life and the death of Christ, the thoughts of men also are brought to view. From the manger to the cross, the life of Jesus was a call to self-surrender, and to fellowship in suffering. It unveiled the purposes of men. Jesus came with the truth of heaven, and all who were listening to the voice of the Holy Spirit were drawn to Him. The worshipers of self belonged to Satan's kingdom. In their attitude toward Christ, all would show on which side they stood. And thus everyone passes judgment on himself.

In the day of final judgment, every lost soul will understand the nature of his own rejection of truth. The cross will be presented, and its real bearing will be seen by every mind that has been blinded by transgression. Before the vision of Calvary with its mysterious Victim, sinners will stand condemned. Every lying excuse will be swept away. Human apostasy will appear in its heinous character. Men will see what their choice has been. Every question of truth and error in the long-standing controversy will then have been made plain. In the judgment of the universe, God will stand clear of blame for the existence or continuance of evil. It will be demonstrated that the divine decrees are not accessory to sin. There was no defect in God's government, no cause for disaffection. When the thoughts of all hearts shall be revealed, both the loyal and the rebellious will unite in declaring, "Just and true are Thy ways, Thou King of saints. Who shall not fear Thee, O Lord, and glorify Thy name? . . .

for Thy judgments are made manifest." Rev. 15:3, 4.

"We Have Seen His Star"

"Now when Jesus was born in Bethlehem of Judea in the days of Herod the king, behold, there came wise men from the East to Jerusalem, saying, Where is He that is born King of the Jews? for we have seen His star in the East, and are come to worship Him."

The wise men from the East were philosophers. They belonged to a large and influential class that included men of noble birth, and comprised much of the wealth and learning of their nation. Among these were many who imposed on the credulity of the people. Others were upright men who studied the indications of Providence in nature, and who were honored for their integrity and wisdom. Of this character were the wise men who came to Jesus.

The light of God is ever shining amid the darkness of heathenism. As these magi studied the starry heavens, and sought to fathom the mystery hidden in their bright paths, they beheld the glory of the Creator. Seeking clearer knowledge, they turned to the Hebrew Scriptures. In their own land were treasured prophetic writings that predicted the coming of a divine teacher. Balaam belonged to the magicians, though at one time a prophet of God; by the Holy Spirit he had foretold the prosperity of Israel and the appearing of the Messiah; and his prophecies had been handed down by tradition from century to century. But in the Old Testament the Saviour's advent was more clearly revealed. The magi learned with joy that His coming was near, and that the whole world was to be filled with a knowledge of the glory of the Lord.

The wise men had seen a mysterious light in the heavens upon that night when the glory of God flooded the hills of Bethlehem. As the light faded, a luminous star appeared, and lingered in the sky. It was not a fixed star nor a planet, and the phenomenon excited the keenest interest. That star was a distant company of shining angels, but of this the wise men were ignorant. Yet they were impressed that the star was of special import to them. They consulted priests and philosophers, and searched the scrolls of the ancient records. The prophecy of Balaam had declared, "There shall come a Star out of Jacob, and a Scepter shall rise out of Israel." Num. 24:17. Could this strange star have been sent as a harbinger of the Promised One? The magi had welcomed the light of heaven-sent truth; now it was shed upon them in brighter rays. Through dreams they were instructed to go in search of the newborn Prince.

As by faith Abraham went forth at the call of God, "not knowing whither he went" (Heb. 11:8); as by faith Israel followed the pillar of cloud to the Promised Land, so did these Gentiles go forth to find the promised Saviour. The Eastern country abounded in precious things, and the magi did not set out empty-handed. It was the custom to offer presents as an act of homage to princes or other personages of rank, and the richest gifts the land afforded were borne as an offering to Him in whom all the families of the earth were to be blessed. It was necessary to journey by night in order to keep the star in view; but the travelers beguiled the hours by repeating traditional sayings and prophetic utterances concerning the One they sought. At every pause for rest they searched the prophecies; and the conviction deepened that they were divinely guided. While they had the star before them as an outward sign, they had also the inward evidence of the Holy Spirit, which was impressing their hearts, and inspiring them with hope. The journey, though long, was a happy one to them.

They have reached the land of Israel, and are descending the Mount of Olives, with Jerusalem in sight, when, lo, the star that has guided them all the weary way rests above the temple, and after a season fades from their view. With eager steps they press onward, confidently expecting the Messiah's birth to be the joyful burden of every tongue. But their inquiries are in vain. Entering the holy city, they repair to the temple. To their amazement they find none who seem to have a knowledge of the newborn king. Their questions call forth no expressions of joy, but rather of surprise and fear, not unmingled with contempt.

The priests are rehearsing traditions. They extol their religion and their own piety, while they denounce the Greeks and Romans as heathen, and sinners above others. The wise men are not idolaters, and in the sight of God they stand far higher than do these, His professed worshipers; yet they are looked upon by the Jews as heathen. Even among the appointed guardians of the Holy Oracles their eager questionings touch no chord of sympathy.

The arrival of the magi was quickly noised throughout Jerusalem. Their strange errand created an excitement among the people, which penetrated to the palace of King Herod. The wily Edomite was aroused at the intimation of a possible rival. Countless murders had stained his pathway to the throne. Being of alien blood, he was hated by the people over whom he ruled. His only security was the favor of Rome. But this new Prince had a higher claim. He was born to the kingdom.

Herod suspected the priests of plotting with the strangers to excite a popular tumult and unseat him from the throne. He concealed his mistrust, however, determined to thwart their schemes by superior cunning. Summoning the chief priests and the scribes, he questioned them as to the teaching of their sacred books in regard to the place of the Messiah's birth.

This inquiry from the usurper of the throne, and made at the request of strangers, stung the pride of the Jewish teachers. The indifference with which they turned to the rolls of prophecy enraged the jealous tyrant. He thought them trying to conceal their knowledge of the matter. With an authority they dared not disregard, he commanded them to make close search, and to declare the birthplace of their expected King. "And they said unto him, In Bethlehem of Judea: for thus it is written by the prophet,

"And thou Bethlehem, land of Judah,
Art in nowise least among the princes of Judah:
For out of thee shall come forth a governor,
Which shall be shepherd of My people Israel."
R. V.

Herod now invited the magi to a private interview. A tempest of wrath and fear was raging in his heart, but he preserved a calm exterior, and received the strangers courteously. He inquired at what time the star had appeared, and professed to hail with joy the intimation of the birth of Christ. He bade his visitors, "Search diligently for the young child; and when ye have found Him, bring me word again, that I may come and worship Him also." So saying, he dismissed them to go on their way to Bethlehem.

The priests and elders of Jerusalem were not as ignorant concerning the birth of Christ as they pretended. The report of the angels' visit to the shepherds had been brought to Jerusalem, but the rabbis had treated it as unworthy of their notice. They themselves might have found Jesus, and might have been ready to lead the magi to His birthplace; but instead of this, the wise men came to call their attention to the birth of the Messiah. "Where is He that is born King of the Jews?" they said; "for we have seen His star in the East, and are come to worship Him."

Now pride and envy closed the door against the light. If the reports brought by the shepherds and the wise men were credited, they would place the priests and rabbis in a most unenviable position, disproving their claim to be the exponents of the truth of God. These learned teachers would not stoop to be instructed by those whom they termed heathen. It could not be, they said, that God had passed them by, to communicate with ignorant shepherds or uncircumcised Gentiles. They determined to show their contempt for the reports that were exciting King Herod and all Jerusalem. They would not even go to Bethlehem to see whether these things were so. And they led the people to regard the interest in Jesus as a fanatical excitement. Here began the rejection of Christ by the priests and rabbis. From this point their pride and stubbornness grew into a settled hatred of the Saviour. While God was opening the door to the Gentiles, the Jewish leaders were closing the door to themselves.

The wise men departed alone from Jerusalem. The shadows of night were falling as they left the gates, but to their great joy they again saw the star, and were directed to Bethlehem. They had received no such intimation of the lowly estate of Jesus as was given to the shepherds. After the long journey they had been disappointed by the indifference of the Jewish leaders, and had left Jerusalem less confident than when they entered the city. At Bethlehem they found no royal guard stationed to protect the newborn King. None of the world's honored men were in attendance. Jesus was cradled in a manger. His parents, uneducated peasants, were His only guardians. Could this be He of whom it was written, that He should "raise up the tribes of Jacob," and "restore the

preserved of Israel;" that He should be "a light to the Gentiles," and for "salvation unto the end of the earth"? Isa. 49:6.

"When they were come into the house, they saw the young child with Mary His mother, and fell down, and worshiped Him." Beneath the lowly guise of Jesus, they recognized the presence of Divinity. They gave their hearts to Him as their Saviour, and then poured out their gifts,—"gold, and frankincense, and myrrh." What a faith was theirs! It might have been said of the wise men from the East, as afterward of the Roman centurion, "I have not found so great faith, no, not in Israel." Matt. 8:10.

The wise men had not penetrated Herod's design toward Jesus. When the object of their journey was accomplished, they prepared to return to Jerusalem, intending to acquaint him with their success. But in a dream they received a divine message to hold no further communication with him. Avoiding Jerusalem, they set out for their own country by another route.

In like manner Joseph received warning to flee into Egypt with Mary and the child. And the angel said, "Be thou there until I bring thee word: for Herod will seek the young child to destroy Him." Joseph obeyed without delay, setting out on the journey by night for greater security.

Through the wise men, God had called the attention of the Jewish nation to the birth of His Son. Their inquiries in Jerusalem, the popular interest excited, and even the jealousy of Herod, which compelled the attention of the priests and rabbis, directed minds to the prophecies concerning the Messiah, and to the great event that had just taken place.

Satan was bent on shutting out the divine light from the world, and he used his utmost cunning to destroy the Saviour. But He who never slumbers nor sleeps was watching over His beloved Son. He who had rained manna from heaven for Israel and had fed Elijah in the time of famine provided in a heathen land a refuge for Mary and the child Jesus. And through the gifts of the magi from a heathen country, the Lord supplied the means for the journey into Egypt and the sojourn in a land of strangers.

The magi had been among the first to welcome the Redeemer. Their gift was the first that was laid at His feet. And through that gift, what privilege of ministry was theirs! The offering from the heart that loves, God delights to honor, giving it highest efficiency in service for Him. If we have given our hearts to Jesus, we also shall bring our gifts to Him. Our gold and silver, our most precious earthly possessions, our highest mental and spiritual endowments, will be freely devoted to Him who loved us, and gave Himself for us.

Herod in Jerusalem impatiently awaited the return of the wise men. As time passed, and they did not appear, his suspicions were roused. The unwillingness of the rabbis to point out the Messiah's birthplace seemed to indicate that they had penetrated his design, and that the magi had purposely avoided him. He was maddened at the thought. Craft had failed, but there was left the resort to force. He would make an example of this child-king. Those haughty Jews should see what they might expect in their attempts to place a monarch on the throne.

Soldiers were at once sent to Bethlehem, with orders to put to death all the children of two years and under. The quiet homes of the city of David witnessed those scenes of horror that, six hundred years before, had been opened to the prophet. "In Ramah was there a voice heard, lamentation, and weeping, and great mourning, Rachel weeping for her children, and would not be comforted, because they are not."

This calamity the Jews had brought upon themselves. If they had been walking in faithfulness and humility before God, He would in a signal manner have made the wrath of the king harmless to them. But they had separated themselves from God by their sins, and had rejected the Holy Spirit, which was their only shield. They had not studied the Scriptures with a desire to conform to the will of God. They had searched for prophecies which could be interpreted to exalt themselves, and to show how God despised all other nations. It was their proud boast that the Messiah was to come as a king, conquering His enemies, and treading down the heathen in His wrath. Thus they had excited the hatred of their rulers. Through their misrepresentation of Christ's mission, Satan had purposed to compass the destruction of the Saviour; but instead of this, it returned upon their own heads.

This act of cruelty was one of the last that darkened the reign of Herod. Soon after the slaughter of the innocents, he was himself compelled to yield to that doom which none can turn aside. He died a fearful death.

Joseph, who was still in Egypt, was now bidden by an angel of God to return to the land of Israel. Regarding Jesus as the heir of David's throne, Joseph desired to make his home in Bethlehem; but learning that Archelaus reigned in Judea in his father's stead, he feared that the father's designs against Christ might be carried out by the son. Of all the sons of Herod, Archelaus most resembled him in character. Already his succession to the government had been marked by a tumult in Jerusalem, and the slaughter of thousands of Jews by the Roman guards.

Again Joseph was directed to a place of safety. He returned to Nazareth, his former home, and here for nearly thirty years Jesus dwelt, "that it might be fulfilled which was spoken by the prophets, He shall be called a Nazarene." Galilee was under the control of a son of Herod, but it had a much larger admixture of foreign inhabitants than Judea. Thus there was less interest in matters relating especially to the Jews, and the claims of Jesus would be less likely to excite the jealousy of those in power.

Such was the Saviour's reception when He came to the earth. There seemed to be no place of rest or safety for the infant Redeemer. God could not trust His beloved Son with men, even while carrying forward His work for their salvation. He commissioned angels to attend Jesus and protect Him till He should accomplish His mission on earth, and die by the hands of those whom He came to save.

As a Child

The childhood and youth of Jesus were spent in a little mountain village. There was no place on earth that would not have been honored by His presence. The palaces of kings would have been privileged in receiving Him as a guest. But He passed by the homes of wealth, the courts of royalty, and the renowned seats of learning, to make His home in obscure and despised Nazareth.

Wonderful in its significance is the brief record of His early life: "The child grew, and waxed strong in spirit, filled with wisdom: and the grace of God was upon Him." In the sunlight of His Father's countenance, Jesus "increased in wisdom and stature, and in favor with God and man." Luke 2:52. His mind was active and penetrating, with a thoughtfulness and wisdom beyond His years. Yet His character was beautiful in its symmetry. The powers of mind and body developed gradually, in keeping with the laws of childhood.

As a child, Jesus manifested a peculiar loveliness of disposition. His willing hands were ever ready to serve others. He manifested a patience that nothing could disturb, and a truthfulness that would never sacrifice integrity. In principle firm as a rock, His life revealed the grace of unselfish courtesy.

With deep earnestness the mother of Jesus watched the unfolding of His powers, and beheld the impress of perfection upon His character. With delight she sought to encourage that bright, receptive mind. Through the Holy Spirit she received wisdom to co-operate with the heavenly agencies in the development of this child, who could claim only God as His Father.

From the earliest times the faithful in Israel had given much care to the education of the youth. The Lord had directed that even from babyhood the children should be taught of His goodness and His greatness, especially as revealed in His law, and shown in the history of Israel. Song and prayer and lessons from the Scriptures were to be adapted to the opening mind. Fathers and mothers were to instruct their children that the law of God is an expression of His character, and that as they received the principles of the law into the heart, the image of God was traced on mind and soul. Much of the teaching was oral; but the youth also learned to read the Hebrew writings; and the parchment rolls of the Old Testament Scriptures were open to their study.

In the days of Christ the town or city that did not provide for the religious instruction of the young was regarded as under the curse of God. Yet the teaching had become formal. Tradition had in a great degree supplanted the Scriptures. True education would lead the youth to "seek the Lord, if haply they might feel after Him, and find Him." Acts 17:27. But the Jewish teachers gave their attention to matters of ceremony. The mind was crowded with material that was worthless to the learner, and that would not be recognized in the higher school of the courts above. The experience which is obtained through a personal acceptance of God's word had no place in the educational system. Absorbed in the round of externals, the students found no quiet hours to spend with God. They did not hear His voice speaking to the heart. In their search after knowledge, they turned away from the Source of wisdom. The great essentials of the service of God were neglected. The principles of the law were obscured. That which was regarded as superior education was the greatest hindrance to real development. Under the training of the rabbis the powers of the youth were repressed. Their minds became cramped and narrow.

The child Jesus did not receive instruction in the synagogue schools. His mother was His first human teacher. From her lips and from the scrolls of the prophets, He learned of heavenly things. The very words which He Himself had spoken to Moses for Israel He was now taught at His mother's knee. As He advanced from childhood to youth, He did not seek the schools of the rabbis. He needed not the education to be obtained from such sources; for God was His instructor.

The question asked during the Saviour's ministry, "How knoweth this man letters, having never learned?" does not indicate that Jesus was unable to read, but merely that He had not received a rabbinical education. John 7:15. Since He gained knowledge as we may do, His intimate acquaintance with the Scriptures shows how diligently His early years were given to the study of God's word. And spread out before Him was the great library of God's created works. He who had made all things studied the lessons which His own hand had written in earth and sea and sky. Apart from the unholy ways of the world, He gathered stores of scientific knowledge from nature. He studied the life of plants and animals, and the life of man. From His earliest years He was possessed of one purpose; He lived to bless others. For this He found resources in nature; new ideas of ways and means flashed into His mind as He studied plant life and animal life. Continually He was seeking to draw from things seen illustrations by which to present the living oracles of God. The parables by which, during His ministry, He loved to teach His lessons of truth show how open His spirit was to the influences of nature, and how He had gathered the spiritual teaching from the surroundings of His daily life.

Thus to Jesus the significance of the word and the works of God was unfolded, as He was trying to understand the reason of things. Heavenly beings were His attendants, and the culture of holy thoughts and communings was His. From the first dawning of intelligence He was constantly growing in spiritual grace and knowledge of truth.

Every child may gain knowledge as Jesus did. As we try to become acquainted with our heavenly Father through His word, angels will draw near, our minds will be strengthened, our characters will be elevated and refined. We shall become more like our Saviour. And as we behold the beautiful and grand in nature, our affections go out after God. While the spirit is awed, the soul is invigorated by coming in contact with the Infinite through His works. Communion with God through prayer develops the mental and moral faculties, and the spiritual powers strengthen as we cultivate thoughts upon spiritual things.

The life of Jesus was a life in harmony with God. While He was a child, He thought and spoke as a child; but no trace of sin marred the image of God within Him. Yet He was not exempt from temptation. The inhabitants of Nazareth were proverbial for their wickedness. The low estimate in which they were generally held is shown by Nathanael's question, "Can there any good thing come out of Nazareth?" John 1:46. Jesus was placed where His character would be tested. It was necessary for Him to be constantly on guard in order to preserve His purity. He was subject to all the conflicts which we have to meet, that He might be an example to us in childhood, youth, and manhood.

Satan was unwearied in his efforts to overcome the Child of Nazareth. From His earliest years Jesus was guarded by heavenly angels, yet His life was one long struggle against the powers of darkness. That there should be upon the earth one life free from the defilement of evil was an offense and a perplexity to the prince of darkness. He left no means untried to ensnare Jesus. No child of humanity will ever be called to live a holy life amid so fierce a conflict with temptation as was our Saviour.

The parents of Jesus were poor, and dependent upon their daily toil. He was familiar with poverty, self-denial, and privation. This experience was a safeguard to Him. In His industrious life there were no idle moments to invite temptation. No aimless hours opened the way for corrupting associations. So far as possible, He closed the door to the tempter. Neither gain nor pleasure, applause nor censure, could induce Him to consent to a wrong act. He was wise to discern evil, and strong to resist it.

Christ was the only sinless one who ever dwelt on earth; yet for nearly thirty years He lived among the wicked inhabitants of Nazareth. This fact is a rebuke to those who think themselves dependent upon place, fortune, or prosperity, in order to live a blameless life. Temptation, poverty, adversity, is the very discipline needed to develop purity and firmness.

Jesus lived in a peasant's home, and faithfully and cheerfully acted His part in bearing the burdens of the household. He had been the Commander of heaven, and angels had delighted to fulfill His word; now He was a willing servant, a loving, obedient son. He learned a trade, and with His own hands worked in the carpenter's shop with Joseph. In the simple garb of a common laborer He walked the streets of the little town, going to and returning from His humble work. He did not employ His divine power to lessen His burdens or to lighten His toil.

As Jesus worked in childhood and youth, mind and body were developed. He did not use His physical powers recklessly, but in such a way as to keep them in health, that He might do the best work in every line. He was not willing to be defective, even in the handling of tools. He was perfect as a workman, as He was perfect in character. By His own example He taught that it is our duty to be industrious, that our work should be performed with exactness and thoroughness, and that such labor is honorable. The exercise that teaches the hands to be useful and trains the young to bear their share of life's burdens gives physical strength, and develops every faculty. All should find something to do that will be beneficial to themselves and helpful to others. God appointed work as a blessing, and only the diligent worker finds the true glory and joy of life. The approval of God rests with loving assurance upon children and youth who cheerfully take their part in the duties of the household, sharing the burdens of father and mother. Such children will go out from the home to be useful members of society.

Throughout His life on earth, Jesus was an earnest and constant worker. He expected much; therefore He attempted much. After He had entered on His ministry, He said, "I must work the works of Him that sent Me, while it is day: the night cometh, when no man can work." John 9:4. Jesus did not shirk care and responsibility, as do many who profess to be His followers. It is because they seek to evade this discipline that so many are weak and inefficient. They may possess precious and amiable traits, but they are nerveless and almost useless when difficulties are to be met or obstacles surmounted. The positiveness and energy, the solidity and strength of character, manifested in Christ are to be developed in us, through the same discipline that He endured. And the grace that He received is for us.

So long as He lived among men, our Saviour shared the lot of the poor. He knew by experience their cares and hardships, and He could comfort and encourage all humble workers. Those who have a true conception of the teaching of His life will never feel that a distinction must be made between classes, that the rich are to be honored above the worthy poor.

Jesus carried into His labor cheerfulness and tact. It requires much patience and spirituality to bring Bible religion into the home life and into the workshop, to bear the strain of worldly business, and yet keep the eye single to the glory of God. This is where Christ was a helper. He was never so full of worldly care as to have no time or thought for heavenly things. Often He expressed the gladness of His heart by singing psalms and heavenly songs. Often the dwellers in Nazareth heard His voice raised in praise and thanksgiving to God. He held communion with heaven in song; and as His companions complained of weariness from labor, they were cheered by the sweet melody from His lips. His praise seemed to banish the evil angels, and, like incense, fill the place with fragrance. The minds of His hearers were carried away from their earthly exile, to the heavenly home.

Jesus was the fountain of healing mercy for the world; and through all those secluded years at Nazareth, His life flowed out in currents of sympathy and tenderness. The aged, the sorrowing, and the sin-burdened, the children at play in their innocent joy, the little creatures of the groves, the patient beasts of burden,—all were happier for His presence. He whose word of power upheld the worlds would stoop to relieve a wounded bird. There was nothing beneath His notice, nothing to which He disdained to minister.

Thus as He grew in wisdom and stature, Jesus increased in favor with God and man. He drew the sympathy of all hearts by showing Himself capable of sympathizing with all. The atmosphere of hope and courage that surrounded Him made Him a blessing in every home. And often in the synagogue on the Sabbath day He was called upon to read the lesson from the prophets, and the hearts of the hearers thrilled as a new light shone out from the familiar words of the sacred text.

Yet Jesus shunned display. During all the years of His stay in Nazareth, He made no exhibition of His miraculous power. He sought no high position and assumed no titles. His quiet and simple life, and even the silence of the Scriptures concerning His early years, teach an important lesson. The more quiet and simple the life of the child,—the more free from artificial excitement, and the more in harmony with nature,—the more favorable is it to physical and mental vigor and to spiritual strength.

Jesus is our example. There are many who dwell with interest upon the period of His public ministry, while they pass unnoticed the teaching of His early years. But it is in His home life that He is the pattern for all children and youth. The Saviour condescended to poverty, that He might teach how closely we in a humble lot may walk with God. He lived to please, honor, and glorify His Father in the common things of life. His work began in consecrating the lowly trade of the craftsmen who toil for their daily bread. He was doing God's service just as much when laboring at the carpenter's bench as when working miracles for the multitude. And every youth who follows Christ's example of faithfulness and obedience in His lowly home may claim those words spoken of Him by the Father through the Holy Spirit, "Behold My Servant, whom I uphold; Mine Elect, in whom My soul delighteth." Isa. 42:1.

The Passover Visit

Among the Jews the twelfth year was the dividing line between childhood and youth. On completing this year a Hebrew boy was called a son of the law, and also a son of God. He was given special opportunities for religious instruction, and was expected to participate in the sacred feasts and observances. It was in accordance with this custom that Jesus in His boyhood made the Passover visit to Jerusalem. Like all devout Israelites, Joseph and Mary went up every year to attend the Passover; and when Jesus had reached the required age, they took Him with them.

There were three annual feasts, the Passover, the Pentecost, and the Feast of Tabernacles, at which all the men of Israel were commanded to appear before the Lord at Jerusalem. Of these feasts the Passover was the most largely attended. Many were present from all countries where the Jews were scattered. From every part of Palestine the worshipers came in great numbers. The journey from Galilee occupied several days, and the travelers united in large companies for companionship and protection. The women and aged men rode upon oxen or asses over the steep and rocky roads. The stronger men and the youth journeyed on foot. The time of the Passover corresponded to the close of March or the beginning of April, and the whole land was bright with flowers, and glad with the song of birds. All along the way were spots memorable in the history of Israel, and fathers and mothers recounted to their children the wonders that God had wrought for His people in ages past. They beguiled their journey with song and music, and when at last the towers of Jerusalem came into view, every voice joined in the triumphant strain,—

"Our feet shall stand
Within thy gates, O Jerusalem. . . .
Peace be within thy walls,
And prosperity within thy palaces."
Ps. 122: 2-7.

The observance of the Passover began with the birth of the Hebrew nation. On the last night of their bondage in Egypt, when there appeared no token of deliverance, God commanded them to prepare for an immediate release. He had warned Pharaoh of the final judgment on the Egyptians, and He directed the Hebrews to gather their families within their own dwellings. Having sprinkled the doorposts with the blood of the slain lamb, they were to eat the lamb, roasted, with unleavened bread and bitter herbs. "And thus shall ye eat it," He said, "with your loins girded, your shoes on your feet, and your staff in your hand; and ye shall eat it in haste: it is the Lord's passover." Ex. 12:11. At midnight all the first-born of the Egyptians were slain. Then the king sent to Israel the message, "Rise up, and get you forth from among my people; . . . and go, serve the Lord, as ye have said." Ex. 12:31. The Hebrews went out from Egypt an independent nation. The Lord had commanded that the Passover should be yearly kept. "It shall come to pass," He said, "when your children shall say unto you, What mean ye by this service? that ye shall say, It is the sacrifice of the Lord's passover, who passed over the houses of the children of Israel in Egypt, when He smote the Egyptians." Thus from generation to generation the story of this wonderful deliverance was to be repeated.

The Passover was followed by the seven days' feast of unleavened bread. On the second day of the feast, the first fruits of the year's harvest, a sheaf of barley, was presented before the Lord. All the ceremonies of the feast were types of the work of Christ. The deliverance of Israel from Egypt was an object lesson of redemption, which the Passover was intended to keep in memory. The slain lamb, the unleavened bread, the sheaf of first fruits, represented the Saviour.

With most of the people in the days of Christ, the observance of this feast had degenerated into formalism. But what was its significance to the Son of God!

For the first time the child Jesus looked upon the temple. He saw the white-robed priests performing their solemn ministry. He beheld the bleeding victim upon the altar of sacrifice. With the worshipers He bowed in prayer, while the cloud of incense ascended before God. He witnessed the impressive rites of the paschal service. Day by day He saw their meaning more clearly. Every act seemed to be bound up with His own life. New impulses were awakening within Him. Silent and absorbed, He seemed to be studying out a great problem. The mystery of His mission was opening to the Saviour.

Rapt in the contemplation of these scenes, He did not remain beside His parents. He sought to be alone. When the paschal services were ended, He still lingered in the temple courts; and when the worshipers departed from Jerusalem, He was left behind.

In this visit to Jerusalem, the parents of Jesus wished to bring Him in connection with the great teachers in Israel. While He was obedient in every particular to the word of God, He did not conform to the rabbinical rites and usages. Joseph and Mary hoped that He might be led to reverence the learned rabbis, and give more diligent heed to their requirements. But Jesus in the temple had been taught by God. That which He had received, He began at once to impart.

At that day an apartment connected with the temple was devoted to a sacred school, after the manner of the schools of the prophets. Here leading rabbis with their pupils assembled, and hither the child Jesus came. Seating Himself at the feet of these grave, learned men, He listened to their instruction. As one seeking for wisdom, He questioned these teachers in regard to the prophecies, and to events then taking place that pointed to the advent of the Messiah.

Jesus presented Himself as one thirsting for a knowledge of God. His questions were suggestive of deep truths which had long been obscured, yet which were vital to the salvation of souls. While showing how narrow and superficial was the wisdom of the wise men, every question put before them a divine lesson, and placed truth in a new aspect. The rabbis spoke of the wonderful elevation which the Messiah's coming would bring to the Jewish nation; but Jesus presented the prophecy of Isaiah, and asked them the meaning of those scriptures that point to the suffering and death of the Lamb of God.

The doctors turned upon Him with questions, and they were amazed at His answers. With the humility of a child He repeated the words of Scripture, giving them a depth of meaning that the wise men had not conceived of. If followed, the lines of truth He pointed out would have worked a reformation in the religion of the day. A deep interest in spiritual things would have been awakened; and when Jesus began His ministry, many would have been prepared to receive Him.

The rabbis knew that Jesus had not been instructed in their schools; yet His understanding of the prophecies far exceeded theirs. In this thoughtful Galilean boy they discerned great promise. They desired to gain Him as a student, that He might become a teacher in Israel. They wanted to have charge of His education, feeling that a mind so original must be brought under their molding.

The words of Jesus had moved their hearts as they had never before been moved by words from human lips. God was seeking to give light to those leaders in Israel, and He used the only means by which they could be reached. In their pride they would have scorned to admit that they could receive instruction from anyone. If Jesus had appeared to be trying to teach them, they would have disdained to listen. But they flattered themselves that they were teaching Him, or at least testing His knowledge of the Scriptures. The youthful modesty and grace of Jesus disarmed their prejudices. Unconsciously their minds were opened to the word of God, and the Holy Spirit spoke to their hearts.

They could not but see that their expectation in regard to the Messiah was not sustained by prophecy; but they would not renounce the theories that had flattered their ambition. They would not admit that they had misapprehended the Scriptures they claimed to teach. From one to another passed the inquiry, How hath this youth knowledge, having never learned? The light was shining in darkness; but "the darkness apprehended it not." John 1:5, R. V.

Meanwhile Joseph and Mary were in great perplexity and distress. In the departure from Jerusalem they had lost sight of Jesus, and they knew not that He had tarried behind. The country was then densely populated, and the caravans from Galilee were very large. There was much confusion as they left the city. On the way the pleasure of traveling with friends and acquaintances absorbed their attention, and they did not notice His absence till night came on. Then as they halted for rest, they missed the helpful hand of their child. Supposing Him to be with their company, they had felt no anxiety. Young as He was, they had trusted Him implicitly, expecting that when needed, He would be ready to assist them, anticipating their wants as He had always done. But now their fears were roused. They searched for Him throughout their company, but in vain. Shuddering they remembered how Herod had tried to destroy Him in His infancy. Dark forebodings filled their hearts. They bitterly reproached themselves.

Returning to Jerusalem, they pursued their search. The next day, as they mingled with the worshipers in the temple, a familiar voice arrested their attention. They could not mistake it; no other voice was like His, so serious and earnest, yet so full of melody.

In the school of the rabbis they found Jesus. Rejoiced as they were, they could not forget their grief and anxiety. When He was with them again, the mother said, in words that implied reproof, "Son, why hast Thou thus dealt with us? Behold, Thy father and I have sought Thee sorrowing."

"How is it that ye sought Me?" answered Jesus. "Wist ye not that I must be about My Father's business?" And as they seemed not to understand His words, He pointed upward. On His face was a light at which they wondered. Divinity was flashing through humanity. On finding Him in the temple, they had listened to what was passing between Him and the rabbis, and they were astonished at His questions and answers.

His words started a train of thought that would never be forgotten.

And His question to them had a lesson. "Wist ye not," He said, "that I must be about My Father's business?" Jesus was engaged in the work that He had come into the world to do; but Joseph and Mary had neglected theirs. God had shown them high honor in committing to them His Son. Holy angels had directed the course of Joseph in order to preserve the life of Jesus. But for an entire day they had lost sight of Him whom they should not have forgotten for a moment. And when their anxiety was relieved, they had not censured themselves, but had cast the blame upon Him.

It was natural for the parents of Jesus to look upon Him as their own child. He was daily with them, His life in many respects was like that of other children, and it was difficult for them to realize that He was the Son of God. They were in danger of failing to appreciate the blessing granted them in the presence of the world's Redeemer. The grief of their separation from Him, and the gentle reproof which His words conveyed, were designed to impress them with the sacredness of their trust.

In the answer to His mother, Jesus showed for the first time that He understood His relation to God. Before His birth the angel had said to Mary, "He shall be great, and shall be called the Son of the Highest: and the Lord God shall give unto Him the throne of His father David: and He shall reign over the house of Jacob forever." Luke 1:32, 33. These words Mary had pondered in her heart; yet while she believed that her child was to be Israel's Messiah, she did not comprehend His mission. Now she did not understand His words; but she knew that He had disclaimed kinship to Joseph, and had declared His Sonship to God.

Jesus did not ignore His relation to His earthly parents. From Jerusalem He returned home with them, and aided them in their life of toil. He hid in His own heart the mystery of His mission, waiting submissively for the appointed time for Him to enter upon His work. For eighteen years after He had recognized that He was the Son of God, He acknowledged the tie that bound Him to the home at Nazareth, and performed the duties of a son, a brother, a friend, and a citizen.

As His mission had opened to Jesus in the temple, He shrank from contact with the multitude. He wished to return from Jerusalem in quietness, with those who knew the secret of His life. By the paschal service, God was seeking to call His people away from their worldly cares, and to remind them of His wonderful work in their deliverance from Egypt. In this work He desired them to see a promise of deliverance from sin. As the blood of the slain lamb sheltered the homes of Israel, so the blood of Christ was to save their souls; but they could be saved through Christ only as by faith they should make His life their own. There was virtue in the symbolic service only as it directed the worshipers to Christ as their personal Saviour. God desired that they should be led to prayerful study and meditation in regard to Christ's mission. But as the multitudes left Jerusalem, the excitement of travel and social intercourse too often absorbed their attention, and the service they had witnessed was forgotten. The Saviour was not attracted to their company.

As Joseph and Mary should return from Jerusalem alone with Jesus, He hoped to direct their minds to the prophecies of the suffering Saviour. Upon Calvary He sought to lighten His mother's grief. He was thinking of her now. Mary was to witness His last agony, and Jesus desired her to understand His mission, that she might be strengthened to endure, when the sword should pierce through her soul. As Jesus had been separated from her, and she had sought Him sorrowing three days, so when He should be offered up for the sins of the world, He would again be lost to her for three days. And as He should come forth from the tomb, her sorrow would again be turned to joy. But how much better she could have borne the anguish of His death if she had understood the Scriptures to which He was now trying to turn her thoughts!

If Joseph and Mary had stayed their minds upon God by meditation and prayer, they would have realized the sacredness of their trust, and would not have lost sight of Jesus. By one day's neglect they lost the Saviour; but it cost them three days of anxious search to find Him. So with us; by idle talk, evilspeaking, or neglect of prayer, we may in one day lose the Saviour's presence, and it may take many days of sorrowful search to find Him, and regain the peace that we have lost.

In our association with one another, we should take heed lest we forget Jesus, and pass along unmindful that He is not with us. When we become absorbed in worldly things so that we have no thought for Him in whom our hope of eternal life is centered, we separate ourselves from Jesus and from the heavenly angels. These holy beings cannot remain where the Saviour's presence is not desired, and His absence is not marked. This is why discouragement so often exists among the professed followers of Christ.

Many attend religious services, and are refreshed and comforted by the word of God; but through neglect of meditation, watchfulness, and prayer, they lose the blessing, and find themselves more destitute than before they received it. Often they feel that God has dealt hardly with them. They do not see that the fault is their own. By separating themselves from Jesus, they have shut away the light of His presence.

It would be well for us to spend a thoughtful hour each day in contemplation of the life of Christ. We should take it point by point, and let the imagination grasp each scene, especially the closing ones. As we thus dwell upon His great sacrifice for us, our confidence in Him will be more constant, our love will be quickened, and we shall be more deeply imbued with His spirit. If we would be saved at last, we must learn the lesson of penitence and humiliation at the foot of the cross.

As we associate together, we may be a blessing to one another. If we are Christ's, our sweetest thoughts will be of Him. We shall love to talk of Him; and as we speak to one another of His love, our hearts will be softened by divine influences. Beholding the beauty of His character, we shall be "changed into the same image from glory to glory." 2 Cor. 3:18.

Days of Conflict

From its earliest years the Jewish child was surrounded with the requirements of the rabbis. Rigid rules were prescribed for every act, down to the smallest details of life. Under the synagogue teachers the youth were instructed in the countless regulations which as orthodox Israelites they were expected to observe. But Jesus did not interest Himself in these matters. From childhood He acted independently of the rabbinical laws. The Scriptures of the Old Testament were His constant study, and the words, "Thus saith the Lord," were ever upon His lips.

As the condition of the people began to open to His mind, He saw that the requirements of society and the requirements of God were in constant collision. Men were departing from the word of God, and exalting theories of their own invention. They were observing traditional rites that possessed no virtue. Their service was a mere round of ceremonies; the sacred truths it was designed to teach were hidden from the worshipers. He saw that in their faithless services they found no peace. They did not know the freedom of spirit that would come to them by serving God in truth. Jesus had come to teach the meaning of the worship of God, and He could not sanction the mingling of human requirements with the divine precepts. He did not attack the precepts or practices of the learned teachers; but when reproved for His own simple habits, He presented the word of God in justification of His conduct.

In every gentle and submissive way, Jesus tried to please those with whom He came in contact. Because He was so gentle and unobtrusive, the scribes and elders supposed that He would be easily influenced by their teaching. They urged Him to receive the maxims and traditions that had been handed down from the ancient rabbis, but He asked for their authority in Holy Writ. He would hear every word that proceeds from the mouth of God; but He could not obey the inventions of men. Jesus seemed to know the Scriptures from beginning to end, and He presented them in their true import. The rabbis were ashamed to be instructed by a child. They claimed that it was their office to explain the Scriptures, and that it was His place to accept their interpretation. They were indignant that He should stand in opposition to their word.

They knew that no authority could be found in Scripture for their traditions. They realized that in spiritual understanding Jesus was far in advance of them. Yet they were angry because He did not obey their dictates. Failing to convince Him, they sought Joseph and Mary, and set before them His course of noncompliance. Thus He suffered rebuke and censure.

At a very early age, Jesus had begun to act for Himself in the formation of His character, and not even respect and love for His parents could turn Him from obedience to God's word.

"It is written" was His reason for every act that varied from the family customs. But the influence of the rabbis made His life a bitter one. Even in His youth He had to learn the hard lesson of silence and patient endurance.

His brothers, as the sons of Joseph were called, sided with the rabbis They insisted that the traditions must be heeded, as if they were the requirements of God. They even regarded the precepts of men more highly than the word of God, and they were greatly annoyed at the clear penetration of Jesus in distinguishing between the false and the true His strict obedience to the law of God they condemned as stubbornness. They were surprised at the knowledge and wisdom He showed in answering the rabbis. They knew that He had not received instruction from the wise men, yet they could not but see that He was an instructor to them. They recognized that His education was of a higher type than their own. But they did not discern that He had access to the tree of life, a source of knowledge of which they were ignorant.

Christ was not exclusive, and He had given special offense to the Pharisees by departing in this respect from their rigid rules. He found the domain of religion fenced in by high walls of seclusion, as too sacred a matter for everyday life. These walls of partition He overthrew. In His contact with men He did not ask, What is your creed? To what church do you belong? He exercised His helping power in behalf of all who needed help. Instead of secluding Himself in a hermit's cell in order to show His heavenly character, He labored earnestly for humanity. He inculcated the principle that Bible religion does not consist in the mortification of the body. He taught that pure and undefiled religion is not meant only for set times and special occasions. At all times and in all places He manifested a loving interest in men, and shed about Him the light of a cheerful piety. All this was a rebuke to the Pharisees. It showed that religion does not consist in selfishness, and that their morbid devotion to personal interest was far from being true godliness. This had roused their enmity against Jesus, so that they tried to enforce His conformity to their regulations.

Jesus worked to relieve every case of suffering that He saw. He had little money to give, but He often denied Himself of food in order to relieve those who appeared more needy than He. His brothers felt that His influence went far to counteract theirs. He possessed a tact which none of them had, or desired to have. When they spoke harshly to poor, degraded beings, Jesus sought out these very ones, and spoke to them words of encouragement. To those who were in need He would give a cup of cold water, and would quietly place His own meal in their hands. As He relieved their sufferings, the truths He taught were associated with His acts of mercy, and were thus riveted in the memory.

All this displeased His brothers. Being older than Jesus, they felt that He should be under their dictation. They charged Him with thinking Himself superior to them, and reproved Him for setting Himself above their teachers and the priests and rulers of the people. Often they threatened and tried to intimidate Him; but He passed on, making the Scriptures His guide.

Jesus loved His brothers, and treated them with unfailing kindness; but they were jealous of Him, and manifested the most decided unbelief and contempt. They could not understand His conduct. Great contradictions presented themselves in Jesus. He was the divine Son of God, and yet a helpless child. The Creator of the worlds, the earth was His possession, and yet poverty marked His life experience at every step. He possessed a dignity and individuality wholly distinct from earthly pride and assumption; He did not strive for worldly greatness, and in even the lowliest position He was content. This angered His brothers. They could not account for His constant serenity under trial and deprivation. They did not know that for our sake He had become poor, that we "through His poverty might be rich." 2 Cor. 8:9. They could understand the mystery of His mission no more than the friends of Job could understand his humiliation and suffering.

Jesus was misunderstood by His brothers because He was not like them. His standard was not their standard. In looking to men they had turned away from God, and they had not His power in their lives. The forms of religion which they observed could not transform the character. They paid "tithe of mint and anise and cummin," but omitted "the weightier matters of the law, judgment, mercy, and faith." Matt. 23:23. The example of Jesus was to them a continual irritation. He hated but one thing in the world, and that was sin. He could not witness a wrong act without pain which it was impossible to disguise. Between the formalists, whose sanctity of appearance concealed the love of sin, and a character in which zeal for God's glory was always paramount, the contrast was unmistakable. Because the life of Jesus condemned evil, He was opposed, both at home and abroad. His unselfishness and integrity were commented on with a sneer. His forbearance and kindness were termed cowardice.

Of the bitterness that falls to the lot of humanity, there was no part which Christ did not taste. There were those who tried to cast contempt upon Him because of His birth, and even in His childhood He had to meet their scornful looks and evil whisperings. If He had responded by an impatient word or look, if He had conceded to His brothers by even one wrong act, He would have failed of being a perfect example. Thus He would have failed of carrying out the plan for our redemption. Had He even admitted that there could be an excuse for sin, Satan would have triumphed, and the world would have been lost. This is why the tempter worked to make His life as trying as possible, that He might be led to sin.

But to every temptation He had one answer, "It is written." He rarely rebuked any wrongdoing of His brothers, but He had a word from God to speak to them. Often He was accused of cowardice for refusing to unite with them in some forbidden act; but His answer was, It is written, "The fear of the Lord, that is wisdom; and to depart from evil is understanding." Job 28:28.

There were some who sought His society, feeling at peace in His presence; but many avoided Him, because they were rebuked by His stainless life. Young companions urged Him to do as they did. He was bright and cheerful; they enjoyed His presence, and welcomed His ready suggestions; but they were impatient at His scruples, and pronounced Him narrow and strait-laced. Jesus answered, It is written, "Wherewithal shall a young man cleanse his way? by taking heed thereto according to Thy word." "Thy word have I hid in mine heart, that I might not sin against Thee." Ps. 119:9, 11.

Often He was asked, Why are you bent on being so singular, so different from us all? It is written, He said, "Blessed are the undefiled in the way, who walk in the law of the Lord. Blessed are they that keep His testimonies, and that seek Him with the whole heart. They also do no iniquity; they walk in His ways." Ps. 119:1-3.

When questioned why He did not join in the frolics of the youth of Nazareth, He said, It is written, "I have rejoiced in the way of Thy testimonies, as much as in all riches. I will meditate in Thy precepts, and have respect unto Thy ways. I will delight myself in Thy statutes; I will not forget Thy word." Ps. 119:14-16.

Jesus did not contend for His rights. Often His work was made unnecessarily severe because He was willing and uncomplaining. Yet He did not fail nor become discouraged. He lived above these difficulties, as if in the light of God's countenance. He did not retaliate when roughly used, but bore insult patiently.

Again and again He was asked, Why do You submit to such despiteful usage, even from Your brothers? It is written, He said, "My son, forget not My law; but let thine heart keep My commandments: for length of days, and long life, and peace, shall they add to thee. Let not mercy and truth forsake thee: bind them about thy neck; write them upon the table of thine heart: so shalt thou find favor and good understanding in the sight of God and man." Prov. 3:1-4.

From the time when the parents of Jesus found Him in the temple, His course of action was a mystery to them. He would not enter into controversy, yet His example was a constant lesson. He seemed as one who was set apart. His hours of happiness were found when alone with nature and with God. Whenever it was His privilege, He turned aside from the scene of His labor, to go into the fields, to meditate in the green valleys, to hold communion with God on the mountainside or amid the trees of the forest. The early morning often found Him in some secluded place, meditating, searching the Scriptures, or in prayer. From these quiet hours He would return to His home to take up His duties again, and to give an example of patient toil.

The life of Christ was marked with respect and love for His mother. Mary believed in her heart that the holy child born of her was the long-promised Messiah, yet she dared not express her faith. Throughout His life on earth she was a partaker in His sufferings. She witnessed with sorrow the trials brought upon Him in His childhood and youth. By her vindication of what she knew to be right in His conduct, she herself was brought into trying positions. She looked upon the associations of the home, and the mother's tender watchcare over her children, as of vital importance in the formation of character. The sons and daughters of Joseph knew this, and by appealing to her anxiety, they tried to correct the practices of Jesus according to their standard.

Mary often remonstrated with Jesus, and urged Him to conform to the usages of the rabbis. But He could not be persuaded to change His habits of contemplating the works of God and seeking to alleviate the suffering of men or even of dumb animals. When the priests and teachers required Mary's aid in controlling Jesus, she was greatly troubled; but peace came to her heart as He presented the statements of Scripture upholding His practices.

At times she wavered between Jesus and His brothers, who did not believe that He was the Sent of God; but evidence was abundant that His was a divine character. She saw Him sacrificing Himself for the good of others. His presence brought a purer atmosphere into the home, and His life was as leaven working amid the elements of society. Harmless and undefiled, He walked among the thoughtless, the rude, the uncourteous; amid the unjust publicans, the reckless prodigals, the unrighteous Samaritans, the heathen soldiers, the rough peasants, and the mixed multitude. He spoke a word of sympathy here and a word there, as He saw men weary, yet compelled to bear heavy burdens. He shared their burdens, and repeated to them the lessons He had learned from nature, of the love, the kindness, the goodness of God.

He taught all to look upon themselves as endowed with precious talents, which if rightly employed would secure for them eternal riches. He weeded all vanity from life, and by His own example taught that every moment of time is fraught with eternal results; that it is to be cherished as a treasure, and to be employed for holy purposes. He passed by no human being as worthless, but sought to apply the saving remedy to every soul. In whatever company He found Himself, He presented a lesson that was appropriate to the time and the circumstances. He sought to inspire with hope the most rough and unpromising, setting before them the assurance that they might become blameless and harmless, attaining such a character as would make them manifest as the children of God. Often He met those who had drifted under Satan's control, and who had no power to break from his snare. To such a one, discouraged, sick, tempted, and fallen, Jesus would speak words of tenderest pity, words that were needed and could be understood. Others He met who were fighting a hand-to-hand battle with the adversary of souls. These He encouraged to persevere, assuring them that they would win; for angels of God were on their side, and would give them the victory. Those whom He thus helped were convinced that here was One in whom they could trust with perfect confidence. He would not betray the secrets they poured into His sympathizing ear.

Jesus was the healer of the body as well as of the soul. He was interested in every phase of suffering that came under His notice, and to every sufferer He brought relief, His kind words having a soothing balm. None could say that He had worked a miracle; but virtue—the healing power of love—went out from Him to the sick and distressed. Thus in an unobtrusive way He worked for the people from His very childhood. And this was why, after His public ministry began, so many heard Him gladly.

Yet through childhood, youth, and manhood, Jesus walked alone. In His purity and His faithfulness, He trod the wine press alone, and of the people there was none with Him. He carried the awful weight of responsibility for the salvation of men. He knew that unless there was a decided change in the principles and purposes of the human race, all would be lost. This was the burden of His soul, and none could appreciate the weight that rested upon Him. Filled with intense purpose, He carried out the design of His life that He Himself should be the light of men.

The Voice in the Wilderness

From among the faithful in Israel, who had long waited for the coming of the Messiah, the forerunner of Christ arose. The aged priest Zacharias and his wife Elisabeth were "both righteous before God;" and in their quiet and holy lives the light of faith shone out like a star amid the darkness of those evil days. To this godly pair was given the promise of a son, who should "go before the face of the Lord to prepare His ways."

Zacharias dwelt in "the hill country of Judea," but he had gone up to Jerusalem to minister for one week in the temple, a service required twice a year from the priests of each course. "And it came to pass, that while he executed the priest's office before God in the order of his course, according to the custom of the priest's office, his lot was to burn incense when he went into the temple of the Lord."

He was standing before the golden altar in the holy place of the sanctuary. The cloud of incense with the prayers of Israel was ascending before God. Suddenly he became conscious of a divine presence. An angel of the Lord was "standing on the right side of the altar." The position of the angel was an indication of favor, but Zacharias took no note of this. For many years he had prayed for the coming of the Redeemer; now heaven had sent its messenger to announce that these prayers were about to be answered; but the mercy of God seemed too great for him to credit. He was filled with fear and self-condemnation.

But he was greeted with the joyful assurance: "Fear not, Zacharias: for thy prayer is heard; and thy wife Elisabeth shall bear thee a son, and thou shalt call his name John. And thou shalt have joy and gladness; and many shall rejoice at his birth. For he shall be great in the sight of the Lord, and shall drink neither wine nor strong drink; and he shall be filled with the Holy Ghost. . . . And many of the children of Israel shall he turn to the Lord their God. And he shall go before Him in the spirit and power of Elias, to turn the hearts of the fathers to the children, and the disobedient to the wisdom of the just; to make ready a people prepared for the Lord. And Zacharias said unto the angel, Whereby shall I know this? for I am an old man, and my wife well stricken in years."

Zacharias well knew how to Abraham in his old age a child was given because he believed Him faithful who had promised. But for a moment the aged priest turns his thought to the weakness of humanity. He forgets that what God has promised, He is able to perform. What a contrast between this unbelief and the sweet, childlike faith of Mary, the maiden of Nazareth, whose answer to the angel's wonderful announcement was, "Behold the handmaid of the Lord; be it unto me according to thy word"! Luke 1:38.

The birth of a son to Zacharias, like the birth of the child of Abraham, and that of Mary, was to teach a great spiritual truth, a truth that we are slow to learn and ready to forget. In ourselves we are incapable of doing any good thing; but that which we cannot do will be wrought by the power of God in every submissive and believing soul. It was through faith that the child of promise was given. It is through faith that spiritual life is begotten, and we are enabled to do the works of righteousness.

To the question of Zacharias, the angel said, "I am Gabriel, that stand in the presence of God; and am sent to speak unto thee, and to show thee these glad tidings." Five hundred years before, Gabriel had made known to Daniel the prophetic period which was to extend to the coming of Christ. The knowledge that the end of this period was near had moved Zacharias to pray for the Messiah's advent. Now the very messenger through whom the prophecy was given had come to announce its fulfillment.

The words of the angel, "I am Gabriel, that stand in the presence of God," show that he holds a position of high honor in the heavenly courts. When he came with a message to Daniel, he said, "There is none that holdeth with me in these things, but Michael your Prince." Dan. 10:21. Of Gabriel the Saviour speaks in the Revelation, saying that "He sent and signified it by His angel unto His servant John." Rev. 1:1. And to John the angel declared, "I am a fellow servant with thee and with thy brethren the prophets." Rev. 22:9, R. V. Wonderful thought—that the angel who stands next in honor to the Son of God is the one chosen to open the purposes of God to sinful men.

Zacharias had expressed doubt of the angel's words. He was not to speak again until they were fulfilled. "Behold," said the angel, "thou shalt be dumb, . . . until the day that these things shall be performed, because thou believest not my words, which shall be fulfilled in their season." It was the duty of the priest in this service to pray for the pardon of public and national sins, and for the coming of the Messiah; but when Zacharias attempted to do this, he could not utter a word.

Coming forth to bless the people, "he beckoned unto them, and remained speechless." They had waited long, and had begun to fear, lest he had been cut down by the judgment of God. But as he came forth from the holy place, his face was shining with the glory of God, "and they perceived that he had seen a vision in the temple." Zacharias communicated to them what he had seen and heard; and "as soon as the days of his ministration were accomplished, he departed to his own house."

Soon after the birth of the promised child, the father's

tongue was loosed, "and he spake, and praised God. And fear came on all that dwelt round about them: and all these sayings were noised abroad throughout all the hill country of Judea. And all they that heard them laid them up in their hearts, saying, What manner of child shall this be!" All this tended to call attention to the Messiah's coming, for which John was to prepare the way.

The Holy Spirit rested upon Zacharias, and in these beautiful words he prophesied of the mission of his son:

"Thou, child, shalt be called the prophet of the Highest;
For thou shalt go before the face of the Lord to prepare His ways;
To give knowledge of salvation unto His people
By the remission of their sins,
Through the tender mercy of our God,
Whereby the Dayspring from on high hath visited us,
To give light to them that sit in darkness and in the shadow of
　death,
To guide our feet into the way of peace."

"And the child grew, and waxed strong in spirit, and was in the deserts till the day of his showing unto Israel." Before the birth of John, the angel had said, "He shall be great in the sight of the Lord, and shall drink neither wine nor strong drink; and he shall be filled with the Holy Ghost." God had called the son of Zacharias to a great work, the greatest ever committed to men. In order to accomplish this work, he must have the Lord to work with him. And the Spirit of God would be with him if he heeded the instruction of the angel.

John was to go forth as Jehovah's messenger, to bring to men the light of God. He must give a new direction to their thoughts. He must impress them with the holiness of God's requirements, and their need of His perfect righteousness. Such a messenger must be holy. He must be a temple for the indwelling Spirit of God. In order to fulfill his mission, he must have a sound physical constitution, and mental and spiritual strength. Therefore it would be necessary for him to control the appetites and passions. He must be able so to control all his powers that he could stand among men as unmoved by surrounding circumstances as the rocks and mountains of the wilderness.

In the time of John the Baptist, greed for riches, and the love of luxury and display had become widespread. Sensuous pleasures, feasting and drinking, were causing physical disease and degeneracy, benumbing the spiritual perceptions, and lessening the sensibility to sin. John was to stand as a reformer. By his abstemious life and plain dress he was to rebuke the excesses of his time. Hence the directions given to the parents of John,—a lesson of temperance by an angel from the throne of heaven.

In childhood and youth the character is most impressible. The power of self-control should then be acquired. By the fireside and at the family board influences are exerted whose results are as enduring as eternity. More than any natural endowment, the habits established in early years decide whether a man will be victorious or vanquished in the battle of life. Youth is the sowing time. It determines the character of the harvest, for this life and for the life to come.

As a prophet, John was "to turn the hearts of the fathers to the children, and the disobedient to the wisdom of the just; to make ready a people prepared for the Lord." In preparing the way for Christ's first advent, he was a representative of those who are to prepare a people for our Lord's second coming. The world is given to self-indulgence. Errors and fables abound. Satan's snares for destroying souls are multiplied. All who would perfect holiness in the fear of God must learn the lessons of temperance and self-control. The appetites and passions must be held in subjection to the higher powers of the mind. This self-discipline is essential to that mental strength and spiritual insight which will enable us to understand and to practice the sacred truths of God's word. For this reason temperance finds its place in the work of preparation for Christ's second coming.

In the natural order of things, the son of Zacharias would have been educated for the priesthood. But the training of the rabbinical schools would have unfitted him for his work. God did not send him to the teachers of theology to learn how to interpret the Scriptures. He called him to the desert, that he might learn of nature and nature's God.

It was a lonely region where he found his home, in the midst of barren hills, wild ravines, and rocky caves. But it was his choice to forgo the enjoyments and luxuries of life for the stern discipline of the wilderness. Here his surroundings were favorable to habits of simplicity and self-denial. Uninterrupted by the clamor of the world, he could here study the lessons of nature, of revelation, and of Providence. The words of the angel to Zacharias had been often repeated to John by his God-fearing parents. From childhood his mission had been kept before him, and he had accepted the holy trust. To him the solitude of the desert was a welcome escape from society in which suspicion, unbelief, and impurity had become well-nigh all-pervading. He distrusted his own power to withstand temptation, and shrank from constant contact with sin, lest he should lose the sense of its exceeding sinfulness.

Dedicated to God as a Nazarite from his birth, he made the vow his own in a life-long consecration. His dress was that of the ancient prophets, a garment of camel's hair, confined by a leather girdle. He ate the "locusts and wild honey" found in the wilderness, and drank the pure water from the hills.

But the life of John was not spent in idleness, in ascetic gloom, or in selfish isolation. From time to time he went forth to mingle with men; and he was ever an interested observer of what was passing in the world. From his quiet retreat he watched the unfolding of events. With vision illuminated by the divine Spirit he studied the characters of men, that he might understand how to reach their hearts with the message of heaven. The burden of his mission was upon him. In solitude, by meditation and prayer, he sought to gird up his soul for the lifework before him.

Although in the wilderness, he was not exempt from temptation. So far as possible, he closed every avenue by which Satan could enter, yet he was still assailed by the tempter. But his spiritual perceptions were clear; he had developed strength and decision of character, and through the aid of the Holy Spirit he was able to detect Satan's approaches, and to resist his power.

John found in the wilderness his school and his sanctuary. Like Moses amid the mountains of Midian, he was shut in by God's presence, and surrounded by the evidences of His power. It was not his lot to dwell, as did Israel's great leader, amid the solemn majesty of the mountain solitudes; but before him were the heights of Moab, beyond Jordan, speaking of Him who had set fast the mountains, and girded them with strength. The gloomy and terrible aspect of nature in his wilderness home vividly pictured the condition of Israel. The fruitful vineyard of the Lord had become a desolate waste. But above the desert the heavens bent bright and beautiful. The clouds that gathered, dark with tempest, were arched by the rainbow of promise. So above Israel's degradation shone the promised glory of the Messiah's reign. The clouds of wrath were spanned by the rainbow of His covenant-mercy.

Alone in the silent night he read God's promise to Abraham of a seed numberless as the stars. The light of dawn, gilding the mountains of Moab, told of Him who should be as "the light of the morning, when the sun riseth, even a morning without clouds." 2 Sam. 23:4. And in the brightness of noontide he saw the splendor of His manifestation, when "the glory of the Lord shall be revealed, and all flesh shall see it together." Isa. 40:5.

With awed yet exultant spirit he searched in the prophetic scrolls the revelations of the Messiah's coming,—the promised seed that should bruise the serpent's head; Shiloh, "the peace giver," who was to appear before a king should cease to reign on David's throne. Now the time had come. A Roman ruler sat in the palace upon Mount Zion. By the sure word of the Lord, already the Christ was born.

Isaiah's rapt portrayals of the Messiah's glory were his study by day and by night,—the Branch from the root of Jesse; a King to reign in righteousness, judging "with equity for the meek of the earth;" "a covert from the tempest; . . . the shadow of a great rock in a weary land;" Israel no longer to be termed "Forsaken," nor her land "Desolate," but to be called of the Lord, "My Delight," and her land "Beulah." Isa. 11:4; 32:2; 62:4, margin. The heart of the lonely exile was filled with the glorious vision.

He looked upon the King in His beauty, and self was forgotten. He beheld the majesty of holiness, and felt himself to be inefficient and unworthy. He was ready to go forth as Heaven's messenger, unawed by the human, because he had looked upon the Divine. He could stand erect and fearless in the presence of earthly monarchs, because he had bowed low before the King of kings.

John did not fully understand the nature of the Messiah's kingdom. He looked for Israel to be delivered from her national foes; but the coming of a King in righteousness, and the establishment of Israel as a holy nation, was the great object of his hope. Thus he believed would be accomplished the prophecy given at his birth,—

"To remember His holy covenant; . . .
That we being delivered out of the hand of our enemies
Might serve Him without fear,
In holiness and righteousness before Him, all the days of our life."

He saw his people deceived, self-satisfied, and asleep in their sins. He longed to rouse them to a holier life. The message that God had given him to bear was designed to startle them from their lethargy, and cause them to tremble because of their great wickedness. Before the seed of the gospel could find lodgment, the soil of the heart must be broken up. Before they would seek healing from Jesus, they must be awakened to their danger from the wounds of sin.

God does not send messengers to flatter the sinner. He delivers no message of peace to lull the unsanctified into fatal security. He lays heavy burdens upon the conscience of the wrongdoer, and pierces the soul with arrows of conviction. The ministering angels present to him the fearful judgments of God to deepen the sense of need, and prompt the cry, "What must I do to be saved?" Then the hand that has humbled in the dust, lifts up the penitent. The voice that has rebuked sin, and put to shame pride and ambition, inquires with tenderest sympathy, "What wilt thou that I shall do unto thee?"

When the ministry of John began, the nation was in a state of excitement and discontent verging on revolution. At the removal of Archelaus, Judea had been brought directly under the control of Rome. The tyranny and extortion of the Roman governors, and their determined efforts to introduce the heathen symbols and customs, kindled revolt, which had been quenched in the blood of thousands of the bravest of Israel. All this intensified the national hatred against Rome, and increased the longing to be freed from her power.

Amid discord and strife, a voice was heard from the wilderness, a voice startling and stern, yet full of hope: "Repent ye; for the kingdom of heaven is at hand." With a new, strange power it moved the people. Prophets had foretold the coming of Christ as an event far in the future; but here was an announcement that it was at hand. John's singular appearance carried the minds of his hearers back to the ancient seers. In his manner and dress he resembled the prophet Elijah. With the spirit and power of Elijah he denounced the national corruption, and rebuked the prevailing sins. His words were plain, pointed, and convincing. Many believed him to be one of the prophets risen from the dead. The whole nation was stirred. Multitudes flocked to the wilderness.

John proclaimed the coming of the Messiah, and called the

people to repentance. As a symbol of cleansing from sin, he baptized them in the waters of the Jordan. Thus by a significant object lesson he declared that those who claimed to be the chosen people of God were defiled by sin, and that without purification of heart and life they could have no part in the Messiah's kingdom.

Princes and rabbis, soldiers, publicans, and peasants came to hear the prophet. For a time the solemn warning from God alarmed them. Many were brought to repentance, and received baptism. Persons of all ranks submitted to the requirement of the Baptist, in order to participate in the kingdom he announced.

Many of the scribes and Pharisees came confessing their sins, and asking for baptism. They had exalted themselves as better than other men, and had led the people to entertain a high opinion of their piety; now the guilty secrets of their lives were unveiled. But John was impressed by the Holy Spirit that many of these men had no real conviction of sin. They were timeservers. As friends of the prophet, they hoped to find favor with the coming Prince. And by receiving baptism at the hands of this popular young teacher, they thought to strengthen their influence with the people.

John met them with the scathing inquiry, "O generation of vipers, who hath warned you to flee from the wrath to come? Bring forth therefore fruits meet for repentance; and think not to say within yourselves, we have Abraham to our father: for I say unto you, that God is able of these stones to raise up children unto Abraham."

The Jews had misinterpreted God's promise of eternal favor to Israel: "Thus saith the Lord, which giveth the sun for a light by day, and the ordinances of the moon and of the stars for a light by night, which divideth the sea when the waves thereof roar; The Lord of hosts is His name: If those ordinances depart from before Me, saith the Lord, then the seed of Israel also shall cease from being a nation before Me forever. Thus saith the Lord; If heaven above can be measured, and the foundations of the earth searched out beneath, I will also cast off all the seed of Israel for all that they have done, saith the Lord." Jer. 31:35-37. The Jews regarded their natural descent from Abraham as giving them a claim to this promise. But they overlooked the conditions which God had specified. Before giving the promise, He had said, "I will put My law in their inward parts, and write it in their hearts; and will be their God, and they shall be My people. . . . For I will forgive their iniquity, and I will remember their sin no more." Jer. 31:33, 34.

To a people in whose hearts His law is written, the favor of God is assured. They are one with Him. But the Jews had separated themselves from God. Because of their sins they were suffering under His judgments. This was the cause of their bondage to a heathen nation. Their minds were darkened by transgression, and because in times past the Lord had shown them so great favor, they excused their sins. They flattered themselves that they were better than other men, and entitled to His blessings.

These things "are written for our admonition, upon whom the ends of the world are come." 1 Cor. 10:11. How often we misinterpret God's blessings, and flatter ourselves that we are favored on account of some goodness in us! God cannot do for us that which He longs to do. His gifts are used to increase our self-satisfaction, and to harden our hearts in unbelief and sin.

John declared to the teachers of Israel that their pride, selfishness, and cruelty showed them to be a generation of vipers, a deadly curse to the people, rather than the children of just and obedient Abraham. In view of the light they had received from God, they were even worse than the heathen, to whom they felt so much superior. They had forgotten the rock whence they were hewn, and the hole of the pit from which they had been digged. God was not dependent upon them for the fulfilling of His purpose. As He had called Abraham out from a heathen people, so He could call others to His service. Their hearts might now appear as lifeless as the stones of the desert, but His Spirit could quicken them to do His will, and receive the fulfillment of His promise.

"And now also," said the prophet, "the ax is laid unto the root of the trees: therefore every tree which bringeth not forth good fruit is hewn down, and cast into the fire." Not by its name, but by its fruit, is the value of a tree determined. If the fruit is worthless, the name cannot save the tree from destruction. John declared to the Jews that their standing before God was to be decided by their character and life. Profession was worthless. If their life and character were not in harmony with God's law, they were not His people.

Under his heart-searching words, his hearers were convicted. They came to him with the inquiry, "What shall we do then?" He answered, "He that hath two coats, let him impart to him that hath none; and he that hath meat, let him do likewise." And he warned the publicans against injustice, and the soldiers against violence.

All who became the subjects of Christ's kingdom, he said, would give evidence of faith and repentance. Kindness, honesty, and fidelity would be seen in their lives. They would minister to the needy, and bring their offerings to God. They would shield the defenseless, and give an example of virtue and compassion. So the followers of Christ will give evidence of the transforming power of the Holy Spirit. In the daily life, justice, mercy, and the love of God will be seen. Otherwise they are like the chaff that is given to the fire.

"I indeed baptize you in water unto repentance," said John; "but He that cometh after me is mightier than I, whose shoes I am not worthy to bear: He shall baptize you with the Holy Ghost and with fire." Matt. 3:11, R. V., margin. The prophet Isaiah had declared that the Lord would cleanse His people from their iniquities "by the spirit of judgment, and by the spirit of burning." The word of the Lord to Israel was, "I will turn My hand upon thee, and purely purge away thy dross, and take away all thy tin." Isa. 4:4; 1:25. To sin, wherever found, "our God is a consuming fire." Heb. 12:29. In all who submit to His power the Spirit of God will consume sin. But if men cling to sin, they become identified with it. Then the glory of God, which destroys sin, must destroy them. Jacob, after his night of wrestling with the Angel, exclaimed, "I have seen God face to face, and my life is preserved." Gen. 32: 30. Jacob had been guilty of a great sin in his conduct toward Esau; but he had repented. His transgression had been forgiven, and his sin purged; therefore he could endure the revelation of God's presence. But wherever men came before God while willfully cherishing evil, they were destroyed. At the second advent of Christ the wicked shall be consumed "with the Spirit of His mouth," and destroyed "with the brightness of His coming." 2 Thess. 2:8. The light of the glory of God, which imparts life to the righteous, will slay the wicked.

In the time of John the Baptist, Christ was about to appear as the revealer of the character of God. His very presence would make manifest to men their sin. Only as they were willing to be purged from sin could they enter into fellowship with Him. Only the pure in heart could abide in His presence.

Thus the Baptist declared God's message to Israel. Many gave heed to his instruction. Many sacrificed all in order to obey. Multitudes followed this new teacher from place to place, and not a few cherished the hope that he might be the Messiah. But as John saw the people turning to him, he sought every opportunity of directing their faith to Him who was to come.

The Baptism

Tidings of the wilderness prophet and his wonderful announcement, spread throughout Galilee. The message reached the peasants in the remotest hill towns, and the fisher folk by the sea, and in these simple, earnest hearts found its truest response. In Nazareth it was told in the carpenter shop that had been Joseph's, and One recognized the call. His time had come. Turning from His daily toil, He bade farewell to His mother, and followed in the steps of His countrymen who were flocking to the Jordan.

Jesus and John the Baptist were cousins, and closely related by the circumstances of their birth; yet they had had no direct acquaintance with each other. The life of Jesus had been spent at Nazareth in Galilee; that of John, in the wilderness of Judea. Amid widely different surroundings they had lived in seclusion, and had had no communication with each other. Providence had ordered this. No occasion was to be given for the charge that they had conspired together to support each other's claims.

John was acquainted with the events that had marked the birth of Jesus. He had heard of the visit to Jerusalem in His boyhood, and of what had passed in the school of the rabbis. He knew of His sinless life, and believed Him to be the Messiah; but of this he had no positive assurance. The fact that Jesus had for so many years remained in obscurity, giving no special evidence of His mission, gave occasion for doubt as to whether He could be the Promised One. The Baptist, however, waited in faith, believing that in God's own time all would be made plain. It had been revealed to him that the Messiah would seek baptism at his hands, and that a sign of His divine character should then be given. Thus he would be enabled to present Him to the people.

When Jesus came to be baptized, John recognized in Him a purity of character that he had never before perceived in any man. The very atmosphere of His presence was holy and awe-inspiring. Among the multitudes that had gathered about him at the Jordan, John had heard dark tales of crime, and had met souls bowed down with the burden of myriad sins; but never had he come in contact with a human being from whom there breathed an influence so divine. All this was in harmony with what had been revealed to John regarding the Messiah. Yet he shrank from granting the request of Jesus. How could he, a sinner, baptize the Sinless One? And why should He who needed no repentance submit to a rite that was a confession of guilt to be washed away?

As Jesus asked for baptism, John drew back, exclaiming, "I have need to be baptized of Thee, and comest Thou to me?" With firm yet gentle authority, Jesus answered, "Suffer it to be so now: for thus it becometh us to fulfill all righteousness." And John, yielding, led the Saviour down into the Jordan, and buried Him beneath the water. "And straightway coming up out of the water," Jesus "saw the heavens opened, and the Spirit like a dove descending upon Him."

Jesus did not receive baptism as a confession of guilt on His own account. He identified Himself with sinners, taking the steps that we are to take, and doing the work that we must do. His life of suffering and patient endurance after His baptism was also an example to us.

Upon coming up out of the water, Jesus bowed in prayer on the river bank. A new and important era was opening before Him. He was now, upon a wider stage, entering on the conflict of His life. Though He was the Prince of Peace, His coming must be as the unsheathing of a sword. The kingdom He had come to establish was the opposite of that which the Jews desired. He who was the foundation of the ritual and economy of Israel would be looked upon as its enemy and destroyer. He who had proclaimed the law upon Sinai would be condemned as a transgressor. He who had come to break the power of Satan would be denounced as Beelzebub. No one upon earth had understood Him, and during His ministry He must still walk alone. Throughout His life His mother and His brothers did not comprehend His mission. Even His disciples did not understand Him. He had dwelt in eternal light, as one with God, but His life on earth must be spent in solitude.

As one with us, He must bear the burden of our guilt and woe. The Sinless One must feel the shame of sin. The peace lover must dwell with strife, the truth must abide with falsehood, purity with vileness. Every sin, every discord, every defiling lust that transgression had brought, was torture to His spirit.

Alone He must tread the path; alone He must bear the burden. Upon Him who had laid off His glory and accepted the weakness of humanity the redemption of the world must rest. He saw and felt it all, but His purpose remained steadfast. Upon His arm depended the salvation of the fallen race, and He reached out His hand to grasp the hand of Omnipotent Love.

The Saviour's glance seems to penetrate heaven as He pours out His soul in prayer. Well He knows how sin has hardened the hearts of men, and how difficult it will be for them to discern His mission, and accept the gift of salvation. He pleads with the Father for power to overcome their unbelief, to break the fetters with which Satan has enthralled them, and in their behalf to conquer the destroyer. He asks for the witness that God accepts humanity in the person of His Son.

Never before have the angels listened to such a prayer. They are eager to bear to their loved Commander a message of assurance and comfort. But no; the Father Himself will answer the petition of His Son. Direct from the throne issue the beams of His glory. The heavens are opened, and upon the Saviour's head descends a dovelike form of purest light,—fit emblem of Him, the meek and lowly One.

Of the vast throng at the Jordan, few except John discerned the heavenly vision. Yet the solemnity of the divine Presence rested upon the assembly. The people stood silently gazing upon Christ. His form was bathed in the light that ever surrounds the throne of God. His upturned face was glorified as they had never before seen the face of man. From the open heavens a voice was heard saying, "This is My beloved Son, in whom I am well pleased."

These words of confirmation were given to inspire faith in those who witnessed the scene, and to strengthen the Saviour for His mission. Notwithstanding that the sins of a guilty world were laid upon Christ, notwithstanding the humiliation of taking upon Himself our fallen nature, the voice from heaven declared Him to be the Son of the Eternal.

John had been deeply moved as he saw Jesus bowed as a suppliant, pleading with tears for the approval of the Father. As the glory of God encircled Him, and the voice from heaven was heard, John recognized the token which God had promised. He knew that it was the world's Redeemer whom he had baptized. The Holy Spirit rested upon him, and with outstretched hand pointing to Jesus, he cried, "Behold the Lamb of God, which taketh away the sin of the world."

None among the hearers, and not even the speaker himself, discerned the import of these words, "the Lamb of God." Upon Mount Moriah, Abraham had heard the question of his son, "My father, . . . where is the lamb for a burnt offering?" The father answered, "My son, God will provide Himself a lamb for a burnt offering." Gen. 22:7, 8. And in the ram divinely provided in the place of Isaac, Abraham saw a symbol of Him who was to die for the sins of men. The Holy Spirit through Isaiah, taking up the illustration, prophesied of the Saviour, "He is brought as a lamb to the slaughter," "and the Lord hath laid on Him the iniquity of us all" (Isa. 53:7, 6); but the people of Israel had not understood the lesson. Many of them regarded the sacrificial offerings much as the heathen looked upon their sacrifices,—as gifts by which they themselves might propitiate the Deity. God desired to teach them that from His own love comes the gift which reconciles them to Himself.

And the word that was spoken to Jesus at the Jordan, "This is My beloved Son, in whom I am well pleased," embraces humanity. God spoke to Jesus as our representative. With all our sins and weaknesses, we are not cast aside as worthless. "He hath made us accepted in the Beloved." Eph. 1:6. The glory that rested upon Christ is a pledge of the love of God for us. It tells us of the power of prayer,—how the human voice may reach the ear of God, and our petitions find acceptance in the courts of heaven. By sin, earth was cut off from heaven, and alienated from its communion; but Jesus has connected it again with the sphere of glory. His love has encircled man, and reached the highest heaven. The light which fell from the open portals upon the head of our Saviour will fall upon us as we pray for help to resist temptation. The voice which spoke to Jesus says to every believing soul, This is My beloved child, in whom I am well pleased.

"Beloved, now are we the sons of God, and it doth not yet appear what we shall be: but we know that, when He shall appear, we shall be like Him; for we shall see Him as He is." 1 John 3:2. Our Redeemer has opened the way so that the most sinful, the most needy, the most oppressed and despised, may find access to the Father. All may have a home in the mansions which Jesus has gone to prepare. "These things saith He that is holy, He that is true, He that hath the key of David, He that openeth, and no man shutteth; and shutteth, and no man openeth; . . . behold, I have set before thee an open door, and no man can shut it." Rev. 3:7, 8.

The Temptation

And Jesus being full of the Holy Ghost returned from Jordan, and was led by the Spirit into the wilderness." The words of Mark are still more significant. He says, "Immediately the Spirit driveth Him into the wilderness. And He was there in the wilderness forty days, tempted of Satan; and was with the wild beasts." "And in those days He did eat nothing."

When Jesus was led into the wilderness to be tempted, He was led by the Spirit of God. He did not invite temptation. He went to the wilderness to be alone, to contemplate His mission and work. By fasting and prayer He was to brace Himself for the bloodstained path He must travel. But Satan knew that the Saviour had gone into the wilderness, and he thought this the best time to approach Him.

Mighty issues for the world were at stake in the conflict between the Prince of light and the leader of the kingdom of darkness. After tempting man to sin, Satan claimed the earth as his, and styled himself the prince of this world. Having conformed to his own nature the father and mother of our race, he thought to establish here his empire. He declared that men had chosen him as their sovereign. Through his control of men, he held dominion over the world. Christ had come to disprove Satan's claim. As the Son of man, Christ would stand loyal to God. Thus it would be shown that Satan had not gained complete control of the human race, and that his claim to the world was false. All who desired deliverance from his power would be set free. The dominion that Adam had lost through sin would be recovered.

Since the announcement to the serpent in Eden, "I will put enmity between thee and the woman, and between thy seed and her seed" (Gen. 3:15), Satan had known that he did not hold absolute sway over the world. There was seen in men the working of a power that withstood his dominion. With intense interest he watched the sacrifices offered by Adam and his sons. In these ceremonies he discerned a symbol of communion between earth and heaven. He set himself to intercept this communion. He misrepresented God, and misinterpreted the rites that pointed to the Saviour. Men were led to fear God as one who delighted in their destruction. The sacrifices that should have revealed His love were offered only to appease His wrath. Satan excited the evil passions of men, in order to fasten his rule upon them. When God's written word was given, Satan studied the prophecies of the Saviour's advent. From generation to generation he worked to blind the people to these prophecies, that they might reject Christ at His coming.

At the birth of Jesus, Satan knew that One had come with a divine commission to dispute his dominion. He trembled at the angel's message attesting the authority of the newborn King. Satan well knew the position that Christ had held in heaven as the Beloved of the Father. That the Son of God should come to this earth as a man filled him with amazement and with apprehension. He could not fathom the mystery of this great sacrifice. His selfish soul could not understand such love for the deceived race. The glory and peace of heaven, and the joy of communion with God, were but dimly comprehended by men; but they were well known to Lucifer, the covering cherub. Since he had lost heaven, he was determined to find revenge by causing others to share his fall. This he would do by causing them to undervalue heavenly things, and to set the heart upon things of earth.

Not without hindrance was the Commander of heaven to win the souls of men to His kingdom. From the time when He was a babe in Bethlehem, He was continually assailed by the evil one. The image of God was manifest in Christ, and in the councils of Satan it was determined that He should be overcome. No human being had come into the world and escaped the power of the deceiver. The forces of the confederacy of evil were set upon His track to engage in warfare against Him, and if possible to prevail over Him.

At the Saviour's baptism, Satan was among the witnesses. He saw the Father's glory overshadowing His Son. He heard the voice of Jehovah testifying to the divinity of Jesus. Ever since Adam's sin, the human race had been cut off from direct communion with God; the intercourse between heaven and earth had been through Christ; but now that Jesus had come "in the likeness of sinful flesh" (Rom. 8:3), the Father Himself

spoke. He had before communicated with humanity through Christ; now He communicated with humanity in Christ. Satan had hoped that God's abhorrence of evil would bring an eternal separation between heaven and earth. But now it was manifest that the connection between God and man had been restored.

Satan saw that he must either conquer or be conquered. The issues of the conflict involved too much to be entrusted to his confederate angels. He must personally conduct the warfare. All the energies of apostasy were rallied against the Son of God. Christ was made the mark of every weapon of hell.

Many look on this conflict between Christ and Satan as having no special bearing on their own life; and for them it has little interest. But within the domain of every human heart this controversy is repeated. Never does one leave the ranks of evil for the service of God without encountering the assaults of Satan. The enticements which Christ resisted were those that we find it so difficult to withstand. They were urged upon Him in as much greater degree as His character is superior to ours. With the terrible weight of the sins of the world upon Him, Christ withstood the test upon appetite, upon the love of the world, and upon that love of display which leads to presumption. These were the temptations that overcame Adam and Eve, and that so readily overcome us.

Satan had pointed to Adam's sin as proof that God's law was unjust, and could not be obeyed. In our humanity, Christ was to redeem Adam's failure. But when Adam was assailed by the tempter, none of the effects of sin were upon him. He stood in the strength of perfect manhood, possessing the full vigor of mind and body. He was surrounded with the glories of Eden, and was in daily communion with heavenly beings. It was not thus with Jesus when He entered the wilderness to cope with Satan. For four thousand years the race had been decreasing in physical strength, in mental power, and in moral worth; and Christ took upon Him the infirmities of degenerate humanity. Only thus could He rescue man from the lowest depths of his degradation.

Many claim that it was impossible for Christ to be overcome by temptation. Then He could not have been placed in Adam's position; He could not have gained the victory that Adam failed to gain. If we have in any sense a more trying conflict than had Christ, then He would not be able to succor us. But our Saviour took humanity, with all its liabilities. He took the nature of man, with the possibility of yielding to temptation. We have nothing to bear which He has not endured.

With Christ, as with the holy pair in Eden, appetite was the ground of the first great temptation. Just where the ruin began, the work of our redemption must begin. As by the indulgence of appetite Adam fell, so by the denial of appetite Christ must overcome. "And when He had fasted forty days and forty nights, He was afterward an hungred. And when the tempter came to Him, he said, If Thou be the Son of God, command that these stones be made bread. But He answered and said, It is written, Man shall not live by bread alone, but by every word that proceedeth out of the mouth of God."

From the time of Adam to that of Christ, self-indulgence had increased the power of the appetites and passions, until they had almost unlimited control. Thus men had become debased and diseased, and of themselves it was impossible for them to overcome. In man's behalf, Christ conquered by enduring the severest test. For our sake He exercised a self-control stronger than hunger or death. And in this first victory were involved other issues that enter into all our conflicts with the powers of darkness.

When Jesus entered the wilderness, He was shut in by the Father's glory. Absorbed in communion with God, He was lifted above human weakness. But the glory departed, and He was left to battle with temptation. It was pressing upon Him every moment. His human nature shrank from the conflict that awaited Him. For forty days He fasted and prayed. Weak and emaciated from hunger, worn and haggard with mental agony, "His visage was so marred more than any man, and His form more than the sons of men." Isa. 52:14. Now was Satan's opportunity. Now he supposed that he could overcome Christ.

There came to the Saviour, as if in answer to His prayers, one in the guise of an angel from heaven. He claimed to have a commission from God to declare that Christ's fast was at an end. As God had sent an angel to stay the hand of Abraham from offering Isaac, so, satisfied with Christ's willingness to enter the bloodstained path, the Father had sent an angel to deliver Him; this was the message brought to Jesus. The Saviour was faint from hunger, He was craving for food, when Satan came suddenly upon Him. Pointing to the stones which strewed the desert, and which had the appearance of loaves, the tempter said, "If Thou be the Son of God, command that these stones be made bread."

Though he appears as an angel of light, these first words betray his character. "If Thou be the Son of God." Here is the insinuation of distrust. Should Jesus do what Satan suggests, it would be an acceptance of the doubt. The tempter plans to overthrow Christ by the same means that were so successful with the human race in the beginning. How artfully had Satan approached Eve in Eden! "Yea, hath God said, Ye shall not eat of every tree of the garden?" Gen 3:1. Thus far the tempter's words were truth; but in his manner of speaking them there was a disguised contempt for the words of God. There was a covert negative, a doubt of the divine truthfulness. Satan sought to instill into the mind of Eve the thought that God would not do as He had said; that the withholding of such beautiful fruit was a contradiction of His love and compassion for man. So now the tempter seeks to inspire Christ with his own sentiments. "If Thou be the Son of God." The words rankle with bitterness in his mind. In the tones of his voice is an expression of utter incredulity. Would God treat His own Son thus? Would He leave Him in the desert with wild beasts, without food, without companions, without comfort? He insinuates that God never meant His Son to be in such a state as this. "If Thou be the Son of God,"

show Thy power by relieving Thyself of this pressing hunger. Command that this stone be made bread.

The words from heaven, "This is My beloved Son, in whom I am well pleased" (Matt. 3:17), were still sounding in the ears of Satan. But he was determined to make Christ disbelieve this testimony. The word of God was Christ's assurance of His divine mission. He had come to live as a man among men, and it was the word that declared His connection with heaven. It was Satan's purpose to cause Him to doubt that word. If Christ's confidence in God could be shaken, Satan knew that the victory in the whole controversy would be his. He could overcome Jesus. He hoped that under the force of despondency and extreme hunger, Christ would lose faith in His Father, and work a miracle in His own behalf. Had He done this, the plan of salvation would have been broken.

When Satan and the Son of God first met in conflict, Christ was the commander of the heavenly hosts; and Satan, the leader of revolt in heaven, was cast out. Now their condition is apparently reversed, and Satan makes the most of his supposed advantage. One of the most powerful of the angels, he says, has been banished from heaven. The appearance of Jesus indicates that He is that fallen angel, forsaken by God, and deserted by man. A divine being would be able to sustain his claim by working a miracle; "if Thou be the Son of God, command this stone that it be made bread." Such an act of creative power, urges the tempter, would be conclusive evidence of divinity. It would bring the controversy to an end.

Not without a struggle could Jesus listen in silence to the arch-deceiver. But the Son of God was not to prove His divinity to Satan, or to explain the reason of His humiliation. By conceding to the demands of the rebel, nothing for the good of man or the glory of God would be gained. Had Christ complied with the suggestion of the enemy, Satan would still have said, Show me a sign that I may believe you to be the Son of God. Evidence would have been worthless to break the power of rebellion in his heart. And Christ was not to exercise divine power for His own benefit. He had come to bear trial as we must do, leaving us an example of faith and submission. Neither here nor at any subsequent time in His earthly life did He work a miracle in His own behalf. His wonderful works were all for the good of others. Though Jesus recognized Satan from the beginning, He was not provoked to enter into controversy with him. Strengthened with the memory of the voice from heaven, He rested in His Father's love. He would not parley with temptation.

Jesus met Satan with the words of Scripture. "It is written," He said. In every temptation the weapon of His warfare was the word of God. Satan demanded of Christ a miracle as a sign of His divinity. But that which is greater than all miracles, a firm reliance upon a "Thus saith the Lord," was a sign that could not be controverted. So long as Christ held to this position, the tempter could gain no advantage.

It was in the time of greatest weakness that Christ was assailed by the fiercest temptations. Thus Satan thought to prevail. By this policy he had gained the victory over men. When strength failed, and the will power weakened, and faith ceased to repose in God, then those who had stood long and valiantly for the right were overcome. Moses was wearied with the forty years' wandering of Israel, when for the moment his faith let go its hold upon infinite power. He failed just upon the borders of the Promised Land. So with Elijah, who had stood undaunted before King Ahab, who had faced the whole nation of Israel, with the four hundred and fifty prophets of Baal at their head. After that terrible day upon Carmel, when the false prophets had been slain, and the people had declared their allegiance to God, Elijah fled for his life before the threats of the idolatrous Jezebel. Thus Satan has taken advantage of the weakness of humanity. And he will still work in the same way. Whenever one is encompassed with clouds, perplexed by circumstances, or afflicted by poverty or distress, Satan is at hand to tempt and annoy. He attacks our weak points of character. He seeks to shake our confidence in God, who suffers such a condition of things to exist. We are tempted to distrust God, to question His love. Often the tempter comes to us as he came to Christ, arraying before us our weakness and infirmities. He hopes to discourage the soul, and to break our hold on God. Then he is sure of his prey. If we would meet him as Jesus did, we should escape many a defeat. By parleying with the enemy, we give him an advantage.

When Christ said to the tempter, "Man shall not live by bread alone, but by every word that proceedeth out of the mouth of God," He repeated the words that, more than fourteen hundred years before, He had spoken to Israel: "The Lord thy God led thee these forty years in the wilderness. . . . And He humbled thee, and suffered thee to hunger, and fed thee with manna, which thou knewest not, neither did thy fathers know; that He might make thee know that man doth not live by bread only, but by every word that proceedeth out of the mouth of the Lord doth man live." Deut. 8:2, 3. In the wilderness, when all means of sustenance failed, God sent His people manna from heaven; and a sufficient and constant supply was given. This provision was to teach them that while they trusted in God and walked in His ways He would not forsake them. The Saviour now practiced the lesson He had taught to Israel. By the word of God succor had been given to the Hebrew host, and by the same word it would be given to Jesus. He awaited God's time to bring relief. He was in the wilderness in obedience to God, and He would not obtain food by following the suggestions of Satan. In the presence of the witnessing universe, He testified that it is a less calamity to suffer whatever may befall than to depart in any manner from the will of God.

"Man shall not live by bread alone, but by every word of God." Often the follower of Christ is brought where he cannot serve God and carry forward his worldly enterprises. Perhaps it appears that obedience to some plain requirement of God will cut off his means of support. Satan would make him believe that he must sacrifice his conscientious convictions. But the only thing in our world upon which we can rely is the word of God. "Seek ye first the kingdom of God, and His righteousness; and all these things shall be added unto you." Matt. 6:33. Even in this life it is not for our good to depart from the will of our Father in heaven. When we learn the power of His word, we shall not follow the suggestions of Satan in order to obtain food or to save our lives. Our only questions will be, What is God's command? and what His promise? Knowing these, we shall obey the one, and trust the other.

In the last great conflict of the controversy with Satan those who are loyal to God will see every earthly support cut off. Because they refuse to break His law in obedience to earthly powers, they will be forbidden to buy or sell. It will finally be decreed that they shall be put to death. See Rev. 13:11-17. But to the obedient is given the promise, "He shall dwell on high: his place of defense shall be the munitions of rocks: bread shall be given him; his waters shall be sure." Isa. 33:16. By this promise the children of God will live. When the earth shall be wasted with famine, they shall be fed. "They shall not be ashamed in the evil time: and in the days of famine they shall be satisfied." Ps. 37:19. To that time of distress the prophet Habakkuk looked forward, and his words express the faith of the church: "Although the fig tree shall not blossom, neither shall fruit be in the vines; the labor of the olive shall fail, and the fields shall yield no meat; the flock shall be cut off from the fold, and there shall be no herd in the stalls: yet I will rejoice in the Lord, I will joy in the God of my salvation." Hab. 3:17,18.

Of all the lessons to be learned from our Lord's first great temptation none is more important than that bearing upon the control of the appetites and passions. In all ages, temptations appealing to the physical nature have been most effectual in corrupting and degrading mankind. Through intemperance, Satan works to destroy the mental and moral powers that God gave to man as a priceless endowment. Thus it becomes impossible for men to appreciate things of eternal worth. Through sensual indulgence, Satan seeks to blot from the soul every trace of likeness to God.

The uncontrolled indulgence and consequent disease and degradation that existed at Christ's first advent will again exist, with intensity of evil, before His second coming. Christ declares that the condition of the world will be as in the days before the Flood, and as in Sodom and Gomorrah. Every imagination of the thoughts of the heart will be evil continually. Upon the very verge of that fearful time we are now living, and to us should come home the lesson of the Saviour's fast. Only by the inexpressible anguish which Christ endured can we estimate the evil of unrestrained indulgence. His example declares that our only hope of eternal life is through bringing the appetites and passions into subjection to the will of God.

In our own strength it is impossible for us to deny the clamors of our fallen nature. Through this channel Satan will bring temptation upon us. Christ knew that the enemy would come to every human being, to take advantage of hereditary weakness, and by his false insinuations to ensnare all whose trust is not in God. And by passing over the ground which man must travel, our Lord has prepared the way for us to overcome. It is not His will that we should be placed at a disadvantage in the conflict with Satan. He would not have us intimidated and discouraged by the assaults of the serpent. "Be of good cheer," He says; "I have overcome the world." John 16:33.

Let him who is struggling against the power of appetite look to the Saviour in the wilderness of temptation. See Him in His agony upon the cross, as He exclaimed, "I thirst." He has endured all that it is possible for us to bear. His victory is ours.

Jesus rested upon the wisdom and strength of His heavenly Father. He declares, "The Lord God will help Me; therefore shall I not be confounded: . . . and I know that I shall not be ashamed. . . . Behold, the Lord God will help Me." Pointing to His own example, He says to us, "Who is among you that feareth the Lord, . . . that walketh in darkness, and hath no light? let him trust in the name of the Lord, and stay upon his God." Isa. 50:7-10.

"The prince of this world cometh," said Jesus, "and hath nothing in Me." John 14:30. There was in Him nothing that responded to Satan's sophistry. He did not consent to sin. Not even by a thought did He yield to temptation. So it may be with us. Christ's humanity was united with divinity; He was fitted for the conflict by the indwelling of the Holy Spirit. And He came to make us partakers of the divine nature. So long as we are united to Him by faith, sin has no more dominion over us. God reaches for the hand of faith in us to direct it to lay fast hold upon the divinity of Christ, that we may attain to perfection of character.

And how this is accomplished, Christ has shown us. By what means did He overcome in the conflict with Satan? By the word of God. Only by the word could He resist temptation. "It is written," He said. And unto us are given "exceeding great and precious promises: that by these ye might be partakers of the divine nature, having escaped the corruption that is in the world through lust." 2 Peter 1:4. Every promise in God's word is ours. "By every word that proceedeth out of the mouth of God" are we to live. When assailed by temptation, look not to circumstances or to the weakness of self, but to the power of the word. All its strength is yours. "Thy word," says the psalmist, "have I hid in mine heart, that I might not sin against Thee." "By the word of Thy lips I have kept me from the paths of the destroyer." Ps. 119:11; 17:4.

The Victory

Then the devil taketh Him up into the holy city, and setteth Him on a pinnacle of the temple, and saith unto Him, If Thou be the Son of God, cast Thyself down: for it is written,—

"He shall give His angels charge concerning Thee:
And in their hands they shall bear Thee up,
Lest at any time Thou dash Thy foot against a stone."

Satan now supposes that he has met Jesus on His own ground. The wily foe himself presents words that proceeded from the mouth of God. He still appears as an angel of light, and he makes it evident that he is acquainted with the Scriptures, and understands the import of what is written. As Jesus before used the word of God to sustain His faith, the tempter now uses it to countenance his deception. He claims that he has been only testing the fidelity of Jesus, and he now commends His steadfastness. As the Saviour has manifested trust in God, Satan urges Him to give still another evidence of His faith.

But again the temptation is prefaced with the insinuation of distrust, "If Thou be the Son of God." Christ was tempted to answer the "if;" but He refrained from the slightest acceptance of the doubt. He would not imperil His life in order to give evidence to Satan.

The tempter thought to take advantage of Christ's humanity, and urge Him to presumption. But while Satan can solicit, he cannot compel to sin. He said to Jesus, "Cast Thyself down," knowing that he could not cast Him down; for God would interpose to deliver Him. Nor could Satan force Jesus to cast Himself down. Unless Christ should consent to temptation, He could not be overcome. Not all the power of earth or hell could force Him in the slightest degree to depart from the will of His Father.

The tempter can never compel us to do evil. He cannot control minds unless they are yielded to his control. The will must consent, faith must let go its hold upon Christ, before Satan can exercise his power upon us. But every sinful desire we cherish affords him a foothold. Every point in which we fail of meeting the divine standard is an open door by which he can enter to tempt and destroy us. And every failure or defeat on our part gives occasion for him to reproach Christ.

When Satan quoted the promise, "He shall give His angels charge over Thee," he omitted the words, "to keep Thee in all Thy ways;" that is, in all the ways of God's choosing. Jesus refused to go outside the path of obedience. While manifesting perfect trust in His Father, He would not place Himself, unbidden, in a position that would necessitate the interposition of His Father to save Him from death. He would not force Providence to come to His rescue, and thus fail of giving man an example of trust and submission.

Jesus declared to Satan, "It is written again, Thou shalt not tempt the Lord thy God." These words were spoken by Moses to the children of Israel when they thirsted in the desert, and demanded that Moses should give them water, exclaiming, "Is the Lord among us, or not?" Exodus 17:7. God had wrought marvelously for them; yet in trouble they doubted Him, and demanded evidence that He was with them. In their unbelief they sought to put Him to the test. And Satan was urging Christ to do the same thing. God had already testified that

Jesus was His Son; and now to ask for proof that He was the Son of God would be putting God's word to the test,—tempting Him. And the same would be true of asking for that which God had not promised. It would manifest distrust, and be really proving, or tempting, Him. We should not present our petitions to God to prove whether He will fulfill His word, but because He will fulfill it; not to prove that He loves us, but because He loves us. "Without faith it is impossible to please Him: for he that cometh to God must believe that He is, and that He is a rewarder of them that diligently seek Him." Heb. 11:6.

But faith is in no sense allied to presumption. Only he who has true faith is secure against presumption. For presumption is Satan's counterfeit of faith. Faith claims God's promises, and brings forth fruit in obedience. Presumption also claims the promises, but uses them as Satan did, to excuse transgression. Faith would have led our first parents to trust the love of God, and to obey His commands. Presumption led them to transgress His law, believing that His great love would save them from the consequence of their sin. It is not faith that claims the favor of Heaven without complying with the conditions on which mercy is to be granted. Genuine faith has its foundation in the promises and provisions of the Scriptures.

Often when Satan has failed of exciting distrust, he succeeds in leading us to presumption. If he can cause us to place ourselves unnecessarily in the way of temptation, he knows that the victory is his. God will preserve all who walk in the path of obedience; but to depart from it is to venture on Satan's ground. There we are sure to fall. The Saviour has bidden us, "Watch ye and pray, lest ye enter into temptation." Mark 14:38. Meditation and prayer would keep us from rushing unbidden into the way of danger, and thus we should be saved from many a defeat.

Yet we should not lose courage when assailed by temptation. Often when placed in a trying situation we doubt that the Spirit of God has been leading us. But it was the Spirit's leading that brought Jesus into the wilderness to be tempted by Satan. When God brings us into trial, He has a purpose to accomplish for our good. Jesus did not presume on God's promises by going unbidden into temptation, neither did He give up to despondency when temptation came upon Him. Nor should we. "God is faithful, who will not suffer you to be tempted above that ye are able; but will with the temptation also make a way to escape, that ye may be able to bear it." He says, "Offer unto God thanksgiving; and pay thy vows unto the Most High: and call upon Me in the day of trouble: I will deliver thee, and thou shalt glorify Me." 1 Cor. 10:13; Ps. 50:14, 15.

Jesus was victor in the second temptation, and now Satan manifests himself in his true character. But he does not appear as a hideous monster, with cloven feet and bat's wings. He is a mighty angel, though fallen. He avows himself the leader of rebellion and the god of this world.

Placing Jesus upon a high mountain, Satan caused the kingdoms of the world, in all their glory, to pass in panoramic view before Him. The sunlight lay on templed cities, marble palaces, fertile fields, and fruit-laden vineyards. The traces of evil were hidden. The eyes of Jesus, so lately greeted by gloom and desolation, now gazed upon a scene of unsurpassed loveliness and prosperity. Then the tempter's voice was heard: "All this power will I give Thee, and the glory of them: for that is delivered unto me; and to whomsoever I will I give it. If Thou therefore wilt worship me, all shall be Thine."

Christ's mission could be fulfilled only through suffering. Before Him was a life of sorrow, hardship, and conflict, and an ignominious death. He must bear the sins of the whole world. He must endure separation from His Father's love. Now the tempter offered to yield up the power he had usurped. Christ might deliver Himself from the dreadful future by acknowledging the supremacy of Satan. But to do this was to yield the victory in the great controversy. It was in seeking to exalt himself above the Son of God that Satan had sinned in heaven. Should he prevail now, it would be the triumph of rebellion.

When Satan declared to Christ, The kingdom and glory of the world are delivered unto me, and to whomsoever I will I give it, he stated what was true only in part, and he declared it to serve his own purpose of deception. Satan's dominion was that wrested from Adam, but Adam was the vicegerent of the Creator. His was not an independent rule. The earth is God's, and He has committed all things to His Son. Adam was to reign subject to Christ. When Adam betrayed his sovereignty into Satan's hands, Christ still remained the rightful King. Thus the Lord had said to King Nebuchadnezzar, "The Most High ruleth in the kingdom of men, and giveth it to whomsoever He will." Dan. 4:17. Satan can exercise his usurped authority only as God permits.

When the tempter offered to Christ the kingdom and glory of the world, he was proposing that Christ should yield up the real kingship of the world, and hold dominion subject to Satan. This was the same dominion upon which the hopes of the Jews were set. They desired the kingdom of this world. If Christ had consented to offer them such a kingdom, they would gladly have received Him. But the curse of sin, with all its woe, rested upon it. Christ declared to the tempter, "Get thee behind Me, Satan: for it is written, Thou shalt worship the Lord thy God, and Him only shalt thou serve."

By the one who had revolted in heaven the kingdoms of this world were offered Christ, to buy His homage to the principles of evil; but He would not be bought; He had come to establish a kingdom of righteousness, and He would not abandon His purpose. With the same temptation Satan approaches men, and here he has better success than with Christ. To men he offers the kingdom of this world on condition that they will acknowledge his supremacy. He requires that they sacrifice integrity, disregard conscience, indulge selfishness. Christ bids them seek first the kingdom of God, and His righteousness; but Satan walks by their side and says: Whatever may be true in regard to life eternal, in order to make a success in this world you must serve me. I hold your welfare in my hands. I can give you riches, pleasures, honor, and happiness. Hearken to my counsel. Do not allow yourselves to be carried away with whimsical notions of honesty or self-sacrifice. I will prepare the way before you." Thus multitudes are deceived. They consent to live for the service of self, and Satan is satisfied. While he allures them with the hope of worldly dominion, he gains dominion over the soul. But he offers that which is not his to bestow, and which is soon to be wrested from him. In return he beguiles them of their title to the inheritance of the sons of God.

Satan had questioned whether Jesus was the Son of God. In his summary dismissal he had proof that he could not gainsay. Divinity flashed through suffering humanity. Satan had no power to resist the command. Writhing with humiliation and rage, he was forced to withdraw from the presence of the world's Redeemer. Christ's victory was as complete as had been the failure of Adam.

So we may resist temptation, and force Satan to depart from us. Jesus gained the victory through submission and faith in God, and by the apostle He says to us, "Submit yourselves therefore to God. Resist the devil, and he will flee from you. Draw nigh to God, and He will draw nigh to you." James 4:7, 8. We cannot save ourselves from the tempter's power; he has conquered humanity, and when we try to stand in our own strength, we shall become a prey to his devices; but "the name of the Lord is a strong tower: the righteous runneth into it, and is safe." Prov. 18:10. Satan trembles and flees before the weakest soul who finds refuge in that mighty name.

After the foe had departed, Jesus fell exhausted to the earth, with the pallor of death upon His face. The angels of heaven had watched the conflict, beholding their loved Commander as He passed through inexpressible suffering to make a way of escape for us. He had endured the test, greater than we shall ever be called to endure. The angels now ministered to the Son of God as He lay like one dying. He was strengthened with food, comforted with the message of His Father's love and the assurance that all heaven triumphed in His victory. Warming to life again, His great heart goes out in sympathy for man, and He goes forth to complete the work He has begun; to rest not until the foe is vanquished, and our fallen race redeemed.

Never can the cost of our redemption be realized until the redeemed shall stand with the Redeemer before the throne of God. Then as the glories of the eternal home burst upon our enraptured senses we shall remember that Jesus left all this for us, that He not only became an exile from the heavenly courts, but for us took the risk of failure and eternal loss. Then we shall cast our crowns at His feet, and raise the song, "Worthy is the Lamb that was slain to receive power, and riches, and wisdom, and strength, and honor, and glory, and blessing." Rev. 5:12.

"We Have Found the Messias"

John the Baptist was now preaching and baptizing at Bethabara, beyond Jordan. It was not far from this spot that God had stayed the river in its flow until Israel had passed over. A little distance from here the stronghold of Jericho had been overthrown by the armies of heaven. The memory of these events was at this time revived, and gave a thrilling interest to the Baptist's message. Would not He who had wrought so wonderfully in ages past again manifest His power for Israel's deliverance? Such was the thought stirring the hearts of the people who daily thronged the banks of the Jordan.

The preaching of John had taken so deep a hold on the nation as to demand the attention of the religious authorities. The danger of insurrection caused every popular gathering to be looked upon with suspicion by the Romans, and whatever pointed toward an uprising of the people excited the fears of the Jewish rulers. John had not recognized the authority of the Sanhedrin by seeking their sanction for his work; and he had reproved rulers and people, Pharisees and Sadducees alike. Yet the people followed him eagerly. The interest in his work seemed to be continually increasing. Though he had not deferred to them, the Sanhedrin accounted that, as a public teacher, he was under their jurisdiction.

This body was made up of members chosen from the priesthood, and from the chief rulers and teachers of the nation. The high priest was usually the president. All its members were to be men advanced in years, though not aged; men of learning, not only versed in Jewish religion and history, but in general knowledge. They were to be without physical blemish, and must be married men, and fathers, as being more likely than others to be humane and considerate. Their place of meeting was an apartment connected with the temple at Jerusalem. In the days of Jewish independence the Sanhedrin was the supreme court of the nation, possessing secular as well as ecclesiastical authority. Though now subordinated by the Roman governors, it still exercised a strong influence in civil as well as religious matters.

The Sanhedrin could not well defer an investigation of John's work. There were some who recalled the revelation made to Zacharias in the temple, and the father's prophecy, that had pointed to his child as the Messiah's herald. In the tumults and changes of thirty years, these things had in a great measure been lost sight of. They were now called to mind by the excitement concerning the ministry of John.

It was long since Israel had had a prophet, long since such a reformation as was now in progress had been witnessed. The demand for confession of sin seemed new and startling. Many among the leaders would not go to hear John's appeals and denunciations, lest they should be led to disclose the secrets of their own lives. Yet his preaching was a direct announcement of the Messiah. It was well known that the seventy weeks of Daniel's prophecy, covering the Messiah's advent, were nearly ended; and all were eager to share in that era of national glory which was then expected. Such was the popular enthusiasm that the Sanhedrin would soon be forced either to sanction or to reject John's work. Already their power over the people was waning. It was becoming a serious question how to maintain their position. In the hope of arriving at some conclusion, they dispatched to the Jordan a deputation of priests and Levites to confer with the new teacher.

A multitude were gathered, listening to his words, when the delegates approached. With an air of authority designed to impress the people and to command the deference of the prophet the haughty rabbis came. With a movement of respect, almost of fear, the crowd opened to let them pass. The great men, in their rich robes, in the pride of rank and power, stood before the prophet of the wilderness.

"Who art thou?" they demanded.

Knowing what was in their thoughts, John answered, "I am not the Christ."

"What then? Art thou Elias?"

"I am not."

"Art thou that prophet?"

"No."

"Who art thou? that we may give an answer to them that sent us. What sayest thou of thyself?"

"I am the voice of one crying in the wilderness, Make straight the way of the Lord, as said the prophet Esaias."

The scripture to which John referred is that beautiful prophecy of Isaiah: "Comfort ye, comfort ye My people, saith your God. Speak ye comfortably to Jerusalem, and cry unto her, that her appointed time is accomplished, that her iniquity is pardoned. . . . The voice of him that crieth in the wilderness, Prepare ye the way of the Lord, make straight in the desert a highway for our God. Every valley shall be exalted, and every mountain and hill shall be made low: and the crooked shall be made straight, and the rough places plain: and the glory of the Lord shall be revealed, and all flesh shall see it together." Isa. 40:1-5, margin.

Anciently, when a king journeyed through the less frequented parts of his dominion, a company of men was sent ahead of the royal chariot to level the steep places and to fill up the hollows, that the king might travel in safety and without hindrance. This custom is employed by the prophet to illustrate the work of the gospel. "Every valley shall be exalted, and every mountain and hill shall be made low." When the Spirit of God, with its marvelous awakening power, touches the soul, it abases human pride. Worldly pleasure and position and power are seen to be worthless. "Imaginations, and every high thing that exalteth itself against the knowledge of God" are cast down; every thought is brought into captivity "to the obedience of Christ." 2 Cor. 10:5. Then humility and self-sacrificing love, so little valued among men, are exalted as alone of worth. This is the work of the gospel, of which John's message was a part.

The rabbis continued their questioning: "Why baptizest thou then, if thou be not that Christ, nor Elias, neither that prophet?" The words "that prophet" had reference to Moses. The Jews had been inclined to the belief that Moses would be raised from the dead, and taken to heaven. They did not know that he had already been raised. When the Baptist began his ministry, many thought that he might be the prophet Moses risen from the dead, for he seemed to have a thorough knowledge of the prophecies and of the history of Israel.

It was believed also that before the Messiah's advent, Elijah would personally appear. This expectation John met in his denial; but his words had a deeper meaning. Jesus afterward said, referring to John, "If ye are willing to receive it, this is Elijah, which is to come." Matt. 11:14, R. V. John came in the spirit and power of Elijah, to do such a work as Elijah did. If the Jews had received him, it would have been accomplished for them. But they did not receive his message. To them he was not Elijah. He could not fulfill for them the mission he came to accomplish.

Many of those gathered at the Jordan had been present at the baptism of Jesus; but the sign then given had been manifest to but few among them. During the preceding months of the Baptist's ministry, many had refused to heed the call to repentance. Thus they had hardened their hearts and darkened their understanding. When Heaven bore testimony to Jesus at His baptism, they perceived it not. Eyes that had never been turned in faith to Him that is invisible beheld not the revelation of the glory of God; ears that had never listened to His voice heard not the words of witness. So it is now. Often the presence of Christ and the ministering angels is manifest in the assemblies of the people, and yet there are many who know it not. They discern nothing unusual. But to some the Saviour's presence is revealed. Peace and joy animate their hearts. They are comforted, encouraged, and blessed.

The deputies from Jerusalem had demanded of John, "Why baptizest thou?" and they were awaiting his answer. Suddenly, as his glance swept over the throng, his eye kindled, his face was lighted up, his whole being was stirred with deep emotion. With outstretched hands he cried, "I baptize in water: in the midst of you standeth One whom ye know not, even He that cometh after me, the latchet of whose shoe I am not worthy to unloose." John 1:27, R. V., margin.

The message was distinct and unequivocal, to be carried back to the Sanhedrin. The words of John could apply to no other than the long-promised One. The Messiah was among them! In amazement priests and rulers gazed about them, hoping to discover Him of whom John had spoken. But He was not distinguishable among the throng.

When at the baptism of Jesus, John pointed to Him as the Lamb of God, a new light was shed upon the Messiah's work. The prophet's mind was directed to the words of Isaiah, "He is brought as a lamb to the slaughter." Isa. 53:7. During the weeks that followed, John with new interest studied the prophecies and the teaching of the sacrificial service. He did not distinguish clearly the two phases of Christ's work,—as a suffering sacrifice and a conquering king,—but he saw that His coming had a deeper significance than priests or people had discerned. When he beheld Jesus among the throng on His return from the desert, he confidently looked for Him to give the people some sign of His true character. Almost impatiently he waited to hear the Saviour declare His mission; but no word was spoken, no sign given. Jesus did not respond to the Baptist's announcement of Him, but mingled with the disciples of John, giving no outward evidence of His special work, and taking no measures to bring Himself to notice.

The next day John sees Jesus coming. With the light of the glory of God resting upon him, the prophet stretches out his hands, declaring, "Behold the Lamb of God, which taketh away the sin of the world! This is He of whom I said, After me cometh a man which is become before me. . . . And I knew Him not; but that He should be made manifest to Israel, for this cause came I baptizing in water. . . . I have beheld the Spirit descending as a dove out of heaven; and it abode upon Him. And I knew Him not: but He that sent me to baptize in water, He said unto me, Upon whomsoever thou shalt see the Spirit descending, and abiding upon Him, the same is He that baptizeth with the Holy Spirit. And I have seen, and have borne witness that this is the Son of God." John 1:29-34, R. V., margin.

Was this the Christ? With awe and wonder the people looked upon the One just declared to be the Son of God. They had been deeply moved by the words of John. He had spoken to them in the name of God. They had listened to him day after day as he reproved their sins, and daily the conviction that he was sent of Heaven had strengthened. But who was this One greater than John the Baptist? In His dress and bearing there was nothing that betokened rank. He was apparently a simple personage, clad like themselves in the humble garments of the poor.

There were in the throng some who at Christ's baptism had beheld the divine glory, and had heard the voice of God. But since that time the Saviour's appearance had greatly changed. At His baptism they had seen His countenance transfigured in the light of heaven; now, pale, worn, and emaciated, He had been recognized only by the prophet John.

But as the people looked upon Him, they saw a face where divine compassion was blended with conscious power. Every glance of the eye, every feature of the countenance, was marked with humility, and expressive of unutterable love. He seemed to be surrounded by an atmosphere of spiritual influence. While His manners were gentle and unassuming, He impressed men with a sense of power that was hidden, yet could not be wholly concealed. Was this the One for whom Israel had so long waited?

Jesus came in poverty and humiliation, that He might be our example as well as our Redeemer. If He had appeared with kingly pomp, how could He have taught humility? how could He have presented such cutting truths as in the Sermon on the Mount? Where would have been the hope of the lowly in life had Jesus come to dwell as a king among men?

To the multitude, however, it seemed impossible that the One designated by John should be associated with their lofty anticipations. Thus many were disappointed, and greatly perplexed.

The words which the priests and rabbis so much desired to hear, that Jesus would now restore the kingdom to Israel, had not been spoken. For such a king they had been waiting and watching; such a king they were ready to receive. But one who sought to establish in their hearts a kingdom of righteousness and peace, they would not accept.

On the following day, while two disciples were standing near, John again saw Jesus among the people. Again the face of the prophet was lighted up with glory from the Unseen, as he cried, "Behold the Lamb of God!" The words thrilled the hearts of the disciples. They did not fully understand them. What meant the name that John had given Him,—"the Lamb of God"? John himself had not explained it.

Leaving John, they went to seek Jesus. One of the two was Andrew, the brother of Simon; the other was John the evangelist. These were Christ's first disciples. Moved by an irresistible impulse, they followed Jesus,—anxious to speak with Him, yet awed and silent, lost in the overwhelming significance of the thought, "Is this the Messiah?"

Jesus knew that the disciples were following Him. They were the first fruits of His ministry, and there was joy in the heart of the divine Teacher as these souls responded to His grace. Yet turning, He asked only, "What seek ye?" He would leave them free to turn back or to speak of their desire.

Of one purpose only were they conscious. One presence filled their thought. They exclaimed, "Rabbi, . . . where dwellest Thou?" In a brief interview by the wayside they could not receive that for which they longed. They desired to be alone with Jesus, to sit at His feet, and hear His words.

"He saith unto them, Come and see. They came and saw where He dwelt, and abode with Him that day."

If John and Andrew had possessed the unbelieving spirit of the priests and rulers, they would not have been found as learners at the feet of Jesus. They would have come to Him as critics, to judge His words. Many thus close the door to the most precious opportunities. But not so did these first disciples. They had responded to the Holy Spirit's call in the preaching of John the Baptist. Now they recognized the voice of the heavenly Teacher. To them the words of Jesus were full of freshness and truth and beauty. A divine illumination was shed upon the teaching of the Old Testament Scriptures. The many-sided themes of truth stood out in new light.

It is contrition and faith and love that enable the soul to receive wisdom from heaven. Faith working by love is the key of knowledge, and everyone that loveth "knoweth God." 1 John 4:7.

The disciple John was a man of earnest and deep affection, ardent, yet contemplative. He had begun to discern the glory of Christ,—not the worldly pomp and power for which he had been taught to hope, but "the glory as of the Only-begotten of the Father, full of grace and truth." John 1:14. He was absorbed in contemplation of the wondrous theme.

Andrew sought to impart the joy that filled his heart. Going in search of his brother Simon, he cried, "We have found the Messias." Simon waited for no second bidding. He also had heard the preaching of John the Baptist, and he hastened to the Saviour. The eye of Christ rested upon him, reading his character and his life history. His impulsive nature, his loving, sympathetic heart, his ambition and self-confidence, the history of his fall, his repentance, his labors, and his martyr death,—the Saviour read it all, and He said, "Thou art Simon the son of Jona: thou shalt be called Cephas, which is by interpretation, A stone."

"The day following Jesus would go forth into Galilee, and findeth Philip, and saith unto him, Follow Me." Philip obeyed the command, and straightway he also became a worker for Christ.

Philip called Nathanael. The latter had been among the throng when the Baptist pointed to Jesus as the Lamb of God. As Nathanael looked upon Jesus, he was disappointed. Could this man, who bore the marks of toil and poverty, be the Messiah? Yet Nathanael could not decide to reject Jesus, for the message of John had brought conviction to his heart.

At the time when Philip called him, Nathanael had withdrawn to a quiet grove to meditate upon the announcement of John and the prophecies concerning the Messiah. He prayed that if the one announced by John was the deliverer, it might be made known to him, and the Holy Spirit rested upon him with assurance that God had visited His people and raised up a horn of salvation for them. Philip knew that his friend was searching the prophecies, and while Nathanael was praying under a fig tree, Philip discovered his retreat. They had often prayed together in this secluded spot hidden by the foliage.

The message, "We have found Him, of whom Moses in the law, and the prophets, did write," seemed to Nathanael a direct answer to his prayer. But Philip had yet a trembling faith. He added doubtfully, "Jesus of Nazareth, the son of Joseph." Again prejudice arose in Nathanael's heart. He exclaimed, "Can there any good thing come out of Nazareth?"

Philip entered into no controversy. He said, "Come and see. Jesus saw Nathanael coming to Him, and saith of him, Behold an Israelite indeed, in whom is no guile!" In surprise Nathanael exclaimed, "Whence knowest Thou me? Jesus answered and said unto him, Before that Philip called thee, when thou wast under the fig tree, I saw thee."

It was enough. The divine Spirit that had borne witness to Nathanael in his solitary prayer under the fig tree now spoke to him in the words of Jesus. Though in doubt, and yielding somewhat to prejudice, Nathanael had come to Christ with an honest desire for truth, and now his desire was met. His faith went beyond that of the one who had brought him to Jesus. He answered and said, "Rabbi, Thou art the Son of God; Thou art the King of Israel."

If Nathanael had trusted to the rabbis for guidance, he would never have found Jesus. It was by seeing and judging for himself that he became a disciple. So in the case of many today whom prejudice withholds from good. How different would be the result if they would "come and see"!

While they trust to the guidance of human authority, none will come to a saving knowledge of the truth. Like Nathanael, we need to study God's word for ourselves, and pray for the enlightenment of the Holy Spirit. He who saw Nathanael under the fig tree will see us in the secret place of prayer. Angels from the world of light are near to those who in humility seek for divine guidance.

With the calling of John and Andrew and Simon, of Philip and Nathanael, began the foundation of the Christian church. John directed two of his disciples to Christ. Then one of these, Andrew, found his brother, and called him to the Saviour. Philip was then called, and he went in search of Nathanael. These examples should teach us the importance of personal effort, of making direct appeals to our kindred, friends, and neighbors. There are those who for a lifetime have professed to be acquainted with Christ, yet who have never made a personal effort to bring even one soul to the Saviour. They leave all the work for the minister. He may be well qualified for his calling, but he cannot do that which God has left for the members of the church.

There are many who need the ministration of loving Christian hearts. Many have gone down to ruin who might have been saved if their neighbors, common men and women, had put forth personal effort for them. Many are waiting to be personally addressed. In the very family, the neighborhood, the town, where we live, there is work for us to do as missionaries for Christ. If we are Christians, this work will be our delight. No sooner is one converted than there is born within him a desire to make known to others what a precious friend he has found in Jesus. The saving and sanctifying truth cannot be shut up in his heart.

All who are consecrated to God will be channels of light. God makes them His agents to communicate to others the riches of His grace. His promise is, "I will make them and the places round about My hill a blessing; and I will cause the shower to come down in his season; there shall be showers of blessing." Ezek. 34:26.

Philip said to Nathanael, "Come and see." He did not ask him to accept another's testimony, but to behold Christ for himself. Now that Jesus has ascended to heaven, His disciples are His representatives among men, and one of the most effective ways of winning souls to Him is in exemplifying His character in our daily life. Our influence upon others depends not so much upon what we say as upon what we are. Men may combat and defy our logic, they may resist our appeals; but a life of disinterested love is an argument they cannot gainsay. A consistent life, characterized by the meekness of Christ, is a power in the world.

The teaching of Christ was the expression of an inwrought conviction and experience, and those who learn of Him become teachers after the divine order. The word of God, spoken by one who is himself sanctified through it, has a life-giving power that makes it attractive to the hearers, and convicts them that it is a living reality. When one has received the truth in the love of it, he will make this manifest in the persuasion of his manner and the tones of his voice. He makes known that which he himself has heard, seen, and handled of the word of life, that others may have fellowship with him through the knowledge of Christ. His testimony, from lips touched with a live coal from off the altar, is truth to the receptive heart, and works sanctification upon the character.

And he who seeks to give light to others will himself be blessed. "There shall be showers of blessing." "He that watereth shall be watered also himself." Prov. 11:25. God could have reached His object in saving sinners without our aid; but in order for us to develop a character like Christ's, we must share in His work. In order to enter into His joy,—the joy of seeing souls redeemed by His sacrifice,—we must participate in His labors for their redemption.

Nathanael's first expression of his faith, so full and earnest and sincere, fell like music on the ears of Jesus. And He "answered and said unto him, Because I said unto thee, I saw thee under the fig tree, believest thou? thou shalt see greater things than these." The Saviour looked forward with joy to His work in preaching good tidings to the meek, binding up the brokenhearted, and proclaiming liberty to the captives of Satan. At thought of the precious blessings He had brought to men, Jesus added, "Verily, verily, I say unto you, Hereafter ye shall see heaven open, and the angels of God ascending and descending upon the Son of man."

Here Christ virtually says, On the bank of the Jordan the heavens were opened, and the Spirit descended like a dove upon Me. That scene was but a token that I am the Son of God. If you believe on Me as such, your faith shall be quickened. You shall see that the heavens are opened, and are never to be closed. I have opened them to you. The angels of God are ascending, bearing the prayers of the needy and distressed to the Father above, and descending, bringing blessing and hope, courage, help, and life, to the children of men.

The angels of God are ever passing from earth to heaven, and from heaven to earth. The miracles of Christ for the afflicted and suffering were wrought by the power of God through the ministration of the angels. And it is through Christ, by the ministration of His heavenly messengers, that every blessing comes from God to us. In taking upon Himself humanity, our Saviour unites His interests with those of the fallen sons and daughters of Adam, while through His divinity He grasps the throne of God. And thus Christ is the medium of communication of men with God, and of God with men.

At the Marriage Feast

Jesus did not begin His ministry by some great work before the Sanhedrin at Jerusalem. At a household gathering in a little Galilean village His power was put forth to add to the joy of a wedding feast. Thus He showed His sympathy with men, and His desire to minister to their happiness. In the wilderness of temptation He Himself had drunk the cup of woe. He came forth to give to men the cup of blessing, by His benediction to hallow the relations of human life.

From the Jordan, Jesus had returned to Galilee. There was to be a marriage at Cana, a little town not far from Nazareth; the parties were relatives of Joseph and Mary; and Jesus, knowing of this family gathering, went to Cana, and with His disciples was invited to the feast.

Again He met His mother, from whom He had for some time been separated. Mary had heard of the manifestation at the Jordan, at His baptism. The tidings had been carried to Nazareth, and had brought to her mind afresh the scenes that for so many years had been hidden in her heart. In common with all Israel, Mary was deeply stirred by the mission of John the Baptist. Well she remembered the prophecy given at his birth. Now his connection with Jesus kindled her hopes anew. But tidings had reached her also of the mysterious departure of Jesus to the wilderness, and she was oppressed with troubled forebodings.

From the day when she heard the angel's announcement in the home at Nazareth Mary had treasured every evidence that Jesus was the Messiah. His sweet, unselfish life assured her that He could be no other than the Sent of God. Yet there came to her also doubts and disappointments, and she had longed for the time when His glory should be revealed. Death had separated her from Joseph, who had shared her knowledge of the mystery of the birth of Jesus. Now there was no one to whom she could confide her hopes and fears. The past two months had been very sorrowful. She had been parted from Jesus, in whose sympathy she found comfort; she pondered upon the words of Simeon, "A sword shall pierce through thy own soul also" (Luke 2:35); she recalled the three days of agony when she thought Jesus lost to her forever; and with an anxious heart she awaited His return.

At the marriage feast she meets Him, the same tender, dutiful son. Yet He is not the same. His countenance is changed. It bears the traces of His conflict in the wilderness, and a new expression of dignity and power gives evidence of His heavenly mission. With Him is a group of young men, whose eyes follow Him with reverence, and who call Him Master. These companions recount to Mary what they have seen and heard at the baptism and elsewhere. They conclude by declaring, "We have found Him, of whom Moses in the law, and the prophets, did write." John 1:45.

As the guests assemble, many seem to be preoccupied with some topic of absorbing interest. A suppressed excitement pervades the company. Little groups converse together in eager but quiet tones, and wondering glances are turned upon the Son of Mary. As Mary had heard the disciples' testimony in regard to Jesus, she had been gladdened with the assurance that her long-cherished hopes were not in vain. Yet she would have been more than human if there had not mingled with this holy joy a trace of the fond mother's natural pride. As she saw the many glances bent upon Jesus, she longed to have Him prove to the company that He was really the Honored of God. She hoped there might be opportunity for Him to work a miracle before them.

It was the custom of the times for marriage festivities to continue several days. On this occasion, before the feast ended it was found that the supply of wine had failed. This discovery caused much perplexity and regret. It was unusual to dispense with wine on festive occasions, and its absence would seem to indicate a want of hospitality. As a relative of the parties, Mary had assisted in the arrangements for the feast, and she now spoke to Jesus, saying, "They have no wine." These words were a suggestion that He might supply their need. But Jesus answered, "Woman, what have I to do with thee? Mine hour is not yet come."

This answer, abrupt as it seems to us, expressed no coldness or discourtesy. The Saviour's form of address to His mother was in accordance with Oriental custom. It was used toward persons to whom it was desired to show respect. Every act of Christ's earthly life was in harmony with the precept He Himself had given, "Honor thy father and thy mother." Ex. 20:12. On the cross, in His last act of tenderness toward His mother, Jesus again addressed her in the same way, as He committed her to the care of His best-loved disciple. Both at the marriage feast and upon the cross, the love expressed in tone and look and manner interpreted His words.

At His visit to the temple in His boyhood, as the mystery of His lifework opened before Him, Christ had said to Mary, "Wist ye not that I must be about My Father's business?" Luke 2:49. These words struck the keynote of His whole life and ministry. Everything was held in abeyance to His work, the great work of redemption which He had come into the world to accomplish. Now He repeated the lesson. There was danger that Mary would regard her relationship to Jesus as giving her a special claim upon Him, and the right, in some degree, to direct Him in His mission. For thirty years He had been to her a loving and obedient son, and His love was unchanged; but He must now go about His Father's work. As Son of the Most High, and Saviour of the world, no earthly ties must hold Him from His mission, or influence His conduct. He must stand free to do the will of God. This lesson is also for us. The claims of God are paramount even to the ties of human relationship. No earthly attraction should turn our feet from the path in which He bids us walk.

The only hope of redemption for our fallen race is in Christ; Mary could find salvation only through the Lamb of God. In herself she possessed no merit. Her connection with Jesus placed her in no different spiritual relation to Him from that of any other human soul. This is indicated in the Saviour's words. He makes clear the distinction between His relation to her as the Son of man and as the Son of God. The tie of kinship between them in no way placed her on an equality with Him.

The words, "Mine hour is not yet come," point to the fact that every act of Christ's life on earth was in fulfillment of the plan that had existed from the days of eternity. Before He came to earth, the plan lay out before Him, perfect in all its details. But as He walked among men, He was guided, step by step, by the Father's will. He did not hesitate to act at the appointed time. With the same submission He waited until the time had come.

In saying to Mary that His hour had not yet come, Jesus was replying to her unspoken thought,—to the expectation she cherished in common with her people. She hoped that He would reveal Himself as the Messiah, and take the throne of Israel. But the time had not come. Not as a King, but as "a Man of Sorrows, and acquainted with grief," had Jesus accepted the lot of humanity.

But though Mary had not a right conception of Christ's mission, she trusted Him implicitly. To this faith Jesus responded. It was to honor Mary's trust, and to strengthen the faith of His disciples, that the first miracle was performed. The disciples were to encounter many and great temptations to unbelief. To them the prophecies had made it clear beyond all controversy that Jesus was the Messiah. They looked for the religious leaders to receive Him with confidence even greater than their own. They declared among the people the wonderful works of Christ and their own confidence in His mission, but they were amazed and bitterly disappointed by the unbelief, the deep-seated prejudice, and the enmity to Jesus, displayed by the priests and rabbis. The Saviour's early miracles strengthened the disciples to stand against this opposition.

In nowise disconcerted by the words of Jesus, Mary said to those serving at table, "Whatsoever He saith unto you, do it." Thus she did what she could to prepare the way for the work of Christ.

Beside the doorway stood six large stone water jars, and Jesus bade the servants fill these with water. It was done. Then as the wine was wanted for immediate use, He said, "Draw out now, and bear unto the governor of the feast." Instead of the water with which the vessels had been filled, there flowed forth wine. Neither the ruler of the feast nor the guests generally were aware that the supply of wine had failed. Upon tasting that which the servants brought, the ruler found it superior to any he had ever before drunk, and very different from that served at the beginning of the feast. Turning to the bridegroom, he said, "Every man at the beginning doth set forth good wine; and when men have well drunk, then that which is worse: but thou hast kept the good wine until now."

As men set forth the best wine first, then afterward that which is worse, so does the world with its gifts. That which it offers may please the eye and fascinate the senses, but it proves to be unsatisfying. The wine turns to bitterness, the gaiety to gloom. That which was begun with songs and mirth ends in weariness and disgust. But the gifts of Jesus are ever fresh and new. The feast that He provides for the soul never fails to give satisfaction and joy. Each new gift increases the capacity of the receiver to appreciate and enjoy the blessings of the Lord. He gives grace for grace. There can be no failure of supply. If you abide in Him, the fact that you receive a rich gift today insures the reception of a richer gift tomorrow. The words of Jesus to Nathanael express the law of God's dealing with the children of faith. With every fresh revelation of His love, He declares to the receptive heart, "Believest thou? thou shalt see greater things than these." John 1:50.

The gift of Christ to the marriage feast was a symbol. The water represented baptism into His death; the wine, the shedding of His blood for the sins of the world. The water to fill the jars was brought by human hands, but the word of Christ alone could impart to it life-giving virtue. So with the rites which point to the Saviour's death. It is only by the power of Christ, working through faith, that they have efficacy to nourish the soul.

The word of Christ supplied ample provision for the feast. So abundant is the provision of His grace to blot out the iniquities of men, and to renew and sustain the soul.

At the first feast He attended with His disciples, Jesus gave them the cup that symbolized His work for their salvation. At the last supper He gave it again, in the institution of that sacred rite by which His death was to be shown forth "till He come." 1 Cor. 11:26. And the sorrow of the disciples at parting from their Lord was comforted with the promise of reunion, as He said, "I will not drink henceforth of this fruit of the vine, until that day when I drink it new with you in My Father's kingdom." Matt. 26:29.

The wine which Christ provided for the feast, and that which He gave to the disciples as a symbol of His own blood, was the pure juice of the grape. To this the prophet Isaiah refers when he speaks of the new wine "in the cluster," and says, "Destroy it not; for a blessing is in it." Isa. 65:8.

It was Christ who in the Old Testament gave the warning to Israel, "Wine is a mocker, strong drink is raging: and whosoever is deceived thereby is not wise." Prov. 20:1. And He Himself provided no such beverage. Satan tempts men to indulgence that will becloud reason and benumb the spiritual perceptions, but Christ teaches us to bring the lower nature into subjection. His whole life was an example of self-denial. In order to break the power of appetite, He suffered in our behalf the severest test that humanity could endure. It was Christ who directed that John the Baptist should drink neither wine nor strong drink. It was He who enjoined similar abstinence upon the wife of Manoah. And He pronounced a curse upon the man who should put the bottle to his neighbor's lips. Christ did not contradict His own teaching. The unfermented wine which He provided for the wedding guests was a wholesome and refreshing drink. Its effect was to bring the taste into harmony with a healthful appetite.

As the guests at the feast remarked upon the quality of the wine, inquiries were made that drew from the servants an account of the miracle. The company were for a time too much amazed to think of Him who had performed the wonderful work. When at length they looked for Him, it was found that He had withdrawn so quietly as to be unnoticed even by His disciples.

The attention of the company was now turned to the disciples. For the first time they had the opportunity of acknowledging their faith in Jesus. They told what they had seen and heard at the Jordan, and there was kindled in many hearts the hope that God had raised up a deliverer for His people. The news of the miracle spread through all that region, and was carried to Jerusalem. With new interest the priests and elders searched the prophecies pointing to Christ's coming. There was eager desire to learn the mission of this new teacher, who appeared among the people in so unassuming a manner.

The ministry of Christ was in marked contrast to that of the Jewish elders. Their regard for tradition and formalism had destroyed all real freedom of thought or action. They lived in continual dread of defilement. To avoid contact with the "unclean," they kept aloof, not only from the Gentiles, but from the majority of their own people, seeking neither to benefit them nor to win their friendship. By dwelling constantly on these matters, they had dwarfed their minds and narrowed the orbit of their lives. Their example encouraged egotism and intolerance among all classes of the people.

Jesus began the work of reformation by coming into close sympathy with humanity. While He showed the greatest reverence for the law of God, He rebuked the pretentious piety of the Pharisees, and tried to free the people from the senseless rules that bound them. He was seeking to break down the barriers which separated the different classes of society, that He might bring men together as children of one family. His attendance at the marriage feast was designed to be a step toward effecting this.

God had directed John the Baptist to dwell in the wilderness, that he might be shielded from the influence of the priests and rabbis, and be prepared for a special mission. But the austerity and isolation of his life were not an example for the people. John himself had not directed his hearers to forsake their former duties. He bade them give evidence of their repentance by faithfulness to God in the place where He had called them.

Jesus reproved self-indulgence in all its forms, yet He was social in His nature. He accepted the hospitality of all classes, visiting the homes of the rich and the poor, the learned and the ignorant, and seeking to elevate their thoughts from questions of commonplace life to those things that are spiritual and eternal. He gave no license to dissipation, and no shadow of worldly levity marred His conduct; yet He found pleasure in scenes of innocent happiness, and by His presence sanctioned the social gathering. A Jewish marriage was an impressive occasion, and its joy was not displeasing to the Son of man. By attending this feast, Jesus honored marriage as a divine institution.

In both the Old and the New Testament, the marriage relation is employed to represent the tender and sacred union that exists between Christ and His people. To the mind of Jesus the gladness of the wedding festivities pointed forward to the rejoicing of that day when He shall bring home His bride to the Father's house, and the redeemed with the Redeemer shall sit down to the marriage supper of the Lamb. He says, "As the bridegroom rejoiceth over the bride, so shall thy God rejoice over thee." "Thou shalt no more be termed Forsaken; . . . but thou shalt be called My Delight; . . . for the Lord delighteth in thee." "He will rejoice over thee with joy; He will rest in His love, He will joy over thee with singing." Isa. 62:5, 4, margin; Zeph. 3:17. When the vision of heavenly things was granted to John the apostle, he wrote: "I heard as it were the voice of a great multitude, and as the voice of many waters, and as the voice of mighty thunderings, saying, Alleluia: for the Lord God omnipotent reigneth. Let us be glad and rejoice, and give honor to Him: for the marriage of the Lamb is come, and His wife hath made herself ready." "Blessed are they which are called unto the marriage supper of the Lamb." Rev. 19:6, 7, 9.

Jesus saw in every soul one to whom must be given the call to His kingdom. He reached the hearts of the people by going among them as one who desired their good. He sought them in the public streets, in private houses, on the boats, in the synagogue, by the shores of the lake, and at the marriage feast. He met them at their daily vocations, and manifested an interest in their secular affairs. He carried His instruction into the household, bringing families in their own homes under the influence of His divine presence. His strong personal sympathy helped to win hearts. He often repaired to the mountains for solitary prayer, but this was a preparation for His labor among men in active life. From these seasons He came forth to relieve the sick, to instruct the ignorant, and to break the chains from the captives of Satan.

It was by personal contact and association that Jesus trained His disciples. Sometimes He taught them, sitting among them on the mountainside; sometimes beside the sea, or walking with them by the way, He revealed the mysteries of the kingdom of God. He did not sermonize as men do today. Wherever hearts were open to receive the divine message, He unfolded the truths of the way of salvation. He did not command His disciples to do this or that, but said, "Follow Me." On His journeys through country and cities He took them with Him, that they might see how He taught the people. He linked their interest with His, and they united with Him in the work.

The example of Christ in linking Himself with the interests of humanity should be followed by all who preach His word, and by all who have received the gospel of His grace. We are not to renounce social communion. We should not seclude ourselves from others. In order to reach all classes, we must meet them where they are. They will seldom seek us of their own accord. Not alone from the pulpit are the hearts of men touched by divine truth. There is another field of labor, humbler, it may be, but fully as promising. It is found in the home of the lowly, and in the mansion of the great; at the hospitable board, and in gatherings for innocent social enjoyment.

As disciples of Christ we shall not mingle with the world from a mere love of pleasure, to unite with them in folly. Such associations can result only in harm. We should never give sanction to sin by our words or our deeds, our silence or our presence. Wherever we go, we are to carry Jesus with us, and to reveal to others the preciousness of our Saviour. But those who try to preserve their religion by hiding it within stone walls lose precious opportunities of doing good. Through the social relations, Christianity comes in contact with the world. Everyone who has received the divine illumination is to brighten the pathway of those who know not the Light of life.

We should all become witnesses for Jesus. Social power, sanctified by the grace of Christ, must be improved in winning souls to the Saviour. Let the world see that we are not selfishly absorbed in our own interests, but that we desire others to share our blessings and privileges. Let them see that our religion does not make us unsympathetic or exacting. Let all who profess to have found Christ, minister as He did for the benefit of men.

We should never give to the world the false impression that Christians are a gloomy, unhappy people. If our eyes are fixed on Jesus, we shall see a compassionate Redeemer, and shall catch light from His countenance. Wherever His Spirit reigns, there peace abides. And there will be joy also, for there is a calm, holy trust in God.

Christ is pleased with His followers when they show that, though human, they are partakers of the divine nature. They are not statues, but living men and women. Their hearts, refreshed by the dews of divine grace, open and expand to the Sun of Righteousness. The light that shines upon them they reflect upon others in works that are luminous with the love of Christ.

In His Temple

"After this He went down to Capernaum, He, and His mother, and His brethren, and His disciples: and they continued there not many days. And the Jews' Passover was at hand, and Jesus went up to Jerusalem."

In this journey, Jesus joined one of the large companies that were making their way to the capital. He had not yet publicly announced His mission, and He mingled unnoticed with the throng. Upon these occasions, the coming of the Messiah, to which such prominence had been given by the ministry of John, was often the theme of conversation. The hope of national greatness was dwelt upon with kindling enthusiasm. Jesus knew that this hope was to be disappointed, for it was founded on a misinterpretation of the Scriptures. With deep earnestness He explained the prophecies, and tried to arouse the people to a closer study of God's word.

The Jewish leaders had instructed the people that at Jerusalem they were to be taught to worship God. Here during the Passover week large numbers assembled, coming from all parts of Palestine, and even from distant lands. The temple courts were filled with a promiscuous throng. Many were unable to bring with them the sacrifices that were to be offered up as typifying the one great Sacrifice. For the convenience of these, animals were bought and sold in the outer court of the temple. Here all classes of people assembled to purchase their offerings. Here all foreign money was exchanged for the coin of the sanctuary.

Every Jew was required to pay yearly a half shekel as "a ransom for his soul;" and the money thus collected was used for the support of the temple. Ex. 30:12-16. Besides this, large sums were brought as freewill offerings, to be deposited in the temple treasury. And it was required that all foreign coin should be changed for a coin called the temple shekel, which was accepted for the service of the sanctuary. The money changing gave opportunity for fraud and extortion, and it had grown into a disgraceful traffic, which was a source of revenue to the priests.

The dealers demanded exorbitant prices for the animals sold, and they shared their profits with the priests and rulers, who thus enriched themselves at the expense of the people. The worshipers had been taught to believe that if they did not offer sacrifice, the blessing of God would not rest on their children or their lands. Thus a high price for the animals could be secured; for after coming so far, the people would not return to their homes without performing the act of devotion for which they had come.

A great number of sacrifices were offered at the time of the Passover, and the sales at the temple were very large. The consequent confusion indicated a noisy cattle market rather than the sacred temple of God. There could be heard sharp bargaining, the lowing of cattle, the bleating of sheep, the cooing of doves, mingled with the chinking of coin and angry disputation. So great was the confusion that the worshipers were disturbed, and the words addressed to the Most High were drowned in the uproar that invaded the temple. The Jews were exceedingly proud of their piety. They rejoiced over their temple, and regarded a word spoken in its disfavor as blasphemy; they were very rigorous in the performance of ceremonies connected with it; but the love of money had overruled their scruples. They were scarcely aware how far they had wandered from the original purpose of the service instituted by God Himself.

When the Lord descended upon Mount Sinai, the place was consecrated by His presence. Moses was commanded to put bounds around the mount and sanctify it, and the word of the Lord was heard in warning: "Take heed to yourselves, that ye go not up into the mount, or touch the border of it: whosoever toucheth the mount shall be surely put to death: there shall not an hand touch it, but he shall surely be stoned, or shot through; whether it be beast or man, it shall not live." Ex. 19:12, 13. Thus was taught the lesson that wherever God manifests His presence, the place is holy. The precincts of God's temple should have been regarded as sacred. But in the strife for gain, all this was lost sight of.

The priests and rulers were called to be the representatives of God to the nation; they should have corrected the abuses of the temple court. They should have given to the people an example of integrity and compassion. Instead of studying their own profit, they should have considered the situation and needs of the worshipers, and should have been ready to assist those who were not able to buy the required sacrifices. But this they did not do. Avarice had hardened their hearts.

There came to this feast those who were suffering, those who were in want and distress. The blind, the lame, the deaf, were there. Some were brought on beds. Many came who were too poor to purchase the humblest offering for the Lord, too poor even to buy food with which to satisfy their own hunger. These were greatly distressed by the statements of the priests. The priests boasted of their piety; they claimed to be the guardians of the people; but they were without sympathy or compassion. The poor, the sick, the dying, made their vain plea for favor. Their suffering awakened no pity in the hearts of the priests.

As Jesus came into the temple, He took in the whole scene. He saw the unfair transactions. He saw the distress of the poor, who thought that without shedding of blood there would be no forgiveness for their sins. He saw the outer court of His temple converted into a place of unholy traffic. The sacred enclosure had become one vast exchange.

Christ saw that something must be done. Numerous ceremonies were enjoined upon the people without the proper instruction as to their import. The worshipers offered their sacrifices without understanding that they were typical of the only perfect Sacrifice. And among them, unrecognized and unhonored, stood the One symbolized by all their service. He had given directions in regard to the offerings. He understood their symbolical value, and He saw that they were now perverted and misunderstood. Spiritual worship was fast disappearing. No link bound the priests and rulers to their God. Christ's work was to establish an altogether different worship.

With searching glance, Christ takes in the scene before Him as He stands upon the steps of the temple court. With prophetic eye He looks into futurity, and sees not only years, but centuries and ages. He sees how priests and rulers will turn the needy from their right, and forbid that the gospel shall be preached to the poor. He sees how the love of God will be concealed from sinners, and men will make merchandise of His grace. As He beholds the scene, indignation, authority, and power are expressed in His countenance. The attention of the people is attracted to Him. The eyes of those engaged in their unholy traffic are riveted upon His face. They cannot withdraw their gaze. They feel that this Man reads their inmost thoughts, and discovers their hidden motives. Some attempt to conceal their faces, as if their evil deeds were written upon their countenances, to be scanned by those searching eyes.

The confusion is hushed. The sound of traffic and bargaining has ceased. The silence becomes painful. A sense of awe overpowers the assembly. It is as if they were arraigned before the tribunal of God to answer for their deeds. Looking upon Christ, they behold divinity flash through the garb of humanity. The Majesty of heaven stands as the Judge will stand at the last day,—not now encircled with the glory that will then attend Him, but with the same power to read the soul. His eye sweeps over the multitude, taking in every individual. His form seems to rise above them in commanding dignity, and a divine light illuminates His countenance. He speaks, and His clear, ringing voice—the same that upon Mount Sinai proclaimed the law that priests and rulers are transgressing—is heard echoing through the arches of the temple: "Take these things hence; make not My Father's house an house of merchandise."

Slowly descending the steps, and raising the scourge of cords gathered up on entering the enclosure, He bids the bargaining company depart from the precincts of the temple. With a zeal and severity He has never before manifested, He overthrows the tables of the money-changers. The coin falls, ringing sharply upon the marble pavement. None presume to question His authority. None dare stop to gather up their ill-gotten gain. Jesus does not smite them with the whip of cords, but in His hand that simple scourge seems terrible as a flaming sword. Officers of the temple, speculating priests, brokers and cattle traders, with their sheep and oxen, rush from the place, with the one thought of escaping from the condemnation of His presence.

A panic sweeps over the multitude, who feel the overshadowing of His divinity. Cries of terror escape from hundreds of blanched lips. Even the disciples tremble. They are awestruck by the words and manner of Jesus, so unlike His usual demeanor. They remember that it is written of Him, "The zeal of Thine house hath eaten Me up." Ps. 69:9. Soon the tumultuous throng with their merchandise are far removed from the temple of the Lord. The courts are free from unholy traffic, and a deep silence and solemnity settles upon the scene of confusion. The presence of the Lord, that of old sanctified the mount, has now made sacred the temple reared in His honor.

In the cleansing of the temple, Jesus was announcing His mission as the Messiah, and entering upon His work. That temple, erected for the abode of the divine Presence, was designed to be an object lesson for Israel and for the world. From eternal ages it was God's purpose that every created being, from the bright and holy seraph to man, should be a temple for the indwelling of the Creator. Because of sin, humanity ceased to be a temple for God. Darkened and defiled by evil, the heart of man no longer revealed the glory of the Divine One. But by the incarnation of the Son of God, the purpose of Heaven is fulfilled. God dwells in humanity, and through saving grace the heart of man becomes again His temple. God designed that the temple at Jerusalem should be a continual witness to the high destiny open to every soul. But the Jews had not understood the significance of the building they regarded with so much pride. They did not yield themselves as holy temples for the Divine Spirit. The courts of the temple at Jerusalem, filled with the tumult of unholy traffic, represented all too truly the temple of the heart, defiled by the presence of sensual passion and unholy thoughts. In cleansing the temple from the world's buyers and sellers, Jesus announced His mission to cleanse the heart from the defilement of sin,—from the earthly desires, the selfish lusts, the evil habits, that corrupt the soul. "The Lord, whom ye seek, shall suddenly come to His temple, even the Messenger of the covenant, whom ye delight in: behold, He shall come, saith the Lord of hosts. But who may abide the day of His coming? and who shall stand when He appeareth? for He is like a refiner's fire, and like fullers' soap: and He shall sit as a refiner and purifier of silver: and He shall purify the sons of Levi, and purge them as gold and silver." Mal. 3:1-3.

"Know ye not that ye are the temple of God, and that the Spirit of God dwelleth in you? If any man defile the temple of God, him shall God destroy; for the temple of God is holy, which temple ye are." 1 Cor. 3:16, 17. No man can of himself cast out the evil throng that have taken possession of the heart. Only Christ can cleanse the soul temple. But He will not force an entrance. He comes not into the heart as to the temple of old; but He says, "Behold, I stand at the door, and knock: if any man hear My voice, and open the door, I will come in to him." Rev. 3:20. He will come, not for one day merely; for He says, "I will dwell in them, and walk in them; . . . and they shall be My people." "He will subdue our iniquities; and Thou wilt cast all their sins into the depths of the sea." 2 Cor. 6:16; Micah 7:19. His presence will cleanse and sanctify the soul, so that it may be a holy temple unto the Lord, and "an habitation of God through the Spirit." Eph. 2:21, 22.

Overpowered with terror, the priests and rulers had fled from the temple court, and from the searching glance that read their hearts. In their flight they met others on their way to the temple, and bade them turn back, telling them what they had seen and heard. Christ looked upon the fleeing men with yearning pity for their fear, and their ignorance of what constituted true worship. In this scene He saw symbolized the dispersion of the whole Jewish nation for their wickedness and impenitence.

And why did the priests flee from the temple? Why did they not stand their ground? He who commanded them to go was a carpenter's son, a poor Galilean, without earthly rank or power. Why did they not resist Him? Why did they leave the gain so ill acquired, and flee at the command of One whose outward appearance was so humble?

Christ spoke with the authority of a king, and in His appearance, and in the tones of His voice, there was that which they had no power to resist. At the word of command they realized, as they had never realized before, their true position as hypocrites and robbers. When divinity flashed through humanity, not only did they see indignation on Christ's countenance; they realized the import of His words. They felt as if before the throne of the eternal Judge, with their sentence passed on them for time and for eternity. For a time they were convinced that Christ was a prophet; and many believed Him to be the Messiah. The Holy Spirit flashed into their minds the utterances of the prophets concerning Christ. Would they yield to this conviction?

Repent they would not. They knew that Christ's sympathy for the poor had been aroused. They knew that they had been guilty of extortion in their dealings with the people. Because Christ discerned their thoughts they hated Him. His public rebuke was humiliating to their pride, and they were jealous of His growing influence with the people. They determined to challenge Him as to the power by which He had driven them forth, and who gave Him this power.

Slowly and thoughtfully, but with hate in their hearts, they returned to the temple. But what a change had taken place during their absence! When they fled, the poor remained behind; and these were now looking to Jesus, whose countenance expressed His love and sympathy. With tears in His eyes, He said to the trembling ones around Him: Fear not; I will deliver thee, and thou shalt glorify Me. For this cause came I into the world.

The people pressed into Christ's presence with urgent, pitiful appeals: Master, bless me. His ear heard every cry. With pity exceeding that of a tender mother He bent over the suffering little ones. All received attention. Everyone was healed of whatever disease he had. The dumb opened their lips in praise; the blind beheld the face of their Restorer. The hearts of the sufferers were made glad.

As the priests and temple officials witnessed this great work, what a revelation to them were the sounds that fell on their ears! The people were relating the story of the pain they had suffered, of their disappointed hopes, of painful days and sleepless nights. When the last spark of hope seemed to be dead, Christ had healed them. The burden was so heavy, one said; but I have found a helper. He is the Christ of God, and I will devote my life to His service. Parents said to their children, He has saved your life; lift up your voice and praise Him. The voices of children and youth, fathers and mothers, friends and spectators, blended in thanksgiving and praise. Hope and gladness filled their hearts. Peace came to their minds. They were restored soul and body, and they returned home, proclaiming everywhere the matchless love of Jesus.

At the crucifixion of Christ, those who had thus been healed did not join with the rabble throng in crying, "Crucify Him, crucify Him." Their sympathies were with Jesus; for they had felt His great sympathy and wonderful power. They knew Him to be their Saviour; for He had given them health of body and soul. They listened to the preaching of the apostles, and the entrance of God's word into their hearts gave them understanding. They became agents of God's mercy, and instruments of His salvation.

The crowd that had fled from the temple court after a time slowly drifted back. They had partially recovered from the panic that had seized them, but their faces expressed irresolution and timidity. They looked with amazement on the works of Jesus, and were convicted that in Him the prophecies concerning the Messiah were fulfilled. The sin of the desecration of the temple rested, in a great degree, upon the priests. It was by their arrangement that the court had been turned into a market place. The people were comparatively innocent. They were impressed by the divine authority of Jesus; but with them the influence of the priests and rulers was paramount. They regarded Christ's mission as an innovation, and questioned His right to interfere with what was permitted by the authorities of the temple. They were offended because the traffic had been interrupted, and they stifled the convictions of the Holy Spirit.

Above all others the priests and rulers should have seen in Jesus the anointed of the Lord; for in their hands were the sacred scrolls that described His mission, and they knew that the cleansing of the temple was a manifestation of more than human power. Much as they hated Jesus, they could not free themselves from the thought that He might be a prophet sent by God to restore the sanctity of the temple. With a deference born of this fear, they went to Him with the inquiry, "What sign showest Thou unto us, seeing that Thou doest these things?"

Jesus had shown them a sign. In flashing light into their hearts, and in doing before them the works which the Messiah was to do, He had given convincing evidence of His character. Now when they asked for a sign, He answered them by a parable, showing that He read their malice, and saw to what lengths it would lead them. "Destroy this temple," He said, "and in three days I will raise it up."

In these words His meaning was twofold. He referred not only to the destruction of the Jewish temple and worship, but to His own death,—the destruction of the temple of His body. This the Jews were already plotting. As the priests and rulers returned to the temple, they had proposed to kill Jesus, and thus rid themselves of the troubler. Yet when He set before them their purpose, they did not understand Him. They took His words as applying only to the temple at Jerusalem, and with indignation exclaimed, "Forty and six years was this temple in building, and wilt Thou rear it up in three days?" Now they felt that Jesus had justified their unbelief, and they were confirmed in their rejection of Him.

Christ did not design that His words should be understood by the unbelieving Jews, nor even by His disciples at this time. He knew that they would be misconstrued by His enemies, and would be turned against Him. At His trial they would be brought as an accusation, and on Calvary they would be flung at Him as a taunt. But to explain them now would give His disciples a knowledge of His sufferings, and bring upon them sorrow which as yet they were not able to bear. And an explanation would prematurely disclose to the Jews the result of their prejudice and unbelief. Already they had entered upon a path which they would steadily pursue until He should be led as a lamb to the slaughter.

It was for the sake of those who should believe on Him that these words of Christ were spoken. He knew that they would be repeated. Being spoken at the Passover, they would come to the ears of thousands, and be carried to all parts of the world. After He had risen from the dead, their meaning would be made plain. To many they would be conclusive evidence of His divinity.

Because of their spiritual darkness, even the disciples of Jesus often failed of comprehending His lessons. But many of these lessons were made plain to them by subsequent events. When He walked no more with them, His words were a stay to their hearts.

As referring to the temple at Jerusalem, the Saviour's words, "Destroy this temple, and in three days I will raise it up," had a deeper meaning than the hearers perceived. Christ was the foundation and life of the temple. Its services were typical of the sacrifice of the Son of God. The priesthood was established to represent the mediatorial character and work of Christ. The entire plan of sacrificial worship was a foreshadowing of the Saviour's death to redeem the world. There would be no efficacy in these offerings when the great event toward which they had pointed for ages was consummated.

Since the whole ritual economy was symbolical of Christ, it had no value apart from Him. When the Jews sealed their rejection of Christ by delivering Him to death, they rejected all that gave significance to the temple and its services. Its sacredness had departed. It was doomed to destruction. From that day sacrificial offerings and the service connected with them were meaningless. Like the offering of Cain, they did not express faith in the Saviour. In putting Christ to death, the Jews virtually destroyed their temple. When Christ was crucified, the inner veil of the temple was rent in twain from top to bottom, signifying that the great final sacrifice had been made, and that the system of sacrificial offerings was forever at an end.

"In three days I will raise it up." In the Saviour's death the powers of darkness seemed to prevail, and they exulted in their victory. But from the rent sepulcher of Joseph, Jesus came forth a conqueror. "Having spoiled principalities and powers, He made a show of them openly, triumphing over them." Col. 2:15. By virtue of His death and resurrection He became the minister of the "true tabernacle, which the Lord pitched, and not man." Heb. 8:2. Men reared the Jewish tabernacle; men builded the Jewish temple; but the sanctuary above, of which the earthly was a type, was built by no human architect. "Behold the Man whose name is The Branch; . . . He shall build the temple of the Lord; and He shall bear the glory, and shall sit and rule upon His throne; and He shall be a priest upon His throne." Zech. 6:12, 13.

The sacrificial service that had pointed to Christ passed away; but the eyes of men were turned to the true sacrifice for the sins of the world. The earthly priesthood ceased; but we look to Jesus, the minister of the new covenant, and "to the blood of sprinkling, that speaketh better things than that of Abel." "The way into the holiest of all was not yet made manifest, while as the first tabernacle was yet standing: . . . but Christ being come an high priest of good things to come, by a greater and more perfect tabernacle, not made with hands, . . . by His own blood He entered in once into the holy place, having obtained eternal redemption for us." Heb. 12:24; 9:8-12.

"Wherefore He is able also to save them to the uttermost that come unto God by Him, seeing He ever liveth to make intercession for them." Heb. 7:25. Though the ministration was to be removed from the earthly to the heavenly temple; though the sanctuary and our great high priest would be invisible to human sight, yet the disciples were to suffer no loss thereby. They would realize no break in their communion, and no diminution of power because of the Saviour's absence. While Jesus ministers in the sanctuary above, He is still by His Spirit the minister of the church on earth. He is withdrawn from the eye of sense, but His parting promise is fulfilled, "Lo, I am with you alway, even unto the end of the world." Matt. 28:20. While He delegates His power to inferior ministers, His energizing presence is still with His church.

"Seeing then that we have a great high priest, . . . Jesus, the Son of God, let us hold fast our profession. For we have not an high priest which cannot be touched with the feeling of our infirmities; but was in all points tempted like as we are, yet without sin. Let us therefore come boldly unto the throne of grace, that we may obtain mercy, and find grace to help in time of need." Heb 4:14-16.

Nicodemus

Nicodemus held a high position of trust in the Jewish nation. He was highly educated, and possessed talents of no ordinary character, and he was an honored member of the national council. With others, he had been stirred by the teaching of Jesus. Though rich, learned, and honored, he had been strangely attracted by the humble Nazarene. The lessons that had fallen from the Saviour's lips had greatly impressed him, and he desired to learn more of these wonderful truths.

Christ's exercise of authority in the cleansing of the temple had roused the determined hatred of the priests and rulers. They feared the power of this stranger. Such boldness on the part of an obscure Galilean was not to be tolerated. They were bent on putting an end to His work. But not all were agreed in this purpose. There were some that feared to oppose One who was so evidently moved upon by the Spirit of God. They remembered how prophets had been slain for rebuking the sins of the leaders in Israel. They knew that the bondage of the Jews to a heathen nation was the result of their stubbornness in rejecting reproofs from God. They feared that in plotting against Jesus the priests and rulers were following in the steps of their fathers, and would bring fresh calamities upon the nation. Nicodemus shared these feelings. In a council of the Sanhedrin, when the course to be pursued toward Jesus was considered, Nicodemus advised caution and moderation. He urged that if Jesus was really invested with authority from God, it would be perilous to reject His warnings. The priests dared not disregard this counsel, and for the time they took no open measures against the Saviour.

Since hearing Jesus, Nicodemus had anxiously studied the prophecies relating to the Messiah; and the more he searched, the stronger was his conviction that this was the One who was to come. With many others in Israel he had been greatly distressed by the profanation of the temple He was a witness of the scene when Jesus drove out the buyers and the sellers; he beheld the wonderful manifestation of divine power; he saw the Saviour receiving the poor and healing the sick; he saw their looks of joy, and heard their words of praise; and he could not doubt that Jesus of Nazareth was the Sent of God.

He greatly desired an interview with Jesus, but shrank from seeking Him openly. It would be too humiliating for a ruler of the Jews to acknowledge himself in sympathy with a teacher as yet so little known. And should his visit come to the knowledge of the Sanhedrin, it would draw upon him their scorn and denunciation. He resolved upon a secret interview, excusing this on the ground that if he were to go openly, others might follow his example. Learning by special inquiry the Saviour's place of retirement in the Mount of Olives, he waited until the city was hushed in slumber, and then sought Him.

In the presence of Christ, Nicodemus felt a strange timidity, which he endeavored to conceal under an air of composure and dignity. "Rabbi," he said, "we know that Thou art a teacher come from God: for no man can do these miracles that Thou doest, except God be with him." By speaking of Christ's rare gifts as a teacher, and also of His wonderful power to perform miracles, he hoped to pave the way for his interview. His words were designed to express and to invite confidence; but they really expressed unbelief. He did not acknowledge Jesus to be the Messiah, but only a teacher sent from God.

Instead of recognizing this salutation, Jesus bent His eyes upon the speaker, as if reading his very soul. In His infinite wisdom He saw before Him a seeker after truth. He knew the object of this visit, and with a desire to deepen the conviction already resting upon His listener's mind, He came directly to the point, saying solemnly, yet kindly, "Verily, verily, I say unto thee, Except a man be born from above, he cannot see the kingdom of God." John 3:3, margin.

Nicodemus had come to the Lord thinking to enter into a discussion with Him, but Jesus laid bare the foundation principles of truth. He said to Nicodemus, It is not theoretical knowledge you need so much as spiritual regeneration. You need not to have your curiosity satisfied, but to have a new heart. You must receive a new life from above before you can appreciate heavenly things. Until this change takes place, making all things new, it will result in no saving good for you to discuss with Me My authority or My mission.

Nicodemus had heard the preaching of John the Baptist concerning repentance and baptism, and pointing the people to One who should baptize with the Holy Spirit. He himself had felt that there was a lack of spirituality among the Jews, that, to a great degree, they were controlled by bigotry and worldly ambition. He had hoped for a better state of things at the Messiah's coming. Yet the heart-searching message of the Baptist had failed to work in him conviction of sin. He was a strict Pharisee, and prided himself on his good works. He was widely esteemed for his benevolence and his liberality in sustaining the temple service, and he felt secure of the favor of God. He was startled at the thought of a kingdom too pure for him to see in his present state.

The figure of the new birth, which Jesus had used, was not wholly unfamiliar to Nicodemus. Converts from heathenism to the faith of Israel were often compared to children just born. Therefore he must have perceived that the words of Christ were not to be taken in a literal sense. But by virtue of his birth as an Israelite he regarded himself as sure of a place in the kingdom of God. He felt that he needed no change. Hence his surprise at the Saviour's words. He was irritated by their close application to himself. The pride of the Pharisee was struggling against the honest desire of the seeker after truth. He wondered that Christ should speak to him as He did, not respecting his position as ruler in Israel.

Surprised out of his self-possession, he answered Christ in words full of irony, "How can a man be born when he is old?" Like many others when cutting truth is brought home to the conscience, he revealed the fact that the natural man receiveth not the things of the Spirit of God. There is in him nothing that responds to spiritual things; for spiritual things are spiritually discerned.

But the Saviour did not meet argument with argument. Raising His hand with solemn, quiet dignity, He pressed the truth home with greater assurance, "Verily, verily, I say unto thee, Except a man be born of water and of the Spirit, he cannot enter into the kingdom of God." Nicodemus knew that Christ here referred to water baptism and the renewing of the heart by the Spirit of God. He was convinced that he was in the presence of the One whom John the Baptist had foretold.

Jesus continued: "That which is born of the flesh is flesh; and that which is born of the Spirit is spirit." By nature the heart is evil, and "who can bring a clean thing out of an unclean? not one." Job 14:4. No human invention can find a remedy for the sinning soul. "The carnal mind is enmity against God: for it is not subject to the law of God, neither indeed can be." "Out of the heart proceed evil thoughts, murders, adulteries, fornications, thefts, false witness, blasphemies." Rom. 8:7; Matt. 15:19. The fountain of the heart must be purified before the streams can become pure. He who is trying to reach heaven by his own works in keeping the law is attempting an impossibility. There is no safety for one who has merely a legal religion, a form of godliness. The Christian's life is not a modification or improvement of the old, but a transformation of nature. There is a death to self and sin, and a new life altogether. This change can be brought about only by the effectual working of the Holy Spirit.

Nicodemus was still perplexed, and Jesus used the wind to illustrate His meaning: "The wind bloweth where it listeth, and thou hearest the sound thereof, but canst not tell whence it cometh, and whither it goeth: so is everyone that is born of the Spirit."

The wind is heard among the branches of the trees, rustling the leaves and flowers; yet it is invisible, and no man knows whence it comes or whither it goes. So with the work of the Holy Spirit upon the heart. It can no more be explained than can the movements of the wind. A person may not be able to tell the exact time or place, or to trace all the circumstances in the process of conversion; but this does not prove him to be unconverted. By an agency as unseen as the wind, Christ is constantly working upon the heart. Little by little, perhaps unconsciously to the receiver, impressions are made that tend to draw the soul to Christ. These may be received through meditating upon Him, through reading the Scriptures, or through hearing the word from the living preacher. Suddenly, as the Spirit comes with more direct appeal, the soul gladly surrenders itself to Jesus. By many this is called sudden conversion; but it is the result of long wooing by the Spirit of God,—a patient, protracted process.

While the wind is itself invisible, it produces effects that are seen and felt. So the work of the Spirit upon the soul will reveal itself in every act of him who has felt its saving power. When the Spirit of God takes possession of the heart, it transforms the life. Sinful thoughts are put away, evil deeds are renounced; love, humility, and peace take the place of anger, envy, and strife. Joy takes the place of sadness, and the countenance reflects the light of heaven. No one sees the hand that lifts the burden, or beholds the light descend from the courts above. The blessing comes when by faith the soul surrenders itself to God. Then that power which no human eye can see creates a new being in the image of God.

It is impossible for finite minds to comprehend the work of redemption. Its mystery exceeds human knowledge; yet he who passes from death to life realizes that it is a divine reality. The beginning of redemption we may know here through a personal experience. Its results reach through the eternal ages.

While Jesus was speaking, some gleams of truth penetrated the ruler's mind. The softening, subduing influence of the Holy Spirit impressed his heart. Yet he did not fully understand the Saviour's words. He was not so much impressed by the necessity of the new birth as by the manner of its accomplishment. He said wonderingly, "How can these things be?"

"Art thou a master of Israel, and knowest not these things?" Jesus asked. Surely one entrusted with the religious instruction of the people should not be ignorant of truths so important. His words conveyed the lesson that instead of feeling irritated over the plain words of truth, Nicodemus should have had a very humble opinion of himself, because of his spiritual ignorance. Yet Christ spoke with such solemn dignity, and both look and tone expressed such earnest love, that Nicodemus was not offended as he realized his humiliating condition.

But as Jesus explained that His mission on earth was to establish a spiritual instead of a temporal kingdom, His hearer was troubled. Seeing this, Jesus added, "If I have told you earthly things, and ye believe not, how shall ye believe, if I tell you of heavenly things?" If Nicodemus could not receive Christ's teaching, illustrating the work of grace upon the heart, how could he comprehend the nature of His glorious heavenly kingdom? Not discerning the nature of Christ's work on earth, he could not understand His work in heaven.

The Jews whom Jesus had driven from the temple claimed to be children of Abraham, but they fled from the Saviour's presence because they could not endure the glory of God which was manifested in Him. Thus they gave evidence that they were not fitted by the grace of God to participate in the sacred services of the temple. They were zealous to maintain an appearance of holiness, but they neglected holiness of heart. While they were sticklers for the letter of the law, they were constantly violating its spirit. Their great need was that very change which Christ had been explaining to Nicodemus,—a new moral birth, a cleansing from sin, and a renewing of knowledge and holiness.

There was no excuse for the blindness of Israel in regard to the work of regeneration. Under the inspiration of the Holy Spirit, Isaiah had written, "We are all as an unclean thing, and all our righteousnesses are as filthy rags." David had prayed, "Create in me a clean heart, O God; and renew a right spirit within me." And through Ezekiel the promise had been given, "A new heart also will I give you, and a new spirit will I put within you: and I will take away the stony heart out of your flesh, and I will give you an heart of flesh. And I will put My Spirit within you, and cause you to walk in My statutes." Isa. 64:6; Ps. 51:10; Ezek. 36:26, 27.

Nicodemus had read these scriptures with a clouded mind; but he now began to comprehend their meaning. He saw that the most rigid obedience to the mere letter of the law as applied to the outward life could entitle no man to enter the kingdom of heaven. In the estimation of men, his life had been just and honorable; but in the presence of Christ he felt that his heart was unclean, and his life unholy.

Nicodemus was being drawn to Christ. As the Saviour explained to him concerning the new birth, he longed to have this change wrought in himself. By what means could it be accomplished? Jesus answered the unspoken question: "As Moses lifted up the serpent in the wilderness, even so must the Son of man be lifted up: that whosoever believeth in Him should not perish, but have eternal life."

Here was ground with which Nicodemus was familiar. The symbol of the uplifted serpent made plain to him the Saviour's mission. When the people of Israel were dying from the sting of the fiery serpents, God directed Moses to make a serpent of brass, and place it on high in the midst of the congregation. Then the word was sounded throughout the encampment that all who would look upon the serpent should live. The people well knew that in itself the serpent had no power to help them. It was a symbol of Christ. As the image made in the likeness of the destroying serpents was lifted up for their healing, so One made "in the likeness of sinful flesh" was to be their Redeemer. Rom. 8:3. Many of the Israelites regarded the sacrificial service as having in itself virtue to set them free from sin. God desired to teach them that it had no more value than that serpent of brass. It was to lead their minds to the Saviour. Whether for the healing of their wounds or the pardon of their sins, they could do nothing for themselves but show their faith in the Gift of God. They were to look and live.

Those who had been bitten by the serpents might have delayed to look. They might have questioned how there could be efficacy in that brazen symbol. They might have demanded a scientific explanation. But no explanation was given. They must accept the word of God to them through Moses. To refuse to look was to perish.

Not through controversy and discussion is the soul enlightened. We must look and live. Nicodemus received the lesson, and carried it with him. He searched the Scriptures in a new way, not for the discussion of a theory, but in order to receive life for the soul. He began to see the kingdom of heaven as he submitted himself to the leading of the Holy Spirit.

There are thousands today who need to learn the same truth that was taught to Nicodemus by the uplifted serpent. They depend on their obedience to the law of God to commend them to His favor. When they are bidden to look to Jesus, and believe that He saves them solely through His grace, they exclaim, "How can these things be?"

Like Nicodemus, we must be willing to enter into life in the same way as the chief of sinners. Than Christ, "there is none other name under heaven given among men, whereby we must be saved." Acts 4:12. Through faith we receive the grace of God; but faith is not our Saviour. It earns nothing. It is the hand by which we lay hold upon Christ, and appropriate His merits, the remedy for sin. And we cannot even repent without the aid of the Spirit of God. The Scripture says of Christ, "Him hath God exalted with His right hand to be a Prince and a Saviour, for to give repentance to Israel, and forgiveness of sins." Acts 5:31. Repentance comes from Christ as truly as does pardon.

How, then, are we to be saved? "As Moses lifted up the serpent in the wilderness," so the Son of man has been lifted up, and everyone who has been deceived and bitten by the serpent may look and live. "Behold the Lamb of God, which taketh away the sin of the world." John 1:29. The light shining from the cross reveals the love of God. His love is drawing us to Himself. If we do not resist this drawing, we shall be led to the foot of the cross in repentance for the sins that have crucified the Saviour. Then the Spirit of God through faith produces a new life in the soul. The thoughts and desires are brought into obedience to the will of Christ. The heart, the mind, are created anew in the image of Him who works in us to subdue all things to Himself. Then the law of God is written in the mind and heart, and we can say with Christ, "I delight to do Thy will, O my God." Ps. 40:8.

In the interview with Nicodemus, Jesus unfolded the plan of salvation, and His mission to the world. In none of His subsequent discourses did He explain so fully, step by step, the work necessary to be done in the hearts of all who would inherit the kingdom of heaven. At the very beginning of His ministry He opened the truth to a member of the Sanhedrin, to the mind that was most receptive, and to an appointed teacher of the people. But the leaders of Israel did not welcome the light. Nicodemus hid the truth in his heart, and for three years there was little apparent fruit.

But Jesus was acquainted with the soil into which He cast the seed. The words spoken at night to one listener in the lonely mountain were not lost. For a time Nicodemus did not publicly acknowledge Christ, but he watched His life, and pondered His teachings. In the Sanhedrin council he repeatedly thwarted the schemes of the priests to destroy Him. When at last Jesus was lifted up on the cross, Nicodemus remembered the teaching upon Olivet: "As Moses lifted up the serpent in the wilderness, even so must the Son of man be lifted up: that whosoever believeth in Him should not perish, but have eternal life." The light from that secret interview illumined the cross upon Calvary, and Nicodemus saw in Jesus the world's Redeemer.

After the Lord's ascension, when the disciples were scattered by persecution, Nicodemus came boldly to the front. He employed his wealth in sustaining the infant church that the Jews had expected to be blotted out at the death of Christ. In the time of peril he who had been so cautious and questioning was firm as a rock, encouraging the faith of the disciples, and furnishing means to carry forward the work of the gospel. He was scorned and persecuted by those who had paid him reverence in other days. He became poor in this world's goods; yet he faltered not in the faith which had its beginning in that night conference with Jesus.

Nicodemus related to John the story of that interview, and by his pen it was recorded for the instruction of millions. The truths there taught are as important today as they were on that solemn night in the shadowy mountain, when the Jewish ruler came to learn the way of life from the lowly Teacher of Galilee.

"He Must Increase"

For a time the Baptist's influence over the nation had been greater than that of its rulers, priests, or princes. If he had announced himself as the Messiah, and raised a revolt against Rome, priests and people would have flocked to his standard. Every consideration that appeals to the ambition of the world's conquerors Satan had stood ready to urge upon John the Baptist. But with the evidence before him of his power, he had steadfastly refused the splendid bribe. The attention which was fixed upon him he had directed to Another.

Now he saw the tide of popularity turning away from himself to the Saviour. Day by day the crowds about him lessened. When Jesus came from Jerusalem to the region about

Jordan, the people flocked to hear Him. The number of His disciples increased daily. Many came for baptism, and while Christ Himself did not baptize, He sanctioned the administration of the ordinance by His disciples. Thus He set His seal upon the mission of His forerunner. But the disciples of John looked with jealousy upon the growing popularity of Jesus. They stood ready to criticize His work, and it was not long before they found occasion. A question arose between them and the Jews as to whether baptism availed to cleanse the soul from sin; they maintained that the baptism of Jesus differed essentially from that of John. Soon they were in dispute with Christ's disciples in regard to the form of words proper to use at baptism, and finally as to the right of the latter to baptize at all.

The disciples of John came to him with their grievances, saying, "Rabbi, He that was with thee beyond Jordan, to whom thou bearest witness, behold, the same baptizeth, and all men come to Him." Through these words, Satan brought temptation upon John. Though John's mission seemed about to close, it was still possible for him to hinder the work of Christ. If he had sympathized with himself, and expressed grief or disappointment at being superseded, he would have sown the seeds of dissension, would have encouraged envy and jealousy, and would seriously have impeded the progress of the gospel.

John had by nature the faults and weaknesses common to humanity, but the touch of divine love had transformed him. He dwelt in an atmosphere uncontaminated with selfishness and ambition, and far above the miasma of jealousy. He manifested no sympathy with the dissatisfaction of his disciples, but showed how clearly he understood his relation to the Messiah, and how gladly he welcomed the One for whom he had prepared the way.

He said, "A man can receive nothing, except it be given him from heaven. Ye yourselves bear me witness, that I said, I am not the Christ, but that I am sent before Him. He that hath the bride is the bridegroom: but the friend of the bridegroom, which standeth and heareth him, rejoiceth greatly because of the bridegroom's voice." John represented himself as the friend who acted as a messenger between the betrothed parties, preparing the way for the marriage. When the bridegroom had received his bride, the mission of the friend was fulfilled. He rejoiced in the happiness of those whose union he had promoted. So John had been called to direct the people to Jesus, and it was his joy to witness the success of the Saviour's work. He said, "This my joy therefore is fulfilled. He must increase, but I must decrease."

Looking in faith to the Redeemer, John had risen to the height of self-abnegation. He sought not to attract men to himself, but to lift their thoughts higher and still higher, until they should rest upon the Lamb of God. He himself had been only a voice, a cry in the wilderness. Now with joy he accepted silence and obscurity, that the eyes of all might be turned to the Light of life.

Those who are true to their calling as messengers for God will not seek honor for themselves. Love for self will be swallowed up in love for Christ. No rivalry will mar the precious cause of the gospel. They will recognize that it is their work to proclaim, as did John the Baptist, "Behold the Lamb of God, which taketh away the sin of the world." John 1:29. They will lift up Jesus, and with Him humanity will be lifted up. "Thus saith the high and lofty One that inhabiteth eternity, whose name is Holy; I dwell in the high and holy place, with him also that is of a contrite and humble spirit, to revive the spirit of the humble, and to revive the heart of the contrite ones." Isa. 57:15.

The soul of the prophet, emptied of self, was filled with the light of the divine. As he witnessed to the Saviour's glory, his words were almost a counterpart of those that Christ Himself had spoken in His interview with Nicodemus. John said, "He that cometh from above is above all: he that is of the earth is earthly, and speaketh of the earth: He that cometh from heaven is above all. . . . For He whom God hath sent speaketh the words of God: for God giveth not the Spirit by measure unto Him." Christ could say, "I seek not Mine own will, but the will of the Father which hath sent Me." John 5:30. To Him it is declared, "Thou hast loved righteousness, and hated iniquity; therefore God, even Thy God, hath anointed Thee with the oil of gladness above Thy fellows." Heb. 1:9. The Father "giveth not the Spirit by measure unto Him."

So with the followers of Christ. We can receive of heaven's light only as we are willing to be emptied of self. We cannot discern the character of God, or accept Christ by faith, unless we consent to the bringing into captivity of every thought to the obedience of Christ. To all who do this the Holy Spirit is given without measure. In Christ "dwelleth all the fullness of the Godhead bodily, and in Him ye are made full." Col. 2:9, 10, R. V.

The disciples of John had declared that all men were coming to Christ; but with clearer insight, John said, "No man receiveth His witness;" so few were ready to accept Him as the Saviour from sin. But "he that hath received His witness hath set his seal to this, that God is true." John 3:33, R. V. "He that believeth on the Son hath everlasting life." No need of disputation as to whether Christ's baptism or John's purified from sin. It is the grace of Christ that gives life to the soul. Apart from Christ, baptism, like any other service, is a worthless form. "He that believeth not the Son shall not see life."

The success of Christ's work, which the Baptist had received with such joy, was reported also to the authorities at Jerusalem. The priests and rabbis had been jealous of John's influence as they saw the people leaving the synagogues and flocking to the wilderness; but here was One who had still greater power to attract the multitudes. Those leaders in Israel were not willing to say with John, "He must increase, but I must decrease." They arose with a new determination to put an end to the work that was drawing the people away from them.

Jesus knew that they would spare no effort to create a division between His own disciples and those of John. He knew that the storm was gathering which would sweep away one of the greatest prophets ever given to the world. Wishing to avoid all occasion for misunderstanding or dissension, He quietly ceased His labors, and withdrew to Galilee. We also, while loyal to truth, should try to avoid all that may lead to discord and misapprehension. For whenever these arise, they result in the loss of souls. Whenever circumstances occur that threaten to cause division, we should follow the example of Jesus and of John the Baptist.

John had been called to lead out as a reformer. Because of this, his disciples were in danger of fixing their attention upon him, feeling that the success of the work depended upon his labors, and losing sight of the fact that he was only an instrument through which God had wrought. But the work of John was not sufficient to lay the foundation of the Christian church. When he had fulfilled his mission, another work was to be done, which his testimony could not accomplish. His disciples did not understand this. When they saw Christ coming in to take the work, they were jealous and dissatisfied.

The same dangers still exist. God calls a man to do a certain work; and when he has carried it as far as he is qualified to take it, the Lord brings in others, to carry it still farther. But, like John's disciples, many feel that the success of the work depends on the first laborer. Attention is fixed upon the human instead of the divine, jealousy comes in, and the work of God is marred. The one thus unduly honored is tempted to cherish self-confidence. He does not realize his dependence on God. The people are taught to rely on man for guidance, and thus they fall into error, and are led away from God.

The work of God is not to bear the image and superscription of man. From time to time the Lord will bring in different agencies, through whom His purpose can best be accomplished. Happy are they who are willing for self to be humbled, saying with John the Baptist, "He must increase, but I must decrease."

At Jacob's Well

On the way to Galilee Jesus passed through Samaria. It was noon when He reached the beautiful Vale of Shechem. At the opening of this valley was Jacob's well. Wearied with His journey, He sat down here to rest while His disciples went to buy food.

The Jews and the Samaritans were bitter enemies, and as far as possible avoided all dealing with each other. To trade with the Samaritans in case of necessity was indeed counted lawful by the rabbis; but all social intercourse with them was condemned. A Jew would not borrow from a Samaritan, nor receive a kindness, not even a morsel of bread or a cup of water. The disciples, in buying food, were acting in harmony with the custom of their nation. But beyond this they did not go. To ask a favor of the Samaritans, or in any way seek to benefit them, did not enter into the thought of even Christ's

disciples.

As Jesus sat by the well side, He was faint from hunger and thirst. The journey since morning had been long, and now the sun of noontide beat upon Him. His thirst was increased by the thought of the cool, refreshing water so near, yet inaccessible to Him; for He had no rope nor water jar, and the well was deep. The lot of humanity was His, and He waited for someone to come to draw.

A woman of Samaria approached, and seeming unconscious of His presence, filled her pitcher with water. As she turned to go away, Jesus asked her for a drink. Such a favor no Oriental would withhold. In the East, water was called "the gift of God." To offer a drink to the thirsty traveler was held to be a duty so sacred that the Arabs of the desert would go out of their way in order to perform it. The hatred between Jews and Samaritans prevented the woman from offering a kindness to Jesus; but the Saviour was seeking to find the key to this heart, and with the tact born of divine love, He asked, not offered, a favor. The offer of a kindness might have been rejected; but trust awakens trust. The King of heaven came to this outcast soul, asking a service at her hands. He who made the ocean, who controls the waters of the great deep, who opened the springs and channels of the earth, rested from His weariness at Jacob's well, and was dependent upon a stranger's kindness for even the gift of a drink of water.

The woman saw that Jesus was a Jew. In her surprise she forgot to grant His request, but tried to learn the reason for it. "How is it," she said, "that Thou, being a Jew, askest drink of me, which am a woman of Samaria?"

Jesus answered, "If thou knewest the gift of God, and who it is that saith to thee, Give Me to drink; thou wouldest have asked of Him, and He would have given thee living water." You wonder that I should ask of you even so small a favor as a draught of water from the well at our feet. Had you asked of Me, I would have given you to drink of the water of everlasting life.

The woman had not comprehended the words of Christ, but she felt their solemn import. Her light, bantering manner began to change. Supposing that Jesus spoke of the well before them, she said, "Sir, Thou hast nothing to draw with, and the well is deep: from whence then hast Thou that living water? Art Thou greater than our father Jacob, which gave us the well, and drank thereof himself?" She saw before her only a thirsty traveler, wayworn and dusty. In her mind she compared Him with the honored patriarch Jacob. She cherished the feeling, which is so natural, that no other well could be equal to that provided by the fathers. She was looking backward to the fathers, forward to the Messiah's coming, while the Hope of the fathers, the Messiah Himself, was beside her, and she knew Him not. How many thirsting souls are today close by the living fountain, yet looking far away for the wellsprings of life! "Say not in thine heart, Who shall ascend into heaven? (that is, to bring Christ down from above:) or, Who shall descend into the deep? (that is, to bring up Christ again from the dead.) . . . The word is nigh thee, even in thy mouth, and in thy heart: . . . if thou shalt confess with thy mouth the Lord Jesus, and shalt believe in thine heart that God hath raised Him from the dead, thou shalt be saved." Rom. 10:6-9.

Jesus did not immediately answer the question in regard to Himself, but with solemn earnestness He said, "Whosoever drinketh of this water shall thirst again: but whosoever drinketh of the water that I shall give him shall never thirst; but the water that I shall give him shall be in him a well of water springing up into everlasting life."

He who seeks to quench his thirst at the fountains of this world will drink only to thirst again. Everywhere men are unsatisfied. They long for something to supply the need of the soul. Only One can meet that want. The need of the world, "The Desire of all nations," is Christ. The divine grace which He alone can impart, is as living water, purifying, refreshing, and invigorating the soul.

Jesus did not convey the idea that merely one draft of the water of life would suffice the receiver. He who tastes of the love of Christ will continually long for more; but he seeks for nothing else. The riches, honors, and pleasures of the world do not attract him. The constant cry of his heart is, More of Thee. And He who reveals to the soul its necessity is waiting to satisfy its hunger and thirst. Every human resource and dependence will fail. The cisterns will be emptied, the pools become dry; but our Redeemer is an inexhaustible fountain. We may drink, and drink again, and ever find a fresh supply. He in whom Christ dwells has within himself the fountain of blessing,—"a well of water springing up into everlasting life." From this source he may draw strength and grace sufficient for all his needs.

As Jesus spoke of the living water, the woman looked upon Him with wondering attention. He had aroused her interest, and awakened a desire for the gift of which He spoke. She perceived that it was not the water of Jacob's well to which He referred; for of this she used continually, drinking, and thirsting again. "Sir," she said, "give me this water, that I thirst not, neither come hither to draw."

Jesus now abruptly turned the conversation. Before this soul could receive the gift He longed to bestow, she must be brought to recognize her sin and her Saviour. He "saith unto her, Go, call thy husband, and come hither." She answered, "I have no husband." Thus she hoped to prevent all questioning in that direction. But the Saviour continued, "Thou hast well said, I have no husband: for thou hast had five husbands; and he whom thou now hast is not thy husband: in that saidst thou truly."

The listener trembled. A mysterious hand was turning the pages of her life history, bringing to view that which she had hoped to keep forever hidden. Who was He that could read the secrets of her life? There came to her thoughts of eternity, of the future Judgment, when all that is now hidden shall be revealed. In its light, conscience was awakened.

She could deny nothing; but she tried to evade all mention of a subject so unwelcome. With deep reverence, she said,

"Sir, I perceive that Thou art a prophet." Then, hoping to silence conviction, she turned to points of religious controversy. If this was a prophet, surely He could give her instruction concerning these matters that had been so long disputed.

Patiently Jesus permitted her to lead the conversation whither she would. Meanwhile He watched for the opportunity of again bringing the truth home to her heart. "Our fathers worshiped in this mountain," she said, "and ye say, that in Jerusalem is the place where men ought to worship." Just in sight was Mount Gerizim. Its temple was demolished, and only the altar remained. The place of worship had been a subject of contention between the Jews and the Samaritans. Some of the ancestors of the latter people had once belonged to Israel; but because of their sins, the Lord suffered them to be overcome by an idolatrous nation. For many generations they were intermingled with idolaters, whose religion gradually contaminated their own. It is true they held that their idols were only to remind them of the living God, the Ruler of the universe; nevertheless the people were led to reverence their graven images.

When the temple at Jerusalem was rebuilt in the days of Ezra, the Samaritans wished to join the Jews in its erection. This privilege was refused them, and a bitter animosity sprang up between the two peoples. The Samaritans built a rival temple on Mount Gerizim. Here they worshiped in accordance with the Mosaic ritual, though they did not wholly renounce idolatry. But disasters attended them, their temple was destroyed by their enemies, and they seemed to be under a curse; yet they still clung to their traditions and their forms of worship. They would not acknowledge the temple at Jerusalem as the house of God, nor admit that the religion of the Jews was superior to their own.

In answer to the woman, Jesus said, "Believe Me, the hour cometh, when ye shall neither in this mountain, nor yet at Jerusalem, worship the Father. Ye worship ye know not what: we know what we worship: for salvation is of the Jews." Jesus had shown that He was free from Jewish prejudice against the Samaritans. Now He sought to break down the prejudice of this Samaritan against the Jews. While referring to the fact that the faith of the Samaritans was corrupted with idolatry, He declared that the great truths of redemption had been committed to the Jews, and that from among them the Messiah was to appear. In the Sacred Writings they had a clear presentation of the character of God and the principles of His government. Jesus classed Himself with the Jews as those to whom God had given a knowledge of Himself.

He desired to lift the thoughts of His hearer above matters of form and ceremony, and questions of controversy. "The hour cometh," He said, "and now is, when the true worshipers shall worship the Father in spirit and in truth: for the Father seeketh such to worship Him. God is a Spirit: and they that worship Him must worship Him in spirit and in truth."

Here is declared the same truth that Jesus had revealed to Nicodemus when He said, "Except a man be born from above, he cannot see the kingdom of God." John 3:3, margin. Not by seeking a holy mountain or a sacred temple are men brought into communion with heaven. Religion is not to be confined to external forms and ceremonies. The religion that comes from God is the only religion that will lead to God. In order to serve Him aright, we must be born of the divine Spirit. This will purify the heart and renew the mind, giving us a new capacity for knowing and loving God. It will give us a willing obedience to all His requirements. This is true worship. It is the fruit of the working of the Holy Spirit. By the Spirit every sincere prayer is indited, and such prayer is acceptable to God. Wherever a soul reaches out after God, there the Spirit's working is manifest, and God will reveal Himself to that soul. For such worshipers He is seeking. He waits to receive them, and to make them His sons and daughters.

As the woman talked with Jesus, she was impressed with His words. Never had she heard such sentiments from the priests of her own people or from the Jews. As the past of her life had been spread out before her, she had been made sensible of her great want. She realized her soul thirst, which the waters of the well of Sychar could never satisfy. Nothing that had hitherto come in contact with her had so awakened her to a higher need. Jesus had convinced her that He read the secrets of her life; yet she felt that He was her friend, pitying and loving her. While the very purity of His presence condemned her sin, He had spoken no word of denunciation, but had told her of His grace, that could renew the soul. She began to have some conviction of His character. The question arose in her mind, Might not this be the long-looked-for Messiah? She said to Him, "I know that Messias cometh, which is called Christ: when He is come, He will tell us all things." Jesus answered, "I that speak unto thee am He."

As the woman heard these words, faith sprang up in her heart. She accepted the wonderful announcement from the lips of the divine Teacher.

This woman was in an appreciative state of mind. She was ready to receive the noblest revelation; for she was interested in the Scriptures, and the Holy Spirit had been preparing her mind to receive more light. She had studied the Old Testament promise, "The Lord thy God will raise up unto thee a Prophet from the midst of thee, of thy brethren, like unto me; unto Him ye shall hearken." Deut. 18:15. She longed to understand this prophecy. Light was already flashing into her mind. The water of life, the spiritual life which Christ gives to every thirsty soul, had begun to spring up in her heart. The Spirit of the Lord was working with her.

The plain statement made by Christ to this woman could not have been made to the self-righteous Jews. Christ was far more reserved when He spoke to them. That which had been withheld from the Jews, and which the disciples were afterward enjoined to keep secret, was revealed to her. Jesus saw that she would make use of her knowledge in bringing others to share His grace.

When the disciples returned from their errand, they were surprised to find their Master speaking with the woman. He had not taken the refreshing draught that He desired, and He did not stop to eat the food His disciples had brought. When the woman had gone, the disciples entreated Him to eat. They saw Him silent, absorbed, as in rapt meditation. His face was beaming with light, and they feared to interrupt His communion with heaven. But they knew that He was faint and weary, and thought it their duty to remind Him of His physical necessities. Jesus recognized their loving interest, and He said, "I have meat to eat that ye know not of."

The disciples wondered who could have brought Him food; but He explained, "My meat is to do the will of Him that sent Me, and to accomplish His work." John 4:34, R. V. As His words to the woman had aroused her conscience, Jesus rejoiced. He saw her drinking of the water of life, and His own hunger and thirst were satisfied. The accomplishment of the mission which He had left heaven to perform strengthened the Saviour for His labor, and lifted Him above the necessities of humanity. To minister to a soul hungering and thirsting for the truth was more grateful to Him than eating or drinking. It was a comfort, a refreshment, to Him. Benevolence was the life of His soul.

Our Redeemer thirsts for recognition. He hungers for the sympathy and love of those whom He has purchased with His own blood. He longs with inexpressible desire that they should come to Him and have life. As the mother watches for the smile of recognition from her little child, which tells of the dawning of intelligence, so does Christ watch for the expression of grateful love, which shows that spiritual life is begun in the soul.

The woman had been filled with joy as she listened to Christ's words. The wonderful revelation was almost overpowering. Leaving her waterpot, she returned to the city, to carry the message to others. Jesus knew why she had gone. Leaving her waterpot spoke unmistakably as to the effect of His words. It was the earnest desire of her soul to obtain the living water; and she forgot her errand to the well, she forgot the Saviour's thirst, which she had purposed to supply. With heart overflowing with gladness, she hastened on her way, to impart to others the precious light she had received.

"Come, see a man, which told me all things that ever I did," she said to the men of the city. "Is not this the Christ?" Her words touched their hearts. There was a new expression on her face, a change in her whole appearance. They were interested to see Jesus. "Then they went out of the city, and came unto Him."

As Jesus still sat at the well side, He looked over the fields of grain that were spread out before Him, their tender green touched by the golden sunlight. Pointing His disciples to the scene, He employed it as a symbol: "Say not ye, There are yet four months, and then cometh harvest? behold, I say unto you, Lift up your eyes, and look on the fields; for they are white already to harvest." And as He spoke, He looked on the groups that were coming to the well. It was four months to the time for harvesting the grain, but here was a harvest ready for the reaper.

"He that reapeth," He said, "receiveth wages, and gathereth fruit unto life eternal: that both he that soweth and he that reapeth may rejoice together. And herein is that saying true, One soweth, and another reapeth." Here Christ points out the sacred service owed to God by those who receive the gospel. They are to be His living agencies. He requires their individual service. And whether we sow or reap, we are working for God. One scatters the seed; another gathers in the harvest; and both the sower and the reaper receive wages. They rejoice together in the reward of their labor.

Jesus said to the disciples, "I sent you to reap that whereon ye bestowed no labor: other men labored, and ye are entered into their labors." The Saviour was here looking forward to the great ingathering on the day of Pentecost. The disciples were not to regard this as the result of their own efforts. They were entering into other men's labors. Ever since the fall of Adam Christ had been committing the seed of the word to His chosen servants, to be sown in human hearts. And an unseen agency, even an omnipotent power, had worked silently but effectually to produce the harvest. The dew and rain and sunshine of God's grace had been given, to refresh and nourish the seed of truth. Christ was about to water the seed with His own blood. His disciples were privileged to be laborers together with God. They were coworkers with Christ and with the holy men of old. By the outpouring of the Holy Spirit at Pentecost, thousands were to be converted in a day. This was the result of Christ's sowing, the harvest of His work.

In the words spoken to the woman at the well, good seed had been sown, and how quickly the harvest was received. The Samaritans came and heard Jesus, and believed on Him. Crowding about Him at the well, they plied Him with questions, and eagerly received His explanations of many things that had been obscure to them. As they listened, their perplexity began to clear away. They were like a people in great darkness tracing up a sudden ray of light till they had found the day. But they were not satisfied with this short conference. They were anxious to hear more, and to have their friends also listen to this wonderful teacher. They invited Him to their city, and begged Him to remain with them. For two days He tarried in Samaria, and many more believed on Him.

The Pharisees despised the simplicity of Jesus. They ignored His miracles, and demanded a sign that He was the Son of God. But the Samaritans asked no sign, and Jesus performed no miracles among them, save in revealing the secrets of her life to the woman at the well. Yet many received Him. In their new joy they said to the woman, "Now we believe, not because of thy saying: for we have heard Him ourselves, and know that this is indeed the Christ, the Saviour of the world."

The Samaritans believed that the Messiah was to come as the Redeemer, not only of the Jews, but of the world. The Holy Spirit through Moses had foretold Him as a prophet sent from God. Through Jacob it had been declared that unto Him should the gathering of the people be; and through Abraham, that in Him all the nations of the earth should be blessed. On these scriptures the people of Samaria based their faith in the Messiah. The fact that the Jews had misinterpreted the later prophets, attributing to the first advent the glory of Christ's second coming, had led the Samaritans to discard all the sacred writings except those given through Moses. But as the Saviour swept away these false interpretations, many accepted the later prophecies and the words of Christ Himself in regard to the kingdom of God.

Jesus had begun to break down the partition wall between Jew and Gentile, and to preach salvation to the world. Though He was a Jew, He mingled freely with the Samaritans, setting at nought the Pharisaic customs of His nation. In face of their prejudices He accepted the hospitality of this despised people. He slept under their roofs, ate with them at their tables,—partaking of the food prepared and served by their hands,—taught in their streets, and treated them with the utmost kindness and courtesy.

In the temple at Jerusalem a low wall separated the outer court from all other portions of the sacred building. Upon this wall were inscriptions in different languages, stating that none but Jews were allowed to pass this boundary. Had a Gentile presumed to enter the inner enclosure, he would have desecrated the temple, and would have paid the penalty with his life. But Jesus, the originator of the temple and its service, drew the Gentiles to Him by the tie of human sympathy, while His divine grace brought to them the salvation which the Jews rejected.

The stay of Jesus in Samaria was designed to be a blessing to His disciples, who were still under the influence of Jewish bigotry. They felt that loyalty to their own nation required them to cherish enmity toward the Samaritans. They wondered at the conduct of Jesus. They could not refuse to follow His example, and during the two days in Samaria, fidelity to Him kept their prejudices under control; yet in heart they were unreconciled. They were slow to learn that their contempt and hatred must give place to pity and sympathy. But after the Lord's ascension, His lessons came back to them with a new meaning. After the outpouring of the Holy Spirit, they recalled the Saviour's look, His words, the respect and tenderness of His bearing toward these despised strangers. When Peter went to preach in Samaria, he brought the same spirit into his own work. When John was called to Ephesus and Smyrna, he remembered the experience at Shechem, and was filled with gratitude to the divine Teacher, who, foreseeing the difficulties they must meet, had given them help in His own example.

The Saviour is still carrying forward the same work as when He proffered the water of life to the woman of Samaria. Those who call themselves His followers may despise and shun the outcast ones; but no circumstance of birth or nationality, no condition of life, can turn away His love from the children of men. To every soul, however sinful, Jesus says, If thou hadst asked of Me, I would have given thee living water.

The gospel invitation is not to be narrowed down, and presented only to a select few, who, we suppose, will do us honor if they accept it. The message is to be given to all. Wherever hearts are open to receive the truth, Christ is ready to instruct them. He reveals to them the Father, and the worship acceptable to Him who reads the heart. For such He uses no parables. To them, as to the woman at the well, He says, "I that speak unto thee am He."

When Jesus sat down to rest at Jacob's well, He had come from Judea, where His ministry had produced little fruit. He had been rejected by the priests and rabbis, and even the people who professed to be His disciples had failed of perceiving His divine character. He was faint and weary; yet He did not neglect the opportunity of speaking to one woman, though she was a stranger, an alien from Israel, and living in open sin.

The Saviour did not wait for congregations to assemble. Often He began His lessons with only a few gathered about Him, but one by one the passers-by paused to listen, until a multitude heard with wonder and awe the words of God through the heaven-sent Teacher. The worker for Christ should not feel that he cannot speak with the same earnestness to a few hearers as to a larger company. There may be only one to hear the message; but who can tell how far-reaching will be its influence? It seemed a small matter, even to His disciples, for the Saviour to spend His time upon a woman of Samaria. But He reasoned more earnestly and eloquently with her than with kings, councilors, or high priests. The lessons He gave to that woman have been repeated to the earth's remotest bounds.

As soon as she had found the Saviour the Samaritan woman brought others to Him. She proved herself a more effective missionary than His own disciples. The disciples saw nothing in Samaria to indicate that it was an encouraging field. Their thoughts were fixed upon a great work to be done in the future. They did not see that right around them was a harvest to be gathered. But through the woman whom they despised, a whole cityful were brought to hear the Saviour. She carried the light at once to her countrymen.

This woman represents the working of a practical faith in Christ. Every true disciple is born into the kingdom of God as a missionary. He who drinks of the living water becomes a fountain of life. The receiver becomes a giver. The grace of Christ in the soul is like a spring in the desert, welling up to refresh all, and making those who are ready to perish eager to drink of the water of life.

"Except Ye See Signs and Wonders"

The Galileans who returned from the Passover brought back the report of the wonderful works of Jesus. The judgment passed upon His acts by the dignitaries at Jerusalem opened His way in Galilee. Many of the people lamented the abuse of the temple and the greed and arrogance of the priests. They hoped that this Man, who had put the rulers to flight, might be the looked-for Deliverer. Now tidings had come that seemed to confirm their brightest anticipations. It was reported that the prophet had declared Himself to be the Messiah.

But the people of Nazareth did not believe on Him. For this reason, Jesus did not visit Nazareth on His way to Cana. The Saviour declared to His disciples that a prophet has no honor in his own country. Men estimate character by that which they themselves are capable of appreciating. The narrow and worldly-minded judged of Christ by His humble birth, His lowly garb, and daily toil. They could not appreciate the purity of that spirit upon which was no stain of sin.

The news of Christ's return to Cana soon spread throughout Galilee, bringing hope to the suffering and distressed. In Capernaum the tidings attracted the attention of a Jewish nobleman who was an officer in the king's service. A son of the officer was suffering from what seemed to be an incurable disease. Physicians had given him up to die; but when the father heard of Jesus, he determined to seek help from Him. The child was very low, and, it was feared, might not live till his return; yet the nobleman felt that he must present the case in person. He hoped that a father's prayers might awaken the sympathy of the Great Physician.

On reaching Cana he found a throng surrounding Jesus. With an anxious heart he pressed through to the Saviour's presence. His faith faltered when he saw only a plainly dressed man, dusty and worn with travel. He doubted that this Person could do what he had come to ask of Him; yet he secured an interview with Jesus, told his errand, and besought the Saviour to accompany him to his home. But already his sorrow was known to Jesus. Before the officer had left his home, the Saviour had beheld his affliction.

But He knew also that the father had, in his own mind, made conditions concerning his belief in Jesus. Unless his petition should be granted, he would not receive Him as the Messiah. While the officer waited in an agony of suspense, Jesus said, "Except ye see signs and wonders, ye will not believe."

Notwithstanding all the evidence that Jesus was the Christ, the petitioner had determined to make his belief in Him conditional on the granting of his own request. The Saviour contrasted this questioning unbelief with the simple faith of the Samaritans, who asked for no miracle or sign. His word, the ever-present evidence of His divinity, had a convincing power that reached their hearts. Christ was pained that His own people, to whom the Sacred Oracles had been committed, should fail to hear the voice of God speaking to them in His Son.

Yet the nobleman had a degree of faith; for he had come to ask what seemed to him the most precious of all blessings. Jesus had a greater gift to bestow. He desired, not only to heal the child, but to make the officer and his household sharers in the blessings of salvation, and to kindle a light in Capernaum, which was so soon to be the field of His own labors. But the nobleman must realize his need before he would desire the grace of Christ. This courtier represented many of his nation. They were interested in Jesus from selfish motives. They hoped to receive some special benefit through His power, and they staked their faith on the granting of this temporal favor; but they were ignorant as to their spiritual disease, and saw not their need of divine grace.

Like a flash of light, the Saviour's words to the nobleman laid bare his heart. He saw that his motives in seeking Jesus were selfish. His vacillating faith appeared to him in its true character. In deep distress he realized that his doubt might cost the life of his son. He knew that he was in the presence of One who could read the thoughts, and to whom all things were possible. In an agony of supplication he cried, "Sir, come down ere my child die." His faith took hold upon Christ as did Jacob, when, wrestling with the Angel, he cried, "I will not let Thee go, except Thou bless me." Gen. 32:26.

Like Jacob he prevailed. The Saviour cannot withdraw from the soul that clings to Him, pleading its great need. "Go thy way," He said; "thy son liveth." The nobleman left the Saviour's presence with a peace and joy he had never known before. Not only did he believe that his son would be restored, but with strong confidence he trusted in Christ as the Redeemer.

At the same hour the watchers beside the dying child in the home at Capernaum beheld a sudden and mysterious change. The shadow of death was lifted from the sufferer's face. The flush of fever gave place to the soft glow of returning health. The dim eyes brightened with intelligence, and strength returned to the feeble, emaciated frame. No signs of his malady lingered about the child. His burning flesh had become soft and moist, and he sank into a quiet sleep. The fever had left him in the very heat of the day. The family were amazed, and great was the rejoicing.

Cana was not so far from Capernaum but that the officer might have reached his home on the evening after his interview with Jesus; but he did not hasten on the homeward journey. It was not until the next morning that he reached Capernaum. What a homecoming was that! When he went to find Jesus, his heart was heavy with sorrow. The sunshine seemed cruel to him, the songs of the birds a mockery. How different his feelings now! All nature wears a new aspect. He sees with new eyes. As he journeys in the quiet of the early morning, all nature seems to be praising God with him. While he is still some distance from his own dwelling, servants come out to meet him, anxious to relieve the suspense they are sure he must feel. He shows no surprise at the news they bring, but with a depth of interest they cannot know he asks at what hour the child began to mend. They answer, "Yesterday at the seventh hour the fever left him." At the very moment when the father's faith grasped the assurance, "Thy son liveth," divine love touched the dying child.

The father hurries on to greet his son. He clasps him to his heart as one restored from the dead, and thanks God again and again for this wonderful restoration.

The nobleman longed to know more of Christ. As he afterward heard His teaching, he and all his household became disciples. Their affliction was sanctified to the conversion of the entire family. Tidings of the miracle spread; and in Capernaum, where so many of His mighty works were performed, the way was prepared for Christ's personal ministry.

He who blessed the nobleman at Capernaum is just as desirous of blessing us. But like the afflicted father, we are often led to seek Jesus by the desire for some earthly good; and upon the granting of our request we rest our confidence in His love. The Saviour longs to give us a greater blessing than we ask; and He delays the answer to our request that He may show us the evil of our own hearts, and our deep need of His grace. He desires us to renounce the selfishness that leads us to seek Him. Confessing our helplessness and bitter need, we are to trust ourselves wholly to His love.

The nobleman wanted to see the fulfillment of his prayer before he should believe; but he had to accept the word of Jesus that his request was heard and the blessing granted. This lesson we also have to learn. Not because we see or feel that God hears us are we to believe. We are to trust in His promises. When we come to Him in faith, every petition enters the heart of God. When we have asked for His blessing, we should believe that we receive it, and thank Him that we have received it. Then we are to go about our duties, assured that the blessing will be realized when we need it most. When we have learned to do this, we shall know that our prayers are answered. God will do for us "exceeding abundantly," "according to the riches of His glory," and "the working of His mighty power." Eph. 3:20, 16; 1:19.

Bethesda and the Sanhedrin

"Now there is at Jerusalem by the sheep market a pool, which is called in the Hebrew tongue Bethesda, having five porches. In these lay a great multitude of impotent folk, of blind, halt, withered, waiting for the moving of the water."

At certain seasons the waters of this pool were agitated, and it was commonly believed that this was the result of supernatural power, and that whoever first after the troubling of the pool stepped into the waters, would be healed of whatever disease he had. Hundreds of sufferers visited the place; but so great was the crowd when the water was troubled that they rushed forward, trampling underfoot men, women, and children, weaker than themselves. Many could not get near the pool. Many who had succeeded in reaching it died upon its brink. Shelters had been erected about the place, that the sick might be protected from the heat by day and the chilliness of the night. There were some who spent the night in these porches, creeping to the edge of the pool day after day, in the vain hope of relief.

Jesus was again at Jerusalem. Walking alone, in apparent meditation and prayer, He came to the pool. He saw the wretched sufferers watching for that which they supposed to be their only chance of cure. He longed to exercise His healing power, and make every sufferer whole. But it was the Sabbath day. Multitudes were going to the temple for worship, and He knew that such an act of healing would so excite the prejudice of the Jews as to cut short His work.

But the Saviour saw one case of supreme wretchedness. It was that of a man who had been a helpless cripple for thirty-eight years. His disease was in a great degree the result of his own sin, and was looked upon as a judgment from God. Alone and friendless, feeling that he was shut out from God's mercy, the sufferer had passed long years of misery. At the time when it was expected that the waters would be troubled, those who pitied his helplessness would bear him to the porches. But at the favored moment he had no one to help him in. He had seen the rippling of the water, but had never been able to get farther than the edge of the pool. Others stronger than he would plunge in before him. He could not contend successfully with the selfish, scrambling crowd. His persistent efforts toward the one object, and his anxiety and continual disappointment, were fast wearing away the remnant of his strength.

The sick man was lying on his mat, and occasionally lifting his head to gaze at the pool, when a tender, compassionate face bent over him, and the words, "Wilt thou be made whole?" arrested his attention. Hope came to his heart. He felt that in some way he was to have help. But the glow of encouragement soon faded. He remembered how often he had tried to reach the pool, and now he had little prospect of living till it should again be troubled. He turned away wearily, saying, "Sir, I have no man, when the water is troubled, to put me into the pool: but while I am coming, another steppeth down before me."

Jesus does not ask this sufferer to exercise faith in Him. He simply says, "Rise, take up thy bed, and walk." But the man's faith takes hold upon that word. Every nerve and muscle thrills with new life, and healthful action comes to his crippled limbs. Without question he sets his will to obey the command of Christ, and all his muscles respond to his will. Springing to his feet, he finds himself an active man.

Jesus had given him no assurance of divine help. The man might have stopped to doubt, and lost his one chance of healing. But he believed Christ's word, and in acting upon it he received strength.

Through the same faith we may receive spiritual healing. By sin we have been severed from the life of God. Our souls are palsied. Of ourselves we are no more capable of living a holy life than was the impotent man capable of walking. There are many who realize their helplessness, and who long for that spiritual life which will bring them into harmony with God; they are vainly striving to obtain it. In despair they cry, "O wretched man that I am! who shall deliver me from this body of death?" Rom. 7:24, margin. Let these desponding, struggling ones look up. The Saviour is bending over the purchase of His blood, saying with inexpressible tenderness and pity, "Wilt thou be made whole?" He bids you arise in health and peace. Do not wait to feel that you are made whole. Believe His word, and it will be fulfilled. Put your will on the side of Christ. Will to serve Him, and in acting upon

His word you will receive strength. Whatever may be the evil practice, the master passion which through long indulgence binds both soul and body, Christ is able and longs to deliver. He will impart life to the soul that is "dead in trespasses." Eph. 2:1. He will set free the captive that is held by weakness and misfortune and the chains of sin.

The restored paralytic stooped to take up his bed, which was only a rug and a blanket, and as he straightened himself again with a sense of delight, he looked around for his Deliverer; but Jesus was lost in the crowd. The man feared that he would not know Him if he should see Him again. As he hurried on his way with firm, free step, praising God and rejoicing in his new-found strength, he met several of the Pharisees, and immediately told them of his cure. He was surprised at the coldness with which they listened to his story.

With lowering brows they interrupted him, asking why he was carrying his bed on the Sabbath day. They sternly reminded him that it was not lawful to bear burdens on the Lord's day. In his joy the man had forgotten that it was the Sabbath; yet he felt no condemnation for obeying the command of One who had such power from God. He answered boldly, "He that made me whole, the same said unto me, Take up thy bed, and walk." They asked who it was that had done this, but he could not tell. These rulers knew well that only One had shown Himself able to perform this miracle; but they wished for direct proof that it was Jesus, that they might condemn Him as a Sabbath-breaker. In their judgment He had not only broken the law in healing the sick man on the Sabbath, but had committed sacrilege in bidding him bear away his bed.

The Jews had so perverted the law that they made it a yoke of bondage. Their meaningless requirements had become a byword among other nations. Especially was the Sabbath hedged in by all manner of senseless restrictions. It was not to them a delight, the holy of the Lord, and honorable. The scribes and Pharisees had made its observance an intolerable burden. A Jew was not allowed to kindle a fire nor even to light a candle on the Sabbath. As a consequence the people were dependent upon the Gentiles for many services which their rules forbade them to do for themselves. They did not reflect that if these acts were sinful, those who employed others to perform them were as guilty as if they had done the work themselves. They thought that salvation was restricted to the Jews, and that the condition of all others, being already hopeless, could be made no worse. But God has given no commandments which cannot be obeyed by all. His laws sanction no unreasonable or selfish restrictions.

In the temple Jesus met the man who had been healed. He had come to bring a sin offering and also a thank offering for the great mercy he had received. Finding him among the worshipers, Jesus made Himself known, with the warning words, "Behold, thou art made whole: sin no more, lest a worse thing come unto thee."

The healed man was overjoyed at meeting his Deliverer. Ignorant of the enmity toward Jesus, he told the Pharisees who had questioned him, that this was He who had performed the cure. "Therefore did the Jews persecute Jesus, and sought to slay Him, because He had done these things on the Sabbath day."

Jesus was brought before the Sanhedrin to answer the charge of Sabbathbreaking. Had the Jews at this time been an independent nation, such a charge would have served their purpose for putting Him to death. This their subjection to the Romans prevented. The Jews had not the power to inflict capital punishment, and the accusations brought against Christ would have no weight in a Roman court. There were other objects, however, which they hoped to secure. Notwithstanding their efforts to counteract His work, Christ was gaining, even in Jerusalem, an influence over the people greater than their own. Multitudes who were not interested in the harangues of the rabbis were attracted by His teaching. They could understand His words, and their hearts were warmed and comforted. He spoke of God, not as an avenging judge, but as a tender father, and He revealed the image of God as mirrored in Himself. His words were like balm to the wounded spirit. Both by His words and by His works of mercy He was breaking the oppressive power of the old traditions and man-made commandments, and presenting the love of God in its exhaustless fullness.

In one of the earliest prophecies of Christ it is written, "The scepter shall not depart from Judah, nor a lawgiver from between his feet, until Shiloh come; and unto Him shall the gathering of the people be." Gen. 49:10. The people were gathering to Christ. The sympathetic hearts of the multitude accepted lessons of love and benevolence in preference to the rigid ceremonies required by the priests. If the priests and rabbis had not interposed, His teaching would have wrought such a reformation as this world has never witnessed. But in order to maintain their own power, these leaders determined to break down the influence of Jesus. His arraignment before the Sanhedrin, and an open condemnation of His teachings, would aid in effecting this; for the people still had great reverence for their religious leaders. Whoever dared to condemn the rabbinical requirements, or attempt to lighten the burdens they had brought upon the people, was regarded as guilty, not only of blasphemy, but of treason. On this ground the rabbis hoped to excite suspicion of Christ. They represented Him as trying to overthrow the established customs, thus causing division among the people, and preparing the way for complete subjugation by the Romans.

But the plans which these rabbis were working so zealously to fulfill originated in another council than that of the Sanhedrin. After Satan had failed to overcome Christ in the wilderness, he combined his forces to oppose Him in His ministry, and if possible to thwart His work. What he could not accomplish by direct, personal effort, he determined to effect by strategy. No sooner had he withdrawn from the conflict in the wilderness than in council with his confederate angels he matured his plans for still further blinding the minds of the Jewish people, that they might not recognize their

Redeemer. He planned to work through his human agencies in the religious world, by imbuing them with his own enmity against the champion of truth. He would lead them to reject Christ and to make His life as bitter as possible, hoping to discourage Him in His mission. And the leaders in Israel became instruments of Satan in warring against the Saviour.

Jesus had come to "magnify the law, and make it honorable." He was not to lessen its dignity, but to exalt it. The scripture says, "He shall not fail nor be discouraged, till He have set judgment in the earth." Isa. 42:21, 4. He had come to free the Sabbath from those burdensome requirements that had made it a curse instead of a blessing.

For this reason He had chosen the Sabbath upon which to perform the act of healing at Bethesda. He could have healed the sick man as well on any other day of the week; or He might simply have cured him, without bidding him bear away his bed. But this would not have given Him the opportunity He desired. A wise purpose underlay every act of Christ's life on earth. Everything He did was important in itself and in its teaching. Among the afflicted ones at the pool He selected the worst case upon whom to exercise His healing power, and bade the man carry his bed through the city in order to publish the great work that had been wrought upon him. This would raise the question of what it was lawful to do on the Sabbath, and would open the way for Him to denounce the restrictions of the Jews in regard to the Lord's day, and to declare their traditions void.

Jesus stated to them that the work of relieving the afflicted was in harmony with the Sabbath law. It was in harmony with the work of God's angels, who are ever descending and ascending between heaven and earth to minister to suffering humanity. Jesus declared, "My Father worketh hitherto, and I work." All days are God's, in which to carry out His plans for the human race. If the Jews' interpretation of the law was correct, then Jehovah was at fault, whose work has quickened and upheld every living thing since first He laid the foundations of the earth; then He who pronounced His work good, and instituted the Sabbath to commemorate its completion, must put a period to His labor, and stop the never-ending routine of the universe.

Should God forbid the sun to perform its office upon the Sabbath, cut off its genial rays from warming the earth and nourishing vegetation? Must the system of worlds stand still through that holy day? Should He command the brooks to stay from watering the fields and forests, and bid the waves of the sea still their ceaseless ebbing and flowing? Must the wheat and corn stop growing, and the ripening cluster defer its purple bloom? Must the trees and flowers put forth no bud nor blossom on the Sabbath?

In such a case, men would miss the fruits of the earth, and the blessings that make life desirable. Nature must continue her unvarying course. God could not for a moment stay His hand, or man would faint and die. And man also has a work to perform on this day. The necessities of life must be attended to, the sick must be cared for, the wants of the needy must be supplied. He will not be held guiltless who neglects to relieve suffering on the Sabbath. God's holy rest day was made for man, and acts of mercy are in perfect harmony with its intent. God does not desire His creatures to suffer an hour's pain that may be relieved upon the Sabbath or any other day.

The demands upon God are even greater upon the Sabbath than upon other days. His people then leave their usual employment, and spend the time in meditation and worship. They ask more favors of Him on the Sabbath than upon other days. They demand His special attention. They crave His choicest blessings. God does not wait for the Sabbath to pass before He grants these requests. Heaven's work never ceases, and men should never rest from doing good. The Sabbath is not intended to be a period of useless inactivity. The law forbids secular labor on the rest day of the Lord; the toil that gains a livelihood must cease; no labor for worldly pleasure or profit is lawful upon that day; but as God ceased His labor of creating, and rested upon the Sabbath and blessed it, so man is to leave the occupations of his daily life, and devote those sacred hours to healthful rest, to worship, and to holy deeds. The work of Christ in healing the sick was in perfect accord with the law. It honored the Sabbath.

Jesus claimed equal rights with God in doing a work equally sacred, and of the same character with that which engaged the Father in heaven. But the Pharisees were still more incensed. He had not only broken the law, according to their understanding, but in calling God "His own Father" had declared Himself equal with God. John 5:18, R. V.

The whole nation of the Jews called God their Father, therefore they would not have been so enraged if Christ had represented Himself as standing in the same relation to God. But they accused Him of blasphemy, showing that they understood Him as making this claim in the highest sense.

These adversaries of Christ had no arguments with which to meet the truths He brought home to their consciences. They could only cite their customs and traditions, and these seemed weak and vapid when compared with the arguments Jesus had drawn from the word of God and the unceasing round of nature. Had the rabbis felt any desire to receive light, they would have been convinced that Jesus spoke the truth. But they evaded the points He made concerning the Sabbath, and sought to stir up anger against Him because He claimed to be equal with God. The fury of the rulers knew no bounds. Had they not feared the people, the priests and rabbis would have slain Jesus on the spot. But the popular sentiment in His favor was strong. Many recognized in Jesus the friend who had healed their diseases and comforted their sorrows, and they justified His healing of the sufferer at Bethesda. So for the time the leaders were obliged to restrain their hatred.

Jesus repelled the charge of blasphemy. My authority, He said, for doing the work of which you accuse Me, is that I am the Son of God, one with Him in nature, in will, and in purpose. In all His works of creation and providence, I co-operate with God. "The Son can do nothing of Himself, but what He seeth the Father do." The priests and rabbis were taking the Son of God to task for the very work He had been sent into the world to do. By their sins they had separated themselves from God, and in their pride were moving independently of Him. They felt sufficient in themselves for all things, and realized no need of a higher wisdom to direct their acts. But the Son of God was surrendered to the Father's will, and dependent upon His power. So utterly was Christ emptied of self that He made no plans for Himself. He accepted God's plans for Him, and day by day the Father unfolded His plans. So should we depend upon God, that our lives may be the simple outworking of His will.

When Moses was about to build the sanctuary as a dwelling place for God, he was directed to make all things according to the pattern shown him in the mount. Moses was full of zeal to do God's work; the most talented, skillful men were at hand to carry out his suggestions. Yet he was not to make a bell, a pomegranate, a tassel, a fringe, a curtain, or any vessel of the sanctuary, except according to the pattern shown him. God called him into the mount, and revealed to him the heavenly things. The Lord covered him with His own glory, that he might see the pattern, and according to it all things were made. So to Israel, whom He desired to make His dwelling place, He had revealed His glorious ideal of character. The pattern was shown them in the mount when the law was given from Sinai, and when the Lord passed by before Moses and proclaimed, "The Lord, The Lord God, merciful and gracious, long-suffering, and abundant in goodness and truth, keeping mercy for thousands, forgiving iniquity and transgression and sin." Ex. 34:6, 7.

Israel had chosen their own ways. They had not builded according to the pattern; but Christ, the true temple for God's indwelling, molded every detail of His earthly life in harmony with God's ideal. He said, "I delight to do Thy will, O My God: yea, Thy law is within My heart." Ps. 40:8. So our characters are to be built "for an habitation of God through the Spirit." Eph. 2:22. And we are to "make all things according to the pattern," even Him who "suffered for us, leaving us an example, that ye should follow His steps." Heb. 8:5; 1 Peter 2:21.

The words of Christ teach that we should regard ourselves as inseparably bound to our Father in heaven. Whatever our position, we are dependent upon God, who holds all destinies in His hands. He has appointed us our work, and has endowed us with faculties and means for that work. So long as we surrender the will to God, and trust in His strength and wisdom, we shall be guided in safe paths, to fulfill our appointed part in His great plan. But the one who depends upon his own wisdom and power is separating himself from God. Instead of working in unison with Christ, he is fulfilling the purpose of the enemy of God and man.

The Saviour continued: "What things soever He doeth, these also doeth the Son likewise. . . . As the Father raiseth up the dead, and quickeneth them; even so the Son quickeneth whom He will." The Sadducees held that there would be no resurrection of the body; but Jesus tells them that one of the greatest works of His Father is raising the dead, and that He Himself has power to do the same work. "The hour is coming, and now is, when the dead shall hear the voice of the Son of God: and they that hear shall live." The Pharisees believed in the resurrection of the dead. Christ declares that even now the power which gives life to the dead is among them, and they are to behold its manifestation. This same resurrection power is that which gives life to the soul "dead in trespasses and sins." Eph. 2:1. That spirit of life in Christ Jesus, "the power of His resurrection," sets men "free from the law of sin and death." Phil. 3:10; Rom. 8:2. The dominion of evil is broken, and through faith the soul is kept from sin. He who opens his heart to the Spirit of Christ becomes a partaker of that mighty power which shall bring forth his body from the grave.

The humble Nazarene asserts His real nobility. He rises above humanity, throws off the guise of sin and shame, and stands revealed, the Honored of the angels, the Son of God, One with the Creator of the universe. His hearers are spellbound. No man has ever spoken words like His, or borne himself with such a kingly majesty. His utterances are clear and plain, fully declaring His mission, and the duty of the world. "For the Father judgeth no man, but hath committed all judgment unto the Son: that all men should honor the Son, even as they honor the Father. He that honoreth not the Son honoreth not the Father which hath sent Him. . . . For as the Father hath life in Himself; so hath He given to the Son to have life in Himself; and hath given Him authority to execute judgment also, because He is the Son of man."

The priests and rulers had set themselves up as judges to condemn Christ's work, but He declared Himself their judge, and the judge of all the earth. The world has been committed to Christ, and through Him has come every blessing from God to the fallen race. He was the Redeemer before as after His incarnation. As soon as there was sin, there was a Saviour. He has given light and life to all, and according to the measure of light given, each is to be judged. And He who has given the light, He who has followed the soul with tenderest entreaty, seeking to win it from sin to holiness, is in one its advocate and judge. From the opening of the great controversy in heaven, Satan has maintained his cause through deception; and Christ has been working to unveil his schemes and to break his power. It is He who has encountered the deceiver, and who through all the ages has been seeking to wrest the captives from his grasp, who will pass judgment upon every soul.

And God "hath given Him authority to execute judgment also, because He is the Son of man." Because He has tasted the very dregs of human affliction and temptation, and understands the frailties and sins of men; because in our behalf He has victoriously withstood the temptations of Satan, and will deal justly and tenderly with the souls that His own blood has been poured out to save,—because of this, the Son of man is appointed to execute the judgment.

But Christ's mission was not for judgment, but for salvation.

"God sent not His Son into the world to condemn the world; but that the world through Him might be saved." John 3:17. And before the Sanhedrin Jesus declared, "He that heareth My word, and believeth Him that sent Me, hath eternal life, and cometh not into judgment, but hath passed out of death into life." John 5:24, R. V.

Bidding His hearers marvel not, Christ opened before them, in still wider view, the mystery of the future. "The hour cometh," He said, "in which all that are in the tombs shall hear His voice, and shall come forth; they that have done good, unto the resurrection of life; and they that have done ill, unto the resurrection of judgment." John 5:28, 29, R. V.

This assurance of the future life was that for which Israel had so long waited, and which they had hoped to receive at the Messiah's advent. The only light that can lighten the gloom of the grave was shining upon them. But self-will is blind. Jesus had violated the traditions of the rabbis, and disregarded their authority, and they would not believe.

The time, the place, the occasion, the intensity of feeling that pervaded the assembly, all combined to make the words of Jesus before the Sanhedrin the more impressive. The highest religious authorities of the nation were seeking the life of Him who declared Himself the restorer of Israel. The Lord of the Sabbath was arraigned before an earthly tribunal to answer the charge of breaking the Sabbath law. When He so fearlessly declared His mission, His judges looked upon Him with astonishment and rage; but His words were unanswerable. They could not condemn Him. He denied the right of the priests and rabbis to question Him, or to interfere with His work. They were invested with no such authority. Their claims were based upon their own pride and arrogance. He refused to plead guilty of their charges, or to be catechized by them.

Instead of apologizing for the act of which they complained, or explaining His purpose in doing it, Jesus turned upon the rulers, and the accused became the accuser. He rebuked them for the hardness of their hearts, and their ignorance of the Scriptures. He declared that they had rejected the word of God, inasmuch as they had rejected Him whom God had sent. "Ye search the Scriptures, because ye think that in them ye have eternal life; and these are they which bear witness of Me." John 5:39, R. V.

In every page, whether history, or precept, or prophecy, the Old Testament Scriptures are irradiated with the glory of the Son of God. So far as it was of divine institution, the entire system of Judaism was a compacted prophecy of the gospel. To Christ "give all the prophets witness." Acts 10:43. From the promise given to Adam, down through the patriarchal line and the legal economy, heaven's glorious light made plain the footsteps of the Redeemer. Seers beheld the Star of Bethlehem, the Shiloh to come, as future things swept before them in mysterious procession. In every sacrifice Christ's death was shown. In every cloud of incense His righteousness ascended. By every jubilee trumpet His name was sounded. In the awful mystery of the holy of holies His glory dwelt.

The Jews had the Scriptures in their possession, and supposed that in their mere outward knowledge of the word they had eternal life. But Jesus said, "Ye have not His word abiding in you." Having rejected Christ in His word, they rejected Him in person. "Ye will not come to Me," He said, "that ye might have life."

The Jewish leaders had studied the teachings of the prophets concerning the kingdom of the Messiah; but they had done this, not with a sincere desire to know the truth, but with the purpose of finding evidence to sustain their ambitious hopes. When Christ came in a manner contrary to their expectations, they would not receive Him; and in order to justify themselves, they tried to prove Him a deceiver. When once they had set their feet in this path, it was easy for Satan to strengthen their opposition to Christ. The very words that should have been received as evidence of His divinity were interpreted against Him. Thus they turned the truth of God into a lie, and the more directly the Saviour spoke to them in His works of mercy, the more determined they were in resisting the light.

Jesus said, "I receive not honor from men." It was not the influence of the Sanhedrin, it was not their sanction He desired. He could receive no honor from their approbation. He was invested with the honor and authority of Heaven. Had He desired it, angels would have come to do Him homage; the Father would again have testified to His divinity. But for their own sake, for the sake of the nation whose leaders they were, He desired the Jewish rulers to discern His character, and receive the blessings He came to bring them.

"I am come in My Father's name, and ye receive Me not: if another shall come in his own name, him ye will receive." Jesus came by the authority of God, bearing His image, fulfilling His word, and seeking His glory; yet He was not accepted by the leaders in Israel; but when others should come, assuming the character of Christ, but actuated by their own will and seeking their own glory, they would be received. And why? Because he who is seeking his own glory appeals to the desire for self-exaltation in others. To such appeals the Jews could respond. They would receive the false teacher because he flattered their pride by sanctioning their cherished opinions and traditions. But the teaching of Christ did not coincide with their ideas. It was spiritual, and demanded the sacrifice of self; therefore they would not receive it. They were not acquainted with God, and to them His voice through Christ was the voice of a stranger.

Is not the same thing repeated in our day? Are there not many, even religious leaders, who are hardening their hearts against the Holy Spirit, making it impossible for them to recognize the voice of God? Are they not rejecting the word of God, that they may keep their own traditions?

"Had ye believed Moses," said Jesus, "ye would have believed Me: for he wrote of Me. But if ye believe not his writings, how shall ye believe My words?" It was Christ who had spoken to Israel through Moses. If they had listened to the divine voice that spoke through their great leader, they would have recognized it in the teachings of Christ. Had they believed Moses, they would have believed Him of whom Moses wrote.

Jesus knew that the priests and rabbis were determined to take His life; yet He clearly explained to them His unity with the Father, and His relation to the world. They saw that their opposition to Him was without excuse, yet their murderous hatred was not quenched. Fear seized them as they witnessed the convincing power that attended His ministry; but they resisted His appeals, and locked themselves in darkness.

They had signally failed to subvert the authority of Jesus or to alienate the respect and attention of the people, many of whom were convicted by His words. The rulers themselves had felt deep condemnation as He had pressed their guilt home upon their consciences; yet this only made them the more bitter against Him. They were determined to take His life. They sent messengers all over the country to warn the people against Jesus as an impostor. Spies were sent to watch Him, and report what He said and did. The precious Saviour was now most surely standing under the shadow of the cross.

Imprisonment and Death of John

John the Baptist had been first in heralding Christ's kingdom, and he was first also in suffering. From the free air of the wilderness and the vast throngs that had hung upon his words, he was now shut in by the walls of a dungeon cell. He had become a prisoner in the fortress of Herod Antipas. In the territory east of Jordan, which was under the dominion of Antipas, much of John's ministry had been spent. Herod himself had listened to the preaching of the Baptist. The dissolute king had trembled under the call to repentance. "Herod feared John, knowing that he was a just man and an holy; . . . and when he heard him, he did many things, and heard him gladly." John dealt with him faithfully, denouncing his iniquitous alliance with Herodias, his brother's wife. For a time Herod feebly sought to break the chain of lust that bound him; but Herodias fastened him the more firmly in her toils, and found revenge upon the Baptist by inducing Herod to cast him into prison.

The life of John had been one of active labor, and the gloom and inaction of his prison life weighed heavily upon him. As week after week passed, bringing no change, despondency and doubt crept over him. His disciples did not forsake him. They were allowed access to the prison, and they brought him tidings of the works of Jesus, and told how the people were flocking to Him. But they questioned why, if this new teacher was the Messiah, He did nothing to effect John's release. How could He permit His faithful herald to be deprived of liberty and perhaps of life?

These questions were not without effect. Doubts which otherwise would never have arisen were suggested to John. Satan rejoiced to hear the words of these disciples, and to see how they bruised the soul of the Lord's messenger. Oh, how often those who think themselves the friends of a good man, and who are eager to show their fidelity to him, prove to be his most dangerous enemies! How often, instead of strengthening his faith, their words depress and dishearten!

Like the Saviour's disciples, John the Baptist did not understand the nature of Christ's kingdom. He expected Jesus to take the throne of David; and as time passed, and the Saviour made no claim to kingly authority, John became perplexed and troubled. He had declared to the people that in order for the way to be prepared before the Lord, the prophecy of Isaiah must be fulfilled; the mountains and hills must be brought low, the crooked made straight, and the rough places plain. He had looked for the high places of human pride and power to be cast down. He had pointed to the Messiah as the One whose fan was in His hand, and who would thoroughly purge His floor, who would gather the wheat into His garner, and burn up the chaff with unquenchable fire. Like the prophet Elijah, in whose spirit and power he had come to Israel, he looked for the Lord to reveal Himself as a God that answereth by fire.

In his mission the Baptist had stood as a fearless reprover of iniquity, both in high places and in low. He had dared to face King Herod with the plain rebuke of sin. He had not counted his life dear unto himself, that he might fulfill his appointed work. And now from his dungeon he watched for the Lion of the tribe of Judah to cast down the pride of the oppressor, and to deliver the poor and him that cried. But Jesus seemed to content Himself with gathering disciples about Him, and healing and teaching the people. He was eating at the tables of the publicans, while every day the Roman yoke rested more heavily upon Israel, while King Herod and his vile paramour worked their will, and the cries of the poor and suffering went up to heaven.

To the desert prophet all this seemed a mystery beyond his fathoming. There were hours when the whisperings of demons tortured his spirit, and the shadow of a terrible fear crept over him. Could it be that the long-hoped-for Deliverer had not yet appeared? Then what meant the message that he himself had been impelled to bear? John had been bitterly disappointed in the result of his mission. He had expected that the message from God would have the same effect as when the law was read in the days of Josiah and of Ezra (2 Chronicles 34; Nehemiah 8, 9); that there would follow a deep-seated work of repentance and returning unto the Lord. For the success of this mission his whole life had been sacrificed. Had it been in vain?

John was troubled to see that through love for him, his own disciples were cherishing unbelief in regard to Jesus. Had his work for them been fruitless? Had he been unfaithful in his mission, that he was now cut off from labor? If the promised Deliverer had appeared, and John had been found true to his calling, would not Jesus now overthrow the oppressor's power, and set free His herald?

But the Baptist did not surrender his faith in Christ. The memory of the voice from heaven and the descending dove, the spotless purity of Jesus, the power of the Holy Spirit that had rested upon John as he came into the Saviour's presence, and the testimony of the prophetic scriptures,—all witnessed that Jesus of Nazareth was the Promised One.

John would not discuss his doubts and anxieties with his companions. He determined to send a message of inquiry to Jesus. This he entrusted to two of his disciples, hoping that an interview with the Saviour would confirm their faith, and bring assurance to their brethren. And he longed for some word from Christ spoken directly for himself.

The disciples came to Jesus with their message, "Art Thou He that should come, or do we look for another?"

How short the time since the Baptist had pointed to Jesus, and proclaimed, "Behold the Lamb of God, which taketh away the sin of the world." "He it is, who coming after me is preferred before me." John 1:29, 27. And now the question, "Art Thou He that should come?" It was keenly bitter and disappointing to human nature. If John, the faithful forerunner, failed to discern Christ's mission, what could be expected from the self-seeking multitude?

The Saviour did not at once answer the disciples' question. As they stood wondering at His silence, the sick and afflicted were coming to Him to be healed. The blind were groping their way through the crowd; diseased ones of all classes, some urging their own way, some borne by their friends, were eagerly pressing into the presence of Jesus. The voice of the mighty Healer penetrated the deaf ear. A word, a touch of His hand, opened the blind eyes to behold the light of day, the scenes of nature, the faces of friends, and the face of the Deliverer. Jesus rebuked disease and banished fever. His voice reached the ears of the dying, and they arose in health and vigor. Paralyzed demoniacs obeyed His word, their madness left them, and they worshiped Him. While He healed their diseases, He taught the people. The poor peasants and laborers, who were shunned by the rabbis as unclean, gathered close about Him, and He spoke to them the words of eternal life.

Thus the day wore away, the disciples of John seeing and hearing all. At last Jesus called them to Him, and bade them go and tell John what they had witnessed, adding, "Blessed is he, whosoever shall find none occasion of stumbling in Me." Luke 7:23, R. V. The evidence of His divinity was seen in its adaptation to the needs of suffering humanity. His glory was shown in His condescension to our low estate.

The disciples bore the message, and it was enough. John recalled the prophecy concerning the Messiah, "The Lord hath anointed Me to preach good tidings unto the meek; He hath sent Me to bind up the brokenhearted, to proclaim liberty to the captives, and the opening of the prison to them that are bound; to proclaim the acceptable year of the Lord." Isa. 61:1, 2. The works of Christ not only declared Him to be the Messiah, but showed in what manner His kingdom was to be established. To John was opened the same truth that had come to Elijah in the desert, when "a great and strong wind rent the mountains, and brake in pieces the rocks before the Lord; but the Lord was not in the wind: and after the wind an earthquake; but the Lord was not in the earthquake: and after the earthquake a fire; but the Lord was not in the fire:" and after the fire, God spoke to the prophet by "a still small voice." 1 Kings 19:11, 12. So Jesus was to do His work, not with the clash of arms and the overturning of thrones and kingdoms, but through speaking to the hearts of men by a life of mercy and self-sacrifice.

The principle of the Baptist's own life of self-abnegation was the principle of the Messiah's kingdom. John well knew how foreign all this was to the principles and hopes of the leaders in Israel. That which was to him convincing evidence of Christ's divinity would be no evidence to them. They were looking for a Messiah who had not been promised. John saw that the Saviour's mission could win from them only hatred and condemnation. He, the forerunner, was but drinking of the cup which Christ Himself must drain to its dregs.

The Saviour's words, "Blessed is he, whosoever shall find none occasion of stumbling in Me," were a gentle reproof to John. It was not lost upon him. Understanding more clearly now the nature of Christ's mission, he yielded himself to God for life or for death, as should best serve the interests of the cause he loved.

After the messengers had departed, Jesus spoke to the people concerning John. The Saviour's heart went out in sympathy to the faithful witness now buried in Herod's dungeon. He would not leave the people to conclude that God had forsaken John, or that his faith had failed in the day of trial. "What went ye out into the wilderness to see?" He said. "A reed shaken with the wind?"

The tall reeds that grew beside the Jordan, bending before every breeze, were fitting representatives of the rabbis who had stood as critics and judges of the Baptist's mission. They were swayed this way and that by the winds of popular opinion. They would not humble themselves to receive the heart-searching message of the Baptist, yet for fear of the people they dared not openly oppose his work. But God's messenger was of no such craven spirit. The multitudes who were gathered about Christ had been witnesses to the work of John. They had heard his fearless rebuke of sin. To the self-righteous Pharisees, the priestly Sadducees, King Herod and his court, princes and soldiers, publicans and peasants, John had spoken with equal plainness. He was no trembling reed, swayed by the winds of human praise or prejudice. In the prison he was the same in his loyalty to God and his zeal for righteousness as when he preached God's message in the wilderness. In his faithfulness to principle he was as firm as a rock.

Jesus continued, "But what went ye out for to see? A man clothed in soft raiment? Behold, they which are gorgeously appareled, and live delicately, are in kings' courts." John had been called to reprove the sins and excesses of his time, and his plain dress and self-denying life were in harmony with the character of his mission. Rich apparel and the luxuries of this life are not the portion of God's servants, but of those who live "in kings' courts," the rulers of this world, to whom pertain its power and its riches. Jesus wished to direct attention to the contrast between the clothing of John, and that worn by the priests and rulers. These officials arrayed themselves in rich robes and costly ornaments. They loved display, and hoped to dazzle the people, and thus command greater consideration. They were more anxious to gain the admiration of men than to obtain the purity of heart which would win the approval of God. Thus they revealed that their allegiance was not given to God, but to the kingdom of this world.

"But what," said Jesus, "went ye out for to see? A prophet? yea, I say unto you, and more than a prophet. For this is he, of whom it is written,—

"Behold, I send My messenger before Thy face,
Which shall prepare Thy way before Thee.

"Verily I say unto you, Among them that are born of women there hath not risen a greater than John the Baptist." In the announcement to Zacharias before the birth of John, the angel had declared, "He shall be great in the sight of the Lord." Luke 1:15. In the estimation of Heaven, what is it that constitutes greatness? Not that which the world accounts greatness; not wealth, or rank, or noble descent, or intellectual gifts, in themselves considered. If intellectual greatness, apart from any higher consideration, is worthy of honor, then our homage is due to Satan, whose intellectual power no man has ever equaled. But when perverted to self-serving, the greater the gift, the greater curse it becomes. It is moral worth that God values. Love and purity are the attributes He prizes most. John was great in the sight of the Lord, when, before the messengers from the Sanhedrin, before the people, and before his own disciples, he refrained from seeking honor for himself, but pointed all to Jesus as the Promised One. His unselfish joy in the ministry of Christ presents the highest type of nobility ever revealed in man.

The witness borne of him after his death, by those who had heard his testimony to Jesus, was, "John did no miracle: but all things that John spake of this Man were true." John 10:41. It was not given to John to call down fire from heaven, or to raise the dead, as Elijah did, nor to wield Moses' rod of power in the name of God. He was sent to herald the Saviour's advent, and to call upon the people to prepare for His coming. So faithfully did he fulfill his mission, that as the people recalled what he had taught them of Jesus, they could say, "All things that John spake of this Man were true." Such witness to Christ every disciple of the Master is called upon to bear.

As the Messiah's herald, John was "much more than a prophet." For while prophets had seen from afar Christ's advent, to John it was given to behold Him, to hear the testimony from heaven to His Messiahship, and to present Him to Israel as the Sent of God. Yet Jesus said, "He that is least in the kingdom of heaven is greater than he."

The prophet John was the connecting link between the two

dispensations. As God's representative he stood forth to show the relation of the law and the prophets to the Christian dispensation. He was the lesser light, which was to be followed by a greater. The mind of John was illuminated by the Holy Spirit, that he might shed light upon his people; but no other light ever has shone or ever will shine so clearly upon fallen man as that which emanated from the teaching and example of Jesus. Christ and His mission had been but dimly understood as typified in the shadowy sacrifices. Even John had not fully comprehended the future, immortal life through the Saviour.

Aside from the joy that John found in his mission, his life had been one of sorrow. His voice had been seldom heard except in the wilderness. His was a lonely lot. And he was not permitted to see the result of his own labors. It was not his privilege to be with Christ and witness the manifestation of divine power attending the greater light. It was not for him to see the blind restored to sight, the sick healed, and the dead raised to life. He did not behold the light that shone through every word of Christ, shedding glory upon the promises of prophecy. The least disciple who saw Christ's mighty works and heard His words was in this sense more highly privileged than John the Baptist, and therefore is said to have been greater than he.

Through the vast throngs that had listened to John's preaching, his fame had spread throughout the land. A deep interest was felt as to the result of his imprisonment. Yet his blameless life, and the strong public sentiment in his favor, led to the belief that no violent measures would be taken against him.

Herod believed John to be a prophet of God, and he fully intended to set him at liberty. But he delayed his purpose from fear of Herodias.

Herodias knew that by direct measures she could never win Herod's consent to the death of John, and she resolved to accomplish her purpose by stratagem. On the king's birthday an entertainment was to be given to the officers of state and the nobles of the court. There would be feasting and drunkenness. Herod would thus be thrown off his guard, and might then be influenced according to her will.

When the great day arrived, and the king with his lords was feasting and drinking, Herodias sent her daughter into the banqueting hall to dance for the entertainment of the guests. Salome was in the first flush of womanhood, and her voluptuous beauty captivated the senses of the lordly revelers. It was not customary for the ladies of the court to appear at these festivities, and a flattering compliment was paid to Herod when this daughter of Israel's priests and princes danced for the amusement of his guests.

The king was dazed with wine. Passion held sway, and reason was dethroned. He saw only the hall of pleasure, with its reveling guests, the banquet table, the sparkling wine and the flashing lights, and the young girl dancing before him. In the recklessness of the moment, he desired to make some display that would exalt him before the great men of his realm. With an oath he promised to give the daughter of Herodias whatever she might ask, even to the half of his kingdom.

Salome hastened to her mother, to know what she should ask. The answer was ready,—the head of John the Baptist. Salome knew not of the thirst for revenge in her mother's heart, and she shrank from presenting the request; but the determination of Herodias prevailed. The girl returned with the terrible petition, "I will that thou forthwith give me in a charger the head of John the Baptist." Mark 6:25, R. V.

Herod was astonished and confounded. The riotous mirth ceased, and an ominous silence settled down upon the scene of revelry. The king was horror-stricken at the thought of taking the life of John. Yet his word was pledged, and he was unwilling to appear fickle or rash. The oath had been made in honor of his guests, and if one of them had offered a word against the fulfillment of his promise, he would gladly have spared the prophet. He gave them opportunity to speak in the prisoner's behalf. They had traveled long distances in order to hear the preaching of John, and they knew him to be a man without crime, and a servant of God. But though shocked at the girl's demand, they were too besotted to interpose a remonstrance. No voice was raised to save the life of Heaven's messenger. These men occupied high positions of trust in the nation, and upon them rested grave responsibilities; yet they had given themselves up to feasting and drunkenness until the senses were benumbed. Their heads were turned with the giddy scene of music and dancing, and conscience lay dormant. By their silence they pronounced the sentence of death upon the prophet of God to satisfy the revenge of an abandoned woman.

Herod waited in vain to be released from his oath; then he reluctantly commanded the execution of the prophet. Soon the head of John was brought in before the king and his guests. Forever sealed were those lips that had faithfully warned Herod to turn from his life of sin. Never more would that voice be heard calling men to repentance. The revels of one night had cost the life of one of the greatest of the prophets.

Oh, how often has the life of the innocent been sacrificed through the intemperance of those who should have been guardians of justice! He who puts the intoxicating cup to his lips makes himself responsible for all the injustice he may commit under its besotting power. By benumbing his senses he makes it impossible for him to judge calmly or to have a clear perception of right and wrong. He opens the way for Satan to work through him in oppressing and destroying the innocent. "Wine is a mocker, strong drink is raging: and whosoever is deceived thereby is not wise." Prov. 20:1. Thus it is that "judgment is turned away backward, . . . and he that departeth from evil maketh himself a prey." Isa. 59:14, 15. Those who have jurisdiction over the lives of their fellow men should be held guilty of a crime when they yield to intemperance. All who execute the laws should be lawkeepers. They should be men of self-control. They need to have full command of their physical, mental, and moral powers, that they may possess vigor of intellect, and a high sense of justice.

The head of John the Baptist was carried to Herodias, who received it with fiendish satisfaction. She exulted in her revenge, and flattered herself that Herod's conscience would no longer be troubled. But no happiness resulted to her from her sin. Her name became notorious and abhorred, while Herod was more tormented by remorse than he had been by the warnings of the prophet. The influence of John's teachings was not silenced; it was to extend to every generation till the close of time.

Herod's sin was ever before him. He was constantly seeking to find relief from the accusings of a guilty conscience. His confidence in John was unshaken. As he recalled his life of self-denial, his solemn, earnest appeals, his sound judgment in counsel, and then remembered how he had come to his death, Herod could find no rest. Engaged in the affairs of the state, receiving honors from men, he bore a smiling face and dignified mien, while he concealed an anxious heart, ever oppressed with the fear that a curse was upon him.

Herod had been deeply impressed by the words of John, that nothing can be hidden from God. He was convinced that God was present in every place, that He had witnessed the revelry of the banqueting room, that He had heard the command to behead John, and had seen the exultation of Herodias, and the insult she offered to the severed head of her reprover. And many things that Herod had heard from the lips of the prophet now spoke to his conscience more distinctly than had the preaching in the wilderness.

When Herod heard of the works of Christ, he was exceedingly troubled. He thought that God had raised John from the dead, and sent him forth with still greater power to condemn sin. He was in constant fear that John would avenge his death by passing condemnation upon him and his house. Herod was reaping that which God had declared to be the result of a course of sin,—"a trembling heart, and failing of eyes, and sorrow of mind: and thy life shall hang in doubt before thee; and thou shalt fear day and night, and shalt have none assurance of thy life: in the morning thou shalt say, Would God it were even! and at even thou shalt say, Would God it were morning! for the fear of thine heart wherewith thou shalt fear, and for the sight of thine eyes which thou shalt see." Deut. 28:65-67. The sinner's own thoughts are his accusers; and there can be no torture keener than the stings of a guilty conscience, which give him no rest day nor night.

To many minds a deep mystery surrounds the fate of John the Baptist. They question why he should have been left to languish and die in prison. The mystery of this dark providence our human vision cannot penetrate; but it can never shake our confidence in God when we remember that John was but a sharer in the sufferings of Christ. All who follow Christ will wear the crown of sacrifice. They will surely be misunderstood by selfish men, and will be made a mark for the fierce assaults of Satan. It is this principle of self-sacrifice that his kingdom is established to destroy, and he will war against it wherever manifested.

The childhood, youth, and manhood of John had been characterized by firmness and moral power. When his voice was heard in the wilderness saying, "Prepare ye the way of the Lord, make His paths straight" (Matt. 3:3), Satan feared for the safety of his kingdom. The sinfulness of sin was revealed in such a manner that men trembled. Satan's power over many who had been under his control was broken. He had been unwearied in his efforts to draw away the Baptist from a life of unreserved surrender to God; but he had failed. And he had failed to overcome Jesus. In the temptation in the wilderness, Satan had been defeated, and his rage was great. Now he determined to bring sorrow upon Christ by striking John. The One whom he could not entice to sin he would cause to suffer.

Jesus did not interpose to deliver His servant. He knew that John would bear the test. Gladly would the Saviour have come to John, to brighten the dungeon gloom with His own presence. But He was not to place Himself in the hands of enemies and imperil His own mission. Gladly would He have delivered His faithful servant. But for the sake of thousands who in after years must pass from prison to death, John was to drink the cup of martyrdom. As the followers of Jesus should languish in lonely cells, or perish by the sword, the rack, or the fagot, apparently forsaken by God and man, what a stay to their hearts would be the thought that John the Baptist, to whose faithfulness Christ Himself had borne witness, had passed through a similar experience!

Satan was permitted to cut short the earthly life of God's messenger; but that life which "is hid with Christ in God," the destroyer could not reach. Col. 3:3. He exulted that he had brought sorrow upon Christ, but he had failed of conquering John. Death itself only placed him forever beyond the power of temptation. In this warfare, Satan was revealing his own character. Before the witnessing universe he made manifest his enmity toward God and man.

Though no miraculous deliverance was granted John, he was not forsaken. He had always the companionship of heavenly angels, who opened to him the prophecies concerning Christ, and the precious promises of Scripture. These were his stay, as they were to be the stay of God's people through the coming ages. To John the Baptist, as to those that came after him, was given the assurance, "Lo, I am with you all the days, even unto the end." Matt. 28:20, R. V., margin.

God never leads His children otherwise than they would choose to be led, if they could see the end from the beginning, and discern the glory of the purpose which they are fulfilling as co-workers with Him. Not Enoch, who was translated to heaven, not Elijah, who ascended in a chariot of fire, was greater or more honored than John the Baptist, who perished alone in the dungeon. "Unto you it is given in the behalf of Christ, not only to believe on Him, but also to suffer for His sake." Phil. 1:29. And of all the gifts that Heaven can bestow upon men, fellowship with Christ in His sufferings is the most weighty trust and the highest honor.

"The Kingdom of God Is at Hand"

"Jesus came into Galilee, preaching the gospel of the kingdom of God, and saying, The time is fulfilled, and the kingdom of God is at hand: repent ye, and believe the gospel." Mark 1:14, 15.

The Messiah's coming had been first announced in Judea. In the temple at Jerusalem the birth of the forerunner had been foretold to Zacharias as he ministered before the altar. On the hills of Bethlehem the angels had proclaimed the birth of Jesus. To Jerusalem the magi had come in search of Him. In the temple Simeon and Anna had testified to His divinity. "Jerusalem, and all Judea" had listened to the preaching of John the Baptist; and the deputation from the Sanhedrin, with the multitude, had heard his testimony concerning Jesus. In Judea, Christ had received His first disciples. Here much of His early ministry had been spent. The flashing forth of His divinity in the cleansing of the temple, His miracles of healing, and the lessons of divine truth that fell from His lips, all proclaimed that which after the healing at Bethesda He had declared before the Sanhedrin,—His Sonship to the Eternal.

If the leaders in Israel had received Christ, He would have honored them as His messengers to carry the gospel to the world. To them first was given the opportunity to become heralds of the kingdom and grace of God. But Israel knew not the time of her visitation. The jealousy and distrust of the Jewish leaders had ripened into open hatred, and the hearts of the people were turned away from Jesus.

The Sanhedrin had rejected Christ's message and was bent upon His death; therefore Jesus departed from Jerusalem, from the priests, the temple, the religious leaders, the people who had been instructed in the law, and turned to another class to proclaim His message, and to gather out those who should carry the gospel to all nations.

As the light and life of men was rejected by the ecclesiastical authorities in the days of Christ, so it has been rejected in every succeeding generation. Again and again the history of Christ's withdrawal from Judea has been repeated. When the Reformers preached the word of God, they had no thought of separating themselves from the established church; but the religious leaders would not tolerate the light, and those that bore it were forced to seek another class, who were longing for the truth. In our day few of the professed followers of the Reformers are actuated by their spirit. Few are listening for the voice of God, and ready to accept truth in whatever guise it may be presented. Often those who follow in the steps of the Reformers are forced to turn away from the churches they love, in order to declare the plain teaching of the word of God. And many times those who are seeking for light are by the same teaching obliged to leave the church of their fathers, that they may render obedience.

The people of Galilee were despised by the rabbis of Jerusalem as rude and unlearned, yet they presented a more favorable field for the Saviour's work. They were more earnest and sincere; less under the control of bigotry; their minds were more open for the reception of truth. In going to Galilee, Jesus was not seeking seclusion or isolation. The province was at this time the home of a crowded population, with a much larger admixture of people of other nations than was found in Judea.

As Jesus traveled through Galilee, teaching and healing, multitudes flocked to Him from the cities and villages. Many came even from Judea and the adjoining provinces. Often He was obliged to hide Himself from the people. The enthusiasm ran so high that it was necessary to take precautions lest the Roman authorities should be aroused to fear an insurrection. Never before had there been such a period as this for the world. Heaven was brought down to men. Hungering and thirsting souls that had waited long for the redemption of Israel now feasted upon the grace of a merciful Saviour.

The burden of Christ's preaching was, "The time is fulfilled, and the kingdom of God is at hand; repent ye, and believe the gospel." Thus the gospel message, as given by the Saviour Himself, was based on the prophecies. The "time" which He declared to be fulfilled was the period made known by the angel Gabriel to Daniel. "Seventy weeks," said the angel, "are determined upon thy people and upon thy holy city, to finish the transgression, and to make an end of sins, and to make reconciliation for iniquity, and to bring in everlasting righteousness, and to seal up the vision and prophecy, and to anoint the most holy." Dan. 9:24. A day in prophecy stands for a year. See Num. 14:34; Ezek. 4:6. The seventy weeks, or four hundred and ninety days, represent four hundred and ninety years. A starting point for this period is given: "Know therefore and understand, that from the going forth of the commandment to restore and to build Jerusalem unto the Messiah the Prince shall be seven weeks, and threescore and two weeks," sixty-nine weeks, or four hundred and eighty-three years. Dan. 9:25. The commandment to restore and build Jerusalem, as completed by the decree of Artaxerxes Longimanus (see Ezra 6:14; 7:1, 9, margin), went into effect in the autumn of B. C. 457. From this time four hundred and eighty-three years extend to the autumn of A. D. 27. According to the prophecy, this period was to reach to the Messiah, the Anointed One. In A. D. 27, Jesus at His baptism received the anointing of the Holy Spirit, and soon afterward began His ministry. Then the message was proclaimed. "The time is fulfilled."

Then, said the angel, "He shall confirm the covenant with many for one week." For seven years after the Saviour entered on His ministry, the gospel was to be preached especially to the Jews; for three and a half years by Christ Himself; and afterward by the apostles. "In the midst of the week He shall cause the sacrifice and the oblation to cease." Dan. 9:27. In the spring of A. D. 31, Christ the true sacrifice was offered on Calvary. Then the veil of the temple was rent in twain, showing that the sacredness and significance of the sacrificial service had departed. The time had come for the earthly sacrifice and oblation to cease.

The one week—seven years—ended in A. D. 34. Then by the stoning of Stephen the Jews finally sealed their rejection of the gospel; the disciples who were scattered abroad by persecution "went everywhere preaching the word" (Acts 8:4); and shortly after, Saul the persecutor was converted, and became Paul, the apostle to the Gentiles.

The time of Christ's coming, His anointing by the Holy Spirit, His death, and the giving of the gospel to the Gentiles, were definitely pointed out. It was the privilege of the Jewish people to understand these prophecies, and to recognize their fulfillment in the mission of Jesus. Christ urged upon His disciples the importance of prophetic study. Referring to the prophecy given to Daniel in regard to their time, He said, "Whoso readeth, let him understand." Matt. 24:15. After His resurrection He explained to the disciples in "all the prophets" "the things concerning Himself." Luke 24:27. The Saviour had spoken through all the prophets. "The Spirit of Christ which was in them" "testified beforehand the sufferings of Christ, and the glory that should follow." 1 Peter 1:11.

It was Gabriel, the angel next in rank to the Son of God, who came with the divine message to Daniel. It was Gabriel, "His angel," whom Christ sent to open the future to the beloved John; and a blessing is pronounced on those who read and hear the words of the prophecy, and keep the things written therein. Rev. 1:3.

"The Lord God will do nothing, but He revealeth His secret unto His servants and prophets." While "the secret things belong unto the Lord our God," "those things which are revealed belong unto us and to our children forever." Amos 3:7; Deut. 29:29. God has given these things to us, and His blessing will attend the reverent, prayerful study of the prophetic scriptures.

As the message of Christ's first advent announced the kingdom of His grace, so the message of His second advent announces the kingdom of His glory. And the second message, like the first, is based on the prophecies. The words of the angel to Daniel relating to the last days were to be understood in the time of the end. At that time, "many shall run to and fro, and knowledge shall be increased." "The wicked shall do wickedly: and none of the wicked shall understand; but the wise shall understand." Dan. 12:4, 10. The Saviour Himself has given signs of His coming, and He says, "When ye see these things come to pass, know ye that the kingdom of God is nigh at hand." "And take heed to yourselves, lest at any time your hearts be overcharged with surfeiting, and drunkenness, and cares of this life, and so that day come upon you unawares." "Watch ye therefore, and pray always, that ye may be accounted worthy to escape all these things that shall come to pass, and to stand before the Son of man." Luke 21:31, 34, 36.

We have reached the period foretold in these scriptures. The time of the end is come, the visions of the prophets are unsealed, and their solemn warnings point us to our Lord's coming in glory as near at hand.

The Jews misinterpreted and misapplied the word of God, and they knew not the time of their visitation. The years of the ministry of Christ and His apostles,—the precious last years of grace to the chosen people,—they spent in plotting the destruction of the Lord's messengers. Earthly ambitions absorbed them, and the offer of the spiritual kingdom came to them in vain. So today the kingdom of this world absorbs men's thoughts, and they take no note of the rapidly fulfilling prophecies and the tokens of the swift-coming kingdom of God.

"But ye, brethren, are not in darkness, that that day should overtake you as a thief. Ye are all the children of light, and the children of the day: we are not of the night, nor of darkness." While we are not to know the hour of our Lord's return, we may know when it is near. "Therefore let us not sleep, as do others; but let us watch and be sober." 1 Thess. 5:4-6.

"Is Not This the Carpenter's Son?"

Across the bright days of Christ's ministry in Galilee, one shadow lay. The people of Nazareth rejected Him. "Is not this the carpenter's son?" they said.

During His childhood and youth, Jesus had worshiped among His brethren in the synagogue at Nazareth. Since the opening of His ministry He had been absent from them, but they had not been ignorant of what had befallen Him. As He again appeared among them, their interest and expectation were excited to the highest pitch. Here were the familiar forms and faces of those whom He had known from infancy. Here were His mother, His brothers and sisters, and all eyes were turned upon Him as He entered the synagogue upon the Sabbath day, and took His place among the worshipers.

In the regular service for the day, the elder read from the prophets, and exhorted the people still to hope for the Coming One, who would bring in a glorious reign, and banish all oppression. He sought to encourage his hearers by rehearsing the evidence that the Messiah's coming was near. He described the glory of His advent, keeping prominent the thought that He would appear at the head of armies to deliver Israel.

When a rabbi was present at the synagogue, he was expected to deliver the sermon, and any Israelite might give the reading from the prophets. Upon this Sabbath Jesus was requested to take part in the service. He "stood up to read. And there was delivered unto Him a roll of the prophet Isaiah." Luke 4:16, 17, R. V., margin. The scripture which He read was one that was understood as referring to the Messiah:

"The Spirit of the Lord is upon Me,
Because He hath anointed Me to preach the gospel to the poor;
He hath sent Me to heal the brokenhearted,
To preach deliverance to the captives,
And recovering of sight to the blind,
To set at liberty them that are bruised,

To preach the acceptable year of the Lord."

"And He closed the roll, and gave it back to the attendant: . . . and the eyes of all in the synagogue were fastened on Him. . . . And all bare Him witness, and wondered at the words of grace which proceeded out of His mouth." Luke 4:20-22, R. V., margin.

Jesus stood before the people as a living expositor of the prophecies concerning Himself. Explaining the words He had read, He spoke of the Messiah as a reliever of the oppressed, a liberator of captives, a healer of the afflicted, restoring sight to the blind, and revealing to the world the light of truth. His impressive manner and the wonderful import of His words thrilled the hearers with a power they had never felt before. The tide of divine influence broke every barrier down; like Moses, they beheld the Invisible. As their hearts were moved upon by the Holy Spirit, they responded with fervent amens and praises to the Lord.

But when Jesus announced, "This day is this scripture fulfilled in your ears," they were suddenly recalled to think of themselves, and of the claims of Him who had been addressing them. They, Israelites, children of Abraham, had been represented as in bondage. They had been addressed as prisoners to be delivered from the power of evil; as in darkness, and needing the light of truth. Their pride was offended, and their fears were roused. The words of Jesus indicated that His work for them was to be altogether different from what they desired. Their deeds might be investigated too closely. Notwithstanding their exactness in outward ceremonies, they shrank from inspection by those clear, searching eyes.

Who is this Jesus? they questioned. He who had claimed for Himself the glory of the Messiah was the son of a carpenter, and had worked at His trade with His father Joseph. They had seen Him toiling up and down the hills, they were acquainted with His brothers and sisters, and knew His life and labors. They had seen Him develop from childhood to youth, and from youth to manhood. Although His life had been spotless, they would not believe that He was the Promised One.

What a contrast between His teaching in regard to the new kingdom and that which they had heard from their elder! Jesus had said nothing of delivering them from the Romans. They had heard of His miracles, and had hoped that His power would be exercised for their advantage, but they had seen no indication of such purpose.

As they opened the door to doubt, their hearts became so much the harder for having been momentarily softened. Satan was determined that blind eyes should not that day be opened, nor souls bound in slavery be set at liberty. With intense energy he worked to fasten them in unbelief. They made no account of the sign already given, when they had been stirred by the conviction that it was their Redeemer who addressed them.

But Jesus now gave them an evidence of His divinity by revealing their secret thoughts. "He said unto them, Doubtless ye will say unto Me this parable, Physician, heal thyself: whatsoever we have heard done at Capernaum, do also here in Thine own country. And He said, Verily I say unto you, No prophet is acceptable in his own country. But of a truth I say unto you, There were many widows in Israel in the days of Elijah, when the heaven was shut up three years and six months, when there came a great famine over all the land; and unto none of them was Elijah sent, but only to Zarephath, in the land of Sidon, unto a woman that was a widow. And there were many lepers in Israel in the time of Elisha the prophet; and none of them was cleansed, but only Naaman, the Syrian." Luke 4:23-27, R. V.

By this relation of events in the lives of the prophets, Jesus met the questionings of His hearers. The servants whom God had chosen for a special work were not allowed to labor for a hardhearted and unbelieving people. But those who had hearts to feel and faith to believe were especially favored with evidences of His power through the prophets. In the days of Elijah, Israel had departed from God. They clung to their sins, and rejected the warnings of the Spirit through the Lord's messengers. Thus they cut themselves off from the channel by which God's blessing could come to them. The Lord passed by the homes of Israel, and found a refuge for His servant in a heathen land, with a woman who did not belong to the chosen people. But this woman was favored because she had followed the light she had received, and her heart was open to the greater light that God sent her through His prophet.

It was for the same reason that in Elisha's time the lepers of Israel were passed by. But Naaman, a heathen nobleman, had been faithful to his convictions of right, and had felt his great need of help. He was in a condition to receive the gifts of God's grace. He was not only cleansed from his leprosy, but blessed with a knowledge of the true God.

Our standing before God depends, not upon the amount of light we have received, but upon the use we make of what we have. Thus even the heathen who choose the right as far as they can distinguish it are in a more favorable condition than are those who have had great light, and profess to serve God, but who disregard the light, and by their daily life contradict their profession.

The words of Jesus to His hearers in the synagogue struck at the root of their self-righteousness, pressing home upon them the bitter truth that they had departed from God and forfeited their claim to be His people. Every word cut like a knife as their real condition was set before them. They now scorned the faith with which Jesus had at first inspired them. They would not admit that He who had sprung from poverty and lowliness was other than a common man.

Their unbelief bred malice. Satan controlled them, and in wrath they cried out against the Saviour. They had turned from Him whose mission it was to heal and restore; now they manifested the attributes of the destroyer.

When Jesus referred to the blessings given to the Gentiles, the fierce national pride of His hearers was aroused, and His words were drowned in a tumult of voices. These people had prided themselves on keeping the law; but now that their prejudices were offended, they were ready to commit murder. The assembly broke up, and laying hands upon Jesus, they thrust Him from the synagogue, and out of the city. All seemed eager for His destruction. They hurried Him to the brow of a precipice, intending to cast Him down headlong. Shouts and maledictions filled the air. Some were casting stones at Him, when suddenly He disappeared from among them. The heavenly messengers who had been by His side in the synagogue were with Him in the midst of that maddened throng. They shut Him in from His enemies, and conducted Him to a place of safety.

So angels protected Lot, and led him out safely from the midst of Sodom. So they protected Elisha in the little mountain city. When the encircling hills were filled with the horses and chariots of the king of Syria, and the great host of his armed men, Elisha beheld the nearer hill slopes covered with the armies of God,—horses and chariots of fire round about the servant of the Lord.

So, in all ages, angels have been near to Christ's faithful followers. The vast confederacy of evil is arrayed against all who would overcome; but Christ would have us look to the things which are not seen, to the armies of heaven encamped about all who love God, to deliver them. From what dangers, seen and unseen, we have been preserved through the interposition of the angels, we shall never know, until in the light of eternity we see the providences of God. Then we shall know that the whole family of heaven was interested in the family here below, and that messengers from the throne of God attended our steps from day to day.

When Jesus in the synagogue read from the prophecy, He stopped short of the final specification concerning the Messiah's work. Having read the words, "To proclaim the acceptable year of the Lord," He omitted the phrase, "and the day of vengeance of our God." Isa. 61:2. This was just as much truth as was the first of the prophecy, and by His silence Jesus did not deny the truth. But this last expression was that upon which His hearers delighted to dwell, and which they were desirous of fulfilling. They denounced judgments against the heathen, not discerning that their own guilt was even greater than that of others. They themselves were in deepest need of the mercy they were so ready to deny to the heathen. That day in the synagogue, when Jesus stood among them, was their opportunity to accept the call of Heaven. He who "delighteth in mercy" (Micah 7:18) would fain have saved them from the ruin which their sins were inviting.

Not without one more call to repentance could He give them up. Toward the close of His ministry in Galilee, He again visited the home of His childhood. Since His rejection there, the fame of His preaching and His miracles had filled the land. None now could deny that He possessed more than human power. The people of Nazareth knew that He went about doing good, and healing all that were oppressed by Satan. About them were whole villages where there was not a moan of sickness in any house; for He had passed through

them, and healed all their sick. The mercy revealed in every act of His life testified to His divine anointing.

Again as they listened to His words the Nazarenes were moved by the Divine Spirit. But even now they would not admit that this Man, who had been brought up among them, was other or greater than themselves. Still there rankled the bitter memory that while He had claimed for Himself to be the Promised One, He had really denied them a place with Israel; for He had shown them to be less worthy of God's favor than a heathen man and woman. Hence though they questioned, "Whence hath this Man this wisdom, and these mighty works?" they would not receive Him as the Christ of God. Because of their unbelief, the Saviour could not work many miracles among them. Only a few hearts were open to His blessing, and reluctantly He departed, never to return.

Unbelief, having once been cherished, continued to control the men of Nazareth. So it controlled the Sanhedrin and the nation. With priests and people, the first rejection of the demonstration of the Holy Spirit's power was the beginning of the end. In order to prove that their first resistance was right, they continued ever after to cavil at the words of Christ. Their rejection of the Spirit culminated in the cross of Calvary, in the destruction of their city, in the scattering of the nation to the winds of heaven.

Oh, how Christ longed to open to Israel the precious treasures of the truth! But such was their spiritual blindness that it was impossible to reveal to them the truths relating to His kingdom. They clung to their creed and their useless ceremonies when the truth of Heaven awaited their acceptance. They spent their money for chaff and husks, when the bread of life was within their reach. Why did they not go to the word of God, and search diligently to know whether they were in error? The Old Testament Scriptures stated plainly every detail of Christ's ministry, and again and again He quoted from the prophets, and declared, "This day is this scripture fulfilled in your ears." If they had honestly searched the Scriptures, bringing their theories to the test of God's word, Jesus need not have wept over their impenitence. He need not have declared, "Behold, your house is left unto you desolate." Luke 13:35. They might have been acquainted with the evidence of His Messiahship, and the calamity that laid their proud city in ruins might have been averted. But the minds of the Jews had become narrowed by their unreasoning bigotry. The lessons of Christ revealed their deficiencies of character, and demanded repentance. If they accepted His teachings, their practices must be changed, and their cherished hopes relinquished. In order to be honored by Heaven, they must sacrifice the honor of men. If they obeyed the words of this new rabbi, they must go contrary to the opinions of the great thinkers and teachers of the time.

Truth was unpopular in Christ's day. It is unpopular in our day. It has been unpopular ever since Satan first gave man a disrelish for it by presenting fables that lead to self-exaltation. Do we not today meet theories and doctrines that have no foundation in the word of God? Men cling as tenaciously to them as did the Jews to their traditions.

The Jewish leaders were filled with spiritual pride. Their desire for the glorification of self manifested itself even in the service of the sanctuary. They loved the highest seats in the synagogue. They loved greetings in the market places, and were gratified with the sound of their titles on the lips of men. As real piety declined, they became more jealous for their traditions and ceremonies.

Because their understanding was darkened by selfish prejudice, they could not harmonize the power of Christ's convicting words with the humility of His life. They did not appreciate the fact that real greatness can dispense with outward show. This Man's poverty seemed wholly inconsistent with His claim to be the Messiah. They questioned, If He was what He claimed to be, why was He so unpretending? If He was satisfied to be without the force of arms, what would become of their nation? How could the power and glory so long anticipated bring the nations as subjects to the city of the Jews? Had not the priests taught that Israel was to bear rule over all the earth? and could it be possible that the great religious teachers were in error?

But it was not simply the absence of outward glory in His life that led the Jews to reject Jesus. He was the embodiment of purity, and they were impure. He dwelt among men an example of spotless integrity. His blameless life flashed light upon their hearts. His sincerity revealed their insincerity. It made manifest the hollowness of their pretentious piety, and discovered iniquity to them in its odious character. Such a light was unwelcome.

If Christ had called attention to the Pharisees, and had extolled their learning and piety, they would have hailed Him with joy. But when He spoke of the kingdom of heaven as a dispensation of mercy for all mankind, He was presenting a phase of religion they would not tolerate. Their own example and teaching had never been such as to make the service of God seem desirable. When they saw Jesus giving attention to the very ones they hated and repulsed, it stirred up the worst passions of their proud hearts. Notwithstanding their boast that under the "Lion of the tribe of Judah" (Rev. 5:5), Israel should be exalted to pre-eminence over all nations, they could have borne the disappointment of their ambitious hopes better than they could bear Christ's reproof of their sins, and the reproach they felt even from the presence of His purity.

The Call by the Sea

Day was breaking over the Sea of Galilee. The disciples, weary with a night of fruitless toil, were still in their fishing boats on the lake. Jesus had come to spend a quiet hour by the waterside. In the early morning He hoped for a little season of rest from the multitude that followed Him day after day. But soon the people began to gather about Him. Their numbers rapidly increased, so that He was pressed upon all sides. Meanwhile the disciples had come to land. In order to escape the pressure of the multitude, Jesus stepped into Peter's boat,

and bade him pull out a little from the shore. Here Jesus could be better seen and heard by all, and from the boat He taught the multitude on the beach.

What a scene was this for angels to contemplate; their glorious Commander, sitting in a fisherman's boat, swayed to and fro by the restless waves, and proclaiming the good news of salvation to the listening throng that were pressing down to the water's edge! He who was the Honored of heaven was declaring the great things of His kingdom in the open air, to the common people. Yet He could have had no more fitting scene for His labors. The lake, the mountains, the spreading fields, the sunlight flooding the earth, all furnished objects to illustrate His lessons and impress them upon the mind. And no lesson of Christ's fell fruitless. Every message from His lips came to some soul as the word of eternal life.

Every moment added to the multitude upon the shore. Aged men leaning upon their staffs, hardy peasants from the hills, fishermen from their toil on the lake, merchants and rabbis, the rich and learned, old and young, bringing their sick and suffering ones, pressed to hear the words of the divine Teacher. To such scenes as this the prophets had looked forward, and they wrote:

"The land of Zebulon and the land of Naphtali,
Toward the sea, beyond Jordan,
Galilee of the Gentiles,
The people which sat in darkness
Saw a great light,
And to them which sat in the region and shadow of death,
To them did light spring up." R. V.

Beside the throng on the shores of Gennesaret, Jesus in His sermon by the sea had other audiences before His mind. Looking down the ages, He saw His faithful ones in prison and judgment hall, in temptation and loneliness and affliction. Every scene of joy and conflict and perplexity was open before Him. In the words spoken to those gathered about Him, He was speaking also to these other souls the very words that would come to them as a message of hope in trial, of comfort in sorrow, and heavenly light in darkness. Through the Holy Spirit, that voice which was speaking from the fisherman's boat on the Sea of Galilee, would be heard speaking peace to human hearts to the close of time.

The discourse ended, Jesus turned to Peter, and bade him launch out into the sea, and let down his net for a draught. But Peter was disheartened. All night he had taken nothing. During the lonely hours he had thought of the fate of John the Baptist, who was languishing alone in his dungeon. He had thought of the prospect before Jesus and His followers, of the ill success of the mission to Judea, and the malice of the priests and rabbis. Even his own occupation had failed him; and as he watched by the empty nets, the future had seemed dark with discouragement. "Master," he said, "we have toiled all the night, and have taken nothing: nevertheless at Thy word I will let down the net."

Night was the only favorable time for fishing with nets in the clear waters of the lake. After toiling all night without success, it seemed hopeless to cast the net by day; but Jesus had given the command, and love for their Master moved the disciples to obey. Simon and his brother together let down the net. As they attempted to draw it in, so great was the quantity of fish enclosed that it began to break. They were obliged to summon James and John to their aid. When the catch was secured, both the boats were so heavily laden that they were in danger of sinking.

But Peter was unmindful now of boats or lading. This miracle, above any other he had ever witnessed, was to him a manifestation of divine power. In Jesus he saw One who held all nature under His control. The presence of divinity revealed his own unholiness. Love for his Master, shame for his own unbelief, gratitude for the condescension of Christ, above all, the sense of his uncleanness in the presence of infinite purity, overwhelmed him. While his companions were securing the contents of the net, Peter fell at the Saviour's feet, exclaiming, "Depart from me; for I am a sinful man, O Lord."

It was the same presence of divine holiness that had caused the prophet Daniel to fall as one dead before the angel of God. He said, "My comeliness was turned in me into corruption, and I retained no strength." So when Isaiah beheld the glory of the Lord, he exclaimed, "Woe is me! for I am undone; because I am a man of unclean lips, and I dwell in the midst of a people of unclean lips: for mine eyes have seen the King, the Lord of hosts." Dan. 10:8; Isa. 6:5. Humanity, with its weakness and sin, was brought in contrast with the perfection of divinity, and he felt altogether deficient and unholy. Thus it has been with all who have been granted a view of God's greatness and majesty.

Peter exclaimed, "Depart from me; for I am a sinful man;" yet he clung to the feet of Jesus, feeling that he could not be parted from Him. The Saviour answered, "Fear not; from henceforth thou shalt catch men." It was after Isaiah has beheld the holiness of God and his own unworthiness that he was entrusted with the divine message. It was after Peter had been led to self-renunciation and dependence upon divine power that he received the call to his work for Christ.

Until this time none of the disciples had fully united as colaborers with Jesus. They had witnessed many of His miracles, and had listened to His teaching; but they had not entirely forsaken their former employment. The imprisonment of John the Baptist had been to them all a bitter disappointment. If such were to be the outcome of John's mission, they could have little hope for their Master, with all the religious leaders combined against Him. Under the circumstances it was a relief to them to return for a short time to their fishing. But now Jesus called them to forsake their former life, and unite their interests with His. Peter had accepted the call. Upon reaching the shore, Jesus bade the three other disciples, "Follow Me, and I will make you fishers of men." Immediately they left all, and followed Him.

Before asking them to leave their nets and fishing boats, Jesus had given them the assurance that God would supply their needs. The use of Peter's boat for the work of the gospel had been richly repaid. He who is "rich unto all that call upon Him," has said, "Give, and it shall be given unto you; good measure, pressed down, and shaken together, and running over." Rom. 10:12; Luke 6:38. In this measure He had rewarded the disciple's service. And every sacrifice that is made in His ministry will be recompensed according to "the exceeding riches of His grace." Eph. 3:20; 2:7.

During that sad night on the lake, when they were separated from Christ, the disciples were pressed hard by unbelief, and weary with fruitless toil. But His presence kindled their faith, and brought them joy and success. So it is with us; apart from Christ, our work is fruitless, and it is easy to distrust and murmur. But when He is near, and we labor under His direction, we rejoice in the evidence of His power. It is Satan's work to discourage the soul; it is Christ's work to inspire with faith and hope.

The deeper lesson which the miracle conveyed for the disciples is a lesson for us also,—that He whose word could gather the fishes from the sea could also impress human hearts, and draw them by the cords of His love, so that His servants might become "fishers of men."

They were humble and unlearned men, those fishers of Galilee; but Christ, the light of the world, was abundantly able to qualify them for the position for which He had chosen them. The Saviour did not despise education; for when controlled by the love of God, and devoted to His service, intellectual culture is a blessing. But He passed by the wise men of His time, because they were so self-confident that they could not sympathize with suffering humanity, and become colaborers with the Man of Nazareth. In their bigotry they scorned to be taught by Christ. The Lord Jesus seeks the co-operation of those who will become unobstructed channels for the communication of His grace. The first thing to be learned by all who would become workers together with God is the lesson of self-distrust; then they are prepared to have imparted to them the character of Christ. This is not to be gained through education in the most scientific schools. It is the fruit of wisdom that is obtained from the divine Teacher alone.

Jesus chose unlearned fishermen because they had not been schooled in the traditions and erroneous customs of their time. They were men of native ability, and they were humble and teachable,—men whom He could educate for His work. In the common walks of life there is many a man patiently treading the round of daily toil, unconscious that he possesses powers which, if called into action, would raise him to an equality with the world's most honored men. The touch of a skillful hand is needed to arouse those dormant faculties. It was such men that Jesus called to be His colaborers; and He gave them the advantage of association with Himself. Never had the world's great men such a teacher. When the disciples came forth from the Saviour's training, they were no longer ignorant and uncultured. They had become like Him in mind and character, and men took knowledge of them that they had been with Jesus.

It is not the highest work of education to communicate knowledge merely, but to impart that vitalizing energy which is received through the contact of mind with mind, and soul with soul. It is only life that can beget life. What privilege, then, was theirs who for three years were in daily contact with that divine life from which has flowed every life-giving impulse that has blessed the world! Above all his companions, John the beloved disciple yielded himself to the power of that wondrous life. He says, "The life was manifested, and we have seen it, and bear witness, and show unto you that eternal life, which was with the Father, and was manifested unto us." "Of His fullness have all we received, and grace for grace." 1 John 1:2; John 1:16.

In the apostles of our Lord there was nothing to bring glory to themselves. It was evident that the success of their labors was due only to God. The lives of these men, the characters they developed, and the mighty work that God wrought through them, are a testimony to what He will do for all who are teachable and obedient.

He who loves Christ the most will do the greatest amount of good. There is no limit to the usefulness of one who, by putting self aside, makes room for the working of the Holy Spirit upon his heart, and lives a life wholly consecrated to God. If men will endure the necessary discipline, without complaining or fainting by the way, God will teach them hour by hour, and day by day. He longs to reveal His grace. If His people will remove the obstructions, He will pour forth the waters of salvation in abundant streams through the human channels. If men in humble life were encouraged to do all the good they could do, if restraining hands were not laid upon them to repress their zeal, there would be a hundred workers for Christ where now there is one.

God takes men as they are, and educates them for His service, if they will yield themselves to Him. The Spirit of God, received into the soul, will quicken all its faculties. Under the guidance of the Holy Spirit, the mind that is devoted unreservedly to God develops harmoniously, and is strengthened to comprehend and fulfill the requirements of God. The weak, vacillating character becomes changed to one of strength and steadfastness. Continual devotion establishes so close a relation between Jesus and His disciple that the Christian becomes like Him in mind and character. Through a connection with Christ he will have clearer and broader views. His discernment will be more penetrative, his judgment better balanced. He who longs to be of service to Christ is so quickened by the life-giving power of the Sun of Righteousness that he is enabled to bear much fruit to the glory of God.

Men of the highest education in the arts and sciences have learned precious lessons from Christians in humble life who were designated by the world as unlearned. But these obscure disciples had obtained an education in the highest of all schools. They had sat at the feet of Him who spoke as "never man spake."

At Capernaum

At Capernaum Jesus dwelt in the intervals of His journeys to and fro, and it came to be known as "His own city." It was on the shores of the Sea of Galilee, and near the borders of the beautiful plain of Gennesaret, if not actually upon it.

The deep depression of the lake gives to the plain that skirts its shores the genial climate of the south. Here in the days of Christ flourished the palm tree and the olive, here were orchards and vineyards, green fields, and brightly blooming flowers in rich luxuriance, all watered by living streams bursting from the cliffs. The shores of the lake, and the hills that at a little distance encircle it, were dotted with towns and villages. The lake was covered with fishing boats. Everywhere was the stir of busy, active life.

Capernaum itself was well adapted to be the center of the Saviour's work. Being on the highway from Damascus to Jerusalem and Egypt, and to the Mediterranean Sea, it was a great thoroughfare of travel. People from many lands passed through the city, or tarried for rest in their journeyings to and fro. Here Jesus could meet all nations and all ranks, the rich and great as well as the poor and lowly, and His lessons would be carried to other countries and into many households. Investigation of the prophecies would thus be excited, attention would be directed to the Saviour, and His mission would be brought before the world.

Notwithstanding the action of the Sanhedrin against Jesus, the people eagerly awaited the development of His mission. All heaven was astir with interest. Angels were preparing the way for His ministry, moving upon men's hearts, and drawing them to the Saviour.

In Capernaum the nobleman's son whom Christ had healed was a witness to His power. And the court official and his household joyfully testified of their faith. When it was known that the Teacher Himself was among them, the whole city was aroused. Multitudes flocked to His presence. On the Sabbath the people crowded the synagogue until great numbers had to turn away, unable to find entrance.

All who heard the Saviour "were astonished at His doctrine: for His word was with power." "He taught them as one having authority, and not as the scribes." Luke 4:32; Matt. 7:29. The teaching of the scribes and elders was cold and formal, like a lesson learned by rote. To them the word of God possessed no vital power. Their own ideas and traditions were substituted for its teaching. In the accustomed round of service they professed to explain the law, but no inspiration from God stirred their own hearts or the hearts of their hearers.

Jesus had nothing to do with the various subjects of dissension among the Jews. It was His work to present the truth. His words shed a flood of light upon the teachings of patriarchs and prophets, and the Scriptures came to men as a new revelation. Never before had His hearers perceived such a depth of meaning in the word of God.

Jesus met the people on their own ground, as one who was acquainted with their perplexities. He made truth beautiful by presenting it in the most direct and simple way. His language was pure, refined, and clear as a running stream. His voice was as music to those who had listened to the monotonous tones of the rabbis. But while His teaching was simple, He spoke as one having authority. This characteristic set His teaching in contrast with that of all others. The rabbis spoke with doubt and hesitancy, as if the Scriptures might be interpreted to mean one thing or exactly the opposite. The hearers were daily involved in greater uncertainty. But Jesus taught the Scriptures as of unquestionable authority. Whatever His subject, it was presented with power, as if His words could not be controverted.

Yet He was earnest, rather than vehement. He spoke as one who had a definite purpose to fulfill. He was bringing to view the realities of the eternal world. In every theme God was revealed. Jesus sought to break the spell of infatuation which keeps men absorbed in earthly things. He placed the things of this life in their true relation, as subordinate to those of eternal interest; but He did not ignore their importance. He taught that heaven and earth are linked together, and that a knowledge of divine truth prepares men better to perform the duties of everyday life. He spoke as one familiar with heaven, conscious of His relationship to God, yet recognizing His unity with every member of the human family.

His messages of mercy were varied to suit His audience. He knew "how to speak a word in season to him that is weary" (Isa. 50:4); for grace was poured upon His lips, that He might convey to men in the most attractive way the treasures of truth. He had tact to meet the prejudiced minds, and surprise them with illustrations that won their attention. Through the imagination He reached the heart. His illustrations were taken from the things of daily life, and although they were simple, they had in them a wonderful depth of meaning. The birds of the air, the lilies of the field, the seed, the shepherd and the sheep,—with these objects Christ illustrated immortal truth; and ever afterward, when His hearers chanced to see these things of nature, they recalled His words. Christ's illustrations constantly repeated His lessons.

Christ never flattered men. He never spoke that which would exalt their fancies and imaginations, nor did He praise them for their clever inventions; but deep, unprejudiced thinkers received His teaching, and found that it tested their wisdom. They marveled at the spiritual truth expressed in the simplest language. The most highly educated were charmed with His words, and the uneducated were always profited. He had a message for the illiterate; and He made even the heathen to understand that He had a message for them.

His tender compassion fell with a touch of healing upon weary and troubled hearts. Even amid the turbulence of angry enemies He was surrounded with an atmosphere of peace. The beauty of His countenance, the loveliness of His character, above all, the love expressed in look and tone, drew to Him all who were not hardened in unbelief. Had it not been for the sweet, sympathetic spirit that shone out in every look and word, He would not have attracted the large congregations that He did. The afflicted ones who came to Him felt that He linked His interest with theirs as a faithful and tender friend, and they desired to know more of the truths He taught. Heaven was brought near. They longed to abide in His presence, that the comfort of His love might be with them continually.

Jesus watched with deep earnestness the changing countenances of His hearers. The faces that expressed interest and pleasure gave Him great satisfaction. As the arrows of truth pierced to the soul, breaking through the barriers of selfishness, and working contrition, and finally gratitude, the Saviour was made glad. When His eye swept over the throng of listeners, and He recognized among them the faces He had before seen, His countenance lighted up with joy. He saw in them hopeful subjects for His kingdom. When the truth, plainly spoken, touched some cherished idol, He marked the change of countenance, the cold, forbidding look, which told that the light was unwelcome. When He saw men refuse the message of peace, His heart was pierced to the very depths.

Jesus in the synagogue spoke of the kingdom He had come to establish, and of His mission to set free the captives of Satan. He was interrupted by a shriek of terror. A madman rushed forward from among the people, crying out, "Let us alone; what have we to do with Thee, Thou Jesus of Nazareth? art Thou come to destroy us? I know Thee who Thou art; the Holy One of God."

All was now confusion and alarm. The attention of the people was diverted from Christ, and His words were unheeded. This was Satan's purpose in leading his victim to the synagogue. But Jesus rebuked the demon, saying, "Hold thy peace, and come out of him. And when the devil had thrown him in the midst, he came out of him, and hurt him not."

The mind of this wretched sufferer had been darkened by Satan, but in the Saviour's presence a ray of light had pierced the gloom. He was roused to long for freedom from Satan's control; but the demon resisted the power of Christ. When the man tried to appeal to Jesus for help, the evil spirit put words into his mouth, and he cried out in an agony of fear. The demoniac partially comprehended that he was in the presence of One who could set him free; but when he tried to come within reach of that mighty hand, another's will held him, another's words found utterance through him. The conflict between the power of Satan and his own desire for freedom was terrible.

He who had conquered Satan in the wilderness of temptation was again brought face to face with His enemy. The demon exerted all his power to retain control of his victim. To lose ground here would be to give Jesus a victory. It seemed that the tortured man must lose his life in the struggle with the foe that had been the ruin of his manhood. But the Saviour spoke with authority, and set the captive free.

The man who had been possessed stood before the wondering people happy in the freedom of self-possession. Even the demon had testified to the divine power of the Saviour.

The man praised God for his deliverance. The eye that had so lately glared with the fire of insanity, now beamed with intelligence, and overflowed with grateful tears. The people were dumb with amazement. As soon as they recovered speech they exclaimed, one to another, "What is this? a new teaching! with authority He commandeth even the unclean spirits, and they obey Him." Mark 1:27, R. V.

The secret cause of the affliction that had made this man a fearful spectacle to his friends and a burden to himself was in his own life. He had been fascinated by the pleasures of sin, and had thought to make life a grand carnival. He did not dream of becoming a terror to the world and the reproach of his family. He thought his time could be spent in innocent folly. But once in the downward path, his feet rapidly descended. Intemperance and frivolity perverted the noble attributes of his nature, and Satan took absolute control of him.

Remorse came too late. When he would have sacrificed wealth and pleasure to regain his lost manhood, he had become helpless in the grasp of the evil one. He had placed himself on the enemy's ground, and Satan had taken possession of all his faculties. The tempter had allured him with many charming presentations; but when once the wretched man was in his power, the fiend became relentless in his cruelty, and terrible in his angry visitations. So it will be with all who yield to evil; the fascinating pleasure of their early career ends in the darkness of despair or the madness of a ruined soul.

The same evil spirit that tempted Christ in the wilderness, and that possessed the maniac of Capernaum, controlled the unbelieving Jews. But with them he assumed an air of piety, seeking to deceive them as to their motives in rejecting the Saviour. Their condition was more hopeless than that of the demoniac, for they felt no need of Christ and were therefore held fast under the power of Satan.

The period of Christ's personal ministry among men was the time of greatest activity for the forces of the kingdom of darkness. For ages Satan with his evil angels had been seeking to control the bodies and the souls of men, to bring upon them sin and suffering; then he had charged all this misery upon God. Jesus was revealing to men the character of God. He was breaking Satan's power, and setting his captives free. New life and love and power from heaven were moving upon the hearts of men, and the prince of evil was aroused to contend for the supremacy of his kingdom. Satan summoned all his forces, and at every step contested the work of Christ.

So it will be in the great final conflict of the controversy between righteousness and sin. While new life and light and power are descending from on high upon the disciples of Christ, a new life is springing up from beneath, and energizing the agencies of Satan. Intensity is taking possession of every earthly element. With a subtlety gained through centuries of conflict, the prince of evil works under a disguise. He appears clothed as an angel of light, and multitudes are "giving heed to seducing spirits, and doctrines of devils." 1 Tim. 4:1.

In the days of Christ the leaders and teachers of Israel were powerless to resist the work of Satan. They were neglecting the only means by which they could have withstood evil spirits. It was by the word of God that Christ overcame the wicked one. The leaders of Israel professed to be the expositors of God's word, but they had studied it only to sustain their traditions, and enforce their man-made observances. By their interpretation they made it express sentiments that God had never given. Their mystical construction made indistinct that which He had made plain. They disputed over insignificant technicalities, and practically denied the most essential truths. Thus infidelity was sown broadcast. God's word was robbed of its power, and evil spirits worked their will.

History is repeating. With the open Bible before them, and professing to reverence its teachings, many of the religious leaders of our time are destroying faith in it as the word of God. They busy themselves with dissecting the word, and set their own opinions above its plainest statements. In their hands God's word loses its regenerating power. This is why infidelity runs riot, and iniquity is rife.

When Satan has undermined faith in the Bible, he directs men to other sources for light and power. Thus he insinuates himself. Those who turn from the plain teaching of Scripture and the convicting power of God's Holy Spirit are inviting the control of demons. Criticism and speculation concerning the Scriptures have opened the way for spiritism and theosophy—those modernized forms of ancient heathenism—to gain a foothold even in the professed churches of our Lord Jesus Christ.

Side by side with the preaching of the gospel, agencies are at work which are but the medium of lying spirits. Many a man tampers with these merely from curiosity, but seeing evidence of the working of a more than human power, he is lured on and on, until he is controlled by a will stronger than his own. He cannot escape from its mysterious power.

The defenses of the soul are broken down. He has no barrier against sin. When once the restraints of God's word and His Spirit are rejected, no man knows to what depths of degradation he may sink. Secret sin or master passion may hold him a captive as helpless as was the demoniac of Capernaum. Yet his condition is not hopeless.

The means by which we can overcome the wicked one is that by which Christ overcame,—the power of the word. God does not control our minds without our consent; but if we desire to know and to do His will, His promises are ours: "Ye shall know the truth, and the truth shall make you free." "If any man willeth to do His will, he shall know of the teaching." John 8:32; 7:17, R. V. Through faith in these promises, every man may be delivered from the snares of error and the control of sin.

Every man is free to choose what power he will have to rule over him. None have fallen so low, none are so vile, but that they can find deliverance in Christ. The demoniac, in place of prayer, could utter only the words of Satan; yet the heart's unspoken appeal was heard. No cry from a soul in need, though it fail of utterance in words, will be unheeded. Those who will consent to enter into covenant relation with the God of heaven are not left to the power of Satan or to the infirmity of their own nature. They are invited by the Saviour, "Let him take hold of My strength, that he may make peace with Me; and he shall make peace with Me." Isa. 27:5. The spirits of darkness will battle for the soul once under their dominion, but angels of God will contend for that soul with prevailing power. The Lord says, "Shall the prey be taken from the mighty, or the lawful captive delivered? . . . Thus saith the Lord, Even the captives of the mighty shall be taken away, and the prey of the terrible shall be delivered: for I will contend with him that contendeth with thee, and I will save thy children." Isa. 49:24, 25.

While the congregation in the synagogue were still spellbound with awe, Jesus withdrew to the home of Peter for a little rest. But here also a shadow had fallen. The mother of Peter's wife lay sick, stricken with a "great fever." Jesus rebuked the disease, and the sufferer arose, and ministered to the wants of the Master and His disciples.

Tidings of the work of Christ spread rapidly throughout Capernaum. For fear of the rabbis, the people dared not come for healing upon the Sabbath; but no sooner had the sun disappeared below the horizon than there was a great commotion. From the homes, the shops, the market places, the inhabitants of the city pressed toward the humble dwelling that sheltered Jesus. The sick were brought upon couches, they came leaning upon staffs, or, supported by friends, they tottered feebly into the Saviour's presence.

Hour after hour they came and went; for none could know whether tomorrow would find the Healer still among them. Never before had Capernaum witnessed a day like this. The air was filled with the voice of triumph and shouts of deliverance. The Saviour was joyful in the joy He had awakened. As He witnessed the sufferings of those who had come to Him, His heart was stirred with sympathy, and He rejoiced in His power to restore them to health and happiness.

Not until the last sufferer had been relieved did Jesus cease His work. It was far into the night when the multitude departed, and silence settled down upon the home of Simon. The long, exciting day was past, and Jesus sought rest. But while the city was still wrapped in slumber, the Saviour, "rising up a great while before day, . . . went out, and departed into a solitary place, and there prayed."

Thus were spent the days in the earthly life of Jesus. He often dismissed His disciples to visit their homes and rest; but He gently resisted their efforts to draw Him away from His labors. All day He toiled, teaching the ignorant, healing the sick, giving sight to the blind, feeding the multitude; and at the eventide or in the early morning, He went away to the sanctuary of the mountains for communion with His Father. Often He passed the entire night in prayer and meditation, returning at daybreak to His work among the people.

Early in the morning, Peter and his companions came to Jesus, saying that already the people of Capernaum were seeking Him. The disciples had been bitterly disappointed at the reception which Christ had met hitherto. The authorities at Jerusalem were seeking to murder Him; even His own townsmen had tried to take His life; but at Capernaum He was welcomed with joyful enthusiasm, and the hopes of the disciples kindled anew. It might be that among the liberty-loving Galileans were to be found the supporters of the new kingdom. But with surprise they heard Christ's words, "I must preach the kingdom of God to other cities also: for therefore am I sent."

In the excitement which then pervaded Capernaum, there was danger that the object of His mission would be lost sight of. Jesus was not satisfied to attract attention to Himself merely as a wonder worker or a healer of physical diseases. He was seeking to draw men to Him as their Saviour. While the people were eager to believe that He had come as a king, to establish an earthly reign, He desired to turn their minds away from the earthly to the spiritual. Mere worldly success would interfere with His work.

And the wonder of the careless crowd jarred upon His spirit. In His life no self-assertion mingled. The homage which the world gives to position, or wealth, or talent, was foreign to the Son of man. None of the means that men employ to win allegiance or command homage did Jesus use. Centuries before His birth, it had been prophesied of Him, "He shall not cry, nor lift up, nor cause His voice to be heard in the street. A bruised reed shall He not break, and the dimly burning flax shall He not quench: He shall bring forth judgment unto truth. He shall not fail nor be discouraged, till He have set judgment in the earth." Isa. 42:2-4, margin.

The Pharisees sought distinction by their scrupulous ceremonialism, and the ostentation of their worship and charities. They proved their zeal for religion by making it the theme of discussion. Disputes between opposing sects were loud and long, and it was not unusual to hear on the streets the voice of angry controversy from learned doctors of the law.

In marked contrast to all this was the life of Jesus. In that life no noisy disputation, no ostentatious worship, no act to gain applause, was ever witnessed. Christ was hid in God, and God was revealed in the character of His Son. To this revelation Jesus desired the minds of the people to be directed, and their homage to be given.

The Sun of Righteousness did not burst upon the world in splendor, to dazzle the senses with His glory. It is written of Christ, "His going forth is prepared as the morning." Hosea 6:3. Quietly and gently the daylight breaks upon the earth, dispelling the shadow of darkness, and waking the world to life. So did the Sun of Righteousness arise, "with healing in His wings." Mal. 4:2.

"Thou Canst Make Me Clean"

Of all diseases known in the East the leprosy was most dreaded. Its incurable and contagious character, and its horrible effect upon its victims, filled the bravest with fear. Among the Jews it was regarded as a judgment on account of sin, and hence was called "the stroke," "the finger of God." Deep-rooted, ineradicable, deadly, it was looked upon as a symbol of sin. By the ritual law, the leper was pronounced unclean. Like one already dead, he was shut out from the habitations of men. Whatever he touched was unclean. The air was polluted by his breath. One who was suspected of having the disease must present himself to the priests, who were to examine and decide his case. If pronounced a leper, he was isolated from his family, cut off from the congregation of Israel, and was doomed to associate with those only who were similarly afflicted. The law was inflexible in its requirement. Even kings and rulers were not exempt. A monarch who was attacked by this terrible disease must yield up the scepter, and flee from society.

Away from his friends and his kindred, the leper must bear the curse of his malady. He was obliged to publish his own calamity, to rend his garments, and sound the alarm, warning all to flee from his contaminating presence. The cry, "Unclean! unclean!" coming in mournful tones from the lonely exile, was a signal heard with fear and abhorrence.

In the region of Christ's ministry, there were many of these sufferers, and the news of His work reached them, kindling a gleam of hope. But since the days of Elisha the prophet, such a thing had never been known as the cleansing of one upon whom this disease had fastened. They dared not expect Jesus to do for them what He had never done for any man. There was one, however, in whose heart faith began to spring up. Yet the man knew not how to reach Jesus. Debarred as he was from contact with his fellow men, how could he present himself to the Healer? And he questioned if Christ would heal him . Would He stoop to notice one believed to be suffering under the judgment of God? Would He not, like the Pharisees, and even the physicians, pronounce a curse upon him, and warn him to flee from the haunts of men? He thought of all that had been told him of Jesus. Not one who had sought His help had been turned away. The wretched man determined to find the Saviour. Though shut out from the cities, it might be that he could cross His path in some byway along the mountain roads, or find Him as He was teaching outside the towns. The difficulties were great, but this was his only hope.

The leper is guided to the Saviour. Jesus is teaching beside the lake, and the people are gathered about Him. Standing afar off, the leper catches a few words from the Saviour's lips. He sees Him laying His hands upon the sick. He sees the lame, the blind, the paralytic, and those dying of various maladies rise up in health, praising God for their deliverance. Faith strengthens in his heart. He draws nearer and yet nearer to the gathered throng. The restrictions laid upon him, the safety of the people, and the fear with which all men regard him are forgotten. He thinks only of the blessed hope of healing.

He is a loathsome spectacle. The disease has made frightful inroads, and his decaying body is horrible to look upon. At sight of him the people fall back in terror. They crowd upon one another in their eagerness to escape from contact with him. Some try to prevent him from approaching Jesus, but in vain. He neither sees nor hears them. Their expressions of loathing are lost upon him. He sees only the Son of God. He hears only the voice that speaks life to the dying. Pressing to Jesus, he casts himself at His feet with the cry, "Lord, if Thou wilt, Thou canst make me clean."

Jesus replied, "I will; be thou made clean," and laid His hand upon him. Matt. 8:3, R. V.

Immediately a change passed over the leper. His flesh became healthy, the nerves sensitive, the muscles firm. The rough, scaly surface peculiar to leprosy disappeared, and a soft glow, like that upon the skin of a healthy child, took its place.

Jesus charged the man not to make known the work that had been wrought, but straightway to present himself with an offering at the temple. Such an offering could not be accepted until the priests had made examination and pronounced the man wholly free from the disease. However unwilling they might be to perform this service, they could not evade an examination and decision of the case.

The words of Scripture show with what urgency Christ enjoined upon the man the necessity of silence and prompt action. "He straitly charged him, and forthwith sent him away; and saith unto him, See thou say nothing to any man: but go thy way, show thyself to the priest, and offer for thy cleansing those things which Moses commanded, for a testimony unto them." Had the priests known the facts concerning the healing of the leper, their hatred of Christ might have led them to render a dishonest sentence. Jesus desired the man to present himself at the temple before any rumors concerning the miracle had reached them. Thus an impartial decision could be secured, and the restored leper would be permitted to unite once more with his family and friends.

There were other objects which Christ had in view in enjoining silence on the man. The Saviour knew that His enemies were ever seeking to limit His work, and to turn the people from Him. He knew that if the healing of the leper were noised abroad, other sufferers from this terrible disease would crowd about Him, and the cry would be raised that the people would be contaminated by contact with them. Many of the lepers would not so use the gift of health as to make it a blessing to themselves or to others. And by drawing the lepers about Him, He would give occasion for the charge that He was breaking down the restrictions of the ritual law. Thus His work in preaching the gospel would be hindered.

The event justified Christ's warning. A multitude of people had witnessed the healing of the leper, and they were eager to learn of the priests' decision. When the man returned to his friends, there was great excitement. Notwithstanding the caution of Jesus, the man made no further effort to conceal the fact of his cure. It would indeed have been impossible to conceal it, but the leper published the matter abroad. Conceiving that it was only the modesty of Jesus which laid this restriction upon him, he went about proclaiming the power of this Great Healer. He did not understand that every such manifestation made the priests and elders more determined to destroy Jesus. The restored man felt that the boon of health was very precious. He rejoiced in the vigor of manhood, and in his restoration to his family and society, and felt it impossible to refrain from giving glory to the Physician who had made him whole. But his act in blazing abroad the matter resulted in hindering the Saviour's work. It caused the people to flock to Him in such multitudes that He was forced for a time to cease His labors.

Every act of Christ's ministry was far-reaching in its purpose. It comprehended more than appeared in the act itself. So in the case of the leper. While Jesus ministered to all who came unto Him, He yearned to bless those who came not. While He drew the publicans, the heathen, and the Samaritans, He longed to reach the priests and teachers who were shut in by prejudice and tradition. He left untried no means by which they might be reached. In sending the healed leper to the priests, He gave them a testimony calculated to disarm their prejudices.

The Pharisees had asserted that Christ's teaching was opposed to the law which God had given through Moses; but His direction to the cleansed leper to present an offering according to the law disproved this charge. It was sufficient testimony for all who were willing to be convinced.

The leaders at Jerusalem had sent out spies to find some pretext for putting Christ to death. He responded by giving them an evidence of His love for humanity, His respect for the law, and His power to deliver from sin and death. Thus He bore witness of them: "They have rewarded Me evil for good, and hatred for My love." Ps. 109:5. He who on the mount gave the precept, "Love your enemies," Himself exemplified the principle, not rendering "evil for evil, or railing for railing: but contrariwise blessing." Matt. 5:44; 1 Peter 3:9.

The same priests who condemned the leper to banishment certified his cure. This sentence, publicly pronounced and registered, was a standing testimony for Christ. And as the healed man was reinstated in the congregation of Israel, upon the priests' own assurance that there was not a taint of the disease upon him, he himself was a living witness for his Benefactor. Joyfully he presented his offering, and magnified the name of Jesus. The priests were convinced of the divine power of the Saviour. Opportunity was granted them to know the truth and to be profited by the light. Rejected, it would pass away, never to return. By many the light was rejected; yet it was not given in vain. Many hearts were moved that for a time made no sign. During the Saviour's life, His mission seemed to call forth little response of love from the priests and teachers; but after His ascension "a great company of the priests were obedient to the faith." Acts 6:7.

The work of Christ in cleansing the leper from his terrible disease is an illustration of His work in cleansing the soul from sin. The man who came to Jesus was "full of leprosy." Its deadly poison permeated his whole body. The disciples sought to prevent their Master from touching him; for he who touched a leper became himself unclean. But in laying His hand upon the leper, Jesus received no defilement. His touch imparted life-giving power. The leprosy was cleansed. Thus it is with the leprosy of sin,—deep-rooted, deadly, and impossible to be cleansed by human power. "The whole head is sick, and the whole heart faint. From the sole of the foot even unto the head there is no soundness in it; but wounds, and bruises, and putrefying sores." Isa. 1:5, 6. But Jesus, coming to dwell in humanity, receives no pollution. His presence has healing virtue for the sinner. Whoever will fall at His feet, saying in faith, "Lord, if Thou wilt, Thou canst make me clean," shall hear the answer, "I will; be thou made clean." Matt. 8:2, 3, R. V.

In some instances of healing, Jesus did not at once grant the blessing sought. But in the case of leprosy, no sooner was the appeal made than it was granted. When we pray for earthly blessings, the answer to our prayer may be delayed, or God may give us something other than we ask, but not so when we ask for deliverance from sin. It is His will to cleanse us from sin, to make us His children, and to enable us to live a holy life. Christ "gave Himself for our sins, that He might deliver us from this present evil world, according to the will of God and our Father." Gal. 1:4. And "this is the confidence that we have in Him, that, if we ask anything according to His will, He heareth us: and if we know that He hear us, whatsoever we ask, we know that we have the petitions that we desired of Him." 1 John 5:14, 15. "If we confess our sins, He is faithful and just to forgive us our sins, and to cleanse us from all unrighteousness." 1 John 1:9.

In the healing of the paralytic at Capernaum, Christ again taught the same truth. It was to manifest His power to forgive sins that the miracle was performed. And the healing of the paralytic also illustrates other precious truths. It is full of hope and encouragement, and from its connection with the caviling Pharisees it has a lesson of warning as well.

Like the leper, this paralytic had lost all hope of recovery. His disease was the result of a life of sin, and his sufferings were embittered by remorse. He had long before appealed to the Pharisees and doctors, hoping for relief from mental suffering and physical pain. But they coldly pronounced him incurable, and abandoned him to the wrath of God. The Pharisees regarded affliction as an evidence of divine displeasure, and they held themselves aloof from the sick and the needy. Yet often these very ones who exalted themselves as holy were more guilty than the sufferers they condemned.

The palsied man was entirely helpless, and, seeing no prospect of aid from any quarter, he had sunk into despair. Then he heard of the wonderful works of Jesus. He was told that others as sinful and helpless as he had been healed; even lepers had been cleansed. And the friends who reported these things encouraged him to believe that he too might be cured if he could be carried to Jesus. But his hope fell when he remembered how the disease had been brought upon him. He feared that the pure Physician would not tolerate him in His presence.

Yet it was not physical restoration he desired so much as relief from the burden of sin. If he could see Jesus, and receive the assurance of forgiveness and peace with Heaven, he would be content to live or die, according to God's will. The cry of the dying man was, Oh that I might come into His presence! There was no time to lose; already his wasted flesh was showing signs of decay. He besought his friends to carry him on his bed to Jesus, and this they gladly undertook to do. But so dense was the crowd that had assembled in and about the house where the Saviour was, that it was impossible for the sick man and his friends to reach Him, or even to come within hearing of His voice.

Jesus was teaching in the house of Peter. According to their custom, His disciples sat close about Him, and "there were Pharisees and doctors of the law sitting by, which were come out of every town of Galilee, and Judea, and Jerusalem." These had come as spies, seeking an accusation against Jesus. Outside of these officials thronged the promiscuous multitude, the eager, the reverent, the curious, and the unbelieving. Different nationalities and all grades of society were represented. "And the power of the Lord was present to heal." The Spirit of life brooded over the assembly, but Pharisees and doctors did not discern its presence. They felt no sense of need, and the healing was not for them. "He hath filled the hungry with good things; and the rich He hath sent empty away." Luke 1:53.

Again and again the bearers of the paralytic tried to push their way through the crowd, but in vain. The sick man looked about him in unutterable anguish. When the longed-for help was so near, how could he relinquish hope? At his suggestion his friends bore him to the top of the house and, breaking up the roof, let him down at the feet of Jesus. The discourse was interrupted. The Saviour looked upon the mournful countenance, and saw the pleading eyes fixed upon Him. He understood the case; He had drawn to Himself that perplexed and doubting spirit. While the paralytic was yet at home, the Saviour had brought conviction to his conscience. When he repented of his sins, and believed in the power of Jesus to make him whole, the life-giving mercies of the Saviour had first blessed his longing heart. Jesus had watched the first glimmer of faith grow into a belief that He was the sinner's only helper, and had seen it grow stronger with every effort to come into His presence.

Now, in words that fell like music on the sufferer's ear, the Saviour said, "Son, be of good cheer; thy sins be forgiven thee."

The burden of despair rolls from the sick man's soul; the peace of forgiveness rests upon his spirit, and shines out upon his countenance. His physical pain is gone, and his whole being is transformed. The helpless paralytic is healed! the guilty sinner is pardoned!

In simple faith he accepted the words of Jesus as the boon of new life. He urged no further request, but lay in blissful silence, too happy for words. The light of heaven irradiated his countenance, and the people looked with awe upon the scene.

The rabbis had waited anxiously to see what disposition Christ would make of this case. They recollected how the man had appealed to them for help, and they had refused him hope or sympathy. Not satisfied with this, they had declared that he was suffering the curse of God for his sins. These things came fresh to their minds when they saw the sick man before them. They marked the interest with which all were watching the scene, and they felt a terrible fear of losing their own influence over the people.

These dignitaries did not exchange words together, but looking into one another's faces they read the same thought in each, that something must be done to arrest the tide of feeling. Jesus had declared that the sins of the paralytic were forgiven. The Pharisees caught at these words as blasphemy, and conceived that they could present this as a sin worthy of death. They said in their hearts, "He blasphemeth: who can forgive sins but One, even God?" Mark 2:7, R. V.

Fixing His glance upon them, beneath which they cowered, and drew back, Jesus said, "Wherefore think ye evil in your hearts? For whether is easier, to say, Thy sins be forgiven thee; or to say, Arise, and walk? But that ye may know that the Son of man hath power on earth to forgive sins," He said, turning to the paralytic, "Arise, take up thy bed, and go unto thine house."

Then he who had been borne on a litter to Jesus rises to his feet with the elasticity and strength of youth. The life-giving blood bounds through his veins. Every organ of his body springs into sudden activity. The glow of health succeeds the pallor of approaching death. "And immediately he arose, took up the bed, and went forth before them all; insomuch that they were all amazed, and glorified God, saying, We never saw it on this fashion."

Oh, wondrous love of Christ, stooping to heal the guilty and the afflicted! Divinity sorrowing over and soothing the ills of suffering humanity! Oh, marvelous power thus displayed to the children of men! Who can doubt the message of salvation? Who can slight the mercies of a compassionate Redeemer?

It required nothing less than creative power to restore health to that decaying body. The same voice that spoke life to man created from the dust of the earth had spoken life to the dying paralytic. And the same power that gave life to the body had renewed the heart. He who at the creation "spake, and it was," who "commanded, and it stood fast," (Ps. 33:9), had spoken life to the soul dead in trespasses and sins. The healing of the body was an evidence of the power that had renewed the heart. Christ bade the paralytic arise and walk, "that ye may know," He said, "that the Son of man hath power on earth to forgive sins."

The paralytic found in Christ healing for both the soul and the body. The spiritual healing was followed by physical restoration. This lesson should not be overlooked. There are today thousands suffering from physical disease, who, like the paralytic, are longing for the message, "Thy sins are forgiven." The burden of sin, with its unrest and unsatisfied desires, is the foundation of their maladies. They can find no relief until they come to the Healer of the soul. The peace which He alone can give, would impart vigor to the mind, and health to the body.

Jesus came to "destroy the works of the devil." "In Him was life," and He says, "I am come that they might have life, and that they might have it more abundantly." He is "a quickening spirit." 1 John 3:8; John 1:4; 10:10; 1 Cor. 15:45. And He still has the same life-giving power as when on earth He healed the sick, and spoke forgiveness to the sinner. He "forgiveth all thine iniquities," He "healeth all thy diseases." Ps. 103:3.

The effect produced upon the people by the healing of the paralytic was as if heaven had opened, and revealed the glories of the better world. As the man who had been cured passed through the multitude, blessing God at every step, and bearing his burden as if it were a feather's weight, the people fell back to give him room, and with awe-stricken faces gazed upon him, whispering softly among themselves, "We have seen strange things today."

The Pharisees were dumb with amazement and overwhelmed with defeat. They saw that here was no opportunity for their jealousy to inflame the multitude. The wonderful work wrought upon the man whom they had given over to the wrath of God had so impressed the people that the rabbis were for the time forgotten. They saw that Christ possessed a power which they had ascribed to God alone; yet the gentle dignity of His manner was in marked contrast to their own haughty bearing. They were disconcerted and abashed, recognizing, but not confessing, the presence of a superior being. The stronger the evidence that Jesus had power on earth to forgive sins, the more firmly they entrenched themselves in unbelief. From the home of Peter, where they had seen the paralytic restored by His word, they went away to invent new schemes for silencing the Son of God.

Physical disease, however malignant and deep-seated, was healed by the power of Christ; but the disease of the soul took a firmer hold upon those who closed their eyes against the light. Leprosy and palsy were not so terrible as bigotry and unbelief.

In the home of the healed paralytic there was great rejoicing when he returned to his family, carrying with ease the couch upon which he had been slowly borne from their presence but a short time before. They gathered round with tears of joy, scarcely daring to believe their eyes. He stood before them in the full vigor of manhood. Those arms that they had seen lifeless were quick to obey his will. The flesh that had been shrunken and leaden-hued was now fresh and ruddy. He walked with a firm, free step. Joy and hope were written in every lineament of his countenance; and an expression of purity and peace had taken the place of the marks of sin and suffering. Glad thanksgiving went up from that home, and God was glorified through His Son, who had restored hope to the hopeless, and strength to the stricken one. This man and his family were ready to lay down their lives for Jesus. No doubt dimmed their faith, no unbelief marred their fealty to Him who had brought light into their darkened home.

Levi-Matthew

Of the Roman officials in Palestine, none were more hated than the publicans. The fact that the taxes were imposed by a foreign power was a continual irritation to the Jews, being a reminder that their independence had departed. And the taxgatherers were not merely the instruments of Roman oppression; they were extortioners on their own account, enriching themselves at the expense of the people. A Jew who accepted this office at the hands of the Romans was looked upon as betraying the honor of his nation. He was despised as an apostate, and was classed with the vilest of society.

To this class belonged Levi-Matthew, who, after the four disciples at Gennesaret, was the next to be called to Christ's service. The Pharisees had judged Matthew according to his employment, but Jesus saw in this man a heart open for the reception of truth. Matthew had listened to the Saviour's teaching. As the convicting Spirit of God revealed his sinfulness, he longed to seek help from Christ; but he was accustomed to the exclusiveness of the rabbis, and had no thought that this Great Teacher would notice him.

Sitting at his toll booth one day, the publican saw Jesus approaching. Great was his astonishment to hear the words addressed to himself, "Follow Me."

Matthew "left all, rose up, and followed Him." There was no hesitation, no questioning, no thought of the lucrative business to be exchanged for poverty and hardship. It was enough for him that he was to be with Jesus, that he might listen to His words, and unite with Him in His work.

So it was with the disciples previously called. When Jesus bade Peter and his companions follow Him, immediately they left their boats and nets. Some of these disciples had friends dependent on them for support; but when they received the Saviour's invitation, they did not hesitate, and inquire, How shall I live, and sustain my family? They were obedient to the call; and when afterward Jesus asked them, "When I sent you without purse, and scrip, and shoes, lacked ye anything?" they could answer, "Nothing." Luke 22:35.

To Matthew in his wealth, and to Andrew and Peter in their poverty, the same test was brought; the same consecration was made by each. At the moment of success, when the nets were filled with fish, and the impulses of the old life were strongest, Jesus asked the disciples at the sea to leave all for the work of the gospel. So every soul is tested as to whether the desire for temporal good or for fellowship with Christ is strongest.

Principle is always exacting. No man can succeed in the service of God unless his whole heart is in the work and he counts all things but loss for the excellency of the knowledge of Christ. No man who makes any reserve can be the disciple of Christ, much less can he be His colaborer. When men appreciate the great salvation, the self-sacrifice seen in Christ's life will be seen in theirs. Wherever He leads the way, they will rejoice to follow.

The calling of Matthew to be one of Christ's disciples excited great indignation. For a religious teacher to choose a publican as one of his immediate attendants was an offense against the religious, social, and national customs. By appealing to the prejudices of the people the Pharisees hoped to turn the current of popular feeling against Jesus.

Among the publicans a widespread interest was created. Their hearts were drawn toward the divine Teacher. In the joy of his new discipleship, Matthew longed to bring his former associates to Jesus. Accordingly he made a feast at his own house, and called together his relatives and friends. Not only were publicans included, but many others who were of doubtful reputation, and were proscribed by their more scrupulous neighbors.

The entertainment was given in honor of Jesus, and He did not hesitate to accept the courtesy. He well knew that this would give offense to the Pharisaic party, and would also compromise Him in the eyes of the people. But no question of policy could influence His movements. With Him external distinctions weighed nothing. That which appealed to His heart was a soul thirsting for the water of life.

Jesus sat as an honored guest at the table of the publicans, by His sympathy and social kindliness showing that He recognized the dignity of humanity; and men longed to become worthy of His confidence. Upon their thirsty hearts His words fell with blessed, life-giving power. New impulses were awakened, and the possibility of a new life opened to these outcasts of society.

At such gatherings as this, not a few were impressed by the Saviour's teaching who did not acknowledge Him until after His ascension. When the Holy Spirit was poured out, and three thousand were converted in a day, there were among them many who first heard the truth at the table of the publicans, and some of these became messengers of the gospel. To Matthew himself the example of Jesus at the feast was a constant lesson. The despised publican became one of the most devoted evangelists, in his own ministry following closely in his Master's steps.

When the rabbis learned of the presence of Jesus at Matthew's feast, they seized the opportunity of accusing Him. But they chose to work through the disciples. By arousing their prejudices they hoped to alienate them from their Master. It was their policy to accuse Christ to the disciples, and the disciples to Christ, aiming their arrows where they would be most likely to wound. This is the way in which Satan has worked ever since the disaffection in heaven; and all who try to cause discord and alienation are actuated by his spirit.

"Why eateth your Master with publicans and sinners?" questioned the envious rabbis.

Jesus did not wait for His disciples to answer the charge, but Himself replied: "They that be whole need not a physician, but they that are sick. But go ye and learn what that meaneth, I will have mercy, and not sacrifice: for I am not come to call the righteous, but sinners to repentance." The Pharisees claimed to be spiritually whole, and therefore in no need of a physician, while they regarded the publicans and Gentiles as perishing from diseases of the soul. Then was it not His work, as a physician, to go to the very class that needed His help?

But although the Pharisees thought so highly of themselves, they were really in a worse condition than the ones they despised. The publicans were less bigoted and self-sufficient, and thus were more open to the influence of truth. Jesus said to the rabbis, "Go ye and learn what that meaneth, I will have mercy, and not sacrifice." Thus He showed that while they claimed to expound the word of God, they were wholly ignorant of its spirit.

The Pharisees were silenced for the time, but only became more determined in their enmity. They next sought out the disciples of John the Baptist, and tried to set them against the Saviour. These Pharisees had not accepted the mission of the Baptist. They had pointed in scorn to his abstemious life, his simple habits, his coarse garments, and had declared him a fanatic. Because he denounced their hypocrisy, they had resisted his words, and had tried to stir up the people against him. The Spirit of God had moved upon the hearts of these scorners, convicting them of sin; but they had rejected the counsel of God, and had declared that John was possessed of a devil.

Now when Jesus came mingling with the people, eating and drinking at their tables, they accused Him of being a glutton and a winebibber. The very ones who made this charge were themselves guilty. As God is misrepresented, and clothed by Satan with his own attributes, so the Lord's messengers were falsified by these wicked men.

The Pharisees would not consider that Jesus was eating with publicans and sinners in order to bring the light of heaven to those who sat in darkness. They would not see that every word dropped by the divine Teacher was a living seed that would germinate and bear fruit to the glory of God. They had determined not to accept the light; and although they had opposed the mission of the Baptist, they were now ready to court the friendship of his disciples, hoping to secure their co-operation against Jesus. They represented that Jesus was setting at nought the ancient traditions; and they contrasted the austere piety of the Baptist with the course of Jesus in feasting with publicans and sinners.

The disciples of John were at this time in great sorrow. It was before their visit to Jesus with John's message. Their beloved teacher was in prison, and they passed their days in mourning. And Jesus was making no effort to release John, and even appeared to cast discredit on his teaching. If John had been sent by God, why did Jesus and His disciples pursue a course so widely different?

The disciples of John had not a clear understanding of Christ's work; they thought there might be some foundation for the charges of the Pharisees. They observed many of the rules prescribed by the rabbis, and even hoped to be justified by the works of the law. Fasting was practiced by the Jews as an act of merit, and the most rigid among them fasted two days in every week. The Pharisees and John's disciples were fasting when the latter came to Jesus with the inquiry, "Why do we and the Pharisees fast oft, but Thy disciples fast not?"

Very tenderly Jesus answered them. He did not try to correct their erroneous conception of fasting, but only to set them right in regard to His own mission. And He did this by employing the same figure that the Baptist himself had used in his testimony to Jesus. John had said, "He that hath the bride is the bridegroom: but the friend of the bridegroom, which standeth and heareth him, rejoiceth greatly because of the bridegroom's voice: this my joy therefore is fulfilled." John 3:29. The disciples of John could not fail to recall these words of their teacher, as, taking up the illustration, Jesus said, "Can ye make the children of the bridechamber fast, while the bridegroom is with them?"

The Prince of heaven was among His people. The greatest gift of God had been given to the world. Joy to the poor; for Christ had come to make them heirs of His kingdom. Joy to the rich; for He would teach them how to secure eternal riches. Joy to the ignorant; He would make them wise unto salvation. Joy to the learned; He would open to them deeper mysteries than they had ever fathomed; truths that had been hidden from the foundation of the world would be opened to men by the Saviour's mission.

John the Baptist had rejoiced to behold the Saviour. What occasion for rejoicing had the disciples who were privileged to walk and talk with the Majesty of heaven! This was not a time for them to mourn and fast. They must open their hearts to receive the light of His glory, that they might shed light upon those who sat in darkness and in the shadow of death.

It was a bright picture which the words of Christ had called up, but across it lay a heavy shadow, which His eye alone discerned. "The days will come," He said, "when the bridegroom shall be taken away from them, and then shall they fast in those days." When they should see their Lord betrayed and crucified, the disciples would mourn and fast. In His last words to them in the upper chamber, He said, "A little while, and ye shall not see Me: and again, a little while, and ye shall see Me. Verily, verily, I say unto you, That ye shall weep and lament, but the world shall rejoice: and ye shall be sorrowful, but your sorrow shall be turned into joy." John 16:19, 20.

When He should come forth from the tomb, their sorrow would be turned to joy. After His ascension He was to be absent in person; but through the Comforter He would still be

with them, and they were not to spend their time in mourning. This was what Satan wanted. He desired them to give the world the impression that they had been deceived and disappointed; but by faith they were to look to the sanctuary above, where Jesus was ministering for them; they were to open their hearts to the Holy Spirit, His representative, and to rejoice in the light of His presence. Yet days of temptation and trial would come, when they would be brought into conflict with the rulers of this world, and the leaders of the kingdom of darkness; when Christ was not personally with them, and they failed to discern the Comforter, then it would be more fitting for them to fast.

The Pharisees sought to exalt themselves by their rigorous observance of forms, while their hearts were filled with envy and strife. "Behold," says the Scripture, "ye fast for strife and debate, and to smite with the fist of wickedness: ye shall not fast as ye do this day, to make your voice to be heard on high. Is it such a fast that I have chosen? a day for a man to afflict his soul? is it to bow down his head as a bulrush, and to spread sackcloth and ashes under him? wilt thou call this a fast, and an acceptable day to the Lord?" Isa. 58:4, 5.

The true fast is no mere formal service. The Scripture describes the fast that God has chosen,—"to loose the bands of wickedness, to undo the heavy burdens, and to let the oppressed go free, and that ye break every yoke;" to "draw out thy soul to the hungry, and satisfy the afflicted soul." Isa. 58:6, 10. Here is set forth the very spirit and character of the work of Christ. His whole life was a sacrifice of Himself for the saving of the world. Whether fasting in the wilderness of temptation or eating with the publicans at Matthew's feast, He was giving His life for the redemption of the lost. Not in idle mourning, in mere bodily humiliation and multitudinous sacrifices, is the true spirit of devotion manifested, but it is shown in the surrender of self in willing service to God and man.

Continuing His answer to the disciples of John, Jesus spoke a parable, saying, "No man putteth a piece of a new garment upon an old; if otherwise, then both the new maketh a rent, and the piece that was taken out of the new agreeth not with the old." The message of John the Baptist was not to be interwoven with tradition and superstition. An attempt to blend the pretense of the Pharisees with the devotion of John would only make more evident the breach between them.

Nor could the principles of Christ's teaching be united with the forms of Pharisaism. Christ was not to close up the breach that had been made by the teachings of John. He would make more distinct the separation between the old and the new. Jesus further illustrated this fact, saying, "No man putteth new wine into old bottles; else the new wine will burst the bottles, and be spilled, and the bottles shall perish." The skin bottles which were used as vessels to contain the new wine, after a time became dry and brittle, and were then worthless to serve the same purpose again. In this familiar illustration Jesus presented the condition of the Jewish leaders. Priests and scribes and rulers were fixed in a rut of ceremonies and traditions. Their hearts had become contracted, like the dried-up wine skins to which He had compared them. While they remained satisfied with a legal religion, it was impossible for them to become the depositaries of the living truth of heaven. They thought their own righteousness all-sufficient, and did not desire that a new element should be brought into their religion. The good will of God to men they did not accept as something apart from themselves. They connected it with their own merit because of their good works. The faith that works by love and purifies the soul could find no place for union with the religion of the Pharisees, made up of ceremonies and the injunctions of men. The effort to unite the teachings of Jesus with the established religion would be vain. The vital truth of God, like fermenting wine, would burst the old, decaying bottles of the Pharisaical tradition.

The Pharisees thought themselves too wise to need instruction, too righteous to need salvation, too highly honored to need the honor that comes from Christ. The Saviour turned away from them to find others who would receive the message of heaven. In the untutored fishermen, in the publican at the market place, in the woman of Samaria, in the common people who heard Him gladly, He found His new bottles for the new wine. The instrumentalities to be used in the gospel work are those souls who gladly receive the light which God sends them. These are His agencies for imparting the knowledge of truth to the world. If through the grace of Christ His people will become new bottles, He will fill them with new wine.

The teaching of Christ, though it was represented by the new wine, was not a new doctrine, but the revelation of that which had been taught from the beginning. But to the Pharisees the truth of God had lost its original significance and beauty. To them Christ's teaching was new in almost every respect, and it was unrecognized and unacknowledged.

Jesus pointed out the power of false teaching to destroy the appreciation and desire for truth. "No man," He said, "having drunk old wine straightway desireth new: for he saith, The old is better." All the truth that has been given to the world through patriarchs and prophets shone out in new beauty in the words of Christ. But the scribes and Pharisees had no desire for the precious new wine. Until emptied of the old traditions, customs, and practices, they had no place in mind or heart for the teachings of Christ. They clung to the dead forms, and turned away from the living truth and the power of God.

It was this that proved the ruin of the Jews, and it will prove the ruin of many souls in our own day. Thousands are making the same mistake as did the Pharisees whom Christ reproved at Matthew's feast. Rather than give up some cherished idea, or discard some idol of opinion, many refuse the truth which comes down from the Father of light. They trust in self, and depend upon their own wisdom, and do not realize their spiritual poverty. They insist on being saved in some way by which they may perform some important work. When they see that there is no way of weaving self into the work, they reject the salvation provided.

A legal religion can never lead souls to Christ; for it is a loveless, Christless religion. Fasting or prayer that is actuated by a self-justifying spirit is an abomination in the sight of God. The solemn assembly for worship, the round of religious ceremonies, the external humiliation, the imposing sacrifice, proclaim that the doer of these things regards himself as righteous, and as entitled to heaven; but it is all a deception. Our own works can never purchase salvation.

As it was in the days of Christ, so it is now; the Pharisees do not know their spiritual destitution. To them comes the message, "Because thou sayest, I am rich, and increased with goods, and have need of nothing; and knowest not that thou art wretched, and miserable, and poor, and blind, and naked: I counsel thee to buy of Me gold tried in the fire, that thou mayest be rich; and white raiment, that thou mayest be clothed, and that the shame of thy nakedness do not appear." Rev. 3:17, 18. Faith and love are the gold tried in the fire. But with many the gold has become dim, and the rich treasure has been lost. The righteousness of Christ is to them as a robe unworn, a fountain untouched. To them it is said, "I have somewhat against thee, because thou hast left thy first love. Remember therefore from whence thou art fallen, and repent, and do the first works; or else I will come unto thee quickly, and will remove thy candlestick out of his place, except thou repent." Rev. 2:4, 5.

"The sacrifices of God are a broken spirit: a broken and a contrite heart, O God, Thou wilt not despise." Ps. 51:17. Man must be emptied of self before he can be, in the fullest sense, a believer in Jesus. When self is renounced, then the Lord can make man a new creature. New bottles can contain the new wine. The love of Christ will animate the believer with new life. In him who looks unto the Author and Finisher of our faith the character of Christ will be manifest.

The Sabbath

The Sabbath was hallowed at the creation. As ordained for man, it had its origin when "the morning stars sang together, and all the sons of God shouted for joy." Job 38:7. Peace brooded over the world; for earth was in harmony with heaven. "God saw everything that He had made, and, behold, it was very good;" and He rested in the joy of His completed work. Gen. 1:31.

Because He had rested upon the Sabbath, "God blessed the seventh day, and sanctified it,"—set it apart to a holy use. He gave it to Adam as a day of rest. It was a memorial of the work of creation, and thus a sign of God's power and His love. The Scripture says, "He hath made His wonderful works to be remembered." "The things that are made," declare "the invisible things of Him since the creation of the world," "even His everlasting power and divinity." Gen. 2:3; Ps. 111:4; Rom. 1:20, R. V.

All things were created by the Son of God. "In the beginning was the Word, and the Word was with God. . . .

All things were made by Him; and without Him was not anything made that was made." John 1: 1-3. And since the Sabbath is a memorial of the work of creation, it is a token of the love and power of Christ.

The Sabbath calls our thoughts to nature, and brings us into communion with the Creator. In the song of the bird, the sighing of the trees, and the music of the sea, we still may hear His voice who talked with Adam in Eden in the cool of the day. And as we behold His power in nature we find comfort, for the word that created all things is that which speaks life to the soul. He "who commanded the light to shine out of darkness, hath shined in our hearts, to give the light of the knowledge of the glory of God in the face of Jesus Christ." 2 Cor. 4:6.

It was this thought that awoke the song,—

"Thou, Lord, hast made me glad through Thy work;
I will triumph in the works of Thy hands.
O Lord, how great are Thy works!
And Thy thoughts are very deep."
Ps. 92:4,5.

And the Holy Spirit through the prophet Isaiah declares: "To whom then will ye liken God? or what likeness will ye compare unto Him? . . . Have ye not known? have ye not heard? hath it not been told you from the beginning? have ye not understood from the foundations of the earth? It is He that sitteth upon the circle of the earth, and the inhabitants thereof are as grasshoppers; that stretcheth out the heavens as a curtain, and spreadeth them out as a tent to dwell in. . . . To whom then will ye liken Me, or shall I be equal? saith the Holy One. Lift up your eyes on high, and behold who hath created these things, that bringeth out their host by number: He calleth them all by names by the greatness of His might, for that He is strong in power; not one faileth. Why sayest thou, O Jacob, and speakest, O Israel, My way is hid from the Lord, and my judgment is passed over from my God? Hast thou not known? hast thou not heard, that the everlasting God, the Lord, the Creator of the ends of the earth, fainteth not, neither is weary? . . . He giveth power to the faint; and to them that have no might He increaseth strength." "Fear thou not; for I am with thee: be not dismayed; for I am thy God: I will strengthen thee; yea, I will help thee; yea, I will uphold thee with the right hand of My righteousness." "Look unto Me, and be ye saved, all the ends of the earth: for I am God, and there is none else." This is the message written in nature, which the Sabbath is appointed to keep in memory. When the Lord bade Israel hallow His Sabbaths, He said, "They shall be a sign between Me and you, that ye may know that I am Jehovah your God." Isa. 40:18-29; 41:10; 45:22; Ezek. 20:20, R. V.

The Sabbath was embodied in the law given from Sinai; but it was not then first made known as a day of rest. The people of Israel had a knowledge of it before they came to Sinai. On the way thither the Sabbath was kept. When some profaned

it, the Lord reproved them, saying, "How long refuse ye to keep My commandments and My laws?" Ex. 16:28.

The Sabbath was not for Israel merely, but for the world. It had been made known to man in Eden, and, like the other precepts of the Decalogue, it is of imperishable obligation. Of that law of which the fourth commandment forms a part, Christ declares, "Till heaven and earth pass, one jot or one tittle shall in nowise pass from the law." So long as the heavens and the earth endure, the Sabbath will continue as a sign of the Creator's power. And when Eden shall bloom on earth again, God's holy rest day will be honored by all beneath the sun. "From one Sabbath to another" the inhabitants of the glorified new earth shall go up "to worship before Me, saith the Lord." Matt. 5:18; Isa. 66:23.

No other institution which was committed to the Jews tended so fully to distinguish them from surrounding nations as did the Sabbath. God designed that its observance should designate them as His worshipers. It was to be a token of their separation from idolatry, and their connection with the true God. But in order to keep the Sabbath holy, men must themselves be holy. Through faith they must become partakers of the righteousness of Christ. When the command was given to Israel, "Remember the Sabbath day, to keep it holy," the Lord said also to them, "Ye shall be holy men unto Me." Ex. 20:8; 22:31. Only thus could the Sabbath distinguish Israel as the worshipers of God.

As the Jews departed from God, and failed to make the righteousness of Christ their own by faith, the Sabbath lost its significance to them. Satan was seeking to exalt himself and to draw men away from Christ, and he worked to pervert the Sabbath, because it is the sign of the power of Christ. The Jewish leaders accomplished the will of Satan by surrounding God's rest day with burdensome requirements. In the days of Christ the Sabbath had become so perverted that its observance reflected the character of selfish and arbitrary men rather than the character of the loving heavenly Father. The rabbis virtually represented God as giving laws which it was impossible for men to obey. They led the people to look upon God as a tyrant, and to think that the observance of the Sabbath, as He required it, made men hard-hearted and cruel. It was the work of Christ to clear away these misconceptions. Although the rabbis followed Him with merciless hostility, He did not even appear to conform to their requirements, but went straight forward, keeping the Sabbath according to the law of God.

Upon one Sabbath day, as the Saviour and His disciples returned from the place of worship, they passed through a field of ripening grain. Jesus had continued His work to a late hour, and while passing through the fields, the disciples began to gather the heads of grain, and to eat the kernels after rubbing them in their hands. On any other day this act would have excited no comment, for one passing through a field of grain, an orchard, or a vineyard, was at liberty to gather what he desired to eat. See Deut. 23:24, 25. But to do this on the Sabbath was held to be an act of desecration. Not only was the gathering of the grain a kind of reaping, but the rubbing of it in the hands was a kind of threshing. Thus, in the opinion of the rabbis, there was a double offense.

The spies at once complained to Jesus, saying, "Behold, Thy disciples do that which is not lawful to do upon the Sabbath day."

When accused of Sabbathbreaking at Bethesda, Jesus defended Himself by affirming His Sonship to God, and declaring that He worked in harmony with the Father. Now that the disciples are attacked, He cites His accusers to examples from the Old Testament, acts performed on the Sabbath by those who were in the service of God.

The Jewish teachers prided themselves on their knowledge of the Scriptures, and in the Saviour's answer there was an implied rebuke for their ignorance of the Sacred Writings. "Have ye not read so much as this," He said, "what David did, when himself was an hungered, and they which were with him; how he went into the house of God, and did take and eat the shewbread, . . . which it is not lawful to eat but for the priests alone?" "And He said unto them, The Sabbath was made for man, and not man for the Sabbath." "Have ye not read in the law, how that on the Sabbath days the priests in the temple profane the Sabbath, and are blameless? But I say unto you, That in this place is one greater than the temple." "The Son of man is Lord also of the Sabbath." Luke 6:3, 4; Mark 2:27, 28; Matt. 12:5, 6.

If it was right for David to satisfy his hunger by eating of the bread that had been set apart to a holy use, then it was right for the disciples to supply their need by plucking the grain upon the sacred hours of the Sabbath. Again, the priests in the temple performed greater labor on the Sabbath than upon other days. The same labor in secular business would be sinful; but the work of the priests was in the service of God. They were performing those rites that pointed to the redeeming power of Christ, and their labor was in harmony with the object of the Sabbath. But now Christ Himself had come. The disciples, in doing the work of Christ, were engaged in God's service, and that which was necessary for the accomplishment of this work it was right to do on the Sabbath day.

Christ would teach His disciples and His enemies that the service of God is first of all. The object of God's work in this world is the redemption of man; therefore that which is necessary to be done on the Sabbath in the accomplishment of this work is in accord with the Sabbath law. Jesus then crowned His argument by declaring Himself the "Lord of the Sabbath,"—One above all question and above all law. This infinite Judge acquits the disciples of blame, appealing to the very statutes they are accused of violating.

Jesus did not let the matter pass with administering a rebuke to His enemies. He declared that in their blindness they had mistaken the object of the Sabbath. He said, "If ye had known what this meaneth, I will have mercy, and not sacrifice, ye would not have condemned the guiltless." Matt. 12:7. Their many heartless rites could not supply the lack of that truthful integrity and tender love which will ever characterize the true worshiper of God.

Again Christ reiterated the truth that the sacrifices were in themselves of no value. They were a means, and not an end. Their object was to direct men to the Saviour, and thus to bring them into harmony with God. It is the service of love that God values. When this is lacking, the mere round of ceremony is an offense to Him. So with the Sabbath. It was designed to bring men into communion with God; but when the mind was absorbed with wearisome rites, the object of the Sabbath was thwarted. Its mere outward observance was a mockery.

Upon another Sabbath, as Jesus entered a synagogue, He saw there a man who had a withered hand. The Pharisees watched Him, eager to see what He would do. The Saviour well knew that in healing on the Sabbath He would be regarded as a transgressor, but He did not hesitate to break down the wall of traditional requirements that barricaded the Sabbath. Jesus bade the afflicted man stand forth, and then asked, "It is lawful to do good on the Sabbath days, or to do evil? to save life, or to kill?" It was a maxim among the Jews that a failure to do good, when one had opportunity, was to do evil; to neglect to save life was to kill. Thus Jesus met the rabbis on their own ground. "But they held their peace. And when He had looked round about on them with anger, being grieved for the hardness of their hearts, He saith unto the man, Stretch forth thine hand. And he stretched it out: and his hand was restored whole as the other." Mark 3:4, 5.

When questioned, "Is it lawful to heal on the Sabbath days?" Jesus answered, "What man shall there be among you, that shall have one sheep, and if it fall into a pit on the Sabbath day, will he not lay hold on it, and lift it out? How much then is a man better than a sheep? Wherefore it is lawful to do well on the Sabbath days." Matt. 12:10-12.

The spies dared not answer Christ in the presence of the multitude, for fear of involving themselves in difficulty. They knew that He had spoken the truth. Rather than violate their traditions, they would leave a man to suffer, while they would relieve a brute because of the loss to the owner if it were neglected. Thus greater care was shown for a dumb animal than for man, who is made in the image of God. This illustrates the working of all false religions. They originate in man's desire to exalt himself above God, but they result in degrading man below the brute. Every religion that wars against the sovereignty of God defrauds man of the glory which was his at the creation, and which is to be restored to him in Christ. Every false religion teaches its adherents to be careless of human needs, sufferings, and rights. The gospel places a high value upon humanity as the purchase of the blood of Christ, and it teaches a tender regard for the wants and woes of man. The Lord says, "I will make a man more precious than fine gold; even a man than the golden wedge of Ophir." Isa. 13:12.

When Jesus turned upon the Pharisees with the question whether it was lawful on the Sabbath day to do good or to do evil, to save life or to kill, He confronted them with their own wicked purposes. They were hunting His life with bitter hatred, while He was saving life and bringing happiness to multitudes. Was it better to slay upon the Sabbath, as they were planning to do, than to heal the afflicted, as He had done? Was it more righteous to have murder in the heart upon God's holy day than love to all men, which finds expression in deeds of mercy?

In the healing of the withered hand, Jesus condemned the custom of the Jews, and left the fourth commandment standing as God had given it. "It is lawful to do well on the Sabbath days," He declared. By sweeping away the senseless restrictions of the Jews, Christ honored the Sabbath, while those who complained of Him were dishonoring God's holy day.

Those who hold that Christ abolished the law teach that He broke the Sabbath and justified His disciples in doing the same. Thus they are really taking the same ground as did the caviling Jews. In this they contradict the testimony of Christ Himself, who declared, "I have kept My Father's commandments, and abide in His love." John 15:10. Neither the Saviour nor His followers broke the law of the Sabbath. Christ was a living representative of the law. No violation of its holy precepts was found in His life. Looking upon a nation of witnesses who were seeking occasion to condemn Him, He could say unchallenged, "Which of you convicteth Me of sin?" John 8:46, R. V.

The Saviour had not come to set aside what patriarchs and prophets had spoken; for He Himself had spoken through these representative men. All the truths of God's word came from Him. But these priceless gems had been placed in false settings. Their precious light had been made to minister to error. God desired them to be removed from their settings of error and replaced in the framework of truth. This work only a divine hand could accomplish. By its connection with error, the truth had been serving the cause of the enemy of God and man. Christ had come to place it where it would glorify God, and work the salvation of humanity.

"The Sabbath was made for man, and not man for the Sabbath," Jesus said. The institutions that God has established are for the benefit of mankind. "All things are for your sakes." "Whether Paul, or Apollos, or Cephas, or the world, or life, or death, or things present, or things to come; all are yours; and ye are Christ's; and Christ is God's." 2 Cor. 4:15; 1 Cor. 3:22, 23. The law of Ten Commandments, of which the Sabbath forms a part, God gave to His people as a blessing. "The Lord commanded us," said Moses, "to do all these statutes, to fear the Lord our God, for our good always, that He might preserve us alive." Deut. 6:24. And through the psalmist the message was given to Israel, "Serve the Lord with gladness: come before His presence with singing. Know ye that the Lord He is God: it is He that hath made us, and not we ourselves; we are His people, and the sheep of His pasture. Enter into His gates with thanksgiving, and into His courts with praise." Ps. 100:2-4. And of all who keep "the Sabbath from polluting it," the Lord declares, "Even them will I bring to My holy mountain, and make them joyful in My house of prayer." Isa. 56:6, 7.

"Wherefore the Son of man is Lord also of the Sabbath." These words are full of instruction and comfort. Because the Sabbath was made for man, it is the Lord's day. It belongs to Christ. For "all things were made by Him; and without Him was not anything made that was made." John 1:3. Since He made all things, He made the Sabbath. By Him it was set apart as a memorial of the work of creation. It points to Him as both the Creator and the Sanctifier. It declares that He who created all things in heaven and in earth, and by whom all things hold together, is the head of the church, and that by His power we are reconciled to God. For, speaking of Israel, He said, "I gave them My Sabbaths, to be a sign between Me and them, that they might know that I am the Lord that sanctify them,"—make them holy. Ezek. 20:12. Then the Sabbath is a sign of Christ's power to make us holy. And it is given to all whom Christ makes holy. As a sign of His sanctifying power, the Sabbath is given to all who through Christ become a part of the Israel of God.

And the Lord says, "If thou turn away thy foot from the Sabbath, from doing thy pleasure on My holy day; and call the Sabbath a delight, the holy of the Lord, honorable; . . . then shalt thou delight thyself in the Lord." Isa. 58:13, 14. To all who receive the Sabbath as a sign of Christ's creative and redeeming power, it will be a delight. Seeing Christ in it, they delight themselves in Him. The Sabbath points them to the works of creation as an evidence of His mighty power in redemption. While it calls to mind the lost peace of Eden, it tells of peace restored through the Saviour. And every object in nature repeats His invitation, "Come unto Me, all ye that labor and are heavy-laden, and I will give you rest." Matt 11:28.

"He Ordained Twelve"

"And He goeth up into a mountain, and calleth unto Him whom He would: and they came unto Him. And He ordained twelve, that they should be with Him, and that He might send them forth to preach."

It was beneath the sheltering trees of the mountainside, but a little distance from the Sea of Galilee, that the twelve were called to the apostolate, and the Sermon on the Mount was given. The fields and hills were the favorite resorts of Jesus, and much of His teaching was given under the open sky, rather than in the temple or the synagogues. No synagogue could have received the throngs that followed Him; but not for this reason only did He choose to teach in the fields and groves. Jesus loved the scenes of nature. To Him each quiet retreat was a sacred temple.

It was under the trees of Eden that the first dwellers on earth had chosen their sanctuary. There Christ had communed with the father of mankind. When banished from Paradise, our first parents still worshiped in the fields and groves, and there Christ met them with the gospel of His grace. It was Christ who spoke with Abraham under the oaks at Mamre; with Isaac as he went out to pray in the fields at the eventide; with Jacob on the hillside at Bethel; with Moses among the mountains of Midian; and with the boy David as he watched his flocks. It was at Christ's direction that for fifteen centuries the Hebrew people had left their homes for one week every year, and had dwelt in booths formed from the green branches "of goodly trees, branches of palm trees, and boughs of thick trees, and willows of the brook." Lev. 23:40.

In training His disciples, Jesus chose to withdraw from the confusion of the city to the quiet of the fields and hills, as more in harmony with the lessons of self-abnegation He desired to teach them. And during His ministry He loved to gather the people about Him under the blue heavens, on some grassy hillside, or on the beach beside the lake. Here, surrounded by the works of His own creation, He could turn the thoughts of His hearers from the artificial to the natural. In the growth and development of nature were revealed the principles of His kingdom. As men should lift up their eyes to the hills of God, and behold the wonderful works of His hands, they could learn precious lessons of divine truth. Christ's teaching would be repeated to them in the things of nature. So it is with all who go into the fields with Christ in their hearts. They will feel themselves surrounded with a holy influence. The things of nature take up the parables of our Lord, and repeat His counsels. By communion with God in nature, the mind is uplifted, and the heart finds rest.

The first step was now to be taken in the organization of the church that after Christ's departure was to be His representative on earth. No costly sanctuary was at their command, but the Saviour led His disciples to the retreat He loved, and in their minds the sacred experiences of that day were forever linked with the beauty of mountain and vale and sea.

Jesus had called His disciples that He might send them forth as His witnesses, to declare to the world what they had seen and heard of Him. Their office was the most important to which human beings had ever been called, and was second only to that of Christ Himself. They were to be workers together with God for the saving of the world. As in the Old Testament the twelve patriarchs stand as representatives of Israel, so the twelve apostles were to stand as representatives of the gospel church.

The Saviour knew the character of the men whom He had chosen; all their weaknesses and errors were open before Him; He knew the perils through which they must pass, the responsibility that would rest upon them; and His heart yearned over these chosen ones. Alone upon a mountain near the Sea of Galilee He spent the entire night in prayer for them, while they were sleeping at the foot of the mountain. With the first light of dawn He summoned them to meet Him; for He had something of importance to communicate to them.

These disciples had been for some time associated with Jesus in active labor. John and James, Andrew and Peter, with Philip, Nathanael, and Matthew, had been more closely connected with Him than the others, and had witnessed more of His miracles. Peter, James, and John stood in still nearer relationship to Him. They were almost constantly with Him, witnessing His miracles, and hearing His words. John pressed into still closer intimacy with Jesus, so that he is distinguished as the one whom Jesus loved. The Saviour loved them all, but John's was the most receptive spirit. He was younger than the others, and with more of the child's confiding trust he opened his heart to Jesus. Thus he came more into sympathy with Christ, and through him the Saviour's deepest spiritual teaching was communicated to His people.

At the head of one of the groups into which the apostles are divided stands the name of Philip. He was the first disciple to whom Jesus addressed the distinct command, "Follow Me." Philip was of Bethsaida, the city of Andrew and Peter. He had listened to the teaching of John the Baptist, and had heard his announcement of Christ as the Lamb of God. Philip was a sincere seeker for truth, but he was slow of heart to believe. Although he had joined himself to Christ, yet his announcement of Him to Nathanael shows that he was not fully convinced of the divinity of Jesus. Though Christ had been proclaimed by the voice from heaven as the Son of God, to Philip He was "Jesus of Nazareth, the son of Joseph." John 1:45. Again, when the five thousand were fed, Philip's lack of faith was shown. It was to test him that Jesus questioned, "Whence shall we buy bread, that these may eat?" Philip's answer was on the side of unbelief: "Two hundred pennyworth of bread is not sufficient for them, that every one of them may take a little." John 6:5, 7. Jesus was grieved. Although Philip had seen His works and felt His power, yet he had not faith. When the Greeks inquired of Philip concerning Jesus, he did not seize upon the opportunity of introducing them to the Saviour, but he went to tell Andrew. Again, in those last hours before the crucifixion, the words of Philip were such as to discourage faith. When Thomas said to Jesus, "Lord, we know not whither Thou goest; and how can we know the way?" the Saviour answered, "I am the Way, the Truth, and the Life. . . . If ye had known Me, ye should have known My Father also." From Philip came the response of unbelief: "Lord, show us the Father, and it sufficeth us." John 14:5-8. So slow of heart, so weak in faith, was that disciple who for three years had been with Jesus.

In happy contrast to Philip's unbelief was the childlike trust of Nathanael. He was a man of intensely earnest nature, one whose faith took hold upon unseen realities. Yet Philip was a student in the school of Christ, and the divine Teacher bore patiently with his unbelief and dullness. When the Holy Spirit was poured out upon the disciples, Philip became a teacher after the divine order. He knew whereof he spoke, and he taught with an assurance that carried conviction to the hearers.

While Jesus was preparing the disciples for their ordination, one who had not been summoned urged his presence among them. It was Judas Iscariot, a man who professed to be a follower of Christ. He now came forward, soliciting a place in this inner circle of disciples. With great earnestness and apparent sincerity he declared, "Master, I will follow Thee whithersoever Thou goest." Jesus neither repulsed nor welcomed him, but uttered only the mournful words: "The foxes have holes, and the birds of the air have nests; but the Son of man hath not where to lay His head." Matt. 8:19, 20. Judas believed Jesus to be the Messiah; and by joining the apostles, he hoped to secure a high position in the new kingdom. This hope Jesus designed to cut off by the statement of His poverty.

The disciples were anxious that Judas should become one of their number. He was of commanding appearance, a man of keen discernment and executive ability, and they commended him to Jesus as one who would greatly assist Him in His work. They were surprised that Jesus received him so coolly.

The disciples had been much disappointed that Jesus had not tried to secure the co-operation of the leaders in Israel. They felt that it was a mistake not to strengthen His cause by securing the support of these influential men. If He had repulsed Judas, they would, in their own minds, have questioned the wisdom of their Master. The after history of Judas would show them the danger of allowing any worldly consideration to have weight in deciding the fitness of men for the work of God. The co-operation of such men as the disciples were anxious to secure would have betrayed the work into the hands of its worst enemies.

Yet when Judas joined the disciples, he was not insensible to the beauty of the character of Christ. He felt the influence of that divine power which was drawing souls to the Saviour. He who came not to break the bruised reed nor quench the smoking flax would not repulse this soul while even one desire was reaching toward the light. The Saviour read the heart of Judas; He knew the depths of iniquity to which, unless delivered by the grace of God, Judas would sink. In connecting this man with Himself, He placed him where he might, day by day, be brought in contact with the outflowing of His own unselfish love. If he would open his heart to Christ, divine grace would banish the demon of selfishness, and even Judas might become a subject of the kingdom of God.

God takes men as they are, with the human elements in their character, and trains them for His service, if they will be disciplined and learn of Him. They are not chosen because they are perfect, but notwithstanding their imperfections, that through the knowledge and practice of the truth, through the grace of Christ, they may become transformed into His image.

Judas had the same opportunities as had the other disciples. He listened to the same precious lessons. But the practice of the truth, which Christ required, was at variance with the desires and purposes of Judas, and he would not yield his ideas in order to receive wisdom from Heaven.

How tenderly the Saviour dealt with him who was to be His betrayer! In His teaching, Jesus dwelt upon principles of benevolence that struck at the very root of covetousness. He presented before Judas the heinous character of greed, and many a time the disciple realized that his character had been portrayed, and his sin pointed out; but he would not confess and forsake his unrighteousness. He was self-sufficient, and instead of resisting temptation, he continued to follow his fraudulent practices. Christ was before him, a living example of what he must become if he reaped the benefit of the divine mediation and ministry; but lesson after lesson fell unheeded on the ears of Judas.

Jesus dealt him no sharp rebuke for his covetousness, but with divine patience bore with this erring man, even while giving him evidence that He read his heart as an open book. He presented before him the highest incentives for right doing; and in rejecting the light of Heaven, Judas would be without excuse.

Instead of walking in the light, Judas chose to retain his defects. Evil desires, revengeful passions, dark and sullen thoughts, were cherished, until Satan had full control of the man. Judas became a representative of the enemy of Christ.

When he came into association with Jesus, he had some precious traits of character that might have been made a blessing to the church. If he had been willing to wear the yoke of Christ, he might have been among the chief of the apostles; but he hardened his heart when his defects were pointed out, and in pride and rebellion chose his own selfish ambitions, and thus unfitted himself for the work that God would have given him to do.

All the disciples had serious faults when Jesus called them to His service. Even John, who came into closest association with the meek and lowly One, was not himself naturally meek and yielding. He and his brother were called "the sons of thunder." While they were with Jesus, any slight shown to Him aroused their indignation and combativeness. Evil temper, revenge, the spirit of criticism, were all in the beloved disciple. He was proud, and ambitious to be first in the kingdom of God. But day by day, in contrast with his own violent spirit, he beheld the tenderness and forbearance of Jesus, and heard His lessons of humility and patience. He opened his heart to the divine influence, and became not only a hearer but a doer of the Saviour's words. Self was hid in Christ. He learned to wear the yoke of Christ and to bear His burden.

Jesus reproved His disciples, He warned and cautioned them; but John and his brethren did not leave Him; they chose Jesus, notwithstanding the reproofs. The Saviour did not withdraw from them because of their weakness and errors. They continued to the end to share His trials and to learn the lessons of His life. By beholding Christ, they became transformed in character.

The apostles differed widely in habits and disposition. There were the publican, Levi-Matthew, and the fiery zealot Simon, the uncompromising hater of the authority of Rome; the generous, impulsive Peter, and the mean-spirited Judas; Thomas, truehearted, yet timid and fearful, Philip, slow of heart, and inclined to doubt, and the ambitious, outspoken sons of Zebedee, with their brethren. These were brought together, with their different faults, all with inherited and cultivated tendencies to evil; but in and through Christ they were to dwell in the family of God, learning to become one in faith, in doctrine, in spirit. They would have their tests, their grievances, their differences of opinion; but while Christ was abiding in the heart, there could be no dissension. His love would lead to love for one another; the lessons of the Master would lead to the harmonizing of all differences, bringing the disciples into unity, till they would be of one mind and one judgment. Christ is the great center, and they would approach one another just in proportion as they approached the center.

When Jesus had ended His instruction to the disciples, He gathered the little band close about Him, and kneeling in the midst of them, and laying His hands upon their heads, He offered a prayer dedicating them to His sacred work. Thus the Lord's disciples were ordained to the gospel ministry.

As His representatives among men, Christ does not choose angels who have never fallen, but human beings, men of like passions with those they seek to save. Christ took upon Himself humanity, that He might reach humanity. Divinity needed humanity; for it required both the divine and the human to bring salvation to the world. Divinity needed humanity, that humanity might afford a channel of communication between God and man. So with the servants and messengers of Christ. Man needs a power outside of and beyond himself, to restore him to the likeness of God, and enable him to do the work of God; but this does not make the human agency unessential. Humanity lays hold upon divine power, Christ dwells in the heart by faith; and through co-operation with the divine, the power of man becomes efficient for good.

He who called the fisherman of Galilee is still calling men to His service. And He is just as willing to manifest His power through us as through the first disciples. However imperfect and sinful we may be, the Lord holds out to us the offer of partnership with Himself, of apprenticeship to Christ. He invites us to come under the divine instruction, that, uniting with Christ, we may work the works of God.

"We have this treasure in earthen vessels, that the exceeding greatness of the power may be of God, and not from ourselves." 2 Cor. 4:7, R. V. This is why the preaching of the gospel was committed to erring men rather than to the angels. It is manifest that the power which works through the weakness of humanity is the power of God; and thus we are encouraged to believe that the power which can help others as weak as ourselves can help us. And those who are themselves "compassed with infirmity" should be able to "have compassion on the ignorant, and on them that are out of the way." Heb. 5:2. Having been in peril themselves, they are acquainted with the dangers and difficulties of the way, and for this reason are called to reach out for others in like peril. There are souls perplexed with doubt, burdened with infirmities, weak in faith, and unable to grasp the Unseen; but a friend whom they can see, coming to them in Christ's stead, can be a connecting link to fasten their trembling faith upon Christ.

We are to be laborers together with the heavenly angels in presenting Jesus to the world. With almost impatient eagerness the angels wait for our co-operation; for man must be the channel to communicate with man. And when we give ourselves to Christ in wholehearted devotion, angels rejoice that they may speak through our voices to reveal God's love.

The Sermon on the Mount

Christ seldom gathered His disciples alone to receive His words. He did not choose for His audience those only who knew the way of life. It was His work to reach the multitudes who were in ignorance and error. He gave His lessons of truth where they could reach the darkened understanding. He Himself was the Truth, standing with girded loins and hands ever outstretched to bless, and in words of warning, entreaty, and encouragement, seeking to uplift all who would come unto Him.

The Sermon on the Mount, though given especially to the disciples, was spoken in the hearing of the multitude. After the ordination of the apostles, Jesus went with them to the seaside. Here in the early morning the people had begun to assemble. Besides the usual crowds from the Galilean towns, there were people from Judea, and even from Jerusalem itself; from Perea, from Decapolis, from Idumea, away to the south of Judea; and from Tyre and Sidon, the Phoenician cities on the shore of the Mediterranean. "When they had heard what great things He did," they "came to hear Him, and to be healed of their diseases: . . . there went virtue out of Him, and healed them all." Mark 3:8; Luke 6:17-19.

The narrow beach did not afford even standing room within reach of His voice for all who desired to hear Him, and Jesus led the way back to the mountainside. Reaching a level space that offered a pleasant gathering place for the vast assembly, He seated Himself on the grass, and the disciples and the multitude followed His example.

The disciples' place was always next to Jesus. The people constantly pressed upon Him, yet the disciples understood that they were not to be crowded away from His presence. They sat close beside Him, that they might not lose a word of His instruction. They were attentive listeners, eager to understand the truths they were to make known to all lands and all ages.

With a feeling that something more than usual might be expected, they now pressed about their Master. They believed that the kingdom was soon to be established, and from the events of the morning they gathered assurance that some announcement concerning it was about to be made. A feeling of expectancy pervaded the multitude also, and eager faces gave evidence of the deep interest. As the people sat upon the green hillside, awaiting the words of the divine Teacher, their hearts were filled with thoughts of future glory. There were scribes and Pharisees who looked forward to the day when they should have dominion over the hated Romans, and possess the riches and splendor of the world's great empire. The poor peasants and fishermen hoped to hear the assurance that their wretched hovels, the scanty food, the life of toil, and fear of want were to be exchanged for mansions of plenty and days of ease. In place of the one coarse garment which was their covering by day, and their blanket at night, they hoped that Christ would give them the rich and costly robes of their conquerors. All hearts thrilled with the proud hope that Israel was soon to be honored before the nations as the chosen of the Lord, and Jerusalem exalted as the head of a universal kingdom.

Christ disappointed the hope of worldly greatness. In the Sermon on the Mount He sought to undo the work that had been wrought by false education, and to give His hearers a right conception of His kingdom and of His own character. Yet He did not make a direct attack on the errors of the people. He saw the misery of the world on account of sin, yet He did not present before them a vivid delineation of their wretchedness. He taught them of something infinitely better than they had known. Without combating their ideas of the kingdom of God, He told them the conditions of entrance therein, leaving them to draw their own conclusions as to its nature. The truths He taught are no less important to us than to the multitude that followed Him. We no less than they need to learn the foundation principles of the kingdom of God.

Christ's first words to the people on the mount were words of blessing. Happy are they, He said, who recognize their spiritual poverty, and feel their need of redemption. The gospel is to be preached to the poor. Not to the spiritually proud, those who claim to be rich and in need of nothing, is it revealed, but to those who are humble and contrite. One fountain only has been opened for sin, a fountain for the poor in spirit.

The proud heart strives to earn salvation; but both our title to heaven and our fitness for it are found in the righteousness of Christ. The Lord can do nothing toward the recovery of man until, convinced of his own weakness, and stripped of all self-sufficiency, he yields himself to the control of God. Then he can receive the gift that God is waiting to bestow. From the soul that feels his need, nothing is withheld. He has unrestricted access to Him in whom all fullness dwells. "For thus saith the high and lofty One that inhabiteth eternity, whose name is Holy; I dwell in the high and holy place, with him also that is of a contrite and humble spirit, to revive the spirit of the humble, and to revive the heart of the contrite ones." Isa. 57:15.

"Blessed are they that mourn: for they shall be comforted." By these words Christ does not teach that mourning in itself has power to remove the guilt of sin. He gives no sanction to pretense or to voluntary humility. The mourning of which He speaks does not consist in melancholy and lamentation. While we sorrow on account of sin, we are to rejoice in the precious privilege of being children of God.

We often sorrow because our evil deeds bring unpleasant consequences to ourselves; but this is not repentance. Real sorrow for sin is the result of the working of the Holy Spirit. The Spirit reveals the ingratitude of the heart that has slighted and grieved the Saviour, and brings us in contrition to the foot of the cross. By every sin Jesus is wounded afresh; and as we look upon Him whom we have pierced, we mourn for the sins that have brought anguish upon Him. Such mourning will lead to the renunciation of sin.

The worldling may pronounce this sorrow a weakness; but it is the strength which binds the penitent to the Infinite One with links that cannot be broken. It shows that the angels of God are bringing back to the soul the graces that were lost through hardness of heart and transgression. The tears of the penitent are only the raindrops that precede the sunshine of holiness. This sorrow heralds a joy which will be a living fountain in the soul. "Only acknowledge thine iniquity, that thou hast transgressed against the Lord thy God;" "and I will not cause Mine anger to fall upon you: for I am merciful, saith the Lord." Jer. 3:13, 12. "Unto them that mourn in Zion," He has appointed to give "beauty for ashes, the oil of joy for mourning, the garment of praise for the spirit of heaviness." Isa. 61:3.

And for those also who mourn in trial and sorrow there is comfort. The bitterness of grief and humiliation is better than the indulgences of sin. Through affliction God reveals to us the plague spots in our characters, that by His grace we may overcome our faults. Unknown chapters in regard to ourselves are opened to us, and the test comes, whether we will accept the reproof and the counsel of God. When brought into trial, we are not to fret and complain. We should not rebel, or worry ourselves out of the hand of Christ. We are to humble the soul before God. The ways of the Lord are obscure to him who desires to see things in a light pleasing to himself. They appear dark and joyless to our human nature. But God's ways are ways of mercy and the end is salvation. Elijah knew not what he was doing when in the desert he said that he had had enough of life, and prayed that he might die. The Lord in His mercy did not take him at his word. There was yet a great work for Elijah to do; and when his work was done, he was not to perish in discouragement and solitude in the wilderness. Not for him the descent into the dust of death, but the ascent in glory, with the convoy of celestial chariots, to the throne on high.

God's word for the sorrowing is, "I have seen his ways, and will heal him: I will lead him also, and restore comforts unto him and to his mourners." "I will turn their mourning into joy, and will comfort them, and make them rejoice from their sorrow." Isa. 57:18; Jer. 31:13.

"Blessed are the meek." The difficulties we have to encounter may be very much lessened by that meekness which hides itself in Christ. If we possess the humility of our Master, we shall rise above the slights, the rebuffs, the annoyances, to which we are daily exposed, and they will cease to cast a gloom over the spirit. The highest evidence of nobility in a

Christian is self-control. He who under abuse or cruelty fails to maintain a calm and trustful spirit robs God of His right to reveal in him His own perfection of character. Lowliness of heart is the strength that gives victory to the followers of Christ; it is the token of their connection with the courts above.

"Though the Lord be high, yet hath He respect unto the lowly." Ps. 138:6. Those who reveal the meek and lowly spirit of Christ are tenderly regarded by God. They may be looked upon with scorn by the world, but they are of great value in His sight. Not only the wise, the great, the beneficent, will gain a passport to the heavenly courts; not only the busy worker, full of zeal and restless activity. No; the poor in spirit, who crave the presence of an abiding Christ, the humble in heart, whose highest ambition is to do God's will,—these will gain an abundant entrance. They will be among that number who have washed their robes and made them white in the blood of the Lamb. "Therefore are they before the throne of God, and serve Him day and night in His temple: and He that sitteth on the throne shall dwell among them." Rev. 7:15.

"Blessed are they which do hunger and thirst after righteousness." The sense of unworthiness will lead the heart to hunger and thirst for righteousness, and this desire will not be disappointed. Those who make room in their hearts for Jesus will realize His love. All who long to bear the likeness of the character of God shall be satisfied. The Holy Spirit never leaves unassisted the soul who is looking unto Jesus. He takes of the things of Christ and shows them unto him. If the eye is kept fixed on Christ, the work of the Spirit ceases not until the soul is conformed to His image. The pure element of love will expand the soul, giving it a capacity for higher attainments, for increased knowledge of heavenly things, so that it will not rest short of the fullness. "Blessed are they which do hunger and thirst after righteousness; for they shall be filled."

The merciful shall find mercy, and the pure in heart shall see God. Every impure thought defiles the soul, impairs the moral sense, and tends to obliterate the impressions of the Holy Spirit. It dims the spiritual vision, so that men cannot behold God. The Lord may and does forgive the repenting sinner; but though forgiven, the soul is marred. All impurity of speech or of thought must be shunned by him who would have clear discernment of spiritual truth.

But the words of Christ cover more than freedom from sensual impurity, more than freedom from that ceremonial defilement which the Jews so rigorously shunned. Selfishness prevents us from beholding God. The self-seeking spirit judges of God as altogether such a one as itself. Until we have renounced this, we cannot understand Him who is love. Only the unselfish heart, the humble and trustful spirit, shall see God as "merciful and gracious, long-suffering, and abundant in goodness and truth." Ex. 34:6.

"Blessed are the peacemakers." The peace of Christ is born of truth. It is harmony with God. The world is at enmity with the law of God; sinners are at enmity with their Maker; and as a result they are at enmity with one another. But the psalmist declares, "Great peace have they which love Thy law: and nothing shall offend them." Ps. 119:165. Men cannot manufacture peace. Human plans for the purification and uplifting of individuals or of society will fail of producing peace, because they do not reach the heart. The only power that can create or perpetuate true peace is the grace of Christ. When this is implanted in the heart, it will cast out the evil passions that cause strife and dissension. "Instead of the thorn shall come up the fir tree, and instead of the brier shall come up the myrtle tree;" and life's desert "shall rejoice, and blossom as the rose." Isa. 55:13; 35:1.

The multitudes were amazed at this teaching, which was so at variance with the precepts and example of the Pharisees. The people had come to think that happiness consisted in the possession of the things of this world, and that fame and the honor of men were much to be coveted. It was very pleasing to be called "Rabbi," and to be extolled as wise and religious, having their virtues paraded before the public. This was regarded as the crown of happiness. But in the presence of that vast throng, Jesus declared that earthly gain and honor were all the reward such persons would ever receive. He spoke with certainty, and a convincing power attended His words. The people were silenced, and a feeling of fear crept over them. They looked at one another doubtfully. Who of them would be saved if this Man's teachings were true? Many were convicted that this remarkable Teacher was actuated by the Spirit of God, and that the sentiments He uttered were divine.

After explaining what constitutes true happiness, and how it may be obtained, Jesus more definitely pointed out the duty of His disciples, as teachers chosen of God to lead others into the path of righteousness and eternal life. He knew that they would often suffer from disappointment and discouragement, that they would meet with decided opposition, that they would be insulted, and their testimony rejected. Well He knew that in the fulfillment of their mission, the humble men who listened so attentively to His words were to bear calumny, torture, imprisonment, and death, and He continued:

"Blessed are they which are persecuted for righteousness' sake: for theirs is the kingdom of heaven. Blessed are ye, when men shall revile you, and persecute you, and shall say all manner of evil against you falsely, for My sake. Rejoice, and be exceeding glad: for great is your reward in heaven: for so persecuted they the prophets which were before you."

The world loves sin, and hates righteousness, and this was the cause of its hostility to Jesus. All who refuse His infinite love will find Christianity a disturbing element. The light of Christ sweeps away the darkness that covers their sins, and the need of reform is made manifest. While those who yield to the influence of the Holy Spirit begin war with themselves, those who cling to sin war against the truth and its representatives.

Thus strife is created, and Christ's followers are accused as troublers of the people. But it is fellowship with God that brings them the world's enmity. They are bearing the reproach of Christ. They are treading the path that has been trodden by the noblest of the earth. Not with sorrow, but with rejoicing, should they meet persecution. Each fiery trial is God's agent for their refining. Each is fitting them for their work as colaborers with Him. Each conflict has its place in the great battle for righteousness, and each will add to the joy of their final triumph. Having this in view, the test of their faith and patience will be cheerfully accepted rather than dreaded and avoided. Anxious to fulfill their obligation to the world, fixing their desire upon the approval of God, His servants are to fulfill every duty, irrespective of the fear or the favor of men.

"Ye are the salt of the earth," Jesus said. Do not withdraw yourselves from the world in order to escape persecution. You are to abide among men, that the savor of the divine love may be as salt to preserve the world from corruption.

Hearts that respond to the influence of the Holy Spirit are the channels through which God's blessing flows. Were those who serve God removed from the earth, and His Spirit withdrawn from among men, this world would be left to desolation and destruction, the fruit of Satan's dominion. Though the wicked know it not, they owe even the blessings of this life to the presence, in the world, of God's people whom they despise and oppress. But if Christians are such in name only, they are like the salt that has lost its savor. They have no influence for good in the world. Through their misrepresentation of God they are worse than unbelievers.

"Ye are the light of the world." The Jews thought to confine the benefits of salvation to their own nation; but Christ showed them that salvation is like the sunshine. It belongs to the whole world. The religion of the Bible is not to be confined between the covers of a book, nor within the walls of a church. It is not to be brought out occasionally for our own benefit, and then to be carefully laid aside again. It is to sanctify the daily life, to manifest itself in every business transaction and in all our social relations.

True character is not shaped from without, and put on; it radiates from within. If we wish to direct others in the path of righteousness, the principles of righteousness must be enshrined in our own hearts. Our profession of faith may proclaim the theory of religion, but it is our practical piety that holds forth the word of truth. The consistent life, the holy conversation, the unswerving integrity, the active, benevolent spirit, the godly example,—these are the mediums through which light is conveyed to the world.

Jesus had not dwelt on the specifications of the law, but He did not leave His hearers to conclude that He had come to set aside its requirements. He knew that spies stood ready to seize upon every word that might be wrested to serve their purpose. He knew the prejudice that existed in the minds of many of His hearers, and He said nothing to unsettle their faith in the religion and institutions that had been committed to them through Moses. Christ Himself had given both the moral and the ceremonial law. He did not come to destroy confidence in

His own instruction. It was because of His great reverence for the law and the prophets that He sought to break through the wall of traditional requirements which hemmed in the Jews. While He set aside their false interpretations of the law, He carefully guarded His disciples against yielding up the vital truths committed to the Hebrews.

The Pharisees prided themselves on their obedience to the law; yet they knew so little of its principles through everyday practice that to them the Saviour's words sounded like heresy. As He swept away the rubbish under which the truth had been buried, they thought He was sweeping away the truth itself. They whispered to one another that He was making light of the law. He read their thoughts, and answered them, saying,—

"Think not that I am come to destroy the law, or the prophets: I am not come to destroy, but to fulfill." Here Jesus refutes the charge of the Pharisees. His mission to the world is to vindicate the sacred claims of that law which they charge Him with breaking. If the law of God could have been changed or abrogated, then Christ need not have suffered the consequences of our transgression. He came to explain the relation of the law to man, and to illustrate its precepts by His own life of obedience.

God has given us His holy precepts, because He loves mankind. To shield us from the results of transgression, He reveals the principles of righteousness. The law is an expression of the thought of God; when received in Christ, it becomes our thought. It lifts us above the power of natural desires and tendencies, above temptations that lead to sin. God desires us to be happy, and He gave us the precepts of the law that in obeying them we might have joy. When at Jesus' birth the angels sang,—

"Glory to God in the highest,
And on earth peace, good will toward men" (Luke 2:14),

they were declaring the principles of the law which He had come to magnify and make honorable.

When the law was proclaimed from Sinai, God made known to men the holiness of His character, that by contrast they might see the sinfulness of their own. The law was given to convict them of sin, and reveal their need of a Saviour. It would do this as its principles were applied to the heart by the Holy Spirit. This work it is still to do. In the life of Christ the principles of the law are made plain; and as the Holy Spirit of God touches the heart, as the light of Christ reveals to men their need of His cleansing blood and His justifying righteousness, the law is still an agent in bringing us to Christ, that we may be justified by faith. "The law of the Lord is perfect, converting the soul." Ps. 19:7.

"Till heaven and earth pass," said Jesus, "one jot or one tittle shall in nowise pass from the law, till all be fulfilled." The sun shining in the heavens, the solid earth upon which you dwell, are God's witnesses that His law is changeless and eternal. Though they may pass away, the divine precepts shall endure. "It is easier for heaven and earth to pass, than one tittle of the law to fail." Luke 16:17. The system of types that pointed to Jesus as the Lamb of God was to be abolished at His death; but the precepts of the Decalogue are as immutable as the throne of God.

Since "the law of the Lord is perfect," every variation from it must be evil. Those who disobey the commandments of God, and teach others to do so, are condemned by Christ. The Saviour's life of obedience maintained the claims of the law; it proved that the law could be kept in humanity, and showed the excellence of character that obedience would develop. All who obey as He did are likewise declaring that the law is "holy, and just, and good." Rom. 7:12. On the other hand, all who break God's commandments are sustaining Satan's claim that the law is unjust, and cannot be obeyed. Thus they second the deceptions of the great adversary, and cast dishonor upon God. They are the children of the wicked one, who was the first rebel against God's law. To admit them into heaven would again bring in the elements of discord and rebellion, and imperil the well-being of the universe. No man who willfully disregards one principle of the law shall enter the kingdom of heaven.

The rabbis counted their righteousness a passport to heaven; but Jesus declared it to be insufficient and unworthy. External ceremonies and a theoretical knowledge of truth constituted Pharisaical righteousness. The rabbis claimed to be holy through their own efforts in keeping the law; but their works had divorced righteousness from religion. While they were punctilious in ritual observances, their lives were immoral and debased. Their so-called righteousness could never enter the kingdom of heaven.

The greatest deception of the human mind in Christ's day was that a mere assent to the truth constitutes righteousness. In all human experience a theoretical knowledge of the truth has been proved to be insufficient for the saving of the soul. It does not bring forth the fruits of righteousness. A jealous regard for what is termed theological truth often accompanies a hatred of genuine truth as made manifest in life. The darkest chapters of history are burdened with the record of crimes committed by bigoted religionists. The Pharisees claimed to be children of Abraham, and boasted of their possession of the oracles of God; yet these advantages did not preserve them from selfishness, malignity, greed for gain, and the basest hypocrisy. They thought themselves the greatest religionists of the world, but their so-called orthodoxy led them to crucify the Lord of glory.

The same danger still exists. Many take it for granted that they are Christians, simply because they subscribe to certain theological tenets. But they have not brought the truth into practical life. They have not believed and loved it, therefore they have not received the power and grace that come through sanctification of the truth. Men may profess faith in the truth; but if it does not make them sincere, kind, patient, forbearing, heavenly-minded, it is a curse to its possessors, and through their influence it is a curse to the world.

The righteousness which Christ taught is conformity of heart and life to the revealed will of God. Sinful men can become righteous only as they have faith in God and maintain a vital connection with Him. Then true godliness will elevate the thoughts and ennoble the life. Then the external forms of religion accord with the Christian's internal purity. Then the ceremonies required in the service of God are not meaningless rites, like those of the hypocritical Pharisees.

Jesus takes up the commandments separately, and explains the depth and breadth of their requirement. Instead of removing one jot of their force, He shows how far-reaching their principles are, and exposes the fatal mistake of the Jews in their outward show of obedience. He declares that by the evil thought or the lustful look the law of God is transgressed. One who becomes a party to the least injustice is breaking the law and degrading his own moral nature. Murder first exists in the mind. He who gives hatred a place in his heart is setting his feet in the path of the murderer, and his offerings are abhorrent to God.

The Jews cultivated a spirit of retaliation. In their hatred of the Romans they gave utterance to hard denunciations, and pleased the wicked one by manifesting his attributes. Thus they were training themselves to do the terrible deeds to which he led them on. In the religious life of the Pharisees there was nothing to recommend piety to the Gentiles. Jesus bade them not to deceive themselves with the thought that they could in heart rise up against their oppressors, and cherish the longing to avenge their wrongs.

It is true there is an indignation that is justifiable, even in the followers of Christ. When they see that God is dishonored, and His service brought into disrepute, when they see the innocent oppressed, a righteous indignation stirs the soul. Such anger, born of sensitive morals, is not a sin. But those who at any supposed provocation feel at liberty to indulge anger or resentment are opening the heart to Satan. Bitterness and animosity must be banished from the soul if we would be in harmony with heaven.

The Saviour goes farther than this. He says, "If thou bring thy gift to the altar, and there rememberest that thy brother hath aught against thee; leave there thy gift before the altar, and go thy way; first be reconciled to thy brother, and then come and offer thy gift." Many are zealous in religious services, while between them and their brethren are unhappy differences which they might reconcile. God requires them to do all in their power to restore harmony. Until they do this, He cannot accept their services. The Christian's duty in this matter is clearly pointed out.

God pours His blessings upon all. "He maketh His sun to rise on the evil and on the good, and sendeth rain on the just and on the unjust." He is "kind unto the unthankful and to the evil." Luke 6:35. He bids us to be like Him. "Bless them that curse you," said Jesus; "do good to them that hate you, . . . that ye may be the children of your Father which is in heaven." These are the principles of the law, and they are the wellsprings of life.

God's ideal for His children is higher than the highest human thought can reach. "Be ye therefore perfect, even as your Father which is in heaven is perfect." This command is a promise. The plan of redemption contemplates our complete recovery from the power of Satan. Christ always separates the contrite soul from sin. He came to destroy the works of the devil, and He has made provision that the Holy Spirit shall be imparted to every repentant soul, to keep him from sinning.

The tempter's agency is not to be accounted an excuse for one wrong act. Satan is jubilant when he hears the professed followers of Christ making excuses for their deformity of character. It is these excuses that lead to sin. There is no excuse for sinning. A holy temper, a Christlike life, is accessible to every repenting, believing child of God.

The ideal of Christian character is Christlikeness. As the Son of man was perfect in His life, so His followers are to be perfect in their life. Jesus was in all things made like unto His brethren. He became flesh, even as we are. He was hungry and thirsty and weary. He was sustained by food and refreshed by sleep. He shared the lot of man; yet He was the blameless Son of God. He was God in the flesh. His character is to be ours. The Lord says of those who believe in Him, "I will dwell in them, and walk in them; and I will be their God, and they shall be My people." 2 Cor. 6:16.

Christ is the ladder that Jacob saw, the base resting on the earth, and the topmost round reaching to the gate of heaven, to the very threshold of glory. If that ladder had failed by a single step of reaching the earth, we should have been lost. But Christ reaches us where we are. He took our nature and overcame, that we through taking His nature might overcome. Made "in the likeness of sinful flesh" (Rom. 8:3), He lived a sinless life. Now by His divinity He lays hold upon the throne of heaven, while by His humanity He reaches us. He bids us by faith in Him attain to the glory of the character of God. Therefore are we to be perfect, even as our "Father which is in heaven is perfect."

Jesus had shown in what righteousness consists, and had pointed to God as its source. Now He turned to practical duties. In almsgiving, in prayer, in fasting, He said, let nothing be done to attract attention or win praise to self. Give in sincerity, for the benefit of the suffering poor. In prayer, let the soul commune with God. In fasting, go not with the head bowed down, and heart filled with thoughts of self. The heart of the Pharisee is a barren and profitless soil, in which no seeds of divine life can flourish. It is he who yields himself most unreservedly to God that will render Him the most acceptable service. For through fellowship with God men become workers together with Him in presenting His character in humanity.

The service rendered in sincerity of heart has great recompense. "Thy Father which seeth in secret Himself shall reward thee openly." By the life we live through the grace of Christ the character is formed. The original loveliness begins to be restored to the soul. The attributes of the character of Christ are imparted, and the image of the Divine begins to shine forth. The faces of men and women who walk and work with God express the peace of heaven. They are surrounded with the atmosphere of heaven. For these souls the kingdom of God has begun. They have Christ's joy, the joy of being a blessing to humanity. They have the honor of being accepted for the Master's use; they are trusted to do His work in His name.

"No man can serve two masters." We cannot serve God with a divided heart. Bible religion is not one influence among many others; its influence is to be supreme, pervading and controlling every other. It is not to be like a dash of color brushed here and there upon the canvas, but it is to pervade the whole life, as if the canvas were dipped into the color, until every thread of the fabric were dyed a deep, unfading hue.

"If therefore thine eye be single, thy whole body shall be full of light. But if thine eye be evil, thy whole body shall be full of darkness." Purity and steadfastness of purpose are the conditions of receiving light from God. He who desires to know the truth must be willing to accept all that it reveals. He can make no compromise with error. To be wavering and halfhearted in allegiance to truth is to choose the darkness of error and satanic delusion.

Worldly policy and the undeviating principles of righteousness do not blend into each other imperceptibly, like the colors of the rainbow. Between the two a broad, clear line is drawn by the eternal God. The likeness of Christ stands out as distinct from that of Satan as midday in contrast with midnight. And only those who live the life of Christ are His co-workers. If one sin is cherished in the soul, or one wrong practice retained in the life, the whole being is contaminated. The man becomes an instrument of unrighteousness.

All who have chosen God's service are to rest in His care. Christ pointed to the birds flying in the heavens, to the flowers of the field, and bade His hearers consider these objects of God's creation. "Are not ye of much more value than they?" He said. Matt. 6:26, R. V. The measure of divine attention bestowed on any object is proportionate to its rank in the scale of being. The little brown sparrow is watched over by Providence. The flowers of the field, the grass that carpets the earth, share the notice and care of our heavenly Father. The great Master Artist has taken thought for the lilies, making them so beautiful that they outshine the glory of Solomon. How much more does He care for man, who is the image and glory of God. He longs to see His children reveal a character after His similitude. As the sunbeam imparts to the flowers their varied and delicate tints, so does God impart to the soul the beauty of His own character.

All who choose Christ's kingdom of love and righteousness and peace, making its interest paramount to all other, are linked to the world above, and every blessing needed for this life is theirs. In the book of God's providence, the volume of life, we are each given a page. That page contains every particular of our history; even the hairs of the head are numbered. God's children are never absent from His mind.

"Be not therefore anxious for the morrow." Matt. 6:34, R. V. We are to follow Christ day by day. God does not bestow help for tomorrow. He does not give His children all the directions for their life journey at once, lest they should become confused. He tells them just as much as they can remember and perform. The strength and wisdom imparted are for the present emergency. "If any of you lack wisdom,"—for today,—"let him ask of God, that giveth to all men liberally, and upbraideth not; and it shall be given him." James 1:5.

"Judge not, that ye be not judged." Do not think yourself better than other men, and set yourself up as their judge. Since you cannot discern motive, you are incapable of judging another. In criticizing him, you are passing sentence upon yourself; for you show that you are a participant with Satan, the accuser of the brethren. The Lord says, "Examine yourselves, whether ye be in the faith; prove your own selves." This is our work. "If we would judge ourselves, we should not be judged." 2 Cor. 13:5; 1 Cor. 11:31.

The good tree will produce good fruit. If the fruit is unpalatable and worthless, the tree is evil. So the fruit borne in the life testifies as to the condition of the heart and the excellence of the character. Good works can never purchase salvation, but they are an evidence of the faith that acts by love and purifies the soul. And though the eternal reward is not bestowed because of our merit, yet it will be in proportion to the work that has been done through the grace of Christ.

Thus Christ set forth the principles of His kingdom, and showed them to be the great rule of life. To impress the lesson He adds an illustration. It is not enough, He says, for you to hear My words. By obedience you must make them the foundation of your character. Self is but shifting sand. If you build upon human theories and inventions, your house will fall. By the winds of temptation, the tempests of trial, it will be swept away. But these principles that I have given will endure. Receive Me; build on My words.

"Everyone therefore which heareth these words of Mine, and doeth them, shall be likened unto a wise man, which built his house upon the rock: and the rain descended, and the floods came, and the winds blew, and beat upon that house; and it fell not: for it was founded upon the rock." Matt. 7:24, 25, R.V.

The Centurion

Christ had said to the nobleman whose son He healed, "Except ye see signs and wonders, ye will not believe." John 4:48. He was grieved that His own nation should require these outward signs of His Messiahship. Again and again He had marveled at their unbelief. But He marveled at the faith of the centurion who came to Him. The centurion did not question the Saviour's power. He did not even ask Him to come in person to perform the miracle. "Speak the word only," he said, "and my servant shall be healed."

The centurion's servant had been stricken with palsy, and lay at the point of death. Among the Romans the servants were slaves, bought and sold in the market places, and treated with abuse and cruelty; but the centurion was tenderly attached to his servant, and greatly desired his recovery. He believed that Jesus could heal him. He had not seen the Saviour, but the reports he heard had inspired him with faith. Notwithstanding the formalism of the Jews, this Roman was convinced that their religion was superior to his own. Already he had broken through the barriers of national prejudice and hatred that separated the conquerors from the conquered people. He had manifested respect for the service of God, and had shown kindness to the Jews as His worshipers. In the teaching of Christ, as it had been reported to him, he found that which met the need of the soul. All that was spiritual within him responded to the Saviour's words. But he felt unworthy to come into the presence of Jesus, and he appealed to the Jewish elders to make request for the healing of his servant. They were acquainted with the Great Teacher, and would, he thought, know how to approach Him so as to win His favor.

As Jesus entered Capernaum, He was met by a delegation of the elders, who told Him of the centurion's desire. They urged "that he was worthy for whom He should do this: for he loveth our nation, and he hath built us a synagogue."

Jesus immediately set out for the officer's home; but, pressed by the multitude, He advanced slowly. The news of His coming preceded Him, and the centurion, in his self-distrust, sent Him the message, "Lord, trouble not Thyself: for I am not worthy that Thou shouldest enter under my roof." But the Saviour kept on His way, and the centurion, venturing at last to approach Him, completed the message, saying, "Neither thought I myself worthy to come unto Thee;" "but speak the word only, and my servant shall be healed. For I am a man under authority, having soldiers under me: and I say to this man, Go, and he goeth; and to another, Come, and he cometh; and to my servant, Do this, and he doeth it." As I represent the power of Rome, and my soldiers recognize my authority as supreme, so dost Thou represent the power of the Infinite God, and all created things obey Thy word. Thou canst command the disease to depart, and it shall obey Thee. Thou canst summon Thy heavenly messengers, and they shall impart healing virtue. Speak but the word, and my servant shall be healed.

"When Jesus heard these things, He marveled at him, and turned Him about, and said unto the people that followed Him, I say unto you, I have not found so great faith, no, not in Israel." And to the centurion He said, "As thou hast believed, so be it done unto thee. And his servant was healed in the selfsame hour."

The Jewish elders who recommended the centurion to Christ had shown how far they were from possessing the spirit of the gospel. They did not recognize that our great need is our only claim on God's mercy. In their self-righteousness they commended the centurion because of the favor he had shown to "our nation." But the centurion said of himself, "I am not worthy." His heart had been touched by the grace of Christ. He saw his own unworthiness; yet he feared not to ask help. He trusted not to his own goodness; his argument was his great need. His faith took hold upon Christ in His true character. He did not believe in Him merely as a worker of miracles, but as the friend and Saviour of mankind.

It is thus that every sinner may come to Christ. "Not by works of righteousness which we have done, but according to His mercy He saved us." Titus 3:5. When Satan tells you that you are a sinner, and cannot hope to receive blessing from God, tell him that Christ came into the world to save sinners. We have nothing to recommend us to God; but the plea that we may urge now and ever is our utterly helpless condition that makes His redeeming power a necessity. Renouncing all self-dependence, we may look to the cross of Calvary and say,—

"In my hand no price I bring;
Simply to Thy cross I cling."

The Jews had been instructed from childhood concerning the work of the Messiah. The inspired utterances of patriarchs and prophets and the symbolic teaching of the sacrificial service had been theirs. But they had disregarded the light; and now they saw in Jesus nothing to be desired. But the centurion, born in heathenism, educated in the idolatry of imperial Rome, trained as a soldier, seemingly cut off from spiritual life by his education and surroundings, and still further shut out by the bigotry of the Jews, and by the contempt of his own countrymen for the people of Israel,—this man perceived the truth to which the children of Abraham were blinded. He did not wait to see whether the Jews themselves would receive the One who claimed to be their Messiah. As the "light, which lighteth every man that cometh into the world" (John 1:9) had shone upon him, he had, though afar off, discerned the glory of the Son of God.

To Jesus this was an earnest of the work which the gospel was to accomplish among the Gentiles. With joy He looked forward to the gathering of souls from all nations to His kingdom. With deep sadness He pictured to the Jews the result of their rejection of His grace: "I say unto you, That many shall come from the east and west, and shall sit down with Abraham, and Isaac, and Jacob, in the kingdom of heaven. But the children of the kingdom shall be cast out into outer darkness: there shall be weeping and gnashing of teeth." Alas, how many are still preparing for the same fatal disappointment! While souls in heathen darkness accept His grace, how many there are in Christian lands upon whom the light shines only to be disregarded.

More than twenty miles from Capernaum, on a tableland overlooking the wide, beautiful plain of Esdraelon, lay the village of Nain, and thither Jesus next bent His steps. Many of His disciples and others were with Him, and all along the way the people came, longing for His words of love and pity, bringing their sick for His healing, and ever with the hope that He who wielded such wondrous power would make Himself known as the King of Israel. A multitude thronged His steps, and it was a glad, expectant company that followed Him up the rocky path toward the gate of the mountain village.

As they draw near, a funeral train is seen coming from the gates. With slow, sad steps it is proceeding to the place of burial. On an open bier carried in front is the body of the dead, and about it are the mourners, filling the air with their wailing cries. All the people of the town seem to have gathered to show their respect for the dead and their sympathy with the bereaved.

It was a sight to awaken sympathy. The deceased was the only son of his mother, and she a widow. The lonely mourner was following to the grave her sole earthly support and comfort. "When the Lord saw her, He had compassion on her." As she moved on blindly, weeping, noting not His presence, He came close beside her, and gently said, "Weep not." Jesus was about to change her grief to joy, yet He could not forbear this expression of tender sympathy.

"He came and touched the bier;" to Him even contact with death could impart no defilement. The bearers stood still, and the lamentations of the mourners ceased. The two companies gathered about the bier, hoping against hope. One was present who had banished disease and vanquished demons; was death also subject to His power?

In clear, authoritative voice the words are spoken, "Young man, I say unto thee, Arise." That voice pierces the ears of the dead. The young man opens his eyes. Jesus takes him by the hand, and lifts him up. His gaze falls upon her who has been weeping beside him, and mother and son unite in a long, clinging, joyous embrace. The multitude look on in silence, as if spellbound. "There came a fear on all." Hushed and reverent they stood for a little time, as if in the very presence of God. Then they "glorified God, saying, That a great prophet is risen up among us; and, That God hath visited His people." The funeral train returned to Nain as a triumphal procession. "And this rumor of Him went forth throughout all Judea, and throughout all the region round about."

He who stood beside the sorrowing mother at the gate of Nain, watches with every mourning one beside the bier. He is touched with sympathy for our grief. His heart, that loved and pitied, is a heart of unchangeable tenderness. His word, that called the dead to life, is no less efficacious now than when spoken to the young man of Nain. He says, "All power is given unto Me in heaven and in earth." Matt. 28:18. That power is not diminished by the lapse of years, nor exhausted by the ceaseless activity of His overflowing grace. To all who believe on Him He is still a living Saviour.

Jesus changed the mother's grief to joy when He gave back her son; yet the youth was but called forth to this earthly life, to endure its sorrows, its toils, and its perils, and to pass again under the power of death. But Jesus comforts our sorrow for the dead with a message of infinite hope: "I am He that liveth, and was dead; and, behold, I am alive forevermore, . .

. and have the keys of hell and of death." "Forasmuch then as the children are partakers of flesh and blood, He also Himself likewise took part of the same; that through death He might destroy him that had the power of death, that is, the devil; and deliver them who through fear of death were all their lifetime subject to bondage." Rev. 1:18; Heb. 2:14, 15.

Satan cannot hold the dead in his grasp when the Son of God bids them live. He cannot hold in spiritual death one soul who in faith receives Christ's word of power. God is saying to all who are dead in sin, "Awake thou that sleepest, and arise from the dead." Eph. 5:14. That word is eternal life. As the word of God which bade the first man live, still gives us life; as Christ's word, "Young man, I say unto thee, Arise," gave life to the youth of Nain, so that word, "Arise from the dead," is life to the soul that receives it. God "hath delivered us from the power of darkness, and hath translated us into the kingdom of His dear Son." Col. 1:13. It is all offered us in His word. If we receive the word, we have the deliverance.

And "if the Spirit of Him that raised up Jesus from the dead dwell in you, He that raised up Christ from the dead shall also quicken your mortal bodies by His Spirit that dwelleth in you." "For the Lord Himself shall descend from heaven with a shout, with the voice of the Archangel, and with the trump of God: and the dead in Christ shall rise first: then we which are alive and remain shall be caught up together with them in the clouds, to meet the Lord in the air: and so shall we ever be with the Lord." Rom. 8:11; 1 Thess. 4:16, 17. This is the word of comfort wherewith He bids us comfort one another.

Who Are My Brethren?

The sons of Joseph were far from being in sympathy with Jesus in His work. The reports that reached them in regard to His life and labors filled them with astonishment and dismay. They heard that He devoted entire nights to prayer, that through the day He was thronged by great companies of people, and did not give Himself time so much as to eat. His friends felt that He was wearing Himself out by His incessant labor; they were unable to account for His attitude toward the Pharisees, and there were some who feared that His reason was becoming unsettled.

His brothers heard of this, and also of the charge brought by the Pharisees that He cast out devils through the power of Satan. They felt keenly the reproach that came upon them through their relation to Jesus. They knew what a tumult His words and works created, and were not only alarmed at His bold statements, but indignant at His denunciation of the scribes and Pharisees. They decided that He must be persuaded or constrained to cease this manner of labor, and they induced Mary to unite with them, thinking that through His love for her they might prevail upon Him to be more prudent.

It was just before this that Jesus had a second time performed the miracle of healing a man possessed, blind and dumb, and the Pharisees had reiterated the charge, "He casteth out devils through the prince of the devils." Matt. 9:34. Christ told them plainly that in attributing the work of the Holy Spirit to Satan, they were cutting themselves off from the fountain of blessing. Those who had spoken against Jesus Himself, not discerning His divine character, might receive forgiveness; for through the Holy Spirit they might be brought to see their error and repent. Whatever the sin, if the soul repents and believes, the guilt is washed away in the blood of Christ; but he who rejects the work of the Holy Spirit is placing himself where repentance and faith cannot come to him. It is by the Spirit that God works upon the heart; when men willfully reject the Spirit, and declare It to be from Satan, they cut off the channel by which God can communicate with them. When the Spirit is finally rejected, there is no more that God can do for the soul.

The Pharisees to whom Jesus spoke this warning did not themselves believe the charge they brought against Him. There was not one of those dignitaries but had felt drawn toward the Saviour. They had heard the Spirit's voice in their own hearts declaring Him to be the Anointed of Israel, and urging them to confess themselves His disciples. In the light of His presence they had realized their unholiness, and had longed for a righteousness which they could not create. But after their rejection of Him it would be too humiliating to receive Him as the Messiah. Having set their feet in the path of unbelief, they were too proud to confess their error. And in order to avoid acknowledging the truth, they tried with desperate violence to dispute the Saviour's teaching. The evidence of His power and mercy exasperated them. They could not prevent the Saviour from working miracles, they could not silence His teaching; but they did everything in their power to misrepresent Him and to falsify His words. Still the convicting Spirit of God followed them, and they had to build up many barriers in order to withstand its power. The mightiest agency that can be brought to bear upon the human heart was striving with them, but they would not yield.

It is not God that blinds the eyes of men or hardens their hearts. He sends them light to correct their errors, and to lead them in safe paths; it is by the rejection of this light that the eyes are blinded and the heart hardened. Often the process is gradual, and almost imperceptible. Light comes to the soul through God's word, through His servants, or by the direct agency of His Spirit; but when one ray of light is disregarded, there is a partial benumbing of the spiritual perceptions, and the second revealing of light is less clearly discerned. So the darkness increases, until it is night in the soul. Thus it had been with these Jewish leaders. They were convinced that a divine power attended Christ, but in order to resist the truth, they attributed the work of the Holy Spirit to Satan. In doing this they deliberately chose deception; they yielded themselves to Satan, and henceforth they were controlled by his power.

Closely connected with Christ's warning in regard to the sin against the Holy Spirit is a warning against idle and evil words. The words are an indication of that which is in the heart. "Out of the abundance of the heart the mouth speaketh." But the words are more than an indication of character; they have power to react on the character. Men are influenced by their own words. Often under a momentary impulse, prompted by Satan, they give utterance to jealousy or evil surmising, expressing that which they do not really believe; but the expression reacts on the thoughts. They are deceived by their words, and come to believe that true which was spoken at Satan's instigation. Having once expressed an opinion or decision, they are often too proud to retract it, and try to prove themselves in the right, until they come to believe that they are. It is dangerous to utter a word of doubt, dangerous to question and criticize divine light. The habit of careless and irreverent criticism reacts upon the character, in fostering irreverence and unbelief. Many a man indulging this habit has gone on unconscious of danger, until he was ready to criticize and reject the work of the Holy Spirit. Jesus said, "Every idle word that men shall speak, they shall give account thereof in the day of judgment. For by thy words thou shalt be justified, and by thy words thou shalt be condemned."

Then He added a warning to those who had been impressed by His words, who had heard Him gladly, but who had not surrendered themselves for the indwelling of the Holy Spirit. It is not only by resistance but by neglect that the soul is destroyed. "When the unclean spirit is gone out of a man," said Jesus, "he walketh through dry places, seeking rest, and findeth none. Then he saith, I will return into my house from whence I came out; and when he is come, he findeth it empty, swept, and garnished. Then goeth he, and taketh with himself seven other spirits more wicked than himself, and they enter in and dwell there."

There were many in Christ's day, as there are today, over whom the control of Satan for the time seemed broken; through the grace of God they were set free from the evil spirits that had held dominion over the soul. They rejoiced in the love of God; but, like the stony-ground hearers of the parable, they did not abide in His love. They did not surrender themselves to God daily, that Christ might dwell in the heart; and when the evil spirit returned, with "seven other spirits more wicked than himself," they were wholly dominated by the power of evil.

When the soul surrenders itself to Christ, a new power takes possession of the new heart. A change is wrought which man can never accomplish for himself. It is a supernatural work, bringing a supernatural element into human nature. The soul that is yielded to Christ becomes His own fortress, which He holds in a revolted world, and He intends that no authority shall be known in it but His own. A soul thus kept in possession by the heavenly agencies is impregnable to the assaults of Satan. But unless we do yield ourselves to the control of Christ, we shall be dominated by the wicked one. We must inevitably be under the control of the one or the other of the two great powers that are contending for the supremacy of the world. It is not necessary for us deliberately to choose the service of the kingdom of darkness in order to come under its dominion. We have only to neglect to ally ourselves with the kingdom of light. If we do not co-operate with the heavenly agencies, Satan will take possession of the heart, and will make it his abiding place. The only defense against evil is the indwelling of Christ in the heart through faith in His righteousness. Unless we become vitally connected with God, we can never resist the unhallowed effects of self-love, self-indulgence, and temptation to sin. We may leave off many bad habits, for the time we may part company with Satan; but without a vital connection with God, through the surrender of ourselves to Him moment by moment, we shall be overcome. Without a personal acquaintance with Christ, and a continual communion, we are at the mercy of the enemy, and shall do his bidding in the end.

"The last state of that man is worse than the first. Even so," said Jesus, "shall it be also unto this wicked generation." There are none so hardened as those who have slighted the invitation of mercy, and done despite to the Spirit of grace. The most common manifestation of the sin against the Holy Spirit is in persistently slighting Heaven's invitation to repent. Every step in the rejection of Christ is a step toward the rejection of salvation, and toward the sin against the Holy Spirit.

In rejecting Christ the Jewish people committed the unpardonable sin; and by refusing the invitation of mercy, we may commit the same error. We offer insult to the Prince of life, and put Him to shame before the synagogue of Satan and before the heavenly universe when we refuse to listen to His delegated messengers, and instead listen to the agents of Satan, who would draw the soul away from Christ. So long as one does this, he can find no hope or pardon, and he will finally lose all desire to be reconciled to God.

While Jesus was still teaching the people, His disciples brought the message that His mother and His brothers were without, and desired to see Him. He knew what was in their hearts, and "He answered and said unto him that told Him, Who is My mother? and who are My brethren? And He stretched forth His hand toward His disciples, and said, Behold My mother and My brethren! For whosoever shall do the will of My Father which is in heaven, the same is My brother, and sister, and mother."

All who would receive Christ by faith were united to Him by a tie closer than that of human kinship. They would become one with Him, as He was one with the Father. As a believer and doer of His words, His mother was more nearly and savingly related to Him than through her natural relationship. His brothers would receive no benefit from their connection with Him unless they accepted Him as their personal Saviour.

What a support Christ would have found in His earthly relatives if they had believed in Him as one from heaven, and had co-operated with Him in doing the work of God! Their unbelief cast a shadow over the earthly life of Jesus. It was a part of the bitterness of that cup of woe which He drained for us.

The enmity kindled in the human heart against the gospel was keenly felt by the Son of God, and it was most painful to Him in His home; for His own heart was full of kindness and love, and He appreciated tender regard in the family relation. His brothers desired that He should concede to their ideas, when such a course would have been utterly out of harmony with His divine mission. They looked upon Him as in need of their counsel. They judged Him from their human point of view, and thought that if He would speak only such things as would be acceptable to the scribes and Pharisees, He would avoid the disagreeable controversy that His words aroused. They thought that He was beside Himself in claiming divine authority, and in placing Himself before the rabbis as a reprover of their sins. They knew that the Pharisees were seeking occasion to accuse Him, and they felt that He had given them sufficient occasion.

With their short measuring line they could not fathom the mission which He came to fulfill, and therefore could not sympathize with Him in His trials. Their coarse, unappreciative words showed that they had no true perception of His character, and did not discern that the divine blended with the human. They often saw Him full of grief; but instead of comforting Him, their spirit and words only wounded His heart. His sensitive nature was tortured, His motives were misunderstood, His work was uncomprehended.

His brothers often brought forward the philosophy of the Pharisees, which was threadbare and hoary with age, and presumed to think that they could teach Him who understood all truth, and comprehended all mysteries. They freely condemned that which they could not understand. Their reproaches probed Him to the quick, and His soul was wearied and distressed. They avowed faith in God, and thought they were vindicating God, when God was with them in the flesh, and they knew Him not.

These things made His path a thorny one to travel. So pained was Christ by the misapprehension in His own home that it was a relief to Him to go where it did not exist. There was one home that He loved to visit,—the home of Lazarus, and Mary, and Martha; for in the atmosphere of faith and love His spirit had rest. Yet there were none on earth who could comprehend His divine mission, or know the burden which He bore in behalf of humanity. Often He could find relief only in being alone, and communing with His heavenly Father.

Those who are called to suffer for Christ's sake, who have to endure misapprehension and distrust, even in their own home, may find comfort in the thought that Jesus has endured the same. He is moved with compassion for them. He bids them find companionship in Him, and relief where He found it, in communion with the Father.

Those who accept Christ as their personal Saviour are not left as orphans, to bear the trials of life alone. He receives them as members of the heavenly family; He bids them call His Father their Father. They are His "little ones," dear to the heart of God, bound to Him by the most tender and abiding

ties. He has toward them an exceeding tenderness, as far surpassing what our father or mother has felt toward us in our helplessness as the divine is above the human.

Of Christ's relation to His people, there is a beautiful illustration in the laws given to Israel. When through poverty a Hebrew had been forced to part with his patrimony, and to sell himself as a bondservant, the duty of redeeming him and his inheritance fell to the one who was nearest of kin. See Lev. 25:25, 47-49; Ruth 2:20. So the work of redeeming us and our inheritance, lost through sin, fell upon Him who is "near of kin" unto us. It was to redeem us that He became our kinsman. Closer than father, mother, brother, friend, or lover is the Lord our Saviour. "Fear not," He says, "for I have redeemed thee, I have called thee by thy name; thou art Mine." "Since thou wast precious in My sight, thou hast been honorable, and I have loved thee: therefore will I give men for thee, and people for thy life." Isa. 43:1, 4.

Christ loves the heavenly beings that surround His throne; but what shall account for the great love wherewith He has loved us? We cannot understand it, but we can know it true in our own experience. And if we do hold the relation of kinship to Him, with what tenderness should we regard those who are brethren and sisters of our Lord! Should we not be quick to recognize the claims of our divine relationship? Adopted into the family of God, should we not honor our Father and our kindred?

The Invitation

"Come unto Me, all ye that labor and are heavy-laden, and I will give you rest."

These words of comfort were spoken to the multitude that followed Jesus. The Saviour had said that only through Himself could men receive a knowledge of God. He had spoken of His disciples as the ones to whom a knowledge of heavenly things had been given. But He left none to feel themselves shut out from His care and love. All who labor and are heavy-laden may come unto Him.

Scribes and rabbis, with their punctilious attention to religious forms, had a sense of want that rites of penance could never satisfy. Publicans and sinners might pretend to be content with the sensual and earthly, but in their hearts were distrust and fear. Jesus looked upon the distressed and heart burdened, those whose hopes were blighted, and who with earthly joys were seeking to quiet the longing of the soul, and He invited all to find rest in Him.

Tenderly He bade the toiling people, "Take My yoke upon you, and learn of Me; for I am meek and lowly in heart: and ye shall find rest unto your souls."

In these words Christ is speaking to every human being. Whether they know it or not, all are weary and heavy-laden. All are weighed down with burdens that only Christ can remove. The heaviest burden that we bear is the burden of sin. If we were left to bear this burden, it would crush us. But the Sinless One has taken our place. "The Lord hath laid on

Him the iniquity of us all." Isa. 53:6. He has borne the burden of our guilt. He will take the load from our weary shoulders. He will give us rest. The burden of care and sorrow also He will bear. He invites us to cast all our care upon Him; for He carries us upon His heart.

The Elder Brother of our race is by the eternal throne. He looks upon every soul who is turning his face toward Him as the Saviour. He knows by experience what are the weaknesses of humanity, what are our wants, and where lies the strength of our temptations; for He was in all points tempted like as we are, yet without sin. He is watching over you, trembling child of God. Are you tempted? He will deliver. Are you weak? He will strengthen. Are you ignorant? He will enlighten. Are you wounded? He will heal. The Lord "telleth the number of the stars;" and yet "He healeth the broken in heart, and bindeth up their wounds." Ps. 147:4, 3. "Come unto Me," is His invitation. Whatever your anxieties and trials, spread out your case before the Lord. Your spirit will be braced for endurance. The way will be opened for you to disentangle yourself from embarrassment and difficulty. The weaker and more helpless you know yourself to be, the stronger will you become in His strength. The heavier your burdens, the more blessed the rest in casting them upon the Burden Bearer. The rest that Christ offers depends upon conditions, but these conditions are plainly specified. They are those with which all can comply. He tells us just how His rest is to be found.

"Take My yoke upon you," Jesus says. The yoke is an instrument of service. Cattle are yoked for labor, and the yoke is essential that they may labor effectually. By this illustration Christ teaches us that we are called to service as long as life shall last. We are to take upon us His yoke, that we may be co-workers with Him.

The yoke that binds to service is the law of God. The great law of love revealed in Eden, proclaimed upon Sinai, and in the new covenant written in the heart, is that which binds the human worker to the will of God. If we were left to follow our own inclinations, to go just where our will would lead us, we should fall into Satan's ranks and become possessors of his attributes. Therefore God confines us to His will, which is high, and noble, and elevating. He desires that we shall patiently and wisely take up the duties of service. The yoke of service Christ Himself has borne in humanity. He said, "I delight to do Thy will, O My God: yea, Thy law is within My heart." Ps. 40:8. "I came down from heaven, not to do Mine own will, but the will of Him that sent Me." John 6:38. Love for God, zeal for His glory, and love for fallen humanity, brought Jesus to earth to suffer and to die. This was the controlling power of His life. This principle He bids us adopt.

There are many whose hearts are aching under a load of care because they seek to reach the world's standard. They have chosen its service, accepted its perplexities, adopted its customs. Thus their character is marred, and their life made a weariness. In order to gratify ambition and worldly desires, they wound the conscience, and bring upon themselves an additional burden of remorse. The continual worry is wearing out the life forces. Our Lord desires them to lay aside this yoke of bondage. He invites them to accept His yoke; He says, "My yoke is easy, and My burden is light." He bids them seek first the kingdom of God and His righteousness, and His promise is that all things needful to them for this life shall be added. Worry is blind, and cannot discern the future; but Jesus sees the end from the beginning. In every difficulty He has His way prepared to bring relief. Our heavenly Father has a thousand ways to provide for us, of which we know nothing. Those who accept the one principle of making the service and honor of God supreme will find perplexities vanish, and a plain path before their feet.

"Learn of Me," says Jesus; "for I am meek and lowly in heart: and ye shall find rest." We are to enter the school of Christ, to learn from Him meekness and lowliness. Redemption is that process by which the soul is trained for heaven. This training means a knowledge of Christ. It means emancipation from ideas, habits, and practices that have been gained in the school of the prince of darkness. The soul must be delivered from all that is opposed to loyalty to God.

In the heart of Christ, where reigned perfect harmony with God, there was perfect peace. He was never elated by applause, nor dejected by censure or disappointment. Amid the greatest opposition and the most cruel treatment, He was still of good courage. But many who profess to be His followers have an anxious, troubled heart, because they are afraid to trust themselves with God. They do not make a complete surrender to Him; for they shrink from the consequences that such a surrender may involve. Unless they do make this surrender, they cannot find peace.

It is the love of self that brings unrest. When we are born from above, the same mind will be in us that was in Jesus, the mind that led Him to humble Himself that we might be saved. Then we shall not be seeking the highest place. We shall desire to sit at the feet of Jesus, and learn of Him. We shall understand that the value of our work does not consist in making a show and noise in the world, and in being active and zealous in our own strength. The value of our work is in proportion to the impartation of the Holy Spirit. Trust in God brings holier qualities of mind, so that in patience we may possess our souls.

The yoke is placed upon the oxen to aid them in drawing the load, to lighten the burden. So with the yoke of Christ. When our will is swallowed up in the will of God, and we use His gifts to bless others, we shall find life's burden light. He who walks in the way of God's commandments is walking in company with Christ, and in His love the heart is at rest. When Moses prayed, "Show me now Thy way, that I may know Thee," the Lord answered him, "My presence shall go with thee, and I will give thee rest." And through the prophets the message was given, "Thus saith the Lord, Stand ye in the ways, and see, and ask for the old paths, where is the good way, and walk therein, and ye shall find rest for your souls." Ex. 33:13, 14; Jer. 6:16. And He says, "O that thou hadst hearkened to My commandments! then had thy peace been as a river, and thy righteousness as the waves of the sea." Isa. 48:18.

Those who take Christ at His word, and surrender their souls to His keeping, their lives to His ordering, will find peace and quietude. Nothing of the world can make them sad when Jesus makes them glad by His presence. In perfect acquiescence there is perfect rest. The Lord says, "Thou wilt keep him in perfect peace, whose mind is stayed on Thee: because he trusteth in Thee." Isa. 26:3. Our lives may seem a tangle; but as we commit ourselves to the wise Master Worker, He will bring out the pattern of life and character that will be to His own glory. And that character which expresses the glory—character—of Christ will be received into the Paradise of God. A renovated race shall walk with Him in white, for they are worthy.

As through Jesus we enter into rest, heaven begins here. We respond to His invitation, Come, learn of Me, and in thus coming we begin the life eternal. Heaven is a ceaseless approaching to God through Christ. The longer we are in the heaven of bliss, the more and still more of glory will be opened to us; and the more we know of God, the more intense will be our happiness. As we walk with Jesus in this life, we may be filled with His love, satisfied with His presence. All that human nature can bear, we may receive here. But what is this compared with the hereafter? There "are they before the throne of God, and serve Him day and night in His temple: and He that sitteth on the throne shall dwell among them. They shall hunger no more, neither thirst any more; neither shall the sun light on them, nor any heat. For the Lamb which is in the midst of the throne shall feed them, and shall lead them unto living fountains of waters: and God shall wipe away all tears from their eyes." Rev. 7:15-17.

"Peace, Be Still"

It had been an eventful day in the life of Jesus. Beside the Sea of Galilee He had spoken His first parables, by familiar illustrations again explaining to the people the nature of His kingdom and the manner in which it was to be established. He had likened His own work to that of the sower; the development of His kingdom to the growth of the mustard seed and the effect of leaven in the measure of meal. The great final separation of the righteous and the wicked He had pictured in the parables of the wheat and tares and the fishing net. The exceeding preciousness of the truths He taught had been illustrated by the hidden treasure and the pearl of great price, while in the parable of the householder He taught His disciples how they were to labor as His representatives.

All day He had been teaching and healing; and as evening came on the crowds still pressed upon Him. Day after day He had ministered to them, scarcely pausing for food or rest. The malicious criticism and misrepresentation with which the Pharisees constantly pursued Him made His labors much more severe and harassing; and now the close of the day found Him so utterly wearied that He determined to seek retirement in some solitary place across the lake.

The eastern shore of Gennesaret was not uninhabited, for there were towns here and there beside the lake; yet it was a desolate region when compared with the western side. It contained a population more heathen than Jewish, and had little communication with Galilee. Thus it offered Jesus the seclusion He sought, and He now bade His disciples accompany Him thither.

After He had dismissed the multitude, they took Him, even "as He was," into the boat, and hastily set off. But they were not to depart alone. There were other fishing boats lying near the shore, and these were quickly crowded with people who followed Jesus, eager still to see and hear Him.

The Saviour was at last relieved from the pressure of the multitude, and, overcome with weariness and hunger, He lay down in the stern of the boat, and soon fell asleep. The evening had been calm and pleasant, and quiet rested upon the lake; but suddenly darkness overspread the sky, the wind swept wildly down the mountain gorges along the eastern shore, and a fierce tempest burst upon the lake.

The sun had set, and the blackness of night settled down upon the stormy sea. The waves, lashed into fury by the howling winds, dashed fiercely over the disciples' boat, and threatened to engulf it. Those hardy fishermen had spent their lives upon the lake, and had guided their craft safely through many a storm; but now their strength and skill availed nothing. They were helpless in the grasp of the tempest, and hope failed them as they saw that their boat was filling.

Absorbed in their efforts to save themselves, they had forgotten that Jesus was on board. Now, seeing their labor vain and only death before them, they remembered at whose command they had set out to cross the sea. In Jesus was their only hope. In their helplessness and despair they cried, "Master, Master!" But the dense darkness hid Him from their sight. Their voices were drowned by the roaring of the tempest, and there was no reply. Doubt and fear assailed them. Had Jesus forsaken them? Was He who had conquered disease and demons, and even death, powerless to help His disciples now? Was He unmindful of them in their distress?

Again they call, but there is no answer except the shrieking of the angry blast. Already their boat is sinking. A moment, and apparently they will be swallowed up by the hungry waters.

Suddenly a flash of lightning pierces the darkness, and they see Jesus lying asleep, undisturbed by the tumult. In amazement and despair they exclaim, "Master, carest Thou not that we perish?" How can He rest so peacefully, while they are in danger and battling with death?

Their cry arouses Jesus. As the lightning's glare reveals Him, they see the peace of heaven in His face; they read in His glance self-forgetful, tender love, and, their hearts turning to Him, cry, "Lord, save us: we perish."

Never did a soul utter that cry unheeded. As the disciples grasp their oars to make a last effort, Jesus rises. He stands in the midst of His disciples, while the tempest rages, the waves break over them, and the lightning illuminates His countenance. He lifts His hand, so often employed in deeds of mercy, and says to the angry sea, "Peace, be still."

The storm ceases. The billows sink to rest. The clouds roll away, and the stars shine forth. The boat rests upon a quiet sea. Then turning to His disciples, Jesus asks sorrowfully, "Why are ye fearful? have ye not yet faith?" Mark 4:40, R.V.

A hush fell upon the disciples. Even Peter did not attempt to express the awe that filled his heart. The boats that had set out to accompany Jesus had been in the same peril with that of the disciples. Terror and despair had seized their occupants; but the command of Jesus brought quiet to the scene of tumult. The fury of the storm had driven the boats into close proximity, and all on board beheld the miracle. In the calm that followed, fear was forgotten. The people whispered among themselves, "What manner of man is this, that even the winds and the sea obey Him?"

When Jesus was awakened to meet the storm, He was in perfect peace. There was no trace of fear in word or look, for no fear was in His heart. But He rested not in the possession of almighty power. It was not as the "Master of earth and sea and sky" that He reposed in quiet. That power He had laid down, and He says, "I can of Mine own self do nothing." John 5:30. He trusted in the Father's might. It was in faith—faith in God's love and care—that Jesus rested, and the power of that word which stilled the storm was the power of God.

As Jesus rested by faith in the Father's care, so we are to rest in the care of our Saviour. If the disciples had trusted in Him, they would have been kept in peace. Their fear in the time of danger revealed their unbelief. In their efforts to save themselves, they forgot Jesus; and it was only when, in despair of self-dependence, they turned to Him that He could give them help.

How often the disciples', experience is ours! When the tempests of temptation gather, and the fierce lightnings flash, and the waves sweep over us, we battle with the storm alone, forgetting that there is One who can help us. We trust to our own strength till our hope is lost, and we are ready to perish. Then we remember Jesus, and if we call upon Him to save us, we shall not cry in vain. Though He sorrowfully reproves our unbelief and self-confidence, He never fails to give us the help we need. Whether on the land or on the sea, if we have the Saviour in our hearts, there is no need of fear. Living faith in the Redeemer will smooth the sea of life, and will deliver us from danger in the way that He knows to be best.

There is another spiritual lesson in this miracle of the stilling of the tempest. Every man's experience testifies to the truth of the words of Scripture, "The wicked are like the troubled sea, when it cannot rest. . . . There is no peace, saith my God, to the wicked." Isa. 57:20, 21. Sin has destroyed our peace. While self is unsubdued, we can find no rest. The masterful passions of the heart no human power can control. We are as helpless here as were the disciples to quiet the raging storm. But He who spoke peace to the billows of Galilee has spoken the word of peace for every soul. However fierce the tempest, those who turn to Jesus with the cry, "Lord, save us," will find deliverance. His grace, that reconciles the soul to God, quiets the strife of human passion, and in His love the heart is at rest. "He maketh the storm a calm, so that the waves thereof are still. Then are they glad because they be quiet; so He bringeth them unto their desired haven." Ps. 107:29, 30. "Being justified by faith, we have peace with God through our Lord Jesus Christ." "The work of righteousness shall be peace; and the effect of righteousness quietness and assurance forever." Rom. 5:1; Isa. 32:17.

In the early morning the Saviour and His companions came to shore, and the light of the rising sun touched sea and land as with the benediction of peace. But no sooner had they stepped upon the beach than their eyes were greeted by a sight more terrible than the fury of the tempest. From some hiding place among the tombs, two madmen rushed upon them as if to tear them in pieces. Hanging about these men were parts of chains which they had broken in escaping from confinement. Their flesh was torn and bleeding where they had cut themselves with sharp stones. Their eyes glared out from their long and matted hair, the very likeness of humanity seemed to have been blotted out by the demons that possessed them, and they looked more like wild beasts than like men.

The disciples and their companions fled in terror; but presently they noticed that Jesus was not with them, and they turned to look for Him. He was standing where they had left Him. He who had stilled the tempest, who had before met Satan and conquered him, did not flee before these demons. When the men, gnashing their teeth, and foaming at the mouth, approached Him, Jesus raised that hand which had beckoned the waves to rest, and the men could come no nearer. They stood raging but helpless before Him.

With authority He bade the unclean spirits come out of them. His words penetrated the darkened minds of the unfortunate men. They realized dimly that One was near who could save them from the tormenting demons. They fell at the Saviour's feet to worship Him; but when their lips were opened to entreat His mercy, the demons spoke through them, crying vehemently, "What have I to do with Thee, Jesus, Thou Son of God most high? I beseech Thee, torment me not."

Jesus asked, "What is thy name?" And the answer was, "My name is Legion: for we are many." Using the afflicted men as mediums of communication, they besought Jesus not to send them out of the country. Upon a mountainside not far distant a great herd of swine was feeding. Into these the demons asked to be allowed to enter, and Jesus suffered them. Immediately a panic seized the herd. They rushed madly down the cliff, and, unable to check themselves upon the shore, plunged into the lake, and perished.

Meanwhile a marvelous change had come over the demoniacs. Light had shone into their minds. Their eyes beamed with intelligence. The countenances, so long deformed into the image of Satan, became suddenly mild, the bloodstained hands were quiet, and with glad voices the men praised God for their deliverance.

From the cliff the keepers of the swine had seen all that had occurred, and they hurried away to publish the news to their employers and to all the people. In fear and amazement the whole population flocked to meet Jesus. The two demoniacs had been the terror of the country. No one had been safe to pass the place where they were; for they would rush upon every traveler with the fury of demons. Now these men were clothed and in their right mind, sitting at the feet of Jesus, listening to His words, and glorifying the name of Him who had made them whole. But the people who beheld this wonderful scene did not rejoice. The loss of the swine seemed to them of greater moment than the deliverance of these captives of Satan.

It was in mercy to the owners of the swine that this loss had been permitted to come upon them. They were absorbed in earthly things, and cared not for the great interests of spiritual life. Jesus desired to break the spell of selfish indifference, that they might accept His grace. But regret and indignation for their temporal loss blinded their eyes to the Saviour's mercy.

The manifestation of supernatural power aroused the superstitions of the people, and excited their fears. Further calamities might follow from having this Stranger among them. They apprehended financial ruin, and determined to be freed from His presence. Those who had crossed the lake with Jesus told of all that had happened on the preceding night, of their peril in the tempest, and how the wind and the sea had been stilled. But their words were without effect. In terror the people thronged about Jesus, beseeching Him to depart from them, and He complied, taking ship at once for the opposite shore.

The people of Gergesa had before them the living evidence of Christ's power and mercy. They saw the men who had been restored to reason; but they were so fearful of endangering their earthly interests that He who had vanquished the prince of darkness before their eyes was treated as an intruder, and the Gift of heaven was turned from their doors. We have not the opportunity of turning from the person of Christ as had the Gergesenes; but still there are many who refuse to obey His word, because obedience would involve the sacrifice of some worldly interest. Lest His presence shall cause them pecuniary loss, many reject His grace, and drive His Spirit from them.

But far different was the feeling of the restored demoniacs. They desired the company of their deliverer. In His presence they felt secure from the demons that had tormented their lives and wasted their manhood. As Jesus was about to enter the boat, they kept close to His side, knelt at His feet, and begged Him to keep them near Him, where they might ever listen to His words. But Jesus bade them go home and tell what great things the Lord had done for them.

Here was a work for them to do,—to go to a heathen home, and tell of the blessing they had received from Jesus. It was hard for them to be separated from the Saviour. Great difficulties were sure to beset them in association with their heathen countrymen. And their long isolation from society seemed to have disqualified them for the work He had indicated. But as soon as Jesus pointed out their duty they were ready to obey. Not only did they tell their own households and neighbors about Jesus, but they went throughout Decapolis, everywhere declaring His power to save, and describing how He had freed them from the demons. In doing this work they could receive a greater blessing than if, merely for benefit to themselves, they had remained in His presence. It is in working to spread the good news of salvation that we are brought near to the Saviour.

The two restored demoniacs were the first missionaries whom Christ sent to preach the gospel in the region of Decapolis. For a few moments only these men had been privileged to hear the teachings of Christ. Not one sermon from His lips had ever fallen upon their ears. They could not instruct the people as the disciples who had been daily with Christ were able to do. But they bore in their own persons the evidence that Jesus was the Messiah. They could tell what they knew; what they themselves had seen, and heard, and felt of the power of Christ. This is what everyone can do whose heart has been touched by the grace of God. John, the beloved disciple, wrote: "That which was from the beginning, which we have heard, which we have seen with our eyes, which we have looked upon, and our hands have handled, of the Word of life; . . . that which we have seen and heard declare we unto you." 1 John 1:1-3. As witnesses for Christ, we are to tell what we know, what we ourselves have seen and heard and felt. If we have been following Jesus step by step, we shall have something right to the point to tell concerning the way in which He has led us. We can tell how we have tested His promise, and found the promise true. We can bear witness to what we have known of the grace of Christ. This is the witness for which our Lord calls, and for want of which the world is perishing.

Though the people of Gergesa had not received Jesus, He did not leave them to the darkness they had chosen. When they bade Him depart from them, they had not heard His words. They were ignorant of that which they were rejecting. Therefore He again sent the light to them, and by those to whom they would not refuse to listen.

In causing the destruction of the swine, it was Satan's purpose to turn the people away from the Saviour, and prevent the preaching of the gospel in that region. But this very occurrence roused the whole country as nothing else could have done, and directed attention to Christ. Though the Saviour Himself departed, the men whom He had healed remained as witnesses to His power. Those who had been mediums of the prince of darkness became channels of light, messengers of the Son of God. Men marveled as they listened to the wondrous news. A door was opened to the gospel throughout that region. When Jesus returned to Decapolis, the people flocked about Him, and for three days, not merely the inhabitants of one town, but thousands from all the surrounding region, heard the message of salvation. Even the power of demons is under the control of our Saviour, and the working of evil is overruled for good.

The encounter with the demoniacs of Gergesa had a lesson for the disciples. It showed the depths of degradation to which Satan is seeking to drag the whole human race, and the mission of Christ to set men free from his power. Those wretched beings, dwelling in the place of graves, possessed by demons, in bondage to uncontrolled passions and loathsome lusts, represent what humanity would become if given up to satanic jurisdiction. Satan's influence is constantly exerted upon men to distract the senses, control the mind for evil, and incite to violence and crime. He weakens the body, darkens the intellect, and debases the soul. Whenever men reject the Saviour's invitation, they are yielding themselves to Satan. Multitudes in every department in life, in the home, in business, and even in the church, are doing this today. It is because of this that violence and crime have overspread the earth, and moral darkness, like the pall of death, enshrouds the habitations of men. Through his specious temptations Satan leads men to worse and worse evils, till utter depravity and ruin are the result. The only safeguard against his power is found in the presence of Jesus. Before men and angels Satan has been revealed as man's enemy and destroyer; Christ, as man's friend and deliverer. His Spirit will develop in man all that will ennoble the character and dignify the nature. It will build man up for the glory of God in body and soul and spirit. "For God hath not given us the spirit of fear; but of power, and of love, and of a sound mind." 2 Tim. 1:7. He has called us "to the obtaining of the glory"—character—"of our Lord Jesus Christ;" has called us to be "conformed to the image of His Son." 2 Thess. 2:14; Rom. 8:29.

And souls that have been degraded into instruments of Satan are still through the power of Christ transformed into messengers of righteousness, and sent forth by the Son of God to tell what "great things the Lord hath done for thee, and hath had compassion on thee."

The Touch of Faith

Returning from Gergesa to the western shore, Jesus found a multitude gathered to receive Him, and they greeted Him with joy. He remained by the seaside for a time, teaching and healing, and then repaired to the house of Levi-Matthew to meet the publicans at the feast. Here Jairus, the ruler of the synagogue, found Him.

This elder of the Jews came to Jesus in great distress, and cast himself at His feet, exclaiming, "My little daughter lieth at the point of death: I pray Thee, come and lay Thy hands on her, that she may be healed; and she shall live."

Jesus set out at once with the ruler for his home. Though the disciples had seen so many of His works of mercy, they were surprised at His compliance with the entreaty of the haughty rabbi; yet they accompanied their Master, and the people followed, eager and expectant.

The ruler's house was not far distant, but Jesus and His companions advanced slowly, for the crowd pressed Him on every side. The anxious father was impatient of delay; but Jesus, pitying the people, stopped now and then to relieve some suffering one, or to comfort a troubled heart.

While they were still on the way, a messenger pressed through the crowd, bearing to Jairus the news that his daughter was dead, and it was useless to trouble the Master further. The word caught the ear of Jesus. "Fear not," He said; "believe only, and she shall be made whole."

Jairus pressed closer to the Saviour, and together they hurried to the ruler's home. Already the hired mourners and flute players were there, filling the air with their clamor. The presence of the crowd, and the tumult jarred upon the spirit of Jesus. He tried to silence them, saying, "Why make ye this ado, and weep? the damsel is not dead, but sleepeth." They were indignant at the words of the Stranger. They had seen the child in the embrace of death, and they laughed Him to scorn. Requiring them all to leave the house, Jesus took with Him the father and mother of the maiden, and the three disciples, Peter, James, and John, and together they entered the chamber of death.

Jesus approached the bedside, and, taking the child's hand in His own, He pronounced softly, in the familiar language of her home, the words, "Damsel, I say unto thee, arise."

Instantly a tremor passed through the unconscious form. The pulses of life beat again. The lips unclosed with a smile. The eyes opened widely as if from sleep, and the maiden gazed with wonder on the group beside her. She arose, and her parents clasped her in their arms, and wept for joy.

On the way to the ruler's house, Jesus had met, in the crowd, a poor woman who for twelve years had suffered from a disease that made her life a burden. She had spent all her means upon physicians and remedies, only to be pronounced incurable. But her hopes revived when she heard of the cures that Christ performed. She felt assured that if she could only go to Him she would be healed. In weakness and suffering she came to the seaside where He was teaching, and tried to press through the crowd, but in vain. Again she followed Him from the house of Levi-Matthew, but was still unable to reach Him. She had begun to despair, when, in making His way through the multitude, He came near where she was.

The golden opportunity had come. She was in the presence of the Great Physician! But amid the confusion she could not speak to Him, nor catch more than a passing glimpse of His figure. Fearful of losing her one chance of relief, she pressed forward, saying to herself, "If I may but touch His garment, I shall be whole." As He was passing, she reached forward, and succeeded in barely touching the border of His garment. But in that moment she knew that she was healed. In that one touch was concentrated the faith of her life, and instantly her pain and feebleness gave place to the vigor of perfect health.

With a grateful heart she then tried to withdraw from the crowd; but suddenly Jesus stopped, and the people halted with Him. He turned, and looking about asked in a voice distinctly heard above the confusion of the multitude, "Who touched Me?" The people answered this query with a look of amazement. Jostled upon all sides, and rudely pressed hither and thither, as He was, it seemed a strange inquiry.

Peter, ever ready to speak, said, "Master, the multitude throng Thee and press Thee, and sayest Thou, Who touched Me?" Jesus answered, "Somebody hath touched Me: for I perceive that virtue is gone out of Me." The Saviour could distinguish the touch of faith from the casual contact of the careless throng. Such trust should not be passed without comment. He would speak to the humble woman words of comfort that would be to her a wellspring of joy,—words that would be a blessing to His followers to the close of time.

Looking toward the woman, Jesus insisted on knowing who had touched Him. Finding concealment vain, she came forward tremblingly, and cast herself at His feet. With grateful tears she told the story of her suffering, and how she had found relief. Jesus gently said, "Daughter, be of good comfort: thy faith hath made thee whole; go in peace." He gave no opportunity for superstition to claim healing virtue for the mere act of touching His garments. It was not through the outward contact with Him, but through the faith which took hold on His divine power, that the cure was wrought.

The wondering crowd that pressed close about Christ realized no accession of vital power. But when the suffering woman put forth her hand to touch Him, believing that she would be made whole, she felt the healing virtue. So in spiritual things. To talk of religion in a casual way, to pray without soul hunger and living faith, avails nothing. A nominal faith in Christ, which accepts Him merely as the Saviour of the world, can never bring healing to the soul. The faith that is unto salvation is not a mere intellectual assent to the truth. He who waits for entire knowledge before he will exercise faith, cannot receive blessing from God. It is not enough to believe about Christ; we must believe in Him. The only faith that will benefit us is that which embraces Him as a personal Saviour; which appropriates His merits to ourselves. Many hold faith as an opinion. Saving faith is a transaction by which those who receive Christ join themselves in covenant relation with God. Genuine faith is life. A living faith means an increase of vigor, a confiding trust, by which the soul becomes a conquering power.

After healing the woman, Jesus desired her to acknowledge the blessing she had received. The gifts which the gospel offers are not to be secured by stealth or enjoyed in secret. So the Lord calls upon us for confession of His goodness. "Ye are My witnesses, saith the Lord, that I am God." Isa. 43:12.

Our confession of His faithfulness is Heaven's chosen agency for revealing Christ to the world. We are to acknowledge His grace as made known through the holy men of old; but that which will be most effectual is the testimony of our own experience. We are witnesses for God as we reveal in ourselves the working of a power that is divine. Every individual has a life distinct from all others, and an experience differing essentially from theirs. God desires that our praise shall ascend to Him, marked by our own individuality. These precious acknowledgments to the praise of the glory of His grace, when supported by a Christ-like life, have an irresistible power that works for the salvation of souls.

When the ten lepers came to Jesus for healing, He bade them go and show themselves to the priest. On the way they were cleansed, but only one of them returned to give Him glory. The others went their way, forgetting Him who had made them whole. How many are still doing the same thing! The Lord works continually to benefit mankind. He is ever imparting His bounties. He raises up the sick from beds of languishing, He delivers men from peril which they do not see, He commissions heavenly angels to save them from calamity, to guard them from "the pestilence that walketh in darkness" and "the destruction that wasteth at noonday" (Ps. 91:6); but their hearts are unimpressed. He has given all the riches of heaven to redeem them, and yet they are unmindful of His great love. By their ingratitude they close their hearts against the grace of God. Like the heath in the desert they know not when good cometh, and their souls inhabit the parched places of the wilderness.

It is for our own benefit to keep every gift of God fresh in our memory. Thus faith is strengthened to claim and to receive more and more. There is greater encouragement for us in the least blessing we ourselves receive from God than in all the accounts we can read of the faith and experience of others. The soul that responds to the grace of God shall be like a watered garden. His health shall spring forth speedily; his light shall rise in obscurity, and the glory of the Lord shall be seen upon him. Let us then remember the loving-kindness of the Lord, and the multitude of His tender mercies. Like the people of Israel, let us set up our stones of witness, and inscribe upon them the precious story of what God has wrought for us. And as we review His dealings with us in our pilgrimage, let us, out of hearts melted with gratitude, declare, "What shall I render unto the Lord for all His benefits toward me? I will take the cup of salvation, and call upon the name of the Lord. I will pay my vows unto the Lord now in the presence of all His people." Ps. 116:12-14.

The First Evangelists

The apostles were members of the family of Jesus, and they had accompanied Him as He traveled on foot through Galilee. They had shared with Him the toils and hardships that overtook them. They had listened to His discourses, they had walked and talked with the Son of God, and from His daily instruction they had learned how to work for the elevation of humanity. As Jesus ministered to the vast multitudes that gathered about Him, His disciples were in attendance, eager to do His bidding and to lighten His labor. They assisted in arranging the people, bringing the afflicted ones to the Saviour, and promoting the comfort of all. They watched for interested hearers, explained the Scriptures to them, and in various ways worked for their spiritual benefit.

They taught what they had learned of Jesus, and were every day obtaining a rich experience. But they needed also an experience in laboring alone. They were still in need of much instruction, great patience and tenderness. Now, while He was personally with them, to point out their errors, and counsel and correct them, the Saviour sent them forth as His representatives.

While they had been with Him, the disciples had often been perplexed by the teaching of the priests and Pharisees, but they had brought their perplexities to Jesus. He had set before them the truths of Scripture in contrast with tradition. Thus He had strengthened their confidence in God's word, and in a great measure had set them free from their fear of the rabbis and their bondage to tradition. In the training of the disciples the example of the Saviour's life was far more effective than any mere doctrinal instruction. When they were separated from Him, every look and tone and word came back to them. Often when in conflict with the enemies of the gospel, they repeated His words, and as they saw their effect upon the people, they rejoiced greatly.

Calling the twelve about Him, Jesus bade them go out two and two through the towns and villages. None were sent forth alone, but brother was associated with brother, friend with friend. Thus they could help and encourage each other, counseling and praying together, each one's strength supplementing the other's weakness. In the same manner He afterward sent forth the seventy. It was the Saviour's purpose that the messengers of the gospel should be associated in this way. In our own time evangelistic work would be far more successful if this example were more closely followed.

The disciples' message was the same as that of John the Baptist and of Christ Himself: "The kingdom of heaven is at hand." They were to enter into no controversy with the people as to whether Jesus of Nazareth was the Messiah; but in His name they were to do the same works of mercy as He had done. He bade them, "Heal the sick, cleanse the lepers, raise the dead, cast out devils: freely ye have received, freely give."

During His ministry Jesus devoted more time to healing the sick than to preaching. His miracles testified to the truth of His words, that He came not to destroy but to save. His righteousness went before Him, and the glory of the Lord was His rearward. Wherever He went, the tidings of His mercy preceded Him. Where He had passed, the objects of His compassion were rejoicing in health, and making trial of their new-found powers. Crowds were collecting around them to hear from their lips the works that the Lord had wrought. His voice was the first sound that many had ever heard, His name the first word they had ever spoken, His face the first they had ever looked upon. Why should they not love Jesus, and sound His praise? As He passed through the towns and cities He was like a vital current, diffusing life and joy wherever He went.

The followers of Christ are to labor as He did. We are to feed the hungry, clothe the naked, and comfort the suffering and afflicted. We are to minister to the despairing, and inspire hope in the hopeless. And to us also the promise will be fulfilled, "Thy righteousness shall go before thee; the glory of the Lord shall be thy rearward." Isa. 58:8. The love of Christ, manifested in unselfish ministry, will be more effective in reforming the evildoer than will the sword or the court of justice. These are necessary to strike terror to the lawbreaker, but the loving missionary can do more than this. Often the heart will harden under reproof; but it will melt under the love of Christ. The missionary cannot only relieve physical maladies, but he can lead the sinner to the Great Physician, who can cleanse the soul from the leprosy of sin. Through His servants, God designs that the sick, the unfortunate, those possessed of evil spirits, shall hear His voice. Through His human agencies He desires to be a Comforter such as the world knows not.

The disciples on their first missionary tour were to go only to "the lost sheep of the house of Israel." If they had now preached the gospel to the Gentiles or the Samaritans, they would have lost their influence with the Jews. By exciting the prejudice of the Pharisees they would have involved themselves in controversy which would have discouraged them at the outset of their labors. Even the apostles were slow to understand that the gospel was to be carried to all nations. Until they themselves could grasp this truth they were not prepared to labor for the Gentiles. If the Jews would receive the gospel, God purposed to make them His messengers to the Gentiles. Therefore they were first to hear the message.

All over the field of Christ's labor there were souls awakened to their need, and hungering and thirsting for the truth. The time had come to send the tidings of His love to these longing hearts. To all these the disciples were to go as His representatives. The believers would thus be led to look upon them as divinely appointed teachers, and when the Saviour should be taken from them they would not be left without instructors.

On this first tour the disciples were to go only where Jesus had been before them, and had made friends. Their preparation for the journey was to be of the simplest kind. Nothing must be allowed to divert their minds from their great work, or in any way excite opposition and close the door for further labor. They were not to adopt the dress of the religious teachers, nor use any guise in apparel to distinguish them from the humble peasants. They were not to enter into the synagogues and call the people together for public service; their efforts were to be put forth in house-to-house labor. They were not to waste time in needless salutations, or in going from house to house for entertainment. But in every place they were to accept the hospitality of those who were worthy, those who would welcome them heartily as if entertaining Christ Himself. They were to enter the dwelling with the beautiful salutation, "Peace be to this house." Luke 10:5. That home would be blessed by their prayers, their songs of praise, and the opening of the Scriptures in the family circle.

These disciples were to be heralds of the truth, to prepare the way for the coming of their Master. The message they had to bear was the word of eternal life, and the destiny of men depended upon their reception or rejection of it. To impress the people with its solemnity, Jesus bade His disciples, "Whosoever shall not receive you, nor hear your words, when ye depart out of that house or city, shake off the dust of your feet. Verily I say unto you, It shall be more tolerable for the land of Sodom and Gomorrah in the day of judgment, than for that city."

Now the Saviour's eye penetrates the future; He beholds the broader fields in which, after His death, the disciples are to be witnesses for Him. His prophetic glance takes in the experience of His servants through all the ages till He shall come the second time. He shows His followers the conflicts they must meet; He reveals the character and plan of the battle. He lays open before them the perils they must encounter, the self-denial that will be required. He desires them to count the cost, that they may not be taken unawares by the enemy. Their warfare is not to be waged against flesh and blood, but "against the principalities, against the powers, against the world rulers of this darkness, against the spiritual hosts of wickedness in the heavenly places." Eph. 6:12, R. V. They are to contend with supernatural forces, but they are assured of supernatural help. All the intelligences of heaven are in this army. And more than angels are in the ranks. The Holy Spirit, the representative of the Captain of the Lord's host, comes down to direct the battle. Our infirmities may be many, our sins and mistakes grievous; but the grace of God is for all who seek it with contrition. The power of Omnipotence is enlisted in behalf of those who trust in God.

"Behold," said Jesus, "I send you forth as sheep in the midst of wolves: be ye therefore wise as serpents, and harmless as doves." Christ Himself did not suppress one word of truth, but He spoke it always in love. He exercised the greatest tact, and thoughtful, kind attention in His intercourse with the people. He was never rude, never needlessly spoke a severe word, never gave needless pain to a sensitive soul. He did not censure human weakness. He fearlessly denounced hypocrisy, unbelief, and iniquity, but tears were in His voice as He uttered His scathing rebukes. He wept over Jerusalem, the city He loved, that refused to receive Him, the Way, the Truth, and the Life. They rejected Him, the Saviour, but He regarded them with pitying tenderness, and sorrow so deep that it broke His heart. Every soul was precious in His eyes. While He always bore Himself with divine dignity, He bowed with tenderest regard to every member of the family of God. In all men He saw fallen souls whom it was His mission to save.

The servants of Christ are not to act out the dictates of the natural heart. They need to have close communion with God, lest, under provocation, self rise up, and they pour forth a torrent of words that are unbefitting, that are not as dew or the still showers that refresh the withering plants. This is what Satan wants them to do; for these are his methods. It is the dragon that is wroth; it is the spirit of Satan that is revealed in anger and accusing. But God's servants are to be representatives of Him. He desires them to deal only in the currency of heaven, the truth that bears His own image and superscription. The power by which they are to overcome evil is the power of Christ. The glory of Christ is their strength. They are to fix their eyes upon His loveliness. Then they can present the gospel with divine tact and gentleness. And the spirit that is kept gentle under provocation will speak more effectively in favor of the truth than will any argument, however forcible.

Those who are brought in controversy with the enemies of truth have to meet, not only men, but Satan and his agents. Let them remember the Saviour's words, "Behold, I send you forth as lambs among wolves." Luke 10:3. Let them rest in the love of God, and the spirit will be kept calm, even under personal abuse. The Lord will clothe them with a divine panoply. His Holy Spirit will influence the mind and heart, so that their voices shall not catch the notes of the baying of the wolves.

Continuing His instruction to His disciples, Jesus said, "Beware of men." They were not to put implicit confidence in those who knew not God, and open to them their counsels; for this would give Satan's agents an advantage. Man's inventions often counterwork God's plans. Those who build the temple of the Lord are to build according to the pattern shown in the mount,—the divine similitude. God is dishonored and the gospel is betrayed when His servants depend on the counsel of men who are not under the guidance of the Holy Spirit. Worldly wisdom is foolishness with God. Those who rely upon it will surely err.

"They will deliver you up to councils, . . . yea and before governors and kings shall ye be brought for My sake, for a testimony to them and to the Gentiles." Matt. 10:17, 18, R. V. Persecution will spread the light. The servants of Christ will be brought before the great men of the world, who, but for this, might never hear the gospel. The truth has been misrepresented to these men. They have listened to false charges concerning the faith of Christ's disciples. Often their only means of learning its real character is the testimony of those who are brought to trial for their faith. Under examination these are required to answer, and their judges to listen to the testimony borne. God's grace will be dispensed to His servants to meet the emergency. "It shall be given you," says Jesus, "in that same hour what ye shall speak. For it is not ye that speak, but the Spirit of your Father which speaketh in you." As the Spirit of God illuminates the minds of His servants, the truth will be presented in its divine power and preciousness. Those who reject the truth will stand to accuse and oppress the disciples. But under loss and suffering, even unto death, the Lord's children are to reveal the meekness of their divine Example. Thus will be seen the contrast between Satan's agents and the representatives of Christ. The Saviour will be lifted up before the rulers and the people.

The disciples were not endowed with the courage and fortitude of the martyrs until such grace was needed. Then the Saviour's promise was fulfilled. When Peter and John testified before the Sanhedrin council, men "marveled; and they took knowledge of them, that they had been with Jesus." Acts 4:13. Of Stephen it is written that "all that sat in the council, looking steadfastly on him, saw his face as it had been the face of an angel." Men "were not able to resist the wisdom and the spirit by which he spake." Acts 6:15, 10. And Paul, writing of his own trial at the court of the Caesars, says, "At my first defense no one took my part, but all forsook me. . . . But the Lord stood by me, and strengthened me; that through me the message might be fully proclaimed, and that all the Gentiles might hear: and I was delivered out of the mouth of the lion." 2 Tim. 4:16, 17, R. V.

The servants of Christ were to prepare no set speech to present when brought to trial. Their preparation was to be made day by day in treasuring up the precious truths of God's word, and through prayer strengthening their faith. When they were brought into trial, the Holy Spirit would bring to their remembrance the very truths that would be needed.

A daily, earnest striving to know God, and Jesus Christ whom He has sent, would bring power and efficiency to the soul. The knowledge obtained by diligent searching of the Scriptures would be flashed into the memory at the right time. But if any had neglected to acquaint themselves with the words of Christ, if they had never tested the power of His grace in trial, they could not expect that the Holy Spirit would bring His words to their remembrance. They were to serve God daily with undivided affection, and then trust Him.

So bitter would be the enmity to the gospel that even the tenderest earthly ties would be disregarded. The disciples of Christ would be betrayed to death by the members of their own households. "Ye shall be hated of all men for My name's sake," He added; "but he that shall endure unto the end, the same shall be saved." Mark 13:13. But He bade them not to expose themselves unnecessarily to persecution. He Himself often left one field of labor for another, in order to escape from those who were seeking His life. When He was rejected at Nazareth, and His own townsmen tried to kill Him, He went down to Capernaum, and there the people were astonished at His teaching; "for His word was with power." Luke 4:32. So His servants were not to be discouraged by persecution, but to seek a place where they could still labor for the salvation of souls.

The servant is not above his master. The Prince of heaven was called Beelzebub, and His disciples will be misrepresented in like manner. But whatever the danger, Christ's followers must avow their principles. They should scorn concealment. They cannot remain uncommitted until assured of safety in confessing the truth. They are set as watchmen, to warn men of their peril. The truth received from Christ must be imparted to all, freely and openly. Jesus said, "What I tell you in darkness, that speak ye in light: and what ye hear in the ear, that preach ye upon the housetops."

Jesus Himself never purchased peace by compromise. His heart overflowed with love for the whole human race, but He was never indulgent to their sins. He was too much their friend to remain silent while they were pursuing a course that would ruin their souls,—the souls He had purchased with His own blood. He labored that man should be true to himself, true to his higher and eternal interest. The servants of Christ are called to the same work, and they should beware lest, in seeking to prevent discord, they surrender the truth. They are to "follow after the things which make for peace" (Rom. 14:19); but real peace can never be secured by compromising principle. And no man can be true to principle without exciting opposition. A Christianity that is spiritual will be opposed by the children of disobedience. But Jesus bade His disciples, "Fear not them which kill the body, but are not able to kill the soul." Those who are true to God need not fear the power of men nor the enmity of Satan. In Christ their eternal life is secure. Their only fear should be lest they surrender the truth, and thus betray the trust with which God has honored them.

It is Satan's work to fill men's hearts with doubt. He leads them to look upon God as a stern judge. He tempts them to sin, and then to regard themselves as too vile to approach their heavenly Father or to excite His pity. The Lord understands all this. Jesus assures His disciples of God's sympathy for them in their needs and weaknesses. Not a sigh is breathed, not a pain felt, not a grief pierces the soul, but the throb vibrates to the Father's heart.

The Bible shows us God in His high and holy place, not in a state of inactivity, not in silence and solitude, but surrounded by ten thousand times ten thousand and thousands of thousands of holy intelligences, all waiting to do His will. Through channels which we cannot discern He is in active communication with every part of His dominion. But it is in this speck of a world, in the souls that He gave His only-begotten Son to save, that His interest and the interest of all heaven is centered. God is bending from His throne to hear the cry of the oppressed. To every sincere prayer He answers, "Here am I." He uplifts the distressed and downtrodden. In all our afflictions He is afflicted. In every temptation and every trial the angel of His presence is near to deliver.

Not even a sparrow falls to the ground without the Father's notice. Satan's hatred against God leads him to hate every object of the Saviour's care. He seeks to mar the handiwork of God, and he delights in destroying even the dumb creatures. It is only through God's protecting care that the birds are preserved to gladden us with their songs of joy. But He does not forget even the sparrows. "Fear ye not therefore, ye are of more value than many sparrows."

Jesus continues: As you confess Me before men, so I will confess you before God and the holy angels. You are to be My witnesses upon earth, channels through which My grace can flow for the healing of the world. So I will be your representative in heaven. The Father beholds not your faulty character, but He sees you as clothed in My perfection. I am the medium through which Heaven's blessings shall come to you. And everyone who confesses Me by sharing My sacrifice for the lost shall be confessed as a sharer in the glory and joy of the redeemed.

He who would confess Christ must have Christ abiding in him. He cannot communicate that which he has not received. The disciples might speak fluently on doctrines, they might repeat the words of Christ Himself; but unless they possessed Christlike meekness and love, they were not confessing Him. A spirit contrary to the spirit of Christ would deny Him, whatever the profession. Men may deny Christ by evilspeaking, by foolish talking, by words that are untruthful or unkind. They may deny Him by shunning life's burdens, by the pursuit of sinful pleasure. They may deny Him by conforming to the world, by uncourteous behavior, by the love of their own opinions, by justifying self, by cherishing doubt, borrowing trouble, and dwelling in darkness. In all these ways they declare that Christ is not in them. And "whosoever shall deny Me before men," He says, "him will I also deny before My Father which is in heaven."

The Saviour bade His disciples not to hope that the world's enmity to the gospel would be overcome, and that after a time its opposition would cease. He said, "I came not to send peace, but a sword." This creating of strife is not the effect of the gospel, but the result of opposition to it. Of all persecution the hardest to bear is variance in the home, the estrangement of dearest earthly friends. But Jesus declares, "He that loveth father or mother more than Me is not worthy of Me: and he that loveth son or daughter more than Me is not worthy of Me. And he that taketh not his cross, and followeth after Me, is not worthy of Me."

The mission of Christ's servants is a high honor, and a sacred trust. "He that receiveth you," He says, "receiveth Me, and he that receiveth Me receiveth Him that sent Me." No act of kindness shown to them in His name will fail to be recognized and rewarded. And in the same tender recognition He includes the feeblest and lowliest of the family of God: "Whosoever shall give to drink unto one of these little ones"—those who are as children in their faith and their knowledge of Christ—"a cup of cold water only in the name of a disciple, verily I say unto you, he shall in nowise lose his reward."

Thus the Saviour ended His instruction. In the name of Christ the chosen twelve went out, as He had gone, "to preach the gospel to the poor, . . . to heal the brokenhearted, to preach deliverance to the captives, and recovering of sight to the blind, to set at liberty them that are bruised, to preach the acceptable year of the Lord." Luke 4:18, 19.

Come Rest Awhile

On returning from their missionary tour, "the apostles gathered themselves together unto Jesus, and told Him all things, both what they had done, and what they had taught. And He said unto them, Come ye yourselves apart into a desert place, and rest awhile: for there were many coming and going, and they had no leisure so much as to eat."

The disciples came to Jesus and told Him all things. Their intimate relationship with Him encouraged them to lay before Him their favorable and unfavorable experiences, their joy at seeing results from their labors, and their sorrow at their failures, their faults, and their weaknesses. They had committed errors in their first work as evangelists, and as they frankly told Christ of their experiences, He saw that they needed much instruction. He saw, too, that they had become weary in their labors, and that they needed to rest.

But where they then were they could not obtain the needed privacy; "for there were many coming and going, and they had no leisure so much as to eat." The people were thronging after Christ, anxious to be healed, and eager to listen to His words. Many felt drawn to Him; for He seemed to them to be the fountain of all blessings. Many of those who then thronged about Christ to receive the precious boon of health accepted Him as their Saviour. Many others, afraid then to confess Him, because of the Pharisees, were converted at the descent of the Holy Spirit, and, before the angry priests and rulers, acknowledged Him as the Son of God.

But now Christ longed for retirement, that He might be with His disciples; for He had much to say to them. In their work they had passed through the test of conflict, and had encountered opposition in various forms. Hitherto they had consulted Christ in everything; but for some time they had been alone, and at times they had been much troubled to know what to do. They had found much encouragement in their work; for Christ did not send them away without His Spirit, and by faith in Him they worked many miracles; but they needed now to feed on the Bread of Life. They needed to go to a place of retirement, where they could hold communion with Jesus and receive instruction for future work.

"And He said unto them, Come ye yourselves apart into a desert place, and rest awhile." Christ is full of tenderness and compassion for all in His service. He would show His disciples that God does not require sacrifice, but mercy. They had been putting their whole souls into labor for the people, and this was exhausting their physical and mental strength. It was their duty to rest.

As the disciples had seen the success of their labors, they were in danger of taking credit to themselves, in danger of cherishing spiritual pride, and thus falling under Satan's temptations. A great work was before them, and first of all they must learn that their strength was not in self, but in God. Like Moses in the wilderness of Sinai, like David among the hills of Judea, or Elijah by the brook Cherith, the disciples needed to come apart from the scenes of their busy activity, to commune with Christ, with nature, and with their own hearts.

While the disciples had been absent on their missionary tour, Jesus had visited other towns and villages, preaching the gospel of the kingdom. It was about this time that He received tidings of the Baptist's death. This event brought vividly before Him the end to which His own steps were tending. The shadows were gathering thickly about His path. Priests and rabbis were watching to compass His death, spies hung upon His steps, and on every hand plots for His ruin were multiplying. News of the preaching of the apostles throughout Galilee reached Herod, calling his attention to Jesus and His work. "This is John the Baptist," he said; "he is risen from the dead;" and he expressed a desire to see Jesus. Herod was in constant fear lest a revolution might be secretly carried forward, with the object of unseating him from the throne, and breaking the Roman yoke from the Jewish nation. Among the people the spirit of discontent and insurrection was rife. It was evident that Christ's public labors in Galilee could not be long continued. The scenes of His suffering were drawing near, and He longed to be apart for a season from the confusion of the multitude.

With saddened hearts the disciples of John had borne his mutilated body to its burial. Then they "went and told Jesus." These disciples had been envious of Christ when He seemed to be drawing the people away from John. They had sided with the Pharisees in accusing Him when He sat with the publicans at Matthew's feast. They had doubted His divine mission because He did not set the Baptist at liberty. But now that their teacher was dead, and they longed for consolation in their great sorrow, and for guidance as to their future work, they came to Jesus, and united their interest with His. They too needed a season of quiet for communion with the Saviour.

Near Bethsaida, at the northern end of the lake, was a lonely region, now beautiful with the fresh green of spring, that offered a welcome retreat to Jesus and His disciples. For this place they set out, going in their boat across the water. Here they would be away from the thoroughfares of travel, and the bustle and agitation of the city. The scenes of nature were in themselves a rest, a change grateful to the senses. Here they could listen to the words of Christ without hearing the angry interruptions, the retorts and accusations of the scribes and Pharisees. Here they could enjoy a short season of precious fellowship in the society of their Lord.

The rest which Christ and His disciples took was not self-indulgent rest. The time they spent in retirement was not devoted to pleasure seeking. They talked together regarding the work of God, and the possibility of bringing greater efficiency to the work. The disciples had been with Christ, and could understand Him; to them He need not talk in parables. He corrected their errors, and made plain to them the right way of approaching the people. He opened more fully to them the precious treasures of divine truth. They were vitalized by divine power, and inspired with hope and courage.

Though Jesus could work miracles, and had empowered His disciples to work miracles, He directed His worn servants to go apart into the country and rest. When He said that the harvest was great, and the laborers were few, He did not urge upon His disciples the necessity of ceaseless toil, but said, "Pray ye therefore the Lord of the harvest, that He will send forth laborers into His harvest." Matt. 9:38. God has appointed to every man his work, according to his ability (Eph. 4:11-13), and He would not have a few weighted with

responsibilities while others have no burden, no travail of soul.

Christ's words of compassion are spoken to His workers today just as surely as they were spoken to His disciples. "Come ye yourselves apart, . . . and rest awhile," He says to those who are worn and weary. It is not wise to be always under the strain of work and excitement, even in ministering to men's spiritual needs; for in this way personal piety is neglected, and the powers of mind and soul and body are overtaxed. Self-denial is required of the disciples of Christ, and sacrifices must be made; but care must also be exercised lest through their overzeal Satan take advantage of the weakness of humanity, and the work of God be marred.

In the estimation of the rabbis it was the sum of religion to be always in a bustle of activity. They depended upon some outward performance to show their superior piety. Thus they separated their souls from God, and built themselves up in self-sufficiency. The same dangers still exist. As activity increases and men become successful in doing any work for God, there is danger of trusting to human plans and methods. There is a tendency to pray less, and to have less faith. Like the disciples, we are in danger of losing sight of our dependence on God, and seeking to make a savior of our activity. We need to look constantly to Jesus, realizing that it is His power which does the work. While we are to labor earnestly for the salvation of the lost, we must also take time for meditation, for prayer, and for the study of the word of God. Only the work accomplished with much prayer, and sanctified by the merit of Christ, will in the end prove to have been efficient for good.

No other life was ever so crowded with labor and responsibility as was that of Jesus; yet how often He was found in prayer! How constant was His communion with God! Again and again in the history of His earthly life are found records such as these: "Rising up a great while before day, He went out, and departed into a solitary place, and there prayed." "Great multitudes came together to hear, and to be healed by Him of their infirmities. And He withdrew Himself into the wilderness, and prayed." "And it came to pass in those days, that He went out into a mountain to pray, and continued all night in prayer to God." Mark 1:35; Luke 5:15, 16; 6:12.

In a life wholly devoted to the good of others, the Saviour found it necessary to withdraw from the thoroughfares of travel and from the throng that followed Him day after day. He must turn aside from a life of ceaseless activity and contact with human needs, to seek retirement and unbroken communion with His Father. As one with us, a sharer in our needs and weaknesses, He was wholly dependent upon God, and in the secret place of prayer He sought divine strength, that He might go forth braced for duty and trial. In a world of sin Jesus endured struggles and torture of soul. In communion with God He could unburden the sorrows that were crushing Him. Here He found comfort and joy.

In Christ the cry of humanity reached the Father of infinite pity. As a man He supplicated the throne of God till His humanity was charged with a heavenly current that should connect humanity with divinity. Through continual communion He received life from God, that He might impart life to the world. His experience is to be ours.

"Come ye yourselves apart," He bids us. If we would give heed to His word, we should be stronger and more useful. The disciples sought Jesus, and told Him all things; and He encouraged and instructed them. If today we would take time to go to Jesus and tell Him our needs, we should not be disappointed; He would be at our right hand to help us. We need more simplicity, more trust and confidence in our Saviour. He whose name is called "The mighty God, The everlasting Father, The Prince of Peace;" He of whom it is written, "The government shall be upon His shoulder," is the Wonderful Counselor. We are invited to ask wisdom of Him. He "giveth to all men liberally, and upbraideth not." Isa. 9:6; James 1:5.

In all who are under the training of God is to be revealed a life that is not in harmony with the world, its customs, or its practices; and everyone needs to have a personal experience in obtaining a knowledge of the will of God. We must individually hear Him speaking to the heart. When every other voice is hushed, and in quietness we wait before Him, the silence of the soul makes more distinct the voice of God. He bids us, "Be still, and know that I am God." Ps. 46:10. Here alone can true rest be found. And this is the effectual preparation for all who labor for God. Amid the hurrying throng, and the strain of life's intense activities, the soul that is thus refreshed will be surrounded with an atmosphere of light and peace. The life will breathe out fragrance, and will reveal a divine power that will reach men's hearts.

"Give Ye Them to Eat"

Christ had retired to a secluded place with His disciples, but this rare season of peaceful quietude was soon broken. The disciples thought they had retired where they would not be disturbed; but as soon as the multitude missed the divine Teacher, they inquired, "Where is He?" Some among them had noticed the direction in which Christ and His disciples had gone. Many went by land to meet them, while others followed in their boats across the water. The Passover was at hand, and, from far and near, bands of pilgrims on their way to Jerusalem gathered to see Jesus. Additions were made to their number, until there were assembled five thousand men besides women and children. Before Christ reached the shore, a multitude were waiting for Him. But He landed unobserved by them, and spent a little time apart with the disciples.

From the hillside He looked upon the moving multitude, and His heart was stirred with sympathy. Interrupted as He was, and robbed of His rest, He was not impatient. He saw a greater necessity demanding His attention as He watched the people coming and still coming. He "was moved with compassion toward them, because they were as sheep not having a shepherd." Leaving His retreat, He found a convenient place where He could minister to them. They received no help from the priests and rulers; but the healing waters of life flowed from Christ as He taught the multitude the way of salvation.

The people listened to the words of mercy flowing so freely from the lips of the Son of God. They heard the gracious words, so simple and so plain that they were as the balm of Gilead to their souls. The healing of His divine hand brought gladness and life to the dying, and ease and health to those suffering with disease. The day seemed to them like heaven upon earth, and they were utterly unconscious of how long it had been since they had eaten anything.

At length the day was far spent. The sun was sinking in the west, and yet the people lingered. Jesus had labored all day without food or rest. He was pale from weariness and hunger, and the disciples besought Him to cease from His toil. But He could not withdraw Himself from the multitude that pressed upon Him.

The disciples finally came to Him, urging that for their own sake the people should be sent away. Many had come from far, and had eaten nothing since morning. In the surrounding towns and villages they might be able to buy food. But Jesus said, "Give ye them to eat," and then, turning to Philip, questioned, "Whence shall we buy bread, that these may eat?" This He said to test the faith of the disciple. Philip looked over the sea of heads, and thought how impossible it would be to provide food to satisfy the wants of such a crowd. He answered that two hundred pennyworth of bread would not be nearly enough to divide among them, so that each might have a little. Jesus inquired how much food could be found among the company. "There is a lad here," said Andrew, "which hath five barley loaves, and two small fishes; but what are they among so many?" Jesus directed that these be brought to Him. Then He bade the disciples seat the people on the grass in parties of fifty or a hundred, to preserve order, and that all might witness what He was about to do. When this was accomplished, Jesus took the food, "and looking up to heaven, He blessed, and brake, and gave the loaves to His disciples, and the disciples to the multitude." "And they did all eat, and were filled. And they took up twelve baskets full of the fragments, and of the fishes."

He who taught the people the way to secure peace and happiness was just as thoughtful of their temporal necessities as of their spiritual need. The people were weary and faint. There were mothers with babes in their arms, and little children clinging to their skirts. Many had been standing for hours. They had been so intensely interested in Christ's words that they had not once thought of sitting down, and the crowd was so great that there was danger of their trampling on one another. Jesus would give them a chance to rest, and He bade them sit down. There was much grass in the place, and all could rest in comfort.

Christ never worked a miracle except to supply a genuine necessity, and every miracle was of a character to lead the people to the tree of life, whose leaves are for the healing of the nations. The simple food passed round by the hands of the disciples contained a whole treasure of lessons. It was humble fare that had been provided; the fishes and barley loaves were the daily food of the fisher folk about the Sea of Galilee. Christ could have spread before the people a rich repast, but food prepared merely for the gratification of appetite would have conveyed no lesson for their good. Christ taught them in this lesson that the natural provisions of God for man had been perverted. And never did people enjoy the luxurious feasts prepared for the gratification of perverted taste as this people enjoyed the rest and the simple food which Christ provided so far from human habitations.

If men today were simple in their habits, living in harmony with nature's laws, as did Adam and Eve in the beginning, there would be an abundant supply for the needs of the human family. There would be fewer imaginary wants, and more opportunities to work in God's ways. But selfishness and the indulgence of unnatural taste have brought sin and misery into the world, from excess on the one hand, and from want on the other.

Jesus did not seek to attract the people to Him by gratifying the desire for luxury. To that great throng, weary and hungry after the long, exciting day, the simple fare was an assurance not only of His power, but of His tender care for them in the common needs of life. The Saviour has not promised His followers the luxuries of the world; their fare may be plain, and even scanty; their lot may be shut in by poverty; but His word is pledged that their need shall be supplied, and He has promised that which is far better than worldly good,—the abiding comfort of His own presence.

In feeding the five thousand, Jesus lifts the veil from the world of nature, and reveals the power that is constantly exercised for our good. In the production of earth's harvests God is working a miracle every day. Through natural agencies the same work is accomplished that was wrought in the feeding of the multitude. Men prepare the soil and sow the seed, but it is the life from God that causes the seed to germinate. It is God's rain and air and sunshine that cause it to put forth, "first the blade, then the ear, after that the full corn in the ear." Mark 4:28. It is God who is every day feeding millions from earth's harvest fields. Men are called upon to co-operate with God in the care of the grain and the preparation of the loaf, and because of this they lose sight of the divine agency. They do not give God the glory due unto His holy name. The working of His power is ascribed to natural causes or to human instrumentality. Man is glorified in place of God, and His gracious gifts are perverted to selfish uses, and made a curse instead of a blessing. God is seeking to change all this. He desires that our dull senses shall be quickened to discern His merciful kindness and to glorify Him for the working of His power. He desires us to recognize Him in His gifts, that they may be, as He intended, a blessing to us. It was to accomplish this purpose that the miracles of Christ were performed.

After the multitude had been fed, there was an abundance of food left. But He who had all the resources of infinite power at His command said, "Gather up the fragments that remain, that nothing be lost." These words meant more than putting the bread into the baskets. The lesson was twofold. Nothing is to be wasted. We are to let slip no temporal advantage. We should neglect nothing that will tend to benefit a human being. Let everything be gathered up that will relieve the necessity of earth's hungry ones. And there should be the same carefulness in spiritual things. When the baskets of fragments were collected, the people thought of their friends at home. They wanted them to share in the bread that Christ had blessed. The contents of the baskets were distributed among the eager throng, and were carried away into all the region round about. So those who were at the feast were to give to others the bread that comes down from heaven, to satisfy the hunger of the soul. They were to repeat what they had learned of the wonderful things of God. Nothing was to be lost. Not one word that concerned their eternal salvation was to fall useless to the ground.

The miracle of the loaves teaches a lesson of dependence upon God. When Christ fed the five thousand, the food was not nigh at hand. Apparently He had no means at His command. Here He was, with five thousand men, besides women and children, in the wilderness. He had not invited the large multitude to follow Him; they came without invitation or command; but He knew that after they had listened so long to His instruction, they would feel hungry and faint; for He was one with them in their need of food. They were far from home, and the night was close at hand. Many of them were without means to purchase food. He who for their sake had fasted forty days in the wilderness would not suffer them to return fasting to their homes. The providence of God had placed Jesus where He was; and He depended on His heavenly Father for the means to relieve the necessity.

And when we are brought into strait places, we are to depend on God. We are to exercise wisdom and judgment in every action of life, that we may not, by reckless movements, place ourselves in trial. We are not to plunge into difficulties, neglecting the means God has provided, and misusing the faculties He has given us. Christ's workers are to obey His instructions implicitly. The work is God's, and if we would bless others His plans must be followed. Self cannot be made a center; self can receive no honor. If we plan according to our own ideas, the Lord will leave us to our own mistakes. But when, after following His directions, we are brought into strait places, He will deliver us. We are not to give up in discouragement, but in every emergency we are to seek help from Him who has infinite resources at His command. Often we shall be surrounded with trying circumstances, and then, in the fullest confidence, we must depend upon God. He will keep every soul that is brought into perplexity through trying to keep the way of the Lord.

Christ has bidden us, through the prophet, "Deal thy bread to the hungry," and "satisfy the afflicted soul;" "when thou seest the naked, that thou cover him," and "bring the poor that are cast out to thy house." Isa. 58:7-10. He has bidden us, "Go ye into all the world, and preach the gospel to every creature." Mark 16:15. But how often our hearts sink, and faith fails us, as we see how great is the need, and how small the means in our hands. Like Andrew looking upon the five barley loaves and the two little fishes, we exclaim, "What are they among so many?" Often we hesitate, unwilling to give all that we have, fearing to spend and to be spent for others. But Jesus has bidden us, "Give ye them to eat." His command is a promise; and behind it is the same power that fed the multitude beside the sea.

In Christ's act of supplying the temporal necessities of a hungry multitude is wrapped up a deep spiritual lesson for all His workers. Christ received from the Father; He imparted to the disciples; they imparted to the multitude; and the people to one another. So all who are united to Christ will receive from Him the bread of life, the heavenly food, and impart it to others.

In full reliance upon God, Jesus took the small store of loaves; and although there was but a small portion for His own family of disciples, He did not invite them to eat, but began to distribute to them, bidding them serve the people. The food multiplied in His hands; and the hands of the disciples, reaching out to Christ Himself the Bread of Life, were never empty. The little store was sufficient for all. After the wants of the people had been supplied, the fragments were gathered up, and Christ and His disciples ate together of the precious, Heaven-supplied food.

The disciples were the channel of communication between Christ and the people. This should be a great encouragement to His disciples today. Christ is the great center, the source of all strength. His disciples are to receive their supplies from Him. The most intelligent, the most spiritually minded, can bestow only as they receive. Of themselves they can supply nothing for the needs of the soul. We can impart only that which we receive from Christ; and we can receive only as we impart to others. As we continue imparting, we continue to receive; and the more we impart, the more we shall receive. Thus we may be constantly believing, trusting, receiving, and imparting.

The work of building up the kingdom of Christ will go forward, though to all appearance it moves slowly and impossibilities seem to testify against advance. The work is of God, and He will furnish means, and will send helpers, true, earnest disciples, whose hands also will be filled with food for the starving multitude. God is not unmindful of those who labor in love to give the word of life to perishing souls, who in their turn reach forth their hands for food for other hungry souls.

In our work for God there is danger of relying too largely upon what man with his talents and ability can do. Thus we lose sight of the one Master Worker. Too often the worker for Christ fails to realize his personal responsibility. He is in danger of shifting his burden upon organizations, instead of relying upon Him who is the source of all strength. It is a great mistake to trust in human wisdom or numbers in the work of God. Successful work for Christ depends not so much on numbers or talent as upon pureness of purpose, the true simplicity of earnest, dependent faith. Personal responsibilities must be borne, personal duties must be taken up, personal efforts must be made for those who do not know Christ. In the place of shifting your responsibility upon someone whom you think more richly endowed than you are, work according to your ability.

When the question comes home to your heart, "Whence shall we buy bread, that these may eat?" let not your answer be the response of unbelief. When the disciples heard the Saviour's direction, "Give ye them to eat," all the difficulties arose in their minds. They questioned, Shall we go away into the villages to buy food? So now, when the people are destitute of the bread of life, the Lord's children question, Shall we send for someone from afar, to come and feed them? But what said Christ? "Make the men sit down," and He fed them there. So when you are surrounded by souls in need, know that Christ is there. Commune with Him. Bring your barley loaves to Jesus.

The means in our possession may not seem to be sufficient for the work; but if we will move forward in faith, believing in the all-sufficient power of God, abundant resources will open before us. If the work be of God, He Himself will provide the means for its accomplishment. He will reward honest, simple reliance upon Him. The little that is wisely and economically used in the service of the Lord of heaven will increase in the very act of imparting. In the hand of Christ the small supply of food remained undiminished until the famished multitude were satisfied. If we go to the Source of all strength, with our hands of faith outstretched to receive, we shall be sustained in our work, even under the most forbidding circumstances, and shall be enabled to give to others the bread of life.

The Lord says, "Give, and it shall be given unto you." "He that soweth sparingly shall reap also sparingly; and he that soweth with blessings shall reap also with blessings. . . . And God is able to make all grace abound unto you; that ye, having always all sufficiency in everything, may abound unto every good work; as it is written,—

"He hath scattered abroad, he hath given to the poor: His righteousness abideth forever.

"And He that supplieth seed to the sower and bread for food, shall supply and multiply your seed for sowing, and increase the fruits of your righteousness: ye being enriched in everything unto all liberality, which worketh through us thanksgiving to God." Luke 6:38; 2 Cor. 9:6-11, R. V., margin.

A Night on the Lake

Seated upon the grassy plain, in the twilight of the spring evening, the people ate of the food that Christ had provided. The words they had heard that day had come to them as the voice of God. The works of healing they had witnessed were such as only divine power could perform. But the miracle of the loaves appealed to everyone in that vast multitude. All were sharers in its benefit. In the days of Moses, God had fed Israel with manna in the desert; and who was this that had fed them that day but He whom Moses had foretold? No human power could create from five barley loaves and two small fishes food sufficient to feed thousands of hungry people. And they said one to another, "This is of a truth that Prophet that should come into the world."

All day the conviction has strengthened. That crowning act is assurance that the long-looked-for Deliverer is among them. The hopes of the people rise higher and higher. This is He who will make Judea an earthly paradise, a land flowing with milk and honey. He can satisfy every desire. He can break the power of the hated Romans. He can deliver Judah and Jerusalem. He can heal the soldiers who are wounded in battle. He can supply whole armies with food. He can conquer the nations, and give to Israel the long-sought dominion.

In their enthusiasm the people are ready at once to crown Him king. They see that He makes no effort to attract attention or secure honor to Himself. In this He is essentially different from the priests and rulers, and they fear that He will never urge His claim to David's throne. Consulting together, they agree to take Him by force, and proclaim Him the king of Israel. The disciples unite with the multitude in declaring the throne of David the rightful inheritance of their Master. It is the modesty of Christ, they say, that causes Him to refuse such honor. Let the people exalt their Deliverer. Let the arrogant priests and rulers be forced to honor Him who comes clothed with the authority of God.

They eagerly arrange to carry out their purpose; but Jesus sees what is on foot, and understands, as they cannot, what would be the result of such a movement. Even now the priests and rulers are hunting His life. They accuse Him of drawing the people away from them. Violence and insurrection would follow an effort to place Him on the throne, and the work of the spiritual kingdom would be hindered. Without delay the movement must be checked. Calling His disciples, Jesus bids them take the boat and return at once to Capernaum, leaving Him to dismiss the people.

Never before had a command from Christ seemed so impossible of fulfillment. The disciples had long hoped for a popular movement to place Jesus on the throne; they could not endure the thought that all this enthusiasm should come to nothing. The multitudes that were assembling to keep the Passover were anxious to see the new prophet. To His followers this seemed the golden opportunity to establish their beloved Master on the throne of Israel. In the glow of this new ambition it was hard for them to go away by themselves, and leave Jesus alone upon that desolate shore. They protested against the arrangement; but Jesus now spoke with an authority He had never before assumed toward them. They knew that further opposition on their part would be useless, and in silence they turned toward the sea.

Jesus now commands the multitude to disperse; and His manner is so decisive that they dare not disobey. The words of praise and exaltation die on their lips. In the very act of advancing to seize Him their steps are stayed, and the glad, eager look fades from their countenances. In that throng are men of strong mind and firm determination; but the kingly bearing of Jesus, and His few quiet words of command, quell the tumult, and frustrate their designs. They recognize in Him a power above all earthly authority, and without a question they submit.

When left alone, Jesus "went up into a mountain apart to pray." For hours He continued pleading with God. Not for Himself but for men were those prayers. He prayed for power to reveal to men the divine character of His mission, that Satan might not blind their understanding and pervert their judgment. The Saviour knew that His days of personal ministry on earth were nearly ended, and that few would receive Him as their Redeemer. In travail and conflict of soul He prayed for His disciples. They were to be grievously tried. Their long-cherished hopes, based on a popular delusion, were to be disappointed in a most painful and humiliating manner. In the place of His exaltation to the throne of David they were to witness His crucifixion. This was to be indeed His true coronation. But they did not discern this, and in consequence strong temptations would come to them, which it would be difficult for them to recognize as temptations. Without the Holy Spirit to enlighten the mind and enlarge the comprehension the faith of the disciples would fail. It was painful to Jesus that their conceptions of His kingdom were, to so great a degree, limited to worldly aggrandizement and honor. For them the burden was heavy upon His heart, and He poured out His supplications with bitter agony and tears.

The disciples had not put off immediately from the land, as Jesus directed them. They waited for a time, hoping that He would come to them. But as they saw that darkness was fast gathering, they "entered into a ship, and went over the sea toward Capernaum." They had left Jesus with dissatisfied hearts, more impatient with Him than ever before since acknowledging Him as their Lord. They murmured because they had not been permitted to proclaim Him king. They blamed themselves for yielding so readily to His command. They reasoned that if they had been more persistent they might have accomplished their purpose.

Unbelief was taking possession of their minds and hearts. Love of honor had blinded them. They knew that Jesus was hated by the Pharisees, and they were eager to see Him exalted as they thought He should be. To be united with a teacher who could work mighty miracles, and yet to be reviled as deceivers, was a trial they could ill endure. Were they always to be accounted followers of a false prophet? Would Christ never assert His authority as king? Why did not He who possessed such power reveal Himself in His true character, and make their way less painful? Why had He not saved John the Baptist from a violent death? Thus the disciples reasoned until they brought upon themselves great spiritual darkness. They questioned, Could Jesus be an impostor, as the Pharisees asserted?

The disciples had that day witnessed the wonderful works of Christ. It had seemed that heaven had come down to the earth. The memory of that precious, glorious day should have filled them with faith and hope. Had they, out of the abundance of their hearts, been conversing together in regard to these things, they would not have entered into temptation. But their disappointment had absorbed their thoughts. The words of Christ, "Gather up the fragments, . . . that nothing be lost," were unheeded. Those were hours of large blessing to the disciples, but they had forgotten it all. They were in the midst of troubled waters. Their thoughts were stormy and unreasonable, and the Lord gave them something else to afflict their souls and occupy their minds. God often does this when men create burdens and troubles for themselves. The disciples had no need to make trouble. Already danger was fast approaching.

A violent tempest had been stealing upon them, and they were unprepared for it. It was a sudden contrast, for the day had been perfect; and when the gale struck them, they were afraid. They forgot their disaffection, their unbelief, their impatience. Everyone worked to keep the boat from sinking. It was but a short distance by sea from Bethsaida to the point where they expected to meet Jesus, and in ordinary weather the journey required but a few hours; but now they were driven farther and farther from the point they sought. Until the fourth watch of the night they toiled at the oars. Then the weary men gave themselves up for lost. In storm and darkness the sea had taught them their own helplessness, and they longed for the presence of their Master.

Jesus had not forgotten them. The Watcher on the shore saw those fear-stricken men battling with the tempest. Not for a moment did He lose sight of His disciples. With deepest solicitude His eyes followed the storm-tossed boat with its precious burden; for these men were to be the light of the world. As a mother in tender love watches her child, so the compassionate Master watched His disciples. When their hearts were subdued, their unholy ambition quelled, and in humility they prayed for help, it was given them.

At the moment when they believe themselves lost, a gleam of light reveals a mysterious figure approaching them upon the water. But they know not that it is Jesus. The One who has come for their help they count as an enemy. Terror overpowers them. The hands that have grasped the oars with muscles like iron let go their hold. The boat rocks at the will of the waves; all eyes are riveted on this vision of a man walking upon the white-capped billows of the foaming sea.

They think it a phantom that omens their destruction, and they cry out for fear. Jesus advances as if He would pass them; but they recognize Him, and cry out, entreating His help. Their beloved Master turns, His voice silences their fear, "Be of good cheer: it is I; be not afraid."

As soon as they could credit the wondrous fact, Peter was almost beside himself with joy. As if he could scarcely yet believe, he cried out, "Lord, if it be Thou, bid me come unto Thee on the water. And He said, Come."

Looking unto Jesus, Peter walks securely; but as in self-satisfaction he glances back toward his companions in the boat, his eyes are turned from the Saviour. The wind is boisterous. The waves roll high, and come directly between him and the Master; and he is afraid. For a moment Christ is hidden from his view, and his faith gives way. He begins to sink. But while the billows talk with death, Peter lifts his eyes from the angry waters, and fixing them upon Jesus, cries, "Lord, save me." Immediately Jesus grasps the outstretched hand, saying, "O thou of little faith, wherefore didst thou doubt?"

Walking side by side, Peter's hand in that of his Master, they stepped into the boat together. But Peter was now subdued and silent. He had no reason to boast over his fellows, for through unbelief and self-exaltation he had very nearly lost his life. When he turned his eyes from Jesus, his footing was lost, and he sank amid the waves.

When trouble comes upon us, how often we are like Peter! We look upon the waves, instead of keeping our eyes fixed upon the Saviour. Our footsteps slide, and the proud waters go over our souls. Jesus did not bid Peter come to Him that he should perish; He does not call us to follow Him, and then forsake us. "Fear not," He says; "for I have redeemed thee, I have called thee by thy name; thou art Mine. When thou passest through the waters, I will be with thee; and through the rivers, they shall not overflow thee: when thou walkest through the fire, thou shalt not be burned; neither shall the flame kindle upon thee. For I am the Lord thy God, the Holy One of Israel, thy Saviour." Isa. 43:1-3.

Jesus read the character of His disciples. He knew how sorely their faith was to be tried. In this incident on the sea He desired to reveal to Peter his own weakness,—to show that his safety was in constant dependence upon divine power. Amid the storms of temptation he could walk safely only as in utter self-distrust he should rely upon the Saviour. It was on the point where he thought himself strong that Peter was weak; and not until he discerned his weakness could he realize his need of dependence upon Christ. Had he learned the lesson that Jesus sought to teach him in that experience on the sea, he would not have failed when the great test came upon him.

Day by day God instructs His children. By the circumstances of the daily life He is preparing them to act their part upon that wider stage to which His providence has appointed them. It is the issue of the daily test that determines their victory or defeat in life's great crisis.

Those who fail to realize their constant dependence upon God will be overcome by temptation. We may now suppose that our feet stand secure, and that we shall never be moved. We may say with confidence, "I know in whom I have believed; nothing can shake my faith in God and in His word." But Satan is planning to take advantage of our hereditary and cultivated traits of character, and to blind our eyes to our own necessities and defects. Only through realizing our own weakness and looking steadfastly unto Jesus can we walk securely.

No sooner had Jesus taken His place in the boat than the wind ceased, "and immediately the ship was at the land whither they went." The night of horror was succeeded by the light of dawn. The disciples, and others who also were on board, bowed at the feet of Jesus with thankful hearts, saying, "Of a truth Thou art the Son of God!"

The Crisis in Galilee

When Christ forbade the people to declare Him king, He knew that a turning point in His history was reached. Multitudes who desired to exalt Him to the throne today would turn from Him tomorrow. The disappointment of their selfish ambition would turn their love to hatred, and their praise to curses. Yet knowing this, He took no measures to avert the crisis. From the first He had held out to His followers no hope of earthly rewards. To one who came desiring to become His disciple He had said, "The foxes have holes, and the birds of the air have nests; but the Son of man hath not where to lay His head." Matt. 8:20. If men could have had the world with Christ, multitudes would have proffered Him their allegiance; but such service He could not accept. Of those now connected with Him there were many who had been attracted by the hope of a worldly kingdom. These must be undeceived. The deep spiritual teaching in the miracle of the loaves had not been comprehended. This was to be made plain. And this new revelation would bring with it a closer test.

The miracle of the loaves was reported far and near, and very early next morning the people flocked to Bethsaida to see Jesus. They came in great numbers, by land and sea. Those who had left Him the preceding night returned, expecting to find Him still there; for there had been no boat by which He could pass to the other side. But their search was fruitless, and many repaired to Capernaum, still seeking Him.

Meanwhile He had arrived at Gennesaret, after an absence of but one day. As soon as it was known that He had landed, the people "ran through that whole region round about, and began to carry about in beds those that were sick, where they heard He was." Mark 6:55.

After a time He went to the synagogue, and there those who had come from Bethsaida found Him. They learned from His disciples how He had crossed the sea. The fury of the storm, and the many hours of fruitless rowing against adverse winds, the appearance of Christ walking upon the water, the fears thus aroused, His reassuring words, the adventure of Peter and its result, with the sudden stilling of the tempest and landing of the boat, were all faithfully recounted to the wondering crowd. Not content with this, however, many gathered about Jesus, questioning, "Rabbi, when camest Thou hither?" They hoped to receive from His own lips a further account of the miracle.

Jesus did not gratify their curiosity. He sadly said, "Ye seek Me, not because ye saw the miracles, but because ye did eat of the loaves, and were filled." They did not seek Him from any worthy motive; but as they had been fed with the loaves, they hoped still to receive temporal benefit by attaching themselves to Him. The Saviour bade them, "Labor not for the meat which perisheth, but for that meat which endureth unto everlasting life." Seek not merely for material benefit. Let it not be the chief effort to provide for the life that now is, but seek for spiritual food, even that wisdom which will endure unto everlasting life. This the Son of God alone can give; "for Him hath God the Father sealed."

For the moment the interest of the hearers was awakened. They exclaimed, "What shall we do, that we might work the works of God?" They had been performing many and burdensome works in order to recommend themselves to God; and they were ready to hear of any new observance by which they could secure greater merit. Their question meant, What shall we do that we may deserve heaven? What is the price we are required to pay in order to obtain the life to come?

"Jesus answered and said unto them, This is the work of God, that ye believe on Him whom He hath sent." The price of heaven is Jesus. The way to heaven is through faith in "the Lamb of God, which taketh away the sin of the world." John 1:29.

But the people did not choose to receive this statement of divine truth. Jesus had done the very work which prophecy had foretold that the Messiah would do; but they had not witnessed what their selfish hopes had pictured as His work. Christ had indeed once fed the multitude with barley loaves; but in the days of Moses Israel had been fed with manna forty years, and far greater blessings were expected from the Messiah. Their dissatisfied hearts queried why, if Jesus could perform so many wondrous works as they had witnessed, could He not give health, strength, and riches to all His people, free them from their oppressors, and exalt them to power and honor? The fact that He claimed to be the Sent of God, and yet refused to be Israel's king, was a mystery which they could not fathom. His refusal was misinterpreted. Many concluded that He dared not assert His claims because He Himself doubted as to the divine character of His mission. Thus they opened their hearts to unbelief, and the seed which Satan had sown bore fruit of its kind, in misunderstanding and defection.

Now, half mockingly, a rabbi questioned, "What sign showest Thou then, that we may see, and believe Thee? what dost Thou work? Our fathers did eat manna in the desert; as it is written, He gave them bread from heaven to eat."

The Jews honored Moses as the giver of the manna, ascribing praise to the instrument, and losing sight of Him by whom the work had been accomplished. Their fathers had murmured against Moses, and had doubted and denied his divine mission. Now in the same spirit the children rejected the One who bore the message of God to themselves. "Then said Jesus unto them, Verily, verily, I say unto you, Moses gave you not that bread from heaven." The giver of the manna was standing among them. It was Christ Himself who had led the Hebrews through the wilderness, and had daily fed them with the bread from heaven. That food was a type of the real bread from heaven. The life-giving Spirit, flowing from the infinite fullness of God, is the true manna. Jesus said, "The bread of God is that which cometh down out of heaven, and giveth life unto the world." John 6:33, R. V.

Still thinking that it was temporal food to which Jesus referred, some of His hearers exclaimed, "Lord, evermore give us this bread." Jesus then spoke plainly: "I am the bread of life."

The figure which Christ used was a familiar one to the Jews. Moses, by the inspiration of the Holy Spirit, had said, "Man doth not live by bread only, but by every word that proceedeth out of the mouth of the Lord." And the prophet Jeremiah had written, "Thy words were found, and I did eat them; and Thy word was unto me the joy and rejoicing of mine heart." Deut. 8:3; Jer. 15:16. The rabbis themselves had a saying, that the eating of bread, in its spiritual significance, was the study of the law and the practice of good works; and it was often said that at the Messiah's coming all Israel would be fed. The teaching of the prophets made plain the deep spiritual lesson in the miracle of the loaves. This lesson Christ was seeking to open to His hearers in the synagogue. Had they understood the Scriptures, they would have understood His words when He said, "I am the bread of life." Only the day before, the great multitude, when faint and weary, had been fed by the bread which He had given. As from that bread they had received physical strength and refreshment, so from Christ they might receive spiritual strength unto eternal life. "He that cometh to Me," He said, "shall never hunger; and he that believeth on Me shall never thirst." But He added, "Ye also have seen Me, and believe not."

They had seen Christ by the witness of the Holy Spirit, by the revelation of God to their souls. The living evidences of His power had been before them day after day, yet they asked for still another sign. Had this been given, they would have remained as unbelieving as before. If they were not convinced by what they had seen and heard, it was useless to show them more marvelous works. Unbelief will ever find excuse for doubt, and will reason away the most positive proof.

Again Christ appealed to those stubborn hearts. "Him that cometh to Me I will in nowise cast out." All who received Him in faith, He said, should have eternal life. Not one could be lost. No need for Pharisees and Sadducees to dispute concerning the future life. No longer need men mourn in hopeless grief over their dead. "This is the will of Him that sent Me, that everyone which seeth the Son, and believeth on Him, may have everlasting life: and I will raise him up at the last day."

But the leaders of the people were offended, "and they said, Is not this Jesus, the son of Joseph, whose father and mother we know? how is it then that He saith, I came down from heaven?" They tried to arouse prejudice by referring scornfully to the lowly origin of Jesus. They contemptuously alluded to

His life as a Galilean laborer, and to His family as being poor and lowly. The claims of this uneducated carpenter, they said, were unworthy of their attention. And on account of His mysterious birth they insinuated that He was of doubtful parentage, thus representing the human circumstances of His birth as a blot upon His history.

Jesus did not attempt to explain the mystery of His birth. He made no answer to the questionings in regard to His having come down from heaven, as He had made none to the questions concerning His crossing the sea. He did not call attention to the miracles that marked His life. Voluntarily He had made Himself of no reputation, and taken upon Him the form of a servant. But His words and works revealed His character. All whose hearts were open to divine illumination would recognize in Him "the Only-begotten of the Father, full of grace and truth." John 1:14.

The prejudice of the Pharisees lay deeper than their questions would indicate; it had its root in the perversity of their hearts. Every word and act of Jesus aroused antagonism in them; for the spirit which they cherished could find in Him no answering chord.

"No man can come to Me, except the Father which hath sent Me draw him: and I will raise him up at the last day. It is written in the prophets, And they shall be all taught of God. Every man therefore that hath heard, and hath learned of the Father, cometh unto Me." None will ever come to Christ, save those who respond to the drawing of the Father's love. But God is drawing all hearts unto Him, and only those who resist His drawing will refuse to come to Christ.

In the words, "They shall be all taught of God," Jesus referred to the prophecy of Isaiah: "All thy children shall be taught of the Lord; and great shall be the peace of thy children." Isa. 54:13. This scripture the Jews appropriated to themselves. It was their boast that God was their teacher. But Jesus showed how vain is this claim; for He said, "Every man therefore that hath heard, and hath learned of the Father, cometh unto Me." Only through Christ could they receive a knowledge of the Father. Humanity could not endure the vision of His glory. Those who had learned of God had been listening to the voice of His Son, and in Jesus of Nazareth they would recognize Him who through nature and revelation has declared the Father.

"Verily, verily, I say unto you, He that believeth on Me hath everlasting life." Through the beloved John, who listened to these words, the Holy Spirit declared to the churches, "This is the record, that God hath given to us eternal life, and this life is in His Son. He that hath the Son hath life." 1 John 5:11, 12. And Jesus said, "I will raise him up at the last day." Christ became one flesh with us, in order that we might become one spirit with Him. It is by virtue of this union that we are to come forth from the grave,—not merely as a manifestation of the power of Christ, but because, through faith, His life has become ours. Those who see Christ in His true character, and receive Him into the heart, have everlasting life. It is through the Spirit that Christ dwells in us; and the Spirit of God, received into the heart by faith, is the beginning of the life eternal. The people had referred Christ to the manna which their fathers ate in the wilderness, as if the furnishing of that food was a greater miracle than Jesus had performed; but He shows how meager was that gift when compared with the blessings He had come to bestow. The manna could sustain only this earthly existence; it did not prevent the approach of death, nor insure immortality; but the bread of heaven would nourish the soul unto everlasting life. The Saviour said, "I am that bread of life. Your fathers did eat manna in the wilderness, and are dead. This is the bread which cometh down from heaven, that a man may eat thereof, and not die. I am the living bread which came down from heaven: if any man eat of this bread, he shall live forever." To this figure Christ now adds another. Only through dying could He impart life to men, and in the words that follow He points to His death as the means of salvation. He says, "The bread that I will give is My flesh, which I will give for the life of the world."

The Jews were about to celebrate the Passover at Jerusalem, in commemoration of the night of Israel's deliverance, when the destroying angel smote the homes of Egypt. In the paschal lamb God desired them to behold the Lamb of God, and through the symbol receive Him who gave Himself for the life of the world. But the Jews had come to make the symbol all-important, while its significance was unnoticed. They discerned not the Lord's body. The same truth that was symbolized in the paschal service was taught in the words of Christ. But it was still undiscerned.

Now the rabbis exclaimed angrily, "How can this Man give us His flesh to eat?" They affected to understand His words in the same literal sense as did Nicodemus when he asked, "How can a man be born when he is old?" John 3:4. To some extent they comprehended the meaning of Jesus, but they were not willing to acknowledge it. By misconstruing His words, they hoped to prejudice the people against Him.

Christ did not soften down His symbolical representation. He reiterated the truth in yet stronger language: "Verily, verily, I say unto you, Except ye eat the flesh of the Son of man, and drink His blood, ye have no life in you. Whoso eateth My flesh, and drinketh My blood, hath eternal life; and I will raise him up at the last day. For My flesh is meat indeed, and My blood is drink indeed. He that eateth My flesh, and drinketh My blood, dwelleth in Me, and I in him."

To eat the flesh and drink the blood of Christ is to receive Him as a personal Saviour, believing that He forgives our sins, and that we are complete in Him. It is by beholding His love, by dwelling upon it, by drinking it in, that we are to become partakers of His nature. What food is to the body, Christ must be to the soul. Food cannot benefit us unless we eat it, unless it becomes a part of our being. So Christ is of no value to us if we do not know Him as a personal Saviour. A theoretical knowledge will do us no good. We must feed upon Him, receive Him into the heart, so that His life becomes our life. His love, His grace, must be assimilated.

But even these figures fail to present the privilege of the believer's relation to Christ. Jesus said, "As the living Father hath sent Me, and I live by the Father: so he that eateth Me, even he shall live by Me." As the Son of God lived by faith in the Father, so are we to live by faith in Christ. So fully was Jesus surrendered to the will of God that the Father alone appeared in His life. Although tempted in all points like as we are, He stood before the world untainted by the evil that surrounded Him. Thus we also are to overcome as Christ overcame.

Are you a follower of Christ? Then all that is written concerning the spiritual life is written for you, and may be attained through uniting yourself to Jesus. Is your zeal languishing? has your first love grown cold? Accept again of the proffered love of Christ. Eat of His flesh, drink of His blood, and you will become one with the Father and with the Son.

The unbelieving Jews refused to see any except the most literal meaning in the Saviour's words. By the ritual law they were forbidden to taste blood, and they now construed Christ's language into a sacrilegious speech, and disputed over it among themselves. Many even of the disciples said, "This is an hard saying; who can hear it?"

The Saviour answered them: "Doth this offend you? What and if ye shall see the Son of man ascend up where He was before? It is the spirit that quickeneth; the flesh profiteth nothing: the words that I speak unto you, they are spirit, and they are life."

The life of Christ that gives life to the world is in His word. It was by His word that Jesus healed disease and cast out demons; by His word He stilled the sea, and raised the dead; and the people bore witness that His word was with power. He spoke the word of God, as He had spoken through all the prophets and teachers of the Old Testament. The whole Bible is a manifestation of Christ, and the Saviour desired to fix the faith of His followers on the word. When His visible presence should be withdrawn, the word must be their source of power. Like their Master, they were to live "by every word that proceedeth out of the mouth of God." Matt. 4:4.

As our physical life is sustained by food, so our spiritual life is sustained by the word of God. And every soul is to receive life from God's word for himself. As we must eat for ourselves in order to receive nourishment, so we must receive the word for ourselves. We are not to obtain it merely through the medium of another's mind. We should carefully study the Bible, asking God for the aid of the Holy Spirit, that we may understand His word. We should take one verse, and concentrate the mind on the task of ascertaining the thought which God has put in that verse for us. We should dwell upon the thought until it becomes our own, and we know "what saith the Lord."

In His promises and warnings, Jesus means me. God so loved the world, that He gave His only-begotten Son, that I by believing in Him, might not perish, but have everlasting life. The experiences related in God's word are to be my experiences. Prayer and promise, precept and warning, are mine. "I am crucified with Christ: nevertheless I live; yet not I, but Christ liveth in me: and the life which I now live in the flesh I live by the faith of the Son of God, who loved me , and gave Himself for me." Gal. 2:20. As faith thus receives and assimilates the principles of truth, they become a part of the being and the motive power of the life. The word of God, received into the soul, molds the thoughts, and enters into the development of character.

By looking constantly to Jesus with the eye of faith, we shall be strengthened. God will make the most precious revelations to His hungering, thirsting people. They will find that Christ is a personal Saviour. As they feed upon His word, they find that it is spirit and life. The word destroys the natural, earthly nature, and imparts a new life in Christ Jesus. The Holy Spirit comes to the soul as a Comforter. By the transforming agency of His grace, the image of God is reproduced in the disciple; he becomes a new creature. Love takes the place of hatred, and the heart receives the divine similitude. This is what it means to live "by every word that proceedeth out of the mouth of God." This is eating the Bread that comes down from heaven.

Christ had spoken a sacred, eternal truth regarding the relation between Himself and His followers. He knew the character of those who claimed to be His disciples, and His words tested their faith. He declared that they were to believe and act upon His teaching. All who received Him would partake of His nature, and be conformed to His character. This involved the relinquishment of their cherished ambitions. It required the complete surrender of themselves to Jesus. They were called to become self-sacrificing, meek and lowly in heart. They must walk in the narrow path traveled by the Man of Calvary, if they would share in the gift of life and the glory of heaven.

The test was too great. The enthusiasm of those who had sought to take Him by force and make Him king grew cold. This discourse in the synagogue, they declared, had opened their eyes. Now they were undeceived. In their minds His words were a direct confession that He was not the Messiah, and that no earthly rewards were to be realized from connection with Him. They had welcomed His miracle-working power; they were eager to be freed from disease and suffering; but they would not come into sympathy with His self-sacrificing life. They cared not for the mysterious spiritual kingdom of which He spoke. The insincere, the selfish, who had sought Him, no longer desired Him. If He would not devote His power and influence to obtaining their freedom from the Romans, they would have nothing to do with Him.

Jesus told them plainly, "There are some of you that believe not;" adding, "Therefore said I unto you, that no man can come unto Me, except it were given unto him of My Father." He wished them to understand that if they were not drawn to Him it was because their hearts were not open to the Holy Spirit. "The natural man receiveth not the things of the Spirit of God: for they are foolishness unto him: neither can he know them, because they are spiritually discerned." 1 Cor. 2:14. It is by faith that the soul beholds the glory of Jesus. This glory is hidden, until, through the Holy Spirit, faith is kindled in the soul.

By the public rebuke of their unbelief these disciples were still further alienated from Jesus. They were greatly displeased, and wishing to wound the Saviour and gratify the malice of the Pharisees, they turned their backs upon Him, and left Him with disdain. They had made their choice,—had taken the form without the spirit, the husk without the kernel. Their decision was never afterward reversed; for they walked no more with Jesus.

"Whose fan is in His hand, and He will throughly purge His floor, and gather His wheat into the garner." Matt. 3:12. This was one of the times of purging. By the words of truth, the chaff was being separated from the wheat. Because they were too vain and self-righteous to receive reproof, too world-loving to accept a life of humility, many turned away from Jesus. Many are still doing the same thing. Souls are tested today as were those disciples in the synagogue at Capernaum. When truth is brought home to the heart, they see that their lives are not in accordance with the will of God. They see the need of an entire change in themselves; but they are not willing to take up the self-denying work. Therefore they are angry when their sins are discovered. They go away offended, even as the disciples left Jesus, murmuring, "This is an hard saying; who can hear it?"

Praise and flattery would be pleasing to their ears; but the truth is unwelcome; they cannot hear it. When the crowds follow, and the multitudes are fed, and the shouts of triumph are heard, their voices are loud in praise; but when the searching of God's Spirit reveals their sin, and bids them leave it, they turn their backs upon the truth, and walk no more with Jesus.

As those disaffected disciples turned away from Christ, a different spirit took control of them. They could see nothing attractive in Him whom they had once found so interesting. They sought out His enemies, for they were in harmony with their spirit and work. They misinterpreted His words, falsified His statements, and impugned His motives. They sustained their course by gathering up every item that could be turned against Him; and such indignation was stirred up by these false reports that His life was in danger.

The news spread swiftly that by His own confession Jesus of Nazareth was not the Messiah. And thus in Galilee the current of popular feeling was turned against Him, as, the year before, it had been in Judea. Alas for Israel! They rejected their Saviour, because they longed for a conqueror who would give them temporal power. They wanted the meat which perishes, and not that which endures unto everlasting life.

With a yearning heart, Jesus saw those who had been His disciples departing from Him, the Life and the Light of men. The consciousness that His compassion was unappreciated, His love unrequited, His mercy slighted, His salvation rejected, filled Him with sorrow that was inexpressible. It was such developments as these that made Him a man of sorrows, and acquainted with grief.

Without attempting to hinder those who were leaving Him, Jesus turned to the twelve and said, "Will ye also go away?"

Peter replied by asking, "Lord, to whom shall we go?" "Thou hast the words of eternal life," he added. "And we believe and are sure that Thou art that Christ, the Son of the living God."

"To whom shall we go?" The teachers of Israel were slaves to formalism. The Pharisees and Sadducees were in constant contention. To leave Jesus was to fall among sticklers for rites and ceremonies, and ambitious men who sought their own glory. The disciples had found more peace and joy since they had accepted Christ than in all their previous lives. How could they go back to those who had scorned and persecuted the Friend of sinners? They had long been looking for the Messiah; now He had come, and they could not turn from His presence to those who were hunting His life, and had persecuted them for becoming His followers.

"To whom shall we go?" Not from the teaching of Christ, His lessons of love and mercy, to the darkness of unbelief, the wickedness of the world. While the Saviour was forsaken by many who had witnessed His wonderful works, Peter expressed the faith of the disciples,—"Thou art that Christ." The very thought of losing this anchor of their souls filled them with fear and pain. To be destitute of a Saviour was to be adrift on a dark and stormy sea.

Many of the words and acts of Jesus appear mysterious to finite minds, but every word and act had its definite purpose in the work for our redemption; each was calculated to produce its own result. If we were capable of understanding His purposes, all would appear important, complete, and in harmony with His mission.

While we cannot now comprehend the works and ways of God, we can discern His great love, which underlies all His dealings with men. He who lives near to Jesus will understand much of the mystery of godliness. He will recognize the mercy that administers reproof, that tests the character, and brings to light the purpose of the heart.

When Jesus presented the testing truth that caused so many of His disciples to turn back, He knew what would be the result of His words; but He had a purpose of mercy to fulfill. He foresaw that in the hour of temptation every one of His beloved disciples would be severely tested. His agony in Gethsemane, His betrayal and crucifixion, would be to them a most trying ordeal. Had no previous test been given, many who were actuated by merely selfish motives would have been connected with them. When their Lord was condemned in the judgment hall; when the multitude who had hailed Him as their king hissed at Him and reviled Him; when the jeering crowd cried, "Crucify Him!"—when their worldly ambitions were disappointed, these self-seeking ones would, by renouncing their allegiance to Jesus, have brought upon the disciples a bitter, heart-burdening sorrow, in addition to their grief and disappointment in the ruin of their fondest hopes. In that hour of darkness, the example of those who turned from Him might have carried others with them. But Jesus brought about this crisis while by His personal presence He could still strengthen the faith of His true followers.

Compassionate Redeemer, who in the full knowledge of the doom that awaited Him, tenderly smoothed the way for the disciples, prepared them for their crowning trial, and strengthened them for the final test!

Tradition

The scribes and Pharisees, expecting to see Jesus at the Passover, had laid a trap for Him. But Jesus, knowing their purpose, had absented Himself from this gathering. "Then came together unto Him the Pharisees, and certain of the scribes." As He did not go to them, they came to Him. For a time it had seemed that the people of Galilee would receive Jesus as the Messiah, and that the power of the hierarchy in that region would be broken. The mission of the twelve, indicating the extension of Christ's work, and bringing the disciples more directly into conflict with the rabbis, had excited anew the jealousy of the leaders at Jerusalem. The spies they sent to Capernaum in the early part of His ministry, who had tried to fix on Him the charge of Sabbathbreaking, had been put to confusion; but the rabbis were bent on carrying out their purpose. Now another deputation was sent to watch His movements, and find some accusation against Him.

As before, the ground of complaint was His disregard of the traditional precepts that encumbered the law of God. These were professedly designed to guard the observance of the law, but they were regarded as more sacred than the law itself. When they came in collision with the commandments given from Sinai, preference was given to the rabbinical precepts.

Among the observances most strenuously enforced was that of ceremonial purification. A neglect of the forms to be observed before eating was accounted a heinous sin, to be punished both in this world and in the next; and it was regarded as a virtue to destroy the transgressor.

The rules in regard to purification were numberless. The period of a lifetime was scarcely sufficient for one to learn them all. The life of those who tried to observe the rabbinical requirements was one long struggle against ceremonial defilement, an endless round of washings and purifications. While the people were occupied with trifling distinctions, and observances which God had not required, their attention was turned away from the great principles of His law.

Christ and His disciples did not observe these ceremonial washings, and the spies made this neglect the ground of their accusation. They did not, however, make a direct attack on Christ, but came to Him with criticism of His disciples. In the presence of the multitude they said, "Why do Thy disciples transgress the tradition of the elders? for they wash not their hands when they eat bread."

Whenever the message of truth comes home to souls with special power, Satan stirs up his agents to start a dispute over some minor question. Thus he seeks to attract attention from the real issue. Whenever a good work is begun, there are cavilers ready to enter into dispute over forms or technicalities, to draw minds away from the living realities. When it appears that God is about to work in a special manner for His people, let them not be enticed into a controversy that will work only ruin of souls. The questions that most concern us are, Do I believe with saving faith on the Son of God? Is my life in harmony with the divine law? "He that believeth on the Son hath everlasting life: and he that believeth not the Son shall not see life." "And hereby we do know that we know Him, if we keep His commandments." John 3:36; 1 John 2:3.

Jesus made no attempt to defend Himself or His disciples. He made no reference to the charges against Him, but proceeded to show the spirit that actuated these sticklers for human rites. He gave them an example of what they were repeatedly doing, and had done just before coming in search of Him. "Full well ye reject the commandment of God," He said, "that ye may keep your own tradition. For Moses said, Honor thy father and thy mother; and, Whoso curseth father or mother, let him die the death: but ye say, If a man shall say to his father or mother, It is Corban, that is to say, a gift, by whatsoever thou mightest be profited by me; he shall be free. And ye suffer him no more to do aught for his father or his mother." They set aside the fifth commandment as of no consequence, but were very exact in carrying out the traditions of the elders. They taught the people that the devotion of their property to the temple was a duty more sacred than even the support of their parents; and that, however great the necessity, it was sacrilege to impart to father or mother any part of what had been thus consecrated. An undutiful child had only to pronounce the word "Corban" over his property, thus devoting it to God, and he could retain it for his own use during his lifetime, and after his death it was to be appropriated to the temple service. Thus he was at liberty, both in life and in death, to dishonor and defraud his parents, under cover of a pretended devotion to God.

Never, by word or deed, did Jesus lessen man's obligation to present gifts and offerings to God. It was Christ who gave all the directions of the law in regard to tithes and offerings. When on earth He commended the poor woman who gave her all to the temple treasury. But the apparent zeal for God on the part of the priests and rabbis was a pretense to cover their desire for self-aggrandizement. The people were deceived by them. They were bearing heavy burdens which God had not imposed. Even the disciples of Christ were not wholly free from the yoke that had been bound upon them by inherited prejudice and rabbinical authority. Now, by revealing the true spirit of the rabbis, Jesus sought to free from the bondage of tradition all who were really desirous of serving God.

"Ye hypocrites," He said, addressing the wily spies, "well did Esaias prophesy of you, saying, This people draweth nigh unto Me with their mouth, and honoreth Me with their lips; but their heart is far from Me. But in vain they do worship Me, teaching for doctrines the commandments of men." The words of Christ were an arraignment of the whole system of Pharisaism. He declared that by placing their requirements above the divine precepts the rabbis were setting themselves above God.

The deputies from Jerusalem were filled with rage. They could not accuse Christ as a violator of the law given from Sinai, for He spoke as its defender against their traditions. The great precepts of the law, which He had presented, appeared in striking contrast to the petty rules that men had devised.

To the multitude, and afterward more fully to His disciples, Jesus explained that defilement comes not from without, but from within. Purity and impurity pertain to the soul. It is the evil deed, the evil word, the evil thought, the transgression of the law of God, not the neglect of external, man-made ceremonies, that defiles a man.

The disciples noted the rage of the spies as their false teaching was exposed. They saw the angry looks, and heard the half-muttered words of dissatisfaction and revenge. Forgetting how often Christ had given evidence that He read the heart as an open book, they told Him of the effect of His words. Hoping that He might conciliate the enraged officials, they said to Jesus, "Knowest Thou that the Pharisees were offended, after they heard this saying?"

He answered, "Every plant, which My heavenly Father hath not planted, shall be rooted up." The customs and traditions so highly valued by the rabbis were of this world, not from heaven. However great their authority with the people, they could not endure the testing of God. Every human invention that has been substituted for the commandments of God will be found worthless in that day when "God shall bring every work into judgment, with every secret thing, whether it be good, or whether it be evil." Eccl. 12:14.

The substitution of the precepts of men for the commandments of God has not ceased. Even among Christians are found institutions and usages that have no better foundation than the traditions of the fathers. Such institutions, resting upon mere human authority, have supplanted those of divine appointment. Men cling to their traditions, and revere their customs, and cherish hatred against those who seek to show them their error. In this day, when we are bidden to call attention to the commandments of God and the faith of Jesus, we see the same enmity as was manifested in the days of Christ. Of the remnant people of God it is written, "The dragon was wroth with the woman, and went to make war with the remnant of her seed, which keep the commandments of God, and have the testimony of Jesus Christ." Rev. 12:17.

But "every plant, which My heavenly Father hath not planted, shall be rooted up." In place of the authority of the so-called fathers of the church, God bids us accept the word of the eternal Father, the Lord of heaven and earth. Here alone is truth unmixed with error. David said, "I have more understanding than all my teachers: for Thy testimonies are my meditation. I understand more than the ancients, because I keep Thy precepts." Ps. 119:99, 100. Let all who accept human authority, the customs of the church, or the traditions of the fathers, take heed to the warning conveyed in the words of Christ, "In vain they do worship Me, teaching for doctrines the commandments of men."

Barriers Broken Down

After the encounter with the Pharisees, Jesus withdrew from Capernaum, and crossing Galilee, repaired to the hill country on the borders of Phoenicia. Looking westward, He could see, spread out upon the plain below, the ancient cities of Tyre and Sidon, with their heathen temples, their magnificent palaces and marts of trade, and the harbors filled with shipping. Beyond was the blue expanse of the Mediterranean, over which the messengers of the gospel were to bear its glad tidings to the centers of the world's great empire. But the time was not yet. The work before Him now was to prepare His disciples for their mission. In coming to this region He hoped to find the retirement He had failed to secure at Bethsaida. Yet this was not His only purpose in taking this journey.

"Behold, a Canaanitish woman came out from those borders, and cried, saying, Have mercy on me, O Lord, Thou Son of David; my daughter is grievously vexed with a devil." Matt. 15:22, R. V. The people of this district were of the old Canaanite race. They were idolaters, and were despised and hated by the Jews. To this class belonged the woman who now came to Jesus. She was a heathen, and was therefore excluded from the advantages which the Jews daily enjoyed. There were many Jews living among the Phoenicians, and the tidings of Christ's work had penetrated to this region. Some of the people had listened to His words and had witnessed His wonderful works. This woman had heard of the prophet, who, it was reported, healed all manner of diseases. As she heard of His power, hope sprang up in her heart. Inspired by a mother's love, she determined to present her daughter's case to Him. It was her resolute purpose to bring her affliction to Jesus. He must heal her child. She had sought help from the heathen gods, but had obtained no relief. And at times she was tempted to think, What can this Jewish teacher do for me? But the word had come, He heals all manner of diseases, whether those who come to Him for help are rich or poor. She determined not to lose her only hope.

Christ knew this woman's situation. He knew that she was longing to see Him, and He placed Himself in her path. By ministering to her sorrow, He could give a living representation of the lesson He designed to teach. For this He had brought His disciples into this region. He desired them to see the ignorance existing in cities and villages close to the land of Israel. The people who had been given every opportunity to understand the truth were without a knowledge of the needs of those around them. No effort was made to help souls in darkness. The partition wall which Jewish pride had erected, shut even the disciples from sympathy with the heathen world. But these barriers were to be broken down.

Christ did not immediately reply to the woman's request. He received this representative of a despised race as the Jews would have done. In this He designed that His disciples should be impressed with the cold and heartless manner in which the Jews would treat such a case, as evinced by His reception of the woman, and the compassionate manner in which He would have them deal with such distress, as manifested by His subsequent granting of her petition.

But although Jesus did not reply, the woman did not lose faith. As He passed on, as if not hearing her, she followed Him, continuing her supplications. Annoyed by her importunities, the disciples asked Jesus to send her away. They saw that their Master treated her with indifference, and they therefore supposed that the prejudice of the Jews against the Canaanites was pleasing to Him. But it was a pitying Saviour to whom the woman made her plea, and in answer to the request of the disciples, Jesus said, "I am not sent but unto the lost sheep of the house of Israel." Although this answer appeared to be in accordance with the prejudice of the Jews, it was an implied rebuke to the disciples, which they afterward understood as reminding them of what He had often told them,—that He came to the world to save all who would accept Him.

The woman urged her case with increased earnestness, bowing at Christ's feet, and crying, "Lord, help me." Jesus, still apparently rejecting her entreaties, according to the unfeeling prejudice of the Jews, answered, "It is not meet to take the children's bread, and to cast it to dogs." This was virtually asserting that it was not just to lavish the blessings brought to the favored people of God upon strangers and aliens from Israel. This answer would have utterly discouraged a less earnest seeker. But the woman saw that her opportunity had come. Beneath the apparent refusal of Jesus, she saw a compassion that He could not hide. "Truth, Lord," she answered, "yet the dogs eat of the crumbs which fall from their masters' table." While the children of the household eat at the father's table, even the dogs are not left unfed. They have a right to the crumbs that fall from the table abundantly supplied. So while there were many blessings given to Israel, was there not also a blessing for her? She was looked upon as a dog, and had she not then a dog's claim to a crumb from His bounty?

Jesus had just departed from His field of labor because the scribes and Pharisees were seeking to take His life. They murmured and complained. They manifested unbelief and bitterness, and refused the salvation so freely offered them. Here Christ meets one of an unfortunate and despised race, that has not been favored with the light of God's word; yet she yields at once to the divine influence of Christ, and has implicit faith in His ability to grant the favor she asks. She begs for the crumbs that fall from the Master's table. If she may have the privilege of a dog, she is willing to be regarded as a dog. She has no national or religious prejudice or pride to influence her course, and she immediately acknowledges Jesus as the Redeemer, and as being able to do all that she asks of Him.

The Saviour is satisfied. He has tested her faith in Him. By His dealings with her, He has shown that she who has been regarded as an outcast from Israel is no longer an alien, but a child in God's household. As a child it is her privilege to share in the Father's gifts. Christ now grants her request, and finishes the lesson to the disciples. Turning to her with a look of pity and love, He says, "O woman, great is thy faith: be it unto thee even as thou wilt." From that hour her daughter became whole. The demon troubled her no more. The woman departed, acknowledging her Saviour, and happy in the granting of her prayer.

This was the only miracle that Jesus wrought while on this journey. It was for the performance of this act that He went to the borders of Tyre and Sidon. He wished to relieve the afflicted woman, and at the same time to leave an example in His work of mercy toward one of a despised people for the benefit of His disciples when He should no longer be with them. He wished to lead them from their Jewish exclusiveness to be interested in working for others besides their own people.

Jesus longed to unfold the deep mysteries of the truth which had been hid for ages, that the Gentiles should be fellow heirs with the Jews, and "partakers of His promise in Christ by the gospel." Eph. 3:6. This truth the disciples were slow to learn, and the divine Teacher gave them lesson upon lesson. In rewarding the faith of the centurion at Capernaum, and preaching the gospel to the inhabitants of Sychar, He had already given evidence that He did not share the intolerance of the Jews. But the Samaritans had some knowledge of God; and the centurion had shown kindness to Israel. Now Jesus brought the disciples in contact with a heathen, whom they regarded as having no reason above any of her people, to expect favor from Him. He would give an example of how such a one should be treated. The disciples had thought that He dispensed too freely the gifts of His grace. He would show that His love was not to be circumscribed to race or nation.

When He said, "I am not sent but unto the lost sheep of the house of Israel," He stated the truth, and in His work for the Canaanite woman He was fulfilling His commission. This woman was one of the lost sheep that Israel should have rescued. It was their appointed work, the work which they had neglected, that Christ was doing.

This act opened the minds of the disciples more fully to the labor that lay before them among the Gentiles. They saw a wide field of usefulness outside of Judea. They saw souls bearing sorrows unknown to those more highly favored. Among those whom they had been taught to despise were souls longing for help from the mighty Healer, hungering for the light of truth, which had been so abundantly given to the Jews.

Afterward, when the Jews turned still more persistently from the disciples, because they declared Jesus to be the Saviour of the world, and when the partition wall between Jew and Gentile was broken down by the death of Christ, this lesson, and similar ones which pointed to the gospel work unrestricted by custom or nationality, had a powerful influence upon the representatives of Christ, in directing their labors.

The Saviour's visit to Phoenicia and the miracle there performed had a yet wider purpose. Not alone for the afflicted woman, nor even for His disciples and those who received their labors, was the work accomplished; but also "that ye might believe that Jesus is the Christ, the Son of God; and that believing ye might have life through His name." John 20:31. The same agencies that barred men away from Christ eighteen hundred years ago are at work today. The spirit which built up the partition wall between Jew and Gentile is still active. Pride and prejudice have built strong walls of separation between different classes of men. Christ and His mission have been misrepresented, and multitudes feel that they are virtually shut away from the ministry of the gospel. But let them not feel that they are shut away from Christ. There are no barriers which man or Satan can erect but that faith can penetrate.

In faith the woman of Phoenicia flung herself against the barriers that had been piled up between Jew and Gentile. Against discouragement, regardless of appearances that might have led her to doubt, she trusted the Saviour's love. It is thus that Christ desires us to trust in Him. The blessings of salvation are for every soul. Nothing but his own choice can prevent any man from becoming a partaker of the promise in Christ by the gospel.

Caste is hateful to God. He ignores everything of this character. In His sight the souls of all men are of equal value. He "hath made of one blood all nations of men for to dwell on all the face of the earth, and hath determined the times before appointed, and the bounds of their habitation; that they should seek the Lord, if haply they might feel after Him, and find Him, though He be not far from every one of us." Without distinction of age, or rank, or nationality, or religious privilege, all are invited to come unto Him and live. "Whosoever believeth on Him shall not be ashamed. For there is no difference." "There is neither Jew nor Greek, there is neither bond nor free." "The rich and poor meet together: the Lord is the Maker of them all." "The same Lord over all is rich unto all that call upon Him. For whosoever shall call upon the name of the Lord shall be saved." Acts 17:26, 27; Gal. 3:28; Prov. 22:2; Rom. 10:11-13.

The True Sign

"Again He went out from the borders of Tyre, and came through Sidon unto the Sea of Galilee, through the midst of the borders of Decapolis." Mark 7:31, R. V.

It was in the region of Decapolis that the demoniacs of Gergesa had been healed. Here the people, alarmed at the destruction of the swine, had constrained Jesus to depart from among them. But they had listened to the messengers He left behind, and a desire was aroused to see Him. As He came again into that region, a crowd gathered about Him, and a deaf, stammering man was brought to Him. Jesus did not, according to His custom, restore the man by a word only. Taking him apart from the multitude, He put His fingers in his ears, and touched his tongue; looking up to heaven, He sighed at thought of the ears that would not be open to the truth, the tongues that refused to acknowledge the Redeemer. At the word, "Be opened," the man's speech was restored, and, disregarding the command to tell no man, he published abroad the story of his cure.

Jesus went up into a mountain, and there the multitude flocked to Him, bringing their sick and lame, and laying them at His feet. He healed them all; and the people, heathen as they were, glorified the God of Israel. For three days they continued to throng about the Saviour, sleeping at night in the open air, and through the day pressing eagerly to hear the words of Christ, and to see His works. At the end of three days their food was spent. Jesus would not send them away hungry, and He called upon His disciples to give them food. Again the disciples revealed their unbelief. At Bethsaida they had seen how, with Christ's blessing, their little store availed for the feeding of the multitude; yet they did not now bring forward their all, trusting His power to multiply it for the hungry crowds. Moreover, those whom He fed at Bethsaida were Jews; these were Gentiles and heathen. Jewish prejudice was still strong in the hearts of the disciples, and they answered Jesus, "Whence can a man satisfy these men with bread here in the wilderness?" But obedient to His word they brought Him what they had,—seven loaves and two fishes. The multitude were fed, seven large baskets of fragments remaining. Four thousand men, besides women and children, were thus refreshed, and Jesus sent them away with glad and grateful hearts.

Then taking a boat with His disciples, He crossed the lake to Magdala, at the southern end of the plain of Gennesaret. In the border of Tyre and Sidon His spirit had been refreshed by the confiding trust of the Syrophoenician woman. The heathen people of Decapolis had received Him with gladness. Now as He landed once more in Galilee, where His power had been most strikingly manifested, where most of His works of mercy had been performed, and His teaching given, He was met with contemptuous unbelief.

A deputation of Pharisees had been joined by representatives from the rich and lordly Sadducees, the party of the priests, the skeptics and aristocracy of the nation. The two sects had been at bitter enmity. The Sadducees courted the favor of the ruling power in order to maintain their own position and authority. The Pharisees, on the other hand, fostered the popular hatred against the Romans, longing for the time when they could throw off the yoke of the conqueror. But Pharisee and Sadducee now united against Christ. Like seeks like; and evil, wherever it exists, leagues with evil for the destruction of the good.

Now the Pharisees and Sadducees came to Christ, asking for a sign from heaven. When in the days of Joshua Israel went out to battle with the Canaanites at Bethhoron, the sun had stood still at the leader's command until victory was gained; and many similar wonders had been manifest in their history. Some such sign was demanded of Jesus. But these signs were not what the Jews needed. No mere external evidence could benefit them. What they needed was not intellectual enlightenment, but spiritual renovation.

"O ye hypocrites," said Jesus, "ye can discern the face of the sky,"—by studying the sky they could foretell the weather,—"but can ye not discern the signs of the times?" Christ's own words, spoken with the power of the Holy Spirit that convicted them of sin, were the sign that God had given for their salvation. And signs direct from heaven had been given to attest the mission of Christ. The song of the angels to the shepherds, the star that guided the wise men, the dove and the voice from heaven at His baptism, were witnesses for Him.

"And He sighed deeply in His spirit, and saith, Why doth this generation seek after a sign?" "There shall no sign be given unto it, but the sign of the prophet Jonas." As Jonah was three days and three nights in the belly of the whale, Christ was to be the same time "in the heart of the earth." And as the preaching of Jonah was a sign to the Ninevites, so Christ's preaching was a sign to His generation. But what a contrast in the reception of the word! The people of the great heathen city trembled as they heard the warning from God. Kings and nobles humbled themselves; the high and the lowly together cried to the God of heaven, and His mercy was granted unto them. "The men of Nineveh shall rise in judgment with this generation," Christ had said, "and shall condemn it: because they repented at the preaching of Jonas; and, behold, a greater than Jonas is here." Matt. 12:40, 41.

Every miracle that Christ performed was a sign of His divinity. He was doing the very work that had been foretold of the Messiah; but to the Pharisees these works of mercy were a positive offense. The Jewish leaders looked with heartless indifference on human suffering. In many cases their selfishness and oppression had caused the affliction that Christ relieved. Thus His miracles were to them a reproach.

That which led the Jews to reject the Saviour's work was the highest evidence of His divine character. The greatest significance of His miracles is seen in the fact that they were for the blessing of humanity. The highest evidence that He came from God is that His life revealed the character of God. He did the works and spoke the words of God. Such a life is the greatest of all miracles.

When the message of truth is presented in our day, there are many who, like the Jews, cry, Show us a sign. Work us a miracle. Christ wrought no miracle at the demand of the Pharisees. He wrought no miracle in the wilderness in answer to Satan's insinuations. He does not impart to us power to vindicate ourselves or to satisfy the demands of unbelief and pride. But the gospel is not without a sign of its divine origin.

Is it not a miracle that we can break from the bondage of Satan? Enmity against Satan is not natural to the human heart; it is implanted by the grace of God. When one who has been controlled by a stubborn, wayward will is set free, and yields himself wholeheartedly to the drawing of God's heavenly agencies, a miracle is wrought; so also when a man who has been under strong delusion comes to understand moral truth. Every time a soul is converted, and learns to love God and keep His commandments, the promise of God is fulfilled, "A new heart also will I give you, and a new spirit will I put within you." Ezek. 36:26. The change in human hearts, the transformation of human characters, is a miracle that reveals an ever-living Saviour, working to rescue souls. A consistent life in Christ is a great miracle. In the preaching of the word of God, the sign that should be manifest now and always is the presence of the Holy Spirit, to make the word a regenerating power to those that hear. This is God's witness before the world to the divine mission of His Son.

Those who desired a sign from Jesus had so hardened their hearts in unbelief that they did not discern in His character the likeness of God. They would not see that His mission was in fulfillment of the Scriptures. In the parable of the rich man and Lazarus, Jesus said to the Pharisees, "If they hear not Moses and the prophets, neither will they be persuaded, though one rose from the dead." Luke 16:31. No sign that could be given in heaven or earth would benefit them.

Jesus "sighed deeply in His spirit," and, turning from the group of cavilers, re-entered the boat with His disciples. In sorrowful silence they again crossed the lake. They did not, however, return to the place they had left, but directed their course toward Bethsaida, near where the five thousand had been fed. Upon reaching the farther side, Jesus said, "Take heed and beware of the leaven of the Pharisees and of the Sadducees." The Jews had been accustomed since the days of Moses to put away leaven from their houses at the Passover season, and they had thus been taught to regard it as a type of sin. Yet the disciples failed to understand Jesus. In their sudden departure from Magdala they had forgotten to take bread, and they had with them only one loaf. To this circumstance they understood Christ to refer, warning them not to buy bread of a Pharisee or a Sadducee. Their lack of faith and spiritual insight had often led them to similar misconception of His words. Now Jesus reproved them for thinking that He who had fed thousands with a few fishes and barley loaves could in that solemn warning have referred merely to temporal food. There was danger that the crafty reasoning of the Pharisees and the Sadducees would leaven His disciples with unbelief, causing them to think lightly of the works of Christ.

The disciples were inclined to think that their Master should have granted the demand for a sign in the heavens. They believed that He was fully able to do this, and that such a sign would put His enemies to silence. They did not discern the hypocrisy of these cavilers.

Months afterward, "when there were gathered together an innumerable multitude of people, insomuch that they trode one upon another," Jesus repeated the same teaching. "He began to say unto His disciples first of all, Beware ye of the leaven of the Pharisees, which is hypocrisy." Luke 12:1.

The leaven placed in the meal works imperceptibly, changing the whole mass to its own nature. So if hypocrisy is allowed to exist in the heart, it permeates the character and the life. A striking example of the hypocrisy of the Pharisees, Christ had already rebuked in denouncing the practice of "Corban," by which a neglect of filial duty was concealed under a pretense of liberality to the temple. The scribes and Pharisees were insinuating deceptive principles. They concealed the real tendency of their doctrines, and improved every occasion to instill them artfully into the minds of their hearers. These false principles, when once accepted, worked like leaven in the meal, permeating and transforming the character. It was this deceptive teaching that made it so hard for the people to receive the words of Christ.

The same influences are working today through those who try to explain the law of God in such a way as to make it conform to their practices. This class do not attack the law openly, but put forward speculative theories that undermine its principles. They explain it so as to destroy its force.

The hypocrisy of the Pharisees was the product of self-seeking. The glorification of themselves was the object of their lives. It was this that led them to pervert and misapply the Scriptures, and blinded them to the purpose of Christ's mission. This subtle evil even the disciples of Christ were in danger of cherishing. Those who classed themselves with the followers of Jesus, but who had not left all in order to become His disciples, were influenced in a great degree by the reasoning of the Pharisees. They were often vacillating between faith and unbelief, and they did not discern the treasures of wisdom hidden in Christ. Even the disciples, though outwardly they had left all for Jesus' sake, had not in heart ceased to seek great things for themselves. It was this spirit that prompted the strife as to who should be greatest. It was this that came between them and Christ, making them so little in sympathy with His mission of self-sacrifice, so slow to comprehend the mystery of redemption. As leaven, if left to complete its work, will cause corruption and decay, so does the self-seeking spirit, cherished, work the defilement and ruin of the soul.

Among the followers of our Lord today, as of old, how widespread is this subtle, deceptive sin! How often our service to Christ, our communion with one another, is marred by the secret desire to exalt self! How ready the thought of self-gratulation, and the longing for human approval! It is the love of self, the desire for an easier way than God has appointed that leads to the substitution of human theories and traditions for the divine precepts. To His own disciples the warning words of Christ are spoken, "Take heed and beware of the leaven of the Pharisees."

The religion of Christ is sincerity itself. Zeal for God's glory is the motive implanted by the Holy Spirit; and only the effectual working of the Spirit can implant this motive. Only the power of God can banish self-seeking and hypocrisy. This change is the sign of His working. When the faith we accept destroys selfishness and pretense, when it leads us to seek God's glory and not our own, we may know that it is of the right order. "Father, glorify Thy name" (John 12:28), was the keynote of Christ's life, and if we follow Him, this will be the keynote of our life. He commands us to "walk, even as He walked;" and "hereby we do know that we know Him, if we keep His commandments."1 John 2:6, 3.

The Foreshadowing of the Cross

The work of Christ on earth was hastening to a close. Before Him, in vivid outline, lay the scenes whither His feet were tending. Even before He took humanity upon Him, He saw the whole length of the path He must travel in order to save that which was lost. Every pang that rent His heart, every insult that was heaped upon His head, every privation that He was called to endure, was open to His view before He laid aside His crown and royal robe, and stepped down from the throne, to clothe His divinity with humanity. The path from the manger to Calvary was all before His eyes. He knew the anguish that would come upon Him. He knew it all, and yet He said, "Lo, I come: in the volume of the Book it is written of Me, I delight to do Thy will, O My God: yea, Thy law is within My heart." Ps. 40:7, 8.

Ever before Him He saw the result of His mission. His earthly life, so full of toil and self-sacrifice, was cheered by the prospect that He would not have all this travail for nought. By giving His life for the life of men, He would win back the world to its loyalty to God. Although the baptism of blood must first be received; although the sins of the world were to weigh upon His innocent soul; although the shadow of an unspeakable woe was upon Him; yet for the joy that was set before Him, He chose to endure the cross, and despised the shame.

From the chosen companions of His ministry the scenes that lay before Him were as yet hidden; but the time was near when they must behold His agony. They must see Him whom they had loved and trusted, delivered into the hands of His enemies, and hung upon the cross of Calvary. Soon He must leave them to face the world without the comfort of His visible presence. He knew how bitter hate and unbelief would persecute them, and He desired to prepare them for their trials.

Jesus and His disciples had now come into one of the towns about Caesarea Philippi. They were beyond the limits of Galilee, in a region where idolatry prevailed. Here the disciples were withdrawn from the controlling influence of Judaism, and brought into closer contact with the heathen worship. Around them were represented forms of superstition that existed in all parts of the world. Jesus desired that a view of these things might lead them to feel their responsibility to the heathen. During His stay in this region, He endeavored to withdraw from teaching the people, and to devote Himself more fully to His disciples.

He was about to tell them of the suffering that awaited Him. But first He went away alone, and prayed that their hearts might be prepared to receive His words. Upon joining them, He did not at once communicate that which He desired to impart. Before doing this, He gave them an opportunity of confessing their faith in Him that they might be strengthened for the coming trial. He asked, "Whom do men say that I the Son of man am?"

Sadly the disciples were forced to acknowledge that Israel had failed to recognize their Messiah. Some indeed, when they saw His miracles, had declared Him to be the Son of David. The multitudes that had been fed at Bethsaida had desired to proclaim Him king of Israel. Many were ready to accept Him as a prophet; but they did not believe Him to be the Messiah.

Jesus now put a second question, relating to the disciples themselves: "But whom say ye that I am?" Peter answered, "Thou art the Christ, the Son of the living God."

From the first, Peter had believed Jesus to be the Messiah. Many others who had been convicted by the preaching of John the Baptist, and had accepted Christ, began to doubt as to John's mission when he was imprisoned and put to death; and they now doubted that Jesus was the Messiah, for whom they had looked so long. Many of the disciples who had ardently expected Jesus to take His place on David's throne left Him when they perceived that He had no such intention. But Peter and his companions turned not from their allegiance. The vacillating course of those who praised yesterday and condemned today did not destroy the faith of the true follower of the Saviour. Peter declared, "Thou art the Christ, the Son of the living God." He waited not for kingly honors to crown his Lord, but accepted Him in His humiliation.

Peter had expressed the faith of the twelve. Yet the disciples were still far from understanding Christ's mission. The opposition and misrepresentation of the priests and rulers, while it could not turn them away from Christ, still caused them great perplexity. They did not see their way clearly. The influence of their early training, the teaching of the rabbis, the power of tradition, still intercepted their view of truth. From time to time precious rays of light from Jesus shone upon them, yet often they were like men groping among shadows. But on this day, before they were brought face to face with the great trial of their faith, the Holy Spirit rested upon them in power. For a little time their eyes were turned away from "the things which are seen," to behold "the things which are not seen." 2 Cor. 4:18. Beneath the guise of humanity they discerned the glory of the Son of God.

Jesus answered Peter, saying, "Blessed art thou, Simon Bar-jona: for flesh and blood hath not revealed it unto thee, but My Father which is in heaven."

The truth which Peter had confessed is the foundation of the believer's faith. It is that which Christ Himself has declared to be eternal life. But the possession of this knowledge was no ground for self-glorification. Through no wisdom or goodness of his own had it been revealed to Peter. Never can humanity, of itself, attain to a knowledge of the divine. "It is as high as heaven; what canst thou do? deeper than hell; what canst thou know?" Job 11:8. Only the spirit of adoption can reveal to us the deep things of God, which "eye hath not seen, nor ear heard, neither have entered into the heart of man." "God hath revealed them unto us by His Spirit: for the Spirit searcheth all things, yea, the deep things of God." 1 Cor. 2:9, 10. "The secret of the Lord is with them that fear Him;" and the fact that Peter discerned the glory of Christ was an evidence that he had been "taught of God." Ps. 25:14; John 6:45. Ah, indeed, "blessed art thou, Simon Bar-jona: for flesh and blood hath not revealed it unto thee."

Jesus continued: "I say also unto thee, That thou art Peter, and upon this rock I will build My church; and the gates of hell shall not prevail against it." The word Peter signifies a stone,—a rolling stone. Peter was not the rock upon which the church was founded. The gates of hell did prevail against him when he denied his Lord with cursing and swearing. The church was built upon One against whom the gates of hell could not prevail.

Centuries before the Saviour's advent Moses had pointed to the Rock of Israel's salvation. The psalmist had sung of "the Rock of my strength." Isaiah had written, "Thus saith the Lord God, Behold, I lay in Zion for a foundation a stone, a tried stone, a precious cornerstone, a sure foundation." Deut. 32:4; Ps. 62:7; Isa. 28:16. Peter himself, writing by inspiration, applies this prophecy to Jesus. He says, "If ye have tasted that the Lord is gracious: unto whom coming, a living stone, rejected indeed of men, but with God elect, precious, ye also, as living stones, are built up a spiritual house." 1 Peter 2:3-5, R. V.

"Other foundation can no man lay than that is laid, which is Jesus Christ." 1 Cor. 3:11. "Upon this rock," said Jesus, "I will build My church." In the presence of God, and all the heavenly intelligences, in the presence of the unseen army of hell, Christ founded His church upon the living Rock. That Rock is Himself,—His own body, for us broken and bruised. Against the church built upon this foundation, the gates of hell shall not prevail.

How feeble the church appeared when Christ spoke these words! There was only a handful of believers, against whom all the power of demons and evil men would be directed; yet the followers of Christ were not to fear. Built upon the Rock of their strength, they could not be overthrown.

For six thousand years, faith has builded upon Christ. For six thousand years the floods and tempests of satanic wrath have beaten upon the Rock of our salvation; but it stands unmoved.

Peter had expressed the truth which is the foundation of the church's faith, and Jesus now honored him as the representative of the whole body of believers. He said, "I will give unto thee the keys of the kingdom of heaven: and whatsoever thou shalt bind on earth shall be bound in heaven: and whatsoever thou shalt loose on earth shall be loosed in heaven."

"The keys of the kingdom of heaven" are the words of Christ. All the words of Holy Scripture are His, and are here included. These words have power to open and to shut heaven. They declare the conditions upon which men are received or rejected. Thus the work of those who preach God's word is a savor of life unto life or of death unto death. Theirs is a mission weighted with eternal results.

The Saviour did not commit the work of the gospel to Peter individually. At a later time, repeating the words that were spoken to Peter, He applied them directly to the church. And the same in substance was spoken also to the twelve as representatives of the body of believers. If Jesus had delegated any special authority to one of the disciples above the others, we should not find them so often contending as to who should be the greatest. They would have submitted to the wish of their Master, and honored the one whom He had chosen.

Instead of appointing one to be their head, Christ said to the disciples, "Be not ye called Rabbi;" "neither be ye called masters: for one is your Master, even Christ." Matt. 23:8, 10.

"The head of every man is Christ." God, who put all things under the Saviour's feet, "gave Him to be the head over all things to the church, which is His body, the fullness of Him that filleth all in all." 1 Cor. 11:3; Eph. 1:22, 23. The church is built upon Christ as its foundation; it is to obey Christ as its head. It is not to depend upon man, or be controlled by man. Many claim that a position of trust in the church gives them authority to dictate what other men shall believe and what they shall do. This claim God does not sanction. The Saviour declares, "All ye are brethren." All are exposed to temptation, and are liable to error. Upon no finite being can we depend for guidance. The Rock of faith is the living presence of Christ in the church. Upon this the weakest may depend, and those who think themselves the strongest will prove to be the weakest, unless they make Christ their efficiency. "Cursed be the man that trusteth in man, and maketh flesh his arm." The Lord "is the Rock, His work is perfect." "Blessed are all they that put their trust in Him." Jer. 17:5; Deut. 32:4; Ps. 2:12.

After Peter's confession, Jesus charged the disciples to tell no man that He was the Christ. This charge was given because of the determined opposition of the scribes and Pharisees. More than this, the people, and even the disciples, had so false a conception of the Messiah that a public announcement of Him would give them no true idea of His character or His work. But day by day He was revealing Himself to them as the Saviour, and thus He desired to give them a true conception of Him as the Messiah.

The disciples still expected Christ to reign as a temporal prince. Although He had so long concealed His design, they believed that He would not always remain in poverty and obscurity; the time was near when He would establish His kingdom. That the hatred of the priests and rabbis would never be overcome, that Christ would be rejected by His own nation, condemned as a deceiver, and crucified as a malefactor,—such a thought the disciples had never entertained. But the hour of the power of darkness was drawing on, and Jesus must open to His disciples the conflict before them. He was sad as He anticipated the trial.

Hitherto He had refrained from making known to them anything relative to His sufferings and death. In His conversation with Nicodemus He had said, "As Moses lifted up the serpent in the wilderness, even so must the Son of man be lifted up: that whosoever believeth in Him should not perish, but have eternal life." John 3:14, 15. But the disciples did not hear this, and had they heard, would not have understood. But now they have been with Jesus, listening to His words, beholding His works, until, notwithstanding the humility of His surroundings, and the opposition of priests and people, they can join in the testimony of Peter, "Thou art the Christ, the Son of the living God." Now the time has come for the veil that hides the future to be withdrawn. "From that time forth began Jesus to show unto His disciples, how that He must go unto Jerusalem, and suffer many things of the elders and chief priests and scribes, and be killed, and be raised again the third day."

Speechless with grief and amazement, the disciples listened. Christ had accepted Peter's acknowledgment of Him as the Son of God; and now His words pointing to His suffering and death seemed incomprehensible. Peter could not keep silent. He laid hold upon his Master, as if to draw Him back from His impending doom, exclaiming, "Be it far from Thee, Lord: this shall not be unto Thee."

Peter loved his Lord; but Jesus did not commend him for thus manifesting the desire to shield Him from suffering. Peter's words were not such as would be a help and solace to Jesus in the great trial before Him. They were not in harmony with God's purpose of grace toward a lost world, nor with the lesson of self-sacrifice that Jesus had come to teach by His own example. Peter did not desire to see the cross in the work of Christ. The impression which his words would make was directly opposed to that which Christ desired to make on the minds of His followers, and the Saviour was moved to utter one of the sternest rebukes that ever fell from His lips: "Get thee behind Me, Satan: thou art an offense unto Me: for thou savorest not the things that be of God, but those that be of men."

Satan was trying to discourage Jesus, and turn Him from His mission; and Peter, in his blind love, was giving voice to the temptation. The prince of evil was the author of the thought. His instigation was behind that impulsive appeal. In the wilderness, Satan had offered Christ the dominion of the world on condition of forsaking the path of humiliation and sacrifice. Now he was presenting the same temptation to the disciple of Christ. He was seeking to fix Peter's gaze upon the earthly glory, that he might not behold the cross to which Jesus desired to turn his eyes. And through Peter, Satan was again pressing the temptation upon Jesus. But the Saviour heeded it not; His thought was for His disciple. Satan had interposed between Peter and his Master, that the heart of the disciple might not be touched at the vision of Christ's humiliation for him. The words of Christ were spoken, not to Peter, but to the one who was trying to separate him from his Redeemer. "Get thee behind Me, Satan." No longer interpose between Me and My erring servant. Let Me come face to face with Peter, that I may reveal to him the mystery of My love.

It was to Peter a bitter lesson, and one which he learned but slowly, that the path of Christ on earth lay through agony and humiliation. The disciple shrank from fellowship with his Lord in suffering. But in the heat of the furnace fire he was to learn its blessing. Long afterward, when his active form was bowed with the burden of years and labors, he wrote, "Beloved, think it not strange concerning the fiery trial which is to try you, as though some strange thing happened unto you: but rejoice, inasmuch as ye are partakers of Christ's sufferings; that, when His glory shall be revealed, ye may be glad also with exceeding joy." 1 Peter 4:12, 13.

Jesus now explained to His disciples that His own life of self-abnegation was an example of what theirs should be. Calling about Him, with the disciples, the people who had been lingering near, He said, "If any man will come after Me, let him deny himself, and take up his cross daily, and follow Me." The cross was associated with the power of Rome. It was the instrument of the most cruel and humiliating form of death. The lowest criminals were required to bear the cross to the place of execution; and often as it was about to be laid upon their shoulders, they resisted with desperate violence, until they were overpowered, and the instrument of torture was bound upon them. But Jesus bade His followers take up the cross and bear it after Him. To the disciples His words, though dimly comprehended, pointed to their submission to the most bitter humiliation,—submission even unto death for the sake of Christ. No more complete self-surrender could the Saviour's words have pictured. But all this He had accepted for them. Jesus did not count heaven a place to be desired while we were lost. He left the heavenly courts for a life of reproach and insult, and a death of shame. He who was rich in heaven's priceless treasure, became poor, that through His poverty we might be rich. We are to follow in the path He trod.

Love for souls for whom Christ died means crucifixion of self. He who is a child of God should henceforth look upon himself as a link in the chain let down to save the world, one with Christ in His plan of mercy, going forth with Him to seek and save the lost. The Christian is ever to realize that he has consecrated himself to God, and that in character he is to reveal Christ to the world. The self-sacrifice, the sympathy, the love, manifested in the life of Christ are to reappear in the life of the worker for God.

"Whosoever will save his life shall lose it; but whosoever shall lose his life for My sake and the gospel's, the same shall save it." Selfishness is death. No organ of the body could live should it confine its service to itself. The heart, failing to send its lifeblood to the hand and the head, would quickly lose its power. As our lifeblood, so is the love of Christ diffused through every part of His mystical body. We are members one of another, and the soul that refuses to impart will perish. And "what is a man profited," said Jesus, "if he shall gain the whole world, and lose his own soul? or what shall a man give in exchange for his soul?"

Beyond the poverty and humiliation of the present, He pointed the disciples to His coming in glory, not in the splendor of an earthly throne, but with the glory of God and the hosts of heaven. And then, He said, "He shall reward every man according to his works." Then for their encouragement He gave the promise, "Verily I say unto you, There be some standing here, which shall not taste of death, till they see the Son of man coming in His kingdom." But the disciples did not comprehend His words. The glory seemed far away. Their eyes were fixed upon the nearer view, the earthly life of poverty, humiliation, and suffering. Must their glowing expectations of the Messiah's kingdom be relinquished? Were they not to see their Lord exalted to the throne of David? Could it be that Christ was to live a humble, homeless wanderer, to be despised, rejected, and put to death? Sadness oppressed their hearts, for they loved their Master. Doubt also harassed their minds, for it seemed incomprehensible that the Son of God should be subjected to such cruel humiliation. They questioned why He should voluntarily go to Jerusalem to meet the treatment which He had told them He was there to receive. How could He resign Himself to such a fate, and leave them in greater darkness than that in which they were groping before He revealed Himself to them?

In the region of Caesarea Philippi, Christ was out of the reach of Herod and Caiaphas, the disciples reasoned. He had nothing to fear from the hatred of the Jews or from the power of the Romans. Why not work there, at a distance from the Pharisees? Why need He give Himself up to death? If He was to die, how was it that His kingdom was to be established so firmly that the gates of hell should not prevail against it? To the disciples this was indeed a mystery.

They were even now journeying along the shores of the Sea of Galilee toward the city where all their hopes were to be crushed. They dared not remonstrate with Christ, but they talked together in low, sorrowful tones in regard to what the future would be. Even amid their questionings they clung to the thought that some unforeseen circumstance might avert the doom which seemed to await their Lord. Thus they sorrowed and doubted, hoped and feared, for six long, gloomy days.

He Was Transfigured

Evening is drawing on as Jesus calls to His side three of His disciples, Peter, James, and John, and leads them across the fields, and far up a rugged path, to a lonely mountainside. The Saviour and His disciples have spent the day in traveling and teaching, and the mountain climb adds to their weariness. Christ has lifted burdens from mind and body of many

sufferers; He has sent the thrill of life through their enfeebled frames; but He also is compassed with humanity, and with His disciples He is wearied with the ascent.

The light of the setting sun still lingers on the mountain top, and gilds with its fading glory the path they are traveling. But soon the light dies out from hill as well as valley, the sun disappears behind the western horizon, and the solitary travelers are wrapped in the darkness of night. The gloom of their surroundings seems in harmony with their sorrowful lives, around which the clouds are gathering and thickening.

The disciples do not venture to ask Christ whither He is going, or for what purpose. He has often spent entire nights in the mountains in prayer. He whose hand formed mountain and valley is at home with nature, and enjoys its quietude. The disciples follow where Christ leads the way; yet they wonder why their Master should lead them up this toilsome ascent when they are weary, and when He too is in need of rest.

Presently Christ tells them that they are now to go no farther. Stepping a little aside from them, the Man of Sorrows pours out His supplications with strong crying and tears. He prays for strength to endure the test in behalf of humanity. He must Himself gain a fresh hold on Omnipotence, for only thus can He contemplate the future. And He pours out His heart longings for His disciples, that in the hour of the power of darkness their faith may not fail. The dew is heavy upon His bowed form, but He heeds it not. The shadows of night gather thickly about Him, but He regards not their gloom. So the hours pass slowly by. At first the disciples unite their prayers with His in sincere devotion; but after a time they are overcome with weariness, and, even while trying to retain their interest in the scene, they fall asleep. Jesus has told them of His sufferings; He has taken them with Him that they might unite with Him in prayer; even now He is praying for them. The Saviour has seen the gloom of His disciples, and has longed to lighten their grief by an assurance that their faith has not been in vain. Not all, even of the twelve, can receive the revelation He desires to give. Only the three who are to witness His anguish in Gethsemane have been chosen to be with Him on the mount. Now the burden of His prayer is that they may be given a manifestation of the glory He had with the Father before the world was, that His kingdom may be revealed to human eyes, and that His disciples may be strengthened to behold it. He pleads that they may witness a manifestation of His divinity that will comfort them in the hour of His supreme agony with the knowledge that He is of a surety the Son of God and that His shameful death is a part of the plan of redemption.

His prayer is heard. While He is bowed in lowliness upon the stony ground, suddenly the heavens open, the golden gates of the city of God are thrown wide, and holy radiance descends upon the mount, enshrouding the Saviour's form. Divinity from within flashes through humanity, and meets the glory coming from above. Arising from His prostrate position, Christ stands in godlike majesty. The soul agony is gone. His countenance now shines "as the sun," and His garments are "white as the light."

The disciples, awaking, behold the flood of glory that illuminates the mount. In fear and amazement they gaze upon the radiant form of their Master. As they become able to endure the wondrous light, they see that Jesus is not alone. Beside Him are two heavenly beings, in close converse with Him. They are Moses, who upon Sinai had talked with God; and Elijah, to whom the high privilege was given—granted to but one other of the sons of Adam—never to come under the power of death.

Upon Mount Pisgah fifteen centuries before, Moses had stood gazing upon the Land of Promise. But because of his sin at Meribah, it was not for him to enter there. Not for him was the joy of leading the host of Israel into the inheritance of their fathers. His agonized entreaty, "I pray Thee, let me go over, and see the good land that is beyond Jordan, that goodly mountain, and Lebanon" (Deut. 3:25), was refused. The hope that for forty years had lighted up the darkness of the desert wanderings must be denied. A wilderness grave was the goal of those years of toil and heart-burdening care. But He who is "able to do exceeding abundantly above all that we ask or think" (Eph. 3:20), had in this measure answered His servant's prayer. Moses passed under the dominion of death, but he was not to remain in the tomb. Christ Himself called him forth to life. Satan the tempter had claimed the body of Moses because of his sin; but Christ the Saviour brought him forth from the grave. Jude 9.

Moses upon the mount of transfiguration was a witness to Christ's victory over sin and death. He represented those who shall come forth from the grave at the resurrection of the just. Elijah, who had been translated to heaven without seeing death, represented those who will be living upon the earth at Christ's second coming, and who will be "changed, in a moment, in the twinkling of an eye, at the last trump;" when "this mortal must put on immortality," and "this corruptible must put on incorruption." 1 Cor. 15:51-53. Jesus was clothed with the light of heaven, as He will appear when He shall come "the second time without sin unto salvation." For He will come "in the glory of His Father with the holy angels." Heb. 9:28; Mark 8:38. The Saviour's promise to the disciples was now fulfilled. Upon the mount the future kingdom of glory was represented in miniature,—Christ the King, Moses a representative of the risen saints, and Elijah of the translated ones.

The disciples do not yet comprehend the scene; but they rejoice that the patient Teacher, the meek and lowly One, who has wandered to and fro a helpless stranger, is honored by the favored ones of heaven. They believe that Elijah has come to announce the Messiah's reign, and that the kingdom of Christ is about to be set up on the earth. The memory of their fear and disappointment they would banish forever. Here, where the glory of God is revealed, they long to tarry. Peter exclaims, "Master, it is good for us to be here: and let us make three tabernacles; one for Thee, and one for Moses, and one for Elias." The disciples are confident that Moses and Elijah have been sent to protect their Master, and to establish His authority as king.

But before the crown must come the cross. Not the inauguration of Christ as king, but the decease to be accomplished at Jerusalem, is the subject of their conference with Jesus. Bearing the weakness of humanity, and burdened with its sorrow and sin, Jesus walked alone in the midst of men. As the darkness of the coming trial pressed upon Him, He was in loneliness of spirit, in a world that knew Him not. Even His loved disciples, absorbed in their own doubt and sorrow and ambitious hopes, had not comprehended the mystery of His mission. He had dwelt amid the love and fellowship of heaven; but in the world that He had created, He was in solitude. Now heaven had sent its messengers to Jesus; not angels, but men who had endured suffering and sorrow, and who could sympathize with the Saviour in the trial of His earthly life. Moses and Elijah had been colaborers with Christ. They had shared His longing for the salvation of men. Moses had pleaded for Israel: "Yet now, if Thou wilt forgive their sin—; and if not, blot me, I pray Thee, out of Thy book which Thou hast written." Ex. 32:32. Elijah had known loneliness of spirit, as for three years and a half of famine he had borne the burden of the nation's hatred and its woe. Alone he had stood for God upon Mount Carmel. Alone he had fled to the desert in anguish and despair. These men, chosen above every angel around the throne, had come to commune with Jesus concerning the scenes of His suffering, and to comfort Him with the assurance of the sympathy of heaven. The hope of the world, the salvation of every human being, was the burden of their interview.

Through being overcome with sleep, the disciples heard little of what passed between Christ and the heavenly messengers. Failing to watch and pray, they had not received that which God desired to give them,—a knowledge of the sufferings of Christ, and the glory that should follow. They lost the blessing that might have been theirs through sharing His self-sacrifice. Slow of heart to believe were these disciples, little appreciative of the treasure with which Heaven sought to enrich them.

Yet they received great light. They were assured that all heaven knew of the sin of the Jewish nation in rejecting Christ. They were given a clearer insight into the work of the Redeemer. They saw with their eyes and heard with their ears things that were beyond the comprehension of man. They were "eyewitnesses of His majesty" (2 Peter 1:16), and they realized that Jesus was indeed the Messiah, to whom patriarchs and prophets had witnessed, and that He was recognized as such by the heavenly universe.

While they were still gazing on the scene upon the mount, "a bright cloud overshadowed them: and behold a voice out of the cloud, which said, This is My beloved Son, in whom I am well pleased; hear ye Him." As they beheld the cloud of glory, brighter than that which went before the tribes of Israel in the wilderness; as they heard the voice of God speak in awful majesty that caused the mountain to tremble, the disciples fell smitten to the earth. They remained prostrate, their faces hidden, till Jesus came near, and touched them, dispelling their fears with His well-known voice, "Arise, and be not afraid." Venturing to lift up their eyes, they saw that the heavenly glory had passed away, the forms of Moses and Elijah had disappeared. They were upon the mount, alone with Jesus.

Ministry

The entire night had been passed in the mountain; and as the sun arose, Jesus and His disciples descended to the plain. Absorbed in thought, the disciples were awed and silent. Even Peter had not a word to say. Gladly would they have lingered in that holy place which had been touched with the light of heaven, and where the Son of God had manifested His glory; but there was work to be done for the people, who were already searching far and near for Jesus.

At the foot of the mountain a large company had gathered, led hither by the disciples who had remained behind, but who knew whither Jesus had resorted. As the Saviour drew near, He charged His three companions to keep silence concerning what they had witnessed, saying, "Tell the vision to no man, until the Son of man be risen again from the dead." The revelation made to the disciples was to be pondered in their own hearts, not to be published abroad. To relate it to the multitudes would excite only ridicule or idle wonder. And even the nine apostles would not understand the scene until after Christ had risen from the dead. How slow of comprehension even the three favored disciples were, is seen in the fact that notwithstanding all that Christ had said of what was before Him, they queried among themselves what the rising from the dead should mean. Yet they asked no explanation from Jesus. His words in regard to the future had filled them with sorrow; they sought no further revelation concerning that which they were fain to believe might never come to pass.

As the people on the plain caught sight of Jesus, they ran to meet Him, greeting Him with expressions of reverence and joy. Yet His quick eye discerned that they were in great perplexity. The disciples appeared troubled. A circumstance had just occurred that had caused them bitter disappointment and humiliation.

While they were waiting at the foot of the mountain, a father had brought to them his son, to be delivered from a dumb spirit that tormented him. Authority over unclean spirits, to cast them out, had been conferred on the disciples when Jesus sent out the twelve to preach through Galilee. As they went forth strong in faith, the evil spirits had obeyed their word. Now in the name of Christ they commanded the torturing spirit to leave his victim; but the demon only mocked them by a fresh display of his power. The disciples, unable to account for their defeat, felt that they were bringing dishonor upon themselves and their Master. And in the crowd there were scribes who made the most of this opportunity to humiliate them. Pressing around the disciples, they plied them with questions, seeking to prove that they and their Master were deceivers. Here, the rabbis triumphantly declared, was an evil spirit that neither the disciples nor Christ Himself could conquer. The people were inclined to side with the scribes, and a feeling of contempt and scorn pervaded the crowd.

But suddenly the accusations ceased. Jesus and the three disciples were seen approaching, and with a quick revulsion of feeling the people turned to meet them. The night of communion with the heavenly glory had left its trace upon the Saviour and His companions. Upon their countenances was a light that awed the beholders. The scribes drew back in fear, while the people welcomed Jesus.

As if He had been a witness of all that had occurred, the Saviour came to the scene of conflict, and fixing His gaze upon the scribes inquired, "What question ye with them?"

But the voices so bold and defiant before were now silent. A hush had fallen upon the entire company. Now the afflicted father made his way through the crowd, and falling at the feet of Jesus, poured out the story of his trouble and disappointment.

"Master," he said, "I have brought unto Thee my son, which hath a dumb spirit; and wheresoever he taketh him, he teareth him: . . . and I spake to Thy disciples that they should cast him out; and they could not."

Jesus looked about Him upon the awe-stricken multitude, the caviling scribes, the perplexed disciples. He read the unbelief in every heart; and in a voice filled with sorrow He exclaimed, "O faithless generation, how long shall I be with you? how long shall I suffer you?" Then He bade the distressed father, "Bring thy son hither."

The boy was brought, and as the Saviour's eyes fell upon him, the evil spirit cast him to the ground in convulsions of agony. He lay wallowing and foaming, rending the air with unearthly shrieks.

Again the Prince of life and the prince of the powers of darkness had met on the field of battle,—Christ in fulfillment of His mission to "preach deliverance to the captives, . . . to set at liberty them that are bruised" (Luke 4:18), Satan seeking to hold his victim under his control. Angels of light and the hosts of evil angels, unseen, were pressing near to behold the conflict. For a moment, Jesus permitted the evil spirit to display his power, that the beholders might comprehend the deliverance about to be wrought.

The multitude looked on with bated breath, the father in an agony of hope and fear. Jesus asked, "How long is it ago since this came unto him?" The father told the story of long years of suffering, and then, as if he could endure no more, exclaimed, "If Thou canst do anything, have compassion on us, and help us." "If Thou canst!" Even now the father questioned the power of Christ.

Jesus answers, "If thou canst believe, all things are possible to him that believeth." There is no lack of power on the part of Christ; the healing of the son depends upon the father's faith. With a burst of tears, realizing his own weakness, the father casts himself upon Christ's mercy, with the cry, "Lord, I believe; help Thou mine unbelief."

Jesus turns to the suffering one, and says, "Thou dumb and deaf spirit, I charge thee, come out of him, and enter no more into him." There is a cry, an agonized struggle. The demon, in passing, seems about to rend the life from his victim. Then the boy lies motionless, and apparently lifeless. The multitude whisper, "He is dead." But Jesus takes him by the hand, and lifting him up, presents him, in perfect soundness of mind and body, to his father. Father and son praise the name of their Deliverer. The multitude are "amazed at the mighty power of God," while the scribes, defeated and crestfallen, turn sullenly away.

"If Thou canst do anything, have compassion on us, and help us." How many a sin-burdened soul has echoed that prayer. And to all, the pitying Saviour's answer is, "If thou canst believe, all things are possible to him that believeth." It is faith that connects us with heaven, and brings us strength for coping with the powers of darkness. In Christ, God has provided means for subduing every sinful trait, and resisting every temptation, however strong. But many feel that they lack faith, and therefore they remain away from Christ. Let these souls, in their helpless unworthiness, cast themselves upon the mercy of their compassionate Saviour. Look not to self, but to Christ. He who healed the sick and cast out demons when He walked among men is the same mighty Redeemer today. Faith comes by the word of God. Then grasp His promise, "Him that cometh to Me I will in no wise cast out." John 6:37. Cast yourself at His feet with the cry, "Lord, I believe; help Thou mine unbelief." You can never perish while you do this—never.

In a brief space of time the favored disciples have beheld the extreme of glory and of humiliation. They have seen humanity as transfigured into the image of God, and as debased into the likeness of Satan. From the mountain where He has talked with the heavenly messengers, and has been proclaimed the Son of God by the voice from the radiant glory, they have seen Jesus descend to meet that most distressing and revolting spectacle, the maniac boy, with distorted countenance, gnashing his teeth in spasms of agony that no human power could relieve. And this mighty Redeemer, who but a few hours before stood glorified before His wondering disciples, stoops to lift the victim of Satan from the earth where he is wallowing, and in health of mind and body restores him to his father and his home.

It was an object lesson of redemption,—the Divine One from the Father's glory stooping to save the lost. It represented also the disciples' mission. Not alone upon the mountaintop with Jesus, in hours of spiritual illumination, is the life of Christ's servants to be spent. There is work for them down in the plain. Souls whom Satan has enslaved are waiting for the word of faith and prayer to set them free.

The nine disciples were yet pondering upon the bitter fact of their own failure; and when Jesus was once more alone with them, they questioned, "Why could not we cast him out?" Jesus answered them,

"Because of your unbelief: for verily I say unto you, If ye have faith as a grain of mustard seed, ye shall say unto this mountain, Remove hence to yonder place; and it shall remove; and nothing shall be impossible unto you. Howbeit this kind goeth not out but by prayer and fasting." Their unbelief, that shut them out from deeper sympathy with Christ, and the carelessness with which they regarded the sacred work committed to them, had caused their failure in the conflict with the powers of darkness.

The words of Christ pointing to His death had brought sadness and doubt. And the selection of the three disciples to accompany Jesus to the mountain had excited the jealousy of the nine. Instead of strengthening their faith by prayer and meditation on the words of Christ, they had been dwelling on their discouragements and personal grievances. In this state of darkness they had undertaken the conflict with Satan.

In order to succeed in such a conflict they must come to the work in a different spirit. Their faith must be strengthened by fervent prayer and fasting, and humiliation of heart. They must be emptied of self, and be filled with the Spirit and power of God. Earnest, persevering supplication to God in faith—faith that leads to entire dependence upon God, and unreserved consecration to His work—can alone avail to bring men the Holy Spirit's aid in the battle against principalities and powers, the rulers of the darkness of this world, and wicked spirits in high places.

"If ye have faith as a grain of mustard seed," said Jesus, "ye shall say unto this mountain, Remove hence to yonder place; and it shall remove." Though the grain of mustard seed is so small, it contains that same mysterious life principle which produces growth in the loftiest tree. When the mustard seed is cast into the ground, the tiny germ lays hold of every element that God has provided for its nutriment, and it speedily develops a sturdy growth. If you have faith like this, you will lay hold upon God's word, and upon all the helpful agencies He has appointed. Thus your faith will strengthen, and will bring to your aid the power of heaven. The obstacles that are piled by Satan across your path, though apparently as insurmountable as the eternal hills, shall disappear before the demand of faith. "Nothing shall be impossible unto you."

Who Is the Greatest?

On returning to Capernaum, Jesus did not repair to the well-known resorts where He had taught the people, but with His disciples quietly sought the house that was to be His temporary home. During the remainder of His stay in Galilee it was His object to instruct the disciples rather than to labor for the multitudes.

On the journey through Galilee, Christ had again tried to prepare the minds of His disciples for the scenes before Him. He told them that He was to go up to Jerusalem to be put to death and to rise again. And He added the strange and solemn announcement that He was to be betrayed into the hands of His enemies. The disciples did not even now comprehend His words. Although the shadow of a great sorrow fell upon them, a spirit of rivalry found a place in their hearts. They disputed among themselves which should be accounted greatest in the kingdom. This strife they thought to conceal from Jesus, and they did not, as usual, press close to His side, but loitered behind, so that He was in advance of them as they entered Capernaum. Jesus read their thoughts, and He longed to counsel and instruct them. But for this He awaited a quiet hour, when their hearts should be open to receive His words.

Soon after they reached the town, the collector of the temple revenue came to Peter with the question, "Doth not your Master pay tribute?"

This tribute was not a civil tax, but a religious contribution, which every Jew was required to pay annually for the support of the temple. A refusal to pay the tribute would be regarded as disloyalty to the temple,—in the estimation of the rabbis a most grievous sin. The Saviour's attitude toward the rabbinical laws, and His plain reproofs to the defenders of tradition, afforded a pretext for the charge that He was seeking to overthrow the temple service. Now His enemies saw an opportunity of casting discredit upon Him. In the collector of the tribute they found a ready ally.

Peter saw in the collector's question an insinuation touching Christ's loyalty to the temple. Zealous for his Master's honor, he hastily answered, without consulting Him, that Jesus would pay the tribute.

But Peter only partially comprehended the purpose of his questioner. There were some classes who were held to be exempt from the payment of the tribute. In the time of Moses, when the Levites were set apart for the service of the sanctuary, they were given no inheritance among the people. The Lord said, "Levi hath no part nor inheritance with his brethren; the Lord is his inheritance." Deut. 10:9. In the days of Christ the priests and Levites were still regarded as especially devoted to the temple, and were not required to make the annual contribution for its support. Prophets also were exempted from this payment. In requiring the tribute from Jesus, the rabbis were setting aside His claim as a prophet or teacher, and were dealing with Him as with any commonplace person. A refusal on His part to pay the tribute would be represented as disloyalty to the temple; while, on the other hand, the payment of it would be taken as justifying their rejection of Him as a prophet.

Only a little before, Peter had acknowledged Jesus as the Son of God; but he now missed an opportunity of setting forth the character of his Master. By his answer to the collector, that Jesus would pay the tribute, he had virtually sanctioned the false conception of Him to which the priests and rulers were trying to give currency.

When Peter entered the house, the Saviour made no reference to what had taken place, but inquired, "What thinkest thou, Simon? of whom do the kings of the earth take custom or tribute? of their own children, or of strangers?"

Peter answered, "Of strangers." And Jesus said, "Then are the children free." While the people of a country are taxed for the maintenance of their king, the monarch's own children are exempt. So Israel, the professed people of God, were required to maintain His service; but Jesus, the Son of God, was under no such obligation. If priests and Levites were exempt because of their connection with the temple, how much more He to whom the temple was His Father's house.

If Jesus had paid the tribute without a protest, He would virtually have acknowledged the justice of the claim, and would thus have denied His divinity. But while He saw good to meet the demand, He denied the claim upon which it was based. In providing for the payment of the tribute He gave evidence of His divine character. It was made manifest that He was one with God, and therefore was not under tribute as a mere subject of the kingdom.

"Go thou to the sea," He directed Peter, "and cast an hook, and take up the fish that first cometh up; and when thou hast opened his mouth, thou shalt find a piece of money: that take, and give unto them for Me and thee."

Though He had clothed His divinity with humanity, in this miracle He revealed His glory. It was evident that this was He who through David had declared, "Every beast of the forest is Mine, and the cattle upon a thousand hills. I know all the fowls of the mountains; and the wild beasts of the field are Mine. If I were hungry, I would not tell thee: for the world is Mine, and the fullness thereof." Ps. 50:10-12.

While Jesus made it plain that He was under no obligation to pay the tribute, He entered into no controversy with the Jews in regard to the matter; for they would have misinterpreted His words, and turned them against Him. Lest He should give offense by withholding the tribute, He did that which He could not justly be required to do. This lesson would be of great value to His disciples. Marked changes were soon to take place in their relation to the temple service, and Christ taught them not to place themselves needlessly in antagonism to established order. So far as possible, they were to avoid giving occasion for misinterpretation of their faith. While Christians are not to sacrifice one principle of truth, they should avoid controversy whenever it is possible to do so.

When Christ and the disciples were alone in the house, while Peter was gone to the sea, Jesus called the others to Him, and asked, "What was it that ye disputed among yourselves by the way?" The presence of Jesus, and His question, put the matter in an entirely different light from that in which it had appeared to them while they were contending by the way. Shame and self-condemnation kept them silent. Jesus had told them that He was to die for their sake, and their selfish ambition was in painful contrast to His unselfish love.

When Jesus told them that He was to be put to death and to rise again, He was trying to draw them into conversation in regard to the great test of their faith. Had they been ready to receive what He desired to make known to them, they would have been saved bitter anguish and despair. His words would have brought consolation in the hour of bereavement and disappointment. But although He had spoken so plainly of what awaited Him, His mention of the fact that He was soon to go to Jerusalem again kindled their hope that the kingdom was about to be set up. This had led to questioning as to who should fill the highest offices. On Peter's return from the sea, the disciples told him of the Saviour's question, and at last one ventured to ask Jesus, "Who is the greatest in the kingdom of heaven?"

The Saviour gathered His disciples about Him, and said to them, "If any man desire to be first, the same shall be last of all, and servant of all." There was in these words a solemnity and impressiveness which the disciples were far from comprehending. That which Christ discerned they could not see. They did not understand the nature of Christ's kingdom, and this ignorance was the apparent cause of their contention. But the real cause lay deeper. By explaining the nature of the kingdom, Christ might for the time have quelled their strife; but this would not have touched the underlying cause. Even after they had received the fullest knowledge, any question of precedence might have renewed the trouble. Thus disaster would have been brought to the church after Christ's departure. The strife for the highest place was the outworking of that same spirit which was the beginning of the great controversy in the worlds above, and which had brought Christ from heaven to die. There rose up before Him a vision of Lucifer, the "son of the morning," in glory surpassing all the angels that surround the throne, and united in closest ties to the Son of God. Lucifer had said, "I will be like the Most High" (Isa. 14:12, 14); and the desire for self-exaltation had brought strife into the heavenly courts, and had banished a multitude of the hosts of God. Had Lucifer really desired to be like the Most High, he would never have deserted his appointed place in heaven; for the spirit of the Most High is manifested in unselfish ministry. Lucifer desired God's power, but not His character. He sought for himself the highest place, and every being who is actuated by his spirit will do the same. Thus alienation, discord, and strife will be inevitable. Dominion becomes the prize of the strongest. The kingdom of Satan is a kingdom of force; every individual regards every other as an obstacle in the way of his own advancement, or a steppingstone on which he himself may climb to a higher place.

While Lucifer counted it a thing to be grasped to be equal with God, Christ, the Exalted One, "made Himself of no reputation, and took upon Him the form of a servant, and was made in the likeness of men: and being found in fashion as a man, He humbled Himself, and became obedient unto death, even the death of the cross." Phil. 2:7, 8. Now the cross was just before Him; and His own disciples were so filled with self-seeking—the very principle of Satan's kingdom—that they could not enter into sympathy with their Lord, or even understand Him as He spoke of His humiliation for them.

Very tenderly, yet with solemn emphasis, Jesus tried to correct the evil. He showed what is the principle that bears sway in the kingdom of heaven, and in what true greatness consists, as estimated by the standard of the courts above. Those who were actuated by pride and love of distinction were thinking of themselves, and of the rewards they were to have, rather than how they were to render back to God the gifts they had received. They would have no place in the kingdom of heaven, for they were identified with the ranks of Satan.

Before honor is humility. To fill a high place before men, Heaven chooses the worker who, like John the Baptist, takes a lowly place before God. The most childlike disciple is the most efficient in labor for God. The heavenly intelligences can co-operate with him who is seeking, not to exalt self, but to save souls. He who feels most deeply his need of divine aid will plead for it; and the Holy Spirit will give unto him glimpses of Jesus that will strengthen and uplift the soul. From communion with Christ he will go forth to work for those who are perishing in their sins. He is anointed for his mission; and he succeeds where many of the learned and intellectually wise would fail.

But when men exalt themselves, feeling that they are a necessity for the success of God's great plan, the Lord causes them to be set aside. It is made evident that the Lord is not dependent upon them. The work does not stop because of their removal from it, but goes forward with greater power.

It was not enough for the disciples of Jesus to be instructed as to the nature of His kingdom. What they needed was a change of heart that would bring them into harmony with its principles. Calling a little child to Him, Jesus set him in the midst of them; then tenderly folding the little one in His arms He said, "Except ye be converted, and become as little children, ye shall not enter into the kingdom of heaven." The simplicity, the self-forgetfulness, and the confiding love of a little child are the attributes that Heaven values. These are the characteristics of real greatness.

Again Jesus explained to the disciples that His kingdom is not characterized by earthly dignity and display. At the feet of Jesus all these distinctions are forgotten. The rich and the poor, the learned and the ignorant, meet together, with no thought of caste or worldly preeminence. All meet as blood-bought souls, alike dependent upon One who has redeemed them to God.

The sincere, contrite soul is precious in the sight of God. He places His own signet upon men, not by their rank, not by their wealth, not by their intellectual greatness, but by their oneness with Christ. The Lord of glory is satisfied with those who are meek and lowly in heart. "Thou hast also given me," said David, "the shield of Thy salvation: . . . and Thy gentleness"—as an element in the human character—"hath made me great." Ps. 18:35.

"Whosoever shall receive one of such children in My name," said Jesus, "receiveth Me: and whosoever shall receive Me, receiveth not Me, but Him that sent Me." "Thus saith the Lord, The heaven is My throne, and the earth is My footstool: . . . but to this man will I look, even to him that is poor and of a contrite spirit, and trembleth at My word." Isa.

66:1, 2.

The Saviour's words awakened in the disciples a feeling of self-distrust. No one had been specially pointed out in the reply; but John was led to question whether in one case his action had been right. With the spirit of a child he laid the matter before Jesus. "Master," he said, "we saw one casting out devils in Thy name, and he followeth not us: and we forbade him, because he followeth not us."

James and John had thought that in checking this man they had had in view their Lord's honor; they began to see that they were jealous for their own. They acknowledged their error, and accepted the reproof of Jesus, "Forbid him not: for there is no man which shall do a miracle in My name, that can lightly speak evil of Me." None who showed themselves in any way friendly to Christ were to be repulsed. There were many who had been deeply moved by the character and the work of Christ, and whose hearts were opening to Him in faith; and the disciples, who could not read motives, must be careful not to discourage these souls. When Jesus was no longer personally among them, and the work was left in their hands, they must not indulge a narrow, exclusive spirit, but manifest the same far-reaching sympathy which they had seen in their Master.

The fact that one does not in all things conform to our personal ideas or opinions will not justify us in forbidding him to labor for God. Christ is the Great Teacher; we are not to judge or to command, but in humility each is to sit at the feet of Jesus, and learn of Him. Every soul whom God has made willing is a channel through which Christ will reveal His pardoning love. How careful we should be lest we discourage one of God's light bearers, and thus intercept the rays that He would have shine to the world!

Harshness or coldness shown by a disciple toward one whom Christ was drawing—such an act as that of John in forbidding one to work miracles in Christ's name—might result in turning the feet into the path of the enemy, and causing the loss of a soul. Rather than for one to do this, said Jesus, "it is better for him that a millstone were hanged about his neck, and he were cast into the sea." And He added, "If thy hand cause thee to stumble, cut it off: it is good for thee to enter into life maimed, rather than having thy two hands to go into hell, into the unquenchable fire. And if thy foot cause thee to stumble, cut it off: it is good for thee to enter into life halt, rather than having thy two feet to be cast into hell." Mark 9:43-45, R. V.

Why this earnest language, than which none can be stronger? Because "the Son of man is come to save that which was lost." Shall His disciples show less regard for the souls of their fellow men than the Majesty of heaven has shown? Every soul has cost an infinite price, and how terrible is the sin of turning one soul away from Christ, so that for him the Saviour's love and humiliation and agony shall have been in vain.

"Woe unto the world because of occasions of stumbling! for it must needs be that the occasions come." Matt. 18:7, R. V.

The world, inspired by Satan, will surely oppose the followers of Christ, and seek to destroy their faith; but woe to him who has taken Christ's name, and yet is found doing this work. Our Lord is put to shame by those who claim to serve Him, but who misrepresent His character; and multitudes are deceived, and led into false paths.

Any habit or practice that would lead into sin, and bring dishonor upon Christ, would better be put away, whatever the sacrifice. That which dishonors God cannot benefit the soul. The blessing of heaven cannot attend any man in violating the eternal principles of right. And one sin cherished is sufficient to work the degradation of the character, and to mislead others. If the foot or the hand would be cut off, or even the eye would be plucked out, to save the body from death, how much more earnest should we be to put away sin, that brings death to the soul!

In the ritual service, salt was added to every sacrifice. This, like the offering of incense, signified that only the righteousness of Christ could make the service acceptable to God. Referring to this practice, Jesus said, "Every sacrifice shall be salted with salt." "Have salt in yourselves, and have peace one with another." All who would present themselves "a living sacrifice, holy, acceptable unto God" (Rom. 12:1), must receive the saving salt, the righteousness of our Saviour. Then they become "the salt of the earth," restraining evil among men, as salt preserves from corruption. Matt. 5:13. But if the salt has lost its savor; if there is only a profession of godliness, without the love of Christ, there is no power for good. The life can exert no saving influence upon the world. Your energy and efficiency in the upbuilding of My kingdom, Jesus says, depend upon your receiving of My Spirit. You must be partakers of My grace, in order to be a savor of life unto life. Then there will be no rivalry, no self-seeking, no desire for the highest place. You will have that love which seeks not her own, but another's wealth.

Let the repenting sinner fix his eyes upon "the Lamb of God, which taketh away the sin of the world" (John 1:29); and by beholding, he becomes changed. His fear is turned to joy, his doubts to hope. Gratitude springs up. The stony heart is broken. A tide of love sweeps into the soul. Christ is in him a well of water springing up unto everlasting life. When we see Jesus, a Man of Sorrows and acquainted with grief, working to save the lost, slighted, scorned, derided, driven from city to city till His mission was accomplished; when we behold Him in Gethsemane, sweating great drops of blood, and on the cross dying in agony,—when we see this, self will no longer clamor to be recognized. Looking unto Jesus, we shall be ashamed of our coldness, our lethargy, our self-seeking. We shall be willing to be anything or nothing, so that we may do heart service for the Master. We shall rejoice to bear the cross after Jesus, to endure trial, shame, or persecution for His dear sake.

"We then that are strong ought to bear the infirmities of the weak, and not to please ourselves." Rom. 15:1. No soul who believes in Christ, though his faith may be weak, and his steps wavering as those of a little child, is to be lightly esteemed. By all that has given us advantage over another,—be it education and refinement, nobility of character, Christian training, religious experience,—we are in debt to those less favored; and, so far as lies in our power, we are to minister unto them. If we are strong, we are to stay up the hands of the weak. Angels of glory, that do always behold the face of the Father in heaven, joy in ministering to His little ones. Trembling souls, who have many objectionable traits of character, are their special charge. Angels are ever present where they are most needed, with those who have the hardest battle with self to fight, and whose surroundings are the most discouraging. And in this ministry Christ's true followers will co-operate.

If one of these little ones shall be overcome, and commit a wrong against you, then it is your work to seek his restoration. Do not wait for him to make the first effort for reconciliation. "How think ye?" said Jesus; "if a man have an hundred sheep, and one of them be gone astray, doth he not leave the ninety and nine, and goeth into the mountains, and seeketh that which is gone astray? And if so be that he find it, verily I say unto you, he rejoiceth more of that sheep, than of the ninety and nine which went not astray. Even so it is not the will of your Father which is in heaven, that one of these little ones should perish."

In the spirit of meekness, "considering thyself, lest thou also be tempted," (Gal. 6:1), go to the erring one, and "tell him his fault between thee and him alone." Do not put him to shame by exposing his fault to others, nor bring dishonor upon Christ by making public the sin or error of one who bears His name. Often the truth must be plainly spoken to the erring; he must be led to see his error, that he may reform. But you are not to judge or to condemn. Make no attempt at self-justification. Let all your effort be for his recovery. In treating the wounds of the soul, there is need of the most delicate touch, the finest sensibility. Only the love that flows from the Suffering One of Calvary can avail here. With pitying tenderness, let brother deal with brother, knowing that if you succeed, you will "save a soul from death," and "hide a multitude of sins." James 5:20.

But even this effort may be unavailing. Then, said Jesus, "take with thee one or two more." It may be that their united influence will prevail where that of the first was unsuccessful. Not being parties to the trouble, they will be more likely to act impartially, and this fact will give their counsel greater weight with the erring one.

If he will not hear them, then, and not till then, the matter is to be brought before the whole body of believers. Let the members of the church, as the representatives of Christ, unite in prayer and loving entreaty that the offender may be restored. The Holy Spirit will speak through His servants, pleading with the wanderer to return to God. Paul the apostle, speaking by inspiration, says, "As though God did beseech you by us: we pray you in Christ's stead, be ye reconciled to God." 2 Cor. 5:20. He who rejects this united overture has broken the tie that binds him to Christ, and thus has severed himself from the fellowship of the church. Henceforth, said Jesus, "let

him be unto thee as an heathen man and a publican." But he is not to be regarded as cut off from the mercy of God. Let him not be despised or neglected by his former brethren, but be treated with tenderness and compassion, as one of the lost sheep that Christ is still seeking to bring to His fold.

Christ's instruction as to the treatment of the erring repeats in more specific form the teaching given to Israel through Moses: "Thou shalt not hate thy brother in thine heart: thou shalt in anywise rebuke thy neighbor, that thou bear not sin for him." Lev. 19:17, margin. That is, if one neglects the duty Christ has enjoined, of trying to restore those who are in error and sin, he becomes a partaker in the sin. For evils that we might have checked, we are just as responsible as if we were guilty of the acts ourselves.

But it is to the wrongdoer himself that we are to present the wrong. We are not to make it a matter of comment and criticism among ourselves; nor even after it is told to the church, are we at liberty to repeat it to others. A knowledge of the faults of Christians will be only a cause of stumbling to the unbelieving world; and by dwelling upon these things, we ourselves can receive only harm; for it is by beholding that we become changed. While we seek to correct the errors of a brother, the Spirit of Christ will lead us to shield him, as far as possible, from the criticism of even his own brethren, and how much more from the censure of the unbelieving world. We ourselves are erring, and need Christ's pity and forgiveness, and just as we wish Him to deal with us, He bids us deal with one another.

"Whatsoever ye shall bind on earth shall be bound in heaven: and whatsoever ye shall loose on earth shall be loosed in heaven." You are acting as the ambassadors of heaven, and the issues of your work are for eternity.

But we are not to bear this great responsibility alone. Wherever His word is obeyed with a sincere heart, there Christ abides. Not only is He present in the assemblies of the church, but wherever disciples, however few, meet in His name, there also He will be. And He says, "If two of you shall agree on earth as touching anything that they shall ask, it shall be done for them of My Father which is in heaven."

Jesus says, " My Father which is in heaven," as reminding His disciples that while by His humanity He is linked with them, a sharer in their trials, and sympathizing with them in their sufferings, by His divinity He is connected with the throne of the Infinite. Wonderful assurance! The heavenly intelligences unite with men in sympathy and labor for the saving of that which was lost. And all the power of heaven is brought to combine with human ability in drawing souls to Christ.

At the Feast of Tabernacles

Three times a year the Jews were required to assemble at Jerusalem for religious purposes. Enshrouded in the pillar of cloud, Israel's invisible Leader had given the directions in regard to these gatherings. During the captivity of the Jews, they could not be observed; but when the people were restored to their own land, the observance of these memorials was once more begun. It was God's design that these anniversaries should call Him to the minds of the people. But with few exceptions, the priests and leaders of the nation had lost sight of this purpose. He who had ordained these national assemblies and understood their significance witnessed their perversion.

The Feast of Tabernacles was the closing gathering of the year. It was God's design that at this time the people should reflect on His goodness and mercy. The whole land had been under His guidance, receiving His blessing. Day and night His watchcare had continued. The sun and rain had caused the earth to produce her fruits. From the valleys and plains of Palestine the harvest had been gathered. The olive berries had been picked, and the precious oil stored in bottles. The palm had yielded her store. The purple clusters of the vine had been trodden in the wine press.

The feast continued for seven days, and for its celebration the inhabitants of Palestine, with many from other lands, left their homes, and came to Jerusalem. From far and near the people came, bringing in their hands a token of rejoicing. Old and young, rich and poor, all brought some gift as a tribute of thanksgiving to Him who had crowned the year with His goodness, and made His paths drop fatness. Everything that could please the eye, and give expression to the universal joy, was brought from the woods; the city bore the appearance of a beautiful forest.

This feast was not only the harvest thanksgiving, but the memorial of God's protecting care over Israel in the wilderness. In commemoration of their tent life, the Israelites during the feast dwelt in booths or tabernacles of green boughs. These were erected in the streets, in the courts of the temple, or on the housetops. The hills and valleys surrounding Jerusalem were also dotted with these leafy dwellings, and seemed to be alive with people.

With sacred song and thanksgiving the worshipers celebrated this occasion. A little before the feast was the Day of Atonement, when, after confession of their sins, the people were declared to be at peace with Heaven. Thus the way was prepared for the rejoicing of the feast. "O give thanks unto the Lord; for He is good: for His mercy endureth forever" (Ps. 106:1) rose triumphantly, while all kinds of music, mingled with shouts of hosanna, accompanied the united singing. The temple was the center of the universal joy. Here was the pomp of the sacrificial ceremonies. Here, ranged on either side of the white marble steps of the sacred building, the choir of Levites led the service of song. The multitude of worshipers, waving their branches of palm and myrtle, took up the strain, and echoed the chorus; and again the melody was caught up by voices near and afar off, till the encircling hills were vocal with praise.

At night the temple and its court blazed with artificial light. The music, the waving of palm branches, the glad hosannas, the great concourse of people, over whom the light streamed from the hanging lamps, the array of the priests, and the majesty of the ceremonies, combined to make a scene that deeply impressed the beholders. But the most impressive ceremony of the feast, one that called forth greatest rejoicing, was one commemorating an event in the wilderness sojourn.

At the first dawn of day, the priests sounded a long, shrill blast upon their silver trumpets, and the answering trumpets, and the glad shouts of the people from their booths, echoing over hill and valley, welcomed the festal day. Then the priest dipped from the flowing waters of the Kedron a flagon of water, and, lifting it on high, while the trumpets were sounding, he ascended the broad steps of the temple, keeping time with the music with slow and measured tread, chanting meanwhile, "Our feet shall stand within thy gates, O Jerusalem." Ps. 122:2.

He bore the flagon to the altar, which occupied a central position in the court of the priests. Here were two silver basins, with a priest standing at each one. The flagon of water was poured into one, and a flagon of wine into the other; and the contents of both flowed into a pipe which communicated with the Kedron, and was conducted to the Dead Sea. This display of the consecrated water represented the fountain that at the command of God had gushed from the rock to quench the thirst of the children of Israel. Then the jubilant strains rang forth, "The Lord Jehovah is my strength and my song;" "therefore with joy shall ye draw water out of the wells of salvation." Isa. 12:2, 3.

As the sons of Joseph made preparation to attend the Feast of Tabernacles, they saw that Christ made no movement signifying His intention of attending. They watched Him with anxiety. Since the healing at Bethesda He had not attended the national gatherings. To avoid useless conflict with the leaders at Jerusalem, He had restricted His labors to Galilee. His apparent neglect of the great religious assemblies, and the enmity manifested toward Him by the priests and rabbis, were a cause of perplexity to the people about Him, and even to His own disciples and His kindred. In His teachings He had dwelt upon the blessings of obedience to the law of God, and yet He Himself seemed to be indifferent to the service which had been divinely established. His mingling with publicans and others of ill repute, His disregard of the rabbinical observances, and the freedom with which He set aside the traditional requirements concerning the Sabbath, all seeming to place Him in antagonism to the religious authorities, excited much questioning. His brothers thought it a mistake for Him to alienate the great and learned men of the nation. They felt that these men must be in the right, and that Jesus was at fault in placing Himself in antagonism to them. But they had witnessed His blameless life, and though they did not rank themselves with His disciples, they had been deeply impressed by His works. His popularity in Galilee was gratifying to their ambition; they still hoped that He would give an evidence of His power which would lead the Pharisees to see that He was what He claimed to be. What if He were the Messiah, the Prince of Israel! They cherished this thought with proud satisfaction.

So anxious were they about this that they urged Christ to go to Jerusalem. "Depart hence," they said, "and go into Judea, that Thy disciples also may see the works that Thou doest. For there is no man that doeth anything in secret, and he himself seeketh to be known openly. If Thou do these things, show Thyself to the world." The "if" expressed doubt and unbelief. They attributed cowardice and weakness to Him. If He knew that He was the Messiah, why this strange reserve and inaction? If He really possessed such power, why not go boldly to Jerusalem, and assert His claims? Why not perform in Jerusalem the wonderful works reported of Him in Galilee? Do not hide in secluded provinces, they said, and perform your mighty works for the benefit of ignorant peasants and fishermen. Present yourself at the capital, win the support of the priests and rulers, and unite the nation in establishing the new kingdom.

These brothers of Jesus reasoned from the selfish motive so often found in the hearts of those ambitious for display. This spirit was the ruling spirit of the world. They were offended because, instead of seeking a temporal throne, Christ had declared Himself to be the bread of life. They were greatly disappointed when so many of His disciples forsook Him. They themselves turned from Him to escape the cross of acknowledging what His works revealed—that He was the Sent of God.

"Then Jesus said unto them, My time is not yet come: but your time is alway ready. The world cannot hate you; but Me it hateth, because I testify of it, that the works thereof are evil. Go ye up unto this feast: I go not up yet unto this feast; for My time is not yet full come. When He had said these words unto them, He abode still in Galilee." His brothers had spoken to Him in a tone of authority, prescribing the course He should pursue. He cast their rebuke back to them, classing them not with His self-denying disciples, but with the world. "The world cannot hate you," He said, "but Me it hateth, because I testify of it, that the works thereof are evil." The world does not hate those who are like it in spirit; it loves them as its own.

The world for Christ was not a place of ease and self-aggrandizement. He was not watching for an opportunity to seize its power and its glory. It held out no such prize for Him. It was the place into which His Father had sent Him. He had been given for the life of the world, to work out the great plan of redemption. He was accomplishing His work for the fallen race. But He was not to be presumptuous, not to rush into danger, not to hasten a crisis. Each event in His work had its appointed hour. He must wait patiently. He knew that He was to receive the world's hatred; He knew that His work would result in His death; but to prematurely expose Himself would not be the will of His Father.

From Jerusalem the report of Christ's miracles had spread wherever the Jews were dispersed; and although for many months He had been absent from the feasts, the interest in Him had not abated. Many from all parts of the world had come up to the Feast of Tabernacles in the hope of seeing Him. At the beginning of the feast many inquiries were made for Him. The Pharisees and rulers looked for Him to come, hoping for an opportunity to condemn Him. They anxiously inquired, "Where is He?" but no one knew. The thought of Him was uppermost in all minds. Through fear of the priests and rulers, none dared acknowledge Him as the Messiah, but everywhere there was quiet yet earnest discussion concerning Him. Many defended Him as one sent from God, while others denounced Him as a deceiver of the people.

Meanwhile Jesus had quietly arrived at Jerusalem. He had chosen an unfrequented route by which to go, in order to avoid the travelers who were making their way to the city from all quarters. Had He joined any of the caravans that went up to the feast, public attention would have been attracted to Him on His entrance into the city, and a popular demonstration in His favor would have aroused the authorities against Him. It was to avoid this that He chose to make the journey alone.

In the midst of the feast, when the excitement concerning Him was at its height, He entered the court of the temple in the presence of the multitude. Because of His absence from the feast, it had been urged that He dared not place Himself in the power of the priests and rulers. All were surprised at His presence. Every voice was hushed. All wondered at the dignity and courage of His bearing in the midst of powerful enemies who were thirsting for His life.

Standing thus, the center of attraction to that vast throng, Jesus addressed them as no man had ever done. His words showed a knowledge of the laws and institutions of Israel, of the sacrificial service and the teachings of the prophets, far exceeding that of the priests and rabbis. He broke through the barriers of formalism and tradition. The scenes of the future life seemed outspread before Him. As one who beheld the Unseen, He spoke of the earthly and the heavenly, the human and the divine, with positive authority. His words were most clear and convincing; and again, as at Capernaum, the people were astonished at His teaching; "for His word was with power." Luke 4:32. Under a variety of representations He warned His hearers of the calamity that would follow all who rejected the blessings He came to bring them. He had given them every possible proof that He came forth from God, and made every possible effort to bring them to repentance. He would not be rejected and murdered by His own nation if He could save them from the guilt of such a deed.

All wondered at His knowledge of the law and the prophecies; and the question passed from one to another, "How knoweth this Man letters, having never learned?" No one was regarded as qualified to be a religious teacher unless he had studied in the rabbinical schools, and both Jesus and John the Baptist had been represented as ignorant because they had not received this training. Those who heard them were astonished at their knowledge of the Scriptures, "having never learned." Of men they had not, truly; but the God of heaven was their teacher, and from Him they had received the highest kind of wisdom.

As Jesus spoke in the temple court, the people were held spellbound. The very men who were the most violent against Him felt themselves powerless to do Him harm. For the time, all other interests were forgotten.

Day after day He taught the people, until the last, "that great day of the feast." The morning of this day found the people wearied from the long season of festivity. Suddenly Jesus lifted up His voice, in tones that rang through the courts of the temple:

"If any man thirst, let him come unto Me, and drink. He that believeth on Me, as the scripture hath said, out of his belly shall flow rivers of living water." The condition of the people made this appeal very forcible. They had been engaged in a continued scene of pomp and festivity, their eyes had been dazzled with light and color, and their ears regaled with the richest music; but there had been nothing in all this round of ceremonies to meet the wants of the spirit, nothing to satisfy the thirst of the soul for that which perishes not. Jesus invited them to come and drink of the fountain of life, of that which would be in them a well of water, springing up unto everlasting life.

The priest had that morning performed the ceremony which commemorated the smiting of the rock in the wilderness. That rock was a symbol of Him who by His death would cause living streams of salvation to flow to all who are athirst. Christ's words were the water of life. There in the presence of the assembled multitude He set Himself apart to be smitten, that the water of life might flow to the world. In smiting Christ, Satan thought to destroy the Prince of life; but from the smitten rock there flowed living water. As Jesus thus spoke to the people, their hearts thrilled with a strange awe, and many were ready to exclaim, with the woman of Samaria, "Give me this water, that I thirst not." John 4:15.

Jesus knew the wants of the soul. Pomp, riches, and honor cannot satisfy the heart. "If any man thirst, let him come unto Me." The rich, the poor, the high, the low, are alike welcome. He promises to relieve the burdened mind, to comfort the sorrowing, and to give hope to the despondent. Many of those who heard Jesus were mourners over disappointed hopes, many were nourishing a secret grief, many were seeking to satisfy their restless longing with the things of the world and the praise of men; but when all was gained, they found that they had toiled only to reach a broken cistern, from which they could not quench their thirst. Amid the glitter of the joyous scene they stood, dissatisfied and sad. That sudden cry, "If any man thirst," startled them from their sorrowful meditation, and as they listened to the words that followed, their minds kindled with a new hope. The Holy Spirit presented the symbol before them until they saw in it the offer of the priceless gift of salvation.

The cry of Christ to the thirsty soul is still going forth, and it appeals to us with even greater power than to those who heard it in the temple on that last day of the feast. The fountain is open for all. The weary and exhausted ones are offered the refreshing draught of eternal life. Jesus is still crying, "If any man thirst, let him come unto Me, and drink." "Let him that is athirst come. And whosoever will, let him take the water of life freely." "Whosoever drinketh of the water that I shall give him shall never thirst; but the water that I shall give him shall be in him a well of water springing up into everlasting life." Rev. 22:17; John 4:14.

Among Snares

All the while Jesus was at Jerusalem during the feast He was shadowed by spies. Day after day new schemes to silence Him were tried. The priests and rulers were watching to entrap Him. They were planning to stop Him by violence. But this was not all. They wanted to humble this Galilean rabbi before the people.

On the first day of His presence at the feast, the rulers had come to Him, demanding by what authority He taught. They wished to divert attention from Him to the question of His right to teach, and thus to their own importance and authority.

"My teaching is not Mine," said Jesus, "but His that sent Me. If any man willeth to do His will, he shall know of the teaching, whether it be of God, or whether I speak from Myself." John 7:16, 17, R. V. The question of these cavilers Jesus met, not by answering the cavil, but by opening up truth vital to the salvation of the soul. The perception and appreciation of truth, He said, depends less upon the mind than upon the heart. Truth must be received into the soul; it claims the homage of the will. If truth could be submitted to the reason alone, pride would be no hindrance in the way of its reception. But it is to be received through the work of grace in the heart; and its reception depends upon the renunciation of every sin that the Spirit of God reveals. Man's advantages for obtaining a knowledge of the truth, however great these may be, will prove of no benefit to him unless the heart is open to receive the truth, and there is a conscientious surrender of every habit and practice that is opposed to its principles. To those who thus yield themselves to God, having an honest desire to know and to do His will, the truth is revealed as the power of God for their salvation. These will be able to distinguish between him who speaks for God, and him who speaks merely from himself. The Pharisees had not put their will on the side of God's will. They were not seeking to know the truth, but to find some excuse for evading it; Christ showed that this was why they did not understand His teaching.

He now gave a test by which the true teacher might be distinguished from the deceiver: "He that speaketh from himself seeketh his own glory: but he that seeketh the glory of Him that sent him, the same is true, and no unrighteousness is in him." John 7:18, R. V. He that seeketh his own glory is speaking only from himself. The spirit of self-seeking betrays its origin. But Christ was seeking the glory of God. He spoke the words of God. This was the evidence of His authority as a teacher of the truth.

Jesus gave the rabbis an evidence of His divinity by showing that He read their hearts. Ever since the healing at Bethesda they had been plotting His death. Thus they were themselves breaking the law which they professed to be defending. "Did not Moses give you the law," He said, "and yet none of you keepeth the law? Why go ye about to kill Me?"

Like a swift flash of light these words revealed to the rabbis the pit of ruin into which they were about to plunge. For an instant they were filled with terror. They saw that they were in conflict with Infinite Power. But they would not be warned. In order to maintain their influence with the people, their murderous designs must be concealed. Evading the question of Jesus, they exclaimed, "Thou hast a devil: who goeth about to kill Thee?" They insinuated that the wonderful works of Jesus were instigated by an evil spirit.

To this insinuation Christ gave no heed. He went on to show that His work of healing at Bethesda was in harmony with the Sabbath law, and that it was justified by the interpretation which the Jews themselves put upon the law. He said, "Moses therefore gave unto you circumcision; . . . and ye on the Sabbath day circumcise a man." According to the law, every child must be circumcised on the eighth day. Should the appointed time fall upon the Sabbath, the rite must then be performed. How much more must it be in harmony with the spirit of the law to make a man "every whit whole on the Sabbath day." And He warned them to "judge not according to the appearance, but judge righteous judgment."

The rulers were silenced; and many of the people exclaimed, "Is not this He, whom they seek to kill? But, lo, He speaketh boldly, and they say nothing unto Him. Do the rulers know indeed that this is the very Christ?"

Many among Christ's hearers who were dwellers at Jerusalem, and who were not ignorant of the plots of the rulers against Him, felt themselves drawn to Him by an irresistible power. The conviction pressed upon them that He was the Son of God. But Satan was ready to suggest doubt; and for this the way was prepared by their own erroneous ideas of the Messiah and His coming. It was generally believed that Christ would be born at Bethlehem, but that after a time He would disappear, and at His second appearance none would know whence He came. There were not a few who held that the Messiah would have no natural relationship to humanity. And because the popular conception of the glory of the Messiah was not met by Jesus of Nazareth, many gave heed to the suggestion, "Howbeit we know this Man whence He is: but when Christ cometh, no man knoweth whence He is."

While they were thus wavering between doubt and faith, Jesus took up their thoughts and answered them: "Ye both know Me, and ye know whence I am: and I am not come of Myself, but He that sent Me is true, whom ye know not." They claimed a knowledge of what the origin of Christ should be, but they were in utter ignorance of it. If they had lived in accordance with the will of God, they would have known His Son when He was manifested to them.

The hearers could not but understand Christ's words. Clearly they were a repetition of the claim He had made in the presence of the Sanhedrin many months before, when He declared Himself the Son of God. As the rulers then tried to compass His death, so now they sought to take Him; but they were prevented by an unseen power, which put a limit to their rage, saying to them, Thus far shalt thou go, and no farther.

Among the people many believed on Him, and they said, "When Christ cometh, will He do more miracles than these which this Man hath done?" The leaders of the Pharisees, who were anxiously watching the course of events, caught the expressions of sympathy among the throng. Hurrying away to the chief priests, they laid their plans to arrest Him. They arranged, however, to take Him when He was alone; for they dared not seize Him in the presence of the people. Again Jesus made it manifest that He read their purpose. "Yet a little while am I with you," He said, "and then I go unto Him that sent Me. Ye shall seek Me, and shall not find Me: and where I am, thither ye cannot come." Soon He would find a refuge beyond the reach of their scorn and hate. He would ascend to the Father, to be again the Adored of the angels; and thither His murderers could never come.

Sneeringly the rabbis said, "Whither will He go, that we shall not find Him? will He go unto the dispersed among the Gentiles, and teach the Gentiles?" Little did these cavilers dream that in their mocking words they were picturing the mission of the Christ! All day long He had stretched forth His hands unto a disobedient and gainsaying people; yet He would be found of them that sought Him not; among a people that had not called upon His name He would be manifest. Rom. 10:20, 21.

Many who were convinced that Jesus was the Son of God were misled by the false reasoning of the priests and rabbis. These teachers had repeated with great effect the prophecies concerning the Messiah, that He would "reign in Mount Zion, and in Jerusalem, and before His ancients gloriously;" that He would "have dominion also from sea to sea, and from the river unto the ends of the earth." Isa. 24:23; Ps. 72:8. Then they made contemptuous comparisons between the glory here pictured and the humble appearance of Jesus. The very words of prophecy were so perverted as to sanction error. Had the people in sincerity studied the word for themselves, they would not have been misled. The sixty-first chapter of Isaiah testifies that Christ was to do the very work He did. Chapter fifty-three sets forth His rejection and sufferings in the world, and chapter fifty-nine describes the character of the priests and rabbis.

God does not compel men to give up their unbelief. Before them are light and darkness, truth and error. It is for them to decide which they will accept. The human mind is endowed with power to discriminate between right and wrong. God designs that men shall not decide from impulse, but from weight of evidence, carefully comparing scripture with scripture. Had the Jews laid by their prejudice and compared written prophecy with the facts characterizing the life of Jesus, they would have perceived a beautiful harmony between the prophecies and their fulfillment in the life and ministry of the lowly Galilean.

Many are deceived today in the same way as were the Jews. Religious teachers read the Bible in the light of their own understanding and traditions; and the people do not search the Scriptures for themselves, and judge for themselves as to what is truth; but they yield up their judgment, and commit their souls to their leaders. The preaching and teaching of His word is one of the means that God has ordained for diffusing light; but we must bring every man's teaching to the test of Scripture. Whoever will prayerfully study the Bible, desiring to know the truth, that he may obey it, will receive divine enlightenment. He will understand the Scriptures. "If any man willeth to do His will, he shall know of the teaching." John 7:17, R. V.

On the last day of the feast, the officers sent out by the priests and rulers to arrest Jesus, returned without Him. They were angrily questioned, "Why have ye not brought Him?" With solemn countenance they answered, "Never man spake like this Man."

Hardened as were their hearts, they were melted by His words. While He was speaking in the temple court, they had lingered near, to catch something that might be turned against Him. But as they listened, the purpose for which they had been sent was forgotten. They stood as men entranced. Christ revealed Himself to their souls. They saw that which priests and rulers would not see,—humanity flooded with the glory of divinity. They returned, so filled with this thought, so impressed by His words, that to the inquiry, "Why have ye not brought Him?" they could only reply, "Never man spake like this Man."

The priests and rulers, on first coming into the presence of Christ, had felt the same conviction. Their hearts were deeply moved, and the thought was forced upon them, "Never man spake like this Man." But they had stifled the conviction of the Holy Spirit. Now, enraged that even the instruments of the law should be influenced by the hated Galilean, they cried, "Are ye also deceived? Have any of the rulers or of the Pharisees believed on Him? But this people who knoweth not the law are cursed."

Those to whom the message of truth is spoken seldom ask, "Is it true?" but, "By whom is it advocated?" Multitudes estimate it by the numbers who accept it; and the question is still asked, "Have any of the learned men or religious leaders believed?" Men are no more favorable to real godliness now than in the days of Christ. They are just as intently seeking earthly good, to the neglect of eternal riches; and it is not an argument against the truth, that large numbers are not ready to accept it, or that it is not received by the world's great men, or even by the religious leaders.

Again the priests and rulers proceeded to lay plans for arresting Jesus. It was urged that if He were longer left at liberty, He would draw the people away from the established leaders, and the only safe course was to silence Him without delay. In the full tide of their discussion, they were suddenly checked. Nicodemus questioned, "Doth our law judge any man, before it hear him, and know what he doeth?" Silence fell on the assembly. The words of Nicodemus came home to their consciences. They could not condemn a man unheard. But it was not for this reason alone that the haughty rulers remained silent, gazing at him who had dared to speak in favor of justice. They were startled and chagrined that one of their own number had been so far impressed by the character of Jesus as to speak a word in His defense. Recovering from their astonishment, they addressed Nicodemus with cutting sarcasm, "Art thou also of Galilee? Search and look: for out of Galilee ariseth no prophet."

Yet the protest resulted in staying the proceedings of the council. The rulers were unable to carry out their purpose and condemn Jesus without a hearing. Defeated for the time, "every man went unto his own house. Jesus went unto the Mount of Olives."

From the excitement and confusion of the city, from the eager crowds and the treacherous rabbis, Jesus turned away to the quiet of the olive groves, where He could be alone with God. But in the early morning He returned to the temple, and as the people gathered about Him, He sat down and taught them.

He was soon interrupted. A group of Pharisees and scribes approached Him, dragging with them a terror-stricken woman, whom with hard, eager voices they accused of having violated the seventh commandment. Having pushed her into the presence of Jesus, they said to Him, with a hypocritical show of respect, "Moses in the law commanded us, that such should be stoned: but what sayest Thou?"

Their pretended reverence veiled a deep-laid plot for His ruin. They had seized upon this opportunity to secure His condemnation, thinking that whatever decision He might make, they would find occasion to accuse Him. Should He acquit the woman, He might be charged with despising the law of Moses. Should He declare her worthy of death, He could be accused to the Romans as one who was assuming authority that belonged only to them.

Jesus looked for a moment upon the scene,—the trembling victim in her shame, the hard-faced dignitaries, devoid of even human pity. His spirit of stainless purity shrank from the spectacle. Well He knew for what purpose this case had been brought to Him. He read the heart, and knew the character and life history of everyone in His presence. These would-be guardians of justice had themselves led their victim into sin, that they might lay a snare for Jesus. Giving no sign that He had heard their question, He stooped, and fixing His eyes upon the ground, began to write in the dust.

Impatient at His delay and apparent indifference, the accusers drew nearer, urging the matter upon His attention. But as their eyes, following those of Jesus, fell upon the pavement at His feet, their countenances changed. There, traced before them, were the guilty secrets of their own lives.

The people, looking on, saw the sudden change of expression, and pressed forward to discover what it was that they were regarding with such astonishment and shame.

With all their professions of reverence for the law, these rabbis, in bringing the charge against the woman, were disregarding its provisions. It was the husband's duty to take action against her, and the guilty parties were to be punished equally. The action of the accusers was wholly unauthorized. Jesus, however, met them on their own ground. The law specified that in punishment by stoning, the witnesses in the case should be the first to cast a stone. Now rising, and fixing His eyes upon the plotting elders, Jesus said, "He that is without sin among you, let him first cast a stone at her." And stooping down, He continued writing on the ground.

He had not set aside the law given through Moses, nor infringed upon the authority of Rome. The accusers had been defeated. Now, their robe of pretended holiness torn from them, they stood, guilty and condemned, in the presence of Infinite Purity. They trembled lest the hidden iniquity of their lives should be laid open to the multitude; and one by one, with bowed heads and downcast eyes, they stole away, leaving their victim with the pitying Saviour.

Jesus arose, and looking at the woman said, "Woman, where are those thine accusers? hath no man condemned thee? She said, No man, Lord. And Jesus said unto her, Neither do I condemn thee: go, and sin no more."

The woman had stood before Jesus, cowering with fear. His words, "He that is without sin among you, let him first cast a stone," had come to her as a death sentence. She dared not lift her eyes to the Saviour's face, but silently awaited her doom. In astonishment she saw her accusers depart speechless and confounded; then those words of hope fell upon her ear, "Neither do I condemn thee: go, and sin no more." Her heart was melted, and she cast herself at the feet of Jesus, sobbing out her grateful love, and with bitter tears confessing her sins.

This was to her the beginning of a new life, a life of purity and peace, devoted to the service of God. In the uplifting of this fallen soul, Jesus performed a greater miracle than in healing the most grievous physical disease; He cured the spiritual malady which is unto death everlasting. This penitent woman became one of His most steadfast followers. With self-sacrificing love and devotion she repaid His forgiving mercy.

In His act of pardoning this woman and encouraging her to live a better life, the character of Jesus shines forth in the beauty of perfect righteousness. While He does not palliate sin, nor lessen the sense of guilt, He seeks not to condemn, but to save. The world had for this erring woman only contempt and scorn; but Jesus speaks words of comfort and hope. The Sinless One pities the weakness of the sinner, and reaches to her a helping hand. While the hypocritical Pharisees denounce, Jesus bids her, "Go, and sin no more."

It is not Christ's follower that, with averted eyes, turns from the erring, leaving them unhindered to pursue their downward course. Those who are forward in accusing others, and zealous in bringing them to justice, are often in their own lives more guilty than they. Men hate the sinner, while they love the sin. Christ hates the sin, but loves the sinner. This will be the spirit of all who follow Him. Christian love is slow to censure, quick to discern penitence, ready to forgive, to encourage, to set the wanderer in the path of holiness, and to stay his feet therein.

"The Light of Life"

Then spake Jesus again unto them, saying, I am the light of the world: he that followeth Me shall not walk in darkness, but shall have the light of life."

When He spoke these words, Jesus was in the court of the temple specially connected with the services of the Feast of Tabernacles. In the center of this court rose two lofty standards, supporting lampstands of great size. After the evening sacrifice, all the lamps were kindled, shedding their light over Jerusalem. This ceremony was in commemoration of the pillar of light that guided Israel in the desert, and was also regarded as pointing to the coming of the Messiah. At evening when the lamps were lighted, the court was a scene of great rejoicing. Gray-haired men, the priests of the temple and the rulers of the people, united in the festive dances to the sound of instrumental music and the chants of the Levites.

In the illumination of Jerusalem, the people expressed their hope of the Messiah's coming to shed His light upon Israel. But to Jesus the scene had a wider meaning. As the radiant lamps of the temple lighted up all about them, so Christ, the source of spiritual light, illumines the darkness of the world. Yet the symbol was imperfect. That great light which His own hand had set in the heavens was a truer representation of the glory of His mission.

It was morning; the sun had just risen above the Mount of Olives, and its rays fell with dazzling brightness on the marble palaces, and lighted up the gold of the temple walls, when Jesus, pointing to it, said, "I am the light of the world."

By one who listened to these words, they were long afterward re-echoed in that sublime passage, "In Him was life; and the life was the light of men. And the light shineth in the darkness; and the darkness apprehended it not." "That was the true light, which lighteth every man that cometh into the world." John 1:4, 5, R. V., 9. And long after Jesus had ascended to heaven, Peter also, writing under the illumination of the divine Spirit, recalled the symbol Christ had used: "We have also a more sure word of prophecy; whereunto ye do well that ye take heed, as unto a light that shineth in a dark place, until the day dawn, and the daystar arise in your hearts." 2 Peter 1:19.

In the manifestation of God to His people, light had ever been a symbol of His presence. At the creative word in the beginning, light had shone out of darkness. Light had been enshrouded in the pillar of cloud by day and the pillar of fire by night, leading the vast armies of Israel. Light blazed with awful grandeur about the Lord on Mount Sinai. Light rested over the mercy seat in the tabernacle. Light filled the temple of Solomon at its dedication. Light shone on the hills of Bethlehem when the angels brought the message of redemption to the watching shepherds.

God is light; and in the words, "I am the light of the world," Christ declared His oneness with God, and His relation to the whole human family. It was He who at the beginning had caused "the light to shine out of darkness." 2 Cor. 4:6. He is the light of sun and moon and star. He was the spiritual light that in symbol and type and prophecy had shone upon Israel. But not to the Jewish nation alone was the light given. As the sunbeams penetrate to the remotest corners of the earth, so does the light of the Sun of Righteousness shine upon every soul.

"That was the true light, which lighteth every man that cometh into the world." The world has had its great teachers, men of giant intellect and wonderful research, men whose utterances have stimulated thought, and opened to view vast fields of knowledge; and these men have been honored as guides and benefactors of their race. But there is One who stands higher than they. "As many as received Him, to them gave He power to become the sons of God." "No man hath seen God at any time; the only-begotten Son, which is in the bosom of the Father, He hath declared Him." John 1:12, 18. We can trace the line of the world's great teachers as far back as human records extend; but the Light was before them. As the moon and the stars of the solar system shine by the reflected light of the sun, so, as far as their teaching is true, do the world's great thinkers reflect the rays of the Sun of Righteousness. Every gem of thought, every flash of the intellect, is from the Light of the world. In these days we hear much about "higher education." The true "higher education" is that imparted by Him "in whom are hid all the treasures of wisdom and knowledge." "In Him was life; and the life was the light of men." Col. 2:3; John 1:4. "He that followeth Me," said Jesus, "shall not walk in darkness, but shall have the light of life."

In the words, "I am the light of the world," Jesus declared Himself the Messiah. The aged Simeon, in the temple where Christ was now teaching, had spoken of Him as "a light to lighten the Gentiles, and the glory of Thy people Israel." Luke 2:32. In these words he was applying to Him a prophecy familiar to all Israel. By the prophet Isaiah, the Holy Spirit had declared, "It is too light a thing that Thou shouldest be My servant to raise up the tribes of Jacob, and to restore the preserved of Israel: I will also give Thee for a light to the Gentiles, that Thou mayest be My salvation unto the end of the earth." Isa. 49:6, R. V. This prophecy was generally understood as spoken of the Messiah, and when Jesus said, "I am the light of the world," the people could not fail to recognize His claim to be the Promised One.

To the Pharisees and rulers this claim seemed an arrogant assumption. That a man like themselves should make such pretensions they could not tolerate. Seeming to ignore His words, they demanded, "Who art Thou?" They were bent upon forcing Him to declare Himself the Christ. His appearance and His work were so at variance with the expectations of the people, that, as His wily enemies believed, a direct announcement of Himself as the Messiah would cause Him to be rejected as an impostor.

But to their question, "Who art Thou?" Jesus replied, "Even that which I have also spoken unto you from the beginning." John 8:25, R.V. That which had been revealed in His words was revealed also in His character. He was the embodiment of the truths He taught. "I do nothing of Myself," He continued; "but as My Father hath taught Me, I speak these things. And He that sent Me is with Me: the Father hath not left Me alone; for I do always those things that please Him." He did not attempt to prove His Messianic claim, but showed His unity with God. If their minds had been open to God's love, they would have received Jesus.

Among His hearers many were drawn to Him in faith, and to them He said, "if ye continue in My word, then are ye My disciples indeed; and ye shall know the truth, and the truth shall make you free."

These words offended the Pharisees. The nation's long subjection to a foreign yoke, they disregarded, and angrily exclaimed, "We be Abraham's seed, and were never in bondage to any man: how sayest Thou, Ye shall be made free?" Jesus looked upon these men, the slaves of malice, whose thoughts were bent upon revenge, and sadly answered, "Verily, verily, I say unto you, Whosoever committeth sin is the servant of sin." They were in the worst kind of bondage,—ruled by the spirit of evil.

Every soul that refuses to give himself to God is under the control of another power. He is not his own. He may talk of freedom, but he is in the most abject slavery. He is not allowed to see the beauty of truth, for his mind is under the control of Satan. While he flatters himself that he is following the dictates of his own judgment, he obeys the will of the prince of darkness. Christ came to break the shackles of sin-slavery from the soul. "If the Son therefore shall make you free, ye shall be free indeed." "The law of the Spirit of life in Christ Jesus" sets us "free from the law of sin and death." Rom. 8:2.

In the work of redemption there is no compulsion. No external force is employed. Under the influence of the Spirit of God, man is left free to choose whom he will serve. In the change that takes place when the soul surrenders to Christ, there is the highest sense of freedom. The expulsion of sin is the act of the soul itself. True, we have no power to free ourselves from Satan's control; but when we desire to be set free from sin, and in our great need cry out for a power out of and above ourselves, the powers of the soul are imbued with the divine energy of the Holy Spirit, and they obey the dictates of the will in fulfilling the will of God.

The only condition upon which the freedom of man is possible is that of becoming one with Christ. "The truth shall make you free;" and Christ is the truth. Sin can triumph only by enfeebling the mind, and destroying the liberty of the soul.

Subjection to God is restoration to one's self,—to the true glory and dignity of man. The divine law, to which we are brought into subjection, is "the law of liberty." James 2:12.

The Pharisees had declared themselves the children of Abraham. Jesus told them that this claim could be established only by doing the works of Abraham. The true children of Abraham would live, as he did, a life of obedience to God. They would not try to kill One who was speaking the truth that was given Him from God. In plotting against Christ, the rabbis were not doing the works of Abraham. A mere lineal descent from Abraham was of no value. Without a spiritual connection with him, which would be manifested in possessing the same spirit, and doing the same works, they were not his children.

This principle bears with equal weight upon a question that has long agitated the Christian world,—the question of apostolic succession. Descent from Abraham was proved, not by name and lineage, but by likeness of character. So the apostolic succession rests not upon the transmission of ecclesiastical authority, but upon spiritual relationship. A life actuated by the apostles' spirit, the belief and teaching of the truth they taught, this is the true evidence of apostolic succession. This is what constitutes men the successors of the first teachers of the gospel.

Jesus denied that the Jews were children of Abraham. He said, "Ye do the deeds of your father." In mockery they answered, "We be not born of fornication; we have one Father, even God." These words, in allusion to the circumstances of His birth, were intended as a thrust against Christ in the presence of those who were beginning to believe on Him. Jesus gave no heed to the base insinuation, but said, "If God were your Father, ye would love Me: for I proceeded forth and came from God."

Their works testified of their relationship to him who was a liar and a murderer. "Ye are of your father the devil," said Jesus, "and the lusts of your father it is your will to do. He was a murderer from the beginning, and stood not in the truth, because there is no truth in him. . . . Because I say the truth, ye believe Me not." John 8:44, 45, R. V. The fact that Jesus spoke the truth, and that with certainty, was why He was not received by the Jewish leaders. It was the truth that offended these self-righteous men. The truth exposed the fallacy of error; it condemned their teaching and practice, and it was unwelcome. They would rather close their eyes to the truth than humble themselves to confess that they had been in error. They did not love the truth. They did not desire it, even though it was truth.

"Which of you convicteth Me of sin? And if I say the truth, why do ye not believe Me?" Day by day for three years His enemies had been following Christ, trying to find some stain in His character. Satan and all the confederacy of evil had been seeking to overcome Him; but they had found nothing in Him by which to gain an advantage. Even the devils were forced to confess, "Thou art the Holy One of God." Mark 1:24. Jesus lived the law in the sight of heaven, in the sight of unfallen worlds, and in the sight of sinful men. Before angels, men, and demons, He had spoken, unchallenged, words that from any other lips would have been blasphemy: "I do always those things that please Him."

The fact that although they could find no sin in Christ the Jews would not receive Him proved that they themselves had no connection with God. They did not recognize His voice in the message of His Son. They thought themselves passing judgment on Christ; but in rejecting Him they were pronouncing sentence upon themselves. "He that is of God," said Jesus, "heareth God's words: ye therefore hear them not, because ye are not of God."

The lesson is true for all time. Many a man who delights to quibble, to criticize, seeking for something to question in the word of God, thinks that he is thereby giving evidence of independence of thought, and mental acuteness. He supposes that he is sitting in judgment on the Bible, when in truth he is judging himself. He makes it manifest that he is incapable of appreciating truths that originate in heaven, and that compass eternity. In presence of the great mountain of God's righteousness, his spirit is not awed. He busies himself with hunting for sticks and straws, and in this betrays a narrow and earthly nature, a heart that is fast losing its capacity to appreciate God. He whose heart has responded to the divine touch will be seeking for that which will increase his knowledge of God, and will refine and elevate the character. As a flower turns to the sun, that the bright rays may touch it with tints of beauty, so will the soul turn to the Sun of Righteousness, that heaven's light may beautify the character with the graces of the character of Christ.

Jesus continued, drawing a sharp contrast between the position of the Jews and that of Abraham: "Your father Abraham rejoiced to see My day: and he saw it, and was glad."

Abraham had greatly desired to see the promised Saviour. He offered up the most earnest prayer that before his death he might behold the Messiah. And he saw Christ. A supernatural light was given him, and he acknowledged Christ's divine character. He saw His day, and was glad. He was given a view of the divine sacrifice for sin. Of this sacrifice he had an illustration in his own experience. The command came to him, "Take now thy son, thine only son Isaac, whom thou lovest, . . . and offer him . . . for a burnt offering." Gen. 22:2. Upon the altar of sacrifice he laid the son of promise, the son in whom his hopes were centered. Then as he waited beside the altar with knife upraised to obey God, he heard a voice from heaven saying, "Lay not thine hand upon the lad, neither do thou anything unto him: for now I know that thou fearest God, seeing thou hast not withheld thy son, thine only son from Me." Gen. 22:12. This terrible ordeal was imposed upon Abraham that he might see the day of Christ, and realize the great love of God for the world, so great that to raise it from its degradation, He gave His only-begotten Son to a most shameful death.

Abraham learned of God the greatest lesson ever given to

mortal. His prayer that he might see Christ before he should die was answered. He saw Christ; he saw all that mortal can see, and live. By making an entire surrender, he was able to understand the vision of Christ, which had been given him. He was shown that in giving His only-begotten Son to save sinners from eternal ruin, God was making a greater and more wonderful sacrifice than ever man could make.

Abraham's experience answered the question: "Wherewith shall I come before the Lord, and bow myself before the high God? Shall I come before Him with burnt offerings, with calves of a year old? Will the Lord be pleased with thousands of rams, or with ten thousands of rivers of oil? shall I give my first-born for my transgression, the fruit of my body for the sin of my soul?" Micah 6:6, 7. In the words of Abraham, "My son, God will provide Himself a lamb for a burnt offering," (Gen. 22:8), and in God's provision of a sacrifice instead of Isaac, it was declared that no man could make expiation for himself. The pagan system of sacrifice was wholly unacceptable to God. No father was to offer up his son or his daughter for a sin offering. The Son of God alone can bear the guilt of the world.

Through his own suffering, Abraham was enabled to behold the Saviour's mission of sacrifice. But Israel would not understand that which was so unwelcome to their proud hearts. Christ's words concerning Abraham conveyed to His hearers no deep significance. The Pharisees saw in them only fresh ground for caviling. They retorted with a sneer, as if they would prove Jesus to be a madman, "Thou art not yet fifty years old, and hast Thou seen Abraham?"

With solemn dignity Jesus answered, "Verily, verily, I say unto you, Before Abraham was, I Am."

Silence fell upon the vast assembly. The name of God, given to Moses to express the idea of the eternal presence, had been claimed as His own by this Galilean Rabbi. He had announced Himself to be the self-existent One, He who had been promised to Israel, "whose goings forth have been from of old, from the days of eternity." Micah 5:2, margin.

Again the priests and rabbis cried out against Jesus as a blasphemer. His claim to be one with God had before stirred them to take His life, and a few months later they plainly declared, "For a good work we stone Thee not; but for blasphemy; and because that Thou, being a man, makest Thyself God." John 10:33. Because He was, and avowed Himself to be, the Son of God, they were bent on destroying Him. Now many of the people, siding with the priests and rabbis, took up stones to cast at Him. "But Jesus hid Himself, and went out of the temple, going through the midst of them, and so passed by."

The Light was shining in darkness; but "the darkness apprehended it not." John 1:5, R. V."

As Jesus passed by, He saw a man which was blind from his birth. And His disciples asked Him, saying, Master, who did sin, this man, or his parents, that he was born blind? Jesus answered, Neither hath this man sinned, nor his parents: but that the works of God should be made manifest in him. . . .

When He had thus spoken, He spat on the ground, and made clay of the spittle, and He anointed the eyes of the blind man with the clay, and said unto him, Go, wash in the pool of Siloam, (which is by interpretation, Sent). He went his way therefore, and washed, and came seeing."

It was generally believed by the Jews that sin is punished in this life. Every affliction was regarded as the penalty of some wrongdoing, either of the sufferer himself or of his parents. It is true that all suffering results from the transgression of God's law, but this truth had become perverted. Satan, the author of sin and all its results, had led men to look upon disease and death as proceeding from God,—as punishment arbitrarily inflicted on account of sin. Hence one upon whom some great affliction or calamity had fallen had the additional burden of being regarded as a great sinner.

Thus the way was prepared for the Jews to reject Jesus. He who "hath borne our griefs, and carried our sorrows" was looked upon by the Jews as "stricken, smitten of God, and afflicted;" and they hid their faces from Him. Isa. 53:4, 3.

God had given a lesson designed to prevent this. The history of Job had shown that suffering is inflicted by Satan, and is overruled by God for purposes of mercy. But Israel did not understand the lesson. The same error for which God had reproved the friends of Job was repeated by the Jews in their rejection of Christ.

The belief of the Jews in regard to the relation of sin and suffering was held by Christ's disciples. While Jesus corrected their error, He did not explain the cause of the man's affliction, but told them what would be the result. Because of it the works of God would be made manifest. "As long as I am in the world," He said, "I am the light of the world." Then having anointed the eyes of the blind man, He sent him to wash in the pool of Siloam, and the man's sight was restored. Thus Jesus answered the question of the disciples in a practical way, as He usually answered questions put to Him from curiosity. The disciples were not called upon to discuss the question as to who had sinned or had not sinned, but to understand the power and mercy of God in giving sight to the blind. It was evident that there was no healing virtue in the clay, or in the pool wherein the blind man was sent to wash, but that the virtue was in Christ.

The Pharisees could not but be astonished at the cure. Yet they were more than ever filled with hatred; for the miracle had been performed on the Sabbath day.

The neighbors of the young man, and those who knew him before in his blindness, said, "Is not this he that sat and begged?" They looked upon him with doubt; for when his eyes were opened, his countenance was changed and brightened, and he appeared like another man. From one to another the question passed. Some said, "This is he;" others, "He is like him." But he who had received the great blessing settled the question by saying, "I am he." He then told them of Jesus, and by what means he had been healed, and they inquired, "Where is He? He said, I know not."

Then they brought him before a council of the Pharisees.

Again the man was asked how he had received his sight. "He said unto them, He put clay upon mine eyes, and I washed, and do see. Therefore said some of the Pharisees, This man is not of God, because He keepeth not the Sabbath day." The Pharisees hoped to make Jesus out to be a sinner, and therefore not the Messiah. They knew not that it was He who had made the Sabbath and knew all its obligation, who had healed the blind man. They appeared wonderfully zealous for the observance of the Sabbath, yet were planning murder on that very day. But many were greatly moved at hearing of this miracle, and were convicted that He who had opened the eyes of the blind was more than a common man. In answer to the charge that Jesus was a sinner because He kept not the Sabbath day, they said, "How can a man that is a sinner do such miracles?"

Again the rabbis appealed to the blind man, "What sayest thou of Him, that He hath opened thine eyes? He said, He is a prophet." The Pharisees then asserted that he had not been born blind and received his sight. They called for his parents, and asked them, saying, "Is this your son, who ye say was born blind?"

There was the man himself, declaring that he had been blind, and had had his sight restored; but the Pharisees would rather deny the evidence of their own senses than admit that they were in error. So powerful is prejudice, so distorting is Pharisaical righteousness.

The Pharisees had one hope left, and that was to intimidate the man's parents. With apparent sincerity they asked, "How then doth he now see?" The parents feared to compromise themselves; for it had been declared that whoever should acknowledge Jesus as the Christ should be "put out of the synagogue;" that is, should be excluded from the synagogue for thirty days. During this time no child could be circumcised nor dead be lamented in the offender's home. The sentence was regarded as a great calamity; and if it failed to produce repentance, a far heavier penalty followed. The great work wrought for their son had brought conviction to the parents, yet they answered, "We know that this is our son, and that he was born blind: but by what means he now seeth, we know not; or who hath opened his eyes, we know not: he is of age; ask him: he shall speak for himself." Thus they shifted all responsibility from themselves to their son; for they dared not confess Christ.

The dilemma in which the Pharisees were placed, their questioning and prejudice, their unbelief in the facts of the case, were opening the eyes of the multitude, especially of the common people. Jesus had frequently wrought His miracles in the open street, and His work was always of a character to relieve suffering. The question in many minds was, Would God do such mighty works through an impostor, as the Pharisees insisted that Jesus was? The controversy was becoming very earnest on both sides.

The Pharisees saw that they were giving publicity to the work done by Jesus. They could not deny the miracle. The blind man was filled with joy and gratitude; he beheld the wondrous things of nature, and was filled with delight at the beauty of earth and sky. He freely related his experience, and again they tried to silence him, saying, "Give God the praise: we know that this Man is a sinner." That is, Do not say again that this Man gave you sight; it is God who has done this.

The blind man answered, "Whether He be a sinner or no, I know not: one thing I know, that, whereas I was blind, now I see."

Then they questioned again, "What did He to thee? how opened He thine eyes?" With many words they tried to confuse him, so that he might think himself deluded. Satan and his evil angels were on the side of the Pharisees, and united their energies and subtlety with man's reasoning in order to counteract the influence of Christ. They blunted the convictions that were deepening in many minds. Angels of God were also on the ground to strengthen the man who had had his sight restored.

The Pharisees did not realize that they had to deal with any other than the uneducated man who had been born blind; they knew not Him with whom they were in controversy. Divine light shone into the chambers of the blind man's soul. As these hypocrites tried to make him disbelieve, God helped him to show, by the vigor and pointedness of his replies, that he was not to be ensnared. He answered, "I have told you already, and ye did not hear: wherefore would ye hear it again? will ye also be His disciples? Then they reviled him, and said, Thou art His disciple; but we are Moses' disciples. We know that God spake unto Moses: as for this fellow, we know not from whence He is."

The Lord Jesus knew the ordeal through which the man was passing, and He gave him grace and utterance, so that he became a witness for Christ. He answered the Pharisees in words that were a cutting rebuke to his questioners. They claimed to be the expositors of Scripture, the religious guides of the nation; and yet here was One performing miracles, and they were confessedly ignorant as to the source of His power, and as to His character and claims. "Why herein is a marvelous thing," said the man, "that ye know not from whence He is, and yet He hath opened mine eyes. Now we know that God heareth not sinners: but if any man be a worshiper of God, and doeth His will, him He heareth. Since the world began was it not heard that any man opened the eyes of one that was born blind. If this Man were not of God, He could do nothing."

The man had met his inquisitors on their own ground. His reasoning was unanswerable. The Pharisees were astonished, and they held their peace,—spellbound before his pointed, determined words. For a few moments there was silence. Then the frowning priests and rabbis gathered about them their robes, as though they feared contamination from contact with him; they shook off the dust from their feet, and hurled denunciations against him,—"Thou wast altogether born in sins, and dost thou teach us?" And they excommunicated him.

Jesus heard what had been done; and finding him soon after,

He said, "Dost thou believe on the Son of God?"

For the first time the blind man looked upon the face of his Restorer. Before the council he had seen his parents troubled and perplexed; he had looked upon the frowning faces of the rabbis; now his eyes rested upon the loving, peaceful countenance of Jesus. Already, at great cost to himself, he had acknowledged Him as a delegate of divine power; now a higher revelation was granted him.

To the Saviour's question, "Dost thou believe on the Son of God?" the blind man replied by asking, "Who is He, Lord, that I might believe on Him?" And Jesus said, "Thou hast both seen Him, and it is He that talketh with thee." The man cast himself at the Saviour's feet in worship. Not only had his natural sight been restored, but the eyes of his understanding had been opened. Christ had been revealed to his soul, and he received Him as the Sent of God.

A group of Pharisees had gathered near, and the sight of them brought to the mind of Jesus the contrast ever manifest in the effect of His words and works. He said, "For judgment I am come into this world, that they which see not might see; and that they which see might be made blind." Christ had come to open the blind eyes, to give light to them that sit in darkness. He had declared Himself to be the light of the world, and the miracle just performed was in attestation of His mission. The people who beheld the Saviour at His advent were favored with a fuller manifestation of the divine presence than the world had ever enjoyed before. The knowledge of God was revealed more perfectly. But in this very revelation, judgment was passing upon men. Their character was tested, their destiny determined.

The manifestation of divine power that had given to the blind man both natural and spiritual sight had left the Pharisees in yet deeper darkness. Some of His hearers, feeling that Christ's words applied to them, inquired, "Are we blind also?" Jesus answered, "If ye were blind, ye should have no sin." If God had made it impossible for you to see the truth, your ignorance would involve no guilt. "But now ye say, We see." You believe yourselves able to see, and reject the means through which alone you could receive sight. To all who realized their need, Christ came with infinite help. But the Pharisees would confess no need; they refused to come to Christ, and hence they were left in blindness,—a blindness for which they were themselves guilty. Jesus said, "Your sin remaineth."

The Divine Shepherd

"I am the Good Shepherd: the good shepherd giveth his life for the sheep." "I am the Good Shepherd, and know My sheep, and am known of Mine. As the Father knoweth Me, even so know I the Father: and I lay down My life for the sheep."

Again Jesus found access to the minds of His hearers by the pathway of their familiar associations. He had likened the Spirit's influence to the cool, refreshing water. He had represented Himself as the light, the source of life and gladness to nature and to man. Now in a beautiful pastoral picture He represents His relation to those that believe on Him. No picture was more familiar to His hearers than this, and Christ's words linked it forever with Himself. Never could the disciples look on the shepherds tending their flocks without recalling the Saviour's lesson. They would see Christ in each faithful shepherd. They would see themselves in each helpless and dependent flock.

This figure the prophet Isaiah had applied to the Messiah's mission, in the comforting words, "O Zion, that bringest good tidings, get thee up into the high mountain; O Jerusalem, that bringest good tidings, lift up thy voice with strength; lift it up, be not afraid; say unto the cities of Judah, Behold your God! . . . He shall feed His flock like a shepherd: He shall gather the lambs with His arm, and carry them in His bosom." Isa. 40:9-11. David had sung, "The Lord is my shepherd; I shall not want." Ps. 23:1. And the Holy Spirit through Ezekiel had declared: "I will set up one Shepherd over them, and He shall feed them." "I will seek that which was lost, and bring again that which was driven away, and will bind up that which was broken, and will strengthen that which was sick." "And I will make with them a covenant of peace." "And they shall no more be a prey to the heathen; . . . but they shall dwell safely, and none shall make them afraid." Ezek. 34:23, 16, 25, 28.

Christ applied these prophecies to Himself, and He showed the contrast between His own character and that of the leaders in Israel. The Pharisees had just driven one from the fold, because he dared to bear witness to the power of Christ. They had cut off a soul whom the True Shepherd was drawing to Himself. In this they had shown themselves ignorant of the work committed to them, and unworthy of their trust as shepherds of the flock. Jesus now set before them the contrast between them and the Good Shepherd, and He pointed to Himself as the real keeper of the Lord's flock. Before doing this, however, He speaks of Himself under another figure.

He said, "He that entereth not by the door into the sheepfold, but climbeth up some other way, the same is a thief and a robber. But he that entereth in by the door is the shepherd of the sheep." The Pharisees did not discern that these words were spoken against them. When they reasoned in their hearts as to the meaning, Jesus told them plainly, "I am the door: by Me if any man enter in, he shall be saved, and shall go in and out, and find pasture. The thief cometh not, but for to steal, and to kill, and to destroy: I am come that they might have life, and that they might have it more abundantly."

Christ is the door to the fold of God. Through this door all His children, from the earliest times, have found entrance. In Jesus, as shown in types, as shadowed in symbols, as manifested in the revelation of the prophets, as unveiled in the lessons given to His disciples, and in the miracles wrought for the sons of men, they have beheld "the Lamb of God, which taketh away the sin of the world" (John 1:29), and through Him they are brought within the fold of His grace.

Many have come presenting other objects for the faith of the world; ceremonies and systems have been devised by which men hope to receive justification and peace with God, and thus find entrance to His fold. But the only door is Christ, and all who have interposed something to take the place of Christ, all who have tried to enter the fold in some other way, are thieves and robbers.

The Pharisees had not entered by the door. They had climbed into the fold by another way than Christ, and they were not fulfilling the work of the true shepherd. The priests and rulers, the scribes and Pharisees, destroyed the living pastures, and defiled the wellsprings of the water of life. Faithfully do the words of inspiration describe those false shepherds: "The diseased have ye not strengthened, neither have ye healed that which was sick, neither have ye bound up that which was broken, neither have ye brought again that which was driven away; . . . but with force and with cruelty have ye ruled them." Ezek. 34:4.

In all ages, philosophers and teachers have been presenting to the world theories by which to satisfy the soul's need. Every heathen nation has had its great teachers and religious systems offering some other means of redemption than Christ, turning the eyes of men away from the Father's face, and filling their hearts with fear of Him who has given them only blessing. The trend of their work is to rob God of that which is His own, both by creation and by redemption. And these false teachers rob man as well. Millions of human beings are bound down under false religions, in the bondage of slavish fear, of stolid indifference, toiling like beasts of burden, bereft of hope or joy or aspiration here, and with only a dull fear of the hereafter. It is the gospel of the grace of God alone that can uplift the soul. The contemplation of the love of God manifested in His Son will stir the heart and arouse the powers of the soul as nothing else can. Christ came that He might re-create the image of God in man; and whoever turns men away from Christ is turning them away from the source of true development; he is defrauding them of the hope and purpose and glory of life. He is a thief and a robber.

"He that entereth in by the door is the shepherd of the sheep." Christ is both the door and the shepherd. He enters in by Himself. It is through His own sacrifice that He becomes the shepherd of the sheep. "To Him the porter openeth; and the sheep hear His voice: and He calleth His own sheep by name, and leadeth them out. And when He putteth forth His own sheep, He goeth before them, and the sheep follow Him: for they know His voice."

Of all creatures the sheep is one of the most timid and helpless, and in the East the shepherd's care for his flock is untiring and incessant. Anciently as now there was little security outside of the walled towns. Marauders from the roving border tribes, or beasts of prey from their hiding places in the rocks, lay in wait to plunder the flocks. The shepherd watched his charge, knowing that it was at the peril of his own life. Jacob, who kept the flocks of Laban in the pasture grounds of Haran, describing his own unwearied labor, said,

"In the day the drought consumed me, and the frost by night; and my sleep departed from mine eyes." Gen. 31:40. And it was while guarding his father's sheep that the boy David, single-handed, encountered the lion and the bear, and rescued from their teeth the stolen lamb.

As the shepherd leads his flock over the rocky hills, through forest and wild ravines, to grassy nooks by the riverside; as he watches them on the mountains through the lonely night, shielding from robbers, caring tenderly for the sickly and feeble, his life comes to be one with theirs. A strong and tender attachment unites him to the objects of his care. However large the flock, the shepherd knows every sheep. Every one has its name, and responds to the name at the shepherd's call.

As an earthly shepherd knows his sheep, so does the divine Shepherd know His flock that are scattered throughout the world. "Ye My flock, the flock of My pasture, are men, and I am your God, saith the Lord God." Jesus says, "I have called thee by thy name; thou art Mine." "I have graven thee upon the palms of My hands." Ezek. 34:31; Isa. 43:1; 49:16.

Jesus knows us individually, and is touched with the feeling of our infirmities. He knows us all by name. He knows the very house in which we live, the name of each occupant. He has at times given directions to His servants to go to a certain street in a certain city, to such a house, to find one of His sheep.

Every soul is as fully known to Jesus as if he were the only one for whom the Saviour died. The distress of every one touches His heart. The cry for aid reaches His ear. He came to draw all men unto Himself. He bids them, "Follow Me," and His Spirit moves upon their hearts to draw them to come to Him. Many refuse to be drawn. Jesus knows who they are. He also knows who gladly hear His call, and are ready to come under His pastoral care. He says, "My sheep hear My voice, and I know them, and they follow Me." He cares for each one as if there were not another on the face of the earth.

"He calleth His own sheep by name, and leadeth them out. . . . And the sheep follow Him: for they know His voice." The Eastern shepherd does not drive his sheep. He depends not upon force or fear; but going before, he calls them. They know his voice, and obey the call. So does the Saviour-Shepherd with His sheep. The Scripture says, "Thou leddest Thy people like a flock by the hand of Moses and Aaron." Through the prophet, Jesus declares, "I have loved thee with an everlasting love: therefore with loving-kindness have I drawn thee." He compels none to follow Him. "I drew them," He says, "with cords of a man, with bands of love." Ps. 77:20; Jer. 31:3; Hosea 11:4.

It is not the fear of punishment, or the hope of everlasting reward, that leads the disciples of Christ to follow Him. They behold the Saviour's matchless love, revealed throughout His pilgrimage on earth, from the manger of Bethlehem to Calvary's cross, and the sight of Him attracts, it softens and subdues the soul. Love awakens in the heart of the beholders. They hear His voice, and they follow Him.

As the shepherd goes before his sheep, himself first encountering the perils of the way, so does Jesus with His people. "When He putteth forth His own sheep, He goeth before them." The way to heaven is consecrated by the Saviour's footprints. The path may be steep and rugged, but Jesus has traveled that way; His feet have pressed down the cruel thorns, to make the pathway easier for us. Every burden that we are called to bear He Himself has borne.

Though now He has ascended to the presence of God, and shares the throne of the universe, Jesus has lost none of His compassionate nature. Today the same tender, sympathizing heart is open to all the woes of humanity. Today the hand that was pierced is reached forth to bless more abundantly His people that are in the world. "And they shall never perish, neither shall any man pluck them out of My hand." The soul that has given himself to Christ is more precious in His sight than the whole world. The Saviour would have passed through the agony of Calvary that one might be saved in His kingdom. He will never abandon one for whom He has died. Unless His followers choose to leave Him, He will hold them fast.

Through all our trials we have a never-failing Helper. He does not leave us alone to struggle with temptation, to battle with evil, and be finally crushed with burdens and sorrow. Though now He is hidden from mortal sight, the ear of faith can hear His voice saying, Fear not; I am with you. "I am He that liveth, and was dead; and, behold, I am alive forevermore." Rev. 1:18. I have endured your sorrows, experienced your struggles, encountered your temptations. I know your tears; I also have wept. The griefs that lie too deep to be breathed into any human ear, I know. Think not that you are desolate and forsaken. Though your pain touch no responsive chord in any heart on earth, look unto Me, and live. "The mountains shall depart, and the hills be removed; but My kindness shall not depart from thee, neither shall the covenant of My peace be removed, saith the Lord that hath mercy on thee." Isa. 54:10.

However much a shepherd may love his sheep, he loves his sons and daughters more. Jesus is not only our shepherd; He is our "everlasting Father." And He says, "I know Mine own, and Mine own know Me, even as the Father knoweth Me, and I know the Father." John 10:14, 15, R. V. What a statement is this!—the only-begotten Son, He who is in the bosom of the Father, He whom God has declared to be "the Man that is My fellow" (Zech. 13:7),—the communion between Him and the eternal God is taken to represent the communion between Christ and His children on the earth!

Because we are the gift of His Father, and the reward of His work, Jesus loves us. He loves us as His children. Reader, He loves you. Heaven itself can bestow nothing greater, nothing better. Therefore trust.

Jesus thought upon the souls all over the earth who were misled by false shepherds. Those whom He longed to gather as the sheep of His pasture were scattered among wolves, and He said, "Other sheep I have, which are not of this fold: them also I must bring, and they shall hear My voice; and they shall become one flock, one shepherd." John 10:16, R. V.

"Therefore doth My Father love Me, because I lay down My life, that I might take it again." That is, My Father has so loved you, that He even loves Me more for giving My life to redeem you. In becoming your substitute and surety, by surrendering My life, by taking your liabilities, your transgressions, I am endeared to My Father.

"I lay down My life, that I might take it again. No man taketh it from Me, but I lay it down of Myself. I have power to lay it down, and I have power to take it again." While as a member of the human family He was mortal, as God He was the fountain of life for the world. He could have withstood the advances of death, and refused to come under its dominion; but voluntarily He laid down His life, that He might bring life and immortality to light. He bore the sin of the world, endured its curse, yielded up His life as a sacrifice, that men might not eternally die. "Surely He hath borne our griefs, and carried our sorrows. . . . He was wounded for our transgressions, He was bruised for our iniquities: the chastisement of our peace was upon Him; and with His stripes we are healed. All we like sheep have gone astray; we have turned every one to his own way; and the Lord hath laid on Him the iniquity of us all." Isa. 53:4-6.

The Last Journey From Galilee

As the close of His ministry drew near, there was a change in Christ's manner of labor. Heretofore He had sought to shun excitement and publicity. He had refused the homage of the people, and had passed quickly from place to place when the popular enthusiasm in His favor seemed kindling beyond control. Again and again He had commanded that none should declare Him to be the Christ.

At the time of the Feast of Tabernacles His journey to Jerusalem was made swiftly and secretly. When urged by His brothers to present Himself publicly as the Messiah, His answer was, "My time is not yet come." John 7:6. He made His way to Jerusalem unobserved, and entered the city unannounced, and unhonored by the multitude. But not so with His last journey. He had left Jerusalem for a season because of the malice of the priests and rabbis. But He now set out to return, traveling in the most public manner, by a circuitous route, and preceded by such an announcement of His coming as He had never made before. He was going forward to the scene of His great sacrifice, and to this the attention of the people must be directed.

"As Moses lifted up the serpent in the wilderness, even so must the Son of man be lifted up." John 3:14. As the eyes of all Israel had been directed to the uplifted serpent, the symbol appointed for their healing, so all eyes must be drawn to Christ, the sacrifice that brought salvation to the lost world.

It was a false conception of the Messiah's work, and a lack of faith in the divine character of Jesus, that had led His brothers to urge Him to present Himself publicly to the people at the Feast of Tabernacles. Now, in a spirit akin to this, the disciples would have prevented Him from making the journey to Jerusalem. They remembered His words concerning what was to befall Him there, they knew the deadly hostility of the religious leaders, and they would fain have dissuaded their Master from going thither.

To the heart of Christ it was a bitter task to press His way against the fears, disappointment, and unbelief of His beloved disciples. It was hard to lead them forward to the anguish and despair that awaited them at Jerusalem. And Satan was at hand to press his temptations upon the Son of man. Why should He now go to Jerusalem, to certain death? All around Him were souls hungering for the bread of life. On every hand were suffering ones waiting for His word of healing. The work to be wrought by the gospel of His grace was but just begun. And He was full of the vigor of manhood's prime. Why not go forward to the vast fields of the world with the words of His grace, the touch of His healing power? Why not take to Himself the joy of giving light and gladness to those darkened and sorrowing millions? Why leave the harvest gathering to His disciples, so weak in faith, so dull of understanding, so slow to act? Why face death now, and leave the work in its infancy? The foe who in the wilderness had confronted Christ assailed Him now with fierce and subtle temptations. Had Jesus yielded for a moment, had He changed His course in the least particular to save Himself, Satan's agencies would have triumphed, and the world would have been lost.

But Jesus had "steadfastly set His face to go to Jerusalem." The one law of His life was the Father's will. In the visit to the temple in His boyhood, He had said to Mary, "Wist ye not that I must be about My Father's business?" Luke 2:49. At Cana, when Mary desired Him to reveal His miraculous power, His answer was, "Mine hour is not yet come." John 2:4. With the same words He replied to His brothers when they urged Him to go to the feast. But in God's great plan the hour had been appointed for the offering of Himself for the sins of men, and that hour was soon to strike. He would not fail nor falter. His steps are turned toward Jerusalem, where His foes have long plotted to take His life; now He will lay it down. He set His face steadfastly to go to persecution, denial, rejection, condemnation, and death.

And He "sent messengers before His face: and they went, and entered into a village of the Samaritans, to make ready for Him." But the people refused to receive Him, because He was on His way to Jerusalem. This they interpreted as meaning that Christ showed a preference for the Jews, whom they hated with intense bitterness. Had He come to restore the temple and worship upon Mount Gerizim, they would gladly have received Him; but He was going to Jerusalem, and they would show Him no hospitality. Little did they realize that they were turning from their doors the best gift of heaven. Jesus invited men to receive Him, He asked favors at their hands, that He might come near to them, to bestow the richest blessings. For every favor manifested toward Him, He requited a more precious grace. But all was lost to the Samaritans because of their prejudice and bigotry.

James and John, Christ's messengers, were greatly annoyed at the insult shown to their Lord. They were filled with indignation because He had been so rudely treated by the Samaritans whom He was honoring by His presence. They had recently been with Him on the mount of transfiguration, and had seen Him glorified by God, and honored by Moses and Elijah. This manifest dishonor on the part of the Samaritans, should not, they thought, be passed over without marked punishment.

Coming to Christ, they reported to Him the words of the people, telling Him that they had even refused to give Him a night's lodging. They thought that a grievous wrong had been done Him, and seeing Mount Carmel in the distance, where Elijah had slain the false prophets, they said, "Wilt Thou that we command fire to come down from heaven, and consume them, even as Elias did?" They were surprised to see that Jesus was pained by their words, and still more surprised as His rebuke fell upon their ears, "Ye know not what manner of spirit ye are of. For the Son of man is not come to destroy men's lives, but to save them." And He went to another village.

It is no part of Christ's mission to compel men to receive Him. It is Satan, and men actuated by his spirit, that seek to compel the conscience. Under a pretense of zeal for righteousness, men who are confederate with evil angels bring suffering upon their fellow men, in order to convert them to their ideas of religion; but Christ is ever showing mercy, ever seeking to win by the revealing of His love. He can admit no rival in the soul, nor accept of partial service; but He desires only voluntary service, the willing surrender of the heart under the constraint of love. There can be no more conclusive evidence that we possess the spirit of Satan than the disposition to hurt and destroy those who do not appreciate our work, or who act contrary to our ideas.

Every human being, in body, soul, and spirit, is the property of God. Christ died to redeem all. Nothing can be more offensive to God than for men, through religious bigotry, to bring suffering upon those who are the purchase of the Saviour's blood.

"And He arose from thence, and cometh into the coasts of Judea by the farther side of Jordan: and the people resort unto Him again; and, as He was wont, He taught them again." Mark 10:1.

A considerable part of the closing months of Christ's ministry was spent in Perea, the province on "the farther side of Jordan" from Judea. Here the multitude thronged His steps, as in His early ministry in Galilee, and much of His former teaching was repeated.

As He had sent out the twelve, so He "appointed seventy others, and sent them two and two before His face into every city and place, whither He Himself was about to come." Luke 10:1, R. V. These disciples had been for some time with Him, in training for their work. When the twelve were sent out on their first separate mission, other disciples accompanied Jesus in His journey through Galilee. Thus they had the privilege of intimate association with Him, and direct personal instruction. Now this larger number also were to go forth on a separate mission.

The directions to the seventy were similar to those that had been given to the twelve; but the command to the twelve, not to enter into any city of the Gentiles or of the Samaritans, was not given to the seventy. Though Christ had just been repulsed by the Samaritans, His love toward them was unchanged. When the seventy went forth in His name, they visited, first of all, the cities of Samaria.

The Saviour's own visit to Samaria, and later, the commendation of the good Samaritan, and the grateful joy of that leper, a Samaritan, who alone of the ten returned to give thanks to Christ, were full of significance to the disciples. The lesson sank deep into their hearts. In His commission to them, just before His ascension, Jesus mentioned Samaria with Jerusalem and Judea as the places where they were first to preach the gospel. This commission His teaching had prepared them to fulfill. When in their Master's name they went to Samaria, they found the people ready to receive them. The Samaritans had heard of Christ's words of commendation and His works of mercy for men of their nation. They saw that, notwithstanding their rude treatment of Him, He had only thoughts of love toward them, and their hearts were won. After His ascension they welcomed the Saviour's messengers, and the disciples gathered a precious harvest from among those who had once been their bitterest enemies. "A bruised reed shall He not break, and the dimly burning flax shall He not quench: He shall bring forth judgment unto truth." "And in His name shall the Gentiles trust." Isa. 42:3, margin; Matt. 12:21.

In sending out the seventy, Jesus bade them, as He had bidden the twelve, not to urge their presence where they were unwelcome. "Into whatsoever city ye enter, and they receive you not," He said, "go your ways out into the streets of the same, and say, Even the very dust of your city, which cleaveth on us, we do wipe off against you: notwithstanding be ye sure of this, that the kingdom of God is come nigh unto you." They were not to do this from motives of resentment or through wounded dignity, but to show how grievous a thing it is to refuse the Lord's message or His messengers. To reject the Lord's servants is to reject Christ Himself.

"I say unto you," Jesus added, "that it shall be more tolerable in that day for Sodom, than for that city." Then His mind reverted to the Galilean towns where so much of His ministry had been spent. In deeply sorrowful accents He exclaimed, "Woe unto thee, Chorazin! woe unto thee, Bethsaida! for if the mighty works had been done in Tyre and Sidon, which have been done in you, they had a great while ago repented, sitting in sackcloth and ashes. But it shall be more tolerable for Tyre and Sidon at the judgment, than for you. And thou, Capernaum, which art exalted to heaven, shalt be thrust down to hell."

To those busy towns about the Sea of Galilee, heaven's richest blessings had been freely offered. Day after day the Prince of life had gone in and out among them. The glory of God, which prophets and kings had longed to see, had shone upon the multitudes that thronged the Saviour's steps. Yet they had refused the heavenly Gift.

With a great show of prudence the rabbis had warned the people against receiving the new doctrines taught by this new teacher; for His theories and practices were contrary to the teachings of the fathers. The people gave credence to what the priests and Pharisees taught, in place of seeking to understand the word of God for themselves. They honored the priests and rulers instead of honoring God, and rejected the truth that they might keep their own traditions. Many had been impressed and almost persuaded; but they did not act upon their convictions, and were not reckoned on the side of Christ. Satan presented his temptations, until the light appeared as darkness. Thus many rejected the truth that would have proved the saving of the soul.

The True Witness says, "Behold, I stand at the door, and knock." Rev. 3:20. Every warning, reproof, and entreaty in the word of God or through His messengers is a knock at the door of the heart. It is the voice of Jesus asking for entrance. With every knock unheeded, the disposition to open becomes weaker. The impressions of the Holy Spirit if disregarded today, will not be as strong tomorrow. The heart becomes less impressible, and lapses into a perilous unconsciousness of the shortness of life, and of the great eternity beyond. Our condemnation in the judgment will not result from the fact that we have been in error, but from the fact that we have neglected heaven-sent opportunities for learning what is truth.

Like the apostles, the seventy had received supernatural endowments as a seal of their mission. When their work was completed, they returned with joy, saying, "Lord, even the devils are subject unto us through Thy name." Jesus answered, "I beheld Satan as lightning fall from heaven."

The scenes of the past and the future were presented to the mind of Jesus. He beheld Lucifer as he was first cast out from the heavenly places. He looked forward to the scenes of His own agony, when before all the worlds the character of the deceiver should be unveiled. He heard the cry, "It is finished" (John 19:30), announcing that the redemption of the lost race was forever made certain, that heaven was made eternally secure against the accusations, the deceptions, the pretensions, that Satan would instigate.

Beyond the cross of Calvary, with its agony and shame, Jesus looked forward to the great final day, when the prince of the power of the air will meet his destruction in the earth so long marred by his rebellion. Jesus beheld the work of evil forever ended, and the peace of God filling heaven and earth.

Henceforward Christ's followers were to look upon Satan as a conquered foe. Upon the cross, Jesus was to gain the victory for them; that victory He desired them to accept as their own. "Behold," He said, "I give unto you power to tread on serpents and scorpions, and over all the power of the enemy: and nothing shall by any means hurt you."

The omnipotent power of the Holy Spirit is the defense of every contrite soul. Not one that in penitence and faith has claimed His protection will Christ permit to pass under the enemy's power. The Saviour is by the side of His tempted and tried ones. With Him there can be no such thing as failure, loss, impossibility, or defeat; we can do all things through Him who strengthens us. When temptations and trials come, do not wait to adjust all the difficulties, but look to Jesus, your helper.

There are Christians who think and speak altogether too much about the power of Satan. They think of their adversary, they pray about him, they talk about him, and he looms up greater and greater in their imagination. It is true that Satan is a powerful being; but, thank God, we have a mighty Saviour, who cast out the evil one from heaven. Satan is pleased when we magnify his power. Why not talk of Jesus? Why not magnify His power and His love?

The rainbow of promise encircling the throne on high is an everlasting testimony that "God so loved the world, that He gave His only-begotten Son, that whosoever believeth in Him should not perish, but have everlasting life." John 3:16. It testifies to the universe that God will never forsake His people in their struggle with evil. It is an assurance to us of strength and protection as long as the throne itself shall endure.

Jesus added, "Notwithstanding in this rejoice not, that the spirits are subject unto you; but rather rejoice, because your names are written in heaven." Rejoice not in the possession of power, lest you lose sight of your dependence upon God. Be careful lest self-sufficiency come in, and you work in your own strength, rather than in the spirit and strength of your Master. Self is ever ready to take the credit if any measure of success attends the work. Self is flattered and exalted, and the impression is not made upon other minds that God is all and in all. The apostle Paul says, "When I am weak, then am I strong." 2 Cor. 12:10. When we have a realization of our weakness, we learn to depend upon a power not inherent. Nothing can take so strong a hold on the heart as the abiding sense of our responsibility to God. Nothing reaches so fully down to the deepest motives of conduct as a sense of the pardoning love of Christ. We are to come in touch with God, then we shall be imbued with His Holy Spirit, that enables us to come in touch with our fellow men. Then rejoice that through Christ you have become connected with God, members of the heavenly family. While you look higher than yourself, you will have a continual sense of the weakness of humanity. The less you cherish self, the more distinct and full will be your comprehension of the excellence of your Saviour. The more closely you connect yourself with the source of light and power, the greater light will be shed upon you, and the greater power will be yours to work for God. Rejoice that you are one with God, one with Christ, and with the whole family of heaven. As the seventy listened to the words of Christ, the Holy Spirit was impressing their minds with living realities, and writing truth upon the tablets of the soul. Though multitudes surrounded them, they were as though shut in with God.

Knowing that they had caught the inspiration of the hour, Jesus "rejoiced in spirit, and said, I thank Thee, O Father, Lord of heaven and earth, that Thou hast hid these things from the wise and prudent, and hast revealed them unto babes: even so, Father; for so it seemed good in Thy sight. All things are delivered to Me of My Father: and no man knoweth who the Son is, but the Father, and who the Father is, but the Son, and he to whom the Son will reveal Him."

The honored men of the world, the so-called great and wise men, with all their boasted wisdom, could not comprehend the character of Christ. They judged Him from outward appearance, from the humiliation that came upon Him as a human being. But to fishermen and publicans it had been given to see the Invisible. Even the disciples failed of understanding all that Jesus desired to reveal to them; but from time to time, as they surrendered themselves to the Holy Spirit's power, their minds were illuminated. They realized that the mighty God, clad in the garb of humanity, was among them. Jesus rejoiced that though this knowledge was not possessed by the wise and prudent, it had been revealed to these humble men. Often as He had presented the Old Testament Scriptures, and showed their application to Himself and His work of atonement, they had been awakened by His Spirit, and lifted into a heavenly atmosphere. Of the spiritual truths spoken by the prophets they had a clearer understanding than had the original writers themselves. Hereafter they would read the Old Testament Scriptures, not as the doctrines of the scribes and Pharisees, not as the utterances of wise men who were dead, but as a new revelation from God. They beheld Him "whom the world cannot receive, because it seeth Him not, neither knoweth Him: but ye know Him; for He dwelleth with you, and shall be in you." John 14:17.

The only way in which we can gain a more perfect apprehension of truth is by keeping the heart tender and subdued by the Spirit of Christ. The soul must be cleansed from vanity and pride, and vacated of all that has held it in possession, and Christ must be enthroned within. Human science is too limited to comprehend the atonement. The plan of redemption is so far-reaching that philosophy cannot explain it. It will ever remain a mystery that the most profound reasoning cannot fathom. The science of salvation cannot be explained; but it can be known by experience. Only he who sees his own sinfulness can discern the preciousness of the Saviour.

Full of instruction were the lessons which Christ taught as He slowly made His way from Galilee toward Jerusalem. Eagerly the people listened to His words. In Perea as in Galilee the people were less under the control of Jewish bigotry than in Judea, and His teaching found a response in their hearts.

During these last months of His ministry, many of Christ's parables were spoken. The priests and rabbis pursued Him with ever-increasing bitterness, and His warnings to them He veiled in symbols. They could not mistake His meaning, yet they could find in His words nothing on which to ground an accusation against Him. In the parable of the Pharisee and the publican, the self-sufficient prayer, "God, I thank Thee that I am not as the rest of men," stood out in sharp contrast to the penitent's plea, "Be merciful to me the sinner." Luke 18:11, 13, R. V., margin. Thus Christ rebuked the hypocrisy of the Jews. And under the figures of the barren fig tree and the great supper He foretold the doom about to fall upon the impenitent nation. Those who had scornfully rejected the invitation to the gospel feast heard His warning words: "I say unto you, That none of those men which were bidden shall taste of My supper." Luke 14:24.

Very precious was the instruction given to the disciples. The parable of the importunate widow and the friend asking for bread at midnight gave new force to His words, "Ask, and it shall be given you; seek, and ye shall find; knock, and it shall be opened unto you." Luke 11:9. And often their wavering faith was strengthened by the memory that Christ had said, "Shall not God do justice for His elect, which cry to Him day and night, and He is long-suffering over them? I say unto you, that He will do them justice speedily." Luke 18:7, 8, R. V., margin.

The beautiful parable of the lost sheep Christ repeated. And He carried its lesson still farther, as He told of the lost piece of silver and the prodigal son. The force of these lessons the disciples could not then fully appreciate; but after the outpouring of the Holy Spirit, as they saw the ingathering of the Gentiles and the envious anger of the Jews, they better understood the lesson of the prodigal son, and could enter into the joy of Christ's words, "It was meet that we should make merry, and be glad;" "for this my son was dead, and is alive again; he was lost, and is found." Luke 15:32, 24. And as they went out in their Master's name, facing reproach and poverty and persecution, they often strengthened their hearts by repeating His injunction, spoken on this last journey, "Fear not, little flock; for it is your Father's good pleasure to give you the kingdom. Sell that ye have, and give alms; provide yourselves bags which wax not old, a treasure in the heavens that faileth not, where no thief approacheth, neither moth corrupteth. For where your treasure is, there will your heart be also." Luke 12:32-34.

The Good Samaritan

In the story of the good Samaritan, Christ illustrates the nature of true religion. He shows that it consists not in systems, creeds, or rites, but in the performance of loving deeds, in bringing the greatest good to others, in genuine goodness.

As Christ was teaching the people, "a certain lawyer stood up, and tempted Him, saying, Master, what shall I do to inherit eternal life?" With breathless attention the large congregation awaited the answer. The priests and rabbis had thought to entangle Christ by having the lawyer ask this question. But the Saviour entered into no controversy. He required the answer from the questioner himself. "What is written in the law?" He said; "how readest thou?" The Jews still accused Jesus of lightly regarding the law given from Sinai; but He turned the question of salvation upon the keeping of God's commandments.

The lawyer said, "Thou shalt love the Lord thy God with all thy heart, and with all thy soul, and with all thy strength, and with all thy mind; and thy neighbor as thyself." Jesus said, "Thou hast answered right: this do, and thou shalt live."

The lawyer was not satisfied with the position and works of the Pharisees. He had been studying the Scriptures with a desire to learn their real meaning. He had a vital interest in the matter, and had asked in sincerity, "What shall I do?" In his answer as to the requirements of the law, he passed by all the mass of ceremonial and ritualistic precepts. For these he claimed no value, but presented the two great principles on which hang all the law and the prophets. This answer, being commended by Christ, placed the Saviour on vantage ground with the rabbis. They could not condemn Him for sanctioning that which had been advanced by an expositor of the law.

"This do, and thou shalt live," Jesus said. He presented the law as a divine unity, and in this lesson taught that it is not possible to keep one precept, and break another; for the same principle runs through them all. Man's destiny will be determined by his obedience to the whole law. Supreme love to God and impartial love to man are the principles to be wrought out in the life.

The lawyer found himself a lawbreaker. He was convicted under Christ's searching words. The righteousness of the law, which he claimed to understand, he had not practiced. He had not manifested love toward his fellow man. Repentance was demanded; but instead of repenting, he tried to justify himself. Rather than acknowledge the truth, he sought to show how difficult of fulfillment the commandment is. Thus he hoped both to parry conviction and to vindicate himself in the eyes of the people. The Saviour's words had shown that his question was needless, since he had been able to answer it himself. Yet he put another question, saying, "Who is my neighbor?"

Among the Jews this question caused endless dispute. They had no doubt as to the heathen and the Samaritans; these were strangers and enemies. But where should the distinction be made among the people of their own nation, and among the different classes of society? Whom should the priest, the rabbi, the elder, regard as neighbor? They spent their lives in a round of ceremonies to make themselves pure. Contact with the ignorant and careless multitude, they taught, would cause defilement that would require wearisome effort to remove. Were they to regard the "unclean" as neighbors?

Again Jesus refused to be drawn into controversy. He did not denounce the bigotry of those who were watching to condemn Him. But by a simple story He held up before His hearers such a picture of the outflowing of heaven-born love as touched all hearts, and drew from the lawyer a confession of the truth.

The way to dispel darkness is to admit light. The best way to deal with error is to present truth. It is the revelation of God's love that makes manifest the deformity and sin of the heart centered in self.

"A certain man," said Jesus, "was going down from Jerusalem to Jericho; and he fell among robbers, which both stripped him and beat him, and departed, leaving him half dead. And by chance a certain priest was going down that way: and when he saw him, he passed by on the other side. And in like manner a Levite also, when he came to the place, and saw him, passed by on the other side." Luke 10:30-32, R. V. This was no imaginary scene, but an actual occurrence, which was known to be exactly as represented. The priest and the Levite who had passed by on the other side were in the company that listened to Christ's words.

In journeying from Jerusalem to Jericho, the traveler had to pass through a portion of the wilderness of Judea. The road led down a wild, rocky ravine, which was infested by robbers, and was often the scene of violence. It was here that the traveler was attacked, stripped of all that was valuable, wounded and bruised, and left half dead by the wayside. As he lay thus, the priest came that way; but he merely glanced toward the wounded man. Then the Levite appeared. Curious to know what had happened, he stopped and looked at the sufferer. He was convicted of what he ought to do; but it was not an agreeable duty. He wished that he had not come that way, so that he need not have seen the wounded man. He persuaded himself that the case was no concern of his.

Both these men were in sacred office, and professed to expound the Scriptures. They were of the class specially chosen to be representatives of God to the people. They were to "have compassion on the ignorant, and on them that are out of the way" (Heb. 5:2), that they might lead men to understand God's great love toward humanity. The work they were called to do was the same that Jesus had described as His own when He said, "The Spirit of the Lord is upon Me, because He hath anointed Me to preach the gospel to the poor; He hath sent Me to heal the brokenhearted, to preach deliverance to the captives, and recovering of sight to the blind, to set at liberty them that are bruised." Luke 4:18.

The angels of heaven look upon the distress of God's family upon the earth, and they are prepared to co-operate with men in relieving oppression and suffering. God in His providence had brought the priest and the Levite along the road where the wounded sufferer lay, that they might see his need of mercy and help. All heaven watched to see if the hearts of these men would be touched with pity for human woe. The Saviour was the One who had instructed the Hebrews in the wilderness; from the pillar of cloud and of fire He had taught a very different lesson from that which the people were now receiving from their priests and teachers. The merciful provisions of the law extended even to the lower animals, which cannot express in words their want and suffering. Directions had been given to Moses for the children of Israel to this effect: "If thou meet thine enemy's ox or his ass going astray, thou shalt surely bring it back to him again. If thou see the ass of him that hateth thee lying under his burden, and wouldest forbear to help him, thou shalt surely help with him." Ex. 23:4, 5. But in the man wounded by robbers, Jesus presented the case of a brother in suffering. How much more should their hearts have been moved with pity for him than for a beast of burden! The message had been given them through Moses that the Lord their God, "a great God, a mighty, and a terrible," "doth execute the judgment of the fatherless and widow, and loveth the stranger." Wherefore He commanded, "Love ye therefore the stranger." "Thou shalt love him as thyself." Deut. 10:17-19; Lev. 19:34.

Job had said, "The stranger did not lodge in the street: but I opened my doors to the traveler." And when the two angels in the guise of men came to Sodom, Lot bowed himself with his face toward the ground, and said, "Behold now, my lords, turn in, I pray you, into your servant's house, and tarry all night." Job 31:32; Gen. 19:2. With all these lessons the priest and the Levite were familiar, but they had not brought them into practical life. Trained in the school of national bigotry, they had become selfish, narrow, and exclusive. When they looked upon the wounded man, they could not tell whether he was of their nation or not. They thought he might be of the Samaritans, and they turned away.

In their action, as Christ had described it, the lawyer saw nothing contrary to what he had been taught concerning the requirements of the law. But now another scene was presented:

A certain Samaritan, in his journey, came where the sufferer was, and when he saw him, he had compassion on him. He did not question whether the stranger was a Jew or a Gentile. If a Jew, the Samaritan well knew that, were their condition reversed, the man would spit in his face, and pass him by with contempt. But he did not hesitate on account of this. He did not consider that he himself might be in danger of violence by tarrying in the place. It was enough that there was before him a human being in need and suffering. He took off his own garment with which to cover him. The oil and wine provided for his own journey he used to heal and refresh the wounded man. He lifted him on his own beast, and moved slowly along with even pace, so that the stranger might not be jarred, and made to suffer increased pain. He brought him to an inn, and cared for him through the night, watching him tenderly. In the morning, as the sick man had improved, the Samaritan ventured to go on his way. But before doing this, he placed him in the care of the innkeeper, paid the charges, and left a deposit for his benefit; and not satisfied even with this, he made provision for any further need, saying to the host, "Take care of him; and whatsoever thou spendest more, when I come again, I will repay thee."

The story ended, Jesus fixed His eyes upon the lawyer, in a glance that seemed to read his soul, and said, "Which of these three, thinkest thou, proved neighbor unto him that fell among the robbers?" Luke 10:36, R. V.

The lawyer would not, even now, take the name Samaritan upon his lips, and he made answer, "He that showed mercy on him." Jesus said, "Go, and do thou likewise."

Thus the question, "Who is my neighbor?" is forever answered. Christ has shown that our neighbor does not mean merely one of the church or faith to which we belong. It has no reference to race, color, or class distinction. Our neighbor is every person who needs our help. Our neighbor is every soul who is wounded and bruised by the adversary. Our neighbor is everyone who is the property of God.

In the story of the good Samaritan, Jesus gave a picture of Himself and His mission. Man had been deceived, bruised, robbed, and ruined by Satan, and left to perish; but the Saviour had compassion on our helpless condition. He left His glory, to come to our rescue. He found us ready to die, and He undertook our case. He healed our wounds. He covered us with His robe of righteousness. He opened to us a refuge of safety, and made complete provision for us at His own charges. He died to redeem us. Pointing to His own example, He says to His followers, "These things I command you, that ye love one another." "As I have loved you, that ye also love one another." John 15:17; 13:34.

The lawyer's question to Jesus had been, "What shall I do?" And Jesus, recognizing love to God and man as the sum of righteousness, had said, "This do, and thou shalt live." The Samaritan had obeyed the dictates of a kind and loving heart, and in this had proved himself a doer of the law. Christ bade the lawyer, "Go, and do thou likewise." Doing, and not saying merely, is expected of the children of God. "He that saith he abideth in Him ought himself also so to walk, even as He walked." 1 John 2:6.

The lesson is no less needed in the world today than when it fell from the lips of Jesus. Selfishness and cold formality have well-nigh extinguished the fire of love, and dispelled the graces that should make fragrant the character. Many who profess His name have lost sight of the fact that Christians are to represent Christ. Unless there is practical self-sacrifice for the good of others, in the family circle, in the neighborhood, in the church, and wherever we may be, then whatever our profession, we are not Christians.

Christ has linked His interest with that of humanity, and He asks us to become one with Him for the saving of humanity. "Freely ye have received," He says, "freely give." Matt. 10:8. Sin is the greatest of all evils, and it is ours to pity and help the sinner. There are many who err, and who feel their shame and their folly. They are hungry for words of encouragement. They look upon their mistakes and errors, until they are driven almost to desperation. These souls we are not to neglect. If we are Christians, we shall not pass by on the other side, keeping as far as possible from the very ones who most need our help. When we see human beings in distress, whether through affliction or through sin, we shall never say, This does not concern me.

"Ye which are spiritual, restore such an one in the spirit of meekness." Gal. 6:1. By faith and prayer press back the power of the enemy. Speak words of faith and courage that will be as a healing balsam to the bruised and wounded one. Many, many, have fainted and become discouraged in the great struggle of life, when one word of kindly cheer would have strengthened them to overcome. Never should we pass by one suffering soul without seeking to impart to him of the comfort wherewith we are comforted of God.

All this is but a fulfillment of the principle of the law,—the principle that is illustrated in the story of the good Samaritan, and made manifest in the life of Jesus. His character reveals the true significance of the law, and shows what is meant by loving our neighbor as ourselves. And when the children of God manifest mercy, kindness, and love toward all men, they also are witnessing to the character of the statutes of heaven. They are bearing testimony to the fact that "the law of the Lord is perfect, converting the soul." Ps. 19:7. And whoever fails to manifest this love is breaking the law which he professes to revere. For the spirit we manifest toward our brethren declares what is our spirit toward God. The love of God in the heart is the only spring of love toward our neighbor. "If a man say, I love God, and hateth his brother, he is a liar: for he that loveth not his brother whom he hath seen, how can he love God whom he hath not seen?" Beloved, "if we love one another, God dwelleth in us, and His love is perfected in us." 1 John 4:20, 12.

Not With Outward Show

Some of the Pharisees had come to Jesus demanding "when the kingdom of God should come." More than three years had passed since John the Baptist gave the message that like a trumpet call had sounded through the land, "The kingdom of heaven is at hand." Matt. 3:2. And as yet these Pharisees saw no indication of the establishment of the kingdom. Many of those who rejected John, and at every step had opposed Jesus, were insinuating that His mission had failed.

Jesus answered, "The kingdom of God cometh not with outward show; neither shall they say, Lo here! or, lo there! for, behold, the kingdom of God is within you." The kingdom of God begins in the heart. Look not here or there for manifestations of earthly power to mark its coming.

"The days will come," He said, turning to His disciples, "when ye shall desire to see one of the days of the Son of man, and ye shall not see it." Because it is not attended by worldly pomp, you are in danger of failing to discern the glory of My mission. You do not realize how great is your present privilege in having among you, though veiled in humanity, Him who is the life and the light of men. The days will come when you will look back with longing upon the opportunities you now enjoy to walk and talk with the Son of God.

Because of their selfishness and earthliness, even the disciples of Jesus could not comprehend the spiritual glory which He sought to reveal unto them. It was not until after Christ's ascension to His Father, and the outpouring of the Holy Spirit upon the believers, that the disciples fully appreciated the Saviour's character and mission. After they had received the baptism of the Spirit, they began to realize that they had been in the very presence of the Lord of glory. As the sayings of Christ were brought to their remembrance, their minds were opened to comprehend the prophecies, and to understand the miracles which He had wrought. The wonders of His life passed before them, and they were as men awakened from a dream. They realized that "the Word was made flesh, and dwelt among us, (and we beheld His glory, the glory as of the Only-begotten of the Father,) full of grace and truth." John 1:14. Christ had actually come from God to a sinful world to save the fallen sons and daughters of Adam. The disciples now seemed, to themselves, of much less importance than before they realized this. They never wearied of rehearsing His words and works. His lessons, which they had but dimly understood, now came to them as a fresh revelation. The Scriptures became to them a new book.

As the disciples searched the prophecies that testified of Christ, they were brought into fellowship with the Deity, and learned of Him who had ascended to heaven to complete the work He had begun on earth. They recognized the fact that in Him dwelt knowledge which no human being, unaided by divine agency, could comprehend. They needed the help of Him whom kings, prophets, and righteous men had foretold. With amazement they read and reread the prophetic delineations of His character and work. How dimly had they comprehended the prophetic scriptures! how slow they had been in taking in the great truths which testified of Christ! Looking upon Him in His humiliation, as He walked a man among men, they had not understood the mystery of His incarnation, the dual character of His nature. Their eyes were holden, so that they did not fully recognize divinity in humanity. But after they were illuminated by the Holy Spirit, how they longed to see Him again, and to place themselves at His feet! How they wished that they might come to Him, and have Him explain the scriptures which they could not comprehend! How attentively would they listen to His words! What had Christ meant when He said, "I have yet many things to say unto you, but ye cannot bear them now"? John 16:12. How eager they were to know it all! They grieved that their faith had been so feeble, that their ideas had been so wide of the mark, that they had so failed of comprehending the reality.

A herald had been sent from God to proclaim the coming of Christ, and to call the attention of the Jewish nation and of the world to His mission, that men might prepare for His reception. The wonderful personage whom John had announced had been among them for more than thirty years, and they had not really known Him as the One sent from God. Remorse took hold of the disciples because they had allowed the prevailing unbelief to leaven their opinions and becloud their understanding. The Light of this dark world had been shining amid its gloom, and they had failed to comprehend whence were its beams. They asked themselves why they had pursued a course that made it necessary for Christ to reprove them. They often repeated His conversations, and said, Why did we allow earthly considerations and the opposition of priests and rabbis to confuse our senses, so that we did not comprehend that a greater than Moses was among us, that One wiser than Solomon was instructing us? How dull were our ears! how feeble was our understanding!

Thomas would not believe until he had thrust his finger into the wound made by the Roman soldiers. Peter had denied Him in His humiliation and rejection. These painful remembrances came before them in distinct lines. They had been with Him, but they had not known or appreciated Him. But how these things now stirred their hearts as they recognized their unbelief!

As priests and rulers combined against them, and they were brought before councils and thrust into prison, the followers of Christ rejoiced "that they were counted worthy to suffer shame for His name." Acts 5:41. They rejoiced to prove, before men and angels, that they recognized the glory of Christ, and chose to follow Him at the loss of all things.

It is as true now as in apostolic days, that without the illumination of the divine Spirit, humanity cannot discern the glory of Christ. The truth and the work of God are unappreciated by a world-loving and compromising Christianity. Not in the ways of ease, of earthly honor or worldly conformity, are the followers of the Master found. They are far in advance, in the paths of toil, and humiliation, and reproach, in the front of the battle "against the principalities, against the powers, against the world rulers of this darkness, against the spiritual hosts of wickedness in the heavenly places." Eph. 6:12, R. V. And now, as in Christ's day, they are misunderstood and reproached and oppressed by the priests and Pharisees of their time.

The kingdom of God comes not with outward show. The gospel of the grace of God, with its spirit of self-abnegation, can never be in harmony with the spirit of the world. The two principles are antagonistic. "The natural man receiveth not the things of the Spirit of God: for they are foolishness unto him: neither can he know them, because they are spiritually discerned." 1 Cor. 2:14.

But today in the religious world there are multitudes who, as they believe, are working for the establishment of the kingdom of Christ as an earthly and temporal dominion. They desire to make our Lord the ruler of the kingdoms of this world, the ruler in its courts and camps, its legislative halls, its palaces and market places. They expect Him to rule through legal enactments, enforced by human authority. Since Christ is not now here in person, they themselves will undertake to act in His stead, to execute the laws of His kingdom. The establishment of such a kingdom is what the Jews desired in the days of Christ. They would have received Jesus, had He been willing to establish a temporal dominion, to enforce what they regarded as the laws of God, and to make them the expositors of His will and the agents of His authority. But He said, "My kingdom is not of this world." John 18:36. He would not accept the earthly throne.

The government under which Jesus lived was corrupt and oppressive; on every hand were crying abuses,—extortion, intolerance, and grinding cruelty. Yet the Saviour attempted no civil reforms. He attacked no national abuses, nor condemned the national enemies. He did not interfere with the authority or administration of those in power. He who was our example kept aloof from earthly governments. Not because He was indifferent to the woes of men, but because the remedy did not lie in merely human and external measures. To be efficient, the cure must reach men individually, and must regenerate the heart.

Not by the decisions of courts or councils or legislative assemblies, not by the patronage of worldly great men, is the kingdom of Christ established, but by the implanting of Christ's nature in humanity through the work of the Holy Spirit. "As many as received Him, to them gave He power to become the sons of God, even to them that believe on His name: which were born, not of blood, nor of the will of the flesh, nor of the will of man, but of God." John 1:12, 13. Here is the only power that can work the uplifting of mankind. And the human agency for the accomplishment of this work is the teaching and practicing of the word of God.

When the apostle Paul began his ministry in Corinth, that populous, wealthy, and wicked city, polluted by the nameless vices of heathenism, he said, "I determined not to know anything among you, save Jesus Christ, and Him crucified." 1 Cor. 2:2. Writing afterward to some of those who had been corrupted by the foulest sins, he could say, "But ye are washed, but ye are sanctified, but ye are justified in the name of the Lord Jesus, and by the Spirit of our God." "I thank my God always on your behalf, for the grace of God which is given you by Jesus Christ." 1 Cor. 6:11; 1:4.

Now, as in Christ's day, the work of God's kingdom lies not with those who are clamoring for recognition and support by earthly rulers and human laws, but with those who are declaring to the people in His name those spiritual truths that will work in the receivers the experience of Paul: "I am crucified with Christ: nevertheless I live; yet not I, but Christ liveth in me." Gal. 2:20. Then they will labor as did Paul for the benefit of men. He said, "Now then we are ambassadors for Christ, as though God did beseech you by us: we pray you in Christ's stead, be ye reconciled to God." 2 Cor. 5:20.

Blessing the Children

Jesus was ever a lover of children. He accepted their childish sympathy and their open, unaffected love. The grateful praise from their pure lips was music in His ears, and refreshed His spirit when oppressed by contact with crafty and hypocritical men. Wherever the Saviour went, the benignity of His countenance, and His gentle, kindly manner won the love and confidence of children.

Among the Jews it was customary for children to be brought to some rabbi, that he might lay his hands upon them in blessing; but the Saviour's disciples thought His work too important to be interrupted in this way. When the mothers came to Him with their little ones, the disciples looked on them with disfavor. They thought these children too young to be benefited by a visit to Jesus, and concluded that He would be displeased at their presence. But it was the disciples with whom He was displeased. The Saviour understood the care and burden of the mothers who were seeking to train their children according to the word of God. He had heard their prayers. He Himself had drawn them into His presence.

One mother with her child had left her home to find Jesus. On the way she told a neighbor her errand, and the neighbor wanted to have Jesus bless her children. Thus several mothers came together, with their little ones. Some of the children had passed beyond the years of infancy to childhood and youth. When the mothers made known their desire, Jesus heard with sympathy the timid, tearful request. But He waited to see how the disciples would treat them. When He saw them send the mothers away, thinking to do Him a favor, He showed them their error, saying, "Suffer the little children to come unto Me, and forbid them not: for of such is the kingdom of God." He took the children in His arms, He laid His hands upon them, and gave them the blessing for which they came.

The mothers were comforted. They returned to their homes strengthened and blessed by the words of Christ. They were encouraged to take up their burden with new cheerfulness, and to work hopefully for their children. The mothers of today are to receive His words with the same faith. Christ is as verily a personal Saviour today as when He lived a man among men. He is as verily the helper of mothers today as when He gathered the little ones to His arms in Judea. The children of our hearths are as much the purchase of His blood as were the children of long ago.

Jesus knows the burden of every mother's heart. He who had a mother that struggled with poverty and privation sympathizes with every mother in her labors. He who made a long journey in order to relieve the anxious heart of a Canaanite woman will do as much for the mothers of today. He who gave back to the widow of Nain her only son, and who in His agony upon the cross remembered His own mother, is touched today by the mother's sorrow. In every grief and every need He will give comfort and help.

Let mothers come to Jesus with their perplexities. They will find grace sufficient to aid them in the management of their children. The gates are open for every mother who would lay her burdens at the Saviour's feet. He who said, "Suffer the little children to come unto Me, and forbid them not," still invites the mothers to lead up their little ones to be blessed by Him. Even the babe in its mother's arms may dwell as under the shadow of the Almighty through the faith of the praying mother. John the Baptist was filled with the Holy Spirit from his birth. If we will live in communion with God, we too may expect the divine Spirit to mold our little ones, even from their earliest moments.

In the children who were brought in contact with Him, Jesus saw the men and women who should be heirs of His grace and subjects of His kingdom, and some of whom would become martyrs for His sake. He knew that these children would listen to Him and accept Him as their Redeemer far more readily than would grown-up people, many of whom were the worldly-wise and hardhearted. In His teaching He came down to their level. He, the Majesty of heaven, did not disdain to answer their questions, and simplify His important lessons to meet their childish understanding. He planted in their minds the seeds of truth, which in after years would spring up, and bear fruit unto eternal life.

It is still true that children are the most susceptible to the teachings of the gospel; their hearts are open to divine influences, and strong to retain the lessons received. The little children may be Christians, having an experience in accordance with their years. They need to be educated in spiritual things, and parents should give them every advantage, that they may form characters after the similitude of the character of Christ.

Fathers and mothers should look upon their children as younger members of the Lord's family, committed to them to educate for heaven. The lessons that we ourselves learn from Christ we should give to our children, as the young minds can receive them, little by little opening to them the beauty of the principles of heaven. Thus the Christian home becomes a school, where the parents serve as underteachers, while Christ Himself is the chief instructor.

In working for the conversion of our children, we should not look for violent emotion as the essential evidence of conviction of sin. Nor is it necessary to know the exact time when they are converted. We should teach them to bring their sins to Jesus, asking His forgiveness, and believing that He pardons and receives them as He received the children when He was personally on earth.

As the mother teaches her children to obey her because they love her, she is teaching them the first lessons in the Christian life. The mother's love represents to the child the love of Christ, and the little ones who trust and obey their mother are learning to trust and obey the Saviour.

Jesus was the pattern for children, and He was also the father's example. He spoke as one having authority, and His word was with power; yet in all His intercourse with rude and violent men He did not use one unkind or discourteous expression. The grace of Christ in the heart will impart a heaven-born dignity and sense of propriety. It will soften whatever is harsh, and subdue all that is coarse and unkind. It will lead fathers and mothers to treat their children as intelligent beings, as they themselves would like to be treated.

Parents, in the training of your children, study the lessons that God has given in nature. If you would train a pink, or rose, or lily, how would you do it? Ask the gardener by what process he makes every branch and leaf to flourish so beautifully, and to develop in symmetry and loveliness. He will tell you that it was by no rude touch, no violent effort; for this would only break the delicate stems. It was by little attentions, often repeated. He moistened the soil, and protected the growing plants from the fierce blasts and from the scorching sun, and God caused them to flourish and to blossom into loveliness. In dealing with your children, follow the method of the gardener. By gentle touches, by loving ministrations, seek to fashion their characters after the pattern of the character of Christ.

Encourage the expression of love toward God and toward one another. The reason why there are so many hardhearted men and women in the world is that true affection has been regarded as weakness, and has been discouraged and repressed. The better nature of these persons was stifled in childhood; and unless the light of divine love shall melt away their cold selfishness, their happiness will be forever ruined. If we wish our children to possess the tender spirit of Jesus, and the sympathy that angels manifest for us, we must encourage the generous, loving impulses of childhood.

Teach the children to see Christ in nature. Take them out into the open air, under the noble trees, into the garden; and in all the wonderful works of creation teach them to see an expression of His love. Teach them that He made the laws which govern all living things, that He has made laws for us, and that these laws are for our happiness and joy. Do not weary them with long prayers and tedious exhortations, but through nature's object lessons teach them obedience to the law of God.

As you win their confidence in you as followers of Christ, it will be easy to teach them of the great love wherewith He has loved us. As you try to make plain the truths of salvation, and point the children to Christ as a personal Saviour, angels will be by your side. The Lord will give to fathers and mothers grace to interest their little ones in the precious story of the Babe of Bethlehem, who is indeed the hope of the world.

When Jesus told the disciples not to forbid the children to come to Him, He was speaking to His followers in all ages,—to officers of the church, to ministers, helpers, and all Christians. Jesus is drawing the children, and He bids us, Suffer them to come; as if He would say, They will come if you do not hinder them.

Let not your un-Christlike character misrepresent Jesus. Do not keep the little ones away from Him by your coldness and harshness. Never give them cause to feel that heaven will not be a pleasant place to them if you are there. Do not speak of religion as something that children cannot understand, or act as if they were not expected to accept Christ in their childhood. Do not give them the false impression that the religion of Christ is a religion of gloom, and that in coming to the Saviour they must give up all that makes life joyful.

As the Holy Spirit moves upon the hearts of the children, co-operate with His work. Teach them that the Saviour is calling them, that nothing can give Him greater joy than for them to give themselves to Him in the bloom and freshness of their years.

The Saviour regards with infinite tenderness the souls whom

He has purchased with His own blood. They are the claim of His love. He looks upon them with unutterable longing. His heart is drawn out, not only to the best-behaved children, but to those who have by inheritance objectionable traits of character. Many parents do not understand how much they are responsible for these traits in their children. They have not the tenderness and wisdom to deal with the erring ones whom they have made what they are. But Jesus looks upon these children with pity. He traces from cause to effect.

The Christian worker may be Christ's agent in drawing these children to the Saviour. By wisdom and tact he may bind them to his heart, he may give them courage and hope, and through the grace of Christ may see them transformed in character, so that of them it may be said, "Of such is the kingdom of God."

"One Thing Thou Lackest"

And when He was gone forth into the way, there came one running, and kneeled to Him, and asked Him, Good Master, what shall I do that I may inherit eternal life?"

The young man who asked this question was a ruler. He had great possessions, and occupied a position of responsibility. He saw the love that Christ manifested toward the children brought to Him; he saw how tenderly He received them, and took them up in His arms, and his heart kindled with love for the Saviour. He felt a desire to be His disciple. He was so deeply moved that as Christ was going on His way, he ran after Him, and kneeling at His feet, asked with sincerity and earnestness the question so important to his soul and to the soul of every human being, "Good Master, what shall I do that I may inherit eternal life?"

"Why callest thou Me good?" said Christ, "there is none good but One, that is, God." Jesus desired to test the ruler's sincerity, and to draw from him the way in which he regarded Him as good. Did he realize that the One to whom he was speaking was the Son of God? What was the true sentiment of his heart?

This ruler had a high estimate of his own righteousness. He did not really suppose that he was defective in anything, yet he was not altogether satisfied. He felt the want of something that he did not possess. Could not Jesus bless him as He blessed the little children, and satisfy his soul want?

In reply to this question Jesus told him that obedience to the commandments of God was necessary if he would obtain eternal life; and He quoted several of the commandments which show man's duty to his fellow men. The ruler's answer was positive: "All these things have I kept from my youth up: what lack I yet?"

Christ looked into the face of the young man, as if reading his life and searching his character. He loved him, and He hungered to give him that peace and grace and joy which would materially change his character. "One thing thou lackest," He said; "go thy way, sell whatsoever thou hast, and give to the poor, and thou shalt have treasure in heaven: and

come, take up the cross, and follow Me."

Christ was drawn to this young man. He knew him to be sincere in his assertion, "All these things have I kept from my youth." The Redeemer longed to create in him that discernment which would enable him to see the necessity of heart devotion and Christian goodness. He longed to see in him a humble and contrite heart, conscious of the supreme love to be given to God, and hiding its lack in the perfection of Christ.

Jesus saw in this ruler just the help He needed if the young man would become a colaborer with Him in the work of salvation. If he would place himself under Christ's guidance, he would be a power for good. In a marked degree the ruler could have represented Christ; for he possessed qualifications, which, if he were united with the Saviour, would enable him to become a divine force among men. Christ, seeing into his character, loved him. Love for Christ was awakening in the ruler's heart; for love begets love. Jesus longed to see him a co-worker with Him. He longed to make him like Himself, a mirror in which the likeness of God would be reflected. He longed to develop the excellence of his character, and sanctify it to the Master's use. If the ruler had then given himself to Christ, he would have grown in the atmosphere of His presence. If he had made this choice, how different would have been his future!

"One thing thou lackest," Jesus said. "If thou wilt be perfect, go and sell that thou hast, and give to the poor, and thou shalt have treasure in heaven: and come and follow Me." Christ read the ruler's heart. Only one thing he lacked, but that was a vital principle. He needed the love of God in the soul. This lack, unless supplied, would prove fatal to him; his whole nature would become corrupted. By indulgence, selfishness would strengthen. That he might receive the love of God, his supreme love of self must be surrendered.

Christ gave this man a test. He called upon him to choose between the heavenly treasure and worldly greatness. The heavenly treasure was assured him if he would follow Christ. But self must yield; his will must be given into Christ's control. The very holiness of God was offered to the young ruler. He had the privilege of becoming a son of God, and a coheir with Christ to the heavenly treasure. But he must take up the cross, and follow the Saviour in the path of self-denial.

Christ's words were verily to the ruler the invitation, "Choose you this day whom ye will serve." Joshua 24:15. The choice was left with him. Jesus was yearning for his conversion. He had shown him the plague spot in his character, and with what deep interest He watched the issue as the young man weighed the question! If he decided to follow Christ, he must obey His words in everything. He must turn from his ambitious projects. With what earnest, anxious longing, what soul hunger, did the Saviour look at the young man, hoping that he would yield to the invitation of the Spirit of God!

Christ made the only terms which could place the ruler where he would perfect a Christian character. His words were words of wisdom, though they appeared severe and exacting. In accepting and obeying them was the ruler's only hope of salvation. His exalted position and his possessions were exerting a subtle influence for evil upon his character. If cherished, they would supplant God in his affections. To keep back little or much from God was to retain that which would lessen his moral strength and efficiency; for if the things of this world are cherished, however uncertain and unworthy they may be, they will become all-absorbing.

The ruler was quick to discern all that Christ's words involved, and he became sad. If he had realized the value of the offered gift, quickly would he have enrolled himself as one of Christ's followers. He was a member of the honored council of the Jews, and Satan was tempting him with flattering prospects of the future. He wanted the heavenly treasure, but he wanted also the temporal advantages his riches would bring him. He was sorry that such conditions existed; he desired eternal life, but he was not willing to make the sacrifice. The cost of eternal life seemed too great, and he went away sorrowful; "for he had great possessions."

His claim that he had kept the law of God was a deception. He showed that riches were his idol. He could not keep the commandments of God while the world was first in his affections. He loved the gifts of God more than he loved the Giver. Christ had offered the young man fellowship with Himself. "Follow Me," He said. But the Saviour was not so much to him as his own name among men or his possessions. To give up his earthly treasure, that was seen, for the heavenly treasure, that was unseen, was too great a risk. He refused the offer of eternal life, and went away, and ever after the world was to receive his worship. Thousands are passing through this ordeal, weighing Christ against the world; and many choose the world. Like the young ruler, they turn from the Saviour, saying in their hearts, I will not have this Man as my leader.

Christ's dealing with the young man is presented as an object lesson. God has given us the rule of conduct which every one of His servants must follow. It is obedience to His law, not merely a legal obedience, but an obedience which enters into the life, and is exemplified in the character. God has set His own standard of character for all who would become subjects of His kingdom. Only those who will become co-workers with Christ, only those who will say, Lord, all I have and all I am is Thine, will be acknowledged as sons and daughters of God. All should consider what it means to desire heaven, and yet to turn away because of the conditions laid down. Think of what it means to say "No" to Christ. The ruler said, No, I cannot give You all. Do we say the same? The Saviour offers to share with us the work God has given us to do. He offers to use the means God has given us, to carry forward His work in the world. Only in this way can He save us.

The ruler's possessions were entrusted to him that he might prove himself a faithful steward; he was to dispense these goods for the blessing of those in need. So God now entrusts men with means, with talents and opportunities, that they may be His agents in helping the poor and the suffering. He who uses his entrusted gifts as God designs becomes a co-worker with the Saviour. He wins souls to Christ, because he is a representative of His character.

To those who, like the young ruler, are in high positions of trust and have great possessions, it may seem too great a sacrifice to give up all in order to follow Christ. But this is the rule of conduct for all who would become His disciples. Nothing short of obedience can be accepted. Self-surrender is the substance of the teachings of Christ. Often it is presented and enjoined in language that seems authoritative, because there is no other way to save man than to cut away those things which, if entertained, will demoralize the whole being.

When Christ's followers give back to the Lord His own, they are accumulating treasure which will be given to them when they shall hear the words, "Well done, good and faithful servant; . . . enter thou into the joy of thy Lord." "Who for the joy that was set before Him endured the cross, despising the shame, and is set down at the right hand of the throne of God." Matt. 25:23; Heb. 12:2. The joy of seeing souls redeemed, souls eternally saved, is the reward of all that put their feet in the footprints of Him who said, "Follow Me."

"Lazarus, Come Forth"

Among the most steadfast of Christ's disciples was Lazarus of Bethany. From their first meeting his faith in Christ had been strong; his love for Him was deep, and he was greatly beloved by the Saviour. It was for Lazarus that the greatest of Christ's miracles was performed. The Saviour blessed all who sought His help; He loves all the human family, but to some He is bound by peculiarly tender associations. His heart was knit by a strong bond of affection to the family at Bethany, and for one of them His most wonderful work was wrought.

At the home of Lazarus, Jesus had often found rest. The Saviour had no home of His own; He was dependent on the hospitality of His friends and disciples, and often, when weary, thirsting for human fellowship, He had been glad to escape to this peaceful household, away from the suspicion and jealousy of the angry Pharisees. Here He found a sincere welcome, and pure, holy friendship. Here He could speak with simplicity and perfect freedom, knowing that His words would be understood and treasured.

Our Saviour appreciated a quiet home and interested listeners. He longed for human tenderness, courtesy, and affection. Those who received the heavenly instruction He was always ready to impart were greatly blessed. As the multitudes followed Christ through the open fields, He unfolded to them the beauties of the natural world. He sought to open the eyes of their understanding, that they might see how the hand of God upholds the world. In order to call out an appreciation of God's goodness and benevolence, He called the attention of His hearers to the gently falling dew, to the soft showers of rain and the bright sunshine, given alike to good and evil. He desired men to realize more fully the regard that God bestows on the human instrumentalities He has created. But the multitudes were slow of hearing, and in the home at Bethany Christ found rest from the weary conflict of public life. Here He opened to an appreciative audience the volume of Providence. In these private interviews He unfolded to His hearers that which He did not attempt to tell to the mixed multitude. He needed not to speak to His friends in parables.

As Christ gave His wonderful lessons, Mary sat at His feet, a reverent and devoted listener. On one occasion, Martha, perplexed with the care of preparing the meal, went to Christ, saying, "Lord, dost Thou not care that my sister hath left me to serve alone? bid her therefore that she help me." This was the time of Christ's first visit to Bethany. The Saviour and His disciples had just made the toilsome journey on foot from Jericho. Martha was anxious to provide for their comfort, and in her anxiety she forgot the courtesy due to her Guest. Jesus answered her with mild and patient words, "Martha, Martha, thou art careful and troubled about many things: but one thing is needful: and Mary hath chosen that good part, which shall not be taken away from her." Mary was storing her mind with the precious words falling from the Saviour's lips, words that were more precious to her than earth's most costly jewels.

The "one thing" that Martha needed was a calm, devotional spirit, a deeper anxiety for knowledge concerning the future, immortal life, and the graces necessary for spiritual advancement. She needed less anxiety for the things which pass away, and more for those things which endure forever. Jesus would teach His children to seize every opportunity of gaining that knowledge which will make them wise unto salvation. The cause of Christ needs careful, energetic workers. There is a wide field for the Marthas, with their zeal in active religious work. But let them first sit with Mary at the feet of Jesus. Let diligence, promptness, and energy be sanctified by the grace of Christ; then the life will be an unconquerable power for good.

Sorrow entered the peaceful home where Jesus had rested. Lazarus was stricken with sudden illness, and his sisters sent to the Saviour, saying, "Lord, behold, he whom Thou lovest is sick." They saw the violence of the disease that had seized their brother, but they knew that Christ had shown Himself able to heal all manner of diseases. They believed that He would sympathize with them in their distress; therefore they made no urgent demand for His immediate presence, but sent only the confiding message, "He whom Thou lovest is sick." They thought that He would immediately respond to their message, and be with them as soon as He could reach Bethany.

Anxiously they waited for a word from Jesus. As long as the spark of life was yet alive in their brother, they prayed and watched for Jesus to come. But the messenger returned without Him. Yet he brought the message, "This sickness is not unto death," and they clung to the hope that Lazarus would live. Tenderly they tried to speak words of hope and encouragement to the almost unconscious sufferer. When Lazarus died, they were bitterly disappointed; but they felt the sustaining grace of Christ, and this kept them from reflecting any blame on the Saviour.

When Christ heard the message, the disciples thought He received it coldly. He did not manifest the sorrow they expected Him to show. Looking up to them, He said, "This sickness is not unto death, but for the glory of God, that the Son of God might be glorified thereby." For two days He remained in the place where He was. This delay was a mystery to the disciples. What a comfort His presence would be to the afflicted household! they thought. His strong affection for the family at Bethany was well known to the disciples, and they were surprised that He did not respond to the sad message, "He whom Thou lovest is sick."

During the two days Christ seemed to have dismissed the message from His mind; for He did not speak of Lazarus. The disciples thought of John the Baptist, the forerunner of Jesus. They had wondered why Jesus, with the power to perform wonderful miracles, had permitted John to languish in prison, and to die a violent death. Possessing such power, why did not Christ save John's life? This question had often been asked by the Pharisees, who presented it as an unanswerable argument against Christ's claim to be the Son of God. The Saviour had warned His disciples of trials, losses, and persecution. Would He forsake them in trial? Some questioned if they had mistaken His mission. All were deeply troubled.

After waiting for two days, Jesus said to the disciples, "Let us go into Judea again." The disciples questioned why, if Jesus were going to Judea, He had waited two days. But anxiety for Christ and for themselves was now uppermost in their minds. They could see nothing but danger in the course He was about to pursue. "Master," they said, "the Jews of late sought to stone Thee; and goest Thou thither again? Jesus answered, Are there not twelve hours in the day?" I am under the guidance of My Father; as long as I do His will, My life is safe. My twelve hours of day are not yet ended. I have entered upon the last remnant of My day; but while any of this remains, I am safe.

"If any man walk in the day," He continued, "he stumbleth not, because he seeth the light of this world." He who does the will of God, who walks in the path that God has marked out, cannot stumble and fall. The light of God's guiding Spirit gives him a clear perception of his duty, and leads him aright till the close of his work. "But if a man walk in the night, he stumbleth, because there is no light in him." He who walks in a path of his own choosing, where God has not called him, will stumble. For him day is turned into night, and wherever he may be, he is not secure.

"These things said He: and after that He saith unto them, Our friend Lazarus sleepeth; but I go that I may awake him out of sleep." "Our friend Lazarus sleepeth." How touching the words! how full of sympathy! In the thought of the peril their Master was about to incur by going to Jerusalem, the disciples had almost forgotten the bereaved family at Bethany. But not so Christ. The disciples felt rebuked. They had been disappointed because Christ did not respond more promptly to the message. They had been tempted to think that He had not the tender love for Lazarus and his sisters that they had thought He had, or He would have hastened back with the messenger. But the words, "Our friend Lazarus sleepeth," awakened right feelings in their minds. They were convinced that Christ had not forgotten His suffering friends.

"Then said His disciples, Lord, if he sleep, he shall do well. Howbeit Jesus spake of his death: but they thought that He had spoken of taking of rest in sleep." Christ represents death as a sleep to His believing children. Their life is hid with Christ in God, and until the last trump shall sound those who die will sleep in Him.

"Then said Jesus unto them plainly, Lazarus is dead. And I am glad for your sakes that I was not there, to the intent ye may believe; nevertheless let us go unto him." Thomas could see nothing but death in store for his Master if he went to Judea; but he girded up his spirit, and said to the other disciples, "Let us also go, that we may die with Him." He knew the hatred of the Jews toward Christ. It was their purpose to compass His death, but this purpose had not succeeded, because some of His allotted time still remained. During this time Jesus had the guardianship of heavenly angels; and even in the regions of Judea, where the rabbis were plotting how they might take Him and put Him to death, no harm could come to Him.

The disciples marveled at Christ's words when He said, "Lazarus is dead. And I am glad . . . that I was not there." Did the Saviour by His own choice avoid the home of His suffering friends? Apparently Mary and Martha and the dying Lazarus were left alone. But they were not alone. Christ beheld the whole scene, and after the death of Lazarus the bereaved sisters were upheld by His grace. Jesus witnessed the sorrow of their rent hearts, as their brother wrestled with his strong foe, death. He felt every pang of anguish, as He said to His disciples, "Lazarus is dead." But Christ had not only the loved ones at Bethany to think of; He had the training of His disciples to consider. They were to be His representatives to the world, that the Father's blessing might embrace all. For their sake He permitted Lazarus to die. Had He restored him from illness to health, the miracle that is the most positive evidence of His divine character, would not have been performed.

Had Christ been in the sickroom, Lazarus would not have died; for Satan would have had no power over him. Death could not have aimed his dart at Lazarus in the presence of the Life-giver. Therefore Christ remained away. He suffered the enemy to exercise his power, that He might drive him back, a conquered foe. He permitted Lazarus to pass under the dominion of death; and the suffering sisters saw their brother laid in the grave. Christ knew that as they looked on the dead face of their brother their faith in their Redeemer would be severely tried. But He knew that because of the struggle through which they were now passing their faith would shine forth with far greater power. He suffered every pang of sorrow

that they endured. He loved them no less because He tarried; but He knew that for them, for Lazarus, for Himself, and for His disciples, a victory was to be gained.

"For your sakes," "to the intent ye may believe." To all who are reaching out to feel the guiding hand of God, the moment of greatest discouragement is the time when divine help is nearest. They will look back with thankfulness upon the darkest part of their way. "The Lord knoweth how to deliver the godly," 2 Peter 2:9. From every temptation and every trial He will bring them forth with firmer faith and a richer experience.

In delaying to come to Lazarus, Christ had a purpose of mercy toward those who had not received Him. He tarried, that by raising Lazarus from the dead He might give to His stubborn, unbelieving people another evidence that He was indeed "the resurrection, and the life." He was loath to give up all hope of the people, the poor, wandering sheep of the house of Israel. His heart was breaking because of their impenitence. In His mercy He purposed to give them one more evidence that He was the Restorer, the One who alone could bring life and immortality to light. This was to be an evidence that the priests could not misinterpret. This was the reason of His delay in going to Bethany. This crowning miracle, the raising of Lazarus, was to set the seal of God on His work and on His claim to divinity.

On His journey to Bethany, Jesus, according to His custom, ministered to the sick and the needy. Upon reaching the town He sent a messenger to the sisters with the tidings of His arrival. Christ did not at once enter the house, but remained in a quiet place by the wayside. The great outward display observed by the Jews at the death of friends or relatives was not in harmony with the spirit of Christ. He heard the sound of wailing from the hired mourners, and He did not wish to meet the sisters in the scene of confusion. Among the mourning friends were relatives of the family, some of whom held high positions of responsibility in Jerusalem. Among these were some of Christ's bitterest enemies. Christ knew their purposes, and therefore He did not at once make Himself known.

The message was given to Martha so quietly that others in the room did not hear. Absorbed in her grief, Mary did not hear the words. Rising at once, Martha went out to meet her Lord, but thinking that she had gone to the place where Lazarus was buried, Mary sat still in her sorrow, making no outcry.

Martha hastened to meet Jesus, her heart agitated by conflicting emotions. In His expressive face she read the same tenderness and love that had always been there. Her confidence in Him was unbroken, but she thought of her dearly loved brother, whom Jesus also had loved. With grief surging in her heart because Christ had not come before, yet with hope that even now He would do something to comfort them, she said, "Lord, if Thou hadst been here, my brother had not died." Over and over again, amid the tumult made by the mourners, the sisters had repeated these words.

With human and divine pity Jesus looked into her sorrowful, careworn face. Martha had no inclination to recount the past; all was expressed by the pathetic words, "Lord, if Thou hadst been here, my brother had not died." But looking into that face of love, she added, "I know, that even now, whatsoever Thou wilt ask of God, God will give it Thee."

Jesus encouraged her faith, saying, "Thy brother shall rise again." His answer was not intended to inspire hope of an immediate change. He carried Martha's thoughts beyond the present restoration of her brother, and fixed them upon the resurrection of the just. This He did that she might see in the resurrection of Lazarus a pledge of the resurrection of all the righteous dead, and an assurance that it would be accomplished by the Saviour's power.

Martha answered, "I know that he shall rise again in the resurrection at the last day."

Still seeking to give a true direction to her faith, Jesus declared, "I am the resurrection, and the life." In Christ is life, original, unborrowed, underived. "He that hath the Son hath life." 1 John 5:12. The divinity of Christ is the believer's assurance of eternal life. "He that believeth in Me," said Jesus, "though he were dead, yet shall he live: and whosoever liveth and believeth in Me shall never die. Believest thou this?" Christ here looks forward to the time of His second coming. Then the righteous dead shall be raised incorruptible, and the living righteous shall be translated to heaven without seeing death. The miracle which Christ was about to perform, in raising Lazarus from the dead, would represent the resurrection of all the righteous dead. By His word and His works He declared Himself the Author of the resurrection. He who Himself was soon to die upon the cross stood with the keys of death, a conqueror of the grave, and asserted His right and power to give eternal life.

To the Saviour's words, "Believest thou?" Martha responded, "Yea, Lord: I believe that Thou art the Christ, the Son of God, which should come into the world." She did not comprehend in all their significance the words spoken by Christ, but she confessed her faith in His divinity, and her confidence that He was able to perform whatever it pleased Him to do.

"And when she had so said, she went her way, and called Mary her sister secretly, saying, The Master is come, and calleth for thee." She delivered her message as quietly as possible; for the priests and rulers were prepared to arrest Jesus when opportunity offered. The cries of the mourners prevented her words from being heard.

On hearing the message, Mary rose hastily, and with an eager look on her face left the room. Thinking that she had gone to the grave to weep, the mourners followed her. When she reached the place where Jesus was waiting, she knelt at His feet, and said with quivering lips, "Lord, if Thou hadst been here, my brother had not died." The cries of the mourners were painful to her; for she longed for a few quiet words alone with Jesus. But she knew of the envy and jealousy cherished in the hearts of some present against Christ, and she was restrained from fully expressing her grief.

"When Jesus therefore saw her weeping, and the Jews also weeping which came with her, He groaned in the spirit, and was troubled." He read the hearts of all assembled. He saw that with many, what passed as a demonstration of grief was only pretense. He knew that some in the company, now manifesting hypocritical sorrow, would erelong be planning the death, not only of the mighty miracle worker, but of the one to be raised from the dead. Christ could have stripped from them their robe of pretended sorrow. But He restrained His righteous indignation. The words He could in all truth have spoken, He did not speak, because of the loved one kneeling at His feet in sorrow, who truly believed in Him.

"Where have ye laid him?" He asked, "They said unto Him, Lord, come and see." Together they proceeded to the grave. It was a mournful scene. Lazarus had been much beloved, and his sisters wept for him with breaking hearts, while those who had been his friends mingled their tears with those of the bereaved sisters. In view of this human distress, and of the fact that the afflicted friends could mourn over the dead while the Saviour of the world stood by,—"Jesus wept." Though He was the Son of God, yet He had taken human nature upon Him, and He was moved by human sorrow. His tender, pitying heart is ever awakened to sympathy by suffering. He weeps with those that weep, and rejoices with those that rejoice.

But it was not only because of His human sympathy with Mary and Martha that Jesus wept. In His tears there was a sorrow as high above human sorrow as the heavens are higher than the earth. Christ did not weep for Lazarus; for He was about to call him from the grave. He wept because many of those now mourning for Lazarus would soon plan the death of Him who was the resurrection and the life. But how unable were the unbelieving Jews rightly to interpret His tears! Some, who could see nothing more than the outward circumstances of the scene before Him as a cause for His grief, said softly, "Behold how He loved him!" Others, seeking to drop the seed of unbelief into the hearts of those present, said derisively, "Could not this Man, which opened the eyes of the blind, have caused that even this man should not have died?" If it were in Christ's power to save Lazarus, why then did He suffer him to die?

With prophetic eye Christ saw the enmity of the Pharisees and the Sadducees. He knew that they were premeditating His death. He knew that some of those now apparently so sympathetic would soon close against themselves the door of hope and the gates of the city of God. A scene was about to take place, in His humiliation and crucifixion, that would result in the destruction of Jerusalem, and at that time none would make lamentation for the dead. The retribution that was coming upon Jerusalem was plainly portrayed before Him. He saw Jerusalem compassed by the Roman legions. He knew that many now weeping for Lazarus would die in the siege of the city, and in their death there would be no hope.

It was not only because of the scene before Him that Christ

wept. The weight of the grief of ages was upon Him. He saw the terrible effects of the transgression of God's law. He saw that in the history of the world, beginning with the death of Abel, the conflict between good and evil had been unceasing. Looking down the years to come, He saw the suffering and sorrow, tears and death, that were to be the lot of men. His heart was pierced with the pain of the human family of all ages and in all lands. The woes of the sinful race were heavy upon His soul, and the fountain of His tears was broken up as He longed to relieve all their distress.

"Jesus therefore again groaning in Himself cometh to the grave." Lazarus had been laid in a cave in a rock, and a massive stone had been placed before the entrance. "Take ye away the stone," Christ said. Thinking that He only wished to look upon the dead, Martha objected, saying that the body had been buried four days, and corruption had already begun its work. This statement, made before the raising of Lazarus, left no room for Christ's enemies to say that a deception had been practiced. In the past the Pharisees had circulated false statements regarding the most wonderful manifestations of the power of God. When Christ raised to life the daughter of Jairus, He had said, "The damsel is not dead, but sleepeth." Mark 5:39. As she had been sick only a short time, and was raised immediately after death, the Pharisees declared that the child had not been dead; that Christ Himself had said she was only asleep. They had tried to make it appear that Christ could not cure disease, that there was foul play about His miracles. But in this case, none could deny that Lazarus was dead.

When the Lord is about to do a work, Satan moves upon someone to object. "Take ye away the stone," Christ said. As far as possible, prepare the way for My work. But Martha's positive and ambitious nature asserted itself. She was unwilling that the decomposing body should be brought to view. The human heart is slow to understand Christ's words, and Martha's faith had not grasped the true meaning of His promise.

Christ reproved Martha, but His words were spoken with the utmost gentleness. "Said I not unto thee, that, if thou wouldest believe, thou shouldest see the glory of God?" Why should you doubt in regard to My power? Why reason in opposition to My requirements? You have My word. If you will believe, you shall see the glory of God. Natural impossibilities cannot prevent the work of the Omnipotent One. Skepticism and unbelief are not humility. Implicit belief in Christ's word is true humility, true self-surrender.

"Take ye away the stone." Christ could have commanded the stone to remove, and it would have obeyed His voice. He could have bidden the angels who were close by His side to do this. At His bidding, invisible hands would have removed the stone. But it was to be taken away by human hands. Thus Christ would show that humanity is to co-operate with divinity. What human power can do divine power is not summoned to do. God does not dispense with man's aid. He strengthens him, co-operating with him as he uses the powers and capabilities given him.

The command is obeyed. The stone is rolled away. Everything is done openly and deliberately. All are given a chance to see that no deception is practiced. There lies the body of Lazarus in its rocky grave, cold and silent in death. The cries of the mourners are hushed. Surprised and expectant, the company stand around the sepulcher, waiting to see what is to follow.

Calmly Christ stands before the tomb. A sacred solemnity rests upon all present. Christ steps closer to the sepulcher. Lifting His eyes to heaven, He says, "Father, I thank Thee that Thou hast heard Me." Not long before this, Christ's enemies had accused Him of blasphemy, and had taken up stones to cast at Him because He claimed to be the Son of God. They accused Him of performing miracles by the power of Satan. But here Christ claims God as His Father, and with perfect confidence declares that He is the Son of God.

In all that He did, Christ was co-operating with His Father. Ever He had been careful to make it evident that He did not work independently; it was by faith and prayer that He wrought His miracles. Christ desired all to know His relationship with His Father. "Father," He said, "I thank Thee that Thou hast heard Me. And I knew that Thou hearest Me always: but because of the people which stand by I said it, that they may believe that Thou hast sent Me." Here the disciples and the people were to be given the most convincing evidence in regard to the relationship existing between Christ and God. They were to be shown that Christ's claim was not a deception.

"And when He thus had spoken, He cried with a loud voice, Lazarus, come forth." His voice, clear and penetrating, pierces the ear of the dead. As He speaks, divinity flashes through humanity. In His face, which is lighted up by the glory of God, the people see the assurance of His power. Every eye is fastened on the entrance to the cave. Every ear is bent to catch the slightest sound. With intense and painful interest all wait for the test of Christ's divinity, the evidence that is to substantiate His claim to be the Son of God, or to extinguish the hope forever.

There is a stir in the silent tomb, and he who was dead stands at the door of the sepulcher. His movements are impeded by the graveclothes in which he was laid away, and Christ says to the astonished spectators, "Loose him, and let him go." Again they are shown that the human worker is to co-operate with God. Humanity is to work for humanity. Lazarus is set free, and stands before the company, not as one emaciated from disease, and with feeble, tottering limbs, but as a man in the prime of life, and in the vigor of a noble manhood. His eyes beam with intelligence and with love for his Saviour. He casts himself in adoration at the feet of Jesus.

The beholders are at first speechless with amazement. Then there follows an inexpressible scene of rejoicing and thanksgiving. The sisters receive their brother back to life as the gift of God, and with joyful tears they brokenly express their thanks to the Saviour. But while brother, sisters, and friends are rejoicing in this reunion, Jesus withdraws from the scene. When they look for the Life-giver, He is not to be found.

Priestly Plottings

Bethany was so near Jerusalem that the news of the raising of Lazarus was soon carried to the city. Through spies who had witnessed the miracle the Jewish rulers were speedily in possession of the facts. A meeting of the Sanhedrin was at once called to decide as to what should be done. Christ had now fully made manifest His control of death and the grave. That mighty miracle was the crowning evidence offered by God to men that He had sent His Son into the world for their salvation. It was a demonstration of divine power sufficient to convince every mind that was under the control of reason and enlightened conscience. Many who witnessed the resurrection of Lazarus were led to believe on Jesus. But the hatred of the priests against Him was intensified. They had rejected all lesser evidence of His divinity, and they were only enraged at this new miracle. The dead had been raised in the full light of day, and before a crowd of witnesses. No artifice could explain away such evidence. For this very reason the enmity of the priests grew deadlier. They were more than ever determined to put a stop to Christ's work.

The Sadducees, though not favorable to Christ, had not been so full of malignity toward Him as were the Pharisees. Their hatred had not been so bitter. But they were now thoroughly alarmed. They did not believe in a resurrection of the dead. Producing so-called science, they had reasoned that it would be an impossibility for a dead body to be brought to life. But by a few words from Christ their theory had been overthrown. They were shown to be ignorant both of the Scriptures and of the power of God. They could see no possibility of removing the impression made on the people by the miracle. How could men be turned away from Him who had prevailed to rob the grave of its dead? Lying reports were put in circulation, but the miracle could not be denied, and how to counteract its effect they knew not. Thus far the Sadducees had not encouraged the plan of putting Christ to death. But after the resurrection of Lazarus they decided that only by His death could His fearless denunciations against them be stopped.

The Pharisees believed in the resurrection, and they could not but see that this miracle was an evidence that the Messiah was among them. But they had ever opposed Christ's work. From the first they had hated Him because He had exposed their hypocritical pretensions. He had torn aside the cloak of rigorous rites under which their moral deformity was hidden. The pure religion that He taught had condemned their hollow professions of piety. They thirsted to be revenged upon Him for His pointed rebukes. They had tried to provoke Him to say or do something that would give them occasion to condemn Him. Several times they had attempted to stone Him, but He had quietly withdrawn, and they had lost sight of Him.

The miracles He performed on the Sabbath were all for the relief of the afflicted, but the Pharisees had sought to condemn Him as a Sabbathbreaker. They had tried to arouse the Herodians against Him. They represented that He was seeking to set up a rival kingdom, and consulted with them how to destroy Him. To excite the Romans against Him, they had represented Him as trying to subvert their authority. They had tried every pretext to cut Him off from influencing the people. But so far their attempts had been foiled. The multitudes who witnessed His works of mercy and heard His pure and holy teachings knew that these were not the deeds and words of a Sabbathbreaker or blasphemer. Even the officers sent by the Pharisees had been so influenced by His words that they could not lay hands on Him. In desperation the Jews had finally passed an edict that any man who professed faith in Jesus should be cast out of the synagogue.

So, as the priests, the rulers, and the elders gathered for consultation, it was their fixed determination to silence Him who did such marvelous works that all men wondered. Pharisees and Sadducees were more nearly united than ever before. Divided hitherto, they became one in their opposition to Christ. Nicodemus and Joseph had, in former councils, prevented the condemnation of Jesus, and for this reason they were not now summoned. There were present at the council other influential men who believed on Jesus, but their influence prevailed nothing against that of the malignant Pharisees.

Yet the members of the council were not all agreed. The Sanhedrin was not at this time a legal assembly. It existed only by tolerance. Some of its number questioned the wisdom of putting Christ to death. They feared that this would excite an insurrection among the people, causing the Romans to withhold further favors from the priesthood, and to take from them the power they still held. The Sadducees were united in their hatred of Christ, yet they were inclined to be cautious in their movements, fearing that the Romans would deprive them of their high standing.

In this council, assembled to plan the death of Christ, the Witness was present who heard the boastful words of Nebuchadnezzar, who witnessed the idolatrous feast of Belshazzar, who was present when Christ in Nazareth announced Himself the Anointed One. This Witness was now impressing the rulers with the work they were doing. Events in the life of Christ rose up before them with a distinctness that alarmed them. They remembered the scene in the temple, when Jesus, then a child of twelve, stood before the learned doctors of the law, asking them questions at which they wondered. The miracle just performed bore witness that Jesus was none other than the Son of God. In their true significance, the Old Testament Scriptures regarding Christ flashed before their minds. Perplexed and troubled, the rulers asked, "What do we?" There was a division in the council. Under the impression of the Holy Spirit, the priests and rulers could not banish the conviction that they were fighting against God.

While the council was at the height of its perplexity, Caiaphas the high priest arose. Caiaphas was a proud and cruel man, overbearing and intolerant. Among his family connections were Sadducees, proud, bold, reckless, full of ambition and cruelty, which they hid under a cloak of pretended righteousness. Caiaphas had studied the prophecies, and although ignorant of their true meaning, he spoke with great authority and assurance: "Ye know nothing at all, nor consider that it is expedient for us, that one man should die for the people, and that the whole nation perish not." Even if Jesus were innocent, urged the high priest, He must be put out of the way. He was troublesome, drawing the people to Himself, and lessening the authority of the rulers. He was only one; it was better that He should die than that the authority of the rulers should be weakened. If the people were to lose confidence in their rulers, the national power would be destroyed. Caiaphas urged that after this miracle the followers of Jesus would likely rise in revolt. The Romans will then come, he said, and will close our temple, and abolish our laws, destroying us as a nation. What is the life of this Galilean worth in comparison with the life of the nation? If He stands in the way of Israel's well-being, is it not doing God a service to remove Him? Better that one man perish than that the whole nation be destroyed.

In declaring that one man should die for the nation, Caiaphas indicated that he had some knowledge of the prophecies, although it was very limited. But John, in his account of this scene, takes up the prophecy, and shows its broad and deep significance. He says, "And not for that nation only, but that also He should gather together in one the children of God that were scattered abroad." How blindly did the haughty Caiaphas acknowledge the Saviour's mission!

On the lips of Caiaphas this most precious truth was turned into a lie. The policy he advocated was based on a principle borrowed from heathenism. Among the heathen, the dim consciousness that one was to die for the human race had led to the offering of human sacrifices. So Caiaphas proposed by the sacrifice of Jesus to save the guilty nation, not from transgression, but in transgression, that they might continue in sin. And by his reasoning he thought to silence the remonstrances of those who might dare to say that as yet nothing worthy of death had been found in Jesus.

At this council Christ's enemies had been deeply convicted. The Holy Spirit had impressed their minds. But Satan strove to gain control of them. He urged upon their notice the grievances they had suffered on account of Christ. How little He had honored their righteousness. He presented a righteousness far greater, which all who would be children of God must possess. Taking no notice of their forms and ceremonies, He had encouraged sinners to go directly to God as a merciful Father, and make known their wants. Thus, in their opinion, He had set aside the priesthood. He had refused to acknowledge the theology of the rabbinical schools. He had exposed the evil practices of the priests, and had irreparably hurt their influence. He had injured the effect of their maxims and traditions, declaring that though they strictly enforced the ritual law, they made void the law of God. All this Satan now brought to their minds.

Satan told them that in order to maintain their authority, they must put Jesus to death. This counsel they followed. The fact that they might lose the power they then exercised, was, they thought, sufficient reason for coming to some decision. With the exception of a few who dared not speak their minds, the Sanhedrin received the words of Caiaphas as the words of God. Relief came to the council; the discord ceased. They resolved to put Christ to death at the first favorable opportunity. In rejecting the proof of the divinity of Jesus, these priests and rulers had locked themselves in impenetrable darkness. They had come wholly under the sway of Satan, to be hurried by him over the brink of eternal ruin. Yet such was their deception that they were well pleased with themselves. They regarded themselves as patriots, who were seeking the nation's salvation.

The Sanhedrin feared, however, to take rash measures against Jesus, lest the people should become incensed, and the violence meditated toward Him should fall upon themselves. On this account the council delayed to execute the sentence they had pronounced. The Saviour understood the plotting of the priests. He knew that they longed to remove Him, and that their purpose would soon be accomplished. But it was not His place to hasten the crisis, and He withdrew from that region, taking the disciples with Him. Thus by His own example Jesus again enforced the instruction He had given to the disciples, "When they persecute you in this city, flee ye into another." Matt. 10:23. There was a wide field in which to work for the salvation of souls; and unless loyalty to Him required it, the Lord's servants were not to imperil their lives.

Jesus had now given three years of public labor to the world. His example of self-denial and disinterested benevolence was before them. His life of purity, of suffering and devotion, was known to all. Yet this short period of three years was as long as the world could endure the presence of its Redeemer.

His life had been one of persecution and insult. Driven from Bethlehem by a jealous king, rejected by His own people at Nazareth, condemned to death without a cause at Jerusalem, Jesus, with His few faithful followers, found a temporary asylum in a strange city. He who was ever touched by human woe, who healed the sick, restored sight to the blind, hearing to the deaf, and speech to the dumb, who fed the hungry and comforted the sorrowful, was driven from the people He had labored to save. He who walked upon the heaving billows, and by a word silenced their angry roaring, who cast out devils that in departing acknowledged Him to be the Son of God, who broke the slumbers of the dead, who held thousands entranced by His words of wisdom, was unable to reach the hearts of those who were blinded by prejudice and hatred, and who stubbornly rejected the light.

The Law of the New Kingdom

The time of the Passover was drawing near, and again Jesus turned toward Jerusalem. In His heart was the peace of perfect oneness with the Father's will, and with eager steps He pressed on toward the place of sacrifice. But a sense of mystery, of doubt and fear, fell upon the disciples. The Saviour "went before them: and they were amazed; and as they followed, they were afraid."

Again Christ called the twelve about Him, and with greater definiteness than ever before, He opened to them His betrayal and sufferings. "Behold," He said, "we go up to Jerusalem, and all things that are written by the prophets concerning the Son of man shall be accomplished. For He shall be delivered unto the Gentiles, and shall be mocked, and spitefully entreated, and spitted on: and they shall scourge Him, and put Him to death: and the third day He shall rise again. And they understood none of these things: and this saying was hid from them, neither knew they the things which were spoken."

Had they not just before proclaimed everywhere, "The kingdom of heaven is at hand"? Had not Christ Himself promised that many should sit down with Abraham and Isaac and Jacob in the kingdom of God? Had He not promised to all who had left aught for His sake a hundredfold in this life, and a part in His kingdom? And had He not given to the twelve the special promise of positions of high honor in His kingdom,—to sit on thrones judging the twelve tribes of Israel? Even now He had said that all things written in the prophets concerning Him should be fulfilled. And had not the prophets foretold the glory of the Messiah's reign? In the light of these thoughts, His words in regard to betrayal, persecution, and death seemed vague and shadowy. Whatever difficulties might intervene, they believed that the kingdom was soon to be established.

John, the son of Zebedee, had been one of the first two disciples who had followed Jesus. He and his brother James had been among the first group who had left all for His service. Gladly they had forsaken home and friends that they might be with Him; they had walked and talked with Him; they had been with Him in the privacy of the home, and in the public assemblies. He had quieted their fears, delivered them from danger, relieved their sufferings, comforted their grief, and with patience and tenderness had taught them, till their hearts seemed linked with His, and in the ardor of their love they longed to be nearest to Him in His kingdom. At every possible opportunity, John took his place next the Saviour, and James longed to be honored with as close connection with Him.

Their mother was a follower of Christ, and had ministered to Him freely of her substance. With a mother's love and ambition for her sons, she coveted for them the most honored place in the new kingdom. For this she encouraged them to make request.

Together the mother and her sons came to Jesus, asking that He would grant a petition on which their hearts were set.

"What would ye that I should do for you?" He questioned.

The mother answered, "Grant that these my two sons may sit, the one on Thy right hand, and the other on the left, in Thy kingdom."

Jesus bears tenderly with them, not rebuking their selfishness in seeking preference above their brethren. He reads their hearts, He knows the depth of their attachment to Him. Their love is not a mere human affection; though defiled by the earthliness of its human channel, it is an outflowing from the fountain of His own redeeming love. He will not rebuke, but deepen and purify. He said, "Are ye able to drink of the cup that I shall drink of, and to be baptized with the baptism that I am baptized with?" They recall His mysterious words, pointing to trial and suffering, yet answer confidently, "We are able." They would count it highest honor to prove their loyalty by sharing all that is to befall their Lord.

"Ye shall drink indeed of My cup, and be baptized with the baptism that I am baptized with," He said; before Him a cross instead of a throne, two malefactors His companions at His right hand and His left. John and James were to share with their Master in suffering; the one, first of the brethren to perish with the sword; the other, longest of all to endure toil, and reproach, and persecution.

"But to sit on My right hand, and on My left," He continued, "is not Mine to give, but it shall be given to them for whom it is prepared of My Father." In the kingdom of God, position is not gained through favoritism. It is not earned, nor is it received through an arbitrary bestowal. It is the result of character. The crown and the throne are the tokens of a condition attained; they are the tokens of self-conquest through our Lord Jesus Christ.

Long afterward, when the disciple had been brought into sympathy with Christ through the fellowship of His sufferings, the Lord revealed to John what is the condition of nearness in His kingdom. "To him that overcometh," Christ said, "will I grant to sit with Me in My throne, even as I also overcame, and am set down with My Father in His throne." "Him that overcometh will I make a pillar in the temple of My God, and he shall go no more out: and I will write upon him the name of My God, . . . and I will write upon him My new name." Rev. 3:21, 12. So Paul the apostle wrote, "I am now ready to be offered, and the time of my departure is at hand. I have fought a good fight, I have finished my course, I have kept the faith: henceforth there is laid up for me a crown of righteousness, which the Lord, the righteous Judge, shall give me at that day." 2 Tim. 4:6-8.

The one who stands nearest to Christ will be he who on earth has drunk most deeply of the spirit of His self-sacrificing love,—love that "vaunteth not itself, is not puffed up, . . . seeketh not her own, is not easily provoked, thinketh no evil" (1 Cor. 13:4, 5),—love that moves the disciple, as it moved our Lord, to give all, to live and labor and sacrifice, even unto death, for the saving of humanity. This spirit was made manifest in the life of Paul. He said, "For to me to live is

Christ;" for his life revealed Christ to men; "and to die is gain,"—gain to Christ; death itself would make manifest the power of His grace, and gather souls to Him. "Christ shall be magnified in my body," he said, "whether it be by life or by death." Phil. 1:21, 20.

When the ten heard of the request of James and John, they were much displeased. The highest place in the kingdom was just what every one of them was seeking for himself, and they were angry that the two disciples had gained a seeming advantage over them.

Again the strife as to which should be greatest seemed about to be renewed, when Jesus, calling them to Him, said to the indignant disciples, "Ye know that they which are accounted to rule over the Gentiles exercise lordship over them; and their great ones exercise authority upon them. But so shall it not be among you."

In the kingdoms of the world, position meant self-aggrandizement. The people were supposed to exist for the benefit of the ruling classes. Influence, wealth, education, were so many means of gaining control of the masses for the use of the leaders. The higher classes were to think, decide, enjoy, and rule; the lower were to obey and serve. Religion, like all things else, was a matter of authority. The people were expected to believe and practice as their superiors directed. The right of man as man, to think and act for himself, was wholly unrecognized.

Christ was establishing a kingdom on different principles. He called men, not to authority, but to service, the strong to bear the infirmities of the weak. Power, position, talent, education, placed their possessor under the greater obligation to serve his fellows. To even the lowliest of Christ's disciples it is said, "All things are for your sakes." 2 Cor. 4:15.

"The Son of man came not to be ministered unto, but to minister, and to give His life a ransom for many." Among His disciples Christ was in every sense a caretaker, a burden bearer. He shared their poverty, He practiced self-denial on their account, He went before them to smooth the more difficult places, and soon He would consummate His work on earth by laying down His life. The principle on which Christ acted is to actuate the members of the church which is His body. The plan and ground of salvation is love. In the kingdom of Christ those are greatest who follow the example He has given, and act as shepherds of His flock.

The words of Paul reveal the true dignity and honor of the Christian life: "Though I be free from all men, yet have I made myself servant unto all," "not seeking mine own profit, but the profit of many, that they may be saved." 1 Cor. 9:19; 10:33.

In matters of conscience the soul must be left untrammeled. No one is to control another's mind, to judge for another, or to prescribe his duty. God gives to every soul freedom to think, and to follow his own convictions. "Every one of us shall give account of himself to God." No one has a right to merge his own individuality in that of another. In all matters where principle is involved, "let every man be fully persuaded in his own mind." Rom. 14:12, 5. In Christ's kingdom there is no lordly oppression, no compulsion of manner. The angels of heaven do not come to the earth to rule, and to exact homage, but as messengers of mercy, to co-operate with men in uplifting humanity.

The principles and the very words of the Saviour's teaching, in their divine beauty, dwelt in the memory of the beloved disciple. To his latest days the burden of John's testimony to the churches was, "This is the message that ye heard from the beginning, that we should love one another." "Hereby perceive we the love of God, because He laid down His life for us: and we ought to lay down our lives for the brethren." 1 John 3:11, 16.

This was the spirit that pervaded the early church. After the outpouring of the Holy Spirit, "the multitude of them that believed were of one heart and of one soul: neither said any of them that aught of the things which he possessed was his own." "Neither was there any among them that lacked." "And with great power gave the apostles witness of the resurrection of the Lord Jesus: and great grace was upon them all." Acts 4:32, 34, 33.

Zacchaeus

On the way to Jerusalem "Jesus entered and passed through Jericho." A few miles from the Jordan, on the western edge of the valley that here spread out into a plain, the city lay in the midst of tropic verdure and luxuriance of beauty. With its palm trees and rich gardens watered by living springs, it gleamed like an emerald in the setting of limestone hills and desolate ravines that interposed between Jerusalem and the city of the plain.

Many caravans on their way to the feast passed through Jericho. Their arrival was always a festive season, but now a deeper interest stirred the people. It was known that the Galilean Rabbi who had so lately brought Lazarus to life was in the throng; and though whispers were rife as to the plottings of the priests, the multitudes were eager to do Him homage.

Jericho was one of the cities anciently set apart for the priests, and at this time large numbers of priests had their residence there. But the city had also a population of a widely different character. It was a great center of traffic, and Roman officials and soldiers, with strangers from different quarters, were found there, while the collection of customs made it the home of many publicans.

"The chief among the publicans," Zacchaeus, was a Jew, and detested by his countrymen. His rank and wealth were the reward of a calling they abhorred, and which was regarded as another name for injustice and extortion. Yet the wealthy customs officer was not altogether the hardened man of the world that he seemed. Beneath the appearance of worldliness and pride was a heart susceptible to divine influences. Zacchaeus had heard of Jesus. The report of One who had borne Himself with kindness and courtesy toward the proscribed classes had spread far and wide. In this chief of the publicans was awakened a longing for a better life. Only a few miles from Jericho, John the Baptist had preached at the Jordan, and Zacchaeus had heard of the call to repentance. The instruction to the publicans, "Exact no more than that which is appointed you" (Luke 3:13), though outwardly disregarded, had impressed his mind. He knew the Scriptures, and was convicted that his practice was wrong. Now, hearing the words reported to have come from the Great Teacher, he felt that he was a sinner in the sight of God. Yet what he had heard of Jesus kindled hope in his heart. Repentance, reformation of life, was possible, even to him; was not one of the new Teacher's most trusted disciples a publican? Zacchaeus began at once to follow the conviction that had taken hold upon him, and to make restitution to those whom he had wronged.

Already he had begun thus to retrace his steps, when the news sounded through Jericho that Jesus was entering the town. Zacchaeus determined to see Him. He was beginning to realize how bitter are the fruits of sin, and how difficult the path of him who tries to return from a course of wrong. To be misunderstood, to be met with suspicion and distrust in the effort to correct his errors, was hard to bear. The chief publican longed to look upon the face of Him whose words had brought hope to his heart.

The streets were crowded, and Zacchaeus, who was small of stature, could see nothing over the heads of the people. None would give way for him; so, running a little in advance of the multitude, to where a wide-branching fig tree hung over the way, the rich tax collector climbed to a seat among the boughs, whence he could survey the procession as it passed below. The crowd comes near, it is going by, and Zacchaeus scans with eager eyes to discern the one figure he longs to see.

Above the clamor of priests and rabbis and the shouts of welcome from the multitude, that unuttered desire of the chief publican spoke to the heart of Jesus. Suddenly, just beneath the fig tree, a group halts, the company before and behind come to a standstill, and One looks upward whose glance seems to read the soul. Almost doubting his senses, the man in the tree hears the words, "Zacchaeus, make haste, and come down; for today I must abide at thy house."

The multitude give way, and Zacchaeus, walking as in a dream, leads the way toward his own home. But the rabbis look on with scowling faces, and murmur in discontent and scorn, "that He was gone to be guest with a man that is a sinner."

Zacchaeus had been overwhelmed, amazed, and silenced at the love and condescension of Christ in stooping to him, so unworthy. Now love and loyalty to his new-found Master unseal his lips. He will make public his confession and his repentance.

In the presence of the multitude, "Zacchaeus stood, and said unto the Lord; Behold, Lord, the half of my goods I give to the poor; and if I have taken anything from any man by false accusation, I restore him fourfold.

"And Jesus said unto him, This day is salvation come to this house, forsomuch as he also is a son of Abraham."

When the rich young ruler had turned away from Jesus, the disciples had marveled at their Master's saying, "How hard is it for them that trust in riches to enter into the kingdom of God!" They had exclaimed one to another, "Who then can be saved?" Now they had a demonstration of the truth of Christ's words, "The things which are impossible with men are possible with God." Mark 10:24, 26; Luke 18:27. They saw how, through the grace of God, a rich man could enter into the kingdom.

Before Zacchaeus had looked upon the face of Christ, he had begun the work that made him manifest as a true penitent. Before being accused by man, he had confessed his sin. He had yielded to the conviction of the Holy Spirit, and had begun to carry out the teaching of the words written for ancient Israel as well as for ourselves. The Lord had said long before, "If thy brother be waxen poor, and fallen in decay with thee; then thou shalt relieve him: yea, though he be a stranger, or a sojourner; that he may live with thee. Take thou no usury of him, or increase: but fear thy God; that thy brother may live with thee. Thou shalt not give him thy money upon usury, nor lend him thy victuals for increase." "Ye shall not therefore oppress one another; but thou shalt fear thy God." Lev. 25:35-37, 17. These words had been spoken by Christ Himself when He was enshrouded in the pillar of cloud, and the very first response of Zacchaeus to the love of Christ was in manifesting compassion toward the poor and suffering.

Among the publicans there was a confederacy, so that they could oppress the people, and sustain one another in their fraudulent practices. In their extortion they were but carrying out what had become an almost universal custom. Even the priests and rabbis who despised them were guilty of enriching themselves by dishonest practices under cover of their sacred calling. But no sooner did Zacchaeus yield to the influence of the Holy Spirit than he cast aside every practice contrary to integrity.

No repentance is genuine that does not work reformation. The righteousness of Christ is not a cloak to cover unconfessed and unforsaken sin; it is a principle of life that transforms the character and controls the conduct. Holiness is wholeness for God; it is the entire surrender of heart and life to the indwelling of the principles of heaven.

The Christian in his business life is to represent to the world the manner in which our Lord would conduct business enterprises. In every transaction he is to make it manifest that God is his teacher. "Holiness unto the Lord" is to be written upon daybooks and ledgers, on deeds, receipts, and bills of exchange. Those who profess to be followers of Christ, and who deal in an unrighteous manner, are bearing false witness against the character of a holy, just, and merciful God. Every converted soul will, like Zacchaeus, signalize the entrance of Christ into his heart by an abandonment of the unrighteous practices that have marked his life. Like the chief publican, he will give proof of his sincerity by making restitution. The Lord says, "If the wicked restore the pledge, give again that he had robbed, walk in the statutes of life, without committing iniquity; . . . none of his sins that he hath committed shall be mentioned unto him: . . . He shall surely live." Ezek. 33:15, 16.

If we have injured others through any unjust business transaction, if we have overreached in trade, or defrauded any man, even though it be within the pale of the law, we should confess our wrong, and make restitution as far as lies in our power. It is right for us to restore not only that which we have taken, but all that it would have accumulated if put to a right and wise use during the time it has been in our possession.

To Zacchaeus the Saviour said, "This day is salvation come to this house." Not only was Zacchaeus himself blessed, but all his household with him. Christ went to his home to give him lessons of truth, and to instruct his household in the things of the kingdom. They had been shut out from the synagogues by the contempt of rabbis and worshipers; but now, the most favored household in all Jericho, they gathered in their own home about the divine Teacher, and heard for themselves the words of life.

It is when Christ is received as a personal Saviour that salvation comes to the soul. Zacchaeus had received Jesus, not merely as a passing guest in his home, but as One to abide in the soul temple. The scribes and Pharisees accused him as a sinner, they murmured against Christ for becoming his guest, but the Lord recognized him as a son of Abraham. For "they which are of faith, the same are the children of Abraham." Gal. 3:7.

The Feast at Simon's House

Simon of Bethany was accounted a disciple of Jesus. He was one of the few Pharisees who had openly joined Christ's followers. He acknowledged Jesus as a teacher, and hoped that He might be the Messiah, but he had not accepted Him as a Saviour. His character was not transformed; his principles were unchanged.

Simon had been healed of the leprosy, and it was this that had drawn him to Jesus. He desired to show his gratitude, and at Christ's last visit to Bethany he made a feast for the Saviour and His disciples. This feast brought together many of the Jews. There was at this time much excitement at Jerusalem. Christ and His mission were attracting greater attention than ever before. Those who had come to the feast closely watched His movements, and some of them with unfriendly eyes.

The Saviour had reached Bethany only six days before the Passover, and according to His custom had sought rest at the home of Lazarus. The crowds of travelers who passed on to the city spread the tidings that He was on His way to Jerusalem, and that He would rest over the Sabbath at Bethany. Among the people there was great enthusiasm. Many flocked to Bethany, some out of sympathy with Jesus, and others from curiosity to see one who had been raised from the dead.

Many expected to hear from Lazarus a wonderful account of scenes witnessed after death. They were surprised that he told them nothing. He had nothing of this kind to tell. Inspiration declares, "The dead know not anything. . . . Their love, and their hatred, and their envy, is now perished." Eccl. 9:5, 6. But Lazarus did have a wonderful testimony to bear in regard to the work of Christ. He had been raised from the dead for this purpose. With assurance and power he declared that Jesus was the Son of God.

The reports carried back to Jerusalem by the visitors to Bethany increased the excitement. The people were eager to see and hear Jesus. There was a general inquiry as to whether Lazarus would accompany Him to Jerusalem, and if the prophet would be crowned king at the Passover. The priests and rulers saw that their hold upon the people was still weakening, and their rage against Jesus grew more bitter. They could hardly wait for the opportunity of removing Him forever from their way. As time passed, they began to fear that after all He might not come to Jerusalem. They remembered how often He had baffled their murderous designs, and they were fearful that He had now read their purposes against Him, and would remain away. They could ill conceal their anxiety, and questioned among themselves, "What think ye, that He will not come to the feast?"

A council of the priests and Pharisees was called. Since the raising of Lazarus the sympathies of the people were so fully with Christ that it would be dangerous to seize upon Him openly. So the authorities determined to take Him secretly, and carry on the trial as quietly as possible. They hoped that when His condemnation became known, the fickle tide of public opinion would set in their favor.

Thus they proposed to destroy Jesus. But so long as Lazarus lived, the priests and rabbis knew that they were not secure. The very existence of a man who had been four days in the grave, and who had been restored by a word from Jesus, would sooner or later cause a reaction. The people would be avenged on their leaders for taking the life of One who could perform such a miracle. The Sanhedrin therefore decided that Lazarus also must die. To such lengths do envy and prejudice lead their slaves. The hatred and unbelief of the Jewish leaders had increased until they would even take the life of one whom infinite power had rescued from the grave.

While this plotting was going on at Jerusalem, Jesus and His friends were invited to Simon's feast. At the table the Saviour sat with Simon, whom He had cured of a loathsome disease, on one side, and Lazarus, whom He had raised from the dead, on the other. Martha served at the table, but Mary was earnestly listening to every word from the lips of Jesus. In His mercy, Jesus had pardoned her sins, He had called forth her beloved brother from the grave, and Mary's heart was filled with gratitude. She had heard Jesus speak of His approaching death, and in her deep love and sorrow she had longed to show Him honor. At great personal sacrifice she had purchased an alabaster box of "ointment of spikenard, very costly," with which to anoint His body. But now many were declaring that He was about to be crowned king. Her grief was turned to joy, and she was eager to be first in honoring her Lord. Breaking her box of ointment, she poured its contents upon the head and feet of Jesus; then, as she knelt weeping, moistening them with her tears, she wiped His feet with her long, flowing hair.

She had sought to avoid observation, and her movements might have passed unnoticed, but the ointment filled the room with its fragrance, and published her act to all present. Judas looked upon this act with great displeasure. Instead of waiting to hear what Christ would say of the matter, he began to whisper his complaints to those near him, throwing reproach upon Christ for suffering such waste. Craftily he made suggestions that would be likely to cause disaffection.

Judas was treasurer for the disciples, and from their little store he had secretly drawn for his own use, thus narrowing down their resources to a meager pittance. He was eager to put into the bag all that he could obtain. The treasure in the bag was often drawn upon to relieve the poor; and when something that Judas did not think essential was bought, he would say, Why is this waste? why was not the cost of this put into the bag that I carry for the poor? Now the act of Mary was in such marked contrast to his selfishness that he was put to shame; and according to his custom, he sought to assign a worthy motive for his objection to her gift. Turning to the disciples, he asked, "Why was not this ointment sold for three hundred pence, and given to the poor? This he said, not that he cared for the poor; but because he was a thief, and had the bag, and bare what was put therein." Judas had no heart for the poor. Had Mary's ointment been sold, and the proceeds fallen into his possession, the poor would have received no benefit.

Judas had a high opinion of his own executive ability. As a financier he thought himself greatly superior to his fellow disciples, and he had led them to regard him in the same light. He had gained their confidence, and had a strong influence over them. His professed sympathy for the poor deceived them, and his artful insinuation caused them to look distrustfully upon Mary's devotion. The murmur passed round the table, "To what purpose is this waste? For this ointment might have been sold for much, and given to the poor."

Mary heard the words of criticism. Her heart trembled within her. She feared that her sister would reproach her for extravagance. The Master, too, might think her improvident. Without apology or excuse she was about to shrink away, when the voice of her Lord was heard, "Let her alone; why trouble ye her?" He saw that she was embarrassed and distressed. He knew that in this act of service she had expressed her gratitude for the forgiveness of her sins, and He brought relief to her mind. Lifting His voice above the murmur of criticism, He said, "She hath wrought a good work on Me. For ye have the poor with you always, and whensoever ye will ye may do them good: but Me ye have not always. She hath done what she could: she is come aforehand to anoint My body to the burying."

The fragrant gift which Mary had thought to lavish upon the dead body of the Saviour she poured upon His living form. At the burial its sweetness could only have pervaded the tomb; now it gladdened His heart with the assurance of her faith and love. Joseph of Arimathaea and Nicodemus offered not their gift of love to Jesus in His life. With bitter tears they brought their costly spices for His cold, unconscious form. The women who bore spices to the tomb found their errand in vain, for He had risen. But Mary, pouring out her love upon the Saviour while He was conscious of her devotion, was anointing Him for the burial. And as He went down into the darkness of His great trial, He carried with Him the memory of that deed, an earnest of the love that would be His from His redeemed ones forever.

Many there are who bring their precious gifts for the dead. As they stand about the cold, silent form, words of love are freely spoken. Tenderness, appreciation, devotion, all are lavished upon one who sees not nor hears. Had these words been spoken when the weary spirit needed them so much, when the ear could hear and the heart could feel, how precious would have been their fragrance!

Mary knew not the full significance of her deed of love. She could not answer her accusers. She could not explain why she had chosen that occasion for anointing Jesus. The Holy Spirit had planned for her, and she had obeyed His promptings. Inspiration stoops to give no reason. An unseen presence, it speaks to mind and soul, and moves the heart to action. It is its own justification.

Christ told Mary the meaning of her act, and in this He gave her more than He had received. "In that she hath poured this ointment on My body," He said, "she did it for My burial." As the alabaster box was broken, and filled the whole house with its fragrance, so Christ was to die, His body was to be broken; but He was to rise from the tomb, and the fragrance of His life was to fill the earth. Christ "hath loved us, and hath given Himself for us an offering and a sacrifice to God for a sweet-smelling savor." Eph. 5:2.

"Verily I say unto you," Christ declared, "Wheresoever this gospel shall be preached throughout the whole world, this also that she hath done shall be spoken of for a memorial of her." Looking into the future, the Saviour spoke with certainty concerning His gospel. It was to be preached throughout the world. And as far as the gospel extended, Mary's gift would shed its fragrance, and hearts would be blessed through her unstudied act. Kingdoms would rise and fall; the names of monarchs and conquerors would be forgotten; but this woman's deed would be immortalized upon the pages of sacred history. Until time should be no more, that broken alabaster box would tell the story of the abundant love of God for a fallen race.

Mary's act was in marked contrast with that which Judas was about to do. What a sharp lesson Christ might have given him who had dropped the seed of criticism and evil thinking into the minds of the disciples! How justly the accuser might have been accused! He who reads the motives of every heart, and understands every action, might have opened before those at the feast dark chapters in the experience of Judas. The hollow pretense on which the traitor based his words might have been laid bare; for, instead of sympathizing with the poor, he was robbing them of the money intended for their relief. Indignation might have been excited against him for his oppression of the widow, the orphan, and the hireling. But had Christ unmasked Judas, this would have been urged as a reason for the betrayal. And though charged with being a thief, Judas would have gained sympathy, even among the disciples. The Saviour reproached him not, and thus avoided giving him an excuse for his treachery.

But the look which Jesus cast upon Judas convinced him that the Saviour penetrated his hypocrisy, and read his base, contemptible character. And in commending Mary's action, which had been so severely condemned, Christ had rebuked Judas. Prior to this, the Saviour had never given him a direct rebuke. Now the reproof rankled in his heart. He determined to be revenged. From the supper he went directly to the palace of the high priest, where he found the council assembled, and he offered to betray Jesus into their hands.

The priests were greatly rejoiced. These leaders of Israel had been given the privilege of receiving Christ as their Saviour, without money and without price. But they refused the precious gift offered them in the most tender spirit of constraining love. They refused to accept that salvation which is of more value than gold, and bought their Lord for thirty pieces of silver.

Judas had indulged avarice until it overpowered every good trait of his character. He grudged the offering made to Jesus. His heart burned with envy that the Saviour should be the recipient of a gift suitable for the monarchs of the earth. For a sum far less than the box of ointment cost, he betrayed his Lord.

The disciples were not like Judas. They loved the Saviour. But they did not rightly appreciate His exalted character. Had they realized what He had done for them, they would have felt that nothing bestowed upon Him was wasted. The wise men from the East, who knew so little of Jesus, had shown a truer appreciation of the honor due Him. They brought precious gifts to the Saviour, and bowed in homage before Him when He was but a babe, and cradled in a manger.

Christ values acts of heartfelt courtesy. When anyone did Him a favor, with heavenly politeness He blessed the actor. He did not refuse the simplest flower plucked by the hand of a child, and offered to Him in love. He accepted the offerings of children, and blessed the givers, inscribing their names in the book of life. In the Scriptures, Mary's anointing of Jesus is mentioned as distinguishing her from the other Marys. Acts of love and reverence for Jesus are an evidence of faith in Him as the Son of God. And the Holy Spirit mentions, as evidences of woman's loyalty to Christ: "If she have washed the saints' feet, if she have relieved the afflicted, if she have diligently followed every good work." 1 Tim. 5:10.

Christ delighted in the earnest desire of Mary to do the will of her Lord. He accepted the wealth of pure affection which His disciples did not, would not, understand. The desire that Mary had to do this service for her Lord was of more value to Christ than all the precious ointment in the world, because it expressed her appreciation of the world's Redeemer. It was the love of Christ that constrained her. The matchless excellence of the character of Christ filled her soul. That ointment was a symbol of the heart of the giver. It was the outward demonstration of a love fed by heavenly streams until it overflowed.

The work of Mary was just the lesson the disciples needed to show them that the expression of their love for Him would be pleasing to Christ. He had been everything to them, and they did not realize that soon they would be deprived of His presence, that soon they could offer Him no token of their gratitude for His great love. The loneliness of Christ, separated from the heavenly courts, living the life of humanity, was never understood or appreciated by the disciples as it should have been. He was often grieved because His disciples did not give Him that which He should have received from them. He knew that if they were under the influence of the heavenly angels that accompanied Him, they too would think no offering of sufficient value to declare the heart's spiritual affection.

Their afterknowledge gave them a true sense of the many things they might have done for Jesus expressive of the love and gratitude of their hearts, while they were near Him. When Jesus was no longer with them, and they felt indeed as sheep without a shepherd, they began to see how they might have shown Him attentions that would have brought gladness to His heart. They no longer cast blame upon Mary, but upon themselves. Oh, if they could have taken back their censuring, their presenting the poor as more worthy of the gift than was Christ! They felt the reproof keenly as they took from the cross the bruised body of their Lord.

The same want is evident in our world today. But few appreciate all that Christ is to them. If they did, the great love of Mary would be expressed, the anointing would be freely bestowed. The expensive ointment would not be called a waste. Nothing would be thought too costly to give for Christ, no self-denial or self-sacrifice too great to be endured for His sake.

The words spoken in indignation, "To what purpose is this waste?" brought vividly before Christ the greatest sacrifice ever made,—the gift of Himself as the propitiation for a lost world. The Lord would be so bountiful to His human family that it could not be said of Him that He could do more. In the gift of Jesus, God gave all heaven. From a human point of view, such a sacrifice was a wanton waste. To human reasoning the whole plan of salvation is a waste of mercies and resources. Self-denial and wholehearted sacrifice meet us everywhere. Well may the heavenly host look with amazement upon the human family who refuse to be uplifted and enriched with the boundless love expressed in Christ. Well may they exclaim, Why this great waste?

But the atonement for a lost world was to be full, abundant, and complete. Christ's offering was exceedingly abundant to reach every soul that God had created. It could not be restricted so as not to exceed the number who would accept the great Gift. All men are not saved; yet the plan of redemption is not a waste because it does not accomplish all that its liberality has provided for. There must be enough and to spare.

Simon the host had been influenced by the criticism of Judas upon Mary's gift, and he was surprised at the conduct of Jesus. His Pharisaic pride was offended. He knew that many of his guests were looking upon Christ with distrust and displeasure. Simon said in his heart, "This Man, if He were a prophet, would have known who and what manner of woman this is that toucheth Him: for she is a sinner."

By curing Simon of leprosy, Christ had saved him from a living death. But now Simon questioned whether the Saviour were a prophet. Because Christ allowed this woman to approach Him, because He did not indignantly spurn her as one whose sins were too great to be forgiven, because He did not show that He realized she had fallen, Simon was tempted to think that He was not a prophet. Jesus knows nothing of this woman who is so free in her demonstrations, he thought, or He would not allow her to touch Him.

But it was Simon's ignorance of God and of Christ that led him to think as he did. He did not realize that God's Son must act in God's way, with compassion, tenderness, and mercy. Simon's way was to take no notice of Mary's penitent service. Her act of kissing Christ's feet and anointing them with ointment was exasperating to his hardheartedness. He thought that if Christ were a prophet, He would recognize sinners and rebuke them.

To this unspoken thought the Saviour answered: "Simon, I have somewhat to say unto thee. . . . There was a certain creditor which had two debtors: the one owed five hundred pence, and the other fifty. And when they had nothing to pay, he frankly forgave them both. Tell Me therefore, which of them will love him most? Simon answered and said, I suppose that he, to whom he forgave most. And He said unto him, Thou hast rightly judged."

As did Nathan with David, Christ concealed His home thrust under the veil of a parable. He threw upon His host the burden of pronouncing sentence upon himself. Simon had led into sin the woman he now despised. She had been deeply wronged by him. By the two debtors of the parable, Simon and the woman were represented. Jesus did not design to teach that different degrees of obligation should be felt by the two persons, for each owed a debt of gratitude that never could be repaid. But Simon felt himself more righteous than Mary, and Jesus desired him to see how great his guilt really was. He would show him that his sin was greater than hers, as much greater as a debt of five hundred pence exceeds a debt of fifty pence.

Simon now began to see himself in a new light. He saw how Mary was regarded by One who was more than a prophet. He saw that with keen prophetic eye Christ read her heart of love and devotion. Shame seized upon him, and he realized that he was in the presence of One superior to himself.

"I entered into thine house," Christ continued, "thou gavest Me no water for My feet;" but with tears of repentance, prompted by love, Mary hath washed My feet, and wiped them with the hair of her head. "Thou gavest Me no kiss: but this woman," whom you despise, "since the time I came in hath not ceased to kiss My feet." Christ recounted the opportunities Simon had had to show his love for his Lord, and his appreciation of what had been done for him. Plainly, yet with delicate politeness, the Saviour assured His disciples that His heart is grieved when His children neglect to show their gratitude to Him by words and deeds of love.

The Heart Searcher read the motive that led to Mary's action, and He saw also the spirit that prompted Simon's words. "Seest thou this woman?" He said to him. She is a sinner. "I say unto thee, Her sins, which are many, are forgiven; for she loved much: but to whom little is forgiven, the same loveth little."

Simon's coldness and neglect toward the Saviour showed how little he appreciated the mercy he had received. He had thought he honored Jesus by inviting Him to his house. But he now saw himself as he really was. While he thought himself reading his Guest, his Guest had been reading him. He saw how true Christ's judgment of him was. His religion had been a robe of Pharisaism. He had despised the compassion of Jesus. He had not recognized Him as the representative of God. While Mary was a sinner pardoned, he was a sinner unpardoned. The rigid rule of justice he had desired to enforce against her condemned him.

Simon was touched by the kindness of Jesus in not openly rebuking him before the guests. He had not been treated as he desired Mary to be treated. He saw that Jesus did not wish to expose his guilt to others, but sought by a true statement of the case to convince his mind, and by pitying kindness to subdue his heart. Stern denunciation would have hardened Simon against repentance, but patient admonition convinced him of his error. He saw the magnitude of the debt which he owed his Lord. His pride was humbled, he repented, and the proud Pharisee became a lowly, self-sacrificing disciple.

Mary had been looked upon as a great sinner, but Christ knew the circumstances that had shaped her life. He might have extinguished every spark of hope in her soul, but He did not. It was He who had lifted her from despair and ruin. Seven times she had heard His rebuke of the demons that controlled her heart and mind. She had heard His strong cries to the Father in her behalf. She knew how offensive is sin to His unsullied purity, and in His strength she had overcome.

When to human eyes her case appeared hopeless, Christ saw in Mary capabilities for good. He saw the better traits of her character. The plan of redemption has invested humanity with great possibilities, and in Mary these possibilities were to be realized. Through His grace she became a partaker of the divine nature. The one who had fallen, and whose mind had been a habitation of demons, was brought very near to the Saviour in fellowship and ministry. It was Mary who sat at His feet and learned of Him. It was Mary who poured upon His head the precious anointing oil, and bathed His feet with her tears. Mary stood beside the cross, and followed Him to the sepulcher. Mary was first at the tomb after His resurrection. It was Mary who first proclaimed a risen Saviour.

Jesus knows the circumstances of every soul. You may say, I am sinful, very sinful. You may be; but the worse you are, the more you need Jesus. He turns no weeping, contrite one away. He does not tell to any all that He might reveal, but He bids every trembling soul take courage. Freely will He pardon all who come to Him for forgiveness and restoration.

Christ might commission the angels of heaven to pour out the vials of His wrath on our world, to destroy those who are filled with hatred of God. He might wipe this dark spot from His universe. But He does not do this. He is today standing at the altar of incense, presenting before God the prayers of those who desire His help.

The souls that turn to Him for refuge, Jesus lifts above the accusing and the strife of tongues. No man or evil angel can impeach these souls. Christ unites them to His own divine-human nature. They stand beside the great Sin Bearer, in the light proceeding from the throne of God. "Who shall lay anything to the charge of God's elect? It is God that justifieth. Who is he that condemneth? It is Christ that died, yea rather, that is risen again, who is even at the right hand of God, who also maketh intercession for us." Rom. 8:33, 34.

"Thy King Cometh"

"Rejoice greatly, O daughter of Zion; shout, O daughter of Jerusalem: behold, thy King cometh unto thee: He is just, and having salvation; lowly, and riding upon an ass, and upon a colt the foal of an ass." Zech. 9:9.

Five hundred years before the birth of Christ, the prophet Zechariah thus foretold the coming of the King to Israel. This prophecy is now to be fulfilled. He who has so long refused royal honors now comes to Jerusalem as the promised heir to David's throne.

It was on the first day of the week that Christ made His triumphal entry into Jerusalem. Multitudes who had flocked to see Him at Bethany now accompanied Him, eager to witness His reception. Many people were on their way to the city to keep the Passover, and these joined the multitude attending Jesus. All nature seemed to rejoice. The trees were clothed with verdure, and their blossoms shed a delicate fragrance on the air. A new life and joy animated the people. The hope of the new kingdom was again springing up.

Purposing to ride into Jerusalem, Jesus had sent two of His disciples to bring to Him an ass and its colt. At His birth the Saviour was dependent upon the hospitality of strangers. The manger in which He lay was a borrowed resting place. Now, although the cattle on a thousand hills are His, He is dependent on a stranger's kindness for an animal on which to enter Jerusalem as its King. But again His divinity is revealed, even in the minute directions given His disciples for this errand. As He foretold, the plea, "The Lord hath need of them," was readily granted. Jesus chose for His use the colt on which never man had sat. The disciples, with glad enthusiasm, spread their garments on the beast, and seated their Master upon it. Heretofore Jesus had always traveled on foot, and the disciples had at first wondered that He should now choose to ride. But hope brightened in their hearts with the joyous thought that He was about to enter the capital, proclaim Himself King, and assert His royal power. While on their errand they communicated their glowing expectations to the friends of Jesus, and the excitement spread far and near, raising the expectations of the people to the highest pitch.

Christ was following the Jewish custom for a royal entry. The animal on which He rode was that ridden by the kings of Israel, and prophecy had foretold that thus the Messiah should come to His kingdom. No sooner was He seated upon the colt than a loud shout of triumph rent the air. The multitude hailed Him as Messiah, their King. Jesus now accepted the homage which He had never before permitted, and the disciples received this as proof that their glad hopes were to be realized by seeing Him established on the throne. The multitude were convinced that the hour of their emancipation was at hand. In imagination they saw the Roman armies driven from Jerusalem, and Israel once more an independent nation. All were happy and excited; the people vied with one another in paying Him homage. They could not display outward pomp and splendor, but they gave Him the worship of happy hearts. They were unable to present Him with costly gifts, but they spread their outer garments as a carpet in His path, and they also strewed the leafy branches of the olive and the palm in the way. They could lead the triumphal procession with no royal standards, but they cut down the spreading palm boughs, Nature's emblem of victory, and waved them aloft with loud acclamations and hosannas.

As they proceeded, the multitude was continually increased by those who had heard of the coming of Jesus and hastened to join the procession. Spectators were constantly mingling with the throng, and asking, Who is this? What does all this commotion signify? They had all heard of Jesus, and expected Him to go to Jerusalem; but they knew that He had heretofore discouraged all effort to place Him on the throne, and they were greatly astonished to learn that this was He. They wondered what could have wrought this change in Him who had declared that His kingdom was not of this world.

Their questionings are silenced by a shout of triumph. Again and again it is repeated by the eager throng; it is taken up by the people afar off, and echoed from the surrounding hills and valleys. And now the procession is joined by crowds from Jerusalem. From the multitudes gathered to attend the Passover, thousands go forth to welcome Jesus. They greet Him with the waving of palm branches and a burst of sacred song. The priests at the temple sound the trumpet for evening service, but there are few to respond, and the rulers say to one another in alarm. "The world is gone after Him."

Never before in His earthly life had Jesus permitted such a demonstration. He clearly foresaw the result. It would bring Him to the cross. But it was His purpose thus publicly to present Himself as the Redeemer. He desired to call attention to the sacrifice that was to crown His mission to a fallen world. While the people were assembling at Jerusalem to celebrate the Passover, He, the antitypical Lamb, by a voluntary act set Himself apart as an oblation. It would be needful for His church in all succeeding ages to make His death for the sins of the world a subject of deep thought and study. Every fact connected with it should be verified beyond a doubt. It was necessary, then, that the eyes of all people should now be directed to Him; the events which preceded His great sacrifice must be such as to call attention to the sacrifice itself. After such a demonstration as that attending His entry into Jerusalem, all eyes would follow His rapid progress to the final scene.

The events connected with this triumphal ride would be the talk of every tongue, and would bring Jesus before every mind. After His crucifixion, many would recall these events in their connection with His trial and death. They would be led to search the prophecies, and would be convinced that Jesus was the Messiah; and in all lands converts to the faith would be multiplied.

In this one triumphant scene of His earthly life, the Saviour might have appeared escorted by heavenly angels, and heralded by the trump of God; but such a demonstration would have been contrary to the purpose of His mission, contrary to the law which had governed His life. He remained true to the humble lot He had accepted. The burden of humanity He must bear until His life was given for the life of the world.

This day, which seemed to the disciples the crowning day of their lives, would have been shadowed with gloomy clouds had they known that this scene of rejoicing was but a prelude to the suffering and death of their Master. Although He had repeatedly told them of His certain sacrifice, yet in the glad triumph of the present they forgot His sorrowful words, and looked forward to His prosperous reign on David's throne.

New accessions were made continually to the procession, and, with few exceptions, all who joined it caught the inspiration of the hour, and helped to swell the hosannas that echoed and re-echoed from hill to hill and from valley to valley. The shouts went up continually, "Hosanna to the Son of David: Blessed is He that cometh in the name of the Lord! Hosanna in the highest."

Never before had the world seen such a triumphal procession. It was not like that of the earth's famous conquerors. No train of mourning captives, as trophies of kingly valor, made a feature of that scene. But about the Saviour were the glorious trophies of His labors of love for sinful man. There were the captives whom He had rescued from Satan's power, praising God for their deliverance. The blind whom He had restored to sight were leading the way.

The dumb whose tongues He had loosed shouted the loudest hosannas. The cripples whom He had healed bounded with joy, and were the most active in breaking the palm branches and waving them before the Saviour. Widows and orphans were exalting the name of Jesus for His works of mercy to them. The lepers whom He had cleansed spread their untainted garments in His path, and hailed Him as the King of glory. Those whom His voice had awakened from the sleep of death were in that throng. Lazarus, whose body had seen corruption in the grave, but who now rejoiced in the strength of glorious manhood, led the beast on which the Saviour rode.

Many Pharisees witnessed the scene, and, burning with envy and malice, sought to turn the current of popular feeling. With all their authority they tried to silence the people; but their appeals and threats only increased the enthusiasm. They feared that this multitude, in the strength of their numbers, would make Jesus king. As a last resort they pressed through the crowd to where the Saviour was, and accosted Him with reproving and threatening words: "Master, rebuke Thy disciples." They declared that such noisy demonstrations were unlawful, and would not be permitted by the authorities. But they were silenced by the reply of Jesus, "I tell you that, if these should hold their peace, the stones would immediately cry out." That scene of triumph was of God's own appointing. It had been foretold by the prophet, and man was powerless to turn aside God's purpose. Had men failed to carry out His plan, He would have given a voice to the inanimate stones, and they would have hailed His Son with acclamations of praise. As the silenced Pharisees drew back, the words of Zechariah were taken up by hundreds of voices: "Rejoice greatly, O daughter of Zion; shout, O daughter of Jerusalem: behold, thy King cometh unto thee: He is just, and having salvation; lowly, and riding upon an ass, and upon a colt the foal of an ass."

When the procession reached the brow of the hill, and was about to descend into the city, Jesus halted, and all the multitude with Him. Before them lay Jerusalem in its glory, now bathed in the light of the declining sun. The temple attracted all eyes. In stately grandeur it towered above all else, seeming to point toward heaven as if directing the people to the only true and living God. The temple had long been the pride and glory of the Jewish nation. The Romans also prided themselves in its magnificence. A king appointed by the Romans had united with the Jews to rebuild and embellish it, and the emperor of Rome had enriched it with his gifts. Its strength, richness, and magnificence had made it one of the wonders of the world.

While the westering sun was tinting and gilding the heavens, its resplendent glory lighted up the pure white marble of the temple walls, and sparkled on its gold-capped pillars. From the crest of the hill where Jesus and His followers stood, it had the appearance of a massive structure of snow, set with golden pinnacles. At the entrance to the temple was a vine of gold and silver, with green leaves and massive clusters of grapes executed by the most skillful artists. This design represented Israel as a prosperous vine. The gold, silver, and living green were combined with rare taste and exquisite workmanship; as it twined gracefully about the white and glistening pillars, clinging with shining tendrils to their golden ornaments, it caught the splendor of the setting sun, shining as if with a glory borrowed from heaven.

Jesus gazes upon the scene, and the vast multitude hush their shouts, spellbound by the sudden vision of beauty. All eyes turn upon the Saviour, expecting to see in His countenance the admiration they themselves feel. But instead of this they behold a cloud of sorrow. They are surprised and disappointed to see His eyes fill with tears, and His body rock to and fro like a tree before the tempest, while a wail of anguish bursts from His quivering lips, as if from the depths of a broken heart. What a sight was this for angels to behold! their loved Commander in an agony of tears! What a sight was this for the glad throng that with shouts of triumph and the waving of palm branches were escorting Him to the glorious city, where they fondly hoped He was about to reign! Jesus had wept at the grave of Lazarus, but it was in a godlike grief in sympathy with human woe. But this sudden sorrow was like a note of wailing in a grand triumphal chorus. In the midst of a scene of rejoicing, where all were paying Him homage, Israel's King was in tears; not silent tears of gladness, but tears and groans of insuppressible agony. The multitude were struck with a sudden gloom. Their acclamations were silenced. Many wept in sympathy with a grief they could not comprehend.

The tears of Jesus were not in anticipation of His own suffering. Just before Him was Gethsemane, where soon the horror of a great darkness would overshadow Him. The sheepgate also was in sight, through which for centuries the beasts for sacrificial offerings had been led. This gate was soon to open for Him, the great Antitype, toward whose sacrifice for the sins of the world all these offerings had pointed. Near by was Calvary, the scene of His approaching agony. Yet it was not because of these reminders of His cruel death that the Redeemer wept and groaned in anguish of spirit. His was no selfish sorrow. The thought of His own agony did not intimidate that noble, self-sacrificing soul. It was the sight of Jerusalem that pierced the heart of Jesus—Jerusalem that had rejected the Son of God and scorned His love, that refused to be convinced by His mighty miracles, and was about to take His life. He saw what she was in her guilt of rejecting her Redeemer, and what she might have been had she accepted Him who alone could heal her wound. He had come to save her; how could He give her up?

Israel had been a favored people; God had made their temple His habitation; it was "beautiful for situation, the joy of the whole earth." Ps. 48:2. The record of more than a thousand years of Christ's guardian care and tender love, such as a father bears his only child, was there. In that temple the prophets had uttered their solemn warnings. There had the burning censers waved, while incense, mingled with the prayers of the worshipers, had ascended to God. There the

blood of beasts had flowed, typical of the blood of Christ. There Jehovah had manifested His glory above the mercy seat. There the priests had officiated, and the pomp of symbol and ceremony had gone on for ages. But all this must have an end.

Jesus raised His hand,—that had so often blessed the sick and suffering,—and waving it toward the doomed city, in broken utterances of grief exclaimed: "If thou hadst known, even thou, at least in this thy day, the things which belong unto thy peace!—" Here the Saviour paused, and left unsaid what might have been the condition of Jerusalem had she accepted the help that God desired to give her,—the gift of His beloved Son. If Jerusalem had known what it was her privilege to know, and had heeded the light which Heaven had sent her, she might have stood forth in the pride of prosperity, the queen of kingdoms, free in the strength of her God-given power. There would have been no armed soldiers standing at her gates, no Roman banners waving from her walls. The glorious destiny that might have blessed Jerusalem had she accepted her Redeemer rose before the Son of God. He saw that she might through Him have been healed of her grievous malady, liberated from bondage, and established as the mighty metropolis of the earth. From her walls the dove of peace would have gone forth to all nations. She would have been the world's diadem of glory.

But the bright picture of what Jerusalem might have been fades from the Saviour's sight. He realizes what she now is under the Roman yoke, bearing the frown of God, doomed to His retributive judgment. He takes up the broken thread of His lamentation: "But now they are hid from thine eyes. For the days shall come upon thee, that thine enemies shall cast a trench about thee, and compass thee round, and keep thee in on every side, and shall lay thee even with the ground, and thy children within thee; and they shall not leave in thee one stone upon another; because thou knewest not the time of thy visitation."

Christ came to save Jerusalem with her children; but Pharisaical pride, hypocrisy, jealousy, and malice had prevented Him from accomplishing His purpose. Jesus knew the terrible retribution which would be visited upon the doomed city. He saw Jerusalem encompassed with armies, the besieged inhabitants driven to starvation and death, mothers feeding upon the dead bodies of their own children, and both parents and children snatching the last morsel of food from one another, natural affection being destroyed by the gnawing pangs of hunger. He saw that the stubbornness of the Jews, as evinced in their rejection of His salvation, would also lead them to refuse submission to the invading armies. He beheld Calvary, on which He was to be lifted up, set with crosses as thickly as forest trees. He saw the wretched inhabitants suffering torture on the rack and by crucifixion, the beautiful palaces destroyed, the temple in ruins, and of its massive walls not one stone left upon another, while the city was plowed like a field. Well might the Saviour weep in agony in view of that fearful scene.

Jerusalem had been the child of His care, and as a tender

father mourns over a wayward son, so Jesus wept over the beloved city. How can I give thee up? How can I see thee devoted to destruction? Must I let thee go to fill up the cup of thine iniquity? One soul is of such value that, in comparison with it, worlds sink into insignificance; but here was a whole nation to be lost. When the fast westering sun should pass from sight in the heavens, Jerusalem's day of grace would be ended. While the procession was halting on the brow of Olivet, it was not yet too late for Jerusalem to repent. The angel of mercy was then folding her wings to step down from the golden throne to give place to justice and swift-coming judgment. But Christ's great heart of love still pleaded for Jerusalem, that had scorned His mercies, despised His warnings, and was about to imbrue her hands in His blood. If Jerusalem would but repent, it was not yet too late. While the last rays of the setting sun were lingering on temple, tower, and pinnacle, would not some good angel lead her to the Saviour's love, and avert her doom? Beautiful and unholy city, that had stoned the prophets, that had rejected the Son of God, that was locking herself by her impenitence in fetters of bondage,—her day of mercy was almost spent!

Yet again the Spirit of God speaks to Jerusalem. Before the day is done, another testimony is borne to Christ. The voice of witness is lifted up, responding to the call from a prophetic past. If Jerusalem will hear the call, if she will receive the Saviour who is entering her gates, she may yet be saved.

Reports have reached the rulers in Jerusalem that Jesus is approaching the city with a great concourse of people. But they have no welcome for the Son of God. In fear they go out to meet Him, hoping to disperse the throng. As the procession is about to descend the Mount of Olives, it is intercepted by the rulers. They inquire the cause of the tumultuous rejoicing. As they question, "Who is this?" the disciples, filled with the spirit of inspiration, answer this question. In eloquent strains they repeat the prophecies concerning Christ:

Adam will tell you, It is the seed of the woman that shall bruise the serpent's head.

Ask Abraham, he will tell you, It is "Melchizedek King of Salem," King of Peace. Gen. 14:18.

Jacob will tell you, He is Shiloh of the tribe of Judah.

Isaiah will tell you, "Immanuel," "Wonderful, Counselor, The mighty God, The everlasting Father, The Prince of Peace." Isa. 7:14; 9:6.

Jeremiah will tell you, The Branch of David, "the Lord our Righteousness." Jer. 23:6.

Daniel will tell you, He is the Messiah.

Hosea will tell you, He is "the Lord God of hosts; the Lord is His memorial." Hosea 12:5.

John the Baptist will tell you, He is "the Lamb of God, which taketh away the sin of the world." John 1:29.

The great Jehovah has proclaimed from His throne, "This is My beloved Son." Matt. 3:17.

We, His disciples, declare, This is Jesus, the Messiah, the Prince of life, the Redeemer of the world.

And the prince of the powers of darkness acknowledges Him, saying, "I know Thee who Thou art, the Holy One of God." Mark 1:24.

A Doomed People

The triumphal ride of Christ into Jerusalem was the dim foreshadowing of His coming in the clouds of heaven with power and glory, amid the triumph of angels and the rejoicing of the saints. Then will be fulfilled the words of Christ to the priests and Pharisees: "Ye shall not see Me henceforth, till ye shall say, Blessed is He that cometh in the name of the Lord." Matt. 23:39. In prophetic vision Zechariah was shown that day of final triumph; and he beheld also the doom of those who at the first advent had rejected Christ: "They shall look upon Me whom they have pierced, and they shall mourn for Him, as one mourneth for his only son, and shall be in bitterness for Him, as one that is in bitterness for his first-born." Zech. 12:10. This scene Christ foresaw when He beheld the city and wept over it. In the temporal ruin of Jerusalem He saw the final destruction of that people who were guilty of the blood of the Son of God.

The disciples saw the hatred of the Jews to Christ, but they did not yet see to what it would lead. They did not yet understand the true condition of Israel, nor comprehend the retribution that was to fall upon Jerusalem. This Christ opened to them by a significant object lesson.

The last appeal to Jerusalem had been in vain. The priests and rulers had heard the prophetic voice of the past echoed by the multitude, in answer to the question, "Who is this?" but they did not accept it as the voice of Inspiration. In anger and amazement they tried to silence the people. There were Roman officers in the throng, and to them His enemies denounced Jesus as the leader of a rebellion. They represented that He was about to take possession of the temple, and reign as king in Jerusalem.

But the calm voice of Jesus hushed for a moment the clamorous throng as He again declared that He had not come to establish a temporal rule; He should soon ascend to His Father, and His accusers would see Him no more until He should come again in glory. Then, too late for their salvation, they would acknowledge Him. These words Jesus spoke with sadness and with singular power. The Roman officers were silenced and subdued. Their hearts, though strangers to divine influence, were moved as they had never been moved before. In the calm, solemn face of Jesus they read love, benevolence, and quiet dignity. They were stirred by a sympathy they could not understand. Instead of arresting Jesus, they were more inclined to pay Him homage. Turning upon the priests and rulers, they charged them with creating the disturbance. These leaders, chagrined and defeated, turned to the people with their complaints, and disputed angrily among themselves.

Meanwhile Jesus passed unnoticed to the temple. All was quiet there, for the scene upon Olivet had called away the people. For a short time Jesus remained at the temple, looking upon it with sorrowful eyes. Then He withdrew with His disciples, and returned to Bethany. When the people sought for Him to place Him on the throne, He was not to be found.

The entire night Jesus spent in prayer, and in the morning He came again to the temple. On the way He passed a fig orchard. He was hungry, "and seeing a fig tree afar off having leaves, He came, if haply He might find anything thereon: and when He came to it, He found nothing but leaves; for the time of figs was not yet."

It was not the season for ripe figs, except in certain localities; and on the highlands about Jerusalem it might truly be said, "The time of figs was not yet." But in the orchard to which Jesus came, one tree appeared to be in advance of all the others. It was already covered with leaves. It is the nature of the fig tree that before the leaves open, the growing fruit appears. Therefore this tree in full leaf gave promise of well-developed fruit. But its appearance was deceptive. Upon searching its branches, from the lowest bough to the topmost twig, Jesus found "nothing but leaves." It was a mass of pretentious foliage, nothing more.

Christ uttered against it a withering curse. "No man eat fruit of thee hereafter forever," He said. The next morning, as the Saviour and His disciples were again on their way to the city, the blasted branches and drooping leaves attracted their attention. "Master," said Peter, "behold, the fig tree which Thou cursedst is withered away."

Christ's act in cursing the fig tree had astonished the disciples. It seemed to them unlike His ways and works. Often they had heard Him declare that He came not to condemn the world, but that the world through Him might be saved. They remembered His words, "The Son of man is not come to destroy men's lives, but to save them." Luke 9:56. His wonderful works had been done to restore, never to destroy. The disciples had known Him only as the Restorer, the Healer. This act stood alone. What was its purpose? they questioned.

God "delighteth in mercy." "As I live, saith the Lord God, I have no pleasure in the death of the wicked." Micah 7:18; Ezek. 33:11. To Him the work of destruction and the denunciation of judgment is a "strange work." Isa. 28:21. But it is in mercy and love that He lifts the veil from the future, and reveals to men the results of a course of sin.

The cursing of the fig tree was an acted parable. That barren tree, flaunting its pretentious foliage in the very face of Christ, was a symbol of the Jewish nation. The Saviour desired to make plain to His disciples the cause and the certainty of Israel's doom. For this purpose He invested the tree with moral qualities, and made it the expositor of divine truth. The Jews stood forth distinct from all other nations, professing allegiance to God. They had been specially favored by Him, and they laid claim to righteousness above every other people. But they were corrupted by the love of the world and the greed of gain. They boasted of their knowledge, but they were ignorant of the requirements of God, and were full of hypocrisy. Like the barren tree, they spread their pretentious branches aloft, luxuriant in appearance, and beautiful to the eye, but they yielded "nothing but leaves." The Jewish religion, with its magnificent temple, its sacred altars, its mitered priests and impressive ceremonies, was indeed fair in outward appearance, but humility, love, and benevolence were lacking.

All the trees in the fig orchard were destitute of fruit; but the leafless trees raised no expectation, and caused no disappointment. By these trees the Gentiles were represented. They were as destitute as were the Jews of godliness; but they had not professed to serve God. They made no boastful pretensions to goodness. They were blind to the works and ways of God. With them the time of figs was not yet. They were still waiting for a day which would bring them light and hope. The Jews, who had received greater blessings from God, were held accountable for their abuse of these gifts. The privileges of which they boasted only increased their guilt.

Jesus had come to the fig tree hungry, to find food. So He had come to Israel, hungering to find in them the fruits of righteousness. He had lavished on them His gifts, that they might bear fruit for the blessing of the world. Every opportunity and privilege had been granted them, and in return He sought their sympathy and co-operation in His work of grace. He longed to see in them self-sacrifice and compassion, zeal for God, and a deep yearning of soul for the salvation of their fellow men. Had they kept the law of God, they would have done the same unselfish work that Christ did. But love to God and man was eclipsed by pride and self-sufficiency. They brought ruin upon themselves by refusing to minister to others. The treasures of truth which God had committed to them, they did not give to the world. In the barren tree they might read both their sin and its punishment. Withered beneath the Saviour's curse, standing forth sere and blasted, dried up by the roots, the fig tree showed what the Jewish people would be when the grace of God was removed from them. Refusing to impart blessing, they would no longer receive it. "O Israel," the Lord says, "thou hast destroyed thyself." Hosea 13:9.

The warning is for all time. Christ's act in cursing the tree which His own power had created stands as a warning to all churches and to all Christians. No one can live the law of God without ministering to others. But there are many who do not live out Christ's merciful, unselfish life. Some who think themselves excellent Christians do not understand what constitutes service for God. They plan and study to please themselves. They act only in reference to self. Time is of value to them only as they can gather for themselves. In all the affairs of life this is their object. Not for others but for themselves do they minister. God created them to live in a world where unselfish service must be performed. He designed them to help their fellow men in every possible way. But self is so large that they cannot see anything else. They are not in touch with humanity. Those who thus live for self are like the fig tree, which made every pretension but was fruitless. They observe the forms of worship, but without repentance or faith. In profession they honor the law of God, but obedience is lacking. They say, but do not. In the sentence pronounced on the fig tree Christ demonstrates how hateful in His eyes is this vain pretense. He declares that the open sinner is less guilty than is he who professes to serve God, but who bears no fruit to His glory.

The parable of the fig tree, spoken before Christ's visit to Jerusalem, had a direct connection with the lesson He taught in cursing the fruitless tree. For the barren tree of the parable the gardener pleaded, Let it alone this year, until I shall dig about it and dress it; and if it bear fruit, well; but if not, then after that thou shalt cut it down. Increased care was to be given the unfruitful tree. It was to have every advantage. But if it remained fruitless, nothing could save it from destruction. In the parable the result of the gardener's work was not foretold. It depended upon that people to whom Christ's words were spoken. They were represented by the fruitless tree, and it rested with them to decide their own destiny. Every advantage that Heaven could bestow was given them, but they did not profit by their increased blessings. By Christ's act in cursing the barren fig tree, the result was shown. They had determined their own destruction.

For more than a thousand years the Jewish nation had abused God's mercy and invited His judgments. They had rejected His warnings and slain His prophets. For these sins the people of Christ's day made themselves responsible by following the same course. In the rejection of their present mercies and warnings lay the guilt of that generation. The fetters which the nation had for centuries been forging, the people of Christ's day were fastening upon themselves.

In every age there is given to men their day of light and privilege, a probationary time in which they may become reconciled to God. But there is a limit to this grace. Mercy may plead for years and be slighted and rejected; but there comes a time when mercy makes her last plea. The heart becomes so hardened that it ceases to respond to the Spirit of God. Then the sweet, winning voice entreats the sinner no longer, and reproofs and warnings cease.

That day had come to Jerusalem. Jesus wept in anguish over the doomed city, but He could not deliver her. He had exhausted every resource. In rejecting the warnings of God's Spirit, Israel had rejected the only means of help. There was no other power by which they could be delivered.

The Jewish nation was a symbol of the people of all ages who scorn the pleadings of Infinite Love. The tears of Christ when He wept over Jerusalem were for the sins of all time. In the judgments pronounced upon Israel, those who reject the reproofs and warnings of God's Holy Spirit, may read their own condemnation.

In this generation there are many who are treading on the same ground as were the unbelieving Jews. They have witnessed the manifestation of the power of God; the Holy Spirit has spoken to their hearts; but they cling to their unbelief and resistance. God sends them warnings and reproof, but they are not willing to confess their errors, and they reject His message and His messenger. The very means He uses for

their recovery becomes to them a stone of stumbling.

The prophets of God were hated by apostate Israel because through them their hidden sins were brought to light. Ahab regarded Elijah as his enemy because the prophet was faithful to rebuke the king's secret iniquities. So today the servant of Christ, the reprover of sin, meets with scorn and rebuffs. Bible truth, the religion of Christ, struggles against a strong current of moral impurity. Prejudice is even stronger in the hearts of men now than in Christ's day. Christ did not fulfill men's expectations; His life was a rebuke to their sins, and they rejected Him. So now the truth of God's word does not harmonize with men's practices and their natural inclination, and thousands reject its light. Men prompted by Satan cast doubt upon God's word, and choose to exercise their independent judgment. They choose darkness rather than light, but they do it at the peril of their souls. Those who caviled at the words of Christ, found ever-increased cause for cavil, until they turned from the Truth and the Life. So it is now. God does not propose to remove every objection which the carnal heart may bring against His truth. To those who refuse the precious rays of light which would illuminate the darkness, the mysteries of God's word remain such forever. From them the truth is hidden. They walk blindly, and know not the ruin before them.

Christ overlooked the world and all ages from the height of Olivet; and His words are applicable to every soul who slights the pleadings of divine mercy. Scorner of His love, He addresses you today. It is "thou, even thou," who shouldest know the things that belong to thy peace. Christ is shedding bitter tears for you, who have no tears to shed for yourself. Already that fatal hardness of heart which destroyed the Pharisees is manifest in you. And every evidence of the grace of God, every ray of divine light, is either melting and subduing the soul, or confirming it in hopeless impenitence.

Christ foresaw that Jerusalem would remain obdurate and impenitent; yet all the guilt, all the consequences of rejected mercy, lay at her own door. Thus it will be with every soul who is following the same course. The Lord declares, "O Israel, thou hast destroyed thyself." "Hear, O earth: behold, I will bring evil upon this people, even the fruit of their thoughts, because they have not hearkened unto My words, nor to My law, but rejected it." Hosea 13:9; Jer. 6:19.

The Temple Cleansed Again

At the beginning of His ministry, Christ had driven from the temple those who defiled it by their unholy traffic; and His stern and godlike demeanor had struck terror to the hearts of the scheming traders. At the close of His mission He came again to the temple, and found it still desecrated as before. The condition of things was even worse than before. The outer court of the temple was like a vast cattle yard. With the cries of the animals and the sharp chinking of coin was mingled the sound of angry altercation between traffickers, and among them were heard the voices of men in sacred office. The dignitaries of the temple were themselves engaged in buying and selling and the exchange of money. So completely were they controlled by their greed of gain that in the sight of God they were no better than thieves.

Little did the priests and rulers realize the solemnity of the work which it was theirs to perform. At every Passover and Feast of Tabernacles, thousands of animals were slain, and their blood was caught by the priests and poured upon the altar. The Jews had become familiar with the offering of blood, and had almost lost sight of the fact that it was sin which made necessary all this shedding of the blood of beasts. They did not discern that it prefigured the blood of God's dear Son, which was to be shed for the life of the world, and that by the offering of sacrifices men were to be directed to a crucified Redeemer.

Jesus looked upon the innocent victims of sacrifice, and saw how the Jews had made these great convocations scenes of bloodshed and cruelty. In place of humble repentance of sin, they had multiplied the sacrifice of beasts, as if God could be honored by a heartless service. The priests and rulers had hardened their hearts through selfishness and avarice. The very symbols pointing to the Lamb of God they had made a means of getting gain. Thus in the eyes of the people the sacredness of the sacrificial service had been in a great measure destroyed. The indignation of Jesus was stirred; He knew that His blood, so soon to be shed for the sins of the world, would be as little appreciated by the priests and elders as was the blood of beasts which they kept incessantly flowing.

Against these practices Christ had spoken through the prophets. Samuel had said, "Hath the Lord as great delight in burnt offerings and sacrifices, as in obeying the voice of the Lord? Behold, to obey is better than sacrifice, and to hearken than the fat of rams." And Isaiah, seeing in prophetic vision the apostasy of the Jews, addressed them as rulers of Sodom and Gomorrah: "Hear the word of the Lord, ye rulers of Sodom; give ear unto the law of our God, ye people of Gomorrah. To what purpose is the multitude of your sacrifices unto Me? saith the Lord: I am full of the burnt offerings of rams, and the fat of fed beasts; and I delight not in the blood of bullocks, or of lambs, or of he-goats. When ye come to appear before Me, who hath required this at your hand, to tread My courts?" "Wash you, make you clean; put away the evil of your doings from before Mine eyes; cease to do evil; learn to do well; seek judgment, relieve the oppressed, judge the fatherless, plead for the widow." 1 Sam. 15:22; Isa. 1:10-12, 16,17.

He who had Himself given these prophecies now for the last time repeated the warning. In fulfillment of prophecy the people had proclaimed Jesus king of Israel. He had received their homage, and accepted the office of king. In this character He must act. He knew that His efforts to reform a corrupt priesthood would be in vain; nevertheless His work must be done; to an unbelieving people the evidence of His divine mission must be given.

Again the piercing look of Jesus swept over the desecrated court of the temple. All eyes were turned toward Him. Priest and ruler, Pharisee and Gentile, looked with astonishment and awe upon Him who stood before them with the majesty of heaven's King. Divinity flashed through humanity, investing Christ with a dignity and glory He had never manifested before. Those standing nearest Him drew as far away as the crowd would permit. Except for a few of His disciples, the Saviour stood alone. Every sound was hushed. The deep silence seemed unbearable. Christ spoke with a power that swayed the people like a mighty tempest: "It is written, My house shall be called the house of prayer; but ye have made it a den of thieves." His voice sounded like a trumpet through the temple. The displeasure of His countenance seemed like consuming fire. With authority He commanded, "Take these things hence." John 2:16.

Three years before, the rulers of the temple had been ashamed of their flight before the command of Jesus. They had since wondered at their own fears, and their unquestioning obedience to a single humble Man. They had felt that it was impossible for their undignified surrender to be repeated. Yet they were now more terrified than before, and in greater haste to obey His command. There were none who dared question His authority. Priests and traders fled from His presence, driving their cattle before them.

On the way from the temple they were met by a throng who came with their sick inquiring for the Great Healer. The report given by the fleeing people caused some of these to turn back. They feared to meet One so powerful, whose very look had driven the priests and rulers from His presence. But a large number pressed through the hurrying crowd, eager to reach Him who was their only hope. When the multitude fled from the temple, many had remained behind. These were now joined by the newcomers. Again the temple court was filled by the sick and the dying, and once more Jesus ministered to them.

After a season the priests and rulers ventured back to the temple. When the panic had abated, they were seized with anxiety to know what would be the next movement of Jesus. They expected Him to take the throne of David. Quietly returning to the temple, they heard the voices of men, women, and children praising God. Upon entering, they stood transfixed before the wonderful scene. They saw the sick healed, the blind restored to sight, and deaf receive their hearing, and the crippled leap for joy. The children were foremost in the rejoicing. Jesus had healed their maladies; He had clasped them in His arms, received their kisses of grateful affection, and some of them had fallen asleep upon His breast as He was teaching the people. Now with glad voices the children sounded His praise. They repeated the hosannas of the day before, and waved palm branches triumphantly before the Saviour. The temple echoed and re-echoed with their acclamations, "Blessed be He that cometh in the name of the Lord!" "Behold, thy King cometh unto thee; He is just, and having salvation!" Ps. 118:26; Zech. 9:9. "Hosanna to the Son of David!"

The sound of these happy, unrestrained voices was an offense to the rulers of the temple. They set about putting a stop to such demonstrations. They represented to the people that the house of God was desecrated by the feet of the children and the shouts of rejoicing. Finding that their words made no impression on the people, the rulers appealed to Christ: "Hearest Thou what these say? And Jesus saith unto them, Yea; have ye never read, Out of the mouth of babes and sucklings Thou hast perfected praise?" Prophecy had foretold that Christ should be proclaimed as king, and that word must be fulfilled. The priests and rulers of Israel refused to herald His glory, and God moved upon the children to be His witnesses. Had the voices of the children been silent, the very pillars of the temple would have sounded the Saviour's praise.

The Pharisees were utterly perplexed and disconcerted. One whom they could not intimidate was in command. Jesus had taken His position as guardian of the temple. Never before had He assumed such kingly authority. Never before had His words and works possessed so great power. He had done marvelous works throughout Jerusalem, but never before in a manner so solemn and impressive. In presence of the people who had witnessed His wonderful works, the priests and rulers dared not show Him open hostility. Though enraged and confounded by His answer, they were unable to accomplish anything further that day.

The next morning the Sanhedrin again considered what course to pursue toward Jesus. Three years before, they had demanded a sign of His Messiahship. Since that time He had wrought mighty works throughout the land. He had healed the sick, miraculously fed thousands of people, walked upon the waves, and spoken peace to the troubled sea. He had repeatedly read the hearts of men as an open book; He had cast out demons, and raised the dead. The rulers had before them the evidences of His Messiahship. They now decided to demand no sign of His authority, but to draw out some admission or declaration by which He might be condemned.

Repairing to the temple where He was teaching, they proceeded to question Him: "By what authority doest Thou these things? and who gave Thee this authority?" They expected Him to claim that His authority was from God. Such an assertion they intended to deny. But Jesus met them with a question apparently pertaining to another subject, and He made His reply to them conditional on their answering this question. "The baptism of John," He said, "whence was it? from heaven, or of men?"

The priests saw that they were in a dilemma from which no sophistry could extricate them. If they said that John's baptism was from heaven, their inconsistency would be made apparent. Christ would say, Why have ye not then believed on him? John had testified of Christ, "Behold the Lamb of God, which taketh away the sin of the world." John 1:29. If the priests believed John's testimony, how could they deny the Messiahship of Christ? If they declared their real belief, that John's ministry was of men, they would bring upon themselves a storm of indignation; for the people believed John to be a prophet.

With intense interest the multitude awaited the decision. They knew that the priests had professed to accept the ministry of John, and they expected them to acknowledge without a question that he was sent from God. But after conferring secretly together, the priests decided not to commit themselves. Hypocritically professing ignorance, they said, "We cannot tell." "Neither tell I you," said Christ, "by what authority I do these things."

Scribes, priests, and rulers were all silenced. Baffled and disappointed, they stood with lowering brows, not daring to press further questions upon Christ. By their cowardice and indecision they had in a great measure forfeited the respect of the people, who now stood by, amused to see these proud, self-righteous men defeated.

All these sayings and doings of Christ were important, and their influence was to be felt in an ever-increasing degree after His crucifixion and ascension. Many of those who had anxiously awaited the result of the questioning of Jesus were finally to become His disciples, first drawn toward Him by His words on that eventful day. The scene in the temple court was never to fade from their minds. The contrast between Jesus and the high priest as they talked together was marked. The proud dignitary of the temple was clothed in rich and costly garments. Upon his head was a glittering tiara. His bearing was majestic, his hair and his long flowing beard were silvered by age. His appearance awed the beholders. Before this august personage stood the Majesty of heaven, without adornment or display. His garments were travel stained; His face was pale, and expressed a patient sadness; yet written there were dignity and benevolence that contrasted strangely with the proud, self-confident, and angry air of the high priest. Many of those who witnessed the words and deeds of Jesus in the temple from that time enshrined Him in their hearts as a prophet of God. But as the popular feeling turned in His favor, the hatred of the priests toward Jesus increased. The wisdom by which He escaped the snares set for His feet, being a new evidence of His divinity, added fuel to their wrath.

In His contest with the rabbis, it was not Christ's purpose to humiliate His opponents. He was not glad to see them in a hard place. He had an important lesson to teach. He had mortified His enemies by allowing them to be entangled in the net they had spread for Him. Their acknowledged ignorance in regard to the character of John's baptism gave Him an opportunity to speak, and He improved the opportunity by presenting before them their real position, adding another warning to the many already given.

"What think ye?" He said. "A certain man had two sons; and he came to the first, and said, Son, go work today in my vineyard. He answered and said, I will not: but afterward he repented, and went. And he came to the second, and said likewise. And he answered and said, I go, sir: and went not. Whether of them twain did the will of his father?"

This abrupt question threw His hearers off their guard. They had followed the parable closely, and now immediately answered, "The first." Fixing His steady eye upon them, Jesus responded in stern and solemn tones: "Verily I say unto you, That the publicans and the harlots go into the kingdom of God before you. For John came unto you in the way of righteousness, and ye believed him not: but the publicans and the harlots believed him: and ye, when ye had seen it, repented not afterward, that ye might believe him."

The priests and rulers could not but give a correct answer to Christ's question, and thus He obtained their opinion in favor of the first son. This son represented the publicans, those who were despised and hated by the Pharisees. The publicans had been grossly immoral. They had indeed been transgressors of the law of God, showing in their lives an absolute resistance to His requirements. They had been unthankful and unholy; when told to go and work in the Lord's vineyard, they had given a contemptuous refusal. But when John came, preaching repentance and baptism, the publicans received his message and were baptized.

The second son represented the leading men of the Jewish nation. Some of the Pharisees had repented and received the baptism of John; but the leaders would not acknowledge that he came from God. His warnings and denunciations did not lead them to reformation. They "rejected the counsel of God against themselves, being not baptized of him." Luke 7:30. They treated his message with disdain. Like the second son, who, when called, said, "I go, sir," but went not, the priests and rulers professed obedience, but acted disobedience. They made great professions of piety, they claimed to be obeying the law of God, but they rendered only a false obedience. The publicans were denounced and cursed by the Pharisees as infidels; but they showed by their faith and works that they were going into the kingdom of heaven before those self-righteous men who had been given great light, but whose works did not correspond to their profession of godliness.

The priests and rulers were unwilling to bear these searching truths; they remained silent, however, hoping that Jesus would say something which they could turn against Him; but they had still more to bear.

"Hear another parable," Christ said: "There was a certain householder, which planted a vineyard, and hedged it round about, and digged a wine press in it, and built a tower, and let it out to husbandmen, and went into a far country: and when the time of the fruit drew near, he sent his servants to the husbandmen, that they might receive the fruits of it. And the husbandmen took his servants, and beat one, and killed another, and stoned another. Again, he sent other servants more than the first: and they did unto them likewise. But last of all he sent unto them his son, saying, They will reverence my son. But when the husbandmen saw the son, they said among themselves, This is the heir; come, let us kill him, and let us seize on his inheritance. And they caught him, and cast him out of the vineyard, and slew him. When the lord therefore of the vineyard cometh, what will he do unto those husbandmen?"

Jesus addressed all the people present; but the priests and rulers answered. "He will miserably destroy those wicked men," they said, "and will let out his vineyard unto other husbandmen, which shall render him the fruits in their seasons." The speakers had not at first perceived the application of the parable, but they now saw that they had pronounced their own condemnation. In the parable the householder represented God, the vineyard the Jewish nation, and the hedge the divine law which was their protection. The tower was a symbol of the temple. The lord of the vineyard had done everything needful for its prosperity. "What could have been done more to my vineyard," he says, "that I have not done in it." Isa. 5:4. Thus was represented God's unwearied care for Israel. And as the husbandmen were to return to the lord a due proportion of the fruits of the vineyard, so God's people were to honor Him by a life corresponding to their sacred privileges. But as the husbandmen had killed the servants whom the master sent to them for fruit, so the Jews had put to death the prophets whom God sent to call them to repentance. Messenger after messenger had been slain. Thus far the application of the parable could not be questioned, and in what followed it was not less evident. In the beloved son whom the lord of the vineyard finally sent to his disobedient servants, and whom they seized and slew, the priests and rulers saw a distinct picture of Jesus and His impending fate. Already they were planning to slay Him whom the Father had sent to them as a last appeal. In the retribution inflicted upon the ungrateful husbandmen was portrayed the doom of those who should put Christ to death.

Looking with pity upon them, the Saviour continued, "Did ye never read in the Scriptures, The stone which the builders rejected, the same is become the head of the corner: this is the Lord's doing, and it is marvelous in our eyes? Therefore say I unto you, The kingdom of God shall be taken from you, and given to a nation bringing forth the fruits thereof. And whosoever shall fall on this stone shall be broken: but on whomsoever it shall fall, it will grind him to powder."

This prophecy the Jews had often repeated in the synagogues, applying it to the coming Messiah. Christ was the cornerstone of the Jewish economy, and of the whole plan of salvation. This foundation stone the Jewish builders, the priests and rulers of Israel, were now rejecting. The Saviour called their attention to the prophecies that would show them their danger. By every means in His power He sought to make plain to them the nature of the deed they were about to do.

And His words had another purpose. In asking the question, "When the lord therefore of the vineyard cometh, what will he do unto those husbandmen?" Christ designed that the Pharisees should answer as they did. He designed that they should condemn themselves. His warnings, failing to arouse them to repentance, would seal their doom, and He wished them to see that they had brought ruin on themselves. He designed to show them the justice of God in the withdrawal of their national privileges, which had already begun, and which would end, not only in the destruction of their temple and their city, but in the dispersion of the nation.

The hearers recognized the warning. But notwithstanding the sentence they themselves had pronounced, the priests and rulers were ready to fill out the picture by saying, "This is the heir; come, let us kill him." "But when they sought to lay hands on Him, they feared the multitude," for the public sentiment was in Christ's favor.

In quoting the prophecy of the rejected stone, Christ referred to an actual occurrence in the history of Israel. The incident was connected with the building of the first temple. While it had a special application at the time of Christ's first advent, and should have appealed with special force to the Jews, it has also a lesson for us. When the temple of Solomon was erected, the immense stones for the walls and the foundation were entirely prepared at the quarry; after they were brought to the place of building, not an instrument was to be used upon them; the workmen had only to place them in position. For use in the foundation, one stone of unusual size and peculiar shape had been brought; but the workmen could find no place for it, and would not accept it. It was an annoyance to them as it lay unused in their way. Long it remained a rejected stone. But when the builders came to the laying of the corner, they searched for a long time to find a stone of sufficient size and strength, and of the proper shape, to take that particular place, and bear the great weight which would rest upon it. Should they make an unwise choice for this important place, the safety of the entire building would be endangered. They must find a stone capable of resisting the influence of the sun, of frost, and of tempest. Several stones had at different times been chosen, but under the pressure of immense weights they had crumbled to pieces. Others could not bear the test of the sudden atmospheric changes. But at last attention was called to the stone so long rejected. It had been exposed to the air, to sun and storm, without revealing the slightest crack. The builders examined this stone. It had borne every test but one. If it could bear the test of severe pressure, they decided to accept it for the cornerstone. The trial was made. The stone was accepted, brought to its assigned position, and found to be an exact fit. In prophetic vision, Isaiah was shown that this stone was a symbol of Christ. He says:

"Sanctify the Lord of hosts Himself; and let Him be your fear, and let Him be your dread. And He shall be for a sanctuary; but for a stone of stumbling and for a rock of offense to both the houses of Israel, for a gin and for a snare to the inhabitants of Jerusalem. And many among them shall stumble, and fall, and be broken, and be snared, and be taken." Carried down in prophetic vision to the first advent, the prophet is shown that Christ is to bear trials and tests of which the treatment of the chief cornerstone in the temple of Solomon was symbolic. "Therefore thus saith the Lord God, Behold, I lay in Zion for a foundation a stone, a tried stone, a precious cornerstone, a sure foundation: he that believeth shall not make haste." Isa. 8:13-15; 28:16.

In infinite wisdom, God chose the foundation stone, and laid it Himself. He called it "a sure foundation." The entire world may lay upon it their burdens and griefs; it can endure them all. With perfect safety they may build upon it. Christ is a "tried stone." Those who trust in Him, He never disappoints. He has borne every test. He has endured the pressure of Adam's guilt, and the guilt of his posterity, and has come off more than conqueror of the powers of evil. He has borne the burdens cast upon Him by every repenting sinner. In Christ the guilty heart has found relief. He is the sure foundation. All who make Him their dependence rest in perfect security.

In Isaiah's prophecy, Christ is declared to be both a sure foundation and a stone of stumbling. The apostle Peter, writing by inspiration of the Holy Spirit, clearly shows to whom Christ is a foundation stone, and to whom a rock of offense:

"If so be ye have tasted that the Lord is gracious. To whom coming, as unto a living stone, disallowed indeed of men, but chosen of God, and precious, ye also, as lively stones, are built up a spiritual house, an holy priesthood, to offer up spiritual sacrifices, acceptable to God by Jesus Christ. Wherefore also it is contained in the Scripture, Behold, I lay in Sion a chief cornerstone, elect, precious: and he that believeth on Him shall not be confounded. Unto you therefore which believe He is precious: but unto them which be disobedient, the stone which the builders disallowed, the same is made the head of the corner, and a stone of stumbling, and a rock of offense, even to them which stumble at the word, being disobedient." 1 Peter 2:3-8.

To those who believe, Christ is the sure foundation. These are they who fall upon the Rock and are broken. Submission to Christ and faith in Him are here represented. To fall upon the Rock and be broken is to give up our self-righteousness and to go to Christ with the humility of a child, repenting of our transgressions, and believing in His forgiving love. And so also it is by faith and obedience that we build on Christ as our foundation.

Upon this living stone, Jews and Gentiles alike may build. This is the only foundation upon which we may securely build. It is broad enough for all, and strong enough to sustain the weight and burden of the whole world. And by connection with Christ, the living stone, all who build upon this foundation become living stones. Many persons are by their own endeavors hewn, polished, and beautified; but they cannot become "living stones," because they are not connected with Christ. Without this connection, no man can be saved. Without the life of Christ in us, we cannot withstand the storms of temptation. Our eternal safety depends upon our building upon the sure foundation. Multitudes are today building upon foundations that have not been tested. When the rain falls, and the tempest rages, and the floods come, their house will fall, because it is not founded upon the eternal Rock, the chief cornerstone Christ Jesus.

"To them which stumble at the word, being disobedient," Christ is a rock of offense. But "the stone which the builders disallowed, the same is made the head of the corner." Like the rejected stone, Christ in His earthly mission had borne neglect and abuse. He was "despised and rejected of men; a man of sorrows, and acquainted with grief: . . . He was despised, and we esteemed Him not." Isa. 53:3. But the time was near when He would be glorified. By the resurrection from the dead He would be declared "the Son of God with power." Rom. 1:4. At His second coming He would be revealed as Lord of heaven and earth. Those who were now about to crucify Him would recognize His greatness. Before the universe the rejected stone would become the head of the corner.

And on "whomsoever it shall fall, it will grind him to powder." The people who rejected Christ were soon to see their city and their nation destroyed. Their glory would be broken, and scattered as the dust before the wind. And what was it that destroyed the Jews? It was the rock which, had they built upon it, would have been their security. It was the goodness of God despised, the righteousness spurned, the mercy slighted. Men set themselves in opposition to God, and all that would have been their salvation was turned to their destruction. All that God ordained unto life they found to be unto death. In the Jews' crucifixion of Christ was involved the destruction of Jerusalem. The blood shed upon Calvary was the weight that sank them to ruin for this world and for the world to come. So it will be in the great final day, when judgment shall fall upon the rejecters of God's grace. Christ, their rock of offense, will then appear to them as an avenging mountain. The glory of His countenance, which to the righteous is life, will be to the wicked a consuming fire. Because of love rejected, grace despised, the sinner will be destroyed.

By many illustrations and repeated warnings, Jesus showed what would be the result to the Jews of rejecting the Son of God. In these words He was addressing all in every age who refuse to receive Him as their Redeemer. Every warning is for them. The desecrated temple, the disobedient son, the false husbandmen, the contemptuous builders, have their counterpart in the experience of every sinner. Unless he repent, the doom which they foreshadowed will be his.

Controversy

The priests and rulers had listened in silence to Christ's pointed rebukes. They could not refute His charges. But they were only the more determined to entrap Him, and with this object they sent to Him spies, "which should feign themselves just men, that they might take hold of His words, that so they might deliver Him unto the power and authority of the governor." They did not send the old Pharisees whom Jesus had often met, but young men, who were ardent and zealous, and whom, they thought, Christ did not know. These were accompanied by certain of the Herodians, who were to hear Christ's words, that they might testify against Him at His trial. The Pharisees and Herodians had been bitter enemies, but they were now one in enmity to Christ.

The Pharisees had ever chafed under the exaction of tribute by the Romans. The payment of tribute they held to be contrary to the law of God. Now they saw opportunity to lay a snare for Jesus. The spies came to Him, and with apparent sincerity, as though desiring to know their duty, said, "Master, we know that Thou sayest and teachest rightly, neither acceptest Thou the person of any, but teachest the way of God truly: is it lawful for us to give tribute unto Caesar, or no?"

The words, "We know that Thou sayest and teachest rightly," had they been sincere, would have been a wonderful admission. But they were spoken to deceive; nevertheless their testimony was true. The Pharisees did know that Christ said and taught rightly, and by their own testimony will they be judged.

Those who put the question to Jesus thought that they had sufficiently disguised their purpose; but Jesus read their hearts as an open book, and sounded their hypocrisy. "Why tempt ye Me?" He said; thus giving them a sign they had not asked, by showing that He read their hidden purpose. They were still more confused when He added, "Show Me a penny." They brought it, and He asked them, "Whose image and superscription hath it? They answered and said, Caesar's." Pointing to the inscription on the coin, Jesus said, "Render therefore unto Caesar the things which are Caesar's; and unto God the things that are God's."

The spies had expected Jesus to answer their question directly, in one way or the other. If He should say, It is unlawful to give tribute to Caesar, He would be reported to the Roman authorities and arrested for inciting rebellion. But in case He should pronounce it lawful to pay the tribute, they designed to accuse Him to the people as opposing the law of God. Now they felt themselves baffled and defeated. Their plans were disarranged. The summary manner in which their question had been settled left them nothing further to say.

Christ's reply was no evasion, but a candid answer to the question. Holding in His hand the Roman coin, upon which were stamped the name and image of Caesar, He declared that since they were living under the protection of the Roman power, they should render to that power the support it claimed, so long as this did not conflict with a higher duty. But while peaceably subject to the laws of the land, they should at all times give their first allegiance to God.

The Saviour's words, "Render . . . unto God the things that are God's," were a severe rebuke to the intriguing Jews. Had they faithfully fulfilled their obligations to God, they would not have become a broken nation, subject to a foreign power. No Roman ensign would have waved over Jerusalem, no Roman sentinel would have stood at her gates, no Roman governor would have ruled within her walls. The Jewish nation was then paying the penalty of its apostasy from God.

When the Pharisees heard Christ's answer, "they marveled, and left Him, and went their way." He had rebuked their hypocrisy and presumption, and in doing this He had stated a great principle, a principle that clearly defines the limits of man's duty to the civil government and his duty to God. In many minds a vexed question had been settled. Ever after they held to the right principle. And although many went away dissatisfied, they saw that the principle underlying the question had been clearly set forth, and they marveled at Christ's far-seeing discernment.

No sooner were the Pharisees silenced than the Sadducees came forward with their artful questions. The two parties stood in bitter opposition to each other. The Pharisees were rigid adherents to tradition. They were exact in outward ceremonies, diligent in washings, fastings, and long prayers, and ostentatious in almsgiving. But Christ declared that they made void the law of God by teaching for doctrines the commandments of men. As a class they were bigoted and hypocritical; yet among them were persons of genuine piety, who accepted Christ's teachings and became His disciples. The Sadducees rejected the traditions of the Pharisees. They professed to believe the greater portion of the Scriptures, and to regard them as the rule of action; but practically they were skeptics and materialists.

The Sadducees denied the existence of angels, the resurrection of the dead, and the doctrine of a future life, with its rewards and punishments. On all these points they differed with the Pharisees. Between the two parties the resurrection was especially a subject of controversy. The Pharisees had been firm believers in the resurrection, but in these discussions their views in regard to the future state became confused. Death became to them an inexplicable mystery. Their inability to meet the arguments of the Sadducees gave rise to continual irritation. The discussions between the two parties usually resulted in angry disputes, leaving them farther apart than before.

In numbers the Sadducees fell far below their opponents, and they had not so strong a hold upon the common people; but many of them were wealthy, and they had the influence which wealth imparts. In their ranks were included most of the priests, and from among them the high priest was usually chosen. This was, however, with the express stipulation that their skeptical opinions should not be made prominent. On account of the numbers and popularity of the Pharisees, it was necessary for the Sadducees to concede outwardly to their doctrines when holding any priestly office; but the very fact that they were eligible to such office gave influence to their errors.

The Sadducees rejected the teaching of Jesus; He was animated by a spirit which they would not acknowledge as manifesting itself thus; and His teaching in regard to God and the future life contradicted their theories. They believed in God as the only being superior to man; but they argued that an overruling providence and a divine foresight would deprive man of free moral agency, and degrade him to the position of a slave. It was their belief, that, having created man, God had left him to himself, independent of a higher influence. They held that man was free to control his own life and to shape the events of the world; that his destiny was in his own hands.

They denied that the Spirit of God works through human efforts or natural means. Yet they still held that, through the proper employment of his natural powers, man could become elevated and enlightened; that by rigorous and austere exactions his life could be purified.

Their ideas of God molded their own character. As in their view He had no interest in man, so they had little regard for one another; there was little union among them. Refusing to acknowledge the influence of the Holy Spirit upon human action, they lacked His power in their lives. Like the rest of the Jews, they boasted much of their birthright as children of Abraham, and of their strict adherence to the requirements of the law; but of the true spirit of the law and the faith and benevolence of Abraham, they were destitute. Their natural sympathies were brought within a narrow compass. They believed it possible for all men to secure the comforts and blessings of life; and their hearts were not touched by the wants and sufferings of others. They lived for themselves.

By His words and His works, Christ testified to a divine power that produces supernatural results, to a future life beyond the present, to God as a Father of the children of men, ever watchful of their true interests. He revealed the working of divine power in benevolence and compassion that rebuked the selfish exclusiveness of the Sadducees. He taught that both for man's temporal and for his eternal good, God moves upon the heart by the Holy Spirit. He showed the error of trusting to human power for that transformation of character which can be wrought only by the Spirit of God.

This teaching the Sadducees were determined to discredit. In seeking a controversy with Jesus, they felt confident of bringing Him into disrepute, even if they could not secure His condemnation. The resurrection was the subject on which they chose to question Him. Should He agree with them, He would give still further offense to the Pharisees. Should He differ with them, they designed to hold His teaching up to ridicule.

The Sadducees reasoned that if the body is to be composed of the same particles of matter in its immortal as in its mortal state, then when raised from the dead it must have flesh and blood, and must resume in the eternal world the life interrupted on earth. In that case they concluded that earthly relationships would be resumed, husband and wife would be reunited, marriages consummated, and all things go on the same as before death, the frailties and passions of this life being perpetuated in the life beyond.

In answer to their questions, Jesus lifted the veil from the future life. "In the resurrection," He said, "they neither marry, nor are given in marriage, but are as the angels of God in heaven." He showed that the Sadducees were wrong in their belief. Their premises were false. "Ye do err," He added, "not knowing the Scriptures, nor the power of God." He did not charge them, as He had charged the Pharisees, with hypocrisy, but with error of belief.

The Sadducees had flattered themselves that they of all men adhered most strictly to the Scriptures. But Jesus showed that they had not known their true meaning. That knowledge must be brought home to the heart by the enlightenment of the Holy Spirit. Their ignorance of the Scriptures and the power of God He declared to be the cause of their confusion of faith and darkness of mind. They were seeking to bring the mysteries of God within the compass of their finite reasoning. Christ called upon them to open their minds to those sacred truths that would broaden and strengthen the understanding. Thousands become infidels because their finite minds cannot comprehend the mysteries of God. They cannot explain the wonderful exhibition of divine power in His providences, therefore they reject the evidences of such power, attributing them to natural agencies which they can comprehend still less. The only key to the mysteries that surround us is to acknowledge in them all the presence and power of God. Men need to recognize God as the Creator of the universe, One who commands and executes all things. They need a broader view of His character, and of the mystery of His agencies.

Christ declared to His hearers that if there were no resurrection of the dead, the Scriptures which they professed to believe would be of no avail. He said, "But as touching the resurrection of the dead, have ye not read that which was spoken unto you by God, saying, I am the God of Abraham, and the God of Isaac, and the God of Jacob? God is not the God of the dead, but of the living." God counts the things that are not as though they were. He sees the end from the beginning, and beholds the result of His work as though it were now accomplished. The precious dead, from Adam down to the last saint who dies, will hear the voice of the Son of God, and will come forth from the grave to immortal life. God will be their God, and they shall be His people. There will be a close and tender relationship between God and the risen saints. This condition, which is anticipated in His purpose, He beholds as if it were already existing. The dead live unto Him.

By the words of Christ the Sadducees were put to silence. They could not answer Him. Not a word had been spoken of which the least advantage could be taken for His condemnation. His adversaries had gained nothing but the contempt of the people.

The Pharisees, however, did not yet despair of driving Him to speak that which they could use against Him. They prevailed upon a certain learned scribe to question Jesus as to which of the ten precepts of the law was of the greatest importance.

The Pharisees had exalted the first four commandments, which point out the duty of man to his Maker, as of far greater consequence than the other six, which define man's duty to his fellow man. As the result, they greatly failed of practical godliness. Jesus had shown the people their great deficiency, and had taught the necessity of good works, declaring that the tree is known by its fruits. For this reason He had been charged with exalting the last six commandments above the first four.

The lawyer approached Jesus with a direct question,

"Which is the first commandment of all?" The answer of Christ is direct and forcible: "The first of all the commandments is, Hear, O Israel; The Lord our God is one Lord: and thou shalt love the Lord thy God with all thy heart, and with all thy soul, and with all thy mind, and with all thy strength: this is the first commandment." The second is like the first, said Christ; for it flows out of it, "Thou shalt love thy neighbor as thyself. There is none other commandment greater than these." "On these two commandments hang all the law and the prophets."

The first four of the Ten Commandments are summed up in the one great precept, "Thou shalt love the Lord thy God with all thy heart." The last six are included in the other, "Thou shalt love thy neighbor as thyself." Both these commandments are an expression of the principle of love. The first cannot be kept and the second broken, nor can the second be kept while the first is broken. When God has His rightful place on the throne of the heart, the right place will be given to our neighbor. We shall love him as ourselves. And only as we love God supremely is it possible to love our neighbor impartially.

And since all the commandments are summed up in love to God and man, it follows that not one precept can be broken without violating this principle. Thus Christ taught His hearers that the law of God is not so many separate precepts, some of which are of great importance, while others are of small importance and may with impunity be ignored. Our Lord presents the first four and the last six commandments as a divine whole, and teaches that love to God will be shown by obedience to all His commandments.

The scribe who had questioned Jesus was well read in the law, and he was astonished at His words. He did not expect Him to manifest so deep and thorough a knowledge of the Scriptures. He had gained a broader view of the principles underlying the sacred precepts. Before the assembled priests and rulers he honestly acknowledged that Christ had given the right interpretation to the law, saying:

"Well, Master, Thou hast said the truth: for there is one God; and there is none other but He: and to love Him with all the heart, and with all the understanding, and with all the soul, and with all the strength, and to love his neighbor as himself, is more than all whole burnt offerings and sacrifices."

The wisdom of Christ's answer had convicted the scribe. He knew that the Jewish religion consisted in outward ceremonies rather than inward piety. He had some sense of the worthlessness of mere ceremonial offerings, and the faithless shedding of blood for expiation of sin. Love and obedience to God, and unselfish regard for man, appeared to him of more value than all these rites. The readiness of this man to acknowledge the correctness of Christ's reasoning, and his decided and prompt response before the people, manifested a spirit entirely different from that of the priests and rulers. The heart of Jesus went out in pity to the honest scribe who had dared to face the frowns of the priests and the threats of the rulers to speak the convictions of his heart. "And when Jesus saw that he answered discreetly, He said unto him, Thou art not far from the kingdom of God."

The scribe was near to the kingdom of God, in that he recognized deeds of righteousness as more acceptable to God than burnt offerings and sacrifices. But he needed to recognize the divine character of Christ, and through faith in Him receive power to do the works of righteousness. The ritual service was of no value, unless connected with Christ by living faith. Even the moral law fails of its purpose, unless it is understood in its relation to the Saviour. Christ had repeatedly shown that His Father's law contained something deeper than mere authoritative commands. In the law is embodied the same principle that is revealed in the gospel. The law points out man's duty and shows him his guilt. To Christ he must look for pardon and for power to do what the law enjoins.

The Pharisees had gathered close about Jesus as He answered the question of the scribe. Now turning He put a question to them: "What think ye of Christ? whose son is He?" This question was designed to test their belief concerning the Messiah,—to show whether they regarded Him simply as a man or as the Son of God. A chorus of voices answered, "The Son of David." This was the title which prophecy had given to the Messiah. When Jesus revealed His divinity by His mighty miracles, when He healed the sick and raised the dead, the people had inquired among themselves, "Is not this the Son of David?" The Syrophoenician woman, blind Bartimaeus, and many others had cried to Him for help, "Have mercy on me, O Lord, Thou Son of David." Matt. 15:22. While riding into Jerusalem He had been hailed with the joyful shout, "Hosanna to the Son of David: Blessed is He that cometh in the name of the Lord." Matt. 21:9. And the little children in the temple had that day echoed the glad ascription. But many who called Jesus the Son of David did not recognize His divinity. They did not understand that the Son of David was also the Son of God.

In reply to the statement that Christ was the Son of David, Jesus said, "How then doth David in Spirit call Him Lord, saying, The Lord said unto my Lord, Sit Thou on My right hand, till I make Thine enemies Thy footstool? If David then call Him Lord, how is He his son? And no man was able to answer Him a word, neither durst any man from that day forth ask Him any more questions."

Woes on the Pharisees

It was the last day of Christ's teaching in the temple. Of the vast throngs that were gathered at Jerusalem, the attention of all had been attracted to Him; the people had crowded the temple courts, watching the contest that had been in progress, and they eagerly caught every word that fell from His lips. Never before had such a scene been witnessed. There stood the young Galilean, bearing no earthly honor or royal badge. Surrounding Him were priests in their rich apparel, rulers with robes and badges significant of their exalted station, and scribes with scrolls in their hands, to which they made frequent reference. Jesus stood calmly before them, with the dignity of a king. As one invested with the authority of heaven, He looked unflinchingly upon His adversaries, who had rejected and despised His teachings, and who thirsted for His life. They had assailed Him in great numbers, but their schemes to ensnare and condemn Him had been in vain. Challenge after challenge He had met, presenting the pure, bright truth in contrast to the darkness and errors of the priests and Pharisees. He had set before these leaders their real condition, and the retribution sure to follow persistence in their evil deeds. The warning had been faithfully given. Yet another work remained for Christ to do. Another purpose was still to be accomplished.

The interest of the people in Christ and His work had steadily increased. They were charmed with His teaching, but they were also greatly perplexed. They had respected the priests and rabbis for their intelligence and apparent piety. In all religious matters they had ever yielded implicit obedience to their authority. Yet they now saw these men trying to cast discredit upon Jesus, a teacher whose virtue and knowledge shone forth the brighter from every assault. They looked upon the lowering countenances of the priests and elders, and there saw discomfiture and confusion. They marveled that the rulers would not believe on Jesus, when His teachings were so plain and simple. They themselves knew not what course to take. With eager anxiety they watched the movements of those whose counsel they had always followed.

In the parables which Christ had spoken, it was His purpose both to warn the rulers and to instruct the people who were willing to be taught. But there was need to speak yet more plainly. Through their reverence for tradition and their blind faith in a corrupt priesthood, the people were enslaved. These chains Christ must break. The character of the priests, rulers, and Pharisees must be more fully exposed.

"The scribes and the Pharisees," He said, "sit in Moses' seat: all therefore whatsoever they bid you observe, that observe and do; but do not ye after their works: for they say, and do not." The scribes and Pharisees claimed to be invested with divine authority similar to that of Moses. They assumed to take his place as expounders of the law and judges of the people. As such they claimed from the people the utmost deference and obedience. Jesus bade His hearers do that which the rabbis taught according to the law, but not to follow their example. They themselves did not practice their own teaching.

And they taught much that was contrary to the Scriptures. Jesus said, "They bind heavy burdens and grievous to be borne, and lay them on men's shoulders; but they themselves will not move them with one of their fingers." The Pharisees enjoined a multitude of regulations, having their foundation in tradition, and unreasonably restricting personal liberty. And certain portions of the law they so explained as to impose upon the people observances which they themselves secretly ignored, and from which, when it served their purpose, they actually claimed exemption.

To make a show of their piety was their constant aim. Nothing was held too sacred to serve this end. To Moses God had said concerning His commandments, "Thou shalt bind them for a sign upon thine hand, and they shall be as frontlets between thine eyes." Deut. 6:8. These words have a deep meaning. As the word of God is meditated upon and practiced, the whole man will be ennobled. In righteous and merciful dealing, the hands will reveal, as a signet, the principles of God's law. They will be kept clean from bribes, and from all that is corrupt and deceptive. They will be active in works of love and compassion. The eyes, directed toward a noble purpose, will be clear and true. The expressive countenance, the speaking eye, will testify to the blameless character of him who loves and honors the word of God. But by the Jews of Christ's day all this was undiscerned. The command given to Moses was construed into a direction that the precepts of Scripture should be worn upon the person. They were accordingly written upon strips of parchment, and bound in a conspicuous manner about the head and wrists. But this did not cause the law of God to take a firmer hold of the mind and heart. These parchments were worn merely as badges, to attract attention. They were thought to give the wearers an air of devotion which would command the reverence of the people. Jesus struck a blow at this vain pretense:

"But all their works they do for to be seen of men: they make broad their phylacteries, and enlarge the borders of their garments, and love the uppermost rooms at feasts, and the chief seats in the synagogues, and greetings in the markets, and to be called of men, Rabbi, Rabbi. But be not ye called Rabbi: for one is your Master, even Christ; and all ye are brethren. And call no man your father upon the earth: for One is your Father, which is in heaven. Neither be ye called master: for One is your Master, even Christ." In such plain words the Saviour revealed the selfish ambition that was ever reaching for place and power, displaying a mock humility, while the heart was filled with avarice and envy. When persons were invited to a feast, the guests were seated according to their rank, and those who were given the most honorable place received the first attention and special favors. The Pharisees were ever scheming to secure these honors. This practice Jesus rebuked.

He also reproved the vanity shown in coveting the title of rabbi, or master. Such a title, He declared, belonged not to men, but to Christ. Priests, scribes, and rulers, expounders and administrators of the law, were all brethren, children of one Father. Jesus impressed upon the people that they were to give no man a title of honor indicating his control of their conscience or their faith.

If Christ were on earth today, surrounded by those who bear the title of "Reverend" or "Right Reverend," would He not repeat His saying, "Neither be ye called masters: for One is your Master, even Christ"? The Scripture declares of God, "Holy and reverend is His name." Ps. 111:9. To what human being is such a title befitting? How little does man reveal of the wisdom and righteousness it indicates! How many of those who assume this title are misrepresenting the name and character of God! Alas, how often have worldly ambition, despotism, and the basest sins been hidden under the broidered garments of a high and holy office! The Saviour continued:

"But he that is greatest among you shall be your servant. And whosoever shall exalt himself shall be abased; and he that shall humble himself shall be exalted." Again and again Christ had taught that true greatness is measured by moral worth. In the estimation of heaven, greatness of character consists in living for the welfare of our fellow men, in doing works of love and mercy. Christ the King of glory was a servant to fallen man.

"Woe unto you, scribes and Pharisees, hypocrites," said Jesus; "for ye shut up the kingdom of heaven against men: for ye neither go in yourselves, neither suffer ye them that are entering to go in." By perverting the Scriptures, the priests and lawyers blinded the minds of those who would otherwise have received a knowledge of Christ's kingdom, and that inward, divine life which is essential to true holiness.

"Woe unto you, scribes and Pharisees, hypocrites! for ye devour widows' houses, and for a pretense make long prayer: therefore ye shall receive the greater damnation." The Pharisees had great influence with the people, and of this they took advantage to serve their own interests. They gained the confidence of pious widows, and then represented it as a duty for them to devote their property to religious purposes. Having secured control of their money, the wily schemers used it for their own benefit. To cover their dishonesty, they offered long prayers in public, and made a great show of piety. This hypocrisy Christ declared would bring them the greater damnation. The same rebuke falls upon many in our day who make a high profession of piety. Their lives are stained by selfishness and avarice, yet they throw over it all a garment of seeming purity, and thus for a time deceive their fellow men. But they cannot deceive God. He reads every purpose of the heart, and will judge every man according to his deeds.

Christ unsparingly condemned abuses, but He was careful not to lessen obligation. He rebuked the selfishness that extorted and misapplied the widow's gifts. At the same time He commended the widow who brought her offering for God's treasury. Man's abuse of the gift could not turn God's blessing from the giver.

Jesus was in the court where were the treasure chests, and He watched those who came to deposit their gifts. Many of the rich brought large sums, which they presented with great ostentation. Jesus looked upon them sadly, but made no comment on their liberal offerings. Presently His countenance lighted as He saw a poor widow approach hesitatingly, as though fearful of being observed. As the rich and haughty swept by, to deposit their offerings, she shrank back as if hardly daring to venture farther. And yet she longed to do something, little though it might be, for the cause she loved.

She looked at the gift in her hand. It was very small in comparison with the gifts of those around her, yet it was her all. Watching her opportunity, she hurriedly threw in her two mites, and turned to hasten away. But in doing this she caught the eye of Jesus, which was fastened earnestly upon her.

The Saviour called His disciples to Him, and bade them mark the widow's poverty. Then His words of commendation fell upon her ear: "Of a truth I say unto you, that this poor widow hath cast in more than they all." Tears of joy filled her eyes as she felt that her act was understood and appreciated. Many would have advised her to keep her pittance for her own use; given into the hands of the well-fed priests, it would be lost sight of among the many costly gifts brought to the treasury. But Jesus understood her motive. She believed the service of the temple to be of God's appointment, and she was anxious to do her utmost to sustain it. She did what she could, and her act was to be a monument to her memory through all time, and her joy in eternity. Her heart went with her gift; its value was estimated, not by the worth of the coin, but by the love to God and the interest in His work that had prompted the deed.

Jesus said of the poor widow, She "hath cast in more than they all." The rich had bestowed from their abundance, many of them to be seen and honored by men. Their large donations had deprived them of no comfort, or even luxury; they had required no sacrifice, and could not be compared in value with the widow's mite.

It is the motive that gives character to our acts, stamping them with ignominy or with high moral worth. Not the great things which every eye sees and every tongue praises does God account most precious. The little duties cheerfully done, the little gifts which make no show, and which to human eyes may appear worthless, often stand highest in His sight. A heart of faith and love is dearer to God than the most costly gift. The poor widow gave her living to do the little that she did. She deprived herself of food in order to give those two mites to the cause she loved. And she did it in faith, believing that her heavenly Father would not overlook her great need. It was this unselfish spirit and childlike faith that won the Saviour's commendation.

Among the poor there are many who long to show their gratitude to God for His grace and truth. They greatly desire to share with their more prosperous brethren in sustaining His service. These souls should not be repulsed. Let them lay up their mites in the bank of heaven. If given from a heart filled with love for God, these seeming trifles become consecrated gifts, priceless offerings, which God smiles upon and blesses.

When Jesus said of the widow, She "hath cast in more than they all," His words were true, not only of the motive, but of the results of her gift. The "two mites which make a farthing" have brought to God's treasury an amount of money far greater than the contributions of those rich Jews. The influence of that little gift has been like a stream, small in its beginning, but widening and deepening as it flowed down through the ages. In a thousand ways it has contributed to the relief of the poor and the spread of the gospel. Her example of self-sacrifice has acted and reacted upon thousands of hearts in every land and in every age. It has appealed to both the rich and the poor, and their offerings have swelled the value of her gift. God's blessing upon the widow's mite has made it the source of great results. So with every gift bestowed and every act performed with a sincere desire for God's glory. It is linked with the purposes of Omnipotence. Its results for good no man can measure.

The Saviour continued His denunciations of the scribes and Pharisees: "Woe unto you, ye blind guides, which say, Whosoever shall swear by the temple, it is nothing; but whosoever shall swear by the gold of the temple, he is a debtor! Ye fools and blind: for whether is greater, the gold, or the temple that sanctifieth the gold? and, Whosoever shall swear by the altar, it is nothing; but whosoever sweareth by the gift that is upon it, he is guilty. Ye fools and blind: for whether is greater, the gift, or the altar that sanctifieth the gift?" The priests interpreted God's requirements according to their own false and narrow standard. They presumed to make nice distinctions as to the comparative guilt of various sins, passing over some lightly, and treating others of perhaps less consequence as unpardonable. For a money consideration they excused persons from their vows. And for large sums of money they sometimes passed over aggravated crimes. At the same time these priests and rulers would in other cases pronounce severe judgment for trivial offenses.

"Woe unto you, scribes and Pharisees, hypocrites! for ye pay tithe of mint and anise and cummin, and have omitted the weightier matters of the law, judgment, mercy, and faith: these ought ye to have done, and not to leave the other undone." In these words Christ again condemns the abuse of sacred obligation. The obligation itself He does not set aside. The tithing system was ordained by God, and it had been observed from the earliest times. Abraham, the father of the faithful, paid tithes of all that he possessed. The Jewish rulers recognized the obligation of tithing, and this was right; but they did not leave the people to carry out their own convictions of duty. Arbitrary rules were laid down for every case. The requirements had become so complicated that it was impossible for them to be fulfilled. None knew when their obligations were met. As God gave it, the system was just and reasonable; but the priests and rabbis had made it a wearisome burden.

All that God commands is of consequence. Christ recognized the payment of tithes as a duty; but He showed that this could not excuse the neglect of other duties. The Pharisees were very exact in tithing garden herbs, such as mint, anise, and rue; this cost them little, and it gave them a reputation for exactness and sanctity. At the same time their useless restrictions oppressed the people and destroyed respect for the sacred system of God's own appointing. They occupied men's minds with trifling distinctions, and turned their attention from essential truths. The weightier matters of the law, justice, mercy, and truth, were neglected. "These," Christ said, "ought ye to have done, and not to leave the other undone."

Other laws had been perverted by the rabbis in like manner. In the directions given through Moses it was forbidden to eat any unclean thing. The use of swine's flesh, and the flesh of certain other animals, was prohibited, as likely to fill the blood with impurities, and to shorten life. But the Pharisees did not leave these restrictions as God had given them. They went to unwarranted extremes. Among other things the people were required to strain all the water used, lest it should contain the smallest insect, which might be classed with the unclean animals. Jesus, contrasting these trivial exactions with the magnitude of their actual sins, said to the Pharisees, "Ye blind guides, which strain at a gnat, and swallow a camel."

"Woe unto you, scribes and Pharisees, hypocrites! for ye are like unto whited sepulchers, which indeed appear beautiful outward, but are within full of dead men's bones, and of all uncleanness." As the whited and beautifully decorated tomb concealed the putrefying remains within, so the outward holiness of the priests and rulers concealed iniquity. Jesus continued:

"Woe unto you, scribes and Pharisees, hypocrites! because ye build the tombs of the prophets, and garnish the sepulchers of the righteous, and say, If we had been in the days of our fathers, we would not have been partakers with them in the blood of the prophets. Wherefore ye be witnesses unto yourselves, that ye are the children of them which killed the prophets." To show their esteem for the dead prophets, the Jews were very zealous in beautifying their tombs; but they did not profit by their teachings, nor give heed to their reproofs.

In the days of Christ a superstitious regard was cherished for the resting places of the dead, and vast sums of money were lavished upon their decoration. In the sight of God this was idolatry. In their undue regard for the dead, men showed that they did not love God supremely, nor their neighbor as themselves. The same idolatry is carried to great lengths today. Many are guilty of neglecting the widow and the fatherless, the sick and the poor, in order to build expensive monuments for the dead. Time, money, and labor are freely spent for this purpose, while duties to the living—duties which Christ has plainly enjoined—are left undone.

The Pharisees built the tombs of the prophets, and adorned their sepulchers, and said one to another, If we had lived in the days of our fathers, we would not have united with them in shedding the blood of God's servants. At the same time they were planning to take the life of His Son. This should be a lesson to us. It should open our eyes to the power of Satan to deceive the mind that turns from the light of truth. Many follow in the track of the Pharisees. They revere those who have died for their faith. They wonder at the blindness of the Jews in rejecting Christ. Had we lived in His day, they declare, we would gladly have received His teaching; we would never have been partakers in the guilt of those who rejected the Saviour. But when obedience to God requires self-denial and humiliation, these very persons stifle their convictions, and refuse obedience. Thus they manifest the same spirit as did the Pharisees whom Christ condemned.

Little did the Jews realize the terrible responsibility involved in rejecting Christ. From the time when the first innocent blood was shed, when righteous Abel fell by the hand of Cain, the same history had been repeated, with increasing guilt. In every age prophets had lifted up their voices against the sins of kings, rulers, and people, speaking the words which God gave them, and obeying His will at the peril of their lives. From generation to generation there had been heaping up a terrible punishment for the rejecters of light and truth. This the enemies of Christ were now drawing down upon their own heads. The sin of the priests and rulers was greater than that of any preceding generation. By their rejection of the Saviour, they were making themselves responsible for the blood of all the righteous men slain from Abel to Christ. They were about to fill to overflowing their cup of iniquity. And soon it was to be poured upon their heads in retributive justice. Of this, Jesus warned them:

"That upon you may come all the righteous blood shed upon the earth, from the blood of righteous Abel unto the blood of Zacharias son of Barachias, whom ye slew between the temple and the altar. Verily I say unto you, All these things shall come upon this generation."

The scribes and Pharisees who listened to Jesus knew that His words were true. They knew how the prophet Zacharias had been slain. While the words of warning from God were upon his lips, a satanic fury seized the apostate king, and at his command the prophet was put to death. His blood had imprinted itself upon the very stones of the temple court, and could not be erased; it remained to bear testimony against apostate Israel. As long as the temple should stand, there would be the stain of that righteous blood, crying to God to be avenged. As Jesus referred to these fearful sins, a thrill of horror ran through the multitude.

Looking forward, Jesus declared that the impenitence of the Jews and their intolerance of God's servants would be the same in the future as it had been in the past:

"Wherefore, behold, I send unto you prophets, and wise men, and scribes: and some of them ye shall kill and crucify; and some of them shall ye scourge in your synagogues, and persecute them from city to city." Prophets and wise men, full of faith and the Holy Ghost,—Stephen, James, and many others,—would be condemned and slain. With hand uplifted to heaven, and a divine light enshrouding His person, Christ spoke as a judge to those before Him. His voice, that had so often been heard in gentleness and entreaty, was now heard in rebuke and condemnation. The listeners shuddered. Never was the impression made by His words and His look to be effaced.

Christ's indignation was directed against the hypocrisy, the gross sins, by which men were destroying their own souls, deceiving the people and dishonoring God. In the specious deceptive reasoning of the priests and rulers He discerned the working of satanic agencies. Keen and searching had been His denunciation of sin; but He spoke no words of retaliation. He had a holy wrath against the prince of darkness; but He manifested no irritated temper. So the Christian who lives in harmony with God, possessing the sweet attributes of love and mercy, will feel a righteous indignation against sin; but he will not be roused by passion to revile those who revile him. Even in meeting those who are moved by a power from beneath to maintain falsehood, in Christ he will still preserve calmness and self-possession.

Divine pity marked the countenance of the Son of God as He cast one lingering look upon the temple and then upon His hearers. In a voice choked by deep anguish of heart and bitter tears He exclaimed, "O Jerusalem, Jerusalem, thou that killest the prophets, and stonest them which are sent unto thee, how often would I have gathered thy children together, even as a hen gathereth her chickens under her wings, and ye would not!" This is the separation struggle. In the lamentation of Christ the very heart of God is pouring itself forth. It is the mysterious farewell of the long-suffering love of the Deity.

Pharisees and Sadducees were alike silenced. Jesus summoned His disciples, and prepared to leave the temple, not as one defeated and forced from the presence of his adversaries, but as one whose work was accomplished. He retired a victor from the contest.

The gems of truth that fell from Christ's lips on that eventful day were treasured in many hearts. For them new thoughts started into life, new aspirations were awakened, and a new history began. After the crucifixion and resurrection of Christ, these persons came to the front, and fulfilled their divine commission with a wisdom and zeal corresponding to the greatness of the work. They bore a message that appealed to the hearts of men, weakening the old superstitions that had long dwarfed the lives of thousands. Before their testimony human theories and philosophies became as idle fables. Mighty were the results flowing from the words of the Saviour to that wondering, awestruck crowd in the temple at Jerusalem.

But Israel as a nation had divorced herself from God. The natural branches of the olive tree were broken off. Looking for the last time upon the interior of the temple, Jesus said with mournful pathos, "Behold, your house is left unto you desolate. For I say unto you, Ye shall not see Me henceforth, till ye shall say, Blessed is He that cometh in the name of the Lord." Hitherto He had called the temple His Father's house; but now, as the Son of God should pass out from those walls, God's presence would be withdrawn forever from the temple built to His glory. Henceforth its ceremonies would be meaningless, its services a mockery.

In the Outer Court

And there were certain Greeks among them that came up to worship at the feast: the same came therefore to Philip, which was of Bethsaida of Galilee, and desired him, saying, Sir, we would see Jesus. Philip cometh and telleth Andrew: and again Andrew and Philip tell Jesus."

At this time Christ's work bore the appearance of cruel defeat. He had been victor in the controversy with the priests and Pharisees, but it was evident that He would never be received by them as the Messiah. The final separation had come. To His disciples the case seemed hopeless. But Christ was approaching the consummation of His work. The great event which concerned not only the Jewish nation, but the whole world, was about to take place. When Christ heard the eager request, "We would see Jesus," echoing the hungering cry of the world, His countenance lighted up, and He said, "The hour is come, that the Son of man should be glorified." In the request of the Greeks He saw an earnest of the results of His great sacrifice.

These men came from the West to find the Saviour at the close of His life, as the wise men had come from the East at the beginning. At the time of Christ's birth the Jewish people were so engrossed with their own ambitious plans that they knew not of His advent. The magi from a heathen land came to the manger with their gifts, to worship the Saviour. So these Greeks, representing the nations, tribes, and peoples of the world, came to see Jesus. So the people of all lands and all ages would be drawn by the Saviour's cross. So shall many "come from the east and west, and shall sit down with Abraham, and Isaac, and Jacob, in the kingdom of heaven." Matt. 8:11.

The Greeks had heard of Christ's triumphal entry into Jerusalem. Some supposed, and had circulated the report, that He had driven the priests and rulers from the temple, and that He was to take possession of David's throne, and reign as king of Israel. The Greeks longed to know the truth in regard to His mission. "We would see Jesus," they said. Their desire was granted. When the request was brought to Jesus, He was in that part of the temple from which all except Jews were excluded, but He went out to the Greeks in the outer court, and had a personal interview with them.

The hour of Christ's glorification had come. He was standing in the shadow of the cross, and the inquiry of the Greeks showed Him that the sacrifice He was about to make would bring many sons and daughters to God. He knew that the Greeks would soon see Him in a position they did not then dream of. They would see Him placed beside Barabbas, a robber and murderer, who would be chosen for release before the Son of God. They would hear the people, inspired by the priests and rulers, making their choice. And to the question, "What shall I do then with Jesus which is called Christ?" the answer would be given, "Let Him be crucified." Matt. 27:22. By making this propitiation for the sins of men, Christ knew that His kingdom would be perfected, and would extend throughout the world. He would work as the Restorer, and His Spirit would prevail. For a moment He looked into futurity, and heard the voices proclaiming in all parts of the earth, "Behold the Lamb of God, which taketh away the sin of the world." John 1:29. In these strangers He saw the pledge of a great harvest, when the partition wall between Jew and Gentile should be broken down, and all nations, tongues, and peoples should hear the message of salvation. The anticipation of this, the consummation of His hopes, is expressed in the words, "The hour is come, that the Son of man should be glorified." But the way in which this glorification must take place was never absent from Christ's mind. The gathering in of the Gentiles was to follow His approaching death. Only by His death could the world be saved. Like a grain of wheat, the Son of man must be cast into the ground and die, and be buried out of sight; but He was to live again.

Christ presented His future, illustrating it by the things of nature, that the disciples might understand. The true result of His mission was to be reached by His death. "Verily, verily, I say unto you," He said, "Except a corn of wheat fall into the ground and die, it abideth alone: but if it die, it bringeth forth much fruit." When the grain of wheat falls into the ground and dies, it springs up, and bears fruit. So the death of Christ would result in fruit for the kingdom of God. In accordance with the law of the vegetable kingdom, life was to be the result of His death.

Those who till the soil have the illustration ever before them. Year by year man preserves his supply of grain by apparently throwing away the choicest part. For a time it must be hidden under the furrow, to be watched over by the Lord. Then appears the blade, then the ear, and then the corn in the ear. But this development cannot take place unless the grain is buried out of sight, hidden, and to all appearance, lost.

The seed buried in the ground produces fruit, and in turn this is planted. Thus the harvest is multiplied. So the death of Christ on the cross of Calvary will bear fruit unto eternal life. The contemplation of this sacrifice will be the glory of those who, as the fruit of it, will live through the eternal ages.

The grain of wheat that preserves its own life can produce no fruit. It abides alone. Christ could, if He chose, save Himself from death. But should He do this, He must abide alone. He could bring no sons and daughters to God. Only by yielding up His life could He impart life to humanity. Only by falling into the ground to die could He become the seed of that vast harvest,—the great multitude that out of every nation, and kindred, and tongue, and people, are redeemed to God.

With this truth Christ connects the lesson of self-sacrifice that all should learn: "He that loveth his life shall lose it; and he that hateth his life in this world shall keep it unto life eternal." All who would bring forth fruit as workers together with Christ must first fall into the ground and die. The life must be cast into the furrow of the world's need. Self-love, self-interest, must perish. And the law of self-sacrifice is the law of self-preservation. The husbandman preserves his grain by casting it away. So in human life. To give is to live. The life that will be preserved is the life that is freely given in service to God and man. Those who for Christ's sake sacrifice their life in this world will keep it unto life eternal.

The life spent on self is like the grain that is eaten. It disappears, but there is no increase. A man may gather all he can for self; he may live and think and plan for self; but his life passes away, and he has nothing. The law of self-serving is the law of self-destruction.

"If any man serve Me," said Jesus, "let him follow Me; and where I am, there shall also My servant be: if any man serve Me, him will My Father honor." All who have borne with Jesus the cross of sacrifice will be sharers with Him of His glory. It was the joy of Christ in His humiliation and pain that His disciples should be glorified with Him. They are the fruit of His self-sacrifice. The outworking in them of His own character and spirit is His reward, and will be His joy throughout eternity. This joy they share with Him as the fruit of their labor and sacrifice is seen in other hearts and lives. They are workers together with Christ, and the Father will honor them as He honors His Son.

The message of the Greeks, foreshadowing as it did the gathering in of the Gentiles, brought to the mind of Jesus His entire mission. The work of redemption passed before Him, from the time when in heaven the plan was laid, to the death that was now so near at hand. A mysterious cloud seemed to enshroud the Son of God. Its gloom was felt by those near Him. He sat rapt in thought. At last the silence was broken by His mournful voice, "Now is My soul troubled; and what shall I say? Father, save Me from this hour?" In anticipation Christ was already drinking the cup of bitterness. His humanity shrank from the hour of abandonment, when to all appearance He would be deserted even by God, when all would see Him stricken, smitten of God, and afflicted. He shrank from public exposure, from being treated as the worst of criminals, from a shameful and dishonored death. A foreboding of His conflict with the powers of darkness, a sense of the awful burden of human transgression, and the Father's wrath because of sin caused the spirit of Jesus to faint, and the pallor of death to overspread His countenance.

Then came divine submission to His Father's will. "For this cause," He said, "came I unto this hour. Father, glorify Thy name." Only through the death of Christ could Satan's kingdom be overthrown. Only thus could man be redeemed, and God be glorified. Jesus consented to the agony, He accepted the sacrifice. The Majesty of heaven consented to suffer as the Sin Bearer. "Father, glorify Thy name," He said. As Christ spoke these words, a response came from the cloud which hovered above His head: "I have both glorified it, and will glorify it again." Christ's whole life, from the manger to the time when these words were spoken, had glorified God; and in the coming trial His divine-human sufferings would indeed glorify His Father's name.

As the voice was heard, a light darted from the cloud, and encircled Christ, as if the arms of Infinite Power were thrown about Him like a wall of fire. The people beheld this scene with terror and amazement. No one dared to speak. With silent lips and bated breath all stood with eyes fixed upon Jesus. The testimony of the Father having been given, the cloud lifted, and scattered in the heavens. For the time the visible communion between the Father and the Son was ended.

"The people therefore, that stood by, and heard it, said that it thundered: others said, An angel spake to Him." But the inquiring Greeks saw the cloud, heard the voice, comprehended its meaning, and discerned Christ indeed; to them He was revealed as the Sent of God.

The voice of God had been heard at the baptism of Jesus at the beginning of His ministry, and again at His transfiguration on the mount. Now at the close of His ministry it was heard for the third time, by a larger number of persons, and under peculiar circumstances. Jesus had just spoken the most solemn truth regarding the condition of the Jews. He had made His last appeal, and pronounced their doom. Now God again set His seal to the mission of His Son. He recognized the One whom Israel had rejected. "This voice came not because of Me," said Jesus, "but for your sakes." It was the crowning evidence of His Messiahship, the signal from the Father that Jesus had spoken the truth, and was the Son of God.

"Now is the judgment of this world," Christ continued; "now shall the prince of this world be cast out. And I, if I be lifted up from the earth, will draw all unto Me. This He said, signifying what death He should die." This is the crisis of the world. If I become the propitiation for the sins of men, the world will be lighted up. Satan's hold upon the souls of men will be broken. The defaced image of God will be restored in humanity, and a family of believing saints will finally inherit the heavenly home. This is the result of Christ's death. The Saviour is lost in contemplation of the scene of triumph called up before Him. He sees the cross, the cruel, ignominious cross, with all its attending horrors, blazing with glory.

But the work of human redemption is not all that is accomplished by the cross. The love of God is manifested to the universe. The prince of this world is cast out. The accusations which Satan has brought against God are refuted. The reproach which he has cast upon heaven is forever removed. Angels as well as men are drawn to the Redeemer. "I, if I be lifted up from the earth," He said, "will draw all unto Me."

Many people were round about Christ as He spoke these words, and one said, "We have heard out of the law that Christ abideth forever: and how sayest Thou, The Son of man must be lifted up? who is this Son of man? Then Jesus said unto them, Yet a little while is the light with you. Walk while ye have the light, lest darkness come upon you: for he that walketh in darkness knoweth not whither he goeth. While ye have light, believe in the light, that ye may be the children of light."

"But though He had done so many miracles before them, yet they believed not on Him." They had once asked the Saviour, "What sign showest Thou then, that we may see, and believe Thee?" John 6:30. Innumerable signs had been given; but they had closed their eyes and hardened their hearts. Now that the Father Himself had spoken, and they could ask for no further sign, they still refused to believe.

"Nevertheless among the chief rulers also many believed on Him; but because of the Pharisees they did not confess Him, lest they should be put out of the synagogue." They loved the praise of men rather than the approval of God. To save themselves from reproach and shame, they denied Christ, and rejected the offer of eternal life. And how many through all the centuries since have been doing the same thing! To them all the Saviour's warning words apply: "He that loveth his life shall lose it." "He that rejecteth Me," said Jesus, "and receiveth not My words, hath one that judgeth him: the word that I have spoken, the same shall judge him in the last day." John 12:48.

Alas for those who knew not the time of their visitation! Slowly and regretfully Christ left forever the precincts of the temple.

On the Mount of Olives

Christ's words to the priests and rulers, "Behold, your house is left unto you desolate" (Matt. 23:38), had struck terror to their hearts. They affected indifference, but the question kept rising in their minds as to the import of these words. An unseen danger seemed to threaten them. Could it be that the magnificent temple, which was the nation's glory, was soon to be a heap of ruins? The foreboding of evil was shared by the disciples, and they anxiously waited for some more definite statement from Jesus. As they passed with Him out of the temple, they called His attention to its strength and beauty. The stones of the temple were of the purest marble, of perfect whiteness, and some of them of almost fabulous size. A portion of the wall had withstood the siege by Nebuchadnezzar's army. In its perfect masonry it appeared like one solid stone dug entire from the quarry. How those mighty walls could be overthrown the disciples could not comprehend.

As Christ's attention was attracted to the magnificence of the temple, what must have been the unuttered thoughts of that Rejected One! The view before Him was indeed beautiful, but He said with sadness, I see it all. The buildings are indeed wonderful. You point to these walls as apparently indestructible; but listen to My words: The day will come when "there shall not be left one stone upon another, that shall not be thrown down."

Christ's words had been spoken in the hearing of a large number of people; but when He was alone, Peter, John, James, and Andrew came to Him as He sat upon the Mount of Olives. "Tell us," they said, "when shall these things be? and what shall be the sign of Thy coming, and of the end of the world?" Jesus did not answer His disciples by taking up separately the destruction of Jerusalem and the great day of His coming. He mingled the description of these two events. Had He opened to His disciples future events as He beheld them, they would have been unable to endure the sight. In mercy to them He blended the description of the two great crises, leaving the disciples to study out the meaning for themselves. When He referred to the destruction of Jerusalem, His prophetic words reached beyond that event to the final conflagration in that day when the Lord shall rise out of His place to punish the world for their iniquity, when the earth shall disclose her blood, and shall no more cover her slain. This entire discourse was given, not for the disciples only, but for those who should live in the last scenes of this earth's history.

Turning to the disciples, Christ said, "Take heed that no man deceive you. For many shall come in My name, saying, I am Christ; and shall deceive many." Many false messiahs will appear, claiming to work miracles, and declaring that the time of the deliverance of the Jewish nation has come. These will mislead many. Christ's words were fulfilled. Between His death and the siege of Jerusalem many false messiahs appeared. But this warning was given also to those who live in this age of the world. The same deceptions practiced prior to the destruction of Jerusalem have been practiced through the ages, and will be practiced again.

"And ye shall hear of wars and rumors of wars: see that ye be not troubled: for all these things must come to pass, but the end is not yet." Prior to the destruction of Jerusalem, men wrestled for the supremacy. Emperors were murdered. Those supposed to be standing next the throne were slain. There were wars and rumors of wars. "All these things must come to pass," said Christ, "but the end is not yet. For nation shall rise against nation, and kingdom against kingdom: and there shall be famines, and pestilences, and earthquakes, in divers places. All these are the beginning of sorrows." Christ said, As the rabbis see these signs, they will declare them to be God's judgments upon the nations for holding in bondage His chosen people. They will declare that these signs are the token of the advent of the Messiah. Be not deceived; they are the beginning of His judgments. The people have looked to themselves. They have not repented and been converted that I should heal them. The signs that they represent as tokens of their release from bondage are signs of their destruction.

"Then shall they deliver you up to be afflicted, and shall kill you: and ye shall be hated of all nations for My name's sake. And then shall many be offended, and shall betray one another, and shall hate one another." All this the Christians suffered. Fathers and mothers betrayed their children. Children betrayed their parents. Friends delivered their friends up to the Sanhedrin. The persecutors wrought out their purpose by killing Stephen, James, and other Christians.

Through His servants, God gave the Jewish people a last opportunity to repent. He manifested Himself through His witnesses in their arrest, in their trial, and in their imprisonment. Yet their judges pronounced on them the death sentence. They were men of whom the world was not worthy, and by killing them the Jews crucified afresh the Son of God. So it will be again. The authorities will make laws to restrict religious liberty. They will assume the right that is God's alone. They will think they can force the conscience, which God alone should control. Even now they are making a beginning; this work they will continue to carry forward till they reach a boundary over which they cannot step. God will interpose in behalf of His loyal, commandment-keeping people.

On every occasion when persecution takes place, those who witness it make decisions either for Christ or against Him. Those who manifest sympathy for the ones wrongly condemned show their attachment for Christ. Others are offended because the principles of truth cut directly across their practice. Many stumble and fall, apostatizing from the faith they once advocated. Those who apostatize in time of trial will, to secure their own safety, bear false witness, and betray their brethren. Christ has warned us of this, that we may not be surprised at the unnatural, cruel course of those who reject the light.

Christ gave His disciples a sign of the ruin to come on Jerusalem, and He told them how to escape: "When ye shall see Jerusalem compassed with armies, then know that the desolation thereof is nigh. Then let them which are in Judea flee to the mountains; and let them which are in the midst of it depart out; and let not them that are in the countries enter thereinto. For these be the days of vengeance, that all things which are written may be fulfilled." This warning was given to be heeded forty years after, at the destruction of Jerusalem. The Christians obeyed the warning, and not a Christian perished in the fall of the city.

"Pray ye that your flight be not in the winter; neither on the Sabbath day," Christ said. He who made the Sabbath did not abolish it, nailing it to His cross. The Sabbath was not rendered null and void by His death. Forty years after His crucifixion it was still to be held sacred. For forty years the disciples were to pray that their flight might not be on the Sabbath day.

From the destruction of Jerusalem, Christ passed on rapidly to the greater event, the last link in the chain of this earth's history,—the coming of the Son of God in majesty and glory. Between these two events, there lay open to Christ's view long centuries of darkness, centuries for His church marked with blood and tears and agony. Upon these scenes His disciples could not then endure to look, and Jesus passed them by with a brief mention. "Then shall be great tribulation," He said, "such as was not since the beginning of the world to this time, no, nor ever shall be. And except those days should be shortened, there should no flesh be saved: but for the elect's sake those days shall be shortened." For more than a thousand years such persecution as the world had never before known was to come upon Christ's followers. Millions upon millions of His faithful witnesses were to be slain. Had not God's hand been stretched out to preserve His people, all would have perished. "But for the elect's sake," He said, "those days shall be shortened."

Now, in unmistakable language, our Lord speaks of His second coming, and He gives warning of dangers to precede His advent to the world. "If any man shall say unto you, Lo, here is Christ, or there; believe it not. For there shall arise false christs, and false prophets, and shall show great signs and wonders; insomuch that, if it were possible, they shall deceive the very elect. Behold, I have told you before. Wherefore if they shall say unto you, Behold, He is in the desert; go not forth: behold, He is in the secret chambers; believe it not. For as the lightning cometh out of the east, and shineth even unto the west; so shall also the coming of the Son of man be." As one of the signs of Jerusalem's destruction, Christ had said, "Many false prophets shall rise, and shall deceive many." False prophets did rise, deceiving the people, and leading great numbers into the desert. Magicians and sorcerers, claiming miraculous power, drew the people after them into the mountain solitudes. But this prophecy was spoken also for the last days. This sign is given as a sign of the second advent. Even now false christs and false prophets are showing signs and wonders to seduce His disciples. Do we not hear the cry, "Behold, He is in the desert"? Have not thousands gone forth into the desert, hoping to find Christ? And from thousands of gatherings where men profess to hold communion with departed spirits is not the call now heard, "Behold, He is in the secret chambers"? This is the very claim that spiritism puts forth. But what says Christ? "Believe it not. For as the lightning cometh out of the east, and shineth even unto the west; so shall also the coming of the Son of man be."

The Saviour gives signs of His coming, and more than this, He fixes the time when the first of these signs shall appear: "Immediately after the tribulation of those days shall the sun be darkened, and the moon shall not give her light, and the stars shall fall from heaven, and the powers of the heavens shall be shaken: and then shall appear the sign of the Son of man in heaven: and then shall all the tribes of the earth mourn, and they shall see the Son of man coming in the clouds of heaven with power and great glory. And He shall send His angels with a great sound of a trumpet, and they shall gather together His elect from the four winds, from one end of heaven to the other."

At the close of the great papal persecution, Christ declared, the sun should be darkened, and the moon should not give her light. Next, the stars should fall from heaven. And He says, "Learn a parable of the fig tree; When his branch is yet tender, and putteth forth leaves, ye know that summer is nigh: so likewise ye, when ye shall see all these things, know that He is near, even at the doors." Matt. 24:32, 33, margin.

Christ has given signs of His coming. He declares that we may know when He is near, even at the doors. He says of those who see these signs, "This generation shall not pass, till all these things be fulfilled." These signs have appeared. Now we know of a surety that the Lord's coming is at hand. "Heaven and earth shall pass away," He says, "but My words shall not pass away."

Christ is coming with clouds and with great glory. A multitude of shining angels will attend Him. He will come to raise the dead, and to change the living saints from glory to glory. He will come to honor those who have loved Him, and kept His commandments, and to take them to Himself. He has not forgotten them nor His promise. There will be a relinking of the family chain. When we look upon our dead, we may think of the morning when the trump of God shall sound, when "the dead shall be raised incorruptible, and we

shall be changed." 1 Cor. 15:52. A little longer, and we shall see the King in His beauty. A little longer, and He will wipe all tears from our eyes. A little longer, and He will present us "faultless before the presence of His glory with exceeding joy." Jude 24. Wherefore, when He gave the signs of His coming He said, "When these things begin to come to pass, then look up, and lift up your heads; for your redemption draweth nigh."

But the day and the hour of His coming Christ has not revealed. He stated plainly to His disciples that He Himself could not make known the day or the hour of His second appearing. Had He been at liberty to reveal this, why need He have exhorted them to maintain an attitude of constant expectancy? There are those who claim to know the very day and hour of our Lord's appearing. Very earnest are they in mapping out the future. But the Lord has warned them off the ground they occupy. The exact time of the second coming of the Son of man is God's mystery.

Christ continues, pointing out the condition of the world at His coming: "As the days of Noah were, so shall also the coming of the Son of man be. For as in the days that were before the Flood they were eating and drinking, marrying and giving in marriage, until the day that Noah entered into the ark, and knew not until the Flood came, and took them all away; so shall also the coming of the Son of man be." Christ does not here bring to view a temporal millennium, a thousand years in which all are to prepare for eternity. He tells us that as it was in Noah's day, so will it be when the Son of man comes again.

How was it in Noah's day? "God saw that the wickedness of man was great in the earth, and that every imagination of the thoughts of his heart was only evil continually." Gen. 6:5. The inhabitants of the antediluvian world turned from Jehovah, refusing to do His holy will. They followed their own unholy imagination and perverted ideas. It was because of their wickedness that they were destroyed; and today the world is following the same way. It presents no flattering signs of millennial glory. The transgressors of God's law are filling the earth with wickedness. Their betting, their horse racing, their gambling, their dissipation, their lustful practices, their untamable passions, are fast filling the world with violence.

In the prophecy of Jerusalem's destruction Christ said, "Because iniquity shall abound, the love of many shall wax cold. But he that shall endure unto the end, the same shall be saved. And this gospel of the kingdom shall be preached in all the world for a witness unto all nations; and then shall the end come." This prophecy will again be fulfilled. The abounding iniquity of that day finds its counterpart in this generation. So with the prediction in regard to the preaching of the gospel. Before the fall of Jerusalem, Paul, writing by the Holy Spirit, declared that the gospel was preached to "every creature which is under heaven." Col. 1:23. So now, before the coming of the Son of man, the everlasting gospel is to be preached "to every nation, and kindred, and tongue, and people." Rev. 14:6, 14. God "hath appointed a day, in the which He will judge the world." Acts 17:31. Christ tells us when that day shall be ushered in. He does not say that all the world will be converted, but that "this gospel of the kingdom shall be preached in all the world for a witness unto all nations; and then shall the end come." By giving the gospel to the world it is in our power to hasten our Lord's return. We are not only to look for but to hasten the coming of the day of God. 2 Peter 3:12, margin. Had the church of Christ done her appointed work as the Lord ordained, the whole world would before this have been warned, and the Lord Jesus would have come to our earth in power and great glory.

After He had given the signs of His coming, Christ said, "When ye see these things come to pass, know ye that the kingdom of God is nigh at hand." "Take ye heed, watch and pray." God has always given men warning of coming judgments. Those who had faith in His message for their time, and who acted out their faith, in obedience to His commandments, escaped the judgments that fell upon the disobedient and unbelieving. The word came to Noah, "Come thou and all thy house into the ark; for thee have I seen righteous before Me." Noah obeyed and was saved. The message came to Lot, "Up, get you out of this place; for the Lord will destroy this city." Gen. 7:1; 19:14. Lot placed himself under the guardianship of the heavenly messengers, and was saved. So Christ's disciples were given warning of the destruction of Jerusalem. Those who watched for the sign of the coming ruin, and fled from the city, escaped the destruction. So now we are given warning of Christ's second coming and of the destruction to fall upon the world. Those who heed the warning will be saved.

Because we know not the exact time of His coming, we are commanded to watch. "Blessed are those servants, whom the Lord when He cometh shall find watching." Luke 12:37. Those who watch for the Lord's coming are not waiting in idle expectancy. The expectation of Christ's coming is to make men fear the Lord, and fear His judgments upon transgression. It is to awaken them to the great sin of rejecting His offers of mercy. Those who are watching for the Lord are purifying their souls by obedience to the truth. With vigilant watching they combine earnest working. Because they know that the Lord is at the door, their zeal is quickened to co-operate with the divine intelligences in working for the salvation of souls. These are the faithful and wise servants who give to the Lord's household "their portion of meat in due season." Luke 12:42. They are declaring the truth that is now specially applicable. As Enoch, Noah, Abraham, and Moses each declared the truth for his time, so will Christ's servants now give the special warning for their generation.

But Christ brings to view another class: "If that evil servant shall say in his heart, My lord delayeth his coming; and shall begin to smite his fellow servants, and to eat and drink with the drunken; the lord of that servant shall come in a day when he looketh not for him."

The evil servant says in his heart, "My lord delayeth his coming." He does not say that Christ will not come. He does not scoff at the idea of His second coming. But in his heart and by his actions and words he declares that the Lord's coming is delayed. He banishes from the minds of others the conviction that the Lord is coming quickly. His influence leads men to presumptuous, careless delay. They are confirmed in their worldliness and stupor. Earthly passions, corrupt thoughts, take possession of the mind. The evil servant eats and drinks with the drunken, unites with the world in pleasure seeking. He smites his fellow servants, accusing and condemning those who are faithful to their Master. He mingles with the world. Like grows with like in transgression. It is a fearful assimilation. With the world he is taken in the snare. "The lord of that servant shall come . . . in an hour that he is not aware of, and shall cut him asunder, and appoint him his portion with the hypocrites."

"If therefore thou shalt not watch, I will come on thee as a thief, and thou shalt not know what hour I will come upon thee." Rev. 3:3. The advent of Christ will surprise the false teachers. They are saying, "Peace and safety." Like the priests and teachers before the fall of Jerusalem, they look for the church to enjoy earthly prosperity and glory. The signs of the times they interpret as foreshadowing this. But what saith the word of Inspiration? "Sudden destruction cometh upon them." 1 Thess. 5:3. Upon all who dwell on the face of the whole earth, upon all who make this world their home, the day of God will come as a snare. It comes to them as a prowling thief.

The world, full of rioting, full of godless pleasure, is asleep, asleep in carnal security. Men are putting afar off the coming of the Lord. They laugh at warnings. The proud boast is made, "All things continue as they were from the beginning." "Tomorrow shall be as this day, and much more abundant." 2 Peter 3:4; Isa. 56:12. We will go deeper into pleasure loving. But Christ says, "Behold, I come as a thief." Rev. 16:15. At the very time when the world is asking in scorn, "Where is the promise of His coming?" the signs are fulfilling. While they cry, "Peace and safety," sudden destruction is coming. When the scorner, the rejecter of truth, has become presumptuous; when the routine of work in the various money-making lines is carried on without regard to principle; when the student is eagerly seeking knowledge of everything but his Bible, Christ comes as a thief.

Everything in the world is in agitation. The signs of the times are ominous. Coming events cast their shadows before. The Spirit of God is withdrawing from the earth, and calamity follows calamity by sea and by land. There are tempests, earthquakes, fires, floods, murders of every grade. Who can read the future? Where is security? There is assurance in nothing that is human or earthly. Rapidly are men ranging themselves under the banner they have chosen. Restlessly are they waiting and watching the movements of their leaders. There are those who are waiting and watching and working for our Lord's appearing. Another class are falling into line under the generalship of the first great apostate. Few believe with heart and soul that we have a hell to shun and a heaven to win.

The crisis is stealing gradually upon us. The sun shines in the heavens, passing over its usual round, and the heavens still declare the glory of God. Men are still eating and drinking, planting and building, marrying, and giving in marriage. Merchants are still buying and selling. Men are jostling one against another, contending for the highest place. Pleasure lovers are still crowding to theaters, horse races, gambling hells. The highest excitement prevails, yet probation's hour is fast closing, and every case is about to be eternally decided. Satan sees that his time is short. He has set all his agencies at work that men may be deceived, deluded, occupied and entranced, until the day of probation shall be ended, and the door of mercy be forever shut.

Solemnly there come to us down through the centuries the warning words of our Lord from the Mount of Olives: "Take heed to yourselves, lest at any time your hearts be overcharged with surfeiting, and drunkenness, and cares of this life, and so that day come upon you unawares." "Watch ye therefore, and pray always, that ye may be accounted worthy to escape all these things that shall come to pass, and to stand before the Son of man."

"The Least of These My Brethren"

When the Son of man shall come in His glory, and all the holy angels with Him, then shall He sit upon the throne of His glory: and before Him shall be gathered all nations: and He shall separate them one from another." Thus Christ on the Mount of Olives pictured to His disciples the scene of the great judgment day. And He represented its decision as turning upon one point. When the nations are gathered before Him, there will be but two classes, and their eternal destiny will be determined by what they have done or have neglected to do for Him in the person of the poor and the suffering.

In that day Christ does not present before men the great work He has done for them in giving His life for their redemption. He presents the faithful work they have done for Him. To those whom He sets upon His right hand He will say, "Come, ye blessed of My Father, inherit the kingdom prepared for you from the foundation of the world: for I was an hungered, and ye gave Me meat: I was thirsty, and ye gave Me drink: I was a stranger, and ye took Me in: naked, and ye clothed Me: I was sick, and ye visited Me: I was in prison, and ye came unto Me." But those whom Christ commends know not that they have been ministering unto Him. To their perplexed inquiries He answers, "Inasmuch as ye have done it unto one of the least of these My brethren, ye have done it unto Me."

Jesus had told His disciples that they were to be hated of all men, to be persecuted and afflicted. Many would be driven from their homes, and brought to poverty. Many would be in distress through disease and privation. Many would be cast into prison. To all who forsook friends or home for His sake He had promised in this life a hundredfold. Now He assured a special blessing to all who should minister to their brethren. In all who suffer for My name, said Jesus, you are to recognize Me. As you would minister to Me, so you are to minister to them. This is the evidence that you are My disciples.

All who have been born into the heavenly family are in a special sense the brethren of our Lord. The love of Christ binds together the members of His family, and wherever that love is made manifest there the divine relationship is revealed. "Everyone that loveth is born of God, and knoweth God." 1 John 4:7.

Those whom Christ commends in the judgment may have known little of theology, but they have cherished His principles. Through the influence of the divine Spirit they have been a blessing to those about them. Even among the heathen are those who have cherished the spirit of kindness; before the words of life had fallen upon their ears, they have befriended the missionaries, even ministering to them at the peril of their own lives. Among the heathen are those who worship God ignorantly, those to whom the light is never brought by human instrumentality, yet they will not perish. Though ignorant of the written law of God, they have heard His voice speaking to them in nature, and have done the things that the law required. Their works are evidence that the Holy Spirit has touched their hearts, and they are recognized as the children of God.

How surprised and gladdened will be the lowly among the nations, and among the heathen, to hear from the lips of the Saviour, "Inasmuch as ye have done it unto one of the least of these My brethren, ye have done it unto Me"! How glad will be the heart of Infinite Love as His followers look up with surprise and joy at His words of approval!

But not to any class is Christ's love restricted. He identifies Himself with every child of humanity. That we might become members of the heavenly family, He became a member of the earthly family. He is the Son of man, and thus a brother to every son and daughter of Adam. His followers are not to feel themselves detached from the perishing world around them. They are a part of the great web of humanity; and Heaven looks upon them as brothers to sinners as well as to saints. The fallen, the erring, and the sinful, Christ's love embraces; and every deed of kindness done to uplift a fallen soul, every act of mercy, is accepted as done to Him.

The angels of heaven are sent forth to minister to those who shall be heirs of salvation. We know not now who they are; it is not yet made manifest who shall overcome, and share the inheritance of the saints in light; but angels of heaven are passing throughout the length and breadth of the earth, seeking to comfort the sorrowing, to protect the imperiled, to win the hearts of men to Christ. Not one is neglected or passed by. God is no respecter of persons, and He has an equal care for all the souls He has created.

As you open your door to Christ's needy and suffering ones, you are welcoming unseen angels. You invite the companionship of heavenly beings. They bring a sacred atmosphere of joy and peace. They come with praises upon their lips, and an answering strain is heard in heaven. Every deed of mercy makes music there. The Father from His throne numbers the unselfish workers among His most precious treasures.

Those on the left hand of Christ, those who had neglected Him in the person of the poor and the suffering, were unconscious of their guilt. Satan had blinded them; they had not perceived what they owed to their brethren. They had been self-absorbed, and cared not for others' needs.

To the rich, God has given wealth that they may relieve and comfort His suffering children; but too often they are indifferent to the wants of others. They feel themselves superior to their poor brethren. They do not put themselves in the poor man's place. They do not understand the temptations and struggles of the poor, and mercy dies out of their hearts. In costly dwellings and splendid churches, the rich shut themselves away from the poor; the means that God has given to bless the needy is spent in pampering pride and selfishness. The poor are robbed daily of the education they should have concerning the tender mercies of God; for He has made ample provision that they should be comforted with the necessities of life. They are compelled to feel the poverty that narrows life, and are often tempted to become envious, jealous, and full of evil surmisings. Those who themselves have not endured the pressure of want too often treat the poor in a contemptuous way, and make them feel that they are looked upon as paupers.

But Christ beholds it all, and He says, It was I who was hungry and thirsty. It was I who was a stranger. It was I who was sick. It was I who was in prison. While you were feasting at your bountifully spread table, I was famishing in the hovel or the empty street. While you were at ease in your luxurious home, I had not where to lay My head. While you crowded your wardrobe with rich apparel, I was destitute. While you pursued your pleasures, I languished in prison.

When you doled out the pittance of bread to the starving poor, when you gave those flimsy garments to shield them from the biting frost, did you remember that you were giving to the Lord of glory? All the days of your life I was near you in the person of these afflicted ones, but you did not seek Me. You would not enter into fellowship with Me. I know you not.

Many feel that it would be a great privilege to visit the scenes of Christ's life on earth, to walk where He trod, to look upon the lake beside which He loved to teach, and the hills and valleys on which His eyes so often rested. But we need not go to Nazareth, to Capernaum, or to Bethany, in order to walk in the steps of Jesus. We shall find His footprints beside the sickbed, in the hovels of poverty, in the crowded alleys of the great city, and in every place where there are human hearts in need of consolation. In doing as Jesus did when on earth, we shall walk in His steps.

All may find something to do. "The poor always ye have with you," (John 12:8), Jesus said, and none need feel that there is no place where they can labor for Him. Millions upon millions of human souls ready to perish, bound in chains of ignorance and sin, have never so much as heard of Christ's love for them. Were our condition and theirs to be reversed, what would we desire them to do for us? All this, so far as lies in our power, we are under the most solemn obligation to do for them. Christ's rule of life, by which every one of us must stand or fall in the judgment, is, "Whatsoever ye would that men should do to you, do ye even so to them." Matt. 7:12.

The Saviour has given His precious life in order to establish a church capable of caring for sorrowful, tempted souls. A company of believers may be poor, uneducated, and unknown; yet in Christ they may do a work in the home, the neighborhood, the church, and even in "the regions beyond," whose results shall be as far-reaching as eternity.

It is because this work is neglected that so many young disciples never advance beyond the mere alphabet of Christian experience. The light which was glowing in their own hearts when Jesus spoke to them, "Thy sins be forgiven thee," they might have kept alive by helping those in need. The restless energy that is so often a source of danger to the young might be directed into channels through which it would flow out in streams of blessing. Self would be forgotten in earnest work to do others good.

Those who minister to others will be ministered unto by the Chief Shepherd. They themselves will drink of the living water, and will be satisfied. They will not be longing for exciting amusements, or for some change in their lives. The great topic of interest will be, how to save the souls that are ready to perish. Social intercourse will be profitable. The love of the Redeemer will draw hearts together in unity.

When we realize that we are workers together with God, His promises will not be spoken with indifference. They will burn in our hearts, and kindle upon our lips. To Moses, when called to minister to an ignorant, undisciplined, and rebellious people, God gave the promise, "My presence shall go with thee, and I will give thee rest." And He said, "Certainly I will be with thee." Ex. 33:14; 3:12. This promise is to all who labor in Christ's stead for His afflicted and suffering ones.

Love to man is the earthward manifestation of the love of God. It was to implant this love, to make us children of one family, that the King of glory became one with us. And when His parting words are fulfilled, "Love one another, as I have loved you" (John 15:12); when we love the world as He has loved it, then for us His mission is accomplished. We are fitted for heaven; for we have heaven in our hearts.

But "if thou forbear to deliver them that are drawn unto death, and those that are ready to be slain; if thou sayest, Behold, we knew it not; doth not He that pondereth the heart consider it? and He that keepeth thy soul, doth not He know it? and shall not He render to every man according to his works?" Prov. 24:11, 12. In the great Judgment day, those who have not worked for Christ, who have drifted along thinking of themselves, caring for themselves, will be placed by the Judge of the whole earth with those who did evil. They receive the same condemnation.

To every soul a trust is given. Of everyone the Chief

Shepherd will demand, "Where is the flock that was given thee, thy beautiful flock?" And "what wilt thou say when He shall punish thee?" Jer. 13:20, 21.

A Servant of Servants

In the upper chamber of a dwelling at Jerusalem, Christ was sitting at table with His disciples. They had gathered to celebrate the Passover. The Saviour desired to keep this feast alone with the twelve. He knew that His hour was come; He Himself was the true paschal lamb, and on the day the Passover was eaten He was to be sacrificed. He was about to drink the cup of wrath; He must soon receive the final baptism of suffering. But a few quiet hours yet remained to Him, and these were to be spent for the benefit of His beloved disciples.

The whole life of Christ had been a life of unselfish service. "Not to be ministered unto, but to minister," (Matt. 20:28), had been the lesson of His every act. But not yet had the disciples learned the lesson. At this last Passover supper, Jesus repeated His teaching by an illustration that impressed it forever on their minds and hearts.

The interviews between Jesus and His disciples were usually seasons of calm joy, highly prized by them all. The Passover suppers had been scenes of special interest; but upon this occasion Jesus was troubled. His heart was burdened, and a shadow rested upon His countenance. As He met the disciples in the upper chamber, they perceived that something weighed heavily upon His mind, and although they knew not its cause, they sympathized with His grief.

As they were gathered about the table, He said in tones of touching sadness, "With desire I have desired to eat this Passover with you before I suffer: for I say unto you, I will not any more eat thereof, until it be fulfilled in the kingdom of God. And He took the cup, and gave thanks, and said, Take this, and divide it among yourselves: for I say unto you, I will not drink of the fruit of the vine, until the kingdom of God shall come."

Christ knew that the time had come for Him to depart out of the world, and go to His Father. And having loved His own that were in the world, He loved them unto the end. He was now in the shadow of the cross, and the pain was torturing His heart. He knew that He would be deserted in the hour of His betrayal. He knew that by the most humiliating process to which criminals were subjected He would be put to death. He knew the ingratitude and cruelty of those He had come to save. He knew how great the sacrifice that He must make, and for how many it would be in vain. Knowing all that was before Him, He might naturally have been overwhelmed with the thought of His own humiliation and suffering. But He looked upon the twelve, who had been with Him as His own, and who, after His shame and sorrow and painful usage were over, would be left to struggle in the world. His thoughts of what He Himself must suffer were ever connected with His disciples. He did not think of Himself. His care for them was uppermost in His mind.

On this last evening with His disciples, Jesus had much to tell them. If they had been prepared to receive what He longed to impart, they would have been saved from heartbreaking anguish, from disappointment and unbelief. But Jesus saw that they could not bear what He had to say. As He looked into their faces, the words of warning and comfort were stayed upon His lips. Moments passed in silence. Jesus appeared to be waiting. The disciples were ill at ease. The sympathy and tenderness awakened by Christ's grief seemed to have passed away. His sorrowful words, pointing to His own suffering, had made little impression. The glances they cast upon each other told of jealousy and contention.

There was "a strife among them, which of them should be accounted the greatest." This contention, carried on in the presence of Christ, grieved and wounded Him. The disciples clung to their favorite idea that Christ would assert His power, and take His position on the throne of David. And in heart each still longed for the highest place in the kingdom. They had placed their own estimate upon themselves and upon one another, and, instead of regarding their brethren as more worthy, they had placed themselves first. The request of James and John to sit on the right and left of Christ's throne had excited the indignation of the others. That the two brothers should presume to ask for the highest position so stirred the ten that alienation threatened. They felt that they were misjudged, that their fidelity and talents were not appreciated. Judas was the most severe upon James and John.

When the disciples entered the supper room, their hearts were full of resentful feelings. Judas pressed next to Christ on the left side; John was on the right. If there was a highest place, Judas was determined to have it, and that place was thought to be next to Christ. And Judas was a traitor.

Another cause of dissension had arisen. At a feast it was customary for a servant to wash the feet of the guests, and on this occasion preparation had been made for the service. The pitcher, the basin, and the towel were there, in readiness for the feet washing; but no servant was present, and it was the disciples' part to perform it. But each of the disciples, yielding to wounded pride, determined not to act the part of a servant. All manifested a stoical unconcern, seeming unconscious that there was anything for them to do. By their silence they refused to humble themselves.

How was Christ to bring these poor souls where Satan would not gain over them a decided victory? How could He show that a mere profession of discipleship did not make them disciples, or insure them a place in His kingdom? How could He show that it is loving service, true humility, which constitutes real greatness? How was He to kindle love in their hearts, and enable them to comprehend what He longed to tell them?

The disciples made no move toward serving one another. Jesus waited for a time to see what they would do. Then He, the divine Teacher, rose from the table. Laying aside the outer garment that would have impeded His movements, He took a towel, and girded Himself. With surprised interest the disciples looked on, and in silence waited to see what was to follow. "After that He poureth water into a basin, and began to wash the disciples' feet, and to wipe them with the towel wherewith He was girded." This action opened the eyes of the disciples. Bitter shame and humiliation filled their hearts. They understood the unspoken rebuke, and saw themselves in altogether a new light.

So Christ expressed His love for His disciples. Their selfish spirit filled Him with sorrow, but He entered into no controversy with them regarding their difficulty. Instead He gave them an example they would never forget. His love for them was not easily disturbed or quenched. He knew that the Father had given all things into His hands, and that He came from God, and went to God. He had a full consciousness of His divinity; but He had laid aside His royal crown and kingly robes, and had taken the form of a servant. One of the last acts of His life on earth was to gird Himself as a servant, and perform a servant's part.

Before the Passover Judas had met a second time with the priests and scribes, and had closed the contract to deliver Jesus into their hands. Yet he afterward mingled with the disciples as though innocent of any wrong, and interested in the work of preparing for the feast. The disciples knew nothing of the purpose of Judas. Jesus alone could read his secret. Yet He did not expose him. Jesus hungered for his soul. He felt for him such a burden as for Jerusalem when He wept over the doomed city. His heart was crying, How can I give thee up? The constraining power of that love was felt by Judas. When the Saviour's hands were bathing those soiled feet, and wiping them with the towel, the heart of Judas thrilled through and through with the impulse then and there to confess his sin. But he would not humble himself. He hardened his heart against repentance; and the old impulses, for the moment put aside, again controlled him. Judas was now offended at Christ's act in washing the feet of His disciples. If Jesus could so humble Himself, he thought, He could not be Israel's king. All hope of worldly honor in a temporal kingdom was destroyed. Judas was satisfied that there was nothing to be gained by following Christ. After seeing Him degrade Himself, as he thought, he was confirmed in his purpose to disown Him, and confess himself deceived. He was possessed by a demon, and he resolved to complete the work he had agreed to do in betraying his Lord.

Judas, in choosing his position at table, had tried to place himself first, and Christ as a servant served him first. John, toward whom Judas had felt so much bitterness, was left till the last. But John did not take this as a rebuke or slight. As the disciples watched Christ's action, they were greatly moved. When Peter's turn came, he exclaimed with astonishment, "Lord, dost Thou wash my feet?" Christ's condescension broke his heart. He was filled with shame to think that one of the disciples was not performing this service. "What I do," Christ said, "thou knowest not now; but thou shalt know hereafter." Peter could not bear to see his Lord,

whom he believed to be the Son of God, acting the part of a servant. His whole soul rose up against this humiliation. He did not realize that for this Christ came into the world. With great emphasis he exclaimed, "Thou shalt never wash my feet."

Solemnly Christ said to Peter, "If I wash thee not, thou hast no part with Me." The service which Peter refused was the type of a higher cleansing. Christ had come to wash the heart from the stain of sin. In refusing to allow Christ to wash his feet, Peter was refusing the higher cleansing included in the lower. He was really rejecting his Lord. It is not humiliating to the Master to allow Him to work for our purification. The truest humility is to receive with thankful heart any provision made in our behalf, and with earnestness do service for Christ.

At the words, "If I wash thee not, thou hast no part with Me," Peter surrendered his pride and self-will. He could not endure the thought of separation from Christ; that would have been death to him. "Not my feet only," he said, "but also my hands and my head. Jesus saith to him, He that is washed needeth not save to wash his feet, but is clean every whit."

These words mean more than bodily cleanliness. Christ is still speaking of the higher cleansing as illustrated by the lower. He who came from the bath was clean, but the sandaled feet soon became dusty, and again needed to be washed. So Peter and his brethren had been washed in the great fountain opened for sin and uncleanness. Christ acknowledged them as His. But temptation had led them into evil, and they still needed His cleansing grace. When Jesus girded Himself with a towel to wash the dust from their feet, He desired by that very act to wash the alienation, jealousy, and pride from their hearts. This was of far more consequence than the washing of their dusty feet. With the spirit they then had, not one of them was prepared for communion with Christ. Until brought into a state of humility and love, they were not prepared to partake of the paschal supper, or to share in the memorial service which Christ was about to institute. Their hearts must be cleansed. Pride and self-seeking create dissension and hatred, but all this Jesus washed away in washing their feet. A change of feeling was brought about. Looking upon them, Jesus could say, "Ye are clean." Now there was union of heart, love for one another. They had become humble and teachable. Except Judas, each was ready to concede to another the highest place. Now with subdued and grateful hearts they could receive Christ's words.

Like Peter and his brethren, we too have been washed in the blood of Christ, yet often through contact with evil the heart's purity is soiled. We must come to Christ for His cleansing grace. Peter shrank from bringing his soiled feet in contact with the hands of his Lord and Master; but how often we bring our sinful, polluted hearts in contact with the heart of Christ! How grievous to Him is our evil temper, our vanity and pride! Yet all our infirmity and defilement we must bring to Him. He alone can wash us clean. We are not prepared for communion with Him unless cleansed by His efficacy.

Jesus said to the disciples, "Ye are clean, but not all." He had washed the feet of Judas, but the heart had not been yielded to Him. It was not purified. Judas had not submitted himself to Christ.

After Christ had washed the disciples' feet, and had taken His garments and sat down again, He said to them, "Know ye what I have done to you? Ye call Me Master and Lord: and ye say well; for so I am. If I then, your Lord and Master, have washed your feet; ye also ought to wash one another's feet. For I have given you an example, that ye should do as I have done to you. Verily, verily, I say unto you, The servant is not greater than his lord; neither he that is sent greater than he that sent him."

Christ would have His disciples understand that although He had washed their feet, this did not in the least detract from His dignity. "Ye call Me Master and Lord: and ye say well; for so I am." And being so infinitely superior, He imparted grace and significance to the service. No one was so exalted as Christ, and yet He stooped to the humblest duty. That His people might not be misled by the selfishness which dwells in the natural heart, and which strengthens by self-serving, Christ Himself set the example of humility. He would not leave this great subject in man's charge. Of so much consequence did He regard it, that He Himself, One equal with God, acted as servant to His disciples. While they were contending for the highest place, He to whom every knee shall bow, He whom the angels of glory count it honor to serve, bowed down to wash the feet of those who called Him Lord. He washed the feet of His betrayer.

In His life and lessons, Christ has given a perfect exemplification of the unselfish ministry which has its origin in God. God does not live for Himself. By creating the world, and by upholding all things, He is constantly ministering for others. "He maketh His sun to rise on the evil and on the good, and sendeth rain on the just and on the unjust." Matt. 5:45. This ideal of ministry God has committed to His Son. Jesus was given to stand at the head of humanity, that by His example He might teach what it means to minister. His whole life was under a law of service. He served all, ministered to all. Thus He lived the law of God, and by His example showed how we are to obey it.

Again and again Jesus had tried to establish this principle among His disciples. When James and John made their request for pre-eminence, He had said, "Whosoever will be great among you, let him be your minister." Matt. 20:26. In My kingdom the principle of preference and supremacy has no place. The only greatness is the greatness of humility. The only distinction is found in devotion to the service of others.

Now, having washed the disciples' feet, He said, "I have given you an example, that ye should do as I have done to you." In these words Christ was not merely enjoining the practice of hospitality. More was meant than the washing of the feet of guests to remove the dust of travel. Christ was here instituting a religious service. By the act of our Lord this humiliating ceremony was made a consecrated ordinance. It was to be observed by the disciples, that they might ever keep in mind His lessons of humility and service.

This ordinance is Christ's appointed preparation for the sacramental service. While pride, variance, and strife for supremacy are cherished, the heart cannot enter into fellowship with Christ. We are not prepared to receive the communion of His body and His blood. Therefore it was that Jesus appointed the memorial of His humiliation to be first observed.

As they come to this ordinance, the children of God should bring to remembrance the words of the Lord of life and glory: "Know ye what I have done to you? Ye call Me Master and Lord: and ye say well; for so I am. If I then, your Lord and Master, have washed your feet; ye also ought to wash one another's feet. For I have given you an example, that ye should do as I have done to you. Verily, verily, I say unto you, The servant is not greater than his lord; neither he that is sent greater than he that sent him. If ye know these things, happy are ye if ye do them." There is in man a disposition to esteem himself more highly than his brother, to work for self, to seek the highest place; and often this results in evil surmisings and bitterness of spirit. The ordinance preceding the Lord's Supper is to clear away these misunderstandings, to bring man out of his selfishness, down from his stilts of self-exaltation, to the humility of heart that will lead him to serve his brother.

The holy Watcher from heaven is present at this season to make it one of soul searching, of conviction of sin, and of the blessed assurance of sins forgiven. Christ in the fullness of His grace is there to change the current of the thoughts that have been running in selfish channels. The Holy Spirit quickens the sensibilities of those who follow the example of their Lord. As the Saviour's humiliation for us is remembered, thought links with thought; a chain of memories is called up, memories of God's great goodness and of the favor and tenderness of earthly friends. Blessings forgotten, mercies abused, kindnesses slighted, are called to mind. Roots of bitterness that have crowded out the precious plant of love are made manifest. Defects of character, neglect of duties, ingratitude to God, coldness toward our brethren, are called to remembrance. Sin is seen in the light in which God views it. Our thoughts are not thoughts of self-complacency, but of severe self-censure and humiliation. The mind is energized to break down every barrier that has caused alienation. Evil thinking and evilspeaking are put away. Sins are confessed, they are forgiven. The subduing grace of Christ comes into the soul, and the love of Christ draws hearts together in a blessed unity.

As the lesson of the preparatory service is thus learned, the desire is kindled for a higher spiritual life. To this desire the divine Witness will respond. The soul will be uplifted. We can partake of the Communion with a consciousness of sins forgiven. The sunshine of Christ's righteousness will fill the chambers of the mind and the soul temple. We "behold the Lamb of God, which taketh away the sin of the world." John 1:29.

To those who receive the spirit of this service, it can never become a mere ceremonial. Its constant lesson will be, "By love serve one another." Gal. 5:13. In washing the feet of His disciples, Christ gave evidence that He would do any service, however humble, that would make them heirs with Him of the eternal wealth of heaven's treasure. His disciples, in performing the same rite, pledge themselves in like manner to serve their brethren. Whenever this ordinance is rightly celebrated, the children of God are brought into a holy relationship, to help and bless each other. They covenant that the life shall be given to unselfish ministry. And this, not only for one another. Their field of labor is as wide as their Master's was. The world is full of those who need our ministry. The poor, the helpless, the ignorant, are on every hand. Those who have communed with Christ in the upper chamber will go forth to minister as He did.

Jesus, the served of all, came to be the servant of all. And because He ministered to all, He will again be served and honored by all. And those who would partake of His divine attributes, and share with Him the joy of seeing souls redeemed, must follow His example of unselfish ministry.

All this was comprehended in the words of Jesus, "I have given you an example, that ye should do as I have done to you." This was the intent of the service He established. And He says, "If ye know these things," if you know the purpose of His lessons, "happy are ye if ye do them."

"In Remembrance of Me"

"The Lord Jesus the same night in which He was betrayed took bread: and when He had given thanks, He brake it, and said, Take, eat: this is My body, which is broken for you: this do in remembrance of Me. After the same manner also He took the cup, when He had supped, saying, This cup is the new testament in My blood: this do ye, as oft as ye drink it, in remembrance of Me. For as often as ye eat this bread, and drink this cup, ye do show the Lord's death till He come." 1 Cor. 11:23-26.

Christ was standing at the point of transition between two economies and their two great festivals. He, the spotless Lamb of God, was about to present Himself as a sin offering, that He would thus bring to an end the system of types and ceremonies that for four thousand years had pointed to His death. As He ate the Passover with His disciples, He instituted in its place the service that was to be the memorial of His great sacrifice. The national festival of the Jews was to pass away forever. The service which Christ established was to be observed by His followers in all lands and through all ages.

The Passover was ordained as a commemoration of the deliverance of Israel from Egyptian bondage. God had directed that, year by year, as the children should ask the meaning of this ordinance, the history should be repeated. Thus the wonderful deliverance was to be kept fresh in the minds of all. The ordinance of the Lord's Supper was given to commemorate the great deliverance wrought out as the result of the death of Christ. Till He shall come the second time in power and glory, this ordinance is to be celebrated. It is the means by which His great work for us is to be kept fresh in our minds.

At the time of their deliverance from Egypt, the children of Israel ate the Passover supper standing, with their loins girded, and with their staves in their hands, ready for their journey. The manner in which they celebrated this ordinance harmonized with their condition; for they were about to be thrust out of the land of Egypt, and were to begin a painful and difficult journey through the wilderness. But in Christ's time the condition of things had changed. They were not now about to be thrust out of a strange country, but were dwellers in their own land. In harmony with the rest that had been given them, the people then partook of the Passover supper in a reclining position. Couches were placed about the table, and the guests lay upon them, resting upon the left arm, and having the right hand free for use in eating. In this position a guest could lay his head upon the breast of the one who sat next above him. And the feet, being at the outer edge of the couch, could be washed by one passing around the outside of the circle.

Christ is still at the table on which the paschal supper has been spread. The unleavened cakes used at the Passover season are before Him. The Passover wine, untouched by fermentation, is on the table. These emblems Christ employs to represent His own unblemished sacrifice. Nothing corrupted by fermentation, the symbol of sin and death, could represent the "Lamb without blemish and without spot." 1 Peter 1:19.

"And as they were eating, Jesus took bread, and blessed it, and brake it, and gave it to the disciples, and said, Take, eat; this is My body. And He took the cup, and gave thanks, and gave it to them, saying, Drink ye all of it; for this is My blood of the new testament, which is shed for many for the remission of sins. But I say unto you, I will not drink henceforth of this fruit of the vine, until that day when I drink it new with you in My Father's kingdom."

Judas the betrayer was present at the sacramental service. He received from Jesus the emblems of His broken body and His spilled blood. He heard the words, "This do in remembrance of Me." And sitting there in the very presence of the Lamb of God, the betrayer brooded upon his own dark purposes, and cherished his sullen, revengeful thoughts.

At the feet washing, Christ had given convincing proof that He understood the character of Judas. "Ye are not all clean" (John 13:11), He said. These words convinced the false disciple that Christ read his secret purpose. Now Christ spoke out more plainly. As they were seated at the table He said, looking upon His disciples, "I speak not of you all: I know whom I have chosen: but that the scripture may be fulfilled, He that eateth bread with Me hath lifted up his heel against Me."

Even now the disciples did not suspect Judas. But they saw that Christ appeared greatly troubled. A cloud settled over them all, a premonition of some dreadful calamity, the nature of which they did not understand. As they ate in silence, Jesus said, "Verily I say unto you, that one of you shall betray Me." At these words amazement and consternation seized them. They could not comprehend how any one of them could deal treacherously with their divine Teacher. For what cause could they betray Him? and to whom? Whose heart could give birth to such a design? Surely not one of the favored twelve, who had been privileged above all others to hear His teachings, who had shared His wonderful love, and for whom He had shown such great regard by bringing them into close communion with Himself!

As they realized the import of His words, and remembered how true His sayings were, fear and self-distrust seized them. They began to search their own hearts to see if one thought against their Master were harbored there. With the most painful emotion, one after another inquired, "Lord, is it I?" But Judas sat silent. John in deep distress at last inquired, "Lord, who is it?" And Jesus answered, "He that dippeth his hand with Me in the dish, the same shall betray Me. The Son of man goeth as it is written of Him: but woe unto that man by whom the Son of man is betrayed! it had been good for that man if he had not been born." The disciples had searched one another's faces closely as they asked, "Lord, is it I?" And now the silence of Judas drew all eyes to him. Amid the confusion of questions and expressions of astonishment, Judas had not heard the words of Jesus in answer to John's question. But now, to escape the scrutiny of the disciples, he asked as they had done, "Master, is it I?" Jesus solemnly replied, "Thou hast said."

In surprise and confusion at the exposure of his purpose, Judas rose hastily to leave the room. "Then said Jesus unto him, That thou doest, do quickly. . . . He then having received the sop went immediately out: and it was night." Night it was to the traitor as he turned away from Christ into the outer darkness.

Until this step was taken, Judas had not passed beyond the possibility of repentance. But when he left the presence of his Lord and his fellow disciples, the final decision had been made. He had passed the boundary line.

Wonderful had been the long-suffering of Jesus in His dealing with this tempted soul. Nothing that could be done to save Judas had been left undone. After he had twice covenanted to betray his Lord, Jesus still gave him opportunity for repentance. By reading the secret purpose of the traitor's heart, Christ gave to Judas the final, convincing evidence of His divinity. This was to the false disciple the last call to repentance. No appeal that the divine-human heart of Christ could make had been spared. The waves of mercy, beaten back by stubborn pride, returned in a stronger tide of subduing love. But although surprised and alarmed at the discovery of his guilt, Judas became only the more determined. From the sacramental supper he went out to complete the work of betrayal.

In pronouncing the woe upon Judas, Christ also had a purpose of mercy toward His disciples. He thus gave them the crowning evidence of His Messiahship. "I tell you before it come," He said, "that, when it is come to pass, ye may believe that I AM." Had Jesus remained silent, in apparent ignorance of what was to come upon Him, the disciples might have thought that their Master had not divine foresight, and had been surprised and betrayed into the hands of the murderous mob. A year before, Jesus had told the disciples that He had chosen twelve, and that one was a devil. Now His words to Judas, showing that his treachery was fully known to his Master, would strengthen the faith of Christ's true followers during His humiliation. And when Judas should have come to his dreadful end, they would remember the woe that Jesus had pronounced upon the betrayer.

And the Saviour had still another purpose. He had not withheld His ministry from him whom He knew to be a traitor. The disciples did not understand His words when He said at the feet washing, "Ye are not all clean," nor yet when at the table He declared, "He that eateth bread with Me hath lifted up his heel against Me." John 13:11, 18. But afterward, when His meaning was made plain, they had something to consider as to the patience and mercy of God toward the most grievously erring.

Though Jesus knew Judas from the beginning, He washed his feet. And the betrayer was privileged to unite with Christ in partaking of the sacrament. A long-suffering Saviour held out every inducement for the sinner to receive Him, to repent, and to be cleansed from the defilement of sin. This example is for us. When we suppose one to be in error and sin, we are not to divorce ourselves from him. By no careless separation are we to leave him a prey to temptation, or drive him upon Satan's battleground. This is not Christ's method. It was because the disciples were erring and faulty that He washed their feet, and all but one of the twelve were thus brought to repentance.

Christ's example forbids exclusiveness at the Lord's Supper. It is true that open sin excludes the guilty. This the Holy Spirit plainly teaches. 1 Cor. 5:11. But beyond this none are to pass judgment. God has not left it with men to say who shall present themselves on these occasions. For who can read the heart? Who can distinguish the tares from the wheat? "Let a man examine himself, and so let him eat of that bread, and drink of that cup." For "whosoever shall eat this bread, and drink this cup of the Lord, unworthily, shall be guilty of the body and blood of the Lord." "He that eateth and drinketh unworthily, eateth and drinketh damnation to himself, not discerning the Lord's body." 1 Cor. 11:28, 27, 29.

When believers assemble to celebrate the ordinances, there are present messengers unseen by human eyes. There may be a Judas in the company, and if so, messengers from the prince of darkness are there, for they attend all who refuse to be controlled by the Holy Spirit. Heavenly angels also are present. These unseen visitants are present on every such occasion. There may come into the company persons who are not in heart servants of truth and holiness, but who may wish to take part in the service. They should not be forbidden.

There are witnesses present who were present when Jesus washed the feet of the disciples and of Judas. More than human eyes beheld the scene.

Christ by the Holy Spirit is there to set the seal to His own ordinance. He is there to convict and soften the heart. Not a look, not a thought of contrition, escapes His notice. For the repentant, brokenhearted one He is waiting. All things are ready for that soul's reception. He who washed the feet of Judas longs to wash every heart from the stain of sin.

None should exclude themselves from the Communion because some who are unworthy may be present. Every disciple is called upon to participate publicly, and thus bear witness that he accepts Christ as a personal Saviour. It is at these, His own appointments, that Christ meets His people, and energizes them by His presence. Hearts and hands that are unworthy may even administer the ordinance, yet Christ is there to minister to His children. All who come with their faith fixed upon Him will be greatly blessed. All who neglect these seasons of divine privilege will suffer loss. Of them it may appropriately be said, "Ye are not all clean."

In partaking with His disciples of the bread and wine, Christ pledged Himself to them as their Redeemer. He committed to them the new covenant, by which all who receive Him become children of God, and joint heirs with Christ. By this covenant every blessing that heaven could bestow for this life and the life to come was theirs. This covenant deed was to be ratified with the blood of Christ. And the administration of the Sacrament was to keep before the disciples the infinite sacrifice made for each of them individually as a part of the great whole of fallen humanity.

But the Communion service was not to be a season of sorrowing. This was not its purpose. As the Lord's disciples gather about His table, they are not to remember and lament their shortcomings. They are not to dwell upon their past religious experience, whether that experience has been elevating or depressing. They are not to recall the differences between them and their brethren. The preparatory service has embraced all this. The self-examination, the confession of sin, the reconciling of differences, has all been done. Now they come to meet with Christ. They are not to stand in the shadow of the cross, but in its saving light. They are to open the soul to the bright beams of the Sun of Righteousness. With hearts cleansed by Christ's most precious blood, in full consciousness of His presence, although unseen, they are to hear His words, "Peace I leave with you, My peace I give unto you: not as the world giveth, give I unto you." John 14:27.

Our Lord says, Under conviction of sin, remember that I died for you. When oppressed and persecuted and afflicted for My sake and the gospel's, remember My love, so great that for you I gave My life. When your duties appear stern and severe, and your burdens too heavy to bear, remember that for your sake I endured the cross, despising the shame. When your heart shrinks from the trying ordeal, remember that your Redeemer liveth to make intercession for you.

The Communion service points to Christ's second coming. It was designed to keep this hope vivid in the minds of the disciples. Whenever they met together to commemorate His death, they recounted how "He took the cup, and gave thanks, and gave it to them, saying, Drink ye all of it; for this is My blood of the new testament, which is shed for many for the remission of sins. But I say unto you, I will not drink henceforth of this fruit of the vine, until that day when I drink it new with you in My Father's kingdom." In their tribulation they found comfort in the hope of their Lord's return. Unspeakably precious to them was the thought, "As often as ye eat this bread, and drink this cup, ye do show the Lord's death till He come." 1 Cor. 11:26.

These are the things we are never to forget. The love of Jesus, with its constraining power, is to be kept fresh in our memory. Christ has instituted this service that it may speak to our senses of the love of God that has been expressed in our behalf. There can be no union between our souls and God except through Christ. The union and love between brother and brother must be cemented and rendered eternal by the love of Jesus. And nothing less than the death of Christ could make His love efficacious for us. It is only because of His death that we can look with joy to His second coming. His sacrifice is the center of our hope. Upon this we must fix our faith.

The ordinances that point to our Lord's humiliation and suffering are regarded too much as a form. They were instituted for a purpose. Our senses need to be quickened to lay hold of the mystery of godliness. It is the privilege of all to comprehend, far more than we do, the expiatory sufferings of Christ. "As Moses lifted up the serpent in the wilderness," even so has the Son of man been lifted up, "that whosoever believeth in Him should not perish, but have eternal life." John 3:14, 15. To the cross of Calvary, bearing a dying Saviour, we must look. Our eternal interests demand that we show faith in Christ.

Our Lord has said, "Except ye eat the flesh of the Son of man, and drink His blood, ye have no life in you. . . . For My flesh is meat indeed, and My blood is drink indeed." John 6:53-55. This is true of our physical nature. To the death of Christ we owe even this earthly life. The bread we eat is the purchase of His broken body. The water we drink is bought by His spilled blood. Never one, saint or sinner, eats his daily food, but he is nourished by the body and the blood of Christ. The cross of Calvary is stamped on every loaf. It is reflected in every water spring. All this Christ has taught in appointing the emblems of His great sacrifice. The light shining from that Communion service in the upper chamber makes sacred the provisions for our daily life. The family board becomes as the table of the Lord, and every meal a sacrament.

And how much more are Christ's words true of our spiritual nature. He declares, "Whoso eateth My flesh, and drinketh My blood, hath eternal life." It is by receiving the life for us poured out on Calvary's cross, that we can live the life of holiness. And this life we receive by receiving His word, by doing those things which He has commanded. Thus we become one with Him. "He that eateth My flesh," He says, "and drinketh My blood, dwelleth in Me, and I in him. As the living Father hath sent Me, and I live by the Father: so he that eateth Me, even he shall live by Me." John 6:54, 56, 57. To the holy Communion this scripture in a special sense applies. As faith contemplates our Lord's great sacrifice, the soul assimilates the spiritual life of Christ. That soul will receive spiritual strength from every Communion. The service forms a living connection by which the believer is bound up with Christ, and thus bound up with the Father. In a special sense it forms a connection between dependent human beings and God.

As we receive the bread and wine symbolizing Christ's broken body and spilled blood, we in imagination join in the scene of Communion in the upper chamber. We seem to be passing through the garden consecrated by the agony of Him who bore the sins of the world. We witness the struggle by which our reconciliation with God was obtained. Christ is set forth crucified among us.

Looking upon the crucified Redeemer, we more fully comprehend the magnitude and meaning of the sacrifice made by the Majesty of heaven. The plan of salvation is glorified before us, and the thought of Calvary awakens living and sacred emotions in our hearts. Praise to God and the Lamb will be in our hearts and on our lips; for pride and self-worship cannot flourish in the soul that keeps fresh in memory the scenes of Calvary.

He who beholds the Saviour's matchless love will be elevated in thought, purified in heart, transformed in character. He will go forth to be a light to the world, to reflect in some degree this mysterious love. The more we contemplate the cross of Christ, the more fully shall we adopt the language of the apostle when he said, "God forbid that I should glory, save in the cross of our Lord Jesus Christ, by whom the world is crucified unto me, and I unto the world." Gal. 6:14.

"Let Not Your Heart Be Troubled"

Looking upon His disciples with divine love and with the tenderest sympathy, Christ said, "Now is the Son of man glorified, and God is glorified in Him." Judas had left the upper chamber, and Christ was alone with the eleven. He was about to speak of His approaching separation from them; but before doing this He pointed to the great object of His mission. It was this that He kept ever before Him. It was His joy that all His humiliation and suffering would glorify the Father's name. To this He first directs the thoughts of His disciples.

Then addressing them by the endearing term, "Little children," He said, "Yet a little while I am with you. Ye shall seek Me: and as I said unto the Jews, Whither I go, ye cannot come; so now I say to you."

The disciples could not rejoice when they heard this. Fear fell upon them. They pressed close about the Saviour. Their Master and Lord, their beloved Teacher and Friend, He was dearer to them than life. To Him they had looked for help in all their difficulties, for comfort in their sorrows and disappointments. Now He was to leave them, a lonely, dependent company. Dark were the forebodings that filled their hearts.

But the Saviour's words to them were full of hope. He knew that they were to be assailed by the enemy, and that Satan's craft is most successful against those who are depressed by difficulties. Therefore He pointed them away from "the things which are seen," to "the things which are not seen." 2 Cor. 4:18. From earthly exile He turned their thoughts to the heavenly home.

"Let not your heart be troubled," He said; "ye believe in God, believe also in Me. In My Father's house are many mansions: if it were not so, I would have told you. I go to prepare a place for you. And if I go and prepare a place for you, I will come again, and receive you unto Myself; that were I am, there ye may be also. And whither I go ye know, and the way ye know." For your sake I came into the world. I am working in your behalf. When I go away, I shall still work earnestly for you. I came into the world to reveal Myself to you, that you might believe. I go to the Father to co-operate with Him in your behalf. The object of Christ's departure was the opposite of what the disciples feared. It did not mean a final separation. He was going to prepare a place for them, that He might come again, and receive them unto Himself. While He was building mansions for them, they were to build characters after the divine similitude.

Still the disciples were perplexed. Thomas, always troubled by doubts, said, "Lord, we know not whither Thou goest; and how can we know the way? Jesus saith unto him, I am the way, the truth, and the life; no man cometh unto the Father, but by Me. If ye had known Me, ye should have known My Father also: and from henceforth ye know Him, and have seen Him."

There are not many ways to heaven. Each one may not choose his own way. Christ says, "I am the way: . . . no man cometh unto the Father, but by Me." Since the first gospel sermon was preached, when in Eden it was declared that the seed of the woman should bruise the serpent's head, Christ had been uplifted as the way, the truth, and the life. He was the way when Adam lived, when Abel presented to God the blood of the slain lamb, representing the blood of the Redeemer. Christ was the way by which patriarchs and prophets were saved. He is the way by which alone we can have access to God.

"If ye had known Me," Christ said, "ye should have known My Father also: and from henceforth ye know Him, and have seen Him." But not yet did the disciples understand. "Lord, show us the Father," exclaimed Philip, "and it sufficeth us."

Amazed at his dullness of comprehension, Christ asked with pained surprise, "Have I been so long time with you, and yet hast thou not known Me, Philip?" Is it possible that you do not see the Father in the works He does through Me? Do you not believe that I came to testify of the Father? "How sayest thou then, Show us the Father?" "He that hath seen Me hath seen the Father." Christ had not ceased to be God when He became man. Though He had humbled Himself to humanity, the Godhead was still His own. Christ alone could represent the Father to humanity, and this representation the disciples had been privileged to behold for over three years.

"Believe Me that I am in the Father, and the Father in Me: or else believe Me for the very works' sake." Their faith might safely rest on the evidence given in Christ's works, works that no man, of himself, ever had done, or ever could do. Christ's work testified to His divinity. Through Him the Father had been revealed.

If the disciples believed this vital connection between the Father and the Son, their faith would not forsake them when they saw Christ's suffering and death to save a perishing world. Christ was seeking to lead them from their low condition of faith to the experience they might receive if they truly realized what He was,—God in human flesh. He desired them to see that their faith must lead up to God, and be anchored there. How earnestly and perseveringly our compassionate Saviour sought to prepare His disciples for the storm of temptation that was soon to beat upon them. He would have them hid with Him in God.

As Christ was speaking these words, the glory of God was shining from His countenance, and all present felt a sacred awe as they listened with rapt attention to His words. Their hearts were more decidedly drawn to Him; and as they were drawn to Christ in greater love, they were drawn to one another. They felt that heaven was very near, and that the words to which they listened were a message to them from their heavenly Father.

"Verily, verily, I say unto you," Christ continued, "He that believeth on Me, the works that I do shall he do also." The Saviour was deeply anxious for His disciples to understand for what purpose His divinity was united to humanity. He came to the world to display the glory of God, that man might be uplifted by its restoring power. God was manifested in Him that He might be manifested in them. Jesus revealed no qualities, and exercised no powers, that men may not have through faith in Him. His perfect humanity is that which all His followers may possess, if they will be in subjection to God as He was.

"And greater works than these shall he do; because I go unto My Father." By this Christ did not mean that the disciples' work would be of a more exalted character than His, but that it would have greater extent. He did not refer merely to miracle working, but to all that would take place under the working of the Holy Spirit.

After the Lord's ascension, the disciples realized the fulfillment of His promise. The scenes of the crucifixion, resurrection, and ascension of Christ were a living reality to them. They saw that the prophecies had been literally fulfilled. They searched the Scriptures, and accepted their teaching with a faith and assurance unknown before. They knew that the divine Teacher was all that He had claimed to be. As they told their experience, and exalted the love of God, men's hearts were melted and subdued, and multitudes believed on Jesus.

The Saviour's promise to His disciples is a promise to His church to the end of time. God did not design that His wonderful plan to redeem men should achieve only insignificant results. All who will go to work, trusting not in what they themselves can do, but in what God can do for and through them, will certainly realize the fulfillment of His promise. "Greater works than these shall ye do," He declares; "because I go unto My Father."

As yet the disciples were unacquainted with the Saviour's unlimited resources and power. He said to them, "Hitherto have ye asked nothing in My name." John 16:24. He explained that the secret of their success would be in asking for strength and grace in His name. He would be present before the Father to make request for them. The prayer of the humble suppliant He presents as His own desire in that soul's behalf. Every sincere prayer is heard in heaven. It may not be fluently expressed; but if the heart is in it, it will ascend to the sanctuary where Jesus ministers, and He will present it to the Father without one awkward, stammering word, beautiful and fragrant with the incense of His own perfection.

The path of sincerity and integrity is not a path free from obstruction, but in every difficulty we are to see a call to prayer. There is no one living who has any power that he has not received from God, and the source whence it comes is open to the weakest human being. "Whatsoever ye shall ask in My name," said Jesus, "that will I do, that the Father may be glorified in the Son. If ye shall ask anything in My name, I will do it."

"In My name," Christ bade His disciples pray. In Christ's name His followers are to stand before God. Through the value of the sacrifice made for them, they are of value in the Lord's sight. Because of the imputed righteousness of Christ they are accounted precious. For Christ's sake the Lord pardons those that fear Him. He does not see in them the vileness of the sinner. He recognizes in them the likeness of His Son, in whom they believe.

The Lord is disappointed when His people place a low estimate upon themselves. He desires His chosen heritage to value themselves according to the price He has placed upon them. God wanted them, else He would not have sent His Son on such an expensive errand to redeem them. He has a use for them, and He is well pleased when they make the very highest demands upon Him, that they may glorify His name. They may expect large things if they have faith in His promises.

But to pray in Christ's name means much. It means that we are to accept His character, manifest His spirit, and work His works. The Saviour's promise is given on condition. "If ye love Me," He says, "keep My commandments." He saves men, not in sin, but from sin; and those who love Him will show their love by obedience.

All true obedience comes from the heart. It was heart work with Christ. And if we consent, He will so identify Himself with our thoughts and aims, so blend our hearts and minds into conformity to His will, that when obeying Him we shall be but carrying out our own impulses. The will, refined and sanctified, will find its highest delight in doing His service. When we know God as it is our privilege to know Him, our life will be a life of continual obedience. Through an appreciation of the character of Christ, through communion with God, sin will become hateful to us.

As Christ lived the law in humanity, so we may do if we will take hold of the Strong for strength. But we are not to place the responsibility of our duty upon others, and wait for them to tell us what to do. We cannot depend for counsel upon humanity. The Lord will teach us our duty just as willingly as He will teach somebody else. If we come to Him in faith, He will speak His mysteries to us personally. Our hearts will often burn within us as One draws nigh to commune with us as He did with Enoch. Those who decide to do nothing in any line that will displease God, will know, after presenting their case before Him, just what course to pursue. And they will receive not only wisdom, but strength. Power for obedience, for service, will be imparted to them, as Christ has promised. Whatever was given to Christ—the "all things" to supply the need of fallen men—was given to Him as the head and representative of humanity. And "whatsoever we ask, we receive of Him, because we keep His commandments, and do those things that are pleasing in His sight." 1 John 3:22.

Before offering Himself as the sacrificial victim, Christ sought for the most essential and complete gift to bestow upon His followers, a gift that would bring within their reach the boundless resources of grace. "I will pray the Father," He said, "and He shall give you another Comforter, that He may abide with you forever; even the Spirit of truth; whom the world cannot receive, because it seeth Him not, neither knoweth Him: but ye know Him; for He dwelleth with you, and shall be in you. I will not leave you orphans: I will come to you." John 14:16-18, margin.

Before this the Spirit had been in the world; from the very beginning of the work of redemption He had been moving upon men's hearts. But while Christ was on earth, the disciples had desired no other helper. Not until they were deprived of His presence would they feel their need of the Spirit, and then He would come.

The Holy Spirit is Christ's representative, but divested of the personality of humanity, and independent thereof. Cumbered with humanity, Christ could not be in every place personally. Therefore it was for their interest that He should go to the Father, and send the Spirit to be His successor on earth. No one could then have any advantage because of his location or his personal contact with Christ. By the Spirit the Saviour would be accessible to all. In this sense He would be nearer to them than if He had not ascended on high.

"He that loveth Me shall be loved of My Father, and I will love him, and will manifest Myself to him." Jesus read the future of His disciples. He saw one brought to the scaffold, one to the cross, one to exile among the lonely rocks of the sea, others to persecution and death. He encouraged them with the promise that in every trial He would be with them. That promise has lost none of its force. The Lord knows all about His faithful servants who for His sake are lying in prison or who are banished to lonely islands. He comforts them with His own presence. When for the truth's sake the believer stands at the bar of unrighteous tribunals, Christ stands by his side. All the reproaches that fall upon him, fall upon Christ. Christ is condemned over again in the person of His disciple. When one is incarcerated in prison walls, Christ ravishes the heart with His love. When one suffers death for His sake, Christ says, "I am He that liveth, and was dead; and, behold, I am alive forevermore, . . . and have the keys of hell and of death." Rev. 1:18. The life that is sacrificed for Me is preserved unto eternal glory.

At all times and in all places, in all sorrows and in all afflictions, when the outlook seems dark and the future perplexing, and we feel helpless and alone, the Comforter will be sent in answer to the prayer of faith. Circumstances may separate us from every earthly friend; but no circumstance, no distance, can separate us from the heavenly Comforter. Wherever we are, wherever we may go, He is always at our right hand to support, sustain, uphold, and cheer.

The disciples still failed to understand Christ's words in their spiritual sense, and again He explained His meaning. By the Spirit, He said, He would manifest Himself to them. "The Comforter, which is the Holy Ghost, whom the Father will send in My name, He shall teach you all things." No more will you say, I cannot comprehend. No longer will you see through a glass, darkly. You shall "be able to comprehend with all saints what is the breadth, and length, and depth, and height; and to know the love of Christ, which passeth knowledge." Eph. 3:18, 19.

The disciples were to bear witness to the life and work of Christ. Through their word He was to speak to all the people on the face of the earth. But in the humiliation and death of Christ they were to suffer great trial and disappointment. That after this experience their word might be accurate, Jesus promised that the Comforter should "bring all things to your remembrance, whatsoever I have said unto you."

"I have yet many things to say unto you," He continued, "but ye cannot bear them now. Howbeit when He, the Spirit of truth, is come, He will guide you into all truth: for He shall not speak of Himself; but whatsoever He shall hear, that shall He speak: and He will show you things to come. He shall glorify Me: for He shall receive of Mine, and shall show it unto you." Jesus had opened before His disciples a vast tract of truth. But it was most difficult for them to keep His lessons distinct from the traditions and maxims of the scribes and Pharisees. They had been educated to accept the teaching of the rabbis as the voice of God, and it still held a power over their minds, and molded their sentiments. Earthly ideas, temporal things, still had a large place in their thoughts. They did not understand the spiritual nature of Christ's kingdom, though He had so often explained it to them. Their minds had become confused. They did not comprehend the value of the scriptures Christ presented. Many of His lessons seemed almost lost upon them. Jesus saw that they did not lay hold of the real meaning of His words. He compassionately promised that the Holy Spirit should recall these sayings to their minds. And He had left unsaid many things that could not be comprehended by the disciples. These also would be opened to them by the Spirit. The Spirit was to quicken their understanding, that they might have an appreciation of heavenly things. "When He, the Spirit of truth, is come," said Jesus, "He will guide you into all truth."

The Comforter is called "the Spirit of truth." His work is to define and maintain the truth. He first dwells in the heart as the Spirit of truth, and thus He becomes the Comforter. There is comfort and peace in the truth, but no real peace or comfort can be found in falsehood. It is through false theories and traditions that Satan gains his power over the mind. By directing men to false standards, he misshapes the character. Through the Scriptures the Holy Spirit speaks to the mind, and impresses truth upon the heart. Thus He exposes error, and expels it from the soul. It is by the Spirit of truth, working through the word of God, that Christ subdues His chosen people to Himself.

In describing to His disciples the office work of the Holy Spirit, Jesus sought to inspire them with the joy and hope that inspired His own heart. He rejoiced because of the abundant help He had provided for His church. The Holy Spirit was the highest of all gifts that He could solicit from His Father for the exaltation of His people. The Spirit was to be given as a regenerating agent, and without this the sacrifice of Christ would have been of no avail. The power of evil had been strengthening for centuries, and the submission of men to this satanic captivity was amazing. Sin could be resisted and overcome only through the mighty agency of the Third Person of the Godhead, who would come with no modified energy, but in the fullness of divine power. It is the Spirit that makes effectual what has been wrought out by the world's Redeemer. It is by the Spirit that the heart is made pure. Through the Spirit the believer becomes a partaker of the divine nature. Christ has given His Spirit as a divine power to overcome all hereditary and cultivated tendencies to evil, and to impress His own character upon His church.

Of the Spirit Jesus said, "He shall glorify Me." The Saviour came to glorify the Father by the demonstration of His love; so the Spirit was to glorify Christ by revealing His grace to the world. The very image of God is to be reproduced in humanity. The honor of God, the honor of Christ, is involved in the perfection of the character of His people.

"When He is come, He will reprove the world of sin, and of righteousness, and of judgment." The preaching of the word will be of no avail without the continual presence and aid of the Holy Spirit. This is the only effectual teacher of divine truth. Only when the truth is accompanied to the heart by the Spirit will it quicken the conscience or transform the life. One might be able to present the letter of the word of God, he might be familiar with all its commands and promises; but unless the Holy Spirit sets home the truth, no souls will fall on the Rock and be broken. No amount of education, no advantages, however great, can make one a channel of light without the co-operation of the Spirit of God. The sowing of the gospel seed will not be a success unless the seed is quickened into life by the dew of heaven. Before one book of the New Testament was written, before one gospel sermon had been preached after Christ's ascension, the Holy Spirit came upon the praying apostles. Then the testimony of their enemies was, "Ye have filled Jerusalem with your doctrine." Acts 5:28.

Christ has promised the gift of the Holy Spirit to His church, and the promise belongs to us as much as to the first disciples. But like every other promise, it is given on conditions. There are many who believe and profess to claim the Lord's promise; they talk about Christ and about the Holy Spirit, yet receive no benefit. They do not surrender the soul to be guided and controlled by the divine agencies. We cannot use the Holy Spirit. The Spirit is to use us. Through the Spirit God works in His people "to will and to do of His good pleasure." Phil. 2:13. But many will not submit to this. They want to manage themselves. This is why they do not receive the heavenly gift. Only to those who wait humbly upon God, who watch for His guidance and grace, is the Spirit given. The power of God awaits their demand and reception. This promised blessing, claimed by faith, brings all other blessings in its train. It is given according to the riches of the grace of Christ, and He is ready to supply every soul according to the capacity to receive.

In His discourse to the disciples, Jesus made no mournful allusion to His own sufferings and death. His last legacy to them was a legacy of peace. He said, "Peace I leave with you, My peace I give unto you: not as the world giveth, give I unto you. Let not your heart be troubled, neither let it be afraid."

Before leaving the upper chamber, the Saviour led His disciples in a song of praise. His voice was heard, not in the strains of some mournful lament, but in the joyful notes of the Passover hallel:

"O praise the Lord, all ye nations:
Praise Him, all ye people.
For His merciful kindness is great toward us:
And the truth of the Lord endureth forever.
Praise ye the Lord." Psalm 117.

After the hymn, they went out. Through the crowded streets they made their way, passing out of the city gate toward the Mount of Olives. Slowly they proceeded, each busy with his own thoughts. As they began to descend toward the mount, Jesus said, in a tone of deepest sadness, "All ye shall be offended because of Me this night: for it is written, I will smite the shepherd, and the sheep of the flock shall be scattered abroad." Matt. 26:31. The disciples listened in sorrow and amazement. They remembered how in the synagogue at Capernaum, when Christ spoke of Himself as the bread of life, many had been offended, and had turned away from Him. But the twelve had not shown themselves unfaithful. Peter, speaking for his brethren, had then declared his loyalty to Christ. Then the Saviour had said, "Have not I chosen you twelve, and one of you is a devil?" John 6:70. In the upper chamber Jesus said that one of the twelve would betray Him, and that Peter would deny Him. But now His words include them all.

Now Peter's voice is heard vehemently protesting, "Although all shall be offended, yet will not I." In the upper chamber he had declared, "I will lay down my life for Thy sake." Jesus had warned him that he would that very night deny his Saviour. Now Christ repeats the warning: "Verily I say unto thee, That this day, even in this night, before the cock crow twice, thou shalt deny Me thrice." But Peter only "spake the more vehemently, If I should die with Thee, I will not deny Thee in anywise. Likewise also said they all." Mark 14:29, 30, 31. In their self-confidence they denied the repeated statement of Him who knew. They were unprepared for the test; when temptation should overtake them, they would understand their own weakness.

When Peter said he would follow his Lord to prison and to death, he meant it, every word of it; but he did not know himself. Hidden in his heart were elements of evil that circumstances would fan into life. Unless he was made conscious of his danger, these would prove his eternal ruin. The Saviour saw in him a self-love and assurance that would overbear even his love for Christ. Much of infirmity, of unmortified sin, carelessness of spirit, unsanctified temper, heedlessness in entering into temptation, had been revealed in his experience. Christ's solemn warning was a call to heart searching. Peter needed to distrust himself, and to have a deeper faith in Christ. Had he in humility received the warning, he would have appealed to the Shepherd of the flock to keep His sheep. When on the Sea of Galilee he was about to sink, he cried, "Lord, save me." Matt. 14:30. Then the hand of Christ was outstretched to grasp his hand. So now if he had cried to Jesus, Save me from myself, he would have been kept. But Peter felt that he was distrusted, and he thought it cruel. He was already offended, and he became more persistent in his self-confidence.

Jesus looks with compassion on His disciples. He cannot save them from the trial, but He does not leave them comfortless. He assures them that He is to break the fetters of the tomb, and that His love for them will not fail. "After I am risen again," He says, "I will go before you into Galilee." Matt. 26:32. Before the denial, they have the assurance of forgiveness. After His death and resurrection, they knew that they were forgiven, and were dear to the heart of Christ.

Jesus and the disciples were on the way to Gethsemane, at the foot of Mount Olivet, a retired spot which He had often visited for meditation and prayer. The Saviour had been explaining to His disciples His mission to the world, and the spiritual relation to Him which they were to sustain. Now He illustrates the lesson. The moon is shining bright, and reveals to Him a flourishing grapevine. Drawing the attention of the disciples to it, He employs it as a symbol.

"I am the true Vine," He says. Instead of choosing the graceful palm, the lofty cedar, or the strong oak, Jesus takes the vine with its clinging tendrils to represent Himself. The palm tree, the cedar, and the oak stand alone. They require no support. But the vine entwines about the trellis, and thus climbs heavenward. So Christ in His humanity was dependent upon divine power. "I can of Mine own self do nothing," He declared. John 5:30.

"I am the true Vine." The Jews had always regarded the vine as the most noble of plants, and a type of all that was powerful, excellent, and fruitful. Israel had been represented as a vine which God had planted in the Promised Land. The Jews based their hope of salvation on the fact of their connection with Israel. But Jesus says, I am the real Vine. Think not that through a connection with Israel you may become partakers of the life of God, and inheritors of His promise. Through Me alone is spiritual life received.

"I am the true Vine, and My Father is the husbandman." On the hills of Palestine our heavenly Father had planted this goodly Vine, and He Himself was the husbandman. Many were attracted by the beauty of this Vine, and declared its heavenly origin. But to the leaders in Israel it appeared as a root out of a dry ground. They took the plant, and bruised it, and trampled it under their unholy feet. Their thought was to destroy it forever. But the heavenly Husbandman never lost sight of His plant. After men thought they had killed it, He took it, and replanted it on the other side of the wall. The vine stock was to be no longer visible. It was hidden from the rude assaults of men. But the branches of the Vine hung over the wall. They were to represent the Vine. Through them grafts might still be united to the Vine. From them fruit has been obtained. There has been a harvest which the passers-by have plucked.

"I am the Vine, ye are the branches," Christ said to His disciples. Though He was about to be removed from them, their spiritual union with Him was to be unchanged. The connection of the branch with the vine, He said, represents the relation you are to sustain to Me. The scion is engrafted into the living vine, and fiber by fiber, vein by vein, it grows into the vine stock. The life of the vine becomes the life of the branch. So the soul dead in trespasses and sins receives life through connection with Christ. By faith in Him as a personal Saviour the union is formed. The sinner unites his weakness to Christ's strength, his emptiness to Christ's fullness, his frailty to Christ's enduring might. Then he has the mind of Christ. The humanity of Christ has touched our humanity, and our humanity has touched divinity. Thus through the agency of the Holy Spirit man becomes a partaker of the divine nature. He is accepted in the Beloved.

This union with Christ, once formed, must be maintained. Christ said, "Abide in Me, and I in you. As the branch cannot bear fruit of itself, except it abide in the vine; no more can ye, except ye abide in Me." This is no casual touch, no off-and-on connection. The branch becomes a part of the living vine. The communication of life, strength, and fruitfulness from the root to the branches is unobstructed and constant. Separated from the vine, the branch cannot live. No more, said Jesus, can you live apart from Me. The life you have received from Me can be preserved only by continual communion. Without Me you cannot overcome one sin, or resist one temptation.

"Abide in Me, and I in you." Abiding in Christ means a constant receiving of His Spirit, a life of unreserved surrender to His service. The channel of communication must be open continually between man and his God. As the vine branch constantly draws the sap from the living vine, so are we to cling to Jesus, and receive from Him by faith the strength and perfection of His own character.

The root sends its nourishment through the branch to the outermost twig. So Christ communicates the current of spiritual strength to every believer. So long as the soul is united to Christ, there is no danger that it will wither or decay.

The life of the vine will be manifest in fragrant fruit on the branches. "He that abideth in Me," said Jesus, "and I in him, the same bringeth forth much fruit: for without Me ye can do nothing." When we live by faith on the Son of God, the fruits of the Spirit will be seen in our lives; not one will be missing.

"My Father is the husbandman. Every branch in Me that beareth not fruit He taketh away." While the graft is outwardly united with the vine, there may be no vital connection. Then there will be no growth or fruitfulness. So there may be an apparent connection with Christ without a real union with Him by faith. A profession of religion places men in the church, but the character and conduct show whether they are in connection with Christ. If they bear no fruit, they are false branches. Their separation from Christ involves a ruin as complete as that represented by the dead branch. "If a man abide not in Me," said Christ, "he is cast forth as a branch, and is withered; and men gather them, and cast them into the fire, and they are burned."

"And every branch that beareth fruit, He purgeth it, that it may bring forth more fruit." From the chosen twelve who had followed Jesus, one as a withered branch was about to be taken away; the rest were to pass under the pruning knife of bitter trial. Jesus with solemn tenderness explained the purpose of the husbandman. The pruning will cause pain, but it is the Father who applies the knife. He works with no wanton hand or indifferent heart. There are branches trailing upon the ground; these must be cut loose from the earthly supports to which their tendrils are fastening. They are to reach heavenward, and find their support in God. The excessive foliage that draws away the life current from the fruit must be pruned off. The overgrowth must be cut out, to give room for the healing beams of the Sun of Righteousness. The husbandman prunes away the harmful growth, that the fruit may be richer and more abundant.

"Herein is My Father glorified," said Jesus, "that ye bear much fruit." God desires to manifest through you the holiness, the benevolence, the compassion, of His own character. Yet the Saviour does not bid the disciples labor to bear fruit. He tells them to abide in Him. "If ye abide in Me," He says, "and My words abide in you, ye shall ask what ye will, and it shall be done unto you." It is through the word that Christ abides in His followers. This is the same vital union that is represented by eating His flesh and drinking His blood. The words of Christ are spirit and life. Receiving them, you receive the life of the Vine. You live "by every word that proceedeth out of the mouth of God." Matt. 4:4. The life of Christ in you produces the same fruits as in Him. Living in Christ, adhering to Christ, supported by Christ, drawing nourishment from Christ, you bear fruit after the similitude of Christ.

In this last meeting with His disciples, the great desire which Christ expressed for them was that they might love one another as He had loved them. Again and again He spoke of this. "These things I command you," He said repeatedly, "that ye love one another." His very first injunction when alone with them in the upper chamber was, "A new commandment I give unto you, That ye love one another; as I have loved you, that ye also love one another." To the disciples this commandment was new; for they had not loved one another as Christ had loved them. He saw that new ideas and impulses must control them; that new principles must be practiced by them; through His life and death they were to receive a new conception of love. The command to love one another had a new meaning in the light of His self-sacrifice. The whole work of grace is one continual service of love, of self-denying, self-sacrificing effort. During every hour of Christ's sojourn upon the earth, the love of God was flowing from Him in irrepressible streams. All who are imbued with His Spirit will love as He loved. The very principle that actuated Christ will actuate them in all their dealing one with another.

This love is the evidence of their discipleship. "By this shall all men know that ye are My disciples," said Jesus, "if ye have love one to another." When men are bound together, not by force or self-interest, but by love, they show the working of an influence that is above every human influence. Where this oneness exists, it is evidence that the image of God is being restored in humanity, that a new principle of life has been implanted. It shows that there is power in the divine nature to withstand the supernatural agencies of evil, and that the grace of God subdues the selfishness inherent in the natural heart.

This love, manifested in the church, will surely stir the wrath of Satan. Christ did not mark out for His disciples an easy path. "If the world hate you," He said, "ye know that it hated Me before it hated you. If ye were of the world, the world would love his own: but because ye are not of the world, but I have chosen you out of the world, therefore the world hateth you. Remember the word that I said unto you, The servant is not greater than his lord. If they have persecuted Me, they will also persecute you; if they have kept My saying, they will keep yours also. But all these things will they do unto you for My name's sake, because they know not Him that sent Me." The gospel is to be carried forward by aggressive warfare, in the midst of opposition, peril, loss, and suffering. But those who do this work are only following in their Master's steps.

As the world's Redeemer, Christ was constantly confronted with apparent failure. He, the messenger of mercy to our world, seemed to do little of the work He longed to do in uplifting and saving. Satanic influences were constantly working to oppose His way. But He would not be discouraged. Through the prophecy of Isaiah He declares, "I have labored in vain, I have spent My strength for nought, and in vain: yet surely My judgment is with the Lord, and My work with My God. . . . Though Israel be not gathered, yet shall I be glorious in the eyes of the Lord, and My God shall be My strength." It is to Christ that the promise is given, "Thus saith the Lord, the Redeemer of Israel, and His Holy One, to Him whom man despiseth, to Him whom the nation abhorreth; . . . thus saith the Lord: . . . I will preserve Thee, and give Thee for a covenant of the people, to establish the earth, to cause to inherit the desolate heritages; that Thou mayest say to the prisoners, Go forth; to them that are in darkness, Show yourselves. . . . They shall not hunger nor thirst; neither shall the heat nor sun smite them: for He that hath mercy on them shall lead them, even by the springs of water shall He guide them." Isa. 49:4, 5, 7-10.

Upon this word Jesus rested, and He gave Satan no advantage. When the last steps of Christ's humiliation were to be taken, when the deepest sorrow was closing about His soul, He said to His disciples, "The prince of this world cometh, and hath nothing in Me." "The prince of this world is judged." Now shall he be cast out. John 14:30; 16:11; 12:31. With prophetic eye Christ traced the scenes to take place in His last great conflict. He knew that when He should exclaim, "It is finished," all heaven would triumph. His ear caught the distant music and the shouts of victory in the heavenly courts. He knew that the knell of Satan's empire would then be sounded, and the name of Christ would be heralded from world to world throughout the universe.

Christ rejoiced that He could do more for His followers than they could ask or think. He spoke with assurance, knowing that an almighty decree had been given before the world was made. He knew that truth, armed with the omnipotence of the Holy Spirit, would conquer in the contest with evil; and that the bloodstained banner would wave triumphantly over His followers. He knew that the life of His trusting disciples would be like His, a series of uninterrupted victories, not seen to be such here, but recognized as such in the great hereafter.

"These things I have spoken unto you," He said, "that in Me ye might have peace. In the world ye shall have tribulation: but be of good cheer; I have overcome the world." Christ did not fail, neither was He discouraged, and His followers are to manifest a faith of the same enduring nature. They are to live as He lived, and work as He worked, because they depend on Him as the great Master Worker. Courage, energy, and perseverance they must possess. Though apparent impossibilities obstruct their way, by His grace they are to go forward. Instead of deploring difficulties, they are called upon to surmount them. They are to despair of nothing, and to hope for everything. With the golden chain of His matchless love Christ has bound them to the throne of God. It is His purpose that the highest influence in the universe, emanating from the source of all power, shall be theirs. They are to have power to resist evil, power that neither earth, nor death, nor hell can master, power that will enable them to overcome as Christ overcame.

Christ designs that heaven's order, heaven's plan of government, heaven's divine harmony, shall be represented in His church on earth. Thus in His people He is glorified. Through them the Sun of Righteousness will shine in undimmed luster to the world. Christ has given to His church ample facilities, that He may receive a large revenue of glory from His redeemed, purchased possession. He has bestowed upon His people capabilities and blessings that they may represent His own sufficiency. The church, endowed with the righteousness of Christ, is His depositary, in which the riches of His mercy, His grace, and His love, are to appear in full and final display. Christ looks upon His people in their purity and perfection, as the reward of His humiliation, and the supplement of His glory,—Christ, the great Center, from whom radiates all glory.

With strong, hopeful words the Saviour ended His instruction. Then He poured out the burden of His soul in prayer for His disciples. Lifting His eyes to heaven, He said, "Father, the hour is come; glorify Thy Son, that Thy Son also may glorify Thee: as Thou hast given Him power over all flesh, that He should give eternal life to as many as Thou hast given Him. And this is life eternal, that they might know Thee the only true God, and Jesus Christ, whom Thou hast sent."

Christ had finished the work that was given Him to do. He had glorified God on the earth. He had manifested the Father's name. He had gathered out those who were to continue His work among men. And He said, "I am glorified in them. And now I am no more in the world, but these are in the world, and I come to Thee. Holy Father, keep through Thine own name those whom Thou hast given Me, that they may be one, as We are." "Neither pray I for these alone, but for them also which shall believe on Me through their word; that they all may be one; . . . I in them, and Thou in Me, that they may be made perfect in one; and that the world may know that Thou hast sent Me, and hast loved them, as Thou hast loved Me."

Thus in the language of one who has divine authority, Christ gives His elect church into the Father's arms. As a consecrated high priest He intercedes for His people. As a faithful shepherd He gathers His flock under the shadow of the Almighty, in the strong and sure refuge. For Him there waits the last battle with Satan, and He goes forth to meet it.

Gethsemane

In company with His disciples, the Saviour slowly made His way to the garden of Gethsemane. The Passover moon, broad and full, shone from a cloudless sky. The city of pilgrims' tents was hushed into silence.

Jesus had been earnestly conversing with His disciples and instructing them; but as He neared Gethsemane, He became strangely silent. He had often visited this spot for meditation and prayer; but never with a heart so full of sorrow as upon this night of His last agony. Throughout His life on earth He had walked in the light of God's presence. When in conflict with men who were inspired by the very spirit of Satan, He could say, "He that sent Me is with Me: the Father hath not left Me alone; for I do always those things that please Him." John 8:29. But now He seemed to be shut out from the light of God's sustaining presence. Now He was numbered with the transgressors. The guilt of fallen humanity He must bear. Upon Him who knew no sin must be laid the iniquity of us all. So dreadful does sin appear to Him, so great is the weight of guilt which He must bear, that He is tempted to fear it will shut Him out forever from His Father's love. Feeling how terrible is the wrath of God against transgression, He exclaims, "My soul is exceeding sorrowful, even unto death."

As they approached the garden, the disciples had marked the change that came over their Master. Never before had they seen Him so utterly sad and silent. As He proceeded, this strange sadness deepened; yet they dared not question Him as to the cause. His form swayed as if He were about to fall. Upon reaching the garden, the disciples looked anxiously for His usual place of retirement, that their Master might rest. Every step that He now took was with labored effort. He groaned aloud, as if suffering under the pressure of a terrible burden. Twice His companions supported Him, or He would have fallen to the earth.

Near the entrance to the garden, Jesus left all but three of the disciples, bidding them pray for themselves and for Him. With Peter, James, and John, He entered its secluded recesses. These three disciples were Christ's closest companions. They had beheld His glory on the mount of transfiguration; they had seen Moses and Elijah talking with Him; they had heard the voice from heaven; now in His great struggle, Christ desired their presence near Him. Often they had passed the night with Him in this retreat. On these occasions, after a season of watching and prayer, they would sleep undisturbed at a little distance from their Master, until He awoke them in the morning to go forth anew to labor. But now He desired them to spend the night with Him in prayer. Yet He could not bear that even they should witness the agony He was to endure.

"Tarry ye here," He said, "and watch with Me."

He went a little distance from them—not so far but that they could both see and hear Him—and fell prostrate upon the ground. He felt that by sin He was being separated from His Father. The gulf was so broad, so black, so deep, that His spirit shuddered before it. This agony He must not exert His divine power to escape. As man He must suffer the consequences of man's sin. As man He must endure the wrath of God against transgression.

Christ was now standing in a different attitude from that in which He had ever stood before. His suffering can best be described in the words of the prophet, "Awake, O sword, against My shepherd, and against the man that is My fellow, saith the Lord of hosts." Zech. 13:7. As the substitute and surety for sinful man, Christ was suffering under divine justice. He saw what justice meant. Hitherto He had been as an intercessor for others; now He longed to have an intercessor for Himself.

As Christ felt His unity with the Father broken up, He feared that in His human nature He would be unable to endure the coming conflict with the powers of darkness. In the wilderness of temptation the destiny of the human race had been at stake. Christ was then conqueror. Now the tempter had come for the last fearful struggle. For this he had been preparing during the three years of Christ's ministry. Everything was at stake with him. If he failed here, his hope of mastery was lost; the kingdoms of the world would finally become Christ's; he himself would be overthrown and cast out. But if Christ could be overcome, the earth would become Satan's kingdom, and the human race would be forever in his power. With the issues of the conflict before Him, Christ's soul was filled with dread of separation from God. Satan told Him that if He became the surety for a sinful world, the separation would be eternal. He would be identified with Satan's kingdom, and would nevermore be one with God.

And what was to be gained by this sacrifice? How hopeless appeared the guilt and ingratitude of men! In its hardest features Satan pressed the situation upon the Redeemer: The people who claim to be above all others in temporal and spiritual advantages have rejected You. They are seeking to destroy You, the foundation, the center and seal of the promises made to them as a peculiar people. One of Your own disciples, who has listened to Your instruction, and has been among the foremost in church activities, will betray You. One of Your most zealous followers will deny You. All will forsake You. Christ's whole being abhorred the thought. That those whom He had undertaken to save, those whom He loved so much, should unite in the plots of Satan, this pierced His soul. The conflict was terrible. Its measure was the guilt of His nation, of His accusers and betrayer, the guilt of a world lying in wickedness. The sins of men weighed heavily upon Christ, and the sense of God's wrath against sin was crushing out His life.

Behold Him contemplating the price to be paid for the human soul. In His agony He clings to the cold ground, as if to prevent Himself from being drawn farther from God. The chilling dew of night falls upon His prostrate form, but He heeds it not. From His pale lips comes the bitter cry, "O My Father, if it be possible, let this cup pass from Me." Yet even now He adds, "Nevertheless not as I will, but as Thou wilt."

The human heart longs for sympathy in suffering. This longing Christ felt to the very depths of His being. In the supreme agony of His soul He came to His disciples with a yearning desire to hear some words of comfort from those whom He had so often blessed and comforted, and shielded in sorrow and distress. The One who had always had words of sympathy for them was now suffering superhuman agony, and He longed to know that they were praying for Him and for themselves. How dark seemed the malignity of sin! Terrible was the temptation to let the human race bear the consequences of its own guilt, while He stood innocent before God. If He could only know that His disciples understood and appreciated this, He would be strengthened.

Rising with painful effort, He staggered to the place where He had left His companions. But He "findeth them asleep." Had He found them praying, He would have been relieved. Had they been seeking refuge in God, that satanic agencies might not prevail over them, He would have been comforted by their steadfast faith. But they had not heeded the repeated warning, "Watch and pray." At first they had been much troubled to see their Master, usually so calm and dignified, wrestling with a sorrow that was beyond comprehension. They had prayed as they heard the strong cries of the sufferer. They did not intend to forsake their Lord, but they seemed paralyzed by a stupor which they might have shaken off if they had continued pleading with God. They did not realize the necessity of watchfulness and earnest prayer in order to withstand temptation.

Just before He bent His footsteps to the garden, Jesus had said to the disciples, "All ye shall be offended because of Me this night." They had given Him the strongest assurance that they would go with Him to prison and to death. And poor, self-sufficient Peter had added, "Although all shall be offended, yet will not I." Mark 14:27, 29. But the disciples trusted to themselves. They did not look to the mighty Helper as Christ had counseled them to do. Thus when the Saviour was most in need of their sympathy and prayers, they were found asleep. Even Peter was sleeping.

And John, the loving disciple who had leaned upon the breast of Jesus, was asleep. Surely, the love of John for his Master should have kept him awake. His earnest prayers should have mingled with those of his loved Saviour in the time of His supreme sorrow. The Redeemer had spent entire nights praying for His disciples, that their faith might not fail. Should Jesus now put to James and John the question He had once asked them, "Are ye able to drink of the cup that I shall drink of, and to be baptized with the baptism that I am baptized with?" they would not have ventured to answer, "We are able." Matt. 20:22.

The disciples awakened at the voice of Jesus, but they hardly knew Him, His face was so changed by anguish. Addressing Peter, Jesus said, "Simon, sleepest thou? couldest not thou watch one hour? Watch ye and pray, lest ye enter into temptation. The spirit truly is ready, but the flesh is weak." The weakness of His disciples awakened the sympathy of Jesus. He feared that they would not be able to endure the test which would come upon them in His betrayal and death. He did not reprove them, but said, "Watch ye and pray, lest ye enter into temptation." Even in His great agony, He was seeking to excuse their weakness. "The spirit truly is ready," He said, "but the flesh is weak."

Again the Son of God was seized with superhuman agony, and fainting and exhausted, He staggered back to the place of His former struggle. His suffering was even greater than before. As the agony of soul came upon Him, "His sweat was as it were great drops of blood falling down to the ground." The cypress and palm trees were the silent witnesses of His anguish. From their leafy branches dropped heavy dew upon His stricken form, as if nature wept over its Author wrestling alone with the powers of darkness.

A short time before, Jesus had stood like a mighty cedar, withstanding the storm of opposition that spent its fury upon Him. Stubborn wills, and hearts filled with malice and subtlety, had striven in vain to confuse and overpower Him. He stood forth in divine majesty as the Son of God. Now He was like a reed beaten and bent by the angry storm. He had approached the consummation of His work a conqueror, having at each step gained the victory over the powers of darkness. As one already glorified, He had claimed oneness with God. In unfaltering accents He had poured out His songs of praise. He had spoken to His disciples in words of courage and tenderness. Now had come the hour of the power of darkness. Now His voice was heard on the still evening air, not in tones of triumph, but full of human anguish. The words of the Saviour were borne to the ears of the drowsy disciples, "O My Father, if this cup may not pass away from Me, except I drink it, Thy will be done."

The first impulse of the disciples was to go to Him; but He had bidden them tarry there, watching unto prayer. When Jesus came to them, He found them still sleeping. Again He had felt a longing for companionship, for some words from His disciples which would bring relief, and break the spell of darkness that well-nigh overpowered Him. But their eyes were heavy; "neither wist they what to answer Him." His presence aroused them. They saw His face marked with the bloody sweat of agony, and they were filled with fear. His anguish of mind they could not understand. "His visage was so marred more than any man, and His form more than the sons of men." Isa. 52:14.

Turning away, Jesus sought again His retreat, and fell prostrate, overcome by the horror of a great darkness. The humanity of the Son of God trembled in that trying hour. He prayed not now for His disciples that their faith might not fail, but for His own tempted, agonized soul. The awful moment had come—that moment which was to decide the destiny of the world. The fate of humanity trembled in the balance. Christ might even now refuse to drink the cup apportioned to guilty man. It was not yet too late. He might wipe the bloody sweat from His brow, and leave man to perish in his iniquity. He might say, Let the transgressor receive the penalty of his sin, and I will go back to My Father. Will the Son of God drink the bitter cup of humiliation and agony? Will the innocent suffer the consequences of the curse of sin, to save the guilty? The words fall tremblingly from the pale lips of Jesus, "O My Father, if this cup may not pass away from Me, except I drink it, Thy will be done."

Three times has He uttered that prayer. Three times has humanity shrunk from the last, crowning sacrifice. But now the history of the human race comes up before the world's Redeemer. He sees that the transgressors of the law, if left to themselves, must perish. He sees the helplessness of man. He sees the power of sin. The woes and lamentations of a doomed world rise before Him. He beholds its impending fate, and His decision is made. He will save man at any cost to Himself. He accepts His baptism of blood, that through Him perishing millions may gain everlasting life. He has left the courts of heaven, where all is purity, happiness, and glory, to save the one lost sheep, the one world that has fallen by transgression. And He will not turn from His mission. He will become the propitiation of a race that has willed to sin. His prayer now breathes only submission: "If this cup may not pass away from Me, except I drink it, Thy will be done."

Having made the decision, He fell dying to the ground from which He had partially risen. Where now were His disciples, to place their hands tenderly beneath the head of their fainting Master, and bathe that brow, marred indeed more than the sons of men? The Saviour trod the wine press alone, and of the people there was none with Him.

But God suffered with His Son. Angels beheld the Saviour's agony. They saw their Lord enclosed by legions of satanic forces, His nature weighed down with a shuddering, mysterious dread. There was silence in heaven. No harp was touched. Could mortals have viewed the amazement of the angelic host as in silent grief they watched the Father separating His beams of light, love, and glory from His beloved Son, they would better understand how offensive in His sight is sin.

The worlds unfallen and the heavenly angels had watched with intense interest as the conflict drew to its close. Satan and his confederacy of evil, the legions of apostasy, watched intently this great crisis in the work of redemption. The powers of good and evil waited to see what answer would come to Christ's thrice-repeated prayer. Angels had longed to bring relief to the divine sufferer, but this might not be. No way of escape was found for the Son of God. In this awful crisis, when everything was at stake, when the mysterious cup trembled in the hand of the sufferer, the heavens opened, a light shone forth amid the stormy darkness of the crisis hour, and the mighty angel who stands in God's presence, occupying the position from which Satan fell, came to the side of Christ. The angel came not to take the cup from Christ's hand, but to strengthen Him to drink it, with the assurance of the Father's love. He came to give power to the divine-human suppliant. He pointed Him to the open heavens, telling Him of the souls that would be saved as the result of His sufferings. He assured Him that His Father is greater and more powerful than Satan, that His death would result in the utter discomfiture of Satan, and that the kingdom of this world would be given to the saints of the Most High. He told Him that He would see of the travail of His soul, and be satisfied, for He would see a multitude of the human race saved, eternally saved.

Christ's agony did not cease, but His depression and discouragement left Him. The storm had in nowise abated, but He who was its object was strengthened to meet its fury. He came forth calm and serene. A heavenly peace rested upon His bloodstained face. He had borne that which no human being could ever bear; for He had tasted the sufferings of death for every man.

The sleeping disciples had been suddenly awakened by the light surrounding the Saviour. They saw the angel bending over their prostrate Master. They saw him lift the Saviour's head upon his bosom, and point toward heaven. They heard his voice, like sweetest music, speaking words of comfort and hope. The disciples recalled the scene upon the mount of transfiguration. They remembered the glory that in the temple had encircled Jesus, and the voice of God that spoke from the cloud. Now that same glory was again revealed, and they had no further fear for their Master. He was under the care of God; a mighty angel had been sent to protect Him. Again the disciples in their weariness yield to the strange stupor that overpowers them. Again Jesus finds them sleeping.

Looking sorrowfully upon them He says, "Sleep on now, and take your rest: behold, the hour is at hand, and the Son of man is betrayed into the hands of sinners."

Even as He spoke these words, He heard the footsteps of the mob in search of Him, and said, "Rise, let us be going: behold, he is at hand that doth betray Me."

No traces of His recent agony were visible as Jesus stepped forth to meet His betrayer. Standing in advance of His disciples He said, "Whom seek ye?" They answered, "Jesus of Nazareth." Jesus replied, "I am He." As these words were spoken, the angel who had lately ministered to Jesus moved between Him and the mob. A divine light illuminated the Saviour's face, and a dovelike form overshadowed Him. In the presence of this divine glory, the murderous throng could not stand for a moment. They staggered back. Priests, elders, soldiers, and even Judas, fell as dead men to the ground.

The angel withdrew, and the light faded away. Jesus had opportunity to escape, but He remained, calm and self-possessed. As one glorified He stood in the midst of that hardened band, now prostrate and helpless at His feet. The disciples looked on, silent with wonder and awe.

But quickly the scene changed. The mob started up. The Roman soldiers, the priests and Judas, gathered about Christ. They seemed ashamed of their weakness, and fearful that He would yet escape. Again the question was asked by the

Redeemer, "Whom seek ye?" They had had evidence that He who stood before them was the Son of God, but they would not be convinced. To the question, "Whom seek ye?" again they answered, "Jesus of Nazareth." The Saviour then said, "I have told you that I am He: if therefore ye seek Me, let these go their way"—pointing to the disciples. He knew how weak was their faith, and He sought to shield them from temptation and trial. For them He was ready to sacrifice Himself.

Judas the betrayer did not forget the part he was to act. When the mob entered the garden, he had led the way, closely followed by the high priest. To the pursuers of Jesus he had given a sign, saying, "Whomsoever I shall kiss, that same is He: hold Him fast." Matt. 26:48. Now he pretends to have no part with them. Coming close to Jesus, he takes His hand as a familiar friend. With the words, "Hail, Master," he kisses Him repeatedly, and appears to weep as if in sympathy with Him in His peril.

Jesus said to him, "Friend, wherefore art thou come?" His voice trembled with sorrow as He added, "Judas, betrayest thou the Son of man with a kiss?" This appeal should have aroused the conscience of the betrayer, and touched his stubborn heart; but honor, fidelity, and human tenderness had forsaken him. He stood bold and defiant, showing no disposition to relent. He had given himself up to Satan, and he had no power to resist him. Jesus did not refuse the traitor's kiss.

The mob grew bold as they saw Judas touch the person of Him who had so recently been glorified before their eyes. They now laid hold of Jesus, and proceeded to bind those precious hands that had ever been employed in doing good.

The disciples had thought that their Master would not suffer Himself to be taken. For the same power that had caused the mob to fall as dead men could keep them helpless, until Jesus and His companions should escape. They were disappointed and indignant as they saw the cords brought forward to bind the hands of Him whom they loved. Peter in his anger rashly drew his sword and tried to defend his Master, but he only cut off an ear of the high priest's servant. When Jesus saw what was done, He released His hands, though held firmly by the Roman soldiers, and saying, "Suffer ye thus far," He touched the wounded ear, and it was instantly made whole. He then said to Peter, "Put up again thy sword into his place: for all they that take the sword shall perish with the sword. Thinkest thou that I cannot now pray to My Father, and He shall presently give Me more than twelve legions of angels?"—a legion in place of each one of the disciples. Oh, why, the disciples thought, does He not save Himself and us? Answering their unspoken thought, He added, "But how then shall the scriptures be fulfilled, that thus it must be?" "The cup which My Father hath given Me, shall I not drink it?"

The official dignity of the Jewish leaders had not prevented them from joining in the pursuit of Jesus. His arrest was too important a matter to be trusted to subordinates; the wily priests and elders had joined the temple police and the rabble in following Judas to Gethsemane. What a company for those

dignitaries to unite with—a mob that was eager for excitement, and armed with all kinds of implements, as if in pursuit of a wild beast!

Turning to the priests and elders, Christ fixed upon them His searching glance. The words He spoke they would never forget as long as life should last. They were as the sharp arrows of the Almighty. With dignity He said: You come out against Me with swords and staves as you would against a thief or a robber. Day by day I sat teaching in the temple. You had every opportunity of laying hands upon Me, and you did nothing. The night is better suited to your work. "This is your hour, and the power of darkness."

The disciples were terrified as they saw Jesus permit Himself to be taken and bound. They were offended that He should suffer this humiliation to Himself and them. They could not understand His conduct, and they blamed Him for submitting to the mob. In their indignation and fear, Peter proposed that they save themselves. Following this suggestion, "they all forsook Him, and fled." But Christ had foretold this desertion, "Behold," He had said, "the hour cometh, yea, is now come, that ye shall be scattered, every man to his own, and shall leave Me alone: and yet I am not alone, because the Father is with Me." John 16:32.

Before Annas and the Court of Caiaphas

Over the brook Kedron, past gardens and olive groves, and through the hushed streets of the sleeping city, they hurried Jesus. It was past midnight, and the cries of the hooting mob that followed Him broke sharply upon the still air. The Saviour was bound and closely guarded, and He moved painfully. But in eager haste His captors made their way with Him to the palace of Annas, the ex-high priest.

Annas was the head of the officiating priestly family, and in deference to his age he was recognized by the people as high priest. His counsel was sought and carried out as the voice of God. He must first see Jesus a captive to priestly power. He must be present at the examination of the prisoner, for fear that the less-experienced Caiaphas might fail of securing the object for which they were working. His artifice, cunning, and subtlety must be used on this occasion; for, at all events, Christ's condemnation must be secured.

Christ was to be tried formally before the Sanhedrin; but before Annas He was subjected to a preliminary trial. Under the Roman rule the Sanhedrin could not execute the sentence of death. They could only examine a prisoner, and pass judgment, to be ratified by the Roman authorities. It was therefore necessary to bring against Christ charges that would be regarded as criminal by the Romans. An accusation must also be found which would condemn Him in the eyes of the Jews. Not a few among the priests and rulers had been convicted by Christ's teaching, and only fear of excommunication prevented them from confessing Him. The priests well remembered the question of Nicodemus, "Doth our law judge any man, before it hear him, and know what he doeth?" John 7:51. This question had for the time broken up the council, and thwarted their plans. Joseph of Arimathaea and Nicodemus were not now to be summoned, but there were others who might dare to speak in favor of justice. The trial must be so conducted as to unite the members of the Sanhedrin against Christ. There were two charges which the priests desired to maintain. If Jesus could be proved a blasphemer, He would be condemned by the Jews. If convicted of sedition, it would secure His condemnation by the Romans. The second charge Annas tried first to establish. He questioned Jesus concerning His disciples and His doctrines, hoping the prisoner would say something that would give him material upon which to work. He thought to draw out some statement to prove that He was seeking to establish a secret society, with the purpose of setting up a new kingdom. Then the priests could deliver Him to the Romans as a disturber of the peace and a creator of insurrection.

Christ read the priest's purpose as an open book. As if reading the inmost soul of His questioner, He denied that there was between Him and His followers any secret bond of union, or that He gathered them secretly and in the darkness to conceal His designs. He had no secrets in regard to His purposes or doctrines. "I spake openly to the world," He answered; "I ever taught in the synagogue, and in the temple, whither the Jews always resort; and in secret have I said nothing."

The Saviour contrasted His own manner of work with the methods of His accusers. For months they had hunted Him, striving to entrap Him and bring Him before a secret tribunal, where they might obtain by perjury what it was impossible to gain by fair means. Now they were carrying out their purpose. The midnight seizure by a mob, the mockery and abuse before He was condemned, or even accused, was their manner of work, not His. Their action was in violation of the law. Their own rules declared that every man should be treated as innocent until proved guilty. By their own rules the priests stood condemned.

Turning upon His questioner, Jesus said, "Why askest thou Me?" Had not the priests and rulers sent spies to watch His movements, and report His every word? Had not these been present at every gathering of the people, and carried to the priests information of all His sayings and doings? "Ask them which heard Me, what I have said unto them," replied Jesus; "behold, they know what I said."

Annas was silenced by the decision of the answer. Fearing that Christ would say something regarding his course of action that he would prefer to keep covered up, he said nothing more to Him at this time. One of his officers, filled with wrath as he saw Annas silenced, struck Jesus on the face, saying, "Answerest Thou the high priest so?"

Christ calmly replied, "If I have spoken evil, bear witness of the evil: but if well, why smitest thou Me?" He spoke no burning words of retaliation. His calm answer came from a heart sinless, patient, and gentle, that would not be provoked.

Christ suffered keenly under abuse and insult. At the hands of the beings whom He had created, and for whom He was making an infinite sacrifice, He received every indignity. And He suffered in proportion to the perfection of His holiness and His hatred of sin. His trial by men who acted as fiends was to Him a perpetual sacrifice. To be surrounded by human beings under the control of Satan was revolting to Him. And He knew that in a moment, by the flashing forth of His divine power, He could lay His cruel tormentors in the dust. This made the trial the harder to bear.

The Jews were looking for a Messiah to be revealed in outward show. They expected Him, by one flash of overmastering will, to change the current of men's thoughts, and force from them an acknowledgment of His supremacy. Thus, they believed, He was to secure His own exaltation, and gratify their ambitious hopes. Thus when Christ was treated with contempt, there came to Him a strong temptation to manifest His divine character. By a word, by a look, He could compel His persecutors to confess that He was Lord above kings and rulers, priests and temple. But it was His difficult task to keep to the position He had chosen as one with humanity.

The angels of heaven witnessed every movement made against their loved Commander. They longed to deliver Christ. Under God the angels are all-powerful. On one occasion, in obedience to the command of Christ, they slew of the Assyrian army in one night one hundred and eighty-five thousand men. How easily could the angels, beholding the shameful scene of the trial of Christ, have testified their indignation by consuming the adversaries of God! But they were not commanded to do this. He who could have doomed His enemies to death bore with their cruelty. His love for His Father, and His pledge, made from the foundation of the world, to become the Sin Bearer, led Him to endure uncomplainingly the coarse treatment of those He came to save. It was a part of His mission to bear, in His humanity, all the taunts and abuse that men could heap upon Him. The only hope of humanity was in this submission of Christ to all that He could endure from the hands and hearts of men.

Christ had said nothing that could give His accusers an advantage; yet He was bound, to signify that He was condemned. There must, however, be a pretense of justice. It was necessary that there should be the form of a legal trial. This the authorities were determined to hasten. They knew the regard in which Jesus was held by the people, and feared that if the arrest were noised abroad, a rescue would be attempted. Again, if the trial and execution were not brought about at once, there would be a week's delay on account of the celebration of the Passover. This might defeat their plans. In securing the condemnation of Jesus they depended largely upon the clamor of the mob, many of them the rabble of Jerusalem. Should there be a week's delay, the excitement would abate, and a reaction would be likely to set in. The better part of the people would be aroused in Christ's favor; many would come forward with testimony in His vindication, bringing to light the mighty works He had done. This would excite popular indignation against the Sanhedrin. Their proceedings would be condemned, and Jesus would be set free, to receive new homage from the multitudes. The priests and rulers therefore determined that before their purpose could become known, Jesus should be delivered into the hands of the Romans.

But first of all, an accusation was to be found. They had gained nothing as yet. Annas ordered Jesus to be taken to Caiaphas. Caiaphas belonged to the Sadducees, some of whom were now the most desperate enemies of Jesus. He himself, though wanting in force of character, was fully as severe, heartless, and unscrupulous as was Annas. He would leave no means untried to destroy Jesus. It was now early morning, and very dark; by the light of torches and lanterns the armed band with their prisoner proceeded to the high priest's palace. Here, while the members of the Sanhedrin were coming together, Annas and Caiaphas again questioned Jesus, but without success.

When the council had assembled in the judgment hall, Caiaphas took his seat as presiding officer. On either side were the judges, and those specially interested in the trial. The Roman soldiers were stationed on the platform below the throne. At the foot of the throne stood Jesus. Upon Him the gaze of the whole multitude was fixed. The excitement was intense. Of all the throng He alone was calm and serene. The very atmosphere surrounding Him seemed pervaded by a holy influence.

Caiaphas had regarded Jesus as his rival. The eagerness of the people to hear the Saviour, and their apparent readiness to accept His teachings, had aroused the bitter jealousy of the high priest. But as Caiaphas now looked upon the prisoner, he was struck with admiration for His noble and dignified bearing. A conviction came over him that this Man was akin to God. The next instant he scornfully banished the thought. Immediately his voice was heard in sneering, haughty tones demanding that Jesus work one of His mighty miracles before them. But his words fell upon the Saviour's ears as though He heard them not. The people compared the excited and malignant deportment of Annas and Caiaphas with the calm, majestic bearing of Jesus. Even in the minds of that hardened multitude arose the question, Is this man of godlike presence to be condemned as a criminal?

Caiaphas, perceiving the influence that was obtaining, hastened the trial. The enemies of Jesus were in great perplexity. They were bent on securing His condemnation, but how to accomplish this they knew not. The members of the council were divided between the Pharisees and the Sadducees. There was bitter animosity and controversy between them; certain disputed points they dared not approach for fear of a quarrel. With a few words Jesus could have excited their prejudices against each other, and thus have averted their wrath from Himself. Caiaphas knew this, and he wished to avoid stirring up a contention. There were plenty of witnesses to prove that Christ had denounced the priests and scribes, that He had called them hypocrites and murderers; but this testimony it was not expedient to bring forward. The Sadducees in their sharp contentions with the Pharisees had used to them similar language. And such testimony would have no weight with the Romans, who were themselves disgusted with the pretensions of the Pharisees. There was abundant evidence that Jesus had disregarded the traditions of the Jews, and had spoken irreverently of many of their ordinances; but in regard to tradition the Pharisees and Sadducees were at swords' points; and this evidence also would have no weight with the Romans. Christ's enemies dared not accuse Him of Sabbathbreaking, lest an examination should reveal the character of His work. If His miracles of healing were brought to light, the very object of the priests would be defeated.

False witnesses had been bribed to accuse Jesus of inciting rebellion and seeking to establish a separate government. But their testimony proved to be vague and contradictory. Under examination they falsified their own statements.

Early in His ministry Christ had said, "Destroy this temple, and in three days I will raise it up." In the figurative language of prophecy, He had thus foretold His own death and resurrection. "He spake of the temple of His body." John 2:19, 21. These words the Jews had understood in a literal sense, as referring to the temple at Jerusalem. Of all that Christ had said, the priests could find nothing to use against Him save this. By misstating these words they hoped to gain an advantage. The Romans had engaged in rebuilding and embellishing the temple, and they took great pride in it; any contempt shown to it would be sure to excite their indignation. Here Romans and Jews, Pharisees and Sadducees, could meet; for all held the temple in great veneration. On this point two witnesses were found whose testimony was not so contradictory as that of the others had been. One of them, who had been bribed to accuse Jesus, declared, "This fellow said, I am able to destroy the temple of God, and to build it in three days." Thus Christ's words were misstated. If they had been reported exactly as He spoke them, they would not have secured His condemnation even by the Sanhedrin. Had Jesus been a mere man, as the Jews claimed, His declaration would only have indicated an unreasonable, boastful spirit, but could not have been construed into blasphemy. Even as misrepresented by the false witnesses, His words contained nothing which would be regarded by the Romans as a crime worthy of death.

Patiently Jesus listened to the conflicting testimonies. No word did He utter in self-defense. At last His accusers were entangled, confused, and maddened. The trial was making no headway; it seemed that their plottings were to fail. Caiaphas was desperate. One last resort remained; Christ must be forced to condemn Himself. The high priest started from the judgment seat, his face contorted with passion, his voice and demeanor plainly indicating that were it in his power he would strike down the prisoner before him. "Answerest Thou nothing?" he exclaimed; "what is it which these witness against Thee?"

Jesus held His peace. "He was oppressed, and He was afflicted, yet He opened not His mouth: He is brought as a lamb to the slaughter, and as a sheep before her shearers is dumb, so He openeth not His mouth." Isaiah 53:7.

At last, Caiaphas, raising his right hand toward heaven, addressed Jesus in the form of a solemn oath: "I adjure Thee by the living God, that Thou tell us whether Thou be the Christ, the Son of God."

To this appeal Christ could not remain silent. There was a time to be silent, and a time to speak. He had not spoken until directly questioned. He knew that to answer now would make His death certain. But the appeal was made by the highest acknowledged authority of the nation, and in the name of the Most High. Christ would not fail to show proper respect for the law. More than this, His own relation to the Father was called in question. He must plainly declare His character and mission. Jesus had said to His disciples, "Whosoever therefore shall confess Me before men, him will I confess also before My Father which is in heaven." Matt. 10:32. Now by His own example He repeated the lesson.

Every ear was bent to listen, and every eye was fixed on His face as He answered, "Thou hast said." A heavenly light seemed to illuminate His pale countenance as He added, "Nevertheless I say unto you, Hereafter shall ye see the Son of man sitting on the right hand of power, and coming in the clouds of heaven."

For a moment the divinity of Christ flashed through His guise of humanity. The high priest quailed before the penetrating eyes of the Saviour. That look seemed to read his hidden thoughts, and burn into his heart. Never in afterlife did he forget that searching glance of the persecuted Son of God.

"Hereafter," said Jesus, "shall ye see the Son of man sitting on the right hand of power, and coming in the clouds of heaven." In these words Christ presented the reverse of the scene then taking place. He, the Lord of life and glory, would be seated at God's right hand. He would be the judge of all the earth, and from His decision there could be no appeal. Then every secret thing would be set in the light of God's countenance, and judgment be passed upon every man according to his deeds.

The words of Christ startled the high priest. The thought that there was to be a resurrection of the dead, when all would stand at the bar of God, to be rewarded according to their works, was a thought of terror to Caiaphas. He did not wish to believe that in future he would receive sentence according to his works. There rushed before his mind as a panorama the scenes of the final judgment. For a moment he saw the fearful spectacle of the graves giving up their dead, with the secrets he had hoped were forever hidden. For a moment he felt as if standing before the eternal Judge, whose eye, which sees all things, was reading his soul, bringing to light mysteries supposed to be hidden with the dead.

The scene passed from the priest's vision. Christ's words cut him, the Sadducee, to the quick. Caiaphas had denied the doctrine of the resurrection, the judgment, and a future life. Now he was maddened by satanic fury. Was this man, a prisoner before him, to assail his most cherished theories? Rending his robe, that the people might see his pretended horror, he demanded that without further preliminaries the prisoner be condemned for blasphemy. "What further need have we of witnesses?" he said; "behold, now ye have heard His blasphemy. What think ye?" And they all condemned Him.

Conviction mingled with passion led Caiaphas to do as he did. He was furious with himself for believing Christ's words, and instead of rending his heart under a deep sense of truth, and confessing that Jesus was the Messiah, he rent his priestly robes in determined resistance. This act was deeply significant. Little did Caiaphas realize its meaning. In this act, done to influence the judges and secure Christ's condemnation, the high priest had condemned himself. By the law of God he was disqualified for the priesthood. He had pronounced upon himself the death sentence.

A high priest was not to rend his garments. By the Levitical law, this was prohibited under sentence of death. Under no circumstances, on no occasion, was the priest to rend his robe. It was the custom among the Jews for the garments to be rent at the death of friends, but this custom the priests were not to observe. Express command had been given by Christ to Moses concerning this. Lev. 10:6.

Everything worn by the priest was to be whole and without blemish. By those beautiful official garments was represented the character of the great antitype, Jesus Christ. Nothing but perfection, in dress and attitude, in word and spirit, could be acceptable to God. He is holy, and His glory and perfection must be represented by the earthly service. Nothing but perfection could properly represent the sacredness of the heavenly service. Finite man might rend his own heart by showing a contrite and humble spirit. This God would discern. But no rent must be made in the priestly robes, for this would mar the representation of heavenly things. The high priest who dared to appear in holy office, and engage in the service of the sanctuary, with a rent robe, was looked upon as having severed himself from God. By rending his garment he cut himself off from being a representative character. He was no longer accepted by God as an officiating priest. This course of action, as exhibited by Caiaphas, showed human passion, human imperfection.

By rending his garments, Caiaphas made of no effect the law of God, to follow the tradition of men. A man-made law provided that in case of blasphemy a priest might rend his garments in horror at the sin, and be guiltless. Thus the law of God was made void by the laws of men.

Each action of the high priest was watched with interest by the people; and Caiaphas thought for effect to display his piety. But in this act, designed as an accusation against Christ, he was reviling the One of whom God had said, "My name is in Him." Ex. 23:21. He himself was committing blasphemy. Standing under the condemnation of God, he pronounced sentence upon Christ as a blasphemer.

When Caiaphas rent his garment, his act was significant of the place that the Jewish nation as a nation would thereafter occupy toward God. The once favored people of God were separating themselves from Him, and were fast becoming a people disowned by Jehovah. When Christ upon the cross cried out, "It is finished" (John 19:30), and the veil of the temple was rent in twain, the Holy Watcher declared that the Jewish people had rejected Him who was the antitype of all their types, the substance of all their shadows. Israel was divorced from God. Well might Caiaphas then rend his official robes, which signified that he claimed to be a representative of the great High Priest; for no longer had they any meaning for him or for the people. Well might the high priest rend his robes in horror for himself and for the nation.

The Sanhedrin had pronounced Jesus worthy of death; but it was contrary to the Jewish law to try a prisoner by night. In legal condemnation nothing could be done except in the light of day and before a full session of the council. Notwithstanding this, the Saviour was now treated as a condemned criminal, and given up to be abused by the lowest and vilest of humankind. The palace of the high priest surrounded an open court in which the soldiers and the multitude had gathered. Through this court, Jesus was taken to the guardroom, on every side meeting with mockery of His claim to be the Son of God. His own words, "sitting on the right hand of power," and, "coming in the clouds of heaven," were jeeringly repeated. While in the guardroom, awaiting His legal trial, He was not protected. The ignorant rabble had seen the cruelty with which He was treated before the council, and from this they took license to manifest all the satanic elements of their nature. Christ's very nobility and godlike bearing goaded them to madness. His meekness, His innocence, His majestic patience, filled them with hatred born of Satan. Mercy and justice were trampled upon. Never was criminal treated in so inhuman a manner as was the Son of God.

But a keener anguish rent the heart of Jesus; the blow that inflicted the deepest pain no enemy's hand could have dealt. While He was undergoing the mockery of an examination before Caiaphas, Christ had been denied by one of His own disciples.

After deserting their Master in the garden, two of the disciples had ventured to follow, at a distance, the mob that had Jesus in charge. These disciples were Peter and John. The priests recognized John as a well-known disciple of Jesus, and admitted him to the hall, hoping that as he witnessed the humiliation of his Leader, he would scorn the idea of such a one being the Son of God. John spoke in favor of Peter, and gained an entrance for him also.

In the court a fire had been kindled; for it was the coldest hour of the night, being just before the dawn. A company drew about the fire, and Peter presumptuously took his place with them. He did not wish to be recognized as a disciple of Jesus. By mingling carelessly with the crowd, he hoped to be taken for one of those who had brought Jesus to the hall.

But as the light flashed upon Peter's face, the woman who kept the door cast a searching glance upon him. She had noticed that he came in with John, she marked the look of dejection on his face, and thought that he might be a disciple of Jesus. She was one of the servants of Caiaphas' household, and was curious to know. She said to Peter, "Art not thou also one of this Man's disciples?" Peter was startled and confused; the eyes of the company instantly fastened upon him. He pretended not to understand her; but she was persistent, and said to those around her that this man was with Jesus. Peter felt compelled to answer, and said angrily, "Woman, I know Him not." This was the first denial, and immediately the cock crew. O Peter, so soon ashamed of thy Master! so soon to deny thy Lord!

The disciple John, upon entering the judgment hall, did not try to conceal the fact that he was a follower of Jesus. He did not mingle with the rough company who were reviling his Master. He was not questioned, for he did not assume a false character, and thus lay himself liable to suspicion. He sought a retired corner secure from the notice of the mob, but as near Jesus as it was possible for him to be. Here he could see and hear all that took place at the trial of his Lord.

Peter had not designed that his real character should be known. In assuming an air of indifference he had placed himself on the enemy's ground, and he became an easy prey to temptation. If he had been called to fight for his Master, he would have been a courageous soldier; but when the finger of scorn was pointed at him, he proved himself a coward. Many who do not shrink from active warfare for their Lord are driven by ridicule to deny their faith. By associating with those whom they should avoid, they place themselves in the way of temptation. They invite the enemy to tempt them, and are led to say and do that of which under other circumstances they would never have been guilty. The disciple of Christ who in our day disguises his faith through dread of suffering or reproach denies his Lord as really as did Peter in the judgment hall.

Peter tried to show no interest in the trial of his Master, but his heart was wrung with sorrow as he heard the cruel taunts, and saw the abuse He was suffering. More than this, he was surprised and angry that Jesus should humiliate Himself and His followers by submitting to such treatment. In order to conceal his true feelings, he endeavored to join with the persecutors of Jesus in their untimely jests. But his appearance was unnatural. He was acting a lie, and while seeking to talk unconcernedly he could not restrain expressions of indignation at the abuse heaped upon his Master.

Attention was called to him the second time, and he was again charged with being a follower of Jesus. He now declared with an oath, "I do not know the Man." Still another opportunity was given him. An hour had passed, when one of the servants of the high priest, being a near kinsman of the man whose ear Peter had cut off, asked him, "Did not I see thee in the garden with Him?" "Surely thou art one of them:

for thou art a Galilean, and thy speech agreeth thereto." At this Peter flew into a rage. The disciples of Jesus were noted for the purity of their language, and in order fully to deceive his questioners, and justify his assumed character, Peter now denied his Master with cursing and swearing. Again the cock crew. Peter heard it then, and he remembered the words of Jesus, "Before the cock crow twice, thou shalt deny Me thrice." Mark 14:30.

While the degrading oaths were fresh upon Peter's lips, and the shrill crowing of the cock was still ringing in his ears, the Saviour turned from the frowning judges, and looked full upon His poor disciple. At the same time Peter's eyes were drawn to his Master. In that gentle countenance he read deep pity and sorrow, but there was no anger there.

The sight of that pale, suffering face, those quivering lips, that look of compassion and forgiveness, pierced his heart like an arrow. Conscience was aroused. Memory was active. Peter called to mind his promise of a few short hours before that he would go with his Lord to prison and to death. He remembered his grief when the Saviour told him in the upper chamber that he would deny his Lord thrice that same night. Peter had just declared that he knew not Jesus, but he now realized with bitter grief how well his Lord knew him, and how accurately He had read his heart, the falseness of which was unknown even to himself.

A tide of memories rushed over him. The Saviour's tender mercy, His kindness and long-suffering, His gentleness and patience toward His erring disciples,—all was remembered. He recalled the caution, "Simon, behold, Satan hath desired to have you, that he may sift you as wheat: but I have prayed for thee, that thy faith fail not." Luke 22:31, 32. He reflected with horror upon his own ingratitude, his falsehood, his perjury. Once more he looked at his Master, and saw a sacrilegious hand raised to smite Him in the face. Unable longer to endure the scene, he rushed, heartbroken, from the hall.

He pressed on in solitude and darkness, he knew not and cared not whither. At last he found himself in Gethsemane. The scene of a few hours before came vividly to his mind. The suffering face of his Lord, stained with bloody sweat and convulsed with anguish, rose before him. He remembered with bitter remorse that Jesus had wept and agonized in prayer alone, while those who should have united with Him in that trying hour were sleeping. He remembered His solemn charge, "Watch and pray, that ye enter not into temptation." Matt. 26:41. He witnessed again the scene in the judgment hall. It was torture to his bleeding heart to know that he had added the heaviest burden to the Saviour's humiliation and grief. On the very spot where Jesus had poured out His soul in agony to His Father, Peter fell upon his face, and wished that he might die.

It was in sleeping when Jesus bade him watch and pray that Peter had prepared the way for his great sin. All the disciples, by sleeping in that critical hour, sustained a great loss. Christ knew the fiery ordeal through which they were to pass. He knew how Satan would work to paralyze their senses that they might be unready for the trial. Therefore it was that He gave them warning. Had those hours in the garden been spent in watching and prayer, Peter would not have been left to depend upon his own feeble strength. He would not have denied his Lord. Had the disciples watched with Christ in His agony, they would have been prepared to behold His suffering upon the cross. They would have understood in some degree the nature of His overpowering anguish. They would have been able to recall His words that foretold His sufferings, His death, and His resurrection. Amid the gloom of the most trying hour, some rays of hope would have lighted up the darkness and sustained their faith.

As soon as it was day, the Sanhedrin again assembled, and again Jesus was brought into the council room. He had declared Himself the Son of God, and they had construed His words into a charge against Him. But they could not condemn Him on this, for many of them had not been present at the night session, and they had not heard His words. And they knew that the Roman tribunal would find in them nothing worthy of death. But if from His own lips they could all hear those words repeated, their object might be gained. His claim to the Messiahship they might construe into a seditious political claim.

"Art Thou the Christ?" they said, "tell us." But Christ remained silent. They continued to ply Him with questions. At last in tones of mournful pathos He answered, "If I tell you, ye will not believe; and if I also ask you, ye will not answer Me, nor let Me go." But that they might be left without excuse He added the solemn warning, "Hereafter shall the Son of man sit on the right hand of the power of God."

"Art Thou then the Son of God?" they asked with one voice. He said unto them, "Ye say that I am." They cried out, "What need we any further witness? for we ourselves have heard of His own mouth."

And so by the third condemnation of the Jewish authorities, Jesus was to die. All that was now necessary, they thought, was for the Romans to ratify this condemnation, and deliver Him into their hands.

Then came the third scene of abuse and mockery, worse even than that received from the ignorant rabble. In the very presence of the priests and rulers, and with their sanction, this took place. Every feeling of sympathy or humanity had gone out of their hearts. If their arguments were weak, and failed to silence His voice, they had other weapons, such as in all ages have been used to silence heretics,—suffering, and violence, and death.

When the condemnation of Jesus was pronounced by the judges, a satanic fury took possession of the people. The roar of voices was like that of wild beasts. The crowd made a rush toward Jesus, crying, He is guilty, put Him to death! Had it not been for the Roman soldiers, Jesus would not have lived to be nailed to the cross of Calvary. He would have been torn in pieces before His judges, had not Roman authority interfered, and by force of arms restrained the violence of the mob.

Heathen men were angry at the brutal treatment of one against whom nothing had been proved. The Roman officers declared that the Jews in pronouncing condemnation upon Jesus were infringing upon the Roman power, and that it was even against the Jewish law to condemn a man to death upon his own testimony. This intervention brought a momentary lull in the proceedings; but the Jewish leaders were dead alike to pity and to shame.

Priests and rulers forgot the dignity of their office, and abused the Son of God with foul epithets. They taunted Him with His parentage. They declared that His presumption in proclaiming Himself the Messiah made Him deserving of the most ignominious death. The most dissolute men engaged in infamous abuse of the Saviour. An old garment was thrown over His head, and His persecutors struck Him in the face, saying, "Prophesy unto us, Thou Christ, Who is he that smote Thee?" When the garment was removed, one poor wretch spat in His face.

The angels of God faithfully recorded every insulting look, word, and act against their beloved Commander. One day the base men who scorned and spat upon the calm, pale face of Christ will look upon it in its glory, shining brighter than the sun.

Judas

The history of Judas presents the sad ending of a life that might have been honored of God. Had Judas died before his last journey to Jerusalem he would have been regarded as a man worthy of a place among the twelve, and one who would be greatly missed. The abhorrence which has followed him through the centuries would not have existed but for the attributes revealed at the close of his history. But it was for a purpose that his character was laid open to the world. It was to be a warning to all who, like him, should betray sacred trusts.

A little before the Passover, Judas had renewed his contract with the priests to deliver Jesus into their hands. Then it was arranged that the Saviour should be taken at one of His resorts for meditation and prayer. Since the feast at the house of Simon, Judas had had opportunity to reflect upon the deed which he had covenanted to perform, but his purpose was unchanged. For thirty pieces of silver—the price of a slave—he sold the Lord of glory to ignominy and death.

Judas had naturally a strong love for money; but he had not always been corrupt enough to do such a deed as this. He had fostered the evil spirit of avarice until it had become the ruling motive of his life. The love of mammon overbalanced his love for Christ. Through becoming the slave of one vice he gave himself to Satan, to be driven to any lengths in sin.

Judas had joined the disciples when multitudes were following Christ. The Saviour's teaching moved their hearts as they hung entranced upon His words, spoken in the synagogue, by the seaside, upon the mount. Judas saw the sick, the lame, the blind, flock to Jesus from the towns and cities. He saw the dying laid at His feet. He witnessed the Saviour's mighty works in healing the sick, casting out devils, and raising the dead. He felt in his own person the evidence of Christ's power. He recognized the teaching of Christ as superior to all that he had ever heard. He loved the Great Teacher, and desired to be with Him. He felt a desire to be changed in character and life, and he hoped to experience this through connecting himself with Jesus. The Saviour did not repulse Judas. He gave him a place among the twelve. He trusted him to do the work of an evangelist. He endowed him with power to heal the sick and to cast out devils. But Judas did not come to the point of surrendering himself fully to Christ. He did not give up his worldly ambition or his love of money. While he accepted the position of a minister of Christ, he did not bring himself under the divine molding. He felt that he could retain his own judgment and opinions, and he cultivated a disposition to criticize and accuse.

Judas was highly regarded by the disciples, and had great influence over them. He himself had a high opinion of his own qualifications, and looked upon his brethren as greatly inferior to him in judgment and ability. They did not see their opportunities, he thought, and take advantage of circumstances. The church would never prosper with such shortsighted men as leaders. Peter was impetuous; he would move without consideration. John, who was treasuring up the truths that fell from Christ's lips, was looked upon by Judas as a poor financier. Matthew, whose training had taught him accuracy in all things, was very particular in regard to honesty, and he was ever contemplating the words of Christ, and became so absorbed in them that, as Judas thought, he could not be trusted to do sharp, far-seeing business. Thus Judas summed up all the disciples, and flattered himself that the church would often be brought into perplexity and embarrassment if it were not for his ability as a manager. Judas regarded himself as the capable one, who could not be overreached. In his own estimation he was an honor to the cause, and as such he always represented himself.

Judas was blinded to his own weakness of character, and Christ placed him where he would have an opportunity to see and correct this. As treasurer for the disciples, he was called upon to provide for the needs of the little company, and to relieve the necessities of the poor. When in the Passover chamber Jesus said to him, "That thou doest, do quickly" (John 13:27), the disciples thought He had bidden him buy what was needed for the feast, or give something to the poor. In ministering to others, Judas might have developed an unselfish spirit. But while listening daily to the lessons of Christ and witnessing His unselfish life, Judas indulged his covetous disposition. The small sums that came into his hands were a continual temptation. Often when he did a little service for Christ, or devoted time to religious purposes, he paid himself out of this meager fund. In his own eyes these pretexts served to excuse his action; but in God's sight he was a thief.

Christ's oft-repeated statement that His kingdom was not of this world offended Judas. He had marked out a line upon which he expected Christ to work. He had planned that John the Baptist should be delivered from prison. But lo, John was left to be beheaded. And Jesus, instead of asserting His royal right and avenging the death of John, retired with His disciples into a country place. Judas wanted more aggressive warfare. He thought that if Jesus would not prevent the disciples from carrying out their schemes, the work would be more successful. He marked the increasing enmity of the Jewish leaders, and saw their challenge unheeded when they demanded from Christ a sign from heaven. His heart was open to unbelief, and the enemy supplied thoughts of questioning and rebellion. Why did Jesus dwell so much upon that which was discouraging? Why did He predict trial and persecution for Himself and for His disciples? The prospect of having a high place in the new kingdom had led Judas to espouse the cause of Christ. Were his hopes to be disappointed? Judas had not decided that Jesus was not the Son of God; but he was questioning, and seeking to find some explanation of His mighty works.

Notwithstanding the Saviour's own teaching, Judas was continually advancing the idea that Christ would reign as king in Jerusalem. At the feeding of the five thousand he tried to bring this about. On this occasion Judas assisted in distributing the food to the hungry multitude. He had an opportunity to see the benefit which it was in his power to impart to others. He felt the satisfaction that always comes in service to God. He helped to bring the sick and suffering from among the multitude to Christ. He saw what relief, what joy and gladness, come to human hearts through the healing power of the Restorer. He might have comprehended the methods of Christ. But he was blinded by his own selfish desires. Judas was first to take advantage of the enthusiasm excited by the miracle of the loaves. It was he who set on foot the project to take Christ by force and make Him king. His hopes were high. His disappointment was bitter.

Christ's discourse in the synagogue concerning the bread of life was the turning point in the history of Judas. He heard the words, "Except ye eat the flesh of the Son of man, and drink His blood, ye have no life in you." John 6:53. He saw that Christ was offering spiritual rather than worldly good. He regarded himself as farsighted, and thought he could see that Jesus would have no honor, and that He could bestow no high position upon His followers. He determined not to unite himself so closely to Christ but that he could draw away. He would watch. And he did watch.

From that time he expressed doubts that confused the disciples. He introduced controversies and misleading sentiments, repeating the arguments urged by the scribes and Pharisees against the claims of Christ. All the little and large troubles and crosses, the difficulties and the apparent hindrances to the advancement of the gospel, Judas interpreted as evidences against its truthfulness. He would introduce texts of Scripture that had no connection with the truths Christ was presenting. These texts, separated from their connection, perplexed the disciples, and increased the discouragement that was constantly pressing upon them. Yet all this was done by Judas in such a way as to make it appear that he was conscientious. And while the disciples were searching for evidence to confirm the words of the Great Teacher, Judas would lead them almost imperceptibly on another track. Thus in a very religious, and apparently wise, way he was presenting matters in a different light from that in which Jesus had given them, and attaching to His words a meaning that He had not conveyed. His suggestions were constantly exciting an ambitious desire for temporal preferment, and thus turning the disciples from the important things they should have considered. The dissension as to which of them should be greatest was generally excited by Judas.

When Jesus presented to the rich young ruler the condition of discipleship, Judas was displeased. He thought that a mistake had been made. If such men as this ruler could be connected with the believers, they would help sustain Christ's cause. If Judas were only received as a counselor, he thought, he could suggest many plans for the advantage of the little church. His principles and methods would differ somewhat from Christ's, but in these things he thought himself wiser than Christ.

In all that Christ said to His disciples, there was something with which, in heart, Judas disagreed. Under his influence the leaven of disaffection was fast doing its work. The disciples did not see the real agency in all this; but Jesus saw that Satan was communicating his attributes to Judas, and thus opening up a channel through which to influence the other disciples. This, a year before the betrayal, Christ declared. "Have not I chosen you twelve," He said, "and one of you is a devil?" John 6:70.

Yet Judas made no open opposition, nor seemed to question the Saviour's lessons. He made no outward murmur until the time of the feast in Simon's house. When Mary anointed the Saviour's feet, Judas manifested his covetous disposition. At the reproof from Jesus his very spirit seemed turned to gall. Wounded pride and desire for revenge broke down the barriers, and the greed so long indulged held him in control. This will be the experience of everyone who persists in tampering with sin. The elements of depravity that are not resisted and overcome, respond to Satan's temptation, and the soul is led captive at his will.

But Judas was not yet wholly hardened. Even after he had twice pledged himself to betray the Saviour, there was opportunity for repentance. At the Passover supper Jesus proved His divinity by revealing the traitor's purpose. He tenderly included Judas in the ministry to the disciples. But the last appeal of love was unheeded. Then the case of Judas was decided, and the feet that Jesus had washed went forth to the betrayer's work.

Judas reasoned that if Jesus was to be crucified, the event

must come to pass. His own act in betraying the Saviour would not change the result. If Jesus was not to die, it would only force Him to deliver Himself. At all events, Judas would gain something by his treachery. He counted that he had made a sharp bargain in betraying his Lord.

Judas did not, however, believe that Christ would permit Himself to be arrested. In betraying Him, it was his purpose to teach Him a lesson. He intended to play a part that would make the Saviour careful thenceforth to treat him with due respect. But Judas knew not that he was giving Christ up to death. How often, as the Saviour taught in parables, the scribes and Pharisees had been carried away with His striking illustrations! How often they had pronounced judgment against themselves! Often when the truth was brought home to their hearts, they had been filled with rage, and had taken up stones to cast at Him; but again and again He had made His escape. Since He had escaped so many snares, thought Judas, He certainly would not now allow Himself to be taken.

Judas decided to put the matter to the test. If Jesus really was the Messiah, the people, for whom He had done so much, would rally about Him, and would proclaim Him king. This would forever settle many minds that were now in uncertainty. Judas would have the credit of having placed the king on David's throne. And this act would secure to him the first position, next to Christ, in the new kingdom.

The false disciple acted his part in betraying Jesus. In the garden, when he said to the leaders of the mob, "Whomsoever I shall kiss, that same is He: hold Him fast" (Matt. 26:48), he fully believed that Christ would escape out of their hands. Then if they should blame him, he could say, Did I not tell you to hold Him fast?

Judas beheld the captors of Christ, acting upon his words, bind Him firmly. In amazement he saw that the Saviour suffered Himself to be led away. Anxiously he followed Him from the garden to the trial before the Jewish rulers. At every movement he looked for Him to surprise His enemies, by appearing before them as the Son of God, and setting at nought all their plots and power. But as hour after hour went by, and Jesus submitted to all the abuse heaped upon Him, a terrible fear came to the traitor that he had sold his Master to His death.

As the trial drew to a close, Judas could endure the torture of his guilty conscience no longer. Suddenly a hoarse voice rang through the hall, sending a thrill of terror to all hearts: He is innocent; spare Him, O Caiaphas!

The tall form of Judas was now seen pressing through the startled throng. His face was pale and haggard, and great drops of sweat stood on his forehead. Rushing to the throne of judgment, he threw down before the high priest the pieces of silver that had been the price of his Lord's betrayal. Eagerly grasping the robe of Caiaphas, he implored him to release Jesus, declaring that He had done nothing worthy of death. Caiaphas angrily shook him off, but was confused, and knew not what to say. The perfidy of the priests was revealed. It was evident that they had bribed the disciple to betray his Master.

"I have sinned," again cried Judas, "in that I have betrayed the innocent blood." But the high priest, regaining his self-possession, answered with scorn, "What is that to us? see thou to that." Matt. 27:4. The priests had been willing to make Judas their tool; but they despised his baseness. When he turned to them with confession, they spurned him.

Judas now cast himself at the feet of Jesus, acknowledging Him to be the Son of God, and entreating Him to deliver Himself. The Saviour did not reproach His betrayer. He knew that Judas did not repent; his confession was forced from his guilty soul by an awful sense of condemnation and a looking for of judgment, but he felt no deep, heartbreaking grief that he had betrayed the spotless Son of God, and denied the Holy One of Israel. Yet Jesus spoke no word of condemnation. He looked pityingly upon Judas, and said, For this hour came I into the world.

A murmur of surprise ran through the assembly. With amazement they beheld the forbearance of Christ toward His betrayer. Again there swept over them the conviction that this Man was more than mortal. But if He was the Son of God, they questioned, why did He not free Himself from His bonds and triumph over His accusers?

Judas saw that his entreaties were in vain, and he rushed from the hall exclaiming, It is too late! It is too late! He felt that he could not live to see Jesus crucified, and in despair went out and hanged himself.

Later that same day, on the road from Pilate's hall to Calvary, there came an interruption to the shouts and jeers of the wicked throng who were leading Jesus to the place of crucifixion. As they passed a retired spot, they saw at the foot of a lifeless tree, the body of Judas. It was a most revolting sight. His weight had broken the cord by which he had hanged himself to the tree. In falling, his body had been horribly mangled, and dogs were now devouring it. His remains were immediately buried out of sight; but there was less mockery among the throng, and many a pale face revealed the thoughts within. Retribution seemed already visiting those who were guilty of the blood of Jesus.

In Pilate's Judgment Hall

In the judgment hall of Pilate, the Roman governor, Christ stands bound as a prisoner. About Him are the guard of soldiers, and the hall is fast filling with spectators. Just outside the entrance are the judges of the Sanhedrin, priests, rulers, elders, and the mob.

After condemning Jesus, the council of the Sanhedrin had come to Pilate to have the sentence confirmed and executed. But these Jewish officials would not enter the Roman judgment hall. According to their ceremonial law they would be defiled thereby, and thus prevented from taking part in the feast of the Passover. In their blindness they did not see that murderous hatred had defiled their hearts. They did not see that Christ was the real Passover lamb, and that, since they had rejected Him, the great feast had for them lost its significance.

When the Saviour was brought into the judgment hall, Pilate looked upon Him with no friendly eyes. The Roman governor had been called from his bedchamber in haste, and he determined to do his work as quickly as possible. He was prepared to deal with the prisoner with magisterial severity. Assuming his severest expression, he turned to see what kind of man he had to examine, that he had been called from his repose at so early an hour. He knew that it must be someone whom the Jewish authorities were anxious to have tried and punished with haste.

Pilate looked at the men who had Jesus in charge, and then his gaze rested searchingly on Jesus. He had had to deal with all kinds of criminals; but never before had a man bearing marks of such goodness and nobility been brought before him. On His face he saw no sign of guilt, no expression of fear, no boldness or defiance. He saw a man of calm and dignified bearing, whose countenance bore not the marks of a criminal, but the signature of heaven.

Christ's appearance made a favorable impression upon Pilate. His better nature was roused. He had heard of Jesus and His works. His wife had told him something of the wonderful deeds performed by the Galilean prophet, who cured the sick and raised the dead. Now this revived as a dream in Pilate's mind. He recalled rumors that he had heard from several sources. He resolved to demand of the Jews their charges against the prisoner.

Who is this Man, and wherefore have ye brought Him? he said. What accusation bring ye against Him? The Jews were disconcerted. Knowing that they could not substantiate their charges against Christ, they did not desire a public examination. They answered that He was a deceiver called Jesus of Nazareth.

Again Pilate asked, "What accusation bring ye against this Man?" The priests did not answer his question, but in words that showed their irritation, they said, "If He were not a malefactor, we would not have delivered Him up unto thee." When those composing the Sanhedrin, the first men of the nation, bring to you a man they deem worthy of death, is there need to ask for an accusation against him? They hoped to impress Pilate with a sense of their importance, and thus lead him to accede to their request without going through many preliminaries. They were eager to have their sentence ratified; for they knew that the people who had witnessed Christ's marvelous works could tell a story very different from the fabrication they themselves were now rehearsing.

The priests thought that with the weak and vacillating Pilate they could carry through their plans without trouble. Before this he had signed the death warrant hastily, condemning to death men they knew were not worthy of death. In his estimation the life of a prisoner was of little account; whether he were innocent or guilty was of no special consequence. The priests hoped that Pilate would now inflict the death penalty on Jesus without giving Him a hearing. This they besought as a favor on the occasion of their great national festival.

But there was something in the prisoner that held Pilate back from this. He dared not do it. He read the purposes of the priests. He remembered how, not long before, Jesus had raised Lazarus, a man that had been dead four days; and he determined to know, before signing the sentence of condemnation, what were the charges against Him, and whether they could be proved.

If your judgment is sufficient, he said, why bring the prisoner to me? "Take ye Him, and judge Him according to your law." Thus pressed, the priests said that they had already passed sentence upon Him, but that they must have Pilate's sentence to render their condemnation valid. What is your sentence? Pilate asked. The death sentence, they answered; but it is not lawful for us to put any man to death. They asked Pilate to take their word as to Christ's guilt, and enforce their sentence. They would take the responsibility of the result.

Pilate was not a just or a conscientious judge; but weak though he was in moral power, he refused to grant this request. He would not condemn Jesus until a charge had been brought against Him.

The priests were in a dilemma. They saw that they must cloak their hypocrisy under the thickest concealment. They must not allow it to appear that Christ had been arrested on religious grounds. Were this put forward as a reason, their proceedings would have no weight with Pilate. They must make it appear that Jesus was working against the common law; then He could be punished as a political offender. Tumults and insurrection against the Roman government were constantly arising among the Jews. With these revolts the Romans had dealt very rigorously, and they were constantly on the watch to repress everything that could lead to an outbreak.

Only a few days before this the Pharisees had tried to entrap Christ with the question, "Is it lawful for us to give tribute unto Caesar?" But Christ had unveiled their hypocrisy. The Romans who were present had seen the utter failure of the plotters, and their discomfiture at His answer, "Render therefore unto Caesar the things which be Caesar's." Luke 20:22-25.

Now the priests thought to make it appear that on this occasion Christ had taught what they hoped He would teach. In their extremity they called false witnesses to their aid, "and they began to accuse Him, saying, We found this fellow perverting the nation, and forbidding to give tribute to Caesar, saying that He Himself is Christ a King." Three charges, each without foundation. The priests knew this, but they were willing to commit perjury could they but secure their end.

Pilate saw through their purpose. He did not believe that the prisoner had plotted against the government. His meek and humble appearance was altogether out of harmony with the charge. Pilate was convinced that a deep plot had been laid to destroy an innocent man who stood in the way of the Jewish dignitaries. Turning to Jesus he asked, "Art Thou the

King of the Jews?" The Saviour answered, "Thou sayest it." And as He spoke, His countenance lighted up as if a sunbeam were shining upon it.

When they heard His answer, Caiaphas and those that were with him called Pilate to witness that Jesus had admitted the crime with which He was charged. With noisy cries, priests, scribes, and rulers demanded that He be sentenced to death. The cries were taken up by the mob, and the uproar was deafening. Pilate was confused. Seeing that Jesus made no answer to His accusers, Pilate said to Him, "Answerest Thou nothing? behold how many things they witness against Thee. But Jesus yet answered nothing."

Standing behind Pilate, in view of all in the court, Christ heard the abuse; but to all the false charges against Him He answered not a word. His whole bearing gave evidence of conscious innocence. He stood unmoved by the fury of the waves that beat about Him. It was as if the heavy surges of wrath, rising higher and higher, like the waves of the boisterous ocean, broke about Him, but did not touch Him. He stood silent, but His silence was eloquence. It was as a light shining from the inner to the outer man.

Pilate was astonished at His bearing. Does this Man disregard the proceedings because He does not care to save His life? he asked himself. As he looked at Jesus, bearing insult and mockery without retaliation, he felt that He could not be as unrighteous and unjust as were the clamoring priests. Hoping to gain the truth from Him and to escape the tumult of the crowd, Pilate took Jesus aside with him, and again questioned, "Art Thou the King of the Jews?"

Jesus did not directly answer this question. He knew that the Holy Spirit was striving with Pilate, and He gave him opportunity to acknowledge his conviction. "Sayest thou this thing of thyself," He asked, "or did others tell it thee of Me?" That is, was it the accusations of the priests, or a desire to receive light from Christ, that prompted Pilate's question? Pilate understood Christ's meaning; but pride arose in his heart. He would not acknowledge the conviction that pressed upon him. "Am I a Jew?" he said. "Thine own nation and the chief priests have delivered Thee unto me: what hast Thou done?"

Pilate's golden opportunity had passed. Yet Jesus did not leave him without further light. While He did not directly answer Pilate's question, He plainly stated His own mission. He gave Pilate to understand that He was not seeking an earthly throne.

"My kingdom is not of this world," He said; "if My kingdom were of this world, then would My servants fight, that I should not be delivered to the Jews: but now is My kingdom not from hence. Pilate therefore said unto Him, Art Thou a king then? Jesus answered, Thou sayest that I am a king. To this end was I born, and for this cause came I into the world, that I should bear witness unto the truth. Everyone that is of the truth heareth My voice."

Christ affirmed that His word was in itself a key which would unlock the mystery to those who were prepared to receive it. It had a self-commending power, and this was the secret of the spread of His kingdom of truth. He desired Pilate to understand that only by receiving and appropriating truth could his ruined nature be reconstructed.

Pilate had a desire to know the truth. His mind was confused. He eagerly grasped the words of the Saviour, and his heart was stirred with a great longing to know what it really was, and how he could obtain it. "What is truth?" he inquired. But he did not wait for an answer. The tumult outside recalled him to the interests of the hour; for the priests were clamorous for immediate action. Going out to the Jews, he declared emphatically, "I find in Him no fault at all."

These words from a heathen judge were a scathing rebuke to the perfidy and falsehood of the rulers of Israel who were accusing the Saviour. As the priests and elders heard this from Pilate, their disappointment and rage knew no bounds. They had long plotted and waited for this opportunity. As they saw the prospect of the release of Jesus, they seemed ready to tear Him in pieces. They loudly denounced Pilate, and threatened him with the censure of the Roman government. They accused him of refusing to condemn Jesus, who, they affirmed, had set Himself up against Caesar.

Angry voices were now heard, declaring that the seditious influence of Jesus was well known throughout the country. The priests said, "He stirreth up the people, teaching throughout all Jewry, beginning from Galilee to this place."

Pilate at this time had no thought of condemning Jesus. He knew that the Jews had accused Him through hatred and prejudice. He knew what his duty was. Justice demanded that Christ should be immediately released. But Pilate dreaded the ill will of the people. Should he refuse to give Jesus into their hands, a tumult would be raised, and this he feared to meet. When he heard that Christ was from Galilee, he decided to send Him to Herod, the ruler of that province, who was then in Jerusalem. By this course, Pilate thought to shift the responsibility of the trial from himself to Herod. He also thought this a good opportunity to heal an old quarrel between himself and Herod. And so it proved. The two magistrates made friends over the trial of the Saviour.

Pilate delivered Jesus again to the soldiers, and amid the jeers and insults of the mob He was hurried to the judgment hall of Herod. "When Herod saw Jesus, he was exceeding glad." He had never before met the Saviour, but "he was desirous to see Him of a long season, because he had heard many things of Him; and he hoped to have seen some miracle done by Him." This Herod was he whose hands were stained with the blood of John the Baptist. When Herod first heard of Jesus, he was terror-stricken, and said, "It is John, whom I beheaded: he is risen from the dead;" "therefore mighty works do show forth themselves in him." Mark 6:16; Matt. 14:2. Yet Herod desired to see Jesus. Now there was opportunity to save the life of this prophet, and the king hoped to banish forever from his mind the memory of that bloody head brought to him in a charger. He also desired to have his curiosity gratified, and thought that if Christ were given any prospect of release, He would do anything that was asked of Him.

A large company of the priests and elders had accompanied Christ to Herod. And when the Saviour was brought in, these dignitaries, all speaking excitedly, urged their accusations against Him. But Herod paid little regard to their charges. He commanded silence, desiring an opportunity to question Christ. He ordered that the fetters of Christ should be unloosed, at the same time charging His enemies with roughly treating Him. Looking with compassion into the serene face of the world's Redeemer, he read in it only wisdom and purity. He as well as Pilate was satisfied that Christ had been accused through malice and envy.

Herod questioned Christ in many words, but throughout the Saviour maintained a profound silence. At the command of the king, the decrepit and maimed were then called in, and Christ was ordered to prove His claims by working a miracle. Men say that Thou canst heal the sick, said Herod. I am anxious to see that Thy widespread fame has not been belied. Jesus did not respond, and Herod still continued to urge: If Thou canst work miracles for others, work them now for Thine own good, and it will serve Thee a good purpose. Again he commanded, Show us a sign that Thou hast the power with which rumor hath accredited Thee. But Christ was as one who heard and saw not. The Son of God had taken upon Himself man's nature. He must do as man must do in like circumstances. Therefore He would not work a miracle to save Himself the pain and humiliation that man must endure when placed in a similar position.

Herod promised that if Christ would perform some miracle in his presence, He should be released. Christ's accusers had seen with their own eyes the mighty works wrought by His power. They had heard Him command the grave to give up its dead. They had seen the dead come forth obedient to His voice. Fear seized them lest He should now work a miracle. Of all things they most dreaded an exhibition of His power. Such a manifestation would prove a deathblow to their plans, and would perhaps cost them their lives. Again the priests and rulers, in great anxiety, urged their accusations against Him. Raising their voices, they declared, He is a traitor, a blasphemer. He works His miracles through the power given Him by Beelzebub, the prince of the devils. The hall became a scene of confusion, some crying one thing and some another.

Herod's conscience was now far less sensitive than when he had trembled with horror at the request of Herodias for the head of John the Baptist. For a time he had felt the keen stings of remorse for his terrible act; but his moral perceptions had become more and more degraded by his licentious life. Now his heart had become so hardened that he could even boast of the punishment he had inflicted upon John for daring to reprove him. And he now threatened Jesus, declaring repeatedly that he had power to release or to condemn Him. But no sign from Jesus gave evidence that He heard a word.

Herod was irritated by this silence. It seemed to indicate utter indifference to his authority. To the vain and pompous king, open rebuke would have been less offensive than to be thus ignored. Again he angrily threatened Jesus, who still remained unmoved and silent.

The mission of Christ in this world was not to gratify idle curiosity. He came to heal the brokenhearted. Could He have spoken any word to heal the bruises of sin-sick souls, He would not have kept silent. But He had no words for those who would but trample the truth under their unholy feet.

Christ might have spoken words to Herod that would have pierced the ears of the hardened king. He might have stricken him with fear and trembling by laying before him the full iniquity of his life, and the horror of his approaching doom. But Christ's silence was the severest rebuke that He could have given. Herod had rejected the truth spoken to him by the greatest of the prophets, and no other message was he to receive. Not a word had the Majesty of heaven for him. That ear that had ever been open to human woe, had no room for Herod's commands. Those eyes that had ever rested upon the penitent sinner in pitying, forgiving love had no look to bestow upon Herod. Those lips that had uttered the most impressive truth, that in tones of tenderest entreaty had pleaded with the most sinful and the most degraded, were closed to the haughty king who felt no need of a Saviour.

Herod's face grew dark with passion. Turning to the multitude, he angrily denounced Jesus as an impostor. Then to Christ he said, If You will give no evidence of Your claim, I will deliver You up to the soldiers and the people. They may succeed in making You speak. If You are an impostor, death at their hands is only what You merit; if You are the Son of God, save Yourself by working a miracle.

No sooner were these words spoken than a rush was made for Christ. Like wild beasts, the crowd darted upon their prey. Jesus was dragged this way and that, Herod joining the mob in seeking to humiliate the Son of God. Had not the Roman soldiers interposed, and forced back the maddened throng, the Saviour would have been torn in pieces.

"Herod with his men of war set Him at nought, and mocked Him, and arrayed Him in a gorgeous robe." The Roman soldiers joined in this abuse. All that these wicked, corrupt soldiers, helped on by Herod and the Jewish dignitaries, could instigate was heaped upon the Saviour. Yet His divine patience failed not.

Christ's persecutors had tried to measure His character by their own; they had represented Him as vile as themselves. But back of all the present appearance another scene intruded itself,—a scene which they will one day see in all its glory. There were some who trembled in Christ's presence. While the rude throng were bowing in mockery before Him, some who came forward for that purpose turned back, afraid and silenced. Herod was convicted. The last rays of merciful light were shining upon his sin-hardened heart. He felt that this was no common man; for divinity had flashed through humanity. At the very time when Christ was encompassed by mockers, adulterers, and murderers, Herod felt that he was beholding a God upon His throne.

Hardened as he was, Herod dared not ratify the condemnation of Christ. He wished to relieve himself of the terrible responsibility, and he sent Jesus back to the Roman judgment hall.

Pilate was disappointed and much displeased. When the Jews returned with their prisoner, he asked impatiently what they would have him do. He reminded them that he had already examined Jesus, and found no fault in Him; he told them that they had brought complaints against Him, but they had not been able to prove a single charge. He had sent Jesus to Herod, the tetrarch of Galilee, and one of their own nation, but he also had found in Him nothing worthy of death. "I will therefore chastise Him," Pilate said, "and release Him."

Here Pilate showed his weakness. He had declared that Jesus was innocent, yet he was willing for Him to be scourged to pacify His accusers. He would sacrifice justice and principle in order to compromise with the mob. This placed him at a disadvantage. The crowd presumed upon his indecision, and clamored the more for the life of the prisoner. If at the first Pilate had stood firm, refusing to condemn a man whom he found guiltless, he would have broken the fatal chain that was to bind him in remorse and guilt as long as he lived. Had he carried out his convictions of right, the Jews would not have presumed to dictate to him. Christ would have been put to death, but the guilt would not have rested upon Pilate. But Pilate had taken step after step in the violation of his conscience. He had excused himself from judging with justice and equity, and he now found himself almost helpless in the hands of the priests and rulers. His wavering and indecision proved his ruin.

Even now Pilate was not left to act blindly. A message from God warned him from the deed he was about to commit. In answer to Christ's prayer, the wife of Pilate had been visited by an angel from heaven, and in a dream she had beheld the Saviour and conversed with Him. Pilate's wife was not a Jew, but as she looked upon Jesus in her dream, she had no doubt of His character or mission. She knew Him to be the Prince of God. She saw Him on trial in the judgment hall. She saw the hands tightly bound as the hands of a criminal. She saw Herod and his soldiers doing their dreadful work. She heard the priests and rulers, filled with envy and malice, madly accusing. She heard the words, "We have a law, and by our law He ought to die." She saw Pilate give Jesus to the scourging, after he had declared, "I find no fault in Him." She heard the condemnation pronounced by Pilate, and saw him give Christ up to His murderers. She saw the cross uplifted on Calvary. She saw the earth wrapped in darkness, and heard the mysterious cry, "It is finished." Still another scene met her gaze. She saw Christ seated upon the great white cloud, while the earth reeled in space, and His murderers fled from the presence of His glory. With a cry of horror she awoke, and at once wrote to Pilate words of warning.

While Pilate was hesitating as to what he should do, a messenger pressed through the crowd, and handed him the letter from his wife, which read:

"Have thou nothing to do with that just Man: for I have suffered many things this day in a dream because of Him."

Pilate's face grew pale. He was confused by his own conflicting emotions. But while he had been delaying to act, the priests and rulers were still further inflaming the minds of the people. Pilate was forced to action. He now bethought himself of a custom which might serve to secure Christ's release. It was customary at this feast to release some one prisoner whom the people might choose. This custom was of pagan invention; there was not a shadow of justice in it, but it was greatly prized by the Jews. The Roman authorities at this time held a prisoner named Barabbas, who was under sentence of death. This man had claimed to be the Messiah. He claimed authority to establish a different order of things, to set the world right. Under satanic delusion he claimed that whatever he could obtain by theft and robbery was his own. He had done wonderful things through satanic agencies, he had gained a following among the people, and had excited sedition against the Roman government. Under cover of religious enthusiasm he was a hardened and desperate villain, bent on rebellion and cruelty. By giving the people a choice between this man and the innocent Saviour, Pilate thought to arouse them to a sense of justice. He hoped to gain their sympathy for Jesus in opposition to the priests and rulers. So, turning to the crowd, he said with great earnestness, "Whom will ye that I release unto you? Barabbas, or Jesus which is called Christ?"

Like the bellowing of wild beasts came the answer of the mob, "Release unto us Barabbas!" Louder and louder swelled the cry, Barabbas! Barabbas! Thinking that the people had not understood his question, Pilate asked, "Will ye that I release unto you the King of the Jews?" But they cried out again, "Away with this Man, and release unto us Barabbas"! "What shall I do then with Jesus which is called Christ?" Pilate asked. Again the surging multitude roared like demons. Demons themselves, in human form, were in the crowd, and what could be expected but the answer, "Let Him be crucified"?

Pilate was troubled. He had not thought it would come to that. He shrank from delivering an innocent man to the most ignominious and cruel death that could be inflicted. After the roar of voices had ceased, he turned to the people, saying, "Why, what evil hath He done?" But the case had gone too far for argument. It was not evidence of Christ's innocence that they wanted, but His condemnation.

Still Pilate endeavored to save Him. "He said unto them the third time, Why, what evil hath He done? I have found no cause of death in Him: I will therefore chastise Him, and let Him go." But the very mention of His release stirred the people to a tenfold frenzy. "Crucify Him, crucify Him," they cried. Louder and louder swelled the storm that Pilate's indecision had called forth.

Jesus was taken, faint with weariness and covered with wounds, and scourged in the sight of the multitude. "And the soldiers led Him away into the hall, called Praetorium, and they call together the whole band. And they clothed Him with purple, and platted a crown of thorns, and put it about His head, and began to salute Him, Hail, King of the Jews! And they . . . did spit upon Him, and bowing their knees worshiped Him." Occasionally some wicked hand snatched the reed that had been placed in His hand, and struck the crown upon His brow, forcing the thorns into His temples, and sending the blood trickling down His face and beard.

Wonder, O heavens! and be astonished, O earth! Behold the oppressor and the oppressed. A maddened throng enclose the Saviour of the world. Mocking and jeering are mingled with the coarse oaths of blasphemy. His lowly birth and humble life are commented upon by the unfeeling mob. His claim to be the Son of God is ridiculed, and the vulgar jest and insulting sneer are passed from lip to lip.

Satan led the cruel mob in its abuse of the Saviour. It was his purpose to provoke Him to retaliation if possible, or to drive Him to perform a miracle to release Himself, and thus break up the plan of salvation. One stain upon His human life, one failure of His humanity to endure the terrible test, and the Lamb of God would have been an imperfect offering, and the redemption of man a failure. But He who by a command could bring the heavenly host to His aid—He who could have driven that mob in terror from His sight by the flashing forth of His divine majesty—submitted with perfect calmness to the coarsest insult and outrage.

Christ's enemies had demanded a miracle as evidence of His divinity. They had evidence far greater than any they had sought. As their cruelty degraded His torturers below humanity into the likeness of Satan, so did His meekness and patience exalt Jesus above humanity, and prove His kinship to God. His abasement was the pledge of His exaltation. The blood drops of agony that from His wounded temples flowed down His face and beard were the pledge of His anointing with "the oil of gladness" (Heb. 1:9.) as our great high priest.

Satan's rage was great as he saw that all the abuse inflicted upon the Saviour had not forced the least murmur from His lips. Although He had taken upon Him the nature of man, He was sustained by a godlike fortitude, and departed in no particular from the will of His Father.

When Pilate gave Jesus up to be scourged and mocked, he thought to excite the pity of the multitude. He hoped they would decide that this was sufficient punishment. Even the malice of the priests, he thought, would now be satisfied. But with keen perception the Jews saw the weakness of thus punishing a man who had been declared innocent. They knew that Pilate was trying to save the life of the prisoner, and they were determined that Jesus should not be released. To please and satisfy us, Pilate has scourged Him, they thought, and if we press the matter to a decided issue, we shall surely gain our end.

Pilate now sent for Barabbas to be brought into the court. He then presented the two prisoners side by side, and pointing to the Saviour he said in a voice of solemn entreaty, "Behold the Man!" "I bring Him forth to you, that ye may know that I find no fault in Him."

There stood the Son of God, wearing the robe of mockery and the crown of thorns. Stripped to the waist, His back showed the long, cruel stripes, from which the blood flowed freely. His face was stained with blood, and bore the marks of exhaustion and pain; but never had it appeared more beautiful than now. The Saviour's visage was not marred before His enemies. Every feature expressed gentleness and resignation and the tenderest pity for His cruel foes. In His manner there was no cowardly weakness, but the strength and dignity of long-suffering. In striking contrast was the prisoner at His side. Every line of the countenance of Barabbas proclaimed him the hardened ruffian that he was. The contrast spoke to every beholder. Some of the spectators were weeping. As they looked upon Jesus, their hearts were full of sympathy. Even the priests and rulers were convicted that He was all that He claimed to be.

The Roman soldiers that surrounded Christ were not all hardened; some were looking earnestly into His face for one evidence that He was a criminal or dangerous character. From time to time they would turn and cast a look of contempt upon Barabbas. It needed no deep insight to read him through and through. Again they would turn to the One upon trial. They looked at the divine sufferer with feelings of deep pity. The silent submission of Christ stamped upon their minds the scene, never to be effaced until they either acknowledged Him as the Christ, or by rejecting Him decided their own destiny.

Pilate was filled with amazement at the uncomplaining patience of the Saviour. He did not doubt that the sight of this Man, in contrast with Barabbas, would move the Jews to sympathy. But he did not understand the fanatical hatred of the priests for Him, who, as the Light of the world, had made manifest their darkness and error. They had moved the mob to a mad fury, and again priests, rulers, and people raised that awful cry, "Crucify Him, crucify Him." At last, losing all patience with their unreasoning cruelty, Pilate cried out despairingly, "Take ye Him, and crucify Him: for I find no fault in Him."

The Roman governor, though familiar with cruel scenes, was moved with sympathy for the suffering prisoner, who, condemned and scourged, with bleeding brow and lacerated back, still had the bearing of a king upon his throne. But the priests declared, "We have a law, and by our law He ought to die, because He made Himself the Son of God."

Pilate was startled. He had no correct idea of Christ and His mission; but he had an indistinct faith in God and in beings superior to humanity. A thought that had once before passed through his mind now took more definite shape. He questioned whether it might not be a divine being that stood before him, clad in the purple robe of mockery, and crowned with thorns.

Again he went into the judgment hall, and said to Jesus, "Whence art Thou?" But Jesus gave him no answer. The Saviour had spoken freely to Pilate, explaining His own

Not a few women are in the crowd that follow the Uncondemned to His cruel death. Their attention is fixed upon Jesus. Some of them have seen Him before. Some have carried to Him their sick and suffering ones. Some have themselves been healed. The story of the scenes that have taken place is related. They wonder at the hatred of the crowd toward Him for whom their own hearts are melting and ready to break.

And notwithstanding the action of the maddened throng, and the angry words of the priests and rulers, these women give expression to their sympathy. As Jesus falls fainting beneath the cross, they break forth into mournful wailing.

This was the only thing that attracted Christ's attention. Although full of suffering, while bearing the sins of the world, He was not indifferent to the expression of grief. He looked upon these women with tender compassion. They were not believers in Him; He knew that they were not lamenting Him as one sent from God, but were moved by feelings of human pity. He did not despise their sympathy, but it awakened in His heart a deeper sympathy for them. "Daughters of Jerusalem," He said, "weep not for Me, but weep for yourselves, and for your children." From the scene before Him, Christ looked forward to the time of Jerusalem's destruction. In that terrible scene, many of those who were now weeping for Him were to perish with their children.

From the fall of Jerusalem the thoughts of Jesus passed to a wider judgment. In the destruction of the impenitent city He saw a symbol of the final destruction to come upon the world. He said, "Then shall they begin to say to the mountains, Fall on us; and to the hills, Cover us. For if they do these things in a green tree, what shall be done in the dry?" By the green tree, Jesus represented Himself, the innocent Redeemer. God suffered His wrath against transgression to fall on His beloved Son. Jesus was to be crucified for the sins of men. What suffering, then, would the sinner bear who continued in sin? All the impenitent and unbelieving would know a sorrow and misery that language would fail to express.

Of the multitude that followed the Saviour to Calvary, many had attended Him with joyful hosannas and the waving of palm branches as He rode triumphantly into Jerusalem. But not a few who had then shouted His praise, because it was popular to do so, now swelled the cry of "Crucify Him, crucify Him." When Christ rode into Jerusalem, the hopes of the disciples had been raised to the highest pitch. They had pressed close about their Master, feeling that it was a high honor to be connected with Him. Now in His humiliation they followed Him at a distance. They were filled with grief, and bowed down with disappointed hopes. How were the words of Jesus verified: "All ye shall be offended because of Me this night: for it is written, I will smite the shepherd, and the sheep of the flock shall be scattered abroad." Matt. 26:31.

Arriving at the place of execution, the prisoners were bound to the instruments of torture. The two thieves wrestled in the hands of those who placed them on the cross; but Jesus made no resistance. The mother of Jesus, supported by John the beloved disciple, had followed the steps of her Son to Calvary. She had seen Him fainting under the burden of the cross, and had longed to place a supporting hand beneath His wounded head, and to bathe that brow which had once been pillowed upon her bosom. But she was not permitted this mournful privilege. With the disciples she still cherished the hope that Jesus would manifest His power, and deliver Himself from His enemies. Again her heart would sink as she recalled the words in which He had foretold the very scenes that were then taking place. As the thieves were bound to the cross, she looked on with agonizing suspense. Would He who had given life to the dead suffer Himself to be crucified? Would the Son of God suffer Himself to be thus cruelly slain? Must she give up her faith that Jesus was the Messiah? Must she witness His shame and sorrow, without even the privilege of ministering to Him in His distress? She saw His hands stretched upon the cross; the hammer and the nails were brought, and as the spikes were driven through the tender flesh, the heart-stricken disciples bore away from the cruel scene the fainting form of the mother of Jesus.

The Saviour made no murmur of complaint. His face remained calm and serene, but great drops of sweat stood upon His brow. There was no pitying hand to wipe the death dew from His face, nor words of sympathy and unchanging fidelity to stay His human heart. While the soldiers were doing their fearful work, Jesus prayed for His enemies, "Father, forgive them; for they know not what they do." His mind passed from His own suffering to the sin of His persecutors, and the terrible retribution that would be theirs. No curses were called down upon the soldiers who were handling Him so roughly. No vengeance was invoked upon the priests and rulers, who were gloating over the accomplishment of their purpose. Christ pitied them in their ignorance and guilt. He breathed only a plea for their forgiveness,—"for they know not what they do."

Had they known that they were putting to torture One who had come to save the sinful race from eternal ruin, they would have been seized with remorse and horror. But their ignorance did not remove their guilt; for it was their privilege to know and accept Jesus as their Saviour. Some of them would yet see their sin, and repent, and be converted. Some by their impenitence would make it an impossibility for the prayer of Christ to be answered for them. Yet, just the same, God's purpose was reaching its fulfillment. Jesus was earning the right to become the advocate of men in the Father's presence.

That prayer of Christ for His enemies embraced the world. It took in every sinner that had lived or should live, from the beginning of the world to the end of time. Upon all rests the guilt of crucifying the Son of God. To all, forgiveness is freely offered. "Whosoever will" may have peace with God, and inherit eternal life.

As soon as Jesus was nailed to the cross, it was lifted by strong men, and with great violence thrust into the place prepared for it. This caused the most intense agony to the Son of God. Pilate then wrote an inscription in Hebrew, Greek, and Latin, and placed it upon the cross, above the head of Jesus. It read, "Jesus of Nazareth the King of the Jews." This inscription irritated the Jews. In Pilate's court they had cried, "Crucify Him." "We have no king but Caesar." John 19:15. They had declared that whoever should acknowledge any other king was a traitor. Pilate wrote out the sentiment they had expressed. No offense was mentioned, except that Jesus was the King of the Jews. The inscription was a virtual acknowledgment of the allegiance of the Jews to the Roman power. It declared that whoever might claim to be the King of Israel would be judged by them worthy of death. The priests had overreached themselves. When they were plotting the death of Christ, Caiaphas had declared it expedient that one man should die to save the nation. Now their hypocrisy was revealed. In order to destroy Christ, they had been ready to sacrifice even their national existence.

The priests saw what they had done, and asked Pilate to change the inscription. They said, "Write not, The King of the Jews; but that He said, I am King of the Jews." But Pilate was angry with himself because of his former weakness, and he thoroughly despised the jealous and artful priests and rulers. He replied coldly, "What I have written I have written."

A higher power than Pilate or the Jews had directed the placing of that inscription above the head of Jesus. In the providence of God it was to awaken thought, and investigation of the Scriptures. The place where Christ was crucified was near to the city. Thousands of people from all lands were then at Jerusalem, and the inscription declaring Jesus of Nazareth the Messiah would come to their notice. It was a living truth, transcribed by a hand that God had guided.

In the sufferings of Christ upon the cross prophecy was fulfilled. Centuries before the crucifixion, the Saviour had foretold the treatment He was to receive. He said, "Dogs have compassed Me: the assembly of the wicked have enclosed Me: they pierced My hands and My feet. I may tell all My bones: they look and stare upon Me. They part My garments among them, and cast lots upon My vesture." Ps. 22:16-18. The prophecy concerning His garments was carried out without counsel or interference from the friends or the enemies of the Crucified One. To the soldiers who had placed Him upon the cross, His clothing was given. Christ heard the men's contention as they parted the garments among them. His tunic was woven throughout without seam, and they said, "Let us not rend it, but cast lots for it, whose it shall be."

In another prophecy the Saviour declared, "Reproach hath broken My heart; and I am full of heaviness: and I looked for some to take pity, but there was none; and for comforters, but I found none. They gave Me also gall for My meat; and in My thirst they gave Me vinegar to drink." Ps. 69:20, 21. To those who suffered death by the cross, it was permitted to give a stupefying potion, to deaden the sense of pain. This was offered to Jesus; but when He had tasted it, He refused it. He would receive nothing that could becloud His mind. His faith must keep fast hold upon God. This was His only strength. To becloud His senses would give Satan an advantage.

The enemies of Jesus vented their rage upon Him as He hung upon the cross. Priests, rulers, and scribes joined with the mob in mocking the dying Saviour. At the baptism and at the transfiguration the voice of God had been heard proclaiming Christ as His Son. Again, just before Christ's betrayal, the Father had spoken, witnessing to His divinity. But now the voice from heaven was silent. No testimony in Christ's favor was heard. Alone He suffered abuse and mockery from wicked men.

"If Thou be the Son of God," they said, "come down from the cross." "Let Him save Himself, if He be Christ, the chosen of God." In the wilderness of temptation Satan had declared, "If Thou be the Son of God, command that these stones be made bread." "If Thou be the Son of God, cast Thyself down" from the pinnacle of the temple. Matt. 4:3, 6. And Satan with his angels, in human form, was present at the cross. The archfiend and his hosts were co-operating with the priests and rulers. The teachers of the people had stimulated the ignorant mob to pronounce judgment against One upon whom many of them had never looked, until urged to bear testimony against Him. Priests, rulers, Pharisees, and the hardened rabble were confederated together in a satanic frenzy. Religious rulers united with Satan and his angels. They were doing his bidding.

Jesus, suffering and dying, heard every word as the priests declared, "He saved others; Himself He cannot save. Let Christ the King of Israel descend now from the cross, that we may see and believe." Christ could have come down from the cross. But it is because He would not save Himself that the sinner has hope of pardon and favor with God.

In their mockery of the Saviour, the men who professed to be the expounders of prophecy were repeating the very words which Inspiration had foretold they would utter upon this occasion. Yet in their blindness they did not see that they were fulfilling the prophecy. Those who in derision uttered the words, "He trusted in God; let Him deliver Him now, if He will have Him: for He said, I am the Son of God," little thought that their testimony would sound down the ages. But although spoken in mockery, these words led men to search the Scriptures as they had never done before. Wise men heard, searched, pondered, and prayed. There were those who never rested until, by comparing scripture with scripture, they saw the meaning of Christ's mission. Never before was there such a general knowledge of Jesus as when He hung upon the cross. Into the hearts of many who beheld the crucifixion scene, and who heard Christ's words, the light of truth was shining.

To Jesus in His agony on the cross there came one gleam of comfort. It was the prayer of the penitent thief. Both the men who were crucified with Jesus had at first railed upon Him; and one under his suffering only became more desperate and defiant. But not so with his companion. This man was not a hardened criminal; he had been led astray by evil associations, but he was less guilty than many of those who stood beside the cross reviling the Saviour. He had seen and heard Jesus, and had been convicted by His teaching, but he had been turned away from Him by the priests and rulers. Seeking to stifle conviction, he had plunged deeper and deeper into sin, until he was arrested, tried as a criminal, and condemned to die on the cross. In the judgment hall and on the way to Calvary he had been in company with Jesus. He had heard Pilate declare, "I find no fault in Him." John 19:4. He had marked His godlike bearing, and His pitying forgiveness of His tormentors. On the cross he sees the many great religionists shoot out the tongue with scorn, and ridicule the Lord Jesus. He sees the wagging heads. He hears the upbraiding speeches taken up by his companion in guilt: "If Thou be Christ, save Thyself and us." Among the passers-by he hears many defending Jesus. He hears them repeat His words, and tell of His works. The conviction comes back to him that this is the Christ. Turning to his fellow criminal he says, "Dost not thou fear God, seeing thou art in the same condemnation?" The dying thieves have no longer anything to fear from man. But upon one of them presses the conviction that there is a God to fear, a future to cause him to tremble. And now, all sin-polluted as it is, his life history is about to close. "And we indeed justly," he moans; "for we receive the due reward of our deeds: but this Man hath done nothing amiss."

There is no question now. There are no doubts, no reproaches. When condemned for his crime, the thief had become hopeless and despairing; but strange, tender thoughts now spring up. He calls to mind all he has heard of Jesus, how He has healed the sick and pardoned sin. He has heard the words of those who believed in Jesus and followed Him weeping. He has seen and read the title above the Saviour's head. He has heard the passers-by repeat it, some with grieved, quivering lips, others with jesting and mockery. The Holy Spirit illuminates his mind, and little by little the chain of evidence is joined together. In Jesus, bruised, mocked, and hanging upon the cross, he sees the Lamb of God, that taketh away the sin of the world. Hope is mingled with anguish in his voice as the helpless, dying soul casts himself upon a dying Saviour. "Lord, remember me," he cries, "when Thou comest into Thy kingdom."

Quickly the answer came. Soft and melodious the tone, full of love, compassion, and power the words: Verily I say unto thee today, Thou shalt be with Me in paradise.

For long hours of agony, reviling and mockery have fallen upon the ears of Jesus. As He hangs upon the cross, there floats up to Him still the sound of jeers and curses. With longing heart He has listened for some expression of faith from His disciples. He has heard only the mournful words, "We trusted that it had been He which should have redeemed Israel." How grateful then to the Saviour was the utterance of faith and love from the dying thief! While the leading Jews deny Him, and even the disciples doubt His divinity, the poor thief, upon the brink of eternity, calls Jesus Lord. Many were ready to call Him Lord when He wrought miracles, and after He had risen from the grave; but none acknowledged Him as He hung dying upon the cross save the penitent thief who was saved at the eleventh hour.

The bystanders caught the words as the thief called Jesus Lord. The tone of the repentant man arrested their attention. Those who at the foot of the cross had been quarreling over Christ's garments, and casting lots upon His vesture, stopped to listen. Their angry tones were hushed. With bated breath they looked upon Christ, and waited for the response from those dying lips.

As He spoke the words of promise, the dark cloud that seemed to enshroud the cross was pierced by a bright and living light. To the penitent thief came the perfect peace of acceptance with God. Christ in His humiliation was glorified. He who in all other eyes appeared to be conquered was a Conqueror. He was acknowledged as the Sin Bearer. Men may exercise power over His human body. They may pierce the holy temples with the crown of thorns. They may strip from Him His raiment, and quarrel over its division. But they cannot rob Him of His power to forgive sins. In dying He bears testimony to His own divinity and to the glory of the Father. His ear is not heavy that it cannot hear, neither His arm shortened that it cannot save. It is His royal right to save unto the uttermost all who come unto God by Him.

I say unto thee today, Thou shalt be with Me in Paradise. Christ did not promise that the thief should be with Him in Paradise that day. He Himself did not go that day to Paradise. He slept in the tomb, and on the morning of the resurrection He said, "I am not yet ascended to My Father." John 20:17. But on the day of the crucifixion, the day of apparent defeat and darkness, the promise was given. "Today" while dying upon the cross as a malefactor, Christ assures the poor sinner, Thou shalt be with Me in Paradise.

The thieves crucified with Jesus were placed "on either side one, and Jesus in the midst." This was done by the direction of the priests and rulers. Christ's position between the thieves was to indicate that He was the greatest criminal of the three. Thus was fulfilled the scripture, "He was numbered with the transgressors." Isa. 53:12. But the full meaning of their act the priests did not see. As Jesus, crucified with the thieves, was placed "in the midst," so His cross was placed in the midst of a world lying in sin. And the words of pardon spoken to the penitent thief kindled a light that will shine to the earth's remotest bounds.

With amazement the angels beheld the infinite love of Jesus, who, suffering the most intense agony of mind and body, thought only of others, and encouraged the penitent soul to believe. In His humiliation He as a prophet had addressed the daughters of Jerusalem; as priest and advocate He had pleaded with the Father to forgive His murderers; as a loving Saviour He had forgiven the sins of the penitent thief.

As the eyes of Jesus wandered over the multitude about Him, one figure arrested His attention. At the foot of the cross stood His mother, supported by the disciple John. She could not endure to remain away from her Son; and John, knowing that the end was near, had brought her again to the cross. In His dying hour, Christ remembered His mother. Looking into her grief-stricken face and then upon John, He said to her, "Woman, behold thy son!" then to John, "Behold thy mother!" John understood Christ's words, and accepted the trust. He at once took Mary to his home, and from that hour cared for her tenderly. O pitiful, loving Saviour; amid all His physical pain and mental anguish, He had a thoughtful care for His mother! He had no money with which to provide for her comfort; but He was enshrined in the heart of John, and He gave His mother to him as a precious legacy. Thus He provided for her that which she most needed,—the tender sympathy of one who loved her because she loved Jesus. And in receiving her as a sacred trust, John was receiving a great blessing. She was a constant reminder of his beloved Master.

The perfect example of Christ's filial love shines forth with undimmed luster from the mist of ages. For nearly thirty years Jesus by His daily toil had helped bear the burdens of the home. And now, even in His last agony, He remembers to provide for His sorrowing, widowed mother. The same spirit will be seen in every disciple of our Lord. Those who follow Christ will feel that it is a part of their religion to respect and provide for their parents. From the heart where His love is cherished, father and mother will never fail of receiving thoughtful care and tender sympathy.

And now the Lord of glory was dying, a ransom for the race. In yielding up His precious life, Christ was not upheld by triumphant joy. All was oppressive gloom. It was not the dread of death that weighed upon Him. It was not the pain and ignominy of the cross that caused His inexpressible agony. Christ was the prince of sufferers; but His suffering was from a sense of the malignity of sin, a knowledge that through familiarity with evil, man had become blinded to its enormity. Christ saw how deep is the hold of sin upon the human heart, how few would be willing to break from its power. He knew that without help from God, humanity must perish, and He saw multitudes perishing within reach of abundant help.

Upon Christ as our substitute and surety was laid the iniquity of us all. He was counted a transgressor, that He might redeem us from the condemnation of the law. The guilt of every descendant of Adam was pressing upon His heart. The wrath of God against sin, the terrible manifestation of His displeasure because of iniquity, filled the soul of His Son with consternation. All His life Christ had been publishing to a fallen world the good news of the Father's mercy and pardoning love. Salvation for the chief of sinners was His theme. But now with the terrible weight of guilt He bears, He cannot see the Father's reconciling face. The withdrawal of the divine countenance from the Saviour in this hour of supreme anguish pierced His heart with a sorrow that can never be fully understood by man. So great was this agony that His physical pain was hardly felt.

Satan with his fierce temptations wrung the heart of Jesus. The Saviour could not see through the portals of the tomb. Hope did not present to Him His coming forth from the grave a conqueror, or tell Him of the Father's acceptance of the sacrifice. He feared that sin was so offensive to God that Their separation was to be eternal. Christ felt the anguish which the sinner will feel when mercy shall no longer plead for the guilty race. It was the sense of sin, bringing the Father's wrath upon Him as man's substitute, that made the cup He drank so bitter, and broke the heart of the Son of God.

With amazement angels witnessed the Saviour's despairing agony. The hosts of heaven veiled their faces from the fearful sight. Inanimate nature expressed sympathy with its insulted and dying Author. The sun refused to look upon the awful scene. Its full, bright rays were illuminating the earth at midday, when suddenly it seemed to be blotted out. Complete darkness, like a funeral pall, enveloped the cross. "There was darkness over all the land unto the ninth hour." There was no eclipse or other natural cause for this darkness, which was as deep as midnight without moon or stars. It was a miraculous testimony given by God that the faith of after generations might be confirmed.

In that thick darkness God's presence was hidden. He makes darkness His pavilion, and conceals His glory from human eyes. God and His holy angels were beside the cross. The Father was with His Son. Yet His presence was not revealed. Had His glory flashed forth from the cloud, every human beholder would have been destroyed. And in that dreadful hour Christ was not to be comforted with the Father's presence. He trod the wine press alone, and of the people there was none with Him.

In the thick darkness, God veiled the last human agony of His Son. All who had seen Christ in His suffering had been convicted of His divinity. That face, once beheld by humanity, was never forgotten. As the face of Cain expressed his guilt as a murderer, so the face of Christ revealed innocence, serenity, benevolence,—the image of God. But His accusers would not give heed to the signet of heaven. Through long hours of agony Christ had been gazed upon by the jeering multitude. Now He was mercifully hidden by the mantle of God.

The silence of the grave seemed to have fallen upon Calvary. A nameless terror held the throng that was gathered about the cross. The cursing and reviling ceased in the midst of half-uttered sentences. Men, women, and children fell prostrate upon the earth. Vivid lightnings occasionally flashed forth from the cloud, and revealed the cross and the crucified Redeemer. Priests, rulers, scribes, executioners, and the mob, all thought that their time of retribution had come. After a while some whispered that Jesus would now come down from the cross. Some attempted to grope their way back to the city, beating their breasts and wailing in fear.

At the ninth hour the darkness lifted from the people, but still enveloped the Saviour. It was a symbol of the agony and horror that weighed upon His heart. No eye could pierce the gloom that surrounded the cross, and none could penetrate the deeper gloom that enshrouded the suffering soul of Christ. The angry lightnings seemed to be hurled at Him as He hung upon the cross. Then "Jesus cried with a loud voice, saying,

Eloi, Eloi, lama sabachthani?" "My God, My God, why hast Thou forsaken Me?" As the outer gloom settled about the Saviour, many voices exclaimed: The vengeance of heaven is upon Him. The bolts of God's wrath are hurled at Him, because He claimed to be the Son of God. Many who believed on Him heard His despairing cry. Hope left them. If God had forsaken Jesus, in what could His followers trust?

When the darkness lifted from the oppressed spirit of Christ, He revived to a sense of physical suffering, and said, "I thirst." One of the Roman soldiers, touched with pity as he looked at the parched lips, took a sponge on a stalk of hyssop, and dipping it in a vessel of vinegar, offered it to Jesus. But the priests mocked at His agony. When darkness covered the earth, they had been filled with fear; as their terror abated, the dread returned that Jesus would yet escape them. His words, "Eloi, Eloi, lama sabachthani?" they had misinterpreted. With bitter contempt and scorn they said, "This man calleth for Elias." The last opportunity to relieve His sufferings they refused. "Let be," they said, "let us see whether Elias will come to save Him."

The spotless Son of God hung upon the cross, His flesh lacerated with stripes; those hands so often reached out in blessing, nailed to the wooden bars; those feet so tireless on ministries of love, spiked to the tree; that royal head pierced by the crown of thorns; those quivering lips shaped to the cry of woe. And all that He endured—the blood drops that flowed from His head, His hands, His feet, the agony that racked His frame, and the unutterable anguish that filled His soul at the hiding of His Father's face—speaks to each child of humanity, declaring, It is for thee that the Son of God consents to bear this burden of guilt; for thee He spoils the domain of death, and opens the gates of Paradise. He who stilled the angry waves and walked the foam-capped billows, who made devils tremble and disease flee, who opened blind eyes and called forth the dead to life,—offers Himself upon the cross as a sacrifice, and this from love to thee. He, the Sin Bearer, endures the wrath of divine justice, and for thy sake becomes sin itself.

In silence the beholders watched for the end of the fearful scene. The sun shone forth; but the cross was still enveloped in darkness. Priests and rulers looked toward Jerusalem; and lo, the dense cloud had settled over the city and the plains of Judea. The Sun of Righteousness, the Light of the world, was withdrawing His beams from the once favored city of Jerusalem. The fierce lightnings of God's wrath were directed against the fated city.

Suddenly the gloom lifted from the cross, and in clear, trumpetlike tones, that seemed to resound throughout creation, Jesus cried, "It is finished." "Father, into Thy hands I commend My spirit." A light encircled the cross, and the face of the Saviour shone with a glory like the sun. He then bowed His head upon His breast, and died.

Amid the awful darkness, apparently forsaken of God, Christ had drained the last dregs in the cup of human woe. In those dreadful hours He had relied upon the evidence of His Father's acceptance heretofore given Him. He was acquainted with the character of His Father; He understood His justice, His mercy, and His great love. By faith He rested in Him whom it had ever been His joy to obey. And as in submission He committed Himself to God, the sense of the loss of His Father's favor was withdrawn. By faith, Christ was victor.

Never before had the earth witnessed such a scene. The multitude stood paralyzed, and with bated breath gazed upon the Saviour. Again darkness settled upon the earth, and a hoarse rumbling, like heavy thunder, was heard. There was a violent earthquake. The people were shaken together in heaps. The wildest confusion and consternation ensued. In the surrounding mountains, rocks were rent asunder, and went crashing down into the plains. Sepulchers were broken open, and the dead were cast out of their tombs. Creation seemed to be shivering to atoms. Priests, rulers, soldiers, executioners, and people, mute with terror, lay prostrate upon the ground.

When the loud cry, "It is finished," came from the lips of Christ, the priests were officiating in the temple. It was the hour of the evening sacrifice. The lamb representing Christ had been brought to be slain. Clothed in his significant and beautiful dress, the priest stood with lifted knife, as did Abraham when he was about to slay his son. With intense interest the people were looking on. But the earth trembles and quakes; for the Lord Himself draws near. With a rending noise the inner veil of the temple is torn from top to bottom by an unseen hand, throwing open to the gaze of the multitude a place once filled with the presence of God. In this place the Shekinah had dwelt. Here God had manifested His glory above the mercy seat. No one but the high priest ever lifted the veil separating this apartment from the rest of the temple. He entered in once a year to make an atonement for the sins of the people. But lo, this veil is rent in twain. The most holy place of the earthly sanctuary is no longer sacred.

All is terror and confusion. The priest is about to slay the victim; but the knife drops from his nerveless hand, and the lamb escapes. Type has met antitype in the death of God's Son. The great sacrifice has been made. The way into the holiest is laid open. A new and living way is prepared for all. No longer need sinful, sorrowing humanity await the coming of the high priest. Henceforth the Saviour was to officiate as priest and advocate in the heaven of heavens. It was as if a living voice had spoken to the worshipers: There is now an end to all sacrifices and offerings for sin. The Son of God is come according to His word, "Lo, I come (in the volume of the Book it is written of Me,) to do Thy will, O God." "By His own blood" He entereth "in once into the holy place, having obtained eternal redemption for us." Heb. 10:7; 9:12.

"It is Finished"

Christ did not yield up His life till He had accomplished the work which He came to do, and with His parting breath He exclaimed, "It is finished." John 19:30. The battle had been won. His right hand and His holy arm had gotten Him the victory. As a Conqueror He planted His banner on the eternal heights. Was there not joy among the angels? All heaven triumphed in the Saviour's victory. Satan was defeated, and knew that his kingdom was lost.

To the angels and the unfallen worlds the cry, "It is finished," had a deep significance. It was for them as well as for us that the great work of redemption had been accomplished. They with us share the fruits of Christ's victory.

Not until the death of Christ was the character of Satan clearly revealed to the angels or to the unfallen worlds. The archapostate had so clothed himself with deception that even holy beings had not understood his principles. They had not clearly seen the nature of his rebellion.

It was a being of wonderful power and glory that had set himself against God. Of Lucifer the Lord says, "Thou sealest up the sum, full of wisdom, and perfect in beauty." Ezek. 28:12. Lucifer had been the covering cherub. He had stood in the light of God's presence. He had been the highest of all created beings, and had been foremost in revealing God's purposes to the universe. After he had sinned, his power to deceive was the more deceptive, and the unveiling of his character was the more difficult, because of the exalted position he had held with the Father.

God could have destroyed Satan and his sympathizers as easily as one can cast a pebble to the earth; but He did not do this. Rebellion was not to be overcome by force. Compelling power is found only under Satan's government. The Lord's principles are not of this order. His authority rests upon goodness, mercy, and love; and the presentation of these principles is the means to be used. God's government is moral, and truth and love are to be the prevailing power.

It was God's purpose to place things on an eternal basis of security, and in the councils of heaven it was decided that time must be given for Satan to develop the principles which were the foundation of his system of government. He had claimed that these were superior to God's principles. Time was given for the working of Satan's principles, that they might be seen by the heavenly universe.

Satan led men into sin, and the plan of redemption was put in operation. For four thousand years, Christ was working for man's uplifting, and Satan for his ruin and degradation. And the heavenly universe beheld it all.

When Jesus came into the world, Satan's power was turned against Him. From the time when He appeared as a babe in Bethlehem, the usurper worked to bring about His destruction. In every possible way he sought to prevent Jesus from developing a perfect childhood, a faultless manhood, a holy ministry, and an unblemished sacrifice. But he was defeated. He could not lead Jesus into sin. He could not discourage Him, or drive Him from a work He had come on earth to do. From the desert to Calvary, the storm of Satan's wrath beat upon Him, but the more mercilessly it fell, the more firmly did the Son of God cling to the hand of His Father, and press on in the bloodstained path. All the efforts of Satan to oppress and overcome Him only brought out in a purer light His spotless character.

All heaven and the unfallen worlds had been witnesses to the controversy. With what intense interest did they follow the closing scenes of the conflict. They beheld the Saviour enter the garden of Gethsemane, His soul bowed down with the horror of a great darkness. They heard His bitter cry, "Father, if it be possible, let this cup pass from Me." Matt. 26:39. As the Father's presence was withdrawn, they saw Him sorrowful with a bitterness of sorrow exceeding that of the last great struggle with death. The bloody sweat was forced from His pores, and fell in drops upon the ground. Thrice the prayer for deliverance was wrung from His lips. Heaven could no longer endure the sight, and a messenger of comfort was sent to the Son of God.

Heaven beheld the Victim betrayed into the hands of the murderous mob, and with mockery and violence hurried from one tribunal to another. It heard the sneers of His persecutors because of His lowly birth. It heard the denial with cursing and swearing by one of His best-loved disciples. It saw the frenzied work of Satan, and his power over the hearts of men. Oh, fearful scene! the Saviour seized at midnight in Gethsemane, dragged to and fro from palace to judgment hall, arraigned twice before the priests, twice before the Sanhedrin, twice before Pilate, and once before Herod, mocked, scourged, condemned, and led out to be crucified, bearing the heavy burden of the cross, amid the wailing of the daughters of Jerusalem and the jeering of the rabble.

Heaven viewed with grief and amazement Christ hanging upon the cross, blood flowing from His wounded temples, and sweat tinged with blood standing upon His brow. From His hands and feet the blood fell, drop by drop, upon the rock drilled for the foot of the cross. The wounds made by the nails gaped as the weight of His body dragged upon His hands. His labored breath grew quick and deep, as His soul panted under the burden of the sins of the world. All heaven was filled with wonder when the prayer of Christ was offered in the midst of His terrible suffering,—"Father, forgive them; for they know not what they do." Luke 23:34. Yet there stood men, formed in the image of God, joining to crush out the life of His only-begotten Son. What a sight for the heavenly universe!

The principalities and powers of darkness were assembled around the cross, casting the hellish shadow of unbelief into the hearts of men. When the Lord created these beings to stand before His throne, they were beautiful and glorious. Their loveliness and holiness were in accordance with their exalted station. They were enriched with the wisdom of God, and girded with the panoply of heaven. They were Jehovah's ministers. But who could recognize in the fallen angels the glorious seraphim that once ministered in the heavenly courts?

Satanic agencies confederated with evil men in leading the people to believe Christ the chief of sinners, and to make Him the object of detestation. Those who mocked Christ as He hung upon the cross were imbued with the spirit of the first great rebel. He filled them with vile and loathsome speeches. He inspired their taunts. But by all this he gained nothing.

Could one sin have been found in Christ, had He in one particular yielded to Satan to escape the terrible torture, the enemy of God and man would have triumphed. Christ bowed His head and died, but He held fast His faith and His submission to God. "And I heard a loud voice saying in heaven, Now is come salvation, and strength, and the kingdom of our God, and the power of His Christ: for the accuser of our brethren is cast down, which accused them before our God day and night." Rev. 12:10.

Satan saw that his disguise was torn away. His administration was laid open before the unfallen angels and before the heavenly universe. He had revealed himself as a murderer. By shedding the blood of the Son of God, he had uprooted himself from the sympathies of the heavenly beings. Henceforth his work was restricted. Whatever attitude he might assume, he could no longer await the angels as they came from the heavenly courts, and before them accuse Christ's brethren of being clothed with the garments of blackness and the defilement of sin. The last link of sympathy between Satan and the heavenly world was broken.

Yet Satan was not then destroyed. The angels did not even then understand all that was involved in the great controversy. The principles at stake were to be more fully revealed. And for the sake of man, Satan's existence must be continued. Man as well as angels must see the contrast between the Prince of light and the prince of darkness. He must choose whom he will serve.

In the opening of the great controversy, Satan had declared that the law of God could not be obeyed, that justice was inconsistent with mercy, and that, should the law be broken, it would be impossible for the sinner to be pardoned. Every sin must meet its punishment, urged Satan; and if God should remit the punishment of sin, He would not be a God of truth and justice. When men broke the law of God, and defied His will, Satan exulted. It was proved, he declared, that the law could not be obeyed; man could not be forgiven. Because he, after his rebellion, had been banished from heaven, Satan claimed that the human race must be forever shut out from God's favor. God could not be just, he urged, and yet show mercy to the sinner.

But even as a sinner, man was in a different position from that of Satan. Lucifer in heaven had sinned in the light of God's glory. To him as to no other created being was given a revelation of God's love. Understanding the character of God, knowing His goodness, Satan chose to follow his own selfish, independent will. This choice was final. There was no more that God could do to save him. But man was deceived; his mind was darkened by Satan's sophistry. The height and depth of the love of God he did not know. For him there was hope in a knowledge of God's love. By beholding His character he might be drawn back to God.

Through Jesus, God's mercy was manifested to men; but mercy does not set aside justice. The law reveals the attributes of God's character, and not a jot or tittle of it could be changed to meet man in his fallen condition. God did not change His law, but He sacrificed Himself, in Christ, for man's redemption. "God was in Christ, reconciling the world unto Himself." 2 Cor. 5:19.

The law requires righteousness,—a righteous life, a perfect character; and this man has not to give. He cannot meet the claims of God's holy law. But Christ, coming to the earth as man, lived a holy life, and developed a perfect character. These He offers as a free gift to all who will receive them. His life stands for the life of men. Thus they have remission of sins that are past, through the forbearance of God. More than this, Christ imbues men with the attributes of God. He builds up the human character after the similitude of the divine character, a goodly fabric of spiritual strength and beauty. Thus the very righteousness of the law is fulfilled in the believer in Christ. God can "be just, and the justifier of him which believeth in Jesus." Rom. 3:26.

God's love has been expressed in His justice no less than in His mercy. Justice is the foundation of His throne, and the fruit of His love. It had been Satan's purpose to divorce mercy from truth and justice. He sought to prove that the righteousness of God's law is an enemy to peace. But Christ shows that in God's plan they are indissolubly joined together; the one cannot exist without the other. "Mercy and truth are met together; righteousness and peace have kissed each other." Ps. 85:10.

By His life and His death, Christ proved that God's justice did not destroy His mercy, but that sin could be forgiven, and that the law is righteous, and can be perfectly obeyed. Satan's charges were refuted. God had given man unmistakable evidence of His love.

Another deception was now to be brought forward. Satan declared that mercy destroyed justice, that the death of Christ abrogated the Father's law. Had it been possible for the law to be changed or abrogated, then Christ need not have died. But to abrogate the law would be to immortalize transgression, and place the world under Satan's control. It was because the law was changeless, because man could be saved only through obedience to its precepts, that Jesus was lifted up on the cross. Yet the very means by which Christ established the law Satan represented as destroying it. Here will come the last conflict of the great controversy between Christ and Satan.

That the law which was spoken by God's own voice is faulty, that some specification has been set aside, is the claim which Satan now puts forward. It is the last great deception that he will bring upon the world. He needs not to assail the whole law; if he can lead men to disregard one precept, his purpose is gained. For "whosoever shall keep the whole law, and yet offend in one point, he is guilty of all." James 2:10. By consenting to break one precept, men are brought under Satan's power. By substituting human law for God's law, Satan will seek to control the world. This work is foretold in prophecy. Of the great apostate power which is the representative of Satan, it is declared, "He shall speak great words against the Most High, and shall wear out the saints of the Most High, and think to change times and laws: and they shall be given into his hand." Dan. 7:25.

Men will surely set up their laws to counterwork the laws of God. They will seek to compel the consciences of others, and in their zeal to enforce these laws they will oppress their fellow men.

The warfare against God's law, which was begun in heaven, will be continued until the end of time. Every man will be tested. Obedience or disobedience is the question to be decided by the whole world. All will be called to choose between the law of God and the laws of men. Here the dividing line will be drawn. There will be but two classes. Every character will be fully developed; and all will show whether they have chosen the side of loyalty or that of rebellion.

Then the end will come. God will vindicate His law and deliver His people. Satan and all who have joined him in rebellion will be cut off. Sin and sinners will perish, root and branch, (Mal. 4:1),—Satan the root, and his followers the branches. The word will be fulfilled to the prince of evil, "Because thou hast set thine heart as the heart of God; . . . I will destroy thee, O covering cherub, from the midst of the stones of fire. . . . Thou shalt be a terror, and never shalt thou be any more." Then "the wicked shall not be: yea, thou shalt diligently consider his place, and it shall not be;" "they shall be as though they had not been." Ezek. 28:6-19; Ps. 37:10; Obadiah 16.

This is not an act of arbitrary power on the part of God. The rejecters of His mercy reap that which they have sown. God is the fountain of life; and when one chooses the service of sin, he separates from God, and thus cuts himself off from life. He is "alienated from the life of God." Christ says, "All they that hate Me love death." Eph. 4:18; Prov. 8:36. God gives them existence for a time that they may develop their character and reveal their principles. This accomplished, they receive the results of their own choice. By a life of rebellion, Satan and all who unite with him place themselves so out of harmony with God that His very presence is to them a consuming fire. The glory of Him who is love will destroy them.

At the beginning of the great controversy, the angels did not understand this. Had Satan and his host then been left to reap the full result of their sin, they would have perished; but it would not have been apparent to heavenly beings that this was the inevitable result of sin. A doubt of God's goodness would have remained in their minds as evil seed, to produce its deadly fruit of sin and woe.

But not so when the great controversy shall be ended. Then, the plan of redemption having been completed, the character of God is revealed to all created intelligences. The precepts of His law are seen to be perfect and immutable. Then sin has made manifest its nature, Satan his character. Then the extermination of sin will vindicate God's love and establish His honor before a universe of beings who delight to do His will, and in whose heart is His law.

Well, then, might the angels rejoice as they looked upon the Saviour's cross; for though they did not then understand all, they knew that the destruction of sin and Satan was forever made certain, that the redemption of man was assured, and that the universe was made eternally secure. Christ Himself fully comprehended the results of the sacrifice made upon Calvary. To all these He looked forward when upon the cross He cried out, "It is finished."

In Joseph's Tomb

At last Jesus was at rest. The long day of shame and torture was ended. As the last rays of the setting sun ushered in the Sabbath, the Son of God lay in quietude in Joseph's tomb. His work completed, His hands folded in peace, He rested through the sacred hours of the Sabbath day.

In the beginning the Father and the Son had rested upon the Sabbath after Their work of creation. When "the heavens and the earth were finished, and all the host of them" (Gen. 2:1), the Creator and all heavenly beings rejoiced in contemplation of the glorious scene. "The morning stars sang together, and all the sons of God shouted for joy." Job 38:7. Now Jesus rested from the work of redemption; and though there was grief among those who loved Him on earth, yet there was joy in heaven. Glorious to the eyes of heavenly beings was the promise of the future. A restored creation, a redeemed race, that having conquered sin could never fall,—this, the result to flow from Christ's completed work, God and angels saw. With this scene the day upon which Jesus rested is forever linked. For "His work is perfect;" and "whatsoever God doeth, it shall be forever." Deut. 32:4; Eccl. 3:14. When there shall be a "restitution of all things, which God hath spoken by the mouth of all His holy prophets since the world began" (Acts 3:21), the creation Sabbath, the day on which Jesus lay at rest in Joseph's tomb, will still be a day of rest and rejoicing. Heaven and earth will unite in praise, as "from one Sabbath to another" (Isa. 66:23) the nations of the saved shall bow in joyful worship to God and the Lamb.

In the closing events of the crucifixion day, fresh evidence was given of the fulfillment of prophecy, and new witness borne to Christ's divinity. When the darkness had lifted from the cross, and the Saviour's dying cry had been uttered, immediately another voice was heard, saying, "Truly this was the Son of God." Matt. 27:54.

These words were said in no whispered tones. All eyes were turned to see whence they came. Who had spoken? It was the centurion, the Roman soldier. The divine patience of the Saviour, and His sudden death, with the cry of victory upon His lips, had impressed this heathen. In the bruised, broken body hanging upon the cross, the centurion recognized the form of the Son of God. He could not refrain from confessing his faith. Thus again evidence was given that our Redeemer was to see of the travail of His soul. Upon the very day of His death, three men, differing widely from one another, had declared their faith,—he who commanded the Roman guard, he who bore the cross of the Saviour, and he who died upon the cross at His side.

As evening drew on, an unearthly stillness hung over Calvary. The crowd dispersed, and many returned to Jerusalem greatly changed in spirit from what they had been in the morning. Many had flocked to the crucifixion from curiosity, and not from hatred toward Christ. Still they believed the accusations of the priests, and looked upon Christ as a malefactor. Under an unnatural excitement they had united with the mob in railing against Him. But when the earth was wrapped in blackness, and they stood accused by their own consciences, they felt guilty of a great wrong. No jest or mocking laughter was heard in the midst of that fearful gloom; and when it was lifted, they made their way to their homes in solemn silence. They were convinced that the charges of the priests were false, that Jesus was no pretender; and a few weeks later, when Peter preached upon the day of Pentecost, they were among the thousands who became converts to Christ.

But the Jewish leaders were unchanged by the events they had witnessed. Their hatred of Jesus had not abated. The darkness that had mantled the earth at the crucifixion was not more dense than that which still enveloped the minds of the priests and rulers. At His birth the star had known Christ, and had guided the wise men to the manger where He lay. The heavenly hosts had known Him, and had sung His praise over the plains of Bethlehem. The sea had known His voice, and had obeyed His command. Disease and death had recognized His authority, and had yielded to Him their prey. The sun had known Him, and at the sight of His dying anguish, had hidden its face of light. The rocks had known Him, and had shivered into fragments at His cry. Inanimate nature had known Christ, and had borne witness to His divinity. But the priests and rulers of Israel knew not the Son of God.

Yet the priests and rulers were not at rest. They had carried out their purpose in putting Christ to death; but they did not feel the sense of victory they had expected. Even in the hour of their apparent triumph, they were harassed with doubts as to what would next take place. They had heard the cry, "It is finished." "Father, into Thy hands I commend My spirit." John 19:30; Luke 23:46. They had seen the rocks rent, and had felt the mighty earthquake, and they were restless and uneasy.

They had been jealous of Christ's influence with the people when living; they were jealous of Him even in death. They dreaded the dead Christ more, far more, than they had ever feared the living Christ. They dreaded to have the attention of the people directed any further to the events attending His crucifixion. They feared the results of that day's work. Not on any account would they have had His body remain on the cross during the Sabbath. The Sabbath was now drawing on, and it would be a violation of its sanctity for the bodies to hang upon the cross. So, using this as a pretext, the leading Jews requested Pilate that the death of the victims might be hastened, and their bodies be removed before the setting of the sun.

Pilate was as unwilling as they for the body of Jesus to remain upon the cross. His consent having been obtained, the legs of the two thieves were broken to hasten their death; but Jesus was found to be already dead. The rude soldiers had been softened by what they had heard and seen of Christ, and they were restrained from breaking His limbs. Thus in the offering of the Lamb of God was fulfilled the law of the Passover, "They shall leave none of it unto the morning, nor break any bone of it: according to all the ordinances of the Passover they shall keep it." Num. 9:12

The priests and rulers were amazed to find that Christ was dead. Death by the cross was a lingering process; it was difficult to determine when life had ceased. It was an unheard-of thing for one to die within six hours of crucifixion. The priests wished to make sure of the death of Jesus, and at their suggestion a soldier thrust a spear into the Saviour's side. From the wound thus made, there flowed two copious and distinct streams, one of blood, the other of water. This was noted by all the beholders, and John states the occurrence very definitely. He says, "One of the soldiers with a spear pierced His side, and forthwith came there out blood and water. And he that saw it bare record, and his record is true: and he knoweth that he saith true, that ye might believe. For these things were done, that the scripture should be fulfilled, A bone of Him shall not be broken. And again another scripture saith, They shall look on Him whom they pierced." John 19:34-37.

After the resurrection the priests and rulers circulated the report that Christ did not die upon the cross, that He merely fainted, and was afterward revived. Another report affirmed that it was not a real body of flesh and bone, but the likeness of a body, that was laid in the tomb. The action of the Roman soldiers disproves these falsehoods. They broke not His legs, because He was already dead. To satisfy the priests, they pierced His side. Had not life been already extinct, this wound would have caused instant death.

But it was not the spear thrust, it was not the pain of the cross, that caused the death of Jesus. That cry, uttered "with a loud voice" (Matt. 27:50; Luke 23:46), at the moment of death, the stream of blood and water that flowed from His side, declared that He died of a broken heart. His heart was broken by mental anguish. He was slain by the sin of the world.

With the death of Christ the hopes of His disciples perished. They looked upon His closed eyelids and drooping head, His hair matted with blood, His pierced hands and feet, and their anguish was indescribable. Until the last they had not believed that He would die; they could hardly believe that He was really dead. Overwhelmed with sorrow, they did not recall His words foretelling this very scene. Nothing that He had said now gave them comfort. They saw only the cross and its bleeding Victim. The future seemed dark with despair. Their faith in Jesus had perished; but never had they loved their Lord as now. Never before had they so felt His worth, and their need of His presence.

Even in death, Christ's body was very precious to His disciples. They longed to give Him an honored burial, but knew not how to accomplish this. Treason against the Roman government was the crime for which Jesus was condemned, and persons put to death for this offense were consigned to a burial ground especially provided for such criminals. The disciple John with the women from Galilee had remained at the cross. They could not leave the body of their Lord to be handled by the unfeeling soldiers, and buried in a dishonored grave. Yet they could not prevent it. They could obtain no favors from the Jewish authorities, and they had no influence with Pilate.

In this emergency, Joseph of Arimathaea and Nicodemus came to the help of the disciples. Both these men were members of the Sanhedrin, and were acquainted with Pilate. Both were men of wealth and influence. They were determined that the body of Jesus should have an honorable burial.

Joseph went boldly to Pilate, and begged from him the body of Jesus. For the first time, Pilate learned that Jesus was really dead. Conflicting reports had reached him in regard to the events attending the crucifixion, but the knowledge of Christ's death had been purposely kept from him. Pilate had been warned by the priests and rulers against deception by Christ's disciples in regard to His body. Upon hearing Joseph's request, he therefore sent for the centurion who had charge at the cross, and learned for a certainty of the death of Jesus. He also drew from him an account of the scenes of Calvary, confirming the testimony of Joseph.

The request of Joseph was granted. While John was troubled about the burial of his Master, Joseph returned with Pilate's order for the body of Christ; and Nicodemus came bringing a costly mixture of myrrh and aloes, of about a hundred pounds' weight, for His embalming. The most honored in all Jerusalem could not have been shown more respect in death. The disciples were astonished to see these wealthy rulers as much interested as they themselves in the burial of their Lord.

Neither Joseph nor Nicodemus had openly accepted the Saviour while He was living. They knew that such a step would exclude them from the Sanhedrin, and they hoped to protect Him by their influence in its councils. For a time they had seemed to succeed; but the wily priests, seeing their favor to Christ, had thwarted their plans. In their absence Jesus had been condemned and delivered to be crucified. Now that He was dead, they no longer concealed their attachment to Him. While the disciples feared to show themselves openly as His followers, Joseph and Nicodemus came boldly to their aid. The help of these rich and honored men was greatly needed at this time. They could do for their dead Master what it was impossible for the poor disciples to do; and their wealth and influence protected them, in a great measure, from the malice of the priests and rulers.

Gently and reverently they removed with their own hands the body of Jesus from the cross. Their tears of sympathy fell fast as they looked upon His bruised and lacerated form.

Joseph owned a new tomb, hewn in a rock. This he was reserving for himself; but it was near Calvary, and he now prepared it for Jesus. The body, together with the spices brought by Nicodemus, was carefully wrapped in a linen sheet, and the Redeemer was borne to the tomb. There the three disciples straightened the mangled limbs, and folded the bruised hands upon the pulseless breast. The Galilean women came to see that all had been done that could be done for the lifeless form of their beloved Teacher. Then they saw the heavy stone rolled against the entrance of the tomb, and the Saviour was left at rest. The women were last at the cross, and last at the tomb of Christ. While the evening shades were gathering, Mary Magdalene and the other Marys lingered about the resting place of their Lord, shedding tears of sorrow over the fate of Him whom they loved. "And they returned, . . . and rested the Sabbath day according to the commandment." Luke 23:56.

That was a never-to-be-forgotten Sabbath to the sorrowing disciples, and also to the priests, rulers, scribes, and people. At the setting of the sun on the evening of the preparation day the trumpets sounded, signifying that the Sabbath had begun. The Passover was observed as it had been for centuries, while He to whom it pointed had been slain by wicked hands, and lay in Joseph's tomb. On the Sabbath the courts of the temple were filled with worshipers. The high priest from Golgotha was there, splendidly robed in his sacerdotal garments. White-turbaned priests, full of activity, performed their duties. But some present were not at rest as the blood of bulls and goats was offered for sin. They were not conscious that type had met antitype, that an infinite sacrifice had been made for the sins of the world. They knew not that there was no further value in the performance of the ritual service. But never before had that service been witnessed with such conflicting feelings. The trumpets and musical instruments and the voices of the singers were as loud and clear as usual. But a sense of strangeness pervaded everything. One after another inquired about a strange event that had taken place. Hitherto the most holy place had been sacredly guarded from intrusion. But now it was open to all eyes. The heavy veil of tapestry, made of pure linen, and beautifully wrought with gold, scarlet, and purple, was rent from top to bottom. The place where Jehovah had met with the high priest, to communicate His glory, the place that had been God's sacred audience chamber, lay open to every eye,—a place no longer recognized by the Lord. With gloomy presentiments the priests ministered before the altar. The uncovering of the sacred mystery of the most holy place filled them with dread of coming calamity.

Many minds were busy with thoughts started by the scenes of Calvary. From the crucifixion to the resurrection many sleepless eyes were constantly searching the prophecies, some to learn the full meaning of the feast they were then celebrating, some to find evidence that Jesus was not what He claimed to be; and others with sorrowful hearts were searching for proofs that He was the true Messiah. Though searching with different objects in view, all were convicted of the same truth,—that prophecy had been fulfilled in the events of the past few days, and that the Crucified One was the world's Redeemer. Many who at that time united in the service never again took part in the paschal rites. Many even of the priests were convicted of the true character of Jesus. Their searching of the prophecies had not been in vain, and after His resurrection they acknowledged Him as the Son of God.

Nicodemus, when he saw Jesus lifted up on the cross, remembered His words spoken by night in the Mount of Olives: "As Moses lifted up the serpent in the wilderness, even so must the Son of man be lifted up: that whosoever believeth in Him should not perish, but have eternal life." John 3:14, 15. On that Sabbath, when Christ lay in the grave, Nicodemus had opportunity for reflection. A clearer light now illuminated his mind, and the words which Jesus had spoken to him were no longer mysterious. He felt that he had lost much by not connecting himself with the Saviour during His life. Now he recalled the events of Calvary. The prayer of Christ for His murderers and His answer to the petition of the dying thief spoke to the heart of the learned councilor. Again he looked upon the Saviour in His agony; again he heard that last cry, "It is finished," spoken like the words of a conqueror. Again he beheld the reeling earth, the darkened heavens, the rent veil, the shivered rocks, and his faith was forever established. The very event that destroyed the hopes of the disciples convinced Joseph and Nicodemus of the divinity of Jesus. Their fears were overcome by the courage of a firm and unwavering faith.

Never had Christ attracted the attention of the multitude as now that He was laid in the tomb. According to their practice, the people brought their sick and suffering ones to the temple courts, inquiring, Who can tell us of Jesus of Nazareth? Many had come from far to find Him who had healed the sick and raised the dead. On every side was heard the cry, We want Christ the Healer! Upon this occasion those who were thought to show indications of the leprosy were examined by the priests. Many were forced to hear their husbands, wives, or children pronounced leprous, and doomed to go forth from the shelter of their homes and the care of their friends, to warn off the stranger with the mournful cry, "Unclean, unclean!" The friendly hands of Jesus of Nazareth, that never refused to touch with healing the loathsome leper, were folded on His breast. The lips that had answered his petition with the comforting words, "I will; be thou clean" (Matt. 8:3), were now silent. Many appealed to the chief priests and rulers for sympathy and relief, but in vain. Apparently they were determined to have the living Christ among them again. With persistent earnestness they asked for Him. They would not be turned away. But they were driven from the temple courts, and soldiers were stationed at the gates to keep back the multitude that came with their sick and dying, demanding entrance.

The sufferers who had come to be healed by the Saviour sank under their disappointment. The streets were filled with mourning. The sick were dying for want of the healing touch of Jesus. Physicians were consulted in vain; there was no skill like that of Him who lay in Joseph's tomb.

The mourning cries of the suffering ones brought home to thousands of minds the conviction that a great light had gone out of the world. Without Christ, the earth was blackness and darkness. Many whose voices had swelled the cry of "Crucify Him, crucify Him," now realized the calamity that had fallen upon them, and would as eagerly have cried, Give us Jesus! had He still been alive.

When the people learned that Jesus had been put to death by the priests, inquiries were made regarding His death. The particulars of His trial were kept as private as possible; but during the time when He was in the grave, His name was on thousands of lips, and reports of His mock trial, and of the inhumanity of the priests and rulers, were circulated everywhere. By men of intellect these priests and rulers were called upon to explain the prophecies of the Old Testament concerning the Messiah, and while trying to frame some falsehood in reply, they became like men insane. The prophecies that pointed to Christ's sufferings and death they could not explain, and many inquirers were convinced that the Scriptures had been fulfilled.

The revenge which the priests had thought would be so sweet was already bitterness to them. They knew that they were meeting the severe censure of the people; they knew that the very ones whom they had influenced against Jesus were now horrified by their own shameful work. These priests had tried to believe Jesus a deceiver; but it was in vain. Some of them had stood by the grave of Lazarus, and had seen the dead brought back to life. They trembled for fear that Christ would Himself rise from the dead, and again appear before them. They had heard Him declare that He had power to lay down His life and to take it again. They remembered that He had said, "Destroy this temple, and in three days I will raise it up." John 2:19. Judas had told them the words spoken by Jesus to the disciples while on the last journey to Jerusalem: "Behold, we go up to Jerusalem; and the Son of man shall be betrayed unto the chief priests and unto the scribes, and they shall condemn Him to death, and shall deliver Him to the Gentiles to mock, and to scourge, and to crucify Him: and the third day He shall rise again." Matt. 20:18, 19. When they heard these words, they had mocked and ridiculed. But now they remembered that Christ's predictions had so far been fulfilled. He had said that He would rise again the third day, and who could say that this also would not come to pass? They longed to shut out these thoughts, but they could not. Like their father, the devil, they believed and trembled.

Now that the frenzy of excitement was past, the image of Christ would intrude upon their minds. They beheld Him as He stood serene and uncomplaining before His enemies, suffering without a murmur their taunts and abuse. All the events of His trial and crucifixion came back to them with an overpowering conviction that He was the Son of God. They felt that He might at any time stand before them, the accused to become the accuser, the condemned to condemn, the slain to demand justice in the death of His murderers.

They could rest little upon the Sabbath. Though they would not step over a Gentile's threshold for fear of defilement, yet they held a council concerning the body of Christ. Death and the grave must hold Him whom they had crucified. "The chief priests and Pharisees came together unto Pilate, saying, Sir, we remember that that deceiver said, while He was yet alive, After three days I will rise again. Command therefore that the sepulcher be made sure until the third day, lest His disciples come by night, and steal Him away, and say unto the people, He is risen from the dead: so the last error shall be worse than the first. Pilate said unto them, Ye have a watch: go your way, make it as sure as ye can." Matt. 27:62-65.

The priests gave directions for securing the sepulcher. A great stone had been placed before the opening. Across this stone they placed cords, securing the ends to the solid rock, and sealing them with the Roman seal. The stone could not be moved without breaking the seal. A guard of one hundred soldiers was then stationed around the sepulcher to prevent it from being tampered with. The priests did all they could to keep Christ's body where it had been laid. He was sealed as securely in His tomb as if He were to remain there through all time.

So weak men counseled and planned. Little did these murderers realize the uselessness of their efforts. But by their action God was glorified. The very efforts made to prevent Christ's resurrection are the most convincing arguments in its proof. The greater the number of soldiers placed around the tomb, the stronger would be the testimony that He had risen. Hundreds of years before the death of Christ, the Holy Spirit had declared through the psalmist, "Why do the heathen rage, and the people imagine a vain thing? The kings of the earth set themselves, and the rulers take counsel together, against the Lord, and against His anointed. . . . He that sitteth in the heavens shall laugh: the Lord shall have them in derision." Ps. 2:1-4. Roman guards and Roman arms were powerless to confine the Lord of life within the tomb. The hour of His release was near.

"The Lord Is Risen"

The night of the first day of the week had worn slowly away. The darkest hour, just before daybreak, had come. Christ was still a prisoner in His narrow tomb. The great stone was in its place; the Roman seal was unbroken; the Roman guards were keeping their watch. And there were unseen watchers. Hosts of evil angels were gathered about the place. Had it been possible, the prince of darkness with his apostate army would have kept forever sealed the tomb that held the Son of God. But a heavenly host surrounded the sepulcher. Angels that excel in strength were guarding the tomb, and waiting to welcome the Prince of life.

"And, behold, there was a great earthquake: for the angel of the Lord descended from heaven." Clothed with the panoply of God, this angel left the heavenly courts. The bright beams of God's glory went before him, and illuminated his pathway. "His countenance was like lightning, and his raiment white as snow: and for fear of him the keepers did shake, and became as dead men."

Now, priests and rulers, where is the power of your guard? Brave soldiers that have never been afraid of human power are now as captives taken without sword or spear. The face they look upon is not the face of mortal warrior; it is the face of the mightiest of the Lord's host. This messenger is he who fills the position from which Satan fell. It is he who on the hills of Bethlehem proclaimed Christ's birth. The earth trembles at his approach, the hosts of darkness flee, and as he rolls away the stone, heaven seems to come down to the earth. The soldiers see him removing the stone as he would a pebble, and hear him cry, Son of God, come forth; Thy Father calls Thee. They see Jesus come forth from the grave, and hear Him proclaim over the rent sepulcher, "I am the resurrection, and the life." As He comes forth in majesty and glory, the angel host bow low in adoration before the Redeemer, and welcome Him with songs of praise.

An earthquake marked the hour when Christ laid down His life, and another earthquake witnessed the moment when He took it up in triumph. He who had vanquished death and the grave came forth from the tomb with the tread of a conqueror, amid the reeling of the earth, the flashing of lightning, and the roaring of thunder. When He shall come to the earth again, He will shake "not the earth only, but also heaven." "The earth shall reel to and fro like a drunkard, and shall be removed like a cottage." "The heavens shall be rolled together as a scroll;" "the elements shall melt with fervent heat, the earth also and the works that are therein shall be burned up." But "the Lord will be the hope of His people, and the strength of the children of Israel." Heb. 12:26; Isa. 24:20; 34:4; 2 Peter 3:10; Joel 3:16.

At the death of Jesus the soldiers had beheld the earth wrapped in darkness at midday; but at the resurrection they saw the brightness of the angels illuminate the night, and heard the inhabitants of heaven singing with great joy and triumph: Thou hast vanquished Satan and the powers of darkness; Thou hast swallowed up death in victory!

Christ came forth from the tomb glorified, and the Roman guard beheld Him. Their eyes were riveted upon the face of Him whom they had so recently mocked and derided. In this glorified Being they beheld the prisoner whom they had seen in the judgment hall, the one for whom they had plaited a crown of thorns. This was the One who had stood unresisting before Pilate and Herod, His form lacerated by the cruel scourge. This was He who had been nailed to the cross, at whom the priests and rulers, full of self-satisfaction, had wagged their heads, saying, "He saved others; Himself He cannot save." Matt. 27:42. This was He who had been laid in Joseph's new tomb. The decree of heaven had loosed the captive. Mountains piled upon mountains over His sepulcher could not have prevented Him from coming forth.

At sight of the angels and the glorified Saviour the Roman guard had fainted and become as dead men. When the heavenly train was hidden from their view, they arose to their feet, and as quickly as their trembling limbs could carry them, made their way to the gate of the garden. Staggering like drunken men, they hurried on to the city, telling those whom they met the wonderful news. They were making their way to Pilate, but their report had been carried to the Jewish authorities, and the chief priests and rulers sent for them to be brought first into their presence. A strange appearance those soldiers presented. Trembling with fear, their faces colorless, they bore testimony to the resurrection of Christ. The soldiers told all, just as they had seen it; they had not had time to think or speak anything but the truth. With painful utterance they said, It was the Son of God who was crucified; we have heard an angel proclaiming Him as the Majesty of heaven, the King of glory.

The faces of the priests were as those of the dead. Caiaphas tried to speak. His lips moved, but they uttered no sound. The soldiers were about to leave the council room, when a voice stayed them. Caiaphas had at last found speech. Wait, wait, he said. Tell no one the things you have seen.

A lying report was then given to the soldiers. "Say ye," said the priests, "His disciples came by night, and stole Him away while we slept." Here the priests overreached themselves. How could the soldiers say that the disciples had stolen the body while they slept? If they were asleep, how could they know? And if the disciples had been proved guilty of stealing Christ's body, would not the priests have been first to condemn them? Or if the sentinels had slept at the tomb, would not the priests have been foremost in accusing them to Pilate?

The soldiers were horrified at the thought of bringing upon themselves the charge of sleeping at their post. This was an offense punishable with death. Should they bear false witness, deceiving the people, and placing their own lives in peril? Had they not kept their weary watch with sleepless vigilance? How could they stand the trial, even for the sake of money, if they perjured themselves?

In order to silence the testimony they feared, the priests promised to secure the safety of the guard, saying that Pilate would not desire to have such a report circulated any more than they did. The Roman soldiers sold their integrity to the Jews for money. They came in before the priests burdened with a most startling message of truth; they went out with a burden of money, and on their tongues a lying report which had been framed for them by the priests.

Meanwhile the report of Christ's resurrection had been carried to Pilate. Though Pilate was responsible for having given Christ up to die, he had been comparatively unconcerned. While he had condemned the Saviour unwillingly, and with a feeling of pity, he had felt no real compunction until now. In terror he now shut himself within his house, determined to see no one. But the priests made their way into his presence, told the story which they had invented, and urged him to overlook the sentinels' neglect of duty. Before consenting to this, he himself privately questioned the guard. They, fearing for their own safety, dared not conceal anything, and Pilate drew from them an account of all that had taken place. He did not prosecute the matter further, but from that time there was no peace for him.

When Jesus was laid in the grave, Satan triumphed. He dared to hope that the Saviour would not take up His life again. He claimed the Lord's body, and set his guard about the tomb, seeking to hold Christ a prisoner. He was bitterly angry when his angels fled at the approach of the heavenly messenger. When he saw Christ come forth in triumph, he knew that his kingdom would have an end, and that he must finally die.

The priests, in putting Christ to death, had made themselves the tools of Satan. Now they were entirely in his power. They were entangled in a snare from which they saw no escape but in continuing their warfare against Christ. When they heard the report of His resurrection, they feared the wrath of the people. They felt that their own lives were in danger. The only hope for them was to prove Christ an impostor by denying that He had risen. They bribed the soldiers, and secured Pilate's silence. They spread their lying reports far and near. But there were witnesses whom they could not silence. Many had heard of the soldiers' testimony to Christ's resurrection. And certain of the dead who came forth with Christ appeared to many, and declared that He had risen. Reports were brought to the priests of persons who had seen these risen ones, and heard their testimony. The priests and rulers were in continual dread, lest in walking the streets, or within the privacy of their own homes, they should come face to face with Christ. They felt that there was no safety for them. Bolts and bars were but poor protection against the Son of God. By day and by night that awful scene in the judgment hall, when they had cried, "His blood be on us, and on our children," was before them. Matt. 27:25. Nevermore would the memory of that scene fade from their minds. Nevermore would peaceful sleep come to their pillows.

When the voice of the mighty angel was heard at Christ's tomb, saying, Thy Father calls Thee, the Saviour came forth from the grave by the life that was in Himself. Now was proved the truth of His words, "I lay down My life, that I might take it again. . . . I have power to lay it down, and I have power to take it again." Now was fulfilled the prophecy He had spoken to the priests and rulers, "Destroy this temple, and in three days I will raise it up." John 10:17, 18; 2:19.

Over the rent sepulcher of Joseph, Christ had proclaimed in triumph, "I am the resurrection, and the life." These words could be spoken only by the Deity. All created beings live by the will and power of God. They are dependent recipients of the life of God. From the highest seraph to the humblest animate being, all are replenished from the Source of life. Only He who is one with God could say, I have power to lay down My life, and I have power to take it again. In His divinity, Christ possessed the power to break the bonds of death.

Christ arose from the dead as the first fruits of those that slept. He was the antitype of the wave sheaf, and His resurrection took place on the very day when the wave sheaf was to be presented before the Lord. For more than a thousand years this symbolic ceremony had been performed. From the harvest fields the first heads of ripened grain were gathered, and when the people went up to Jerusalem to the Passover, the sheaf of first fruits was waved as a thank offering before the Lord. Not until this was presented could the sickle be put to the grain, and it be gathered into sheaves. The sheaf dedicated to God represented the harvest. So Christ the first fruits represented the great spiritual harvest to be gathered for the kingdom of God. His resurrection is the type and pledge of the resurrection of all the righteous dead. "For if we believe that Jesus died and rose again, even so them also which sleep in Jesus will God bring with Him." 1 Thess. 4:14.

As Christ arose, He brought from the grave a multitude of captives. The earthquake at His death had rent open their graves, and when He arose, they came forth with Him. They were those who had been co-laborers with God, and who at the cost of their lives had borne testimony to the truth. Now they were to be witnesses for Him who had raised them from the dead.

During His ministry, Jesus had raised the dead to life. He had raised the son of the widow of Nain, and the ruler's daughter and Lazarus. But these were not clothed with immortality. After they were raised, they were still subject to death. But those who came forth from the grave at Christ's resurrection were raised to everlasting life. They ascended with Him as trophies of His victory over death and the grave. These, said Christ, are no longer the captives of Satan; I have redeemed them. I have brought them from the grave as the first fruits of My power, to be with Me where I am, nevermore to see death or experience sorrow.

These went into the city, and appeared unto many, declaring, Christ has risen from the dead, and we be risen with Him. Thus was immortalized the sacred truth of the resurrection. The risen saints bore witness to the truth of the words, "Thy dead men shall live, together with My dead body shall they arise." Their resurrection was an illustration of the fulfillment of the prophecy, "Awake and sing, ye that dwell in dust: for thy dew is as the dew of herbs, and the earth shall cast out the dead." Isa. 26:19.

To the believer, Christ is the resurrection and the life. In our Saviour the life that was lost through sin is restored; for He has life in Himself to quicken whom He will. He is invested with the right to give immortality. The life that He laid down in humanity, He takes up again, and gives to humanity. "I am come," He said, "that they might have life, and that they might have it more abundantly." "Whosoever drinketh of the water that I shall give him shall never thirst; but the water that I shall give him shall be in him a well of water springing up into everlasting life." "Whoso eateth My flesh, and drinketh My blood, hath eternal life; and I will raise him up at the last day." John 10:10; 4:14; 6:54.

To the believer, death is but a small matter. Christ speaks of it as if it were of little moment. "If a man keep My saying, he shall never see death," "he shall never taste of death." To the Christian, death is but a sleep, a moment of silence and darkness. The life is hid with Christ in God, and "when Christ, who is our life, shall appear, then shall ye also appear with Him in glory." John 8:51, 52; Col. 3:4.

The voice that cried from the cross, "It is finished," was heard among the dead. It pierced the walls of sepulchers, and summoned the sleepers to arise. Thus will it be when the voice of Christ shall be heard from heaven. That voice will penetrate the graves and unbar the tombs, and the dead in Christ shall arise. At the Saviour's resurrection a few graves were opened, but at His second coming all the precious dead shall hear His voice, and shall come forth to glorious, immortal life. The same power that raised Christ from the dead will raise His church, and glorify it with Him, above all principalities, above all powers, above every name that is named, not only in this world, but also in the world to come.

"Why Weepest Thou?"

The women who had stood by the cross of Christ waited and watched for the hours of the Sabbath to pass. On the first day of the week, very early, they made their way to the tomb, taking with them precious spices to anoint the Saviour's body. They did not think about His rising from the dead. The sun of their hope had set, and night had settled down on their hearts. As they walked, they recounted Christ's works of mercy and His words of comfort. But they remembered not His words, "I will see you again." John 16:22.

Ignorant of what was even then taking place, they drew near the garden, saying as they went, "Who shall roll us away the stone from the door of the sepulcher?" They knew that they could not remove the stone, yet they kept on their way. And lo, the heavens were suddenly alight with glory that came not from the rising sun. The earth trembled. They saw that the great stone was rolled away. The grave was empty.

The women had not all come to the tomb from the same direction. Mary Magdalene was the first to reach the place; and upon seeing that the stone was removed, she hurried away to tell the disciples. Meanwhile the other women came up. A light was shining about the tomb, but the body of Jesus was not there. As they lingered about the place, suddenly they saw that they were not alone. A young man clothed in shining garments was sitting by the tomb. It was the angel who had rolled away the stone. He had taken the guise of humanity that he might not alarm these friends of Jesus. Yet about him the light of the heavenly glory was still shining, and the women were afraid. They turned to flee, but the angel's words stayed their steps. "Fear not ye," he said; "for I know that ye seek Jesus, which was crucified. He is not here: for He is risen, as He said. Come, see the place where the Lord lay. And go quickly, and tell His disciples that He is risen from the dead."

Again they look into the tomb, and again they hear the wonderful news. Another angel in human form is there, and he says, "Why seek ye the living among the dead? He is not here, but is risen: remember how He spake unto you when He was yet in Galilee, saying, The Son of man must be delivered into the hands of sinful men, and be crucified, and the third day rise again."

He is risen, He is risen! The women repeat the words again and again. No need now for the anointing spices. The Saviour is living, and not dead. They remember now that when speaking of His death He said that He would rise again. What a day is this to the world! Quickly the women departed from the sepulcher "with fear and great joy; and did run to bring His disciples word."

Mary had not heard the good news. She went to Peter and John with the sorrowful message, "They have taken away the Lord out of the sepulcher, and we know not where they have laid Him." The disciples hurried to the tomb, and found it as Mary had said. They saw the shroud and the napkin, but they did not find their Lord. Yet even here was testimony that He had risen. The graveclothes were not thrown heedlessly aside, but carefully folded, each in a place by itself. John "saw, and believed." He did not yet understand the scripture that Christ must rise from the dead; but he now remembered the Saviour's words foretelling His resurrection.

It was Christ Himself who had placed those graveclothes with such care. When the mighty angel came down to the tomb, he was joined by another, who with his company had been keeping guard over the Lord's body. As the angel from heaven rolled away the stone, the other entered the tomb, and unbound the wrappings from the body of Jesus. But it was the Saviour's hand that folded each, and laid it in its place. In His sight who guides alike the star and the atom, there is nothing unimportant. Order and perfection are seen in all His work.

Mary had followed John and Peter to the tomb; when they returned to Jerusalem, she remained. As she looked into the empty tomb, grief filled her heart. Looking in, she saw the two angels, one at the head and the other at the foot where Jesus had lain. "Woman, why weepest thou?" they asked her. "Because they have taken away my Lord," she answered, "and I know not where they have laid Him."

Then she turned away, even from the angels, thinking that she must find someone who could tell her what had been done with the body of Jesus. Another voice addressed her, "Woman, why weepest thou? whom seekest thou?" Through her tear-dimmed eyes, Mary saw the form of a man, and thinking that it was the gardener, she said, "Sir, if thou have borne Him hence, tell me where thou hast laid Him, and I will take Him away." If this rich man's tomb was thought too honorable a burial place for Jesus, she herself would provide a place for Him. There was a grave that Christ's own voice had made vacant, the grave where Lazarus had lain. Might she not there find a burial place for her Lord? She felt that to care for His precious crucified body would be a great consolation to her in her grief.

But now in His own familiar voice Jesus said to her, "Mary." Now she knew that it was not a stranger who was addressing her, and turning she saw before her the living Christ. In her joy she forgot that He had been crucified. Springing toward Him, as if to embrace His feet, she said, "Rabboni." But Christ raised His hand, saying, Detain Me not; "for I am not yet ascended to My Father: but go to My brethren, and say unto them, I ascend unto My Father, and your Father; and to My God, and your God." And Mary went her way to the disciples with the joyful message.

Jesus refused to receive the homage of His people until He had the assurance that His sacrifice was accepted by the Father. He ascended to the heavenly courts, and from God Himself heard the assurance that His atonement for the sins of men had been ample, that through His blood all might gain eternal life. The Father ratified the covenant made with Christ, that He would receive repentant and obedient men, and would love them even as He loves His Son. Christ was to complete His work, and fulfill His pledge to "make a man more precious than fine gold; even a man than the golden wedge of Ophir." Isa. 13:12. All power in heaven and on earth was given to the Prince of Life, and He returned to His followers in a world of sin, that He might impart to them of His power and glory.

While the Saviour was in God's presence, receiving gifts for His church, the disciples thought upon His empty tomb, and mourned and wept. The day that was a day of rejoicing to all heaven was to the disciples a day of uncertainty, confusion, and perplexity. Their unbelief in the testimony of the women gives evidence of how low their faith had sunk. The news of Christ's resurrection was so different from what they had anticipated that they could not believe it. It was too good to be true, they thought. They had heard so much of the doctrines and the so-called scientific theories of the Sadducees that the impression made on their minds in regard to the resurrection was vague. They scarcely knew what the resurrection from the dead could mean. They were unable to take in the great subject.

"Go your way," the angels had said to the women, "tell His disciples and Peter that He goeth before you into Galilee: there shall ye see Him, as He said unto you." These angels had been with Christ as guardian angels throughout His life on earth. They had witnessed His trial and crucifixion. They had heard His words to His disciples. This was shown by their message to the disciples, and should have convinced them of its truth. Such words could have come only from the messengers of their risen Lord.

"Tell His disciples and Peter," the angels said. Since the death of Christ, Peter had been bowed down with remorse. His shameful denial of the Lord, and the Saviour's look of love and anguish, were ever before him. Of all the disciples he had suffered most bitterly. To him the assurance is given that his repentance is accepted and his sin forgiven. He is mentioned by name.

"Tell His disciples and Peter that He goeth before you into Galilee: there shall ye see Him." All the disciples had forsaken Jesus, and the call to meet Him again includes them all. He has not cast them off. When Mary Magdalene told them she had seen the Lord, she repeated the call to the meeting in Galilee. And a third time the message was sent to them. After He had ascended to the Father, Jesus appeared to the other women, saying, "All hail. And they came and held Him by the feet, and worshiped Him. Then said Jesus unto them, Be not afraid: go tell My brethren that they go into Galilee, and there shall they see Me."

Christ's first work on earth after His resurrection was to convince His disciples of His undiminished love and tender regard for them. To give them proof that He was their living Saviour, that He had broken the fetters of the tomb, and could no longer be held by the enemy death; to reveal that He had the same heart of love as when He was with them as their beloved Teacher, He appeared to them again and again. He would draw the bonds of love still closer around them. Go tell My brethren, He said, that they meet Me in Galilee.

As they heard this appointment, so definitely given, the disciples began to think of Christ's words to them foretelling His resurrection. But even now they did not rejoice. They could not cast off their doubt and perplexity. Even when the women declared that they had seen the Lord, the disciples would not believe. They thought them under an illusion.

Trouble seemed crowding upon trouble. On the sixth day of the week they had seen their Master die; on the first day of the next week they found themselves deprived of His body, and they were accused of having stolen it away for the sake of deceiving the people. They despaired of ever correcting the false impressions that were gaining ground against them. They feared the enmity of the priests and the wrath of the people. They longed for the presence of Jesus, who had helped them in every perplexity.

Often they repeated the words, "We trusted that it had been He which should have redeemed Israel." Lonely and sick at heart they remembered His words, "If they do these things in a green tree, what shall be done in the dry?" Luke 24:21; 23:31. They met together in the upper chamber, and closed and fastened the doors, knowing that the fate of their beloved Teacher might at any time be theirs.

And all the time they might have been rejoicing in the knowledge of a risen Saviour. In the garden, Mary had stood weeping, when Jesus was close beside her. Her eyes were so blinded by tears that she did not discern Him. And the hearts of the disciples were so full of grief that they did not believe the angels' message or the words of Christ Himself.

How many are still doing what these disciples did! How many echo Mary's despairing cry, "They have taken away the Lord, . . . and we know not where they have laid Him"! To how many might the Saviour's words be spoken, "Why weepest thou? whom seekest thou?" He is close beside them, but their tear-blinded eyes do not discern Him. He speaks to them, but they do not understand.

Oh that the bowed head might be lifted, that the eyes might be opened to behold Him, that the ears might listen to His voice! "Go quickly, and tell His disciples that He is risen." Bid them look not to Joseph's new tomb, that was closed with a great stone, and sealed with the Roman seal. Christ is not there. Look not to the empty sepulcher. Mourn not as those who are hopeless and helpless. Jesus lives, and because He lives, we shall live also. From grateful hearts, from lips touched with holy fire, let the glad song ring out, Christ is risen! He lives to make intercession for us. Grasp this hope, and it will hold the soul like a sure, tried anchor. Believe, and thou shalt see the glory of God.

The Walk to Emmaus

Late in the afternoon of the day of the resurrection, two of the disciples were on their way to Emmaus, a little town eight miles from Jerusalem. These disciples had had no prominent place in Christ's work, but they were earnest believers in Him. They had come to the city to keep the Passover, and were greatly perplexed by the events that had recently taken place. They had heard the news of the morning in regard to the removal of Christ's body from the tomb, and also the report of the women who had seen the angels and had met Jesus. They were now returning to their homes to meditate and pray. Sadly they pursued their evening walk, talking over the scenes of the trial and the crucifixion. Never before had they been so utterly disheartened. Hopeless and faithless, they were walking in the shadow of the cross.

They had not advanced far on their journey when they were joined by a stranger, but they were so absorbed in their gloom and disappointment that they did not observe him closely. They continued their conversation, expressing the thoughts of their hearts. They were reasoning in regard to the lessons that Christ had given, which they seemed unable to comprehend. As they talked of the events that had taken place, Jesus longed to comfort them. He had seen their grief; He understood the conflicting, perplexing ideas that brought to their minds the thought, Can this Man, who suffered Himself to be so humiliated, be the Christ? Their grief could not be restrained, and they wept. Jesus knew that their hearts were bound up with Him in love, and He longed to wipe away their tears, and fill them with joy and gladness. But He must first give them lessons they would never forget.

"He said unto them, What manner of communications are these that ye have one to another, as ye walk, and are sad? And the one of them, whose name was Cleopas, answering said unto Him, Art Thou only a stranger in Jerusalem, and hast not known the things which are come to pass there in these days?" They told Him of their disappointment in regard to their Master, "which was a prophet mighty in deed and word before God and all the people;" but "the chief priests and our rulers," they said, "delivered Him to be condemned to death, and have crucified Him." With hearts sore with disappointment, and with quivering lips, they added, "We trusted that it had been He which should have redeemed Israel: and beside all this, today is the third day since these things were done."

Strange that the disciples did not remember Christ's words, and realize that He had foretold the events which had come to pass! They did not realize that the last part of His disclosure would be just as verily fulfilled as the first part, that the third day He would rise again. This was the part they should have remembered. The priests and rulers did not forget this. On the day "that followed the day of the preparation, the chief priests and Pharisees came together unto Pilate, saying, Sir, we remember that that deceiver said, while He was yet alive, After three days I will rise again." Matt. 27:62, 63. But the disciples did not remember these words.

"Then He said unto them, O fools, and slow of heart to believe all that the prophets have spoken: ought not Christ to have suffered these things, and to enter into His glory?" The disciples wondered who this stranger could be, that He should penetrate to their very souls, and speak with such earnestness, tenderness, and sympathy, and with such hopefulness. For the first time since Christ's betrayal, they began to feel hopeful. Often they looked earnestly at their companion, and thought that His words were just the words that Christ would have spoken. They were filled with amazement, and their hearts began to throb with joyful expectation.

Beginning at Moses, the very Alpha of Bible history, Christ expounded in all the Scriptures the things concerning Himself. Had He first made Himself known to them, their hearts would have been satisfied. In the fullness of their joy they would have hungered for nothing more. But it was necessary for them to understand the witness borne to Him by the types and prophecies of the Old Testament. Upon these their faith must be established. Christ performed no miracle to convince them, but it was His first work to explain the Scriptures. They had looked upon His death as the destruction of all their hopes. Now He showed from the prophets that this was the very strongest evidence for their faith.

In teaching these disciples, Jesus showed the importance of the Old Testament as a witness to His mission. Many professed Christians now discard the Old Testament, claiming that it is no longer of any use. But such is not Christ's teaching. So highly did He value it that at one time He said, "If they hear not Moses and the prophets, neither will they be persuaded, though one rose from the dead." Luke 16:31.

It is the voice of Christ that speaks through patriarchs and prophets, from the days of Adam even to the closing scenes of time. The Saviour is revealed in the Old Testament as clearly as in the New. It is the light from the prophetic past that brings out the life of Christ and the teachings of the New Testament with clearness and beauty. The miracles of Christ are a proof of His divinity; but a stronger proof that He is the world's Redeemer is found in comparing the prophecies of the Old Testament with the history of the New.

Reasoning from prophecy, Christ gave His disciples a correct idea of what He was to be in humanity. Their expectation of a Messiah who was to take His throne and kingly power in accordance with the desires of men had been misleading. It would interfere with a correct apprehension of His descent from the highest to the lowest position that could be occupied. Christ desired that the ideas of His disciples might be pure and true in every specification. They must understand as far as possible in regard to the cup of suffering that had been apportioned to Him. He showed them that the awful conflict which they could not yet comprehend was the fulfillment of the covenant made before the foundation of the world was laid. Christ must die, as every transgressor of the law must die if he continues in sin. All this was to be, but it was not to end in defeat, but in glorious, eternal victory. Jesus told them that every effort must be made to save the world from sin. His followers must live as He lived, and work as He worked, with intense, persevering effort.

Thus Christ discoursed to His disciples, opening their minds that they might understand the Scriptures. The disciples were weary, but the conversation did not flag. Words of life and assurance fell from the Saviour's lips. But still their eyes were holden. As He told them of the overthrow of Jerusalem, they looked upon the doomed city with weeping. But little did they yet suspect who their traveling companion was. They did not think that the subject of their conversation was walking by their side; for Christ referred to Himself as though He were another person. They thought that He was one of those who had been in attendance at the great feast, and who was now returning to his home. He walked as carefully as they over the rough stones, now and then halting with them for a little rest. Thus they proceeded along the mountainous road, while the One who was soon to take His position at God's right hand, and who could say, "All power is given unto Me in heaven and in earth," walked beside them. Matt. 28:18.

During the journey the sun had gone down, and before the travelers reached their place of rest, the laborers in the fields had left their work. As the disciples were about to enter their home, the stranger appeared as though He would continue His journey. But the disciples felt drawn to Him. Their souls hungered to hear more from Him. "Abide with us," they said. He did not seem to accept the invitation, but they pressed it upon Him, urging, "It is toward evening, and the day is far spent." Christ yielded to this entreaty and "went in to tarry with them."

Had the disciples failed to press their invitation, they would not have known that their traveling companion was the risen Lord. Christ never forces His company upon anyone. He interests Himself in those who need Him. Gladly will He enter the humblest home, and cheer the lowliest heart. But if men are too indifferent to think of the heavenly Guest, or ask Him to abide with them, He passes on. Thus many meet with great loss. They do not know Christ any more than did the disciples as He walked with them by the way.

The simple evening meal of bread is soon prepared. It is placed before the guest, who has taken His seat at the head of the table. Now He puts forth His hands to bless the food. The disciples start back in astonishment. Their companion spreads forth His hands in exactly the same way as their Master used to do. They look again, and lo, they see in His hands the print of nails. Both exclaim at once, It is the Lord Jesus! He has risen from the dead!

They rise to cast themselves at His feet and worship Him, but He has vanished out of their sight. They look at the place which had been occupied by One whose body had lately lain in the grave, and say to each other, "Did not our heart burn within us, while He talked with us by the way, and while He opened to us the Scriptures?"

But with this great news to communicate they cannot sit and talk. Their weariness and hunger are gone. They leave their meal untasted, and full of joy immediately set out again on the same path by which they came, hurrying to tell the tidings to the disciples in the city. In some parts the road is not safe, but they climb over the steep places, slipping on the smooth rocks. They do not see, they do not know, that they have the protection of Him who has traveled the road with them. With their pilgrim staff in hand, they press on, desiring to go faster than they dare. They lose their track, but find it again. Sometimes running, sometimes stumbling, they press forward, their unseen Companion close beside them all the way.

The night is dark, but the Sun of Righteousness is shining upon them. Their hearts leap for joy. They seem to be in a new world. Christ is a living Saviour. They no longer mourn over Him as dead. Christ is risen—over and over again they repeat it. This is the message they are carrying to the sorrowing ones. They must tell them the wonderful story of the walk to Emmaus. They must tell who joined them by the way. They carry the greatest message ever given to the world, a message of glad tidings upon which the hopes of the human family for time and for eternity depend.

"Peace Be Unto You"

On reaching Jerusalem the two disciples enter at the eastern gate, which is open at night on festal occasions. The houses are dark and silent, but the travelers make their way through the narrow streets by the light of the rising moon. They go to the upper chamber where Jesus spent the hours of the last evening before His death. Here they know that their brethren are to be found. Late as it is, they know that the disciples will not sleep till they learn for a certainty what has become of the body of their Lord. They find the door of the chamber securely barred. They knock for admission, but no answer comes. All is still. Then they give their names. The door is carefully unbarred, they enter, and Another, unseen, enters with them. Then the door is again fastened, to keep out spies.

The travelers find all in surprised excitement. The voices of those in the room break out into thanksgiving and praise, saying, "The Lord is risen indeed, and hath appeared to Simon." Then the two travelers, panting with the haste with which they have made their journey, tell the wondrous story

of how Jesus has appeared to them. They have just ended, and some are saying that they cannot believe it, for it is too good to be true, when behold, another Person stands before them. Every eye is fastened upon the stranger. No one has knocked for entrance. No footstep has been heard. The disciples are startled, and wonder what it means. Then they hear a voice which is no other than the voice of their Master. Clear and distinct the words fall from His lips, "Peace be unto you."

"But they were terrified and affrighted, and supposed that they had seen a spirit. And He said unto them, Why are ye troubled? and why do thoughts arise in your hearts? Behold My hands and My feet, that it is I Myself: handle Me, and see; for a spirit hath not flesh and bones, as ye see Me have. And when He had thus spoken, He showed them His hands and His feet."

They beheld the hands and feet marred by the cruel nails. They recognized His voice, like no other they had ever heard. "And while they yet believed not for joy, and wondered, He said unto them, Have ye here any meat? And they gave Him a piece of a broiled fish, and of an honeycomb. And He took it, and did eat before them." "Then were the disciples glad, when they saw the Lord." Faith and joy took the place of unbelief, and with feelings which no words could express they acknowledged their risen Saviour.

At the birth of Jesus the angel announced, Peace on earth, and good will to men. And now at His first appearance to the disciples after His resurrection, the Saviour addressed them with the blessed words, "Peace be unto you." Jesus is ever ready to speak peace to souls that are burdened with doubts and fears. He waits for us to open the door of the heart to Him, and say, Abide with us. He says, "Behold, I stand at the door, and knock: if any man hear My voice, and open the door, I will come in to him, and will sup with him, and he with Me." Rev. 3:20.

The resurrection of Jesus was a type of the final resurrection of all who sleep in Him. The countenance of the risen Saviour, His manner, His speech, were all familiar to His disciples. As Jesus arose from the dead, so those who sleep in Him are to rise again. We shall know our friends, even as the disciples knew Jesus. They may have been deformed, diseased, or disfigured, in this mortal life, and they rise in perfect health and symmetry; yet in the glorified body their identity will be perfectly preserved. Then shall we know even as also we are known. 1 Cor. 13:12. In the face radiant with the light shining from the face of Jesus, we shall recognize the lineaments of those we love.

When Jesus met with His disciples, He reminded them of the words He had spoken to them before His death, that all things must be fulfilled which were written in the law of Moses, and in the prophets, and in the Psalms concerning Him. "Then opened He their understanding, that they might understand the Scriptures, and said unto them, Thus it is written, and thus it behooved Christ to suffer, and to rise from the dead the third day: and that repentance and remission of sins should be preached in His name among all nations, beginning at Jerusalem. And ye are witnesses of these things."

The disciples began to realize the nature and extent of their work. They were to proclaim to the world the wonderful truths which Christ had entrusted to them. The events of His life, His death and resurrection, the prophecies that pointed to these events, the sacredness of the law of God, the mysteries of the plan of salvation, the power of Jesus for the remission of sins,—to all these things they were witnesses, and they were to make them known to the world. They were to proclaim the gospel of peace and salvation through repentance and the power of the Saviour.

"And when He had said this, He breathed on them, and saith unto them, Receive ye the Holy Ghost: Whosesoever sins ye remit, they are remitted unto them; and whosesoever sins ye retain, they are retained." The Holy Spirit was not yet fully manifested; for Christ had not yet been glorified. The more abundant impartation of the Spirit did not take place till after Christ's ascension. Not until this was received could the disciples fulfill the commission to preach the gospel to the world. But the Spirit was now given for a special purpose. Before the disciples could fulfill their official duties in connection with the church, Christ breathed His Spirit upon them. He was committing to them a most sacred trust, and He desired to impress them with the fact that without the Holy Spirit this work could not be accomplished.

The Holy Spirit is the breath of spiritual life in the soul. The impartation of the Spirit is the impartation of the life of Christ. It imbues the receiver with the attributes of Christ. Only those who are thus taught of God, those who possess the inward working of the Spirit, and in whose life the Christ-life is manifested, are to stand as representative men, to minister in behalf of the church.

"Whosesoever sins ye remit," said Christ, "they are remitted; . . . and whosesoever sins ye retain, they are retained." Christ here gives no liberty for any man to pass judgment upon others. In the Sermon on the Mount He forbade this. It is the prerogative of God. But on the church in its organized capacity He places a responsibility for the individual members. Toward those who fall into sin, the church has a duty, to warn, to instruct, and if possible to restore. "Reprove, rebuke, exhort," the Lord says, "with all long-suffering and doctrine." 2 Tim. 4:2. Deal faithfully with wrongdoing. Warn every soul that is in danger. Leave none to deceive themselves. Call sin by its right name. Declare what God has said in regard to lying, Sabbathbreaking, stealing, idolatry, and every other evil. "They which do such things shall not inherit the kingdom of God." Gal. 5:21. If they persist in sin, the judgment you have declared from God's word is pronounced upon them in heaven. In choosing to sin, they disown Christ; the church must show that she does not sanction their deeds, or she herself dishonors her Lord. She must say about sin what God says about it. She must deal with it as God directs, and her action is ratified in heaven. He who despises the authority of the church despises the authority of Christ Himself.

But there is a brighter side to the picture. "Whosesoever sins ye remit, they are remitted." Let this thought be kept uppermost. In labor for the erring, let every eye be directed to Christ. Let the shepherds have a tender care for the flock of the Lord's pasture. Let them speak to the erring of the forgiving mercy of the Saviour. Let them encourage the sinner to repent, and believe in Him who can pardon. Let them declare, on the authority of God's word, "If we confess our sins, He is faithful and just to forgive us our sins, and to cleanse us from all unrighteousness." 1 John 1:9. All who repent have the assurance, "He will have compassion upon us; He will subdue our iniquities; and Thou wilt cast all their sins into the depths of the sea." Micah 7:19.

Let the repentance of the sinner be accepted by the church with grateful hearts. Let the repenting one be led out from the darkness of unbelief into the light of faith and righteousness. Let his trembling hand be placed in the loving hand of Jesus. Such a remission is ratified in heaven.

Only in this sense has the church power to absolve the sinner. Remission of sins can be obtained only through the merits of Christ. To no man, to no body of men, is given power to free the soul from guilt. Christ charged His disciples to preach the remission of sins in His name among all nations; but they themselves were not empowered to remove one stain of sin. The name of Jesus is the only "name under heaven given among men, whereby we must be saved." Acts 4:12.

When Jesus first met the disciples in the upper chamber, Thomas was not with them. He heard the reports of the others, and received abundant proof that Jesus had risen; but gloom and unbelief filled his heart. As he heard the disciples tell of the wonderful manifestations of the risen Saviour, it only plunged him in deeper despair. If Jesus had really risen from the dead, there could be no further hope of a literal earthly kingdom. And it wounded his vanity to think that his Master should reveal Himself to all the disciples except him. He was determined not to believe, and for a whole week he brooded over his wretchedness, which seemed all the darker in contrast with the hope and faith of his brethren.

During this time he repeatedly declared, "Except I shall see in His hands the print of the nails, and put my finger into the print of the nails, and thrust my hand into His side, I will not believe." He would not see through the eyes of his brethren, or exercise faith which was dependent upon their testimony. He ardently loved his Lord, but he had allowed jealousy and unbelief to take possession of his mind and heart.

A number of the disciples now made the familiar upper chamber their temporary home, and at evening all except Thomas gathered here. One evening Thomas determined to meet with the others. Notwithstanding his unbelief, he had a faint hope that the good news was true. While the disciples were taking their evening meal, they talked of the evidences which Christ had given them in the prophecies. "Then came Jesus, the doors being shut, and stood in the midst, and said, Peace be unto you."

Turning to Thomas He said, "Reach hither thy finger, and

behold My hands; and reach hither thy hand, and thrust it into My side: and be not faithless, but believing." These words showed that He was acquainted with the thoughts and words of Thomas. The doubting disciple knew that none of his companions had seen Jesus for a week. They could not have told the Master of his unbelief. He recognized the One before him as his Lord. He had no desire for further proof. His heart leaped for joy, and he cast himself at the feet of Jesus crying, "My Lord and my God."

Jesus accepted his acknowledgment, but gently reproved his unbelief: "Thomas, because thou hast seen Me, thou hast believed: blessed are they that have not seen, and yet have believed." The faith of Thomas would have been more pleasing to Christ if he had been willing to believe upon the testimony of his brethren. Should the world now follow the example of Thomas, no one would believe unto salvation; for all who receive Christ must do so through the testimony of others.

Many who are given to doubt excuse themselves by saying that if they had the evidence which Thomas had from his companions, they would believe. They do not realize that they have not only that evidence, but much more. Many who, like Thomas, wait for all cause of doubt to be removed, will never realize their desire. They gradually become confirmed in unbelief. Those who educate themselves to look on the dark side, and murmur and complain, know not what they do. They are sowing the seeds of doubt, and they will have a harvest of doubt to reap. At a time when faith and confidence are most essential, many will thus find themselves powerless to hope and believe.

In His treatment of Thomas, Jesus gave a lesson for His followers. His example shows how we should treat those whose faith is weak, and who make their doubts prominent. Jesus did not overwhelm Thomas with reproach, nor did He enter into controversy with him. He revealed Himself to the doubting one. Thomas had been most unreasonable in dictating the conditions of his faith, but Jesus, by His generous love and consideration, broke down all the barriers. Unbelief is seldom overcome by controversy. It is rather put upon self-defense, and finds new support and excuse. But let Jesus, in His love and mercy, be revealed as the crucified Saviour, and from many once unwilling lips will be heard the acknowledgment of Thomas, "My Lord and my God."

By the Sea Once More

Jesus had appointed to meet His disciples in Galilee; and soon after the Passover week was ended, they bent their steps thither. Their absence from Jerusalem during the feast would have been interpreted as disaffection and heresy, therefore they remained till its close; but this over, they gladly turned homeward to meet the Saviour as He had directed.

Seven of the disciples were in company. They were clad in the humble garb of fishermen; they were poor in worldly goods, but rich in the knowledge and practice of the truth, which in the sight of Heaven gave them the highest rank as teachers. They had not been students in the schools of the prophets, but for three years they had been taught by the greatest Educator the world has ever known. Under His instruction they had become elevated, intelligent, and refined, agents through whom men might be led to a knowledge of the truth.

Much of the time of Christ's ministry had been passed near the Sea of Galilee. As the disciples gathered in a place where they were not likely to be disturbed, they found themselves surrounded by reminders of Jesus and His mighty works. On this sea, when their hearts were filled with terror, and the fierce storm was hurrying them to destruction, Jesus had walked upon the billows to their rescue. Here the tempest had been hushed by His word. Within sight was the beach where above ten thousand persons had been fed from a few small loaves and fishes. Not far distant was Capernaum, the scene of so many miracles. As the disciples looked upon the scene, their minds were full of the words and deeds of their Saviour.

The evening was pleasant, and Peter, who still had much of his old love for boats and fishing, proposed that they should go out upon the sea and cast their nets. In this plan all were ready to join; they were in need of food and clothing, which the proceeds of a successful night's fishing would supply. So they went out in their boat, but they caught nothing. All night they toiled, without success. Through the weary hours they talked of their absent Lord, and recalled the wonderful events they had witnessed in His ministry beside the sea. They questioned as to their own future, and grew sad at the prospect before them.

All the while a lone watcher upon the shore followed them with His eye, while He Himself was unseen. At length the morning dawned. The boat was but a little way from the shore, and the disciples saw a stranger standing upon the beach, who accosted them with the question, "Children, have ye any meat?" When they answered, "No," "He said unto them, Cast the net on the right side of the ship, and ye shall find. They cast therefore, and now they were not able to draw it for the multitude of fishes."

John recognized the stranger, and exclaimed to Peter, "It is the Lord." Peter was so elated and so glad that in his eagerness he cast himself into the water and was soon standing by the side of his Master. The other disciples came in their boat, dragging the net with fishes. "As soon then as they were come to land, they saw a fire of coals there, and fish laid thereon, and bread."

They were too much amazed to question whence came the fire and the food. "Jesus saith unto them, Bring of the fish which ye have now caught." Peter rushed for the net, which he had dropped, and helped his brethren drag it to the shore. After the work was done, and the preparation made, Jesus bade the disciples come and dine. He broke the food, and divided it among them, and was known and acknowledged by all the seven. The miracle of feeding the five thousand on the mountainside was now brought to their minds; but a mysterious awe was upon them, and in silence they gazed upon the risen Saviour.

Vividly they recalled the scene beside the sea when Jesus had bidden them follow Him. They remembered how, at His command, they had launched out into the deep, and had let down their net, and the catch had been so abundant as to fill the net, even to breaking. Then Jesus had called them to leave their fishing boats, and had promised to make them fishers of men. It was to bring this scene to their minds, and to deepen its impression, that He had again performed the miracle. His act was a renewal of the commission to the disciples. It showed them that the death of their Master had not lessened their obligation to do the work He had assigned them. Though they were to be deprived of His personal companionship, and of the means of support by their former employment, the risen Saviour would still have a care for them. While they were doing His work, He would provide for their needs. And Jesus had a purpose in bidding them cast their net on the right side of the ship. On that side He stood upon the shore. That was the side of faith. If they labored in connection with Him,—His divine power combining with their human effort,—they could not fail of success.

Another lesson Christ had to give, relating especially to Peter. Peter's denial of his Lord had been in shameful contrast to his former professions of loyalty. He had dishonored Christ, and had incurred the distrust of his brethren. They thought he would not be allowed to take his former position among them, and he himself felt that he had forfeited his trust. Before being called to take up again his apostolic work, he must before them all give evidence of his repentance. Without this, his sin, though repented of, might have destroyed his influence as a minister of Christ. The Saviour gave him opportunity to regain the confidence of his brethren, and, so far as possible, to remove the reproach he had brought upon the gospel.

Here is given a lesson for all Christ's followers. The gospel makes no compromise with evil. It cannot excuse sin. Secret sins are to be confessed in secret to God; but, for open sin, open confession is required. The reproach of the disciple's sin is cast upon Christ. It causes Satan to triumph, and wavering souls to stumble. By giving proof of repentance, the disciple, so far as lies in his power, is to remove this reproach.

While Christ and the disciples were eating together by the seaside, the Saviour said to Peter, "Simon, son of Jonas, lovest thou Me more than these?" referring to his brethren. Peter had once declared, "Though all men shall be offended because of Thee, yet will I never be offended." Matt. 26:33. But he now put a truer estimate upon himself. "Yea, Lord," he said, "Thou knowest that I love Thee." There is no vehement assurance that his love is greater than that of his brethren. He does not express his own opinion of his devotion. To Him who can read all the motives of the heart he appeals to judge as to his sincerity,—"Thou knowest that I love Thee." And Jesus bids him, "Feed My lambs."

Again Jesus applied the test to Peter, repeating His former words: "Simon, son of Jonas, lovest thou Me?" This time He did not ask Peter whether he loved Him better than did his brethren. The second response was like the first, free from extravagant assurance: "Yea, Lord; Thou knowest that I love Thee." Jesus said to him, "Feed My sheep." Once more the Saviour put the trying question: "Simon, son of Jonas, lovest thou Me?" Peter was grieved; he thought that Jesus doubted his love. He knew that his Lord had cause to distrust him, and with an aching heart he answered, "Lord, Thou knowest all things; Thou knowest that I love Thee." Again Jesus said to him, "Feed My sheep."

Three times Peter had openly denied his Lord, and three times Jesus drew from him the assurance of his love and loyalty, pressing home that pointed question, like a barbed arrow to his wounded heart. Before the assembled disciples Jesus revealed the depth of Peter's repentance, and showed how thoroughly humbled was the once boasting disciple.

Peter was naturally forward and impulsive, and Satan had taken advantage of these characteristics to overthrow him. Just before the fall of Peter, Jesus had said to him, "Satan hath desired to have you, that he may sift you as wheat: but I have prayed for thee, that thy faith fail not: and when thou art converted, strengthen thy brethren." Luke 22:31, 32. That time had now come, and the transformation in Peter was evident. The close, testing questions of the Lord had not called out one forward, self-sufficient reply; and because of his humiliation and repentance, Peter was better prepared than ever before to act as shepherd to the flock.

The first work that Christ entrusted to Peter on restoring him to the ministry was to feed the lambs. This was a work in which Peter had little experience. It would require great care and tenderness, much patience and perseverance. It called him to minister to those who were young in the faith, to teach the ignorant, to open the Scriptures to them, and to educate them for usefulness in Christ's service. Heretofore Peter had not been fitted to do this, or even to understand its importance. But this was the work which Jesus now called upon him to do. For this work his own experience of suffering and repentance had prepared him.

Before his fall, Peter was always speaking unadvisedly, from the impulse of the moment. He was always ready to correct others, and to express his mind, before he had a clear comprehension of himself or of what he had to say. But the converted Peter was very different. He retained his former fervor, but the grace of Christ regulated his zeal. He was no longer impetuous, self-confident, and self-exalted, but calm, self-possessed, and teachable. He could then feed the lambs as well as the sheep of Christ's flock.

The Saviour's manner of dealing with Peter had a lesson for him and for his brethren. It taught them to meet the transgressor with patience, sympathy, and forgiving love. Although Peter had denied his Lord, the love which Jesus bore him never faltered. Just such love should the undershepherd feel for the sheep and lambs committed to his care. Remembering his own weakness and failure, Peter was to deal with his flock as tenderly as Christ had dealt with him.

The question that Christ had put to Peter was significant. He mentioned only one condition of discipleship and service. "Lovest thou Me?" He said. This is the essential qualification. Though Peter might possess every other, yet without the love of Christ he could not be a faithful shepherd over the Lord's flock. Knowledge, benevolence, eloquence, gratitude, and zeal are all aids in the good work; but without the love of Jesus in the heart, the work of the Christian minister is a failure.

Jesus walked alone with Peter, for there was something which He wished to communicate to him only. Before His death, Jesus had said to him, "Whither I go, thou canst not follow Me now; but thou shalt follow Me afterwards." To this Peter had replied, "Lord, why cannot I follow Thee now? I will lay down my life for Thy sake." John 13:36, 37. When he said this, he little knew to what heights and depths Christ's feet would lead the way. Peter had failed when the test came, but again he was to have opportunity to prove his love for Christ. That he might be strengthened for the final test of his faith, the Saviour opened to him his future. He told him that after living a life of usefulness, when age was telling upon his strength, he would indeed follow his Lord. Jesus said, "When thou wast young, thou girdedst thyself, and walkedst whither thou wouldest: but when thou shalt be old, thou shalt stretch forth thy hands, and another shall gird thee, and carry thee whither thou wouldest not. This spake He, signifying by what death he should glorify God."

Jesus thus made known to Peter the very manner of his death; He even foretold the stretching forth of his hands upon the cross. Again He bade His disciple, "Follow Me." Peter was not disheartened by the revelation. He felt willing to suffer any death for his Lord.

Heretofore Peter had known Christ after the flesh, as many know Him now; but he was no more to be thus limited. He knew Him no more as he had known Him in his association with Him in humanity. He had loved Him as a man, as a heaven-sent teacher; he now loved Him as God. He had been learning the lesson that to him Christ was all in all. Now he was prepared to share in his Lord's mission of sacrifice. When at last brought to the cross, he was, at his own request, crucified with his head downward. He thought it too great an honor to suffer in the same way as his Master did.

To Peter the words "Follow Me" were full of instruction. Not only for his death, but for every step of his life, was the lesson given. Hitherto Peter had been inclined to act independently. He had tried to plan for the work of God, instead of waiting to follow out God's plan. But he could gain nothing by rushing on before the Lord. Jesus bids him, "Follow Me." Do not run ahead of Me. Then you will not have the hosts of Satan to meet alone. Let Me go before you, and you will not be overcome by the enemy.

As Peter walked beside Jesus, he saw that John was following. A desire came over him to know his future, and he "saith to Jesus, Lord, and what shall this man do? Jesus saith unto him, If I will that he tarry till I come, what is that to thee? follow thou Me." Peter should have considered that his Lord would reveal to him all that it was best for him to know. It is the duty of everyone to follow Christ, without undue anxiety as to the work assigned to others. In saying of John, "If I will that he tarry till I come," Jesus gave no assurance that this disciple should live until the Lord's second coming. He merely asserted His own supreme power, and that even if He should will this to be so, it would in no way affect Peter's work. The future of both John and Peter was in the hands of their Lord. Obedience in following Him was the duty required of each.

How many today are like Peter! They are interested in the affairs of others, and anxious to know their duty, while they are in danger of neglecting their own. It is our work to look to Christ and follow Him. We shall see mistakes in the lives of others, and defects in their character. Humanity is encompassed with infirmity. But in Christ we shall find perfection. Beholding Him, we shall become transformed.

John lived to be very aged. He witnessed the destruction of Jerusalem, and the ruin of the stately temple,—a symbol of the final ruin of the world. To his latest days John closely followed his Lord. The burden of his testimony to the churches was, "Beloved, let us love one another;" "he that dwelleth in love, dwelleth in God, and God in him." 1 John 4:7, 16.

Peter had been restored to his apostleship, but the honor and authority he received from Christ had not given him supremacy over his brethren. This Christ had made plain when in answer to Peter's question, "What shall this man do?" He had said, "What is that to thee? follow thou Me." Peter was not honored as the head of the church. The favor which Christ had shown him in forgiving his apostasy, and entrusting him with the feeding of the flock, and Peter's own faithfulness in following Christ, won for him the confidence of his brethren. He had much influence in the church. But the lesson which Christ had taught him by the Sea of Galilee Peter carried with him throughout his life. Writing by the Holy Spirit to the churches, he said:

"The elders which are among you I exhort, who am also an elder, and a witness of the sufferings of Christ, and also a partaker of the glory that shall be revealed: Feed the flock of God which is among you, taking the oversight thereof, not by constraint, but willingly; not for filthy lucre, but of a ready mind; neither as being lords over God's heritage, but being ensamples to the flock. And when the Chief Shepherd shall appear, ye shall receive a crown of glory that fadeth not away." 1 Peter 5:1-4.

Go Teach All Nations

Standing but a step from His heavenly throne, Christ gave the commission to His disciples. "All power is given unto Me in heaven and in earth," He said. "Go ye therefore, and teach all nations." "Go ye into all the world, and preach the gospel to every creature." Mark 16:15. Again and again the words were repeated, that the disciples might grasp their significance. Upon all the inhabitants of the earth, high and low, rich and poor, was the light of heaven to shine in clear, strong rays. The disciples were to be colaborers with their Redeemer in the work of saving the world.

The commission had been given to the twelve when Christ met with them in the upper chamber; but it was now to be given to a larger number. At the meeting on a mountain in Galilee, all the believers who could be called together were assembled. Of this meeting Christ Himself, before His death, had designated the time and place. The angel at the tomb reminded the disciples of His promise to meet them in Galilee. The promise was repeated to the believers who were gathered at Jerusalem during the Passover week, and through them it reached many lonely ones who were mourning the death of their Lord. With intense interest all looked forward to the interview. They made their way to the place of meeting by circuitous routes, coming in from every direction, to avoid exciting the suspicion of the jealous Jews. With wondering hearts they came, talking earnestly together of the news that had reached them concerning Christ.

At the time appointed, about five hundred believers were collected in little knots on the mountainside, eager to learn all that could be learned from those who had seen Christ since His resurrection. From group to group the disciples passed, telling all they had seen and heard of Jesus, and reasoning from the Scriptures as He had done with them. Thomas recounted the story of his unbelief, and told how his doubts had been swept away. Suddenly Jesus stood among them. No one could tell whence or how He came. Many who were present had never before seen Him; but in His hands and feet they beheld the marks of the crucifixion; His countenance was as the face of God, and when they saw Him, they worshiped Him.

But some doubted. So it will always be. There are those who find it hard to exercise faith, and they place themselves on the doubting side. These lose much because of their unbelief.

This was the only interview that Jesus had with many of the believers after His resurrection. He came and spoke to them saying, "All power is given unto Me in heaven and in earth." The disciples had worshiped Him before He spoke, but His words, falling from lips that had been closed in death, thrilled them with peculiar power. He was now the risen Saviour. Many of them had seen Him exercise His power in healing the sick and controlling satanic agencies. They believed that He possessed power to set up His kingdom at Jerusalem, power to quell all opposition, power over the elements of nature. He had stilled the angry waters; He had walked upon the white-crested billows; He had raised the dead to life. Now He declared that "all power" was given to Him. His words carried the minds of His hearers above earthly and temporal things to the heavenly and eternal. They were lifted to the highest conception of His dignity and glory.

Christ's words on the mountainside were the announcement that His sacrifice in behalf of man was full and complete. The conditions of the atonement had been fulfilled; the work for which He came to this world had been accomplished. He was on His way to the throne of God, to be honored by angels, principalities, and powers. He had entered upon His mediatorial work. Clothed with boundless authority, He gave His commission to the disciples: "Go ye therefore, and teach all nations," "baptizing them into the name of the Father and of the Son and of the Holy Spirit: teaching them to observe all things whatsoever I commanded you: and lo, I am with you always, even unto the end of the world." Matt. 28:19, 20, R. V.

The Jewish people had been made the depositaries of sacred truth; but Pharisaism had made them the most exclusive, the most bigoted, of all the human race. Everything about the priests and rulers—their dress, customs, ceremonies, traditions—made them unfit to be the light of the world. They looked upon themselves, the Jewish nation, as the world. But Christ commissioned His disciples to proclaim a faith and worship that would have in it nothing of caste or country, a faith that would be adapted to all peoples, all nations, all classes of men.

Before leaving His disciples, Christ plainly stated the nature of His kingdom. He called to their minds what He had previously told them concerning it. He declared that it was not His purpose to establish in this world a temporal, but a spiritual kingdom. He was not to reign as an earthly king on David's throne. Again He opened to them the Scriptures, showing that all He had passed through had been ordained in heaven, in the councils between the Father and Himself. All had been foretold by men inspired by the Holy Spirit. He said, You see that all I have revealed to you concerning My rejection as the Messiah has come to pass. All I have said in regard to the humiliation I should endure and the death I should die, has been verified. On the third day I rose again. Search the Scriptures more diligently, and you will see that in all these things the specifications of prophecy concerning Me have been fulfilled.

Christ commissioned His disciples to do the work He had left in their hands, beginning at Jerusalem. Jerusalem had been the scene of His amazing condescension for the human race. There He had suffered, been rejected and condemned. The land of Judea was His birthplace. There, clad in the garb of humanity, He had walked with men, and few had discerned how near heaven came to the earth when Jesus was among them. At Jerusalem the work of the disciples must begin.

In view of all that Christ had suffered there, and the unappreciated labor He had put forth, the disciples might have pleaded for a more promising field; but they made no such plea. The very ground where He had scattered the seed of truth was to be cultivated by the disciples, and the seed would spring up and yield an abundant harvest. In their work the disciples would have to meet persecution through the jealousy and hatred of the Jews; but this had been endured by their Master, and they were not to flee from it. The first offers of mercy must be made to the murderers of the Saviour.

And there were in Jerusalem many who had secretly believed on Jesus, and many who had been deceived by the priests and rulers. To these also the gospel was to be presented. They were to be called to repentance. The wonderful truth that through Christ alone could remission of sins be obtained was to be made plain. While all Jerusalem was stirred by the thrilling events of the past few weeks, the preaching of the gospel would make the deepest impression.

But the work was not to stop here. It was to be extended to the earth's remotest bounds. To His disciples Christ said, You have been witnesses of My life of self-sacrifice in behalf of the world. You have witnessed My labors for Israel. Although they would not come unto Me that they might have life, although priests and rulers have done to Me as they listed, although they have rejected Me as the Scriptures foretold, they shall have still another opportunity of accepting the Son of God. You have seen that all who come to Me, confessing their sins, I freely receive. Him that cometh to Me I will in nowise cast out. All who will, may be reconciled to God, and receive everlasting life. To you, My disciples, I commit this message of mercy. It is to be given to Israel first, and then to all nations, tongues, and peoples. It is to be given to Jews and Gentiles. All who believe are to be gathered into one church.

Through the gift of the Holy Spirit the disciples were to receive a marvelous power. Their testimony was to be confirmed by signs and wonders. Miracles would be wrought, not only by the apostles, but by those who received their message. Jesus said, "In My name shall they cast out devils; they shall speak with new tongues; they shall take up serpents; and if they drink any deadly thing, it shall not hurt them; they shall lay hands on the sick, and they shall recover." Mark 16:17, 18.

At that time poisoning was often practiced. Unscrupulous men did not hesitate to remove by this means those who stood in the way of their ambition. Jesus knew that the life of His disciples would thus be imperiled. Many would think it doing God service to put His witnesses to death. He therefore promised them protection from this danger.

The disciples were to have the same power which Jesus had to heal "all manner of sickness and all manner of disease among the people." By healing in His name the diseases of the body, they would testify to His power for the healing of the soul. Matt. 4:23; 9:6. And a new endowment was now promised. The disciples were to preach among other nations, and they would receive power to speak other tongues. The apostles and their associates were unlettered men, yet through the outpouring of the Spirit on the day of Pentecost, their speech, whether in their own or a foreign language, became pure, simple, and accurate, both in word and in accent.

Thus Christ gave His disciples their commission. He made full provision for the prosecution of the work, and took upon Himself the responsibility for its success. So long as they obeyed His word, and worked in connection with Him, they could not fail. Go to all nations, He bade them. Go to the farthest part of the habitable globe, but know that My presence will be there. Labor in faith and confidence, for the time will never come when I will forsake you.

The Saviour's commission to the disciples included all the believers. It includes all believers in Christ to the end of time. It is a fatal mistake to suppose that the work of saving souls depends alone on the ordained minister. All to whom the heavenly inspiration has come are put in trust with the gospel. All who receive the life of Christ are ordained to work for the salvation of their fellow men. For this work the church was established, and all who take upon themselves its sacred vows are thereby pledged to be co-workers with Christ.

"The Spirit and the bride say, Come. And let him that heareth say, Come." Rev. 22:17. Everyone who hears is to repeat the invitation. Whatever one's calling in life, his first interest should be to win souls for Christ. He may not be able to speak to congregations, but he can work for individuals. To them he can communicate the instruction received from his Lord. Ministry does not consist alone in preaching. Those minister who relieve the sick and suffering, helping the needy, speaking words of comfort to the desponding and those of little faith. Nigh and afar off are souls weighed down by a sense of guilt. It is not hardship, toil, or poverty that degrades humanity. It is guilt, wrongdoing. This brings unrest and dissatisfaction. Christ would have His servants minister to sin-sick souls.

The disciples were to begin their work where they were. The hardest and most unpromising field was not to be passed by. So every one of Christ's workers is to begin where he is. In our own families may be souls hungry for sympathy, starving for the bread of life. There may be children to be trained for Christ. There are heathen at our very doors. Let us do faithfully the work that is nearest. Then let our efforts be extended as far as God's hand may lead the way. The work of many may appear to be restricted by circumstances; but, wherever it is, if performed with faith and diligence it will be felt to the uttermost parts of the earth. Christ's work when upon earth appeared to be confined to a narrow field, but multitudes from all lands heard His message. God often uses the simplest means to accomplish the greatest results. It is His plan that every part of His work shall depend on every other part, as a wheel within a wheel, all acting in harmony. The humblest worker, moved by the Holy Spirit, will touch invisible chords, whose vibrations will ring to the ends of the earth, and make melody through eternal ages.

But the command, "Go ye into all the world," is not to be lost sight of. We are called upon to lift our eyes to the "regions beyond." Christ tears away the wall of partition, the dividing prejudice of nationality, and teaches a love for all the human family. He lifts men from the narrow circle which their selfishness prescribes; He abolishes all territorial lines and artificial distinctions of society. He makes no difference between neighbors and strangers, friends and enemies. He teaches us to look upon every needy soul as our brother, and the world as our field.

When the Saviour said, "Go, . . . teach all nations," He said also, "These signs shall follow them that believe; In My name shall they cast out devils; they shall speak with new tongues; they shall take up serpents; and if they drink any deadly thing, it shall not hurt them; they shall lay hands on the sick, and they shall recover." The promise is as far-reaching as the commission. Not that all the gifts are imparted to each believer. The Spirit divides "to every man severally as He will." 1 Cor. 12:11. But the gifts of the Spirit are promised to every believer according to his need for the Lord's work. The promise is just as strong and trustworthy now as in the days of the apostles. "These signs shall follow them that believe." This is the privilege of God's children, and faith should lay hold on all that it is possible to have as an indorsement of faith.

"They shall lay hands on the sick, and they shall recover." This world is a vast lazar house, but Christ came to heal the sick, to proclaim deliverance to the captives of Satan. He was in Himself health and strength. He imparted His life to the sick, the afflicted, those possessed of demons. He turned away none who came to receive His healing power. He knew that those who petitioned Him for help had brought disease upon themselves; yet He did not refuse to heal them. And when virtue from Christ entered into these poor souls, they were convicted of sin, and many were healed of their spiritual disease, as well as of their physical maladies. The gospel still possesses the same power, and why should we not today witness the same results?

Christ feels the woes of every sufferer. When evil spirits rend a human frame, Christ feels the curse. When fever is burning up the life current, He feels the agony. And He is just as willing to heal the sick now as when He was personally on earth. Christ's servants are His representatives, the channels for His working. He desires through them to exercise His healing power.

In the Saviour's manner of healing there were lessons for His disciples. On one occasion He anointed the eyes of a blind man with clay, and bade him, "Go, wash in the pool of Siloam. . . . He went his way therefore, and washed, and came seeing." John 9:7. The cure could be wrought only by the power of the Great Healer, yet Christ made use of the simple agencies of nature. While He did not give countenance to drug medication, He sanctioned the use of simple and natural remedies.

To many of the afflicted ones who received healing, Christ said, "Sin no more, lest a worse thing come unto thee." John 5:14. Thus He taught that disease is the result of violating God's laws, both natural and spiritual. The great misery in the world would not exist did men but live in harmony with the Creator's plan.

Christ had been the guide and teacher of ancient Israel, and He taught them that health is the reward of obedience to the laws of God. The Great Physician who healed the sick in Palestine had spoken to His people from the pillar of cloud, telling them what they must do, and what God would do for them. "If thou wilt diligently hearken to the voice of the Lord thy God," He said, "and wilt do that which is right in His sight, and wilt give ear to His commandments, and keep all His statutes, I will put none of these diseases upon thee, which I have brought upon the Egyptians: for I am the Lord that healeth thee." Ex. 15:26. Christ gave to Israel definite instruction in regard to their habits of life, and He assured them, "The Lord will take away from thee all sickness." Deut. 7:15. When they fulfilled the conditions, the promise was verified to them. "There was not one feeble person among their tribes." Ps. 105:37.

These lessons are for us. There are conditions to be observed by all who would preserve health. All should learn what these conditions are. The Lord is not pleased with ignorance in regard to His laws, either natural or spiritual. We are to be workers together with God for the restoration of health to the body as well as to the soul.

And we should teach others how to preserve and to recover health. For the sick we should use the remedies which God has provided in nature, and we should point them to Him who alone can restore. It is our work to present the sick and suffering to Christ in the arms of our faith. We should teach them to believe in the Great Healer. We should lay hold on His promise, and pray for the manifestation of His power. The very essence of the gospel is restoration, and the Saviour would have us bid the sick, the hopeless, and the afflicted take hold upon His strength.

The power of love was in all Christ's healing, and only by partaking of that love, through faith, can we be instruments for His work. If we neglect to link ourselves in divine connection with Christ, the current of life-giving energy cannot flow in rich streams from us to the people. There were places where the Saviour Himself could not do many mighty works because of their unbelief. So now unbelief separates the church from her divine Helper. Her hold upon eternal realities is weak. By her lack of faith, God is disappointed, and robbed of His glory.

It is in doing Christ's work that the church has the promise of His presence. Go teach all nations, He said; "and, lo, I am with you alway, even unto the end of the world." To take His yoke is one of the first conditions of receiving His power. The very life of the church depends upon her faithfulness in fulfilling the Lord's commission. To neglect this work is surely to invite spiritual feebleness and decay. Where there is no active labor for others, love wanes, and faith grows dim.

Christ intends that His ministers shall be educators of the church in gospel work. They are to teach the people how to seek and save the lost. But is this the work they are doing? Alas, how many are toiling to fan the spark of life in a church that is ready to die! How many churches are tended like sick lambs by those who ought to be seeking for the lost sheep! And all the time millions upon millions without Christ are perishing.

Divine love has been stirred to its unfathomable depths for the sake of men, and angels marvel to behold in the recipients of so great love a mere surface gratitude. Angels marvel at man's shallow appreciation of the love of God. Heaven stands indignant at the neglect shown to the souls of men. Would we know how Christ regards it? How would a father and mother feel, did they know that their child, lost in the cold and the snow, had been passed by, and left to perish, by those who might have saved it? Would they not be terribly grieved, wildly indignant? Would they not denounce those murderers with wrath hot as their tears, intense as their love? The sufferings of every man are the sufferings of God's child, and those who reach out no helping hand to their perishing fellow beings provoke His righteous anger. This is the wrath of the Lamb. To those who claim fellowship with Christ, yet have been indifferent to the needs of their fellow men, He will declare in the great Judgment day, "I know you not whence ye are; depart from Me, all ye workers of iniquity." Luke 13:27.

In the commission to His disciples, Christ not only outlined their work, but gave them their message. Teach the people, He said, "to observe all things whatsoever I have commanded you." The disciples were to teach what Christ had taught. That which He had spoken, not only in person, but through all the prophets and teachers of the Old Testament, is here included. Human teaching is shut out. There is no place for tradition, for man's theories and conclusions, or for church legislation. No laws ordained by ecclesiastical authority are included in the commission. None of these are Christ's servants to teach. "The law and the prophets," with the record of His own words and deeds, are the treasure committed to the disciples to be given to the world. Christ's name is their watchword, their badge of distinction, their bond of union, the authority for their course of action, and the source of their success. Nothing that does not bear His superscription is to be recognized in His kingdom.

The gospel is to be presented, not as a lifeless theory, but as a living force to change the life. God desires that the receivers of His grace shall be witnesses to its power. Those whose course has been most offensive to Him He freely accepts; when they repent, He imparts to them His divine Spirit, places them in the highest positions of trust, and sends them forth into the camp of the disloyal to proclaim His boundless mercy. He would have His servants bear testimony to the fact that through His grace men may possess Christlikeness of character, and may rejoice in the assurance of His great love. He would have us bear testimony to the fact that He cannot be satisfied until the human race are reclaimed and reinstated in their holy privileges as His sons and daughters.

In Christ is the tenderness of the shepherd, the affection of the parent, and the matchless grace of the compassionate Saviour. His blessings He presents in the most alluring terms. He is not content merely to announce these blessings; He presents them in the most attractive way, to excite a desire to possess them. So His servants are to present the riches of the glory of the unspeakable Gift. The wonderful love of Christ will melt and subdue hearts, when the mere reiteration of doctrines would accomplish nothing. "Comfort ye, comfort ye My people, saith your God." "O Zion, that bringest good tidings, get thee up into the high mountain; O Jerusalem, that bringest good tidings, lift up thy voice with strength; lift it up,

be not afraid; say unto the cities of Judah, Behold your God! . . . He shall feed His flock like a shepherd: He shall gather the lambs with His arm, and carry them in His bosom." Isa. 40:1, 9-11. Tell the people of Him who is "the Chiefest among ten thousand," and the One "altogether lovely." The Song of Solomon 5:10, 16. Words alone cannot tell it. Let it be reflected in the character and manifested in the life. Christ is sitting for His portrait in every disciple. Every one God has predestinated to be "conformed to the image of His Son." Rom. 8:29. In every one Christ's long-suffering love, His holiness, meekness, mercy, and truth are to be manifested to the world.

The first disciples went forth preaching the word. They revealed Christ in their lives. And the Lord worked with them, "confirming the word with signs following." Mark 16:20. These disciples prepared themselves for their work. Before the day of Pentecost they met together, and put away all differences. They were of one accord. They believed Christ's promise that the blessing would be given, and they prayed in faith. They did not ask for a blessing for themselves merely; they were weighted with the burden for the salvation of souls. The gospel was to be carried to the uttermost parts of the earth, and they claimed the endowment of power that Christ had promised. Then it was that the Holy Spirit was poured out, and thousands were converted in a day.

So it may be now. Instead of man's speculations, let the word of God be preached. Let Christians put away their dissensions, and give themselves to God for the saving of the lost. Let them in faith ask for the blessing, and it will come. The outpouring of the Spirit in apostolic days was the "former rain," and glorious was the result. But the "latter rain" will be more abundant. Joel 2:23.

All who consecrate soul, body, and spirit to God will be constantly receiving a new endowment of physical and mental power. The inexhaustible supplies of heaven are at their command. Christ gives them the breath of His own spirit, the life of His own life. The Holy Spirit puts forth its highest energies to work in heart and mind. The grace of God enlarges and multiplies their faculties, and every perfection of the divine nature comes to their assistance in the work of saving souls. Through co-operation with Christ they are complete in Him, and in their human weakness they are enabled to do the deeds of Omnipotence.

The Saviour longs to manifest His grace and stamp His character on the whole world. It is His purchased possession, and He desires to make men free, and pure, and holy. Though Satan works to hinder this purpose, yet through the blood shed for the world there are triumphs to be achieved that will bring glory to God and the Lamb. Christ will not be satisfied till the victory is complete, and "He shall see of the travail of His soul, and shall be satisfied." Isa. 53:11. All the nations of the earth shall hear the gospel of His grace. Not all will receive His grace; but "a seed shall serve Him; it shall be accounted to the Lord for a generation." Ps. 22:30. "The kingdom and dominion, and the greatness of the kingdom under the whole heaven, shall be given to the people of the saints of the Most High," and "the earth shall be full of the knowledge of the Lord, as the waters cover the sea." "So shall they fear the name of the Lord from the west, and His glory from the rising of the sun." Dan. 7:27; Isa. 11:9; 59:19.

"How beautiful upon the mountains are the feet of him that bringeth good tidings, that publisheth peace; that bringeth good tidings of good, that publisheth salvation; that saith unto Zion, Thy God reigneth! . . . Break forth into joy, sing together, ye waste places: . . . for the Lord hath comforted His people. . . . The Lord hath made bare His holy arm in the eyes of all the nations; and all the ends of the earth shall see the salvation of our God." Isa. 52:7-10.

"To My Father, and Your Father"

The time had come for Christ to ascend to His Father's throne. As a divine conqueror He was about to return with the trophies of victory to the heavenly courts. Before His death He had declared to His Father, "I have finished the work which Thou gavest Me to do." John 17:4. After His resurrection He tarried on earth for a season, that His disciples might become familiar with Him in His risen and glorified body. Now He was ready for the leave-taking. He had authenticated the fact that He was a living Saviour. His disciples need no longer associate Him with the tomb. They could think of Him as glorified before the heavenly universe.

As the place of His ascension, Jesus chose the spot so often hallowed by His presence while He dwelt among men. Not Mount Zion, the place of David's city, not Mount Moriah, the temple site, was to be thus honored. There Christ had been mocked and rejected. There the waves of mercy, still returning in a stronger tide of love, had been beaten back by hearts as hard as rock. Thence Jesus, weary and heart-burdened, had gone forth to find rest in the Mount of Olives. The holy Shekinah, in departing from the first temple, had stood upon the eastern mountain, as if loath to forsake the chosen city; so Christ stood upon Olivet, with yearning heart overlooking Jerusalem. The groves and glens of the mountain had been consecrated by His prayers and tears. Its steeps had echoed the triumphant shouts of the multitude that proclaimed Him king. On its sloping descent He had found a home with Lazarus at Bethany. In the garden of Gethsemane at its foot He had prayed and agonized alone. From this mountain He was to ascend to heaven. Upon its summit His feet will rest when He shall come again. Not as a man of sorrows, but as a glorious and triumphant king He will stand upon Olivet, while Hebrew hallelujahs mingle with Gentile hosannas, and the voices of the redeemed as a mighty host shall swell the acclamation, "Crown Him Lord of all!

Now with the eleven disciples Jesus made His way toward the mountain. As they passed through the gate of Jerusalem, many wondering eyes looked upon the little company, led by One whom a few weeks before the rulers had condemned and crucified. The disciples knew not that this was to be their last

interview with their Master. Jesus spent the time in conversation with them, repeating His former instruction. As they approached Gethsemane, He paused, that they might call to mind the lessons He had given them on the night of His great agony. Again He looked upon the vine by which He had then represented the union of His church with Himself and His Father; again He repeated the truths He had then unfolded. All around Him were reminders of His unrequited love. Even the disciples who were so dear to His heart, had, in the hour of His humiliation, reproached and forsaken Him.

Christ had sojourned in the world for thirty-three years; He had endured its scorn, insult, and mockery; He had been rejected and crucified. Now, when about to ascend to His throne of glory,—as He reviews the ingratitude of the people He came to save,—will He not withdraw from them His sympathy and love? Will not His affections be centered upon that realm where He is appreciated, and where sinless angels wait to do His bidding? No; His promise to those loved ones whom He leaves on earth is, "I am with you alway, even unto the end of the world." Matt. 28:20.

Upon reaching the Mount of Olives, Jesus led the way across the summit, to the vicinity of Bethany. Here He paused, and the disciples gathered about Him. Beams of light seemed to radiate from His countenance as He looked lovingly upon them. He upbraided them not for their faults and failures; words of the deepest tenderness were the last that fell upon their ears from the lips of their Lord. With hands outstretched in blessing, and as if in assurance of His protecting care, He slowly ascended from among them, drawn heavenward by a power stronger than any earthly attraction. As He passed upward, the awe-stricken disciples looked with straining eyes for the last glimpse of their ascending Lord. A cloud of glory hid Him from their sight; and the words came back to them as the cloudy chariot of angels received Him, "Lo, I am with you alway, even unto the end of the world." At the same time there floated down to them the sweetest and most joyous music from the angel choir.

While the disciples were still gazing upward, voices addressed them which sounded like richest music. They turned, and saw two angels in the form of men, who spoke to them, saying, "Ye men of Galilee, why stand ye gazing up into heaven? this same Jesus, which is taken up from you into heaven, shall so come in like manner as ye have seen Him go into heaven."

These angels were of the company that had been waiting in a shining cloud to escort Jesus to His heavenly home. The most exalted of the angel throng, they were the two who had come to the tomb at Christ's resurrection, and they had been with Him throughout His life on earth. With eager desire all heaven had waited for the end of His tarrying in a world marred by the curse of sin. The time had now come for the heavenly universe to receive their King. Did not the two angels long to join the throng that welcomed Jesus? But in sympathy and love for those whom He had left, they waited to give them comfort. "Are they not all ministering spirits, sent forth to minister for them who shall be heirs of salvation?" Heb. 1:14.

Christ had ascended to heaven in the form of humanity. The disciples had beheld the cloud receive Him. The same Jesus who had walked and talked and prayed with them; who had broken bread with them; who had been with them in their boats on the lake; and who had that very day toiled with them up the ascent of Olivet,—the same Jesus had now gone to share His Father's throne. And the angels had assured them that the very One whom they had seen go up into heaven, would come again even as He had ascended. He will come "with clouds; and every eye shall see Him." "The Lord Himself shall descend from heaven with a shout, with the voice of the Archangel, and with the trump of God: and the dead in Christ shall rise." "The Son of man shall come in His glory, and all the holy angels with Him, then shall He sit upon the throne of His glory." Rev. 1:7; 1 Thess. 4:16; Matt. 25:31. Thus will be fulfilled the Lord's own promise to His disciples: "If I go and prepare a place for you, I will come again, and receive you unto Myself; that where I am, there ye may be also." John 14:3. Well might the disciples rejoice in the hope of their Lord's return.

When the disciples went back to Jerusalem, the people looked upon them with amazement. After the trial and crucifixion of Christ, it had been thought that they would appear downcast and ashamed. Their enemies expected to see upon their faces an expression of sorrow and defeat. Instead of this there was only gladness and triumph. Their faces were aglow with a happiness not born of earth. They did not mourn over disappointed hopes, but were full of praise and thanksgiving to God. With rejoicing they told the wonderful story of Christ's resurrection and His ascension to heaven, and their testimony was received by many.

The disciples no longer had any distrust of the future. They knew that Jesus was in heaven, and that His sympathies were with them still. They knew that they had a friend at the throne of God, and they were eager to present their requests to the Father in the name of Jesus. In solemn awe they bowed in prayer, repeating the assurance, "Whatsoever ye shall ask the Father in My name, He will give it you. Hitherto have ye asked nothing in My name: ask, and ye shall receive, that your joy may be full." John 16:23, 24. They extended the hand of faith higher and higher, with the mighty argument, "It is Christ that died, yea rather, that is risen again, who is even at the right hand of God, who also maketh intercession for us." Rom. 8:34. And Pentecost brought them fullness of joy in the presence of the Comforter, even as Christ had promised.

All heaven was waiting to welcome the Saviour to the celestial courts. As He ascended, He led the way, and the multitude of captives set free at His resurrection followed. The heavenly host, with shouts and acclamations of praise and celestial song, attended the joyous train.

As they drew near to the city of God, the challenge is given by the escorting angels,—

"Lift up your heads, O ye gates;
And be ye lift up, ye everlasting doors;
And the King of glory shall come in."

Joyfully the waiting sentinels respond,—

"Who is this King of glory?"

This they say, not because they know not who He is, but because they would hear the answer of exalted praise,—

"The Lord strong and mighty,
The Lord mighty in battle!
Lift up your heads, O ye gates;
Even lift them up, ye everlasting doors;
And the King of glory shall come in."

Again is heard the challenge, "Who is this King of glory?" for the angels never weary of hearing His name exalted. The escorting angels make reply,—

"The Lord of hosts;
He is the King of glory." Ps. 24:7-10.

Then the portals of the city of God are opened wide, and the angelic throng sweep through the gates amid a burst of rapturous music.

There is the throne, and around it the rainbow of promise. There are cherubim and seraphim. The commanders of the angel hosts, the sons of God, the representatives of the unfallen worlds, are assembled. The heavenly council before which Lucifer had accused God and His Son, the representatives of those sinless realms over which Satan had thought to establish his dominion,—all are there to welcome the Redeemer. They are eager to celebrate His triumph and to glorify their King.

But He waves them back. Not yet; He cannot now receive the coronet of glory and the royal robe. He enters into the presence of His Father. He points to His wounded head, the pierced side, the marred feet; He lifts His hands, bearing the print of nails. He points to the tokens of His triumph; He presents to God the wave sheaf, those raised with Him as representatives of that great multitude who shall come forth from the grave at His second coming. He approaches the Father, with whom there is joy over one sinner that repents; who rejoices over one with singing. Before the foundations of the earth were laid, the Father and the Son had united in a covenant to redeem man if he should be overcome by Satan. They had clasped Their hands in a solemn pledge that Christ should become the surety for the human race. This pledge Christ has fulfilled. When upon the cross He cried out, "It is finished," He addressed the Father. The compact had been fully carried out. Now He declares: Father, it is finished. I have done Thy will, O My God. I have completed the work of redemption. If Thy justice is satisfied, "I will that they also, whom Thou hast given Me, be with Me where I am." John

19:30; 17:24.

The voice of God is heard proclaiming that justice is satisfied. Satan is vanquished. Christ's toiling, struggling ones on earth are "accepted in the Beloved." Eph. 1:6. Before the heavenly angels and the representatives of unfallen worlds, they are declared justified. Where He is, there His church shall be. "Mercy and truth are met together; righteousness and peace have kissed each other." Ps. 85:10. The Father's arms encircle His Son, and the word is given, "Let all the angels of God worship Him." Heb. 1:6.

With joy unutterable, rulers and principalities and powers acknowledge the supremacy of the Prince of life. The angel host prostrate themselves before Him, while the glad shout fills all the courts of heaven, "Worthy is the Lamb that was slain to receive power, and riches, and wisdom, and strength, and honor, and glory, and blessing." Rev. 5:12.

Songs of triumph mingle with the music from angel harps, till heaven seems to overflow with joy and praise. Love has conquered. The lost is found. Heaven rings with voices in lofty strains proclaiming, "Blessing, and honor, and glory, and power, be unto Him that sitteth upon the throne, and unto the Lamb forever and ever." Rev. 5:13.

From that scene of heavenly joy, there comes back to us on earth the echo of Christ's own wonderful words, "I ascend unto My Father, and your Father; and to My God, and your God." John 20:17. The family of heaven and the family of earth are one. For us our Lord ascended, and for us He lives. "Wherefore He is able also to save them to the uttermost that come unto God by Him, seeing He ever liveth to make intercession for them." Heb. 7:25.

The Acts of the Apostles

CONTENTS

God's Purpose for His Church

The church is God's appointed agency for the salvation of men. It was organized for service, and its mission is to carry the gospel to the world. From the beginning it has been God's plan that through His church shall be reflected to the world His fullness and His sufficiency. The members of the church, those whom He has called out of darkness into His marvelous light, are to show forth His glory. The church is the repository of the riches of the grace of Christ; and through the church will eventually be made manifest, even to "the principalities and powers in heavenly places," the final and full display of the love of God. Ephesians 3:10.

Many and wonderful are the promises recorded in the Scriptures regarding the church. "Mine house shall be called an house of prayer for all people." Isaiah 56:7. "I will make them and the places round about My hill a blessing; and I will cause the shower to come down in his season; there shall be showers of blessing." "And I will raise up for them a plant of renown, and they shall be no more consumed with hunger in the land, neither bear the shame of the heathen any more. Thus shall they know that I the Lord their God am with them, and that they, even the house of Israel, are My people, saith the Lord God. And ye My flock, the flock of My pasture, are men, and I am your God, saith the Lord God." Ezekiel 34:26, 29-31.

"Ye are My witnesses, saith the Lord, and My servant whom I have chosen: that ye may know and believe Me, and understand that I am He: before Me there was no God formed, neither shall there be after Me. I, even I, am the Lord; and beside Me there is no Saviour. I have declared, and have saved, and I have showed, when there was no strange god among you: therefore ye are My witnesses." "I the Lord have called thee in righteousness, and will hold thine hand, and will keep thee, and give thee for a covenant of the people, for a light of the Gentiles; to open the blind eyes, to bring out the prisoners from the prison, and them that sit in darkness out of the prison house." Isaiah 43:10-12; 42:6, 7.

"In an acceptable time have I heard thee, and in a day of salvation have I helped thee: and I will preserve thee, and give thee for a covenant of the people, to establish the earth, to cause to inherit the desolate heritages; that thou mayest say to the prisoners, Go forth; to them that are in darkness, Show yourselves. They shall feed in the ways, and their pastures shall be in all high places. They shall not hunger nor thirst; neither shall the heat nor sun smite them: for He that hath mercy on them shall lead them, even by the springs of water shall He guide them. And I will make all My mountains a way, and My highways shall be exalted. . . .

"Sing, O heavens; and be joyful, O earth; and break forth into singing, O mountains: for the Lord hath comforted His people, and will have mercy upon His afflicted. But Zion said, The Lord hath forsaken me, and my Lord hath forgotten me. Can a woman forget her sucking child, that she should not have compassion on the son of her womb? yea, they may forget, yet will I not forget thee. Behold, I have graven thee upon the palms of My hands; thy walls are continually before Me." Isaiah 49:8-16.

The church is God's fortress. His city of refuge, which He holds in a revolted world. Any betrayal of the church is treachery to Him who has bought mankind with the blood of His only-begotten Son. From the beginning, faithful souls have constituted the church on earth. In every age the Lord has had His watchmen, who have borne a faithful testimony to the generation in which they lived. These sentinels gave the message of warning; and when they were called to lay off their armor, others took up the work. God brought these witnesses into covenant relation with Himself, uniting the church on earth with the church in heaven. He has sent forth His angels to minister to His church, and the gates of hell have not been able to prevail against His people.

Through centuries of persecution, conflict, and darkness, God has sustained His church. Not one cloud has fallen upon it that He has not prepared for; not one opposing force has risen to counterwork His work, that He has not foreseen. All has taken place as He predicted. He has not left His church forsaken, but has traced in prophetic declarations what would occur, and that which His Spirit inspired the prophets to foretell has been brought about. All His purposes will be fulfilled. His law is linked with His throne, and no power of evil can destroy it. Truth is inspired and guarded by God; and it will triumph over all opposition.

During ages of spiritual darkness the church of God has been as a city set on a hill. From age to age, through successive generations, the pure doctrines of heaven have been unfolding within its borders. Enfeebled and defective as it may appear, the church is the one object upon which God bestows in a special sense His supreme regard. It is the theater of His grace, in which He delights to reveal His power to transform hearts.

"Whereunto," asked Christ, "shall we liken the kingdom of God? or with what comparison shall we compare it?" Mark 4:30. He could not employ the kingdoms of the world as a similitude. In society He found nothing with which to compare it. Earthly kingdoms rule by the ascendancy of physical power; but from Christ's kingdom every carnal weapon, every instrument of coercion, is banished. This kingdom is to uplift and ennoble humanity. God's church is the court of Holy life, filled with varied gifts and endowed with the Holy Spirit. The members are to find their happiness in the happiness of those whom they help and bless.

Wonderful is the work which the Lord designs to accomplish through His church, that His name may be glorified. A picture of this work is given in Ezekiel's vision of the river of healing: "These waters issue out toward the east country, and go down into the desert, and go into the sea: which being brought forth into the sea, the waters shall be healed. And it shall come to pass, that everything that liveth, which moveth, whithersoever the rivers shall come, shall live: . . . and by the river upon the bank thereof, on this side and on that side, shall grow all trees for meat, whose leaf shall not fade, neither shall the fruit thereof be consumed: it shall bring forth new fruit according to his months, because their waters they issued out of the sanctuary: and the fruit thereof shall be for meat, and the leaf thereof for medicine." Ezekiel 47:8-12.

From the beginning God has wrought through His people to bring blessing to the world. To the ancient Egyptian nation God made Joseph a fountain of life. Through the integrity of Joseph the life of that whole people was preserved. Through Daniel God saved the life of all the wise men of Babylon. And these deliverances are as object lessons; they illustrate the spiritual blessings offered to the world through connection with the God whom Joseph and Daniel worshiped. Everyone in whose heart Christ abides, everyone who will show forth His love to the world, is a worker together with God for the blessing of humanity. As he receives from the Saviour grace to impart to others, from his whole being flows forth the tide of spiritual life.

God chose Israel to reveal His character to men. He desired them to be as wells of salvation in the world. To them were committed the oracles of heaven, the revelation of God's will. In the early days of Israel the nations of the world, through corrupt practices, had lost the knowledge of God. They had once known Him; but because "they glorified Him not as God, neither were thankful; but became vain in their imaginations, . . . their foolish heart was darkened." Romans 1:21. Yet in His mercy God did not blot them out of existence. He purposed to give them an opportunity of again becoming acquainted with Him through His chosen people. Through the teachings of the sacrificial service, Christ was to be uplifted before all nations, and all who would look to Him should live. Christ was the foundation of the Jewish economy. The whole system of types and symbols was a compacted prophecy of the gospel, a presentation in which were bound up the promises of redemption.

But the people of Israel lost sight of their high privileges as God's representatives. They forgot God and failed to fulfill their holy mission. The blessings they received brought no blessing to the world. All their advantages they appropriated for their own glorification. They shut themselves away from the world in order to escape temptation. The restrictions that God had placed upon their association with idolaters as a means of preventing them from conforming to the practices of the heathen, they used to build up a wall of separation between themselves and all other nations. They robbed God of the service He required of them, and they robbed their fellow men of religious guidance and a holy example.

Priests and rulers became fixed in a rut of ceremonialism. They were satisfied with a legal religion, and it was impossible for them to give to others the living truths of heaven. They thought their own righteousness all-sufficient, and did not desire that a new element should be brought into their religion. The good will of God to men they did not accept as something apart from themselves, but connected it with their own merit because of their good works. The faith that works by love and purifies the soul could find no place for union with the religion of the Pharisees, made up of ceremonies and the injunctions of men.

Of Israel God declared: "I had planted thee a noble vine, wholly a right seed: how then art thou turned into the degenerate plant of a strange vine unto Me?" Jeremiah 2:21. "Israel is an empty vine, he bringeth forth fruit unto himself." Hosea 10:1. "And now, O inhabitants of Jerusalem, and men of Judah, judge, I pray you, betwixt Me and My vineyard. What could have been done more to My vineyard, that I have not done in it? wherefore, when I looked that it should bring forth grapes, brought it forth wild grapes?

"And now go to; I will tell you what I will do to My vineyard: I will take away the hedge thereof, and it shall be eaten up; and break down the wall thereof, and it shall be trodden down: and I will lay it waste: it shall not be pruned, nor digged; but there shall come up briers and thorns: I will also command the clouds that they rain no rain upon it. For the vineyard of the Lord of hosts is the house of Israel, and the men of Judah His pleasant plant: and He looked for judgment, but behold oppression; for righteousness, but behold a cry." Isaiah 5:3-7. "The diseased have ye not strengthened, neither have ye healed that which was sick, neither have ye bound up that which was broken, neither have ye brought again that which was driven away, neither have ye sought that which was lost; but with force and with cruelty have ye ruled them." Ezekiel 34:4.

The Jewish leaders thought themselves too wise to need instruction, too righteous to need salvation, too highly honored to need the honor that comes from Christ. The Saviour turned from them to entrust to others the privileges they had abused and the work they had slighted. God's glory must be revealed, His word established. Christ's kingdom must be set up in the world. The salvation of God must be made known in the cities of the wilderness; and the disciples were called to do the work that the Jewish leaders had failed to do.

The Training of the Twelve

For the carrying on of His work, Christ did not choose the learning or eloquence of the Jewish Sanhedrin or the power of Rome. Passing by the self-righteous Jewish teachers, the Master Worker chose humble, unlearned men to proclaim the truths that were to move the world. These men He purposed to train and educate as the leaders of His church. They in turn were to educate others and send them out with the gospel message. That they might have success in their work they were to be given the power of the Holy Spirit. Not by human might or human wisdom was the gospel to be proclaimed, but by the power of God.

For three years and a half the disciples were under the instruction of the greatest Teacher the world has ever known. By personal contact and association, Christ trained them for His service. Day by day they walked and talked with Him, hearing His words of cheer to the weary and heavy-laden, and seeing the manifestation of His power in behalf of the sick and the afflicted. Sometimes He taught them, sitting among them on the mountainside; sometimes beside the sea or walking by the way, He revealed the mysteries of the kingdom of God. Wherever hearts were open to receive the divine message, He unfolded the truths of the way of salvation. He did not command the disciples to do this or that, but said, "Follow Me." On His journeys through country and cities, He took them with Him, that they might see how He taught the people. They traveled with Him from place to place. They shared His frugal fare, and like Him were sometimes hungry and often weary. On the crowded streets, by the lakeside, in the lonely desert, they were with Him. They saw Him in every phase of life.

It was at the ordination of the Twelve that the first step was taken in the organization of the church that after Christ's departure was to carry on His work on the earth. Of this ordination the record says, "He goeth up into a mountain, and calleth unto Him whom He would: and they came unto Him. And He ordained twelve, that they should be with Him, and that He might send them forth to preach." Mark 3:13, 14.

Look upon the touching scene. Behold the Majesty of heaven surrounded by the Twelve whom He has chosen. He is about to set them apart for their work. By these feeble agencies, through His word and Spirit, He designs to place salvation within the reach of all.

With gladness and rejoicing, God and the angels beheld this scene. The Father knew that from these men the light of heaven would shine forth; that the words spoken by them as they witnessed for His Son, would echo from generation to generation till the close of time.

The disciples were to go forth as Christ's witnesses, to declare to the world what they had seen and heard of Him. Their office was the most important to which human beings had ever been called, second only to that of Christ Himself. They were to be workers together with God for the saving of men. As in the Old Testament the twelve patriarchs stood as representatives of Israel, so the twelve apostles stand as representatives of the gospel church.

During His earthly ministry Christ began to break down the partition wall between Jew and Gentile, and to preach salvation to all mankind. Though He was a Jew, He mingled freely with the Samaritans, setting at nought the Pharisaic customs of the Jews with regard to this despised people. He slept under their roofs, ate at their tables, and taught in their streets.

The Saviour longed to unfold to His disciples the truth regarding the breaking down of the "middle wall of partition" between Israel and the other nations—the truth that "the Gentiles should be fellow heirs" with the Jews and "partakers of His promise in Christ by the gospel." Ephesians 2:14; 3:6. This truth was revealed in part at the time when He rewarded the faith of the centurion at Capernaum, and also when He preached the gospel to the inhabitants of Sychar. Still more plainly was it revealed on the occasion of His visit to Phoenicia, when He healed the daughter of the Canaanite woman. These experiences helped the disciples to understand that among those whom many regarded as unworthy of salvation, there were souls hungering for the light of truth.

Thus Christ sought to teach the disciples the truth that in God's kingdom there are no territorial lines, no caste, no aristocracy; that they must go to all nations, bearing to them the message of a Saviour's love. But not until later did they realize in all its fullness that God "hath made of one blood all nations of men for to dwell on all the face of the earth, and hath determined the times before appointed, and the bounds of their habitation; that they should seek the Lord, if haply they might feel after Him, and find Him, though He be not far from every one of us." Acts 17:26, 27.

In these first disciples was presented marked diversity. They were to be the world's teachers, and they represented widely varied types of character. In order successfully to carry forward the work to which they had been called, these men, differing in natural characteristics and in habits of life, needed to come into unity of feeling, thought, and action. This unity it was Christ's object to secure. To this end He sought to bring them into unity with Himself. The burden of His labor for them is expressed in His prayer to His Father, "That they all may be one; as Thou, Father, art in Me, and I in Thee, that they also may be one in Us;" "that the world may know that Thou has sent Me, and hast loved them, as Thou hast loved Me." John 17:21, 23. His constant prayer for them was that they might be sanctified through the truth; and He prayed with assurance, knowing that an Almighty decree had been given before the world was made. He knew that the gospel of the kingdom would be preached to all nations for a witness; He knew that truth armed with the omnipotence of the Holy Spirit, would conquer in the battle with evil, and that the bloodstained banner would one day wave triumphantly over His followers.

As Christ's earthly ministry drew to a close, and He realized that He must soon leave His disciples to carry on the work without His personal supervision, He sought to encourage them and to prepare them for the future. He did not deceive them with false hopes. As an open book He read what was to be. He knew He was about to be separated from them, to leave them as sheep among wolves. He knew that they would suffer persecution, that they would be cast out of the synagogues, and would be thrown into prison. He knew that for witnessing to Him as the Messiah, some of them would suffer death. And something of this He told them. In speaking of their future, He was plain and definite, that in their coming trial they might remember His words and be strengthened to believe in Him as the Redeemer.

He spoke to them also words of hope and courage. "Let not your heart be troubled," He said; "ye believe in God, believe also in Me. In My Father's house are many mansions: if it were not so, I would have told you. I go to prepare a place for you. And if I go and prepare a place for you, I will come again, and receive you unto Myself; that where I am, there ye may be also. And whither I go ye know, and the way ye know." John 14:1-4. For your sake I came into the world; for you I have been working. When I go away I shall still work earnestly for you. I came to the world to reveal Myself to you, that you might believe. I go to My Father and yours to co-operate with Him in your behalf.

"Verily, verily, I say unto you, He that believeth on Me, the works that I do shall he do also; and greater works than these shall he do; because I go unto My Father." John 14:12. By this, Christ did not mean that the disciples would make more exalted exertions than He had made, but that their work would have greater magnitude. He did not refer merely to miracle working, but to all that would take place under the agency of the Holy Spirit. "When the Comforter is come," He said, "whom I will send unto you from the Father, even the Spirit of truth, which proceedeth from the Father, He shall testify of Me: and ye also shall bear witness, because ye have been with Me from the beginning." John 15:26, 27.

Wonderfully were these words fulfilled. After the descent of the Holy Spirit, the disciples were so filled with love for Him and for those for whom He died, that hearts were melted by the words they spoke and the prayers they offered. They spoke in the power of the Spirit; and under the influence of that power, thousands were converted.

As Christ's representatives the apostles were to make a decided impression on the world. The fact that they were humble men would not diminish their influence, but increase it; for the minds of their hearers would be carried from them to the Saviour, who, though unseen, was still working with them. The wonderful teaching of the apostles, their words of courage and trust, would assure all that it was not in their own power that they worked, but in the power of Christ. Humbling themselves, they would declare that He whom the Jews had crucified was the Prince of life, the Son of the living God, and that in His name they did the works that He had done.

In His parting conversation with His disciples on the night before the crucifixion the Saviour made no reference to the suffering that He had endured and must yet endure. He did not speak of the humiliation that was before Him, but sought to bring to their minds that which would strengthen their faith, leading them to look forward to the joys that await the overcomer. He rejoiced in the consciousness that He could and would do more for His followers than He had promised; that from Him would flow forth love and compassion, cleansing the soul temple, and making men like Him in character; that His truth, armed with the power of the Spirit, would go forth conquering and to conquer.

"These things I have spoken unto you," He said, "that in Me ye might have peace. In the world ye shall have tribulation: but be of good cheer; I have overcome the world." John 16:33. Christ did not fail, neither was He discouraged; and the disciples were to show a faith of the same enduring nature. They were to work as He had worked, depending on Him for strength. Though their way would be obstructed by apparent impossibilities, yet by His grace they were to go forward, despairing of nothing and hoping for everything.

Christ had finished the work that was given Him to do. He had gathered out those who were to continue His work among men. And He said: "I am glorified in them. And now I am no more in the world, but these are in the world, and I come to Thee. Holy Father, keep through Thine own name those whom Thou hast given Me, that they may be one, as We are." "Neither pray I for these alone, but for them also which shall believe on Me through their word; that they all may be one; . . . I in them and Thou in Me, that they may be made perfect in one; and that the world may know that Thou hast sent Me, and hast loved them, as Thou hast loved Me." John 17:10, 11, 20-23.

The Great Commission

After the death of Christ the disciples were well-nigh overcome by discouragement. Their Master had been rejected, condemned, and crucified. The priests and rulers had declared scornfully, "He saved others; Himself He cannot save. If He be the King of Israel, let Him now come down from the cross, and we will believe Him." Matthew 27:42. The sun of the disciples' hope had set, and night settled down upon their hearts. Often they repeated the words, "We trusted that it had been He which should have redeemed Israel." Luke 24:21. Lonely and sick at heart, they remembered His words, "If they do these things in a green tree, what shall be done in the dry?" Luke 23:31.

Jesus had several times attempted to open the future to His disciples, but they had not cared to think about what He said. Because of this His death had come to them as a surprise; and afterward, as they reviewed the past and saw the result of their unbelief, they were filled with sorrow.

When Christ was crucified, they did not believe that He would rise. He had stated plainly that He was to rise on the third day, but they were perplexed to know what He meant. This lack of comprehension left them at the time of His death in utter hopelessness. They were bitterly disappointed. Their faith did not penetrate beyond the shadow that Satan had cast athwart their horizon. All seemed vague and mysterious to them. If they had believed the Saviour's words, how much sorrow they might have been spared!

Crushed by despondency, grief, and despair, the disciples met together in the upper chamber, and closed and fastened the doors, fearing that the fate of their beloved Teacher might be theirs. It was here that the Saviour, after His resurrection, appeared to them.

For forty days Christ remained on the earth, preparing the disciples for the work before them and explaining that which heretofore they had been unable to comprehend. He spoke of the prophecies concerning His advent, His rejection by the Jews, and His death, showing that every specification of these prophecies had been fulfilled. He told them that they were to regard this fulfillment of prophecy as an assurance of the power that would attend them in their future labors. "Then opened He their understanding," we read, "that they might understand the Scriptures, and said unto them, Thus it is written, and thus it behooved Christ to suffer, and to rise from the dead the third day: and that repentance and remission of sins should be preached in His name among all nations, beginning at Jerusalem."

And He added, "Ye are witnesses of these things." Luke 24:45-48.

During these days that Christ spent with His disciples, they gained a new experience. As they heard their beloved Master explaining the Scriptures in the light of all that had happened, their faith in Him was fully established. They reached the place where they could say, "I know whom I have believed." 2 Timothy 1:12. They began to realize the nature and extent of their work, to see that they were to proclaim to the world the truths entrusted to them. The events of Christ's life, His death and resurrection, the prophecies pointing to these events, the mysteries of the plan of salvation, the power of Jesus for the remission of sins—to all these things they had been witnesses, and they were to make them known to the world. They were to proclaim the gospel of peace and salvation through repentance and the power of the Saviour.

Before ascending to heaven, Christ gave His disciples their commission. He told them that they were to be the executors of the will in which He bequeathed to the world the treasures of eternal life. You have been witnesses of My life of sacrifice in behalf of the world, He said to them. You have seen My labors for Israel. And although My people would not come to Me that they might have life, although priests and rulers have done unto Me as they listed, although they have rejected Me, they shall have still another opportunity of accepting the Son of God. You have seen that all who come to Me confessing their sins, I freely receive. Him that cometh to Me I will in no wise cast out. To you, My disciples, I commit this message of mercy. It is to be given to both Jews and Gentiles—to Israel, first, and then to all nations, tongues, and peoples. All who believe are to be gathered into one church.

The gospel commission is the great missionary charter of Christ's kingdom. The disciples were to work earnestly for souls, giving to all the invitation of mercy. They were not to wait for the people to come to them; they were to go to the people with their message.

The disciples were to carry their work forward in Christ's name. Their every word and act was to fasten attention on His name, as possessing that vital power by which sinners may be saved. Their faith was to center in Him who is the source of mercy and power. In His name they were to present their petitions to the Father, and they would receive answer. They were to baptize in the name of the Father, the Son, and the Holy Spirit. Christ's name was to be their watchword, their badge of distinction, their bond of union, the authority for their course of action, and the source of their success. Nothing was to be recognized in His kingdom that did not bear His name and superscription.

When Christ said to the disciples, Go forth in My name to gather into the church all who believe, He plainly set before them the necessity of maintaining simplicity. The less ostentation and show, the greater would be their influence for good. The disciples were to speak with the same simplicity with which Christ had spoken. They were to impress upon their hearers the lessons He had taught them.

Christ did not tell His disciples that their work would be easy. He showed them the vast confederacy of evil arrayed against them. They would have to fight "against principalities, against powers, against the rulers of the darkness of this world, against spiritual wickedness in high places." Ephesians 6:12. But they would not be left to fight alone. He assured them that He would be with them; and that if they would go forth in faith, they should move under the shield of Omnipotence. He bade them be brave and strong; for One mightier than angels would be in their ranks—the General of the armies of heaven. He made full provision for the prosecution of their work and took upon Himself the responsibility of its success. So long as they obeyed His word, and worked in connection with Him, they could not fail. Go to all nations, He bade them. Go to the farthest part of the habitable globe and be assured that My presence will be with you even there. Labor in faith and confidence; for the time will never come when I will forsake you. I will be with you always, helping you to perform your duty, guiding, comforting, sanctifying, sustaining you, giving you success in speaking words that shall draw the attention of others to heaven.

Christ's sacrifice in behalf of man was full and complete. The condition of the atonement had been fulfilled. The work for which He had come to this world had been accomplished. He had won the kingdom. He had wrested it from Satan and had become heir of all things. He was on His way to the throne of God, to be honored by the heavenly host. Clothed with boundless authority, He gave His disciples their commission, "Go ye therefore, and teach all nations, baptizing them in the name of the Father, and of the Son, and of the Holy Ghost: teaching them to observe all things whatsoever I have commanded you: and, lo, I am with you alway, even unto the end." Matthew 28:19, 20.

Just before leaving His disciples, Christ once more plainly stated the nature of His kingdom. He recalled to their remembrance things He had previously told them regarding it. He declared that it was not His purpose to establish in this world a temporal kingdom. He was not appointed to reign as an earthly monarch on David's throne. When the disciples asked Him, "Lord, wilt Thou at this time restore again the kingdom to Israel?" He answered, "It is not for you to know the times or the seasons, which the Father hath put in His own power." Acts 1:6, 7. It was not necessary for them to see farther into the future than the revelations He had made enabled them to see. Their work was to proclaim the gospel message.

Christ's visible presence was about to be withdrawn from the disciples, but a new endowment of power was to be theirs. The Holy Spirit was to be given them in its fullness, sealing them for their work. "Behold," the Saviour said, "I send the promise of My Father upon you: but tarry ye in the city of Jerusalem, until ye be endued with power from on high." Luke 24:49. "For John truly baptized with water; but ye shall be baptized with the Holy Ghost not many days hence." "Ye shall receive power, after that the Holy Ghost is come upon you: and ye shall be witnesses unto Me both in Jerusalem, and in all Judea, and in Samaria, and unto the uttermost part of the earth." Acts 1:5, 8.

The Saviour knew that no argument, however logical, would melt hard hearts or break through the crust of worldliness and selfishness. He knew that His disciples must receive the heavenly endowment; that the gospel would be effective only as it was proclaimed by hearts made warm and lips made eloquent by a living knowledge of Him who is the way, the truth, and the life. The work committed to the disciples would require great efficiency; for the tide of evil ran deep and strong against them. A vigilant, determined leader was in command of the forces of darkness, and the followers of Christ could battle for the right only through the help that God, by His Spirit, would give them.

Christ told His disciples that they were to begin their work at Jerusalem. That city had been the scene of His amazing sacrifice for the human race. There, clad in the garb of humanity, He had walked and talked with men, and few had discerned how near heaven came to earth. There He had been condemned and crucified. In Jerusalem were many who secretly believed Jesus of Nazareth to be the Messiah, and many who had been deceived by priests and rulers. To these the gospel must be proclaimed. They were to be called to repentance. The wonderful truth that through Christ alone could remission of sins be obtained, was to be made plain. And it was while all Jerusalem was stirred by the thrilling events of the past few weeks, that the preaching of the disciples would make the deepest impression.

During His ministry, Jesus had kept constantly before the disciples the fact that they were to be one with Him in His work for the recovery of the world from the slavery of sin. When He sent forth the Twelve and afterward the Seventy, to proclaim the kingdom of God, He was teaching them their duty to impart to others what He had made known to them. In all His work He was training them for individual labor, to be extended as their numbers increased, and eventually to reach to the uttermost parts of the earth. The last lesson He gave His followers was that they held in trust for the world the glad tidings of salvation.

When the time came for Christ to ascend to His Father, He led the disciples out as far as Bethany. Here He paused, and they gathered about Him. With hands outstretched in blessing, as if in assurance of His protecting care, He slowly ascended from among them. "It came to pass, while He blessed them, He was parted from them, and carried up into heaven." Luke 24:51.

While the disciples were gazing upward to catch the last glimpse of their ascending Lord, He was received into the rejoicing ranks of heavenly angels. As these angels escorted Him to the courts above, they sang in triumph, "Sing unto God, ye kingdoms of the earth; O sing praises unto the Lord, to Him that rideth upon the heavens of heavens. . . . Ascribe ye strength unto God: His excellency is over Israel, and His strength is in the heavens." Psalm 68:32-34, margin.

The disciples were still looking earnestly toward heaven when, "behold, two men stood by them in white apparel; which also said, Ye men of Galilee, why stand ye gazing up into heaven? this same Jesus, which is taken up from you into heaven, shall so come in like manner as ye have seen Him go into heaven." Acts 1:10, 11.

The promise of Christ's second coming was ever to be kept fresh in the minds of His disciples. The same Jesus whom they had seen ascending into heaven, would come again, to take to Himself those who here below give themselves to His service. The same voice that had said to them, "Lo, I am with you alway, even unto the end," would bid them welcome to His presence in the heavenly kingdom.

As in the typical service the high priest laid aside his pontifical robes and officiated in the white linen dress of an ordinary priest; so Christ laid aside His royal robes and garbed Himself with humanity and offered sacrifice, Himself the priest, Himself the victim. As the high priest, after performing his service in the holy of holies, came forth to the waiting congregation in his pontifical robes; so Christ will come the second time, clothed in garments of whitest white, "so as no fuller on earth can white them." Mark 9:3. He will come in His own glory, and in the glory of His Father, and all the angelic host will escort Him on His way.

Thus will be fulfilled Christ's promise to His disciples, "I will come again, and receive you unto Myself." John 14:3. Those who have loved Him and waited for Him, He will crown with glory and honor and immortality. The righteous dead will come forth from their graves, and those who are alive will be caught up with them to meet the Lord in the air. They will hear the voice of Jesus, sweeter than any music that ever fell on mortal ear, saying to them, Your warfare is accomplished. "Come, ye blessed of My Father, inherit the kingdom prepared for you from the foundation of the world." Matthew 25;34.

Well might the disciples rejoice in the hope of their Lord's return.

Pentecost

As the disciples returned from Olivet to Jerusalem, the people looked on them, expecting to see on their faces expressions of sorrow, confusion, and defeat; but they saw there gladness and triumph. The disciples did not now mourn over disappointed hopes. They had seen the risen Saviour, and the words of His parting promise echoed constantly in their ears.

In obedience to Christ's command, they waited in Jerusalem for the promise of the Father—the outpouring of the Spirit. They did not wait in idleness. The record says that they were "continually in the temple, praising and blessing God." Luke 24:53. They also met together to present their requests to the Father in the name of Jesus. They knew that they had a Representative in heaven, an Advocate at the throne of God. In solemn awe they bowed in prayer, repeating the assurance, "Whatsoever ye shall ask the Father in My name, He will give it you. Hitherto have ye asked nothing in My name: ask, and ye shall receive, that your joy may be full." John 16:23, 24. Higher and still higher they extended the hand of faith, with the mighty argument, "It is Christ that died, yea rather, that is risen again, who is even at the right hand of God, who also maketh intercession for us." Romans 8:34.

As the disciples waited for the fulfillment of the promise, they humbled their hearts in true repentance and confessed their unbelief. As they called to remembrance the words that Christ had spoken to them before His death they understood more fully their meaning. Truths which had passed from their memory were again brought to their minds, and these they repeated to one another. They reproached themselves for their misapprehension of the Saviour. Like a procession, scene after scene of His wonderful life passed before them. As they meditated upon His pure, holy life they felt that no toil would be too hard, no sacrifice too great, if only they could bear witness in their lives to the loveliness of Christ's character. Oh, if they could but have the past three years to live over, they thought, how differently they would act! If they could only see the Master again, how earnestly they would strive to show Him how deeply they loved Him, and how sincerely they sorrowed for having ever grieved Him by a word or an act of unbelief! But they were comforted by the thought that they were forgiven. And they determined that, so far as possible, they would atone for their unbelief by bravely confessing Him before the world.

The disciples prayed with intense earnestness for a fitness to meet men and in their daily intercourse to speak words that would lead sinners to Christ. Putting away all differences, all desire for the supremacy, they came close together in Christian fellowship. They drew nearer and nearer to God, and as they did this they realized what a privilege had been theirs in being permitted to associate so closely with Christ. Sadness filled their hearts as they thought of how many times they had grieved Him by their slowness of comprehension, their failure to understand the lessons that, for their good, He was trying to teach them.

These days of preparation were days of deep heart searching. The disciples felt their spiritual need and cried to the Lord for the holy unction that was to fit them for the work of soul saving. They did not ask for a blessing for themselves merely. They were weighted with the burden of the salvation of souls. They realized that the gospel was to be carried to the world, and they claimed the power that Christ had promised.

During the patriarchal age the influence of the Holy Spirit had often been revealed in a marked manner, but never in its fullness. Now, in obedience to the word of the Saviour, the disciples offered their supplications for this gift, and in heaven Christ added His intercession. He claimed the gift of the Spirit, that He might pour it upon His people.

"And when the Day of Pentecost was fully come, they were all with one accord in one place. And suddenly there came a sound from heaven as of a rushing mighty wind, and it filled all the house where they were sitting."

The Spirit came upon the waiting, praying disciples with a fullness that reached every heart. The Infinite One revealed Himself in power to His church. It was as if for ages this influence had been held in restraint, and now Heaven rejoiced in being able to pour out upon the church the riches of the Spirit's grace. And under the influence of the Spirit, words of penitence and confession mingled with songs of praise for sins forgiven. Words of thanksgiving and of prophecy were heard. All heaven bent low to behold and to adore the wisdom of matchless, incomprehensible love. Lost in wonder, the apostles exclaimed, "Herein is love." They grasped the imparted gift. And what followed? The sword of the Spirit, newly edged with power and bathed in the lightnings of heaven, cut its way through unbelief. Thousands were converted in a day.

"It is expedient for you that I go away," Christ had said to His disciples; "for If I go not away, the Comforter will not come unto you; but if I depart, I will send Him unto you." "When He, the Spirit of truth, is come, He will guide you into all truth: for He shall not speak of Himself; but whatsoever He shall hear, that shall He speak: and He will show you things to come." John 16:7, 13.

Christ's ascension to heaven was the signal that His followers were to receive the promised blessing. For this they were to wait before they entered upon their work. When Christ passed within the heavenly gates, He was enthroned amidst the adoration of the angels. As soon as this ceremony was completed, the Holy Spirit descended upon the disciples in rich currents, and Christ was indeed glorified, even with the glory which He had with the Father from all eternity. The Pentecostal outpouring was Heaven's communication that the Redeemer's inauguration was accomplished. According to His promise He had sent the Holy Spirit from heaven to His followers as a token that He had, as priest and king, received all authority in heaven and on earth, and was the Anointed One over His people.

"And there appeared unto them cloven tongues like as of fire, and it sat upon each of them. And they were all filled with the Holy Ghost, and began to speak with other tongues, as the Spirit gave them utterance." The Holy Spirit, assuming the form of tongues of fire, rested upon those assembled. This was an emblem of the gift then bestowed on the disciples, which enabled them to speak with fluency languages with which they had heretofore been unacquainted. The appearance of fire signified the fervent zeal with which the apostles would labor and the power that would attend their work.

"There were dwelling at Jerusalem Jews, devout men, out of every nation under heaven." During the dispersion the Jews had been scattered to almost every part of the inhabited world, and in their exile they had learned to speak various languages. Many of these Jews were on this occasion in Jerusalem, attending the religious festivals then in progress.

Every known tongue was represented by those assembled. This diversity of languages would have been a great hindrance to the proclamation of the gospel; God therefore in a miraculous manner supplied the deficiency of the apostles. The Holy Spirit did for them that which they could not have accomplished for themselves in a lifetime. They could now proclaim the truths of the gospel abroad, speaking with accuracy the languages of those for whom they were laboring. This miraculous gift was a strong evidence to the world that their commission bore the signet of Heaven. From this time forth the language of the disciples was pure, simple, and accurate, whether they spoke in their native tongue or in a foreign language.

"Now when this was noised abroad, the multitude came together, and were confounded, because that every man heard them speak in his own language. And they were all amazed and marveled, saying one to another, Behold, are not all these which speak Galileans? and how hear we every man in our own tongue, wherein we were born?"

The priests and rulers were greatly enraged at this wonderful manifestation, but they dared not give way to their malice, for fear of exposing themselves to the violence of the people. They had put the Nazarene to death; but here were His servants, unlettered men of Galilee, telling in all the languages then spoken, the story of His life and ministry. The priests, determined to account for the miraculous power of the disciples in some natural way, declared that they were drunken from partaking largely of the new wine prepared for the feast. Some of the most ignorant of the people present seized upon this suggestion as the truth, but the more intelligent knew it to be false; and those who understood the different languages testified to the accuracy with which these languages were used by the disciples.

In answer to the accusation of the priests Peter showed that this demonstration was in direct fulfillment of the prophecy of Joel, wherein he foretold that such power would come upon men to fit them for a special work. "Ye men of Judea, and all ye that dwell at Jerusalem," he said, "be this known unto you, and hearken to my words: for these are not drunken, as ye suppose, seeing it is but the third hour of the day. But this is that which was spoken by the prophet Joel: And it shall come to pass in the last days, saith God, I will pour out of My Spirit upon all flesh: and your sons and your daughters shall prophesy, and your young men shall see visions, and your old men shall dream dreams: and on My servants and on My handmaidens I will pour out in those days of My Spirit; and they shall prophesy."

With clearness and power Peter bore witness of the death and resurrection of Christ: "Ye men of Israel, hear these words: Jesus of Nazareth, a man approved of God among you by miracles and wonders and signs, which God did by Him in the midst of you, as ye yourselves also know: Him . . . ye have taken, and by wicked hands have crucified and slain: whom God hath raised up, having loosed the pains of death: because it was not possible that He should be holden of it."

Peter did not refer to the teachings of Christ to prove his position, because he knew that the prejudice of his hearers was so great that his words on this subject would be of no effect. Instead, he spoke to them of David, who was regarded by the Jews as one of the patriarchs of their nation. "David speaketh concerning Him," he declared: "I foresaw the Lord always before My face, for He is on My right hand, that I should not be moved: therefore did My heart rejoice, and My tongue was glad; moreover also My flesh shall rest in hope: because Thou wilt not leave My soul in hell, neither wilt Thou suffer Thine Holy One to see corruption. . . .

"Men and brethren, let me freely speak unto you of the patriarch David, that he is both dead and buried, and his sepulcher is with us unto this day." "He . . . spake of the resurrection of Christ, that His soul was not left in hell, neither His flesh did see corruption. This Jesus hath God raised up, whereof we all are witnesses."

The scene is one full of interest. Behold the people coming from all directions to hear the disciples witness to the truth as it is in Jesus. They press in, crowding the temple. Priests and rulers are there, the dark scowl of malignity still on their faces, their hearts still filled with abiding hatred against Christ, their hands uncleansed from the blood shed when they crucified the world's Redeemer. They had thought to find the apostles cowed with fear under the strong hand of oppression and murder, but they find them lifted above all fear and filled with the Spirit, proclaiming with power the divinity of Jesus of Nazareth. They hear them declaring with boldness that the One so recently humiliated, derided, smitten by cruel hands, and crucified, is the Prince of life, now exalted to the right hand of God.

Some of those who listened to the apostles had taken an active part in the condemnation and death of Christ. Their voices had mingled with the rabble in calling for His crucifixion. When Jesus and Barabbas stood before them in the judgment hall and Pilate asked, "Whom will ye that I release unto you?" they had shouted, "Not this Man, but Barabbas!" Matthew 27:17; John 18:40. When Pilate delivered Christ to them, saying, "Take ye Him, and crucify Him: for I find no fault in Him;" "I am innocent of the blood of this just Person," they had cried, "His blood be on us, and on our children." John 19:6; Matthew 27:24, 25.

Now they heard the disciples declaring that it was the Son of God who had been crucified. Priests and rulers trembled. Conviction and anguish seized the people. "They were pricked in their heart, and said unto Peter and to the rest of the apostles, Men and brethren, what shall we do?" Among those who listened to the disciples were devout Jews, who were sincere in their belief. The power that accompanied the words of the speaker convinced them that Jesus was indeed the Messiah.

"Then Peter said unto them, Repent, and be baptized every one of you in the name of Jesus Christ for the remission of sins, and ye shall receive the gift of the Holy Ghost. For the promise is unto you, and to your children, and to all that are afar off, even as many as the Lord our God shall call."

Peter urged home upon the convicted people the fact that they had rejected Christ because they had been deceived by priests and rulers; and that if they continued to look to these men for counsel, and waited for them to acknowledge Christ before they dared to do so, they would never accept Him. These powerful men, though making a profession of godliness, were ambitious for earthly riches and glory. They were not willing to come to Christ to receive light.

Under the influence of this heavenly illumination the scriptures that Christ had explained to the disciples stood out before them with the luster of perfect truth. The veil that had prevented them from seeing to the end of that which had been abolished, was now removed, and they comprehended with perfect clearness the object of Christ's mission and the nature of His kingdom. They could speak with power of the Saviour; and as they unfolded to their hearers the plan of salvation, many were convicted and convinced. The traditions and superstitions inculcated by the priests were swept away from their minds, and the teachings of the Saviour were accepted.

"Then they that gladly received his word were baptized: and the same day there were added unto them about three thousand souls."

The Jewish leaders had supposed that the work of Christ would end with His death; but, instead of this, they witnessed the marvelous scenes of the Day of Pentecost. They heard the disciples, endowed with a power and energy hitherto unknown, preaching Christ, their words confirmed by signs and wonders. In Jerusalem, the stronghold of Judaism, thousands openly declared their faith in Jesus of Nazareth as the Messiah.

The disciples were astonished and overjoyed at the greatness of the harvest of souls. They did not regard this wonderful ingathering as the result of their own efforts; they realized that they were entering into other men's labors. Ever since the fall of Adam, Christ had been committing to chosen servants the seed of His word, to be sown in human hearts. During His life on this earth He had sown the seed of truth and had watered it with His blood. The conversions that took place on the Day of Pentecost were the result of this sowing, the harvest of Christ's work, revealing the power of His teaching.

The arguments of the apostles alone, though clear and convincing, would not have removed the prejudice that had withstood so much evidence. But the Holy Spirit sent the arguments home to hearts with divine power. The words of the apostles were as sharp arrows of the Almighty, convicting men of their terrible guilt in rejecting and crucifying the Lord of glory.

Under the training of Christ the disciples had been led to feel their need of the Spirit. Under the Spirit's teaching they received the final qualification, and went forth to their lifework. No longer were they ignorant and uncultured. No longer were they a collection of independent units or discordant, conflicting elements. No longer were their hopes set on worldly greatness. They were of "one accord," "of one heart and of one soul." Acts. 2:46; 4:32. Christ filled their thoughts; the advancement of His kingdom was their aim. In mind and character they had become like their Master, and men "took knowledge of them, that they had been with Jesus." Acts 4:13.

Pentecost brought them the heavenly illumination. The truths they could not understand while Christ was with them were now unfolded. With a faith and assurance that they had never before known, they accepted the teachings of the Sacred Word. No longer was it a matter of faith with them that Christ was the Son of God. They knew that, although clothed with humanity, He was indeed the Messiah, and they told their experience to the world with a confidence which carried with it the conviction that God was with them.

They could speak the name of Jesus with assurance; for was He not their Friend and Elder Brother? Brought into close communion with Christ, they sat with Him in heavenly places. With what burning language they clothed their ideas as they bore witness for Him! Their hearts were surcharged with a benevolence so full, so deep, so far-reaching, that it impelled them to go to the ends of the earth, testifying to the power of Christ. They were filled with an intense longing to carry forward the work He had begun. They realized the greatness of their debt to heaven and the responsibility of their work. Strengthened by the endowment of the Holy Spirit, they went forth filled with zeal to extend the triumphs of the cross. The Spirit animated them and spoke through them. The peace of Christ shone from their faces. They had consecrated their lives to Him for service, and their very features bore evidence to the surrender they had made.

The Gift of the Spirit

When Christ gave His disciples the promise of the Spirit, He was nearing the close of His earthly ministry. He was standing in the shadow of the cross, with a full realization of the load of guilt that was to rest upon Him as the Sin Bearer. Before offering Himself as the sacrificial victim, He instructed His disciples regarding a most essential and complete gift which He was to bestow upon His followers—the gift that would bring within their reach the boundless resources of His grace. "I will pray the Father," He said, "and He shall give you another Comforter, that He may abide with you forever; even the Spirit of truth; whom the world cannot receive, because it seeth Him not, neither knoweth Him: but ye know Him; for He dwelleth with you, and shall be in you." John 14:16, 17. The Saviour was pointing forward to the time when the Holy Spirit should come to do a mighty work as His representative. The evil that had been accumulating for centuries was to be resisted by the divine power of the Holy Spirit.

What was the result of the outpouring of the Spirit on the Day of Pentecost? The glad tidings of a risen Saviour were carried to the uttermost parts of the inhabited world. As the disciples proclaimed the message of redeeming grace, hearts yielded to the power of this message. The church beheld converts flocking to her from all directions. Backsliders were reconverted. Sinners united with believers in seeking the pearl of great price. Some who had been the bitterest opponents of the gospel became its champions. The prophecy was fulfilled, "He that is feeble. . . shall be as David; and the house of David . . . as the angel of the Lord." Zechariah 12:8. Every Christian saw in his brother a revelation of divine love and benevolence. One interest prevailed; one subject of emulation swallowed up all others. The ambition of the believers was to reveal the likeness of Christ's character and to labor for the enlargement of His kingdom.

"With great power gave the apostles witness of the resurrection of the Lord Jesus: and great grace was upon them all." Acts 4:33. Under their labors were added to the church chosen men, who, receiving the word of truth, consecrated their lives to the work of giving to others the hope that filled their hearts with peace and joy. They could not be restrained or intimidated by threatenings. The Lord spoke through them, and as they went from place to place, the poor had the gospel preached to them, and miracles of divine grace were wrought.

So mightily can God work when men give themselves up to the control of His Spirit.

The promise of the Holy Spirit is not limited to any age or to any race. Christ declared that the divine influence of His Spirit was to be with His followers unto the end. From the Day of Pentecost to the present time, the Comforter has been sent to all who have yielded themselves fully to the Lord and to His service. To all who have accepted Christ as a personal Saviour, the Holy Spirit has come as a counselor, sanctifier, guide, and witness. The more closely believers have walked with God, the more clearly and powerfully have they testified of their Redeemer's love and of His saving grace. The men and women who through the long centuries of persecution and trial enjoyed a large measure of the presence of the Spirit in their lives, have stood as signs and wonders in the world. Before angels and men they have revealed the transforming power of redeeming love.

Those who at Pentecost were endued with power from on high, were not thereby freed from further temptation and trial. As they witnessed for truth and righteousness they were repeatedly assailed by the enemy of all truth, who sought to rob them of their Christian experience. They were compelled to strive with all their God-given powers to reach the measure of the stature of men and women in Christ Jesus. Daily they prayed for fresh supplies of grace, that they might reach higher and still higher toward perfection. Under the Holy Spirit's working even the weakest, by exercising faith in God, learned to improve their entrusted powers and to become sanctified, refined, and ennobled. As in humility they submitted to the molding influence of the Holy Spirit, they received of the fullness of the Godhead and were fashioned in the likeness of the divine.

The lapse of time has wrought no change in Christ's parting promise to send the Holy Spirit as His representative. It is not because of any restriction on the part of God that the riches of His grace do not flow earthward to men. If the fulfillment of the promise is not seen as it might be, it is because the promise is not appreciated as it should be. If all were willing, all would be filled with the Spirit. Wherever the need of the Holy Spirit is a matter little thought of, there is seen spiritual drought, spiritual darkness, spiritual declension and death. Whenever minor matters occupy the attention, the divine power which is necessary for the growth and prosperity of the church, and which would bring all other blessings in its train, is lacking, though offered in infinite plenitude.

Since this is the means by which we are to receive power, why do we not hunger and thirst for the gift of the Spirit? Why do we not talk of it, pray for it, and preach concerning it? The Lord is more willing to give the Holy Spirit to those who serve Him than parents are to give good gifts to their children. For the daily baptism of the Spirit every worker should offer his petition to God. Companies of Christian workers should gather to ask for special help, for heavenly wisdom, that they may know how to plan and execute wisely. Especially should they pray that God will baptize His chosen ambassadors in mission fields with a rich measure of His Spirit. The presence of the Spirit with God's workers will give the proclamation of truth a power that not all the honor or glory of the world could give.

With the consecrated worker for God, in whatever place he may be, the Holy Spirit abides. The words spoken to the disciples are spoken also to us. The Comforter is ours as well as theirs. The Spirit furnishes the strength that sustains striving, wrestling souls in every emergency, amidst the hatred of the world, and the realization of their own failures and mistakes. In sorrow and affliction, when the outlook seems dark and the future perplexing, and we feel helpless and alone,—these are the times when, in answer to the prayer of faith, the Holy Spirit brings comfort to the heart.

It is not a conclusive evidence that a man is a Christian because he manifests spiritual ecstasy under extraordinary circumstances. Holiness is not rapture: it is an entire surrender of the will to God; it is living by every word that proceeds from the mouth of God; it is doing the will of our heavenly Father; it is trusting God in trial, in darkness as well as in the light; it is walking by faith and not by sight; it is relying on God with unquestioning confidence, and resting in His love.

It is not essential for us to be able to define just what the Holy Spirit is. Christ tells us that the Spirit is the Comforter, "the Spirit of truth, which proceedeth from the Father." It is plainly declared regarding the Holy Spirit that, in His work of guiding men into all truth, "He shall not speak of Himself." John 15:26; 16:13.

The nature of the Holy Spirit is a mystery. Men cannot explain it, because the Lord has not revealed it to them. Men having fanciful views may bring together passages of Scripture and put a human construction on them, but the acceptance of these views will not strengthen the church. Regarding such mysteries, which are too deep for human understanding, silence is golden.

The office of the Holy Spirit is distinctly specified in the words of Christ: "When He is come, He will reprove the world of sin, and of righteousness, and of judgment." John 16:8. It is the Holy Spirit that convicts of sin. If the sinner responds to the quickening influence of the Spirit, he will be brought to repentance and aroused to the importance of obeying the divine requirements.

To the repentant sinner, hungering and thirsting for righteousness, the Holy Spirit reveals the Lamb of God that taketh away the sin of the world. "He shall receive of Mine, and shall show it unto you," Christ said. "He shall teach you all things, and bring all things to your remembrance, whatsoever I have said unto you." John 16:14; 14:26.

The Spirit is given as a regenerating agency, to make effectual the salvation wrought by the death of our Redeemer. The Spirit is constantly seeking to draw the attention of men to the great offering that was made on the cross of Calvary, to unfold to the world the love of God, and to open to the convicted soul the precious things of the Scriptures.

Having brought conviction of sin, and presented before the mind the standard of righteousness, the Holy Spirit withdraws the affections from the things of this earth and fills the soul with a desire for holiness. "He will guide you into all truth" (John 16:13), the Saviour declared. If men are willing to be molded, there will be brought about a sanctification of the whole being. The Spirit will take the things of God and stamp them on the soul. By His power the way of life will be made so plain that none need err therein.

From the beginning, God has been working by His Holy Spirit through human instrumentalities for the accomplishment of His purpose in behalf of the fallen race. This was manifest in the lives of the patriarchs. To the church in the wilderness also, in the time of Moses, God gave His "good Spirit to instruct them." Nehemiah 9:20. And in the days of the apostles He wrought mightily for His church through the agency of the Holy Spirit. The same power that sustained the patriarchs, that gave Caleb and Joshua faith and courage, and that made the work of the apostolic church effective, has upheld God's faithful children in every succeeding age. It was through the power of the Holy Spirit that during the Dark Ages the Waldensian Christians helped to prepare the way for the Reformation. It was the same power that made successful the efforts of the noble men and women who pioneered the way for the establishment of modern missions and for the translation of the Bible into the languages and dialects of all nations and peoples.

And today God is still using His church to make known His purpose in the earth. Today the heralds of the cross are going from city to city, and from land to land, preparing the way for the second advent of Christ. The standard of God's law is being exalted. The Spirit of the Almighty is moving upon men's hearts, and those who respond to its influence become witnesses for God and His truth. In many places consecrated men and women may be seen communicating to others the light that has made plain to them the way of salvation through Christ. And as they continue to let their light shine, as did those who were baptized with the Spirit on the Day of Pentecost, they receive more and still more of the Spirit's power. Thus the earth is to be lightened with the glory of God.

On the other hand, there are some who, instead of wisely improving present opportunities, are idly waiting for some special season of spiritual refreshing by which their ability to enlighten others will be greatly increased. They neglect present duties and privileges, and allow their light to burn dim, while they look forward to a time when, without any effort on their part, they will be made the recipients of special blessing, by which they will be transformed and fitted for service.

It is true that in the time of the end, when God's work in the earth is closing, the earnest efforts put forth by consecrated believers under the guidance of the Holy Spirit are to be accompanied by special tokens of divine favor. Under the figure of the early and the latter rain, that falls in Eastern lands at seedtime and harvest, the Hebrew prophets foretold the bestowal of spiritual grace in extraordinary measure upon God's church. The outpouring of the Spirit in the days of the apostles was the beginning of the early, or former, rain, and glorious was the result. To the end of time the presence of the Spirit is to abide with the true church.

But near the close of earth's harvest, a special bestowal of spiritual grace is promised to prepare the church for the coming of the Son of man. This outpouring of the Spirit is likened to the falling of the latter rain; and it is for this added power that Christians are to send their petitions to the Lord of the harvest "in the time of the latter rain." In response, "the Lord shall make bright clouds, and give them showers of rain." "He will cause to come down . . . the rain, the former rain, and the latter rain," Zechariah 10:1; Joel 2:23.

But unless the members of God's church today have a living connection with the Source of all spiritual growth, they will not be ready for the time of reaping. Unless they keep their lamps trimmed and burning, they will fail of receiving added grace in times of special need.

Those only who are constantly receiving fresh supplies of grace, will have power proportionate to their daily need and their ability to use that power. Instead of looking forward to some future time when, through a special endowment of spiritual power, they will receive a miraculous fitting up for soul winning, they are yielding themselves daily to God, that He may make them vessels meet for His use. Daily they are improving the opportunities for service that lie within their reach. Daily they are witnessing for the Master wherever they may be, whether in some humble sphere of labor in the home, or in a public field of usefulness.

To the consecrated worker there is wonderful consolation in

the knowledge that even Christ during His life on earth sought His Father daily for fresh supplies of needed grace; and from this communion with God He went forth to strengthen and bless others. Behold the Son of God bowed in prayer to His Father! Though He is the Son of God, He strengthens His faith by prayer, and by communion with heaven gathers to Himself power to resist evil and to minister to the needs of men. As the Elder Brother of our race He knows the necessities of those who, compassed with infirmity and living in a world of sin and temptation, still desire to serve Him. He knows that the messengers whom He sees fit to send are weak, erring men; but to all who give themselves wholly to His service He promises divine aid. His own example is an assurance that earnest, persevering supplication to God in faith—faith that leads to entire dependence upon God, and unreserved consecration to His work—will avail to bring to men the Holy Spirit's aid in the battle against sin.

Every worker who follows the example of Christ will be prepared to receive and use the power that God has promised to His church for the ripening of earth's harvest. Morning by morning, as the heralds of the gospel kneel before the Lord and renew their vows of consecration to Him, He will grant them the presence of His Spirit, with its reviving, sanctifying power. As they go forth to the day's duties, they have the assurance that the unseen agency of the Holy Spirit enables them to be "laborers together with God."

At the Temple Gate

The disciples of Christ had a deep sense of their own inefficiency, and with humiliation and prayer they joined their weakness to His strength, their ignorance to His wisdom, their unworthiness to His righteousness, their poverty to His exhaustless wealth. Thus strengthened and equipped, they hesitated not to press forward in the service of the Master.

A short time after the descent of the Holy Spirit, and immediately after a season of earnest prayer, Peter and John, going up to the temple to worship, saw at the gate Beautiful a cripple, forty years of age, whose life, from his birth, had been one of pain and infirmity. This unfortunate man had long desired to see Jesus, that he might be healed; but he was almost helpless, and was far removed from the scene of the great Physician's labors. His pleadings at last induced some friends to bear him to the gate of the temple, but upon arriving there, he found that the One upon whom his hopes were centered, had been put to a cruel death.

His disappointment excited the sympathy of those who knew for how long he had eagerly hoped to be healed by Jesus, and daily they brought him to the temple, in order that passers-by might be induced by pity to give him a trifle to relieve his wants. As Peter and John passed, he asked an alms from them. The disciples regarded him compassionately, and Peter said, "Look on us. And he gave heed unto them, expecting to receive something of them. Then Peter said,

Silver and gold have I none." As Peter thus declared his poverty, the countenance of the cripple fell; but it grew bright with hope as the apostle continued, "But such as I have give I thee: In the name of Jesus Christ of Nazareth rise up and walk.

"And he took him by the right hand, and lifted him up: and immediately his feet and anklebones received strength. And he leaping up stood, and walked, and entered with them into the temple, walking, and leaping, and praising God. And all the people saw him walking and praising God: and they knew that it was he which sat for alms at the Beautiful Gate of the temple: and they were filled with wonder and amazement at that which had happened."

"And as the lame man which was healed held Peter and John, all the people ran together unto them in the porch that is called Solomon's, greatly wondering." They were astonished that the disciples could perform miracles similar to those performed by Jesus. Yet here was this man, for forty years a helpless cripple, now rejoicing in the full use of his limbs, free from pain, and happy in believing in Jesus.

When the disciples saw the amazement of the people, Peter asked, "Why marvel ye at this? or why look ye so earnestly on us, as though by our own power or holiness we had made this man to walk?" He assured them that the cure had been wrought in the name and through the merits of Jesus of Nazareth, whom God had raised from the dead. "His name through faith in His name," the apostle declared, "hath made this man strong, whom ye see and know: yea, the faith which is by Him hath given him this perfect soundness in the presence of you all."

The apostles spoke plainly of the great sin of the Jews in rejecting and putting to death the Prince of life; but they were careful not to drive their hearers to despair. "Ye denied the Holy One and the Just," Peter said, "and desired a murderer to be granted unto you; and killed the Prince of life, whom God hath raised from the dead; whereof we are witnesses." "And now, brethren, I wot that through ignorance ye did it, as did also your rulers. But those things, which God before had showed by the mouth of all His prophets, that Christ should suffer, He hath so fulfilled." He declared that the Holy Spirit was calling upon them to repent and be converted, and assured them that there was no hope of salvation except through the mercy of the One whom they had crucified. Only through faith in Him could their sins be forgiven.

"Repent ye therefore, and be converted," he cried, "that your sins may be blotted out, when the times of refreshing shall come from the presence of the Lord."

"Ye are the children of the prophets, and of the covenant which God made with our fathers, saying unto Abraham, And in thy seed shall all the kindreds of the earth be blessed. Unto you first God, having raised up His Son Jesus, sent Him to bless you, in turning away every one of you from his iniquities."

Thus the disciples preached the resurrection of Christ. Many among those who listened were waiting for this testimony, and when they heard it they believed. It brought to their minds the words that Christ had spoken, and they took their stand in the ranks of those who accepted the gospel. The seed that the Saviour had sown sprang up and bore fruit.

While the disciples were speaking to the people, "the priests, and the captain of the temple, and the Sadducees, came upon them, being grieved that they taught the people, and preached through Jesus the resurrection from the dead."

After Christ's resurrection the priests had spread far and near the lying report that His body had been stolen by the disciples while the Roman guard slept. It is not surprising that they were displeased when they hear Peter and John preaching the resurrection of the One they had murdered. The Sadducees especially were greatly aroused. They felt that their most cherished doctrine was in danger, and their reputation at stake.

Converts to the new faith were rapidly increasing, and both Pharisees and Sadducees agreed that if these new teachers were suffered to go unchecked, their own influence would be in greater danger than when Jesus was upon the earth. Accordingly, the captain of the temple, with the help of a number of Sadducees, arrested Peter and John, and put them in prison, as it was too late that day for them to be examined.

The enemies of the disciples could not but be convinced that Christ had risen from the dead. The evidence was too clear to be doubted. Nevertheless, they hardened their hearts, refusing to repent of the terrible deed they had committed in putting Jesus to death. Abundant evidence that the apostles were speaking and acting under divine inspiration had been given the Jewish rulers, but they firmly resisted the message of truth. Christ had not come in the manner that they expected, and though at times they had been convinced that He was the Son of God, yet they had stifled conviction, and crucified Him. In mercy God gave them still further evidence, and now another opportunity was granted them to turn to Him. He sent the disciples to tell them that they had killed the Prince of life, and in this terrible charge He gave them another call to repentance. But feeling secure in their own righteousness, the Jewish teachers refused to admit that the men charging them with crucifying Christ were speaking by the direction of the Holy Spirit.

Having committed themselves to a course of opposition to Christ, every act of resistance became to the priests an additional incentive to pursue the same course. Their obstinacy became more and more determined. It was not that they could not yield; they could, but would not. It was not alone because they were guilty and deserving of death, not alone because they had put to death the Son of God, that they were cut off from salvation; it was because they armed themselves with opposition to God. They persistently rejected light and stifled the convictions of the Spirit. The influence that controls the children of disobedience worked in them, leading them to abuse the men through whom God was working. The malignity of their rebellion was intensified by each successive act of resistance against God and the message He had given His servants to declare. Every day, in their refusal to repent, the Jewish leaders took up their rebellion afresh, preparing to reap that which they had sown.

The wrath of God is not declared against unrepentant sinners merely because of the sins they have committed, but because, when called to repent, they choose to continue in resistance, repeating the sins of the past in defiance of the light given them. If the Jewish leaders had submitted to the convicting power of the Holy Spirit, they would have been pardoned; but they were determined not to yield. In the same way, the sinner, by continued resistance, places himself where the Holy Spirit cannot influence him.

On the day following the healing of the cripple, Annas and Caiaphas, with the other dignitaries of the temple, met together for the trial, and the prisoners were brought before them. In that very room and before some of those very men, Peter had shamefully denied his Lord. This came distinctly to his mind as he appeared for his own trial. He now had an opportunity of redeeming his cowardice.

Those present who remembered the part that Peter had acted at the trial of his Master, flattered themselves that he could now be intimidated by the threat of imprisonment and death. But the Peter who denied Christ in the hour of His greatest need was impulsive and self-confident, differing widely from the Peter who was brought before the Sanhedrin for examination. Since his fall he had been converted. He was no longer proud and boastful, but modest and self-distrustful. He was filled with the Holy Spirit, and by the help of this power he was resolved to remove the stain of his apostasy by honoring the name he had once disowned.

Hitherto the priests had avoided mentioning the crucifixion or the resurrection of Jesus. But now, in fulfillment of their purpose, they were forced to inquire of the accused how the cure of the impotent man had been accomplished. "By what power, or by what name, have ye done this?" they asked.

With holy boldness and in the power of the Spirit Peter fearlessly declared: "Be it known unto you all, and to all the people of Israel, that by the name of Jesus Christ of Nazareth, whom ye crucified, whom God raised from the dead, even by Him doth this man stand here before you whole. This is the stone which was set at nought of you builders, which is become the head of the corner. Neither is there salvation in any other: for there is none other name under heaven given among men, whereby we must be saved."

This courageous defense appalled the Jewish leaders. They had supposed that the disciples would be overcome with fear and confusion when brought before the Sanhedrin. But, instead, these witnesses spoke as Christ had spoken, with a convincing power that silenced their adversaries. There was no trace of fear in Peter's voice as he declared of Christ, "This is the stone which was set at nought of you builders, which is become the head of the corner."

Peter here used a figure of speech familiar to the priests. The prophets had spoken of the rejected stone; and Christ Himself, speaking on one occasion to the priests and elders, said: "Did ye never read in the Scriptures, The stone which the builders rejected, the same is become the head of the corner: this is the Lord's doing, and it is marvelous in our eyes? Therefore say I unto you, The kingdom of God shall be taken from you, and given to a nation bringing forth the fruits thereof. And whosoever shall fall on this stone shall be broken: but on whomsoever it shall fall, it will grind him to powder." Matthew 21:42-44.

As the priests listened to the apostles' fearless words, "they took knowledge of them, that they had been with Jesus."

Of the disciples after the transfiguration of Christ it is written that at the close of that wonderful scene "they saw no man, save Jesus only." Matthew 17:8. "Jesus only"— in these words is contained the secret of the life and power that marked the history of the early church. When the disciples first heard the words of Christ, they felt their need of Him. They sought, they found, they followed Him. They were with Him in the temple, at the table, on the mountainside, in the field. They were as pupils with a teacher, daily receiving from Him lessons of eternal truth.

After the Saviour's ascension, the sense of the divine presence, full of love and light, was still with them. It was a personal presence. Jesus, the Saviour, who had walked and talked and prayed with them, who had spoken hope and comfort to their hearts, had, while the message of peace was upon His lips, been taken from them into heaven. As the chariot of angels received Him, His words had come to them, "Lo, I am with you alway, even unto the end." Matthew 28:20. He had ascended to heaven in the form of humanity. They knew that He was before the throne of God, their Friend and Saviour still; that His sympathies were unchanged; that He would forever be identified with suffering humanity. They knew that He was presenting before God the merit of His blood, showing His wounded hands and feet as a remembrance of the price He had paid for His redeemed ones; and this thought strengthened them to endure reproach for His sake. Their union with Him was stronger now than when He was with them in person. The light and love and power of an indwelling Christ shone out through them, so that men, beholding, marveled.

Christ placed His seal on the words that Peter spoke in His defense. Close beside the disciple, as a convincing witness, stood the man who had been so miraculously healed. The appearance of this man, a few hours before a helpless cripple, but now restored to soundness of health, added a weight of testimony to Peter's words. Priests and rulers were silent. They were unable to refute Peter's statement, but they were nonetheless determined to put a stop to the teaching of the disciples.

Christ's crowning miracle—the raising of Lazarus—had sealed the determination of the priests to rid the world of Jesus and His wonderful works, which were fast destroying their influence over the people. They had crucified Him; but here was a convincing proof that they had not put a stop to the working of miracles in His name, nor to the proclamation of the truth He taught. Already the healing of the cripple and the preaching of the apostles had filled Jerusalem with excitement.

In order to conceal their perplexity, the priests and rulers ordered the apostles to be taken away, that they might counsel among themselves. They all agreed that it would be useless to deny that the man had been healed. Gladly would they have covered up the miracle by falsehoods; but this was impossible, for it had been wrought in the full light of day, before a multitude of people, and had already come to the knowledge of thousands. They felt that the work of the disciples must be stopped or Jesus would gain many followers. Their own disgrace would follow, for they would be held guilty of the murder of the Son of God.

But notwithstanding their desire to destroy the disciples, the priests dared not do more than threaten them with the severest punishment if they continued to speak or to work in the name of Jesus. Calling them again before the Sanhedrin, they commanded them not to speak or teach in the name of Jesus. But Peter and John answered: "Whether it be right in the sight of God to hearken unto you more than unto God, judge ye. For we cannot but speak the things which we have seen and heard."

Gladly would the priests have punished these men for their unswerving fidelity to their sacred calling, but they feared the people; "for all men glorified God for that which was done." So, with repeated threats and injunctions, the apostles were set at liberty.

While Peter and John were prisoners, the other disciples, knowing the malignity of the Jews, had prayed unceasingly for their brethren, fearing that the cruelty shown to Christ might be repeated. As soon as the apostles were released, they sought the rest of the disciples and reported to them the result of the examination. Great was the joy of the believers. "They lifted up their voice to God with one accord, and said, Lord, Thou art God, which hast made heaven, and earth, and the sea, and all that in them is: who by the mouth of Thy servant David hast said, Why did the heathen rage, and the people imagine vain things? The kings of the earth stood up, and the rulers were gathered together against the Lord, and against His Christ. For of a truth against Thy Holy Child Jesus, whom Thou hast anointed, both Herod, and Pontius Pilate, with the Gentiles, and the people of Israel, were gathered together, for to do whatsoever Thy hand and Thy counsel determined before to be done.

"And now, Lord, behold their threatenings: and grant unto Thy servants, that with all boldness they may speak Thy word, by stretching forth Thine hand to heal; and that signs and wonders may be done by the name of Thy Holy Child Jesus."

The disciples prayed that greater strength might be imparted to them in the work of the ministry; for they saw that they would meet the same determined opposition that Christ had encountered when upon the earth. While their united prayers were ascending in faith to heaven, the answer came. The place where they were assembled was shaken, and they were endowed anew with the Holy Spirit. Their hearts filled with courage, they again went forth to proclaim the word of God in Jerusalem. "With great power gave the apostles witness of the resurrection of the Lord Jesus," and God marvelously blessed their efforts.

The principle for which the disciples stood so fearlessly when, in answer to the command not to speak any more in the name of Jesus, they declared, "Whether it be right in the sight of God to hearken unto you more than unto God, judge ye," is the same that the adherents of the gospel struggled to maintain in the days of the Reformation. When in 1529 the German princes assembled at the Diet of Spires, there was presented the emperor's decree restricting religious liberty, and prohibiting all further dissemination of the reformed doctrines. It seemed that the hope of the world was about to be crushed out. Would the princes accept the decree? Should the light of the gospel be shut out from the multitudes still in darkness? Mighty issues for the world were at stake. Those who had accepted the reformed faith met together, and their unanimous decision was, "Let us reject this decree. In matters of conscience the majority has no power."—Merle d'Aubigne, History of the Reformation, b. 13, ch. 5.

This principle we in our day are firmly to maintain. The banner of truth and religious liberty held aloft by the founders of the gospel church and by God's witnesses during the centuries that have passed since then, has, in this last conflict, been committed to our hands. The responsibility for this great gift rests with those whom God has blessed with a knowledge of His word. We are to receive this word as supreme authority. We are to recognize human government as an ordinance of divine appointment, and teach obedience to it as a sacred duty, within its legitimate sphere. But when its claims conflict with the claims of God, we must obey God rather than men. God's word must be recognized as above all human legislation. A "Thus saith the Lord" is not to be set aside for a "Thus saith the church" or a "Thus saith the state." The crown of Christ is to be lifted above the diadems of earthly potentates.

We are not required to defy authorities. Our words, whether spoken or written, should be carefully considered, lest we place ourselves on record as uttering that which would make us appear antagonistic to law and order. We are not to say or do anything that would unnecessarily close up our way. We are to go forward in Christ's name, advocating the truths committed to us. If we are forbidden by men to do this work, then we may say, as did the apostles, "Whether it be right in the sight of God to hearken unto you more than unto God, judge ye. For we cannot but speak the things which we have seen and heard."

A Warning Against Hypocrisy

As The disciples proclaimed the truths of the gospel in Jerusalem, God bore witness to their word, and a multitude believed. Many of these early believers were immediately cut off from family and friends by the zealous bigotry of the Jews, and it was necessary to provide them with food and shelter.

The record declares, "Neither was there any among them that lacked," and it tells how the need was filled. Those among the believers who had money and possessions cheerfully sacrificed them to meet the emergency. Selling their houses or their lands, they brought the money and laid it at the apostles' feet, "and distribution was made unto every man according as he had need."

This liberality on the part of the believers was the result of the outpouring of the Spirit. The converts to the gospel were "of one heart and of one soul." One common interest controlled them—the success of the mission entrusted to them; and covetousness had no place in their lives. Their love for their brethren and the cause they had espoused, was greater than their love of money and possessions. Their works testified that they accounted the souls of men of higher value them earthly wealth.

Thus it will ever be when the Spirit of God takes possession of the life. Those whose hearts are filled with the love of Christ, will follow the example of Him who for our sake became poor, that through His poverty we might be made rich. Money, time, influence—all the gifts they have received from God's hand, they will value only as a means of advancing the work of the gospel. Thus it was in the early church; and when in the church of today it is seen that by the power of the Spirit the members have taken their affections from the things of the world, and that they are willing to make sacrifices in order that their fellow men may hear the gospel, the truths proclaimed will have a powerful influence upon the hearers.

In sharp contrast to the example of benevolence shown by the believers, was the conduct of Ananias and Sapphira, whose experience, traced by the pen of Inspiration, has left a dark stain upon the history of the early church. With others, these professed disciples had shared the privilege of hearing the gospel preached by the apostles. They had been present with other believers when, after the apostles had prayed, "the place was shaken where they were assembled together; and they were all filled with the Holy Ghost." Acts 4:31. Deep conviction had rested upon all present, and under the direct influence of the Spirit of God, Ananias and Sapphira had made a pledge to give to the Lord the proceeds from the sale of certain property.

Afterward, Ananias and Sapphira grieved the Holy Spirit by yielding to feelings of covetousness. They began to regret their promise and soon lost the sweet influence of the blessing that had warmed their hearts with a desire to do large things in behalf of the cause of Christ. They thought they had been too hasty, that they ought to reconsider their decision. They talked the matter over, and decided not to fulfill their pledge. They saw, however, that those who parted with their possessions to supply the needs of their poorer brethren, were held in high esteem among the believers; and ashamed to have their brethren know that their selfish souls grudged that which they had solemnly dedicated to God, they deliberately decided to sell their property and pretend to give all the proceeds into the general fund, but really to keep a large share for themselves. Thus they would secure their living from the common store and at the same time gain the high esteem of their brethren.

But God hates hypocrisy and falsehood. Ananias and Sapphira practiced fraud in their dealing with God; they lied to the Holy Spirit, and their sin was visited with swift and terrible judgment. When Ananias came with his offering, Peter said: "Ananias, why hath Satan filled thine heart to lie to the Holy Ghost, and to keep back part of the price of the land? Whiles it remained, was it not thine own? and after it was sold, was it not in thine own power? why hast thou conceived this thing in thine heart? thou hast not lied unto men, but unto God."

"Ananias hearing these words fell down, and gave up the ghost: and great fear came on all them that heard these things."

"Whiles it remained, was it not thine own?" Peter asked. No undue influence had been brought to bear upon Ananias to compel him to sacrifice his possessions to the general good. He had acted from choice. But in attempting to deceive the disciples, he had lied to the Almighty.

"It was about the space of three hours after, when his wife, not knowing what was done, came in. And Peter answered unto her, Tell me whether ye sold the land for so much? And she said, Yea, for so much. Then Peter said unto her, How is it that ye have agreed together to tempt the Spirit of the Lord? behold, the feet of them which have buried thy husband are at the door, and shall carry thee out. Then fell she down straightway at his feet, and yielded up the ghost: and the young men came in, and found her dead, and, carrying her forth, buried her by her husband. And great fear came upon all the church, and upon as many as heard these things."

Infinite Wisdom saw that this signal manifestation of the wrath of God was necessary to guard the young church from becoming demoralized. Their numbers were rapidly increasing. The church would have been endangered if, in the rapid increase of converts, men and women had been added who, while professing to serve God, were worshiping mammon. This judgment testified that men cannot deceive God, that He detects the hidden sin of the heart, and that He will not be mocked. It was designed as a warning to the church, to lead them to avoid pretense and hypocrisy, and to beware of robbing God.

Not to the early church only, but to all future generations, this example of God's hatred of covetousness, fraud, and hypocrisy, was given as a danger-signal. It was covetousness that Ananias and Sapphira had first cherished. The desire to retain for themselves a part of that which they had promised to the Lord, led them into fraud and hypocrisy.

God has made the proclamation of the gospel dependent upon the labors and the gifts of His people. Voluntary offerings and the tithe constitute the revenue of the Lord's work. Of the means entrusted to man, God claims a certain portion,—the tenth. He leaves all free to say whether or not they will give more than this. But when the heart is stirred by the influence of the Holy Spirit, and a vow is made to give a certain amount, the one who vows has no longer any right to the consecrated portion. Promises of this kind made to men would be looked upon as binding; are those not more binding that are made to God? Are promises tried in the court of conscience less binding than written agreements of men?

When divine light is shining into the heart with unusual clearness and power, habitual selfishness relaxes its grasp and there is a disposition to give to the cause of God. But none need think that they will be allowed to fulfill the promises then made, without a protest on the part of Satan. He is not pleased to see the Redeemer's kingdom on earth built up. He suggests that the pledge made was too much, that it may cripple them in their efforts to acquire property or gratify the desires of their families.

It is God who blesses men with property, and He does this that they may be able to give toward the advancement of His cause. He sends the sunshine and the rain. He causes vegetation to flourish. He gives health and the ability to acquire means. All our blessings come from His bountiful hand. In turn, He would have men and women show their gratitude by returning Him a portion in tithes and offerings—in thank offerings, in freewill offerings, in trespass offerings. Should means flow into the treasury in accordance with this divinely appointed plan,—a tenth of all the increase, and liberal offerings,—there would be an abundance for the advancement of the Lord's work.

But the hearts of men become hardened through selfishness, and, like Ananias and Sapphira, they are tempted to withhold part of the price, while pretending to fulfill God's requirements. Many spend money lavishly in self-gratification. Men and women consult their pleasure and gratify their taste, while they bring to God, almost unwillingly, a stinted offering. They forget that God will one day demand a strict account of how His goods have been used, and that He will no more accept the pittance they hand into the treasury than He accepted the offering of Ananias and Sapphira.

From the stern punishment meted out to those perjurers, God would have us learn also how deep is His hatred and contempt for all hypocrisy and deception. In pretending that they had given all, Ananias and Sapphira lied to the Holy Spirit, and, as a result, they lost this life and the life that is to come. The same God who punished them, today condemns all falsehood. Lying lips are an abomination to Him. He declares that into the Holy City "there shall in no wise enter . . . anything that defileth, neither whatsoever worketh abomination, or maketh a lie." Revelation 21:27. Let truth telling be held with no loose hand or uncertain grasp. Let it become a part of the life. Playing fast and loose with truth, and dissembling to suit one's own selfish plans, means shipwreck of faith. "Stand therefore, having your loins girt about with truth." Ephesians 6:14. He who utters untruths sells his soul in a cheap market. His falsehoods may seem to serve in emergencies; he may thus seem to make business advancement that he could not gain by fair dealing; but he finally reaches the place where he can trust no one. Himself a falsifier, he has no confidence in the word of others.

In the case of Ananias and Sapphira, the sin of fraud against God was speedily punished. The same sin was often repeated in the after history of the church and is committed by many in our time. But though it may not be attended by the visible manifestation of God's displeasure, it is no less heinous in His sight now than in the apostles' time. The warning has been given; God has clearly manifested His abhorrence of this sin; and all who give themselves up to hypocrisy and covetousness may be sure that they are destroying their own souls.

Before the Sanhedrin

It was the cross, that instrument of shame and torture, which brought hope and salvation to the world. The disciples were but humble men, without wealth, and with no weapon but the word of God; yet in Christ's strength they went forth to tell the wonderful story of the manger and the cross, and to triumph over all opposition. Without earthly honor or recognition, they were heroes of faith. From their lips came words of divine eloquence that shook the world.

In Jerusalem, where the deepest prejudice existed, and where the most confused ideas prevailed in regard to Him who had been crucified as a malefactor, the disciples continued to speak with boldness the words of life, setting before the Jews the work and mission of Christ, His crucifixion, resurrection, and ascension. Priests and rulers heard with amazement the clear, bold testimony of the apostles. The power of the risen Saviour had indeed fallen on the disciples, and their work was accompanied by signs and miracles that daily increased the number of believers. Along the streets where the disciples were to pass, the people laid their sick "on beds and couches, that at the least the shadow of Peter passing by might overshadow some of them." Here also were brought those vexed with unclean spirits. The crowds gathered round them, and those who were healed shouted the praises of God and glorified the name of the Redeemer.

The priests and rulers saw that Christ was extolled above them. As the Sadducees, who did not believe in a resurrection, heard the apostles declaring that Christ had risen from the dead, they were enraged, realizing that if the apostles were allowed to preach a risen Saviour, and to work miracles in His name, the doctrine that there would be no resurrection would be rejected by all, and the sect of the Sadducees would soon become extinct. The Pharisees were angry as they perceived that the tendency of the disciples' teaching was to undermine the Jewish ceremonies, and make the sacrificial offerings of no effect.

Hitherto all the efforts made to suppress this new teaching had been in vain; but now both Sadducees and Pharisees determined that the work of the disciples should be stopped, for it was proving them guilty of the death of Jesus. Filled with indignation, the priests laid violent hands on Peter and John, and put them in the common prison.

The leaders in the Jewish nation had signally failed of fulfilling God's purpose for His chosen people. Those whom the Lord had made the depositaries of truth had proved unfaithful to their trust, and God chose others to do His work. In their blindness these leaders now gave full sway to what they called righteous indignation against the ones who were setting aside their cherished doctrines. They would not admit even the possibility that they themselves did not rightly understand the word, or that they had misinterpreted or misapplied the Scriptures. They acted like men who had lost their reason. What right have these teachers, they said, some of them mere fishermen, to present ideas contrary to the doctrines that we have taught the people? Being determined to suppress the teaching of these ideas, they imprisoned those who were presenting them.

The disciples were not intimidated or cast down by this treatment. The Holy Spirit brought to their minds the words spoken by Christ: "The servant is not greater than his lord. If they have persecuted Me, they will also persecute you; if they have kept My saying, they will keep yours also. But all these things will they do unto you for My name's sake, because they know not Him that sent Me." "They shall put you out of the synagogues: yea, the time cometh, that whosoever killeth you will think that he doeth God service." "These things have I told you, that when the time shall come, ye may remember that I told you of them." John 15:20, 21; 16:2, 4.

The God of heaven, the mighty Ruler of the universe, took the matter of the imprisonment of the disciples into His own hands, for men were warring against His work. By night the angel of the Lord opened the prison doors and said to the disciples, "Go, stand and speak in the temple to the people all the words of this life." This command was directly contrary to the order given by the Jewish rulers; but did the apostles say, We cannot do this until we have consulted the magistrates and received permission from them? No; God had said, "Go," and they obeyed. "They entered into the temple early in the morning, and taught."

When Peter and John appeared among the believers and recounted how the angel had led them directly through the band of soldiers guarding the prison, bidding them resume the work that had been interrupted, the brethren were filled with amazement and joy.

In the meantime the high priest and those with him had "called the council together, and all the senate of the children of Israel." The priests and rulers had decided to fix upon the disciples the charge of insurrection, to accuse them of murdering Ananias and Sapphira, and of conspiring to deprive the priests of their authority. They hoped so to excite the mob that it would take the matter in hand and deal with the disciples as it had dealt with Jesus. They were aware that many who did not accept the teachings of Christ were weary of the arbitrary rule of the Jewish authorities and anxious for some change. The priests feared that if these dissatisfied ones were to accept the truths proclaimed by the apostles, and were to acknowledge Jesus as the Messiah, the anger of the entire people would be raised against the religious leaders, who would then be made to answer for the murder of Christ. They decided to take strong measures to prevent this.

When they sent for the prisoners to be brought before them, great was their amazement at the word brought back that the prison doors were found to be securely bolted and the guard stationed before them, but that the prisoners were nowhere to be found.

Soon the astonishing report came, "Behold, the men whom ye put in prison are standing in the temple, and teaching the people. Then went the captain with the officers, and brought them without violence: for they feared the people, lest they should have been stoned."

Although the apostles were miraculously delivered from prison, they were not safe from examination and punishment. Christ had said when He was with them, "Take heed to yourselves: for they shall deliver you up to councils." Mark 13:9. By sending an angel to deliver them, God had given them a token of His love and an assurance of His presence. It was now their part to suffer for the sake of the One whose gospel they were preaching.

In the history of prophets and apostles, are many noble examples of loyalty to God. Christ's witnesses have endured imprisonment, torture, and death itself, rather than break God's commands. The record left by Peter and John is as heroic as any in the gospel dispensation. As they stood for the second time before the men who seemed bent on their destruction, no fear or hesitation could be discerned in their words or attitude. And when the high priest said, "Did we not straitly command you that ye should not teach in this name? and, behold, ye have filled Jerusalem with your doctrine, and intend to bring this Man's blood upon us," Peter answered, "We ought to obey God rather than men." It was an angel from heaven who delivered them from prison and bade them teach in the temple. In following his directions they were obeying the divine command, and this they must continue to do at whatever cost to themselves.

Then the Spirit of Inspiration came upon the disciples; the accused became the accusers, charging the murder of Christ upon those who composed the council. "The God of our fathers raised up Jesus," Peter declared, "whom ye slew and hanged on a tree. Him hath God exalted with His right hand to be a Prince and a Saviour, for to give repentance to Israel, and forgiveness of sins. And we are His witnesses of these things; and so is also the Holy Ghost, whom God hath given to them that obey Him."

So enraged were the Jews at these words that they decided to take the law into their own hands and without further trial, or without authority from the Roman officers, to put the prisoners to death. Already guilty of the blood of Christ, they were no eager to stain their hands with the blood of His disciples.

But in the council there was one man who recognized the voice of God in the words spoken by the disciples. This was Gamaliel, a Pharisee of good reputation and a man of learning and high position. His clear intellect saw that the violent step contemplated by the priests would lead to terrible consequences. Before addressing those present, he requested that the prisoners be removed. He well knew the elements he had to deal with; he knew that the murderers of Christ would hesitate at nothing in order to carry out their purpose.

He then spoke with great deliberation and calmness, saying: "Ye men of Israel, take heed to yourselves what ye intend to do as touching these men. For before these days rose up Theudas, boasting himself to be somebody; to whom a number of men, about four hundred, joined themselves: who was slain; and all, as many as obeyed him, were scattered, and brought to nought. After this man rose up Judas of Galilee in the days of the taxing, and drew away much people after him: he also perished; and all, even as many as obeyed him, were dispersed. And now I say unto you, Refrain from these men, and let them alone: for if this counsel or this work be of men, it will come to nought: but if it be of God, ye cannot overthrow it; lest haply ye be found even to fight against God."

The priests saw the reasonableness of these views, and were obliged to agree with Gamaliel. Yet their prejudice and hatred could hardly be restrained. Very reluctantly, after beating the disciples and charging them again at the peril of their lives to preach no more in the name of Jesus, they released them. "And they departed from the presence of the council, rejoicing that they were counted worthy to suffer shame for His name. And daily in the temple, and in every house, they ceased not to teach and preach Jesus Christ."

Shortly before His crucifixion Christ had bequeathed to His disciples a legacy of peace. "Peace I leave with you," He said, "My peace I give unto you: not as the world giveth, give I unto you. Let not your heart be troubled, neither let it be afraid." John 14:27. This peace is not the peace that comes through conformity to the world. Christ never purchased peace by compromise with evil. The peace that Christ left His disciples is internal rather than external and was ever to remain with His witnesses through strife and contention.

Christ said of Himself, "Think not that I am come to send peace on earth: I came not to send peace, but a sword." Matthew 10:34. The Prince of Peace, He was yet the cause of division. He who came to proclaim glad tidings and to create hope and joy in the hearts of the children of men, opened a controversy that burns deep and arouses intense passion in the human heart. And He warns His followers, "In the world ye shall have tribulation." "They shall lay their hands on you, and persecute you, delivering you up to the synagogues, and into prisons, being brought before kings and rulers for My name's sake." "Ye shall be betrayed both by parents, and brethren, and kinsfolks, and friends; and some of you shall they cause to be put to death." John 16:33; Luke 21:12, 16.

This prophecy has been fulfilled in a marked manner. Every indignity, reproach, and cruelty that Satan could instigate human hearts to devise, has been visited upon the followers of Jesus. And it will be again fulfilled in a marked manner; for the carnal heart is still at enmity with the law of God, and will not be subject to its commands. The world is no more in harmony with the principles of Christ today than it was in the days of the apostles. The same hatred that prompted the cry, "Crucify Him! crucify Him!" the same hatred that led to the persecution of the disciples, still works in the children of disobedience. The same spirit which in the Dark Ages consigned men and women to prison, to exile, and to death, which conceived the exquisite torture of the Inquisition, which planned and executed the Massacre of St. Bartholomew, and which kindled the fires of Smithfield, is still at work with malignant energy in unregenerate hearts. The history of truth has ever been the record of a struggle between right and wrong. The proclamation of the gospel has ever been carried forward in this world in the face of opposition, peril, loss, and suffering.

What was the strength of those who in the past have suffered persecution for Christ's sake? It was union with God, union with the Holy Spirit, union with Christ. Reproach and persecution have separated many from earthly friends, but never from the love of Christ. Never is the tempest-tried soul more dearly loved by His Saviour than when he is suffering reproach for the truth's sake. "I will love him," Christ said, "and will manifest Myself to him." John 14:21. When for the truth's sake the believer stands at the bar of earthly tribunals, Christ stands by his side. When he is confined within prison walls, Christ manifests Himself to him and cheers his heart with His love. When he suffers death for Christ's sake, the Saviour says to him, They may kill the body, but they cannot hurt the soul. "Be of good cheer; I have overcome the world." "Fear thou not; for I am with thee: be not dismayed; for I am thy God: I will strengthen thee; yea, I will help thee; yea, I will uphold thee with the right hand of My righteousness." John 16:33; Isaiah 41:10.

"They that trust in the Lord shall be as Mount Zion, which cannot be removed, but abideth forever. As the mountains are round about Jerusalem, so the Lord is round about His people from henceforth even forever." "He shall redeem their soul from deceit and violence: and precious shall their blood be in His sight." Psalms 125:1-3; 72:14.

"The Lord of hosts shall defend them; . . . the Lord their God shall save them in that day as the flock of His people: for they shall be as the stones of a crown, lifted up as an ensign upon His land." Zechariah 9:15, 16.

The Seven Deacons

In those days, when the number of the disciples was multiplied, there arose a murmuring of the Grecians against the Hebrews, because their widows were neglected in the daily ministration."

The early church was made up of many classes of people, of various nationalities. At the time of the outpouring of the Holy Spirit at Pentecost, "there were dwelling at Jerusalem Jews, devout men, out of every nation under heaven." Acts 2:5. Among those of the Hebrew faith who were gathered at Jerusalem were some commonly known as Grecians, between whom and the Jews of Palestine there had long existed distrust and even antagonism.

The hearts of those who had been converted under the labors of the apostles, were softened and united by Christian love. Despite former prejudices, all were in harmony with one another. Satan knew that so long as this union continued to exist, he would be powerless to check the progress of gospel truth; and he sought to take advantage of former habits of thought, in the hope that thereby he might be able to introduce into the church elements of disunion.

Thus it came to pass that as disciples were multiplied, the enemy succeeded in arousing the suspicions of some who had formerly been in the habit of looking with jealousy on their brethren in the faith and of finding fault with their spiritual leaders, and so "there arose a murmuring of the Grecians against the Hebrews." The cause of complaint was an alleged neglect of the Greek widows in the daily distribution of assistance. Any inequality would have been contrary to the spirit of the gospel, yet Satan had succeeded in arousing suspicion. Prompt measures must now be taken to remove all occasion for dissatisfaction, lest the enemy triumph in his effort to bring about a division among the believers.

The disciples of Jesus had reached a crisis in their experience. Under the wise leadership of the apostles, who labored unitedly in the power of the Holy Spirit, the work committed to the gospel messengers was developing rapidly. The church was continually enlarging, and this growth in membership brought increasingly heavy burdens upon those in charge. No one man, or even one set of men, could continue to bear these burdens alone, without imperiling the future prosperity of the church. There was necessity for a further distribution of the responsibilities which had been borne so faithfully by a few during the earlier days of the church. The apostles must now take an important step in the perfecting of gospel order in the church by laying upon others some of the burdens thus far borne by themselves.

Summoning a meeting of the believers, the apostles were led by the Holy Spirit to outline a plan for the better organization of all the working forces of the church. The time had come, the apostles stated, when the spiritual leaders having the oversight of the church should be relieved from the task of distributing to the poor and from similar burdens, so that they might be free to carry forward the work of preaching the gospel. "Wherefore, brethren," they said, "look ye out among you seven men of honest report, full of the Holy Ghost and wisdom, whom we may appoint over this business. But we will give ourselves continually to prayer, and to the ministry of the word." This advice was followed, and by prayer and the laying on of hands, seven chosen men were solemnly set apart for their duties as deacons.

The appointment of the seven to take the oversight of special lines of work, proved a great blessing to the church. These officers gave careful consideration to individual needs as well as to the general financial interests of the church, and by their prudent management and their godly example they were an important aid to their fellow officers in binding together the various interests of the church into a united whole.

That this step was in the order of God, is revealed in the immediate results for good that were seen. "The word of God increased; and the number of the disciples multiplied in Jerusalem greatly; and a great company of the priests were obedient to the faith." This ingathering of souls was due both to the greater freedom secured by the apostles and to the zeal and power shown by the seven deacons. The fact that these brethren had been ordained for the special work of looking after the needs of the poor, did not exclude them from teaching the faith. On the contrary, they were fully qualified to instruct others in the truth, and they engaged in the work with great earnestness and success.

To the early church had been entrusted a constantly enlarging work—that of establishing centers of light and blessing wherever there were honest souls willing to give themselves to the service of Christ. The proclamation of the gospel was to be world-wide in its extent, and the messengers of the cross could not hope to fulfill their important mission unless they should remain united in the bonds of Christian unity, and thus reveal to the world that they were one with Christ in God. Had not their divine Leader prayed to the Father, "Keep through Thine own name those whom Thou hast given Me, that they may be one, as We are"? And had He not declared of His disciples, "The world hath hated them, because they are not of the world"? Had He not pleaded with the Father that they might be "made perfect in one," "that the world may believe that Thou hast sent Me"? John 17:11, 14, 23, 21. Their spiritual life and power was dependent on a close connection with the One by whom they had been commissioned to preach the gospel.

Only as they were united with Christ could the disciples hope to have the accompanying power of the Holy Spirit and the co-operation of angels of heaven. With the help of these divine agencies they would present before the world a united front and would be victorious in the conflict they were compelled to wage unceasingly against the powers of darkness. As they should continue to labor unitedly, heavenly messengers would go before them, opening the way; hearts would be prepared for the reception of truth, and many would be won to Christ. So long as they remained united, the church would go forth "fair as the moon, clear as the sun, and terrible as an army with banners." Song of Solomon 6:10. Nothing could withstand her onward progress. The church would advance from victory to victory, gloriously fulfilling her divine mission of proclaiming the gospel to the world.

The organization of the church at Jerusalem was to serve as a model for the organization of churches in every other place where messengers of truth should win converts to the gospel. Those to whom was given the responsibility of the general oversight of the church were not to lord it over God's heritage, but, as wise shepherds, were to "feed the flock of God,. . . being ensamples to the flock" (1 Peter 5:2, 3); and the deacons were to be "men of honest report, full of the Holy Ghost and wisdom." These men were to take their position unitedly on the side of right and to maintain it with firmness and decision. Thus they would have a uniting influence upon the entire flock.

Later in the history of the early church, when in various parts of the world many groups of believers had been formed into churches, the organization of the church was further perfected, so that order and harmonious action might be maintained. Every member was exhorted to act well his part. Each was to make a wise use of the talents entrusted to him. Some were endowed by the Holy Spirit with special gifts —"first apostles, secondarily prophets, thirdly teachers, after that miracles, then gifts of healings, helps, governments, diversities of tongues." 1 Corinthians 12:28. But all these classes of workers were to labor in harmony.

"There are diversities of gifts, but the same Spirit. And there are differences of administrations, but the same Lord. And there are diversities of operations, but it is the same God which worketh all in all. But the manifestation of the Spirit is given to every man to profit withal. For to one is given by the Spirit the word of wisdom; to another the word of knowledge by the same Spirit; to another faith by the same Spirit; to another the gifts of healing by the same Spirit; to another the working of miracles; to another prophecy; to another discerning of spirits; to another divers kinds of tongues; to another the interpretation of tongues: but all these worketh that one and the selfsame Spirit, dividing to every man severally as He will. For as the body is one, and hath many members, and all the members of that one body, being many, are one body: so also is Christ." 1 Corinthians 12:4-12.

Solemn are the responsibilities resting upon those who are called to act as leaders in the church of God on earth. In the days of the theocracy, when Moses was endeavoring to carry alone burdens so heavy that he would soon have worn away under them, he was counseled by Jethro to plan for a wise distribution of responsibilities. "Be thou for the people to Godward," Jethro advised, "that thou mayest bring the causes unto God: and thou shalt teach them ordinances and laws, and shalt show them the way wherein they must walk, and the work that they must do." Jethro further advised that men be appointed to act as "rulers of thousands, and rulers of hundreds, rulers of fifties, and rulers of tens." These were to be "able men, such as fear God, men of truth, hating covetousness." They were to "judge the people at all seasons," thus relieving Moses of the wearing responsibility of giving consideration to many minor matters that could be dealt with wisely by consecrated helpers.

The time and strength of those who in the providence of God have been placed in leading positions of responsibility in the church, should be spent in dealing with the weightier matters demanding special wisdom and largeness of heart. It is not in the order of God that such men should be appealed to for the adjustment of minor matters that others are well qualified to handle. "Every great matter they shall bring unto thee," Jethro proposed to Moses, "but every small matter they shall judge: so shall it be easier for thyself, and they shall bear the burden with thee. If thou shalt do this thing, and God command thee so, then thou shalt be able to endure, and all this people shall also go to their place in peace."

In harmony with this plan, "Moses chose able men out of all Israel, and made them heads over the people, rulers of thousands, rulers of hundreds, rulers of fifties, and rulers of tens. And they judged the people at all seasons: the hard causes they brought unto Moses, but every small matter they judged themselves." Exodus 18:19-26.

Later, when choosing seventy elders to share with him the responsibilities of leadership, Moses was careful to select, as his helpers, men possessing dignity, sound judgment, and experience. In his charge to these elders at the time of their ordination, he outlined some of the qualifications that fit a man to be a wise ruler in the church. "Hear the causes between your brethren," said Moses, "and judge righteously between every man and his brother, and the stranger that is with him. Ye shall not respect persons in judgment; but ye shall hear the small as well as the great; ye shall not be afraid of the face of man; for the judgment is God's." Deuteronomy 1:16, 17.

King David, toward the close of his reign, delivered a solemn charge to those bearing the burden of the work of God in his day. Summoning to Jerusalem "all the princes of Israel, the princes of the tribes, and the captains of the companies that ministered to the king by course, and the captains over the thousands, and captains over the hundreds, and the stewards over all the substance and possession of the king, and of his sons, with the officers, and with the mighty men, and with all the valiant men," the aged king solemnly charged them, "in the sight of all Israel the congregation of the Lord, and in the audience of our God," to "keep and seek for all the commandments of the Lord your God." I Chronicles 28:1, 8.

To Solomon, as one called to occupy a position of leading responsibility, David gave a special charge: "Thou, Solomon my son, know thou the God of thy father, and serve Him with a perfect heart and with a willing mind: for the Lord searcheth all hearts, and understandeth all the imaginations of the thoughts: if thou seek Him, He will be found of thee; but if thou forsake Him, He will cast thee off forever. Take heed now; for the Lord hath chosen thee: . . . be strong." I Chronicles 28:9, 10.

The same principles of piety and justice that were to guide the rulers among God's people in the time of Moses and of David, were also to be followed by those given the oversight of the newly organized church of God in the gospel dispensation. In the work of setting things in order in all the churches, and ordaining suitable men to act as officers, the apostles held to the high standards of leadership outlined in the Old Testament Scriptures. They maintained that he who is called to stand in a position of leading responsibility in the church "must be blameless, as the steward of God; not self-willed, not soon angry, not given to wine, no striker, not given to filthy lucre; but a lover of hospitality, a lover of good men, sober, just, holy, temperate; holding fast the faithful word as he hath been taught, that he may be able by sound doctrine both to exhort and to convince the gainsayers." Titus 1:7-9.

The order that was maintained in the early Christian church made it possible for them to move forward solidly as a well-disciplined army clad with the armor of God. The companies of believers, though scattered over a large territory, were all members of one body; all moved in concert and in harmony with one another. When dissension arose in a local church, as later it did arise in Antioch and elsewhere, and the believers were unable to come to an agreement among themselves, such matters were not permitted to create a division in the church, but were referred to a general council of the entire body of believers, made up of appointed delegates from the various local churches, with the apostles and elders in positions of leading responsibility. Thus the efforts of Satan to attack the church in isolated places were met by concerted action on the part of all, and the plans of the enemy to disrupt and destroy were thwarted.

"God is not the author of confusion, but of peace, as in all churches of the saints." I Corinthians 14:33. He requires that order and system be observed in the conduct of church affairs today no less than in the days of old. He desires His work to be carried forward with thoroughness and exactness so that He may place upon it the seal of His approval. Christian is to be united with Christian, church with church, the human instrumentality co-operating with the divine, every agency subordinate to the Holy Spirit, and all combined in giving to the world the good tidings of the grace of God.

The First Christian Martyr

Stephen, the foremost of the seven deacons, was a man of deep piety and broad faith. Though a Jew by birth, he spoke the Greek language and was familiar with the customs and manners of the Greeks. He therefore found opportunity to preach the gospel in the synagogues of the Greek Jews. He was very active in the cause of Christ and boldly proclaimed his faith. Learned rabbis and doctors of the law engaged in public discussion with him, confidently expecting an easy victory. But "they were not able to resist the wisdom and the spirit by which he spake." Not only did he speak in the power of the Holy Spirit, but it was plain that he was a student of the prophecies and learned in all matters of the law. He ably defended the truths that he advocated and utterly defeated his opponents. To him was the promise fulfilled, "Settle it therefore in your hearts, not to meditate before what ye shall answer: for I will give you a mouth and wisdom, which all your adversaries shall not be able to gainsay nor resist." Luke 21:14, 15.

As the priests and rulers saw the power that attended the

preaching of Stephen, they were filled with bitter hatred. Instead of yielding to the evidence that he presented, they determined to silence his voice by putting him to death. On several occasions they had bribed the Roman authorities to pass over without comment instances where the Jews had taken the law into their own hands and had tried, condemned, and executed prisoners in accordance with their national custom. The enemies of Stephen did not doubt that they could again pursue such a course without danger to themselves. They determined to risk the consequences and therefore seized Stephen and brought him before the Sanhedrin council for trial.

Learned Jews from the surrounding countries were summoned for the purpose of refuting the arguments of the prisoner. Saul of Tarsus was present and took a leading part against Stephen. He brought the weight of eloquence and the logic of the rabbis to bear upon the case, to convince the people that Stephen was preaching delusive and dangerous doctrines; but in Stephen he met one who had a full understanding of the purpose of God in the spreading of the gospel to other nations.

Because the priests and rulers could not prevail against the clear, calm wisdom of Stephen, they determined to make an example of him; and while thus satisfying their revengeful hatred, they would prevent others, through fear, from adopting his belief. Witnesses were hired to bear false testimony that they had heard him speak blasphemous words against the temple and the law. "We have heard him say," these witnesses declared, "that this Jesus of Nazareth shall destroy this place, and shall change the customs which Moses delivered us."

As Stephen stood face to face with his judges to answer to the charge of blasphemy, a holy radiance shone upon his countenance, and "all that sat in the council, looking steadfastly on him, saw his face as it had been the face of an angel." Many who beheld this light trembled and veiled their faces, but the stubborn unbelief and prejudice of the rulers did not waver.

When Stephen was questioned as to the truth of the charges against him, he began his defense in a clear, thrilling voice, which rang through the council hall. In words that held the assembly spellbound, he proceeded to rehearse the history of the chosen people of God. He showed a thorough knowledge of the Jewish economy and the spiritual interpretation of it now made manifest through Christ. He repeated the words of Moses that foretold of the Messiah: "A Prophet shall the Lord your God raise up unto you of your brethren, like unto me; Him shall ye hear." He made plain his own loyalty to God and to the Jewish faith, while he showed that the law in which the Jews trusted for salvation had not been able to save Israel from idolatry. He connected Jesus Christ with all the Jewish history. He referred to the building of the temple by Solomon, and to the words of both Solomon and Isaiah: "Howbeit the Most High dwelleth not in temples made with hands; as saith the prophet, Heaven is My throne,

and earth is My footstool: what house will ye build Me? saith the Lord: or what is the place of My rest? Hath not My hand made all these things?"

When Stephen reached this point, there was a tumult among the people. When he connected Christ with the prophecies and spoke as he did of the temple, the priest, pretending to be horror-stricken, rent his robe. To Stephen this act was a signal that his voice would soon be silenced forever. He saw the resistance that met his words and knew that he was giving his last testimony. Although in the midst of his sermon, he abruptly concluded it.

Suddenly breaking away from the train of history that he was following, and turning upon his infuriated judges, he cried: "Ye stiff-necked and uncircumcised in heart and ears, ye do always resist the Holy Ghost: as your fathers did, so do ye. Which of the prophets have not your fathers persecuted? and they have slain them which showed before of the coming of the Just One; of whom ye have been now the betrayers and murderers: who have received the law by the disposition of angels, and have not kept it."

At this, priests and rulers were beside themselves with anger. Acting more like beasts of prey than human beings, they rushed upon Stephen, gnashing their teeth. In the cruel faces about him the prisoner read his fate; but he did not waver. For him the fear of death was gone. For him the enraged priests and the excited mob had no terror. The scene before him faded from his vision. To him the gates of heaven were ajar, and, looking in, he saw the glory of the courts of God, and Christ, as if just risen from His throne, standing ready to sustain His servant. In words of triumph Stephen exclaimed, "Behold, I see the heavens opened, and the Son of man standing on the right hand of God."

As he described the glorious scene upon which his eyes were gazing, it was more than his persecutors could endure. Stopping their ears, that they might not hear his words, and uttering loud cries, they ran furiously upon him with one accord "and cast him out of the city." "And they stoned Stephen, calling upon God, and saying, Lord Jesus, receive my spirit. And he kneeled down, and cried with a loud voice, Lord, lay not this sin to their charge. And when he had said this, he fell asleep."

No legal sentence had been passed upon Stephen, but the Roman authorities were bribed by large sums of money to make no investigation into the case.

The martyrdom of Stephen made a deep impression upon all who witnessed it. The memory of the signet of God upon his face; his words, which touched the very souls of those who heard them, remained in the minds of the beholders, and testified to the truth of that which he had proclaimed. His death was a sore trial to the church, but it resulted in the conviction of Saul, who could not efface from his memory the faith and constancy of the martyr, and the glory that had rested on his countenance.

At the scene of Stephen's trial and death, Saul had seemed to be imbued with a frenzied zeal. Afterward he was angered by his own secret conviction that Stephen had been honored by God at the very time when he was dishonored by men. Saul continued to persecute the church of God, hunting them down, seizing them in their houses, and delivering them up to the priests and rulers for imprisonment and death. His zeal in carrying forward this persecution brought terror to the Christians at Jerusalem. The Roman authorities made no special effort to stay the cruel work and secretly aided the Jews in order to conciliate them and to secure their favor.

After the death of Stephen, Saul was elected a member of the Sanhedrin council in consideration of the part he had acted on that occasion. For a time he was a mighty instrument in the hands of Satan to carry out his rebellion against the Son of God. But soon this relentless persecutor was to be employed in building up the church that he was now tearing down. A Mightier than Satan had chosen Saul to take the place of the martyred Stephen, to preach and suffer for His name, and to spread far and wide the tidings of salvation through His blood.

The Gospel in Samaria

After the death of Stephen there arose against the believers in Jerusalem a persecution so relentless that "they were all scattered abroad throughout the regions of Judea and Samaria." Saul "made havoc of the church, entering into every house, and haling men and women committed them to prison." Of his zeal in this cruel work he said at a later date: "I verily thought with myself, that I ought to do many things contrary to the name of Jesus of Nazareth. Which thing I also did in Jerusalem: and many of the saints did I shut up in prison. . . . And I punished them oft in every synagogue, and compelled them to blaspheme; and being exceedingly mad against them, I persecuted them even unto strange cities." That Stephen was not the only one who suffered death may be seen from Saul's own words, "And when they were put to death, I gave my voice against them." Acts 26:9-11.

At this time of peril Nicodemus came forward in fearless avowal of his faith in the crucified Saviour. Nicodemus was a member of the Sanhedrin and with others had been stirred by the teaching of Jesus. As he had witnessed Christ's wonderful works, the conviction had fastened itself upon his mind that this was the Sent of God. Too proud openly to acknowledge himself in sympathy with the Galilean Teacher, he had sought a secret interview. In this interview Jesus had unfolded to him the plan of salvation and His mission to the world, yet still Nicodemus had hesitated. He hid the truth in his heart, and for three years there was little apparent fruit. But while Nicodemus had not publicly acknowledged Christ, he had in the Sanhedrin council repeatedly thwarted the schemes of the priests to destroy Him. When at last Christ had been lifted up on the cross, Nicodemus remembered the words that He had spoken to him in the night interview on the Mount of Olives, "As Moses lifted up the serpent in the wilderness, even so must the Son of man be lifted up" (John 3:14); and he saw in Jesus the world's Redeemer.

With Joseph of Arimathea, Nicodemus had borne the expense of the burial of Jesus. The disciples had been afraid to show themselves openly as Christ's followers, but Nicodemus and Joseph had come boldly to their aid. The help of these rich and honored men was greatly needed in that hour of darkness. They had been able to do for their dead Master what it would have been impossible for the poor disciples to do; and their wealth and influence had protected them, in a great measure, from the malice of the priests and rulers.

Now, when the Jews were trying to destroy the infant church, Nicodemus came forward in its defense. No longer cautious and questioning, he encouraged the faith of the disciples and used his wealth in helping to sustain the church at Jerusalem and in advancing the work of the gospel. Those who in other days had paid him reverence, now scorned and persecuted him, and he became poor in this world's goods; yet he faltered not in the defense of his faith.

The persecution that came upon the church in Jerusalem resulted in giving a great impetus to the work of the gospel. Success had attended the ministry of the word in that place, and there was danger that the disciples would linger there too long, unmindful of the Saviour's commission to go to all the world. Forgetting that strength to resist evil is best gained by aggressive service, they began to think that they had no work so important as that of shielding the church in Jerusalem from the attacks of the enemy. Instead of educating the new converts to carry the gospel to those who had not heard it, they were in danger of taking a course that would lead all to be satisfied with what had been accomplished. To scatter His representatives abroad, where they could work for others, God permitted persecution to come upon them. Driven from Jerusalem, the believers "went everywhere preaching the word."

Among those to whom the Saviour had given the commission, "Go ye therefore, and teach all nations" (Matthew 28:19), were many from the humbler walks of life—men and women who had learned to love their Lord and who had determined to follow His example of unselfish service. To these lowly ones, as well as to the disciples who had been with the Saviour during His earthly ministry, had been given a precious trust. They were to carry to the world the glad tidings of salvation through Christ.

When they were scattered by persecution they went forth filled with missionary zeal. They realized the responsibility of their mission. They knew that they held in their hands the bread of life for a famishing world; and they were constrained by the love of Christ to break this bread to all who were in need. The Lord wrought through them. Wherever they went, the sick were healed and the poor had the gospel preached unto them.

Philip, one of the seven deacons, was among those driven from Jerusalem. He "went down to the city of Samaria, and preached Christ unto them. And the people with one accord gave heed unto those things which Philip spake, hearing and seeing the miracles while he did. For unclean spirits . . . came out of many that were possessed with them: and many taken with palsies, and that were lame, were healed. And there was great joy in that city."

Christ's message to the Samaritan woman with whom He had talked at Jacob's well had borne fruit. After listening to His words, the woman had gone to the men of the city, saying, "Come, see a man, which told me all things that ever I did: is not this the Christ? They went with her, heard Jesus, and believed on Him. Anxious to hear more, they begged Him to remain. For two days He stayed with them, "and many more believed because of His own word." John 4:29, 41.

And when His disciples were driven from Jerusalem, some found in Samaria a safe asylum. The Samaritans welcomed these messengers of the gospel, and the Jewish converts gathered a precious harvest from among those who had once been their bitterest enemies.

Philip's work in Samaria was marked with great success, and, thus encouraged, he sent to Jerusalem for help. The apostles now perceived more fully the meaning of the words of Christ, "Ye shall be witnesses unto Me both in Jerusalem, and in all Judea, and in Samaria, and unto the uttermost part of the earth." Acts 1:8.

While Philip was still in Samaria, he was directed by a heavenly messenger to "go toward the south unto the way that goeth down from Jerusalem unto Gaza. . . . And he arose and went." He did not question the call, nor did he hesitate to obey; for he had learned the lesson of conformity to God's will.

"And, behold, a man of Ethiopia, a eunuch of great authority under Candace queen of the Ethiopians, who had the charge of all her treasure, and had come to Jerusalem for to worship, was returning, and sitting in his chariot read Esaias the prophet." This Ethiopian was a man of good standing and of wide influence. God saw that when converted he would give others the light he had received and would exert a strong influence in favor of the gospel. Angels of God were attending this seeker for light, and he was being drawn to the Saviour. By the ministration of the Holy Spirit the Lord brought him into touch with one who could lead him to the light.

Philip was directed to go to the Ethiopian and explain to him the prophecy that he was reading. "Go near," the Spirit said, "and join thyself to this chariot." As Philip drew near, he asked the eunuch, "Understandest thou what thou readest? And he said, How can I, except some man should guide me? And he desired Philip that he would come up and sit with him." The scripture that he was reading was the prophecy of Isaiah relating to Christ: "He was led as a sheep to the slaughter; and like a lamb dumb before his shearer, so opened He not His mouth: in His humiliation His judgment was taken away: and who shall declare His generation? for His life is taken from the earth."

"Of whom speaketh the prophet this?" the eunuch asked, "of himself, or of some other man?" Then Philip opened to him the great truth of redemption. Beginning at the same

scripture, he "preached unto him Jesus."

The man's heart thrilled with interest as the Scriptures were explained to him; and when the disciple had finished, he was ready to accept the light given. He did not make his high worldly position an excuse for refusing the gospel. "As they went on their way, they came unto a certain water: and the eunuch said, See, here is water; what doth hinder me to be baptized? And Philip said, If thou believest with all thine heart, thou mayest. And he answered and said, I believe that Jesus Christ is the Son of God. And he commanded the chariot to stand still: and they went down both into the water, both Philip and the eunuch; and he baptized him.

"And when they were come up out of the water, the Spirit of the Lord caught away Philip, that the eunuch saw him no more: and he went on his way rejoicing. But Philip was found at Azotus: and passing through he preached in all the cities, till he came to Caesarea."

This Ethiopian represented a large class who need to be taught by such missionaries as Philip—men who will hear the voice of God and go where He sends them. There are many who are reading the Scriptures who cannot understand their true import. All over the world men and women are looking wistfully to heaven. Prayers and tears and inquiries go up from souls longing for light, for grace, for the Holy Spirit. Many are on the verge of the kingdom, waiting only to be gathered in.

An angel guided Philip to the one who was seeking for light and who was ready to receive the gospel, and today angels will guide the footsteps of those workers who will allow the Holy Spirit to sanctify their tongues and refine and ennoble their hearts. The angel sent to Philip could himself have done the work for the Ethiopian, but this is not God's way of working. It is His plan that men are to work for their fellow men.

In the trust given to the first disciples, believers in every age have shared. Everyone who has received the gospel has been given sacred truth to impart to the world. God's faithful people have always been aggressive missionaries, consecrating their resources to the honor of His name and wisely using their talents in His service.

The unselfish labor of Christians in the past should be to us an object lesson and an inspiration. The members of God's church are to be zealous of good works, separating from worldly ambition and walking in the footsteps of Him who went about doing good. With hearts filled with sympathy and compassion, they are to minister to those in need of help, bringing to sinners a knowledge of the Saviour's love. Such work calls for laborious effort, but it brings a rich reward. Those who engage in it with sincerity of purpose will see souls won to the Saviour, for the influence that attends the practical carrying out of the divine commission is irresistible.

Not upon the ordained minister only rests the responsibility of going forth to fulfill this commission. Everyone who has received Christ is called to work for the salvation of his fellow men. "The Spirit and the bride say, Come. And let him that heareth say, Come." Revelation 22:17. The charge to give this invitation includes the entire church. Everyone who has heard the invitation is to echo the message from hill and valley, saying, "Come."

It is fatal mistake to suppose that the work of soul-saving depends alone upon the ministry. The humble, consecrated believer upon whom the Master of the vineyard places a burden for souls is to be given encouragement by the men upon whom the Lord has laid larger responsibilities. Those who stand as leaders in the church of God are to realize that the Saviour's commission is given to all who believe in His name. God will send forth into His vineyard many who have not been dedicated to the ministry by the laying on of hands.

Hundreds, yea, thousands, who have heard the message of salvation are still idlers in the market place, when they might be engaged in some line of active service. To these Christ is saying, "Why stand ye here all the day idle?" and He adds, "Go ye also into the vineyard." Matthew 20:6, 7. Why is it that many more do not respond to the call? Is it because they think themselves excused in that they do not stand in the pulpit? Let them understand that there is a large work to be done outside the pulpit by thousands of consecrated lay members.

Long has God waited for the spirit of service to take possession of the whole church so that everyone shall be working for Him according to his ability. When the members of the church of God do their appointed work in the needy fields at home and abroad, in fulfillment of the gospel commission, the whole world will soon be warned and the Lord Jesus will return to this earth with power and great glory. "This gospel of the kingdom shall be preached in all the world for a witness unto all nations; and then shall the end come." Matthew 24:14.

From Persecutor to Disciple

Prominent among the Jewish leaders who became thoroughly aroused by the success attending the proclamation of the gospel, was Saul of Tarsus. A Roman citizen by birth, Saul was nevertheless a Jew by descent and had been educated in Jerusalem by the most eminent of the rabbis. "Of the stock of Israel, of the tribe of Benjamin," Saul was "a Hebrew of the Hebrews; as touching the law, a Pharisee; concerning zeal, persecuting the church; touching the righteousness which is in the law, blameless." Philippians 3:5, 6. He was regarded by the rabbis as a young man of great promise, and high hopes were cherished concerning him as an able and zealous defender of the ancient faith. His elevation to membership in the Sanhedrin council placed him in a position of power.

Saul had taken a prominent part in the trial and conviction of Stephen, and the striking evidences of God's presence with the martyr had led Saul to doubt the righteousness of the cause he had espoused against the followers of Jesus. His mind was deeply stirred. In his perplexity he appealed to those in whose wisdom and judgment he had full confidence. The arguments of the priests and rulers finally convinced him that Stephen was a blasphemer, that the Christ whom the martyred disciple had preached was an impostor, and that those ministering in holy office must be right.

Not without severe trial did Saul come to this conclusion. But in the end his education and prejudices, his respect for his former teachers, and his pride of popularity braced him to rebel against the voice of conscience and the grace of God. And having fully decided that the priests and scribes were right, Saul became very bitter in his opposition to the doctrines taught by the disciples of Jesus. His activity in causing holy men and women to be dragged before tribunals, where some were condemned to imprisonment and some even to death, solely because of their faith in Jesus, brought sadness and gloom to the newly organized church, and caused many to seek safety in flight.

Those who were driven from Jerusalem by this persecution "went everywhere preaching the word." Acts 8:4. Among the cities to which they went was Damascus, where the new faith gained many converts.

The priests and rulers had hoped that by vigilant effort and stern persecution the heresy might be suppressed. Now they felt that they must carry forward in other places the decided measures taken in Jerusalem against the new teaching. For the special work that they desired to have done at Damascus, Saul offered his services. "Breathing out threatenings and slaughter against the disciples of the Lord," he "went unto the high priest, and desired of him letters to Damascus to the synagogues, that if he found any of this way, whether they were men or women, he might bring them bound unto Jerusalem." Thus "with authority and commission from the chief priests" (Acts 26:12), Saul of Tarsus, in the strength and vigor of manhood, and fired with mistaken zeal, set out on that memorable journey, the strange occurrences of which were to change the whole current of his life.

On the last day of the journey, "at midday," as the weary travelers neared Damascus, they came within full view of broad stretches of fertile lands, beautiful gardens, and fruitful orchards, watered by cool streams from the surrounding mountains. After the long journey over desolate wastes such scenes were refreshing indeed. While Saul, with his companions, gazed with admiration on the fruitful plain and the fair city below, "suddenly," as he afterward declared, there shone "round about me and them which journeyed with me" "a light from heaven, above the brightness of the sun" (Acts 26:13), too glorious for mortal eyes to bear. Blinded and bewildered, Saul fell prostrate to the ground.

While the light continued to shine round about them, Saul heard, "a voice speaking . . . in the Hebrew tongue" (Acts 26:14), "saying unto him, Saul, Saul, why persecutest thou Me? And he said, Who art Thou, Lord? And the Lord said, I am Jesus whom thou persecutest: it is hard for thee to kick against the pricks."

Filled with fear, and almost blinded by the intensity of the light, the companions of Saul heard a voice, but saw no man. But Saul understood the words that were spoken, and to him was clearly revealed the One who spoke —even the Son of God. In the glorious Being who stood before him he saw the Crucified One. Upon the soul of the stricken Jew the image of the Saviour's countenance was imprinted forever. The words spoken struck home to his heart with appalling force. Into the darkened chambers of his mind there poured a flood of light, revealing the ignorance and error of his former life and his present need of the enlightenment of the Holy Spirit.

Saul now saw that in persecuting the followers of Jesus he had in reality been doing the work of Satan. He saw that his convictions of right and of his own duty had been based largely on his implicit confidence in the priests and rulers. He had believed them when they told him that the story of the resurrection was an artful fabrication of the disciples. Now that Jesus Himself stood revealed, Saul was convinced of the truthfulness of the claims made by the disciples.

In that hour of heavenly illumination Saul's mind acted with remarkable rapidity. The prophetic records of Holy Writ were opened to his understanding. He saw that the rejection of Jesus by the Jews, His crucifixion, resurrection, and ascension, had been foretold by the prophets and proved Him to be the promised Messiah. Stephen's sermon at the time of his martyrdom was brought forcibly to Saul's mind, and he realized that the martyr had indeed beheld "the glory of God" when he said, "Behold, I see the heavens opened, and the Son of man standing on the right hand of God." Acts 7:55, 56. The priests had pronounced these words blasphemy, but Saul now knew them to be truth.

What a revelation was all this to the persecutor! Now Saul knew for a certainty that the promised Messiah had come to this earth as Jesus of Nazareth and that He had been rejected and crucified by those whom He came to save. He knew also that the Saviour had risen in triumph from the tomb and had ascended into the heavens. In that moment of divine revelation Saul remembered with terror that Stephen, who had borne witness of a crucified and risen Saviour, had been sacrificed by his consent, and that later, through his instrumentality, many other worthy followers of Jesus had met their death by cruel persecution.

The Saviour had spoken to Saul through Stephen, whose clear reasoning could not be controverted. The learned Jew had seen the face of the martyr reflecting the light of Christ's glory—appearing as if "it had been the face of an angel." Acts 6:15. He had witnessed Stephen's forbearance toward his enemies and his forgiveness of them. He had also witnessed the fortitude and cheerful resignation of many whom he had caused to be tormented and afflicted. He had seen some yield up even their lives with rejoicing for the sake of their faith.

All these things had appealed loudly to Saul and at times had thrust upon his mind an almost overwhelming conviction that Jesus was the promised Messiah. At such times he had struggled for entire nights against this conviction, and always he had ended the matter by avowing his belief that Jesus was not the Messiah and that His followers were deluded fanatics.

Now Christ had spoken to Saul with His own voice, saying, "Saul, Saul, why persecutest thou Me?" And the question, "Who art Thou, Lord?" was answered by the same voice, "I am Jesus whom thou persecutest." Christ here identifies Himself with His people. In persecuting the followers of Jesus, Saul had struck directly against the Lord of heaven. In falsely accusing and testifying against them, he had falsely accused and testified against the Saviour of the world.

No doubt entered the mind of Saul that the One who spoke to him was Jesus of Nazareth, the long-looked-for Messiah, the Consolation and Redeemer of Israel. "Trembling and astonished," he inquired, "Lord, what wilt Thou have me to do? And the Lord said unto him, Arise, and go into the city, and it shall be told thee what thou must do."

When the glory was withdrawn, and Saul arose from the ground, he found himself totally deprived of sight. The brightness of Christ's glory had been too intense for his mortal eyes; and when it was removed, the blackness of night settled upon his vision. He believed that this blindness was a punishment from God for his cruel persecution of the followers of Jesus. In terrible darkness he groped about, and his companions, in fear and amazement, "led him by the hand, and brought him into Damascus."

On the morning of that eventful day, Saul had neared Damascus with feelings of self-satisfaction because of the confidence that had been placed in him by the chief priest. To him had been entrusted grave responsibilities. He was commissioned to further the interests of the Jewish religion by checking, if possible, the spread of the new faith in Damascus. He had determined that his mission should be crowned with success and had looked forward with eager anticipation to the experiences that he expected were before him.

But how unlike his anticipations was his entrance into the city? Stricken with blindness, helpless, tortured by remorse, knowing not what further judgment might be in store for him, he sought out the home of the disciple Judas, where, in solitude, he had ample opportunity for reflection and prayer.

For three days Saul was "without sight, and neither did eat nor drink." These days of soul agony were to him as years. Again and again he recalled, with anguish of spirit, the part he had taken in the martyrdom of Stephen. With horror he thought of his guilt in allowing himself to be controlled by the malice and prejudice of the priests and rulers, even when the face of Stephen had been lighted up with the radiance of heaven. In sadness and brokenness of spirit he recounted the many times he had closed his eyes and ears against the most striking evidences and had relentlessly urged on the persecution of the believers in Jesus of Nazareth.

These days of close self-examination and of heart humiliation were spent in lonely seclusion. The believers, having been given warning of the purpose of Saul in coming to Damascus, feared that he might be acting a part, in order the more readily to deceive them; and they held themselves aloof, refusing him their sympathy. He had no desire to appeal to the unconverted Jews, with whom he had planned to unite in persecuting the believers; for he knew that they would not even listen to his story. Thus he seemed to be shut away from all human sympathy. His only hope of help was in a merciful God, and to Him he appealed in brokenness of heart.

During the long hours when Saul was shut in with God alone, he recalled many of the passages of Scripture referring to the first advent of Christ. Carefully he traced down the prophecies, with a memory sharpened by the conviction that had taken possession of his mind. As he reflected on the meaning of these prophecies he was astonished at his former blindness of understanding and at the blindness of the Jews in general, which had led to the rejection of Jesus as the promised Messiah. To his enlightened vision all now seemed plain. He knew that his former prejudice and unbelief had clouded his spiritual perception and had prevented him from discerning in Jesus of Nazareth the Messiah of prophecy.

As Saul yielded himself fully to the convicting power of the Holy Spirit, he saw the mistakes of his life and recognized the far-reaching claims of the law of God. He who had been a proud Pharisee, confident that he was justified by his good works, now bowed before God with the humility and simplicity of a little child, confessing his own unworthiness and pleading the merits of a crucified and risen Saviour. Saul longed to come into full harmony and communion with the Father and the Son; and in the intensity of his desire for pardon and acceptance he offered up fervent supplications to the throne of grace.

The prayers of the penitent Pharisee were not in vain. The inmost thoughts and emotions of his heart were transformed by divine grave; and his nobler faculties were brought into harmony with the eternal purposes of God. Christ and His righteousness became to Saul more than the whole world.

The conversion of Saul is a striking evidence of the miraculous power of the Holy Spirit to convict men of sin. He had verily believed that Jesus of Nazareth had disregarded the law of God and had taught His disciples that it was of no effect. But after his conversion, Saul recognized Jesus as the one who had come into the world for the express purpose of vindicating His Father's law. He was convinced that Jesus was the originator of the entire Jewish system of sacrifices. He saw that at the crucifixion type had met antitype, that

Jesus had fulfilled the Old Testament prophecies concerning the Redeemer of Israel.

In the record of the conversion of Saul important principles are given us, which we should ever bear in mind. Saul was brought directly into the presence of Christ. He was one whom Christ intended for a most important work, one who was to be a "chosen vessel" unto Him; yet the Lord did not at once tell him of the work that had been assigned him. He arrested him in his course and convicted him of sin; but when Saul asked, "What wilt Thou have me to do?" the Saviour placed the inquiring Jew in connection with His church, there to obtain a knowledge of God's will concerning him.

The marvelous light that illumined the darkness of Saul was the work of the Lord; but there was also a work that was to be done for him by the disciples. Christ had performed the work of revelation and conviction; and now the penitent was in a condition to learn from those whom God had ordained to teach His truth.

While Saul in solitude at the house of Judas continued in prayer and supplication, the Lord appeared in vision to "a certain disciple at Damascus, named Ananias," telling him that Saul of Tarsus was praying and in need of help. "Arise, and go into the street which is called Straight," the heavenly messenger said, "and inquire in the house of Judas for one called Saul, of Tarsus: for, behold, he prayeth, and hath seen in a vision a man named Ananias coming in, and putting his hand on him, that he might receive his sight."

Ananias could scarcely credit the words of the angel; for the reports of Saul's bitter persecution of the saints at Jerusalem had spread far and wide. He presumed to expostulate: "Lord, I have heard by many of this man, how much evil he hath done to Thy saints at Jerusalem: and here he hath authority from the chief priests to bind all that call on Thy name." But the command was imperative: "Go thy way: for he is a chosen vessel unto Me, to bear My name before the Gentiles, and kings, and the children of Israel."

Obedient to the direction of the angel, Ananias sought out the man who had but recently breathed out threatenings against all who believed on the name of Jesus; and putting his hands on the head of the penitent sufferer, he said, "Brother Saul, the Lord, even Jesus, that appeared unto thee in the way as thou camest, hath sent me, that thou mightest receive thy sight, and be filled with the Holy Ghost.

"And immediately there fell from his eyes as it had been scales: and he received sight forthwith, and arose, and was baptized."

Thus Jesus gave sanction to the authority of His organized church and placed Saul in connection with His appointed agencies on earth. Christ had now a church as His representative on earth, and to it belonged the work of directing the repentant sinner in the way of life.

Many have an idea that they are responsible to Christ alone for their light and experience, independent of His recognized followers on earth. Jesus is the friend of sinners, and His heart is touched with their woe. He has all power, both in heaven and on earth; but He respects the means that He has ordained for the enlightenment and salvation of men; He directs sinners to the church, which He has made a channel of light to the world.

When, in the midst of his blind error and prejudice, Saul was given a revelation of the Christ whom he was persecuting, he was placed in direct communication with the church, which is the light of the world. In this case Ananias represents Christ, and also represents Christ's ministers upon the earth, who are appointed to act in His stead. In Christ's stead Ananias touches the eyes of Saul, that they may receive sight. In Christ's stead he places his hands upon him, and, as he prays in Christ's name, Saul receives the Holy Ghost. All is done in the name and by the authority of Christ. Christ is the fountain; the church is the channel of communication.

Days of Preparation

After his baptism, Paul broke his fast and remained "certain days with the disciples which were at Damascus. And straightway he preached Christ in the synagogues, that He is the Son of God." Boldly he declared Jesus of Nazareth to be the long-looked-for Messiah, who "died for our sins according to the Scriptures; . . . was buried, and . . . rose again the third day," after which He was seen by the Twelve and by others. "And last of all," Paul added, "He was seen of me also, as of one born out of due time." I Corinthians 15:3, 4, 8. His arguments from prophecy were so conclusive, and his efforts were so manifestly attended by the power of God, that the Jews were confounded and unable to answer him.

The news of Paul's conversion had come to the Jews as a great surprise. He who had journeyed to Damascus "with authority and commission from the chief priests" (Acts 26:12) to apprehend and persecute the believers was now preaching the gospel of a crucified and risen Saviour, strengthening the hands of those who were already its disciples, and continually bringing in new converts to the faith he had once so bitterly opposed.

Paul had formerly been known as a zealous defender of the Jewish religion and an untiring persecutor of the followers of Jesus. Courageous, independent, persevering, his talents and training would have enabled him to serve in almost any capacity. He could reason with extraordinary clearness, and by his withering sarcasm could place an opponent in no enviable light. And now the Jews saw this young man of unusual promise united with those whom he formerly persecuted, and fearlessly preaching in the name of Jesus.

A general slain in battle is lost to his army, but his death gives no additional strength to the enemy. But when a man of prominence joins the opposing force, not only are his services lost, but those to whom he joins himself gain a decided advantage. Saul of Tarsus, on his way to Damascus, might easily have been struck dead by the Lord, and much strength would have been withdrawn from the persecuting power. But God in His providence not only spared Saul's life, but converted him, thus transferring a champion from the side of the enemy to the side of Christ. An eloquent speaker and a severe critic, Paul, with his stern purpose and undaunted courage, possessed the very qualifications needed in the early church.

As Paul preached Christ in Damascus, all who heard him were amazed and said, "Is not this he that destroyed them which called on this name in Jerusalem, and came hither for that intent, that he might bring them bound unto the chief priests?" Paul declared that his change of faith had not been prompted by impulse or fanaticism, but had been brought about by overwhelming evidence. In his presentation of the gospel he sought to make plain the prophecies relating to the first advent of Christ. He showed conclusively that these prophecies had been literally fulfilled in Jesus of Nazareth. The foundation of his faith was the sure word of prophecy.

As Paul continued to appeal to his astonished hearers to "repent and turn to God, and do works meet for repentance" (Acts 26:20), he "increased the more in strength, and confounded the Jews which dwelt at Damascus, proving that this is very Christ." But many hardened their hearts, refusing to respond to his message, and soon their astonishment at his conversion was changed into intense hatred like that which they had shown toward Jesus.

The opposition grew so fierce that Paul was not allowed to continue his labors at Damascus. A messenger from heaven bade him leave for a time, and he "went into Arabia" (Galatians 1:17), where he found a safe retreat.

Here, in the solitude of the desert, Paul had ample opportunity for quiet study and meditation. He calmly reviewed his past experience and made sure work of repentance. He sought God with all his heart, resting not until he knew for a certainty that his repentance was accepted and his sin pardoned. He longed for the assurance that Jesus would be with him in his coming ministry. He emptied his soul of the prejudices and traditions that had hitherto shaped his life, and received instruction from the Source of truth. Jesus communed with him and established him in the faith, bestowing upon him a rich measure of wisdom and grace.

When the mind of man is brought into communion with the mind of God, the finite with the Infinite, the effect on body and mind and soul is beyond estimate. In such communion is found the highest education. It is God's own method of development. "Acquaint now thyself with Him" (Job 22:21), is His message to mankind.

The solemn charge that had been given Paul on the occasion of his interview with Ananias, rested with increasing weight upon his heart. When, in response to the word, "Brother Saul, receive thy sight," Paul had for the first time looked upon the face of this devout man, Ananias under the inspiration of the Holy Spirit said to him: "The God of our fathers hath chosen thee, that thou shouldest know His will, and see that Just One, and shouldest hear the voice of His mouth. For thou shalt be His witness unto all men of what thou hast seen and heard. And now why tarriest thou? arise, and be baptized, and wash away thy sins, calling on the name of the Lord." Acts 22:13-16.

These words were in harmony with the words of Jesus Himself, who, when He arrested Saul on the journey to Damascus, declared: "I have appeared unto thee for this purpose, to make thee a minister and a witness both of these things which thou hast seen, and of those things in the which I will appear unto thee; delivering thee from the people, and from the Gentiles, unto whom now I send thee, to open their eyes, and to turn them from darkness to light, and from the power of Satan unto God, that they may receive forgiveness of sins, and inheritance among them which are sanctified by faith that is in Me." Acts 26:16-18.

As he pondered these things in his heart, Paul understood more and more clearly the meaning of his call "to be an apostle of Jesus Christ through the will of God." 1 Corinthians 1:1. His call had come, "not of men, neither by man, but by Jesus Christ, and God the Father." Galatians 1:1. The greatness of the work before him led him to give much study to the Holy Scriptures, in order that he might preach the gospel "not with wisdom of words, lest the cross of Christ should be made of none effect," "but in demonstration of the Spirit and of power," that the faith of all who heard "should not stand in the wisdom of men, but in the power of God." 1 Corinthians 1:17; 2:4, 5.

As Paul searched the Scriptures, he learned that throughout the ages "not many wise men after the flesh, not many mighty, not many noble, are called: but God hath chosen the foolish things of the world to confound the wise; and God hath chosen the weak things of the world to confound the things which are mighty; and base things of the world, and things which are despised, hath God chosen, yea, and things which are not, to bring to nought things that are: that no flesh should glory in His presence." 1 Corinthians 1:26-29. And so, viewing the wisdom of the world in the light of the cross, Paul "determined not to know anything, . . . save Jesus Christ, and Him crucified." 1 Corinthians 2:2.

Throughout his later ministry, Paul never lost sight of the Source of his wisdom and strength. Hear him, years afterward, still declaring, "For to me to live is Christ." Philippians 1:21. And again: "I count all things but loss for the excellency of the knowledge of Christ Jesus my Lord: for whom I have suffered the loss of all things, . . . that I may win Christ, and be found in Him, not having mine own righteousness, which is of the law, but that which is through the faith of Christ, the righteousness which is of God by faith: that I may know Him, and the power of His resurrection, and the fellowship of His sufferings." Philippians 3:8-10.

From Arabia Paul "returned again unto Damascus" (Galatians 1:17), and "preached boldly . . . in the name of Jesus." Unable to withstand the wisdom of his arguments, "the Jews took counsel to kill him." The gates of the city were diligently guarded day and night to cut off his escape. This crisis led the disciples to seek God earnestly, and finally they "took him by night, and let him down through the wall, lowering him in a basket." Acts 9:25, R.V.

After his escape from Damascus, Paul went to Jerusalem, about three years having passed since his conversion. His chief object in making this visit, as he himself declared afterward, was "to see Peter." Galatians 1:18. Upon arriving in the city where he had once been well known as "Saul the persecutor," "he assayed to join himself to the disciples: but they were all afraid of him, and believed not that he was a disciple." It was difficult for them to believe that so bigoted a Pharisee, and one who had done so much to destroy the church, could become a sincere follower of Jesus. "But Barnabas took him, and brought him to the apostles, and declared unto them how he had seen the Lord in the way, and that He had spoken to him, and how he had preached boldly at Damascus in the name of Jesus."

Upon hearing this, the disciples received him as one of their number. Soon they had abundant evidence as to the genuineness of his Christian experience. The future apostle to the Gentiles was now in the city where many of his former associates lived, and to these Jewish leaders he longed to make plain the prophecies concerning the Messiah, which had been fulfilled by the advent of the Saviour. Paul felt sure that these teachers in Israel, with whom he had once been so well acquainted, were as sincere and honest as he had been. But he had miscalculated the spirit of his Jewish brethren, and in the hope of their speedy conversion he was doomed to bitter disappointment. Although "he spake boldly in the name of the Lord Jesus, and disputed against the Grecians," those who stood at the head of the Jewish church refused to believe, but "went about to slay him." Sorrow filled his heart. He would willingly have yielded up his life if by that means he might bring some to a knowledge of the truth. With shame he thought of the active part he had taken in the martyrdom of Stephen, and now in his anxiety to wipe out the stain resting upon one so falsely accused, he sought to vindicate the truth for which Stephen had given his life.

Burdened in behalf of those who refused to believe, Paul was praying in the temple, as he himself afterward testified, when he fell into a trance; whereupon a heavenly messenger appeared before him and said, "Make haste, and get thee quickly out of Jerusalem: for they will not receive thy testimony concerning Me." Acts 22:18.

Paul was inclined to remain at Jerusalem, where he could face the opposition. To him it seemed an act of cowardice to flee, if by remaining he might be able to convince some of the obstinate Jews of the truth of the gospel message, even if to remain should cost him his life. And so he answered, "Lord, they know that I imprisoned and beat in every synagogue them that believed on Thee: and when the blood of Thy martyr Stephen was shed, I was also standing by, and consenting unto his death, and kept the raiment of them that slew him." But it was not in harmony with the purpose of God that His servant should needlessly expose his life; and the heavenly messenger replied, "Depart: for I will send thee far hence unto the Gentiles." Acts 22:19-21.

Upon learning of this vision, the brethren hastened Paul's secret escape from Jerusalem, for fear of his assassination. "They brought him down to Caesarea, and sent him forth to Tarsus." The departure of Paul suspended for a time the violent opposition of the Jews, and the church had a period of rest, in which many were added to the number of believers.

A Seeker for Truth

In the course of his ministry the apostle Peter visited the believers at Lydda. Here he healed Aeneas, who for eight years had been confined to his bed with palsy. "Aeneas, Jesus Christ maketh thee whole," the apostle said; "arise, and make thy bed." "He arose immediately. And all that dwelt at Lydda and Saron saw him, and turned to the Lord."

At Joppa, which was near Lydda, there lived a woman named Dorcas, whose good deeds had made her greatly beloved. She was a worthy disciple of Jesus, and her life was filled with acts of kindness. She knew who needed comfortable clothing and who needed sympathy, and she freely ministered to the poor and the sorrowful. Her skillful fingers were more active than her tongue.

"And it came to pass in those days, that she was sick, and died." The church in Joppa realized their loss, and hearing that Peter was at Lydda, the believers sent messengers to him, "desiring him that he would not delay to come to them. Then Peter arose and went with them. When he was come, they brought him into the upper chamber: and all the widows stood by him weeping, and showing the coats and garments which Dorcas made, while she was with them." In view of the life of service that Dorcas had lived, it is little wonder that they mourned, that warm teardrops fell upon the inanimate day.

The apostle's heart was touched with sympathy as he beheld their sorrow. Then, directing that the weeping friends be sent from the room, he kneeled down and prayed fervently to God to restore Dorcas to life and health. Turning to the body, he said, "Tabitha, arise. And she opened her eyes: and when she saw Peter, she sat up." Dorcas had been of great service to the church, and God saw fit to bring her back from the land of the enemy, that her skill and energy might still be a blessing to others, and also that by this manifestation of His power the cause of Christ might be strengthened.

It was while Peter was still at Joppa that he was called by God to take the gospel to Cornelius, in Caesarea.

Cornelius was a Roman centurion. He was a man of wealth and noble birth, and his position was one of trust and honor. A heathen by birth, training, and education, through contact with the Jews he had gained a knowledge of God, and he worshiped Him with a true heart, showing the sincerity of his faith by compassion to the poor. He was known far and near for his beneficence, and his righteous life made him of good repute among both Jews and Gentiles. His influence was a blessing to all with whom he came in contact. The inspired record describes him as "a devout man, and one that feared God with all his house, which gave much alms to the people, and prayed to God alway."

Believing in God as the Creator of heaven and earth, Cornelius revered Him, acknowledged His authority, and sought His counsel in all the affairs of life. He was faithful to Jehovah in his home life and in his official duties. He had erected the altar of God in his home, for he dared not attempt to carry out his plans or to bear his responsibilities without the help of God.

Though Cornelius believed the prophecies and was looking for the Messiah to come, he had not a knowledge of the gospel as revealed in the life and death of Christ. He was not a member of the Jewish church and would have been looked upon by the rabbis as a heathen and unclean. But the same Holy Watcher who said of Abraham, "I know him," knew

Cornelius also, and sent a message direct from heaven to him.

The angel appeared to Cornelius while he was at prayer. As the centurion heard himself addressed by name, he was afraid, yet he knew that the messenger had come from God, and he said, "What is it, Lord?" The angel answered, "Thy prayers and thine alms are come up for a memorial before God. And now send men to Joppa, and call for one Simon, whose surname is Peter: he lodgeth with one Simon a tanner, whose house is by the seaside."

The explicitness of these directions, in which was named even the occupation of the man with whom Peter was staying, shows that Heaven is acquainted with the history and business of men in every station of life. God is familiar with the experience and work of the humble laborer, as well as with that of the king upon his throne.

"Send men to Joppa, and call for one Simon." Thus God gave evidence of His regard for the gospel ministry and for His organized church. The angel was not commissioned to tell Cornelius the story of the cross. A man subject, even as the centurion himself, to human frailties and temptations, was to be the one to tell him of the crucified and risen Saviour.

As His representatives among men, God does not choose angels who have never fallen, but human beings, men of like passions with those they seek to save. Christ took humanity that He might reach humanity. A divine-human Saviour was needed to bring salvation to the world. And to men and women has been committed the sacred trust of making known "the unsearchable riches of Christ." Ephesians 3:8.

In His wisdom the Lord brings those who are seeking for truth into touch with fellow beings who know the truth. It is the plan of Heaven that those who have received light shall impart it to those in darkness. Humanity, drawing its efficiency from the great Source of wisdom, is made the instrumentality, the working agency, through which the gospel exercises its transforming power on mind and heart.

Cornelius was gladly obedient to the vision. When the angel had gone, the centurion "called two of his household servants, and a devout soldier of them that waited on him continually; and when he had declared all these things unto them, he sent them to Joppa."

The angel, after his interview with Cornelius, went to Peter, in Joppa. At the time, Peter was praying upon the housetop of his lodging, and we read that he "became very hungry, and would have eaten: but while they made ready, he fell into a trance." It was not for physical food alone that Peter hungered. As from the housetop he viewed the city of Joppa and the surrounding country be hungered for the salvation of his countrymen. He had an intense desire to point out to them from the Scriptures the prophecies relating to the sufferings and death of Christ.

In the vision Peter "saw heaven opened, and a certain vessel descending unto them, as it had been a great sheet knit at the four corners, and let down to the earth: wherein were all manner of four-footed beasts of the earth, and wild beasts, and creeping things, and fowls of the air. And there came a voice to him, Rise, Peter; kill, and eat. But Peter said, Not so, Lord; for I have never eaten anything that is common or unclean. And the voice spake unto him again the second time, What God hath cleansed, that call not thou common. This was done thrice: and the vessel was received up again into heaven."

This vision conveyed to Peter both reproof and instruction. It revealed to him the purpose of God—that by the death of Christ the Gentiles should be made fellow heirs with the Jews to the blessings of salvation. As yet none of the disciples had preached the gospel to the Gentiles. In their minds the middle wall of partition, broken down by the death of Christ, still existed, and their labors had been confined to the Jews, for they had looked upon the Gentiles as excluded from the blessings of the gospel. Now the Lord was seeking to teach Peter the world-wide extent of the divine plan.

Many of the Gentiles had been interested listeners to the preaching of Peter and the other apostles, and many of the Greek Jews had become believers in Christ, but the conversion of Cornelius was to be the first of importance among the Gentiles.

The time had come for an entirely new phase of work to be entered upon by the church of Christ. The door that many of the Jewish converts had closed against the Gentiles was now to be thrown open. And the Gentiles who accepted the gospel were to be regarded as on an equality with the Jewish disciples, without the necessity of observing the rite of circumcision.

How carefully the Lord worked to overcome the prejudice against the Gentiles that had been so firmly fixed in Peter's mind by his Jewish training! By the vision of the sheet and its contents He sought to divest the apostle's mind of this prejudice and to teach the important truth that in heaven there is no respect of persons; that Jew and Gentile are alike precious in God's sight; that through Christ the heathen may be made partakers of the blessings and privileges of the gospel.

While Peter was meditating on the meaning of the vision, the men sent from Cornelius arrived in Joppa and stood before the gate of his lodginghouse. Then the Spirit said to him, "Behold, three men seek thee. Arise therefore, and get thee down, and go with them, doubting nothing: for I have sent them."

To Peter this was a trying command, and it was with reluctance at every step that he undertook the duty laid upon him; but he dared not disobey. He "went down to the men which were sent unto him from Cornelius; and said, Behold, I am he whom ye seek: what is the cause wherefore ye are come?" They told him of their singular errand, saying, "Cornelius the centurion, a just man, and one that feareth God, and of good report among all the nation of the Jews, was warned from God by a holy angel to send for thee into his house, and to hear words of thee."

In obedience to the directions just received from God, the apostle promised to go with them. On the following morning he set out for Caesarea, accompanied by six of his brethren.

These were to be witnesses of all that he should say or do while visiting the Gentiles, for Peter knew that he would be called to account for so direct a violation of the Jewish teachings.

As Peter entered the house of the Gentile, Cornelius did not salute him as an ordinary visitor, but as one honored of Heaven and sent to him by God. It is an Eastern custom to bow before a prince or other high dignitary and for children to bow before their parents; but Cornelius, overwhelmed with reverence for the one sent by God to teach him, fell at the apostle's feet and worshiped him. Peter was horror-stricken, and he lifted the centurion up, saying, "Stand up; I myself also am a man."

While the messengers of Cornelius had been gone upon their errand, the centurion "had called together his kinsmen and near friends," that they as well as he might hear the preaching of the gospel. When Peter arrived, he found a large company eagerly waiting to listen to his words.

To those assembled, Peter spoke first of the custom of the Jews, saying that it was looked upon as unlawful for Jews to mingle socially with the Gentiles, that to do this involved ceremonial defilement. "Ye know," he said, "how that it is an unlawful thing for a man that is a Jew to keep company, or come unto one of another nation; but God hath showed me that I should not call any man common or unclean. Therefore came I unto you without gainsaying, as soon as I was sent for: I ask therefore for what intent ye have sent for me?"

Cornelius then related his experience and the words of the angel, saying in conclusion, "Immediately therefore I sent to thee; and thou hast well done that thou art come. Now therefore are we all here present before God, to hear all things that are commanded thee of God."

Peter said, "Of a truth I perceive that God is no respecter of persons: but in every nation he that feareth Him, and worketh righteousness, is accepted with Him."

Then to that company of attentive hearers the apostle preached Christ—His life, His miracles, His betrayal and crucifixion, His resurrection and ascension, and His work in heaven as man's representative and advocate. As Peter pointed those present to Jesus as the sinner's only hope, he himself understood more fully the meaning of the vision he had seen, and his heart glowed with the spirit of the truth that he was presenting.

Suddenly the discourse was interrupted by the descent of the Holy Spirit. "While Peter yet spake these words, the Holy Ghost fell on all them which heard the world. And they of the circumcision which believed were astonished, as many as came with Peter, because that on the Gentiles also was poured out the gift of the Holy Ghost. For they heard them speak with tongues, and magnify God.

"Then answered Peter, Can any man forbid water, that these should not be baptized, which have received the Holy Ghost as well as we? And he commanded them to be baptized in the name of the Lord."

Thus was the gospel brought to those who had been strangers and foreigners, making them fellow citizens with the saints, and members of the household of God. The conversion of Cornelius and his household was but the first fruits of a harvest to be gathered in. From this household a wide-spread work of grace was carried on in that heathen city.

Today God is seeking for souls among the high as well as the lowly. There are many like Cornelius, men whom the Lord desires to connect with His work in the world. Their sympathies are with the Lord's people, but the ties that bind them to the world hold them firmly. It requires moral courage for them to take their position for Christ. Special efforts should be made for these souls, who are in so great danger, because of their responsibilities and associations.

God calls for earnest, humble workers, who will carry the gospel to the higher class. There are miracles to be wrought in genuine conversions,—miracles that are not now discerned. The greatest men of this earth are not beyond the power of a wonder-working God. If those who are workers together with Him will be men of opportunity, doing their duty bravely and faithfully, God will convert men who occupy responsible positions, men of intellect and influence. Through the power of the Holy Spirit many will accept the divine principles. Converted to the truth, they will become agencies in the hand of God to communicate the light. They will have a special burden for other souls of this neglected class. Time and money will be consecrated to the work of the Lord, and new efficiency and power will be added to the church.

Because Cornelius was living in obedience to all the instruction he had received, God so ordered events that he was given more truth. A messenger from the courts of heaven was sent to the Roman officer and to Peter in order that Cornelius might be brought into touch with one who could lead him into greater light.

There are in our world many who are nearer the kingdom of God than we suppose. In this dark world of sin the Lord has many precious jewels, to whom He will guide His messengers. Everywhere there are those who will take their stand for Christ. Many will prize the wisdom of God above any earthly advantage, and will become faithful light bearers. Constrained by the love of Christ, they will constrain others to come to Him.

When the brethren in Judea heard that Peter had gone to the house of a Gentile and preached to those assembled, they were surprised and offended. They feared that such a course, which looked to them presumptuous, would have the effect of counteracting his own teaching. When they next saw Peter they met him with severe censure, saying, "Thou wentest in to men uncircumcised, and didst eat with them."

Peter laid the whole matter before them. He related his experience in regard to the vision and pleaded that it admonished him to observe no longer the ceremonial distinction of circumcision and uncircumcision, nor to look upon the Gentiles as unclean. He told them of the command given him to go to the Gentiles, of the coming of the messengers, of his journey to Caesarea, and of the meeting with Cornelius. He recounted the substance of his interview with the centurion, in which the latter had told him of the vision by which he had been directed to send for Peter.

"As I began to speak," he said, in relating his experience, "the Holy Ghost fell on them, as on us at the beginning. Then remembered I the word of the Lord, how that He said, John indeed baptized with water; but ye shall be baptized with the Holy Ghost. Forasmuch then as God gave them the like gift as He did unto us, who believed on the Lord Jesus Christ; what was I, that I could withstand God?"

On hearing this account, the brethren were silenced. Convinced that Peter's course was in direct fulfillment of the plan of God, and that their prejudices and exclusiveness were utterly contrary to the spirit of the gospel, they glorified God, saying, "Then hath God also to the Gentiles granted repentance unto life."

Thus, without controversy, prejudice was broken down, the exclusiveness established by the custom of ages was abandoned, and the way was opened for the gospel to be proclaimed to the Gentiles.

Delivered From Prison

"Now about that time Herod the king stretched forth his hands to vex certain of the church." The government of Judea was then in the hands of Herod Agrippa, subject to Claudius, the Roman emperor. Herod also held the position of tetrarch of Galilee. He was professedly a proselyte to the Jewish faith, and apparently very zealous in carrying out the ceremonies of the Jewish law. Desirous of obtaining the favor of the Jews, hoping thus to make secure his offices and honors, he proceeded to carry out their desires by persecuting the church of Christ, spoiling the houses and goods of the believers, and imprisoning the leading members of the church. He cast James, the brother of John, into prison, and sent an executioner to kill him with the sword, as another Herod had caused the prophet John to be beheaded. Seeing that the Jews were well pleased with these efforts, he imprisoned Peter also.

It was during the Passover that these cruelties were practiced. While the Jews were celebrating their deliverance from Egypt and pretending great zeal for the law of God, they were at the same time transgressing every principle of that law by persecuting and murdering the believers in Christ.

The death of James caused great grief and consternation among the believers. When Peter also was imprisoned, the entire church engaged in fasting and prayer.

Herod's act in putting James to death was applauded by the Jews, though some complained of the private manner in which it was accomplished, maintaining that a public execution would have more thoroughly intimidated the believers and those sympathizing with them. Herod therefore held Peter in custody, meaning still further to gratify the Jews by the public spectacle of his death. But it was suggested that it would not be safe to bring the veteran apostle out for execution before all the people then assembled in Jerusalem.

It was feared that the sight of him being led out to die might excite the pity of the multitude.

The priests and elders also feared lest Peter might make one of those powerful appeals which had frequently aroused the people to study the life and character of Jesus—appeals which they, with all their arguments, had been unable to controvert. Peter's zeal in advocating the cause of Christ had led many to take their stand for the gospel, and the rulers feared that should he be given an opportunity to defend his faith in the presence of the multitude who had come to the city to worship, his release would be demanded at the hands of the king.

While, upon various pretexts, the execution of Peter was being delayed until after the Passover, the members of the church had time for deep searching of heart and earnest prayer. They prayed without ceasing for Peter, for they felt that he could not be spared from the cause. They realized that they had reached a place where, without the special help of God, the church of Christ would be destroyed.

Meanwhile worshipers from every nation sought the temple which had been dedicated to the worship of God. Glittering with gold and precious stones, it was a vision of beauty and grandeur. But Jehovah was no longer to be found in that palace of loveliness. Israel as a nation had divorced herself from God. When Christ, near the close of His earthly ministry, looked for the last time upon the interior of the temple, He said, "Behold, your house is left unto you desolate." Matthew 23:38. Hitherto He had called the temple His Father's house; but as the Son of God passed out from those walls, God's presence was withdrawn forever from the temple built to His glory.

The day of Peter's execution was at last appointed, but still the prayers of the believers ascended to heaven; and while all their energies and sympathies were called out in fervent appeals for help, angels of God were watching over the imprisoned apostle.

Remembering the former escape of the apostles from prison, Herod on this occasion had taken double precautions. To prevent all possibility of release, Peter had been put under the charge of sixteen soldiers, who, in different watches, guarded him day and night. In his cell he was placed between two soldiers and was bound by two chains, each chain being fastened to the wrist of one of the soldiers. He was unable to move without their knowledge. With the prison doors securely fastened, and a strong guard before them, all chance of rescue or escape through human means was cut off. But man's extremity is God's opportunity.

Peter was confined in a rock-hewn cell, the doors of which were strongly bolted and barred; and the soldiers on guard were made answerable for the safekeeping of the prisoner. But the bolts and bars and the Roman guard, which effectually cut off all possibility of human aid, were but to make more complete the triumph of God in the deliverance of Peter. Herod was lifting his hand against Omnipotence, and he was to be utterly defeated. By the putting forth of His might, God was about to save the precious life that the Jews were plotting to destroy.

It is the last night before the proposed execution. A mighty angel is sent from heaven to rescue Peter. The strong gates that shut in the saint of God open without the aid of human hands. The angel of the Most High passes through, and the gates close noiselessly behind him. He enters the cell, and there lies Peter, sleeping the peaceful sleep of perfect trust.

The light that surrounds the angel fills the cell, but does not rouse the apostle. Not until he feels the touch of the angel's hand and hears a voice saying, "Arise up quickly," does he awaken sufficiently to see his cell illuminated by the light of heaven, and an angel of great glory standing before him. Mechanically he obeys the word spoken to him, and as in rising he lifts his hands he is dimly conscious that the chains have fallen from his wrists.

Again the voice of the heavenly messenger bids him, "Gird thyself, and bind on thy sandals," and again Peter mechanically obeys, keeping his wondering gaze riveted upon his visitor and believing himself to be dreaming or in a vision. Once more the angel commands, "Cast thy garment about thee, and follow me." He moves toward the door, followed by the usually talkative Peter, now dumb from amazement. They step over the guard and reach the heavily bolted door, which of its own accord swings open and closes again immediately, while the guards within and without are motionless at their post.

The second door, also guarded within and without, is reached. It opens as did the first, with no creaking of hinges or rattling of iron bolts. They pass through, and it closes again as noiselessly. In the same way they pass through the third gateway and find themselves in the open street. No word is spoken; there is no sound of footsteps. The angel glides on in front, encircled by a light of dazzling brightness, and Peter, bewildered, and still believing himself to be in a dream, follows his deliverer. Thus they pass on through one street, and then, the mission of the angel being accomplished, he suddenly disappears.

The heavenly light faded away, and Peter felt himself to be in profound darkness; but as his eyes became accustomed to the darkness, it gradually seemed to lessen, and he found himself alone in the silent street, with the cool night air blowing upon his brow. He now realized that he was free, in a familiar part of the city; he recognized the place as one that he had often frequented and had expected to pass on the morrow for the last time.

He tried to recall the events of the past few moments. He remembered falling asleep, bound between two soldiers, with his sandals and outer garments removed. He examined his person and found himself fully dressed and girded. His wrists, swollen from wearing the cruel irons, were free from the manacles. He realized that his freedom was no delusion, no dream or vision, but a blessed reality. On the morrow he was to have been led forth to die; but, lo, an angel had delivered him from prison and from death. "And when Peter was come to himself, he said, Now I know of a surety, that the Lord hath sent His angel, and hath delivered me out of the hand of Herod, and from all the expectation of the people of the Jews."

The apostle made his way at once to the house where his brethren were assembled and where they were at that moment engaged in earnest prayer for him. "As Peter knocked at the door of the gate, a damsel came to hearken, named Rhoda. And when she knew Peter's voice, she opened not the gate for gladness, but ran in, and told how Peter stood before the gate. And they said unto her, Thou art mad. But she constantly affirmed that it was even so. Then said they, It is his angel."

"But Peter continued knocking: and when they had opened the door, and saw him, they were astonished. But he, beckoning unto them with the hand to hold their peace, declared unto them how the Lord had brought him out of the prison." And Peter "departed, and went into another place." Joy and praise filled the hearts of the believers, because God had heard and answered their prayers and had delivered Peter from the hands of Herod.

In the morning a large concourse of people gathered to witness the execution of the apostle. Herod sent officers to the prison for Peter, who was to be brought with a great display of arms and guards in order not only to ensure against his escape, but to intimidate all sympathizers and to show the power of the king.

When the keepers before the door found that Peter had escaped, they were seized with terror. It had been expressly stated that their lives would be required for the life of their charge, and because of this they had been especially vigilant. When the officers came for Peter, the soldiers were still at the door of the prison, the bolts and bars were still fast, the chains were still secured to the wrists of the two soldiers; but the prisoner was gone.

When the report of Peter's escape was brought to Herod, he was exasperated and enraged. Charging the prison guard with unfaithfulness, he ordered them to be put to death. Herod knew that no human power had rescued Peter, but he was determined not to acknowledge that a divine power had frustrated his design, and he set himself in bold defiance against God.

Not long after Peter's deliverance from prison, Herod went to Caesarea. While there he made a great festival designed to excite the admiration and gain the applause of the people. This festival was attended by pleasure lovers from all quarters, and there was much feasting and wine drinking. With great pomp and ceremony Herod appeared before the people and addressed them in an eloquent oration. Clad in a robe sparkling with silver and gold, which caught the rays of the sun in its glittering folds and dazzled the eyes of the beholders, he was a gorgeous figure. The majesty of his appearance and the force of his well-chosen language swayed the assembly with a mighty power. Their senses already perverted by feasting and wine drinking, they were dazzled by Herod's decorations and charmed by his deportment and oratory; and wild with enthusiasm they showered adulation upon him, declaring that no mortal could present such an appearance or command such startling eloquence. They further declared that while they had ever respected him as a ruler, henceforth they should worship him as a god.

Some of those whose voices were now heard glorifying a vile sinner had but a few years before raised the frenzied cry, Away with Jesus! Crucify Him, crucify Him! The Jews had refused to receive Christ, whose garments, coarse and often travel-stained, covered a heart of divine love. Their eyes could not discern, under the humble exterior, the Lord of life and glory, even though Christ's power was revealed before them in works that no mere man could do. But they were ready to worship as a god the haughty king whose splendid garments of silver and gold covered a corrupt, cruel heart.

Herod knew that he deserved none of the praise and homage offered him, yet he accepted the idolatry of the people as his due. His heart bounded with triumph, and a glow of gratified pride overspread his countenance as he heard the shout ascend, "It is the voice of a god, and not of a man."

But suddenly a terrible change came over him. His face became pallid as death and distorted with agony. Great drops of sweat started from his pores. He stood for a moment as if transfixed with pain and terror; then turning his blanched and livid face to his horror-stricken friends, he cried in hollow, despairing tones, He whom you have exalted as a god is stricken with death.

Suffering the most excruciating anguish, he was borne from the scene of revelry and display. A moment before he had been the proud recipient of the praise and worship of that vast throng; now he realized that he was in the hands of a Ruler mightier than himself. Remorse seized him; he remembered his relentless persecution of the followers of Christ; he remembered his cruel command to slay the innocent James, and his design to put to death the apostle Peter; he remembered how in his mortification and disappointed rage he had wreaked an unreasoning vengeance upon the prison guards. He felt that God was now dealing with him, the relentless persecutor. He found no relief from pain of body or anguish of mind, and he expected none.

Herod was acquainted with the law of God, which says, "Thou shalt have no other gods before Me" (Exodus 20:3); and he knew that in accepting the worship of the people he had filled up the measure of his iniquity and brought upon himself the just wrath of Jehovah.

The same angel who had come from the royal courts to rescue Peter, had been the messenger of wrath and judgment to Herod. The angel smote Peter to arouse him from slumber; it was with a different stroke that he smote the wicked king, laying low his pride and bringing upon him the punishment of the Almighty. Herod died in great agony of mind and body, under the retributive judgment of God.

This demonstration of divine justice had a powerful influence upon the people. The tidings that the apostle of Christ had been miraculously delivered from prison and death, while his persecutor had been stricken down by the curse of God, were borne to all lands and became the means of leading many to a belief in Christ.

The experience of Philip, directed by an angel from heaven to go to the place where he met one seeking for truth; of Cornelius, visited by an angel with a message from God; of Peter, in prison and condemned to death, led by an angel forth to safety—all show the closeness of the connection between heaven and earth.

To the worker for God the record of these angel visits should bring strength and courage. Today, as verily as in the days of the apostles, heavenly messengers are passing through the length and breadth of the land, seeking to comfort the sorrowing, to protect the impenitent, to win the hearts of men to Christ. We cannot see them personally; nevertheless they are with us, guiding, directing, protecting.

Heaven is brought near to earth by that mystic ladder, the base of which is firmly planted on the earth, while the topmost round reaches the throne of the Infinite. Angels are constantly ascending and descending this ladder of shining brightness, bearing the prayers of the needy and distressed to the Father above, and bringing blessing and hope, courage and help, to the children of men. These angels of light create a heavenly atmosphere about the soul, lifting us toward the unseen and the eternal. We cannot behold their forms with our natural sight; only by spiritual vision can we discern heavenly things. The spiritual ear alone can hear the harmony of heavenly voices.

"The angel of the Lord encampeth round about them that fear Him, and delivereth them." Psalm 34:7. God commissions His angels to save His chosen ones from calamity, to guard them from "the pestilence that walketh in darkness" and "the destruction that wasteth at noonday." Psalm 91:6. Again and again have angels talked with men as a man speaketh with a friend, and led them to places of security. Again and again have the encouraging words of angels renewed the drooping spirits of the faithful and, carrying their minds above the things of earth, caused them to behold by faith the white robes, the crowns, the palm branches of victory, which overcomers will receive when they surround the great white throne.

It is the work of the angels to come close to the tried, the suffering, the tempted. They labor untiringly in behalf of those for whom Christ died. When sinners are led to give themselves to the Saviour, angels bear the tidings heavenward, and there is great rejoicing among the heavenly host. "Joy shall be in heaven over one sinner that repenteth, more than over ninety and nine just persons, which need no repentance." Luke 15:7. A report is borne to heaven of every successful effort on our part to dispel the darkness and to spread abroad the knowledge of Christ. As the deed is recounted before the Father, joy thrills through all the heavenly host.

The principalities and powers of heaven are watching the warfare which, under apparently discouraging circumstances,

God's servants are carrying on. New conquests are being achieved, new honors won, as the Christians, rallying round the banner of their Redeemer, go forth to fight the good fight of faith. All the heavenly angels are at the service of the humble, believing people of God; and as the Lord's army of workers here below sing their songs of praise, the choir above join with them in ascribing praise to God and to His Son.

We need to understand better than we do the mission of the angels. It would be well to remember that every true child of God has the co-operation of heavenly beings. Invisible armies of light and power attend the meek and lowly ones who believe and claim the promises of God. Cherubim and seraphim, and angels that excel in strength, stand at God's right hand, "all ministering spirits, sent forth to minister for them who shall be heirs of salvation." Hebrews 1:14.

The Gospel Message in Antioch

After the disciples had been driven from Jerusalem by persecution, the gospel message spread rapidly through the regions lying beyond the limits of Palestine; and many small companies of believers were formed in important centers. Some of the disciples "traveled as far as Phenice, and Cyprus, and Antioch, preaching the word." Their labors were usually confined to the Hebrew and Greek Jews, large colonies of whom were at this time to be found in nearly all the cities of the world.

Among the places mentioned where the gospel was gladly received is Antioch, at that time the metropolis of Syria. The extensive commerce carried on from that populous center brought to the city many people of various nationalities. Besides, Antioch was favorably known as a resort for lovers of ease and pleasure, because of its healthful situation, its beautiful surroundings, and the wealth, culture, and refinement to be found there. In the days of the apostles it had become a city of luxury and vice.

The gospel was publicly taught in Antioch by certain disciples from Cyprus and Cyrene, who came "preaching the Lord Jesus." "The hand of the Lord was with them," and their earnest labors were productive of fruit. "A great number believed, and turned unto the Lord."

"Tidings of these things came unto the ears of the church which was in Jerusalem: and they sent forth Barnabas, that he should go as far as Antioch." Upon arrival in his new field of labor, Barnabas saw the work that had already been accomplished by divine grace, and he "was glad, and exhorted them all, that with purpose of heart they would cleave unto the Lord."

The labors of Barnabas in Antioch were richly blessed, and many were added to the number of believers there. As the work developed, Barnabas felt the need of suitable help in order to advance in the opening providences of God, and he went to Tarsus to seek for Paul, who, after his departure from Jerusalem some time before, had been laboring in "the regions of Syria and Cilicia," proclaiming "the faith which once he destroyed." Galatians 1:21, 23. Barnabas was successful in finding Paul and in persuading him to return with him as a companion in ministry.

In the populous city of Antioch, Paul found an excellent field of labor. His learning, wisdom, and zeal exerted a powerful influence over the inhabitants and frequenters of that city of culture; and he proved just the help that Barnabas needed. For a year the two disciples labored unitedly in faithful ministry, bringing to many a saving knowledge of Jesus of Nazareth, the world's Redeemer.

It was in Antioch that the disciples were first called Christians. The name was given them because Christ was the main theme of their preaching, their teaching, and their conversation. Continually they were recounting the incidents that had occurred during the days of His earthly ministry, when His disciples were blessed with His personal presence. Untiringly they dwelt upon His teachings and His miracles of healing. With quivering lips and tearful eyes they spoke of His agony in the garden, His betrayal, trial, and execution, the forbearance and humility with which He had endured the contumely and torture imposed upon Him by His enemies, and the Godlike pity with which He had prayed for those who persecuted Him. His resurrection and ascension, and His work in heaven as the Mediator for fallen man, were topics on which they rejoiced to dwell. Well might the heathen call them Christians, since they preached Christ and addressed their prayers to God through Him.

It was God who gave to them the name of Christian. This is a royal name, given to all who join themselves to Christ. It was of this name that James wrote later, "Do not rich men oppress you, and draw you before the judgment seats? Do not they blaspheme that worthy name by the which ye are called?" James 2:6, 7. And Peter declared, "If any man suffer as a Christian, let him not be ashamed; but let him glorify God on this behalf." "If ye be reproached for the name of Christ, happy are ye; for the spirit of glory and of God resteth upon you." 1 Peter 4:16, 14.

The believers at Antioch realized that God was willing to work in their lives "both to will and to do of His good pleasure." Philippians 2:13. Living, as they were, in the midst of a people who seemed to care but little for the things of eternal value, they sought to arrest the attention of the honest in heart, and to bear positive testimony concerning Him whom they loved and served. In their humble ministry they learned to depend upon the power of the Holy Spirit to make effective the word of life. And so, in the various walks of life, they daily bore testimony of their faith in Christ.

The example of the followers of Christ at Antioch should be an inspiration to every believer living in the great cities of the world today. While it is in the order of God that chosen workers of consecration and talent should be stationed in important centers of population to lead out in public efforts, it is also His purpose that the church members living in these cities shall use their God-given talents in working for souls. There are rich blessings in store for those who surrender fully to the call of God. As such workers endeavor to win souls to Jesus, they will find that many who never could have been reached in any other way are ready to respond to intelligent personal effort.

The cause of God in the earth today is in need of living representatives of Bible truth. The ordained ministers alone are not equal to the task of warning the great cities. God is calling not only upon ministers, but also upon physicians, nurses, colporteurs, Bible workers, and other consecrated laymen of varied talent who have a knowledge of the word of God and who know the power of His grace, to consider the needs of the unwarned cities. Time is rapidly passing, and there is much to be done. Every agency must be set in operation, that present opportunities may be wisely improved.

Paul's labors at Antioch, in association with Barnabas, strengthened him in his conviction that the Lord had called him to do a special work for the Gentile world. At the time of Paul's conversion, the Lord had declared that he was to be made a minister to the Gentiles, "to open their eyes, and to turn them from darkness to light, and from the power of Satan unto God, that they may receive forgiveness of sins, and inheritance among them which are sanctified by faith that is in Me." Acts 26:18. The angel that appeared to Ananias had said of Paul, "He is a chosen vessel unto Me, to bear My name before the Gentiles, and kings, and the children of Israel." Acts 9:15. And Paul himself, later in his Christian experience, while praying in the temple at Jerusalem, had been visited by an angel from heaven, who bade him, "Depart: for I will send thee far hence unto the Gentiles." Acts 22:21.

Thus the Lord had given Paul his commission to enter the broad missionary field of the Gentile world. To prepare him for this extensive and difficult work, God had brought him into close connection with Himself and had opened before his enraptured vision views of the beauty and glory of heaven. To him had been given the ministry of making known "the mystery" which had been "kept secret since the world began" (Romans 16:25),—"the mystery of His will" (Ephesians 1:9), "which in other ages was not made known unto the sons of men, as it is now revealed unto His holy apostles and prophets by the Spirit; that the Gentiles should be fellow heirs, and of the same body, and partakers of His promise in Christ by the gospel: whereof," declares Paul, "I was made a minister. . . . Unto me, who am less than the least of all saints, is this grace given, that I should preach among the Gentiles the unsearchable riches of Christ; and to make all men see what is the fellowship of the mystery, which from the beginning of the world hath been hid in God, who created all things by Jesus Christ: to the intent that now unto the principalities and powers in heavenly places might be known by the church the manifold wisdom of God, according to the eternal purpose which He purposed in Christ Jesus our Lord." Ephesians 3:5-11.

God had abundantly blessed the labors of Paul and Barnabas during the year they remained with the believers in Antioch. But neither of them had as yet been formally ordained to the gospel ministry. They had now reached a point in their Christian experience when God was about to entrust them with the carrying forward of a difficult missionary enterprise, in the prosecution of which they would need every advantage that could be obtained through the agency of the church.

"There were in the church that was at Antioch certain prophets and teachers; as Barnabas, and Simeon that was called Niger, and Lucius of Cyrene, and Manaen, . . . and Saul. As they ministered to the Lord, and fasted, the Holy Ghost said, Separate Me Barnabas and Saul for the work whereunto I have called them." Before being sent forth as missionaries to the heathen world, these apostles were solemnly dedicated to God by fasting and prayer and the laying on of hands. Thus they were authorized by the church, not only to teach the truth, but to perform the rite of baptism and to organize churches, being invested with full ecclesiastical authority.

The Christian church was at this time entering upon an important era. The work of proclaiming the gospel message among the Gentiles was now to be prosecuted with vigor; and as a result the church was to be strengthened by a great ingathering of souls. The apostles who had been appointed to lead out in this work would be exposed to suspicion, prejudice, and jealousy. Their teachings concerning the breaking down of "the middle wall of partition" (Ephesians 2:14) that had so long separated the Jewish and the Gentile world, would naturally subject them to the charge of heresy, and their authority as ministers of the gospel would be questioned by many zealous, believing Jews. God foresaw the difficulties that His servants would be called to meet, and, in order that their work should be above challenge, He instructed the church by revelation to set them apart publicly to the work of the ministry. Their ordination was a public recognition of their divine appointment to bear to the Gentiles the glad tidings of the gospel.

Both Paul and Barnabas had already received their commission from God Himself, and the ceremony of the laying on of hands added no new grace or virtual qualification. It was an acknowledged form of designation to an appointed office and a recognition of one's authority in that office. By it the seal of the church was set upon the work of God.

To the Jew this form was a significant one. When a Jewish father blessed his children, he laid his hands reverently upon their heads. When an animal was devoted to sacrifice, the hand of the one invested with priestly authority was laid upon the head of the victim. And when the ministers of the church of believers in Antioch laid their hands upon Paul and Barnabas, they, by that action, asked God to bestow His blessing upon the chosen apostles in their devotion to the specific work to which they had been appointed.

At a later date the rite of ordination by the laying on of hands was greatly abused; unwarrantable importance was attached to the act, as if a power came at once upon those who received such ordination, which immediately qualified them for any and all ministerial work. But in the setting apart of these two apostles, there is no record indicating that any virtue was imparted by the mere act of laying on of hands. There is only the simple record of their ordination and of the bearing that it had on their future work.

The circumstances connected with the separation of Paul and Barnabas by the Holy Spirit to a definite line of service show clearly that the Lord works through appointed agencies in His organized church. Years before, when the divine purpose concerning Paul was first revealed to him by the Saviour Himself, Paul was immediately afterward brought into contact with members of the newly organized church at Damascus. Furthermore, the church at that place was not long left in darkness as to the personal experience of the converted Pharisee. And now, when the divine commission given at that time was to be more fully carried out, the Holy Spirit, again bearing witness concerning Paul as a chosen vessel to bear the gospel to the Gentiles, laid upon the church the work of ordaining him and his fellow laborer. As the leaders of the church in Antioch "ministered to the Lord, and fasted, the Holy Ghost said, Separate Me Barnabas and Saul for the work whereunto I have called them."

God has made His church on the earth a channel of light, and through it He communicates His purposes and His will. He does not give to one of His servants an experience independent of and contrary to the experience of the church itself. Neither does He give one man a knowledge of His will for the entire church while the church—Christ's body —is left in darkness. In His providence He places His servants in close connection with His church in order that they may have less confidence in themselves and greater confidence in others whom He is leading out to advance His work.

There have ever been in the church those who are constantly inclined toward individual independence. They seem unable to realize that independence of spirit is liable to lead the human agent to have too much confidence in himself and to trust in his own judgment rather than to respect the counsel and highly esteem the judgment of his brethren, especially of those in the offices that God has appointed for the leadership of His people. God has invested His church with special authority and power which no one can be justified in disregarding and despising, for he who does this despises the voice of God.

Those who are inclined to regard their individual judgment as supreme are in grave peril. It is Satan's studied effort to separate such ones from those who are channels of light, through whom God has wrought to build up and extend His work in the earth. To neglect or despise those whom God has appointed to bear the responsibilities of leadership in connection with the advancement of the truth, is to reject the means that He has ordained for the help, encouragement, and strength of His people. For any worker in the Lord's cause to pass these by, and to think that his light must come through

no other channel than directly from God, is to place himself in a position where he is liable to be deceived by the enemy and overthrown. The Lord in His wisdom has arranged that by means of the close relationship that should be maintained by all believers, Christian shall be united to Christian and church to church. Thus the human instrumentality will be enabled to co-operate with the divine. Every agency will be subordinate to the Holy Spirit, and all the believers will be united in an organized and well-directed effort to give to the world the glad tidings of the grace of God.

Paul regarded the occasion of his formal ordination as marking the beginning of a new and important epoch in his lifework. It was from this time that he afterward dated the beginning of his apostleship in the Christian church.

While the light of the gospel was shining brightly at Antioch, an important work was continued by the apostles who had remained in Jerusalem. Every year, at the time of the festivals, many Jews from all lands came to Jerusalem to worship at the temple. Some of these pilgrims were men of fervent piety and earnest students of the prophecies. They were looking and longing for the advent of the promised Messiah, the hope of Israel. While Jerusalem was filled with these strangers, the apostles preached Christ with unflinching courage, though they knew that in so doing they were placing their lives in constant jeopardy. The Spirit of God set its seal upon their labors; many converts to the faith were made; and these, returning to their homes in different parts of the world, scattered the seeds of truth through all nations and among all classes of society.

Prominent among the apostles who engaged in this work were Peter, James, and John, who felt confident that God had appointed them to preach Christ among their countrymen at home. Faithfully and wisely they labored, testifying of the things they had seen and heard, and appealing to "a more sure word of prophecy" (2 Peter 1:19), in an effort to persuade "the house of Israel. . . that God hath made that same Jesus, whom" the Jews "crucified, both Lord and Christ" (Acts 2:36).

Heralds of the Gospel

"Sent forth by the Holy Ghost," Paul and Barnabas, after their ordination by the brethren in Antioch, "departed unto Seleucia; and from thence they sailed to Cyprus." Thus the apostles began their first missionary journey.

Cyprus was one of the places to which the believers had fled from Jerusalem because of the persecution following the death of Stephen. It was from Cyprus that certain men had journeyed to Antioch, "preaching the Lord Jesus." Acts 11:20. Barnabas himself was "of the country of Cyprus" (Acts 4:36); and now he and Paul, accompanied by John Mark, a kinsman of Barnabas, visited this island field.

Mark's mother was a convert to the Christian religion, and her home at Jerusalem was an asylum for the disciples. There they were always sure of a welcome and a season of rest. It was during one of these visits of the apostles to his mother's home, that Mark proposed to Paul and Barnabas that he should accompany them on their missionary tour. He felt the favor of God in his heart and longed to devote himself entirely to the work of the gospel ministry.

Arriving at Salamis, the apostles "preached the word of God in the synagogues of the Jews. . . . And when they had gone through the isle unto Paphos, they found a certain sorcerer, a false prophet, a Jew, whose name was Bar-Jesus: which was with the deputy of the country, Sergius Paulus, a prudent man; who called for Barnabas and Saul, and desired to hear the word of God. But Elymas the sorcerer (for so is his name by interpretation) withstood them, seeking to turn away the deputy from the faith."

Not without a struggle does Satan allow the kingdom of God to be built up in the earth. The forces of evil are engaged in unceasing warfare against the agencies appointed for the spread of the gospel, and these powers of darkness are especially active when the truth is proclaimed before men of repute and sterling integrity. Thus it was when Sergius Paulus, the deputy of Cyprus, was listening to the gospel message. The deputy had sent for the apostles, that he might be instructed in the message they had come to bear, and now the forces of evil, working through the sorcerer Elymas, sought with their baleful suggestions to turn him from the faith and so thwart the purpose of God.

Thus the fallen foe ever works to keep in his ranks men of influence who, if converted, might render effective service in God's cause. But the faithful gospel worker need not fear defeat at the hand of the enemy; for it is his privilege to be endued with power from above to withstand every satanic influence.

Although sorely beset by Satan, Paul had the courage to rebuke the one through whom the enemy was working. "Filled with the Holy Ghost," the apostle "set his eyes on him, and said, O full of all subtlety and all mischief, thou child of the devil, thou enemy of all righteousness, wilt thou not cease to pervert the right ways of the Lord? And now, behold, the hand of the Lord is upon thee, and thou shalt be blind, not seeing the sun for a season. And immediately there fell on him a mist and a darkness; and he went about seeking some to lead him by the hand. Then the deputy, when he saw what was done, believed, being astonished at the doctrine of the Lord."

The sorcerer had closed his eyes to the evidences of gospel truth, and the Lord, in righteous anger, caused his natural eyes to be closed, shutting out from him the light of day. This blindness was not permanent, but only for a season, that he might be warned to repent and seek pardon of the God whom he had so grievously offended. The confusion into which he was thus brought made of no effect his subtle arts against the doctrine of Christ. The fact that he was obliged to grope about in blindness proved to all that the miracles which the apostles had performed, and which Elymas had denounced as sleight of hand, were wrought by the power of God. The deputy, convinced of the truth of the doctrine taught by the apostles, accepted the gospel.

Elymas was not a man of education, yet he was peculiarly fitted to do the work of Satan. Those who preach the truth of God will meet the wily foe in many different forms. Sometimes it will be in the person of learned, but more often of ignorant, men, whom Satan has trained to be successful instruments to deceive souls. It is the duty of the minister of Christ to stand faithful at his post, in the fear of God and in the power of His might. Thus he may put to confusion the hosts of Satan and may triumph in the name of the Lord.

Paul and his company continued their journey, going to Perga, in Pamphylia. Their way was toilsome; they encountered hardships and privations, and were beset with dangers on every side. In the towns and cities through which they passed, and along the lonely highways, they were surrounded by dangers seen and unseen. But Paul and Barnabas had learned to trust God's power to deliver. Their hearts were filled with fervent love for perishing souls. As faithful shepherds in search of the lost sheep, they gave no thought to their own ease and convenience. Forgetful of self, they faltered not when weary, hungry, and cold. They had in view but one object—the salvation of those who had wandered far from the fold.

It was here that Mark, overwhelmed with fear and discouragement, wavered for a time in his purpose to give himself wholeheartedly to the Lord's work. Unused to hardships, he was disheartened by the perils and privations of the way. He had labored with success under favorable circumstances; but now, amidst the opposition and perils that so often beset the pioneer worker, he failed to endure hardness as a good soldier of the cross. He had yet to learn to face danger and persecution and adversity with a brave heart. As the apostles advanced, and still greater difficulties were apprehended, Mark was intimidated and, losing all courage, refused to go farther and returned to Jerusalem.

This desertion caused Paul to judge Mark unfavorably, and even severely, for a time. Barnabas, on the other hand, was inclined to excuse him because of his inexperience. He felt anxious that Mark should not abandon the ministry, for he saw in him qualifications that would fit him to be a useful worker for Christ. In after years his solicitude in Mark's behalf was richly rewarded, for the young man gave himself unreservedly to the Lord and to the work of proclaiming the gospel message in difficult fields. Under the blessing of God, and the wise training of Barnabas, he developed into a valuable worker.

Paul was afterward reconciled to Mark and received him as a fellow laborer. He also recommended him to the Colossians as one who was a fellow worker "unto the kingdom of God," and "a comfort unto me." Colossians 4:11. Again, not long before his own death, he spoke of Mark as "profitable" to him "for the ministry." 2 Timothy 4:11.

After the departure of Mark, Paul and Barnabas visited Antioch in Pisidia and on the Sabbath day went into the Jewish synagogue and sat down. "After the reading of the law and the prophets the rulers of the synagogue sent unto them, saying, Ye men and brethren, if ye have any word of exhortation for the people, say on." Being thus invited to speak, "Paul stood up, and beckoning with his hand said, Men of Israel, and ye that fear God, give audience." Then followed a wonderful discourse. He proceeded to give a history of the manner in which the Lord had dealt with the Jews from the time of their deliverance from Egyptian bondage, and how a Saviour had been promised, of the seed of David, and he boldly declared that "of this man's seed hath God according to His promise raised unto Israel a Saviour, Jesus: when John had first preached before His coming the baptism of repentance to all the people of Israel. And as John fulfilled his course, he said, Whom think ye that I am? I am not He. But, behold, there cometh One after me, whose shoes of His feet I am not worthy to loose." Thus with power he preached Jesus as the Saviour of men, the Messiah of prophecy.

Having made this declaration, Paul said, "Men and brethren, children of the stock of Abraham, and whosoever among you feareth God, to you is the word of this salvation sent. For they that dwell at Jerusalem, and their rulers, because they knew Him not, nor yet the voices of the prophets which are read every Sabbath day, they have fulfilled them in condemning Him."

Paul did not hesitate to speak the plain truth concerning the rejection of the Saviour by the Jewish leaders. "Though they found no cause of death in Him," the apostle declared, "yet desired they Pilate that He should be slain. And when they had fulfilled all that was written of Him, they took Him down from the tree, and laid Him in a sepulcher. But God raised Him from the dead: and He was seen many days of them which came up with Him from Galilee to Jerusalem, who are His witnesses unto the people."

"We declare unto you glad tidings," the apostle continued, "how that the promise which was made unto the fathers, God hath fulfilled the same unto us their children, in that He hath raised up Jesus again; as it is also written in the second psalm, Thou art My Son, this day have I begotten Thee. And as concerning that He raised Him up from the dead, now no more to return to corruption, He said on this wise, I will give you the sure mercies of David. Wherefore He saith also in another psalm, Thou shalt not suffer Thine Holy One to see corruption. For David, after he had served his own generation by the will of God, fell on sleep, and was laid unto his fathers, and saw corruption: but He, whom God raised again, saw no corruption."

And now, having spoken plainly of the fulfillment of familiar prophecies concerning the Messiah, Paul preached unto them repentance and the remission of sin through the merits of Jesus their Saviour. "Be it known unto you," he said, "that through this Man is preached unto you the forgiveness of sins: and by Him all that believe are justified from all things, from which ye could not be justified by the law of Moses."

The Spirit of God accompanied the words that were spoken, and hearts were touched. The apostle's appeal to Old Testament prophecies, and his declaration that these had been fulfilled in the ministry of Jesus of Nazareth, carried conviction to many a soul longing for the advent of the promised Messiah. And the speaker's words of assurance that the "glad tidings" of salvation were for Jew and Gentile alike, brought hope and joy to those who had not been numbered among the children of Abraham according to the flesh.

"When the Jews were gone out of the synagogue, the Gentiles besought that these words might be preached to them the next Sabbath." The congregation having finally broken up, "many of the Jews and religious proselytes," who had accepted the glad tidings borne to them that day, "followed Paul and Barnabas: who, speaking to them, persuaded them to continue in the grace of God."

The interest aroused in Antioch of Pisidia by Paul's discourse brought together on the next Sabbath day, "almost the whole city . . . to hear the word of God. But when the Jews saw the multitudes, they were filled with envy, and spake against those things which were spoken by Paul, contradicting and blaspheming."

"Then Paul and Barnabas waxed bold, and said, It was necessary that the word of God should first have been spoken to you: but seeing ye put it from you, and judge yourselves unworthy of everlasting life, lo, we turn to the Gentiles. For so hath the Lord commanded us, saying, I have set thee to be a light of the Gentiles, that thou shouldest be for salvation unto the ends of the earth."

"When the Gentiles heard this, they were glad, and glorified the word of the Lord: and as many as were ordained to eternal life believed." They rejoiced exceedingly that Christ recognized them as the children of God, and with grateful hearts they listened to the word preached. Those who believed were zealous in communicating the gospel message to others, and thus "the word of the Lord was published throughout all the region."

Centuries before, the pen of inspiration had traced this ingathering of the Gentiles; but those prophetic utterances had been but dimly understood. Hosea had said: "Yet the number of the children of Israel shall be as the sand of the sea, which cannot be measured nor numbered; and it shall come to pass, that in the place where it was said unto them, Ye are not My people, there it shall be said unto them, Ye are the sons of the living God." And again: I will sow her unto Me in the earth; and I will have mercy upon her that had not obtained mercy; and I will say to them which were not My people, Thou art My people; and they shall say, Thou art my God." Hosea 1:10; 2:23.

The Saviour Himself, during His earthly ministry, foretold the spread of the gospel among the Gentiles. In the parable of the vineyard He declared to the impenitent Jews, "The kingdom of God shall be taken from you, and given to a nation bringing forth the fruits thereof." Matthew 21:43. And after His resurrection He commissioned His disciples to go "into all the world" and "teach all nations." They were to leave none unwarned, but were to "preach the gospel to every creature." Matthew 28:19; Mark 16:15.

In turning to the Gentiles in Antioch of Pisidia, Paul and Barnabas did not cease laboring for the Jews elsewhere, wherever there was a favorable opportunity to gain a hearing. Later, in Thessalonica, in Corinth, in Ephesus, and in other important centers, Paul and his companions in labor preached the gospel to both Jews and Gentiles. But their chief energies were henceforth directed toward the building up of the kingdom of God in heathen territory, among peoples who had but little or no knowledge of the true God and of His Son.

The hearts of Paul and his associate workers were drawn out in behalf of those who were "without Christ, being aliens from the commonwealth of Israel, and strangers from the covenants of promise, having no hope, and without God in the world." Through the untiring ministrations of the apostles to the Gentiles, the "strangers and foreigners," who "sometimes were far off," learned that they had been "made nigh by the blood of Christ," and that through faith in His atoning sacrifice they might become "fellow citizens with the saints, and of the household of God." Ephesians 2:12, 13, 19.

Advancing in faith, Paul labored unceasingly for the upbuilding of God's kingdom among those who had been neglected by the teachers in Israel. Constantly he exalted Christ Jesus as "the King of kings, and Lord of lords" (1 Timothy 6:15), and exhorted the believers to be "rooted and built up in Him, and stablished in the faith." Colossians 2:7.

To those who believe, Christ is a sure foundation. Upon this living stone, Jews and Gentiles alike may build. It is broad enough for all and strong enough to sustain the weight and burden of the whole world. This is a fact plainly recognized by Paul himself. In the closing days of his ministry, when addressing a group of Gentile believers who had remained steadfast in their love of the gospel truth, the apostle wrote, "Ye . . .are built upon the foundation of the apostles and prophets, Jesus Christ Himself being the chief cornerstone." Ephesians 2:19, 20.

As the gospel message spread in Pisidia, the unbelieving Jews of Antioch in their blind prejudice "stirred up the devout and honorable women, and the chief men of the city, and raised persecution against Paul and Barnabas, and expelled them" from that district.

The apostles were not discouraged by this treatment; they remembered the words of their Master: "Blessed are ye, when men shall revile you, and persecute you, and shall say all manner of evil against you falsely, for My sake. Rejoice, and be exceeding glad: for great is your reward in heaven: for so persecuted they the prophets which were before you." Matthew 5:11, 12.

The gospel message was advancing, and the apostles had every reason for feeling encouraged. Their labors had been richly blessed among the Pisidians at Antioch, and the believers whom they left to carry forward the work alone for a time, "were filled with joy, and with the Holy Ghost."

Preaching Among the Heathen

From Antioch in Pisidia, Paul and Barnabas went to Iconium. In this place, as at Antioch, they began their labors in the synagogue of their own people. They met with marked success; "a great multitude both of the Jews and also of the Greeks believed." But in Iconium, as in other places where the apostles labored, "the unbelieving Jews stirred up the Gentiles, and made their minds evil affected against the brethren."

The apostles, however, were not turned aside from their mission, for many were accepting the gospel of Christ. In the face of opposition, envy, and prejudice they went on with their work, "speaking boldly in the Lord," and God "gave testimony unto the word of His grace, and granted signs and wonders to be done by their hands." These evidences of divine approval had a powerful influence on those whose minds were open to conviction, and converts to the gospel multiplied.

The increasing popularity of the message borne by the apostles, filled the unbelieving Jews with envy and hatred, and they determined to stop the labors of Paul and Barnabas at once. By means of false and exaggerated reports they led the authorities to fear that the entire city was in danger of being incited to insurrection. They declared that large numbers were attaching themselves to the apostles and suggested that it was for secret and dangerous designs.

In consequence of these charges the disciples were repeatedly brought before the authorities; but their defense was so clear and sensible, and their statement of what they were teaching so calm and comprehensive, that a strong influence was exerted in their favor. Although the magistrates were prejudiced against them by the false statements they had heard, they dared not condemn them. They could but acknowledge that the teachings of Paul and Barnabas tended to make men virtuous, law-abiding citizens, and that the morals and order of the city would improve if the truths taught by the apostles were accepted.

Through the opposition that the disciples met, the message of truth gained great publicity; the Jews saw that their efforts to thwart the work of the new teachers resulted only in adding greater numbers to the new faith. "The multitude of the city was divided: and part held with the Jews, and part with the apostles."

So enraged were the leaders among the Jews by the turn that matters were taking, that they determined to gain their ends by violence. Arousing the worst passions of the ignorant, noisy mob, they succeeded in creating a tumult, which they attributed to the teaching of the disciples. By this false charge they hoped to gain the help of the magistrates in carrying out their purpose. They determined that the apostles should have no opportunity to vindicate themselves and that the mob should interfere by stoning Paul and Barnabas, thus putting an end to their labors.

Friends of the apostles, though unbelievers, warned them of

the malicious designs of the Jews and urged them not to expose themselves needlessly to the fury of the mob, but to escape for their lives. Paul and Barnabas accordingly departed in secret from Iconium, leaving the believers to carry on the work alone for a time. But they by no means took final leave; they purposed to return after the excitement had abated, and complete the work begun.

In every age and in every land, God's messengers have been called upon to meet bitter opposition from those who deliberately chose to reject the light of heaven. Often, by misrepresentation and falsehood, the enemies of the gospel have seemingly triumphed, closing the doors by which God's messengers might gain access to the people. But these doors cannot remain forever closed, and often, as God's servants have returned after a time to resume their labors, the Lord has wrought mightily in their behalf, enabling them to establish memorials to the glory of His name.

Driven by persecution from Iconium, the apostles went to Lystra and Derbe, in Lycaonia. These towns were inhabited largely by a heathen, superstitious people, but among them were some who were willing to hear and accept the gospel message. In these places and in the surrounding country the apostles decided to labor, hoping to avoid Jewish prejudice and persecution.

In Lystra there was no Jewish synagogue, though a few Jews were living in the town. Many of the inhabitants of Lystra worshiped at a temple dedicated to Jupiter. When Paul and Barnabas appeared in the town and, gathering the Lystrians about them, explained the simple truths of the gospel, many sought to connect these doctrines with their own superstitious belief in the worship of Jupiter.

The apostles endeavored to impart to these idolaters a knowledge of God the Creator and of His Son, the Saviour of the human race. They first directed attention to the wonderful works of God—the sun, the moon, and the stars, the beautiful order of the recurring seasons, the mighty snow-capped mountains, the lofty trees, and other varied wonders of nature, which showed a skill beyond human comprehension. Through these works of the Almighty, the apostles led the minds of the heathen to a contemplation of the great Ruler of the universe.

Having made plain these fundamental truths concerning the Creator, the apostles told the Lystrians of the Son of God, who came from heaven to our world because He loved the children of men. They spoke of His life and ministry, His rejection by those He came to save, His trial and crucifixion, His resurrection, and His ascension to heaven, there to act as man's advocate. Thus, in the Spirit and power of God, Paul and Barnabas preached the gospel in Lystra.

At one time, while Paul was telling the people of Christ's work as a healer of the sick and afflicted, he saw among his hearers a cripple whose eyes were fastened on him and who received and believed his words. Paul's heart went out in sympathy toward the afflicted man, in whom he discerned one who "had faith to be healed." In the presence of the idolatrous assembly Paul commanded the cripple to stand upright on his feet. Heretofore the sufferer had been able to take a sitting posture only, but now he instantly obeyed Paul's command and for the first time in his life stood on his feet. Strength came with this effort of faith, and he who had been a cripple "leaped and walked."

"When the people saw what Paul had done, they lifted up their voices, saying in the speech of Lycaonia, The gods are come down to us in the likeness of men." This statement was in harmony with a tradition of theirs that the gods occasionally visited the earth. Barnabas they called Jupiter, the father of gods, because of his venerable appearance, his dignified bearing, and the mildness and benevolence expressed in his countenance. Paul they believe to be Mercury, "because he was the chief speaker," earnest and active, and eloquent with words of warning and exhortation.

The Lystrians, eager to show their gratitude, prevailed upon the priest of Jupiter to do the apostles honor, and he "brought oxen and garlands unto the gates, and would have done sacrifice with the people." Paul and Barnabas, who had sought retirement and rest, were not aware of these preparations. Soon, however, their attention was attracted by the sound of music and the enthusiastic shouting of a large crowd who had come to the house where they were staying.

When the apostles ascertained the cause of this visit and its attendant excitement, "they rent their clothes, and ran in among the people" in the hope of preventing further proceedings. In a loud, ringing voice, which rose above the shouting of the people, Paul demanded their attention; and as the tumult suddenly ceased, he said: "Sirs, why do ye these things? We also are men of like passions with you, and preach unto you that ye should turn from these vanities unto the living God, which made heaven, and earth, and the sea, and all things that are therein: who in times past suffered all nations to walk in their own ways. Nevertheless He left not Himself without witness, in that He did good, and gave us rain from heaven, and fruitful seasons, filling our hearts with food and gladness."

Notwithstanding the positive denial of the apostles that they were divine, and notwithstanding Paul's endeavors to direct the minds of the people to the true God as the only object worthy of adoration, it was almost impossible to turn the heathen from their intention to offer sacrifice. So firm had been their belief that these men were indeed gods, and so great their enthusiasm, that they were loath to acknowledge their error. The record says that they were "scarce restrained."

The Lystrians reasoned that they had beheld with their own eyes the miraculous power exercised by the apostles. They had seen a cripple who had never before been able to walk, made to rejoice in perfect health and strength. It was only after much persuasion on the part of Paul, and careful explanation regarding the mission of himself and Barnabas as representatives of the God of heaven and of His Son, the great Healer, that the people were persuaded to give up their purpose.

The labors of Paul and Barnabas at Lystra were suddenly checked by the malice of "certain Jews from Antioch and Iconium," who, upon learning of the success of the apostles' work among the Lycaonians, had determined to follow them and persecute them. On arriving at Lystra, these Jews soon succeeded in inspiring the people with the same bitterness of spirit that actuated their own minds. By words of misrepresentation and calumny those who had recently regarded Paul and Barnabas as divine beings were persuaded that in reality the apostles were worse than murderers and were deserving of death.

The disappointment that the Lystrians had suffered in being refused the privilege of offering sacrifice to the apostles, prepared them to turn against Paul and Barnabas with an enthusiasm approaching that with which they had hailed them as gods. Incited by the Jews, they planned to attack the apostles by force. The Jews charged them not to allow Paul an opportunity to speak, alleging that if they were to grant him this privilege, he would bewitch the people.

Soon the murderous designs of the enemies of the gospel were carried out. Yielding to the influence of evil, the Lystrians became possessed with a satanic fury and, seizing Paul, mercilessly stoned him. The apostle thought that his end had come. The martyrdom of Stephen, and the cruel part that he himself had acted upon that occasion, came vividly to his mind. Covered with bruises and faint with pain, he fell to the ground, and the infuriated mob "drew him out of the city, supposing he had been dead."

In this dark and trying hour the company of Lystrian believers, who through the ministry of Paul and Barnabas had been converted to the faith of Jesus, remained loyal and true. The unreasoning opposition and cruel persecution by their enemies served only to confirm the faith of these devoted brethren; and now, in the face of danger and scorn, they showed their loyalty by gathering sorrowfully about the form of him whom they believed to be dead.

What was their surprise when in the midst of their lamentations the apostle suddenly lifted up his head and rose to his feet with the praise of God upon his lips. To the believers this unexpected restoration of God's servant was regarded as a miracle of divine power and seemed to set the signet of Heaven upon their change of belief. They rejoiced with inexpressible gladness and praised God with renewed faith.

Among those who had been converted at Lystra, and who were eyewitnesses of the sufferings of Paul, was one who was afterward to become a prominent worker for Christ and who was to share with the apostle the trials and the joys of pioneer service in difficult fields. This was a young man named Timothy. When Paul was dragged out of the city, this youthful disciple was among the number who took their stand beside his apparently lifeless body and who saw him arise, bruised and covered with blood, but with praises upon his lips because he had been permitted to suffer for the sake of Christ.

The day following the stoning of Paul, the apostles departed for Derbe, where their labors were blessed, and many souls were led to receive Christ as the Saviour. But "when they had preached the gospel to that city, and had taught many," neither Paul nor Barnabas was content to take up work elsewhere without confirming the faith of the converts whom they had been compelled to leave alone for a time in the places where they had recently labored. And so, undaunted by danger, "they returned again to Lystra, and to Iconium, and Antioch, confirming the souls of the disciples, and exhorting them to continue in the faith." Many had accepted the glad tidings of the gospel and had thus exposed themselves to reproach and opposition. These the apostles sought to establish in the faith in order that the work done might abide.

As an important factor in the spiritual growth of the new converts the apostles were careful to surround them with the safeguards of gospel order. Churches were duly organized in all places in Lycaonia and Pisidia where there were believers. Officers were appointed in each church, and proper order and system were established for the conduct of all the affairs pertaining to the spiritual welfare of the believers.

This was in harmony with the gospel plan of uniting in one body all believers in Christ, and this plan Paul was careful to follow throughout his ministry. Those who in any place were by his labor led to accept Christ as the Saviour were at the proper time organized into a church. Even when the believers were but few in number, this was done. The Christians were thus taught to help one another, remembering the promise, "Where two or three are gathered together in My name, there am I in the midst of them." Matthew 18:20.

And Paul did not forget the churches thus established. The care of these churches rested on his mind as an ever-increasing burden. However small a company might be, it was nevertheless the object of his constant solicitude. He watched over the smaller churches tenderly, realizing that they were in need of special care in order that the members might be thoroughly established in the truth and taught to put forth earnest, unselfish efforts for those around them.

In all their missionary endeavors Paul and Barnabas sought to follow Christ's example of willing sacrifice and faithful, earnest labor for souls. Wide-awake, zealous, untiring, they did not consult inclination or personal ease, but with prayerful anxiety and unceasing activity they sowed the seed of truth. And with the sowing of the seed, the apostles were careful to give to all who took their stand for the gospel, practical instruction that was of untold value. This spirit of earnestness and godly fear made upon the minds of the new disciples a lasting impression regarding the importance of the gospel message.

When men of promise and ability were converted, as in the case of Timothy, Paul and Barnabas sought earnestly to show them the necessity of laboring in the vineyard. And when the apostles left for another place, the faith of these men did not fail, but rather increased. They had been faithfully instructed in the way of the Lord, and had been taught how to labor unselfishly, earnestly, perseveringly, for the salvation of their fellow men. This careful training of new converts was an important factor in the remarkable success that attended Paul and Barnabas as they preached the gospel in heathen lands.

The first missionary journey was fast drawing to a close. Commending the newly organized churches to the Lord, the apostles went to Pamphylia, "and when they had preached the word in Perga, they went down into Attalia, and thence sailed to Antioch."

Jew and Gentile

On reaching Antioch in Syria, from which place they had been sent forth on their mission, Paul and Barnabas took advantage of an early opportunity to assemble the believers and rehearse "all that God had done with them, and how He had opened the door of faith unto the Gentiles." Acts 14:27. The church at Antioch was a large and growing one. A center of missionary activity, it was one of the most important of the groups of Christian believers. Its membership was made up of many classes of people from among both Jews and Gentiles.

While the apostles united with the ministers and lay members at Antioch in an earnest effort to win many souls to Christ, certain Jewish believers from Judea "of the sect of the Pharisees" succeeded in introducing a question that soon led to wide-spread controversy in the church and brought consternation to the believing Gentiles. With great assurance these Judaizing teachers asserted that in order to be saved, one must be circumcised and must keep the entire ceremonial law.

Paul and Barnabas met this false doctrine with promptness and opposed the introduction of the subject to the Gentiles. On the other hand, many of the believing Jews of Antioch favored the position of the brethren recently come from Judea.

The Jewish converts generally were not inclined to move as rapidly as the providence of God opened the way. From the result of the apostles' labors among the Gentiles it was evident that the converts among the latter people would far exceed the Jewish converts in number. The Jews feared that if the restrictions and ceremonies of their law were not made obligatory upon the Gentiles as a condition of church fellowship, the national peculiarities of the Jews, which had hitherto kept them distinct from all other people, would finally disappear from among those who received the gospel message.

The Jews had always prided themselves upon their divinely appointed services, and many of those who had been converted to the faith of Christ still felt that since God had once clearly outlined the Hebrew manner of worship, it was improbable that He would ever authorize a change in any of its specifications. They insisted that the Jewish laws and ceremonies should be incorporated into the rites of the Christian religion. They were slow to discern that all the sacrificial offerings had but prefigured the death of the Son of God, in which type met antitype, and after which the rites and ceremonies of the Mosaic dispensation were no longer binding.

Before his conversion Paul had regarded himself as blameless "touching the righteousness which is in the law." Philippians 3:6. But since his change of heart he had gained a clear conception of the mission of the Saviour as the Redeemer of the entire race, Gentile as well as Jew, and had learned the difference between a living faith and a dead formalism. In the light of the gospel the ancient rites and ceremonies committed to Israel had gained a new and deeper significance. That which they shadowed forth had come to pass, and those who were living under the gospel dispensation had been freed from their observance. God's unchangeable law of Ten Commandments, however, Paul still kept in spirit as well as in letter.

In the church at Antioch the consideration of the question of circumcision resulted in much discussion and contention. Finally, the members of the church, fearing that a division among them would be the outcome of continued discussion, decided to send Paul and Barnabas, with some responsible men from the church, to Jerusalem to lay the matter before the apostles and elders. There they were to meet delegates from the different churches and those who had come to Jerusalem to attend the approaching festivals. Meanwhile all controversy was to cease until a final decision should be given in general council. This decision was then to be universally accepted by the different churches throughout the country.

On the way to Jerusalem the apostles visited the believers in the cities through which they passed, and encouraged them by relating their experience in the work of God and the conversion of the Gentiles.

At Jerusalem the delegates from Antioch met the brethren of the various churches, who had gathered for a general meeting, and to them they related the success that had attended their ministry among the Gentiles. They then gave a clear outline of the confusion that had resulted because certain converted Pharisees had gone to Antioch declaring that, in order to be saved, the Gentile converts must be circumcised and keep the law of Moses.

This question was warmly discussed in the assembly. Intimately connected with the question of circumcision were several others demanding careful study. One was the problem as to what attitude should be taken toward the use of meats offered to idols. Many of the Gentile converts were living among ignorant and superstitious people who made frequent sacrifices and offerings to idols. The priests of this heathen worship carried on an extensive merchandise with the offerings brought to them, and the Jews feared that the Gentile converts would bring Christianity into disrepute by purchasing that which had been offered to idols, thereby sanctioning, in some measure, idolatrous customs.

Again, the Gentiles were accustomed to eat the flesh of animals that has been strangled, while the Jews had been divinely instructed that when beasts were killed for food, particular care was to be taken that the blood should flow from the body; otherwise the meat would not be regarded as wholesome. God had given these injunctions to the Jews for the purpose of preserving their health. The Jews regarded it as sinful to use blood as an article of diet. They held that the blood was the life, and that the shedding of blood was in consequence of sin.

The Gentiles, on the contrary, practiced catching the blood that flowed from the sacrificial victim and using it in the preparation of food. The Jews could not believe that they ought to change the customs they had adopted under the special direction of God. Therefore, as things then stood, if Jew and Gentile should attempt to eat at the same table, the former would be shocked and outraged by the latter.

The Gentiles, and especially the Greeks, were extremely licentious, and there was danger that some, unconverted in heart, would make a profession of faith without renouncing their evil practices. The Jewish Christians could not tolerate the immorality that was not even regarded as criminal by the heathen. The Jews therefore held it as highly proper that circumcision and the observance of the ceremonial law should be enjoined on the Gentile converts as a test of their sincerity and devotion. This, they believed, would prevent the addition to the church of those who, adopting the faith without true conversion of heart, might afterward bring reproach upon the cause by immorality and excess.

The various points involved in the settlement of the main question at issue seemed to present before the council insurmountable difficulties. But the Holy Spirit had, in reality, already settled this question, upon the decision of which seemed to depend the prosperity, if not the very existence, of the Christian church.

"When there had been much disputing, Peter rose up, and said unto them, Men and brethren, ye know how that a good while ago God made choice among us, that the Gentiles by my mouth should hear the word of the gospel, and believe." He reasoned that the Holy Spirit had decided the matter under dispute by descending with equal power upon the uncircumcised Gentiles and the circumcised Jews. He recounted his vision, in which God had presented before him a sheet filled with all manner of four-footed beasts and had bidden him kill and eat. When he refused, affirming that he had never eaten that which was common or unclean, the answer had been, "What God hath cleansed, that call not thou common." Acts 10:15.

Peter related the plain interpretation of these words, which was given him almost immediately in his summons to go to the centurion and instruct him in the faith of Christ. This message showed that God was no respecter of persons, but accepted and acknowledged all who feared Him. Peter told of his astonishment when, in speaking the words of truth to those assembled at the home of Cornelius, he witnessed the Holy Spirit taking possession of his hearers, Gentiles as well as Jews. The same light and glory that was reflected upon the circumcised Jews shone also upon the faces of the uncircumcised Gentiles. This was God's warning that Peter was not to regard one as inferior to the other, for the blood of Christ could cleanse from all uncleanness.

Once before, Peter had reasoned with his brethren concerning the conversion of Cornelius and his friends, and his fellowship with them. As he on that occasion related how the Holy Spirit fell on the Gentiles he declared, "Forasmuch then as God gave them the like gift as He did unto us, who believed on the Lord Jesus Christ; what was I, that I could withstand God?" Acts 11:17. Now, with equal fervor and force, he said: "God, which knoweth the hearts, bare them witness, giving them the Holy Ghost, even as He did unto us; and put no difference between us and them, purifying their hearts by faith. Now therefore why tempt ye God, to put a yoke upon the neck of the disciples, which neither our fathers nor we were able to bear?" This yoke was not the law of Ten Commandments, as some who oppose the binding claims of the law assert; Peter here referred to the law of ceremonies, which was made null and void by the crucifixion of Christ.

Peter's address brought the assembly to a point where they could listen with patience to Paul and Barnabas, who related their experience in working for the Gentiles. "All the multitude kept silence, and gave audience to Barnabas and Paul, declaring what miracles and wonders God had wrought among the Gentiles by them."

James also bore his testimony with decision, declaring that it was God's purpose to bestow upon the Gentiles the same privileges and blessings that had been granted to the Jews.

The Holy Spirit saw good not to impose the ceremonial law on the Gentile converts, and the mind of the apostles regarding this matter was as the mind of the Spirit of God. James presided at the council, and his final decision was, "Wherefore my sentence is, that we trouble not them, which from among the Gentiles are turned to God."

This ended the discussion. In this instance we have a refutation of the doctrine held by the Roman Catholic Church that Peter was the head of the church. Those who, as popes, have claimed to be his successors, have no Scriptural foundation for their pretensions. Nothing in the life of Peter gives sanction to the claim that he was elevated above his brethren as the vicegerent of the Most High. If those who are declared to be the successors of Peter had followed his example, they would always have been content to remain on an equality with their brethren.

In this instance James seems to have been chosen as the one to announce the decision arrived at by the council. It was his sentence that the ceremonial law, and especially the ordinance of circumcision, should not be urged upon the Gentiles, or even recommended to them. James sought to impress the minds of his brethren with the fact that, in turning to God, the Gentiles had made a great change in their lives and that much caution should be used not to trouble them with perplexing and doubtful questions of minor importance, lest they be discouraged in following Christ.

The Gentile converts, however, were to give up the customs that were inconsistent with the principles of Christianity. The apostles and elders therefore agreed to instruct the Gentiles by letter to abstain from meats offered to idols, from fornication, from things strangled, and from blood. They were to be urged to keep the commandments and to lead holy lives. They were also to be assured that the men who had declared circumcision to be binding were not authorized to do so by the apostles.

Paul and Barnabas were recommended to them as men who had hazarded their lives for the Lord. Judas and Silas were sent with these apostles to declare to the Gentiles by word of mouth the decision of the council: "It seemed good to the Holy Ghost, and to us, to lay upon you no greater burden than these necessary things; that ye abstain from meats offered to idols, and from blood, and from things strangled, and from fornication: from which if ye keep yourselves, ye shall do well." The four servants of God were sent to Antioch with the epistle and message that was to put an end to all controversy; for it was the voice of the highest authority upon the earth.

The council which decided this case was composed of apostles and teachers who had been prominent in raising up the Jewish and Gentile Christian churches, with chosen delegates from various places. Elders from Jerusalem and deputies from Antioch were present, and the most influential churches were represented. The council moved in accordance with the dictates of enlightened judgment, and with the dignity of a church established by the divine will. As a result of their deliberations they all saw that God Himself had answered the question at issue by bestowing upon the Gentiles the Holy Ghost; and they realized that it was their part to follow the guidance of the Spirit.

The entire body of Christians was not called to vote upon the question. The "apostles and elders," men of influence and judgment, framed and issued the decree, which was thereupon generally accepted by the Christian churches. Not all, however, were pleased with the decision; there was a faction of ambitious and self-confident brethren who disagreed with it. These men assumed to engage in the work on their own responsibility. They indulged in much murmuring and faultfinding, proposing new plans and seeking to pull down the work of the men whom God had ordained to teach the gospel message. From the first the church has had such obstacles to meet and ever will have till the close of time.

Jerusalem was the metropolis of the Jews, and it was there that the greatest exclusiveness and bigotry were found. The Jewish Christians living within sight of the temple naturally allowed their minds to revert to the peculiar privileges of the Jews as a nation. When they saw the Christian church departing from the ceremonies and traditions of Judaism, and perceived that the peculiar sacredness with which the Jewish customs had been invested would soon be lost sight of in the light of the new faith, many grew indignant with Paul as the one who had, in a large measure, caused this change. Even the disciples were not all prepared to accept willingly the decision of the council. Some were zealous for the ceremonial law, and they regarded Paul with disfavor because they thought that his principles in regard to the obligations of the Jewish law were lax.

The broad and far-reaching decisions of the general council brought confidence into the ranks of the Gentile believers, and the cause of God prospered. In Antioch the church was favored with the presence of Judas and Silas, the special messengers who had returned with the apostles from the meeting in Jerusalem. "Being prophets also themselves," Judas and Silas, "exhorted the brethren with many words, and confirmed them." These godly men tarried in Antioch for a time. "Paul also and Barnabas continued in Antioch, teaching and preaching the word of the Lord, with many others also."

When Peter, at a later date, visited Antioch, he won the confidence of many by his prudent conduct toward the Gentile converts. For a time he acted in accordance with the light given from heaven. He so far overcame his natural prejudice as to sit at table with the Gentile converts. But when certain Jews who were zealous for the ceremonial law, came from Jerusalem, Peter injudiciously changed his deportment toward the converts from paganism. A number of the Jews "dissembled likewise with him; insomuch that Barnabas also was carried away with their dissimulation." This revelation of weakness on the part of those who had been respected and loved as leaders, left a most painful impression on the minds of the Gentile believers. The church was threatened with division. But Paul, who saw the subverting influence of the wrong done to the church through the double part acted by Peter, openly rebuked him for thus disguising his true sentiments. In the presence of the church, Paul inquired of Peter, "If thou, being a Jew, livest after the manner of Gentiles, and not as do the Jews, why compellest thou the Gentiles to live as do the Jews?" Galatians 2:13, 14.

Peter saw the error into which he had fallen, and immediately set about repairing the evil that had been wrought, so far as was in his power. God, who knows the end from the beginning, permitted Peter to reveal this weakness of character in order that the tried apostle might see that there was nothing in himself whereof he might boast. Even the best of men, if left to themselves, will err in judgment. God also saw that in time to come some would be so deluded as to claim for Peter and his pretended successors the exalted prerogatives that belong to God alone. And this record of the apostle's weakness was to remain as a proof of his fallibility and of the fact that he stood in no way above the level of the other apostles.

The history of this departure from right principles stands as a solemn warning to men in positions of trust in the cause of God, that they may not fail in integrity, but firmly adhere to principle. The greater the responsibilities placed upon the human agent, and the larger his opportunities to dictate and control, the more harm he is sure to do if he does not carefully follow the way of the Lord and labor in harmony with the decisions arrived at by the general body of believers in united council.

After all Peter's failures; after his fall and restoration, his long course of service, his intimate acquaintance with Christ, his knowledge of the Saviour's straightforward practice of right principles; after all the instruction he had received, all the gifts and knowledge and influence he had gained by preaching and teaching the word—is it not strange that he should dissemble and evade the principles of the gospel through fear of man, or in order to gain esteem? Is it not strange that he should waver in his adherence to right? May God give every man a realization of his helplessness, his inability to steer his own vessel straight and safe into the harbor.

In his ministry, Paul was often compelled to stand alone. He was specially taught of God and dared make no concessions that would involve principle. At times the burden was heavy, but Paul stood firm for the right. He realized that the church must never be brought under the control of human power. The traditions and maxims of men must not take the place of revealed truth. The advance of the gospel message must not be hindered by the prejudices and preferences of men, whatever might be their position in the church.

Paul had dedicated himself and all his powers to the service of God. He had received the truths of the gospel direct from heaven, and throughout his ministry he maintained a vital connection with heavenly agencies. He had been taught by God regarding the binding of unnecessary burdens upon the Gentile Christians; thus when the Judaizing believers introduced into the Antioch church the question of circumcision, Paul knew the mind of the Spirit of God concerning such teaching and took a firm and unyielding position which brought to the churches freedom from Jewish rites and ceremonies.

Notwithstanding the fact that Paul was personally taught by God, he had no strained ideas of individual responsibility. While looking to God for direct guidance, he was ever ready to recognize the authority vested in the body of believers united in church fellowship. He felt the need of counsel, and when matters of importance arose, he was glad to lay these before the church and to unite with his brethren in seeking God for wisdom to make right decisions. Even "the spirits of the prophets," he declared, "are subject to the prophets. For God is not the author of confusion, but of peace, as in all churches of the saints." 1 Corinthians 14:32, 33. With Peter, he taught that all united in church capacity should be "subject one to another." 1 Peter 5:5.

Exalting the Cross

After spending some time in ministry at Antioch, Paul proposed to his fellow worker that they set forth on another missionary journey. "Let us go again," he said to Barnabas, "and visit our brethren in every city where we have preached the word of the Lord, and see how they do."

Both Paul and Barnabas had a tender regard for those who had recently accepted the gospel message under their ministry, and they longed to see them once more. This solicitude Paul never lost. Even when in distant mission fields, far from the scene of his earlier labors, he continued to bear upon his heart the burden of urging these converts to

remain faithful, "perfecting holiness in the fear of God." 2 Corinthians 7:1. Constantly he tried to help them to become self-reliant, growing Christians, strong in faith, ardent in zeal, and wholehearted in their consecration to God and to the work of advancing His kingdom.

Barnabas was ready to go with Paul, but wished to take with them Mark, who had again decided to devote himself to the ministry. To this Paul objected. He "thought not good to take . . . with them" one who during their first missionary journey had left them in a time of need. He was not inclined to excuse Mark's weakness in deserting the work for the safety and comforts of home. He urged that one with so little stamina was unfitted for a work requiring patience, self-denial, bravery, devotion, faith, and a willingness to sacrifice, if need be, even life itself. So sharp was the contention that Paul and Barnabas separated, the latter following out his convictions and taking Mark with him. "So Barnabas took Mark, and sailed unto Cyprus; and Paul chose Silas, and departed, being recommended by the brethren unto the grace of God."

Journeying through Syria and Cilicia, where they strengthened the church, Paul and Silas at length reached Derbe and Lystra in the province of Lycaonia. It was at Lystra that Paul had been stoned, yet we find him again on the scene of his former danger. He was anxious to see how those who through his labors had accepted the gospel were enduring the test of trial. He was not disappointed, for he found that the Lystrian believers had remained firm in the face of violent opposition.

Here Paul again met Timothy, who had witnessed his sufferings at the close of his first visit to Lystra and upon whose mind the impression then made had deepened with the passing of time until he was convinced that it was his duty to give himself fully to the work of the ministry. His heart was knit with the heart of Paul, and he longed to share the apostle's labors by assisting as the way might open.

Silas, Paul's companion in labor, was a tried worker, gifted with the spirit of prophecy; but the work to be done was so great that there was need of training more laborers for active service. In Timothy Paul saw one who appreciated the sacredness of the work of a minister; who was not appalled at the prospect of suffering and persecution; and who was willing to be taught. Yet the apostle did not venture to take the responsibility of giving Timothy, an untried youth, a training in the gospel ministry, without first fully satisfying himself in regard to his character and his past life.

Timothy's father was a Greek and his mother a Jewess. From a child he had known the Scriptures. The piety that he saw in his home life was sound and sensible. The faith of his mother and his grandmother in the sacred oracles was to him a constant reminder of the blessing in doing God's will. The word of God was the rule by which these two godly women had guided Timothy. The spiritual power of the lessons that he had received from them kept him pure in speech and unsullied by the evil influences with which he was surrounded. Thus his home instructors had co-operated with God in preparing him to bear burdens.

Paul saw that Timothy was faithful, steadfast, and true, and he chose him as a companion in labor and travel. Those who had taught Timothy in his childhood were rewarded by seeing the son of their care linked in close fellowship with the great apostle. Timothy was a mere youth when he was chosen by God to be a teacher, but his principles had been so established by his early education that he was fitted to take his place as Paul's helper. And though young, he bore his responsibilities with Christian meekness.

As a precautionary measure, Paul wisely advised Timothy to be circumcised—not that God required it, but in order to remove from the minds of the Jews that which might be an objection to Timothy's ministration. In his work Paul was to journey from city to city, in many lands, and often he would have opportunity to preach Christ in Jewish synagogues, as well as in other places of assembly. If it should be known that one of his companions in labor was uncircumcised, his work might be greatly hindered by the prejudice and bigotry of the Jews. Everywhere the apostle met determined opposition and severe persecution. He desired to bring to his Jewish brethren, as well as to the Gentiles, a knowledge of the gospel, and therefore he sought, so far as was consistent with the faith, to remove every pretext for opposition. Yet while he conceded this much to Jewish prejudice, he believed and taught circumcision or uncircumcision to be nothing and the gospel of Christ everything.

Paul loved Timothy, his "own son in the faith." 1 Timothy 1:2. The great apostle often drew the younger disciple out, questioning him in regard to Scripture history, and as they traveled from place to place, he carefully taught him how to do successful work. Both Paul and Silas, in all their association with Timothy, sought to deepen the impression that had already been made upon his mind, of the sacred, serious nature of the work of the gospel minister.

In his work, Timothy constantly sought Paul's advice and instruction. He did not move from impulse, but exercised consideration and calm thought, inquiring at every step, Is this the way of the Lord? The Holy Spirit found in him one who could be molded and fashioned as a temple for the indwelling of the divine Presence.

As the lessons of the Bible are wrought into the daily life, they have a deep and lasting influence upon the character. These lessons Timothy learned and practiced. He had no specially brilliant talents, but his work was valuable because he used his God-given abilities in the Master's service. His knowledge of experimental piety distinguished him from other believers and gave him influence.

Those who labor for souls must attain to a deeper, fuller, clearer knowledge of God than can be gained by ordinary effort. They must throw all their energies into the work of the Master. They are engaged in a high and holy calling, and if they gain souls for their hire they must lay firm hold upon God, daily receiving grace and power from the Source of all blessing. "For the grace of God that bringeth salvation hath appeared to all men, teaching us that, denying ungodliness and worldly lusts, we should live soberly, righteously, and godly, in this present world; looking for that blessed hope, and the glorious appearing of the great God and our Saviour Jesus Christ; who gave Himself for us, that He might redeem us from all iniquity, and purify unto Himself a peculiar people, zealous of good works." Titus 2:11-14.

Before pressing forward into new territory, Paul and his companions visited the churches that had been established in Pisidia and the regions round about. "As they went through the cities, they delivered them the decrees for to keep, that were ordained of the apostles and elders which were at Jerusalem. And so were the churches established in the faith, and increased in number daily."

The apostle Paul felt a deep responsibility for those converted under his labors. Above all things, he longed that they should be faithful, "that I may rejoice in the day of Christ," he said, "that I have not run in vain, neither labored in vain." Philippians 2:16. He trembled for the result of his ministry. He felt that even his own salvation might be imperiled if he should fail of fulfilling his duty and the church should fail of co-operating with him in the work of saving souls. He knew that preaching alone would not suffice to educate the believers to hold forth the word of life. He knew that line upon line, precept upon precept, here a little and there a little, they must be taught to advance in the work of Christ.

It is a universal principle that whenever one refuses to use his God-given powers, these powers decay and perish. Truth that is not lived, that is not imparted, loses its life-giving power, its healing virtue. Hence the apostle's fear that he might fail of presenting every man perfect in Christ. Paul's hope of heaven grew dim when he contemplated any failure on his part that would result in giving the church the mold of the human instead of the divine. His knowledge, his eloquence, his miracles, his view of eternal scenes when caught up to the third heaven—all would be unavailing if through unfaithfulness in his work those for whom he labored should fail of the grace of God. And so, by word of mouth and by letter, he pleaded with those who had accepted Christ, to pursue a course that would enable them to be "blameless and harmless, the sons of God, without rebuke, in the midst of a crooked and perverse nation, . . . as lights in the world, holding forth the word of life." Philippians 2:15, 16.

Every true minister feels a heavy responsibility for the spiritual advancement of the believers entrusted to his care, a longing desire that they shall be laborers together with God. He realizes that upon the faithful performance of his God-given work depends in a large degree the well-being of the church. Earnestly and untiringly he seeks to inspire the believers with a desire to win souls for Christ, remembering that every addition to the church should be one more agency for the carrying out of the plan of redemption.

Having visited the churches in Pisidia and the neighboring region, Paul and Silas, with Timothy, pressed on into "Phrygia and the region of Galatia," where with mighty power they proclaimed the glad tidings of salvation. The Galatians were given up to the worship of idols; but, as the apostles preached to them, they rejoiced in the message that promised freedom from the thralldom of sin. Paul and his fellow workers proclaimed the doctrine of righteousness by faith in the atoning sacrifice of Christ. They presented Christ as the one who, seeing the helpless condition of the fallen race, came to redeem men and women by living a life of obedience to God's law and by paying the penalty of disobedience. And in the light of the cross many who had never before known of the true God, began to comprehend the greatness of the Father's love.

Thus the Galatians were taught the fundamental truths concerning "God the Father" and "our Lord Jesus Christ, who gave Himself for our sins, that He might deliver us from this present evil world, according to the will of God and our Father." "By the hearing of faith" they received the Spirit of God and became "the children of God by faith in Christ." Galatians 1:3, 4; 3:2, 26.

Paul's manner of life while among the Galatians was such that he could afterward say, "I beseech you, be as I am." Galatians 4:12. His lips had been touched with a live coal from off the altar, and he was enabled to rise above bodily infirmities and to present Jesus as the sinner's only hope. Those who heard him knew that he had been with Jesus. Endued with power from on high, he was able to compare spiritual things with spiritual and to tear down the strongholds of Satan. Hearts were broken by his presentation of the love of God, as revealed in the sacrifice of His only-begotten Son, and many were led to inquire, What must I do to be saved?

This method of presenting the gospel characterized the labors of the apostle throughout his ministry among the Gentiles. Always he kept before them the cross of Calvary. "We preach not ourselves," he declared in the later years of his experience, "but Christ Jesus the Lord; and ourselves your servants for Jesus' sake. For God, who commanded the light to shine out of darkness, hath shined in our hearts, to give the light of the knowledge of the glory of God in the face of Jesus Christ." 2 Corinthians 4:5, 6.

The consecrated messengers who in the early days of Christianity carried to a perishing world the glad tidings of salvation, allowed no thought of self-exaltation to mar their presentation of Christ and Him crucified. They coveted neither authority nor pre-eminence. Hiding self in the Saviour, they exalted the great plan of salvation, and the life of Christ, the Author and Finisher of this plan. Christ, the same yesterday, today, and forever, was the burden of their teaching.

If those who today are teaching the word of God, would uplift the cross of Christ higher and still higher, their ministry would be far more successful. If sinners can be led to give one earnest look at the cross, if they can obtain a full view of the crucified Saviour, they will realize the depth of God's compassion and the sinfulness of sin.

Christ's death proves God's great love for man. It is our pledge of salvation. To remove the cross from the Christian would be like blotting the sun from the sky. The cross brings us near to God, reconciling us to Him. With the relenting compassion of a father's love, Jehovah looks upon the suffering that His Son endured in order to save the race from eternal death, and accepts us in the Beloved.

Without the cross, man could have no union with the Father. On it depends our every hope. From it shines the light of the Saviour's love, and when at the foot of the cross the sinner looks up to the One who died to save him, he may rejoice with fullness of joy, for his sins are pardoned. Kneeling in faith at the cross, he has reached the highest place to which man can attain.

Through the cross we learn that the heavenly Father loves us with a love that is infinite. Can we wonder that Paul exclaimed, "God forbid that I should glory, save in the cross of our Lord Jesus Christ"? Galatians 6:14. It is our privilege also to glory in the cross, our privilege to give ourselves wholly to Him who gave Himself for us. Then, with the light that streams from Calvary shining in our faces, we may go forth to reveal this light to those in darkness.

In the Regions Beyond

The time had come for the gospel to be proclaimed beyond the confines of Asia Minor. The way was preparing for Paul and his fellow workers to cross over into Europe. At Troas, on the borders of the Mediterranean Sea, "a vision appeared to Paul in the night: There stood a man of Macedonia, and prayed him, saying, Come over into Macedonia, and help us."

The call was imperative, admitting of no delay. "After he had seen the vision," declares Luke, who accompanied Paul and Silas and Timothy on the journey across to Europe, "immediately we endeavored to go into Macedonia, assuredly gathering that the Lord had called us for to preach the gospel unto them. Therefore loosing from Troas, we came with a straight course to Samothracia, and the next day to Neapolis; and from thence to Philippi, which is the chief city of that part of Macedonia, and a colony."

"On the Sabbath," Luke continues, "we went out of the city by a riverside, where prayer was wont to be made; and we sat down, and spake unto the women which resorted thither. And a certain woman named Lydia, a seller of purple, of the city of Thyatira, which worshiped God, heard us: whose heart the Lord opened." Lydia received the truth gladly. She and her household were converted and baptized, and she entreated the apostles to make her house their home.

As the messengers of the cross went about their work of teaching, a woman possessed of a spirit of divination followed them, crying, "These men are the servants of the most high God, which show unto us the way of salvation. And this did she many days."

This woman was a special agent of Satan and had brought to her masters much gain by soothsaying. Her influence had helped to strengthen idolatry. Satan knew that his kingdom was being invaded, and he resorted to this means of opposing the work of God, hoping to mingle his sophistry with the truths taught by those who were proclaiming the gospel message. The words of recommendation uttered by this woman were an injury to the cause of truth, distracting the minds of the people from the teachings of the apostles and bringing disrepute upon the gospel, and by them many were led to believe that the men who spoke with the Spirit and power of God were actuated by the same spirit as this emissary of Satan.

For some time the apostles endured this opposition; then under the inspiration of the Holy Ghost Paul commanded the evil spirit to leave the woman. Her immediate silence testified that the apostles were the servants of God and that the demon had acknowledged them to be such and had obeyed their command.

Dispossessed of the evil spirit and restored to her right mind, the woman chose to become a follower of Christ. Then her masters were alarmed for their craft. They saw that all hope of receiving money from her divinations and soothsayings was at an end and that their source of income would soon be entirely cut off if the apostles were allowed to continue the work of the gospel.

Many others in the city were interested in gaining money through satanic delusions, and these, fearing the influence of a power that could so effectually stop their work, raised a mighty cry against the servants of God. They brought the apostles before the magistrates with the charge: "These men, being Jews, do exceedingly trouble our city, and teach customs, which are not lawful for us to receive, neither to observe, being Romans."

Stirred by a frenzy of excitement, the multitude rose against the disciples. A mob spirit prevailed and was sanctioned by the authorities, who tore the outer garments from the apostles and commanded that they should be scourged. "And when they had laid many stripes upon them, they cast them into prison, charging the jailer to keep them safely: who, having received such a charge, thrust them into the inner prison, and made their feet fast in the stocks."

The apostles suffered extreme torture because of the painful position in which they were left, but they did not murmur. Instead, in the utter darkness and desolation of the dungeon, they encouraged each other by words of prayer and sang praises to God because they were found worthy to suffer shame for His sake. Their hearts were cheered by a deep and earnest love for the cause of their Redeemer. Paul thought of the persecution he had been instrumental in bringing upon the disciples of Christ, and he rejoiced that his eyes had been opened to see, and his heart to feel, the power of the glorious truths which once he despised.

With astonishment the other prisoners heard the sound of prayer and singing issuing from the inner prison. They had been accustomed to hear shrieks and moans, cursing and swearing, breaking the silence of the night; but never before had they heard words of prayer and praise ascending from that gloomy cell. Guards and prisoners marveled and asked themselves who these men could be, who, cold, hungry, and tortured, could yet rejoice.

Meanwhile the magistrates returned to their homes, congratulating themselves that by prompt and decisive measures they had quelled a tumult. But on the way they heard further particulars concerning the character and work of the men they had sentenced to scourging and imprisonment. They saw the woman who had been freed from satanic influence and were struck by the change in her countenance and demeanor. In the past she had caused the city much trouble; now she was quiet and peaceable. As they realized that in all probability they had visited upon two innocent men the rigorous penalty of the Roman law they were indignant with themselves and decided that in the morning they would command that the apostles be privately released and escorted from the city, beyond the danger of violence from the mob.

But while men were cruel and vindictive, or criminally negligent of the solemn responsibilities devolving upon them, God had not forgotten to be gracious to His servants. All heaven was interested in the men who were suffering for Christ's sake, and angels were sent to visit the prison. At their tread the earth trembled. The heavily bolted prison doors were thrown open; the chains and fetters fell from the hands and feet of the prisoners; and a bright light flooded the prison.

The keeper of the jail had heard with amazement the prayers and songs of the imprisoned apostles. When they were led in, he had seen their swollen and bleeding wounds, and had himself caused their feet to be fastened in the stocks. He had expected to hear from them bitter groans and imprecations, but he heard instead songs of joy and praise. With these sounds in his ears the jailer had fallen into a sleep from which he was awakened by the earthquake and the shaking of the prison walls.

Starting up in alarm, he saw with dismay that all the prison doors were open, and the fear flashed upon him that the prisoners had escaped. He remembered with what explicit charge Paul and Silas had been entrusted to his care the night before, and he was certain that death would be the penalty of his apparent unfaithfulness. In the bitterness of his spirit he felt that it was better for him to die by his own hand than to submit to a disgraceful execution. Drawing his sword, he was about to kill himself, when Paul's voice was heard in the words of cheer, "Do thyself no harm: for we are all here." Every man was in his place, restrained by the power of God exerted through one fellow prisoner.

The severity with which the jailer had treated the apostles had not aroused their resentment. Paul and Silas had the spirit of Christ, not the spirit of revenge. Their hearts, filled with the love of the Saviour, had no room for malice against their persecutors.

The jailer dropped his sword and, calling for lights, hastened into the inner dungeon. He would see what manner of men these were who repaid with kindness the cruelty with which they had been treated. Reaching the place where the apostles were, and casting himself before them, he asked their forgiveness. Then, bringing them out into the open court, he inquired, "Sirs, what must I do to be saved?"

The jailer had trembled as he beheld the wrath of God manifested in the earthquake; when he thought that the prisoners had escaped he had been ready to die by his own hand; but now all these things seemed of little consequence compared with the new, strange dread that agitated his mind, and his desire to possess the tranquillity and cheerfulness shown by the apostles under suffering and abuse. He saw in their countenances the light of heaven; he knew that God had interposed in a miraculous manner to save their lives; and with peculiar force the words of the spirit-possessed woman came to his mind: "These men are the servants of the most high God, which show unto us the way of salvation."

With deep humility he asked the apostles to show him the way of life. "Believe on the Lord Jesus Christ, and thou shalt be saved, and thy house," they answered; and "they spake unto him the word of the Lord, and to all that were in his house." The jailer then washed the wounds of the apostles and ministered to them, after which he was baptized by them, with all his household. A sanctifying influence diffused itself among the inmates of the prison, and the minds of all were opened to listen to the truths spoken by the apostles. They were convinced that the God whom these men served had miraculously released them from bondage.

The citizens of Philippi had been greatly terrified by the earthquake, and when in the morning the officers of the prison told the magistrates of what had occurred during the night, they were alarmed and sent the sergeants to liberate the apostles. But Paul declared, "They have beaten us openly uncondemned, being Romans, and have cast us into prison; and now do they thrust us out privily? nay verily; but let them come themselves and fetch us out."

The apostles were Roman citizens, and it was unlawful to scourge a Roman, save for the most flagrant crime, or to deprive him of his liberty without a fair trial. Paul and Silas had been publicly imprisoned, and they now refused to be privately released without the proper explanation on the part of the magistrates.

When this word was brought to the authorities, they were alarmed for fear that the apostles would complain to the emperor, and going at once to the prison, they apologized to Paul and Silas for the injustice and cruelty done them and personally conducted them out of the prison, entreating them to depart from the city. The magistrates feared the apostles' influence over the people, and they also feared the Power that had interposed in behalf of these innocent men.

Acting upon the instruction given by Christ, the apostles would not urge their presence where it was not desired. "They went out of the prison, and entered into the house of Lydia: and when they had seen the brethren, they comforted them, and departed."

The apostles did not regard as in vain their labors in Philippi. They had met much opposition and persecution; but the intervention of Providence in their behalf, and the conversion of the jailer and his household, more than atoned for the disgrace and suffering they had endured. The news of their unjust imprisonment and miraculous deliverance became known through all that region, and this brought the work of the apostles to the notice of a large number who otherwise would not have been reached.

Paul's labors at Philippi resulted in the establishment of a church whose membership steadily increased. His zeal and devotion, and, above all, his willingness to suffer for Christ's sake, exerted a deep and lasting influence upon the converts. They prized the precious truths for which the apostles had sacrificed so much, and gave themselves with wholehearted devotion to the cause of their Redeemer.

That this church did not escape persecution is shown by an expression in Paul's letter to them. He says, "Unto you it is given in the behalf of Christ, not only to believe on Him, but also to suffer for His sake; having the same conflict which ye saw in me." Yet such was their steadfastness in the faith that he declares, "I thank my God upon every remembrance of you, always in every prayer of mine for you all making request with joy, for your fellowship in the gospel from the first day until now." Philippians 1:29, 30, 3-5.

Terrible is the struggle that takes place between the forces of good and of evil in important centers where the messengers of truth are called upon to labor. "We wrestle not against flesh and blood," declares Paul, "but against principalities, against powers, against the rulers of the darkness of this world." Ephesians 6:12. Till the close of time there will be a conflict between the church of God and those who are under the control of evil angels.

The early Christians were often called to meet the powers of darkness face to face. By sophistry and by persecution the enemy endeavored to turn them from the true faith. At the present time, when the end of all things earthly is rapidly approaching, Satan is putting forth desperate efforts to ensnare the world. He is devising many plans to occupy minds and to divert attention from the truths essential to salvation. In every city his agencies are busily organizing into parties those who are opposed to the law of God. The archdeceiver is at work to introduce elements of confusion and rebellion, and men are being fired with a zeal that is not according to knowledge.

Wickedness is reaching a height never before attained, and yet many ministers of the gospel are crying, "Peace and safety." But God's faithful messengers are to go steadily forward with their work. Clothed with the panoply of heaven, they are to advance fearlessly and victoriously, never ceasing their warfare until every soul within their reach shall have received the message of truth for this time.

Thessalonica

After leaving Philippi, Paul and Silas made their way to Thessalonica. Here they were given the privilege of addressing large congregations in the Jewish synagogue. Their appearance bore evidence of the shameful treatment they had recently received, and necessitated an explanation of what had taken place. This they made without exalting themselves, but magnified the One who had wrought their deliverance.

In preaching to the Thessalonians, Paul appealed to the Old Testament prophecies concerning the Messiah. Christ in His ministry had opened the minds of His disciples to these prophecies; "beginning at Moses and all the prophets, He expounded unto them in all the Scriptures the things concerning Himself." Luke 24:27. Peter in preaching Christ had produced his evidence from the Old Testament. Stephen had pursued the same course. And Paul also in his ministry appealed to the scriptures foretelling the birth, sufferings, death, resurrection, and ascension of Christ. By the inspired testimony of Moses and the prophets he clearly proved the identity of Jesus of Nazareth with the Messiah and showed that from the days of Adam it was the voice of Christ which had been speaking through patriarchs and prophets.

Plain and specific prophecies had been given regarding the appearance of the Promised One. To Adam was given an assurance of the coming of the Redeemer. The sentence pronounced on Satan, "I will put enmity between thee and the woman, and between thy seed and her seed; it shall bruise thy head, and thou shalt bruise his heel" (Genesis 3:15), was to our first parents a promise of the redemption to be wrought out through Christ.

To Abraham was given the promise that of his line of Saviour of the world should come: "In thy seed shall all the nations of the earth be blessed." "He saith not, And to seeds, as of many; but as of one, And to thy seed, which is Christ." Genesis 22:18; Galatians 3:16.

Moses, near the close of his work as a leader and teacher of Israel, plainly prophesied of the Messiah to come. "The Lord thy God," he declared to the assembled hosts of Israel, "will raise up unto thee a Prophet from the midst of thee, of thy brethren, like unto me; unto Him ye shall hearken." And Moses assured the Israelites that God Himself had revealed this to him while in Mount Horeb, saying, "I will raise them up a Prophet from among their brethren, like unto thee, and will put My words in His mouth; and He shall speak unto them all that I shall command Him." Deuteronomy 18:15, 18.

The Messiah was to be of the royal line, for in the prophecy uttered by Jacob the Lord said, "The scepter shall not depart from Judah, nor a lawgiver from between his feet, until Shiloh come; and unto Him shall the gathering of the people be." Genesis 49:10.

Isaiah prophesied: "There shall come forth a rod out of the stem of Jesse, and a Branch shall grow out of his roots." "Incline your ear, and come unto Me: hear, and your soul shall live; and I will make an everlasting covenant with you, even the sure mercies of David. Behold, I have given Him for a witness to the people, a leader and commander to the people. Behold, thou shalt call a nation that thou knowest not, and nations that knew not thee shall run unto thee

because of the Lord thy God, and for the Holy One of Israel; for He hath glorified thee." Isaiah 11:1; 55:3-5.

Jeremiah also bore witness of the coming Redeemer as a Prince of the house of David: "Behold, the days come, saith the Lord, that I will raise unto David a righteous Branch, and a King shall reign and prosper, and shall execute judgment and justice in the earth. In His days Judah shall be saved, and Israel shall dwell safely: and this is His name whereby He shall be called, The Lord Our Righteousness." And again: "Thus saith the Lord: David shall never want a man to sit upon the throne of the house of Israel; neither shall the priests the Levites want a man before Me to offer burnt offerings, and to kindle meat offerings, and to do sacrifice continually." Jeremiah 23:5, 6; 33:17, 18.

Even the birthplace of the Messiah was foretold: "Thou, Bethlehem Ephratah, though thou be little among the thousands of Judah, yet out of thee shall He come forth unto Me that is to be Ruler in Israel; whose goings forth have been from of old, from everlasting." Micah 5:2.

The work that the Saviour was to do on the earth had been fully outlined: "The Spirit of the Lord shall rest upon Him, the spirit of wisdom and understanding, the spirit of counsel and might, the spirit of knowledge and of the fear of the Lord; and shall make Him of quick understanding in the fear of the Lord." The One thus anointed was "to preach good tidings unto the meek; . . . to bind up the brokenhearted, to proclaim liberty to the captives, and the opening of the prison to them that are bound; to proclaim the acceptable year of the Lord, and the day of vengeance of our God; to comfort all that mourn; to appoint unto them that mourn in Zion, to give unto them beauty for ashes, the oil of joy for mourning, the garment of praise for the spirit of heaviness; that they might be called trees of righteousness, the planting of the Lord, that He might be glorified." Isaiah 11:2, 3; 61:1-3.

"Behold My servant, whom I uphold; Mine elect, in whom My soul delighteth; I have put My Spirit upon Him: He shall bring forth judgment to the Gentiles. He shall not cry, nor lift up, nor cause His voice to be heard in the street. A bruised reed shall He not break, and the smoking flax shall He not quench: He shall bring forth judgment unto truth. He shall not fail nor be discouraged, till He have set judgment in the earth: and the isles shall wait for His law." Isaiah 42:1-4.

With convincing power Paul reasoned from the Old Testament Scriptures that "Christ must needs have suffered, and risen again from the dead." Had not Micah prophesied, "They shall smite the Judge of Israel with a rod upon the cheek"? Micah 5:1. And had not the Promised One, through Isaiah, prophesied of Himself, "I gave My back to the smiters, and My cheeks to them that plucked off the hair: I hid not My face from shame and spitting"? Isaiah 50:6. Through the psalmist Christ had foretold the treatment that He should receive from men: "I am . . . a reproach of men, and despised of the people. All they that see Me laugh Me to scorn: they shoot out the lip, they shake the head, saying, He trusted on the Lord that He would deliver Him: let Him deliver Him, seeing He delighted in Him." "I may tell all My bones: they look and stare upon Me. They part My garments among them, and cast lots upon My vesture." "I am become a stranger unto My brethren, and an alien unto My mother's children. For the zeal of Thine house hath eaten Me up; and the reproaches of them that reproached Thee are fallen upon Me." "Reproach hath broken My heart; and I am full of heaviness: and I looked for some to take pity, but there was none; and for comforters, but I found none." Psalms 22:6-8, 17, 18; 69:8, 9, 20.

How unmistakably plain were Isaiah's prophecies of Christ's sufferings and death! "Who hath believed our report? "the prophet inquires, "and to whom is the arm of the Lord revealed? For He shall grow up before Him as a tender plant, and as a root out of a dry ground: He hath no form nor comeliness; and when we shall see Him, there is no beauty that we should desire Him. He is despised and rejected of men; a man of sorrows, and acquainted with grief: and we hid as it were our faces from Him; He was despised, and we esteemed Him not.

"Surely He hath borne our griefs, and carried our sorrows: yet we did esteem Him stricken, smitten of God, and afflicted. But He was wounded for our transgressions, He was bruised for our iniquities: the chastisement of our peace was upon Him; and with His stripes we are healed.

"All we like sheep have gone astray; we have turned everyone to his own way; and the Lord hath laid on Him the iniquity of us all. He was oppressed, and he was afflicted, yet He opened not His mouth: He is brought as a lamb to the slaughter, and as a sheep before her shearers is dumb, so He openeth not His mouth. He was taken from prison and from judgment: and who shall declare His generation? for He was cut off out of the land of the living: for the transgression of my people was He stricken." Isaiah 53:1-8.

Even the manner of His death had been shadowed forth. As the brazen serpent had been uplifted in the wilderness, so was the coming Redeemer to be lifted up, "that whosoever believeth in Him should not perish, but have everlasting life." John 3:16.

"One shall say unto Him, What are these wounds in Thine hands? Then He shall answer, Those with which I was wounded in the house of My friends." Zechariah 13:6.

"He made His grave with the wicked, and with the rich in His death; because He had done no violence, neither was any deceit in His mouth. Yet it pleased the Lord to bruise Him; He hath put Him to grief." Isaiah 53:9, 10.

But He who was to suffer death at the hands of evil men was to rise again as a conqueror over sin and the grave. Under the inspiration of the Almighty the Sweet Singer of Israel had testified of the glories of the resurrection morn. "My flesh also," he joyously proclaimed, "shall rest in hope. For Thou wilt not leave My soul in hell; neither wilt Thou suffer Thine Holy One to see corruption." Psalm 16:9, 10.

Paul showed how closely God had linked the sacrificial service with the prophecies relating to the One who was to be "brought as a lamb to the slaughter." The Messiah was to give His life as "an offering for sin." Looking down through the centuries to the scenes of the Saviour's atonement, the prophet Isaiah had testified that the Lamb of God "poured out His soul unto death: and He was numbered with the transgressors; and He bare the sin of many, and made intercession for the transgressors." Isaiah 53:7, 10, 12.

The Saviour of prophecy was to come, not as a temporal king, to deliver the Jewish nation from earthly oppressors, but as a man among men, to live a life of poverty and humility, and at last to be despised, rejected, and slain. The Saviour foretold in the Old Testament Scriptures was to offer Himself as a sacrifice in behalf of the fallen race, thus fulfilling every requirement of the broken law. In Him the sacrificial types were to meet their antitype, and His death on the cross was to lend significance to the entire Jewish economy.

Paul told the Thessalonian Jews of his former zeal for the ceremonial law and of his wonderful experience at the gate of Damascus. Before his conversion he had been confident in a hereditary piety, a false hope. His faith had not been anchored in Christ; he had trusted instead in forms and ceremonies. His zeal for the law had been disconnected from faith in Christ and was of no avail. While boasting that he was blameless in the performance of the deeds of the law, he had refused the One who made the law of value.

But at the time of his conversion all had been changed. Jesus of Nazareth, whom he had been persecuting in the person of His saints, appeared before him as the promised Messiah. The persecutor saw Him as the Son of God, the one who had come to the earth in fulfillment of the prophecies and who in His life had met every specification of the Sacred Writings.

As with holy boldness Paul proclaimed the gospel in the synagogue at Thessalonica, a flood of light was thrown upon the true meaning of the rites and ceremonies connected with the tabernacle service. He carried the minds of his hearers beyond the earthly service and the ministry of Christ in the heavenly sanctuary, to the time when, having completed His mediatorial work, Christ would come again in power and great glory, and establish His kingdom on the earth. Paul was a believer in the second coming of Christ; so clearly and forcibly did he present the truths concerning this event, that upon the minds of many who heard there was made an impression which never wore away.

For three successive Sabbaths Paul preached to the Thessalonians, reasoning with them from the Scriptures regarding the life, death, resurrection, office work, and future glory of Christ, the "Lamb slain from the foundation of the world." Revelation 13:8. He exalted Christ, the proper understanding of whose ministry is the key that unlocks the Old Testament Scriptures, giving access to their rich treasures.

As the truths of the gospel were thus proclaimed in Thessalonica with mighty power, the attention of large congregations was arrested. "Some of them believed, and consorted with Paul and Silas; and of the devout Greeks a great multitude, and of the chief women not a few."

As in the places formerly entered, the apostles met with determined opposition. "The Jews which believed not" were "moved with envy." These Jews were not then in favor with the Roman power, because, not long before, they had raised an insurrection in Rome. They were looked upon with suspicion, and their liberty was in a measure restricted. They now saw an opportunity to take advantage of circumstances to re-establish themselves in favor and at the same time to throw reproach upon the apostles and the converts to Christianity.

This they set about doing by uniting with "certain lewd fellows of the baser sort," by which means they succeeded in setting "all the city on an uproar." In the hope of finding the apostles, they "assaulted the house of Jason;" but they could find neither Paul nor Silas. And "when they found them not," the mob in their mad disappointment "drew Jason and certain brethren unto the rulers of the city, crying, These that have turned the world upside down are come hither also; whom Jason hath received: and these all do contrary to the decrees of Caesar, saying that there is another king, one Jesus."

As Paul and Silas were not to be found, the magistrates put the accused believers under bonds to keep the peace. Fearing further violence, "the brethren immediately sent away Paul and Silas by night unto Berea."

Those who today teach unpopular truths need not be discouraged if at times they meet with no more favorable reception, even from those who claim to be Christians, than did Paul and his fellow workers from the people among whom they labored. The messengers of the cross must arm themselves with watchfulness and prayer, and move forward with faith and courage, working always in the name of Jesus. They must exalt Christ as man's mediator in the heavenly sanctuary, the One in whom all the sacrifices of the Old Testament dispensation centered, and through whose atoning sacrifice the transgressors of God's law may find peace and pardon.

Berea and Athens

At Berea Paul found Jews who were willing to investigate the truths he taught. Luke's record declares of them: "These were more noble than those in Thessalonica, in that they received the word with all readiness of mind, and searched the Scriptures daily, whether those things were so. Therefore many of them believed; also of honorable women which were Greeks, and of men, not a few."

The minds of the Bereans were not narrowed by prejudice. They were willing to investigate the truthfulness of the doctrines preached by the apostles. They studied the Bible, not from curiosity, but in order that they might learn what had been written concerning the promised Messiah. Daily they searched the inspired records, and as they compared scripture with scripture, heavenly angels were beside them, enlightening their minds and impressing their hearts.

Wherever the truths of the gospel are proclaimed, those who honestly desire to do right are led to a diligent searching of the Scriptures. If, in the closing scenes of this earth's history, those to whom testing truths are proclaimed would follow the example of the Bereans, searching the Scriptures daily, and comparing with God's word the messages brought them, there would today be a large number loyal to the precepts of God's law, where now there are comparatively few. But when unpopular Bible truths are presented, many refuse to make this investigation. Though unable to controvert the plain teachings of Scripture, they yet manifest the utmost reluctance to study the evidences offered. Some assume that even if these doctrines are indeed true, it matters little whether or not they accept the new light, and they cling to pleasing fables which the enemy uses to lead souls astray. Thus their minds are blinded by error, and they become separated from heaven.

All will be judged according to the light that has been given. The Lord sends forth His ambassadors with a message of salvation, and those who hear He will hold responsible for the way in which they treat the words of His servants. Those who are sincerely seeking for truth will make a careful investigation, in the light of God's word, of the doctrines presented to them.

The unbelieving Jews of Thessalonica, filled with jealousy and hatred of the apostles, and not content with having driven them from their own city, followed them to Berea and aroused against them the excitable passions of the lower class. Fearing that violence would be done to Paul if he remained there, the brethren sent him to Athens, accompanied by some of the Bereans who had newly accepted the faith.

Thus persecution followed the teachers of truth from city to city. The enemies of Christ could not prevent the advancement of the gospel, but they succeeded in making the work of the apostles exceedingly hard. Yet in the face of opposition and conflict, Paul pressed steadily forward, determined to carry out the purpose of God as revealed to him in the vision at Jerusalem: "I will send thee far hence unto the Gentiles." Acts 22:21.

Paul's hasty departure from Berea deprived him of the opportunity he had anticipated of visiting the brethren at Thessalonica.

On arriving at Athens, the apostle sent the Berean brethren back with a message to Silas and Timothy to join him immediately. Timothy had come to Berea prior to Paul's departure, and with Silas had remained to carry on the work so well begun there, and to instruct the new converts in the principles of the faith.

The city of Athens was the metropolis of heathendom. Here Paul did not meet with an ignorant, credulous populace, as at Lystra, but with a people famous for their intelligence and culture. Everywhere statues of their gods and of the deified heroes of history and poetry met the eye, while magnificent architecture and paintings represented the national glory and the popular worship of heathen deities. The senses of the people were entranced by the beauty and splendor of art. On every hand sanctuaries and temples, involving untold expense, reared their massive forms. Victories of arms and deeds of celebrated men were commemorated by sculpture, shrines, and tablets. All these made Athens a vast gallery of art.

As Paul looked upon the beauty and grandeur surrounding him, and saw the city wholly given to idolatry, his spirit was stirred with jealousy for God, whom he saw dishonored on every side, and his heart was drawn out in pity for the people of Athens, who, notwithstanding their intellectual culture, were ignorant of the true God.

The apostle was not deceived by that which he saw in this center of learning. His spiritual nature was so alive to the attraction of heavenly things that the joy and glory of the riches which will never perish made valueless in his eyes the pomp and splendor with which he was surrounded. As he saw the magnificence of Athens he realized its seductive power over lovers of art and science, and his mind was deeply impressed with the importance of the work before him.

In this great city, where God was not worshiped, Paul was oppressed by a feeling of solitude, and he longed for the sympathy and aid of his fellow laborers. So far as human friendship was concerned, he felt himself to be utterly alone. In his epistle to the Thessalonians he expresses his feelings in the words, "Left at the Athens alone." 1 Thessalonians 3:1. Obstacles that were apparently insurmountable presented themselves before him, making it seem almost hopeless for him to attempt to reach the hearts of the people.

While waiting for Silas and Timothy, Paul was not idle. He "disputed . . . in the synagogue with the Jews, and with the devout persons, and in the market daily with them that met with him." But his principal work in Athens was to bear the tidings of salvation to those who had no intelligent conception of God and of His purpose in behalf of the fallen race. The apostle was soon to meet paganism in its most subtle, alluring form.

The great men of Athens were not long in learning of the presence in their city of a singular teacher who was setting before the people doctrines new and strange. Some of these men sought Paul out and entered into conversation with him. Soon a crowd of listeners gathered about them. Some were prepared to ridicule the apostle as one who was far beneath them both socially and intellectually, and these said jeeringly among themselves, "What will this babbler say?" Others, "because he preached unto them Jesus, and the resurrection," said, "He seemeth to be a setter forth of strange gods."

Among those who encountered Paul in the market place were "certain philosophers of the Epicureans, and of the Stoics;" but they, and all others who came in contact with him, soon saw that he had a store of knowledge even greater than their own. His intellectual power commanded the respect of the learned; while his earnest, logical reasoning and the power of his oratory held the attention of all in the audience. His hearers recognized the fact that he was no novice, but was able to meet all classes with convincing arguments in support of the doctrines he taught. Thus the apostle stood undaunted, meeting his opposers on their own ground, matching logic with logic, philosophy with philosophy, eloquence with eloquence.

His heathen opponents called his attention to the fate of Socrates, who, because he was a setter forth of strange gods, had been condemned to death, and they counseled Paul not to endanger his life in the same way. But the apostle's discourses riveted the attention of the people, and his unaffected wisdom commanded their respect and admiration. He was not silenced by the science or the irony of the philosophers, and satisfying themselves that he was determined to accomplish his errand among them, and, at all hazards, to tell his story, they decided to give him a fair hearing.

They accordingly conducted him to Mars' Hill. This was one of the most sacred spots in all Athens, and its recollections and associations were such as to cause it to be regarded with a superstitious reverence that in the minds of some amounted to dread. It was in this place that matters connected with religion were often carefully considered by men who acted as final judges on all the more important moral as well as civil questions.

Here, away from the noise and bustle of crowded thoroughfares, and the tumult of promiscuous discussion, the apostle could be heard without interruption. Around him gathered poets, artists, and philosophers—the scholars and sages of Athens, who thus addressed him: "May we know what this new doctrine, whereof thou speakest, is? for thou bringest certain strange things to our ears: we would know thereof what these things mean."

In that hour of solemn responsibility, the apostle was calm and self-possessed. His heart was burdened with an important message, and the words that fell from his lips convinced his hearers that he was no idle babbler. "Ye men of Athens," he said, "I perceive that in all things ye are too superstitious. For as I passed by, and beheld your devotions, I found an altar with this inscription, To the Unknown God. Whom therefore ye ignorantly worship, Him declare I unto you." With all their intelligence and general knowledge, they were ignorant of the God who created the universe. Yet there were some who were longing for greater light. They were reaching out toward the Infinite.

With hand outstretched toward the temple crowded with idols, Paul poured out the burden of his soul, and exposed the fallacies of the religion of the Athenians. The wisest of his hearers were astonished as they listened to his reasoning. He showed himself familiar with their works of art, their literature, and their religion. Pointing to their statuary and idols, he declared that God could not be likened to forms of man's devising. These graven images could not, in the faintest sense, represent the glory of Jehovah. He reminded them that these images had no life, but were controlled by human power, moving only when the hands of men moved them; and therefore those who worshiped them were in every way superior to that which they worshiped.

Paul drew the minds of his idolatrous hearers beyond the limits of their false religion to a true view of the Deity, whom they had styled the "Unknown God." This Being, whom he now declared unto them, was independent of man, needing nothing from human hands to add to His power and glory.

The people were carried away with admiration for Paul's earnest and logical presentation of the attributes of the true God—of His creative power and the existence of His overruling providence. With earnest and fervid eloquence the apostle declared, "God that made the world and all things therein, seeing that He is Lord of heaven and earth, dwelleth not in temples made with hands; neither is worshiped with men's hands, as though He needed anything, seeing He giveth to all life, and breath, and all things." The heavens were not large enough to contain God, how much less were the temples made by human hands!

In that age of caste, when the rights of men were often unrecognized, Paul set forth the great truth of human brotherhood, declaring that God "hath made of one blood all nations of men for to dwell on all the face of the earth." In the sight of God all are on an equality, and to the Creator every human being owes supreme allegiance. Then the apostle showed how, through all God's dealings with man, His purpose of grace and mercy runs like a thread of gold. He "hath determined the times before appointed, and the bounds of their habitation; that they should seek the Lord, if haply they might feel after Him, and find Him, though He be not far from every one of us."

Pointing to the noble specimens of manhood about him, with words borrowed from a poet of their own he pictured the infinite God as a Father, whose children they were. "In Him we live, and move, and have our being," he declared; "as certain also of your own poets have said, For we are also His offspring. Forasmuch then as we are the offspring of God, we ought not to think that the Godhead is like unto gold, or silver, or stone, graven by art and man's device.

"And the times of this ignorance God winked at; but now commandeth all men everywhere to repent." In the ages of darkness that had preceded the advent of Christ, the divine Ruler had passed lightly over the idolatry of the heathen; but now, through His Son, He had sent men the light of truth; and He expected from all repentance unto salvation, not only from the poor and humble, but from the proud philosopher and the princes of the earth. "Because He hath appointed a day, in the which He will judge the world in righteousness by that Man whom He hath ordained; whereof He hath given assurance unto all men, in that He hath raised Him from the dead." As Paul spoke of the resurrection from the dead, "some mocked: and others said, We will hear thee again of this matter."

Thus closed the labors of the apostle at Athens, the center of heathen learning, for the Athenians, clinging persistently to their idolatry, turned from the light of the true religion. When a people are wholly satisfied with their own attainments, little more need be expected of them. Though boasting of learning and refinement, the Athenians were constantly becoming more corrupt and more content with the vague mysteries of idolatry.

Among those who listened to the words of Paul were some to whose minds the truths presented brought conviction, but they would not humble themselves to acknowledge God and to accept the plan of salvation. No eloquence of words, no force of argument, can convert the sinner. The power of God alone can apply the truth to the heart. He who persistently turns from this power cannot be reached. The Greeks sought after wisdom, yet the message of the cross was to them foolishness because they valued their own wisdom more highly than the wisdom that comes from above.

In their pride of intellect and human wisdom may be found the reason why the gospel message met with comparatively little success among the Athenians. The worldly-wise men who come to Christ as poor lost sinners, will become wise unto salvation; but those who come as distinguished men, extolling their own wisdom, will fail of receiving the light and knowledge that He alone can give.

Thus Paul met the paganism of his day. His labors in Athens were not wholly in vain. Dionysius, one of the most prominent citizens, and some others, accepted the gospel message and united themselves fully with the believers.

Inspiration has given us this glance into the life of the Athenians, who, with all their knowledge, refinement, and art, were yet sunken in vice, that it might be seen how God, through His servant, rebuked idolatry and the sins of a proud, self-sufficient people. The words of the apostle, and the description of his attitude and surroundings, as traced by the pen of inspiration, were to be handed down to all coming generations, bearing witness of his unshaken confidence, his courage in loneliness and adversity, and the victory he gained for Christianity in the very heart of paganism.

Paul's words contain a treasure of knowledge for the church. He was in a position where he might easily have said that which would have irritated his proud listeners and brought himself into difficulty. Had his oration been a direct attack upon their gods and the great men of the city, he would have been in danger of meeting the fate of Socrates. But with a tact born of divine love, he carefully drew their minds away from heathen deities, by revealing to them the true God, who was to them unknown.

Today the truths of Scripture are to be brought before the great men of the world in order that they may choose between obedience to God's law and allegiance to the prince of evil. God sets everlasting truth before them—truth that will make them wise unto salvation, but He does not force them to accept it. If they turn from it, He leaves them to themselves, to be filled with the fruit of their own doings.

"The preaching of the cross is to them that perish foolishness; but unto us which are saved it is the power of God. For it is written, I will destroy the wisdom of the wise, and will bring to nothing the understanding of the prudent."

"God hath chosen the foolish things of the world to confound the wise; and God hath chosen the weak things of the world to confound the things which are mighty; and base things of the world, and things which are despised, hath God chosen, yea, and things which are not, to bring to nought things that are." 1 Corinthians 1:18, 19, 27, 28. Many of the greatest scholars and statesmen, the world's most eminent men, will in these last days turn from the light because the world by wisdom knows not God. Yet God's servants are to improve every opportunity to communicate the truth to these men. Some will acknowledge their ignorance of the things of God and will take their place as humble learners at the feet of Jesus, the Master Teacher.

In every effort to reach the higher classes, the worker for God needs strong faith. Appearances may seem forbidding, but in the darkest hour there is light above. The strength of those who love and serve God will be renewed day by day. The understanding of the Infinite is placed at their service, that in carrying out His purposes they may not err. Let these workers hold the beginning of their confidence firm unto the end, remembering that the light of God's truth is to shine amid the darkness that enshrouds our world. There is to be no despondency in connection with God's service. The faith of the consecrated worker is to stand every test brought to bear upon it. God is able and willing to bestow upon His servants all the strength they need and to give them the wisdom that their varied necessities demand. He will more than fulfill the highest expectations of those who put their trust in Him.

Corinth

During the first century of the Christian Era, Corinth was one of the leading cities, not only of Greece, but of the world. Greeks, Jews, and Romans, with travelers from every land, thronged its streets, eagerly intent on business and pleasure. A great commercial center, situated within easy access of all parts of the Roman Empire, it was an important place in which to establish memorials for God and His truth.

Among the Jews who had taken up their residence in Corinth were Aquila and Priscilla, who afterward became distinguished as earnest workers for Christ. Becoming acquainted with the character of these persons, Paul "abode with them."

At the very beginning of his labors in this thoroughfare of travel, Paul saw on every hand serious obstacles to the progress of his work. The city was almost wholly given up to idolatry. Venus was the favorite goddess, and with the worship of Venus were connected many demoralizing rites and ceremonies. The Corinthians had become conspicuous, even among the heathen, for their gross immorality. They seemed to have little thought or care beyond the pleasures and gaieties of the hour.

In preaching the gospel in Corinth, the apostle followed a course different from that which had marked his labors at Athens. While in the latter place, he had sought to adapt his style to the character of his audience; he had met logic with logic, science with science, philosophy with philosophy. As he thought of the time thus spent, and realized that his teaching in Athens had been productive of but little fruit, he decided to follow another plan of labor in Corinth in his efforts to arrest the attention of the careless and the indifferent. He determined to avoid elaborate arguments and discussions, and "not to know anything" among the Corinthians "save Jesus Christ, and Him crucified." He would preach to them "not with enticing words of man's wisdom, but in demonstration of the Spirit and of power." 1 Corinthians 2:2, 4.

Jesus, whom Paul was about to present before the Greeks in Corinth as the Christ, was a Jew of lowly origin, reared in a town proverbial for its wickedness. He had been rejected by His own nation and at last crucified as a malefactor. The Greeks believed that there was need of elevating the human race, but they regarded the study of philosophy and science as the only means of attaining to true elevation and honor. Could Paul lead them to believe that faith in the power of this obscure Jew would uplift and ennoble every power of the being?

To the minds of multitudes living at the present time, the cross of Calvary is surrounded by sacred memories. Hallowed associations are connected with the scenes of the crucifixion. But in Paul's day the cross was regarded with feelings of repulsion and horror. To uphold as the Saviour of mankind one who had met death on the cross, would naturally call forth ridicule and opposition.

Paul well knew how his message would be regarded by both the Jews and the Greeks of Corinth. "We preach Christ crucified," he admitted, "unto the Jews a stumbling block, and unto the Greeks foolishness." 1 Corinthians 1:23. Among his Jewish hearers there were many who would be angered by the message he was about to proclaim. In the estimation of the Greeks his words would be absurd folly. He would be looked upon as weak-minded for attempting to show how the cross could have any connection with the elevation of the race or the salvation of mankind.

But to Paul the cross was the one object of supreme interest. Ever since he had been arrested in his career of persecution against the followers of the crucified Nazarene he had never ceased to glory in the cross. At that time there had been given him a revelation of the infinite love of God, as revealed in the death of Christ; and a marvelous transformation had been wrought in his life, bringing all his plans and purposes into harmony with heaven. From that hour he had been a new man in Christ. He knew by personal experience that when a sinner once beholds the love of the Father, as seen in the sacrifice of His Son, and yields to the divine influence, a change of heart takes place, and henceforth Christ is all and in all.

At the time of his conversion, Paul was inspired with a longing desire to help his fellow men to behold Jesus of Nazareth as the Son of the living God, mighty to transform and to save. Henceforth his life was wholly devoted to an effort to portray the love and power of the Crucified One. His great heart of sympathy took in all classes. "I am debtor," he declared, "both to the Greeks, and to the barbarians; both to the wise, and to the unwise." Romans 1:14. Love for the Lord of glory, whom he had so relentlessly persecuted in the person of His saints, was the actuating principle of his conduct, his motive power. If ever his ardor in the path of duty flagged, one glance at the cross and the amazing love there revealed, was enough to cause him to gird up the loins of his mind and press forward in the path of self-denial.

Behold the apostle preaching in the synagogue at Corinth, reasoning from the writings of Moses and the prophets, and bringing his hearers down to the advent of the promised Messiah. Listen as he makes plain the work of the Redeemer as the great high priest of mankind—the One who through the sacrifice of His own life was to make atonement for sin once for all, and was then to take up His ministry in the heavenly sanctuary. Paul's hearers were made to understand that the Messiah for whose advent they had been longing, had already come; that His death was the antitype of all the sacrificial offerings, and that His ministry in the sanctuary in heaven was the great object that cast its shadow backward and made clear the ministry of the Jewish priesthood.

Paul "testified to the Jews that Jesus was Christ." From the Old Testament Scriptures he showed that according to the prophecies and the universal expectation of the Jews, the Messiah would be of the lineage of Abraham and of David; then he traced the descent of Jesus from the patriarch Abraham through the royal psalmist. He read the testimony of the prophets regarding the character and work of the promised Messiah, and His reception and treatment on the earth; then he showed that all these predictions had been fulfilled in the life, ministry, and death of Jesus of Nazareth.

Paul showed that Christ had come to offer salvation first of all to the nation that was looking for the Messiah's coming as the consummation and glory of their national existence. But that nation had rejected Him who would have given them life, and had chosen another leader, whose reign would end in death. He endeavored to bring home to his hearers the fact that repentance alone could save the Jewish nation from impending ruin. He revealed their ignorance concerning the meaning of those Scriptures which it was their chief boast and glory that they fully understood. He rebuked their worldliness, their love of station, titles, and display, and their inordinate selfishness.

In the power of the Spirit, Paul related the story of his own miraculous conversion and of his confidence in the Old Testament Scriptures, which had been so completely fulfilled in Jesus of Nazareth. His words were spoken with solemn earnestness, and his hearers could not but discern that he loved with all his heart the crucified and risen Saviour. They saw that his mind was centered in Christ, that his whole life was bound up with his Lord. So impressive were his words, that only those who were filled with the bitterest hatred against the Christian religion could stand unmoved by them.

But the Jews of Corinth closed their eyes to the evidence so clearly presented by the apostle, and refused to listen to his appeals. The same spirit that had led them to reject Christ, filled them with wrath and fury against His servant; and had not God especially protected him, that he might continue to bear the gospel message to the Gentiles, they would have put an end to his life.

"And when they opposed themselves, and blasphemed, he shook his raiment, and said unto them, Your blood be upon your own heads; I am clean: from henceforth I will go unto the Gentiles. And he departed thence, and entered into a certain man's house, named Justus, one that worshiped God, whose house joined hard to the synagogue."

Silas and Timothy had "come from Macedonia" to help Paul, and together they labored for the Gentiles. To the heathen, as well as to the Jews, Paul and his companions preached Christ as the Saviour of the fallen race. Avoiding complicated, far-fetched reasoning, the messengers of the cross dwelt upon the attributes of the Creator of the world, the Supreme Ruler of the universe. Their hearts aglow with the love of God and of His Son, they appealed to the heathen to behold the infinite sacrifice made in man's behalf. They knew that if those who had long been groping in the darkness of heathenism could but see the light streaming from Calvary's cross, they would be drawn to the Redeemer. "I, if I be lifted up," the Saviour had declared, "will draw all men unto Me." John 12:32.

The gospel workers in Corinth realized the terrible dangers threatening the souls of those for whom they were laboring; and it was with a sense of the responsibility resting on them that they presented the truth as it is in Jesus. Clear, plain, and decided was their message—a savor of life unto life, or of death unto death. And not only in their words, but in the daily life, was the gospel revealed. Angels co-operated with them, and the grace and power of God was shown in the conversion of many. "Crispus, the chief ruler of the synagogue, believed on the Lord with all his house; and many of the Corinthians hearing believed, and were baptized."

The hatred with which the Jews had always regarded the apostles was now intensified. The conversion and baptism of Crispus had the effect of exasperating instead of convincing these stubborn opposers. They could not bring arguments to disprove Paul's preaching, and for lack of such evidence they resorted to deception and malignant attack. They blasphemed the gospel and the name of Jesus. In their blind anger no words were too bitter, no device too low, for them to use. They could not deny that Christ had worked miracles; but they declared that He had performed them through the power of Satan; and they boldly affirmed that the wonderful works wrought by Paul were accomplished through the same agency.

Though Paul had a measure of success in Corinth, yet the wickedness that he saw and heard in that corrupt city almost disheartened him. The depravity that he witnessed among the Gentiles, and the contempt and insult that he received from the Jews, caused him great anguish of spirit. He doubted the wisdom of trying to build up a church from the material that he found there.

As he was planning to leave the city for a more promising field, and seeking earnestly to understand his duty, the Lord appeared to him in a vision and said, "Be not afraid, but speak, and hold not thy peace: for I am with thee, and no man shall set on thee to hurt thee: for I have much people in this city." Paul understood this to be a command to remain in Corinth and a guarantee that the Lord would give increase to the seed sown. Strengthened and encouraged, he continued to labor there with zeal and perseverance.

The apostle's efforts were not confined to public speaking; there were many who could not have been reached in that way. He spent much time in house-to-house labor, thus availing himself of the familiar intercourse of the home circle. He visited the sick and the sorrowing, comforted the afflicted, and lifted up the oppressed. And in all that he said and did he magnified the name of Jesus. Thus he labored, "in weakness, and in fear, and in much trembling." 1 Corinthians 2:3. He trembled lest his teaching should reveal the impress of the human rather than the divine.

"We speak wisdom among them that are perfect," Paul afterward declared; "yet not the wisdom of this world, nor of the princes of this world, that come to nought: but we speak the wisdom of God in a mystery, even the hidden wisdom, which God ordained before the world unto our glory: which none of the princes of this world knew: for had they known it, they would not have crucified the Lord of glory. But as it is written, Eye hath not seen, nor ear heard, neither have entered into the heart of man, the things which God hath prepared for them that love Him. But God hath revealed them unto us by His Spirit: for the Spirit searcheth all things, yea, the deep things of God. For what man knoweth the things of a man, save the spirit of man which is in him? even so the things of God knoweth no man, but the Spirit of God.

"Now we have received, not the spirit of the world, but the spirit which is of God; that we might know the things that are freely given to us of God. Which things also we speak, not in the words which man's wisdom teacheth, but which the Holy Ghost teacheth; comparing spiritual things with spiritual." 1 Corinthians 2:6-13.

Paul realized that his sufficiency was not in himself, but in the presence of the Holy Spirit, whose gracious influence filled his heart, bringing every thought into subjection to Christ. He spoke of himself as "always bearing about in the body the dying of the Lord Jesus, that the life also of Jesus might be made manifest in our body." 2 Corinthians 4:10. In the apostle's teachings Christ was the central figure. "I live," he declared, "yet not I, but Christ liveth in me." Galatians 2:20. Self was hidden; Christ was revealed and exalted.

Paul was an eloquent speaker. Before his conversion he had often sought to impress his hearers by flights of oratory. But now he set all this aside. Instead of indulging in poetic descriptions and fanciful representations, which might please the senses and feed the imagination, but which would not touch the daily experience, Paul sought by the use of simple language to bring home to the heart the truths that are of vital importance. Fanciful representations of truth may cause an ecstasy of feeling, but all too often truths presented in this way do not supply the food necessary to strengthen and fortify the believer for the battles of life. The immediate needs, the present trials, of struggling souls—these must be met with sound, practical instruction in the fundamental principles of Christianity.

Paul's efforts in Corinth were not without fruit. Many turned from the worship of idols to serve the living God, and a large church was enrolled under the banner of Christ. Some were rescued from among the most dissipated of the Gentiles and became monuments of the mercy of God and the efficacy of the blood of Christ to cleanse from sin.

The increased success that Paul had in presenting Christ, roused the unbelieving Jews to more determined opposition. They rose in a body and "made insurrection with one accord against Paul, and brought him to the judgment seat" of Gallio, who was then proconsul of Achaia. They expected that the authorities, as on former occasions, would side with them; and with loud, angry voices they uttered their complaints against the apostle, saying, "This fellow persuadeth men to worship God contrary to the law."

The Jewish religion was under the protection of the Roman power, and the accusers of Paul thought that if they could fasten upon him the charge of violating the laws of their religion, he would probably be delivered to them for trial and sentence. They hoped thus to compass his death. But Gallio was a man of integrity, and he refused to become the dupe of the jealous, intriguing Jews. Disgusted with their bigotry and self-righteousness, he would take no notice of the charge. As Paul prepared to speak in self-defense, Gallio told him that it was not necessary. Then turning to the angry accusers, he said, "If it were a matter of wrong or wicked lewdness, O ye Jews, reason would that I should bear with you: but if it be a question of words and names, and of your law, look ye to it; for I will be no judge of such matters. And he drave them from the judgment seat."

Both Jews and Greeks had waited eagerly for Gallio's decision; and his immediate dismissal of the case, as one that had no bearing upon the public interest, was the signal for the Jews to retire, baffled and angry. The proconsul's decided course opened the eyes of the clamorous crowd who had been abetting the Jews. For the first time during Paul's labors in Europe, the mob turned to his side; under the very eye of the proconsul, and without interference from him, they violently beset the most prominent accusers of the apostle. "All the Greeks took Sosthenes, the chief ruler of the synagogue, and beat him before the judgment seat. And Gallio cared for none of those things." Thus Christianity obtained a signal victory.

"Paul after this tarried there yet a good while." If the apostle had at this time been compelled to leave Corinth, the converts to the faith of Jesus would have been placed in a perilous position. The Jews would have endeavored to follow up the advantage gained, even to the extermination of Christianity in that region.

The Thessalonian Letters

The arrival of Silas and Timothy from Macedonia, during Paul's sojourn in Corinth, had greatly cheered the apostle. They brought him "good tidings" of the "faith and charity" of those who had accepted the truth during the first visit of the gospel messengers to Thessalonica. Paul's heart went out in tender sympathy toward these believers, who, in the midst of trial and adversity, had remained true to God. He longed to visit them in person, but as this was not then possible, he wrote to them.

In this letter to the church at Thessalonica the apostle expresses his gratitude to God for the joyful news of their increase of faith. "Brethren," he wrote, "we were comforted over you in all our affliction and distress by your faith: for now we live, if ye stand fast in the Lord. For what thanks can we render to God again for you, for all the joy wherewith we joy for your sakes before our God; night and day praying exceedingly that we might see your face, and might perfect that which is lacking in your faith?"

"We give thanks to God always for you all, making mention of you in our prayers; remembering without ceasing your work of faith, and labor of love, and patience of hope in our Lord Jesus Christ, in the sight of God and our Father."

Many of the believers in Thessalonica had "turned . . . from idols to serve the living and true God." They had "received the word in much affliction;" and their hearts were filled with "joy of the Holy Ghost." The apostle declared that in their faithfulness in following the Lord they were "ensamples to all that believe in Macedonia and Achaia." These words of commendation were not unmerited; "for from you," he wrote, "sounded out the word of the Lord not only in Macedonia and Achaia, but also in every place your faith to Godward is spread abroad."

The Thessalonian believers were true missionaries. Their hearts burned with zeal for their Saviour, who had delivered them from fear of "the wrath to come." Through the grace of Christ a marvelous transformation had taken place in their lives, and the word of the Lord, as spoken through them, was accompanied with power. Hearts were won by the truths presented, and souls were added to the number of believers.

In this first epistle, Paul referred to his manner of labor among the Thessalonians. He declared that he had not sought to win converts through deception or guile. "As we were allowed of God to be put in trust with the gospel, even so we speak; not as pleasing men, but God, which trieth our hearts. For neither at any time used we flattering words, as ye know, nor a cloak of covetousness; God is witness: nor of men sought we glory, neither of you, nor yet of others, when we might have been burdensome, as the apostles of Christ. But we were gentle among you, even as a nurse cherisheth her children: so being affectionately desirous of you, we were willing to have imparted unto you, not the gospel of God only, but also our own souls, because ye were dear unto us."

"Ye are witnesses, and God also," the apostle continued, "how holily and justly and unblamably we behaved ourselves among you that believe: as ye know how we exhorted and comforted and charged every one of you, as a father doth his children, that ye would walk worthy of God, who hath called you unto His kingdom and glory.

"For this cause also thank we God without ceasing, because, when ye receive the word of God which ye heard of us, ye received it not as the word of men, but as it is in truth, the word of God, which effectually worketh also in you that believe." "What is our hope, or joy, or crown of rejoicing? Are not even ye in the presence of our Lord Jesus Christ at His coming? For ye are our glory and joy."

In his first epistle to the Thessalonian believers, Paul endeavored to instruct them regarding the true state of the dead. He spoke of those who die as being asleep—in a state of unconsciousness: "I would not have you to be ignorant, brethren, concerning them which are asleep, that ye sorrow not, even as others which have no hope. For if we believe that Jesus died and rose again, even so them also which sleep in Jesus will God bring with Him. . . . For the Lord Himself shall descend from heaven with a shout, with the voice of the Archangel, and with the trump of God: and the dead in Christ shall rise first: then we which are alive and remain shall be caught up together with them in the clouds, to meet the Lord in the air: and so shall we ever be with the Lord."

The Thessalonians had eagerly grasped the idea that Christ was coming to change the faithful who were alive, and to take them to Himself. They had carefully guarded the lives of their friends, lest they should die and lose the blessing which they looked forward to receiving at the coming of their Lord. But one after another their loved ones had been taken from them, and with anguish the Thessalonians had looked for the last time upon the faces of their dead, hardly daring to hope to meet them in a future life.

As Paul's epistle was opened and read, great joy and consolation was brought to the church by the words revealing the true state of the dead. Paul showed that those living when Christ should come would not go to meet their Lord in advance of those who had fallen asleep in Jesus. The voice of the Archangel and the trump of God would reach the sleeping ones, and the dead in Christ should rise first, before the touch of immortality should be given to the living. "Then we which are alive and remain shall be caught up together with them in the clouds, to meet the Lord in the air: and so shall we ever be with the Lord. Wherefore comfort one another with these words."

The hope and joy that this assurance brought to the young church at Thessalonica can scarcely be appreciated by us. They believed and cherished the letter sent to them by their father in the gospel, and their hearts went out in love to him. He had told them these things before; but at that time their minds were striving to grasp doctrines that seemed new and strange, and it is not surprising that the force of some points had not been vividly impressed on their minds. But they were hungering for truth, and Paul's epistle gave them new hope and strength, and a firmer faith in, and a deeper affection for, the One who through His death had brought life and immortality to light.

Now they rejoiced in the knowledge that their believing friends would be raised from the grave to live forever in the kingdom of God. The darkness that had enshrouded the resting place of the dead was dispelled. A new splendor crowned the Christian faith, and they saw a new glory in the life, death, and resurrection of Christ.

"Even so them also which sleep in Jesus will God bring with Him," Paul wrote. Many interpret this passage to mean that the sleeping ones will be brought with Christ from heaven; but Paul meant that as Christ was raised from the dead, so God will call the sleeping saints from their graves and take them with Him to heaven. Precious consolation! glorious hope! not only to the church of Thessalonica, but to all Christians wherever they may be.

While laboring at Thessalonica, Paul had so fully covered the subject of the signs of the times, showing what events would occur prior to the revelation of the Son of man in the clouds of heaven, that he did not think it necessary to write at length regarding this subject. He, however, pointedly referred to his former teachings. "Of the times and the seasons," he said, "ye have no need that I write unto you. For yourselves know perfectly that the day of the Lord so cometh as a thief in the night. For when they shall say, Peace and safety; then sudden destruction cometh upon them."

There are in the world today many who close their eyes to the evidences that Christ has given to warn men of His coming. They seek to quiet all apprehension, while at the same time the signs of the end are rapidly fulfilling, and the world is hastening to the time when the Son of man shall be revealed in the clouds of heaven. Paul teaches that it is sinful to be indifferent to the signs which are to precede the second coming of Christ. Those guilty of this neglect he calls children of the night and of darkness. He encourages the vigilant and watchful with these words: "But ye, brethren, are not in darkness, that that day should overtake you as a thief. Ye are all the children of light, and the children of the day: we are not of the night, nor of darkness. Therefore let us not sleep, as do others; but let us watch and be sober."

Especially important to the church in our time are the teachings of the apostle upon this point. To those living so near the great consummation, the words of Paul should come with telling force: "Let us, who are of the day, be sober, putting on the breastplate of faith and love; and for a helmet, the hope of salvation. For God hath not appointed us to wrath, but to obtain salvation by our Lord Jesus Christ, who died for us, that, whether we wake or sleep, we should live together with Him."

The watchful Christian is a working Christian, seeking zealously to do all in his power for the advancement of the gospel. As love for his Redeemer increases, so also does love for his fellow men. He has severe trials, as had his Master; but he does not allow affliction to sour his temper or destroy his peace of mind. He knows that trial, if well borne, will refine and purify him, and bring him into closer fellowship with Christ. Those who are partakers of Christ's sufferings will also be partakers of His consolation and at last sharers of His glory.

"We beseech you, brethren," Paul continued in his letter to the Thessalonians, "to know them which labor among you, and are over you in the Lord, and admonish you; and to esteem them very highly in love for their work's sake. And be at peace among yourselves."

The Thessalonian believers were greatly annoyed by men coming among them with fanatical ideas and doctrines. Some were "disorderly, working not at all, but . . . busy-bodies." The church had been properly organized, and officers had been appointed to act as ministers and deacons. But there were some, self-willed and impetuous, who refused to be subordinate to those who held positions of authority in the church. They claimed not only the right of private judgment, but that of publicly urging their views upon the church. In view of this, Paul called the attention of the Thessalonians to the respect and deference due to those who had been chosen to occupy positions of authority in the church.

In his anxiety that the believers at Thessalonica should walk in the fear of God, the apostle pleaded with them to reveal practical godliness in the daily life. "We beseech you, brethren," he wrote, "and exhort you by the Lord Jesus, that as ye have received of us how ye ought to walk and to please God, so ye would abound more and more. For ye know what commandments we gave you by the Lord Jesus. For this is the will of God, even your sanctification, that ye should abstain from fornication." "For God hath not called us unto uncleanness, but unto holiness."

The apostle felt that he was to a large extent responsible for the spiritual welfare of those converted under his labors. His desire for them was that they might increase in a knowledge of the only true God, and Jesus Christ, whom He had sent. Often in his ministry he would meet with little companies of men and women who loved Jesus, and bow with them in prayer, asking God to teach them how to maintain a living connection with Him. Often he took counsel with them as to the best methods of giving to others the light of gospel truth. And often, when separated from those for whom he had thus labored, he pleaded with God to keep them from evil and help them to be earnest, active missionaries.

One of the strongest evidences of true conversion is love to God and man. Those who accept Jesus as their Redeemer have a deep, sincere love for others of like precious faith. Thus it was with the believers at Thessalonica. "As touching brotherly love," the apostle wrote, "ye need not that I write unto you: for ye yourselves are taught of God to love one another. And indeed ye do it toward all the brethren which are in all Macedonia: but we beseech you, brethren, that ye increase more and more; and that ye study to be quiet, and to do your own business, and to work with your own hands, as we commanded you; that ye may walk honestly toward them that are without, and that ye may have lack of nothing."

"The Lord make you to increase and abound in love one toward another, and toward all men, even as we do toward you: to the end He may stablish your hearts unblamable in holiness before God, even our Father, at the coming of our Lord Jesus Christ with all His saints."

"Now we exhort you, brethren, warn them that are unruly, comfort the feeble-minded, support the weak, be patient toward all men. See that none render evil for evil unto any man; but ever follow that which is good, both among yourselves, and to all men. Rejoice evermore. Pray without ceasing. In everything give thanks: for this is the will of God in Christ Jesus concerning you." The apostle cautioned the Thessalonians not to despise the gift of prophecy, and in the words, "Quench not the Spirit; despise not prophesyings; prove all things; hold fast that which is good," he enjoined a careful discrimination in distinguishing the false from the true. He besought them to "abstain from all appearance of evil;" and closed his letter with the prayer that God would sanctify them wholly, that in "Spirit and soul and body" they might "be preserved blameless unto the coming of our Lord Jesus Christ. Faithful is He that calleth you," he added, "who also will do it."

The instruction that Paul sent the Thessalonians in his first epistle regarding the second coming of Christ, was in perfect harmony with his former teaching. Yet his words were misapprehended by some of the Thessalonian brethren. They understood him to express the hope that he himself would live to witness the Saviour's advent. This belief served to increase their enthusiasm and excitement. Those who had previously neglected their responsibilities and duties, now became more persistent in urging their erroneous views.

In his second letter Paul sought to correct their misunderstanding of his teaching and to set before them his true position. He again expressed his confidence in their integrity, and his gratitude that their faith was strong, and that their love abounded for one another and for the cause of their Master. He told them that he presented them to other churches as an example of the patient, persevering faith that bravely withstands persecution and tribulation, and he carried their minds forward to the time of the second coming of Christ, when the people of God shall rest from all their cares and perplexities.

"We ourselves," he wrote, "glory in you in the churches of God for your patience and faith in all your persecutions and tribulations that ye endure: . . . and to you who are troubled rest with us, when the Lord Jesus shall be revealed from heaven with His mighty angels, in flaming fire taking vengeance on them that know not God, and that obey not the gospel of our Lord Jesus Christ: who shall be punished with everlasting destruction from the presence of the Lord, and from the glory of His power. . . . Wherefore also we pray always for you, that our God would count you worthy of this calling, and fulfill all the good pleasure of His goodness, and the work of faith with power: that the name of our Lord Jesus Christ may be glorified in you, and ye in Him, according to the grace of our God and the Lord Jesus Christ."

But before the coming of Christ, important developments in the religious world, foretold in prophecy, were to take place. The apostle declared: "Be not soon shaken in mind, or be troubled, neither by spirit, nor by word, nor by letter as from us, as that the day of Christ is at hand. Let no man deceive you by any means: for that day shall not come, except there come a falling away first, and that man of sin be revealed, the son of perdition; who opposeth and exalteth himself above all that is called God, or that is worshiped; so that he as God sitteth in the temple of God, showing himself that he is God."

Paul's words were not to be misinterpreted. It was not to be taught that he, by special revelation, had warned the Thessalonians of the immediate coming of Christ. Such a position would cause confusion of faith; for disappointment often leads to unbelief. The apostle therefore cautioned the brethren to receive no such message as coming from him, and he proceeded to emphasize the fact that the papal power, so clearly described by the prophet Daniel, was yet to rise and wage war against God's people. Until this power should have performed its deadly and blasphemous work, it would be in vain for the church to look for the coming of their Lord. "Remember ye not," Paul inquired, "that, when I was yet with you, I told you these things?"

Terrible were the trials that were to beset the true church. Even at the time when the apostle was writing, the "mystery of iniquity" had already begun to work. The developments that were to take place in the future were to be "after the working of Satan with all power and signs and lying wonders, and with all deceivableness of unrighteousness in them that perish."

Especially solemn is the apostle's statement regarding those who should refuse to receive "the love of the truth." "For this cause," he declared of all who should deliberately reject the messages of truth, "God shall send them strong delusion, that they should believe a lie: that they all might be damned who believed not the truth, but had pleasure in unrighteousness." Men cannot with impunity reject the warnings that God in mercy sends them. From those who persist in turning from these warnings, God withdraws His Spirit, leaving them to the deceptions that they love.

Thus Paul outlined the baleful work of that power of evil which was to continue through long centuries of darkness and persecution before the second coming of Christ. The Thessalonian believers had hoped for immediate deliverance; now they were admonished to take up bravely and in the fear of God the work before them. The apostle charged them not to neglect their duties or resign themselves to idle waiting. After their glowing anticipations of immediate deliverance the round of daily life and the opposition that they must meet would appear doubly forbidding. He therefore exhorted them to steadfastness in the faith:

"Stand fast, and hold the traditions which ye have been taught, whether by word, or our epistle. Now our Lord Jesus Christ Himself, and God, even our Father, which hath loved us, and hath given us everlasting consolation and good hope through grace, comfort your hearts, and stablish you in every good work and work." "The Lord is faithful, who shall stablish you, and keep you from evil. And we have confidence in the Lord touching you, that ye both do and will do the things which we command you. And the Lord direct your hearts into the love of God, and into the patient waiting for Christ."

The work of the believers had been given them by God. By their faithful adherence to the truth they were to give to others the light which they had received. The apostle bade them not to become weary in well-doing, and pointed them to his own example of diligence in temporal matters while laboring with untiring zeal in the cause of Christ. He reproved those who had given themselves up to sloth and aimless excitement, and directed that "with quietness they work, and eat their own bread." He also enjoined upon the church to separate from their fellowship anyone who should persist in disregarding the instruction given by God's ministers. "Yet," he added, "count him not as an enemy, but admonish him as a brother."

This epistle also Paul concluded with a prayer that amidst life's toils and trials the peace of God and the grace of the Lord Jesus Christ might be their consolation and support.

Apollos at Corinth

After leaving Corinth, Paul's next scene of labor was Ephesus. He was on his way to Jerusalem to attend an approaching festival, and his stay at Ephesus was necessarily brief. He reasoned with the Jews in the synagogue, and so favorable was the impression made upon them that they entreated him to continue his labors among them. His plan to visit Jerusalem prevented him from tarrying then, but he promised to return to them, "if God will." Aquila and Priscilla had accompanied him to Ephesus, and he left them there to carry on the work that he had begun.

It was at this time that "a certain Jew named Apollos, born at Alexandria, an eloquent man, and mighty in the Scriptures, came to Ephesus." He had heard the preaching of John the Baptist, had received the baptism of repentance, and was a living witness that the work of the prophet had not been in vain. The Scripture record of Apollos is that he "was instructed in the way of the Lord; and being fervent in the spirit, he spake and taught diligently the things of the Lord, knowing only the baptism of John."

While in Ephesus, Apollos "began to speak boldly in the synagogue." Among his hearers were Aquila and Priscilla, who, perceiving that he had not yet received the full light of the gospel, "took him unto them, and expounded unto him the way of God more perfectly." Through their teaching he obtained a clearer understanding of the Scriptures and became one of the ablest advocates of the Christian faith.

Apollos was desirous of going on into Achaia, and the brethren at Ephesus "wrote, exhorting the disciples to receive him" as a teacher in full harmony with the church of Christ. He went to Corinth, where, in public labor and from house to house, "he mightily convinced the Jews, . . . showing by the Scriptures that Jesus was Christ." Paul had planted the seed of truth; Apollos now watered it. The success that attended Apollos in preaching the gospel led some of the believers to exalt his labors above those of Paul. This comparison of man with man brought into the church a party spirit that threatened to hinder greatly the progress of the gospel.

During the year and a half that Paul had spent in Corinth, he had purposely presented the gospel in its simplicity. "Not with excellency of speech or of wisdom" had he come to the Corinthians; but with fear and trembling, and "in demonstration of the Spirit and of power," had he declared "the testimony of God," that their "faith should not stand in the wisdom of men, but in the power of God." 1 Corinthians 2:1, 4, 5.

Paul had necessarily adapted his manner to teaching to the condition of the church. "I, brethren could not speak unto you as unto spiritual," he afterward explained to them, "but as unto carnal, even as unto babes in Christ. I have fed you with milk, and not with meat: for hitherto ye were not able to bear it, neither yet now are ye able." 1 Corinthians 3:1, 2. Many of the Corinthian believers had been slow to learn the lessons that he was endeavoring to teach them. Their advancement in spiritual knowledge had not been proportionate to their privileges and opportunities. When they should have been far advanced in Christian experience, and able to comprehend and to practice the deeper truths of the word, they were standing where the disciples stood when Christ said to them, "I have yet many things to say unto you, but ye cannot bear them now." John 16:12. Jealousy, evil surmising, and accusation had closed the hearts of many of the Corinthian believers against the full working of the Holy Spirit, which "searcheth all things, yea, the deep things of God." 1 Corinthians 2:10. However wise they might be in worldly knowledge, they were but babes in the knowledge of Christ.

It had been Paul's work to instruct the Corinthian converts in the rudiments, the very alphabet, of the Christian faith. He had been obliged to instruct them as those who were ignorant of the operations of divine power upon the heart. At that time they were unable to comprehend the mysteries of salvation; for "the natural man receiveth not the things of the Spirit of God: for they are foolishness unto him: neither can he know them, because they are spiritually discerned." Verse 14. Paul had endeavored to sow the seed, which others must water. Those who followed him must carry forward the work from the point where he had left it, giving spiritual light and knowledge in due season, as the church was able to bear it.

When the apostle took up his work in Corinth, he realized that he must introduce most carefully the great truths he wished to teach. He knew that among his hearers would be proud believers in human theories, and exponents of false systems of worship, who were groping with blinds eyes, hoping to find in the book of nature theories that would contradict the reality of the spiritual and immortal life as revealed in the Scriptures. He also knew that critics would endeavor to controvert the Christian interpretation of the revealed word, and that skeptics would treat the gospel of Christ with scoffing and derision.

As he endeavored to lead souls to the foot of the cross, Paul did not venture to rebuke, directly, those who were licentious, or to show how heinous was their sin in the sight of a holy God. Rather he set before them the true object of life and tried to impress upon their minds the lessons of the divine Teacher, which, if received, would lift them from worldliness and sin to purity and righteousness. He dwelt especially upon practical godliness and the holiness to which those must attain who shall be accounted worthy of a place in God's kingdom. He longed to see the light of the gospel of Christ piercing the darkness of their minds, that they might see how offensive in the sight of God were their immoral practices. Therefore the burden of his teaching among them was Christ and Him crucified. He sought to show them that their most earnest study and their greatest joy must be the wonderful truth of salvation through repentance toward God and faith in the Lord Jesus Christ.

The philosopher turns aside from the light of salvation, because it puts his proud theories to shame; the worldling refuses to receive it, because it would separate him from his earthly idols. Paul saw that the character of Christ must be understood before men could love Him or view the cross with the eye of faith. Here must begin that study which shall be the science and the song of the redeemed through all eternity. In the light of the cross alone can the true value of the human soul be estimated.

The refining influence of the grace of God changes the natural disposition of man. Heaven would not be desirable to the carnal-minded; their natural, unsanctified hearts would feel no attraction toward that pure and holy place, and if it were possible for them to enter, they would find there nothing congenial. The propensities that control the natural heart must be subdued by the grace of Christ before fallen man is fitted to enter heaven and enjoy the society of the pure, holy angels. When man dies to sin and is quickened to new life in Christ, divine love fills his heart; his understanding is sanctified; he drinks from an inexhaustible fountain of joy and knowledge, and the light of an eternal day shines upon his path, for with him continually is the Light of life.

Paul had sought to impress upon the minds of his Corinthian brethren the fact that he and the ministers associated with him were but men commissioned by God to teach the truth, that they were all engaged in the same work, and that they were alike dependent upon God for success in their labors. The discussion that had arisen in the church regarding the relative merits of different ministers was not in the order of God, but was the result of cherishing the attributes of the natural heart. "While one saith, I am of Paul; and another, I am of Apollos; are ye not carnal? Who then is Paul, and who is Apollos, but ministers by whom ye believed, even as the Lord gave to every man? I have planted, Apollos watered; but God gave the increase. So then neither is he that planteth anything, neither he that watereth; but God that giveth the increase." 1 Corinthians 3:4-7.

It was Paul who had first preached the gospel in Corinth, and who had organized the church there. This was the work that the Lord had assigned him. Later, by God's direction, other workers were brought in, to stand in their lot and place. The seed sown must be watered, and this Apollos was to do. He followed Paul in his work, to give further instruction, and to help the seed sown to develop. He won his way to the hearts of the people, but it was God who gave the increase. It is not human, but divine power, that works transformation of character. Those who plant and those who water do not cause the growth of the seed; they work under God, as His appointed agencies, co-operating with Him in His work. To the Master Worker belongs the honor and glory that comes with success.

God's servants do not all possess the same gifts, but they are all His workmen. Each is to learn of the Great Teacher, and is then to communicate what he has learned. God has given to each of His messengers an individual work. There is a diversity of gifts, but all the workers are to blend in harmony, controlled by the sanctifying influence of the Holy Spirit. As they make known the gospel of salvation, many will be convicted and converted by the power of God. The human instrumentality is hid with Christ in God, and Christ appears as the chiefest among ten thousand, the One altogether lovely.

"Now he that planteth and he that watereth are one: and every man shall receive his own reward according to his own labor. For we are laborers together with God: ye are God's husbandry, ye are God's building." Verses 8, 9. In this scripture the apostle compares the church to a cultivated field, in which the husbandmen labor, caring for the vines of the Lord's planting; and also to a building, which is to grow into a holy temple for the Lord. God is the Master Worker, and He has appointed to each man his work. All are to labor under His supervision, letting Him work for and through His workmen. He gives them tact and skill, and if they heed His instruction, crowns their efforts with success.

God's servants are to work together, blending in kindly, courteous order, "in honor preferring one another." Romans 12:10. There is to be no unkind criticism, no pulling to pieces of another's work; and there are to be no separate parties. Every man to whom the Lord has entrusted a message has his specific work. Each one has an individuality of his own, which he is not to sink in that of any other man. Yet each is to work in harmony with his brethren. In their service God's workers are to be essentially one. No one is to set himself up as a criterion, speaking disrespectfully of his fellow workers or treating them as inferior. Under God each is to do his appointed work, respected, loved, and encouraged by the other laborers. Together they are to carry the work forward to completion.

These principles are dwelt upon at length in Paul's first letter to the Corinthian church. The apostle refers to "the ministers of Christ" as "stewards of the mysteries of God," and of their work he declares: "It is required in stewards, that a man be found faithful. But with me it is a very small thing that I should be judged of you, or of man's judgment: yea, I judge not mine own self. For I know nothing by myself; yet I am not hereby justified: but He that judgeth me is the Lord. Therefore judge nothing before the time, until the Lord come, who both will bring to light the hidden things of darkness, and will make manifest the counsels of the hearts: and then shall every man have praise of God." 1 Corinthians 4:1-5.

It is not given to any human being to judge between the different servants of God. The Lord alone is the judge of man's work, and He will give to each his just reward.

The apostle, continuing, referred directly to the comparisons that had been made between his labors and those of Apollos: "These things, brethren, I have in a figure transferred to myself and to Apollos for your sakes; that ye might learn in us not to think of men above that which is written, that no one of you be puffed up for one against another. For who maketh thee to differ from another? and what hast thou that thou didst not receive? now if thou didst receive it, why dost thou glory, as if thou hadst not received it?" Verses 6, 7.

Paul plainly set before the church the perils and the hardships that he and his associates had patiently endured in their service for Christ. "Even unto this present hour," he declared, "we both hunger, and thirst, and are naked, and are buffeted, and have no certain dwelling place; and labor, working with our own hands: being reviled, we bless; being persecuted, we suffer it: being defamed, we entreat: we are made as the filth of the world, and are the offscouring of all things unto this day. I write not these things to shame you, but as my beloved sons I warn you. For though ye have ten thousand instructors in Christ, yet have ye not many fathers: for in Christ Jesus I have begotten you through the gospel." Verses 11-15.

He who sends forth gospel workers as His ambassadors is dishonored when there is manifested among the hearers so strong an attachment to some favorite minister that there is an unwillingness to accept the labors of some other teacher. The Lord sends help to His people, not always as they may choose, but as they need; for men are shortsighted and cannot discern what is for their highest good. It is seldom that one minister has all the qualifications necessary to perfect a church in all the requirements of Christianity; therefore God often sends to them other ministers, each possessing some qualifications in which the others were deficient.

The church should gratefully accept these servants of Christ, even as they would accept the Master Himself. They should seek to derive all the benefit possible from the instruction which each minister may give them from the word of God. The truths that the servants of God bring are to be accepted and appreciated in the meekness of humility, but no minister is to be idolized.

Through the grace of Christ, God's ministers are made messengers of light and blessing. As by earnest, persevering prayer they obtain the endowment of the Holy Spirit and go forth weighted with the burden of soulsaving, their hearts filled with zeal to extend the triumphs of the cross, they will see fruit of their labors. Resolutely refusing to display human wisdom or to exalt self, they will accomplish a work that will withstand the assaults of Satan. Many souls will be turned from darkness to light, and many churches will be established. Men will be converted, not to the human instrumentality, but to Christ. Self will be kept in the background; Jesus only, the Man of Calvary, will appear.

Those who are working for Christ today may reveal the same distinguishing excellencies revealed by those who in the apostolic age proclaimed the gospel. God is just as ready to give power to His servants today as He was to give power to Paul and Apollos, to Silas and Timothy, to Peter, James, and John.

In the apostles' day there were some misguided souls who claimed to believe in Christ, yet refused to show respect to His ambassadors. They declared that they followed no human teacher, but were taught directly by Christ without the aid of the ministers of the gospel. They were independent in spirit and unwilling to submit to the voice of the church. Such men were in grave danger of being deceived.

God has placed in the church, as His appointed helpers, men of varied talents, that through the combined wisdom of many the mind of the Spirit may be met. Men who move in accordance with their own strong traits of character, refusing to yoke up with others who have had a long experience in the work of God, will become blinded by self-confidence, unable to discern between the false and the true. It is not safe for such ones to be chosen as leaders in the church; for they would follow their own judgment and plans, regardless of the judgment of their brethren. It is easy for the enemy to work through those who, themselves needing counsel at every step, undertake the guardianship of souls in their own strength, without having learned the lowliness of Christ.

Impressions alone are not a safe guide to duty. The enemy often persuades men to believe that it is God who is guiding them, when in reality they are following only human impulse. But if we watch carefully, and take counsel with our brethren, we shall be given an understanding of the Lord's will; for the promise is, "The meek will He guide in judgment: and the meek will He teach His way." Psalm 25:9.

In the early Christian church there were some who refused to recognize either Paul or Apollos, but held that Peter was their leader. They affirmed that Peter had been most intimate with Christ when the Master was upon the earth, while Paul had been a persecutor of the believers. Their views and feelings were bound about by prejudice. They did not show the liberality, the generosity, the tenderness, which reveals that Christ is abiding in the heart.

There was danger that this party spirit would result in great evil to the Christian church, and Paul was instructed by the Lord to utter words of earnest admonition and solemn protest. Of those who were saying, "I am of Paul; and I of Apollos; and I of Cephas; and I of Christ," the apostle inquired, "Is Christ divided? was Paul crucified for you? or were ye baptized in the name of Paul?" "Let no man glory in men," he pleaded. "For all things are yours; whether Paul, or Apollos, or Cephas, or the world, or life, or death, or things present, or things to come; all are yours; and ye are Christ's; and Christ is God's." 1 Corinthians 1:12, 13; 3:21-23.

Paul and Apollos were in perfect harmony. The latter was disappointed and grieved because of the dissension in the church at Corinth; he took no advantage of the preference shown to himself, nor did he encourage it, but hastily left the field of strife. When Paul afterward urged him to revisit Corinth, he declined and did not again labor there until long afterward when the church had reached a better spiritual state.

Ephesus

While Apollos was preaching at Corinth, Paul fulfilled his promise to return to Ephesus. He had made a brief visit to Jerusalem and had spent some time at Antioch, the scene of his early labors. Thence he traveled through Asia Minor, "over all the country of Galatia and Phrygia" (Acts 18:23), visiting the churches which he himself had established, and strengthening the faith of the believers.

In the time of the apostles the western portion of Asia Minor was known as the Roman province of Asia. Ephesus, the capital, was a great commercial center. Its harbor was crowded with shipping, and its streets were thronged with people from every country. Like Corinth, it presented a promising field for missionary effort.

The Jews, now widely dispersed in all civilized lands, were generally expecting the advent of the Messiah. When John the Baptist was preaching, many, in their visits to Jerusalem at the annual feasts, had gone out to the banks of the Jordan to listen to him. There they had heard Jesus proclaimed as the Promised One, and they had carried the tidings to all parts of the world. Thus had Providence prepared the way for the labors of the apostles.

On his arrival at Ephesus, Paul found twelve brethren, who, like Apollos, had been disciples of John the Baptist, and like him had gained some knowledge of the mission of Christ. They had not the ability of Apollos, but with the same sincerity and faith they were seeking to spread abroad the knowledge they had received.

These brethren knew nothing of the mission of the Holy Spirit. When asked by Paul if they had received the Holy Ghost, they answered, "We have not so much as heard whether there be any Holy Ghost." "Unto what then were ye baptized?" Paul inquired, and they said, "Unto John's baptism."

Then the apostle set before them the great truths that are the foundation of the Christian's hope. He told them of Christ's life on this earth and of His cruel death of shame. He told them how the Lord of life had broken the barriers of the tomb and risen triumphant over death. He repeated the Saviour's commission to His disciples: "All power is given unto Me in heaven and in earth. Go ye therefore, and teach all nations, baptizing them in the name of the Father, and of the Son, and of the Holy Ghost." Matthew 28:18, 19. He told them also of Christ's promise to send the Comforter, through whose power mighty signs and wonders would be wrought, and he described how gloriously this promise had been fulfilled on the Day of Pentecost.

With deep interest and grateful, wondering joy the brethren listened to Paul's words. By faith they grasped the wonderful truth of Christ's atoning sacrifice and received Him as their Redeemer. They were then baptized in the name of Jesus, and as Paul "laid his hands upon them," they received also the baptism of the Holy Spirit, by which they were enabled to speak the languages of other nations and to prophesy. Thus they were qualified to labor as missionaries in Ephesus and its vicinity and also to go forth to proclaim the gospel in Asia Minor.

It was by cherishing a humble, teachable spirit that these men gained the experience that enabled them to go out as workers into the harvest field. Their example presents to Christians a lesson of great value. There are many who make but little progress in the divine life because they are too self-sufficient to occupy the position of learners. They are content with a superficial knowledge of God's word. They do not wish to change their faith or practice and hence make no effort to obtain greater light.

If the followers of Christ were but earnest seekers after wisdom, they would be led into rich fields of truth as yet wholly unknown to them. He who will give himself fully to God will be guided by the divine hand. He may be lowly and apparently ungifted; yet if with a loving, trusting heart he obeys every intimation of God's will, his powers will be purified, ennobled, energized, and his capabilities will be increased. As he treasures the lessons of divine wisdom, a sacred commission will be entrusted to him; he will be enabled to make his life an honor to God and a blessing to the world. "The entrance of Thy words giveth light; it giveth understanding unto the simple." Psalm 119:130.

There are today many as ignorant of the Holy Spirit's work upon the heart as were those believers in Ephesus; yet no truth is more clearly taught in the word of God. Prophets and apostles have dwelt upon this theme. Christ Himself calls our attention to the growth of the vegetable world as an illustration of the agency of His Spirit in sustaining spiritual life. The sap of the vine, ascending from the root, is diffused to the branches, sustaining growth and producing blossoms and fruit. So the life-giving power of the Holy Spirit, proceeding from the Saviour, pervades the soul, renews the motives and affections, and brings even the thoughts into obedience to the will of God, enabling the receiver to bear the precious fruit of holy deeds.

The Author of this spiritual life is unseen, and the exact method by which that life is imparted and sustained, it is beyond the power of human philosophy to explain. Yet the operations of the Spirit are always in harmony with the written word. As in the natural, so in the spiritual world. The natural life is preserved moment by moment by divine power; yet it is not sustained by a direct miracle, but through the use of blessings placed within our reach. So the spiritual life is sustained by the use of those means that Providence has supplied. If the follower of Christ would grow up "unto a perfect man, unto the measure of the stature of the fullness of Christ" (Ephesians 4:13), he must eat of the bread of life and drink of the water of salvation. He must watch and pray and work, in all things giving heed to the instructions of God in His word.

There is still another lesson for us in the experience of those Jewish converts. When they received baptism at the hand of John they did not fully comprehend the mission of Jesus as the Sin Bearer. They were holding serious errors. But with clearer light, they gladly accepted Christ as their Redeemer, and with this step of advance came a change in their obligations. As they received a purer faith, there was a corresponding change in their life. In token of this change, and as an acknowledgment of their faith in Christ, they were rebaptized in the name of Jesus.

As was his custom, Paul had begun his work at Ephesus by preaching in the synagogue of the Jews. He continued to labor there for three months, "disputing and persuading the things concerning the kingdom of God." At first he met with a favorable reception; but as in other fields, he was soon violently opposed. "Divers were hardened, and believed not, but spake evil of that way before the multitude." As they persisted in their rejection of the gospel, the apostle ceased to preach in the synagogue.

The Spirit of God had wrought with and through Paul in his labors for his countrymen. Sufficient evidence had been presented to convince all who honestly desired to know the truth. But many permitted themselves to be controlled by prejudice and unbelief, and refused to yield to the most conclusive evidence. Fearing that the faith of the believers would be endangered by continued association with these opposers of the truth, Paul separated from them and gathered the disciples into a distinct body, continuing his public instructions in the school of Tyrannus, a teacher of some note.

Paul saw that "a great door and effectual" was opening before him, although there were "many adversaries." 1 Corinthians 16:9. Ephesus was not only the most magnificent, but the most corrupt, of the cities of Asia. Superstition and sensual pleasure held sway over her teeming population. Under the shadow of her temples, criminals of every grade found shelter, and the most degrading vices flourished.

Ephesus was a popular center for the worship of Diana. The fame of the magnificent temple of "Diana of the Ephesians" extended throughout all Asia and the world. Its surpassing splendor made it the pride, not only of the city, but of the nation. The idol within the temple was declared by tradition to have fallen from the sky. Upon it were inscribed symbolic characters, which were believed to possess great power. Books had been written by the Ephesians to explain the meaning and use of these symbols.

Among those who gave close study to these costly books were many magicians, who wielded a powerful influence over the minds of the superstitious worshipers of the image within the temple.

The apostle Paul, in his labors at Ephesus, was given special tokens of divine favor. The power of God accompanied his efforts, and many were healed of physical maladies. "God wrought special miracles by the hands of Paul: so that from his body were brought unto the sick handkerchiefs or aprons, and the diseases departed from them, and the evil spirits went out of them." These manifestations of supernatural power were far more potent than had ever before been witnessed in Ephesus, and were of such a character that they could not be imitated by the skill of the juggler or the enchantments of the sorcerer. As these miracles were wrought in the name of Jesus of Nazareth, the people had opportunity to see that the God of heaven was more powerful than the magicians who were worshipers of the goddess Diana. Thus the Lord exalted His servant, even before the idolaters themselves, immeasurably above the most powerful and favored of the magicians.

But the One to whom all the spirits of evil are subject and who had given His servants authority over them, was about to bring still greater shame and defeat upon those who despised and profaned His holy name. Sorcery had been prohibited by the Mosaic law, on pain of death, yet from time to time it had been secretly practiced by apostate Jews. At the time of Paul's visit to Ephesus there were in the city "certain of the vagabond Jews, exorcists," who, seeing the wonders wrought by him, "took upon them to call over them which had evil spirits the name of the Lord Jesus." An attempt was made by "seven sons of one Sceva, a Jew, and chief of the priests." Finding a man possessed with a demon, they addressed him, "We adjure you by Jesus whom Paul preacheth." But "the evil spirit answered and said, Jesus I know, and Paul I know; but who are ye? And the man in whom the evil spirit was leaped on them, and overcame them, and prevailed against them, so that they fled out of that house naked and wounded."

Thus unmistakable proof was given of the sacredness of the name of Christ, and the peril which they incurred who should invoke it without faith in the divinity of the Saviour's mission. "Fear fell on them all, and the name of the Lord Jesus was magnified."

Facts which had previously been concealed were now brought to light. In accepting Christianity, some of the believers had not fully renounced their superstitions. To some extent they still continued the practice of magic. Now, convinced of their error, "many that believed came, and confessed, and showed their deeds." Even to some of the sorcerers themselves the good work extended; and "many of them also which used curious arts brought their books together, and burned them before all men: and they counted the price of them, and found it fifty thousand pieces of silver. So mightily grew the word of God and prevailed."

By burning their books on magic, the Ephesian converts showed that the things in which they had once delighted they now abhorred. It was by and through magic that they had especially offended God and imperiled their souls; and it was against magic that they showed such indignation. Thus they gave evidence of true conversion.

These treatises on divination contained rules and forms of communication with evil spirits. They were the regulations of the worship of Satan—directions for soliciting his help and obtaining information from him. By retaining these books the disciples would have exposed themselves to temptation; by selling them they would have placed temptation in the way of others. They had renounced the kingdom of darkness, and to destroy its power they did not hesitate at any sacrifice. Thus truth triumphed over men's prejudices and their love of money.

By this manifestation of the power of Christ, a mighty victory for Christianity was gained in the very stronghold of superstition. The influence of what had taken place was more widespread than even Paul realized. From Ephesus the news was widely circulated, and a strong impetus was given to the cause of Christ. Long after the apostle himself had finished his course, these scenes lived in the memory of men and were the means of winning converts to the gospel.

It is fondly supposed that heathen superstitions have disappeared before the civilization of the twentieth century. But the word of God and the stern testimony of facts declare that sorcery is practiced in this age as verily as in the days of the old-time magicians. The ancient system of magic is, in reality, the same as what is now known as modern spiritualism. Satan is finding access to thousands of minds by presenting himself under the guise of departed friends. The Scriptures declare that "the dead know not anything." Ecclesiastes 9:5. Their thoughts, their love, their hatred, have perished. The dead do not hold communion with the living. But true to his early cunning, Satan employs this device in order to gain control of minds.

Through spiritualism many of the sick, the bereaved, the curious, are communicating with evil spirits. All who venture to do this are on dangerous ground. The word of truth declares how God regards them. In ancient times He pronounced a stern judgment on a king who had sent for counsel to a heathen oracle: "Is it not because there is not a God in Israel, that ye go to inquire of Baal-zebub the god of Ekron? Now therefore thus saith the Lord, Thou shalt not come down from that bed on which thou art gone up, but shalt surely die." 2 Kings 1:3, 4.

The magicians of heathen times have their counterpart in the spiritualistic mediums, the clairvoyants, and the fortune-tellers of today. The mystic voices that spoke at Endor and at Ephesus are still by their lying words misleading the children of men. Could the veil be lifted from before our eyes, we should see evil angels employing all their arts to deceive and to destroy. Wherever an influence is exerted to cause men to forget God, there Satan is exercising his bewitching power. When men yield to his influence, ere they are aware the mind is bewildered and the soul polluted. The apostle's admonition to the Ephesian church should be heeded by the people of God today: "Have no fellowship with the unfruitful works of darkness, but rather reprove them." Ephesians 5:11.

Days of Toil and Trial

For over three years Ephesus was the center of Paul's work. A flourishing church was raised up here, and from this city the gospel spread throughout the province of Asia, among both Jews and Gentiles.

The apostle had now for some time had been contemplating another missionary journey. He "purposed in the spirit, when he had passed through Macedonia and Achaia, to go to Jerusalem, saying, After I have been there, I must also see Rome." In harmony with this plan "he sent into Macedonia two of them that ministered unto him, Timotheus and Erastus;" but feeling that the cause in Ephesus still demanded his presence, he decided to remain until after Pentecost. An event soon occurred, however, which hastened his departure.

Once a year, special ceremonies were held at Ephesus in honor of the goddess Diana. These attracted great numbers of people from all parts of the province. Throughout this period, festivities were conducted with the utmost pomp and splendor.

This gala season was a trying time for those who had newly come to the faith. The company of believers who met in the school of Tyrannus were an inharmonious note in the festive chorus, and ridicule, reproach, and insult were freely heaped upon them. Paul's labors had given the heathen worship a telling blow, in consequence of which there was a perceptible falling off in the attendance at the national festival and in the enthusiasm of the worshipers. The influence of his teachings extended far beyond the actual converts to the faith. Many who had not openly accepted the new doctrines became so far enlightened as to lose all confidence in their heathen gods.

There existed also another cause of dissatisfaction. An extensive and profitable business had grown up at Ephesus from the manufacture and sale of small shrines and images, modeled after the temple and the image of Diana. Those interested in this industry found their gains diminishing, and all united in attributing the unwelcome change to Paul's labors.

Demetrius, a manufacturer of silver shrines, calling together the workmen of his craft, said: "Sirs, ye know that by this craft we have our wealth. Moreover ye see and hear, that not alone at Ephesus, but almost throughout all Asia, this Paul hath persuaded and turned away much people, saying that they be no gods, which are made with hands: so that not only this our craft is in danger to be set at nought; but also that the temple of the great goddess Diana should be despised, and her magnificence should be destroyed, whom all Asia and the world worshipeth." These words roused the excitable passions of the people. "They were full of wrath, and cried out, saying, Great is Diana of the Ephesians."

A report of this speech was rapidly circulated. "The whole city was filled with confusion." Search was made for Paul, but the apostle was not to be found. His brethren, receiving an intimation of the danger, had hurried him from the place. Angels of God had been sent to guard the apostle; his time to die a martyr's death had not yet come.

Failing to find the object of their wrath, the mob seized "Gaius and Aristarchus, men of Macedonia, Paul's companions in travel," and with these "they rushed with one accord into the theater."

Paul's place of concealment was not far distant, and he soon learned of the peril of his beloved brethren. Forgetful of his own safety, he desired to go at once to the theater to address the rioters. But "the disciples suffered him not." Gaius and Aristarchus were not the prey the people sought; no serious harm to them was apprehended. But should the apostle's pale, care-worn face be seen, it would arouse at once the worst passions of the mob and there would not be the least human possibility of saving his life.

Paul was still eager to defend the truth before the multitude, but he was at last deterred by a message of warning from the theater. "Certain of the chief of Asia, which were his friends, sent unto him, desiring him that he would not adventure himself into the theater."

The tumult in the theater was continually increasing. "Some . . . cried one thing, and some another: for the assembly was confused; and the more part knew not wherefore they were come together." The fact that Paul and some of his companions were of Hebrew extraction made the Jews anxious to show plainly that they were not sympathizers with him and his work. They therefore brought forward one of their own number to set the matter before the people. The speaker chosen was Alexander, one of the craftsmen, a coppersmith, to whom Paul afterward referred as having done him much evil. 2 Timothy 4:14. Alexander was a man of considerable ability, and he bent all his energies to direct the wrath of the people exclusively against Paul and his companions. But the crowd, seeing that Alexander was a Jew, thrust him aside, and "all with one voice about the space of two hours cried out, Great is Diana of the Ephesians."

At last, from sheer exhaustion, they ceased, and there was a momentary silence. Then the recorder of the city arrested the attention of the crowd, and by virtue of his office obtained a hearing. He met the people on their own ground and showed that there was no cause for the present tumult. He appealed to their reason. "Ye men of Ephesus," he said, "what man is there that knoweth not how that the city of the Ephesians is a worshiper of the great goddess Diana, and of the image which fell down from Jupiter? Seeing then that these things cannot be spoken against, ye ought to be quiet, and to do nothing rashly. For ye have brought hither these men, which are neither robbers of churches, nor yet blasphemers of your goddess. Wherefore if Demetrius, and the craftsmen which are with him, have a matter against any man, the law is open, and there are deputies: let them implead one another. But if ye inquire anything concerning other matters, it shall be determined in a lawful assembly. For we are in danger to be called in question for this day's uproar, there being no cause whereby we may give an account of this concourse. And when he had thus spoken, he dismissed the assembly."

In his speech Demetrius had said, "This our craft is in danger." These words reveal the real cause of the tumult at Ephesus, and also the cause of much of the persecution which followed the apostles in their work. Demetrius and his fellow craftsmen saw that by the teaching and spread of the gospel the business of image making was endangered. The income of pagan priests and artisans was at stake, and for this reason they aroused against Paul the most bitter opposition.

The decision of the recorder and of others holding honorable offices in the city had set Paul before the people as one innocent of any unlawful act. This was another triumph of Christianity over error and superstition. God had raised up a great magistrate to vindicate His apostle and hold the tumultuous mob in check. Paul's heart was filled with gratitude to God that his life had been preserved and that Christianity had not been brought into disrepute by the tumult at Ephesus.

"After the uproar was ceased, Paul called unto him the disciples, and embraced them, and departed for to go into Macedonia." On this journey he was accompanied by two faithful Ephesian brethren, Tychicus and Trophimus.

Paul's labors in Ephesus were concluded. His ministry there had been a season of incessant labor, of many trials, and of deep anguish. He had taught the people in public and from house to house, with many tears instructing and warning them. Continually he had been opposed by the Jews, who lost no opportunity to stir up the popular feeling against him.

And while thus battling against opposition, pushing forward with untiring zeal the gospel work, and guarding the interests of a church yet young in the faith, Paul was bearing upon his soul a heavy burden for all the churches.

News of apostasy in some of the churches of his planting caused him deep sorrow. He feared that his efforts in their behalf might prove to be in vain. Many a sleepless night was spent in prayer and earnest thought as he learned of the methods employed to counteract his work. As he had opportunity and as their condition demanded, he wrote to the churches, giving reproof, counsel, admonition, and encouragement. In these letters the apostle does not dwell on his own trials, yet there are occasional glimpses of his labors and sufferings in the cause of Christ. Stripes and imprisonment, cold and hunger and thirst, perils by land and by sea, in the city and in the wilderness, from his own countrymen, from the heathen, and from false brethren— all this he endured for the sake of the gospel. He was "defamed," "reviled," made "the offscouring of all things," "perplexed," "persecuted," "troubled on every side," "in jeopardy every hour," "alway delivered unto death for Jesus' sake."

Amidst the constant storm of opposition, the clamor of enemies, and the desertion of friends the intrepid apostle almost lost heart. But he looked back to Calvary and with new ardor pressed on to spread the knowledge of the Crucified. He was but treading the blood-stained path that Christ had trodden before him. He sought no discharge from the warfare till he should lay off his armor at the feet of his Redeemer.

A Message of Warning and Entreaty

The first epistle to the Corinthian church was written by the apostle Paul during the latter part of his stay at Ephesus. For no others had he felt a deeper interest or put forth more untiring effort than for the believers in Corinth. For a year and a half he had labored among them, pointing them to a crucified and risen Saviour as the only means of salvation, and urging them to rely implicitly on the transforming power of His grace. Before accepting into church fellowship those who made a profession of Christianity, he had been careful to give them special instruction as to the privileges and duties of the Christian believer, and he had earnestly endeavored to help them to be faithful to their baptismal vows.

Paul had a keen sense of the conflict which every soul must wage with the agencies of evil that are continually seeking to deceive and ensnare, and he had worked untiringly to strengthen and confirm those who were young in the faith. He had entreated them to make an entire surrender to God; for he knew that when the soul fails to make this surrender, then sin is not forsaken, the appetites and passions still strive for the mastery, and temptations confuse the conscience.

The surrender must be complete. Every weak, doubting, struggling soul who yields fully to the Lord is placed in direct touch with agencies that enable him to overcome. Heaven is near to him, and he has the support and help of angels of mercy in every time of trial and need.

The members of the church at Corinth were surrounded by idolatry and sensuality of the most alluring form. While the apostle was with them, these influences had but little power over them. Paul's firm faith, his fervent prayers and earnest words of instruction, and, above all, his godly life had helped them to deny self for Christ's sake rather than to enjoy the pleasures of sin.

After the departure of Paul, however, unfavorable conditions arose; tares that had been sown by the enemy appeared among the wheat, and erelong these began to bring forth their evil fruit. This was a time of severe trial to the Corinthian church. The apostle was no longer with them to quicken their zeal and aid them in their endeavors to live in harmony with God, and little by little many became careless and indifferent, and allowed natural tastes and inclinations to control them. He who had so often urged them to high ideals of purity and uprightness was no longer with them, and not a few who, at the time of their conversion, had put away their evil habits, returned to the debasing sins of heathenism.

Paul had written briefly to the church, admonishing them "not to company" with members who should persist in profligacy; but many of the believers perverted the apostle's meaning, quibbled over his words, and excused themselves for disregarding his instruction.

A letter was sent to Paul by the church, asking for counsel concerning various matters, but saying nothing of the grievous sins existing among them. The apostle was, however, forcibly impressed by the Holy Spirit that the true state of the church had been concealed and that this letter was an attempt to draw from him statements which the writers could construe to serve their own purposes.

About this time there came to Ephesus members of the household of Chloe, a Christian family of high repute in Corinth. Paul asked them regarding the condition of things, and they told him that the church was rent by divisions. The dissensions that had prevailed at the time of Apollos's visit had greatly increased. False teachers were leading the members to despise the instructions of Paul. The doctrines and ordinances of the gospel had been perverted. Pride, idolatry, and sensualism, were steadily increasing among those who had once been zealous in the Christian life.

As this picture was presented before him, Paul saw that his worst fears were more than realized. But he did not because of this give way to the thought that his work had been a failure. With "anguish of heart" and with "many tears" he sought counsel from God. Gladly would he have visited Corinth at once, had this been the wisest course to pursue. But he knew that in their present condition the believers would not profit by his labors, and therefore he sent Titus to prepare the way for a visit from himself later on. Then, putting aside all personal feelings over the course of those whose conduct revealed such strange perverseness, and keeping his soul stayed upon God, the apostle wrote to the church at Corinth one of the richest, most instructive, most powerful of all his letters.

With remarkable clearness he proceeded to answer the various questions brought forward by the church, and to lay down general principles, which, if heeded, would lead them to a higher spiritual plane. They were in peril, and he could not bear the thought of failing at this critical time to reach their hearts. Faithfully he warned them of their dangers and reproved them for their sins. He pointed them again to Christ and sought to kindle anew the fervor of their early devotion.

The apostle's great love for the Corinthian believers was revealed in his tender greeting to the church. He referred to their experience in turning from idolatry to the worship and service of the true God. He reminded them of the gifts of the

Holy Spirit which they had received, and showed that it was their privilege to make continual advancement in the Christian life until they should attain to the purity and holiness of Christ. "In everything ye are enriched by Him," he wrote, "in all utterance, and in all knowledge; even as the testimony of Christ was confirmed in you: so that ye come behind in no gift; waiting for the coming of our Lord Jesus Christ: who shall also confirm you unto the end, that ye may be blameless in the day of our Lord Jesus Christ."

Paul spoke plainly of the dissensions that had arisen in the Corinthian church, and exhorted the members to cease from strife. "I beseech you, brethren," he wrote, "by the name of our Lord Jesus Christ, that ye all speak the same thing, and that there be no divisions among you; but that ye be perfectly joined together in the same mind and in the same judgment."

The apostle felt at liberty to mention how and by whom he had been informed of the divisions in the church. "It hath been declared unto me of you, my brethren, by them which are of the house of Chloe, that there are contentions among you."

Paul was an inspired apostle. The truths he taught to others he had received "by revelation;" yet the Lord did not directly reveal to him at all times just the condition of His people. In this instance those who were interested in the prosperity of the church at Corinth, and who had seen evils creeping in, had presented the matter before the apostle, and from divine revelations which he had formerly received he was prepared to judge of the character of these developments. Notwithstanding the fact that the Lord did not give him a new revelation for that special time, those who were really seeking for light accepted his message as expressing the mind of Christ. The Lord had shown him the difficulties and dangers which would arise in the churches, and, as these evils developed, the apostle recognized their significance. He had been set for the defense of the church. He was to watch for souls as one who must render account to God, and was it not consistent and right for him to take notice of the reports concerning the anarchy and divisions among them? Most assuredly; and the reproof he sent them was as certainly written under the inspiration of the Spirit of God as were any of his other epistles.

The apostle made no mention of the false teachers who were seeking to destroy the fruit of his labor. Because of the darkness and division in the church, he wisely forbore to irritate them by such references, for fear of turning some entirely from the truth. He called attention to his own work among them as that of "a wise master builder," who had laid the foundation upon which others had built. But he did not thereby exalt himself; for he declared, "We are laborers together with God." He claimed no wisdom of his own, but acknowledged that divine power alone had enabled him to present the truth in a manner pleasing to God. United with Christ, the greatest of all teachers, Paul had been enabled to communicate lessons of divine wisdom, which met the necessities of all classes, and which were to apply at all times, in all places, and under all conditions.

Among the more serious of the evils that had developed among the Corinthian believers, was that of a return to many of the debasing customs of heathenism. One former convert had so far backslidden that his licentious course was a violation of even the low standard of morality held by the Gentile world. The apostle pleaded with the church to put away from among them "that wicked person." "Know ye not," he admonished them, "that a little leaven leaveneth the whole lump? Purge out therefore the old leaven, that ye may be a new lump, as ye are unleavened."

Another grave evil that had arisen in the church was that of brethren going to law against one another. Abundant provision had been made for the settlement of difficulties among believers. Christ Himself had given plain instruction as to how such matters were to be adjusted. "If thy brother shall trespass against thee," the Saviour had counseled, "go and tell him his fault between thee and him alone: if he shall hear thee, thou hast gained thy brother. But if he will not hear thee, then take with thee one or two more, that in the mouth of two or three witnesses every word may be established. And if he shall neglect to hear them, tell it unto the church: but if he neglect to hear the church, let him be unto thee as a heathen man and a publican. Verily I say unto you, Whatsoever ye shall bind on earth shall be bound in heaven: and whatsoever ye shall loose on earth shall be loosed in heaven." Matthew 18:15-18.

To the Corinthian believers who had lost sight of this plain counsel, Paul wrote in no uncertain terms of admonition and rebuke. "Dare any of you," he asked, "having a matter against another, go to law before the unjust, and not before the saints? Do ye not know that the saints shall judge the world? and if the world shall be judged by you, are ye unworthy to judge the smallest matters? Know ye not that we shall judge angels? how much more things that pertain to this life? If then ye have judgments of things pertaining to this life, set them to judge who are least esteemed in the church. I speak to your shame. Is it so, that there is not a wise man among you? no, not one that shall be able to judge between his brethren? But brother goeth to law with brother, and that before the unbelievers. Now therefore there is utterly a fault among you, because ye go to law one with another. Why do ye not rather take wrong? . . . Nay, ye do wrong, and defraud, and that your brethren. Know ye not that the unrighteous shall not inherit the kingdom of God?"

Satan is constantly seeking to introduce distrust, alienation, and malice among God's people. We shall often be tempted to feel that our rights are invaded, even when there is no real cause for such feelings. Those whose love for self is stronger than their love for Christ and His cause will place their own interests first and will resort to almost any expedient to guard and maintain them. Even many who appear to be conscientious Christians are hindered by pride and self-esteem from going privately to those whom they think in error, that they may talk with them in the spirit of Christ and pray together for one another. When they think themselves injured by their brethren, some will even go to law instead of following the Saviour's rule.

Christians should not appeal to civil tribunals to settle differences that may arise among church members. Such differences should be settled among themselves, or by the church, in harmony with Christ's instruction. Even though injustice may have been done, the follower of the meek and lowly Jesus will suffer himself "to be defrauded" rather than open before the world the sins of his brethren in the church.

Lawsuits between brethren are a reproach to the cause of truth. Christians who go to law with one another expose the church to the ridicule of her enemies and cause the powers of darkness to triumph. They are wounding Christ afresh and putting Him to open shame. By ignoring the authority of the church, they show contempt for God, who gave to the church its authority.

In this letter to the Corinthians Paul endeavored to show them Christ's power to keep them from evil. He knew that if they would comply with the conditions laid down, they would be strong in the strength of the Mighty One. As a means of helping them to break away from the thralldom of sin and to perfect holiness in the fear of the Lord, Paul urged upon them the claims of Him to whom they had dedicated their lives at the time of their conversion. "Ye are Christ's," he declared. "Ye are not your own. . . . Ye are bought with a price: therefore glorify God in your body, and in your spirit, which are God's."

The apostle plainly outlined the result of turning from a life of purity and holiness to the corrupt practices of heathenism. "Be not deceived," he wrote; "neither fornicators, nor idolaters, nor adulterers, . . . nor thieves, nor covetous, nor drunkards, nor revilers, nor extortioners, shall inherit the kingdom of God." He begged them to control the lower passions and appetites. "Know ye not," he asked, "that your body is the temple of the Holy Ghost which is in you, which ye have of God?"

While Paul possessed high intellectual endowments, his life revealed the power of a rarer wisdom, which gave him quickness of insight and sympathy of heart, and brought him into close touch with others, enabling him to arouse their better nature and inspire them to strive for a higher life. His heart was filled with an earnest love for the Corinthian believers. He longed to see them revealing an inward piety that would fortify them against temptation. He knew that at every step in the Christian pathway they would be opposed by the synagogue of Satan and that they would have to engage in conflicts daily. They would have to guard against the stealthy approach of the enemy, forcing back old habits and natural inclinations, and ever watching unto prayer. Paul knew that the higher Christian attainments can be reached only through much prayer and constant watchfulness, and this he tried to instill into their minds. But he knew also that in Christ crucified they were offered power sufficient to convert the soul and divinely adapted to enable them to resist all temptations to evil. With faith in God as their armor, and with His word as their weapon of warfare, they would be supplied with an inner power that would enable them to turn aside the attacks of the enemy.

The Corinthian believers needed a deeper experience in the things of God. They did not know fully what it meant to behold His glory and to be changed from character to character. They had seen but the first rays of the early dawn of that glory. Paul's desire for them was that they might be filled with all the fullness of God, following on to know Him whose going forth is prepared as the morning, and continuing to learn of Him until they should come into the full noontide of a perfect gospel faith.

Called to Reach a Higher Standard

In the hope of impressing vividly upon the minds of the Corinthian believers the importance of firm self-control, strict temperance, and unflagging zeal in the service of Christ, Paul in his letter to them made a striking comparison between the Christian warfare and the celebrated foot races held at stated intervals near Corinth. Of all the games instituted among the Greeks and the Romans, the foot races were the most ancient and the most highly esteemed. They were witnessed by kings, nobles, and statesmen. Young men of rank and wealth took part in them and shrank from no effort or discipline necessary to obtain the prize.

The contests were governed by strict regulations, from which there was no appeal. Those who desired their names entered as competitors for the prize had first to undergo a severe preparatory training. Harmful indulgence of appetite, or any other gratification that would lower mental or physical vigor, was strictly forbidden. For one to have any hope of success in these trials of strength and speed, the muscles must be strong and supple, and the nerves well under control. Every movement must be certain, every step swift and unswerving; the physical powers must reach the highest mark.

As the contestants in the race made their appearance before the waiting multitude, their names were heralded, and the rules of the race were distinctly stated. Then they all started together, the fixed attention of the spectators inspiring them with a determination to win. The judges were seated near the goal, that they might watch the race from its beginning to its close and give the prize to the true victor. If a man reached the goal first by taking an unlawful advantage, he was not awarded the prize.

In these contests great risks were run. Some never recovered from the terrible physical strain. It was not unusual for men to fall on the course, bleeding at the mouth and nose, and sometimes a contestant would drop dead when about to seize the prize. But the possibility of lifelong injury or of death was not looked upon as too great a risk to run for the sake of the honor awarded the successful contestant.

As the winner reached the goal, the applause of the vast multitude of onlookers rent the air and awoke the echoes of the surrounding hills and mountains. In full view of the spectators, the judge presented him with the emblems of victory—a laurel crown and a palm branch to carry in his right hand. His praise was sung throughout the land; his parents received their share of honor; and even the city in which he lived was held in high esteem for having produced so great an athlete.

In referring to these races as a figure of the Christian warfare, Paul emphasized the preparation necessary to the success of the contestants in the race—the preliminary discipline, the abstemious diet, the necessity for temperance. "Every man that striveth for the mastery," he declared, "is temperate in all things." The runners put aside every indulgence that would tend to weaken the physical powers, and by severe and continuous discipline trained their muscles to strength and endurance, that when the day of the contest should arrive, they might put the heaviest tax upon their powers. How much more important that the Christian, whose eternal interests are at stake, bring appetite and passion under subjection to reason and the will of God! Never must he allow his attention to be diverted by amusements, luxuries, or ease. All his habits and passions must be brought under the strictest discipline. Reason, enlightened by the teachings of God's word and guided by His Spirit, must hold the reins of control.

And after this has been done, the Christian must put forth the utmost exertion in order to gain the victory. In the Corinthian games the last few strides of the contestants in the race were made with agonizing effort to keep up undiminished speed. So the Christian, as he nears the goal, will press onward with even more zeal and determination than at the first of his course.

Paul presents the contrast between the chaplet of fading laurel received by the victor in the foot races, and the crown of immortal glory that will be given to him who runs with triumph the Christian race. "They do it," he declares, "to obtain a corruptible crown; but we an incorruptible." To win a perishable prize, the Grecian runners spared themselves no toil or discipline. We are striving for a prize infinitely more valuable, even the crown of everlasting life. How much more careful should be our striving, how much more willing our sacrifice and self-denial!

In the epistle to the Hebrews is pointed out the single-hearted purpose that should characterize the Christian's race for eternal life: "Let us lay aside every weight, and the sin which doth so easily beset us, and let us run with patience the race that is set before us, looking unto Jesus the author and finisher of our faith." Hebrews 12:1, 2. Envy, malice, evil thinking, evilspeaking, covetousness—these are weights that the Christian must lay aside if he would run successfully the race for immortality. Every habit or practice that leads into sin and brings dishonor upon Christ must be put away, whatever the sacrifice. The blessing of heaven cannot attend any man in violating the eternal principles of right. One sin cherished is sufficient to work degradation of character and to mislead others.

"If thy hand cause thee to stumble," the Saviour said, "Cut it off: it is good for thee to enter into life maimed, rather than having thy two hands to go into hell, into the unquenchable fire. And if thy foot cause thee to stumble, cut it off: it is good for thee to enter into life halt, rather than having thy two feet to be cast into hell." Mark 9:43-45, R.V. If to save the body from death, the foot or the hand should be cut off, or even the eye plucked out, how much more earnest should the Christian be to put away sin, which brings death to the soul!

The competitors in the ancient games, after they had submitted to self-denial and rigid discipline, were not even then sure of the victory. "Know ye not," Paul asked, "that they which run in a race run all, but one receiveth the prize?" However eagerly and earnestly the runners might strive, the prize could be awarded to but one. One hand only could grasp the coveted garland. Some might put forth the utmost effort to obtain the prize, but as they reached forth the hand to secure it, another, an instant before them, might grasp the coveted treasure.

Such is not the case in the Christian warfare. Not one who complies with the conditions will be disappointed at the end of the race. Not one who is earnest and persevering will fail of success. The race is not to the swift, nor the battle to the strong. The weakest saint, as well as the strongest, may wear the crown of immortal glory. All may win who, through the power of divine grace, bring their lives into conformity to the will of Christ. The practice, in the details of life, of the principles laid down in God's word, is too often looked upon as unimportant—a matter too trivial to demand attention. But in view of the issue at stake, nothing is small that will help or hinder. Every act casts its weight into the scale that determines life's victory or defeat. And the reward given to those who win will be in proportion to the energy and earnestness with which they have striven.

The apostle compared himself to a man running in a race, straining every nerve to win the prize. "I therefore so run," he says, "not as uncertainly; so fight I, not as one that beateth the air: but I keep under my body, and bring it into subjection: lest that by any means, when I have preached to others, I myself should be a castaway." That he might not run uncertainly or at random in the Christian race, Paul subjected himself to severe training. The words, "I keep under my body," literally mean to beat back by severe discipline the desires, impulses, and passions.

Paul feared lest, having preached to others, he himself should be a castaway. He realized that if he did not carry out in his life the principles he believed and preached, his labors in behalf of others would avail him nothing. His conversation, his influence, his refusal to yield to self-gratification, must show that his religion was not a profession merely, but a daily, living connection with God. One goal he kept ever before him, and strove earnestly to reach— "the righteousness which is of God by faith." Philippians 3:9.

Paul knew that his warfare against evil would not end so long as life should last. Ever he realized the need of putting a strict guard upon himself, that earthly desires might not overcome spiritual zeal. With all his power he continued to strive against natural inclinations. Ever he kept before him the ideal to be attained, and this ideal he strove to reach by willing obedience to the law of God. His words, his practices, his passions—all were brought under the control of the Spirit of God.

It was this singlehearted purpose to win the race for eternal life that Paul longed to see revealed in the lives of the Corinthian believers. He knew that in order to reach Christ's ideal for them, they had before them a life struggle from which there would be no release. He entreated them to strive lawfully, day by day seeking for piety and moral excellence. He pleaded with them to lay aside every weight and to press forward to the goal of perfection in Christ.

Paul pointed the Corinthians to the experience of ancient Israel, to the blessings that rewarded their obedience, and to the judgments that followed their transgressions. He reminded them of the miraculous way in which the Hebrews were led from Egypt under the protection of the cloud by day and the pillar of fire by night. Thus they were safely conducted through the Red Sea, while the Egyptians, essaying to cross in like manner, were all drowned. By these acts God had acknowledged Israel as His church. They "did all eat the same spiritual meat; and did all drink the same spiritual drink: for they drank of that spiritual Rock that followed them: and that Rock was Christ." The Hebrews, in all their travels, had Christ as a leader. The smitten rock typified Christ, who was to be wounded for men's transgressions, that the stream of salvation might flow to all.

Notwithstanding the favor that God showed to the Hebrews, yet because of their lust for the luxuries left behind in Egypt, and because of their sin and rebellion, the judgments of God came upon them. The apostle enjoined the Corinthian believers to heed the lesson contained in Israel's experience. "Now these things were our examples," he declared, "to the intent we should not lust after evil things, as they also lusted." He showed how love of ease and pleasure had prepared the way for sins that called forth the signal vengeance of God. It was when the children of Israel sat down to eat and drink, and rose up to play, that they threw off the fear of God, which they had felt as they listened to the giving of the law; and, making a golden calf to represent God, they worshiped it. And it was after enjoying a luxurious feast connected with the worship of Baalpeor, that many of the Hebrews fell through licentiousness. The anger of God was aroused, and at His command "three and twenty thousand" were slain by the plague in one day.

The apostle adjured the Corinthians, "Let him that thinketh he standeth take heed lest he fall." Should they become boastful and self-confident, neglecting to watch and pray, they would fall into grievous sin, calling down upon themselves the wrath of God. Yet Paul would not have them yield to despondency or discouragement. He gave them the assurance: "God is faithful, who will not suffer you to be tempted above that ye are able; but will with the temptation also make a way of escape, that ye may be able to bear it."

Paul urged his brethren to ask themselves what influence their words and deeds would have upon others and to do nothing, however innocent in itself, that would seem to sanction idolatry or offend the scruples of those who might be weak in the faith. "Whether therefore ye eat, or drink, or whatsoever ye do, do all to the glory of God. Give none offense, neither to the Jews, nor to the Gentiles, nor to the church of God."

The apostle's words of warning to the Corinthian church are applicable to all time and are especially adapted to our day. By idolatry he meant not only the worship of idols, but self-serving, love of ease, the gratification of appetite and passion. A mere profession of faith in Christ, a boastful knowledge of the truth, does not make a man a Christian. A religion that seeks only to gratify the eye, the ear, and the taste, or that sanctions self-indulgence, is not the religion of Christ.

By a comparison of the church with the human body, the apostle aptly illustrated the close and harmonious relationship that should exist among all members of the church of Christ. "By one Spirit," he wrote, "are well all baptized into one body, whether we be Jews or Gentiles, whether we be bond or free; and have been all made to drink into one Spirit. For the body is not one member, but many. If the foot shall say, Because I am not the hand, I am not of the body; is it therefore not of the body? And if the ear shall say, Because I am not the eye, I am not of the body; is it therefore not of the body? If the whole body were an eye, where were the hearing? If the whole were hearing, where were the smelling? But now hath God set the members every one of them in the body, as it hath pleased Him. And if they were all one member, where were the body?

But now are they many members, yet but one body. And the eye cannot say unto the hand, I have no need of thee: nor again the head to the feet, I have no need of you. . . . God hath tempered the body together, having given more abundant honor to that part which lacked: that there should be no schism in the body; but that the members should have the same care one for another. And whether one member suffer, all the members suffer with it; or one member be honored, all the members rejoice with it. Now ye are the body of Christ, and members in particular."

And then, in words which from that day to this have been to men and women a source of inspiration and encouragement, Paul set forth the importance of that love which should be cherished by the followers of Christ: "Though I speak with the tongues of men and of angels, and have not charity, I am become as sounding brass, or a tinkling cymbal. And though I have the gift of prophecy, and understand all mysteries, and all knowledge; and though I have all faith, so that I could remove mountains, and have not charity, I am nothing. And though I bestow all my goods to feed the poor, and though I give my body to be burned, and have not charity, it profiteth me nothing."

No matter how high the profession, he whose heart is not filled with love for God and his fellow men is not a true disciple of Christ. Though he should possess great faith and have power even to work miracles, yet without love his faith would be worthless. He might display great liberality; but should he, from some other motive than genuine love, bestow all his goods to feed the poor, the act would not commend him to the favor of God. In his zeal he might even meet a martyr's death, yet if not actuated by love, he would be regarded by God as a deluded enthusiast or an ambitious hypocrite.

"Charity suffereth long, and is kind; charity envieth not; charity vaunteth not itself, is not puffed up." The purest joy springs from the deepest humiliation. The strongest and noblest characters are built on the foundation of patience, love, and submission to God's will.

Charity "doth not behave itself unseemly, seeketh not her own, is not easily provoked, thinketh no evil." Christ-like love places the most favorable construction on the motives and acts of others. It does not needlessly expose their faults; it does not listen eagerly to unfavorable reports, but seeks rather to bring to mind the good qualities of others.

Love "rejoiceth not in iniquity, but rejoiceth in the truth; beareth all things, believeth all things, hopeth all things, endureth all things." This love "never faileth." It can never lose its value; it is a heavenly attribute. As a precious treasure, it will be carried by its possessor through the portals of the city of God.

"And now abideth faith, hope, charity, these three; but the greatest of these is charity."

In the lowering of the moral standard among the Corinthian believers, there were those who had given up some of the fundamental features of their faith. Some had gone so far as to deny the doctrine of the resurrection. Paul met this heresy with a very plain testimony regarding the unmistakable evidence of the resurrection of Christ. He declared that Christ, after His death, "rose again the third day according to the Scriptures," after which "He was seen of Cephas, then of the Twelve: after that, He was seen of above five hundred brethren at once; of whom the greater part remain unto this present, but some are fallen asleep. After that, He was seen of James; then of all the apostles. And last of all He was seen of me also."

With convincing power the apostle set forth the great truth of the resurrection. "If there be no resurrection of the dead," he argued, "then is Christ not risen: and if Christ be not risen, then is our preaching vain, and your faith is also vain. Yea, and we are found false witnesses of God; because we have testified of God that He raised up Christ: whom He raised not up, if so be that the dead rise not. For if the dead rise not, then is not Christ raised: and if Christ be not raised, your faith is vain; ye are yet in your sins. Then they also which are fallen asleep in Christ are perished. If in this life only we have hope in Christ, we are of all men most miserable. But now is Christ risen from the dead, and become the first fruits of them that slept."

The apostle carried the minds of the Corinthian brethren forward to the triumphs of the resurrection morn, when all the sleeping saints are to be raised, henceforth to live forever with their Lord. "Behold," the apostle declared, "I show you a mystery: We shall not all sleep, but we shall all be changed, in a moment, in the twinkling of an eye, at the last trump: for the trumpet shall sound, and the dead shall be raised incorruptible, and we shall be changed. For this corruptible must put on incorruption, and this mortal must put on immortality. So when this corruptible shall have put on incorruption, and this mortal shall have put on immortality, then shall be brought to pass the saying that is written, Death is swallowed up in victory. O death, where is thy sting? O grave, where is thy victory? . . . Thanks be to God, which giveth us the victory through our Lord Jesus Christ."

Glorious is the triumph awaiting the faithful. The apostle, realizing the possibilities before the Corinthian believers, sought to set before them that which uplifts from the selfish and the sensual, and glorifies life with the hope of immortality. Earnestly he exhorted them to be true to their high calling in Christ. "My beloved brethren," he pleaded, "be ye steadfast, unmovable, always abounding in the work of the Lord, forasmuch as ye know that your labor is not in vain in the Lord."

Thus the apostle, in the most decided and impressive manner, endeavored to correct the false and dangerous ideas and practices that were prevailing in the Corinthian church. He spoke plainly, yet in love for their souls. In his warnings and reproofs, light from the throne of God was shining upon them, to reveal the hidden sins that were defiling their lives. How would it be received?

After the letter had been dispatched, Paul feared lest that which he had written might wound too deeply those whom he desired to benefit. He keenly dreaded a further alienation and sometimes longed to recall his words. Those who, like the apostle, have felt a responsibility for beloved churches or institutions, can best appreciate his depression of spirit and self-accusing. The servants of God who bear the burden of His work for this time know something of the same experience of labor, conflict, and anxious care that fell to the lot of the great apostle. Burdened by divisions in the church, meeting with ingratitude and betrayal from some to whom he looked for sympathy and support, realizing the peril of the churches that harbored iniquity, compelled to bear a close, searching testimony in reproof of sin, he was at the same time weighed down with fear that he might have dealt with too great severity. With trembling anxiety he waited to receive some tidings as to the reception of his message.

The Message Heeded

From Ephesus Paul set forth on another missionary tour, during which he hoped to visit once more the scenes of his former labors in Europe. Tarrying for a time at Troas, "to preach Christ's gospel," he found some who were ready to listen to his message. "A door was opened unto me of the Lord," he afterward declared of his labors in this place. But successful as were his efforts at Troas, he could not remain there long. "The care of all the churches," and particularly of the church at Corinth, rested heavily on his heart. He had hoped to meet Titus at Troas and to learn from him how the words of counsel and reproof sent to the Corinthian brethren had been received, but in this he was disappointed. "I had no rest in my spirit," he wrote concerning this experience, "because I found not Titus my brother." He therefore left Troas and crossed over to Macedonia, where, at Philippi he met Timothy.

During this time of anxiety concerning the church at Corinth, Paul hoped for the best; yet at times feelings of deep sadness would sweep over his soul, lest his counsels and admonitions might be misunderstood. "Our flesh had no rest," he afterward wrote, "but we were troubled on every side; without were fightings, within were fears. Nevertheless God, that comforteth those that are cast down, comforted us by the coming of Titus."

This faithful messenger brought the cheering news that a wonderful change had taken place among the Corinthian believers. Many had accepted the instruction contained in Paul's letter and had repented of their sins. Their lives were no longer a reproach to Christianity, but exerted a powerful influence in favor of practical godliness.

Filled with joy, the apostle sent another letter to the Corinthian believers, expressing his gladness of heart because of the good work wrought in them: "Though I made you sorry with a letter, I do not repent, though I did repent." When tortured by the fear that his words would be despised, he had sometimes regretted that he had written so decidedly and severely. "Now I rejoice," he continued, "not that ye were made sorry, but that ye sorrowed to repentance: for ye were made sorry after a godly manner, that ye might receive damage by us in nothing. For godly sorrow worketh repentance to salvation not to be repented of." That repentance which is produced by the influence of divine grace upon the heart will lead to confession and forsaking of sin. Such were the fruits which the apostle declared had been seen in the lives of the Corinthian believers. "What carefulness it wrought in you, yea, what clearing of yourselves, yea, what indignation, yea, what fear, yea, what vehement desire, yea, what zeal."

For some time Paul had been carrying a burden of soul for the churches—a burden so heavy that he could scarcely endure it. False teachers had sought to destroy his influence among the believers and to urge their own doctrines in the place of gospel truth. The perplexities and discouragements with which Paul was surrounded are revealed in the words, "We were pressed out of measure, above strength, insomuch that we despaired even of life."

But now one cause of anxiety was removed. At the tidings of the acceptance of his letter to the Corinthians, Paul broke forth into words of rejoicing: "Blessed be God, even the Father of our Lord Jesus Christ, the Father of mercies, and the God of all comfort; who comforteth us in all our tribulation, that we may be able to comfort them which are in any trouble, by the comfort wherewith we ourselves are comforted of God. For as the sufferings of Christ abound in us, so our consolation also aboundeth by Christ. And whether we be afflicted, it is for your consolation and salvation, which is effectual in the enduring of the same sufferings which we also suffer: or whether we be comforted, it is for your consolation and salvation. And our hope of you is steadfast, knowing, that as ye are partakers of the sufferings, so shall ye be also of the consolation."

In expressing his joy over their reconversion and their growth in grace, Paul ascribed to God all the praise for this transformation of heart and life. "Thanks be unto God," he exclaimed, "which always causeth us to triumph in Christ, and maketh manifest the savor of His knowledge by us in every place. For we are unto God a sweet savor of Christ, in them that are saved, and in them that perish." It was the custom of the day for a general victorious in warfare to bring with him on his return a train of captives. On such occasions incense bearers were appointed, and as the army marched triumphantly home, the fragrant odor was to the captives appointed to die, a savor of death, showing that they were nearing the time of their execution; but to those of the prisoners who had found favor with their captors, and whose lives were to be spared, it was a savor of life, in that it showed them that their freedom was near.

Paul was now full of faith and hope. He felt that Satan was not to triumph over the work of God in Corinth, and in words of praise he poured forth the gratitude of his heart. He and his fellow laborers would celebrate their victory over the enemies of Christ and the truth, by going forth with new zeal to extend the knowledge of the Saviour. Like incense the fragrance of the gospel was to be diffused throughout the world. To those who should accept Christ, the message would be a savor of life unto life; but to those who should persist in unbelief, a savor of death unto death.

Realizing the overwhelming magnitude of the work, Paul exclaimed, "Who is sufficient for these things?" Who is able to preach Christ in such a way that His enemies shall have no just cause to despise the messenger or the message that he bears? Paul desired to impress upon believers the solemn responsibility of the gospel ministry. Faithfulness in preaching the word, united with a pure, consistent life, can alone make the efforts of ministers acceptable to God and profitable to souls. Ministers of our day, burdened with a sense of the greatness of the work, may well exclaim with the apostle, "Who is sufficient for these things?"

There were those who had charged Paul with self-commendation in writing his former letter. The apostle now referred to this by asking the members of the church if they thus judged his motives. "Do we begin again to commend ourselves?" he inquired; "or need we, as some others, epistles of commendation to you, or letters of commendation from you?" Believers moving to a new place often carried with them letters of commendation from the church with which they had formerly been united; but the leading workers, the founders of these churches, had no need of such commendation. The Corinthian believers, who had been led from the worship of idols to the faith of the gospel, were themselves all the recommendation that Paul needed. Their reception of the truth, and the reformation wrought in their lives, bore eloquent testimony to the faithfulness of his labors and to his authority to counsel, reprove, and exhort as a minister of Christ.

Paul regarded the Corinthian brethren as his testimonial. "Ye are our epistle," he said, "written in our hearts, known and read of all men: forasmuch as ye are manifestly declared to be the epistle of Christ ministered by us, written not with ink, but with the Spirit of the living God; not in tables of stone, but in fleshy tables of the heart."

The conversion of sinners and their sanctification through the truth is the strongest proof a minister can have that God has called him to the ministry. The evidence of his apostleship is written upon the hearts of those converted, and is witnessed to by their renewed lives. Christ is formed within, the hope of glory. A minister is greatly strengthened by these seals of his ministry.

Today the ministers of Christ should have the same witness as that which the Corinthian church bore to Paul's labors. But though in this age there are many preachers, there is a great scarcity of able, holy ministers—men filled with the love that dwelt in the heart of Christ. Pride, self-confidence, love of the world, faultfinding, bitterness, envy, are the fruit borne by many who profess the religion of Christ. Their lives, in sharp contrast to the life of the Saviour, often bear sad testimony to the character of the ministerial labor under which they were converted.

A man can have no greater honor than to be accepted by God as an able minister of the gospel. But those whom the Lord blesses with power and success in His work do not boast. They acknowledge their entire dependence on Him, realizing that of themselves they have no power. With Paul they say, "Not that we are sufficient of ourselves to think anything as of ourselves; but our sufficiency is of God; who also hath made us able ministers of the new testament."

A true minister does the work of the Master. He feels the importance of his work, realizing that he sustains to the church and to the world a relation similar to that which Christ sustained. He works untiringly to lead sinners to a nobler, higher life, that they may obtain the reward of the overcomer. His lips are touched with a live coal from the altar, and he uplifts Jesus as the sinner's only hope. Those who hear him know that he has drawn near to God in fervent, effectual prayer. The Holy Spirit has rested upon him, his soul has felt the vital, heavenly fire, and he is able to compare spiritual things with spiritual. Power is given him to tear down the strongholds of Satan. Hearts are broken by his presentation of the love of God, and many are led to inquire, "What must I do to be saved?"

"Therefore seeing we have this ministry, as we have received mercy, we faint not; but have renounced the hidden things of dishonesty, not walking in craftiness, nor handling the word of God deceitfully; but by manifestation of the truth commending ourselves to every man's conscience in the sight of God. But if our gospel be hid, it is hid to them that are lost: in whom the god of this world hath blinded the minds of them which believe not, lest the light of the glorious gospel of Christ, who is the image of God, should shine unto them. For we preach not ourselves, but Christ Jesus the Lord; and ourselves your servants for Jesus' sake. For God, who commanded the light to shine out of darkness, hath shined in our hearts, to give the light of the knowledge of the glory of God in the face of Jesus Christ."

Thus the apostle magnified the grace and mercy of God, shown in the sacred trust committed to him as a minister of Christ. By God's abundant mercy he and his brethren had been sustained in difficulty, affliction, and danger. They had not modeled their faith and teaching to suit the desires of their hearers, nor kept back truths essential to salvation in order to make their teaching more attractive. They had presented the truth with simplicity and clearness, praying for the conviction and conversion of souls. And they had endeavored to bring their conduct into harmony with their teaching, that the truth presented might commend itself to every man's conscience.

"We have this treasure," the apostle continued, "in earthen vessels, that the excellency of the power may be of God, and not of us." God could have proclaimed His truth through sinless angels, but this is not His plan. He chooses human beings, men compassed with infirmity, as instruments in the working out of His designs. The priceless treasure is placed in earthen vessels. Through men His blessings are to be conveyed to the world. Through them His glory is to shine forth into the darkness of sin. In loving ministry they are to meet the sinful and the needy, and lead them to the cross. And in all their work they are to ascribe glory, honor, and praise to Him who is above all and over all.

Referring to his own experience, Paul showed that in choosing the service of Christ he had not been prompted by selfish motives, for his pathway had been beset by trial and temptation. "We are troubled on every side," he wrote, "yet not distressed; we are perplexed, but not in despair; persecuted, but not forsaken; cast down, but not destroyed; always bearing about in the body the dying of the Lord Jesus, that the life also of Jesus might be made manifest in our body."

Paul reminded his brethren that as Christ's messengers he and his fellow laborers were continually in peril. The hardships they endured were wearing away their strength. "We which live," he wrote, "are alway delivered unto death for Jesus' sake, that the life also of Jesus might be made manifest in our mortal flesh. So then death worketh in us, but life in you." Suffering physically through privation and toil, these ministers of Christ were conforming to His death. But that which was working death in them was bringing spiritual life and health to the Corinthians, who by a belief in the truth were being made partakers of life eternal. In view of this, the followers of Jesus were to be careful not to increase, by neglect and disaffection, the burdens and trials of the laborers.

"We having the same spirit of faith," Paul continued, "according as it is written, I believed, and therefore have I spoken; we also believe, and therefore speak." Fully convinced of the reality of the truth entrusted to him, nothing could induce Paul to handle the word of God deceitfully or to conceal the convictions of his soul. He would not purchase wealth, honor, or pleasure by conformity to the opinions of the world. Though in constant danger of martyrdom for the faith that he had preached to the Corinthians, he was not intimidated, for he knew that He who had died and risen again would raise him from the grave and present him to the Father.

"All things are for your sakes," he said, "that the abundant grace might through the thanksgiving of many redound to the glory of God." Not for self-aggrandizement did the apostles preach the gospel. It was the hope of saving souls that led them to devote their lives to this work. And it was this hope that kept them from ceasing their efforts because of threatened danger or actual suffering.

"For which cause," Paul declared, "we faint not; but though our outward man perish, yet the inward man is renewed day by day." Paul felt the power of the enemy; but though his physical strength was declining, yet faithfully and unflinchingly he declared the gospel of Christ. Clad in the whole armor of God, this hero of the cross pressed forward in the conflict. His voice of cheer proclaimed him triumphant in the combat. Fixing his gaze on the reward of the faithful, he exclaimed in tones of victory, "Our light affliction, which is but for a moment, worketh for us a far more exceeding and eternal weight of glory; while we look not at the things which are seen, but at the things which are not seen: for the things which are seen are temporal; but the things which are not seen are eternal."

Very earnest and touching is the apostle's appeal that his Corinthian brethren consider anew the matchless love of their Redeemer. "Ye know the grace of our Lord Jesus Christ," he wrote, "that, though He was rich, yet for your sakes He became poor, that ye through His poverty might be rich." You know the height from which He stooped, the depth of humiliation to which He descended. Having once entered upon the path of self-denial and sacrifice, he turned not aside until He had given His life. There was no rest for Him between the throne and the cross.

Point after point Paul lingered over, in order that those who should read his epistle might fully comprehend the wonderful condescension of the Saviour in their behalf. Presenting Christ as He was when equal with God and with Him receiving the homage of the angels, the apostle traced His course until He had reached the lowest depths of humiliation. Paul was convinced that if they could be brought to comprehend the amazing sacrifice made by the Majesty of heaven, all selfishness would be banished from their lives. He showed how the Son of God had laid aside His glory, voluntarily subjecting Himself to the conditions of human nature, and then had humbled Himself as a servant, becoming obedient unto death, "even the death of the cross" (Philippians 2:8), that He might lift fallen man from degradation to hope and joy and heaven.

When we study the divine character in the light of the cross we see mercy, tenderness, and forgiveness blended with equity and justice. We see in the midst of the throne One bearing in hands and feet and side the marks of the suffering endured to reconcile man to God. We see a Father, infinite, dwelling in light unapproachable, yet receiving us to Himself through the merits of His Son. The cloud of vengeance that threatened only misery and despair, in the light reflected from the cross reveals the writing of God: Live, sinner, live! ye penitent, believing souls, live! I have paid a ransom.

In the contemplation of Christ we linger on the shore of a love that is measureless. We endeavor to tell of this love, and language fails us. We consider His life on earth, His sacrifice for us, His work in heaven as our advocate, and the mansions He is preparing for those who love Him, and we can only exclaim, O the height and depth of the love of Christ! "Herein is love, not that we loved God, but that He loved us, and sent His Son to be the propitiation for our sins." "Behold, what manner of love the Father hath bestowed upon us, that we should be called the sons of God." 1 John 4:10; 3:1.

In every true disciple this love, like sacred fire, burns on the altar of the heart. It was on the earth that the love of God was revealed through Christ. It is on the earth that His children are to reflect this love through blameless lives. Thus sinners will be led to the cross to behold the Lamb of God.

A Liberal Church

In his first letter to the church at Corinth, Paul gave the believers instruction regarding the general principles underlying the support of God's work in the earth. Writing of his apostolic labors in their behalf, he inquired:

"Who goeth a warfare any time at his own charges? who planteth a vineyard, and eateth not of the fruit thereof? or who feedeth a flock, and eateth not of the milk of the flock? Say I these things as a man? or saith not the law the same also? For it is written in the law of Moses, Thou shalt not muzzle the mouth of the ox that treadeth out the corn. Doth God take care for oxen? or saith He it altogether for our sakes? For our sakes, no doubt, this is written: that he that ploweth should plow in hope; and that he that thresheth in hope should be partaker of his hope.

"If we have sown unto you spiritual things," the apostle further inquired, "is it a great thing if we shall reap your carnal things? If others be partakers of this power over you, are not we rather? Nevertheless we have not used this power; but suffer all things, lest we should hinder the gospel of Christ. Do ye not know that they which minister about holy things live of the things of the temple? and they which wait at the altar are partakers with the altar? Even so hath the Lord ordained that they which preach the gospel should live of the gospel." 1 Corinthians 9:7-14.

The apostle here referred to the Lord's plan for the maintenance of the priests who ministered in the temple. Those who were set apart to this holy office were supported by their brethren, to whom they ministered spiritual blessings. "Verily they that are of the sons of Levi, who receive the office of the priesthood, have a commandment to take tithes of the people according to the law." Hebrews 7:5. The tribe of Levi was chosen by the Lord for the sacred offices pertaining to the temple and the priesthood. Of the priest it was said, "The Lord thy God hath chosen him . . . to stand to minister in the name of the Lord." (Deuteronomy 18:5.) One tenth of all the increase was claimed by the Lord as His own, and to withhold the tithe was regarded by Him as robbery.

It was to this plan for the support of the ministry that Paul referred when he said, "Even so hath the Lord ordained that they which preach the gospel should live of the gospel." And later, in writing to Timothy, the apostle said, "The laborer is worthy of his reward." 1 Timothy 5:18.

The payment of the tithe was but a part of God's plan for the support of His service. Numerous gifts and offerings were divinely specified. Under the Jewish system the people were taught to cherish a spirit of liberality both in sustaining the cause of God and in supplying the wants of the needy. For special occasions there were freewill offerings. At the harvest and the vintage, the first fruits of the field—corn, wine, and oil—were consecrated as an offering to the Lord. The gleanings and the corners of the field were reserved for the poor. The first fruits of the wool when the sheep were shorn, of the grain when the wheat was threshed, were set apart for God. So also were the first-born of all animals, and a redemption price was paid for the first-born son. The first fruits were to be presented before the Lord at the sanctuary and were then devoted to the use of the priests.

By this system of benevolence the Lord sought to teach Israel that in everything He must be first. Thus they were reminded that God was the proprietor of their fields, their flocks, and their herds; that it was He who sent them the sunshine and the rain that developed and ripened the harvest. Everything that they possessed was His; they were but the stewards of His goods.

It is not God's purpose that Christians, whose privileges far exceed those of the Jewish nation, shall give less freely than they gave. "Unto whomsoever much is given," the Saviour declared, "of him shall be much required." Luke 12:48. The liberality required of the Hebrews was largely to benefit their own nation; today the work of God extends over all the earth. In the hands of His followers, Christ has placed the treasures of the gospel, and upon them He has laid the responsibility of giving the glad tidings of salvation to the world. Surely our obligations are much greater than were those of ancient Israel.

As God's work extends, calls for help will come more and more frequently. That these calls may be answered, Christians should heed the command, "Bring ye all the tithes into the storehouse, that there may be meat in Mine house." Malachi 3:10. If professing Christians would faithfully bring to God their tithes and offerings, His treasury would be full. There would then be no occasion to resort to fairs, lotteries, or parties of pleasure to secure funds for the support of the gospel.

Men are tempted to use their means in self-indulgence, in the gratification of appetite, in personal adornment, or in the embellishment of their homes. For these objects many church members do not hesitate to spend freely and even extravagantly. But when asked to give to the Lord's treasury, to carry forward His work in the earth, they demur. Perhaps, feeling that they cannot well do otherwise, they dole out a sum far smaller than they often spend for needless indulgence. They manifest no real love for Christ's service, no earnest interest in the salvation of souls. What marvel that the Christian life of such ones is but a dwarfed, sickly existence!

He whose heart is aglow with the love of Christ will regard it as not only a duty, but a pleasure, to aid in the advancement of the highest, holiest work committed to man—the work of presenting to the world the riches of goodness, mercy, and truth.

It is the spirit of covetousness which leads men to keep for gratification of self means that rightfully belong to God, and this spirit is as abhorrent to Him now as when through His prophet He sternly rebuked His people, saying, "Will a man rob God? Yet ye have robbed Me. But ye say, Wherein have we robbed Thee? In tithes and offerings. Ye are cursed with a curse: for ye have robbed Me, even this whole nation." Malachi 3:8, 9.

The spirit of liberality is the spirit of heaven. This spirit finds its highest manifestation in Christ's sacrifice on the cross. In our behalf the Father gave His only-begotten Son; and Christ, having given up all that He had, then gave Himself, that man might be saved. The cross of Calvary should appeal to the benevolence of every follower of the Saviour. The principle there illustrated is to give, give. "He that saith he abideth in Him ought himself also so to walk, even as He walked." 1 John 2:6.

On the other hand, the spirit of selfishness is the spirit of Satan. The principle illustrated in the lives of worldlings is to get, get. Thus they hope to secure happiness and ease, but the fruit of their sowing is misery and death.

Not until God ceases to bless His children will they cease to be under bonds to return to Him the portion that He claims. Not only should they render the Lord the portion that belongs to Him, but they should bring also to His treasury, as a gratitude offering, a liberal tribute. With joyful hearts they should dedicate to the Creator the first fruits of their bounties—their choicest possessions, their best and holiest service. Thus they will gain rich blessings. God Himself will make their souls like a watered garden whose waters fail not. And when the last great harvest is gathered in, the sheaves that they are enabled to bring to the Master will be the recompense of their unselfish use of the talents lent them.

God's chosen messengers, who are engaged in aggressive labor, should never be compelled to go a warfare at their own charges, unaided by the sympathetic and hearty support of their brethren. It is the part of church members to deal liberally with those who lay aside their secular employment that they may give themselves to the ministry. When God's ministers are encouraged, His cause is greatly advanced. But when, through the selfishness of men, their rightful support is withheld, their hands are weakened, and often their usefulness is seriously crippled.

The displeasure of God is kindled against those who claim to be His followers, yet allow consecrated workers to suffer for the necessities of life while engaged in active ministry. These selfish ones will be called to render an account, not only for the misuse of their Lord's money, but for the depression and heartache which their course has brought upon His faithful servants. Those who are called to the work of the ministry, and at the call of duty give up all to engage in God's service, should receive for their self-sacrificing efforts wages sufficient to support themselves and their families.

In the various departments of secular labor, mental and physical, faithful workmen can earn good wages. Is not the work of disseminating truth, and leading souls to Christ, of more importance than any ordinary business? And are not those who faithfully engage in this work justly entitled to ample remuneration? By our estimate of the relative value of labor for moral and for physical good, we show our appreciation of the heavenly in contrast with the earthly.

That there may be funds in the treasury for the support of the ministry, and to meet the calls for assistance in missionary enterprises, it is necessary that the people of God give cheerfully and liberally. A solemn responsibility rests upon ministers to keep before the churches the needs of the cause of God and to educate them to be liberal. When this is neglected, and the churches fail to give for the necessities of others, not only does the work of the Lord suffer, but the blessing that should come to believers is withheld.

Even the very poor should bring their offerings to God. They are to be sharers of the grace of Christ by denying self to help those whose need is more pressing than their own. The poor man's gift, the fruit of self-denial, comes up before God as fragrant incense. And every act of self-sacrifice strengthens the spirit of beneficence in the giver's heart, allying him more closely to the One who was rich, yet for our sakes became poor, that we through His poverty might be rich.

The act of the widow who cast two mites—all that she had—into the treasury, is placed on record for the encouragement of those who, struggling with poverty, still desire by their gifts to aid the cause of God. Christ called the attention of the disciples to this woman, who had given "all

her living." Mark 12:44. He esteemed her gift of more value than the large offerings of those whose alms did not call for self-denial. From their abundance they had given a small portion. To make her offering, the widow had deprived herself of even the necessities of life, trusting God to supply her needs for the morrow. Of her the Saviour declared, "Verily I say unto you, That this poor widow hath cast more in, than all they which have cast into the treasury." Verse 43. Thus He taught that the value of the gift is estimated not by the amount, but by the proportion that is given and the motive that actuates the giver.

The apostle Paul in his ministry among the churches was untiring in his efforts to inspire in the hearts of the new converts a desire to do large things for the cause of God. Often he exhorted them to the exercise of liberality. In speaking to the elders of Ephesus of his former labors among them, he said, "I have showed you all things, how that so laboring ye ought to support the weak, and to remember the words of the Lord Jesus, how He said, It is more blessed to give than to receive." "He which soweth sparingly," he wrote to the Corinthians, "shall reap also sparingly; and he which soweth bountifully shall reap also bountifully. Every man according as he purposeth in his heart, so let him give; not grudgingly, or of necessity: for God loveth a cheerful giver." Acts 20:35; 2 Corinthians 9:6, 7.

Nearly all the Macedonian believers were poor in this world's goods, but their hearts were overflowing with love for God and His truth, and they gladly gave for the support of the gospel. When general collections were taken up in the Gentile churches for the relief of the Jewish believers, the liberality of the converts in Macedonia was held up as an example to other churches. Writing to the Corinthian believers, the apostle called their attention to "the grace of God bestowed on the churches of Macedonia; how that in a great trial of affliction the abundance of their joy and their deep poverty abounded unto the riches of their liberality. For to their power, . . . yea, and beyond their power they were willing of themselves; praying us with much entreaty that we would receive the gift, and take upon us the fellowship of the ministering to the saints." 2 Corinthians 8:1-4.

The willingness to sacrifice on the part of the Macedonian believers came as a result of wholehearted consecration. Moved by the Spirit of God, they "first gave their own selves to the Lord" (2 Corinthians 8:5), then they were willing to give freely of their means for the support of the gospel. It was not necessary to urge them to give; rather, they rejoiced in the privilege of denying themselves even of necessary things in order to supply the needs of others. When the apostle would have restrained them, they importuned him to accept their offering. In their simplicity and integrity, and in their love for the brethren, they gladly denied self, and thus abounded in the fruit of benevolence.

When Paul sent Titus to Corinth to strengthen the believers there, he instructed him to build up that church in the grace of giving, and in a personal letter to the believers he also added his own appeal. "As ye abound in everything," he pleaded, "in faith, and utterance, and knowledge, and in all diligence, and in your love to us, see that ye abound in this grace also," "Now therefore perform the doing of it; that as there was a readiness to will, so there may be a performance also out of that which ye have. For if there be first a willing mind, it is accepted according to that a man hath, and not according to that he hath not." "And God is able to make all grace abound toward you; that ye, always having all sufficiency in all things, may abound to every good work: . . . . being enriched in everything to all bountifulness, which causeth through us thanksgiving to God." 2 Corinthians 8:7, 11, 12; 9:8-11.

Unselfish liberality threw the early church into a transport of joy; for the believers knew that their efforts were helping to send the gospel message to those in darkness. Their benevolence testified that they had not received the grace of God in vain. What could produce such liberality but the sanctification of the Spirit? In the eyes of believers and unbelievers it was a miracle of grace.

Spiritual prosperity is closely bound up with Christian liberality. The followers of Christ should rejoice in the privilege of revealing in their lives the beneficence of their Redeemer. As they give to the Lord they have the assurance that their treasure is going before them to the heavenly courts. Would men make their property secure? Let them place it in the hands that bear the marks of the crucifixion. Would they enjoy their substance? Let them use it to bless the needy and suffering. Would they increase their possessions? Let them heed the divine injunction, "Honor the Lord with thy substance, and with the first fruits of all thine increase: so shall thy barns be filled with plenty, and thy presses shall burst out with new wine." Proverbs 3:9, 10. Let them seek to retain their possessions for selfish purposes, and it will be to their eternal loss. But let their treasure be given to God, and from that moment it bears His inscription. It is sealed with His immutability.

God declares, "Blessed are ye that sow beside all waters." Isaiah 32:20. A continual imparting of God's gifts wherever the cause of God or the needs of humanity demand our aid, does not tend to poverty. "There is that scattereth, and yet increaseth; and there is that withholdeth more than is meet, but it tendeth to poverty." Proverbs 11:24. The sower multiplies his seed by casting it away. So it is with those who are faithful in distributing God's gifts. By imparting they increase their blessings. "Give, and it shall be given unto you," God has promised; "good measure, pressed down, and shaken together, and running over, shall men give into your bosom." Luke 6:38.

Laboring Under Difficulties

While Paul was careful to set before his converts the plain teaching of Scripture regarding the proper support of the work of God, and while he claimed for himself as a minister of the gospel the "power to forbear working" (1 Corinthians 9:6) at secular employment as a means of self-support, yet at various times during his ministry in the great centers of civilization he wrought at a handicraft for his own maintenance.

Among the Jews physical toil was not thought strange or degrading. Through Moses the Hebrews had been instructed to train their children to industrious habits, and it was regarded as a sin to allow the youth to grow up in ignorance of physical labor. Even though a child was to be educated for holy office, a knowledge of practical life was thought essential. Every youth, whether his parents were rich or poor, was taught some trade. Those parents who neglected to provide such a training for their children were looked upon as departing from the instruction of the Lord. In accordance with this custom, Paul had early learned the trade of tentmaking.

Before he became a disciple of Christ, Paul had occupied a high position and was not dependent upon manual labor for support. But afterward, when he had used all his means in furthering the cause of Christ, he resorted at times to his trade to gain a livelihood. Especially was this the case when he labored in places where his motives might have been misunderstood.

It is at Thessalonica that we first read of Paul's working with his hands in self-supporting labor while preaching the word. Writing to the church of believers there, he reminded them that he "might have been burdensome" to them, and added: "Ye remember, brethren, our labor and travail: for laboring night and day, because we would not be chargeable unto any of you, we preached unto you the gospel of God." 1 Thessalonians 2:6, 9. And again, in his second epistle to them, he declared that he and his fellow laborer while with them had not eaten "any man's bread for nought." Night and day we worked, he wrote, "that we might not be chargeable to any of you: not because we have not power, but to make ourselves an ensample unto you to follow us." 2 Thessalonians 3:8, 9.

At Thessalonica Paul had met those who refused to work with their hands. It was of this class that he afterward wrote: "There are some which walk among you disorderly, working not at all, but are busybodies. Now them that are such we command and exhort by our Lord Jesus Christ, that with quietness they work, and eat their own bread." While laboring in Thessalonica, Paul had been careful to set before such ones a right example. "Even when we were with you," he wrote, "this we commanded you, that if any would not work, neither should he eat." Verses 11, 12, 10.

In every age Satan has sought to impair the efforts of God's servants by introducing into the church a spirit of fanaticism. Thus it was in Paul's day, and thus it was in later centuries during the time of the Reformation. Wycliffe, Luther, and many others who blessed the world by their influence and their faith, encountered the wiles by which the enemy seeks to lead into fanaticism overzealous, unbalanced, and unsanctified minds. Misguided souls have taught that the attainment of true holiness carries the mind above all earthly thoughts and leads men to refrain wholly from labor. Others, taking extreme views of certain texts of Scripture, have taught that it is a sin to work—that Christians should take no thought concerning the temporal welfare of themselves or their families, but should devote their lives wholly to spiritual things. The teaching and example of the apostle Paul are a rebuke to such extreme views.

Paul was not wholly dependent upon the labor of his hands for support while at Thessalonica. Referring later to his experiences in that city, he wrote to the Philippian believers in acknowledgment of the gifts he had received from them while there, saying, "Even in Thessalonica ye sent once and again unto my necessity." Philippians 4:16. Notwithstanding the fact that he received this help he was careful to set before the Thessalonians an example of diligence, so that none could rightfully accuse him of covetousness, and also that those who held fanatical views regarding manual labor might be given a practical rebuke.

When Paul first visited Corinth, he found himself among a people who were suspicious of the motives of strangers. The Greeks on the seacoast were keen traders. So long had they trained themselves in sharp business practices, that they had come to believe that gain was godliness, and that to make money, whether by fair means or foul, was commendable. Paul was acquainted with their characteristics, and he would give them no occasion for saying that he preached the gospel in order to enrich himself. He might justly have claimed support from his Corinthian hearers; but this right he was willing to forgo, lest his usefulness and success as a minister should be injured by the unjust suspicion that he was preaching the gospel for gain. He would seek to remove all occasion for misrepresentation, that the force of his message might not be lost.

Soon after his arrival at Corinth, Paul found "a certain Jew named Aquila, born in Pontus, lately come from Italy, with his wife Priscilla." These were "of the same craft" with himself. Banished by the decree of Claudius, which commanded all Jews to leave Rome, Aquila and Priscilla had come to Corinth, where they established a business as manufacturers of tents. Paul made inquiry concerning them, and learning that they feared God and were seeking to avoid the contaminating influences with which they were surrounded, "he abode with them, and wrought. . . . And he reasoned in the synagogue every Sabbath, and persuaded the Jews and the Greeks." Acts 18:2-4.

Later, Silas and Timothy joined Paul at Corinth. These brethren brought with them funds from the churches in Macedonia, for the support of the work.

In his second letter to the believers in Corinth, written after he had raised up a strong church there, Paul reviewed his manner of life among them. "Have I committed an offense," he asked, "in abasing myself that ye might be exalted, because I have preached to you the gospel of God freely? I robbed other churches, taking wages of them, to do you service. And when I was present with you, and wanted, I was chargeable to no man: for that which was lacking to me the brethren which came from Macedonia supplied: and in all things I have kept myself from being burdensome unto you, and so will I keep myself. As the truth of Christ is in me, no man shall stop me of this boasting in the regions of Achaia." 2 Corinthians 11:7-10.

Paul tells why he had followed this course in Corinth. It was that he might give no cause for reproach to "them which desire occasion." 2 Corinthians 11:12. While he had worked at tentmaking he had also labored faithfully in the proclamation of the gospel. He himself declares of his labors, "Truly the signs of an apostle were wrought among you in all patience, in signs, and wonders, and mighty deeds." And he adds, "For what is it wherein ye were inferior to other churches, except it be that I myself was not burdensome to you? Forgive me this wrong. Behold, the third time I am ready to come to you; and I will not be burdensome to you: for I seek not yours, but you. . . . And I will very gladly spend and be spent for you." 2 Corinthians 12:12-15.

During the long period of his ministry in Ephesus, where for three years he carried forward an aggressive evangelistic effort throughout that region, Paul again worked at his trade. In Ephesus, as in Corinth, the apostle was cheered by the presence of Aquila and Priscilla, who had accompanied him on his return to Asia at the close of his second missionary journey.

There were some who objected to Paul's toiling with his hands, declaring that it was inconsistent with the work of a gospel minister. Why should Paul, a minister of the highest rank, thus connect mechanical work with the preaching of the word? Was not the laborer worthy of his hire? Why should he spend in making tents time that to all appearance could be put to better account?

But Paul did not regard as lost the time thus spent. As he worked with Aquila he kept in touch with the Great Teacher, losing no opportunity of witnessing for the Saviour, and of helping those who needed help. His mind was ever reaching out for spiritual knowledge. He gave his fellow workers instruction in spiritual things, and he also set an example of industry and thoroughness. He was a quick, skillful worker, diligent in business, "fervent in spirit, serving the Lord." Romans 12:11. As he worked at his trade, the apostle had access to a class of people that he could not otherwise have reached. He showed his associates that skill in the common arts is a gift from God, who provides both the gift and the wisdom to use it aright. He taught that even in everyday toil God is to be honored. His toil-hardened hands detracted nothing from the force of his pathetic appeals as a Christian minister.

Paul sometimes worked night and day, not only for his own support, but that he might assist his fellow laborers. He shared his earnings with Luke, and he helped Timothy. He even suffered hunger at times, that he might relieve the necessities of others. His was an unselfish life. Toward the close of his ministry, on the occasion of his farewell talk to the elders of

Ephesus, at Miletus, he could lift up before them his toilworn hands, and say, "I have coveted no man's silver, or gold, or apparel. Yea, ye yourselves know, that these hands have ministered unto my necessities, and to them that were with me. I have showed you all things, how that so laboring ye ought to support the weak, and to remember the words of the Lord Jesus, how He said, It is more blessed to give than to receive." Acts 20:33-35.

If ministers feel that they are suffering hardship and privation in the cause of Christ, let them in imagination visit the workshop where Paul labored. Let them bear in mind that while this chosen man of God is fashioning the canvas, he is working for bread which he has justly earned by his labors as an apostle.

Work is a blessing, not a curse. A spirit of indolence destroys godliness and grieves the Spirit of God. A stagnant pool is offensive, but a pure, flowing stream spreads health and gladness over the land. Paul knew that those who neglect physical work soon become enfeebled. He desired to teach young ministers that by working with their hands, by bringing into exercise their muscles and sinews, they would become strong to endure the toils and privations that awaited them in the gospel field. And he realized that his own teachings would lack vitality and force if he did not keep all parts of the system properly exercised.

The indolent forfeit the invaluable experience gained by a faithful performance of the common duties of life. Not a few, but thousands of human beings exist only to consume the benefits which God in His mercy bestows upon them. They forget to bring to the Lord gratitude offerings for the riches He has entrusted to them. They forget that by trading wisely on the talents lent them they are to be producers as well as consumers. If they comprehended the work that the Lord desires them to do as His helping hand they would not shun responsibility.

The usefulness of young men who feel that they are called by God to preach, depends much upon the manner in which they enter upon their labors. Those who are chosen of God for the work of the ministry will give proof of their high calling and by every possible means will seek to develop into able workmen. They will endeavor to gain an experience that will fit them to plan, organize, and execute. Appreciating the sacredness of their calling, they will, by self-discipline, become more and still more like their Master, revealing His goodness, love, and truth. And as they manifest earnestness in improving the talents entrusted to them, the church should help them judiciously.

Not all who feel that they have been called to preach, should be encouraged to throw themselves and their families at once upon the church for continuous financial support. There is danger that some of limited experience may be spoiled by flattery, and by unwise encouragement to expect full support independent of any serious effort on their part. The means dedicated to the extension of the work of God should not be consumed by men who desire to preach only that they may receive support and thus gratify a selfish ambition for an easy life.

Young men who desire to exercise their gifts in the work of the ministry, will find a helpful lesson in the example of Paul at Thessalonica, Corinth, Ephesus, and other places. Although an eloquent speaker, and chosen by God to do a special work, he was never above labor, nor did he ever weary of sacrificing for the cause he loved. "Even unto this present hour," he wrote to the Corinthians, "we both hunger, and thirst, and are naked, and are buffeted, and have no certain dwelling place; and labor, working with our own hands: being reviled, we bless; being persecuted, we suffer it." 1 Corinthians 4:11, 12.

One of the greatest of human teachers, Paul cheerfully performed the lowliest as well as the highest duties. When in his service for the Master circumstances seemed to require it, he willingly labored at his trade. Nevertheless, he ever held himself ready to lay aside his secular work, in order to meet the opposition of the enemies of the gospel, or to improve a special opportunity to win souls to Jesus. His zeal and industry are a rebuke to indolence and desire for ease.

Paul set an example against the sentiment, then gaining influence in the church, that the gospel could be proclaimed successfully only by those who were wholly freed from the necessity of physical toil. He illustrated in a practical way what might be done by consecrated laymen in many places where the people were unacquainted with the truths of the gospel. His course inspired many humble toilers with a desire to do what they could to advance the cause of God, while at the same time they supported themselves in daily labor. Aquila and Priscilla were not called to give their whole time to the ministry of the gospel, yet these humble laborers were used by God to show Apollos the way of truth more perfectly. The Lord employs various instrumentalities for the accomplishment of His purpose, and while some with special talents are chosen to devote all their energies to the work of teaching and preaching the gospel, many others, upon whom human hands have never been laid in ordination, are called to act an important part in soulsaving.

There is a large field open before the self-supporting gospel worker. Many may gain valuable experiences in ministry while toiling a portion of the time at some form of manual labor, and by this method strong workers may be developed for important service in needy fields.

The self-sacrificing servant of God who labors untiringly in word and doctrine, carries on his heart a heavy burden. He does not measure his work by hours. His wages do not influence him in his labor, nor is he turned from his duty because of unfavorable conditions. From heaven he received his commission, and to heaven he looks for his recompense when the work entrusted to him is done.

It is God's design that such workers shall be freed from unnecessary anxiety, that they may have full opportunity to obey the injunction of Paul to Timothy, "Meditate upon these things; give thyself wholly to them." 1 Timothy 4:15. While they should be careful to exercise sufficiently to keep mind and body vigorous, yet it is not God's plan that they should be compelled to spend a large part of their time at secular employment.

These faithful workers, though willing to spend and be spent for the gospel, are not exempt from temptation. When hampered and burdened with anxiety because of a failure on the part of the church to give them proper financial support, some are fiercely beset by the tempter. When they see their labors so lightly prized, they become depressed. True, they look forward to the time of the judgment for their just award, and this buoys them up; but meanwhile their families must have food and clothing. If they could feel that they were released from their divine commission they would willingly labor with their hands. But they realize that their time belongs to God, notwithstanding the shortsightedness of those who should provide them with sufficient funds. They rise above the temptation to enter into pursuits by which they could soon place themselves beyond the reach of want, and they continue to labor for the advancement of the cause that is dearer to them than life itself. In order to do this, they may, however, be forced to follow the example of Paul and engage for a time in manual labor while continuing to carry forward their ministerial work. This they do to advance not their own interests, but the interests of God's cause in the earth.

There are times when it seems to the servant of God impossible to do the work necessary to be done, because of the lack of means to carry on a strong, solid work. Some are fearful that with the facilities at their command they cannot do all that they feel it their duty to do. But if they advance in faith, the salvation of God will be revealed, and prosperity will attend their efforts. He who has bidden His followers go into all parts of the world will sustain every laborer who in obedience to His command seeks to proclaim His message.

In the upbuilding of His work the Lord does not always make everything plain before His servants. He sometimes tries the confidence of His people by bringing about circumstances which compel them to move forward in faith. Often He brings them into strait and trying places, and bids them advance when their feet seem to be touching the waters of Jordan. It is at such times, when the prayers of His servants ascend to Him in earnest faith, that God opens the way before them and brings them out into a large place.

When God's messengers recognize their responsibilities toward the needy portions of the Lord's vineyard, and in the spirit of the Master Worker labor untiringly for the conversion of souls, the angels of God will prepare the way before them, and the means necessary for the carrying forward of the work will be provided. Those who are enlightened will give freely to support the work done in their behalf. They will respond liberally to every call for help, and the Spirit of God will move upon their hearts to sustain the Lord's cause not only in the home fields, but in the regions beyond. Thus strength will come to the working forces in other places, and the work of the Lord will advance in His own appointed way.

A Consecrated Ministry

In His life and lessons Christ has given a perfect exemplification of the unselfish ministry which has its origin in God. God does not live for Himself. By creating the world, and by upholding all things, He is constantly ministering to others. "He maketh His sun to rise on the evil and on the good, and sendeth rain on the just and on the unjust." Matthew 5:45. This ideal of ministry the Father committed to His Son. Jesus was given to stand at the head of humanity, by His example to teach what it means to minister. His whole life was under a law of service. He served all, ministered to all.

Again and again Jesus tried to establish his principle among His disciples. When James and John made their request for pre-eminence, He said, "Whosoever will be great among you, let him be your minister; and whosoever will be chief among you, let him be your servant: even as the Son of man came not to be ministered unto, but to minister, and to give His life a ransom for many." Matthew 20:26-28.

Since His ascension Christ has carried forward His work on the earth by chosen ambassadors, through whom He speaks to the children of men and ministers to their needs. The great Head of the church superintends His work through the instrumentality of men ordained by God to act as His representatives.

The position of those who have been called of God to labor in word and doctrine for the upbuilding of His church, is one of grave responsibility. In Christ's stead they are to beseech men and women to be reconciled to God, and they can fulfill their mission only as they receive wisdom and power from above.

Christ's ministers are the spiritual guardians of the people entrusted to their care. Their work has been likened to that of watchmen. In ancient times sentinels were often stationed on the walls of cities, where, from points of vantage, they could overlook important posts to be guarded, and give warning of the approach of an enemy. Upon their faithfulness depended the safety of all within. At stated intervals they were required to call to one another, to make sure that all were awake and that no harm had befallen any. The cry of good cheer or of warning was borne from one to another, each repeating the call till it echoed round the city.

To every minister the Lord declares: "O son of man, I have set thee a watchman unto the house of Israel; therefore thou shalt hear the word at My mouth, and warn them from Me. When I say unto the wicked, O wicked man, thou shalt surely die; if thou dost not speak to warn the wicked from his way, that wicked man shall die in his iniquity; but his blood will I require at thine hand. Nevertheless, if thou warn the wicked of his way to turn from it, . . . thou hast delivered thy soul." Ezekiel 33:7-9.

The words of the prophet declare the solemn responsibility of those who are appointed as guardians of the church of God, stewards of the mysteries of God. They are to stand as watchmen on the walls of Zion, to sound the note of alarm at the approach of the enemy. Souls are in danger of falling under temptation, and they will perish unless God's ministers are faithful to their trust. If for any reason their spiritual senses become so benumbed that they are unable to discern danger, and through their failure to give warning the people perish, God will require at their hands the blood of those who are lost.

It is the privilege of the watchmen on the walls of Zion to live so near to God, and to be susceptible to the impressions of His Spirit, that He can work through them to tell men and women of their peril and point them to the place of safety. Faithfully are they to warn them of the sure result of transgression, and faithfully are they to safeguard the interests of the church. At no time may they relax their vigilance. Theirs is a work requiring the exercise of every faculty of the being. In trumpet tones their voices are to be lifted, and never are they to sound one wavering, uncertain note. Not for wages are they to labor, but because they cannot do otherwise, because they realize that there is a woe upon them if they fail to preach the gospel. Chosen of God, sealed with the blood of consecration, they are to rescue men and women from impending destruction.

The minister who is a co-worker with Christ will have a deep sense of the sacredness of his work and of the toil and sacrifice required to perform it successfully. He does not study his own ease or convenience. He is forgetful of self. In his search for the lost sheep he does not realize that he himself is weary, cold, and hungry. He has but one object in view—the saving of the lost.

He who serves under the bloodstained banner of Immanuel will have that to do which will call for heroic effort and patient endurance. But the soldier of the cross stands unshrinkingly in the forefront of the battle. As the enemy presses the attack against him, he turns to the stronghold for aid, and as he brings to the Lord the promises of the word, he is strengthened for the duties of the hour. He realizes his need of strength from above. The victories that he gains do not lead to self exaltation, but cause him to lean more and more heavily on the Mighty One. Relying upon that Power, he is enabled to present the message of salvation so forcibly that it vibrates in other minds.

He who teaches the word must himself live in conscious, hourly communion with God through prayer and a study of His word, for here is the source of strength. Communion with God will impart to the minister's efforts a power greater than the influence of his preaching. Of this power he must not allow himself to be deprived. With an earnestness that cannot be denied, he must plead with God to strengthen and fortify him for duty and trial, and to touch his lips with living fire. All too slight is the hold that Christ's ambassadors often have upon eternal realities. If men will walk with God, He will hide them in the cleft of the Rock. Thus hidden, they can see God, even as Moses saw Him. By the power and light that He imparts they can comprehend more and accomplish more than their finite judgment had seemed possible.

Satan's craft is most successfully used against those who are depressed. When discouragement threatens to overwhelm the minister, let him spread out before God his necessities. It was when the heavens were as brass over Paul that he trusted most fully in God. More than most men, he knew the meaning of affliction; but listen to his triumphant cry as, beset by temptation and conflict, his feet press heavenward: "Our light affliction, which is but for a moment, worketh for us a far more exceeding and eternal weight of glory; while we look not at the things which are seen, but at the things which are not seen." 2 Corinthians 4:17, 18. Paul's eyes were ever fastened on the unseen and eternal. Realizing that he was fighting against supernatural powers, he placed this dependence on God, and in this lay his strength. It is by seeing Him who is invisible that strength and vigor of soul are gained and the power of earth over mind and character is broken.

A pastor should mingle freely with the people for whom he labors, that by becoming acquainted with them he may know how to adapt his teaching to their needs. When a minister has preached a sermon, his work has but just begun. There is personal work for him to do. He should visit the people in their homes, talking and praying with them in earnestness and humility. There are families who will never be reached by the truths of God's word unless the stewards of His grace enter their homes and point them to the higher way. But the hearts of those who do this work must throb in unison with the heart of Christ.

Much is comprehended in the command, "Go out into the highways and hedges, and compel them to come in, that My house may be filled." Luke 14:23. Let ministers teach the truth in families, drawing close to those for whom they labor, and as they thus co-operate with God, He will clothe them with spiritual power. Christ will guide them in their work, giving them words to speak that will sink deep into the hearts of the listeners. It is the privilege of every minister to be able to say with Paul, "I have not shunned to declare unto you all the counsel of God." "I kept back nothing that was profitable unto you, but have showed you, and have taught you publicly, and from house to house,... repentance toward God, and faith toward our Lord Jesus Christ." Acts 20:27, 20, 21.

The Saviour went from house to house, healing the sick, comforting the mourners, soothing the afflicted, speaking peace to the disconsolate. He took the little children in His arms and blessed them, and spoke words of hope and comfort to the weary mothers. With unfailing tenderness and gentleness He met every form of human woe and affliction. Not for Himself but for others did He labor. He was the servant of all. It was His meat and drink to bring hope and strength to all with whom He came in contact. And as men and women listened to the truths that fell from His lips, so different from the traditions and dogmas taught by the rabbis, hope sprang up in their hearts. In His teaching there was an earnestness that sent His words home with convicting power.

God's ministers are to learn Christ's method of laboring, that they may bring from the storehouse of His word that which will supply the spiritual needs of those for whom they labor. Thus only can they fulfill their trust. The same Spirit that dwelt in Christ as He imparted the instruction He was constantly receiving, is to be the source of their knowledge and the secret of their power in carrying on the Saviour's work in the world.

Some who have labored in the ministry have failed of attaining success because they have not given their undivided interest to the Lord's work. Ministers should have no engrossing interests aside from the great work of leading souls to the Saviour. The fishermen whom Christ called, straightway left their nets and followed Him. Ministers cannot do acceptable work for God and at the same time carry the burden of large personal business enterprises. Such a division of interest dims their spiritual perception. The mind and heart are occupied with earthly things, and the service of Christ takes a second place. They seek to shape their work for God by their circumstances, instead of shaping circumstances to meet the demands of God.

The energies of the minister are all needed for his high calling. His best powers belong to God. He should not engage in speculation or in any other business that would turn him aside from his great work. "No man that warreth," Paul declared, "entangleth himself with the affairs of this life; that he may please him who hath chosen him to be a soldier." 2 Timothy 2:4. Thus the apostle emphasized the minister's need of unreserved consecration to the Master's service. The minister who is wholly consecrated to God refuses to engage in business that would hinder him from giving himself fully to his sacred calling. He is not striving for earthly honor or riches; his one purpose is to tell others of the Saviour, who gave Himself to bring to human beings the riches of eternal life. His highest desire is not to lay up treasure in this world, but to bring to the attention of the indifferent and the disloyal the realities of eternity. He may be asked to engage in enterprises which promise large worldly gain, but to such temptations he returns the answer, "What shall it profit a man, if he shall gain the whole world, and lose his own soul?" Mark 8:36.

Satan presented this inducement to Christ, knowing that if He accepted it, the world would never be ransomed. And under different guises he presents the same temptation to God's ministers today, knowing that those who are beguiled by it will be false to their trust.

It is not God's will that His ministers should seek to be rich. Regarding this, Paul wrote to Timothy: "The love of money is the root of all evil: which while some coveted after, they have erred from the faith, and pierced themselves through with many sorrows. But thou, O man of God, flee these things; and follow after righteousness, godliness, faith, love, patience, meekness." By example as well as by precept, the ambassador for Christ is to "charge them that are rich in this world, that they be not high-minded, nor trust in uncertain riches, but in the living God, who giveth us richly all things to enjoy; that they do good, that they be rich in

good works, ready to distribute, willing to communicate; laying up in store for themselves a good foundation against the time to come, that they may lay hold on eternal life." 1 Timothy 6:10, 11, 17-19.

The experiences of the apostle Paul and his instruction regarding the sacredness of the minister's work are a source of help and inspiration to those engaged in the gospel ministry. Paul's heart burned with a love for sinners, and he put all his energies into the work of soul winning. There never lived a more self-denying, persevering worker. The blessings he received he prized as so many advantages to be used in blessing others. He lost no opportunity of speaking of the Saviour or of helping those in trouble. From place to place he went, preaching the gospel of Christ and establishing churches. Wherever he could find a hearing, he sought to counteract wrong, and to turn the feet of men and women into the path of righteousness.

Paul did not forget the churches that he had established. After making a missionary tour, he and Barnabas retraced their steps and visited the churches they had raised up, choosing from them men whom they could train to unite in proclaiming the gospel.

This feature of Paul's work contains an important lesson for ministers today. The apostle made it a part of his work to educate young men for the office of the ministry. He took them with him on his missionary journeys, and thus they gained an experience that later enabled them to fill positions of responsibility. When separated from them, he still kept in touch with their work, and his letters to Timothy and to Titus are evidences of how deep was his desire for their success.

Experienced workers today do a noble work when, instead of trying to carry all the burdens themselves, they train younger workers and place burdens on their shoulders.

Paul never forgot the responsibility resting on him as a minister of Christ, or that if souls were lost through unfaithfulness on his part, God would hold him accountable. "Whereof I am made a minister," he declared of the gospel, "according to the dispensation of God which is given to me for you, to fulfill the word of God; even the mystery which hath been hid from ages and from generations, but now is made manifest to His saints: to whom God would make known what is the riches of the glory of this mystery among the Gentiles; which is Christ in you, the hope of glory: whom we preach, warning every man, and teaching every man in all wisdom; that we may present every man perfect in Christ Jesus: whereunto I also labor, striving according to His working, which worketh in me mightily." Colossians 1:25-29.

These words present before the worker for Christ a high attainment, yet this attainment all can reach who, putting themselves under the control of the Great Teacher, learn daily in the school of Christ. The power at God's command is limitless, and the minister who in his great need shuts himself in with the Lord may be assured that he will receive that which will be to his hearers a savor of life unto life.

Paul's writings show that the gospel minister should be an

example of the truths that he teaches, "giving no offense in anything, that the ministry be not blamed." Of his own work he has left us a picture in his letter to the Corinthian believers: "In all things approving ourselves as the ministers of God, in much patience, in afflictions, in necessities, in distresses, in stripes, in imprisonments, in tumults, in labors, in watchings, in fastings; but pureness, by knowledge, by long suffering, by kindness, by the Holy Ghost, by love unfeigned, by the word of truth, by the power of God, by the armor of righteousness on the right hand and on the left, by honor and dishonor, by evil report and good report: as deceivers, and yet true; as unknown, and yet well known; as dying, and, behold, we live; as chastened, and not killed; as sorrowful, yet alway rejoicing; as poor, yet making many rich." 2 Corinthians 6:3, 4-10.

To Titus he wrote: "Young men likewise exhort to be sober-minded. In all things showing thyself a pattern of good works: in doctrine showing uncorruptness, gravity, sincerity, sound speech, that cannot be condemned; that he that is of the contrary part may be ashamed, having no evil thing to say of you." Titus 2:6-8.

There is nothing more precious in the sight of God than His ministers, who go forth into the waste places of the earth to sow the seeds of truth, looking forward to the harvest. None but Christ can measure the solicitude of His servants as they seek for the lost. He imparts His Spirit to them, and by their efforts souls are led to turn from sin to righteousness.

God is calling for men who are willing to leave their farms, their business, if need be their families, to become missionaries for Him. And the call will be answered. In the past there have been men who, stirred by the love of Christ and the needs of the lost, have left the comforts of home and the society of friends, even that of wife and children, to go into foreign lands, among idolaters and savages, to proclaim the message of mercy. Many in the attempt have lost their lives, but others have been raised up to carry on the work. Thus step by step the cause of Christ has progressed, and the seed sown in sorrow has yielded a bountiful harvest. The knowledge of God has been widely extended and the banner of the cross planted in heathen lands.

For the conversion of one sinner the minister should tax his resources to the utmost. The soul that God has created and Christ has redeemed is of great value because of the possibilities before it, the spiritual advantages that have been granted it, the capabilities that it may possess if vitalized by the word of God, and the immortality it may gain through the hope presented in the gospel. And if Christ left the ninety and nine that He might seek and save one lost sheep, can we be justified in doing less? Is not a neglect to work as Christ worked, to sacrifice as He sacrificed, a betrayal of sacred trusts, an insult to God?

The heart of the true minister is filled with an intense longing to save souls. Time and strength are spent, toilsome effort is not shunned; for others must hear the truths that brought to his own soul such gladness and peace and joy. The Spirit of Christ rests upon him. He watches for souls as one that must give an account. With his eyes fixed on the cross of Calvary, beholding the uplifted Saviour, relying on His grace, believing that He will be with him until the end, as his shield, his strength, his efficiency, he works for God. With invitations and pleadings, mingled with the assurances of God's love, he seeks to win souls to Jesus, and in heaven he is numbered among those who are "called, and chosen, and faithful." Revelation 17:14.

Salvation to the Jews

After many unavoidable delays, Paul at last reached Corinth, the scene of so much anxious labor in the past, and for a time the object of deep solicitude. He found that many of the early believers still regarded him with affection as the one who had first borne to them the light of the gospel. As he greeted these disciples and saw the evidences of their fidelity and zeal he rejoiced that his work in Corinth had not been in vain.

The Corinthian believers, once so prone to lose sight of their high calling in Christ, had developed strength of Christian character. Their words and acts revealed the transforming power of the grace of God, and they were now a strong force for good in that center of heathenism and superstition. In the society of his beloved companions and these faithful converts the apostle's worn and troubled spirit found rest.

During his sojourn at Corinth, Paul found time to look forward to new and wider fields of service. His contemplated journey to Rome especially occupied his thoughts. To see the Christian faith firmly established at the great center of the known world was one of his dearest hopes and most cherished plans. A church had already been established in Rome, and the apostle desired to secure the co-operation of the believers there in the work to be accomplished in Italy and in other countries. To prepare the way for his labors among these brethren, many of whom were as yet strangers to him, he sent them a letter announcing his purpose of visiting Rome and his hope of planting the standard of the cross in Spain.

In his epistle to the Romans, Paul set forth the great principles of the gospel. He stated his position on the questions which were agitating the Jewish and the Gentile churches, and showed that the hopes and promises which had once belonged especially to the Jews were now offered to the Gentiles also.

With great clearness and power the apostle presented the doctrine of justification by faith in Christ. He hoped that other churches also might be helped by the instruction sent to the Christians at Rome; but how dimly could he foresee the far-reaching influence of his words! Through all the ages the great truth of justification by faith has stood as a mighty beacon to guide repentant sinners into the way of life. It was this light that scattered the darkness which enveloped Luther's mind and revealed to him the power of the blood of

Christ to cleanse from sin. The same light has guided thousands of sin-burdened souls to the true Source of pardon and peace. For the epistle to the church at Rome, every Christian has reason to thank God.

In this letter Paul gave free expression to his burden in behalf of the Jews. Ever since his conversion, he had longed to help his Jewish brethren to gain a clear understanding of the gospel message. "My heart's desire and prayer to God for Israel is," he declared, "that they might be saved."

It was no ordinary desire that the apostle felt. Constantly he was petitioning God to work in behalf of the Israelites who had failed to recognize Jesus of Nazareth as the promised Messiah. "I say the truth in Christ," he assured the believers at Rome, "my conscience also bearing me witness in the Holy Ghost, that I have great heaviness and continual sorrow in my heart. For I could wish that myself were accursed from Christ for my brethren, my kinsmen according to the flesh: who are Israelites, to whom pertaineth the adoption, and the glory, and the covenants, and the giving of the law, and the service of God, and the promises; whose are the fathers, and of whom as concerning the flesh Christ came, who is over all, God blessed forever."

The Jews were God's chosen people, through whom He had purposed to bless the entire race. From among them God had raised up many prophets. These had foretold the advent of a Redeemer who was to be rejected and slain by those who should have been the first to recognize Him as the Promised One.

The prophet Isaiah, looking down through the centuries and witnessing the rejection of prophet after prophet and finally of the Son of God, was inspired to write concerning the acceptance of the Redeemer by those who had never before been numbered among the children of Israel. Referring to this prophecy, Paul declares: "Esaias is very bold, and saith, I was found of them that sought Me not; I was made manifest unto them that asked not after Me. But to Israel He saith, All day long I have stretched forth My hands unto a disobedient and gainsaying people."

Even though Israel rejected His Son, God did not reject them. Listen to Paul as he continues the argument: "I say then, Hath God cast away His people? God forbid. For I also am an Israelite, of the seed of Abraham, of the tribe of Benjamin. God hath not cast away His people which He foreknew. Wot ye not what the Scripture saith of Elias? how he maketh intercession to God against Israel, saying, Lord, they have killed Thy prophets, and digged down Thine altars; and I am left alone, and they seek my life. But what saith the answer of God unto him? I have reserved to Myself seven thousand men, who have not bowed the knee to the image of Baal. Even so then at this present time also there is a remnant according to the election of grace."

Israel had stumbled and fallen, but this did not make it impossible for them to rise again. In answer to the question, "Have they stumbled that they should fall?" the apostle replies: "God forbid: but rather through their fall salvation is come unto the Gentiles, for to provoke them to jealousy. Now if the fall of them be the riches of the world, and the diminishing of them the riches of the Gentiles; how much more their fullness? For I speak to you Gentiles, inasmuch as I am the apostle of the Gentiles, I magnify mine office: if by any means I may provoke to emulation them which are my flesh, and might save some of them. For if the casting away of them be the reconciling of the world, what shall the receiving of them be, but life from the dead?"

It was God's purpose that His grace should be revealed among the Gentiles as well as among the Israelites. This had been plainly outlined in Old Testament prophecies. The apostle uses some of these prophecies in his argument. "Hath not the potter power over the clay," he inquires, "of the same lump to make one vessel unto honor, and another unto dishonor? What if God, willing to show His wrath, and to make His power known, endured with much long-suffering the vessels of wrath fitted to destruction: and that He might make known the riches of His glory on the vessels of mercy, which He had afore prepared unto glory, even us, whom He hath called, not of the Jews only, but also of the Gentiles? As He saith also in Osee, I will call them My people, which were not My people; and her beloved, which was not beloved. And it shall come to pass, that in the place where it was said unto them, Ye are not My people; there shall they be called the children of the living God." See Hosea 1:10.

Notwithstanding Israel's failure as a nation, there remained among them a goodly remnant of such as should be saved. At the time of the Saviour's advent there were faithful men and women who had received with gladness the message of John the Baptist, and had thus been led to study anew the prophecies concerning the Messiah. When the early Christian church was founded, it was composed of these faithful Jews who recognized Jesus of Nazareth as the one for whose advent they had been longing. It is to this remnant that Paul refers when he writes, "If the first fruit be holy, the lump is also holy: and if the root be holy, so are the branches."

Paul likens the remnant in Israel to a noble olive tree, some of whose branches have been broken off. He compares the Gentiles to branches from a wild olive tree, grafted into the parent stock. "If some of the branches be broken off," he writes to the Gentile believers, "and thou, being a wild olive tree, wert grafted in among them, and with them partakest of the root and fatness of the olive tree; boast not against the branches. But if thou boast, thou barest not the root, but the root thee. Thou wilt say then, The branches were broken off, that I might be grafted in. Well; because of unbelief they were broken off, and thou standest by faith. Be not high-minded, but fear: for if God spared not the natural branches, take heed lest He also spare not thee. Behold therefore the goodness and severity of God: on them which fell, severity; but toward thee, goodness, if thou continue in His goodness: otherwise thou also shalt be cut off."

Through unbelief and the rejection of Heaven's purpose for her, Israel as a nation had lost her connection with God. But the branches that had been separated from the parent stock God was able to reunite with the true stock of Israel —the remnant who had remained true to the God of their fathers. "They also," the apostle declares of these broken branches, "if they abide not still in unbelief, shall be grafted in: for God is able to graft them in again." "If thou," he writes to the Gentiles, "wert cut out of the olive tree which is wild by nature, and wert grafted contrary to nature into a good olive tree: how much more shall these, which be the natural branches, be grafted into their own olive tree? For I would not, brethren, that ye should be ignorant of this mystery, lest ye should be wise in your own conceits; that blindness in part is happened to Israel, until the fullness of the Gentiles be come in.

"And so all Israel shall be saved: as it is written, There shall come out of Sion the Deliverer, and shall turn away ungodliness from Jacob: for this is My covenant unto them, when I shall take away their sins. As concerning the gospel, they are enemies for your sakes: but as touching the election, they are beloved for the father's sakes. For the gifts and calling of God are without repentance. For as ye in times past have not believed God, yet have now obtained mercy through their unbelief: even so have these also now not believed, that through your mercy they also may obtain mercy. For God had concluded them all in unbelief, that He might have mercy upon all.

"O the depth of the riches both of the wisdom and knowledge of God! how unsearchable are His judgments, and His ways past finding out! For who hath known the mind of the Lord? or who hath been His counselor? or who hath first given to Him, and it shall be recompensed unto him again? For of Him, and through Him, and to Him, are all things: to whom be glory forever."

Thus Paul shows that God is abundantly able to transform the hearts of Jew and Gentile alike, and to grant to every believer in Christ the blessings promised to Israel. He repeats Isaiah's declaration concerning God's people: "Though the number of children of Israel be as the sand of the sea, a remnant shall be saved: for He will finish the work, and cut it short in righteousness: because a short work will the Lord make upon the earth. And as Esaias said before, Except the Lord of Sabaoth had left us a seed, we had been as Sodoma and been made like unto Gomorrah."

At the time when Jerusalem was destroyed and the temple laid in ruins, many thousands of the Jews were sold to serve as bondmen in heathen lands. Like wrecks on a desert shore they were scattered among the nations. For eighteen hundred years the Jews have wandered from land to land throughout the world, and in no place have they been given the privilege of regaining their ancient prestige as a nation. Maligned, hated, persecuted, from century to century theirs has been a heritage of suffering.

Notwithstanding the awful doom pronounced upon the Jews as a nation at the time of their rejection of Jesus of Nazareth, there have lived from age to age many noble, God-fearing Jewish men and women who have suffered in silence. God has comforted their hearts in affliction and has beheld with pity their terrible situation. He has heard the agonizing prayers of those who have sought Him with all the heart for a right understanding of His word. Some have learned to see in the lowly Nazarene whom their forefathers rejected and crucified, the true Messiah of Israel. As their minds have grasped the significance of the familiar prophecies so long obscured by tradition and misinterpretation, their hearts have been filled with gratitude to God for the unspeakable gift He bestows upon every human being who chooses to accept Christ as a personal Saviour.

It is to this class that Isaiah referred in his prophecy, "A remnant shall be saved." From Paul's day to the present time, God by His Holy Spirit has been calling after the Jew as well as the Gentile. "There is no respect of persons with God," declared Paul. The apostle regarded himself as "debtor both to the Greeks, and to the barbarians," as well as to the Jews; but he never lost sight of the decided advantages possessed by the Jews over others, "chiefly, because that unto them were committed the oracles of God." "The gospel," he declared, "is the power of God unto salvation to everyone that believeth; to the Jew first, and also to the Greek. For therein is the righteousness of God revealed from faith to faith: as it is written, The just shall live by faith." It is of this gospel of Christ, equally efficacious for Jew and Gentile, that Paul in his epistle to the Romans declared he was not ashamed.

When this gospel shall be presented in its fullness to the Jews, many will accept Christ as the Messiah. Among Christian ministers there are only a few who feel called upon to labor for the Jewish people; but to those who have been often passed by, as well as to all others, the message of mercy and hope in Christ is to come.

In the closing proclamation of the gospel, when special work is to be done for classes of people hitherto neglected, God expects His messengers to take particular interest in the Jewish people whom they find in all parts of the earth. As the Old Testament Scriptures are blended with the New in an explanation of Jehovah's eternal purpose, this will be to many of the Jews as the dawn of a new creation, the resurrection of the soul. As they see the Christ of the gospel dispensation portrayed in the pages of the Old Testament Scriptures, and perceive how clearly the New Testament explains the Old, their slumbering faculties will be aroused, and they will recognize Christ as the Saviour of the world. Many will by faith receive Christ as their Redeemer. To them will be fulfilled the words, "As many as received Him, to them gave He power to become the sons of God, even to them that believe on His name." John 1:12.

Among the Jews are some who, like Saul of Tarsus, are mighty in the Scriptures, and these will proclaim with wonderful power the immutability of the law of God. The God of Israel will bring this to pass in our day. His arm is not shortened that it cannot save. As His servants labor in faith for those who have long been neglected and despised, His salvation will be revealed.

"Thus saith the Lord, who redeemed Abraham, concerning the house of Jacob, Jacob shall not now be ashamed, neither shall his face now wax pale. But when he seeth his children, the work of Mine hands, in the midst of him, they shall sanctify My name, and sanctify the Holy One of Jacob, and shall fear the God of Israel. They also that erred in spirit shall come to understanding, and they that murmured shall learn doctrine." Isaiah 29:22-24.

Apostasy in Galatia

While tarrying at Corinth, Paul had cause for serious apprehension concerning some of the churches already established. Through the influence of false teachers who had arisen among the believers in Jerusalem, division, heresy, and sensualism were rapidly gaining ground among the believers in Galatia. These false teachers were mingling Jewish traditions with the truths of the gospel. Ignoring the decision of the general council at Jerusalem, they urged upon the Gentile converts the observance of the ceremonial law.

The situation was critical. The evils that had been introduced threatened speedily to destroy the Galatian churches.

Paul was cut to the heart, and his soul was stirred by this open apostasy on the part of those to whom he had faithfully taught the principles of the gospel. He immediately wrote to the deluded believers, exposing the false theories that they had accepted and with great severity rebuking those who were departing from the faith. After saluting the Galatians in the words, "Grace be to you and peace from God the Father, and from our Lord Jesus Christ," he addressed to them these words of sharp reproof:

"I marvel that ye are so soon removed from Him that called you into the grace of Christ unto another gospel: which is not another; but there be some that trouble you, and would pervert the gospel of Christ. But though we, or an angel from heaven, preach any other gospel unto you than that which we have preached unto you, let him be accursed." Paul's teachings had been in harmony with the Scriptures, and the Holy Spirit had witnessed to his labors; therefore he warned his brethren not to listen to anything that contradicted the truths he had taught them.

The apostle bade the Galatian believers consider carefully their first experience in the Christian life. "O foolish Galatians," he exclaimed, "who hath bewitched you, that ye should not obey the truth, before whose eyes Jesus Christ hath been evidently set forth, crucified among you? This only would I learn of you, Received ye the Spirit by the works of the law, or by the hearing of faith? Are ye so foolish? having begun in the Spirit, are ye now made perfect by the flesh? Have ye suffered so many things in vain? if it be yet in vain. He therefore that ministereth to you the Spirit, and worketh miracles among you, doeth he it by the works of the law, or by the hearing of faith?"

Thus Paul arraigned the believers in Galatia before the tribunal of their own conscience and sought to arrest them in their course. Relying on the power of God to save, and refusing to recognize the doctrines of the apostate teachers, the apostle endeavored to lead the converts to see that they had been grossly deceived, but that by returning to their former faith in the gospel they might yet defeat the purpose of Satan. He took his position firmly on the side of truth and righteousness; and his supreme faith and confidence in the message he bore, helped many whose faith had failed, to return to their allegiance to the Saviour.

How different from Paul's manner of writing to the Corinthian church was the course he pursued toward the Galatians! The former he rebuked with caution and tenderness, the latter with words of unsparing reproof. The Corinthians had been overcome by temptation. Deceived by the ingenious sophistry of teachers who presented errors under the guise of truth, they had become confused and bewildered. To teach them to distinguish the false from the true, called for caution and patience. Harshness or injudicious haste on Paul's part would have destroyed his influence over many of those whom he longed to help.

In the Galatian churches, open, unmasked error was supplanting the gospel message. Christ, the true foundation of the faith, was virtually renounced for the obsolete ceremonies of Judaism. The apostle saw that if the believers in Galatia were saved from the dangerous influences which threatened them, the most decisive measures must be taken, the sharpest warnings given.

An important lesson for every minister of Christ to learn is that of adapting his labors to the condition of those whom he seeks to benefit. Tenderness, patience, decision, and firmness are alike needful; but these are to be exercised with proper discrimination. To deal wisely with different classes of minds, under varied circumstances and conditions, is a work requiring wisdom and judgment enlightened and sanctified by the Spirit of God.

In his letter to the Galatian believers Paul briefly reviewed the leading incidents connected with his own conversion and early Christian experience. By this means he sought to show that it was through a special manifestation of divine power that he had been led to see and grasp the great truths of the gospel. It was through instruction received from God Himself that Paul was led to warn and admonish the Galatians in so solemn and positive a manner. He wrote, not in hesitancy and doubt, but with the assurance of settled conviction and absolute knowledge. He clearly outlined the difference between being taught by man and receiving instruction direct from Christ.

The apostle urged the Galatians to leave the false guides by whom they had been misled, and to return to the faith that had been accompanied by unmistakable evidences of divine approval. The men who had attempted to lead them from their belief in the gospel were hypocrites, unholy in heart and corrupt in life. Their religion was made up of a round of ceremonies, through the performance of which they expected to gain the favor of God. They had no desire for a gospel that called for obedience to the word, "Except a man be born again, he cannot see the kingdom of God." John 3:3. They felt that a religion based on such a doctrine, required too great a sacrifice, and they clung to their errors, deceiving themselves and others.

To substitute external forms of religion for holiness of heart and life is still as pleasing to the unrenewed nature as it was in the days of these Jewish teachers. Today, as then, there are false spiritual guides, to whose doctrines many listen eagerly. It is Satan's studied effort to divert minds from the hope of salvation through faith in Christ and obedience to the law of God. In every age the archenemy adapts his temptations to the prejudices or inclinations of those whom he is seeking to deceive. In apostolic times he led the Jews to exalt the ceremonial law and reject Christ; at the present time he induces many professing Christians, under pretense of honoring Christ, to cast contempt on the moral law and to teach that its precepts may be transgressed with impunity. It is the duty of every servant of God to withstand firmly and decidedly these perverters of the faith and by the word of truth fearlessly to expose their errors.

In his effort to regain the confidence of his brethren in Galatia, Paul ably vindicated his position as an apostle of Christ. He declared himself to be an apostle, "not of men, neither by man, but by Jesus Christ, and God the Father, who raised Him from the dead." Not from men, but from the highest Authority in heaven, had he received his commission. And his position had been acknowledged by a general council at Jerusalem, with the decisions of which Paul had complied in all his labors among the Gentiles.

It was not to exalt self, but to magnify the grace of God, that Paul thus presented to those who were denying his apostleship, proof that he was "not a whit behind the very chiefest apostles." 2 Corinthians 11:5. Those who sought to belittle his calling and his work were fighting against Christ, whose grace and power were manifested through Paul. The apostle was forced, by the opposition of his enemies, to take a decided stand in maintaining his position and authority.

Paul pleaded with those who had once known in their lives the power of God, to return to their first love of gospel truth. With unanswerable arguments he set before them their privilege of becoming free men and women in Christ, through whose atoning grace all who make full surrender are clothed with the robe of His righteousness. He took the position that every soul who would be saved must have a genuine, personal experience in the things of God.

The apostle's earnest words of entreaty were not fruitless. The Holy Spirit wrought with mighty power, and many whose feet had wandered into strange paths, returned to their former faith in the gospel. Henceforth they were steadfast in the liberty wherewith Christ had made them free. In their lives were revealed the fruits of the Spirit—"love, joy, peace, long-suffering, gentleness, goodness, faith, meekness, temperance." The name of God was glorified, and many were added to the number of believers throughout that region.

Paul's Last Journey to Jerusalem

Paul greatly desired to reach Jerusalem before the Passover as he would thus have an opportunity to meet those who should come from all parts of the world to attend the feast. Ever he cherished the hope that in some way he might be instrumental in removing the prejudice of his unbelieving countrymen, so that they might be led to accept the precious light of the gospel. He also desired to meet the church at Jerusalem and bear to them the gifts sent by the Gentile churches to the poor brethren in Judea. And by this visit he hoped to bring about a firmer union between the Jewish and the Gentile converts to the faith.

Having completed his work at Corinth, he determined to sail directly for one of the ports on the coast of Palestine. All the arrangements had been made, and he was about to step on board the ship, when he was told of a plot laid by the Jews to take his life. In the past these opposers of the faith had been foiled in all their efforts to put an end to the apostle's work.

The success attending the preaching of the gospel aroused the anger of the Jews anew. From every quarter were coming accounts of the spread of the new doctrine by which Jews were released from the observance of the rites of the ceremonial law and Gentiles were admitted to equal privileges with the Jews as children of Abraham. Paul, in his preaching at Corinth, presented the same arguments which he urged so forcibly in his epistles. His emphatic statement, "There is neither Greek nor Jew, circumcision nor uncircumcision" (Colossians 3:11), was regarded by his enemies as daring blasphemy, and they determined that his voice should be silenced.

Upon receiving warning of the plot, Paul decided to go around by way of Macedonia. His plan to reach Jerusalem in time for the Passover services had to be given up, but he hoped to be there at Pentecost.

Accompanying Paul and Luke were "Sopater of Berea; and of the Thessalonians, Aristarchus and Secundus; and Gaius of Derbe, and Timotheus; and of Asia, Tychicus and Trophimus." Paul had with him a large sum of money from the Gentile churches, which he purposed to place in the hands of the brethren in charge of the work in Judea; and because of this he made arrangements for these representative brethren from various contributing churches, to accompany him to Jerusalem.

At Philippi Paul tarried to keep the Passover. Only Luke remained with him, the other members of the company passing on to Troas to await him there. The Philippians were the most loving and truehearted of the apostle's converts, and during the eight days of the feast he enjoyed peaceful and happy communion with them.

Sailing from Philippi, Paul and Luke reached their companions at Troas five days later, and remained for seven days with the believers in that place.

Upon the last evening of his stay the brethren "came together to break bread." The fact that their beloved teacher was about to depart, had called together a larger company than usual. They assembled in an "upper chamber" on the third story. There, in the fervency of his love and solicitude for them, the apostle preached until midnight.

In one of the open windows sat a youth named Eutychus. In this perilous position he went to sleep and fell to the court below. At once all was alarm and confusion. The youth was taken up dead, and many gathered about him with cries and mourning. But Paul, passing through the frightened company, embraced him and offered up an earnest prayer that God would restore the dead to life. His petition was granted. Above the sound of mourning and lamentation the apostle's voice was heard, saying, "Trouble not yourselves; for his life is in him." With rejoicing the believers again assembled in the upper chamber. They partook of the Communion, and then Paul "talked a long while, even till break of day."

The ship on which Paul and his companions were to continue their journey, was about to sail, and the brethren hastened on board. The apostle himself, however, chose to take the nearer route by land between Troas and Assos, meeting his companions at the latter city. This gave him a short season for meditation and prayer. The difficulties and dangers connected with his coming visit to Jerusalem, the attitude of the church there toward him and his work, as well as the condition of the churches and the interests of the gospel work in other fields, were subjects of earnest, anxious thought, and he took advantage of this special opportunity to seek God for strength and guidance.

As the travelers sailed southward from Assos, they passed the city of Ephesus, so long the scene of the apostle's labors. Paul had greatly desired to visit the church there, for he had important instruction and counsel to give them. But upon consideration he determined to hasten on, for he desired, "if it were possible for him, to be at Jerusalem the Day of Pentecost." On arriving at Miletus, however, about thirty miles from Ephesus, he learned that it might be possible to communicate with the church before the ship should sail. He therefore immediately sent a message to the elders, urging them to hasten to Miletus, that he might see them before continuing his journey.

In answer to his call they came, and he spoke to them strong, touching words of admonition and farewell. "Ye know," he said, "from the first day that I came into Asia, after what manner I have been with you at all seasons, serving the Lord with all humility of mind, and with many tears, and temptations, which befell me by the lying in wait of the Jews: and how I kept back nothing that was profitable unto you, but have showed you, and have taught you publicly, and from house to house, testifying both to the Jews, and also to the Greeks, repentance toward God, and faith toward our Lord Jesus Christ."

Paul had ever exalted the divine law. He had shown that in the law there is no power to save men from the penalty of disobedience. Wrongdoers must repent of their sins and humble themselves before God, whose just wrath they have incurred by breaking His law, and they must also exercise faith in the blood of Christ as their only means of pardon. The Son of God had died as their sacrifice and had ascended to heaven to stand before the Father as their advocate. By repentance and faith they might be freed from the condemnation of sin and through the grace of Christ be enabled henceforth to render obedience to the low of God.

"And now, behold," Paul continued, "I go bound in the spirit unto Jerusalem, not knowing the things that shall befall me there: save that the Holy Ghost witnesseth in every city, saying that bonds and afflictions abide me. But none of these things move me, neither count I my life dear unto myself, so that I might finish my course with joy, and the ministry, which I have received of the Lord Jesus, to testify the gospel of the grace of God. And now, behold, I know that ye all, among whom I have gone preaching the kingdom of God, shall see my face no more."

Paul had no designed to bear this testimony; but, while he was speaking, the Spirit of Inspiration came upon him, confirming his fears that this would be his last meeting with his Ephesian brethren.

"Wherefore I take you to record this day, that I am pure from the blood of all men. For I have not shunned to declare unto you all the counsel of God." No fear of giving offense, no desire for friendship or applause, could lead Paul to withhold the words that God had given him for their instruction, warning, or correction. From His servants today God requires fearlessness in preaching the word and in carrying out its precepts. The minister of Christ is not to present to the people only those truths that are the most pleasing, while he withholds others that might cause them pain. He should watch with deep solicitude the development of character. If he sees that any of his flock are cherishing sin he must as a faithful shepherd give them from God's word the instruction that is applicable to their case. Should he permit them in their self-confidence to go on unwarned, he would be held responsible for their souls. The pastor who fulfills his high commission must give his people faithful instruction on every point of the Christian faith, showing them what they must be and do in order to stand perfect in the day of God. He only who is a faithful teacher of the truth will at the close of his work be able to say with Paul, "I am pure from the blood of all men."

"Take heed therefore unto yourselves," the apostle admonished his brethren, "and to all the flock, over the which the Holy Ghost hath made you overseers, to feed the church of God, which He hath purchased with His own blood." If ministers of the gospel were to bear constantly in mind the fact that they are dealing with the purchase of the blood of Christ, they would have a deeper sense of the importance of their work. They are to take heed to themselves and to their flock. Their own example is to illustrate and enforce their instructions. As teachers of the way of life they should give no occasion for the truth to be evil spoken of. As representatives of Christ they are to maintain the honor of His name. By their devotion, their purity of life, their godly conversation, they are to prove themselves worthy of their high calling.

The dangers that would assail the church at Ephesus were revealed to the apostle. "I know this," he said, "that after my departing shall grievous wolves enter in among you, not sparing the flock. Also of your own selves shall men arise, speaking perverse things, to draw away disciples after them." Paul trembled for the church as, looking into the future, he saw the attacks which she must suffer from both external and internal foes. With solemn earnestness he bade his brethren guard vigilantly their sacred trusts. For an example he pointed them to his own unwearied labors among them: "Therefore watch, and remember, that by the space of three years I ceased not to warn everyone night and day with tears.

"And now, brethren," he continued, "I commend you to God, and to the word of His grace, which is able to build you up, and to give you an inheritance among all them which are sanctified. I have coveted no man's silver, or gold, or apparel." Some of the Ephesian brethren were wealthy, but Paul had never sought personal benefit from them. It was no part of his message to call attention to his own wants. "These hands," he declared, "have ministered unto my necessities, and to them that were with me." Amidst his arduous labors and extensive journeys for the cause of Christ, he was able, not only to supply his own wants, but to spare something for the support of his fellow laborers and the relief of the worthy poor. This he accomplished only by unremitting diligence and the closest economy. Well might he point to his own example as he said, "I have showed you all things, how that so laboring ye ought to support the weak, and to remember the words of the Lord Jesus, how He said, It is more blessed to give than to receive.

"And when he had thus spoken, he kneeled down, and prayed with them all. And they all wept sore, and fell on Paul's neck, and kissed him, sorrowing most of all for the words which he spake, that they should see his face no more. And they accompanied him unto the ship."

From Miletus the travelers sailed in "a straight course unto Coos, and the day following unto Rhodes, and from thence unto Patara," on the southwest shore of Asia Minor, where, "finding a ship sailing over unto Phoenicia," they "went aboard, and set forth." At Tyre, where the ship was unloaded, they found a few disciples, with whom they were permitted to tarry seven days. Through the Holy Spirit these disciples were warned of the perils awaiting Paul at Jerusalem, and they urged him "that he should not go up to Jerusalem." But the apostle allowed not the fear of affliction and imprisonment to turn him from his purpose.

At the close of the week spent in Tyre, all the brethren, with their wives and children, went with Paul to the ship, and before he stepped on board, they knelt upon the shore and prayed, he for them, and they for him.

Pursuing their journey southward, the travelers arrived at Caesarea and "entered into the house of Philip the evangelist, which was one of the seven; and abode with him." Here Paul spent a few peaceful, happy days—the last of perfect freedom that he was to enjoy for a long time.

While Paul tarried at Caesarea, "there came down from Judea a certain prophet, named Agabus. And when he was come unto us," Luke says, "he took Paul's girdle, and bound his own hands and feet, and said, Thus saith the Holy Ghost, So shall the Jews at Jerusalem bind the man that owneth this girdle, and shall deliver him into the hands of the Gentiles."

"When we heard these things," Luke continues, "both we, and they of that place, besought him not to go up to Jerusalem." But Paul would not swerve from the path of duty. He would follow Christ if need be to prison and to death. "What mean ye to weep and to break mine heart?" he exclaimed; "for I am ready not to be bound only, but also to die at Jerusalem for the name of the Lord Jesus." Seeing that they caused him pain without changing his purpose, the brethren ceased their importunity, saying only, "The will of the Lord be done."

The time soon came for the brief stay at Caesarea to end, and, accompanied by some of the brethren, Paul and his company set out for Jerusalem, their hearts deeply shadowed by the presentiment of coming evil.

Never before had the apostle approached Jerusalem with so sad a heart. He knew that he would find few friends and many enemies. He was nearing the city which had rejected and slain the Son of God and over which now hung the threatenings of divine wrath. Remembering how bitter had been his own prejudice against the followers of Christ, he felt the deepest pity for his deluded countrymen. And yet how little could he hope that he would be able to help them! The same blind wrath which had once burned in his own heart, was now with untold power kindling the hearts of a whole nation against him.

And he could not count upon the sympathy and support of even his own brethren in the faith. The unconverted Jews who had followed so closely upon his track, had not been slow to circulate the most unfavorable reports at Jerusalem, both personally and by letter, concerning him and his work; and some, even of the apostles and elders, had received these reports as truth, making no attempt to contradict them, and manifesting no desire to harmonize with him.

Yet in the midst of discouragements the apostle was not in despair. He trusted that the Voice which had spoken to his own heart would yet speak to the hearts of his countrymen, and that the Master whom his fellow disciples loved and served would yet unite their hearts with his in the work of the gospel.

Paul A Prisoner

When we were come to Jerusalem, the brethren received us gladly. And the day following Paul went in with us unto James; and all the elders were present."

On this occasion, Paul and his companions formally presented to the leaders of the work at Jerusalem the contributions forwarded by the Gentile churches for the support of the poor among their Jewish brethren. The gathering of these contributions had cost the apostle and his fellow workers much time, anxious thought, and wearisome labor. The sum, which far exceeded the expectations of the elders at Jerusalem, represented many sacrifices and even severe privations on the part of the Gentile believers.

These freewill offerings betokened the loyalty of the Gentile converts to the organized work of God throughout the world and should have been received by all with grateful acknowledgment, yet it was apparent to Paul and his companions that even among those before whom they now stood were some who were unable to appreciate the spirit of brotherly love that had prompted the gifts.

In the earlier years of the gospel work among the Gentiles some of the leading brethren at Jerusalem, clinging to former prejudices and habits of thought, had not co-operated heartily with Paul and his associates. In their anxiety to preserve a few meaningless forms and ceremonies, they had lost sight of the blessing that would come to them and to the cause they loved, through an effort to unite in one all parts of the Lord's work. Although desirous of safeguarding the best interests of the Christian church, they had failed to keep step with the advancing providences of God, and in their human wisdom attempted to throw about workers many unnecessary restrictions. Thus there arose a group of men who were unacquainted personally with the changing circumstances and peculiar needs met by laborers in distant fields, yet who insisted that they had the authority to direct their brethren in these fields to follow certain specified methods of labor. They felt as if the work of preaching the gospel should be carried forward in harmony with their opinions.

Several years had passed since the brethren in Jerusalem, with representatives from other leading churches, gave careful consideration to the perplexing questions that had arisen over methods followed by those who were laboring for the Gentiles. As a result of this council, the brethren had united in making definite recommendations to the churches concerning certain rites and customs, including circumcision. It was at this general council that the brethren had also united in commending to the Christian churches Barnabas and Paul as laborers worthy of the full confidence of every believer.

Among those present at this meeting, were some who had severely criticized the methods of labor followed by the apostles upon whom rested the chief burden of carrying the gospel to the Gentile world. But during the council their views of God's purpose had broadened, and they had united with their brethren in making wise decisions which made possible the unification of the entire body of believers.

Afterward, when it became apparent that the converts among the Gentiles were increasing rapidly, there were a few of the leading brethren at Jerusalem who began to cherish anew their former prejudices against the methods of Paul and his associates. These prejudices strengthened with the passing of the years, until some of the leaders determined that the work of preaching the gospel must henceforth be conducted in accordance with their own ideas. If Paul would conform his methods to certain policies which they advocated they would acknowledge and sustain his work; otherwise they could no longer look upon it with favor or grant it their support.

These men had lost sight of the fact that God is the teacher of His people; that every worker in His cause is to obtain an individual experience in following the divine Leader, not looking to man for direct guidance; that His workers are to be molded and fashioned, not after man's ideas, but after the similitude of the divine.

In his ministry the apostle Paul had taught the people "not with enticing words of man's wisdom, but in demonstration of the Spirit and of power." The truths that he proclaimed had been revealed to him by the Holy Spirit, "for the Spirit searcheth all things, yea, the deep things of God. For what man knoweth the things of a man, save the spirit of man which is in him? even so the things of God knoweth no man, but the Spirit of God. . . . Which things," declared Paul, "we speak, not in the words which man's wisdom teacheth, but which the Holy Ghost teacheth; comparing spiritual things with spiritual." 1 Corinthians 2:4, 10-13.

Throughout his ministry, Paul had looked to God for direct guidance. At the same time, he had been very careful to labor in harmony with the decisions of the general council at Jerusalem, and as a result the churches were "established in the faith, and increased in number daily." Acts 16:5. And now, notwithstanding the lack of sympathy shown him by some, he found comfort in the consciousness that he had done his duty in encouraging in his converts a spirit of loyalty, generosity, and brotherly love, as revealed on this occasion in the liberal contributions which he was enabled to place before the Jewish elders.

After the presentation of the gifts, Paul "declared particularly what things God had wrought among the Gentiles by his ministry." This recital of facts brought to the hearts of all, even of those who had been doubting, the conviction that the blessing of heaven had accompanied his labors. "When they heard it, they glorified the Lord." They felt that the methods of labor pursued by the apostle bore the signet of Heaven. The liberal contributions lying before them added weight to the testimony of the apostle concerning the faithfulness of the new churches established among the Gentiles. The men who, while numbered among those who were in charge of the work at Jerusalem, had urged that arbitrary measures of control be adopted, saw Paul's ministry in a new light and were convinced that their own course had been wrong, that they had been held in bondage by Jewish customs and traditions, and that the work of the gospel had been greatly hindered by their failure to recognize that the wall of partition between Jew and Gentile had been broken down by the death of Christ.

This was the golden opportunity for all the leading brethren to confess frankly that God had wrought through Paul, and that at times they had erred in permitting the reports of his enemies to arouse their jealousy and prejudice. But instead of uniting in an effort to do justice to the one who had been injured, they gave him counsel which showed that they still cherished a feeling that Paul should be held largely responsible for the existing prejudice. They did not stand nobly in his defense, endeavoring to show the disaffected ones where they were wrong, but sought to effect a compromise by counseling him to pursue a course which in their opinion would remove all cause for misapprehension.

"Thou seest, brother," they said, in response to his testimony, "how many thousands of Jews there are which believe; and they are all zealous of the law: and they are informed of thee, that thou teachest all the Jews which are among the Gentiles to forsake Moses, saying that they ought not to circumcise their children, neither to walk after the customs. What is it therefore? the multitude must needs come together: for they will hear that thou art come. Do therefore this that we say to thee: We have four men which have a vow on them; them take, and purify thyself with them, and be at charges with them, that they may shave their heads: and all may know that those things, whereof they were informed concerning thee, are nothing; but that thou thyself also walkest orderly, and keepest the law. As touching the Gentiles which believe, we have written and concluded that they observe no such thing, save only that they keep themselves from things offered to idols, and from blood, and from strangled, and from fornication."

The brethren hoped that Paul, by following the course suggested, might give a decisive contradiction to the false reports concerning him. They assured him that the decision of the former council concerning the Gentile converts and the ceremonial law, still held good. But the advice now given was not consistent with that decision. The Spirit of God did not prompt this instruction; it was the fruit of cowardice. The leaders of the church in Jerusalem knew that by non-conformity to the ceremonial law, Christians would bring upon themselves the hatred of the Jews and expose themselves to persecution. The Sanhedrin was doing its utmost to hinder the progress of the gospel. Men were chosen by this body to follow up the apostles, especially Paul, and in every possible way to oppose their work. Should the believers in Christ be condemned before the Sanhedrin as breakers of the law, they would suffer swift and severe punishment as apostates from the Jewish faith.

Many of the Jews who had accepted the gospel still cherished a regard for the ceremonial law and were only too willing to make unwise concessions, hoping thus to gain the confidence of their countrymen, to remove their prejudice, and to win them to faith in Christ as the world's Redeemer. Paul realized that so long as many of the leading members of the church at Jerusalem should continue to cherish prejudice against him, they would work constantly to counteract his influence. He felt that if by any reasonable concession he could win them to the truth he would remove a great obstacle to the success of the gospel in other places. But he was not authorized of God to concede as much as they asked.

When we think of Paul's great desire to be in harmony with his brethren, his tenderness toward the weak in the faith, his reverence for the apostles who had been with Christ, and for James, the brother of the Lord, and his purpose to become all things to all men so far as he could without sacrificing principle—when we think of all this, it is less surprising that he was constrained to deviate from the firm, decided course that he had hitherto followed. But instead of accomplishing the desired object, his efforts for conciliation only precipitated the crisis, hastened his predicted sufferings, and resulted in separating him from his brethren, depriving the church of one of its strongest pillars, and bringing sorrow to Christian hearts in every land.

On the following day Paul began to carry out the counsel of the elders. The four men who were under the Nazarite vow (Numbers 6), the term of which had nearly expired, were taken by Paul into the temple, "to signify the accomplishment of the days of purification, until that an offering should be offered for every one of them." Certain costly sacrifices for purification were yet to be offered.

Those who advised Paul to take this step had not fully considered the great peril to which he would thus be exposed. At this season, Jerusalem was filled with worshipers from many lands. As, in fulfillment of the commission given him by God, Paul had borne the gospel to the Gentiles, he had visited many of the world's largest cities, and he was well known to thousands who from foreign parts had come to Jerusalem to attend the feast. Among these were men whose hearts were filled with bitter hatred for Paul, and for him to enter the temple on a public occasion was to risk his life. For several days he passed in and out among the worshipers, apparently unnoticed; but before the close of the specified period, as he was talking with a priest concerning the sacrifices to be offered, he was recognized by some of the Jews from Asia.

With the fury of demons they rushed upon him, crying, "Men of Israel, help: This is the man, that teacheth all men everywhere against the people, and the law, and this place." And as the people responded to the call for help, another accusation was added—"and further brought Greeks also into the temple, and hath polluted this holy place."

By the Jewish law it was a crime punishable with death for an uncircumcised person to enter the inner courts of the sacred edifice. Paul had been seen in the city in company with Trophimus, an Ephesian, and it was conjectured that he had brought him into the temple. This he had not done; and being himself a Jew, his act in entering the temple was no violation of the law. But though the charge was wholly false, it served to arouse the popular prejudice. As the cry was taken up and borne through the temple courts, the throngs gathered there were thrown into wild excitement. The news quickly spread through Jerusalem, "and all the city was moved, and the people ran together."

That an apostate from Israel should presume to profane the temple at the very time when thousands had come there from all parts of the world to worship, excited the fiercest passions of the mob. "They took Paul, and drew him out of the temple: and forthwith the doors were shut."

"As they went about to kill him, tidings came unto the chief captain of the band, that all Jerusalem was in an uproar." Claudius Lysias well knew the turbulent elements with which he had to deal, and he "immediately took soldiers and centurions, and ran down unto them: and when they saw the chief captain and the soldiers, they left beating of Paul." Ignorant of the cause of the tumult, but seeing that the rage of the multitude was directed against Paul, the Roman captain concluded that he must be a certain Egyptian rebel of whom he had heard, who had thus far escaped capture. He therefore "took him, and commanded him to be bound with two chains; and demanded who he was, and what he had done." At once many voices were raised in loud and angry accusation; "some cried one thing, some another, among the multitude: and when he could not know the certainty for the tumult, he commanded him to be carried into the castle. And when he came upon the stairs, so it was, that he was borne of the soldiers for the violence of the people. For the multitude of the people followed after, crying, Away with him."

In the midst of the tumult the apostle was calm and self-possessed. His mind was stayed upon God, and he knew that angels of heaven were about him. He felt unwilling to leave the temple without making an effort to set the truth before his countrymen. As he was about to be led into the castle he said to the chief captain, "May I speak unto thee?" Lysias responded, "Canst thou speak Greek? Art not thou that Egyptian, which before these days madest an uproar, and leddest out into the wilderness four thousand men that were murderers?" In reply Paul said, "I am a man which am a Jew of Tarsus, a city in Cilicia, a citizen of no mean city: and, I beseech thee, suffer me to speak unto the people."

The request was granted, and "Paul stood on the stairs, and beckoned with the hand unto the people." The gesture attracted their attention, while his bearing commanded respect. "And when there was made a great silence, he spake unto them in the Hebrew tongue, saying, Men, brethren, and fathers, hear ye my defense which I make now unto you." At the sound of the familiar Hebrew words, "they kept the more silence," and in the universal hush he continued:

"I am verily a man which am a Jew, born in Tarsus, a city in Cilicia, yet brought up in this city at the feet of Gamaliel, and taught according to the perfect manner of the law of the fathers, and was zealous toward God, as ye all are this day." None could deny the apostle's statements, as the facts that he referred to were well known to many who were still living in Jerusalem. He then spoke of his former zeal in persecuting the disciples of Christ, even unto death; and he narrated the circumstances of his conversion, telling his hearers how his own proud heart had been led to bow to the crucified

Nazarene. Had he attempted to enter into argument with his opponents, they would have stubbornly refused to listen to his words; but the relation of his experience was attended with a convincing power that for the time seemed to soften and subdue their hearts.

He then endeavored to show that his work among the Gentiles had not been entered upon from choice. He had desired to labor for his own nation; but in that very temple the voice of God had spoken to him in holy vision, directing his course "far hence upon the Gentiles."

Hitherto the people had listened with close attention, but when Paul reached the point in his history where he was appointed Christ's ambassador to the Gentiles, their fury broke forth anew. Accustomed to look upon themselves as the only people favored by God, they were unwilling to permit the despised Gentiles to share the privileges which had hitherto been regarded as exclusively their own. Lifting their voices above the voice of the speaker, they cried, "Away with such a fellow from the earth: for it is not fit that he should live."

"As they cried out, and cast off their clothes, and threw dust into the air, the chief captain commanded him to be brought into the castle, and bade that he should be examined by scourging; that he might know wherefore they cried so against him.

"And as they bound him with thongs, Paul said unto the centurion that stood by, Is it lawful for you to scourge a man that is a Roman, and uncondemned? When the centurion heard that, he went and told the chief captain, saying, Take heed what thou doest: for this man is a Roman. Then the chief captain came, and said unto him, Tell me, art thou a Roman? He said, Yea. And the chief captain answered, With a great sum obtained I this freedom. And Paul said, But I was freeborn. Then straightway they departed from him which should have examined him: and the chief captain also was afraid, after he knew that he was a Roman, and because he had bound him.

"On the morrow, because he would have known the certainty wherefore he was accused of the Jews, he loosed him from his bands, and commanded the chief priests and all their council to appear, and brought Paul down, and set him before them."

The apostle was now to be tried by the same tribunal of which he himself had been a member before his conversion. As he stood before the Jewish rulers, his bearing was calm, and his countenance revealed the peace of Christ. "Earnestly beholding the council," he said, "Men and brethren, I have lived in all good conscience before God until this day." Upon hearing these words, their hatred was kindled afresh; "and the high priest Ananias commanded them that stood by him to smite him on the mouth." At this inhuman command, Paul exclaimed, "God shall smite thee, thou whited wall: for sittest thou to judge me after the law, and commandest me to be smitten contrary to the law?" "They that stood by said, Revilest thou God's high priest?" With his usual courtesy Paul answered, "I wish not, brethren, that he was the high priest:

for it is written, Thou shalt not speak evil of the ruler of thy people.

"But when Paul perceived that the one part were Sadducees, and the other Pharisees, he cried out in the council, Men and brethren, I am a Pharisee, the son of a Pharisee: of the hope and resurrection of the dead I am called in question.

"And when he had so said, there arose a dissension between the Pharisees and the Sadducees: and the multitude was divided. For the Sadducees say that there is no resurrection, neither angel, nor spirit: but the Pharisees confess both." The two parties began to dispute between themselves, and thus the strength of their opposition against Paul was broken. "The scribes that were of the Pharisees' part arose, and strove, saying, We find no evil in this man: but if a spirit or an angel hath spoken to him, let us not fight against God."

In the confusion that followed, the Sadducees were eagerly striving to gain possession of the apostle, that they might put him to death; and the Pharisees were as eager in striving to protect him. "The chief captain, fearing lest Paul should have been pulled in pieces of them, commanded the soldiers to go down, and to take him by force from among them, and to bring him into the castle."

Later, while reflecting on the trying experiences of the day, Paul began to fear that his course might not have been pleasing to God. Could it be that he had made a mistake after all in visiting Jerusalem? Had his great desire to be in union with his brethren led to this disastrous result?

The position which the Jews as God's professed people occupied before an unbelieving world, caused the apostle intense anguish of spirit. How would those heathen officers look upon them?—claiming to be worshipers of Jehovah, and assuming sacred office, yet giving themselves up to the control of blind, unreasoning anger, seeking to destroy even their brethren who dared to differ with them in religious faith, and turning their most solemn deliberative council into a scene of strife and wild confusion. Paul felt that the name of his God had suffered reproach in the eyes of the heathen.

And now he was in prison, and he knew that his enemies, in their desperate malice, would resort to any means to put him to death. Could it be that his work for the churches was ended and that ravening wolves were to enter in now? The cause of Christ was very near to Paul's heart, and with deep anxiety he thought of the perils of the scattered churches, exposed as they were to the persecutions of just such men as he had encountered in the Sanhedrin council. In distress and discouragement he wept and prayed.

In this dark hour the Lord was not unmindful of His servant. He had guarded him from the murderous throng in the temple courts; He had been with him before the Sanhedrin council; He was with him in the fortress; and He revealed Himself to His faithful witness in response to the earnest prayers of the apostle for guidance. "The night following the Lord stood by him, and said, Be of good cheer, Paul: for as thou hast testified of Me in Jerusalem, so must thou bear witness also at Rome."

Paul had long looked forward to visiting Rome; he greatly desired to witness for Christ there, but had felt that his purposes were frustrated by the enmity of the Jews. He little thought, even now, that it would be as a prisoner that he would go.

While the Lord encouraged His servant, Paul's enemies were eagerly plotting his destruction. "And when it was day, certain of the Jews banded together, and bound themselves under a curse, saying that they would neither eat nor drink till they had killed Paul. And they were more than forty which had made this conspiracy." Here was a fast such as the Lord through Isaiah had condemned—a fast "for strife and debate, and to smite with the fist of wickedness." Isaiah 58:4.

The conspirators "came to the chief priests and elders, and said, We have bound ourselves under a great curse, that we will eat nothing until we have slain Paul. Now therefore ye with the council signify to the chief captain that he bring him down unto you tomorrow, as though ye would inquire something more perfectly concerning him: and we, or ever he come near, are ready to kill him."

Instead of rebuking this cruel scheme, the priests and rulers eagerly agreed to it. Paul had spoken the truth when he compared Ananias to a whited sepulcher.

But God interposed to save the life of His servant. Paul's sister's son, hearing of the "lying in wait" of the assassins, "went and entered into the castle, and told Paul. Then Paul called one of the centurions unto him, and said, Bring this young man unto the chief captain: for he hath a certain thing to tell him. So he took him, and brought him to the chief captain, and said, Paul the prisoner called me unto him, and prayed me to bring this young man unto thee, who hath something to say unto thee."

Claudius Lysias received the youth kindly, and taking him aside, asked, "What is that thou hast to tell me?" The youth replied: "The Jews have agreed to desire thee that thou wouldest bring down Paul tomorrow into the council, as though they would inquire somewhat of him more perfectly. But do not thou yield unto them: for there lie in wait for him of them more than forty men, which have bound themselves with an oath, that they will neither eat nor drink till they have killed him: and now are they ready, looking for a promise from thee."

"The chief captain then let the young man depart, and charged him, See thou tell no man that thou hast showed these things to me."

Lysias at once decided to transfer Paul from his jurisdiction to that of Felix the procurator. As a people, the Jews were in a state of excitement and irritation, and tumults were of frequent occurrence. The continued presence of the apostle in Jerusalem might lead to consequences dangerous to the city and even to the commandant himself. He therefore "called unto him two centurions, saying, Make ready two hundred soldiers to go to Caesarea, and horsemen threescore and ten, and spearmen two hundred, at the third hour of the night;

and provide them beasts, that they may set Paul on, and bring him safe unto Felix the governor."

No time was to be lost in sending Paul away. "The soldiers, as it was commanded them, took Paul, and brought him by night to Antipatris." From that place the horsemen went on with the prisoner to Caesarea, while the four hundred soldiers returned to Jerusalem.

The officer in charge of the detachment delivered his prisoner to Felix, also presenting a letter with which he had been entrusted by the chief captain:

"Claudius Lysias unto the most excellent governor Felix sendeth greeting. This man was taken of the Jews, and should have been killed of them: then came I with an army, and rescued him, having understood that he was a Roman. And when I would have known the cause wherefore they accused him, I brought him forth into their council: whom I perceived to be accused of questions of their law, but to have nothing laid to his charge worthy of death or of bonds. And when it was told me how that the Jews laid wait for the man, I sent straightway to thee, and gave commandment to his accusers also to say before thee what they had against him. Farewell."

After reading the communication, Felix inquired to what province the prisoner belonged, and being informed that he was of Cilicia, said: "I will hear thee . . . when thine accusers are also come. And he commanded him to be kept in Herod's judgment hall."

The case of Paul was not the first in which a servant of God had found among the heathen an asylum from the malice of the professed people of Jehovah. In their rage against Paul the Jews had added another crime to the dark catalogue which marked the history of that people. They had still further hardened their hearts against the truth and had rendered their doom more certain.

Few realize the full meaning of the words that Christ spoke when, in the synagogue at Nazareth, He announced Himself as the Anointed One. He declared His mission to comfort, bless, and save the sorrowing and the sinful; and then, seeing that pride and unbelief controlled the hearts of His hearers, He reminded them that in time past God had turned away from His chosen people because of their unbelief and rebellion, and had manifested Himself to those in heathen lands who had not rejected the light of heaven. The widow of Sarepta and Naaman the Syrian had lived up to all the light they had; hence they were accounted more righteous than God's chosen people who had backslidden from Him and had sacrificed principle to convenience and worldly honor.

Christ told the Jews at Nazareth a fearful truth when He declared that with backsliding Israel there was no safety for the faithful messenger of God. They would not know his worth or appreciate his labors. While the Jewish leaders professed to have great zeal for the honor of God and the good of Israel, they were enemies of both. By precept and example they were leading the people farther and farther from obedience to God—leading them where He could not be their defense in the day of trouble.

The Saviour's words of reproof to the men of Nazareth applied, in the case of Paul, not only to the unbelieving Jews, but to his own brethren in the faith. Had the leaders in the church fully surrendered their feeling of bitterness toward the apostle, and accepted him as one specially called of God to bear the gospel to the Gentiles, the Lord would have spared him to them. God had not ordained that Paul's labors should so soon end, but He did not work a miracle to counteract the train of circumstances to which the course of the leaders in the church at Jerusalem had given rise.

The same spirit is still leading to the same results. A neglect to appreciate and improve the provisions of divine grace has deprived the church of many a blessing. How often would the Lord have prolonged the work of some faithful minister, had his labors been appreciated! But if the church permits the enemy of souls to pervert the understanding, so that they misrepresent and misinterpret the words and acts of the servant of Christ; if they allow themselves to stand in his way and hinder his usefulness, the Lord sometimes removes from them the blessing which He gave.

Satan is constantly working through his agents to dishearten and destroy those whom God has chosen to accomplish a great and good work. They may be ready to sacrifice even life itself for the advancement of the cause of Christ, yet the great deceiver will suggest to their brethren doubts concerning them which, if entertained, would undermine confidence in their integrity of character, and thus cripple their usefulness. Too often he succeeds in bringing upon them, through their own brethren, such sorrow of heart that God graciously interposes to give His persecuted servants rest. After the hands are folded upon the pulseless breast, when the voice of warning and encouragement is silent, then the obdurate may be aroused to see and prize the blessings they have cast from them. Their death may accomplish that which their life has failed to do.

The Trial at Caesarea

Five days after Paul's arrival at Caesarea his accusers came from Jerusalem, accompanied by Tertullus, an orator whom they had engaged as their counsel. The case was granted a speedy hearing. Paul was brought before the assembly, and Tertullus "began to accuse him." Judging that flattery would have more influence upon the Roman governor than the simple statements of truth and justice, the wily orator began his speech by praising Felix: "Seeing that by thee we enjoy great quietness, and that very worthy deeds are done unto this nation by thy providence, we accept it always, and in all places, most noble Felix, with all thankfulness."

Tertullus here descended to barefaced falsehood; for the character of Felix was base and contemptible. It was said of him, that "in the practice of all kinds of lust and cruelty, he exercised the power of a king with the temper of a slave." —Tacitus, History, ch. 5, par. 9. Those who heard Tertullus knew that his flattering words were untrue, but their desire to secure the condemnation of Paul was stronger than their love of truth.

In his speech, Tertullus charged Paul with crimes which, if proved, would have resulted in his conviction for high treason against the government. "We have found this man a pestilent fellow," declared the orator, "and a mover of sedition among all the Jews throughout the world, and a ringleader of the sect of the Nazarenes: who also hath gone about to profane the temple." Tertullus then stated that Lysias, the commandant of the garrison at Jerusalem, had violently taken Paul from the Jews when they were about to judge him by their ecclesiastical law, and had thus forced them to bring the matter before Felix. These statements were made with the design of inducing the procurator to deliver Paul over to the Jewish court. All the charges were vehemently supported by the Jews present, who made no effort to conceal their hatred of the prisoner.

Felix had sufficient penetration to read the disposition and character of Paul's accusers. He knew from what motive they had flattered him, and he saw also that they had failed to substantiate their charges against Paul. Turning to the accused, he beckoned to him to answer for himself. Paul wasted no words in compliments, but simply stated that he could the more cheerfully defend himself before Felix, since the latter had been so long a procurator, and therefore had so good an understanding of the laws and customs of the Jews. Referring to the charges brought against him, he plainly showed that not one of them was true. He declared that he had caused no disturbance in any part of Jerusalem, nor had he profaned the sanctuary. "They neither found me in the temple disputing with any man," he said, "neither raising up the people, neither in the synagogues, nor in the city: neither can they prove the things whereof they now accuse me."

While confessing that "after the way which they call heresy" he had worshiped the God of his fathers, he asserted that he had always believed "all things which are written in the law and in the prophets;" and that in harmony with the plain teaching of the Scriptures, he held the faith of the resurrection of the dead. And he further declared that the ruling purpose of his life was to "have always a conscience void of offense toward God, and toward men."

In a candid, straightforward manner he stated the object of his visit to Jerusalem, and the circumstances of his arrest and trial: "Now after many years I came to bring alms to my nation, and offerings. Whereupon certain Jews from Asia found me purified in the temple, neither with multitude, nor with tumult. Who ought to have been here before thee, and object, if they had aught against me. Or else let these same here say, if they have found any evil doing in me, while I stood before the council, except it be for this one voice, that I cried standing among them, Touching the resurrection of the dead I am called in question by you this day."

The apostle spoke with earnestness and evident sincerity, and his words carried with them a weight of conviction. Claudius Lysias, in his letter to Felix, had borne a similar testimony in regard to Paul's conduct. Moreover, Felix himself had a better knowledge of the Jewish religion than many supposed. Paul's plain statement of the facts in the case enabled Felix to understand still more clearly the motives by which the Jews were governed in attempting to convict the apostle of sedition and treasonable conduct. The governor would not gratify them by unjustly condemning a Roman citizen, neither would he give him up to them to be put to death without a fair trial. Yet Felix knew no higher motive than self-interest, and he was controlled by love of praise and a desire for promotion. Fear of offending the Jews held him back from doing full justice to a man whom he knew to be innocent. He therefore decided to suspend the trial until Lysias should be present, saying, "When Lysias the chief captain shall come down, I will know the uttermost of your matter."

The apostle remained a prisoner, but Felix commanded the centurion who had been appointed to keep Paul, "to let him have liberty," and to "forbid none of his acquaintance to minister or come unto him."

It was not long after this that Felix and his wife, Drusilla, sent for Paul in order that in a private interview they might hear from him "concerning the faith in Christ." They were willing and even eager to listen to these new truths —truths which they might never hear again and which, if rejected, would prove a swift witness against them in the day of God.

Paul regarded this as a God-given opportunity, and faithfully he improved it. He knew that he stood in the presence of one who had power to put him to death or to set him free; yet he did not address Felix and Drusilla with praise or flattery. He knew that his words would be to them a savor of life or of death, and, forgetting all selfish considerations, he sought to arouse them to a sense of their peril.

The apostle realized that the gospel had a claim upon whoever might listen to his words; that one day they would stand either among the pure and holy around the great white throne, or with those to whom Christ would say, "Depart from Me, ye that work iniquity." Matthew 7: 23. He knew that he must meet every one of his hearers before the tribunal of heaven and must there render an account, not only for all that he had said and done, but for the motive and spirit of his words and deeds.

So violent and cruel had been the course of Felix that few had ever before dared even to intimate to him that his character and conduct were not faultless. But Paul had no fear of man. He plainly declared his faith in Christ, and the reasons for that faith, and was thus led to speak particularly of those virtues essential to Christian character, but of which the haughty pair before him were so strikingly destitute.

He held up before Felix and Drusilla the character of God—His righteousness, justice, and equity, and the nature of His law. He clearly showed that it is man's duty to live a life of sobriety and temperance, keeping the passions under the control of reason, in conformity to God's law, and preserving the physical and mental powers in a healthy condition. He declared that there would surely come a day of judgment when all would be rewarded according to the deeds done in the body, and when it would be plainly revealed that wealth, position, or titles are powerless to gain for man the favor of God or to deliver him from the results of sin. He showed that this life is man's time of preparation for the future life. Should he neglect present privileges and opportunities he would suffer an eternal loss; no new probation would be given him.

Paul dwelt especially upon the far-reaching claims of God's law. He showed how it extends to the deep secrets of man's moral nature and throws a flood of light upon that which has been concealed from the sight and knowledge of men. What the hands may do or the tongue may utter —what the outer life reveals—but imperfectly shows man's moral character. The law searches his thoughts, motives, and purposes. The dark passions that lie hidden from the sight of men, the jealousy, hatred, lust, and ambition, the evil deeds meditated upon in the dark recesses of the soul, yet never executed for want of opportunity—all these God's law condemns.

Paul endeavored to direct the minds of his hearers to the one great Sacrifice for sin. He pointed to the sacrifices that were shadows of good things to come, and then presented Christ as the antitype of all those ceremonies—the object to which they pointed as the only source of life and hope for fallen man. Holy men of old were saved by faith in the blood of Christ. As they saw the dying agonies of the sacrificial victims they looked across the gulf of ages to the Lamb of God that was to take away the sin of the world.

God justly claims the love and obedience of all His creatures. He has given them in His law a perfect standard of right. But many forget their Maker and choose to follow their own way in opposition to His will. They return enmity for love that is as high as heaven and as broad as the universe. God cannot lower the requirements of His law to meet the standard of wicked men; neither can man in his own power meet the demands of the law. Only by faith in Christ can the sinner be cleansed from guilt and be enabled to render obedience to the law of his Maker.

Thus Paul, the prisoner, urged the claims of the divine law upon Jew and Gentile, and presented Jesus, the despised Nazarene, as the Son of God, the world's Redeemer.

The Jewish princess well understood the sacred character of that law which she had so shamelessly transgressed, but her prejudice against the Man of Calvary steeled her heart against the word of life. But Felix had never before listened to the truth, and as the Spirit of God sent conviction to his soul, he became deeply agitated. Conscience, now aroused, made her voice heard, and Felix felt that Paul's words were true. Memory went back over the guilty past. With terrible distinctness there came up before him the secrets of his early life of profligacy and bloodshed, and the black record of his later years. He saw himself licentious, cruel, rapacious. Never before had the truth been thus brought home to his heart. Never before had his soul been so filled with terror. The thought that all the secrets of his career of crime were open before the eye of God, and that he must be judged according to his deeds, caused him to tremble with dread.

But instead of permitting his convictions to lead him to repentance, he sought to dismiss these unwelcome reflections. The interview with Paul was cut short. "Go thy way for this time," he said; "when I have a convenient season, I will call for thee."

How wide the contrast between the course of Felix and that of the jailer of Philippi! The servants of the Lord were brought in bonds to the jailer, as was Paul to Felix. The evidence they gave of being sustained by a divine power, their rejoicing under suffering and disgrace, their fearlessness when the earth was reeling with the earthquake shock, and their spirit of Christlike forgiveness, sent conviction to the jailer's heart, and with trembling he confessed his sins and found pardon. Felix trembled, but he did not repent. The jailer joyfully welcomed the Spirit of God to his heart and to his home; Felix bade the divine Messenger depart. The one chose to become a child of God and an heir of heaven; the other cast his lot with the workers of iniquity.

For two years no further action was taken against Paul, yet he remained a prisoner. Felix visited him several times and listened attentively to his words. But the real motive for this apparent friendliness was a desire for gain, and he intimated that by the payment of a large sum of money Paul might secure his release. The apostle, however, was of too noble a nature to free himself by a bribe. He was not guilty of any crime, and he would not stoop to commit a wrong in order to gain freedom. Furthermore, he was himself too poor to pay such a ransom, had he been disposed to do so, and he would not, in his own behalf, appeal to the sympathy and generosity of his converts. He also felt that he was in the hands of God, and he would not interfere with the divine purposes respecting himself.

Felix was finally summoned to Rome because of gross wrongs committed against the Jews. Before leaving Caesarea in answer to this summons, he thought to "show the Jews a pleasure" by allowing Paul to remain in prison. But Felix was not successful in his attempt to regain the confidence of the Jews. He was removed from office in disgrace, and Porcius Festus was appointed to succeed him, with headquarters at Caesarea.

A ray of light from heaven had been permitted to shine upon Felix, when Paul reasoned with him concerning righteousness, temperance, and a judgment to come. That was his heaven-sent opportunity to see and to forsake his sins. But he said to the messenger of God, "Go thy way for this time; when I have a convenient season, I will call for thee." He had slighted his last offer of mercy. Never was he to receive another call from God.

Paul Appeals to Caesar

"When Festus was come into the province, after three days he ascended from Caesarea to Jerusalem. Then the high priest and the chief of the Jews informed him against Paul, and besought him, and desired favor against him, that he would send for him to Jerusalem." In making this request they purposed to waylay Paul along the road to Jerusalem and murder him. But Festus had a high sense of the responsibility of his position, and courteously declined to send for Paul. "It is not the manner of the Romans," he declared, "to deliver any man to die, before that he which is accused have the accusers face to face, and have license to answer for himself concerning the crime laid against him." He stated that "he himself would depart shortly" for Caesarea. "Let them there . . . which among you are able, go down with me, and accuse this man, if there be any wickedness in him."

This was not what the Jews wanted. They had not forgotten their former defeat at Caesarea. In contrast with the calm bearing and forcible arguments of the apostle, their own malignant spirit and baseless accusations would appear in the worst possible light. Again they urged that Paul be brought to Jerusalem for trial, but Festus held firmly to his purpose of giving Paul a fair trial at Caesarea. God in His providence controlled the decision of Festus, that the life of the apostle might be lengthened.

Their purposes defeated, the Jewish leaders at once prepared to witness against Paul at the court of the procurator. Upon returning to Caesarea, after a few days' sojourn at Jerusalem, Festus "the next day sitting on the judgment seat commanded Paul to be brought." "The Jews which came down from Jerusalem stood round about, and laid many and grievous complaints against Paul, which they could not prove." Being on this occasion without a lawyer, the Jews preferred their charges themselves. As the trial proceeded, the accused with calmness and candor clearly showed the falsity of their statements.

Festus discerned that the question in dispute related wholly to Jewish doctrines, and that, rightly understood, there was nothing in the charges against Paul, could they be proved, that would render him subject to sentence of death, or even to imprisonment. Yet he saw clearly the storm of rage that would be created if Paul were not condemned or delivered into their hands. And so, "willing to do the Jews a pleasure," Festus turned to Paul, and asked if he was willing to go to Jerusalem under his protection, to be tried by the Sanhedrin.

The apostle knew that he could not look for justice from the people who by their crimes were bringing down upon themselves the wrath of God. He knew that, like the prophet Elijah, he would be safer among the heathen than with those who had rejected light from heaven and hardened their hearts against the gospel. Weary of strife, his active spirit could ill endure the repeated delays and wearing suspense of his trial and imprisonment. He therefore decided to exercise his privilege, as a Roman citizen, of appealing to Caesar.

In answer to the governor's question, Paul said: "I stand at Caesar's judgment seat, where I ought to be judged: to the Jews have I done no wrong, as thou very well knowest. For if I be an offender, or have committed anything worthy of death, I refuse not to die: but if there be none of these things whereof these accuse me, no man may deliver me unto them. I appeal unto Caesar."

Festus knew nothing of the conspiracies of the Jews to murder Paul, and he was surprised at this appeal to Caesar. However, the words of the apostle put a stop to the proceedings of the court. "Festus, when he had conferred with the council, answered, Hast thou appealed unto Caesar? unto Caesar shalt thou go."

Thus it was that once more, because of hatred born of bigotry and self-righteousness, a servant of God was driven to turn for protection to the heathen. It was this same hatred that forced the prophet Elijah to flee for succor to the widow of Sarepta; and that forced the heralds of the gospel to turn from the Jews to proclaim their message to the Gentiles. And this hatred the people of God living in this age have yet to meet. Among many of the professing followers of Christ there is the same pride, formalism, and selfishness, the same spirit of oppression, that held so large a place in the Jewish heart. In the future, men claiming to be Christ's representatives will take a course similar to that followed by the priests and rulers in their treatment of Christ and the apostles. In the great crisis through which they are soon to pass, the faithful servants of God will encounter the same hardness of heart, the same cruel determination, the same unyielding hatred.

All who in that evil day would fearlessly serve God according to the dictates of conscience, will need courage, firmness, and a knowledge of God and His word; for those who are true to God will be persecuted, their motives will be impugned, their best efforts misinterpreted, and their names cast out as evil. Satan will work with all his deceptive power to influence the heart and becloud the understanding, to make evil appear good, and good evil. The stronger and purer the faith of God's people, and the firmer their determination to obey Him, the more fiercely will Satan strive to stir up against them the rage of those who, while claiming to be righteous, trample upon the law of God. It will require the firmest trust, the most heroic purpose, to hold fast the faith once delivered to the saints.

God desires His people to prepare for the soon-coming crisis. Prepared or unprepared, they must all meet it; and those only who have brought their lives into conformity to the divine standard, will stand firm at that time of test and trial. When secular rulers unite with ministers of religion to dictate in matters of conscience, then it will be seen who really fear and serve God. When the darkness is deepest, the light of a godlike character will shine the brightest. When every other trust fails, then it will be seen who have an abiding trust in Jehovah. And while the enemies of truth are on every side, watching the Lord's servants for evil, God will watch over them for good. He will be to them as the shadow of a great rock in a weary land.

"Almost Thou Persuadest Me"

Paul had appealed to Caesar, and Festus could not do otherwise than send him to Rome. But some time passed before a suitable ship could be found; and as other prisoners were to be sent with Paul, the consideration of their cases also occasioned delay. This gave Paul opportunity to present the reasons of his faith before the principal men of Caesarea, and also before King Agrippa II, the last of the Herods.

"After certain days King Agrippa and Bernice came unto Caesarea to salute Festus. And when they had been there many days, Festus declared Paul's cause unto the king, saying, There is a certain man left in bonds by Felix: about whom, when I was at Jerusalem, the chief priests and the elders of the Jews informed me, desiring to have judgment against him." He outlined the circumstances that led to the prisoner's appeal to Caesar, telling of Paul's recent trial before him, and saying that the Jews had brought against Paul no accusation such as he had supposed they would bring, but "certain questions . . . of their own superstition, and of one Jesus, which was dead, whom Paul affirmed to be alive."

As Festus told his story, Agrippa became interested and said, "I would also hear the man myself." In harmony with his wish, a meeting was arranged for the following day. "And on the morrow, when Agrippa was come, and Bernice, with great pomp, and was entered into the place of hearing, with the chief captains, and principal men of the city, at Festus' commandment Paul was brought forth."

In honor of his visitors, Festus had sought to make this an occasion of imposing display. The rich robes of the procurator and his guests, the swords of the soldiers, and the gleaming armor of their commanders, lent brilliancy to the scene.

And now Paul, still manacled, stood before the assembled company. What a contrast was here presented! Agrippa and Bernice possessed power and position, and because of this they were favored by the world. But they were destitute of the traits of character that God esteems. They were transgressors of His law, corrupt in heart and life. Their course of action was abhorred by heaven.

The aged prisoner, chained to his soldier guard, had in his appearance nothing that would lead the world to pay him homage. Yet in this man, apparently without friends or wealth or position, and held a prisoner for his faith in the Son of God, all heaven was interested. Angels were his attendants. Had the glory of one of those shining messengers flashed forth, the pomp and pride of royalty would have paled; king and courtiers would have been stricken to the earth, as were the Roman guards at the sepulcher of Christ.

Festus himself presented Paul to the assembly with the words: "King Agrippa, and all men which are here present with us, ye see this man, about whom all the multitude of the Jews have dealt with me, both at Jerusalem, and also here, crying that he ought not to live any longer. But when I found that he had committed nothing worthy of death, and that he himself hath appealed to Augustus, I have determined to send him. Of whom I have no certain thing to write unto my lord. Wherefore I have brought him forth before you, and specially before thee, O King Agrippa, that, after examination had, I might have somewhat to write. For it seemeth to me unreasonable to send a prisoner, and not withal to signify the crimes laid against him."

King Agrippa now gave Paul liberty to speak for himself. The apostle was not disconcerted by the brilliant display or the high rank of his audience; for he knew of how little worth are worldly wealth and position. Earthly pomp and power could not for a moment daunt his courage or rob him of his self-control.

"I think myself happy, King Agrippa," he declared, "because I shall answer for myself this day before thee touching all the things whereof I am accused of the Jews: especially because I know thee to be expert in all customs and questions which are among the Jews: wherefore I beseech thee to hear me patiently."

Paul related the story of his conversion from stubborn unbelief to faith in Jesus of Nazareth as the world's Redeemer. He described the heavenly vision that at first had filled him with unspeakable terror, but afterward proved to be a source of the greatest consolation—a revelation of divine glory, in the midst of which sat enthroned He whom he had despised and hated, whose followers he was even then seeking to destroy. From that hour Paul had been a new man, a sincere and fervent believer in Jesus, made such by transforming mercy.

With clearness and power Paul outlined before Agrippa the leading events connected with the life of Christ on earth. He testified that the Messiah of prophecy had already appeared in the person of Jesus of Nazareth. He showed how the Old Testament Scriptures had declared that the Messiah was to appear as a man among men, and how in the life of Jesus had been fulfilled every specification outlined by Moses and the prophets. For the purpose of redeeming a lost world, the divine Son of God had endured the cross, despising the shame, and had ascended to heaven triumphant over death and the grave.

Why, Paul reasoned, should it seem incredible that Christ should rise from the dead? Once it had thus seemed to him, but how could he disbelieve that which he himself had seen and heard? At the gate of Damascus he had verily looked upon the crucified and risen Christ, the same who had walked the streets of Jerusalem, died on Calvary, broken the bands of death, and ascended to heaven. As verily as had Cephas, James, John, or any others of the disciples, he had seen and talked with Him. The Voice had bidden him proclaim the gospel of a risen Saviour, and how could he disobey? In Damascus, in Jerusalem, throughout all Judea, and in the regions afar off, he had borne witness of Jesus the Crucified, showing all classes "that they should repent and turn to God, and do works meet for repentance.

"For these causes," the apostle declared, "the Jews caught me in the temple, and went about to kill me. Having therefore obtained help of God, I continue unto this day, witnessing both to small and great, saying none other things than those which the prophets and Moses did say should come: that Christ should suffer, and that He should be the first that should rise from the dead, and should show light unto the people, and to the Gentiles."

The whole company had listened spellbound to Paul's account of his wonderful experiences. The apostle was dwelling upon his favorite theme. None who heard him could doubt his sincerity. But in the full tide of his persuasive eloquence he was interrupted by Festus, who cried out, "Paul, thou art beside thyself; much learning doth make thee mad."

The apostle replied, "I am not mad, most noble Festus; but speak forth the words of truth and soberness. For the king knoweth of these things, before whom also I speak freely: for I am persuaded that none of these thing are hidden from him; for this thing was not done in a corner." Then, turning to Agrippa, he addressed him directly, "King Agrippa, believest thou the prophets? I know that thou believest."

Deeply affected, Agrippa for the moment lost sight of his surroundings and the dignity of his position. Conscious only of the truths which he had heard, seeing only the humble prisoner standing before him as God's ambassador, he answered involuntarily, "Almost thou persuadest me to be a Christian."

Earnestly the apostle made answer, "I would to God, that not only thou, but also all that hear me this day, were both almost, and altogether such as I am," adding, as he raised his fettered hands, "except these bonds."

Festus, Agrippa, and Bernice might in justice have worn the fetters that bound the apostle. All were guilty of grievous crimes. These offenders had that day heard the offer of salvation through the name of Christ. One, at least, had been almost persuaded to accept the grace and pardon offered. But Agrippa put aside the proffered mercy, refusing to accept the cross of a crucified Redeemer.

The king's curiosity was satisfied, and, rising from his seat, he signified that the interview was at an end. As the assembly dispersed, they talked among themselves, saying, "This man doeth nothing worthy of death or of bonds."

Though Agrippa was a Jew, he did not share the bigoted zeal and blind prejudice of the Pharisees. "This man," he said to Festus, "might have been set at liberty, if he had not appealed unto Caesar." But the case had been referred to that higher tribunal, and it was now beyond the jurisdiction of either Festus or Agrippa.

The Voyage and Shipwreck

At last Paul was on his way to Rome. "When it was determined," Luke writes, "that we should sail into Italy, they delivered Paul and certain other prisoners unto one named Julius, a centurion of Augustus' band. And entering into a ship of Adramyttium, we launched, meaning to sail by the coasts of Asia; one Aristarchus, a Macedonian of Thessalonica, being with us."

In the first century of the Christian Era traveling by sea was attended with peculiar hardship and peril. Mariners directed their course largely by the position of the sun and stars; and when these did not appear, and there were indications of storm, the owners of vessels were fearful of venturing into the open sea. During a portion of the year, safe navigation was almost impossible.

The apostle Paul was now called upon to endure the trying experiences that would fall to his lot as a prisoner in chains during the long and tedious voyage to Italy. One circumstance greatly lightened the hardship of his lot—he was permitted the companionship of Luke and Aristarchus. In his letter to the Colossians he afterward referred to the latter as his "fellow prisoner" (Colossians 4:10); but it was from choice that Aristarchus shared Paul's bondage, that he might minister to him in his afflictions.

The voyage began prosperously. The following day they cast anchor in the harbor of Sidon. Here Julius, the centurion, "courteously entreated Paul," and being informed that there were Christians in the place, "gave him liberty to go unto his friends to refresh himself." This permission was greatly appreciated by the apostle, who was in feeble health.

Upon leaving Sidon, the ship encountered contrary winds; and being driven from a direct course, its progress was slow. At Myra, in the province of Lycia, the centurion found a large Alexandrian ship, bound for the coast of Italy, and to this he immediately transferred his prisoners. But the winds were still contrary, and the ship's progress was difficult. Luke writes, "When we had sailed slowly many days, and scarce were come over against Cnidus, the wind not suffering us, we sailed under Crete, over against Salmone; and, hardly passing it, came unto a place which is called the Fair Havens."

At Fair Havens they were compelled to remain for some time, waiting for favoring winds. Winter was approaching rapidly; "sailing was now dangerous;" and those in charge of the vessel had to give up hope of reaching their destination before the season for travel by sea should be closed for the year. The only question now to be decided was, whether to remain at Fair Havens, or attempt to reach a more favorable place in which to winter.

This question was earnestly discussed, and was finally referred by the centurion to Paul, who had won the respect of both sailors and soldiers. The apostle unhesitatingly advised remaining where they were. "I perceive," he said, "that this voyage will be with hurt and much damage, not only of the lading and ship, but also of our lives." But "the master and the owner of the ship," and the majority of passengers and crew, were unwilling to accept this counsel. Because the haven in which they had anchored "was not commodious to winter in, the more part advised to depart thence also, if by any means they might attain to Phenice, and there to winter; which is an haven of Crete, and lieth toward the southwest and northwest."

The centurion decided to follow the judgment of the majority. Accordingly, "when the south wind blew softly," they set sail from Fair Havens, in the hope that they would soon reach the desired harbor. "But not long after there arose . . . a tempestuous wind;" "the ship was caught, and could not bear up into the wind."

Driven by the tempest, the vessel neared the small island of Clauda, and while under its shelter the sailors made ready for the worst. The lifeboat, their only means of escape in case the ship should founder, was in tow and liable to be dashed in pieces any moment. Their first work was to hoist this boat on board. All possible precautions were then taken to strengthen the ship and prepare it to withstand the tempest. The scant protection afforded by the little island did not avail them long, and soon they were again exposed to the full violence of the storm.

All night the tempest raged, and notwithstanding the precautions that had been taken, the vessel leaked. "The next day they lightened the ship." Night came again, but the wind did not abate. The storm-beaten ship, with its shattered mast and rent sails, was tossed hither and thither by the fury of the gale. Every moment it seemed that the groaning timbers must give way as the vessel reeled and quivered under the tempest's shock. The leak increased rapidly, and passengers and crew worked continually at the pumps. There was not a moment's rest for any on board. "The third day," writes Luke, "we cast out with our own hands the tackling of the ship. And when neither sun nor stars in many days appeared, and no small tempest lay on us, all hope that we should be saved was then taken away."

For fourteen days they drifted under a sunless and starless heaven. The apostle, though himself suffering physically, had words of hope for the darkest hour, a helping hand in every emergency. He grasped by faith the arm of Infinite Power, and his heart was stayed upon God. He had no fears for himself; he knew that God would preserve him to witness at Rome for the truth of Christ. But his heart yearned with pity for the poor souls around him, sinful, degraded, and unprepared to die. As he earnestly pleaded with God to spare their lives, it was revealed to him that his prayer was granted.

Taking advantage of a lull in the tempest, Paul stood forth on the deck and, lifting up his voice, said: "Sirs, ye should have hearkened unto me, and not have loosed from Crete, and to have gained this harm and loss. And now I exhort you to be of good cheer: for there shall be no loss of any man's life among you, but of the ship. For there stood by me this night the angel of God, whose I am, and whom I serve, saying, Fear not, Paul; thou must be brought before Caesar: and, lo, God hath given thee all them that sail with thee. Wherefore, sirs, be of good cheer: for I believe God, that it shall be even as it was told me. Howbeit we must be cast upon a certain island."

At these words, hope revived. Passengers and crew roused from their apathy. There was much yet to be done, and every effort within their power must be put forth to avert destruction.

It was on the fourteenth night of tossing on the black, heaving billows, that "about midnight" the sailors, hearing the sound of breakers, "deemed that they drew near to some country; and sounded, and found it twenty fathoms: and when they had gone a little further, they sounded again, and found it fifteen fathoms. Then fearing," Luke writes, "lest we should have fallen upon rocks, they cast four anchors out of the stern, and wished for the day."

At break of day the outlines of the stormy coast were dimly visible, but no familiar landmarks could be seen. So gloomy was the outlook that the heathen sailors, losing all courage, "were about to flee out of the ship," and feigning to make preparations for casting "anchors out of the foreship," they had already let down the lifeboat, when Paul, perceiving their base design, said to the centurion and the soldiers, "Except these abide in the ship, ye cannot be saved." The soldiers immediately "cut off the ropes of the boat, and let her fall off" into the sea.

The most critical hour was still before them. Again the apostle spoke words of encouragement, and entreated all, both sailors and passengers, to take some food, saying, "This day is the fourteenth day that ye have tarried and continued fasting, having taken nothing. Wherefore I pray you to take some meat: for this is for your health: for there shall not a hair fall from the head of any of you."

"When he had thus spoken, he took bread, and gave thanks to God in presence of them all: and when he had broken it, he began to eat." Then that worn and discouraged company of two hundred and seventy-five souls, who but for Paul would have become desperate, joined with the apostle in partaking of food. "And when they had eaten enough, they lightened the ship, and cast out the wheat into the sea."

Daylight had now fully come, but they could see nothing by which to determine their whereabouts. However, "they discovered a certain creek with a shore, into the which they were minded, if it were possible, to thrust in the ship. And when they had taken up the anchors, they committed themselves unto the sea, and loosed the rudder bands, and hoisted up the mainsail to the wind, and made toward shore. And falling into a place where two seas met, they ran the ship aground; and the fore part stuck fast, and remained unmovable, but the hinder part was broken with the violence of the waves."

Paul and the other prisoners were now threatened by a fate more terrible than shipwreck. The soldiers saw that while endeavoring to reach land it would be impossible for them to keep their prisoners in charge. Every man would have all he could do to save himself. Yet if any of the prisoners were missing, the lives of those who were responsible for them would be forfeited. Hence the soldiers desired to put all the prisoners to death. The Roman law sanctioned this cruel policy, and the plan would have been executed at once, but for him to whom all alike were under deep obligation. Julius the centurion knew that Paul had been instrumental in saving the lives of all on board, and, moreover, convinced that the Lord was with him, he feared to do him harm. He therefore "commanded that they which could swim should cast themselves first into the sea, and get to land: and the rest, some on boards, and some on broken pieces of the ship. And so it came to pass, that they escaped all safe to land." When the roll was called, not one was missing.

The shipwrecked crew were kindly received by the barbarous people of Melita. "They kindled a fire," Luke writes, "and received us everyone, because of the present rain, and because of the cold." Paul was among those who were active in ministering to the comfort of others. Having gathered "a bundle of sticks," he "laid them on the fire," when a viper came forth "out of the heat, and fastened on his hand." The bystanders were horror-stricken; and seeing by his chain that Paul was a prisoner, they said to one another, "No doubt this man is a murderer, whom, though he hath escaped the sea, yet vengeance suffereth not to live." But Paul shook off the creature into the fire and felt no harm. Knowing its venomous nature, the people looked for him to fall down at any moment in terrible agony. "But after they had looked a great while, and saw no harm come to him, they changed their minds, and said that he was a god."

During the three months that the ship's company remained at Melita, Paul and his fellow laborers improved many opportunities to preach the gospel. In a remarkable manner the Lord wrought through them. For Paul's sake the entire shipwrecked company were treated with great kindness; all their wants were supplied, and upon leaving Melita they were liberally provided with everything needful for their voyage. The chief incidents of their stay are thus briefly related by Luke:

"In the same quarters were possessions of the chief man of the island, whose name was Publius; who received us, and lodged us three days courteously. And it came to pass, that the father of Publius lay sick of a fever and of a bloody flux: to whom Paul entered in, and prayed, and laid his hands on him, and healed him. So when this was done, others also, which had diseases in the island, came, and were healed: who also honored us with many honors; and when we departed, they laded us with such things as were necessary."

In Rome

With the opening of navigation, the centurion and his prisoners set out on their journey to Rome. An Alexandrian ship, the "Castor and Pollux," had wintered at Melita on her way westward, and in this the travelers embarked. Though somewhat delayed by contrary winds, the voyage was safely accomplished, and the ship cast anchor in the beautiful harbor of Puteoli, on the coast of Italy.

In this place there were a few Christians, and they entreated the apostle to remain with them for seven days, a privilege kindly granted by the centurion. Since receiving Paul's epistle to the Romans, the Christians of Italy had eagerly looked forward to a visit from the apostle. They had not thought to see him come as a prisoner, but his sufferings only endeared him to them the more. The distance from

Puteoli to Rome being but a hundred and forty miles, and the seaport being in constant communication with the metropolis, the Roman Christians were informed of Paul's approach, and some of them started to meet and welcome him.

On the eighth day after landing, the centurion and his prisoners set out for Rome. Julius willingly granted the apostle every favor which it was in his power to bestow; but he could not change his condition as a prisoner, or release him from the chain that bound him to his soldier guard. It was with a heavy heart that Paul went forward to his long-expected visit to the world's metropolis. How different the circumstances from those he had anticipated! How was he, fettered and stigmatized, to proclaim the gospel? His hopes of winning many souls to the truth in Rome, seemed destined to disappointment.

At last the travelers reach Appii Forum, forty miles from Rome. As they make their way through the crowds that throng the great thoroughfare, the gray-haired old man, chained with a group of hardened-looking criminals, receives many a glance of scorn and is made the subject of many a rude, mocking jest.

Suddenly a cry of joy is heard, and a man springs from the passing throng and falls upon the prisoner's neck, embracing him with tears and rejoicing, as a son would welcome a long-absent father. Again and again is the scene repeated as, with eyes made keen by loving expectation, many discern in the chained captive the one who at Corinth, at Philippi, at Ephesus, had spoken to them the words of life.

As the warmhearted disciples eagerly flock around their father in the gospel, the whole company is brought to a standstill. The soldiers are impatient of delay, yet they have not the heart to interrupt this happy meeting; for they, too, have learned to respect and esteem their prisoner. In that worn, pain-stricken face, the disciples see reflected the image of Christ. They assure Paul that they have not forgotten him nor ceased to love him; that they are indebted to him for the joyful hope which animates their lives and gives them peace toward God. In the ardor of their love they would bear him upon their shoulders the whole way to the city, could they but have the privilege.

Few realize the significance of those words of Luke, that when Paul saw his brethren, "he thanked God, and took courage." In the midst of the weeping, sympathizing company of believers, who were not ashamed of his bonds, the apostle praised God aloud. The cloud of sadness that had rested upon his spirit was swept away. His Christian life had been a succession of trials, sufferings, and disappointments, but in that hour he felt abundantly repaid. With firmer step and joyful heart he continued on his way. He would not complain of the past, nor fear for the future. Bonds and afflictions awaited him, he knew; but he knew also that it had been his to deliver souls from a bondage infinitely more terrible, and he rejoiced in his sufferings for Christ's sake.

At Rome the centurion Julius delivered up his prisoners to the captain of the emperor's guard. The good account which he gave of Paul, together with the letter from Festus, caused the apostle to be favorably regarded by the chief captain, and, instead of being thrown into prison, he was permitted to live in his own hired house. Although still constantly chained to a soldier, he was at liberty to receive his friends and to labor for the advancement of the cause of Christ.

Many of the Jews who had been banished from Rome some years previously, had been allowed to return, so that large numbers were now to be found there. To these, first of all, Paul determined to present the facts concerning himself and his work, before his enemies should have opportunity to embitter them against him. Three days after his arrival in Rome, therefore, he called together their leading men and in a simple, direct manner stated why he had come to Rome as a prisoner.

"Men and brethren," he said, "though I have committed nothing against the people, or customs of our fathers, yet was I delivered prisoner from Jerusalem into the hands of the Romans. Who, when they had examined me, would have let me go, because there was no cause of death in me. But when the Jews spake against it, I was constrained to appeal unto Caesar; not that I had aught to accuse my nation of. For this cause therefore have I called for you, to see you, and to speak with you: because that for the hope of Israel I am bound with this chain."

He said nothing of the abuse which he had suffered at the hands of the Jews, or of their repeated plots to assassinate him. His words were marked with caution and kindness. He was not seeking to win personal attention or sympathy, but to defend the truth and to maintain the honor of the gospel.

In reply, his hearers stated that they had received no charges against him by letters public or private, and that none of the Jews who had come to Rome had accused him of any crime. They also expressed a strong desire to hear for themselves the reasons of his faith in Christ. "As concerning this sect," they said, "we know that everywhere it is spoken against."

Since they themselves desired it, Paul bade them set a day when he could present to them the truths of the gospel. At the time appointed, many came together, "to whom he expounded and testified the kingdom of God, persuading them concerning Jesus, both out of the law of Moses, and out of the prophets, from morning till evening." He related his own experience, and presented arguments from the Old Testament Scriptures with simplicity, sincerity, and power.

The apostle showed that religion does not consist in rites and ceremonies, creeds and theories. If it did, the natural man could understand it by investigation, as he understands worldly things. Paul taught that religion is a practical, saving energy, a principle wholly from God, a personal experience of God's renewing power upon the soul.

He showed how Moses had pointed Israel forward to Christ as that Prophet whom they were to hear; how all the prophets had testified of Him as God's great remedy for sin, the guiltless One who was to bear the sins of the guilty. He did not find fault with their observance of forms and ceremonies, but showed that while they maintained the ritual service with great exactness, they were rejecting Him who was the antitype of all that system.

Paul declared that in his unconverted state he had known Christ, not by personal acquaintance, but merely by the conception which he, in common with others, cherished concerning the character and work of the Messiah to come. He had rejected Jesus of Nazareth as an impostor because He did not fulfill this conception. But now Paul's views of Christ and His mission were far more spiritual and exalted, for he had been converted. The apostle asserted that he did not present to them Christ after the flesh. Herod had seen Christ in the days of His humanity; Annas had seen Him; Pilate and the priests and rulers had seen Him; the Roman soldiers had seen Him. But they had not seen Him with the eye of faith; they had not seen Him as the glorified Redeemer. To apprehend Christ by faith, to have a spiritual knowledge of Him, was more to be desired than a personal acquaintance with Him as He appeared on the earth. The communion with Christ which Paul now enjoyed was more intimate, more enduring, than a mere earthly and human companionship.

As Paul spoke of what he knew, and testified of what he had seen, concerning Jesus of Nazareth as the hope of Israel, those who were honestly seeking for truth were convinced. Upon some minds, at least, his words made an impression that was never effaced. But others stubbornly refused to accept the plain testimony of the Scriptures, even when presented to them by one who had the special illumination of the Holy Spirit. They could not refute his arguments, but they refused to accept his conclusions.

Many months passed by after Paul's arrival in Rome, before the Jews of Jerusalem appeared in person to present their accusations against the prisoner. They had been repeatedly thwarted in their designs; and now that Paul was to be tried before the highest tribunal of the Roman Empire, they had no desire to risk another defeat. Lysias, Felix, Festus, and Agrippa had all declared their belief in his innocence. His enemies could hope for success only in seeking by intrigue to influence the emperor in their favor. Delay would further their object, as it would afford them time to perfect and execute their plans, and so they waited for a while before preferring their charges in person against the apostle.

In the providence of God this delay resulted in the furtherance of the gospel. Through the favor of those who had Paul in charge, he was permitted to dwell in a commodious house, where he could meet freely with his friends and also present the truth daily to those who came to hear. Thus for two years he continued his labors, "preaching the kingdom of God, and teaching those things which concern the Lord Jesus Christ, will all confidence, no man forbidding him."

During this time the churches that he had established in many lands were not forgotten. Realizing the dangers that threatened the converts to the new faith, the apostle sought so far as possible to meet their needs by letters of warning and practical instruction. And from Rome he sent out consecrated workers to labor not only for these churches, but in fields that he himself had not visited. These workers, as wise shepherds, strengthened the work so well begun by Paul; and the apostle, kept informed of the condition and dangers of the churches by constant communication with them, was enabled to exercise a wise supervision over all.

Thus, while apparently cut off from active labor, Paul exerted a wider and more lasting influence than if he had been free to travel among the churches as in former years. As a prisoner of the Lord, he had a firmer hold upon the affections of his brethren; and his words, written by one under bonds for the sake of Christ, commanded greater attention and respect than they did when he was personally with them. Not until Paul was removed from them, did the believers realize how heavy were the burdens he had borne in their behalf. Heretofore they had largely excused themselves from responsibility and burden bearing because they lacked his wisdom, tact, and indomitable energy; but now, left in their inexperience to learn the lessons they had shunned, they prized his warnings, counsels, and instructions as they had not prized his personal work. And as they learned of his courage and faith during his long imprisonment they were stimulated to greater fidelity and zeal in the cause of Christ.

Among Paul's assistants at Rome were many of his former companions and fellow workers. Luke, "the beloved physician," who had attended him on the journey to Jerusalem, through the two years' imprisonment at Caesarea, and upon his perilous voyage to Rome, was with him still. Timothy also ministered to his comfort. Tychicus, "a beloved brother, and a faithful minister and fellow servant in the Lord," stood nobly by the apostle. Demas and Mark were also with him. Aristarchus and Epaphras were his "fellow prisoners." Colossians 4:7-14.

Since the earlier years of his profession of faith, Mark's Christian experience had deepened. As he had studied more closely the life and death of Christ he had obtained clearer views of the Saviour's mission, its toils and conflicts. Reading in the scars in Christ's hands and feet the marks of His service for humanity, and the length to which self-abnegation leads to save the lost and perishing, Mark had become willing to follow the Master in the path of self-sacrifice. Now, sharing the lot of Paul the prisoner, he understood better than ever before that it is infinite gain to win Christ, infinite loss to win the world and lose the soul for whose redemption the blood of Christ was shed. In the face of severe trial and adversity, Mark continued steadfast, a wise and beloved helper of the apostle.

Demas, steadfast for a time, afterward forsook the cause of Christ. In referring to this, Paul wrote, "Demas hath forsaken me, having loved this present world." 2 Timothy 4:10. For worldly gain, Demas bartered every high and noble consideration. How shortsighted the exchange! Possessing only worldly wealth or honor, Demas was poor indeed, however much he might proudly call his own; while Mark, choosing to suffer for Christ's sake, possessed eternal riches,

being accounted in heaven an heir of God and a joint heir with His Son.

Among those who gave their hearts to God through the labors of Paul in Rome was Onesimus, a pagan slave who had wronged his master, Philemon, a Christian believer in Colosse, and had escaped to Rome. In the kindness of his heart, Paul sought to relieve the poverty and distress of the wretched fugitive and then endeavored to shed the light of truth into his darkened mind. Onesimus listened to the words of life, confessed his sins, and was converted to the faith of Christ.

Onesimus endeared himself to Paul by his piety and sincerity, no less than by his tender care for the apostle's comfort, and his zeal in promoting the work of the gospel. Paul saw in him traits of character that would render him a useful helper in missionary labor, and he counseled him to return without delay to Philemon, beg his forgiveness, and plan for the future. The apostle promised to hold himself responsible for the sum of which Philemon had been robbed. Being about to dispatch Tychicus with letters to various churches in Asia Minor, he sent Onesimus with him. It was a severe test for this servant thus to deliver himself up to the master he had wronged; but he had been truly converted, and he did not turn aside from his duty.

Paul made Onesimus the bearer of a letter to Philemon, in which, with his usual tact and kindness, the apostle pleaded the cause of the repentant slave and expressed a desire to retain his services in the future. The letter began with an affectionate greeting to Philemon as a friend and fellow laborer:

"Grace to you, and peace, from God our Father and the Lord Jesus Christ. I thank my God, making mention of thee always in my prayers, hearing of thy love and faith, which thou hast toward the Lord Jesus, and toward all saints; that the communication of thy faith may become effectual by the acknowledging of every good thing which is in you in Christ Jesus." The apostle reminded Philemon that every good purpose and trait of character which he possessed was due to the grace of Christ; this alone made him different from the perverse and the sinful. The same grace could make the debased criminal a child of God and a useful laborer in the gospel.

Paul might have urged upon Philemon his duty as a Christian; but he chose rather the language of entreaty: "As Paul the aged, and now also a prisoner of Jesus Christ, I beseech thee for my son Onesimus, whom I have begotten in my bonds; which in time past was to thee unprofitable, but now profitable to thee and to me."

The apostle asked Philemon, in view of the conversion of Onesimus, to receive the repentant slave as his own child, showing him such affection that he would choose to dwell with his former master, "not now as a servant, but above a servant, a brother beloved." He expressed his desire to retain Onesimus as one who could minister to him in his bonds as Philemon himself would have done, though he did not desire his services unless Philemon should of his own accord set the slave free.

The apostle well knew the severity which masters exercised toward their slaves, and he knew also that Philemon was greatly incensed because of the conduct of his servant. He tried to write to him in a way that would arouse his deepest and tenderest feelings as a Christian. The conversion of Onesimus had made him a brother in the faith, and any punishment inflicted on this new convert would be regarded by Paul as inflicted on himself.

Paul voluntarily proposed to assume the debt of Onesimus in order that the guilty one might be spared the disgrace of punishment, and might again enjoy the privileges he had forfeited. "If thou count me therefore a partner," he wrote to Philemon, "receive him as myself. If he hath wronged thee, or oweth thee aught, put that on mine account; I Paul have written it with mine own hand, I will repay it."

How fitting an illustration of the love of Christ for the repentant sinner! The servant who had defrauded his master had nothing with which to make restitution. The sinner who has robbed God of years of service has no means of canceling the debt. Jesus interposes between the sinner and God, saying, I will pay the debt. Let the sinner be spared; I will suffer in his stead.

After offering to assume the debt of Onesimus, Paul reminded Philemon how greatly he himself was indebted to the apostle. He owed him his own self, since God had made Paul the instrument of his conversion. Then, in a tender, earnest appeal, he besought Philemon that as he had by his liberalities refreshed the saints, so he would refresh the spirit of the apostle by granting him this cause of rejoicing. "Having confidence in thy obedience," he added, "I wrote unto thee, knowing that thou wilt also do more than I say."

Paul's letter to Philemon shows the influence of the gospel upon the relation between master and servant. Slave-holding was an established institution throughout the Roman Empire, and both masters and slaves were found in most of the churches for which Paul labored. In the cities, where slaves often greatly outnumbered the free population, laws of terrible severity were regarded as necessary to keep them in subjection. A wealthy Roman often owned hundreds of slaves, of every rank, of every nation, and of every accomplishment. With full control over the souls and bodies of these helpless beings, he could inflict upon them any suffering he chose. If one of them in retaliation or self-defense ventured to raise a hand against his owner, the whole family of the offender might be inhumanly sacrificed. The slightest mistake, accident, or carelessness was often punished without mercy.

Some masters, more humane than others, were more indulgent toward their servants; but the vast majority of the wealthy and noble, given up without restraint to the indulgence of lust, passion, and appetite, made their slaves the wretched victims of caprice and tyranny. The tendency of the whole system was hopelessly degrading.

It was not the apostle's work to overturn arbitrarily or suddenly the established order of society. To attempt this would be to prevent the success of the gospel. But he taught principles which struck at the very foundation of slavery and which, if carried into effect, would surely undermine the whole system. "Where the Spirit of the Lord is, there is liberty," he declared. 2 Corinthians 3:17. When converted, the slave became a member of the body of Christ, and as such was to be loved and treated as a brother, a fellow heir with his master to the blessings of God and the privileges of the gospel. On the other hand, servants were to perform their duties, "not with eyeservice, as men pleasers; but as the servants of Christ, doing the will of God from the heart." Ephesians 6:6.

Christianity makes a strong bond of union between master and slave, king and subject, the gospel minister and the degraded sinner who has found in Christ cleansing from sin. They have been washed in the same blood, quickened by the same Spirit; and they are made one in Christ Jesus.

Caesar's Household

The gospel has ever achieved its greatest success among the humbler classes. "Not many wise men after the flesh, not many mighty, not many noble, are called." 1 Corinthians 1:26. It could not be expected that Paul, a poor and friendless prisoner, would be able to gain the attention of the wealthy and titled classes of Roman citizens. To them vice presented all its glittering allurements and held them willing captives. But from among the toilworn, want-stricken victims of their oppression, even from among the poor slaves, many gladly listened to the words of Paul and in the faith of Christ found a hope and peace that cheered them under the hardships of their lot.

Yet while the apostle's work began with the humble and the lowly, its influence extended until it reached the very palace of the emperor.

Rome was at this time the metropolis of the world. The haughty Caesars were giving laws to nearly every nation upon the earth. King and courtier were either ignorant of the humble Nazarene or regarded Him with hatred and derision. And yet in less than two years the gospel found its way from the prisoner's lowly home into the imperial halls. Paul is in bonds as an evildoer; but "the word of God is not bound." 2 Timothy 2:9.

In former years the apostle had publicly proclaimed the faith of Christ with winning power, and by signs and miracles he had given unmistakable evidence of its divine character. With noble firmness he had risen up before the sages of Greece and by his knowledge and eloquence had put to silence the arguments of proud philosophy. With undaunted courage he had stood before kings and governors, and reasoned of righteousness, temperance, and judgment to come, until the haughty rulers trembled as if already beholding the terrors of the day of God.

No such opportunities were now granted the apostle, confined as he was to his own dwelling, and able to proclaim the truth to those only who sought him there. He had not, like Moses and Aaron, a divine command to go before the profligate king and in the name of the great I AM rebuke his cruelty and oppression. Yet it was at this very time, when its chief advocate was apparently cut off from public labor, that a great victory was won for the gospel; for from the very household of the king, members were added to the church.

Nowhere could there exist an atmosphere more uncongenial to Christianity than in the Roman court. Nero seemed to have obliterated from his soul the last trace of the divine, and even of the human, and to bear the impress of Satan. His attendants and courtiers were in general of the same character as himself—fierce, debased, and corrupt. To all appearance it would be impossible for Christianity to gain a foothold in the court and palace of Nero.

Yet in this case, as in so many others, was proved the truth of Paul's assertion that the weapons of his warfare were "mighty through God to the pulling down of strongholds," 2 Corinthians 10:4. Even in Nero's household, trophies of the cross were won. From the vile attendants of a viler king were gained converts who became sons of God. These were not Christians secretly, but openly. They were not ashamed of their faith.

And by what means was an entrance achieved and a firm footing gained for Christianity where even its admission seemed impossible? In his epistle to the Philippians, Paul ascribed to his own imprisonment his success in winning converts to the faith from Nero's household. Fearful lest it might be thought that his afflictions had impeded the progress of the gospel, he assured them: "I would ye should understand, brethren, that the things which happened unto me have fallen out rather unto the furtherance of the gospel." Philippians 1:12.

When the Christian churches first learned that Paul was to visit Rome, they looked forward to a signal triumph of the gospel in that city. Paul had borne the truth to many lands; he had proclaimed it in great cities. Might not this champion of the faith succeed in winning souls to Christ even in the metropolis of the world? But their hopes were crushed by the tidings that Paul had gone to Rome as a prisoner. They had confidently hoped to see the gospel, once established at this great center, extend rapidly to all nations and become a prevailing power in the earth. How great their disappointment! Human expectations had failed, but not the purpose of God.

Not by Paul's sermon's, but by his bonds, was the attention of the court attracted to Christianity. It was as a captive that he broke from so many souls the bonds that held them in the slavery of sin. Nor was this all. He declared: "Many of the brethren in the Lord, waxing confident by my bonds, are much more bold to speak the word without fear." Philippians 1:14.

Paul's patience and cheerfulness during his long and unjust imprisonment, his courage and faith, were a continual sermon. His spirit, so unlike the spirit of the world, bore witness that a power higher than that of earth was abiding with him. And by his example, Christians were impelled to greater energy as advocates of the cause from the public labors of which Paul had been withdrawn. In these ways were the apostle's bonds influential, so that when his power and usefulness seemed cut off, and to all appearance he could do the least, then it was that he gathered sheaves for Christ in fields from which he seemed wholly excluded.

Before the close of that two years' imprisonment, Paul was able to say, "My bonds in Christ are manifest in all the palace, and in all other places," and among those who sent greetings to the Philippians he mentions chiefly them "that are of Caesar's household." Verse 13; 4:22.

Patience as well as courage has its victories. By meekness under trial, no less than by boldness in enterprise, souls may be won to Christ. The Christian who manifests patience and cheerfulness under bereavement and suffering, who meets even death itself with the peace and calmness of an unwavering faith, may accomplish for the gospel more than he could have effected by a long life of faithful labor. Often when the servant of God is withdrawn from active duty, the mysterious providence which our shortsighted vision would lament is designed by God to accomplish a work that otherwise would never have been done.

Let not the follower of Christ think, when he is no longer able to labor openly and actively for God and His truth, that he has no service to render, no reward to secure. Christ's true witnesses are never laid aside. In health and sickness, in life and death, God uses them still. When through Satan's malice the servants of Christ have been persecuted, their active labors hindered, when they have been cast into prison, or dragged to the scaffold or to the stake, it was that truth might gain a greater triumph. As these faithful ones sealed their testimony with their blood, souls hitherto in doubt and uncertainty were convinced of the faith of Christ and took their stand courageously for Him. From the ashes of the martyrs has sprung an abundant harvest for God.

The zeal and fidelity of Paul and his fellow workers, no less than the faith and obedience of these converts to Christianity, under circumstances so forbidding, rebuke slothfulness and lack of faith in the minister of Christ. The apostle and his associate workers might have argued that it would be vain to call to repentance and faith in Christ the servants of Nero, subjected, as they were, to fierce temptations, surrounded by formidable hindrances, and exposed to bitter opposition. Even should they be convinced of the truth, how could they render obedience? But Paul did not reason thus; in faith he presented the gospel to these souls, and among those who heard were some who decided to obey at any cost. Notwithstanding obstacles and dangers, they would accept the light, and trust God to help them let their light shine forth to others.

Not only were converts won to the truth in Caesar's household, but after their conversion they remained in that household. They did not feel at liberty to abandon their post of duty because their surroundings were no longer congenial. The truth had found them there, and there they remained, by their changed life and character testifying to the transforming power of the new faith.

Are any tempted to make their circumstances an excuse for failing to witness for Christ? Let them consider the situation of the disciples in Caesar's household—the depravity of the emperor, the profligacy of the court. We can hardly imagine circumstances more unfavorable to a religious life, and entailing greater sacrifice or opposition, than those in which these converts found themselves. Yet amidst difficulties and dangers they maintained their fidelity. Because of obstacles that seem insurmountable, the Christian may seek to excuse himself from obeying the truth as it is in Jesus; but he can offer no excuse that will bear investigation. Could he do this he would prove God unjust in that He had made for His children conditions of salvation with which they could not comply.

He whose heart is fixed to serve God will find opportunity to witness for Him. Difficulties will be powerless to hinder him who is determined to seek first the kingdom of God and His righteousness. In the strength gained by prayer and a study of the word, he will seek virtue and forsake vice. Looking to Jesus, the Author and Finisher of the faith, who endured the contradiction of sinners against Himself, the believer will willingly brave contempt and derision. And help and grace sufficient for every circumstances are promised by Him whose word is truth. His everlasting arms encircle the soul that turns to Him for aid. In His care we may rest safely, saying, "What time I am afraid, I will trust in Thee." Psalm 56:3. To all who put their trust in Him, God will fulfill His promise.

By His own example the Saviour has shown that His followers can be in the world and yet not of the world. He came not to partake of its delusive pleasures, to be swayed by its customs, and to follow its practices, but to do His Father's will, to seek and save the lost. With this object before him the Christian may stand uncontaminated in any surroundings. Whatever his station or circumstances, exalted or humble, he will manifest the power of true religion in the faithful performance of duty.

Not in freedom from trial, but in the midst of it, is Christian character developed. Exposure to rebuffs and opposition leads the follower of Christ to greater watchfulness and more earnest prayer to the mighty Helper. Severe trial endured by the grace of God develops patience, vigilance, fortitude, and a deep and abiding trust in God. It is the triumph of the Christian faith that it enables its followers to suffer and be strong; to submit, and thus to conquer; to be killed all the day long, and yet to live; to bear the cross, and thus to win the crown of glory.

Written From Rome

The apostle Paul early in his Christian experience was given special opportunities to learn the will of God concerning the followers of Jesus. He was "caught up to the third heaven," "into paradise, and heard unspeakable words, which it is not lawful for a man to utter." He himself acknowledged that many "visions and revelations" had been given him "of the Lord." His understanding of the principles of gospel truth was equal to that of "the very chiefest apostles." 2 Corinthians 12:2, 4, 1, 11. He had a clear, full comprehension of "the breadth, and length, and depth, and height" of "the love of Christ, which passeth knowledge." Ephesians 3:18, 19.

Paul could not tell all that he had seen in vision; for among his hearers were some who would have misapplied his words. But that which was revealed to him enabled him to labor as a leader and a wise teacher, and also molded the messages that he in later years sent to the churches. The impression that he received when in vision was ever with him, enabling him to give a correct representation of Christian character. By word of mouth and by letter he bore a message that ever since has brought help and strength to the church of God. To believers today this message speaks plainly of the dangers that will threaten the church, and the false doctrines that they will have to meet.

The apostle's desire for those to whom he addressed his letters of counsel and admonition was that they should "be no more children, tossed to and fro, and carried about with every wind of doctrine;" but that they should all come into "the unity of the faith, and of the knowledge of the Son of God, unto a perfect man, unto the measure of the stature of the fullness of Christ." He entreated those who were followers of Jesus in heathen communities not to walk "as other Gentiles walk, in the vanity of their mind, having the understanding darkened, being alienated from the life of God . . . because of the blindness of their heart," but "circumspectly, not as fools, but as wise, redeeming the time." Ephesians 4:14, 13, 17, 18; 5:15, 16. He encouraged the believers to look forward to the time when Christ, who "loved the church, and gave Himself for it," would "present it to Himself a glorious church, not having spot, or wrinkle, or any such thing" —a church "holy and without blemish." Ephesians 5:25, 27.

These messages, written with a power not of man but of God, contain lessons which should be studied by all and which may with profit be often repeated. In them practical godliness is outlined, principles are laid down that should be followed in every church, and the way that leads to life eternal is made plain.

In his letter to "the saints and faithful brethren in Christ which are at Colosse," written while he was a prisoner in Rome, Paul makes mention of his joy over their steadfastness in the faith, tidings of which had been brought him by Epaphras, who, the apostle wrote, "declared unto us your love in the Spirit. For this cause," he continued, "we also, since the day we heard it, do not cease to pray for you, and to desire that ye might be filled with the knowledge of His will in all wisdom and spiritual understanding; that ye might walk worthy of the Lord unto all pleasing, being fruitful in every good work, and increasing in the knowledge of God;

strengthened with all might, according to His glorious power, unto all patience and long-suffering with joyfulness."

Thus Paul put into words his desire for the Colossian believers. How high the ideal that these words hold before the follower of Christ! They show the wonderful possibilities of the Christian life and make it plain that there is no limit to the blessings that the children of God may receive. Constantly increasing in a knowledge of God, they may go on from strength to strength, from height to height in Christian experience, until by "His glorious power" they are made "meet to be partakers of the inheritance of the saints in light."

The apostle exalted Christ before his brethren as the One by whom God had created all things and by whom He had wrought out their redemption. He declared that the hand that sustains the worlds in space, and holds in their orderly arrangements and tireless activity all things throughout the universe of God, is the hand that was nailed to the cross for them. "By Him were all things created," Paul wrote, "that are in heaven, and that are in earth, visible and invisible, whether they be thrones, or dominions, or principalities, or powers: all things were created by Him, and for Him: and He is before all things, and by Him all things consist." "And you, that were sometime alienated and enemies in your mind by wicked works, yet now hath He reconciled in the body of His flesh through death, to present you holy and unblamable and unreprovable in His sight."

The Son of God stooped to uplift the fallen. For this He left the sinless worlds on high, the ninety and nine that loved Him, and came to this earth to be "wounded for our transgressions" and "bruised for our iniquities." Isaiah 53:5. He was in all things made like unto His brethren. He became flesh, even as we are. He knew what it meant to be hungry and thirsty and weary. He was sustained by food and refreshed by sleep. He was a stranger and a sojourner on the earth—in the world, but not of the world; tempted and tried as men and women of today are tempted and tried, yet living a life free from sin. Tender, compassionate, sympathetic, ever considerate of others, He represented the character of God. "The Word was made flesh, and dwelt among us, . . . full of grace and truth." John 1:14.

Surrounded by the practices and influences of heathenism, the Colossian believers were in danger of being drawn away from the simplicity of the gospel, and Paul, in warning them against this, pointed them to Christ as the only safe guide. "I would that ye knew," he wrote, "what great conflict I have for you, and for them at Laodicea, and for as many as have not seen my face in the flesh; that their hearts might be comforted, being knit together in love, and unto all riches of the full assurance of understanding, to the acknowledgment of the mystery of God, and of the Father, and of Christ; in whom are hid all the treasures of wisdom and knowledge.

"And this I say, lest any man should beguile you with enticing words. . . . As ye have therefore received Christ Jesus the Lord, so walk ye in Him: rooted and built up in Him, and stablished in the faith, as ye have been taught, abounding

therein with thanksgiving. Beware lest any man spoil you through philosophy and vain deceit, after the tradition of men, after the rudiments of the world, and not after Christ. For in Him dwelleth all the fullness of the Godhead bodily. And ye are complete in Him, which is the head of all principality and power."

Christ had foretold that deceivers would arise, through whose influence "iniquity" should "abound," and "the love of many" should "wax cold." Matthew 24:12. He had warned the disciples that the church would be in more danger from this evil than from the persecution of her enemies. Again and again Paul warned the believers against these false teachers. This peril, above all others, they must guard against; for by receiving false teachers, they would open the door to errors by which the enemy would dim the spiritual perceptions and shake the confidence of those newly come to the faith of the gospel. Christ was the standard by which they were to test the doctrines presented. All that was not in harmony with His teachings they were to reject. Christ crucified for sin, Christ risen from the dead, Christ ascended on high—this was the science of salvation that they were to learn and teach.

The warnings of the word of God regarding the perils surrounding the Christian church belong to us today. As in the days of the apostles men tried by tradition and philosophy to destroy faith in the Scriptures, so today, by the pleasing sentiments of higher criticism, evolution, spiritualism, theosophy, and pantheism, the enemy of righteousness is seeking to lead souls into forbidden paths. To many the Bible is as a lamp without oil, because they have turned their minds into channels of speculative belief that bring misunderstanding and confusion. The work of higher criticism, in dissecting, conjecturing, reconstructing, is destroying faith in the Bible as a divine revelation. It is robbing God's word of power to control, uplift, and inspire human lives. By spiritualism, multitudes are taught to believe that desire is the highest law, that license is liberty, and that man is accountable only to himself.

The follower of Christ will meet with the "enticing words" against which the apostle warned the Colossian believers. He will meet with spiritualistic interpretations of the Scriptures, but he is not to accept them. His voice is to be heard in clear affirmation of the eternal truths of the Scriptures. Keeping his eyes fixed on Christ, he is to move steadily forward in the path marked out, discarding all ideas that are not in harmony with His teaching. The truth of God is to be the subject for his contemplation and meditation. He is to regard the Bible as the voice of God speaking directly to him. Thus he will find the wisdom which is divine.

The knowledge of God as revealed in Christ is the knowledge that all who are saved must have. This is the knowledge that works transformation of character. Received into the life, it will re-create the soul in the image of Christ. This is the knowledge that God invites His children to receive, beside which all else is vanity and nothingness.

In every generation and in every land the true foundation

for character building has been the same—the principles contained in the word of God. The only safe and sure rule is to do what God says. "The statutes of the Lord are right," and "he that doeth these things shall never be moved." Psalms 19:8; 15:5. It was with the word of God that the apostles met the false theories of their day, saying, "Other foundation can no man lay than that is laid." 1 Corinthians 3:11.

At the time of their conversion and baptism the Colossian believers pledged themselves to put away beliefs and practices that had hitherto been a part of their lives, and to be true to their allegiance to Christ. In his letter, Paul reminded them of this, and entreated them not to forget that in order to keep their pledge they must put forth constant effort against the evils that would seek for mastery over them. "If ye then be risen with Christ," he said, "seek those things which are above, where Christ sitteth on the right hand of God. Set your affection on things above, not on things on the earth. For ye are dead, and your life is hid with Christ in God."

"If any man be in Christ, he is a new creature: old things are passed away; behold, all things are become new." 2 Corinthians 5:17. Through the power of Christ, men and women have broken the chains of sinful habit. They have renounced selfishness. The profane have become reverent, the drunken sober, the profligate pure. Souls that have borne the likeness of Satan have become transformed into the image of God. This change is in itself the miracle of miracles. A change wrought by the Word, it is one of the deepest mysteries of the Word. We cannot understand it; we can only believe, as declared by the Scriptures, it is "Christ in you, the hope of glory."

When the Spirit of God controls mind and heart, the converted soul breaks forth into a new song; for he realizes that in his experience the promise of God has been fulfilled, that his transgression has been forgiven, his sin covered. He has exercised repentance toward God for the violation of the divine law, and faith toward Christ, who died for man's justification. "Being justified by faith," he has "peace with God through our Lord Jesus Christ." Romans 5:1.

But because this experience is his, the Christian is not therefore to fold his hands, content with that which has been accomplished for him. He who has determined to enter the spiritual kingdom will find that all the powers and passions of unregenerate nature, backed by the forces of the kingdom of darkness, are arrayed against him. Each day he must renew his consecration, each day do battle with evil. Old habits, hereditary tendencies to wrong, will strive for the mastery, and against these he is to be ever on guard, striving in Christ's strength for victory.

"Mortify therefore your members which are upon the earth," Paul wrote to the Colossians; "in the which ye also walked sometime, when ye lived in them. But now ye also put off all these: anger, wrath, malice, blasphemy, filthy communication out of your mouth. . . . Put on therefore, as the elect of God, holy and beloved, bowels of mercies, kindness, humbleness of mind, meekness, long-suffering;

forbearing one another, and forgiving one another, if any man have a quarrel against any: even as Christ forgave you, so also do ye. And above all these things put on charity, which is the bond of perfectness. And let the peace of God rule in your hearts, to the which also ye are called in one body; and be ye thankful."

The letter to the Colossians is filled with lessons of highest value to all who are engaged in the service of Christ, lessons that show the singleness of purpose and the loftiness of aim which will be seen in the life of him who rightly represents the Saviour. Renouncing all that would hinder him from making progress in the upward way or that would turn the feet of another from the narrow path, the believer will reveal in his daily life mercy, kindness, humility, meekness, forbearance, and the love of Christ.

The power of a higher, purer, nobler life is our great need. The world has too much of our thought, and the kingdom of heaven too little.

In his efforts to reach God's ideal for him, the Christian is to despair of nothing. Moral and spiritual perfection, through the grace and power of Christ, is promised to all. Jesus is the source of power, the fountain of life. He brings us to His word, and from the tree of life presents to us leaves for the healing of sin-sick souls. He leads us to the throne of God, and puts into our mouth a prayer through which we are brought into close contact with Himself. In our behalf He sets in operation the all-powerful agencies of heaven. At every step we touch His living power.

God fixes no limit to the advancement of those who desire to be "filled with the knowledge of His will in all wisdom and spiritual understanding." Through prayer, through watchfulness, through growth in knowledge and understanding, they are to be " strengthened with all might, according to His glorious power." Thus they are prepared to work for others. It is the Saviour's purpose that human beings, purified and sanctified, shall be His helping hand. For this great privilege let us give thanks to Him who "hath made us meet to be partakers of the inheritance of the saints in light: who hath delivered us from the power of darkness, and hath translated us into the kingdom of His dear Son."

Paul's letter to the Philippians, like the one to the Colossians, was written while he was a prisoner at Rome. The church at Philippi had sent gifts to Paul by the hand of Epaphroditus, whom Paul calls "my brother, and companion in labor, and fellow soldier, but your messenger, and he that ministered to my wants." While in Rome, Epaphroditus was sick, "nigh unto death: but God had mercy on him," Paul wrote, "and not on him only, but on me also, lest I should have sorrow upon sorrow." Hearing of the sickness of Epaphroditus, the believers at Philippi were filled with anxiety regarding him, and he decided to return to them. "He longed after you all," Paul wrote, "and was full of heaviness, because that ye had heard that he had been sick. . . . I sent him therefore the more carefully, that, when ye see him again, ye may rejoice, and that I may be the less sorrowful. Receive him therefore in the Lord with all gladness; and hold such in reputation: because for the work of Christ he was nigh unto death, not regarding his life, to supply your lack of service toward me."

By Epaphroditus, Paul sent the Philippian believers a letter, in which he thanked them for their gifts to him. Of all the churches, that of Philippi had been the most liberal in supplying Paul's wants. "Now ye Philippians know also," the apostle said in his letter, "that in the beginning of the gospel, when I departed from Macedonia, no church communicated with me as concerning giving and receiving, but ye only. For even in Thessalonica ye sent once and again unto my necessity. Not because I desire a gift: but I desire fruit that may abound to your account. But I have all, and abound: I am full, having received of Epaphroditus the things which were sent from you, an odor of a sweet smell, a sacrifice acceptable, well-pleasing to God."

"Grace be unto you, and peace, from God our Father, and from the Lord Jesus Christ. I thank my God upon every remembrance of you, always in every prayer of mine for you all making request with joy, for your fellowship in the gospel from the first day until now; being confident of this very thing, that He which hath begun a good work in you will perform it until the day of Jesus Christ: even as it is meet for me to think this of you all, because I have you in my heart; inasmuch as both in my bonds, and in the defense and confirmation of the gospel, ye all are partakers of my grace. For God is my record, how greatly I long after you all. . . . And this I pray, that your love may abound yet more and more in knowledge and in all judgment; that ye may approve things that are excellent; that ye may be sincere and without offense till the day of Christ; being filled with the fruits of righteousness, which are by Jesus Christ, unto the glory and praise of God."

The grace of God sustained Paul in his imprisonment, enabling him to rejoice in tribulation. With faith and assurance he wrote to his Philippian brethren that his imprisonment had resulted in the furtherance of the gospel. "I would ye should understand, brethren," he declared, "that the things which happened unto me have fallen out rather unto the furtherance of the gospel; so that my bonds with Christ are manifest in all the palace, and in all other places; and many of the brethren in the Lord, waxing confident by my bonds, are much more bold to speak the word without fear."

There is a lesson for us in this experience of Paul's, for it reveals God's way of working. The Lord can bring victory out of that which may seem to us discomfiture and defeat. We are in danger of forgetting God, of looking at the things which are seen, instead of beholding by the eye of faith the things which are unseen. When misfortune or calamity comes, we are ready to charge God with neglect or cruelty. If He sees fit to cut off our usefulness in some line, we mourn, not stopping to think that thus God may be working for our good. We need to learn that chastisement is a part of His great plan and that under the rod of affliction the Christian may sometimes do more for the Master than when engaged in active service.

As their example in the Christian life, Paul pointed the Philippians to Christ, who, "being in the form of God, thought it not robbery to be equal with God: but made Himself of no reputation, and took upon Him the form of a servant, and was made in the likeness of men: and being found in a fashion as a man, He humbled Himself, and became obedient unto death, even the death of the cross."

"Wherefore, my beloved," he continued, "as ye have always obeyed, not as in my presence only, but now much more in my absence, work out your own salvation with fear and trembling. For it is God which worketh in you both to will and to do His good pleasure. Do all things without murmurings and disputings: that ye may be blameless and harmless, the sons of God, without rebuke, in the midst of a crooked and perverse nation, among whom ye shine as lights in the world; holding forth the word of life; that I may rejoice in the day of Christ, that I have not run in vain, neither labored in vain."

These words were recorded for the help of every striving soul. Paul holds up the standard of perfection and shows how it may be reached. "Work out your own salvation," he says, "for it is God which worketh in you."

The work of gaining salvation is one of copartnership, a joint operation. There is to be co-operation between God and the repentant sinner. This is necessary for the formation of right principles in the character. Man is to make earnest efforts to overcome that which hinders him from attaining to perfection. But he is wholly dependent upon God for success. Human effort of itself is not sufficient. Without the aid of divine power it avails nothing. God works and man works. Resistance of temptation must come from man, who must draw his power from God. On the one side there is infinite wisdom, compassion, and power; on the other, weakness, sinfulness, absolute helplessness.

God wishes us to have the mastery over ourselves. But He cannot help us without our consent and co-operation. The divine Spirit works through the powers and faculties given to man. Of ourselves, we are not able to bring the purposes and desires and inclinations into harmony with the will of God; but if we are "willing to be made willing," the Saviour will accomplish this for us, "Casting down imaginations, and every high thing that exalteth itself against the knowledge of God, and bringing into captivity every thought to the obedience of Christ." 2 Corinthians 10:5.

He who would build up a strong, symmetrical character, he who would be a well-balanced Christian, must give all and do all for Christ; for the Redeemer will not accept divided service. Daily he must learn the meaning of self-surrender. He must study the word of God, learning its meaning and obeying its precepts. Thus he may reach the standard of Christian excellence. Day by day God works with him, perfecting the character that is to stand in the time of final test. And day by day the believer is working out before men and angels a sublime experiment, showing what the gospel can do for fallen human beings.

"I count not myself to have apprehended," Paul wrote; "but this one thing I do, forgetting those things which are behind, and reaching forth unto those things which are before, I press toward the mark for the prize of the high calling of God in Christ Jesus."

Paul did many things. From the time that he gave his allegiance to Christ, his life was filled with untiring service. From city to city, from country to country, he journeyed, telling the story of the cross, winning converts to the gospel, and establishing churches. For these churches he had a constant care, and he wrote many letters of instruction to them. At times he worked at his trade to earn his daily bread. But in all the busy activities of his life, Paul never lost sight of one great purpose—to press toward the prize of his calling. One aim he kept steadfastly before him —to be faithful to the One who at the gate of Damascus had revealed Himself to him. From this aim nothing had power to turn him aside. To exalt the cross of Calvary— this was the all-absorbing motive that inspired his words and acts.

The great purpose that constrained Paul to press forward in the face of hardship and difficulty should lead every Christian worker to consecrate himself wholly to God's service. Worldly attractions will be presented to draw his attentions from the Saviour, but he is to press on toward the goal, showing to the world, to angels, and to men that the hope of seeing the face of God is worth all the effort and sacrifice that the attainment of this hope demands.

Though he was a prisoner, Paul was not discouraged. Instead, a note of triumph rings through the letters that he wrote from Rome to the churches. "Rejoice in the Lord alway," he wrote to the Philippians, "and again I say, Rejoice. . . . Be careful for nothing; but in everything by prayer and supplication with thanksgiving let your requests be made known unto God. And the peace of God, which passeth all understanding, shall keep your hearts and minds through Christ Jesus. Finally, brethren, whatsoever things are true, whatsoever things are honest, whatsoever things are just, whatsoever things are pure, whatsoever things are lovely, whatsoever things are of good report; if there be any virtue, and if there be any praise, think on these things."

"My God shall supply all your need according to His riches in glory by Christ Jesus. . . . The grace of our Lord Jesus Christ be with you all."

At Liberty

While Paul's labors in Rome were being blessed to the conversion of many souls and the strengthening and encouragement of the believers, clouds were gathering that threatened not only his own safety, but also the prosperity of the church. On his arrival in Rome he had been placed in charge of the captain of the imperial guards, a man of justice and integrity, by whose clemency he was left comparatively free to pursue the work of the gospel. But before the close of the two years' imprisonment, this man was replaced by an official from whom the apostle could expect no special favor.

The Jews were now more active than ever in their efforts against Paul, and they found an able helper in the profligate woman whom Nero had made his second wife, and who, being a Jewish proselyte, lent all her influence to aid their murderous designs against the champion of Christianity.

Paul could hope for little justice from the Caesar to whom he had appealed. Nero was more debased in morals, more frivolous in character, and at the same time capable of more atrocious cruelty, than any ruler who had preceded him. The reins of government could not have been entrusted to a more despotic ruler. The first year of his reign had been marked by the poisoning of his young stepbrother, the rightful heir to the throne. From one depth of vice and crime to another, Nero had descended, until he had murdered his own mother, and then his wife. There was no atrocity which he would not perpetrate, no vile act to which he would not stoop. In every noble mind he inspired only abhorrence and contempt.

The details of the iniquity practiced in his court are too degrading, too horrible, for description. His abandoned wickedness created disgust and loathing, even in many who were forced to share his crimes. They were in constant fear as to what enormities he would suggest next. Yet even such crimes as Nero's did not shake the allegiance of his subjects. He was acknowledged as the absolute ruler of the whole civilized world. More than this, he was made the recipient of divine honors and was worshiped as a god.

From the viewpoint of human judgment, Paul's condemnation before such a judge was certain. But the apostle felt that so long as he was loyal to God, he had nothing to fear. The One who in the past had been his protector could shield him still from the malice of the Jews and from the power of Caesar.

And God did shield His servant. At Paul's examination the charges against him were not sustained, and, contrary to the general expectation, and with a regard for justice wholly at variance with his character, Nero declared the prisoner guiltless. Paul's bonds were removed; he was again a free man.

Had his trial been longer deferred, or had he from any cause been detained in Rome until the following year, he would doubtless have perished in the persecution which then took place. During Paul's imprisonment the converts to Christianity had become so numerous as to attract the attention and arouse the enmity of the authorities. The anger of the emperor was especially excited by the conversion of members of his own household, and he soon found a pretext to make the Christians the objects of his merciless cruelty.

About this time a terrible fire occurred in Rome by which nearly one half of the city was burned. Nero himself, it was rumored, had caused the flames to be kindled, but to avert suspicion he made a pretense of great generosity by assisting the homeless and destitute. He was, however, accused of the crime. The people were excited and enraged, and in order to clear himself, and also to rid the city of a class whom he feared and hated, Nero turned the accusation upon the Christians. His device succeeded, and thousands of the followers of Christ—men, women, and children— were cruelly put to death.

From this terrible persecution Paul was spared, for soon after his release he had left Rome. This last interval of freedom he diligently improved in laboring among the churches. He sought to establish a firmer union between the Greek and the Eastern churches and to fortify the minds of the believers against the false doctrines that were creeping in to corrupt the faith.

The trials and anxieties that Paul had endured had preyed upon his physical powers. The infirmities of age were upon him. He felt that he was now doing his last work, and, as the time of his labor grew shorter, his efforts became more intense. There seemed to be no limit to his zeal. Resolute in purpose, prompt in action, strong in faith, he journeyed from church to church, in many lands, and sought by every means within his power to strengthen the hands of the believers, that they might do faithful work in winning souls to Jesus, and that in the trying times upon which they were even then entering, they might remain steadfast to the gospel, bearing faithful witness for Christ.

The Final Arrest

Paul's work among the churches after his acquittal at Rome, could not escape the observation of his enemies. Since the beginning of the persecution under Nero the Christians had everywhere been a proscribed sect. After a time the unbelieving Jews conceived the idea of fastening upon Paul the crime of instigating the burning of Rome. Not one of them thought for a moment that he was guilty; but they knew that such a charge, made with the faintest show of plausibility, would seal his doom. Through their efforts, Paul was again arrested, and hurried away to his final imprisonment.

On his second voyage to Rome, Paul was accompanied by several of his former companions; others earnestly desired to share his lot, but he refused to permit them thus to imperil their lives. The prospect before him was far less favorable than at the time of his former imprisonment. The persecution under Nero had greatly lessened the number of Christians in Rome. Thousands had been martyred for their faith, many had left the city, and those who remained were greatly depressed and intimidated.

Upon his arrival at Rome, Paul was placed in a gloomy dungeon, there to remain until his course should be finished. Accused of instigating one of the basest and most terrible of crimes against the city and the nation, he was the object of universal execration.

The few friends who had shared the burdens of the apostle, now began to leave him, some by desertion, and others on missions to the various churches. Phygellus and Hermogenes were the first to go. Then Demas, dismayed by the thickening clouds of difficulty and danger, forsook the persecuted apostle. Crescens was sent by Paul to the churches of Galatia, Titus to Dalmatia, Tychicus to Ephesus. Writing to Timothy of this experience, Paul said, "Only Luke is with me." 2 Timothy 4:11. Never had the apostle needed the ministrations of his brethren as now, enfeebled as he was by age, toil, and infirmities, and confined in the damp, dark vaults of a Roman prison. The services of Luke, the beloved disciple and faithful friend, were a great comfort to Paul and enabled him to communicate with his brethren and the world without.

In this trying time Paul's heart was cheered by frequent visits from Onesiphorus. This warmhearted Ephesian did all in his power to lighten the burden of the apostle's imprisonment. His beloved teacher was in bonds for the truth's sake, while he himself went free, and he spared himself no effort to make Paul's lot more bearable.

In the last letter that the apostle ever wrote, he speaks thus of this faithful disciple: "The Lord give mercy unto the house of Onesiphorus; for he oft refreshed me, and was not ashamed of my chain; but, when he was in Rome, he sought me out very diligently, and found me. The Lord grant unto him that he may find mercy of the Lord in that day." 2 Timothy I:16-18.

The desire for love and sympathy is implanted in the heart by God Himself. Christ, in His hour of agony in Gethsemane, longed for the sympathy of His disciples. And Paul, though apparently indifferent to hardship and suffering, yearned for sympathy and companionship. The visit of Onesiphorus, testifying to his fidelity at a time of loneliness and desertion, brought gladness and cheer to one who had spent his life in service for others.

Paul Before Nero

When Paul was summoned to appear before the emperor Nero for trial, it was with the near prospect of certain death. The serious nature of the crime charged against him, and the prevailing animosity toward Christians, left little ground for hope of a favorable issue.

Among the Greeks and Romans it was customary to allow

an accused person the privilege of employing an advocate to plead in his behalf before courts of justice. By force of argument, by impassioned eloquence, or by entreaties, prayers, and tears, such an advocate often secured a decision in favor of the prisoner or, failing in this, succeeded in mitigating the severity of the sentence. But when Paul was summoned before Nero, no man ventured to act as his counsel or advocate; no friend was at hand even to preserve a record of the charges brought against him, or of the arguments that he urged in his own defense. Among the Christians at Rome there was not one who came forward to stand by him in that trying hour.

The only reliable record of the occasion is given by Paul himself, in his second letter to Timothy. "At my first answer," the apostle wrote, "no man stood with me, but all men forsook me: I pray God that it may not be laid to their charge. Notwithstanding the Lord stood with me, and strengthened me; that by me the preaching might be fully known, and that all the Gentiles might hear: and I was delivered out of the mouth of the lion." 2 Timothy 4:16, 17.

Paul before Nero—how striking the contrast! The haughty monarch before whom the man of God was to answer for his faith, had reached the height of earthly power, authority, and wealth, as well as the lowest depths of crime and iniquity. In power and greatness he stood unrivaled. There were none to question his authority, none to resist his will. Kings laid their crowns at his feet. Powerful armies marched at his command, and the ensigns of his navies betokened victory. His statue was set up in the halls of justice, and the decrees of senators and the decisions of judges were but the echo of his will. Millions bowed in obedience to his mandates. The name of Nero made the world tremble. To incur his displeasure was to lose property, liberty, life; and his frown was more to be dreaded than a pestilence.

Without money, without friends, without counsel, the aged prisoner stood before Nero—the countenance of the emperor bearing the shameful record of the passions that raged within; the face of the accused telling of a heart at peace with God. Paul's experience had been one of poverty, self-denial, and suffering. Notwithstanding constant misrepresentation, reproach, and abuse, by which his enemies had endeavored to intimidate him, he had fearlessly held aloft the standard of the cross. Like his Master, he had been a homeless wanderer, and like Him, he had lived to bless humanity. How could Nero, a capricious, passionate, licentious tyrant, understand or appreciate the character and motives of this son of God?

The vast hall was thronged by an eager, restless crowd that surged and pressed to the front to see and hear all that should take place. The high and the low were there, the rich and the poor, the learned and the ignorant, the proud and the humble, all alike destitute of a true knowledge of the way of life and salvation.

The Jews brought against Paul the old charges of sedition and heresy, and both Jews and Romans accused him of instigating the burning of the city. While these accusations were urged against him, Paul preserved an unbroken serenity.

The people and the judges looked at him in surprise. They had been present at many trials and had looked upon many a criminal, but never had they seen a man wear a look of such holy calmness as did the prisoner before them. The keen eyes of the judges, accustomed to read the countenances of prisoners, searched Paul's face in vain for some evidence of guilt. When he was permitted to speak in his own behalf, all listened with eager interest.

Once more Paul has an opportunity to uplift before a wondering multitude the banner of the cross. As he gazes upon the throng before him,—Jews, Greeks, Romans, with strangers from many lands,—his soul is stirred with an intense desire for their salvation. He loses sight of the occasion, of the perils surrounding him, of the terrible fate that seems so near. He sees only Jesus, the Intercessor, pleading before God in behalf of sinful men. With more than human eloquence and power, Paul presents the truths of the gospel. He points his hearers to the sacrifice made for the fallen race. He declares that an infinite price has been paid for man's redemption. Provision has been made for him to share the throne of God. By angel messengers, earth is connected with heaven, and all the deeds of men, whether good or evil, are open to the eye of Infinite Justice.

Thus pleads the advocate of truth. Faithful among the faithless, loyal among the disloyal, he stands as God's representative, and his voice is as a voice from heaven. There is no fear, no sadness, no discouragement in word or look. Strong in a consciousness of innocence, clothed in the panoply of truth, he rejoices that he is a son of God. His words are as a shout of victory above the roar of battle. He declares the cause to which he has devoted his life, to be the only cause that can never fail. Though he may perish, the gospel will not perish. God lives, and His truth will triumph.

Many who that day looked upon him "saw his face as it had been the face of an angel." Acts 6:15.

Never before had that company listened to words like these. They struck a cord that vibrated in the hearts of even the most hardened. Truth, clear and convincing, overthrew error. Light shone into the minds of many who afterward gladly followed its rays. The truths spoken on that day were destined to shake nations and to live through all time, influencing the hearts of men when the lips that had uttered them should be silent in a martyr's grave.

Never before had Nero heard the truth as he heard it on this occasion. Never before had the enormous guilt of his own life been so revealed to him. The light of heaven pierced the sin-polluted chambers of his soul, and he trembled with terror at the thought of a tribunal before which he, the ruler of the world, would finally be arraigned, and his deeds receive their just award. He feared the apostle's God, and he dared not pass sentence upon Paul, against whom no accusation had been sustained. A sense of awe restrained for a time his bloodthirsty spirit.

For a moment, heaven was opened to the guilty and hardened Nero, and its peace and purity seemed desirable.

That moment the invitation of mercy was extended even to him. But only for a moment was the thought of pardon welcomed. Then the command was issued that Paul be taken back to his dungeon; and as the door closed upon the messenger of God, the door of repentance closed forever against the emperor of Rome. No ray of light from heaven was ever again to penetrate the darkness that enveloped him. Soon he was to suffer the retributive judgments of God.

Not long after this, Nero sailed on his infamous expedition to Greece, where he disgraced himself and his kingdom by contemptible and debasing frivolity. Returning to Rome with great pomp, he surrounded himself with his courtiers and engaged in scenes of revolting debauchery. In the midst of this revelry a voice of tumult in the streets was heard. A messenger dispatched to learn the cause, returned with the appalling news that Galba, at the head of an army, was marching rapidly upon Rome, that insurrection had already broken out in the city, and that the streets were filled with an enraged mob, which, threatening death to the emperor and all his supporters, was rapidly approaching the palace.

In this time of peril, Nero had not, like the faithful Paul, a powerful and compassionate God on whom to rely. Fearful of the suffering and possible torture he might be compelled to endure at the hands of the mob, the wretched tyrant thought to end his life by his own hand, but at the critical moment his courage failed. Completely unmanned, he fled ignominiously from the city and sought shelter at a countryseat a few miles distant, but to no avail. His hiding place was soon discovered, and as the pursuing horsemen drew near, he summoned a slave to his aid and inflicted on himself a mortal wound. Thus perished the tyrant Nero, at the early age of thirty-two.

Paul's Last Letter

From the judgment hall of Caesar, Paul returned to his cell, realizing that he had gained for himself only a brief respite. He knew that his enemies would not rest until they had compassed his death. But he knew also that for a time truth had triumphed. To have proclaimed a crucified and risen Saviour before the vast crowd who had listened to him, was in itself a victory. That day a work had begun which would grow and strengthen, and which Nero and all other enemies of Christ would seek in vain to hinder or destroy.

Sitting day after day in his gloomy cell, knowing that at a word or a nod from Nero his life might be sacrificed, Paul thought of Timothy and determined to send for him. To Timothy had been committed the care of the church at Ephesus, and he had therefore been left behind when Paul made his last journey to Rome. Paul and Timothy were bound together by an affection unusually deep and strong. Since his conversion, Timothy had shared Paul's labors and sufferings, and the friendship between the two had grown stronger, deeper, and more sacred, until all that a son could be to a loved and honored father, Timothy was to the aged, toilworn apostle. It is little wonder that in his loneliness and solitude, Paul longed to see him.

Under the most favorable circumstances several months must pass before Timothy could reach Rome from Asia Minor. Paul knew that his life was uncertain, and he feared that Timothy might arrive too late to see him. He had important counsel and instruction for the young man, to whom so great responsibility had been entrusted; and while urging him to come without delay, he dictated the dying testimony that he might not be spared to utter. His soul filled with loving solicitude for his son in the gospel and for the church under his care, Paul sought to impress Timothy with the importance of fidelity to his sacred trust.

Paul began his letter with the salutation: "To Timothy, my dearly beloved son: Grace, mercy, and peace, from God the Father and Christ Jesus our Lord. I thank God, whom I serve from my forefathers with pure conscience, that without ceasing I have remembrance of thee in my prayers night and day."

The apostle then urged upon Timothy the necessity of steadfastness in the faith. "I put thee in remembrance," he wrote, "that thou stir up the gift of God, which is in thee by the putting on of my hands. For God hath not given us the spirit of fear; but of power, and of love, and of a sound mind. Be not thou therefore ashamed of the testimony of our Lord, nor of me His prisoner: but be thou partaker of the afflictions of the gospel according to the power of God." Paul entreated Timothy to remember that he had been called "with a holy calling" to proclaim the power of Him who had "brought life and immortality to light through the gospel: whereunto," he declared, "I am appointed a preacher, and an apostle, and a teacher of the Gentiles. For the which cause I also suffer these things: nevertheless I am not ashamed: for I know whom I have believed, and am persuaded that He is able to keep that which I have committed unto Him against that day."

Through his long term of service, Paul had never faltered in his allegiance to his Saviour. Wherever he was—whether before scowling Pharisees, or Roman authorities; before the furious mob at Lystra, or the convicted sinners in the Macedonian dungeon; whether reasoning with the panic-stricken sailors on the shipwrecked vessel, or standing alone before Nero to plead for his life—he had never been ashamed of the cause he was advocating. The one great purpose of his Christian life had been to serve Him whose name had once filled him with contempt; and from this purpose no opposition or persecution had been able to turn him aside. His faith, made strong by effort and pure by sacrifice, upheld and strengthened him.

"Thou therefore, my son," Paul continued, "be strong in the grace that is in Christ Jesus. And the things that thou hast heard of me among many witnesses, the same commit thou to faithful men, who shall be able to teach others also. Thou therefore endure hardness, as a good soldier of Jesus Christ."

The true minister of God will not shun hardship or responsibility. From the Source that never fails those who sincerely seek for divine power, he draws strength that enables him to meet and overcome temptation, and to perform the duties that God places upon him. The nature of the grace that he receives, enlarges his capacity to know God and His Son. His soul goes out in longing desire to do acceptable service for the Master. And as he advances in the Christian pathway he becomes "strong in the grace that is in Christ Jesus." This grace enables him to be a faithful witness of the things that he has heard. He does not despise or neglect the knowledge that he has received from God, but commits this knowledge to faithful men, who in their turn teach others.

In this his last letter to Timothy, Paul held up before the younger worker a high ideal, pointing out the duties devolving on him as a minister of Christ. "Study to show thyself approved unto God," the apostle wrote, "a workman that needeth not to be ashamed, rightly dividing the word of truth." "Flee also youthful lusts: but follow righteousness, faith, charity, peace, with them that call on the Lord out of a pure heart. But foolish and unlearned questions avoid, knowing that they do gender strifes. And the servant of the Lord must not strive; but be gentle unto all men, apt to teach, patient, in meekness instructing those that oppose themselves; if God peradventure will give them repentance to the acknowledging of the truth."

The apostle warned Timothy against the false teachers who would seek to gain entrance into the church. "This know also," he declared, "that in the last days perilous times shall come. For men shall be lovers of their own selves, covetous, boasters, proud, blasphemers, disobedient to parents, unthankful, unholy; . . . having a form of godliness, but denying the power thereof: from such turn away."

"Evil men and seducers shall wax worse and worse," he continued, "deceiving, and being deceived. But continue thou in the things which thou hast learned and hast been assured of, knowing of whom thou hast learned them; and that from a child thou hast known the Holy Scriptures, which are able to make thee wise unto salvation. . . . All Scripture is given by inspiration of God, and is profitable for doctrine, for reproof, for correction, for instruction in righteousness: that the man of God may be perfect, throughly furnished unto all good works." God has provided abundant means for successful warfare against the evil that is in the world. The Bible is the armory where we may equip for the struggle. Our loins must be girt about with truth. Our breastplate must be righteousness. The shield of faith must be in our hand, the helmet of salvation on our brow; and with the sword of the Spirit, which is the word of God, we are to cut our way through the obstructions and entanglements of sin.

Paul knew that there was before the church a time of great peril. He knew that faithful, earnest work would have to be done by those left in charge of the churches; and he wrote to Timothy, "I charge thee therefore before God, and the Lord Jesus Christ, who shall judge the quick and the dead at His appearing and His kingdom; Preach the word; be instant in season, out of season; reprove, rebuke, exhort with all long-suffering and doctrine."

This solemn charge to one so zealous and faithful as was Timothy is a strong testimony to the importance and responsibility of the work of the gospel minister. Summoning Timothy before the bar of God, Paul bids him preach the word, not the sayings and customs of men; to be ready to witness for God whenever opportunity should present itself—before large congregations and private circles, by the way and at the fireside, to friends and to enemies, whether in safety or exposed to hardship and peril, reproach and loss.

Fearing that Timothy's mild, yielding disposition might lead him to shun an essential part of his work, Paul exhorted him to be faithful in reproving sin and even to rebuke with sharpness those who were guilty of gross evils. Yet he was to do this "with all long-suffering and doctrine." He was to reveal the patience and love of Christ, explaining and enforcing his reproofs by the truths of the word.

To hate and reprove sin, and at the same time to show pity and tenderness for the sinner, is a difficult attainment. The more earnest our own efforts to attain to holiness of heart and life, the more acute will be our perception of sin and the more decided our disapproval of any deviation from the right. We must guard against undue severity toward the wrongdoer, but we must also be careful not to lose sight of the exceeding sinfulness of sin. There is need of showing Christlike patience and love for the erring one, but there is also danger of showing so great toleration for his error that he will look upon himself as undeserving of reproof, and will reject it as uncalled for and unjust.

Ministers of the gospel sometimes do great harm by allowing their forbearance toward the erring to degenerate into toleration of sins and even participation in them. Thus they are led to excuse and palliate that which God condemns, and after a time they become so blinded as to commend the very ones whom God commands them to reprove. He who has blunted his spiritual perceptions by sinful leniency toward those whom God condemns, will erelong commit a greater sin by severity and harshness toward those whom God approves.

By the pride of human wisdom, by contempt for the influence of the Holy Spirit, and by disrelish for the truths of God's word, many who profess to be Christians, and who feel competent to teach others, will be led to turn away from the requirements of God. Paul declared to Timothy, "The time will come when they will not endure sound doctrine; but after their own lusts shall they heap to themselves teachers, having itching ears; and they shall turn away their ears from the truth, and shall be turned unto fables."

The apostle does not here refer to the openly irreligious, but to the professing Christians who make inclination their guide, and thus become enslaved by self. Such are willing to listen to those doctrines only that do not rebuke their sins or condemn their pleasure-loving course. They are offended by the plain words of the faithful servants of Christ and choose teachers who praise and flatter them. And among professing ministers there are those who preach the opinions of men instead of the word of God. Unfaithful to their trust, they lead astray those who look to them for spiritual guidance.

In the precepts of His holy law, God has given a perfect rule of life; and He has declared that until the close of time this law, unchanged in a single jot or tittle, is to maintain its claim upon human beings. Christ came to magnify the law and make it honorable. He showed that it is based upon the broad foundation of love to God and love to man, and that obedience to its precepts comprises the whole duty of man. In His own life He gave an example of obedience to the law of God. In the Sermon on the Mount He showed how its requirements extend beyond the outward acts and take cognizance of the thoughts and intents of the heart.

The law, obeyed, leads men to deny "ungodliness and worldly lusts," and to "live soberly, righteously, and godly, in this present world." Titus 2:12. But the enemy of all righteousness has taken the world captive and has led men and women to disobey the law. As Paul foresaw, multitudes have turned from the plain, searching truths of God's word and have chosen teachers who present to them the fables they desire. Many among both ministers and people are trampling under their feet the commandments of God. Thus the Creator of the world is insulted, and Satan laughs in triumph at the success of his devices.

With the growing contempt for God's law there is an increasing distaste for religion, an increase of pride, love of pleasure, disobedience to parents, and self-indulgence; and thoughtful minds everywhere are anxiously inquiring, What can be done to correct these alarming evils? The answer is found in Paul's exhortation to Timothy, "Preach the word." In the Bible are found the only safe principles of action. It is a transcript of the will of God, an expression of divine wisdom. It opens to man's understanding the great problems of life, and to all who heed its precepts it will prove an unerring guide, keeping them from wasting their lives in misdirected effort.

God has made known His will, and it is folly for man to question that which has gone out of His lips. After Infinite Wisdom has spoken, there can be no doubtful questions for man to settle, no wavering possibilities for him to adjust. All that is required of him is a frank, earnest concurrence in the expressed will of God. Obedience is the highest dictate of reason as well as of conscience.

Paul continued his charge: "Watch thou in all things, endure afflictions, do the work of an evangelist, make full proof of thy ministry." Paul was about to finish his course, and he desired Timothy to take his place, guarding the church from the fables and heresies by which the enemy, in various ways, would endeavor to lead them from the simplicity of the gospel. He admonished him to shun all temporal pursuits and entanglements that would prevent him from giving himself wholly to his work for God; to endure with cheerfulness the opposition, reproach, and persecution to which his faithfulness would expose him; to make full proof of his ministry by employing every means within his reach of doing good to those for whom Christ died.

Paul's life was an exemplification of the truths he taught, and herein lay his power. His heart was filled with a deep, abiding sense of his responsibility, and he labored in close communion with Him who is the fountain of justice, mercy, and truth. He clung to the cross of Christ as his only guarantee of success. The love of the Saviour was the undying motive that upheld him in his conflicts with self and in his struggles against evil as in the service of Christ he pressed forward against the unfriendliness of the world and the opposition of his enemies.

What the church needs in these days of peril is an army of workers who, like Paul, have educated themselves for usefulness, who have a deep experience in the things of God, and who are filled with earnestness and zeal. Sanctified, self-sacrificing men are needed; men who will not shun trial and responsibility; men who are brave and true; men in whose hearts Christ is formed "the hope of glory," and who with lips touched with holy fire will "preach the word." For want of such workers the cause of God languishes, and fatal errors, like a deadly poison, taint the morals and blight the hopes of a large part of the human race.

As the faithful, toilworn standard-bearers are offering up their lives for the truth's sake, who will come forward to take their place? Will our young men accept the holy trust at the hands of their fathers? Are they preparing to fill the vacancies made by the death of the faithful? Will the apostle's charge be heeded, the call to duty be heard, amidst the incitements to selfishness and ambition that allure the youth?

Paul concluded his letter with personal messages to different ones and again repeated the urgent request that Timothy come to him soon, if possible before the winter. He spoke of his loneliness, caused by the desertion of some of his friends and the necessary absence of others; and lest Timothy should hesitate, fearing that the church at Ephesus might need his labors, Paul stated that he had already dispatched Tychicus to fill the vacancy.

After speaking of the scene of his trial before Nero, the desertion of his brethren, and the sustaining grace of a covenant-keeping God, Paul closed his letter by commending his beloved Timothy to the guardianship of the Chief Shepherd, who, though the undershepherds might be stricken down, would still care for His flock.

Condemned to Die

During Paul's final trial before Nero, the emperor had been so strongly impressed with the force of the apostle's words that he deferred the decision of the case, neither acquitting nor condemning the accused servant of God. But the emperor's malice against Paul soon returned. Exasperated by his inability to check the spread of the Christian religion, even in the imperial household, he determined that as soon as a plausible pretext could be found, the apostle should be put to death. Not long afterward Nero pronounced the decision that condemned Paul to a martyr's death. Inasmuch as a Roman citizen could not be subjected to torture, he was sentenced to be beheaded.

Paul was taken in a private manner to the place of execution. Few spectators were allowed to be present; for his persecutors, alarmed at the extent of his influence, feared that converts might be won to Christianity by the scenes of his death. But even the hardened soldiers who attended him listened to his words and with amazement saw him cheerful and even joyous in the prospect of death. To some who witnessed his martyrdom, his spirit of forgiveness toward his murderers and his unwavering confidence in Christ till the last, proved a savor of life unto life. More than one accepted the Saviour whom Paul preached, and erelong fearlessly sealed their faith with their blood.

Until his latest hour the life of Paul testified to the truth of his words to the Corinthians: "God, who commanded the light to shine out of darkness, hath shined in our hearts, to give the light of the knowledge of the glory of God in the face of Jesus Christ. But we have this treasure in earthen vessels, that the excellency of the power may be of God, and not of us. We are troubled on every side, yet not distressed; we are perplexed, but not in despair; persecuted, but not forsaken; cast down, but not destroyed; always bearing about in the body the dying of the Lord Jesus, that the life also of Jesus might be made manifest in our body." 2 Corinthians 4:6-10. His sufficiency was not in himself, but in the presence and agency of the divine Spirit that filled his soul and brought every thought into subjection to the will of Christ. The prophet declares, "Thou wilt keep him in perfect peace, whose mind is stayed on Thee: because he trusteth in Thee." Isaiah 26:3. The heaven-born peace expressed on Paul's countenance won many a soul to the gospel.

Paul carried with him the atmosphere of heaven. All who associated with him felt the influence of his union with Christ. The fact that his own life exemplified the truth he proclaimed, gave convincing power to his preaching. Here lies the power of truth. The unstudied, unconscious influence of a holy life is the most convincing sermon that can be given in favor of Christianity. Argument, even when unanswerable, may provoke only opposition; but a godly example has a power that it is impossible wholly to resist.

The apostle lost sight of his own approaching sufferings in his solicitude for those whom he was about to leave to cope with prejudice, hatred, and persecution. The few Christians who accompanied him to the place of execution he endeavored to strengthen and encourage by repeating the promises given for those who are persecuted for righteousness' sake. He assured them that nothing would fail of all that the Lord had spoken concerning His tried and faithful children. For a little season they might be in heaviness through manifold temptations; they might be destitute of earthly comforts; but they could encourage their hearts with the assurance of God's faithfulness, saying, "I know whom I have believed, and am persuaded that He is able to keep that which I have committed unto Him." 2 Timothy 1:12. Soon the night of trial and suffering would end, and then would dawn the glad morning of peace and perfect day.

The apostle was looking into the great beyond, not with uncertainty or dread, but with joyous hope and longing expectation. As he stands at the place of martyrdom he sees not the sword of the executioner or the earth so soon to receive his blood; he looks up through the calm blue heaven of that summer day to the throne of the Eternal.

This man of faith beholds the ladder of Jacob's vision, representing Christ, who has connected earth with heaven, and finite man with the infinite God. His faith is strengthened as he calls to mind how patriarchs and prophets have relied upon the One who is his support and consolation, and for whom he is giving his life. From these holy men who from century to century have borne testimony for their faith, he hears the assurance that God is true. His fellow apostles, who, to preach the gospel of Christ, went forth to meet religious bigotry and heathen superstition, persecution, and contempt, who counted not their lives dear unto themselves that they might bear aloft the light of the cross amidst the dark mazes of infidelity—these he hears witnessing to Jesus as the Son of God, the Saviour of the world. From the rack, the stake, the dungeon, from dens and caves of the earth, there falls upon his ear the martyr's shout of triumph. He hears the witness of steadfast souls, who, though destitute, afflicted, tormented, yet bear fearless, solemn testimony for the faith, declaring, "I know whom I have believed." These, yielding up their lives for the faith, declare to the world that He in whom they have trusted is able to save to the uttermost.

Ransomed by the sacrifice of Christ, washed from sin in His blood, and clothed in His righteousness, Paul has the witness in himself that his soul is precious in the sight of his Redeemer. His life is hid with Christ in God, and he is persuaded that He who has conquered death is able to keep that which is committed to His trust. His mind grasps the Saviour's promise, "I will raise him up at the last day." John 6:40. His thoughts and hopes are centered on the second coming of his Lord. And as the sword of the executioner descends and the shadows of death gather about the martyr, his latest thought springs forward, as will his earliest in the great awakening, to meet the Life-giver, who shall welcome him to the joy of the blest.

Well-nigh a score of centuries have passed since Paul the aged poured out his blood as a witness for the word of God and the testimony of Jesus Christ. No faithful hand recorded for the generations to come the last scenes in the life of this holy man, but Inspiration has preserved for us his dying testimony. Like a trumpet peal his voice has rung out through all the ages since, nerving with his own courage thousands of witnesses for Christ and wakening in thousands of sorrow-stricken hearts the echo of his own triumphant joy: "I am now ready to be offered, and the time of my departure is at hand. I have fought a good fight, I have finished my course, I have kept the faith: henceforth there is laid up for me a crown of righteousness, which the Lord, the righteous Judge, shall give me at that day: and not to me only, but unto all them also that love His appearing." 2 Timothy 4:6-8.

A Faithful Undershepherd

Little mention is made in the book of Acts of the later work of the apostle Peter. During the busy years of ministry that followed the outpouring of the Spirit on the Day of Pentecost, he was among those who put forth untiring efforts to reach the Jews who came to Jerusalem to worship at the time of the annual festivals.

As the number of believers multiplied in Jerusalem and in other places visited by the messengers of the cross, the talents possessed by Peter proved of untold value to the early Christian church. The influence of his testimony concerning Jesus of Nazareth extended far and wide. Upon him had been laid a double responsibility. He bore positive witness concerning the Messiah before unbelievers, laboring earnestly for their conversion; and at the same time he did a special work for believers, strengthening them in the faith of Christ.

It was after Peter had been led to self-renunciation and entire reliance upon divine power, that he received his call to act as an undershepherd. Christ had said to Peter, before his denial of Him, "When thou art converted, strengthen thy brethren." Luke 22:32. These words were significant of the wide and effectual work which this apostle was to do in the future for those who should come to the faith. For this work, Peter's own experience of sin and suffering and repentance had prepared him. Not until he had learned his weakness, could he know the believer's need of dependence on Christ. Amid the storm of temptation he had come to understand that man can walk safely only as in utter self-distrust he relies upon the Saviour.

At the last meeting of Christ with His disciples by the sea, Peter, tested by the thrice-repeated question, "Lovest thou Me?" (John 21:15-17), had been restored to his place among the Twelve. His work had been appointed him; he was to feed the Lord's flock. Now, converted and accepted, he was not only to seek to save those without the fold, but was to be a shepherd of the sheep.

Christ mentioned to Peter only one condition of service —"Lovest thou Me?" This is the essential qualification. Though Peter might possess every other, yet without the love of Christ he could not be a faithful shepherd over the flock of God. Knowledge, benevolence, eloquence, zeal— all are essential in the good work; but without the love of Christ in the heart, the work of the Christian minister is a failure.

The love of Christ is not a fitful feeling, but a living principle, which is to be made manifest as an abiding power in the heart. If the character and deportment of the shepherd is an exemplification of the truth he advocates, the Lord will set the seal of His approval to the work. The shepherd and the flock will become one, united by their common hope in Christ.

The Saviour's manner of dealing with Peter had a lesson for him and his brethren. Although Peter had denied his Lord, the love which Jesus bore him had never faltered. And as the apostle should take up the work of ministering the word to others, he was to meet the transgressor with patience, sympathy, and forgiving love. Remembering his own weakness and failure, he was to deal with the sheep and lambs committed to his care as tenderly as Christ had dealt with him.

Human beings, themselves given to evil, are prone to deal untenderly with the tempted and the erring. They cannot read the heart; they know not its struggle and its pain. Of the rebuke that is love, of the blow that wounds to heal, of the warning that speaks hope, they have need to learn.

Throughout his ministry, Peter faithfully watched over the flock entrusted to his care, and thus proved himself worthy of the charge and responsibility given him by the Saviour. Ever he exalted Jesus of Nazareth as the Hope of Israel, the Saviour of mankind. He brought his own life under the discipline of the Master Worker. By every means within his power he sought to educate the believers for active service. His godly example and untiring activity inspired many young men of promise to give themselves wholly to the work of the ministry. As time went on, the apostle's influence as an educator and leader increased; and while he never lost his burden to labor especially for the Jews, yet he bore his testimony in many lands and strengthened the faith of multitudes in the gospel.

In the later years of his ministry, Peter was inspired to write to the believers "scattered throughout Pontus, Galatia, Cappadocia, Asia, and Bithynia." His letters were the means of reviving the courage and strengthening the faith of those who were enduring trial and affliction, and of renewing to good works those who through manifold temptations were in danger of losing their hold upon God. These letters bear the impress of having been written by one in whom the sufferings of Christ and also His consolation had been made to abound; one whose entire being had been transformed by grace, and whose hope of eternal life was sure and steadfast.

At the very beginning of his first letter the aged servant of God ascribed to his Lord a tribute of praise and thanksgiving. "Blessed be the God and Father of our Lord Jesus Christ," he exclaimed, "which according to His abundant mercy hath begotten us again unto a lively hope by the resurrection of Jesus Christ from the dead, to an inheritance incorruptible, and undefiled, and that fadeth not away, reserved in heaven for you, who are kept by the power of God through faith unto salvation ready to be revealed in the last time."

In this hope of a sure inheritance in the earth made new, the early Christians rejoiced, even in times of severe trial and affliction. "Ye greatly rejoice," Peter wrote, "though now for a season, if need be, ye are in heaviness through manifold temptations: that the trial of your faith, being much more precious than of gold that perisheth, though it be tried with fire, might be found unto praise and honor and glory at the appearing of Jesus Christ: whom having not seen, ye love; in whom, though now ye see Him not, . . . ye rejoice with joy unspeakable and full of glory: receiving the end of your faith, even the salvation of your souls."

The apostle's words were written for the instruction of believers in every age, and they have a special significance for those who live at the time when "the end of all things is at hand." His exhortations and warnings, and his words of faith and courage, are needed by every soul who would maintain his faith "steadfast unto the end." Hebrews 3:14.

The apostle sought to teach the believers how important it is to keep the mind from wandering to forbidden themes or from spending its energies on trifling subjects. Those who would not fall a prey to Satan's devices, must guard well the avenues of the soul; they must avoid reading, seeing, or hearing that which will suggest impure thoughts. The mind must not be left to dwell at random upon every subject that the enemy of souls may suggest. The heart must be faithfully sentineled, or evils without will awaken evils within, and the soul will wander in darkness. "Gird up the loins of your mind," Peter wrote, "be sober, and hope to the end for the grace that is to be brought unto you at the revelation of Jesus Christ; . . . not fashioning yourselves according to the former lusts in your ignorance: but as He which hath called you is holy, so be ye holy in all manner of conversation; because it is written, Be ye holy; for I am holy."

"Pass the time of your sojourning here in fear: forasmuch as ye know that ye were not redeemed with corruptible things, as silver and gold, from your vain conversation received by tradition from your fathers; but with the precious blood of Christ, as of a Lamb without blemish and without spot: who verily was foreordained before the foundation of the world, but was manifest in these last times for you, who by Him do believe in God, that raised Him up from the dead, and gave Him glory; that your faith and hope might be in God."

Had silver and gold been sufficient to purchase the salvation of men, how easily might it have been accomplished by Him who says, "The silver is Mine, and the gold is Mine." Haggai 2:8. But only by the precious blood of the Son of God could the transgressor be redeemed. The plan of salvation was laid in sacrifice. The apostle Paul wrote, "Ye know the grace of our Lord Jesus Christ, that, though He was rich, yet for your sakes He became poor, that ye through His poverty might be rich." 2 Corinthians 8:9. Christ gave Himself for us that He might redeem us from all iniquity. And as the crowning blessing of salvation, "the gift of God is eternal life through Jesus Christ our Lord." Romans 6:23.

"Seeing ye have purified your souls in obeying the truth through the Spirit unto unfeigned love of the brethren," Peter continued, "see that ye love one another with a pure heart fervently." The word of God—the truth—is the channel through which the Lord manifests His Spirit and power. Obedience to the word produces fruit of the required quality —"unfeigned love of the brethren." This love is heaven-born and leads to high motives and unselfish actions.

When truth becomes an abiding principle in the life, the soul is "born again, not of corruptible seed, but of incorruptible, by the word of God, which liveth and abideth forever." This new birth is the result of receiving Christ as the Word of God. When by the Holy Spirit divine truths are impressed upon the heart, new conceptions are awakened, and the energies hitherto dormant are aroused to co-operate with God.

Thus it had been with Peter and his fellow disciples. Christ was the revealer of truth to the world. By Him the incorruptible seed—the word of God—was sown in the hearts of men. But many of the most precious lessons of the Great Teacher were spoken to those who did not then understand them. When, after His ascension, the Holy Spirit brought His teachings to the remembrance of the disciples, their slumbering senses awoke. The meaning of these truths flashed upon their minds as a new revelation, and truth, pure and unadulterated, made a place for itself. Then the wonderful experience of His life became theirs. The Word bore testimony through them, the men of His appointment, and they proclaimed the mighty truth, "The Word was made flesh, and dwelt among us, . . . full of grace and truth." "And of His fullness have all we received, and grace for grace." John 1:14, 16.

The apostles exhorted the believers to study the Scriptures, through a proper understanding of which they might make sure work for eternity. Peter realized that in the experience of every soul who is finally victorious there would be scenes of perplexity and trial; but he knew also that an understanding of the Scriptures would enable the tempted one to bring to mind promises that would comfort the heart and strengthen faith in the Mighty One.

"All flesh is as grass," he declared, "and all the glory of man as the flower of grass. The grass withereth, and the flower thereof falleth away: but the word of the Lord endureth forever. And this is the word which by the gospel is preached unto you. Wherefore laying aside all malice, and all guile, and hypocrisies, and envies, and all evilspeakings, as newborn babes, desire the sincere milk of the word, that ye may grow thereby: if so be ye have tasted that the Lord is gracious."

Many of the believers to whom Peter addressed his letters, were living in the midst of heathen, and much depended on their remaining true to the high calling of their profession. The apostle urged upon them their privileges as followers of Christ Jesus. "Ye are a chosen generation," he wrote, "a royal priesthood, an holy nation, a peculiar people; that ye should show forth the praises of Him who hath called you out of darkness into His marvelous light: which in time past were not a people, but are now the people of God: which had not obtained mercy, but now have obtained mercy.

"Dearly beloved, I beseech you as strangers and pilgrims, abstain from fleshly lusts, which war against the soul; having your conversation honest among the Gentiles: that, whereas they speak against you as evildoers, they may by your good works, which they shall behold, glorify God in the day of visitation."

The apostle plainly outlined the attitude that believers

should sustain toward the civil authorities: "Submit yourselves to every ordinance of man for the Lord's sake: whether it be to the king, as supreme; or unto governors, as unto them that are sent by him for the punishment of evildoers, and for the praise of them that do well. For so is the will of God, that with well-doing ye may put to silence the ignorance of foolish men: as free, and not using your liberty for a cloak of maliciousness, but as the servants of God. Honor all men. Love the brotherhood. Fear God. Honor the king."

Those who were servants were advised to remain subject to their masters "with all fear; not only to the good and gentle, but also to the froward. For this is thankworthy," the apostle explained, "if a man for conscience toward God endure grief, suffering wrongfully. For what glory is it, if, when ye be buffeted for your faults, ye shall take it patiently? but if, when ye do well, and suffer for it, ye take it patiently, this is acceptable with God. For even hereunto were ye called: because Christ also suffered for us, leaving us an example, that ye should follow His steps: who did no sin, neither was guile found in His mouth: who, when He was reviled, reviled not again; when He suffered, He threatened not; but committed Himself to Him that judgeth righteously: who His own self bare our sins in His own body on the tree, that we, being dead to sins, should live unto righteousness: by whose stripes ye were healed. For ye were as sheep going astray; but are now returned unto the Shepherd and Bishop of your souls."

The apostle exhorted the women in the faith to be chaste in conversation and modest in dress and deportment. "Whose adorning," he counseled, "let it not be that outward adorning of plaiting the hair, and of wearing of gold, or of putting on of apparel; but let it be the hidden man of the heart, in that which is not corruptible, even the ornament of a meek and quiet spirit, which is in the sight of God of great price."

The lesson applies to believers in every age. "By their fruits ye shall know them." Matthew 7:20. The inward adorning of a meek and quiet spirit is priceless. In the life of the true Christian the outward adorning is always in harmony with the inward peace and holiness. "If any man will come after Me," Christ said, "let him deny himself, and take up his cross, and follow Me." Matthew 16:24. Self-denial and sacrifice will mark the Christian's life. Evidence that the taste is converted will be seen in the dress of all who walk in the path cast up for the ransomed of the Lord.

It is right to love beauty and to desire it; but God desires us to love and seek first the highest beauty, that which is imperishable. No outward adorning can compare in value or loveliness with that "meek and quiet spirit," the "fine linen, white and clean" (Revelation 19:14), which all the holy ones of earth will wear. This apparel will make them beautiful and beloved here, and will hereafter be their badge of admission to the palace of the King. His promise is, "They shall walk with Me in white: for they are worthy." Revelation 3:4.

Looking forward with prophetic vision to the perilous times into which the church of Christ was to enter, the apostle exhorted the believers to steadfastness in the face of trial and suffering. "Beloved," he wrote, "think it not strange concerning the fiery trial which is to try you."

Trial is part of the education given in the school of Christ, to purify God's children from the dross of earthliness. It is because God is leading His children that trying experiences come to them. Trials and obstacles are His chosen methods of discipline, and His appointed conditions of success. He who reads the hearts of men knows their weaknesses better than they themselves can know them. He sees that some have qualifications which, if rightly directed, could be used in the advancement of His work. In His providence He brings these souls into different positions and varied circumstances, that they may discover the defects that are concealed form their own knowledge. He gives them opportunity to overcome these defects and to fit themselves for service. Often He permits the fires of affliction to burn, that they may be purified.

God's care for His heritage is unceasing. He suffers no affliction to come upon His children but such as is essential for their present and eternal good. He will purify His church, even as Christ purified the temple during His ministry on earth. All that He brings upon His people in test and trial comes that they may gain deeper piety and greater strength to carry forward the triumphs of the cross.

There had been a time in Peter's experience when he was unwilling to see the cross in the work of Christ. When the Saviour made known to the disciples His impending sufferings and death, Peter exclaimed, "Be it far from Thee, Lord: this shall not be unto Thee." Matthew 16:22. Self-pity, which shrank from fellowship with Christ in suffering, prompted Peter's remonstrance. It was to the disciple a bitter lesson, and one which he learned but slowly, that the path of Christ on earth lay through agony and humiliation. But in the heat of the furnace fire he was to learn its lesson. Now, when his once active form was bowed with the burden of years and labors, he could write, "Beloved, think it not strange concerning the fiery trial which is to try you, as though some strange thing happened unto you: but rejoice, inasmuch as ye are partakers of Christ's sufferings; that, when His glory shall be revealed, ye may be glad also with exceeding joy."

Addressing the church elders regarding their responsibilities as undershepherds of Christ's flock, the apostle wrote: "Feed the flock of God which is among you, taking the oversight thereof, not by constraint, but willingly; not for filthy lucre, but of a ready mind; neither as being lords over God's heritage, but being ensamples to the flock. And when the Chief Shepherd shall appear, ye shall receive a crown of glory that fadeth not away."

Those who occupy the position of undershepherds are to exercise a watchful diligence over the Lord's flock. This is not to be a dictatorial vigilance, but one that tends to encourage and strengthen and uplift. Ministry means more than sermonizing; it means earnest, personal labor. The church on earth is composed of erring men and women, who need patient, painstaking effort that they may be trained and disciplined to work with acceptance in this life, and in the future life to be crowned with glory and immortality. Pastors are needed—faithful shepherds—who will not flatter God's people, nor treat them harshly, but who will feed them with the bread of life—men who in their lives feel daily the converting power of the Holy Spirit and who cherish a strong, unselfish love toward those for whom they labor.

There is tactful work for the undershepherd to do as he is called to meet alienation, bitterness, envy, and jealousy in the church, and he will need to labor in the spirit of Christ to set things in order. Faithful warnings are to be given, sins rebuked, wrongs made right, not only by the minister's work in the pulpit, but by personal labor. The wayward heart may take exception to the message, and the servant of God may be misjudged and criticized. Let him then remember that "the wisdom that is from above is first pure, then peaceable, gentle, and easy to be entreated, full of mercy and good fruits, without partiality, and without hypocrisy. And the fruit of righteousness is sown in peace of them that make peace." James 3:17, 18.

The work of the gospel minister is "to make all men see what is the fellowship of the mystery, which from the beginning of the world hath been hid in God." Ephesians 3:9. If one entering upon this work chooses the least self-sacrificing part, contenting himself with preaching, and leaving the work of personal ministry for someone else, his labors will not be acceptable to God. Souls for whom Christ died are perishing for want of well-directed, personal labor; and he has mistaken his calling who, entering upon the ministry, is unwilling to do the personal work that the care of the flock demands.

The spirit of the true shepherd is one of self-forgetfulness. He loses sight of self in order that he may work the works of God. By the preaching of the word and by personal ministry in the homes of the people, he learns their needs, their sorrows, their trials; and, co-operating with the great Burden Bearer, he shares their afflictions, comforts their distresses, relieves their soul hunger, and wins their hearts to God. In this work the minister is attended by the angels of heaven, and he himself is instructed and enlightened in the truth that maketh wise unto salvation.

In connection with his instruction to those in positions of trust in the church, the apostle outlined some general principles that were to be followed by all who were associated in church fellowship. The younger members of the flock were urged to follow the example of their elders in the practice of Christlike humility: "Likewise, ye younger, submit yourselves unto the elder. Yea, all of you be subject one to another, and be clothed with humility: for God resisteth the proud, and giveth grace to the humble. Humble yourselves therefore under the mighty hand of God, that He may exalt you in due time: casting all your care upon Him; for He careth for you. Be sober, be vigilant; because your adversary the devil, as a roaring lion, walketh about, seeking whom he may devour: whom resist steadfast in the faith."

Thus Peter wrote to the believers at a time of peculiar trial to the church. Many had already become partakers of Christ's sufferings, and soon the church was to undergo a period of terrible persecution. Within a few brief years many those who had stood as teachers and leaders in the church were to lay down their lives for the gospel. Soon grievous wolves were to enter in, not sparing the flock. But none of these things were to bring discouragement to those whose hopes were centered in Christ. With words of encouragement and good cheer Peter directed the minds of the believers from present trials and future scenes of suffering "to an inheritance incorruptible, and undefiled, and that fadeth not away." "The God of all grace," he fervently prayed, "who hath called us unto His eternal glory by Christ Jesus, after that ye have suffered awhile, make you perfect, stablish, strengthen, settle you. To Him be glory and dominion for ever and ever. Amen."

Steadfast Unto the End

In the second letter addressed by peter to those who had obtained "like precious faith" with himself, the apostle sets forth the divine plan for the development of Christian character. He writes:

"Grace and peace be multiplied unto you through the knowledge of God, and of Jesus our Lord, according as His divine power hath given unto us all things that pertain unto life and godliness, through the knowledge of Him that hath called us to glory and virtue: whereby are given unto us exceeding great and precious promises: that by these ye might be partakers of the divine nature, having escaped the corruption that is in the world through lust.

"And beside this, giving all diligence, add to your faith virtue; and to virtue knowledge; and to knowledge temperance; and to temperance patience; and to patience godliness; and to godliness brotherly kindness; and to brotherly kindness charity. For if these things be in you, and abound, they make you that ye shall neither be barren nor unfruitful in the knowledge of our Lord Jesus Christ."

These words are full of instruction, and strike the keynote of victory. The apostle presents before the believers the ladder of Christian progress, every step of which represents advancement in the knowledge of God, and in the climbing of which there is to be no standstill. Faith, virtue, knowledge, temperance, patience, godliness, brotherly kindness, and charity are the rounds of the ladder. We are saved by climbing round after round, mounting step after step, to the height of Christ's ideal for us. Thus He is made unto us wisdom, and righteousness, and sanctification, and redemption.

God has called His people to glory and virtue, and these will be manifest in the lives of all who are truly connected with Him. Having become partakers of the heavenly gift, they are to go unto perfection, being "kept by the power of God through faith." 1 Peter 1:5. It is the glory of God to give His virtue to His children. He desires to see men and women reaching the highest standard; and when by faith they lay hold of the power of Christ, when they plead His unfailing promises, and claim them as their own, when with an importunity that will not be denied they seek for the power of the Holy Spirit, they will be made complete in Him.

Having received the faith of the gospel, the next work of the believer is to add to his character virtue, and thus cleanse the heart and prepare the mind for the reception of the knowledge of God. This knowledge is the foundation of all true education and of all true service. It is the only real safeguard against temptation; and it is this alone that can make one like God in character. Through the knowledge of God and of His Son Jesus Christ, are given to the believer "all things that pertain unto life and godliness." No good gift is withheld from him who sincerely desires to obtain the righteousness of God.

"This is life eternal," Christ said, "that they might know Thee the only true God, and Jesus Christ, whom Thou hast sent." John 17:3. And the prophet Jeremiah declared: "Let not the wise man glory in his wisdom, neither let the mighty man glory in his might, let not the rich man glory in his riches: but let him that glorieth glory in this, that he understandeth and knoweth Me, that I am the Lord which exercise loving-kindness, judgment, and righteousness, in the earth: for in these things I delight, saith the Lord." Jeremiah 9:23, 24. Scarcely can the human mind comprehend the breadth and depth and height of the spiritual attainments of him who gains this knowledge.

None need fail of attaining, in his sphere, to perfection of Christian character. By the sacrifice of Christ, provision has been made for the believer to receive all things that pertain to life and godliness. God calls upon us to reach the standard of perfection and places before us the example of Christ's character. In His humanity, perfected by a life of constant resistance of evil, the Saviour showed that through co-operation with Divinity, human beings may in this life attain to perfection of character. This is God's assurance to us that we, too, may obtain complete victory.

Before the believer is held out the wonderful possibility of being like Christ, obedient to all the principles of the law. But of himself man is utterly unable to reach this condition. The holiness that God's word declares he must have before he can be saved is the result of the working of divine grace as he bows in submission to the discipline and restraining influences of the Spirit of truth. Man's obedience can be made perfect only by the incense of Christ's righteousness, which fills with divine fragrance every act of obedience. The part of the Christian is to persevere in overcoming every fault. Constantly he is to pray to the Saviour to heal the disorders of his sin-sick soul. He has not the wisdom or the strength to overcome; these belong to the Lord, and He bestows them on those who in humiliation and contrition seek Him for help.

The work of transformation from unholiness to holiness is a continuous one. Day by day God labors for man's sanctification, and man is to co-operate with Him, putting forth persevering efforts in the cultivation of right habits. He is to add grace to grace; and as he thus works on the plan of addition, God works for him on the plan of multiplication. Our Saviour is always ready to hear and answer the prayer of the contrite heart, and grace and peace are multiplied to His faithful ones. Gladly He grants them the blessings they need in their struggle against the evils that beset them.

There are those who attempt to ascend the ladder of Christian progress; but as they advance they begin to put their trust in the power of man, and soon lose sight of Jesus, the Author and Finisher of their faith. The result is failure— the loss of all that has been gained. Sad indeed is the condition of those who, becoming weary of the way, allow the enemy of souls to rob them of the Christian graces that have been developing in their hearts and lives. "He that lacketh these things," declares the apostle, "is blind, and cannot see afar off, and hath forgotten that he was purged from his old sins."

The apostle Peter had had a long experience in the things of God. His faith in God's power to save had strengthened with the years, until he had proved beyond question that there is no possibility of failure before the one who, advancing by faith, ascends round by round, ever upward and onward, to the topmost round of the ladder that reaches even to the portals of heaven.

For many years Peter had been urging upon the believers the necessity of a constant growth in grace and in a knowledge of the truth; and now, knowing that soon he would be called to suffer martyrdom for his faith, he once more drew attention to the precious privileges within the reach of every believer. In the full assurance of his faith the aged disciple exhorted his brethren to steadfastness of purpose in the Christian life. "Give diligence," he pleaded, "to make your calling and election sure: for if ye do these things, ye shall never fall: for so an entrance shall be ministered unto you abundantly into the everlasting kingdom of our Lord and Saviour Jesus Christ." Precious assurance! Glorious is the hope before the believer as he advances by faith toward the heights of Christian perfection!

"I will not be negligent," the apostle continued, "to put you always in remembrance of these things, though ye know them, and be established in the present truth. Yea, I think it meet, as long as I am in this tabernacle, to stir you up by putting you in remembrance; knowing that shortly I must put off this my tabernacle, even as our Lord Jesus Christ hath showed me. Moreover I will endeavor that ye may be able after my decease to have these things always in remembrance."

The apostle was well qualified to speak of the purposes of God concerning the human race; for during the earthly ministry of Christ he had seen and heard much that pertained to the kingdom of God. "We have not followed cunningly devised fables," he reminded the believers, "when we made known unto you the power and coming of our Lord Jesus Christ, but were eyewitnesses of His majesty. For He received from God the Father honor and glory, when there came such a voice to Him from the excellent glory, This is My beloved Son, in whom I am well pleased. And this voice which came from heaven we heard, when we were with Him in the holy mount."

Yet convincing as was this evidence of the certainty of the believers' hope, there was another still more convincing in the witness of prophecy, through which the faith of all might be confirmed and securely anchored. "We have also," Peter declared, "a more sure word of prophecy; whereunto ye do well that ye take heed, as unto a light that shineth in a dark place, until the day dawn, and the daystar arise in your hearts: knowing this first, that no prophecy of the Scripture is of any private interpretation. For the prophecy came not in old time by the will of man: but holy men of God spake as they were moved by the Holy Ghost."

While exalting the "sure word of prophecy" as a safe guide in times of peril, the apostle solemnly warned the church against the torch of false prophecy, which would be uplifted by "false teachers," who would privily bring in "damnable heresies, even denying the Lord." These false teachers, arising in the church and accounted true by many of their brethren in the faith, the apostle compared to "wells without water, clouds that are carried with a tempest; to whom the mist of darkness is reserved forever." "The latter end is worse with them," he declared, "than the beginning. For it had been better for them not to have known the way of righteousness, than, after they have known it, to turn from the holy commandment delivered unto them."

Looking down through the ages to the close of time, Peter was inspired to outline conditions that would exist in the world just prior to the second coming of Christ. "There shall come in the last days scoffers," he wrote, "walking after their own lusts, and saying, Where is the promise of His coming? for since the fathers fell asleep, all things continue as they were from the beginning of the creation." But "when they shall say, Peace and safety; then sudden destruction cometh upon them." 1 Thessalonians 5:3. Not all, however, would be ensnared by the enemy's devices. As the end of all things earthly should approach, there would be faithful ones able to discern the signs of the times. While a large number of professing believers would deny their faith by their works, there would be a remnant who would endure to the end.

Peter kept alive in his heart the hope of Christ's return, and he assured the church of the certain fulfillment of the Saviour's promise, "If I go and prepare a place for you, I will come again, and receive you unto Myself." John 14:3. To the tried and faithful ones the coming might seem long delayed, but the apostle assured them: "The Lord is not slack concerning His promise, as some men count slackness; but is long-suffering to usward, not willing that any should perish, but that all should come to repentance. But the day of the Lord will come as a thief in the night; in the which the heavens shall pass away with a great noise, and the elements shall melt with fervent heat, the earth also and the works that are therein shall be burned up.

"Seeing then that all these things shall be dissolved, what manner of persons ought ye to be in all holy conversation and godliness, looking for and hasting unto the coming of the day of God, wherein the heavens being on fire shall be dissolved, and the elements shall melt with fervent heat? Nevertheless we, according to His promise, look for new heavens and a new earth, wherein dwelleth righteousness.

"Wherefore, beloved, seeing that ye look for such things, be diligent that ye may be found of Him in peace, without spot, and blameless. And account that the long-suffering of our Lord is salvation; even as our beloved brother Paul also according to the wisdom given unto him hath written unto you. . . . Ye therefore, beloved, seeing ye know these things before, beware lest ye also, being led away with the error of the wicked, fall from your own steadfastness. But grow in grace, and in the knowledge of our Lord and Saviour Jesus Christ."

In the providence of God, Peter was permitted to close his ministry in Rome, where his imprisonment was ordered by the emperor Nero about the time of Paul's final arrest. Thus the two veteran apostles, who for many years had been widely separated in their labors, were to bear their last witness for Christ in the world's metropolis, and upon its soil to shed their blood as the seed of a vast harvest of saints and martyrs.

Since his reinstatement after his denial of Christ, Peter had unflinchingly braved danger and had shown a noble courage in preaching a crucified, risen, and ascended Saviour. As he lay in his cell he called to mind the words that Christ had spoken to him: "Verily, verily, I say unto thee, When thou wast young, thou girdedst thyself, and walkedst whither thou wouldest: but when thou shalt be old, thou shalt stretch forth thy hands, and another shall gird thee, and carry thee whither thou wouldest not." John 21:18. Thus Jesus had made known to the disciple the very manner of his death, and even foretold the stretching of his hands upon the cross.

Peter, as a Jew and a foreigner, was condemned to be scourged and crucified. In prospect of this fearful death, the apostle remembered his great sin in denying Jesus in the hour of His trial. Once so unready to acknowledge the cross, he now counted it a joy to yield up his life for the gospel, feeling only that, for him who had denied his Lord, to die in the same manner as his Master died was too great an honor. Peter had sincerely repented of that sin and had been forgiven by Christ, as is shown by the high commission given him to feed the sheep and lambs of the flock. But he could never forgive himself. Not even the thought of the agonies of the last terrible scene could lessen the bitterness of his sorrow and repentance. As a last favor he entreated his executioners that he might be nailed to the cross with his head downward. The request was granted, and in this manner died the great apostle Peter.

John the Beloved

John is distinguished above the other apostles as "the disciple whom Jesus loved." John 21:20. He seems to have enjoyed to a pre-eminent degree the friendship of Christ, and he received many tokens of the Saviour's confidence and love. He was one of the three permitted to witness Christ's glory upon the mount of transfiguration and His agony in Gethsemane, and it was to his care that our Lord confided His mother in those last hours of anguish upon the cross.

The Saviour's affection for the beloved disciple was returned with all the strength of ardent devotion. John clung to Christ as the vine clings to the stately pillar. For his Master's sake he braved the dangers of the judgment hall and lingered about the cross, and at the tidings that Christ had risen, he hastened to the sepulcher, in his zeal out-stripping even the impetuous Peter.

The confiding love and unselfish devotion manifested in the life and character of John present lessons of untold value to the Christian church. John did not naturally possess the loveliness of character that his later experience revealed. By nature he had serious defects. He was not only proud, self-assertive, and ambitious for honor, but impetuous, and resentful under injury. He and his brother were called "sons of thunder." Evil temper, the desire for revenge, the spirit of criticism, were all in the beloved disciple. But beneath all this the divine Teacher discerned the ardent, sincere, loving heart. Jesus rebuked this self-seeking, disappointed his ambitions, tested his faith. But He revealed to him that for which his soul longed—the beauty of holiness, the transforming power of love.

The defects in John's character came strongly to the front on several occasions during his personal association with the Saviour. At one time Christ sent messengers before Him into a village of the Samaritans, requesting the people to prepare refreshments for Him and His disciples. But when the Saviour approached the town, He appeared to be desirous of passing on toward Jerusalem. This aroused the envy of the Samaritans, and instead of inviting Him to tarry with them, they withheld the courtesies which they would have given to a common wayfarer. Jesus never urges His presence upon any, and the Samaritans lost the blessing which would have been granted them had they solicited Him to be their guest.

The disciples knew that it was the purpose of Christ to bless the Samaritans by His presence; and the coldness, jealousy, and disrespect shown to their Master filled them with surprise and indignation. James and John especially were aroused. That He whom they so highly reverenced should be thus treated, seemed to them a wrong too great to be passed over without immediate punishment. In their zeal they said, "Lord, wilt Thou that we command fire to come down from heaven, and consume them, even as Elias did?" referring to the destruction of the Samaritan captains and their companies sent out to take the prophet Elijah. They were surprised to see that Jesus was pained by their words, and still more surprised as His rebuke fell upon their ears: "Ye know not what manner of spirit ye are of. For the Son of man is not come to destroy men's lives, but to save them." Luke 9:54-56.

It is no part of Christ's mission to compel men to receive Him. It is Satan, and men actuated by his spirit, who seek to compel the conscience. Under a pretense of zeal for righteousness, men who are confederated with evil angels sometimes bring suffering upon their fellow men in order to convert them to their ideas of religion; but Christ is ever showing mercy, ever seeking to win by the revealing of His love. He can admit no rival in the soul, nor accept of partial service; but He desires only voluntary service, the willing surrender of the heart under the constraint of love.

On another occasion James and John presented through their mother a petition requesting that they might be permitted to occupy the highest positions of honor in Christ's kingdom. Notwithstanding Christ's repeated instruction concerning the nature of His kingdom, these young disciples still cherished the hope for a Messiah who would take His throne and kingly power in accordance with the desires of men. The mother, coveting with them the place of honor in this kingdom for her sons, asked, "Grant that these my two sons may sit, the one on Thy right hand, and the other on the left, in Thy kingdom."

But the Saviour answered, "Ye know not what ye ask. Are ye able to drink of the cup that I shall drink of, and to be baptized with the baptism that I am baptized with?" They recalled His mysterious words pointing to trial and suffering, yet answered confidently, "We are able." They would count it highest honor to prove their loyalty by sharing all that was to befall their Lord.

"Ye shall drink indeed of My cup, and be baptized with the baptism that I am baptized with," Christ declared— before Him a cross instead of a throne, two malefactors His companions at His right hand and at His left. James and John were to be sharers with their Master in suffering—the one, destined to swift-coming death by the sword; the other, longest of all the disciples to follow his Master in labor and reproach and persecution. "But to sit on My right hand, and on My left," He continued, "is not Mine to give, but it shall be given to them for whom it is prepared of My Father." Matthew 20:21-23.

Jesus understood the motive that prompted the request and thus reproved the pride and ambition of the two disciples: "The princes of the Gentiles exercise dominion over them, and they that are great exercise authority upon them. But it shall not be so among you: but whosoever will be great among you, let him be your minister; and whosoever will be chief among you, let him be your servant: even as the Son of man came not to be ministered unto, but to minister, and to give His life a ransom for many." Matthew 20:25-28.

In the kingdom of God, position is not gained through favoritism. It is not earned, nor is it received through an arbitrary bestowal. It is the result of character. The crown and the throne are the tokens of a condition attained—tokens of self-conquest through the grace of our Lord Jesus Christ.

Long afterward, when John had been brought into sympathy with Christ through the fellowship of His sufferings, the Lord Jesus revealed to him what is the condition of nearness to His kingdom. "To him that overcometh," Christ said, "will I grant to sit with Me in My throne, even as I also overcame, and am set down with My Father in His throne." Revelation 3:21. The one who stands nearest to Christ will be he who has drunk most deeply of His spirit of self-sacrificing love,—love that "vaunteth not itself, is not puffed up, . . . seeketh not her own, is not easily provoked, thinketh no evil" (1 Corinthians 13:4, 5),—love that moves the disciple, as it moved our Lord, to give all, to live and labor and sacrifice even unto death, for the saving of humanity.

At another time during their early evangelistic labors, James and John met one who, while not an acknowledged follower of Christ, was casting out devils in His name. The disciples forbade the man to work and thought they were right in doing this. But when they laid the matter before Christ, He reproved them, saying, "Forbid him not: for there is no man which shall do a miracle in My name, that can lightly speak evil of Me." Mark 9:39. None who showed themselves in any way friendly to Christ were to be repulsed. The disciples must not indulge a narrow, exclusive spirit, but must manifest the same far-reaching sympathy which they had seen in their Master. James and John had thought that in checking this man they had in view the Lord's honor; but they began to see that they were jealous for their own. They acknowledged their error and accepted the reproof.

The lessons of Christ, setting forth meekness and humility and love as essential to growth in grace and a fitness for His work, were of the highest value to John. He treasured every lesson and constantly sought to bring his life into harmony with the divine pattern. John had begun to discern the glory of Christ—not the worldly pomp and power for which he had been taught to hope, but "the glory as of the Only Begotten of the Father, full of grace and truth." John 1:14.

The depth and fervor of John's affection for his Master was not the cause of Christ's love for him, but the effect of that love. John desired to become like Jesus, and under the transforming influence of the love of Christ he did become meek and lowly. Self was hid in Jesus. Above all his companions, John yielded himself to the power of that wondrous life. He says, "The life was manifested, and we have seen it." "And of His fullness have all we received, and grace for grace." 1 John 1:2; John 1:16. John knew the Saviour by an experimental knowledge. His Master's lessons were graven on his soul. When he testified of the Saviour's grace, his simple language was eloquent with the love that pervaded his whole being.

It was John's deep love for Christ which led him always to desire to be close by His side. The Saviour loved all the Twelve, but John's was the most receptive spirit. He was younger than the others, and with more of the child's confiding trust he opened his heart to Jesus. Thus he came more into sympathy with Christ, and through him the Saviour's deepest spiritual teaching was communicated to the people.

Jesus loves those who represent the Father, and John could talk of the Father's love as no other of the disciples could. He revealed to his fellow men that which he felt in his own soul, representing in his character the attributes of God. The glory of the Lord was expressed in his face. The beauty of holiness which had transformed him shone with a Christlike radiance from his countenance. In adoration and love he beheld the Saviour until likeness to Christ and fellowship with Him became his one desire, and in his character was reflected the character of his Master.

"Behold," he said, "what manner of love the Father hath bestowed upon us, that we should be called the sons of God. ... Beloved, now are we the sons of God, and it doth not yet appear what we shall be: but we know that, when He shall appear, we shall be like Him; for we shall see Him as He is." 1 John 3:1, 2.

A Faithful Witness

After the ascension of Christ, John stands forth as a faithful, earnest laborer for the Master. With the other disciples he enjoyed the outpouring of the Spirit on the Day of Pentecost, and with fresh zeal and power he continued to speak to the people the words of life, seeking to lead their thoughts to the Unseen. He was a powerful preacher, fervent, and deeply in earnest. In beautiful language and with a musical voice he told of the words and works of Christ, speaking in a way that impressed the hearts of those who heard him. The simplicity of his words, the sublime power of the truths he uttered, and the fervor that characterized his teachings, gave him access to all classes.

The apostle's life was in harmony with his teachings. The love for Christ which glowed in his heart led him to put forth earnest, untiring labor for his fellow men, especially for his brethren in the Christian church.

Christ had bidden the first disciples love one another as He had loved them. Thus they were to bear testimony to the world that Christ was formed within, the hope of glory. "A new commandment I give unto you," He had said, "That ye love one another; as I have loved you, that ye also love one another." John 13:34. At the time when these words were spoken, the disciples could not understand them; but after they had witnessed the sufferings of Christ, after His crucifixion and resurrection, and ascension to heaven, and after the Holy Spirit had rested on them at Pentecost, they had a clearer conception of the love of God and of the nature of that love which they must have for one another. Then John could say to his fellow disciples:

"Hereby perceive we the love of God, because He laid down His life for us: and we ought to lay down our lives for the brethren."

After the descent of the Holy Spirit, when the disciples went forth to proclaim a living Saviour, their one desire was the salvation of souls. They rejoiced in the sweetness of communion with saints. They were tender, thoughtful, self-denying, willing to make any sacrifice for the truth's sake. In their daily association with one another, they revealed the love that Christ had enjoined upon them. By unselfish words and deeds they strove to kindle this love in other hearts.

Such a love the believers were ever to cherish. They were to go forward in willing obedience to the new commandment. So closely were they to be united with Christ that they would be enabled to fulfill all His requirements. Their lives were to magnify the power of a Saviour who could justify them by His righteousness.

But gradually a change came. The believers began to look for defects in others. Dwelling upon mistakes, giving place to unkind criticism, they lost sight of the Saviour and His love. They became more strict in regard to outward ceremonies, more particular about the theory than the practice of the faith. In their zeal to condemn others, they overlooked their own errors. They lost the brotherly love that Christ had enjoined, and, saddest of all, they were unconscious of their loss. They did not realize that happiness and joy were going out of their lives and that, having shut the love of God out of their hearts, they would soon walk in darkness.

John, realizing that brotherly love was waning in the church, urged upon believers the constant need of this love. His letters to the church are full of this thought. "Beloved, let us love one another," he writes; "for love is of God; and everyone that loveth is born of God, and knoweth God. He that loveth not knoweth not God; for God is love. In this was manifested the love of God toward us, because that God sent His only-begotten Son into the world, that we might live through Him. Herein is love, not that we loved God, but that He loved us, and sent His Son to be the propitiation for our sins. Beloved, if God so loved us, we ought also to love one another."

Of the special sense in which this love should be manifested by believers, the apostle writes: "A new commandment I write unto you, which thing is true in Him and in you: because the darkness is past, and the true light now shineth. He that saith he is in the light, and hateth his brother, is in darkness even until now. He that loveth his brother abideth in the light, and there is none occasion of stumbling in him. But he that hateth his brother is in darkness, and walketh in darkness, and knoweth not whither he goeth, because that darkness hath blinded his eyes." "This is the message that ye heard from the beginning, that we should love one another." "He that loveth not his brother abideth in death. Whosoever hateth his brother is a murderer: and ye know that no murderer hath eternal life abiding in him. Hereby perceive we the love of God, because He laid down His life for us: and we ought to lay down our lives for the brethren."

It is not the opposition of the world that most endangers the church of Christ. It is the evil cherished in the hearts of believers that works their most grievous disaster and most surely retards the progress of God's cause. There is no surer way of weakening spirituality than by cherishing envy, suspicion, faultfinding, and evil surmising. On the other hand, the strongest witness that God has sent His Son into the world is the existence of harmony and union among men of varied dispositions who form His church. This witness it is the privilege of the followers of Christ to bear. But in order to do this, they must place themselves under Christ's command. Their characters must be conformed to His character and their wills to His will.

"A new commandment I give unto you," Christ said, "That ye love one another; as I have loved you, that ye also love one another." John 13:34. What a wonderful statement; but, oh, how poorly practiced! In the church of God today brotherly love is sadly lacking. Many who profess to love the Saviour do not love one another. Unbelievers are watching to see if the faith of professed Christians is exerting a sanctifying influence upon their lives; and they are quick to discern the defects in character, the inconsistencies in action. Let Christians not make it possible for the enemy to point to them and say, Behold how these people, standing under the banner of Christ, hate one another. Christians are all members of one family, all children of the same heavenly Father, with the same blessed hope of immortality. Very close and tender should be the tie that binds them together.

Divine love makes its most touching appeals to the heart when it calls upon us to manifest the same tender compassion that Christ manifested. That man only who has unselfish love for his brother has true love for God. The true Christian will not willingly permit the soul in peril and need to go unwarned, uncared for. He will not hold himself aloof from the erring, leaving them to plunge farther into unhappiness and discouragement or to fall on Satan's battleground.

Those who have never experienced the tender, winning love of Christ cannot lead others to the fountain of life. His love in the heart is a constraining power, which leads men to reveal Him in the conversation, in the tender, pitiful spirit, in the uplifting of the lives of those with whom they associate. Christian workers who succeed in their efforts must know Christ; and in order to know Him, they must know His love. In heaven their fitness as workers is measured by their ability to love as Christ loved and to work as He worked.

"Let us not love in word," the apostle writes, "but in deed and in truth." The completeness of Christian character is attained when the impulse to help and bless others springs constantly from within. It is the atmosphere of this love surrounding the soul of the believer that makes him a savor of life unto life and enables God to bless his work.

Supreme love for God and unselfish love for one another —this is the best gift that our heavenly Father can bestow. This love is not an impulse, but a divine principle, a permanent power. The unconsecrated heart cannot originate or produce it. Only in the heart where Jesus reigns is it found. "We love Him, because He first loved us." In the heart renewed by divine grace, love is the ruling principle of action. It modifies the character, governs the impulses, controls the passions, and ennobles the affections. This love, cherished in the soul, sweetens the life and sheds a refining influence on all around.

John strove to lead the believers to understand the exalted privileges that would come to them through the exercise of the spirit of love. This redeeming power, filling the heart, would control every other motive and raise its possessors above the corrupting influences of the world. And as this love was allowed full sway and became the motive power in the life, their trust and confidence in God and His dealing with them would be complete. They could then come to Him in full confidence of faith, knowing that they would receive from Him everything needful for their present and eternal good. "Herein is our love made perfect," he wrote, "that we may have boldness in the day of judgment: because as He is, so are we in this world. There is no fear in love; but perfect love casteth out fear." "And this is the confidence that we have in Him, that, if we ask anything according to His will, He heareth us: and if we know that He hear us, . . . we know that we have the petitions that we desired of Him."

"And if any man sin, we have an advocate with the Father, Jesus Christ the righteous: and He is the propitiation for our sins: and not for ours only, but also for the sins of the whole world." "If we confess our sins, He is faithful and just to forgive us our sins, and to cleanse us from all unrighteousness." The conditions of obtaining mercy from God are simple and reasonable. The Lord does not require us to do some grievous thing in order to gain forgiveness. We need not make long and wearisome pilgrimages, or perform painful penances, to commend our souls to the God of heaven or to expiate our transgression. He that "confesseth and forsaketh" his sin "shall have mercy." Proverbs 28:13.

In the courts above, Christ is pleading for His church—pleading for those for whom He has paid the redemption price of His blood. Centuries, ages, can never lessen the efficacy of His atoning sacrifice. Neither life nor death, height nor depth, can separate us from the love of God which is in Christ Jesus; not because we hold Him so firmly, but because He holds us so fast. If our salvation depended on our own efforts, we could not be saved; but it depends on the One who is behind all the promises. Our grasp on Him may seem feeble, but His love is that of an elder brother; so long as we maintain our union with Him, no one can pluck us out of His hand.

As the years went by and the number of believers grew, John labored with increasing fidelity and earnestness for his brethren. The times were full of peril for the church. Satanic delusions existed everywhere. By misrepresentation and falsehood the emissaries of Satan sought to arouse opposition against the doctrines of Christ, and in consequence dissensions and heresies were imperiling the church. Some who professed Christ claimed that His love released them from obedience to the law of God. On the other hand, many taught that it was necessary to observe the Jewish customs and ceremonies; that a mere observance of the law, without faith in the blood of Christ, was sufficient for salvation. Some held that Christ was a good man, but denied His divinity. Some who pretended to be true to the cause of God were deceivers, and in practice they denied Christ and His gospel. Living themselves in transgression, they were bringing heresies into the church. Thus many were being led into the mazes of skepticism and delusion.

John was filled with sadness as he saw these poisonous errors creeping into the church. He saw the dangers to which the church was exposed, and he met the emergency with promptness and decision. The epistles of John breathe the spirit of love. It seems as if he wrote with a pen dipped in love. But when he came in contact with those who were breaking the law of God, yet claiming that they were living without sin, he did not hesitate to warn them of their fearful deception.

Writing to a helper in the gospel work, a woman of good repute and wide influence, he said: "Many deceivers are entered into the world, who confess not that Jesus Christ is come in the flesh. This is a deceiver and an antichrist. Look to yourselves, that we lose not those things which we have wrought, but that we receive a full reward. Whosoever transgresseth, and abideth not in the doctrine of Christ, hath not God. He that abideth in the doctrine of Christ, he hath both the Father and the Son. If there come any unto you, and bring not this doctrine, receive him not into your house, neither bid him Godspeed: for he that biddeth him Godspeed is partaker of his evil deeds."

We are authorized to hold in the same estimation as did the beloved disciple those who claim to abide in Christ while living in transgression of God's law. There exist in these last days evils similar to those that threatened the prosperity of the early church; and the teachings of the apostle John on these points should be carefully heeded. "You must have charity," is the cry heard everywhere, especially from those who profess sanctification. But true charity is too pure to cover an unconfessed sin. While we are to love the souls for whom Christ died, we are to make no compromise with evil. We are not to unite with the rebellious and call this charity. God requires His people in this age of the world to stand for the right as unflinchingly as did John in opposition to soul-destroying errors.

The apostle teaches that while we should manifest Christian courtesy we are authorized to deal in plain terms with sin and sinners; that this is not inconsistent with true charity. "Whosoever committeth sin," he writes, "transgresseth also the law: for sin is the transgression of the law. And ye know that He was manifested to take away our sins; and in Him is no sin. Whosoever abideth in Him sinneth not: whosoever sinneth hath not seen Him, neither known Him."

As a witness for Christ, John entered into no controversy, no wearisome contention. He declared what he knew, what he had seen and heard. He had been intimately associated with Christ, had listened to His teachings, had witnessed His mighty miracles. Few could see the beauties of Christ's character as John saw them. For him the darkness had passed away; on him the true light was shining. His testimony in regard to the Saviour's life and death was clear and forcible.

Out of the abundance of a heart overflowing with love for the Saviour he spoke; and no power could stay his words.

"That which was from the beginning," he declared, "which we have heard, which we have seen with our eyes, which we have looked upon, and our hands have handled, of the Word of life; . . . that which we have seen and heard declare we unto you, that ye also may have fellowship with us: and truly our fellowship is with the Father, and with His Son Jesus Christ."

So may every true believer be able, through his own experience, to "set to his seal that God is true." John 3:33. He can bear witness to that which he has seen and heard and felt of the power of Christ.

Transformed by Grace

In the life of the disciple John true sanctification is exemplified. During the years of his close association with Christ, he was often warned and cautioned by the Saviour; and these reproofs he accepted. As the character of the Divine One was manifested to him, John saw his own deficiencies, and was humbled by the revelation. Day by day, in contrast with his own violent spirit, he beheld the tenderness and forbearance of Jesus, and heard His lessons of humility and patience. Day by day his heart was drawn out to Christ, until he lost sight of self in love for his Master. The power and tenderness, the majesty and meekness, the strength and patience, that he saw in the daily life of the Son of God, filled his soul with admiration. He yielded his resentful, ambitious temper to the molding power of Christ, and divine love wrought in him a transformation of character.

In striking contrast to the sanctification worked out in the life of John is the experience of his fellow disciple, Judas. Like his associate, Judas professed to be a disciple of Christ, but he possessed only a form of godliness. He was not insensible to the beauty of the character of Christ; and often, as he listened to the Saviour's words, conviction came to him, but he would not humble his heart or confess his sins. By resisting the divine influence he dishonored the Master whom he professed to love. John warred earnestly against his faults; but Judas violated his conscience and yielded to temptation, fastening upon himself more securely his habits of evil. The practice of the truths that Christ taught was at variance with his desires and purposes, and he could not bring himself to yield his ideas in order to receive wisdom from heaven. Instead of walking in the light, he chose to walk in darkness. Evil desires, covetousness, revengeful passions, dark and sullen thoughts, were cherished until Satan gained full control of him.

John and Judas are representatives of those who profess to be Christ's followers. Both these disciples had the same opportunities to study and follow the divine Pattern. Both were closely associated with Jesus and were privileged to listen to His teaching. Each possessed serious defects of character; and each had access to the divine grace that transforms character. But while one in humility was learning of Jesus, the other revealed that he was not a doer of the word, but a hearer only. One, daily dying to self and overcoming sin, was sanctified through the truth; the other, resisting the transforming power of grace and indulging selfish desires, was brought into bondage to Satan.

Such transformation of character as is seen in the life of John is ever the result of communion with Christ. There may be marked defects in the character of an individual, yet when he becomes a true disciple of Christ, the power of divine grace transforms and sanctifies him. Beholding as in a glass the glory of the Lord, he is changed from glory to glory, until he is like Him whom he adores.

John was a teacher of holiness, and in his letters to the church he laid down unerring rules for the conduct of Christians. "Every man that hath this hope in him," he wrote, "purifieth himself, even as He is pure." "He that saith he abideth in Him ought himself also so to walk, even as He walked." 1 John 3:3; 2:6. He taught that the Christian must be pure in heart and life. Never should he be satisfied with an empty profession. As God is holy in His sphere, so fallen man, through faith in Christ, is to be holy in his sphere.

"This is the will of God," the apostle Paul wrote, "even your sanctification." 1 Thessalonians 4:3. The sanctification of the church is God's object in all His dealings with His people. He has chosen them from eternity, that they might be holy. He gave His Son to die for them, that they might be sanctified through obedience to the truth, divested of all the littleness of self. From them Her requires a personal work, a personal surrender. God can be honored by those who profess to believe in Him, only as they are conformed to His image and controlled by His Spirit. Then, as witnesses for the Saviour, they may make known what divine grace has done for them.

True sanctification comes through the working out of the principle of love. "God is love; and he that dwelleth in love dwelleth in God, and God in him." 1 John 4:16. The life of him in whose heart Christ abides, will reveal practical godliness. The character will be purified, elevated, ennobled, and glorified. Pure doctrine will blend with works of righteousness; heavenly precepts will mingle with holy practices.

Those who would gain the blessing of sanctification must first learn the meaning of self-sacrifice. The cross of Christ is the central pillar on which hangs the "far more exceeding and eternal weight of glory." "If any man will come after Me," Christ says, "let him deny himself, and take up his cross, and follow Me." 2 Corinthians 4:17; Matthew 16:24. It is the fragrance of our love for our fellow men that reveals our love for God. It is patience in service that brings rest to the soul. It is through humble, diligent, faithful toil that the welfare of Israel is promoted. God upholds and strengthens the one who is willing to follow in Christ's way.

Sanctification is not the work of a moment, an hour, a day, but of a lifetime. It is not gained by a happy flight of feeling, but is the result of constantly dying to sin, and constantly living for Christ. Wrongs cannot be righted nor reformations wrought in the character by feeble, intermittent efforts. It is only by long, persevering effort, sore discipline, and stern conflict, that we shall overcome. We know not one day how strong will be our conflict the next. So long as Satan reigns, we shall have self to subdue, besetting sins to overcome; so long as life shall last, there will be no stopping place, no point which we can reach and say, I have fully attained. Sanctification is the result of lifelong obedience.

None of the apostles and prophets ever claimed to be without sin. Men who have lived the nearest to God, men who would sacrifice life itself rather than knowingly commit a wrong act, men whom God has honored with divine light and power, have confessed the sinfulness of their nature. They have put no confidence in the flesh, have claimed no righteousness of their own, but have trusted wholly in the righteousness of Christ.

So will it be with all who behold Christ. The nearer we come to Jesus, and the more clearly we discern the purity of His character, the more clearly shall we see the exceeding sinfulness of sin, and the less shall we feel like exalting ourselves. There will be a continual reaching out of the soul after God, a continual, earnest, heartbreaking confession of sin and humbling of the heart before Him. At every advance step in our Christian experience our repentance will deepen. We shall know that our sufficiency is in Christ alone and shall make the apostle's confession our own: "I know that in me (that is, in my flesh,) dwelleth no good thing." "God forbid that I should glory, save in the cross of our Lord Jesus Christ, by whom the world is crucified unto me, and I unto the world." Romans 7:18; Galatians 6:14.

Let the recording angels write the history of the holy struggles and conflicts of the people of God; let them record their prayers and tears; but let not God be dishonored by the declaration from human lips, "I am sinless; I am holy." Sanctified lips will never give utterance to such presumptuous words.

The apostle Paul had been caught up to the third heaven and had seen and heard things that could not be uttered, and yet his unassuming statement is: "Not as though I had already attained, either were already perfect: but I follow after." Philippians 3:12. Let the angels of heaven write of Paul's victories in fighting the good fight of faith. Let heaven rejoice in his steadfast tread heavenward, and that, keeping the prize in view, he counts every other consideration dross. Angels rejoice to tell his triumphs, but Paul makes no boast of his attainments. The attitude of Paul is the attitude that every follower of Christ should take as he urges his way onward in the strife for the immortal crown.

Let those who feel inclined to make a high profession of holiness look into the mirror of God's law. As they see its far-reaching claims, and understand its work as a discerner of the thoughts and intents of the heart, they will not boast of sinlessness. "If we," says John, not separating himself from his brethren, "say that we have no sin, we deceive ourselves, and the truth is not in us." "If we say that we have not sinned, we make Him a liar, and His word is not in us." "If we confess our sins, He is faithful and just to forgive us our sins, and to cleanse us from all unrighteousness." 1 John 1:8, 10, 9.

There are those who profess holiness, who declare that they are wholly the Lord's, who claim a right to the promises of God, while refusing to render obedience to His commandments. These transgressors of the law claim everything that is promised to the children of God; but this is presumption on their part, for John tells us that true love for God will be revealed in obedience to all His commandments. It is not enough to believe the theory of truth, to make a profession of faith in Christ, to believe that Jesus is no impostor, and that the religion of the Bible is no cunningly devised fable. "He that saith, I know Him, and keepeth not His commandments," John wrote, "is a liar, and the truth is not in him. But whoso keepeth His word, in him verily is the love of God perfected: hereby know we that we are in Him." "He that keepeth His commandments dwelleth in Him, and He in him." 1 John 2:4, 5; 3:24.

John did not teach that salvation was to be earned by obedience; but that obedience was the fruit of faith and love. "Ye know that He was manifested to take away our sins," he said, "and in Him is no sin. Whosoever abideth in Him sinneth not: whosoever sinneth hath not seen Him, neither known Him." 1 John 3:5, 6. If we abide in Christ, if the love of God dwells in the heart, our feelings, our thoughts, our actions, will be in harmony with the will of God. The sanctified heart is in harmony with the precepts of God's law.

There are many who, though striving to obey God's commandments, have little peace or joy. This lack in their experience is the result of a failure to exercise faith. They walk as it were in a salt land, a parched wilderness. They claim little, when they might claim much; for there is no limit to the promises of God. Such ones do not correctly represent the sanctification that comes through obedience to the truth. The Lord would have all His sons and daughters happy, peaceful, and obedient. Through the exercise of faith the believer comes into possession of these blessings. Through faith, every deficiency of character may be supplied, every defilement cleansed, every fault corrected, every excellence developed.

Prayer is heaven's ordained means of success in the conflict with sin and the development of Christian character. The divine influences that come in answer to the prayer of faith will accomplish in the soul of the suppliant all for which he pleads. For the pardon of sin, for the Holy Spirit, for a Christlike temper, for wisdom and strength to do His work, for any gift He has promised, we may ask; and the promise is, "Ye shall receive."

It was in the mount with God that Moses beheld the pattern of that wonderful building that was to be the abiding place of His glory. It is in the mount with God—in the secret place of communion—that we are to contemplate His glorious ideal for humanity. In all ages, through the medium of communion with heaven, God has worked out His purpose for

His children, by unfolding gradually to their minds the doctrines of grace. His manner of imparting truth is illustrated in the words, "His going forth is prepared as the morning." Hosea 6:3. He who places himself where God can enlighten him, advances, as it were, from the partial obscurity of dawn to the full radiance of noonday.

True sanctification means perfect love, perfect obedience, perfect conformity to the will of God. We are to be sanctified to God through obedience to the truth. Our conscience must be purged from dead works to serve the living God. We are not yet perfect; but it is our privilege to cut away from the entanglements of self and sin, and advance to perfection. Great possibilities, high and holy attainments, are placed within the reach of all.

The reason many in this age of the world make no greater advancement in the divine life is because they interpret the will of God to be just what they will to do. While following their own desires, they flatter themselves that they are conforming to God's will. These have no conflicts with self. There are others who for a time are successful in the struggle against their selfish desire for pleasure and ease. They are sincere and earnest, but grow weary of protracted effort, of daily death, of ceaseless turmoil. Indolence seems inviting, death to self repulsive; and they close their drowsy eyes and fall under the power of temptation instead of resisting it.

The directions laid down in the word of God leave no room for compromise with evil. The Son of God was manifested that He might draw all men unto Himself. He came not to lull the world to sleep, but to point out the narrow path in which all must travel who reach at last the gates of the City of God. His children must follow where He has led the way; at whatever sacrifice of ease or selfish indulgence, at whatever cost of labor or suffering, they must maintain a constant battle with self.

The greatest praise that men can bring to God is to become consecrated channels through whom He can work. Time is rapidly passing into eternity. Let us not keep back from God that which is His own. Let us not refuse Him that which, though it cannot be given with merit, cannot be denied without ruin. He asks for a whole heart; give it to Him; it is His, both by creation and by redemption. He asks for your intellect; give it to Him; it is His. He asks for your money; give it to Him; it is His. "Ye are not your own, for ye are bought with a price." 1 Corinthians 6: 19, 20. God requires the homage of a sanctified soul, which has prepared itself, by the exercise of the faith that works by love, to serve Him. He holds up before us the highest ideal, even perfection. He asks us to be absolutely and completely for Him in this world as He is for us in the presence of God.

"This is the will of God" concerning you, "even your sanctification." 1 Thessalonians 4:3. Is it your will also? Your sins may be as mountains before you; but if you humble your heart and confess your sins, trusting in the merits of a crucified and risen Saviour, He will forgive and will cleanse you from all unrighteousness. God demands of you entire conformity to His law. This law is the echo of His voice saying to you, Holier, yes, holier still. Desire the fullness of the grace of Christ. Let your heart be filled with an intense longing for His righteousness, the work of which God's word declares is peace, and its effect quietness and assurance forever.

As your soul yearns after God, you will find more and still more of the unsearchable riches of His grace. As you contemplate these riches you will come into possession of them and will reveal the merits of the Saviour's sacrifice, the protection of His righteousness, the fullness of His wisdom, and His power to present you before the Father "without spot, and blameless." 2 Peter 3:14.

Patmos

More than half a century had passed since the organization of the Christian church. During that time the gospel message had been constantly opposed. Its enemies had never relaxed their efforts, and had at last succeeded in enlisting the power of the Roman emperor against the Christians.

In the terrible persecution that followed, the apostle John did much to confirm and strengthen the faith of the believers. He bore a testimony which his adversaries could not controvert and which helped his brethren to meet with courage and loyalty the trials that came upon them. When the faith of the Christians would seem to waver under the fierce opposition they were forced to meet, the old, tried servant of Jesus would repeat with power and eloquence the story of the crucified and risen Saviour. He steadfastly maintained his faith, and from his lips came ever the same glad message: "That which was from the beginning, which we have heard, which we have seen with our eyes, which we have looked upon, and our hands have handled, of the Word of life; . . . that which we have seen and heard declare we unto you.: 1 John 1:1-3.

John lived to be very old. He witnessed the destruction of Jerusalem and the ruin of the stately temple. The last survivor of the disciples who had been intimately connected with the Saviour, his message had great influence in setting forth the fact that Jesus was the Messiah, the Redeemer of the world. No one could doubt his sincerity, and through his teachings many were led to turn from unbelief.

The rulers of the Jews were filled with bitter hatred against John for his unwavering fidelity to the cause of Christ. They declared that their efforts against the Christians would avail nothing so long as John's testimony kept ringing in the ears of the people. In order that the miracles and teachings of Jesus might be forgotten, the voice of the bold witness must be silenced.

John was accordingly summoned to Rome to be tried for his faith. Here before the authorities the apostle's doctrines were misstated. False witnesses accused him of teaching seditious heresies. By these accusations his enemies hoped to bring about the disciple's death.

John answered for himself in a clear and convincing

manner, and with such simplicity and candor that his words had a powerful effect. His hearers were astonished at his wisdom and eloquence. But the more convincing his testimony, the deeper was the hatred of his opposers. The emperor Domitian was filled with rage. He could neither dispute the reasoning of Christ's faithful advocate, nor match the power that attended his utterance of truth; yet he determined that he would silence his voice.

John was cast into a caldron of boiling oil; but the Lord preserved the life of His faithful servant, even as He preserved the three Hebrews in the fiery furnace. As the words were spoken, Thus perish all who believe in that deceiver, Jesus Christ of Nazareth, John declared, My Master patiently submitted to all that Satan and his angels could devise to humiliate and torture Him. He gave His life to save the world. I am honored in being permitted to suffer for His sake. I am a weak, sinful man. Christ was holy, harmless, undefiled. He did no sin, neither was guile found in His mouth.

These words had their influence, and John was removed from the caldron by the very men who had cast him in.

Again the hand of persecution fell heavily upon the apostle. By the emperor's decree John was banished to the Isle of Patmos, condemned "for the word of God, and for the testimony of Jesus Christ." Revelation 1:9. Here, his enemies thought, his influence would no longer be felt, and he must finally die of hardship and distress.

Patmos, a barren, rocky island in the Aegean Sea, had been chosen by the Roman government as a place of banishment for criminals; but to the servant of God this gloomy abode became the gate of heaven. Here, shut away from the busy scenes of life, and from the active labors of former years, he had the companionship of God and Christ and the heavenly angels, and from them he received instruction for the church for all future time. The events that would take place in the closing scenes of this earth's history were outlined before him; and there he wrote out the visions he received from God. When his voice could no longer testify to the One whom he loved and served, the messages given him on that barren coast were to go forth as a lamp that burneth, declaring the sure purpose of the Lord concerning every nation on the earth.

Among the cliffs and rocks of Patmos, John held communion with his Maker. He reviewed his past life, and at thought of the blessings he had received, peace filled his heart. He had lived the life of a Christian, and he could say in faith, "We know that we have passed from death unto life." 1 John 3:14. Not so the emperor who had banished him. He could look back only on fields of warfare and carnage, on desolated homes, on weeping widows and orphans, the fruit of his ambitious desire for pre-eminence.

In his isolated home John was able to study more closely than ever before the manifestations of divine power as recorded in the book of nature and in the pages of inspiration. To him it was a delight to meditate on the work of creation and to adore the divine Architect. In former years his eyes had been greeted by the sight of forest-covered hills, green valleys, and fruitful plains; and in the beauties of nature it had ever been his delight to trace the wisdom and skill of the Creator. He was now surrounded by scenes that to many would appear gloomy and uninteresting; but to John it was otherwise. While his surroundings might be desolate and barren, the blue heavens that bent above him were as bright and beautiful as the skies above his loved Jerusalem. In the wild, rugged rocks, in the mysteries of the deep, in the glories of the firmament, he read important lessons. All bore the message of God's power and glory.

All around him the apostle beheld witnesses to the Flood that had deluged the earth because the inhabitants ventured to transgress the law of God. The rocks thrown up from the great deep and from the earth by the breaking forth of the waters, brought vividly to his mind the terrors of that awful outpouring of God's wrath. In the voice of many waters—deep calling unto deep—the prophet heard the voice of the Creator. The sea, lashed to fury by the merciless winds, represented to him the wrath of an offended God. The mighty waves, in their terrible commotion, restrained within limits appointed by an invisible hand, spoke of the control of an infinite Power. And in contrast he realized the weakness and folly of mortals, who, though but worms of the dust, glory in their supposed wisdom and strength, and set their hearts against the Ruler of the universe, as if God were altogether such a one as themselves. By the rocks he was reminded of Christ, the Rock of his strength, in whose shelter he could hide without fear. From the exiled apostle on rocky Patmos there went up the most ardent longing of soul after God, the most fervent prayers.

The history of John affords a striking illustration of the way in which God can use aged workers. When John was exiled to the Isle of Patmos, there were many who thought him to be past service, an old and broken reed, ready to fall at any time. But the Lord saw fit to use him still. Though banished from the scenes of his former labor, he did not cease to bear witness to the truth. Even in Patmos he made friends and converts. His was a message of joy, proclaiming a risen Saviour who on high was interceding for His people until He should return to take them to Himself. And it was after John had grown old in the service of his Lord that he received more communications from heaven than he had received during all the former years of his life.

The most tender regard should be cherished for those whose life interest has been bound up with the work of God. These aged workers have stood faithful amid storm and trial. They may have infirmities, but they still possess talents that qualify them to stand in their place in God's cause. Though worn, and unable to bear the heavier burdens that younger men can and should carry, the counsel they can give is of the highest value.

They may have made mistakes, but from their failures they have learned to avoid errors and dangers, and are they not therefore competent to give wise counsel? They have borne test and trial, and though they have lost some of their vigor, the Lord does not lay them aside. He gives them special grace and wisdom.

Those who have served their Master when the work went hard, who endured poverty and remained faithful when there were few to stand for truth, are to be honored and respected. The Lord desires the younger laborers to gain wisdom, strength, and maturity by association with these faithful men. Let the younger men realize that in having such workers among them they are highly favored. Let them give them an honored place in their councils.

As those who have spent their lives in the service of Christ draw near to the close of their earthly ministry, they will be impressed by the Holy Spirit to recount the experiences they have had in connection with the work of God. The record of His wonderful dealings with His people, of His great goodness in delivering them from trial, should be repeated to those newly come to the faith. God desires the old and tried laborers to stand in their place, doing their part to save men and women from being swept downward by the mighty current of evil, He desires them to keep the armor on till He bids them lay it down.

In the experience of the apostle John under persecution, there is a lesson of wonderful strength and comfort for the Christian. God does not prevent the plottings of wicked men, but He causes their devices to work for good to those who in trial and conflict maintain their faith and loyalty. Often the gospel laborer carries on his work amid storms of persecution, bitter opposition, and unjust reproach. At such times let him remember that the experience to be gained in the furnace of trial and affliction is worth all the pain it costs. Thus God brings His children near to Him, that He may show them their weakness and His strength. He teaches them to lean on Him. Thus He prepares them to meet emergencies, to fill positions of trust, and to accomplish the great purpose for which their powers were given them.

In all ages God's appointed witnesses have exposed themselves to reproach and persecution for the truth's sake. Joseph was maligned and persecuted because he preserved his virtue and integrity. David, the chosen messenger of God, was hunted like a beast of prey by his enemies. Daniel was cast into a den of lions because he was true to his allegiance to heaven. Job was deprived of his worldly possessions, and so afflicted in body that he was abhorred by his relatives, and friends; yet he maintained his integrity. Jeremiah could not be deterred from speaking the words that God had given him to speak; and his testimony so enraged the king and princes that he was cast into a loathsome pit. Stephen was stoned because he preached Christ and Him crucified. Paul was imprisoned, beaten with rods, stoned, and finally put to death because he was a faithful messenger for God to the Gentiles. And John was banished to the Isle of Patmos "for the word of God, and for the testimony of Jesus Christ."

These examples of human steadfastness bear witness to the faithfulness of God's promises—of His abiding presence and sustaining grace. They testify to the power of faith to withstand the powers of the world. It is the work of faith to rest in God in the darkest hour, to feel, however sorely tried and tempest-tossed, that our Father is at the helm. The eye of faith alone can look beyond the things of time to estimate aright the worth of the eternal riches.

Jesus does not present to His followers the hope of attaining earthly glory and riches, of living a life free from trial. Instead He calls upon them to follow Him in the path of self-denial and reproach. He who came to redeem the world was opposed by the united forces of evil. In an unpitying confederacy, evil men and evil angels arrayed themselves against the Prince of Peace. His every word and act revealed divine compassion, and His unlikeness to the world provoked the bitterest hostility.

So it will be with all who will live godly in Christ Jesus. Persecution and reproach await all who are imbued with the Spirit of Christ. The character of the persecution changes with the times, but the principle—the spirit that underlies it—is the same that has slain the chosen of the Lord ever since the days of Abel.

In all ages Satan has persecuted the people of God. He has tortured them and put them to death, but in dying they became conquerors. They bore witness to the power of One mightier than Satan. Wicked men may torture and kill the body, but they cannot touch the life that is hid with Christ in God. They can incarcerate men and women in prison walls, but they cannot bind the spirit.

Through trial and persecution the glory—the character— of God is revealed in His chosen ones. The believers in Christ, hated and persecuted by the world, are educated and disciplined in the school of Christ. On earth they walk in narrow paths; they are purified in the furnace of affliction. They follow Christ through sore conflicts; they endure self-denial and experience bitter disappointments; but thus they learn the guilt and woe of sin, and they look upon it with abhorrence. Being partakers of Christ's sufferings, they can look beyond the gloom to the glory, saying, "I reckon that the sufferings of this present time are not worthy to be compared with the glory which shall be revealed in us." Romans 8:18.

The Revelation

In the days of the apostles the Christian believers were filled with earnestness and enthusiasm. So untiringly did they labor for their Master that in a comparatively short time, notwithstanding fierce opposition, the gospel of the kingdom was sounded to all the inhabited parts of the earth. The zeal manifested at this time by the followers of Jesus has been recorded by the pen of inspiration for the encouragement of believers in every age. Of the church at Ephesus, which the Lord Jesus used as a symbol of the entire Christian church in the apostolic age, the faithful and true Witness declared:

"I know thy works, and thy labor, and thy patience, and how thou canst not bear them which are evil: and thou hast tried them which say they are apostles, and are not, and hast found them liars: and hast borne, and hast patience, and for My name's sake hast labored, and hast not fainted." Revelation 2:2, 3.

At the first the experience of the church at Ephesus was marked with childlike simplicity and fervor. The believers sought earnestly to obey every word of God, and their lives revealed an earnest, sincere love for Christ. They rejoiced to do the will of God because the Saviour was in their hearts as an abiding presence. Filled with love for their Redeemer, their highest aim was to win souls to Him. They did not think of hoarding the precious treasure of the grace of Christ. They felt the importance of their calling; and, weighted with the message, "On earth peace, good will toward men," they burned with desire to carry the glad tidings of salvation to earth's remotest bounds. And the world took knowledge of them that they had been with Jesus. Sinful men, repentant, pardoned, cleansed, and sanctified, were brought into partnership with God through His Son.

The members of the church were united in sentiment and action. Love for Christ was the golden chain that bound them together. They followed on to know the Lord more and still more perfectly, and in their lives were revealed the joy and peace of Christ. They visited the fatherless and widows in their affliction, and kept themselves unspotted from the world, realizing that a failure to do this would be a contradiction of their profession and a denial of their Redeemer.

In every city the work was carried forward. Souls were converted, who in their turn felt that they must tell of the inestimable treasure they had received. They could not rest till the light which had illumined their minds was shining upon others. Multitudes of unbelievers were made acquainted with the reasons of the Christian's hope. Warm, inspired personal appeals were made to the erring, to the outcast, and to those who, while professing to know the truth, were lovers of pleasure more than lovers of God.

But after a time the zeal of the believers began to wane, and their love for God and for one another grew less. Coldness crept into the church. Some forgot the wonderful manner in which they had received the truth. One by one the old standard-bearers fell at their post. Some of the younger workers, who might have shared the burdens of these pioneers, and thus have been prepared for wise leadership, had become weary of oft-repeated truths. In their desire for something novel and startling they attempted to introduce new phases of doctrine, more pleasing to many minds, but not in harmony with the fundamental principles of the gospel. In their self-confidence and spiritual blindness they failed to discern that these sophistries would cause many to question the experiences of the past, and would thus lead to confusion and unbelief.

As these false doctrines were urged, differences sprang up, and the eyes of many were turned from beholding Jesus as the Author and Finisher of their faith. The discussion of unimportant points of doctrine, and the contemplation of pleasing fables of man's invention, occupied time that should

have been spent in proclaiming the gospel. The masses that might have been convicted and converted by a faithful presentation of the truth were left unwarned. Piety was rapidly waning, and Satan seemed about to gain the ascendancy over those who claimed to be followers of Christ.

It was at this critical time in the history of the church that John was sentenced to banishment. Never had his voice been needed by the church as now. Nearly all his former associates in the ministry had suffered martyrdom. The remnant of believers was facing fierce opposition. To all outward appearance the day was not far distant when the enemies of the church of Christ would triumph.

But the Lord's hand was moving unseen in the darkness. In the providence of God, John was placed where Christ could give him a wonderful revelation of Himself and of divine truth for the enlightenment of the churches.

In exiling John, the enemies of truth had hoped to silence forever the voice of God's faithful witness; but on Patmos the disciple received a message, the influence of which was to continue to strengthen the church till the end of time. Though not released from the responsibility of their wrong act, those who banished John became instruments in the hands of God to carry out Heaven's purpose; and the very effort to extinguish the light placed the truth in bold relief.

It was on the Sabbath that the Lord of glory appeared to the exiled apostle. The Sabbath was as sacredly observed by John on Patmos as when he was preaching to the people in the towns and cities of Judea. He claimed as his own the precious promises that had been given regarding that day. "I was in the Spirit on the Lord's day," John writes, "and heard behind me a great voice, as of a trumpet, saying, I am Alpha and Omega, the first and the last. . . . And I turned to see the voice that spake with me. And being turned, I saw seven golden candlesticks; and in the midst of the seven candlesticks One like unto the Son of man." Revelation 1:10-13.

Richly favored was this beloved disciple. He had seen his Master in Gethsemane, His face marked with the blood drops of agony, His "visage . . . marred more than any man, and His form more than the sons of men." Isaiah 52:14. He had seen Him in the hands of the Roman soldiers, clothed with an old purple robe and crowned with thorns. He had seen Him hanging on the cross of Calvary, the object of cruel mockery and abuse. Now John is once more permitted to behold his Lord. But how changed is His appearance! He is no longer a Man of Sorrows, despised and humiliated by men. He is clothed in a garment of heavenly brightness. "His head and His hairs" are "white like wool, as white as snow; and His eyes . . . as a flame of fire; and His feet like unto fine brass, as if they burned in a furnace." Revelation 1:14, 15, 17. His voice is like the music of many waters. His countenance shines as the sun. In His hand are seven stars, and out of His mouth issues a sharp two-edged sword, an emblem of the power of His word. Patmos is made resplendent with the glory of the risen Lord.

"And when I saw Him," John writes, "I fell at His feet as

dead. And He laid His right hand upon me, saying unto me, Fear not." Verse 17.

John was strengthened to live in the presence of his glorified Lord. Then before his wondering vision were opened the glories of heaven. He was permitted to see the throne of God and, looking beyond the conflicts of earth, to behold the white-robed throng of the redeemed. He heard the music of the heavenly angels and the triumphant songs of those who had overcome by the blood of the Lamb and the word of their testimony. In the revelation given to him there was unfolded scene after scene of thrilling interest in the experience of the people of God, and the history of the church foretold to the very close of time. In figures and symbols, subjects of vast importance were presented to John, which he was to record, that the people of God living in his age and in future ages might have an intelligent understanding of the perils and conflicts before them.

This revelation was given for the guidance and comfort of the church throughout the Christian dispensation. Yet religious teachers have declared that it is a sealed book and its secrets cannot be explained. Therefore many have turned from the prophetic record, refusing to devote time and study to its mysteries. But God does not wish His people to regard the book thus. It is "the revelation of Jesus Christ, which God gave unto Him, to show unto His servants things which must shortly come to pass." "Blessed is he that readeth," the Lord declares, "and they that hear the words of this prophecy, and keep those things which are written therein: for the time is at hand." Verses 1, 3. "I testify unto every man that heareth the words of the prophecy of this book, If any man shall add unto these things, God shall add unto him the plagues that are written in this book: and if any man shall take away from the words of the book of this prophecy, God shall take away his part out of the book of life, and out of the Holy City, and from the things which are written in this book. He which testifieth these things saith, Surely I come quickly." Revelation 22:18-20.

In the Revelation are portrayed the deep things of God. The very name given to its inspired pages, "the Revelation," contradicts the statement that this is a sealed book. A revelation is something revealed. The Lord Himself revealed to His servant the mysteries contained in this book, and He designs that they shall be open to the study of all. Its truths are addressed to those living in the last days of this earth's history, as well as to those living in the days of John. Some of the scenes depicted in this prophecy are in the past, some are now taking place; some bring to view the close of the great conflict between the powers of darkness and the Prince of heaven, and some reveal the triumphs and joys of the redeemed in the earth made new.

Let none think, because they cannot explain the meaning of every symbol in the Revelation, that it is useless for them to search this book in an effort to know the meaning of the truth it contains. The One who revealed these mysteries to John will give to the diligent searcher for truth a foretaste of heavenly things. Those whose hearts are open to the reception of truth will be enabled to understand its teachings, and will be granted the blessing promised to those who "hear the words of this prophecy, and keep those things which are written therein."

In the Revelation all the books of the Bible meet and end. Here is the complement of the book of Daniel. One is a prophecy; the other a revelation. The book that was sealed is not the Revelation, but that portion of the prophecy of Daniel relating to the last days. The angel commanded, "But thou, O Daniel, shut up the words, and seal the book, even to the time of the end." Daniel 12:4.

It was Christ who bade the apostle record that which was to be opened before him. "What thou seest, write in a book," He commanded, "and send it unto the seven churches which are in Asia; unto Ephesus, and unto Smyrna, and unto Pergamos, and unto Thyatira, and unto Sardis, and unto Philadelphia, and unto Laodicea." "I am He that liveth, and was dead; and, behold, I am alive for evermore. . . . Write the things which thou hast seen, and the things which are, and the things which shall be hereafter; the mystery of the seven stars which thou sawest in My right hand, and the seven golden candlesticks. The seven stars are the angels of the seven churches: and the seven candlesticks which thou sawest are the seven churches." Revelation 1:11, 18-20.

The names of the seven churches are symbolic of the church in different periods of the Christian Era. The number 7 indicates completeness, and is symbolic of the fact that the messages extend to the end of time, while the symbols used reveal the condition of the church at different periods in the history of the word.

Christ is spoken of as walking in the midst of the golden candlesticks. Thus is symbolized His relation to the churches. He is in constant communication with His people. He knows their true state. He observes their order, their piety, their devotion. Although He is high priest and mediator in the sanctuary above, yet He is represented as walking up and down in the midst of His churches on the earth. With untiring wakefulness and unremitting vigilance, He watches to see whether the light of any of His sentinels is burning dim or going out. If the candlesticks were left to mere human care, the flickering flame would languish and die; but He is the true watchman in the Lord's house, the true warden of the temple courts. His continued care and sustaining grace are the source of life and light.

Christ is represented as holding the seven stars in His right hand. This assures us that no church faithful to its trust need fear coming to nought, for not a star that has the protection of Omnipotence can be plucked out of the hand of Christ.

"These things saith He that holdeth the seven stars in His right hand." Revelation 2:1. These words are spoken to the teachers in the church—those entrusted by God with weighty responsibilities. The sweet influences that are to be abundant in the church are bound up with God's ministers, who are to reveal the love of Christ. The stars of heaven are under His control. He fills them with light. He guides and directs their movements. If He did not do this, they would become fallen stars. So with His ministers. They are but instruments in His hands, and all the good they accomplish is done through His power. Through them His light is to shine forth. The Saviour is to be their efficiency. If they will look to Him as He looked to the Father they will be enabled to do His work. As they make God their dependence, He will give them His brightness to reflect to the world.

Early in the history of the church the mystery of iniquity foretold by the apostle Paul began its baleful work; and as the false teachers concerning whom Peter had warned the believers, urged their heresies, many were ensnared by false doctrines. Some faltered under trial and were tempted to give up the faith. At the time when John was given this revelation, many had lost their first love of gospel truth. But in His mercy God did not leave the church to continue in a backslidden state. In a message of infinite tenderness He revealed His love for them and His desire that they should make sure work for eternity. "Remember," He pleaded, "from whence thou art fallen, and repent, and do the first works." Verse 5.

The church was defective and in need of stern reproof and chastisement, and John was inspired to record messages of warning and reproof and entreaty to those who, losing sight of the fundamental principles of the gospel, should imperil their hope of salvation. But always the words of rebuke that God finds it necessary to send are spoken in tender love and with the promise of peace to every penitent believer. "Behold, I stand at the door, and knock," the Lord declares; "if any man hear My voice, and open the door, I will come in to him, and will sup with him, and he with Me." Revelation 3:20.

And for those who in the midst of conflict should maintain their faith in God, the prophet was given the words of commendation and promise: "I know thy works: behold, I have set before thee an open door, and no man can shut it: for thou hast a little strength, and hast kept My word, and hast not denied My name." "Because thou hast kept the word of My patience, I also will keep thee from the hour of temptation, which shall come upon all the world, to try them that dwell upon the earth." The believers were admonished: "Be watchful, and strengthen the things which remain, that are ready to die." "Behold, I come quickly: hold that fast which thou hast, that no man take thy crown." Verses 8, 10, 2, 11.

It was through one who declared himself to be a "brother, and companion in tribulation" (Revelation 1:9), that Christ revealed to His church the things that they must suffer for His sake. Looking down through long centuries of darkness and superstition, the aged exile saw multitudes suffering martyrdom because of their love for the truth. But he saw also that He who sustained His early witnesses would not forsake His faithful followers during the centuries of persecution that they must pass through before the close of time. "Fear none of those things which thou shalt suffer," the Lord declared; "behold, the devil shall cast some of you into prison, that ye may be tried; and ye shall have tribulation: . . . be thou faithful unto death, and I will give thee a crown of life." Revelation 2:10.

And to all the faithful ones who were striving against evil, John heard the promises made: "To him that overcometh will I give to eat of the tree of life, which is in the midst of the Paradise of God." "He that overcometh, the same shall be clothed in white raiment; and I will not blot out his name out of the book of life, but I will confess his name before My Father, and before His angels." "To him that overcometh will I grant to sit with Me in My throne, even as I also overcame, and am set down with My Father in His throne." Verse 7; 3:5, 21.

John saw the mercy, the tenderness, and the love of God blending with His holiness, justice, and power. He saw sinners finding a Father in Him of whom their sins had made them afraid. And looking beyond the culmination of the great conflict, he beheld upon Zion "them that had gotten the victory . . . stand on the sea of glass, having the harps of God," and singing "the song of Moses" and the Lamb. Revelation 15:2, 3.

The Saviour is presented before John under the symbols of "the Lion of the tribe of Judah" and of "a Lamb as it had been slain." Revelation 5:5, 6. These symbols represent the union of omnipotent power and self-sacrificing love. The Lion of Judah, so terrible to the rejectors of His grace, will be the Lamb of God to the obedient and faithful. The pillar of fire that speaks terror and wrath to the transgressor of God's law is a token of light and mercy and deliverance to those who have kept His commandments. The arm strong to smite the rebellious will be strong to deliver the loyal. Everyone who is faithful will be saved. "He shall send His angels with a great sound of a trumpet, and they shall gather together His elect from the four winds, from one end of heaven to the other." Matthew 24:31.

In comparison with the millions of the world, God's people will be, as they have ever been, a little flock; but if they stand for the truth as revealed in His word, God will be their refuge. They stand under the broad shield of Omnipotence. God is always a majority. When the sound of the last trump shall penetrate the prison house of the dead, and the righteous shall come forth with triumph, exclaiming, "O death, where is thy sting? O grave, where is thy victory?" (1 Corinthians 15:55)—standing then with God, with Christ, with the angels, and with the loyal and true of all ages, the children of God will be far in the majority.

Christ's true disciples follow Him through sore conflicts, enduring self-denial and experiencing bitter disappointment; but this teaches them the guilt and woe of sin, and they are led to look upon it with abhorrence. Partakers of Christ's sufferings, they are destined to be partakers of His glory. In holy vision the prophet saw the ultimate triumph of God's remnant church. He writes:

"I saw as it were a sea of glass mingled with fire: and them that had gotten the victory . . . stand on the sea of glass, having the harps of God. And they sing the song of Moses the servant of God, and the song of the Lamb, saying, Great and marvelous are Thy works, Lord God Almighty; just and true are Thy ways, Thou King of saints." Revelation 15:2, 3.

"And I looked, and, lo, a Lamb stood on the Mount Sion, and with Him a hundred forty and four thousand, having His Father's name written in their foreheads." Revelation 14:1. In this world their minds were consecrated to God; they served Him with the intellect and with the heart; and now He can place His name "in their foreheads." "And they shall reign for ever and ever." Revelation 22:5. They do not go in and out as those who beg a place. They are of that number to whom Christ says, "Come, ye blessed of My Father, inherit the kingdom prepared for you from the foundation of the world." He welcomes them as His children, saying, "Enter thou into the joy of thy Lord." Matthew 25:34, 21.

"These are they which follow the Lamb withersoever He goeth. These were redeemed from among men, being the first fruits unto God and to the Lamb." Revelation 14:4. The vision of the prophet pictures them as standing on Mount Zion, girt for holy service, clothed in white linen, which is the righteousness of the saints. But all who follow the Lamb in heaven must first have followed Him on earth, not fretfully or capriciously, but in trustful, loving, willing obedience, as the flock follows the shepherd.

"I heard the voice of harpers harping with their harps: and they sung as it were a new song before the throne: ... and no man could learn that song but the hundred and forty and four thousand, which were redeemed from the earth.... In their mouth was found no guile: for they are without fault before the throne of God." Verses 2-5.

"And I John saw the Holy City, New Jerusalem, coming down from God out of heaven, prepared as a bride adorned for her husband." "Her light was like unto a stone most precious, even like a jasper stone, clear as crystal; and had a wall great and high, and had twelve gates, and at the gates twelve angels, and names written thereon, which are the names of the twelve tribes of the children of Israel." "The twelve gates were twelve pearls; every several gate was of one pearl: and the street of the city was pure gold, as it were transparent glass. And I saw no temple therein: for the Lord God Almighty and the Lamb are the temple of it." Revelation 21:2, 11, 12, 21, 22.

"And there shall be no more curse: but the throne of God and of the Lamb shall be in it; and His servants shall serve Him: and they shall see His face; and His name shall be in their foreheads. And there shall be no night there; and they need no candle, neither light of the sun; for the Lord God giveth them light." Revelation 22:3-5.

"He showed me a pure river of water of life, clear as crystal, proceeding out of the throne of God and of the Lamb. In the midst of the street of it, and on either side of the river, was there the tree of life, which bare twelve manner of fruits, and yielded her fruit every month: and the leaves of the tree were for the healing of the nations." "Blessed are they that do His commandments, that they may have right to the tree of life, and may enter in through the gates into the city." Verses 1, 2, 14.

"And I heard a great voice out of heaven saying,
"Behold, the tabernacle of God is with men,
And He will dwell with them,
And they shall be His people,
And God Himself shall be with them,
And be their God." Revelation 21:3.

The Church Triumphant

More than eighteen centuries have passed since the apostles rested from their labors, but the history of their toils and sacrifices for Christ's sake is still among the most precious treasures of the church. This history, written under the direction of the Holy Spirit, was recorded in order that by it the followers of Christ in every age might be impelled to greater zeal and earnestness in the cause of the Saviour.

The commission that Christ gave to the disciples, they fulfilled. As these messengers of the cross went forth to proclaim the gospel, there was such a revelation of the glory of God as had never before been witnessed by mortal man. By the co-operation of the divine Spirit, the apostles did a work that shook the world. To every nation was the gospel carried in a single generation.

Glorious were the results that attended the ministry of the chosen apostles of Christ. At the beginning of their ministry some of them were unlearned men, but their consecration to the cause of their Master was unreserved, and under His instruction they gained a preparation for the great work committed to them. Grace and truth reigned in their hearts, inspiring their motives and controlling their actions. Their lives were hid with Christ in God, and self was lost sight of, submerged in the depths of infinite love.

The disciples were men who knew how to speak and pray sincerely, men who could take hold of the might of the Strength of Israel. How closely they stood by the side of God, and bound their personal honor to His throne! Jehovah was their God. His honor was their honor. His truth was their truth. Any attack made upon the gospel was as if cutting deep into their souls, and with every power of their being they battled for the cause of Christ. They could hold forth the word of life because they had received the heavenly anointing. They expected much, and therefore they attempted much. Christ had revealed Himself to them, and to Him they looked for guidance. Their understanding of truth and their power to withstand opposition were proportionate to their conformity to God's will. Jesus Christ, the wisdom and power of God, was the theme of every discourse. His name—the only name given under heaven whereby men can be saved—was by them exalted. As they proclaimed the completeness of Christ, the risen Saviour, their words moved hearts, and men and women were won to the gospel. Multitudes who had reviled the Saviour's name and despised His power now confessed themselves disciples of the Crucified.

Not in their own power did the apostles accomplish their mission, but in the power of the living God. Their work was not easy. The opening labors of the Christian church were attended by hardship and bitter grief. In their work the disciples constantly encountered privation, calumny, and persecution; but they counted not their lives dear unto themselves and rejoiced that they were called to suffer for Christ. Irresolution, indecision, weakness of purpose, found no place in their efforts. They were willing to spend and be spent. The consciousness of the responsibility resting on them purified and enriched their experience, and the grace of heaven was revealed in the conquests they achieved for Christ. With the might of omnipotence God worked through them to make the gospel triumphant.

Upon the foundation that Christ Himself had laid, the apostles built the church of God. In the Scriptures the figure of the erection of a temple is frequently used to illustrate the building of the church. Zechariah refers to Christ as the Branch that should build the temple of the Lord. He speaks of the Gentiles as helping in the work: "They that are far off shall come and build in the temple of the Lord;" and Isaiah declares, "The sons of strangers shall build up thy walls." Zechariah 6:12, 15; Isaiah 60:10.

Writing of the building of this temple, Peter says, "To whom coming, as unto a living stone, disallowed indeed of men, but chosen of God, and precious, ye also, as lively stones, are built up a spiritual house, an holy priesthood, to offer up spiritual sacrifices, acceptable to God by Jesus Christ." 1 Peter 2:4, 5.

In the quarry of the Jewish and the Gentile world the apostles labored, bringing out stones to lay upon the foundation. In his letter to the believers at Ephesus, Paul said, "Now therefore ye are no more strangers and foreigners, but fellow citizens with the saints, and of the household of God; and are built upon the foundation of the apostles and prophets, Jesus Christ Himself being the Chief Cornerstone; in whom all the building fitly framed together groweth unto an holy temple in the Lord: in whom ye also are builded together for an habitation of God through the Spirit." Ephesians 2:19-22.

And to the Corinthians he wrote: "According to the grace of God which is given unto me, as a wise master builder, I have laid the foundation, and another buildeth thereon. But let every man take heed how he buildeth thereupon. For other foundation can no man lay than that is laid, which is Jesus Christ. Now if any man build upon this foundation gold, silver, precious stones, wood, hay, stubble; every man's work shall be made manifest: for the day shall declare it, because it shall be revealed by fire; and the fire shall try every man's work of what sort it is." 1 Corinthians 3:10-13.

The apostles built upon a sure foundation, even the Rock of Ages. To this foundation they brought the stones that they quarried from the world. Not without hindrance did the builders labor. Their work was made exceedingly difficult by the opposition of the enemies of Christ. They had to contend against the bigotry, prejudice, and hatred of those who were building upon a false foundation. Many who wrought as builders of the church could be likened to the builders of the wall in Nehemiah's day, of whom it is written: "They which builded on the wall, and they that bare burdens, with those that laded, everyone with one of his hands wrought in the work, and with the other hand held a weapon." Nehemiah 4:17.

Kings and governors, priests and rulers, sought to destroy the temple of God. But in the face of imprisonment, torture, and death, faithful men carried the work forward; and the structure grew, beautiful and symmetrical. At times the workmen were almost blinded by the mists of superstition that settled around them. At times they were almost overpowered by the violence of their opponents. But with unfaltering faith and unfailing courage they pressed on with the work.

One after another the foremost of the builders fell by the hand of the enemy. Stephen was stoned; James was slain by the sword; Paul was beheaded; Peter was crucified; John was exiled. Yet the church grew. New workers took the place of those who fell, and stone after stone was added to the building. Thus slowly ascended the temple of the church of God.

Centuries of fierce persecution followed the establishment of the Christian church, but there were never wanting men who counted the work of building God's temple dearer than life itself. Of such it is written: "Others had trial of cruel mockings and scourgings, yea, moreover of bonds and imprisonment: they were stoned, they were sawn asunder, were tempted, were slain with the sword: they wandered about in sheepskins and goatskins; being destitute, afflicted, tormented; (of whom the world was not worthy:) they wandered in deserts, and in mountains, and in dens and caves of the earth." Hebrews 11:36-38.

The enemy of righteousness left nothing undone in his effort to stop the work committed to the Lord's builders. But God "left not Himself without witness." Acts 14:17. Workers were raised up who ably defended the faith once delivered to the saints. History bears record to the fortitude and heroism of these men. Like the apostles, many of them fell at their post, but the building of the temple went steadily forward. The workmen were slain, but the work advanced. The Waldenses, John Wycliffe, Huss and Jerome, Martin Luther and Zwingli, Cranmer, Latimer, and Knox, the Huguenots, John and Charles Wesley, and a host of others brought to the foundation material that will endure throughout eternity. And in later years those who have so nobly endeavored to promote the circulation of God's word, and those who by their service in heathen lands have prepared the way for the proclamation of the last great message— these also have helped to rear the structure.

Through the ages that have passed since the days of the apostles, the building of God's temple has never ceased. We may look back through the centuries and see the living stones of which it is composed gleaming like jets of light through the darkness of error and superstition. Throughout eternity these precious jewels will shine with increasing luster, testifying to the power of the truth of God. The flashing light of these polished stones reveals the strong contrast between light and darkness, between the gold of truth and the dross of error.

Paul and the other apostles, and all the righteous who have lived since then, have acted their part in the building of the temple. But the structure is not yet complete. We who are living in this age have a work to do, a part to act. We are to bring to the foundation material that will stand the test of fire—gold, silver, and precious stones, "polished after the similitude of a palace." Psalm 144:12. To those who thus build for God, Paul speaks words of encouragement and warning: "If any man's work abide which he hath built thereupon, he shall receive a reward. If any man's work shall be burned, he shall suffer loss: but he himself shall be saved; yet so as by fire." 1 Corinthians 3:14, 15. The Christian who faithfully presents the word of life, leading men and women into the way of holiness and peace, is bringing to the foundation material that will endure, and in the kingdom of God he will be honored as a wise builder.

Of the apostles it is written, "They went forth, and preached everywhere, the Lord working with them, and confirming the word with signs following." Mark 16:20. As Christ sent forth His disciples, so today He sends forth the members of His church. The same power that the apostles had is for them. If they will make God their strength, He will work with them, and they shall not labor in vain. Let them realize that the work in which they are engaged is one upon which the Lord has placed His signet. God said to Jeremiah, "Say not, I am a child: for thou shalt go to all that I shall send thee, and whatsoever I command thee thou shalt speak. Be not afraid of their faces: for I am with thee to deliver thee." Then the Lord put forth His hand and touched His servant's mouth, saying, "Behold, I have put My words in thy mouth." Jeremiah 1:7-9. And He bids us go forth to speak the words He gives us, feeling His holy touch upon our lips.

Christ has given to the church a sacred charge. Every member should be a channel through which God can communicate to the world the treasures of His grace, the unsearchable riches of Christ. There is nothing that the Saviour desires so much as agents who will represent to the world His Spirit and His character. There is nothing that the world needs so much as the manifestation through humanity of the Saviour's love. All heaven is waiting for men and women through whom God can reveal the power of Christianity.

The church is God's agency for the proclamation of truth, empowered by Him to do a special work; and if she is loyal to Him, obedient to all His commandments, there will dwell within her the excellency of divine grace. If she will be true to her allegiance, if she will honor the Lord God of Israel, there is no power that can stand against her.

Zeal for God and His cause moved the disciples to bear witness to the gospel with mighty power. Should not a like zeal fire our hearts with a determination to tell the story of redeeming love, of Christ and Him crucified? It is the privilege of every Christian, not only to look for, but to hasten the coming of the Saviour.

If the church will put on the robe of Christ's righteousness, withdrawing from all allegiance with the world, there is before her the dawn of a bright and glorious day. God's promise to her will stand fast forever. He will make her an eternal excellency, a joy of many generations. Truth, passing by those who despise and reject it, will triumph. Although at times apparently retarded, its progress has never been checked. When the message of God meets with opposition, He gives it additional force, that it may exert greater influence. Endowed with divine energy, it will cut its way through the strongest barriers and triumph over every obstacle.

What sustained the Son of God during His life of toil and sacrifice? He saw the results of the travail of His soul and was satisfied. Looking into eternity, He beheld the happiness of those who through His humiliation had received pardon and everlasting life. His ear caught the shout of the redeemed. He heard the ransomed ones singing the song of Moses and the Lamb.

We may have a vision of the future, the blessedness of heaven. In the Bible are revealed visions of the future glory, scenes pictured by the hand of God, and these are dear to His church. By faith we may stand on the threshold of the eternal city, and hear the gracious welcome given to those who in this life co-operate with Christ, regarding it as an honor to suffer for His sake. As the words are spoken, "Come, ye blessed of My Father," they cast their crowns at the feet of the Redeemer, exclaiming, "Worthy is the Lamb that was slain to receive power, and riches, and wisdom, and strength, and honor, and glory, and blessing. . . . Honor, and glory, and power, be unto Him that sitteth upon the throne, and unto the Lamb for ever and ever." Matthew 25:34; Revelation 5:12, 13.

There the redeemed greet those who led them to the Saviour, and all unite in praising Him who died that human beings might have the life that measures with the life of God. The conflict is over. Tribulation and strife are at an end. Songs of victory fill all heaven as the ransomed ones take up the joyful strain, Worthy, worthy is the Lamb that was slain, and lives again, a triumphant conqueror.

"I beheld, and, lo, a great multitude, which no man could number, of all nations, and kindreds, and people, and tongues, stood before the throne, and before the Lamb, clothed with white robes, and palms in their hands; and cried with a loud voice, saying, Salvation to our God which sitteth upon the throne, and unto the Lamb." Revelation 7:9, 10.

"These are they which came out of great tribulation, and have washed their robes, and made them white in the blood of the Lamb. Therefore are they before the throne of God, and serve Him day and night in His temple: and He that sitteth on the throne shall dwell among them. They shall hunger no more, neither thirst any more; neither shall the sun light on them, nor any heat. For the Lamb which is in the midst of the throne shall feed them, and shall lead them unto living fountains of waters: and God shall wipe away all tears from their eyes." "And there shall be no more death, neither sorrow, nor crying, neither shall there be any more pain: for the former things are passed away." Revelation 7:14-17; 21:4.

The Great Controversy Between Christ and Satan

CONTENTS

The Fall of Satan

The Lord has shown me that Satan was once an honored angel in heaven, next to Jesus Christ. His countenance was mild, expressive of happiness like the other angels. His forehead was high and broad, and showed great intelligence. His form was perfect. He had a noble, majestic bearing. And I saw that when God said to his Son, Let us make man in our image, Satan was jealous of Jesus. He wished to be consulted concerning the formation of man. He was filled with envy, jealousy and hatred. He wished to be the highest in heaven, next to God, and receive the highest honors. Until this time all heaven was in order, harmony and perfect subjection to the government of God.

It was the highest sin to rebel against the order and will of God. All heaven seemed in commotion. The angels were marshaled in companies with a commanding angel at their head. All the angels were astir. Satan was insinuating against the government of God, ambitious to exalt himself, and unwilling to submit to the authority of Jesus. Some of the angels sympathized with Satan in his rebellion, and others strongly contended for the honor and wisdom of God in giving authority to his Son. And there was contention with the angels. Satan and his affected ones, who were striving to reform the government of God, wished to look into his unsearchable wisdom to ascertain his purpose in exalting Jesus, and endowing him with such unlimited power and command. They rebelled against the authority of the Son of God, and all the angels were summoned to appear before the Father, to have their cases decided. And it was decided that Satan should be expelled from heaven, and that the angels, all who joined with Satan in the rebellion, should be turned out with him. Then there was war in heaven. Angels were engaged in the battle; Satan wished to conquer the Son of God, and those who were submissive to his will. But the good and true angels prevailed, and Satan, with his followers, was driven from heaven.

After Satan was shut out of heaven, with those who fell with him, he realized that he had lost all the purity and glory of heaven forever. Then he repented and wished to be reinstated again in heaven. He was willing to take his proper place, or any place that might be assigned him. But no, heaven must not be placed in jeopardy. All heaven might be marred should he be taken back; for sin originated with him, and the seeds of rebellion were within him. Satan had obtained followers, those who sympathized with him in his rebellion. He and his followers repented, wept and implored to be taken back into the favor of God. But no, their sin, their hate, their envy and jealousy, had been so great that God could not blot it out. It must remain to receive its final punishment.

When Satan became fully conscious that there was no possibility of his being brought again into favor with God, then his malice and hatred began to be manifest. He consulted with his angels, and a plan was laid to still work against God's government. When Adam and Eve were placed in the beautiful garden, Satan was laying plans to destroy them. A consultation was held with his evil angels. In no way could this happy couple be deprived of their happiness if they obeyed God. Satan could not exercise his power upon them unless they should first disobey God, and forfeit his favor. They must devise some plan to lead them to disobedience that they might incur God's frown and be brought under the more direct influence of Satan and his angels. It was decided that Satan should assume another form, and manifest an interest for man. He must insinuate against God's truthfulness, create doubt whether God did mean as he said, next, excite their curiosity, and lead them to pry into the unsearchable plans of God, which Satan had been guilty of, and reason as to the cause of his restrictions in regard to the tree of knowledge.

See Ezekiel 28:1-19; Isaiah 14:12-20; Revelation 12:7-9

The Fall of Man

I saw that the holy angels often visited the garden, and gave instruction to Adam and Eve concerning their employment, and also taught them concerning the rebellion of Satan and his fall. The angels warned them of Satan, and cautioned them not to separate from each other in their employment, for they might be brought in contact with this fallen foe. The angels enjoined upon them to closely follow the directions God had given them, for in perfect obedience only were they safe. And if they were obedient, this fallen foe could have no power over them.

Satan commenced his work with Eve, to cause her to disobey. She first erred in wandering from her husband, next, in lingering around the forbidden tree, and next in listening to the voice of the tempter, and even daring to doubt what God had said -- In the day that thou eatest thereof thou shalt surely die. She thought, Perhaps it does not mean just as the Lord said. She ventured to disobey. She put forth her hand, took of the fruit, and ate. It was pleasing to the eye, and pleasant to the taste. She was jealous that God had withheld from them what was really for their good. She offered the fruit to her husband, thereby tempting him. She related to Adam all that the serpent had said, and expressed her astonishment that he had the power of speech.

I saw a sadness came over Adam fs countenance. He appeared afraid and astonished. A struggle appeared to be going on in his mind. He felt sure that this was the foe which they had been warned against, and that his wife must die. They must be separated. His love for Eve was strong. And in utter discouragement he resolved to share her fate. He seized the fruit, and quickly ate it. Then Satan exulted. He had rebelled in heaven, and had sympathizers who loved him, and followed him in his rebellion. He fell, and caused others to fall with him. And he had now tempted the woman to distrust God, to inquire into his wisdom, and to seek to penetrate his all-wise plans. Satan knew the woman would not fall alone. Adam, through his love for Eve, disobeyed the command of God and fell with her.

The news of man fs fall spread through heaven. Every harp was hushed. The angels cast their crowns from their heads in sorrow. All heaven was in agitation. A counsel was held to decide what must be done with the guilty pair. The angels feared that they would put forth the hand, and eat of the tree of life, and be immortal sinners. But God said that he would drive the transgressors from the garden. Angels were commissioned immediately to guard the way of the tree of life. It had been Satan fs studied plan that Adam and Eve should disobey God, receive his frown, and then be led on to partake of the tree of life, that they might live forever in sin and disobedience, and thus sin be immortalized. But holy angels were sent to drive them out of the garden, while another company of angels were commissioned to guard the way to the tree of life. Each of these mighty angels appeared to have something in their right hand, which looked like a glittering sword.

Then Satan triumphed. Others he had made to suffer by his fall. He had been shut out of heaven, they out of Paradise.

See Genesis 3.

The Plan of Salvation

Sorrow filled heaven, as it was realized that man was lost, and the world that God created was to be filled with mortals doomed to misery, sickness and death, and there was no way of escape for the offender. The whole family of Adam must die. I saw the lovely Jesus, and beheld an expression of sympathy and sorrow upon his countenance. Soon I saw him approach the exceeding bright light which enshrouded the Father. Said my accompanying angel, He is in close converse with His Father. The anxiety of the angels seemed to be intense while Jesus was communing with his Father. Three times he was shut in by the glorious light about the Father, and the third time he came from the Father, his person could be seen. His countenance was calm, free from all perplexity and trouble, and shone with benevolence and loveliness, such as words cannot express. He then made known to the angelic host that a way of escape had been made for lost man. He told them that he had been pleading with his Father, and had offered to give his life a ransom, and take the sentence of death upon himself, that through him man might find pardon. That through the merits of his blood, and obedience to the law of God, they could have the favor of God, and be brought into the beautiful garden, and eat of the fruit of the tree of life.

At first the angels could not rejoice, for their commander concealed nothing from them, but opened before them the plan of salvation. Jesus told them that he would stand between the wrath of his Father and guilty man, that he would bear iniquity and scorn, and but few would receive him as the Son of God. Nearly all would hate and reject him. He would leave all his glory in heaven, appear upon earth as a man, humble himself as a man, become acquainted by His own experience with the various temptations with which man would be beset, that he might know how to succor those who should be tempted; and that finally, after his mission as a teacher should be accomplished, he would be delivered into the hands of men, and endure almost every cruelty and suffering that Satan and his angels could inspire wicked men to inflict; that he should die the cruelest of deaths, hung up between the heavens and the earth as a guilty sinner; that he should suffer dreadful hours of agony, which even angels could not look upon, but would vail their faces from the sight. Not merely agony of body would he suffer; but mental agony, that with which bodily suffering could in no wise be compared. The weight of the sins of the whole world would be upon him. He told them he would die and rise again the third day, and should ascend to his Father to intercede for wayward, guilty man.

The angels prostrated themselves before him. They offered their lives. Jesus said to them that he should by his death save many; that the life of an angel could not pay the debt. His life alone could be accepted of his Father as a ransom for man.

Jesus also told them that they should have a part to act, to be with him, and at different times strengthen him. That he should take man fs fallen nature, and his strength would not be even equal with theirs. And they should be witnesses of his humiliation and great sufferings. And as they should witness his sufferings, and the hate of men towards him, they would be stirred with the deepest emotions, and through their love for him, would wish to rescue, and deliver him from his murderers; but that they must not interfere to prevent anything they should behold; and that they should act a part in his resurrection; that the plan of salvation was devised, and his Father had accepted the plan.

With a holy sadness, Jesus comforted and cheered the angels, and informed them that hereafter those whom he should redeem would be with him, and ever dwell with him; and that by his death he should ransom many, and destroy him who had the power of death. And his Father would give him the kingdom, and the greatness of the kingdom under the whole heaven, and he should possess it forever and ever. Satan and sinners should be destroyed, never more to disturb heaven, or the purified, new earth. Jesus bid the heavenly host be reconciled to the plan that his Father accepted, and rejoice that fallen man could be exalted again through his death, to obtain favor with God and enjoy heaven.

Then joy, inexpressible joy, filled heaven. And the heavenly host sung a song of praise and adoration. They touched their harps and sung a note higher than they had done before, for the great mercy and condescension of God in yielding up his dearly Beloved to die for a race of rebels. Praise and adoration were poured forth for the self-denial and sacrifice of Jesus; that he would consent to leave the bosom of his Father, and choose a life of suffering and anguish, and die an ignominious death to give life to others.

Said the angel, Think ye that the Father yielded up his dearly beloved Son without a struggle? No, no. It was even a struggle with the God of heaven, whether to let guilty man perish, or to give his beloved Son to die for them. Angels were so interested for man fs salvation that there could be found among them those who would yield their glory, and give their life for perishing man. But, said my accompanying angel, that would avail nothing. The transgression was so great that an angel fs life would not pay the debt. Nothing but the death and intercessions of his Son would pay the debt, and save lost man from hopeless sorrow and misery.

But the work of the angels was assigned them, to ascend and descend with strengthening balm from glory to soothe the Son of God in his sufferings, and administer unto him. Also, their work would be to guard and keep the subjects of grace from the evil angels, and the darkness constantly thrown around them by Satan. I saw that it was impossible for God to alter or change his law, to save lost, perishing man; therefore he suffered his beloved Son to die for man fs transgression.

Satan again rejoiced with his angels that he could, by causing man fs fall, pull down the Son of God from his exalted position. He told his angels that when Jesus should take fallen man fs nature, he could overpower him, and hinder the accomplishment of the plan of salvation.

I was then shown Satan as he was, a happy, exalted angel. Then I was shown him as he now is. He still bears a kingly form. His features are still noble, for he is an angel fallen. But the expression of his countenance is full of anxiety, care, unhappiness, malice, hate, mischief, deceit, and every evil. That brow which was once so noble, I particularly noticed. His forehead commenced from his eyes to recede backward. I saw that he had demeaned himself so long, that every good quality was debased, and every evil trait was developed. His eyes were cunning, sly, and showed great penetration. His frame was large, but the flesh hung loosely about his hands and face. As I beheld him, his chin was resting upon his left hand. He appeared to be in deep thought. A smile was upon his countenance, which made me tremble, it was so full of evil, and Satanic slyness. This smile is the one he wears just before he makes sure of his victim, and as he fastens the victim in his snare, this smile grows horrible.

See Isaiah 53.

The First Advent of Christ

Then I was carried down to the time when Jesus was to take upon himself man fs nature, humble himself as a man, and suffer the temptations of Satan.

His birth was without worldly grandeur. He was born in a stable, cradled in a manger; yet his birth was honored far above any of the sons of men. Angels from heaven informed the shepherds of the advent of Jesus, while the light and glory from God accompanied their testimony. The heavenly host touched their harps and glorified God. They triumphantly heralded the advent of the Son of God to a fallen world to accomplish the work of redemption, and by his death bring peace, happiness, and everlasting life to man. God honored the advent of his Son. Angels worshiped him.

Angels of God hovered over the scene of his baptism, and the Holy Spirit descended in the shape of a dove, and lighted upon him, and as the people stood greatly amazed, with their eyes fastened upon him, the Father fs voice was heard from heaven, saying, Thou art my beloved Son, in thee I am well pleased.

John was not certain that it was the Saviour who came to be baptized of him in Jordan. But God had promised him a sign by which he should know the Lamb of God. That sign was given as the heavenly Dove rested upon Jesus, and the glory of God shone round about him. John reached forth his hand, pointing to Jesus, and with a loud voice cried out, Behold the Lamb of God which taketh away the sin of the world.

John informed his disciples that Jesus was the promised Messiah, the Saviour of the world. As his work was closing, he taught his disciples to look to Jesus, and follow him as the great teacher. John fs life was without pleasure. It was sorrowful and self-denying. He heralded the first advent of Christ, and then was not permitted to witness the miracles, and enjoy the power manifested by him. He knew that when Jesus should establish himself as a teacher, he must die. His voice was seldom heard, except in the wilderness. His life was lonely. He did not cling to his father fs family, to enjoy their society, but left them in order to fulfill his mission. Multitudes left the busy cities and villages, and flocked to the wilderness to hear the words of the wonderful, singular Prophet. John laid the axe at the root of the tree. He reproved sin fearless of consequences, and prepared the way for the Lamb of God.

Herod was affected as he listened to the powerful, pointed testimonies of John. With deep interest he inquired what he must do to become his disciple. John was acquainted with the fact that he was about to marry his brother fs wife, while her husband was yet living, and faithfully told Herod that it was not lawful. Herod was not willing to make any sacrifice. He married his brother fs wife, and, through her influence, seized John and put him in prison. But Herod intended to release him again. While there confined, John heard through his disciples of the mighty works of Jesus. He could not listen to his gracious words. But the disciples informed him, and comforted him with what they had heard. Soon John was beheaded through the influence of Herod fs wife. I saw that the least disciple that followed Jesus, witnessed his miracles, and heard the comforting words which fell from his lips, was greater than John the Baptist. That is, they were more exalted and honored, and had more pleasure in their lives.

John came in the spirit and power of Elijah, to proclaim the first advent of Jesus. I was pointed down to the last days, and saw that John was to represent those who should go forth in the spirit and power of Elijah, to herald the day of wrath, and the second advent of Jesus.

After the baptism of Jesus in Jordan, he was led by the Spirit into the wilderness, to be tempted of the Devil. The Holy Spirit had fitted him for that special scene of fierce temptations. Forty days he was tempted of the Devil, and in those days he ate nothing. Everything around Jesus was unpleasant, from which human nature would be led to shrink. He was with the wild beasts, and the Devil, in a desolate, lonely place. I saw that the Son of God was pale and emaciated through fasting and suffering. But his course was marked out, and he must fulfill the work he came to do.

Satan took advantage of the sufferings of the Son of God, and prepared to beset him with manifold temptations, hoping he should obtain the victory over him, because he had humbled himself as a man. Satan came with this temptation, If thou be the Son of God, command that this stone be made bread. He tempted Jesus to condescend to him, and give him proof of his being the Messiah, by exercising his divine power. Jesus mildly answered him, It is written, Man shall not live by bread alone, but by every word of God.

Satan was seeking a dispute with Jesus concerning his being the Son of God. He referred to his weak, suffering condition, and boastingly affirmed that he was stronger than Jesus. But the word spoken from heaven, Thou art my beloved Son, in thee I am well pleased, was sufficient to sustain Jesus through all his sufferings. I saw that in all his mission he had nothing to do in convincing Satan of his power, and of his being the Saviour of the world, Satan had sufficient evidence of his exalted station and authority. His unwillingness to yield to Jesus f authority, shut him out of heaven.

Satan, to manifest his strength, carried Jesus to Jerusalem, and set him upon a pinnacle of the temple, and again tempted him, that if he was the Son of God, to give him evidence of it by casting himself down from the dizzy height upon which he had placed him. Satan came with the words of inspiration. For it is written, He shall give his angels charge over thee, and in their hands they shall bear thee up, lest at any time thou dash thy foot against a stone. Jesus answering said unto him, It is said, Thou shalt not tempt the Lord thy God. Satan wished to cause Jesus to presume upon the mercy of his Father, and risk his life before the fulfillment of his mission. He had hoped that the plan of salvation would fail; but I saw that the plan was laid too deep to be thus overthrown, or marred by Satan.

I saw that Christ was the example for all christians when tempted, or their rights disputed. They should bear it patiently. They should not feel that they have a right to call upon God to display his power, that they may obtain a victory over their enemies, unless there is a special object in view, that God can be directly honored and glorified by it. I saw that if Jesus had cast himself from the pinnacle, it would not have glorified his Father; for none would witness the act but Satan, and the angels of God. And it would be tempting the Lord to display his power to his bitterest foe. It would have been condescending to the one whom Jesus came to conquer.

gAnd the Devil, taking him up into a high mountain, showed unto him all the kingdoms of the world in a moment of time. And the Devil said unto him, All this power will I give thee, and the glory of them: for that is delivered unto me; and to whomsoever I will I give it. If thou, therefore, wilt worship me, all shall be thine. And Jesus answered and said unto him, Get thee behind me, Satan; for it is written, Thou shalt worship the Lord thy God, and him only shalt thou serve. h

Here Satan showed Jesus the kingdoms of the world. They were presented in the most attractive light. He offered them to Jesus if he would there worship him. He told Jesus that he would relinquish his claims of the possessions of earth. Satan knew that his power must be limited, and finally taken away, if the plan of salvation should be carried out. He knew that if Jesus should die to redeem man, his power would end after a

season, and he would be destroyed. Therefore it was his studied plan to prevent, if possible, the completion of the great work which had been commenced by the Son of God. If the plan of man fs redemption should fail, he would retain the kingdom which he then claimed. And if he should succeed, he flattered himself that he would reign in opposition to the God of heaven.

Satan exulted when Jesus left heaven, and left his power and glory there. He thought that the Son of God was placed in his power. The temptation took so easily with the holy pair in Eden, that he hoped he could with his satanic cunning and power overthrow even the Son of God, and thereby save his life and kingdom. If he could tempt Jesus to depart from the will of his Father, then his object would be gained. Jesus bid Satan get behind him. He was to bow only to his Father. The time was to come when Jesus should redeem the possessions of Satan by his own life, and, after a season, all in heaven and earth should submit to him. Satan claimed the kingdoms of earth as his, and he insinuated to Jesus that all his sufferings might be saved. He need not die to obtain the kingdoms of this world. But he might have the entire possessions of earth, and the glory of reigning over them, if he would worship him. Jesus was steadfast. He chose his life of suffering, his dreadful death, and, in the way appointed by his Father, to become a lawful heir to the kingdoms of earth, and have them given into his hands as an everlasting possession. Satan also will be given into his hands to be destroyed by death, never more to annoy Jesus, or the saints in glory.

See Luke 2; 3:1-22; 4.

The Ministry of Christ

After Satan had ended his temptations, he departed from Jesus for a season, and angels prepared him food in the wilderness, and strengthened him, and the blessing of his Father rested upon him. Satan had failed in his fiercest temptations, yet he looked forward to the period of Jesus' ministry, when he should at different times try his cunning against him. He still hoped to prevail against him by stirring up those who would not receive Jesus, to hate and seek to destroy him. Satan held a special counsel with his angels. They were disappointed and enraged that they had prevailed nothing against the Son of God. They decided that they must be more cunning, and use their power to the utmost to inspire unbelief in the minds of his own nation as to his being the Saviour of the world, and in this way discourage Jesus in his mission. No matter how exact the Jews might be in their ceremonies and sacrifices, if they could keep their eyes blinded as to the prophecies, and make them believe that it was a mighty, worldly king who was to fulfill these prophecies, they would keep their minds on the stretch for a Messiah to come.

I was then shown that Satan and his angels were very busy during Christ's ministry, inspiring men with unbelief, hate and scorn. Often when Jesus uttered some cutting truth reproving their sins, they would become enraged. Satan and his angels urged them on to take the life of the Son of God. Once they took up stones to cast at him, but angels guarded him, and bore him away from the angry multitude to a place of safety. Again as the plain truth dropped from his holy lips, the multitude laid hold of him, and led him to the brow of a hill, intending to thrust him down. A contention arose among themselves as to what they should do with him, when the angels again hid him from the sight of the multitude, and he, passing through the midst of them, went his way.

Satan still hoped the great plan of salvation would fail. He exerted all his power to make the hearts of all people hard, and their feelings bitter against Jesus. He hoped that the number who would receive him as the Son of God would be so few, that Jesus would consider his sufferings and sacrifice too great to make for so small a company. But I saw that if there had been but two who would have accepted Jesus as the Son of God, to believe in him to the saving of their souls, he would have carried out the plan.

Jesus commenced his work by breaking the power which Satan held over the suffering. He healed those who had suffered by his evil power. He restored the sick to health, healed the lame, and caused them to leap in the gladness of their hearts, and glorify God. He gave sight to the blind, restored to health by his power those who had been infirm and bound by Satan's cruel power many years. The weak, the trembling, and desponding, he comforted with gracious words. He raised the dead to life, and they glorified God for the mighty display of his power. He wrought mightily for all who believed on him. And the feeble suffering ones whom Satan held in triumph, Jesus wrenched from his grasp, and brought to them by his power, soundness of body, and great joy and happiness.

The life of Christ was full of benevolence, sympathy and love. He was ever attentive to listen to, and relieve the woes of those who came to him. Multitudes carried the evidences in their own persons of his divine power. Yet many of them soon after the work was accomplished were ashamed of the humble, yet mighty teacher. Because the rulers did not believe on him, they were not willing to suffer with Jesus. He was a man of sorrows and acquainted with grief. But few could endure to be governed by his sober, self-denying life. They wished to enjoy the honor which the world bestows. Many followed the Son of God, and listened to his instructions, feasting upon the words which fell so graciously from his lips. His words were full of meaning, yet so plain that the weakest could understand.

Satan and his angels were busy. They blinded the eyes and darkened the understanding of the Jews. Satan stirred up the chief of the people and the rulers to take his life. They sent officers to bring Jesus unto them, and as they came near where he was, they were greatly amazed. They saw Jesus stirred to sympathy and compassion, as he witnessed human woe. They saw him in love and tenderness speak encouragingly to the weak and afflicted. They also heard him, in a voice of authority, rebuke the power of Satan, and bid the captives held by him, go free. They listened to the words of wisdom that fell from his lips, and they were captivated. They could not lay hands on him. They returned to the priests and elders without Jesus. They inquired of the officers, Why have ye not brought him? They related what they had witnessed of his miracles, and the holy words of wisdom, love and knowledge which they had heard, and ended with saying, Never man spake like this man. The chief priests accused them of being also deceived. Some were ashamed that they had not brought him. The chief priests inquired in a ridiculing manner if any of the rulers had believed on him. I saw that many of the magistrates and elders did believe on Jesus. But Satan kept them from acknowledging it. They feared the reproach of the people more than they feared God.

Thus far the cunning and hatred of Satan had not broken up the plan of salvation. The time for the accomplishment of the object for which Jesus came into the world was drawing on. Satan and his angels consulted together, and decided to inspire Christ ƒs own nation to cry eagerly for his blood, and invent cruelty and scorn to be heaped upon him. He hoped that Jesus would resent such treatment, and not maintain his humility and meekness.

While Satan was laying his plans, Jesus was carefully opening to his disciples the sufferings he must pass through. That he should be crucified, and that he would rise again the third day. But their understanding seemed dull. They could not comprehend what he told them.

See John 7:45,46; John 8:59; Luke 4:29, 24:6-8

The Transfiguration

I saw that the faith of the disciples was greatly strengthened at the transfiguration. God chose to give the followers of Jesus strong proof that he was the promised Messiah, that in their bitter sorrow and disappointment they should not entirely cast away their confidence. At the transfiguration the Lord sent Moses and Elias to talk with Jesus concerning his sufferings and death. Instead of choosing angels to converse with his Son, God chose those who had an experience in the trials of earth. A few of his followers were permitted to be with him and behold his face lighted up with divine glory, and witness his raiment white and glistening, and hear the voice of God, in fearful majesty, saying, This is my beloved Son, hear him.

Elijah had walked with God. His work had not been pleasant. God, through him, had reproved sin. He was a prophet of God, and had to flee from place to place to save his life. He was hunted like the wild beasts that they might destroy him. God translated Elijah. Angels bore him in glory and triumph to heaven.

Moses had been a man greatly honored of God. He was greater than any who had lived before him. He was privileged to talk with God face to face as a man speaketh with a friend. He was permitted to see the bright light and excellent glory that enshrouded the Father. Through Moses the Lord delivered the children of Israel from Egyptian bondage. Moses was a mediator for the children of Israel. He often stood between them and the wrath of God. When the wrath of God was greatly kindled against Israel for their unbelief, their murmurings, and their grievous sins, Moses f love for them was tested. God promised him that if he would let Israel go, let them be destroyed, he would make of him a mighty nation. Moses showed his love for Israel by his earnest pleading. In his distress he prayed God to turn from his fierce anger, and forgive Israel, or blot his name out of his book.

When Israel murmured against God and against Moses, because they could get no water, they accused him of leading them out to kill them and their children. God heard their murmurings, and bade Moses smite the rock, that the children of Israel might have water. Moses smote the rock in wrath, and took the glory to himself. The continual waywardness and murmuring of the children of Israel had caused him the keenest sorrow, and for a little he forgot how much God had borne with them, and that their murmuring was not against Moses, but against God. He thought only of himself, how deeply he was wronged, and how little gratitude they manifested in return, for his deep love for them.

As Moses smote the rock, he failed to honor God, and magnify him before the children of Israel, that they might glorify God. And the Lord was displeased with Moses, and said that he should not enter the promised land. It was God fs plan to often prove Israel by bringing them into strait places, and then in their great necessity exhibit his power, that he might live in their memory, and they glorify him.

When Moses came down from the mount with the two tables of stone, and saw Israel worshiping the golden calf, his anger was greatly kindled, and he threw down the tables of stone, and broke them. I saw that Moses did not sin in this. He was wroth for God, jealous for his glory. But when he yielded to the natural feelings of the heart, and took glory to himself, which was due to God, he sinned, and for that sin, God would not suffer him to enter the promised land.

Satan had been trying to find something wherewith to accuse Moses before the angels. Satan triumphed in that he had caused him to displease God, and he exulted, and told the angels that when the Saviour of the world should come to redeem man, he could overcome him. For this transgression Moses came under the power of Satan -- the dominion of death. Had he remained steadfast, and not sinned in taking glory to himself, the Lord would have brought him to the promised land, and then translated him to heaven without seeing death.

I saw that Moses passed through death, but Michael came down and gave him life before he saw corruption. Satan claimed the body as his, but Michael resurrected Moses, and took him to heaven. The Devil tried to hold his body, and railed out bitterly against God, denounced him as unjust, in taking from him his prey. But Michael did not rebuke the Devil, although it was through his temptation and power that God fs servant had fallen. Christ meekly referred him to his Father, saying, The Lord rebuke thee.

Jesus told his disciples that there were some standing with him who should not taste of death till they should see the kingdom of God come with power. At the transfiguration this promise was fulfilled. The fashion of Jesus f countenance was changed, and shone like the sun. His raiment was white and glistening. Moses was present, and represented those who will be raised from the dead at the second appearing of Jesus. And Elias, who was translated without seeing death, represented those who will be changed to immortality at Christ fs second coming, and without seeing death will be translated to heaven. The disciples beheld with fear and astonishment the excellent majesty of Jesus, and the cloud that overshadowed them, and heard the voice of God in terrible majesty, saying, This is my beloved Son, hear him.

See Matthew 17; Mark 9; Exodus 32:32; Numbers 20:11; Jude 9

The Betrayal of Christ

I was then carried down to the time when Jesus ate the Passover supper with his disciples. Satan had deceived Judas, and led him to think he was one of Christ fs true disciples; but his heart had ever been carnal. He had seen the mighty works of Jesus, he had been with him through his ministry, and yielded to the overpowering evidences that he was the Messiah; but he was close and covetous. He loved money. He complained in anger of the costly ointment poured upon Jesus. Mary loved her Lord. He had forgiven her sins which were many, and had raised from the dead her much loved brother, and she felt that nothing was too dear to bestow upon Jesus. The more costly and precious the ointment, the better could Mary express her gratitude to her Saviour, by devoting it to him. Judas, as an excuse for his covetousness, said that the ointment might have been sold and given to the poor. But it was not because he had any care for the poor; for he was selfish, and often appropriated to his own use that which was entrusted to his care to be given to the poor. Judas had not been attentive to the comforts and wants of Jesus, and to excuse his covetousness, he often referred to the poor. And this act of generosity on the part of Mary was a most cutting rebuke of his covetous disposition.

The way was prepared for the temptation of Satan to find a ready reception in Judas f heart. The Jews hated Jesus; but multitudes thronged him to listen to his words of wisdom, and to witness his mighty works. This drew the attention of the people from the chief priests and elders, for the people were stirred with the deepest interest, and anxiously followed Jesus, and listened to the instructions of this wonderful teacher. Many of the chief rulers believed on Jesus, but were afraid to confess it, fearing they would be put out of the synagogue. The priests and elders decided that something must be done to draw the attention of the people from Jesus. They feared that all men would believe on him. They could see no safety for themselves. They must lose their position, or put Jesus to death. And after they should put him to death, there were still those who were living monuments of his power. Jesus had raised Lazarus from the dead. And they feared that if they should kill Jesus, Lazarus would testify of his mighty power. The people were flocking to see him who was raised from the dead, and the rulers determined to slay Lazarus also, and put down the excitement. Then they would turn the people to the traditions and doctrines of men, to tithe mint and rue, and again have influence over them. They agreed to take Jesus when he was alone; for if they should attempt to take him in a crowd, when the minds of the people were all interested in him, they would be stoned.

Judas knew how anxious they were to obtain Jesus, and offered to betray him to the chief priests and elders for a few pieces of silver. His love of money led him to agree to betray his Lord into the hands of his bitterest enemies. Satan was working directly through Judas, and in the midst of the impressive scene of the last supper, he was contriving plans to betray Jesus. Jesus sorrowfully told his disciples that all of them would be offended because of him, that night. But Peter ardently affirmed that although all should be offended because of him, he would not. Jesus said to Peter, Satan hath desired to have you, that he may sift you as wheat; but I have prayed for thee, that thy faith fail not; and when thou art converted, strengthen thy brethren.

I then viewed Jesus in the garden with his disciples. In deep sorrow he bade them watch and pray lest they should enter into temptation. Jesus knew that their faith was to be tried, and their hopes disappointed, and that they would need all the strength they could obtain by close watching and fervent prayer. With strong cries and weeping, Jesus prayed, Father, if thou be willing, remove this cup from me, nevertheless, not my will, but thine be done. The Son of God prayed in agony. Large drops of sweat like blood came out of his face, and fell upon the ground. Angels were hovering over the place, witnessing the scene, while only one was commissioned to go and strengthen the Son of God in his agony. The angels in heaven cast their crowns and harps from them, and with the deepest interest silently watched Jesus. There was no joy in heaven. They wished to surround the Son of God, but the commanding angels suffered them not, lest, as they should behold his betrayal, they would deliver him; for the plan was laid out, and it must be fulfilled.

After Jesus had prayed, he came to see his disciples. They were sleeping. He had not the comfort and prayers of even his disciples in that dreadful hour. Peter who was so zealous a little before, was heavy with sleep. Jesus reminded him of his positive declarations, and said unto him, What! could ye not watch with me one hour? Three times the Son of God prayed in agony, when Judas, with his band of men, was at hand. He met Jesus as usual to salute him. The band surrounded Jesus; but there he manifested his divine power, as he said, Whom seek ye? I am he. They fell backward to the ground. Jesus made this inquiry that they might witness his power, and have evidence that he could deliver himself from their hands if he would.

The disciples began to hope as they saw the multitude with their staves and swords fall so quickly. As they arose and again surrounded the Son of God, Peter drew the sword and cut off an ear. Jesus bid him put up the sword, and said unto him, Thinkest thou that I cannot now pray to my Father, and he shall presently give me more than twelve legions of angels? I saw that as these words were spoken, the countenances of the angels were animated. They wished then, and there, to surround their commander, and disperse that angry mob. But again sadness settled upon them as Jesus added, But how then shall the scriptures be fulfilled, that thus it must be? The hearts of the disciples sunk again in despair and bitter disappointment, as Jesus suffered them to lead him away.

The disciples were afraid of their own lives, and fled one this way, and the other that, and Jesus was left alone. O what triumph of Satan then! And what sadness and sorrow with the angels of God! Many companies of holy angels, with each a tall commanding angel at their head, were sent to witness the scene. They were to record every act, every insult and cruelty imposed upon the Son of God, and to register every pang of anguish which Jesus should suffer; for the very men should see it all again in living characters.

See Matthew 26; Mark 14; John 13.

The Trial of Christ

The angels as they left heaven, in sadness laid off their glittering crowns. They could not wear them while their commander was suffering, and was to wear a crown of thorns. Satan and his angels were busy in that judgment hall to destroy humanity and sympathy. The very atmosphere was heavy and polluted by their influence. The chief priests and elders were inspired by them to abuse and insult Jesus, in a manner the most difficult for human nature to bear. Satan hoped that such insult and sufferings would call forth from the Son of God some complaint or murmur; or that he would manifest his divine power, and wrench himself from the grasp of the multitude, and thus the plan of salvation at last fail.

Peter followed his Lord after his betrayal. He was anxious to see what would be done with Jesus. And when he was accused of being one of his disciples, he denied it. He was afraid of his life, and when charged with being one of them, he declared that he knew not the man. The disciples were noted for the purity of their words, and Peter, to deceive, and convince them that he was not one of Christ's disciples, denied it the third time with cursing and swearing. Jesus, who was some distance from Peter, turned a sorrowful reproving gaze upon him. Then he remembered the words which Jesus had spoken to him in the upper chamber, and also his zealous assertion, Though all men shall be offended because of thee, yet will I never be offended. He denied his Lord, even with cursing and swearing; but that look of Jesus melted Peter at once, and saved him. He bitterly wept and repented of his great sin, and was converted, and then was prepared to strengthen his brethren.

The multitude were clamorous for the blood of Jesus. They cruelly scourged him, and put an old purple, kingly robe upon him, and bound his sacred head with a crown of thorns. They put a reed in his hand, and mockingly bowed to him, and saluted him with, Hail king of the Jews! They then took the reed from his hand, and smote him with it upon the head, causing the thorns to penetrate his temples, sending the trickling blood down his face and beard.

It was difficult for the angels to endure the sight. They would have delivered Jesus out of their hands; but the commanding angels forbade them, and said that it was a great ransom that was to be paid for man; but it would be complete, and would cause the death of him who had the power of death. Jesus knew that angels were witnessing the scene of his humiliation. I saw that the feeblest angel could have caused that multitude to fall powerless, and delivered Jesus. He knew that if he should desire it of his Father, angels would instantly release him. But it was necessary that Jesus should suffer many things of wicked men, in order to carry out the plan of salvation.

There stood Jesus, meek and humble before the infuriated multitude, while they offered him the meanest abuse. They spit in his face -- that face which they will one day desire to be hid from, which will give light to the city of God, and shine brighter than the sun -- but not an angry look did he cast upon the offenders. He meekly raised his hand, and wiped it off. They covered his head with an old garment; blindfolded him, and then struck him in the face, and cried out, Prophesy unto us who it was that smote thee. There was commotion among the angels. They would have rescued him instantly; but their commanding angel restrained them.

The disciples had gained confidence to enter where Jesus was, and witness his trial. They expected that he would manifest his divine power, and deliver himself from the hands of his enemies, and punish them for their cruelty towards him. Their hopes would rise and fall as the different scenes transpired. Sometimes they doubted, and feared they had been deceived. But the voice heard at the mount of transfiguration, and the glory they there witnessed, strengthened them that he was the Son of God. They called to mind the exciting scenes which they had witnessed, the miracles they had seen Jesus do in healing the sick, opening the eyes of the blind, unstopping the deaf ears, rebuking and casting out devils, raising the dead to life, and even rebuking the wind, and it obeyed him. They could not believe that he would die. They hoped he would yet rise in power, and with his commanding voice disperse that blood-thirsty multitude, as when he entered the temple and drove out those who were making the house of God a place of merchandise; when they fled before him, as though a company of armed soldiers were pursuing them. The disciples hoped that Jesus would manifest his power, and convince all that he was the King of Israel.

Judas was filled with bitter remorse and shame at his treacherous act in betraying Jesus. And when he witnessed the abuse he suffered, he was overcome. He had loved Jesus, but loved money more. He did not think that Jesus would suffer himself to be taken by the mob which he had led on. He thought that Jesus would work a miracle, and deliver himself from them. But when he saw the infuriated multitude in the judgment hall, thirsting for his blood, he deeply felt his guilt, and while many were vehemently accusing Jesus, Judas rushed through the multitude, confessing that he had sinned in betraying innocent blood. He offered them the money, and begged of them to release Jesus, declaring that he was entirely innocent. Vexation and confusion kept the priests for a short time silent. They did not wish the people to know that they had hired one of Jesus f professed followers to betray him into their hands. Their hunting Jesus like a thief and taking him secretly, they wished to hide. But the confession of Judas, his haggard and guilty appearance, exposed the priests before the multitude, showing that it was hatred that had caused them to take Jesus. As Judas loudly declared Jesus to be innocent, the priests replied, What is that to us? See thou to that. They had Jesus in their power, and they were determined to make sure of him. Judas, overwhelmed with anguish, threw the money that he now despised at the feet of those who had hired him, and in anguish and horror at his crime, went and hung himself.

Jesus had many sympathizers in that company, and his answering nothing to the many questions put to him amazed the throng. To all the insults and mockery not a frown, not a troubled expression was upon his features. He was dignified and composed. He was of perfect and noble form. The spectators looked upon him with wonder. They compared his perfect form, his firm, dignified bearing, with those who sat in judgment against him, and said to one another that he appeared more like a king to be entrusted with a kingdom than any of the rulers. He bore no marks of being a criminal. His eye was mild, clear and undaunted, his forehead broad and high. Every feature was strongly marked with benevolence and noble principle. His patience and forbearance were so unlike man, that many trembled. Even Herod and Pilate were greatly troubled at his noble, God-like bearing.

Pilate from the first was convicted that he was no common man, but an excellent character. He believed him to be entirely innocent. The angels who were witnessing the whole scene noticed the convictions of Pilate, and marked his sympathy and compassion for Jesus; and to save him from engaging in the awful act of delivering Jesus to be crucified, an angel was sent to Pilate fs wife, and gave her information through a dream that it was the Son of God in whose trial Pilate was engaged, and that he was an innocent sufferer. She immediately sent word to Pilate that she had suffered many things in a dream on account of Jesus, and warned him to have nothing to do with that holy man. The messenger bearing the communication pressed hastily through the crowd, and handed it to Pilate. As he read it he trembled and turned pale. He at once thought he would have nothing to do in the matter; that if they would have the blood of Jesus he would not give his influence to it, but would labor to deliver him.

When Pilate heard that Herod was at Jerusalem he was glad, and hoped to free himself from the disagreeable matter altogether, and have nothing to do in condemning Jesus. He sent him, with his accusers, to Herod. Herod was hardened. His murdering John left a stain upon his conscience which he could not free himself from, and when he heard of Jesus, and the mighty works done by him, he thought it was John risen from the dead. He feared and trembled, for he bore a guilty conscience. Jesus was placed in Herod fs hands by Pilate. Herod considered this act an acknowledgment from Pilate of his power, authority and judgment. They had previously been enemies, but then they were made friends. Herod was glad to see Jesus, for he expected that he would work some mighty miracle for his satisfaction. But it was not the work of Jesus to gratify his curiosity. His divine and miraculous power was to be exercised for the salvation of others, but not in his own behalf.

Jesus answered nothing to the many questions put to him by Herod; neither did he regard his enemies who were vehemently accusing him. Herod was enraged because Jesus did not appear to fear his power, and with his men of war, derided, mocked and abused the Son of God. Herod was astonished at the noble, God-like appearance of Jesus, when shamefully abused, and feared to condemn him, and he sent him again to Pilate.

Satan and his angels were tempting Pilate, and trying to lead him on to his own ruin. They suggested to him that if he did not take any part in condemning Jesus, others would; the multitude were thirsting for his blood; and if he did not deliver Jesus to be crucified, he would lose his power and worldly honor, and would be denounced as a believer on the impostor, as they termed him. Pilate, through fear of losing his power and authority, consented to the death of Jesus. And notwithstanding he placed the blood of Jesus upon his accusers, and the multitude received it, crying, His blood be on us and on our children, yet Pilate was not clear; he was guilty of the blood of Christ. For his own selfish interest, and love of honor from the great men of earth, he delivered an innocent man to die. If Pilate had followed his conviction, he would have had nothing to do with condemning Jesus.

The trial and condemnation of Jesus were working on the minds of many; and impressions were being made which were to appear after his resurrection; and many were to be added to the Church whose experience and conviction should be dated from the time of Jesus f trial.

Satan fs rage was great as he saw that all the cruelty which he had led the chief priests to inflict on Jesus had not called forth from him the least murmur. I saw that, although Jesus had taken man fs nature, a power and fortitude that was God-like sustained him, and he did not depart from the will of his Father in the least.

See Matthew 27.

The Crucifixion of Christ

The Son of God was delivered to the people to be crucified. They led the dear Saviour away. He was weak and feeble through pain and suffering, caused by the scourging and blows which he had received, yet they laid on him the heavy cross upon which they were soon to nail him. But Jesus fainted beneath the burden. Three times they laid on him the heavy cross, and three times he fainted. They then seized one of his followers, a man who had not openly professed faith in Christ, yet believed on him. They laid on him the cross, and he bore it to the fatal spot. Companies of angels were marshaled in the air above the place. A number of his disciples followed him to Calvary in sorrow, and with bitter weeping. They called to mind Jesus f riding triumphantly into Jerusalem, and they following him, crying, Hosanna in the highest! and strewing their garments in the way, and the beautiful palm branches. They thought that he was then to take the kingdom and reign a temporal prince over Israel. How changed the scene! How blighted their prospects! They followed Jesus; not with rejoicing; not with bounding hearts and cheerful hopes; but with hearts stricken with fear and despair they slowly, sadly followed him who had been disgraced and humbled, and who was about to die.

The mother of Jesus was there. Her heart was pierced with anguish, such as none but a fond mother can feel. Her stricken heart still hoped, with the disciples, that her Son would work some mighty miracle, and deliver himself from his murderers. She could not endure the thought that he would suffer himself to be crucified. But the preparations were made, and they laid Jesus upon the cross. The hammer and the nails were brought. The heart of his disciples fainted within them. The mother of Jesus was agonized, almost beyond endurance, and as they stretched Jesus upon the cross, and were about to fasten his hands with the cruel nails to the wooden arms, the disciples bore the mother of Jesus from the scene, that she might not hear the crashing of the nails, as they were driven through the bone and muscle of his tender hands and feet. Jesus murmured not; but groaned in agony. His face was pale, and large drops of sweat stood upon his brow. Satan exulted in the sufferings which the Son of God was passing through, yet feared that his kingdom was lost, and that he must die.

They raised the cross after they had nailed Jesus to it, and with great force thrust it into the place prepared for it in the ground, tearing the flesh, and causing the most intense suffering. They made his death as shameful as possible. With him they crucified two thieves, one on either side of Jesus. The thieves were taken by force, and after much resistance on their part, their arms were thrust back and nailed to their crosses. But Jesus meekly submitted. He needed no one to force his arms back upon the cross. While the thieves were cursing their executioners, Jesus in agony prayed for his enemies, Father, forgive them, for they know not what they do. It was not merely agony of body which Jesus endured, but the sins of the whole world were upon him.

As Jesus hung upon the cross, some who passed by reviled him, wagging their heads, as though bowing to a king, and said to him, Thou that destroyest the temple and buildest it in three days, save thyself. If thou be the Son of God, come down from the cross. The Devil used the same words to Christ in the wilderness, If thou be the Son of God. The chief priests and elders and scribes mockingly said, He saved others, himself he cannot save. If he be the King of Israel, let him now come down from the cross, and we will believe him. The angels who hovered over the scene of Christ fs crucifixion were moved to indignation as the rulers derided him, and said, If he be the Son of God let him deliver himself. They wished there to come to the rescue of Jesus, and deliver him; but they were not suffered to do so. The object of his mission was almost accomplished. As Jesus hung upon the cross those dreadful hours of agony, he did not forget his mother. She could not remain away from the suffering scene. Jesus f last lesson was one of compassion and humanity. He looked upon his mother, whose heart was well nigh bursting with grief, and then upon his beloved disciple John. He said to his mother, Woman, behold thy Son. Then said he to John, Behold thy mother. And from that hour John took her to his own house.

Jesus thirsted in his agony; but they heaped upon him additional insult, by giving him vinegar and gall to drink. The angels had viewed the horrid scene of the crucifixion of their loved commander, until they could behold no longer; and veiled their faces from the sight. The sun refused to look upon the dreadful scene. Jesus cried with a loud voice, which struck terror to the hearts of his murderers, It is finished. Then the veil of the temple was rent from the top to the bottom, the earth shook, and the rocks rent. Great darkness was upon the face of the earth. The last hope of the disciples seemed swept away as Jesus died. Many of his followers witnessed the scene of his sufferings and death, and their cup of sorrow was full.

Satan did not then exult as he had done. He had hoped that he could break up the plan of salvation; but it was laid too deep. And now by Jesus f death, he knew that he must finally die, and his kingdom be taken away and given to Jesus. He held a council with his angels. He had prevailed nothing against the Son of God, and now they must increase their efforts, and with their cunning and power turn to Jesus f followers. They must prevent all they could from receiving salvation purchased for them by Jesus. By so doing Satan could still work against the government of God. Also it would be for his own interest to keep from Jesus all he could. For the sins of those who are redeemed by the blood of Christ, and overcome, at last will be rolled back upon the originator of sin, the Devil, and he will have to bear their sins, while those who do not accept salvation through Jesus will bear their own sins.

Jesus f life was without worldly grandeur, or extravagant show. His humble, self-denying life was a great contrast to the lives of the priests and elders, who loved ease and worldly honor, and the strict and holy life of Jesus was a continual reproof to them, on account of their sins. They despised him for his humbleness, holiness and purity. But those who despised him here, will one day see him in the grandeur of heaven, and the unsurpassed glory of his Father. He was surrounded with enemies in the judgment hall, who were thirsting for his blood; but those hardened ones who cried out, His blood be on us and on our children, will behold him an honored King. All the heavenly host will escort him on his way with songs of victory, majesty and might, to him that was slain, yet lives again a mighty conqueror. Poor, weak, miserable man spit in the face of the King of glory, while a shout of brutal triumph arose from the mob at the degrading insult. They marred that face with blows and cruelty which filled all heaven with admiration. They will behold that face again, bright as the noonday sun, and will seek to flee from before it. Instead of that shout of brutal triumph, in terror they will wail because of him. Jesus will present his hands with the marks of his crucifixion. The marks of this cruelty he will ever bear. Every print of the nails will tell the story of man fs wonderful redemption, and the dear price that purchased it. The very men who thrust the spear into the side of the Lord of life, will behold the print of the spear, and will lament with deep anguish the part they acted in marring his body. His murderers were greatly annoyed by the superscription, The King of the Jews, placed upon the cross above his head. But then they will be obliged to see him in all his glory and kingly power. They will behold on his vesture and on his thigh, written in living characters, King of Kings, and Lord of Lords. They cried to him mockingly, as he hung upon the cross, Let Christ the King of Israel descend from the cross, that we may see and believe. They will behold him then with kingly power and authority. They will demand no evidence then of his being the King of Israel; but overwhelmed with a sense of his majesty and exceeding glory, they will be compelled to acknowledge, Blessed is he that cometh in the name of the Lord.

The shaking of the earth, the rending of the rocks, the darkness spread over the earth, and the loud, strong cry of Jesus, It is finished, as he yielded up his life, troubled his enemies, and made his murderers tremble. The disciples wondered at these singular manifestations; but their hopes were all crushed. They were afraid the Jews would seek to destroy them also. Such hate manifested against the Son of God they thought would not end there. Lonely hours the disciples spent in sorrow, weeping over their disappointment. They expected that he would reign a temporal prince; but their hopes died with Jesus. They doubted in their sorrow and disappointment whether Jesus had not deceived them. His mother was humbled, and even her faith wavered in his being the Messiah.

But notwithstanding the disciples had been disappointed in their hopes concerning Jesus, yet they loved him, and respected and honored his body, but knew not how to obtain it. Joseph of Arimathea, an honorable counsellor, had influence, and was one of Jesus f true disciples. He went privately, yet boldly, to Pilate and begged his body. He dared not go openly; for the hatred of the Jews was so great that the disciples feared that an effort would be made by them to prevent the body of Jesus having an honored resting place. But Pilate granted his request, and as they took the body of Jesus down from the cross, their sorrows were renewed, and they mourned over their blighted hopes in deep anguish. They wrapped Jesus in fine linen, and Joseph laid him in his own new sepulchre. The women who had been his humble followers while he lived still kept near him after his death, and would not leave him until they saw his sacred body laid in the sepulchre, and a stone of great weight rolled at the door, lest his enemies should seek to obtain his body. But they need not have feared; for I beheld the angelic host watching with untold interest the resting place of Jesus. They guarded the sepulchre, earnestly waiting the command to act their part in liberating the King of glory from his prison house.

Christ fs murderers were afraid that he might yet come to life and escape them. They begged of Pilate a watch to guard the sepulchre until the third day. Pilate granted them armed soldiers to guard the sepulchre, sealing the stone at the door, lest his disciples should steal him away, and say that he had risen from the dead.

See Matthew 27.

The Resurrection of Christ

The disciples rested on the Sabbath, sorrowing for the death of their Lord, while Jesus, the King of glory, rested in the sepulchre. The night had worn slowly away, and while it was yet dark, the angels hovering over the sepulchre knew that the time of the release of God fs dear Son, their loved commander, had nearly come. And as they were waiting with the deepest emotion the hour of his triumph, a strong and mighty angel came flying swiftly from heaven. His face was like the lightning, and his garments white as snow. His light dispersed the darkness from his track, and caused the evil angels who had triumphantly claimed the body of Jesus, to flee in terror from his brightness and glory. One of the angelic host who had witnessed the scene of Jesus f humiliation, and was watching his sacred resting place, joined the angel from heaven, and together they came down to the sepulchre. The earth shook and trembled as they approached, and there was a mighty earthquake. The strong and mighty angel laid hold of the stone and quickly rolled it away from the door of the sepulchre, and sat upon it.

Terrible fear seized the guard. Where was now their power to keep the body of Jesus? They did not think of their duty, or of the disciples stealing him away. They were amazed and affrighted, as the exceeding bright light of the angels shone all around brighter than the sun. The Roman guard saw the angels, and fell as dead men to the ground. One angel rolled back the stone in triumph, and with a clear and mighty voice, cried out, Thou Son of God! Thy Father calls thee! Come forth! Death could hold dominion over him no longer. Jesus arose from the dead. The other angel entered the sepulchre,

and as Jesus arose in triumph, he unbound the napkin which was about his head, and Jesus walked forth a victorious conqueror. In solemn awe the angelic host gazed upon the scene. And as Jesus walked forth from the sepulchre in majesty, those shining angels prostrated themselves to the ground and worshiped him; then hailed him with songs of victory and triumph, that death could hold its divine captive no longer. Satan did not now triumph. His angels had fled before the bright, penetrating light of the heavenly angels. They bitterly complained to their king, that their prey had been taken violently from them, and that he whom they so much hated had risen from the dead.

Satan and his angels had enjoyed a little moment of triumph that their power over fallen man had caused the Lord of life, to be laid in the grave; but short was their hellish triumph. For as Jesus walked forth from his prison house a majestic conqueror, Satan knew that after a season he must die, and his kingdom pass unto him whose right it was. He lamented and raged that notwithstanding all his efforts and power, Jesus had not been overcome, but had laid open a way of salvation for man, and whosoever would, might walk in it and be saved.

For a little, Satan seemed sad and showed distress. He held a council with his angels to consider what they should engage in next to work against the government of God. Said Satan, You must hasten to the chief priests and elders. We succeeded in deceiving them and blinding their eyes, and hardening their hearts against Jesus. We made them believe he was an impostor. That Roman guard will carry the hateful news that Christ is risen. We led the priests and elders on to hate Jesus, and to murder him. Now hold it before them in a bright light, that as they were his murderers, if it becomes known that Jesus is risen, they will be stoned to death by the people, in that they killed an innocent man.

I saw the Roman guard, as the angelic host passed back to heaven, and the light and glory passed away, raise themselves to see if it were safe for them to look around. They were filled with amazement as they saw that the great stone was rolled from the door of the sepulchre, and Jesus was risen. They hastened to the chief priests and elders with the wonderful story of what they had seen; and as those murderers heard the marvelous report, paleness sat upon every face. Horror seized them at what they had done. They then realized that if the report was correct, they were lost. For a little they were stupefied, and looked one to the other in silence, not knowing what to do or say. They were placed where they could not believe unless it be to their own condemnation. They went aside by themselves to consult what should be done. They decided that if it should be spread abroad that Jesus had risen, and the report of such amazing glory, which caused the guard to fall like dead men, should come to the people, they would surely be enraged, and would slay them. They decided to hire the soldiers to keep the matter secret. They offered them much money, saying, Say ye, His disciples came by night and stole him away while we slept. And when the guard inquired what should be done with them for sleeping at their post, the priests and elders said that they would persuade the governor and save them. For the sake of money the Roman guard sold their honor, and agreed to follow the counsel of the priests and elders.

When Jesus as he hung upon the cross, cried out, It is finished, the rocks rent, the earth shook, and some of the graves were shaken open; for when Jesus arose from the dead, and conquered death and the grave; when he walked forth from his prison house a triumphant conqueror; while the earth was reeling and shaking, and the excellent glory of heaven clustered around the sacred spot, obedient to his call, many of the righteous dead came forth as witnesses that he had risen. Those favored, resurrected saints came forth glorified. They were a few chosen and holy ones who had lived in every age from creation, even down to the days of Christ. And while the chief priests and Pharisees were seeking to cover up the resurrection of Christ, God chose to bring up a company from their graves to testify that Jesus had risen, and to declare his glory.

Those who were resurrected were of different stature and form. I was informed that the inhabitants of earth had been degenerating, losing their strength and comeliness. Satan has the power of disease and death, and in every age the curse has been more visible, and the power of Satan more plainly seen. Some of those raised were more noble in appearance and form than others. I was informed that those who lived in the days of Noah and Abraham were more like the angels in form, in comeliness and strength. But every generation has been growing weaker, and more subject to disease, and their lives of shorter duration. Satan has been learning how to annoy men, and to enfeeble the race.

Those holy ones who came forth after the resurrection of Jesus appeared unto many, telling them that the sacrifice for man was completed, that Jesus, whom the Jews crucified, had risen from the dead, and added, We be risen with him. They bore testimony that it was by his mighty power that they had been called forth from their graves. Notwithstanding the lying reports circulated, the matter could not be concealed by Satan, his angels, or the chief priests; for this holy company, brought forth from their graves, spread the wonderful, joyful news; also Jesus showed himself unto his sorrowing, heart-broken disciples, dispelling their fears, and causing them gladness and joy.

As the news spread from city to city, and from town to town, the Jews in their turn were afraid for their lives, and concealed the hate they cherished towards the disciples. Their only hope was to spread their lying report. And those who wished this lie to be true, believed it. Pilate trembled. He believed the strong testimony given, that Jesus was risen from the dead, and that many others he had brought up with him, and his peace left him forever. For the sake of worldly honor; for fear of losing his authority, and his life, he delivered Jesus to die. He was now fully convinced that it was not merely a common, innocent man of whose blood he was guilty but the blood of the Son of God. Miserable was the life of Pilate; miserable to its close. Despair and anguish crushed every hopeful, joyful feeling. He refused to be comforted, and died a most miserable death.

Herod fs heart grew still harder, and when he heard that Jesus had arisen, he was not much troubled. He took the life of James; and when he saw that this pleased the Jews, he took Peter also, intending to put him to death. But God had a work for Peter to do, and sent his angel and delivered him. Herod was visited with judgment. God smote him in the sight of a great multitude as he was exalting himself before them, and he died a horrible death.

Early in the morning before it was yet light, the holy women came to the sepulchre, bringing sweet spices to anoint the body of Jesus, when lo! they found the heavy stone rolled away from the door of the sepulchre, and the body of Jesus was not there. Their hearts sunk within them, and they feared that their enemies had taken away the body. And, behold, two angels in white apparel stood by them; their faces were bright and shining. They understood the errand of the holy women, and immediately told them that they were seeking Jesus, but he was not there, he had risen, and they could behold the place where he lay. They bid them go tell his disciples that he would go before them into Galilee. But the women were frightened and astonished. They hastily ran to the disciples who were mourning, and could not be comforted because their Lord had been crucified; they hurriedly told them the things which they had seen and heard. The disciples could not believe that he had risen, but, with the women who had brought the report, ran hastily to the sepulchre, and found that truly Jesus was not there. There were his linen clothes, but they could not believe the good news that Jesus had risen from the dead. They returned home marveling at the things they had seen, also at the report brought them by the women. But Mary chose to linger around the sepulchre, thinking of what she had seen, and distressed with the thought that she might have been deceived. She felt that new trials awaited her. Her grief was renewed, and she broke forth in bitter weeping. She stooped down to look again into the sepulchre, and beheld two angels clothed in white. Their countenances were bright and shining. One was sitting at the head, the other at the feet, where Jesus had lain. They spoke to her tenderly, and asked her why she wept. She replied, They have taken away my Lord, and I know not where they have laid him.

And as she turned from the sepulchre, she saw Jesus standing by her; but knew him not. Jesus spoke tenderly to Mary, and inquired the cause of her sorrow, and asked her whom she was seeking. She supposed he was the gardener, and begged of him, if he had borne away her Lord, to tell her where he had laid him, and she would take him away. Jesus spoke to her with his own heavenly voice, and said, Mary. She was acquainted with the tones of that dear voice, and quickly answered, Master! and with joy and gladness was about to embrace him; but Jesus stood back, and said, Touch me not, for I am not yet ascended to my Father; but go to my brethren and say unto them, I ascend unto my Father, and your Father, and to my God, and your God. Joyfully she hastened to the disciples with the good news. Jesus quickly ascended up to his Father to hear from his lips that he accepted the sacrifice, and that he had done all things well, and to receive all power in heaven, and upon earth, from his Father.

Angels like a cloud surrounded the Son of God, and bid the everlasting gates be lifted up, that the King of glory might come in. I saw that while Jesus was with that bright, heavenly host, and in the presence of his Father, and the excellent glory of God surrounded him, he did not forget his poor disciples upon earth; but received power from his Father, that he might return unto them, and while with them impart power unto them. The same day he returned, and showed himself to his disciples. He suffered them then to touch him, for he had ascended to his Father, and had received power.

But at this time Thomas was not present. He would not humbly receive the report of the disciples; but firmly, and self-confidently affirmed that he would not believe, unless he should put his fingers in the prints of the nails, and his hand in his side where the cruel spear was thrust. In this he showed a lack of confidence in his brethren. And if all should require the same evidence, but few would receive Jesus, and believe in his resurrection. But it was the will of God that the report of the disciples should go from one to the other, and many receive it from the lips of those who had seen and heard. God was not well pleased with such unbelief. And when Jesus met with his disciples again, Thomas was with them. The moment he beheld Jesus he believed. But he had declared that he would not be satisfied without the evidence of feeling added to sight, and Jesus gave him the evidence he had desired. Thomas cried out, my Lord and my God. But Jesus reproved Thomas for his unbelief. He said to him, Thomas, because thou hast seen me, thou hast believed; blessed are they that have not seen and yet have believed.

So, I saw, that those who had no experience in the first and second angels' messages1 must receive them from those who had an experience, and followed down through the messages. As Jesus was crucified, so I saw that these messages have been crucified. And as the disciples declared that there was salvation in no other name under heaven, given among men; so, also, should the servants of God faithfully and fearlessly declare that those who embrace but a part of the truths connected with the third message2 must gladly embrace the first, second and third messages as God has given them, or have no part nor lot in the matter.

I was shown that while the holy women were carrying the report that Jesus had risen, the Roman guard were circulating the lie that had been put in their mouths by the chief priests and elders, that the disciples came by night, while they slept, and stole the body of Jesus. Satan had put this lie into the hearts and mouths of the chief priests, and the people stood ready to receive their word. But God had made this matter sure, and placed this important event, upon which hangs salvation, beyond all doubt, and where it was impossible for priests and elders to cover it up. Witnesses were raised from the dead to testify to Christ fs resurrection.

Jesus remained with his disciples forty days, causing them joy and gladness of heart, and opening to them more fully the realities of the kingdom of God. He commissioned them to bear testimony to the things which they had seen and heard, concerning his sufferings, death and resurrection; that he had made a sacrifice for sin, that all who would, might come unto him and find life. He with faithful tenderness told them that they would be persecuted and distressed; but they would find relief in referring to their experience, and remembering the words he had spoken to them. He told them that he had overcome the temptations of the Devil, and maintained the victory through trials and suffering, that Satan could have no more power over him, but would more directly bring his temptations and power to bear upon them, and upon all who should believe in his name. He told them that they could overcome, as he had overcome. Jesus endowed his disciples with power to do miracles, and he told them that although wicked men should have power over their bodies, he would at certain times send his angels and deliver them; that their lives could not be taken from them until their mission should be accomplished. And when their testimony should be finished, their lives might be required to seal the testimonies which they had borne. His anxious followers gladly listened to his teachings. They eagerly feasted upon every word which fell from his holy lips. Then they certainly knew that he was the Saviour of the world. Every word sunk with deep weight into their hearts, and they sorrowed that they must be parted from their blessed, heavenly teacher; that after a little they should no more hear comforting, gracious words from his lips. But again their hearts were warmed with love and exceeding joy, as Jesus told them that he would go and prepare mansions for them, and come again and receive them, that they might ever be with him. He told them that he would send them the Comforter, the Holy Spirit, to guide, bless and lead them into all truth; and he lifted up his hands and blessed them.

See Matthew 27:52-53, chap.28; Mark 16:1-18; Luke 24:1-50; John chap.20; Acts chap.12

1 See Revelation 14:6-8. Explained in chapter 23&24 of this book.

2 See Revelation 14:9-12. Explained in chapter 28 of this book.

The Ascension of Christ

All heaven was waiting the hour of triumph when Jesus should ascend to his Father. Angels came to receive the King of glory, and to escort him triumphantly to heaven. After Jesus had blessed his disciples, he was parted from them, and taken up. And as he led the way upward, the multitude of captives who were raised at his resurrection followed. A multitude of the heavenly host was in attendance; while in heaven an innumerable number of angels awaited his coming. As they ascended up to the holy city, the angels who escorted Jesus cried out, Lift up your heads, O ye gates, and be ye lift up, ye everlasting doors, and the King of glory shall come in. With rapture the angels in the city, who awaited his coming, cried out, who is this King of glory? The escorting angels with triumph answered, The Lord strong and mighty! The Lord mighty in battle! Lift up your heads, O ye gates! even lift them up, ye everlasting doors, and the King of glory shall come in. Again the heavenly host cried out, Who is this King of glory? The escorting angels in melodious strains answered, The Lord of hosts! He is the King of Glory! And the heavenly train passed into the city. Then all the heavenly host surrounded the Son of God, their majestic commander, and with the deepest adoration bowed, casting their glittering crowns at his feet. And then they touched their golden harps, and in sweet, melodious strains, filled all heaven with their rich music and songs to the Lamb who was slain, yet lives again in majesty and glory.

Next I was shown the disciples as they sorrowfully gazed towards heaven to catch the last glimpse of their ascending Lord. Two angels clothed in white apparel stood by them, and said unto them, Ye men of Galilee, why stand ye gazing up into heaven? This same Jesus, which is taken up from you into heaven, shall so come in like manner as ye have seen him go into heaven. The disciples, with the mother of Jesus, witnessed the ascension of the Son of God, and they spent that night in talking over his wonderful acts, and the strange and glorious things which had transpired within a short time.

Satan counselled with his angels, and with bitter hatred against God's government, told them that while he retained his power and authority upon earth, their efforts must be tenfold stronger against the followers of Jesus. They had prevailed nothing against Jesus; but his followers they must overthrow if possible, and carry on his work through every generation, to ensnare those who should believe in Jesus, his resurrection and ascension. Satan related to his angels that Jesus had given his disciples power to cast them out, rebuke them, and heal those whom he should afflict. Then Satan's angels went forth like roaring lions, seeking to destroy the followers of Jesus.

See Psalms 24:7-10, Acts1:1-11.

The Disciples of Christ

With mighty power the disciples preached a crucified and risen Saviour. They healed the sick, even one who had always been lame was restored to perfect soundness, and entered with them into the temple, walking and leaping and praising God in the sight of all the people. The news spread, and the people began to press around the disciples. Many ran together, greatly astonished and amazed at the cure that had been wrought.

When Jesus died the chief priests thought that there would be no more miracles wrought among them, that the excitement would die, and that the people would again turn to the traditions of men. But, lo! right in their midst, the disciples were working miracles, and the people were filled with amazement, and gazed with wonder upon them. Jesus had been crucified, and they wondered where the disciples had obtained this power. When he was alive they thought that he imparted power to his disciples; when Jesus died, they expected those miracles would end. Peter understood their perplexity, and said to them, Ye men of Israel, why marvel ye at this? or why look ye so earnestly on us, as though by our own power or holiness we had made this man to walk? The God of Abraham, and of Isaac, and of Jacob, the God of our fathers hath glorified his Son Jesus, whom ye delivered up, and denied him in the presence of Pilate, when he was determined to let him go. But ye denied the Holy One, and the Just, and desired a murderer to be granted unto you, and killed the Prince of life, whom God hath raised from the dead, whereof we are witnesses. Peter told them that it was faith in Jesus that had caused this perfect soundness of a man who was before a cripple.

The chief priests and elders could not bear these words. They laid hold of the disciples and put them in confinement. But thousands were converted, and believed in the resurrection and ascension of Christ, by hearing only one discourse from the disciples. The chief priests and elders were troubled. They had slain Jesus that the minds of the people might be turned to themselves; but the matter was now worse than before. They were openly accused by the disciples of being the murderers of the Son of God, and they could not determine to what extent these things might grow, or how they themselves would be regarded by the people. They would gladly have put the disciples to death; but dared not for fear the people would stone them. They called for the disciples, who were brought before the council. The very men who eagerly cried for the blood of the Just One were there. They had heard Peter's cowardly denial of Jesus, with cursing and swearing, as he was accused of being one of his disciples. They thought to intimidate Peter; but he was now converted. An opportunity was here given Peter to exalt Jesus. He once denied him; but he could now remove the stain of that hasty, cowardly denial, and honor the name he had denied. No cowardly fears reigned in the breast of Peter then; but with holy boldness, and in the power of the Holy Spirit, he fearlessly declared unto them that by the name of Jesus Christ of Nazareth, whom ye crucified, whom God raised from the dead, even by him doth this man stand here before you whole. This is the stone which was set at naught of you builders, which has become the head stone of the corner. Neither is there salvation in any other; for there is none other name under heaven given among men, whereby we must be saved.

The people were astonished at the boldness of Peter and John. They took knowledge of them that they had been with Jesus; for their noble, fearless conduct compared well with the appearance of Jesus when he was persecuted by his murderers. Jesus, by one look of pity and sorrow, reproved Peter after he had denied him, and now as he boldly acknowledged his Lord,

Peter was approved and blessed. As a token of the approbation of Jesus, he was filled with the Holy Spirit.

The chief priests dared not manifest the hate they felt towards the disciples. They commanded them to go aside out of the council, and they conferred among themselves, saying, What shall we do to these men? for that indeed a notable miracle hath been done by them is manifest to all them that dwell in Jerusalem, and we cannot deny it. They were afraid to have this good work spread. If it should spread, their power would be lost, and they would be looked upon as the murderers of Jesus. All that they dared to do was to threaten them, and command them to speak no more in the name of Jesus lest they die. But Peter declared boldly that they could but speak the things which they had seen and heard.

By the power of Jesus the disciples continued to heal every one of the afflicted and the sick which were brought to them. The high priests and elders, and those particularly engaged with them, were alarmed. Hundreds were enlisting daily under the banner of a crucified, risen and ascended Saviour. They shut the apostles up in prison, and hoped that the excitement would subside. Satan triumphed, and the evil angels exulted; but the angels of God were sent and opened the prison doors, and, contrary to the command of the high priest and elders, bade them go into the temple, and speak all the words of this life. The council assembled and sent for their prisoners. The officers unclosed the prison doors; but the prisoners whom they sought were not there. They returned to the priests and elders, and said to them, The prison truly found we shut with all safety, and the keepers standing without before the doors; but when we had opened we found no man within. Then came one and told them, saying, Behold the men whom ye put in prison are standing in the temple, and teaching the people. Then went the captain with the officers, and brought them without violence; for they feared the people lest they should have been stoned. And when they had brought them, they set them before the council; and the high priest asked them, Did not we straitly command you, that ye should not teach in this name? and, behold, ye have filled Jerusalem with your doctrine, and intend to bring this man's blood upon us.

They were hypocrites, and loved the praise of men more than they loved God. Their hearts were hardened, and the most mighty acts wrought by the apostles only enraged them. They knew that if the disciples preached Jesus, his crucifixion, resurrection and ascension, it would fasten guilt upon them, and proclaim them his murderers. They were not as willing to receive the blood of Jesus as when they vehemently cried, His blood be on us, and on our children.

The apostles boldly declared that they ought to obey God rather than man. Said Peter, The God of our fathers raised up Jesus, whom ye slew and hanged on a tree. Him hath God exalted with his right hand to be a Prince and a Saviour, for to give repentance to Israel, and forgiveness of sins. And we are his witnesses of these things, and so is also the Holy Spirit whom God hath given to them that obey him. Then were those murderers enraged. They wished to imbrue their hands in blood again by slaying the apostles. They were planning how to do this, when an angel from God was sent to Gamaliel to move upon his heart to counsel the chief priest and rulers. Said Gamaliel, Refrain from these men, and let them alone; for if this counsel or this work be of men, it will come to naught; but if it be of God ye cannot overthrow it; lest haply ye be found even to fight against God. The evil angels were moving upon the priests and elders to put the apostles to death; but God sent his angel to prevent it, by raising up a voice in favor of the disciples in their own ranks.

The work of the apostles was not finished. They were to be brought before kings, to witness to the name of Jesus, and to testify to the things which they had seen and heard. But before these chief priests and elders let them go, they beat them, and commanded them to speak no more in the name of Jesus. They departed from the council praising God that they were accounted worthy to suffer for his dear name. They continued their mission, preaching in the temple and in every house where they were invited. The word of God grew and multiplied. Satan had moved upon the chief priests and elders to hire the Roman guard to falsely say that the disciples stole Jesus while they slept. Through this lie they hoped to conceal the facts; but, lo, springing up all around them were the mighty evidences of Jesus' resurrection. The disciples boldly declared it, and testified to the things which they had seen and heard, and through the name of Jesus they performed mighty miracles. They boldly placed the blood of Jesus upon those who were so willing to receive it, when they were permitted to have power over the Son of God.

I saw that the angels of God were commissioned to have a special care, and guard the sacred, important truths which were to serve as an anchor to hold the disciples of Christ through every generation.

The Holy Spirit especially rested upon the apostles, who were witnesses of Jesus' crucifixion, resurrection and ascension -- -important truths which were to be the hope of Israel. All were to look to the Saviour of the world as their only hope, and walk in the way Jesus opened by the sacrifice of his own life, and keep God's law and live. I saw the wisdom and goodness of Jesus in giving power to the disciples to carry on the same work which caused the Jews to hate and slay him. They had power given them over the works of Satan. They wrought signs and wonders through the name of Jesus, who was despised, and by wicked hands slain. A halo of light and glory clustered about the time of Jesus' death and resurrection, immortalizing the sacred facts that he was the Saviour of the world.

See Acts 3; Acts 4.

The Death of Stephen

Disciples multiplied greatly in Jerusalem. The word of God increased, and many of the priests were obedient unto the faith. Stephen, full of faith, was doing great wonders and miracles among the people. Many were angry; for the priests were turning from their traditions, and from the sacrifices and offerings, and were accepting Jesus as the great sacrifice. Stephen, with power from on high, reproved the priests and elders, and exalted Jesus before them. They could not withstand the wisdom and power by which he spoke, and as they found that they could prevail nothing against him, they hired men to falsely swear that they had heard him speak blasphemous words against Moses and against God. They stirred up the people, and took Stephen, and, through false witnesses, accused him of speaking against the temple and the law. They testified that they had heard him say that this Jesus of Nazareth would destroy the customs which Moses gave them.

All who sat in judgment against Stephen saw the light of the glory of God in his countenance. His countenance was lighted up like the face of an angel. He stood up full of faith and the Holy Spirit, and, beginning at the prophets, he brought them down to the advent of Jesus, his crucifixion, his resurrection and ascension, and showed them that the Lord dwelt not in temples made with hands. They worshiped the temple. Anything spoken against the temple filled them with greater indignation than if spoken against God. The spirit of Stephen was stirred with heavenly indignation as he cried out against them for being wicked, and uncircumcised in heart. Ye do always resist the Holy Spirit. They observed the outward ordinances, while their hearts were corrupt, and full of deadly evil. Stephen referred them to the cruelty of their fathers in persecuting the prophets, saying, Ye have slain them which showed before the coming of the Just One, of whom ye have been now the betrayers and murderers.

The chief priests and the rulers were enraged as the plain, cutting truths were spoken; and they rushed upon Stephen. The light of heaven shone upon him, and as he looked up steadfastly into heaven, a vision of God's glory was given him, and angels hovered around him. He cried out, Behold, I see the heavens opened, and the Son of man standing on the right hand of God. The people would not hear him. They cried out with a loud voice, and stopped their ears, and ran upon him with one accord, and cast him out of the city, and stoned him. And Stephen kneeled down, and cried with a loud voice, Lord, lay not this sin to their charge.

I saw that Stephen was a mighty man of God, especially raised up to fill an important place in the church. Satan exulted as he was stoned to death; for he knew that the disciples would greatly feel his loss. But Satan's triumph was short; for there was one standing in that company, witnessing the death of Stephen, to whom Jesus was to reveal himself. Although he took no part in casting the stones at Stephen, yet he consented to his death. Saul was zealous in persecuting the church of God, hunting them, seizing them in their houses, and delivering them to those who would slay them. Satan was using Saul effectually. But God can break the Devil's power, and set free those who are led captive by him. Saul was a learned man, and Satan was triumphantly employing his talents to help carry out his rebellion against

the Son of God, and those who believed in him. But Jesus selected Saul as a chosen vessel to preach his name, to strengthen the disciples in their work, and more than fill the place of Stephen. Saul was greatly esteemed by the Jews. His zeal and his learning pleased them, and terrified many of the disciples.

See Acts 6; Acts 7.

The Conversion of Saul

As Saul journeyed to Damascus with letters of authority to take men or women who were preaching Jesus, and to bring them bound unto Jerusalem, evil angels exulted around him. But as he journeyed, suddenly a light from heaven shone around him, which made the evil angels flee, and caused Saul to fall quickly to the ground. He heard a voice saying, Saul, Saul, why persecutest thou me? Saul inquired, Who art thou, Lord? And the Lord said, I am Jesus whom thou persecutest. It is hard for thee to kick against the pricks. And Saul trembling and astonished said, Lord, what wilt thou have me to do? And the Lord said, Arise and go into the city, and it shall be told thee what thou must do.

The men who were with him stood speechless, hearing a voice, but saw no man. As the light passed away, and Saul arose from the earth, and opened his eyes, he saw no man. The glory of the light of heaven had blinded him. They led him by the hand, and brought him to Damascus, and he was three days without sight, neither did he eat or drink. The Lord then sent his angel to one of the very men whom Saul hoped to make captive, and revealed to him in vision that he should go into the street called straight, and inquire in the house of Judas for one called Saul of Tarsus; for, behold, he prayeth, and hath seen in a vision a man named Ananias coming in, and putting his hands on him, that he might receive his sight.

Ananias feared that there was some mistake in this matter, and began to relate to the Lord what he had heard of Saul. But the Lord said unto Ananias, Go thy way; for he is a chosen vessel unto me, to bear my name before the Gentiles, and kings, and the children of Israel. For I will show him how great things he must suffer for my name's sake. Ananias followed the directions of the Lord, and entered into the house, and putting his hands on him, said, Brother Saul, the Lord, even Jesus, that appeared unto thee in the way as thou camest, hath sent me, that thou mightest receive thy sight, and be filled with the Holy Spirit.

Immediately Saul received sight, and arose, and was baptized. He then preached Christ in the synagogues, that he was the Son of God. All who heard him were amazed, and inquired, Is not this he that destroyed them which called on this name in Jerusalem? and come hither on that intent, that he might bring them bound unto the chief priests. But Saul increased the more in strength, and confounded the Jews. They were again in trouble. Saul told his experience in the power of the Holy Spirit. All were acquainted with the fact of Saul's opposition to Jesus, and his zeal in hunting out and delivering up to death all who believed on his name. His miraculous conversion convinced many that Jesus was the Son of God. Saul related his experience, that as he was persecuting unto the death, binding and delivering into prison, both men and women, as he journeyed to Damascus, suddenly a great light from heaven shone round about him, and Jesus revealed himself to him, and taught him that he was the Son of God. As Saul boldly preached Jesus, he carried a powerful influence with him. He had knowledge of the scriptures, and after his conversion a divine light shone upon the prophecies concerning Jesus, which enabled him to clearly and boldly present the truth, and to correct any perversion of the scriptures. With the Spirit of God resting upon him, he would in a clear and forcible manner carry his hearers down through the prophecies to the time of Christ's first advent, and show them that the scriptures had been fulfilled, which referred to Christ's sufferings, death and resurrection.

See Acts 9.

The Jews Decided to Kill Paul

The chief priests and rulers were moved with hatred against Paul, as they witnessed the effect of the relation of his experience. They saw that he boldly preached Jesus, and wrought miracles in his name, and that multitudes listened to him, and turned from their traditions, and looked upon them as being the murderers of the Son of God. Their anger was kindled, and they assembled to consult as to what was best to be done to put down the excitement. They agreed that the only safe course for them was to put Paul to death. But God knew of their intention, and angels were commissioned to guard him, that he might live to fulfill his mission, and to suffer for the name of Jesus.

Paul was informed that the Jews were seeking his life. Satan led the unbelieving Jews to watch the gates of Damascus day and night, that as Paul should pass out of the gates; they might immediately kill him. But the disciples in the night let him down by the wall in a basket. Here the Jews were made ashamed of their failure, and Satan's object was defeated. And Paul went to Jerusalem to join himself to the disciples; but they were all afraid of him. They could not believe that he was a disciple. His life had been hunted by the Jews in Damascus, and his own brethren would not receive him; but Barnabas took him, and brought him to the apostles, and declared unto them how he had seen the Lord in the way, and that he had preached boldly at Damascus in the name of Jesus.

But Satan was stirring up the Jews to destroy Paul, and Jesus bade him leave Jerusalem. And as he went into other cities preaching Jesus, and working miracles, many were converted, and as one man was healed who had always been lame, the people who worshiped idols were about to sacrifice to the disciples. Paul was grieved, and told them that they were only men, and that they must worship God who made heaven and earth, and the sea, and all things that are therein. Paul exalted God before them; but he could scarcely restrain the people.

The first knowledge of faith in the true God, and the worship and honor due to him, were being formed in their minds; and as they were listening to Paul, Satan urged on the unbelieving Jews of other cities to follow after Paul to destroy the good work wrought through him. The Jews stirred up, and inflamed the minds of those idolaters by false reports against Paul. The wonder and admiration of the people now changed to hate, and they who a short time before were ready to worship the disciples, stoned Paul, and drew him out of the city, supposing that he was dead. But as the disciples were standing about Paul, and mourning over him, to their joy he rose up, and went with them into the city.

As Paul preached Jesus, a certain woman possessed with a spirit of divination, followed them, crying, These men are the servants of the most high God, which show unto us the way of salvation. Thus she followed the disciples many days. But Paul was grieved; for this crying after them diverted the minds of the people from the truth. Satan's object in leading her to do this was to disgust the people, and destroy the influence of the disciples. But Paul's spirit was stirred within him, and he turned to the woman, and said to the spirit, I command thee in the name of Jesus Christ to come out of her, and the evil spirit was rebuked, and left her.

Her masters were pleased that she cried after the disciples; but when the evil spirit had left her, and they saw her a meek disciple of Christ, they were enraged. They had gathered much money by her fortune-telling, and now the hope of their gain was gone. Satan's object was defeated; but his servants caught Paul and Silas, and drew them into the market place, unto the rulers, and to the magistrates, saying, These men being Jews do exceedingly trouble our city. And the multitude rose up together against them, and the magistrates tore off their clothes, and commanded to beat them. And when they had laid many stripes upon them, they cast them into prison, charging the jailer to keep them safely, who, having received such a charge, thrust them into the inner prison and made their feet fast in the stocks. But the angels of God accompanied them within the prison walls. Their imprisonment told to the glory of God, and showed to the people that God was in the work, and with his chosen servants, and that prison walls could be shaken, and strong iron bars could easily be opened by him.

At midnight Paul and Silas prayed, and sung praises unto God, and suddenly there was a great earthquake, so that the foundations of the prison were shaken; and I saw that immediately the angel of God loosed everyone's bands. The keeper of the prison awoke and was affrighted as he saw the prison doors open. He thought that the prisoners had escaped, and that he must be punished with death. As he was about to kill himself, Paul cried with a loud voice, saying, Do thyself no harm, for we are all here. The power of God convicted the keeper. He called for a light, and sprang in, and came trembling, and fell down before Paul and Silas, and brought them out, and said, Sirs, what must I do to be saved? And they said, Believe on the Lord Jesus Christ, and thou shalt be saved, and thy house. The jailer then assembled his whole household, and Paul preached unto them Jesus. The jailer's heart was united to those brethren, and he washed their stripes, and he, and all his house, were baptized that night. He then set meat before them, and rejoiced, believing in God, with all his house.

The wonderful news was spread abroad of the glorious power of God which had been manifest in opening the prison doors, and the conversion and baptism of the jailer and his family. The rulers heard of these things, and were afraid, and sent to the jailer, requesting him to let Paul and Silas go. But Paul would not leave the prison in a private manner. He said unto them, They have beaten us openly uncondemned, being Romans, and have cast us into prison; and now do they thrust us out privily? Nay, verily; but let them come themselves, and fetch us out. Paul and Silas were not willing that the manifestation of the power of God should be concealed. The sergeants told these words unto the magistrates; and they feared when they heard that they were Romans. And they came and besought them, and brought them out, and desired them to depart out of the city.

See Acts 13; Acts 16.

Paul Visited Jerusalem

Shortly after Paul's conversion he visited Jerusalem, and preached Jesus, and the wonders of his grace. He related his miraculous conversion, which enraged the priests, and rulers, and they sought to take his life. But that his life might be saved, Jesus appeared to him again in a vision while he was praying, saying unto him, Get thee quickly out of Jerusalem; for they will not receive thy testimony concerning me. Paul earnestly plead with Jesus, Lord, they know that I imprisoned and beat in every synagogue them that believed on thee. And when the blood of thy martyr Stephen was shed, I also was standing by and consenting unto his death, and kept the raiment of them that slew him. Paul thought the Jews in Jerusalem could not resist his testimony; that they would consider that the great change in him could only be wrought by the power of God. But Jesus said unto him, Depart, for I will send thee far hence unto the Gentiles.

In Paul's absence from Jerusalem, he wrote many letters to different places, relating his experience, and bearing a powerful testimony. But some strove to destroy the influence of those letters. They had to admit that his letters were weighty and powerful; but declared that his bodily presence was weak, and his speech contemptible.

I saw that Paul was a man of great learning, and his wisdom and manners charmed his hearers. Learned men were pleased with his knowledge, and many of them believed on Jesus. When before kings and large assemblies, he would pour forth such eloquence as would bear down all before him. This greatly enraged the priests and elders. Paul could readily enter into deep reasoning, and soar up, and carry the people with him, in the most exalted trains of thought, and bring to view the deep riches of the grace of God, and portray before them the amazing love of Christ. Then with simplicity he would come down to the understanding of the common people, and in a most powerful manner relate his experience, which called forth from them ardent desires to be the disciples of Christ.

The Lord revealed to Paul that he must again go up to Jerusalem; that he would there be bound and suffer for his name. And although he was a prisoner for a great length of time, yet the Lord was carrying forward his special work through him. Paul's bonds were to be the means of spreading the knowledge of Christ, and thus glorifying God. As he was sent from city to city for his trial, the testimony concerning Jesus, and the interesting incidents of his conversion were related before kings and governors, that they should not be left without testimony concerning Jesus. Thousands believed on him and rejoiced in his name. I saw that God's special purpose was fulfilled in the journey of Paul upon the water, that the ship's crew might witness the power of God through Paul, and that the heathen also might hear the name of Jesus, and many be converted through his teaching, and by witnessing the miracles he wrought. Kings and governors were charmed by his reasoning, and as, with zeal and the power of the Holy Spirit, he preached Jesus, and related the interesting events of his experience, conviction fastened upon them that Jesus was the Son of God; and while some wondered with amazement as they listened to Paul, one cried out, Almost thou persuadest me to be a Christian. Yet they thought that at some future time they would consider what they had heard. Satan took advantage of the delay, and as they neglected that opportunity when their hearts were softened, it was forever. Their hearts became hardened.

I was shown the work of Satan in first blinding the eyes of the Jews so that they would not receive Jesus as their Saviour; and next in leading them, through envy because of his mighty works, to desire his life. Satan entered one of Jesus' own followers, and led him on to betray him into their hands, and they crucified the Lord of life and glory. After Jesus arose from the dead, the Jews added sin to sin as they sought to hide the fact of the resurrection, by hiring for money the Roman guard to testify to a falsehood. But the resurrection of Jesus was made doubly sure by the resurrection of a multitude of witnesses who arose with him. Jesus appeared to his disciples, and to above five hundred at once, while those whom he brought up with him appeared unto many declaring that Jesus had risen.

Satan had caused the Jews to rebel against God, by refusing to receive his Son, and in staining their hands with most precious blood in crucifying him. No matter how powerful the evidence given of Jesus' being the Son of God, the Redeemer of the world; they had murdered him, and could not receive any evidence in his favor. Their only hope and consolation, like Satan's after his fall, was in trying to prevail against the Son of God. They continued their rebellion by persecuting the disciples of Christ, and putting them to death. Nothing fell so harshly on their ears as the name of Jesus whom they had crucified; and they were determined not to listen to any evidence in his favor. As in the case of Stephen, as the Holy Spirit through him declared the mighty evidence of his being the Son of God, they stopped their ears lest they should be convinced. And while Stephen was wrapped up in God's glory, they stoned him to death. Satan had the murderers of Jesus fast in his grasp. By wicked works they had yielded themselves his willing subjects, and through them he was at work to trouble and annoy the believers of Christ. He worked through the Jews to stir up the Gentiles against the name of Jesus, and against those who followed him, and believed on his name. But God sent his angels to strengthen the disciples for their work, that they might testify of the things they had seen and heard, and at last in their steadfastness, seal their testimony with their blood.

Satan rejoiced that the Jews were safe in his snare. They still continued their useless forms, their sacrifices and ordinances. As Jesus hung upon the cross, and cried, It is finished, the vail of the temple was rent in twain, from the top to the bottom, to signify that God would no longer meet with the priests in the temple, to accept their sacrifices and ordinances; and also to show that the partition wall was broken down between the Jews and the Gentiles. Jesus had made an offering of himself for both, and if saved at all, both must believe in Jesus as the only offering for sin, and the Saviour of the world.

While Jesus hung upon the cross, as the soldier pierced his side with a spear, there came out blood and water, in two distinct streams, one of blood, the other of clear water. The blood was to wash away the sins of those who should believe in his name. The water represents that living water which is obtained from Jesus to give life to the believer.

See Acts 24-26.

The Great Apostasy

I was carried forward to the time when the heathen idolators cruelly persecuted the Christians, and killed them. Blood flowed in torrents. The noble, the learned, and the common people, were alike slain without mercy. Wealthy families were reduced to poverty because they would not yield their religion. Notwithstanding the persecution and sufferings those Christians endured, they would not lower the standard. They kept their religion pure. I saw that Satan exulted and triumphed over the sufferings of God's people. But God looked with great approbation upon his faithful martyrs, and the Christians who lived in that fearful time were greatly beloved of him; for they were willing to suffer for his sake. Every suffering endured by them increased their reward in heaven. But although Satan rejoiced because the saints suffered, yet he was not satisfied. He wanted control of the mind as well as the body. The sufferings those Christians endured drove them closer to the Lord, and led them to love one another, and caused them to fear more than ever to offend him. Satan wished to lead them to displease God; then they would lose their strength, fortitude and firmness.

Although thousands were slain, yet others were springing up to supply their place. Satan saw that he was losing his subjects, and although they suffered persecution and death, yet they were secured to Jesus Christ, to be the subjects of his kingdom, and he laid his plans to more successfully fight against the government of God, and overthrow the church. He led on those heathen idolators to embrace part of the Christian faith. They professed to believe in the crucifixion and resurrection of Christ, without a change of heart, and proposed to unite with the followers of Jesus. O the fearful danger of the church! It was a time of mental anguish. Some thought that if they should come down and unite with those idolators who had embraced a portion of the Christian faith, it would be the means of their conversion. Satan was seeking to corrupt the doctrines of the Bible. At last I saw the standard lowered, and those heathen were uniting with Christians. They had been worshipers of idols, and although they professed to be Christians, they brought along with them their idolatry. They changed the objects only of their worship, to images of saints, and even the image of Christ, and Mary the mother of Jesus. Christians gradually united with them, and the Christian religion was corrupted, and the church lost its purity and power. Some refused to unite with them and they preserved their purity, and worshiped God alone. They would not bow down to any image of anything in the heavens above, or in the earth beneath.

Satan exulted over the fall of so many; and then he stirred up the fallen church to force those who would preserve the purity of their religion, to either yield to their ceremonies and image worship, or to put them to death. The fires of persecution were again kindled against the true church of Jesus Christ, and millions were slain without mercy.

It was presented before me in the following manner: A large company of heathen idolators bore a black banner upon which were figures of the sun, moon and stars. The company seemed to be very fierce and angry. I was then shown another company bearing a pure white banner, and upon it was written Purity, and Holiness unto the Lord. Their countenances were marked with firmness and heavenly resignation. I saw the heathen idolators approach them, and there was a great slaughter. The Christians melted away before them; and yet the Christian company pressed the more closely together, and held the banner more firmly. As many fell, others rallied around the banner and filled their places.

I saw the company of idolators consulting together. They failed to make the Christians yield, and they agreed to another plan. I saw them lower their banner, and they approached that firm Christian company, and made propositions to them. At first their propositions were utterly refused. Then I saw the Christian company consulting together. Some said that they would lower the banner, accept the propositions, and save their lives, and at last they could gain strength to raise their banner among those heathen idolators. But some would not yield to this plan, but firmly chose to die holding their banner, rather than lower it. Then I saw many of that Christian company lower the banner, and unite with the heathen; while the firm and steadfast seized the banner, and bore it high again. I saw individuals continually leaving the company of those bearing the pure banner, and joining the idolators, and they united together under the black banner, to persecute those bearing the white banner, and many were slain; yet the white banner was held high, and individuals were raised up to rally around it.

The Jews who first started the rage of the heathen against Jesus, were not to escape. In the judgment hall the infuriated Jews cried, as Pilate hesitated to condemn Jesus, His blood be on us and on our children. The race of the Jews experienced the fulfillment of this terrible curse which they called down upon their own heads. Heathen and those called Christians were alike their foes. Those professed Christians, in their zeal for the cross of Christ, because the Jews had crucified Jesus, thought that the more suffering they could bring upon them, the better could they please God; and many of those unbelieving Jews were killed, while others were driven from place to place, and were punished in almost every manner.

The blood of Christ, and of the disciples, whom they had put to death, was upon them, and in terrible judgments were they visited. The curse of God followed them, and they were a by-word and a derision to the heathen and to Christians. They were shunned, degraded and detested, as though the brand of Cain was upon them. Yet I saw that God marvelously preserved this people, and had scattered them over the world, that they might be looked upon as especially visited by a curse from God. I saw that God had forsaken the Jews as a nation; yet there was a portion of them who would be enabled to tear away the veil from their hearts. Some will yet see that prophecy has been fulfilled concerning them, and they will receive Jesus as the Savior of the world, and see the great sin of their nation in rejecting Jesus, and crucifying him. Individuals among the Jews will be converted; but as a nation they are forever forsaken of God.

Mystery of Iniquity

It has ever been the design of Satan to draw the minds of the people from Jesus to man, and to destroy individual accountability. Satan failed in his design when he tempted the Son of God. He succeeded better as he came to fallen man. The doctrine of Christianity was corrupted. Popes and priests presumed to take an exalted position, and taught the people to look to them to pardon their sins, instead of looking to Christ for themselves. The Bible was kept from them, in order to conceal the truths which would condemn them.

The people were entirely deceived. They were taught that the popes and priests were Christ's representatives, when in fact they were the representatives of Satan; and when they bowed to them, they worshiped Satan. The people called for the Bible; but the priests considered it dangerous to let them have the word of God to read for themselves, lest they become enlightened, and their sins be exposed. The people were taught to look to these deceivers, and receive every word from them, as from the mouth of God. They held that power over the mind, which God alone should hold. And if any dared to follow their own convictions, the same hate which Satan and the Jews exercised towards Jesus would be kindled against them, and those in authority would thirst for their blood. I was shown a time when Satan especially triumphed. Multitudes of Christians were slain in a dreadful manner because they would preserve the purity of their religion.

The Bible was hated, and efforts were made to rid the earth of the precious word of God. The Bible was forbidden to be read on pain of death, and all the copies of the holy Book which could be found were burned. But I saw that God had a special care for his word. He protected it. At different periods there were but a very few copies of the Bible in existence, yet God would not suffer his word to be lost. And in the last days, copies of the Bible were to be so multiplied that every family could possess it. I saw that when there were but a very few copies of the Bible, it was precious and comforting to the persecuted followers of Jesus. It was read in the most secret manner, and those who had this exalted privilege felt that they had had an interview with God, with his Son Jesus, and with his disciples. But this blessed privilege cost many of them their lives. If discovered, they were taken from reading the sacred Word to the chopping block, the stake, or to the dungeon to die from starvation.

Satan could not hinder the plan of salvation. Jesus was crucified, and arose again the third day. He told his angels that he would make even the crucifixion and resurrection tell to his advantage. He was willing that those who professed faith in Jesus should believe that the laws regulating the Jewish sacrifices and offerings ceased at the death of Christ, if he could push them further, and make them believe that the law of ten commandments died also with Christ.

I saw that many readily yielded to this device of Satan. All heaven was moved with indignation, as they saw the holy law of God trampled under foot. Jesus and all the heavenly host were acquainted with the nature of God's law; they knew that he would not change or abolish it. The hopeless condition of man caused the deepest sorrow in heaven, and moved Jesus to offer to die for the transgressors of God's holy law. If his law could be abolished, man might have been saved without the death of Jesus. The death of Christ did not destroy the law of his Father; but magnified and honored it, and enforces obedience to all its holy precepts. Had the church remained pure and steadfast, Satan could not have deceived them, and led them to trample on the law of God. In this bold plan, Satan strikes directly against the foundation of God's government in heaven and on earth. His rebellion caused him to be expelled from heaven. After he rebelled, in order to save himself, he wished God to change his law; but God told Satan, before the whole heavenly host, that his law was unalterable. Satan knows that if he can cause others to violate God's law he is sure of them; for every transgressor of his law must die.

Satan decided to go still further. He told his angels that some would be so jealous of God's law that they could not be caught in this snare; that the ten commandments were so plain that many would believe that they were still binding; therefore he must seek to corrupt the fourth commandment which brings to view the living God. He led on his representatives to attempt to change the Sabbath, and alter the only commandment of the ten which brings to view the true God, the maker of the heavens and the earth. Satan presented before them the glorious resurrection of Jesus, and told them that by his rising on the first day of the week, he changed the Sabbath from the seventh to the first day of the week. Thus Satan used the resurrection to serve his purpose. He and his angels rejoiced that the errors they had prepared took so well with the professed friends of Christ. What one might look upon with religious horror, another would receive. The different errors would be received, and with zeal defended. The will of God plainly revealed in his word, was covered up with error and tradition, which have been taught as the commandments of God. But although this heaven-daring deception was to be suffered to be carried on down through time until the second appearing of Jesus, yet through all this time of error and deception, God has not been left without a witness. There have been true and faithful witnesses keeping all of God commandments through the darkness and persecution of the church.

I saw that angels were filled with amazement as they beheld the sufferings and death of the King of glory. But I saw that it was no marvel to the angelic host that the Lord of life and glory, who filled all heaven with joy and splendor, should break the bands of death, and walk forth from his prison house a triumphant conqueror. And if either of these events should be commemorated by a day of rest, it is the crucifixion. But, I saw that neither of those events were designed to alter or abolish God's law; but they give the strongest proof of its immutability.

Both of these important events have their memorials. By partaking of the Lord's supper, the broken bread and the fruit of the vine, we show forth the Lord's death until he comes. By observing this memorial, the scenes of his sufferings and death are brought fresh to our minds. The resurrection of Christ is commemorated by our being buried with him by baptism, and raised up out of the watery grave in likeness of his resurrection, to live in newness of life.

I was shown that the law of God would stand fast forever, and exist in the new earth to all eternity. At the creation, when the foundations of the earth were laid, the sons of God looked with admiration upon the work of the Creator, and all the heavenly host shouted for joy. It was then that the foundation of the Sabbath was laid. At the close of the six days of creation, God rested on the seventh day from all his work which he had made; and he blessed the seventh day and sanctified it, because that in it he had rested from all his work. The Sabbath was instituted in Eden before the fall, and was observed by Adam and Eve, and all the heavenly host. God rested on the seventh day, and blessed and hallowed it; and I saw that the Sabbath would never be done away; but the redeemed saints, and all the angelic host, will observe it in honor of the great Creator to all eternity.

See II Thessalonians 2:7; Daniel 7:25.

Death, Not Eternal Life in Misery

Satan commenced his deception in Eden. He said to Eve, Thou shalt not surely die. This was Satan's first lesson upon the immortality of the soul; and he has carried on this deception from that time to the present, and will carry it on until the captivity of God's children shall be turned. I was pointed to Adam and Eve in Eden. They partook of the forbidden tree, and then the flaming sword was placed around the tree of life, and they were driven from the Garden, lest they should partake of the tree of life, and be immortal sinners. The tree of life was to perpetuate immortality. I heard an angel ask, Who of the family of Adam have passed that flaming sword, and have partaken of the tree of life? I heard another angel answer, Not one of the family of Adam have passed that flaming sword, and partaken of that tree; therefore there is not an immortal sinner. The soul that sinneth it shall die an everlasting death; a death that will last forever, where there will be no hope of a resurrection; and then the wrath of God will be appeased.

It was a marvel to me that Satan could succeed so well in making men believe that the words of God, The soul that sinneth it shall die, mean that the soul that sinneth it shall not die, but live eternally in misery. Said the angel, Life is life, whether it is in pain or happiness. Death is without pain, without joy, without hatred.

Satan told his angels to make a special effort to spread the deception and lie first repeated to Eve in Eden, Thou shalt not surely die. And as the error was received by the people, and they believed that man was immortal, Satan led them still further to believe that the sinner would live in eternal misery. Then the way was prepared for Satan to work through his representatives, and hold up God before the people as a revengeful tyrant; that those who do not please him, he will plunge into hell, and cause them ever to feel his wrath; and that they will suffer unutterable anguish, while he will look down upon them with satisfaction, as they writhe in horrible sufferings and eternal flames. Satan knew that if this error should be received, God would be dreaded and hated by very many, instead of being loved and admired; and that many would be led to believe that the threatenings of God's word would not be literally fulfilled; for it would be against his character of benevolence and love, to plunge beings whom he had created into eternal torments. Satan has led them to another extreme, to entirely overlook the justice of God, and the threatenings in his Word, and represent him as being all mercy, and that not one will perish, but all, both saint and sinner, will at last be saved in his kingdom. In consequence of the popular error of the immortality of the soul, and endless misery, Satan takes advantage of another class, and leads them on to regard the Bible as an uninspired book. They think it teaches many good things; but they cannot rely upon it and love it; because they have been taught that it declares the doctrine of eternal misery.

Satan takes advantage of still another class, and leads them still further to deny the existence of God. They can see no consistency in the character of the God of the Bible, if he will torment a portion of the human family to all eternity in horrible tortures; and they deny the Bible and its Author, and regard death as an eternal sleep.

Then Satan leads another class who are fearful and timid to commit sin; and after they have sinned, he holds up before them that the wages of sin is (not death, but) an eternal life in horrible torments, to be endured through the endless ages of eternity. Satan improves the opportunity, and magnifies before their feeble minds the horrors of an endless hell, and takes charge of their minds, and they lose their reason. Then Satan and his angels exult, and the infidel and atheist join in casting reproach upon Christianity. They regard these evil consequences of the reception of popular heresy, as the natural results of believing in the Bible and its Author.

I saw that the heavenly host was filled with indignation at this bold work of Satan. I inquired why all these delusions should be suffered to take effect upon the minds of men, when the angels of God were powerful, and if commissioned, could easily break the enemy's power. Then I saw that God knew that Satan would try every art to destroy man; therefore he had caused his Word to be written out, and had made his designs to man so plain that the weakest need not err. Then, after he had given his Word to man, he had carefully preserved it, so that Satan and his angels, through any agent or representative, could not destroy it. While other books might be destroyed, this holy Book was to be immortal. And down near the close of time, when the delusions of Satan should increase, the copies of this Book were to be so multiplied, that all who desired it might have a copy of God's revealed will to man, and, if they would, might arm themselves against the deceptions and lying wonders of Satan.

I saw that God had especially guarded the Bible, yet learned men, when the copies were few, had changed the words in some instances, thinking that they were making it more plain, when they were mystifying that which was plain, in causing it to lean to their established views, governed by tradition. But I saw that the word of God, as a whole, is a perfect chain, one portion of scripture explaining another. True seekers for truth need not err; for not only is the word of God plain and simple in declaring the way to life, but the Holy Spirit is given to guide in understanding the way of life revealed in his Word.

I saw that the angels of God were never to control the will. God sets before man life and death. He can have his choice. Many desire life, but continue to walk in the broad road, because they have not chosen life.

I saw the mercy and compassion of God in giving his Son to die for guilty man. Those who will not choose to accept salvation which has been so dearly purchased for them, must be punished. Beings whom God created have chosen to rebel against his government; but I saw that God did not shut them up in hell to endure endless misery. He could not take them to heaven; for to bring them into the company of the pure and holy would make them perfectly miserable. God will not take them to heaven, neither will he cause them to suffer eternally. He will destroy them utterly, and cause them to be as though they had not been, and then his justice will be satisfied. He formed man out of the dust of the earth, and the disobedient and unholy will be consumed by fire, and return to dust again. I saw that the benevolence and compassion of God in this, should lead all to admire his character, and to adore him; and after the wicked shall be destroyed from off the earth, all the heavenly host will say, Amen!

Satan looked with great satisfaction upon those who professed the name of Christ, and were closely adhering to these delusions formed by himself. His work is to still form new delusions. His power increases, and he grows more artful. He led on his representatives, the popes and the priests, to exalt themselves, and to stir up the people to bitterly persecute those who loved God, and were not willing to yield to his delusions, introduced through them. Satan moved upon his agents to destroy Christ's devoted followers. O the sufferings and agony, which they made the precious of God to endure! Angels have kept a faithful record of it all. But Satan and his evil angels exulted, and told the angels who administered to, and strengthened those suffering saints, that they would kill them, so that there would not be left a true Christian upon the earth. I saw that the church of God was then pure. There was no danger of men with corrupt hearts coming into the church of God then; for the true Christian, who dared to declare his faith, was in danger of the rack, the stake, and every torture which Satan and his evil angels could invent, and put into the mind of man.

See Genesis 3; Isaiah 47:13-14, John 17:17; John 3:16; Ecclesiastes 9:5, 12:7.

The Reformation

But notwithstanding all the persecution and the putting to death of the saints, yet living witnesses were raised up on every hand. The angels of God were doing the work committed to their trust. They were searching in the darkest places, and were selecting out of the darkness, men who were honest at heart. They were all buried up in error, yet God selected them as he did Saul, as chosen vessels to bear his truth, and raise their voices against the sins of his professed people. The angels of God moved upon Martin Luther, Melancthon, and others in different places, to thirst for the living testimony of the word of God. The enemy had come in like a flood, and the standard must be raised up against him. Luther was chosen to breast the storm, and stand up against the ire of a fallen church, and strengthen the few who were faithful to their holy profession. He was ever fearful of offending God. He tried through works to obtain the favor of God; but he was not satisfied until a gleam of light from heaven drove the darkness from his mind, and led him to trust, not in works, but in the merits of the blood of Christ; and to come to God for himself, not through popes nor confessors, but through Jesus Christ alone. O how precious was this knowledge to Luther! He prized this new and precious light which had dawned upon his dark understanding, and had driven away his superstition, higher than the richest earthly treasure. The word of God was new. Every thing was changed. The Book he had dreaded because he could not see beauty in it, was life, LIFE to him. It was his joy, his consolation, his blessed teacher. Nothing could induce him to leave its study. He had feared death; but as he read the word of God, all his terrors disappeared, and he admired the character of God, and loved him. He searched the word of God for himself. He feasted upon the rich treasures it contained, and then he searched it for the church. He was disgusted with the sins of those in whom he had trusted for salvation. He saw very many enshrouded in the same darkness which had covered him. He anxiously sought an opportunity to point them to the Lamb of God, who alone taketh away the sin of the world. He raised his voice against the errors and sins of the Papal church, and earnestly longed to break the chain of darkness which was confining thousands, and causing them to trust in works for salvation. He longed to be enabled to open to their minds the true riches of the grace of God, and the excellence of salvation obtained through Jesus Christ. He raised his voice zealously, and in the power of the Holy Spirit, cried against the existing sins of the leaders of the church; and as he met the storm of opposition from the priests, his courage did not fail; for he firmly relied upon the strong arm of God, and confidently trusted in him for victory. And as he pushed the battle closer and closer, the rage of the priests was kindled against him. They did not wish to be reformed. They chose to be left in ease, in wanton pleasure, in wickedness. They wished the church kept in darkness.

I saw that Luther was ardent and zealous, fearless and bold in reproving sin, and advocating the truth. He cared not for wicked men and devils. He knew that he had One with him mightier than they all. Luther possessed fire, zeal, courage and boldness, and at times might go too far; but God raised up Melancthon, who was just the opposite in character, to aid Luther, and carry on the work of reformation. Melancthon was timid, fearful, cautious, and possessed great patience. He was greatly beloved of God. His knowledge was great in the Scriptures, and his judgment and wisdom was excellent. His love for the cause of God was equal to Luther's. These hearts, the Lord knit together; they were friends which were never to be separated. Luther was a great help to Melancthon when he was in danger of being fearful and slow, and Melancthon was also a great help to Luther to keep him from moving too fast. Melancthon's far-seeing cautiousness often averted trouble which would have come upon the cause, if the work had been left alone to Luther; and the work would often have failed in

being pushed forward, if it had been left to Melancthon alone. I was shown the wisdom of God in choosing these two men, of different characters to carry on the work of reformation.

I was then carried back to the days of the apostles, and saw that God chose as companions an ardent and zealous Peter, and a mild, patient, meek John. Sometimes Peter was impetuous. And the beloved disciple often checked Peter, when his zeal and ardor led him too far; but it did not reform him. But after Peter had denied his Lord, and repented, and was converted, all he needed was a mild caution from John to check his ardor and zeal. The cause of Christ would often have suffered had it been left alone to John. Peter's zeal was needed. His boldness and energy often delivered them from difficulty, and silenced their enemies. John was winning. He gained many to the cause of Christ by his patient forbearance, and deep devotedness.

God raised up men to cry against the existing sins of the Papal church, and carry forward the reformation. Satan sought to destroy these living witnesses; but God made a hedge about them. Some, for the glory of his name, were permitted to seal the testimony they had borne with their blood; but there were other powerful men, like Luther and Melancthon, who could best glorify God by living and crying aloud against the sins of popes, priests and kings. They trembled before the voice of Luther. Through those chosen men, rays of light began to scatter the darkness, and very many joyfully received the light and walked in it. And when one witness was slain, two or more were raised up to fill his place.

But Satan was not satisfied. He could only have power over the body. He could not make believers yield their faith and hope. And even in death they triumphed with a bright hope of immortality at the resurrection of the just. They had more than mortal energy. They dared not sleep for a moment. They kept the Christian armor girded about them, prepared for a conflict, not merely with spiritual foes, but with Satan in the form of men, whose constant cry was, Give up your faith, or die. Those few Christians were strong in God, and more precious in his sight than half a world bearing the name of Christ, yet cowards in his cause. While the church was persecuted, they were united and loving. They were strong in God. Sinners were not permitted to unite themselves with it; neither the deceiver nor the deceived. Those only who were willing to forsake all for Christ could be his disciples. They loved to be poor, humble and Christ-like.

For further study see an encyclopedia on the Reformation.

The Church and World United

Satan then consulted with his angels, and they there considered what they had gained. It was true that they had kept some timid souls through fear of death, from embracing the truth; but many, even of the most timid, received the truth, and immediately their fears and timidity left them, and as they witnessed the death of their brethren, and saw their firmness and patience, they knew that God and angels assisted them to endure such sufferings, and they grew bold and fearless. And when called to yield their own lives, they maintained their faith with such patience and firmness as caused even their murderers to tremble. Satan and his angels decided that there was a more successful way to destroy souls, and more certain in the end. They saw that although they caused Christians to suffer, their steadfastness, and the bright hope that cheered them, caused the weakest to grow strong, and that the rack and the flames could not daunt them. They imitated the noble bearing of Christ when before his murderers, and many were convinced of the truth by witnessing their constancy, and the glory of God which rested upon them. Satan decided that he must come in a milder form. He had corrupted the doctrines of the Bible; and traditions which were to ruin millions were taking deep root. He restrained his hate, and decided not to urge on his subjects to such bitter persecution; but lead on the church to contend, not for the faith once delivered to the saints, but, for various traditions. As he led on the church to receive favors and honors of the world, under the false pretense of benefiting them, she began to lose favor with God. Gradually the church lost her power, as she shunned to declare the straight truths which shut out the lovers of pleasure and friends of the world.

The church is not the separate and peculiar people she was when the fires of persecution were kindled against her. How is the gold become dim? How is the most fine gold changed?

I saw that if the church had always retained her holy and peculiar character, the power of the Holy Spirit which was imparted to the disciples would be with her. The sick would be healed, devils would be rebuked and cast out, and she would be mighty, and a terror to her enemies.

I saw that a very large company professed the name of Christ, but God does not recognize them as his. He has no pleasure in them. Satan seemed to assume a religious character, and was very willing that the people should think they were Christians. He was very willing that they should believe in Jesus, his crucifixion, and his resurrection. Satan and his angels fully believed all this themselves, and trembled. But if this faith does not provoke to good works, and lead those who profess it to imitate the self-denying life of Christ, he is not disturbed; for they merely assume the Christian name, while their hearts are still carnal; and he can use them in his service better than if they made no profession. Under the name of Christian they hide their deformity. They pass along with their unsanctified natures, and their evil passions unsubdued. This gives occasion for the unbeliever to throw their imperfections in the face of Jesus Christ, to reproach him, and to cause those who do possess pure and undefiled religion to be brought into disrepute.

The ministers preach smooth things to suit carnal professors. This is just as Satan would have it. They dare not preach Jesus and the cutting truths of the Bible; for if they should, these carnal professors would not hear them. Many of them are wealthy and must be retained in the church, although they are no more fit to be there than Satan and his angels. The religion of Jesus is made to appear popular and honorable in the eyes of the world. The people are told that those who profess religion will be more honored by the world. Very widely do such teachings differ from the teachings of Christ. His doctrine and the world could not be at peace. Those who followed him had to renounce the world. These smooth things originated with Satan and his angels. They formed the plan, and nominal professors have carried it out. Hypocrites and sinners unite with the church. Pleasing fables are taught, and readily received. But if the truth should be preached in its purity, it would soon shut out hypocrites and sinners. But there is no difference between the professed followers of Christ and the world. I saw that if the false covering could be torn off from the members of the churches, there would be revealed such iniquity, vileness and corruption, that the most diffident child of God would have no hesitancy in calling them by their right name, children of their father, the Devil; for his works they do. Jesus and all the heavenly host looked with disgust upon the scene; yet God had a message for the church that was sacred and important. If received, it would make a thorough reformation in the church, revive the living testimony that would purge out hypocrites and sinners, and bring the church again into favor with God.

See Revelation 3:14-22.

William Miller

I saw that God sent his angel to move upon the heart of a farmer who had not believed the Bible, and led him to search the prophecies. Angels of God repeatedly visited that chosen one, and guided his mind, and opened his understanding to prophecies which had ever been dark to God's people. The commencement of the chain of truth was given him, and he was led on to search for link after link, until he looked with wonder and admiration upon the word of God. He saw there a perfect chain of truth. That Word which he had regarded as uninspired, now opened before his vision with beauty and glory. He saw that one portion of scripture explained another, and when one portion was closed to his understanding, he found in another portion of the Word that which explained it. He regarded the sacred word of God with joy, and with the deepest respect and awe.

As he followed down the prophecies, he saw that the inhabitants of earth were living in the closing scenes of this world's history, and they knew it not. He looked at the corruptions of the churches, and saw that their love was taken from Jesus, and placed on the world, and that they were seeking for worldly honor instead of that honor which cometh from above; ambitious for worldly riches, instead of laying up their treasure in heaven. Hypocrisy, darkness and death he could see everywhere. His spirit was stirred within him. God called him to leave his farm, as Elisha was called to leave his oxen and the field of his labor to follow Elijah. With trembling, William Miller began to unfold the mysteries of the kingdom of God to the people. He gained strength with every effort. He carried the people down through the prophecies to the second advent of Christ. As John the Baptist heralded the first advent of Jesus, and prepared the way for his coming, so also, Wm. Miller and those who joined with him, proclaimed the second advent of the Son of God.

I was carried back to the days of the disciples, and was shown the beloved John, that God had a special work for him to accomplish. Satan was determined to hinder this work, and he led on his servants to destroy John. But God sent his angel and wonderfully preserved him. All who witnessed the great power of God manifested in the deliverance of John, were astonished, and many were convinced that God was with him, and that the testimony which he bore concerning Jesus was correct. Those who sought to destroy him were afraid to again attempt to take his life, and he was permitted to suffer on for Jesus. He was falsely accused by his enemies, and was shortly banished to a lonely island, where the Lord sent his angel to reveal to him things which were to take place upon the earth, and the state of the church down through to the end; her backslidings, and the position the church should occupy if she would please God, and finally overcome. The angel from heaven came to John in majesty. His countenance beamed with the excellent glory of heaven. He revealed to John scenes of deep and thrilling interest concerning the church of God, and brought before him the perilous conflicts they were to endure. John saw them pass through fiery trials, and made white and tried, and, finally, victorious overcomers, gloriously saved in the kingdom of God. The countenance of the angel grew radiant with joy, and was exceeding glorious, as he showed to John the final triumph of the church of God. John was enraptured as he beheld the final deliverance of the church, and as he was carried away with the glory of the scene, with deep reverence and awe he fell at the feet of the angel to worship him. The angel instantly raised him up, and gently reproved him, saying, See thou do it not; I am thy fellow-servant, and of thy brethren that have the testimony of Jesus; worship God; for the testimony of Jesus is the spirit of prophecy. The angel then showed John the heavenly city with all its splendor and dazzling glory. John was enraptured and overwhelmed with the glory of the city. He did not bear in mind his former reproof from the angel, but again fell to worship before the feet of the angel, who again gave the gentle reproof, See thou do it not; for I am thy fellow-servant, and of thy brethren the prophets, and of them that keep the sayings of this book; worship God.

Preachers and people have looked upon the book of Revelation as mysterious, and of less importance than other portions of the sacred Scriptures. But I saw that this book is indeed a revelation given for the especial benefit of those who should live in the last days, to guide them in ascertaining their true position, and their duty. God led the mind of Wm. Miller into the prophecies, and gave him great light upon the book of Revelation.

If Daniel's visions had been understood, the people could better have understood the visions of John. But at the right time, God moved upon his chosen servant, who with clearness and in the power of the Holy Spirit, opened the prophecies, and showed the harmony of the visions of Daniel and John, and other portions of the Bible, and pressed home upon the hearts of the people the sacred, fearful warnings of the Word, to prepare for the coming of the Son of man. Deep and solemn convictions rested upon the minds of those who heard him, and ministers and people, sinners and infidels, turned to the Lord, to seek a preparation to stand in the judgment.

Angels of God accompanied Wm. Miller in his mission. He was firm and undaunted. He fearlessly proclaimed the message committed to his trust. A world lying in wickedness, and a cold, worldly church were enough to call into action his energy, and lead him to willingly endure toil, privation and suffering. Although opposed by professed Christians and the world, and buffeted by Satan and his angels, he ceased not to preach the everlasting gospel to crowds wherever he was invited, and sound the cry, Fear God and give glory to him; for the hour of his judgment is come.

See Daniel 8:14; Revelation 19:10.

The First Angel's Message

I saw that God was in the proclamation of the time in 1843. It was his design to arouse the people, and bring them to a testing point where they should decide. Ministers were convicted and convinced of the correctness of the positions taken on the prophetic periods, and they left their pride, their salaries, and their churches, to go forth from place to place and proclaim the message. But as the message from heaven could find a place in the hearts of but a very few of the professed ministers of Christ, the work was laid upon many who were not preachers. Some left their fields to sound the message, while others were called from their shops and their merchandise. And even some professional men were compelled to leave their professions to engage in the unpopular work of giving the first angel's message. Ministers laid aside their sectarian views and feelings, and united in proclaiming the coming of Jesus. The people were moved everywhere the message reached them. Sinners repented, wept and prayed for forgiveness, and those whose lives had been marked with dishonesty, were anxious to make restitution.

Parents felt the deepest solicitude for their children. Those who received the message, labored with their unconverted friends and relatives, and with their souls bowed with the weight of the solemn message, warned and entreated them to prepare for the coming of the Son of man. Those cases were the most hardened that would not yield to such a weight of evidence set home by heart-felt warnings. This soul-purifying work led the affections away from worldly things, to a consecration never before experienced. Thousands were led to embrace the truth preached by Wm. Miller, and servants of God were raised up in the spirit and power of Elijah to proclaim the message. Those who preached this solemn message, like John the forerunner of Jesus, felt compelled to lay the axe at the root of the tree, and call upon men to bring forth fruits meet for repentance. Their testimony was calculated to arouse and powerfully affect the churches, and manifest their real character. And as they raised the solemn warning to flee from the wrath to come, many who were united with the churches received the healing message; they saw their backslidings, and, with bitter tears of repentance, and deep agony of soul, humbled themselves before God. And as the Spirit of God rested upon them, they helped to sound the cry, Fear God, and give glory to him, for the hour of his judgment is come.

The preaching of definite time called forth great opposition from all classes, from the minister in the pulpit, down to the most reckless, heaven-daring sinner. No man knoweth the day and the hour, was heard from the hypocritical minister and the bold scoffer. Neither would be instructed and corrected on the use made of the text by those who were pointing to the year when they believed the prophetic periods would run out, and to the signs which showed Christ near, even at the doors. Many shepherds of the flock, who professed to love Jesus, said they had no opposition to the preaching of Christ's coming; but they objected to the definite time. God's all-seeing eye read their hearts. They did not love Jesus near. They knew that their unchristian lives would not stand the test; for they were not walking in the humble path laid out by him. These false shepherds stood in the way of the work of God. The truth spoken in its convincing power to the people aroused them, and like the jailer, they began to inquire, What must I do to be saved. But these shepherds stepped between the truth and the people, and preached smooth things to lead them from the truth. They united with Satan and his angels, and cried, Peace, peace, when there was no peace. I saw that angels of God had marked it all, and the garments of those unconsecrated shepherds were covered with the blood of souls. Those who loved their ease, and were content with their distance from God, would not be aroused from their carnal security.

Many ministers would not accept this saving message themselves, and those who would receive it, they hindered. The blood of souls is upon them. Preachers and people joined to oppose this message from heaven. They persecuted Wm. Miller, and those who united with him in the work. Falsehoods were circulated to injure his influence, and at different times after he had plainly declared the counsel of God, applying cutting truths to the hearts of his hearers, great rage was kindled against him, and as he left the place of meeting, some waylaid him in order to take his life. But angels of God were sent to preserve his life, and they led him safely away from the angry mob. His work was not yet finished.

The most devoted gladly received the message. They knew it was from God, and that it was delivered at the right time. Angels were watching with the deepest interest the result of the heavenly message, and when the churches turned from and rejected it, they in sadness consulted with Jesus. He turned his face from the churches, and bid his angels to faithfully watch over the precious ones who did not reject the testimony, for another light was yet to shine upon them.

I saw that if professed Christians had loved their Saviour's appearing, if their affections were placed on him, if they felt that there was none upon earth to be compared with him, they would have hailed with joy the first intimation of his coming. But the dislike they manifested, as they heard of their Lord's coming, was a decided proof that they did not love him. Satan and his angels triumphed, and cast it in the face of Jesus Christ and his holy angels, that his professed people had so little love for Jesus that they did not desire his second appearing.

I saw the people of God, joyful in expectation, looking for their Lord. But God designed to prove them. His hand covered a mistake in the reckoning of the prophetic periods. Those who were looking for their Lord did not discover it, and the most learned men who opposed the time also failed to see the mistake. God designed that his people should meet with a disappointment. The time passed, and those who had looked with joyful expectation for their Saviour were sad and disheartened, while those who had not loved the appearing of Jesus, but embraced the message through fear, were pleased that he did not come at the time of expectation. Their profession had not affected their hearts, and purified their lives. The passing of the time was well calculated to reveal such hearts. They were the first to turn and ridicule the sorrowful, disappointed ones, who really loved the appearing of their Saviour. I saw the wisdom of God in proving his people, and giving them a searching test to discover those who would shrink and turn back in the hour of trial.

Jesus and all the heavenly host looked with sympathy and love upon those who had with sweet expectation longed to see him whom their souls loved. Angels were hovering around them, to sustain them in the hour of their trial. Those who had neglected to receive the heavenly message were left in darkness, and God's anger was kindled against them, because they would not receive the light he had sent them from heaven. Those faithful, disappointed ones, who could not understand why their Lord did not come, were not left in darkness. Again they were led to their Bibles to search the prophetic periods. The hand of the Lord was removed from the figures, and the mistake was explained. They saw that the prophetic periods reached to 1844, and that the same evidence they had presented to show that the prophetic periods closed in 1843, proved that they would terminate in 1844. Light from the word of God shone upon their position, and they discovered a tarrying time. -- If the vision tarry, wait for it. -- In their love for Jesus' immediate coming, they had overlooked the tarrying of the vision, which was calculated to manifest the true waiting ones. Again they had a point of time. Yet I saw that many of them could not rise above their severe disappointment, to possess that degree of zeal and energy which had marked their faith in 1843.

Satan and his angels triumphed over them, and those who would not receive the message, congratulated themselves upon their far-seeing judgment and wisdom in not receiving the delusion, as they called it. They realized not that they were rejecting the counsel of God against themselves, and that they were working in union with Satan and his angels to perplex God's people, who were living out the heaven-born message.

The believers in this message were oppressed in the churches. Fear had held them for a time, so that they did not act out the sentiments of their heart, but the passing of the time revealed their true feelings. They wished to silence the testimony which the believers felt compelled to bear, that the prophetic periods extended to 1844. With clearness they explained their mistake, and gave their reasons why they expected their Lord in 1844. The opposers could not bring any arguments against the powerful reasons offered. The anger of the churches was kindled against them. They were determined not to listen to any evidence, and to shut their testimony out of the churches, so that others could not hear it. Those who dared not withhold from others the light God had given them, were shut out of the churches; but Jesus was with them, and they were joyful in the light of his countenance. They were prepared to receive the message of the second angel.

See Malachi 3; John 14:1-3; Revelation 14:6.

The Second Angel's Message

The churches would not receive the light of the first angel's message, and as they rejected the light from heaven they fell from the favor of God. They trusted in their own strength, and placed themselves by their opposition to the first message where they could not see the light of the second angel's message. But the beloved of God, who were oppressed, answered to the message, Babylon is fallen, and left the fallen churches.

Near the close of the second angel's message, I saw a great light from heaven shining upon the people of God. The rays of this light seemed bright as the sun. And I heard the voices of angels crying, Behold the Bridegroom cometh, go ye out to meet him!

The midnight cry was given to give power to the second angel's message. Angels were sent from heaven to wake up the discouraged saints, and prepare them for the great work before them. The most talented men were not the first to receive this message. Angels were sent to the humble, devoted ones, and constrained them to raise the cry, Behold the Bridegroom cometh, go ye out to meet him. Those entrusted with the cry made haste, and in the power of the Holy Spirit spread the cry, and aroused their discouraged brethren. This cry did not stand in the wisdom and learning of men, but in the power of God, and his saints who heard the cry could not resist it. The most spiritual received this message first, and those who had formerly led in the work were the last to receive and help swell the cry, Behold the Bridegroom cometh, go ye out to meet him.

In every part of the land, light was given upon the second angel's message, and the cry was melting down thousands. It went from city to city, and from village to village, until the waiting people of God were fully aroused. Many would not permit this message to enter the churches, and a large company who had the living testimony within them left the fallen churches. A mighty work was accomplished by the midnight cry. The message was heart-searching, and led the believers to seek a living experience for themselves. They knew that they could not lean upon one another.

The saints anxiously waited for their Lord with fasting, watching and almost constant prayer. Even some sinners looked forward to the time with terror, while the great mass seemed to be stirred against this message, and manifested the spirit of Satan. They mocked and scoffed, and everywhere was heard, No man knoweth the day and the hour. Evil angels exulted around them, urging them on to harden their hearts, and to reject every ray of light from heaven, that they might fasten them in the snare. Many professed to be looking for their Lord, who had neither part nor lot in the matter. The glory of God they had witnessed, the humility and deep devotion of the waiting ones, and the overwhelming weight of evidence, caused them to profess to receive the truth. But they were not converted. They were not ready. A spirit of solemn and earnest prayer was everywhere felt by the saints. A holy solemnity was resting upon them. Angels with the deepest interest had watched the result, and were elevating those who received the heavenly message, and were drawing them from earthly things to obtain large supplies from salvation's fountain. God's people were then accepted with him. Jesus looked upon them with pleasure. His image was reflected in them. They had made a full sacrifice, an entire consecration, and expected to be changed to immortality. But they were destined to be again sadly disappointed. The time to which they looked, expecting deliverance, passed. They were still upon the earth, and the effects of the curse never seemed more visible. They had placed their affections on heaven, and in sweet anticipation, had tasted immortal deliverance; but their hopes were not realized.

The fear that had rested upon many of the people did not at once disappear. They did not immediately triumph over the disappointed ones. But as no visible wrath of God was felt by them, they recovered from the fear they had felt, and commenced their ridicule, their mocking, and scoffing. The people of God were again proved, and tested. The world laughed, and mocked, and reproached them; and those who had believed without a doubt that Jesus would then come and raise the dead, and change the living saints, and take the kingdom, and possess it forever, felt like the disciples of Christ. They have taken away my Lord, and I know not where they have laid him.

See Revelation 14:8.

Advent Movement Illustrated

I saw a number of companies who seemed to be bound together by cords. Many in these companies were in total darkness. Their eyes were directed downward to the earth, and there seemed to be no connection between them and Jesus. I saw individuals scattered through these different companies whose countenances looked light, and whose eyes were raised upward to heaven. Beams of light from Jesus, like rays of light from the sun, were imparted to them. An angel bid me look carefully, and I saw an angel watching over every one of those who had a ray of light, while evil angels surrounded those who were in darkness. I heard the voice of an angel cry, Fear God and give glory to him, for the hour of his judgment is come.

A glorious light rested down upon these companies, to enlighten all who would receive it. Some of those who were in darkness received the light and rejoiced; while others resisted the light from heaven, and said that it was deception to lead them astray. The light passed away from them, and they were left in darkness. Those who had received the light from Jesus, joyfully cherished the increase of precious light which was shed upon them. Their faces lighted up, and beamed with holy joy, while their gaze was directed upward to Jesus with intense interest, and their voices were heard in harmony with the voice of the angel, Fear God and give glory to him, for the hour of his judgment is come. As they raised this cry, I saw those who were in darkness thrusting them with side and with shoulder. Then many of those who cherished the sacred light, broke the cords which confined them, and stood out separate from those companies. And as many were breaking the cords which bound them, men belonging to these different companies, who were revered by them, passed through the companies, and some with pleasing words, and others with wrathful looks and threatening gestures, fastened the cords which were weakening, and were constantly saying, God is with us. We stand in the light. We have the truth. I inquired who these men were. I was told that they were ministers, and leading men, who had rejected the light themselves, and were unwilling that others should receive it. I saw those who cherished the light looking with interest and ardent desire upward, expecting Jesus to come and take them to himself. Soon a cloud passed over those who rejoiced in the light, and their faces looked sorrowful. I inquired the cause of this cloud. I was shown that it was their disappointment. The time when they expected their Saviour had passed, and Jesus had not come. Discouragement settled upon them, and those men I had before noticed, the ministers and leading men, rejoiced. Those who had rejected the light, triumphed greatly, while Satan and his evil angels also exulted around them.

Then I heard the voice of another angel, saying, Babylon is fallen! is fallen! A light shone upon those desponding ones, and with ardent desires for his appearing, they again fixed their eyes upon Jesus. Then I saw a number of angels conversing with the second angel, who had cried, Babylon is fallen, is fallen, and these angels raised their voices with the second angel, and cried, Behold the Bridegroom cometh! go ye out to meet him! The musical voices of these angels seemed to reach everywhere. An exceeding bright and glorious light shone around those who had cherished the light which had

been imparted to them. Their faces shone with excellent glory, and they united with the angels in the cry, Behold, the Bridegroom cometh! And as they harmoniously raised the cry among these different companies, those who rejected the light, pushed them, and with angry looks, scorned and derided them. But the angels of God wafted their wings over the persecuted ones, while Satan and his angels were seeking to press their darkness around them, to lead them to reject the light from heaven.

Then I heard a voice saying to those who had been pushed and derided, come out from among them, and touch not the unclean. A large number broke the cords which bound them, and they obeyed the voice, and left those who were in darkness, and united with those who had previously broken the cords, and they joyfully united their voices with them. I heard the voice of earnest, agonizing prayer from a few who still remained with the companies who were in darkness. The ministers and leading men were passing around in these different companies, fastening the cords stronger; but still I heard this voice of earnest prayer. Then I saw those who had been praying reach out their hands for help towards that united company who were free, rejoicing in God. The answer from them, as they earnestly looked to heaven, and pointed upward, was, Come out from among them, and be separate. I saw individuals struggling for freedom, and at last they broke the cords that bound them. They resisted the efforts which were made to fasten the cords tighter, and would not heed the repeated assertions, God is with us, We have the truth with us. Individuals continued to leave the companies who were in darkness, and joined the free company, who appeared to be in an open field raised above the earth. Their gaze was upward, and the glory of God rested upon them, and they shouted the praises of God. They were united, and seemed to be wrapt in the light of heaven. Around this company were some who came under the influence of the light, but who were not particularly united to the company. All who cherished the light shed upon them were gazing upward with intense interest. Jesus looked upon them with sweet approbation. They expected Jesus to come. They longed for his appearing. They did not cast one lingering look to earth. Again I saw a cloud settle upon the waiting ones. I saw them turn their weary eyes downward. I inquired the cause of this change. Said my accompanying angel, They are again disappointed in their expectations. Jesus cannot yet come to earth. They must yet suffer for Jesus and endure greater trials. They must give up errors and traditions received from men, and turn wholly to God and his word. They must be purified, made white and tried. And those who endure that bitter trial will obtain an eternal victory.

Jesus did not come to earth as the waiting, joyful company expected, to cleanse the Sanctuary, by purifying the earth by fire. I saw that they were correct in their reckoning of the prophetic periods. Prophetic time closed in 1844. Their mistake consisted in not understanding what the Sanctuary was, and the nature of its cleansing. Jesus did enter the Most

Holy place to cleanse the Sanctuary at the ending of the days. I looked again at the waiting, disappointed company. They looked sad. They carefully examined the evidences of their faith, and followed down through the reckoning of the prophetic periods, and could discover no mistake. Time was fulfilled, but where was their Saviour? They had lost him.

I was then shown the disappointment of the disciples as they came to the sepulchre and found not the body of Jesus. Said Mary, They have taken away my Lord, and I know not where they have laid him. Angels told the sorrowing disciples that their Lord had risen, and would go before them into Galilee.

I saw that as Jesus looked upon the disappointed ones with the deepest compassion, he sent his angels to direct their minds that they might find him, and follow him where he was; that they might understand that the earth is not the Sanctuary; that he must needs enter the Most Holy place of the heavenly Sanctuary to cleanse it; to make a special atonement for Israel, and to receive the kingdom of his Father, and then return to earth and take them to dwell with him forever. The disappointment of the disciples well represents the disappointment of those who expected their Lord in 1844. I was carried back to the time when Christ triumphantly rode into Jerusalem. The joyful disciples believed that he was then to take the kingdom, and reign a temporal prince. They followed their King with high hopes. They cut down the beautiful palm branches, and took off their outer garments, and with enthusiastic zeal spread them in the way; and some went before, and others followed crying, Hosanna to the Son of David! Blessed is he that cometh in the name of the Lord! Hosanna in the highest! The excitement disturbed the Pharisees, and they wished Jesus to rebuke his disciples. But he said unto them, If these should hold their peace, the stones would immediately cry out. The prophecy of Zechariah 9:9, must be fulfilled, yet, I saw, the disciples were doomed to a bitter disappointment. In a few days they followed Jesus to Calvary, and beheld him bleeding and mangled upon the cruel cross. They witnessed his agonizing death, and laid him in the tomb. Their hearts sunk with grief. Their expectations were not realized in a single particular. Their hopes died with Jesus. But as he arose from the dead, and appeared to his sorrowing disciples, their hopes revived. They had lost their Saviour; but again they had found him.

I saw that the disappointment of those who believed in the coming of the Lord in 1844, was not equal to the disappointment of the disciples. Prophecy was fulfilled in the first and second angels' messages. They were given at the right time, and accomplished the work God designed they should.

See Habakkuk 2:1-3.

Another Illustration

I was shown the interest which all heaven had taken in the work which had been going on upon the earth. Jesus commissioned a strong and mighty angel to descend and warn the inhabitants of earth to get ready for his second appearing.

I saw the mighty angel leave the presence of Jesus in heaven. Before him went an exceedingly bright and glorious light. I was told that his mission was to lighten the earth with his glory, and warn man of the coming wrath of God. Multitudes received the light. Some seemed to be very solemn, while others were joyful and enraptured. The light was shed upon all, but some merely came under the influence of the light, and did not heartily receive it. But all who received it, turned their faces upward to heaven, and glorified God. Many were filled with great wrath. Ministers and people united with the vile, and stoutly resisted the light shed by the mighty angel. But all who received it withdrew from the world, and were closely united together.

Satan and his angels were busily engaged in seeking to attract the minds of all they could from the light. The company who rejected it were left in darkness. I saw the angel watching with the deepest interest the professed people of God, to record the character they developed, as the message of heavenly origin was introduced to them. And as very many who professed love for Jesus turned from the heavenly message with scorn, derision and hatred, an angel with a parchment in his hand, made the shameful record. All heaven was filled with indignation, because Jesus was slighted by his professed followers.

I saw the disappointment of the trusting ones. They did not see their Lord at the expected time. It was God's purpose to conceal the future, and bring his people to a point of decision. Without this point of time the work designed of God would not have been accomplished. Satan was leading the minds of very many far ahead in the future. A period of time proclaimed for Christ's appearing must bring the mind to earnestly seek for a present preparation. As the time passed, those who had not fully received the light of the angel, united with those who had despised the heavenly message, and they turned upon the disappointed ones in ridicule. I saw the angels in heaven consulting with Jesus. They had marked the situation of Christ's professed followers. The passing of the definite time had tested and proved them, and very many were weighed in the balance and found wanting. They all loudly professed to be Christians, yet failed in following Christ in almost every particular. Satan exulted at the state of the professed followers of Christ. He had them in his snare. He had led the majority to leave the straight path, and they were attempting to climb up to heaven some other way. Angels saw the pure, the clean, and holy, all mixed up with sinners in Zion, and the world-loving hypocrite. They had watched over the true lovers of Jesus; but the corrupt were affecting the holy.

Those whose hearts burned with a longing, intense desire to see Jesus, were forbidden by their professed brethren to speak of his coming. Angels viewed the whole scene, and sympathized with the remnant, who loved the appearing of Jesus. Another mighty angel was commissioned to descend to earth. Jesus placed in his hand a writing, and as he came to earth, he cried, Babylon is fallen! is fallen! Then I saw the disappointed ones again look cheerful, and raise their eyes to heaven, looking with faith and hope for their Lord's appearing. But many seemed to remain in a stupid state, as if asleep; yet I could see the trace of deep sorrow upon their countenances. The disappointed ones saw from the Bible that they were in the tarrying time, and that they must patiently wait the fulfillment of the vision. The same evidence which led them to look for their Lord in 1843, led them to expect him in 1844. I saw that the majority did not possess that energy which marked their faith in 1843. Their disappointment had dampened their faith. But as the disappointed ones united in the cry of the second angel, the heavenly host looked with the deepest interest, and marked the effect of the message. They saw those who bore the name of Christians turn with derision and scorn upon those who had been disappointed. As the words fell from the mocker's lips, You have not gone up yet! an angel wrote them. Said the angel, They mock God.

I was pointed back to the translation of Elijah. His mantle fell on Elisha, and wicked children (or young people) followed him, mocking, crying, Go up thou bald head! Go up thou bald head! They mocked God, and met their punishment there. They had learned it of their parents. And those who have scoffed and mocked at the idea of the saints' going up, will be visited with the plagues of God, and will realize that it is not a small thing to trifle with him.

Jesus commissioned other angels to fly quickly to revive and strengthen the drooping faith of his people, and prepare them to understand the message of the second angel, and of the important move which was soon to be made in heaven. I saw these angels receive great power and light from Jesus, and fly quickly to earth to fulfill their commission to aid the second angel in his work. A great light shone upon the people of God as the angels cried, Behold the Bridegroom cometh, go ye out to meet him. Then I saw those disappointed ones rise, and in harmony with the second angel, proclaim, Behold the Bridegroom cometh, go ye out to meet him. The light from the angels penetrated the darkness everywhere. Satan and his angels sought to hinder this light from spreading, and having its designed effect. They contended with the angels of God, and told them that God had deceived the people, and that with all their light and power, they could not make the people believe that Jesus was coming. The angels of God continued their work, although Satan strove to hedge up the way, and draw the minds of the people from the light. Those who received it looked very happy. They fixed their eyes up to heaven, and longed for the appearing of Jesus. Some were in great distress, weeping and praying. Their eyes seemed to be fixed upon themselves, and they dared not look upward.

A precious light from heaven parted the darkness from them, and their eyes, which had been fixed in despair upon themselves, were turned upward, while gratitude and holy joy were expressed upon every feature. Jesus and all the angelic host looked with approbation upon the faithful, waiting ones.

Those who rejected and opposed the light of the first angel's message, lost the light of the second, and could not be benefited by the power and glory which attended the message, Behold the Bridegroom cometh. Jesus turned from them with a frown. They had slighted and rejected him. Those who received the message were wrapt in a cloud of glory. They waited and watched and prayed to know the will of God. They greatly feared to offend him. I saw Satan and his angels seeking to shut this divine light from the people of God; but as long as the waiting ones cherished the light, and kept their eyes raised from earth to Jesus, Satan could have no power to deprive them of this precious light. The message given from heaven enraged Satan and his angels, and those who professed to love Jesus, but despised his coming, scorned and derided the faithful, trusting ones. But an angel marked every insult, every slight, every abuse they received from their professed brethren. Very many raised their voices to cry, Behold the Bridegroom cometh, and left their brethren who did not love the appearing of Jesus, and who would not suffer them to dwell upon his second coming. I saw Jesus turn his face from those who rejected and despised his coming, and then he bade angels lead his people out from among the unclean, lest they should be defiled. Those obedient to the messages stood out free and united. A holy and excellent light shone upon them. They renounced the world, tore their affections from it, and sacrificed their earthly interests. They gave up their earthly treasure and their anxious gaze was directed to heaven, expecting to see their loved Deliverer. A sacred, holy joy beamed upon their countenances, and told of the peace and joy which reigned within. Jesus bade his angels go and strengthen them, for the hour of their trial drew on. I saw that these waiting ones were not yet tried as they must be. They were not free from errors. And I saw the mercy and goodness of God in sending a warning to the people of earth, and repeated messages to bring them up to a point of time, to lead them to a diligent search of themselves, that they might divest themselves of errors which have been handed down from the heathen and papists. Through these messages God has been bringing out his people where he can work for them in greater power, and where they can keep all his commandments.

See Matthew 25:6; Revelation 3:14-16, 18:1, 22:14.

The Sanctuary

I was then shown the grievous disappointment of the people of God. They did not see Jesus at the expected time. They knew not why their Saviour did not come. They could see no evidence why prophetic time had not ended. Said an angel, Has God's word failed? Has God failed to fulfill his promises? No: he has fulfilled all he promised. Jesus has risen up, and has shut the door of the Holy place of the heavenly Sanctuary, and has opened a door into the Most Holy place, and has entered in to cleanse the Sanctuary. Said the angel, All who wait patiently shall understand the mystery. Man has erred; but there has been no failure on the part of God. All was accomplished that God promised; but man erroneously looked to the earth, believing it to be the Sanctuary to be cleansed at the end of the prophetic periods. Man's expectations have failed; but God's promise not at all. Jesus sent his angels to direct the disappointed ones, to lead their minds into the Most Holy place where he had gone to cleanse the Sanctuary, and make a special atonement for Israel. Jesus told the angels that all who found him would understand the work which he was to perform. I saw that while Jesus was in the Most Holy place he would be married to the New Jerusalem, and after his work should be accomplished in the Holiest, he would descend to earth in kingly power and take the precious ones to himself who had patiently waited his return.

I was then shown what did take place in heaven as the prophetic periods ended in 1844. I saw that as the ministration of Jesus in the Holy place ended, and he closed the door of that apartment, a great darkness settled upon those who had heard, and had rejected the messages of Christ's coming, and they lost sight of him. Jesus then clothed himself with precious garments. Around the bottom of his robe was a bell and a pomegranate, a bell and a pomegranate. He had suspended from his shoulders a breastplate of curious work. And as he moved, it glittered like diamonds, magnifying letters which looked like names written, or engraven upon the breastplate. After he was fully attired, with something upon his head which looked like a crown, angels surrounded him, and in a flaming chariot he passed within the second vail. I was then bid to take notice of the two apartments of the heavenly Sanctuary. The curtain, or door, was opened, and I was permitted to enter. In the first apartment I saw the candlestick with seven lamps, which looked rich and glorious; also the table on which was the shew-bread, and the altar of incense, and the censer. All the furniture of this apartment looked like purest gold, and reflected the image of the one who entered that place. The curtain which separated these two apartments looked glorious. It was of different colors and material, with a beautiful border, with figures of gold wrought upon it, representing angels. The vail was lifted, and I looked into the second apartment. I saw there an ark which had the appearance of being of the finest gold. As a border around the top of the ark, was most beautiful work representing crowns. It was of fine gold. In the ark were the tables of stone containing the ten commandments. On each end of the ark was a lovely cherub with their wings spread out over it. Their wings were raised on high, and touched each other above the head of Jesus, as he stood by the ark. Their faces were turned towards each other, and they looked downwards to the ark, representing all the angelic host looking with interest at the law of God. Between the cherubim was a golden censer. And as the prayers of the saints in faith came up to Jesus, and he offered them to his Father, a sweet fragrance arose from the incense. It looked like smoke of most beautiful colors. Above the place where Jesus stood, before the ark, I saw an exceeding bright glory that I could not look upon. It appeared like a throne where God dwelt. As the incense ascended up to the Father, the excellent glory came from the Father's throne

to Jesus, and from Jesus it was shed upon those whose prayers had come up like sweet incense. Light and glory poured upon Jesus in rich abundance, and overshadowed the mercy-seat, and the train of the glory filled the temple. I could not long look upon the glory. No language can describe it. I was overwhelmed, and turned from the majesty and glory of the scene.

I was shown a Sanctuary upon earth containing two apartments. It resembled the one in heaven. I was told that it was the earthly Sanctuary, a figure of the heavenly. The furniture of the first apartment of the earthly Sanctuary was like that in the first apartment of the heavenly. The vail was lifted, and I looked into the Holy of Holies, and saw that the furniture was the same as in the Most Holy place of the heavenly Sanctuary. The priests ministered in both apartments of the earthly. In the first apartment he ministered every day in the year, and entered the Most Holy but once in a year, to cleanse it from the sins which had been conveyed there. I saw that Jesus ministered in both apartments of the heavenly Sanctuary. He entered into the heavenly Sanctuary by the offering of his own blood. The earthly priests were removed by death, therefore they could not continue long; but Jesus, I saw, was a priest forever. Through the sacrifices and offerings brought to the earthly Sanctuary, the children of Israel were to lay hold of the merits of a Saviour to come. And in the wisdom of God the particulars of this work were given us that we might look back to them, and understand the work of Jesus in the heavenly Sanctuary.

At the crucifixion, as Jesus died on Calvary, he cried, It is finished, and the vail of the temple was rent in twain, from the top to the bottom. This was to show that the services of the earthly Sanctuary were forever finished, and that God would no more meet with them in their earthly temple, to accept their sacrifices. The blood of Jesus was then shed, which was to be ministered by himself in the heavenly Sanctuary. As the priests in the earthly Sanctuary entered the Most Holy once a year to cleanse the Sanctuary, Jesus entered the Most Holy of the heavenly, at the end of the 2300 days of Daniel 8, in 1844, to make a final atonement for all who could be benefited by his mediation, and to cleanse the Sanctuary.

See Jeremiah 3:14; Hebrews 9; Revelation 3:8, 4:1, 21:2.

The Third Angel's Message

As the ministration of Jesus closed in the Holy place, and he passed into the Holiest, and stood before the ark containing the law of God, he sent another mighty angel to earth with the third message. He placed a parchment in the angel's hand, and as he descended to earth in majesty and power, he proclaimed a fearful warning, the most terrible threatening ever borne to man. This message was designed to put the children of God upon their guard, and show them the hour of temptation and anguish that was before them. Said the angel, They will be brought into close combat with the beast and his image. Their only hope of eternal life is to remain steadfast. Although their lives are at stake, yet they must hold fast the truth. The third angel closes his message with these words, Here is the patience of the saints; here are they that keep the commandments of God, and the faith of Jesus. As he repeated these words he pointed to the heavenly Sanctuary. The minds of all who embrace this message are directed to the Most Holy place where Jesus stands before the ark, making his final intercession for all those for whom mercy still lingers, and for those who have ignorantly broken the law of God. This atonement is made for the righteous dead as well as for the righteous living. Jesus makes an atonement for those who died, not receiving the light upon God's commandments, who sinned ignorantly.

After Jesus opened the door of the Most Holy the light of the Sabbath was seen, and the people of God were to be tested and proved, as God proved the children of Israel anciently, to see if they would keep his law. I saw the third angel pointing upward, showing the disappointed ones the way to the Holiest of the heavenly Sanctuary. They followed Jesus by faith into the Most Holy. Again they have found Jesus, and joy and hope spring up anew. I saw them looking back reviewing the past, from the proclamation of the second advent of Jesus, down through their travels to the passing of the time in 1844. They see their disappointment explained, and joy and certainty again animate them. The third angel has lighted up the past, present and future, and they know that God has indeed led them by his mysterious providence.

It was represented to me that the remnant followed Jesus into the Most Holy place, and beheld the ark, and the mercy-seat, and were captivated with their glory. Jesus raised the cover of the ark, and behold! the tables of stone, with the ten commandments written upon them. They trace down the lively oracles; but they start back with trembling when they see the fourth commandment living among the ten holy precepts, while a brighter light shines upon it than upon the other nine, and a halo of glory is all around it. They find nothing there informing them that the Sabbath has been abolished, or changed to the first day of the week. It reads as when spoken by the mouth of God in solemn and awful grandeur upon the mount, while the lightnings flashed and the thunders rolled, and when written with his own holy finger in the tables of stone. Six days shalt thou labor and do all thy work; but the seventh day is the Sabbath of the Lord thy God. They are amazed as they behold the care taken of the ten commandments. They see them placed close by Jehovah, overshadowed and protected by his holiness. They see that they have been trampling upon the fourth commandment of the decalogue, and have observed a day handed down by the heathen and papists, instead of the day sanctified by Jehovah. They humble themselves before God, and mourn over their past transgressions.

I saw the incense in the censer smoke as Jesus offered their confessions and prayers to his Father. And as it ascended, a bright light rested upon Jesus, and upon the mercy-seat; and

the earnest, praying ones, who were troubled because they had discovered themselves to be transgressors of God's law, were blest, and their countenances lighted up with hope and joy. They joined in the work of the third angel, and raised their voices and proclaimed the solemn warning. But few at first received the message, yet they continued with energy to proclaim the warning. Then I saw many embrace the message of the third angel, and unite their voices with those who had first proclaimed the warning, and they exalted God and magnified him by observing his sanctified Rest-day.

Many who embraced the third message had not an experience in the two former messages. Satan understood this, and his evil eye was upon them to overthrow them; but the third angel was pointing them to the Most Holy place, and those who had an experience in the past messages were pointing them the way to the heavenly Sanctuary. Many saw the perfect chain of truth in the angels' messages, and gladly received it. They embraced them in their order, and followed Jesus by faith into the heavenly Sanctuary. These messages were represented to me as an anchor to hold the body. And as individuals receive and understand them, they are shielded against the many delusions of Satan.

After the great disappointment in 1844, Satan and his angels were busily engaged in laying snares to unsettle the faith of the body. He was affecting the minds of individuals who had a personal experience in these things. They had an appearance of humility. They changed the first and second messages, and pointed to the future for their fulfilment, while others pointed far back in the past, declaring that they had been there fulfilled. These individuals were drawing the minds of the inexperienced away, and unsettling their faith. Some were searching the Bible to try to build up a faith of their own, independent of the body. Satan exulted in all this; for he knew that those who broke loose from the anchor, he could affect by different errors and drive about with winds of doctrine. Many who had led in the first and second messages, denied them, and division and scattering was throughout the body. I then saw Wm. Miller. He looked perplexed, and was bowed with sorrow and distress for his people. He saw the company who were united and loving in 1844, losing their love for each other, and opposing one another. He saw them fall back into a cold, backslidden state. Grief wasted his strength. I saw leading men watching Wm. Miller, and fearing lest he should embrace the third angel's message and the commandments of God. And as he would lean towards the light from heaven, these men would lay some plan to draw his mind away. I saw a human influence exerted to keep his mind in darkness, and to retain his influence among them. At length Wm. Miller raised his voice against the light from heaven. He failed in not receiving the message which would have fully explained his disappointment, and cast a light and glory on the past, which would have revived his exhausted energies, brightened up his hope, and led him to glorify God. But he leaned to human wisdom instead of divine, and being broken with arduous labor in his Master's cause, and by age, he was not as accountable as those who kept him from the truth. They are responsible, and the sin rests upon them. If Wm. Miller could have seen the light of the third message, many things which looked dark and mysterious to him would have been explained. His brethren professed such deep love and interest for him, he thought he could not tear away from them. His heart would incline towards the truth; but then he looked at his brethren. They opposed it. Could he tear away from those who had stood side and shoulder with him in proclaiming Jesus' coming? He thought they surely would not lead him astray.

God suffered him to come under the power of Satan, and death to have dominion over him. He hid him in the grave, away from those who were constantly drawing him from God. Moses erred just as he was about to enter the promised land. So also, I saw that Wm. Miller erred as he was soon to enter the heavenly Canaan, in suffering his influence to go against the truth. Others led him to this. Others must account for it. But angels watch the precious dust of this servant of God, and he will come forth at the sound of the last trump.

See Exodus 20:1-17, 31:18; 1Thessalonians 4:16; Revelation 14:9-12.

A Firm Platform

I saw a company who stood well guarded and firm, and would give no countenance to those who would unsettle the established faith of the body. God looked upon them with approbation. I was shown three steps -- one, two and three -- the first, second and third angels' messages. Said the angel, Woe to him who shall move a block, or stir a pin in these messages. The true understanding of these messages is of vital importance. The destiny of souls hangs upon the manner in which they are received. I was again brought down through these messages, and saw how dearly the people of God had purchased their experience. It had been obtained through much suffering and severe conflict. Step by step had God brought them along, until he had placed them upon a solid, immovable platform. Then I saw individuals as they approached the platform, before stepping upon it examine the foundation. Some with rejoicing immediately stepped upon it. Others commenced to find fault with the laying of the foundation of the platform. They wished improvements made, and then the platform would be more perfect, and the people much happier. Some stepped off the platform and examined it, then found fault with it, declaring it to be laid wrong. I saw that nearly all stood firm upon the platform, and exhorted others who had stepped off to cease their complaints, for God was the master builder, and they were fighting against him. They recounted the wonderful work of God, which had led them to the firm platform, and in union nearly all raised their eyes to heaven, and with a loud voice glorified God. This affected some of those who had complained, and left the platform, and again they with humble look stepped upon it.

I was pointed back to the proclamation of the first advent of Christ. John was sent in the spirit and power of Elijah to prepare the way for Jesus' coming. Those who rejected the testimony of John were not benefited by the teachings of Jesus. Their opposition to the proclamation of his first advent placed them where they could not readily receive the strongest evidence of his being the Messiah. Satan led on those who rejected the message of John to go still further, to reject Jesus and crucify him. In doing this, they placed themselves where they could not receive the blessing on the day of Pentecost, which would have taught them the way into the heavenly Sanctuary. The rending of the vail of the temple showed that the Jewish sacrifices and ordinances would no longer be received. The great Sacrifice had been offered, and had been accepted, and the Holy Spirit which descended on the day of Pentecost carried the minds of the disciples from the earthly Sanctuary to the heavenly, where Jesus had entered by his own blood, and shed upon his disciples the benefits of his atonement. The Jews were left in complete deception and total darkness. They lost all the light they might have had upon the plan of salvation, and still trusted in their useless sacrifices and offerings. They could not be benefited by the mediation of Christ in the Holy place. The heavenly Sanctuary had taken the place of the earthly, yet they had no knowledge of the way to the heavenly.

Many look with horror at the course the Jews pursued toward Jesus in rejecting and crucifying him. And as they read the history of his shameful abuse, they think they love Christ, and would not have denied him like Peter, or crucified him like the Jews. But God who has witnessed their professed sympathy for his Son, has proved them, and has brought to the test that love which they professed for Jesus.

All heaven watched with the deepest interest the reception of the message. But many who profess to love Jesus, and who shed tears as they read the story of the cross, instead of receiving the message with gladness, are stirred with anger, and deride the good news of Jesus' coming, and declare it to be delusion. They would not fellowship those who loved his appearing, but hated them, and shut them out of the churches. Those who rejected the first message could not be benefited by the second, and were not benefited by the midnight cry, which was to prepare them to enter with Jesus by faith into the Most Holy place of the heavenly Sanctuary. And by rejecting the two former messages, they can see no light in the third angel's message, which shows the way into the Most Holy place. I saw that the nominal churches, as the Jews crucified Jesus, had crucified these messages, and therefore they have no knowledge of the move made in heaven, or of the way into the Most Holy, and they cannot be benefited by the intercession of Jesus there. Like the Jews, who offered their useless sacrifices, they offer up their useless prayers to the apartment which Jesus has left, and Satan, pleased with the deception of the professed followers of Christ, fastens them in his snare, and assumes a religious character, and leads the minds of these professed Christians to himself, and works with his power, his signs and lying wonders. Some he deceives in one way and some in another. He has different delusions prepared to affect different minds. Some look with horror upon one deception, while they readily receive another. Satan deceives some with Spiritualism. He also comes as an angel of light, and spreads his influence over the land. I saw false reformations everywhere. The churches were elated, and considered that God was marvelously working for them, when it was another spirit. It will die away and leave the world and the church in a worse condition than before.

I saw that God had honest children among the nominal Adventists, and the fallen churches, and ministers and people will yet be called out from these churches, before the plagues shall be poured out, and they will gladly embrace the truth. Satan knows this, and before the loud cry of the third angel, raises an excitement in these religious bodies, that those who have rejected the truth may think God is with them. He hopes to deceive the honest, and lead them to think that God is still working for the churches. But the light will shine, and every one of the honest ones will leave the fallen churches, and take their stand with the remnant.

See Revelation 22:16-21.

Spiritualism

I saw the rapping delusion. Satan has power to bring the appearance of forms before us purporting to be our relatives and friends that now sleep in Jesus. It will be made to appear as if they were present, the words they uttered while here, which we were familiar with, will be spoken, and the same tone of voice which they had while living will fall upon the ear. All this is to deceive the world, and ensnare them into the belief of this delusion.

I saw that the saints must have a thorough understanding of the present truth, which they will have to maintain from the Scriptures. They must understand the state of the dead; for the spirits of devils will yet appear to them, professing to be beloved friends and relatives, who will declare to them unscriptural doctrines. They will do all in their power to excite sympathy, and work miracles before them, to confirm what they declare. The people of God must be prepared to withstand these spirits with the Bible truth that the dead know not anything, and that they are the spirits of devils.

I saw that we must examine well the foundation of our hope, for we shall have to give a reason for it from the Scriptures; for we shall see this delusion spreading, and we shall have to contend with it face to face. And unless we are prepared for it, we shall be ensnared and overcome. But if we do what we can on our part to be ready for the conflict that is just before us, God will do his part, and his all-powerful arm will protect us. He would sooner send every angel out of glory to make a hedge about faithful souls, than that they should be deceived and led away by the lying wonders of Satan.

I saw the rapidity with which this delusion was spreading. A train of cars was shown me, going with the speed of lightning. The angel bade me look carefully. I fixed my eyes upon the train. It seemed that the whole world was on board. Then he showed me the conductor, who looked like a stately fair person, whom all the passengers looked up to and reverenced. I was perplexed, and asked my attending angel who it was. Said he, It is Satan. He is the conductor in the form of an angel of light. He has taken the world captive. They are given over to strong delusions, to believe a lie that they may be damned. His agent, the next highest in order to him, is the engineer, and others of his agents are employed in different offices as he may need them, and they are all going with lightning speed to perdition. I asked the angel if there were none left. He bade me look in an opposite direction, and I saw a little company traveling a narrow pathway. All seemed to be firmly united, and bound together by the truth.

This little company looked care-worn, as though they had passed through severe trials and conflicts. And it seemed as if the sun had just appeared from behind the cloud, and shone upon their countenances, and caused them to look triumphant, as though their victories were nearly won.

I saw that the Lord had given the world opportunity to discover the snare. This one thing was evidence enough for the Christian if there were no other. There is no difference made between the precious and the vile.

Thomas Paine, whose body has mouldered to dust, and who is to be called forth at the end of the 1000 years, at the second resurrection, to receive his reward, and suffer the second death, is purported by Satan to be in heaven, and highly exalted there. Satan used him on earth as long as he could, and now he is carrying on the same work through pretensions of having Thomas Paine so much exalted and honored; and as he taught on earth, Satan is making it appear that he is teaching in heaven. And some on earth who have looked with horror at his life and death, and his corrupt teachings while living, now submit to be taught by him who was one of the vilest and most corrupt of men; one who despised God and his law.

He who is the father of lies, blinds and deceives the world by sending his angels forth to speak for the apostles, and make it appear that they contradict what they wrote when on earth, which was dictated by the Holy Ghost. These lying angels make the apostles to corrupt their own teachings and declare them to be adulterated. By so doing he can throw professed Christians, who have a name to live and are dead, and all the world, into uncertainty about the word of God; for that cuts directly across his track, and is likely to thwart his plans. Therefore he gets them to doubt the divine origin of the Bible, and then sets up the infidel Thomas Paine, as though he was ushered into heaven when he died, and with the holy apostles whom he hated on earth, is united, and appears to be teaching the world.

Satan assigns each one of his angels their part to act. He enjoins upon them to be cunning, artful and sly. He instructs some of them to act the part of the apostles, and speak for them, while others are to act out infidels and wicked men who died cursing God, but now appear to be very religious. There is no difference made between the most holy apostles and the vilest infidel. They are both made to teach the same thing. It matters not who Satan makes to speak, if his object is only accomplished. He was so intimately connected with Paine upon earth, and so aided him, that it is an easy thing for him to know the very words he used, and the very hand-writing of one of his devoted children who served him so faithfully, and accomplished his purposes so well. Satan dictated much of his writings, and it is an easy thing for him to dictate sentiments through his angels now, and make it appear that it comes through Thomas Paine, who was his devoted servant while he lived. But this is the masterpiece of Satan. All this teaching purporting to be from apostles, and saints, and wicked men who have died, comes directly from his Satanic majesty.

This should be enough to remove the vail from every mind and discover unto all the dark, mysterious works of Satan;--that he has got one whom he loved so well, and who hated God so perfectly, with the holy apostles and angels in glory: virtually saying to the world and infidels, No matter how wicked you are; no matter whether you believe in God or the Bible, or disbelieve; live as you please, heaven is your home; -- for everyone knows that if Thomas Paine is in heaven, and so exalted, they will surely get there. This is so glaring that all may see if they will. Satan is doing now what he has been trying to do since his fall, through individuals like Thomas Paine. He is, through his power and lying wonders, tearing away the foundation of the Christians' hope, and putting out their sun that is to lighten them in the narrow way to heaven. He is making the world believe that the Bible is no better than a story-book, uninspired, while he holds out something to take its place; namely, Spiritual Manifestations!

Here is a channel wholly devoted to himself, under his control, and he can make the world believe what he will. The Book that is to judge him and his followers, he puts back into the shade, just where he wants it. The Saviour of the world he makes to be no more than a common man; and as the Roman guard that watched the tomb of Jesus, spread the false and lying report that the chief priests and elders put in their mouth, so will the poor, deluded followers of these pretended spiritual manifestations, repeat, and try to make it appear, that there is nothing miraculous about our Saviour's birth, death and resurrection; and they put Jesus with the Bible, back into the shade, where they want him, and then get the world to look to them and their lying wonders and miracles, which they declare far exceed the works of Christ. Thus the world is taken in the snare, and lulled to security; not to find out their awful deception, until the seven last plagues are poured out. Satan laughs as he sees his plan succeed so well, and the whole world in the snare.

See Revelation 16:14, 18:2.

Covetousness

I saw Satan and his angels consulting together. He bade his angels go and lay their snares especially for those who were looking for Christ's second appearing, and who were keeping all God's commandments. Satan told his angels that the churches were all asleep. He would increase his power and lying wonders, and he could hold them. But the sect of Sabbath-keepers we hate. They are continually working against us, and taking from us our subjects, to keep that hated law of God.

Go, make the possessors of lands and money drunk with cares. If you can make them place their affections upon these things, we have them yet. They may profess what they please, only make them care more for money than the success of Christ's kingdom, or the spread of the truths we hate. Present the world before them in the most attractive light, that they may love and idolize it. We must keep all the means in our ranks we can. The more means they have, the more will they injure our kingdom by getting our subjects. And as they appoint meetings in different places, then we are in danger. Be very vigilant then. Cause all the distraction you can. Destroy love for each other. Discourage and dishearten their ministers; for we hate them. Hold up every plausible excuse to those that have means, lest they hand it out. Control the money matters if you can, and drive their ministers to want, and distress. This will weaken their courage and zeal. Battle every inch of ground. Make

and love of earthly treasures the ruling traits of their character. As long as these traits rule, salvation and grace stand back. Crowd all you can around them to attract them, and they will be surely ours. Not only are we sure of them, but their hateful influence will not be exercised toward others to lead them to heaven. And those who shall attempt to give, put within them a grudging disposition, that it may be sparingly.

I saw that Satan carried out his plans well. And as the servants of God appointed meetings, Satan and his angels understood their business, and were on the ground to hinder the work of God, and he was constantly putting suggestions into the minds of God's people. Some he leads in one way, and some in another, always taking advantage of evil traits in the brethren and sisters, exciting and stirring up their natural besetments. If they are disposed to be selfish and covetous, Satan is well pleased to take his stand by their side, and then with all his power he seeks to lead them to manifest their besetting sins. If the grace of God and the light of truth melt away these covetous, selfish feelings for a little, and they do not obtain entire victory over them, when they are not under a saving influence, Satan comes in and withers up every noble, generous principle, and they think that they have to do too much. They become weary of well-doing and forget all about the great sacrifice Jesus made for them, to redeem them from the power of Satan, and hopeless misery.

Satan took advantage of Judas' covetous, selfish disposition, and led him to murmur against the ointment Mary dedicated to Jesus. Judas looked upon it as a great waste; it might have been sold and given to the poor. He cared not for the poor, but considered the liberal offering to Jesus extravagant. Judas prized his Lord just enough to sell him for a few pieces of silver. And I saw that there were some like Judas among those who profess to be waiting for their Lord. Satan has the control over them, but they know it not. Not a particle of

or selfishness can God approbate. He hates it, and he despises the prayers and exhortations of those who possess it. As Satan sees his time is short, he leads them on to be more and more selfish, more and more covetous, and then exults as he sees them wrapt up in themselves, close, penurious and selfish. If the eyes of such could be opened, they would see Satan in hellish triumph, exulting over them, and laughing at the folly of those who accept his suggestions, and enter his snares. Then he and his angels take the mean and covetous acts of these individuals, and present them to Jesus and the holy angels, and reproachfully say, These are Christ's followers! They are getting ready to be translated! Satan marks their deviating course, and then compares it with the Bible, with passages which plainly rebuke such things, and then presents it to annoy the heavenly angels, saying, These are following Christ and his word! These are the fruits of Christ's sacrifice and redemption! Angels turn in disgust from the scene. God requires a constant doing on the part of his people, and when they become weary of well and generous doing, he becomes weary of them. I saw that God was greatly displeased with the least manifestation of selfishness on the part of his professed people, for whom Jesus has not spared his own precious life. Every selfish, covetous individual will fall out by the way. Like Judas, who sold his Lord, they will sell good principles, and a noble, generous disposition for a little of earth's gain. All such will be sifted out from God's people. Those who want heaven, must, with every energy they possess, be encouraging the principles of heaven. And instead of their souls withering up with selfishness, they should be expanding with benevolence, and every opportunity should be improved in doing good to one another, and increasing and growing more and more into the principles of heaven. Jesus was held up to me as the perfect pattern. His life was without selfish interest, and was marked with disinterested benevolence.

See I John 2:15; Luke 12:15; Col. 3:5,6

The Shaking

I saw some with strong faith and agonizing cries, pleading with God. Their countenances were pale, and marked with deep anxiety, which expressed their internal struggle. There were firmness and great earnestness expressed in their countenances, while large drops of perspiration rose upon their foreheads, and fell. Now and then their faces would light up with the marks of God's approbation, and again the same solemn, earnest, anxious look settled upon them.

Evil angels crowded around them, pressing their darkness upon them, to shut out Jesus from their view, that their eyes might be drawn to the darkness that surrounded them, and they distrust God, and next murmur against him. Their only

safety was in keeping their eyes directed upward. Angels were having the charge over the people of God, and as the poisonous atmosphere from these evil angels was pressed around these anxious ones, the angels, which had the charge over them, were continually wafting their wings over them to scatter the thick darkness that surrounded them.

Some, I saw, did not participate in this work of agonizing and pleading. They seemed indifferent and careless. They were not resisting the darkness around them, and it shut them in like a thick cloud. The angels of God left them, and went to the aid of those earnest, praying ones. I saw the angels of God hasten to the assistance of all those who were struggling with all their energies to resist those evil angels, and trying to help themselves by calling upon God with perseverance. But the angels left those who made no effort to help themselves, and I lost sight of them.

As these praying ones continued their earnest cries, at times a ray of light from Jesus came to them, and encouraged their hearts, and lighted up their countenances.

I asked the meaning of the shaking I had seen. I was shown that it would be caused by the straight testimony called forth by the counsel of the true Witness to the Laodiceans. It will have its effect upon the heart of the receiver of the testimony, and it will lead him to exalt the standard and pour forth the straight truth. This straight testimony some will not bear. They will rise up against it, and this will cause a shaking among God's people.

I saw that the testimony of the True Witness has not been half heeded. The solemn testimony upon which the destiny of the church hangs, has been lightly esteemed, if not entirely disregarded. This testimony must work deep repentance, and all that truly receive it, will obey it, and be purified.

Said the angel, List ye! Soon I heard a voice that sounded like many musical instruments, all sounding in perfect strains, sweet and harmonious. It surpassed any music I had ever heard. It seemed to be so full of mercy, compassion, and elevating, holy joy. It thrilled through my whole being. Said the angel, Look ye! My attention was then turned to the company I had seen before, who were mightily shaken. I was shown those whom I had before seen weeping, and praying with agony of spirit. I saw that the company of guardian angels around them had doubled, and they were clothed with an armor from their head to their feet. They moved in exact order, firm like a company of soldiers. Their countenances expressed the severe conflict which they had endured, the agonizing struggle they had passed through. Yet their features, marked with severe internal anguish, shone now with the light and glory of heaven. They had obtained the victory, and it called forth from them the deepest gratitude, and holy, sacred joy.

The numbers of this company had lessened. Some had been shaken out, and left by the way. The careless and indifferent who did not join with those who prized victory and salvation enough to agonize, persevere, and plead for it, did not obtain it, and they were left behind in darkness, and their numbers were immediately made up by others taking hold of the truth, and coming into the ranks. Still the evil angels pressed around them, but they could have no power over them.

I heard those clothed with the armor speak forth the truth in great power. It had effect. I saw those who had been bound; some wives had been bound by their husbands, and some children had been bound by their parents. The honest who had been held or prevented from hearing the truth, now eagerly laid hold of the truth spoken. All fear of their relatives was gone. The truth alone was exalted to them. It was dearer and more precious than life. They had been hungering and thirsting for truth. I asked what had made this great change. An angel answered, It is the latter rain; the refreshing from the presence of the Lord; the loud cry of the third angel.

Great power was with these chosen ones. Said the angel, Look ye! My attention was turned to the wicked, or unbelievers. They were all astir. The zeal and power with the people of God had aroused and enraged them. Confusion, confusion, was on every side. I saw measures taken against this company, who were having the power and light of God. Darkness thickened around them, yet there they stood, approved of God, and trusting in him. I saw them perplexed. Next I heard them crying unto God earnestly. Through the day and night their cry ceased not. I heard these words, Thy will, O God, be done! If it can glorify thy name, make a way of escape for thy people! Deliver us from the heathen round about us! They have appointed us unto death; but thine arm can bring salvation. These are all the words I can bring to mind. They seemed to have a deep sense of their unworthiness, and manifested entire submission to the will of God, Yet everyone, without an exception, was earnestly pleading, and wrestling like Jacob for deliverance.

Soon after they had commenced their earnest cry, the angels, in sympathy would have gone to their deliverance. But a tall, commanding angel suffered them not. Said he, The will of God is not yet fulfilled. They must drink of the cup. They must be baptized with the baptism.

Soon I heard the voice of God, which shook the heavens and the earth. There was a mighty earthquake. Buildings were shaken down, and fell on every side. I then heard a triumphant shout of victory, loud, musical and clear. I looked upon this company who, a short time before were in such distress and bondage. Their captivity was turned. A glorious light shone upon them. How beautiful they then looked. All weariness and marks of care were gone. Health and beauty were seen in every counte-nance. Their enemies, the heathen around them, fell like dead men. They could not endure the light that shone upon the delivered, holy ones. This light and glory remained upon them, until Jesus was seen in the clouds of heaven, and the faithful, tried company was changed in a moment, in the twinkling of an eye, from glory to glory. And the graves were opened and the saints came forth, clothed with immortality, crying victory over death and the grave, and together with the living saints, were caught up to meet their Lord in the air; while the rich, musical shouts of glory and victory were upon every immortal tongue, and proceeding from every sanctified, holy lip.

See Joel 2:12-17; Zechariah 12:10; Revelation 1:5.

The Sins of Babylon

I saw the state of the different churches since the second angel proclaimed their fall. They have been growing more and more corrupt; yet they bear the name of being Christ's followers. It is impossible to distinguish them from the world. Their ministers take their text from the Word, but preach smooth things. The natural heart feels no objection to this. It is only the spirit and power of the truth, and the salvation of Christ, that is hateful to the carnal heart. There is nothing in the popular ministry that stirs the wrath of Satan, makes the sinner tremble, or applies to the heart and conscience the fearful realities of a judgment soon to come. Wicked men are generally pleased with a form without true godliness, and they will aid and support such a religion. Said the angel, Nothing less than the whole armor of righteousness can overcome, and retain the victory over the powers of darkness. Satan has taken full possession of the churches as a body. The sayings and doings of men are dwelt upon instead of the plain cutting truths of the word of God. Said the angel, The friendship and spirit of the world are at enmity with God. When truth in its simplicity and strength, as it is in Jesus, is brought to bear against the spirit of the world, it awakens the spirit of persecution at once. Many, very many, who profess to be Christians, have not known God. The character of the natural heart has not been changed, and the carnal mind remains at enmity with God. They are Satan's own faithful servants, notwithstanding they have assumed another name.

I saw that since Jesus had left the Holy place of the heavenly Sanctuary, and had entered within the second vail, the churches were left as were the Jews; and they have been filling up with every unclean and hateful bird. I saw great iniquity and vileness in the churches; yet they profess to be Christians. Their profession, their prayers and their exhortations, are an abomination in the sight of God. Said the angel, God will not smell in their assemblies. Selfishness, fraud and deceit are practiced by them without the reprovings of conscience. And over all these evil traits they throw the cloak of religion. I was shown the pride of the nominal churches. God was not in their thoughts; but their carnal minds dwell upon themselves. They decorate their poor mortal bodies, and then look upon themselves with satisfaction and pleasure. Jesus and the angels looked upon them in anger. Said the angel, Their sins and pride have reached unto heaven. Their portion is prepared. Justice and judgment have slumbered long, but will soon awake. Vengeance is mine, and I will repay, saith the Lord. The fearful threatenings of the third angel are to be realized, and they will drink the wrath of God. An innumerable host of evil angels are spreading themselves over the whole land. The churches and religious bodies are crowded with them. And they look upon the religious bodies with exultation; for the cloak of religion covers the greatest crimes and iniquity.

All heaven beholds with indignation, human beings, the workmanship of God, reduced to the lowest depths of degradation, and placed on a level with the brute creation by their fellow men. And professed followers of that dear Saviour whose compassion was ever moved as he witnessed human woe, heartily engage in this enormous and grievous sin, and deal in slaves and souls of men. Angels have recorded it all. It is written in the book. The tears of the pious bond-men and bond-women, of fathers, mothers and children, brothers and sisters, are all bottled up in heaven. Agony, human agony, is carried from place to place, and bought and sold. God will restrain his anger but a little longer. His anger burns against this nation, and especially against the religious bodies who have sanctioned, and have themselves engaged in this terrible merchandise. Such injustice, such oppression, such sufferings, many professed followers of the meek and lowly Jesus can witness with heartless indifference. And many of them can inflict with hateful satisfaction, all this indescribable agony themselves, and yet dare to worship God. It is solemn mockery, and Satan exults over it, and reproaches Jesus and his angels with such inconsistency, saying, with hellish triumph, Such are Christ's followers!

These professed Christians read of the sufferings of the martyrs, and tears course down their cheeks. They wonder that men could ever possess hearts so hardened as to practice such inhuman cruelties towards their fellow-men, while at the same time they hold their fellow-men in slavery. And this is not all. They sever the ties of nature, and cruelly oppress from day to day their fellow-men. They can inflict most inhuman tortures with relentless cruelty, which would well compare with the cruelty papists and heathens exercised towards Christ's followers. Said the angel, It will be more tolerable for the heathen and for papists in the day of the execution of God's judgment than for such men. The cries and sufferings of the oppressed have reached unto heaven, and angels stand amazed at the hard-hearted, untold, agonizing suffering, man in the image of his Maker, causes his fellow-man. Said the angel, The names of such are written in blood, crossed with stripes, and flooded with agonizing, burning tears of suffering. God's anger will not cease until he has caused the land of light to drink the dregs of the cup of his fury, and until he has rewarded unto Babylon double. Reward her even as she rewarded you, double unto her double according to her works: in the cup which she hath filled, fill to her double.

I saw that the slave-master would have to answer for the soul of his slave whom he has kept in ignorance; and all the sins of the slave will be visited upon the master. God cannot take the slave to heaven, who has been kept in ignorance and degradation, knowing nothing of God, or the Bible, fearing nothing but his master's lash, and not holding so elevated a position as his master's brute beasts. But he does the best thing for him that a compassionate God can do. He lets him be as though he had not been; while the master has to suffer the seven last plagues, and then come up in the second resurrection, and suffer the second, most awful death. Then the wrath of God will be appeased.

See Revelation 18, Amos 5:21.

The Loud Cry

I saw angels hurrying to and fro in heaven. They were descending to earth, and again ascending to heaven, preparing for the fulfilment of some important event. Then I saw another mighty angel commissioned to descend to earth, and unite his voice with the third angel, and give power and force to his message. Great power and glory were imparted to the angel, and as he descended, the earth was lightened with his glory. The light which went before and followed after this angel, penetrated everywhere, as he cried mightily, with a strong voice, saying, Babylon the great is fallen, is fallen, and is become the habitation of devils, and the hold of every foul spirit, and a cage of every unclean and hateful bird. The message of the fall of Babylon, as given by the second angel, is again given, with the addition of the corruptions which have been entering the churches since 1844. The work of this angel comes in at the right time, and joins in the last great work of the third angel's message, as it swells into a loud cry. And the people of God are fitted up everywhere to stand in the hour of temptation which they are soon to meet. I saw a great light resting upon them, and they united in the message, and fearlessly proclaimed with great power the third angel's message.

Angels were sent to aid the mighty angel from heaven, and I heard voices which seemed to sound everywhere, Come out of her, my people, that ye be not partakers of her sins, and that ye receive not of her plagues; for her sins have reached unto heaven, and God hath remembered her iniquities. This message seemed to be an addition to the third message, and joined it, as the midnight cry joined the second angel's message in 1844. The glory of God rested upon the patient, waiting saints, and they fearlessly gave the last solemn warning, proclaiming the fall of Babylon, and calling upon God's people to come out of her; that they might escape her fearful doom.

The light that was shed upon the waiting ones penetrated everywhere, and those who had any light in the churches, who had not heard and rejected the three messages, answered to the call, and left the fallen churches. Many had come to years of accountability since these messages had been given, and the light shone upon them, and they were privileged to choose life or death. Some chose life, and took their stand with those looking for their Lord, and keeping all his commandments. The third message was to do its work; all were to be tested upon it, and the precious ones were to be called out from the religious bodies. A compelling power moves the honest, while the manifestation of the power of God holds in fear and restraint relatives and friends, and they dare not, neither have they power to, hinder those who feel the work of the Spirit of God upon them. The last call is carried even to the poor slaves, and the pious among them, with humble expressions, pour forth their songs of extravagant joy at the prospect of their happy deliverance, and their masters cannot check them; for a fear and astonishment keep them silent. Mighty miracles are wrought, the sick are healed, and signs and wonders follow the believers. God is in the work, and every saint, fearless of consequences, follows the convictions of his own conscience, and unites with those who are keeping all the commandments of God; and they sound abroad the third message with power. I saw that the third message would close with power and strength far exceeding the midnight cry.

Servants of God, endowed with power from on high, with their faces lighted up, and shining with holy consecration, went forth fulfilling their work, and proclaiming the message from heaven. Souls that were scattered all through the religious bodies answered to the call, and the precious were hurried out of the doomed churches, as Lot was hurried out of Sodom before her destruction. God's people were fitted up and strengthened by the excellent glory which fell upon them in rich abundance, preparing them to endure the hour of temptation. A multitude of voices I heard everywhere, saying, Here is the patience of the saints; here are they that keep the commandments of God, and the faith of Jesus.

See Revelation 14:12, Revelation 18, Joel 2:9-11.

The Third Message Closed

I was pointed down to the time when the third angel's message was closing. The power of God had rested upon his people. They had accomplished their work, and were prepared for the trying hour before them. They had received the latter rain, or refreshing from the presence of the Lord, and the living testimony had been revived. The last great warning had sounded everywhere, and it had stirred up and enraged the inhabitants of earth, who would not receive the message.

I saw angels hurrying to and fro in heaven. An angel returned from the earth with a writer's ink-horn by his side, and reported to Jesus that his work was done, that the saints were numbered and sealed. Then I saw Jesus, who had been ministering before the ark containing the ten commandments, throw down the censer. He raised his hands upward, and with a loud voice said, It is done. And all the angelic host laid off their crowns as Jesus made the solemn declaration, He that is unjust, let him be unjust still; and he which is filthy, let him be filthy still; and he that is righteous, let him be righteous still; and he that is holy, let him be holy still.

I saw that every case was then decided for life or death. Jesus had blotted out the sins of his people. He had received his kingdom, and the atonement had been made for the subjects of his kingdom. While Jesus had been ministering in the Sanctuary, the judgment had been going on for the righteous dead, and then for the righteous living. The subjects of the kingdom were made up. The marriage of the Lamb was finished. And the kingdom, and the greatness of the kingdom under the whole heaven, was given to Jesus, and the heirs of salvation, and Jesus was to reign as King of kings, and Lord of lords.

As Jesus moved out of the Most Holy place, I heard the tinkling of the bells upon his garment, and as he left, a cloud of darkness covered the inhabitants of the earth. There was then no mediator between guilty man, and an offended God. While Jesus had been standing between God and guilty man, a restraint was upon the people; but when Jesus stepped out from between man and the Father, the restraint was removed, and Satan had the control of man. It was impossible for the plagues to be poured out while Jesus officiated in the Sanctuary; but as his work there is finished, as his intercession closes, there is nothing to stay the wrath of God, and it breaks with fury upon the shelterless head of the guilty sinner, who has slighted salvation, and hated reproof. The saints in that fearful time, after the close of Jesus' mediation, were living in the sight of a holy God, without an intercessor. Every case was decided, every jewel numbered. Jesus tarried a moment in the outer apartment of the heavenly Sanctuary, and the sins which had been confessed while he was in the Most Holy place, he placed back upon the originator of sin, the Devil. He must suffer the punishment of these sins.

Then I saw Jesus lay off his priestly attire, and clothe himself with his most kingly robes -- upon his head were many crowns, a crown within a crown -- and surrounded by the angelic host, he left heaven. The plagues were falling upon the inhabitants of the earth. Some were denouncing God, and cursing him. Others rushed to the people of God, and begged to be taught how they should escape the judgments of God. But the saints had nothing for them. The last tear for sinners had been shed, the last agonizing prayer offered, the last burden had been borne. The sweet voice of mercy was no more to invite them. The last note of warning had been given. When the saints, and all heaven were interested for their salvation, they had no interest for themselves. Life and death had been set before them. Many desired life; but did not make any effort to obtain it. They did not choose life, and now there was no atoning blood to cleanse the sinner. No compassionate Saviour to plead for them, and cry, Spare, spare the sinner a little longer. All heaven had united with Jesus, as they heard the fearful words, It is done, It is finished. The plan of salvation had been accomplished. But few had chosen to accept the plan. And as mercy's sweet voice died away, a fearfulness and horror seized them. With terrible distinctness they hear, Too late! too late!

Those who had not prized God's word were hurrying to and fro. They wandered from sea to sea, and from the north to the east, to seek the word of the Lord. Said the angel, They shall not find it. There is a famine in the land; not a famine of bread, nor a thirst for water, but of hearing the words of the Lord. What would they not give for one word of approval from God? but no, they must hunger and thirst on. Day after day have they slighted salvation, and prized earthly pleasure, and earthly riches, higher than any heavenly inducement and treasure. They have rejected Jesus, and despised his saints. The filthy must remain filthy forever.

A great portion of the wicked were greatly enraged, as they suffered the effects of the plagues. It was a scene of fearful agony. Parents were bitterly reproaching their children, and children reproaching their parents, brothers their sisters, and sisters their brothers. Loud wailing cries were heard in every direction, It was you who kept me from receiving the truth, which would have saved me from this awful hour. The people turned upon the ministers with bitter hate, and reproached them, telling them, You have not warned us. You told us all the world was to be converted, and cried, Peace, peace, to quiet every fear that was aroused. You have not told us of this hour, and those who warned us of it you said were fanatics, and evil men, who would ruin us. But the ministers, I saw, did not escape the wrath of God. Their sufferings were ten-fold greater than their people's.

See Ezekiel 9:2-11; Revelation 22:11.

The Time of Jacob's Trouble

I saw the saints leaving the cities and villages, and associating in companies together, and living in the most solitary places. Angels provided them food and water; but the wicked were suffering with hunger and thirst. Then I saw the leading men of earth consulting together, and Satan and his angels were busy around them. I saw a writing, and copies of it scattered in different parts of the land, giving orders, that unless the saints should yield their peculiar faith, give up the Sabbath, and observe the first day, they were at liberty, after such a time, to put them to death. But in this time the saints were calm and composed, trusting in God, and leaning upon his promise, that a way of escape would be made for them. In some places, before the time for the writing to be executed, the wicked rushed upon the saints to slay them; but angels in the form of men of war fought for them. Satan wished to have the privilege of destroying the saints of the Most High; but Jesus bade his angels watch over them, for God would be honored by making a covenant with those who had kept his law in the sight of the heathen round about them; and Jesus would be honored by translating the faithful, waiting ones, who had so long expected him, without their seeing death.

Soon I saw the saints suffering great mental anguish. They seemed to be surrounded with the wicked inhabitants of earth. Every appearance was against them. Some began to fear that God had left them at last to perish by the hand of the wicked. But if their eyes could have been opened, they would have seen themselves surrounded by angels of God. Next came the multitude of the angry wicked, and next a mass of evil angels, hurrying on the wicked to slay the saints. But as they would attempt to approach them, they would first have to pass this company of mighty, holy angels, which was impossible. The angels of God were causing them to recede, and also causing the evil angels who were pressing around them, to fall back. It was an hour of terrible, fearful agony to the saints. They cried day and night unto God for deliverance. To outward appearance there was no possibility of their escape. The wicked had already commenced their triumphing, and were crying out, Why don't your God deliver you out of our hands? Why don't you go up, and save your lives? The saints heeded them not. They were wrestling with God like Jacob. The angels longed to deliver them; but they must wait a little longer, and drink of the cup, and be baptized with the baptism. The angels, faithful to their trust, kept their watch. The time had about come when God was to manifest his mighty power, and gloriously deliver them. God would not suffer his name to be reproached among the heathen. For his name's glory he would deliver every one of those who had patiently waited for him, and whose names were written in the book.

I was pointed back to faithful Noah. The rain descended, the floods came. Noah and his family had entered the ark, and God shut them in. Noah had faithfully warned the inhabitants of the old world, while they had mocked and derided him. And as the waters descended upon the earth, and as one after another were being drowned, they beheld that ark that they had made so much sport of, riding safely upon the waters, preserving the faithful Noah and his family. So I saw that the people of God, who had warned the world of his coming wrath, would be delivered. They had faithfully warned the inhabitants of the earth, and God would not suffer the wicked to destroy those who were expecting translation, and who would not bow to the decree of the beast, or receive his mark. I saw that if the wicked were permitted to slay the saints, Satan and all his evil host, and all who hate God, would be gratified. And O, what a time of triumph it would be for his Satanic majesty, to have power, in the last closing struggle, over those who had so long waited to behold Him whom they loved. Those who have mocked at the idea of the saints going up, will witness the care of God for his people, and their glorious deliverance.

As the saints left the cities and villages, they were pursued by the wicked. They raised their swords to kill the saints, but they broke, and fell as powerless as a straw. Angels of God shielded the saints. As they cried day and night for deliverance, their cry came up before God.

See Genesis 7:1; Isaiah 33:16, 49:10; Revelation 14:14.

Deliverance of the Saints

It was at midnight that God chose to deliver his people. As the wicked were mocking around them, suddenly the sun appeared, shining in his strength, and the moon stood still. The wicked beheld the scene with amazement. Signs and wonders followed in quick succession. Everything seemed turned out of its natural course. The saints beheld the tokens of their deliverance with solemn joy.

The streams ceased to flow. Dark, heavy clouds came up, and clashed against each other. But there was one clear place of settled glory, from whence came the voice of God, like many waters, which shook the heavens and the earth. There was a mighty earthquake. The graves were shaken open, and those who had died in faith under the third angel's message, keeping the Sabbath, came forth from their dusty beds, glorified, to hear the covenant of peace that God was to make with those who had kept his law.

The sky opened and shut, and was in commotion. The mountains shook like a reed in the wind, and cast out ragged rocks all around. The sea boiled like a pot, and cast out stones upon the land. And as God spake the day and hour of Jesus' coming, and delivered the everlasting covenant to his people, he spake one sentence, and then paused, while the words were rolling through the earth. The Israel of God stood with their eyes fixed upwards, listening to the words as they came from the mouth of Jehovah, and rolled through the earth like peals of loudest thunder. It was awfully solemn. At the end of every sentence the saints shouted, Glory! Hallelujah! Their countenances were lighted up with the glory of God; and they shone with the glory as did Moses' face when he came down from Sinai. The wicked could not look on them for the glory. And when the never-ending blessing was pronounced on those who had honored God, in keeping his Sabbath holy, there was a mighty shout of victory over the beast, and over his image.

Then commenced the jubilee, when the land should rest. I saw the pious slave rise in triumph and victory, and shake off the chains that bound him, while his wicked master was in confusion, and knew not what to do; for the wicked could not understand the words of the voice of God. Soon appeared the great white cloud. On it sat the Son of man.

This cloud when it first appeared in the distance, looked very small. The angel said that it was the sign of the Son of man. And as the cloud approached nearer to the earth, we could behold the excellent glory and majesty of Jesus as he rode forth to conquer. A holy retinue of angels, with their bright, glittering crowns upon their heads, escorted him on his way. No language can describe the glory of the scene. The living cloud of majesty, and unsurpassed glory, came still nearer, and we could clearly behold the lovely person of Jesus. He did not wear a crown of thorns; but a crown of glory decked his holy brow. Upon his vesture and thigh was a name written, KING OF KINGS AND LORD OF LORDS. His eyes were as a flame of fire, his feet had the appearance of fine brass, and his voice sounded like many musical instruments. His countenance was as bright as the noon-day sun. The earth trembled before him, and the heavens departed as a scroll when it is rolled together, and every mountain and island were moved out of their places. And the kings of the earth, and the great men, and the rich men, and the chief captains, and the mighty men, and every bondman, and every freeman, hid themselves in the dens and in the rocks of the mountains. And said to the mountains and rocks, Fall on us, and hide us from the face of him that sitteth on the throne, and from the wrath of the Lamb: for the great day of his wrath is come; and who shall be able to stand?

Those who a little before would have destroyed God's faithful children from the earth, had to witness the glory of God which rested upon them. They had seen them glorified. And amid all the terrible scenes they had heard the voices of the saints in joyful strains, saying, Lo, this is our God, we have waited for him, and he will save us. The earth mightily shook as the voice of the Son of God called forth the sleeping saints. They responded to the call, and came forth clothed with glorious immortality, crying, Victory! victory! over death and the grave. O death, where is thy sting? O grave, where is thy victory? Then the living saints, and the resurrected ones, raised their voices in a long, transporting shout of victory. Those sickly bodies that had gone down into the grave came up in immortal health and vigor. The living saints were changed in a moment, in the twinkling of an eye, and caught up with the resurrected ones, and together they meet their Lord in the air. O what a glorious meeting. Friends whom death had separated, were united, never more to part.

On either side of the cloudy chariot were wings, and beneath it were living wheels; and as the cloudy chariot rolled upward, the wheels cried, Holy, and the wings, as they moved, cried, Holy, and the retinue of holy angels around the cloud cried, Holy, Holy, Holy, Lord God Almighty. And the saints in the cloud cried, Glory, Alleluia. And the chariot rolled upward to the holy city. Before entering the holy city, the saints were arranged in a perfect square, with Jesus in the midst. He was head and shoulders high above the saints, and head and shoulders above the angels. His majestic form, and lovely countenance, could be seen by all in the square.

See Revelation 15:1-4, 6:12-17.

The Saints' Reward

Then I saw a very great number of angels bring from the city glorious crowns; a crown for every saint with his name written thereon; and as Jesus called for the crowns, angels presented them to him, and the lovely Jesus, with his own right hand, placed the crowns on the heads of the saints. In the same manner, the angels brought the harps, and Jesus presented them also to the saints. The commanding angels first struck the note, and then every voice was raised in grateful, happy praise, and every hand skillfully swept over the strings of the harp, sending forth melodious music in rich and perfect strains. Then I saw Jesus lead the redeemed company to the gate of the city. He laid hold of the gate and swung it back on its glittering hinges, and bade the nations who had kept the truth to enter in. There was everything in the city to feast the eye. Rich glory they beheld everywhere. Then Jesus looked upon his redeemed saints; their countenances were radiant with glory; and as he fixed his loving eyes upon them, he said, with his rich, musical voice, I behold the travail of my soul, and am satisfied. This rich glory is yours to enjoy eternally. Your sorrows are ended. There shall be no more death, neither sorrow, nor crying, neither shall there be any more pain. I saw the redeemed host bow and cast their glittering crowns at the feet of Jesus, and then, as his lovely hand raised them up, they touched their golden harps, and filled all heaven with their rich music, and songs to the Lamb.

I then saw Jesus leading the redeemed host to the tree of life, and again we heard his lovely voice, richer than any music that ever fell on mortal ear, saying, The leaves of this tree are for the healing of the nations. Eat ye all of it. Upon the tree of life was most beautiful fruit, which the saints could partake of freely. There was a most glorious throne in the City, and from under the throne proceeded a pure river of water of life, as clear as crystal. On either side of this river of life was the tree of life. On the banks of the river were beautiful trees bearing fruit which was good for food. Language is altogether too feeble to attempt a description of heaven. As the scene rises before me I am lost in amazement; and carried away with the surpassing splendor and the excellent glory, I lay down the pen, and exclaim, O what love! What wondrous love! The most exalted language cannot describe the glory of heaven, nor the matchless depths of a Saviour's love.

See Revelation 2:10, 21:4, 22:1-6; Isaiah 65:17-25.

The Earth Desolated

I then beheld the earth. The wicked were dead, and their bodies were lying upon the face of the earth. The inhabitants of earth had suffered the wrath of God in the seven last plagues. They had gnawed their tongues for pain and had cursed God. The false shepherds were signal objects of Jehovah's wrath. Their eyes had consumed away in their holes, and their tongues in their mouths, while they stood upon their feet. After the saints were delivered by the voice of God, the rage of the wicked multitude was turned upon each other. The earth seemed to be deluged with blood, and dead bodies were from one end of the earth to the other.

The earth was in a most desolate condition. Cities and villages, shaken down by the earthquake, lay in heaps. Mountains were moved out of their places, leaving large caverns. The sea had thrown out ragged rocks upon the earth, and rocks had been torn out of the earth, and were scattered all over its surface. The earth looked like a desolate wilderness. Large trees were rooted up, and were strewn over the land. Here is Satan's home, with his evil angels, through the 1000 years. Here they will be confined, and wander up and down over the broken surface of the earth, and see the effects of his rebellion against God's law. The effects of the curse which he has caused, he can enjoy through the 1000 years. Limited alone to the earth, he will have no privilege of ranging around to other planets, to tempt and annoy those who have not fallen. Satan suffers in this time extremely. Since his fall his evil traits have been in constant exercise. He is then deprived of his power, and left to reflect upon the part he has acted since his fall, and to look forward with trembling and terror to the dreadful future, when he must suffer for all the evil he has done, and be punished for all the sins he has caused to be committed.

Then I heard shouts of triumph from the angels, and from the redeemed saints, which sounded like ten thousand musical instruments, because they were to be no more annoyed and tempted by the Devil, and the inhabitants of other worlds were delivered from his presence and his temptations.

Then I saw thrones, and Jesus and the redeemed saints sat upon them; and the saints reigned as kings and priests unto God, and the wicked dead were judged, and their acts were compared with the statute book, the word of God, and they were judged according to the deeds done in the body. Jesus, in union with the saints, meted out to the wicked the portion they must suffer, according to their works; and it was written in the book of death, and set off against their names. Satan and his angels were also judged by Jesus and the saints. Satan's punishment was to be far greater than that of those whom he had deceived. It so far exceeded their punishment that it could not be compared with theirs. After all those whom he had deceived had perished, Satan was to still live and suffer on much longer.

After the judgment of the wicked dead was finished, at the end of the one thousand years, Jesus left the City, and a train of the angelic host followed him. The saints also went with him. Jesus descended upon a great and mighty mountain, which, as soon as his feet touched it, parted asunder, and became a mighty plain. Then we looked up and saw the great and beautiful City, with twelve foundations, twelve gates, three on each side, and an angel at each gate. We cried out, The City! The great City! It is coming down from God out of heaven! And it came down in all its splendor, and dazzling glory, and settled in the mighty plain which Jesus had prepared for it.

See Revelation 16:1-21, 20:2, 7:15.

The Second Resurrection

Then Jesus and all the holy retinue of angels, and all the redeemed saints, left the City. The holy angels surrounded Jesus, and escorted him on his way, and the train of redeemed saints followed. Then Jesus in terrible, fearful majesty called forth the wicked dead; and as they came up with the same feeble, sickly bodies that went into the grave, what a spectacle! what a scene! At the first resurrection all came forth in immortal bloom; but at the second, the marks of the curse are visible on all. Kings and the noble men of earth come forth with the mean and the low, learned and unlearned together. All behold the Son of man; and those very men who despised and mocked Jesus, and smote him with the reed, and that put the crown of thorns upon his sacred brow, behold him in all his kingly majesty. Those who spit upon him in the hour of his trial, now turn from his piercing gaze, and from the glory of his countenance. Those who drove the nails through his hands and his feet, now look upon the marks of his crucifixion. Those who thrust the spear into his side, behold the marks of their cruelty on his body. And they know that he is the very One whom they crucified, and derided in his expiring agony. And then there arises one long protracted wail of agony, as they flee to hide from the presence of the King of kings and Lord of lords.

All are seeking to hide in the rocks, and shield themselves from the terrible glory of him whom they once despised. As all are overwhelmed and pained with his majesty and his exceeding glory, they with one accord raise their voices, and with terrible distinctness exclaim, Blessed is he who cometh in the name of the Lord.

Then Jesus and the holy angels, accompanied by all the saints, again go to the City, and the bitter lamentations and wailings of the doomed wicked fill the air. Then I saw that Satan again commenced his work. He passed around among his subjects, and made the feeble and weak strong, and then he told them that he and his angels were powerful. He then pointed to the countless millions who had been raised. There were mighty warriors and kings who were well skilled in battle, and who had conquered kingdoms. And there were mighty giants, and men who were valiant, and had never lost a battle. There was the proud, ambitious Napoleon whose approach had caused kingdoms to tremble. There stood men of very high stature, and of dignified, lofty bearing, who had fallen in battle. They fell while thirsting to conquer. As they come forth from their graves, they resume the current of their thoughts where it ceased in death. They possess the same spirit to conquer which ruled when they fell. Satan consults with his angels, and then with those kings and conquerors and mighty men. Then he looks over the vast army and tells them that the company in the City is small and feeble, and that they can go up and take that City, and cast out its inhabitants, and possess its riches and glory themselves.

Satan succeeds in deceiving them, and all immediately commence to fit themselves for battle. They construct weapons of war; for there are many skillful men in that vast army. And then with Satan at their head, the multitude move on. Kings and warriors follow close after Satan, and the multitude follow after in companies. Every company has a leader, and order is observed as they march over the broken surface of the earth to the holy City. Jesus closes the gates of the City, and this vast army surround it and place themselves in battle array. They have prepared all kinds of implements of war, expecting to have a fierce conflict. They arrange themselves around the City. Jesus and all the angelic host with the glittering crowns upon their heads, and all the saints with their bright crowns, ascend to the top of the wall of the City. Jesus speaks with majesty and says, Behold, ye sinners, the reward of the just! And behold ye my redeemed, the reward of the wicked! The vast multitude behold the glorious company on the walls of the City. And as they witness the splendor of their glittering crowns, and see their faces radiant with glory, expressing the image of Jesus, and then behold the unsurpassed glory and majesty of the King of kings, and Lord of lords, their courage fails. The sense of the treasure and glory which they have lost, rushes upon them, and they have a realizing sense that the wages of sin is death. They see the holy, happy company whom they have despised, clothed with glory, honor, immortality and eternal life, while they are outside of the City with every mean and abominable thing.

See I Thessalonians 4:16,17; Revelation 6:15,16, 20:7-9.

The Second Death

Satan rushes into the midst, and tries to stir up the multitude to action. But fire from God out of heaven is rained upon them, and the great men, and the mighty men, and the noble, and poor and miserable men, are all consumed together. I saw that some were quickly destroyed, while others suffered longer. They were punished according to the deeds done in the body. Some were many days consuming, and just as long as there was a portion of them unconsumed, all the sense of suffering was there. Said the angel, The worm of life shall not die; their fire shall not be quenched as long as there is the least particle for it to prey upon.

But Satan and his angels suffered long. Satan not only bore the weight and punishment of his sins, but the sins of all the redeemed host had been placed upon him; and he must also suffer for the ruin of the souls which he had caused. Then I saw that Satan, and all the wicked host, were consumed, and the justice of God was satisfied; and all the angelic host, and all the redeemed saints, with a loud voice said, Amen!

Said the angel, Satan is the root, his children are the branches. They are now consumed root and branch. They have died an everlasting death. They will never have a resurrection, and God will have a clean universe. I then looked, and saw the fire which had consumed the wicked, burning up the rubbish and purifying the earth. Again I looked and saw the earth purified. There was not a single sign of the curse. The broken up, and uneven surface of the earth now looked like a level, extensive plain. God's entire universe was clean, and the great controversy was forever ended. Everywhere we looked, everything the eye rested upon, was beautiful and holy. And all the redeemed host, old and young, great and small, cast their glittering crowns at the feet of their Redeemer, and prostrated themselves in adoration before him, and worshiped him that liveth forever and ever. The beautiful New Earth, with all its glory, was the eternal inheritance of the saints. The kingdom, and dominion, and greatness of the kingdom under the whole heaven, was then given to the saints of the Most High who were to possess it forever, even forever and ever.

See Daniel 7:26,27; Mark 9:44,48; II Peter 3:9-13; Revelation 20:6-10.

Printed in the USA
CPSIA information can be obtained
at www.ICGtesting.com
LVHW080549071223
765731LV00006B/30